# THE HISTORY OF MIDDLE-EARTH I

TOLKIEN

# The History
# of Middle-earth I

I The Book of Lost Tales, Part One
II The Book of Lost Tales, Part Two
III The Lays of Beleriand
IV The Shaping of Middle-earth
V The Lost Road and other writings

CHRISTOPHER TOLKIEN

HarperCollins*Publishers*

HarperCollins*Publishers*
77–85 Fulham Palace Road,
Hammersmith, London W6 8JB

www.tolkien.co.uk

This edition published by HarperCollins*Publishers* 2002
5

First published by HarperCollins*Publishers* 2000

*The Book of Lost Tales I* first published in Great Britain by
George Allen & Unwin 1983
*The Book of Lost Tales II* first published in Great Britain by
George Allen & Unwin 1984
*The Lays of Beleriand* first published in Great Britain by
George Allen & Unwin 1985
*The Shaping of Middle-earth* first published in Great Britain by
George Allen & Unwin 1986
*The Lost Road and other writings* first published in Great Britain by
Unwin Hyman 1987

ISBN-13   978 0 00 714915 5
ISBN-10   0 00 714915 8

Set in Imprint

Printed in Great Britain by
Clays Ltd, St Ives plc

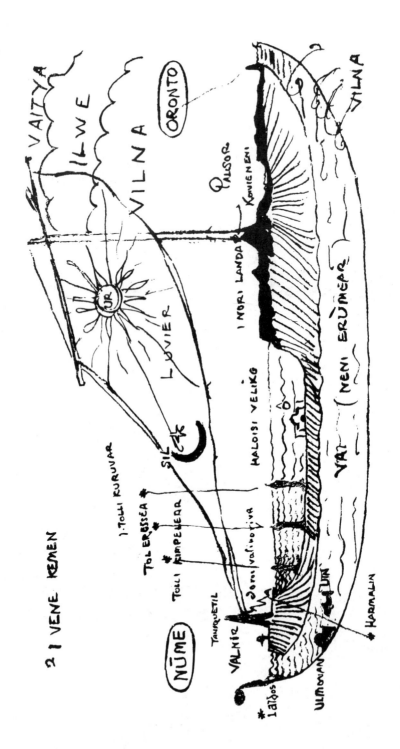

# THE BOOK OF LOST TALES

## PART I

# J. R. R. TOLKIEN

# The
# Book of Lost Tales

## PART I

Christopher Tolkien

# CONTENTS

# FOREWORD

*The Book of Lost Tales*, written between sixty and seventy years ago, was the first substantial work of imaginative literature by J. R. R. Tolkien, and the first emergence in narrative of the Valar, of the Children of Ilúvatar, Elves and Men, of the Dwarves and the Orcs, and of the lands in which their history is set, Valinor beyond the western ocean, and Middle-earth, the 'Great Lands' between the seas of east and west. Some fifty-seven years after my father ceased to work on the *Lost Tales*, *The Silmaril-lion*,* profoundly transformed from its distant forerunner, was published; and six years have passed since then. This Foreword seems a suitable opportunity to remark on some aspects of both works.

*The Silmarillion* is commonly said to be a 'difficult' book, needing explanation and guidance on how to 'approach' it; and in this it is con-trasted to *The Lord of the Rings*. In Chapter 7 of his book *The Road to Middle-earth* Professor T. A. Shippey accepts that this is so ('*The Silmarillion* could never be anything but hard to read', p. 201), and expounds his view of why it should be. A complex discussion is not treated justly when it is extracted, but in his view the reasons are essentially two (p. 185). In the first place, there is in *The Silmarillion* no 'mediation' of the kind provided by the hobbits (so, in *The Hobbit*, 'Bilbo acts as the link between modern times and the archaic world of dwarves and dragons'). My father was himself well aware that the absence of hobbits would be felt as a lack, were 'The Silmarillion' to be published – and not only by readers with a particular liking for them. In a letter written in 1956 (*The Letters of J. R. R. Tolkien*, p. 238), soon after the publication of *The Lord of the Rings*, he said:

> I do not think it would have the appeal of the L.R. – no hobbits! Full of mythology, and elvishness, and all that 'heigh stile' (as Chaucer might say), which has been so little to the taste of many reviewers.

In 'The Silmarillion' the draught is pure and unmixed; and the reader is worlds away from such 'mediation', such a deliberate collison (far more than a matter of styles) as that produced in the meeting between King Théoden and Pippin and Merry in the ruins of Isengard:

> 'Farewell, my hobbits! May we meet again in my house! There you shall sit beside me and tell me all that your hearts desire: the deeds of

---

* When the name is printed in italics, I refer to the work as published; when in inverted commas, to the work in a more general way, in any or all of its forms.

your grandsires, as far as you can reckon them . . .'
The hobbits bowed low. 'So that is the King of Rohan!' said Pippin
in an undertone. 'A fine old fellow. Very polite.'

In the second place,

> Where *The Silmarillion* differs from Tolkien's earlier works is in its
> refusal to accept novelistic convention. Most novels (including *The
> Hobbit* and *The Lord of the Rings*) pick a character to put in the fore-
> ground, like Frodo and Bilbo, and then tell the story as it happens to
> him. The novelist of course is inventing the story, and so retains
> omniscience: he can explain, or show, what is 'really' happening and
> contrast it with the limited perception of his character.

There is, then, and very evidently, a question of literary 'taste' (or
literary 'habituation') involved; and also a question of literary 'disappointment' – the '(mistaken) disappointment in those who wanted a second
*Lord of the Rings*' to which Professor Shippey refers. This has even produced a sense of outrage – in one case formulated to me in the words
'It's like *the Old Testament*!': a dire condemnation against which, clearly,
there can be no appeal (though this reader cannot have got very far
before being overcome by the comparison). Of course, 'The Silmarillion'
was intended to move the heart and the imagination, directly, and without
peculiar effort or the possession of unusual faculties; but its mode is
inherent, and it may be doubted whether any 'approach' to it can greatly
aid those who find it unapproachable.
There is a third consideration (which Professor Shippey does not indeed
advance in the same context):

> One quality which [*The Lord of the Rings*] has in abundance is the
> Beowulfian 'impression of depth', created just as in the old epic by
> songs and digressions like Aragorn's lay of Tinúviel, Sam Gamgee's
> allusions to the Silmaril and the Iron Crown, Elrond's account of
> Celebrimbor, and dozens more. This, however, is a quality of *The
> Lord of the Rings*, not of the inset stories. To tell these in their own right
> and expect them to retain the charm they got from their larger setting
> would be a terrible error, an error to which Tolkien would be more
> sensitive than any man alive. As he wrote in a revealing letter dated
> 20 September 1963:

> > I am doubtful myself about the undertaking [to write *The Silmarillion*].
> > Part of the attraction of The L.R. is, I think, due to the glimpses of
> > a large history in the background: an attraction like that of viewing
> > far off an unvisited island, or seeing the towers of a distant city
> > gleaming in a sunlit mist. To go there is to destroy the magic, unless
> > new unattainable vistas are again revealed. (*Letters*, p. 333)

*To go there is to destroy the magic.* As for the revealing of 'new un-attainable vistas', the problem there – as Tolkien must have thought many times – was that in *The Lord of the Rings* Middle-earth was already old, with a vast weight of history behind it. *The Silmarillion*, though, in its longer form, was bound to begin at the beginning. How could 'depth' be created when you had nothing to reach further back to?

The letter quoted here certainly shows that my father felt this, or perhaps rather one should say, at times felt this, to be a problem. Nor was it a new thought: while he was writing *The Lord of the Rings*, in 1945, he said in a letter to me (*Letters*, p. 110):

A story must be told or there'll be no story, yet it is the untold stories that are most moving. I think you are moved by *Celebrimbor* because it conveys a sudden sense of endless *untold* stories: mountains seen far away, never to be climbed, distant trees (like Niggle's) never to be approached – or if so only to become 'near trees' . . .

This matter is perfectly illustrated for me by Gimli's song in Moria, where great names out of the ancient world appear utterly remote:

> The world was fair, the mountains tall,
> In Elder Days before the fall
> Of mighty kings in Nargothrond
> And Gondolin, who now beyond
> The Western Seas have passed away . . .

'I like that!' said Sam. 'I should like to learn it. *In Moria, in Khazad-dûm.* But it makes the darkness seem heavier, thinking of all those lamps.' By his enthusiastic 'I like that!' Sam not only 'mediates' (and engagingly 'Gamgifies') the 'high', the mighty kings of Nargothrond and Gondolin, Durin on his carven throne, but places them at once at an even remoter distance, a magical distance that it might well seem (*at that moment*) destructive to traverse.

Professor Shippey says that 'to tell [the stories that are only alluded to in *The Lord of the Rings*] in their own right and expect them to retain the charm they got from their larger setting would be a terrible error'. The 'error' presumably lies in the holding of such an expectation, if the stories were told, not in the telling of the stories at all; and it is apparent that Professor Shippey sees my father as wondering, in 1963, whether he should or should not put pen to paper, for he expands the words of the letter, 'I am doubtful myself about the undertaking', to mean 'the undertaking to write *The Silmarillion*'. But when my father said this he was not – most emphatically not – referring to the work itself, which was in any case already written, and much of it many times over (the allusions in *The Lord of the Rings* are not illusory): what was in question for him, as he said earlier in this same letter, was its *presentation*, in a publication, *after* the appearance of *The Lord of the Rings*, when, as he thought, the right time to make it known was already gone.

I am afraid all the same that the presentation will need a lot of work, and I work so slowly. The legends have to be worked over (they were written at different times, some many years ago) and made consistent; and they have to be integrated with The L.R.; and they have to be given some progressive shape. No simple device, like a journey and a quest, is available.

I am doubtful myself about the undertaking . . .

When after his death the question arose of publishing 'The Silmarillion' in some form, I attached no importance to this doubt. The effect that 'the glimpses of a large history in the background' have in *The Lord of the Rings* is incontestable and of the utmost importance, but I did not think that the 'glimpses' used there with such art should preclude all further knowledge of the 'large history'.

The literary 'impression of depth . . . created by songs and digressions' cannot be made a criterion by which a work in a wholly different mode is measured: this would be to treat the history of the Elder Days as of value primarily or even solely in the artistic use made of it in *The Lord of the Rings*. Nor should the device of a backward movement in imagined time to dimly apprehended events, whose attraction lies in their very dimness, be understood mechanically, as if a fuller account of the mighty kings of Nargothrond and Gondolin would imply a dangerously near approach to the bottom of the well, while an account of the Creation would signify the striking of the bottom and a definitive running-out of 'depth' – 'nothing to reach further back to'.

This, surely, is not how things work, or at least not how they need work. 'Depth' in this sense implies a relation between different temporal layers or levels within the same world. Provided that the reader has a place, a point of vantage, *in the imagined time* from which to look back, the extreme oldness of the extremely old can be made apparent and made to be felt continuously. And the very fact that *The Lord of the Rings* establishes such a powerful sense of a real time-structure (far more powerful than can be done by mere chronological assertion, tables of dates) provides this necessary vantage-point. To read *The Silmarillion* one must place oneself imaginatively at the time of the ending of the Third Age – within Middle-earth, looking back: at the temporal point of Sam Gamgee's 'I like that!' – adding, 'I should like to know more about it'. Moreover the compendious or epitomising form and manner of *The Silmarillion*, with its suggestion of ages of poetry and 'lore' behind it, strongly evokes a sense of 'untold tales', even in the telling of them; 'distance' is never lost. There is no narrative urgency, the pressure and fear of the immediate and unknown event. We do not actually see the Silmarils as we see the Ring. The maker of 'The Silmarillion', as he himself said of the author of *Beowulf*, 'was telling of things already old and weighted with regret, and he expended his art in making keen that touch upon the heart which sorrows have that are both poignant and remote'.

As has now been fully recorded, my father greatly desired to publish 'The Silmarillion' together with *The Lord of the Rings*. I say nothing of its practicability at the time, nor do I make any guesses at the subsequent fate of such a much longer combined work, quadrilogy or tetralogy, or at the different courses that my father might then have taken – for the further development of 'The Silmarillion' itself, the history of the Elder Days, would have been arrested. But by its posthumous publication nearly a quarter of a century later the natural order of presentation of the whole 'Matter of Middle-earth' was inverted; and it is certainly debatable whether it was wise to publish in 1977 a version of the primary 'legendarium' standing on its own and claiming, as it were, to be self-explanatory. The published work has no 'framework', no suggestion of what it is and how (within the imagined world) it came to be. This I now think to have been an error.

The letter of 1963 quoted above shows my father pondering the mode in which the legends of the Elder Days might be presented. The original mode, that of *The Book of Lost Tales*, in which a Man, Eriol, comes after a great voyage over the ocean to the island where the Elves dwell and learns their history from their own lips, had (by degrees) fallen away. When my father died in 1973 'The Silmarillion' was in a characteristic state of disarray: the earlier parts much revised or largely rewritten, the concluding parts still as he had left them some twenty years before; but in the latest writing there is no trace or suggestion of any 'device' or 'framework' in which it was to be set. I think that in the end he concluded that nothing would serve, and no more would be said beyond an explanation of how (within the imagined world) it came to be recorded.

In the original edition of *The Lord of the Rings* Bilbo gave to Frodo at Rivendell as his parting gift 'some books of lore that he had made at various times, written in his spidery hand, and labelled on their red backs: *Translations from the Elvish, by B.B.*' In the second edition (1966) 'some books' was changed to 'three books', and in the *Note on the Shire Records* added to the Prologue in that edition my father said that the content of 'the three large volumes bound in red leather' was preserved in that copy of the Red Book of Westmarch which was made in Gondor by the King's Writer Findegil in the year 172 of the Fourth Age; and also that

These three volumes were found to be a work of great skill and learning in which . . . [Bilbo] had used all the sources available to him in Rivendell, both living and written. But since they were little used by Frodo, being almost entirely concerned with the Elder Days, no more is said of them here.

In *The Complete Guide to Middle-earth* Robert Foster says: '*Quenta Silmarillion* was no doubt one of Bilbo's *Translations from the Elvish* preserved in the Red Book of Westmarch.' So also I have assumed: the 'books of lore' that Bilbo gave to Frodo provided in the end the solution: they were 'The Silmarillion'. But apart from the evidence cited here, there is, so far as I know, no other statement on this matter anywhere in my father's writings; and (wrongly, as I think now) I was reluctant to step into the breach and make definite what I only surmised.

The choice before me, in respect of 'The Silmarillion', was threefold. I could withhold it indefinitely from publication, on the ground that the work was incomplete and incoherent between its parts. I could accept the nature of the work as it stood, and, to quote my Foreword to the book, 'attempt to present the diversity of the materials − to show "The Silmarillion" as in truth a continuing and evolving creation extending over more than half a century'; and that, as I have said in *Unfinished Tales* (p. 1), would have entailed 'a complex of divergent texts interlinked by commentary' − a far larger undertaking than those words suggest. In the event, I chose the third course, 'to work out a single text, selecting and arranging in such a way as seemed to me to produce the most coherent and internally self-consistent narrative'. Having come, at length, to that decision, all the editorial labour of myself and of Guy Kay who assisted me was directed to the end that my father had stated in the letter of 1963: 'The legends have to be worked over . . . and made consistent; and they have to be integrated with the L.R.' Since the object was to present 'The Silmarillion' as 'a completed and cohesive entity' (though that could not in the nature of the case be entirely successful), it followed that there would be in the published book no exposition of the complexities of its history.

Whatever may be thought of this matter, the result, which I by no means foresaw, has been to add a further dimension of obscurity to 'The Silmarillion', in that uncertainty about the age of the work, whether it is to be regarded as 'early' or 'late' or in what proportions, and about the degree of editorial intrusion and manipulation (or even invention), is a stumbling-block and a source of much misapprehension. Professor Randel Helms, in *Tolkien and the Silmarils* (p. 93), has stated the question thus:

Anyone interested, as I am, in the growth of *The Silmarillion* will want to study *Unfinished Tales*, not only for its intrinsic value but also because its relationship to the former provides what will become a classic example of a long-standing problem in literary criticism: what, really, *is* a literary work? Is it what the author intended (or may have intended) it to be, or is it what a later editor makes of it? The problem becomes especially intense for the practising critic when, as happened with *The Silmarillion*, a writer dies before finishing his work and leaves more than one version of some of its parts, which then find publication elsewhere. Which version will the critic approach as the 'real' story?

But he also says: 'Christopher Tolkien has helped us in this instance by honestly pointing out that *The Silmarillion* in the shape that we have it is the invention of the son not the father'; and this is a serious mis-apprehension to which my words have given rise.

Again, Professor Shippey, while accepting (p. 169) my assurance that a 'very high proportion' of the 1937 'Silmarillion' text remained into the published version, is nonetheless elsewhere clearly reluctant to see it as other than a 'late' work, even the latest work of its author. And in an article entitled 'The Text of *The Hobbit*: Putting Tolkien's Notes in Order' (English Studies in Canada, VII, 2, Summer 1981) Constance B. Hieatt concludes that 'it is very clear indeed that we shall never be able to see the progressive steps of authorial thinking behind *The Silmarillion*'.

But beyond the difficulties and the obscurities, what is certain and very evident is that for the begetter of Middle-earth and Valinor there was a deep coherence and vital interrelation between all its times, places, and beings, whatever the literary modes, and however protean some parts of the conception might seem when viewed over a long lifetime. He himself understood very well that many who read *The Lord of the Rings* with enjoyment would never wish to regard Middle-earth as more than the mise-en-scène of the story, and would delight in the sensation of 'depth' without wishing to explore the deep places. But the 'depth' is not of course an illusion, like a line of imitation book-backs with no books inside them; and Quenya and Sindarin are comprehensive structures. There are explorations to be conducted in this world with perfect right quite irrespec-tive of literary-critical considerations; and it is proper to attempt to comprehend its structure in its largest extent, from the myth of its Creation. Every person, every feature of the imagined world that seemed significant to its author is then worthy of attention in its own right, Manwë or Fëanor no less than Gandalf or Galadriel, the Silmarils no less than the Rings; the Great Music, the divine hierarchies, the abodes of the Valar, the fates of the Children of Ilúvatar, are essential elements in the perception of the whole. Such enquiries are in no way illegitimate in principle; they arise from an acceptance of the imagined world as an object of contemplation or study valid as many other objects of contemplation or study in the all too unimaginary world. It was in this opinion and in the knowledge that others shared it that I made the collection called *Unfinished Tales*.

But the author's vision of his own vision underwent a continual slow shifting, shedding and enlarging: only in *The Hobbit* and *The Lord of the Rings* did parts of it emerge to become fixed in print, in his own lifetime. The study of Middle-earth and Valinor is thus complex; for the object of the study was not stable, but exists, as it were 'longitudinally' in time (the author's lifetime), and not only 'transversely' in time, as a printed book that undergoes no essential further change. By the publication of 'The Silmarillion' the 'longitudinal' was cut 'transversely', and a kind of finality imposed.

★

This rather rambling discussion is an attempt to explain my primary motives in offering *The Book of Lost Tales* for publication. It is the first step in presenting the 'longitudinal' view of Middle-earth and Valinor: when the huge geographical expansion, swelling out from the centre and (as it were) thrusting Beleriand into the west, was far off in the future; when there were no 'Elder Days' ending in the drowning of Beleriand, for there were as yet no other Ages of the World; when the Elves were still 'fairies', and even Rúmil the learned Noldo was far removed from the magisterial 'loremasters' of my father's later years. In *The Book of Lost Tales* the princes of the Noldor have scarcely emerged, nor the Grey-elves of Beleriand; Beren is an Elf, not a Man, and his captor, the ultimate precursor of Sauron in that rôle, is a monstrous cat inhabited by a fiend; the Dwarves are an evil people; and the historical relations of Quenya and Sindarin were quite differently conceived. These are a few especially notable features, but such a list could be greatly prolonged. On the other hand, there was already a firm underlying structure that would endure. Moreover in the history of the history of Middle-earth the development was seldom by outright rejection – far more often it was by subtle transformation in stages, so that the growth of the legends (the process, for instance, by which the Nargothrond story made contact with that of Beren and Lúthien, a contact not even hinted at in the *Lost Tales*, though both elements were present) can seem like the growth of legends among peoples, the product of many minds and generations.

*The Book of Lost Tales* was begun by my father in 1916–17 during the First War, when he was 25 years old, and left incomplete several years later. It is the starting-point, at least in fully-formed narrative, of the history of Valinor and Middle-earth; but before the *Tales* were complete he turned to the composition of long poems, the *Lay of Leithian* in rhyming couplets (the story of Beren and Lúthien), and *The Children of Húrin* in alliterative verse. The prose form of the 'mythology' began again from a new starting-point* in a quite brief synopsis, or 'Sketch' as he called it, written in 1926 and expressly intended to provide the necessary background of knowledge for the understanding of the alliterative poem. The further written development of the prose form proceeded from that 'Sketch' in a direct line to the version of 'The Silmarillion' which was nearing completion towards the end of 1937, when my father broke off to send it as it stood to Allen and Unwin in November of that year; but there were also important side-branches and subordinate texts composed in the 1930s, as the *Annals of Valinor* and the *Annals of Beleriand* (fragments of which are extant also in the Old English translations made by Ælfwine (Eriol)), the cosmological account called *Ambarkanta*, the

---

* Only in the case of *The Music of the Ainur* was there a direct development, manuscript to manuscript, from *The Book of Lost Tales* to the later forms; for *The Music of the Ainur* became separated off and continued as an independent work.

Shape of the World, by Rúmil, and the *Lhammas* or 'Account of Tongues', by Pengolod of Gondolin. Thereafter the history of the First Age was laid aside for many years, until *The Lord of the Rings* was completed, but in the years preceding its actual publication my father returned to 'The Silmarillion' and associated works with great vigour.

This edition of the *Lost Tales* in two parts is to be, as I hope, the beginning of a series that will carry the history further through these later writings, in verse and prose; and in this hope I have applied to this present book an 'overriding' title intended to cover also those that may follow it, though I fear that 'The History of Middle-earth' may turn out to have been over-ambitious. In any case this title does not imply a 'History' in the conventional sense: my intention is to give complete or largely complete texts, so that the books will be more like a series of editions. I do not set myself as a primary object the unravelling of many single and separate threads, but rather the making available of works that can and should be read as wholes.

The tracing of this long evolution is to me of deep interest, and I hope that it may prove so to others who have a taste for this kind of enquiry: whether the major transformations of plot or cosmological theory, or such a detail as the premonitory appearance of Legolas Greenleaf the keen-sighted in the tale of *The Fall of Gondolin*. But these old manuscripts are by no means of interest only for the study of origins. Much is to be found there that my father never (so far as one can tell) expressly rejected, and it is to be remembered that 'The Silmarillion', from the 1926 'Sketch' onwards, was written as an abridgement or epitome, giving the substance of much longer works (whether existing in fact, or not) in a smaller compass. The highly archaic manner devised for his purpose was no fustian: it had range and great vigour, peculiarly apt to convey the magical and eerie nature of the early Elves, but as readily turned to the sarcastic, sneering Melko or the affairs of Ulmo and Ossë. These last approach at times a comic conception, and are delivered in a rapid and lively language that did not survive in the gravity of my father's later 'Silmarillion' prose (so Ossë 'fares about in a foam of business' as he anchors the islands to the sea-bed, the cliffs of Tol Eressëa new-filled with the first sea-birds 'are full of a chattering and a smell of fish, and great conclaves are held upon its ledges', and when the Shoreland Elves are at last drawn over the sea to Valinor Ulmo marvellously 'fares at the rear in his fishy car and trumpets loudly for the discomfiture of Ossë').

The *Lost Tales* never reached or even approached a form in which my father could have considered their publication before he abandoned them; they were experimental and provisional, and the tattered notebooks in which they were written were bundled away and left unlooked at as the years passed. To present them in a printed book has raised many thorny editorial problems. In the first place, the manuscripts are intrinsically very difficult: partly because much of the text was written rapidly in pencil and is now in places extremely hard to read, requiring a magnifying glass and much patience, not always rewarded. But also in some of the *Tales* my father erased the original pencilled text and wrote a revised version over it in ink – and since at this period he used bound notebooks rather than loose sheets, he was liable to find himself short of space: so detached portions of tales were written in the middle of other tales, and in places a fearsome textual jigsaw puzzle was produced.

Secondly, the *Lost Tales* were not all written progressively one after the other in the sequence of the narrative; and (inevitably) my father began a new arrangement and revision of the *Tales* while the work was still in progress. *The Fall of Gondolin* was the first of the tales told to Eriol to be composed, and the *Tale of Tinúviel* the second, but the events of those tales take place towards the end of the history; on the other hand the extant texts are later revisions. In some cases nothing earlier than the revised form can now be read; in some both forms are extant for all, or a part, of their length; in some there is only a preliminary draft; and in some there is no formed narrative at all, but only notes and projections. After much experimentation I have found that no method of presentation is feasible but to set out the *Tales* in the sequence of the narrative.

And finally, as the writing of the *Tales* progressed, relations were changed, new conceptions entered, and the development of the languages *pari passu* with the narrative led to continual revision of names.

An edition that takes account of such complexities, as this does, rather than attempt to smooth them artificially away, is liable to be an intricate and crabbed thing, in which the reader is never left alone for a moment. I have attempted to make the *Tales* themselves accessible and uncluttered while providing a fairly full account, for those who want it, of the actual textual evidences. To achieve this I have drastically reduced the quantity of annotation to the texts in these ways: the many changes made to names are all recorded, but they are lumped together at the end of each tale, not recorded individually at each occurrence (the places where the names occur can be found from the Index); almost all annotation concerned with content is taken up into, or boiled down into, a commentary or short essay following each tale; and almost all linguistic comment (primarily the etymology of names) is collected in an Appendix on Names at the end of the book, where will be found a great deal of information relating to the earliest stages of the 'Elvish' languages. In this way the numbered notes are very largely restricted to variants and divergences found in other texts, and the reader who does not wish to trouble with these can read the *Tales* knowing that that is almost all that he is missing.

The commentaries are limited in their scope, being mostly concerned to discuss the implications of what is said within the context of the *Tales* themselves, and to compare them with the published *Silmarillion*. I have eschewed parallels, sources, influences; and have mostly avoided the complexities of the development between the *Lost Tales* and the published work (since to indicate these even cursorily would, I think, be distracting), treating the matter in a simplified way, as between two fixed points. I do not suppose for one moment that my analyses will prove either altogether just or altogether accurate, and there must be clues to the solution of puzzling features in the *Tales* which I have failed to observe. There is also included a short glossary of words occurring in the *Tales* and poems that are obsolete, archaic, or rare.

The texts are given in a form very close to that of the original manuscripts. Only the most minor and obvious slips have been silently corrected; where sentences fall awkwardly, or where there is a lack of grammatical cohesion, as is sometimes the case in the parts of the *Tales* that never got beyond a first rapid draft, I have let them stand. I have allowed myself greater freedom in providing punctuation, for my father when writing at speed often punctuated erratically or not at all; and I have gone further than he did in consistency of capitalisation. I have adopted, though hesitantly, a consistent system of accentuation for Elvish names. My father wrote, for instance: *Palúrien, Palúrien, Palurien*; *Ōnen, Onen*; *Kôr, Kor*. I have used the acute accent for macron, circumflex, and acute (and occasional grave) accents of the original texts, but the circumflex on monosyllables – thus *Palúrien, Ónen, Kôr*: the same system, at least to the eye, as in later Sindarin.

Lastly, the division of this edition into two parts is entirely due to the length of the *Tales*. The edition is conceived as a whole, and I hope that the second part will appear within a year of the first; but each part has its own Index and Appendix on Names. The second part contains what are in many respects the most interesting of the *Tales*: *Tinúviel, Turambar* (Túrin), *The Fall of Gondolin*, and the *Tale of the Nauglafring* (the Necklace of the Dwarves); outlines for the *Tale of Eärendel* and the conclusion of the work; and *Ælfwine of England*.

# I

# THE COTTAGE OF LOST PLAY

On the cover of one of the now very battered 'High School Exercise Books' in which some of the *Lost Tales* were composed my father wrote: *The Cottage of Lost Play, which introduceth [the] Book of Lost Tales*; and on the cover is also written, in my mother's hand, her initials, E.M.T., and a date, Feb. 12th 1917. In this book the tale was written out by my mother; and it is a fair copy of a very rough pencilled manuscript of my father's on loose sheets, which were placed inside the cover. Thus the date of the actual composition of this tale could have been, but probably was not, earlier than the winter of 1916–17. The fair copy follows the original text precisely; some further changes, mostly slight (other than in the matter of names), were then made to the fair copy. The text follows here in its final form.

Now it happened on a certain time that a traveller from far countries, a man of great curiosity, was by desire of strange lands and the ways and dwellings of unaccustomed folk brought in a ship as far west even as the Lonely Island, Tol Eressëa in the fairy speech, but which the Gnomes[1] call Dor Faidwen, the Land of Release, and a great tale hangs thereto.

Now one day after much journeying he came as the lights of evening were being kindled in many a window to the feet of a hill in a broad and woody plain. He was now near the centre of this great island and for many days had wandered its roads, stopping each night at what dwelling of folk he might chance upon, were it hamlet or good town, about the hour of eve at the kindling of candles. Now at that time the desire of new sights is least, even in one whose heart is that of an explorer; and then even such a son of Eärendel as was this wayfarer turns his thoughts rather to supper and to rest and the telling of tales before the time of bed and sleep is come.

Now as he stood at the foot of the little hill there came a faint breeze and then a flight of rooks above his head in the clear even light. The sun had some time sunk beyond the boughs of the elms that stood as far as eye could look about the plain, and some time had its last gold faded through the leaves and slipped across the glades to sleep beneath the roots and dream till dawn.

Now these rooks gave voice of home-coming above him, and with a swift turn came to their dwelling in the tops of some high elms at the summit of this hill. Then thought Eriol (for thus did the people of the island after call him, and its purport is 'One who dreams alone', but of his former names the story nowhere tells): 'The hour of rest is at hand, and though I know not even the name of this fair-seeming town upon a little hill here I will seek rest and lodging and go no further till the morrow, nor go even then perchance, for the place seems fair and its breezes of a good savour. To me it has the air of holding many secrets of old and wonderful and beautiful things in its treasuries and noble places and in the hearts of those that dwell within its walls.'

Now Eriol was coming from the south and a straight road ran before him bordered at one side with a great wall of grey stone topped with many flowers, or in places overhung with great dark yews. Through them as he climbed the road he could see the first stars shine forth, even as he afterwards sang in the song which he made to that fair city.

Now was he at the summit of the hill amidst its houses, and stepping as if by chance he turned aside down a winding lane, till, a little down the western slope of the hill, his eye was arrested by a tiny dwelling whose many small windows were curtained snugly, yet only so that a most warm and delicious light, as of hearts content within, looked forth. Then his heart yearned for kind company, and the desire for wayfaring died in him – and impelled by a great longing he turned aside at this cottage door, and knocking asked one who came and opened what might be the name of this house and who dwelt therein. And it was said to him that this was Mar Vanwa Tyaliéva, or the Cottage of Lost Play, and at that name he wondered greatly. There dwelt within, 'twas said, Lindo and Vairë who had built it many years ago, and with them were no few of their folk and friends and children. And at this he wondered more than before, seeing the size of the cottage; but he that opened to him, perceiving his mind, said: 'Small is the dwelling, but smaller still are they that dwell here – for all who enter must be very small indeed, or of their own good wish become as very little folk even as they stand upon the threshold.'

Then said Eriol that he would dearly desire to come therein and seek of Vairë and Lindo a night's guest-kindliness, if so they would, and if he might of his own good wish become small enough there upon the threshold. Then said the other, 'Enter', and Eriol stepped in, and behold, it seemed a house of great spaciousness and very great delight, and the lord of it, Lindo, and his wife, Vairë, came forth to greet him; and his heart was more glad within him than it had yet been in all his wanderings, albeit since his landing in the Lonely Isle his joy had been great enough.

And when Vairë had spoken the words of welcome, and Lindo had asked of him his name and whence he came and whither he might be seeking, and he had named himself the Stranger and said that he came from the Great Lands,[2] and that he was seeking whitherso his desire for travel led him, then was the evening meal set out in the great hall and Eriol bidden thereto. Now in this hall despite the summertide were three great fires – one at the far end and one on either side of the table, and save for their light as Eriol entered all was in a warm gloom. But at that moment many folk came in bearing candles of all sizes and many shapes in sticks of strange pattern: many were of carven wood and others of beaten metal, and these were set at hazard about the centre table and upon those at the sides.

At that same moment a great gong sounded far off in the house with a sweet noise, and a sound followed as of the laughter of many voices mingled with a great pattering of feet. Then Vairë said to Eriol, seeing his face filled with a happy wonderment: 'That is the voice of Tombo, the Gong of the Children, which stands outside the Hall of Play Regained, and it rings once to summon them to this hall at the times for eating and drinking, and three times to summon them to the Room of the Log Fire for the telling of tales,' and added Lindo: 'If at his ringing once there be laughter in the corridors and a sound of feet, then do the walls shake with mirth and stamping at the three strokes in an evening. And the sounding of the three strokes is the happiest moment in the day of Littleheart the Gong-warden, as he himself declares who has known happiness enough of old; and ancient indeed is he beyond count in spite of his merriness of soul. He sailed in Wingilot with Eärendel in that last voyage wherein they sought for Kôr. It was the ringing of this Gong on the Shadowy Seas that awoke the Sleeper in the Tower of Pearl that stands far out to west in the Twilit Isles.'

To these words did Eriol's mind so lean, for it seemed to him that a new world and very fair was opening to him, that he heard naught else till he was bidden by Vairë to be seated. Then he looked up, and lo, the hall and all its benches and chairs were filled with children of every aspect, kind, and size, while sprinkled among them were folk of all manners and ages. In one thing only were all alike, that a look of great happiness lit with a merry expectation of further mirth and joy lay on every face. The soft light of candles too was upon them all; it shone on bright tresses and gleamed about dark hair, or here and there set a pale fire in locks gone grey. Even as he gazed all arose and with one voice sang the song of the Bringing in of the Meats. Then was the food brought in and set before them, and thereafter the bearers and those that served and those that waited, host and hostess, children and guest, sat down: but Lindo first blessed both food and company. As they ate Eriol fell into speech with Lindo and his wife, telling them tales of his old days and of his adventures, especially those he had encountered upon the journey that had brought him to the Lonely Isle, and asking in return many things concerning the fair land, and most of all of that fair city wherein he now found himself.

Lindo said to him: 'Know then that today, or more like 'twas yesterday, you crossed the borders of that region that is called Alalminórë or the "Land of Elms", which the Gnomes call Gar Lossion, or the "Place of Flowers". Now this region is accounted the centre of the island, and its fairest realm; but above all the towns and villages of Alalminórë is held Koromas, or as some call it, Kortirion, and this city is the one wherein you now find yourself. Both because it stands at the heart of the island, and from the height of its mighty tower, do those that speak of it with love call it the Citadel of the Island, or of the World itself. More reason is there thereto than even great love, for all the island looks to the dwellers here for wisdom and leadership, for song and lore; and here in a great *korin* of elms dwells Meril-i-Turinqi. (Now a *korin* is a great circular hedge, be it of stone or of thorn or even of trees, that encloses a green sward.) Meril comes of the blood of Inwë, whom the Gnomes call Inwithiel, he that was King of all the Eldar when they dwelt in Kôr. That was in the days before hearing the lament of the world Inwë led them forth to the lands of Men: but those great and sad things and how the Eldar came to this fair and lonely island, maybe I will tell them another time.

'But after many days Ingil son of Inwë, seeing this place to be very fair, rested here and about him gathered most of the fairest and the wisest, most of the merriest and the kindest, of all the Eldar.[3] Here among those many came my father Valwë who went with Noldorin to find the Gnomes, and the father of Vairë my wife, Tulkastor. He was of Aulë's kindred, but had dwelt long with the Shoreland Pipers, the Solosimpi, and so came among the earliest to the island.

'Then Ingil builded the great tower[4] and called the town Koromas, or "the Resting of the Exiles of Kôr", but by reason of that tower it is now mostly called Kortirion.'

Now about this time they drew nigh the end of the meal; then did Lindo fill his cup and after him Vairë and all those in the hall, but to Eriol he said: 'Now this which we put into our cups is *limpë*, the drink of the Eldar both young and old, and drinking, our hearts keep youth and our mouths grow full of song, but this drink I may not administer: Turinqi only may give it to those not of the Eldar race, and those that drink must dwell always with the Eldar of the Island until such time as they fare forth to find the lost families of the kindred.' Then he filled Eriol's cup, but filled it with golden wine from ancient casks of the Gnomes; and then all rose and drank 'to the Faring Forth and the Rekindling of the Magic Sun'. Then sounded the Gong of the Children thrice, and a glad clamour arose in the hall, and some swung back big oaken doors at the hall's end – at that end which had no hearth. Then many seized those candles that were set in tall wooden sticks and held them aloft while others laughed and chattered, but all made a lane midmost of the company down which went Lindo and Vairë and Eriol, and as they passed the doors the throng followed them.

Eriol saw now that they were in a short broad corridor whose walls half-way up were arrassed; and on those tapestries were many stories pictured whereof he knew not at that time the purport. Above the tapestries it seemed there were paintings, but he could not see for gloom, for the candle-bearers were behind, and before him the only light came from an open door through which poured a red glow as of a big fire. 'That,' said Vairë, 'is the Tale-fire blazing in the Room of Logs; there does it burn all through the year, for 'tis a magic fire, and greatly aids the teller in his tale – but thither we now go,' and Eriol said that that seemed better to him than aught else.

Then all that company came laughing and talking into the room whence came the red glow. A fair room it was as might be felt even by the fire-flicker which danced upon the walls and low ceiling, while deep shadows lay in the nooks and corners. Round the great hearth was a multitude of soft rugs and yielding cushions strewn; and a little to one side was a deep chair with carven arms and feet. And so it was that Eriol felt at that time and at all others whereon he entered there at the hour of tale-telling, that whatso the number of the folk and children the room felt ever just great enough but not large, small enough but not overthronged.

Then all sat them down where they would, old and young, but Lindo in the deep chair and Vairë upon a cushion at his feet, and Eriol rejoicing in the red blaze for all that it was summer stretched nigh the hearthstone.

Then said Lindo: 'Of what shall the tales be tonight? Shall they be of the Great Lands, and of the dwellings of Men; of the Valar and Valinor; of the West and its mysteries, of the East and its glory, of the South and its untrodden wilds, of the North and its power and strength; or of this island and its folk; or of the old days of Kôr where our folk once dwelt? For that this night we entertain a guest, a man of great and excellent travel, a son meseems of Eärendel, shall it be of voyaging, of beating about in a boat, of winds and the sea?'[5]

But to this questioning some answered one thing and some another, till Eriol said: 'I pray you, if it be to the mind of the others, for this time tell me of this island, and of all this island most eagerly would I learn of this goodly house and this fair company of maids and boys, for of all houses this seems to me the most lovely and of all gatherings the sweetest I have gazed upon.'

Then said Vairë: 'Know then that aforetime, in the days of[6] Inwë (and farther back it is hard to go in the history of the Eldar), there was a place of fair gardens in Valinor beside a silver sea. Now this place was near the confines of the realm but not far from Kôr, yet by reason of its distance from the sun-tree Lindelos there was a light there as of summer evening, save only when the silver lamps were kindled on the hill at dusk, and then little lights of white would dance and quiver on the paths, chasing black shadow-dapples under the trees. This was a time of joy to the children, for it was mostly at this hour that a new comrade would come down the lane called Olórë Mallë or the Path of Dreams. It has been said to me, though the truth I know not, that that lane ran by devious routes to the homes of Men, but that way we never trod when we fared thither ourselves. It was a lane of deep banks and great overhanging hedges, beyond which stood many tall trees wherein a perpetual whisper seemed to live; but not seldom great glow-worms crept about its grassy borders.

'Now in this place of gardens a high gate of lattice-work that shone golden in the dusk opened upon the lane of dreams, and from there led winding paths of high box to the fairest of all the gardens, and amidmost of the garden stood a white cottage. Of what it was built, nor when, no one knew, nor now knows, but it was said to me that it shone with a pale light, as it was of pearl, and its roof was a thatch, but a thatch of gold.

'Now on one side of the cot stood a thicket of white lilac and at the other end a mighty yew, from whose shoots the children fashioned bows or clambered by his branches upon the roof. But in the lilacs every bird that ever sang sweetly gathered and sang. Now the walls

of the cottage were bent with age and its many small lattice windows
were twisted into strange shapes. No one, 'tis said, dwelt in the
cottage, which was however guarded secretly and jealously by the
Eldar so that no harm came nigh it, and that yet might the children
playing therein in freedom know of no guardianship. This was the
Cottage of the Children, or of the Play of Sleep, and not of Lost
Play, as has wrongly been said in song among Men – for no play was
lost then, and here alas only and now is the Cottage of Lost Play.

'These too were the earliest children – the children of the fathers
of the fathers of Men that came there; and for pity the Eldar sought
to guide all who came down that lane into the cottage and the garden,
lest they strayed into Kôr and became enamoured of the glory of
Valinor; for then would they either stay there for ever, and great
grief fall on their parents, or would they wander back and long for
ever vainly, and become strange and wild among the children of
Men. Nay, some even who wandered on to the edge of the rocks of
Eldamar and there strayed, dazzled by the fair shells and the fishes
of many colours, the blue pools and the silver foam, they drew back
to the cottage, alluring them gently with the odour of many flowers.
Yet even so there were a few who heard on that beach the sweet
piping of the Solosimpi afar off and who played not with the other
children but climbed to the upper windows and gazed out, straining
to see the far glimpses of the sea and the magic shores beyond the
shadows and the trees.

'Now for the most part the children did not often go into the house,
but danced and played in the garden, gathering flowers or chasing
the golden bees and butterflies with embroidered wings that the
Eldar set within the garden for their joy. And many children have
there become comrades, who after met and loved in the lands of
Men, but of such things perchance Men know more than I can tell
you. Yet some there were who, as I have told, heard the Solosimpi
piping afar off, or others who straying again beyond the garden
caught a sound of the singing of the Telelli on the hill, and even
some who reaching Kôr afterwards returned home, and their minds
and hearts were full of wonder. Of the misty aftermemories of these,
of their broken tales and snatches of song, came many strange legends
that delighted Men for long, and still do, it may be; for of such were
the poets of the Great Lands.[7]

'Now when the fairies left Kôr that lane was blocked for ever
with great impassable rocks, and there stands of a surety the cottage
empty and the garden bare to this day, and will do until long after
the Faring Forth, when if all goes well the roads through Arvalin

to Valinor shall be thronged with the sons and daughters of Men. But seeing that no children came there for refreshment and delight, sorrow and greyness spread amongst them and Men ceased almost to believe in, or think of, the beauty of the Eldar and the glory of the Valar, till one came from the Great Lands and besought us to relieve the darkness.

'Now there is alas no safe way for children from the Great Lands hither, but Meril-i-Turinqi hearkened to his boon and chose Lindo my husband to devise some plan of good. Now Lindo and I, Vairë, had taken under our care the children – the remainder of those who found Kôr and remained with the Eldar for ever: and so here we builded of good magic this Cottage of Lost Play: and here old tales, old songs, and elfin music are treasured and rehearsed. Ever and anon our children fare forth again to find the Great Lands, and go about among the lonely children and whisper to them at dusk in early bed by night-light and candle-flame, or comfort those that weep. Some I am told listen to the complaints of those that are punished or chidden, and hear their tales and feign to take their part, and this seems to me a quaint and merry service.

'Yet all whom we send return not and that is great grief to us, for it is by no means out of small love that the Eldar held children from Kôr, but rather of thought for the homes of Men; yet in the Great Lands, as you know well, there are fair places and lovely regions of much allurement, wherefore it is only for the great necessity that we adventure any of the children that are with us. Yet the most come back hither and tell us many stories and many sad things of their journeys – and now I have told most of what is to tell of the Cottage of Lost Play.'

Then Eriol said: 'Now these are tidings sad and yet good to hear, and I remember me of certain words that my father spake in my early boyhood. It had long, said he, been a tradition in our kindred that one of our father's fathers would speak of a fair house and magic gardens, of a wondrous town, and of a music full of all beauty and longing – and these things he said he had seen and heard as a child, though how and where was not told. Now all his life was he restless, as if a longing half-expressed for unknown things dwelt within him; and 'tis said that he died among rocks on a lonely coast on a night of storm – and moreover that most of his children and their children since have been of a restless mind – and methinks I know now the truth of the matter.'

And Vairë said that 'twas like to be that one of his kindred had found the rocks of Eldamar in those old days.

## NOTES

1 *Gnomes*: the Second Kindred, the *Noldoli* (later *Noldor*). For the use of the word *Gnomes* see p. 43; and for the linguistic distinction made here see pp. 50–1.

2 The 'Great Lands' are the lands East of the Great Sea. The term 'Middle-earth' is never used in the *Lost Tales*, and in fact does not appear until writings of the 1930s.

3 In both MSS the words 'of all the Eldar' are followed by: 'for of most noble there were none, seeing that to be of the blood of the Eldar is equal and sufficient'; but this was struck out in the second MS.

4 The original reading was 'the great Tirion', changed to 'the great tower'.

5 This sentence, from 'a son meseems . . .', replaced in the original MS an earlier reading: 'shall it be of Eärendel the wanderer, who alone of the sons of Men has had great traffic with the Valar and Elves, who alone of their kindred has seen beyond Taniquetil, even he who sails for ever in the firmament?'

6 The original reading was 'before the days of', changed to 'in the first days of', and then to the reading given.

7 This last phrase was an addition to the second MS.

### Changes made to names in
*The Cottage of Lost Play*

The names were at this time in a very fluid state, reflecting in part the rapid development of the languages that was then taking place. Changes were made to the original text, and further changes, at different times, to the second text, but it seems unnecessary in the following notes to go into the detail of when and where the changes were made. The names are given in the order of their occurrence in the tale. The signs 〉 and 〈 are used to mean 'changed to' and 'changed from'.

*Dor Faidwen* The Gnomish name of Tol Eressëa was changed many times: *Gar Eglos* 〉 *Dor Edloth* 〉 *Dor Usgwen* 〉 *Dor Uswen* 〉 *Dor Faidwen*.

*Mar Vanwa Tyaliéva* In the original text a space was left for the Elvish name, subsequently filled in as *Mar Vanwa Taliéva*.

*Great Lands* Throughout the tale *Great Lands* is an emendation of *Outer Lands*, when the latter was given a different meaning (lands West of the Great Sea).

*Wingilot* 〈 *Wingelot*.

*Gar Lossion* 〈 *Losgar*.

*Koromas* ⟨ *Kormas.*
*Meril-i-Turinqi*  The first text has only *Turinqi*, with in one place a space left for a personal name.
*Inwë* ⟨ *Ing* at each occurrence.
*Inwithiel* ⟨ *Gim Githil*, which was in turn ⟨ *Githil.*
*Ingil* ⟨ *Ingilmo.*
*Valwë* ⟨ *Manwë.* It seems possible that *Manwë* as the name of Lindo's father was a mere slip.
*Noldorin*  The original reading was *Noldorin whom the Gnomes name Goldriel*; *Goldriel* was changed to *Golthadriel*, and then the reference to the Gnomish name was struck out, leaving only *Noldorin.*
*Tulkastor* ⟨ *Tulkassë* ⟨ *Turenbor.*
*Solosimpi* ⟨ *Solosimpë* at each occurrence.
*Lindelos* ⟨ *Lindeloksë* ⟨ *Lindelokte Singing Cluster (Glingol).*
*Telelli* ⟨ *Telellë.*
*Arvalin* ⟨ *Harmalin* ⟨ *Harwalin.*


## Commentary on
## *The Cottage of Lost Play*

The story of Eriol the mariner was central to my father's original conception of the mythology. In those days, as he recounted long after in a letter to his friend Milton Waldman,* the primary intention of his work was to satisfy his desire for a specifically and recognizably *English* literature of 'faerie':

> I was from early days grieved by the poverty of my own beloved country: it had no stories of its own (bound up with its tongue and soil), not of the quality that I sought, and found (as an ingredient) in legends of other lands. There was Greek, and Celtic, and Romance, Germanic, Scandinavian, and Finnish (which greatly affected me); but nothing English, save impoverished chap-book stuff.

In his earliest writings the mythology was anchored in the ancient legendary history of England; and more than that, it was peculiarly associated with certain places in England.

Eriol, himself close kin of famous figures in the legends of North-western Europe, came at last on a voyage westward over the ocean to Tol Eressëa, the Lonely Isle, where Elves dwelt; and from them he learned 'The Lost Tales of Elfinesse'. But his rôle was at first to be more important in the structure of the work than (what it afterwards became) simply that of a man of later days who came to 'the land of the Fairies' and there acquired

---

* *The Letters of J. R. R. Tolkien*, ed. Humphrey Carpenter, 1981, p. 144. The letter was almost certainly written in 1951.

lost or hidden knowledge, which he afterwards reported in his own tongue: at first, Eriol was to be an important element in the fairy-history itself – the witness of the ruin of Elvish Tol Eressëa. The element of ancient English history or 'historical legend' was at first not merely a framework, isolated from the great tales that afterwards constituted 'The Silmarillion', but an integral part of their ending. The elucidation of all this (so far as elucidation is possible) must necessarily be postponed to the end of the *Tales*; but here something at least must be said of the history of Eriol up to the time of his coming to Tol Eressëa, and of the original significance of the Lonely Isle.

The 'Eriol-story' is in fact among the knottiest and most obscure matters in the whole history of Middle-earth and Aman. My father abandoned the writing of the *Lost Tales* before he reached their end, and when he abandoned them he had also abandoned his original ideas for their conclusion. Those ideas can indeed be discerned from his notes; but the notes were for the most part pencilled at furious speed, the writing now rubbed and faint and in places after long study scarcely decipherable, on little slips of paper, disordered and dateless, or in a little notebook in which, during the years when he was composing the *Lost Tales*, he jotted down thoughts and suggestions (see p. 171). The common form of these notes on the 'Eriol' or 'English' element is that of short outlines, in which salient narrative features, often without clear connection between them, are set down in the manner of a list; and they vary constantly among themselves.

In what must be, at any rate, among the very earliest of these outlines, found in this little pocket-book, and headed 'Story of Eriol's Life', the mariner who came to Tol Eressëa is brought into relation with the tradition of the invasion of Britain by Hengest and Horsa in the fifth century A.D. This was a matter to which my father gave much time and thought; he lectured on it at Oxford and developed certain original theories, especially in connection with the appearance of Hengest in *Beowulf*.*

From these jottings we learn that Eriol's original name was *Ottor*, but that he called himself *Wǽfre* (an Old English word meaning 'restless, wandering') and lived a life on the waters. His father was named *Eoh* (a word of the Old English poetic vocabulary meaning 'horse'); and Eoh was slain by his brother *Beorn* (in Old English 'warrior', but originally meaning 'bear', as does the cognate word *björn* in Old Norse; cf. Beorn the shape-changer in *The Hobbit*). Eoh and Beorn were the sons of *Heden* 'the leather and fur clad', and Heden (like many heroes of Northern legend) traced his ancestry to the god Wóden. In other notes there are other connections and combinations, and since none of this story was written as a coherent narrative these names are only of significance as showing the direction of my father's thought at that time.

Ottor Wǽfre settled on the island of Heligoland in the North Sea, and

* J. R. R. Tolkien, *Finn and Hengest*, ed. Alan Bliss, 1982.

he wedded a woman named *Cwén* (Old English: 'woman', 'wife'); they had two sons named 'after his father' *Hengest* and *Horsa* 'to avenge Eoh' (*hengest* is another Old English word for 'horse').

Then sea-longing gripped Ottor Wǽfre: he was a son of *Eärendel*, born under his beam. If a beam from Eärendel fall on a child new-born he becomes 'a child of Eärendel' and a wanderer. (So also in *The Cottage of Lost Play* Eriol is called both by the author and by Lindo a 'son of Eärendel'.) After the death of Cwén Ottor left his young children. Hengest and Horsa avenged Eoh and became great chieftains; but Ottor Wǽfre set out to seek, and find, Tol Eressëa, here called in Old English *se uncúþa holm*, 'the unknown island'.

Various things are told in these notes about Eriol's sojourn in Tol Eressëa which do not appear in *The Book of Lost Tales*, but of these I need here only refer to the statements that 'Eriol adopted the name of *Angol*' and that he was named by the Gnomes (the later Noldor, see below p. 43) *Angol* 'after the regions of his home'. This certainly refers to the ancient homeland of the 'English' before their migration across the North Sea to Britain: Old English *Angel, Angul*, modern German *Angeln*, the region of the Danish peninsula between the Flensburg fjord and the river Schlei, south of the modern Danish frontier. From the west coast of the peninsula it is no very great distance to the island of Heligoland.

In another place *Angol* is given as the Gnomish equivalent of *Eriollo*, which names are said to be those of 'the region of the northern part of the Great Lands, "between the seas", whence Eriol came'. (On these names see further under *Eriol* in the Appendix on Names.)

It is not to be thought that these notes represent in all respects the story of Eriol as my father conceived it when he wrote *The Cottage of Lost Play* – in any case, it is said expressly there that *Eriol* means 'One who dreams alone', and that 'of his former names the story nowhere tells' (p. 14). But what is important is that (according to the view that I have formed of the earliest conceptions, apparently the best explanation of the very difficult evidence) this was still the leading idea when it was written: *Eriol came to Tol Eressëa from the lands to the East of the North Sea*. He belongs to the period preceding the Anglo-Saxon invasions of Britain (as my father, for his purposes, wished to represent it).

Later, his name changed to *Ælfwine* ('Elf-friend'), the mariner became an Englishman of the 'Anglo-Saxon period' of English history, who sailed west over sea to Tol Eressëa – he sailed from England out into the Atlantic Ocean; and from this later conception comes the very remarkable story of *Ælfwine of England*, which will be given at the end of the *Lost Tales*. But in the earliest conception he was not an Englishman of England: England in the sense of the land of the English did not yet exist; for the cardinal fact (made quite explicit in extant notes) of this conception is that *the Elvish isle to which Eriol came was England* – that is to say, Tol Eressëa would become England, the land of the English, at the end of the story. Koromas or Kortirion, the town in the centre of Tol Eressëa to which Eriol comes in *The Cottage of Lost Play*, would become in after days Warwick (and the elements *Kor-* and *War-* were etymologically connected);* Alalminórë, the Land of Elms, would be Warwickshire; and Tavrobel, where Eriol sojourned for a while in Tol Eressëa, would afterwards be the Staffordshire village of Great Haywood.

None of this is explicit in the written *Tales*, and is only found in notes independent of them; but it seems certain that it was still present when *The Cottage of Lost Play* was written (and indeed, as I shall try to show later, underlies all the *Tales*). The fair copy that my mother made of it was dated February 1917. From 1913 until her marriage in March 1916 she lived in Warwick and my father visited her there from Oxford; after their marriage she lived for a while at Great Haywood (east of Stafford), since it was near the camp where my father was stationed, and after his return from France he was at Great Haywood in the winter of 1916–17. Thus the identification of Tol Eressëan Tavrobel with Great Haywood cannot be earlier than 1916, and the fair copy of *The Cottage of Lost Play* (and quite possibly the original composition of it) was actually done there.

In November 1915 my father wrote a poem entitled *Kortirion among the Trees* which was dedicated to Warwick.† To the first fair copy of the poem there is appended a prose introduction, as follows:

Now on a time the fairies dwelt in the Lonely Isle after the great wars with Melko and the ruin of Gondolin; and they builded a fair city amidmost of that island, and it was girt with trees. Now this city they called Kortirion, both in memory of their ancient dwelling of Kôr in Valinor, and because this city stood also upon a hill and had a great tower tall and grey that Ingil son of Inwë their lord let raise.

Very beautiful was Kortirion and the fairies loved it, and it became rich in song and poesy and the light of laughter; but on a time the great Faring Forth was made, and the fairies had rekindled once more the Magic Sun of Valinor but for the treason and faint hearts of Men. But so it is that the Magic Sun is dead and the Lonely Isle drawn back unto the confines of the Great Lands, and the fairies are scattered through all the wide unfriendly pathways of the world; and now Men dwell even on this faded isle, and care nought or know nought of its ancient days. Yet still there be some of the Eldar and the Noldoli‡ of old who linger in the island, and their songs are heard about the shores of the land that once was the fairest dwelling of the immortal folk.

* The great tower or *tirion* that Ingil son of Inwe built (p. 16) and the great tower of Warwick Castle are not identified, but at least it is certain that Koromas had a great tower because Warwick has one.

† This poem is given, in three different texts, on pp. 33–43. – A poem written at Étaples in the Pas de Calais in June 1916 and entitled 'The Lonely Isle' is explicitly addressed to England. See *Letters*, p. 437, note 4 to letter 43.

‡ For the distinction between *Eldar* and *Noldoli* see pp. 50–1.

And it seems to the fairies and it seems to me who know that town
and have often trodden its disfigured ways that autumn and the falling
of the leaf is the season of the year when maybe here or there a heart
among Men may be open, and an eye perceive how is the world's estate
fallen from the laughter and the loveliness of old. Think on Kortirion
and be sad – yet is there not hope?

Both here and in *The Cottage of Lost Play* there are allusions to events
still in the future when Eriol came to Tol Eressëa; and though the full
exposition and discussion of them must wait until the end of the *Tales*
it needs to be explained here that 'the Faring Forth' was a great expedition
made from Tol Eressëa for the rescue of the Elves who were still wandering
in the Great Lands – cf. Lindo's words (p. 17): 'until such time as they
fare forth to find the lost families of the kindred'. At that time Tol Eressëa
was uprooted, by the aid of Ulmo, from the sea-bottom and dragged near
to the western shores of the Great Lands. In the battle that followed the
Elves were defeated, and fled into hiding in Tol Eressëa; Men entered the
isle, and the fading of the Elves began. The subsequent history of Tol
Eressëa is the history of England; and Warwick is 'disfigured Kortirion',
itself a memory of ancient Kôr (the later Tirion upon Túna, city of the
Elves in Aman; in the *Lost Tales* the name Kôr is used both of the city
and the hill).

Inwë, referred to in *The Cottage of Lost Play* as 'King of all the Eldar
when they dwelt in Kôr', is the forerunner of Ingwë King of the Vanyar
Elves in *The Silmarillion*. In a story told later to Eriol in Tol Eressëa
Inwë reappears as one of the three Elves who went first to Valinor after
the Awakening, as was Ingwë in *The Silmarillion*; his kindred and descendants were the *Inwir*, of whom came Meril-i-Turinqi, the Lady of Tol
Eressëa (see p. 50). Lindo's references to Inwë's hearing 'the lament of
the world' (i.e. of the Great Lands) and to his leading the Eldar forth to
the lands of Men (p. 16) are the germ of the story of the coming of the
Hosts of the West to the assault on Thangorodrim: 'The host of the Valar
prepared for battle; and beneath their white banners marched the Vanyar,
the people of Ingwë . . .' (*The Silmarillion*, p. 251). Later in the *Tales* it is
said to Eriol by Meril-i-Turinqi that 'Inwë was the eldest of the Elves,
and had lived yet in majesty had he not perished in that march into the
world; but Ingil his son went long ago back to Valinor and is with Manwë'.
In *The Silmarillion*, on the other hand, it is said of Ingwë that 'he entered
into Valinor [in the beginning of the days of the Elves] and sits at the feet
of the Powers, and all Elves revere his name; but he came never back, nor
looked again upon Middle-earth' (p. 53).

Lindo's words about the sojourn of Ingil in Tol Eressëa 'after many
days', and the interpretation of the name of his town Koromas as 'the
Resting of the Exiles of Kôr', refer to the return of the Eldar from the
Great Lands after the war on Melko (Melkor, Morgoth) for the deliverance
of the enslaved Noldoli. His words about his father Valwë 'who went with

Noldorin to find the Gnomes' refer to an element in this story of the expedition from Kôr.*

It is important to see, then, that (if my general interpretation is correct) in *The Cottage of Lost Play* Eriol comes to Tol Eressëa *in the time after* the Fall of Gondolin and the march of the Elves of Kôr into the Great Lands for the defeat of Melko, when the Elves who had taken part in it had returned over the sea to dwell in Tol Eressëa; but *before the time* of the 'Faring Forth' and the removal of Tol Eressëa to the geographical position of England. This latter element was soon lost in its entirety from the developing mythology.

★

Of the 'Cottage' itself it must be said at once that very little light can be cast on it from other writings of my father's; for the entire conception of the Children who went to Valinor was to be abandoned almost without further trace. Later in the *Lost Tales*, however, there are again references to Olóre Mallë. After the description of the Hiding of Valinor, it is told that at the bidding of Manwë (who looked on the event with sorrow) the Valar Oromë and Lórien devised strange paths from the Great Lands to Valinor, and the way of Lórien's devising was Olórë Mallë, the Path of Dreams; by this road, when 'Men were yet but new-wakened on the earth', 'the children of the fathers of the fathers of Men' came to Valinor in their sleep (pp. 211, 213). There are two further mentions in tales to be given in Part II: the teller of the *Tale of Tinúviel* (a child of Mar Vanwa Tyaliéva) says that she saw Tinúviel and her mother with her own eyes 'when journeying by the Way of Dreams in long past days', and the teller of the *Tale of Turambar* says that he 'trod Olórë Mallë in the days before the fall of Gondolin'.

There is also a poem on the subject of the Cottage of Lost Play, which has many of the details of the description in the prose text. This poem, according to my father's notes, was composed at 59 St John's Street, Oxford, his undergraduate lodgings, on 27–28 April 1915 (when he was 23). It exists (as is constantly the case with the poems) in several versions, each modified in detail from the preceding one, and the end of the poem was twice entirely rewritten. I give it here first in the earliest form, with changes made to this in notes at the foot of the page, and then in the final version, the date of which cannot be certainly determined. I suspect that it was very much later – and may indeed have been one of the revisions made to old poems when the collection *The Adventures of Tom Bombadil* (1962) was being prepared, though it is not mentioned in my father's correspondence on that subject.

The original title was: *You and Me | and the Cottage of Lost Play* (with

---

* A little light on Lindo's references to the ringing of the Gong on the Shadowy Seas and the Sleeper in the Tower of Pearl will be shed when the story of Eärendel is reached at the end of the *Tales*.

an Old English rendering *Þæt húsincel ǽrran gamenes*), which was changed
to *Mar Vanwa Tyaliéva, The Cottage of Lost Play*; in the final version it
is *The Little House of Lost Play: Mar Vanwa Tyaliéva.* The verse-lines
are indented as in the original texts.

You & Me
and the Cottage of Lost Play

You and me – we know that land
  And often have been there
In the long old days, old nursery days,
  A dark child and a fair.
5  Was it down the paths of firelight dreams
  In winter cold and white,
Or in the blue-spun twilit hours
Of little early tucked-up beds
  In drowsy summer night,
10  That You and I got lost in Sleep
  And met each other there –
Your dark hair on your white nightgown,
  And mine was tangled fair?

We wandered shyly hand in hand,
15    Or rollicked in the fairy sand
And gathered pearls and shells in pails,
    While all about the nightingales
    Were singing in the trees.
We dug for silver with our spades
20    By little inland sparkling seas,
Then ran ashore through sleepy glades
  And down a warm and winding lane
  We never never found again
    Between high whispering trees.

25  The air was neither night or day,
    But faintly dark with softest light,
When first there glimmered into sight
    The Cottage of Lost Play.
'Twas builded very very old
30    White, and thatched with straws of gold,
  And pierced with peeping lattices
    That looked toward the sea;

 1  You and I
 3  In the long old days, the shining days,
15  in the golden sand
23  That now we cannot find again
25  night nor day
29  New-built it was, yet very old,

And our own children's garden-plots
Were there – our own forgetmenots,
35          Red daisies, cress and mustard,
And blue nemophilë.
O! all the borders trimmed with box
Were full of favourite flowers – of phlox,
Of larkspur, pinks, and hollyhocks
40          Beneath a red may-tree:
And all the paths were full of shapes,
Of tumbling happy white-clad shapes,
And with them You and Me.
And some had silver watering-cans
45          And watered all their gowns,
Or sprayed each other; some laid plans
To build them houses, fairy towns,
Or dwellings in the trees;
And some were clambering on the roof;
50          Some crooning lonely and aloof;
And some were dancing fairy-rings
And weaving pearly daisy-strings,
Or chasing golden bees;
But here and there a little pair
55          With rosy cheeks and tangled hair
Debated quaint old childish things – *
And we were one of these.

37   And all the borders
43   That laughed with You and Me.
47   little towns
56   Debated ancient childish things

Lines 58–65 (p. 30) were subsequently rewritten:

But why it was there came a time
When we could take the road no more,
Though long we looked, and high would climb,
Or gaze from many a seaward shore
To find the path between sea and sky
To those old gardens of delight;
And how it goes now in that land,
If there the house and gardens stand,
Still filled with children clad in white –
We know not, You and I.

---

\* This seems to echo the lines of Francis Thompson's poem *Daisy*:

Two children did we stray and talk
Wise, idle, childish things.

My father acquired the Works of Francis Thompson in 1913 and 1914.

> And why it was Tomorrow came
>     And with his grey hand led us back;
> 60  And why we never found the same
>     Old cottage, or the magic track
>     That leads between a silver sea
> And those old shores and gardens fair
> Where all things are, that ever were –
> 65      We know not, You and Me.

This is the final version of the poem:

### The Little House of Lost Play
#### *Mar Vanwa Tyaliéva*

> We knew that land once, You and I,
>     and once we wandered there
> in the long days now long gone by,
>     a dark child and a fair.
> 5  Was it on the paths of firelight thought
>     in winter cold and white,
> or in the blue-spun twilit hours
> of little early tucked-up beds
>     in drowsy summer night,
> 10  that you and I in Sleep went down
>     to meet each other there,
> your dark hair on your white nightgown
>     and mine was tangled fair?
>
> We wandered shyly hand in hand,
> 15  small footprints in the golden sand,
> and gathered pearls and shells in pails,
> while all about the nightingales
>     were singing in the trees.
> We dug for silver with our spades,
> 20  and caught the sparkle of the seas,
> then ran ashore to greenlit glades,
> and found the warm and winding lane
> that now we cannot find again,
>     between tall whispering trees.
>
> 25   The air was neither night nor day,
>     an ever-eve of gloaming light,
> when first there glimmered into sight
>     the Little House of Play.
> New-built it was, yet very old,

62  That leads between the sea and sky
63  To those old shores
65  We know not, You and I.

30             white, and thatched with straws of gold,
                and pierced with peeping lattices
                    that looked toward the sea;
            and our own children's garden-plots
            were there: our own forgetmenots,
35             red daisies, cress and mustard,
                and radishes for tea.
            There all the borders, trimmed with box,
            were filled with favourite flowers, with phlox,
            with lupins, pinks, and hollyhocks,
40                 beneath a red may-tree;
            and all the gardens full of folk
            that their own little language spoke,
                but not to You and Me.

            For some had silver watering-cans
45                 and watered all their gowns,
            or sprayed each other; some laid plans
            to build their houses, little towns
            and dwellings in the trees.
            And some were clambering on the roof;
50             some crooning lonely and aloof;
            some dancing round the fairy-rings
            all garlanded in daisy-strings,
                while some upon their knees
            before a little white-robed king
55             crowned with marigold would sing
                their rhymes of long ago.
            But side by side a little pair
            with heads together, mingled hair,
                went walking to and fro
60             still hand in hand; and what they said,
            ere Waking far apart them led,
                that only we now know.

It is notable that the poem was called *The Cottage*, or *The Little House of Lost Play*, whereas what is described is the Cottage of the Children in Valinor, near the city of Kôr; but this, according to Vairë (p. 19), 'the Cottage of the Play of Sleep', was 'not of Lost Play, as has wrongly been said in song among Men'.

I shall not attempt any analysis or offer any elucidation of the ideas embodied in the 'Cottages of the Children'. The reader, however he interprets them, will in any case not need to be assisted in his perception of the personal and particular emotions in which all was still anchored.

As I have said, the conception of the coming of mortal children in sleep to the gardens of Valinor was soon to be abandoned in its entirety, and in the developed mythology there would be no place for it – still less for the idea that in some possible future day 'the roads through Arvalin to Valinor shall be thronged with the sons and daughters of Men'. Likewise, all the 'elfin' diminutiveness soon disappeared. The idea of the Cottage of the Children was already in being in 1915, as the poem *You and Me* shows; and it was in the same year, indeed on the same days of April, that *Goblin Feet* (or *Cumap pá Nihtielfas*) was written, concerning which my father said in 1971: 'I wish the unhappy little thing, representing all that I came (so soon after) to fervently dislike, could be buried for ever.'* Yet it is to be observed that in early notes Elves and Men are said to have been 'of a size' in former days, and the smallness (and filminess and transparency) of the 'fairies' is an aspect of their 'fading', and directly related to the domination of Men in the Great Lands. To this matter I shall return later. In this connection, the diminutiveness of the Cottage is very strange, since it seems to be a diminutiveness peculiar to itself: Eriol, who has travelled for many days through Tol Eressëa, is astonished that the dwelling can hold so many, and he is told that all who enter it must be, or must become, very small. But Tol Eressëa is an island inhabited by Elves.

I give now three texts of the poem *Kortirion among the Trees* (later *The Trees of Kortirion*). The very earliest workings (November 1915) of this poem are extant,† and there are many subsequent texts. The prose introduction to the early form has been cited on pp. 25–6. A major revision was made in 1937, and another much later; by this time it was almost a different poem. Since my father sent it to Rayner Unwin in February 1962 as a possible candidate for inclusion in *The Adventures of Tom Bombadil*, it seems virtually certain that the final version dates from that time.‡

I give the poem first in its pre-1937 form, when only slight changes had yet been made. In one of the earliest copies it bears a title in Old English: *Cor Tirion pára béama on middes*, and is 'dedicated to Warwick'; but in another the second title is in Elvish (the second word is not perfectly legible): *Narquelion la . . tu y aldalin Kortirionwen* (i.e. 'Autumn (among) the trees of Kortirion').

---

* He had been asked for his permission to include the poem in an anthology, as it had been several times previously. See Humphrey Carpenter, *Biography*, p. 74, where (a part only) of the poem is printed, and also his bibliography *ibid.* (year 1915).

† According to my father's notes, the original composition dates from November 21–28, 1915, and was written in Warwick on 'a week's leave from camp'. This is not precisely accurate, since letters to my mother survive that were written from the camp on November 25 and 26, in the second of which he says that he has 'written out a pencil copy of "Kortirion" '.

‡ In his letter my father said: '*The Trees* is too long and too ambitious, and even if considered good enough would probably upset the boat.'

*Kortirion among the Trees*

*The First Verses*

O fading town upon a little hill,
    Old memory is waning in thine ancient gates,
The robe gone gray, thine old heart almost still;
    The castle only, frowning, ever waits

5    And ponders how among the towering elms
    The Gliding Water leaves these inland realms
        And slips between long meadows to the western sea –
    Still bearing downward over murmurous falls
        One year and then another to the sea;

10   And slowly thither have a many gone
    Since first the fairies built Kortirion.

O spiry town upon a windy hill
    With sudden-winding alleys shady-walled
(Where even now the peacocks pace a stately drill,

15     Majestic, sapphirine, and emerald),
Behold thy girdle of a wide champain
Sunlit, and watered with a silver rain,
    And richly wooded with a thousand whispering trees
That cast long shadows in many a bygone noon,

20     And murmured many centuries in the breeze.
Thou art the city of the Land of Elms,
Alalminórë in the Faery Realms.

Sing of thy trees, old, old Kortirion!
    Thine oaks, and maples with their tassels on,

25   Thy singing poplars; and the splendid yews
    That crown thine agéd walls and muse
        Of sombre grandeur all the day –
    Until the twinkle of the early stars
    Is tangled palely in their sable bars;

30   Until the seven lampads of the Silver Bear
    Swing slowly in their shrouded hair
        And diadem the fallen day.
    O tower and citadel of the world!
    When bannered summer is unfurled

35   Most full of music are thine elms –
    A gathered sound that overwhelms
        The voices of all other trees.
    Sing then of elms, belov'd Kortirion,
    How summer crowds their full sails on,

40   Like clothéd masts of verdurous ships,
    A fleet of galleons that proudly slips
        Across long sunlit seas.

*The Second Verses*

Thou art the inmost province of the fading isle
Where linger yet the Lonely Companies.
45    Still, undespairing, do they sometimes slowly file
Along thy paths with plaintive harmonies:
The holy fairies and immortal elves
That dance among the trees and sing themselves
A wistful song of things that were, and could be yet.
50    They pass and vanish in a sudden breeze,
A wave of bowing grass – and we forget
Their tender voices like wind-shaken bells
Of flowers, their gleaming hair like golden asphodels.

Spring still hath joy: thy spring is ever fair
55    Among the trees; but drowsy summer by thy streams
Already stoops to hear the secret player
Pipe out beyond the tangle of her forest dreams
The long thin tune that still do sing
The elvish harebells nodding in a jacinth ring
60    Upon the castle walls;
Already stoops to listen to the clear cold spell
Come up her sunny aisles and perfumed halls:
A sad and haunting magic note,
A strand of silver glass remote.

65    Then all thy trees, old town upon a windy bent,
Do loose a long sad whisper and lament;
For going are the rich-hued hours, th'enchanted nights
When flitting ghost-moths dance like satellites
Round tapers in the moveless air;
70    And doomed already are the radiant dawns,
The fingered sunlight dripping on long lawns;
The odour and the slumbrous noise of meads,
When all the sorrel, flowers, and pluméd weeds
Go down before the scyther's share.
75    Strange sad October robes her dewy furze
In netted sheen of gold-shot gossamers,
And then the wide-umbraged elm begins to fail;
Her mourning multitudes of leaves go pale
Seeing afar the icy shears
80    Of Winter, and his blue-tipped spears
Marching unconquerable upon the sun
Of bright All-Hallows. Then their hour is done,
And wanly borne on wings of amber pale
They beat the wide airs of the fading vale
85    And fly like birds across the misty meres.

*The Third Verses*

Yet is this season dearest to my heart,
Most fitting to the little faded town
With sense of splendid pomps that now depart
In mellow sounds of sadness echoing down
90    The paths of stranded mists. O! gentle time
When the late mornings are bejewelled with rime,
And the blue shadows gather on the distant woods.
The fairies know thy early crystal dusk
And put in secret on their twilit hoods
95    Of grey and filmy purple, and long bands
Of frosted starlight sewn by silver hands.

They know the season of the brilliant night,
When naked elms entwine in cloudy lace
The Pleiades, and long-armed poplars bar the light
100    Of golden-rondured moons with glorious face.
O fading fairies and most lonely elves
Then sing ye, sing ye to yourselves
A woven song of stars and gleaming leaves;
Then whirl ye with the sapphire-wingéd winds;
105    Then do ye pipe and call with heart that grieves
To sombre men: 'Remember what is gone –
The magic sun that lit Kortirion!'

Now are thy trees, old, old Kortirion,
Seen rising up through pallid mists and wan,
110    Like vessels floating vague and long afar
Down opal seas beyond the shadowy bar
Of cloudy ports forlorn:
They leave behind for ever havens throng'd
Wherein their crews a while held feasting long
115    And gorgeous ease, who now like windy ghosts
Are wafted by slow airs to empty coasts;
There are they sadly glimmering borne
Across the plumbless ocean of oblivion.
Bare are thy trees become, Kortirion,
120    And all their summer glory swiftly gone.
The seven lampads of the Silver Bear
Are waxen to a wondrous flare
That flames above the fallen year.
Though cold thy windy squares and empty streets;
125    Though elves dance seldom in thy pale retreats
(Save on some rare and moonlit night,
A flash, a whispering glint of white),
Yet would I never need depart from here.

*The Last Verse*

130
        I need not know the desert or red palaces
        Where dwells the sun, the great seas or the magic isles,
        The pinewoods piled on mountain-terraces;
        And calling faintly down the windy miles
        Touches my heart no distant bell that rings
        In populous cities of the Earthly Kings.

135
        Here do I find a haunting ever-near content
        Set midmost of the Land of withered Elms
        (Alalmínórë of the Faery Realms);
        Here circling slowly in a sweet lament
        Linger the holy fairies and immortal elves

140
        Singing a song of faded longing to themselves.


                        ★


I give next the text of the poem as my father rewrote it in 1937, in the
later of slightly variant forms.

                *Kortirion among the Trees*

                        I

        O fading town upon an inland hill,
            Old shadows linger in thine ancient gate,
        Thy robe is grey, thine old heart now is still;
            Thy towers silent in the mist await

5
        Their crumbling end, while through the storeyed elms
        The Gliding Water leaves these inland realms,
            And slips between long meadows to the Sea,
        Still bearing downward over murmurous falls
            One day and then another to the Sea;

10
        And slowly thither many years have gone,
        Since first the Elves here built Kortirion.

        O climbing town upon thy windy hill
            With winding streets, and alleys shady-walled
        Where now untamed the peacocks pace in drill

15
            Majestic, sapphirine, and emerald;
        Amid the girdle of this sleeping land,
        Where silver falls the rain and gleaming stand
            The whispering host of old deep-rooted trees
        That cast long shadows in many a bygone noon,

20
            And murmured many centuries in the breeze;
        Thou art the city of the Land of Elms,
        Alalmínórë in the Faery Realms.

Sing of thy trees, Kortirion, again:
The beech on hill, the willow in the fen,
25     The rainy poplars, and the frowning yews
Within thine agéd courts that muse
    In sombre splendour all the day;
Until the twinkle of the early stars
Comes glinting through their sable bars,
30 And the white moon climbing up the sky
Looks down upon the ghosts of trees that die
    Slowly and silently from day to day.
O Lonely Isle, here was thy citadel,
Ere bannered summer from his fortress fell.
35 Then full of music were thine elms:
Green was their armour, green their helms,
    The Lords and Kings of all thy trees.
Sing, then, of elms, renowned Kortirion,
That under summer crowds their full sail on,
40 And shrouded stand like masts of verdurous ships,
A fleet of galleons that proudly slips
    Across long sunlit seas.

## II

Thou art the inmost province of the fading isle,
    Where linger yet the Lonely Companies;
45 Still, undespairing, here they slowly file
    Along thy paths with solemn harmonies:
The holy people of an elder day,
Immortal Elves, that singing fair and fey
    Of vanished things that were, and could be yet,
50 Pass like a wind among the rustling trees,
    A wave of bowing grass, and we forget
Their tender voices like wind-shaken bells
Of flowers, their gleaming hair like golden asphodels.

Once Spring was here with joy, and all was fair
55     Among the trees; but Summer drowsing by the stream
Heard trembling in her heart the secret player
    Pipe, out beyond the tangle of her forest dream,
The long-drawn tune that elvish voices made
Foreseeing Winter through the leafy glade;
60     The late flowers nodding on the ruined walls
Then stooping heard afar that haunting flute
    Beyond the sunny aisles and tree-propped halls;
For thin and clear and cold the note,
As strand of silver glass remote.

65    Then all thy trees, Kortirion, were bent,
      And shook with sudden whispering lament:
      For passing were the days, and doomed the nights
      When flitting ghost-moths danced as satellites
          Round tapers in the moveless air;
70    And doomed already were the radiant dawns,
      The fingered sunlight drawn across the lawns;
      The odour and the slumbrous noise of meads,
      Where all the sorrel, flowers, and pluméd weeds
          Go down before the scyther's share.
75    When cool October robed her dewy furze
      In netted sheen of gold-shot gossamers,
      Then the wide-umbraged elms began to fail;
      Their mourning multitude of leaves grew pale,
          Seeing afar the icy spears
80    Of Winter marching blue behind the sun
      Of bright All-Hallows. Then their hour was done,
      And wanly borne on wings of amber pale
      They beat the wide airs of the fading vale,
      And flew like birds across the misty meres.


                          III

85    This is the season dearest to the heart,
          And time most fitting to the ancient town,
      With waning musics sweet that slow depart
          Winding with echoed sadness faintly down
      The paths of stranded mist. O gentle time,
90    When the late mornings are begemmed with rime,
          And early shadows fold the distant woods!
      The Elves go silent by, their shining hair
          They cloak in twilight under secret hoods
      Of grey, and filmy purple, and long bands
95    Of frosted starlight sewn by silver hands.

      And oft they dance beneath the roofless sky,
          When naked elms entwine in branching lace
      The Seven Stars, and through the boughs the eye
          Stares golden-beaming in the round moon's face.
100   O holy Elves and fair immortal Folk,
      You sing then ancient songs that once awoke
          Under primeval stars before the Dawn;
      You whirl then dancing with the eddying wind,
          As once you danced upon the shimmering lawn
105   In Elvenhome, before we were, before
      You crossed wide seas unto this mortal shore.

Now are thy trees, old grey Kortirion,
Through pallid mists seen rising tall and wan,
Like vessels floating vague, and drifting far
110    Down opal seas beyond the shadowy bar
    Of cloudy ports forlorn;
Leaving behind for ever havens loud,
Wherein their crews a while held feasting proud
And lordly ease, they now like windy ghosts
115    Are wafted by slow airs to windy coasts,
    And glimmering sadly down the tide are borne.
Bare are thy trees become, Kortirion;
The rotted raiment from their bones is gone.
The seven candles of the Silver Wain,
120    Like lighted tapers in a darkened fane,
    Now flare above the fallen year.
Though court and street now cold and empty lie,
And Elves dance seldom neath the barren sky,
Yet under the white moon there is a sound
125    Of buried music still beneath the ground.
    When winter comes, I would meet winter here.

I would not seek the desert, or red palaces
    Where reigns the sun, nor sail to magic isles,
Nor climb the hoary mountains' stony terraces;
130    And tolling faintly over windy miles
To my heart calls no distant bell that rings
In crowded cities of the Earthly Kings.
    For here is heartsease still, and deep content,
Though sadness haunt the Land of withered Elms
135    (Alalminórë in the Faery Realms);
    And making music still in sweet lament
The Elves here holy and immortal dwell,
And on the stones and trees there lies a spell.

★

I give lastly the final poem, in the second of two slightly different versions;
composed (as I believe) nearly half a century after the first.

### The Trees of Kortirion

#### I

#### Alalminórë

O ancient city on a leaguered hill!
Old shadows linger in your broken gate,

Your stones are grey, your old halls now are still,
   Your towers silent in the mist await
5     Their crumbling end, while through the storeyed elms
The River Gliding leaves these inland realms
   And slips between long meadows to the Sea,
Still bearing down by weir and murmuring fall
   One day and then another to the Sea;
10    And slowly thither many days have gone
Since first the Edain built Kortirion.

Kortirion! Upon your island hill
   With winding streets, and alleys shadow-walled
Where even now the peacocks pace in drill
15    Majestic, sapphirine and emerald,
Once long ago amid this sleeping land
Of silver rain, where still year-laden stand
   In unforgetful earth the rooted trees
That cast long shadows in the bygone noon,
20    And whispered in the swiftly passing breeze,
Once long ago, Queen of the Land of Elms,
High City were you of the Inland Realms.

Your trees in summer you remember still:
   The willow by the spring, the beech on hill;
25    The rainy poplars, and the frowning yews
Within your aged courts that muse
   In sombre splendour all the day,
Until the firstling star comes glimmering,
And flittermice go by on silent wing;
30    Until the white moon slowly climbing sees
In shadow-fields the sleep-enchanted trees
   Night-mantled all in silver-grey.
Alalminor! Here was your citadel,
Ere bannered summer from his fortress fell;
35    About you stood arrayed your host of elms:
Green was their armour, tall and green their helms,
   High lords and captains of the trees.
But summer wanes. Behold, Kortirion!
The elms their full sail now have crowded on
40    Ready to the winds, like masts amid the vale
Of mighty ships too soon, too soon, to sail
   To other days beyond these sunlit seas.

## II

### *Narquelion**

Alalminórë! Green heart of this Isle
Where linger yet the Faithful Companies!
45 Still undespairing here they slowly file
Down lonely paths with solemn harmonies:
The Fair, the first-born in an elder day,
Immortal Elves, who singing on their way
Of bliss of old and grief, though men forget,
50 Pass like a wind among the rustling trees,
A wave of bowing grass, and men forget
Their voices calling from a time we do not know,
Their gleaming hair like sunlight long ago.

A wind in the grass! The turning of the year.
55 A shiver in the reeds beside the stream,
A whisper in the trees – afar they hear,
Piercing the heart of summer's tangled dream,
Chill music that a herald piper plays
Foreseeing winter and the leafless days.
60 The late flowers trembling on the ruined walls
Already stoop to hear that elven-flute.
Through the wood's sunny aisles and tree-propped halls
Winding amid the green with clear cold note
Like a thin strand of silver glass remote.

65 The high-tide ebbs, the year will soon be spent;
And all your trees, Kortirion, lament.
At morn the whetstone rang upon the blade,
At eve the grass and golden flowers were laid
To wither, and the meadows bare.
70 Now dimmed already comes the tardier dawn,
Paler the sunlight fingers creep across the lawn.
The days are passing. Gone like moths the nights
When white wings fluttering danced like satellites
Round tapers in the windless air.
75 Lammas is gone. The Harvest-moon has waned.
Summer is dying that so briefly reigned.
Now the proud elms at last begin to quail,
Their leaves uncounted tremble and grow pale,
Seeing afar the icy spears

---

* With the name *Narquelion* (which appears also in the title in Elvish of
the original poem, see p. 32) cf. *Narquelië* 'Sun-fading', name of the tenth
month in Quenya (*The Lord of the Rings*, Appendix D).

80      Of winter march to battle with the sun.
        When bright All-Hallows fades, their day is done,
        And borne on wings of amber wan they fly
        In heedless winds beneath the sullen sky,
            And fall like dying birds upon the meres.

### III

*Hrívion**

85      Alas! Kortirion, Queen of Elms, alas!
            This season best befits your ancient town
        With echoing voices sad that slowly pass,
            Winding with waning music faintly down
        The paths of stranded mist. O fading time,
90      When morning rises late all hoar with rime,
            And early shadows veil the distant woods!
        Unseen the Elves go by, their shining hair
            They cloak in twilight under secret hoods
        Of grey, their dusk-blue mantles gird with bands
95      Of frosted starlight sewn by silver hands.

        At night they dance beneath the roofless sky,
            When naked elms entwine in branching lace
        The Seven Stars, and through the boughs the eye
            Stares down cold-gleaming in the high moon's face.
100     O Elder Kindred, fair immortal folk!
        You sing now ancient songs that once awoke
            Under primeval stars before the Dawn;
        You dance like shimmering shadows in the wind,
            As once you danced upon the shining lawn
105     Of Elvenhome, before we were, before
        You crossed wide seas unto this mortal shore.

        Now are your trees, old grey Kortirion,
        Through pallid mists seen rising tall and wan,
        Like vessels vague that slowly drift afar
110     Out, out to empty seas beyond the bar
            Of cloudy ports forlorn;
        Leaving behind for ever havens loud,
        Wherein their crews a while held feasting proud
        In lordly ease, they now like windy ghosts
115     Are wafted by cold airs to friendless coasts,
            And silent down the tide are borne.
        Bare has your realm become, Kortirion,

* Cf. *hrívë* 'winter', *The Lord of the Rings*, Appendix D.

Stripped of its raiment, and its splendour gone.
Like lighted tapers in a darkened fane
120 The funeral candles of the Silver Wain
Now flare above the fallen year.
Winter is come. Beneath the barren sky
The Elves are silent. But they do not die!
Here waiting they endure the winter fell
125 And silence. Here I too will dwell;
Kortirion, I will meet the winter here.


IV

*Mettanyë**

I would not find the burning domes and sands
Where reigns the sun, nor dare the deadly snows,
Nor seek in mountains dark the hidden lands
130 Of men long lost to whom no pathway goes;
I heed no call of clamant bell that rings
Iron-tongued in the towers of earthly kings.
Here on the stones and trees there lies a spell
Of unforgotten loss, of memory more blest
135 Than mortal wealth. Here undefeated dwell
The Folk Immortal under withered elms,
Alalminórë once in ancient realms.


★

I conclude this commentary with a note on my father's use of the word
*Gnomes* for the *Noldor*, who in the *Lost Tales* are called *Noldoli*. He con-
tinued to use it for many years, and it still appeared in earlier editions of
*The Hobbit*.†

In a draft for the final paragraph of Appendix F to *The Lord of the
Rings* he wrote:

I have sometimes (not in this book) used 'Gnomes' for *Noldor* and
'Gnomish' for *Noldorin*. This I did, for whatever Paracelsus may have
thought (if indeed he invented the name) to some 'Gnome' will still

---

* *Mettanyë* contains *metta* 'ending', as in *Ambar-metta*, the ending of the
world (*The Return of the King*, VI.5).

† In Chapter 3, *A Short Rest*, 'swords of the High Elves of the West'
replaced 'swords of the elves that are now called Gnomes'; and in Chapter
8, *Flies and Spiders*, the phrase 'There the Light-elves and the Deep-elves
and the Sea-elves went and lived for ages' replaced 'There the Light-elves
and the Deep-elves (or Gnomes) and the Sea-elves lived for ages'.

suggest knowledge.* Now the High-elven name of this people, Noldor, signifies Those who Know; for of the three kindreds of the Eldar from their beginning the Noldor were ever distinguished both by their knowledge of things that are and were in this world, and by their desire to know more. Yet they in no way resembled the Gnomes either of learned theory or popular fancy; and I have now abandoned this rendering as too misleading. For the Noldor belonged to a race high and beautiful, the elder Children of the world, who now are gone. Tall they were, fair-skinned and grey-eyed, and their locks were dark, save in the golden house of Finrod . . .

In the last paragraph of Appendix F *as published* the reference to 'Gnomes' was removed, and replaced by a passage explaining the use of the word *Elves* to translate *Quendi* and *Eldar* despite the diminishing of the English word. This passage – referring to the Quendi as a whole – continues however with the same words as in the draft: 'They were a race high and beautiful, and among them the Eldar were as kings, who now are gone: the People of the Great Journey, the People of the Stars. They were tall, fair of skin and grey-eyed, though their locks were dark, save in the golden house of Finrod . . .' Thus these words describing characters of face and hair were actually written of the Noldor only, and *not* of all the Eldar: indeed the Vanyar had golden hair, and it was from Finarfin's Vanyarin mother Indis that he, and Finrod Felagund and Galadriel his children, had their golden hair that marked them out among the princes of the Noldor. But I am unable to determine how this extraordinary perversion of meaning arose.†

* Two words are in question: (1) Greek *gnōmē* 'thought, intelligence' (and in the plural 'maxims, sayings', whence the English word *gnome*, a maxim or aphorism, and adjective *gnomic*); and (2) the word *gnome* used by the 16th-century writer Paracelsus as a synonym of *pygmaeus*. Paracelsus 'says that the beings so called have the earth as their element . . . through which they move unobstructed as fish do through water, or birds and land animals through air' (*Oxford English Dictionary* s.v. *Gnome*²). The *O.E.D.* suggests that whether Paracelsus invented the word himself or not it was intended to mean 'earth-dweller', and discounts any connection with the other word *Gnome*. (This note is repeated from that in *The Letters of J. R. R. Tolkien*, p. 449; see the letter (no. 239) to which it refers.)

† The name *Finrod* in the passage at the end of Appendix F is now in error: Finarfin was Finrod, and Finrod was Inglor, until the second edition of *The Lord of the Rings*, and in this instance the change was overlooked.

# II

# THE MUSIC OF THE AINUR

In another notebook identical to that in which *The Cottage of Lost Play* was written out by my mother, there is a text in ink in my father's hand (and all the other texts of the *Lost Tales* are in his hand, save for a fair copy of *The Fall of Gondolin*\*) entitled: *Link between Cottage of Lost Play and (Tale 2) Music of Ainur*. This follows on directly from Vairë's last words to Eriol on p. 20, and in turn links on directly to *The Music of the Ainur* (in a third notebook identical to the other two). The only indication of date for the *Link* and the *Music* (which were, I think, written at the same time) is a letter of my father's of July 1964 (*Letters* p. 345), in which he said that while in Oxford 'employed on the staff of the then still incomplete great Dictionary' he 'wrote a cosmogonical myth, "The Music of the Ainur"'. He took up the post on the Oxford Dictionary in November 1918 and relinquished it in the spring of 1920 (*Biography* pp. 99, 102). If his recollection was correct, and there is no evidence to set against it, some two years or more elapsed between *The Cottage of Lost Play* and *The Music of the Ainur*.

The *Link* between the two exists in only one version, for the text in ink was written over a draft in pencil that was wholly erased. In this case I follow the *Link* with a brief commentary, before giving *The Music of the Ainur*.

'But,' said Eriol, 'still are there many things that remain dark to me. Indeed I would fain know who be these Valar; are they the Gods?'

'So be they,' said Lindo, 'though concerning them Men tell many strange and garbled tales that are far from the truth, and many strange names they call them that you will not hear here'; but Vairë said: 'Nay then, Lindo, be not drawn into more tale-telling tonight, for the hour of rest is at hand, and for all his eagerness our guest is way-worn. Send now for the candles of sleep, and more tales to his head's filling and his heart's satisfying the wanderer shall have on the morrow.' But to Eriol she said: 'Think not that you must leave our house tomorrow of need; for none do so – nay, all may remain while a tale remains to tell which they desire to hear.'

Then said Eriol that all desire of faring abroad had left his heart

---

\* The actual title of this tale is *Tuor and the Exiles of Gondolin*, but my father referred to it as *The Fall of Gondolin* and I do likewise.

and that to be a guest there a while seemed to him fairest of all things. Thereupon came in those that bore the candles of sleep, and each of that company took one, and two of the folk of the house bade Eriol follow them. One of these was the door-ward who had opened to his knocking before. He was old in appearance and grey of locks, and few of that folk were so; but the other had a weather-worn face and blue eyes of great merriment, and was very slender and small, nor might one say if he were fifty or ten thousand. Now that was Ilverin or Littleheart. These two guided him down the corridor of broidered stories to a great stair of oak, and up this he followed them. It wound up and round until it brought them to a passage lit by small pendent lamps of coloured glass, whose swaying cast a spatter of bright hues upon the floors and hangings.

In this passage the guides turned round a sudden corner, then going down a few dark steps flung open a door before him. Now bowing they wished him good sleep, and said Littleheart: 'dreams of fair winds and good voyages in the great seas', and then they left him; and he found that he stood in a chamber that was small, and had a bed of fairest linen and deep pillows set nigh the window – and here the night seemed warm and fragrant, although he had but now come from rejoicing in the blaze of the Tale-fire logs. Here was all the furniture of dark wood, and as his great candle flickered its soft rays worked a magic with the room, till it seemed to him that sleep was the best of all delights, but that fair chamber the best of all for sleep. Ere he laid him down however Eriol opened the window and scent of flowers gusted in therethrough, and a glimpse he caught of a shadow-filled garden that was full of trees, but its spaces were barred with silver lights and black shadows by reason of the moon; yet his window seemed very high indeed above those lawns below, and a nightingale sang suddenly in a tree nearby.

Then slept Eriol, and through his dreams there came a music thinner and more pure than any he heard before, and it was full of longing. Indeed it was as if pipes of silver or flutes of shape most slender-delicate uttered crystal notes and threadlike harmonies beneath the moon upon the lawns; and Eriol longed in his sleep for he knew not what.

When he awoke the sun was rising and there was no music save that of a myriad of birds about his window. The light struck through the panes and shivered into merry glints, and that room with its fragrance and its pleasant draperies seemed even sweeter than before; but Eriol arose, and robing himself in fair garments laid ready for him that he might shed his raiment stained with travel went forth

and strayed about the passages of the house, until he chanced upon
a little stairway, and going down this he came to a porch and a sunny
court. Therein was a lattice-gate that opened to his hand and led
into that garden whose lawns were spread beneath the window of
his room. There he wandered breathing the airs and watching the
sun rise above the strange roofs of that town, when behold the aged
door-ward was before him, coming along a lane of hazel-bushes.
He saw not Eriol, for he held his head as ever bent towards the earth,
and muttered swiftly to himself; but Eriol spake bidding him good
morrow, and thereat he started.

Then said he: 'Your pardon, sir! I marked you not, for I was
listening to the birds. Indeed sir you find me in a sour temper; for
lo! here I have a black-winged rogue fat with impudence who singeth
songs before unknown to me, and in a tongue that is strange! It
irks me sir, it irks me, for methought at least I knew the simple
speeches of all birds. I have a mind to send him down to Mandos
for his pertness!' At this Eriol laughed heartily, but said the door-ward:
'Nay sir, may Tevildo Prince of Cats harry him for daring to perch
in a garden that is in the care of Rúmil. Know you that the Noldoli
grow old astounding slow, and yet have I grey hairs in the study of
all the tongues of Valar and of Eldar. Long ere the fall of Gondolin,
good sir, I lightened my thraldom under Melko in learning the speech
of all monsters and goblins – have I not conned even the speeches
of beasts, disdaining not the thin voices of the voles and mice? – have
I not cadged a stupid tune or two to hum of the speechless beetles?
Nay, I have worried at whiles even over the tongues of Men, but
Melko take them! they shift and change, change and shift, and when
you have them are but a hard stuff whereof to labour songs or tales.
Wherefore is it that this morn I felt as Ómar the Vala who knows
all tongues, as I hearkened to the blending of the voices of the birds
comprehending each, recognising each well-loved tune, when *tiripti
lirilla* here comes a bird, an imp of Melko – but I weary you sir,
with babbling of songs and words.'

'Nay, not so,' quoth Eriol, 'but I beg of you be not disheartened
by one fat imp of an ousel. If my eyes deceive not, for a good age of
years you have cared for this garden. Then must you know store of
songs and tongues sufficient to comfort the heart of the greatest of
all sages, if indeed this be the first voice that you have heard therein,
and lacked its interpretation. Is it not said that the birds of every
district, nay almost of every nest, speak unalike?'

''Tis said so, and said truly,' quoth Rúmil, 'and all the songs of
Tol Eressëa are to be heard at times within this garden.'

'More than heart-content am I,' said Eriol, 'to have learned that one fair tongue which the Eldar speak about this isle of Tol Eressëa – but I marvelled to hear you speak as if there were many speeches of the Eldar: are there so?'

'Aye,' said Rúmil, 'for there is that tongue to which the Noldoli cling yet – and aforetime the Teleri, the Solosimpi, and the Inwir had all their differences. Yet these were slighter and are now merged in that tongue of the island Elves which you have learnt. Still are there the lost bands too that dwell wandering sadly in the Great Lands, and maybe they speak very strangely now, for it was ages gone that that march was made from Kôr, and as I hold 'twas but the long wandering of the Noldoli about the Earth and the black ages of their thraldom while their kin dwelt yet in Valinor that caused the deep sundering of their speech. Akin nonetheless be assuredly Gnome-speech and Elfin of the Eldar, as my lore teacheth me – but lo! I weary you again. Never have I found another ear yet in the world that grew not tired ere long of such discourse. "Tongues and speeches," they will say, "one is enough for me" – and thus said Littleheart the Gong-warden once upon a time: "Gnome-speech," said he, "is enough for me – did not that one Eärendel and Tuor and Bronweg my father (that mincingly ye miscall Voronwë) speak it and no other?" Yet he had to learn the Elfin in the end, or be doomed either to silence or to leave Mar Vanwa Tyaliéva – and neither fate would his heart suffer. Lo! now he is chirping Eldar like a lady of the Inwir, even Meril-i-Turinqi our queen herself – Manwë care for her. But even these be not all – there is beside the secret tongue in which the Eldar wrote many poesies and books of wisdom and histories of old and earliest things, and yet speak not. This tongue do only the Valar use in their high counsels, and not many of the Eldar of these days may read it or solve its characters. Much of it I learnt in Kôr, a lifetime gone, of the goodness of Aulë, and thereby I know many matters: very many matters.'

'Then,' quoth Eriol, 'maybe you can tell me of things that I greatly desire to know since the words by the Tale-fire yester-eve. Who be the Valar – Manwë, Aulë, and the ones ye name – and wherefore came ye Eldar from that home of loveliness in Valinor?'

Now came those two to a green arbour and the sun was up and warm, and the birds sang mightily, but the lawns were spread with gold. Then Rúmil sat upon a seat there of carven stone grown with moss, and said he: 'Very mighty are the things that you ask, and their true answer delves beyond the uttermost confines of the wastes of time, whither even the sight of Rúmil the aged of the Noldoli may not see; and all the tales of the Valar and the Elves are so knit together that one may scarce expound any one without needing to set forth the whole of their great history.'

'Yet', said Eriol, 'tell me, Rúmil, I beg, some of what you know even of the first beginnings, that I may begin to understand those things that are told me in this isle.'

But Rúmil said: 'Ilúvatar was the first beginning, and beyond that no wisdom of the Valar or of Eldar or of Men can go.'

'Who was Ilúvatar?' said Eriol. 'Was he of the Gods?'

'Nay,' said Rúmil, 'that he was not, for he made them. Ilúvatar is the Lord for Always who dwells beyond the world; who made it and is not of it or in it, but loves it.'

'This have I never heard elsewhere,' said Eriol.

'That may be,' said Rúmil, 'for 'tis early days in the world of Men as yet, nor is the Music of the Ainur much spoken of.'

'Tell me,' said Eriol, 'for I long to learn, what was the Music of the Ainur?'

## Commentary on the Link between The Cottage of Lost Play and The Music of the Ainur

Thus it was that the *Ainulindalë* was first to be heard by mortal ears, as Eriol sat in a sunlit garden in Tol Eressëa. Even after Eriol (or Ælfwine) had fallen away, Rúmil remained, the great Noldorin sage of Tirion 'who first achieved fitting signs for the recording of speech and song' (*The Silmarillion* p. 63), and *The Music of the Ainur* continued to be ascribed to him, though invested with the gravity of a remote time he moved far away from the garrulous and whimsical philologist of Kortirion. It is to be noted that in this account Rúmil had been a slave under Melko.

Here the Exile of the Noldor from Valinor appears, for it is to this that Rúmil's words about the march from Kôr undoubtedly refer, rather than to Inwë's 'march into the world' (pp. 16, 26); and something is said also of the languages, and of those who spoke them.

In this link-passage Rúmil asserts:

(1) that the *Teleri*, *Solosimpi*, and *Inwir* had linguistic differences in the past;

(2) but that these dialects are now merged in the 'tongue of the island Elves';

(3) that the tongue of the *Noldoli* (Gnomes) was deeply sundered through their departure into the Great Lands and their captivity under Melko;

(4) that those Noldoli who now dwell in Tol Eressëa have learnt the tongue of the island Elves; but others remain in the Great Lands. (When Rúmil spoke of 'the lost bands that dwell wandering sadly in the Great

Lands' who 'maybe speak very strangely now' he seems to have been referring to remnants of the Noldorin exiles from Kôr who had not come to Tol Eressëa (as he himself had done), rather than to Elves who never went to Valinor.)*

In the *Lost Tales* the name given to the Sea-elves afterwards called the *Teleri* – the third of the three 'tribes' – is *Solosimpi* ('Shoreland Pipers'). It must now be explained that, confusingly enough, the first of the tribes, that led by King Inwë, were called the *Teleri* (the *Vanyar* of *The Silmarillion*). Who then were the *Inwir*? Eriol was told later by Meril-i-Turinqi (p. 115) that the Teleri were those that followed Inwë, 'but his kindred and descendants are that royal folk the Inwir of whose blood I am.' The Inwir were then a 'royal' clan *within the Teleri*; and the relation between the old conception and that of *The Silmarillion* can be shown thus:

|     | *Lost Tales*       |           | *The Silmarillion* |
| --- | ------------------ | --------- | ------------------ |
| I   | Teleri             | .. .. .. .. | Vanyar             |
|     | (including Inwir)  |           |                    |
| II  | Noldoli            | .. .. .. .. | Noldor             |
|     | (Gnomes)           |           |                    |
| III | Solosimpi          | .. .. .. .. | Teleri             |

In this link-passage Rúmil seems to say that the 'Eldar' are distinct from the 'Gnomes' – 'akin nonetheless be assuredly Gnome-speech and Elfin of the Eldar'; and 'Eldar' and 'Noldoli' are opposed in the prose preamble to *Kortirion among the Trees* (p. 25). Elsewhere 'Elfin', as a language, is used in opposition to 'Gnomish', and 'Eldar' is used of a word of form in contradistinction to 'Gnomish'. It is in fact made quite explicit in the *Lost Tales* that the Gnomes were themselves Eldar – for instance, 'the Noldoli, who were the sages of the Eldar' (p. 58); but on the other hand we read that after the Flight of the Noldoli from Valinor Aulë 'gave still his love to those few faithful Gnomes who remained still about his halls, yet did he name them thereafter "Eldar"' (p. 176). This is not so purely contradictory as appears at first sight. It seems that (on the one hand) the opposition of 'Eldar' or 'Elfin' to 'Gnomish' arose because Gnomish had become a language apart; and while the Gnomes were certainly themselves Eldar, their language was not. But (on the other hand) the Gnomes had long ago left Kôr, and thus came to be seen as not 'Koreldar', and therefore not 'Eldar'. The word *Eldar* had thus narrowed its meaning, but might at any moment be expanded again to the older sense in which the Noldoli were 'Eldar'.

If this is so, the narrowed sense of *Eldar* reflects the situation in after days in Tol Eressëa; and indeed, in the tales that follow, where the

* On the other hand it is possible that by 'the lost bands' he did in fact mean the Elves who were lost on the journey from the Waters of Awakening (see p. 118); i.e. the implication is: 'if the sundering of the speech of the Noldoli from that of the Eldar who remained in Valinor is very deep, how much more so must be the speech of those who never crossed the sea'.

narrative is concerned with the time before the rebellion of the Noldoli and their departure from Valinor, they are firmly 'Eldar'. *After* the rebellion, in the passage cited above, Aulë would not call the Noldoli who remained in Valinor by that name – and, by implication, he would not call those who had departed 'Eldar'.

The same ambiguity is present in the words *Elves* and *Elfin*. Rúmil here calls the language of the Eldar 'Elfin' in opposition to 'Gnomish'; the teller of the *Tale of Tinúviel* says: 'This is my tale, and 'tis a tale of the Gnomes, wherefore I beg that thou fill not Eriol's ear with thy Elfin names', and in the same passage 'Elves' are specifically opposed to 'Gnomes'. But, again, in the tales that follow in this book, *Elves* and *Eldar* and *Eldalië* are used interchangeably of the Three Kindreds (see for instance the account of the debate of the Valar concerning the summoning of the Elves to Valinor, pp. 116–18). And finally, an apparently similar variation is seen in the word 'fairy'; thus Tol Eressëa is the name 'in the fairy speech', while 'the Gnomes call it Dor Faidwen' (p. 13), but on the other hand Gilfanon, a Gnome, is called 'one of the oldest of the fairies' (p. 175).

It will be seen from Rúmil's remarks that the 'deep sundering' of the speech of the Elves into two branches was at this time given an historical basis wholly different from that which afterwards caused the division. Here, Rúmil ascribes it to 'the long wandering of the Noldoli about the Earth and the black ages of their thraldom while their kin dwelt yet in Valinor' – in later terms, 'the Exile of the Noldor'. In *The Silmarillion* (see especially pp. 113, 129) the Noldor brought the Valinórean tongue to Middle-earth but abandoned it (save among themselves), and adopted instead the language of Beleriand, *Sindarin* of the Grey-elves, who had never been to Valinor: Quenya and Sindarin were of common origin, but their 'deep sundering' had been brought about through vast ages of separation. In the *Lost Tales*, on the other hand, the Noldor still brought the Elvish speech of Valinor to the Great Lands, but they retained it, and there it itself changed and became wholly different. In other words, in the original conception the 'second tongue' only split off from the parent speech through the departure of the Gnomes from Valinor into the Great Lands; whereas afterwards the 'second tongue' separated from the 'first tongue' near the very beginning of Elvish existence in the world. Nonetheless, Gnomish *is* Sindarin, in the sense that Gnomish is *the actual language* that ultimately, as the whole conception evolved, became that of the Grey-elves of Beleriand.

With Rúmil's remarks about the secret tongue which the Valar use and in which the Eldar once wrote poetry and books of wisdom, but few of them now know it, cf. the following note found in the little *Lost Tales* pocket-book referred to on p. 23:

The Gods understood the language of the Elves but used it not among themselves. The wiser of the Elves learned much of the speech of the

Gods and long treasured that knowledge among both Teleri and Noldoli, but by the time of the coming to Tol Eressëa none knew it save the Inwir, and now that knowledge is dead save in Meril's house.

Some new persons appear in this passage. Ómar the Vala 'who knows all tongues' did not survive the *Lost Tales*; a little more is heard of him subsequently, but he is a divinity without much substance. Tuor and Bronweg appear from the tale of *The Fall of Gondolin*, which was already written; *Bronweg* is the Gnomish form of *Voronwë*, that same Voronwë who accompanied Tuor from Vinyamar to Gondolin in the later legend. Tevildo Prince of Cats was a demonic servant of Melko and the remote forerunner of Sauron; he is a principal actor in the original story of Beren and Tinúviel, which was also already written (the *Tale of Tinúviel*).

Littleheart the Gong-warden, son of Bronweg, now receives an Elvish name, *Ilverin* (an emendation from *Elwenildo*).

### The Music of the Ainur

The original hastily pencilled and much emended draft text of *The Music of the Ainur* is still extant, on loose sheets placed inside the cover of the notebook that contains a fuller and much more finished text written in ink. This second version was however closely based on the first, and changed it chiefly by additions. The text given here is the second, but some passages where the two differ notably are annotated (few of the differences between the two texts are in my opinion of much significance). It will be seen from passages of the first draft given in the notes that the plural was originally *Ainu*, not *Ainur*, and that *Ilúvatar* was originally *Ilu* (but *Ilúvatar* also occurs in the draft).

Then said Rúmil:

'Hear now things that have not been heard among Men, and the Elves speak seldom of them; yet did Manwë Súlimo, Lord of Elves and Men, whisper them to the fathers of my father in the deeps of time.[1] Behold, Ilúvatar dwelt alone. Before all things he sang into being the Ainur first, and greatest is their power and glory of all his creatures within the world and without. Thereafter he fashioned them dwellings in the void, and dwelt among them, teaching them all manner of things, and the greatest of these was music.

Now he would speak propounding to them themes of song and joyous hymn, revealing many of the great and wonderful things that he devised ever in his mind and heart, and now they would make music unto him, and the voices of their instruments rise in splendour about his throne.

Upon a time Ilúvatar propounded a mighty design of his heart to the Ainur, unfolding a history whose vastness and majesty had never been equalled by aught that he had related before, and the glory of its beginning and the splendour of its end amazed the Ainur, so that they bowed before Ilúvatar and were speechless.

Then said Ilúvatar: "The story that I have laid before you, and that great region of beauty that I have described unto you as the place where all that history might be unfolded and enacted, is related only as it were in outline. I have not filled all the empty spaces, neither have I recounted to you all the adornments and things of loveliness and delicacy whereof my mind is full. It is my desire now that ye make a great and glorious music and a singing of this theme; and (seeing that I have taught you much and set brightly the Secret Fire within you)[2] that ye exercise your minds and powers in adorning the theme to your own thoughts and devising. But I will sit and hearken and be glad that through you I have made much beauty to come to Song."

Then the harpists, and the lutanists, the flautists and pipers, the organs and the countless choirs of the Ainur began to fashion the theme of Ilúvatar into great music; and a sound arose of mighty melodies changing and interchanging, mingling and dissolving amid the thunder of harmonies greater than the roar of the great seas, till the places of the dwelling of Ilúvatar and the regions of the Ainur were filled to overflowing with music, and the echo of music, and the echo of the echoes of music which flowed even into the dark and empty spaces far off. Never was there before, nor has there been since, such a music of immeasurable vastness of splendour; though it is said that a mightier far shall be woven before the seat of Ilúvatar by the choirs of both Ainur and the sons of Men after the Great End. Then shall Ilúvatar's mightiest themes be played aright; for then Ainur and Men will know his mind and heart as well as may be, and all his intent.

But now Ilúvatar sat and hearkened, and for a great while it seemed very good to him, for the flaws in that music were few, and it seemed to him the Ainur had learnt much and well. But as the great theme progressed it came into the heart of Melko to interweave matters of his own vain imagining that were not fitting to that great theme of Ilúvatar. Now Melko had among the Ainur been given some of the greatest gifts of power and wisdom and knowledge by Ilúvatar; and he fared often alone into the dark places and the voids seeking the Secret Fire that giveth Life and Reality (for he had a very hot desire to bring things into being of his own); yet he found it not, for it dwelleth with Ilúvatar, and that he knew not till afterward.[3]

There had he nonetheless fallen to thinking deep cunning thoughts of his own, all of which he showed not even to Ilúvatar. Some of these devisings and imaginings he now wove into his music, and straightway harshness and discordancy rose about him, and many of those that played nigh him grew despondent and their music feeble, and their thoughts unfinished and unclear, while many others fell to attuning their music to his rather than to the great theme wherein they began.

In this way the mischief of Melko spread darkening the music, for those thoughts of his came from the outer blackness whither Ilúvatar had not yet turned the light of his face; and because his secret thoughts had no kinship with the beauty of Ilúvatar's design its harmonies were broken and destroyed. Yet sat Ilúvatar and hearkened till the music reached a depth of gloom and ugliness unimaginable; then did he smile sadly and raised his left hand, and immediately, though none clearly knew how, a new theme began among the clash, like and yet unlike the first, and it gathered power and sweetness. But the discord and noise that Melko had aroused started into uproar against it, and there was a war of sounds, and a clangour arose in which little could be distinguished.

Then Ilúvatar raised his right hand, and he no longer smiled but wept; and behold a third theme, and it was in no way like the others, grew amid the turmoil, till at the last it seemed there were two musics progressing at one time about the feet of Ilúvatar, and these were utterly at variance. One was very great and deep and beautiful, but it was mingled with an unquenchable sorrow, while the other was now grown to unity and a system of its own, but was loud and vain and arrogant, braying triumphantly against the other as it thought to drown it, yet ever, as it essayed to clash most fearsomely, finding itself but in some manner supplementing or harmonising with its rival.

At the midmost of this echoing struggle, whereat the halls of Ilúvatar shook and a tremor ran through the dark places, Ilúvatar raised up both his hands, and in one unfathomed chord, deeper then the firmament, more glorious than the sun, and piercing as the light of Ilúvatar's glance, that music crashed and ceased.

Then said Ilúvatar: "Mighty are the Ainur, and glorious, and among them is Melko the most powerful in knowledge; but that he may know, and all the Ainur, that I am Ilúvatar, those things that ye have sung and played, lo! I have caused to be — not in the musics that ye make in the heavenly regions, as a joy to me and a play unto yourselves, alone, but rather to have shape and reality even as have ye Ainur, whom I have made to share in the reality of Ilúvatar myself. Maybe I shall love these things that come of my song even as I love the Ainur who are of my thought,[4] and maybe more. Thou Melko shalt see that no theme can be played save it come in the end of Ilúvatar's self, nor can any alter the music in Ilúvatar's despite. He that attempts this finds himself in the end but aiding me in devising a thing of still greater grandeur and more complex wonder: – for lo! through Melko have terror as fire, and sorrow like dark waters, wrath like thunder, and evil as far from my light as the depths of the uttermost of the dark places, come into the design that I laid before you. Through him has pain and misery been made in the clash of overwhelming musics; and with confusion of sound have cruelty, and ravening, and darkness, loathly mire and all putrescence of thought or thing, foul mists and violent flame, cold without mercy, been born, and death without hope. Yet is this through him and not by him; and he shall see, and ye all likewise, and even shall those beings, who must now dwell among his evil and endure through Melko misery and sorrow, terror and wickedness, declare in the end that it redoundeth only to my great glory, and doth but make the theme more worth the hearing, Life more worth the living, and the World so much the more wonderful and marvellous, that of all the deeds of Ilúvatar it shall be called his mightiest and his loveliest."

Then the Ainur feared and comprehended not all that was said, and Melko was filled with shame and the anger of shame; but Ilúvatar seeing their amaze arose in glory and went forth from his dwellings, past those fair regions he had fashioned for the Ainur, out into the dark places; and he bade the Ainur follow him.

Now when they reached the midmost void they beheld a sight of surpassing beauty and wonder where before had been emptiness; but Ilúvatar said: "Behold your choiring and your music! Even as ye played so of my will your music took shape, and lo! even now the world unfolds and its history begins as did my theme in your hands. Each one herein will find contained within the design that is mine the adornments and embellishments that he himself devised; nay, even Melko will discover those things there which he thought to contrive of his own heart, out of harmony with my mind, and he will find them but a part of the whole and tributary to its glory. One thing only have I added, the fire that giveth Life and Reality" – and behold, the Secret Fire burnt at the heart of the world.

Then the Ainur marvelled to see how the world was globed amid the void and yet separated from it; and they rejoiced to see light, and found it was both white and golden, and they laughed for the pleasure of colours, and for the great roaring of the ocean they were filled with longing. Their hearts were glad because of air and the winds, and the matters whereof the Earth was made – iron and stone and silver and gold and many substances: but of all these water was held the fairest and most goodly and most greatly praised. Indeed there liveth still in water a deeper echo of the Music of the Ainur than in any substance else that is in the world, and at this latest day many of the Sons of Men will hearken unsatedly to the voice of the Sea and long for they know not what.

Know then that water was for the most part the dream and invention of Ulmo, an Ainu whom Ilúvatar had instructed deeper than all others in the depths of music; while the air and winds and the ethers of the firmament had Manwë Súlimo devised, greatest and most noble of the Ainur. The earth and most of its goodly substances did Aulë contrive, whom Ilúvatar had taught many things of wisdom scarce less than Melko, yet was there much therein that was nought of his.[5]

Now Ilúvatar spake to Ulmo and said: "Seest thou not how Melko hath bethought him of biting colds without moderation, yet hath not destroyed the beauty of thy crystal waters nor of all thy limpid pools. Even where he has thought to conquer utterly, behold snow has been made, and frost has wrought his exquisite works; ice has reared his castles in grandeur."

Again said Ilúvatar: "Melko hath devised undue heats, and fires without restraint, and yet hath not dried up thy desire nor utterly quelled the music of thy seas. Rather behold now the height and glory of the clouds and the magic that dwells in mist and vapours; listen to the whisper of rains upon the earth."

Then said Ulmo: "Yea truly is water fairer now than was my best devising before. Snow is of a loveliness beyond my most secret thoughts, and if there is little music therein, yet rain is beautiful indeed and hath a music that filleth my heart, so glad am I that my ears have found it, though its sadness is among the saddest of all things. Lo! I will go seek Súlimo of the air and winds, that he and I play melodies for ever and ever to thy glory and rejoicing."

Now Ulmo and Manwë have been great friends and allies in almost all matters since then.[6]

Now even as Ilúvatar spake to Ulmo, the Ainur beheld how the world unfolded, and that history which Ilúvatar had propounded to them as a great music was already being carried out. It is of their gathered memories of the speech of Ilúvatar and the knowledge, incomplete it may be, that each has of their music, that the Ainur know so much of the future that few things are unforeseen by them – yet are there some that be hidden even from these.[7] So the Ainur gazed; until long before the coming of Men – nay, who does not know that it was countless ages before even the Eldar arose and sang their first song and made the first of all the gems, and were seen by both Ilúvatar and the Ainur to be of exceeding loveliness – there grew a contention among them, so enamoured did they become of the glory of the world as they gazed upon it, and so enthralled by the history enacted therein to which the beauty of the world was but the background and the scene.

Now this was the end, that some abode still with Ilúvatar beyond the world – and these were mostly those who had been engrossed in their playing with thoughts of Ilúvatar's plan and design, and cared only to set it forth without aught of their own devising to adorn it; but some others, and among them many of the most beautiful and wisest of the Ainur, craved leave of Ilúvatar to dwell within the world. For said they: "We would have the guarding of those fair things of our dreams, which of thy might have now attained to reality and surpassing beauty; and we would instruct both Eldar and Men in their wonder and uses whenso the times come that those appear upon Earth by your intent, first the Eldar and at length the fathers of the fathers of Men." And Melko feigned that he desired to control the violence of the heats and turmoils he had set in the Earth, but of a truth purposed deep in his heart to usurp the power of the other Ainur and make war upon Eldar and Men, for he was wroth at those great gifts which Ilúvatar had purposed to give to these races.[8]

Now Eldar and Men were of Ilúvatar's devising only, nor, for they comprehended not fully when Ilúvatar first propounded their being, did any of the Ainur dare in their music to add anything to their fashion; and these races are for that reason named rightly the Children of Ilúvatar. This maybe is the cause wherefore many others of the Ainur, beside Melko, have ever been for meddling with both Elves and Men, be it of good or evil intent; yet seeing that Ilúvatar made the Eldar most like in nature if not in power and stature to the Ainur, while to Men he gave strange gifts, their dealings have been chiefly with the Elves.[9]

Knowing all their hearts, still did Ilúvatar grant the desire of the Ainur, nor is it said he was grieved thereat. So entered these great ones into the world, and these are they whom we now call the Valar (or the Vali, it matters not).[10] They dwelt in Valinor, or in the firmament; and some on earth or in the deeps of the Sea. There Melko ruled both fires and the cruellest frost, both the uttermost colds and the deepest furnaces beneath the hills of flame; and whatso is violent or excessive, sudden or cruel, in the world is laid to his charge, and for the most part with justice. But Ulmo dwells in the outer ocean and controls the flowing of all waters and the courses of rivers, the replenishment of springs and the distilling of rains and dews throughout the world. At the bottom of the sea he bethinks him of music deep and strange yet full ever of a sorrow: and therein he has aid from Manwë Súlimo.

The Solosimpi, what time the Elves came and dwelt in Kôr, learnt much of him, whence cometh the wistful allurement of their piping and their love to dwell ever by the shore. Salmar there was with him, and Ossë and Ónen to whom he gave the control of the waves and lesser seas, and many another.

But Aulë dwelt in Valinor and fashioned many things; tools and instruments he devised and was busied as much in the making of webs as in the beating of metals; tillage too and husbandry was his delight as much as tongues and alphabets, or broideries and painting. Of him did the Noldoli, who were the sages of the Eldar and thirsted ever after new lore and fresh knowledge, learn uncounted wealth of crafts, and magics and sciences unfathomed. From his teaching, whereto the Eldar brought ever their own great beauty of mind and heart and imagining, did they attain to the invention and making of gems; and these were not in the world before the Eldar, and the finest of all gems were Silmarilli, and they are lost.

Yet was the greatest and chief of those four great ones Manwë Súlimo; and he dwelt in Valinor and sate in a glorious abode upon a throne of wonder on the topmost pinnacle of Taniquetil that towers up upon the world's edge. Hawks flew ever to and fro about that abode, whose eyes could see to the deeps of the sea or penetrate the most hidden caverns and profoundest darkness of the world. These brought him news from everywhere of everything, and little escaped him – yet did some matters lie hid even from the Lord of the Gods. With him was Varda the Beautiful, and she became his spouse and is Queen of the Stars, and their children were Fionwë-Úrion and Erinti most lovely. About them dwell a great host of fair spirits, and their happiness is great; and men love Manwë even more than mighty Ulmo, for he hath never of intent done ill to them nor is he so fain of honour or so jealous of his power as that ancient one

of Vai. The Teleri whom Inwë ruled were especially beloved of
him, and got of him poesy and song; for if Ulmo hath a power of
musics and of voices of instruments Manwë hath a splendour of
poesy and song beyond compare.

Lo, Manwë Súlimo clad in sapphires, ruler of the airs and wind,
is held lord of Gods and Elves and Men, and the greatest bulwark
against the evil of Melko.'[11]

Then said Rúmil again:
'Lo! After the departure of these Ainur and their vassalage all
was quiet for a great age while Ilúvatar watched. Then on a sudden
he said: "Behold I love the world, and it is a hall of play for Eldar
and Men who are my beloved. But when the Eldar come they will
be the fairest and the most lovely of all things by far; and deeper in
the knowledge of beauty, and happier than Men. But to Men I will
give a new gift, and a greater." Therefore he devised that Men
should have a free virtue whereby within the limits of the powers
and substances and chances of the world they might fashion and
design their life beyond even the original Music of the Ainur that
is as fate to all things else. This he did that of their operations everything should in shape and deed be completed, and the world fulfilled
unto the last and smallest.[12] Lo! Even we Eldar have found to our
sorrow that Men have a strange power for good or ill and for turning
things despite Gods and Fairies to their mood in the world; so that
we say: "Fate may not conquer the Children of Men, but yet are
they strangely blind, whereas their joy should be great."

Now Ilúvatar knew that Men set amid the turmoils of the Ainur
would not be ever of a mind to use that gift in harmony with his
intent, but thereto he said: "These too in their time shall find that
all they have done, even the ugliest of deeds or works, redounds at
the end only to my glory, and is tributary to the beauty of my world."
Yet the Ainur say that the thought of Men is at times a grief even to
Ilúvatar; wherefore if the giving of that gift of freedom was their
envy and amazement, the patience of Ilúvatar at its misuse is a
matter of the greatest marvelling to both Gods and Fairies. It is
however of one with this gift of power that the Children of Men
dwell only a short time in the world alive, yet do not perish utterly
for ever, whereas the Eldar dwell till the Great End[13] unless they be
slain or waste in grief (for to both of these deaths are they subject),
nor doth eld subdue their strength, except it may be in ten thousand
centuries; and dying they are reborn in their children, so that their
number minishes not, nor grows. Yet while the Sons of Men will

after the passing of things of a certainty join in the Second Music
of the Ainur, what Ilúvatar has devised for the Eldar beyond the
world's end he has not revealed even to the Valar, and Melko has
not discovered it.'

## NOTES

1   This opening sentence is lacking in the draft.
2   The reference to the setting of the Secret Fire within the Ainur is
    lacking in the draft.
3   This passage, from 'Now Melko had among the Ainur...', is developed
    from one much briefer in the draft: 'Melko had among the Ainu fared
    most often alone into the dark places and the voids [*added afterwards*:
    seeking the secret fires].'
4   The words 'my song' and 'my thought' were in the text as written in
    reversed positions, and were emended afterwards in pencil to the
    reading given. At the beginning of the text occurs the phrase:
    'Before all things he sang into being the Ainur first.' Cf. the opening
    of the *Ainulindalë* in *The Silmarillion*: 'The Ainur . . . that were the
    offspring of his thought.'
5   There is no reference here in the draft to Manwë or Aulë.
6   This sentence concerning the friendship and alliance of Manwë and
    Ulmo is lacking in the draft.
7   This passage was quite different in the draft text:
    And even as Ilu was speaking to Ulmo the Ainu beheld how the
    great history which Ilu had propounded to them to their amaze-
    ment and whereto all his glory was but the hall of its enactment −
    how it was unfolding in myriad complexities even as had been the
    music they played about the feet of Ilu, how beauty was whelmed
    in uproar and tumult and again new beauty arose therefrom, how the
    earth changed and stars went out and stars were kindled, and the
    air swept about the firmament, and the sun and moon were
    loosened on their courses and had life.
8   This sentence concerning Melko is lacking in the draft.
9   In the draft this paragraph reads:
    Now Eldar and Men were of Ilu's devising alone, nor had any of
    the Ainu nor even Melko aught to do with their fashioning, though
    in truth his music of old and his deeds in the world mightily
    affected their history thereafter. For this reason maybe, Melko and
    many of the Ainu out of good or evil mind would ever be for
    meddling with them, but seeing that Ilu had made the Eldar too
    alike in nature if not in stature to the Ainu their dealings have been
    chiefly with Men.
    The conclusion of this passage seems to be the only place where the
    second text is in direct contradiction of the draft.

10  The draft has: 'and these are they whom ye and we now call the Valur and Valir.'

11  The entire passage following the mention of the Solosimpi and 'their love to dwell ever by the shore' is lacking in the draft.

12  For this passage the draft has:

". . . but to Men I will appoint a task and give a great gift." And he devised that they should have free will and the power of fashioning and designing beyond the original music of the Ainu, that by reason of their operations all things shall in shape and deed be fulfilled, and the world that comes of the music of the Ainu be completed unto the last and smallest.

13  'whereas the Eldar dwell for ever' draft text.

## Changes made to names in
## *The Music of the Ainur*

*Ainur*   Always *Ainu* in the draft text.

*Ilúvatar*   Usually *Ilu* in the draft text, but also *Ilúvatar*.

*Ulmo*   In the draft text Ulmo is thus named but also *Linqil* (corrected to *Ulmo*).

*Solosimpi* ⟨ *Solosimpë*.

*Valar or Vali*   Draft text *Valur and Valir* (these appear to be masculine and feminine forms).

*Ónen* ⟨ *Ówen*.

*Vai* ⟨ *Ulmonan*.

## Commentary on
## *The Music of the Ainur*

A linking passage continues the text of *The Music of the Ainur* and leads into the story of *The Building of Valinor* without any break in the narrative; but I postpone this link until the next chapter. The actual written text is likewise continuous between the two tales, and there is no suggestion or indication that the composition of *The Building of Valinor* did not follow that of *The Music of the Ainur*.

In later years the Creation myth was revised and rewritten over and over again; but it is notable that in this case only and in contrast to the development of the rest of the mythology there is a direct tradition, manuscript to manuscript, from the earliest draft to the final version: each text is directly based on the one preceding.* Moreover, and most

* For comparison with the published text in *The Silmarillion* it should be noted that some of the matter of the early version does not appear in the *Ainulindalë* itself but at the end of Chapter 1, *Of the Beginning of Days* (pp. 39–42).

remarkably, the earliest version, written when my father was 27 or 28 and embedded still in the context of the Cottage of Lost Play, was so evolved in its conception that it underwent little change of an essential kind. There were indeed very many changes, which can be followed stage by stage through the successive texts, and much new matter came in; but the fall of the original sentences can continually be recognized in the last version of the *Ainulindalë*, written more than thirty years later, and even many phrases survived.

It will be seen that the great theme that Ilúvatar propounded to the Ainur was originally made somewhat more explicit ('The story that I have laid before you,' p. 53), and that the words of Ilúvatar to the Ainur at the end of the Music contained a long declaration of what Melko had brought about, of what he had introduced into the world's history (p. 55). But by far the most important difference is that in the early form the Ainur's first sight of the World was in its actuality ('even now the world unfolds and its history begins', p. 55), not as a Vision that was taken away from them and only given existence in the words of Ilúvatar: *Eä! Let these things Be!* (*The Silmarillion* p. 20).

Yet when all differences have been observed, they are much less remarkable than the solidity and completeness with which the myth of the Creation emerged at its first beginning.

In this 'Tale', also, many specific features of less general import make their appearance; and many of them were to survive. Manwë, called 'lord of Gods and Elves and Men', is surnamed *Súlimo*, 'ruler of the airs and wind'; he is clad in sapphires, and hawks of penetrating sight fly from his dwelling on Taniquetil (*The Silmarillion* p. 40); he loves especially the Teleri (the later Vanyar), and from him they received their gifts of poetry and song; and his spouse is Varda, Queen of the Stars.

Manwë, Melko, Ulmo, and Aulë are marked out as 'the four great ones'; ultimately the great Valar, the *Aratar*, came to be numbered nine, but there was much shifting in the membership of the hierarchy before this was reached. The characteristic concerns of Aulë, and his particular association with the Noldoli, emerge here as they were to remain, though there is attributed to him a delight in 'tongues and alphabets', whereas in *The Silmarillion* (p. 39), while this is not denied, it seems to be implied that this was rather the peculiar endowment and skill of the Noldorin Elves; later in the *Lost Tales* (p. 141) it is said that Aulë himself 'aided by the Gnomes contrived alphabets and scripts'. Ulmo, specially associated with the Solosimpi (the later Teleri), is here presented as more 'fain of his honour and jealous of his power' than Manwë; and he dwells in Vai. Vai is an emendation of Ulmonan; but this is not simply a replacement of one name by another: Ulmonan was the name of Ulmo's halls, which were in Vai, the Outer Ocean. The significance of Vai, an important element in the original cosmology, will emerge in the next chapter.

Other divine beings now appear. Manwë and Varda have offspring, Fionwë-Úrion and Erinti. Erinti later became Ilmarë 'handmaid of Varda'

(*The Silmarillion* p. 30), but nothing was ever told of her (see p. 202). Fionwë, his name long afterwards changed to Eönwë, endured to become the Herald of Manwë, when the idea of 'the Children of the Valar' was abandoned. Beings subordinate to Ulmo, Salmar, Ossë, and Ónen (later Uinen) appear; though these all survived in the pantheon, the conception of Maiar did not emerge for many years, and Ossë was long numbered among the Valar. The Valar are here referred to as 'Gods' (indeed when Eriol asked 'are they the Gods?' Lindo replied that they were, p. 45), and this usage survived until far on in the development of the mythology.

The idea of Elvish rebirth in their own children is here formally stated, and the different fates of Elves and Men. In this connection, the following curious matter may be mentioned. Early in the text just given (p. 53) occurs the sentence: 'It is said that a mightier [music] far shall be woven before the seat of Ilúvatar by the choirs of both Ainur *and the sons of Men* after the Great End'; and in the concluding sentence of the text: 'Yet while *the sons of Men* will after the passing of things of a certainty join in the Second Music of the Ainur, what Ilúvatar has devised for the Eldar beyond the world's end he has not revealed even to the Valar, and Melko has not discovered it.' Now in the first revision of the *Ainulindalë* (which dates from the 1930s) the first of these sentences was changed to read: '. . . by the choirs of the Ainur *and the Children of Ilúvatar* after the end of days'; whereas the second remained, in this essential, unchanged. This remained the case right through to the final version. It is possible that the change in the first passage was unintentional, the substitution of another common phrase, and that this was never subsequently picked up. However, in the published work (pp. 15, 42) I left the two passages as they stand.

# III

# THE COMING OF THE VALAR
# AND THE BUILDING OF VALINOR

As I have already noticed, the next tale is linked to *The Music of the Ainur* without narrative break; and it has no title in the text. It is contained in three separate books (the *Lost Tales* were written in the most bewildering fashion, with sections from different tales interleaved with each other); and on the cover of the book that has the opening section, following on *The Music of the Ainur*, is written: 'containeth also the Coming of the Valar and beginneth the Building of Valinor'. The text is in ink, written over an erased pencil manuscript.

Then when Rúmil finished and fell silent Eriol said after a pause: 'Great are these tidings and very new and strange in my ears, yet doth it seem that most whereof you have yet told happened outside this world, whereas if I know now wherefrom comes its life and motion and the ultimate devising of its history, I would still hear many things of the earliest deeds within its borders; of the labours of the Valar I would know, and the great beings of most ancient days. Whereof, tell me, are the Sun or the Moon or the Stars, and how came their courses and their stations? Nay more – whence are the continents of the earth, the Outer Lands, the great seas, and the Magic Isles? Even of the Eldar and their arising and of the coming of Men I would listen to your tales of wisdom and wonder.'

Then answered Rúmil: 'Nay, but your questions are nigh as long and wordy as my tales – and the thirst of your curiosity would dry a well deeper than even my lore, an I let you drink and come again unstinted to your liking. Indeed you know not what you ask nor the length and complexity of the stories you would hear. Behold, the sun is well above the roofs and this is no hour of the day for the telling of tales. Rather is it time already, and something more, for the breaking of the fast.' With these words Rúmil went down that lane of hazels, and passing a space of sunlight entered the house at great speed, for all that he looked ever before his toes as he went.

But Eriol sat musing in that arbour, pondering what he had heard, and many questions came into his mind that he desired to ask, until he forgot that he fasted still. But now comes Littleheart and another bearing covers and fair linen, and they say to him: 'It is the words of

Rúmil the Sage that you are fainting in the Arbour of the Thrushes for hunger and for weariness of his garrulous tongue – and thinking that very like to be, we are come to aid thee.'

Then Eriol thanked them, and breaking his fast spent the remainder of that fair day hidden in the quiet alleys of that garden deep in thought; nor did he have lack of pleasance, for although it seemed enclosed within great stone walls covered with fruit-trees or with climbing plants whose golden and red blossoms shone beneath the sun, yet were the nooks and corners of the garden, its coppices and lawns, its shady ways and flowering fields, without end, and exploration discovered always something new. Nonetheless even greater was his joy when that night again the toast was drunk to the 'Rekindling of the Magic Sun' and the candles held aloft and the throng went once more to the room where the Tale-fire burnt.

There said Lindo: 'Is it to be tales, as of custom, again this night, or shall it be musics and the singing of songs?' And the most said songs and music, and thereat skilled ones arose who sang old melodies or maybe roused dead minstrelsy of Valinor to life amid the flicker of that firelit room. Some too spake poesies concerning Kôr, and Eldamar, short snatches of the wealth of old; but soon the song and music died down and there was a quiet, while those there thought of the departed beauty and longed eagerly for the Rekindling of the Magic Sun.

Now at length spake Eriol to Lindo, saying: 'One Rúmil the doorward, and, methought, a great sage, did this morning in the garden relate to me the beginning of the world and the coming of the Valar. Now fain would I hear of Valinor!'

Then said Rúmil, for he sat upon a stool in a deep-shadowed nook: 'Then with the leave of Lindo and of Vairë I will begin the tale, else will you go on asking for ever; and may the company have pardon if they hear old tales again.' But Vairë said that those words concerning the oldest things were far from stale yet in the ears of the Eldar.

Then said Rúmil:

'Behold, Manwë Súlimo and Varda the Beautiful arose. Varda it was who at the playing of the Music had thought much of light that was of white and silver, and of stars. Those twain gathered now wings of power to themselves and fared swiftly through the three airs. Vaitya is that which is wrapped dark and sluggish about the world and without it, but Ilwë is blue and clear and flows among the stars, and last came they to Vilna that is grey and therein may the birds fly safely.

With them came many of those lesser Vali who loved them and

had played nigh them and attuned their music to theirs, and these are the Mánir and the Súruli, the sylphs of the airs and of the winds.

Now swiftly as they fared Melko was there before them, having rushed headlong flaming through the airs in the impetuosity of his speed, and there was a tumult of the sea where he had dived and the mountains above him spouted flames and the earth gaped and rocked; but Manwë beholding this was wroth.

Thereafter came Ulmo and Aulë, and with Ulmo were none, save Salmar only who was after known as ¡Noldorin, for good though the heart of that mighty one he thought ever deep thoughts alone, and was silent and aloof and haughty even to the Ainur; but with Aulë was that great lady Palúrien whose delights were richness and fruits of the earth, for which reason has she long been called Yavanna among the Eldar. About them fared a great host who are the sprites of trees and woods, of dale and forest and mountain-side, or those that sing amid the grass at morning and chant among the standing corn at eve. These are the Nermir and the Tavari, Nandini and Orossi, brownies, fays, pixies, leprawns, and what else are they not called, for their number is very great: yet must they not be confused with the Eldar, for they were born before the world and are older than its oldest, and are not of it, but laugh at it much, for had they not somewhat to do with its making, so that it is for the most part a play for them; but the Eldar are of the world and love it with a great and burning love, and are wistful in all their happiness for that reason.

Now behind those greatest chieftains came Falman-Ossë of the waves of the sea and Ónen his consort, and with them the troops of the Oarni and Falmaríni and the long-tressed Wingildi, and these are the spirits of the foam and the surf of ocean. Now Ossë was a vassal and subordinate to Ulmo, and was so for fear and reverence and not for love. Behind him there came Tulkas Poldórëa rejoicing in his strength, and those brethren the Fánturi, Fantur of Dreams who is Lórien Olofántur, and Fantur of Death who is Vefántur Mandos, and those twain also who are named Tári for they are ladies of great worship, queens of the Valar. The one was the spouse of Mandos, and is known to all as Fui Nienna by reason of her glooms, and she is fain of mourning and tears. Many other names has she that are spoken seldom and all are grievous, for she is Núri who sighs and Heskil who breedeth winter, and all must bow before her as Qalmë-Tári the mistress of death. But lo, the other was the spouse of Oromë the hunter who is named Aldaron king of forests, who shouts for joy upon mountain-tops and is nigh as lusty as that perpetual youth Tulkas. Oromë is the son of Aulë and Palúrien, and that Tári who is his wife is known to all as Vána the fair and loveth mirth and youth and beauty, and is happiest of all beings, for she is Tuilérë or as the Valar said Vána Tuivána who bringeth spring, and all sing her praises as Tári-Laisi mistress of life.

Yet even when all these had crossed the confines of the world and Vilna was in uproar with their passing, there came still hurrying late Makar and his fierce sister Meássë; and it had been better had they not found the world but remained for ever with the Ainur beyond Vaitya and the stars, for both were spirits of quarrelsome mood, and with some other lesser ones who came now with them had been the first and chief to join in the discords of Melko and to aid in the spreading of his music.

Last of all came Ómar who is called Amillo, youngest of the great Valar, and he sang songs as he came.

Then when all these great spirits were gathered together within the confines of the world Manwë spake to them, saying: "Lo now! How may the Valar abide in this fair place or be happy and rejoice in its goodness, if Melko be suffered to destroy it, and make fire and turmoil, so that we have not where to sit in peace, nor may the earth blossom or the designs of Ilúvatar come to being?"

Then all the Valar were angered with Melko, and Makar alone spoke against Manwë; but the rest chose certain of their number to seek out the wrongdoer, and these were Mandos and Tulkas, Mandos for that of his dread aspect was Melko more in fear than of aught else save it were the strength of Tulkas' arm, and Tulkas was the other.

Now those two sought him out and constrained him to come before Manwë, and Tulkas whose heart misliked the crooked guile of Melko gave him a blow with his fist, and he abode that then but did not forget. Yet did he speak the Gods fair, and said how he did scant harm, revelling only a while in the newness of the world; nor, said he, would he ever seek to do aught against the lordship of Manwë or the dignity of those chiefs Aulë and Ulmo, nor indeed to the hurt of any beside. Rather was it his counsel that each of the Valar should now depart and dwell amid those things that he loved upon Earth, nor should any seek to extend his sway beyond its just boundaries. In this there was some covert reflection upon Manwë and Ulmo, but of the Gods some took his words in faith and would use his advice, but others distrusted; and in the midst of their debate Ulmo arose and went to the Outermost Seas that were set beyond the Outer Lands. He loved not high words nor concourse of folk, and in those deep waters moveless and empty he purposed to dwell, leaving the governance of the Great and lesser seas to Ossë and Ónen his vassals. Yet ever of his magic deep in his outermost sea-halls of Ulmonan he controlled the faint stirrings of the Shadowy Seas, and ruled the lakes and springs and rivers of the world.

Now this was the manner of the Earth in those days, nor has it since changed save by the labours of the Valar of old. Mightiest of regions are the Great Lands where Men do dwell and wander now, and the Lost Elves sing and dance upon the hills; but beyond their westernmost limits lie the Great Seas, and in that vast water of the West are many smaller lands and isles, ere the lonely seas are found whose waves whisper about the Magic Isles. Farther even than this, and few are the boats of mortal men that have dared so far, are set the Shadowy Seas whereon there float the Twilit Isles and the Tower of Pearl rises pale upon their most western cape; but as yet it was not built, and the Shadowy Seas stretched dark away till their uttermost shore in Eruman.                                                  ·

Now the Twilit Isles are reckoned the first of the Outer Lands, which are these and Eruman and Valinor. Eruman or Arvalin is to the southward, but the Shadowy Seas run even to the edges of Eldamar to the north; yet must ships sail farther to reach these silver strands, for beyond Eruman stand the Mountains of Valinor in a great ring curving westward, and the Shadowy Seas to north of Eruman bend a vast bay inward, so that waves beat even upon the feet of the great cliffs and the Mountains stand beside the sea. There is Taniquetil glorious to behold, loftiest of all mountains, clad in purest snow, and he looks from the bay's head southward across Eruman and northward across the Bay of Faëry; indeed all the Shadowy Seas, even the sails of ships upon the sunlit waters of the great ocean and the throngs about westward havens in the lands of Men could afterward be seen therefrom, albeit that distance is counted out in unimagined leagues. But as yet the Sun had not risen and the Mountains of Valinor had not been raised, and the vale of Valinor lay wide and cold. Beyond Valinor I have never seen or heard, save that of a surety there are the dark waters of the Outer Seas, that have no tides, and they are very cool and thin, that no boat can sail upon their bosom or fish swim within their depths, save the enchanted fish of Ulmo and his magic car.

Thither is he now gone, but the Gods hold council concerning the words of Melko. It was the rede of Aulë and of his wife Palúrien, for they were the most grieved by the mischief of Melko's turmoils and trusted his promises not at all, that the Gods should not separate as he bid, lest he take it into his heart perchance to attack them singly or do hurt to their possessions. "Is he not," said they, "more powerful than any one of us save Manwë only? Rather let us build a dwelling wherein we may abide in joy together, faring only at need to the care and survey of our goods and fiefs. There even such as be of other mind may dwell at times, and find rest and pleasance after labours in the world." Now Aulë's mind and fingers itched already to be making things, and he urged this matter the more for that; and to most of the Gods it seemed a good counsel, and they fared about the world seeking a place to dwell in. Those were the days of Gloaming (Lomendánar), for light there was, silver and golden, but it was not gathered together but flowed and quivered in uneven streams about the airs, or at times fell gently to the earth in glittering rain and ran like water on the ground; and at that time Varda in her playing had set but a few stars within the sky.

In this dimness the Gods stalked North and South and could see little; indeed in the deepest of these regions they found great cold and solitude and the rule of Melko already fortified in strength; but Melko and his servants were delving in the North, fashioning the grim halls of Utumna, for he had no thought to dwell amongst the others, howso he might feign peace and friendship for the time.

Now because of the darkness Aulë suaded Melko to build two towers to the North and South, for he purposed to set upon them mighty lamps one upon each. These did Aulë himself fashion of gold and silver, and the pillars were raised by Melko and were very tall, and shone like pale blue crystal; and when Aulë smote them with his hand they rang like metal. They sprang up through the lower air even to Ilwë and the stars, and Melko said they were of an imperishable substance of great strength that he had devised; and he lied, for he knew that they were of ice. That one of the North he named Ringil and of the South Helkar, and the lamps were made ready and set upon them, being filled with gathered light, silver to the North and golden to the South. This light had Manwë and Varda gathered lavishly from the sky, that the Gods might the better explore the regions of the world, and choose the fairest for their home.

Now in that flaming light did they fare East and West, and East was a waste of tumbled lands and West great seas of darkness, for indeed they were gathered now upon those Twilit Isles and stood there gazing westward, when lo! the lamps to North and South flickered and fell, and as they fell the waters rose about the isles. Now these things they did not then understand, but it so happened that the blaze of those lights had melted the treacherous ice of the pillars of Melko, Ringil and Helkar, and great floods of water had poured from them into the Shadowy Seas. So great was their thaw that whereas those seas were at first of no great size but clear and warm, now were they black and wide and vapours lay upon them and deep shades, for the great cold rivers that poured into them. Thus were the mighty lamps unseated from on high and the clangour of their fall shook the stars, and some of their light was spilled again into the air, but much flowed upon the earth and made fires and deserts for its great volume ere it gathered into lakes and pools.

Then was the time of first night and it was very long; but the Valar were sorely wroth at the treachery of Melko and were like to be whelmed in the shadowy seas that now arose and sucked about their feet, covering many of the islands in their waves.

Then Ossë, for Ulmo was not there, gathered to him the Oarni, and putting forth their might they dragged that island whereon stood the Valar westward from the waters till they came to Eruman, whose high shores held the angry flood – and that was the first tide.

Then said Manwë: "Now will we make a dwelling speedily and a bulwark against evil." So they fared over Arvalin and saw a wide open space beyond, reaching for unknown leagues even to the Outer Seas. There, said Aulë, would be a place well suited to great building and to a fashioning of realms of delight; wherefore the Valar and all their folk first gathered the most mighty rocks and stones from Arvalin and reared therewith huge mountains between it and that plain which now they name Valinor, or the land of the Gods. Aulë indeed it was himself who laboured for seven ages at Manwë's bidding in the piling of Taniquetil, and the world rumbled in the gloom and Melko heard the noises of their labour. By reason of their great masonry is Erumáni now very broad and bare and of a marvellous level, for they removed all the stone and rock that was there; but the Mountains of Valinor are rugged and of impregnable height. Seeing at length that these towered mightily between Valinor and the world the Gods drew breath; but Aulë and Tulkas fared abroad with many of their folk and brought back all they might of marbles and good stones, of iron and gold and silver and bronze and all manner of substances. These they heaped amid the plain, and straightway Aulë began to labour mightily.

At last he says: "It is ill working in this gloom, and 'twas an evil deed of Melko's that brought to ruin those fair lamps." But Varda answering said: "Still is there much light remaining both in the airs and that which floweth spilled upon the earth", and she wished to gather new store and set a beacon on Taniquetil. But Manwë

suffered not more radiance to be gleaned from heaven, for that the
dark was already that of night, but at his asking Ulmo rose from his
deeps and fared to the blazing lakes and the pools of brilliance.
Therefrom he drew rivers of light into vast vessels, pouring back
waters in their place, and with these he got him back to Valinor.
There was all the light poured into two great cauldrons that Aulë
fashioned in the gloom against his return, and those are called
Kulullin and Silindrin.

Now in the midmost vale they digged two great pits, and those
are leagues asunder yet nigh together beside the vastness of that
plain. In the one did Ulmo set seven rocks of gold brought from
the most silent deeps of the sea, and a fragment was cast thereafter
of the lamp that had burned awhile upon Helkar in the South. Then
was the pit covered with rich earths that Palúrien devised, and Vána
came who loveth life and sunlight and at whose song the flowers
arise and open, and the murmur of her maidens round her was like
to the merry noise of folk that stir abroad for the first time on a bright
morning. There sang she the song of spring upon the mound, and
danced about it, and watered it with great streams of that golden
light that Ulmo had brought from the spilled lakes – yet was Kulullin
almost o'erflowing at the end.

But in the other pit they cast three huge pearls that Ossë found in
the Great Sea, and a small star Varda cast after them, and they
covered it with foams and white mists and thereafter sprinkled
lightly earth upon it, but Lórien who loveth twilights and flittering
shadows, and sweet scents borne upon evening winds, who is the
lord of dreams and imaginings, sat nigh and whispered swift noiseless words, while his sprites played half-heard tunes beside him like
music stealing out into the dark from distant dwellings; and the Gods
poured upon that place rivers of the white radiance and silver light
which Silindrin held even to the brim – and after their pouring was
Silindrin yet well nigh full.

Then came Palúrien, even Kémi the Earth-lady, wife of Aulë,
mother of the lord of forests, and she wove spells about those two
places, deep enchantments of life and growth and putting forth of
leaf, blossoming and yielding of fruit – but she mingled no word of
fading in her song. There having sung she brooded for a great while,
and the Valar sat in a circle about, and the plain of Valinor was dark.
Then after a time there came at last a bright gleam of gold amid
the gloom, and a cry of joy and praise was sent up by the Valar and
all their companies. Behold from that place that had been watered
from Kulullin rose a slender shoot, and from its bark pale gold

effulgence poured; yet did that plant grow apace so that in seven hours there was a tree of mighty stature, and all the Valar and their folk might sit beneath its branches. Of a great shapeliness and goodly growth was that stock, and nought was there to break its smooth rind, which glowed faintly with a yellow light, for a vast height above the earth. Then did fair boughs thrust overhead in all directions, and golden buds swelled from all the twigs and lesser branches, and from these burst leaves of a rich green whose edges shone. Already was the light that that tree gave wide and fair, but as the Valar gazed it put forth blossom in exceeding great profusion, so that all its boughs were hidden by long swaying clusters of gold flowers like a myriad hanging lamps of flame, and light spilled from the tips of these and splashed upon the ground with a sweet noise. Then did the Gods praise Vána and Palúrien and rejoice in the light, saying to them: "Lo, this is a very fair tree indeed, and must have a name unto itself," and Kémi said: "Let it be called Laurelin, for the brightness of its blossom and the music of its dew," but Vána would call it Lindelóksë, and both names remain.

Now was it twelve hours since Lindelóksë had first sprouted, and at that hour did a glint of silver pierce the yellow blaze, and behold the Valar saw a shoot arise in that place whereto the pools of Silindrin had been poured. It had a bark of tender white that gleamed like pearls and it grew even as swiftly as had Laurelin, and as it grew the glory of Laurelin abated and its blossom shone less, till that tree glowed only gently as in sleep: but, behold, the other waxed now to a stature even as lofty as Laurelin, and its stock was yet more shapely and more slender, and its rind like silk, but its boughs above were thicker and more tangled and its twigs denser, and they put forth masses of bluish green leaves like spearheads.

Then did the Valar stare in wonder, but Palúrien said: "Not yet has this tree ceased its growing", and behold as she spake it blossomed, and its blossoms did not hang in clusters but were like separate flowers growing each on fine stems that swung together, and were as silver and pearls and glittering stars and burnt with a white light; and it seemed as if the tree's heart throbbed, and its radiance wavered thereto waxing and waning. Light like liquid silver distilled from its bole and dripped to earth, and it shed a very great illumination about the plain, yet was that not as wide as the light of the tree of gold, and by reason also of its great leaves and of the throb of its inward life it cast a continual flutter of shadows among the pools of its brightness, very clear and black; whereat Lórien could not contain his joy, and even Mandos smiled. But Lórien said: "Lo! I will give this tree a name and call it Silpion", and that has ever been its name since. Then Palúrien arose and said to the Gods: "Gather ye now all the light that drips in liquid shape from this fair tree and store it in Silindrin, and let it fare thence but very sparingly. Behold, this tree, when the twelve hours of its fullest light are past, will wane again, and thereat will Laurelin blaze forth once more; but that it may not be exhausted water it ever gently from the cauldron of Kulullin at the hour when Silpion grows dim, but to Silpion do ye in the same manner, pouring back the gathered light from deep Silindrin at every waning of the tree of gold. Light is the sap of these trees and their sap is light!"

And in these words did she signify that albeit these trees must needs be watered with light to have sap and live, yet of their growth and being did they ever make light in great abundance still over and beyond that which their roots sucked in; but the Gods hearkened to her bidding, and Vána caused one of her own maidens, even Urwen, to care ever for this task of watering Laurelin, while Lórien bade Silmo, a youth he loved, to be ever mindful of the refreshing of Silpion. Wherefore is it said that at either watering of the trees there was a wondrous gloaming of gold and silver and mingled lights great beauty ere one tree quite faded or the other came to its full glory.

Now because of the bright trees had Aulë light in plenty for his works, and he set about many tasks, and Tulkas aided him much, and Palúrien mother of magic was at his side. First upon Taniquetil was a great abode raised up for Manwë and a watchtower set. Thence did he speed his darting hawks and receive them on his return, and thither fared often in later days Sorontur King of Eagles whom Manwë gave much might and wisdom.

That house was builded of marbles white and blue and stood amid the fields of snow, and its roofs were made of a web of that blue air called *ilwë* that is above the white and grey. This web did Aulë and his wife contrive, but Varda spangled it with stars, and Manwë dwelt thereunder; but in the plain in the full radiance of the trees was a cluster of dwellings built like a fair and smiling town, and that town was named Valmar. No metal and no stone, nor any wood of mighty trees was spared to their raising. Their roofs were of gold and their floors silver and their doors of polished bronze; they were lifted with spells and their stones were bound with magic. Separate from these and bordering upon the open vale was a great court, and this was Aulë's house, and it was filled with magic webs woven of the light of Laurelin and the sheen of Silpion and the glint of stars; but others there were made of threads of gold and silver and iron and bronze beaten to the thinness of a spider's filament, and all were woven with beauty to stories of the musics of the Ainur, picturing those things that were and shall be, or such as have only been in the glory of the mind of Ilúvatar.

In this court were some of all the trees that after grew upon the earth, and a pool of blue water lay among them. There fruits fell throughout the day, thudding richly to the earth upon the grass of its margin, and were gathered by Palúrien's maids for her feasting and her lord's.

Ossë too had a great house, and dwelt therein whenso a conclave of the Valar was held or did he grow weary of the noise of the waves upon his seas. Ónen and the Oarni brought thousands of pearls for its building, and its floors were of sea-water, and its tapestries like the glint of the silver skins of fishes, and it was roofed with foam. Ulmo dwelt not in Valmar and fared back after its building to the Outer Seas, and did he have need ever of sojourn in Valinor he would go as guest to the halls of Manwë; – but this was not often. Lórien too dwelt far away, and his hall was great and dimly lit and had wide gardens. The place of his dwelling he called Murmuran, which Aulë made of mists gathered beyond Arvalin upon the Shadowy Seas. 'Twas set in the South by the feet of the Mountains of Valinor upon the confines of the realm, but its gardens wandered marvellously about, winding nigh to the feet of Silpion whose shining lit them strangely. They were full of labyrinths and mazes, for Palúrien had given Lórien great wealth of yewtrees and cedars, and of pines that exuded drowsy odours in the dusk; and these hung over deep pools. Glowworms crept about their borders and Varda had set stars within their depths for the pleasure of Lórien, but his sprites sang wonderfully in these gardens and the scent of nightflowers and the songs of sleepy nightingales filled them with great loveliness. There too grew the poppies glowing redly in the dusk, and those the Gods called *fumellar* the flowers of sleep – and Lórien used them much in his enchantments. Amidmost of those pleasances was set within a ring of shadowy cypress towering high that deep vat Silindrin. There it lay in a bed of pearls, and its surface unbroken was shot with silver flickerings, and the shadows of the trees lay on it, and the Mountains of Valinor could see their faces mirrored there. Lórien gazing upon it saw many visions of mystery pass across its face, and that he suffered never to be stirred from its sleep save when Silmo came noiselessly with a silver urn to draw a draught of its shimmering cools, and fared softly thence to water the roots of Silpion ere the tree of gold grew hot.

Otherwise was the mind of Tulkas, and he dwelt amidmost of Valmar. Most youthful is he and strong of limb and lusty, and for that is he named Poldórëa who loveth games and twanging of bows and boxing, wrestling, running, and leaping, and songs that go with a swing and a toss of a well-filled cup. Nonetheless is he no wrangler or striker of blows unprovoked as is Makar, albeit there are none of Valar or Úvanimor (who are monsters, giants, and ogres) that do not fear the sinews of his arm and the buffet of his iron-clad fist, when he has cause for wrath. His was a house of mirth and revelry; and it sprang high into the air with many storeys, and had a tower of bronze and pillars of copper in a wide arcade. In its court men played and rivalled one another in doughty feats, and there at times would that fair maiden Nessa wife of Tulkas bear goblets of the goodliest wine and cooling drinks among the players. But most she loved to retire unto a place of fair lawns whose turf Oromë her brother had culled from the richest of all his forest glades, and Palúrien had planted it with spells that it was always green and smooth. There danced she among her maidens as long as Laurelin was in bloom, for is she not greater in the dance than Vána herself?

In Valmar too dwelt Noldorin known long ago as Salmar, playing now upon his harps and lyres, now sitting beneath Laurelin and raising sweet music with an instrument of the bow. There sang Amillo joyously to his playing, Amillo who is named Ómar, whose voice is the best of all voices, who knoweth all songs in all speeches; but whiles if he sang not to his brother's harp then would he be trilling in the gardens of Oromë when after a time Nielíqui, little maiden, danced about its woods.

Now Oromë had a vast domain and it was beloved by him, and no less by Palúrien his mother. Behold, the groves of trees they planted upon the plain of Valinor and even upon the foothills of the mountains have no compare on Earth. Beasts revelled there, deer among the trees, and herds of kine among its spaces and wide grass-lands; bison there were, and horses roaming unharnessed, but these strayed never into the gardens of the Gods, yet were they in peace and had no fear, for beasts of prey dwelt not among them, nor did Oromë fare to hunting in Valinor. Much indeed as he loves those realms yet is he very often in the world without; more often even than Ossë and as often as Palúrien, and then does he become the greatest of all huntsmen. But in Valmar his halls are wide and low, and skins and fells of great richness and price are strewn there without end upon the floor or hung upon the walls, and spears and bows and knives thereto. In the midst of each room and hall a living tree grows and holds up the roof, and its bole is hung with trophies and with antlers. Here is all Oromë's folk in green and brown and there is a noise of boisterous mirth, and the lord of forests makes lusty cheer; but Vána his wife so often as she may steals thence. Far away from the echoing courts of that house lie her gardens, fenced stoutly from the wilder lands with whitethorn of great size that blossoms like everlasting snow. Its innermost solitude is walled with roses, and this is the place best beloved of that fair lady of the Spring. Amidmost of this place of odorous air did Aulë set long ago that cauldron, gold Kulullin, filled ever with the radiance of Laurelin like shining water, and thereof he contrived a fountain so that all the garden was full of the health and happiness of its pure light. Birds sang there all the year with the full throat of spring, and flowers grew in a riot of blossom and of glorious life. Yet was none ever of that splendour spilled from the vat of gold save when Vána's maidens led by Urwen left that garden at the waxing of Silpion to water the roots of the tree of flame; but by the fountain it was always light with the amber light of day, as bees made busy about the roses, and there trod Vána lissomly while larks sang above her golden head.

So fair were these abodes and so great the brilliance of the trees of Valinor that Vefántur and Fui his wife of tears might not endure to stay there long, but fared away far to the northward of those regions, where beneath the roots of the most cold and northerly of the Mountains of Valinor, that rise here again almost to their height nigh Arvalin, they begged Aulë to delve them a hall. Wherefore, that all the Gods might be housed to their liking, he did so, and they and all their shadowy folk aided him. Very vast were those caverns that they made stretching even down under the Shadowy Seas, and they are full of gloom and filled with echoes, and all that deep abode is known to Gods and Elves as Mandos. There in a sable hall sat Vefántur, and he called that hall with his own name Vê. It was lit only with a single vessel placed in the centre, wherein there lay some gleaming drops of the pale dew of Silpion: it was draped with dark vapours and its floors and columns were of jet. Thither in after days fared the Elves of all the clans who were by illhap slain with weapons or did die of grief for those that were slain – and only so might the Eldar die, and then it was only for a while. There Mandos spake their doom, and there they waited in the darkness, dreaming of their past deeds, until such time as he appointed when they might again be born into their children, and go forth to laugh and sing again. To Vê Fui came not much, for she laboured rather at the distilling of salt humours whereof are tears, and black clouds she wove and floated up that they were caught in the winds and went about the world, and their lightless webs settled ever and anon upon those that dwelt therein. Now these tissues were despairs and hopeless mourning, sorrows and blind grief. The hall that she loved best was one yet wider and more dark than Vê, and she too named it with her own name, calling it Fui. Therein before her black chair burnt a brazier with a single flickering coal, and the roof was of bats' wings, and the pillars that upheld it and the walls about were made of basalt. Thither came the sons of Men to hear their doom, and thither are they brought by all the multitude of ills that Melko's evil music set within the world. Slaughters and fires, hungers and mishaps, diseases and blows dealt in the dark, cruelty and bitter cold and anguish and their own folly bring them here; and Fui reads their hearts. Some then she keeps in Mandos beneath the mountains and some she drives forth beyond the hills and Melko seizes them and bears them to Angamandi, or the Hells of Iron, where they have evil days. Some too, and these are the many, she sends aboard the black ship Mornië, who lieth ever and anon in a dark harbour of the North awaiting those times when the sad pomp winds to the beach down slow rugged paths from Mandos.

Then, when she is laden, of her own accord she spreads her sable sails and before a slow wind coasts down those shores. Then do all aboard as they come South cast looks of utter longing and regret to that low place amid the hills where Valinor may just be glimpsed upon the far off plain; and that opening is nigh Taniquetil where is the strand of Eldamar. No more do they ever see of that bright place, but borne away dwell after on the wide plains of Arvalin. There do they wander in the dusk, camping as they may, yet are they not utterly without song, and they can see the stars, and wait in patience till the Great End come.

Few are they and happy indeed for whom at a season doth Nornorë the herald of the Gods set out. Then ride they with him in chariots or upon good horses down into the vale of Valinor and feast in the halls of Valmar, dwelling in the houses of the Gods until the Great End come. Far away are they from the black mountains of the North or the misty plains of Arvalin, and music and fair light is theirs, and joy.

And lo! Now have I recounted the manner of the dwellings of all the great Gods which Aulë of his craftsmanship raised in Valinor, but Makar and his fierce sister Meássë built them a dwelling of themselves, aided only by their own folk, and a grim hall it was.

Upon the confines of the Outer Lands did it stand, nor was it very far from Mandos. Of iron was it made, and unadorned. There fought the vassals of Makar clad in armour, and a clash there was and a shouting and a braying of trumps, but Meásse fared among the warriors and egged them to more blows, or revived the fainting with strong wine that they might battle still; and her arms were reddened to the elbow dabbling in that welter.

None of the Gods fared ever there, save Tulkas, and did they seek to visit Mandos they went thither by circuitous paths to avoid passing nigh to that clamorous hall; but Tulkas would at times wrestle there with Makar or deal sledge-blows among the fighters, and this he did that he might not grow soft in his fair living, for he loved not that company nor in sooth did they love him and his great unangered strength. Now the battle of the courts of Makar was waged unceasingly save when men gathered in the halls for feasting, or at those times when Makar and Meásse were far abroad hunting together in the black mountains wolves and bears. But that house was full of weapons of battle in great array, and shields of great size and brightness of polish were on the walls. It was lit with torches, and fierce songs of victory, of sack and harrying, were there sung, and the torches' red light was reflected in the blades of naked swords. There sit often Makar and his sister listening to the songs, and Makar has a huge bill across his knees and Meásse holds a spear. But in those days ere the closing of Valinor did these twain fare mostly about the Earth and were often far from the land, for they loved the unbridled turmoils which Melko roused throughout the world.

Therefore is Valinor now built, and there is great peace there, and the Gods in joy, for those quarrelsome spirits dwell not much among them, and Melko comes not nigh.'

Then said a child among the company, a great drinker-in of both tales and poesies: 'And would that he had never come there since, and would that I might have seen that land still gleaming new as Aulë left it.' Now she had heard Rúmil tell his tale before and was much in thought of it, but to the most of the company it was new, even as it was to Eriol, and they sat amazed. Then said Eriol: 'Very mighty and glorious are the Valar, and I would fain hear yet more of those oldest days, did I not see the glimmer of the Candles of Sleep that fare now hither'; but another child spoke from a cushion nigh Lindo's chair and said: 'Nay, 'tis in the halls of Makar I would fain be, and get perchance a sword or knife to wear; yet in Valmar methinks 'twould be good to be a guest of Oromë', and Lindo laughing said: ''Twould be good indeed,' and thereat he arose, and the tale-telling was over for that night.

## NOTES

### Changes made to names in
### The Coming of the Valar and the Building of Valinor

*Ónen*  〈 *Ówen* (at the first occurrence only; subsequently *Ónen* is the name as first written).

*Eruman* and *Arvalin*  The names of this region were originally written *Habbanan* and *Harmalin*, but were emended throughout the tale (except in two cases where *Habbanan* was overlooked) to *Eruman* (once *Erumáni*, p. 70) and *Arvalin*. (In the last three occurrences *Habbanan* 〉 *Arvalin*, whereas in the earlier ones *Habbanan* 〉 *Eruman*; but the difference is presumably without significance, since the names *Habbanan* / *Harmalin* and later *Eruman* / *Arvalin* were interchangeable.) In *The Cottage of Lost Play* the changes were *Harwalin* 〉 *Harmalin* 〉 *Arvalin* (p. 22).

*Lomendánar*  〈 *Lome Danar*.

*Silindrin*  〈 *Telimpë* (*Silindrin*) (at the first occurrence only; subsequently *Silindrin* is the name as first written).

*Lindeloksë*  〈 *Lindelótë* (cf. p. 22).

### Commentary on
### The Coming of the Valar and the Building of Valinor

The abundant instruction provided by Rúmil on this occasion is best discussed in sections, and I begin with:

#### (i) The Coming of the Valar and their encounter with Melko
#### (pp. 65–7)

The description of the entry of the Valar into the world was not retained, though the account of them in this passage is the ultimate origin of that in the *Valaquenta* (*The Silmarillion* pp. 25–9): not, however, by continuous manuscript progression. The passage is of much interest, for here appear all at once many figures of the mythology who were to endure, beside others who were not. It is remarkable how many of the names of the Valar in the earliest writings were never afterwards displaced or reshaped: *Yavanna, Tulkas, Lórien, Nienna, Oromë, Aldaron, Vána, Nessa*, first appearing in this tale, and *Manwë, Súlimo, Varda, Ulmo, Aulë, Mandos, Ossë, Salmar*, who have appeared previously. Some were retained in a modified form: *Melkor* for *Melko*, *Uinen* (which appears already later in the *Lost Tales*) for *Ónen*, *Fëanturi* for *Fánturi*; while yet others, as Yavanna *Palúrien* and Tulkas *Poldórëa*, survived long in the 'Silmarillion' tradition before being displaced by *Kementári* (but cf. *Kémi* 'Earth-lady' in this tale) and *Astaldo*. But some of these early Valar had disappeared by the next stage or phase after the *Lost Tales*: Ómar-Amillo, and the barbaric war-gods Makar and Meássë.

Here appear also certain relations that survived to the latest form. Thus Lórien and Mandos were from the beginning 'brethren', each with his special association, of 'dreams' and 'death'; and Nienna stood from the beginning in a close relationship with them, here as 'the spouse of Mandos', though afterwards as the sister of the Fëanturi. The original conception of Nienna was indeed darker and more fearful, a death-goddess in close association with Mandos, than it afterwards became. Ossë's uncertain relations with Ulmo are seen to go back to the beginnings; but Ulmo's haughtiness and aloofness subsequently disappeared, at least as a feature of his divine 'character' explicitly described. Vána was already the spouse of Oromë, but Oromë was the son of Aulë and (Yavanna) Palúrien; in the later evolution of the myths Vána sank down in relation to Nienna, whereas Oromë rose, becoming finally one of the great Valar, the *Aratar*.

Particularly interesting is the passage concerning the host of lesser spirits who accompanied Aulë and Palúrien, from which one sees how old is the conception of the Eldar as quite dissimilar in essential nature from 'brownies, fays, pixies, leprawns', since the Eldar are 'of the world' and bound to it, whereas those others are beings from before the world's making. In the later work there is no trace of any such explanation of the 'pixie' element in the world's population: the Maiar are little referred to, and certainly not said to include such beings as 'sing amid the grass at morning and chant among the standing corn at eve'.*

Salmar, companion of Ulmo, who has appeared in *The Music of the Ainur* (p. 58), is now identified with Noldorin, who was mentioned by Vairë in *The Cottage of Lost Play* (p. 16); such of his story as can be discerned will appear later. Subsequent writings say nothing of him save that he came with Ulmo and made his horns (*The Silmarillion* p. 40).

In the later development of this narrative there is no mention of Tulkas (or Mandos!) going off to round up Melkor at the very outset of the history of the Valar in Arda. In *The Silmarillion* we learn rather of the great war between the Valar and Melkor 'before Arda was full-shaped', and how it was the coming of Tulkas from 'the far heaven' that routed him, so that he fled from Arda and 'brooded in the outer darkness'.

---

* Cf. *The Silmarillion* p. 30: 'With the Valar came other spirits whose being also began before the world, of the same order as the Valar but of less degree. These are the Maiar, the people of the Valar, and their servants and helpers. Their number is not known to the Elves, and few have names in any of the tongues of the Children of Ilúvatar.' An earlier version of this passage reads: 'Many lesser spirits they [the Valar] brought in their train, both great and small, and some of these Men have confused with the Eldar or Elves; but wrongly, for they were before the world, but Elves and Men awoke first in the world after the coming of the Valar.'

(ii) The earliest conception of the Western Lands, and the Oceans

In *The Cottage of Lost Play* the expression 'Outer Lands' was used of the lands to the east of the Great Sea, later Middle-earth; this was then changed to 'Great Lands' (p. 21). The 'Outer Lands' are now defined as

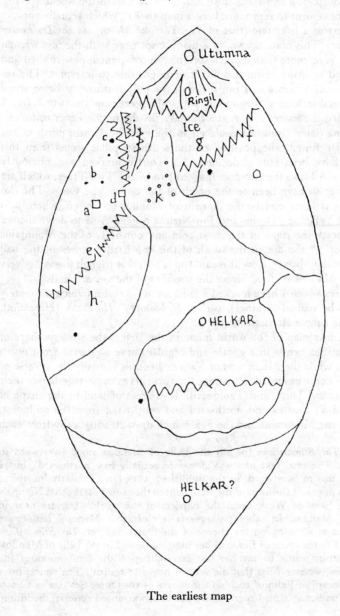

The earliest map

the Twilit Isles, Eruman (or Arvalin), and Valinor (p. 68). A curious usage, which often appears in the *Lost Tales*, is the equation of 'the world' with the Great Lands, or with the whole surface of the earth east of the Outer Lands; so the mountains 'towered mightily between Valinor and the world' (p. 70), and King Inwë heard 'the lament of the world' (p. 16). It is convenient to reproduce here a map (p. 81), which actually appears in the text of a later tale (that of *The Theft of Melko and the Darkening of Valinor*). This map, drawn on a manuscript page with the text written round it, is no more than a quick scribble, in soft pencil, now rubbed and faded, and in many features difficult or impossible to interpret. The redrawing is as accurate as I can make it, the only feature lost being some indecipherable letters (beginning with M) preceding the word *Ice*. I have added the letters *a*, *b*, *c*, etc. to make the discussion easier to follow.

Utumna (later Utumno) is placed in the extreme North, north of the lamp-pillar Ringil; the position of the southern pillar seems from this map to have been still undecided. The square marked *a* is obviously Valmar, and I take the two dots marked *b* to be the Two Trees, which are stated later to have been to the north of the city of the Gods. The dot marked *c* is fairly clearly the domain of Mandos (cf. p. 76, where it is said that Vefántur Mandos and Fui Nienna begged Aulë to delve them a hall 'beneath the roots of the most cold and northerly of the Mountains of Valinor');* the dot to the south of this can hardly represent the hall of Makar and Meássë, since it is said (pp. 77-8) that though it was not very far from Mandos it stood 'upon the confines of the Outer Lands'.

The area which I have marked *h* is Eruman / Arvalin (which ultimately came to be named Avathar), earlier *Habbanan* / *Harmalin* (*Harwalin*), which are simple alternatives (see p. 79).

Later, in a map of the world made in the 1930s, the western shore of the Great Sea bends in a gentle and regular curve westward from north to south, while the Mountains of Valinor bend in virtually the reverse of the same curve eastward, )(; where the two curves come together at their midpoints are Túna, and Taniquetil. Two areas of land in the shape of elongated Vs thus extend northward and southward from the midpoint, between the Mountains and the Sea, which draw steadily away from each

---

* In *The Silmarillion* (p. 28) the halls of Mandos stood 'westward in Valinor'. The final text of the *Valaquenta* actually has 'northward', but I changed this to 'westward' in the published work (and similarly 'north' to 'west' on p. 52) on the basis of the statement in the same passage that Nienna's halls are 'west of West, upon the borders of the world', but are near to those of Mandos. In other passages it is clear that Mandos' halls were conceived as standing on the shores of the Outer Sea; cf. *The Silmarillion* p. 186: 'For the spirit of Beren at her bidding tarried in the halls of Mandos, until Lúthien came to say her last farewell upon the dim shores of the Outer Sea, whence Men that die set out never to return'. The conceptions of 'northward in Valinor' and 'on the shores of the Outer Sea' are not however contradictory, and I regret this piece of unwarranted editorial meddling.

other; and these are named Eruman (to the northward) and Arvalin (to the southward).

In the little primitive map the line of the mountains is already thus, and it is described in the text as 'a great ring curving westward' (the curve is westward if the extremities are considered rather than the central portion) But the curve of the coast is different. Unhappily the little map is here very obscure, for there are several lines (marked *j*) extending northwards from Kôr (marked *d*), and it is impossible to make out whether marks on them are directions for erasure or whether they represent parallel mountain-chains. But I think that in fact these lines merely represent variant ideas for the curve of the Mountains of Valinor in the north; and I have little doubt that at this time my father had no conception of a region of 'waste' north of Kôr and east of the mountains. This interpretation of the map agrees well with what is said in the tale (p. 68): 'the Shadowy Seas to north of Eruman bend a vast bay inwards, so that waves beat even upon the feet of the great cliffs, and the Mountains stand beside the sea', and 'Taniquetil looks from the bay's head southward across Eruman and northward across the Bay of Faëry'. On this view the name *Eruman* (later *Araman*), at first an alternative to *Arvalin*, was taken over for the northern waste when the plan of the coastal regions became more symmetrical.

It is said in the tale (p. 68) that 'in that vast water of the West are many smaller lands and isles, ere the lonely seas are found whose waves whisper about the Magic Isles'. The little circles on the map (marked *k*) are evidently a schematic representation of these archipelagoes (of the Magic Isles more will be told later). The Shadowy Seas, as will emerge more clearly later, were a region of the Great Sea west of Tol Eressëa. The other letters on the map refer to features that have not yet entered the narrative.

In this tale we meet the important cosmological idea of the Three Airs, Vaitya, Ilwë, and Vilna, and of the Outer Ocean, tideless, cold, and 'thin'. It has been said in *The Music of the Ainur* (p. 58) that Ulmo dwells in the Outer Ocean and that he gave to Ossë and Ónen 'control of the waves and lesser seas'; he is there called 'the ancient one of Vai' (emended from Ulmonan). It is now seen that *Ulmonan* is the name of his halls in the Outer Ocean, and also that the 'lesser seas' controlled by Ossë and Ónen include the Great Sea (p. 68).

There exists a very early and very remarkable drawing, in which the world is seen in section, and is presented as a huge 'Viking' ship, with mast arising from the highest point of the Great Lands, single sail on which are the Sun and Moon, sailropes fastened to Taniquetil and to a great mountain in the extreme East, and curved prow (the black marks on the sail are an ink-blot). This drawing was done fairly rapidly in soft pencil on a small sheet; and it is closely associated with the cosmology of the *Lost Tales*.

I give here a list of the names and words written on the drawing with,

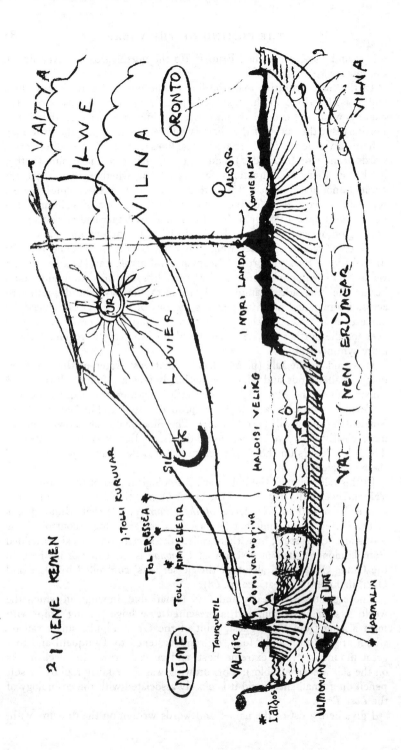

so far as possible, their meanings (but without any etymological detail, for which see the Appendix on Names, where names and words occurring only on this drawing are given separate entries).

*I Vene Kemen*   This is clearly the title of the drawing; it might mean 'The Shape of the Earth' or 'The Vessel of the Earth' (see the Appendix on Names, entry *Glorvent*).

*Nūme*   'West'.

*Valinor*; *Taniquetil*   (The vast height of Taniquetil, even granting the formalisation of this drawing, is noteworthy: it is described in the tale as being so high that 'the throngs about westward havens in the lands of Men could be seen therefrom' (p. 68). Its fantastic height is conveyed in my father's painting, dating from 1927–8 (*Pictures by J. R. R. Tolkien*, no. 31).)

*Harmalin*   Earlier name of *Arvalin* (see p. 79).

*i aldas*   'The Trees' (standing to the west of Taniquetil).

*Toros valinoriva*   *Toros* is obscure, but in any case the first letter of the first word, if it is a T, is a very uncharacteristic one. The reference seems to be to the Mountains of Valinor.

*Tolli Kimpelear*   These must be the Twilit Isles, but I have found no other occurrence of *Kimpelear* or anything similar.

*Tol Eressëa*   'The Lonely Isle'.

*I Tolli Kuruvar*   'The Magic Isles'.

*Haloisi Velike*   'The Great Sea'.

*Ō*   'The Sea'. (What is the structure at the sea-bottom shown below the name *Ō*? It must surely be the dwelling of Ossë beneath the Great Sea that is referred to in the next tale (p. 106).)

*I Nori Landar*   Probably means 'The Great Lands'.

*Koivienéni*   The precursor of *Cuiviénen*, the Waters of Awakening.

*Palisor*   The land where the Elves awoke.

*Sil*   'Moon'.

*Ūr*   'Sun'.

*Luvier*   'Clouds'.

*Oronto*   'East'.

*Vaitya*, *Ilwë*, and *Vilna* appear in the three layers described in the tale (p. 65), and *Vilna* reappears in the bottom right-hand corner of the drawing. There is nothing said in the *Lost Tales* to explain this last feature, nor is it at all evident what is represented by the curled lines in the same place (see p. 86).

*Ulmonan*   The halls of Ulmo.

*Uin*   The Great Whale, who appears later in the *Tales*.

*Vai*   The Outer Ocean.

*Neni Erùmear*   'Outermost Waters'= *Vai*.

It is seen from the drawing that the world floats in and upon Vai. This is indeed how Ulmo himself describes it to the Valar in a later tale (p. 214):

Lo, there is but one Ocean, and that is Vai, for those that Ossë esteemeth as oceans are but seas, waters that lie in the hollows of the rock . . . In this vast water floateth the wide Earth upheld by the word of Ilúvatar . . .

In the same passage Ulmo speaks of the islands in the seas, and says that ('save some few that swim still unfettered') they 'stand now like pinnacles from their weedy depths', as is also well seen in the drawing.

It might seem a plausible idea that there was some connection (physical as well as etymological) between *Vai* and *Vaitya*, the outermost of the Three Airs, 'wrapped dark and sluggish about the world and without it' (at a later point in the *Tales*, p. 181, there is a reference to 'the dark and tenuous realm of Vaitya that is outside all'). In the next 'phase' of the mythical cosmology (dating from the 1930s, and very clearly and fully documented and illustrated in a work called *Ambarkanta*, The Shape of the World) the whole world is contained within *Vaiya*, a word meaning 'fold, envelope'; Vaiya 'is more like to sea below the Earth and more like to air above the Earth' (which chimes with the description of the waters of Vai (p. 68) as very 'thin', so that no boat can sail on them nor fish swim in them, save the enchanted fish of Ulmo and his car); and in Vaiya below the Earth dwells Ulmo. Thus Vaiya is partly a development of Vaitya and partly of Vai.

Now since in the earliest word-list of the Qenya tongue (see the Appendix on Names) both *Vaitya* ('the outermost air beyond the world') and *Vai* ('the outer ocean') are derived from a root *vaya-* 'enfold', and since Vaitya in the present tale is said to be 'wrapped about the world and without it', one might think that Vaitya-Vai already in the early cosmology was a continuous enfolding substance, and that the later cosmology, in this point, only makes explicit what was present but un-expressed in the *Lost Tales*. But there is certainly no actual suggestion of this idea in any early writing; and when we look again at the drawing it seems untenable. For Vai is obviously *not* continuous with Vaitya; and if the appearance of Vilna in the bottom of the drawing is taken to mean that the Earth, *and* the ocean Vai in and on which it floats, were contained within the Three Airs, of which we see the reappearance of the innermost (Vilna) below the earth and Vai, then the suggestion that Vaitya–Vai were continuous is still more emphatically confounded.

There remains the baffling question of the representation of the world as a ship. In only one place is there a suggestion that my father conceived the world in such a way: the passage that I have cited above, in which Ulmo addresses the Valar on the subject of Vai, concludes:

O Valar, ye know not all wonders, and many secret things are there *beneath the Earth's dark keel*, even where I have my mighty halls of Ulmonan, that ye have never dreamed on.

But in the drawing Ulmonan is not beneath the ship's keel, it is within the ship's hull; and I am inclined to think that Ulmo's words 'beneath the Earth's dark keel' refer to the shape of the Earth itself, which is certainly ship-like. Moreover, close examination of the original drawing strongly suggests to me that the mast and sail, and still more clearly the curved prow, *were added afterwards.* Can it be that the shape of the Earth and of Vai as he had drawn them – with the appearance of a ship's hull – prompted my father to add mast, sail, and prow as a *jeu d'esprit,* without deeper significance? That seems uncharacteristic and unlikely, but I have no other explanation to offer.*

(iii) The Lamps (pp. 69–70)

In this part of the narrative the tale differs remarkably from the later versions. Here there is no mention of the dwelling of the Valar on the Isle of Almaren after the making of the Lamps (*The Silmarillion* p. 35), nor of course of the return of Melko from 'outside' – because here Melko not only did not leave the world after entering it, but actually himself made the pillars of the Lamps. In this story, though Melko was distrusted by some, his guileful co-operation (even to the extent of contributing names for the pillars) was accepted, whereas in the later story his hostility and malice were known and manifest to the Valar, even though they did not know of his return to Arda and the building of Utumno until too late. In the present tale there is a tricksiness, a low cunning, in Melko's behaviour that could not survive (yet the story of his deceitful making of the pillars out of ice survived into the versions of the 1930s).

Later, it was the Lamps themselves that were named (ultimately, after intervening forms had been devised and discarded, *Illuin* the northern Lamp and *Ormal* the southern). In *The Silmarillion* Ringil (containing *ring* 'cold') survived only as the name of Fingolfin's sword, but Helcar is that of the Inland Sea which 'stood where aforetime the roots of the mountain of Illuin had been' (p. 49). In the present tale Helcar was the name of the southern, not the northern, pillar. Now *helkar* meant 'utter cold' (see the Appendix on Names), which shows that Helcar was originally in the extreme south (as it is in one of the two positions given for it on the little map, p. 81), just as Ringil was in the extreme north. In the tale there is no mention of the formation of Inland Seas at the fall of the Lamps; this idea appeared later, but it seems virtually certain that it arose from the story of the melting pillars of ice.

There is no later reference to the building of the Mountains of Valinor from great rocks gathered in Eruman / Arvalin, so that the region became flat and stoneless.

* If this is so, and if *I Vene Kemen* means 'The Earth-Ship', then this title must have been added to the drawing at the same time as the mast, sail, and prow. – In the little notebook referred to on p. 23 there is an isolated note: 'Map of the Ship of the World.'

## (iv) The Two Trees (pp. 71–3)

This earliest account of the uprising of the Two Trees illuminates some elements of later versions more concentrated in expression. The enduring feature that the ground beneath Silpion (Telperion) was 'dappled with the shadows of his fluttering leaves' (*The Silmarillion* p. 38) is seen to have had its origin in the 'throbbing of the tree's heart'. The conception of light as a liquid substance that 'splashed upon the ground', that ran in rivers and was poured in cauldrons, though not lost in the published work (pp. 38–9), is here more strongly and physically expressed. Some features were never changed, as the clustered flowers of Laurelin and the shining edges of its leaves.

On the other hand there are notable differences between this and the later accounts: above all perhaps that Laurelin was in origin the Eldar Tree. The Two Trees had here periods of twelve hours, not as later seven;* and the preparations of the Valar for the birth of the Trees, with all their detail of physical 'magic', were afterwards abandoned. The two great 'cauldrons' Kulullin and Silindrin survived in the 'great vats like shining lakes' in which Varda hoarded 'the dews of Telperion and the rain that fell from Laurelin' (*ibid.* p. 39), though the names disappeared, as did the need to 'water' the Trees with the light gathered in the vats or cauldrons – or at any rate it is not mentioned later. Urwen ('Sun-maiden') was the forebear of Arien, Maia of the Sun; and Tilion, steersman of the Moon in *The Silmarillion*, who 'lay in dreams by the pools of Estë [Lórien's wife], in Telperion's flickering beams', perhaps owes something to the figure of Silmo, whom Lórien loved.

As I noted earlier, 'in the later evolution of the myths Vána sank down in relation to Nienna', and here it is Vána and (Yavanna) Palúrien who are the midwives of the birth of the Trees, not as afterwards Yavanna and Nienna.

As regards the names of the Trees, *Silpion* was for long the name of the White Tree; *Telperion* did not appear till long after, and even then *Silpion* was retained and is mentioned in *The Silmarillion* (p. 38) as one of its names. *Laurelin* goes back to the beginning and was never changed, but its other name in the *Lost Tales*, *Lindeloksë* and other similar forms, was not retained.

## (v) The Dwellings of the Valar (pp. 73 ff.)

This account of the mansions of the Valar was very largely lost in the subsequent versions. In the published work nothing is told of Manwë's dwelling, save the bare fact that his halls were 'above the everlasting snow, upon Oiolossë, the uttermost tower of Taniquetil' (p. 26). Here

---

* Palúrien's words (p. 73) 'This tree, *when the twelve hours of its fullest light are past,* will wane again' seem to imply a longer space than twelve hours; but probably the period of waning was not allowed for. In an annotated list of names to the tale of *The Fall of Gondolin* it is said that Silpion lit all Valinor with silver light 'for half the twenty-four hours'.

now appears Sorontur King of Eagles, a visitor to Manwë's halls (cf.
*The Silmarillion* p. 110: 'For Manwë to whom all birds are dear, and to
whom they bring news upon Taniquetil from Middle-earth, had sent
forth the race of Eagles'); he had in fact appeared already in the tale of
*The Fall of Gondolin*, as 'Thorndor [the Gnomish name] King of Eagles
whom the Eldar name Ramandur', Ramandur being subsequently emended
to Sorontur.

Of Valmar and the dwellings of the Valar in the city scarcely anything
survived in later writing, and there remain only phrases here and there
(the 'golden streets' and 'silver domes' of Valmar, 'Valmar of many bells')
to suggest the solidity of the original description, where Tulkas' house of
many storeys had a tower of bronze and Oromë's halls were upheld by
living trees with trophies and antlers hung upon their trunks. This is not
to say that all such imagining was definitively abandoned: as I have said
in the Foreword, the *Lost Tales* were followed by a version so compressed
as to be no more than a résumé (as was its purpose), and the later development of the mythology proceeded from that – a process of re-expansion.
Many things never referred to again after the *Lost Tales* may have continued to exist in a state of suspension, as it were. Valmar certainly
remained a city, with gates, streets, and dwellings. But in the context of
the later work one could hardly conceive of the tempestuous Ossë being
possessed of a house in Valmar, even if its floor were of seawater and its
roof of foam; and of course the hall of Makar and Meássë (where the life
described owes something to the myths of the Unending Battle in ancient
Scandinavia) disappeared with the disappearance of those divinities – a
'Melko-faction' in Valinor that was bound to prove an embarrassment.

Several features of the original descriptions endured: the rarity of
Ulmo's visits to Valmar (cf. *The Silmarillion* p. 40), the frequency with
which Palúrien and Oromë visit 'the world without' (*ibid.* pp. 29, 41, 47),
the association of the gardens of Lórien with Silpion and of the gardens
of Vána with Laurelin (*ibid.* p. 99); and much that is said here of the
divine 'characters' can be seen to have remained, even if differently
expressed. Here also appears Nessa, already as the wife of Tulkas and
the sister of Oromë, excelling in the dance; and Ómar-Amillo is now named
the brother of Noldorin-Salmar. It appears elsewhere (see p. 93) that
Nielíqui was the daughter of Oromë and Vána.

### (vi) The Gods of Death and the Fates of Elves and Men
### (pp. 76–7)

This section of the tale contains its most surprising and difficult elements.
Mandos and his wife Nienna appear in the account of the coming of the
Valar into the world at the beginning of the tale (p. 66), where they are
named 'Fantur of Death, Vefántur Mandos' and 'Fui Nienna', 'mistress
of death'. In the present passage it is said that Vefántur named his dwelling
Vê by his own name, whereas afterwards (*The Silmarillion* p. 28) he was

called by the name of his dwelling; but in the early writing there is a distinction between the region (Mandos) and the halls (Vê and Fui) within the region. There is here no trace of Mandos as the 'Doomsman of the Valar', who 'pronounces his dooms and his judgements only at the bidding of Manwë', one of the most notable aspects of the later conception of this Vala; nor, since Nienna is the wife of Mandos, has Vairë the Weaver, his wife in the later story, appeared, with her tapestries that portray 'all things that have ever been in Time' and clothe the halls of Mandos 'that ever widen as the ages pass' – in the Lost Tales the name Vairë is given to an Elf of Tol Eressëa. Tapestries 'picturing those things that were and shall be' are found here in the halls of Aulë (p. 74).

Most important in the passage concerning Mandos is the clear statement about the fate of Elves who die: that they wait in the halls of Mandos until Vefántur decrees their release, to be reborn in their own children. This latter idea has already appeared in the tale of The Music of the Ainur (p. 59), and it remained my father's unchanged conception of Elvish 'immortality' for many years; indeed the idea that the Elves might die only from the wounds of weapons or from grief was never changed – it also has appeared in The Music of the Ainur (ibid.): 'the Eldar dwell till the Great End unless they be slain or waste in grief', a passage that survived with little alteration in The Silmarillion (p. 42).

With the account of Fui Nienna, however, we come upon ideas in deep contradiction to the central thought of the later mythology (and in this passage, also, there is a strain of another kind of mythic conception, in the 'conceits' of 'the distilling of salt humours whereof are tears', and the black clouds woven by Nienna which settle on the world as 'despairs and hopeless mourning, sorrows and blind grief'). Here we learn that Nienna is the judge of Men in her halls named Fui after her own name; and some she keeps in the region of Mandos (where is her hall), while the greater number board the black ship Mornië – which does no more than ferry these dead down the coast to Arvalin, where they wander in the dusk until the end of the world. But yet others are driven forth to be seized by Melko and taken to endure 'evil days' in Angamandi (in what sense are they dead, or mortal?); and (most extraordinary of all) there are a very few who go to dwell among the Gods in Valinor. We are far away here from the Gift of Ilúvatar, whereby Men are not bound to the world, but leave it, none know where;* and this is the true meaning of Death (for

---

* Cf. The Silmarillion p. 104: 'Some say that they [Men] too go to the halls of Mandos; but their place of waiting there is not that of the Elves, and Mandos under Ilúvatar alone save Manwë knows whither they go after the time of recollection in those silent halls beside the Outer Sea.' Also ibid. p. 186: 'For the spirit of Beren at her bidding tarried in the halls of Mandos, unwilling to leave the world, until Lúthien came to say her last farewell upon the dim shores of the Outer Sea, whence Men that die set out never to return.'

the death of the Elves is a 'seeming death', *The Silmarillion* p. 42): the final and inescapable exit.

But a little illumination, if of a very misty kind, can be shed on the idea of Men, after death, wandering in the dusk of Arvalin, where they 'camp as they may' and 'wait in patience till the Great End'. I must refer here to the details of the changed names of this region, which have been given on p. 79. It is clear from the early word-lists or dictionaries of the two languages (for which see the Appendix on Names) that the meaning of *Harwalin* and *Arvalin* (and probably *Habbanan* also) was 'nigh Valinor' or 'nigh the Valar'. From the Gnomish dictionary it emerges that the meaning of *Eruman* was 'beyond the abode of the Mánir' (i.e. south of Taniquetil, where dwelt Manwë's spirits of the air), and this dictionary also makes it clear that the word *Mánir* was related to Gnomish *manos*, defined as 'a spirit that has gone to the Valar or to Erumáni', and *mani* 'good, holy'. The significance of these etymological connections is very unclear.

But there is also a very early poem on the subject of this region. This, according to my father's notes, was written at Brocton Camp, Staffordshire, in December 1915 or at Étaples in June 1916; and it is entitled *Habbanan beneath the Stars*. In one of the three texts (in which there are no variants) there is a title in Old English: *þā gebletsode* ['blessed'] *felda under þām steorrum*, and in two of them *Habbanan* in the title was emended to *Eruman*; in the third *Eruman* stood from the first. The poem is preceded by a short prose preamble.

### Habbanan beneath the Stars

Now Habbanan is that region where one draws nigh to the places that are not of Men. There is the air very sweet and the sky very great by reason of the broadness of the Earth.

> In Habbanan beneath the skies
> Where all roads end however long
> There is a sound of faint guitars
> And distant echoes of a song,
> For there men gather into rings
> Round their red fires while one voice sings –
> And all about is night.

★

> Not night as ours, unhappy folk,
> Where nigh the Earth in hazy bars,
> A mist about the springing of the stars,
> There trails a thin and wandering smoke
> Obscuring with its veil half-seen
> The great abysmal still Serene.

★

A globe of dark glass faceted with light
Wherein the splendid winds have dusky flight;
Untrodden spaces of an odorous plain
That watches for the moon that long has lain
And caught the meteors' fiery rain –
Such there is night.

★

There on a sudden did my heart perceive
That they who sang about the Eve,
Who answered the bright-shining stars
With gleaming music of their strange guitars,
These were His wandering happy sons
Encamped upon those aëry leas
Where God's unsullied garment runs
In glory down His mighty knees.

★

A final evidence comes from the early Qenya word-list. The original
layer of entries in this list dates (as I believe, see the Appendix on Names)
from 1915, and among these original entries, under a root *mana* (from
which *Manwë* is derived), is given a word *manimo* which means a soul who
is in *manimuine* 'Purgatory'.

This poem, and this entry in the word-list, offer a rare and very suggestive glimpse of the mythic conception in its earliest phase; for here
ideas that are drawn from Christian theology are explicitly present. It is
disconcerting to perceive that they are still present in this tale. For in the
tale there is an account of the fates of dead Men after judgement in the
black hall of Fui Nienna. Some ('and these are the many') are ferried by
the death-ship to (Habbanan) Eruman, where they wander in the dusk
and wait in patience till the Great End; some are seized by Melko and
tormented in Angamandi 'the Hells of Iron'; and some few go to dwell
with the Gods in Valinor. Taken with the poem and the evidence of the
early 'dictionaries', can this be other than a reflection of Purgatory, Hell,
and Heaven?

This becomes all the more extraordinary if we refer to the concluding
passage of the tale of *The Music of the Ainur* (p. 59), where Ilúvatar said:
'To Men I will give a new gift and a greater', the gift that they might
'fashion and design their life beyond even the original Music of the Ainur
that is as fate to all things else', and where it is said that 'it is one with
this gift of power that the Children of Men dwell only for a short time in
the world alive, yet do not perish utterly for ever . . .' In the final form
given in *The Silmarillion* pp. 41–2 this passage was not very greatly
changed. The early version does not, it is true, have the sentences:

But the sons of Men die indeed, and leave the world; wherefore they are called the Guests, or the Strangers. Death is their fate, the gift of Ilúvatar, which as Time wears even the Powers shall envy.

Even so, it seems clear that this central idea, the Gift of Death, was already present. This matter I must leave, as a conundrum that I cannot solve. The most obvious explanation of the conflict of ideas within these tales would be to suppose *The Music of the Ainur* later than *The Coming of the Valar and the Building of Valinor*; but as I have said (p. 61) all the appearances are to the contrary.

Lastly may be noticed the characteristic linguistic irony whereby *Eruman* ultimately became *Araman*. For *Arvalin* meant simply 'near Valinor', and it was the other name *Eruman* that had associations with spirits of the dead; but *Araman* almost certainly simply means 'beside Aman'. And yet the same element *man-* 'good' remains, for *Aman* was derived from it ('the Unmarred State').

Two minor matters in the conclusion of the tale remain to be noticed. Here Nornorë is the Herald of the Gods; afterwards this was Fionwë (later Eonwë), see p. 63. And in the reference to 'that low place amid the hills where Valinor may just be glimpsed', near to Taniquetil, we have the first mention of the gap in the Mountains of Valinor where was the hill of the city of the Elves.

On blank pages near the end of the text of this tale my father wrote a list of secondary names of the Valar (as Manwë *Súlimo*, etc.). Some of these names appear in the text of the *Tales*; those that do not are given in the Appendix on Names under the primary names. It emerges from this list that Ómar-Amillo is the twin of Salmar-Noldorin (they are named as brothers in the tale, p. 75); that Nielíqui (p. 75) is the daughter of Oromë and Vána; and that Melko has a son ('by Ulbandi') called Kosomot: this, it will emerge later, was Gothmog Lord of Balrogs, whom Ecthelion slew in Gondolin.

# IV

# THE CHAINING OF MELKO

Following the end of Rúmil's tale of *The Coming of the Valar and the Building of Valinor* there is a long interlude before the next one, though the manuscript continues without even interrupting the paragraph. But on the cover of the notebook *The Chaining of Melko* is given as a separate title, and I have adopted this. The text continues in ink over an erased pencil manuscript.

That night Eriol heard again in his sleep the music that had so moved him on the first night; and the next morning he went again into the gardens early. There he met Vairë, and she called him *Eriol*: 'that was the first making and uttering of that name'. Eriol told Vairë of the 'dream-musics' he had heard, and she said that it was no dream-music, but rather the flute of Timpinen, 'whom those Gnomes Rúmil and Littleheart and others of my house call Tinfang'. She told him that the children called him Tinfang Warble; and that he played and danced in summer dusks for joy of the first stars: 'at every note a new one sparkles forth and glisters. The Noldoli say that they come out too soon if Tinfang Warble plays, and they love him, and the children will watch often from the windows lest he tread the shadowy lawns unseen.' She told Eriol that he was 'shier than a fawn – swift to hide and dart away as any vole: a footstep on a twig and he is away, and his fluting will come mocking from afar'.

'And a marvel of wizardry liveth in that fluting,' said Eriol, 'if that it be indeed which I have heard now for two nights here.'

'There be none,' said Vairë, 'not even of the Solosimpi, who can rival him therein, albeit those same pipers claim him as their kin; yet 'tis said everywhere that this quaint spirit is neither wholly of the Valar nor of the Eldar, but is half a fay of the woods and dells, one of the great companies of the children of Palúrien, and half a Gnome or a Shoreland Piper.[1] Howso that be he is a wondrous wise and strange creature, and he fared hither away with the Eldar long ago, marching nor resting among them but going always ahead piping strangely or whiles sitting aloof. Now does he play about the gardens of the land; but Alalminórë he loves the best, and this garden best of all. Ever and again we miss his piping for long months, and we say: "Tinfang Warble has gone heart-breaking in the Great Lands, and many a one in those far regions will hear his piping in the dusk outside tonight." But on a sudden will his flute be heard again at an hour of gentle gloaming, or will he play beneath a goodly moon and the stars go bright and blue.'

'Aye,' said Eriol, 'and the hearts of those that hear him go beating with a quickened longing. Meseemed 'twas my desire to open the window and leap forth, so sweet was the air that came to me from without, nor might I drink deep enough, but as I listened I wished to follow I know not whom, I know not whither, out into the magic of the world beneath the stars.'

'Then of a sooth 'twas Timpinen who played to you,' said Vairë, 'and honoured are you, for this garden has been empty of his melody many a night. Now, however, for such is the eeriness of that sprite, you will ever love the evenings of summer and the nights of stars, and their magic will cause your heart to ache unquenchably.'

'But have you not all heard him many times and often, that dwell here,' said Eriol, 'yet do not seem to me like those who live with a longing that is half understood and may not be fulfilled.'

'Nor do we so, for we have *limpë*,' said she, '*limpë* that alone can cure, and a draught of it giveth a heart to fathom all music and song.'

'Then,' said Eriol, 'would I might drain a goblet of that good drink'; but Vairë told him that that might only be if he sought out Meril the queen.

Of this converse of Eriol and Vairë upon the lawn that fair day-tide came it that Eriol set out not many days thereafter – and Tinfang Warble had played to him many times by dusk, by starry light and moongleam, till his heart was full. In that was Littleheart his guide, and he sought the dwellings of Meril-i-Turinqui in her *korin* of elms.

Now the house of that fair lady was in that very city, for at the foot of the great tower which Ingil had built was a wide grove of the most ancient and beautiful elms that all that Land of Elms possessed. High to heaven they rose in three lessening storeys of bright foliage, and the sunlight that filtered through was very cool – a golden green. Amidst of these was a great green sward of grass smooth as a web of stuffs, and about it those trees stood in a circle, so that shades were heavy at its edge but the gaze of the sun fell all day on its middle. There stood a beautiful house, and it was builded all of white and of a whiteness that shone, but its roof was so o'ergrown with mosses and with houseleek and many curious clinging plants that of what it was once fashioned might not be seen for the glorious maze of colours, golds and red-russets, scarlets and greens.

Innumerable birds chattered in its eaves; and some sang upon the housetops, while doves and pigeons circled in flights about the *korin*'s borders or swooped to settle and sun upon the sward. Now all that dwelling was footed in flowers. Blossomy clusters were about it, ropes and tangles, spikes and tassels all in bloom, flowers in panicles and umbels or with great wide faces gazing at the sun. There did they loose upon the faintly stirring airs their several odours blended to a great fragrance of exceeding marvellous enchantment, but their hues and colours were scattered and gathered seemingly as chance and the happiness of their growth directed them. All day long there went a hum of bees among those flowers: bees fared about the roof and all the scented beds and ways; even about the cool porches of the house. Now Littleheart and Eriol climbed the hill and it was late afternoon, and the sun shone brazen upon the western side of Ingil's tower. Soon came they to a mighty wall of hewn stone blocks, and this leaned outward, but grasses grew atop of it, and harebells, and yellow daisies.

A wicket they found in the wall, and beyond was a glade beneath the elms, and there ran a pathway bordered of one side with bushes while of the other flowed a little running water whispering over a brown bed of leafy mould. This led even to the sward's edge, and coming thither said Littleheart pointing to that white house: 'Behold the dwelling of Meril-i-Turinqui, and as I have no errand with so great a lady I will get me back again.' Then Eriol went over the sunny lawn alone until he was nigh shoulder-high in the tall flowers that grew before the porches of the door; and as he drew near a sound of music came to him, and a fair lady amid many maidens stepped forth as it were to meet him. Then said she smiling: 'Welcome, O mariner of many seas – wherefore do you seek the pleasure of my quiet gardens and their gentle noise, when the salt breezes of the sea and the snuff of winds and a swaying boat should rather be your joy?'

For a while Eriol might say nought thereto, being tongue-tied by the beauty of that lady and the loveliness of that place of flowers; yet at length he muttered that he had known sea enough, but of this most gracious land he might never be sated. 'Nay,' said she, 'on a day of autumn will come the winds and a driven gull, maybe, will wail overhead, and lo! you will be filled with desire, remembering the black coasts of your home.'[2] 'Nay, lady,' said Eriol, and now he spoke with eager voice, 'nay, not so, for the spirit that flutes upon twilit lawns has filled my heart with music, and I thirst for a draught of *limpë*!'

Then straightway did the smiling face of Meril grow grave, and bidding her maidens depart she prayed Eriol follow her to a space nigh to the house, and this was of cool grass but not very short. Fruit-trees grew there, and about the roots of one, an apple-tree of great girth and age, the soil was piled so that there was now a broad seat around its bole, soft and grass-covered. There sat Meril and she gazed upon Eriol and said: 'Know you then what it is that you ask?' and he said: 'I know nought save that I desire to know the soul of every song and of all music and to dwell always in fellowship and kinship with this wondrous people of the Eldar of the Isle, and to be free of unquenchable longing even till the Faring Forth, even till the Great End!'

But Meril said: 'Fellowship is possible, maybe, but kinship not so, for Man is Man and Elda Elda, and what Ilúvatar has made unalike may not become alike while the world remains. Even didst thou dwell here till the Great End and for the health of *limpë* found no death, yet then must thou die and leave us, for Man must die once. And hearken, O Eriol, think not to escape unquenchable longing with a draught of *limpë* – for only wouldst thou thus exchange desires, replacing thy old ones with new and deeper and more keen. Desire unsatisfied dwells in the hearts of both those races that are called the Children of Ilúvatar, but with the Eldar most, for their hearts arc filled with a vision of beauty in great glory.' 'Yet, O Queen,' said Eriol thereto, 'let me but taste of this drink and become an agelong fellow of your people: O queen of the Eldalië, that I may be as the happy children of Mar Vanwa Tyaliéva.' 'Nay, not yet can I do that,' said Meril, 'for 'tis a graver matter far to give this drink to one who has known life and days already in the lands of Men than for a child to drink who knows but little else; yet even these did we keep a long while ere we gave them the wine of song, teaching them first much lore and testing their hearts and souls. Therefore I bid you now bide still longer and learn all that you may in this our isle. Lo, what do you know of the world, or of the ancient days of Men, or of the roots which those things that now are have far back in time, or what of the Eldalië and all their wisdom, that you should claim our cup of youth and poesy?'

'The tongue of Tol Eressëa do I know, and of the Valar have I heard, and the great world's beginning, and the building of Valinor; to musics have I hearkened and to poesy and the laughter of the Elves, and all I have found true and good, and my heart knows and it saith to me that these shall I always henceforth love, and love alone' – thus answered Eriol, and his heart was sore for the refusal of the Queen.

'Yet nothing do you know of the coming of the Elves, of the fates wherein they move, nor their nature and the place that Ilúvatar has given to them. Little do you reck of that great splendour of their home in Eldamar upon the hill of Kôr, nor all the sorrow of our parting. What know you of our travail down all the dark ways of the world, and the anguish we have known because of Melko; of the sorrows we have suffered, and do yet, because of Men, of all the fears that darken our hopes because of Men? Know you the wastes of tears that lie between our life in Tol Eressëa and that time of laughter that we knew in Valinor? O child of Men who wouldst be sharer of the fates of the Eldalië, what of our high desires and all those things we look for still to be – for lo! if you drink this drink all these must you know and love, having one heart with us – nay, even at the Faring Forth, should Eldar and Men fall into war at the last, still must you stand by us against the children of your kith and kin, but until then never may you fare away home though longings gnaw you – and the desires that at whiles consume a full-grown man who drinketh *limpë* are a fire of unimagined torture – knew you these things, O Eriol, when you fared hither with your request?'

'Nay, I knew them not,' said Eriol sadly, 'though often have I questioned folk thereof.'

'Then lo!' said Meril, 'I will begin a tale, and tell you some of it ere the long afternoon grows dim – but then must you fare hence again in patience'; and Eriol bowed his head.

'Then,' said Meril, 'now I will tell you of a time of peace the world once knew, and it is known as "Melko's Chains".³ Of the Earth I will tell you as the Eldar found it and of the manner of their awakening into it.

Behold, Valinor is built, and the Gods dwell in peace, for Melko is far in the world delving deep and fortifying himself in iron and cold, but Makar and Meássë ride upon the gales and rejoice in earthquakes and the overmastering furies of the ancient seas. Light and beautiful is Valinor, but there is a deep twilight upon the world, for the Gods have gathered so much of that light that had before flowed about the airs. Seldom now falls the shimmering rain as it was used, and there reigns a gloom lit with pale streaks or shot with red where Melko spouts to heaven from a fire-torn hill.

Then Palúrien Yavanna fared forth from her fruitful gardens to survey the wide lands of her domain, and wandered the dark continents sowing seed and brooding upon hill and dale. Alone in that agelong gloaming she sang songs of the utmost enchantment, and of such deep magic were they that they floated about the rocky places and their echoes lingered for years of time in hill and empty plain, and all the good magics of all later days are whispers of the memories of her echoing song.

Then things began to grow there, fungus and strange growths heaved in damp places and lichens and mosses crept stealthily across the rocks and ate their faces, and they crumbled and made dust, and the creeping plants died in the dust, and there was mould, and ferns and warted plants grew in it silently, and strange creatures thrust their heads from crannies and crept over the stones. But Yavanna wept, for this was not the fair vigour that she had thought of – and thereupon Oromë came to her leaping in the dusk, but Tuivána would not leave the radiance of Kulullin nor Nessa the green swards of her dancing.

Then Oromë and Palúrien put forth all their might, and Oromë blew great blasts upon his horn as though he would awake the grey rocks to life and lustihead. Behold, at these blasts the great forest reared and moaned about the hills, and all the trees of dark leaf came to being, and the world was shaggy with a growth of pines and odorous with resinous trees, and firs and cedars hung their blue and olive draperies about the slopes, and yews began the centuries of their growth. Now was Oromë less gloomy and Palúrien was comforted, seeing the beauty of the first stars of Varda gleaming in the pale heavens through the shadows of the first trees' boughs, and hearing the murmur of the dusky forests and the creaking of the branches when Manwë stirred the airs.

At that time did many strange spirits fare into the world, for there were pleasant places dark and quiet for them to dwell in. Some came from Mandos, aged spirits that journeyed from Ilúvatar with him who are older than the world and very gloomy and secret, and some from the fortresses of the North where Melko then dwelt in the deep dungeons of Utumna. Full of evil and unwholesome were they; luring and restlessness and horror they brought, turning the dark into an ill and fearful thing, which it was not before. But some few danced thither with gentle feet exuding evening scents, and these came from the gardens of Lórien.

Still is the world full of these in the days of light, lingering alone in shadowy hearts of primeval forests, calling secret things across a starry waste, and haunting caverns in the hills that few have found: – but the pinewoods are yet too full of these old unelfin and inhuman spirits for the quietude of Eldar or of Men.

When this great deed was done then Palúrien would fain rest from her long labours and return to taste the sweet fruits of Valinor, and be refreshed beneath the tree of Laurelin whose dew is light, and Oromë was for beechwoods on the plains of the great Gods; but Melko who long time had delved in fear because of the wrath of the

Valar at his treacherous dealing with their lamps burst forth now into a great violence, for he had thought the world abandoned by the Gods to him and his. Beneath the very floors of Ossë he caused the Earth to quake and split and his lower fires to mingle with the sea. Vaporous storms and a great roaring of uncontrolled sea-motions burst upon the world, and the forests groaned and snapped. The sea leapt upon the land and tore it, and wide regions sank beneath its rage or were hewn into scattered islets, and the coast was dug into caverns. The mountains rocked and their hearts melted, and stone poured like liquid fire down their ashen sides and flowed even to the sea, and the noise of the great battles of the fiery beaches came roaring even through the Mountains of Valinor and drowned the singing of the Gods. Then rose Kémi Palúrien, even Yavanna that giveth fruits, and Aulë who loveth all her works and the substances of the earth, and they climbed to the halls of Manwë and spake to him, saying that all that goodliness was going utterly to wreck for the fiery evil of Melko's untempered heart, and Yavanna pleaded that all her agelong labour in the twilight be not drowned and buried. Thither, as they spake, came Ossë raging like a tide among the cliffs, for he was wroth at the upheaval of his realm and feared the displeasure of Ulmo his overlord. Then arose Manwë Súlimo, Lord of Gods and Elves, and Varda Tinwetári was beside him, and he spake in a voice of thunder from Taniquetil, and the Gods in Valmar heard it, and Vefántur knew the voice in Mandos, and Lórien was aroused in Murmuran.

Then was a great council held between the Two Trees at the mingling of the lights, and Ulmo came thither from the outer deeps; and of the redes there spoken the Gods devised a plan of wisdom, and the thought of Ulmo was therein and much of the craft of Aulë and the wide knowledge of Manwë.

Behold, Aulë now gathered six metals, copper, silver, tin, lead, iron, and gold, and taking a portion of each made with his magic a seventh which he named therefore *tilkal*,* and this had all the properties of the six and many of its own. Its colour was bright green or red in varying lights and it could not be broken, and Aulë alone could forge it. Thereafter he forged a mighty chain, making it of all seven metals welded with spells to a substance of uttermost hardness and brightness and smoothness, but of *tilkal* he had not sufficient to add more than a little to each link. Nonetheless he made two manacles of *tilkal* only and four fetters likewise. Now the chain was

* Footnote in the manuscript: '*T(ambë) I(lsa) L(atúken) K(anu) A(nga) L(aurë)*. *ilsa* and *laurë* are the 'magic' names of ordinary *telpë* and *kulu*.'

named *Angaino*, the oppressor, and the manacles *Vorotemnar* that bind for ever, but the fetters *Ilterendi* for they might not be filed or cleft.

But the desire of the Gods was to seek out Melko with great power – and to entreat him, if it might be, to better deeds; yet did they purpose, if naught else availed, to overcome him by force or guile, and set him in a bondage from which there should be no escape.

Now as Aulë smithied the Gods arrayed themselves in armour, which they had of Makar, and he was fain to see them putting on weapons and going as to war, howso their wrath be directed against Melko. But when the great Gods and all their folk were armed, then Manwë climbed into his blue chariot whose three horses were the whitest that roamed in Oromë's domain, and his hand bore a great white bow that would shoot an arrow like a gust of wind across the widest seas. Fionwë his son stood behind him and Nornorë who was his herald ran before; but Oromë rode alone upon a chestnut horse and had a spear, and Tulkas strode mightily beside his stirrup, having a tunic of hide and a brazen belt and no weapon save a gauntlet upon his right hand, iron-bound. Telimektar his son but just war-high was by his shoulder with a long sword girt about his waist by a silver girdle. There rode the Fánturi upon a car of black, and there was a black horse upon the side of Mandos and a dappled grey upon the side of Lórien, and Salmar and Ómar came behind running speedily, but Aulë who was late tarrying overlong at his smithy came last, and he was not armed, but caught up his long-handled hammer as he left his forge and fared hastily to the borders of the Shadowy Sea, and the fathoms of his chain were borne behind by four of his smithy-folk.

Upon those shores Falman-Ossë met them and drew them across on a mighty raft whereon he himself sat in shimmering mail; but Ulmo Vailimo was far ahead roaring in his deep-sea car and trumpeting in wrath upon a horn of conches. Thus was it that the Gods got them over the sea and through the isles, and set foot upon the wide lands, and marched in great power and anger ever more to the North. Thus they passed the Mountains of Iron and Hisilómë that lies dim beyond, and came to the rivers and hills of ice. There Melko shook the earth beneath them, and he made snow-capped heights to belch forth flame, yet for the greatness of their array his vassals who infested all their ways availed nothing to hinder them on their journey. There in the deepest North beyond even the shattered pillar Ringil they came upon the huge gates of deep Utumna, and Melko shut them with great clangour before their faces.

Then Tulkas angered smote them thunderously with his great fist, and they rang and stirred not, but Oromë alighting grasped his horn and blew such a blast thereon that they fled open instantly, and Manwë raised his immeasurable voice and bade Melko come forth. But though deep down within those halls Melko heard him and was in doubt, he would not come, but sent Langon his servant and said by him that "Behold, he was rejoiced and in wonder to see the Gods before his gates. Now would he gladly welcome them, yet for the poverty of his abode not more than two of them could he fitly entertain; and he begged that neither Manwë nor Tulkas be of the two, for the one merited and the other demanded hospitality of great cost and richness. Should this not be to their mind then would he fain hearken to Manwë's herald and learn what it were the Gods so greatly desired that they must leave their soft couches and indolence of Valinor for the bleak places where Melko laboured humbly and did his toilsome work."

Then Manwë and Ulmo and all the Gods were exceeding wroth at the subtlety and fawning insolence of his words, and Tulkas would have started straightway raging down the narrow stairs that descended out of sight beyond the gates, but the others withheld him, and Aulë gave counsel that it was clear from Melko's words that he was awake and wary in this matter, and it could most plainly be seen which of the Gods he was most in fear of and desired least to see standing in his halls - "therefore," said he, "let us devise how these twain may come upon him unawares and how fear may perchance drive him into betterment of ways." To this Manwë assented, saying that all their force might scarce dig Melko from his stronghold, whereas that deceit must be very cunningly woven that would ensnare the master of guile. "Only by his pride is Melko assailable," quoth Manwë, "or by such a struggle as would rend the earth and bring evil upon us all," and Manwë sought to avoid all strife twixt Ainur and Ainur. When therefore the Gods had concerted a plan to catch Melko in his overweening pride they wove cunning words purporting to come from Manwë himself, and these they put in the mouth of Nornorë, who descended and spoke them before the seat of Melko. "Behold," said he, "the Gods be come to ask the pardon of Melko, for seeing his great anger and the rending of the world beneath his rage they have said one to another: 'Lo! wherefore is Melko displeased?' and one to another have answered beholding the tumults of his power: 'Is he not then the greatest among us - why dwells not the mightiest of the Valar in Valinor? Of a surety he has cause for indignation. Let us get us to Utumna and beseech him to dwell in

Valinor that Valmar be not empty of his presence.' To this," said he, "Tulkas alone would not assent, but Manwë bowed to the common voice (this the Gods said knowing the rancour that Melko had for Poldórëa) and now have they come constraining Tulkas with violence to beg thee to pardon them each one and to fare home with them and complete their glory, dwelling, if it be thy pleasure, in the halls of Makar, until such time as Aulë can build thee a great house; and its towers shall overtop Taniquetil." To this did Melko answer eagerly, for already his boundless pride surged up and drowned his cunning.

"At last do the Gods speak fair words and just, but ere I grant their boon my heart must be appeased for old affronts. Therefore must they come putting aside their weapons at the gate, and do homage to me in these my deep halls of Utumna: – but lo! Tulkas I will not see, and if I come to Valinor then will I thrust him out." These things did Nornorë report, and Tulkas smote his hands in wrath, but Manwë returned answer that the Gods would do as Melko's heart desired, yet would Tulkas come and that in chains and be given to Melko's power and pleasure; and this was Melko eager to grant for the humiliation of the Valar, and the chaining of Tulkas gave him great mirth.

Then the Valar laid aside their weapons at the gates, setting however folk to guard them, and placed the chain Angaino about the neck and arms of Tulkas, and even he might scarce support its great weight alone; and now they follow Manwë and his herald into the caverns of the North. There sat Melko in his chair, and that chamber was lit with flaming braziers and full of evil magic, and strange shapes moved with feverish movement in and out, but snakes of great size curled and uncurled without rest about the pillars that upheld that lofty roof. Then said Manwë: "Behold, we have come and salute you here in your own halls; come now and be in Valinor."

But Melko might not thus easily forgo his sport. "Nay first," said he, "wilt thou come Manwë and kneel before me, and after you all the Valar; but last shall come Tulkas and kiss my foot, for I have in mind something for which I owe Poldórëa no great love." Now he purposed to spurn Tulkas in the mouth in payment of that buffet long ago, but the Valar had foreseen something of this and did but make play of humiliation that Melko might thereby be lured from his stronghold of Utumna. In sooth Manwë hoped even to the end for peace and amity, and the Gods would at his bidding indeed have received Melko into Valinor under truce and pledges of friendship, had not his pride been insatiate and his obstinacy in evil unconquerable. Now however was scant mercy left for him within their hearts, seeing that he abode in his demand that Manwë should do homage and Tulkas bend to those ruthless feet; nonetheless the Lord of Gods and Elves approaches now the chair of Melko and makes to kneel, for such was their plan the more to ensnare that evil one; but lo, so fiercely did wrath blaze up in the hearts of Tulkas and Aulë at that sight that Tulkas leapt across the hall at a bound despite Angaino, and Aulë was behind him and Oromë followed his father and the hall was full of tumult. Then Melko sprang to his feet shouting in a loud voice and his folk came through all those dismal passages to his aid. Then lashed he at Manwë with an iron flail he bore, but Manwë breathed gently upon it and its iron tassels were blown backward, and thereupon Tulkas smote Melko full in his teeth with his fist of iron, and he and Aulë grappled with him, and straight he was wrapped thirty times in the fathoms of Angaino. ·

Then said Oromë: "Would that he might be slain" – and it would have been well indeed, but the great Gods may not yet be slain.[4] Now is Melko held in dire bondage and beaten to his knees, and he is constrained to command all his vassalage that they molest not the Valar – and indeed the most of these, affrighted at the binding of their lord, fled away to the darkest places.

Tulkas indeed dragged Melko out before the gates, and there Aulë set upon each wrist one of the Vorotemnar and upon each ankle twain of the Ilterendi, and *tilkal* went red at the touch of Melko, and those bands have never since been loosened from his hands and feet. Then the chain is smithied to each of these and Melko borne thus helpless away, while Tulkas and Ulmo break the gates of Utumna and pile hills of stone upon them. And the saps and cavernous places beneath the surface of the earth are full yet of the dark spirits that were prisoned that day when Melko was taken, and yet many are the ways whereby they find the outer world from time to time – from fissures where they shriek with the voices of the tide on rocky coasts, down dark water-ways that wind unseen for many leagues, or out of the blue arches where the glaciers of Melko find their end.

After these things did the Gods return to Valmar by long ways and dark, guarding Melko every moment, and he gnawed his consuming rage. His lip was split and his face has had a strange leer upon it since that buffet dealt him by Tulkas, who even of policy could not endure to see the majesty of Manwë bow before the accursed one.

Now is a court set upon the slopes of Taniquetil and Melko arraigned before all the Vali[5] great and small, lying bound before the silver chair of Manwë. Against him speaketh Ossë, and Oromë, and Ulmo in deep ire, and Vána in abhorrence, proclaiming his deeds of cruelty and violence; yet Makar still spake for him, although not warmly, for said he: "'Twere an ill thing if peace were for always: already no blow echoes ever in the eternal quietude of Valinor, wherefore, if one might neither see deed of battle nor riotous joy even in the world without, then 'twould be irksome indeed, and I for one long not for such times!" Thereat arose Palúrien in sorrow and tears, and told of the plight of Earth and of the great beauty of her designs and of those things she desired dearly to bring forth; of all the wealth of flower and herbage, of tree and fruit and grain that the world might bear if it had but peace. "Take heed, O Valar, that both Elves and Men be not devoid of all solace whenso the times come for them to find the Earth"; but Melko writhed in rage at the name of Eldar and of Men and at his own impotence.

Now Aulë mightily backed her in this and after him many else of the Gods, yet Mandos and Lórien held their peace, nor do they ever speak much at the councils of the Valar or indeed at other times, but Tulkas arose angrily from the midst of the assembly and went from among them, for he could not endure parleying where he thought the guilt to be clear. Liever would he have unchained Melko and fought him then and there alone upon the plain of Valinor, giving him many a sore buffet in meed of his illdoings, rather than making high debate of them. Howbeit Manwë sate and listened and was moved by the speech of Palúrien, yet was it his thought that Melko was an Ainu and powerful beyond measure for the future good or evil of the world; wherefore he put away harshness and his doom was this. For three ages during the displeasure of the Gods should Melko be chained in a vault of Mandos by that chain Angaino, and thereafter should he fare into the light of the Two Trees, but only so that he might for four ages yet dwell as a servant in the house of Tulkas, and obey him in requital of his ancient malice. "Thus," said Manwë, "and yet but hardly, mayst thou win favour again sufficient that the Gods suffer thee to abide thereafter in an house of thine own and to have some slight estate among them as befitteth a Vala and a lord of the Ainur."

Such was the doom of Manwë, and even to Makar and Meássë it seemed good, albeit Tulkas and Palúrien thought it merciful to peril. Now doth Valinor enter upon its greatest time of peace, and all the earth beside, while Melko bideth in the deepest vaults of Mandos and his heart grows black within him.

Behold the tumults of the sea abate slowly, and the fires beneath the mountains die; the earth quakes no more and the fierceness of the cold and the stubbornness of the hills and rivers of ice is melted to the uttermost North and to the deepest South, even to the regions about Ringil and Helkar. Then Palúrien goes once more out over the Earth, and the forests multiply and spread, and often is Oromë's horn heard behind her in the dimness: now do nightshade and bryony begin to creep about the brakes, and holly and ilex are seen upon the earth. Even the faces of the cliffs are grown with ivies and trailing plants for the calm of the winds and the quietude of the sea, and all the caverns and the shores are festooned with weeds, and great sea-growths come to life swaying gently when Ossë moves the waters.

Now came that Vala and sat upon a headland of the Great Lands, having leisure in the stillness of his realm, and he saw how Palúrien was filling the quiet dusk of the Earth with flitting shapes. Bats and owls whom Vefántur set free from Mandos swooped about the sky, and nightingales sent by Lórien from Valinor trilled beside still waters. Far away a nightjar croaked, and in dark places snakes that slipped from Utumna when Melko was bound moved noiselessly about; a frog croaked upon a bare pool's border.

Then he sent word to Ulmo of the new things that were done, and Ulmo desired not that the waters of the inner seas be longer un-peopled, but came forth seeking Palúrien, and she gave him spells, and the seas began to gleam with fish or strange creatures crawled at bottom; yet the shellfish and the oysters no-one of Valar or of Elves knows whence they are, for already they gaped in the silent waters or ever Melko plunged therein from on high, and pearls there were before the Eldar thought or dreamed of any gem.

Three great fish luminous in the dark of the sunless days went ever with Ulmo, and the roof of Ossë's dwelling beneath the Great Sea shone with phosphorescent scales. Behold that was a time of great peace and quiet, and life struck deep roots into the new-made soils of Earth, and seeds were sown that waited only for the light to come, and it is known and praised as the age of "Melko's Chains".'

## NOTES

1   The following passage was added here, apparently very soon after the writing of the text, but was later firmly struck through:

The truth is that he is a son of Linwë Tinto King of the Pipers who was lost of old upon the great march from Palisor, and wandering in Hisilómë found the lonely twilight spirit (Tindriel) Wendelin dancing in a glade of beeches. Loving her he was content to leave his folk and dance for ever in the shadows, but his children Timpinen and Tinúviel long after joined the Eldar again, and tales there are concerning them both, though they are seldom told.

The name *Tindriel* stood alone in the manuscript as written, but it was then bracketed and *Wendelin* added in the margin. These are the first references in the consecutive narrative to Thingol (Linwë Tinto), Hithlum (Hisilómë), Melian (Tindriel, Wendelin), and Lúthien Tinúviel; but I postpone discussion of these allusions.

2  Cf. the explanation of the names *Eriol* and *Angol* as 'ironcliffs' referred to in the Appendix on Names (entry *Eriol*).

3  Associated with the story of the sojourn of Eriol (Ælfwine) in Tol Eressëa, and the 'Lost Tales' that he heard there, are two 'schemes' or synopses setting out the plan of the work. One of these is, for much of its length, a résumé of the *Tales* as they are extant; the other, certainly the later, is divergent. In this second scheme, in which the voyager is called Ælfwine, the tale on the second night by the Tale-fire is given to 'Evromord the Door-ward', though the narrative-content was to be the same (The Coming of the Gods; the World-fashioning and the Building of Valinor; the Planting of the Two Trees). After this is written (a later addition): 'Ælfwine goes to beg *limpë* of Meril; she sends him back.' The third night by the Tale-fire is thus described:

The Door-ward continues of the Primeval Twilight. The Furies of Melko. Melko's Chains and the awakening of the Elves. (How Fankil and many dark shapes escape into the world.) [Given to Meril but to be placed as here and much abridged.]

It seems certain that this was a revision in intention only, never achieved. It is notable that in the actual text, as also in the first of these two 'schemes', Rúmil's function in the house is that of door-ward – and Rúmil, not Evromord, was the name that was preserved long after as the recounter of The Music of the Ainur.

4  The text as originally written read: 'but the great Gods may not be slain, though their children may and all those lesser people of the Vali, albeit only at the hands of some one of the Valar.'

5  *Vali* is an emendation from *Valar*. Cf. Rúmil's words (p. 58): 'they whom we now call the Valar (or Vali, it matters not).'

Commentary on
*The Chaining of Melko*

In the interlude between this tale and the last we encounter the figure of Timpinen or Tinfang. This being had existed in my father's mind for some years, and there are two poems about him. The first is entitled *Tinfang Warble*; it is very brief, but exists in three versions. According to a note by my father the original was written at Oxford in 1914, and it was rewritten at Leeds in '1920–23'. It was finally published in 1927 in a further altered form, which I give here.*

### Tinfang Warble

O the hoot! O the hoot!
How he trillups on his flute!
O the hoot of Tinfang Warble!

Dancing all alone,
Hopping on a stone,
Flitting like a fawn,
In the twilight on the lawn,
And his name is Tinfang Warble!

The first star has shown
And its lamp is blown
to a flame of flickering blue.
He pipes not to me,
He pipes not to thee,
He whistles for none of you.
His music is his own,
The tunes of Tinfang Warble!

In the earliest version Tinfang is called a 'leprawn', and in the early glossary of the Gnomish speech he is a 'fay'.

The second poem is entitled *Over Old Hills and Far Away*. This exists in five texts, of which the earliest bears an Old English title as well (of the same meaning): ʒeond fyrne beorgas ⁊ heonan feor. Notes by my father state that it was written at Brocton Camp in Staffordshire between December 1915 and February 1916, and rewritten at Oxford in 1927. The final version given here differs in many details of wording and in places whole lines from earlier versions, from which I note at the end a few interesting readings.

### Over Old Hills and Far Away

It was early and still in the night of June,
And few were the stars, and far was the moon,
The drowsy trees drooping, and silently creeping
Shadows woke under them while they were sleeping.

5    I stole to the window with stealthy tread
Leaving my white and unpressed bed;
And something alluring, aloof and queer,
Like perfume of flowers from the shores of the mere

* Publication was in a periodical referred to in the cutting preserved from it as 'I.U.M[agazine]').

That in Elvenhome lies, and in starlit rains
10 Twinkles and flashes, came up to the panes
Of my high lattice-window. Or was it a sound?
I listened and marvelled with eyes on the ground.
For there came from afar a filtered note
Enchanting sweet, now clear, now remote,
15 As clear as a star in a pool by the reeds,
As faint as the glimmer of dew on the weeds.

Then I left the window and followed the call
Down the creaking stairs and across the hall
Out through a door that swung tall and grey,
20 And over the lawn, and away, away!

It was Tinfang Warble that was dancing there,
Fluting and tossing his old white hair,
Till it sparkled like frost in a winter moon;
And the stars were about him, and blinked to his tune
25 Shimmering blue like sparks in a haze,
As always they shimmer and shake when he plays.

My feet only made there the ghost of a sound
On the shining white pebbles that ringed him round,
Where his little feet flashed on a circle of sand,
30 And the fingers were white on his flickering hand.
In the wink of a star he had leapt in the air
With his fluttering cap and his glistening hair;
And had cast his long flute right over his back,
Where it hung by a ribbon of silver and black.

35 His slim little body went fine as a shade,
And he slipped through the reeds like a mist in the glade;
And he laughed like thin silver, and piped a thin note,
As he flapped in the shadows his shadowy coat.
O! the toes of his slippers were twisted and curled,
40 But he danced like a wind out into the world.

He is gone, and the valley is empty and bare
Where lonely I stand and lonely I stare.
Then suddenly out in the meadows beyond,
Then back in the reeds by the shimmering pond,
45 Then afar from a copse where the mosses are thick
A few little notes came trillaping quick.

I leapt o'er the stream and I sped from the glade,
For Tinfang Warble it was that played;
I must follow the hoot of his twilight flute

50     Over reed, over rush, under branch, over root,
       And over dim fields, and through rustling grasses
       That murmur and nod as the old elf passes,
       Over old hills and far away
       Where the harps of the Elvenfolk softly play.

*Earlier readings:*

1–2    'Twas a very quiet evening once in June –
       And I thought that stars had grown bright too soon –
       Cf. the prose text, p. 94: 'The Noldoli say that [the stars] come
       out too soon if Tinfang Warble plays'.

8      from the shores of the mere] by the fairies' mere

9      Elvenhome] emendation made on the text of the final version,
       replacing 'Fairyland'.

24     Till the stars came out, as it seemed, too soon.
       Cf. the note to line 2.

25–6   They always come out when he warbles and plays,
       And they shine bright blue as long as he stays.
       Cf. the prose text, p. 95: 'or will he play beneath a goodly moon
       and the stars go bright and blue.'

54     Elvenfolk] emendation made on the text of the final version,
       replacing 'fairies'.

★

The first part of this story of *The Chaining of Melko* came to have a very
different form in later versions, where (*The Silmarillion* p. 35) it was
during the sojourn of the Valar on the Isle of Almaren, under the light of
the Two Lamps, that 'the seeds that Yavanna had sown began swiftly to
sprout and to burgeon, and there arose a multitude of growing things
great and small, mosses and grasses and great ferns, and trees whose tops
were crowned with cloud'; and that 'beasts came forth and dwelt in the
grassy plains, or in the rivers and the lakes, or walked in the shadows of
the woods'. This was the Spring of Arda; but after the coming of Melkor
and the delving of Utumno 'green things fell sick and rotted, and rivers
were choked with weeds and slime, and fens were made, rank and poisonous, the breeding place of flies; and forests grew dark and perilous,
the haunts of fear; and beasts became monsters of horn and ivory and
dyed the earth with blood'. Then came the fall of the Lamps, and 'thus
ended the Spring of Arda' (p. 37). After the building of Valinor and the
arising of the Two Trees 'Middle-earth lay in a twilight beneath the
stars' (p. 39), and Yavanna and Oromë alone of the Valar returned there
at times: 'Yavanna would walk there in the shadows, grieving because the
growth and promise of the Spring of Arda was stayed. And she set a sleep
upon many things that had arisen in the Spring, so that they should not

age, but should wait for a time of awakening that yet should be' (p. 47).
'But already the oldest living things had arisen: in the seas the great weeds,
and on earth the shadow of great trees; and in the valleys of the night-clad
hills there were dark creatures old and strong.'

In this earliest narrative, on the other hand, there is no mention of the
beginning of growth during the time when the Lamps shone (see p. 69),
and the first trees and low plants appeared under Yavanna's spells in the
twilight after their overthrow. Moreover in the last sentence of this tale
'seeds were sown', in that time of 'quiet dusk' while Melko was chained,
'that waited only for the light to come'. Thus in the early story Yavanna
sows in the dark with a view (it seems) to growth and flowering in later
days of sunlight, whereas in all the subsequent versions the goddess in
the time of darkness sows no more, but rather lays a sleep on many things
that had arisen beneath the light of the Lamps in the Spring of Arda.
But both in the early tale and in *The Silmarillion* there is a suggestion that
Yavanna foresees that light will come in the end to the Great Lands, to
Middle-earth.

The conception of a flowing, liquid light in the airs of Earth is again
very marked, and it seems that in the original idea the twilight ages of the
world east of the sea were still illumined by the traces of this light
('Seldom now falls the shimmering rain as it was used, and there reigns a
gloom lit with pale streaks', p. 98) as well as by the stars of Varda, even
though 'the Gods have gathered so much of that light that had before
flowed about the airs' (*ibid.*).

The renewed cosmic violence is conceivably the precursor of the great
Battle of the Powers in the later mythology (*The Silmarillion* p. 51); but
in this earliest tale Melko's upheavals are the cause of the Valar's visitation,
whereas the Battle of the Powers, in which the shape of Middle-earth was
changed, resulted from it. In *The Silmarillion* it was the discovery of the
newly-awakened Elves by Oromë that led the Valar to the assault on
Utumno.

In its rich narrative detail, as in its 'primitive' air, the tale told by
Meril-i-Turinqi of the capture of Melko bears little relation to the later
narrative; while the tone of the encounter at Utumna, and the treacherous
shifts of the Valar to ensnare him, is foreign to it likewise. But some
elements survived: the chain Angainor forged by Aulë (if not the marvellous metal *tilkal* with its most uncharacteristically derived name), the
wrestling of Tulkas with Melko, his imprisonment in Mandos for 'three
ages', and the idea that his fortress was not destroyed to its foundations.
It emerges too that the clement and trustful character of Manwë was
early defined; while the reference to Mandos' seldom speaking is possibly
a foreshadowing of his pronouncing his judgements only at the bidding
of Manwë (see p. 90). The origin of nightingales in the domain of Lórien
in Valinor is already present.

Lastly, it may seem from the account of the journey of the Valar in
this tale that Hisilómë (which survived without any further change as the

Quenya name of Hithlum) was here a quite distinct region from the later Hithlum, since it is placed *beyond* the Mountains of Iron: in *The Silmaril-lion* the Mountains of Iron are said to have been reared by Melkor 'as a fence to his citadel of Utumno': 'they stood upon the borders of the regions of everlasting cold, in a great curve from east to west' (p. 118). But in fact the 'Mountains of Iron' here correspond to the later 'Mountains of Shadow' (*Ered Wethrin*). In an annotated list of names accompanying the tale of *The Fall of Gondolin* the name *Dor Lómin* is thus defined:

> *Dor Lómin* or the 'Land of Shadow' was that region named of the Eldar *Hisilómë* (and this means 'Shadowy Twilights') . . . and it is so called by reason of the scanty sun which peeps little over the Iron Mountains to the east and south of it.

On the little map given on p. 81 the line of peaks which I have marked *f* almost certainly represents these mountains, and the region to the north of them, marked *g*, is then Hisilómë.

The manuscript continues, from the point where I have ended the text in this chapter, with no break; but this point is the end of a section in the mythological narrative (with a brief interruption by Eriol), and the remainder of Meril-i-Turinqi's tale is reserved to the next chapter. Thus I make two tales of one.

# V

# THE COMING OF THE ELVES
# AND THE MAKING OF KÔR

I take this title from the cover of the book (which adds also 'How the
Elves did fashion Gems'), for as I have already remarked the narrative
continues without a new heading.

Then said Eriol: 'Sad was the unchaining of Melko, methinks, even
did it seem merciful and just – but how came the Gods to do this
thing?'

Then Meril[1] continuing said:

'Upon a time thereafter was the third period of Melko's prison-
ment beneath the halls of Mandos come nearly to its ending. Manwë
sat upon the top of the mountain and gazed with his piercing eyes
into the shades beyond Valinor, and hawks flew to him and from him
bearing many great tidings, but Varda was singing a song and looking
upon the plain of Valinor. Silpion was at that time glimmering and
the roofs of Valmar below were black and silver beneath its rays;
and Varda was joyous, but on a sudden Manwë spake, saying:
"Behold, there is a gleam of gold beneath the pine-trees, and the
deepest gloaming of the world is full of a patter of feet. The Eldar
have come, O Taniquetil!" Then Varda arose swiftly and stretched
her arms out North and South, and unbraided her long hair, and
lifted up the Song of the Valar, and Ilwë was filled with the loveliness
of her voice.

Then did she descend to Valmar and to the abode of Aulë; and
he was making vessels of silver for Lórien. A bason filled with the
radiance of Telimpë[2] was by his side, and this he used cunningly in
his craft, but now Varda stood before him and said: "The Eldar have
come!" and Aulë flung down his hammer saying: "Then Ilúvatar
hath sent them at last," and the hammer striking some ingots of
silver upon the floor did of its magic smite silver sparks to life, that
flashed from his windows out into the heavens. Varda seeing this
took of that radiance in the bason and mingled it with molten silver
to make it more stable, and fared upon her wings of speed, and set
stars about the firmament in very great profusion, so that the skies
grew marvellously fair and their glory was doubled; and those stars

that she then fashioned have a power of slumbers, for the silver of their bodies came of the treasury of Lórien and their radiance had lain in Telimpë long time in his garden.

Some have said that the Seven Stars were set at that time by Varda to commemorate the coming of the Eldar, and that Morwinyon who blazes above the world's edge in the west was dropped by her as she fared in great haste back to Valinor. Now this is indeed the true beginning of Morwinyon and his beauty, yet the Seven Stars were not set by Varda, being indeed the sparks from Aulë's forge whose brightness in the ancient heavens urged Varda to make their rivals; yet this did she never achieve.

But now even as Varda is engaged in this great work, behold, Oromë pricks over the plain, and drawing rein he shouts aloud so that all the ears in Valmar may hear him: "*Tulielto! Tulielto!* They have come – they have come!" Then he stands midway between the Two Trees and winds his horn, and the gates of Valmar are opened, and the Vali troop into the plain, for they guess that tidings of wonder have come into the world. Then spake Oromë: "Behold the woods of the Great Lands, even in Palisor the midmost region where the pinewoods murmur unceasingly, are full of a strange noise. There did I wander, and lo! 'twas as if folk arose betimes beneath the latest stars. There was a stir among the distant trees and words were spoken suddenly, and feet went to and fro. Then did I say what is this deed that Palúrien my mother has wrought in secret, and I sought her out and questioned her, and she answered: 'This is no work of mine, but the hand of one far greater did this. Ilúvatar hath awakened his children at the last – ride home to Valinor and tell the Gods that the Eldar have come indeed!' "

Then shouted all the people of Valinor: "*I·Eldar tulier* – the Eldar have come" – and it was not until that hour that the Gods knew that their joy had contained a flaw, or that they had waited in hunger for its completion, but now they knew that the world had been an empty place beset with loneliness having no children for her own.

Now once more is council set and Manwë sitteth before the Gods there amid the Two Trees – and those had now borne light for four ages. Every one of the Vali fare thither, even Ulmo Vailimo in great haste from the Outer Seas, and his face is eager and glad.

On that day Manwë released Melko from Angaino before the full time of his doom, but the manacles and the fetters of *tilkal* were not unloosed, and he bore them yet upon wrist and ankle. Great joy blindeth even the forewisdom of the Gods. Last of all came Palúrien Yavanna hasting from Palisor, and the Valar debated concerning the

Eldar; but Melko sat at the feet of Tulkas and feigned a glad and humble cheer. At length it is the word of the Gods that some of the new-come Eldar be bidden to Valinor, there to speak to Manwë and his people, telling of their coming into the world and of the desires that it awakened in them.

Then does Nornorë, whose feet flash invisibly for the greatness of their speed, hurtle from Valinor bearing the embassy of Manwë, and he goes unstaying over both land and sea to Palisor. There he finds a place deep in a vale surrounded by pine-clad slopes; its floor is a pool of wide water and its roof the twilight set with Varda's stars. There had Oromë heard the awaking of the Eldar, and all songs name that place Koivië-néni or the Waters of Awakening.

Now all the slopes of that valley and the bare margin of the lake, even the rugged fringes of the hills beyond, are filled with a concourse of folk who gaze in wonder at the stars, and some sing already with voices that are very beautiful. But Nornorë stood upon a hill and was amazed for the beauty of that folk, and because he was a Vala they seemed to him marvellously small and delicate and their faces wistful and tender. Then did he speak in the great voice of the Valar and all those shining faces turned towards his voice.

"Behold O Eldalië, desired are ye for all the age of twilight, and sought for throughout the ages of peace, and I come even from Manwë Súlimo Lord of the Gods who abides upon Taniquetil in peace and wisdom to you who are the Children of Ilúvatar, and these are the words he put into my mouth to speak: Let now some few of you come back with me – for am I not Nornorë herald of the Valar – and enter Valinor and speak with him, that he may learn of your coming and of all your desires."

Great was the stir and wonder now about the waters of Koivië, and its end was that three of the Eldar came forward daring to go with Nornorë, and these he bore now back to Valinor, and their names as the Elves of Kôr have handed them on were Isil Inwë, and Finwë Nólemë who was Turondo's father, and Tinwë Lintö father of Tinúviel – but the Noldoli call them Inwithiel, Golfinweg, and Tinwelint. Afterward they became very great among the Eldar, and the Teleri were those who followed Isil, but his kindred and descendants are that royal folk the Inwir of whose blood I am. Nolemë was lord of the Noldoli, and of his son Turondo (or Turgon as they called him) are great tales told, but Tinwë[3] abode not long with his people, and yet 'tis said lives still lord of the scattered Elves of Hisilómë, dancing in its twilight places with Wendelin his spouse, a sprite come long long ago from the quiet gardens of Lórien; yet greatest of all the Elves did Isil Inwë become, and folk reverence his mighty name to this day.

Behold now brought by Nornorë the three Elves stood before the Gods, and it was at that time the changing of the lights, and Silpion was waning but Laurelin was awakening to his greatest glory, even as Silmo emptied the urn of silver about the roots of the other Tree. Then those Elves were utterly dazed and astonied by the splendour of the light, whose eyes knew only the dusk and had yet seen no brighter things than Varda's stars, but the beauty and majestic strength of the Gods in conclave filled them with awe, and the roofs of Valmar blazing afar upon the plain made them tremble, and they bowed in reverence – but Manwë said to them: "Rise, O Children of Ilúvatar, for very glad are the Gods of your coming! Tell us how ye came; how found ye the world; what seemeth it to you who are its first offspring, or with what desires doth it fill you."

But Nólemë answering said: "Lo! Most mighty one, whence indeed come we! For meseems I awoke but now from a sleep eternally profound, whose vast dreams already are forgotten." And Tinwë said thereto that his heart told him that he was new-come from illimitable regions, yet he might not recollect by what dark and strange paths he had been brought; and last spake Inwë, who had been gazing upon Laurelin while the others spake, and he said: "Knowing neither whence I come nor by what ways nor yet whither I go, the world that we are in is but one great wonderment to me, and methinks I love it wholly, yet it fills me altogether with a desire for light."

Then Manwë saw that Ilúvatar had wiped from the minds of the Eldar all knowledge of the manner of their coming, and that the Gods might not discover it; and he was filled with deep astonishment; but Yavanna who hearkened also caught her breath for the stab of the words of Inwë, saying that he desired light. Then she looked upon Laurelin and her heart thought of the fruitful orchards in Valmar, and she whispered to Tuivána who sat beside her, gazing upon the tender grace of those Eldar; then those twain said to Manwë: "Lo! the Earth and its shadows are no place for creatures so fair, whom only the heart and mind of Ilúvatar have conceived. Fair are the pine-forests and the thickets, but they are full of unelfin spirits and Mandos' children walk abroad and vassals of Melko lurk in strange places – and we ourselves would not be without the sight of this sweet folk. Their distant laughter has filtered to our ears from Palisor, and we would have it echo always about us in our halls and pleasaunces in Valmar. Let the Eldar dwell among us, and the well of our joy be filled from new springs that may not dry up."

Then arose a clamour among the Gods and the most spake for Palúrien and Vána, whereas Makar said that Valinor was builded for the Valar – "and already is it a rose-garden of fair ladies rather than an abode of men. Wherefore do ye desire to fill it with the children of the world?" In this Meássë backed him, and Mandos and Fui were cold to the Eldar as to all else; yet was Varda vehement in support of Yavanna and Tuivána, and indeed her love for the Eldar has ever been the greatest of all the folk of Valinor; and Aulë and Lórien, Oromë and Nessa and Ulmo most mightily proclaimed their desire for the bidding of the Eldar to dwell among the Gods. Wherefore, albeit Ossë spake cautiously against it – belike out of that ever-smouldering jealousy and rebellion he felt against Ulmo – it was the voice of the council that the Eldar should be bidden, and the Gods awaited but the judgement of Manwë. Behold even Melko seeing where was the majority insinuated his guileful voice into the pleading, and has nonetheless since those days maligned the Valar, saying they did but summon the Eldar as to a prison out of covetice and jealousy of their beauty. Thus often did he lie to the Noldoli afterwards when he would stir their restlessness, adding beside all truth that he alone had withstood the general voice and spoken for the freedom of the Elves.

Maybe indeed had the Gods decided otherwise the world had been a fairer place now and the Eldar a happier folk, but never would they have achieved such glory, knowledge, and beauty as they did of old, and still less would any of Melko's redes have benefited them.

Now having hearkened to all that was said Manwë gave judgement and was glad, for indeed his heart leaned of itself to the leading of the Eldar from the dusky world to the light of Valinor. Turning to the three Eldar he said: "Go ye back now to your kindreds and Nornorë shall bring you swiftly there, even to Koivië-néni in Palisor. Behold, this is the word of Manwë Súlimo, and the voice of the Valar's desire, that the people of the Eldalië, the Children of Ilúvatar, fare to Valinor, and there dwell in the splendour of Laurelin and the radiance of Silpion and know the happiness of the Gods. An abode of surpassing beauty shall they possess, and the Gods will aid them in its building."

Thereto answered Inwë: "Fain are we indeed of thy bidding, and who of the Eldalië that have already longed for the beauty of the stars will stay or rest till his eyes have feasted on the blessed light of Valinor!" Thereafter Nornorë guided those Elves back to the bare margins of Koivië-néni, and standing upon a boulder Inwë spake the embassy to all those hosts of the Eldalië that Ilúvatar waked first upon the Earth, and all such as heard his words were filled with desire to see the faces of the Gods.

When Nornorë returning told the Valar that the Elves were indeed coming and that Ilúvatar had set already a great multitude upon the Earth, the Gods made mighty preparation. Behold Aulë gathers his tools and stuffs and Yavanna and Tuivána wander about the plain even to the foothills of the mountains and the bare coasts of the Shadowy Seas, seeking them a home and an abiding-place; but Oromë goeth straightway out of Valinor into the forests whose every darkling glade he knew and every dim path had traversed, for he purposed to guide the troops of the Eldar from Palisor over all the wide lands west till they came to the confines of the Great Sea.

To those dark shores fared Ulmo, and strange was the roaring of the unlit sea in those most ancient days upon that rocky coast that bore still the scars of the tumultuous wrath of Melko. Falman-Ossë was little pleased to see Ulmo in the Great Seas, for Ulmo had taken that island whereon Ossë himself had drawn the Gods to Arvalin, saving them from the rising waters when Ringil and Helkar thawed beneath their blazing lamps. That was many ages past in the days when the Gods were new-come strangers in the world, and during all that time the island had floated darkly in the Shadowy Seas, desolate save when Ossë climbed its beaches on his journeys in the deeps; but now Ulmo had come upon his secret island and harnessed thereto a host of the greatest fish, and amidmost was Uin the mightiest and most ancient of whales; and he bid these put forth their strength, and they drew the island mightily to the very shores of the Great Lands, even to the coast of Hisilómë northward of the Iron Mountains whither all the deepest shades withdrew when the Sun first arose.

Now Ulmo stands there and there comes a glint in the woods that marched even down to the sea-foam in those quiet days, and behold! he hears the footsteps of the Teleri crackle in the forest, and Inwë is at their head beside the stirrup of Oromë. Grievous had been their march, and dark and difficult the way through Hisilómë the land of shade, despite the skill and power of Oromë. Indeed long after the joy of Valinor had washed its memory faint the Elves sang still sadly of it, and told tales of many of their folk whom they said and say were lost in those old forests and ever wandered there in sorrow. Still were they there long after when Men were shut in Hisilómë by Melko, and still do they dance there when

Men have wandered far over the lighter places of the Earth. Hisilómë did Men name Aryador, and the Lost Elves did they call the Shadow Folk, and feared them.

Nonetheless the most of the great companies of the Teleri came now to the beaches and climbed therefrom upon the island that Ulmo had brought. Ulmo counselled them that they wait not for the other kindreds, and though at first they will not yield, weeping at the thought, at last are they persuaded, and straightway are drawn with utmost speed beyond the Shadowy Seas and the wide bay of Arvalin to the strands of Valinor. There does the distant beauty of the trees shining down the opening in the hills enchant their hearts, and yet do they stand gazing back across the waters they have passed, for they know not where those other kindreds of their folk may be, and not even the loveliness of Valinor do they desire without them.

Then leaving them silent and wondering on the shore Ulmo draws back that great island-car to the rocks of Hisilómë, and behold, warmed by the distant gleam of Laurelin that lit upon its western edge as it lay in the Bay of Faëry, new and more tender trees begin to grow upon it, and the green of herbage is seen upon its slopes.

Now Ossë raises his head above the waves in wrath, deeming himself slighted that his aid was not sought in the ferrying of the Elves, but his own island taken unasked. Fast does he follow in Ulmo's wake and yet is left far behind, for Ulmo set the might of the Valar in Uin and the whales. Upon the cliffs there stand already the Noldoli in anguish, thinking themselves deserted in the gloom, and Nóleme Finwë who had led them thither hard upon the rear of the Teleri went among them enheartening them. Full of travail their journey too had been, for the world is wide and nigh half across it had they come from most distant Palisor, and in those days neither sun shone nor moon gleamed, and pathways were there none be it of Elves or of Men. Oromë too was far ahead riding before the Teleri upon the march and was now gone back into the lands. There the Solosimpi were astray in the forests stretching deep behind, and his horn wound faintly in the ears of those upon the shore, from whence that Vala sought them up and down the dark vales of Hisilómë.

Therefore now coming Ulmo thinks to draw the Noldoli swiftly to the strand of Valinor, returning once again for those others when Oromë shall have led them to the coast. This does he, and Falman beholds that second ferrying from afar and spumes in rage, but great is the joy of the Teleri and Noldoli upon that shore where the lights are those of late summer afternoons for the distant glow of Lindeloksë. There may I leave them for a while and tell of the strange happenings that befell the Solosimpi by reason of Ossë's wrath, and of the first dwelling upon Tol Eressëa.

Fear falls upon them in that old darkness, and beguiled by the fair music of the fay Wendelin, as other tales set forth more fully elsewhere, their leader Tinwë Linto was lost, and long they sought him, but it was in vain, and he came never again among them.[4] When therefore they heard the horn of Oromë ringing in the forest great was their joy, and gathering to its sound soon are they led to the cliffs, and hear the murmur of the sunless sea. Long time they waited there, for Ossë cast storms and shadows about the return of Ulmo, so that he drove by devious ways, and his great fish faltered in their going; yet at the last do they too climb upon that island and are drawn towards Valinor; and one Ellu they chose in place of Tinwë, and he has ever since been named the Lord of the Solosimpi.[5]

Behold now less than half the distance have they traversed, and the Twilit Isles float still far aloof, when Ossë and Ónen waylay them in the western waters of the Great Sea ere yet the mists of the Shadowy Seas are reached. Then Ossë seizes that island in his great hand, and all the great strength of Uin may scarcely drag it onward, for at swimming and in deeds of bodily strength in the water none of the Valar, not even Ulmo's self, is Ossë's match, and indeed Ulmo was not at hand, for he was far ahead piloting the great craft in the glooms that Ossë had gathered, leading it onward with the music of his conches. Now ere he can return Ossë with Ónen's aid had brought the isle to a stand, and was anchoring it even to the sea-bottom with giant ropes of those leather-weeds and polyps that in those dark days had grown already in slow centuries to unimagined girth about the pillars of his deep-sea house. Thereto as Ulmo urges the whales to put forth all their strength and himself aids with all his godlike power, Ossë piles rocks and boulders of huge mass that Melko's ancient wrath had strewn about the seafloor, and builds these as a column beneath the island.

Vainly doth Ulmo trumpet and Uin with the flukes of his un-measured tail lash the seas to wrath, for thither Ossë now brings every kind of deep sea creature that buildeth itself a house and dwelling of stony shell; and these he planted about the base of the island: corals there were of every kind and barnacles and sponges like stone. Nonetheless for a very great while did that struggle endure, until at length Ulmo returned to Valmar in wrath and dismay. There did he warn the other Valar that the Solosimpi may not yet be brought thither, for that the isle has grown fast in the most lonely waters of the world.

There stands that island yet – indeed thou knowest it, for it is called "the Lonely Isle" – and no land may be seen for many leagues' sail from its cliffs, for the Twilit Isles upon the bosom of the Shadowy Seas are deep in the dim West, and the Magic Isles lie backward in the East. Now therefore do the Gods bid the Elves build a dwelling, and Aulë aided them in that, but Ulmo fares back to the Lonely Island, and lo! it stands now upon a pillar of rock upon the seas' floor, and Ossë fares about it in a foam of business anchoring all the scattered islands of his domain fast to the ocean-bed. Hence came the first dwelling of the Solosimpi on the Lonely Island, and the deeper sundering of that folk from the others both in speech and customs; for know that all these great deeds of the past that make but a small tale now were not lightly achieved and in a moment of time, but rather would very many men have grown and died betwixt the binding of the Islands and the making of the Ships.

Twice now had that isle of their dwelling caught the gleam of the glorious Trees of Valinor, and so was it already fairer and more fertile and more full of sweet plants and grasses than the other places of all the world beside where great light had not been seen; indeed the Solosimpi say that birches grew there already, and many reeds, and turf there was upon the western slopes. There too were many caverns, and there was a stretching shoreland of white sand about the feet of black and purple cliffs, and here was the dwelling even in those deepest days of the Solosimpi.

There Ulmo sate upon a headland and spake to them words of comfort and of the deepest wisdom; and all sea-lore he told them, and they hearkened; and music he taught them, and they made slender pipes of shells. By reason of that labour of Ossë there are no strands so strewn with marvellous shells as were the white beaches and the sheltered coves of Tol Eressëa, and the Solosimpi dwelt much in caves, and adorned them with those sea-treasures, and the sound of their wistful piping might be heard for many a long day come faintly down the winds.

Then Falman-Ossë's heart melted towards them and he would have released them, save for the new joy and pride he had that their beauty dwelt thus amidmost of his realm, so that their pipes gave perpetual pleasure to his ear, and Uinen[6] and the Oarni and all the spirits of the waves were enamoured of them.

So danced the Solosimpi upon the waves' brink, and the love of the sea and rocky coasts entered in their hearts, even though they gazed in longing towards the happy shores whither long ago the Teleri and Noldoli had been borne.

Now these after a season took hope and their sorrow grew less bitter, learning how their kindred dwelt in no unkindly land, and Ulmo had them under his care and guardianship. Wherefore they heeded now the Gods' desire and turned to the building of their home; and Aulë taught them very much lore and skill, and Manwë also. Now Manwë loved more the Teleri, and from him and from Ómar did they learn deeper of the craft of song and poesy than all the Elves beside; but the Noldoli were beloved most by Aulë, and they learned much of his science, till their hearts became unquiet for the lust of more knowing, but they grew to great wisdom and to great subtlety of skill.

Behold there is a low place in that ring of mountains that guards Valinor, and there the shining of the Trees steals through from the plain beyond and gilds the dark waters of the bay of Arvalin,[7] but a great beach of finest sand, golden in the blaze of Laurelin, white in the light of Silpion, runs inland there, where in the trouble of the ancient seas a shadowy arm of water had groped in toward Valinor, but now there is only a slender water fringed with white. At the head of this long creek there stands a lonely hill which gazes at the loftier mountains. Now all the walls of that inlet of the seas are luxuriant with a marvellous vigour of fair trees, but the hill is covered only with a deep turf, and harebells grow atop of it ringing softly in the gentle breath of Súlimo.

Here was the place that those fair Elves bethought them to dwell, and the Gods named that hill Kôr by reason of its roundness and its smoothness. Thither did Aulë bring all the dust of magic metals that his great works had made and gathered, and he piled it about the foot of that hill, and most of this dust was of gold, and a sand of gold stretched away from the feet of Kôr out into the distance where the Two Trees blossomed. Upon the hill-top the Elves built fair abodes of shining white – of marbles and stones quarried from the Mountains of Valinor that glistened wondrously,[8] silver and gold and a substance of great hardness and white lucency that they contrived of shells melted in the dew of Silpion, and white streets there were bordered with dark trees that wound with graceful turns or climbed with flights of delicate stairs up from the plain of Valinor to topmost Kôr; and all those shining houses clomb each shoulder higher than the others till the house of Inwë was reached that was the uppermost, and had a slender silver tower shooting skyward like a needle, and a white lamp of piercing ray was set therein that shone upon the shadows of the bay, but every window of the city on the hill of Kôr looked out toward the sea.

Fountains there were of great beauty and frailty and roofs and pinnacles of bright glass and amber that was made by Palúrien and Ulmo, and trees stood thick on the white walls and terraces, and their golden fruit shone richly.

Now at the building of Kôr the Gods gave to Inwë and to Nólemë a shoot each of either of those glorious trees, and they grew to very small and slender elfin trees, but blossomed both eternally without abating, and those of the courts of Inwë were the fairest, and about them the Teleri sang songs of happiness, but others singing also fared up and down the marble flights and the wistful voices of the Noldoli were heard about the courts and chambers; but yet the Solosimpi dwelt far off amid the sea and made windy music on their pipes of shell.

Now is Ossë very fain of those Solosimpi, the shoreland pipers, and if Ulmo be not nigh he sits upon a reef at sea and many of the Oarni are by him, and hearkens to their voice and watches their flitting dances on this shore, but to Valmar he dare not fare again for the power of Ulmo in the councils of the Valar and . . . . . . . . . . the wrath of that mighty one at the anchoring of the islands.

Indeed war had been but held off by the Gods, who desired peace and would not suffer Ulmo to gather the folk of the Valar and assail Ossë and rend the islands from their new roots. Therefore does Ossë sometimes ride the foams out into the bay of Arvalin[9] and gaze upon the glory on the hills, and he longs for the light and happiness upon the plain, but most for the song of birds and the swift movement of their wings into the clear air, grown weary of his silver and dark fish silent and strange amid the deep waters.

But on a day some birds came flying high from the gardens of Yavanna, and some were white and some black and some both black and white; and being dazed among the shadows they had not where to settle, and Ossë coaxed them, and they settled about his mighty shoulders, and he taught them to swim and gave them great strength of wing, for of such strength of shoulder he had more than any [?other] being and was the greatest of swimmers; and he poured fishy oils upon their feathers that they might bear the waters, and he fed them on small fish.

Then did he turn away to his own seas, and they swam about him or fared above him on low wing crying and piping; and he showed them dwellings on the Twilit Isles and even about the cliffs of Tol Eressëa, and the manner of diving and of spearing fish they learned there, and their voices became harsh for the rugged places of their life far from the soft regions of Valinor or wailing for the music of the Solosimpi and sighing of the sea. And now have all that great folk of gulls and seamews and petrels come into their kingdom; and puffins are there, and eider-duck, and cormorants, and gannets, and rock-doves, and the cliffs are full of a chattering and a smell of fish, and great conclaves are held upon their ledges, or among spits and reefs among the waters. But the proudest of all these birds were the swans, and these Ossë let dwell in Tol Eressëa, [?flying] along its coasts or paddling inland up its streams; and he set them there as a gift and joy to the Solosimpi. But when Ulmo heard of these new deeds he was ill-pleased for the havoc wrought amid the fishes where-with he had filled the waters with the aid of Palúrien.

Now do the Solosimpi take great joy of [?their] birds, new creatures to them, and of swans, and behold upon the lakes of Tol Eressëa already they fare on rafts of fallen timber, and some harness thereto swans and speed across the waters; but the more hardy dare out upon the sea and the gulls draw them, and when Ulmo saw that he was very glad. For lo! the Teleri and Noldoli complain much to Manwë of the separation of the Solosimpi, and the Gods desire them to be drawn to Valinor; but Ulmo cannot yet think of any device save by help of Ossë and the Oarni, and will not be humbled to this. But now does he fare home in haste to Aulë, and those twain got them speedily to Tol Eressëa, and Oromë was with them, and there is the first hewing of trees that was done in the world outside Valinor. Now does Aulë of the sawn wood of pine and oak make great vessels like to the bodies of swans, and these he covers with the bark of silver birches, or . . . . . with gathered feathers of the oily plumage of Ossë's birds, and they are nailed and [?sturdily] riveted and fastened with silver, and he carves prows for them like the upheld necks of swans, but they are hollow and have no feet; and by cords of great strength and slimness are gulls and petrels harnessed to them, for they were tame to the hands of the Solosimpi, because their hearts were so turned by Ossë.

Now are the beaches upon the western shores of Tol Eressëa, even at Falassë Númëa (Western Surf), thronged with that people of the Elves, and drawn up there is a very great host indeed of those swanships, and the cry of the gulls above them is unceasing. But the Solosimpi arise in great numbers and climb into the hollow bodies of these new things of Aulë's skill, and more of their kin fare ever to the shores, marching to the sound of innumerable pipes and flutes.

Now all are embarked and the gulls fare mightily into the twilit sky, but Aulë and Oromë are in the foremost galley and the mightiest, and seven hundred gulls are harnessed thereto and it gleams with silver and white feathers, and has a beak of gold and eyes of jet and amber. But Ulmo fares at the rear in his fishy car and trumpets loudly for the discomfiture of Ossë and the rescue of the Shoreland Elves.

But Ossë seeing how these birds have been to his undoing is very downcast, yet for the presence of those three Gods and indeed for his love of the Solosimpi that had grown by now very great he molested not their white fleet, and they came thus over the grey leagues of the ocean, through the dim sounds, and the mists of the Shadowy Seas, even to the first dark waters of the bay of Arvalin.

Know then that the Lonely Island is upon the confines of the Great Sea. Now that Great Sea or the Western Water is beyond the westernmost limits of the Great Lands, and in it are many lands and islands ere beyond their anchorage you reach the Magic Isles, and beyond these still lies Tol Eressëa. But beyond Tol Eressëa is the misty wall and those great sea glooms beneath which lie the Shadowy Seas, and thereon float the Twilit Isles whither only pierced at clearest times the faintest twinkle of the far gleam of Silpion. But in the westernmost of these stood the Tower of Pearl built in after days and much sung in song; but the Twilit Isles are held the first of the Outer Lands, which are these and Arvalin and Valinor, and Tol Eressëa is held neither of the Outer Lands or of the Great Lands where Men after roamed. But the farthest shore of those Shadowy Seas is Arvalin or Erumáni to the far south, but more northerly do they lap the very coasts of Eldamar, and here are they broader to one faring west. Beyond Arvalin tower those huge Mountains of Valinor which are in a great ring bending slowly west, but the Shadowy Seas make a vast bay to the north of Arvalin running right up to the black feet of the mountains, so that here they border upon the waters and not upon the lands, and there at the bay's innermost stands Taniquetil, glorious to behold, loftiest of all mountains clad in purest snow, looking across Arvalin half south and half north across that mighty Bay of Faëry, and so beyond the Shadowy Seas themselves, even so that all the sails upon the sunlit waters of the Great Sea in after days (when the Gods had made that lamp) and all the throngs about the western havens of the Lands of Men could be seen from its summit; and yet is that distance counted only in unimagined leagues.

But now comes that strange fleet nigh these regions and eager eyes look out. There stands Taniquetil and he is purple and dark of one side with gloom of Arvalin and of the Shadowy Seas, and lit in glory of the other by reason of the light of the Trees of Valinor. Now where the seas lapped those shores of old their waves long ere their breaking were suddenly lit by Laurelin were it day or by Silpion were it night, and the shadows of the world ceased almost abruptly and the waves laughed. But an opening in the mountains on those shores let through a glimpse of Valinor, and there stood the hill of Kôr, and the white sand runs up the creek to meet it, but its feet are in green water, and behind the sand of gold fares away farther than eye can guess, and indeed beyond Valinor who has heard or seen anything save Ulmo, yet of a certainty here spread the dark waters of the Outer Seas: tideless are they and very cool, and so thin that no boat can float upon their bosom, and few fish swim beneath their depths.

But now upon the hill of Kôr is a running and a joyous concourse, and all the people of the Teleri and Noldoli fare out of the gates and wait to welcome the coming of the fleet upon the shore. And now those ships leave the shadows and now are caught in the bright gleam about the inner bay, and now are they beached high and the Solosimpi dance and pipe, and mingle with the singing of the Teleri and the Noldoli's faint music.

Far behind lay Tol Eressëa in silence and its woods and shores were still, for nearly all that host of sea-birds had flown after the Eldar and wailed now about the shores of Eldamar: but Ossë dwelt in despondency and his silver halls in Valmar abode long empty, for he came no nearer to them for a great while than the shadow's edge, whither came the wailing of his sea-birds far away.

Now the Solosimpi abode not much in Kôr but had strange dwellings among the shoreland rocks, and Ulmo came and sat among them as aforetime in Tol Eressëa, and that was his time of greatest mirth and gentleness, and all his lore and love of music he poured out to them, and they drank it eagerly. Musics did they make and weave catching threads of sound whispered by waters in caverns or by wave-tops brushed by gentle winds; and these they twined with the wail of gulls and the echoes of their own sweet voices in the places of their home. But the Teleri and Inwir gathered [?harvest] of poesy and song, and were oftenest among the Gods, dancing in the skiey halls of Manwë for the joy of Varda of the Stars, or filling the streets and courts of Valmar with the strange loveliness of their pomps and revelry; for Oromë and for Nessa they danced upon green swards, and the glades of Valinor knew them as they flitted among the gold-lit trees, and Palúrien was very merry for the sight of them. Often were the Noldoli with them and made much music for the multitude of their harps and viols was very sweet, and Salmar loved them; but their greatest delight was in the courts of Aulë, or in their own dear homes in Kôr, fashioning many beautiful things and weaving many stories. With paintings and broidered hangings and carvings of great delicacy they filled all their city, and even did Valmar grow more fair beneath their skilful hands.

Now is to tell how the Solosimpi fared often about the near seas in their swanships, or drawn by the birds, or paddling themselves with great oars that they had made to the likeness of the webs of swan or duck; and they dredged the sea-beds and won wealth of the slim shells of those magic waters and uncounted store of pearls of a most pure and starry lustre: and these were both their glory and delight and the envy of the other Eldar who longed for them to shine in the adornment of the city of Kôr.

But those of the Noldoli whom Aulë had most deeply taught laboured in secret unceasingly, and of Aulë they had wealth of metals and of stones and marbles, and of the leave of the Valar much store too was granted to them of the radiance of Kulullin and of Telimpë held in hidden bowls. Starlight they had of Varda and strands of the bluest *ilwë* Manwë gave them; water of the most limpid pools in that creek of Kôr, and crystal drops from all the sparkling founts in the courts of Valmar. Dews did they gather in the woods of Oromë, and flower-petals of all hues and honeys in Yavanna's gardens, and they chased the beams of Laurelin and Silpion amongst the leaves. But when all this wealth of fair and radiant things was gathered, they got of the Solosimpi many shells white and pink, and purest foam, and lastly some few pearls. These pearls were their model, and the lore of Aulë and the magic of the Valar were their tools, and all the most lovely things of the substance of the Earth the matters of their craft – and therefrom did the Noldoli with great labour invent and fashion the first gems. Crystals did they make of the waters of the springs shot with the lights of Silpion; amber and chrysoprase and topaz glowed beneath their hands, and garnets and rubies they wrought, making their glassy substance as Aulë had taught them but dyeing them with the juices of roses and red flowers, and to each they gave a heart of fire. Emeralds some made of the water of the creek of Kôr and glints among the grassy glades of-Valinor, and sapphires did they fashion in great profusion, [?tingeing] them with the airs of Manwë; amethysts there were and moonstones, beryls and onyx, agates of blended marbles and many lesser stones, and their hearts were very glad, nor were they content with a few, but made them jewels in immeasurable number till all the fair substances were well nigh exhausted and the great piles of those gems might not be concealed but blazed in the light like beds of brilliant flowers. Then took they those pearls that had and some of wellnigh all their jewels and made a new gem of a milky pallor shot with gleams like echoes of all other stones, and this they thought very fair, and they were opals; but still some laboured on, and of starlight and the purest water-drops, of the dew of Silpion, and the thinnest air, they made diamonds, and challenged any to make fairer.

Then arose Fëanor of the Noldoli and fared to the Solosimpi and begged a great pearl, and he got moreover an urn full of the most luminous phosphor-light gathered of foam in dark places, and with these he came home, and he took all the other gems and did gather their glint by the light of white lamps and silver candles, and he took the sheen of pearls and the faint half-colours of opals, and he [?bathed] them in phosphorescence and the radiant dew of Silpion, and but a single tiny drop of the light of Laurelin did he let fall therein, and giving all those magic lights a body to dwell in of such perfect glass as he alone could make nor even Aulë compass, so great was the slender dexterity of the fingers of Fëanor, he made a jewel – and it shone of its own . . . . . . . . .[10] radiance in the uttermost dark; and he set it therein and sat a very long while and gazed at its beauty. Then he made two more, and had no more stuffs: and he fetched the others to behold his handiwork, and they were utterly amazed, and those jewels he called Silmarilli, or as we say the name in the speech of the Noldoli today Silubrilthin.[11] Wherefore though the Solosimpi held ever that none of the gems of the Noldoli, not even that majestic shimmer of diamonds, overpassed their tender pearls, yet have all held who ever saw them that the Silmarils of Fëanor were the most beautiful jewels that ever shone or [?glowed].

Now Kôr is lit with this wealth of gems and sparkles most marvellously, and all the kindred of the Eldalië are made rich in their loveliness by the generosity of the Noldoli, and the Gods' desire of their beauty is sated to the full. Sapphires in great [?wonder] were given to Manwë and his raiment was crusted with them, and Oromë had a belt of emeralds, but Yavanna loved all the gems, and Aulë's delight was in diamonds and amethysts. Melko alone was given none of them, for that he had not expiated his many crimes, and he lusted after them exceedingly, yet said nought, feigning to hold them of lesser worth than metals.

But now all the kindred of the Eldalië has found its greatest bliss, and the majesty and glory of the Gods and their home is augmented to the greatest splendour that the world has seen, and the Trees shone on Valinor, and Valinor gave back their light in a thousand scintillations of splintered colours; but the Great Lands were still and dark and very lonesome, and Ossë sat without the precincts and saw the moongleam of Silpion twinkle on the pebbles of diamonds and of crystals which the Gnomes cast in prodigality about the margin of the seas, and the glassy fragments splintered in their labouring glittered about the seaward face of Kôr; but the pools amid the dark rocks were filled with jewels, and the Solosimpi whose robes were sewn with pearls danced about them, and that was the fairest of all shores, and the music of the waters about those silver strands was beyond all sounds enchanting.

These were the rocks of Eldamar, and I saw them long ago, for Inwë was my grandsire's sire[12]; and [?even] he was the eldest of the Elves and had lived yet in majesty had he not perished in that march into the world, but Ingil his son went long ago back to Valinor and is with Manwë. And I am also akin to the shoreland dancers, and these things that I tell you I know they are true; and the magic and the wonder of the Bay of Faëry is such that none who have seen it as it was then can speak without a catch of the breath and a sinking of the voice.'

Then Meril the Queen ceased her long tale, but Eriol said nought, gazing at the long radiance of the westering sun gleaming through the apple boles, and dreaming of Faëry. At length said Meril: 'Fare now home, for the afternoon has waned, and the telling of the tale has set a weight of desire in my heart and in thine. But be in patience and bide yet ere ye seek fellowship with that sad kindred of the Island Elves.'

But Eriol said: 'Even now I know not and it passes my heart to guess how all that loveliness came to fading, or the Elves might be prevailed to depart from Eldamar.'

But Meril said: 'Nay, I have lengthened the tale too much for love of those days, and many great things lie between the making of the gems and the coming back to Tol Eressëa: but these things many know as well as I, and Lindo or Rúmil of Mar Vanwa Tyaliéva would tell them more skilfully than I.' Then did she and Eriol fare back to the house of flowers, and Eriol took his leave ere the western face of Ingil's tower was yet grown grey with dusk.

## NOTES

1  The manuscript has *Vairë*, but this can only be a slip.
2  The occurrence of the name *Telimpë* here, and again later in the tale, as also in that of *The Sun and Moon*, is curious; in the tale of *The*

*Coming of the Valar and the Building of Valinor* the name was changed at its first appearance from *Telimpë* (*Silindrin*) to *Silindrin*, and at subsequent occurrences *Silindrin* was written from the first (p. 79).

3  The manuscript has *Linwë* here, and again below; see under *Tinwë Linto* in 'Changes made to names' at the end of these notes.

4  This sentence, from 'and beguiled . . .', was added after, though not to all appearance much after, the writing of the text.

5  This sentence, from 'and one Ellu . . .', was added at the same time as that referred to in note 4.

6  The first occurrence of the form *Uinen*, and so written at the time of composition (i.e. not corrected from *Ónen*).

7  *Arvalin*: thus written at the time of composition, not emended from *Habbanan* or *Harmalin* as previously.

8  When my father wrote these texts, he wrote first in pencil, and then subsequently wrote over the top of it in ink, erasing the pencilled text – of which bits can be read here and there, and from which one can see that he altered the pencilled original somewhat as he went along. At the words 'glistened wondrously', however, he abandoned the writing of the new text in ink, and from this point we have only the original pencilled manuscript, which is in places exceedingly difficult to read, being more hasty, and also soft and smudged in the course of time. In deciphering this text I have been in places defeated, and I use brackets and question-marks to indicate uncertain readings, and rows of dots to show roughly the length of illegible words.

It is to be emphasized therefore that from here on there is only a *first draft*, and one written very rapidly, dashed onto the page.

9  *Arvalin*: here and subsequently emended from *Habbanan*; see note 7. The explanation is clearly that the name *Arvalin* came in at or before the time of the rewriting in ink over the pencilled text; though further on in the narrative we are here at an earlier stage of composition.

10  The word might be read as 'wizardous'.

11  Other forms (beginning *Sigm-*) preceded *Silubrilthin* which cannot be read with certainty. Meril speaks as if the Gnomish name was the form used in Tol Eressëa, but it is not clear why.

12  'my grandsire's sire': the original reading was 'my grandsire'.

Changes made to names in<br>*The Coming of the Elves and the Making of Kôr*

**Tinwë Linto** ⟨ *Linwë Tinto* (this latter is the form of the name in an interpolated passage in the preceding tale, see p. 106 note 1). At two subsequent occurrences of *Linwë* (see note 3 above) the name was

not changed, clearly through oversight; in the two added passages
where the name occurs (see notes 4 and 5 above) the form is *Tinwë*
(*Linto*).
*Inwithiel* 〈 *Gim-githil* (the same change in *The Cottage of Lost Play*, see
p. 22).
*Tinwelint* 〈 *Tintoglin*.
*Wendelin* 〈 *Tindriel* (cf. the interpolated passage in the previous tale,
p. 106 note 1).
*Arvalin* 〈 *Habbanan* throughout the tale except once, where the name
was written *Arvalin* from the first; see notes 7 and 9 above.
*Lindeloksë* 〈 *Lindelótë* (the same change in *The Coming of the Valar and
the Building of Valinor*, see p. 79).
*Erumáni* 〈 *Harwalin*.

## Commentary on
### The Coming of the Elves and the Making of Kôr

I have already (p. 111) touched on the great difference in the structure of
the narrative at the beginning of this tale, namely that here the Elves
awoke *during* Melko's captivity in Valinor, whereas in the later story it
was the very fact of the Awakening that brought the Valar to make war
on Melkor, which led to his imprisonment in Mandos. Thus the ultimately
very important matter of the capture of the Elves about Cuiviénen by
Melkor (*The Silmarillion* pp. 49–50) is necessarily entirely absent. The
release of Melko from Mandos here takes place far earlier, before the
coming of the Elvish 'ambassadors' to Valinor, and Melko plays a part in
the debate concerning the summons.

The story of Oromë's coming upon the newly-awakened Elves is seen
to go back to the beginnings (though here Yavanna Palúrien was also
present, as it appears), but its singular beauty and force is the less for the
fact of their coming being known independently to Manwë, so that the
great Valar did not need to be told of it by Oromë. The name *Eldar* was
already in existence in Valinor before the Awakening, and the story of
its being given by Oromë ('the People of the Stars') had not arisen – as
will be seen from the Appendix on Names, *Eldar* had a quite different
etymology at this time. The later distinction between the *Eldar* who
followed Oromë on the westward journey to the ocean and the *Avari*,
the Unwilling, who would not heed the summons of the Valar, is not
present, and indeed in this tale there is no suggestion that any Elves who
heard the summons refused it; there were however, according to another
(later) tale, Elves who never left Palisor (pp. 231, 234).

Here it is Nornorë, Herald of the Gods, not Oromë, who brought the
three Elves to Valinor and afterwards returned them to the Waters of
Awakening (and it is notable that even in this earliest version, given more

than the later to 'explanations', there is no hint of how they passed from the distant parts of the Earth to Valinor, when afterwards the Great March was only achieved with such difficulty). The story of the questioning of the three Elves by Manwë concerning the nature of their coming into the world, and their loss of all memory of what preceded their awakening, did not survive the *Lost Tales*. A further important shift in the structure is seen in Ulmo's eager support of the party favouring the summoning of the Elves to Valinor; in *The Silmarillion* (p. 52) Ulmo was the chief of those who 'held that the Quendi should be left free to walk as they would in Middle-earth'.

I set out here the early history of the names of the chief Eldar.

*Elu Thingol* (Quenya *Elwë Singollo*) began as *Linwë Tinto* (also simply *Linwë*); this was changed to *Tinwë Linto* (*Tinwë*). His Gnomish name was at first *Tintoglin*, then *Tinwelint*. He was the leader of the Solosimpi (the later Teleri) on the Great Journey, but he was beguiled in Hisilómë by the 'fay' (*Tindriel* ⟩) *Wendelin* (later *Melian*), who came from the gardens of Lórien in Valinor; he became lord of the Elves of Hisilómë, and their daughter was *Tinúviel*. The leader of the Solosimpi in his place was, confusingly, *Ellu* (afterwards *Olwë*, brother of Elwë).

The lord of the Noldoli was *Finwë Nólemë* (also *Nólemë Finwë*, and most commonly simply *Nólemë*); the name *Finwë* remained throughout the history. In the Gnomish speech he was *Golfinweg*. His son was *Turondo*, in Gnomish *Turgon* (later Turgon became Finwë's grandson, being the son of Finwë's son Fingolfin).

The lord of the Teleri (afterwards the Vanyar) was (*Ing* ⟩) *Inwë*, here called *Isil Inwë*, named in Gnomish (*Gim-githil* ⟩) *Inwithiel*. His son, who built the great tower of Kortirion, was (*Ingilmo* ⟩) *Ingil*. The 'royal clan' of the Teleri were the Inwir. Thus:

| *Lost Tales* (later forms of names) | *The Silmarillion* |
|---|---|
| Isil Inwë (Gnomish Inwithiel) lord of the Teleri    ..  ..  ..  .. | Ingwë lord of the Vanyar |
| (his son Ingil) | |
| Finwë Nólemë (Gnomish Golfinweg) lord of the Noldoli    ..  .. | Finwë lord of the Noldor |
| (his son Turondo, Gnomish Turgon) | (his grandson Turgon) |
| Tinwë Linto (Gnomish Tinwelint) lord of the Solosimpi, later lord of the Elves of Hisilómë | Elwë Singollo (Sindarin Elu Thingol) lord of the Teleri, later lord of the Grey-elves of Beleriand |
| Wendelin    ..  ..  ..  ..  .. | Melian |
| (their daughter Tinúviel)  ..  ..  .. | (their daughter Lúthien Tinúviel) |

Ellu, lord of the Solosimpi after          Olwë, lord of the Teleri
   the loss of Tinwë Linto                     after the loss of his
                                               brother Elwë Singollo

★

In *The Silmarillion* (p. 48) is described the second star-making of Varda
before and in preparation for the coming of the Elves:

> Then Varda went forth from the council, and she looked out from the
> height of Taniquetil, and beheld the darkness of Middle-earth beneath
> the innumerable stars, faint and far. Then she began a great labour,
> greatest of all the works of the Valar since their coming into Arda.
> She took the silver dews from the vats of Telperion, and therewith she
> made new stars and brighter against the coming of the First-born . . .

In the earliest version we see the conception already present that the stars
were created in two separate acts – that a new star-making by Varda
celebrated the coming of the Elves, even though here the Elves were
already awakened; and that the new stars were derived from the liquid
light fallen from the Moon-tree, Silpion. The passage just cited from
*The Silmarillion* goes on to tell that it was at the time of the second star-
making that Varda 'high in the north as a challenge to Melkor set the
crown of seven mighty stars to swing, Valacirca, the Sickle of the Valar
and sign of doom'; but here this is denied, and a special origin is claimed
for the Great Bear, whose stars were not of Varda's contriving but were
sparks that escaped from Aulë's forge. In the little notebook mentioned
on p. 23, which is full of disjointed jottings and hastily noted projects, a
different form of this myth appears:

The Silver Sickle
The seven butterflies
Aulë was making a silver sickle. Melko interrupted his work telling him
a lie concerning the lady Palúrien. Aulë so wroth that he broke the
sickle with a blow. Seven sparks leapt up and winged into the heavens.
Varda caught them and gave them a place in the heavens as a sign of
Palúrien's honour. They fly now ever in the shape of a sickle round and
round the pole.

There can be no doubt, I think, that this note is earlier than the present
text.

The star Morwinyon, 'who blazes above the world's edge in the west',
is Arcturus; see the Appendix on Names. It is nowhere explained why
Morwinyon-Arcturus is mythically conceived to be always in the west.

Turning now to the Great March and the crossing of the ocean, the origin of Tol Eressëa in the island on which Ossë drew the Gods to the western lands at the time of the fall of the Lamps (see p. 70) was necessarily lost afterwards with the loss of that story, and Ossë ceased to have any proprietary right upon it. The idea that the Eldar came to the shores of the Great Lands in three large and separated companies (in the order Teleri – Noldori – Solosimpi, as later Vanyar – Noldor – Teleri) goes back to the beginning; but here the first people and the second people each crossed the ocean alone, whereas afterwards they crossed together. In *The Silmarillion* (p. 58) 'many years' elapsed before Ulmo returned for the last of the three kindreds, the Teleri, so long a time that they came to love the coasts of Middle-earth, and Ossë was able to persuade some of them to remain (Círdan the Shipwright and the Elves of the Falas, with their havens at Brithombar and Eglarest). Of this there is no trace in the earliest account, though the germ of the idea of the long wait of the lastcomers for Ulmo's return is present. In the published version the cause of Ossë's rage against the transportation of the Eldar on the floating island has disappeared, and his motive for anchoring the island in the ocean is wholly different: indeed he did this at the bidding of Ulmo (*ibid.* p. 59), who was opposed to the summoning of the Eldar to Valinor in any case. But the anchoring of Tol Eressëa as a rebellious act of Ossë's long remained an element in the story. It is not made clear what other 'scattered islands of his domain' (p. 121) Ossë anchored to the sea-bottom; but since on the drawing of the World-Ship the Lonely Isle, the Magic Isles, and the Twilit Isles are all shown in the same way as 'standing like pinnacles from the weedy depths' (see pp. 84-6) it was probably these that Ossë now established (though Rúmil and Meril still speak of the Twilit Isles as 'floating' on the Shadowy Seas, pp. 68, 125).

In the old story it is made very clear that Tol Eressëa was made fast far out in the mid-ocean, and 'no land may be seen for many leagues' sail from its cliffs'. That was indeed the reason for its name, which was diminished when the Lonely Isle came to be set in the Bay of Eldamar. But the words used of Tol Eressëa, 'the Lonely Isle, that looks both west and east', in the last chapter of *The Silmarillion* (relatively very little worked on and revised), undoubtedly derive from the old story; in the tale of *Ælfwine of England* is seen the origin of this phrase: 'the Lonely Island looking East to the Magic Archipelago and to the lands of Men beyond it, and West into the Shadows beyond which afar off is glimpsed the Outer Land, the kingdom of the Gods'. The deep sundering of the speech of the Solosimpi from that of the other kindreds, referred to in this tale (p. 121), is preserved in *The Silmarillion*, but the idea arose in the days when Tol Eressëa was far further removed from Valinor.

As is very often to be observed in the evolution of these myths, an early idea survived in a wholly altered context: here, the growth of trees and plants on the westward slopes of the floating island began with its twice lying in the Bay of Faëry and catching the light of the Trees when the Teleri and Noldoli disembarked, and its greater beauty and fertility remained from those times after it was anchored far away from Valinor in the midst of the ocean; afterwards, this idea survived in the context of the light of the Trees passing through the Calacirya and falling on Tol Eressëa near at hand in the Bay of Eldamar. Similarly, it seems that Ulmo's instruction of the Solosimpi in music and sea-lore while sitting 'upon a headland' of Tol Eressëa after its binding to the sea-bottom was shifted to Ossë's instruction of the Teleri 'in all manner of sea-lore and sea-music' sitting on a rock off the coast of Middle-earth (*The Silmarillion* p. 58). Very noteworthy is the account given here of the gap in the Mountains of Valinor. In *The Silmarillion* the Valar made this gap, the Calacirya or Pass of Light, only after the coming of the Eldar to Aman, for 'even among the radiant flowers of the Tree-lit gardens of Valinor they [the Vanyar and Noldor] longed still at times to see the stars' (p. 59); whereas in this tale it was a 'natural' feature, associated with a long creek thrust in from the sea.

From the account of the coming of the Elves to the shores of the Great Lands it is seen (p. 118) that Hisilómë was a region bordering the Great Sea, agreeing with its identification as the region marked *g* on the earliest map, see pp. 81, 112; and most remarkably we meet here the idea that Men were shut in Hisilómë by Melko, an idea that survived right through to the final form in which the Easterling Men were rewarded after the Nirnaeth Arnoediad for their treacherous service to Morgoth by being confined in Hithlum (*The Silmarillion* p. 195).

In the description of the hill and city of Kôr appear several features that were never lost in the later accounts of Tirion upon Túna. Cf. *The Silmarillion* p. 59:

> Upon the crown of Túna the city of the Elves was built, the white walls and terraces of Tirion; and the highest of the towers of that city was the Tower of Ingwë, Mindon Eldaliéva, whose silver lamp shone far out into the mists of the sea.

The dust of gold and 'magic metals' that Aulë piled about the feet of Kôr powdered the shoes and clothing of Eärendil when he climbed the 'long white stairs' of Tirion (*ibid.* p. 248).

It is not said here whether the shoots of Laurelin and Silpion that the Gods gave to Inwë and Nólemë, which 'blossomed both eternally without abating', were also givers of light, but later in the *Lost Tales* (p. 213), after the Flight of the Noldoli, the Trees of Kôr are again referred to, and there the trees given to Inwë 'shone still', while the trees given to Nólemë had been uprooted and 'were gone no one knew whither.' In *The Silmarillion* it is said that Yavanna made for the Vanyar and the Noldor 'a tree like to a lesser image of Telperion, save that it did not give light of its own being'; it was 'planted in the courts beneath the Mindon and there flourished, and its seedlings were many in Eldamar'. Thence came the Tree of Tol Eressëa.

In connection with this description of the city of the Elves in Valinor I give here a poem entitled *Kôr*. It was written on April 30th, 1915 (two days after *Goblin Feet* and *You and Me*, see pp. 27, 32), and two texts of it are extant: the first, in manuscript, has a subtitle 'In a City Lost and Dead'. The second, a typescript, was apparently first entitled *Kôr*, but this was changed to *The City of the Gods*, and the subtitle erased; and with this title the poem was published at Leeds in 1923.* No changes were made to the text except that in the penultimate line 'no bird sings' was altered already in the manuscript to 'no voice stirs'. It seems possible, especially in view of the original subtitle, that the poem described Kôr after the Elves had left it.

### Kôr

#### In a City Lost and Dead

A sable hill, gigantic, rampart-crowned
Stands gazing out across an azure sea
Under an azure sky, on whose dark ground
Impearled as 'gainst a floor of porphyry
Gleam marble temples white, and dazzling halls;
And tawny shadows fingered long are made
In fretted bars upon their ivory walls
By massy trees rock-rooted in the shade
Like stony chiselled pillars of the vault
With shaft and capital of black basalt.
There slow forgotten days for ever reap
The silent shadows counting out rich hours;
And no voice stirs; and all the marble towers
White, hot and soundless, ever burn and sleep.

The story of the evolution of sea-birds by Ossë, and of how the Solosimpi went at last to Valinor in ships of swan-shape drawn by gulls, to the chagrin of Ossë, is greatly at variance with the account in *The Silmarillion* (p. 61):

Through a long age they [the Teleri] dwelt in Tol Eressëa; but slowly their hearts were changed, and were drawn towards the light that flowed out over the sea to the Lonely Isle. They were torn between the love of the music of the waves upon their shores, and the desire to see

* Publication was in a magazine called *The Microcosm*, edited by Dorothy Ratcliffe, Volume VIII no. 1, Spring 1923.

again their kindred and to look upon the splendour of Valinor; but in the end desire of the light was the stronger. Therefore Ulmo, submitting to the will of the Valar, sent to them Ossë, their friend, and he though grieving taught them the craft of ship-building; and when their ships were built he brought them as his parting gift many strong-winged swans. Then the swans drew the white ships of the Teleri over the windless sea; and thus at last and latest they came to Aman and the shores of Eldamar.

But the swans remained as a gift of Ossë to the Elves of Tol Eressëa, and the ships of the Teleri retained the form of the ships built by Aulë for the Solosimpi: they 'were made in the likeness of swans, with beaks of gold and eyes of gold and jet' (ibid.).

The passage of geographical description that follows (p. 125) is curious; for it is extremely similar to (and even in some phrases identical with) that in the tale of The Coming of the Valar and the Building of Valinor, p. 68. An explanation of this repetition is suggested below. This second version gives in fact little new information, its chief difference of substance being the mention of Tol Eressëa. It is now made clear that the Shadowy Seas were a region of the Great Sea west of Tol Eressëa. In The Silmarillion (p. 102) the conception had changed, with the change in the anchorage of Tol Eressëa: at the time of the Hiding of Valinor

the Enchanted Isles were set, and all the seas about them were filled with shadows and bewilderment. And these isles were strung as a net in the Shadowy Seas from the north to the south, before Tol Eressëa, the Lonely Isle, is reached by one sailing west.

There is a further element of repetition in the account of the gap in the Mountains of Valinor and the hill of Kôr at the head of the creek (p. 126), which have already been described earlier in this same tale (p. 122). The explanation of this repetition is almost certainly to be found in the two layers of composition in this tale (see note 8 above); for the first of these passages is in the revised portion and the second in the original, pencilled text. My father in his revision had, I think, simply taken in earlier the passage concerning the gap in the Mountains, the hill and the creek, and if he had continued the revision of the tale to its end the second passage would have been excised. This explanation may be suggested also for the repetition of the passage concerning the islands in the Great Sea and the coast of Valinor from the tale of The Coming of the Valar and the Building of Valinor; but in that case the implication must be that the revision in ink over the original pencilled manuscript was carried out when the latter was already far ahead in the narrative.

In *The Silmarillion* the entire account of the making of gem-stones by the Noldoli has become compressed into these words (p. 60):

And it came to pass that the masons of the house of Finwë, quarrying in the hills after stone (for they delighted in the building of high towers), first discovered the earth-gems, and brought them forth in countless myriads; and they devised tools for the cutting and shaping of gems, and carved them in many forms. They hoarded them not, but gave them freely, and by their labour enriched all Valinor.

Thus the rhapsodic account at the end of this tale of the making of gems out of 'magic' materials – starlight, and *ilwë*, dews and petals, glassy substances dyed with the juice of flowers – was abandoned, and the Noldor became miners, skilful indeed, but mining only what was there to be found in the rocks of Valinor. On the other hand, in an earlier passage in *The Silmarillion* (p. 39), the old idea is retained: 'The Noldor also it was who first achieved the making of gems.' It need not be said that everything was to be gained by the discretion of the later writing; in this early narrative the Silmarils are not strongly marked out from the accumulated wonder of all the rest of the gems of the Noldoli's making.

Features that remained are the generosity of the Noldor in the giving of their gems and the scattering of them on the shores (cf. *The Silmarillion* p. 61: 'Many jewels the Noldor gave them [the Teleri], opals and diamonds and pale crystals, which they strewed upon the shores and scattered in the pools'); the pearls that the Teleri got from the sea (*ibid.*); the sapphires that the Noldor gave to Manwë ('His sceptre was of sapphire, which the Noldor wrought for him', *ibid.* p. 40); and, of course, Fëanor as the maker of the Silmarils – although, as will be seen in the next tale, Fëanor was not yet the son of Finwë (Nólemë).

★

I conclude this commentary with another early poem that bears upon the matter of this tale. It is said in the tale (p. 119) that Men in Hisilómë feared the Lost Elves, calling them the Shadow Folk, and that their name for the land was *Aryador*. The meaning of this is given in the early Gnomish word-list as 'land or place of shadow' (cf. the meanings of *Hisilómë* and *Dor Lómin*, p. 112).

The poem is called *A Song of Aryador*, and is extant in two copies; according to notes on these it was written in an army camp near Lichfield on September 12th, 1915. It was never, to my knowledge, printed. The first copy, in manuscript, has the title also in Old English: *An léoþ Éargedores*; the second, in typescript, has virtually no differences in the text, but it may be noted that the first word of the third verse, 'She', is an emendation from 'He' in both copies.

*A Song of Aryador*

In the vales of Aryador
By the wooded inland shore
Green the lakeward bents and meads
Sloping down to murmurous reeds
That whisper in the dusk o'er Aryador:

'Do you hear the many bells
Of the goats upon the fells
Where the valley tumbles downward from the pines?
Do you hear the blue woods moan
When the Sun has gone alone
To hunt the mountain-shadows in the pines?

She is lost among the hills
And the upland slowly fills
With the shadow-folk that murmur in the fern;
And still there are the bells
And the voices on the fells
While Eastward a few stars begin to burn.

Men are kindling tiny gleams
Far below by mountain-streams
Where they dwell among the beechwoods near the shore,
But the great woods on the height
Watch the waning western light
And whisper to the wind of things of yore,

When the valley was unknown,
And the waters roared alone,
And the shadow-folk danced downward all the night,
When the Sun had fared abroad
Through great forests unexplored
And the woods were full of wandering beams of light.

Then were voices on the fells
And a sound of ghostly bells
And a march of shadow-people o'er the height.
In the mountains by the shore
In forgotten Aryador
There was dancing and was ringing;
There were shadow-people singing
Ancient songs of olden gods in Aryador.'

# VI

# THE THEFT OF MELKO
# AND THE DARKENING OF VALINOR

This title is again taken from the cover of the book containing the text; the narrative, still written rapidly in pencil (see note 8 to the last chapter), with some emendations from the same time or later, continues without a break.

Now came Eriol home to the Cottage of Lost Play, and his love for all the things that he saw about him and his desire to understand them all became more deep. Continually did he thirst to know yet more of the history of the Eldar; nor did he ever fail to be among those who fared each evening to the Room of the Tale-fire; and so on a time when he had already sojourned some while as a guest of Vairë and Lindo it so passed that Lindo at his entreaty spake thus from his deep chair:

'Listen then, O Eriol, if thou wouldst [know] how it so came that the loveliness of Valinor was abated, or the Elves might ever be constrained to leave the shores of Eldamar. It may well be that you know already that Melko dwelt in Valmar as a servant in the house of Tulkas in those days of the joy of the Eldalië; there did he nurse his hatred of the Gods, and his consuming jealousy of the Eldar, but it was his lust for the beauty of the gems for all his feigned indifference that in the end overbore his patience and caused him to design deep and evilly.

Now the Noldoli alone at those times had the art of fashioning these beautiful things, and despite their rich gifts to all whom they loved the treasure they possessed of them was beyond count the greatest, wherefore Melko whenever he may consorteth with them, speaking cunning words. In this way for long he sought to beg gifts of jewels for himself, and maybe also catching the unwary to learn something of their hidden art, but when none of these devices succeeded he sought to sow evil desires and discords among the Gnomes, telling them that lie concerning the Council when the Eldar were first bidden to Valinor.[1] "Slaves are ye," he would say, "or children, an you will, bidden play with toys and seek not to stray or know too much. Good days mayhap the Valar give you, as ye say; seek but to cross their walls and ye shall know the hardness of their hearts. Lo, they use your skill, and to your beauty they hold fast as an adornment of their realms. This is not love, but selfish desire – make test of it. Ask for your inheritance that Ilúvatar designed for you – the whole wide world to roam, with all its mysteries to explore, and all its substances to be material of such mighty crafts as never can be realised in these narrow gardens penned by the mountains, hemmed in by the impassable sea."

Hearing these things, despite the true knowledge which Nólemë had and spread abroad, there were many who hearkened with half their hearts to Melko, and restlessness grew amongst them, and Melko poured oil on their smouldering desires. From him they learnt many things it were not good for any but the great Valar to know, for being half-comprehended such deep and hidden things slay happiness; and besides many of the sayings of Melko were cunning lies or were but partly true, and the Noldoli ceased to sing, and their viols fell silent upon the hill of Kôr, for their hearts grew somewhat older as their lore grew deeper and their desires more swollen, and the books of their wisdom were multiplied as the leaves of the forest. For know that in those days Aulë aided by the Gnomes contrived alphabets and scripts, and on the walls of Kôr were many dark tales written in pictured symbols, and runes of great beauty were drawn there too or carved upon stones, and Eärendel read many a wondrous tale there long ago, and mayhap still is many a one still there to read, if it be not corrupted into dust. The other Elves heeded these things not over much, and were at times sad and fearful at the lessened gladness of their kinsmen. Great mirth had Melko at this and wrought in patience biding his time, yet no nearer did he get to his end, for despite all his labours the glory of the Trees and the beauty of the gems and the memory of the dark ways from Palisor held back the Noldoli – and ever Nólemë spake against Melko, calming their restlessness and discontents.

At length so great became his care that he took counsel with Fëanor, and even with Inwë and Ellu Melemno (who then led the Solosimpi), and took their rede that Manwë himself be told of the dark ways of Melko.

And Melko knowing this was in great anger against the Gnomes, and going first before Manwë bowed very low, and said how the Noldoli dared murmur to his ears against Manwë's lordship, claiming that in skill and beauty they (whom Ilúvatar had destined to possess all the earth) far surpassed the Valar, for whom they must labour unrecompensed. Heavy was Manwë's heart at these words, for he had feared long that that great amity of the Valar and Eldar be ever perchance broken, knowing that the Elves were children of the world and must one day return to her bosom. Nay, who shall say but that all these deeds, even the seeming needless evil of Melko, were but a portion of the destiny of old? Yet cold was the Lord of the Gods to the informer, and lo! even as he questioned him further the embassy of Nólemë came thither, and being granted leave spake the truth before him. By reason of the presence of Melko perchance they spoke somewhat less skilfully in their own cause than they might, and perchance even the heart of Manwë Súlimo was tainted with the poison of Melko's words, for that venom of Melko's malice is very strong and subtle indeed.

Howbeit, both Melko and the Noldoli were chidden and dismissed. Melko indeed was bidden get him back to Mandos and there dwell awhile in penitence, nor dare to walk in Valmar for many moons, not until the great festival that now approached had come and gone; but Manwë fearing lest the pollution of their discontent spread among the other kindreds commanded Aulë to find other places and thither lead the Noldoli, and build them a new town where they might dwell.

Great was the sorrow upon the hill of Kôr when those tidings were brought thither, and though all were wroth with the treachery of Melko, yet was there now a new bitterness against the Gods, and the murmuring louder than before.

A little stream, and its name was *Híri*, ran down from the hills, northward of the opening to the coast where Kôr was built, and it wandered thence across the plain no one knew whither. Maybe it found the Outer Seas, for north of the roots of Silpion it dived into the earth and there was a rugged place and a rock-ringed dale; and here the Noldoli purposed to abide, or rather to await the passing of wrath from Manwë's heart, for in no way as yet would they accept the thought of leaving Kôr for ever.

Caves they made in the walls of that dale, and thither they bore their wealth of gems, of gold and silver and fair things; but their ancient homes in Kôr were empty of their voices, filled only with their paintings and their books of lore, and the streets of Kôr and all the ways of Valmar shone still with [?gems] and carven marbles telling of the days of the happiness of the Gnomes that cometh now upon its waning.

Now Melko gets him gone to Mandos, and far from Valinor he plans rebellion and vengeance upon both Gnomes and Gods. Indeed, dwelling for nigh three ages in the vaults of Mandos Melko had made

friends to himself of certain gloomy spirits there and perverted them
to ill, promising them great lands and regions on the Earth for their
[?having] if they aided him when he called on them in need; and
now he gathers them to him in the dark ravines of the mountains
about Mandos. Thence sends he spies, invisible as fleeting shades
when Silpion is in bloom, and learns of those doings of the Noldoli
and of all that passes in the plain. Now soon after it chanced indeed
that the Valar and Eldar held a great feast, even that one that Manwë
had spoken of, bidding Melko rid Valmar of his presence at that time;
for know that they made merry on one day every seventh year to
celebrate the coming of the Eldar into Valinor, and every third year
a lesser feast to commemorate the coming of the white fleet of the
Solosimpi to the shores of Eldamar; but at every twenty-first year
when both these feasts fell together they held one of the greatest
magnificence, and it endured for seven days, and for this cause such
years were called "Years of Double Mirth";* and these feasts all
the Koreldar wherever they now may be in the wide world still do
celebrate. Now that feast that approacheth is one of Double Mirth,
and all the hosts of the Gods and Elves made ready to celebrate it
most gloriously. Pomps there were and long processions of the
Elves, dancing and singing, that wound from Kôr to Valmar's gates.
A road had been laid against this festival from the westward gate of
Kôr even to the turrets of the mighty arch which opened in the walls
of Valmar northward towards the Trees. Of white marble it was and
many a gentle stream flowing from the far mountains crossed its
path. Here it would leap into slender bridges marvellously fenced
with delicate balustrades that shone like pearls; scarcely did these
clear the water, so that lilies of great beauty growing upon the bosom
of the streams that fared but gently in the plain thrust their wide
blossoms about its borders and iris marched along its flanks; for
by cunning delving runnels of clearest water were made to flow from
stream to stream bordering that whole long way with the cool noise
of rippling water. At places mighty trees grew on either side, or at
places the road would open to a glade and fountains spring by magic
high into the air for the refreshment of all who sped that way.

Now came the Teleri led by the white-robed people of the Inwir,
and the throbbing of their congregated harps beat the air most
sweetly; and after them went the Noldoli mingling once more with
their own dear folk by Manwë's clemency, that his festival might be
duly kept, but the music that their viols and instruments awoke was
now more sweetly sad than ever before. And last came the people

* Added in the margin here: *Samírien*.

of the shores, and their piping blent with voices brought the sense of tides and murmurous waves and the wailing cry of the coast-loving birds thus inland deep upon the plain.

Then was all that host marshalled before the gate of Valmar, and at the word and sign from Inwë as one voice they burst in unison into the Song of Light. This had Lirillo² written and taught them, and it told of the longing of the Elves for light, of their dread journey through the dark world led by the desire of the Two Trees, and sang of their utmost joy beholding the faces of the Gods and their renewed desire once more to enter Valmar and tread the Valar's blessed courts. Then did the gates of Valmar open and Nornorë bid them enter, and all that bright company passed through. There Varda met them, standing amid the companies of the Mánir and the Súruli, and all the Gods made them welcome, and feasts there were in all the great halls thereafter.

Now their custom was on the third day to robe themselves all in white and blue and ascend to the heights of Taniquetil, and there would Manwë speak to them as he thought fit of the Music of the Ainur and the glory of Ilúvatar, and of things to be and that had been. And on that day would Kôr and Valmar be silent and still, but the roof of the world and the slope of Taniquetil shine with the gleaming raiment of the Gods and Elves, and all the mountains echo with their speech − but afterward on the last day of merriment the Gods would come to Kôr and sit upon the slopes of its bright hill, gazing in love upon that slender town, and thereafter blessing it in the name of Ilúvatar would depart ere Silpion came to bloom; and so would end the days of Double Mirth.

But in this fateful year Melko dared of his blasphemous heart to choose that very day of Manwë's speech upon Taniquetil for the carrying out of his designs; for then would Kôr and Valmar and the rock-ringed dale of Sirnúmen be unguarded: for against whom indeed had Elf or Vala need to guard in those old days?

Creeping then down with his dark people on the third day of Samírien, as that feast was named, he passed the dark halls of Makar's abode (for even that wild Vala had gone to Valmar to honour the time, and indeed all of the Gods went there saving Fui and Vefántur only, and Ossë even was there, dissembling for those seven days his feud and jealousy with Ulmo). Here does a thought come to Melko's heart, and he arms himself and his band stealthily with swords very sharp and cruel, and this was well for them: for now do they all steal into the vale of Sirnúmen where the Noldoli had their present dwelling, and behold the Gnomes by reason of the workings in their hearts of Melko's own teaching had become wary and suspicious beyond the wont of the Eldar of those days. Guards of some strength were set over the treasures there that went not to the feast, albeit this was contrary to the customs and ordinances of the Gods. Now is there suddenly bitter war awake in the heart of Valinor and those guards are slain, even while the peace and gladness upon Taniquetil afar is very great – indeed for that reason none heard their cries. Now Melko knew that it was indeed war for ever between himself and all those other folk of Valinor, for he had slain the Noldoli – guests of the Valar – before the doors of their own homes. With his own hand indeed he slew Bruithwir father of Fëanor,[3] and bursting into that rocky house that he defended laid hands upon those most glorious gems, even the Silmarils, shut in a casket of ivory. Now all that great treasury of gems he despoiled, and lading himself and all his companions to the utmost he seeks how he may escape.

Know then that Oromë had great stables and a breeding ground of good horses not so far from this spot, where a wild forest land had grown up. Thither Melko steals, and a herd of black horses he captures, cowing them with the terror that he could wield. Astride those his whole company of thieves rides far away, after destroying what things of lesser value they deemed it impossible to carry thence. Making a wide circuit and faring with the speed of hurricanes such as only the divine horses of Oromë ridden by the children of the Gods could compass they pass far to the west of Valmar in the un-tracked regions where the light of the Trees was thin. Long ere the folk had come down from Taniquetil and long ere the end of the feast or ever the Noldoli fared back to find their homes despoiled, Melko and his [?thieves] were ridden to the deep south, and finding there a low place in the hills they passed into the plains of Eruman. Well might Aulë and Tulkas bemoan their carelessness in leaving that low place long ago when they reared those hills to fend all evil from the plain – for that was the place where they were accustomed to enter Valinor after their quarryings in the fields of Arvalin.[4] It is said indeed that this riding in a half-circle, laborious and perilous as it was, was at first no part of Melko's design, for rather had he purposed to get to northward over the passes nigh to Mandos; but this he was warned might not be done, for Mandos and Fui never left those realms, and all the ravines and chasms of the northward mountains were infested with their folk, nor for all his gloom was Mandos any rebel against Manwë or an abetter of evil deeds. Far to the north if one may endure the colds as Melko could it is said in ancient lore that the Great Seas narrow to a little thing, and without aid of ships Melko and his company might thus have got into the world safely; but this was not done, and the sad tale took its appointed course, or the Two Trees might yet have shone and the Elves sung still in Valinor.

At length that daytide of festival is over and the Gods are turned back towards Valmar, treading the white road from Kôr. The lights twinkle in the city of the Elves and peace dwells there, but the Noldoli fare over the plain to Sirnúmen sadly. Silpion is gleaming in that hour, and ere it wanes the first lament for the dead that was heard in Valinor rises from that rocky vale, for Fëanor laments the death of Bruithwir; and many of the Gnomes beside find that the spirits of their dead have winged their way to Vê. Then messengers ride hastily to Valmar bearing tidings of the deeds, and there they find Manwë, for he has not yet left that town for his abode upon Taniquetil.

"Alas, O Manwë Súlimo," they cry, "evil has pierced the Mountains of Valinor and fallen upon Sirnúmen of the Plain. There lies Bruithwir sire of Fëanor[5] dead and many of the Noldoli beside, and all our treasury of gems and fair things and the loving travail of our hands and hearts through many years is stolen away. Whither O Manwë whose eyes see all things? Who has done this evil, for the Noldoli cry for vengeance, O most [?just] one!"

Then said Manwë to them: "Behold O Children of the Noldoli, my heart is sad towards you, for the poison of Melko has already changed you, and covetice has entered your hearts. Lo! had ye not thought your gems and fabrics[6] of better worth than the festival of the folk or the ordinances of Manwë your lord, this had not been, and Bruithwir go-Maidros and those other hapless ones still had lived, and your jewels been in no greater peril. Nay, my wisdom teaches me that because of the death of Bruithwir and his comrades shall the greatest evils fall on Gods and Elves, and Men to be. Without the Gods who brought you to the light and gave you all the materials of your craft, teaching your first ignorance, none of these fair things you love now so well ever would have been; what has been done may again be done, for the power of the Valar does not change; but of more worth than all the glory of Valinor and all the grace and beauty of Kôr is peace and happiness and wisdom, and these once lost are harder to recapture. Cease then to murmur and to speak against the Valar, or to set yourselves in your hearts as equals to their majesty; rather depart now in penitence knowing full well that Melko has wrought this evil against you, and that your secret trafficking with him has brought you all this loss and sorrow. Trust him not again therefore, nor any others that whisper secret words of discontent among you, for its fruit is humiliation and dismay."

And the embassy was abashed and afraid and went back unto Sirnúmen utterly cast down; yet was Manwë's heart heavier than theirs, for things had gone ill indeed, and yet he foresaw that worse would be; and so did the destinies of the Gods work out, for lo! to the Noldoli Manwë's words seemed cold and heartless, and they knew not his sorrow and his tenderness; and Manwë thought them strangely changed and turned to covetice, who longed but for comfort, being like children very full of the loss of their fair things.

Now Melko findeth himself in the wastes of Arvalin and knoweth not how he may escape, for the gloom there is very great, and he knoweth not those regions that stretch there unto the utmost south. Therefore he sent a messenger claiming the inviolable right of a herald (albeit this was a renegade servant of Mandos whom Melko had perverted) over the pass to Valinor, and there standing before the gates of Valmar[7] he demanded audience of the Gods; and it was asked of him whence he came, and he said from Ainu Melko, and Tulkas would have hurled stones at him from the walls and slain him, but the others as yet suffered him not to be mishandled, but despite their anger and loathing they admitted him to the great square of gold that was before Aulë's courts. And at the same hour riders were sent to Kôr and to Sirnúmen summoning the Elves, for it was guessed that this matter touched them near. When all was made ready the messenger took stand beside the needle of pure gold whereon Aulë had written the story of the kindling of the Tree of gold (in Lórien's courts stood one of silver with another tale), and on a sudden Manwë said: "Speak!" and his voice was as a clap of wrathful thunder, and the courts rang, but the envoy unabashed uttered his message, saying:

"The Lord Melko, ruler of the world from the darkest east to the outer slopes of the Mountains of Valinor unto his kinsmen the Ainur. Behold, in compensation for divers grievous affronts and for long times of unjust imprisonment despite his noble estate and blood that he has at your hands suffered, now has he taken, as is due to him, certain small treasures held by the Noldoli, your slaves. Great grief is it to him that of these he has slain some, in that they would do him hurt in the evil of their hearts; yet their blasphemous intent will he now put from memory, and all the past injuries that ye the

Gods have wrought him will he so far forget as once again to show his presence in that place that is called Valmar, if ye will hearken to his conditions and fulfil them. For know that the Noldoli shall be his servants and shall adorn him a house; moreover of right he does demand –" but hereon even as the herald lifted up his voice yet louder swelling with his words of insolence, so great became the wrath of the Valar that Tulkas and several of his house leapt down and seizing him stopped his mouth, and the place of council was in uproar. Indeed Melko had not thought to gain aught but time and the confusion of the Valar by this embassage of insolence.

Then Manwë bid him unhand the herald, but the Gods arose crying with one voice: "This is no herald, but a rebel, a thief, and a murderer." "He hath defiled the sanctity of Valinor," shouted Tulkas, "and cast his insolence in our teeth." Now the mind of all the Elves was as one in this matter. Hope they had none of the recovery of the jewels save by the capture of Melko, which was now a matter beyond hope, but they would have no parley with Melko whatsoever and would treat him as an outlaw and all his folk. (And this was the meaning of Manwë, saying that the death of Bruithwir would be the root of the greatest evil, for it was that slaying that most inflamed both Gods and Elves.)[8]

To this end they spoke in the ears of Varda and Aulë, and Varda befriended their cause before Manwë, and Aulë yet more stoutly, for his heart was sore too for the theft of so many things of exquisite craft and workmanship; but Tulkas Poldórëa needed no pleading, being hot with ire. Now these great advocates moved the council with their words, so that in the end it is Manwë's doom that word he sent back to Melko rejecting him and his words and outlawing him and all his followers from Valinor for ever. These words would he now speak to the envoy, bidding him begone to his master with them, but the folk of the Vali and the Elves would have none of it, and led by Tulkas they took that renegade to the topmost peak of Taniquetil, and there declaring him no herald and taking the mountain and the stars to witness of the same they cast him to the boulders of Arvalien so that he was slain, and Mandos received him into his deepest caves.

Then Manwë seeing in this rebellion and their violent deed the seed of bitterness cast down his sceptre and wept; but the others spake unto Sorontur King of Eagles upon Taniquetil and by him were the words of Manwë sent to Melko: "Begone for ever, O accursed, nor dare to parley more with Gods or Elves. Neither shall thy foot nor that of any who serve thee tread the soil of Valinor again while the world endures." And Sorontur sought out Melko and said as he was bidden, and of the death of his envoy he told [?too]. Then Melko would have slain Sorontur, being mad with anger at the death of his messenger; and verily this deed was not in accord with the strict justice of the Gods, yet was the anger of those at Valmar sorely tempted; but Melko has ever cast it against the Gods most bitterly, twisting it into a black tale of wrong; and between that evil one and Sorontur has there ever since been hate and war, and that was most bitter when Sorontur and his folk fared to the Iron Mountains and there abode, watching all that Melko did.

Now Aulë goeth to Manwë and speaketh enheartening words, saying how Valmar still stands and the Mountains are high and a sure bulwark against evil. "Lo! if Melko sets once more turmoils in the world, was he not bound in chains aforetime, and so may be again: – but behold, soon will I and Tulkas fill that pass that leads to Erumáni and the seas, that Melko come not ever that way hither again."

But Manwë and Aulë plan to set guards about all those mountains until such time as Melko's deeds and places of abode without become known.

Then does Aulë fall to speech with Manwë concerning the Noldoli, and he pleads much for them, saying that Manwë wrought with anxiety has done hardly by them, for that of Melko in sooth alone is the evil come, whereas the Eldar are not slaves nor servants but beings of a wondrous sweetness and beauty – that they were guests for ever of the Gods. Therefore does Manwë bid them now, an they will, go back to Kôr, and, if they so desire, busy themselves in fashioning gems and fabrics anew, and all things of beauty and cost that they may need in their labour shall be given to them even more lavishly than before.

But when Fëanor heard this saying, he said: "Yea, but who shall give us back the joyous heart without which works of loveliness and magic cannot be? – and Bruithwir is dead, and my heart also." Many nonetheless went then back to Kôr, and some semblance of old joy is then restored, though for the lessened happiness of their hearts their labours do not bring forth gems of the old lustre and glory. But Fëanor dwelt in sorrow with a few folk in Sirnúmen, and though he sought day and night to do so he could in no wise make other jewels like to the Silmarils of old, that Melko snatched away; nor indeed has any craftsman ever done so since. At length does he abandon the attempt, sitting rather beside the tomb of Bruithwir, that is called the Mound of the First Sorrow,* and is well named for

* In the margin are written Gnomish names: 'Cùm a Gumlaith or Cùm a Thegranaithos'.

all the woe that came from the death of him who was laid there. There brooded Fëanor bitter thoughts, till his brain grew dazed by the black vapours of his heart, and he arose and went to Kôr. There did he speak to the Gnomes, dwelling on their wrongs and sorrows and their minished wealth and glory – bidding them leave this prison-house and get them into the world. "As cowards have the Valar become; but the hearts of the Eldar are not weak, and we will see what is our own, and if we may not get it by stealth we will do so by violence. There shall be war between the Children of Ilúvatar and Ainu Melko. What if we perish in our quest? The dark halls of Vê be little worse than this bright prison . . . ."⁹ And he prevailed thus upon some to go before Manwë with himself and demand that the Noldoli be suffered to leave Valinor in peace and set safely by the Gods upon the shores of the world whence they had of old been ferried.

Then Manwë was grieved by their request and forbade the Gnomes to utter such words in Kôr if they desired still to dwell there among the other Elves; but then changing from harshness he told them many things concerning the world and its fashion and the dangers that were already there, and the worse that might soon come to be by reason of Melko's return. "My heart feels, and my wisdom tells me," said he, "that no great age of time will now elapse ere those other Children of Ilúvatar, the fathers of the fathers of Men, do come into the world – and behold it is of the unalterable Music of the Ainur that the world come in the end for a great while under the sway of Men; yet whether it shall be for happiness or sorrow Ilúvatar has not revealed, and I would not have strife or fear or anger come ever between the different Children of Ilúvatar, and fain would I for many an age yet leave the world empty of beings who might strive against the new-come Men and do hurt to them ere their clans be grown to strength, while the nations and peoples of the Earth are yet infants." To this he added many words concerning Men and their nature and the things that would befall them, and the Noldoli were amazed, for they had not heard the Valar speak of Men, save very seldom; and had not then heeded overmuch, deeming these creatures weak and blind and clumsy and beset with death, nor in any ways likely to match the glory of the Eldalië. Now therefore, although Manwë had unburdened his heart in this way hoping that the Noldoli, seeing that he did not labour without a purpose or a reason, would grow calmer and more trustful of his love, rather were they astonished to discover that the Ainur made the thought of Men so great a matter, and Manwë's words achieved the opposite of his wish; for Fëanor in his misery twisted them into an evil semblance, when standing again before the throng of Kôr he spake these words:

"Lo, now do we know the reason of our transportation hither as it were cargoes of fair slaves! Now at length are we told to what end we are guarded here, robbed of our heritage in the world, ruling not the wide lands, lest perchance we yield them not to a race unborn. To these foresooth – a sad folk, beset with swift mortality, a race of burrowers in the dark, clumsy of hand, untuned to songs or musics, who shall dully labour at the soil with their rude tools, to these whom still he says are of Ilúvatar would Manwë Súlimo lordling of the Ainur give the world and all the wonders of its land, all its hidden substances – give it to these, that is our inheritance. Or what is this talk of the dangers of the world? A trick to deceive us; a mask of words! O all ye children of the Noldoli, whomso will no longer be house-thralls of the Gods however softly held, arise I bid ye and get you from Valinor, for now is the hour come and the world awaits."

In sooth it is a matter for great wonder, the subtle cunning of Melko – for in those wild words who shall say that there lurked not a sting of the minutest truth, nor fail to marvel seeing the very words of Melko pouring from Fëanor his foe, who knew not nor remembered whence was the fountain of these thoughts; yet perchance the [?outmost] origin of these sad things was before Melko himself, and such things must be – and the mystery of the jealousy of Elves and Men is an unsolved riddle, one of the sorrows at the world's dim roots.

Howso these deep things be, the fierce words of Fëanor got him instantly a mighty following, for a veil there seemed before the hearts of the Gnomes – and mayhap even this was not without the knowledge of Ilúvatar. Yet would Melko have been rejoiced to hear it, seeing his evil giving fruit beyond his hopes. Now however that evil one wanders the dark plains of Eruman, and farther south than anyone had yet penetrated he found a region of the deepest gloom, and it seemed to him a good place wherein for the time to hide his stolen treasure.

Therefore he seeks until he finds a dark cavern in the hills, and webs of darkness lie about so that the black air might be felt heavy and choking about one's face and hands. Very deep and winding were those ways having a subterranean outlet on the sea as the ancient books say, and here on a time were the Moon and Sun imprisoned afterward;[10] for here dwelt the primeval spirit Móru whom even the Valar know not whence or when she came, and the folk of Earth have given her many names. Mayhap she was bred of mists and darkness on the confines of the Shadowy Seas, in that utter dark that came between the overthrow of the Lamps and the kindling of the Trees, but more like she has always been; and she it is who loveth still to dwell in that black place taking the guise of an unlovely spider, spinning a clinging gossamer of gloom that catches in its mesh stars and moons and all bright things that sail the airs. Indeed it was because of her labours that so little of that overflowing light of the Two Trees flowed ever into the world, for she sucked light greedily, and it fed her, but she brought forth only that darkness that is a denial of all light. Ungwë Lianti the great spider who enmeshes did the Eldar call her, naming her also Wirilómë or Gloomweaver, whence still do the Noldoli speak of her as Ungoliont the spider or as Gwerlum the Black.

Now between Melko and Ungwë Lianti was there friendship from the first, when she found him and his comrades straying in her caves, but Gloomweaver was ahungered of the brightness of that hoard of jewels so soon as she saw them.

Now Melko having despoiled the Noldoli and brought sorrow and confusion into the realm of Valinor through less of that hoard than aforetime, having now conceived a darker and deeper plan of aggrandisement; therefore seeing the lust of Ungwë's eyes he offers her all that hoard, saving only the three Silmarils, if she will abet him in his new design. This she granteth readily, and so came all that treasury of most lovely gems fairer than any others that the world has seen into the foul keeping of Wirilómë, and was wound in webs of darkness and hidden deep in the caverns of the eastern slopes of the great hills that are the southern boundary of Eruman.

Deeming that now is the time to strike while Valinor is yet in uproar nor waiting for Aulë and Tulkas to block the passage in the hills, Melko and Wirilómë crept into Valinor and lay hidden in a valley of the foothills until Silpion was in bloom; but all the while was Gloomweaver spinning her most lightless webs and ill-enchanted shades. These she lets float down so that in place of the fair silver light of Silpion all about the western plain of Valinor there creeps now a dim uncertain darkness and faint lights waver in it. Then does she throw a black cloak of invisibility about Melko and herself and they steal across the plain, and the Gods are in wonder and the Elves in Kôr are afraid; nonetheless they do not as yet suspect the hand of Melko in this, thinking rather it is some work of Ossë's, who at times with his storms caused great mists and darkness to be wafted off the Shadowy Seas, encroaching even the bright airs of Valinor;

though in this he met the anger both of Ulmo and of Manwë. Then Manwë sent forth a sweet westerly breath wherewith he was accustomed at such times to blow all sea-humours back eastward over the waters, but such gentle breathing availed nothing against the woven night heavy and clinging that Wirilómë had spread far abroad. Thus was it that unmarked Melko and the Spider of Night reached the roots of Laurelin, and Melko summoning all his godlike might thrust a sword into its beauteous stock, and the fiery radiance that spouted forth assuredly had consumed him even as it did his sword, had not Gloomweaver cast herself down and lapped it thirstily, plying even her lips to the wound in the tree's bark and sucking away its life and strength.

By accursed fortune this deed was not straightway marked, for it was the time of Laurelin's accustomed deepest repose; and now behold, never more would it wake to glory, scattering beauty and joy upon the faces of the Gods. Because of that great draught of light suddenly pride surged in Gwerlum's heart, and she heeded not Melko's warnings, but sate herself now nigh to the roots of Silpion and spouted forth evil fumes of night that flowed like rivers of blackness even to the gates of Valmar. Now Melko takes the weapon that remains to him, a knife, and will injure the bole of Silpion as much as time will allow; but a Gnome called Daurin (Tórin) wandering from Sirnúmen in great boding of ill sees him and makes for him, crying aloud. So great was the onrush of that impetuous Gnome that ere Melko is aware he has hewn at Wirilómë where in the likeness of a spider she sprawls upon the ground. Now the slender blade that Daurin wielded came from the forge of Aulë and was steeped in *miruvor*, or never had he done harm to that secret [?being], but now he cleaves one of her great legs, and his blade is stained with her black gore, a poison to all [?things] whose life is light. Then Wirilómë writhing throws a thread about him and he may not get free, and Melko ruthless stabs him. Then wresting that bright slender blade from his dying grasp he thrusts it deep into Silpion's trunk, and the poison of Gwerlum black upon it dried the very sap and essence of the tree, and its light died suddenly to a dismal glow lost in impenetrable dusk.

Then did Melko and Wirilómë turn in flight, nor is it too soon, for some that were behind Daurin seeing his fate fled in terror both to Kôr and Valmar, stumbling madly in the darkness, but indeed already the Valar are riding forth upon the plain speeding as fast as may be yet too late to defend the Trees which they now know to be in danger.

Now do those Noldoli confirm their fears, saying how Melko is indeed the author of the mischief, and they have but one desire and that is to lay hands upon him and his accomplices ere they can escape beyond the mountains.

Tulkas is in the van of that great hunt leaping surefooted in the dimness, and Oromë may not keep up with him, for even his divine steed cannot rush as headlong in the gathering night as does Poldórëa in the fire of his wrath. Ulmo hears the shouting in his house in Vai, and Ossë [?thrusteth] his head above the Shadowy Seas and seeing no longer any light come down the valley of Kôr he leaps upon the beach of Eldamar and runs in haste to join the Ainur in their hunt. Now is the only light place left in Valinor that garden where the golden fountain sprang from Kulullin, and then were Vána and Nessa and Urwen and many maids and ladies of the Valar in tears, but Palúrien girds her lord as he stands impatiently, and Varda has ridden forth from Taniquetil by her lord's side bearing a blazing star before him as a torch.

Telimektar son of Tulkas is with those noble ones, and his face and weapons gleam as silver in the dark, but now all the Gods and all their folk ride this way and that, and some have [?hasty] torches in their hands, so that the plain is full of pale wandering lights and the sound of voices hallooing in the dusk.

Even as Melko speeds away a vanguard of the chase sweeps by the Trees, and well nigh the Vali faint for anguish at the ruin they see there; but now Melko and certain of his comrades, aforetime children of Mandos, are separated from Ungwë, who wrapped in night gets her gone southward and over the mountains to her home, nor does that chase ever draw nigh to her; but the others flee northward with great speed, for Melko's comrades have knowledge of the mountains there, and hope to get [?him] through. There came a place at length where the shadow-veils were thin and they were viewed by a scattered band of the Vali, and Tulkas was amongst them; who now with a great roar leaps at them. Indeed it might have come to battle upon the plain betwixt Tulkas and Melko had not the distance been overgreat, so that even as Tulkas gained to within spearcast of Melko a belt of mist took the fugitives again and the mocking laugh of Melko seems to come first from one side and then from the other, now from his elbow almost, now from far ahead, and Tulkas turns wildly about and Melko slips away.

Then Makar and Meássë rode in all haste north with their folk, arousing Mandos and ordering the guarding of the mountain paths, but either Makar was too late or Melko's cunning defeated him –

and the mind of Makar was not oversubtle, for no glimpse of that Ainu did they see, though assuredly he did escape that way, and worked much evil after in the world, yet none are there whom I have heard tell ever of the manner of his perilous flight back to the ice-kingdoms of the North.'

# NOTES

1 See p. 117.
2 *Lirillo* appears in the list of secondary names of the Valar referred to on p. 93 as a name of Salmar-Noldorin.
3 'father of Fëanor' is the final reading after a prolonged hesitation between 'son of Fëanor' and 'brother of Fëanor'.
4 For the story of the taking of rock and stone from Arvalin (Eruman) for the raising of the Mountains of Valinor see p. 70.
5 'sire of Fëanor' is an emendation from 'son of Fëanor'; see note 3.
6 After the word 'fabrics' there stood the following sentence, which was struck through: 'which the Gods could an they listed have created in an hour' – a sentence notable in itself and also for its excision.
7 The MS page beginning with the words 'before the gates of Valmar' and ending with 'unabashed uttered his message, saying' is written round the little world-map reproduced and described on pp. 81 ff.
8 In this part of the tale the manuscript consists of detached passages, with directions from one to another; the place of this sentence is not perfectly clear, but seems most probably to belong here.
9 The dots are in the original.
10 'afterward' is an emendation from 'of old'. A question mark is written in the margin against this sentence.

## Changes made to names in
## The Theft of Melko and the Darkening of Valinor

*Ellu Melemno* ⟨ *Melemno* (in Chapter V, p. 120, in an added sentence, the leader of the Solosimpi is *Ellu*).

*Sirnúmen* ⟨ *Numessir* (at the first two occurrences; subsequently *Sirnúmen* was the form first written).

*Eruman* ⟨ *Harmalin* (pp. 145, 152), ⟨ *Habbanan* (p. 151).

*Arvalin* ⟨ *Harvalien* ⟨ *Habbanan* (p. 145), ⟨ *Harvalien* ⟨ *Harmalin* (p. 147); *Arvalien* thus first written p. 148.

*Bruithwir* replaces an earlier name, probably *Maron*.

*Bruithwir go-Maidros* ⟨ *Bruithwir go-Fëanor. go-* is a patronymic, 'son of'. See notes 3 and 5 above.

*Móru*   This name could equally well be read, as also at its occasional
occurrences elsewhere, as *Morn* (see the Appendix on Names). It
replaces here another name, probably *Mordi.*

*Ungoliont* ⟨ *Gungliont.*

*Daurin (Tórin)*   The original reading at the first occurence was *Fëanor,*
changed to (?)*Daurlas* . . . . . . . . *akin to Fëanor,* and then to *a Gnome
called Daurin (Tórin).* The subsequent occurrences of *Daurin* are
emendations of *Fëanor.*


Commentary on
*The Theft of Melko and the Darkening of Valinor*


The story of the corruption of the Noldoli by Melko was ultimately told
quite differently; for there entered the matter of the strife between Finwë's
sons Fëanor and Fingolfin (*The Silmarillion* p. 69), of which in the tale
there is no trace, and where in any case Fëanor is not the son of Finwë
Nólemë but of one Bruithwir. The primary motive in the later story of
Melkor's desire for the Silmarils (*ibid.* p. 67) is here represented only by
a lust for the gems of the Noldoli in general: it is indeed a remarkable
feature of the original mythology that though the Silmarils were present
they were of such relatively small importance. There is essential agreement with the later story in its being the Noldoli at whom Melko aimed his
attack, and there is a quite close, if limited, similarity in the arguments he
used: the confinement of the Elves in Valinor by the Valar, and the broad
realms in the East that were rightly theirs – but notably absent from Melko's
words is any reference to the coming of Men: this element is in the tale
introduced later and quite differently, by Manwë himself (p. 150). Moreover the particular association of the Noldoli with the evil Vala arises
from his desire for their gems: in *The Silmarillion* (p. 66) the Noldor
turned to him for the instruction he could give, while the other kindreds
held aloof.

From this point the narratives diverge altogether; for the secret evil
of Melkor was in *The Silmarillion* laid bare as a result of the enquiry
held into the quarrel of the Noldorin princes, whereas here its revelation
came about more simply from the anxiety of Finwë Nólemë about the
unrest of his people. The later story is of course far superior, in that
Melkor was sought by the Valar as a known enemy as soon as his machinations were uncovered (though he escaped), whereas in the tale, despite
there being now every evidence that he was by no means reformed, he
was merely told to go and think things over in Mandos. The germ of the
story in *The Silmarillion* of Fëanor's banishment to Formenos, where he
was accompanied by Finwë, is present, though here the entire people of
the Noldoli are ordered to leave Kôr for the rugged dale northwards
where the stream Híri plunged underground, and the command to do so

seems to have been less a punishment meted out to them by Manwë than a precaution and a safeguard.

In connection with the place of the banishment of the Noldoli, here called *Sirnúmen* ('Western Stream'), it may be mentioned that in an isolated note found in the little book referred to on p. 23 it is stated: 'The river of the second rocky dwelling of the Gnomes in Valinor was *kelusindi* and the spring at its source *kapalinda*.'

Very remarkable is the passage (p. 142) where Manwë is said to know that 'the Elves were children of the world and must one day return to her bosom'. As I have noticed earlier (p. 82) 'the world' is often equated with the Great Lands, and this usage occurs repeatedly in the present tale, but it is not clear to me whether this sense is intended here. I incline to think that the meaning of the phrase is that at 'the Great End' the Eldar, being bound to the Earth, cannot return with the Valar and spirits that were 'before the world' (p. 66) to the regions whence they came (cf. the conclusion of the original *Music of the Ainur*, p. 60).

Coming to the account of the theft of the jewels, the structure of the narrative is again radically different from the later story, in that there Melkor's attack on the Noldor of Formenos, the theft of the Silmarils and the slaying of Finwë, was accomplished *after* his meeting with Ungoliant in the South and the destruction of the Two Trees; Ungoliant was with him at Formenos. Nor in the earliest version is there any mention of Melko's previous visit to Formenos (*The Silmarillion* pp. 71–2), after which he passed through the Calacirya and went northwards up the coast, returning later in secret to Avathar (Arvalin, Eruman) to seek out Ungoliant.

On the other hand the great festival was already the occasion for Melko's theft of the Silmarils from the dwelling of the Noldoli, though the festival was wholly different in having a purely commemorative purpose (see *The Silmarillion* pp. 74–5), and it was a necessary part of that purpose that the Solosimpi should be present (in *The Silmarillion* 'Only the Teleri beyond the mountains still sang upon the shores of the sea; for they recked little of seasons or times . . .').

Of Melko's dark accomplices out of Mandos (some of them said to be 'aforetime children of Mandos', p. 154) there is no trace later, nor of his theft of Oromë's horses; and while Melko is here said to have wished to leave Valinor by passes over the northern mountains, but to have thought better of it (leading to a reflection on what might have been the fate of Valinor had he not), in the later story his movement northwards was a feint. But it is interesting to observe the germ of the one in the other, the underlying idea never lost of a northward and then a southward movement, even though it takes place at a different point in the narrative and has a different motivation.

Interesting also is the emergence of the idea that a close kinsman of Fëanor's – only after much hesitation between brother and son becoming fixed on the father – was slain by Melkor in the dwelling of the Noldoli, Sirnúmen, precursor of Formenos; but the father had yet to be identified with the lord of the Noldoli.

In this passage there are some slight further geographical indications. The Two Trees stood to the north of the city of Valmar (p. 143), as they are shown on the map (see pp. 81–2); and, again in agreement with the map, the Great Lands and the Outer Lands came very close together in the far North (p. 146). Most notably, the gap in the Mountains of Valinor shown on the map and which I marked with the letter *e* is now explained: 'the low place in the hills' by which Melko and his following passed out of Valinor into Arvalin-Eruman, a gap left by Tulkas and Aulë for their own entry into Valinor at the time of the raising of the mountains (p. 145).

Of the next part of this tale (pp. 146–9) almost nothing survived. Manwë's lecture to the Noldoli disappeared (but some of its content is briefly expressed at another place in the narrative of *The Silmarillion*, p. 68: 'The Noldor began to murmur against [the Valar], and many became filled with pride, forgetting how much of what they had and knew came to them in gift from the Valar'). Manwë's naming of Fëanor's father Bruithwir by the patronymic *go-Maidros* is notable: though the name *Maidros* was subsequently to be that of Fëanor's eldest son, not of his grandfather, it was from the outset associated with the 'Fëanorians'. There is no trace later of the strange story of the renegade servant of Mandos, who brought Melko's outrageous message to the Valar, and who was hurled to his death from Taniquetil by the irrepressible Tulkas in direct disobedience to Manwë; nor of the sending of Sorontur to Melko as the messenger of the Gods (it is not explained how Sorontur knew where to find him). It is said here that afterwards 'Sorontur and his folk fared to the Iron Mountains and there abode, watching all that Melko did'. I have noticed in commenting (pp. 111–12) on *The Chaining of Melko* that the Iron Mountains, said to be south of Hisilómë (pp. 101, 118), there correspond to the later Mountains of Shadow (*Ered Wethrin*). On the other hand, in the *Tale of the Sun and Moon* (p. 176) Melko after his escape from Valinor makes himself 'new dwellings in that region of the North where stand the Iron Mountains very high and terrible to see'; and in the original *Tale of Turambar** it is said that Angband lay beneath the roots of the northernmost fastnesses of the Iron Mountains, and that these mountains were so named from 'the Hells of Iron' beneath them. The statement in the present tale that Sorontur 'watched all that Melko did' from his abode in the Iron Mountains obviously implies likewise that Angband was beneath them; and the story that Sorontur (Thorondor) had his eyries on Thangorodrim before he removed them to Gondolin survived long in the 'Silmarillion' tradition (see *Unfinished Tales* p. 43 and note 25). There is thus, apparently, a contradictory usage of the term

---

* The actual title of this tale is *The Tale of Turambar and the Foalókë*, the *Foalókë* being the Dragon.

'Iron Mountains' within the *Lost Tales*; unless it can be supposed that these mountains were conceived as a continuous range, the southerly extension (the later Mountains of Shadow) forming the southern fence of Hisilómë, while the northern peaks, being above Angband, gave the range its name. Evidence that this is so will appear later.

In the original story the Noldoli of Sirnúmen were given permission (through the intercession of Aulë) to return to Kôr, but Fëanor remained there in bitterness with a few others; and thus the situation of the later narrative – the Noldor in Tirion, but Fëanor at Formenos – is achieved, with the element absent of Fëanor's banishment and unlawful return to the city of the Elves. An underlying difference to be noted is that in *The Silmarillion* (pp. 61–2) the Vanyar had long since departed from Tirion and gone to dwell on Taniquetil or in Valinor: of this there is no suggestion in the old tale; and of course there is the central structural difference between the early and late narratives – when Fëanor raises his standard of rebellion the Trees are still shining in Valinor.

In the tale, a good while seems to elapse after the loss of the treasures of the Noldoli, during which they set to work again with lessened joy and Fëanor sought in vain to remake the Silmarils: this element must of course disappear in the later, much tauter structure, where Fëanor (refusing to hand over the Silmarils to the Valar for the healing of the Trees and not yet knowing that Melko has taken them) knows without attempting it that he cannot remake them any more than Yavanna can remake the Trees.

The embassage of Fëanor and other Noldoli to Manwë, demanding that the Gods ferry them back to the Great Lands, was excised, and with it Manwë's remarkable instruction to them concerning the coming of Men – and his expressed reluctance to have the Eldar return to 'the world' while Men were still in their infancy. No such idea is represented in *The Silmarillion* as being in Manwë's mind (nor is there any suggestion that Manwë's knowledge was so great); and indeed, where in the old story it was Manwë's very description of Men and account of his policy with regard to them that gave rise to Fëanor's rhetoric against them, and which gave strong colour to his assertion of the Valar's true motive for bringing the Eldar to Valinor, in *The Silmarillion* (p. 68) these ideas are a part of the lies of Melkor (I have noticed above that in Melko's persuasions of the Noldoli in the tale there is no reference to the coming of Men).

An otherwise unknown element in the Music of the Ainur is revealed in Manwë's words: that the world shall come in the end for a great while under the sway of Men. In the original version there are several suggestions in reflective asides that all was fated: so here 'the jealousy of Elves and Men' is seen as perhaps a necessary part of the unfolding of the history of the world, and earlier in the tale (p. 142) it is asked: 'Who shall say but that all these deeds, even the seeming needless evil of Melko, were but a portion of the destiny of old?'

But for all the radical changes in the narrative the characteristic note of Fëanor's rhetoric remained; his speech to the Noldoli of Kôr rises in the same rhythms as his speech by torchlight to the Noldor of Tirion (*The Silmarillion* pp. 82–3).

In the story of Melko and Ungoliont it is seen that essential elements were present *ab initio*: the doubt as to her origin, her dwelling in the desolate regions in the south of the Outer Lands, her sucking in of light to bring forth webs of darkness; her alliance with Melko, his rewarding her with the gems stolen from the Noldoli (though this was differently treated later), the piercing of the Trees by Melko and Ungoliont's sucking up the light; and the great hunt mounted by the Valar, which failed of its object through darkness and mist, allowing Melko to escape out of Valinor by the northward ways.

Within this structure there are as almost always a great many points of difference between the first story and the later versions. In *The Silmarillion* (p. 73) Melkor went to Avathar because he knew of Ungoliant's dwelling there, whereas in the tale she found him wandering there seeking a way of escape. In the tale her origin is unknown, and though this element may be said to have remained in *The Silmarillion* ('The Eldar know not whence she came', *ibid.*), by the device of 'Some have said . . .' a clear explanation is in fact given: she was a being from 'before the world', perverted by Melkor, who had been her lord, though she denied him. The original idea of 'the primeval spirit Móru' (p. 151) is made explicit in an entry in the early word-list of the Gnomish language, where the name *Muru* is defined as 'a name of the Primeval Night personified as Gwerlum or Gungliont'.*

The old story markedly lacks the quality of the description in *The Silmarillion* of the descent of Melkor and Ungoliant from Mount Hyarmentir into the plain of Valinor; and there too the great festival of the Valar and Eldar was in progress at the time: here it is long since over. In *The Silmarillion* the assault on the Trees came at the time of the mingling of the lights (p. 75), while here Silpion was in full bloom; and the detail of the account of the destruction of the Trees is rendered quite different through the presence of the Gnome Daurin, afterwards abandoned without trace. Thus in the old story it is not actually said that Ungoliont drank the light of Silpion, but only that the tree died from her poison on Daurin's blade, with which Melko stabbed its trunk; and in *The Silmarillion* Ungoliant went to 'the Wells of Varda' and drank them dry also. It is puzzling that the Gnome was first named Fëanor, since he was slain by Melko. It would seem that my father was at least momentarily entertaining the idea that Fëanor would play no part in the story of the Noldoli in the Great Lands; but in outlines for a later tale (pp. 238–9) he died in Mithrim. In this passage is the first appearance of *miruvor*, defined in the early Qenya word-list as 'nectar, drink of the Valar'; with this cf. *The Road Goes Ever On*, p. 61, where my father stated that it was the name given by the Valar to the drink poured at their festivals,

* In the tale (see p. 156) the name *Gungliont* was originally written, but was emended to *Ungoliont*.

and compared it to the nectar of the Olympian Gods (in the translation of *Namárië* he rendered *miruvórë* 'nectar', *ibid.* p. 58).

Most important of the differences in the tale is the immediate return of Ungoliont to her lair in the south, so that all the story in *The Silmarillion* (pp. 80–1) of 'the Thieves' Quarrel', the rescue of Melkor by the Balrogs, and Ungoliant's coming into Nan Dungortheb, is absent from the narrative in the *Lost Tales*; the surrender of the gems of the Noldoli to Ungoliont takes place in the early version at the time of her first meeting with Melko – in *The Silmarillion* he did not then possess them, for the attack on Formenos had not yet taken place.

# VII

# THE FLIGHT OF THE NOLDOLI

There is no break in Lindo's narrative, which continues on in the same hastily-pencilled form (and near this point passes to another similar notebook, clearly with no break in composition), but I have thought it convenient to introduce a new chapter, or a new 'Tale', here, again taking the title from the cover of the book.

'Nonetheless the Gods did not give up hope, but many a time would meet beneath the ruined tree of Laurelin and thence break and scour the land of Valinor once more unwearyingly, desiring fiercely to avenge the hurts done to their fair realm; and now the Eldar at their summons aided in the chase that labours not only in the plain but toils both up and down the slopes of the mountains, for there is no escape from Valinor to west, where lie the cold waters of the Outer Seas.

But Fëanor standing in the square about Inwë's house in topmost Kôr will not be silenced, and cries out that all the Noldoli shall gather about him and hearken, and many thousands of them come to hear his words bearing slender torches, so that that place is filled with a lurid light such as has never before shone on those white walls. Now when they are gathered there and Fëanor sees that far the most of the company is of the kin of the Noldor[1] he exhorts them to seize now this darkness and confusion and the weariness of the Gods to cast off the yoke – for thus demented he called the days of bliss in Valinor – and get them hence carrying with them what they might or listed. "If all your hearts be too faint to follow, behold I Fëanor go now alone into the wide and magic world to seek the gems that are my own, and perchance many great and strange adventures will there befall me more worthy of a child of Ilúvatar than a servant of the Gods."[2]

Then is there a great rush of those who will follow him at once, and though wise Nólemë speaks against this rashness they will not hear him, and ever the tumult groweth wilder. Again Nólemë pleads that at least they send an embassy to Manwë to take due farewell and maybe get his goodwill and counsel for their journeying, but Fëanor persuades them to cast away even such moderate wisdom, saying that to do so were but to court refusal, and that Manwë would forbid them and prevent them: "What is Valinor to us," say they, "now that its light is come to little – as lief and liever would we have the untrammeled world." Now then they arm themselves as best they may – for nor Elves nor Gods in those days bethought themselves overmuch of weapons – and store of jewels they took and stuffs of raiment; but all their books of their lore they left behind, and indeed there was not much therein that the wise men among them could not match from memory. But Nólemë seeing that his counsel prevailed not would not be separated from his folk, and went with them and aided them in all their preparations. Then did they get them down the hill of Kôr lit by the flame of torches, and so faring in haste along the creek and the shores of that arm of the Shadowy Sea that encroached here upon the hills they found the seaward dwellings of the Solosimpi.

The next short section of the text was struck through afterwards, the words 'Insert the Battle of Kópas Alqalunten' written across it, and replaced by a rider. The rejected section reads:

The most of that folk were gone a-hunting with the Gods, but some of those that remained they suaded to cast in their lot with them, as already had some of the Teleri, but of the Inwir none would hearken to their words. Now having nigh as many maids and women as of men and boys (albeit many especially of the youngest children were left in Kôr and Sirnúmen) they were at a loss, and in this extremity, being distraught with sorrows and wildered in mind, the Noldoli did those deeds which afterwards they most bitterly rued – for by them was the displeasure laid heavily on all their folk and the hearts even of their kindred were turned against them for a while.

Coming upon Cópas where was a haven of great quiet beloved of the Solosimpi they seized all the ships of that people and embarked thereon their womenfolk and children and some few [?others] wherewith were those of the Solosimpi who had joined them, for these had a skill in navigation. In this way marching endlessly along the beach that grew wilder and more evil going as it trended to the North, while the fleet coasted beside them not far out to sea, it has been said to me that the Noldoli got them from Valinor; however I know not the matter deeply, and maybe there are tales known to none of the Gnome-kin that relate more clearly the sad happenings of that time. Moreover have I heard say

The rider that replaces this passage was written carefully and very legibly in ink on separate sheets, at how great an interval of time I cannot say.

## The Kinslaughter
### (Battle of Kópas Alqalunten)

The most of that folk were gone a-hunting with the Gods, but many there were gathered about the beaches before their dwellings and dismay was abroad among them, yet still were no few busy about the places of their ships, and the chief of these was that one they named Kópas, or more fully Kópas Alqaluntë, the Haven of the Swanships.* Now Swanhaven was like a bason of quiet waters, save that towards the eastward and the seas the ring of rocks that enclosed it sank somewhat, and there did the sea pierce through, so that there was a mighty arch of living stone. So great was this that save of the mightiest ships two might pass therethrough, one going out maybe and another seeking inward to the quiet blue waters of the haven, nor would the mast-tops come nigh to grazing on the rock. Not much of the light of the Trees came thither aforetime by reason of the wall, wherefore was it lit ever with a ring of lamps of gold, and lanterns there were too of many colours tokening the wharves and landings of the different houses; but through the arch the pale waters of the Shadowy Seas might distantly be glimpsed, lit faintly with the shining of the Trees. Very beautiful was that harbour to gaze upon, what time the white fleets came shimmering home and the troubled waters broke the mirrored radiance of the lamps into rippling lights, weaving strange patterns of many twinkling lines. But now were all those vessels lying still, and a deep gloom was settled on the place at the fading of the Trees.

Of the Solosimpi none would hearken to the wild words of the Noldoli, save a few that might be counted on two hands; and so did that folk wander unhappily northward along the shores of Eldamar, even till they came to the cliff-tops that gazed down upon Swanhaven, and therefrom had the Solosimpi of old cut winding stairs in the rock leading down to the harbour's edge. Now northward thence the way was very rugged and evil, and the Noldoli had with them nigh as many maids and women as of men and boys (albeit many especially of the youngest children were left in Kôr and in Sirnúmen and many tears were shed thereat); wherefore were they now at a loss, and in this extremity, distraught with sorrows and wildered in mind, they here wrought those deeds which afterwards they have most bitterly

---

* In the margin is written *Ielfethýþ*. This is Old English, representing the interpretation of the Elvish name made by Eriol in his own language: the first element meaning 'swan' (*ielfetu*), and the second (later 'hithe') meaning 'haven, landing-place'.

repented – for by them was for a while the displeasure of the Gods laid heavily upon all their folk and the hearts even of the Eldalië were turned against them.

Behold, the counsel of Fëanor is that by no means can that host hope to win swiftly along the coast save by the aid of ships; "and these," said he, "an the shore-elves will not give them, we must take". Wherefore going down to the harbour they essayed to go upon those ships that there lay, but the Solosimpi said them nay, yet for the great host of the Gnome-folk they did not as yet resist; but a new wrath awoke there between Eldar and Eldar. So did the Noldoli embark all their womenfolk and children and a great host beside upon those ships, and casting them loose they oared them with a great multitude of oars towards the seas. Then did a great anger blaze in the hearts of the Shoreland Pipers, seeing the theft of those vessels that their cunning and long labours had fashioned, and some there were that the Gods had made of old on Tol Eressëa as has been recounted, wondrous and magic boats, the first that ever were. So sprang up suddenly a voice among them: "Never shall these thieves leave the Haven in our ships", and all those of the Solosimpi that were there ran swiftly atop of the cliff-wall to where the archway was wherethrough that fleet must pass, and standing there they shouted to the Gnomes to return; but these heeded them not and held ever on their course, and the Solosimpi threatened them with rocks and strung their elfin bows.

Seeing this and believing war already to be kindled came now those of the Gnomes who might not fare aboard the ships but whose part it was to march along the shores, and they sped behind the Solosimpi, until coming suddenly upon them nigh the Haven's gate they slew them bitterly or cast them in the sea; and so first perished the Eldar neath the weapons of their kin, and that was a deed of horror. Now the number of the Solosimpi that fell was very many, and of the Gnomes not a few, for they had to fight hard to win their way back from those narrow cliff-top paths, and many of the shoreland folk hearing the affray were gathered in their rear.

At length however it is done, and all those ships have passed out to the wide seas, and the Noldoli fared far away, but the little lamps are broken and the Haven is dark and very still, save for the faint sound of tears. Of like kind were all the works of Melko in this world.

Now tells the tale that as the Solosimpi wept and the Gods scoured all the plain of Valinor or sat despondent neath the ruined Trees a great age passed and it was one of gloom, and during that time the Gnome-folk suffered the very greatest evils and all the unkindliness of the world beset them. For some marched endlessly along that shore until Eldamar was dim and forgotten far behind, and wilder grew the ways and more impassable as it trended to the North, but the fleet coasted beside them not far out to sea and the shore-farers might often see them dimly in the gloom, for they fared but slowly in those sluggish waves.

Yet of all the sorrows that walked those ways I know not the full tale, nor have any told it, for it would be an ill tale, and though the Gnomes relate many things concerning those days more clearly than I can, yet do they in no wise love to dwell upon the sad happenings of that time and will not often awake its memory. Nonetheless have I heard it said

The inserted rider ends here and we return to the original roughly-pencilled text:

that never would they have made the dreadful passage of the Qerkaringa³ had they or yet been subject to weariness, sickness, and the many weaknesses that after became their lot dwelling far from Valinor. Still was the blessed food of the Gods and their drink rich in their veins and they were half-divine – but no *limpë* had they as yet to bring away, for that was not given to the fairies until long after, when the March of Liberation was undertaken, and the evils of the world which Melko poisoned with his presence soon fell upon them.'

'Nay, if thou wilt forgive me bursting in upon thy tale,' quoth Eriol, 'what meaneth thy saying "the dread passage of the Qerkaringa"?'

'Know then,' said Lindo, 'that the trend of the coasts of Eldamar and those coasts that continue that strand northward beyond the wide haven of Kópas is ever to the East, so that after uncounted miles, more northward even than the Mountains of Iron and upon the confines of the Icy Realms, the Great Seas aided by a westerly bend of the shores of the Great Lands dwindle to a narrow sound. Now the passage of that water is of impassable peril, for it is full of evil currents and eddies of desperate strength, and islands of floating ice swim therein, grinding and crashing together with a dread noise and destroying both great fish and vessels, do any ever dare to venture there. In those days however a narrow neck, which the Gods after destroyed, ran out from the western land almost to the eastern shores, yet it was of ice and snow [?pillared] and torn into gaps and cliffs and was all but untraversable, and that was the

Helkaraksë or Icefang,[4] and it was a remnant of the old and terrible
ices that crept throughout those regions ere Melko was chained and
the North became clement for a while, and it maintained itself there
by reason of the narrowness of the seas and the [?jamming] of the
ice-isles floating down from the deepest North whither winter had
withdrawn. Now that strip of water that flowed still between Icefang's
tip and the Great Lands was called Qerkaringa or Chill Gulf.[5]

Had Melko indeed known of the Gnomes' wild attempt to cross
it he might have overwhelmed them all in that ill place or done
whatso he willed, but many months had gone since he himself had
fled perchance by that very way, and he was now far afield. Say I not
well, Rúmil, with regard to these things?'

'Thou hast told the true tale,' said Rúmil, 'yet hast thou not said
how ere they came to Helkaraksë the host passed by that place
where Mornië is wont to be beached, for there a steep and rugged
path winds down from Mandos deep in the mountains that the souls
whom Fui sends to Arvalin must tread.[6] There did a servant of
Vefántur spy them and asking what might that wayfaring mean pled
with them to return, but they answered him scornfully, so that
standing upon a high rock he spoke to them aloud and his voice
came even to the fleet upon the waves; and he foretold to them many
of the evil adventures that after came to them, warning them against
Melko, and at last he said: "Great is the fall of Gondolin", and none
there understood, for Turondo son of Nólemë[7] was not yet upon the
Earth. But the wise men stored his sayings, for Mandos and all his
people have a power of prophecy, and these words were treasured
long among them as the Prophecies of Amnos, for thus was the place
where they were spoken called at that time, which now is Hanstovánen[8] or the beaching place of Mornië.

After that the Noldoli journeyed slowly, and when the awful
isthmus of Helkaraksë was before them some were for ferrying all
the host, part at a time, across the sea, venturing rather over the
perilous waters than seeking to find passage over the gulfs and
treacherous crevasses of the isthmus of ice. This they tried, and a
great ship was lost with all aboard by reason of a certain fearsome
eddy that was in the bay nigh where Helkaraksë jutted from the
western mainland; and that eddy at times spins around like a vast
top and shrieks with a loud wailing noise most terrible to hear, and
such things as approach are sucked down to its monstrous deep and
crushed there upon jags of ice and rock; and the name of the eddy
is Wiruin. Wherefore are the Noldoli in great anguish and perplexity,
for even could they find a way through the terrors of the Helkaraksë,

behold they cannot even so reach the inner world, for still there lies that gap at the far end, and though but narrow the screech of water rushing therethrough can be heard thus far away, and the boom of ice splitting from the cape came to them, and the crash and buffet of the ice-isles that thrust down from the North through that dreadful strait.

Now the presence of those floating isles of ice no doubt was due to the presence of Melko once more in the far North, for winter had retreated to the uttermost North and South, so that almost it had no foothold in the world remaining in those days of peace that are called Melko's Chains; but nonetheless it was this very activity of Melko that in the end proved the salvation of the Noldoli, for behold they now are constrained to lead all their womenfolk and the mariners of their host out of the ships, and there on those bleak shores they beach them and set now a miserable encampment.

Songs name that dwelling[9] the Tents of Murmuring, for there arose much lamentation and regret, and many blamed Fëanor bitterly, as indeed was just, yet few deserted the host for they suspected that there was no welcome ever again for them back to Valinor – and this some few who sought to return indeed found, though this entereth not into this tale.

When their woes are now at the blackest and scarce any look for return of any joy again, behold winter unfurls her banners again and marches slowly south clad in ice with spears of frost and lashes of hail. Yet so great is the cold that the floating ice packs and jams and piles like hills between the end of Helkaraksë[10] and the Eastern land, and in the end does it become so strong that the current moves it not. Then abandoning their stolen ships they leave their sorrowful encampment and strive to cross the terrors of the Qerkaringa. Who shall tell of their misery in that march or of those numbers who were lost, falling into great pits of ice where far below hidden water boiled, or losing their way until cold overcame them – for evil as it was so many and desperate things befell them after in the Great Lands that it was lessened in their minds to a thing of less worth, and in sooth tales that told of the leaving of Valinor were never sweet in the ears of the Noldoli after, were they thralls or citizens of Gondolin. Yet even so such things may not slay the Gnome-kin, and of those there lost still 'tis said some wander sadly there among the icehills, unknowing of all things that have befallen their folk, and some essayed to get them back to Valinor, and Mandos has them, and some following after found in long days their unhappy kin again. Howso it be, a gaunt and lessened band indeed did in the end reach the rocky soil of the Eastern lands, and there stood looking backward over the ice of Helkaraksë and of Qerkaringa at the spurs of hills beyond the sea, for far away in the gathering southward mists rose those most glorious heights of Valinor, fencing them for ever from their kindred and their homes.

Thus came the Noldoli into the world.'

And with those words of Rúmil's the story of the darkening of Valinor was at an end.

'Great was the power of Melko for ill,' saith Eriol, 'if he could indeed destroy with his cunning the happiness and glory of the Gods and of the Elves, darkening the light of their hearts no less than of their dwelling, and bringing all their love to naught! This must surely be the worst deed that ever he has done.'

'Of a truth never has such evil again been done in Valinor,' said Lindo, 'but Melko's hand has laboured at worse things in the world, and the seeds of his evil have waxen since those days to a great and terrible growth.'

'Nay,' said Eriol, 'yet can my heart not think of other griefs, for sorrow at the destruction of those most fair Trees and the darkness of the world.'

## NOTES

1 The manuscript seems certainly to have the form *Noldor* here. – It is to be remembered that in the old story the Teleri (i.e. the later Vanyar) had not departed from Kôr; see p. 159.

2 At the top of the manuscript page and fairly clearly referring to Fëanor's words my father wrote: 'Increase the element of the desire for Silmarils'. Another note refers to the section of the narrative that begins here and says that it 'wants a lot of revision: the [?thirst ?lust] for jewels – especially for the sacred Silmarils – wants emphasizing. And the all-important battle of Cópas Alqaluntë where the Gnomes slew the Solosimpi must be inserted.' This note was then struck through and marked 'done', but only the latter direction was in fact followed: this is the rider on the Kinslaughter given on pp. 164–6.

3 Against this my father wrote in the margin: '*Helkaraksë* Icefang *Qerkaringa* the water'; see note 5.

4 *Helkaraksë or Icefang*: earlier reading *Qerkaringa*; see note 5.

5 This passage, from ' "Know then," said Lindo . . .', replaces an earlier version which I do not give, for it contains almost nothing that is not in the replacement; and the last sentence of the replacement is a later addition still. It is to be noted however that in the first version the neck of land is called *Qerkaringa* (as also in the replacement passage at first, see note 4), with the remark that 'the name has also

been given to the sound beyond'. This then was the earlier idea: *Qerkaringa* the name primarily of the neck of land, but extended also to the sound (presumably at that stage *querka* did not mean 'gulf'). My father than decided that *Qerkaringa* was the name of the sound and introduced the name *Helkaraksë* for the neck of land; hence the marginal annotation given in note 3 above. At this point he added the last sentence of the replacement passage, 'Now that strip of water that flowed still between Icefang's tip and the Great Lands was called Qerkaringa or Chill Gulf', and emended *Qerkaringa* in the body of the passage (note 4) to *Helkaraksë or Icefang*, carrying this change through the rest of the tale (on p. 169 *of Qerkaringa* ⟩ *of Helkaraksë and of Qerkaringa*).

6  For the path down from Mandos, the black ship Mornië, and its journey down the coast to Arvalin, see pp. 77, 90 ff.

7  Turondo or Turgon, son of Nólemë, has been named previously, p. 115.

8  The reading *Hanstovánen* is slightly uncertain, and another name 'or . . . . . . *Mornien*' follows it. See under 'Changes made to names' below.

9  After the word 'dwelling' there is a space left for the insertion of an Elvish name.

10  MS *Qerkaringa* unemended, but clearly the western promontory (the Icefang) is referred to, and I therefore read *Helkaraksë* in the text (see note 5).

## Changes made to names in
## The Flight of the Noldoli

*Helkaraksë* ⟨ *Qerkaringa* (for the details of, and the explanation of this change see note 5 above).

*Arvalin* ⟨ *Habbanan*.

*Amnos* ⟨ *Emnon* ⟨ *Morniento*.

*Hanstovánen* The name of 'the beaching place of Mornië' was first written *Mornielta* (last letters uncertain), then *Vane* (or *Vone*) *Hansto*; this latter was not struck out, but the form in the text (which may also be read as *Hanstavánen*) seems to be the final one. After *Hanstovánen* follows 'or . . . . . . *Mornien*'.

## Commentary on
## The Flight of the Noldoli

In this 'tale' (in reality the conclusion of the long tale of 'The Theft of Melko and the Darkening of Valinor' told by Lindo and finished by

Rúmil) is found the oldest account of the departure of the Gnomes out of Valinor. Here the Gods continue the vain pursuit and search long after Melko has escaped, and moreover are aided in it by the Eldar (including the Solosimpi, who as the later Teleri portrayed in *The Silmarillion* would hardly have left their shores and their ships). Fëanor's return to Kôr and his haranguing of the Noldoli (and, in this account, others) by the light of their torches is seen to be an original feature; but his sons have not yet appeared, nor indeed any of the Noldorin princes descended from Finwë save Turondo (Turgon), of whom it is specifically stated (p. 167) that he was 'not yet upon the Earth'. There is no Oath of Fëanor, and the later story of the divided counsels of the Noldor appears only in the attempt of Nólemë (Finwë) to calm the people – Nólemë thus playing the later part of Finarfin (*The Silmarillion* p. 83). In *The Silmarillion*, after the Kinslaying at Alqualondë and the Prophecy of the North, Finarfin and many of his people returned to Valinor and were pardoned by the Valar (p. 88); but here those few who went back found there was no welcome for them, or else 'Mandos has them' (p. 168).

In the rejected section given on p. 163, which was replaced by the account of the battle of Kópas Alqualunten, the reference to 'those deeds which afterwards the Noldoli most bitterly rued' must be simply to the theft of the ships of the Solosimpi, since there is no suggestion of any worse actions (in the replacement passage almost the same words are used of the Kinslaying). The actual emergence of the idea that the Noldoli were guilty of worse than theft at Kópas is seen in a note in the little book (see p. 23) that my father used to jot down thoughts and suggestions – many of these being no more than single sentences, or mere isolated names, serving as reminders of work to be done, stories to be told, or changes to be made. This note reads:

> The wrath of the Gods and Elves very great – even let some Noldoli slay some Solosimpi at Kópas – and let Ulmo plead for them (? if Ulmo so fond of the Solosimpi).

This was struck through and marked 'done', and the recommendation here that Ulmo should plead for the Noldoli is found in the tale of *The Hiding of Valinor* (p. 209).

In the description of Kópas the 'mighty arch of living stone' survived into the 'arch of living rock sea-carved' in the much briefer description of Alqualondë in *The Silmarillion* (p. 61); and we see here the reason for the Haven's being 'lit with many lamps' (*ibid.*) – because little light came there from the Two Trees on account of the rock-wall around it (though the darkness of Alqualondë is implied by the statement in *The Silmarillion* that it 'lay upon the confines of Eldamar, north of the Calacirya, where the light of the stars was bright and clear').

The events at the Haven were differently conceived in detail from the later story, but still with much general agreement; and though the storm raised by Uinen (*ibid.* p. 87) does not appear in the original version, the picture of the Noldoli journeying northward some along the shore and some in the vessels remained.

There are interesting indications of the geography of the northern regions. There is no suggestion of a great wasteland (later Araman) between the northern Mountains of Valinor and the sea, a conclusion reached earlier (p. 83), and supported incidentally by the accounts of the steep path from Mandos in the mountains down to the beaching place of the black ship Mornië (pp. 77, 167). The name *Helkaraksë*, 'Icefang', first appearing in emendations to the text and given to the neck or promontory running out from the western land, was afterwards re-applied to what is here called *Qerkaringa*, the strait filled with ice-floes that 'grind and crash together'; but this was when the *Helcaraxë*, 'the Grinding Ice', had come to have a quite different geographical significance in the much more sophisticated world-picture that my father evolved during the next 'phase' of the mythology.

In *The Silmarillion* (p. 87) there is a suggestion that the speaker of the Prophecy of the North was Mandos himself 'and no lesser herald of Manwë', and its gravity, indeed its centrality in the mythology, is far greater; here there is no suggestion of a 'doom' or 'curse', but only a foretelling. This foretelling included the dark words 'Great is the fall of Gondolin'. In the tale of *The Fall of Gondolin* (but in an interpolated sentence very possibly later than the present tale) Turgon, standing upon the stairs of his palace amid the destruction of the city, uttered these same words, 'and men shuddered, for such were the words of Amnon the prophet of old'. Here *Amnon* (rather than *Amnos* as in the present text, itself an emendation from *Emnon*) is not a place but a person (the servant of Vefántur who uttered the prophecy?). In the little notebook referred to above occurs the following jotting:

> Prophecy of Amnon. Great is the fall of Gondolin. Lo Turgon shall not fade till the lily of the valley fadeth.

In some other notes for the *Lost Tales* this takes the form:

> Prophecy of Amnon. 'Great is the fall of Gondolin' and 'When the lily of the valley withers then shall Turgon fade'.

In these notes *Amnon* might be either place or person. The 'lily of the valley' is Gondolin itself, one of whose Seven Names was *Losengriol*, later *Lothengriol*, which is translated 'flower of the vale or lily of the valley'.

There is an interesting statement in the old story (p. 166) that the Noldoli would never have passed the ice if they had yet been subject to the 'weariness, sickness, and the many weaknesses that after became their lot dwelling far from Valinor', but 'still was the blessed food of the Gods and their drink rich in their veins and they were half-divine'. This is echoed in the words of *The Silmarillion* (p. 90) that the Noldor were 'but new-come from the Blessed Realm, and not yet weary with the weariness of Earth'. On the other hand it was specifically said in the Prophecy of the North (*ibid.* p. 88) that 'though Eru appointed you to die not in Eä, *and no sickness may assail you*, yet slain ye may be, and slain ye shall be,' &c.

Of the treachery of the Fëanorians, sailing away in the ships and leaving the host of Fingolfin on the shores of Araman, there is of course in the old story no trace; but the blaming of Fëanor was already present ('the Tents of Murmuring', p. 168). It is a remarkable aspect of the earliest version of the mythology that while so much of the narrative structure was firm and was to endure, the later 'genealogical' structure had scarcely emerged. Turgon existed as the son of (Finwë) Nólemë, but there is no suggestion that Fëanor was close akin to the lord of the Noldoli, and the other princes, Fingolfin, Finarfin, Fingon, Felagund, do not appear at all, in any form, or by any name.

# VIII

# THE TALE OF THE SUN AND MOON

The *Tale of the Sun and Moon* is introduced by an 'Interlude' (as it is called in the manuscript) in which there appears, as a guest at Mar Vanwa Tyaliéva, one Gilfanon of Tavrobel. This interlude exists also in a rejected earlier version.

The tale itself is for most of its length a manuscript in ink over an erased pencilled original, but towards its end (see note 19) it becomes a primary manuscript in ink with the pencilled draft extant in another book.

The *Tale of the Sun and Moon* is very long, and I have shortened it in places in brief paraphrase, without omitting any detail of interest. (A note of my father's refers to this tale as 'in need of great revision, cutting-down, and [?reshaping]'.)

## Gilfanon a·Davrobel

Now it is not to be thought that as Eriol hearkened to many tales which spake of divers sorrows of the Elves that the thirst for *limpë* grew less within him, for it was not so, and ever as the throng sat about the Tale-fire he was an eager questioner, seeking to learn all the history of the folk even down to those days that then were, when the elfin people dwelt again together in the isle.

Knowing now therefore something of the glorious fashion of their ancient home and of the splendour of the Gods, he pondered often on the coming of the days of Sunlight and of Moonsheen, and of the doings of the Elves in the world without, and of their adventures there with Men ere Melko compassed their estrangement; wherefore one night he said, sitting before the Tale-fire: 'Whence be the Sun and Moon, O Lindo? For as yet have I heard only of the Two Trees and their sad fading, but of the coming of Men, or of the deeds of the Elves beyond Valinor has no one told me.'

Now there happened that night to be present a guest both at their board and at their tale-telling, and his name was Gilfanon, and all named him beside Gilfanon a·Davrobel,[1] for he came from that region of the isle where stands the Tower of Tavrobel beside the rivers,[2] and about it dwelt the Gnome-folk still as one people, naming the places in their own tongue. That region was Gilfanon wont to name the fairest of all the isle, and the Gnome-kin its best folk, albeit ere the coming of the folk thither long had he dwelt away from the Noldoli, faring with Ilkorins in Hisilómë and Artanor,[3] and thereto had he become as few Elves did a great friend and companion of the Children of Men of those days. To their legends and their memories he added his own knowledge, for he had been deep-versed in many lores and tongues once in the far days of Kôr, and experience had he beside of many very ancient deeds, being indeed one of the oldest of the fairies[4] and the most aged that now dwelt in the isle, albeit Meril held the title of Lady of the Isle by reason of her blood.

Therefore said Lindo now, answering Eriol: 'Behold, Gilfanon here can tell thee much of such matters, and it were well if you fared hence away with him to sojourn awhile in Tavrobel. – Nay, look not thus,' he laughed, seeing Eriol's face, 'for we do not banish thee yet – but of a sooth he who would drink of *limpë* were wise first to seek the guestkindliness of Gilfanon, in whose ancient house – the House of the Hundred Chimneys, that stands nigh the bridge of Tavrobel[5] – may many things be heard of both past and that are to come.'

'Methinks,' said Gilfanon to Eriol, 'that Lindo seeks to rid himself of two guests at once; howso he may not do so yet, for I purpose to stay in Kortirion a sennight yet, and moreover to feast at his good board meanwhile, and stretch me by the Tale-fire too – thereafter maybe thou and I will fare away and thou shalt see the full loveliness of the fairies' isle – but now let Lindo raise up his voice and tell us yet more of the splendour of the Gods and their works, a theme that never wearies him!'

At that was Lindo well-pleased, for of a truth he loved to tell such tales and sought often an occasion for recalling them, and said he: 'Then will I tell the story of the Sun and Moon and of the Stars, that Eriol may hearken to his desire,' and Eriol was well pleased, but Gilfanon said: 'Speak on, my Lindo – yet lengthen not the tale for ever.'

Then did Lindo lift up his voice,[6] and it was the most pleasant to hearken to of all tale-tellers, and he said:*

'A tale I tell of that time of the first flight of the Gnomes, and behold they are but newly fled. Now came that grievous news to the Gods and the other Elves, and at first none believed. Nonetheless the tidings came still unto them, and by many different messengers. Some were of the Teleri, who had heard the speech of Fëanor in the square of Kôr and had seen the Noldoli depart thence with all

* Written in the margin: 'Beginning of The Sun and Moon'.

the goods they might convey; others were of the Solosimpi, and these brought the dire tidings of the swanships' rape and the dread kinslaughter of the Haven, and the blood that lay on the white shores of Alqaluntë.

Lastly came some hotfoot from Mandos who had gazed upon that sad throng nigh the strands of Amnor, and the Gods knew that the Gnomes were far abroad, and Varda and all the Elves wept, for now seemed the darkness black indeed and that more than the outward light of the fair Trees was slain.

Strange is to tell that albeit Aulë had loved the Noldoli above all the Elves and had taught them all they knew and given them great stores of wealth, now was his heart most turned against them, for he deemed them ingrate in that they had bidden him no farewell, and for their ill deeds among the Solosimpi he was grieved to the heart. "Speak not," said he, "the name of the Noldoli ever again unto me," and albeit he gave still his love to those few faithful Gnomes who remained still about his halls, yet did he name them thereafter "Eldar".

But the Teleri and the Solosimpi having wept at first, when the onslaught of the Haven became known to all dried their tears and horror and anguish held their hearts, and they too spake seldom of the Noldoli, save sadly or in whispers behind closed doors; and those few of the Noldoli that remained behind were named the Aulenossë or kindred of Aulë, or were taken into the other kindreds, and the Gnome-folk has no place or name remaining now in all Valinor.

Now is it to tell that after a great while it seemed to Manwë that the hunt of the Gods availed nothing, and that surely Melko is now escaped out of Valinor; wherefore he sent Sorontur into the world, and Sorontur came not back for long, and still Tulkas and many others ranged the land, but Manwë stood beside the darkened Trees and his heart was very heavy as he pondered deep and gloomily, but at that time could he see little light of hope. Suddenly there is a sound of wings in that place, for Sorontur King of Eagles is come again on strong wings through the dusk, and behold alighting on the boughs of darkened Silpion he tells how Melko is now broken into the world and many evil spirits are gathered to him: "but," quoth he, "methinks never more will Utumna open unto him, and already is he busy making himself new dwellings in that region of the North where stand the Iron Mountains very high and terrible to see. Yet O Manwë Lord of the Air, other tidings have I also for thy ear, for lo! as I winged my way homeward hither over the black seas and over the unkindly lands a sight I saw of greatest wonder and amaze:

a fleet of white ships that drifted empty in the gales, and some were
burning with bright fires, and as I marvelled behold I saw a great
concourse of folk upon the shores of the Great Lands, and they
gazed all westward, but some were still wandering in the ice – for
know, this was at that place where are the crags of Helkaraksë and
the murderous waters of Qerkaringa flowed of old, which now are
stopped with ice. Swooping methought I heard the sound of wailing
and of sad words spoken in the Eldar tongue; and this tale do I
bring to thee for thy unravelling.''

But Manwë knew thereby that the Noldoli were gone for ever
and their ships burned or abandoned, and Melko too was in the
world, and the hunt of no avail; and belike it is in memory of those
deeds that it has ever been a saying in the mouths of Elves and Men
that those burn their boats who put all hope from them of change of
mind or counsel. Therefore now Manwë lifted up his unmeasurable
voice calling to the Gods, and all those about the wide lands of
Valinor hearkened and returned.

There first came Tulkas weary and dust-covered, for none had
leapt about that plain as he. Seven times had he encompassed all its
width and thrice had he scaled the mountain-wall, and all those
measureless slopes and pastures, meads and forests, he had traversed,
burnt by his desire to punish the spoiler of Valinor. There came
Lórien and leaned against the withered bole of Silpion, and wept the
wrack of his quiet gardens by the trampling hunt; there too was
Meássë and with her Makar, and his hand was red for he had come
upon twain of Melko's comrades as they fled, and he slew them as they
ran, and he alone had aught of joy in those ill times. Ossë was there
and his beard of green was torn and his eyes were dim, and he gasped
leaning on a staff and was very much athirst, for mighty as he was
about the seas and tireless, such desperate travail on the bosom of
Earth spent his vigour utterly.

Salmar and Ómar stood by and their instruments of music made
no sound and they were heavy of heart, yet not so bitterly as was
Aulë, lover of the earth and of all things made or gained by good
labour therefrom, for of all the Gods he had loved Valmar most
wholly and Kôr and all their treasures, and the smile of the fair
plains without, and its ruin cut his heart. With him was Yavanna,
Earth-queen, and she had hunted with the Gods and was spent; but
Vána and Nessa wept as maidens still beside the founts of gold
Kulullin.

Ulmo alone came not to the Trees, but went down to the beach
of Eldamar, and there he stood gazing into the gloom far out to

sea, and he called often with his most mighty voice as though he would draw back those truants to the bosom of the Gods, and whiles he played deep longing music on his magic conches, and to him alone, lest it be[7] Varda lady of the stars, was the going of the Gnomes a greater grief than even the ruin of the Trees. Aforetime had Ulmo loved the Solosimpi very dearly, yet when he heard of their slaughter by the Gnomes he grieved indeed but anger hardened not his heart, for Ulmo was foreknowing more than all the Gods, even than great Manwë, and perchance he saw many of the things that should spring from that flight and the dread pains of the unhappy Noldoli in the world, and the anguish wherewith they would expiate the blood of Kópas, and he would that it need not be.

Now when all were thus come together, then spake Manwë to them and told the tidings of Sorontur and how the chase had failed, but at that time the Gods were wildered in the gloom and had little counsel, and sought each one his home and places of old delight now dead, and there sat in silence and dark pondering. Yet some fared ever and anon out upon the plain and gazed wistfully at the faded Trees as though those withered boughs would one day burgeon with new light: but this came not to pass, and Valinor was full of shadows and of gloom, and the Elves wept and could not be comforted, and the Noldoli had bitter sorrow in the northern lands.

Thereafter in a great time it pierced the grief and the weariness of the Gods that light is gone from Valinor for ever, and that never again will those Trees bloom again at their appointed times. Only the light of the stars remained, save where a glow lay about the fountain of Kulullin playing still or a pale gleam lingered nigh deep Telimpë,[8] vat of dreams. Yet even these were dimmed and tarnished, for the Trees bore dew no more for their replenishment.

Wherefore does Vána arise and seek Lórien, and with them go Urwendi and Silmo[9] and many of both Vali and the Elves; and they gather much light of gold and silver in great vessels and fare sadly to the ruined Trees. There singeth Lórien most wistful songs of magic and enchantment about the stock of Silpion, and he bid water his roots with the radiance of Telimpë; and this was lavishly done, albeit small store thereof remained now in the dwellings of the Gods. In like manner doth Vána, and she sings old golden songs of the happier days, and bids her maidens dance their bright dances even such as they were used to dance upon the sward of the rose-gardens nigh Kulullin, and as they danced she flooded the roots of Laurelin with streams from out her golden jars.

Yet all their singing and enchantment is of little worth, and though the roots of the Trees seem to drink all that they may pour yet can they see no stir of life renewed nor faintest gleam of light; nor withered leaf glows with sap nor blossom lifts its drooping stem. Indeed in the frenzy of their grief they had poured out all the last remaining stores of brightness that the Gods retained, had not of a fortune Manwë and Aulë come upon them in that hour, being drawn thither by their singing in the gloom, and stayed them, saying: "Lo, O Vána, and thou O Lórien, what is this rashness? And wherefore did ye not first take counsel of your brethren? For know ye not that that which ye spill unthinking upon the earth is become more precious than all the things the world contains; and when it is gone perchance not all the wisdom of the Gods may get us more."

Then Vána said: "Pardon, O Manwë Súlimo, and let my sorrow and my tears be my excuse; yet aforetime did this draught fail never to refresh the heart of Laurelin, and she bare ever in return a fruit of light more plentiful than we gave; and methought the Gods sat darkly in their halls and for the weight of their grief essayed no remedy of their ills. But behold now have Lórien and I put forth our spells and nought may they avail," and Vána wept.

Now was it the thought of many that those twain Lórien and Vána might not avail to heal the wounds of Laurelin and Silpion, in that no word of the Earth-lady, mother of magics, was mingled in their spells. Therefore many said: "Let us seek Palúrien, for of her magic maybe these Trees shall again know some portion of their ancient glory – and then if light be renewed Aulë and his craftsmen may repair the hurts of our fair realm, and happiness will be once more twixt Erumáni and the Sea"[10] – but of the darkness and ill days that had long been without the hills few recked or thought.

Now therefore they called for Yavanna, and she came and asked them what they would, and hearing she wept and spake before them, saying: "Know ye, O Valar, and ye sons and daughters of the Eldar, Children of Ilúvatar, first offspring of the forests of the Earth, that never may these Two Trees bloom again, and others like them may not be brought to life for many many ages of the world. Many things shall be done and come to pass, and the Gods grow old, and the Elves come nigh to fading, ere ye shall see the rekindling of these Trees or the Magic Sun relit," and the Gods knew not what she meant, speaking of the Magic Sun, nor did for a long while after. But Tulkas hearing said: "Why speakest thou these words, O Kémi Palúrien, for foretelling is not thy wont, and that of evil least of all?" And others there were who said: "Ay, and never before has Kémi the Earth-lady been hard of counsel or lacked a spell of deepest virtue," and they besought her to put forth her power. But Yavanna said: " 'Tis of fate and the Music of the Ainur. Such marvels as those Trees of gold and silver may even the Gods make but once, and that in the youth of the world; nor may all my spells avail to do what ye now ask."

Then said Vána: "How then sayest thou, Aulë, mighty contriver, who art called *i·Talka Marda* – Smith of the World – for the might of thy works, how are we to obtain light that is needful to our joy? For what is Valinor without light, or what art thou an thou losest thy skill, as, meseems, in this hour thy spouse has done?"

"Nay," said Aulë, "light may not be fashioned by smithcraft, O Vána-Laisi, nor can any even of the Gods devise it, if the sap of the Trees of wonder be dried for ever." But Palúrien answering also said: "Lo, O Tuivána, and ye beside of the Vali and of the Elves, think ye only and always of Valinor, forgetting the world without? – for my heart saith to me that already were it time for the Gods to take up once more the battle for the world and expel therefrom the powers of Melko ere they be waxen to o'erwhelming strength." But Vána comprehended not Palúrien's mind, thinking only of her Tree of gold, and she abode ill-content; but Manwë and Varda, and with them Aulë and Yavanna, fared thence, and in secret conclave they took deep and searching counsel one of another, and at the last they bethought them of a rede of hope. Then did Manwë call together all the folk of Valinor once more; and that great throng was gathered even in Vána's bower amidst her roses, where Kulullin's fountains were, for the plain without lay now all cold and dark. There came even the leaders of the Elves and sat at the feet of the Gods, nor had that before been done; but when all were come together Aulë arose and said: "Hearken ye all. A rede has Manwë Súlimo Valatúru* to declare, and the mind of the Earth-lady and of the Queen of the Stars is therein, nor yet is my counsel absent."

Then was there a great silence that Manwë might speak, and he said: "Behold O my people, a time of darkness has come upon us, and yet I have it in mind that this is not without the desire of Ilúvatar. For the Gods had well-nigh forgot the world that lies without expectant of better days, and of Men, Ilúvatar's younger sons that soon must come. Now therefore are the Trees withered that so filled our land with loveliness and our hearts with mirth that wider desires came not into them, and so behold, we must turn now

---

* In margin: 'also *Valahíru*'.

our thoughts to new devices whereby light may be shed upon both the world without and Valinor within."

Then told he them concerning those stores of radiance they still possessed; for of silver light they had no great store save only that that yet lay in Telimpë, and a lesser measure that Aulë had in basons in his smithy. Some indeed had the Eldar lovingly saved in tiny vessels as it flowed and wasted in the soils about the stricken bole, but it was little enough.

Now the smallness of their store of white light was due to many causes, in that Varda had used greatly of it when she kindled mighty stars about the heavens, both at the coming of the Eldar and at other times. Moreover that Tree Silpion bore dew of light less richly far than Laurelin had been wont to do, and nonetheless, for it was less hot and fiery-subtle, did the Gods and Elves have need of it always in their magic crafts, and had mingled it with all manner of things that they devised, and in this were the Noldoli the chief.

Now golden light not even the Gods could tame much to their uses, and had suffered it to gather in the great vat Kulullin to the great increase of its fountains, or in other bright basons and wide pools about their courts, for the health and glory of its radiance was very great. 'Tis said indeed that those first makers of jewels, of whom Fëanor has the greatest fame, alone of the Eldar knew the secret of subtly taming golden light to their uses, and they dared use their knowledge but very sparingly, and now is that perished with them out of the Earth. Yet even of this golden radiance was there no unfailing source, now that Laurelin dripped her sweet dew no more. Of this necessity did Manwë shape his plan, and it was caught from that very sowing of the stars that Varda did of yore; for to each of the stars had she given a heart of silver flame set in vessels of crystals and pale glass and unimagined substances of faintest colours: and these vessels were some made like to boats, and buoyed by their hearts of light they fared ever about Ilwë, yet could they not soar into the dark and tenuous realm of Vaitya that is outside all. Now winged spirits of the utmost purity and beauty – even the most ethereal of those bright choirs of the Mánir and the Súruli who fare about the halls of Manwë on Taniquetil or traverse all the airs that move upon the world – sate in those starry boats and guided them on mazy courses high above the Earth, and Varda gave them names, but few of these are known.

Others there were whose vessels were like translucent lamps set quivering above the world, in Ilwë or on the very confines of Vilna and the airs we breathe, and they flickered and waned for the stirring of the upper winds, yet abode where they hung and moved not; and of these some were very great and beautiful and the Gods and Elves among all their riches loved them; and thence indeed the jewel-makers catch their inspiration. Not least did they love Morwinyon of the west, whose name meaneth the glint at dusk, and of his setting in the heavens much has been told; and of Nielluin too, who is the Bee of Azure, Nielluin whom still may all men see in autumn or in winter burning nigh the foot of Telimektar son of Tulkas whose tale is yet to tell.

But lo! (said Lindo) the beauty of the stars hath drawn me far afield, and yet I doubt not in that great speech, the mightiest Manwë ever spake before the Gods, mention he made of them yet more loving than was mine. For behold, he desired in this manner to bring the hearts of the Gods to consider his design, and having spoken of the stars he shaped thus his final words: "Behold," said Manwë, "this is now the third essay of the Gods to bring light into dark places, and both the Lamps of the North and South, and the Trees of the plain, Melko hath brought to ruin. Now in the air only hath Melko no power for ill, wherefore it is my rede that we build a great vessel brimming with golden light and the hoarded dews of Laurelin, and this do set afloat like a mighty ship high above the dark realms of the Earth. There shall it thread far courses through the airs and pour its light on all the world twixt Valinórë and the Eastern shores."

Now Manwë designed the course of the ship of light to be between the East and West, for Melko held the North and Ungweliant the South, whereas in the West was Valinor and the blessed realms, and in the East great regions of dark lands that craved for light.

Now it is said (quoth Lindo) that, whereas certain of the Gods of their divine being might, an they wished, fare with a great sudden-ness of speed through Vilna and the low airs, yet might none even of the Valar, not Melko himself, nor any other save Manwë and Varda and their folk alone avail to pass beyond: for this was the word of Ilúvatar when he sped them to the world at their desire, that they should dwell for ever within the world if once they entered it, nor should leave it, until its Great End came, being woven about it in the threads of its fate and becoming part thereof. Yet more, to Manwë alone, knowing the purity and glory of his heart, did Ilúvatar grant the power of visiting the uttermost heights; and breathing the great clear Serene which lies so far above the world that no finest dust of it, nor thinnest odour of its lives, nor faintest echo of its song or sorrow comes there; but far below it gleams palely beneath the stars and the shadows of the Sun and Moon faring back and forth from Valinor flutter upon its face. There walks Manwë Súlimo often far out beyond the stars and watches it with love, and he is very near the heart of Ilúvatar.

But this has ever been and is yet the greatest bitterness to Melko, for in no wise of himself could he now forsake the bosom of the Earth, and belike ye shall yet hear how mightily his envy was increased when the great vessels of radiance set sail; but now is it to tell that so moving were the words and so great their wisdom that[11] the most part of the Gods thought his purpose good, and they said: "Let Aulë busy himself then with all his folk in the fashioning of this ship of light", and few said otherwise, though 'tis told that Lórien was little pleased, fearing lest shadow and quiet and secret places ceased to be, and of a surety Vána might think of little else for the greatness of her vain desire to see the rekindling of the Trees.

Then said Aulë: "The task ye set me is of the utmost difficulty, yet will I do all that I may therein," and he begged the aid of Varda the starfashioner, and those twain departed and were lost in the gloom a great while.

The narrative continues with an account of the failure of Aulë and Varda to devise any substance that was not 'too gross to swim the airs or too frail to bear the radiance of Kulullin'; and when this was made known Vána and Lórien asked that, since Manwë's design had failed, he should command Yavanna to attempt the healing of the Trees.

At length therefore did Manwë bid Yavanna to put forth her power, and she was loath, but the clamour of the folk constrained her, and she begged for some of the radiance of white and gold; but of this would Manwë and Aulë spare only two small phials, saying that if the draught of old had power to heal the Trees already had they been blooming, for Vána and Lórien had poured it unstintingly upon their roots. Then sorrowfully Yavanna stood upon the plain and her form trembled and her face was very pale for the greatness of the effort that her being put forth, striving against fate. The phial of gold she held in her right hand and the silver in her left, and standing between the Trees she lifted them on high, and flames of red and of white arose from each like flowers, and the ground shook, and the earth opened, and a growth of flowers and plants leapt up therefrom about her feet, white and blue about her left side and red and gold about her right, and the Gods sat still and in amaze. Then going she cast each phial upon its proper Tree and sang the songs of unfading growth and a song of resurrection after death and wither-ing; and suddenly she sang no more. Midway she stood between the

Trees and utter silence fell, then there was a great noise heard and none knew what passed, but Palúrien lay swooning on the Earth; but many leapt beside her and raised her from the ground, and she trembled and was afraid.

"Vain, O children of the Gods," she cried, "is all my strength. Lo, at your desire I have poured my power upon the Earth like water, and like water the Earth has sucked it from me – it is gone and I can do no more." And the Trees stood still gaunt and stark, and all the companies wept beholding her, but Manwë said: "Weep not, O children of the Gods, the irreparable harm, for many fair deeds may be yet to do, and beauty hath not perished on the earth nor all the counsels of the Gods been turned to nought"; but nonetheless folk left that place in sorrow, save Vána only, and she clung to the bole of Laurelin and wept.

Now was the time of faintest hope and darkness most profound fallen on Valinor that was ever yet; and still did Vána weep, and she twined her golden hair about the bole of Laurelin and her tears dropped softly at its roots; and even as the dew of her gentle love touched that tree, behold, a sudden pale gleam was born in those dark places. Then gazed Vána in wonder, and even where her first tears fell a shoot sprang from Laurelin, and it budded, and the buds were all of gold, and there came light therefrom like a ray of sunlight beneath a cloud.

Then sped Vána a little way out upon the plain, and she lifted up her sweet voice with all her power and it came trembling faintly to the gates of Valmar, and all the Valar heard. Then said Ómar: "'Tis the voice of Vána's lamentation," but Salmar said: "Nay, listen more, for rather is there joy in that sound," and all that stood by hearkened, and the words they heard were *I·kal'antúlien*, Light hath returned.

Loud then was the murmur about the streets of Valmar, and folk sped thronging over the plain, and when they beheld Vána beneath the Tree and the new shoot of gold then suddenly did a song of very mighty praise and joy burst forth on every tongue; and Tulkas said: "Lo, mightier have the spells of Yavanna proved than her foretelling!" But Yavanna gazing upon Vána's face said: "Alas, 'tis not so, for in this have my spells played but a lesser part, and more potent has the gentle love of Vána been and her falling tears a dew more healing and more tender than all the radiance of old: yet as for my foretelling, soon wilt thou see, O Tulkas, if thou dost but watch."

Then did all the folk gaze on Laurelin, and behold, those buds opened and put forth leaves, and these were of finest gold and of other kind to those of old, and even as they watched the branch bore golden blossom, and it was thronged with flowers. Now as swiftly as its blossoms opened full it seemed a gust of wind came suddenly and shook them from their slender stems, blowing them about the heads of those that watched like jets of fire, and folk thought there was evil in that; but many of the Eldar chased those shining petals far and wide and gathered them in baskets, yet save such as were of golden threads or of other metals these might not contain those ardent blooms and were all consumed and burnt, that the petals were lost again.

One flower there was however greater than the others, more shining, and more richly golden, and it swayed to the winds but fell not; and it grew, and as it grew of its own radiant warmth it fructified. Then as its petals fell and were treasured a fruit there was of great beauty hanging from that bough of Laurelin, but the leaves of the bough grew sere and they shrivelled and shone no more. Even as they dropped to earth the fruit waxed wonderfully, for all the sap and radiance of the dying Tree were in it, and the juices of that fruit were like quivering flames of amber and of red and its pips like shining gold, but its rind was of a perfect lucency smooth as a glass whose nature is transfused with gold and therethrough the moving of its juices could be seen within like throbbing furnace-fires. So great became the light and richness of that growth and the weight of its fruitfulness that the bough bent thereunder, and it hung as a globe of fires before their eyes.

Then said Yavanna to Aulë: "Bear thou up the branch, my lord, lest it snap and the fruit of wonder be dashed rudely to the ground; and the greatest ruth would that be, for know ye all that this is the last flame of life that Laurelin shall show." But Aulë had stood by as one lost in sudden thought since first that fruit came to ripening, and he answered now saying: "Very long indeed did Varda and I seek through the desolate homes and gardens for materials of our craft. Now do I know that Ilúvatar has brought my desire into my hand." Then calling to Tulkas to aid him he severed the stem of that fruit, and they that behold gasped and were astonied at his ruthlessness.

Loudly they murmured, and some cried: "Woe to him that ravishes anew our Tree," and Vána was in great ire. Yet did none dare to draw nigh, for those twain Aulë and Tulkas might scarcely bear up even upon their godlike shoulders that great globe of flame and were tottering beneath it. Hearing their anger indeed Aulë stayed, saying: "Cease ye of little wisdom and have a patience," but even with those words his foot went astray and he stumbled, and even Tulkas might not bear that fruit alone, so that it fell, and striking stony ground burst asunder. Straightway such a blinding radiance leapt forth as even the full bloom of Laurelin had not yielded of old, and the darkened eyes of the Vali were dazzled so that they fell back stunned; but a pillar of light rose from that place smiting the heavens that the stars paled above it and the face of Taniquetil went red afar off, and Aulë alone of all those there was unmoved by sorrow. Then said Aulë: "Of this can I make a ship of light – surpassing even the desire of Manwë," and now Varda and many others, even Vána, understood his purpose and were glad. But they made a mighty corbel of twisted gold, and strewing it with ardent petals of its own bloom they laid therein the halves of the fruit of noon and uplifting it with many hands bore it away with much singing and great hope. Then coming to the courts of Aulë they set it down, and thereupon began the great smithying of the Sun; and this was the most cunning-marvellous of all the works of Aulë Talkamarda, whose works are legion. Of that perfect rind a vessel did he make, diaphanous and shining, yet of a tempered strength, for with spells of his own he overcame its brittleness, nor in any way was its subtle delicacy thereby diminished.

Now the most ardent radiance poured therein neither spilled nor dimmed, nor did that vessel receive any injury therefrom, yet would it swim the airs more lightly than a bird; and Aulë was overjoyed, and he fashioned that vessel like a great ship broad of beam, laying one half of the rind within the other so that its strength might not be broken.

There follows an account of how Vána, repenting of her past murmurings, cut short her golden hair and gave it to the Gods, and from her hair they wove sails and ropes 'more strong than any mariner hath seen, yet of the slenderness of gossamer'. The masts and spars of the ship were all of gold.

Then that the Ship of the Heavens might be made ready unto the last, the unfading petals of the latest flower of Laurelin were gathered like a star at her prow, and tassels and streamers of glancing light were hung about her bulwarks, and a flash of lightning was caught in her mast to be a pennant; but all that vessel was filled to the brim with the blazing radiance of gold Kulullin and mingled therein drops of the juices of the fruit of noon, and these were very hot, and thereafter scarcely might the bosom of the Earth withhold her, and she leapt at her cords like a captive bird that listeth for the airs.

Then did the Gods name that ship, and they called her Sári which

is the Sun, but the Elves Úr which is fire;[12] but many other names
does she bear in legend and in poesy. The Lamp of Vána is she
named among the Gods in memory of Vána's tears and her sweet
tresses that she gave; and the Gnomes call her Galmir the goldgleamer[13] and Glorvent the ship of gold, and Bráglorin the blazing
vessel, and many a name beside; and her names among Men no man
has counted them.

Behold now it is to be told how while that galleon was a-building
others nigh to where the Two Trees once grew fashioned a great
bason and folk laboured mightily at it. Its floor they made of gold
and its walls of polished bronze, and an arcade of golden pillars
topped with fires engirdled it, save only on the East; but Yavanna
set a great and nameless spell around it, so that therein was poured
the most of the waters of the fruit of noon and it became a bath
of fire. Indeed is it not called Tanyasalpë, the bowl of fire, even
Faskalanúmen, the Bath of the Setting Sun, for here when Urwendi
after returned from the East and the first sunset came on Valinor the
ship was drawn down and its radiance refreshed against new voyagings
on the morrow while the Moon held High Heaven.

Now the making of this place of fire is more wondrous than seems,
for so subtle were those radiances that set in the air they spilled not
nor sank, nay rather they rose and floated away far above Vilna,
being of the utmost buoyancy and lightness; yet now did nought
escape from Faskalan which burnt amid the plain, and light came to
Valinor therefrom, yet by reason of the deepness of the bason it
fared not far abroad and the ring of shadows stood close in.

Then said Manwë, looking upon the glory of that ship as it strained
to be away: "Who shall steer us this boat and guide its course above
the realms of Earth, for even the holy bodies of the Valar, meseems,
may not for long endure to bathe in this great light."

But a great thought came into the heart of Urwendi, and she said
that she was not adread, and begged leave to become the mistress
of the Sun and to make herself ready for that office as Ilúvatar set it
in her heart to do. Then did she bid a many of her maidens follow
her, even of those who had aforetime watered the roots of Laurelin
with light, and casting aside their raiment they went down into that
pool Faskalan as bathers into the sea, and its golden foams went over
their bodies, and the Gods saw them not and were afraid. But after
a while they came again to the brazen shores and were not as before,
for their bodies were grown lucent and shone as with an ardour
within, and light flashed from their limbs as they moved, nor might
any raiment endure to cover their glorious bodies any more. Like

air were they, and they trod as lightly as does sunlight on the earth, and saying no word they climbed upon the ship, and that vessel heaved against its great cords and all the folk of Valinor might scarce restrain it.

Now at last by Manwë's command do they climb the long slopes of Taniquetil and draw i·Kalaventë the Ship of Light along with them, nor is that any great task; and now do they stand on the wide space before great Manwë's doors, and the ship is on the western slope of the mountain trembling and tugging at its bonds, and already so great is its glory become that sunbeams pour out over the shoulders of Taniquetil and a new light is in the sky, and the waters of the Shadowy Seas beyond are touched with such fire as they never yet had seen. In that hour 'tis said that all creatures that wandered in the world stood still and wondered, even as Manwë going spake to Urwendi and said: "Go now, most wondrous maiden washed in fire, and steer the ship of divine light above the world, that joy may search out its narrowest crannies and all the things that sleep within its bosom may awake";[14] but Urwendi answered not, looking only eagerly to the East, and Manwë bade cast the ropes that held her, and straightway the Ship of the Morning arose above Taniquetil and the bosom of the air received it.

Ever as it rose it burned the brighter and the purer till all Valinor was filled with radiance, and the vales of Erúmáni and the Shadowy Seas were bathed in light, and sunshine was spilled on the dark plain of Arvalin, save only where Ungweliantë's clinging webs and darkest fumes still lay too thick for any radiance to filter through.

Then all looking up saw that heaven was blue, and very bright and beautiful, but the stars fled as that great dawn came upon the world; and a gentle wind blew from the cold lands to meet the vessel and filled its gleaming sails, and white vapours mounted from off the misty seas below toward her, that her prow seemed to cleave a white and airy foam. Yet did she waver not, for the Mánir that fared about her drew her by golden cords, and higher and higher the Sun's great galleon arose, until even to the sight of Manwë it was but a disc of fire wreathed in veils of splendour that slowly and majestically wandered from the West.

Now ever as it drew further on its way so grew the light in Valinor more mellow, and the shadows of the houses of the Gods grew long, slanting away towards the waters of the Outer Seas, but Taniquetil threw a great westering shadow that waxed ever longer and deeper, and it was afternoon in Valinor.'

Then said Gilfanon laughing: 'Nay, but, good sir, you lengthen the tale mightily, for methinks you love to dwell upon the works and deeds of the great Gods, but an you set not a measure to your words our stranger here will live not to hear of those things that happened in the world when at length the Gods gave to it the light they so long had withholden – and such tales, methinks, were a variety pleasing to hear.'

But Eriol had of a sooth been listening very eagerly to the sweet voice of Lindo, and he said: 'But a little while agone, a day perchance the Eldar would esteem it, did I come hither, yet no longer do I love the name of stranger, neither will Lindo ever lengthen the tale beyond my liking, whatsoever he tells, but behold this history is all to my heart.'

But Lindo said: 'Nay, nay, I have indeed more to tell; yet, O Eriol, the things that Gilfanon hath upon his lips are well worth the hearing – indeed never have I nor any here heard a full count of these matters. As soon therefore as may be will I wind up my tale and make an end, but three nights hence let us have another tale-telling, and it shall be one of greater ceremony, and musics there shall be, and all the children of the House of Lost Play shall here be gathered together at his feet to hear Gilfanon relate the travail of the Noldoli and the coming of Mankind.'

Now these words mightily pleased Gilfanon and Eriol, and many beside were glad, but now doth Lindo proceed:

'Know then that to such vast heights did the Sunship climb, and climbing blazed ever hotter and brighter, that ere long its glory was wider than ever the Gods conceived of when that vessel was still harboured in their midst. Everywhere did its great light pierce and all the vales and darkling woods, the bleak slopes and rocky streams, lay dazzled by it, and the Gods were amazed. Great was the magic and wonder of the Sun in those days of bright Urwendi, yet not so tender and so delicately fair as had the sweet Tree Laurelin once been; and thus whisper of new discontent awoke in Valinor, and words ran among the children of the Gods, for Mandos and Fui were wroth, saying that Aulë and Varda would for ever be meddling with the due order of the world, making it a place where no quiet or peaceful shadow could remain; but Lórien sat and wept in a grove of trees beneath the shade of Taniquetil and looked upon his gardens stretching beneath, still disordered by the great hunt of the Gods, for he had not had the heart for their mending. There the nightin-gales were silent for the heat danced above the trees, and his poppies were withered, and his evening flowers drooped and gave no scent; and Silmo stood sadly by Telimpë that gleamed wanly as still waters rather than the shining dew of Silpion, so overmastering was the great light of day. Then Lórien arose and said to Manwë: "Call back your glittering ship, O Lord of the Heavens, for the eyes of us ache by reason of its flaming, and beauty and soft sleep is driven far away. Rather the darkness and our memories than this, for this is not the old loveliness of Laurelin, and Silpion is no more." Nor were any of the Gods utterly content, knowing in their hearts that they had done a greater thing than they at first knew, and never again would Valinor see such ages as had passed; and Vána said that Kulullin's fount was dulled and her garden wilted in the heat, and her roses lost their hues and fragrance, for the Sun then sailed nearer to the Earth than it now does.

Then Manwë chid them for their fickleness and discontent, but they were not appeased; and suddenly spake Ulmo, coming from outer Vai: "Lord Manwë, neither are their counsels nor thine to be despised. Have ye then not yet understood, O Valar, wherein lay much of the great beauty of the Trees of old? — In change, and in slow alternation of fair things, the passing blending sweetly with that which was to come."

But Lórien said suddenly: "O Valatúru, the Lord of Vai speaketh words wiser than ever before, and they fill me with a great longing," and he left them thereupon and went out upon the plain, and it was then three daytimes, which is the length of three blossomings of Laurelin of old, since the Ship of Morning was unmoored. Then for four daytimes more sate Lórien beside the stock of Silpion and the shadows gathered shyly round him, for the Sun was far to the East, beating about the heavens where it listed, since Manwë had not as yet ruled its course and Urwendi was bidden fare as seemed good to her. Yet even so Lórien is not appeased, not though the darkness of the mountains creep across the plain, and a mist bloweth in from off the sea and a vague and flitting twilight gathers once more in Valinor, but long he sits pondering why the spells of Yavanna wrought only upon Laurelin.

Then Lórien sang to Silpion, saying that the Valar were lost 'in a wilderness of gold and heat, or else in shadows full of death and unkindly glooms,' and he touched the wound in the bole of the Tree.

Lo, even as he touched that cruel hurt, a light glowed faintly there as if radiant sap still stirred within, but a low branch above Lórien's bowed head burgeoned suddenly, and leaves of a very dark green, long and oval, budded and unfolded upon it, yet was all the Tree beside bare and dead and has ever been so since. Now it was at that time seven times seven days since the fruit of noon was born upon Laurelin, and many of the Eldar and of the sprites and of the Gods were drawn nigh, listening to Lórien's song; but he heeded them not, gazing upon the Tree.

Lo, its new leaves were crusted with a silver moisture, and their undersides were white and set with pale gleaming filaments. Buds there were of flowers also upon the bough, and they opened, but a dark mist of the sea gathered about the tree, and the air grew bitterly cold as it never before had been in Valinor, and those blossoms faded and fell and none heeded them. One only was there at the branch's end that opening shone of its own light and no mist or cold harmed it, but indeed waxing it seemed to suck the very vapours and transform them subtly to the silver substance of its body; and it grew to be a very pale and wondrous glistering flower, nor did even the purest snow upon Taniquetil gleaming in the light of Silpion outrival it, and its heart was of white flame and it throbbed, waxing and waning marvellously. Then said Lórien for the joy of his heart: "Behold the Rose of Silpion", and that rose grew till the fruit of Laurelin had been but little greater, and ten thousand crystal petals were in that flower, and it was drenched in a fragrant dew like honey and this dew was light. Now Lórien would suffer none to draw near, and this will he rue for ever: for the branch upon which the Rose hung yielded all its sap and withered, nor even yet would he suffer that blossom to be plucked gently down, being enamoured of its loveliness and lusting to see it grow mightier than the fruit of noon, more glorious than the Sun.

Then snapped the withered bough and the Rose of Silpion fell, and some of its dewy light was roughly shaken from it, and here and there a petal was crushed and tarnished, and Lórien cried aloud and sought to lift it gently up, but it was too great. Therefore did the Gods let send to Aulë's halls, for there was a great silver charger, like to a table of the giants, and they set the latest bloom of Silpion upon it, and despite its hurts its glory and fragrance and pale magic were very great indeed.

Now when Lórien had mastered his grief and ruth he spake the counsel that Ulmo's words had called to his heart: that the Gods build another vessel to match the galleon of the Sun, "and it shall be made from the Rose of Silpion," said he, "and in memory of the waxing and waning of these Trees for twelve hours shall the Sunship sail the heavens and leave Valinor, and for twelve shall Silpion's pale bark mount the skies, and there shall be rest for tired eyes and weary hearts."

This then was the manner of the shaping of the Moon, for Aulë would not dismember the loveliness of the Rose of Silver, and he called rather to him certain of those Eldar of his household who were of the Noldoli of old[15] and had consorted with the jewel-makers. Now these revealed to him much store of crystals and delicate glasses that Fëanor and his sons[16] had laid up in secret places in Sirnúmen, and with the aid of those Elves and of Varda of the stars, who gave even of the light of those frail boats of hers to give limpid clearness to their fashioning, he brought to being a substance thin as a petal of a rose, clear as the most transparent elfin glass, and very smooth, yet might Aulë of his skill bend it and fashion it, and naming it he called it *virin*. Of *virin* now he built a marvellous vessel, and often have men spoken of the Ship of the Moon, yet is it scarce like to any bark that sailed or sea or air. Rather was it like an island of pure glass, albeit not very great, and tiny lakes there were bordered with snowy flowers that shone, for the water of those pools that gave them sap was the radiance of Telimpë. Midmost of that shim-mering isle was wrought a cup of that crystalline stuff that Aulë made and therein the magic Rose was set, and the glassy body of the vessel sparkled wonderfully as it gleamed therein. Rods there were and perchance they were of ice, and they rose upon it like aëry masts, and sails were caught to them by slender threads, and Uinen wove them of white mists and foam, and some were sprent with glinting scales of silver fish, some threaded with tiniest stars like points of light – sparks caught in snow when Nielluin was shining.

Thus was the Ship of the Moon, the crystal island of the Rose, and the Gods named it Rána, the Moon, but the fairies Sil, the Rose,[17] and many a sweet name beside. Ilsaluntë or the silver shallop has it been called, and thereto the Gnomes have called it Minethlos or the argent isle and Crithosceleg the disc of glass.

Now Silmo begged to sail upon the oceans of the firmament therein, but he might not, for neither was he of the children of the air nor might he find a way to cleanse his being of its earthwardness as had Urwendi[18] done, and little would it have availed to enter Faskalan had he dared essay it, for then would Rána have shrivelled before him. Manwë bade therefore Ilinsor, a spirit of the Súruli who loved the snows and the starlight and aided Varda in many of her works, to pilot this strange-gleaming boat, and with him went many another spirit of the air arrayed in robes of silver and white, or else of palest gold; but an aged Elf with hoary locks stepped upon the Moon unseen and hid him in the Rose, and there dwells he ever since and tends that flower, and a little white turret has he builded on the Moon where often he climbs and watches the heavens, or the world beneath, and that is Uolë Kúvion who sleepeth never. Some indeed have named him the Man in the Moon, but Ilinsor is it rather who hunts the stars.

Now is to tell how the plan that Lórien devised was changed, for the white radiance of Silpion is by no means so buoyant and ethereal as is the flame of Laurelin, nor *virin* so little weighty as the rind of the bright fruit of noon; and when the Gods laded the white ship with light and would launch it upon the heavens, behold, it would not rise above their heads. Moreover, behold, that living Rose continued to give forth a honey as of light that distills upon the isle of glass, and a dew of moonbeams glistens there, yet rather does this weigh the vessel than buoy it as did the increase of the Sunship's flames. So is it that Ilinsor must return at times, and that overflowing radiance of the Rose is stored in Valinor against dark days – and it is to tell that such days come ever and anon, for then the white flower of the isle wanes and scarcely shines, and then must it be refreshed and watered with its silver dew, much as Silpion was wont of old to be.

Hence was it that a pool was builded hard by the dark southern wall of Valmar, and of silver and white marbles were its walls, but dark yews shut it in, being planted in a maze most intricate about it. There Lórien hoarded the pale dewy light of that fair Rose, and he named it the Lake Irtinsa.

So comes it that for fourteen nights men may see Rána's bark float upon the airs, and for other fourteen the heavens know it not; while even on those fair nights when Rána fares abroad it showeth not ever the same aspect as doth Sári the glorious, for whereas that bright galleon voyageth even above Ilwë and beyond the stars and cleaveth a dazzling way blinding the heavens, highest of all things recking little of winds or motions of the airs, yet Ilinsor's bark is heavier and less filled with magic and with power, and fareth never above the skies but saileth in the lower folds of Ilwë threading a white swathe among the stars. For this reason the high winds trouble it at times, tugging at its misty shrouds; and often are these torn and scattered, and the Gods renew them. At times too are the petals of the Rose ruffled, and its white flames blown hither and thither like a silver candle guttering in the wind. Then doth Rána heave and toss about the air, as often you may see him, and mark the slender curve of his bright keel, his prow now dipping, now his stern; and whiles again he sails serenely to the West, and up through the pure lucency of his frame the wide Rose of Silpion is seen, and some say the aged form of Uolë Kúvion beside.

Then indeed is the Ship of the Moon very fair to look upon, and the Earth is filled with slender lights and deep quick-moving shadows, and radiant dreams go with cool wings about the world, but Lórien has ruth amid his gladness, because his flower bears yet, and will for ever, the faint marks of its bruising and its fall; and all men can see them clearly.

But[19] lo,' saith Lindo, 'I run on ahead, for yet have I only told that the silver ship is newly built, and Ilinsor yet but first stepped aboard – and now do the Gods draw that vessel once again up the steep sides of old Taniquetil singing as they go songs of Lórien's folk that long have been dumb in Valinor. Slower was that wayfaring than the lifting of the Ship of Morn, and all the folk strain lustily at the ropes, until Oromë coming harnesses thereto a herd of wild white horses, and thus comes the vessel to the topmost place.

Then behold, the galleon of the Sun is seen afar beating golden from the East, and the Valar marvel to descry the glowing peaks of many a mountain far away, and isles glimmering green in seas once dark. Then cried Ossë: "Look, O Manwë, but the sea is blue, as blue wellnigh as Ilwë that thou lovest!" and "Nay," said Manwë, "envy we not Ilwë, for the sea is not blue alone, but grey and green and purple, and most beauteous-flowered with foaming white. Nor jade nor amethyst nor porphyry set with diamonds and with pearls outrival the waters of the Great and little seas when the sunlight drenches them."

So saying Manwë sent Fionwë his son, swiftest of all to move about the airs, and bade him say to Urwendi that the bark of the Sun come back awhile to Valinor, for the Gods have counsels for her ear; and Fionwë fled most readily, for he had conceived a great love for that bright maiden long ago, and her loveliness now, when bathed in fire she sate as the radiant mistress of the Sun, set him aflame with the eagerness of the Gods. So was it that Urwendi brought her ship unwilling above Valinor, and Oromë cast a noose of gold about it, and it was drawn slowly down upon the Earth, and behold, the woods upon Taniquetil glowed once more in the mingled light of silver and of gold, and all were minded of the ancient blending of the Trees; but Ilsaluntë paled before the galleon of the Sun till almost it seemed to burn no more. So ended the first day upon the world, and it was very long and full of many marvellous deeds that Gilfanon may tell; but now the Gods beheld the evening deepen over the world as the Sunship was drawn down and the glow upon the mountains faded, and the sparkle of the seas went out. Then the primeval darkness crept out again once more from many stealthy lairs, but Varda was glad to see the steady shining of the stars. Far upon the plain was Sári drawn, and when she was gone Ilsaluntë was haled upon the topmost peak so that his white lucency fell out thence over the wide world and the first night was come. Indeed in these days darkness is no more within the borders of the world, but only night, and night is another and a different thing, by reason of the Rose of Silpion.

Now however does Aulë fill the brimming vessel of that flower with white radiance, and many of the Súruli white-winged glide beneath and bear it slowly up and set it among the company of the stars. There does it swim slowly, a pale and glorious thing, and Ilinsor and his comrades sit them upon its rim and with shimmering oars urge it bravely through the sky; and Manwë breathed upon its bellying sails till it was wafted far away, and the beat of the unseen oars against the winds of night faded and grew faint.

Of this manner was the first rising of the Moon above Taniquetil, and Lórien rejoiced, but Ilinsor was jealous of the supremacy of the Sun, and he bade the starry mariners flee before him and the constellate lamps go out, but many would not, and often he set sail in chase of them, and the little ships of Varda fled before the huntsman of the firmament, and were not caught: – and that, said Lindo, 'is all, methinks, I know to tell of the building of those marvellous ships and their launching on the air.'[20]

'But,' said Eriol, 'nay, surely that is not so, for at the tale's beginning methought you promised us words concerning the present courses of the Sun and Moon and their rising in the East, and I for one, by the leave of the others here present am not minded to release you of your word.'

Then quoth Lindo laughing, 'Nay, I remember not the promise, and did I make it then it was rash indeed, for the things you ask are nowise easy to relate, and many matters concerning the deeds in those days in Valinor are hidden from all save only the Valar. Now however am I fain rather to listen, and thou Vairë perchance will take up the burden of the tale.'

Thereat did all rejoice, and the children clapped their hands, for dearly did they love those times when Vairë was the teller of the tale; but Vairë said:

'Lo, tales I tell of the deep days, and the first is called *The Hiding of Valinor.*'

## NOTES

1 The manuscript has here *Gilfan a·Davrobel*, but in the rejected

earlier version of this passage the reading is *Gilfanon a·Davrobel,* suggesting that *Gilfan* was not intentional.

2  See pp. 24–5 on the relation of Tavrobel to the Staffordshire village of Great Haywood. At Great Haywood the river Sow joins the Trent.

3  In the rejected version of this 'interlude' Gilfanon's history is differently recounted: 'he was long before an Ilkorin and had dwelt ages back in Hisilómë'; 'he came to Tol Eressëa after the great march [i.e. Inwë's 'march into the world', the great expedition from Kôr, see p. 26], for he had adopted blood-kinship with the Noldoli.' – This is the first occurrence of the term *Ilkorin,* which refers to Elves who were 'not of Kôr' (cf. the later term *Úmanyar,* Elves 'not of Aman'). *Artanor* is the precursor of Doriath.

4  Gilfanon, a Gnome, is here called the oldest of the *fairies;* see p. 51.

5  No explanation of 'the House of the Hundred Chimneys', near the bridge of Tavrobel, is known to me, but I have never visited Great Haywood, and it may be that there was (or is) a house there that gave rise to it.

6  The rejected form of the 'interlude' is quite different in its latter part:

> Therefore said Lindo in answer to Eriol: 'Behold, Gilfanon here can tell you much of such matters, but first of all must you be told of the deeds that were done in Valinor when Melko slew the Trees and the Gnomes marched away into the darkness. 'Tis a long tale but well worth the hearkening.' For Lindo loved to tell such tales and sought often an occasion for recalling them; but Gilfanon said: 'Speak on, my Lindo, but methinks the tale will not be told tonight or for many a night after, and I shall have fared long back to Tavrobel.' 'Nay,' said Lindo, 'I will not make the tale overlong, and tomorrow shall be all your own.' And so saying Gilfanon sighed, but Lindo lifted up his voice . . .

7  'lest it be': this curious expression is clear in the manuscript; the usage seems wholly unrecorded, but the meaning intended must be 'unless it be', i.e. 'to him alone, unless also to Varda . . .'

8  On *Telimpë* as the name of the 'Moon-cauldron', rather than *Silindrin,* see pp. 79 and 129 note 2.

9  See pp. 73, 88. At previous occurrences the name is *Urwen,* not *Urwendi.*

10  'twixt Erumáni and the Sea': i.e., the Outer Sea, Vai, the western bound of Valinor.

11  The passage beginning 'For behold, he desired in this manner . . .' on p. 182 and continuing to this point was added on a detached sheet and replaced a very much shorter passage in which Manwë briefly declared his plan, and nothing was said about the powers of the Valar. But I do not think that the replacement was composed significantly later than the body of the text.

12  The earlier reading here was: 'Then did the Gods name that ship, and they called her Ûr which is the Sun', etc.

13  The earlier reading here was: 'and the Gnomes call her Aur the Sun, and Galmir the goldgleamer', etc.

14  An isolated note refers to the coming forth of more wholesome
    creatures when the Sun arose (i.e. over the Great Lands), and says
    that 'all the birds sang in the first dawn'.

15  The Aulenossë: see p. 176.

16  This is the first appearance of the Sons of Fëanor.

17  Earlier reading: 'the silver rose'.

18  *Urwendi*: manuscript *Urwandi*, but I think that this was probably
    unintended.

19  From this point the text of the *Tale of the Sun and Moon* ceases to
    be written over an erased pencilled original, and from the same
    point the original text is extant in another book. In fact, to the end
    of the *Tale of the Sun and Moon* the differences are slight, no more
    than alterations of wording; but the original text does explain the
    fact that at the first occurrence of the name *Gilfanon* on p. 189
    the original reading was *Ailios*. One would guess in any case that
    this was a slip, a reversion to an earlier name, and that this is so is
    shown by the first version, which has, for 'many marvellous deeds
    that Gilfanon may tell' (p. 194), 'many marvellous deeds as Ailios
    shall tell'.

20  From this point the second version diverges sharply from the first.
    The first reads as follows:

    And that is all, methinks,' said Lindo, 'that I know to tell of those
    fairest works of the Gods'; but Ailios said: 'Little doth it cost thee
    to spin the tale, an it be of Valinor; it is a while since ye offered
    us a . . . . . tale concerning the rising of the Sun and Moon in the
    East, and a flow of speech has poured from thee since then, but
    now art thou minded to [?tease], and no word of that promise.'
    Of a truth Ailios beneath his roughness liked the words of Lindo
    as well as any, and he was eager to learn of the matter.
       'That is easy told,' said Lindo . . .

    What follows in the original version relates to the matter of the
    next chapter (see p. 220 note 2).
       Ailios here claims that a promise made by Lindo has not been
    fulfilled, just as does Eriol, more politely, in the second version.
    The beginning of the tale in the first version is not extant, and
    perhaps as it was originally written Lindo did make this promise;
    but in the second he says no such thing (indeed Eriol's question
    was 'Whence be the Sun and Moon?'), and at the end of his tale
    denies that he had done so, when Eriol asserts it.

## Changes made to names in
## *The Tale of the Sun and Moon*

*Amnor* ⟨ *Amnos* (*Amnos* is the form in *The Flight of the Noldoli*, ⟨ *Emnon*;
    the form *Amnon* also occurs, see p. 172).

For changes in the passage on the names of the Sun see notes 12 and 13.
*Gilfanon* ⟨ *Ailios* (p. 189, at the first occurrence only, see note 19).
*Minethlos* ⟨ *Mainlos*.
*Uolë Kúvion* ⟨ *Uolë Mikúmi*, only at the second occurrence on p. 193;
    at the first occurrence, *Uolë Mikúmi* was left unchanged, though
    I have given *Uolë Kúvion* in the text.
*Ship of Morning* ⟨ *Kalaventë* (p. 190; *i·Kalaventë* 'the Ship of Light'
    occurs unemended in the text on p. 188).
*the Sunship's flames* ⟨ *the flames of Kalaventë* (p. 193).
*Sári* ⟨ *Kalavénë* (pp. 193, 195. *Kalavénë* is the form in the original
    version, see note 19).

## Commentary on
### The Tale of the Sun and Moon

The effect of the opening of this tale is undoubtedly to emphasize more
strongly than in the later accounts the horror aroused by the deeds of
the Noldoli (notable is Aulë's bitterness against them, of which nothing
is said afterwards), and also the finality and absoluteness of their exclusion
from Valinor. But the idea that some Gnomes remained in Valinor (the
Aulenossë, p. 176) survived; cf. *The Silmarillion* p. 84:

> And of all the Noldor in Valinor, who were grown now to a great
> people, but one tithe refused to take the road: some for the love that
> they bore to the Valar (and to Aulë not least), some for the love of
> Tirion and the many things that they had made; none for fear of peril
> by the way.

Sorontur's mission and the tidings that he brought back were to be
abandoned. Very striking is his account of the empty ships drifting, of
which 'some were burning with bright fires': the origin of Fëanor's burning
of the ships of the Teleri at Losgar in *The Silmarillion* (p. 90), where
however there is a more evident reason for doing so. That Melko's second
dwelling-place in the Great Lands was distinct from Utumna is here
expressly stated, as also that it was in the Iron Mountains (cf. pp. 149,
158); the name *Angamandi* 'Hells of Iron' has occurred once in the *Lost
Tales*, in the very strange account of the fate of Men after death (p. 77).
In later accounts Angband was built on the site of Utumno, but finally
they were separated again, and in *The Silmarillion* Angband had existed
from ancient days before the captivity of Melkor (p. 47). It is not explained
in the present tale why 'never more will Utumna open to him' (p. 176),
but doubtless it was because Tulkas and Ulmo broke its gates and piled
hills of stone upon them (p. 104).
    In the next part of the tale (pp. 177 ff.) much light is cast on my father's
early conception of the powers and limitations of the great Valar. Thus

Yavanna and Manwë (brought to this realization by Yavanna?) are shown
to believe that the Valar have done ill, or at least failed to achieve the
wider designs of Ilúvatar ('I have it in mind that this [time of darkness]
is not without the desire of Ilúvatar'): the idea of 'selfish', inward-looking
Gods is plainly expressed, Gods content to tend their gardens and devise
their devisings behind their mountains, leaving 'the world' to shape itself
as it may. And this realization is an essential element in their conceiving
the making of the Sun and Moon, which are to be such bodies as may light
not only 'the blessed realms' (an expression which occurs here for the
first time, p. 182) but all the rest of the dark Earth. Of all this there is
only a trace in *The Silmarillion* (p. 99):

> These things the Valar did, recalling in their twilight the darkness of
> the lands of Arda; and they resolved now to illumine Middle-earth and
> with light to hinder the deeds of Melkor.

Of much interest also is the 'theological' statement in the early narrative
concerning the binding of the Valar to the World as the condition of their
entering it (p. 182); cf. *The Silmarillion* p. 20:

> But this condition Ilúvatar made, or it is the necessity of their love,
> that their power should thenceforward be contained and bounded in
> the World, to be within it for ever, until it is complete, so that they are
> its life and it is theirs.

In the tale this condition is an express physical limitation: none of the
Valar, save Manwë and Varda and their attendant spirits, could pass into
the higher airs above Vilna, though they could move at great speed within
the lowest air.

From the passage on p. 178, where it is said that Ulmo, despite his love
for the Solosimpi and grief at the Kinslaying, was yet not filled with anger
against the Noldoli, for he 'was foreknowing more than all the Gods,
even than great Manwë', it is seen that Ulmo's peculiar concern for the
exiled Eldar – which plays such an important if mysterious part in the
development of the story – was there from the beginning; as also was
Yavanna's thought, expressed in *The Silmarillion* p. 78:

> Even for those who are mightiest under Ilúvatar there is some work
> that they may accomplish once, and once only. The Light of the Trees
> I brought into being, and within Eä I can do so never again.

Yavanna's reference to the Magic Sun and its relighting (which has appeared
in the toast drunk in the evening in the Cottage of Lost Play, pp. 17, 65)
is obviously intended to be obscure at this stage.

There is no later reference to the story of the wastage of light by Lórien
and Vána, pouring it over the roots of the Trees unavailingly.

Turning to Lindo's account of the stars (pp. 181–2), *Morwinyon* has appeared in an earlier tale (p. 114), with the story that Varda dropped it 'as she fared in great haste back to Valinor', and that it 'blazes above the world's edge in the west'; in the present tale Morwinyon (which according to both the Qenya and Gnomish word-lists is Arcturus) is again strangely represented as being a luminary always of the western sky. It is said here that while some of the stars were guided by the Mánir and the Súruli 'on mazy courses', others, including Morwinyon and Nielluin, 'abode where they hung and moved not'. Is the explanation of this that in the ancient myths of the Elves there was a time when the regular apparent movement of all the heavenly bodies from East to West had not yet begun? This movement is nowhere explained mythically in my father's cosmology.

Nielluin ('Blue Bee') is Sirius (in *The Silmarillion* called *Helluin*), and this star had a place in the legend of Telimektar son of Tulkas, though the story of his conversion into the constellation of Orion was never clearly told (cf. *Telumehtar* 'Orion' in *The Lord of the Rings* Appendix E, I). Nielluin was Inwë's son Ingil, who followed Telimektar 'in the likeness of a great bee bearing honey of flame' (see the Appendix on Names under *Ingil* and *Telimektar*).

The course of the Sun and Moon between East and West (rather than in some other direction) is here given a rationale, and the reason for avoiding the South is Ungweliant's presence there. This seems to give Ungweliant a great importance and also a vast area subject to her power of absorbing light. It is not made clear in the tale of *The Darkening of Valinor* where her dwelling was. It is said (p. 151) that Melko wandered 'the dark plains of Eruman, and farther south than anyone yet had penetrated he found a region of the deepest gloom' – the region where he found the cavern of Ungweliant, which had 'a subterranean outlet on the sea'; and after the destruction of the Trees Ungweliant 'gets her gone southward and over the mountains to her home' (p. 154). It is impossible to tell from the vague lines on the little map (p. 81) what was at this time the configuration of the southern lands and seas.

In comparison with the last part of the tale, concerning the last fruit of Laurelin and the last flower of Silpion, the making from them of the Sun and Moon, and the launching of their vessels (pp. 183–95), Chapter XI of *The Silmarillion* (constituted from two later versions not greatly dissimilar the one from the other) is extremely brief. Despite many differences the later versions read in places almost as summaries of the early story, but it is often hard to say whether the shortening depends rather on my father's feeling (certainly present, see p. 174) that the description was too long, was taking too large a place in the total structure, or an actual rejection of some of the ideas it contains, and a desire to diminish the extreme 'concreteness' of its images. Certainly there is here a revelling in materials of 'magic' property, gold, silver, crystal, glass, and above all light conceived as a liquid element, or as dew, as honey, an element that can be bathed in and gathered into vessels, that has quite

largely disappeared from *The Silmarillion* (although, of course, the idea
of light as liquid, dripping down, poured and hoarded, sucked up by
Ungoliant, remained essential to the conception of the Trees, this idea
becomes in the later writing less palpable and the divine operations are
given less 'physical' explanation and justification).

As a result of this fullness and intensity of description, the origin of the
Sun and Moon in the last fruit and last flower of the Trees has less of
mystery than in the succinct and beautiful language of *The Silmarillion*;
but also much is said here to emphasize the great size of the 'Fruit of
Noon', and the increase in the heat and brilliance of the Sunship after its
launching, so that the reflection rises less readily that if the Sun that
brilliantly illumines the whole Earth was but one fruit of Laurelin then
Valinor must have been painfully bright and hot in the days of the Trees.
In the early story the last outpourings of life from the dying Trees are
utterly strange and 'enormous', those of Laurelin portentous, even
ominous; the Sun is astoundingly bright and hot even to the Valar, who are
awestruck and disquieted by what has been done (the Gods knew 'that
they had done a greater thing than they at first knew', p. 190); and the anger
and distress of certain of the Valar at the burning light of the Sun enforces
the feeling that in the last fruit of Laurelin a terrible and unforeseen power
has been released. This distress does indeed survive in *The Silmarillion*
(p. 100), in the reference to 'the prayers of Lórien and Estë, who said that
sleep and rest had been banished from the Earth, and the stars were
hidden'; but in the tale the blasting power of the new Sun is intensely
conveyed in the images of 'the heat dancing above the trees' in the gardens
of Lórien, the silent nightingales, the withered poppies and the drooping
evening flowers.

In the old story there is a mythical explanation of the Moon's phases
(though not of eclipses), and of the markings on its face through the
story of the breaking of the withered bough of Silpion and the fall of the
Moonflower – a story altogether at variance with the explanation given in
*The Silmarillion* (*ibid.*). In the tale the fruit of Laurelin also fell to the
ground, when Aulë stumbled and its weight was too great for Tulkas to
bear alone: the significance of this event is not made perfectly clear, but
it seems that, had the Fruit of Noon not burst asunder, Aulë would not
have understood its structure and conceived that of the Sunship.

To whatever extent the great differences between the versions in this
part of the Mythology may be due to later compression, there remain a
good many actual contradictions, of which I note here only some of the
more important, in addition to that concerning the markings on the Moon
already mentioned. Thus in *The Silmarillion* the Moon rose first, 'and
was the elder of the new lights as was Telperion of the Trees' (*ibid.*); in
the old story the reverse is true both of the Trees and of the new lights.
Again, in *The Silmarillion* it is Varda who decides their motions, and she
changes these from her first plan at the plea of Lórien and Estë, whereas
here it is Lórien's very distress at the coming of Sunlight that leads to the

last blossoming of Silpion and the making of the Moon. The Valar indeed play different roles throughout; and here far greater importance attaches to the acts of Vána and Lórien, whose relations with the Sun and Moon are at once deeper and more explicit than they afterwards became, as they had been with the Trees (see p. 71); in *The Silmarillion* it was Nienna who watered the Trees with her tears (p. 98). In *The Silmarillion* the Sun and Moon move nearer to Arda than 'the ancient stars' (p. 99), but here they move at quite different levels in the firmament.

But a feature in which later compression can be certainly discerned is the elaborate description in the tale of the Moon as 'an island of pure glass', 'a shimmering isle', with little lakes of the light from Telimpë bordered with shining flowers and a crystalline cup amidmost in which was set the Moonflower; only from this is explicable the reference in *The Silmarillion* to Tilion's steering 'the island of the Moon'. The aged Elf Uolë Kúvion (whom 'some indeed have named the Man in the Moon') seems almost to have strayed in from another conception; his presence gives difficulty in any case, since we have just been told (p. 192) that Silmo could not sail in the Moonship because he was not of the children of the air and could not 'cleanse his being of its earthwardness'. – An isolated heading 'Uolë and Erinti' in the little pocket-book used among things for suggestions of stories to be told (see p. 171) no doubt implies that a tale was preparing on the subject of Uolë; cf. the Tale of Qorinómi concerning Urwendi and Erinti's brother Fionwë (p. 215). No traces of these tales are to be found and they were presumably never written. Another note in the pocket-book calls Uolë Mikúmi (the earlier name of Uolë Kúvion, see p. 198) 'King of the Moon'; and a third refers to a poem 'The Man in the Moon' which is to be sung by Eriol, 'who says he will sing them a song of a legend touching Uolë Mikúmi as Men have it'. My father wrote a poem about the Man in the Moon in March 1915, but if it was this that he was thinking of including it would have startled the company of Mar Vanwa Tyaliéva – and he would have had to change its references to places in England which were not yet in existence. Although it is very probable that he had something quite different in mind, I think it may be of interest to give this poem in an early form (see p. 204).

As the mythology evolved and changed, the Making of the Sun and Moon became the element of greatest difficulty; and in the published *Silmarillion* this chapter does not seem of a piece with much of the rest of the work, and could not be made to be so. Towards the end of his life my father was indeed prepared to dismantle much of what he had built, in the attempt to solve what he undoubtedly felt to be a fundamental problem.

## Note on the order of the Tales

The development of the *Lost Tales* is here in fact extremely complex. After the concluding words of *The Flight of the Noldoli*, 'the story of the darkening of Valinor was at an end' (p. 169), my father wrote: 'See on beyond in other books', but in fact he added subsequently the short dialogue between Lindo and Eriol ('Great was the power of Melko for ill . . .') which is given at the end of *The Flight of the Noldoli*.

The page-numbering of the notebooks shows that the next tale was to be the *Tale of Tinúviel*, which is written in another book. This long story (to be given in Part II), the oldest extant version of 'Beren and Lúthien', begins with a long *Link* passage; and the curious thing is that this *Link* begins with the very dialogue between Lindo and Eriol just referred to, in almost identical wording, and this can be seen to be its original place; but here it was struck through.

I have mentioned earlier (p. 45) that in a letter written by my father in 1964 he said that he wrote *The Music of the Ainur* while working in Oxford on the staff of the Dictionary, a post that he took up in November 1918 and relinquished in the spring of 1920. In the same letter he said that he wrote ' "The Fall of Gondolin" during sick-leave from the army in 1917', and 'the original version of the "Tale of Lúthien Tinúviel and Beren" later in the same year'. There is nothing in the manuscripts to suggest that the tales that follow *The Music of the Ainur* to the point we have now reached were not written consecutively and continuously from *The Music*, while my father was still in Oxford.

At first sight, then, there is a hopeless contradiction in the evidence: for the *Link* in question refers explicitly to the Darkening of Valinor, a tale written *after* his appointment in Oxford at the end of 1918, but is a link to the *Tale of Tinúviel*, which he said that he wrote in 1917. But the *Tale of Tinúviel* (and the *Link* that precedes it) is in fact a text in ink written over an erased pencilled original. It is, I think, certain that this *rewriting* of *Tinúviel* was considerably later. It was linked to *The Flight of the Noldoli* by the speeches of Lindo and Eriol (the link-passage is integral and continuous with the *Tale of Tinúviel* that follows it, and was not added afterwards). At this stage my father must have felt that the *Tales* need not necessarily be told in the actual sequence of the narrative (for *Tinúviel* belongs of course to the time after the making of the Sun and Moon).

The rewritten *Tinúviel* was followed with no break by a first form of the 'interlude' introducing Gilfanon of Tavrobel as a guest in the house, and this led into the *Tale of the Sun and Moon*. But subsequently my father changed his mind, and so struck out the dialogue of Lindo and Eriol from the beginning of the *Link* to *Tinúviel*, which was not now to follow *The Flight of the Noldoli*, and wrote it out again in the other book at the end of that tale. At the same time he rewrote the Gilfanon 'interlude' in an extended form, and placed it at the end of *The Flight of the Noldoli*. Thus:

| | |
|---|---|
| Flight of the Noldoli | Flight of the Noldoli |
| Words of Lindo and Eriol | Words of Lindo and Eriol |

That the rewriting of *Tinúviel* was one of the latest elements in the composition of the *Lost Tales* seems clear from the fact that it is followed by the first form of the Gilfanon 'interlude', written at the same time: for Gilfanon replaced Ailios, and Ailios, not Gilfanon, is the guest in the house in the earlier versions of the *Tale of the Sun and Moon* and *The Hiding of Valinor*, and is the teller of the *Tale of the Nauglafring*.

The poem about the Man in the Moon exists in many texts, and was published at Leeds in 1923;* long after and much changed it was included in *The Adventures of Tom Bombadil* (1962). I give it here in a form close to the earlier published version, but with a few (mostly very minor) alterations made subsequently. The 1923 version was only a little retouched from the earliest workings – where it has the title 'Why the Man in the Moon came down too soon: an East Anglian phantasy'; in the first finished text the title is 'A Faërie: Why the Man in the Moon came down too soon', together with one in Old English: *Se Móncyning*.

Why the Man in the Moon
came down too soon

The Man in the Moon had silver shoon
   And his beard was of silver thread;
He was girt with pale gold and inaureoled
   With gold about his head.                                    4
Clad in silken robe in his great white globe
   He opened an ivory door
With a crystal key, and in secrecy
   He stole o'er a shadowy floor;                             8

Down a filigree stair of spidery hair
   He slipped in gleaming haste,
And laughing with glee to be merry and free
   He swiftly earthward raced.                               12
He was tired of his pearls and diamond twirls;
   Of his pallid minaret
Dizzy and white at its lunar height
   In a world of silver set;                                  16

---

* '*A Northern Venture*: verses by members of the Leeds University English School Association' (Leeds, at the Swan Press, 1923). I have not seen this publication and take these details from Humphrey Carpenter, *Biography*, p. 269.

And adventured this peril for ruby and beryl
    And emerald and sapphire,
And all lustrous gems for new diadems,
    Or to blazon his pale attire.          20
He was lonely too with nothing to do
    But to stare at the golden world,
Or strain for the hum that would distantly come
    As it gaily past him whirled;        24

And at plenilune in his argent moon
    He had wearily longed for Fire –
Not the limpid lights of wan selenites,
    But a red terrestrial pyre        28
With impurpurate glows of crimson and rose
    And leaping orange tongue;
For great seas of blues and the passionate hues
    When a dancing dawn is young;        32

For the meadowy ways like chrysoprase
    By winding Yare and Nen.
How he longed for the mirth of the populous Earth
    And the sanguine blood of men;        36
And coveted song and laughter long
    And viands hot and wine,
Eating pearly cakes of light snowflakes
    And drinking thin moonshine.        40

He twinkled his feet as he thought of the meat,
    Of the punch and the peppery brew,
Till he tripped unaware on his slanting stair,
    And fell like meteors do;        44
As the whickering sparks in splashing arcs
    Of stars blown down like rain
From his laddery path took a foaming bath
    In the Ocean of Almain;        48

And began to think, lest he melt and stink,
    What in the moon to do,
When a Yarmouth boat found him far afloat,
    To the mazement of the crew        52
Caught in their net all shimmering wet
    In a phosphorescent sheen
Of bluey whites and opal lights
    And delicate liquid green.        56

With the morning fish – 'twas his regal wish –
  They packed him to Norwich town,
To get warm on gin in a Norfolk inn,
  And dry his watery gown.               60
Though Saint Peter's knell waked many a bell
  In the city's ringing towers
To shout the news of his lunatic cruise
  In the early morning hours,          64

No hearths were laid, not a breakfast made,
  And no one would sell him gems;
He found ashes for fire, and his gay desire
  For chorus and brave anthems      68
Met snores instead with all Norfolk abed,
  And his round heart nearly broke,
More empty and cold than above of old,
  Till he bartered his fairy cloak      72

With a half-waked cook for a kitchen nook,
  And his belt of gold for a smile,
And a priceless jewel for a bowl of gruel,
  A sample cold and vile          76
Of the proud plum-porridge of Anglian Norwich –
  He arrived so much too soon
For unusual guests on adventurous quests
  From the Mountains of the Moon.     80

It seems very possible that the 'pallid minaret' reappears in the 'little white turret' which Uolë Kúvion built on the Moon, 'where often he climbs and watches the heavens, or the world beneath'. The minaret of the Man in the Moon survives in the final version.

The Ocean of Almain is the North Sea (*Almain* or *Almany* was a name of Germany in earlier English); the Yare is a Norfolk river which falls into the sea at Yarmouth, and the Nene (pronounced also with a short vowel) flows into the Wash.

# IX

# THE HIDING OF VALINOR

The link to this tale, which is told by Vairë, has been given at the end of the last (p. 195). The manuscript continues as in the latter part of *The Tale of the Sun and Moon* (see p. 197 note 19), with an earlier draft also extant, to which reference is made in the notes.

'Lo, tales I tell of the deep days, and the first is called *The Hiding of Valinor*.

Already have ye heard,' said she, 'of the setting forth of the Sun and Moon upon their wayward journeyings, and many things are there to tell concerning the awakening of the Earth beneath their light; but hear now of the thoughts and deeds of the dwellers in Valinor in those mighty days.

Now is it to tell that so wide were the wanderings of those boats of light that the Gods found it no easy thing to govern all their comings and their goings as they had purposed at the first, and Ilinsor was loath to yield the heaven to Urwendi, and Urwendi set sail often before Ilinsor's due return, being eager and hot of mood. Wherefore were both vessels often far afloat at one and the same time, and the glory of them sailing most nigh to the very bosom of the Earth, as often they did at that time, was very great and very terrible to see.

Then did a vague uneasiness begin to stir anew in Valinor, and the hearts of the Gods were troubled, and the Eldar spake one to another, and this was their thought.

"Lo, all the world is grown clear as the courtyards of the Gods, straight to walk upon as are the avenues of Vansamírin or the terraces of Kôr; and Valinor no longer is safe, for Melko hates us without ceasing, and he holds the world without and many and wild are his allies there" – and herein in their hearts they[1] numbered even the Noldoli, and wronged them in their thought unwittingly, nor did they forget Men, against whom Melko had lied of old. Indeed in the joy of the last burgeoning of the Trees and the great and glad labour of that fashioning of ships the fear of Melko had been laid aside, and the bitterness of those last evil days and of the Gnome-folk's flight was fallen into slumber – but now when Valinor had peace once more and its lands and gardens were mended of their hurts memory awoke their anger and their grief again.

Indeed if the Gods forgot not the folly of the Noldoli and hardened their hearts, yet more wroth were the Elves, and the Solosimpi were full of bitterness against their kin, desiring never more to see their faces in the pathways of their home. Of these the chief were those whose kin had perished at the Haven of the Swans, and their leader was one Ainairos who had escaped from that fray leaving his brother dead; and he sought unceasingly with his words to persuade the Elves to greater bitterness of heart.

Now this was a grief to Manwë, yet did he see that as yet his design was not complete, and that the wisdom of the Valar must needs be bent once more to the more perfect government of the Sun and Moon. Wherefore he summoned the Gods and Elves in conclave, that their counsel might better his design, and moreover he hoped with soft words of wisdom to calm their anger and uneasiness ere evil came of it. For clearly he saw herein the poison of Melko's lies that live and multiply wherever he may cast them more fruitfully than any seed that is sown upon the Earth; and already it was reported to him that the ancient murmuring of the Elves was begun anew concerning their freedom, and that pride made some full of folly, so that they might not endure the thought of the coming of Mankind.

Now then sat Manwë in heavy mood before Kulullin and looked searchingly upon the Valar gathered nigh and upon the Eldar about his knees, but he opened not his full mind, saying to them only that he had called them in council once more to determine the courses of the Sun and Moon and devise an order and wisdom in their paths. Then straightway spake Ainairos before him saying that other matters were deeper in their hearts than this, and he laid before the Gods the mind of the Elves concerning the Noldoli and of the nakedness of the land of Valinor toward the world beyond. Thereat arose much tumult and many of the Valar and their folk supported him loudly, and some others of the Eldar cried out that Manwë and Varda had caused their kindred to dwell in Valinor promising them unfailing joy therein – now let the Gods see to it that their gladness was not minished to a little thing, seeing that Melko held the world and they dared not fare forth to the places of their awakening even an they would. The most of the Valar moreover were fain of their ancient ease and desired only peace, wishing neither rumour of Melko and his violence nor murmur of the restless Gnomes to come ever again among them to disturb their happiness; and for such reasons they also clamoured for the concealment of the land. Not the

least among these were Vána and Nessa, albeit most even of the
great Gods were of one mind. In vain did Ulmo of his foreknowing
plead before them for pity and pardon on the Noldoli, or Manwë
unfold the secrets of the Music of the Ainur and the purpose of the
world; and long and very full of that noise was that council, and
more filled with bitterness and burning words than any that had
been; wherefore did Manwë Súlimo depart at length from among
them, saying that no walls or bulwarks might now fend Melko's
evil from them which lived already among them and clouded all
their minds.

So came it that the enemies of the Gnomes carried the council of
the Gods and the blood of Kópas began already its fell work; for
now began that which is named the Hiding of Valinor, and Manwë
and Varda and Ulmo of the Seas had no part therein, but none others
of the Valar or the Elves held aloof therefrom, albeit Yavanna and
Oromë her son were uneasy in their hearts.

Now Lórien and Vána led the Gods and Aulë lent his skill and
Tulkas his strength, and the Valar went not at that time forth to
conquer Melko, and the greatest ruth was that to them thereafter,
and yet is; for the great glory of the Valar by reason of that error
came not to its fullness in many ages of the Earth, and still doth the
world await it.[2]

In those days however they were unwitting of these things, and
they set them to new and mighty labours such as had not been seen
among them since the days of the first building of Valinor. The
encircling mountains did they make more utterly impassable of their
eastern side than ever were they before, and such earth-magics did
Kémi weave about their precipices and inaccessible peaks that of all
the dread and terrible places in the mighty Earth was that rampart
of the Gods that looked upon Eruman the most dire and perilous,
and not Utumna nor the places of Melko in the Hills of Iron were so
filled with insuperable fear. Moreover even upon the plains about
their eastward . . .[3] were heaped those impenetrable webs of clinging
dark that Ungweliantë sloughed in Valinor at the Trees' destroying.
Now did the Gods cast them forth from their bright land, that they
might entangle utterly the steps of all who fared that way, and they
flowed and spread both far and wide, lying even upon the bosom of
the Shadowy Seas until the Bay of Faëry grew dim and no radiance
of Valinor filtered there, and the twinkling of the lamps of Kôr died
or ever it passed the jewelled shores. From North to South marched
the enchantments and inaccessible magic of the Gods, yet were they

not content; and they said: Behold, we will cause all the paths that fare to Valinor both known and secret to fade utterly from the world, or wander treacherously into blind confusion.

This then they did, and no channel in the seas was left that was not beset with perilous eddies or with streams of overmastering strength for the confusion of all ships. And spirits of sudden storms and winds unlooked-for brooded there by Ossë's will, and others of inextricable mist. Neither did they forget even the long circuitous ways that messengers of the Gods had known and followed through the dark wildernesses of the North and the deepest South; and when all was done to their mind Lórien said: "Now doth Valinor stand alone, and we have peace," and Vána sang once more about her garden in the lightness of her heart.

Alone among all did the hearts of the Solosimpi misgive them, and they stood upon the coasts nigh to their ancient homes and laughter came not easily again amongst them, and they looked upon the Sea and despite its peril and its gloom they feared it lest it still might bring evil into the land. Then did some of them going speak to Aulë and to Tulkas who stood nigh, saying: "O great ones of the Valar, full well and wondrously have the Gods laboured, yet do we think in our hearts that something is yet lacking; for we have not heard that the way of the escape of the Noldoli, even the dread passage of Helkaraksë's cliffs, is destroyed. Yet where the children of the Eldar have trodden so may the sons of Melko return, despite all your enchantments and deceits; neither are we in peace at heart by reason of the undefended sea."

Thereat did Tulkas laugh, saying that naught might come now to Valinor save only by the topmost airs, "and Melko hath no power there; neither have ye, O little ones of the Earth". Nonetheless at Aulë's bidding he fared with that Vala to the bitter places of the sorrow of the Gnomes, and Aulë with the mighty hammer of his forge smote that wall of jagged ice, and when it was cloven even to the chill waters Tulkas rent it asunder with his great hands and the seas roared in between, and the land of the Gods was sundered utterly from the realms of Earth.[4]

This did they at the Shoreland Elves' behest, yet by no means would the Gods suffer that low place in the hills beneath Taniquetil that lets upon the Bay of Faëry to be piled with rocks as the Solosimpi desired, for there had Oromë many pleasant woods and places of delight, and the Teleri[5] would not endure that Kôr should be destroyed or pressed too nearly by the gloomy mountain walls.

Then spake the Solosimpi to Ulmo, and he would not listen to them, saying that never had they learnt such bitterness of heart of his music, and that rather had they been listening to whispers of Melko the accursed. And going from Ulmo some were abashed, but others went and sought out Ossë, and he aided them in Ulmo's despite; and of Ossë's labour in those days are come the Magic Isles; for Ossë set them in a great ring about the western limits of the mighty sea, so that they guarded the Bay of Faëry, and albeit in those days the huge glooms of that far water overreached all the Shadowy Seas and stretched forth tongues of darkness towards them, still were they themselves surpassing fair to look upon. And such ships as fare that way must needs espy them or ever they reach the last waters that wash the elfin shores, and so alluring were they that few had power to pass them by, and did any essay to then sudden storms drove them perforce against those beaches whose pebbles shone like silver and like gold. Yet all such as stepped thereon came never thence again, but being woven in the nets of Oinen's[6] hair the Lady of the Sea, and whelmed in agelong slumber that Lórien set there, lay upon the margin of the waves, as those do who being drowned are cast up once more by the movements of the sea; yet rather did these hapless ones sleep unfathomably and the dark waters laved their limbs, but their ships rotted, swathed in weeds, on those enchanted sands, and sailed never more before the winds of the dim West.[7]

Now when Manwë gazing in sorrow from high Taniquetil saw all these things done he sent for Lórien and for Oromë, thinking them less stubborn of heart than the others, and when they were come he spoke earnestly with them; yet he would not that the labour of the Gods be undone, for he thought it not altogether ill, but he prevailed on those twain to do his bidding in certain matters. And in this manner did they so; for Lórien wove a way of delicate magic, and it fared by winding roads most secret from the Eastern lands and all the great wildernesses of the world even to the walls of Kôr, and it ran past the Cottage of the Children of the Earth[8] and thence down the "lane of whispering elms" until it reached the sea.

But the gloomy seas and all the straits it bridged with slender bridges resting on the air and greyly gleaming as it were of silken mists lit by a thin moon, or of pearly vapours; yet beside the Valar and the Elves have no Man's eyes beheld it save in sweet slumbers in their heart's youth. Longest of all ways is it and few are there ever reach its end, so many lands and marvellous places of allurement and of loveliness doth it pass ere it comes to Elfinesse, yet smooth is it to the feet and none tire ever who fare that way.

Such,' then said Vairë, 'was and still is the manner of Olórë
Mallë, the Path of Dreams; but of far other sort was the work of
Oromë, who hearing the words of Manwë went speedily to Vána his
wife, and begged of her a tress of her long golden hair. Now the hair
of Vána the fair had become more long and radiant still since the
days of her offering to Aulë, and she gave to Oromë of its golden
threads. Then did he dip these in the radiance of Kulullín, but
Vána wove them cunningly to a leash immeasurable, and therewith
Oromë strode swiftly to the gatherings of Manwë on the mountain.

Then calling loudly that Manwë and Varda and all their folk
come forth he held before their eyes his thong of gold, and they
knew not his purpose; but Oromë bid them cast their eyes on that
Hill that is called Kalormë standing hugely in the lands most distant from Valinor, and is held most lofty save Taniquetil, yet
seemeth therefrom a dim thing fading afar off. Even as they watched
Oromë stepped back, and putting all his cunning and his strength
thereto he made a mighty cast, and that golden cord sped in a curve
through the sky until its noose caught Kalormë's topmost pinnacle.
Then by the magic of its making and the cunning of Oromë's hand
it stayed a bright golden curve and neither drooped nor sagged; but
Oromë fastened its hither end to a pillar in Manwë's courts, and
turning to those who gazed upon him said: "Who then listeth to
wander in the Great Lands, let him follow me," and thereat he set
foot upon the thong and sped like the wind out over the gulf even to
Kalormë, while all upon Taniquetil were silent in amaze. Now did
Oromë loosen the thong from Kalormë's peak and run as swiftly
back, ravelling it as he came, until once more he stood before Manwë.
Then said he: "Lo, O Súlimo Lord of the Airs, a way I have devised
whereby any of the Valar of good heart may fare whithersoever they
list in the Great Lands; for whither they wish I will cast my slender
bridge, and its hither end wilt thou securely guard."

And of this work of Oromë's came that mighty wonder of the
heavens that all men look upon and marvel at, and some fear much,
pondering what it may portend. Yet doth that bridge wear a different
aspect at different times and in various regions of the Earth, and
seldom is it visible to Men and Elves. Now because it glistens most
marvellously in the slanting rays of the Sun, and when the rains of
heaven moisten it it shines most magically therein and the gold light
breaks upon its dripping cords to many hues of purple, green, and
red, so do men most often name it the Rainbow, but many other
names have they fashioned also, and the fairies call it Ilweran the
Bridge of Heaven.

Now living Men may not tread the swaying threads of Ilweran and few of the Eldar have the heart, yet other paths for Elves and Men to fare to Valinor are there none since those days save one alone, and it is very dark; yet is it very short, the shortest and swiftest of all roads, and very rough, for Mandos made it and Fui set it in its place. Qalvanda is it called, the Road of Death, and it leads only to the halls of Mandos and Fui. Twofold is it, and one way tread the Elves and the other the souls of Men, and never do they mingle.[9]

'Thus,' said Vairë, 'was the Hiding of Valinor achieved, and the Valar let slip the chance of a glory more splendid and enduring even than that great glory which was theirs and still is. Nonetheless are there still very mighty tidings of those days to tell, of which perchance I may now recount to you a few; and one I will name *The Haven of the Sun*.

Behold, now are the hearts of all set at rest by the truce[10] of Manwë and the Valar, and while the Gods feast in Valmar and the heaven is full of the ungoverned glory of the Ships of Light the Elves go back at last to rebuild the happiness of Kôr; and there they seek to forget all the sorrows and all the labours that had come among them since the Release of Melko. Now does Kôr become the fairest and most delicate-lovely of all the realms of Valinor, for in the courtyard of Inwë those two elfin trees shone still tenderly; and they were shoots of the glorious Trees now dead given by the Gods to Inwë in the first days of that town's building. Others too had been given to Nólemë, but these were uprooted and were gone no one knew whither, and more had there never been.[11]

Yet even though the Elves trusted the Valar to shield the land and weave protection about them, and though the days of sorrow faring into the past grew dim, still could they not yet utterly shake away the memory of their unhappiness; nor did they ever so, until after the magic way of Lórien was complete and the children of the fathers of the fathers of Men first were suffered to come there in sweet sleep; then did a new joy burn very brightly in their hearts, but these things were not yet come to pass and Men were yet but new-wakened on the Earth.

But Manwë and Ulmo knowing their hour was come held high councils for their protection. Many designs they made therein, and they were weighed down by the thought of Melko and the wandering of the Gnomes; yet did the other folk of Valinor trouble themselves little with such matters yet. Nonetheless Manwë ventured to speak once more to the Valar, albeit he uttered no word of Men, and he

reminded them that in their labours for the concealment of their
land they had let slip from thought the waywardness of the Sun
and Moon. Now it was the fear of Manwë lest the Earth become
unbearable by reason of the great light and heat of those bright
things, and Yavanna's heart was in accord with him in that, but the
most of the Valar and the Elves saw good in his design because in
the lifting of the Sun and Moon to higher paths they thought to set
a final end to all their labours, removing those piercing beams more
far, that all those hills and regions of their abode be not too bright
illumined, and that none might ever again espy them afar off.

Wherefore said some: "Let us send now messengers to discover
the fashion of the world in the uttermost East beyond even the
sight of Manwë from the Mountain of the World." Then arose
Oromë: "That I can tell you, for I have seen. In the East beyond the
tumbled lands there is a silent beach and a dark and empty sea."
And the Gods marvelled at these tidings, yet never before had any
save Oromë listed to see or hear such things, not even Yavanna the
Earth-lady. Nought do I say of Ulmo Vailimo, Lord of Vai, for of
a truth all such matters he knew from the beginning of the Earth.
Now therefore did that ancient one follow Oromë, expounding to the
Valar what was the secret nature of the Earth, and he said:

"Lo, there is but one Ocean, and that is Vai, for those that Ossë
esteemeth as oceans are but seas, waters that lie in the hollows of
the rock; but Vai runneth from the Wall of Things unto the Wall
of Things whithersoever you may fare. Now to the North is it so
cold that even its pale waters are frozen to a depth beyond thought
or sounding, and to the South is such utter darkness and deceit by
reason of Ungoliont[12] that none save I alone may find a way. In
this vast water floateth the wide Earth upheld by the word of Ilúvatar,
for nought else or fish or bark will swim therein to whom I have not
spoken the great word that Ilúvatar said to me and bound them
with the spell; but of the wide Earth is even Valinor a part, and the
substance of the Earth is stone and metal, and the seas are pools in
its hollows, and the islands save some few that swim still unfettered
stand now like pinnacles from their weedy depths. Know then that
somewhat nearer stands Valinor to the great Wall of Things wherein
Ilúvatar hath enclosed us than doth that furthest Eastern shore:
and this do I know, for diving beneath the world often have I
visited those unharboured beaches; for lo, O Valar, ye know not all
wonders, and many secret things are there beneath the Earth's dark
keel, even where I have my mighty halls of Ulmonan, that ye have
never dreamed on."

But said Manwë: "True is that, O Ulmo Vailimo; but what is it to our present purpose?" And Ulmo answered: "Lo, I will take Aulë the Smith with me and convey him safe and swift beneath the waters of Vai in my deep-sea car, even to the Eastern shores, and there will he and I build havens for the Ships, and from the East hereafter shall they arise and give their fullest light and glory to Men who need them, and to the unhappy Noldoli, following one the other over the sky, and coming home to Valinor. Here, when their hearts wax faint by reason of their journeyings, shall they rest awhile upon the Outer Seas and Urwendi bathe in Faskalan and Ilinsor drink of the quiet waters of the Lake Irtinsa, ere ever they return again."

Now this speech had Manwë and Ulmo designed in collusion, and the Valar and Eldar hearkened for divers reasons as before; wherefore was Aulë sped now with Ulmo, and they builded great havens in the East beside the soundless sea; and the haven of the Sun was wide and golden, but the haven of the Moon was set within the same harbourage, and it was white, having gates of silver and of pearl that shone faintly so soon as the Sun sank from the heavens into Valinor; at that hour do those gates open of themselves before the issuing Moon, but none of the Eldar have seen these things save Uolë Kúvion, and he has told no tale.

Now at first the Valar purposed to draw the Sun and Moon beneath the Earth, hallowing them with Ulmo's spell that Vai harm them not, each at its appointed time; yet in the end they found that Sári[13] might not, even so, safely come beneath the world, for it was too frail and lissom; and much precious radiance was spilled in their attempts about the deepest waters, and escaped to linger as secret sparks in many an unknown ocean cavern. These have many elfin divers, and divers of the fays, long time sought beyond the outmost East, even as is sung in the song of the Sleeper in the Tower of Pearl.[14]

Indeed for a while mishap fell even upon bright Urwendi, that she wandered the dark grots and endless passages of Ulmo's realm until Fionwë found her and brought her back to Valinor – but the full tale is called the Tale of Qorinómi and may not here be told.[15]

Thus came it that the Gods dared a very great deed, the most mighty of all their works; for making a fleet of magic rafts and boats with Ulmo's aid – and otherwise had none of these endured to sail upon the waters of Vai – they drew to the Wall of Things, and there they made the Door of Night (Moritarnon or Tarn Fui as the Eldar name it in their tongues): There it still stands, utterly black and huge against the deep-blue walls. Its pillars are of the mightiest basalt and its lintel likewise, but great dragons of black stone are carved thereon, and shadowy smoke pours slowly from their jaws. Gates it has unbreakable, and none know how they were made or set, for the Eldar were not suffered to be in that dread building, and it is the last secret of the Gods; and not the onset of the world will force that door, which opens to a mystic word alone. That word Urwendi only knows and Manwë who spake it to her; for beyond the Door of Night is the outer dark, and he who passes therethrough may escape the world and death and hear things not yet for the ears of Earth-dwellers, and this may not be.

In the East however was the work of the Gods of other sort, for there was a great arch made, and, 'tis said, 'tis all of shining gold and barred with silver gates, yet few have beheld it even of the Gods for the wealth of glowing vapours that are often swathed about it. Now the Gates of Morn open also before Urwendi only, and the word she speaks is the same that she utters at the Door of Night, but it is reversed.

So comes it that ever now, as the Ship of the Moon leaves his haven in the East and his gates of pearl, Ulmo draws the galleon of the Sun before the Door of Night. Then speaks Urwendi the mystic word, and they open outward before her, and a gust of darkness sweeps in but perishes before her blazing light; and the galleon of the Sun goes out into the limitless dark, and coming behind the world finds the East again. There doth Sári filled with the lightness of the morning ride through the gates and Urwendi and her maidens make a sound of golden horns, and dawn is spilt upon the eyes of Men.[16]

Yet many a time and oft a tiny star-ship of Varda that has dipped into the Outer Seas, as often they will, is sucked through that Door of Night behind the Sun; and some track her galleon through the starless vast back unto the Eastern Wall, and some are lost for ever, and some glimmer beyond the Door until the Sunship issues forth again.[17] Then do these leap back and rush up into the sky again, or flee across its spaces; and this is a very beautiful thing to see – the Fountains of the Stars.

Behold, the Moon dares not the utter loneliness of the outer dark by reason of his lesser light and majesty, and he journeys still beneath the world and many are the chances of that way; wherefore is it that he is often less timely than the Sun and is more fickle. Sometimes he comes not after Sári at all, and other times is late and maketh but a little voyage or even dares the heavens while Urwendi still is there. Then smile the Gods wistfully and say: "It is the mingling of the lights once more."[18]

Long was this indeed the manner of the ships' guidance, and long was it after those days that the Gods grew afraid once more for the Sun and Moon because of certain tidings of those days, which perchance may after be told; and because of their fear a new and strange thing befell. Now the manner of this mayhap I may tell before I make an end; and it is called *The Weaving of the Days and Months and of the Years.*

For know that even as the great Gods sat in conclave pondering how they might fetter the lamps of heaven ever to their hand and guide their goings even as a charioteer doth guide his galloping horses, behold three aged men stood before them and saluted Manwë.

But Manwë asked them who they were, "for well I know," quoth he, "that ye are not of the glad folk that dwell in Valmar or the gardens of the Gods," and the Valar marvelled how they came unaided to their land. Now those men were of strange aspect, seeming aged beyond count albeit of strength untamed. And one that stood at the left was exceeding small and short, and another amidmost of middle stature, and the third was long and tall; and the first had short hair and a small beard, and the other's was neither long nor short, but the beard of the third swept the earth before his feet as he walked. Now after a while he that was short and small spake in answer to Manwë, and he said: "Brothers are we; and men of exceeding subtle craft"; and the other answered: "Lo, Danuin, Ranuin, and Fanuin are we called,* and I am Ranuin, and Danuin has spoken." Then said Fanuin: "And we will offer thee our skill in your perplexity – yet who we are and whence we come or whither we go that we will tell to you only if ye accept our rede and after we have wrought as we desire."

Then some of the Gods said them nay, fearing a trick (even perhaps of Melko), and others would grant their request, and such was the counsel that in the end prevailed because of the great perplexity of the time. Then did those three Danuin and Ranuin and Fanuin beg that a room might be set apart for them; and this was done in Aulë's house. There did they spin and weave in secret, and after a space of twice twelve hours Danuin came forth and spake to Manwë, saying: "Behold my handicraft!"; and none knew his intent, for his hands were empty. But when the Ship of the Sun returned then went Danuin to her stern, and laying his hand thereon he bid Ulmo draw her, as was his wont, over the waters to the Door of Night; and when Ulmo was gone a little way from the further

* In the margin is written *Dōgor Mōnaþ 7 Missére*, Old English words meaning 'Day, Month, and Year'.

shore of Valinor Danuin stepped back, and behold Ulmo might not draw the Sunship further, not though he put forth all his strength. Then were Manwë and Ulmo and all that beheld afraid, but Danuin after released the Sun and went from among them, and they might not find him; but after twenty nights and eight came forth Ranuin and he said also: "Behold my handicraft!" and yet no more could be seen in his outstretched hands than before in those of Danuin. Now Ranuin waited until Ilinsor brought the Rose of Silpion unto Valinor, and then going he set his hands against a jag of glass upon that isle, and thereafter might no man stir Ilinsor's bark far from Ranuin against his will; but again Ranuin spake no word and went from among them; then Rána was released, but Ranuin no man could find.

Now the Gods pondered long what this might portend, but nought more betid until thirteen times had Rána waxed and waned. Then came forth Fanuin, and he bid the Gods detain Ilinsor that at Sári's coming both ships might stand in Valinor at once. But when this was done he begged aid of the Gods, "for," said he, "I have fashioned somewhat of great weight that I would fain show to you, yet cannot of my own strength hale it forth." And seven of the stoutest from the halls of Tulkas went to the place of Fanuin's labouring and could not see aught therein; but he bid them stoop, and them seemed they laid hands upon a mighty cable and staggered beneath it as they laid it upon their shoulders, yet could they not see it.

Then going unto Sári and to Rána in turn Fanuin moved his hands as though he were making fast a great rope to each of those vessels; but when all was done he said to Manwë: "Lo, O Súlimo Lord of the Gods, the work is wrought and the ships of light are set in the unbreakable fetters of time, which neither ye, nor they, may ever break, nor may they escape therefrom, albeit these fetters are invisible to all beings that Ilúvatar has made; for nonetheless are they the strongest of things."

Then suddenly behold Danuin and Ranuin stood beside him, and Danuin going to Manwë placed in his hand a slender cord, but Manwë saw it not. "Herewith," said Danuin, "O Manwë Súlimo, canst thou govern the goings and comings of the Sun, and never may she be brought beyond the guidance of your hand, and such is the virtue of this cord that the goings and returnings of the Sun shall be accounted the most timely and inevitable of all things on Earth." Thereafter did Ranuin in like manner, and behold Manwë felt a stout rope within his palm invisible. "Herewith," said Ranuin, "shalt thou hold and steer the wayward Moon, as well as may be, and so great is the virtue of the 'thong of Ranuin' that even the fickle and untimely Moon shall be a measure of time to Elves and Men." Lastly did Fanuin bid bear his mighty cable's end to Manwë, and Manwë touched it, and it was made fast to a great rock upon Taniquetil (that is called therefore Gonlath), and Fanuin said: "Now doth this mightiest cable hold both the Moon and Sun in tow; and herewith mayest thou coordinate their motions and interweave their fates; for the rope of Fanuin is the Rope of Years, and Urwendi issuing through the Door of Night shall wind it all tangled with the daycord's slender meshes, round and about the Earth until the Great End come – and so shall all the world and the dwellers within it, both Gods and Elves and Men, and all the creatures that go and the things that have roots thereon, be bound about in the bonds of Time."

Then were all the Gods afraid, seeing what was come, and knowing that hereafter even they should in counted time be subject to slow eld and their bright days to waning, until Ilúvatar at the Great End calls them back. But Fanuin said: "Nay, it is but the Music of the Ainur: for behold, who are we, Danuin, Ranuin, and Fanuin, Day and Month and Year, but the children of Aluin, of Time, who is the oldest of the Ainur, and is beyond, and subject to Ilúvatar; and thence came we, and thither go we now." Then did those three vanish from Valinor; but of such is the framing of the moveless courses of the Sun and Moon, and the subjection of all things within the world to time and change.

But as for the Ships of Light themselves, behold! O Gilfanon and all that hearken, I will end the tale of Lindo and Vairë concerning the building of the Sun and Moon with that great foreboding that was spoken among the Gods when first the Door of Night was opened. For 'tis said that ere the Great End come Melko shall in some wise contrive a quarrel between Moon and Sun, and Ilinsor shall seek to follow Urwendi through the Gates, and when they are gone the Gates of both East and West will be destroyed, and Urwendi and Ilinsor shall be lost. So shall it be that Fionwë Úrion, son of Manwë, of love for Urwendi shall in the end be Melko's bane, and shall destroy the world to destroy his foe, and so shall all things then be rolled away.'[19]

And thus ended Vairë, and the great tale fell silent in the room.

## NOTES

1  'they': original reading 'the Solosimpi'.

2   The rejected draft text of the tale to this point is remarkably brief,
    and reads as follows (following on from Ailios' remarks given on p. 197,
    note 20):

> 'That is easy told,' said Lindo; 'for the murmurings that I have
> spoken of grew ever louder, and came to speech at that council
> which was now summoned to fix the courses of the Sun and Moon;
> and all the ancient grievance that had flamed before at Melko's
> instigation concerning the freedom of the Elves – even that strife
> that ended in the Exile of the Noldoli – grew sore again. Yet
> were few now in pity of the Gnomes, and such of the Eldar whom
> the newlit world allured dared not for the power of Melko break
> from Valinor; wherefore in the end the enemies of the Gnomes,
> despite all that Ulmo might say or plead, and despite the clemency
> of Manwë, carried the counsels of the Gods – and so came that
> which stories name the [Closing >] Hiding of Valinor. And the
> Gods went not at that time forth to fight Melko, and their greatest
> opportunity for glory and eternal honour was let slip, [even as the
> Music of Ilúvatar had foreboded – and they little understood it –
> and who knows if the salvation of the world and the freeing of
> Men and Elves shall ever come from them again? Some there are
> who whisper that it is not so, and hope dwelleth only in a far
> land of Men, but how so that may be I do not know.]

    The concluding passage is thus bracketed in the manuscript, with a
    question-mark against it.
3   The word looks like 'east'. The word 'eastward' was added to the
    text, and it may be that my father intended to change 'east' to
    'eastward edge' or something similar.
4   Here 'Earth' is clearly used, if strangely so, in the same way as is
    'the world', to mean the Great Lands as distinguished from the
    Outer Lands of the West.
5   The Teleri (i.e. the later Vanyar) had not in the old story departed
    from Kôr (see p. 159).
6   Originally *Ówen* and then *Ónen*, the name of Ossë's wife has already
    appeared in the final form *Uinen* (pp. 121, 192); but *Oinen* here is
    clear, and clearly intended.
7   In the draft text the account of the Hiding of Valinor is very brief,
    and moves on quickly to the Path of Dreams. The webs of darkness
    laid on the eastward slopes of the mountains were not those 'sloughed
    in Valinor' by Ungweliantë, but are merely compared to 'the most
    clinging that ever Ungweliantë wove'. Helkaraksë and the Magic Isles
    are only mentioned in a marginal direction that they are to be included.
8   'Earth' is again used in the sense of the Great Lands (see note 4).
    The draft has here 'Children of the World'.
9   While there are no differences of any substance in the account of the
    Olórë Mallë in the two texts, in the first there is no mention of Oromë's

Path of the Rainbow. – An isolated note, obviously written before the present Tale, says: 'When the Gods close Valinor . . . Lórien leaves a path across the mountains called Olórë Mallë, and Manwë the Rainbow where he walks to survey the world. It is only visible after rain, for then it is wet.'

10 .'truce': earlier reading 'compromise'. It is notable how Manwë is portrayed as *primus inter pares* rather than as ruler over the other Valar.

11 On the Trees of Kôr see pp. 123, 135.

12 See p. 200.

13 *Sári* is here (and subsequently) the name as written, not an emendation from *Kalavénë*, the name in the draft texts of *The Sun and Moon* and *The Hiding of Valinor* (see p. 198). The reading of the draft in this place is 'the Sunship', itself an alteration from 'the ships', for my father first wrote that neither ship could safely be drawn beneath the Earth.

14 The Sleeper in the Tower of Pearl is named in *The Cottage of Lost Play*, p. 15. The song of the sleeper is virtually certainly the poem *The Happy Mariners*, originally written in 1915 and published in 1923 (see Humphrey Carpenter, *Biography*, Appendix C, p. 269); this will be given in two versions in connection with the materials for the *Tale of Eärendel* in the second part of the *Lost Tales*. The poem contains a reference to the boats that pass the Tower of Pearl, piled 'with hoarded sparks of orient fire / that divers won in waters of the unknown Sun'.

15 The original draft has here: 'but that is the tale of Qorinómi and I dare not tell it here, for friend Ailios is watching me' (see p. 197, notes 19 and 20).

16 The draft text had here at first: 'and the galleon of the Sun goes out into the dark, and coming behind the world finds the East again, but there there is no door and the Wall of Things is lower; and filled with the lightness of the morning Kalavénë rides above it and dawn is split upon the Eastern hills and falls upon the eyes of Men.' Part of this, from 'but there there is no door', was bracketed, and the passage about the great arch in the East and the Gates of Morn introduced. In the following sentence, the draft had 'back over the Eastern Wall', changed to the reading of the second text, 'back unto the Eastern Wall'. For the name *Kalavénë* see p. 198.

17 I.e., until the Sunship issues forth, through the Door of Night, into the outer dark; as the Sunship leaves, the shooting stars pass back into the sky.

18 The second version of this part of Vairë's tale, 'The Haven of the Sun', follows the original draft (as emended) fairly closely, with no differences of any substance; but the part of her tale that now follows, 'The Weaving of the Days and Months and Years', is wholly absent from the draft text.

19   This concluding passage differs in several points from the original
     version. In that, Ailios appears again, for Gilfanon; the 'great fore-
     boding' was spoken among the Gods 'when they designed first to
     build the Door of Night'; and when Ilinsor has followed Urwendi
     through the Gates 'Melko will destroy the Gates and raise the Eastern
     Wall beyond the [?skies] and Urwendi and Ilinsor shall be lost'.

Changes made to names in
*The Hiding of Valinor*

*Vansamírin*   < *Samírien's road* (*Samírien* occurs as the name of the Feast
     of Double Mirth, pp. 143-4).
*Kôr*   < *Kortirion* (p. 207). Afterwards, though *Kôr* was not struck out,
     my father wrote above it *Tûn*, with a query, and the same at the
     occurrence of *Kôr* on p. 210. This is the first appearance in the
     text of the *Lost Tales* of this name, which ultimately gave rise to
     *Túna* (the hill on which Tirion was built).
*Ainairos*   < *Oivárin.*
*Moritarnon*, *Tarn Fui*   The original draft of the tale has '*Móritar* or
     *Tarna Fui*'.
*Sári*   The original draft has *Kalavéné* (see p. 198 and note 13 above).
At the first occurrence of the names of the three Sons of Time the sequence
     of forms was:
     *Danuin*   < *Danos* < an illegible form *Dan..*
     *Ranuin*   < *Ranos* < *Ranoth* < *Rôn*
     *Fanuin*   < *Lathos* < *Lathweg*
     Throughout the remainder of the passage: *Danuin* < *Dana; Ranuin* <
     *Ranoth; Fanuin* < *Lathweg.*
*Aluin*   < *Lúmin.*

Commentary on
*The Hiding of Valinor*

The account of the Council of the Valar and Eldar in the opening of this
tale (greatly developed from the preliminary draft given in note 2) is
remarkable and important in the history of my father's ideas concerning
the Valar and their motives. In *The Silmarillion* (p. 102) the Hiding of
Valinor sprang from the assault of Melkor on the steersman of the Moon:

> But seeing the assault upon Tilion the Valar were in doubt, fearing
> what the malice and cunning of Morgoth might yet contrive against
> them. Being unwilling to make war upon him in Middle-earth, they
> remembered nonetheless the ruin of Almaren; and they resolved that
> the like should not befall Valinor.

A little earlier in *The Silmarillion* (p. 99) reasons are given for the unwillingness of the Valar to make war:

It is said indeed that, even as the Valar made war upon Melkor for the sake of the Quendi, so now for that time they forbore for the sake of the Hildor, the Aftercomers, the younger Children of Ilúvatar. For so grievous had been the hurts of Middle-earth in the war upon Utumno that the Valar feared lest even worse should now befall; whereas the Hildor should be mortal, and weaker than the Quendi to withstand fear and tumult. Moreover it was not revealed to Manwë where the beginning of Men should be, north, south, or east. Therefore the Valar sent forth light, but made strong the land of their dwelling.

In *The Silmarillion* there is no vestige of the tumultuous council, no suggestion of a disagreement among the Valar, with Manwë, Varda and Ulmo actively disapproving the work and holding aloof from it; no mention, equally, of any pleading for pity on the Noldor by Ulmo, nor of Manwë's disgust. In the old story it was the hostility of some of the Eldar towards the Noldoli, led by an Elf of Kópas (Alqualondë) – who likewise disappeared utterly: in the later account there is never a word about the feelings of the Elves of Valinor for the exiled Noldor – that was the starting-point of the Hiding of Valinor; and it is most curious to observe that the action of the Valar here sprang essentially from indolence mixed with fear. Nowhere does my father's early conception of the *fainéant* Gods appear more clearly. He held moreover quite explicitly that their failure to make war upon Melko then and there was a deep error, diminishing themselves, and (as it appears) irreparable. In his later writing the Hiding of Valinor remained indeed, but only as a great fact of mythological antiquity; there is no whisper of its condemnation.

The blocking-up and utter isolation of Valinor from the world without is perhaps even more strongly emphasized in the early narrative. The cast-off webs of Ungweliant and the use to which the Valar put them disappeared in the later story. Most notable is the different explanation of the fact that the gap in the encircling heights (later named the Calacirya) was not blocked up. In *The Silmarillion* (p. 102) it is said that the pass was not closed

because of the Eldar that were faithful, and in the city of Tirion upon the green hill Finarfin yet ruled the remnant of the Noldor in the deep cleft of the mountains. For all those of elven-race, even the Vanyar and Ingwë their lord, must breathe at times the outer air and the wind that comes over the sea from the lands of their birth; and the Valar would not sunder the Teleri wholly from their kin.

The old motive of the Solosimpi (> Teleri) wishing this to be done (sufficiently strange, for did the Shoreland Pipers wish to abandon the shores?) disappeared in the general excision of their bitter resentment against the Noldoli, as did Ulmo's refusal to aid them, and Ossë's willingness to do so in Ulmo's despite. The passage concerning the Magic Isles, made by Ossë, is the origin of the conclusion of Chapter XI of *The Silmarillion*:

And in that time, which songs call *Nurtalë Valinoréva*, the Hiding of Valinor, the Enchanted Isles were set, and all the seas about them were filled with shadows and bewilderment. And these isles were strung as a net in the Shadowy Seas from the north to the south, before Tol Eressëa, the Lonely Isle, is reached by one sailing west. Hardly might any vessel pass between them, for in the dangerous sounds the waves sighed for ever upon dark rocks shrouded in mist. And in the twilight a great weariness came upon mariners and a loathing of the sea; but all that ever set foot upon the islands were there entrapped, and slept until the Change of the World.

It is clear from this passage in the tale that the Magic Isles were set to the east of the Shadowy Seas, though 'the huge glooms . . . . stretched forth tongues of darkness towards them'; while in an earlier passage (p. 125) it is said that beyond Tol Eressëa (which was itself beyond the Magic Isles) 'is the misty wall and those great sea-glooms beneath which lie the Shadowy Seas'. The later 'Enchanted Isles' certainly owe much as a conception to the Magic Isles, but in the passage just cited from *The Silmarillion* they were set in the Shadowy Seas and were in twilight. It is possible therefore that the Enchanted Isles derive also from the Twilit Isles (pp. 68, 125).

The account of the works of Tulkas and Aulë in the northern regions (p. 210) does not read as perfectly in accord with what has been said previously, though a real contradiction is unlikely. On pp. 166-7 it is plainly stated that there was a strip of water (Qerkaringa, the Chill Gulf) between the tip of the 'Icefang' (Helkaraksë) and the Great Lands at the time of the crossing of the Noldoli. In this same passage the Icefang is referred to as 'a narrow neck, which the Gods after destroyed'. The Noldoli were able to cross over to the Great Lands despite 'that gap at the far end' (p. 168) because in the great cold the sound had become filled with unmoving ice. The meaning of the present passage may be, however, that by the destruction of the Icefang a much wider gap was made, so that there was now no possibility of any crossing by that route.

Of the three 'roads' made by Lórien, Oromë, and Mandos there is no vestige in my father's later writing. The Rainbow is never mentioned, nor is there ever any hint of an explanation of how Men and Elves pass to the halls of Mandos. But it is difficult to interpret this conception of the 'roads' — to know to what extent there was a purely figurative content in the idea.

For the road of Lórien, Olórë Mallë the Path of Dreams, which is described by Vairë in *The Cottage of Lost Play*, see pp. 18, 27 ff. There Vairë told that Olórë Mallë came from the lands of Men, that it was 'a lane of deep banks and great overhanging hedges, beyond which stood many tall trees wherein a perpetual whisper seemed to live', and that from this lane a high gate led to the Cottage of the Children or of the Play of Sleep. This was not far from Kôr, and to it came 'the children of the fathers of the fathers of Men'; the Eldar guided them into the Cottage and its garden if they could, 'lest they strayed into Kôr and became enamoured of the glory of Valinor'. The accounts in the two tales seem to be in general agreement, though it is difficult to understand the words in the present passage 'it ran past the Cottage of the Children of the Earth and *thence* down the "lane of whispering elms" *until it reached* the sea'. It is very notable that still at this stage in the development of the mythology, when so much more had been written since the coming of Eriol to Tol Eressëa, the conception of the children of Men coming in sleep by a mysterious 'road' to a cottage in Valinor had by no means fallen away.

In the account of Oromë's making of the Rainbow-bridge, the noose that he cast caught on the summit of the great mountain Kalormë ('Sun-rising-hill') in the remotest East. This mountain is seen on the 'World-Ship' drawing, p. 84.

The story that Vairë named 'The Haven of the Sun' (pp. 213 ff.) provides the fullest picture of the structure of the world that is to be found in the earliest phase of the mythology. The Valar, to be sure, seem strangely ignorant on this subject – the nature of the world that came into being so largely from their own devising, if they needed Ulmo to acquaint them with such fundamental truths. A possible explanation of this ignorance may be found in the radical difference in the treatment of the Creation of the World between the early and later forms of *The Music of the Ainur*. I have remarked earlier (p. 62) that originally the Ainur's first sight of the world was already in its actuality, and Ilúvatar said to them: 'even now the world unfolds and its history begins'; whereas in the developed form it was a vision that was taken away from them, and only given existence in the word of Ilúvatar: *Eä! Let these things Be!* It is said in *The Silmarillion* (p. 20) that

> when the Valar entered into Eä they were at first astounded and at a loss, for it was as if naught was yet made which they had seen in vision, and all was but on point to begin and yet unshaped . . .

and there follows (pp. 21–2) an account of the vast labours of the Valar in the actual 'construction' of the world:

> They built lands and Melkor destroyed them; valleys they delved and Melkor raised them up; mountains they carved and Melkor threw them down; seas they hollowed and Melkor spilled them . . .

In the old version there is none of this, and one gains the impression (though nothing is explicit) that the Valar came into a world that was already 'made', and unknown to them ('the Gods stalked north and south and could see little; indeed in the deepest of these regions they found great cold and solitude . . .', p. 69). Although the conception of the world was indeed derived in large measure from their own playing in the Music, its reality came from the creative act of Ilúvatar ('We would have the guarding of those fair things of our dreams, which of thy might have now attained to reality', p. 57); and the knowledge possessed by the Valar of the actual properties and dimensions of their habitation was correspondingly smaller (so we may perhaps assume) than it was afterwards conceived to be.

But this is to lean rather heavily on the matter. More probably, the ignorance of the Valar is to be attributed to their curious collective isolation and indifference to the world beyond their mountains that is so much emphasized in this tale.

However this may be, Ulmo at this time informed the Valar that the whole world is an Ocean, Vai, on which the Earth floats, 'upheld by the word of Ilúvatar'; and all the seas of the Earth, even that which divides Valinor from the Great Lands, are hollows in the Earth's surface, and are thus distinct from Vai, which is of another nature. All this we have already seen (pp. 84 ff.); and in an earlier tale something has been said (p. 68) of the nature of the upholding waters:

> Beyond Valinor I have never seen or heard, save that of a surety there are the dark waters of the Outer Seas, that have no tides, and they are very cool and thin, that no boat can sail upon their bosom or fish swim within their depths, save the enchanted fish of Ulmo and his magic car.

So here Ulmo says that neither fish nor boat will swim in its waters 'to whom I have not spoken the great word that Ilúvatar said to me and bound them with the spell'.

At the outer edge of Vai stands the Wall of Things, which is described as 'deep-blue' (p. 215). Valinor is nearer to the Wall of Things than is the eastern shore of the Great Lands, which must mean that Vai is narrower in the West than in the East. In the Wall of Things the Gods at this time made two entrances, in the West the Door of Night and in the East the Gates of Morn; and what lies beyond these entrances in the Wall is called 'the starless vast' and 'the outer dark'. It is not made clear how the outer air ('the dark and tenuous realm of Vaitya that is outside all', p. 181) is to be related to the conception of the Wall of Things or the Outer Dark. In the rejected preliminary text of this tale my father wrote at first (see note 16 above) that in the East 'the Wall of Things is lower', so that when the Sun returns from the Outer Dark it does not enter the eastern sky by a door but 'rides above' the Wall. This was then changed, and the idea of the Door in the Eastern Wall, the Gates of Morn, introduced; but the implication seems clear that the Walls were originally conceived like the walls of terrestrial cities, or gardens – walls with a top: a 'ring-fence'. In the cosmological essay of the 1930s, the *Ambarkanta*, the Walls are quite other:

> About the World are the *Ilurambar*, or Walls of the World. They are as ice and glass and steel, being above all imagination of the Children of Earth cold, transparent, and hard. They cannot be seen, nor can they be passed, save by the Door of Night.
>   Within these walls the Earth is globed: above, below, and upon all sides is *Vaiya*, the Enfolding Ocean. But this is more like to sea below the Earth and more like to air above the Earth.

See further p. 86.

The Tale of Qorinómi (p. 215) was never in fact told – in the first version of the present tale (see note 15 above) it seems that Vairë would have liked to tell it, but felt the beady eye of the captious Ailios upon her. In the early Qenya word-list *Qorinómi* is defined as 'the name of the Sun', literally 'Drowned in the Sea', the name being a derivative from a root meaning 'choke, suffocate, drown', with this explanation: 'The Sun, after fleeing from the Moon, dived into the sea and wandered in the caverns of the Oaritsi.' *Oaritsi* is not given in the word-list, but *oaris* = 'mermaid'. Nothing is said in the *Lost Tales* of the Moon giving chase to the Sun; it was the stars of Varda that Ilinsor, 'huntsman of the firmament', pursued, and he was 'jealous of the supremacy of the Sun' (p. 195).

The conclusion of Vairë's tale, 'The Weaving of Days, Months, and Years', shows (as it seems to me) my father exploring a mode of mythical imagining that was for him a dead end. In its formal and explicit symbolism it stands quite apart from the general direction of his thought, and he excised it without trace. It raises, also, a strange question. In what possible sense were the Valar 'outside Time' before the weavings of Danuin, Ranuin, and Fanuin? In *The Music of the Ainur* (p. 55) Ilúvatar said: 'even now the world unfolds *and its history begins*'; in the final version (*The Silmarillion* p. 20) it is said that

> The Great Music had been but the growth and flowering of thought in the Timeless Halls, and the Vision only a foreshowing; but now they had entered in at the beginning of Time . . .

(It is also said in *The Silmarillion* (p. 39) that when the Two Trees of Valinor began to shine there began the Count of Time; this refers to the beginning of the measurement of Time from the waxing and the waning of the Trees.)

In the present tale the works of Danuin, Ranuin, and Fanuin are said to be the cause of 'the subjection of all things within the world to time and change'. But the very notion of a history, a consecutive story, self-evidently implies time and change; how then can Valinor be said only now to come under the necessity of change, with the ordering of the motions of the Sun and Moon, when it has undergone vast changes in the course of the story of the *Lost Tales*? Moreover the Gods now know 'that *hereafter* even they should in counted time be subject to slow eld and their bright days to waning'. But the very statement (for instance) that Ómar-Amillo was 'the youngest of the great Valar' who entered the world (p. 67) is an assertion that the other Valar, older than he, were 'subject to eld'. 'Age' has of course for mortal beings two aspects, which draw always closer: time passes, and the body decays. But of the 'natural' immortality of the Eldar it is said (p. 59): 'nor doth eld subdue their strength, unless it may be in ten thousand centuries'. Thus they 'age' (so Gilfanon is 'the most aged that now dwelt in the isle' and is 'one of the oldest of the fairies', p. 175), but they do not 'age' (do not become enfeebled). Why then do the Gods know that 'hereafter' they will be 'subject to slow eld' – which can only mean ageing in the latter sense? It may well be that there is a deeper thought here than I can fathom; but certainly I cannot explain it.

Finally, at the end of all the early writing concerning it, it may be remarked how major a place was taken in my father's original conception by the creation of the Sun and the Moon and the government of their motions: the astronomical myth is central to the whole. Afterwards it was steadily diminished, until in the end, perhaps, it would have disappeared altogether.

# X

# GILFANON'S TALE: THE TRAVAIL OF THE NOLDOLI AND THE COMING OF MANKIND

The rejected draft text of *The Hiding of Valinor* continues a little way beyond the end of Vairë's tale, thus:

> Now after the telling of this tale no more was there of speaking for that night, but Lindo begged Ailios to consent to a tale-telling of ceremony to be held the next night or as soon as might be; but Ailios would not agree, pleading matters that he must needs journey to a distant village to settle. So was it that the tale-telling was fixed ere the candles of sleep were lit for a sevennight from that time – and that was the day of Turuhalmë[1] or the Logdrawing. "Twill be a fitting day,' saith Lindo, 'for the sports of the morning in the snow and the gathering of the logs from the woods and the songs and drinking of Turuhalmë will leave us of right mood to listen to old tales beside this fire.'

As I have noticed earlier (p. 204), the original form of the *Tale of the Sun and Moon* and *The Hiding of Valinor* belonged to the phase before the entry of Gilfanon of Tavrobel, replacing Ailios.

Immediately following this rejected draft text, on the same manuscript page, the text in ink of the *Tale of Turambar* (Túrin) begins, with these words:

> When then Ailios had spoken his fill the time for the lighting of candles was at hand, and so came the first day of Turuhalmë to an end; but on the second night Ailios was not there, and being asked by Lindo one Eltas began a tale . . .

What was Ailios' tale to have been? (for I think it certain that it was never written). The answer becomes clear from a separate short text, very rough, which continues on from the discussion at the end of *The Hiding of Valinor*, given above. This tells that at length the day of Turuhalmë was come, and the company from Mar Vanwa Tyaliéva went into the snowy woods to bring back firewood on sleighs. Never was the Tale-fire allowed to go out or to die into grey ash, but on the eve of Turuhalmë it sank always to a smaller blaze until Turuhalmë itself, when great logs were brought into the Room of the Tale-fire and being blessed by Lindo with ancient magic roared and flared anew upon the hearth. Vairë blessed the door and lintel of the hall and gave the key to Rúmil, making him once again the Doorward, and to Littleheart was given the hammer of his gong. Then Lindo said, as he said each year:

> 'Lift up your voices, O Pipers of the Shore, and ye Elves of Kôr sing aloud; and all ye Noldoli and hidden fairies of the world dance ye and sing, sing and dance O little children of Men that the House of Memory resound with your voices . . .'

Then was sung a song of ancient days that the Eldar made when they dwelt beneath the wing of Manwë and sang on the great road from Kôr to the city of the Gods (see pp. 143-4).

It was now six months since Eriol went to visit Meril-i-Turinqi beseeching a draught of *limpë* (see pp. 96–8), and that desire had for a time fallen from him; but on this night he said to Lindo: 'Would I might drink with thee!' To this Lindo replied that Eriol should not 'think to overpass the bounds that Ilúvatar hath set', but also that he should consider that 'not yet hath Meril denied thee thy desire for ever'. Then Eriol was sad, for he guessed in his deepest heart that 'the savour of *limpë* and the blessedness of the Elves might not be his for ever'.

The text ends with Ailios preparing to tell a tale:

'I tell but as I may those things I have seen and known of very ancient days within the world when the Sun rose first, and there was travail and much sorrow, for Melko reigned unhampered and the power and strength that went forth from Angamandi reached almost to the ends of the great Earth.'

It is clear that no more was written. If it had been completed it would have led into the opening of *Turambar* cited above ('When then Ailios had spoken his fill . . .'); and it would have been central to the history of the Great Lands, telling of the coming of the Noldoli from Valinor, the Awakening of Men, and the Battle of Unnumbered Tears.

The text just described, linking *The Hiding of Valinor* to Ailios' unwritten tale, was not struck out, and my father later wrote on it: 'To come after the Tale of Eärendel and before Eriol fares to Tavrobel – after Tavrobel he drinks of *limpë*.' This is puzzling, since he cannot have intended the story of the Coming of Men to follow that of Eärendel; but it may be that he intended only to use the substance of this short text, describing the Turuhalmë ceremonies, without its ending.

However this may be, he devised a new framework for the telling of these tales, though he did not carry it through, and the revised account of the arranging of the next tale-telling has appeared in the *Tale of the Sun and Moon*, where after Gilfanon's interruption (p. 189) it was agreed that three nights after that on which *The Sun and Moon* and *The Hiding of Valinor* were told by Lindo and Vairë there should be a more ceremonial occasion, on which Gilfanon should relate 'the travail of the Noldoli and the coming of Mankind'.

Gilfanon's tale follows on, with consecutive page-numbers, from the second version of Vairë's tale of *The Hiding of Valinor*; but Gilfanon here tells it on the night following, not three days later. Unhappily Gilfanon was scarcely better served than Ailios had been, for if Ailios scarcely got started Gilfanon stops abruptly after a very few pages. What there is of his tale is very hastily written in pencil, and it is quite clear that it ends where it does because my father wrote no more of it. It was here that my father abandoned the *Lost Tales* – or, more accurately, abandoned those that still waited to be written; and the effects of this withdrawal never ceased to be felt throughout the history of 'The Silmarillion'. The major stories to follow Gilfanon's, those of Beren and Tinúviel, Túrin Turambar, the Fall of Gondolin, and the Necklace of the Dwarves, had been written and (in the first three cases) rewritten; and the last of these was to lead on to 'the great tale of Eärendel'. But that was not even begun. Thus the *Lost Tales* lack their middle, and their end.

I give here the text of Gilfanon's Tale so far as it goes.

Now when Vairë made an end, said Gilfanon: 'Complain not if on the morrow I weave a long tale, for the things I tell of cover many years of time, and I have waited long to tell them,' and Lindo laughed, saying he might tell to his heart's desire all that he knew.

But on the morrow Gilfanon sat in the chair and in this wise he began:

'Now many of the most ancient things of the Earth are forgotten, for they were lost in the darkness that was before the Sun, and no lore may recover them; yet mayhap this is new to the ears of many here that when the Teleri, the Noldoli, and the Solosimpi fared after Oromë and afterward found Valinor, yet was that not all of the race of the Eldalië that marched from Palisor, and those who remained behind are they whom many call the Qendi, the lost fairies of the world, but ye Elves of Kôr name Ilkorins, the Elves that never saw the light of Kôr. Of these some fell out upon the way, or were lost in the trackless glooms of those days, being wildered and but newly awakened on the Earth, but the most were those who left not Palisor at all, and a long time they dwelt in the pine-woods of Palisor, or sat in silence gazing at the mirrored stars in the pale still Waters of Awakening. Such great ages fared over them that the coming of Nornorë among them faded to a distant legend, and they said one to another that their brethren had gone westward to the Shining Isles. There, said they, do the Gods dwell, and they called them the Great Folk of the West, and thought they dwelt on firelit islands in the sea; but many had not even seen the great waves of that mighty water.

Now the Eldar or Qendi had the gift of speech direct from Ilúvatar, and it is but the sunderance of their fates that has altered them and made them unlike; yet is none so little changed as the tongue of the Dark Elves of Palisor.[2]

Now the tale tells of a certain fay, and names him Tû the wizard, for he was more skilled in magics than any that have dwelt ever yet beyond the land of Valinor; and wandering about the world he found the . . .[3] Elves and he drew them to him and taught them many deep things, and he became as a mighty king among them, and their tales name him the Lord of Gloaming and all the fairies of his realm Hisildi or the twilight people. Now the places about Koivië-néni the Waters of Awakening are rugged and full of mighty rocks, and the stream that feeds that water falls therein down a deep cleft . . . . a pale and slender thread, but the issue of the dark lake was beneath the earth into many endless caverns falling ever more deeply into the bosom of the world. There was the dwelling of Tû the wizard, and fathomless hollow are those places, but their doors have long been sealed and none know now the entry.

There was . . . . a pallid light of blue and silver flickering ever, and many strange spirits fared in and out beside the [?numbers] of the Elves. Now of those Elves there was one Nuin, and he was very wise, and he loved much to wander far abroad, for the eyes of the Hisildi were become exceeding keen, and they might follow very faint paths in those dim days. On a time did Nuin wander far to the east of Palisor, and few of his folk went with him, nor did Tû send them ever to those regions on his business, and strange tales were told concerning them; but now[4] curiosity overcame Nuin, and journeying far he came to a strange and wonderful place the like of which he had not seen before. A mountainous wall rose up before him, and long time he sought a way thereover, till he came upon a passage, and it was very dark and narrow, piercing the great cliff and winding ever down. Now daring greatly he followed this slender way, until suddenly the walls dropped upon either hand and he saw that he had found entrance to a great bowl set in a ring of unbroken hills whose compass he could not determine in the gloom.

Suddenly about him there gushed the sweetest odours of the Earth – nor were more lovely fragrances ever upon the airs of Valinor, and he stood drinking in the scents with deep delight, and amid the fragrance of [?evening] flowers came the deep odours that many pines loosen upon the midnight airs.

Suddenly afar off down in the dark woods that lay above the valley's bottom a nightingale sang, and others answered palely afar off, and Nuin well-nigh swooned at the loveliness of that dreaming place, and he knew that he had trespassed upon Murmenalda or the "Vale of Sleep", where it is ever the time of first quiet dark beneath young stars, and no wind blows.

Now did Nuin descend deeper into the vale, treading softly by reason of some unknown wonder that possessed him, and lo, beneath the trees he saw the warm dusk full of sleeping forms, and some were twined each in the other's arms, and some lay sleeping gently all alone, and Nuin stood and marvelled, scarce breathing.

Then seized with a sudden fear he turned and stole from that hallowed place, and coming again by the passage through the mountain he sped back to the abode of Tû; and coming before that oldest of wizards he said unto him that he was new come from the Eastward Lands, and Tû was little pleased thereat; nor any the more when Nuin made an end of his tale, telling of all he there saw – "and methought," said he, "that all who slumbered there were children, yet was their stature that of the greatest of the Elves."

Then did Tû fall into fear of Manwë, nay even of Ilúvatar the Lord of All, and he said to Nuin:

Here *Gilfanon's Tale* breaks off. The wizard Tû and the Dark Elf Nuin disappeared from the mythology and never appear again, together with the marvellous story of Nuin's coming upon the forms of the Fathers of Mankind still asleep in the Vale of Murmenalda – though from the nature of the work and the different degrees of attention that my father later gave to its different parts one cannot always distinguish between elements definitively abandoned and elements held in 'indefinite abeyance'. And unhappy though it is that this tale should have been abandoned, we are nonetheless by no means entirely in the dark as to how the narrative would have proceeded.

I have referred earlier (p. 107, note 3) to the existence of two 'schemes' or outlines setting out the plan of the *Lost Tales*; and I have said that one of these is a résumé of the *Tales* as they are extant, while the other is divergent, a project for a revision that was never undertaken. There is no doubt that the former of these, which for the purposes of this chapter I will call 'B', was composed when the *Lost Tales* had reached their furthest point of development, as represented by the latest texts and arrangements given in this book. Now when this outline comes to the matter of *Gilfanon's Tale* it becomes at once very much fuller, but then contracts again to cursory references for the tales of Tinúviel, Túrin, Tuor, and the Necklace of the Dwarves, and once more becomes fuller for the tale of Eärendel. It is clear, therefore, that B is the preliminary form, according to the method that my father regularly used in those days, of *Gilfanon's Tale*, and indeed the part of the tale that was written as a proper narrative is obviously following the outline quite closely, while substantially expanding it.

There is also an extremely rough, though full, outline of the matter of *Gilfanon's Tale* which though close to B has things that B does not, and vice versa; this is virtually certainly the predecessor of B, and in this chapter will be called 'A'.

The second outline referred to above, an unrealized project for the revision of the whole work, introduces features that need not be discussed here; it is sufficient to say that the mariner was now Ælfwine, not Eriol, and that his previous history was changed, but that the general plan of the *Tales* themselves was largely intact (with several notes to the effect that they needed abridging or recasting). This outline I shall call 'D'. How much time elapsed between B and D cannot be said, but I think probably not much. It seems possible that this new scheme was associated with the sudden breaking-off of *Gilfanon's Tale*. As with B, D suddenly expands to a much fuller account when this point is reached.

Lastly, a much briefer and more cursory outline, which however adds one or two interesting points, also has Ælfwine instead of Eriol; this followed B and preceded D, and is here called 'C'.

I shall not give all these outlines *in extenso*, which is unnecessary in view of the amount of overlap between them; on the other hand to combine them all into one would be both inaccurate and confusing. But since A and B are very close they can be readily combined into one; and I follow this account by that of D, with C in so far as it adds anything of note. And since in the matter of *Gilfanon's Tale* the outlines are clearly divided into two parts, the Awakening of Men and the history of the Gnomes in the Great Lands, I treat the narrative in each case in these two parts, separately.

There is no need to give the material of the outlines in the opening passage of *Gilfanon's Tale* that was actually written, but there are some points of difference between the outlines and the tale to be noted.

A and B call the wizard-king Túvo, not Tù; in C he is not named, and in D he is Tù 'the fay', as in the tale. Evil associations of this being appear in A: 'Melko meets with Túvo in the halls of Mandos during his enchainment. He teaches Túvo much black magic.' This was struck out, and nothing else is said of the matter; but both A and B say that it was after the escape of Melko and the ruin of the Trees that Túvo entered the world and 'set up a wizard kingship in the middle lands'.

In A, only, the Elves who remained behind in Palisor are said to have been of the people of the Teleri (the later Vanyar). This passage of *Gilfanon's Tale* is the first indication we have had that there were any such Elves (see p. 131); and I incline to think that the conception of the Dark Elves (the later Avari) who never undertook the journey from the Waters of Awakening only emerged in the course of the composition of the *Lost Tales*. But the name *Qendi*, which here first appears in the early narratives, is used somewhat ambiguously. In the fragment of the written tale, the words 'those who remained behind are they whom many call the Qendi, the lost fairies of the world,[5] but ye Elves of Kôr name Ilkorins' seem an altogether explicit statement that Qendi=Dark Elves; but a little later Gilfanon speaks of 'the Eldar or Qendi', and in the outline B it is said that 'a number of the original folk called Qendi (the name Eldar being given by the Gods) remained in Palisor'. These latter statements seem to show equally clearly that *Qendi* was intended as a term for all Elves.

The contradiction is however only apparent. *Qendi* was indeed the original name of all the Elves, and *Eldar* the name given by the Gods and adopted by the Elves of Valinor; those who remained behind preserved the old name *Qendi*. The early word-list of the Gnomish tongue states explicitly that the name *Elda* was given to the 'fairies' by the Valar and was 'adopted largely by them; the Ilkorins still preserved the old name *Qendi*, and this was adopted as the name of the reunited clans in Tol Eressëa'.[6]

In both A and B it is added that 'the Gods spoke not among themselves the tongues of the Eldalië, but could do so, and they comprehended all tongues. The wiser of the Elves learned the secret speech of the Gods and long treasured it, but after the coming to Tol Eressëa none remembered it save the Inwir, and now that knowledge has died save in the house of Meril.' With this compare Rúmil's remarks to Eriol, p. 48: 'There is beside the secret tongue in which the Eldar wrote many poesies and books of wisdom and histories of old and earliest things, and yet speak not. This tongue do only the Valar use in their high counsels, and not many of the Eldar of these days may read it or solve its characters.'

Nuin's words to Tû on the stature of the sleepers in the Vale of Murmenalda are curious. In A is added: 'Men were almost of a stature at first with Elves, the fairies being far greater and Men smaller than now. As the power of Men has grown the fairies have dwindled and Men waxed somewhat.' Other early statements indicate that Men and Elves were originally of very similar stature, and that the diminishing in that of the Elves was closely related to the coming of, and the dominance of, Men. Nuin's words are therefore puzzling, especially since in A they immediately precede the comment on the original similarity of size; for he can surely only mean that the sleepers in Murmenalda were very large by comparison with the Elves. That the sleepers were in fact children, not merely likened in some way to children, is made clear in D: 'Nuin finds the Slumbrous Dale (Murmenalda) where countless sleeping children lie.'

We come now to the point where the narrative is carried forward only in the outlines.

## The Awakening of Men
### according to the earlier outlines

The wizard Túvo told Nuin that the sleepers he had found were the new Children of Ilúvatar, and that they were waiting for light. He forbade

any of the Elves to wake them or to visit those places, being frightened of
the wrath of Ilúvatar; but despite this Nuin went there often and watched,
sitting on a rock. Once he stumbled against a sleeper, who stirred but did
not wake. At last, overcome by curiosity, he awakened two, named Ermon
and Elmir; they were dumb and very much afraid, but he taught them
much of the Ilkorin tongue, for which reason he is called Nuin Father of
Speech. Then came the First Dawn; and Ermon and Elmir alone of Men
saw the first Sun rise in the West and come over to the Eastward Haven.
Now Men came forth from Murmenalda as 'a host of sleepy children'.

(In the tale of *The Hiding of Valinor* it was long after the first rising of
the Sunship from Valinor that its Haven in the East was built; see pp.
214–15. It is interesting that the first Men, Ermon and Elmir, were woken
by Nuin before the first rising of the Sun, and although it was known to
Túvo that Men were 'waiting for light' no connection is made between
Nuin's act and the Sunrise. But of course one cannot judge the inner
tenor of the narrative from such summaries. It is notable also that whereas
the tongue of the Elves, in origin one and the same, was a direct gift of
Ilúvatar (p. 232), Men were born into the world without language and
received it from the instruction of an Ilkorin. Cf. *The Silmarillion*, p. 141:
'It is said also that these Men [the people of Bëor] had long had dealings
with the Dark Elves east of the mountains, and from them had learned
much of their speech; and since all the languages of the Quendi were of
one origin, the language of Bëor and his folk resembled the Elven-tongue
in many words and devices.')

At this point in the story the agents of Melko appear, the Úvanimor,
'bred in the earth' by him (Úvanimor, 'who are monsters, giants, and
ogres', have been mentioned in an earlier tale, p. 75); and Túvo protected
Men and Elves from them and from 'evil fays'. A makes mention of Orcs
besides.

A servant of Melko named 'Fúkil or Fangli' entered the world, and
coming among Men perverted them, so that they fell treacherously upon
the Ilkorins; there followed the Battle of Palisor, in which the people of
Ermon fought beside Nuin. According to A 'the fays and those Men
that aided them were defeated', but B calls it an 'undecided battle';
and the Men corrupted by Fangli fled away and became 'wild and
savage tribes', worshipping Fangli and Melko. Thereafter (in A only)
Palisor was possessed by 'Fangli and his hosts of Nauglath (or Dwarves)'.
(In the early writings the Dwarves are always portrayed as an evil
people.)

From this outline it is seen that the corruption of certain Men in the
beginning of their days by the agency of Melko was a feature of the
earliest phase of the mythology; but of all the story here sketched
there is no more than a hint or suggestion, at most, in *The Silmarillion*
(p. 141): ' "A darkness lies behind us," Bëor said; "and we have turned
our backs upon it, and we do not desire to return thither even in
thought." '[7]

## The Awakening of Men
### according to the later outline

Here it is told at the beginning of the narrative that Melko's Úvanimor had escaped when the Gods broke the Fortress of the North, and were wandering in the forests; Fankil servant of Melko dwelt uncaptured in the world. (Fankil = Fangli / Fúkil of A and B. In C he is called 'child of Melko'. Fankil has been mentioned at an earlier point in D, when at the time of the Awakening of the Elves 'Fankil and many dark shapes escaped into the world'; see p. 107, note 3.)

Nuin 'Father of Speech', who went again and again to Murmenalda despite the warnings of Tû (which are not here specified), woke Ermon and Elmir, and taught them speech and many things else. Ermon and Elmir alone of Mankind saw the Sun arising in the West, and the seeds of Palúrien bursting forth into leaf and bud. The hosts of Men came forth as sleepy children, raising a dumb clamour at the Sun; they followed it westward when it returned, and were grievously afraid of the first Night. Nuin and Ermon and Elmir taught them speech.

Men grew in stature, and gathered knowledge of the Dark Elves,[8] but Tû faded before the Sun and hid in the bottomless caverns. Men dwelt in the centre of the world and spread thence in all directions; and a very great age passed.

Fankil with the Dwarves and Goblins went among Men, and bred estrangement between them and the Elves; and many Men aided the Dwarves. The folk of Ermon alone stood by the fairies in the first war of Goblins and Elves (Goblins is here an emendation from Dwarves, and that from Men), which is called the War of Palisor. Nuin died at the hands of the Goblins through the treachery of Men. Many kindreds of Men were driven to the eastern deserts and the southern forests, whence came dark and savage peoples.

The hosts of Tareg the Ikorin marched North-west hearing a rumour of the Gnomes; and many of the lost kindreds joined him.

## The History of the Exiled Gnomes
### according to the earlier outlines

The Gnomes, after the passage of Helkaraksë, spread into Hisilómë, where they had 'trouble' with the ancient Shadow Folk in that land – in A called 'fay-people', in B '*Úvalear* fays'. (We have met the Shadow Folk of Hisilómë before, in the tale of *The Coming of the Elves*, p. 119, but there this is a name given by Men, after they were shut in Hisilómë by Melko, to the Lost Elves who remained there after straying on the march from Palisor. It will be seen in the later outlines that these Shadow Folk were an unknown people wholly distinct from Elves; and it seems therefore that the name was preserved while given a new interpretation.)

The Gnomes found the Waters of Asgon* and encamped there; then took place the Counting of the Folk, the birth of Turgon with 'prophecies', and the death of Fëanor. On this last matter the outlines are divergent. In A it was Nólemë, called also Fingolma, who died: 'his bark vanishes down a hidden way – said to be the way that Tuor after escaped by. He sailed to offer sacrifice in the islanded rock in Asgon.' (To whom was he sacrificing?) In B, as first written, it was likewise 'Fingolma (Nólemë)' who died, but this was emended to Fëanor; 'his bark vanished down a hidden [way] – said to be that opening that the Noldoli after enlarged and fashioned to a path, so that Tuor escaped that way. He sailed to the Islanded Rock in Asgon because he saw something brightly glitter there and sought his jewels.'

Leaving Asgon the Gnomes passed the Bitter Hills and fought their first battle with Orcs in the foothills of the Iron Mountains. (For the Iron Mountains as the southern border of Hisilómë see pp. 111-12, 158-9.) In the *Tale of Tinúviel* Beren came from Hisilómë, from 'beyond the Bitter Hills', and 'through the terrors of the Iron Mountains', and it thus seems clear that the Bitter Hills and the Iron Mountains may be equated.)

The next camp of the Gnomes was 'by Sirion' (which here first appears); and here the Gnomes first met the Ilkorins – A adding that these Ilkorins were originally of the Noldoli, and had been lost on the march from Palisor. The Gnomes learned from them of the coming of Men and of the Battle of Palisor; and they told the Ilkorins of the tidings in Valinor, and of their search for the jewels.

Now appears for the first time Maidros son of Fëanor (previously, in the tale of *The Theft of Melko*, the name was given to Fëanor's grandfather, pp. 146, 158). Maidros, guided by Ilkorins, led a host into the hills, either 'to seek for the jewels' (A), or 'to search the dwellings of Melko' (B – this should perhaps read 'search for the dwellings of Melko', the reading of C), but they were driven back with slaughter from the doors of Angamandi; and Maidros himself was taken alive, tortured – because he would not reveal the secret arts of the Noldoli in the making of jewels – and sent back to the Gnomes maimed. (In A, which still had Nólemë rather than Fëanor die in the Waters of Asgon, it was Fëanor himself who led the host against Melko, and it was Fëanor who was captured, tortured, and maimed.)

Then the Seven Sons of Fëanor swore an oath of enmity for ever against any that should hold the Silmarils. (This is the first appearance of the Seven Sons, and of the Oath, though that Fëanor had sons is mentioned in the *Tale of the Sun and Moon*, p. 192.)

The hosts of Melko now approached the camp of the Gnomes by Sirion, and they fled south, and dwelt then at Gorfalon, where they made the acquaintance of Men, both good and bad, but especially those of Ermon's folk; and an embassy was sent to Túvo, to Tinwelint (i.e. Thingol,

---

* later Lake Mithrim.

see p. 132), and to Ermon.[9] A great host was arrayed of Gnomes, Ilkorins, and Men, and Fingolma (Nólemë) marshalled it in the Valley of the Fountains, afterwards called the Vale of Weeping Waters. But Melko himself went into the tents of Men and beguiled them, and some of them fell treacherously on the rear of the Gnomes even as Melko's host attacked them; others Melko persuaded to abandon their friends, and these, together with others that he led astray with mists and wizardries, he beguiled into the Land of Shadows. (With this cf. the reference in the tale of *The Coming of the Elves* to the shutting of Men in Hisilómë by Melko, p. 118.)

Then took place 'the terrible Battle of Unnumbered Tears'. The Children of Úrin* (Sons of Úrin, A) alone of Men fought to the last, and none (save two messengers) came out of the fray; Turgon and a great regiment, seeing the day lost, turned and cut their way out, and rescued a part of the women and children. Turgon was pursued, and there is a reference to 'Mablon the Ilkorin's sacrifice to save the host'; Maidros and the other sons of Fëanor quarrelled with Turgon – because they wanted the leadership, A – and departed into the south. The remainder of the survivors and fugitives were surrounded, and swore allegiance to Melko; and he was wrathful, because he could not discover whither Turgon had fled.

After a reference to 'the Mines of Melko' and 'the Spell of Bottomless Dread' (the spell that Melko cast upon his slaves), the story concludes with 'the Building of Gondolin' and 'the estrangement of Men and Elves in Hisilómë, owing to the Battle of Unnumbered Tears': Melko fostered distrust and kept them spying on each other, so that they should not combine against him; and he fashioned the false-fairies or Kaukareldar in their likeness, and these deceived and betrayed Men.[10]

Since the outlines at this point return to mere headings for the tales of Tinúviel, Túrin, etc., it is clear that *Gilfanon's Tale* would have ended here.

## The History of the Exiled Gnomes
### according to the later outline

The Gnomes sojourned in the Land of Shadows (i.e. Hisilómë), and had dealings with the Shadow Folk. These were fays (C); no one knows whence they came: they are not of the Valar nor of Melko, but it is thought that they came from the outer void and primeval dark when the world was first fashioned. The Gnomes found 'the Waters of Mithrim (Asgon)', and here Fëanor died, drowned in the Waters of Mithrim. The Gnomes devised weapons for the first time, and quarried the dark hills. (This is curious, for it has been said in the account of the Kinslaughter at Alqaluntë that 'so first perished the Eldar neath the weapons of their kin', p. 165.

* later Húrin.

The first acquisition of weapons by the Eldar remained a point of uncertainty for a long time.)

The Gnomes now fought for the first time with the Orcs and captured the pass of the Bitter Hills; thus they escaped out of the Land of Shadows, to Melko's fear and amazement. They entered the Forest of Artanor (later Doriath) and the Region of the Great Plains (perhaps the forerunner of the later Talath Dirnen, the Guarded Plain of Nargothrond); and the host of Nólemë grew to a vast size. They practised many arts, but would dwell no longer in settled abodes. The chief camp of Nólemë was about the waters of Sirion; and the Gnomes drove the Orcs to the foothills of the Iron Mountains. Melko gathered his power in secret wrath.

Turgon was born to Nólemë.

Maidros, 'chief son of Fëanor', led a host against Angband, but was driven back with fire from its gates, and he was taken alive and tortured — according to C, repeating the story of the earlier outline, because he would not reveal the secret arts of jewel-making. (It is not said here that Maidros was freed and returned, but it is implied in the Oath of the Seven Sons that follows.)

The Seven Sons of Fëanor swore their terrible oath of hatred for ever against all, Gods or Elves or Men, who should hold the Silmarils; and the Children of Fëanor left the host of Nólemë and went back into Dor Lómin, where they became a mighty and a fierce race.

The hosts of Tareg the Ilkorin (see p. 237) found the Gnomes at the Feast of Reunion; and the Men of Ermon first saw the Gnomes. Then Nólemë's host, swollen by that of Tareg and by the sons of Ermon, prepared for battle; and messengers were sent out North, South, East, and West. Tinwelint alone refused the summons, and he said: 'Go not into the hills.' Úrin and Egnor* marched with countless battalions.

Melko withdrew all his forces and Nólemë believed that he was afraid. The hosts of Elfinesse drew into the Tumbled Lands and encamped in the Vale of Fountains (Gorfalong), or as it was afterwards called the Valley of Weeping Waters.

(The outline D differs in its account of the events before the Battle of Unnumbered Tears from that in the earlier ones, here including C. In the earlier, the Gnomes fled from the camp by Sirion when Melko's hosts approached, and retreated to Gorfalon, where the great host of Gnomes, Ilkorins, and Men was gathered, and arrayed in the Valley of the Fountains. In D, there is no mention of any retreat by Nólemë's hosts: rather, it seems, they advanced from the camp by Sirion into the Vale of Fountains (Gorfalong). But from the nature of these outlines they cannot be too closely pressed. The outline C, which ends here, says that when the Gnomes first encountered Men at Gorfalon the Gnomes taught them crafts — and this was one of the starting-points, no doubt, of the later Elf-friends of Beleriand.)

* The father of Beren.

Certain Men suborned by Melko went among the camp as minstrels and betrayed it. Melko fell upon them at early dawn in a grey rain, and the terrible Battle of Unnumbered Tears followed, of which no full tale is told, for no Gnome will ever speak of it. (In the margin here my father wrote: 'Melko himself was there?' In the earlier outline Melko himself entered the camp of his enemies.)

In the battle Nólemë was isolated and slain, and the Orcs cut out his heart; but Turgon rescued his body and his heart, and it became his emblem.[11] Nearly half of all the Gnomes and Men who fought there were slain.

Men fled, and the sons of Úrin alone stood fast until they were slain; but Úrin was taken. Turgon was terrible in his wrath, and his great battalion hewed its way out of the fight by sheer prowess.

Melko sent his host of Balrogs after them, and Mablon the Ilkorin died to save them when pursued. Turgon fled south along Sirion, gathering women and children from the camps, and aided by the magic of the stream escaped into a secret place and was lost to Melko.

The Sons of Fëanor came up too late and found a stricken field: they slew the spoilers who were left, and burying Nólemë they built the greatest cairn in the world over him and the [?Gnomes]. It was called the Hill of Death.

There followed the Thraldom of the Noldoli. The Gnomes were filled with bitterness at the treachery of Men, and the ease with which Melko beguiled them. The outline concludes with references to 'the Mines of Melko' and 'the Spell of Bottomless Dread', and the statement that all the Men of the North were shut in Hisilómë.

The outline D then turns to the story of Beren and Tinúviel, with a natural connection from the tale just sketched: 'Beren son of Egnor wandered out of Dor Lómin* into Artanor . . .' This is to be the next story told by the Tale-fire (as also in outline B); in D the matter of *Gilfanon's Tale* is to take four nights.

★

If certain features are selected from these outlines, and expressed in such a way as to emphasize agreement rather than disagreement, the likeness to the narrative structure of *The Silmarillion* is readily apparent. Thus:

- The Noldoli cross the Helkaraksë and spread into Hisilómë, making their encampment by Asgon (Mithrim);
- They meet Ilkorin Elves (=Úmanyar);
- Fëanor dies;
- First battle with Orcs;
- A Gnomish army goes to Angband;

* i.e. Hisilómë; see p. 112.

- Maidros captured, tortured, and maimed;
- The Sons of Fëanor depart from the host of the Elves (in D only);
- A mighty battle called the Battle of Unnumbered Tears is fought between Elves and Men and the hosts of Melko;
- Treachery of Men, corrupted by Melko, at that battle;
- But the people of Úrin (Húrin) are faithful, and do not survive it;
- The leader of the Gnomes is isolated and slain (in D only);
- Turgon and his host cut their way out, and go to Gondolin;
- Melko is wrathful because he cannot discover where Turgon has gone;
- The Fëanorians come late to the battle (in D only);
- A great cairn is piled (in D only).

These are essential features of the story that were to survive. But the unlikenesses are many and great. Most striking of all is that the entire later history of the long years of the Siege of Angband, ending with the Battle of Sudden Flame (Dagor Bragollach), of the passage of Men over the Mountains into Beleriand and their taking service with the Noldorin Kings, had yet to emerge; indeed these outlines give the effect of only a brief time elapsing between the coming of the Noldoli from Kôr and their great defeat. This effect may be to some extent the result of the compressed nature of these outlines, and indeed the reference in the last of them, D, to the practice of many arts by the Noldoli (p. 240) somewhat counteracts the impression – in any case, Turgon, born when the Gnomes were in Hisilómë or (according to D) when they were encamped by Sirion, is full grown at the Battle of Unnumbered Tears.[12] Even so, the picture in *The Silmarillion* of a period of centuries elapsing while Morgoth was straitly confined in Angband and 'behind the guard of their armies in the north the Noldor built their dwellings and their towers' is emphatically not present. In later 'phases' of the history my father steadily expanded the period between the rising of the Sun and Moon and the Battle of Unnumbered Tears. It is essential, also, to the old conception that Melko's victory was so complete and overwhelming: vast numbers of the Noldoli became his thralls, and wherever they went lived in the slavery of his spell; in Gondolin alone were they free – so in the old tale of *The Fall of Gondolin* it is said that the people of Gondolin 'were that kin of the Noldoli who alone escaped Melko's power, when at the Battle of Unnumbered Tears he slew and enslaved their folk and wove spells about them and caused them to dwell in the Hells of Iron, faring thence at his will and bidding only'. Moreover Gondolin was not founded until *after* the Battle of Unnumbered Tears.[13]

Of Fëanor's death in the early conception we can discern little; but at least it is clear that it bore no relation to the story of his death in *The Silmarillion* (p. 107). In these early outlines the Noldoli, leaving Hisilómë, had their first affray with the Orcs in the foothills of the Iron Mountains or in the pass of the Bitter Hills, and these heights pretty clearly correspond to the later Mountains of Shadow, Ered Wethrin (see pp. 158, 238);

but in *The Silmarillion* (p. 106) the first encounter of the Noldor with the Orcs was in Mithrim.

The meeting of Gnomes and Ilkorins survived in the meeting of the new-come Noldor with the Grey-elves of Mithrim (*ibid.* p. 108); but the Noldor heard rather of the power of King Thingol of Doriath than of the Battle of Palisor.

Whereas in these outl:nes Maidros son of Fëanor led an attack on Angband which was repulsed with slaughter and his own capture, in *The Silmarillion* it was Fingolfin who appeared before Angband, and being met with silence prudently withdrew to Mithrim (p. 109). Maidros (Maedhros) had been already taken at a meeting with an embassage of Morgoth's that was supposed to be a parley, and he heard the sound of Fingolfin's trumpets from his place of torment on Thangorodrim – where Morgoth set him until, as he said, the Noldor forsook their war and departed. Of the divided hosts of the Noldor there is of course no trace in the old story; and the rescue of Maedhros by Fingon, who cut off his hand in order to save him, does not appear in any form: rather is he set free by Melko, though maimed, and without explanation given. But it is very characteristic that the maiming of Maidros – an important 'moment' in the legends – should never itself be lost, though it came to be given a wholly different setting and agency.

The Oath of the Sons of Fëanor was here sworn after the coming of the Gnomes from Valinor, and after the death of their father; and in the later outline D they then left the host of (Finwë) Nólemë, Lord of the Noldoli, and returned to Dor Lómin (Hisilómë). In this and in other features that appear only in D the story is moved nearer to its later form. In the return to Dor Lómin is the germ of the departure of the Fëanorians from Mithrim to the eastern parts of Beleriand (*The Silmarillion* p. 112); in the Feast of Reunion that of Mereth Aderthad, the Feast of Reuniting, held by Fingolfin for the Elves of Beleriand (*ibid.* p. 113), though the participants are necessarily greatly different; in the latecoming of the Fëanorians to the stricken field of Unnumbered Tears that of the delayed arrival of the host of Maedhros (*ibid.* pp. 190–2); in the cutting-off and death of (Finwë) Nólemë in the battle that of the slaying of Fingon (*ibid.* p. 193 – when Finwë came to be Fëanor's father, and thus stepped into the place of Bruithwir, killed by Melko in Valinor, his position as leader of the hosts in the Battle of Unnumbered Tears was taken by Fingon); and in the great cairn called the Hill of Death, raised by the Sons of Fëanor, that of the Haudh-en-Ndengin or Hill of Slain, piled by Orcs in Anfauglith (*ibid.* p. 197). Whether the embassy to Túvo, Tinwelint, and Ermon (which in D becomes the sending of messengers) remotely anticipates the Union of Maedhros (*ibid.* pp. 188–9) is not clear, though Tinwelint's refusal to join forces with Nólemë survived in Thingol's rejection of Maedhros' approaches (p. 189). I cannot certainly explain Tinwelint's words 'Go not into the hills', but I suspect that 'the hills' are the Mountains of Iron (in *The Hiding of Valinor*, p. 209, called 'the Hills of Iron') above

Angband, and that he warned against an attack on Melko; in the old *Tale of Turambar* Tinwelint said: 'Of the wisdom of my heart and the fate of the Valar did I not go with my folk to the Battle of Unnumbered Tears.'

Other elements in the story of the battle that survived – the steadfastness of the folk of Úrin (Húrin), the escape of Turgon – already existed at this time in a tale that had been written (that of Túrin).

The geographical indications are slight, and there is no map of the Great Lands for the earliest period of the legends; in any case these questions are best left until the tales that take place in those lands. The Vale (or Valley) of the Fountains, afterwards the Valley (or Vale) of Weeping Waters, is in D explicitly equated with Gorfalong, which in the earlier outlines is given as Gorfalon, and seems to be distinct; but in any case neither these, nor 'the Tumbled Lands', can be brought into relation with any places or names in the later geography – unless (especially since in D Turgon is said to have fled 'south down Sirion') it may be supposed that something like the later picture of the Pass of Sirion was already in being, and that the Vale of the Fountains, or of Weeping Waters, was a name for it.

## NOTES

1   Above *Turuhalmë* are written *Duruchalm* (struck out) and *Halmadhurwion*.

2   This paragraph is marked with queries.

3   The word may be read equally well as 'dim' or 'dun'.

4   The original reading here was: 'and few of his folk went with him, and this Tû forbade to his folk, fearing the wrath of Ilúvatar and Manwë; yet did' (sc. curiosity overcome Nuin, etc.).

5   Earlier in the *Tales*, 'the Lost Elves' are those who were lost from the great journey and wandered in Hisilómë (see p. 118).

6   In the tale the 'fairies' of Tû's dominion (i.e. the Dark Elves) are given the name *Hisildi*, the twilight people; in outlines A and B, in addition to *Hisildi*, other names are given: *Humarni, Kaliondi, Lómëarni*.

7   Cf. also Sador's words to Túrin in his boyhood (*Unfinished Tales* p. 61): 'A darkness lies behind us, and out of it few tales have come. The fathers of our fathers may have had things to tell, but they did not tell them. Even their names are forgotten. The Mountains stand between us and the life that they came from, flying from no man now knows what.'

8   Cf. *The Silmarillion* p. 104: 'It is told that ere long they met Dark Elves in many places, and were befriended by them; and Men became the companions and disciples in their childhood of these ancient folk, wanderers of the Elven-race who never set out upon the paths to Valinor, and knew of the Valar only as a rumour and a distant name.'

9   Above *Ermon* is written, to all appearance, the Old English word *Æsc* ('ash'). It seems conceivable that this is an anglicizing of Old Norse *Askr* ('ash'), in the northern mythology the name of the first man, who with the first woman (*Embla*) were made by the Gods out of two trees that they found on the seashore (Völuspá strophe 17; Snorra Edda, Gylfaginning §8).

10  The text has here the bracketed word '(Gongs)'. This might be thought to be a name for the *Kaukareldar* or 'false-fairies', but in the Gnomish word-list *Gong* is defined as 'one of a tribe of the Orcs, a goblin'.

11  The cutting out of Nólemë's heart by the Orcs, and its recapture by Turgon his son, is referred to in an isolated early note, which says also that Turgon encased it in gold; and the emblem of the King's Folk in Gondolin, the Scarlet Heart, is mentioned in the tale of *The Fall of Gondolin*.

12  Cf. p. 167: 'Turondo son of Nólemë was not yet upon the Earth.' *Turgon* was the Gnomish name of *Turondo* (p. 115). In the later story Turgon was a leader of the Noldor from Valinor.

13  After the story was changed, and the founding of Gondolin was placed far earlier, the concluding part of *The Silmarillion* was never brought into harmony; and this was a main source of difficulty in the preparation of the published work.

# APPENDIX
## NAMES IN THE *LOST TALES* – PART I

There exist two small books, contemporary with the *Lost Tales*, which contain the first 'lexicons' of the Elvish languages; and both of them are very difficult documents.

One is concerned with the language called, in the book, *Qenya*, and I shall refer to this book as 'QL' (Qenya Lexicon). A good proportion of the entries in the first half of the alphabet were made at one time, when the work was first begun; these were very carefully written, though the pencil is now faint. Among these original entries is this group:

*Lemin* 'five'
*Lempe* 'ten'
*Leminkainen* '23'

The choice of '23' suggests that this was my father's age at the time, and that the book was begun therefore in 1915. This is supported by some of the statements made in the first layer of entries about certain figures of the mythology, statements that are at odds with everything that is said elsewhere, and which give glimpses of a stage even earlier than the *Lost Tales*.

The book naturally continued in use, and many entries (virtually all of those in the second part of the alphabet) are later than this first layer, though nothing more definite can be said than that all entries belong to the period of (or not long preceding) the *Lost Tales*.

The words in QL are arranged according to 'roots', and a note at the beginning states:

Roots are in capitals, and are not words in use at all, but serve as an elucidation of the words grouped together and a connection between them.

There is a good deal of uncertainty, expressed by queries, in the formulation of the roots, and in the ascription of words to one root or another, as my father moved among different etymological ideas; and in some cases it seems clear that the word was 'there', so to speak, but its etymology remained to be certainly defined, and not vice versa. The roots themselves are often difficult to represent, since certain consonants carry diacritic marks that are not defined. The notes on names that follow inevitably give a slightly more positive impression than does the book itself.

The other book is a dictionary of the Gnomish language, *Goldogrin*, and I shall refer to this as 'GL' (Goldogrin, or Gnomish, Lexicon). This is not arranged historically, by roots (though occasionally roots are given), but rather, in plan at least, as a conventional dictionary; and it contains a remarkable number of words. The book is entitled *i·Lam na·Ngoldathon* (i.e. 'the tongue of the Gnomes'): *Goldogrin*, with a date: 1917. Written beneath the title is *Eriol Sarothron* (i.e. 'Eriol the Voyager'), *who else is called Angol but in his own folk Ottor Wǽfre* (see p. 23).*

The great difficulty in this case is the intensity with which my father used this diminutive book, emending, rejecting, adding, in layer upon layer, so that in places it has become very hard to interpret. Moreover later changes to the forms in one entry were not necessarily made in related entries; thus the stages of a rapidly expanding linguistic conception are very confused in their representation. These little books were working materials, by no means the setting-out of finished ideas (it is indeed quite clear that GL in particular closely accompanied the actual composition of the *Tales*). Further, the languages changed even while the first 'layer' was being entered in GL; for example, the word *mô* 'sheep' was changed later to *moth*, but later in the dictionary *uimoth* 'sheep of the waves' was the form first written.

It is immediately obvious that an already extremely sophisticated and phonetically intricate historical structure lies behind the languages at this stage; but it seems that (unhappily and frustratingly) very little indeed in the way of phonological or grammatical description now survives from those days. I have found nothing, for instance, that sets out even in the sketchiest way the phonological relations between the two languages. Some early phonological description does exist for Qenya, but this became through later alterations and substitutions such a baffling muddle (while the material is in any case intrinsically extremely complex) that I have been unable to make use of it.

To attempt to use later materials for the elucidation of the linguistic ideas of the earliest period would in this book be quite impractical. But the perusal of these two vocabularies shows in the clearest possible way how deeply involved were the developments in the mythology and in the languages, and it would be seriously misleading to publish the *Lost Tales* without some attempt to show the etymological connections of the names that appear in them. I give therefore as much information, derived from these books, as is possible, but without any speculation beyond them. It is evident, for instance, that a prime element in the etymological constructions was slight variation in ancient 'roots' (caused especially by differences in the formation of consonants) that in the course of ages yielded very complex semantic situations; or again, that an old vocalic 'ablaut' (variation, in length or quality, of vowels in series) was present;

---

* The note concerning *Angol* and *Eriollo* referred to on p. 24 is written inside the cover of GL.

but I have thought it best merely to try to present the content of the dictionaries as clearly as I can.

It is noteworthy that my father introduced a kind of 'historical punning' here and there: so for instance the root SAHA 'be hot' yields (beside *saiwa* 'hot' or *sára* 'fiery') *Sahóra* 'the South', and from NENE 'flow' come *nen* 'river', *nénu* 'yellow water-lily', and *nénuvar* 'pool of lilies' – cf. *nenuphar* 'water-lily', modern French *nénufar*. There are also several resemblances to early English that are obviously not fortuitous, as *hôr* 'old', HERE 'rule', *rûm* 'secret (whisper)'.

It will be seen that a great many elements in the later languages, Quenya and Sindarin, as they are known from the published works, go back to the beginning; the languages, like the legends, were a continuous evolution, expansion, and refinement. But the historical status and relationship of the two languages as they were conceived at this time was radically changed later on: see p. 51.

The arrangement of the material has proved difficult, and indeed without a better understanding of relationships and their shifting formulations could scarcely be made satisfactory. The system I have adopted is to give etymologically-connected groups of words, in both Qenya and Gnomish, under an important name that contains one of them; to this entry other occurrences of a word in the group are referred (e.g. *glor-* in *Glorvent*, *Bráglorin* is referred to the entry *Laurelin*, where the etymological associations of Qenya *laurë* 'gold' are given).* Every name in the *Lost Tales* of this volume is given – that is, if any contemporary etymological information is to be found concerning it: any name not found in the following list is either quite opaque to me, or at least cannot be identified with any certainty. Rejected names are also included, on the same basis, but are given under the names that replaced them (e.g. *Dor Uswen* under *Dor Faidwen*).

The list of secondary names of the Valar which is written out on blank facing pages in the tale of *The Coming of the Valar* (see p. 93) is referred to as 'the Valar name-list'. The sign ⟨ is used only where it is used in the Gnomish dictionary, as *alfa* ⟨ *alchwa*, meaning that the one was historically derived from the other: it is not used in this Appendix to refer to alterations made by my father in the dictionaries themselves.

★

**Ainur**   Among the original entries in QL are *ainu* 'a pagan god' and *aini* 'a pagan goddess', together with *áye* 'hail!' and *Ainatar* 'Ilúvatar, God'. (Of course no one *within* the context of the mythology can call

---

* Later Quenya and Sindarin forms are only exceptionally mentioned. For such words see the vocabularies given in *An Introduction to Elvish*, ed. J. Allan, Bran's Head Books, 1978; also the Appendix to *The Silmarillion*.

the Ainur 'pagan'.) GL has *Ain*: 'also with distinctive masc. and fem. forms *Ainos* and *Ainil*, a God, i.e. one of the Great Valar'.

**Alalminórë**  See *Aldaron*, *Valinor*. In QL *Alalminórë* is glossed 'Land of Elms, one of the provinces of Inwinórë in which is situated Kortirion (Warwickshire)'; i.e. *Alalminórë* = Warwickshire (see p. 25). Gnomish words are *lalm* or *larm*, also *lalmir*, 'elm'.

**Aldaron**  In QL is a root ALA 'spread', with derivatives *alda* 'tree', *aldëa* 'tree-shadowed', *aldëon* 'avenue of trees', and *alalmë* 'elm' (see *Alalminórë*). In GL this name of Oromë appears as *Aldor* and *Ormaldor* (*Oromë* is *Orma* in Gnomish); *ald* 'wood (material)', later altered to *âl*.

**Alqaluntë**  QL *alqa* 'swan'; GL *alcwi*, with the corresponding word in Qenya here given as *alqë*, *alcwi* changed later to *alfa* ⟨ *alchwa*.

QL *luntë* 'ship' from root LUTU, with other derivatives *lúto* 'flood' and verb *lutta-*, *lutu-* 'flow, float' (cf. *Ilsaluntë*). GL has correspondingly *lunta* 'ship', *lud-* 'flow, stream, float'.

**Aluin**  See *Lúmin*.

**Amillo**  This appears in QL but with no indication of meaning; *Amillion* is Amillo's month, February (one of the most 'primitive' entries).

**Angaino**  Together with *angayassë* 'misery', *angaitya* 'torment', *Angaino* is given in QL separately from the 'iron' words (see *Angamandi*) and was first defined as 'a giant', emended to 'the great chain'. In GL Melko has a name *Angainos*, with a note: 'Do not confuse Gnomish *Angainos* with Qenya *Angaino* (Gnomish *Gainu*), the great chain of *tilkal*.' Under *Gainu* there is a later note: 'popularly connected with *ang* "iron" but really = "tormentor".'

**Angamandi**  QL has *anga* 'iron' (which is the *a* of *tilkal*, p. 100), *angaina* 'of iron', *Angaron(ti)* 'Mountains of Iron', and *Angamandu* or *Eremandu* 'Hells of Iron' (added later: 'or *Angamandi*, plural'). The Gnomish forms are *ang* 'iron' (as in *Angol*, see under *Eriol*), *angrin* 'of iron', *Angband* – which, strangely, is said in GL to be 'Melko's great fortress after the battle of Countless Lamentation down to the battle of the Twilit Pool' (when Tulkas finally overthrew Melko). See *Mandos*.

**Angol**  See *Eriol*.

**Arvalin**  See *Eruman*.

**Aryador**  This is said (p. 119) to be the name among Men of Hisilómë; but according to GL it was a word of Ilkorin origin, meaning 'land or place of shadow'; QL *Arëandor*, *Arëanor* 'name of a mountainous district, the abode of the Shadow Folk' (see p. 237). See *Eruman*.

**Asgon**  GL has *Asgon* 'name of a lake in Dor Lómin (Hisilómë), Q. *Aksanda*'; QL has *aksa* 'waterfall', of which the Gnomish equivalent is given as *acha* of the same meaning. (No light is cast on the later name *Mithrim* in the dictionaries.)

**Aulë**  A word *aulë* 'shaggy' is given in QL as a derivative from a root OWO (whence also *oa* 'wool', *uë* 'fleece'), but without any indication that this is to be connected with the name of the Vala. The Gnomish form of his name is *Óla*, changed to *Óli*, without further information. In the Valar name-list Aulë is called also *Tamar* or *Tamildo*. These are given in QL without translation under root TAMA 'smelt, forge', with *tambë* 'copper' (the *t* of *tilkal*, p. 100), *tambina* 'of copper', *tamin* 'forge'; Gnomish words are *tam* 'copper', *tambin* 'of copper', *tambos* 'cauldron'. For other names of Aulë see *Talka Marda*.

**Aulenossë** For *nossë* 'kin, people' see *Valinor*.

**Aur** Gnomish name of the Sun; see *Úr*.

**Balrog** GL defines *Balrog* as 'a kind of fire-demon; creatures and servants of Melko'. With the article the form is *i'Malrog*, plural *i'Malraugin*. Separate entries give *bal* 'anguish' (original initial consonant *mb-*), *balc* 'cruel'; and *graug* 'demon'. Qenya forms are mentioned: *araukë* and *Malkaraukë*. In QL *Malkaraukë* with other words such as *malkanë* 'torture' are given under a root MALA (MBALA) '(crush), hurt, damage', but the relation of this to MALA 'crush, squeeze' (see *Olórë Mallë*) was apparently not decided. There are also *Valkaraukë* and *valkanë* 'torture', but again the relationship is left obscure.

**Bráglorin** Defined in the text (p. 187) as 'the blazing vessel', but translated in GL as 'Golden Wain, a name of the Sun', with a note: 'also in analytical form *i·Vreda 'Loriol*'; *brada* 'waggon, wain'. For *-glorin* see *Laurelin*.

**Bronweg** GL has *Bronweg* '(the constant one), name of a famous Gnome', with related words as *brod, bronn* 'steadfast', *bronweth* 'constancy'. In QL *Voronwë* (see p. 48) 'the faithful' is derived from the root VORO, with *vor, voro* 'ever', *voronda* 'faithful', *vorima* 'everlasting', etc. Cf. *Vorotemnar*.

The common ending *-weg* is not given in GL, but cf. *gweg* 'man', plural *gwaith*.

**Cûm a Gumlaith** 'The Mound of the First Sorrow', tomb of Bruithwir, p. 149. GL *cûm* 'mound, especially burial-mound' (also *cum-* 'lie', *cumli* 'couch'); *gumlaith* 'weariness of spirit, grief' (*blaith* 'spirit').

**Cûm a Thegranaithos** See preceding entry. GL *thegra* 'first, foremost', *thegor* 'chief'; *naitha-* 'lament, weep, wail for', *naithol* 'miserable'.

**Danuin** GL has *dana* 'day (24 hours)', with reference to Qenya *sana* (not in QL); *Dana* was an earlier reading for *Danuin* (p. 222). The same element appears in *Lomendánar* 'Days of Gloaming'.

**Dor Faidwen** Gnomish *dôr* (< *ndor-*) '(inhabited) land, country, people of the land'; see *Valinor*.

*Dor Faidwen* is translated in the text 'Land of Release' (p. 13); GL has *faidwen* 'freedom' and many related words, as *fair* 'free', *faith* 'liberty', etc. In QL under root FAYA appear *fairë* 'free', *fairië* 'freedom', *fainu-* 'release'.

*Dor Faidwen* was the final Gnomish name of Tol Eressëa after many changes (p. 21), but little light can be cast on the earlier forms. *Gar* in *Gar Eglos* is a Gnomish word meaning 'place, district'. *Dor Us(g)wen*: GL gives the stem *us-* 'leave, depart' (also *uthwen* 'way out, exit'), and QL under root USU 'escape' has *uswë* 'issue, escape' and *usin* 'he escapes'.

**Dor Lómin**  See *Valinor, Hisilómë*.

**Eärendel**  In an annotated list of names accompanying *The Fall of Gondolin* there is a suggestion, attributed to Littleheart son of Voronwë, that *Eärendel* had 'some kinship to the Elfin *ea* and *earen* "eagle" and "eyrie" ', and in QL these words (both given the meaning 'eagle') are placed with *Eärendel*, though not explicitly connected. In the tale itself it is said that 'there are many interpretations both among Elves and Men' of the name *Eärendel*, with a suggestion that it was a word of 'some secret tongue' spoken by the people of Gondolin.

GL has an entry: *Ioringli* 'true Gnomish form of Eärendel's name, though the Eldar-form has been also adopted and often is met in transition state as *Iarendel, Iorendel*' (on the distinction between 'Gnomish' and 'Eldar' see p. 50). Gnomish words for 'eagle' are *ior, ioroth*.

In QL is an entry *Eärendilyon* 'son of Eärendel (used of any mariner)'; cf. p. 13.

**Eldamar**  For the first element see *Eldar*. – In QL the following words are given in a group: *mar* (*mas-*) 'dwelling of men, the Earth, -land', *mardo* 'dweller', *masto* 'village', and *-mas* equivalent to English *-ton*, *-by* in place-names (cf. *Mar Vanwa Tyaliéva*; *Koromas*; *i·Talka Marda* 'Smith of the World', Aulë). In GL are *bar* 'home' (< *mbar-*), and derivatives, as *baros* 'hamlet', also *-bar* as suffix 'dweller', or 'home, -ham'.

The Gnomish equivalent of *Eldamar* was *Eglobar* (Gnomish *Egla* = Qenya *Elda*): '*Eglobar* "Elfinesse" = Q. *Eldamar*, i.e. Elfhome; the land on the edge of Valinor where the fairies dwelt and built Côr. Also in forms *Eglabar, Eglamar, Eglomar*.' In QL *Eldamar* is said, in a very early entry, to be 'the rocky beach in western Inwinórë (Faëry)'; 'upon this rock was the white town built called Kôr'.

**Eldar**  In QL *Elda* is given separately, without etymological connections, and defined as 'a beach-fay or *Solosimpë* (shore-piper)'. This is a glimpse of an earlier conception than that found in the *Lost Tales*: the *Eldar* were originally the Sea-elves. GL has the entry *Egla* ' "a being from outside", name of the fairies given by the Valar and largely adopted by them, =Q. *Elda*' (see p. 235); also *eg, êg* 'far away, distant'. The association of *Eldar* with the stars does not go back to the beginning.

**Erinti**  She appears in QL in an isolated, early entry (afterwards struck through). Nothing is ever told of Erinti in the *Lost Tales*, but in this note she is called the Vala of love, music, and beauty, also named *Lotessë* and *Akairis* ('bride'), sister of Noldorin and Amillo. These three alone (i.e. of the Valar) have left Valinor, and dwell in Inwenórë (Tol Eressëa); she herself dwells in Alalminórë in a *korin* of elms guarded by the fairies. The second half of the month of *avestalis* (January) is called *Erintion*.

There is no trace of this elsewhere; but clearly, when Erinti became the daughter of Manwë and Varda her dwelling in Alalmínórë was taken over by Meril-i-Turinqi, the Lady of Tol Eressëa.

In the Valar name-list Erinti is called also *Kalainis*; this word appears in QL with the meaning 'May', one of many derivatives from the root KALA (see *Galmir*).

**Eriol**  In *The Cottage of Lost Play* (p. 14) *Eriol* is translated 'One who dreams alone'. In QL the elements of this interpretation are given under the roots ERE 'remain alone' (see *Tol Eressëa*) and LORO 'slumber' (see *Lórien*). In GL appears the note cited on p. 24 that Gnomish *Angol* and Qenya *Eriollo* were the names of the region 'between the seas' whence Eriol came (=Angeln in the Danish peninsula); and in an isolated note elsewhere *Angol* is derived from *ang* 'iron' and *ól* 'cliff', while Eriol is said to mean the same – 'this being the name of the fairies for the parts [*sic*] of his home (ironcliffs)'. Meril refers to 'the black coasts of your home' (p. 96). In this note the interpretation 'One who dreams alone' is said to be a pun on Lindo's part.

For *ang* 'iron' see *Angamandi*. GL has *ol, óla* 'cliff, seaward precipice', with Qenya forms *ollo, oldō. ere(n)* 'iron or steel' is given in QL, and this element appears also in the alternative name *Eremandu* for *Angamandu*, 'Hells of Iron'.

**Eruman**  The names of this region are as difficult as the original conception of the region itself (see pp. 91 ff.). The form *Erumáni* (which occurs in the *Tales* as well as *Eruman*) appears in QL under ERE 'out' (cf. *Neni Erúmëar*) without further information. GL has a long entry under *Edhofon*, which=Q. *Erumáni*: it is a 'dark land outside Valinor and to the south of the Bay of Faëry, that ran right up to the bases of the western side of the Mountains of Valinor; its farthest northern point touched upon the roots of Taniquetil, hence *Edhofon* ⟨ *Eðusmānī*-, i.e. beyond the abode of the Mánir. Hence also the Q. title *Afalinan* or *Arvalion*, i.e. nigh Valinor.' The implication of this seems to be that Taniquetil was 'the abode of the Mánir', as is comprehensible, since the Mánir were particularly associated with Manwë (the Gnomish words *móna, móni* are defined as 'spirits of the air, children of Manwë'), and therefore Eruman was beyond (south of) their abode. See *Mánir*.

GL also states that Edhofon was called *Garioth*; and *Garioth* is 'the true Gnome form' of the name *Aryador* (a word of Ilkorin origin) 'land of shadow', though applied not to Hisilómë but to Edhofon / Eruman.

According to QL *Harwalin* 'near the Valar' contains *har(e)* 'near'; the entries in GL are too confusing to cite, for the forms of *Harwalin / Arvalin* were changed over and over again. A late entry in GL gives a prefix *ar-* 'beside, along with'. For *Habbanan* see *Valar*.

**Falassë Númëa**   Translated in the text (p. 124) as 'Western Surf'; see *Falman, Númë*.

**Falman**   In QL the root FALA has derivatives *falma* 'foam', *falmar* 'wave as it breaks', *falas(s)* 'shore, beach', *Falman*=Ossë; cf. *Falassë Númea, Falmaríni*. GL has *falm* 'breaker, wave', *falos* 'sea-marge, surf', *Falmon* or *Falathron* 'names of Otha [Ossë], =Q. *Falman* and *Falassar*'.

**Falmaríni**   See *Falman*.

**Fanturi**   In QL *fantur*, without translation but with reference to Lórien and Mandos, is given under root FANA, with several derivatives all referring to visions, dreams, falling asleep. In GL (a late entry) the form is *Fanthor*, plural *i·Fanthaurin* 'the name of each of the two brothers, of sleep, of death'.

**Fanuin**   GL has *fann* 'a year'. For the rejected names *Lathos, Lathweg* (p. 222) see *Gonlath*.

**Faskala-númen, Faskalan**   Translated in the text (p. 187) as 'Bath of the Setting Sun'. GL has *fas-* 'wash', *fasc* 'clean', *fasca-* 'splash, sprinkle', *fôs* 'bath'. For *-númen* see *Númë*.

**Fëanor**   The only evidence for the meaning of this name is given under *Fionwë-Úrion*.

**Fingolma**   See *Nólemë*.

**Finwë**   As a proper name this is not in the dictionaries, but GL gives a common noun *finweg* 'craftsman, man of skill' (with *fim* 'clever; right hand' and other related words); for *-weg* see *Bronweg*. In QL derivatives of root FINI are *finwa* 'sagacious', *finië, findë* 'cunning'. See *Nólemë*.

**Fionwë-Úrion**   *Fion* 'son' is given separately in QL (a hurried later addition), with the note 'especially Fion(wë) the Vala'. In Gnomish he is '*Auros Fionweg*, or *Fionaur Fionor*'. In a later entry in GL '*Fionaur (Fionor)*=Q. *Fëanor* (goblet-smith)', and among the original entries is *fion* 'bowl, goblet'. There is no indication that this refers to Fëanor the Gnome.

For the second element (*Úrion, Auros*) see *Ûr*. In the Valar name-list Fionwë is called *Kalmo*; see *Galmir*.

**Fui**   In QL are *hui* 'fog, dark, murk, night' and *huiva* 'murky', and also '*Fui* (=*hui*) wife of Vê'. In Gnomish she is *Fuil* 'Queen of the Dark', and related words are *fui* 'night', *fuin* 'secret, dark'.

**fumellar**   The 'flowers of sleep' (poppies) in Lórien's gardens (p. 74). QL under root FUMU 'sleep' has *fúmë* 'sleep' (noun), *fúmella, fúmellot* 'poppy'.

**Galmir**   Translated in the text (p. 187) as 'the goldgleamer' (a name of the Sun). This is a derivative of Gnomish *gal-* 'shine', which in Qenya is KALA 'shine golden', and of which a great many derivatives are given in QL, as *kala-* 'shine', *kálë* 'morning', *kalma* 'daylight', *Kalainis* 'May' (see *Erinti*), *kalwa* 'beautiful', etc. Cf. *Kalormë*, *Kalaventë*, and *i·kal'antúlien* 'Light hath returned' (p. 184).

**Gar Lossion**   Translated in the text (p. 16) as 'Place of Flowers' (Gnomish name of Alalminórë). For *Gar* see *Dor Faidwen*. GL gives *lost* 'blossom' and *lôs* 'flower', but it is noted that they are probably unconnected and that *lôs* is more likely to be related to *lass* 'leaf', also used to mean 'petal'. (QL has *lassë* 'leaf', *lasselanta* 'the Fall, Autumn'.) See *Lindelos*.

**Glorvent**   For the element *Glor-* see *Laurelin.* – GL had *Glorben(d)* 'ship of gold', changed later to *Glorvent* 'boat of gold'; *benn* 'shape, cut, fashion', *benc, bent* 'small boat'. QL has the root VENE 'shape, cut out, scoop', with derivatives *venië, venwë* 'shape, cut' and *venë* 'small boat, vessel, dish'. Cf. the title of the 'World-Ship' drawing, *I Vene Kemen* (see p. 85), and the Sun's name *i·Kalaventë* (*Kalavénë*).

**Golfinweg**   See *Nólemë, Finwë.*

**Gondolin**   QL does not give this name, but *ondo* 'stone' appears under root ONO 'hard'. In GL *Gondolin* is said to=Qenya *Ondolin* (changed to *Ondolinda*) 'singing stone'. There is also an entry *gond* 'great stone, rock'; later this was changed to *gonn*, and a note added that *Gondolin*= *Gonn Dolin*, together with an entry *dólin* 'song'. See *Lindelos*.

**Gong**   GL gives no other information beyond that cited on p. 245, note 10, but compares *sithagong* 'dragonfly' (*sitha* 'fly', *Sithaloth* or *Sithaloctha* ('fly-cluster'), the Pleiades).

**Gonlath**   This is the name of the great rock on Taniquetil to which Fanuin's cable was tied (p. 219); the second element must therefore be Gnomish *lath* 'a year', which appears also in the rejected names for Fanuin, *Lathos* and *Lathweg* (p. 222). For *Gon-* see *Gondolin.*

**Gwerlum**   This is given in GL with the translation 'Gloomweaver'; *gwer-* 'wind, turn, bend', but also used in the sense of the root *gwidh-* 'plait, weave'. QL has a root GWERE 'whirl, twirl, twist', but the name *Wirilómë* of the great Spider is placed under the root GWIÐI, whence also *windelë* 'loom', *winda* 'woof', *wistë* 'weft'. The name of the great eddy *Wiruin* (p. 167), not in the dictionaries, must belong here. For the element *-lómë, -lum* see *Hisilómë.*

**Haloisi Velikë**   (On the 'World-Ship' drawing, p. 84.) In QL *haloisi* 'the sea (in storm)' is given under a root HALA, with other derivatives *haloitë* 'leaping', *halta-* 'to leap'.

　　To Qenya *velikë* 'great' corresponds Gnomish *beleg* 'mighty, great' (as in Beleg the Bowman in the tale of Túrin).

**Helkar**   QL under root HELE has *helkë* 'ice', *helka* 'ice-cold', *hilkin* 'it freezes', *halkin* 'frozen'. GL has *helc, heleg* 'ice', *hel-* 'freeze', *heloth* 'frost', etc., and *helcor* 'arctic cold, utter frost'; this last was changed to read *helchor* 'antarctic cold, utter frost of the South (the pillar of the Southern Lamp). Q. *Helkar*.'

**Helkaraksë** See *Helkar*; *Helkaraksë* is not in either dictionary and the second element is obscure, unless it is to be connected with Q. *aksa* 'waterfall' (see *Asgon*).

**Heskil** The root HESE 'winter' in QL has derivatives *Heskil* 'winter one', *Hesin* 'winter', *hessa* 'dead, withered', *hesta-* 'wither'. In GL are *Hess* 'winter, especially as name of Fuil', and *hesc* 'withered, dead; chill'. For another name of Fui Nienna see *Vailimo*.

**Hisildi** See *Hisilómë*.

**Hisilómë** Under the root HISI QL gives *hisë*, *histë* 'dusk', *Hisinan* 'Land of Twilight'. For the translation of *Hisilómë* as 'Shadowy Twilights' see p. 112.

The root LOMO has many derivatives, as *lómë* 'dusk, gloom, darkness', *lómëar* 'child of gloom' (cf. *Lómëarni*), *lómin* 'shade, shadow', *lomir* 'I hide', *lomba* 'secret'. Cf. *Wirilómë*. Gnomish words are *lôm* 'gloom, shade', *lómin* 'shadowy, gloomy' and noun 'gloom': so *Dor Lómin*. The same element occurs in *Lomendánar* 'Days of Gloaming'.

**Ilinsor** A late entry in GL gives *Glinthos*=Qenya *Ilinsor*, Helmsman of the Moon. The first element is probably *glint* 'crystal'. *Ilinsor* does not appear in QL.

**Ilkorin** A negative prefix *il-* is given in both dictionaries; in GL it is said that *il-* 'denotes the opposite, the reversal, i.e. more than the mere negation'. See *Kôr*.

**Ilsaluntë** (Name of the Moon.) *Ilsa* is given in QL as 'the mystic name of silver, as *laurë* of gold'; it is the *i* of *tilkal*, p. 100. For *luntë* 'ship' see *Alqaluntë*. The Gnomish name is *Gilthalont*; *giltha* 'white metal' is said to be properly the same as *celeb* 'silver' (Q. *telpë*), but now including *gais* 'steel', *ladog* 'tin', etc., as opposed to *culu* 'gold'; and *culu* is said to be a poetic word for 'gold' but 'also used mythically as a class name of all red and yellow metals, as *giltha* of white and grey'. See *Telimpë*.

**Ilterendi** In the text the fetters are called *Ilterendi* 'for they might not be filed or cleft' (p. 101); but root TERE in QL has derivatives with a sense of 'boring' (*tereva* 'piercing', *teret* 'auger, gimlet').

**Ilúvatar** There can be no doubt that the original meaning of *Ilúvatar* was 'Sky-father' (in QL is found *atar* 'father'); see *Ilwë*.

**Ilverin** Elvish name of Littleheart son of Bronweg. The rejected name *Elwenildo* (p. 52) contains the word *elwen* 'heart' given in QL; GL gives the word *ilf* 'heart (especially used of feelings)', and several names (*Ilfin(g)*, *Ilfiniol*, *Ilfrith*) corresponding to Qenya *Ilwerin*.

**Ilwë** In QL the word *ilu* is glossed 'ether, the slender airs among the stars', while in GL the Gnomish name *Ilon* of Illúvatar is said to= Qenya *Ilu*. In QL *ilwë* was first glossed 'sky, heavens', with a later addition 'the blue air that is about the stars, the middle layers'; to this in Gnomish corresponds *ilwint* – concerning which it is explained in GL that the true form *ilwi* or *ilwin* was perverted to *ilwint* through association with *gwint* 'face', as if it meant 'face of God'. Other words found in Gnomish are *Ilbar*, *Ilbaroth* 'heaven, the uttermost region beyond the world'; *Ilador*, *Ilathon=Ilúvatar*; *ilbrant* 'rainbow' (see *Ilweran*).

**Ilweran**    QL gives *Ilweran*, *Ilweranta* 'rainbow' (another word for the rainbow in Qenya is *Iluqinga*, in which *qinga* means 'bow'; *qingi-* 'twang, of strings, harp'). In Gnomish the corresponding forms are *Ilbrant* or *Ilvrant*, which are said in GL to be falsely associated with *brant* 'bow (for shooting)'; the second element is related rather to *rantha* 'arch, bridge', as Q. *Ilweran(ta)* shows.

**Ingil**    In GL the Gnomish names of Inwë's son are *Gilweth* and *Githilma*; *Gil* is the star Sirius, and is said to be the name of Gilweth after he rose into the heavens and 'in the likeness of a great bee bearing honey of flame followed Daimord [Telimektar, Orion]'; see entries *Nielluin*, *Telimektar*. No explanation of these names is given, but *Gil(weth)* is clearly connected with *gil-* 'gleam', *gilm* 'moonlight', *giltha* 'white metal' (see *Ilsaluntë*). For *Githilma* see *Isil*.

**Inwë**    In QL this, the name of 'the ancient king of the fairies who led them to the world', is a derivative of a root INI 'small', whence also the adjective *inya* and the names *Inwilis*, *Inwinórë* 'Faëry' and 'England' (the latter struck out). Tol Eressëa was here said to have been named *Inwinórë* after Inwë, but this was changed to say that it was named *Ingilnórë* after his son Ingil. These entries relate to a very early conception (see *Alalminórë*, *Eldamar*). For other names of Inwë see *Inwithiel*, *Isil*.

**Inwir**    See *Inwë*. In GL the 'noble clan of the Tilthin' (Teleri) are called *Imrim*, singular *Im* (see *Inwithiel*).

**Inwithiel**    In the texts *Inwithiel*, Gnomish name of King Inwë, is an emendation from *(Gim)Githil* (pp. 22, 131). In GL these names *Inwithiel*, *Githil* are given as additional to his proper names *Inweg* or *Im*. See *Isil*.

**Isil**    In the tale of *The Coming of the Elves* (p. 115) Inwë is called *Isil Inwë*, and in GL the Gnomish form corresponding to *Isil* is *Githil* (to the name of his son *Githilma* corresponds Qenya *Isilmo*). In QL is a root ISI (*iska* 'pale', *is* 'light snow'), of which the Gnomish equivalent is given as *ith-* or *gith-*; GL has a word *ith* 'fine snow'.

**Kalaventë**    See *Galmir*, *Glorvent*.

**Kalormë**    This appears in QL among the derivatives of root KALA (see *Galmir*), with the meaning 'hill-crest over which the Sun rises'. *ormë*='summit, crest', from a root ORO with apparently a base sense of 'rise': *or* 'on', *oro* 'hill', *oro-* 'rise', *orto-* 'raise', *oronta* 'steep', *orosta* 'ascension', etc.; Gnomish *or* 'on, onto, on top', *orod*, *ort* 'mountain', *orm* 'hill-top', *oros, orost-* 'rising'. Cf. *Oromë, Orossi, Tavrobel.*

**Kapalinda**  (The source of the river in the place of the banishment of the Noldoli in Valinor, p. 157.) QL has *kapalinda* 'spring of water' among derivatives of root KAPA 'leap, spring'; *linda* is obscure.

**Kaukareldar**  Under the root KAWA 'stoop' in QL are derivations *kauka* 'crooked, bent, humped', *kauko* 'humpback', *kawin* 'I bow', *kaurë* 'fear', *kaurëa* 'timid'.

**Kelusindi**  (The river in the place of the banishment of the Noldoli in Valinor, p. 157; in the text called *Sirnúmen.*) In QL under root KELE, KELU 'flow, trickle, ooze' are given many derivatives including *kelusindi* 'a river', also *kelu, kelumë* 'stream', *kektelë* 'fountain' (also in the form *ektelë*), etc. For *-sindi* see *Sirion.*

**Kémi**  QL gives *kemi* 'earth, soil, land' and *kemen* 'soil', from root KEME. The Gnomish name is *Címir*, which=Q. *Kémi* 'Mother Earth'. There is also a Gnomish word *grosgen* 'soil' in which *-gen* is said to= Q. *kémi.*

**Koivië-néni**  'Waters of Awakening.' In QL under root KOYO 'have life' are derivatives *koi, koirë* 'life', *koitë* 'living being', *koina, koirëa* 'alive', *koiva* 'awake', *koivië* 'awakening'. In GL are *cuil* 'life', *cuith* 'life, living body', etc.; *cwiv-* 'be awake', *cwivra-* 'awaken', *cuivros* 'awakening': *Nenin a Gwivros* 'Waters of Awakening'. For *-néni, Nenin* see *Neni Erúmëar.*

**Kópas**  QL has *kópa* 'harbour', the only word given under root KOPO 'keep, guard'. GL has *gobos* 'haven', with a reference to Q. *kópa, kópas*; also *gob* 'hollow of hand', *gobli* 'dell'.

**Kôr**  In QL this name is given under the root KORO 'revere?', with the note 'the ancient town built above the rocks of Eldamar, whence the fairies marched into the world'; also placed here are *korda* 'temple', *kordon* 'idol'. The Gnomish form is here given as *Côr*, but in GL *Côr* ('the hill of the fairies and the town thereon near the shores of the Bay of Faëry') was replaced by *Gwâr, Goros* '=Q. *Kôr* the town on the round hill'. This interpretation of the name *Kôr* clearly replaces that in QL, which belongs with the earliest layer of entries. See further under *korin.*

**korin**  See *Kôr.* In QL there is a second root KORO (i.e. distinct from that which gave *Kôr*); this has the meaning 'be round, roll', and has such derivatives as *korima* 'round', *kornë* 'loaf', also *korin* 'a circular enclosure, especially on a hill-top'. At the same time as *Côr* was replaced by *Gwâr, Goros* in GL the word *gorin* (*gwarin*) 'circle of trees', =Q. *korin*' was entered, and all these forms derive from the same root (*gwas-* or *gor-* ‹ *guor*=Q. *kor-*), which would seem to signify 'roundness'; so in the tale of *The Coming of the Elves* 'the Gods named that hill Kôr by reason of its roundness and its smoothness' (p. 122).

**Koromas**  A separate and early entry in QL defines *Kormas* (the form in the text before emendation to *Koromas*, p. 22) thus: 'the new capital of the fairies after their retreat from the hostile world to Tol Eressëa, now Inwinórë. It was named in memory of Kôr and because of its great tower was called also *Kortirion*.' For -*mas* see *Eldamar*.

**Kortirion**  The word *tirion* 'a mighty tower, a city on a hill' is given in QL under root TIRI 'stick up', with *tinda* 'spike', *tirin* 'tall tower', *tirios* 'a town with walls and towers'. There is also another root TIRI, differing in the nature of the medial consonant, with meaning 'watch, guard, keep; look at, observe', whence *tiris* 'watch, vigil', etc. In GL are *tir-* 'look out for, await', *tirin* (poetic form *tirion*) 'watch-tower, turret', *Tirimbrithla* 'the Tower of Pearl' (see *Silmarilli*).

**Kosomot**  Son of Melko (see p. 93). With a different second element, *Kosomoko*, this name is found in QL under root MOKO 'hate' (*mokir* 'I hate'), and the corresponding Gnomish form is there said to be *Gothmog*. The first element is from root KOSO 'strive', in Gnomish *goth* 'war, strife', with many derivative words.

**Kulullin**  This name is not among the derivatives of KULU 'gold' in QL, nor does it appear with the Gnomish words (mostly names of the Sun) containing *culu* in GL. For the meaning of *culu* in Gnomish see *Ilsaluntë*.

**Laisi**  See *Tári-Laisi*.

**Laurelin**  QL has *laurë* 'gold (much the same as *kulu*)', *laurina* 'golden'. *laurë* is the final *l* of *tilkal* (p. 100, where it is said to be the 'magic' name of gold, as *ilsa* of silver). The Gnomish words are *glôr* 'gold', *glôrin*, *glôriol* 'golden', but GL gives no names of the Golden Tree. Cf. *Bráglorin, Glorvent*.

**limpë**  *limpë* 'drink of the fairies' is given in QL under root LIPI, with *lipte-* 'to drip', *liptë* 'a little drop', *lipil* 'little glass'. Corresponding forms in GL are *limp* or *limpelis* 'the drink of the fairies', *lib-* 'to drip', *lib* 'a drop', *libli* 'small glass'.

**Lindeloksë**  At one occurrence in the texts an emendation from *Lindeloktë* and itself emended to *Lindelos* (p. 22), at others an emendation from *Lindelótë* and itself allowed to stand (pp. 79, 131). See *Lindelos*.

**Lindelos**  *Linde-* is one of many derivatives from the root LIRI 'sing', as *lin* 'melody', *lindelë* 'song, music', *lindelëa* 'melodious', *lirit* 'poem', *lirilla* 'lay, song' (cf. Rúmil's *tiripti lirilla*, p. 47), and the name of the Vala *Lirillo*. GL has *lir-* 'sing' and *glîr* 'song, poem'. *Lindelos* is not given in QL, which has the name rejected in the text *Lindeloktë* (p. 22), here translated 'singing cluster, laburnum'.

*Loktë* 'blossom (of flowers in bunches or clusters)' is derived from a root LOHO, with *lokta-* 'sprout, put forth leaves or flowers'. This is said to be an extended form of root OLO 'tip', whence *olë* 'three', *olma* 'nine', *ólemë* 'elbow'. Another extended form of this root is LO'O, from which are derived *lótë* 'a flower' (and *-lot* 'the common form in compounds') and many other words; cf. *Lindelótë*, another rejected name of the Golden Tree (pp. 79, 131), *Wingilot*. For Gnomish words see *Gar Lossion*. No Gnomish name of the Golden Tree is found in GL, but it was in fact *Glingol* (which originally appeared in the text, see p. 22); GL has *glin* 'sound, voice, utterance' (also *lin* 'sound'), with the note that *-glin, -grin* is a suffix in the names of languages, as *Goldogrin* Gnomish.

**Lirillo** (A name of Salmar-Noldorin, p. 144.) See *Lindelos*.

**Lómëarni** (A name of the Dark Elves, p. 244 note 6.) See *Hisilómë.*

**Lomendánar** 'Days of Gloaming' (p. 69). See *Hisilómë, Danuin.*

**Lórien** A derivative of the root LORO 'slumber', with *lor-* 'to slumber', *lorda* 'drowsy, slumbrous'; also *olor, olórë* 'dream', *olórëa* 'dreamy'. (For much later formulation of words from this root, including *Olórin* (Gandalf), see *Unfinished Tales* p. 396.) In GL are given *lúr* 'slumber', *Lúriel* changed to *Lúrin*=Qenya *Lórien*, and also *olm, oloth, olor* 'dream, apparition, vision', *oltha* 'appear as an apparition'. Cf. *Eriol, Olofantur, Olórë Mallë*.

**Lúmin** (Rejected name for Aluin 'Time', p. 222.) GL has *lúm* 'time', *luin* 'gone, past', *lu* 'occasion, time', *lútha* 'pass (of time), come to pass'. *Aluin* perhaps belongs here also.

**Luvier** I have translated this word on the 'World-Ship' drawing as 'Clouds' (p. 85) on the basis of words in QL derived from the root LUVU: *luvu-* 'lower, brood', *lumbo* 'dark lowering cloud', *lúrë* 'dark weather', *lúrëa* 'dark, overcast'. GL has *lum* 'cloud', *lumbri* 'foul weather', *lumbrin, lumba* 'overcast', *lur-* 'hang, lower, of clouds'.

**Makar** Given in QL ('God of battle') under root MAKA, with *mak-* 'slay', *makil* 'sword'. His Gnomish name is *Magron* or *Magorn*, with related words *mactha-* 'slay', *macha* 'slaughter, battle', *magli* 'a great sword'. See *Meássë*.

In the Valar name-list Makar is called also *Ramandor*. This was the original name of the King of the Eagles in *The Fall of Gondolin*, replaced by *Sorontur*. In QL under root RAMA (*rama-* 'to shout', *rambë* 'a shout', *ran* 'noise') *Ramandor* is translated 'the Shouter, =Makar'.

**Mandos** This name is defined in QL as 'the halls of Vê and Fui (hell)', and a comparison made with *-mandu* in *Angamandu* 'Hells of Iron'. In GL is the following entry: '*Bandoth* [later changed to *Bannoth*] (cf. *Angband*)=Mandos (1) the region of the waiting souls of the dead (2) the God who judged the dead Elves and Gnomes (3) improperly used exclusively of his hall, properly called *Gwê* [changed to *Gwi*] or *Ingwi*'. For this distinction between the region *Mandos*, in which dwelt the death-gods, and their halls *Vê* and *Fui*, see pp. 76, 89-90.

**Mánir** Not in QL; but GL has '*móna* or *móni*: the spirits of the air, children of Manweg'. Further relations are indicated in the following entry: '*manos* (plural *manossin*): a spirit that has gone to the Valar or to Erumáni (Edhofon). Cf. *móna*, Q. *mánë.*' See *Eruman* and pp. 91 ff. Other words are *mani* 'good (of men and character only), holy' (QL *manë* 'good (moral)'), *mandra* 'noble', and *Manweg* (Q. *Manwë*).

**Manwë**  See *Mánir*. The Gnomish names are *Man* and *Manweg* (for *-weg* see *Bronweg*).

**Mar Vanwa Tyaliéva**  For *Mar* see *Eldamar*, and for *Vanwa* see *Qalvanda*. *Tyalië* 'play, game' is an isolated entry in QL under root TYALA.

**Meássë**  A late, hasty entry in QL adds *Meássë* 'sister of Makar, Amazon with bloody arms' to the root MEHE 'ooze?', whence *mear* 'gore'. In GL she is *Mechos* and *Mechothli* (*mechor* 'gore'), and is also called *Magrintha* 'the red-handed' (*magru=macha* 'slaughter, battle', *magrusaig* 'bloodthirsty'). In the Valar name-list she is called *Rávë* or *Ravenni*; in QL the root RAVA has many derivatives, as *rauta-* 'to hunt', *raust* 'hunting, preying', *Raustar* a name of Oromë, *rau* (plural *rávi*) 'lion', *ravennë* 'she-lion', *Rávi* a name of Meássë. Very similar forms are given in GL: *rau* 'lion', *rausta* 'to hunt', *raust* 'hunt'.

**Melko**  The name is entered in QL but without etymological affinity. In GL the corresponding name is *Belca*, changed to *Belcha*, with a note referring to Qenya *velka* 'flame'. In the Valar name-list he is called *Yelur* (root DYELE, whence Qenya *yelwa* 'cold', *Yelin* 'winter'); the Gnomish form is *Geluim*, *Gieluim*, 'name of Belcha when exercising his opposite functions of extreme cold, Q. *Yeloimu*', cf. *Gilim* 'winter'. Melko is also called in the name-list *Ulban(d)*, which is found in QL glossed 'monster', under the negative prefix UL-; his son Kosomot (Gothmog) was 'by Ulbandi' (p. 93). Other names for him in Gnomish are *Uduvrin* (see *Utumna*) and *Angainos* (see *Angaino*).

**Meril-i-Turinqi**  *Meril* is not in QL, but *turinqi* 'queen' is given with a great many other derivatives of the root TURU 'be strong', including *Turambar* (*Turumarto*), and *tur* 'king'. In GL are *tur-* 'can, have power to', *tûr* 'king', *turwin* 'queen', *turm* 'authority, rule; strength', *turinthi* 'princess, especially title of Gwidhil'. Cf. *Sorontur*, *Valatúru*, *Tuor*.

There are also these later additions in GL: '*Gwidhil-i-Durinthi=Meril-i-Turinqi* Queen of Flowers'; *gwethra* 'bloom, flourish'; and the stem *gwedh-* is here compared to Qenya *mer-*, which is not in QL.

**Minethlos**  GL *min* 'one, single', *mindon* 'tower, properly an isolated turret or peak', *mineth* 'island', *Minethlos* 'Argent Isle (Moon)' – the same translation is given in the text, p. 192. Under root MĪ QL has *mir* 'one', *minqë* 'eleven'; and under root MINI *mindon* 'turret'. The second element of *Minethlos* must in fact be *lós* 'flower' (see *Gar Lossion*).

**Miruvor** QL *miruvórë* 'nectar, drink of the Valar' (see p. 161), with *miru* 'wine'; GL *mirofor* (or *gurmir*) 'drink of the Gods', *mîr*, *miros* 'wine'.

**Moritarnon** 'Door of Night' (see *Mornië*). GL gives *tarn* 'gate', *tarnon* 'porter'. Cf. *Tarn Fui*.

**Mornië** Not in QL, but one of the many derivatives of root MORO, as *moru-* 'to hide', *mori* 'night', *morna*, *morqa* 'black', *morion* 'son of the dark'. (A curious item is *Morwen* 'daughter of the dark', Jupiter. In the original tale of Túrin his mother was not named Morwen.) The Gnomish name of the death-ship is *Mornir*, a later addition to original entries *morn* 'dark, black', *morth* 'darkness', *mortha* 'dim', with the note 'the black ship that plies between Mandos and Erumáni, Q. *Mornië* (Black Grief)'. The second element is therefore *nîr* 'grief' (‹ *niēr-*), to which Qenya *nyérë* is said to correspond. Cf. *Moritarnon*, *Móru*, *Morwinyon*.

**Móru** GL in a later addition gives *Muru* 'a name of the Primeval Night personified as Gwerlum or Gungliont', hence my reading in the text *Móru* rather than *Morn* (p. 156). Among the original entries in GL is *múri* 'darkness, night'. See *Mornië*.

**Morwinyon** This name of the star Arcturus is translated in the text (p. 182) as 'the glint at dusk', and QL, giving it under root MORO (see *Mornië*), renders it 'glint in the dark'. QL has a root GWINI with derivative word *wintil* 'a glint'.

The Gnomish name is *Morwinthi*; presumably connected are *gwim*, *gwinc* 'spark, flash', *gwimla* 'wink, twinkle'.

**Murmenalda** Translated in the text as 'Vale of Sleep', 'the Slumbrous Dale' (pp. 233, 235). QL under root MURU gives *muru-* 'to slumber', *murmë* 'slumber', *murmëa* 'slumbrous'. The second element is from a root NĻDĻ, of which the derivatives in QL are *nal(lë)* 'dale, dell' and *nalda* 'valley' used as an adjective. In Gnomish occur *nal* 'dale, vale', *nal* 'down, downwards', *nalos* 'sinking, setting, slope', *Nalosaura* 'sunset', etc. Cf. *Murmuran*.

**Murmuran** See *Murmenalda*. GL gives the Gnomish form corresponding to Qenya *Murmuran* as *Mormaurien* 'abode of Lúriel', but this seems to be of different etymology: cf. *Malmaurien*=*Olórë Mallë*, the Path of Dreams, *maur* 'dream, vision'.

**Nandini** On an isolated paper that gives a list of the different clans of 'fays' the *Nandini* are 'fays of the valleys'. QL gives a root NARA with derivatives *nan(d)* 'woodland', *nandin* 'dryad'; GL has *nandir* 'fay of the country', Q. *nandin*', together with *nand* 'field, acre' (plural *nandin* 'country'), *nandor* 'farmer', etc.

**Nauglath** GL gives the following words: *naug* and *naugli* 'dwarf', *naugla* 'of the dwarves', *nauglafel* 'dwarf-natured, i.e. mean, avaricious' (see p. 236). QL has nothing corresponding, but in GL the Qenya equivalent of *naug* is said to be *nauka*.

**Neni Erúmëar**  (On the 'World-Ship' drawing, where I have translated it 'Outermost Waters', p. 85.) QL under root NENE 'flow' has *nen* 'river, water', and the same form occurs in Gnomish. *Erúmëa* 'outer, outermost' is given in QL as a derivative of ERE 'out', as in *Eruman*. Cf. *Koivië-néni*.

**Nermir**  In the list of fays referred to under *Nandini* the *Nermir* are 'fays of the meads'. QL has an isolated entry *Nermi* 'a field-spirit', and GL has *Nermil* 'a fay that haunts meadows and river-banks'.

**Nessa**  This name does not appear in the dictionaries. – In the Valar name-list she is called *Helinyetillë* and *Melesta*. In QL, among the very early entries, *helin* is the name of the violet or pansy, and *Helinyetillë* is glossed 'Eyes of Heartsease' (that being a name of the pansy); cf. *yéta* 'look at'. But in QL this is a name of Erinti. There was clearly much early shifting among the goddesses of Spring, the ascription of names and rôles (see *Erinti*). *Melesta* is doubtless from root MELE 'love' (*meles(së)* 'love', *melwa* 'lovely', etc.; Gnomish *mel-* 'to love', *meleth* 'love', *melon*, *meltha* 'beloved', etc.).

**Nielíqui**  In QL this name (*Nieliqi*, also *Nielikki*, *Nyelikki*) is derived from the root NYEHE 'weep' (see *Nienna*). Where her tears fell snow-drops (*nieninqë*, literally 'white tear') sprang. See the poem *Nieninqë* in J. R. R. Tolkien, *The Monsters and the Critics and Other Essays*, 1983, p. 215. For *ninqë* see *Taniquetil*.

The second element of *Nieliqui* is presumably from the root LIQI, whence *linqë* 'water', *liqin* 'wet', *liqis* 'transparence', etc. (see *Ulmo*).

**Nielluin**  This name of the star Sirius is translated in the text (p. 182) as 'the Bee of Azure' (see *Ingil*). The first element is from the root NEHE, whence *nektë* 'honey', *nier* (< *neier* < *neχier*) 'honey-bee', *nierwes* 'hive'. The name of Sirius is given in QL as *Niellúnë* or *Nierninwa*; both *ninwa* and *lúnë* are Qenya words meaning 'blue'. In Gnomish the name of the star is *Niothluimi*, = Qenya *Nielluin*: *nio*, *nios* 'bee' and many related words, *luim* 'blue'.

**Nienna**  In QL *Nyenna* the goddess is given under a root NYE(NE) 'bleat', whence *nyéni* 'she-goat', *nyéna-* 'lament', etc.; but there is a note 'or all to root NYEHE'. This means 'weep': *nië* 'tear' (cf. *Nielíqui*), *nyenyë* 'weeping'. In GL the forms of the name are *Nenni(r)*, *Nenir*, *Ninir*, without etymological connections given, but cf. *nín* 'tear'.

**Noldoli**  The root NOL 'know' in QL has derivatives *Noldo* 'Gnome' and *Noldorinwa* adjective, *Noldomar* 'Gnomeland', and *Noldorin* 'who dwelt awhile in Noldomar and brought the Gnomes back to Inwenórë'. It seems that *Noldomar* means the Great Lands. But it is very curious that in these entries, which are among the earliest, 'Gnome' is an emendation of 'Goblin'; cf. the poem *Goblin Feet* (1915), and its Old English title *Cumaþ þá Nihtielfas* (p. 32).

In Gnomish 'Gnome' is *Golda* ('i.e. wise one'); *Goldothrim* 'the people of the Gnomes', *Goldogrin* their tongue, *Goldobar*, *Goldomar* 'Gnomeland'. The equivalent of *Noldorin* in GL is *Goldriel*, which was the form antecedent to *Golthadriel* in the text before both were struck out (p. 22). See *Nólemë*.

**Noldorin** See *Noldoli*.

**Nólemë** This is given in QL as a common noun, 'deep lore, wisdom' (see *Noldoli*). The Gnomish name of Finwë Nólemë, *Golfinweg* (p. 115), contains the same element, as must also the name *Fingolma* given to him in outlines for *Gilfanon's Tale* (pp. 238-9).

**I Nori Landar** (On the 'World-Ship' drawing, probably meaning 'the Great Lands', pp. 84-5.) For *nori* see *Valinor*. Nothing similar to *landar* appears in QL; GL gives a word *land* (*lann*) 'broad'.

**Nornorë** In QL this name has the form *Nornoros* 'herald of the Gods', and with the verb *nornoro-* 'run on, run smoothly' is derived from a root NORO 'run, ride, spin, etc.'. GL has similar words, *nor-* run', roll', *norn* 'wheel', *nûr* 'smooth, rolling free'. The name corresponding to Qenya *Nornorë* is here *Drondor* 'messenger of the Gods' (*drond* 'race, course, track' and *drô* 'wheel-track, rut'); *Drondor* was later changed to *Dronúrin* (< *Noronōr-*) and *drond* to *dronn*.

**Númë** (On the 'World-Ship' drawing.) In QL *númë* 'West' is derived from root NUHU 'bow, bend down, stoop, sink'; other words are *núta-* 'stoop, sink', *númeta-*, *numenda-* 'get low (of the Sun)', *númëa* 'in the West'. Gnomish *num-* 'sink, descend', *númin* 'in the West', *Auranúmin* 'sunset', *numbros* 'incline, slope', *nunthi* 'downward'. Cf. *Falassë Númëa, Faskala-númen, Sirnúmen*.

**Núri** Name of Fui Nienna: 'Núri who sighs', p. 66. This is given without translation in QL under root NURU, with *núru-* 'growl (of dogs), grumble', *nur* 'growl, complaint'. In Gnomish she is *Nurnil*, with associated words *nur-* 'growl, grumble', *nurn* 'lament', *nurna-* 'bewail, lament'.

**Ô** (On the 'World-Ship' drawing: 'the Sea', pp. 84-5.) See *Ónen*.

**Oarni** See *Ónen*.

**Olofantur** See *Lórien, Fanturi*.

**Olórë Mallë** For *Olórë* see *Lórien*. *mallë* 'street' appears in QL under root MALA 'crush' (see *Balrog*); the Gnomish form is *mal* 'paved way, road', and the equivalent of *Olórë Mallë* is *Malmaurien* (see *Murmuran*).

**Ónen** The root 'o'o in QL has derivatives *Ô*, a poetic word, 'the sea', *oar* 'child of the sea, merchild', *oaris* (*-ts*), *oarwen* 'mermaid', and *Ossë*; the name *Ówen* (antecedent of *Ónen* in the text, pp. 61, 79) also appears, and evidently means the same as *oarwen* (for *-wen* see *Urwen*). The later form *Uinen* in the Tales is apparently Gnomish; GL *Únen* 'Lady of the Sea', changed later to *Uinen*. A form *Oinen* also occurs (p. 211).

In the Valar name-list Ónen is called also *Solórë* (see *Solosimpi*) and *Ui Oarista*. This latter appears in QL, with the definition 'Queen of the Mermaids', together with *Uin* 'the primeval whale'; but how these relate to the other names is obscure.

**Orc**   QL *ork* (*orq-*) 'monster, demon'. GL *orc* 'goblin', plural *orcin*, *orchoth* (*hoth* 'folk, people', *hothri* 'army', *hothron* 'captain').

**Oromë**   In QL *Oromë* 'son of Aulë' is placed under a root ORO that is distinct (apparently because of the nature of the consonant) from ORO (with meaning of 'steepness, rising') given under *Kalormë*; but these roots are said to be 'much confused'. This second root yields *órë* 'the dawn, Sunrise, East', *órëa* 'of the dawn, Eastern', *orontë*, *oronto* 'Sunrise', *osto* 'the gates of the Sun', and *Ostor* 'the East, the Sun when she issues from her white gates'. It is noted that *Oromë* should perhaps be placed under the other root, but there is no indication of the connections of the name. In *The Hiding of Valinor* (p. 214) Oromë has a particular knowledge of the East of the world. His name in Gnomish is *Orma*; and in the Valar name-list he is also called *Raustar*, for which see *Meássë*.

**Oronto**   (On the 'World-Ship' drawing, 'East'.) See *Oromë*.

**Orossi**   In the list of fays referred to under *Nandini* the *Orossi* are 'fays of the mountains', and this name is thus a derivative from the root ORO seen in *Kalormë*.

**Ossë**   See *Ónen*. His Gnomish name is *Otha* or *Oth*.

**Palisor**   See *Palúrien*.

**Palúrien**   An early entry in QL gives *Palurin* 'the wide world' under a root PALA, whose derivatives have a common general sense of 'flatness', among them *palis* 'sward, lawn', whence no doubt *Palisor*. In GL the corresponding name is *Belaurin*, *B(a)laurin*; but she is also called *Bladorwen* 'the wide earth, the world and its plants and fruits, Mother Earth' (related words are *blant* 'flat, open, expansive, candid', *blath* 'floor', *bladwen* 'a plain'). See *Yavanna*.

**Poldórëa**   Not in QL, but GL gives several corresponding forms: *Polodweg*=Tulcus (*polod* 'power, might, authority'); *polodrin* 'mighty, also in poetic form *Poldurin* or *Poldorin* which is especially used as epithet of Tulcus; Q. *Poldórëa*'.

**Qalmë-Tári**   The root is QALA 'die', whence *qalmë* 'death', *qalin* 'dead', and other words of the same meaning. *Tári* is from TAHA: *tâ* 'high', *tára* 'lofty', *tári* 'queen', etc.; Gnomish *dâ* 'high', *dara* 'lofty', *daroth* 'summit, peak'. Cf. *Taniquetil*.

**Qalvanda**   'The Road of Death' (p. 213). See *Qalmë-Tári*. The second element is from root VAHA: whence *vâ* past tense 'went', *vand-* 'way, path', *vandl* 'staff', *vanwa* 'gone on the road, past, over, lost' (as in *Mar Vanwa Tyaliéva*). Cf. *Vansamírin*.

**Qerkaringa**   The first element is obscure; for *-ringa* see *Ringil*.

**Qorinómi**   See p. 227. The root is QORO/QOSO, whence *qoro-* 'choke, suffocate', *qorin* 'drowned, choked', etc.

**Rána**   Not in QL, but GL has *Rân* 'the Moon (Q. *Rána*)' and *ranoth* 'month' (*Ranoth* was a rejected name preceding *Ranuin*, p. 222).

In the text (p. 192) it is said that the Gods named the Moon *Rána*.

**Ranuin**  See *Rána*.

**Ringil**  QL gives *ringa* 'damp, cold, chilly', *ringwë* 'rime, frost', *rin* 'dew'; GL *rî* 'coolness', *ring* 'cool, cold, a sudden breeze or cold breath', and (a later addition) *Ringli* 'the arctic colds, the North Pole (see the tale of the Coming of the Ainur)'. Cf. *Qerkaringa*.

**Rúmil**  This name is not found in either dictionary, but seems likely to be connected with words given in GL: *rû* and *rûm* 'secret, mystery', *ruim* 'secret, mysterious', *rui* 'whisper', *ruitha* 'to whisper'.

**Salmar**  This name must belong with derivatives of the root SALA: *salma* 'lyre', *salmë* 'harp-playing', etc.

**Samírien**  ('The Feast of Double Mirth', p. 143.) Presumably derived from the root MIRI 'smile'; *sa-* is referred to in QL as an 'intensive prefix'. Cf. *Vansamírin*.

**Sári**  Not in either dictionary, but in QL the root SAHA/SAHYA yields *sâ* 'fire', *saiwa* 'hot', *Sahóra* 'the South'; GL has *sâ* 'fire' (poetic form *sai*), *sairin* 'fiery', *saiwen* 'summer', and other words.

**Sil**  Under the root SILI QL gives a long list of words beginning with *Sil* 'Moon' and all with meanings of whiteness or white light, but neither *Silpion* nor *Silmaril* occurs in it. In GL *Sil* 'properly="Rose of Silpion", see Tale of the Making of the Sun and Moon, but often used poetically=Whole Moon or Rân'. In this tale (p. 192) it is said that the fairies named the Moon 'Sil, the Rose' (earlier reading 'the silver rose').

**Silindrin**  The 'Moon-cauldron' does not appear in either dictionary; the nearest form is *Silindo* in QL, which is a name of Jupiter. See *Sil*.

**Silmarilli**  See *Sil*. In GL the equivalent of 'Q. *Silmaril*' is *silubrill-(silum(b)aril-)*, plural *silubrilthin* (which occurs in the text, p. 128); a later addition compares *brithla* 'pearl', Qenya *marilla* (not in QL). The Tower of Pearl was named in Gnomish *Tirimbrithla*.

**Silmo**  See *Sil*. In QL *Silmo* is translated 'the Moon', and in GL *Silma* is given as the Gnomish equivalent of Qenya *Silmo*.

**Silpion**  See *Sil*. The Gnomish names are *Silpios* or *Piosil*, but no meaning is given.

**Silubrilthin**  See *Silmarilli*.

**Sirion**  QL root SIRI 'flow', with derivatives *sindi* 'river' (cf. *Kelusindi*), *sírë* 'stream', *sírima* 'liquid, flowing'. In GL are given *sîr* 'river', *siriol* 'flowing', and *Sirion* (poetic word) 'river, properly name of the famous magic river that flowed through Garlisgion and Nantathrin' (*Garlisgion* 'the Place of Reeds' survived in *Lisgardh* 'the land of reeds at the Mouths of Sirion', *Unfinished Tales* p. 34). Cf. *Sirnúmen*, and the name it replaced, *Numessir*.

**Sirnúmen**  See *Sirion*, *Númë*.

**Solosimpi**  QL gives *Solosimpë* 'the Shoreland Pipers', of which the first element is from root SOLO: *solmë* 'wave', *solor*, *solossë* 'surf, surge' (cf. *Solórë*, name of Ónen), and the second from SIPI 'whistle, pipe': *simpa*, *simpina* 'pipe, flute', *simpisë* 'piping', *simpetar* 'piper'. In GL the Gnomish name of the Solosimpi is *Thlossibin* or *Thlossibrim*, from *thloss* 'breaker', with a variant *Flossibrim*. The word *floss* is said to have been formed from *thloss* by influence of *flass* 'seamarge, surf; margin, fringe'.

**Sorontur**   Derived from a root SORO 'eagle': *sor*, *sornë* 'eagle', *sornion* 'eyrie', *Sorontur* 'King of Eagles'. For *-tur* see *Meril-i-Turinqi*. The Gnomish forms are *thorn* 'eagle', *thrond* '(eyrie), pinnacle', *Thorndor* and *Throndor* 'King of Eagles'.

**Súlimo**   In QL under the three root-forms SUHYU, SUHU, SUFU 'air, breathe, exhale, puff' are given *sû* 'noise of wind', *súlimë* 'wind', and *Súlimi, -o* 'Vali of Wind=Manwë and Varda'. This probably means that Manwë was *Súlimo* and Varda *Súlimi*, since Varda is called *Súlimi* in the Valar name-list; but in GL it is said that Manwë and Varda were together called *i·Súlimi*. GL has *sû* 'noise of wind', *súltha* 'blow (of wind)', but Manwë's wind-name is *Saulmoth* (*saul* 'a great wind'), which is said to be an older form of later *Solmoth*; and this '=Q. *Súlimo*'.

In Gnomish he is also called *Gwanweg* (*gwâ* 'wind', *gwam* 'gust of wind'), often combined with *Man* (see *Manwë*) as *Man 'Wanweg*=Q. *Manwë Súlimo*. The root GWĀ appears in QL: *wâ* 'wind', *wanwa* 'great gale', *wanwavoitë* 'windy'; and in the Valar name-list Manwë and Varda are together called *Wanwavoisi*.

**Súruli**   See *Súlimo*. *Súruli* is not in QL, but GL has *Sulus* (plurals *Sulussin* and *Suluthrim*) 'one of Manwë's two clans of air-spirits, Q. *Súru* plural *Súruli*'.

**Talka Marda**   This title of Aulë, translated in the text (p. 180) as 'Smith of the World', is not found in QL, but GL gives '*Martaglos*, correctly *Maltagros*, title of Óla, Smith of the World' as the equivalent of Qenya *Talka Marwa*; also *tagros*, *taglos* 'smith'. He is also called *Óla Mar*; and in the Valar name-list *Aulë Mar*. (Long afterwards this title of Aulë reappeared. In a very late note he is given the name *mbartanō* 'world-artificer' > Quenya *Martamo*, Sindarin *Barthan*.)

**Taniquetil**   Under the root TAHA (see *Qalmë-Tári*) *Taniqetil* is given in QL with the meaning 'lofty snowcap'. The second element is from root NIQI (*ninqë* 'white', *niqis* 'snow', *niqetil* 'snowcap'; cf. *nieninqë* 'white tear' (snowdrop) in entry *Nieliqui*).

The Gnomish form is *Danigwethil* (*dâ* 'high'), but the second element seems to be different, since GL gives a word *nigweth* 'storm (properly of snow, but that sense has evaporated)'.

**Tanyasalpë**   Translated in the text 'the bowl of fire' (p. 187). *salpa* 'bowl' is given in QL under a root SḶPḶ, with *sulp-* 'lick', *salpa* 'take a sup of', *sulpa* 'soup'. *Tanya* is not in QL; GL has *tan* 'firewood', *tantha-* 'kindle', *tang* 'flame, flash', and *Tanfa* 'the lowest of all airs, the hot air of the deep places'.

**Tári-Laisi** For *Tári* see *Qalmë-Tári*. In QL the root LAYA 'be alive, flourish' has derivatives *lairë* 'meadow', *laiqa* 'green', *laito* and *laisi* both meaning 'youth, vigour, new life'. The Gnomish words are *laib* (also *glaib*) 'green', *laigos* 'greenness', =Q. *laiqassë*, *lair* (also *glair*) 'meadow'. The following note is of great interest: 'Note *Laigolas*=green-leaf [see *Gar Lossion*], becoming archaic because of final form becoming *laib*, gave *Legolast* i.e. keen-sight [*last* 'look, glance', *leg*, *lêg* 'keen, piercing']. But perhaps both were his names, as the Gnomes delighted to give two similar-sounding names of dissimilar meaning, as *Laigolas Legolast*, *Túrin Turambar*, etc. *Legolas* the ordinary form is a confusion of the two.' (Legolas Green-leaf appears in the tale of *The Fall of Gondolin*; he was an Elf of Gondolin, and being night-sighted he led the fugitives from the city over the plain in the dark. A note associated with the tale says that 'he liveth still in Tol Eressëa named by the Eldar there *Laiqalassë*'.)

**Tarn Fui** See *Moritarnon*, *Fui*.

**Tavari** In the list of fays referred to under *Nandini* the *Tavari* are 'fays of the woods'. In QL *tavar* (*tavarni*) 'dale-sprites' is derived from a root TAVA, whence also *tauno* 'forest', *taulë* 'great tree', *tavas* 'woodland'. GL has *tavor* 'a wood-fay', *taur*, *tavros* 'forest' (*Tavros* also a proper name, 'chief wood-fay, the Blue Spirit of the Woods'. Later, *Tavros* became a name of Oromë, leading through *Tauros* to the form *Tauron* in *The Silmarillion*).

**Tavrobel** This is given in GL with the translation 'wood-home' (see *Tavari*). The element *pel* is said to be 'usual only in such place-names as *Tavrobel*', and means 'village, hamlet, -ham'. In a separate note elsewhere an additional Gnomish name *Tavrost* is given, and Qenya names *Tavaros(së)*, *Taurossë*. *Tavrost* evidently contains *rost* 'slope, hillside, ascent', with associated words *rosta* 'ascent' (*Rost'aura* 'Sunrise'), *ront* 'high, steep', ascribed to a stem *rō-*, *oro-*. These are etymological variants of words given under *Kalormë*.

**Telelli** This term, which occurs once only in the Tales (p. 19), is obscure. In QL, in early entries, a complex of words is given all of which mean 'little elf': these include *Teler* and *Telellë*, and the adjectives *telerëa* and *telella*. There is no suggestion of any distinction between them. An isolated note states that young Elves of all clans who dwelt in Kôr to perfect their arts of singing and poetry were called *Telelli*; but in another place *Telellin*, a dialect, appears to be used instead of *Telerin*. See *Teleri*.

**Teleri** See *Telelli*. In GL appears *Tilith* 'an elf, a member of the first of the three tribes of the fairies or Eldar; plural *Tilthin*'. The later meaning of *Teleri*, when it became the name of the Third Tribe, was already potentially present: QL gives a root TEL + U with derivatives *telu-* 'to finish, end', *telu* (noun), *telwa* 'last, late', with the suggestion that this was perhaps an extension of root TELE 'cover in' (see *Telimek-*

*tar*). In GL these meanings 'cover in – close – finish' are expressly assigned to the root TEL-: *telm* 'roof, sky', *teloth* 'roofing, canopy, shelter', *telu-* 'to close, end, finish', *telu* 'end'.

**Telimektar**  In QL *Telimektar*, *Telimbektar* is glossed 'Orion, literally Swordsman of Heaven', and is given under the root TELE 'cover in', together with *tel* 'roof', *telda* 'having a roof', *telimbo* 'canopy; sky', etc. *-mektar* probably derives from the root MAKA, see *Makar*. The Gnomish form is *Telumaithar*.

In the Valar name-list he is called also *Taimondo*. There are substantial notes on this name in both dictionaries, which appear to have been entered at the same time. In QL *Taimondo* and *Taimordo*, names of Telimektar, together with *Taimë*, *Taimië* 'the sky', were entered under the root TAHA (see *Qalmë-Tári*). The Gnomish equivalent is *Daimord* (*dai*, *daimoth* 'sky, heaven'), who appears also in the GL entry concerning Inwë's son Ingil (Gil, Sirius): he rose into the heavens in the likeness of a great bee and 'followed Daimord' (see *Ingil*). But the word *mordo* 'warrior, hero' in Qenya was actually a borrowing from Gnomish *mord*, and the true Quenya equivalent of *mord* was *mavar* 'shepherd' – this being the original meaning of the Gnomish word also, which developed that of 'man, warrior' through its use in poetry after it had become obsolete in prose and speech. Thus *Daimord* originally meant 'Shepherd of the Sky', as did the original Qenya name *Taimavar*, altered under the influence of the Gnomish name to *Taimondo*, *Taimordo*.

**Telimpë**  Not in QL under root TELPE, which has however *telempë= telpë* 'silver'. Gnomish words are *celeb* 'silver', *celebrin* 'of silver', *Celebron*, *Celioth* names of the Moon. See *Ilsaluntë*.

**Tevildo**  Given in QL under root TEFE (with derivatives *teve-* 'to hate', *tevin*, *tevië* 'hatred') and explained as 'the Lord of Cats' (see p. 47). The Gnomish form is *Tifil*, 'Prince of Cats'.

**Tilkal**  A name made up of the initial sounds of six names of metals (see p. 100 and footnote). For *tambë* 'copper' see *Aulë*, and for *ilsa* 'silver' see *Ilsaluntë*. *Latúken* 'tin' is given as a separate entry in QL, with *latukenda* 'of tin'; the Gnomish form is *ladog*. *Kanu* 'lead', *kanuva* 'leaden' are placed under a root KANA in QL. For *anga* 'iron' see *Angamandi*, and for *laurë* 'gold' see *Laurelin*.

**Timpinen**  The name stands in QL as the only derivative of a root TIFI, but under root TIPI are given *timpë* 'fine rain', *timpinë* 'spray', etc. See *Tinfang*.

**Tinfang**  The entry in GL is: '*Tinfing* or *Tinfang* the fluter (surnamed *Gwarbilin* or *Birdward*), a fay; cf. Q. *timpinen* a fluter (*Timpando*, *Varavilindo*)'. Other Gnomish words are *tif-* 'whistle', *timpa-* 'ring, jingle', *timpi* 'little bell', *timp* 'hoot, note of a flute', *tifin* 'small flute'. The first element in *Gwarbilin* is seen also in *Amon Gwareth* 'Hill of Watch', which occurs in the tale of *The Fall of Gondolin*; the second is *bilin(c)* 'sparrow, small bird'.

**Tinwë Linto, Tinwelint** GL has: '*Tinweg* (also *Lintinweg*) and more usually *Tinwelint*, =Q. *Tinwë Linto*; originally leader of the Solosimpi (after led by Ellu), but became King of the Lost Elves of Artanor'. The first element of the name is derived from TIN-, with such derivatives as *tim* 'spark, gleam, (star)', *tintiltha-* 'twinkle', *tinwithli* 'star-cluster, constellation'. The second element is possibly Gnomish *lint* 'quick, nimble, light' – which my father referred to in his essay 'A Secret Vice' (*The Monsters and the Critics and Other Essays*, 1983, p. 205) as a word he remembered from a very early stage of his linguistic constructions. The name is not in QL either in the earlier form (*Linwë Tinto*, p. 130) or the later, but under root TINI are *tinwë* 'star', *tint* '(silver) spark', etc., and also *lintitinwë* 'having many stars', the first element of this being a multiplicative prefix *li-*, *lin-*. Cf. *Tinwetári*.

**Tinwetári** 'Queen of Stars'. For the elements of this name see *Tinwë Linto*, *Qalmë-Tári*. The corresponding Gnomish name is *Tinturwin* with a different second element (see *Meril-i-Turinqi*). Varda is also called *Timbridhil*, *Timfiril*, with the same first element (*Bridhil* being the Gnomish name of Varda), and *Gailbridh(n)ir*, which contains *gail* 'star' (corresponding to Qenya *ílë* in *Ílivarda*, not found in QL).

**Tol Eressëa** Under root TOLO QL has derivatives *tol* 'island; any rise standing alone in water, plain of green, etc.', *tolmen* 'boss (of shield), isolated round hill, etc.', *tolos* 'knob, lump', *tólë* 'centre', and other words. GL gives *tol* 'an isle with high steep coasts'.

   *Eressëa* is given in QL under root ERE (distinct from that seen in *Eruman*) 'remain alone': *er* 'only, but, still', *eressë* 'singly, only, alone', *eressëa* 'lonely', *erda* 'solitary, deserted', *erin* 'remains'. In Gnomish the Lonely Isle is *Tol Erethrin* (*er* 'one', *ereth* 'solitude', *erethrin* 'solitary, lonely', etc.)

**Tolli Kuruvar** (On the 'World-Ship' drawing, 'the Magic Isles', pp. 84–5.) For *Tolli* see *Tol Eressëa*. QL has a group *kuru* 'magic, wizardry', *kuruvar* 'wizard', *kuruni* 'witch', with a note: 'of the good magic'. GL has *curu* 'magic', *curug* 'wizard', *curus* 'witch'.

**Tombo** *Tombo* 'gong' is derived in QL from a root TUMU 'swell (with idea of hollowness)', together with *tumbë* 'trumpet', *tumbo* 'dark vale', *tumna* 'deep, profound, dark or hidden' (see *Utumna*). Words in Gnomish are *tûm* 'valley', *tum* 'hollow', *tumli* 'dale', *tumbol* 'valley-like, hollow', *tumla-* 'hollow out'.

**Tuilérë** QL root TUYU: *tuilë* 'Spring, literally a budding – also collectively: buds, new shoots, fresh green', *Tuilérë* 'Spring', and several other words, as *tuilindo* '(spring-singer), swallow'. Gnomish forms are *tuil*, *tuilir* 'Spring' (with the note that *Tuilir*=Vána); but Vána is also called *Hairen* 'Spring', presumably connected with *hair* 'punctual, timely', *hai* 'punctually', *haidri* 'forenoon'.

**Tuivána** See *Tuilérë*, *Vána*.

**tulielto, &c.**   *Tulielto* is translated 'they have come' (p. 114), and *I·Eldar tulier* 'the Eldar have come' (*ibid.*); *I·kal'antúlien* is translated 'Light hath returned' (p. 184). QL under root TULU 'fetch, bring, bear; move, come' has the verb *tulu-* of the same meaning, also *tulwë* 'pillar, standard, pole', *tulma* 'bier'. GL has *tul-* 'bring; come', *tultha-* 'lift, carry'.

**Tulkas**   QL gives the name under root TULUK, with *tulunka* 'steady, firm', *tulka-* 'fix, set up, establish'. The Gnomish form is *Tulcus* (*-os*), with related words *tulug* 'steady, firm', *tulga-* 'make firm, settle, steady, comfort'.

**Tulkastor**   The name does not appear in the dictionaries (nor the precedent forms, *Tulkassë*, *Turenbor*, p. 22); see *Tulkas*, *Meril-i-Turinqi*.

**Tuor**   *Tuor* is not given in the dictionaries, but it is probably derived (since the name is also written *Túr*) from the root TURU 'be strong'; see *Meril-i-Turinqi*.

**Turgon**   Neither *Turondo* nor Gnomish *Turgon* are given in the dictionaries, and beyond the likelihood that the first element is from the root TURU (see *Meril-i-Turinqi*) these names cannot be explained.

**Turuhalmë**   'The Logdrawing' (p. 229). A second root TURU (TUSO) 'kindle' in QL (differing in the medial consonant from TURU 'be strong') has many derivatives: *turu-*, *tunda-* 'kindle', *turu* 'properly = firewood, but used of wood in general', *turúva* 'wooden', *tusturë* 'tinder', etc. In GL are *duru* 'wood: pole, beam, or log', *durog* 'wooden'.

The second element is in Gnomish *halm* 'drawing, draught (of fishes etc.)'. The name of the festival is *Duruchalmo(s)=Halm na-dhuruthon* (*Duruchalm* was written in the text and struck out, p. 244), translated 'Yule'; this was changed later to *Durufui* 'Yule (night), i.e. Log-night' (see *Fui*).

**Uin**   See *Ónen*. In GL *uin* is a common noun, 'whale', named after *Uin* 'Gulma's great whale' (*Gulma=Ulmo*); but apparently (though this entry is rather obscure) the original meaning of *uin*, preserved in poetry, was 'wave'. Another Gnomish word for 'whale' is *uimoth* 'sheep of the waves' (*moth* 'sheep', also '1000', probably originally 'flock'; *mothweg* 'shepherd').

**Uinen**   See *Ónen*.

**Ulmo**   *Ulmo* is given in QL under the root ULU 'pour, flow fast', together with *ulu-* and *ulto-* 'pour', in transitive and intransitive senses. His name in Gnomish is *Gulma*, with corresponding verbs *gul-* and *gulta-*. In the draft text of *The Music of the Ainur* he is also called *Linqil*: see *Nieliqui*. For other names see *Vailimo*.

**Ulmonan**   See *Ulmo*; the second element of this name is not explained.

**Ungoliont**   See *Ungwë Lianti*.

**Ungwë Lianti, Ungweliant(ë)**   Under a queried root GUNGU QL gives *ungwë* 'spider, especially *Ungwë* the Gloomweaver, usually *Ungwelianti*'. The second element is from root LI+*ya* 'entwine', with derivatives *lia* 'twine', *liantë* 'tendril', *liantassë* 'vine'. In GL the name as originally entered was *Gungliont*, as also first written in the text (p. 156); later this was changed to '*Ungweliont* or *Ungoliont*'. The second element is assigned to root *lī-* (*lind* 'twine').

**Uolë Kúvion** *Kúvion* was changed from *Mikúmi* (p. 198). The name is not in QL under the root KUVU 'bend, bow', which has derivatives *kú* 'crescent Moon', *kúnë* 'crescent, bow'. GL gives *cû* 'bow, crescent; the waxing or waning Moon', and also '*Cuvonweg: Ûl Cuvonweg* (=Q. *Ólë Kúmion*), the Moonking'. Under *Ûl* the Qenya equivalent is however *Uolë*, and here it is said that the name *Ûl* is usually in the phrase *Ûl·a·Rinthilios*; while *Rinthilios* is glossed 'the orbed Moon, name of the Moon-elf' (*rinc* 'circular', noun 'disc'; *rin-* 'revolve, return').

**Ûr** The root URU/USU in QL has derivatives *uru* 'fire', *úrin* 'blazing hot', *uruvoitë* 'fiery', *urúva* 'like fire', *urwa* 'on fire', *Ûr* 'the Sun' (with other forms *Úri*, *Úrinki*, *Urwen*), *Úrion* 'a name of Fionwë', *urna* 'oven', *usta-*, *urya-* 'burn' (transitive and intransitive). The Gnomish form is *Aur* (*aurost* 'dawn'), and also a poetic word *Uril*. See *Fionwë-Úrion*, *Urwen*.

**Urwen, Urwendi** In the earlier tales in this book the form is *Urwen*, becoming *Urwendi* in the *Tale of the Sun and Moon*. The original entry in GL was '*Urwendi* and *Urwin* (Q. *Urwen*) the maiden of the Sun-ship', but this was later changed to read '*Urwedhin* and *Urwin* (Q. *Urwendi*)'. In QL (see *Ûr*) *Urwen* appears as a name of the Sun. In the Valar name-list the Sun-maiden is also called *Úrinki*, and this also appears in QL as a name of the Sun.

The element *-wen* is given in QL under root GWENE: *wen* and *wendi* 'maid, girl', *-wen* feminine patronymic, like masculine *-ion*, *wendelë* 'maidenhood' (see *Wendelin*). In GL the forms were much changed and confused. The words given have stems in *gwin-*, *gwen-*, *gweth*, with meanings 'woman', 'girl', etc.; the root seems to have been changed from *gweni-* to *gwedhe-*, with reference both to Qenya *meril* (see *Meril-i-Turinqi*) and Qenya *wendi*.

**Utumna** In QL the root of *Utumna* ('lower regions of gloom and darkness in the North, Melko's first dwelling') is not given, but cf. the word *tumna* 'deep, profound, dark or hidden' cited under *Tombo*. In Gnomish the forms are *Udum* and *Uduvna*; Belcha (Melko) is called *Uduvrin*.

**Úvanimor** See *Vána*.

**Vai** The root VAYA 'enfold' in QL yields *Vai* 'the Outer Ocean', *Vaimo* or *Vailimo* 'Ulmo as Ruler of Vai', *vaima* 'robe', *vainë* 'sheath', *vainolë* 'quiver', *vaita-* 'to wrap', *Vaitya* 'the outermost airs beyond the world', etc. In Gnomish the form is *Bai*, with related words

*Baithon* 'the outer airs', *baith* 'garment', *baidha* 'to clothe', *bain* 'clad (Q. *vaina*)'.

**Vailimo**   See *Vai*. In Gnomish the form is *Belmoth* (< *Bailmoth*); there is also a poetic name *Bairos*. Ulmo is also called in Gnomish *i Chorweg a·Vai*, i.e. 'the old one of Vai' (*hôr* 'old, ancient (only of things still existing)', *hortha-* 'grow old', *horoth* 'old age', *Hôs* 'old age', a name of Fuil). For *-weg* see *Bronweg*.

**Vaitya**   See *Vai*.

**Valahíru**   (Marginal addition in the text against *Valatúru*, p. 180.) Not in the dictionaries, but probably to be associated with QL root HERE 'rule, have power': *heru-* 'to rule', *heru* 'lord', *heri* 'lady', *hérë* 'lordship'.

**Valar**   In QL '*Valar* or *Vali*' is derived from root VALA, with masc. singular *Valon* or *Valmo* and fem. singular *Valis* or *Valdë*; other words are *valin, valimo* 'happy', *vald-* 'blessedness, happiness'.

The Gnomish words are complicated and curious. As first written, there was *Ban* 'a god, one of the great Valar', plural *Banin*, and '*Dor'Vanion=Dor Banion=Gwalien* (or *Valinor*)'. All this was struck out. Elsewhere in GL is given the root GWAL 'fortune, happiness': *Gwala* 'one of the gods, including their divine folk and children, hence often used of one of the lesser folk as opposed to *Ban*'; *Gwalon* and *Gwalthi* corresponding to Qenya *Valon, Valsi*; *gwalt* 'good luck – any providential occurrence or thought: "the luck of the Valar", *i·walt ne Vanion* (Q. *valto*)'; and other abstract words, as *gwalweth* 'fortune, happiness'. Of the later interpretation of *Valar* there is thus no suggestion. See further under *Vána*.

**Valatúru**   See *Valar, Meril-i-Turinqi*.

**Valinor**   In QL two forms are given, *Valinor* and *Valinórë* (the latter also occurs in the text, p. 182), both glossed 'Asgard' (i.e. the City of the Gods in Norse mythology). For the Gnomish names (*Gwalien*, etc.) see *Valar*.

*nórë* is found in QL under the root NŌ 'become, be born', and is glossed 'native land, nation, family, country', also *-nor*, 'the form in compounds'. Other words are *nosta-* 'give birth', *nosta* 'birth, birthday', *nostalë* 'species, kind', *nossë* 'kin, people' (as in *Aulenossë*). The Gnomish form is *dôr*: see *Dor Faidwen*.

**Valmar**   See *Valar, Eldamar*.

**Vána**   A derivative of QL root VANA, together with *vanë* 'fair', *vanessë* 'beauty', *vanima* 'proper, right, fair', *úvanimo* 'monster' (*ú-* = 'not'), etc. Here also are given *Vanar* and *Vani=Valar, Vali*, with the note: 'cf. Gnomish *Ban-*'. See *Valar*.

Vána's name in Gnomish was *Gwân* or *Gwani* (changed later to *Gwann* or *Gwannuin*); *gwant, gwandra* 'beautiful', *gwanthi* 'beauty'.

**Vána-Laisi**   See Vána, *Tári-Laisi*.

**Vansamírin**   This name replaced *Samírien's road* in the text (p. 222). See *Qalvanda, Samírien*.

**Varda**  In QL the name is given with *vard-* 'rule, govern', *vardar* 'king', *varni* 'queen'. In Gnomish *Varda* was called *Bridhil* (and *Timbridhil*, see *Tinwetári*), which is cognate with Qenya *vard-*.

**Vê**  QL gives *Vê* 'name of Fantur' under root VEHE, but without meaning ascribed or other derivatives. The form in GL is *Gwê*, changed to *Gwî*: 'name of the hall of Bandoth, Q. *Vê*'. See *Mandos*, *Vefántur*.

**Vefántur**  In GL the Vala himself is called *Bandoth Gwê* (changed to *Bannoth Gwî*), *Gwefantur* (changed to *Gwifanthor*), and *Gwivannoth*.

**Vene Kemen**  See *Glorvent*, *Kémi*.

**Vilna**  In QL the root VILI (without meaning given) has derivatives *Vilna* (changed later to *Vilya*) '(lower) air', *Vilmar* 'dwelling of Manwë – the upper airs (but not *ilu*)', *vilin* 'airy, breezy', *vílë* 'gentle breeze'. The words 'but not *ilu*' refer to the definition of *ilu* in the sense of *ilwë*, the middle air among the stars (see *ilwë*). Manwë's dwelling *Vilmar* is not named elsewhere.

The Gnomish names for the lowest air were *Gwilfa* or *Fâ*; the latter is said to be of unknown etymology. The corresponding Qenya names are given in GL as *Fâ* and *Favilna*, and these appear in QL under a root FAGA without translation, merely as equivalents of *Vilna*. Other Gnomish words are *gwil-* 'sail, float, fly', *gwilith* 'breeze', *gwilbrin* 'butterfly': these correspond to words in QL under a root GWILI, *wili-* 'sail, float, fly', *wilin* 'bird', *wilwarin* 'butterfly'. Another name of Manweg as Lord of the Winds, *Famfir*, is given in GL.

**Voronwë**  See *Bronweg*.

**Vorotemnar**  For *voro* 'ever' see *Bronweg*. *Temnar* must be from root TEME 'tie', of which no derivative words are listed in QL.

**Wendelin**  This is not in QL, but GL gives *Gwendeling* (changed later to *Gwedhiling*) as the Gnomish name corresponding to Qenya *Wendelin*; 'Queen of the Woodland Elves, mother of Tinúviel' (the only occurrence of the name *Tinúviel* in the dictionaries). The name must be related to Qenya *wen* 'maid, girl' and the Gnomish forms given under *Urwen*.

**Wingildi**  See *Wingilot*.

**Wingilot**  Under the root GWINGI/GWIGI in QL are *wingë* 'foam, spindrift', *wingilot* 'foamflower, Eärendel's boat', and *wingild-* 'nymph' (cf. *Wingildi*). For the element *-lot* see *Lindelos*.

GL has the entry: '*Gwingalos* or *Gwingli*=*Lothwinga* or Foamflower, the name of Eärendel's (Ioringli's) boat'; also *lothwing* 'foamflower', *gwing* 'wavecrest, foam', and *gwingil* 'foam-maiden (mermaid, one of the attendants of Uinen)'.

**Wirilómë**  See *Gwerlum*.

**Wiruin**  See *Gwerlum*.

**Yavanna**  In QL this name is given under the root YAVA, together with *yavin* 'bears fruit', *yáva* 'fruit', *yávan* 'harvest, autumn'. The Gnomish form is *Ifon*, *Ivon*, 'especially in the combinations *Ivon Belaurin*, *Ivon Címir*, *Ivon i·Vladorwen*'; see *Kémi*, *Palúrien*.

# SHORT GLOSSARY OF OBSOLETE, ARCHAIC, AND RARE WORDS

**an**  if, 64, 140, 149, 155, 165, 180, 182, 189, 197, 208
**arrassed**  covered with arras (rich figured tapestry), 17
**astonied**  stunned, astonished, 116, 185
**bason**  formerly a common spelling of *basin*, 164 etc.
**bent**  open place covered with grass, 34
**brakes**  thickets, 106
**charger**  large dish, 191
**clamant**  clamorous, noisy, 43
**clomb**  old past tense of *climb*, 122
**constellate**  formed into a constellation, 195
**cools**  coolnesses, 74
**corbel**  basket, 186
**covetice**  (inordinate) desire, 117; covetousness, 146–7
**eld**  old age, 59, 219, 228
**fain**  gladly, 45, 150; disposed, desirous, 195; **fain of** well-pleased with, 117, 208
**fane**  temple, 39, 43
**fey**  37. The old senses were 'fated, approaching death; presaging death'. It seems very unlikely that the later sense 'possessing or displaying magical, fairylike, or unearthly qualities' (O.E.D. Supplement) was intended.
**flittermice**  bats, 40
**go**  move, in the phrase *all the creatures that go* 219
**houseleek**  a fleshy plant that grows on the walls and roofs of houses, 95
**inaureoled**  surrounded with a halo, 204 (the word is only recorded in the O.E.D. in a poem by Francis Thompson, 1897).
**jacinth**  blue, 34
**lampads**  35. The word is only recorded in the O.E.D. (first used by Coleridge) of the seven lamps of fire burning before the throne of God in the Book of Revelation, iv.5.
**lets upon**  gives on to, opens on to, 210
**lief**  gladly, willingly, 163; **liever** more gladly, more willingly, rather, 105, 163
**lustihead**  vigour, 99
**meed**  requital, 105
**minished**  reduced, diminished, 150, 208
**or . . . or**  either . . . or, 127, 192, 214
**or yet**  apparently means 'already', 166
**ousel**  blackbird, 47 (now spelt *ouzel*, in *Ring-ouzel* and other bird-names).

**pleasance**  'A pleasure-ground, usually attached to a mansion; sometimes a secluded part of a garden, but more often a separate enclosure laid out with shady walks, trees and shrubs . . .' (O.E.D.) This sense is present in *pleasa(u)nces* 74, 116, but in *rest and pleasance* 69 the sense is 'enjoyment, pleasure'; in *nor did he have lack of pleasance* 65 either meaning may be intended, but I think probably the former.

**pled**  old past tense of *plead*, 167

**plenilune**  the time of full moon, 205 (see *Letters* p. 310).

**pricks**  (spurs his horse), rides fast, 114. *Oromë pricks over the plain* echoes the first line of *The Faerie Queene*, *A Gentle Knight was pricking on the plaine*.

**recked**  troubled, cared, 179

**rede**  counsel, advice, 141, 182, 217; plan, 180; **redes** counsels, 117

**rondured**  (in **golden-rondured**)  35. *Rondure* 'circle, rounded form'; *rondured* is not recorded.

**ruth**  matter of sorrow, calamity, 185; distress, grief, 191; remorse, 194; in *the greatest ruth was that to [the Valar] thereafter* 209 the sense is unclear: 'matter of sorrow or regret', or possibly 'harm, ill'.

**saps**  deep diggings, 104

**sate**  old past tense of *sit*, 58, 105, 153, 181, 190, 194

**seamews**  seagulls, 124

**selenites**  inhabitants of the Moon, 205

**shallop**  192. This word had precise applications to particular kinds of boat, but here apparently means 'open boat propelled by oars and sail'.

**share**  34, 38. *share*=ploughshare, but used here of the blade of a scythe.

**sledge-blows**  blows as of a *sledge*, a large heavy hammer, 78

**sprent**  past participle of the lost verb *sprenge* 'sprinkle, scatter', 192

**sprite(s)**  spirit(s), 71, 74, 95, 115, 191

**suaded**  persuaded, 69, 163

**trillups**  108, **trillaping** 109. This word is not recorded in any dictionary available to me.

**umbraged**  (in **wide-umbraged**)  34, 38. *Umbraged* 'shaded, shadowed', but here in the sense 'shadowing', 'casting a shade'.

**web(s)**  woven fabric, 58, 73, 95 (also used in senses 'webbed feet' 127, 'cobwebs' 77, etc.)

**whickering**  205 (*whickering sparks*). The verb *whicker* meant to laugh or titter, or of a horse to whinny, but the O.E.D. cites a line from Masefield *the wall-top grasses whickered in the breeze*, and the 1920 Supplement to the Dictionary gives a meaning 'to make a hurtling sound', with a single citation where the word is used of a thunderbolt *whickering* through the sky. In the 1962 version of *The Man in the Moon* the word *flickering* occurs in this verse.

**whitethorn**  hawthorn, 76

**wildered**  perplexed, bewildered, 163–4, 178, 231

**wrack**  devastation, ruin, 177 (cf. (*w*)*rack and ruin*).

# INDEX

This index provides (in intention) complete page-references to all entries with the exception of *Eldar/Elves*, *Gods/Valar*, and *Valinor*; the entries include the rejected name-forms given in the Notes, but the Appendix on Names is not covered.

Occasionally references are given to pages where a person or place is not actually named, as 'the door-ward' p. 46 under *Rúmil*. References are given to mentions of Tales that will appear in Part II, but not to mentions of those in this book. The explanatory statements are kept very brief, and names defined in the Index to *The Silmarillion* are not as a rule explained here.

156–9, 162, 172, 176–84, 186–8, 190, 192, 194–6, 199, 208–9, 211–21, 223, 230, 233, 244; called *Lord of the Air* 176, *of the Heavens* 190, *of Gods and Elves and Men, of the Gods, of Gods and Elves, of Elves and Men* 52, 58–9, 62, 100, 104, 115, 142, 218. See *Súlimo, Valahíru, Valatúru; Valwë.*

**March of Liberation** The great expedition from Kôr. 166; *march into the world* 26, 129, 196

**Mar Vanwa Tyaliéva** The Cottage of Lost Play in Kortirion. 14, 21 (also *Taliéva*), 27–8, 30, 48, 97, 129, 174, 202, 229; in title of poem 28, 30

**Meássë** Warrior goddess. 67, 77–8, 80, 82, 89, 98, 105, 117, 154, 177

**Melemno, Ellu Melemno** See *Ellu.*

**Melian** 107, 132–3. See *Tindriel, Wendelin.*

**Melko** 25–7, 47, 49, 52–60, 62–3, 66–70, 77–9, 87, 89–90, 92–3, 98–107, 111, 113–18, 120, 128, 131, 133, 135, 140–54, 156–60, 165–9, 171, 174, 176–7, 180, 182–3, 196, 198, 200, 203, 207–11, 213, 217, 219–20, 222–3, 230, 234, 236–44; *son(s) of Melko* 93, 210, *child of Melko* 237; *Melko's Chains* 98, 107, 168; *Mines of Melko* 239, 241. See *Melkor, Morgoth.*

**Melkor** 26, 79–80, 110, 112, 131, 133, 156–61, 198–9, 222–3, 225

**Men, Mankind** 16, 18–20, 25–7, 31–2, 45, 47, 49, 52–3, 56–7, 59–61, 63–4, 68, 77, 80, 82, 90–3, 97–9, 105, 118–19, 125, 134–5, 138–9, 146, 150, 156, 159, 174–5, 177, 180, 187, 189, 198, 207–8, 211–13, 215–16, 219–21, 223–5, 230, 233–42, 244. On the nature and fate of Men see especially 59–61, 77, 90–3, 150–1

**Mereth Aderthad** The Feast of Reuniting. 243

**Meril-i-Turinqi** The Lady of Tol Eressëa; also *Meril, Turinqi.* 16–17, 20, 22, 26, 48, 50, 52, 95–8, 107, 111–13, 129–30, 134, 175, 230, 235; *Lady of the Isle* 175

**Mettanyë** The last part of the poem *The Trees of Kortirion.* 43

**Middle-earth** 21, 23, 26, 51, 81, 89, 110–11, 132–5, 199, 222–3

**Middle lands** 234

**Mindon Eldaliéva** 135

**Minethlos** A name of the Moon (Gnomish). 192, 198. (Replaced *Mainlos.*)

**Miruvor** 153, 160; *miruvórë* 161

**Mithrim** (lake and region) 160, 238–9, 241, 243. See *Asgon.*

**Moon, The** 60, 64, 83, 85, 88, 119, 151, 174–5, 182, 187, 192–3, 195, 197, 199–203, 206–8, 214–20, 227–8, 242; *Ship of the Moon* 192, 194, 216; *Man in the Moon* 193, 202; *King of the Moon* 202; *Harvest Moon* 41. See *Haven of the Moon*; and for other names of the Moon see 192.

**Morgoth** 26, 135, 222, 242–3

**Moritarnon** 'The Door of Night'. 215, 222; *Móritar* 222. See *Door of Night, Tarn Fui.*

**Mornië** The black ship that ferries the dead from Mandos. 77, 90, 92, 167, 170, 172

# THE BOOK OF LOST TALES

## PART II

# J. R. R. TOLKIEN

# The
# Book of Lost Tales

## PART II

Christopher Tolkien

# CONTENTS

A page from the *Tale of Tinúviel*

# PREFACE

This second part of *The Book of Lost Tales* is arranged on the same lines and with the same intentions as the first part, as described in the Foreword to it, pages 10–11. References to the first part are given in the form 'I. 240', to the second as 'p. 240', except where a reference is made to both, e.g. 'I. 222, II. 292'.

As before, I have adopted a consistent (if not necessarily 'correct') system of accentuation for names; and in the cases of *Mim* and *Niniel*, written thus throughout, I give *Mîm* and *Níniel*.

The two pages from the original manuscripts are reproduced with the permission of the Bodleian Library, Oxford, and I wish to express my thanks to the staff of the Department of Western Manuscripts at the Bodleian for their assistance. The correspondence of the original pages to the printed text in this book is as follows:

(1) The page from the manuscript of *The Tale of Tinúviel*. Upper part: printed text page 24 (7 lines up, *the sorest dread*) to page 25 (line 3, *so swiftly."*). Lower part: printed text page 25 (11 lines up, *the harsh voice*) to page 26 (line 7, *but Tevildo*).

(2) The page from the manuscript of *The Fall of Gondolin*. Upper part: printed text page 189 (line 12, *"Now," therefore said Galdor* to line 20 *if no further."*). Lower part: printed text page 189 (line 27, *But the others, led by one Legolas Greenleaf*) to page 190 (line 11, *leaving the main company to follow he*).

For differences in the printed text of *The Fall of Gondolin* from the page reproduced see page 201, notes 34–36, and page 203, *Bad Uthwen*; some other small differences not referred to in the notes are also due to later changes made to the text B of the Tale (see pages 146–7).

These pages illustrate the complicated 'jigsaw' of the manuscripts of the *Lost Tales* described in the Foreword to Part I, page 10.

The third volume in this 'History' will contain the alliterative *Lay of the Children of Húrin* (c.1918–1925) and the *Lay of Leithian* (1925–1931), together with the commentary on a part of the latter by C. S. Lewis, and the rewriting of the poem that my father embarked on after the completion of *The Lord of the Rings*.

# I
# THE TALE OF TINÚVIEL

The *Tale of Tinúviel* was written in 1917, but the earliest extant text is later, being a manuscript in ink over an erased original in pencil; and in fact my father's rewriting of this tale seems to have been one of the last completed elements in the *Lost Tales* (see I. 203–4).

There is also a typescript version of the *Tale of Tinúviel*, later than the manuscript but belonging to the same 'phase' of the mythology: my father had the manuscript before him and changed the text as he went along. Significant differences between the two versions of the tale are given on pp. 41 ff.

In the manuscript the tale is headed: 'Link to the Tale of Tinúviel, also the Tale of Tinúviel.' The *Link* begins with the following passage:

> 'Great was the power of Melko for ill,' said Eriol, 'if he could indeed destroy with his cunning the happiness and glory of the Gods and Elves, darkening the light of their dwelling and bringing all their love to naught. This must surely be the worst deed that ever he has done.'
>
> 'Of a truth never has such evil again been done in Valinor,' said Lindo, 'but Melko's hand has laboured at worse things in the world, and the seeds of his evil have waxen since to a great and terrible growth.'
>
> 'Nay,' said Eriol, 'yet can my heart not think of other griefs, for sorrow at the destruction of those most fair Trees and the darkness of the world.'

This passage was struck out, and is not found in the typescript text, but it reappears in almost identical form at the end of *The Flight of the Noldoli* (I. 169). The reason for this was that my father decided that the *Tale of the Sun and Moon*, rather than *Tinúviel*, should follow *The Darkening of Valinor* and *The Flight of the Noldoli* (see I. 203–4, where the complex question of the re-ordering of the *Tales* at this point is discussed). The opening words of the next part of the *Link*, 'Now in the days soon after the telling of this tale', referred, when they were written, to the tale of *The Darkening of Valinor* and *The Flight of the Noldoli*; but it is never made plain to what tale they were to refer when *Tinúviel* had been removed from its earlier position.

The two versions of the *Link* are at first very close, but when Eriol speaks of his own past history they diverge. For the earlier part I give the typescript text alone, and when they diverge I give them both in succession. All discussion of this story of Eriol's life is postponed to Chapter VI.

Now in the days soon after the telling of this tale, behold, winter approached the land of Tol Eressëa, for now had Eriol forgetful of his wandering mood abode some time in old Kortirion. Never in those months did he fare beyond the good tilth that lay without the grey walls of that town, but many a hall of the kindreds of the Inwir and the Teleri received him as their glad guest, and ever more skilled in the tongues of the Elves did he become, and more deep in knowledge of their customs, of their tales and songs.

Then was winter come sudden upon the Lonely Isle, and the lawns and gardens drew on a sparkling mantle of white snows; their fountains were still, and all their bare trees silent, and the far sun glinted pale amid the mist or splintered upon facets of long hanging ice. Still fared Eriol not away, but watched the cold moon from the frosty skies look down upon Mar Vanwa Tyaliéva, and when above the roofs the stars gleamed blue he would listen, yet no sound of the flutes of Timpinen heard he now; for the breath of summer is that sprite, and or ever autumn's secret presence fills the air he takes his grey magic boat, and the swallows draw him far away.

Even so Eriol knew laughter and merriment and musics too, and song, in the dwellings of Kortirion – even Eriol the wanderer whose heart before had known no rest. Came now a grey day, and a wan afternoon, but within was firelight and good warmth and dancing and merry children's noise, for Eriol was making a great play with the maids and boys in the Hall of Play Regained. There at length tired with their mirth they cast themselves down upon the rugs before the hearth, and a child among them, a little maid, said: 'Tell me, O Eriol, a tale!'

'What then shall I tell, O Vëannë?' said he, and she, clambering upon his knee, said: 'A tale of Men and of children in the Great Lands, or of thy home – and didst thou have a garden there such as we, where poppies grew and pansies like those that grow in my corner by the Arbour of the Thrushes?'

I give now the manuscript version of the remainder of the Link passage:

Then Eriol told her of his home that was in an old town of Men girt with a wall now crumbled and broken, and a river ran thereby over which a castle with a great tower hung. 'A very high tower indeed,' said he, 'and the moon climbed high or ever he thrust his face above it.' 'Was it then as high as Ingil's Tirin?' said Vëannë, but Eriol said that that he could not guess, for 'twas very many years agone since he had seen that castle or its tower, for 'O Vëannë,' said he, 'I lived there but a while, and not after I was grown to be a boy. My father came of a coastward folk, and the love of the sea that I had never seen was in my bones, and my father whetted my desire, for he told me tales that his father had told him before. Now my mother died in a cruel and hungry siege of that old town, and my father was slain in bitter fight about the walls, and in the end I Eriol escaped to the shoreland of the Western Sea, and mostly have lived upon the bosom of the waves or by its side since those far days.'

Now the children about were filled with sadness at the sorrows that fell on those dwellers in the Great Lands, and at the wars and death, and Vëannë clung to Eriol, saying: 'O Melinon, go never to a war – or hast thou ever yet?'

'Aye, often enough,' said Eriol, 'but not to the great wars of the earthly kings and mighty nations which are cruel and bitter, and many fair lands and lovely things and even women and sweet maids such as thou Vëannë Melinir are whelmed by them in ruin; yet gallant affrays have I seen wherein small bands of brave men do sometimes meet and swift blows are dealt. But behold, why speak we of these things, little one; wouldst not hear rather of my first ventures on the sea?'

Then was there much eagerness alight, and Eriol told them of his wanderings about the western havens, of the comrades he made and the ports he knew, of how he was wrecked upon far western islands until at last upon one lonely one he came on an ancient sailor who gave him shelter, and over a fire within his lonely cabin told him strange tales of things beyond the Western Seas, of the Magic Isles and that most lonely one that lay beyond. Long ago had he once sighted it shining afar off, and after had he sought it many a day in vain.

'Ever after,' said Eriol, 'did I sail more curiously about the western isles seeking more stories of the kind, and thus it is indeed that after many great voyages I came myself by the blessing of the Gods to Tol Eressëa in the end – wherefore I now sit here talking to thee, Vëannë, till my words have run dry.'

Then nonetheless did a boy, Ausir, beg him to tell more of ships and the sea, but Eriol said: 'Nay – still is there time ere Ilfiniol ring the gong for evening meat: come, one of you children, tell me a tale that you have heard!' Then Vëannë sat up and clapped her hands, saying: 'I will tell you the Tale of Tinúviel.'

The typescript version of this passage reads as follows:

Then Eriol told of his home of long ago, that was in an ancient town of Men girt with a wall now crumbled and broken, for the folk that dwelt there had long known days of rich and easy peace. A river ran thereby, o'er which a castle with a great tower hung. 'There dwelt a mighty duke,' said he, 'and did he gaze from the topmost battlements never might he see the bounds of his wide domain, save where far to east the blue shapes of the great mountains lay – yet was that tower held the most lofty that stood in the lands of Men.' 'Was it as high as great Ingil's Tirin?' said Vëannë, but said Eriol: 'A very high tower indeed was it, and the moon climbed far or ever he thrust his face above it, yet may I not now guess how high, O Vëannë, for 'tis many years agone since last I saw that castle or its steep tower. War fell suddenly on that town amid its slumbrous peace, nor were its crumbled walls able to withstand the onslaught of the wild men from the Mountains of the East. There perished my mother in that cruel and hungry siege, and my father was slain fighting bitterly about the walls in the last sack. In those far days was I not yet war-high, and a bondslave was I made.

'Know then that my father was come of a coastward folk ere he wandered to that place, and the longing for the sea that I had never seen was in my bones; which often had my father whetted, telling me tales of the wide waters and recalling lore that he had learned of his father aforetime. Small need to tell of my travail thereafter in thraldom, for in the end I brake my bonds and got me to the shoreland of the Western Sea – and mostly have I lived upon the bosom of its waves or by its side since those old days.'

Now hearing of the sorrows that fell upon the dwellers in the Great Lands, the wars and death, the children were filled with sadness, and Vëannë clung to Eriol, saying: 'O Melinon, go thou never to a war – or hast thou ever yet?'

'Aye, often enough,' said Eriol, 'yet not to the great wars of the earthly kings and mighty nations, which are cruel and bitter, whelming in their ruin all the beauty both of the earth and of those fair things that men fashion with their hands in times of peace – nay, they spare not sweet women and tender maids, such as thou, Vëannë Melinir, for then are men drunk with wrath and the lust of blood, and Melko fares abroad. But gallant affrays have I seen wherein brave men did sometimes meet, and swift blows were dealt, and strength of body and of heart was proven – but, behold, why speak we of these things, little one? Wouldst not hear rather of my ventures on the sea?'

Then was there much eagerness alight, and Eriol told them of his first wanderings about the western havens, of the comrades he made, and the ports he knew; of how he was one time wrecked upon far western islands and there upon a lonely eyot found an ancient mariner who dwelt for ever solitary in a cabin on the shore, that he had fashioned of the timbers of his boat. 'More wise was he,' said Eriol, 'in all matters of the sea than any other I have met, and much of wizardry was there in his lore. Strange things he told me of regions far beyond the Western Sea, of the Magic Isles and that most lonely one that lies behind. Once long ago, he said, he had sighted it glimmering afar off, and after had he sought it many a day in vain. Much lore he taught me of the hidden seas, and the dark and trackless waters, and without this never had I found this sweetest land, or this dear town or the Cottage of Lost Play – yet it was not without long and grievous search thereafter, and many a weary voyage, that I came myself by the blessing of the Gods to Tol Eressëa at the last – wherefore I now sit here talking to thee, Vëannë, till my words have run dry.'

Then nevertheless did a boy, Ausir, beg him to tell more of ships and the sea, saying: 'For knowest thou not, O Eriol, that that ancient mariner beside the lonely sea was none other than Ulmo's self, who appeareth not seldom thus to those voyagers whom he loves – yet he who has spoken with Ulmo must have many a tale to tell that will not be stale in the ears even of those that dwell here in Kortirion.' But Eriol at that time believed not that saying of Ausir's, and said: 'Nay, pay me your debt ere Ilfrin ring the gong for evening meat – come, one of you shall tell me a tale that you have heard.'

Then did Vëannë sit up and clap her hands, crying: 'I will tell thee the Tale of Tinúviel.'

★

## The Tale of Tinúviel

I give now the text of the *Tale of Tinúviel* as it appears in the manuscript. The *Link* is not in fact distinguished or separated in any way from the tale proper, and Vëannë makes no formal opening to it.

'Who was then Tinúviel?' said Eriol. 'Know you not?' said Ausir; 'Tinúviel was the daughter of Tinwë Linto.' 'Tinwelint', said Vëannë, but said the other: ''Tis all one, but the Elves of this house who love the tale do say Tinwë Linto, though Vairë hath said that Tinwë alone is his right name ere he wandered in the woods.'

'Hush thee, Ausir,' said Vëannë, 'for it is my tale and I will tell it to Eriol. Did I not see Gwendeling and Tinúviel once with my own eyes when journeying by the Way of Dreams in long past days?'[1]

'What was Queen Wendelin like (for so do the Elves call her),[2] O Vëannë, if thou sawest her?' said Ausir.

'Slender and very dark of hair,' said Vëannë, 'and her skin was white and pale, but her eyes shone and seemed deep, and she was clad in filmy garments most lovely yet of black, jet-spangled and girt with silver. If ever she sang, or if she danced, dreams and slumbers passed over your head and made it heavy. Indeed she was a sprite that escaped from Lórien's gardens before even Kôr was built, and she wandered in the wooded places of the world, and nightingales went with her and often sang about her. It was the song of these birds that smote the ears of Tinwelint, leader of that tribe of the Eldar that after were the Solosimpi the pipers of the shore, as he fared with his companions behind the horse of Oromë from Palisor. Ilúvatar had set a seed of music in the hearts of all that kindred, or so Vairë saith, and she is of them, and it blossomed after very wondrously, but now the song of Gwendeling's nightingales was the most beautiful music that Tinwelint had ever heard, and he strayed aside for a moment, as he thought, from the host, seeking in the dark trees whence it might come.

And it is said that it was not a moment he hearkened, but many years, and vainly his people sought him, until at length they followed Oromë and were borne upon Tol Eressëa far away, and he saw them never again. Yet after a while as it seemed to him he came upon Gwendeling lying in a bed of leaves gazing at the stars above her and hearkening also to her birds. Now Tinwelint stepping softly stooped and looked upon her, thinking "Lo, here is a fairer being even than the most beautiful of my own folk" – for indeed Gwendeling was not elf or woman but of the children of the Gods; and bending further to touch a tress of her hair he snapped a twig with his foot. Then Gwendeling was up and away laughing softly, sometimes singing distantly or dancing ever just before him, till a swoon of fragrant slumbers fell upon him and he fell face downward neath the trees and slept a very great while.

Now when he awoke he thought no more of his people (and indeed it had been vain, for long now had those reached Valinor) but desired only to see the twilight-lady; but she was not far, for she had remained nigh at hand and watched over him. More of their story I know not, O Eriol, save that in the end she became his wife, for Tinwelint and Gwendeling very long indeed were king and queen of the Lost Elves of Artanor or the Land Beyond, or so it is said here.

Long, long after, as thou knowest, Melko brake again into the world from Valinor, and all the Eldar both those who remained in the dark or had been lost upon the march from Palisor and those Noldoli too who fared back into the world after him seeking their stolen treasury fell beneath his power as thralls. Yet it is told that many there were who escaped and wandered in the woods and empty places, and of these many a wild and woodland clan rallied beneath King Tinwelint. Of those the most were Ilkorindi – which is to say Eldar that never had beheld Valinor or the Two Trees or dwelt in Kôr – and eerie they were and strange beings, knowing little of light or loveliness or of musics save it be dark songs and chantings of a rugged wonder that faded in the wooded places or echoed in deep caves. Different indeed did they become when the Sun arose, and indeed before that already were their numbers mingled with a many wandering Gnomes, and wayward sprites too there were of Lórien's host that dwelt in the courts of Tinwelint, being followers of Gwendeling, and these were not of the kindreds of the Eldalië.

Now in the days of Sunlight and Moonsheen still dwelt Tinwelint in Artanor, and nor he nor the most of his folk went to the Battle of Unnumbered Tears, though that story toucheth not this tale. Yet was his lordship greatly increased after that unhappy field by fugitives that fled to his protection. Hidden was his dwelling from the vision and knowledge of Melko by the magics of Gwendeling the fay, and she wove spells about the paths thereto that none but the Eldar might tread them easily, and so was the king secured from all dangers save it be treachery alone. Now his halls were builded in a deep cavern of great size, and they were nonetheless a kingly and a fair abode. This cavern was in the heart of the mighty forest of Artanor that is the mightiest of forests, and a stream ran before its doors, but none could enter that portal save across the stream, and a bridge spanned it narrow and well-guarded. Those places were not ill albeit the Iron Mountains were not utterly distant beyond whom lay Hisilómë where dwelt Men, and thrall-Noldoli laboured, and few free-Eldar went.

Lo, now I will tell you of things that happened in the halls of Tinwelint after the arising of the Sun indeed but long ere the unforgotten Battle of Unnumbered Tears. And Melko had not completed his designs nor had he unveiled his full might and cruelty.

Two children had Tinwelint then, Dairon and Tinúviel, and Tinúviel was a maiden, and the most beautiful of all the maidens of the hidden Elves, and indeed few have been so fair, for her mother was a fay, a daughter of the Gods; but Dairon was then a boy strong and merry, and above all things he delighted to play upon a pipe of reeds or other woodland instruments, and he is named now among the three most magic players of the Elves, and the others are Tinfang Warble and Ivárë who plays beside the sea. But Tinúviel's joy was rather in the dance, and no names are set with hers for the beauty and subtlety of her twinkling feet.

Now it was the delight of Dairon and Tinúviel to fare away from the cavernous palace of Tinwelint their father and together spend long times amid the trees. There often would Dairon sit upon a tussock or a tree-root and make music while Tinúviel danced thereto, and when she danced to the playing of Dairon more lissom was she than Gwendeling, more magical than Tinfang Warble neath the moon, nor may any see such lilting save be it only in the rose gardens of Valinor where Nessa dances on the lawns of never-fading green.

Even at night when the moon shone pale still would they play and dance, and they were not afraid as I should be, for the rule of Tinwelint and of Gwendeling held evil from the woods and Melko troubled them not as yet, and Men were hemmed beyond the hills.

Now the place that they loved the most was a shady spot, and elms grew there, and beech too, but these were not very tall, and some chestnut trees there were with white flowers, but the ground was moist and a great misty growth of hemlocks rose beneath the trees. On a time of June they were playing there, and the white umbels of the hemlocks were like a cloud about the boles of the trees, and there Tinúviel danced until the evening faded late, and there were many white moths abroad. Tinúviel being a fairy minded them not as many of the children of Men do, although she loved not beetles, and spiders will none of the Eldar touch because of Ungweliantë – but now the white moths flittered about her head and Dairon trilled an eerie tune, when suddenly that strange thing befell.

Never have I heard how Beren came thither over the hills; yet was he braver than most, as thou shalt hear, and 'twas the love of wandering maybe alone that had sped him through the terrors of the Iron Mountains until he reached the Lands Beyond.

Now Beren was a Gnome, son of Egnor the forester who hunted in the darker places³ in the north of Hisilómë. Dread and suspicion was between the Eldar and those of their kindred that had tasted the slavery of Melko, and in this did the evil deeds of the Gnomes at the Haven of the Swans revenge itself. Now the lies of Melko ran among Beren's folk so that they believed evil things of the secret Elves, yet now did he see Tinúviel dancing in the twilight, and Tinúviel was in a silver-pearly dress, and her bare white feet were twinkling among the hemlock-stems. Then Beren cared not whether she were Vala or Elf or child of Men and crept near to see; and he leant against a young elm that grew upon a mound so that he might look down into the little glade where she was dancing, for the enchantment made him faint. So slender was she and so fair that at length he stood heedlessly in the open the better to gaze upon her, and at that moment the full moon came brightly through the boughs and Dairon caught sight of Beren's face. Straightway did he perceive that he was none of their folk, and all the Elves of the woodland thought of the Gnomes of Dor Lómin as treacherous creatures, cruel and faithless, wherefore Dairon dropped his instrument and crying "Flee, flee, O Tinúviel, an enemy walks this wood" he was gone swiftly through the trees. Then Tinúviel in her amaze followed not straightway, for she understood not his words at once, and knowing she could not run or leap so hardily as her brother she slipped suddenly down among the white hemlocks and hid herself beneath a very tall flower with many spreading leaves; and here she looked in her white raiment like a spatter of moonlight shimmering through the leaves upon the floor.

Then Beren was sad, for he was lonely and was grieved at their fright, and he looked for Tinúviel everywhere about, thinking her not fled. Thus suddenly did he lay his hand upon her slender arm beneath the leaves, and with a cry she started away from him and flitted as fast as she could in the wan light, in and about the tree-trunks and the hemlock-stalks. The tender touch of her arm made Beren yet more eager than before to find her, and he followed swiftly and yet not swiftly enough, for in the end she escaped him, and reached the dwellings of her father in fear; nor did she dance alone in the woods for many a day after.

This was a great sorrow to Beren, who would not leave those places, hoping to see that fair elfin maiden dance yet again, and he wandered in the wood growing wild and lonely for many a day and searching for Tinúviel. By dawn and dusk he sought her, but ever more hopefully when the moon shone bright. At last one night he caught a sparkle afar off, and lo, there she was dancing alone on a little treeless knoll and Dairon was not there. Often and often she came there after and danced and sang to herself, and sometimes Dairon would be nigh, and then Beren watched from the wood's edge afar, and sometimes he was away and Beren crept then closer. Indeed for long Tinúviel knew of his coming and feigned otherwise, and for long her fear had departed by reason of the wistful hunger of his face lit by the moonlight; and she saw that he was kind and in love with her beautiful dancing.

Then Beren took to following Tinúviel secretly through the woods even to the entrance of the cave and the bridge's head, and when she was gone in he would cry across the stream, softly saying "Tinúviel", for he had caught the name from Dairon's lips; and although he knew it not Tinúviel often hearkened from within the shadows of the cavernous doors and laughed softly or smiled. At length one day as she danced alone he stepped out more boldly and said to her: "Tinúviel, teach me to dance." "Who art thou?" said she. "Beren. I am from across the Bitter Hills." "Then if thou wouldst dance, follow me," said the maiden, and she danced before Beren away, and away into the woods, nimbly and yet not so fast that he could not follow, and ever and anon she would look back and laugh at him stumbling after, saying "Dance, Beren, dance! as they dance beyond the Bitter Hills!" In this way they came by winding paths to the abode of Tinwelint, and Tinúviel beckoned Beren beyond the stream, and he followed her wondering down into the cave and the deep halls of her home.

When however Beren found himself before the king he was abashed, and of the stateliness of Queen Gwendeling he was in great awe, and behold when the king said: "Who art thou that stumbleth into my halls unbidden?" he had nought to say. Tinúviel answered therefore for him, saying: "This, my father, is Beren, a wanderer from beyond the hills, and he would learn to dance as the Elves of Artanor can dance," and she laughed, but the king frowned when he heard whence Beren came, and he said: "Put away thy light words, my child, and say has this wild Elf of the shadows sought to do thee any harm?"

"Nay, father," said she, "and I think there is not evil in his heart at all, and be thou not harsh with him, unless thou desirest to see thy daughter Tinúviel weep, for more wonder has he at my dancing than any that I have known." Therefore said Tinwelint now: "O Beren son of the Noldoli, what dost thou desire of the Elves of the wood ere thou returnest whence thou camest?"

So great was the amazed joy of Beren's heart when Tinúviel spake thus for him to her father that his courage rose within him, and his adventurous spirit that had brought him out of Hisilómë and over the Mountains of Iron awoke again, and looking boldly upon Tinwelint he said: "Why, O king, I desire thy daughter Tinúviel, for she is the fairest and most sweet of all maidens I have seen or dreamed of."

Then was there a silence in the hall, save that Dairon laughed, and all who heard were astounded, but Tinúviel cast down her eyes, and the king glancing at the wild and rugged aspect of Beren burst also into laughter, whereat Beren flushed for shame, and Tinúviel's heart was sore for him. "Why! wed my Tinúviel fairest of the maidens of the world, and become a prince of the woodland Elves – 'tis but a little boon for a stranger to ask," quoth Tinwelint. "Haply I may with right ask somewhat in return. Nothing great shall it be, a token only of thy esteem. Bring me a Silmaril from the Crown of Melko, and that day Tinúviel weds thee, an she will."

Then all in that place knew that the king treated the matter as an uncouth jest, having pity on the Gnome, and they smiled, for the fame of the Silmarils of Fëanor was now great throughout the world, and the Noldoli had told tales of them, and many that had escaped from Angamandi had seen them now blazing lustrous in the iron crown of Melko. Never did this crown leave his head, and he treasured those jewels as his eyes, and no one in the world, or fay or elf or man, could hope ever to set finger even on them and live. This indeed did Beren know, and he guessed the meaning of their mocking smiles, and aflame with anger he cried: "Nay, but 'tis too small a gift to the father of so sweet a bride. Strange nonetheless seem to me the customs of the woodland Elves, like to the rude laws of the folk of Men, that thou shouldst name the gift unoffered, yet lo! I Beren, a huntsman of the Noldoli,[4] will fulfil thy small desire," and with that he burst from the hall while all stood astonished; but Tinúviel wept suddenly. "'Twas ill done, O my father," she cried, "to send one to his death with thy sorry jesting – for now methinks he will attempt the deed, being maddened by thy scorn, and Melko will slay him, and none will look ever again with such love upon my dancing."

Then said the king: "'Twill not be the first of Gnomes that Melko has slain and for less reason. It is well for him that he lies not bound here in grievous spells for his trespass in my halls and for his insolent speech"; yet Gwendeling said nought, neither did she chide Tinúviel or question her sudden weeping for this unknown wanderer.

Beren however going from before the face of Tinwelint was carried by his wrath far through the woods, until he drew nigh to the lower hills and treeless lands that warned of the approach of the bleak Iron Mountains. Only then did he feel his weariness and stay his march, and thereafter did his greater travails begin. Nights of deep despondency were his and he saw no hope whatever in his quest, and indeed there was little, and soon, as he followed the Iron Mountains till he drew nigh to the terrible regions of Melko's abode, the greatest fears assailed him. Many poisonous snakes were in those places and wolves roamed about, and more fearsome still were the wandering bands of the goblins and the Orcs – foul broodlings of Melko who fared abroad doing his evil work, snaring and capturing beasts, and Men, and Elves, and dragging them to their lord.

Many times was Beren near to capture by the Orcs, and once he escaped the jaws of a great wolf only after a combat wherein he was armed but with an ashen club, and other perils and adventures did he know each day of his wandering to Angamandi. Hunger and thirst too tortured him often, and often he would have turned back had not that been well nigh as perilous as going on; but the voice of Tinúviel pleading with Tinwelint echoed in his heart, and at night time it seemed to him that his heart heard her sometimes weeping softly for him far away in the woodlands of her home: – and this was indeed true.

One day he was driven by great hunger to search amid a deserted camping of some Orcs for scraps of food, but some of these returned unawares and took him prisoner, and they tormented him but did not slay him, for their captain seeing his strength, worn though he was with hardships, thought that Melko might perchance be pleasured if he was brought before him and might set him to some heavy thrall-work in his mines or in his smithies. So came it that Beren was dragged before Melko, and he bore a stout heart within him nonetheless, for it was a belief among his father's kindred that the power of Melko would not abide for ever, but the Valar would hearken at last to the tears of the Noldoli, and would arise and bind Melko and open Valinor once more to the weary Elves, and great joy should come back upon Earth.

Melko however looking upon him was wroth, asking how a Gnome, a thrall by birth of his, had dared to fare away into the woods unbidden, but Beren answered that he was no runagate but came of a kindred of Gnomes that dwelt in Aryador and mingled much there among the folk of Men. Then was Melko yet more angry, for he sought ever to destroy the friendship and intercourse of Elves and Men, and said that evidently here was a plotter of deep treacheries against Melko's lordship, and one worthy of the tortures of the Balrogs; but Beren seeing his peril answered: "Think not, O most mighty Ainu Melko, Lord of the World, that this can be true, for an it were then should I not be here unaided and alone. No friendship has Beren son of Egnor for the kindred of Men; nay indeed, wearying utterly of the lands infested by that folk he has wandered out of Aryador. Many a great tale has my father made to me aforetime of thy splendour and glory, wherefore, albeit I am no renegade thrall, I do desire nothing so much as to serve thee in what small manner I may," and Beren said therewith that he was a great trapper of small animals and a snarer of birds, and had become lost in the hills in these pursuits until after much wandering he had come into strange lands, and even had not the Orcs seized him he would indeed have had no other rede of safety but to approach the majesty of Ainu Melko and beg him to grant him some humble office – as a winner of meats for his table perchance.

Now the Valar must have inspired that speech, or perchance it was a spell of cunning words cast on him in compassion by Gwendeling, for indeed it saved his life, and Melko marking his hardy frame believed him, and was willing to accept him as a thrall of his kitchens. Flattery savoured ever sweet in the nostrils of that Ainu, and for all his unfathomed wisdom many a lie of those whom he despised deceived him, were they clothed sweetly in words of praise; therefore now he gave orders for Beren to be made a thrall of Tevildo Prince of Cats*. Now Tevildo was a

---

* Footnote in the manuscript: *Tifil (Bridhon) Miaugion or Tevildo (Vardo) Meoita.*

mighty cat — the mightiest of all — and possessed of an evil sprite, as some say, and he was in Melko's constant following; and that cat had all cats subject to him, and he and his subjects were the chasers and getters of meat for Melko's table and for his frequent feasts. Wherefore is it that there is hatred still between the Elves and all cats even now when Melko rules no more, and his beasts are become of little account.

When therefore Beren was led away to the halls of Tevildo, and these were not utterly distant from the place of Melko's throne, he was much afraid, for he had not looked for such a turn in things, and those halls were ill-lighted and were full of growling and of monstrous purrings in the dark. All about shone cats' eyes glowing like green lamps or red or yellow where Tevildo's thanes sat waving and lashing their beautiful tails, but Tevildo himself sat at their head and he was a mighty cat and coal-black and evil to look upon. His eyes were long and very narrow and slanted, and gleamed both red and green, but his great grey whiskers were as stout and as sharp as needles. His purr was like the roll of drums and his growl like thunder, but when he yelled in wrath it turned the blood cold, and indeed small beasts and birds were frozen as to stone, or dropped lifeless often at the very sound. Now Tevildo seeing Beren narrowed his eyes until they seemed to shut, and said: "I smell dog", and he took dislike to Beren from that moment. Now Beren had been a lover of hounds in his own wild home.

"Why," said Tevildo, "do ye dare to bring such a creature before me, unless perchance it is to make meat of him?" But those who led Beren said: "Nay, 'twas the word of Melko that this unhappy Elf wear out his life as a catcher of beasts and birds in Tevildo's employ." Then indeed did Tevildo screech in scorn and said: "Then in sooth was my lord asleep or his thoughts were settled elsewhere, for what use think ye is a child of the Eldar to aid the Prince of Cats and his thanes in the catching of birds or of beasts — as well had ye brought some clumsy-footed Man, for none are there either of Elves or Men that can vie with us in our pursuit." Nonetheless he set Beren to a test, and he bade him go catch three mice, "for my hall is infested with them," said he. This indeed was not true, as might be imagined, yet a certain few there were — a very wild, evil, and magic kind that dared to dwell there in dark holes, but they were larger than rats and very fierce, and Tevildo harboured them for his own private sport and suffered not their numbers to dwindle.

Three days did Beren hunt them, but having nothing wherewith to devise a trap (and indeed he did not lie to Melko saying that he had cunning in such contrivances) he hunted in vain getting nothing better than a bitten finger for all his labour. Then was Tevildo scornful and in great anger, but Beren got no harm of him or his thanes at that time because of Melko's bidding other than a few scratches. Evil however were his days thereafter in the dwellings of Tevildo. They made him a scullion, and his days passed miserably in the washing of floors and vessels, in the scrubbing of tables and the hewing of wood and the drawing of water. Often too would he be set to the turning of spits whereon birds and fat mice were daintily roasted for the cats, yet seldom did he get food or sleep himself, and he became haggard and unkempt, and wished often that never straying out of Hisilómë he had not even caught sight of the vision of Tinúviel.

Now that fair maiden wept for a very great while after Beren's departure and danced no more about the woods, and Dairon grew angry and could not understand her, but she had grown to love the face of Beren peeping through the branches and the crackle of his feet as they followed her through the wood; and his voice that called wistfully "Tinúviel, Tinúviel" across the stream before her father's doors she longed to hear again, and she would not now dance when Beren was fled to the evil halls of Melko and maybe had already perished. So bitter did this thought become at last that that most tender maiden went to her mother, for to her father she dared not go nor even suffer him to see her weep.

"O Gwendeling, my mother," said she, "tell me of thy magic, if thou canst, how doth Beren fare. Is all yet well with him. Is all yet well with him?" "Nay," said Gwendeling. "He lives indeed, but in an evil captivity, and hope is dead in his heart, for behold, he is a slave in the power of Tevildo Prince of Cats."

"Then," said Tinúviel, "I must go and succour him, for none else do I know that will."

Now Gwendeling laughed not, for in many matters she was wise, and forewise, yet it was a thing unthought in a mad dream that any Elf, still less a maiden, the daughter of the king, should fare untended to the halls of Melko, even in those earlier days before the Battle of Tears when Melko's power had not grown great and he veiled his designs and spread his net of lies. Wherefore did Gwendeling softly bid her not to speak such folly; but Tinúviel said: "Then must thou plead with my father for aid, that he send warriors to Angamandi and demand the freedom of Beren from Ainu Melko."

This indeed did Gwendeling do, of love for her daughter, and so wroth was Tinwelint that Tinúviel wished that never had her desire been made known; and Tinwelint bade her nor speak nor think of Beren more, and swore he would slay him an he trod those halls again. Now then Tinúviel pondered much what she might do, and going to Dairon she begged him to aid her, or indeed to fare away with her to Angamandi an he would; but Dairon thought with little love of Beren, and he said: "Wherefore should I go into the direst peril that there is in the world for the sake of a wandering Gnome of the woods? Indeed I have no love for him, for he has destroyed our play together, our music and our dancing." But Dairon moreover told the king of what Tinúviel had desired of him – and this he did not of ill intent but fearing lest Tinúviel fare away to her death in the madness of her heart.

Now[5] when Tinwelint heard this he called Tinúviel and said: "Wherefore, O maiden of mine, does thou not put this folly away from thee, and seek to do my bidding?" But Tinúviel would not answer, and the king bade her promise him that neither would she think more on Beren, nor would she seek in her folly to follow after him to the evil lands whether alone or tempting any of his folk with her. But Tinúviel said that the first she would not promise and the second only in part, for she would not tempt any of the folk of the woodlands to go with her.

Then was her father mightily angry, and beneath his anger not a little amazed and afraid, for he loved Tinúviel; but this was the plan he devised, for he might not shut his daughter for ever in the caverns where only a dim and flickering light ever came. Now above the portals of his cavernous hall was a steep slope falling to the river, and there grew mighty beeches; and one there was that was named Hirilorn, the Queen of Trees, for she was very mighty, and so deeply cloven was her bole that it seemed as if three shafts sprang from the ground together and they were of like size, round and straight, and their grey rind was smooth as silk, unbroken by branch or twig for a very great height above men's heads.

Now Tinwelint let build high up in that strange tree, as high as men could fashion their longest ladders to reach, a little house of wood, and it was above the first branches and was sweetly veiled in leaves. Now that house had three corners and three windows in each wall, and at each corner was one of the shafts of Hirilorn. There then did Tinwelint bid Tinúviel dwell until she would consent to be wise, and when she fared up the ladders of tall pine these were taken from beneath and no way had she to get down again. All that she required was brought to her, and folk would scale the ladders and give her food or whatever else she wished for, and then descending again take away the ladders, and the king promised death to any who left one leaning against the tree or who should try by stealth to place one there at night. A guard therefore was set nigh the tree's foot, and yet came Dairon often thither in sorrow at what he had brought to pass, for he was lonely without Tinúviel; but Tinúviel had at first much pleasure in her house among the leaves, and would gaze out of her little window while Dairon made his sweetest melodies beneath.

But one night a dream of the Valar came to Tinúviel and she dreamt of Beren, and her heart said: "Let me be gone to seek him whom all others have forgot"; and waking, the moon was shining through the trees, and she pondered very deeply how she might escape. Now Tinúviel daughter of Gwendeling was not ignorant of magics or of spells, as may well be believed, and after much thought she devised a plan. The next day she asked those who came to her to bring, if they would, some of the clearest water of the stream below, "but this," she said, "must be drawn at midnight in a silver bowl, and brought to my hand with no word spoken," and after that she desired wine to be brought, "but this," she said, "must be borne hither in a flagon of gold at noon, and he who brings it must sing as he comes," and they did as they were bid, but Tinwelint was not told.

Then said Tinúviel, "Go now to my mother and say to her that her daughter desires a spinning wheel to pass her weary hours," but Dairon secretly she begged fashion her a tiny loom, and he did this even in the little house of Tinúviel in the tree. "But wherewith will you spin and wherewith weave?" said he; and Tinúviel answered: "With spells and magics," but Dairon knew not her design, nor said more to the king or to Gwendeling.

Now Tinúviel took the wine and water when she was alone, and singing a very magical song the while, she mingled them together, and as they lay in the bowl of gold she sang a song of growth, and as they lay in the bowl of silver she sang another song, and the names of all the tallest and longest things upon Earth were set in that song; the beards of the Indravangs, the tail of Karkaras, the body of Glorund, the bole of Hirilorn, and the sword of Nan she named, nor did she forget the chain Angainu that Aulë and Tulkas made or the neck of Gilim the giant, and last and longest of all she spake of the hair of Uinen the lady of the sea that is spread through all the waters. Then did she lave her head with the mingled water and wine, and as she did so she sang a third song, a song of uttermost sleep, and the hair of Tinúviel which was dark and finer than the most delicate threads of twilight began suddenly to grow very fast indeed, and after twelve hours had passed it nigh filled the little room, and then Tinúviel was very pleased and she lay down to rest; and when she awoke the room was full as with a black mist and she was deep hidden under it, and lo! her hair was trailing out of the windows and blowing about the tree boles in the morning. Then with difficulty she found her little shears and cut the threads of that growth nigh to her head, and after that her hair grew only as it was wont before.

Then was the labour of Tinúviel begun, and though she laboured with the deftness of an Elf long was she spinning and longer weaving still, and did any come and hail her from below she bid them be gone, saying: "I am abed, and desire only to sleep," and Dairon was much amazed, and called often up to her, but she did not answer.

Now of that cloudy hair Tinúviel wove a robe of misty black soaked with drowsiness more magical far than even that one that her mother had worn and danced in long long ago before the Sun arose, and therewith she covered her garments of shimmering white, and magic slumbers filled the airs about her; but of what remained she twisted a mighty strand, and this she fastened to the bole of the tree within her house, and then was her labour ended, and she looked out of her window westward to the river. Already the sunlight was fading in the trees, and as dusk filled the woods she began a song very soft and low, and as she sung she cast out her long hair from the window so that its slumbrous mist touched the heads and faces of the guards below, and they listening to her voice fell suddenly into a fathomless sleep. Then did Tinúviel clad in her garments of darkness slip down that rope of hair light as a squirrel, and away she danced to the bridge, and before the bridgewards could cry out she was among them dancing; and as the hem of her black robe touched them they fell asleep, and Tinúviel fled very far away as fast as her dancing feet would flit.

Now when the escape of Tinúviel reached the ears of Tinwelint great was his mingled grief and wrath, and all his court was in uproar, and all the woods ringing with the search, but Tinúviel was already far away drawing nigh to the gloomy foothills where the Mountains of Night begin; and 'tis said that Dairon following after her became utterly lost, and came never back to Elfinesse, but turned towards Palisor, and there plays[6] subtle magic musics still, wistful and lonely in the woods and forests of the south.

Yet ere long as Tinúviel went forward a sudden dread overtook her at the thought of what she had dared to do and what lay before; then did she turn back for a while, and she wept, wishing Dairon was with her, and it is said that he indeed was not far off, but was wandering lost in the great pines, the Forest of Night, where afterward Túrin slew Beleg by mishap.[7] Nigh was Tinúviel now to those places, but she entered not that dark region, and regaining heart pressed on, and by reason of the greater magic of her being and because of the spell of wonder and of sleep that fared about her no such dangers assailed her as did Beren before; yet was it a long and evil and weary journey for a maiden to tread.

Now is it to be told to thee, Eriol, that in those days Tevildo had but one trouble in the world, and that was the kindred of the Dogs. Many indeed of these were neither friends nor foes of the Cats, for they had become subject to Melko and were as savage and cruel as any of his animals; indeed from the most cruel and most savage he bred the race of wolves, and they were very dear indeed to him. Was it not the great grey wolf Karkaras Knife-fang, father of wolves, who guarded the gates of Angamandi in those days and long had done so? Many were there however who would neither bow to Melko nor live wholly in fear of him, but dwelt either in the dwellings of Men and guarded them from much evil that had otherwise befallen them or roamed the woods of Hisilómë or passing the mountainous places fared even at times into the region of Artanor and the lands beyond and to the south.

Did ever any of these view Tevildo or any of his thanes or subjects, then there was a great baying and a mighty chase, and albeit seldom was any cat slain by reason of their skill in climbing and in hiding and because of the protecting might of Melko, yet was great enmity between them, and some of those hounds were held in dread among the cats. None however did Tevildo fear, for he was as strong as any among them, and more agile and more swift save only than Huan Captain of Dogs. So swift was Huan that on a time he had tasted the fur of Tevildo, and though Tevildo had paid him for that with a gash from his great claws, yet was the pride of the Prince of Cats unappeased and he lusted to do a great harm to Huan of the Dogs.

Great therefore was the good fortune that befell Tinúviel in meeting with Huan in the woods, although at first she was mortally afraid and fled. But Huan overtook her in two leaps, and speaking soft and deep the tongue of the Lost Elves he bid her be not afraid, and "Wherefore," said he, "do I see an Elfin maiden, and one most fair, wandering alone so nigh to the abodes of the Ainu of Evil? Knowst thou not these are very evil places to be in, little one, even with a companion, and they are death to the lonely?"

"That know I," said she, "and I am not here for the love of wayfaring, but I seek only Beren."

"What knowest thou then," said Huan, "of Beren — or indeed meanest thou Beren son of the huntsman of the Elves, Egnor bo-Rimion, a friend of mine since very ancient days?"

"Nay, I know not even whether my Beren be thy friend, for I seek only Beren from beyond the Bitter Hills, whom I knew in the woods near to my father's home. Now is he gone, and my mother Gwendeling says of her wisdom that he is a thrall in the cruel house of Tevildo Prince of Cats; and whether this be true or yet worse be now befallen him I do not know, and I go to discover him — though plan I have none."

"Then will I make thee one," said Huan, "but do thou trust in me, for I am Huan of the Dogs, chief foe of Tevildo. Rest thee now with me a while within the shadows of the wood, and I will think deeply."

Then Tinúviel did as he said, and indeed she slept long while Huan watched, for she was very weary. But after a while awakening she said: "Lo, I have tarried over long. Come, what is thy thought, O Huan?"

And Huan said: "A dark and difficult matter is this, and no other rede can I devise but this. Creep now if thou hast the heart to the abiding place of that Prince while the sun is high, and Tevildo and the most of his household drowze upon the terraces before his gates. There discover in what manner thou mayst whether Beren be indeed within, as thy mother said to thee. Now I will lie not far hence in the woods, and thou wilt do me a pleasure and aid thy own desires an going before Tevildo, be Beren there or be he not, thou tellest him how thou hast stumbled upon Huan of the Dogs lying sick in the woods at this place. Do not indeed direct him hither, for thou must guide him, if it may be, thyself. Then wilt thou see what I contrive for thee and for Tevildo. Methinks that bearing such tidings Tevildo will not entreat thee ill within his halls nor seek to hold thee there."

In this way did Huan design both to do Tevildo a hurt, or perchance if it might so be to slay him, and to aid Beren whom he guessed in truth to be that Beren son of Egnor whom the hounds of Hisilómë loved. Indeed hearing the name of Gwendeling and knowing thereby that this maiden was a princess of the woodland fairies he was eager to aid her, and his heart warmed to her sweetness.

Now Tinúviel taking heart stole near to the halls of Tevildo, and Huan wondered much at her courage, following unknown to her, as far as he might for the success of his design. At length however she passed beyond his sight, and leaving the shelter of the trees came to a region of long grass dotted with bushes that sloped ever upward toward a shoulder of the hills. Now upon that rocky spur the sun shone, but over all the hills and mountains at its back a black cloud brooded, for there was Angamandi; and Tinúviel fared on not daring to look up at that gloom, for fear oppressed her, and as she went the ground rose and the grass grew more scant and rock-strewn until it came even to a cliff, sheer of one side, and there upon a stony shelf was the castle of Tevildo. No pathway led thereto, and the place where it stood fell towards the woods in terrace after terrace so that none might reach its gates save by many great leaps, and those became ever steeper as the castle drew more nigh. Few were the windows of the house and upon the ground there were none – indeed the very gate was in the air where in the dwellings of Men are wont to be the windows of the upper floor; but the roof had many wide and flat spaces open to the sun.

Now does Tinúviel wander disconsolate upon the lowest terrace and look in dread at the dark house upon the hill, when behold, she came at a bend in the rock upon a lone cat lying in the sun and seemingly asleep. As she approached he opened a yellow eye and blinked at her, and thereupon rising and stretching he stepped up to her and said: "Whither away, little maid – dost not know that you trespass on the sunning ground of his highness Tevildo and his thanes?"

Now Tinúviel was very much afraid, but she made as bold an answer as she was able, saying: "That know I, my lord" – and this pleased the old cat greatly, for he was in truth only Tevildo's doorkeeper – "but I would indeed of your goodness be brought to Tevildo's presence now – nay, even if he sleeps," said she, for the doorkeeper lashed his tail in astonished refusal. "I have words of immediate import for his private ear. Lead me to him, my lord," she pleaded, and thereat the cat purred so loudly that she dared to stroke his ugly head, and this was much larger than her own, being greater than that of any dog that is now on Earth. Thus entreated,

Umuiyan, for such was his name, said: "Come then with me," and seizing Tinúviel suddenly by her garments at the shoulder to her great terror he tossed her upon his back and leaped upon the second terrace. There he stopped, and as Tinúviel scrambled from his back he said: "Well is it for thee that this afternoon my lord Tevildo lieth upon this lowly terrace far from his house, for a great weariness and a desire for sleep has come upon me, so that I fear me I should not be willing to carry thee much farther"; now Tinúviel was robed in her robe of sable mist.

So saying Umuiyan* yawned mightily and stretched himself before he led her along that terrace to an open space, where upon a wide couch of baking stones lay the horrible form of Tevildo himself, and both his evil eyes were shut. Going up to him the doorcat Umuiyan spoke in his ear softly, saying: "A maiden awaits thy pleasure, my lord, who hath news of importance to deliver to thee, nor would she take my refusal." Then did Tevildo angrily lash his tail, half opening an eye – "What is it – be swift," said he, "for this is no hour to come desiring audience of Tevildo Prince of Cats."

"Nay, lord," said Tinúviel trembling, "be not angry; nor do I think that thou wilt when thou hearest, yet is the matter such that it were better not even whispered here where the breezes blow," and Tinúviel cast a glance as it were of apprehension toward the woods.

"Nay, get thee gone," said Tevildo, "thou smellest of dog, and what news of good came ever to a cat from a fairy that had had dealings with the dogs?"

"Why, sir, that I smell of dogs is no matter of wonder, for I have just escaped from one – and it is indeed of a certain very mighty dog whose name thou knowest that I would speak." Then up sat Tevildo and opened his eyes, and he looked all about him, and stretched three times, and at last bade the doorcat lead Tinúviel within; and Umuiyan caught her upon his back as before. Now was Tinúviel in the sorest dread, for having gained what she desired, a chance of entering Tevildo's stronghold and maybe of discovering whether Beren were there, she had no plan more, and knew not what would become of her – indeed had she been able she would have fled; yet now do those cats begin to ascend the terraces towards the castle, and one leap does Umuiyan make bearing Tinúviel upwards and then another, and at the third he

* Written above *Umuiyan* here is the name *Gumniow*, enclosed within brackets.

stumbled so that Tinúviel cried out in fear, and Tevildo said: "What ails thee, Umuiyan, thou clumsy-foot? It is time that thou left my employ if age creeps on thee so swiftly." But Umuiyan said: "Nay, lord, I know not what it is, but a mist is before mine eyes and my head is heavy," and he staggered as one drunk, so that Tinúviel slid from his back, and thereupon he laid him down as if in a dead sleep; but Tevildo was wroth and seized Tinúviel and none too gently, and himself bore her to the gates. Then with a mighty leap he sprang within, and bidding that maiden alight he set up a yell that echoed fearsomely in the dark ways and passages. Forthwith they hastened to him from within, and some he bid descend to Umuiyan and bind him and cast him from the rocks "on the northern side where they fall most sheer, for he is of no use more to me," he said, "for age has robbed him of his sureness of foot"; and Tinúviel quaked to hear the ruthlessness of this beast. But even as he spake he himself yawned and stumbled as with a sudden drowziness, and he bid others to lead Tinúviel away to a certain chamber within, and that was the one where Tevildo was accustomed to sit at meat with his greatest thanes. It was full of bones and smelt evilly; no windows were there and but one door; but a hatchway gave from it upon the great kitchens, and a red light crept thence and dimly lit the place.

Now so adread was Tinúviel when those catfolk left her there that she stood a moment unable to stir, but soon becoming used to the darkness she looked about and espying the hatchway that had a wide sill she sprang thereto, for it was not over high and she was a nimble Elf. Now gazing therethrough, for it was ajar, she saw the wide vaulted kitchens and the great fires that burnt there, and those that toiled always within, and the most were cats – but behold, there by a great fire stooped Beren, and he was grimed with labour, and Tinúviel sat and wept, but as yet dared nothing. Indeed even as she sat the harsh voice of Tevildo sounded suddenly within that chamber: "Nay, where then in Melko's name has that mad Elf fled," and Tinúviel hearing shrank against the wall, but Tevildo caught sight of her where she was perched and cried: "Then the little bird sings not any more; come down or I must fetch thee, for behold, I will not encourage the Elves to seek audience of me in mockery."

Then partly in fear, and part in hope that her clear voice might carry even to Beren, Tinúviel began suddenly to speak very loud and to tell her tale so that the chambers rang; but "Hush, dear maiden," said Tevildo, "if the matter were secret without it is not

one for bawling within." Then said Tinúviel: "Speak not thus to
me, O cat, mighty Lord of Cats though thou be, for am I not
Tinúviel Princess of Fairies that have stepped out of my way to do
thee a pleasure?" Now at those words, and she had shouted them
even louder than before, a great crash was heard in the kitchens as
of a number of vessels of metal and earthenware let suddenly fall,
but Tevildo snarled: "There trippeth that fool Beren the Elf.
Melko rid me of such folk" – yet Tinúviel, guessing that Beren had
heard and been smitten with astonishment, put aside her fears and
repented her daring no longer. Tevildo nonetheless was very
wroth at her haughty words, and had he not been minded first to
discover what good he might get from her tale, it had fared ill with
Tinúviel straightway. Indeed from that moment was she in great
peril, for Melko and all his vassals held Tinwelint and his folk as
outlaws, and great was their joy to ensnare them and cruelly
entreat them, so that much favour would Tevildo have gained had
he taken Tinúviel before his lord. Indeed, so soon as she named
herself, this did he purpose to do when his own business had
been done, but of a truth his wits were drowzed that day, and he
forgot to marvel more why Tinúviel sat perched upon the sill of
the hatchway; nor did he think more of Beren, for his mind was
bent only to the tale Tinúviel bore to him. Wherefore said he,
dissembling his evil mood, "Nay, Lady, be not angry, but come,
delay whetteth my desire – what is it that thou hast for my ears, for
they twitch already."

But Tinúviel said: "There is a great beast, rude and violent, and
his name is Huan" – and at that name Tevildo's back curved, and
his hair bristled and crackled, and the light of his eyes was red –
"and," she went on, "it seems to me a shame that such a brute be
suffered to infest the woods so nigh even to the abode of the
powerful Prince of Cats, my lord Tevildo"; but Tevildo said:
"Nor is he suffered, and cometh never there save it be by stealth."

"Howso that may be," said Tinúviel, "there he is now, yet
methinks that at last may his [life] be brought utterly to an end, for
lo, as I was going through the woods I saw where a great animal lay
upon the ground moaning as in sickness – and behold, it was
Huan, and some evil spell or malady has him in its grip, and still he
lies helpless in a dale not a mile westward in the woods from this
hall. Now with this perhaps I would not have troubled your ears,
had not the brute when I approached to succour him snarled upon
me and essayed to bite me, and meseems that such a creature
deserves whatever come to him."

A page from the *Tale of Tinúviel*

A page from the tale of *The Fall of Gondolin*

Now all this that Tinúviel spake was a great lie in whose devising Huan had guided her, and maidens of the Eldar are not wont to fashion lies; yet have I never heard that any of the Eldar blamed her therein nor Beren afterward, and neither do I, for Tevildo was an evil cat and Melko the wickedest of all beings, and Tinúviel was in dire peril at their hands. Tevildo however, himself a great and skilled liar, was so deeply versed in the lies and subtleties of all the beasts and creatures that he seldom knew whether to believe what was said to him or not, and was wont to disbelieve all things save those he wished to believe true, and so was he often deceived by the more honest. Now the story of Huan and his helplessness so pleased him that he was fain to believe it true, and determined at least to test it; yet at first he feigned indifference, saying this was a small matter for such secrecy and might have been spoken outside without further ado. But Tinúviel said she had not thought that Tevildo Prince of Cats needed to learn that the ears of Huan heard the slightest sounds a league away, and the voice of a cat further than any sound else.

Now therefore Tevildo sought to discover from Tinúviel under pretence of mistrusting her tale where exactly Huan might be found, but she made only vague answers, seeing in this her only hope of escaping from the castle, and at length Tevildo, overcome by curiosity and threatening evil things if she should prove false, summoned two of his thanes to him, and one was Oikeroi, a fierce and warlike cat. Then did the three set out with Tinúviel from that place, but Tinúviel took off her magical garment of black and folded it, so that for all its size and density it appeared no more than the smallest kerchief (for so was she able), and thus was she borne down the terraces upon the back of Oikeroi without mishap, and no drowziness assailed her bearer. Now crept they through the woods in the direction she had named, and soon does Tevildo smell dog and bristles and lashes his great tail, but after he climbs a lofty tree and looks down from thence into that dale that Tinúviel had shown to them. There he does indeed see the great form of Huan lying prostrate groaning and moaning, and he comes down in much glee and haste, and indeed in his eagerness he forgets Tinúviel, who now in great fear for Huan lies hidden in a bank of fern. The design of Tevildo and his two companions was to enter that dale silently from different quarters and so come all suddenly upon Huan unawares and slay him, or if he were too stricken to make fight to make sport of him and torment him. This did they now, but even as they leapt out upon him Huan sprang up into the

air with a mighty baying, and his jaws closed in the back close to
the neck of that cat Oikeroi, and Oikeroi died; but the other thane
fled howling up a great tree, and so was Tevildo left alone face to
face with Huan, and such an encounter was not much to his mind,
yet was Huan upon him too swiftly for flight, and they fought
fiercely in that glade, and the noise that Tevildo made was very
hideous; but at length Huan had him by the throat, and that cat
might well have perished had not his claws as he struck out blindly
pierced Huan's eye. Then did Huan give tongue, and Tevildo
screeching fearsomely got himself loose with a great wrench and
leapt up a tall and smooth tree that stood by, even as his companion
had done. Despite his grievous hurt Huan now leaps beneath that
tree baying mightily, and Telvido curses him and casts evil words
upon him from above.

Then said Huan: "Lo, Tevildo, these are the words of Huan
whom thou thoughtest to catch and slay helpless as the miserable
mice it is thy wont to hunt — stay for ever up thy lonely tree and
bleed to death of thy wounds, or come down and feel again my
teeth. But if neither are to thy liking, then tell me where is
Tinúviel Princess of Fairies and Beren son of Egnor, for these are
my friends. Now these shall be set as ransom against thee — though
it be valuing thee far over thy worth."

"As for that cursed Elf, she lies whimpering in the ferns yonder,
an my ears mistake not," said Tevildo, "and Beren methinks is
being soundly scratched by Miaulë my cook in the kitchens of my
castle for his clumsiness there an hour ago."

"Then let them be given to me in safety," said Huan, "and thou
mayest return thyself to thy halls and lick thyself unharmed."

"Of a surety my thane who is here with me shall fetch them for
thee," said Tevildo, but growled Huan: "Ay, and fetch also all thy
tribe and the hosts of the Orcs and the plagues of Melko. Nay, I
am no fool; rather shalt thou give Tinúviel a token and she shall
fetch Beren, or thou shalt stay here if thou likest not the other
way." Then was Tevildo forced to cast down his golden collar — a
token no cat dare dishonour, but Huan said: "Nay, more yet is
needed, for this will arouse all thy folk to seek thee," and this
Tevildo knew and had hoped. So was it that in the end weariness
and hunger and fear prevailed upon that proud cat, a prince of the
service of Melko, to reveal the secret of the cats and the spell that
Melko had entrusted to him; and those were words of magic
whereby the stones of his evil house were held together, and
whereby he held all beasts of the catfolk under his sway, filling

them with an evil power beyond their nature; for long has it been said that Tevildo was an evil fay in beastlike shape. When therefore he had told it Huan laughed till the woods rang, for he knew that the days of the power of the cats were over.

Now sped Tinúviel with the golden collar of Tevildo back to the lowest terrace before the gates, and standing she spake the spell in her clear voice. Then behold, the air was filled with the voices of cats and the house of Tevildo shook; and there came therefrom a host of indwellers and they were shrunk to puny size and were afeared of Tinúviel, who waving the collar of Tevildo spake before them certain of the words that Tevildo had said in her hearing to Huan, and they cowered before her. But she said: "Lo, let all those of the folk of the Elves or of the children of Men that are bound within these halls be brought forth," and behold, Beren was brought forth, but of other thralls there were none, save only Gimli, an aged Gnome, bent in thraldom and grown blind, but whose hearing was the keenest that has been in the world, as all songs say. Gimli came leaning upon a stick and Beren aided him, but Beren was clad in rags and haggard, and he had in his hand a great knife he had caught up in the kitchen, fearing some new ill when the house shook and all the voices of the cats were heard; but when he beheld Tinúviel standing amid the host of cats that shrank from her and saw the great collar of Tevildo, then was he[8] amazed utterly, and knew not what to think. But Tinúviel was very glad, and spoke saying: "O Beren from beyond the Bitter Hills, wilt thou now dance with me – but let it not be here." And she led Beren far away, and all those cats set up a howling and wailing, so that Huan and Tevildo heard it in the woods, but none followed or molested them, for they were afraid, and the magic of Melko was fallen from them.

This indeed they rued afterward when Tevildo returned home followed by his trembling comrade, for Tevildo's wrath was terrible, and he lashed his tail and dealt blows at all who stood nigh. Now Huan of the dogs, though it might seem a folly, when Beren and Tinúviel came to that glade had suffered that evil Prince to return without further war, but the great collar of gold he had set about his own neck, and at this was Tevildo more angry than all else, for a great magic of strength and power lay therein. Little to Huan's liking was it that Tevildo lived still, but now no longer did he fear the cats, and that tribe has fled before the dogs ever since, and the dogs hold them still in scorn since the humbling of Tevildo in the woods nigh Angamandi; and Huan has not done any greater deed. Indeed afterward Melko heard all and he cursed Tevildo and his folk and banished them, nor have they since that day had lord or master or any friend, and their voices wail and screech for their hearts are very lonely and bitter and full of loss, yet there is only darkness therein and no kindliness.

At the time however whereof the tale tells it was Tevildo's chief desire to recapture Beren and Tinúviel and to slay Huan, that he might regain the spell and magic he had lost, for he was in great fear of Melko, and he dared not seek his master's aid and reveal his defeat and the betrayal of his spell. Unwitting of this Huan feared those places, and was in great dread lest those doings come swiftly to Melko's ear, as did most things that came to pass in the world; wherefore now Tinúviel and Beren wandered far away with Huan, and they became great in friendship with him, and in that life Beren grew strong again and his thraldom fell from him, and Tinúviel loved him.

Yet wild and rugged and very lonely were those days, for never a face of Elf or of Man did they see, and Tinúviel grew at last to long sorely for Gwendeling her mother and the songs of sweet magic she was used to sing to her children as twilight fell in the woodlands by their ancient halls. Often she half fancied she heard the flute of Dairon her brother, in pleasant glades' wherein they sojourned, and her heart grew heavy. At length she said to Beren and to Huan: "I must return home," and now is it Beren's heart that is overcast with sorrow, for he loved that life in the woods with the dogs (for by now many others had become joined to Huan), yet not if Tinúviel were not there.

Nonetheless said he: "Never may I go back with thee to the land of Artanor — nor come there ever after to seek thee, sweet Tinúviel, save only bearing a Silmaril; nor may that ever now be achieved, for am I not a fugitive from the very halls of Melko, and in danger of the most evil pains do any of his servants spy me." Now this he said in the grief of his heart at parting with Tinúviel, and she was torn in mind, abiding not the thought of leaving Beren nor yet of living ever thus in exile. So sat she a great while in sad thought and she spoke not, but Beren sat nigh and at length said: "Tinúviel, one thing only can we do — go get a Silmaril"; and she sought thereupon Huan, asking his aid and advice, but he was very grave and saw nothing but folly in the matter. Yet in the end Tinúviel begged of him the fell of Oikeroi that he slew in the affray of the glade; now Oikeroi was a very mighty cat and Huan carried that fell with him as a trophy.

Now doth Tinúviel put forth her skill and fairy-magic, and she sews Beren into this fell and makes him to the likeness of a great cat, and she teaches him how to sit and sprawl, to step and bound and trot in the semblance of a cat, till Huan's very whiskers bristled at the sight, and thereat Beren and Tinúviel laughed. Never however could Beren learn to screech or wail or to purr like any cat that ever walked, nor could Tinúviel awaken a glow in the dead eyes of the catskin – "but we must put up with that," said she, "and thou hast the air of a very noble cat if thou but hold thy tongue."

Then did they bid farewell to Huan and set out for the halls of Melko by easy journeys, for Beren was in great discomfort and heat within the fur of Oikeroi, and Tinúviel's heart became lighter awhile than it had been for long, and she stroked Beren or pulled his tail, and Beren was angry because he could not lash it in answer as fiercely as he wished. At length however they drew near to Angamandi, as indeed the rumblings and deep noises, and the sound of mighty hammerings of ten thousand smiths labouring unceasingly, declared to them. Nigh were the sad chambers where the thrall-Noldoli laboured bitterly under the Orcs and goblins of the hills, and here the gloom and darkness was great so that their hearts fell, but Tinúviel arrayed her once more in her dark garment of deep sleep. Now the gates of Angamandi were of iron wrought hideously and set with knives and spikes, and before them lay the greatest wolf the world has ever seen, even Karkaras Knife-fang who had never slept; and Karkaras growled when he saw Tinúviel approach, but of the cat he took not much heed, for he thought little of cats and they were ever passing in and out.

"Growl not, O Karkaras," said she, "for I go to seek my lord Melko, and this thane of Tevildo goeth with me as escort." Now the dark robe veiled all her shimmering beauty, and Karkaras was not much troubled in mind, yet nonetheless he approached as was his wont to snuff the air of her, and the sweet fragrance of the Eldar that garment might not hide. Therefore straightway did Tinúviel begin a magic dance, and the black strands of her dark veil she cast in his eyes so that his legs shook with a drowziness and he rolled over and was asleep. But not until he was fast in dreams of great chases in the woods of Hisilómë when he was yet a whelp did Tinúviel cease, and then did those twain enter that black portal, and winding down many shadowy ways they stumbled at length into the very presence of Melko.

In that gloom Beren passed well enough as a very thane of

Tevildo, and indeed Oikeroi had aforetime been much about the halls of Melko, so that none heeded him and he slunk under the very chair of the Ainu unseen, but the adders and evil things there lying set him in great fear so that he durst not move.

Now all this fell out most fortunately, for had Tevildo been with Melko their deceit would have been discovered – and indeed of that danger they had thought, not knowing that Tevildo sat now in his halls and knew not what to do should his discomfiture become noised in Angamandi; but behold, Melko espieth Tinúviel and saith: "Who art thou that flittest about my halls like a bat? How camest thou in, for of a surety thou dost not belong here?"

"Nay, that I do not yet," saith Tinúviel, "though I may perchance hereafter, of thy goodness, my lord Melko. Knowest thou not that I am Tinúviel daughter of Tinwelint the outlaw, and he hath driven me from his halls, for he is an overbearing Elf and I give not my love at his command."

Now in truth was Melko amazed that the daughter of Tinwelint came thus of her free will to his dwelling, Angamandi the terrible, and suspecting something untoward he asked what was her desire: "for knowest thou not," saith he, "that there is no love here for thy father or his folk, nor needst thou hope for soft words and good cheer from me."

"So hath my father said," saith she, "but wherefore need I believe him? Behold, I have a skill of subtle dances, and I would dance now before you, my lord, for then methinks I might readily be granted some humble corner of your halls wherein to dwell until such times as you should call for the little dancer Tinúviel to lighten your cares."

"Nay," saith Melko, "such things are little to my mind; but as thou hast come thus far to dance, dance, and after we will see," and with that he leered horribly, for his dark mind pondered some evil.

Then did Tinúviel begin such a dance as neither she nor any other sprite or fay or elf danced ever before or has done since, and after a while even Melko's gaze was held in wonder. Round the hall she fared, swift as a swallow, noiseless as a bat, magically beautiful as only Tinúviel ever was, and now she was at Melko's side, now before him, now behind, and her misty draperies touched his face and waved before his eyes, and the folk that sat about the walls or stood in that place were whelmed one by one in sleep, falling down into deep dreams of all that their ill hearts desired.

Beneath his chair the adders lay like stones, and the wolves before his feet yawned and slumbered, and Melko gazed on enchanted, but he did not sleep. Then began Tinúviel to dance a yet swifter dance before his eyes, and even as she danced she sang in a voice very low and wonderful a song which Gwendeling had taught her long ago, a song that the youths and maidens sang beneath the cypresses of the gardens of Lórien when the Tree of Gold had waned and Silpion was gleaming. The voices of nightingales were in it, and many subtle odours seemed to fill the air of that noisome place as she trod the floor lightly as a feather in the wind; nor has any voice or sight of such beauty ever again been seen there, and Ainu Melkó for all his power and majesty succumbed to the magic of that Elf-maid, and indeed even the eyelids of Lórien had grown heavy had he been there to see. Then did Melko fall forward drowzed, and sank at last in utter sleep down from his chair upon the floor, and his iron crown rolled away.

Suddenly Tinúviel ceased. In the hall no sound was heard save of slumbrous breath; even Beren slept beneath the very seat of Melko, but Tinúviel shook him so that he awoke at last. Then in fear and trembling he tore asunder his disguise and freeing himself from it leapt to his feet. Now does he draw that knife that he had from Tevildo's kitchens and he seizes the mighty iron crown, but Tinúviel could not move it and scarcely might the thews of Beren avail to turn it. Great is the frenzy of their fear as in that dark hall of sleeping evil Beren labours as noiselessly as may be to prise out a Silmaril with his knife. Now does he loosen the great central jewel and the sweat pours from his brow, but even as he forces it from the crown lo! his knife snaps with a loud crack.

Tinúviel smothers a cry thereat and Beren springs away with the one Silmaril in his hand, and the sleepers stir and Melko groans as though ill thoughts disturbed his dreams, and a black look comes upon his sleeping face. Content now with that one flashing gem those twain fled desperately from the hall, stumbling wildly down many dark passages till from the glimmering of grey light they knew they neared the gates – and behold! Karkaras lies across the threshold, awake once more and watchful.

Straightway Beren thrust himself before Tinúviel although she said him nay, and this proved in the end ill, for Tinúviel had not time to cast her spell of slumber over the beast again, ere seeing Beren he bared his teeth and growled angrily. "Wherefore this surliness, Karkaras?" said Tinúviel. "Wherefore this Gnome[10] who entered not and yet now issueth in haste?" quoth Knife-fang, and with that he leapt upon Beren, who struck straight between the wolf's eyes with his fist, catching for his throat with the other hand.

Then Karkaras seized that hand in his dreadful jaws, and it was the hand wherein Beren clasped the blazing Silmaril, and both hand and jewel Karkaras bit off and took into his red maw. Great was the agony of Beren and the fear and anguish of Tinúviel, yet even as they expect to feel the teeth of the wolf a new thing strange and terrible comes to pass. Behold now that Silmaril blazeth with a white and hidden fire of its own nature and is possessed of a fierce and holy magic — for did it not come from Valinor and the blessed realms, being fashioned with spells of the Gods and Gnomes before evil came there; and it doth not tolerate the touch of evil flesh or of unholy hand. Now cometh it into the foul body of Karkaras, and suddenly that beast is burnt with a terrible anguish and the howling of his pain is ghastly to hear as it echoeth in those rocky ways, so that all that sleeping court within awakes. Then did Tinúviel and Beren flee like the wind from the gates, yet was Karkaras far before them raging and in madness as a beast pursued by Balrogs; and after when they might draw breath Tinúviel wept over the maimed arm of Beren kissing it often, so that behold it bled not, and pain left it, and was healed by the tender healing of her love; yet was Beren ever after surnamed among all folk Ermabwed the One-handed, which in the language of the Lonely Isle is Elmavoitë.

Now however must they bethink them of escape — if such may be their fortune, and Tinúviel wrapped part of her dark mantle about Beren, and so for a while flitting by dusk and dark amid the hills they were seen by none, albeit Melko had raised all his Orcs of terror against them; and his fury at the rape of that jewel was greater than the Elves had ever seen it yet.

Even so it seems soon to them that the net of the hunters drew ever more tightly upon them, and though they had reached the edge of the more familiar woods and passed the glooms of the forest of Taurfuin, still were there many leagues of peril yet to pass between them and the caverns of the king, and even did they reach ever there it seemed like they would but draw the chase behind them thither and Melko's hate upon all that woodland folk. So great indeed was the hue and cry that Huan learnt of it far away, and he marvelled much at the daring of those twain, and still more that ever they had escaped from Angamandi.

Now goes he with many dogs through the woods hunting Orcs

and thanes of Tevildo, and many hurts he got thus, and many of them he slew or put to fear and flight, until one even at dusk the Valar brought him to a glade in that northward region of Artanor that was called afterward Nan Dumgorthin, the land of the dark idols, but that is a matter that concerns not this tale. Howbeit it was even then a dark land and gloomy and foreboding, and dread wandered beneath its lowering trees no less even than in Taurfuin; and those two Elves Tinúviel and Beren were lying therein weary and without hope, and Tinúviel wept but Beren was fingering his knife.

Now when Huan saw them he would not suffer them to speak or to tell any of their tale, but straightway took Tinúviel upon his mighty back and bade Beren run as best he could beside him, "for," said he, "a great company of the Orcs are drawing swiftly hither, and wolves are their trackers and their scouts." Now doth Huan's pack run about them, and they go very swiftly along quick and secret paths towards the homes of the folk of Tinwelint far away. Thus was it that they eluded the host of their enemies, but had nonetheless many an encounter afterward with wandering things of evil, and Beren slew an Orc that came nigh to dragging off Tinúviel, and that was a good deed. Seeing then that the hunt still pressed them close, once more did Huan lead them by winding ways, and dared not yet straightly to bring them to the land of the woodland fairies. So cunning however was his leading that at last after many days the chase fell far away, and no longer did they see or hear anything of the bands of Orcs; no goblins waylaid them nor did the howling of any evil wolves come upon the airs at night, and belike that was because already they had stepped within the circle of Gwendeling's magic that hid the paths from evil things and kept harm from the regions of the woodelves.

Then did Tinúviel breathe freely once more as she had not done since she fled from her father's halls, and Beren rested in the sun far from the glooms of Angband until the last bitterness of thraldom left him. Because of the light falling through green leaves and the whisper of clean winds and the song of birds once more are they wholly unafraid.

At last came there nevertheless a day whereon waking out of a deep slumber Beren started up as one who leaves a dream of happy things coming suddenly to his mind, and he said: "Farewell, O Huan, most trusty comrade, and thou, little Tinúviel, whom I love, fare thee well. This only I beg of thee, get thee now straight to the safety of thy home, and may good Huan lead thee. But I – lo,

I must away into the solitude of the woods, for I have lost that
Silmaril which I had, and never dare I draw near to Angamandi
more, wherefore neither will I enter the halls of Tinwelint." Then
he wept to himself, but Tinúviel who was nigh and had hearkened
to his musing came beside him and said: "Nay, now is my heart
changed," and if thou dwellest in the woods, O Beren Ermabwed,
then so will I, and if thou wilt wander in the wild places there will I
wander also, or with thee or after thee: — yet never shall my father
see me again save only if thou takest me to him." Then indeed was
Beren glad at her sweet words, and fain would he have dwelt with
her as a huntsman of the wild, but his heart smote him for all that
she had suffered for him, and for her he put away his pride.
Indeed she reasoned with him, saying it would be folly to be
stubborn, and that her father would greet them with nought but
joy, being glad to see his daughter yet alive – and "maybe," said
she, "he will have shame that his jesting has given thy fair hand to
the jaws of Karkaras." But Huan also she implored to return with
them a space, for "my father owes thee a very great reward, O
Huan," saith she, "an he loves his daughter at all."

So came it that those three set forward once again together, and
came at last back to the woodlands that Tinúviel knew and loved
nigh to the dwellings of her folk and to the deep halls of her home.
Yet even as they approach they find fear and tumult among that
people such as had not been for a long age, and asking some that
wept before their doors they learned that ever since the day of
Tinúviel's secret flight ill-fortune had befallen them. Lo, the king
had been distraught with grief and had relaxed his ancient wariness
and cunning; indeed his warriors had been sent hither and thither
deep into the unwholesome woods searching for that maiden, and
many had been slain or lost for ever, and war there was with
Melko's servants about all their northern and eastern borders, so
that the folk feared mightily lest that Ainu upraise his strength
and come utterly to crush them and Gwendeling's magic have not
the strength to withhold the numbers of the Orcs. "Behold,"
said they, "now is the worst of all befallen, for long has Queen
Gwendeling sat aloof and smiled not nor spoken, looking as it were
to a great distance with haggard eyes, and the web of her magic has
blown thin about the woods, and the woods are dreary, for Dairon
comes not back, neither is his music heard ever in the glades.
Behold now the crown of all our evil tidings, for know that there
has broken upon us raging from the halls of Evil a great grey wolf
filled with an evil spirit, and he fares as though lashed by some

hidden madness, and none are safe. Already has he slain many as he runs wildly snapping and yelling through the woods, so that the very banks of the stream that flows before the king's halls has become a lurking-place of danger. There comes the awful wolf oftentimes to drink, looking as the evil Prince himself with bloodshot eyes and tongue lolling out, and never can he slake his desire for water as though some inward fire devours him."

Then was Tinúviel sad at the thought of the unhappiness that had come upon her folk, and most of all was her heart bitter at the story of Dairon, for of this she had not heard any murmur before. Yet could she not wish Beren had come never to the lands of Artanor, and together they made haste to Tinwelint; and already to the Elves of the wood it seemed that the evil was at an end now that Tinúviel was come back among them unharmed. Indeed they scarce had hoped for that.

In great gloom do they find King Tinwelint, yet suddenly is his sorrow melted to tears of gladness, and Gwendeling sings again for joy when Tinúviel enters there and casting away her raiment of dark mist she stands before them in her pearly radiance of old. For a while all is mirth and wonder in that hall, and yet at length the king turns his eyes to Beren and says: "So thou hast returned too – bringing a Silmaril, beyond doubt, in recompense for all the ill thou hast wrought my land; or an thou hast not, I know not wherefore thou art here."

Then Tinúviel stamped her foot and cried so that the king and all about him wondered at her new and fearless mood: "For shame, my father – behold, here is Beren the brave whom thy jesting drove into dark places and foul captivity and the Valar alone saved from a bitter death. Methinks 'twould rather befit a king of the Eldar to reward him than revile him."

"Nay," said Beren, "the king thy father hath the right. Lord," said he, "I have a Silmaril in my hand even now."

"Show me then," said the king in amaze.

"That I cannot," said Beren, "for my hand is not here"; and he held forth his maimed arm.

Then was the king's heart turned to him by reason of his stout and courteous demeanour, and he bade Beren and Tinúviel relate to him all that had befallen either of them, and he was eager to hearken, for he did not fully comprehend the meaning of Beren's words. When however he had heard all yet more was his heart turned to Beren, and he marvelled at the love that had awakened in the heart of Tinúviel so that she had done greater deeds and more daring than any of the warriors of his folk.

"Never again," said he, "O Beren I beg of thee, leave this court nor the side of Tinúviel, for thou art a great Elf and thy name will ever be great among the kindreds." Yet Beren answered him proudly, and said: "Nay, O King, I hold to my word and thine, and I will get thee that Silmaril or ever I dwell in peace in thy halls." And the king entreated him to journey no more into the dark and unknown realms, but Beren said: "No need is there thereof, for behold that jewel is even now nigh to thy caverns," and he made clear to Tinwelint that that beast that ravaged his land was none other than Karkaras, the wolfward of Melko's gates – and this was not known to all, but Beren knew it taught by Huan, whose cunning in the reading of track and slot was greatest among all the hounds, and therein are none of them unskilled. Huan indeed was with Beren now in the halls, and when those twain spoke of a chase and a great hunt he begged to be in that deed; and it was granted gladly. Now do those three prepare themselves to harry that beast, that all the folk be rid of the terror of the wolf, and Beren kept his word, bringing a Silmaril to shine once more in Elfinesse. King Tinwelint himself led that chase, and Beren was beside him, and Mablung the heavy-handed, chief of the king's thanes, leaped up and grasped a spear[12] – a mighty weapon captured in battle with the distant Orcs – and with those three stalked Huan mightiest of dogs, but others they would not take according to the desire of the king, who said: "Four is enough for the slaying even of the Hell-wolf" – but only those who had seen knew how fearsome was that beast, nigh as large as a horse among Men, and so great was the ardour of his breath that it scorched whatsoever it touched. About the hour of sunrise they set forth, and soon after Huan espied a new slot beside the stream, not far from the king's doors, "and," quoth he, "this is the print of Karkaras." Thereafter they followed that stream all day, and at many places its banks were new-trampled and torn and the water of the pools that lay about it was fouled as though some beasts possessed of madness had rolled and fought there not long before.

Now sinks the sun and fades beyond the western trees and darkness is creeping down from Hisilómë so that the light of the forest dies. Even so come they to a place where the spoor swerves from the stream or perchance is lost in its waters and Huan may no longer follow it; and here therefore they encamp, sleeping in turns beside the stream, and the early night wears away.

Suddenly in Beren's watch a sound of great terror leaped up from far away – a howling as of seventy maddened wolves – then lo! the brushwood cracks and saplings snap as the terror draweth near, and Beren knows that Karkaras is upon them. Scarce had he time to rouse the others, and they were but just sprung up and half-awake, when a great form loomed in the wavering moonlight filtering there, and it was fleeing like one mad, and its course was bent towards the water. Thereat Huan gave tongue, and straightway the beast swerved aside towards them, and foam was dripping from his jaws and a red light shining from his eyes, and his face was marred with mingled terror and with wrath. No sooner did he leave the trees than Huan rushed upon him fearless of heart, but he with a mighty leap sprang right over that great dog, for all his fury was kindled suddenly against Beren whom he recognized as he stood behind, and to his dark mind it seemed that there was the cause of all his agony. Then Beren thrust swiftly upward with a spear into his throat, and Huan leapt again and had him by a hind leg, and Karkaras fell as a stone, for at that same moment the king's spear found his heart, and his evil spirit gushed forth and sped howling faintly as it fared over the dark hills to Mandos; but Beren lay under him crushed beneath his weight. Now they roll back that carcase and fall to cutting it open, but Huan licks Beren's face whence blood is flowing. Soon is the truth of Beren's words made clear, for the vitals of the wolf are half-consumed as though an inner fire had long been smouldering there, and suddenly the night is filled with a wondrous lustre, shot with pale and secret colours, as Mablung[13] draws forth the Silmaril. Then holding it out he said: "Behold O King,"[14] but Tinwelint said: "Nay, never will I handle it save only if Beren give it to me." But Huan said: "And that seems like never to be, unless ye tend him swiftly, for methinks he is hurt sorely"; and Mablung and the king were ashamed.

Therefore now they raised Beren gently up and tended him and washed him, and he breathed, but he spoke not nor opened his eyes, and when the sun arose and they had rested a little they bore him as softly as might be upon a bier of boughs back through the woodlands; and nigh midday they drew near the homes of the folk again, and then were they deadly weary, and Beren had not moved nor spoken, but groaned thrice.

There did all the people flock to meet them when their approach was noised among them, and some bore them meat and cool drinks and salves and healing things for their hurts, and but for the harm that Beren had met great indeed had been their joy. Now then they covered the leafy boughs whereon he lay with soft raiment, and they bore him away to the halls of the king, and there was Tinúviel awaiting them in great distress; and she fell upon Beren's breast and wept and kissed him, and he awoke and knew her, and after Mablung gave him that Silmaril, and he lifted it above him gazing at its beauty, ere he said slowly and with pain: "Behold, O King, I give thee the wondrous jewel thou didst desire, and it is but a little thing found by the wayside, for once methinks thou hadst one beyond thought more beautiful, and she is now mine." Yet even as he spake the shadows of Mandos lay upon his face, and his spirit fled in that hour to the margin of the world, and Tinúviel's tender kisses called him not back.'

Then did Vëannë suddenly cease speaking, and Eriol sadly said: 'A tale of ruth for so sweet a maid to tell'; but behold, Vëannë wept, and not for a while did she say: 'Nay, that is not all the tale; but here endeth all that I rightly know,' and other children there spake, and one said: 'Lo, I have heard that the magic of Tinúviel's tender kisses healed Beren, and recalled his spirit from the gates of Mandos, and long time he dwelt among the Lost Elves wandering the glades in love with sweet Tinúviel.' But another said: 'Nay, that was not so, O Ausir, and if thou wilt listen I will tell the true and wondrous tale; for Beren died there in Tinúviel's arms even as Vëannë has said, and Tinúviel crushed with sorrow and finding no comfort or light in all the world followed him swiftly down those dark ways that all must tread alone. Now her beauty and tender loveliness touched even the cold heart of Mandos, so that he suffered her to lead Beren forth once more into the world, nor has this ever been done since to Man or Elf, and many songs and stories are there of the prayer of Tinúviel before the throne of Mandos that I remember not right well. Yet said Mandos to those twain: "Lo, O Elves, it is not to any life of perfect joy that I dismiss you, for such may no longer be found in all the world where sits Melko of the evil heart — and know ye that ye will become mortal even as Men, and when ye fare hither again it will be for ever, unless the Gods summon you indeed to Valinor." Nonetheless those twain departed hand in hand, and they fared together through the northern woods, and oftentimes were they seen dancing magic dances down the hills, and their name became heard far and wide.'

And thereat that boy ceased, and Vëannë said: 'Aye, and they did more than dance, for their deeds afterward were very great, and many tales are there thereof that thou must hear, O Eriol Melinon, upon another time of tale-telling. For those twain it is that stories name i·Cuilwarthon, which is to say the dead that live again, and they became mighty fairies in the lands about the north of Sirion. Behold now all is ended – and doth it like thee?' But Eriol said: 'Indeed 'tis a wondrous tale, such as I looked not to hear from the lips of the little maids of Mar Vanwa Tyaliéva,' but Vëannë answered him: 'Nay, but I fashioned it not with words of myself; but it is dear to me – and indeed all the children know of the deeds that it relates – and I have learned it by heart, reading it in the great books, and I do not comprehend all that is set therein.'

'Neither do I,' said Eriol – but suddenly cried Ausir: 'Behold, Eriol, Vëannë has never told thee what befell Huan; nor how he would take no rewards from Tinwelint nor dwell nigh him, but wandered forth again grieving for Tinúviel and Beren. On a time he fell in with Mablung[15] who aided in the chase, and was now fallen much to hunting in lonely parts; and the twain hunted together as friends until the days of Glorund the Drake and of Túrin Turambar, when once more Huan found Beren and played his part in the great deeds of the Nauglafring, the Necklace of the Dwarves.'

'Nay, how could I tell all this,' said Vëannë, 'for behold it is time for the evening meat already'; and soon after the great gong rang.

### The second version of the Tale of Tinúviel

As already mentioned (p. 3), there exists a revised version of part of the tale in a typescript (made by my father). This follows the manuscript version closely or very closely on the whole, and in no way alters the style or air of the former; it is therefore unnecessary to give this second version *in extenso*. But the typescript does in places introduce interesting changes, and these are given below (the pages of the corresponding passages in the manuscript version are given in the margin).

The title in the typescript (which begins with the *Link* passage already given, pp. 4–7) was originally 'The Tale of Tynwfiel, Princess of Dor Athro', which was changed to 'The Tale of Tinúviel, the Dancer of Doriath'.

(8)    'Who then was Tinúviel?' said Eriol. 'Knowst thou not,' said Ausir, 'she was the daughter of Singoldo, king of Artanor?' 'Hush

thee, Ausir,' said Vëannë, 'this is my tale, and 'tis a tale of the
Gnomes, wherefore I beg that thou fill not Eriol's ear with thy
Elfin names. Lo! I will tell this tale only, for did I not see Melian
and Tinúviel once long ago with my own eyes when journeying by
the Way of Dreams?'

'What then was Queen Melian like,' quoth Eriol, 'if thou hast
seen her, O Vëannë?'

'Slender and very dark of hair,' said she, 'and her skin was white
and pale, but her eyes shone seeming to hold great depths. Clad
she was in filmy garments most lovely yet of the hue of night,
jet-spangled and girt with silver. If ever she sang or if ever
she danced, dreams and slumbers passed over the heads of those
that were nigh, making them heavy as it were with a strong wine
of sleep. Indeed she was a sprite that, escaping from Lórien's
gardens before even Kôr was built, wandered in the wild places of
the world and in every lonely wood. Nightingales fared with her
singing about her as she went – and 'twas the song of these birds
that smote the ears of Thingol as he marched at the head of that
second[16] tribe of the Eldalië which afterward became the Shoreland Pipers, the Solosimpi of the Isle. Now had they come a great
way from dim Palisor, and wearily the companies laboured behind
the swift-footed horse of Oromë, wherefore the music of the magic
birds of Melian seemed to him full of all solace, more beautiful
than other melodies of Earth, and he strayed aside for a moment,
as he thought, from the host, seeking in the dark trees whence it
might come.

And it is said that it was not a moment that he hearkened, but
many years, and vainly his people sought him, until at length they
must perforce follow Oromë upon Tol Eressëa, and be borne
thereon far away leaving him listening to the birds enchanted in
the woods of Aryador. That was the first sorrow of the Solosimpi,
that after were many; but Ilúvatar in memory of Thingol set a seed
of music in the hearts of that folk above all kindreds of the Earth
save only the Gods, and after, as all story tells, it blossomed
wondrously upon the isle and in glorious Valinor.

Little sorrow, however, had Thingol; for after a little, as him
seemed, he came upon Melian lying on a bed of leaves . . .

*

(9)     Long thereafter, as now thou knowest, Melko brake once more
into the world from Valinor, and wellnigh all beings therein came
under his foul thraldom; nor were the Lost Elves free, nor the
errant Gnomes that wandered the mountainous places seeking
their stolen treasury. Yet some few there were that led by mighty
kings still defied that evil one in fast and hidden places, and if

Turgon King of Gondolin was the most glorious of these, for a while the most mighty and the longest free was Thingol of the Woods.

Now in the after-days of Sunshine and Moonsheen still dwelt Thingol in Artanor and ruled a numerous and hardy folk drawn from all the tribes of ancient Elfinesse – for neither he nor his people went to the dread Battle of Unnumbered Tears – a matter which toucheth not this tale. Yet was his lordship greatly increased after that most bitter field by fugitives seeking a leader and a home. Hidden was his dwelling thereafter from the vision and knowledge of Melko by the cunning magics of Melian the fay, and she wove spells about all the paths that led thereto, so that none but the children of the Eldalië might tread them without straying. Thus was the king guarded against all evils save treachery alone; his halls were built in a deep cavern, vaulted immeasurable, that knew no other entrance than a rocky door, mighty, pillared with stone, and shadowed by the loftiest and most ancient trees in all the shaggy forests of Artanor. A great stream was there that fared a dark and silent course in the deep woods, and this flowed wide and swift before that doorway, so that all who would enter that portal must first cross a bridge hung by the Noldoli of Thingol's service across that water – and narrow it was and strongly guarded. In no wise ill were those forest lands, although not utterly distant were the Iron Mountains and black Hisilómë beyond them where dwelt the strange race of Men, and thrall-Noldoli laboured, and few free-Eldar went.

Two children had Thingol then, Dairon and Tinúviel . . .

\*

(10)     'her mother was a fay, a child of Lórien' for manuscript 'her mother was a fay, a daughter of the Gods'.

\*

(11)     'Now Beren was a Gnome, son of Egnor the forester' as in manuscript; but *Egnor* changed to *Barahir*. This however was a much later and as it were casual change; Beren's father was still Egnor in 1925.

\*

(11)     Manuscript version 'and all the Elves of the woodland thought of the Gnomes of Dor Lómin as treacherous creatures, cruel and faithless' is omitted in the typescript.

\*

(13)     *Angband* for manuscript *Angamandi*, and throughout.

\*

(14)     Many a combat and an escape had he in those days, and he slew
therein more than once both wolf and the Orc that rode thereon
with nought but an ashen club that he bore; and other perils and
adventures . . .

*

(15)     But Melko looking wroth upon him asked: "How hast thou, O
thrall, dared to fare thus out of the land where thy folk dwells at
my behest, and to wander in the great woods unbidden, leaving
the labours to which thou hast been set?" Then answered Beren
that he was no runagate thrall, but came of a kindred of the
Gnomes that dwelt in Aryador where were many of the folk of
Men. Then was Melko yet more wroth, saying: "Here have we a
plotter of deep treacheries against Melko's lordship, and one
worthy of the tortures of the Balrogs" – for he sought ever to
destroy the friendship and intercourse of Elves and Men, lest they
forget the Battle of Unnumbered Tears and once more arise in
wrath against him. But Beren seeing his peril answered: "Think
not, O most mighty Belcha Morgoth (for such be his names
among the Gnomes), that could be so; for, an it were, then should
I not be here unaided and alone. No friendship has Beren son of
Egnor for the kindred of Men; nay indeed, wearying utterly of the
lands infested by that folk he has wandered out of Aryador.
Whither then should he go but to Angband? For many a great tale
has his father made to him aforetime of thy splendour and thy
glory. Lo, lord, albeit I am no renegade thrall, still do I desire
nothing so much as to serve thee in what small manner I may."
Little of truth was therein, and indeed his father Egnor was the
chiefest foe of Melko in all the kin of the Gnomes that still were
free, save only Turgon king of Gondolin and the sons of Fëanor,
and long days of friendship had he known with the folk of Men,
what time he was brother in arms to Úrin the steadfast; but in
those days he bore another name and Egnor was nought for
Melko. The truth, however, did Beren then tell, saying that he
was a great huntsman, swift and cunning to shoot or snare or to
outrun all birds and beasts. "I was lost unawares in a part of the
hills that were not known to me, O lord," he said, "the while I was
hunting; and wandering far I came to strange lands and knew no
other rede of safety save to fare to Angband, that all can find who
see the black hills of the north from afar. I would myself have fared
to thee and begged of thee some humble office (as a winner of
meats for thy table, perchance) had not these Orcs seized me and
tormented me unjustly."
     Now the Valar must have inspired that speech, or maybe it was
a spell of cunning words cast upon him in compassion by Melian as
he fled from the hall; for indeed it saved his life . . .

Subsequently a part of this passage was emended on the typescript, to read:

. . . and long days of friendship had he known with the folk of
Men (as had Beren himself thereafter as brother in arms to Úrin
the Steadfast); but in those days the Orcs named him Rog the
Fleet, and the name of Egnor was nought to Melko.

At the same time the words 'Now the Valar must have inspired
that speech' were changed to 'Now the Valar inspired that speech'.

*

(15)    Thus was Beren set by Melko as a thrall to The Prince of Cats,
whom the Gnomes have called Tiberth Bridhon Miaugion, but
the Elves Tevildo.

Subsequently *Tiberth* appears for MS *Tevildo* throughout,
and in one place the full name *Tiberth Bridhon Miaugion* appears
again. In the MS the Gnomish name is *Tifil*.

*

(17)    . . . getting nought but a bitten finger for his toil. Then was
Tiberth wroth, and said: "Thou hast lied to my lord, O Gnome,
and art fitter to be a scullion than a huntsman, who canst not catch
even the mice about my halls." Evil thereafter were his days in the
power of Tiberth; for a scullion they made him, and unending
labour he had in the hewing of wood and drawing of water, and in
the menial services of that noisome abode. Often too was he
tormented by the cats and other evil beasts of their company, and
when, as happened at whiles, there was an Orc-feast in those halls,
he would ofttimes be set to the roasting of birds and other meats
upon spits before the mighty fires in Melko's dungeons, until he
swooned for the overwhelming heat; yet he knew himself fortunate
beyond all hope in being yet alive among those cruel foes of Gods
and Elves. Seldom got he food or sleep himself, and he became
haggard and half-blind, so that he wished often that never straying
out of the wild free places of Hisilómë he had not even caught sight
afar off of the vision of Tinúviel.

*

(17)    But Melian laughed not, nor said aught thereto; for in many
things was she wise and forewise – yet nonetheless it was a thing
unthought in a mad dream that any Elf, still less a maiden, the
daughter of that king who had longest defied Melko, should fare
alone even to the borders of that sorrowful country amid which
lies Angband and the Hells of Iron. Little love was there between
the woodland Elves and the folk of Angband even in those days
before the Battle of Unnumbered Tears when Melko's power was
not grown to its full, and he veiled his designs, and spread his net

of lies. "No help wilt thou get therein of me, little one," said she; "for even if magic and destiny should bring thee safe out of that foolhardiness, yet should many and great things come thereof, and on some many sorrows, and my rede is that thou tell never thy father of thy desire."

But this last word of Melian's did Thingol coming unaware overhear, and they must perforce tell him all, and he was so wroth when he heard it that Tinúviel wished that never had her thoughts been revealed even to her mother.

\*

(18)    Indeed I have no love for him, for he has destroyed our play together, our music and our dancing." But Tinúviel said: "I ask it not for him, but for myself, and for that very play of ours together aforetime." And Dairon said: "And for thy sake I say thee nay"; and they spake no more thereof together, but Dairon told the king of what Tinúviel had desired of him, fearing lest that dauntless maiden fare away to her death in the madness of her heart.

\*

(18)    . . . he might not shut his daughter for ever in the caves, where the light was only that of torches dim and flickering.

\*

(19)    The names of all the tallest and longest things upon Earth were set in that song: the beards of the Indrafangs, the tail of Carcaras, the body of Glorund the drake, the bole of Hirilorn, and the sword of Nan she named, nor did she forget the chain Angainu that Aulë and Tulkas made, or the neck of Gilim the giant that is taller than many elm trees; . . .

Carcaras is spelt thus subsequently in the typescript.

\*

(20)    . . . as fast as her dancing feet would flit.

Now when the guards awoke it was late in the morning, and they fled away nor dared to bear the tidings to their lord; and Dairon it was bore word of the escape of Tinúviel to Thingol, for he had met the folk that ran in amazement from the ladders which each morning were lifted to her door. Great was the mingled grief and wrath of the king, and all the deep places of his court were in uproar, and all the woods were ringing with the search; but Tinúviel was already far away dancing madly through the dark woods towards the gloomy foothills and the Mountains of Night. 'Tis said that Dairon sped swiftest and furthest in pursuit, but was wrapped in the deceit of those far places, and became utterly lost, and came never back to Elfinesse, but turned towards Palisor; and there he plays subtle magic musics still, wistful and lonely in the woods and forests of the south.

Now fared Tinúviel forward, and a sudden dread overtook her at the thought of what she had dared to do, and of what lay before her. Then did she turn back for a while, and wept, wishing that Dairon were with her. It is said that he was not indeed at that time far off, and wandered lost in Taurfuin, the Forest of Night, where after Túrin slew Beleg by mishap. Nigh was Tinúviel to those evil places; but she entered not that dark region, and the Valar set a new hope in her heart, so that she pressed on once more.

\*

(21)  Seldom was any of the cats slain indeed; for in those days they were mightier far in valour and in strength than they have been since those things befell that thou art soon to learn, mightier even than the tawny cats of the southern lands where the sun burns hot. No less too was their skill in climbing and in hiding, and their fleetness was that of an arrow, yet were the free dogs of the northern woods marvellously valiant and knew no fear, and great enmity was between them, and some of those hounds were held in dread even by the greatest of the cats. None, however, did Tiberth fear save only Huan the lord of the Hounds of Hisilómë. So swift was Huan that on a time he had fallen upon Tiberth as he hunted alone in the woods, and pursuing him had overtaken him and nigh rent the fur of his neck from him ere he was rescued by a host of Orcs that heard his cries. Huan got him many hurts in that battle ere he won away, but the wounded pride of Tiberth lusted ever for his death.

Great therefore was the good fortune that befell Tinúviel in meeting with Huan in the woods; and this she did in a little glade nigh to the forest's borders, where the first grasslands begin that are nourished by the upper waters of the river Sirion. Seeing him she was mortally afraid and turned to flee; but in two swift leaps Huan overtook her. Speaking softly the deep tongue of the Lost Elves he bade her be not afeared, and "wherefore," said he, "do I see an Elfin maiden, and one most fair, wandering thus nigh to the places of the Prince of Evil Heart?

\*

(22)  What is thy thought, O Huan?"

"Little counsel have I for thee," said he, "save that thou goest with all speed back to Artanor and thy father's halls, and I will accompany thee all the way, until those lands be reached that the magic of Melian the Queen does encompass." "That will I never do," said she, "while Beren liveth here, forgotten of his friends." "I thought that such would be thy answer," said he, "but if thou wilt still go forward with thy mad quest, then no counsel have I for thee save a desperate and a perilous one: we must make now all speed towards the ill places of Tiberth's abiding that are yet far off. I will guide thee thither by the most secret ways, and when we are come there thou must creep alone, if thou hast the heart, to the dwelling of that prince at an hour nigh noon when he and most of his household lie drowsing upon the terraces before his gates. There thou mayst perchance discover, if fortune is very kind, whether Beren be indeed within that ill place as thy mother said to thee. But lo, I will lie not far from the foot of the mount whereon Tiberth's hall is built, and thou must say to Tiberth so soon as thou seest him, be Beren there or be he not, that thou hast stumbled upon Huan of the Dogs lying sick of great wounds in a withered dale without his gates. Fear not overmuch, for herein wilt thou both do my pleasure and further thine own desires, as well as may be; nor do I think that when Tiberth hears thy tidings thou wilt be in any peril thyself for a time. Only do thou not direct him to the place that I shall show to thee; thou must offer to guide him thither thyself. Thus thou shalt get free again of his evil house, and shalt see what I contrive for the Prince of Cats." Then did Tinúviel shudder at the thought of what lay before, but she said that this rede would she sooner take than to return home, and they set forth straightway by secret pathways through the woods, and by winding trails over the bleak and stony lands that lay beyond.

At last on a day at morn they came to a wide dale hollowed like a bowl among the rocks. Deep were its sides, but nought grew there save low bushes of scanty leaves and withered grass. "This is the Withered Dale that I spake of," said Huan. "Yonder is the cave where the great

Here the typescript version of the *Tale of Tinúviel* ends, at the foot of a page. I think it is improbable that any more of this version was made.

## NOTES

1   For earlier references to Olórë Mallë, the Way of Dreams, see I.18, 27; 211, 225.

2   The distinction made here between the Elves (who call the queen *Wendelin*) and, by implication, the Gnomes (who call her

*Gwendeling*) is even more explicit in the typescript version, p. 42 ('tis a tale of the *Gnomes*, wherefore I beg that thou fill not Eriol's ears with thy *Elfin* names') and p. 45 ('The Prince of Cats, whom the *Gnomes* have called Tiberth Bridhon Miaugion, but the *Elves* Tevildo'). See I.50–1.

3  The manuscript as originally written read: 'Now Beren was a Gnome, son of a thrall of Melko's, some have said, that laboured in the darker places . . .' See note 4.

4  The manuscript as originally written read: 'I Beren of the Noldoli, son of Egnor the huntsman . . .' See note 3.

5  From this point, and continuing to the words 'forests of the south' on p. 21, the text is written on detached pages placed in the notebook. There is no rejected material corresponding to this passage. It is possible that it existed, and was removed from the book and lost; but, though the book is in a decayed state, it does not seem that any pages were removed here, and I think it more likely that my father simply found himself short of space, as he wrote over the original, erased, version, and (almost certainly) expanded it as he went.

6  The text as originally written read: 'came never back to Ellu, but plays . . .' (for *Ellu* see *Changes to Names* below). As a result of the interpolation 'but turned towards Palisor' Palisor is placed in the south of the world. In the tale of *The Coming of the Elves* (I.114) Palisor is called 'the midmost region' (see also the drawing of the 'World-Ship', I.84), and it seems possible that the word 'south' should have been changed; but it remains in the typescript (p. 47).

7  The *Tale of Turambar*, though composed after the *Tale of Tinúviel*, was in existence when *Tinúviel* was rewritten (see p. 69).

8  From 'amazed utterly' to 'if Tinúviel were not there' (p. 30) the text is written on an inserted page; see note 5 – here also the underlying textual situation is obscure.

9  A short passage of earlier text in pencil becomes visible here, ending: '. . . and Tinúviel grew to long sorely for Wendelin her mother and for the sight of Linwë and for Kapalen making music in pleasant glades.' *Kapalen* must be a name preceding *Tifanto*, itself preceding *Dairon* (see *Changes to Names* below).

10 *this Gnome*: original reading *this man*. This was a slip, but a significant slip (see p. 52), in all probability. It is possible that 'man' was used here, as occasionally elsewhere (e.g. p. 18 'as high as men could fashion their longest ladders', where the reference is to the Elves of Artanor), to mean 'male Elf', but in that case there would seem no reason to change it.

11 Struck out here in the manuscript: 'Beren of the Hills'.

12 'Mablung the heavy-handed, chief of the king's thanes, leaped up and grasped a spear' replaced the original reading 'Tifanto cast aside his pipe and grasped a spear'. Originally the name of Tinúviel's

brother was *Tifanto* throughout the tale. See notes 13–15, and the Commentary, p. 59.

13  *Mablung* replaced *Tifanto*, and again immediately below; see note 12.

14  'O King' replaced 'O father'; see note 12.

15  In this place *Mablung* was the form as first written; see the Commentary, p. 59.

16  It is essential to the narrative of the Coming of the Elves that the Solosimpi were the third and last of the three tribes; 'second' here can only be a slip, if a surprising one.

Changes made to names in
*The Tale of Tinúviel*

(i)  Manuscript Version

*Ilfiniol* < *Elfriniol*. In the typescript text the name is *Ilfrin*. See pp. 201–2.

*Tinwë Linto, Tinwelint*  In the opening passage of the tale (p. 8), where Ausir and Vëannë differ on the forms of Tinwelint's name, the MS is very confused and it is impossible to understand the succeeding stages. Throughout the tale, as originally written, Vëannë calls Tinwelint *Tinto Ellu* or *Ellu*, but in the argument at the beginning it is Ausir who calls him *Tinto Ellu* while Vëannë calls him *Tinto'ellon*. *(Tinto) Ellu* is certainly an 'Elvish' form, but it is corrected throughout the tale to the Gnomish *Tinwelint*, while Ausir's *Tinto Ellu* at the beginning is corrected to *Tinwë Linto*. (At the third occurrence of *Tinwë* in the opening passage the name as originally written was *Linwë*: see I.130.)

In the tales of *The Coming of the Elves* and *The Theft of Melko* in Part One *Ellu* is the name of the second lord of the Solosimpi chosen in Tinwelint's place (afterwards Olwë), but at both occurrences (I.120, 141) this is a later addition (I.130 note 5, 155). Many years later *Ellu* again became Thingol's name (Sindarin *Elu Thingol*, Quenya *Elwë Singollo*, in *The Silmarillion*).

*Gwendeling*  As the tale was originally written, *Wendelin* was the name throughout (*Wendelin* is found in tales given in Part One, emended from *Tindriel*: I.106–7, 131). It was later changed throughout to the Gnomish form *Gwendeling* (found in the early Gnomish dictionary, I.273, itself changed later to *Gwedhiling*) except in the mouth of Ausir, who uses the 'Elvish' form *Wendelin* (p. 8).

*Dairon*  < *Tifanto* throughout. For the change of *Tifanto* > *Mablung* at the end of the tale (notes 12–14 above) see the Commentary, p. 59, and for the name *Kapalen* preceding *Tifanto* see note 9.

*Dor Lómin*  < *Aryador* (p. 11). In the tale of *The Coming of the*

*Elves* it is said (I.119) that Aryador was the name of Hisilómë among Men; for *Dor Lómin – Hisilómë* see I.112. At subsequent occurrences in this tale *Aryador* was not changed.

*Angband* was originally twice written, and in one of these cases it was changed to *Angamandi*, in the other (p. 35) allowed to stand; in all other instances *Angamandi* was the form first written. In the manuscript version of the tale Vëannë does not make consistent use of Gnomish or 'Elvish' forms: thus she says *Tevildo* (not *Tifil*), *Angamandi*, *Gwendeling* (< *Wendelin*), *Tinwelint* (< *Tinto* (*Ellu*)). In the typescript version, on the other hand, Vëannë says *Tiberth*, *Angband*, *Melian* (< *Gwenethlin*), *Thingol* (< *Tinwelint*).

*Hirilorn, the Queen of Trees* < *Golosbrindi, the Queen of the Forest* (p. 18); *Hirilorn* < *Golosbrindi* at subsequent occurrences.

*Uinen* < *Onen* (or possibly *Únen*).

*Egnor bo-Rimion* < *Egnor go-Rimion*. In the tales previously given the patronymic prefix is *go-* (I.146, 155).

*Tinwelint* < *Tinthellon* (p. 35, the only case). Cf. *Tinto'ellon* mentioned above under *Tinwë Linto*.

*i·Cuilwarthon* < *i·Guilwarthon*.

## (ii) Typescript Version

*Tinúviel* < *Tynwfiel* in the title and at every occurrence until the passage corresponding to MS version p. 11 'yet now did he see Tinúviel dancing in the twilight'; there and subsequently the form typed was *Tinúviel*.

*Singoldo* < *Tinwë Linto* (p. 41).

*Melian* < *Gwenethlin* at every occurrence until the passage corresponding to MS version p. 12 'the stateliness of Queen Gwendeling'; there and subsequently the form typed was *Melian*.

*Thingol* < *Tinwelint* at every occurrence until the passage corresponding to MS version p. 12 'by winding paths to the abode of Tinwelint'; there and subsequently the form typed was *Thingol*.

For *Egnor* > *Barahir* see p. 43.

## Commentary on
## The Tale of Tinúviel

### §1. The primary narrative

In this section I shall consider only the conduct of the main story, and leave for the moment such questions as the wider history implied in it, Tinwelint's people and his dwelling, or the geography of the lands that appear in the story.

The story of Beren's coming upon Tinúviel in the moonlit glade in its earliest recorded form (pp. 11–12) was never changed in its central image; and it should be noticed that the passage in *The Silmarillion* (p. 165) is an extremely concentrated and exalted rendering of the scene: many elements not mentioned there were never in fact lost. In a very late reworking of the passage in the *Lay of Leithian** the hemlocks and the white moths still appear, and Daeron the minstrel is present when Beren comes to the glade. But there are nonetheless the most remarkable differences; and the chief of these is of course that Beren was here no mortal Man, but an Elf, one of the Noldoli, and the absolutely essential element of the story of Beren and Lúthien is not present. It will be seen later (pp. 71–2, 139) that this was not originally so, however: in the now lost (because erased) first form of the *Tale of Tinúviel* he had been a Man (it is for this reason that I have said that the reading *man* in the manuscript (see p. 33 and note 10), later changed to *Gnome*, is a 'significant slip'). Several years after the composition of the tale in the form in which we have it he became a Man again, though at that time (1925–6) my father appears to have hesitated long on the matter of the elvish or mortal nature of Beren.

In the tale there is, necessarily, a quite different reason for the hostility and distrust shown to Beren in Artanor (Doriath) − namely that 'the Elves of the woodland thought of the Gnomes of Dor Lómin as treacherous creatures, cruel and faithless' (see below, p. 65). It seems clear that at this time the history of Beren and his father (Egnor) was only very sketchily devised; there is in any case no hint of the story of the outlaw band led by his father and its betrayal by Gorlim the Unhappy (*The Silmarillion* pp. 162ff.) before the first form of the *Lay of Leithian*, where the story appears fully formed (the Lay was in being to rather beyond this point by the late summer of 1925). But an association of Beren's father (changed to Beren himself) with Úrin (Húrin) as 'brother in arms' is mentioned in the typescript version of the tale (pp. 44–5); according to the latest of the outlines for *Gilfanon's Tale* (I.240) 'Úrin and Egnor marched with countless battalions' (against the forces of Melko).

In the old story, Tinúviel had no meetings with Beren before the day when he boldly accosted her at last, and it was at that very time that she led him to Tinwelint's cave; they were not lovers, Tinúviel knew nothing of Beren but that he was enamoured of her dancing, and it seems that she brought him before her father as a matter of courtesy, the natural thing to do. The betrayal of Beren to Thingol by Daeron (*The Silmarillion* p. 166) therefore has no place in the old story − there is nothing to betray; and indeed it is not shown in the tale that Dairon knew anything

---

* The long unfinished poem in rhyming couplets in which is told the story of Beren and Lúthien Tinúviel; composed in 1925-31, but parts of it substantially rewritten many years later.

whatsoever of Beren before Tinúviel led him into the cave, beyond having once seen his face in the moonlight.

Despite these radical differences in the narrative structure, it is remarkable how many features of the scene in Tinwelint's hall (pp.12–13), when Beren stood before the king, endured, while all the inner significance was shifted and enlarged. To the beginning go back, for instance, Beren's abashment and silence, Tinúviel's answering for him, the sudden rising of his courage and uttering of his desire without preamble or hesitation. But the tone is altogether lighter and less grave than it afterwards became; in the jeering laughter of Tinwelint, who treats the matter as a jest and Beren as a benighted fool, there is no hint of what is explicit in the later story: 'Thus he wrought the doom of Doriath, and was ensnared within the curse of Mandos' (*The Silmarillion* p. 167). The Silmarils are indeed famous, and they have a holy power (p. 34), but the fate of the world is not bound up with them (*The Silmarillion* p. 67); Beren is an Elf, if of a feared and distrusted people, and his request lacks the deepest dimension of outrage; and he and Tinúviel are not lovers.

In this passage is the first mention of the Iron Crown of Melko, and the setting of the Silmarils in the Crown; and here again is a detail that was never lost: 'Never did this crown leave his head' (cf. *The Silmarillion* p. 81: 'That crown he never took from his head, though its weight became a deadly weariness').

But from this point Vëannë's story diverges in an altogether unexpected fashion from the later narrative. At no other place in the *Lost Tales* is the subsequent transformation more remarkable than in this, the precursor of the story of the capture of Beren and Felagund and their companions by Sauron the Necromancer, the imprisonment and death of all save Beren in the dungeons of Tol-in-Gaurhoth (the Isle of Werewolves in the river Sirion), and the rescue of Beren and overthrow of Sauron by Lúthien and Huan.

Most notably, what may be referred to as 'the Nargothrond Element' is entirely absent, and in so far as it already existed had as yet made no contact with the story of Beren and Tinúviel (for Nargothrond, not yet so named, at this period see pp. 81, 123–4). Beren has no ring of Felagund, he has no companions on his northward journey, and there is no relationship between (on the one hand) the story of his capture, his speech with Melko, and his dispatch to the house of Tevildo, and (on the other) the events of the later narrative whereby Beren and the band of Elves out of Nargothrond found themselves in Sauron's dungeon. Indeed, all the complex background of legend, of battles and rivalries, oaths and alliances, out of which the story of Beren and Lúthien arises in *The Silmarillion*, is very largely absent. The castle of the Cats 'is' the tower of Sauron on Tol-in-Gaurhoth, but only in the sense that it occupies the same 'space' in the narrative: beyond this there is no point in seeking even shadowy resemblances between the two establishments. The monstrous gormandising cats, their kitchens and their sunning terraces, and their

engagingly Elvish-feline names (*Miaugion*, *Miaulë*, *Meoita*) all disappeared without trace. Did Tevildo? It would scarcely be true, I think,
to say even that Sauron 'originated' in a cat: in the next phase of the
legends the Necromancer (Thû) has no feline attributes. On the other
hand it would be wrong to regard it as a simple matter of *replacement*
(Thû stepping into the narrative place vacated by Tevildo) without any
element of *transformation* of what was previously there. Tevildo's
immediate successor is 'the Lord of Wolves', himself a werewolf, and he
retains the Tevildo-trait of hating Huan more than any other creature in
the world. Tevildo was 'an evil fay in beastlike shape' (p. 29); and the
battle between the two great beasts, the hound against the werewolf
(originally the hound against the demon in feline form) was never lost.

When the tale returns to Tinúviel in Artanor the situation is quite the
reverse: for the story of her imprisonment in the house in Hirilorn and
her escape from it never underwent any significant change. The passage
in *The Silmarillion* (p. 172) is indeed very brief, but its lack of detail is
due to compression rather than to omission based on dissatisfaction; the
*Lay of Leithian*, from which the prose account in *The Silmarillion*
directly derives, is in this passage so close, in point of narrative detail, to
the *Tale of Tinúviel* as to be almost identical with it.

It may be observed that in this part of the story the earliest version had
a strength that was diminished later, in that the duration of Tinúviel's
imprisonment and her journey to Beren's rescue relates readily enough to
that of Beren's captivity, which was intended by his captors to be
unending; whereas in the later story there is a great deal of event and
movement (with the addition of Lúthien's captivity in Nargothrond) to
be fitted into the time when Beren was awaiting his death in the dungeon
of the Necromancer.

While the strong element of 'explanatory' beast-fable (concerning cats
and dogs) was to be entirely eliminated, and Tevildo Prince of Cats
replaced by the Necromancer, Huan nonetheless remained from it as the
great Hound of Valinor. His encounter with Tinúviel in the woods, her
inability to escape from him, and indeed his love for her from the
moment of their meeting (suggested in the tale, p. 23, explicit in
*The Silmarillion* p. 173), were already present, though the context
of their encounter and the motives of Huan were wholly different from
the absence of 'the Nargothrond Element' (Felagund, Celegorm and
. Curufin).

In the story of the defeat of Tevildo and the rescue of Beren the germ
of the later legend is clearly seen, though for the most part only in broad
structural resemblances. It is curious to observe that the loud speaking of
Tinúviel sitting perched on the sill of the kitchen hatch in the castle of the
Cats, so that Beren might hear, is the precursor of her singing on the
bridge of Tol-in-Gaurhoth the song that Beren heard in his dungeon
(*The Silmarillion* p. 174). Tevildo's intention to hand her over to Melko
remained in Sauron's similar purpose (*ibid.*); the killing of the cat

Oikeroi (p. 28) is the germ of Huan's fight with Draugluin – the skin of
Huan's dead opponent is put to the same use in either case (pp. 30–1,
*The Silmarillion* pp. 178–9); the battle of Tevildo and Huan was to
become that of Huan and Wolf-Sauron, and with essentially the same
outcome: Huan released his enemy when he yielded the mastery of his
dwelling. This last is very notable: the utterance by Tinúviel of the spell
which bound stone to stone in the evil castle (p. 29). Of course, when this
was written the castle of Tevildo was an adventitious feature in the story
– it had no previous history: it was an evil place through and through,
and the spell (deriving from Melko) that Tevildo was forced to reveal was
the secret of Tevildo's own power over his creatures as well as the magic
that held the stones together. With the entry of Felagund into the
developing legend and the Elvish watchtower on Tol Sirion (*Minas
Tirith: The Silmarillion* pp. 120, 155–6) captured by the Necromancer,
the spell is displaced: for it cannot be thought to be the work of Felagund,
who built the fortress, since if it had been he would have been able to
pronounce it in the dungeon and bring the place down over their heads –
a less evil way for them to die. This element in the legend remained,
however, and is fully present in *The Silmarillion* (p. 175), though since
my father did not actually say there that Sauron told Huan and Lúthien
what the words were, but only that he 'yielded himself', one may miss the
significance of what happened:

> And she said: 'There everlastingly thy naked self shall endure the
> torment of his scorn, pierced by his eyes, unless thou yield to me the
> mastery of thy tower.'
> Then Sauron yielded himself, and Lúthien took the mastery of the
> isle and all that was there. . . .
> Then Lúthien stood upon the bridge, and declared her power: and
> the spell was loosed that bound stone to stone, and the gates were
> thrown down, and the walls opened, and the pits laid bare.

Here again the actual matter of the narrative is totally different in the
early and late forms of the legend: in *The Silmarillion* 'many thralls and
captives came forth in wonder and dismay . . . for they had lain long in
the darkness of Sauron', whereas in the tale the inmates who emerged
from the shaken dwelling (other than Beren and the apparently inconse-
quent figure of the blind slave-Gnome Gimli) were a host of cats,
reduced by the breaking of Tevildo's spell to 'puny size'. (If my father
had used in the tale names other than Huan, Beren, and Tinúviel, and in
the absence of all other knowledge, including that of authorship, it would
not be easy to demonstrate from a simple comparison between this part of
the Tale and the story as told in *The Silmarillion* that the resemblances
were more than superficial and accidental.)

A more minor narrative point may be noticed here. The typescript
version would presumably have treated the fight of Huan and Tevildo

somewhat differently, for in the manuscript Tevildo and his companion can flee up great trees (p. 28), whereas in the typescript nothing grew in the Withered Dale (where Huan was to lie feigning sick) save 'low bushes of scanty leaves' (p. 48).

In the remainder of the story the congruence between early and late forms is far closer. The narrative structure in the tale may be summarised thus:

- Beren is attired for disguise in the fell of the dead cat Oikeroi.
- He and Tinúviel journey together to Angamandi.
- Tinúviel lays a spell of sleep on Karkaras the wolf-ward of Angamandi.
- They enter Angamandi, Beren slinks in his beast-shape beneath the seat of Melko, and Tinúviel dances before Melko.
- All the host of Angamandi and finally Melko himself are cast into sleep, and Melko's iron crown rolls from his head.
- Tinúviel rouses Beren, who cuts a Silmaril from the crown, and the blade snaps.
- The sleepers stir, and Beren and Tinúviel flee back to the gates, but find Karkaras awake again.
- Karkaras bites off Beren's outthrust hand holding the Silmaril.
- Karkaras becomes mad with the pain of the Silmaril in his belly, for the Silmaril is a holy thing and sears evil flesh.
- Karkaras goes raging south to Artanor.
- Beren and Tinúviel return to Artanor; they go before Tinwelint and Beren declares that a Silmaril is in his hand.
- The hunting of the wolf takes place, and Mablung the Heavy-handed is one of the hunters.
- Beren is slain by Karkaras, and is borne back to the cavern of Tinwelint on a bier of boughs; dying he gives the Silmaril to Tinwelint.
- Tinúviel follows Beren to Mandos, and Mandos permits them to return into the world.

Changing the catskin of Oikeroi to the wolfskin of Draugluin, and altering some other names, this would do tolerably well as a précis of the story in *The Silmarillion*! But of course it is devised as a summary of similarities. There are major differences as well as a host of minor ones that do not appear in it.

Again, most important is the absence of 'the Nargothrond Element'. When this combined with the Beren legend it introduced Felagund as Beren's companion, Lúthien's imprisonment in Nargothrond by Celegorm and Curufin, her escape with Huan the hound of Celegorm, and the attack on Beren and Lúthien as they returned from Tol-in-Gaurhoth by Celegorm and Curufin, now fleeing from Nargothrond (*The Silmarillion* pp. 173–4, 176–8).

The narrative after the conclusion of the episode of 'the Thraldom of Beren' is conducted quite differently in the old story (pp. 30–1), in that here Huan is with Beren and Tinúviel; Tinúviel longs for her home, and Beren is grieved because he loves the life in the woods with the dogs, but he resolves the impasse by determining to obtain a Silmaril, and though Huan thinks their plan is folly he gives them the fell of Oikeroi, clad in which Beren sets out with Tinúviel for Angamandi. In *The Silmarillion* (p. 177) likewise, Beren, after long wandering in the woods with Lúthien (though not with Huan), resolves to set forth again on the quest of the Silmaril, but Lúthien's stance in the matter is different:

'You must choose, Beren, between these two: to relinquish the quest and your oath and seek a life of wandering upon the face of the earth; or to hold to your word and challenge the power of darkness upon its throne. But on either road I shall go with you, and our doom shall be alike.'

There then intervened the attack on Beren and Lúthien by Celegorm and Curufin, when Huan, deserting his master, joined himself to them; they returned together to Doriath, and when they got there Beren left Lúthien sleeping and went back northwards by himself, riding Curufin's horse. He was overtaken on the edge of Anfauglith by Huan bearing Lúthien on his back and bringing from Tol-in-Gaurhoth the skins of Draugluin and of Sauron's bat-messenger Thuringwethil (of whom in the old story there is no trace); attired in these Beren and Lúthien went to Angband. Huan is here their active counsellor.

The later legend is thus more full of movement and incident in this part than is the *Tale of Tinúviel* (though the final form was not achieved all at one stroke, as may be imagined); and in the *Silmarillion* form this is the more marked from the fact that the account is a compression and a summary of the long *Lay of Leithian*.*

In the *Tale of Tinúviel* the account of Beren's disguise is characteristically detailed: his instruction by Tinúviel in feline behaviour, his heat and discomfort inside the skin. Tinúviel's disguise as a bat has however not yet emerged, and whereas in *The Silmarillion* when confronted by

---

* Cf. Professor T. A. Shippey, *The Road to Middle-earth*, 1982, p. 193: 'In "Beren and Lúthien" as a whole there is too much plot. The other side of that criticism is that on occasion Tolkien has to be rather brisk with his own inventions. Celegorm wounds Beren, and the hound Huan turns on his master and pursues him; "returning he brought to Lúthien a herb out of the forest. With that leaf she staunched Beren's wound, and by her arts and her love she healed him. . . ." The motif of the healing herb is a common one, the centre for instance of the Breton *lai* of *Eliduc* (turned into *conte* by Marie de France). But in that it occupies a whole scene, if not a whole poem. In *The Silmarillion* it appears only to be dismissed in two lines, while Beren's wound is inflicted and healed in five. Repeatedly one has this sense of summary . . .' This sense is eminently justified! In the *Lay of Leithian* the wounding and the healing with the herb occupy some 64 lines. (Cf. my Foreword to *The Silmarillion*, p. 8.)

Carcharoth she 'cast back her foul raiment' and 'commanded him to sleep', here she used once more the magical misty robe spun of her hair: 'the black strands of her dark veil she cast in his eyes' (p. 31). The indifference of Karkaras to the false Oikeroi contrasts with Carcharoth's suspicion of the false Druagluin, of whose death he had heard tidings: in the old story it is emphasised that no news of the discomfiture of Tevildo (and the death of Oikeroi) had yet reached Angamandi.

The encounter of Tinúviel with Melko is given with far more detail than in *The Silmarillion* (here much compressed from its source); notable is the phrase (p. 32) 'he leered horribly, for his dark mind pondered some evil', forerunner of that in *The Silmarillion* (p. 180):

> Then Morgoth looking upon her beauty conceived in his thought an evil lust, and a design more dark than any that had yet come into his heart since he fled from Valinor.

We are never told anything more explicit.

Whether Melko's words to Tinúviel, 'Who art thou that flittest about my halls like a bat?', and the description of her dancing 'noiseless as a bat', were the germ of her later bat-disguise cannot be said, though it seems possible.

The knife with which Beren cut the Silmaril from the Iron Crown has a quite different provenance in the *Tale of Tinúviel*, being a kitchen-knife that Beren took from Tevildo's castle (pp. 29, 33); in *The Silmarillion* it was Angrist, the famous knife made by Telchar which Beren took from Curufin. The sleepers of Angamandi are here disturbed by the sound of the snapping of the knife-blade; in *The Silmarillion* it is the shard flying from the snapped knife and striking Morgoth's cheek that makes him groan and stir.

There is a minor difference in the accounts of the meeting with the wolf as Beren and Tinúviel fled out. In *The Silmarillion* 'Lúthien was spent, and she had not time nor strength to quell the wolf'; in the tale it seems that she might have done so if Beren had not been precipitate. Much more important, there appears here for the first time the conception of the holy power of the Silmarils that burns unhallowed flesh.*

The escape of Tinúviel and Beren from Angamandi and their return to Artanor (pp. 34–6) is treated quite differently in the *Tale of Tinúviel*. In *The Silmarillion* (pp. 182–3) they were rescued by the Eagles and set down on the borders of Doriath; and far more is made of the healing of Beren's wound, in which Huan plays a part. In the old story Huan comes to them later, after their long southward flight on foot. In both accounts there is a discussion between them as to whether or not they should return to her father's hall, but it is quite differently conducted – in the tale it is she who persuades Beren to return, in *The Silmarillion* it is Beren who persuades her.

---

* In an early note there is a reference to 'the sacred Silmarils': I.169, note 2.

There is a curious feature in the story of the Wolf-hunt (pp. 38–9) which may be considered here (see p. 50, notes 12–15). At first, it was Tinúviel's brother who took part in the hunt with Tinwelint, Beren, and Huan, and his name is here *Tifanto*, which was the name throughout the tale before its replacement by *Dairon*.* Subsequently 'Tifanto' – without passing through the stage of 'Dairon' – was replaced by 'Mablung the heavy-handed, chief of the king's thanes', who here makes his first appearance, as the fourth member of the hunt. But earlier in the tale it is told that Tifanto > Dairon, leaving Artanor to seek Tinúviel, became utterly lost, 'and came never back to Elfinesse' (p. 21), and the loss of Tifanto > Dairon is referred to again when Beren and Tinúviel returned to Artanor (pp. 36–7).

Thus on the one hand Tifanto was lost, and it is a grief to Tinúviel on her return to learn of it, but on the other he was present at the Wolf-hunt. *Tifanto* was then changed to *Dairon* throughout the tale, except in the story of the Wolf-hunt, where *Tifanto* was replaced by a new character, *Mablung*. This shows that *Tifanto* was removed from the hunt before the change of name to *Dairon*, but does not explain how, under the name *Tifanto*, he was both lost in the wilds and present at the hunt. Since there is nothing in the MS itself to explain this puzzle, I can only conclude that my father did, in fact, write at first that Tifanto was lost and never came back, and also that he took part in the Wolf-hunt; but observing this contradiction he introduced Mablung in the latter rôle (and probably did this even before the tale was completed, since at the last appearance of Mablung his name was written thus, not emended from *Tifanto*: see note 15). It was subsequent to this that *Tifanto* was emended, wherever it still stood, to *Dairon*.

In the tale the hunt is differently managed from the story in *The Silmarillion* (where, incidentally, Beleg Strongbow was present). It is curious that all (including, as it appears, Huan!) save Beren were asleep when Karkaras came on them ('in Beren's watch', p. 39). In *The Silmarillion* Huan slew Carcharoth and was slain by him, whereas here Karkaras met his death from the king's spear, and the boy Ausir tells at the end that Huan lived on to find Beren again at the time of 'the great deeds of the Nauglafring' (p. 41). Of Huan's destiny, that he should not die 'until he encountered the mightiest wolf that would ever walk the world', and of his being permitted 'thrice only ere his death to speak with words' (*The Silmarillion* p. 173), there is nothing here.

The most remarkable feature of the *Tale of Tinúviel* remains the fact that in its earliest extant form Beren was an Elf; and in this connection very notable are the words of the boy at the end (p. 40):

---

* The idea that Timpinen (Tinfang Warble) was the son of Tinwelint and sister of Tinúviel (see I.106, note 1) had been abandoned. Tifanto/Dairon is now named with Tinfang and Ivárë as 'the three most magic players of the Elves' (p. 10).

Yet said Mandos to those twain: 'Lo, O Elves, it is not to any life of perfect joy that I dismiss you, for such may no longer be found in all the world where sits Melko of the evil heart – and know ye that *ye will become mortal even as Men*, and when ye fare hither again it will be for ever, unless the Gods summon you indeed to Valinor.'

In the tale of *The Coming of the Valar and the Building of Valinor* there occurs the following passage (I.76; commentary I.90):

Thither [i.e. to Mandos] in after days fared the Elves of all the clans who were by illhap slain with weapons or did die of grief for those that were slain – and only so might the Eldar die, and then it was only for a while. There Mandos spake their doom, and there they waited in the darkness, dreaming of their past deeds, until such time as he appointed when they might again be born into their children, and go forth to laugh and sing again.

The same idea occurs in the tale of *The Music of the Ainur* (I.59). The peculiar dispensation of Mandos in the case of Beren and Tinúviel as here conceived is therefore that their whole 'natural' destiny as Elves was changed: having died as Elves might die (from wounds or from grief) they were not reborn as new beings, but returned from Mandos in their own persons – yet now 'mortal even as Men'. The earliest eschatology is too unclear to allow of a satisfactory interpretation of this 'mortality', and the passage in *The Building of Valinor* on the fates of Men (I.77) is particularly hard to understand (see the commentary on it, I.90ff.). But it seems possible that the words 'even as Men' in the address of Mandos to Beren and Tinúviel were included to stress the finality of whatever second deaths they might undergo; their departure would be as final as that of Men, there would be no second return in their own persons, and no reincarnation. They will remain in Mandos ('when ye fare hither again it will be for ever') – unless they are summoned by the Gods to dwell in Valinor. These last words should probably be related to the passage in *The Building of Valinor* concerning the fate of certain Men (I.77):

Few are they and happy indeed for whom at a season doth Nornorë the herald of the Gods set out. Then ride they with him in chariots or upon good horses down into the vale of Valinor and feast in the halls of Valmar, dwelling in the houses of the Gods until the Great End come.

## §2.   *Places and peoples in the Tale of Tinúviel*

To consider first what can be learned of the geography of the Great Lands from this tale: the early 'dictionary' of the Gnomish language makes it clear that the meaning of *Artanor* was 'the Land Beyond', as it is interpreted in the text (p. 9). Several passages in the *Lost Tales* cast light on this expression. In an outline for Gilfanon's untold tale (I.240) the Noldoli exiled from Valinor

> now fought for the first time with the Orcs and captured the pass of the Bitter Hills; thus they escaped from the Land of Shadows . . . They entered the Forest of Artanor and the Region of the Great Plains . . .

(which latter, I suggested, may be the forerunner of the later Talath Dirnen, the Guarded Plain of Nargothrond). The tale to follow Gilfanon's, according to the projected scheme (I.241), was to be that of Tinúviel, and this outline begins: 'Beren son of Egnor wandered out of Dor Lómin [i.e. Hisilómë, see I.112] into Artanor . . .' In the present tale, it is said that Beren came 'through the terrors of the Iron Mountains until he reached the Lands Beyond' (p. 11), and also (p. 21) that some of the Dogs 'roamed the woods of Hisilómë or passing the mountainous places fared even at times into the region of Artanor and the lands beyond and to the south'. And finally, in the *Tale of Turambar* (p. 72) there is a reference to 'the road over the dark hills of Hithlum into the great forests of the Land Beyond where in those days Tinwelint the hidden king had his abode'.

It is quite clear, then, that Artanor, afterwards called Doriath (which appears in the title to the typescript text of the *Tale of Tinúviel*, together with an earlier form *Dor Athro*, p. 41), lay in the original conception in much the same relation to Hisilómë (the Land of Shadow(s), Dor Lómin, Aryador) as does Doriath to Hithlum (Hisilómë) in *The Silmarillion*: to the south, and divided from it by a mountain-range, the Iron Mountains or Bitter Hills.

In commenting on the tale of *The Theft of Melko and the Darkening of Valinor* I have noticed (I.158–9) that whereas in the *Lost Tales* Hisilómë is declared to be beyond the Iron Mountains, it is also said (in the *Tale of Turambar*, p. 77) that these mountains were so named from Angband, the Hells of Iron, which lay beneath 'their northernmost fastnesses', and that therefore there seems to be a contradictory usage of the term 'Iron Mountains' within the *Lost Tales* – 'unless it can be supposed that these mountains were conceived as a continuous range, the southerly extension (the later Mountains of Shadow) forming the southern fence of Hisilómë, while the northern peaks, being above Angband, gave the range its name'.

Now in the *Tale of Tinúviel* Beren, journeying north from Artanor, 'drew nigh to the lower hills and treeless lands that warned of the approach of the bleak Iron Mountains' (p. 14). These he had previously traversed, coming out of Hisilómë; but now 'he followed the Iron Mountains till he drew nigh to the terrible regions of Melko's abode'.

This seems to support the suggestion that the mountains fencing Hisilómë from the Lands Beyond were continuous with those above Angband; and we may compare the little primitive map (I.81), where the mountain range *f* isolates Hisilómë (*g*): see I.112, 135. The implication is that 'dim' or 'black' Hisilómë had no defence against Melko.

There appear now also the Mountains of Night (pp. 20, 46–7), and it seems clear that the great pinewoods of Taurfuin, the Forest of Night, grew upon those heights (in *The Silmarillion* Dorthonion 'Land of Pines', afterwards named Taur-nu-Fuin). Dairon was lost there, but Tinúviel, though she passed near, did not enter 'that dark region'. There is nothing to show that it was not placed then as it was later – to the east of Ered Wethrin, the Mountains of Shadow. It is also at least possible that the description (in the manuscript version only, p. 23) of Tinúviel, on departing from Huan, leaving 'the shelter of the trees' and coming to 'a region of long grass' is a first intimation of the great plain of Ard-galen (called after its desolation Anfauglith and Dor-nu-Fauglith), especially if this is related to the passage in the typescript version telling of Tinúviel's meeting with Huan 'in a little glade nigh to the forest's borders, where the first grasslands begin that are nourished by the upper waters of the river Sirion' (p. 47).

After their escape from Angamandi Huan found Beren and Tinúviel 'in that northward region of Artanor that was called afterward Nan Dumgorthin, the land of the dark idols' (p. 35). In the Gnomish dictionary *Nan Dumgorthin* is defined as 'a land of dark forest east of Artanor where on a wooded mountain were hidden idols sacrificed to by some evil tribes of renegade men' (*dum* 'secret, not to be spoken', *dumgort*, *dungort* 'an (evil) idol'). In the *Lay of the Children of Húrin* in alliterative verse Túrin and his companion Flinding (later Gwindor), fleeing after the death of Beleg Strongbow, came to this land:

> There the twain enfolded    phantom twilight
> and dim mazes    dark, unholy,
> in Nan Dungorthin    where nameless gods
> have shrouded shrines    in shadows secret,
> more old than Morgoth    or the ancient lords
> the golden Gods    of the guarded West.
> But the ghostly dwellers    of that grey valley
> hindered nor hurt them,    and they held their course
> with creeping flesh    and quaking limb.
> Yet laughter at whiles    with lingering echo,
> as distant mockery    of demon voices
> there harsh and hollow    in the hushed twilight
> Flinding fancied,    fell, unwholesome . . .

There are, I believe, no other references to the gods of Nan Dumgorthin. In the poem the land was placed west of Sirion; and finally, as Nan

Dungortheb 'the Valley of Dreadful Death', it becomes in *The Sil-marillion* (pp. 81, 121) a 'no-land' between the Girdle of Melian and Ered Gorgoroth, the Mountains of Terror. But the description of it in the *Tale of Tinúviel* as a 'northward region of Artanor' clearly does not imply that it lay within the protective magic of Gwendeling, and it seems that this 'zone' was originally less distinctly bounded, and less extensive, than 'the Girdle of Melian' afterwards became. Probably *Artanor* was conceived at this time as a great region of forest in the heart of which was Tinwelint's cavern, and only his immediate domain was protected by the power of the queen:

> Hidden was his dwelling from the vision and knowledge of Melko by the magics of Gwendeling the fay, and she wove spells about the paths thereto that none but the Eldar might tread them easily, and so was the king secured from all dangers save it be treachery alone. (p. 9).

It seems, also, that her protection was originally by no means so complete and so mighty a wall of defence as it became. Thus, although Orcs and wolves disappeared when Beren and Tinúviel 'stepped within the circle of Gwendeling's magic that hid the paths from evil things and kept harm from the regions of the woodelves' (p. 35), the fear is expressed that even if Beren and Tinúviel reached the cavern of King Tinwelint 'they would but draw the chase behind them thither' (p. 34), and Tinwelint's people feared that Melko would 'upraise his strength and come utterly to crush them and Gwendeling's magic have not the strength to withhold the numbers of the Orcs' (p. 36).

The picture of Menegroth beside Esgalduin, accessible only by the bridge (*The Silmarillion* pp. 92–3) goes back to the beginning, though neither cave nor river are named in the tale. But (as will be seen more emphatically in later tales in this book) Tinwelint, the wood-fairy in his cavern, had a long elevation before him, to become ultimately Thingol of the Thousand Caves ('the fairest dwelling of any king that has ever been east of the Sea'). In the beginning, Tinwelint's dwelling was not a subterranean city full of marvels, silver fountains falling into basins of marble and pillars carved like trees, but a rugged cave; and if in the typescript version the cave comes to be 'vaulted immeasureable', it is still illuminated only by the dim and flickering light of torches (pp. 43, 46).

There have been earlier references in the *Lost Tales* to Tinwelint and the place of his dwelling. In a passage added to, but then rejected from, the tale of *The Chaining of Melko* (I. 106, note 1) it is said that he was lost in Hisilómë and met Wendelin there; 'loving her he was content to leave his folk and dance for ever in the shadows'. In *The Coming of the Elves* (I. 115) 'Tinwë abode not long with his people, and yet 'tis said lives still lord of the scattered Elves of Hisilómë'; and in the same tale (I. 118–19) the 'Lost Elves' were still there 'long after when Men were shut in Hisilómë by Melko', and Men called them the Shadow Folk, and feared them. But in the *Tale of Tinúviel* the conception has changed. Tinwelint is now a king ŕuling, not in Hisilómë, but in Artanor.* (It is not said where it was that he came upon Gwendeling.)

In the account (manuscript version only, see pp. 9, 42) of Tinwelint's people there is mention of Elves 'who remained in the dark'; and this obviously refers to Elves who never left the Waters of Awakening. (Of course those who were lost on the march from Palisor also never left 'the dark' (i.e. they never came to the light of the Trees), but the distinction made in this sentence is not between the darkness and the light but between those who *remained* and those who *set out*). On the emergence of this idea in the course of the writing of the *Lost Tales* see I.234. Of Tinwelint's subjects 'the most werc Ilkorindi', and they must be those who 'had been lost upon the march from Palisor' (earlier, 'the Lost Elves of Hisilómë').

Here, a major difference in essential conception between the old legend and the form in *The Silmarillion* is apparent. These Ilkorindi of Tinwelint's following ('eerie and strange beings' whose 'dark songs and chantings . . . faded in the wooded places or echoed in deep caves') are described in terms applicable to the wi!d Avari ('the Unwilling') of *The Silmarillion*; but they are of course actually the precursors of the Grey-elves of Doriath. The term *Eldar* is here equivalent to *Elves* ('all the Eldar both *those who remained in the dark* or had been lost upon the march from Palisor') and is not restricted to those who made, or at least embarked on, the Great Journey; all were Ilkorindi – Dark Elves – if they never passed over the Sea. The later significance of the Great Journey in conferring 'Eldarin' status was an aspect of the elevation of the Grey-elves of Beleriand, bringing about a distinction of the utmost importance within the category of the *Moriquendi* or 'Elves of the Darkness' – the *Avari* (who were not Eldar) and the *Úmanyar* (the Eldar who were 'not of Aman'): see the table 'The Sundering of the Elves' given in *The Silmarillion*. Thus:

|  | *Lost Tales* |  | *Silmarillion* |  |  |
|---|---|---|---|---|---|
|  | of Kôr | Avari |  |  |  |
| Eldar | of the Great Lands (the Darkness): Ilkorindi | Eldar (of the Great Journey) |  | of Aman | |
|  |  |  |  | of Middle-earth (Úmanyar) | |

But among Tinwelint's subjects there were also *Noldoli*, Gnomes. This matter is somewhat obscure, but at least it may be observed that the

* In the outlincs for *Gilfanon's Tale* the 'Shadow Folk' of Hisilómë have ceased to be Elves and become 'fays' whose origin is unknown: I.237, 239.

manuscript and typescript versions of the *Tale of Tinúviel* do not
envisage precisely the same situation.

The manuscript text is perhaps not perfectly explicit on the subject,
but it is said (p. 9) that of Tinwelint's subjects '*the most* were Ilkorindi',
and that before the rising of the Sun 'already were their numbers mingled
with a many wandering Gnomes'. Yet Dairon fled from the apparition of
Beren in the forest because 'all the Elves of the woodland thought of the
Gnomes of Dor Lómin as treacherous creatures, cruel and faithless'
(p. 11); and 'Dread and suspicion was between the Eldar and those of
their kindred that had tasted the slavery of Melko, and in this did the evil
deeds of the Gnomes at the Haven of the Swans revenge itself' (p. 11).
The hostility of the Elves of Artanor to Gnomes was, then, specifically a
hostility to the Gnomes of Hisilómë (Dor Lómin), who were suspected
of being under the will of Melko (and this is probably a foreshadowing of
the suspicion and rejection of Elves escaped from Angband described in
*The Silmarillion* p. 156). In the manuscript it is said (p. 9) that *all* the
Elves of the Great Lands (those who remained in Palisor, those who were
lost on the march, and the Noldoli returned from Valinor) fell beneath the
power of Melko, though many escaped and wandered in the wild; and as
the manuscript text was first written (see p. 11 and note 3) Beren was 'son
of a thrall of Melko's . . . that laboured in the darker places in the north
of Hisilómë'. This conception seems reasonably clear, so far as it goes.

In the typescript version it is expressly stated that there were Gnomes
'in Tinwelint's service' (p. 43): the bridge over the forest river, leading to
Tinwelint's door, was hung by them. It is not now stated that all the
Elves of the Great Lands fell beneath Melko; rather there are named
several centres of resistance to his power, in addition to Tinwelint/
Thingol in Artanor: Turgon of Gondolin, the Sons of Fëanor, and
Egnor of Hisilómë (Beren's father) – one of the chiefest foes of Melko 'in
all the kin of the Gnomes that still were free' (p. 44). Presumably this led
to the exclusion in the typescript of the passage telling that the woodland
Elves thought of the Gnomes of Dor Lómin as treacherous and faithless
(see p. 43), while that concerning the distrust of those who had been
Melko's slaves was retained. The passage concerning Hisilómë 'where
dwelt Men, and thrall-Noldoli laboured, and few free-Eldar went' (p. 10)
was also retained; but Hisilómë, in Beren's wish that he had never
strayed out of it, becomes 'the wild free places of Hisilómë' (pp. 17, 45).

This leads to an altogether baffling question, that of the references to
the Battle of Unnumbered Tears; and several of the passages just cited
bear on it.

The story of 'The Travail of the Noldoli and the Coming of Mankind'
that was to have been told by Gilfanon, but which after its opening pages
most unhappily never got beyond the stage of outline projections, was to
be followed by that of Beren and Tinúviel (see I. 241). After the Battle of
Unnumbered Tears there is mention of the Thraldom of the Noldoli, the
Mines of Melko, the Spell of Bottomless Dread, the shutting of Men in

Hisilómë, and *then* 'Beren son of Egnor wandered out of Dor Lómin into Artanor . . .' (In *The Silmarillion* the deeds of Beren and Lúthien preceded the Battle of Unnumbered Tears.)

Now in the *Tale of Tinúviel* there is a reference, in both versions, to the 'thrall-Noldoli' who laboured in Hisilómë and of Men dwelling there; and as the passage introducing Beren was first written in the manuscript his father was one of these slaves. It is said, again in both versions, that neither Tinwelint nor the most part of his people went to the battle, but that his lordship was greatly increased by fugitives from it (p. 9); and to the following statement that his dwelling was hidden by the magic of Gwendeling/Melian the typescript adds the word 'thereafter' (p. 43), i.e. after the Battle of Unnumbered Tears. In the changed passage in the typescript referring to Egnor he is one of the chiefest foes of Melko 'in all the kin of the Gnomes *that still were free*'.

All this seems to allow of only one conclusion: the events of the *Tale of Tinúviel* took place *after* the great battle; and this seems to be clinched by the express statement in the typescript: where the manuscript (p. 15) says that Melko 'sought ever to destroy the friendship and intercourse of Elves and Men', the second version adds (p. 44): '*lest they forget the Battle of Unnumbered Tears* and once more arise in wrath against him'.

It is very odd, therefore, that Vëannë should say at the beginning (in the manuscript only, p. 10 and see p. 43) that she will tell 'of things that happened in the halls of Tinwelint *after the arising of the Sun indeed but long ere the unforgotten Battle of Unnumbered Tears*'. (This in any case seems to imply a much longer period between the two events than is suggested in the outlines for *Gilfanon's Tale*: see I.242). This is repeated later (p. 17): 'it was a thing unthought . . . that any Elf . . . should fare untended to the halls of Melko, *even in those earlier days before the Battle of Tears* when Melko's power had not grown great . . .' But it is stranger still that this second sentence is retained in the typescript (p. 45). The typescript version has thus two inescapably contradictory statements:

Melko 'sought ever to destroy the friendship and intercourse of Elves and Men, lest they forget the Battle of Unnumbered Tears' (p. 44);

'Little love was there between the woodland Elves and the folk of Angband even in those days before the Battle of Unnumbered Tears' (p. 45).

Such a radical contradiction within a single text is in the highest degree unusual, perhaps unique, in all the writings concerned with the First Age. But I can see no way to explain it, other than simply accepting it as a radical contradiction; nor indeed can I explain those statements in both versions that the events of the tale took place *before* the battle, since virtually all indications point to the contrary.*

---

* In the *Tale of Turambar* the story of Beren and Tinúviel clearly and necessarily took place *before* the Battle of Unnumbered Tears (pp. 71–2, 140).

## §3. *Miscellaneous Matters*

### (i) *Morgoth*

Beren addresses Melko as 'most mighty Belcha Morgoth', which are said to be his names among the Gnomes (p. 44). In the Gnomish dictionary *Belcha* is given as the Gnomish form corresponding to *Melko* (see I.260), but *Morgoth* is not found in it: indeed this is the first and only appearance of the name in the *Lost Tales*. The element *goth* is given in the Gnomish dictionary with the meaning 'war, strife'; but if *Morgoth* meant at this period 'Black Strife' it is perhaps strange that Beren should use it in a flattering speech. A name-list made in the 1930s explains *Morgoth* as 'formed from his Orc-name *Goth* "Lord or Master" with *mor* "dark or black" prefixed', but it seems very doubtful that this etymology is valid for the earlier period. This name-list explains *Gothmog* 'Captain of Balrogs' as containing the same Orc-element ('Voice of *Goth* (Morgoth)'); but in the name-list to the tale of *The Fall of Gondolin* (p. 216) the name *Gothmog* is said to mean 'Strife-and-hatred' (*mog-* 'detest, hate' appears in the Gnomish dictionary), which supports the interpretation of *Morgoth* in the present tale as 'Black Strife'.*

### (ii) *Orcs and Balrogs*

Despite the reference to 'the wandering bands of the goblins *and* the Orcs' (p. 14, retained in the typescript version), the terms are certainly synonymous in the *Tale of Turambar*. The Orcs are described in the present tale (*ibid.*) as 'foul broodlings of Melko'. In the second version (p. 44) wolf-rider Orcs appear.

Balrogs, mentioned in the tale (p. 15), have appeared in one of the outlines for *Gilfanon's Tale* (I.241); but they had already played an important part in the earliest of the *Lost Tales*, that of *The Fall of Gondolin* (see pp. 212–13).

### (iii) *Tinúviel's 'lengthening spell'*

Of the 'longest things' named in this spell (pp. 19–20, 46) two, 'the sword of Nan' and 'the neck of Gilim the giant', seem now lost beyond recall, though they survived into the spell in the *Lay of Leithian*, where the sword of Nan is itself named, *Glend*, and Gilim is called 'the giant of

---

* Nothing is said in any text to suggest that Gothmog played such a role in relation to Morgoth as the interpretation 'Voice of *Goth*' implies, but nor is anything said to contradict it, and he was from the beginning an important figure in the evil realm and in especial relation to Melko (see p. 216). There is perhaps a reminiscence of 'the Voice of Morgoth' in 'the Mouth of Sauron', the Black Númenórean who was the Lieutenant of Barad-dûr (*The Return of the King* V. 10)..

Eruman'. *Gilim* in the Gnomish dictionary means 'winter' (see I.260, entry *Melko*), which does not seem particularly appropriate: though a jotting, very difficult to read, in the little notebook used for memoranda in connection with the *Lost Tales* (see I.171) seems to say that Nan was a 'giant of summer of the South', and that he was like an elm.

The *Indravangs* (*Indrafangs* in the typescript) are the 'Longbeards'; this is said in the Gnomish dictionary to be 'a special name of the Nauglath or Dwarves' (see further the *Tale of the Nauglafring*, p. 247).

*Karkaras* (*Carcaras* in the typescript) 'Knife-fang' is named in the spell since he was originally conceived as the 'father of wolves, who guarded the gates of Angamandi in those days *and long had done so*' (p. 21). In *The Silmarillion* (p. 180) he has a different history: chosen by Morgoth 'from among the whelps of the race of Draugluin' and reared to be the death of Huan, he was set before the gates of Angband in that very time. In *The Silmarillion* (*ibid.*) Carcharoth is rendered 'the Red Maw', and this expression is used in the text of the tale (p. 34): 'both hand and jewel Karkaras bit off and took into his red maw'.

*Glorund* is the name of the dragon in the *Tale of Turambar* (*Glaurung* in *The Silmarillion*).

In the tale of *The Chaining of Melko* there is no suggestion that Tulkas had any part in the making of the chain (there in the form *Angaino*): I.100.

### (iv)   *The influence of the Valar*

There is frequent suggestion that the Valar in some way exercised a direct influence over the minds and hearts of the distant Elves in the Great Lands. Thus it is said (p. 15) that the Valar must have inspired Beren's ingenious speech to Melko, and while this may be no more than a 'rhetorical' flourish, it is clear that Tinúviel's dream of Beren is meant to be accepted as 'a dream of the Valar' (p. 19). Again, 'the Valar set a new hope in her heart' (p. 47); and later in Vëannë's tale the Valar are seen as active 'fates', guiding the destinies of the characters — so the Valar 'brought' Huan to find Beren and Tinúviel in Nan Dumgorthin (p. 35), and Tinúviel says to Tinwelint that 'the Valar alone saved Beren from a bitter death' (p. 37).

# II

# TURAMBAR AND THE FOALÓKË

The *Tale of Turambar*, like that of *Tinúviel*, is a manuscript written in ink over a wholly erased original in pencil. But it seems certain that the *extant* form of *Turambar* preceded the *extant* form of *Tinúviel*. This can be deduced in more ways than one, but the order of composition is clearly exemplified in the forms of the name of the King of the Woodland Elves (Thingol). Throughout the manuscript of *Turambar* he was originally *Tintoglin* (and this appears also in the tale of *The Coming of the Elves*, where it was changed to *Tinwelint*, I.115, 131). A note on the manuscript at the beginning of the tale says: 'Tintoglin's name must be altered throughout to *Ellon* or *Tinthellon* = Q. *Ellu*', but the note was struck out, and all through the tale *Tintoglin* was in fact changed to *Tinwelint*.

Now in the *Tale of Tinúviel* the king's name was first given as *Ellu* (or *Tinto Ellu*), and once as *Tinthellon* (pp. 50–1); subsequently it was changed throughout to *Tinwelint*. It is clear that the direction to change *Tintoglin* to '*Ellon* or *Tinthellon* = Q. *Ellu*' belongs to the time when the *Tale of Tinúviel* was being, or had been, rewritten, and that the extant *Tale of Turambar* already existed.

There is also the fact that the rewritten *Tinúviel* was followed, at the same time of composition, by the first form of the 'interlude' in which Gilfanon appears (see I.203), whereas at the beginning of *Turambar* there is a reference to Ailios (who was replaced by Gilfanon) concluding the previous tale. On the different arrangement of the tale-telling at this point that my father subsequently introduced but failed to carry through see I.229–30. According to the earlier arrangement, Ailios told his tale on the first night of the feast of Turuhalmë or the Logdrawing, and Eltas followed with the *Tale of Turambar* on the second.

There is evidence that the *Tale of Turambar* was in existence at any rate by the middle of 1919. Humphrey Carpenter discovered a passage, written on a scrap of proof for the Oxford English Dictionary, in an early alphabet of my father's devising; and transliterating it he found it to be from this tale, not far from the beginning. He has told me that my father was using this version of the 'Alphabet of Rúmil' about June 1919 (see *Biography*, p. 100).

When then Ailios had spoken his fill the time for the lighting of candles was at hand, and so came the first day of Turuhalmë to an end; but on the second night Ailios was not there, and being asked by Lindo one Eltas began a tale, and said:

'Now all folk gathered here know that this is the story of Turambar and the Foalókë, and it is,' said he, 'a favourite tale among Men, and tells of very ancient days of that folk before the Battle of Tasarinan when first Men entered the dark vales of Hisilómë.

In these days many such stories do Men tell still, and more have they told in the past especially in those kingdoms of the North that once I knew. Maybe the deeds of other of their warriors have become mingled therein, and many matters beside that are not in the most ancient tale – but now I will tell to you the true and lamentable tale, and I knew it long ere I trod Olórë Mallë in the days before the fall of Gondolin.

In those days my folk dwelt in a vale of Hisilómë and that land did Men name Aryador in the tongues they then used, but they were very far from the shores of Asgon and the spurs of the Iron Mountains were nigh to their dwellings and great woods of very gloomy trees. My father said to me that many of our older men venturing afar had themselves seen the evil worms of Melko and some had fallen before them, and by reason of the hatred of our people for those creatures and of the evil Vala often was the story of Turambar and the Foalókë in their mouths – but rather after the fashion of the Gnomes did they say Turumart and the Fuithlug.

For know that before the Battle of Lamentation and the ruin of the Noldoli there dwelt a lord of Men named Úrin, and hearkening to the summons of the Gnomes he and his folk marched with the Ilkorindi against Melko, but their wives and children they left behind them in the woodlands, and with them was Mavwin wife of Úrin, and her son remained with her, for he was not yet war-high. Now the name of that boy was Túrin and is so in all tongues, but Mavwin do the Eldar call Mavoinë.

Now Úrin and his followers fled not from that battle as did most of the kindreds of Men, but many of them were slain fighting to the last, and Úrin was made captive. Of the Noldoli who fought there all the companies were slain or captured or fled away in rout, save that of Turondo (Turgon) only, and he and his folk cut a path for themselves out of that fray and come not into this tale. Nonetheless the escape of that great company marred the complete victory that otherwise had Melko won over his adversaries, and he desired very greatly to discover whither they had fled; and this he might not do, for his spies availed nothing, and no tortures at that time had power to force treacherous knowledge from the captive Noldoli.

Knowing therefore that the Elves of Kôr thought little of Men, holding them in scant fear or suspicion for their blindness and lack of skill, he would constrain Úrin to take up his employ and go seek after Turondo as a spy of Melko. To this however neither threats of torture nor promises of rich reward would bring Úrin to consent, for he said: "Nay, do as thou wilt, for to no evil work of thine wilt thou ever constrain me, O Melko, thou foe of Gods and Men."

"Of a surety," said Melko in anger, "to no work of mine will I bid thee again, nor yet will I force thee thereto, but upon deeds of mine that will be little to thy liking shalt thou sit here and gaze, nor be able to move foot or hand against them." And this was the torture he devised for the affliction of Úrin the Steadfast, and setting him in a lofty place of the mountains he stood beside him and cursed him and his folk with dread curses of the Valar, putting a doom of woe and a death of sorrow upon them; but to Úrin he gave a measure of vision, so that much of those things that befell his wife and children he might see and be helpless to aid, for magic held him in that high place. "Behold!" said Melko, "the life of Túrin thy son shall be accounted a matter for tears wherever Elves or Men are gathered for the telling of tales"; but Úrin said: "At least none shall pity him for this, that he had a craven for father."

Now after that battle Mavwin got her in tears into the land of Hithlum or Dor Lómin where all Men must now dwell by the word of Melko, save some wild few that yet roamed without. There was Nienóri born to her, but her husband Úrin languished in the thraldom of Melko, and Túrin being yet a small boy Mavwin knew not in her distress how to foster both him and his sister, for Úrin's men had all perished in the great affray, and the strange men who dwelt nigh knew not the dignity of the Lady Mavwin, and all that land was dark and little kindly.

The next short section of the text was struck through afterwards and replaced by a rider on an attached slip. The rejected passage reads:

At that time the rumour [*written above*: memory] of the deeds of Beren Ermabwed had become noised much in Dor Lómin, wherefore it came into the heart of Mavwin, for lack of better counsel, to send Túrin to the court of Tintoglin,[1] begging him to foster this orphan for the memory of Beren, and to teach him the wisdom of fays and of Eldar; now Egnor[2] was akin to Mavwin and he was the father of Beren the One-handed.

The replacement passage reads:

> Amended passage to fit better with the story of Tinúviel and
> the afterhistory of the Nauglafring:

The tale tells however that Úrin had been a friend of the Elves,
and in this he was different from many of his folk. Now great had
his friendship been with Egnor, the Elf of the greenwood, the
huntsman of the Gnomes, and Beren Ermabwed son of Egnor he
knew and had rendered him a service once in respect of Damrod
his son; but the deeds of Beren of the One Hand in the halls of
Tinwelint³ were remembered still in Dor Lómin. Wherefore it
came into the heart of Mavwin, for lack of other counsel, to send
Túrin her son to the court of Tinwelint, begging him to foster this
orphan for the memory of Úrin and of Beren son of Egnor.⁴

Very bitter indeed was that sundering, and for long [?time]
Túrin wept and would not leave his mother, and this was the first
of the many sorrows that befell him in life. Yet at length when his
mother had reasoned with him he gave way and prepared him in
anguish for that journey. With him went two old men, retainers
aforetime of his father Úrin, and when all was ready and the
farewells taken they turned their feet towards the dark hills, and
the little dwelling of Mavwin was lost in the trees, and Túrin blind
with tears could see her no more. Then ere they passed out of
earshot he cried out: "O Mavwin my mother, soon will I come
back to thee" – but he knew not that the doom of Melko lay
between them.

Long and very weary and uncertain was the road over the dark
hills of Hithlum into the great forests of the Land Beyond where in
those days Tinwelint the hidden king had his abode; and Túrin
son of Úrin⁵ was the first of Men to tread that way, nor have many
trodden it since. In perils were Túrin and his guardians of wolves
and wandering Orcs that at that time fared even thus far from
Angband as the power of Melko waxed and spread over the
kingdoms of the North. Evil magics were about them, that often
missing their way they wandered fruitlessly for many days, yet in
the end did they win through and thanked the Valar therefor – yet
maybe it was but part of the fate that Melko wove about their feet,
for in after time Túrin would fain have perished as a child there in
the dark woods.

Howso that may be, this was the manner of their coming to

Tinwelint's halls; for in the woodlands beyond the mountains they became utterly lost, until at length having no means of sustenance they were like to die, when they were discovered by a wood-ranger, a huntsman of the secret Elves, and he was called Beleg, for he was of great stature and girth as such was among that folk. Then Beleg led them by devious paths through many dark and lonely forestlands to the banks of that shadowed stream before the cavernous doors of Tinwelint's halls. Now coming before that king they were received well for the memory of Úrin the Steadfast, and when also the king heard of the bond tween Úrin and Beren the One-handed[6] and of the plight of that lady Mavwin his heart became softened and he granted her desire, nor would he send Túrin away, but rather said he: "Son of Úrin, thou shalt dwell sweetly in my woodland court, nor even so as a retainer, but behold as a second child of mine shalt thou be, and all the wisdoms of Gwedheling and of myself shalt thou be taught."

After a time therefore when the travellers had rested he despatched the younger of the two guardians of Túrin back unto Mavwin, for such was that man's desire to die in the service of the wife of Úrin, yet was an escort of Elves sent with him, and such comfort and magics for the journey as could be devised, and moreover these words did he bear from Tinwelint to Mavwin: "Behold O Lady Mavwin wife of Úrin the Steadfast, not for love nor for fear of Melko but of the wisdom of my heart and the fate of the Valar did I not go with my folk to the Battle of Unnumbered Tears, who now am become a safety and a refuge for all who fearing evil may find the secret ways that lead to the protection of my halls. Perchance now is there no other bulwark left against the arrogance of the Vala of Iron, for men say Turgon is not slain, but who knoweth the truth of it or how long he may escape? Now therefore shall thy son Túrin be fostered here as my own child until he is of age to succour thee – then, an he will, he may depart." More too he bid the Lady Mavwin, might she o'ercome the journey, fare back also to his halls, and dwell there in peace; but this when she heard she did not do, both for the tenderness of her little child Nienóri, and for that rather would she dwell poor among Men than live sweetly as an almsguest even among the woodland Elves. It may be too that she clung to that dwelling that Úrin had set her in ere he went to the great war, hoping still faintly for his return, for none of the messengers that had borne the lamentable tidings from that field might say that he was dead, reporting only that none knew where he might be – yet in truth those messengers were few and half-distraught, and now the years were slowly passing since the last blow fell on that most grievous day. Indeed in after days she yearned to look again upon Túrin, and maybe in the end, when Nienóri had grown, had cast aside her pride and fared over the hills, had not these become impassable for the might and great magic of Melko, who hemmed all Men in Hithlum and slew such as dared beyond its walls.

Thus came to pass the dwelling of Túrin in the halls of Tinwelint; and with him was suffered to dwell Gumlin the aged who had fared with him out of Hithlum, and had no heart or strength for the returning. Very much joy had he in that sojourn, yet did the sorrow of his sundering from Mavwin fall never quite away from him; great waxed his strength of body and the stoutness of his feats got him praise wheresoever Tinwelint was held as lord, yet he was a silent boy and often gloomy, and he got not love easily and fortune did not follow him, for few things that he desired greatly came to him and many things at which he laboured went awry. For nothing however did he grieve so much as the ceasing of all messengers between Mavwin and himself, when after a few years as has been told the hills became untraversable and the ways were shut. Now Túrin was seven years old when he fared to the woodland Elves, and seven years he dwelt there while tidings came ever and anon to him from his mother, so that he heard how his sister Nienóri grew to a slender maid and very fair, and how things grew better in Hithlum and his mother more in peace; and then all words ceased, and the years passed.

To ease his sorrow and the rage of his heart, that remembered always how Úrin and his folk had gone down in battle against Melko, Túrin was for ever ranging with the most warlike of the folk of Tinwelint far abroad, and long ere he was grown to first manhood he slew and took hurts in frays with the Orcs that prowled unceasingly upon the confines of the realm and were a menace to the Elves. Indeed but for his prowess much hurt had that folk sustained, and he held the wrath of Melko from them for many years, and after his days they were harassed sorely, and in the end must have been cast into thraldom had not such great and dread events befallen that Melko forgot them.

Now about the courts of Tinwelint there dwelt an Elf called Orgof, and he, as were the most of that king's folk, was an Ilkorin, yet he had Gnome-blood also. Of his mother's side he was nearly akin to the king himself, and was in some favour being a good hunter and an Elf of prowess, yet was he somewhat loose with his tongue and overweening by reason of his favour with the king; yet of nothing was he so fain as of fine raiment and of jewels and of gold and silver ornament, and was ever himself clad most bravely. Now Túrin lying continually in the woods and travailing in far and lonely places grew to be uncouth of raiment and wild of locks, and Orgof made jest of him whensoever the twain sat at the king's board; but Túrin said never a word to his foolish jesting, and indeed at no time did he give much heed to words that were spoken to him, and the eyes beneath his shaggy brows oftentimes looked as to a great distance – so that he seemed to see far things and to listen to sounds of the woodland that others heard not.

On a time Túrin sate at meat with the king, and it was that day twelve years since he had gazed through his tears upon Mavwin standing before the doors and weeping as he made his way among the trees, until their stems had taken her from his sight, and he was moody, speaking curt answers to those that sat nigh him, and most of all to Orgof.

But this fool would not give him peace, making a laugh of his rough clothes and tangled hair, for Túrin had then come new from a long abiding in the woods, and at length he drew forth daintily a comb of gold that he had and offered it to Túrin; and having drunk well, when Túrin deigned not to notice him he said: "Nay, an thou knowst not how to use a comb, hie thee back to thy mother, for she perchance will teach thee – unless in sooth the women of Hithlum be as ugly as their sons and as little kempt." Then a fierce anger born of his sore heart and these words concerning the lady Mavwin blazed suddenly in Túrin's breast, so that he seized a heavy drinking-vessel of gold that lay by his right hand and unmindful of his strength he cast it with great force in Orgof's teeth, saying: "Stop thy mouth therewith, fool, and prate no more." But Orgof's face was broken and he fell back with great weight, striking his head upon the stone of the floor and dragging upon him the table and all its vessels, and he spake nor prated again, for he was dead.

Then all men rose in silence, but Túrin, gazing aghast upon the body of Orgof and the spilled wine upon his hand, turned on his heel and strode into the night; and some that were akin to Orgof drew their weapons half from their sheaths, yet none struck, for the king gave no sign but stared stonily upon the body of Orgof, and very great amaze was in his face. But Túrin laved his hands in the stream without the doors and burst there into tears, saying:

"Lo! Is there a curse upon me, for all I do is ill, and now is it so turned that I must flee the house of my fosterfather an outlaw guilty of blood – nor look upon the faces of any I love again." And in his heart he dared not return to Hithlum lest his mother be bitterly grieved at his disgrace, or perchance he might draw the wrath of the Elves behind him to his folk; wherefore he got himself far away, and when men came to seek him he might not be found.

Yet they did not seek his harm, although he knew it not, for Tinwelint despite his grief and the ill deed pardoned him, and the most of his folk were with him in that, for Túrin had long held his peace or returned courtesy to the folly of Orgof, though stung often enough thereby, for that Elf being not a little jealous was used to barb his words; and now therefore the near kinsmen of Orgof were constrained by fear of Tinwelint and by many gifts to accept the king's doom.

Yet Túrin in unhappiness, believing the hand of all against him and the heart of the king become that of a foe, crept to the uttermost bounds of that woodland realm. There he hunted for his subsistence, being a good shot with the bow, yet he rivalled not the Elves at that, for rather at the wielding of the sword was he mightier than they. To him gathered a few wild spirits, and amongst them was Beleg the huntsman, who had rescued Gumlin and Túrin in the woods aforetime. Now in many adventures were those twain together, Beleg the Elf and Túrin the Man, which are not now told or remembered but which once were sung in many a place. With beast and with goblin they warred and fared at times into far places unknown to the Elves, and the fame of the hidden hunters of the marches began to be heard among Orcs and Elves, so that perchance Tinwelint would soon have become aware of the place of Túrin's abiding, had not upon a time all that band of Túrin's fallen into desperate encounter with a host of Orcs who outnumbered them three times. All were there slain save Túrin and Beleg, and Beleg escaped with wounds, but Túrin was overborne and bound, for such was the will of Melko that he be brought to him alive; for behold, dwelling in the halls of Linwë[7] about which had that fay Gwedheling the queen woven much magic and mystery and such power of spells as can come only from Valinor, whence indeed long time agone she once had brought them, Túrin had been lost out of his sight, and he feared lest he cheat the doom that was devised for him. Therefore now he purposed to entreat him grievously before the eyes of Úrin; but Úrin had called upon the Valar of the West, being taught much concerning them by the

Eldar of Kôr – the Gnomes he had encountered – and his words came, who shall say how, to Manwë Súlimo upon the heights of Taniquetil, the Mountain of the World. Nonetheless was Túrin dragged now many an evil league in sore distress, a captive of the pitiless Orcs, and they made slow journeying, for they followed ever the line of dark hills toward those regions where they rise high and gloomy and their heads are shrouded in black vapours. There are they called Angorodin or the Iron Mountains, for beneath the roots of their northernmost fastnesses lies Angband, the Hells of Iron, most grievous of all abodes – and thither were they now making laden with booty and with evil deeds.

Know then that in those days still was Hithlum and the Lands Beyond full of the wild Elves and of Noldoli yet free, fugitives of the old battle; and some wandered ever wearily, and others had secret and hidden abodes in caves or woodland fastnesses, but Melko sought untiringly after them and most pitilessly did he entreat them of all his thralls did he capture them. Orcs and dragons and evil fays were loosed against them and their lives were full of sorrow and travail, so that those who found not in the end the realms of Tinwelint nor the secret stronghold of the king of the city of stone* perished or were enslaved.

Noldoli too there were who were under the evil enchantments of Melko and wandered as in a dream of fear, doing his ill bidding, for the spell of bottomless dread was on them and they felt the eyes of Melko burn them from afar. Yet often did these sad Elves both thrall and free hear the voice of Ulmo in the streams or by the sea-marge where the waters of Sirion mingled with the waves; for Ulmo, of all the Valar, still thought of them most tenderly and designed with their slender aid to bring Melko's evil to ruin. Then remembering the blessedness of Valinor would they at times cast away their fear, doing good deeds and aiding both Elves and Men against the Lord of Iron.

Now was it that it came into the heart of Beleg the hunter of the Elves to seek after Túrin so soon as his own hurts were healed. This being done in no great number of days, for he had a skill of healing, he made all speed after the band of Orcs, and he had need of all his craft as tracker to follow that trail, for a band of the goblins of Melko go cunningly and very light. Soon was he far beyond any regions known to him, yet for love of Túrin he pressed on, and in this did he show courage greater than the most of that

* Gondolin.

woodland folk, and indeed there are none who may now measure the depth of fear and anguish that Melko set in the hearts of Men and of Elves in those sad days. Thus did it fall out that Beleg became lost and benighted in a dark and perilous region so thick with pines of giant growth that none but the goblins might find a track, having eyes that pierced the deepest gloom, yet were many even of these lost long time in those regions; and they were called by the Noldoli Taurfuin, the Forest of Night. Now giving himself up for lost Beleg lay with his back to a mighty tree and listened to the wind in the gaunt tops of the forest many fathoms above him, and the moaning of the night airs and the creaking of the branches was full of sorrow and foreboding, and his heart became utterly weary.

On a sudden he noticed a little light afar among the trees steady and pale as it were of a glowworm very bright, yet thinking it might scarce be glowworm in such a place he crept towards it. Now the Noldoli that laboured in the earth and aforetime had skill of crafts in metals and gems in Valinor were the most valued of the thralls of Melko, and he suffered them not to stray far away, and so it was that Beleg knew not that these Elves had little lanterns of strange fashion, and they were of silver and of crystal and a flame of a pale blue burnt forever within, and this was a secret and the jewel-makers among them alone knew it nor would they reveal it even to Melko, albeit many jewels and many magic lights they were constrained to make for him.

Aided by these lamps the Noldoli fared much at night, and seldom lost a path had they but once trodden it before. So it was that drawing near Beleg beheld one of the hill-gnomes stretched upon the needles beneath a great pine asleep, and his blue lantern stood glimmering nigh his head. Then Beleg awakened him, and that Elf started up in great fear and anguish, and Beleg learned that he was a fugitive from the mines of Melko and named himself Flinding bo-Dhuilin of an ancient house of the Gnomes. Now falling into talk Flinding was overjoyed to have speech with a free Noldo, and told many tales of his flight from the uttermost fastness of the mines of Melko; and at length said he: "When I thought myself all but free, lo, I strayed at night unwarily into the midmost of an Orc-camp, and they were asleep and much spoil and weighted packs they had, and many captive Elves I thought I descried: and one there was that lay nigh to a trunk to which he was bound most grievously, and he moaned and cried out bitterly against Melko, calling on the names of Úrin and Mavwin; and though at that time being a craven from long captivity I fled heedlessly, now do I marvel much, for who of the thralls of Angband has not known of Úrin the Steadfast who alone of Men defies Melko chained in torment upon a bitter peak?"

Then was Beleg in great eagerness and sprang to his feet shouting: "'Tis Túrin, fosterson of Tinwelint, even he whom I seek, who was the son of Úrin long ago. – Nay, lead me to this camp, O son of Duilin, and soon shall he be free," but Flinding was much afeared, saying: "Softer words, my Beleg, for the Orcs have ears of cats, and though a day's march lies between me and that encampment who knows whether they be not followed after."

Nonetheless hearing the story of Túrin from Beleg, despite his dread he consented to lead Beleg to that place, and long ere the sun rose on the day or its fainting beams crept into that dark forest they were upon the road, guided by the dancing light of Flinding's swinging lamp. Now it happened that in their journeying their paths crossed that of the Orcs who now were renewing their march, but in a direction other than that they had for long pursued, for now fearing the escape of their prisoner they made for a place where they knew the trees were thinner and a track ran for many a league easy to pursue; wherefore that evening, or ever they came to the spot that Flinding sought, they heard a shouting and a rough singing that was afar in the woods but drawing near; nor did they hide too soon ere the whole of that Orc-band passed nigh to them, and some of the captains were mounted upon small horses, and to one of these was Túrin tied by the wrists so that he must trot or be dragged cruelly. Then did Beleg and Flinding follow timorously after as dusk fell on the forest, and when that band encamped they lurked near until all was quiet save the moaning of the captives. Now Flinding covered his lamp with a pelt and they crept near, and behold the goblins slept, for it was not their wont to keep fire or watch in their bivouacs, and for guard they trusted to certain fierce wolves that went always with their bands as dogs with Men, but slept not when they camped, and their eyes shone like points of red light among the trees. Now was Flinding in sore dread, but Beleg bid him follow, and the two crept between the wolves at a point where there was a great gap between them, and as the luck of the Valar had it Túrin was lying nigh, apart from the others, and Beleg came unseen to his side and would cut his bonds, when he found his knife had dropped from his side in his creeping and his sword he had left behind without the camp. Therefore now, for they dare not risk the creeping forth and back again, do Beleg and Flinding both stout men essay to carry him sleeping soundly in utter weariness stealthily from the camp, and this they did, and it has ever been thought a great feat, and few have done the like in passing the wolf guards of the goblins and despoiling their camps.

Now in the woods at no great distance from the camp they laid him down, for they might not bear him further, seeing that he was a Man and of greater stature than they;[8] but Beleg fetched his sword and would cut his bonds forthwith. The bonds about his wrists he severed first and was cutting those upon the ankles when blundering in the dark he pricked Túrin's foot deeply, and Túrin awoke in fear. Now seeing a form bend over him in the gloom sword in hand and feeling the smart of his foot he thought it was one of the Orcs come to slay him or to torment him – and this they did often, cutting him with knives or hurting him with spears; but now Túrin feeling his hand free leapt up and flung all his weight suddenly upon Beleg, who fell and was half-crushed, lying speechless on the ground; but Túrin at the same time seized the sword and struck it through Beleg's throat or ever Flinding might know what had betid. Then Túrin leapt back and shouting out curses upon the goblins bid them come and slay him or taste of his sword, for he fancied himself in the midst of their camp, and thought not of flight but only of selling his life dear. Now would he have made at Flinding, but that Gnome sprang back, dropping his lamp, so that its cover slipped and the light of it shone forth, and he called out in the tongue of the Gnomes that Túrin should hold his hand and slay not his friends – then did Túrin hearing his speech pause, and as he stood, by the light of the lamp he saw the white face of Beleg lying nigh his feet with pierced throat, and he stood as one stricken to stone, and such was the look upon his face that Flinding dared not speak for a long while. Indeed little mind had he for words, for by that light had he also seen the fate of Beleg and was very bitter in heart. At length however it seemed to Flinding that the Orcs were astir, and so it was, for the shouts of Túrin had come to them; wherefore he said to Túrin: "The Orcs are upon us, let us flee," but Túrin answered not, and Flinding shook him, bidding him gather his wits or perish, and then Túrin did as he was bid but yet as one dazed, and stooping he raised Beleg and kissed his mouth.

Then did Flinding guide Túrin as well as he might swiftly from those regions, and Túrin wandered with him following as he led, and at length for a while they had shaken off pursuit and could breathe again. Now then did Flinding have space to tell Túrin all he knew and of his meeting with Beleg, and the floods of Túrin's tears were loosed, and he wept bitterly, for Beleg had been his comrade often in many deeds; and this was the third anguish that befell Túrin, nor did he lose the mark of that sorrow utterly in all his life; and long he wandered with Flinding caring little whither he went, and but for that Gnome soon would he have been recaptured or lost, for he thought only of the stark face of Beleg the huntsman, lying in the dark forest slain by his hand even as he cut the bonds of thraldom from him.

In that time was Túrin's hair touched with grey, despite his few years. Long time however did Túrin and the Noldo journey together, and by reason of the magic of that lamp fared by night and hid by day and were lost in the hills, and the Orcs found them not.

Now in the mountains there was a place of caves above a stream, and that stream ran down to feed the river Sirion, but grass grew before the doors of the caves, and these were cunningly concealed by trees and such magics as those scattered bands that dwelt therein remembered still. Indeed at this time this place had grown to be a strong dwelling of the folk and many a fugitive swelled them, and there the ancient arts and works of the Noldoli came once more to life albeit in a rude and rugged fashion.

There was smithying in secret and forging of good weapons, and even fashioning of some fair things beside, and the women spun once more and wove, and at times was gold quarried privily in places nigh, where it was found, so that deep in those caverns might vessels of beauty be seen in the flame of secret lights, and old songs were faintly sung. Yet did the dwellers in the caves flee always before the Orcs and never give battle unless compelled by mischance or were they able to so entrap them that all might be slain and none escape alive; and this they did of policy that no tidings reach Melko of their dwelling nor might he suspect any numerous gathering of folk in those parts.

This place however was known to the Noldo Flinding who fared with Túrin; indeed he was once of that people long since, before the Orcs captured him and he was held in thraldom. Thither did he now wend being sure that the pursuit came no longer nigh them, yet went he nonetheless by devious ways, so that it was long ere they drew nigh to that region, and the spies and watchers of the Rodothlim (for so were that folk named) gave warning of their approach, and the folk withdrew before them, such as were abroad from their dwelling. Then they closed their doors and hoped that the strangers might not discover their caves, for they feared and mistrusted all unknown folk of whatever race, so evil were the lessons of that dreadful time.

Now then Flinding and Túrin dared even to the caves' mouths, and perceiving that these twain knew now the paths thereto the Rodothlim sallied and made them prisoners and drew them within their rocky halls, and they were led before the chief, Orodreth. Now the free Noldoli at that time feared much those of their kin who had tasted thraldom, for compelled by fear and torture and spells much treachery had they wrought; even thus did the evil deeds of the Gnomes at Cópas Alqalunten find vengeance,⁹ setting Gnome against Gnome, and the Noldoli cursed the day that ever they first hearkened to the deceit of Melko, rueing utterly their departure from the blessed realm of Valinor.

Nonetheless when Orodreth heard the tale of Flinding and knew it to be true he welcomed him with joy back among the folk, yet was that Gnome so changed by the anguish of his slavery that few knew him again; but for Flinding's sake Orodreth hearkened to the tale of Túrin, and Túrin told of his travails and named Úrin as his sire, nor had the Gnomes yet forgot that name. Then was the heart of Orodreth made kind and he bade them dwell among the Rodothlim and be faithful to him. So came the sojourn of Túrin among the people of the caves, and he dwelt with Flinding bo-Dhuilin and laboured much for the good of the folk, and slew many a wandering Orc, and did doughty deeds in their defence. In return much did he learn of new wisdom from them, for memories of Valinor burnt yet deep in their wild hearts, and greater still was their wisdom than that of such Eldar as had seen never the blest faces of the Gods.

Among that people was a very fair maiden and she was named Failivrin, and her father was Galweg; and this Gnome had a liking for Túrin and aided him much, and Túrin was often with him in ventures and good deeds. Now many a tale of these did Galweg make beside his hearth and Túrin was often at his board, and the heart of Failivrin became moved at the sight of him, and wondered often at his gloom and sadness, pondering what sorrow lay locked in his breast, for Túrin went not gaily being weighted with the death of Beleg that he felt upon his head, and he suffered not his heart to be moved, although he was glad of her sweetness; but he deemed himself an outlawed man and one burdened with a heavy doom of ill. Therefore did Failivrin become sorrowful and wept in secret, and she grew so pale that folk marvelled at the whiteness and delicacy of her face and her bright eyes that shone therein.

Now came a time when the Orc-bands and the evil things of Melko drew ever nigher to the dwelling of this folk, and despite the good spells that ran in the stream beneath it seemed like that their abode would remain no longer hidden. It is said however that during all this time the dwelling of Túrin in the caves and his deeds among the Rodothlim were veiled from Melko's eyes, and that he infested not the Rodothlim for Túrin's sake nor out of design, but rather it was the ever increasing numbers of these creatures and their growing power and fierceness that brought them so far afield. Nonetheless the blindness and ill-fortune that he wove of old clung yet to Túrin, as may be seen.

Each day grew the brows of the chiefs of the Rodothlim more dark, and dreams came to them[10] bidding them arise and depart swiftly and secretly, seeking, if it might be, after Turgon, for with him might yet salvation be found for the Gnomes. Whispers too there were in the stream at eve, and those among them skilled to hear such voices added their foreboding at the councils of the folk. Now at these councils had Túrin won him a place by dint of many valorous deeds, and he gainsaid their fears, trusting in his strength, for he lusted ever for war with the creatures of Melko, and he upbraided the men of the folk, saying: "Lo! Ye have weapons of great excellence of workmanship, and yet are the most of them clean of your foes' blood. Remember ye the Battle of Uncounted Tears and forget not your folk that there fell, nor seek ever to flee, but fight and stand."

Now despite the wisdom of their wisest such bitter words confused their counsels and delayed them, and there were no few of the stout-hearted that found hope in them, being sad at the thought of abandoning those places where they had begun to make an abiding place of peace and goodliness; but Túrin begged Orodreth for a sword, and he had not wielded a sword since the slaying of Beleg, but rather had he been contented with a mighty club. Now then Orodreth let fashion for him a great sword, and it was made by magic to be utterly black save at its edges, and those were shining bright and sharp as but Gnome-steel may be. Heavy it was, and was sheathed in black, and it hung from a sable belt, and Túrin named it Gurtholfin the Wand of Death; and often that blade leapt in his hand of its own lust, and it is said that at times it spake dark words to him. Therewith did he now range the hills, and slew unceasingly, so that Blacksword of the Rodothlim became a name of terror to the Orcs, and for a great season all evil was fended from the caverns of the Gnomes. Hence comes that name of Túrin's among the Gnomes, calling him Mormagli or Mormakil according to their speech, for these names signify black sword.

The greater however did Túrin's valour become so grew the love of Failivrin more deep, and did men murmur against him in his absence she spake for him, and sought ever to minister to him, and her he treated ever courteously and happily, saying he had found a fair sister in the Gnome-lands. By Túrin's deeds however was the ancient counsel of the Rodothlim set aside and their abode made known far and wide, nor was Melko ignorant of it, yet many of the Noldoli now fled to them and their strength waxed and Túrin was held in great honour among them. Then were days of great happiness and for a while men lived openly again and might fare far abroad from their homes in safety, and many boasted of the salvation of the Noldoli, while Melko gathered in secret his great hordes. These did he loose suddenly upon them at unawares, and they gathered their warriors in great haste and went against him, but behold, an army of Orcs descended upon them, and wolves, and Orcs mounted upon wolves; and a great worm was with them whose scales were polished bronze and whose breath was a mingled fire and smoke, and his name was Glorund.[11] All the men of the Rodothlim fell or were taken in that battle, for the foe was numberless, and that was the most bitter affray since the evil field of Nínin-Udathriol.* Orodreth was there sorely hurt and Túrin bore him out of the fight ere yet all was ended, and with the aid of Flinding whose wounds were not great[12] he got him to the caves.

There died Orodreth, reproaching Túrin that he had ever withstood his wise counsels, and Túrin's heart was bitter at the ruin of the folk that was set to his account.[13] Then leaving Lord Orodreth dead Túrin went to the places of Galweg's abiding, and there was Failivrin weeping bitterly at the tidings of her father's death, but Túrin sought to comfort her, and for the pain of her heart and the sorrow of her father's death and of the ruin of her folk she swooned upon his breast and cast her arms about

---

* At the bottom of the manuscript page is written:

'*Nieriltasinwa*    the battle of unnumbered tears
*Glorund    Laurundo* or *Undolaurë*'

Later *Glorund* and *Laurundo* were emended to *Glorunt* and *Laurunto*.

him. So deep was the ruth of Túrin's heart that in that hour he deemed he loved her very dearly; yet were now he and Flinding alone save for a few aged carles and dying men, and the Orcs having despoiled the field of dead were nigh upon them.

Thus stood Túrin before the doors with Gurtholfin in hand, and Flinding was beside him; and the Orcs fell on that place and ransacked it utterly, dragging out all the folk that lurked therein and all their goods, whatsoever of great or little worth might there lie hid. But Túrin denied the entrance of Galweg's dwelling to them, and they fell thick about him, until a company of their archers standing at a distance shot a cloud of arrows at him. Now he wore chainmail such as all the warriors of the Gnomes have ever loved and still do wear, yet it turned not all those ill shafts, and already was he sore hurt when Flinding fell pierced suddenly through the eye; and soon too had he met his death – and his weird had been the happier thereby – had not that great drake coming now upon the sack bidden them cease their shooting; but with the power of his breath he drove Túrin from those doors and with the magic of his eyes he bound him hand and foot.

Now those drakes and worms are the evillest creatures that Melko has made, and the most uncouth, yet of all are they the most powerful, save it be the Balrogs only. A great cunning and wisdom have they, so that it has been long said amongst Men that whosoever might taste the heart of a dragon would know all tongues of Gods or Men, of birds or beasts, and his ears would catch whispers of the Valar or of Melko such as never had he heard before. Few have there been that ever achieved a deed of such prowess as the slaying of a drake, nor might any even of such doughty ones taste their blood and live, for it is as a poison of fires that slays all save the most godlike in strength. Howso that may be, even as their lord these foul beasts love lies and lust after gold and precious things with a great fierceness of desire, albeit they may not use nor enjoy them.

Thus was it that this *lókë* (for so do the Eldar name the worms of Melko) suffered the Orcs to slay whom they would and to gather whom they listed into a very great and very sorrowful throng of women, maids, and little children, but all the mighty treasure that they had brought from the rocky halls and heaped glistering in the sun before the doors he coveted for himself and forbade them set finger on it, and they durst not withstand him, nor could they have done so an they would.

In that sad band stood Failivrin in horror, and she stretched out

her arms towards Túrin, but Túrin was held by the spell of the
drake, for that beast had a foul magic in his glance, as have many
others of his kind, and he turned the sinews of Túrin as it were to
stone, for his eye held Túrin's eye so that his will died, and he
could not stir of his own purpose, yet might he see and hear.

Then did Glorund taunt Túrin nigh to madness, saying that lo!
he had cast away his sword nor had the heart to strike a blow for his
friends – now Túrin's sword lay at his feet whither it had slipped
from his unnervéd grasp. Great was the agony of Túrin's heart
thereat, and the Orcs laughed at him, and of the captives some
cried bitterly against him. Even now did the Orcs begin to drive
away that host of thralls, and his heart broke at the sight, yet he
moved not; and the pale face of Failivrin faded afar, and her voice
was borne to him crying: "O Túrin Mormakil, where is thy heart;
O my beloved, wherefore dost thou forsake me?" So great then
became Túrin's anguish that even the spell of that worm might not
restrain it, and crying aloud he reached for the sword at his feet
and would wound the drake with it, but the serpent breathed a
foul and heated breath upon him, so that he swooned and thought
that it was death.

A long time thereafter, and the tale telleth not how long,
he came to himself, and he was lying gazing at the sun before
the doors, and his head rested against a heap of gold even as the
ransackers had left it. Then said the drake, who was hard by:
"Wonderest thou not wherefore I have withheld death from thee,
O Túrin Mormakil, who wast once named brave?" Then Túrin
remembered all his griefs and the evil that had fallen upon him,
and he said: "Taunt me not, foul worm, for thou knowest I would
die; and for that alone, methinks, thou slayest me not."

But the drake answered saying: "Know then this, O Túrin son
of Úrin, that a fate of evil is woven about thee, and thou mayst not
untangle thy footsteps from it whitherever thou goest. Yea indeed,
I would not have thee slain, for thus wouldst thou escape very
bitter sorrows and a weird of anguish." Then Túrin leaping
suddenly to his feet and avoiding that beast's baleful eye raised
aloft his sword and cried: "Nay, from this hour shall none name
me Túrin if I live. Behold, I will name me a new name and it shall
be Turambar!" Now this meaneth Conqueror of Fate, and the
form of the name in the Gnome-speech is Turumart. Then uttering
these words he made a second time at the drake, thinking indeed to
force the drake to slay him and to conquer his fate by death, but
the dragon laughed, saying: "Thou fool! An I would, I had slain

thee long since and could do so here and now, and if I will not thou
canst not do battle with me waking, for my eye can cast once more
the binding spell upon thee that thou stand as stone. Nay, get thee
gone, O Turambar Conqueror of Fate! First thou must meet thy
doom an thou wouldst o'ercome it." But Turambar was filled with
shame and anger, and perchance he had slain himself, so great was
his madness, although thus might he not hope that ever his spirit
would be freed from the dark glooms of Mandos or stray into the
pleasant paths of Valinor;[14] but amidst his misery he bethought
him of Failivrin's pallid face and he bowed his head, for the
thought came into his heart to seek back through all the woods
after her sad footsteps even be it to Angamandi and the Hills of
Iron. Maybe in that desperate venture he had found a kindly and
swift death or perchance an ill one, and maybe he had rescued
Failivrin and found happiness, yet not thus was he fated to earn
the name he had taken anew, and the drake reading his mind
suffered him not thus lightly to escape his tide of ill.

"Hearken to me, O son of Úrin," said he; "ever wast thou a
coward at heart, vaunting thyself falsely before men. Perchance
thou thinkest it a gallant deed to go follow after a maiden of strange
kin, recking little of thine own that suffer now terrible things?
Behold, Mavwin who loves thee long has eagerly awaited thy
return, knowing that thou hast found manhood a while ago, and
she looks for thy succour in vain, for little she knows that her son is
an outlaw stained with the blood of his comrades, a defiler of his
lord's table. Ill do men entreat her, and behold the Orcs infest now
those parts of Hithlum, and she is in fear and peril and her
daughter Nienóri thy sister with her."

Then was Turambar aflame with sorrow and with shame for the
lies of that worm were barbed with truth, and for the spell of his
eyes he believed all that was said. Therefore his old desire to see
once more Mavwin his mother and to look upon Nienóri whom he
had never seen since his first days[15] grew hot within him, and with
a heart torn with sorrow for the fate of Failivrin he turned his feet
towards the hills seeking Dor Lómin, and his sword was sheathed.
And truly is it said: "Forsake not for anything thy friends – nor
believe those who counsel thee to do so" – for of his abandoning of
Failivrin in danger that he himself could see came the very direst
evil upon him and all he loved; and indeed his heart was confounded and wavered, and he left those places in uttermost shame
and weariness. But the dragon gloated upon the hoard and lay
coiled upon it, and the fame of that great treasure of golden vessels

and of unwrought gold that lay by the caves above the stream fared
far and wide about; yet the great worm slept before it, and evil
thoughts he had as he pondered the planting of his cunning lies
and the sprouting thereof and their growth and fruit, and fumes of
smoke went up from his nostrils as he slept.

On a time therefore long afterward came Turambar with great
travail into Hisilómë, and found at length the place of the abode of
his mother, even the one whence he had been sundered as a child,
but behold, it was roofless and the tilth about it ran wild. Then his
heart smote him, but he learned of some that dwelt nigh that
lighting on better days the Lady Mavwin had departed some years
agone to places not far distant where was a great and prosperous
dwelling of men, for that region of Hisilómë was fertile and men
tilled the land somewhat and many had flocks and herds, though
for the most part in the dark days after the great battle men feared
to dwell in settled places and ranged the woods and hunted or
fished, and so it was with those kindreds about the waters of Asgon
whence after arose Tuor son of Peleg.

Hearing these words however Turambar was amazed, and
questioned them concerning the wandering into those regions of
Orcs and other fierce folk of Melko, but they shook their heads,
and said that never had such creatures come hither deep into the
land of Hisilómë.[16] "If thou wishest for Orcs then go to the hills
that encompass our land about," said they, "and thou wilt not
search long. Scarce may the wariest fare in and out so constant is
their watch, and they infest the rocky gates of the land that the
Children of Men be penned for ever in the Land of Shadows; but
men say 'tis the will of Melko that they trouble us not here – and
yet it seems to us that thou hast come from afar, and at this we
marvel, for long is it since one from other lands might tread this
way." Then Turambar was in perplexity at this and he doubted
the deceit of the dragon's words, yet he went now in hope to the
dwelling of men and the house of his mother, and coming upon
homesteads of men he was easily directed thither. Now men
looked strangely at his questioning, and indeed they had reason,
yet were such as he spoke to in great awe and wonder at him and
shrank back from speech with him, for his garb was of the wild
woods and his hair was long and his face haggard and drawn as
with unquenchable sorrows, and therein burnt fiercely his dark
eyes beneath dark brows. A collar of fine gold he wore and his
mighty sword was at his side, and men marvelled much at him;

and did any dare to question him he named himself Turambar son of the weary forest,* and that seemed but the more strange to them.

Now came he to the dwelling of Mavwin, and behold it was a fair house, but none dwelt there, and grass was high in the gardens, and there were no kine in the byres nor horses in the sheds, and the pastures about were silent and empty. Only the swallows had dwelling beneath the timbers of the eaves and these made a noise and a bustle as if departure for autumn was at hand, and Turambar sat before the carven doors and wept. And one who was passing on to other dwellings, for a track passed nigh to that homestead, espied him, and coming asked him his grief, and Turambar said that it was bitter for a son sundered for many years from his home to give up all that was dear and dare the dangers of the infested hills to find only the halls of his kindred empty when he returned at last.

"Nay, then this is a very trick of Melko's," said the other, "for of a truth here dwelt the Lady Mavwin wife of Úrin, and yet is she gone two years past very secretly and suddenly, and men say that she seeks her son who is lost, and that her daughter Nienóri goes with her, but I know not the story. This however I know, and many about here do likewise, and cry shame thereon, for know that the guardianship of all her goods and land she gave to Brodda, a man whom she trusted, and he is lord of these regions by men's consent and has to wife a kinswoman of hers. But now she is long away he has mingled her herds and flocks, small as they were, with his mighty ones, branding them with his own marks, yet the dwelling and stead of Mavwin he suffereth to fall to ruin, and men think ill of it but move not, for the power of Brodda has grown to be great."

Then Turambar begged him to set his feet upon the paths to Brodda's halls, and the man did as he desired, so that Turambar striding thither came upon them just as night fell and men sat to meat in that house. Great was the company that night and the light of many torches fell upon them, but the Lady Airin was not there, for men drank overmuch at Brodda's feasts and their songs were fierce and quarrels blazed about the hall, and those things she loved not. Now Turambar smote upon the gates and his heart was black and a great wrath was in him, for the words of the stranger before his mother's doors were bitter to him.

* A note on the manuscript referring to this name reads: '*Turumart go-Dhrauthodauros* [emended to *bo-Dhrauthodavros*] or *Turambar Rúsitaurion*.'

Then did some open to his knocking and Turambar strode into
that hall, and Brodda bade him be seated and ordered wine and
meats to be set before him, but Turambar would neither eat nor
drink, so that men looking askance upon his sullenness asked him
who he might be. Then Turambar stepping out into the midst of
them before the high place where Brodda sat said: "Behold, I
am Turambar son of the forest", and men laughed thereat, but
Turambar's eyes were full of wrath. Then said Brodda in doubt:
"What wilt thou of me, O son of the wild forest?" But Turambar
said: "Lord Brodda, I am come to repay thy stewardship of others'
goods," and silence fell in that place; but Brodda laughed, saying
again: "But who art thou?" And thereupon Turambar leapt upon
the high place and ere Brodda might foresee the act he drew
Gurtholfin and seizing Brodda by the locks all but smote his head
from off his body, crying aloud: "So dieth the rich man who
addeth the widow's little to his much. Lo, men die not all in the
wild woods, and am I not in truth the son of Úrin, who having
sought back unto his folk findeth an empty hall despoiled." Then
was there a great uproar in that hall, and indeed though he was
burdened overmuch with his many griefs and wellnigh distraught,
yet was this deed of Turambar violent and unlawful. Some were
there nonetheless that would not unsheathe their weapons, saying
that Brodda was a thief and died as one, but many there were that
leapt with swords against Turambar and he was hard put to it, and
one man he slew, and it was Orlin. Then came Airin of the long
hair in great fear into the halls and at her voice men stayed their
hands; but great was her horror when she saw the deeds that were
done, and Turambar turned his face away and might not look
upon her, for his wrath was grown cold and he was sick and weary.

But she hearing the tale said: "Nay, grieve not for me, son
of Úrin, but for thyself; for my lord was a hard lord and cruel
and unjust, and men might say somewhat in thy defence, yet
behold thou hast slain him now at his board being his guest, and
Orlin thou hast slain who is of thy mother's kin; and what shall be
thy doom?" At those words some were silent and many shouted
"death", but Airin said that it was not wholly in accord with the
laws of that place, "for," said she, "Brodda was slain wrongfully,
yet just was the wrath of the slayer, and Orlin too did he slay in
defence, though it were in the hall of a feast. Yet now I fear that
this man must get him swiftly from among us nor ever set foot
upon these lands again, else shall any man slay him; but those
lands and goods that were Úrin's shall Brodda's kin hold, save only

do Mavwin and Nienóri return ever from their wandering, yet even so may Túrin son of Úrin inherit nor part nor parcel of them ever." Now this doom seemed just to all save Turambar, and they marvelled at the equity of Airin whose lord lay slain, and they guessed not at the horror of her life aforetime with that man; but Turambar cast his sword upon the floor and bade them slay him, yet they would not for the words of Airin whom they loved, and Airin suffered it not for the love of Mavwin, hoping yet to join those twain mother and son in happiness, and her doom she had made to satisfy men's anger and save Túrin from death. "Nay," said she, "three days do I give thee to get thee out of the land, wherefore go!" and Turambar lifting his sword wiped it, saying: "Would I were clean of his blood," and he went forth into the night. In the folly of his heart now did he deem himself cut off in truth for ever from Mavwin his mother, thinking that never again would any he loved be fain to look upon him. Then did he thirst for news of his mother and sister and of none might he ask, but wandered back over the hills knowing only that they sought him still perchance in the forests of the Lands Beyond, and no more did he know for a long while.

Of his wanderings thereafter has no tale told, save that after much roaming his sorrow grew dulled and his heart dead, until at last in places very far away many a journey beyond the river of the Rodothlim he fell in with some huntsmen of the woods, and these were Men. Some of that company were thanes of Úrin, or sons of them, and they had wandered darkly ever since that Battle of Tears, but now did Turambar join their number, and built his life anew so well as he might. Now that people had houses in a more smiling region of the woods in lands that were not utterly far from Sirion or the grassy hills of that river's middle course, and they were hardy men and bowed not to Melko, and Turambar got honour among them.

Now is it to tell that far other had matters fallen out with Mavwin than the Foalókë had said to Túrin, for her days turning to better she had peace and honour among the men of those regions. Nonetheless her grief at the loss of her son by reason of the cutting off of all messengers deepened only with the years, albeit Nienóri grew to a most fair and slender maid. At the time of Túrin's flight from the halls of Tinwelint she was already twelve[17] years old and tall and beautiful.

Now the tale tells not the number of days that Turambar

sojourned with the Rodothlim but these were very many, and during that time Nienóri grew to the threshold of womanhood, and often was there speech between her and her mother of Túrin that was lost. In the halls of Tinwelint too the memory of Túrin lived still, and there still abode Gumlin, now decrepit in years, who aforetime had been the guardian of Túrin's childhood upon that first journey to the Lands Beyond. Now was Gumlin white-haired and the years were heavy on him, but he longed sorely for a sight once more of the folk of Men and of the Lady Mavwin his mistress. On a time then Gumlin learnt of the with-drawal from the hills of the greater number of those Orc-bands and other fierce beings of Melko's that had for so long made them impassable to Elves and Men. Now for a space were the hills and the paths that led over them far and wide free of his evil, for Melko had at that time a great and terrible project afoot, and that was the destruction of the Rodothlim and of many dwellings of the Gnomes beside, that his spies had revealed,[18] yet all the folk of those regions breathed the freer for a while, though had they known all perchance they had not done so.

Then Gumlin the aged fell to his knees before Tinwelint and begged that he suffer him to depart homeward, that he might see his mistress of old ere death took him to the halls of Mandos − if indeed that lady had not fared thither before him. Then the king[19] said yea, and for his journey he gave him two guides for the succouring of his age; yet those three, Gumlin and the woodland Elves, made a very hard journey, for it was late winter, and yet would Gumlin by no means abide until spring should come.

Now as they drew nigh to that region of Hisilómë where afore-time Mavwin had dwelt and nigh where she dwelt yet a great snow fell, as happened oft in those parts on days that should rather have been ones of early spring. Therein was Gumlin whelmed, and his guides seeking aid came unawares upon Mavwin's house, and calling for aid of her were granted it. Then by the aid of the folk of Mavwin was Gumlin found and carried to the house and warmed back to life, and coming to himself at length he knew Mavwin and was very joyful.

Now when he was in part healed he told his tale to Mavwin, and as he recounted the years and the doughtiest of the feats of Túrin she was glad, but great was her sorrow and dismay at the tidings of his sundering from Linwë[20] and the manner of it, and going from Gumlin she wept bitterly. Indeed for long and since ever she knew that Túrin, an he lived, had grown to manhood she had wondered that he sought not back to her, and often dread had filled her heart lest attempting this he had perished in the hills; but now the truth was bitter to bear and she was desolate for a great while, nor might Nienóri comfort her.

Now by reason of the unkindness of the weather those guides that had brought Gumlin out of Tinwelint's realms abode as her guests until spring came, but with spring's first coming Gumlin died.

Then arose Mavwin and going to several of the chiefs of those places she besought their aid, telling them the tale of Túrin's fate as Gumlin had told it to her. But some laughed, saying she was deceived by the babblings of a dying man, and the most said that she was distraught with grief, and that it would be a fool's counsel to seek beyond the hills a man who had been lost for years agone: "nor," said they, "will we lend man or horse to such a quest, for all our love for thee, O Mavwin wife of Úrin."

Then Mavwin departed in tears but railed not at them, for she had scant hope in her plea and knew that wisdom was in their words. Nonetheless being unable to rest she came now to those guides of the Elves, who chafed already to be away beneath the sun; and she said to them: "Lead me now to your lord," and they would dissuade her, saying that the road was no road for a woman's feet to tread; yet she did not heed them. Rather did she beg of her friend whose name was Airin Faiglindra* (long-tressed) and was wed to Brodda a lord of that region, and rich and powerful, that Nienóri might be taken under the guardianship of her husband and all her goods thereto. This did Airin obtain of Brodda without great pleading, and when she knew this she would take farewell of her daughter; but her plan availed little, for Nienóri stood before her mother and said: "Either thou goest not, O Mavwin my mother, or go we both," nor would anything turn her from those words. Therefore in the end did both mother and daughter make them ready for that sore journey, and the guides murmured much thereat. Yet it so happened that the season which followed that bitter winter was very kindly, and despite the forebodings of the guides the four passed the hills and made their long journey with no greater evils than hunger and thirst.

Coming therefore at length before Tinwelint Mavwin cast herself down and wept, begging pardon for Túrin and compassion and aid for herself and Nienóri; but Tinwelint bade her arise and

* In the margin is written *Firilanda*.

seat herself beside Gwedheling his queen, saying: "Long years ago was Túrin thy son forgiven, aye, even as he left these halls, and many a weary search have we made for him. No outlawry of mine was it that took him from this realm, but remorse and bitterness drew him to the wilds, and there, methinks, evil things o'ertook him, or an he lives yet I fear me it is in bondage to the Orcs." Then Mavwin wept again and implored the king to give her aid, for she said: "Yea verily I would fare until the flesh of my feet were worn away, if haply at the journey's end I might see the face of Túrin son of Úrin my well-beloved." But the king said that he knew not whither she might seek her son save in Angamandi, and thither he might not send any of his lieges, not though his heart were full of ruth for the sorrow of Úrin's folk. Indeed Tinwelint spoke but as he believed just, nor meant he to add to Mavwin's sorrow save only to restrain her from so mad and deadly a quest, but Mavwin hearing him spake no word more, and going from him went out into the woods and suffered no one to stay her, and only Nienóri followed her whithersoever she went.

Now the folk of Tinwelint looked with pity on those twain and with kindness, and secretly they watched them, and unbeknown kept much harm from them, so that the wandering ladies of the woods became familiar among them and dear to many, yet were they a sight of ruth, and folk swore hatred to Melko and his works who saw them pass. Thus came it that after many moons Mavwin fell in with a band of wandering Gnomes, and entering into discourse with them the tale was told to her of the Rodothlim, such as those Gnomes knew of it, and of the dwelling of Túrin among them. Of the whelming of that abode of folk by the hosts of Melko and by the dragon Glorund they told too, for those deeds were then new and their fame went far and wide. Now Túrin they named not by name, calling him Mormakil, a wild man who fled from the face of Tinwelint and escaped thereafter from the hands of the Orcs.

Then was the heart of Mavwin filled with hope and she questioned them more, but the Noldoli said that they had not heard that any came alive out of that ransacking save such as were haled to Angamandi, and then again was Mavwin's hope dashed low. Yet did she nonetheless get her back to the king's halls, and telling her tale besought his aid against the Foalókë. Now it was Mavwin's thought that perchance Túrin dwelt yet in the thraldom of the dragon and it might fall to them in some manner to liberate him, or again should the prowess of the king's men suffice then might they slay the worm in vengeance for his evils, and so at his death might he speak words of knowledge concerning the fate of Túrin, were he indeed no longer nigh the caverns of the Rodothlim. Of the mighty hoard that that worm guarded Mavwin recked little, but she spake much of it to Tinwelint, even as the Noldoli had spoken of it to her. Now the folk of Tinwelint were of the woodlands and had scant wealth, yet did they love fair and beauteous things, gold and silver and gems, as do all the Eldar but the Noldoli most of all; nor was the king of other mind in this, and his riches were small, save it be for that glorious Silmaril that many a king had given all his treasury contained if he might possess it.

Therefore did Tinwelint answer: "Now shalt thou have aid, O Mavwin most steadfast, and, openly I say it to thee, it is not for hope of freeing Túrin thereby that I grant it to thee, for such hope I do not see in this tale, but rather the death of hope. Yet it is a truth that I have need and desire of treasury, and it may be that such shall come to me by this venture; yet half of the spoil shalt thou have O Mavwin for the memory of Úrin and Túrin, or else shalt thou ward it for Nienóri thy daughter." Then said Mavwin: "Nay, give me but a woodman's cot and my son," and the king answered: "That I cannot, for I am but a king of the wild Elves, and no Vala of the western isles."

Then Tinwelint gathered a picked band of his warriors and hunters and told them his bidding, and it seemed that the name of the Foalókë was known already among them, and there were many who could guide the band unto the regions of his dwelling, yet was that name a terror to the stoutest and the places of his abode a land of accursed dread. Now the ancient dwellings of the Rodothlim were not utterly distant from the realm of Tinwelint, albeit far enough, but the king said to Mavwin: "Bide now and Nienóri also with me, and my men shall fare against the drake, and all that they do and find in those places will they faithfully report," – and his men said: "Yea, we will do thy bidding, O King," but fear stood in their eyes.

Then Mavwin seeing it said: "Yea, O King, let Nienóri my daughter bide indeed at the feet of Gwedheling the Queen, but I who care not an I die or live will go look upon the dragon and find my son"; and Tinwelint laughed, yet Gwedheling and Nienóri fearing that she spake no jest pled earnestly with her. But she was as adamant, fearing lest this her last hope of rescuing Túrin come to nought through the terror of Tinwelint's men, and none might move her. "Of love, I know," said she, "come all the words ye speak, yet give me rather a horse to ride and if ye will a sharp knife for my own death at need, and let me be gone." Now these words struck amazement into those Elves that heard, for indeed the wives and daughters of Men in those days were hardy and their youth lasted a great span, yet did this seem a madness to all.

Madder yet did it seem when Nienóri, seeing the obstinacy of her mother, said before them all: "Then I too will go; whither my mother Mavwin goeth thither more easily yet shall I, Nienóri daughter of Úrin, fare"; but Gwedheling said to the king that he allow it not, for she was a fay and perchance foresaw dimly what might be.

Then had Mavwin ended the dispute and departed from the king's presence into the woods, had not Nienóri caught at her robe and stayed her, and so did all plead with Mavwin, till at length it was agreed that the king send a strong party against the Foalókë and that Nienóri and Mavwin ride with them until the regions of the beast be found. Then should they seek a high place whence they might see something of the deeds yet in safety and secrecy, while the warriors crept upon the worm to slay it. Now of this high place a woodsman told, and often had he gazed therefrom upon the dwelling of the worm afar. At length was that band of dragon-slayers got ready, and they were mounted upon goodly horses swift and sure-going, albeit few of those beasts were possessed by the folk of the woods. Horses too were found for Nienóri and for Mavwin, and they rode at the head of the warriors, and folk marvelled much to see their bearing, for the men of Úrin and those amongst whom Nienóri was nurtured were much upon horses, and both knave and maid among them rode even in tender years.

After many days' going came now that cavalcade within view of a place that once had been a fair region, and through it a swift river ran over a rocky bed, and of one side was the brink of it high and tree-grown and of the other the land was more level and fertile and broad-swelling, but beyond the high bank of the river the hills drew close. Thither as they looked they saw that the land had become all barren and was blasted for a great distance about the ancient caverns of the Rodothlim, and the trees were crushed to the earth or snapped. Toward the hills a black heath stretched and the lands were scored with the great slots that that loathly worm made in his creeping.

Many are the dragons that Melko has loosed upon the world and some are more mighty than others. Now the least mighty – yet were they very great beside the Men of those days – are cold as is

the nature of snakes and serpents, and of them a many having
wings go with the uttermost noise and speed; but the mightier are
hot and very heavy and slow-going, and some belch flame, and fire
flickereth beneath their scales, and the lust and greed and cunning
evil of these is the greatest of all creatures: and such was the
Foalókë whose burning there set all the places of his habitation in
waste and desolation. Already greater far had this worm waxen
than in the days of the onslaught upon the Rodothlim, and greater
too was his hoarded treasure, for Men and Elves and even Orcs he
slew, or enthralled that they served him, bringing him food to
slake his lust [?on] precious things, and spoils of their harryings to
swell his hoard.

Now was that band aghast as they looked upon that region from
afar, yet they prepared them for battle, and drawing lots sent one
of their number with Nienóri and Mavwin to that high place[21]
upon the confines of the withered land that had been named, and it
was covered with trees, and might be reached by hidden paths.
Even as those three rode thither and the warriors crept stealthily
toward the caves, leaving their horses that were already in a sweat
of fear, behold the Foalókë came from his lair, and sliding down
the bank lay across the stream, as often was his wont. Straightway
great fog and steams leapt up and a stench was mingled therein, so
that that band was whelmed in vapours and well-nigh stifled, and
they crying to one another in the mist displayed their presence to
the worm; and he laughed aloud. At that most awful of all sounds
of beasts they fled wildly in the mists, and yet they could not
discover their horses, for these in an extremity of terror broke
loose and fled.

Then Nienóri hearing far cries and seeing the great mist roll
toward them from the river turned back with her mother to the
place of sundering, and there alighting waited in great doubt.
Suddenly came that blind mist upon them as they stood, and with
it came flying madly the dim horses of the huntsmen. Then their
own catching their terror trampled to death that Elf who was their
escort as he caught at the flying bridles, and wild with fear they
sped to the dark woods and never more bore Man or Elf upon their
saddles; but Mavwin and Nienóri were left alone and succourless
upon the borders of the places of fear. Very perilous indeed was
their estate, and long they groped in the mist and knew not where
they were nor saw they ever any of the band again, and only pale
voices seemed to pass them by afar crying out as in dread, and then
all was silent. Now did they cling together and being weary

stumbled on heedless whither their steps might go, till on a sudden the sun gleamed thin above them, and hope returned to them; and behold the mists lifted and the airs became clearer and they stood not far from the river. Even now it smoked as it were hot, and behold the Foalókë lay there and his eyes were upon them.

No word did he speak nor did he move, but his baleful eye held their gaze until the strength seemed to leave their knees and their minds grew dim. Then did Nienóri drag herself by a might of will from that influence for a while, and "Behold," she cried, "O serpent of Melko, what wilt thou with us – be swift to say or do, for know that we seek not thee nor thy gold but one Túrin who dwelt here upon a time." Then said the drake, and the earth quaked at him: "Thou liest – glad had ye been at my death, and glad thy band of cravens who now flee gibbering in the woods might they have despoiled me. Fools and liars, liars and cravens, how shall ye slay or despoil Glorund the Foalókë, who ere his power had waxen slew the hosts of the Rodothlim and Orodreth their lord, devouring all his folk."

"Yet perchance," said Nienóri, "one Túrin got him from that fray and dwells still here beneath thy bonds, an he has not escaped thee and is now far hence," and this she said at a venture, hoping against hope, but said the evil one: "Lo! the names of all who dwelt here before the taking of the caves of my wisdom I know, and I say to thee that none who named himself Túrin went hence alive." And even so was Túrin's boast subtly turned against him, for these beasts love ever to speak thus, doubly playing with cunning words.[22]

"Then was Túrin slain in this evil place," said Mavwin, but the dragon answered: "Here did the name of Túrin fade for ever from the earth – but weep not, woman, for it was the name of a craven that betrayed his friends." "Foul beast, cease thy evil sayings," said Mavwin; "slayer of my son, revile not the dead, lest thine own bane come upon thee." "Less proud must be thy words, O Mavwin, an thou wilt escape torment or thy daughter with thee," did that drake answer, but Mavwin cried: "O most accursed, lo! I fear thee not. Take me an thou wilt to thy torments and thy bondage, for of a truth I desired thy death, but suffer only Nienóri my daughter to go back to the dwellings of Men: for she came hither constrained by me, and knowing not the purposes of our journey."

"Seek not to cajole me, woman," sneered that evil one. "Liever would I keep thy daughter and slay thee or send thee back to thy hovels, but I have need of neither of you." With those words he opened full his evil eyes, and a light shone in them, and Mavwin and Nienóri quaked beneath them and a swoon came upon their minds, and them seemed that they groped in endless tunnels of darkness, and there they found not one another ever again, and calling only vain echoes answered and there was no glimmer of light.

When however after a time that she remembered not the blackness left the mind of Nienóri, behold the river and the withered places of the Foalókë were no more about her, but the deep woodlands, and it was dusk. Now she seemed to herself to awake from dreams of horror nor could she recall them, but their dread hung dark behind her mind, and her memory of all past things was dimmed. So for a long while she strayed lost in the woods, and haply the spell alone kept life in her, for she hungered bitterly and was athirst, and by fortune it was summer, for her garments became torn and her feet unshod and weary, and often she wept, and she went she knew not whither.

Now on a time in an opening in the wood she descried a campment as it were of Men, and creeping nigh by reason of hunger to espy it she saw that they were creatures of a squat and unlovely stature that dwelt there, and most evil faces had they, and their voices and their laughter was as the clash of stone and metal. Armed they were with curved swords and bows of horn, and she was possessed with fear as she looked upon them, although she knew not that they were Orcs, for never had she seen those evil ones before. Now did she turn and flee, but was espied, and one let fly a shaft at her that quivered suddenly in a tree beside her as she ran, and others seeing that it was a woman young and fair gave chase whooping and calling hideously. Now Nienóri ran as best she might for the density of the wood, but soon was she spent and capture and dread thraldom was very near, when one came crashing through the woods as though in answer to her lamentable cries.

Wild and black was his hair yet streaked with grey, and his face was pale and marked as with deep sorrows of the past, and in his hand he bare a great sword whereof all but the very edge was black. Therewith he leapt against the following Orcs and hewed them, and they soon fled, being taken aback, and though some shot arrows at random amidst the trees they did little scathe, and five of them were slain.

Then sat Nienóri upon a stone and for weariness and the

lessened strain of fear sobs shook her and she could not speak; but her rescuer stood beside her awhile and marvelled at her fairness and that she wandered thus lonely in the woods, and at length he said: "O sweet maiden of the woods, whence comest thou, and what may be thy name?"

"Nay, these things I know not," said she. "Yet methinks I stray very far from my home and folk, and many very evil things have fallen upon me in the way, whereof nought but a cloud hangs upon my memory – nay, whence I am or whither I go I know not" – and she wept afresh, but that man spake, saying: "Then behold, I will call thee Níniel, or little one of tears," and thereat she raised her face towards his, and it was very sweet though marred with weeping, and she said with a look of wonderment: "Nay, not Níniel, not Níniel." Yet more might she not remember, and her face filled with distress, so that she cried: "Nay, who art thou, warrior of the woods; why troublest thou me?" "Turambar am I called," said he, "and no home nor kindred have I nor any past to think on, but I wander for ever," and again at that name that maiden's wonder stirred.

"Now," said Turambar, "dry thy tears, O Níniel, for thou hast come upon such safety as these words afford. Lo, one am I now of a small folk of the forest, and a sweet dwelling in a clearing have we far from hence, but today as thy fortune would we fared a-hunting, – aye, and Orc-harrying too, for we are hard put to it to fend those evil ones from our homes."

Then did Níniel (for thus Turambar called her ever, and she learnt to call it her name) fare away with him to his comrades, and they asking little got them upon horses, and Turambar set Níniel before him, and thus they fared as swift as they might from the danger of the Orcs.

Now at the time of the affray of Turambar with the pursuing Orcs was half the day already spent, yet were they already leagues upon their way ere they dismounted once more, and it was then early night. Already at the sunset had it seemed to Níniel that the woods were lighter and less gloomy and the air less evil-laden than behind. Now did they make a camp in a glade and the stars shone clear above where the tree-roof was thin, but Níniel lay a little apart and they gave her many fells to keep her from the night chills, and thus she slept more softly than for many a night and the breezes kissed her face, but Turambar told his comrades of the meeting in the wood and they wondered who she might be or how she came wandering thither as one under a spell of blind forgetfulness.

Next day again they pressed on and so for many journeys more beside until at length weary and fain for rest they came one noon to a woodland stream, and this they followed for some way until, behold, they came to a place where it might be forded by reason of its shallowness and of the rocks that stood up in its course; but on their right it dived in a great fall and fell into a chasm, and Turambar pointing said: "Now are we nigh to home, for this is the fall of the Silver Bowl," but Níniel not knowing why was filled with a dread and could not look upon the loveliness of that foaming water. Now soon came they to places of thinner trees and to a slope whereon but few grew save here and there an ancient oak of great girth, and the grass about their feet was soft, for the clearing had been made many years and was very wide. There stood also a cluster of goodly houses of timber, and a tilth was about them and trees of fruit. To one of these houses that was adorned with strange rude carvings, and flowers bloomed bright about it, did Turambar lead now Níniel. "Behold," said he, "my abode – there an thou listest thou shalt abide for now, but methinks it is a lonely hall, and there be houses of this folk beside where there are maidens and womenfolk, and there wouldst thou liever and better be." So came it afterward that Nienóri dwelt with the wood-rangers,* and after a while entered the house of Bethos, a stout man who had fought though then but a boy in the Battle of Unnumbered Tears. Thence did he escape, but his wife was a Noldo-maiden, as the tale telleth, and very fair, and fair also were his sons and daughters save only his eldest son Tamar Lamefoot.

Now as the days passed Turambar grew to love Níniel very greatly indeed, and all the folk beside loved her for her great loveliness and sweetness, yet was she ever half-sorrowful and often distraught of mind, as one that seeks for something mislaid that soon she must discover, so that folk said: "Would that the Valar would lift the spell that lies upon Níniel." Nonetheless for the most part she was happy indeed among the folk and in the house of Bethos, and each day she grew ever fairer, and Tamar Lamefoot who was held of little account loved her though in vain.

Now came days when life once more seemed to contain joy to Turambar, and the bitterness of the past grew dim and far away, and a fresh love was in his heart. Then did he think to put his fate

* In the margin, apparently with reference to the word 'wood-rangers', is written *Vettar*.

for ever from him and live out his life there in the woodland homes
with children about him, and looking upon Níniel he desired to
wed her. Then did he often press his suit with her, yet though he
was a man of valiance and renown she delayed him, saying nor yea
nor no, yet herself she knew not why, for it seemed to her heart
that she loved him deeply, fearing for him were he away, and
knowing happiness when he was nigh.

Now it was a custom of that folk to obey a chief, and he was
chosen by them from their stoutest men, and that office did he
hold until of his own will he laid it down again being sick or gone in
years, or were he slain. And at that time Bethos was their chief;
but he was slain by evil luck in a foray not long after – for despite
his years he still rode abroad – and it fell out that a new captain
must be chosen. In the end then did they name Turambar, for his
lineage, in that it was known among them that he was son of Úrin,
was held in esteem among those stout rebels against Melko,
whereas[21] he had beside become a very mighty man in all deeds and
one of wisdom great beyond his years, by reason of his far wanderings and his dealings with the Elves.

Seeing therefore the love of their new chief for Níniel and
thinking they knew that she loved him also in return, those men
began to say how they would lief see their lord wed, and that it was
folly to delay for no good cause; but this word came to the ears of
Níniel, and at length she consented to be the wife of Turambar,
and all were fain thereat. A goodly feast was made and there was
song and mirth, and Níniel became lady of the woodland-rangers
and dwelt thereafter in Turambar's house. There great was their
happiness, though there lay at times a chill foreboding upon
Níniel's heart, but Turambar was in joy and said in his heart:
"'Twas well that I did name myself Turambar, for lo! I have
overcome the doom of evil that was woven about my feet." The
past he laid aside and to Níniel he spoke not overmuch of bygone
things, save of his father and mother and the sister he had not
seen, but always was Níniel troubled at such talk and he knew not
why.[24] But of his flight from the halls of Tinwelint and the death of
Beleg and of his seeking back to Hisilómë he said never a word,
and the thought of Failivrin lay locked in his deepest heart well-
nigh forgotten.

Naught ever might Níniel tell him of her days before, and did he
ask her distress was written on her face as though he troubled the
surface of dark dreams, and he grieved at times thereat, but it
weighed not much upon him.

Now fare the days by and Níniel and Turambar dwell in peace, but Tamar Lamefoot wanders the woods thinking the world an ill and bitter place, and he loved Níniel very greatly nor might he stifle his love. But behold, in those days the Foalókë waxed fat, and having many bands of Noldoli and of Orcs subject to him he thought to extend his dominion far and wide. Indeed in many places in those days these beasts of Melko's did in like manner, setting up kingdoms of terror of their own that flourished beneath the evil mantle of Melko's lordship. So it was that the bands of Glorund the drake harried the folk of Tinwelint very grievously, and at length there came some nigh even to those woods and glades that were beloved of Turambar and his folk.

Now those woodmen fled not but dealt stoutly with their foes, and the wrath of Glorund the worm was very great when tidings were brought to him of a brave folk of Men that dwelt far beyond the river and that his marauders might not subdue them. It is told indeed that despite the cunning of his evil designs he did not yet know where was the dwelling of Turambar or of Nienóri; and of truth in those days it seemed that fortune smiled on Turambar awhile, for his people waxed and they became prosperous, and many escaped even from uttermost Hisilómë and came unto him, and store of wealth and good things he gathered, for all his battles brought him victory and booty. Like a king and queen did Turambar and Níniel become, and there was song and mirth in those glades of their dwelling, and much happiness in their halls. And Níniel conceived.[25]

Much of this did spies report to the Foalókë, and his wrath was terrible. Moreover his greed was mightily kindled, so that after pondering much he set a guard that he might trust to watch his dwelling and his treasury, and the captain of these was Mîm the dwarf.[26] Then leaving the caves and the places of his sleep he crossed the streams and drew into the woods, and they blazed before his face. Tidings of this came swiftly to Turambar, but he feared not as yet nor indeed heeded the tale much, for it was a very great way from the home of the woodmen to the caverns of the worm. But now sank Níniel's heart, and though she knew not wherefore a weight of dread and sorrow lay upon her, and seldom after the coming of that word did she smile, so that Turambar wondered and was sad.

Now draweth the Foalókë during that time through the deep woods and a path of desolation lies behind, and yet in his creeping a very great while passes, until, behold, suddenly a party of the

woodmen come upon him unawares sleeping in the woods among
the broken trees. Of these several were overcome by the noxious
breath of the beast and after were slain; but two making their
utmost speed brought tidings to their lord that the tale aforetime
had not been vain, and indeed now was the drake crept even
within the confines of his realm; and so saying they fell fainting
before his feet.

Now the place where the dragon lay was low-lying and a little
hill there was, not far distant, islanded among the trees but itself
not much wooded, whence might be espied albeit afar off much of
that region now torn by the passage of the drake. A stream there
was too that ran through the forest in that part between the drake
and the dwellings of the woodmen, but its course ran very nigh to
the dragon and it was a narrow stream with banks deep-cloven and
o'erhung with trees. Wherefore Turambar purposed now to take
his stoutest men to that knoll and watch if they could the dragon's
movements in secret, that perchance they might fall upon him at
some disadvantage and contrive to slay him, for in this lay their
best hope. This band he suffered not to be very great, and the rest
at his bidding took arms and scoured about, fearing that hosts of
the Orcs were come with the worm their lord. This indeed was not
so, and he came alone trusting in his overwhelming power.

Now when Turambar made ready to depart then Níniel begged
to ride beside him and he consented, for he loved her and it was his
thought that if he fell and the drake lived then might none of that
people be saved, and he would liever have Níniel by him, hoping
perchance to snatch her at the least from the clutches of the worm,
by death at his own or one of his liege's hands.

So rode forth together Turambar and Níniel, as that folk knew
them, and behind were a score of good men. Now the distance to
that knoll among the woods they compassed in a day's journey,
and after them though it were against the bidding and counsel of
Turambar there stole a great concourse of his folk, even women
and children. The lure of a strange dread held them, and some
thought to see a great fight, and others went with the rest thinking
little, nor did any think to see what in the end their eyes saw; and
they followed not far behind, for Turambar's party went slowly
and warily. When first then Turambar suffered her to ride beside
him Níniel was blither than for long she had been, and she
brightened the foreboding of those men's hearts; but soon they
came to a place not far from the foot of the knoll, and there her
heart sank, and indeed a gloom fell upon all.

Yet very fair was that place, for here flowed that same stream that further down wound past the dragon's lair in a deep bed cloven deep into the earth; and it came rushing cold from the hills beyond the woodmen's homes, and it fell over a great fall where the water-worn rock jutted smooth and grey from amid the grass. Now this was the head of that force which the woodmen named the Silver Bowl, and aforetime Turambar and Níniel had passed it by, faring home first from the rescuing of Níniel. The height of that fall was very great and the waters had a loud and musical voice, splashing into a silver foam far below where they had worn a great hollow in the rocks; and this hollow was o'ershadowed by trees and bushes, but the sun gleamed through upon the spray; and about the head of the fall there was an open glade and a green sward where grew a wealth of flowers, and men loved that spot.

Here did Níniel of a sudden weep, and casting herself upon Turambar begged him tempt not fate but rather fly with her and all his folk, leading them into distant lands. But looking at her he said: "Nay, Níniel mine, nor thou nor I die this day, nor yet tomorrow, by the evil of the dragon or by the foemen's swords," but he knew not the fulfilment of his words; and hearing them Níniel quelled her weeping and was very still. Having therefore rested a while here those warriors afterward climbed the hill and Níniel fared with them. Afar off they might see from its summit a wide tract where all the trees were broken and the lands were hurt[27] and scorched and the earth black, yet nigh the edge of the trees that were still unharmed, and that was not far from the lip of the deep river-chasm, there arose a thin smoke of great blackness, and men said: "There lieth the worm."

Then were counsels of many a kind spoken upon that hill-top, and men feared to go openly against the dragon by day or by night or whether he waked or slept, and seeing their dread Turambar gave them a rede, and it was taken, and these were his words: "Well have ye said, O huntsmen of the woods, that not by day or by night shall men hope to take a dragon of Melko unawares, and behold this one hath made a waste about him, and the earth is beaten flat so that none may creep near and be hidden. Wherefore whoso hath the heart shall come with me and we will go down the rocks to the foot of the fall, and so gaining the path of the stream perchance we may come as nigh to the drake as may be. Then must we climb if we are able up under the near bank and so wait, for methinks the Foalókë will rest not much longer ere he draweth on towards our dwellings. Thus must he either cross this deep stream or turn far out of his ways, for he is grown too mighty to creep along its bed. Now I think not that he will turn aside, for it is but a ditch, a narrow rut filled with trickling water, to the great Foalókë of the golden caves. If however he belie my counsel and come not on by this path, some few of you must take courage in your hearts, striving to decoy him warily back across the stream, that there we who lie hid may give him his bane stabbing from beneath, for the armour of these vile worms is of little worth upon their bellies."

Now of that band were there but six that stood forward readily to go with Turambar, and he seeing that said that he had thought there were more than six brave men among his folk, yet after that he would not suffer any of the others to go with him, saying that better were the six without the hindrance of the fearful. Then did Turambar take farewell of Níniel and they kissed upon the hilltop, and it was then late afternoon, but Níniel's heart went as to stone with grief; and all that company descended to the head of Silver Bowl, and there she beheld her lord climb to the fall's bottom with his six companions. Now when he was vanished far below she spake bitterly to those who had dared not to go, and they for shame answered not but crept back unto the hill-top and gazed out towards the dragon's lair, and Níniel sat beside the water looking before her, and she wept not but was in anguish.

None stayed beside her save Tamar alone who had fared unbidden with that company, and he had loved her since first she dwelt in Bethos' halls, and once had thought to win her ere Turambar took her. The lameness of Tamar was with him from childhood, yet was he both wise and kindly, though held of little account among those folk, to whom strength was safety and valour the greatest pride of men. Now however did Tamar bear a sword, and many had scoffed at him for that, yet he took joy at the chance of guarding Níniel, albeit she noticed him not.

Now is it to tell that Turambar reached the place of his design after great labour in the rocky bed of the stream, and with his men clambered with difficulty up the steep side of that ravine. Just below the lip of it they were lodged in certain overhanging trees, and not far off they might hear the great breathing of the beast, and some of his companions fell in dread.

Already had darkness come and all the night they clung there, and there was a strange flickering where the dragon lay and dread noises and a quaking if he stirred, and when dawn came Turambar saw that he had but three companions, and he cursed the others for their cravenhood, nor doth any tale tell whither those unfaithful ones fled. On this day did all come to pass as Turambar had thought, for the drake bestirring himself drew slowly to the chasm's edge and turned not aside, but sought to overcreep it and come thus at the homes of the woodmen. Now the terror of his oncoming was very great, for the earth shook, and those three feared lest the trees that upheld them should loosen their roots and fall into the rocky stream below. The leaves too of those trees that grew nigh were shrivelled in the serpent's breath, yet were they not hurt because of the shelter of the bank.

At length did the drake reach the stream-edge and the sight of his evil head and dripping jaws was utterly hideous, and these they saw clearly and were in terror lest he too espy them, for he crossed not over at the spot where Turambar had chosen to lie hid because of the narrowness here of the chasm and its lesser depth. Rather he began to heave himself now across the ravine a little below them, and so slipping from their places Turambar and his men reached as swiftly as might be the stream's bed and came beneath the belly of the worm. Here was the heat so great and so vile the stench that his men were taken with a sore dread and durst not climb the bank again. Then in his wrath Turambar would have turned his sword against them, but they fled, and so was it that alone he scaled the wall until he came close beneath the dragon's body, and he reeled by reason of the heat and of the stench and clung to a stout bush.

Then abiding until a very vital and unfended spot was within stroke, he heaved up Gurtholfin his black sword and stabbed with all his strength above his head, and that magic blade of the Rodothlim went into the vitals of the dragon even to the hilt, and the yell of his death-pain rent the woods and all that heard it were aghast.

Then did that drake writhe horribly and the huge spires of his contortions were terrible to see, and all the trees he brake that stood nigh to the place of his agony. Almost had he crossed the chasm when Gurtholfin pierced him, and now he cast himself upon its farther bank and laid all waste about him, and lashed and coiled and made a yelling and a bellowing such that the stoutest blenched and turned to flee. Now those afar thought that this was the fearsome noise of battle betwixt the seven, Turambar and his comrades,[28] and little they hoped ever to see any of them return, and Níniel's heart died within her at the sounds; but below in the ravine those three cravens who had watched Turambar from afar fled now in terrror back towards the fall, and Turambar clung nigh to the lip of the chasm white and trembling, for he was spent.

At length did those noises of horror cease, and there arose a great smoking, for Glorund was dying. Then in utter hardihood did Turambar creep out alone from his hiding, for in the agony of the Foalókë his sword was dragged from his hand ere he might withdraw it, and he cherished Gurtholfin beyond all his possessions, for all things died, or man or beast, whom once its edges bit. Now Turambar saw where the dragon lay, and he was stretched out stiff upon his side, and Gurtholfin stood yet in his belly; but he breathed still.

Nonetheless Turambar creeping up set his foot upon his body and withdrew Gurtholfin hardly with all his strength, and as he did so he said in the triumph of his heart: "Now do we meet again, O Glorund, thou and I, Turambar, who was once named brave";[29] but even as he spake the evil blood spouted from that wound upon his hand and burnt it, and it was withered, so that for the sudden pain he cried aloud. Then the Foalókë opening his dread eyes looked upon him, and he fell in a swoon beside the drake and his sword was under him.

Thus did the day draw on and there came no tidings to the hill-top, nor could Níniel longer bear her anguish but arose and made as to leave that glade above the waterfall, and Tamar Lamefoot said: "What dost thou seek to do?" but she: "I would seek my lord and lay me in death beside him, for methinks he is dead", and he sought to dissuade her but without avail. And even as evening fell that fair lady crept through the woods and she would not that Tamar should follow her, but seeing that he did so she fled blindly through the trees, tearing her clothes and marring her face in places of thorny undergrowth, and Tamar being lame could not keep up with her. So fell night upon the woods and all was still, and a great dread for Níniel fell upon Tamar, so that he cursed his weakness and his heart was bitter, yet did he cease not to follow so swiftly as he might, and losing sight of her he bent his course towards that part of the forest nigh to the ravine where had been fought the worm's last fight, for indeed that might be perceived by the watchers on the hill. Now rose a bright moon when the night was old, and Tamar, wandering often alone far and wide from the woodmen's homes, knew those places, and came at last to the edge of that desolation that the dragon had made in his agony; but the moonlight was very bright, and staying among the bushes near the edge of that place Tamar heard and saw all that there betid.

Behold now Níniel had reached those places not long before

him, and straightway did she run fearless into the open for love of
her lord, and so found him lying with his withered hand in a swoon
across his sword; but the beast that lay hugely stretched beside she
heeded not at all, and falling beside Turambar she wept, and
kissed his face, and put salve upon his hand, for such she had
brought in a little box when first they sallied forth, fearing that
many hurts would be gotten ere men wended home.

Yet Turambar woke not at her touch, nor stirred, and she cried
aloud, thinking him now surely dead: "O Turambar, my lord,
awake, for the serpent of wrath is dead and I alone am near!" But
lo! at those words the drake stirred his last, and turning his baleful
eyes upon her ere he shut them for ever said: "O thou Nienóri
daughter of Mavwin, I give thee joy that thou hast found thy
brother at the last, for the search hath been weary – and now is he
become a very mighty fellow and a stabber of his foes unseen"; but
Nienóri sat as one stunned, and with that Glorund died, and with
his death the veil of his spells fell from her, and all her memory
grew crystal clear, neither did she forget any of those things that had
befallen her since first she fell beneath the magic of the worm; so
that her form shook with horror and anguish. Then did she start to
her feet, standing wanly in the moon, and looking upon Turambar
with wide eyes thus spake she aloud: "Then is thy doom spent at
last. Well art thou dead, O most unhappy," but distraught with
her woe suddenly she fled from that place and fared wildly away as
one mad whithersoever her feet led her.

But Tamar whose heart was numbed with grief and ruth followed
as he might, recking little of Turambar, for wrath at the fate of
Nienóri filled all his heart. Now the stream and the deep chasm lay
across her path, but it so chanced that she turned aside ere she
came to its banks and followed its winding course through stony
and thorny places until she came once again to the glade at the
head of the great roaring fall, and it was empty as the first grey
light of a new day filtered through the trees.

There did she stay her feet and standing spake as to herself: "O
waters of the forest whither do ye go? Wilt thou take Nienóri,
Nienóri daughter of Úrin, child of woe? O ye white foams, would
that ye might lave me clean – but deep, deep must be the waters
that would wash my memory of this nameless curse. O bear me
hence, far far away, where are the waters of the unremembering
sea. O waters of the forest whither do ye go?" Then ceasing
suddenly she cast herself over the fall's brink, and perished where
it foams about the rocks below; but at that moment the sun arose

above the trees and light fell upon the waters, and the waters roared unheeding above the death of Nienóri.

Now all this did Tamar behold, and to him the light of the new sun seemed dark, but turning from those places he went to the hill-top and there was already gathered a great concourse of folk, and among them were those three that had last deserted Turambar, and they made a story for the ears of the folk. But Tamar coming stood suddenly before them, and his face was terrible to see, so that a whisper ran among them: "He is dead"; but others said: "What then has befallen the little Níniel?" – but Tamar cried aloud: "Hear, O my people, and say if there is a fate like unto the one I tell unto thee, or a woe so heavy. Dead is the drake, but at his side lieth also Turambar dead, even he who was first called Túrin son of Úrin,[30] and that is well; aye very well," and folk murmured, wondering at his speech, and some said that he was mad. But Tamar said: "For know, O people, that Níniel the fair beloved of you all and whom I love dearer than my heart is dead, and the waters roar above her, for she has leapt o'er the falls of Silver Bowl desiring never more to see the light of day. Now endeth all that evil spell, now is the doom of the folk of Úrin terribly fulfilled, for she that ye called Níniel was even Nienóri daughter of Úrin, and this did she know or ever she died, and this did she tell to the wild woods, and their echo came to me."

At those words did the hearts of all who stood there break for sorrow and for dread, yet did none dare to go to the place of the anguish of that fair lady, for a sad spirit abideth there yet and none sets foot upon its sward; but a great remorse pierced the hearts of those three cravens, and creeping from the throng they went to seek their lord's body, and behold they found him stirring and alive, for when the dragon died the swoon had left him, and he slept a deep sleep of weariness, yet now was he awakening and was in pain. Even as those three stood by he spake and said "Níniel", and at that word they hid their faces for ruth and horror, and could not look upon his face, but afterward they roused him, and behold he was very fain of his victory; yet suddenly marking his hand he said: "Lo! one has been that has tended my hurt with skill – who think ye that it was?" – but they answered him not, for they guessed. Now therefore was Turambar borne weary and hurt back among his folk, and one sped before and cried that their lord lived, but men knew not if they were glad; and as he came among them many turned aside their faces to hide their hearts' perplexity and their tears, and none durst speak.

But Turambar said to those that stood nigh: "Where is Níniel, my Níniel – for I had thought to find her here in gladness – yet if she has returned rather to my halls then is it well", but those that heard could no longer restrain their weeping, and Turambar rose crying: "What new ill is this – speak, speak, my people, and torment me not!" But one said: "Níniel alas is dead my lord," but Turambar cried out bitterly against the Valar and his fate of woe, and at last another said: "Aye, she is dead, for she fell even into the depths of Silver Bowl," but Tamar who stood by muttered: "Nay, she cast herself thither." Then Turambar catching those words seized him by the arm and cried: "Speak, thou club-foot, speak, say what meaneth thy foul speech, or thou shalt lose thy tongue," for his misery was terrible to see.

Now was Tamar's heart in a great turmoil of pain for the dread things that he had seen and heard, and the long hopelessness of his love for Níniel, so did rage against Turambar kindle suddenly within him, and shaking off his touch he said: "A maid thou foundest in the wild woods and gave her a jesting name, that thou and all the folk called her Níniel, the little one of tears. Ill was that jest, Turambar, for lo! she has cast herself away blind with horror and with woe, desiring never to see thee again, and the name she named herself in death was Nienóri daughter of Úrin, child of woe, nor may all the waters of the Silver Bowl as they drop into the deep shed the full tale of tears o'er Níniel."

Then Turambar with a roar took his throat and shook him, saying: "Thou liest – thou evil son of Bethos" – but Tamar gasped "Nay, accursed one; so spake Glorund the drake, and Níniel hearing knew that it was true." But Turambar said: "Then go commune in Mandos with thy Glorund," and he slew him before the face of the people, and fared after as one mad, shouting "He lieth, he lieth"; and yet being free now of blindness and of dreams in his deep heart he knew that it was true and that now his weird was spent at last.

So did he leave the folk behind and drive heedless through the woods calling ever the name of Níniel, till the woods rang most dismally with that word, and his going led him by circuitous ways ever to the glade of Silver Bowl, and none had dared to follow him. There shone the sun of afternoon, and lo, were all the trees grown sere although it was high summer still, and noise there was as of dying autumn in the leaves. Withered were all the flowers and the grass, and the voice of the falling water was sadder than tears for the death of the white maiden Nienóri daughter of Úrin that there had been. There stood Turambar spent at last, and there he drew his sword, and said: "Hail, Gurtholfin, wand of death, for thou art all men's bane and all men's lives fain wouldst thou drink, knowing no lord or faith save the hand that wields thee if it be strong. Thee only have I now – slay me therefore and be swift, for life is a curse, and all my days are creeping foul, and all my deeds are vile, and all I love is dead." And Gurtholfin said: "That will I gladly do, for blood is blood, and perchance thine is not less sweet than many a one's that thou hast given me ere now"; and Turambar cast himself then upon the point of Gurtholfin, and the dark blade took his life.

But later some came timidly and bore him away and laid him in a place nigh, and raised a great mound over him, and thereafter some drew a great rock there with a smooth face, and on it were cut strange signs such as Turambar himself had taught them in dead days, bringing that knowledge from the caves of the Rodothlim, and that writing said:

> Turambar slayer of Glorund the Worm
> who also was Túrin Mormakil
> Son of Úrin of the Woods

and beneath that was carven the word "Níniel" (or child of tears); but she was not there, nor where the waters have laid her fair form doth any man know.'

Now thereupon did Eltas cease his speaking, and suddenly all who hearkened wept; but he said thereto: 'Yea, 'tis an unhappy tale, for sorrow hath fared ever abroad among Men and doth so still, but in the wild days were very terrible things done and suffered; and yet hath Melko seldom devised more cruelty, nor do I know a tale that is more pitiful.'

Then after a time some questioned him concerning Mavwin and Úrin and after happenings, and he said: 'Now of Mavwin hath no sure record been preserved like unto the tale of Túrin Turambar her son, and many things are said and some of them differ from one another; but this much can I tell to ye, that after those dread deeds the woodfolk had no heart for their abiding place and departed to other valleys of the wood, and yet did a few linger sadly nigh their old homes; and once came an aged dame wandering through the woods, and she chanced upon that carven rock. To her did one of those woodmen read the meaning of the signs, and he told her all the tale as he remembered it – but she was silent, and nor spoke nor moved. Then said he: "Thy heart is heavy, for it is a tale to move all men to tears." But she said: "Ay, sad indeed is my heart, for I am Mavwin, mother of those twain," and that man perceived that not yet had that long tale of sorrow reached its ending – but Mavwin arose and went out into the woods crying in anguish, and for long time she haunted that spot so that the woodman and his folk fled and came never back, and none may say whether indeed it was Mavwin that came there or her dark shade that sought not back to Mandos by reason of her great unhappiness.[31]

Yet it is said that all these dread happenings Úrin saw by the magic of Melko, and was continually tempted by that Ainu to yield to his will, and he would not; but when the doom of his folk was utterly fulfilled then did Melko think to use Úrin in another and more subtle way, and he released him from that high and bitter place where he had sat through many years in torment of heart. But Melko went to him and spoke evilly of the Elves to him, and especially did he accuse Tinwelint[32] of weakness and cravenhood. "Never can I comprehend," said he, "wherefore it is that there be still great and wise Men who trust to the friendship of the Elves, and becoming fools enough to resist my might do treble their folly in looking for sure help therein from Gnomes or Fairies. Lo, O Úrin, but for the faint heart of Tinwelint of the woodland how could my designs have come to pass, and perchance now had Nienóri lived and Mavwin thy wife had wept not, being glad for the recovery of her son. Go therefore, O foolish one, and return to eat the bitter bread of almsgiving in the halls of thy fair friends."

Then did Úrin bowed with years and sorrow depart unmolested from Melko's realms and came unto the better lands, but ever as he went he pondered Melko's saying and the cunning web of woven truth and falsity clouded his heart's eye, and he was very bitter in spirit. Now therefore he gathered to him a band of wild Elves,[33] and they were waxen a fierce and lawless folk that dwelt not with their kin, who thrust them into the hills to live or die as they might. On a time therefore Úrin led them to the caves of the Rodothlim, and behold the Orcs had fled therefrom at the death of Glorund, and one only dwelt there still, an old misshapen dwarf who sat ever on the pile of gold singing black songs of enchantment to himself. But none had come nigh till then to despoil him, for the terror of the drake lived longer than he, and none had ventured thither again for dread of the very spirit of Glorund the worm.[34] Now therefore when those Elves approached the dwarf stood before the doors of the cave that was once the abode of Galweg, and he cried: "What will ye with me, O outlaws of the hills?" But Úrin answered: "We come to take what is not thine." Then said that dwarf, and his name was Mîm: "O Úrin, little did I think to see thee, a lord of Men, with such a rabble. Hearken now to the words of Mîm the fatherless, and depart, touching not this gold no more than were it venomous fires. For has not Glorund lain long years upon it, and the evil of the drakes of Melko is on it, and no good can it bring to Man or Elf, but I, only I, can ward it, Mîm the dwarf, and by many a dark spell have I bound it to myself." Then Úrin wavered, but his men were wroth at that, so that he bid them seize it all, and Mîm stood by and watched, and he broke forth into terrible and evil curses. Thereat did Úrin smite him, saying: "We came but to take what was not thine – now for thy evil words we will take what is thine as well, even thy life."

But Mîm dying said unto Úrin: "Now Elves and Men shall rue this deed, and because of the death of Mîm the dwarf shall death follow this gold so long as it remain on Earth, and a like fate shall every part and portion share with the whole." And Úrin shuddered, but his folk laughed.

Now Úrin caused his followers to bear this gold to the halls of Tinwelint, and they murmured at that, but he said: "Are ye become as the drakes of Melko, that would lie and wallow in gold and seek no other joy? A sweeter life shall ye have in the court of that king of greed, an ye bear such treasury to him, than all the gold of Valinor can get you in the empty woods."

Now his heart was bitter against Tinwelint, and he desired to have a vengeance on him, as may be seen. So great was that hoard that great though Úrin's company might be scarce could they bear it to the caves of Tinwelint the king, and some 'tis said was left behind and some was lost upon the way, and evil has followed its finders for ever.

Yet in the end that laden host came to the bridge before the doors, and being asked by the guards Úrin said: "Say to the king that Úrin the Steadfast is come bearing gifts," and this was done. Then Úrin let bear all that magnificence before the king, but it was hidden in sacks or shut in boxes of rough wood; and Tinwelint greeted Úrin with joy and with amaze and bid him thrice welcome, and he and all his court arose in honour of that lord of Men; but Úrin's heart was blind by reason of his tormented years and of the lies of Melko, and he said: "Nay, O King, I do not desire to hear such words – but say only, where is Mavwin my wife, and knowest

thou what death did Nienóri my daughter die?" And Tinwelint
said that he knew not.

Then did Úrin fiercely tell that tale, and the king and all his folk
about him hid their faces for great ruth, but Úrin said: "Nay,[35] had
you such a heart as have the least of Men, never would they have
been lost; but lo, I bring you now a payment in full for the troubles
of your puny band that went against Glorund the drake, and
deserting gave up my dear ones to his power. Gaze, O Tinwelint,
sweetly on my gifts, for methinks the lustre of gold is all your heart
contains."

Then did men cast down that treasury at the king's feet, uncovering it so that all that court were dazzled and amazed – but
Úrin's men understood now what was forward and were little
pleased. "Behold the hoard of Glorund," said Úrin, "bought by
the death of Nienóri with the blood of Túrin slayer of the worm.
Take it, O craven king, and be glad that some Men be brave to win
thee riches."

Then were Úrin's words more than Tinwelint could endure,
and he said: "What meanest thou, child of Men, and wherefore
upbraidest thou me?[36] Long did I foster thy son and forgave him
the evil of his deeds, and afterward thy wife I succoured, giving
way against my counsel to her wild desires. Melko it is that hates
thee and not I. Yet what is it to me – and wherefore dost thou of
the uncouth race of Men endure to upbraid a king of the Eldalië?
Lo! in Palisor my life began years uncounted before the first of
Men awoke. Get thee gone, O Úrin, for Melko hath bewitched
thee, and take thy riches with thee" – but he forebore to slay or to
bind Úrin in spells, remembering his ancient valiance in the
Eldar's cause.

Then Úrin departed, but would not touch the gold, and stricken
in years he reached Hisilómë and died among Men, but his words
living after him bred estrangement between Elves and Men. Yet it
is said that when he was dead his shade fared into the woods
seeking Mavwin, and long those twain haunted the woods about
the fall of Silver Bowl bewailing their children. But the Elves of
Kôr have told, and they know, that at last Úrin and Mavwin fared
to Mandos, and Nienóri was not there nor Túrin their son.
Turambar indeed had followed Nienóri along the black pathways
to the doors of Fui, but Fui would not open to them, neither
would Vefántur. Yet now the prayers of Úrin and Mavwin came
even to Manwë, and the Gods had mercy on their unhappy fate, so
that those twain Túrin and Nienóri entered into Fôs'Almir, the

bath of flame, even as Urwendi and her maidens had done in ages past before the first rising of the Sun, and so were all their sorrows and stains washed away, and they dwelt as shining Valar among the blessed ones, and now the love of that brother and sister is very fair; but Turambar indeed shall stand beside Fionwë in the Great Wrack, and Melko and his drakes shall curse the sword of Mormakil.'

And so saying Eltas made an end, and none asked further.

## NOTES

1   The passage was rejected before the change of *Tintoglin* to *Tinwelint*; see p. 69.

2   Above the name *Egnor* is written 'Damrod the Gnome'; see Commentary, pp. 139–40.

3   Here and immediately below the name as first written was *Tinthellon*; this rider must belong to the same time as the note on the MS directing that *Tintoglin* be changed to *Ellon* or *Tinthellon* (p. 69). See note 32.

4   Associated with this replacement is a note on the manuscript reading: 'If Beren be a Gnome (as now in the story of Tinúviel) the references to Beren must be altered.' In the rejected passage Egnor father of Beren 'was akin to Mavwin', i.e. Egnor was a Man. See notes 5 and 6, and the Commentary, p. 139.

5   'Túrin son of Úrin': original reading 'Beren Ermabwed'. See notes 4 and 6.

6   Original reading 'and when also the king heard of the kinship between Mavwin and Beren'. See notes 4 and 5.

7   *Linwë (Tinto)* was the king's original 'Elvish' name, and belongs to the same 'layer' of names as *Tintoglin* (see I.115, 131). Its retention here (not changed to *Tinwë*) is clearly a simple oversight. See notes 19 and 20.

8   Original reading 'seeing that he was a Man of great size'.

9   With this passage cf. that in the *Tale of Tinúviel* p. 11, which is closely similar. That the passage in *Turambar* is the earlier (to be presumed in any case) is shown by the fact that that in *Tinúviel* is only relevant if Beren is a Gnome, not a Man (see note 4).

10   'dreams came to them': original reading 'dreams the Valar sent to them'.

11   'and his name was Glorund' was added later, as were the subsequent occurrences of the name on pp. 86, 94, 98; but from the first on p. 103 onwards *Glorund* appears in the manuscript as first written.

12   'with the aid of Flinding whose wounds were not great': original reading 'with the aid of a lightly wounded man'. All the subsequent references to Flinding in this passage were added.

13 Original reading 'Túrin's heart was bitter, and so it was that he and that other alone returned from that battle'. – In the phrase 'reproaching Túrin that he had ever withstood his wise counsels' 'ever' means 'always': Túrin had always resisted Orodreth's counsels.

14 Original reading 'although all folk at that time held such a deed grievous and cowardly'.

15 Original reading 'and to look upon Nienóri again'. This was emended to 'and to look upon Nienóri whom he had never seen'. The words 'since his first days' were added still later.

16 The following passage was struck out, apparently at the time of writing:

"Indeed," said they, "it is the report of men of travel and rangers of the hills that for many and many moons have even the farthest marches been free of them and unwonted safe, and so have many men fared out of Hisilómë to the Lands Beyond." And this was the truth that during the life of Turambar as an exile from the court of Tintoglin or hidden amongst the Rothwarin Melko had troubled Hisilómë little and the paths thereto.

(*Rothwarin* was the original form throughout, replaced later by *Rodothlim*.) See p. 92, where the situation described in the rejected passage is referred to the earlier time (before the destruction of the Rodothlim) when Mavwin and Nienóri left Hisilómë.

17 Original reading 'twice seven'. When Túrin fled from the land of Tinwelint it was exactly 12 years since he had left his mother's house (p. 75), and Nienóri was born before that, but just how long before is not stated.

18 After 'a great and terrible project afoot' the original reading was 'the story of which entereth not into this tale'. I do not know whether this means that when my father first wrote here of Melko's 'project' he did not have the destruction of the Rodothlim in mind.

19 'the king': original reading 'Linwë'. See note 7.

20 *Linwë*: an oversight. See note 7.

21 'that high place': original reading 'a hill'.

22 This sentence, 'And even so was Túrin's boast . . .', was added in pencil later. The reference is to Túrin's naming himself *Turambar* – 'from this hour shall none name me Túrin if I live', p. 86.

23 This sentence, from 'for his lineage . . .' to approximately this point, is very lightly struck through. On the opposite page of the MS is hastily scribbled: 'Make Turambar never tell new folk of his lineage (will bury the past) – this avoids chance (as cert.) of Níniel hearing his lineage from any.' See Commentary, p. 131.

24 Against this sentence there is a pencilled question-mark in the margin. See note 23 and the Commentary, p. 131.

25 'And Níniel conceived' was added in pencil later. See Commentary, p. 135.

26  'and the captain of these was Mîm the dwarf' added afterwards in pencil. See Commentary p. 137.

27  The word *tract* may be read as *track*, and the word *hurt* (but with less probability) as *burnt*.

28  As it stands this sentence can hardly mean other than that the people thought that the men were fighting among themselves; but why should they think such a thing? More likely, my father inadvertently missed out the end of the sentence: 'betwixt the seven, Turambar and his comrades, and the dragon.'

29  Turambar refers to Glorund's words to him before the caves of the Rodothlim: 'O Túrin Mormakil, who wast once named brave' (p. 86).

30  These words, from 'even he who . . .', were added later in pencil. *Úrin* may also be read as *Húrin*.

31  From this point to the end of Eltas' tale the original text was struck through, and is followed in the manuscript book by two brief narrative outlines, these being rejected also. The text given here (from 'Yet it is said . . .') is found on slips placed in the book. For the rejected material see the Commentary, pp. 135–7.

32  Throughout the final portion of the text (that written on slips, see note 31) the king's name was first written *Tinthellon*, not *Tintoglin* (see note 3).

33  'Elves': original reading 'men'. The same change was made below ('Now therefore when those Elves approached'), and a little later 'men' was removed in two places ('his folk laughed', 'Úrin caused his followers to bear the gold', p. 114); but several occurrences of 'men' were retained, possibly through oversight, though 'men' is used of Elves very frequently in the *Tale of Turambar* (e.g. 'Beleg and Flinding both stout men', p. 80).

34  This sentence, from 'But none had come nigh . . .', was added later in pencil.

35  This sentence, from 'Then did Úrin fiercely . . .', was added later, replacing 'Then said Úrin: "Yet had you such a heart . . ."'

36  This sentence, from "What meanest thou . . .", replaces the original reading "Begone, and take thy filth with thee."

Changes made to names in
*The Tale of Turambar*

*Fuithlug*  < *Fothlug* < *Fothlog*

*Nienóri*  At the first occurrence (p. 71) my father originally wrote *Nyenòre (Nienor)*. Afterwards he struck out *Nyenòre*, removed the brackets round *Nienor*, and added *-i*, giving *Nienóri*. At subsequent occurrences the name was written both *Nienor* and

*Nienóri*, but *Nienor* was changed to *Nienóri* later throughout the earlier part of the tale. Towards the end, and in the text written on slips that concludes it, the form is *Nienor*. I have given *Nienóri* throughout.

*Tinwelint < Tinthellon* (p. 72, twice). See p. 69 and note 3. *Tinwelint < Tinthellon* also in the concluding portion of the text, see note 32.

*Tinwelint < Tintoglin* throughout the tale, except as just noted (where *Tinwelint < Tinthellon* in passages added later); see p. 69.

*Gwedheling < Gwendeling* at all occurrences (*Gwendeling* unchanged at p. 76, but this is obviously an oversight: I read *Gwedheling* in the text). In the Gnomish dictionary the form *Gwendeling* was changed to *Gwedhiling*; see p. 50.

*Flinding bo-Dhuilin < Flinding go-Dhuilin* This change, made at the occurrence on p. 78, was not made at p. 82, but this was clearly because the form was missed, and I read *bo-Dhuilin* in both cases; the same change from *go-* to *bo-* in the *Tale of Tinúviel*, see p. 51. The form *Dhuilin* is taken by the name when the patronymic is prefixed (cf. *Duilin* p. 79).

*Rodothlim < Rothwarin* at every occurrence.

*Gurtholfin < Gortholfin* at the first occurrences, but from p. 90 *Gurtholfin* was the form first written.

Commentary on<br>
*The Tale of Turambar*

§1. *The primary narrative*

In commenting on this long tale it is convenient to break it into short sections. In the course of this commentary I frequently refer to the long (though incomplete) prose narrative, the *Narn i Hîn Húrin*, given in *Unfinished Tales* pp. 57ff., often in preference to the briefer account in *The Silmarillion*, chapter XXI; and in reference to the former I cite '*Narn*' and the page-number in *Unfinished Tales*.

(i) *The capture of Úrin and Túrin's childhood in Hisilómë* (pp. 70–2).

At the outset of the tale, it would be interesting to know more of the teller, Eltas. He is a puzzling figure: he seems to be a Man (he says that 'our people' called Turambar *Turumart* 'after the fashion of the Gnomes') living in Hisilómë after the days of Turambar but before the fall of Gondolin, and he 'trod Olórë Mallë', the Path of Dreams. Is he then a child, one of 'the children of the fathers of the fathers of Men', who 'found Kôr and remained with the Eldar for ever' (*The Cottage of Lost Play*, I.19–20)?

The opening passage agrees in almost all essentials with the ultimate form of the story. Thus there go back to the beginning of the 'tradition' (or at least to its earliest extant form) the departure of Húrin to the Battle of Unnumbered Tears at the summons of the Noldor, while his wife (Mavwin = Morwen) and young son Túrin remained behind; the great stand of Húrin's men, and Húrin's capture by Morgoth; the reason for Húrin's torture (Morgoth's wish to learn the whereabouts of Turgon) and the mode of it, and Morgoth's curse; the birth of Nienor shortly after the great battle.

That Men were shut in Hisilómë (or Hithlum, the Gnomish form, which here first appears, equated with Dor Lómin, p. 71) after the Battle of Unnumbered Tears is stated in *The Coming of the Elves* (I.118) and in the last of the outlines for *Gilfanon's Tale* (I.241); later on this was transformed into the confinement of the treacherous Easterling Men in Hithlum (*The Silmarillion* p. 195), and their ill-treatment of the survivors of the House of Hador became an essential element in the story of Túrin's childhood. But in the *Tale of Turambar* the idea is already present that 'the strange men who dwelt nigh knew not the dignity of the Lady Mavwin'. It is not in fact clear where Úrin dwelt: it is said here that after the battle 'Mavwin got her in tears into the land of Hithlum or Dor Lómin where all Men must now dwell', which can only mean that she went there, on account of Melko's command, from wherever she had dwelt with Úrin before; on the other hand, a little later in the tale (p. 73), and in apparent contradiction to this, Mavwin would not accept the invitation of Tinwelint to come to Artanor partly because (it is suggested) 'she clung to that dwelling that Úrin had set her in *ere he went to the great war*'.

In the later story Morwen resolved to send Túrin away from fear that he would be enslaved by the Easterlings (*Narn* p. 70), whereas here all that is said is that Mavwin 'knew not in her distress how to foster both him and his sister' (which presumably reflects her poverty). This in turn reflects a further difference, namely that here Nienóri was born before Túrin's departure (but see p. 131); in the later legend he and his companions left Dor-lómin in the autumn of the Year of Lamentation and Nienor was born early in the following year – thus he had never seen her, even as an infant.

An important underlying difference is the absence in the tale of the motive that Húrin had himself visited Gondolin, a fact known to Morgoth and the reason for his being taken alive (*The Silmarillion* pp. 158–9, 196–7); this element in the story arose much later, when the founding of Gondolin was set far back and long before the Battle of Unnumbered Tears.

(ii)    *Túrin in Artanor* (pp. 72–6)

From the original story of Túrin's journey the two old men who accom-

panied him, one of whom returned to Mavwin while the older remained
with Túrin, were never lost; and the cry of Túrin as they set out
reappears in the *Narn* (p. 73): 'Morwen, Morwen, when shall I see you
again?'

Beleg was present from the beginning, as was the meaning of his name:
'he was called Beleg *for* he was of great stature' (see I.254, entry *Haloisi
velikë*, and the Appendix to *The Silmarillion*, entry *beleg*); and he
plays the same rôle in the old story, rescuing the travellers starving in the
forest and taking them to the king.

In the later versions there is no trace of the remarkable message sent by
Tinwelint to Mavwin, and indeed his curiously candid explanation, that
he held aloof from the Battle of Unnumbered Tears because in his
wisdom he foresaw that Artanor could become a refuge if disaster befell,
is hardly in keeping with his character as afterwards conceived. There
were of course quite other reasons for his conduct (*The Silmarillion*
p. 189). On the other hand, Mavwin's motives for not herself leaving
Hithlum remained unchanged (see the passage in the *Narn*, p. 70, where
the word 'almsguest' is an echo of the old tale); but the statement is
puzzling that Mavwin might, when Nienóri was grown, have put aside
her pride and passed over the mountains, had they not become impassable
– clearly suggesting that she never left Hithlum. Perhaps the meaning is,
however, that she might have made the journey *earlier* (while Túrin was
still in Artanor) than she in fact did (when for a time the ways became
easier, but Túrin had gone).

The character of Túrin as a boy reappears in every stroke of the
description in the *Narn* (p. 77):

It seemed that fortune was unfriendly to him, so that often what he
designed went awry, and what he desired he did not gain; neither did
he win friendship easily, for he was not merry, and laughed seldom,
and a shadow lay on his youth.

(It is a notable point that is added in the tale: 'at no time did he give
much heed to words that were spoken to him'). And the ending of all
word between Túrin and his mother comes about in the same way –
increased guard on the mountains (*Narn* p. 78).

While the story of Túrin and Saeros as told in *The Silmarillion*, and in
far more detail in the *Narn*, goes back in essentials to the *Tale of
Turambar*, there are some notable differences – the chief being that as
the story was first told Túrin's tormentor was slain outright by the
thrown drinking-cup. The later complications of Saeros' treacherous
assault on Túrin the following day and his chase to the death, of the trial
of Túrin in his absence for this deed and of the testimony of Nellas (this
last only in the *Narn*) are entirely absent, necessarily; nor does Mablung
appear – indeed it seems clear that Mablung first emerged at the end of
the *Tale of Tinúviel* (see p. 59). Some details survived (as the comb

which Orgof/Saeros offered tauntingly to Túrin, *Narn* p. 80), while others were changed or neglected (as that it was the anniversary of Túrin's departure from his home – though the figure of twelve years agrees with the later story, and that the king was present in the hall, contrast *Narn* p. 79). But the taunt that roused Túrin to murderous rage remained essentially the same, in that it touched on his mother; and the story was never changed that Túrin came into the hall tousled and roughly clad, and that he was mocked for this by his enemy.

Orgof is not greatly distinct from Saeros, if less developed. He was in the king's favour, proud, and jealous of Túrin; in the later story he was a Nandorin Elf while here he is an Ilkorin with some Gnomish blood (for Gnomes in Artanor see p. 65), but doubtless some peculiarity in his origin was part of the 'tradition'. In the old story he is explicitly a fop and a fool, and he is not given the motives of hatred for Túrin that are ascribed to him in the *Narn* (p. 77).

Though far simpler in narrative, the essential element of Túrin's ignorance of his pardon was present from the outset. The tale provides an explanation, not found later, of why Túrin did not, on leaving Artanor, return to Hithlum; cf. the *Narn* p. 87: 'to Dor-lómin he did not dare, for it was closely beset, and one man alone could not hope at that time, as he thought, to come through the passes of the Mountains of Shadow.'

Túrin's prowess against the Orcs during his sojourn in Artanor is given a more central or indeed unique importance in the tale ('he held the wrath of Melko from them for many years') especially as Beleg, his companion-in-arms in the later versions, is not here mentioned (and in this passage the power of the queen to withstand invasion of the kingdom seems again (see p. 63) less than it afterwards became).

(iii)    *Túrin and Beleg* (pp. 76–81)

That part of the Túrin saga following on his days in Artanor/Doriath underwent a large development later ('Túrin among the Outlaws'), and indeed my father never brought this part of the story to finality. In the oldest version there is a much more rapid development of the plot: Beleg joins Túrin's band, and the destruction of the band and capture of Túrin by the Orcs follows (in terms of the narrative) almost immediately. There is no mention of 'outlaws' but only of 'wild spirits', no long search for Túrin by Beleg, no capture and maltreatment of Beleg by the band, and no betrayal of the camp by a traitor (the part ultimately taken by Mîm the Dwarf). Beleg indeed (as already noticed) is not said to have been Túrin's companion in the earlier time, before the slaying of Orgof, and they only take up together after Túrin's self-imposed exile.

Beleg is called a Noldo (p. 78), and if this single reference is to be given full weight (and there seems no reason not to: it is explicit in the *Tale of Tinúviel* that there were Noldoli in Artanor, and Orgof had Gnomish blood) then it is to be observed that Beleg as originally conceived was an Elf of Kôr. He is not here marked out as a great bowman (neither his name Cúthalion 'Strongbow' nor his great bow Belthronding appear); he is described at his first appearance (p. 73) as 'a wood-ranger, a huntsman of the secret Elves', but not as the chief of the marchwardens of the realm.

But from the capture of Túrin to the death of Beleg the old tale was scarcely changed afterwards in any really important respect, though altered in many details: such as Beleg's shooting of the wolf-sentinels silently in the darkness in the later story, and the flash of lightning that illuminated Beleg's face – but the blue-shining lamps of the Noldor appear again in much later writings: one was borne by the Elves Gelmir and Arminas who guided Tuor through the Gate of the Noldor on his journey to the sea (see *Unfinished Tales* pp. 22, 51 note 2). In my father's painting (probably dating from 1927 or 1928) of the meeting between Beleg and Flinding in Taur-nu-Fuin (reproduced in *Pictures by J. R. R. Tolkien*, no. 37) Flinding's lamp is seen beside him. The plot of the old story is very precisely contrived in such details as the reason for the carrying of Túrin, still sleeping, out of the Orc-camp, and for Beleg's using his sword, rather than a knife, to cut Túrin's bonds; perhaps also in the crushing of Beleg by Túrin so that he was winded and could not speak his name before Túrin gave him his death-blow.

The story of Túrin's madness after the slaying of Beleg, the guidance of Gwindor, and the release of Túrin's tears at Eithel Ivrin, is here in embryo. Of the peculiar nature of Beleg's sword there is no suggestion.

(iv)   *Túrin among the Rodothlim; Túrin and Glorund* (pp. 81–8)

In this passage is found (so far as written record goes, for it is to be remembered that a wholly erased text underlies the manuscript) the origin of Nargothrond, as yet unnamed. Among many remarkable features the chief is perhaps that Orodreth was there before Felagund, Lord of Caves, with whom in the later legend Nargothrond was identified, as its founder and deviser. (In *The Silmarillion* Orodreth was one of Finrod Felagund's brothers (the sons of Finarfin), to whom Felagund gave the command of Minas Tirith on Tol Sirion after the making of Nargothrond (p. 120), and Orodreth became King of Nargothrond after Felagund's death.) In the tale this cave-dwelling of exiled Noldoli is a simpler and rougher place, and (as is suggested) short-lived against the overwhelming power of Melko; but, as so often, there were many features that were never altered, even though in a crucial respect the history of Nargothrond was to be greatly modified by contact with the legend of Beren and Tinúviel. Thus the site was from the start 'above a stream' (the later Narog) that 'ran down to feed the river Sirion', and as is seen later (p. 96) the bank of the river on the side of the caves was higher and the hills drew close: cf. *The Silmarillion* p. 114: 'the caves under the

High Faroth in its steep western shore'. The policy of secrecy and refusal of open war pursued by the Elves of Nargothrond was always an essential element (cf. *The Silmarillion* pp. 168, 170),* as was the overturning of that policy by the confidence and masterfulness of Túrin (though in the tale there is no mention of the great bridge that he caused to be built). Here, however, the fall of the redoubt is perhaps more emphatically attributed to Túrin, his coming there seen more simply as a curse, and the disaster as more inevitably proceeding from his unwisdom: at least in the fragments of this part of the *Narn* (pp. 155–7) Túrin's case against Gwindor, who argued for the continuation of secrecy, is seemingly not without substance, despite the outcome. But the essential story is the same: Túrin's policy revealed Nargothrond to Morgoth, who came against it with overwhelming strength and destroyed it.

In relation to the earliest version the roles of Flinding (Gwindor), Failivrin (Finduilas),† and Orodreth were to undergo a remarkable set of transferences. In the old tale Flinding had been of the Rodothlim before his capture and imprisonment in Angband, just as afterwards Gwindor came from Nargothrond (but with a great development in his story, see *The Silmarillion* pp. 188, 191–2), and on his return was so changed as to be scarcely recognisable (I pass over such enduring minor features as the taking of Túrin and Flinding/Gwindor prisoner on their coming to the caves). The beautiful Failivrin is already present, and her unrequited love for Túrin, but the complication of her former relation with Gwindor is quite absent, and she is not the daughter of Orodreth the King but of one Galweg (who was to disappear utterly). Flinding is not shown as opposed to Túrin's policies; and in the final battle he aids Túrin in bearing Orodreth out of the fight. Orodreth dies (after being carried back to the caves) reproaching Túrin for what he has brought to pass – as does Gwindor dying in *The Silmarillion* (p. 213), with the added bitterness of his relation with Finduilas. But Failivrin's father Galweg is slain in the battle, as is Finduilas' father Orodreth in *The Silmarillion*. Thus in the evolution of the legend Orodreth took over the rôle of Galweg, while Gwindor took over in part the rôle of Orodreth.

As I have noticed earlier, there is no mention in the tale of any peculiarity attaching to Beleg's sword, and though the Black Sword is already present it was made for Túrin on the orders of Orodreth, and its blackness and its shining pale edges were of its first making (see *The Silmarillion* pp. 209–10). Its power of speech ('it is said that at times it spake dark words to him') remained afterwards in its dreadful words to Túrin before his death (*Narn* p. 145) – a motive that appears already

---

* From the first of these passages it seems that when Beren came to Nargothrond the 'secret' policy was already pursued under Felagund; but from the second it seems that it came into being from the potent rhetoric of Curufin after Beren went there.

† In *The Silmarillion* she is named Finduilas, and the name Faelivrin 'which is the gleam of the sun on the pools of Ivrin' was given to her by Gwindor (pp. 209–10).

in the tale, p. 112; and Túrin's name derived from the sword (here *Mormagli*, *Mormakil*, later *Mormegil*) was already devised. But of Túrin's disguising of his true name in Nargothrond there is no suggestion: indeed it is explicitly stated that he said who he was.

Of Gelmir and Arminas and the warning they brought to Nargothrond from Ulmo (*Narn* pp. 159–62) the germ can perhaps be seen in the 'whispers in the stream at eve', which undoubtedly implies messages from Ulmo (see p. 77).

The dragon Glorund is named in the 'lengthening spell' in the *Tale of Tinúviel* (pp. 19, 46), but the actual name was only introduced in the course of the writing of the *Tale of Turambar* (see note 11). There is no suggestion that he had played any previous part in the history, or indeed that he was the first of his kind, the Father of Dragons, with a long record of evil already before the Sack of Nargothrond. Of great interest is the passage in which the nature of the dragons of Melko is defined: their evil wisdom, their love of lies and gold (which 'they may not use or enjoy'), and the knowledge of tongues that Men say would come from eating a dragon's heart (with evident reference to the legend in the Norse Edda of Sigurd Fafnisbane, who was enabled to understand, to his own great profit, the speech of birds when he ate the heart of the dragon Fafnir, roasting it on a spit).

The story of the sack of Nargothrond is somewhat differently treated in the old story, although the essentials were to remain of the driving away of Failivrin/Finduilas among the captives and of the powerlessness of Túrin to aid her, being spellbound by the dragon. Minor differences (such as the later arrival of Glorund on the scene: in *The Silmarillion* Túrin only came back to Nargothrond after Glaurung had entered the caves and the sack was 'well nigh achieved') and minor agreements (such as the denial of the plunder to the Orcs) may here be passed over; most interesting is the account of Túrin's words with the dragon. Here the whole issue of Túrin's escaping or not escaping his doom is introduced, and it is significant that he takes the name *Turambar* at this juncture, whereas in the later legend he takes it when he joins the Woodmen in Brethil, and less is made of it. The old version is far less powerfully and concisely expressed, and the dragon's words are less subtle and ingeniously untrue. Here too the moral is very explicitly pointed, that Túrin *should not* have abandoned Failivrin 'in danger that he himself could see' – does this not suggest that, even under the dragon's spell as he was, there was a weakness (a 'blindness', see p. 83) in Túrin which the dragon touched? As the story is told in *The Silmarillion* the moral would seem uncalled for: Túrin was opposed by an adversary too powerful for his mind and will.

There is here a remarkable passage in which suicide is declared a sin, depriving such a one of all hope 'that ever his spirit would be freed from the dark glooms of Mandos or stray into the pleasant paths of Valinor'. This seems to go with the perplexing passage in the tale of *The Coming of the Valar and the Building of Valinor* concerning the fates of Men: see p. 60.

Finally, it is strange that in the old story the gold and treasure was carried out from the caves by the Orcs and remained there (it 'lay by the caves above the stream'), and the dragon most uncharacteristically 'slept before it' in the open. In *The Silmarillion* Glaurung 'gathered all the hoard and riches of Felagund and heaped them, and lay upon them in the innermost hall'.

### (v)   *Túrin's return to Hithlum* (pp. 88–91)

In this passage the case is much as in previous parts of the tale: the large structure of the story was not greatly changed afterwards, but there are many important differences nonetheless.

In the *Tale of Turambar* it is clear that the house of Mavwin was not imagined as standing near to the hills or mountains that formed the barrier between Hithlum and the Lands Beyond: Túrin was told that never did Orcs 'come hither deep into the land of Hisilómë', in contrast to the *Narn* (p. 68), where 'Húrin's house stood in the south-east of Dor-lómin, and the mountains were near; Nen Lalaith indeed came down from a spring under the shadow of Amon Darthir, over whose shoulder there was a steep pass'. The removal of Mavwin from one house to another in Hithlum, visited in turn by Túrin as he sought for her, was afterwards rejected, to the improvement of the story. Here Túrin comes back to his old home in the late summer, whereas in *The Silmarillion* the fall of Nargothrond took place in the late autumn ('the leaves fell from the trees in a great wind as they went, for the autumn was passing to a dire winter,' p. 213) and Túrin came to Dor-lómin in the Fell Winter (p. 215).

The names Brodda and Airin (later spelled Aerin) remained; but Brodda is here the lord of the land, and Airin plays a more important part in the scene in the hall, dealing justice with vigour and wisdom, than she does later. It is not said here that she had been married by force, though her life with Brodda is declared to have been very evil; but of course the situation in the later narratives is far more clear-cut – the Men of Hithlum were 'Easterlings', 'Incomers' hostile to the Elves and the remnant of the House of Hador, whereas in the early story no differentiation is made among them, and indeed Brodda was 'a man whom Mavwin trusted'. The motive of Brodda's ill-treatment of Mavwin is already present, but only to the extent that he embezzled her goods after her departure; in the *Narn* it seems from Aerin's words to Túrin (p. 107) that the oppression of Morwen by Brodda and others was the cause of her going at last to Doriath. In the brief account in *The Silmarillion* (p. 215) it is not indeed made explicit that Brodda in particular deserved Túrin's hatred.

Túrin's conduct in the hall is in the tale essentially simpler: the true story has been told to him by a passer-by, he enters to exact vengeance on Brodda for thieving Mavwin's goods, and he does so with dispatch. As told in the *Narn*, where Túrin's eyes are only finally opened to the deception that has been practised upon him by the words of Aerin, who is present in the hall, his rage is more passionate, crazed, and bitter, and indeed more comprehensible: and the moral observation that Túrin's deed was 'violent and unlawful' is not made. The story of Airin's judgement on these doings, made in order to save Túrin, was afterwards removed; and Túrin's solitary departure was expanded, with the addition also of the firing of Brodda's hall by Aerin (*Narn* p. 109).

Some details survived all the changes: in the *Narn* Túrin still seizes Brodda by the hair, and just as in the tale his rage suddenly expired after the deed of violence ('his wrath was grown cold'), so in the *Narn* 'the fire of his rage was as ashes'. It may be noticed here that while in the old story Túrin does not rename himself so often, his tendency to do so is already present.

The story of how Túrin came among the Woodmen and delivered them from Orcs is not found in the *Tale of Turambar*; nor is there any mention of the Mound of Finduilas near the Crossings of Teiglin nor any account of her fate.

(vi)    *The return of Gumlin to Hithlum and the departure of Mavwin and Nienóri to Artanor* (pp. 91–3)

In the later story the elder of Túrin's guardians (Gumlin in the tale, Grithnir in the *Narn*) plays no part after his bringing Túrin to Doriath: it is only said that he stayed there till he died (*Narn* p. 74); and Morwen had no tidings out of Doriath before leaving her home – indeed she only learnt that Túrin had left Thingol's realm when she got there (*The Silmarillion* p. 211; cf. Aerin's words in the *Narn*, p. 107: 'She looked to find her son there awaiting her.') This whole section of the tale does no more than explain with what my father doubtless felt (since he afterwards rejected it almost in its entirety) to be unnecessary complication why Mavwin went to Tinwelint. I think it is clear, however, that the difference between the versions here depends on the different views of Mavwin's (Morwen's) condition in Hithlum. In the old story she is not suffering hardship and oppression; she trusts Brodda to the extent of entrusting not only her goods to him but even her daughter, and is said indeed to have 'peace and honour among the men of those regions'; the chieftains speak of the love they bear her. A motive for her departure is found in the coming of Gumlin and the news he brings of Túrin's flight from the lands of Tinwelint. In the later story, on the other hand, Brodda's character as tyrant and oppressor is extended, and it is Morwen's very plight at his hands that leads her to depart. (The news that came to Túrin in Doriath that 'Morwen's plight was eased' (*Narn* p. 77, cf. *The Silmarillion* p. 199) is probably a survival from the old story; nothing is said in the later narratives to explain how this came about, and ceased.) In either case her motive for leaving is coupled with the fact of the increased safety of the lands; but whereas in the later story the reason for this was the prowess of the Black Sword of Nargothrond, in the tale it was the 'great and terrible project' of Melko that was afoot – the assault on the caves of the Rodothlim (see note 18).

It is curious that in this passage Airin and Brodda are introduced as if for the first time. It is perhaps significant that the part of the tale extending from the dragon's words 'Hearken to me, O son of Úrin . . .' on p. 87 to '. . . fell to his knees before Tinwelint' on p. 92 was written in a separate part of the manuscript book: possibly this replaced an earlier text in which Brodda and Airin did not appear. But many such questions arise from the earliest manuscripts, and few can now be certainly unravelled.

(vii)   *Mavwin and Nienóri in Artanor and their meeting with Glorund* (pp. 93–9)

The next essential step in the development of the plot – the learning by Mavwin/Morwen of Túrin's sojourn in Nargothrond – is more neatly and naturally handled in *The Silmarillion* (p. 217) and the *Narn* (p. 112), where news is brought to Thingol by fugitives from the sack, in contrast to the *Tale of Turambar*, where Mavwin and Nienóri only learn of the destruction of the Elves of the Caves from a band of Noldoli while themselves wandering aimlessly in the forest. It is odd that these Noldoli did not name Túrin by his name but only as the *Mormakil*: it seems that they did not know who he was, but they knew enough of his history to make his identity plain to Mavwin. As noted above, Túrin declared his name and lineage to the Elves of the Caves. In the later narrative, on the other hand, Túrin did conceal it in Nargothrond, calling himself Agarwaen, but all those who brought news of the fall to Doriath 'declared that it was known to many in Nargothrond ere the end that the Mormegil was none other than Túrin son of Húrin of Dor-lómin'.

As often, unneeded complication in the early story was afterwards cleared away: thus the elaborate argumentation needed to get Tinwelint's warriors and Mavwin and Nienóri on the road together is gone from *The Silmarillion* and the *Narn*. In the tale the ladies and the Elvish warriors all set off together with the full intention that the former shall watch developments from a high place (afterwards Amon Ethir, the Hill of Spies); in the later story Morwen simply rides off, and the party of Elves, led by Mablung, follows after her, with Nienor among them in disguise.

Particularly notable is the passage in the tale in which Mavwin holds out the great gold-hoard of the Rodothlim as a bait to Tinwelint, and Tinwelint unashamedly admits that (as a wild Elf of the woods) it is this, not any hope of aiding Túrin, that moves him to send out a party. The majesty, power, and pride of Thingol rose with the development of the conception of the Grey-elves of Beleriand; as I have said earlier (p. 63) 'In the beginning, Tinwelint's dwelling was not a subterranean city full of marvels . . . but a rugged cave', and here he is seen planning a foray to augment his slender wealth in precious things – a far cry from the description of his vast treasury in the *Narn* (p. 76):

> Now Thingol had in Menegroth deep armouries filled with great wealth of weapons: metal wrought like fishes' mail and shining like water in the moon; swords and axes, shields and helms, wrought by Telchar himself or by his master Gamil Zirak the old, or by elven-wrights more skilful still. For some things he had received in gift that came out of Valinor and were wrought by Fëanor in his mastery, than whom no craftsman was greater in all the days of the world.

Great as are the differences from the later legend in the encounter with the dragon, the stinking vapours raised by his lying in the river as the cause of the miscarriage of the plan, the maddened flight of the horses, and the enspelling of Nienor so that all memory of her past was lost, are already present. Most striking perhaps of the many differences is the fact that Mavwin was present at the conversation with Glorund; and of these speeches there is no echo in the *Narn* (pp. 118–19), save that Nienor's naming of Túrin as the object of their quest revealed her identity to the dragon (this is explicit in the *Narn*, and may probably be surmised from the tale). The peculiar tone of Glaurung in the later narrative, sneering and curt, knowing and self-possessed, and unfathomably wicked, can be detected already in the words of Glorund, but as he evolved he gained immeasurably in dread by becoming more laconic.

The chief difference of structure lies in the total absence of the 'Mablung-element' from the tale, nor is there any foreshadowing of it. There is no suggestion of an exploration of the sacked dwellings in the dragon's absence (indeed he does not, as it appears, go any distance from them); the purpose of the expedition from Artanor was expressly warlike ('a strong party against the Foalókë', 'they prepared them for battle'), since Tinwelint had hopes of laying hands on the treasure, whereas afterwards it became purely a scouting foray, for Thingol 'desired greatly to know more of the fate of Nargothrond' (*Narn* p. 113).

A curious point is that though Mavwin and Nienóri were to be stationed on the tree-covered 'high place' that was afterward called the Hill of Spies, and where they were in fact so stationed in *The Silmarillion* and the *Narn*, it seems that in the old story they never got there, but were ensnared by Glorund where he lay in, or not far from, the river. Thus the 'high place' had in the event almost no significance in the tale.

### (viii)   *Turambar and Níniel* (pp. 99–102)

In the later legend Nienor was found by Mablung after her enspelling by Glaurung, and with three companions he led her back towards the borders of Doriath. The chase after Nienor by the band of Orcs (*Narn* p. 120) is present in the tale, but it does not have its later narrative function of leading to Nienor's flight and loss by Mablung and the other Elves (who do not appear): rather it leads directly to her rescue by Turambar, now dwelling among the Woodmen. In the *Narn* (p. 122) the Woodmen of Brethil did indeed come past the spot where they found her on their return from a foray against Orcs; but the circumstances of her finding are altogether different, most especially since there is in the tale no mention of the Haudh-en-Elleth, the Mound of Finduilas.

An interesting detail concerns Nienor's response to Turambar's naming her *Níniel*. In *The Silmarillion* and the *Narn* 'she shook her head, but said: Níniel'; in the present text she said: 'Not Níniel, not Níniel.' One has the impression that in the old story what impressed her darkened mind was only the resemblance of *Níniel* to her own forgotten name *Nienóri* (and of *Turambar* to *Túrin*), whereas in the later she both denied and in some way accepted the name *Níniel*.

An original element in the legend is the Woodmen's bringing of Níniel to a place ('Silver Bowl') where there was a great waterfall (afterwards Dimrost, the Rainy Stair, where the stream of Celebros 'fell towards Teiglin'): and these falls were near to the dwellings of the Woodmen – but the place where they found Níniel was much further off in the forest (several days' journey) than were the Crossings of Teiglin from Dimrost. When she came there she was filled with dread, a foreboding of what was to happen there afterwards, and this is the origin of her shuddering fit in the later narratives, from which the place was renamed Nen Girith, the Shuddering Water (see *Narn* p. 149, note 24).

The utter darkness imposed on Níniel's mind by the dragon's spell is less emphasized in the tale, and there is no suggestion that she needed to relearn her very language; but it is interesting to observe the recurrence in a changed context of the simile of 'one that seeks for something mislaid': in the *Narn* (p. 123) Níniel is said to have taken great delight in the relearning of words, 'as one that finds again treasures great and small that were mislaid'.

The lame man, here called Tamar, and his vain love of Níniel already appear; unlike his later counterpart Brandir he was not the chief of the Woodmen, but he was the son of the chief. He was also Half-elven! Most extraordinary is the statement that the wife of Bethos the chieftain and mother of Tamar was an Elf, a woman of the Noldoli: this is mentioned in passing, as if the great significance and rarity of the union of Elf and Mortal had not yet emerged – but in a Name-list associated with the tale of *The Fall of Gondolin* Eärendel is said to be 'the only being that is half of the kindred of the Eldalië and half of Men' (p. 215).*

---

* In a later rewriting of a passage in that tale (p. 164 and note 22) it is said of Tuor and Idril of Gondolin: 'Thus was first wed a child of Men with a daughter of Elfinesse, nor was Tuor the last.'

The initial reluctance of Níniel to receive Turambar's suit is given no explanation in the tale: the implication must be that some instinct, some subconscious appreciation of the truth, held her back. In *The Silmarillion* (p. 220)

> for that time she delayed in spite of her love. For Brandir foreboded he knew not what, and sought to restrain her, rather for her sake than his own or rivalry with Turambar; and he revealed to her that Turambar was Túrin son of Húrin, and though she knew not the name a shadow fell upon her mind.

In the final version as in the oldest, the Woodmen knew who Turambar was. My father's scribbled directions for the alteration of the story cited in note 23 ('Make Turambar never tell new folk of his lineage . . .') are puzzling: for since Níniel had lost all memory of her past she would not know the names Túrin son of Húrin even if it were told to her that Turambar was he. It is however possible that when my father wrote this he imagined Níniel's lost knowledge of herself and her family as being nearer the surface of her mind, and capable of being brought back by hearing the names – in contrast to the later story where she did not consciously recognise the name of Túrin even when Brandir told it to her. Clearly the question-mark against the reference in the text of the tale to Turambar's speaking to Níniel 'of his father and mother and the sister he had not seen' and Níniel's distress at his words (see note 24) depends on the same train of thought. The statement here that Turambar had never seen his sister is at variance with what is said earlier in the tale, that he did not leave Hithlum until after Nienóri's birth (p. 71); but my father was uncertain on this point, as is clearly seen from the succession of readings, changed back and forth between the two ideas, given in note 15.

## (ix)   *The slaying of Glorund* (pp. 103–8)

In this section I follow the narrative of the tale as far as Túrin's swoon when the dying dragon opened his eyes and looked at him. Here the later story runs very close to the old, but there are many interesting differences.

In the tale Glorund is said to have had bands of both Orcs and Noldoli subject to him, but only the Orcs remained afterwards; cf. the *Narn* p. 125:

> Now the power and malice of Glaurung grew apace, and he waxed fat [cf. 'the Foalókë waxed fat'], and he gathered Orcs to him, and ruled as a dragon-King, and all the realm of Nargothrond that had been was laid under him.

The mention in the tale that Tinwelint's people were 'grievously harried' by Glorund's bands suggests once again that the magic of the Queen was no very substantial protection; while the statement that 'at length there came some [Orcs] nigh even to those woods and glades that were beloved of Turambar and his folk' seems at variance with Turambar's saying to Níniel earlier that 'we are hard put to it to fend those evil ones from our homes' (p. 100). There is no mention here of Turambar's pledge to Níniel that he would go to battle only if the homes of the Woodmen were assailed (*Narn* pp. 125–6); and there is no figure corresponding to Dorlas of the later versions. Tamar's character, briefly described (p. 106), is in accord so far as it goes with what is later told of Brandir, but the relationship of Brandir to Níniel, who called him her brother (*Narn* p. 124), had not emerged. The happiness and prosperity of the Woodmen under Turambar's chieftainship is much more strongly emphasized in the tale (afterwards he was not indeed the chieftain, at least not in name); and it leads in fact to Glorund's greed as a motive for his assault on them.

The topographical indications in this passage, important to the narrative, are readily enough accommodated to the later accounts, with one major exception: it is clear that in the old story the stream of the waterfall that fell down to the Silver Bowl was the same as that which ran through the gorge where Turambar slew Glorund:

Here flowed that same stream that further down wound past the dragon's lair [*lair* = the place where he was lying] in a deep bed cloven deep into the earth (p. 105).

Thus Turambar and his companions, as he said,

will go down the rocks to the foot of the fall, and so gaining the path of the stream perchance we may come as nigh to the drake as may be (*ibid.*).

In the final story, on the other hand, the falling stream (Celebros) was a tributary of Teiglin; cf. the *Narn* p. 127:

Now the river Teiglin . . . flowed down from Ered Wethrin swift as Narog, but at first between low shores, until after the Crossings, gathering power from other streams, it clove a way through the feet of the highlands upon which stood the Forest of Brethil. Thereafter it ran in deep ravines, whose great sides were like walls of rock, but pent at the bottom the waters flowed with great force and noise. And right in the path of Glaurung there lay now one of these gorges, by no means the deepest, but the narrowest, just north of the inflow of Celebros.

The pleasant place ('a green sward where grew a wealth of flowers')
survived; cf. the Narn p. 123: 'There was a wide greensward at the
head of the falls, and birches grew about it.' So also did the 'Silver
Bowl', though the name was lost: 'the stream [Celebros] went over a
lip of worn stone, and fell down by many foaming steps into a rocky bowl
far below' (Narn, ibid.; cf. the tale p. 105: 'it fell over a great fall where
the water-worn rock jutted smooth and grey from amid the grass'). The
'little hill' or 'knoll', 'islanded among the trees', from which Turambar
and his companions looked out is not so described in the Narn, but the
picture of a high place and lookout near the head of the falls remained, as
may be seen from the statement in the Narn (p. 123) that from Nen
Girith 'there was a wide view towards the ravines of Teiglin'; later (Narn
p. 128) it is said that it was Turambar's intention to 'ride to the high fall of
Nen Girith . . . whence he could look far across the lands'. It seems
certain, then, that the old image never faded, and was only a little
changed.

While in both old and late accounts a great concourse of the people
follow Turambar to the head of the falls against his bidding, in the late
his motive for commanding them not to come is explicit: they are to
remain in their homes and prepare for flight. Here on the other hand
Níniel rides with Turambar to the head of Silver Bowl and says farewell
to him there. But a detail of the old story survived: Turambar's words to
Níniel 'Nor thou nor I die this day, nor yet tomorrow, by the evil of the
dragon or by the foemen's swords' are closely paralleled by his words to
her in the Narn (p. 129): 'Neither you nor I shall be slain by this Dragon,
nor by any foe of the North'; and in the one account Níniel 'quelled her
weeping and was very still', while in the other she 'ceased to weep and fell
silent'. The situation is generally simpler in the tale, in that the Woodmen
are scarcely characterised; Tamar is not as Brandir the titular head of the
people, and this motive for bitterness against Turambar is absent, nor is
there a Dorlas to insult him or a Hunthor to rebuke Dorlas. Tamar is
however present with Níniel at the same point in the story, having girded
himself with a sword: 'and many scoffed at him for that', just as it is
afterwards said of Brandir that he had seldom done so before (Narn
p. 132).

Turambar here set out from the head of the falls with six companions,
all of whom proved in the end fainthearted, whereas later he had only
two, Dorlas and Hunthor, and Hunthor remained staunch, though killed
by a falling stone in the gorge. But the result is the same, in that
Turambar must climb the further cliff of the gorge alone. Here the
dragon remained where he lay near the brink of the cliff all night,
and only moved with the dawn, so that his death and the events that
immediately followed it took place by daylight. But in other respects
the killing of the dragon remained even in many details much as it
was originally written, more especially if comparison is made with the
Narn (p. 134), where there reappears the need for Turambar and his

companion(s) to move from their first station in order to come up directly under the belly of the beast (this is passed over in *The Silmarillion*).

Two notable points in this section remain to be mentioned; both are afterthoughts pencilled into the manuscript. In the one we meet for the first time Mîm the Dwarf as the captain of Glorund's guard over his treasure during his absence − a strange choice for the post, one would think. On this matter see p. 137 below. In the other it is said that Níniel conceived a child by Turambar, which, remarkably enough, is not said in the text as originally written; on this see p. 135.

(x)    *The deaths of Túrin and Nienóri* (pp. 108−12)

In the conclusion of the story the structure remained the same from the old tale to the *Narn*: the moonlight, the tending of Turambar's burnt hand, the cry of Níniel that stirred the dragon to his final malice, the accusation by the dragon that Turambar was a stabber of foes unseen, Turambar's naming Tamar/Brandir 'Club-foot' and sending him to consort with the dragon in death, the sudden withering of the leaves at the place of Nienor's leap as if it were already the end of autumn, the invocation of Nienor to the waters and of Turambar to his sword, the raising of Túrin's mound and the inscription in 'strange signs' upon it. Many other features could be added. But there are also many differences; here I refer only to some of the most important.

Mablung being absent from the old story, it is only Turambar's intuition ('being free now of blindness' − the blindness that Melko 'wove of old', p. 83)* that informs him that Tamar was telling the truth. The slaying of Glaurung and all its aftermath is in the late story compassed in the course of a single night and the morning of the next day, whereas in the tale it is spread over two nights, the intervening day, and the morning of the second. Turambar is carried back to the people on the hill-top by the three deserters who had left him in the ravine, whereas in the late story he comes himself. (Of the slaying of Dorlas by Brandir there is no trace in the tale, and the taking of a sword by Tamar has no issue.)

Particularly interesting is the result of the changing of the place where Túrin and Nienóri died. In the tale there is only one river, and Níniel follows the stream up through the woods and casts herself over the falls of Silver Bowl (in the place afterwards called Nen Girith), and here too, in the glade above the falls, Turambar slew himself; in the developed story her death-leap was into the ravine of Teiglin at Cabed-en-Aras, the Deer's Leap, near the spot where Turambar lay beside Glaurung, and here Turambar's death took place also. Thus Níniel's sense of dread when she first came to Silver Bowl with the Woodmen who rescued her

---

* Cf. his words to Mablung in the *Narn*, p. 144: 'For see, I am blind! Did you not know? Blind, blind, groping since childhood in a dark mist of Morgoth!'

(p. 101) foreboded her own death in that place, but in the changed story there is less reason for a foreknowledge of evil to come upon her there. But while the place was changed, the withering of the leaves remained, and the awe of the scene of their deaths, so that none would go to Cabed-en-Aras after, as they would not set foot on the grass above Silver Bowl.

The most remarkable feature of the earliest version of the story of Turambar and Níniel is surely that as my father first wrote it he did *not* say that she had conceived a child by him (note 25); and thus there is nothing in the old story corresponding to Glaurung's words to her: 'But the worst of all his deeds thou shalt feel in thyself' (*Narn* p. 138). The fact that above all accounts for Nienor's utter horror and despair was added to the tale later.

In concluding this long analysis of the *Tale of Turambar* proper the absence of place-names in the later part of it may be remarked. The dwelling of the Rodothlim is not named, nor the river that flowed past it; no name is given to the forest where the Woodmen dwelt, to their village, or even to the stream of such central importance at the end of the story (contrast Nargothrond, Narog, Tumhalad, Amon Ethir, Brethil, Amon Obel, Ephel Brandir, Teiglin, Celebros of the later narratives).

## §2. *The further narrative of Eltas (after the death of Túrin)*

My father struck out the greater part of this continuation, allowing it to stand only as far as the words 'by reason of her great unhappiness' on p. 113 (see note 31). From the brief passage that was retained it is seen that the story of Morwen's coming to the stone on Túrin's mound goes back to the beginning, though in the later story she met Húrin there (*The Silmarillion*, p. 229).

The rejected part continues as follows:

Yet it is said also that when the doom of his folk was utterly fulfilled then was Úrin released by Melko, and bowed with age he fared back into the better lands. There did he gather some few to him, and they went and found the caverns of the Rothwarin [*earlier form for* Rodothlim, *see p.* 119] empty, and none guarded them, and a mighty treasury lay there still for none had found it, in that the terror of the drake lived longer than he and none had ventured thither again. But Úrin let bear the gold even before Linwë [i.e. Tinwelint], and casting it before his feet bade him bitterly to take his vile reward, naming him a craven by whose faint heart had much evil fallen to his house that might never have been; and in this began a new estrangement between Elves and Men, for Linwë was wroth at Úrin's words and bid him begone, for said he: "Long did I foster Túrin thy son and forgave him the evil of his deeds, and afterward thy wife I succoured, giving way against my counsel to her wild desires. Yet what is it to me – and wherefore dost thou, O son of the uncouth race of Men, endure to upbraid a king of the Eldalië, whose life began in Palisor ages uncounted before Men were born?" And then Úrin would have gone, but his men were not willing to leave the gold there, and a dissension arose between them and the Elves, and of this grew bitter blows, and Tintoglin [i.e. Tinwelint] might not stay them.

There then was Úrin's band slain in his halls, and they stained with their blood the dragon's hoard; but Úrin escaped and cursed that gold with a dread curse so that none might enjoy it, and he that held any part of it found evil and death to come of it. But Linwë hearing that curse caused the gold to be cast into a deep pool of the river before his doors, and not for very long did any see it again save for the Ring of Doom [*emended to:* the Necklace of the Dwarves], and that tale belongs not here, although therein did the evil of the worm Glorund find its last fulfilment.

(The last phrase is an addition to the text.) The remainder of this rejected narrative, concerning the final fates of Úrin and Mavwin and their children, is essentially the same as in the replacement text given on p. 115 ('Then Úrin departed . . .') and need not be given.

Immediately following the rejected narrative there is a short outline headed 'Story of the Nauglafring or the Necklace of the Dwarves', and this also was struck through. Here there is no mention of Úrin at all, but it is told that the Orcs (emended from *Gongs*, see I.245 note 10) who guarded the treasury of Glorund went in search of him when he did not come back to the caves, and in their absence Tintoglin (i.e. Tinwelint), learning of Glorund's death, sent Elves to steal the hoard of the Rothwarin (i.e. Rodothlim). The Orcs returning cursed the thieves, and they cursed the gold also.

Linwë (i.e. Tinwelint) guarded the gold, and he had a great necklace made by certain Úvanimor (Nautar or Nauglath). (*Úvanimor* have been defined in an earlier tale as 'monsters, giants, and ogres', see I.75, 236; *Nauglath* are Dwarves, I.236). In this Necklace the Silmaril was set; but the curse of the gold was on him, and he defrauded them of part of their reward. The Nauglath plotted, and got aid of Men; Linwë was slain in a raid, and the gold carried away.

There follows another rejected outline, headed 'The Necklace of the Dwarves', and this combines features of the preceding outline with features of the rejected ending of Eltas' narrative (pp. 135–6). Here Úrin gathers a band of Elves and Men who are wild and fierce, and they go to the caves, which are lightly guarded because the 'Orqui' (i.e. Orcs) are abroad seeking Glorund. They carry off the treasure, and the Orcs returning curse it. Úrin casts the treasure before the king and reproaches him (saying that he might have sent a greater company to the caves to secure the treasure, if not to aid Mavwin in her distress); 'Tintoglin would not touch it and bid Úrin hold what he had won, but Úrin would depart with bitter words'. Úrin's men were not willing to leave it, and they sneaked back; there was an affray in the king's halls, and much blood was spilt on the gold. The outline concludes thus:

> The Gongs sack Linwë's halls and Linwë is slain and the gold is carried far away. Beren Ermabwed falls upon them at a crossing of Sirion and the treasure is cast into the water, and with it the Silmaril of Fëanor. The Nauglath that dwell nigh dive after the gold but only one mighty necklace of gold (and that Silmaril is on it) do they find. This becomes a mark of their king.

These two outlines are partly concerned with the story of the Nauglafring and show my father pondering that story before he wrote it; there is no need to consider these elements here. It is evident that he was in great doubt as to the further course of the story after the release of Úrin – what happened to the dragon's hoard? Was it guarded or unguarded, and if guarded by whom? How did it come at last into Tinwelint's hands? Who cursed it, and at what point in the story? If it was Úrin and his band that seized it, were they Men or Elves or both?

In the final text, written on slips placed in the manuscript book and given above pp. 113–16, these questions were resolved thus: Úrin's band was at first Men, then changed to Elves (see note 33); the treasure was guarded by the dwarf Mîm, whom Úrin slew, and it was he who cursed the gold as he died; Úrin's band became a baggage-train to carry the treasure to Tinwelint in sacks and wooden boxes (and they got it to the bridge before the king's door in the heart of the forest without, apparently, any difficulty). In this text there is no hint of what happened to the treasure after Úrin's departure (because the *Tale of the Nauglafring* begins at that point).

Subsequent to the writing of the *Tale of Turambar* proper, my father inserted Mîm into the text at an earlier point in the story (see pp. 103, 118 note 26), making him the captain of the guard appointed by Glorund to watch the treasure in his absence; but whether this was written in before or after the appearance of Mîm at the end (pp. 113–14) – whether it represents a different idea, or is an explanation of how Mîm came to be there – I cannot say.

In *The Silmarillion* (pp. 230–2) the story is wholly changed, in that the treasure remained in Nargothrond, and Húrin after the slaying of Mîm (for a far better reason than that in the early narrative) brought nothing from it to Doriath save the Necklace of the Dwarves.

Of the astonishing feature at the end of Eltas' narrative (pp. 115–16) of the 'deification' of Túrin Turambar and Nienóri (and the refusal of the Gods of Death to open their doors to them) it must be said that nowhere is there any explanation given – though in much later versions of the mythology Túrin Turambar appears in the Last Battle and smites Morgoth with his black sword. The purifying bath into which Túrin and Nienóri entered, called *Fôs'Almir* in the final text, was in the rejected text named *Fauri*; in the *Tale of the Sun and Moon* it has been described (I. 187), but is there given other names: *Tanyasalpë*, *Faskalanúmen*, and *Faskalan*.

There remains one further scrap of text to be considered. The second of the rejected outlines given above (pp. 136–7) was written in ink over a pencilled outline that was *not* erased, and I have been able to disinter a good deal of it from beneath the later writing. The two passages have nothing to do with each other; for some reason my father did not trouble in this case to erase earlier writing. The underlying text, so far as I can make it out, reads:

Tirannë and Vainóni fall in with the evil magician Kurúki who gives them a baneful drink. They forget their names and wander distraught in the woods. Vainóni is lost. She meets Turambar who saves her from Orcs and aids in her search for her mother. They are wed and live in happiness. Turambar becomes lord of rangers of the woods and a harrier of the Orcs. He goes to seek out the Foalókë which ravages his land. The treasure-heap – and flight of his band. He slays the Foalókë and is wounded. Vainóni succours him, but the dragon in dying tells her all, lifting the veil Kurúki has set over them. Anguish of Turambar and Vainóni. She flees into the woods and casts herself over a waterfall. Madness of Turambar who dwells alone . . . . . . . . . Úrin escapes from Angamandi and seeks Tirannë. Turambar flees from him and falls upon his sword. . . . . . . . . . . . . . . . . . . . . . . . Úrin builds a cairn and . . . . . . . . . . . doom of Melko. Tirannë dies of grief and Úrin reaches Hisilómë. . . . . . . . . . . . . . . . . . . . . . . . . . . . . . . . . . . . . Purification of Turambar and Vainóni who fare shining about the world and go with the hosts of Tulkas against Melko.

Detached jottings follow this, doubtless written at the same time:

Úrin escapes. Tirannë learns of Túrin. Both wander distraught . . . in the wood.
Túrin leaves Linwë for in a quarrel he slew one of Linwë's kin (accidentally).
Introduce Failivrin element into the story?
Turambar unable to fight because of Foalókë's eyes. Sees Failivrin depart.

This can only represent some of my father's very earliest meditations on the story of Túrin Turambar. (That it appears in the notebook at the *end* of the fully-written Tale may seem surprising, but he clearly used these books in a rather eccentric way.) Nienóri is here called *Vainóni*, and Mavwin *Tirannë*; the spell of forgetfulness is here laid by a magician named *Kurúki*, although it is the dragon who lifts the veil that the magician set over them. Túrin's two encounters with the dragon seem to have emerged from an original single one.

As I have mentioned before, the *Tale of Turambar*, like others of the *Lost Tales*, is written in ink over a wholly erased pencilled text, and the extant form of the tale is such that it could only be derived from a rougher draft preceding it; but the underlying text is so completely erased that there is no clue as to what stage it had reached in the development of the legend. It may well be – I think it is extremely probable – that in this outline concerning Vainóni, Tirannë, and Kurúki we glimpse by an odd chance a 'layer' in the Túrin-saga older even than the erased text underlying the extant version.

### §3. *Miscellaneous Matters*

#### (i) *Beren*

The rejected passage given on p. 71, together with the marginal note 'If Beren be a Gnome (as now in the story of Tinúviel) the references to Beren must be altered' (note 4), is the basis for my assertion (p. 52) that in the earliest, now lost, form of the *Tale of Tinúviel* Beren was a Man. I have shown, I hope, that the extant form of the *Tale of Turambar* preceded the extant form of the *Tale of Tinúviel* (p. 69). Beren was a Man, *and akin to Mavwin*, when the extant *Turambar* was written; he became a Gnome in the extant *Tinúviel*; and this change was then written into *Turambar*. What the replacement passage on p. 72 does is to change the relation of Egnor and Beren from kinship with Úrin's wife to friendship with Úrin. (A correction to the typescript version of *Tinúviel*, p. 45, is later: making the comradeship of Úrin with Beren rather than with Egnor.) Two further changes to the text of Turambar consequent on the change in Beren from Man to Elf are given in notes 5 and 6. – It is interesting to observe that in the developed genealogy of *The Silmarillion*, when Beren was of course again a Man, he was also again akin to Morwen: for Beren was first cousin to Morwen's father Baragund.

In the rejected passage on p. 71 my father wrote against the name Egnor 'Damrod the Gnome' (note 2), and in the amended passage he wrote that Úrin had known Beren 'and had rendered him a service once in respect of Damrod his son'. There is no clue anywhere as to what this service may have been; but in the second of the 'schemes' for *The Book of Lost Tales* (see I.233–4) the outline for the *Tale of the Nauglafring* refers to the son of Beren and Tinúviel, the father of Elwing, by the name *Daimord*, although in the actual tale as written the son is as he was to remain *Dior*. Presumably *Daimord* is to be equated with *Damrod*.

I cannot explain the insertion of 'Damrod the Gnome' against 'Egnor' in the rejected passage – possibly it was no more than a passing idea, to give the name *Damrod* to Beren's father.

It may be noticed here that both the rejected and the replacement passages make it very clear that the events of the story of Beren and Tinúviel took place *before* the Battle of Unnumbered Tears; see pp. 65–6.

### (ii)   *The Battle of Tasarinan*

It is said at the beginning of the present tale (p. 70) that it 'tells of very ancient days of that folk [Men] before the Battle of Tasarinan when first Men entered the dark vales of Hisilómë'.

On the face of it this offers an extreme contradiction, since it is said many times that Men were shut in Hisilómë at the time of the Battle of Unnumbered Tears, and the *Tale of Turambar* takes place – must take place – after that battle. The solution lies, however, in an ambiguity in the sentence just cited. My father did not mean that this was a tale of Men in ancient days of that folk before they entered Hisilómë; he meant 'this is a tale of the ancient days *when* Men first entered Hisilómë – long before the Battle of Tasarinan'.

*Tasarinan* is the Land of Willows, *Nan-tathren* in *The Silmarillion*; the early word-lists or dictionaries give the 'Elvish' form *tasarin* 'willow' and the Gnomish *tathrin*.* The Battle of Tasarinan took place long after, in the course of the great expedition from Valinor for the release of the enslaved Noldoli in the Great Lands. See pp. 219–20.

### (iii)   *The geography of the Tale of Turambar*

The passage describing the route of the Orcs who captured Túrin (p. 77) seems to give further support to the idea that 'the mountains fencing Hisilómë from the Lands Beyond were continuous with those above Angband' (p. 62); for it is said here that the Orcs 'followed ever the line of dark hills toward those regions where they rise high and gloomy and their heads are shrouded in black vapours', and '*there* are they called Angorodin or the Iron Mountains, for beneath the roots of their northernmost fastnesses lies Angband'.

The site of the caves of the Rodothlim, agreeing well with what is said later of Nargothrond, has been discussed already (p. 123), as has the topography of the Silver Bowl and the ravine in which Turambar slew Glorund, in relation to the later Teiglin, Celebros, and Nen Girith (pp. 132–3). There are in addition some indications in the tale of how the caves of the Rodothlim related to Tinwelint's kingdom and to the land

---

* *Tasarinan* survived as the Quenya name without change: 'the willow-meads of Tasarinan' in Treebeard's song in *The Two Towers*, III.4.

where the Woodmen dwelt. It is said (p. 95) that 'the dwellings of the Rodothlim were not utterly distant from the realm of Tinwelint, albeit far enough'; while the Woodmen dwelt 'in lands that were not utterly far from Sirion or the grassy hills of that river's middle course' (p. 91), which may be taken to agree tolerably with the situation of the Forest of Brethil. The region where they lived is said in the same passage to have been 'very far away many a journey beyond the river of the Rodothlim', and Glorund's wrath was great when he heard of 'a brave folk of Men that dwelt far beyond the river' (p. 103); this also can be accommodated quite well to the developed geographical conception – Brethil was indeed a good distance beyond the river (Narog) for one setting out from Nargothrond.

My strong impression is that though the geography of the west of the Great Lands *may* have been still fairly vague, it already had, in many important respects, the same essential structure and relations as those seen on the map accompanying *The Silmarillion*.

## (iv) *The influence of the Valar*

As in the *Tale of Tinúviel* (see p. 68), in the *Tale of Turambar* also there are several references to the power of the Valar in the affairs of Men and Elves in the Great Lands – and to prayers, both of thanksgiving and request, addressed to them: thus Túrin's guardians 'thanked the Valar' that they accomplished the journey to Artanor (p. 72), and more remarkably, Úrin 'called upon the Valar of the West, being taught much concerning them by the Eldar of Kôr – the Gnomes he had encountered – and his words came, who shall say how, to Manwë Súlimo upon the heights of Taniquetil' (p. 77). (Úrin was already an 'Elf-friend', instructed by the Noldoli; cf. the replacement passage on p. 72.) Was his prayer 'answered'? Possibly this is the meaning of the very strange expression 'as the luck of the Valar had it' (p. 79), when Flinding and Beleg found Túrin lying near the point where they entered the Orc-camp.*

Dreams sent by the Valar came to the chieftains of the Rodothlim, though this was changed later and the reference to the Valar removed (p. 83 and note 10); the Woodmen said 'Would that the Valar would lift the spell that lies upon Níniel' (p. 101); and Túrin 'cried out bitterly against the Valar and his fate of woe' (p. 111).

An interesting reference to the Valar (and their power) occurs in Tinwelint's reply (p. 95) to Mavwin's words 'Give me but a woodman's cot and my son'. The king said: 'That I cannot, for I am but a king of the wild Elves, *and no Vala of the western isles.*' In the small part of *Gilfanon's Tale* that was actually written it is told (I. 231) of the Dark Elves who remained in Palisor that they said that 'their brethren had gone

---

* The Gnomish dictionary has the entry: *gwalt* 'good luck – any providential occurrence or thought: "the luck of the Valar", *i-gwalt ne Vanion*' (I. 272).

westward to the Shining Isles. There, said they, do the Gods dwell, and they called them the Great Folk of the West, and thought they dwelt on firelit islands in the sea.'

### (v)   Túrin's age

According to the *Tale of Turambar*, when Túrin left Mavwin he was seven years old, and it was after he had dwelt among the woodland Elves for seven years that all tidings from his home ceased (p. 74); in the *Narn* the corresponding years are eight and nine, and Túrin was seventeen, not fourteen, when 'his grief was renewed' (pp. 68, 76–7). It was exactly twelve years to the day of his departure from Mavwin when he slew Orgof and fled from Artanor (p. 75), when he was nineteen; in the *Narn* (p. 79) it was likewise twelve years since he left Hithlum when he hunted Saeros to his death, but he was twenty.

'The tale tells not the number of days that Turambar sojourned with the Rodothlim but these were very many, and during that time Nienóri grew to the threshold of womanhood' (pp. 91–2). Nienóri was seven years younger than Túrin: she was twelve when he fled from Artanor (*ibid.*). He cannot then have dwelt among the Rodothlim for more than (say) five or six years; and it is said that when he was chosen chieftain of the Woodmen he possessed 'wisdom great beyond his years'.

Bethos, chieftain of the Woodmen before Túrin, 'had fought *though then but a boy* in the Battle of Unnumbered Tears' (p. 101), but he was killed in a foray, since '*despite his years* he still rode abroad'. But it is impossible to relate Bethos' span (from 'a boy' at the Battle of Unnumbered Tears to his death on a foray at an age sufficiently ripe to be remarked on) to Túrin's; for the events after the destruction of the Rodothlim, culminating in Túrin's rescue of Níniel after her first encounter with Glorund, cannot cover any great length of time. What is clear and certain is that in the old story Túrin died when still a very young man. According to the precise dating provided in much later writing, he was 35 years old at his death.

### (vi)   The stature of Elves and Men

The Elves are conceived to be of slighter build and stature than Men: so Beleg 'was of great stature and girth *as such was among that folk*' (p. 73), and Túrin 'was a Man and of greater stature than they', i.e. Beleg and Flinding (p. 80) – this sentence being an emendation from 'he was a Man of great size' (note 8). See on this matter I. 32, 235.

### (vii)   Winged Dragons

At the end of *The Silmarillion* (p. 252) Morgoth 'loosed upon his foes the last desperate assault that he had prepared, and out of the pits of Angband there issued the winged dragons, that had not before been seen'. The suggestion is that winged dragons were a refinement of Morgoth's original design (embodied in Glaurung, Father of Dragons who went upon his belly). According to the *Tale of Turambar* (pp. 96–7), on the other hand, among Melko's many dragons some were smaller, cold like snakes, and of these many were flying creatures; while others, the mightier, were hot and heavy, fire-dragons, and these were unwinged. As already noted (p. 125) there is no suggestion in the tale that Glorund was the first of his kind.

# III

# THE FALL' OF GONDOLIN

At the end of Eltas' account of Úrin's visit to Tinwelinc and of the strange fates of Úrin and Mavwin, Túrin and Nienóri (p. 116), the manuscript written on loose sheets in fact continues with a brief interlude in which the further course of the tale-telling is discussed in Mar Vanwa Tyaliéva.

And so saying Eltas made an end, and none asked further. But Lindo bid all thank him for his tale, and thereto he said: 'Nay, if you will, there is much yet to tell concerning the gold of Glorund, and how the evil of that worm found its last fulfilment – but behold, that is the story of the Nauglafring or the Necklace of the Dwarves and must wait a while – and other stories of lighter and more happy things I have to tell if you would liefer listen to them.'

Then arose many voices begging Eltas to tell the tale of the Nauglafring on the morrow, but he said: 'Nay! For who here knows the full tale of Tuor and the coming of Eärendel, or who was Beren Ermabwed, and what were his deeds, for such things is it better to know rightly first.' And all said that Beren Ermabwed they knew well, but of the coming of Eärendel little enough had ever been told.

'And great harm is that,' said Lindo, 'for it is the greatest of the stories of the Gnomes, and even in this house is Ilfiniol son of Bronweg, who knows those deeds more truly than any that are now on Earth.'

About that time Ilfiniol the Gong-warden entered indeed, and Lindo said to him: 'Behold, O Littleheart son of Bronweg, it is the desire of all that you tell us the tales of Tuor and of Eärendel as soon as may be.' And Ilfiniol was fain of that, but said he: 'It is a mighty tale, and seven times shall folk fare to the Tale-fire ere it be rightly told; and so twined is it with those stories of the Nauglafring and of the Elf-march[1] that I would fain have aid in that telling of Ailios here and of Meril the Lady of the Isle, for long is it since she sought this house.'

Therefore were messengers sent on the next day to the *korin*[2] of high elms, and they said that Lindo and Vairë would fain see the face of their lady among them, for they purposed to make a festival and to hold a great telling of Elfin tales, ere Eriol their guest fared awhile to Tavrobel. So was it that for three days that room heard no more tales and the folk of Vanwa Tyaliéva made great preparations, but on the fourth night Meril fared there amid her company of maidens, and full of light and mirth was that place; but after the evening meat a great host sat before Tôn a Gwedrin,[3] and the maidens of Meril sang the most beautiful songs that island knew.[4]

And of those one did afterward Heorrenda turn to the language of his folk, and it is thus.[5]

But when those songs had fallen into silence then said Meril, who sate in the chair of Lindo: 'Come now, O Ilfiniol, begin thou the tale of tales, and tell it more fully than thou hast ever done.'

Then said Littleheart son of Bronweg . . . (Tale of Gondolin). [sic]

This then is the *Link* between the *Tale of Turambar* and *The Fall of Gondolin* (an earlier 'preface' to the tale is given below). It seems that my father hesitated as to which tale was to follow *Turambar* (see note 4), but decided that it was time to introduce *The Fall of Gondolin*, which had been in existence for some time.

In this *Link*, Ailios (later Gilfanon) is present ('I would fain have aid . . . of Ailios here') at the end of Eltas' tale of Turambar, but at the beginning of Eltas' tale (p. 70) it is expressly said that he was not present that night. On the proposal that Eriol should 'fare awhile' to Tavrobel (as the guest of Gilfanon) see I.175.

The fact that Eltas speaks of the tale of Beren Ermabwed as if he did not know that it had only recently been told in Mar Vanwa Tyaliéva is no doubt to be explained by that tale not having been told before the Tale-fire (see pp. 4–7).

The teller of the tale of *The Fall of Gondolin*, Littleheart the Gong-warden of Mar Vanwa Tyaliéva, has appeared several times in the *Lost Tales*, and his Elvish name(s) have many different forms (see under *Changes made to names* at the end of the text of the tale). In *The Cottage of Lost Play* he is said (I.15) to be 'ancient beyond count', and to have 'sailed in Wingilot with Eärendel in that last voyage wherein they sought for Kôr'; and in the *Link* to *The Music of the Ainur* (I.46) he 'had a weather-worn face and blue eyes of great merriment, and was very slender and small, nor might one say if he were fifty or ten thousand'. He is a Gnome, the son of Bronweg/Voronwë (Voronwë of *The Silmarillion*) (I.48, 94).

*The texts of 'The Fall of Gondolin'*

The textual history of *The Fall of Gondolin*, if considered in detail, is extremely complex; but though I will set it out here, as I understand it, there is no need in fact for it to complicate the reading of the tale.

In the first place, there is a very difficult manuscript contained in two school exercise-books, where the title of the tale is *Tuor and the Exiles of Gondolin (which bringeth in the great tale of Eärendel)*. (This is the only title actually found in the early texts, but my father always later referred to it as *The Fall of Gondolin*.) This manuscript is (or rather, was) the original text of the tale, dating from 1916–17 (see I. 203 and *Unfinished Tales* p. 4), and I will call it here for convenience *Tuor A*. My father's treatment of it subsequently was unlike that of *Tinúviel* and *Turambar* (where the original text was erased and a new version written in its place); in this tale he did not set down a complete new text, but allowed a good deal of the old to stand, at least in the earlier part of it: as the revision progressed the rewriting in ink over the top of the pencilled text did become almost continuous, and though the pencil was not erased the ink effectively obliterates it. But even after the second version becomes continuous there are several places where the old narrative was not over-written but merely struck through, and remains legible. Thus, while *Tuor A* is on the same footing as *Tinúviel* and *Turambar* (and others of the *Lost Tales*) in that it is a later revision, a second version, my father's method in *Gondolin* allows it to be seen that here at least the revision was by no means a complete recasting (still less a re-imagining); for if those passages in the later parts of the tale which can still be compared in the two versions shew that he was following the old fairly closely, the same is quite probably true in those places where no comparison can be made.

From Tuor A, as it was *when all changes had been made to it* (i.e. when it was in the form that it has now), my mother made a fair copy (*Tuor B*), which considering the difficulty of the original is extremely exact, with only very occasional errors of transcription. I have said in *Unfinished Tales* (p. 5) that this copy was made 'apparently in 1917', but this now seems to me improbable.* Such conceptions as the Music of the Ainur, which is referred to by later addition in *Tuor A* (p. 163), *may* of course have been in my father's mind a good while before he wrote that tale in Oxford while working on the Dictionary (I. 45), but it seems more likely that the revision of *Tuor A* (and therefore also *Tuor B* copied from it after its revision) belongs to that period also.

Subsequently my father took his pencil to *Tuor B*, emending it fairly heavily, though mostly in the earlier part of the tale, and almost entirely

---

* Humphrey Carpenter in his *Biography* (p. 92) says that the tale 'was written out during Tolkien's convalescence at Great Haywood early in 1917', but he is doubtless referring to the original pencilled text of *Tuor A*.

for stylistic rather than narrative reasons; but these emendations, as will be seen, were not all made at the same time. Some of them are written out on separate slips, and of these several have on their reverse sides parts of an etymological discussion of certain Germanic words for the Butcherbird or Shrike, material which appears in the Oxford Dictionary in the entry *Wariangle*. Taken with the fact that one of the slips with this material on the reverse clearly contains a direction for the shortening of the tale when delivered orally (see note 21), it is virtually certain that a good deal of the revision of *Tuor B* was made before my father read it to the Essay Club of Exeter College in the spring of 1920 (see *Unfinished Tales* p. 5).

That not all the emendations to *Tuor B* were made at the same time is shown by the existence of a typescript (*Tuor C*), without title, which extends only so far as 'your hill of vigilance against the evil of Melko' (p. 161). This was taken from *Tuor B* when some changes had been made to it, but not those which I deduce to have been made before the occasion when it was read aloud. An odd feature of this text is that blanks were left for many of the names, and only some were filled in afterwards. Towards the end of it there is a good deal of independent variation from *Tuor B*, but it is all of a minor character and none has narrative significance. I conclude that this was a side-branch that petered out.

The textual history can then be represented thus:

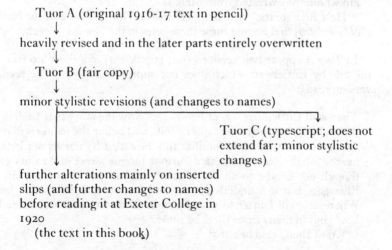

Tuor A (original 1916-17 text in pencil)
↓
heavily revised and in the later parts entirely overwritten
↓
Tuor B (fair copy)
↓
minor stylistic revisions (and changes to names)

Tuor C (typescript; does not extend far; minor stylistic changes)

further alterations mainly on inserted slips (and further changes to names) before reading it at Exeter College in 1920
    (the text in this book)

Since the narrative itself underwent very little change of note in the course of this history (granted that substantial parts of the original text *Tuor A* are almost entirely illegible), the text that follows here is that of *Tuor B* in its final form, with some interesting earlier readings given in the Notes. It seems that my father did not check the fair copy *Tuor B* against the original, and did not in every case pick up the errors of transcription it contains; when he did, he emended them anew, according to the sense, and not by reference back to *Tuor A*. In a very few cases I have gone back to *Tuor A* where this is clearly correct (as 'a wall of water rose nigh to the cliff-top', p. 151, where *Tuor B* and the typescript *Tuor C* have 'high to the cliff-top').

Throughout the typescript Tuor is called *Tûr*. In *Tuor B* the name is sometimes emended from *Tuor* to *Tûr* in the earlier part of the tale (it appears as *Tûr* in the latest revisions), but by no means in every case. My father apparently decided to change the name but ultimately decided against it; and I give *Tuor* throughout.

An interesting document accompanies the Tale: this is a substantial though incomplete list of names (with explanations) that occur in it, now in places difficult or impossible to read. The names are given in alphabetical order but go only as far as L. Linguistic information from this list is incorporated in the Appendix on Names, but the head-note to the list may be cited here:

Here is set forth by Eriol at the teaching of Bronweg's son Elfrith [*emended from* Elfriniel] or Littleheart (and he was so named for the youth and wonder of his heart) those names and words that are used in these tales from either the tongue of the Elves of Kôr as at that time spoken in the Lonely Isle, or from that related one of the Noldoli their kin whom they wrested from Melko.

Here first are they which appear in *The Tale of Tuor and the Exiles of Gondolin*, first among these those ones in the Gnome-speech.

In *Tuor A* appear two versions (one struck out) of a short 'preface' to the tale by Littleheart which does not appear in *Tuor B*. The second version reads:

Then said Littleheart son of Bronweg: 'Now the story that I tell is of the Noldoli, who were my father's folk, and belike the names will ring strange in your ears and familiar folk be called by names not before heard, for the Noldoli speak a curious tongue sweet still to my ears though not maybe to all the Eldar. Wise folk see it as close kin to Eldarissa, but it soundeth not so, and I know nought of such lore. Wherefore will I utter to you the right Eldar names where there be such, but in many cases there be none.

Know then,' said he, 'that

The earlier version (headed 'Link between *Tuor* and tale before') begins in the same way but then diverges:

... and it is sweet to my ears still, though lest it be not so to all else of Eldar and Men here gathered I will use no more of it than I must, and that is in the names of those folk and things whereof the tale tells but for which, seeing they passed away ere ever the rest of the Eldar came from Kôr, the Elves have no true names. Know then,' said he, 'that Tuor

This 'preface' thus connects to the opening of the tale. There here appears, in the second version, the name *Eldarissa* for the language of the *Eldar* or *Elves*, as opposed to *Noldorissa* (a term found in the Name-list); on the distinction involved see I.50–1. With Littleheart's words here compare what Rúmil said to Eriol about him (I.48):

'"Tongues and speeches," they will say, "one is enough for me" – and thus said Littleheart the Gong-warden once upon a time: "Gnome-speech," said he, "is enough for me – did not that one Eärendel and Tuor and Bronweg my father (that mincingly ye miscall Voronwë) speak it and no other?" Yet he had to learn the Elfin in the end, or be doomed either to silence or to leave Mar Vanwa Tyaliéva . . .'

After these lengthy preliminaries I give the text of the Tale.

★

### Tuor and the Exiles of Gondolin
*(which bringeth in the great tale of Eärendel)*

Then said Littleheart son of Bronweg: 'Know then that Tuor was a man who dwelt in very ancient days in that land of the North called Dor Lómin or the Land of Shadows, and of the Eldar the Noldoli know it best.

Now the folk whence Tuor came wandered the forests and fells and knew not and sang not of the sea; but Tuor dwelt not with them, and lived alone about that lake called Mithrim, now hunting in its woods, now making music beside its shores on his rugged harp of wood and the sinews of bears. Now many hearing of the power of his rough songs came from near and far to hearken to his harping, but Tuor left his singing and departed to lonely places. Here he learnt many strange things and got knowledge of the wandering Noldoli, who taught him much of their speech and lore; but he was not fated to dwell for ever in those woods.

Thereafter 'tis said that magic and destiny led him on a day to a cavernous opening down which a hidden river flowed from Mithrim. And Tuor entered that cavern seeking to learn its secret, but the waters of Mithrim drove him forward into the heart of the rock and he might not win back into the light. And this, 'tis said, was the will of Ulmo Lord of Waters at whose prompting the Noldoli had made that hidden way.

Then came the Noldoli to Tuor and guided him along dark passages amid the mountains until he came out in the light once more, and saw that the river flowed swiftly in a ravine of great depth with sides unscalable. Now Tuor desired no more to return but went ever forward, and the river led him always toward the west.[6]

The sun rose behind his back and set before his face, and where the water foamed among many boulders or fell over falls there were at times rainbows woven across the ravine, but at evening its smooth sides would glow in the setting sun, and for these reasons Tuor called it Golden Cleft or the Gully of the Rainbow Roof, which is in the speech of the Gnomes Glorfalc or Cris Ilbranteloth.

Now Tuor journeyed here for three days,[7] drinking the waters of the secret river and feeding on its fish; and these were of gold and blue and silver and of many wondrous shapes. At length the ravine widened, and ever as it opened its sides became lower and more rough, and the bed of the river more impeded with boulders against which the waters foamed and spouted. Long times would Tuor sit and gaze at the splashing water and listen to its voice, and then he would rise and leap onward from stone to stone singing as he went; or as the stars came out in the narrow strip of heaven above the gully he would raise echoes to answer the fierce twanging of his harp.

One day after a great journey of weary going Tuor at deep evening heard a cry, and he might not decide of what creature it came. Now he said: "It is a fay-creature", now, "Nay, 'tis but some small beast that waileth among the rocks"; or again it seemed to him that an unknown bird piped with a voice new to his ears and strangely sad – and because he had not heard the voice of any bird in all his wandering down Golden Cleft he was glad of the sound although it was mournful. On the next day at an hour of the morning he heard the same cry above his head, and looking up beheld three great white birds beating back up the gully on strong wing, and uttering cries like to the ones he had heard amid the dusk. Now these were the gulls, the birds of Ossë.[8]

In this part of that riverway there were islets of rock amid the currents, and fallen rocks fringed with white sand at the gully-side, so that it was ill-going, and seeking a while Tuor found a spot where he might with labour scale the cliffs at last. Then came a fresh wind against his face, and he said: "This is very good and like the drinking of wine," but he knew not that he was near the confines of the Great Sea.

As he went along above the waters that ravine again drew together and the walls towered up, so that he fared on a high cliff-top, and there came a narrow neck, and this was full of noise. Then Tuor looking downward saw the greatest of marvels, for it seemed that a flood of angry water would come up the narrows and flow back against the river to its source, but that water which had come down from distant Mithrim would still press on, and a wall of water rose nigh to the cliff-top, and it was crowned with foam and twisted by the winds. Then the waters of Mithrim were overthrown and the incoming flood swept roaring up the channel and whelmed the rocky islets and churned the white sand – so that Tuor fled and was afraid, who did not know the ways of the sea; but the Ainur put it into his heart to climb from the gully when he did, or had he been whelmed in the incoming tide, and that was a fierce one by reason of a wind from the west. Then Tuor found himself in a rugged country bare of trees, and swept by a wind coming from the set of the sun, and all the shrubs and bushes leaned to the dawn because of that prevalence of that wind. And here for a while he wandered till he came to the black cliffs by the sea and saw the ocean and its waves for the first time, and at that hour the sun sank beyond the rim of Earth far out to sea, and he stood on the cliff-top with outspread arms, and his heart was filled with a longing very great indeed. Now some say that he was the first of Men to reach the Sea and look upon it and know the desire it brings; but I know not if they say well.

In those regions he set up his abode, dwelling in a cove sheltered by great sable rocks, whose floor was of white sand, save when the high flood partly overspread it with blue water; nor did foam or froth come there save at times of the direst tempest. There long he sojourned alone and roamed about the shore or fared over the rocks at the ebb, marvelling at the pools and the great weeds, the dripping caverns and the strange sea-fowl that he saw and came to know; but the rise and fall of the water and the voice of the waves was ever to him the greatest wonder and ever did it seem a new and unimaginable thing.

Now on the quiet waters of Mithrim over which the voice of the duck or moorhen would carry far he had fared much in a small boat with a prow fashioned like to the neck of a swan, and this he had lost on the day of his finding the hidden river. On the sea he adventured not as yet, though his heart was ever egging him with a strange longing thereto, and on quiet evenings when the sun went down beyond the edge of the sea it grew to a fierce desire.

Timber he had that came down the hidden river; a goodly wood it was, for the Noldoli hewed it in the forests of Dor Lómin and floated it to him of a purpose. But he built not as yet aught save a dwelling in a sheltered place of his cove, which tales among the Eldar since name Falasquil. This by slow labour he adorned with fair carvings of the beasts and trees and flowers and birds that he knew about the waters of Mithrim, and ever among them was the Swan the chief, for Tuor loved this emblem and it became the sign of himself, his kindred and folk thereafter. There he passed a very great while until the loneliness of the empty sea got into his heart, and even Tuor the solitary longed for the voice of Men. Herewith the Ainur[9] had something to do: for Ulmo loved Tuor.

One morning while casting his eye along the shore – and it was then the latest days of summer – Tuor saw three swans flying high and strong from the northward. Now these birds he had not before seen in these regions, and he took them for a sign, and said: "Long has my heart been set on a journey far from here; lo! now at length I will follow these swans." Behold, the swans dropped into the water of his cove and there swimming thrice about rose again and winged slowly south along the coast, and Tuor bearing his harp and spear followed them.

'Twas a great day's journey Tuor put behind him that day; and he came ere evening to a region where trees again appeared, and the manner of the land through which he now fared differed greatly from those shores about Falasquil. There had Tuor known mighty cliffs beset with caverns and great spoutholes, and deep-walled coves, but from the cliff-tops a rugged land and flat ran bleakly back to where a blue rim far to the east spake of distant hills. Now however did he see a long and sloping shore and stretches of sand, while the distant hills marched ever nearer to the margin of the sea, and their dark slopes were clad with pine or fir and about their feet sprang birches and ancient oaks. From the feet of the hills fresh torrents rushed down narrow chasms and so found the shores and the salt waves. Now some of these clefts Tuor might not overleap, and often was it ill-going in these places, but still he laboured on, for the swans fared ever before him, now circling suddenly, now speeding forward, but never coming to earth, and the rush of their strong-beating wings encouraged him.

'Tis told that in this manner Tuor fared onward for a great

number of days, and that winter marched from the north somewhat speedier than he for all his tirelessness. Nevertheless came he
without scathe of beast or weather at a time of first spring to a river
mouth. Now here was the land less northerly and more kindly
than about the issuing of Golden Cleft, and moreover by a trend of
the coast was the sea now rather to the south of him than to the
west, as he could mark by the sun and stars; but he had kept his
right hand always to the sea.

This river flowed down a goodly channel and on its banks were
rich lands: grasses and moist meadow to the one side and tree-
grown slopes of the other; its waters met the sea sluggishly and
fought not as the waters of Mithrim in the north. Long tongues of
land lay islanded in its course covered with reeds and bushy
thicket, until further to seaward sandy spits ran out; and these
were places beloved by such a multitude of birds as Tuor had
nowhere yet encountered. Their piping and wailing and whistling
filled the air; and here amid their white wings Tuor lost sight of
the three swans, nor saw he them again.

Then did Tuor grow for a season weary of the sea, for the
buffeting of his travel had been sore. Nor was this without Ulmo's
devising, and that night the Noldoli came to him and he arose
from sleep. Guided by their blue lanterns he found a way beside
the river border, and strode so mightily inland that when dawn
filled the sky to his right hand lo! the sea and its voice were far
behind him, and the wind came from before him so that its odour
was not even in the air. Thus came he soon to that region that has
been called Arlisgion "the place of reeds", and this is in those lands
that are to the south of Dor Lómin and separated therefrom by the
Iron Mountains whose spurs run even to the sea. From those
mountains came this river, and of a great clearness and marvellous
chill were its waters even at this place. Now this is a river most
famous in the histories of Eldar and Noldoli and in all tongues is it
named Sirion. Here Tuor rested awhile until driven by desire he
arose once more to journey further and further by many days'
marches along the river borders. Full spring had not yet brought
summer when he came to a region yet more lovely. Here the song
of small birds shrilled about him with a music of loveliness, for
there are no birds that sing like the songbirds of the Land of
Willows; and to this region of wonder he had now come. Here the
river wound in wide curves with low banks through a great plain of
the sweetest grass and very long and green; willows of untold age
were about its borders, and its wide bosom was strewn with

waterlily leaves, whose flowers were not yet in the earliness of the year, but beneath the willows the green swords of the flaglilies were drawn, and sedges stood, and reeds in embattled array. Now there dwelt in these dark places a spirit of whispers, and it whispered to Tuor at dusk and he was loth to depart; and at morn for the glory of the unnumbered buttercups he was yet more loth, and he tarried.

Here saw he the first butterflies and was glad of the sight; and it is said that all butterflies and their kindred were born in the valley of the Land of Willows. Then came the summer and the time of moths and the warm evenings, and Tuor wondered at the multitude of flies, at their buzzing and the droning of the beetles and the hum of bees; and to all these things he gave names of his own, and wove the names into new songs on his old harp; and these songs were softer than his singing of old.

Then Ulmo grew in dread lest Tuor dwell for ever here and the great things of his design come not to fulfilment. Therefore he feared longer to trust Tuor's guidance to the Noldoli alone, who did service to him in secret, and out of fear of Melko wavered much. Nor were they strong against the magic of that place of willows, for very great was its enchantment. Did not even after the days of Tuor Noldorin and his Eldar come there seeking for Dor Lómin and the hidden river and the caverns of the Gnomes' imprisonment; yet thus nigh to their quest's end were like to abandon it? Indeed sleeping and dancing here, and making fair music of river sounds and the murmur of grass, and weaving rich fabrics of gossamer and the feathers of winged insects, they were whelmed by the goblins sped by Melko from the Hills of Iron and Noldorin made bare escape thence. But these things were not as yet.

Behold now Ulmo leapt upon his car before the doorway of his palace below the still waters of the Outer Sea; and his car was drawn by narwhal and sealion and was in fashion like a whale; and amidst the sounding of great conches he sped from Ulmonan. So great was the speed of his going that in days, and not in years without count as might be thought, he reached the mouth of the river. Up this his car might not fare without hurt to its water and its banks; therefore Ulmo, loving all rivers and this one more than most, went thence on foot, robed to the middle in mail like the scales of blue and silver fishes; but his hair was a bluish silver and his beard to his feet was of the same hue, and he bore neither helm nor crown. Beneath his mail fell the skirts of his kirtle of shimmering greens, and of what substance these were woven is not known, but whoso looked into the depths of their subtle colours seemed to behold the faint movements of deep waters shot with the stealthy lights of phosphorescent fish that live in the abyss. Girt was he with a rope of mighty pearls, and he was shod with mighty shoes of stone.

Thither he bore too his great instrument of music; and this was of strange design, for it was made of many long twisted shells pierced with holes. Blowing therein and playing with his long fingers he made deep melodies of a magic greater than any other among musicians hath ever compassed on harp or lute, on lyre or pipe, or instruments of the bow. Then coming along the river he sate among the reeds at twilight and played upon his thing of shells; and it was nigh to those places where Tuor tarried. And Tuor hearkened and was stricken dumb. There he stood knee-deep in the grass and heard no more the hum of insects, nor the murmur of the river borders, and the odour of flowers entered not into his nostrils; but he heard the sound of waves and the wail of sea-birds, and his soul leapt for rocky places and the ledges that reek of fish, for the splash of the diving cormorant and those places where the sea bores into the black cliffs and yells aloud.

Then Ulmo arose and spake to him and for dread he came near to death, for the depth of the voice of Ulmo is of the uttermost depth: even as deep as his eyes which are the deepest of all things. And Ulmo said: "O Tuor of the lonely heart, I will not that thou dwell for ever in fair places of birds and flowers; nor would I lead thee through this pleasant land,[10] but that so it must be. But fare now on thy destined journey and tarry not, for far from hence is thy weird set. Now must thou seek through the lands for the city of the folk called Gondothlim or the dwellers in stone, and the Noldoli shall escort thee thither in secret for fear of the spies of Melko. Words I will set to your mouth there, and there you shall abide awhile. Yet maybe thy life shall turn again to the mighty waters; and of a surety a child shall come of thee than whom no man shall know more of the uttermost deeps, be it of the sea or of the firmament of heaven." Then spake Ulmo also to Tuor some of his design and desire, but thereof Tuor understood little at that time and feared greatly.

Then Ulmo was wrapped in a mist as it were of sea air in those inland places, and Tuor, with that music in his ears, would fain return to the regions of the Great Sea; yet remembering his bidding turned and went inland along the river, and so fared till day. Yet he that has heard the conches of Ulmo hears them call him till death, and so did Tuor find.

When day came he was weary and slept till it was nigh dusk again, and the Noldoli came to him and guided him. So fared he many days by dusk and dark and slept by day, and because of this it came afterwards that he remembered not over well the paths that he traversed in those times. Now Tuor and his guides held on untiring, and the land became one of rolling hills and the river wound about their feet, and there were many dales of exceeding pleasantness; but here the Noldoli became ill at ease. "These," said they, "are the confines of those regions which Melko infesteth with his Goblins, the people of hate. Far to the north — yet alas not far enough, would they were ten thousand leagues — lie the Mountains of Iron where sits the power and terror of Melko, whose thralls we are. Indeed in this guiding of thee we do in secret from him, and did he know all our purposes the torment of the Balrogs would be ours."

Falling then into such fear the Noldoli soon after left him and he fared alone amid the hills, and their going proved ill afterwards, for "Melko has many eyes", 'tis said, and while Tuor fared with the Gnomes they took him twilight ways and by many secret tunnels through the hills. But now he became lost, and climbed often to the tops of knolls and hills scanning the lands about. Yet he might not see signs of any dwelling of folk, and indeed the city of the Gondothlim was not found with ease, seeing that Melko and his spies had not even yet discovered it. 'Tis said nonetheless that at this time those spies got wind thus that the strange foot of Man had been set in those lands, and that for that Melko doubled his craft and watchfulness.

Now when the Gnomes out of fear deserted Tuor, one Voronwë or Bronweg followed afar off despite his fear, when chiding availed not to enhearten the others. Now Tuor had fallen into a great weariness and was sitting beside the rushing stream, and the sea-longing was about his heart, and he was minded once more to follow this river back to the wide waters and the roaring waves. But this Voronwë the faithful came up with him again, and standing by his ear said: "O Tuor, think not but that thou shalt again one day see thy desire; arise now, and behold, I will not leave thee. I am not of the road-learned of the Noldoli, being a craftsman and maker of things made by hand of wood and of metal, and I joined not the band of escort till late. Yet of old have I heard whispers and sayings said in secret amid the weariness of thraldom, concerning a city where Noldoli might be free could they find the hidden way thereto; and we twain may without a doubt [11] find the road to the City of Stone, where is that freedom of the Gondothlim."

Know then that the Gondothlim were that kin of the Noldoli who alone escaped Melko's power when at the Battle of Unnumbered Tears he slew and enslaved their folk [12] and wove spells about them and caused them to dwell in the Hells of Iron, faring thence at his will and bidding only.

Long time did Tuor and Bronweg [13] seek for the city of that folk, until after many days they came upon a deep dale amid the hills. Here went the river over a very stony bed with much rush and noise, and it was curtained with a heavy growth of alders; but the walls of the dale were sheer, for they were nigh to some mountains which Voronwë knew not. There in the green wall that Gnome found an opening like a great door with sloping sides, and this was cloaked with thick bushes and long-tangled undergrowth; yet Voronwë's piercing sight might not be deceived. Nonetheless 'tis said that such a magic had its builders set about it (by aid of Ulmo whose power ran in that river even if the dread of Melko fared upon its banks) that none save of the blood of the Noldoli might light on it thus by chance; nor would Tuor have found it ever but for the steadfastness of that Gnome Voronwë. [14] Now the Gondothlim made their abode thus secret out of dread of Melko; yet even so no few of the braver Noldoli would slip down the river Sirion from those mountains, and if many perished so by Melko's evil, many finding this magic passage came at last to the City of Stone and swelled its people.

Greatly did Tuor and Voronwë rejoice to find this gate, yet entering they found there a way dark, rough-going, and circuitous; and long time they travelled faltering within its tunnels. It was full of fearsome echoes, and there a countless stepping of feet would come behind them, so that Voronwë became adread, and said: "It is Melko's goblins, the Orcs of the hills." Then would they run, falling over stones in the blackness, till they perceived it was but the deceit of the place. Thus did they come, after it seemed a measureless time of fearful groping, to a place where a far light glimmered, and making for this gleam they came to a gate like that by which they had entered, but in no way overgrown. Then they passed into the sunlight and could for a while see nought, but instantly a great gong sounded and there was a clash of armour, and behold, they were surrounded by warriors in steel.

Then they looked up and could see, and lo! they were at the foot of steep hills, and these hills made a great circle wherein lay a wide plain, and set therein, not rightly at the midmost but rather nearer to that place where they stood, was a great hill with a level top, and upon that summit rose a city in the new light of the morning.

Then Voronwë spake to the Guard of the Gondothlim, and his speech they comprehended, for it was the sweet tongue of the Gnomes.[15] Then spake Tuor also and questioned where they might be, and who might be the folk in arms who stood about, for he was somewhat in amaze and wondered much at the goodly fashion of their weapons. Then 'twas said to him by one of that company: "We are the guardians of the issue of the Way of Escape. Rejoice that ye have found it, for behold before you the City of Seven Names where all who war with Melko may find hope."

Then said Tuor: "What be those names?" And the chief of the Guard made answer: "'Tis said and 'tis sung: 'Gondobar am I called and Gondothlimbar, City of Stone and City of the Dwellers in Stone; Gondolin the Stone of Song and Gwarestrin am I named, the Tower of Guard, Gar Thurion or the Secret Place, for I am hidden from the eyes of Melko; but they who love me most greatly call me Loth, for like a flower am I, even Lothengriol the flower that blooms on the plain.' Yet," said he, "in our daily speech we speak and we name it mostly Gondolin." Then said Voronwë: "Bring us thither, for we fain would enter," and Tuor said that his heart desired much to tread the ways of that fair city.

Then said the chief of the Guard that they themselves must abide here, for there were yet many days of their moon of watch to pass, but that Voronwë and Tuor might pass on to Gondolin; and moreover that they would need thereto no guide, for "Lo, it stands fair to see and very clear, and its towers prick the heavens above the Hill of Watch in the midmost plain." Then Tuor and his companion fared over the plain that was of a marvellous level, broken but here and there by boulders round and smooth which lay amid a sward, or by pools in rocky beds. Many fair pathways lay across that plain, and they came after a day's light march to the foot of the Hill of Watch (which is in the tongue of the Noldoli Amon Gwareth). Then did they begin to ascend the winding stairways which climbed up to the city gate; nor might any one reach that city save on foot and espied from the walls. As the westward gate was golden in the last sunlight did they come to the long stair's head, and many eyes gazed[16] upon them from the battlements and towers.

But Tuor looked upon the walls of stone, and the uplifted towers, upon the glistering pinnacles of the town, and he looked upon the stairs of stone and marble, bordered by slender balustrades and cooled by the leap of threadlike waterfalls seeking the plain from the fountains of Amon Gwareth, and he fared as one in some dream of the Gods, for he deemed not such things were seen by men in the visions of their sleep, so great was his amaze at the glory of Gondolin.

Even so came they to the gates, Tuor in wonder and Voronwë in great joy that daring much he had both brought Tuor hither in the will of Ulmo and had himself thrown off the yoke of Melko for ever. Though he hated him no wise less, no longer did he dread that Evil One[17] with a binding terror (and of a sooth that spell which Melko held over the Noldoli was one of bottomless dread, so that he seemed ever nigh them even were they far from the Hells of Iron, and their hearts quaked and they fled not even when they could; and to this Melko trusted often).

Now is there a sally from the gates of Gondolin and a throng comes about these twain in wonder, rejoicing that yet another of the Noldoli has fled hither from Melko, and marvelling at the stature and the gaunt limbs of Tuor, his heavy spear barbed with fish bone and his great harp. Rugged was his aspect, and his locks were unkempt, and he was clad in the skins of bears. 'Tis written that in those days the fathers of the fathers of Men were of less stature than Men now are, and the children of Elfinesse of greater growth, yet was Tuor taller than any that stood there. Indeed the Gondothlim were not bent of back as some of their unhappy kin became, labouring without rest at delving and hammering for Melko, but small were they and slender and very lithe.[18] They were swift of foot and surpassing fair; sweet and sad were their mouths, and their eyes had ever a joy within quivering to tears; for in those times the Gnomes were exiles at heart, haunted with a desire for their ancient home that faded not. But fate and unconquerable eagerness after knowledge had driven them into far places, and now were they hemmed by Melko and must make their abiding as fair as they might by labour and by love.

How it came ever that among Men the Noldoli have been confused with the Orcs who are Melko's goblins, I know not, unless it be that certain of the Noldoli were twisted to the evil of Melko and mingled among these Orcs, for all that race were bred by Melko of the subterranean heats and şlime. Their hearts were of granite and their bodies deformed; foul their faces which smiled

not, but their laugh that of the clash of metal, and to nothing were
they more fain than to aid in the basest of the purposes of Melko.
The greatest hatred was between them and the Noldoli, who
named them Glamhoth, or folk of dreadful hate.

Behold, the armed' guardians of the gate pressed back the
thronging folk that gathered about the wanderers, and one among
them spake saying: "This is a city of watch and ward, Gondolin on
Amon Gwareth, where all may be free who are of true heart, but
none may be free to enter unknown. Tell me then your names."
But Voronwë named himself Bronweg of the Gnomes, come
hither[19] by the will of Ulmo as guide to this son of Men; and Tuor
said: "I am Tuor son of Peleg son of Indor of the house of the
Swan of the sons of the Men of the North who live far hence, and I
fare hither by the will of Ulmo of the Outer Oceans."

Then all who listened grew silent, and his deep and rolling voice
held them in amaze, for their own voices were fair as the plash of
fountains. Then a saying arose among them: "Lead him before the
king."

Then did the throng return within the gates and the wanderers
with them, and Tuor saw they were of iron and of great height
and strength. Now the streets of Gondolin were paved with
stone and wide, kerbed with marble, and fair houses and courts
amid gardens of bright flowers were set about the ways, and many
towers of great slenderness and beauty builded of white marble
and carved most marvellously rose to the heaven. Squares there
were lit with fountains and the home of birds that sang amid the
branches of their aged trees, but of all these the greatest was that
place where stood the king's palace, and the tower thereof was the
loftiest in the city, and the fountains that played before the doors
shot twenty fathoms and seven in the air and fell in a singing rain
of crystal: therein did the sun glitter splendidly by day, and the
moon most magically shimmered by night. The birds that dwelt
there were of the whiteness of snow and their voices sweeter than a
lullaby of music.

On either side of the doors of the palace were two trees, one
that bore blossom of gold and the other of silver, nor did
they ever fade, for they were shoots of old from the glorious Trees
of Valinor that lit those places before Melko and Gloomweaver
withered them: and those trees the Gondothlim named Glingol
and Bansil.

Then Turgon king of Gondolin robed in white with a belt of
gold, and a coronet of garnets was upon his head, stood before

his doors and spake from the head of the white stairs that led thereto. "Welcome, O Man of the Land of Shadows. Lo! thy coming was set in our books of wisdom, and it has been written that there would come to pass many great things in the homes of the Gondothlim whenso thou faredst hither."

Then spake Tuor, and Ulmo set power in his heart and majesty in his voice. "Behold, O father of the City of Stone, I am bidden by him who maketh deep music in the Abyss, and who knoweth the mind of Elves and Men, to say unto thee that the days of Release draw nigh. There have come to the ears of Ulmo whispers of your dwelling and your hill of vigilance against the evil of Melko, and he is glad: but his heart is wroth and the hearts of the Valar are angered who sit in the mountains of Valinor and look upon the world from the peak of Taniquetil, seeing the sorrow of the thraldom of the Noldoli and the wanderings of Men; for Melko ringeth them in the Land of Shadows beyond hills of iron. Therefore have I been brought by a secret way to bid you number your hosts and prepare for battle, for the time is ripe."

Then spake Turgon: "That will I not do, though it be the words of Ulmo and all the Valar. I will not adventure this my people against the terror of the Orcs, nor emperil my city against the fire of Melko."

Then spake Tuor: "Nay, if thou dost not now dare greatly then will the Orcs dwell for ever and possess in the end most of the mountains of the Earth, and cease not to trouble both Elves and Men, even though by other means the Valar contrive hereafter to release the Noldoli; but if thou trust now to the Valar, though terrible the encounter, then shall the Orcs fall, and Melko's power be minished to a little thing."

But Turgon said that he was king of Gondolin and no will should force him against his counsel to emperil the dear labour of long ages gone; but Tuor said, for thus was he bidden by Ulmo who had feared the reluctance of Turgon: "Then am I bidden to say that men of the Gondothlim repair swiftly and secretly down the river Sirion to the sea, and there build them boats and go seek back to Valinor: lo! the paths thereto are forgotten and the highways faded from the world, and the seas and mountains are about it, yet still dwell there the Elves on the hill of Kôr and the Gods sit in Valinor, though their mirth is minished for sorrow and fear of Melko, and they hide their land and weave about it inaccessible magic that no evil come to its shores. Yet still might thy messengers win there and turn their hearts that they rise in wrath and smite Melko, and destroy the Hells of Iron that he has wrought beneath the Mountains of Darkness."

Then said Turgon: "Every year at the lifting of winter have messengers repaired swiftly and by stealth down the river that is called Sirion to the coasts of the Great Sea, and there builded them boats whereto have swans and gulls been harnessed or the strong wings of the wind, and these have sought back beyond the moon and sun to Valinor; but the paths thereto are forgotten and the highways faded from the world, and the seas and mountains are about it, and they that sit within in mirth reck little of the dread of Melko or the sorrow of the world, but hide their land and weave about it inaccessible magic, that no tidings of evil come ever to their ears. Nay, enough of my people have for years untold gone out to the wide waters never to return, but have perished in the deep places or wander now lost in the shadows that have no paths; and at the coming of next year no more shall fare to the sea, but rather will we trust to ourselves and our city for the warding off of Melko; and thereto have the Valar been of scant help aforetime."

Then Tuor's heart was heavy, and Voronwë wept; and Tuor sat by the great fountain of the king and its splashing recalled the music of the waves, and his soul was troubled by the conches of Ulmo and he would return down the waters of Sirion to the sea. But Turgon, who knew that Tuor, mortal as he was, had the favour of the Valar, marking his stout glance and the power of his voice sent to him and bade him dwell in Gondolin and be in his favour, and abide even within the royal halls if he would.

Then Tuor, for he was weary, and that place was fair, said yea; and hence cometh the abiding of Tuor in Gondolin. Of all Tuor's deeds among the Gondothlim the tales tell not, but 'tis said that many a time would he have stolen thence, growing weary of the concourses of folk, and thinking of empty forest and fell or hearing afar the sea-music of Ulmo, had not his heart been filled with love for a woman of the Gondothlim, and she was a daughter of the king.

Now Tuor learnt many things in those realms taught by Voronwë whom he loved, and who loved him exceeding greatly in return; or else was he instructed by the skilled men of the city and the wise men of the king. Wherefore he became a man far mightier than aforetime and wisdom was in his counsel; and many things became clear to him that were unclear before, and many things known that are still unknown to mortal Men. There he heard concerning that city of Gondolin and how

unstaying labour through ages of years had not sufficed to its
building and adornment whereat folk [20] travailed yet; of the delving of that hidden tunnel he heard, which the folk named the Way
of Escape, and how there had been divided counsels in that
matter, yet pity for the enthralled Noldoli had prevailed in the end
to its making; of the guard without ceasing he was told, that
was held there in arms and likewise at certain low places in the
encircling mountains, and how watchers dwelt ever vigilant on
the highest peaks of that range beside builded beacons ready
for the fire; for never did that folk cease to look for an onslaught
of the Orcs did their stronghold become known.

Now however was the guard of the hills maintained rather by
custom than necessity, for the Gondothlim had long ago with
unimagined toil levelled and cleared and delved all that plain
about Amon Gwareth, so that scarce Gnome or bird or beast or
snake could approach but was espied from many leagues off, for
among the Gondothlim were many whose eyes were keener than
the very hawks of Manwë Súlimo Lord of Gods and Elves who
dwells upon Taniquetil; and for this reason did they call that
vale Tumladin or the valley of smoothness. Now this great work
was finished to their mind, and folk were the busier about the
quarrying of metals and the forging of all manner of swords and
axes, spears and bills, and the fashioning of coats of mail,
byrnies and hauberks, greaves and vambraces, helms and shields.
Now 'twas said to Tuor that already the whole folk of Gondolin
shooting with bows without stay day or night might not expend
their hoarded arrows in many years, and that yearly their fear of
the Orcs grew the less for this.

There learnt Tuor of building with stone, of masonry and the
hewing of rock and marble; crafts of weaving and spinning,
broidure and painting, did he fathom, and cunning in metals.
Musics most delicate he there heard; and in these were they who
dwelt in the southern city the most deeply skilled, for there played
a profusion of murmuring founts and springs. Many of these
subtleties Tuor mastered and learned to entwine with his songs to
the wonder and heart's joy of all who heard. Strange stories of the
Sun and Moon and Stars, of the manner of the Earth and its
elements, and of the depths of heaven, were told to him; and the
secret characters of the Elves he learnt, and their speeches and old
tongues, and heard tell of Ilúvatar, the Lord for Always, who
dwelleth beyond the world, of the great music of the Ainur about
Ilúvatar's feet in the uttermost deeps of time, whence came the

making of the world and the manner of it, and all therein and their governance.[21]

Now for his skill and his great mastery over all lore and craft whatsoever, and his great courage of heart and body, did Tuor become a comfort and stay to the king who had no son; and he was beloved by the folk of Gondolin. Upon a time the king caused his most cunning artificers to fashion a suit of armour for Tuor as a great gift, and it was made of Gnome-steel overlaid with silver; but his helm was adorned with a device of metals and jewels like to two swan-wings, one on either side, and a swan's wing was wrought on his shield; but he carried an axe rather than a sword, and this in the speech of the Gondothlim he named Dramborleg, for its buffet stunned and its edge clove all armour.

A house was built for him upon the southern walls, for he loved the free airs and liked not the close neighbourhood of other dwellings. There it was his delight often to stand on the battlements at dawn, and folk rejoiced to see the new light catch the wings of his helm – and many murmured and would fain have backed him into battle with the Orcs, seeing that the speeches of those two, Tuor and Turgon, before the palace were known to many; but this matter went not further for reverence of Turgon, and because at this time in Tuor's heart the thought of the words of Ulmo seemed to have grown dim and far off.

Now came days when Tuor had dwelt among the Gondothlim many years. Long had he known and cherished a love for the king's daughter, and now was his heart full of that love. Great love too had Idril for Tuor, and the strands of her fate were woven with his even from that day when first she gazed upon him from a high window as he stood a way-worn suppliant before the palace of the king. Little cause had Turgon to withstand their love, for he saw in Tuor a kinsman of comfort and great hope. Thus was first wed a child of Men with a daughter of Elfinesse, nor was Tuor the last. Less bliss have many had than they, and their sorrow in the end was great. Yet great was the mirth of those days when Idril and Tuor were wed before the folk in Gar Ainion, the Place of the Gods, nigh to the king's halls. A day of merriment was that wedding to the city of Gondolin, and of[22] the greatest happiness to Tuor and Idril. Thereafter dwelt they in joy in that house upon the walls that looked out south over Tumladin, and this was good to the hearts of all in the city save Meglin alone. Now that Gnome was come of an ancient house, though now were its numbers less

than others, but he himself was nephew to the king by his mother
the king's sister Isfin; and that tale of Isfin and Eöl may not here be
told.[23]

Now the sign of Meglin was a sable Mole, and he was great
among quarrymen and a chief of the delvers after ore; and many of
these belonged to his house. Less fair was he than most of this
goodly folk, swart and of none too kindly mood, so that he won
small love, and whispers there were that he had Orc's blood in his
veins, but I know not how this could be true. Now he had bid
often with the king for the hand of Idril, yet Turgon finding her
very loth had as often said nay, for him seemed Meglin's suit was
caused as much by the desire of standing in high power beside the
royal throne as by love of that most fair maid. Fair indeed was
she and brave thereto; and the people called her Idril of the
Silver Feet* in that she went ever barefoot and bareheaded, king's
daughter as she was, save only at pomps of the Ainur; and Meglin
gnawed his anger seeing Tuor thrust him out.

In these days came to pass the fulfilment of the time of the
desire of the Valar and the hope of [the] Eldalië, for in great love
Idril bore to Tuor a son and he was called Eärendel. Now thereto
there are many interpretations both among Elves and Men, but
belike it was a name wrought of some secret tongue among the
Gondothlim[24] and that has perished with them from the dwellings
of the Earth.

Now this babe was of greatest beauty; his skin of a shining white
and his eyes of a blue surpassing that of the sky in southern lands –
bluer than the sapphires of the raiment of Manwë;[25] and the envy
of Meglin was deep at his birth, but the joy of Turgon and all the
people very great indeed.

Behold now many years have gone since Tuor was lost amid the
foothills and deserted by those Noldoli; yet many years too have
gone since to Melko's ears came first those strange tidings – faint
were they and various in form – of a Man wandering amid the
dales of the waters of Sirion. Now Melko was not much afraid of
the race of Men in those days of his great power, and for this
reason did Ulmo work through one of this kindred for the better
deceiving of Melko, seeing that no Valar and scarce any of the
Eldar or Noldoli might stir unmarked of his vigilance. Yet nonetheless foreboding smote that ill heart at the tidings, and he got
together a mighty army of spies: sons of the Orcs were there with

---

* Faintly pencilled above in *Tuor B: Idril Talceleb.*

eyes of yellow and green like cats that could pierce all glooms and
see through mist or fog or night; snakes that could go everywhither
and search all crannies or the deepest pits or the highest peaks,
listen to every whisper that ran in the grass or echoed in the hills;
wolves there were and ravening dogs and great weasels full of the
thirst of blood whose nostrils could take scent moons old through
running water, or whose eyes find among shingle footsteps that
had passed a lifetime since; owls came and falcons whose keen
glance might descry by day or night the fluttering of small birds in
all the woods of the world, and the movement of every mouse or
vole or rat that crept or dwelt throughout the Earth. All these he
summoned to his Hall of Iron, and they came in multitudes.
Thence he sent them over the Earth to seek this Man who had
escaped from the Land of Shadows, but yet far more curiously and
intently to search out the dwelling of the Noldoli that had escaped
his thraldom; for these his heart burnt to destroy or to enslave.

Now while Tuor dwelt in happiness and in great increase of
knowledge and might in Gondolin, these creatures through the
years untiring nosed among the stones and rocks, hunted
the forests and the heaths, espied the airs and lofty places,
tracked all paths about the dales and plains, and neither let
nor stayed. From this hunt they brought a wealth of tidings to
Melko – indeed among many hidden things that they dragged
to light they discovered that Way of Escape whereby Tuor
and Voronwë entered aforetime. Nor had they done so save by
constraining some of the less stout of the Noldoli with dire threats
of torment to join in that great ransacking; for because of the
magic about that gate no folk of Melko unaided by the Gnomes
could come to it. Yet now they had pried of late far into its
tunnels and captured within many of the Noldoli creeping there to
flee from thraldom. They had scaled too the Encircling Hills*
at certain places and gazed upon the beauty of the city of
Gondolin and the strength of Amon Gwareth from afar; but into
the plain they could not win for the vigilance of its guardians and
the difficulty of those mountains. Indeed the Gondothlim were
mighty archers, and bows they made of a marvel of power.
Therewith might they shoot an arrow into heaven seven times as
far as could the best bowman among Men shoot at a mark upon the
ground; and they would have suffered no falcon to hover long over
their plain or snake to crawl therein; for they liked not creatures of
blood, broodlings of Melko.

* Pencilled above in *Tuor B: Heborodin.*

Now in those days was Eärendel one year old when these ill tidings came to that city of the spies of Melko and how they encompassed the vale of Tumladin around. Then Turgon's heart was saddened, remembering the words of Tuor in past years before the palace doors; and he caused the watch and ward to be thrice strengthened at all points, and engines of war to be devised by his artificers and set upon the hill. Poisonous fires and hot liquids, arrows and great rocks, was he prepared to shoot down on any who would assail those gleaming walls; and then he abode as well content as might be, but Tuor's heart was heavier than the king's, for now the words of Ulmo came ever to his mind, and their purport and gravity he understood more deeply than of old; nor did he find any great comfort in Idril, for her heart boded more darkly even than his own.

Know then that Idril had a great power of piercing with her thought the darkness of the hearts of Elves and Men, and the glooms of the future thereto – further even than is the common power of the kindreds of the Eldalië; therefore she spake thus on a day to Tuor: "Know, my husband, that my heart misgives me for doubt of Meglin, and I fear that he will bring an ill on this fair realm, though by no means may I see how or when – yet I dread lest all that he knows of our doings and preparations become in some manner known to the Foe, so that he devise a new means of whelming us, against which we have thought of no defence. Lo! I dreamed on a night that Meglin builded a furnace, and coming at us unawares flung therein Eärendel our babe, and would after thrust in thee and me; but that for sorrow at the death of our fair child I would not resist."

And Tuor answered: "There is reason for thy fear, for neither is my heart good towards Meglin; yet is he the nephew of the king and thine own cousin, nor is there charge against him, and I see nought to do but to abide and watch."

But Idril said: "This is my rede thereto: gather thou in deep secret those delvers and quarrymen who by careful trial are found to hold least love for Meglin by reason of the pride and arrogance of his dealings among them. From these thou must choose trusty men to keep watch upon Meglin whenso he fares to the outer hills, yet I counsel thee to set the greater part of those in whose secrecy thou canst confide at a hidden delving, and to devise with their aid – howsoever cautious and slow that labour be – a secret way from thy house here beneath the rocks of this hill unto the vale below. Now this way must not lead toward the Way of Escape, for my heart bids me trust it not, but even to that far distant pass, the Cleft of Eagles in the southern mountains; and the further this delving reach thitherward beneath the plain so much the better would I esteem it — yet let all this labour be kept dark save from a few."

Now there are none such delvers of earth or rock as the Noldoli (and this Melko knows), but in those places is the earth of a great hardness; and Tuor said: "The rocks of the hill of Amon Gwareth are as iron, and only with much travail may they be cloven; yet if this be done in secret then must great time and patience be added; but the stone of the floor of the Vale of Tumladin is as forgéd steel, nor may it be hewn without the knowledge of the Gondothlim save in moons and years."

Idril said then: "Sooth this may be, but such is my rede, and there is yet time to spare." Then Tuor said that he might not see all its purport, "but 'better is any plan than a lack of counsel', and I will do even as thou sayest".

Now it so chanced that not long after Meglin went to the hills for the getting of ore, and straying in the mountains alone was taken by some of the Orcs prowling there, and they would do him evil and terrible hurt, knowing him to be a man of the Gondothlim. This was however unknown of Tuor's watchers. But evil came into the heart of Meglin, and he said to his captors: "Know then that I am Meglin son of Eöl who had to wife Isfin sister of Turgon king of the Gondothlim." But they said: "What is that to us?" And Meglin answered: "Much is it to you; for if you slay me, be it speedy or slow, ye will lose great tidings concerning the city of Gondolin that your master would rejoice to hear." Then the Orcs stayed their hands, and said they would give him life if the matters he opened to them seemed to merit that; and Meglin told them of all the fashion of that plain and city, of its walls and their height and thickness, and the valour of its gates; of the host of men at arms who now obeyed Turgon he spake, and the countless hoard of weapons gathered for their equipment, of the engines of war and the venomous fires.

Then the Orcs were wroth, and having heard these matters were yet for slaying him there and then as one who impudently enlarged the power of his miserable folk to the mockery of the great might and puissance of Melko; but Meglin catching at a straw said: "Think ye not that ye would rather pleasure your master if ye bore to his feet so noble a captive, that he might hear my tidings of himself and judge of their verity?"

Now this seemed good to the Orcs, and they returned from the mountains about Gondolin to the Hills of Iron and the dark halls of Melko; thither they haled Meglin with them, and now was he in a sore dread. But when he knelt before the black throne of Melko in terror of the grimness of the shapes about him, of the wolves that sat beneath that chair and of the adders that twined about its legs, Melko bade him speak. Then told he those tidings, and Melko hearkening spake very fair to him, that the insolence of his heart in great measure returned.

Now the end of this was that Melko aided by the cunning of Meglin devised a plan for the overthrow of Gondolin. For this Meglin's reward was to be a great captaincy among the Orcs – yet Melko purposed not in his heart to fulfil such a promise – but Tuor and Eärendel should Melko burn, and Idril be given to Meglin's arms – and such promises was that evil one fain to redeem. Yet as meed of treachery did Melko threaten Meglin with the torment of the Balrogs. Now these were demons with whips of flame and claws of steel by whom he tormented those of the Noldoli who durst withstand him in anything – and the Eldar have called them Malkarauki. But the rede that Meglin gave to Melko was that not all the host of the Orcs nor the Balrogs in their fierceness might by assault or siege hope ever to overthrow the walls and gates of Gondolin even if they availed to win unto the plain without. Therefore he counselled Melko to devise out of his sorceries a succour for his warriors in their endeavour. From the greatness of his wealth of metals and his powers of fire he bid him make beasts like snakes and dragons of irresistible might that should overcreep the Encircling Hills and lap that plain and its fair city in flame and death.

Then Meglin was bidden fare home lest at his absence men suspect somewhat; but Melko wove about him the spell of bottomless dread, and he had thereafter neither joy nor quiet in his heart. Nonetheless he wore a fair mask of good liking and gaiety, so that men said: "Meglin is softened", and he was held in less disfavour; yet Idril feared him the more. Now Meglin said: "I have laboured much and am minded to rest, and to join in the dance and the song and the merrymakings of the folk", and he went no more quarrying stone or ore in the hills: yet in sooth he sought herein to drown his fear and disquiet. A dread possessed him that Melko was ever at hand, and this came of the spell; and he durst never again wander amid the mines lest he again fall in with the Orcs and be bidden once more to the terrors of the halls of darkness.

Now the years fare by, and egged by Idril Tuor keepeth ever at his secret delving; but seeing that the leaguer of spies hath grown thinner Turgon dwelleth more at ease and in less fear. Yet these years are filled by Melko in the utmost ferment of labour, and all the thrall-folk of the Noldoli must dig unceasingly for metals while Melko sitteth and deviseth fires and calleth flames and smokes to come from the lower heats, nor doth he suffer any of the Noldoli to stray ever a foot from their places of bondage. Then on a time Melko assembled all his most cunning smiths and sorcerers, and of iron and flame they wrought a host of monsters such as have only at that time been seen and shall not again be till the Great End. Some were all of iron so cunningly linked that they might flow like slow rivers of metal or coil themselves around and above all obstacles before them, and these were filled in their innermost depths with the grimmest of the Orcs with scimitars and spears; others of bronze and copper were given hearts and spirits of blazing fire, and they blasted all that stood before them with the terror of their snorting or trampled whatso escaped the ardour of their breath; yet others were creatures of pure flame that writhed like ropes of molten metal, and they brought to ruin whatever fabric they came nigh, and iron and stone melted before them and became as water, and upon them rode the Balrogs in hundreds; and these were the most dire of all those monsters which Melko devised against Gondolin.

Now when the seventh summer had gone since the treason of Meglin, and Eärendel was yet of very tender years though a valorous child, Melko withdrew all his spies, for every path and corner of the mountains was now known to him; yet the Gondothlim thought in their unwariness that Melko would no longer seek against them, perceiving their might and the impregnable strength of their dwelling.

But Idril fell into a dark mood and the light of her face was clouded, and many wondered thereat; yet Turgon reduced the watch and ward to its ancient numbers, and to somewhat less, and as autumn came and the gathering of fruits was over folk turned with glad hearts to the feasts of winter: but Tuor stood upon the battlements and gazed upon the Encircling Hills.

Now behold, Idril stood beside him, and the wind was in her hair, and Tuor thought that she was exceeding beautiful, and stooped to kiss her; but her face was sad, and she said: "Now come the days when thou must make choice," and Tuor knew not what she said. Then drawing him within their halls she said to him how her heart misgave her for fear concerning Eärendel her son, and for boding that some great evil was nigh, and that Melko would be at the bottom of it. Then Tuor would comfort her, but might not, and she questioned him concerning the secret delving, and he said how it now led a league into the plain, and at that was her heart somewhat lightened. But still she counselled that the delving be pressed on, and that henceforth should speed weigh more than secrecy, "because now is the time very near". And another rede she gave him, and this he took also, that certain of the bravest and most true among the lords and warriors of the Gondothlim be chosen with care and told of that secret way and its issue. These she counselled him to make into a stout guard and to give them his emblem to wear that they become his folk, and to do thus under pretext of the right and dignity of a great lord, kinsman to the king. "Moreover," said she, "I will get my father's favour to that." In secret too she whispered to folk that if the city came to its last stand or Turgon be slain that they rally about Tuor and her son, and to this they laughed a yea, saying however that Gondolin would stand as long as Taniquetil or the Mountains of Valinor.

Yet to Turgon she spoke not openly, nor suffered Tuor to do so, as he desired, despite their love and reverence for him – a great and a noble and a glorious king he was – seeing that he trusted in Meglin and held with blind obstinacy his belief in the impregnable might of the city and that Melko sought no more against it, perceiving no hope therein. Now in this he was ever strengthened by the cunning sayings of Meglin. Behold, the guile of that Gnome was very great, for he wrought much in the dark, so that folk said: "He doth well to bear the sign of a sable mole"; and by reason of the folly of certain of the quarrymen, and yet more by reason of the loose words of certain among his kin to whom word was somewhat unwarily spoken by Tuor, he gathered a knowledge of the secret work and laid against that a plan of his own.

So winter deepened, and it was very cold for those regions, so that frost fared about the plain of Tumladin and ice lay on its pools; yet the fountains played ever on Amon Gwareth and the two trees blossomed, and folk made merry till the day of terror that was hidden in the heart of Melko.

In these ways that bitter winter passed, and the snows lay deeper than ever before on the Encircling Hills; yet in its time a spring of wondrous glory melted the skirts of those white mantles and the valley drank the waters and burst into flowers. So came

and passed with revelry of children the festival of Nost-na-Lothion
or the Birth of Flowers, and the hearts of the Gondothlim were
uplifted for the good promise of the year; and now at length is that
great feast Tarnin Austa or the Gates of Summer near at hand.
For know that on a night it was their custom to begin a solemn
ceremony at midnight, continuing it even till the dawn of Tarnin
Austa broke, and no voice was uttered in the city from midnight
till the break of day, but the dawn they hailed with ancient songs.
For years uncounted had the coming of summer thus been greeted
with music of choirs, standing upon their gleaming eastern wall;
and now comes even the night of vigil and the city is filled with
silver lamps, while in the groves upon the new-leaved trees lights
of jewelled colours swing, and low musics go along the ways, but
no voice sings until the dawn.

The sun has sunk beyond the hills and folk array them for the
festival very gladly and eagerly – glancing in expectation to the
East. Lo! even when she had gone and all was dark, a new light
suddenly began, and a glow there was, but it was beyond the
northward heights,[26] and men marvelled, and there was a thronging
of the walls and battlements. Then wonder grew to doubt as that
light waxed and became yet redder, and doubt to dread as men saw
the snow upon the mountains dyed as it were with blood. And thus
it was that the fire-serpents of Melko came upon Gondolin.

Then came over the plain riders who bore breathless tidings
from those who kept vigil on the peaks; and they told of the fiery
hosts and the shapes like dragons, and said: "Melko is upon us."
Great was the fear and anguish within that beauteous city, and the
streets and byeways were filled with the weeping of women and
the wailing of children, and the squares with the mustering of
soldiers and the ring of arms. There were the gleaming banners
of all the great houses and kindreds of the Gondothlim. Mighty
was the array of the house of the king and their colours were white
and gold and red, and their emblems the moon and the sun and the
scarlet heart.[27] Now in the midmost of these stood Tuor above all
heads, and his mail of silver gleamed; and about him was a press of
the stoutest of the folk. Lo! all these wore wings as it were of swans
or gulls upon their helms, and the emblem of the White Wing was
upon their shields. But the folk of Meglin were drawn up in the
same place, and sable was their harness, and they bore no sign or
emblem, but their round caps of steel were covered with moleskin,
and they fought with axes two-headed like mattocks. There Meglin
prince of Gondobar gathered many warriors of dark countenance

and lowering gaze about him, and a ruddy glow shone upon their faces and gleamed about the polished surfaces of their accoutrement. Behold, all the hills to the north were ablaze, and it was as if rivers of fire ran down the slopes that led to the plain of Tumladin, and folk might already feel the heat thereof.

And many other kindreds were there, the folk of the Swallow and the Heavenly Arch, and from these folk came the greatest number and the best of the bowmen, and they were arrayed upon the broad places of the walls. Now the folk of the Swallow bore a fan of feathers on their helms, and they were arrayed in white and dark blue and in purple and black and showed an arrowhead on their shields. Their lord was Duilin, swiftest of all men to run and leap and surest of archers at a mark. But they of the Heavenly Arch being a folk of uncounted wealth were arrayed in a glory of colours, and their arms were set with jewels that flamed in the light now over the sky. Every shield of that battalion was of the blue of the heavens and its boss a jewel built of seven gems, rubies and amethysts and sapphires, emeralds, chrysoprase, topaz, and amber, but an opal of great size was set in their helms. Egalmoth was their chieftain, and wore a blue mantle upon which the stars were broidered in crystal, and his sword was bent – now none else of the Noldoli bore curved swords – yet he trusted rather to the bow, and shot therewith further than any among that host.

There too were the folk of the Pillar and of the Tower of Snow, and both these kindreds were marshalled by Penlod, tallest of Gnomes. There were those of the Tree, and they were a great house, and their raiment was green. They fought with iron-studded clubs or with slings, and their lord Galdor was held the most valiant of all the Gondothlim save Turgon alone. There stood the house of the Golden Flower who bare a rayed sun upon their shield, and their chief Glorfindel bare a mantle so broidered in threads of gold that it was diapered with celandine as a field in spring; and his arms were damascened with cunning gold.

Then came there from the south of the city the people of the Fountain, and Ecthelion was their lord, and silver and diamonds were their delight; and swords very long and bright and pale did they wield, and they went into battle to the music of flutes. Behind them came the host of the Harp, and this was a battalion of brave warriors; but their leader Salgant was a craven, and he fawned upon Meglin. They were dight with tassels of silver and tassels of gold, and a harp of silver shone in their blazonry upon a field of black; but Salgant bore one of gold, and he alone rode into battle of all the sons of the Gondothlim, and he was heavy and squat.

Now the last of the battalions was furnished by the folk of the Hammer of Wrath, and of these came many of the best smiths and craftsmen, and all that kindred reverenced Aulë the Smith more than all other Ainur. They fought with great maces like hammers, and their shields were heavy, for their arms were very strong. In older days they had been much recruited by Noldoli who escaped from the mines of Melko, and the hatred of this house for the works of that evil one and the Balrogs his demons was exceeding great. Now their leader was Rog, strongest of the Gnomes, scarce second in valour to that Galdor of the Tree. The sign of this people was the Stricken Anvil, and a hammer that smiteth sparks about it was set on their shields, and red gold and black iron was their delight. Very numerous was that battalion, nor had any amongst them a faint heart, and they won the greatest glory of all those fair houses in that struggle against doom; yet were they ill-fated, and none ever fared away from that field, but fell about Rog and vanished from the Earth; and with them much craftsmanship and skill has been lost for ever.[28]

This was the fashion and the array of the eleven houses of the Gondothlim with their signs and emblems, and the bodyguard of Tuor, the folk of the Wing, was accounted the twelfth. Now is the face of that chieftain grim and he looks not to live long – and there in his house upon the walls Idril arrays herself in mail, and seeks Eärendel. And that child was in tears for the strange lights of red that played about the walls of the chamber where he slept; and tales that his nurse Meleth had woven him concerning fiery Melko at times of his waywardness came to him and troubled him. But his mother coming set about him a tiny coat of mail that she had let fashion in secret, and at that time he was glad and exceeding proud, and he shouted for pleasure. Yet Idril wept, for much had she cherished in her heart the fair city and her goodly house, and the love of Tuor and herself that had dwelt therein; but now she saw its destroying nigh at hand, and feared that her contriving would fail against this overwhelming might of the terror of the serpents.

It was now four hours still from middle night, and the sky was red in the north and in the east and west; and those serpents of iron had reached the levels of Tumladin, and those fiery ones were among the lowest slopes of the hills, so that the guards were taken and set in evil torment by the Balrogs that scoured all about, saving only to the furthest south where was Cristhorn the Cleft of Eagles.

Then did King Turgon call a council, and thither fared Tuor and Meglin as royal princes; and Duilin came with Egalmoth and Penlod the tall, and Rog strode thither with Galdor of the Tree and golden Glorfindel and Ecthelion of the voice of music. Thither too fared Salgant atremble at the tidings, and other nobles beside of less blood but better heart.

Then spake Tuor and this was his rede, that a mighty sally be made forthwith, ere the light and heat grew too great in the plain; and many backed him, being but of different minds as to whether the sally should be made by the entire host with the maids and wives and children amidmost, or by diverse bands seeking out in many directions; and to this last Tuor leaned.

But Meglin and Salgant alone held other counsel and were for holding to the city and seeking to guard those treasures that lay within. Out of guile did Meglin speak thus, fearing lest any of the Noldoli escape the doom that he had brought upon them for the saving of his skin, and he dreaded lest his treason become known and somehow vengeance find him in after days. But Salgant spake both echoing Meglin and being grievously afraid of issuing from the city, for he was fain rather to do battle from an impregnable fortress than to risk hard blows upon the field.

Then the lord of the house of the Mole played upon the one weakness of Turgon, saying: "Lo! O King, the city of Gondolin contains a wealth of jewels and metals and stuffs and of things wrought by the hands of the Gnomes to surpassing beauty, and all these thy lords – more brave meseems than wise – would abandon to the Foe. Even should victory be thine upon the plain thy city will be sacked and the Balrogs get hence with a measureless booty"; and Turgon groaned, for Meglin had known his great love for the wealth and loveliness of that burg[29] upon Amon Gwareth. Again said Meglin, putting fire in his voice: "Lo! Hast thou for nought laboured through years uncounted at the building of walls of impregnable thickness and in the making of gates whose valour may not be overthrown; is the power of the hill Amon Gwareth become as lowly as the deep vale, or the hoard of weapons that lie upon it and its unnumbered arrows of so little worth that in the hour of peril thou wouldst cast all aside and go naked into the open against enemies of steel and fire, whose trampling shakes the earth and the Encircling Mountains ring with the clamour of their footsteps?"

And Salgant quaked to think of it and spake noisily, saying: "Meglin speaks well, O King, hear thou him." Then the king took the counsel of those twain though all the lords said otherwise, nay rather the more for that: therefore at his bidding does all that folk abide now the assault upon their walls. But Tuor wept and left the king's hall, and gathering the men of the Wing went through the streets seeking his home; and by that hour was the light great and lurid and there was stifling heat and a black smoke and stench arose about the pathways to the city.

And now came the Monsters across the valley and the white towers of Gondolin reddened before them; but the stoutest were in dread seeing those dragons of fire and those serpents of bronze and iron that fare already about the hill of the city; and they shot unavailing arrows at them. Then is there a cry of hope, for behold, the snakes of fire may not climb the hill for its steepness and for its glassiness, and by reason of the quenching waters that fall upon its sides; yet they lie about its feet and a vast steam arises where the streams of Amon Gwareth and the flames of the serpents drive together. Then grew there such a heat that women became faint and men sweated to weariness beneath their mail, and all the springs of the city, save only the fountain of the king, grew hot and smoked.

But now Gothmog lord of Balrogs, captain of the hosts of Melko, took counsel and gathered all his things of iron that could coil themselves around and above all obstacles before them. These he bade pile themselves before the northern gate; and behold, their great spires reached even to its threshold and thrust at the towers and bastions about it, and by reason of the exceeding heaviness of their bodies those gates fell, and great was the noise thereof: yet the most of the walls around them still stood firm. Then the engines and the catapults of the king poured darts and boulders and molten metals on those ruthless beasts, and their hollow bellies clanged beneath the buffeting, yet it availed not for they might not be broken, and the fires rolled off them. Then were the topmost opened about their middles, and an innumerable host of the Orcs, the goblins of hatred, poured therefrom into the breach; and who shall tell of the gleam of their scimitars or the flash of the broad-bladed spears with which they stabbed?

Then did Rog shout in a mighty voice, and all the people of the Hammer of Wrath and the kindred of the Tree with Galdor the valiant leapt at the foe. There the blows of their great hammers and the dint of their clubs rang to the Encircling Mountains and the Orcs fell like leaves; and those of the Swallow and the Arch poured arrows like the dark rains of autumn upon them, and both

Orcs and Gondothlim fell thereunder for the smoke and the confusion. Great was that battle, yet for all their valour the Gondothlim by reason of the might of ever increasing numbers were borne slowly backwards till the goblins held part of the northernmost city.

At this time is Tuor at the head of the folk of the Wing struggling in the turmoil of the streets, and now he wins through to his house and finds that Meglin is before him. Trusting in the battle now begun about the northern gate and in the uproar in the city, Meglin had looked to this hour for the consummation of his designs. Learning much of the secret delving of Tuor (yet only at the last moment had he got this knowledge and he could not discover all) he said nought to the king or any other, for it was his thought that of a surety that tunnel would go in the end toward the Way of Escape, this being the most nigh to the city, and he had a mind to use this to his good, and to the ill of the Noldoli. Messengers by great stealth he despatched to Melko to set a guard about the outer issue of that Way when the assault was made; but he himself thought now to take Eärendel and cast him into the fire beneath the walls, and seizing Idril he would constrain her to guide him to the secrets of the passage, that he might win out of this terror of fire and slaughter and drag her withal along with him to the lands of Melko. Now Meglin was afeared that even the secret token which Melko had given him would fail in that direful sack, and was minded to help that Ainu to the fulfilment of his promises of safety. No doubt had he however of the death of Tuor in that great burning, for to Salgant he had confided the task of delaying him in the king's halls and egging him straight thence into the deadliest of the fight – but lo! Salgant fell into a terror unto death, and he rode home and lay there now aquake on his bed; but Tuor fared home with the folk of the Wing.

Now Tuor did this, though his valour leapt to the noise of war, that he might take farewell of Idril and Eärendel, and speed them with a bodyguard down the secret way ere he returned himself to the battle throng to die if must be: but he found a press of the Mole-folk about his door, and these were the grimmest and least good-hearted of folk that Meglin might get in that city. Yet were they free Noldoli and under no spell of Melko's like their master, wherefore though for the lordship of Meglin they aided not Idril, no more would they touch of his purpose despite all his curses.

Now then Meglin had Idril by the hair and sought to drag her to the battlements out of cruelty of heart, that she might see the fall of Eärendel to the flames; but he was cumbered by that child, and she fought, alone as she was, like a tigress for all her beauty and slenderness. There he now struggles and delays amid oaths while that folk of the Wing draw nigh – and lo! Tuor gives a shout so great that the Orcs hear it afar and waver at the sound of it. Like a crash of tempest the guard of the Wing were amid the men of the Mole, and these were stricken asunder. When Meglin saw this he would stab Eärendel with a short knife he had; but that child bit his left hand, that his teeth sank in, and he staggered, and stabbed weakly, and the mail of the small coat turned the blade aside; and thereupon Tuor was upon him and his wrath was terrible to see. He seized Meglin by that hand that held the knife and broke the arm with the wrench, and then taking him by the middle leapt with him upon the walls, and flung him far out. Great was the fall of his body, and it smote Amon Gwareth three times ere it pitched in the midmost of the flames; and the name of Meglin has gone out in shame from among Eldar and Noldoli.

Then the warriors of the Mole being more numerous than those few of the Wing, and loyal to their lord, came at Tuor, and there were great blows, but no man might stand before the wrath of Tuor, and they were smitten and driven to fly into what dark holes they might, or flung from the walls. Then Tuor and his men must get them to the battle of the Gate, for the noise of it has grown very great, and Tuor has it still in his heart that the city may stand; yet with Idril he left there Voronwë against his will and some other swordsmen to be a guard for her till he returned or might send tidings from the fray.

Now was the battle at that gate very evil indeed, and Duilin of the Swallow as he shot from the walls was smitten by a fiery bolt of the Balrogs who leapt about the base of Amon Gwareth; and he fell from the battlements and perished. Then the Balrogs continued to shoot darts of fire and flaming arrows like small snakes into the sky, and these fell upon the roofs and gardens of Gondolin till all the trees were scorched, and the flowers and grass burned up, and the whiteness of those walls and colonnades was blackened and seared: yet a worse matter was it that a company of those demons climbed upon the coils of the serpents of iron and thence loosed unceasingly from their bows and slings till a fire began to burn in the city to the back of the main army of the defenders.

Then said Rog in a great voice: "Who now shall fear the Balrogs for all their terror? See before us the accursed ones who for ages have tormented the children of the Noldoli, and who now set a fire at our backs with their shooting. Come ye of the Hammer of Wrath and we will smite them for their evil." Thereupon he lifted his mace, and its handle was long; and he made a way before him by the wrath of his onset even unto the fallen gate: but all the people of the Stricken Anvil ran behind like a wedge, and sparks came from their eyes for the fury of their rage. A great deed was that sally, as the Noldoli sing yet, and many of the Orcs were borne backward into the fires below; but the men of Rog leapt even upon the coils of the serpents and came at those Balrogs and smote them grievously, for all they had whips of flame and claws of steel, and were in stature very great. They battered them into nought, or catching at their whips wielded these against them, that they tore them even as they had aforetime torn the Gnomes; and the number of Balrogs that perished was a marvel and dread to the hosts of Melko, for ere that day never had any of the Balrogs been slain by the hand of Elves or Men.

Then Gothmog Lord of Balrogs gathered all his demons that were about the city and ordered them thus: a number made for the folk of the Hammer and gave before them, but the greater company rushing upon the flank contrived to get to their backs, higher upon the coils of the drakes and nearer to the gates, so that Rog might not win back save with great slaughter among his folk. But Rog seeing this essayed not to win back, as was hoped, but with all his folk fell on those whose part was to give before him; and they fled before him now of dire need rather than of craft. Down into the plain were they harried, and their shrieks rent the airs of Tumladin. Then that house of the Hammer fared about smiting and hewing the astonied bands of Melko till they were hemmed at the last by an overwhelming force of the Orcs and the Balrogs, and a fire-drake was loosed upon them. There did they perish about Rog hewing to the last till iron and flame overcame them, and it is yet sung that each man of the Hammer of Wrath took the lives of seven foemen to pay for his own. Then did dread fall more heavily still upon the Gondothlim at the death of Rog and the loss of his battalion, and they gave back further yet into the city, and Penlod perished there in a lane with his back to the wall, and about him many of the men of the Pillar and many of the Tower of Snow.

Now therefore Melko's goblins held all the gate and a great part of the walls on either side, whence numbers of the Swallow and those of the Rainbow were thrust to doom; but within the city they had won a great space reaching nigh to the centre, even to the Place of the Well that adjoined the Square of the Palace. Yet about those ways and around the gate their dead were piled in uncounted heaps, and they halted therefore and took counsel, seeing that for the valour of the Gondothlim they had lost many more than they had hoped and far more than those defenders. Fearful too they were for that slaughter Rog had done amid the Balrogs, because of those demons they had great courage and confidence of heart.

Now then the plan that they made was to hold what they had won, while those serpents of bronze and with great feet for trampling climbed slowly over those of iron, and reaching the walls there opened a breach wherethrough the Balrogs might ride upon the dragons of flame: yet they knew this must be done with speed, for the heats of those drakes lasted not for ever, and might only be plenished from the wells of fire that Melko had made in the fastness of his own land.

But even as their messengers were sped they heard a sweet music that was played amid the host of the Gondothlim and they feared what it might mean; and lo! there came Ecthelion and the people of the Fountain whom Turgon till now had held in reserve, for he watched the most of that affray from the heights of his tower. Now marched these folk to a great playing of their flutes, and the crystal and silver of their array was most lovely to see amid the red light of the fires and the blackness of the ruins.

Then on a sudden their music ceased and Ecthelion of the fair voice shouted for the drawing of swords, and before the Orcs might foresee his onslaught the flashing of those pale blades was amongst them. 'Tis said that Ecthelion's folk there slew more of the goblins than fell ever in all the battles of the Eldalië with that race, and that his name is a terror among them to this latest day, and a warcry to the Eldar.

Now it is that Tuor and the men of the Wing fare into the fight and range themselves beside Ecthelion and those of the Fountain, and the twain strike mighty blows and ward each many a thrust from the other, and harry the Orcs so that they win back almost to the gate. But there behold a quaking and a trampling, for the dragons labour mightily at beating a path up Amon Gwareth and at casting down the walls of the city; and already there is a gap therein and a confusion of masonry where the ward-towers have fallen in ruin. Bands of the Swallow and of the Arch of Heaven there fight bitterly amid the wreck or contest the walls to east and west with the foe; but even as Tuor comes nigh driving the Orcs, one of those brazen snakes heaves against the western wall and a great mass of it shakes and falls, and behind comes a creature of fire and Balrogs upon it. Flames gust from the jaws of that worm and folk wither before it, and the wings of the helm of Tuor are blackened, but he stands and gathers about him his guard and all of the Arch and Swallow he can find, whereas on his right Ecthelion rallies the men of the Fountain of the South.

Now the Orcs again take heart from the coming of the drakes, and they mingle with the Balrogs that pour about the breach, and they assail the Gondothlim grievously. There Tuor slew Othrod a lord of the Orcs cleaving his helm, and Balcmeg he hewed asunder, and Lug he smote with his axe that his limbs were cut from beneath him at the knee, but Ecthelion shore through two captains of the goblins at a sweep and cleft the head of Orcobal their chiefest champion to his teeth; and by reason of the great doughtiness of those two lords they came even unto the Balrogs. Of those demons of power Ecthelion slew three, for the brightness of his sword cleft the iron of them and did hurt to their fire, and they writhed; yet of the leap of that axe Dramborleg that was swung by the hand of Tuor were they still more afraid, for it sang like the rush of eagle's wings in the air and took death as it fell, and five of them went down before it.

But so it is that few cannot fight always against the many, and Ecthelion's left arm got a sore rent from a whip of the Balrog's and his shield fell to earth even as that dragon of fire drew nigh amid the ruin of the walls. Then Ecthelion must lean on Tuor, and Tuor might not leave him, though the very feet of the trampling beast were upon them, and they were like to be overborne: but Tuor hewed at a foot of the creature so that flame spouted forth, and that serpent screamed, lashing with its tail; and many of both Orcs and Noldoli got their death therefrom. Now Tuor gathered his might and lifted Ecthelion, and amid a remnant of the folk got thereunder and escaped the drake; yet dire was the killing of men that beast had wrought, and the Gondothlim were sorely shaken.

Thus it was that Tuor son of Peleg gave before the foe, fighting as he yielded ground, and bore from that battle Ecthelion of the Fountain, but the drakes and the foemen held half the city and all the north of it. Thence marauding bands fared about the streets and did much ransacking, or slew in the dark men and women and children, and many, if occasion let, they bound and led back and flung in the iron chambers amid the dragons of iron, that they might drag them afterward to be thralls of Melko.

Now Tuor reached the Square of the Folkwell by a way entering from the north, and found there Galdor denying the western entry by the Arch of Inwë to a horde of the goblins, but about him was now but a few of those men of the Tree. There did Galdor become the salvation of Tuor, for he fell behind his men stumbling beneath Ecthelion over a body that lay in the dark, and the Orcs had taken them both but for the sudden rush of that champion and the dint of his club.

There were the scatterlings of the guard of the Wing and of the houses of the Tree and the Fountain, and of the Swallow and the Arch, welded to a good battalion, and by the counsel of Tuor they gave way out of that Place of the Well, seeing that the Square of the King that lay next was the more defensible. Now that place had aforetime contained many beautiful trees, both oak and poplar, around a great well of vast depth and great purity of water; yet at that hour it was full of the riot and ugliness of those hideous people of Melko, and those waters were polluted with their carcases.

Thus comes the last stout gathering of those defenders in the Square of the Palace of Turgon. Among them are many wounded and fainting, and Tuor is weary for the labours of the night and the weight of Ecthelion who is in a deadly swoon. Even as he led that battalion in by the Road of Arches from the north-west (and they had much ado to prevent any foe getting behind their backs) a noise arose at the eastward of the square, and lo! Glorfindel is driven in with the last of the men of the Golden Flower.

Now these had sustained a terrible conflict in the Great Market to the east of the city, where a force of Orcs led by Balrogs came on them at unawares as they marched by a circuitous way to the fight about the gate. This they did to surprise the foe upon his left flank, but were themselves ambuscaded; there fought they bitterly for hours till a fire-drake new-come from the breach overwhelmed them, and Glorfindel cut his way out very hardly and with few men; but that place with its stores and its goodly things of fine workmanship was a waste of flames.

The story tells that Turgon had sent the men of the Harp to their aid because of the urgency of messengers from Glorfindel, but Salgant concealed this bidding from them, saying they were to garrison the square of the Lesser Market to the south where he dwelt, and they fretted thereat. Now however they brake from Salgant and were come before the king's hall; and that was very timely, for a triumphant press of foemen was at Glorfindel's heels. On these the men of the Harp unbidden fell with great eagerness and utterly redeemed the cravenhood of their lord, driving the enemy back into the market, and being leaderless fared even over wrathfully, so that many of them were trapped in the flames or sank before the breath of the serpent that revelled there.

Tuor now drank of the great fountain and was refreshed, and loosening Ecthelion's helm gave him to drink, splashing his face that his swoon left him. Now those lords Tuor and Glorfindel clear the square and withdraw all the men they may from the entrances and bar them with barriers, save as yet on the south. Even from that region comes now Egalmoth. He had had charge of the engines on the wall; but long since deeming matters to call rather for handstrokes about the streets than shooting upon the battlements he gathered some of the Arch and of the Swallow about him, and cast away his bow. Then did they fare about the city dealing good blows whenever they fell in with bands of the enemy. Thereby he rescued many bands of captives and gathered no few wandering and driven men, and so got to the King's Square with hard fighting; and men were fain to greet him for they had feared him dead. Now are all the women and children that had gathered there or been brought in by Egalmoth stowed in the king's halls, and the ranks of the houses made ready for the last. In that host of survivors are some, be it however few, of all the kindreds save of the Hammer of Wrath alone; and the king's house is as yet untouched. Nor is this any shame, for their part was ever to bide fresh to the last and defend the king.

But now the men of Melko have assembled their forces, and seven dragons of fire are come with Orcs about them and Balrogs upon them down all the ways from north, east, and west, seeking the Square of the King. Then there was carnage at the barriers, and Egalmoth and Tuor went from place to place of the defence, but Ecthelion lay by the fountain; and that stand was the most stubborn-valiant that is remembered in all the songs or in any tale. Yet at long last a drake bursts the barrier to the north – and there had once been the issue of the Alley of Roses and a fair place to see or to walk in, but now there is but a lane of blackness and it is filled with noise.

Tuor stood then in the way of that beast, but was sundered from Egalmoth, and they pressed him backward even to the centre of the square nigh the fountain. There he became weary from the strangling heat and was beaten down by a great demon, even Gothmog lord of Balrogs, son of Melko. But lo! Ecthelion, whose face was of the pallor of grey steel and whose shield-arm hung limp at his side, strode above him as he fell; and that Gnome drave at the demon, yet did not give him his death, getting rather a wound to his sword-arm that his weapon left his grasp. Then leapt Ecthelion lord of the Fountain, fairest of the Noldoli, full at Gothmog even as he raised his whip, and his helm that had a spike upon it he drave into that evil breast, and he twined his legs about his foeman's thighs; and the Balrog yelled and fell forward; but those two dropped into the basin of the king's fountain which was very deep. There found that creature his bane; and Ecthelion sank steel-laden into the depths, and so perished the lord of the Fountain after fiery battle in cool waters.[30]

Now Tuor had arisen when the assault of Ecthelion gave him space, and seeing that great deed he wept for his love of that fair Gnome of the Fountain, but being wrapped in battle he scarce cut his way to the folk about the palace. There seeing the wavering of the enemy by reason of the dread of the fall of Gothmog the marshal of the hosts, the royal house laid on and the king came down in splendour among them and hewed with them, that they swept again much of the square, and of the Balrogs slew even two score, which is a very great prowess indeed: but greater still did they do, for they hemmed in one of the Fire-drakes for all his flaming, and forced him into the very waters of the fountain that he perished therein. Now this was the end of that fair water; and its pools turned to steam and its spring was dried up, and it shot no more into the heaven, but rather a vast column of vapour arose to the sky and the cloud therefrom floated over all the land.

Then dread fell on all for the doom of the fountain, and the square was filled with mists of scalding heat and blinding fogs, and the people of the royal house were killed therein by heat and by the foe and by the serpents and by one another: but a body of them saved the king, and there was a rally of men beneath Glingol and Bansil.

Then said the king: "Great is the fall of Gondolin", and men shuddered, for such were the words of Amnon the prophet of old;[31] but Tuor speaking wildly for ruth and love of the king cried: "Gondolin stands yet, and Ulmo will not suffer it to perish!" Now were they at that time standing, Tuor by the Trees and the king upon the Stairs, as they had stood aforetime when Tuor spake the embassy of Ulmo. But Turgon said: "Evil have I brought upon the Flower of the Plain in despite of Ulmo, and now he leaveth it to wither in the fire. Lo! hope is no more in my heart for my city of loveliness, but the children of the Noldoli shall not be worsted for ever."

Then did the Gondothlim clash their weapons, for many stood

nigh, but Turgon said: "Fight not against doom, O my children!
Seek ye who may safety in flight, if perhaps there be time yet: but
let Tuor have your lealty." But Tuor said: "Thou art king"; and
Turgon made answer: "Yet no blow will I strike more", and he
cast his crown at the roots of Glingol. Then did Galdor who stood
there pick it up, but Turgon accepted it not, and bare of head
climbed to the topmost pinnacle of that white tower that stood
nigh his palace. There he shouted in a voice like a horn blown
among the mountains, and all that were gathered beneath the
Trees and the foemen in the mists of the square heard him: "Great
is the victory of the Noldoli!" And 'tis said that it was then middle
night, and that the Orcs yelled in derision.

Then did men speak of a sally, and were of two minds. Many
held that it were impossible to burst through, nor might they even
so get over the plain or through the hills, and that it were better
therefore to die about the king. But Tuor might not think well of
the death of so many fair women and children, were it at the hands
of their own folk in the last resort, or by the weapons of the enemy,
and he spake of the delving and of the secret way. Therefore did he
counsel that they beg Turgon to have other mind, and coming
among them lead that remnant southward to the walls and the
entry of that passage; but he himself burnt with desire to fare
thither and know how Idril and Eärendel might be, or to get
tidings hence to them and bid them begone speedily, for Gondolin
was taken. Now Tuor's plan seemed to the lords desperate indeed
– seeing the narrowness of the tunnel and the greatness of the
company that must pass it – yet would they fain take this rede in
their straits. But Turgon hearkened not, and bid them fare now
ere it was too late, and "Let Tuor," said he, "be your guide and
your chieftain. But I Turgon will not leave my city, and will burn
with it." Then sped they messengers again to the tower, saying:
"Sire, who are the Gondothlim if thou perish? Lead us!" But he
said: "Lo! I abide here"; and a third time, and he said: "If I am
king, obey my behests, and dare not to parley further with my
commands." After that they sent no more and made ready for the
forlorn attempt. But the folk of the royal house that yet lived
would not budge a foot, but gathered thickly about the base of the
king's tower. "Here," said they, "we will stay if Turgon goes not
forth"; and they might not be persuaded.

Now was Tuor torn sorely between his reverence for the king
and the love for Idril and his child, wherewith his heart was sick;
yet already serpents fare about the square trampling upon dead

and dying, and the foe gathers in the mists for the last onslaught; and the choice must be made. Then because of the wailing of the women in the halls of the palace and the greatness of his pity for that sad remainder of the peoples of Gondolin, he gathered all that rueful company, maids, children and mothers, and setting them amidmost marshalled as well as he might his men around them. Deepest he set them at flank and at rear, for he purposed falling back southward fighting as best he might with the rearguard as he went; and thus if it might so be to win down the Road of Pomps to the Place of the Gods ere any great force be sent to circumvent him. Thence was it his thought to go by the Way of Running Waters past the Fountains of the South to the walls and to his home; but the passage of the secret tunnel he doubted much. Thereupon espying his movement the foe made forthwith a great onslaught upon his left flank and his rear – from east and north – even as he began to withdraw; but his right was covered by the king's hall and the head of that column drew already into the Road of Pomps.

Then some of the hugest of the drakes came on and glared in the fog, and he must perforce bid the company to go at a run, fighting on the left at haphazard; but Glorfindel held the rear manfully and many more of the Golden Flower fell there. So it was that they passed the Road of Pomps and reached Gar Ainion, the Place of the Gods; and this was very open and at its middle the highest ground of all the city. Here Tuor looks for an evil stand and it is scarce in his hope to get much further; but behold, the foe seems already to slacken and scarce any follow them, and this is a wonder. Now comes Tuor at their head to the Place of Wedding, and lo! there stands Idril before him with her hair unbraided as on that day of their marriage before; and great is his amaze. By her stood Voronwë and none other, but Idril saw not even Tuor, for her gaze was set back upon the Place of the King that now lay somewhat below them. Then all that host halted and looked back whither her eyes gazed and their hearts stood still; for now they saw why the foe pressed them so little and the reason of their salvation. Lo! a drake was coiled even on the very steps of the palace and defiled their whiteness; but swarms of the Orcs ransacked within and dragged forth forgotten women and children or slew men that fought alone. Glingol was withered to the stock and Bansil was blackened utterly, and the king's tower was beset. High up could they descry the form of the king, but about the base a serpent of iron spouting flame lashed and rowed with his tail, and

Balrogs were round him; and there was the king's house in great anguish, and dread cries carried up to the watchers. So was it that the sack of the halls of Turgon and that most valiant stand of the royal house held the mind of the foe, so that Tuor got thence with his company, and stood now in tears upon the Place of the Gods.

Then said Idril: "Woe is me whose father awaiteth doom even upon his topmost pinnacle; but seven times woe whose lord hath gone down before Melko and will stride home no more!" – for she was distraught with the agony of that night.

Then said Tuor: "Lo! Idril, it is I, and I live; yet now will I get thy father hence, be it from the Hells of Melko!" With that he would make down the hill alone, maddened by the grief of his wife; but she coming to her wits in a storm of weeping clasped his knees saying: "My lord! My lord!" and delayed him. Yet even as they spake a great noise and a yelling rose from that place of anguish. Behold, the tower leapt into a flame and in a stab of fire it fell, for the dragons crushed the base of it and all who stood there. Great was the clangour of that terrible fall, and therein passed Turgon King of the Gondothlim, and for that hour the victory was to Melko.

Then said Idril heavily: "Sad is the blindness of the wise"; but Tuor said: "Sad too is the stubbornness of those we love – yet 'twas a valiant fault," then stooping he lifted and kissed her, for she was more to him than all the Gondothlim; but she wept bitterly for her father. Then turned Tuor to the captains, saying: "Lo, we must get hence with all speed, lest we be surrounded"; and forthwith they moved onward as swiftly as they might and got them far from thence ere the Orcs tired of sacking the palace and rejoicing at the fall of the tower of Turgon.

Now are they in the southward city and meet but scattered bands of plunderers who fly before them; yet do they find fire and burning everywhere for the ruthlessness of that enemy. Women do they meet, some with babes and some laden with chattels, but Tuor would not let them bear away aught save a little food. Coming now at length to a greater quiet Tuor asked Voronwë for tidings, in that Idril spake not and was well-nigh in a swoon; and Voronwë told him of how she and he had waited before the doors of the house while the noise of those battles grew and shook their hearts; and Idril wept for lack of tidings from Tuor. At length she had sped the most part of her guard down the secret way with Eärendel, constraining them to depart with imperious words, yet was her grief great at that sundering. She herself would bide, said she, nor seek to live after her lord; and then she fared about gathering womenfolk and wanderers and speeding them down the tunnel, and smiting marauders with her small band; nor might they dissuade her from bearing a sword.

At length they had fallen in with a band somewhat too numerous, and Voronwë had dragged her thence but by the luck of the Gods, for all else with them perished, and their foe burned Tuor's house; yet found not the secret way. "Therewith," said Voronwë, "thy lady became distraught of weariness and grief, and fared into the city wildly to my great fear – nor might I get her to sally from the burning."

About the saying of these words were they come to the southern walls and nigh to Tuor's house, and lo! it was cast down and the wreckage was asmoke; and thereat was Tuor bitterly wroth. But there was a noise that boded the approach of Orcs, and Tuor despatched that company as swiftly as might be down that secret way.

Now is there great sorrow upon that staircase as those exiles bid farewell to Gondolin; yet are they without much hope of further life beyond the hills, for how shall any slip from the hand of Melko?

Glad is Tuor when all have passed the entrance and his fear lightens; indeed by the luck of the Valar only can all those folk have got therein unspied of the Orcs. Some now are left who casting aside their arms labour with picks from within and block up the entry of the passage, faring then after the host as they might; but when that folk had descended the stairway to a level with the valley the heat grew to a torment for the fire of the dragons that were about the city; and they were indeed nigh, for the delving was there at no great depth in the earth. Boulders were loosened by the tremors of the ground and falling crushed many, and fumes were in the air so that their torches and lanterns went out. Here they fell over bodies of some that had gone before and perished, and Tuor was in fear for Eärendel; and they pressed on in great darkness and anguish. Nigh two hours were they in that tunnel of the earth, and towards its end it was scarce finished, but rugged at the sides and low.[32]

Then came they at the last lessened by wellnigh a tithe to the tunnel's opening, and it debouched cunningly in a large basin where once water had lain, but it was now full of thick bushes. Here were gathered no small press of mingled folk whom Idril and Voronwë sped down the hidden way before them, and they

were weeping softly in weariness and sorrow, but Eärendel was
not there. Thereat were Tuor and Idril in anguish of heart.[33]
Lamentation was there too among all those others, for amidmost
of the plain about them loomed afar the hill of Amon Gwareth
crowned with flames, where had stood the gleaming city of their
home. Fire-drakes are about it and monsters of iron fare in and
out of its gates, and great is that sack of the Balrogs and Orcs.
Somewhat of comfort has this nonetheless for the leaders, for they
judge the plain to be nigh empty of Melko's folk save hard by
the city, for thither have fared all his evil ones to revel in that
destruction.

"Now," therefore said Galdor, "we must get as far hence toward
the Encircling Mountains as may be ere dawn come upon us, and
that giveth no great space of time, for summer is at hand."[34] Thereat
rose a dissension, for a number said that it were folly to make for
Cristhorn as Tuor purposed. "The sun," say they, "will be up long
ere we win the foothills, and we shall be whelmed in the plain by
those drakes and those demons. Let us fare to Bad Uthwen, the
Way of Escape, for that is but half the journeying, and our weary
and our wounded may hope to win so far if no further."

Yet Idril spake against this, and persuaded the lords that they
trust not to the magic of that way that had aforetime shielded it
from discovery: "for what magic stands if Gondolin be fallen?"
Nonetheless a large body of men and women sundered from Tuor
and fared to Bad Uthwen, and there into the jaws of a monster who
by the guile of Melko at Meglin's rede sat at the outer issue that
none came through. But the others, led by one Legolas Greenleaf
of the house of the Tree, who knew all that plain by day or by dark,
and was night-sighted, made much speed over the vale for all their
weariness, and halted only after a great march. Then was all the
Earth spread with the grey light of that sad dawn which looked no
more on the beauty of Gondolin; but the plain was full of mists –
and that was a marvel, for no mist or fog came there ever before,
and this perchance had to do with the doom of the fountain of the
king. Again they rose, and covered by the vapours fared long past
dawn in safety, till they were already too far away for any to descry
them in those misty airs from the hill or from the ruined walls.

Now the Mountains or rather their lowest hills were on that side
seven leagues save a mile from Gondolin, and Cristhorn the Cleft
of Eagles two leagues of upward going from the beginning of the
Mountains, for it was at a great height; wherefore they had yet two
leagues and part of a third to traverse amid the spurs and foothills,

and they were very weary.[35] By now the sun hung well above a saddle in the eastern hills, and she was very red and great; and the mists nigh them were lifted, but the ruins of Gondolin were utterly hidden as in a cloud. Behold then at the clearing of the airs they saw, but a few furlongs off, a knot of men that fled on foot, and these were pursued by a strange cavalry, for on great wolves rode Orcs, as they thought, brandishing spears. Then said Tuor: "Lo! there is Eärendel my son; behold, his face shineth as a star in the waste,[36] and my men of the Wing are about him, and they are in sore straits." Forthwith he chose fifty of the men that were least weary, and leaving the main company to follow he fared over the plain with that troop as swiftly as they had strength left. Coming now to carry of voice Tuor shouted to the men about Eärendel to stand and flee not, for the wolfriders were scattering them and slaying them piecemeal, and the child was upon the shoulders of one Hendor, a house-carle of Idril's, and he seemed like to be left with his burden. Then they stood back to back and Hendor and Eärendel amidmost; but Tuor soon came up, though all his troop were breathless.

Of the wolfriders there were a score, and of the men that were about Eärendel but six living; therefore had Tuor opened his men into a crescent of but one rank, and hoped so to envelop the riders, lest any escaping bring tidings to the main foe and draw ruin upon the exiles. In this he succeeded, so that only two escaped, and therewithal wounded and without their beasts, wherefore were their tidings brought too late to the city.

Glad was Eärendel to greet Tuor, and Tuor most fain of his child; but said Eärendel: "I am thirsty, father, for I have run far − nor had Hendor need to bear me." Thereto his father said nought, having no water, and thinking of the need of all that company that he guided; but Eärendel said again: "'Twas good to see Meglin die so, for he would set arms about my mother − and I liked him not; but I would travel in no tunnels for all Melko's wolfriders." Then Tuor smiled and set him upon his shoulders. Soon after this the main company came up, and Tuor gave Eärendel to his mother who was in a great joy; but Eärendel would not be borne in her arms, for he said: "Mother Idril, thou art weary, and warriors in mail ride not among the Gondothlim, save it be old Salgant!" and his mother laughed amid her sorrow; but Eärendel said: "Nay, where is Salgant?" − for Salgant had told him quaint tales or played drolleries with him at times, and Eärendel had much laughter of the old Gnome in those days when he came many a day to the house of Tuor, loving the good wine and fair repast he there received. But none could say where Salgant was, nor can they now. Mayhap he was whelmed by fire upon his bed; yet some have it that he was taken captive to the halls of Melko and made his buffoon – and this is an ill fate for a noble of the good race of the Gnomes. Then was Eärendel sad at that, and walked beside his mother in silence.

Now came they to the foothills and it was full morning but still grey, and there nigh to the beginning of the upward road folk stretched them and rested in a little dale fringed with trees and with hazel-bushes, and many slept despite their peril, for they were utterly spent. Yet Tuor set a strict watch, and himself slept not. Here they made one meal of scanty food and broken meats; and Eärendel quenched his thirst and played beside a little brook. Then said he to his mother: "Mother Idril, I would we had good Ecthelion of the Fountain here to play to me on his flute, or make me willow-whistles! Perchance he has gone on ahead?" But Idril said nay, and told what she had heard of his end. Then said Eärendel that he cared not ever to see the streets of Gondolin again, and he wept bitterly; but Tuor said that he would not again see those streets, "for Gondolin is no more".

Thereafter nigh to the hour of sundown behind the hills Tuor bade the company arise, and they pressed on by rugged paths. Soon now the grass faded and gave way to mossy stones, and trees fell away, and even the pines and firs grew sparse. About the set of the sun the way so wound behind a shoulder of the hills that they might not again look toward Gondolin. There all that company turned, and lo! the plain is clear and smiling in the last light as of old; but afar off as they gazed a great flare shot up against the darkened north – and that was the fall of the last tower of Gondolin, even that which had stood hard by the southern gate, and whose shadow fell oft across the walls of Tuor's house. Then sank the sun, and they saw Gondolin no more.

Now the pass of Cristhorn, that is the Eagles' Cleft, is one of dangerous going, and that host had not ventured it by dark, lanternless and without torches, and very weary and cumbered with women and children and sick and stricken men, had it not been for their great fear of Melko's scouts, for it was a great company and might not fare very secretly. Darkness gathered rapidly as they approached that high place, and they must string out into a long and straggling line. Galdor and a band of men spear-armed went ahead, and Legolas was with them, whose eyes were like cats' for the dark, yet could they see further. Thereafter followed the least weary of the women supporting the sick and the wounded that could go on foot. Idril was with these, and Eärendel who bore up well, but Tuor was in the midmost behind them with all his men of the Wing, and they bare some who were grievously hurt, and Egalmoth was with him, but he had got a hurt in that sally from the square. Behind again came many women with babes, and girls, and lamed men, yet was the going slow enough for them. At the rearmost went the largest band of men battle-whole, and there was Glorfindel of the golden hair.

Thus were they come to Cristhorn, which is an ill place by reason of its height, for this is so great that spring nor summer come ever there, and it is very cold. Indeed while the valley dances in the sun, there all the year snow dwells in those bleak places, and even as they came there the wind howled, coming from the north behind them, and it bit sorely. Snow fell and whirled in wind-eddies and got into their eyes, and this was not good, for there the path is narrow, and of the right or westerly hand a sheer wall rises nigh seven chains from the way, ere it bursts atop into jagged pinnacles where are many eyries. There dwells Thorndor King of Eagles, Lord of the Thornhoth, whom the Eldar named Sorontur. But of the other hand is a fall not right sheer yet dreadly steep, and it has long teeth of rock up-pointing so that one may climb down – or fall maybe – but by no means up. And from that deep is no escape at either end any more than by the sides, and Thorn Sir runs at bottom. He falls therein from the south over a great precipice but with a slender water, for he is a thin stream in those heights, and he issues to the north after flowing but a rocky mile above ground down a narrow passage that goes into the mountain, and scarce a fish could squeeze through with him.

Galdor and his men were come now to the end nigh to where Thorn Sir falls into the abyss, and the others straggled, for all Tuor's efforts, back over most of the mile of the perilous way between chasm and cliff, so that Glorfindel's folk were scarce come to its beginning, when there was a yell in the night that echoed in that grim region. Behold, Galdor's men were beset in the dark suddenly by shapes leaping from behind rocks where they had lain hidden even from the glance of Legolas. It was Tuor's thought that they had fallen in with one of Melko's ranging companies, and he feared no more than a sharp brush in the dark, yet he sent the women and sick around him rearward and joined his men to Galdor's, and there was an affray upon the perilous path. But now rocks fell from above, and things looked ill, for they did grievous hurt; but matters seemed to Tuor yet worse when the noise of arms came from the rear, and tidings were said to him by a man of the Swallow that Glorfindel was ill bested by men from behind, and that a Balrog was with them.

Then was he sore afraid of a trap, and this was even what had in truth befallen; for watchers had been set by Melko all about the encircling hills. Yet so many did the valour of the Gondothlim draw off to the assault ere the city could be taken that these were but thinly spread, and were at the least here in the south. Nonetheless one of these had espied the company as they started the upward going from the dale of hazels, and as many bands were got together against them as might be, and devised to fall upon the exiles to front and rear even upon the perilous way of Cristhorn. Now Galdor and Glorfindel held their own despite the surprise of assault, and many of the Orcs were struck into the abyss; but the falling of the rocks was like to end all their valour, and the flight from Gondolin to come to ruin. The moon about that hour rose above the pass, and the gloom somewhat lifted, for his pale light filtered into dark places; yet it lit not the path for the height of the walls. Then arose Thorndor, King of Eagles, and he loved not Melko, for Melko had caught many of his kindred and chained them against sharp rocks to squeeze from them the magic words whereby he might learn to fly (for he dreamed of contending even against Manwë in the air); and when they would not tell he cut off their wings and sought to fashion therefrom a mighty pair for his use, but it availed not.

Now when the clamour from the pass rose to his great eyrie he said: "Wherefore are these foul things, these Orcs of the hills, climbed near to my throne; and why do the sons of the Noldoli cry out in the low places for fear of the children of Melko the accursed? Arise O Thornhoth, whose beaks are of steel and whose talons swords!"

Thereupon there was a rushing like a great wind in rocky places, and the Thornhoth, the people of the Eagles, fell on those Orcs who had scaled above the path, and tore their faces and their hands and flung them to the rocks of Thorn Sir far below. Then were the Gondothlim glad, and they made in after days the Eagle a sign of their kindred in token of their joy, and Idril bore it, but Eärendel loved rather the Swan-wing of his father. Now unhampered Galdor's men bore back those that opposed them, for they were not very many and the onset of the Thornhoth affrighted them much; and the company fared forward again, though Glorfindel had fighting enough in the rear. Already the half had passed the perilous way and the falls of Thorn Sir, when that Balrog that was with the rearward foe leapt with great might on certain lofty rocks that stood into the path on the left side upon the lip of the chasm, and thence with a leap of fury he was past Glorfindel's men and among the women and the sick in front, lashing with his whip of flame. Then Glorfindel leapt forward upon him and his golden armour gleamed strangely in the moon, and he hewed at that demon that it leapt again upon a great boulder and Glorfindel after. Now there was a deadly combat upon that high rock above the folk; and these, pressed behind and hindered ahead, were grown so close that well nigh all could see, yet was it over ere Glorfindel's men could leap to his side. The ardour of Glorfindel drave that Balrog from point to point, and his mail fended him from its whip and claw. Now had he beaten a heavy swinge upon its iron helm, now hewn off the creature's whip-arm at the elbow. Then sprang the Balrog in the torment of his pain and fear full at Glorfindel, who stabbed like a dart of a snake; but he found only a shoulder, and was grappled, and they swayed to a fall upon the crag-top. Then Glorfindel's left hand sought a dirk, and this he thrust up that it pierced the Balrog's belly nigh his own face (for that demon was double his stature); and it shrieked, and fell backwards from the rock, and falling clutched Glorfindel's yellow locks beneath his cap, and those twain fell into the abyss.

Now was this a very grievous thing, for Glorfindel was most dearly beloved – and lo! the dint of their fall echoed about the hills, and the abyss of Thorn Sir rang. Then at the death-cry of the Balrog the Orcs before and behind wavered and were slain or fled far away, and Thorndor himself, a mighty bird, descended to the abyss and brought up the body of Glorfindel; but the Balrog lay, and the water of Thorn Sir ran black for many a day far below in Tumladin.

Still do the Eldar say when they see good fighting at great odds of power against a fury of evil: "Alas! 'Tis Glorfindel and the Balrog", and their hearts are still sore for that fair one of the Noldoli. Because of their love, despite the haste and their fear of the advent of new foes, Tuor let raise a great stone-cairn over Glorfindel just there beyond the perilous way by the precipice of Eagle-stream, and Thorndor has let not yet any harm come thereto, but yellow flowers have fared thither and blow ever now

about that mound in those unkindly places; but the folk of the
Golden Flower wept at its building and might not dry their tears.

Now who shall tell of the wanderings of Tuor and the exiles of
Gondolin in the wastes that lie beyond the mountains to the south
of the vale of Tumladin? Miseries were theirs and death, colds and
hungers, and ceaseless watches. That they won ever through those
regions infested by Melko's evil came from the great slaughter and
damage done to his power in that assault, and from the speed and
wariness with which Tuor led them; for of a certain Melko knew of
that escape and was furious thereat. Ulmo had heard tidings in the
far oceans of the deeds that were done, but he could not yet aid
them for they were far from waters and rivers – and indeed they
thirsted sorely, and they knew not the way.

But after a year and more of wandering, in which many a time
they journeyed long tangled in the magic of those wastes only to
come again upon their own tracks, once more the summer came,
and nigh to its height[37] they came at last upon a stream, and
following this came to better lands and were a little comforted.
Here did Voronwë guide them, for he had caught a whisper of
Ulmo's in that stream one late summer's night – and he got ever
much wisdom from the sound of waters. Now he led them even till
they came down to Sirion which that stream fed, and then both
Tuor and Voronwë saw that they were not far from the outer issue
of old of the Way of Escape, and were once more in that deep
dale of alders. Here were all the bushes trampled and the trees
burnt, and the dale-wall scarred with flame, and they wept, for
they thought they knew the fate of those who sundered aforetime
from them at the tunnel-mouth.

Now they journeyed down that river but were again in fear from
Melko, and fought affrays with his Orc-bands and were in peril
from the wolfriders, but his firedrakes sought not at them, both
for the great exhaustion of their fires in the taking of Gondolin,
and the increasing power of Ulmo as the river grew. So came they
after many days – for they went slowly and got their sustenance
very hardly – to those great heaths and morasses above the Land of
Willows, and Voronwë knew not those regions. Now here goes
Sirion a very great way under earth, diving at the great cavern of
the Tumultuous Winds, but running clear again above the Pools
of Twilight, even where Tulkas[38] after fought with Melko's self.
Tuor had fared over these regions by night and dusk after Ulmo
came to him amid the reeds, and he remembered not the ways. In

places that land is full of deceits and very marshy; and here the host had long delay and was vexed by sore flies, for it was autumn still, and agues and fevers fared amongst them, and they cursed Melko.

Yet came they at last to the great pools and the edges of that most tender Land of Willows; and the very breath of the winds thereof brought rest and peace to them, and for the comfort of that place the grief was assuaged of those who mourned the dead in that great fall. There women and maids grew fair again and their sick were healed, and old wounds ceased to pain; yet they alone who of reason feared their folk living still in bitter thraldom in the Hells of Iron sang not, nor did they smile.

Here they abode very long indeed, and Eärendel was a grown boy ere the voice of Ulmo's conches drew the heart of Tuor, that his sea-longing returned with a thirst the deeper for years of stifling; and all that host arose at his bidding, and got them down Sirion to the Sea.

Now the folk that had passed into the Eagles' Cleft and who saw the fall of Glorfindel had been nigh eight hundreds — a large wayfaring, yet was it a sad remnant of so fair and numerous a city. But they who arose from the grasses of the Land of Willows in years after and fared away to sea, when spring set celandine in the meads and they had held sad festival in memorial of Glorfindel, these numbered but three hundreds and a score of men and man-children, and two hundreds and three score of women and maid-children. Now the number of women was few because of their hiding or being stowed by their kinsfolk in secret places in the city. There they were burned or slain or taken and enthralled, and the rescue-parties found them too seldom; and it is the greatest ruth to think of this, for the maids and women of the Gondothlim were as fair as the sun and as lovely as the moon and brighter than the stars. Glory dwelt in that city of Gondolin of the Seven Names, and its ruin was the most dread of all the sacks of cities upon the face of Earth. Nor Bablon, nor Ninwi, nor the towers of Trui, nor all the many takings of Rûm that is greatest among Men, saw such terror as fell that day upon Amon Gwareth in the kindred of the Gnomes; and this is esteemed the worst work that Melko has yet thought of in the world.

Yet now those exiles of Gondolin dwelt at the mouth of Sirion by the waves of the Great Sea. There they take the name of Lothlim, the people of the flower, for Gondothlim is a name too sore to their hearts; and fair among the Lothlim Eärendel grows in the house of his father,[39] and the great tale of Tuor is come to its waning.'

Then said Littleheart son of Bronweg: 'Alas for Gondolin.'

And no one in all the Room of Logs spake or moved for a great while.

# NOTES

1 Not of course the great journey to the Sea from the Waters of Awakening, but the expedition of the Elves of Kôr for the rescue of the Gnomes (see I.26).

2 A *korin* is defined in *The Cottage of Lost Play* (I.16) as 'a great circular hedge, be it of stone or of thorn or even of trees, that encloses a green sward'; Meril-i-Turinqi dwelt 'in a great *korin* of elms'.

3 *Tôn a Gwedrin* is the Tale-fire.

4 There is here a direction: 'See hereafter the Nauglafring', but this is struck out.

5 On Heorrenda see pp. 290ff, 323. A small space is left after the words 'it is thus' to mark the place of the poem in Old English that was to be inserted, but there is no indication of what it was to be.

*(In the following notes 'the original reading' refers to the text of Tuor A, and of Tuor B before the emendation in question. It does not imply that the reading of Tuor A was, or was not, found in the original pencilled text (in the great majority of cases this cannot be said).)*

6 This passage, beginning with the words 'And Tuor entered that cavern . . .' on p. 149, is a late replacement written on a slip (see p. 147). The original passage was largely similar in meaning, but contained the following:

Now in delving that riverway beneath the hills the Noldoli worked unknown to Melko who in those deep days held them yet hidden and thralls beneath his will. Rather were they prompted by Ulmo who strove ever against Melko; and through Tuor he hoped to devise for the Gnomes release from the terror of the evil of Melko.

7 'three days': 'three years' all texts, but 'days?' pencilled above 'years' in *Tuor B*.

8 The 'evolution' of sea-birds through Ossë is described in the tale of *The Coming of the Elves*, I.123; but the sentence here derives from the original pencilled text of *Tuor A*.

9 In the typescript *Tuor C* a blank was left here (see p. 147) and subsequently filled in with 'Ulmo', not 'Ainur'.

10    The original reading was: 'Thou Tuor of the lonely heart the Valar
      will not to dwell for ever in fair places of birds and flowers; nor
      would they lead thee through this pleasant land . . .'

11    *Tuor C* adds here: 'with Ulmo's aid'.

12    The reference to the Battle of Unnumbered Tears is a later addition
      to *Tuor B*. The original reading was: 'who alone escaped Melko's
      power when he caught their folk . . .'

13    In *Tuor A* and *B Voronwë* is used throughout, but this phrase, with
      the form *Bronweg*, is an addition to *Tuor B* (replacing the original
      'Now after many days these twain found a deep dale').

14    The typescript *Tuor C* has here:

      . . . that none, were they not of the blood of the Noldoli, might
      light on it, neither by chance nor agelong search. Thus was
      it secure from all ill hap save treachery alone, and never would
      Tûr have won thereto but for the steadfastness of that Gnome
      Voronwë.

      In the next sentence *Tuor C* has 'yet even so no few of the bolder of
      the Gnomes enthralled would slip down the river Sirion from the
      fell mountains'.

15    The original reading was: 'his speech they comprehended, though
      somewhat different was the tongue of the free Noldoli by those days
      to that of the sad thralls of Melko.' The typescript *Tuor C* has: 'they
      comprehended him for they were Noldoli. Then spake Tûr also in
      the same tongue . . .'

16    The original reading was: 'It was early morn when they drew near
      the gates and many eyes gazed . . .' But when Tuor and Voronwë
      first saw Gondolin it was 'in the new light of the morning' (p. 158),
      and it was 'a day's light march' across the plain; hence the change
      made later to *Tuor B*.

17    'Evil One': original reading 'Ainu'.

18    This passage, from 'Rugged was his aspect . . .', is a replacement on
      a separate slip; the original text was:

      Tuor was goodly in countenance but rugged and unkempt
      of locks and clad in the skins of bears, yet his stature
      was not overgreat among his own folk, but the Gondothlim,
      though not bent as were no few of their kin who laboured at
      ceaseless delving and hammering for Melko, were small and
      slender and lithe.

      In the original passage Men are declared to be of their nature taller
      than the Elves of Gondolin. See pp. 142, 220.

19    'come hither': 'escaped from Melko' *Tuor C*.

20    'folk': original reading 'men'. This is the only place where 'men' in
      reference to Elves is changed. The use is constant in *The Fall of
      Gondolin*, and even occurs once in an odd-sounding reference to

the hosts of Melko: 'But now the men of Melko have assembled their forces' (p. 183).

21   The passage ending here and beginning with the words 'Then Tuor's heart was heavy . . .' on p. 162 was bracketed by my father in *Tuor B*, and on a loose slip referring to this bracketed passage he wrote:

> (If nec[essary]): Then is told how Idril daughter of the king added her words to the king's wisdom so that Turgon bid Tuor rest himself awhile in Gondolin, and being forewise prevailed on him [to] abide there in the end. How he came to love the daughter of the king, Idril of the Silver Feet, and how he was taught deeply in the lore of that great folk and learned of its history and the history of the Elves. How Tuor grew in wisdom and mighty in the counsels of the Gondothlim.

The only narrative difference here from the actual text lies in the introduction of the king's daughter Idril as an influence on Tuor's decision to remain in Gondolin. The passage is otherwise an extremely abbreviated summary of the account of Tuor's instruction in Gondolin, with omission of what is said in the text about the preparations of the Gondothlim against attack; but I do not think that this was a proposal for shortening the written tale. Rather, the words 'If necessary' suggest strongly that my father had in mind only a reduction for oral delivery – and that was when it was read to the Exeter College Essay Club in the spring of 1920; see p. 147. Another proposed shortening is given in note 32.

22   This passage, beginning 'Great love too had Idril for Tuor . . .', was written on a separate slip and replaced the original text as follows:

> The king hearing of this, and finding that his child Idril, whom the Eldar speak of as Irildë, loved Tuor in return, he consented to their being wed, seeing that he had no son, and Tuor was like to make a kinsman of strength and consolation. There were Idril and Tuor wed before the folk in that Place of the Gods, Gar Ainion, nigh the king's palace; and that was a day of mirth to the city of Gondolin, but of (&c.)

The replacement states that the marriage of Tuor and Idril was the first but not the last of the unions of Man and Elf, whereas it is said in the Name-list to *The Fall of Gondolin* that Eärendel was 'the only being that is half of the kindred of the Eldalië and half of Men' (see p. 215).

23   The phrase 'and that tale of Isfin and Eöl may not here be told' was added to *Tuor B*. See p. 220.

24   Original reading: 'a name wrought of the tongue of the Gondothlim'.

25   The sapphires given to Manwë by the Noldoli are referred to in the

tale of *The Coming of the Elves*, I.128. The original pencilled text of *Tuor A* can be read here: 'bluer than the sapphires of Súlimo'.

26    The passage ending here and beginning with 'In these ways that bitter winter passed . . .' is inserted on a separate sheet in *Tuor B* (but is not part of the latest layer of emendation); it replaces a much shorter passage going back to the primary text of *Tuor A*:

> Now on midwinter's day at early even the sun sank betimes beyond the mountains, and lo! when she had gone a light arose beyond the hills to the north, and men marvelled (&c.)

See notes 34 and 37.

27    The Scarlet Heart: the heart of Finwë Nólemë, Turgon's father, was cut out by Orcs in the Battle of Unnumbered Tears, but it was regained by Turgon and became his emblem; see I. 241 and note 11.

28    This passage describing the array and the emblems of the houses of the Gondothlim was relatively very little affected by the later revision of *Tuor A*; the greater part of it is in the original pencilled text, which was allowed to stand, and all the names appear to be original.

29    The word 'burg' is used in the Old English sense of a walled and fortified town.

30    The death of Ecthelion in the primary text of *Tuor A* is legible; the revision introduced a few changes of wording, but no more.

31    This sentence, from 'and men shuddered', was added to *Tuor B*. On the prophecy see I.172.

32    *Tuor B* is bracketed from 'Now comes Tuor at their head to the Place of Wedding' on p. 186 to this point, and an inserted slip relating to this bracketing reads:

> How Tuor and his folk came upon Idril wandering distraught in the Place of the Gods. How Tuor and Idril from that high place saw the sack of the King's Hall and the ruin of the King's Tower and the passing of the king, for which reason the foe followed not after. How Tuor heard tidings of Voronwë that Idril had sent Eärendel and her guard down the hidden way, and fared into the city in search of her husband; how in peril from the enemy they had rescued many that fled and sent them down the secret way. How Tuor led his host with the luck of the Gods to the mouth of that passage, and how all descended into the plain, sealing the entrance utterly behind them. How the sorrowful company issued into a dell in the vale of Tumladin.

This is simply a summary of the text as it stands; I suppose it was a cut proposed for the recitation of the tale if that seemed to be taking too long (see note 21).

33    This passage, from 'Here were gathered . . .', replaced in *Tuor B* the original reading: 'Here they are fain to rest, but finding no signs of

Eärendel and his escort Tuor is downcast, and Idril weeps.' This was rewritten partly for narrative reasons, but also to put it into the past tense. In the next sentence the text was emended from 'Lamentation is there . . .' and 'about them looms . . .' But the sentence following ('Fire-drakes are about it . . .') was left untouched; and I think that it was my father's intention, only casually indicated and never carried through, to reduce the amount of 'historical present' in the narrative.

34  'for summer is at hand': the original reading was 'albeit it is winter'. See notes 26 and 37.

35  The original reading was:

> Now the Mountains were on that side seven leagues save a mile from Gondolin, and Cristhorn the Cleft of Eagles another league of upward going from the beginning of the Mountains; wherefore they were now yet two leagues and part of a third from the pass, and very weary thereto.

36  'Behold, his face shineth as a star in the waste' was added to *Tuor B*.

37  This passage, from 'But after a year and more of wandering . . .', replaced the original reading 'But after a half-year's wandering, nigh midsummer'. This emendation depends on the changing of the time of the attack on Gondolin from midwinter to the 'Gates of Summer' (see notes 26 and 34). Thus in the revised version summer is retained as the season when the exiles came to the lands about Sirion, but they spent a whole year and more, rather than a half-year, to reach them.

38  'even where Tulkas': original reading: 'even where Noldorin and Tulkas'. See pp. 278–9.

39  The original pencilled text of *Tuor A* had 'Fair among the Lothlim grows Eärendel in Sornontur the house of Tuor'. The fourth letter of this name could as well be read as a *u*.

### Changes made to names in
### *The Fall of Gondolin*

*Ilfiniol* < *Elfriniol* in the first three occurrences of the name in the initial linking passage, *Ilfiniol* so written at the fourth.

(In *The Cottage of Lost Play* (I.15) the Gong-warden of Mar Vanwa Tyaliéva is named only *Littleheart*; in the *Link* to *The Music of the Ainur* his Elvish name is *Ilverin* < *Elwenildo* (I.46, 52); and in the *Link* to the *Tale of Tinúviel* he is *Ilfiniol* < *Elfriniol* as here, while the typescript has *Ilfrin* (p. 7).

In the head-note to the Name-list to *The Fall of Gondolin* he is *Elfrith* < *Elfriniel*, and this is the only place where the meaning of the name 'Littleheart' is explained (p. 148); the Name-list has an

entry 'Elf meaneth "heart" (as Elfin Elben): Elfrith is Littleheart'
(see I.255, entry Ilverin). In another projected list of names,
abandoned after only a couple of entries had been made, we meet
again the form Elfrith, and also Elbenil > Elwenil.

This constant changing of name is to be understood in relation to
swiftly changing phonological ideas and formulations, but even so is
rather extraordinary.)

> In the following notes it is to be understood, for brevity's
> sake, that names in Tuor B (before emendation) are found
> in the same form in Tuor A; e.g. 'Mithrim < Asgon in Tuor B'
> implies that Tuor A has Asgon (unchanged).

Tuor    Although sometimes emended to Tûr in Tuor B, and invariably
written Tûr in the typescript Tuor C, I give Tuor throughout; see
p. 148.

Dor Lómin    This name was so written from the first in Tuor B. Tuor A
has, at the first three occurrences, Aryador > Mathusdor; at the
fourth, Aryador > Mathusdor > Dor Lómin.

Mithrim    < Asgon throughout Tuor B; Tuor C has Asgon unchanged.

Glorfalc or Cris Ilbranteloth (p. 150)    Tuor A has Glorfalc or Teld
Quing Ilon; Tuor B as written had no Elvish names, Glorfalc or
Cris Ilbranteloth being a later addition.

Ainur    As in the first draft of The Music of the Ainur (I.61) the
original text of Tuor A had Ainu plural.

Falasquil    At both occurrences (p. 152) in Tuor A this replaces the
original name now illegible but beginning with Q; in Tuor B my
mother left blanks and added the name later in pencil; in Tuor C
blanks are left in the typescript and not filled in.

Arlisgion    This name was added later to Tuor B.

Orcs    Tuor A and B had Orqui throughout; my father emended this in
Tuor B to Orcs, but not consistently, and in the later part of the
tale not at all. In one place only (p. 193, in Thorndor's speech)
both texts have Orcs (also Orc-bands p. 195). As with the name
Tuor/Tûr I give throughout the form that was to prevail.

At the only occurrence of the singular the word is written with a k
in both Tuor A and B ('Ork's blood', p. 165).

Gar Thurion    < Gar Furion in Tuor B (Gar Furion in Tuor C).

Loth    < Lôs in Tuor B (Lôs in Tuor C).

Lothengriol    < Lósengriol in Tuor B (Lósengriol in Tuor C).

Taniquetil    At the occurrence on p. 161 there was added in the original
text of Tuor A: (Danigwiel), but this was struck out.

Kôr    Against this name (p. 161) is pencilled in Tuor B: Tûn. See I.222,
II.292.

Gar Ainion    < Gar Ainon in Tuor B (p. 164; at the occurrence on
p. 186 not emended, but I read Gar Ainion in both places).

Nost-na-Lothion    < Nost-na-Lossion in Tuor B.

*Duilin*   At the first occurrence (p. 173) < *Duliglin* in the original text of *Tuor A*.

*Rog*   In *Tuor A* spelt *Rôg* in the earlier occurrences, *Rog* in the later; in *Tuor B* spelt *Rôg* throughout but mostly emended later to *Rog*.

*Dramborleg*   At the occurrence on p. 181 < *Drambor* in the original text of *Tuor A*.

*Bansil*   At the occurrence on p. 184 only, *Bansil* > *Banthil* in *Tuor B*.

*Cristhorn*   From the first occurrence on p. 189 written *Cristhorn* (not *Cris Thorn*) in *Tuor A*; *Cris Thorn Tuor B* throughout.

*Bad Uthwen*   < *Bad Uswen* in *Tuor B*. The original reading in *Tuor A* was (apparently) *Bad Usbran*.

*Sorontur*   < *Ramandur* in *Tuor B*.

*Bablon, Ninwi, Trui, Rûm*   The original text of *Tuor A* had *Babylon, Nineveh, Troy,* and (probably) *Rome*. These were changed to the forms given in the text, except *Nineveh* > *Ninwë*, changed to *Ninwi* in *Tuor B*.


Commentary on
*The Fall of Gondolin*

§1.   *The primary narrative*

As with the *Tale of Turambar* I break my commentary on this tale into sections. I refer frequently to the much later version (which extends only to the coming of Tuor and Voronwë to sight of Gondolin across the plain) printed in *Unfinished Tales* pp. 17–51 ('Of Tuor and his Coming to Gondolin'); this I shall call here 'the later *Tuor*'.


(i)   *Tuor's journey to the Sea and the visitation of Ulmo* (pp. 149–56)

In places the later *Tuor* (the abandonment of which is one of the saddest facts in the whole history of incompletion) is so close in wording to *The Fall of Gondolin*, written more than thirty years before, as to make it almost certain that my father had it in front of him, or at least had recently reread it. Striking examples from the late version (pp. 23–4) are: 'The sun rose behind his back and set before his face, and where the water foamed among the boulders or rushed over sudden falls, at morning and evening rainbows were woven across the stream'; 'Now he said: "It is a fay-voice," now: "Nay, it is a small beast that is wailing in the waste"'; '[Tuor] wandered still for some days in a rugged country bare of trees; and it was swept by a wind from the sea, and all that grew there, herb or bush, leaned ever to the dawn because of the prevalence of that wind from the West' – which are very closely similar to or almost identical with passages in the tale (pp. 150–1). But the differences in the narrative are profound.

Tuor's origin is left vague in the old story. There is a reference in the *Tale of Turambar* (p. 88) to 'those kindreds about the waters of Asgon whence after arose Tuor son of Peleg', but here it is said that Tuor did not dwell with his people (who 'wandered the forests and fells') but 'lived alone about that lake called Mithrim [< Asgon]', on which he journeyed in a small boat with a prow made like the neck of a swan. There is indeed scarcely any linking reference to other events, and of course no trace of the Grey-elves of Hithlum who in the later story fostered him, or of his outlawry and hunting by the Easterlings; but there are 'wandering Noldoli' in Dor Lómin (Hisilómë, Hithlum) − on whom see p. 65 − from whom Tuor learnt much, including their tongue, and it was they who guided him down the dark river-passage under the mountains. There is in this a premonition of Gelmir and Arminas, the Noldorin Elves who guided Tuor through the Gate of the Noldor (later *Tuor* pp. 21–2), and the story that the Noldoli 'made that hidden way at the prompting of Ulmo' survived in the much richer historical context of the later legend, where 'the Gate of the Noldor . . . was made by the skill of that people, long ago in the days of Turgon' (later *Tuor* p. 18).

The later *Tuor* becomes very close to the old story for a time when Tuor emerges out of the tunnel into the ravine (later called Cirith Ninniach, but still a name of Tuor's own devising); many features recur, such as the stars shining in the 'dark lane of sky above him', the echoes of his harping (in the tale of course without the literary echoes of Morgoth's cry and the voices of Fëanor's host that landed there), his doubt concerning the mournful calling of the gulls, the narrowing of the ravine where the incoming tide (fierce because of the west wind) met the water of the river, and Tuor's escape by climbing to the cliff-top (but in the tale the connection between Tuor's curiosity concerning the gulls and the saving of his life is not made: he climbed the cliff in response to the prompting of the Ainur). Notable is the retention of the idea that Tuor was the first of Men to reach the Sea, standing on the cliff-top with outspread arms, and of his 'sea-longing' (later *Tuor* p. 25). But the story of his dwelling in the cove of Falasquil and his adornment of it with carvings (and of course the floating of timber down the river to him by the Noldoli of Dor Lómin) was abandoned; in the later legend Tuor finds on the coast ruins of the ancient harbour-works of the Noldor from the days of Turgon's lordship in Nevrast, and of Turgon's former dwelling in these regions before he went to Gondolin there is in the old story no trace. Thus the entire Vinyamar episode is absent from it, and despite the frequent reminder that Ulmo was guiding Tuor as the instrument of his designs, the essential element in the later legend of the arms left for him by Turgon on Ulmo's instruction (*The Silmarillion* pp. 126, 238–9) is lacking.

The southward-flying swans (seven, not three, in the later *Tuor*) play essentially the same part in both narratives, drawing Tuor to continue his journey; but the emblem of the Swan was afterwards given a different origin, as 'the token of Annael and his foster-folk', the Grey-elves of Mithrim (later *Tuor* p. 25).

Both in the route taken (for the geography see p. 217) and in the seasons of the year my father afterwards departed largely from the original story of Tuor's journey to Gondolin. In the later *Tuor* it was the Fell Winter after the fall of Nargothrond, the winter of Túrin's return to Hithlum, when he and Voronwë journeyed in snow and bitter cold eastwards beneath the Mountains of Shadow. Here the journey takes far longer: he left Falasquil in 'the latest days of summer' (as still in the later *Tuor*) but he went down all the coast of Beleriand to the mouths of Sirion, and it was the summer of the following year when he lingered in the Land of Willows. (Doubtless the geography was less definite than it afterwards became, but its general resemblance to the later map seems assured by the description (p. 153) of the coast's trending after a time eastwards rather than southwards.)

Only in its place in the narrative structure is there resemblance between Ulmo's visitation of Tuor in the Land of Willows in a summer twilight and his tremendous epiphany out of the rising storm on the coast at Vinyamar. It is however most remarkable that the old vision of the Land of Willows and its drowsy beauty of river-flowers and butterflies was not lost, though afterwards it was Voronwë, not Tuor, who wandered there, devising names, and who stood enchanted 'knee-deep in the grass' (p. 155; later *Tuor* p. 35), until his fate, or Ulmo Lord of Waters, carried him down to the Sea. Possibly there is a faint reminiscence of the old story in Ulmo's words (later *Tuor* p. 28): 'Haste thou must learn, and *the pleasant road that I designed for thee* must be changed.'

In the tale, Ulmo's speech to Tuor (or at least that part of it that is reported) is far more simple and brief, and there is no suggestion there of Ulmo's 'opposing the will of his brethren, the Lords of the West'; but two essential elements of his later message are present, that Tuor will find the words to speak when he stands before Turgon, and the reference to Tuor's unborn son (in the later *Tuor* much less explicit: 'But it is not for thy valour only that I send thee, but to bring into the world a hope beyond thy sight, and a light that shall pierce the darkness').

(ii)   *The journey of Tuor and Voronwë to Gondolin* (pp. 156–8)

Of Tuor's journey to Gondolin, apart from his sojourn in the Land of Willows, little is told in the tale, and Voronwë only appears late in its course as the one Noldo who was not too fearful to accompany him further; of Voronwë's history as afterwards related there is no word, and he is not an Elf of Gondolin.

It is notable that the Noldoli who guided Tuor northwards from the Land of Willows call themselves thralls of Melko. On this matter the *Tales* present a consistent picture. It is said in the *Tale of Tinúviel* (p. 9) that

> all the Eldar both those who remained in the dark or who had been lost upon the march from Palisor and those Noldoli too who fared back into the world after [Melko] seeking their stolen treasury fell beneath his power as thralls.

In *The Fall of Gondolin* it is said that the Noldoli did their service to Ulmo in secret, and 'out of fear of Melko wavered much' (p. 154), and Voronwë spoke to Tuor of 'the weariness of thraldom' (pp. 156–7); Melko sent out his army of spies 'to search out the dwelling of the Noldoli that had escaped his thraldom' (p. 166). These 'thrall-Noldoli' are represented as moving as it were freely about the lands, even to the mouths of Sirion, but they 'wandered as in a dream of fear, doing [Melko's] ill bidding, for the spell of bottomless dread was on them and they felt the eyes of Melko burn them from afar' (*Tale of Turambar*, p. 77). This expression is often used: Voronwë rejoiced in Gondolin that he no longer dreaded Melko with 'a binding terror' – 'and of a sooth that spell which Melko held over the Noldoli was one of bottomless dread, so that he seemed ever nigh them even were they far from the Hells of Iron, and their hearts quaked and they fled not even when they could' (p. 159). The spell of bottomless dread was laid too on Meglin (p. 169).

There is little in all this that cannot be brought more or less into harmony with the later narratives, and indeed one may hear an echo in the words of *The Silmarillion* (p. 156):

> But ever the Noldor feared most the treachery of those of their own kin, who had been thralls in Angband; for Morgoth used some of these for his evil purposes, and feigning to give them liberty sent them abroad, but their wills were chained to his, and they strayed only to come back to him again.

Nonetheless one gains the impression that at that time my father pictured the power of Melko when at its height as operating more diffusedly and intangibly, and perhaps also more universally, in the Great Lands. Whereas in *The Silmarillion* the Noldor who are not free are prisoners in Angband (whence a few may escape, and others with enslaved wills may be sent out), here all save the Gondothlim are 'thralls', controlled by Melko from afar, and Melko asserts that the Noldoli are all, by their very existence in the Great Lands, his slaves by right. It is a difference difficult to define, but that there is a difference may be seen in the improbability, for the later story, of Tuor being guided on his way to Gondolin by Noldor who were in any sense slaves of Morgoth.

The entrance to Gondolin has some general similarity to the far fuller and more precisely visualised account in the later *Tuor*: a deep river-gorge, tangled bushes, a cave-mouth – but the river is certainly Sirion (see the passage at the end of the tale, p. 195, where the exiles come back to the entrance), and the entrance to the secret way is in one of the steep river banks, quite unlike the description of the Dry River whose ancient bed was itself the secret way (later *Tuor* pp. 43–4). The long tunnel which Tuor and Voronwë traverse in the tale leads them at length not only to the Guard but also to sunlight, and they are 'at the foot of steep hills' and can see the city: in other words there is a simple conception of a plain, a ring-wall of mountains, and a tunnel through them leading to the outer world. In the later *Tuor* the approach to the city is much stranger: for the tunnel of the Guard leads to the ravine of Orfalch Echor, a great rift from top to bottom of the Encircling Mountains ('sheer as if axe-cloven', p. 46), up which the road climbed through the successive gates until it came to the Seventh Gate, barring the rift at the top. Only when this last gate was opened and Tuor passed through was he able to see Gondolin; and we must suppose (though the narrative does not reach this point) that the travellers had to descend again from the Seventh Gate in order to reach the plain.

It is notable that Tuor and Voronwë are received by the Guard without any of the suspicion and menace that greeted them in the later story (p. 45).

### (iii)   *Tuor in Gondolin* (pp. 159–64)

With this section of the narrative compare *The Silmarillion*, p. 126:

> Behind the circle of the mountains the people of Turgon grew and throve, and they put forth their skill in labour unceasing, so that Gondolin upon Amon Gwareth became fair indeed and fit to compare even with Elven Tirion beyond the sea. High and white were its walls, and smooth its stairs, and tall and strong was the Tower of the King. There shining fountains played, and in the courts of Turgon stood images of the Trees of old, which Turgon himself wrought with elven-craft; and the Tree which he made of gold was named Glingal, and the Tree whose flowers he made of silver was named Belthil.

The image of Gondolin was enduring, and it reappears in the glimpses given in notes for the continuation of the later *Tuor* (*Unfinished Tales* p. 56): 'the stairs up to its high platform, and its great gate . . . the Place of the Fountain, the King's tower on a pillared arcade, the King's house . . .' Indeed the only real difference that emerges from the original account concerns the Trees of Gondolin, which in the former were unfading, 'shoots of old from the glorious Trees of Valinor', but in *The Silmarillion* were images made of the precious metals. On the Trees of Gondolin see the entries *Bansil* and *Glingol* from the Name-list, given below pp. 214–16. The gift by the Gods of these 'shoots' (which 'blossomed eternally without abating') to Inwë and Nólemë at the time of the building of Kôr, each being given a shoot of either Tree, is mentioned in *The Coming of the Elves* (I.123), and in *The Hiding of Valinor* there is a reference to the uprooting of those given to Nólemë, which 'were gone no one knew whither, and more had there never been' (I.213).

But a deep underlying shift in the history of Gondolin separates the earlier and later accounts: for whereas in the *Lost Tales* (and later) Gondolin was only discovered *after* the Battle of Unnumbered Tears when the host of Turgon retreated southwards down Sirion, in *The Silmarillion* it had been found by Turgon of Nevrast more than four hundred years before (442 years before Tuor came to Gondolin in the Fell Winter after the fall of Nargothrond in the year 495 of the Sun). In the tale my father imagined a great age passing *between* the Battle of Unnumbered Tears and the destruction of the city ('unstaying labour *through ages of years* had not sufficed to its building and adornment whereat folk travailed yet', p. 163); afterwards, with radical changes in the chronology of the First Age after the rising of the Sun and Moon, this period was reduced to no more than (in the last extant version of 'The Tale of Years' of the First Age) thirty-eight years. But the old conception can still be felt in the passage on p. 240 of *The Silmarillion* describing the withdrawal of the people of Gondolin from all concern with the world outside after the Nirnaeth Arnoediad, with its air of long years passing.*

In *The Silmarillion* it is explicit that Turgon devised the city to be 'a memorial of Tirion upon Túna' (p. 125), and it became 'as beautiful as a memory of Elven Tirion' (p. 240). This is not said in the old story, and indeed in the *Lost Tales* Turgon himself had never known Kôr (he was born in the Great Lands after the return of the Noldoli from Valinor, I.167, 238, 240); one may feel nonetheless that the tower of the King, the fountains and stairs, the white marbles of Gondolin embody a recollection of Kôr as it is described in *The Coming of the Elves and the Making of Kôr* (I.122–3).

I have said above that 'despite the frequent reminder that Ulmo was guiding Tuor as the instrument of his designs, the essential element in the later legend of the arms left for him by Turgon on Ulmo's instruction is lacking'. Now however we seem to see the germ of this conception in Turgon's words to Tuor (p. 161): 'Thy coming was set in our books of wisdom, and it has been written that there would come to pass many great things in the homes of the Gondothlim whenso thou faredst hither.' Yet it is clear from Tuor's reply that as yet the establishment of Gondolin was no part of Ulmo's design, since 'there have come to the ears of Ulmo whispers of your dwelling and your hill of vigilance against the evil of Melko, and he is glad'.

---

* Of the story of Gondolin from Tuor's coming to its destruction my father wrote nothing after the version of 'The Silmarillion' made (very probably) in 1930; and in this the old conception of its history was still present. This was the basis for much of Chapter 23 in the published work.

In the tale, Ulmo foresaw that Turgon would be unwilling to take up arms against Melko, and he fell back, through the mouth of Tuor, on a second counsel: that Turgon send Elves from Gondolin down Sirion to the coasts, there to build ships to carry messages to Valinor. To this Turgon replied, decisively and unanswerably, that he had sent messengers down the great river with this very purpose 'for years untold', and since all had been unavailing he would now do so no more. Now this clearly relates to a passage in *The Silmarillion* (p. 159) where it is said that Turgon, after the Dagor Bragollach and the breaking of the Siege of Angband,

> sent companies of the Gondolindrim in secret to the mouths of Sirion and the Isle of Balar. There they built ships, and set sail into the uttermost West upon Turgon's errand, seeking for Valinor, to ask for pardon and aid of the Valar; and they besought the birds of the sea to guide them. But the seas were wild and wide, and shadow and enchantment lay upon them; and Valinor was hidden. Therefore none of the messengers of Turgon came into the West, and many were lost and few returned.

Turgon did indeed do so once more, after the Battle of Unnumbered Tears (*The Silmarillion* p. 196), and the only survivor of that last expedition into the West was Voronwë of Gondolin. Thus, despite profound changes in chronology and a great development in the narrative of the last centuries of the First Age, the idea of the desperate attempts of Turgon to get a message through to Valinor goes back to the beginning.

Another aboriginal feature is that Turgon had no son; but (curiously) no mention whatsoever is made in the tale of his wife, the mother of Idril. In *The Silmarillion* (p. 90) his wife Elenwë was lost in the crossing of the Helcaraxë, but obviously this story belongs to a later period, when Turgon was born in Valinor.

The tale of Tuor's sojourn in Gondolin survived into the brief words of *The Silmarillion* (p. 241):

> And Tuor remained in Gondolin, for its bliss and its beauty and the wisdom of its people held him enthralled; and he became mighty in stature and in mind, and learned deeply of the lore of the exiled Elves.

In the present tale he 'heard tell of Ilúvatar, the Lord for Always, who dwelleth beyond the world', and of the Music of the Ainur. Knowledge of the very existence of Ilúvatar was, it seems, a prerogative of the Elves; long afterwards in the garden of Mar Vanwa Tyaliéva (I. 49) Eriol asked Rúmil: 'Who was Ilúvatar? Was he of the Gods?' and Rúmil answered: 'Nay, that he was not; for he made them. Ilúvatar is the Lord for Always, who dwells beyond the world.'

(iv)   *The encirclement of Gondolin;*
*the treachery of Meglin* (pp. 164–71)

The king's daughter was from the first named 'Idril of the Silver Feet' (Irildë in the language of the 'Eldar', note 22); Meglin (later Maeglin) was his nephew, though the name of his mother (Turgon's sister) Isfin was later changed.

In this section of the narrative the story in *The Silmarillion* (pp. 241–2) preserved all the essentials of the original version, with one major exception. The wedding of Tuor and Idril took place with the consent and full favour of the king, and there was great joy in Gondolin among all save Maeglin (whose love of Idril is told earlier in *The Silmarillion*, p. 139, where the barrier of his being close kin to her, not mentioned in the tale, is emphasised). Idril's power of foreseeing and her foreboding of evil to come; the secret way of her devising (but in the tale this led south from the city, and the Eagles' Cleft was in the southern mountains); the loss of Meglin in the hills while seeking for ore; his capture by Orcs, his treacherous purchase of life, and his return to Gondolin to avert suspicion (with the detail of his changed mood thereafter and 'smiling face') – all this remained. Much is of course absent (whether rejected or merely passed over) in the succinct account devised for *The Silmarillion* – where there is no mention, for example, of Idril's dream concerning Meglin, the watch set on him when he went to the hills, the formation on Idril's advice of a guard bearing Tuor's emblem, the refusal of Turgon to doubt the invulnerability of the city and his trust in Meglin, Meglin's discovery of the secret way,* or the remarkable story that it was Meglin himself who conceived the idea of the monsters of fire and iron and communicated it to Melko – a valuable defector indeed!

The great difference between the versions lies of course in the nature of Melko/Morgoth's knowledge of Gondolin. In the tale, he had by means of a vast army of spies† already discovered it before ever Meglin was captured, and creatures of Melko had found the 'Way of Escape' and looked down on Gondolin from the surrounding heights. Meglin's treachery in the old story lay in his giving an exact account of the structure of the city and the preparations made for its defence – and in his advice to Melko concerning the monsters of flame. In *The Silmarillion*, on the other hand, there is the element, devised much later, of the unconscious betrayal by Húrin to Morgoth's spies of the general region in which Gondolin must be sought, in 'the mountainous land between

---

* This is in fact specifically denied in *The Silmarillion*: 'she contrived it that the work was known but to few, and no whisper of it came to Maeglin's ears.'

† It seems that the 'creatures of blood' (said to be disliked by the people of Gondolin, p. 166), snakes, wolves, weasels, owls, falcons, are here regarded as the natural servants and allies of Melko.

Anach and the upper waters of Sirion, whither [Morgoth's] servants had never passed' (p. 241); but 'still no spy or creature out of Angband could come there because of the vigilance of the eagles' – and of this rôle of the eagles of the Encircling Mountains (though hostile to Melko, p. 193) there is in the original story no suggestion.

Thus in *The Silmarillion* Morgoth remained in ignorance until Maeglin's capture of the precise location of Gondolin, and Maeglin's information was of correspondingly greater value to him, as it was also of greater damage to the city. The history of the last years of Gondolin has thus a somewhat different atmosphere in the tale, for the Gondothlim are informed of the fact that Melko has 'encompassed the vale of Tumladin around' (p. 167), and Turgon makes preparations for war and strengthens the watch on the hills. The withdrawal of all Melko's spies shortly before the attack on Gondolin did indeed bring about a renewal of optimism among the Gondothlim, and in Turgon not least, so that when the attack came the people were unprepared; but in the later story the shock of the sudden assault is much greater, for there has never been any reason to suppose that the city is in immediate danger, and Idril's foreboding is peculiar to herself and more mysterious.

### (v) *The array of the Gondothlim* (pp. 171–4)

Though the central image of this part of the story – the people of Gondolin looking out from their walls to hail the rising sun on the feast of the Gates of Summer, but seeing a red light rising in the north and not in the east – survived, of all the heraldry in this passage scarcely anything is found in later writings. Doubtless, if my father had continued the later *Tuor*, much would have re-emerged, however changed, if we judge by the rich 'heraldic' descriptions of the great gates and their guards in the Orfalch Echor (pp. 46–50). But in the concise account in *The Silmarillion* the only vestiges are the titles Ecthelion 'of the Fountain'* and Glorfindel 'chief of the House of the Golden Flower of Gondolin'. Ecthelion and Glorfindel are named also in *The Silmarillion* (p. 194) as Turgon's captains who guarded the flanks of the host of Gondolin in their retreat down Sirion from the Nirnaeth Arnoediad, but of other captains named in the tale there is no mention afterwards† – though it is significant that the eighteenth Ruling Steward of Gondor was named Egalmoth, as the

---

* In the later *Tuor* (p. 50) he is 'Lord of the Fountains', plural (the reading in the manuscript is certain).

† In the version of 'The Silmarillion' made in 1930 (see footnote on p. 208), the last account of the Fall of Gondolin to be written and the basis for that in chapter 23 of the published work, the text actually reads: '. . . much is told in *The Fall of Gondolin*: of the death of Rog without the walls, and of the battle of Ecthelion of the Fountain ', &c. I removed the reference to Rog (*The Silmarillion* p. 242) on the grounds that it was absolutely certain that my father would not have retained this name as that of a lord of Gondolin.

seventeenth and twenty-fifth were named Ecthelion (*The Lord of the Rings*, Appendix A (I,ii)).*

Glorfindel 'of the golden hair' (p. 192) remains 'yellow-haired Glorfindel' in *The Silmarillion*, and this was from the beginning the meaning of his name.

## (vi)   *The battle of Gondolin* (pp. 174–88)

Virtually the entire history of the fighting in Gondolin is unique in the tale of *The Fall of Gondolin*; the whole story is summarised in *The Silmarillion* (p. 242) in a few lines:

> Of the deeds of desperate valour there done, by the chieftains of the noble houses and their warriors, and not least by Tuor, much is told in *The Fall of Gondolin*: of the battle of Ecthelion of the Fountain with Gothmog Lord of Balrogs in the very square of the King, where each slew the other, and of the defence of the tower of Turgon by the people of his household, until the tower was overthrown: and mighty was its fall and the fall of Turgon in its ruin.
>
> Tuor sought to rescue Idril from the sack of the city, but Maeglin had laid hands on her, and on Eärendil; and Tuor fought with Maeglin on the walls, and cast him far out, and his body as it fell smote the rocky slopes of Amon Gwareth thrice ere it pitched into the flames below. Then Tuor and Idril led such remnants of the people of Gondolin as they could gather in the confusion of the burning down the secret way which Idril had prepared.

(In this highly compressed account the detail that Maeglin's body struck the slopes of Amon Gwareth three times before it 'pitched' into the flames was retained.) It would seem from *The Silmarillion* account that Maeglin's attempt on Idril and Eärendil took place much later in the fighting, and indeed shortly before the escape of the fugitives down the tunnel; but I think that this is far more likely to be the result of compression than of a change in the narrative of the battle.

In the tale Gondolin is very clearly visualised as a city, with its markets and its great squares, of which there are only vestiges in later writing (see above, p. 207); and there is nothing vague in the description of the fighting. The early conception of the Balrogs makes them less terrible, and certainly more destructible, than they afterwards became: they

---

* In a very late note written on one of the texts that constitute chapter 16 of *The Silmarillion* ('Of Maeglin') my father was thinking of making the 'three lords of his household' whom Turgon appointed to ride with Aredhel from Gondolin (p. 131) Glorfindel, Ecthelion, and Egalmoth. He notes that Ecthelion and Egalmoth 'are derived from the primitive F[all of]G[ondolin]', but that they 'are well-sounding and have been in print' (with reference to the names of the Stewards of Gondor). Subsequently he decided against naming Aredhel's escort.

existed in 'hundreds' (p. 170),* and were slain by Tuor and the Gondothlim in large numbers: thus five fell before Tuor's great axe Dramborleg, three before Ecthelion's sword, and two score were slain by the warriors of the king's house. The Balrogs are 'demons of power' (p. 181); they are capable of pain and fear (p. 194); they are attired in iron armour (pp. 181, 194), and they have whips of flame (a character they never lost) and claws of steel (pp. 169, 179).

In *The Silmarillion* the dragons that came against Gondolin were 'of the brood of Glaurung', which 'were become now many and terrible'; whereas in the tale the language employed (p. 170) suggests that some at least of the 'Monsters' were inanimate 'devices', the construction of smiths in the forges of Angband. But even the 'things of iron' that 'opened about their middles' to disgorge bands of Orcs are called 'ruthless beasts', and Gothmog 'bade' them 'pile themselves' (p. 176); those made of bronze or copper 'were given hearts and spirits of blazing fire'; while the 'fire-drake' that Tuor hewed screamed and lashed with its tail (p. 181).

A small detail of the narrative is curious: what 'messengers' did Meglin send to Melko to warn him to guard the outer entrance of the Way of Escape (where he guessed that the secret tunnel must lead in the end)? Whom could Meglin trust sufficiently? And who would dare to go?

(vii)    *The escape of the fugitives and the battle in Cristhorn* (pp. 188–95)

The story as told in *The Silmarillion* (p. 243) is somewhat fuller in its account of the escape of the fugitives from the city and the ambush in the Eagles' Cleft (there called Cirith Thoronath) than in that of the assault and sack itself, but only in one point are the two narratives actually at variance – as already noticed, the Eagles' Cleft was afterwards moved from the southern parts of the Encircling Mountains to the northern, and Idril's tunnel led north from the city (the comment is made that it was not thought 'that any fugitives would take a path towards the north and the highest parts of the mountains and the nighest to Angband'). The tale provides a richness of detail and an immediacy that is lacking in the short version, where such things as the tripping over dead bodies in the hot and reeking underground passage have disappeared; and there is no mention of the Gondothlim who against the counsel of Idril and Tuor went to the Way of Escape and were there destroyed by the dragon lying in wait,† or of the fight to rescue Eärendel.

* The idea that Morgoth disposed of a 'host' of Balrogs endured long, but in a late note my father said that only very few ever existed – 'at most seven'.

† This element in the story was in fact still present in the 1930 'Silmarillion' (see footnote on p. 208), but I excluded it from the published work on account of evidence in a much later text that the old entrance to Gondolin had by this time been blocked up – a fact which was then written into the text in chapter 23 of *The Silmarillion*.

In the tale appears the keen-sighted Elf Legolas Greenleaf, first of the names of the Fellowship of the Ring to appear in my father's writings (see p. 217 on this earlier Legolas), followed by Gimli (an Elf) in the *Tale of Tinúviel*.

In one point the story of the ambush in Cristhorn seems difficult to follow: this is the statement on p. 193 that the moon 'lit not the path for the height of the walls'. The fugitives were moving southwards through the Encircling Mountains, and the sheer rockwall above the path in the Eagles' Cleft was 'of the right or westerly hand', while on the left there was 'a fall . . . dreadly steep'. Surely then the moon rising in the east would illuminate the path?

The name *Cristhorn* appears in my father's drawing of 'Gondolin and the Vale of Tumladin from Cristhorn', September 1928 (*Pictures by J. R. R. Tolkien*, 1979, no. 35).

### (viii)   *The wanderings of the Exiles of Gondolin* (pp. 195–7)

In *The Silmarillion* (p. 243) it is said that 'led by Tuor son of Huor the remnant of Gondolin passed over the mountains, and came down into the Vale of Sirion'. One would suppose that they came down into Dimbar, and so 'fleeing southward by weary and dangerous marches they came at length to Nan-tathren, the Land of Willows'. It seems strange in the tale that the exiles were wandering in the wilderness for more than a year, and yet achieved only to the outer entrance of the Way of Escape; but the geography of this region may have been vaguer when *The Fall of Gondolin* was written.

In *The Silmarillion* when Tuor and Idril went down from Nan-tathren to the mouths of Sirion they 'joined their people to the company of Elwing, Dior's daughter, that had fled thither but a little while before'. Of this there is no mention here; but I postpone consideration of this part of the narrative.

### §2   *Entries in the Name-list to The Fall of Gondolin*

On this list see p. 148, where the head-note to it is given. Specifically linguistic information from the list, including meanings, is incorporated in the Appendix on Names, but I collect here some statements of other kind (arranged in alphabetical order) that are contained in it.

*Bablon* 'was a city of Men, and more rightly *Babylon*, but such is the Gnomes' name as they now shape it, and they got it from Men aforetime.'

*Bansil* 'Now this name had the Gondothlim for that tree before their king's door which bore silver blossom and faded not – and its name had Elfriniel from his father Voronwë; and it meaneth "Fairgleam". Now that tree of which it was a shoot (brought in the deep ages out of Valinor by the Noldoli) had like properties, but greater, seeing that for half the twenty-four hours it lit all Valinor with silver light. This the Eldar still tell of as *Silpion* or "Cherry-moon", for its blossom was like that of a cherry in spring – but of that tree in Gondolin they know no name, and the Noldoli tell of it alone.'

*Dor Lómin* 'or the "Land of Shadows" was that region named of the Eldar Hisilómë (and this means Shadowy Twilights) where Melko shut Men, and it is so called by reason of the scanty sun which peeps little over the Iron Mountains to the east and south of it – there dwell now the Shadow Folk. Thence came Tuor to Gondolin.'

*Eärendel* 'was the son of Tuor and Idril and 'tis said the only being that is half of the kindred of the Eldalië and half of Men. He was the greatest and first of all mariners among Men, and saw regions that Men have not yet found nor gazed upon for all the multitude of their boats. He rideth now with Voronwë upon the winds of the firmament nor comes ever further back than Kôr, else would he die like other Men, so much of the mortal is in him.'

(For these last statements about Eärendel see pp. 264–5. The statement that Eärendel was 'the only being that is half of the kindred of the Eldalië and half of Men' is very notable. Presumably this was written when Beren was an Elf, not a Man (see p. 139); Dior son of Beren and Tinúviel appears in the *Tale of the Nauglafring*, but there Beren is an Elf, and Dior is not Half-elven. In the tale of *The Fall of Gondolin* itself it is said, but in a later replacement passage (p. 164 and note 22), that Tuor was the first but not the last to wed 'a daughter of Elfinesse'. On the extraordinary statement in the *Tale of Turambar* that Tamar Lamefoot was Half-elven see p. 130.)

*Ecthelion* 'was that lord of the house of the Fountain, who had the fairest voice and was most skilled in musics of all the Gondothlim. He won renown for ever by his slaying of Gothmog son of Melko, whereby Tuor was saved from death but Ecthelion was drowned with his foe in the king's fountain.'

*Egalmoth* was 'lord of the house of the Heavenly Arch, and got even out of the burning of Gondolin, and dwelt after at the mouth of Sirion, but was slain in a dire battle there when Melko seized Elwing'. (See p. 258.)

*Galdor* 'was that valiant Gnome who led the men of the Tree in many a charge and yet won out of Gondolin and even the onslaught of Melko upon the dwellers at Sirion's mouth and went back to the ruins with Eärendel. He dwelleth yet in Tol Eressëa (said Elfriniel), and still do some of his folk name themselves *Nos Galdon*, for *Galdon* is a tree, and thereto Galdor's name akin.' The last phrase was emended to read: '*Nos nan Alwen*, for *Alwen* is a Tree.'

(For Galdor's return to the ruins of Gondolin with Eärendel see p. 258.)

*Glingol* 'meaneth "singing-gold" ('tis said), and this name was that which the Gondothlim had for that other of the two unfading trees in the king's square which bore golden bloom. It also was a shoot from the trees of Valinor (see rather where Elfrith has spoken of Bansil), but of Lindeloktë (which is "singing-cluster") or Laurelin [*emended from* Lindelaurë] (which is "singing-gold") which lit all Valinor with golden light for half the 24 hours.'

(For the name *Lindeloktë* see I. 22, 258 (entry *Lindelos*).)

*Glorfindel* 'led the Golden Flower and was the best beloved of the Gondothlim, save it be Ecthelion, but who shall choose. Yet he was hapless and fell slaying a Balrog in the great fight in Cristhorn. His name meaneth Goldtress for his hair was golden, and the name of his house in Noldorissa *Los'lóriol'* (emended from *Los Glóriol*).

*Gondolin* 'meaneth stone of song (whereby figuratively the Gnomes meant stone that was carven and wrought to great beauty), and this was the name most usual of the Seven Names they gave to their city of secret refuge from Melko in those days before the release.'

*Gothmog* 'was a son of Melko and the ogress Fluithuin and his name is Strife-and-hatred, and he was Captain of the Balrogs and lord of Melko's hosts ere fair Ecthelion slew him at the taking of Gondolin. The Eldar named him *Kosmoko* or *Kosomok(o)*, but 'tis a name that fitteth their tongue no way and has an ill sound even in our own rougher speech, said Elfrith [*emended from* Elfriniel].'

(In a list of names of the Valar associated with the tale of *The Coming of the Valar* (I.93) it is said that Melko had a son 'by Ulbandi' called *Kosomot*; the early 'Qenya' dictionary gives *Kosomoko* = Gnomish *Gothmog*, I.258. In the tale Gothmog is called the 'marshal' of the hosts of Melko (p. 184).)

In the later development of the legends Gothmog was the slayer of Fëanor, and in the Battle of Unnumbered Tears it was he who slew Fingon and captured Húrin (*The Silmarillion* pp. 107, 193, 195). He is not of course called later 'son of Melkor'; the 'Children of the Valar' was a feature of the earlier mythology that my father discarded.

In the Third Age *Gothmog* was the name of the lieutenant of Minas Morgul (*The Return of the King* V.6).)

*Hendor* 'was a house-carle of Idril's and was aged, but bore Eärendel down the secret passage.'

*Idril* 'was that most fair daughter of the king of Gondolin whom Tuor loved when she was but a little maid, and who bare him Eärendel. Her the Elves name *Irildë*; and we speak of as *Idril Tal-Celeb* or Idril of the Silver Feet, but they *Irildë Taltelepta*.'

See the Appendix on Names, entry *Idril*.

*Indor* 'was the name of the father of Tuor's father, wherefore did the Gnomes name Eärendel *Gon Indor* and the Elves *Indorildo* or *Indorion*.'

*Legolas* 'or Green-leaf was a man of the Tree, who led the exiles over Tumladin in the dark, being night-sighted, and he liveth still in Tol Eressëa named by the Eldar there *Laiqalassë*; but the book of Rúmil saith further hereon.'
(See I. 267, entry *Tári-Laisi*.)

## §3  *Miscellaneous Matters*

### (i)  *The geography of The Fall of Gondolin*

I have noticed above (p. 205) that in Tuor's journey all along the coast of what was afterwards Beleriand to the mouths of Sirion there is an unquestionable resemblance to the later map, in the trend of the coast from north-south to east-west. It is also said that after he left Falasquil 'the distant hills marched ever nearer to the margin of the sea', and that the spurs of the Iron Mountains 'run even to the sea' (pp. 152–3). These statements can likewise be readily enough related to the map, where the long western extension of the Mountains of Shadow (Ered Wethrin), forming the southern border of Nevrast, reached the sea at Vinyamar (for the equation of the Mountains of Iron and the Mountains of Shadow see I. 111–12).

Arlisgion, 'the place of reeds' (p. 153) above the mouths of Sirion, survived in Lisgardh 'the land of reeds at the Mouths of Sirion' in the later *Tuor* (p. 34); and the feature that the great river passed underground for a part of its course goes back to the earliest period, as does that of the Meres of Twilight, Aelin-uial ('the Pools of Twilight', p. 195). There is here however a substantial difference in the tale from *The Silmarillion* (p. 122), where Aelin-uial was the region of great pools and marshes where 'the flood of Sirion was stayed'; *south of the Meres* the river 'fell from the north in a mighty fall . . . and then he plunged suddenly underground into great tunnels that the weight of his falling waters delved'. Here on the other hand the Pools of Twilight are clearly *below* the 'cavern of the Tumultuous Winds' (never mentioned later) where Sirion dives underground. But the Land of Willows, below the region of Sirion's underground passage, is placed as it was to remain.

Thus the view I expressed (p. 141) of the geographical indications in the *Tale of Turambar* can be asserted also of those of *The Fall of Gondolin*.

### (ii)  *Ulmo and the other Valar in The Fall of Gondolin*

In the speech of Tuor inspired by Ulmo that he uttered at his first meeting with Turgon (p. 161) he said: 'the hearts of the Valar are angered . . . seeing the sorrow of the thraldom of the Noldoli and the wanderings of Men.' This is greatly at variance with what is told in *The Hiding of Valinor*, especially the following (I. 208–9):*

> The most of the Valar moreover were fain of their ancient ease and desired only peace, wishing neither rumour of Melko and his violence nor murmur of the restless Gnomes to come ever again among them to disturb their happiness; and for such reasons they also clamoured for the concealment of the land. Not the least among these were Vána and Nessa, albeit most even of the great Gods were of one mind. In vain did Ulmo of his foreknowing plead before them for pity and pardon on the Noldoli . . .

Subsequently Tuor said (p. 161): 'the Gods sit in Valinor, though their mirth is minished for sorrow and fear of Melko, and they hide their land and weave about it inaccessible magic that no evil come to its shores.' Turgon in his reply ironically echoed and altered the words: 'they that sit within [*i.e. in Valinor*] reck little of the dread of Melko or the sorrow of the world, but hide their land and weave about it inaccessible magic, that no tidings of evil come ever to their ears.'

How is this to be understood? Was this Ulmo's 'diplomacy'? Certainly Turgon's understanding of the motives of the Valar chimes better with what is said of them in *The Hiding of Valinor*.

But the Gnomes of Gondolin reverenced the Valar. There were 'pomps of the Ainur' (p. 165); a great square of the city and its highest point was Gar Ainion, the Place of the Gods, where weddings were celebrated (pp. 164, 186); and the people of the Hammer of Wrath 'reverenced Aulë the Smith more than all other Ainur' (p. 174).

Of particular interest is the passage (p. 165) in which a reason is given for Ulmo's choice of a Man as the agent of his designs: 'Now Melko was not much afraid of the race of Men in those days of his great power, and for this reason did Ulmo work through one of this kindred for the better deceiving of Melko, seeing that no Valar and scarce any of the Eldar or Noldoli might stir unmarked of his vigilance.' This is the only place where a reason is expressly offered, save for an isolated early note, where two reasons are given:

(1) 'the wrath of the Gods' (i.e. against the Gnomes);

(2) 'Melko did not fear Men – had he thought that any messengers were getting to Valinor he would have redoubled his vigilance and evil and hidden the Gnomes away utterly.'

---

* It also seems to be at variance with the story that all Men were shut in Hithlum by Melko's decree after the Battle of Unnumbered Tears; but 'wanderings' is a strange word in the context, since the next words are 'for Melko ringeth them in the Land of Shadows'.

But this is too oblique to be helpful.

The conception of 'the luck of the Gods' occurs again in this tale (pp. 188, 200 note 32), as it does in the *Tale of Turambar*: see p. 141. The Ainur 'put it into Tuor's heart' to climb the cliff out of the ravine of Golden Cleft for the saving of his life (p. 151).

Very strange is the passage concerning the birth of Eärendel (p. 165): 'In these days came to pass the fulfilment of the time of the desire of the Valar and the hope of the Eldalië, for in great love Idril bore to Tuor a son and he was called Eärendel.' Is it to be understood that the union of Elf and mortal Man, and the birth of their offspring, was 'the desire of the Valar' – that the Valar foresaw it, or hoped for it, as the fulfilment of a design of Ilúvatar from which great good should come? There is no hint or suggestion of such an idea elsewhere.

### (iii)   *Orcs*

There is a noteworthy remark in the tale (p. 159) concerning the origin of the Orcs (or *Orqui* as they were called in *Tuor A*, and in *Tuor B* as first written): 'all that race were bred of the subterranean heats and slime.' There is no trace yet of the later view that 'naught that had life of its own, nor the semblance of life, could ever Melkor make since his rebellion in the Ainulindalë before the Beginning', or that the Orcs were derived from enslaved Quendi after the Awakening (*The Silmarillion* p. 50). Conceivably there is a first hint of this idea of their origin in the words of the tale in the same passage: 'unless it be that certain of the Noldoli were twisted to the evil of Melko and mingled among these Orcs', although of course this is as it stands quite distinct from the idea that the Orcs were actually bred from Elves.

Here also occurs the name *Glamhoth* of the Orcs, a name that reappears in the later *Tuor* (pp. 39 and 54 note 18).

On Balrogs and Dragons in *The Fall of Gondolin* see pp. 212–13.

### (iv)   *Noldorin in the Land of Willows*

'Did not even after the days of Tuor Noldorin and his Eldar come there seeking for Dor Lómin and the hidden river and the caverns of the Gnomes' imprisonment; yet thus nigh to their quest's end were like to abandon it? Indeed sleeping and dancing here . . . they were whelmed by the goblins sped by Melko from the Hills of Iron and Noldorin made bare escape thence' (p. 154). This was the Battle of Tasarinan, mentioned in the *Tale of Turambar* (pp. 70, 140), at the time of the great expedition of the Elves from Kôr. Cf. Lindo's remark in *The Cottage of Lost Play* (I.16) that his father Valwë 'went with Noldorin to find the Gnomes'.

Noldorin (Salmar, companion of Ulmo) is also said in the tale to have fought beside Tulkas at the Pools of Twilight against Melko himself, though his name was struck out (p. 195 and note 38); this was after the Battle of Tasarinan. On these battles see pp. 278 ff.

### (v)   The stature of Elves and Men

The passage concerning Tuor's stature on p. 159, before it was rewritten (see note 18), can only mean that while Tuor was not himself unusually tall for a Man he was nonetheless taller than the Elves of Gondolin, and thus agrees with statements made in the *Tale of Turambar* (see p. 142). As emended, however, the meaning is rather that Men and Elves were not greatly distinct in stature.

### (vi)   Isfin and Eöl

The earliest version of this tale is found in the little *Lost Tales* notebook (see I.171), as follows:

#### Isfin and Eöl

Isfin daughter of Fingolma loved from afar by Eöl (Arval) of the Mole-kin of the Gnomes. He is strong and in favour with Fingolma and with the Sons of Fëanor (to whom he is akin) because he is a leader of the Miners and searches after hidden jewels, but he is illfavoured and Isfin loathes him.

(Fingolma as a name for Finwë Nólemë appears in outlines for *Gilfanon's Tale*, I.238–9.) We have here an illfavoured miner named Eöl 'of the Mole' who loves Isfin but is rejected by her with loathing; and this is obviously closely parallel to the illfavoured miner Meglin with the sign of the sable mole seeking the hand of Idril, who rejects him, in *The Fall of Gondolin*. It is difficult to know how to interpret this. The simplest explanation is that the story adumbrated in the little notebook is actually earlier than that in *The Fall of Gondolin*; that Meglin did not yet exist; and that subsequently the image of the 'ugly miner – unsuccessful suitor' became that of the son, the object of desire becoming Idril (niece of Isfin), while a new story was developed for the father, Eöl the dark Elf of the forest who ensnared Isfin. But it is by no means clear where Eöl the miner was when he 'loved from afar' Isfin daughter of Fingolma. There seems to be no reason to think that he was associated with Gondolin; more probably the idea of the miner bearing the sign of the Mole entered Gondolin with Meglin.

# IV

# THE NAUGLAFRING

We come now to the last of the original *Lost Tales* to be given consecutive narrative form. This is contained in a separate notebook, and it bears the title *The Nauglafring: The Necklace of the Dwarves*.

The beginning of this tale is somewhat puzzling. Before the telling of *The Fall of Gondolin* Lindo told Littleheart that 'it is the desire of all that you tell us the tales of Tuor and of Eärendel as soon as may be' (p. 144), and Littleheart replied: 'It is a mighty tale, and seven times shall folk fare to the Tale-fire ere it be rightly told; and so twined is it with those stories of the Nauglafring and of the Elf-march that I would fain have aid in that telling of Ailios here . . .' Thus Littleheart's surrender of the chair of the tale-teller to Ailios at the beginning of the present text, so that Ailios should tell of the Nauglafring, fits the general context well; but we should not expect the new tale to be introduced with the words 'But after a while silence fell', since *The Fall of Gondolin* ends 'And no one in all the Room of Logs spake or moved for a great while.' In any case, after the very long *Fall of Gondolin* the next tale would surely have waited till the following evening.

This tale is once again a manuscript in ink over a wholly erased original in pencil, but only so far as the words 'sate his greed' on page 230. From this point to the end there is only a primary manuscript in pencil in the first stage of composition, written in haste – in places hurled on to the page, with a good many words not certainly decipherable; and a part of this was extensively rewritten while the tale was still in progress (see note 13).

### The Nauglafring
### The Necklace of the Dwarves

But after a while silence fell, and folk murmured 'Eärendel', but others said 'Nay – what of the Nauglafring, the Necklace of the Dwarves.' Therefore said Ilfiniol, leaving the chair of the tale-teller: 'Yea, better would the tale be told if Ailios would relate the matters concerning that necklace,' and Ailios being nowise unwilling thus began, looking upon the company.

'Remember ye all how Úrin the Steadfast cast the gold of Glorund before the feet of Tinwelint, and after would not touch it again, but went in sorrow back to Hisilómë, and there died?' And all said that that tale was still fresh in their hearts.

'Behold then,' said Ailios, 'in great grief gazed the king upon Úrin as he left the hall, and he was weary for the evil of Melko that thus deceived all hearts; yet tells the tale that so potent were the spells that Mîm the fatherless had woven about that hoard that, even as it lay upon the floor of the king's halls shining strangely in the light of the torches that burnt there, already were all who looked upon it touched by its subtle evil.

Now therefore did those of Úrin's band murmur, and one said to the king: "Lo, lord, our captain Úrin, an old man and mad, has departed, but we have no mind to forego our gain."

Then said Tinwelint, for neither was he untouched by the golden spell: "Nay then, know ye not that this gold belongs to the kindred of the Elves in common, for the Rodothlim who won it from the earth long time ago are no more, and no one has especial claim[1] to so much as a handful save only Úrin by reason of his son Túrin, who slew the Worm, the robber of the Elves; yet Túrin is dead and Úrin will have none of it; and Túrin was my man."

At those words the outlaws fell into great wrath, until the king said: "Get ye now gone, and seek not O foolish ones to quarrel with the Elves of the forest, lest death or the dread enchantments of Valinor find you in the woods. Neither revile ye the name of Tinwelint their king, for I will reward you richly enough for your travail and the bringing of the gold. Let each one now approach and take what he may grasp with either hand, and then depart in peace."

Now were the Elves of the wood in turn displeased, who long had stood nigh gazing on the gold; but the wild folk did as they were bid, and yet more, for some went into the hoard twice and thrice, and angry cries were raised in that hall. Then would the woodland Elves hinder them of their thieving, and a great dissension arose, so that though the king would stay them none heeded him. Then did those outlaws being fierce and fearless folk draw swords and deal blows about them, so that soon there was a great fight even upon the steps of the high-seat of the king. Doughty were those outlaws and great wielders of sword and axe from their warfare with Orcs,[2] so that many were slain ere the king, seeing that peace and pardon might no longer be, summoned a host of his warriors, and those outlaws being wildered with the stronger magics of the king[3] and confused in the dark ways of the halls of Tinwelint were all slain fighting bitterly; but the king's hall ran with gore, and the gold that lay before his throne, scattered and spurned by trampling feet, was drenched with blood. Thus did the curse of Mîm the Dwarf begin its course; and yet another sorrow sown by the Noldoli of old in Valinor was come to fruit.[4]

Then were the bodies of the outlaws cast forth, but the woodland Elves that were slain Tinwelint let bury nigh to the knoll of Tinúviel, and 'tis said that the great mound stands there still in Artanor, and for long the fairies called it Cûm an-Idrisaith, the Mound of Avarice.

Now came Gwenniel to Tinwelint and said: "Touch not this gold, for my heart tells me it is trebly cursed. Cursed indeed by the dragon's breath, and cursed by thy lieges' blood that moistens it, and the death of those[5] they slew; but some more bitter and more binding ill methinks hangs over it that I may not see."

Then, remembering the wisdom of Gwenniel his wife, the king was minded to hearken to her, and he bade gather it up and cast it into the stream before the gates. Yet even so he might not shake off its spell, and he said to himself: "First will I gaze my last upon its loveliness ere I fling it from me for ever." Therefore he let wash it clean of its stains of blood in clear waters, and display it before him. Now such mighty heaps of gold have never since been gathered in one place; and some thereof was wrought to cups, to basons, and to dishes, and hilts there were for swords, and scabbards, and sheaths for daggers; but the most part was of red gold unwrought lying in masses and in bars. The value of that hoard no man could count, for amid the gold lay many gems, and these were very beautiful to look upon, for the fathers of the Rodothlim had brought them out of Valinor, a portion of that boundless treasury the Noldoli had there possessed.

Now as he gazed Tinwelint said: "How glorious is this treasure! And I have not a tithe thereof, and of the gems of Valinor none save that Silmaril that Beren won from Angamandi." But Gwenniel who stood by said: "And that were worth all that here lies, were it thrice as great."

Then arose one from among the company, and that was Ufedhin, a Gnome; but more had he wandered about the world than any of the king's folk, and long had he dwelt with the Nauglath and the Indrafangs their kin. The Nauglath are a strange race and none know surely whence they be; and they serve not Melko nor Manwë and reck not for Elf or Man, and some say that they have not heard of Ilúvatar, or hearing disbelieve.

Howbeit in crafts and sciences and in the knowledge of the virtues of all things that are in the earth[6] or under the water none excel them; yet they dwell beneath the ground in caves and tunnelled towns, and aforetime Nogrod was the mightiest of these. Old are they, and never comes a child among them, nor do they laugh. They are squat in stature, and yet are strong, and their beards reach even to their toes, but the beards of the Indrafangs are the longest of all, and are forked, and they bind them about their middles when they walk abroad. All these creatures have Men called 'Dwarves', and say that their crafts and cunning surpass that of the Gnomes in marvellous contrivance, but of a truth there is little beauty in their works of themselves, for in those things of loveliness that they have wrought in ages past such renegade Gnomes as was Ufedhin have ever had a hand. Now long had that Gnome forsaken his folk, becoming leagued with the Dwarves of Nogrod, and was at that time come to the realms of Tinwelint with certain other Noldoli of like mind bearing swords and coats of mail and other smithyings of exquisite skill in which the Nauglath in those days did great traffic with the free Noldoli, and, 'tis said, with the Orcs and soldiers of Melko also.

As he stood in that place the spell of the gold had pierced the heart of Ufedhin more deeply than the heart of any there, and he could not endure that it should all be cast away, and these were his words: "An evil deed is this that Tinwelint the king intends; or who hereafter shall say that the kindreds of the Eldalië love things of beauty if a king of the Eldar cast so great a store of loveliness into the dark woodland waters where none but the fishes may after behold it? Rather than this should be, I beg of thee, O King, to suffer the craftsmen of the Dwarves to try their skill upon this unwrought gold, that the name of the golden treasury of Tinwelint become heard in all lands and places. This will they do, I promise thee, for small guerdon, might they but save the hoard from ruin."

Then looked the king upon the gold and he looked upon Ufedhin, and that Gnome was clad very richly, having a tunic of golden web and a belt of gold set with tiny gems; and his sword was damasked in strange wise,[7] but a collar of gold and silver interlaced most intricate was round his neck, and Tinwelint's raiment could in no wise compare with that of the wayfarer in his halls. Again looked Tinwelint upon the gold, and it shone yet more alluring fair, nor ever had the sparkle of the gems seemed so brilliant, and Ufedhin said again: "Or in what manner, O King, dost thou guard that Silmaril of which all the world hath heard?"

Now Gwenniel warded it in a casket of wood bound with iron, and Ufedhin said it was shame so to set a jewel that should not touch aught less worthy than the purest gold. Then was Tinwelint abashed, and yielded, and this was the agreement that he made with Ufedhin. Half the gold should the king measure and give to the hands of Ufedhin and his company, and they should bear it away to Nogrod and the dwellings of the Dwarves. Now those were a very long journey southward beyond the wide forest on the borders of those great heaths nigh Umboth-muilin the Pools of Twilight, on the marches of Tasarinan. Yet after but seven full moons back would the Nauglath fare bearing the king's loan all wrought to works of greatest cunning, yet in no wise would the weight and purity of the gold be minished. Then would they speak to Tinwelint, and an he liked not the handiwork then would they return and say no more; yet if it seemed good to him then of that which remained would they fashion such marvellous things for his adornment and for Gwenniel the Queen as never had Gnome or Dwarf made yet.

"For," said Ufedhin, "the cunning of the Nauglath have I learnt, and the beauty of design that only can the Noldoli compass do I know – yet shall the wages of our labour be small indeed, and we will name it before thee when all is done."

Then by reason of the glamour of the gold the king repented his agreement with Ufedhin, and he liked not altogether his words, and he would not suffer so great a store of gold to be borne without surety out of his sight for seven moons to the distant dwellings of the Dwarves; yet was he minded nonetheless to profit by their skill. Therefore suddenly he let seize Ufedhin, and his folk, and he said unto them: "Here shall ye remain as hostages in my halls until I see again my treasury." Now Tinwelint thought in his heart that Ufedhin and his Gnomes were of the utmost service to the Dwarves, and no covetice would be strong enough to bring them to forsake him; but that Gnome was very wroth, saying: "The Nauglath are no thieves, O King, nor yet their friends"; but Tinwelint said: "Yet the light of overmuch gold has made many thieves, who were not so before," and Ufedhin perforce consented, yet he forgave not Tinwelint in his heart.

Therefore was the gold now borne to Nogrod by folk of the king guided by one only of Ufedhin's companions, and the agreement of Ufedhin and Tinwelint spoken to Naugladur, the king of those places.

Now during the time of waiting Ufedhin was kindly entreated

in the courts of Tinwelint, yet was he idle perforce, and he fretted inwardly. In his leisure he pondered ever what manner of lovely thing of gold and jewels he would after fashion for Tinwelint, but this was only for the greater ensnaring of the king, for already he began to weave dark plots most deep of avarice and revenge.

On the very day of the fullness of the seventh moon thereafter the watchers on the king's bridge cried: "Lo! there comes a great company through the wood, and all it seems are aged men, and they bear very heavy burdens on their backs." But the king hearing said: "It is the Nauglath, who keep their tryst: now mayst thou go free, Ufedhin, and take my greeting to them, and lead them straightway to my hall"; and Ufedhin sallied forth gladly, but his heart forgot not its resentment. Therefore having speech privily with the Nauglath he prevailed upon them to demand at the end a very great reward, and one thereto that the king might not grant unhumbled; and more of his designs also did he unfold, whereby that gold might fare in the end to Nogrod for ever.

Now come the Dwarves nonetheless over the bridge and before the chair of Tinwelint, and behold, the things of their workmanship they had conveyed thither in silken cloths, and boxes of rare woods carven cunningly. In other wise had Úrin haled the treasure thither, and half thereof lay yet in his rude sacks and clumsy chests; yet when the gold was once more revealed, then did a cry of wonder arise, for the things the Nauglath had made were more wondrous far than the scanty vessels and the ornaments that the Rodothlim wrought of old. Cups and goblets did the king behold, and some had double bowls or curious handles interlaced, and horns there were of strange shape, dishes and trenchers, flagons and ewers, and all appurtenances of a kingly feast. Candlesticks there were and sconces for the torches, and none might count the rings and armlets, the bracelets and collars, and the coronets of gold; and all these were so subtly made and so cunningly adorned that Tinwelint was glad beyond the hope of Ufedhin.

But as yet the designs of Ufedhin came to nought, for in no wise would Tinwelint suffer or him or those of the Nauglath to depart to Nogrod with or without that portion of the unwrought gold that yet remained, and he said: "How shall it be thought that after the weariness of your burdened journeys hither I should let you so soon be gone, to noise the lack of courtesy of Tinwelint abroad in Nogrod? Stay now awhile and rest and feast, and afterward shall ye have the gold that remains to work your pleasure on; nor shall aught of help that I or my folk may afford be wanting in your labour, and a reward rich and more than just awaits you at the end."

But they knew nonetheless that they were prisoners, and trying the exits privily found them strongly warded. Being therefore without counsel they bowed before the king, and the faces of the Dwarf-folk show seldom what they think. Now after a time of rest was that last smithying begun in a deep place of Tinwelint's abode which he caused to be set apart for their uses, and what their hearts lacked therein fear supplied, and in all that work Ufedhin had a mighty part.

A golden crown they made for Tinwelint, who yet had worn nought but a wreath of scarlet leaves, and a helm too most glorious they fashioned; and a sword of dwarven steel brought from afar was hilted with bright gold and damascened in gold and silver with strange figurings wherein was pictured clear the wolf-hunt of Karkaras Knife-fang, father of wolves. That was a more wonderful sword than any Tinwelint had seen before, and outshone the sword in Ufedhin's belt the king had coveted. These things were of Ufedhin's cunning, but the Dwarves made a coat of linked mail of steel and gold for Tinwelint, and a belt of gold. Then was the king's heart gladdened, but they said: "All is not finished," and Ufedhin made a silver crown for Gwenniel, and aided by the Dwarves contrived slippers of silver crusted with diamonds, and the silver thereof was fashioned in delicate scales, so that it yielded as soft leather to the foot, and a girdle he made too of silver blended with pale gold. Yet were those things but a tithe of their works, and no tale tells a full count of them.

Now when all was done and their smithcraft given to the king, then said Ufedhin: "O Tinwelint, richest of kings, dost thou think these things fair?" And he said: "Yea"; but Ufedhin said: "Know then that great store of thy best and purest gold remaineth still, for we have husbanded it, having a boon to ask of thee, and it is this: we would make thee a carcanet and to its making lay all the skill and cunning that we have, and we desire that this should be the most marvellous ornament that the Earth has seen, and the greatest of the works of Elves and Dwarves. Therefore we beg of thee to let us have that Silmaril that thou treasurest, that it may shine wondrously amid the Nauglafring, the Necklace of the Dwarves."

Then again did Tinwelint doubt Ufedhin's purpose, yet did he yield the boon, an they would suffer him to be present at that smithying.

None are that yet live,' quoth Ailios,[8] 'who have seen that most glorious thing, save only[9] Littleheart son of Bronweg, yet are many things told thereof. Not only was it wrought with the greatest skill and subtlety in the world but it had a magic power, and there was no throat so great or so slender whereon it sat not with grace and loveliness. Albeit a weight beyond belief of gold was used in the making, lightly it hung upon its wearer as a strand of flax; and all such as clasped it about their necks seemed, as it hung upon their breasts, to be of goodly countenance, and women seemed most fair. Gems uncounted were there in that carcanet of gold, yet only as a setting that did prepare for its great central glory, and led the eye thereto, for amidmost hung like a little lamp of limpid fire the Silmaril of Fëanor, jewel of the Gods. Yet alas, even had that gold of the Rodothlim held no evil spell still had that carcanet been a thing of little luck, for the Dwarves were full of bitterness, and all its links were twined with baleful thoughts. Now however did they bear it before the king in its new-gleaming splendour; and then was the joy of Tinwelint king of the woodland Elves come to its crowning, and he cast the Nauglafring about his throat, and straightway the curse of Mîm fell upon him. Then said Ufedhin: "Now, O Lord, that thou art pleased beyond thy hope, perchance thou wilt grant the craftsmen thy kingly reward, and suffer them to depart also in joy to their own lands."

But Tinwelint, bewildered by the golden spell and the curse of Mîm, liked not the memory of his tryst; yet dissembling he bid the craftsmen come before him, and he praised their handiwork with royal words. At length said he: "'Twas said to me by one Ufedhin that at the end such reward as ye wished ye would name before me, yet would it be small enough, seeing that the labour was of love and of Ufedhin's desire that the golden hoard be not cast away and lost. What then do ye wish that I may grant?"

Then said Ufedhin scornfully: "For myself, nothing, O Lord; indeed the guestkindliness of thy halls for seven moons and three is more than I desire." But the Dwarves said: "This do we ask. For our labours during seven moons each seven jewels of Valinor, and seven robes of magic that only Gwendelin[10] can weave, and each a sack of gold; but for our great labour during three moons in thy halls unwilling, we ask each three sacks of silver, and each a cup of gold wherein to pledge thy health, O King, and each a fair maiden of the woodland Elves to fare away with us to our homes."

Then was King Tinwelint wroth indeed, for what the Dwarves had asked was of itself a goodly treasury, seeing that their company was very great; and he had no mind thus to devour the dragon's hoard, but never could he deliver maidens of the Elves unto illshapen Dwarves without undying shame.

Now that demand they had made only by the design of Ufedhin, yet seeing the anger of the king's face they said: "Nay, but this is not all, for in payment of Ufedhin's captivity for seven moons seven stout Elves must come with us and abide seven times seven years among us as bondsmen and menials in our labour."

Thereat arose Tinwelint from his seat, and calling summoned his weaponed thanes and warriors, that these surrounded the Nauglath and those Gnomes. Then said he: "For your insolence each three stripes with stinging withes shall ye receive, and Ufedhin seven, and afterwards will we speak of recompense."

When this was done, and a flame of bitter vengeance lit in those deep hearts, he said: "Lo, for your labour of seven months six pieces of gold and one of silver each shall have, and for your labours in my halls each three pieces of gold and some small gem that I can spare. For your journey hither a great feast shall ye eat and depart with good store against your return, and ere ye go ye shall drink to Tinwelint in elfin wine; yet, mark ye, for the sustenance of Ufedhin seven idle months about my halls shall ye each pay a piece of gold, and of silver two, for he has not aught himself and shall not receive since he desires it not, yet methinks he is at the bottom of your arrogance."

Then were the Dwarves paid their reward like common smiths of bronze and iron, and constrained to yield once more therefrom payment for Ufedhin – "else," said the king, "never shall ye get him hence." Then sat they to a great feast and dissembled their mood; yet at the end the time of their going came, and they drank to Tinwelint in elfin wine, but they cursed him in their beards, and Ufedhin swallowed not and spat the wine from his mouth upon the threshold.

Now tells the tale that the Nauglath fared home again, and if their greed had been kindled when first the gold was brought to Nogrod now was it a fierce flame of desire, and moreover they burnt under the insults of the king. Indeed all that folk love gold and silver more dearly than aught else on Earth, while that treasury was haunted by a spell and by no means were they armed against it. Now one there had been, Fangluin* the aged, who had counselled them from the first never to return the king's loan, for

* In the margin of the manuscript is written: *Fangluin: Bluebeard.*

said he: "Ufedhin we may later seek by guile to release, if it seem good," but at that time this seemed not policy to Naugladur their lord, who desired not warfare with the Elves.Yet now did Fangluin jeer at them mightily on their return, saying they had flung away their labour for a botcher's wage and a draught of wine and gotten dishonour thereto, and he played upon their lust, and Ufedhin joined his bitter words thereto. Therefore did Naugladur hold a secret council of the Dwarves of Nogrod, and sought how he might both be avenged upon Tinwelint, and sate his greed.[11]

Yet after long pondering he saw not how he might achieve his purpose save by force, and there was little hope therein, both by reason of the great strength of numbers of the Elves of Artanor in those days, and of the woven magic of Gwenniel that guarded all those regions, so that men of hostile heart were lost and came not to those woods; nor indeed could any such come thither unaided by treachery from within.

Now even as those aged ones sat in their dark halls and gnawed their beards, behold a sound of horns, and messengers were come from Bodruith of the Indrafangs, a kindred of the Dwarves that dwelt in other realms. Now these brought tidings of the death of Mîm the fatherless at the hand of Úrin and the rape of Glorund's gold, which tale had but new come to Bodruith's ears. Now hitherto the Dwarves knew not the full tale concerning that hoard, nor more than Ufedhin might tell hearing the speech in Tinwelint's halls, and Úrin had not spoken the full count thereof ere he departed. Hearing therefore these tidings new wrath was added to their lust and a clamour arose among them, and Naugladur vowed to rest not ere Mîm was thrice avenged – "and more," said he, "meseems the gold belongs of right to the people of the Dwarves."

This then was the design; and by his deeds have the Dwarves been severed in feud for ever since those days with the Elves, and drawn more nigh in friendship to the kin of Melko. Secretly he let send to the Indrafangs that they prepare their host against a day that he would name, whenso the time should be ripe; and a hidden forging of bitter steel then was in Belegost the dwelling of the Indrafangs. Moreover he gathered about him a great host of the Orcs, and wandering goblins, promising them a good wage, and the pleasure of their Master moreover, and a rich booty at the end; and all these he armed with his own weapons. Now came unto Naugladur an Elf, and he was one of Tinwelint's folk, and he offered to lead that host through the magics of Gwendelin, for he was bitten by the gold-lust of Glorund's hoard, and so did the curse of Mîm come upon Tinwelint and treachery first arose among the Elves of Artanor. Then did Naugladur [?smile] bitterly, for he knew that the time was ripe and Tinwelint delivered to him. Now each year about the time of the great wolf-hunt of Beren Tinwelint was wont to keep the memory of that day by a hunt in the woods, and it was a very mighty chase and thronged with very many folk, and nights of merriment and feasting were there in the forest. Now Naugladur learnt of that Elf Narthseg, whose name is bitter to the Eldar yet, that the king would fare a-hunting at the next high moon but one, and straightway he sent the trysted sign, a bloodstained knife, to Bodruith at Belegost. Now all that host assembled on the confines of the woods, and no word came yet unto the king.

Now tells the tale that one came unto Tinwelint, and Tinwelint knew him not for the wild growth of his hair – and lo! it was Mablung, and he said: "Lo, even in the depths of the forest have we heard that this year you will celebrate the death of Karkaras with a high-tide greater than even before, O King – and behold I have returned to bear you company." And the king was full of mirth and fain to greet Mablung the brave; and at the words of Mablung that Huan captain of Dogs was come also into Artanor was he glad indeed.

Behold now Tinwelint the king rode forth a-hunting, and more glorious was his array than ever aforetime, and the helm of gold was above his flowing locks, and with gold were the trappings of his steed adorned; and the sunlight amid the trees fell upon his face, and it seemed to those that beheld it like to the glorious face of the sun at morning; for about his throat was clasped the Nauglafring, the Necklace of the Dwarves. Beside him rode Mablung the Heavyhand in the place of honour by reason of his deeds at that great hunt aforetime – but Huan of the Dogs was ahead of the hunters, and men thought that great dog bore him strangely, but mayhap there was something in the wind that day he liked not.

Now is the king far in the woods with all his company, and the horns grow faint in the deep forest, but Gwendelin sits in her bower and foreboding is in her heart and eyes. Then said an Elfmaid, Nielthi: "Wherefore, O Lady, art thou sorrowful at the hightide of the king?" And Gwendelin said: "Evil seeks our land, and my heart misgives me that my days in Artanor are speeding to their end, yet if I should lose Tinwelint then would I wish never to have wandered forth from Valinor." But Nielthi said: "Nay, O Lady Gwendelin, hast thou not woven great magic all about us, so that we fear not?" But the queen made answer: "Yet meseems there is a rat that gnaws the threads and all the web has come unwoven." Even at that word there was a cry about the doors, and suddenly it grew to a fierce noise . . . by the clash of steel. Then went Gwendelin unafraid forth from her bower, and behold, a sudden multitude of Orcs and Indrafangs held the bridge, and there was war within the cavernous gates; but that place ran with blood, and a great heap of slain lay there, for the onset had been secret and all unknown.

Then did Gwendelin know well that her foreboding was true, and that treachery had found her realm at last, yet did she hearten those few guards that remained to her and had fared not to the hunt, and valiantly they warded the palace of the king until the tide of numbers bore them back [and] fire and blood found all the halls and deep ways of that great fortress of the Elves.

Then did those Orcs and Dwarves ransack all the chambers seeking for treasure, and lo! one came and sate him in the high seat of the king laughing loud, and Gwendelin saw that it was Ufedhin, and mocking he bid her be seated in her ancient seat beside the king's. Then Gwendelin gazed upon him so that his glance fell, and she said: "Wherefore, O renegade, dost thou defile my lord's seat? Little had I thought to see any of the Elves sit there, a robber, stained with murder, a league-fellow of the truceless enemies of his kin. Or thinkest thou it is a glorious deed to assail an ill-armed house what time its lord is far away?" But Ufedhin said nought, shunning the bright eyes of Gwendelin, wherefore said she anew: "Get thee now gone with thy foul Orcs, lest Tinwelint coming repay thee bitterly."

Then at last did Ufedhin answer, and he laughed, but ill at ease, and he looked not at the queen, but he said listening to a sound without: "Nay, but already is he come." And behold, Naugladur entered now and a host of the Dwarves were about him, but he bore the head of Tinwelint crowned and helmed in gold; but the necklace of all wonder was clasped about the throat of Naugladur. Then did Gwendelin see in her heart all that had befallen, and how the curse of the gold had fallen on the realm of Artanor, and never has she danced or sung since that dark hour; but Naugladur bid gather all things of gold or silver or of precious stones and bear them to Nogrod – "and whatso remains of goods or folk may the

Orcs keep, or slay, as they desire. Yet the Lady Gwendelin Queen of Artanor shall fare with me."

Then said Gwendelin: "Thief and murderer, child of Melko, yet art thou a fool, for thou canst not see what hangs over thine own head." By reason of the anguish of her heart was her sight grown very clear, and she read by her fay-wisdon the curse of Mîm and much of what would yet betide.

Then did Naugladur in his triumph laugh till his beard shook, and bid seize her: but none might do so, for as they came towards her they groped as if in sudden dark, or stumbled and fell tripping each the other, and Gwendelin went forth from the places of her abode, and her bitter weeping filled the forest. Now did a great darkness fall upon her mind and her counsel and lore forsook her, that she wandered she knew not whither for a great while; and this was by reason of her love for Tinwelint the king, for whom she had chosen never to fare back to Valinor and the beauty of the Gods, dwelling always in the wild forests of the North; and now did there seem to her neither beauty nor joy be it in Valinor or in the Lands Without. Many of the scattered Elves in her wayward journeyings she met, and they took pity on her, but she heeded them not. Tales had they told her, but she hearkened not over much since Tinwelint was dead; nonetheless must ye know how even in the hour that Ufedhin's host brake the palace and despoiled it, and other companies as great and as terrible of the Orcs and Indrafangs fell with death and fire upon all the realm of Tinwelint, behold the brave hunt of the king were resting amid mirth and laughter, but Huan stalked apart. Then suddenly were the woods filled with noise and Huan bayed aloud; but the king and his company were all encircled with armed foes. Long they fought bitterly there among the trees, and the Nauglath – for such were their foes – had great scathe of them or ever they were slain. Yet in the end were they all fordone, and Mablung and the king fell side by side – but Naugladur it was who swept off the head of Tinwelint after he was dead, for living he dared not so near to his bright sword or the axe of Mablung.[12]

Now doth the tale know no more to tell of Huan, save that even while the swords still sang that great dog was speeding through the land, and his way led him as the [?wind] to the land of i·Guilwarthon, the living-dead, where reigned Beren and Tinúviel the daughter of Tinwelint. Not in any settled abode did those twain dwell, nor had their realm boundaries well-marked – and indeed no other messenger save Huan alone to whom all ways were known had ever found Beren and obtained his aid so soon.[13] Indeed the tale tells that even as that host of the Orcs were burning all the land of Tinwelint and the Nauglath and the Indrafangin were wending homeward burdened utterly with spoils of gold and precious things, came Huan to Beren's lodge, and it was dusk. Lo, Beren sat upon a tree root and Tinúviel danced on a green sward in the gloaming as he gazed upon her, when suddenly stood Huan before them, and Beren gave a cry of joy and wonder, for it was long since he and Huan had hunted together. But Tinúviel looking upon Huan saw that he bled, and there was a tale to read in his great eyes. And she said suddenly: "What evil then has fallen upon Artanor?" and Huan said: "Fire and death and the terror of Orcs; but Tinwelint is slain."

Then did both Beren and Tinúviel weep bitter tears; nor did the full tale of Huan dry their eyes. When then it was told to the end leapt Beren to his feet in white wrath, and seizing a horn that hung at his belt he blew a clear blast thereon that rang round all the neighbouring hills, and an elfin folk all clad in green and brown sprang as it were by magic towards him from every glade and coppice, stream and fell.

Now not even Beren knew the tale of those myriad folk that followed his horn in the woods of Hisilómë, and or ever the moon was high above the hills the host assembled in the glade of his abiding was very great, yet were they lightly armed and the most bore only knives and bows. "Yet," said Beren, "speed is that which now we need the most"; and certain Elves at his bidding fared like deer before him, seeking news of the march of the Dwarves and Indrafangs, but at dawn he followed at the head of the green Elves, and Tinúviel abode in the glade and wept unto herself for the death of Tinwelint, and Gwendelin also she mourned as dead.

Now is to tell that the laden host of the Dwarves fared from the place of their ransacking, and Naugladur was at their head, and beside him Ufedhin and Bodruith; and ever as he rode Ufedhin sought to put the dread eyes of Gwendelin from his mind and could not, and all happiness was fled from his heart that shrivelled under the memory of that glance; nor was this the only disquiet that tortured him, for if ever he raised his eyes lo! they lighted on the Necklace of the Dwarves shining about the aged neck of Naugladur, and then all other thoughts save bottomless desire of its beauty were banished.

Thus did those three fare and with them all their host, but so great became the torment of Ufedhin's mind that in the end he might not endure it more, but at night when a halt was called he crept stealthily to the place where Naugladur slept, and coming upon that aged one wrapt in slumbers would slay that Dwarf and lay hands upon the wondrous Nauglafring. Now even as he sought to do so, behold one seized his throat suddenly from behind, and it was Bodruith, who filled with the same lust sought also to make that lovely thing his own; but coming upon Ufedhin would slay him by reason of his kinship to Naugladur. Then did Ufedhin stab suddenly backward at hazard in the dark with a keen knife long and slender that he had with him for the bane of Naugladur, and that knife pierced the vitals of Bodruith Lord of Belegost so that he fell dying upon Naugladur, and the throat of Naugladur and the magic carcanet were drenched anew with blood.

Thereat did Naugladur awake with a great cry, but Ufedhin fled gasping from that place, for the long fingers of the Indrafang had well-nigh choked him. Now when some bore torches swiftly to that place Naugladur thought that Bodruith alone had sought to rob him of the jewel, and marvelled how he had thus been timely slain, and he proclaimed a rich reward to the slayer of Bodruith if that man would come forward telling all that he had seen. Thus was it that none perceived the flight of Ufedhin for a while, and wrath awoke between the Dwarves of Nogrod and the Indrafangs, and many were slain ere the Indrafangs being in less number were scattered and got them as best they might to Belegost, bearing scant treasury with them. Of this came the agelong feud between those kindreds of the Dwarves that has spread to many lands and caused many a tale, whereof the Elves know little tidings and Men have seldom heard. Yet may it be seen how the curse of Mîm came early home to rest among his own kin, and would indeed it had gone no further and had visited the Eldar never more.

Lo, when the flight of Ufedhin came also to light then was Naugladur in wrath, and he let kill all the Gnomes that remained in the host. Then said he: "Now are we rid of Indrafangs and Gnomes and all traitors, and nought more do I fear at all."

But Ufedhin ranged the wild lands in great fear and anguish, for him seemed that he had become a traitor to his kin, blood-guilty to the Elves, and haunted with the [?burning] eyes of Gwendelin the queen, for nought but exile and misery, and no smallest part nor share had he in the gold of Glorund, for all his heart was afire with lust; yet few have pitied him.

Now tells the tale that he fell in with the rangers of Beren's folk, and these gaining from him sure knowledge of all the host and

array of Naugladur and the ways he purposed to follow, they sped
back like wind among the trees unto their lord; but Ufedhin
revealed not to them who he was, feigning to be an Elf of Artanor
escaped from bondage in their host. Now therefore they entreated
him well, and he was sent back to Beren that their captain might
. . . . . . . . . . . his words, and albeit Beren marvelled at his
[?cowardly] . . . . . .[14] and downward glance it seemed to him that
he brought safe word, and he set a trap for Naugladur.

No longer did he march hotly on the trail of the Dwarves, but
knowing that they would essay the passage of the river Aros at a
certain time he turned aside, faring swiftly with his light-footed
Elves by straighter paths that he might reach Sarnathrod the
Stony Ford before them. Now the Aros is a fierce stream – and is it
not that very water that more near its spring runs swiftly past the
aged doors of the Rodothlim's caves and the dark lairs of Glorund[15]
– and in those lower regions by no means can be crossed by a great
host of laden men save at this ford, nor is it overeasy here. Never
would Naugladur have taken that way had he knowledge of Beren
– yet blinded by the spell and the dazzling gold he feared nought
either within or without his host, and he was in haste to reach
Nogrod and its dark caverns, for the Dwarves list not long to abide
in the bright light of day.

Now came all that host to the banks of Aros, and their array was
thus: first a number of unladen Dwarves most fully armed, and
amidmost the great company of those that bore the treasury of
Glorund, and many a fair thing beside that they had haled from
Tinwelint's halls; and behind these was Naugladur, and he bestrode
Tinwelint's horse, and a strange figure did he seem, for the legs of
the Dwarves are short and crooked, but two Dwarves led that
horse for it went not willingly and it was laden with spoil. But
behind these came again a mass of armed men but little laden; and
in this array they sought to cross Sarnathrod on their day of doom.

Morn was it when they reached the hither bank and high noon
saw them yet passing in long-strung lines and wading slowly the
shallow places of the swift-running stream. Here doth it widen out
.and fare down narrow channels filled with boulders atween long
spits of shingle and stones less great. Now did Naugladur slip
from his burdened horse and prepare to get him over, for the
armed host of the vanguard had climbed already the further bank,
and it was great and sheer and thick with trees, and the bearers of
the gold were some already stepped thereon and some amidmost
of the stream, but the armed men of the rear were resting awhile.

Suddenly is all that place filled with the sound of elfin horns, and one . . . . .[16] with a clearer blast above the rest, and it is the horn of Beren, the huntsman of the woods. Then is the air thick with the slender arrows of the Eldar that err not neither doth the wind bear them aside, and lo, from every tree and boulder do the brown Elves and the green spring suddenly and loose unceasingly from full quivers. Then was there a panic and a noise in the host of Naugladur, and those that waded in the ford cast their golden burdens in the waters and sought affrighted to either bank, but many were stricken with those pitiless darts and fell with their gold into the currents of the Aros, staining its clear waters with their dark blood.

Now were the warriors on the far bank [?wrapped] in battle and rallying sought to come at their foes, but these fled nimbly before them, while [?others] poured still the hail of arrows upon them, and thus got the Eldar few hurts and the Dwarf-folk fell dead unceasingly. Now was that great fight of the Stony Ford . . . . . . nigh to Naugladur, for even though Naugladur and his captains led their bands stoutly never might they grip their foe, and death fell like rain upon their ranks until the most part broke and fled, and a noise of clear laughter echoed from the Elves thereat, and they forebore to shoot more, for the illshapen figures of the Dwarves as they fled, their white beards torn by the wind, filled them [with] mirth. But now stood Naugladur and few were about him, and he remembered the words of Gwendelin, for behold, Beren came towards him and he cast aside his bow, and drew a bright sword; and Beren was of great stature among the Eldar, albeit not of the girth and breadth of Naugladur of the Dwarves.

Then said Beren: "Ward thy life an thou canst, O crook-legged murderer, else will I take it," and Naugladur bid him even the Nauglafring, the necklace of wonder, that he be suffered to go unharmed; but Beren said: "Nay, that may I still take when thou art slain," and thereat he made alone upon Naugladur and his companions, and having slain the foremost of these the others fled away amid elfin laughter, and so Beren came upon Naugladur, slayer of Tinwelint. Then did that aged one defend himself doughtily, and 'twas a bitter fight, and many of the Elves that watched for love and fear of their captain fingered their bow-strings, but Beren called even as he fought that all should stay their hands.

Now little doth the tale tell of wounds and blows of that affray, save that Beren got many hurts therein, and many of his shrewdest

blows did little harm to Naugladur by reason of the [?skill] and
magic of his dwarfen mail; and it is said that three hours they
fought and Beren's arms grew weary, but not those of Naugladur
accustomed to wield his mighty hammer at the forge, and it is
more than like that otherwise would the issue have been but for the
curse of Mîm; for marking how Beren grew faint Naugladur
pressed him ever more nearly, and the arrogance that was of
that grievous spell came into his heart, and he thought: "I will
slay this Elf, and his folk will flee in fear before me," and
grasping his sword he dealt a mighty blow and cried: "Take here
thy bane, O stripling of the woods," and in that moment his
foot found a jagged stone and he stumbled forward, but Beren
slipped aside from that blow and catching at his beard his hand
found the carcanet of gold, and therewith he swung Naugladur
suddenly off his feet upon his face: and Naugladur's sword was
shaken from his grasp, but Beren seized it and slew him therewith,
for he said: "I will not sully my bright blade with thy dark blood,
since there is no need." But the body of Naugladur was cast into
the Aros.

Then did he unloose the necklace, and he gazed in wonder at it —
and beheld the Silmaril, even the jewel he won from Angband and
gained undying glory by his deed; and he said: "Never have mine
eyes beheld thee O Lamp of Faëry burn one half so fair as now
thou dost, set in gold and gems and the magic of the Dwarves";
and that necklace he caused to be washed of its stains, and he cast it
not away, knowing nought of its power, but bore it with him back
into the woods of Hithlum.

But the waters of Aros flowed on for ever above the drowned
hoard of Glorund, and so do still, for in after days Dwarves came
from Nogrod and sought for it, and for the body of Naugladur;
but a flood arose from the mountains and therein the seekers
perished; and so great now is the gloom and dread of that Stony
Ford that none seek the treasure that it guards nor dare ever to
cross the magic stream at that enchanted place.

But in the vales of Hithlum was there gladness at the home-
coming of the Elves, and great was the joy of Tinúviel to see her
lord once more returning amidst his companies, but little did it
ease her grief for the death of Tinwelint that Naugladur was
slain and many Dwarves beside. Then did Beren seek to comfort
her, and taking her in his arms he set the glorious Nauglafring
about her neck, and all were blinded by the greatness of her
beauty; and Beren said: "Behold the Lamp of Fëanor that thou

and I did win from Hell," and Tinúviel smiled, remembering the first days of their love and those days of travail in the wild.

Now is it to be said that Beren sent for Ufedhin and well rewarded him for his words of true guidance whereof the Dwarves had been overcome, and he bid him dwell in . . . . among his folk, and Ufedhin was little loth; yet on a time, no great space thereafter, did that thing betide which he least desired. For came there a sound of very sorrowful singing in the woods, and behold, it was Gwendelin wandering distraught, and her feet bore her to the midmost of a glade where sat Beren and Tinúviel; and at that hour it was new morning, but at the sound all nigh ceased their speaking and were very still. Then did Beren gaze in awe upon Gwendelin, but Tinúviel cried suddenly in sorrow mixed with joy: "O mother Gwendelin, whither do thy feet bear thee, for methought thee dead"; but the greeting of those twain upon the greensward was very sweet. And Ufedhin fled from among the Elves, for he could not endure to look upon the eyes of Gwendelin, and madness took him, and none may say what was his unhappy weird thereafter; and little but a tortured heart got he from the Gold of Glorund.

Now hearing the cries of Ufedhin Gwendelin looked in wonder after him, and stayed her tender words; and memory came back into her eyes so that she cried as in amaze beholding the Necklace of the Dwarves that hung about the white throat of Tinúviel. Then wrathfully she asked of Beren what it might portend, and wherefore he suffered the accursed thing to touch Tinúviel; and told Beren[17] all that tale such as Huan had told him, in deed or guess, and of the pursuit and fighting at the ford he told also, saying at the end: "Nor indeed do I see who, now that Lord Tinwelint is fared to Valinor, should so fittingly wear that jewel of the Gods as Tinúviel." But Gwendelin told of the dragon's ban upon the gold and the [?staining] of blood in the king's halls, "and yet another and more potent curse, whose arising I know not, is woven therewith," said she, "nor methinks was the labour of the Dwarves free from spells of the most enduring malice." But Beren laughed, saying that the glory of the Silmaril and its holiness might overcome all such evils, even as it burnt the [?foul] flesh of Karkaras. "Nor," said he, "have I seen ever my Tinúviel so fair as now she is, clasped in the loveliness of this thing of gold"; but Gwendelin said: "Yet the Silmaril abode in the Crown of Melko, and that is the work of baleful smiths indeed."

Then said Tinúviel that she desired not things of worth or precious stones but the elfin gladness of the forest, and to pleasure Gwendelin she cast it from her neck; but Beren was little pleased and he would not suffer it to be flung away, but warded it in his . . . . . . . .[18]

Thereafter did Gwendelin abide a while in the woods among them and was healed; and in the end she fared wistfully back to the land of Lórien and came never again into the tales of the dwellers of Earth; but upon Beren and Tinúviel fell swiftly that doom of mortality that Mandos had spoken when he sped them from his halls — and in this perhaps did the curse of Mîm have [?potency] in that it came more soon upon them; nor this time did those twain fare the road together, but when yet was the child of those twain, Dior[19] the Fair, a little one, did Tinúviel slowly fade, even as the Elves of later days have done throughout the world, and she vanished in the woods, and none have seen her dancing ever there again. But Beren searched all the lands of Hithlum and of Artanor ranging after her; and never has any of the Elves had more loneliness than his, or ever he too faded from life, and Dior his son was left ruler of the brown Elves and the green, and Lord of the Nauglafring.

Mayhap what all Elves say is true, that those twain hunt now in the forest of Oromë in Valinor, and Tinúviel dances on the green swards of Nessa and of Vána daughters of the Gods for ever more; yet great was the grief of the Elves when the Guilwarthon went from among them, and being leaderless and lessened of magic their numbers minished; and many fared away to Gondolin, the rumour of whose growing power and glory ran in secret whispers among all the Elves.

Still did Dior when come to manhood rule a numerous folk, and he loved the woods even as Beren had done; and songs name him mostly Ausir the Wealthy for his possession of that wondrous gem set in the Necklace of the Dwarves. Now the tales of Beren and Tinúviel grew dim in his heart, and he took to wearing it about his neck and to love its loveliness most dearly; and the fame of that jewel spread like fire through all the regions of the North, and the Elves said one to another: "A Silmaril of Fëanor burns in the woods of Hisilómë."

Now fare the long days of Elfinesse unto that time when Tuor dwelt in Gondolin; and children then had Dior the Elf,[20] Auredhir and Elwing, and Auredhir was most like to his forefather Beren, and all loved him, yet none so dearly as did Dior; but Elwing the fairy have all poesies named as beautiful as Tinúviel if that indeed may be, yet hard is it to say seeing the great loveliness of the elfin folk of yore. Now those were days of happiness in the vales of Hithlum, for there was peace with Melko and the Dwarves who had but one thought as they plotted against Gondolin, and Angband was full of labour; yet is it to tell that bitterness entered into the hearts of the seven sons of Fëanor, remembering their oath. Now Maidros, whom Melko maimed, was their leader; and he called to his brethren Maglor and Dinithel, and to Damrod, and to Celegorm, to Cranthor and to Curufin the Crafty, and he said to them how it was now known to him that a Silmaril of those their father Fëanor had made was now the pride and glory of Dior of the southern vales, "and Elwing his daughter bears it whitherso she goes – but do you not forget," said he, "that we swore to have no peace with Melko nor any of his folk, nor with any other of Earth-dwellers that held the Silmarils of Fëanor from us. For what," said Maidros, "do we suffer exile and wandering and rule over a scant and forgotten folk, if others gather to their hoard the heirlooms that are ours?"

Thus was it that they sent Curufin the Crafty to Dior, and told him of their oath, and bid him give that fair jewel back unto those whose right it was; but Dior gazing on the loveliness of Elwing would not do so, and he said that he could not endure that the Nauglafring, fairest of earthly craft, be so despoiled. "Then," said Curufin, "must the Nauglafring unbroken be given to the sons of Fëanor," and Dior waxed wroth, bidding him be gone, nor dare to claim what his sire Beren the Onehanded won with his hand from the [?jaws] of Melko – "other twain are there in the selfsame place," said he, "an your hearts be bold enow."

Then went Curufin unto his brethren, and because of their unbreakable oath and of their [?thirst] for that Silmaril (nor indeed was the spell of Mîm and of the dragon wanting) they planned war upon Dior – and the Eldar cry shame upon them for that deed, the first premeditated war of elfin folk upon elfin folk, whose name otherwise were glorious among the Eldalië for their sufferings. Little good came thereby to them; for they fell unawares upon Dior, and Dior and Auredhir were slain, yet behold, Evranin the nurse of Elwing, and Gereth a Gnome, took her unwilling in a flight swift and sudden from those lands, and they bore with them the Nauglafring, so that the sons of Fëanor saw it not; but a host of Dior's folk, coming with all speed yet late unto the fray, fell suddenly on their rear, and there was a great battle, and Maglor was slain with swords, and Mai . . . .[21] died of wounds in the wild, and Celegorm was pierced with a hundred

arrows, and Cranthor beside him. Yet in the end were the sons of
Fëanor masters of the field of slain, and the brown Elves and the
green were scattered over all the lands unhappy, for they would
not hearken to Maidros the maimed, nor to Curufin and Damrod
who had slain their lord; and it is said that even on the day of
that battle of the Elves Melko sought against Gondolin, and the
fortunes of the Elves came to their uttermost waning.

Now was naught left of the seed of Beren Ermabwed son of
Egnor save Elwing the Lovely, and she wandered in the woods,
and of the brown Elves and the green a few gathered to her, and
they departed for ever from the glades of Hithlum and got them to
the south towards Sirion's deep waters, and the pleasant lands.

And thus did all the fates of the fairies weave then to one strand,
and that strand is the great tale of Eärendel; and to that tale's true
beginning are we now come.'

Then said Ailios: 'And methinks that is tale enow for this time
of telling.'

## NOTES

1    This sentence is a rewriting of the text, which had originally:

"Nay then, know ye not that this gold belongs to the kindred of
the Elves, who won it from the earth long time ago, and no one
among Men has claim . . ."

The remainder of this scene, ending with the slaughter of Úrin's
band, was rewritten at many points, with the same object as in the
passage just cited – to convert Úrin's band from Men to Elves, as
was done also at the end of Eltas' tale (see p. 118 note 33). Thus
original 'Elves' was changed to 'Elves of the wood, woodland Elves',
and original 'Men' to 'folk, outlaws'; and see notes 2, 3, 5.

2    The original sentence here was:

Doughty were those Men and great wielders of sword and axe,
and still in those unfaded days might mortal weapons wound the
bodies of the elfin-folk.

See note 1.

3    The original sentence here was: 'and those Men being wildered with
magics'. See note 1.

4    This sentence, from 'and yet another sorrow . . .', was added to the
text later.

5    'those': the text has 'the Men', obviously left unchanged through
oversight. See note 1.

6   'in the earth' is an emendation of the original reading 'on the earth'.

7   'damasked in strange wise', i.e. 'damascened', ornamentally inlaid with designs in gold and silver. The word 'damascened' is used of the sword of Tinwelint made by the Dwarves, on which were seen images of the wolf-hunt (p. 227), and of Glorfindel's arms (p. 173).

8   The text has 'Eltas', but with 'Ailios' written above in pencil. Since Ailios appears as the teller at the beginning of the tale, and not as the result of emendation, 'Eltas' here was probably no more than a slip.

9   'save only' is a later emendation of the original 'not even'. See p. 256.

10   It is odd that *Gwendelin* appears here, not *Gwenniel* as hitherto in this tale. Since the first part of the tale is in ink over an erased pencil text, the obvious explanation is that the erased text had *Gwendelin* and that my father changed this to *Gwenniel* as he went along, overlooking it in this one instance. But the matter is probably more complex – one of those small puzzles with which the texts of the *Lost Tales* abound – for after the manuscript in ink ceases the form *Gwenniel* occurs, though once only, and *Gwendelin* is then used for all the rest of the tale. See *Changes made to Names*, p. 244.

11   Here the manuscript in ink ends; see p. 221.

12   Against this sentence my father wrote a direction that the story was to be that the Nauglafring caught in the bushes and held the king.

13   A rejected passage in the manuscript here gives an earlier version of the events, according to which it was Gwendelin, not Huan, who brought the news to Beren:

> . . . and her bitter weeping filled the forest. Now there did Gwendeling [*sic*] gather to her many of the scattered woodland Elves and of them did she hear how matters had fared even as she had guessed: how the hunting party had been surrounded and o'erwhelmed by the Nauglath while the Indrafangs and Orcs fell suddenly with death and fire upon all the realm of Tinwelint, and not the least host was that of Ufedhin that slew the guardians of the bridge; and it was said that Naugladur had slain Tinwelint when he was borne down by numbers, and folk thought Narthseg a wild Elf had led the foemen hither, and he had been slain in the fighting.
>
> Then seeing no hope Gwendelin and her companions fared with the utmost speed out of that land of sorrow, even to the kingdom of i·Guilwarthon in Hisilómë, where reigned Beren and Tinúviel her daughter. Now Beren and Tinúviel lived not in any settled abode, nor had their realm boundaries well-marked, and no other messenger save Gwendelin daughter of the Vali had of a surety found those twain the living-dead so soon.

It is clear from the manuscript that the return of Mablung and Huan to Artanor and their presence at the hunt (referred to in general terms at the end of the *Tale of Tinúviel*, p. 41) was added to the tale, and with this new element went the change in Gwendelin's movements immediately after the disaster. But though the textual history is here extremely hard to interpet, what with erasures and additions on loose pages, I think it is almost certain that this reshaping was done while the original composition of the tale was still in progress.

14　The first of these lacunae that I have left in the text contains two words, the first possibly 'believe' and the second probably 'best'. In the second lacuna the word might conceivably be 'pallor'.

15　This sentence, from 'and is it not that very water . . .', is struck through and bracketed, and in the margin my father scribbled: 'No [?that] is Narog.'

16　The illegible word might be 'brays': the word 'clearer' is an emendation from 'hoarser'.

17　'and told Beren': i.e., 'and Beren told'. The text as first written had 'Then told Beren . . .'

18　The illegible word might just possibly be 'treasury', but I do not think that it is.

19　*Dior* replaced the name *Ausir*, which however occurs below as another name for Dior.

20　'Dior the Elf' is an emendation from 'Dior then an aged Elf'.

21　The latter part of this name is quite unclear: it might be read as *Maithog*, or as *Mailweg*. See *Changes made to Names* under *Dinithel*.

### Changes made to names in
### The Tale of the Nauglafring

*Ilfiniol* (p. 221) here so written from the first: see p. 201.

*Gwenniel* is used throughout the revised section of the tale except at the last occurrence (p. 228), where the form is *Gwendelin*; in the pencilled part of the tale at the first occurrence of the queen's name it is again *Gwenniel* (p. 230), but thereafter always *Gwendelin* (see note 10).

　　The name of the queen in the *Lost Tales* is as variable as that of Littleheart. In *The Chaining of Melko* and *The Coming of the Elves* she is *Tindriel* > *Wendelin*. In the *Tale of Tinúviel* she is *Wendelin* > *Gwendeling* (see p. 50); in the type-script text of *Tinúviel Gwenethlin* > *Melian*; in the *Tale of Turambar Gwendeling* > *Gwedheling*; in the present tale *Gwendelin/Gwenniel* (the form *Gwendeling* occurs in the rejected passage given in note 13); and in the Gnomish dictionary *Gwendeling* > *Gwedhiling*.

*Belegost*　At the first occurrence (p. 230) the manuscript has *Ost Belegost*, with *Ost* circled as if for rejection, and *Belegost* is the reading subsequently.

(*i·*)*Guilwarthon*   In the *Tale of Tinúviel*, p. 41, the form is
   *i·Cuilwarthon*. At the occurrence on p. 240 the ending of the
   name does not look like -*on*, but as I cannot say what it is I give
   *Guilwarthon* in the text.

*Dinithel* could also be read as *Durithel* (p. 241). This name was written
   in later in ink over an earlier name in pencil now scarcely legible,
   though clearly the same as that beginning *Mai* . . . . which appears
   for this son of Fëanor subsequently (see note 21).

Commentary on
*The Tale of the Nauglafring*

In this commentary I shall not compare in detail the *Tale of the
Nauglafring* with the story told in *The Silmarillion* (Chapter 22, *Of the
Ruin of Doriath*). The stories are profoundly different in essential
features – above all, in the reduction of the treasure brought by Húrin
from Nargothrond to a single object, the Necklace of the Dwarves, which
had long been in existence (though not, of course, containing the
Silmaril); while the whole history of the relation between Thingol and
the Dwarves is changed. My father never again wrote any part of this
story on a remotely comparable scale, and the formation of the published
text was here of the utmost difficulty; I hope later to give an account of it.

While it is often difficult to differentiate what my father omitted in his
more concise versions (in order to keep them concise) from what he
rejected, it seems clear that a large part of the elaborate narrative of the
*Tale of the Nauglafring* was early abandoned. In subsequent writing
the story of the fighting between Úrin's band and Tinwelint's Elves
disappeared, and there is no trace afterwards of Ufedhin or the other
Gnomes that lived among the Dwarves, of the story that the Dwarves
took half the unwrought gold ('the king's loan') away to Nogrod to
make precious objects from it, of the keeping of Ufedhin hostage, of
Tinwelint's refusal to let the Dwarves depart, of their outrageous
demands, of their scourging and their insulting payment.

We meet here again the strong emphasis on Tinwelint's love of treasure
and lack of it, in contrast to the later conception of his vast wealth (see my
remarks, pp. 128–9). The Silmaril is kept in a wooden casket (p. 225),
Tinwelint has no crown but a wreath of scarlet leaves (p. 227), and he
is far less richly clad and accoutred than 'the wayfarer in his halls'
(Ufedhin). This is very well in itself – the Woodland Elf corrupted by
the lure of golden splendour, but it need not be remarked again how
strangely at variance is this picture with that of Thingol Lord of
Beleriand, who had a vast treasury in his marvellous underground realm
of Menegroth, the Thousand Caves – itself largely contrived by the
Dwarves of Belegost in the distant past (*The Silmarillion* pp. 92–3), and
who most certainly did not need the aid of Dwarves at this time to make

him a crown and a fine sword, or vessels to adorn his banquets. Thingol in the later conception is proud, and stern; he is also wise, and powerful, and greatly increased in stature and in knowledge through his union with a Maia. Could such a king have sunk to the level of miserly swindling that is portrayed in the *Tale of the Nauglafring*?

Great stress is indeed placed on the enormous size of the hoard – 'such mighty heaps of gold have never since been gathered in one place', p. 223 – which is made so vast that it becomes hard to believe that a band of wandering outlaws could have brought it to the halls of the woodland Elves, even granting that 'some was lost upon the way' (p. 114). There is perhaps some difference here from the account of the Rodothlim and their works in the *Tale of Turambar* (p. 81), where there is certainly no suggestion that the Rodothlim possessed treasures coming out of Valinor – though this idea remained through all the vicissitudes of this part of the story: it is said of the Lord of Nargothrond in *The Silmarillion* (p. 114) that 'Finrod had brought more treasures out of Tirion than any other of the princes of the Noldor'.

More important, the elements of 'spell' and 'curse' are dominant in this tale, to such a degree that they might almost be said to be the chief actors in it. The curse of Mîm on the gold is felt at every turn of the narrative. Vengeance for him is one motive in Naugladur's decision to attack the Elves of Artanor (p. 230). His curse is fulfilled in the 'agelong feud' between the kindreds of the Dwarves (p. 235) – of which all trace was afterwards effaced, with the loss of the entire story of Ufedhin's intent to steal the Necklace from Naugladur sleeping, the killing of Bodruith Lord of Belegost, and the fighting between the two clans of Dwarves. Naugladur was 'blinded by the spell' in taking so imprudent a course out of Artanor (p. 236); and the curse of Mîm is made the 'cause' of his stumbling on a stone in his fight with Beren (p. 238). It is even, and most surprisingly, suggested as a reason for the short second lives of Beren and Tinúviel (p. 240); and finally 'the spell of Mîm' is an element in the attack on Dior by the Fëanorians (p. 241). An important element also in the tale is the baleful nature of the Nauglafring, for the Dwarves made it with bitterness; and into the complex of curses and spells is introduced also 'the dragon's ban upon the gold' (p. 239) or 'the spell of the dragon' (p. 241). It is not said in the *Tale of Turambar* that Glorund had cursed the gold or enspelled it; but Mîm said to Úrin (p. 114): 'Has not Glorund lain long years upon it, and the evil of the drakes of Melko is on it, and no good can it bring to Man or Elf.' Most notably, Gwendelin implies, against Beren's assertion that 'its holiness might overcome all such evils', that the Silmaril itself is unhallowed, since it 'abode in the Crown of Melko' (p. 239). In the later of the two 'schemes' for the *Lost Tales* (see I. 107 note 3) it is said that the Nauglafring 'brought sickness to Tinúviel'.*

---

* It is said in the Gnomish dictionary that the curse of Mîm was 'appeased' when the Nauglafring was lost in the sea; see the Appendix on Names, entry *Nauglafring*.

But however much the chief actors in this tale are 'enspelled' or blindly carrying forward the mysterious dictates of a curse, there is no question but that the Dwarves in the original conception were altogether more ignoble than they afterwards became, more prone to evil to gain their ends, and more exclusively impelled by greed; that Doriath should be laid waste by mercenary Orcs under Dwarvish paymasters (p. 230) was to become incredible and impossible later. It is even said that by the deeds of Naugladur 'have the Dwarves been severed in feud for ever since those days with the Elves, and drawn more nigh in friendship to the kin of Melko' (p. 230); and in the outlines for *Gilfanon's Tale* the Nauglath are an evil people, associates of goblins (I. 236–7). In a rejected outline for the *Tale of the Nauglafring* (p. 136) the Necklace was made 'by certain Úvanimor (Nautar or Nauglath)', Úvanimor being defined elsewhere as 'monsters, giants, and ogres'. With all this compare *The Lord of the Rings*, Appendix F (I): 'They [the Dwarves] are not evil by nature, and few ever served the Enemy of free will, whatever the tales of Men may have alleged.'

The account of the Dwarves in this tale is of exceptional interest in other respects. 'The beards of the Indrafangs' have been named in Tinúviel's 'lengthening spell' (pp. 19, 46); but this is the first description of the Dwarves in my father's writings – already with the spelling that he maintained against the unceasing opposition of proof-readers – and they are eminently recognisable in their dour and hidden natures, in their 'unloveliness' (*The Silmarillion* p. 113), and in their 'marvellous skill with metals' (*ibid.* p. 92). The strange statement that 'never comes a child among them' is perhaps to be related to 'the foolish opinion among Men' referred to in *The Lord of the Rings*, Appendix A (III), 'that there are no Dwarf-women, and that the Dwarves "grow out of stone".' In the same place it is said that 'it is because of the fewness of women among them that the kind of the Dwarves increases slowly'.

It is also said in the tale that it is thought by some that the Dwarves 'have not heard of Ilúvatar'; on knowledge of Ilúvatar among Men see p. 209.

According to the Gnomish dictionary *Indrafang* was 'a special name of the Longbeards or Dwarves', but in the tale it is made quite plain that the Longbeards were on the contrary the Dwarves of Belegost; the Dwarves of Nogrod were the Nauglath, with their king Naugladur. It must be admitted however that the use of the terms is sometimes confusing, or confused: thus the description of the Nauglath on pp. 223–4 seems to be a description of all Dwarves, and to include the Indrafangs, though this cannot have been intended. The reference to 'the march of the Dwarves and Indrafangs' (p. 234) must be taken as an ellipse, i.e. 'the Dwarves of Nogrod and the Indrafangs'. Naugladur of Nogrod and Bodruith of Belegost are said to have been akin (p. 235), though this perhaps only means that they were both Dwarves whereas Ufedhin was an Elf.

The Dwarf-city of Nogrod is said in the tale to lie 'a very long journey southward beyond the wide forest on the borders of those great heaths nigh Umboth-muilin the Pools of Twilight, on the marches of Tasarinan' (p. 225). This could be interpreted to mean that Nogrod was itself 'on the borders of those great heaths nigh Umboth-muilin'; but I think that this is out of the question. It would be a most improbable place for Dwarves, who 'dwell beneath the earth in caves and tunnelled towns, and aforetime Nogrod was the mightiest of these' (p. 224). Though mountains are not specifically mentioned here in connection with Dwarves, I think it extremely likely that my father at this time conceived their cities to be in the mountains, as they were afterwards. Further, there seems nothing to contradict the view that the configuration of the lands in the *Lost Tales* was essentially similar to that of the earliest and later 'Silmarillion' maps; and on them, 'a very long journey southward' is totally inappropriate to that between the Thousand Caves and the Pools of Twilight.

The meaning must therefore be, simply, 'a very long journey southward beyond the wide forest', and what follows places the wide forest, not Nogrod; the forest being, in fact, the Forest of Artanor.

The Pools of Twilight are described in *The Fall of Gondolin*, but the Elvish name does not there appear (see pp. 195–6, 217).

Whether Belegost was near to or far from Nogrod is not made plain; it is said in this passage that the gold should be borne away 'to Nogrod and the dwellings of the Dwarves', but later (p. 230) the Indrafangs are 'a kindred of the Dwarves that dwelt in other realms'.

In his association with the Dwarves Ufedhin is reminiscent of Eöl, Maeglin's father, of whom it is said in *The Silmarillion* (p. 133) that 'for the Dwarves he had more liking than any other of the Elvenfolk of old'; cf. *ibid.* p. 92: 'Few of the Eldar went ever to Nogrod or Belegost, save Eöl of Nan Elmoth and Maeglin his son.' In the early forms of the story of Eöl and Isfin (referred to in *The Fall of Gondolin*, p. 165) Eöl has no association with Dwarves. In the present tale there is mention (p. 224) of 'great traffic' carried on by the Dwarves 'with the free Noldoli' (with Melko's servants also) in those days: we may wonder who these free Noldoli were, since the Rodothlim had been destroyed, and Gondolin was hidden. Perhaps the sons of Fëanor are meant, or Egnor Beren's father (see p. 65).

The idea that it was the Dwarves of Nogrod who were primarily involved survived into the later narrative, but they became exclusively so, and those of Belegost specifically denied all aid to them (*The Silmarillion* p. 233).

Turning now to the Elves, Beren is here of course still an Elf (see p. 139), and in his second span of life he is the ruler, in Hithlum–Hisilómë, of an Elvish people so numerous that 'not even Beren knew the tale of those myriad folk' (p. 234); they are called 'the green Elves' and 'the brown Elves and the green', for they were 'clad in green and brown', and Dior ruled them in Hithlum after the final departure of Beren and Tinúviel. Who were they? It is far from clear how they are to be set into the conception of the Elves of the Great Lands as it appears in other Tales. We may compare the passage in *The Coming of the Elves* (I.118–19):

> Long after the joy of Valinor had washed its memory faint [i.e., the memory of the journey through Hisilómë] the Elves sang still sadly of it, and told tales of many of their folk whom they said and say were lost in those old forests and ever wandered there in sorrow. Still were they there long after when Men were shut in Hisilómë by Melko, and still do they dance there when Men have wandered far over the lighter places of the Earth. Hisilómë did Men name Aryador, and the Lost Elves did they call the Shadow Folk, and feared them.

But in that tale the conception still was that Tinwelint ruled 'the scattered Elves of Hisilomë', and in the outlines for *Gilfanon's Tale* the 'Shadow Folk' of Hisilómë had ceased to be Elves (see p. 64). In any case, the expression 'green Elves', coupled with the fact that it was the Green-elves of Ossiriand whom Beren led to the ambush of the Dwarves at Sarn Athrad in the later story (*The Silmarillion* p. 235), shows which Elvish people they were to become, even though there is as yet no trace of Ossiriand beyond the river Gelion and the story of the origin of the Laiquendi (*ibid.* pp. 94, 96).

It was inevitable that 'the land of the dead that live' should cease to be in Hisilómë (which seems to have been in danger of having too many inhabitants), and a note on the manuscript of the *Tale of the Nauglafring* says: 'Beren must be in "Doriath beyond Sirion" on a . . . . . not in Hithlum.' Doriath beyond Sirion was the region called in *The Silmarillion* (p. 122) Nivrim, the West March, the woods on the west bank of the river between the confluence of Teiglin and Sirion and Aelin-uial, the Meres of Twilight. In the *Tale of Tinúviel* Beren and Tinúviel, called i·Cuilwarthon, 'became mighty fairies in the lands about the north of Sirion' (p. 41).

Gwendelin/Gwenniel appears a somewhat faint and ineffective figure by comparison with the Melian of *The Silmarillion*. Conceivably, an aspect of this is the far slighter protection afforded to the realm of Artanor by her magic than that of the impenetrable wall and deluding mazes of the Girdle of Melian (see p. 63). But the nature of the protection in the old conception is very unclear. In the *Tale of the Nauglafring* the coming of the Dwarves from Nogrod is only known when they approach the bridge before Tinwelint's caves (p. 226); on the other hand, it is said (p. 230) that the 'woven magic' of the queen was a defence against 'men of hostile heart', who could never make their way through the woods unless aided by treachery from within. Perhaps this provides an explanation of a sort of how the Dwarves bringing treasure from Nogrod were able to penetrate to the halls of Tinwelint without hindrance and apparently undetected (cf. also the coming of Úrin's band in the *Tale of Turambar*, p. 114). In the event, the protective magic was easily – too easily – overthrown by the simple device of a single treacherous Elf of Artanor who 'offered to lead the host through the magics of Gwendelin'. This was evidently unsatisfactory; but I shall not enter further into this question here. Extraordinary difficulties of narrative structure were caused by this element of the inviolability of Doriath, as I hope to describe at a future date.

It might be thought that the story of the drowning of the treasure at the Stony Ford (falling into the waters of the river with the Dwarves who bore it) was evolved from that in the rejected conclusion of the *Tale of Turambar* (p. 136) – Tinwelint 'hearing that curse [set on the treasure by Úrin] caused the gold to be cast into a deep pool of the river before his doors'. In the *Tale of the Nauglafring*, however, Tinwelint, influenced by the queen's foreboding words, still has the intention of doing this, but does not fulfil his intention (p. 223).

The account of the second departure of Beren and Tinúviel (p. 240) raises again the extremely difficult question of the peculiar fate that was decreed for them by the edict of Mandos, which I have discussed on pp. 59–60. There I have suggested that

> the peculiar dispensation of Mandos in the case of Beren and Tinúviel as here conceived is therefore that their whole 'natural' destiny as Elves was changed: having died as Elves might die (from wounds or from grief) they were not reborn as new beings, but returned in their own persons – yet now 'mortal even as Men'.

Here however Tinúviel 'faded', and vanished in the woods; and Beren searched all Hithlum and Artanor for her, until he too 'faded from life'. Since this fading is here quite explicitly the mode in which 'that doom of mortality that Mandos had spoken' came upon them (p. 240), it is very notable that it is likened to, and even it seems identified with, the fading of 'the Elves of later days throughout the world' – as though in the original idea Elvish fading was a form of mortality. This is in fact made explicit in a later version.

The seven Sons of Fëanor, their oath (sworn not in Valinor but after the coming of the Noldoli to the Great Lands), and the maiming of Maidros appear in the outlines for *Gilfanon's Tale*; and in the latest of these outlines the Fëanorians are placed in Dor Lómin (= Hisilómë, Hithlum), see I. 238, 240, 243. Here, in the *Tale of the Nauglafring*, appear for the first time the names of the Sons of Fëanor, five of them (Maidros, Maglor, Celegorm, Cranthor, Curufin) in the forms, or almost the forms, they were to retain, and Curufin already with his sobriquet 'the Crafty'. The names Amrod and Amras in *The Silmarillion* were a late change; for long these two sons of Fëanor were Damrod (as here) and Díriel (here Dinithel or Durithel, see *Changes made to Names*, p. 245).

Here also appear Dior the Fair, also called Ausir the Wealthy, and his daughter Elwing; his son Auredhir early disappeared in the development of the legends. But Dior ruled in 'the southern vales' (p. 241) of Hisilómë, not in Artanor, and there is no suggestion of any renewal of Tinwelint's kingdom after his death, in contrast to what was told later (*The Silmarillion* p. 236); moreover the Fëanorians, as noted above, dwelt also in Hisilómë – and how all this is to be related to what is said elsewhere of the inhabitants of that region I am unable to say: cf. the *Tale of Tinúviel*, p. 10: 'Hisilómë where dwelt Men, and thrall-Noldoli laboured, and few free-Eldar went.'

A very curious statement is made in this concluding part of the tale, that 'those were days of happiness in the vales of Hithlum, for there was peace with Melko and the Dwarves who had but one thought as they plotted against Gondolin' (p. 241). Presumably 'peace with Melko' means no more than that Melko had averted his attention from those lands; but nowhere else is there any reference to the Dwarves' plotting against Gondolin.

In the typescript version of the *Tale of Tinúviel* (p. 43) it is said that if Turgon King of Gondolin was the most glorious of the kings of the Elves who defied Melko, 'for a while the most mighty *and the longest free* was Thingol of the Woods'. The most natural interpretation of this expression is surely that Gondolin fell before Artanor; whereas in *The Silmarillion* (p. 240) 'Tidings were brought by Thorondor Lord of Eagles of the fall of Nargothrond, and after of the slaying of Thingol and of Dior his heir, and of the ruin of Doriath; but Turgon shut his ear to word of the woes without.' In the present tale we see the same chronology, in that many of the Elves who followed Beren went after his departure to Gondolin, 'the rumour of whose growing power and glory ran in secret whispers among all the Elves' (p. 240), though here the destruction of Gondolin is said to have taken place on the very day that Dior was attacked by the Sons of Fëanor (p. 242). To evade the discrepancy therefore we must interpret the passage in the *Tale of Tinúviel* to mean that Thingol remained free for a longer period of years than did Turgon, irrespective of the dates of their downfalls.

Lastly, the statements that Cûm an-Idrisaith, the Mound of Avarice, 'stands there still in Artanor' (p. 223), and that the waters of Aros still flow above the drowned hoard (p. 238), are noteworthy as indications that nothing analogous to the Drowning of Beleriand was present in the original conception.

# V

# THE TALE OF EÄRENDEL

The 'true beginning' of the *Tale of Eärendel* was to be the dwelling at Sirion's mouth of the Lothlim (the point at which *The Fall of Gondolin* ends: 'and fair among the Lothlim Eärendel grows in the house of his father', pp. 196–7) and the coming there of Elwing (the point at which the *Tale of the Nauglafring* ends: 'they departed for ever from the glades of Hithlum and got them to the south towards Sirion's deep waters, and the pleasant lands. And thus did all the fates of the fairies weave then to one strand, and that strand is the great tale of Eärendel; and to that tale's true beginning are we now come', p. 242). The matter is complicated, however, as will be seen in a moment, by my father's also making the *Nauglafring* the first part of the *Tale of Eärendel*.

But the great tale was never written; and for the story as he then conceived it we are wholly dependent on highly condensed and often contradictory outlines. There are also many isolated notes; and there are the very early Eärendel poems. While the poems can be precisely dated, the notes and outlines can not; and it does not seem possible to arrange them in order so as to provide a clear line of development.

One of the outlines for the *Tale of Eärendel* is the earlier of the two 'schemes' for the *Lost Tales* which are the chief materials for *Gilfanon's Tale*; and I will repeat here what I said of this in the first part (I.233):

> There is no doubt that [the earlier of the two schemes] was composed when the *Lost Tales* had reached their furthest point of development, as represented by the latest texts and arrangements given in this book. Now when this outline comes to the matter of *Gilfanon's Tale* it becomes at once very much fuller, but then contracts again to cursory references for the tales of Tinúviel, Túrin, Tuor, and the Necklace of the Dwarves, and once more becomes fuller for the tale of Eärendel.

This scheme B (as I will continue to call it) provides a coherent if very rough narrative plan, and divides the story into seven parts, of which the first (marked 'Told') is 'The Nauglafring down to the flight of Elwing'. This sevenfold division is referred to by Littleheart at the beginning of *The Fall of Gondolin* (p. 144):

> It is a mighty tale, and seven times shall folk fare to the Tale-fire ere it be rightly told; and so twined is it with those stories of the Nauglafring and of the Elf-march that I would fain have aid in that telling . . .

If the six parts following the *Tale of the Nauglafring* were each to be of comparable length, the whole *Tale of Eärendel* would have been somewhere near half the length of all the tales that were in fact written; but my father never afterwards returned to it on any ample scale.

I give now the concluding part of Scheme B.

Tale of Eärendel begins, with which is interwoven the Nauglafring and the March of the Elves. For further details see Notebook C.*

*First part.* The tale of the Nauglafring down to the flight of Elwing.

*Second part.* The dwelling at Sirion. Coming thither of Elwing, and the love of her and Eärendel as girl and boy. Ageing of Tuor – his secret sailing after the conches of Ulmo in Swanwing.

Eärendel sets sail to the North to find Tuor, and if needs be Mandos. Sails in Eärámë. Wrecked. Ulmo appears. Saves him, bidding him sail to Kôr – 'for for this hast thou been brought out of the Wrack of Gondolin'.

*Third part.* Second attempt of Eärendel to Mandos. Wreck of Falasquil and rescue by the Oarni.[1] He sights the Isle of Seabirds 'whither do all the birds of all waters come at whiles'. Goes back by land to Sirion.

Idril has vanished (she set sail at night). The conches of Ulmo call Eärendel. Last farewell of Elwing. Building of Wingilot.

*Fourth part.* Eärendel sails for Valinor. His many wanderings, occupying several years.

*Fifth part.* Coming of the birds of Gondolin to Kôr with tidings. Uproar of the Elves. Councils of the Gods. March of the Inwir (death of Inwë), Teleri, and Solosimpi.

Raid upon Sirion and captivity of Elwing.

Sorrow and wrath of Gods, and a veil dropped between Valmar and Kôr, for the Gods will not destroy it but cannot bear to look upon it.

Coming of the Eldar. Binding of Melko. Faring to Lonely Isle. Curse of the Nauglafring and death of Elwing.

*Sixth part.* Eärendel reaches Kôr and finds it empty. Fares home in sorrow (and sights Tol Eressëa and the fleet of the Elves, but a great wind and darkness carries him away, and he misses his way and has a voyage eastward).

Arriving at length at Sirion finds it empty. Goes to the ruins of Gondolin. Hears of tidings. Sails to Tol Eressëa. Sails to the Isle of Seabirds.

*Seventh part.* His voyage to the firmament.

* For 'Notebook C' see p. 254.

Written at the end of the text is: 'Rem[ainder] of Scheme in Notebook
C'. These references in Scheme B to 'Notebook C' are to the little
pocket-book which goes back to 1916–17 but was used for notes and
suggestions throughout the period of the *Lost Tales* (see I.171). At the
beginning of it there is an outline (here called 'C') headed 'Eärendel's
Tale, Tuor's son', which is in fair harmony with Scheme B:

> Eärendel dwells with Tuor and Irildë[2] at Sirion's mouth by the sea (on
> the Isles of Sirion). Elwing of the Gnomes of Artanor[3] flees to them
> with the Nauglafring. Eärendel and Elwing love one another as boy
> and girl.
>     Great love of Eärendel and Tuor. Tuor ages, and Ulmo's conches
> far out west over the sea call him louder and louder, till one evening he
> sets sail in his twilit boat with purple sails, Swanwing, Alqarámë.[4]
> Idril sees him too late. Her song on the beach of Sirion.
>     When he does not return grief of Eärendel and Idril. Eärendel
> (urged also by Idril who is immortal) desires to set sail and search even
> to Mandos. [*Marginal addition*:] Curse of Nauglafring rests on his
> voyages. Ossë his enemy.
>     Fiord of the Mermaid. Wreck. Ulmo appears at wreck and saves
> them, telling them he must go to Kôr and is saved for that.
>     Elwing's grief when she learns Ulmo's bidding. 'For no man may
> tread the streets of Kôr or look upon the places of the Gods and dwell
> in the Outer Lands in peace again.'
>     Eärendel departs all the same and is wrecked by the treachery of
> Ossë and saved only by the Oarni (who love him) with Voronwë and
> dragged to Falasquil.
>     Eärendel makes his way back by land with Voronwë. Finds that
> Idril has vanished.[5] His grief. Prays to Ulmo and hears the conches.
> Ulmo bids him build a new and wonderful ship of the wood of Tuor
> from Falasquil. Building of Wingilot.

There are four items headed 'Additions' on this page of the notebook:

> Building of Eärámë (Eaglepinion).
> Noldoli add their pleading to Ulmo's bidding.
> Eärendel surveys the first dwelling of Tuor at Falasquil.
> The voyage to Mandos and the Icy Seas.

The outline continues:

> Voronwë and Eärendel set sail in Wingilot. Driven south. Dark
> regions. Fire mountains. Tree-men. Pygmies. Sarqindi or cannibal-
> ogres.
>     Driven west. Ungweliantë. Magic Isles. Twilit Isle [*sic*]. Little-
> heart's gong awakes the Sleeper in the Tower of Pearl.[6]

Kôr is found. Empty. Eärendel reads tales and prophecies in the waters. Desolation of Kôr. Eärendel's shoes and self powdered with diamond dust so that they shine brightly.

Homeward adventures. Driven east – the deserts and red palaces where dwells the Sun.[7]

Arrives at Sirion, only to find it sacked and empty. Eärendel distraught wanders with Voronwë and comes to the ruins of Gondolin. Men are encamped there miserably. Also Gnomes searching still for lost gems (or some Gnomes gone back to Gondolin).

Of the binding of Melko.[8] The wars with Men and the departure to Tol Eressëa (the Eldar unable to endure the strife of the world). Eärendel sails to Tol Eressëa and learns of the sinking of Elwing and the Nauglafring. Elwing became a seabird. His grief is very great. His garments and body shine like diamonds and his face is in silver flame for the grief and . . . . . . . . .

He sets sail with Voronwë and dwells on the Isle of Seabirds in the northern waters (not far from Falasquil) – and there hopes that Elwing will return among the seabirds, but she is seeking him wailing along all the shores and especially among wreckage.

After three times seven years he sails again for halls of Mandos with Voronwë – he gets there because [?only] those who still . . . . . . . . . . and had suffered may do so – Tuor is gone to Valinor and nought is known of Idril or of Elwing.

Reaches bar at margin of the world and sets sail on oceans of the firmament in order to gaze over the Earth. The Moon mariner chases him for his brightness and he dives through the Door of Night. How he cannot now return to the world or he will die.

He will find Elwing at the Faring Forth.

Tuor and Idril some say sail now in Swanwing and may be seen going swift down the wind at dawn and dusk.

### The Co-events to Eärendel's Tale

Raid upon Sirion by Melko's Orcs and the captivity of Elwing.

Birds tell Elves of the Fall of Gondolin and the horrors of the fate of the Gnomes. Counsels of the Gods and uproar of the Elves. March of the Inwir and Teleri. The Solosimpi go forth also but fare along all the beaches of the world, for they are loth to fare far from the sound of the sea – and only consent to go with the Teleri under these conditions – for the Noldoli slew some of their kin at Kópas.

This outline then goes on to the events after the coming of the Elves of Valinor into the Great Lands, which will be considered in the next chapter.

Though very much fuller, there seems to be little in C that is certainly contradictory to what is said in B, and there are elements in the latter that are absent from the former. In discussing these outlines I follow the divisions of the tale made in B.

*Second part.* A little more is told in C of Tuor's departure from Sirion (in B there is no mention of Idril); and there appears the motive of Ossë's hostility to Eärendel and the curse of the Nauglafring as instrumental in his shipwrecks. The place of the first wreck is called the Fiord of the Mermaid. The word 'them' rather than 'him' in 'Ulmo saves them, telling them he must go to Kôr' is certain in the manuscript, which possibly suggests that Idril or Elwing (or both) were with Eärendel.

*Third part.* In B Eärendel's second voyage, like the first, is explicitly an attempt to reach Mandos (seeking his father), whereas in C it seems that the second is undertaken rather in order to fulfil Ulmo's bidding that he sail to Kôr (to Elwing's grief). In C Voronwë is named as Eärendel's companion on the second voyage which ended at Falasquil; but the Isle of Seabirds is not mentioned at this point. In C Wingilot is built 'of the wood of Tuor from Falasquil'; in *The Fall of Gondolin* Tuor's wood was hewed for him by the Noldoli in the forests of Dor Lómin and floated down the hidden river (p. 152).

*Fourth part.* Whereas B merely refers to Eärendel's 'many wanderings, occupying several years' in his quest for Valinor, C gives some glimpses of what they were to be, as Wingilot was driven to the south and then into the west. The encounter with Ungweliantë on the western voyage is curious; it is said in *The Tale of the Sun and Moon* that 'Melko held the North and Ungweliant the South' (see I.182, 200).

In C we meet again the Sleeper in the Tower of Pearl (said to be Idril, though this was struck out, note 6) awakened by Littleheart's gong; cf. the account of Littleheart in *The Cottage of Lost Play* (I.15):

> He sailed in Wingilot with Eärendel in that last voyage wherein they sought for Kôr. It was the ringing of this Gong on the Shadowy Seas that awoke the Sleeper in the Tower of Pearl that stands far out to west in the Twilit Isles.

In *The Coming of the Valar* it is said that the Twilit Isles 'float' on the Shadowy Seas 'and the Tower of Pearl rises pale upon their most western cape' (I.68; cf. I.125). But there is no other mention in C of Littleheart, Voronwë's son, as a companion of Eärendel, though he was named earlier in the outline, in a rejected phrase, as present at the Mouths of Sirion (see note 5), and in the *Tale of the Nauglafring* (p. 228) Ailios says that none still living have seen the Nauglafring 'save only Littleheart son of Bronweg' (where 'save only' is an emendation from 'not even').

*Fifth and sixth parts.* In C we meet the image of Eärendel's shoes shining from the dust of diamonds in Kör, an image that was to survive (*The Silmarillion* p. 248):

> He walked in the deserted ways of Tirion, and the dust upon his raiment and his shoes was a dust of diamonds, and he shone and glistened as he climbed the long white stairs.

But in *The Silmarillion* Tirion was deserted because it was 'a time of festival, and wellnigh all the Elvenfolk were gone to Valimar, or were gathered in the halls of Manwë upon Taniquetil'; here on the other hand it seems at least strongly implied, in both B and C, that Kôr was empty because the Elves of Valinor had departed into the Great Lands, as a result of the tidings brought by the birds of Gondolin. In these very early narrative schemes there is no mention of Eärendel's speaking to the Valar, as the ambassador of Elves and Men (*The Silmarillion* p. 249), and we can only conclude, extraordinary as the conclusion is, that Eärendel's great western voyage, though he attained his goal, was fruitless, that he was not the agent of the aid that did indeed come out of Valinor to the Elves of the Great Lands, and (most curious of all) that Ulmo's designs for Tuor had no issue. In fact, my father actually wrote in the 1930 version of 'The Silmarillion':

> Thus it was that the many emissaries of the Gnomes in after days came never back to Valinor – save one: and he came too late.

The words 'and he came too late' were changed to 'the mightiest mariner of song', and this is the phrase that is found in *The Silmarillion*, p. 102. It is unfortunately never made clear in the earliest writings what was Ulmo's purpose in bidding Eärendel sail to Kôr, for which he had been saved from the ruin of Gondolin. What would he have achieved, had he come to Kôr 'in time', more than in the event did take place after the coming of tidings from Gondolin – the March of the Elves into the Great Lands? In a curious note in C, not associated with the present outline, my father asked: 'How did King Turgon's messengers get to Valinor or gain the Gods' consent?' and answered: 'His messengers never got there. Ulmo [*sic*] but the birds brought tidings to the Elves of the fate of Gondolin (the doves and pigeons of Turgon) and they [?arm and march away].'

The coming of the message was followed by 'the councils (counsels C) of the Gods and the uproar of the Elves', but in C nothing is said of 'the sorrow and wrath of the Gods' or 'the veil dropped between Valmar and Kôr' referred to in B: where the meaning can surely only be that the March of the Elves from Valinor was undertaken in direct opposition to the will of the Valar, that the Valar were bitterly opposed to the intervention of the Elves of Valinor in the affairs of the Great Lands. There may well be a connection here with Vairë's words (I. 19): 'When the fairies left

Kôr that lane [i.e. Olórë Mallë that led past the Cottage of Lost Play] *was blocked for ever with great impassable rocks'*. Elsewhere there is only one other reference to the effect of the message from across the sea, and that is in the words of Lindo to Eriol in *The Cottage of Lost Play* (I.16):

> Inwë, whom the Gnomes call Inwithiel . . . . . was King of all the Eldar when they dwelt in Kôr. That was in the days before hearing the lament of the world [i.e. the Great Lands] Inwë led them forth to the lands of Men.

Later, Meril-i-Turinqi told Eriol (I.129) that Inwë, her grandsire's sire, 'perished in that march into the world', but Ingil his son 'went long ago back to Valinor and is with Manwë'; and there is a reference to Inwë's death in B.

In C the Solosimpi only agreed to accompany the expedition on condition that they remain by the sea, and the reluctance of the Third Kindred, on account of the Kinslaying at Swanhaven, survived (*The Silmarillion* p. 251). But there is no suggestion that the Elves of Valinor were transported by ship, indeed the reverse, for the Solosimpi 'fare along all the beaches of the world', and the expedition is a 'March'; though there is no indication of how they came to the Great Lands.

Both outlines refer to Eärendel being driven eastwards on his homeward voyage from Kôr, and to his finding the dwellings at Sirion's mouth ravaged when he finally returned there; but B does not say who carried out the sack and captured Elwing. In C it was a raid by Orcs of Melko; cf. the entry in the Name-list to *The Fall of Gondolin* (p. 215): '*Egalmoth* . . . got even out of the burning of Gondolin, and dwelt after at the mouth of Sirion, but was slain in a dire battle there when Melko seized Elwing'.

Neither outline refers to Elwing's escape from captivity. Both mention Eärendel's going back to the ruins of Gondolin – in C he returns there with Voronwë and finds Men and Gnomes; another entry in the Name-list to *The Fall of Gondolin* (p. 215) bears on this: '*Galdor* . . . won out of Gondolin and even the onslaught of Melko upon the dwellers at Sirion's mouth and went back to the ruins with Eärendel.'

Both outlines mention the departure of the Elves from the Great Lands, after the binding of Melko, to Tol Eressëa, C adding a reference to 'wars with Men' and to the Eldar being 'unable to endure the strife of the world', and both refer to Eärendel's going there subsequently, but the order of events seems to be different: in B Eärendel on his way back from Kôr 'sights Tol Eressëa and the fleet of the Elves' (presumably the fleet returning from the Great Lands), whereas in C the departure of the Elves is not mentioned until after Eärendel's return to Sirion. But the nature of these outlines is not conveyed in print: they were written at great speed, catching fugitive thoughts, and cannot be pressed hard. However, with the fate of Elwing B and C seem clearly to part company:

in B there is a simple reference to her death, apparently associated with
the curse of the Nauglafring, and from the order in which the events are
set down it may be surmised that her death took place on the journey to
Tol Eressëa; C specifically refers to the 'sinking' of Elwing and the
Nauglafring – but says that Elwing became a seabird, an idea that
survived (*The Silmarillion* p. 247). This perhaps gives more point to
Eärendel's going to the Isle of Seabirds, mentioned in both B and C: in
the latter he 'hopes that Elwing will return among the seabirds'.

*Seventh part.* In B the concluding part of the tale is merely summarised in the words 'His voyage to the firmament', with a reference to
the other outline C, and in the latter we get some glimpses of a narrative.
It seems to be suggested that the brightness of Eärendel (quite unconnected with the Silmaril) arose from the 'diamond dust' of Kôr, but also
in some sense from the exaltation of his grief. An isolated jotting elsewhere in C asks: 'What became of the Silmarils after the capture of
Melko?' My father at this time gave no answer to the question; but the
question is itself a testimony to the relatively minor importance of
the jewels of Fëanor, if also, perhaps, a sign of his awareness that they
would not always remain so, that in them lay a central meaning of the
mythology, yet to be discovered.

It seems too that Eärendel sailed into the sky in continuing search for
Elwing ('he sets sail on the oceans of the firmament in order to gaze over
the Earth'); and that his passing through the Door of Night (the entrance
made by the Gods in the Wall of Things in the West, see I.215–16) did
not come about through any devising, but because he was hunted by the
Moon. With this last idea, cf. I.193, where Ilinsor, steersman of
the Moon, is said to 'hunt the stars'.

The later of the two schemes for the *Lost Tales*, which gives a quite
substantial outline for *Gilfanon's Tale*, where I have called it 'D' (see
I.234), here fails us, for the concluding passage is very condensed, in
part erased, and ends abruptly early in the *Tale of Eärendel*. I give it
here, beginning at a slightly earlier point in the narrative:

> Of the death of Tinwelint and the flight of Gwenethlin [see p. 51].
> How Beren avenged Tinwelint and how the Necklace became his.
> How it brought sickness to Tinúviel [see p. 246], and how Beren and
> Tinúviel faded from the Earth. How their sons [*sic*] dwelt after them
> and how the sons of Fëanor came up against them with a host because
> of the Silmaril. How all were slain but Elwing daughter of Daimord
> [see p. 139] son of Beren fled with the Necklace.
> Of Tuor's vessel with white sails.
>
> How folk of the Lothlim dwelt at Sirion's Mouth. Eärendel grew
> fairest of all Men that were or are. How the mermaids (Oarni) loved

him. How Elwing came to the Lothlim and of the love of Elwing and Eärendel. How Tuor fell into age, and how Ulmo beckoned to him at eve, and he set forth on the waters and was lost. How Idril swam after him.

(In the following passage my father seems at first to have written: 'Eärendel . . . . . . . Oarni builded Wingilot and set forth in search of . . . . leaving Voronwë with Elwing', where the first lacuna perhaps said 'with the aid of', though nothing is now visible; but then he wrote 'Eärendel built Swanwing', and then partly erased the passage: it is impossible to see now what his intention was.)

Elwing's lament. How Ulmo forbade his quest but Eärendel would yet sail to find a passage to Mandos. How Wingilot was wrecked at Falasquil and how Eärendel found the carven house of Tuor there.

Here Scheme D ends. There is also a reference at an earlier point in it to 'the messengers sent from Gondolin. The doves of Gondolin fly to Valinor at the fall of that town.'

This outline seems to show a move to reduce the complexity of the narrative, with Wingilot being the ship in which Eärendel attempted to sail to Mandos and in which he was wrecked at Falasquil; but the outline is too brief and stops too soon to allow any certain conclusions to be drawn.

A fourth outline, which I will call 'E', is found on a detached sheet; in this Tuor is called Tûr (see p. 148).

Fall of Gondolin. The feast of Glorfindel. The dwelling by the waters of Sirion's mouth. The mermaids come to Eärendel.

Tûr groweth sea-hungry – his song to Eärendel. One evening he calls Eärendel and they go to the shore. There is a skiff. Tûr bids farewell to Eärendel and bids him thrust it off – the skiff fares away into the West. Eärendel hears a great song swelling from the sea as Tûr's skiff dips over the world's rim. His passion of tears upon the shore. The lament of Idril.

The building of Earum.[9] The coming of Elwing. Eärendel's reluctance. The whetting of Idril. The voyage and foundering of Earum in the North, and the vanishing of Idril. How the seamaids rescued Eärendel, and brought him to Tûr's bay. His coastwise journey.

The rape of Elwing. Eärendel discovers the ravaging of Sirion's mouth.

The building of Wingelot. He searches for Elwing and is blown far to the South. Wirilómë. He escapes eastward. He goes back westward; he descries the Bay of Faëry. The Tower of Pearl, the magic isles, the great shadows. He finds Kôr empty; he sails back, crusted with dust and his face afire. He learns of Elwing's foundering. He sitteth on the Isle of Seabirds. Elwing as a seamew comes to him. He sets sail over the margent of the world.

Apart from the fuller account of Tuor's departure from the mouths of Sirion, not much can be learned from this – it is too condensed. But even allowing for speed and compression, there seem to be essential differences from B and C. Thus in this outline (E) Elwing, as it appears, comes to Sirion at a later point in the story, after the departure of Tuor; but the raid and capture of Elwing seems to take place at an earlier point, while Eärendel is on his way back to Sirion from his shipwreck in the North (not, as in B and C, while he is on the great voyage in Wingilot that took him to Kôr). Here, it seems, there was to be only one northward journey, ending in the shipwreck of Earámë/Earum near Falasquil. Though it cannot be demonstrated, I incline to think that E was subsequent to B and C: partly because the reduction of two northward voyages ending in shipwreck to one seems more likely than the other way about, and partly because of the form *Tûr*, which, though it did not survive, replaced *Tuor* for a time (p. 148).

One or two other points may be noticed in this outline. The great spider, called *Ungweliantë* in C but here *Wirilómë* ('Gloomweaver', see I.152), is here encountered by Eärendel in the far South, not as in C on his westward voyage: see p. 256. Elwing in this version comes to Eärendel as a seabird (as she does in *The Silmarillion*, p. 247), which is not said in C and even seems to be denied.

Another isolated page (associated with the poem 'The Bidding of the Minstrel', see pp. 269–70 below) gives a very curious account of Eärendel's great voyage:

Eärendel's boat goes through North. Iceland. [*Added in margin*: back of North Wind.] Greenland, and the wild islands: a mighty wind and crest of great wave carry him to hotter climes, to back of West Wind. Land of strange men, land of magic. The home of Night. The Spider. He escapes from the meshes of Night with a few comrades, sees a great mountain island and a golden city [*added in margin*: Kôr] – wind blows him southward. Tree-men, Sun-dwellers, spices, fire-mountains, red sea: Mediterranean (loses his boat (travels afoot through wilds of Europe?)) or Atlantic.* Home. Waxes aged. Has a new boat builded. Bids adieu to his north land. Sails west again to the lip of the world, just as the Sun is diving into the sea. He sets sail upon the sky and returns no more to earth.

The golden city was Kôr and he had caught the music of the Solosimpë, and returns to find it, only to find that the fairies have departed from Eldamar. See little book. Dusted with diamond dust climbing the deserted streets of Kôr.

* The words in this passage ('Tree-men, Sun-dwellers . . .') are clear but the punctuation is not, and the arrangement here may not be that intended.

One would certainly suppose this account to be earlier than anything so far considered (both from the fact that Eärendel's history after his return from the great voyage seems to bear no relation to that in B and C, and from his voyage being set in the lands and oceans of the known world), were it not for the reference to the 'little book', which must mean 'Notebook C', from which the outline C above is taken (see p. 254). But I think it very probable (and the appearance of the MS rather supports this) that the last paragraph ('The golden city was Kôr . . .') was added later, and that the rest of the outline belongs with the earliest writing of the poem, in the winter of 1914.

It is notable that only here in the earliest writings is it made clear that the 'diamond dust' that coated Eärendel came from the streets of Kôr (cf. the passage from *The Silmarillion* cited on p. 257).

Another of the early Eärendel poems, 'The Shores of Faëry', has a short prose preface, which if not as old as the first composition of the poem itself (July 1915, see p. 271) is certainly not much later:

Eärendel the Wanderer who beat about the Oceans of the World in his white ship Wingelot sat long while in his old age upon the Isle of Seabirds in the Northern Waters ere he set forth upon a last voyage.

He passed Taniquetil and even Valinor, and drew his bark over the bar at the margin of the world, and launched it on the Oceans of the Firmament. Of his ventures there no man has told, save that hunted by the orbed Moon he fled back to Valinor, and mounting the towers of Kôr upon the rocks of Eglamar he gazed back upon the Oceans of the World. To Eglamar he comes ever at plenilune when the Moon sails a-harrying beyond Taniquetil and Valinor.*

Both here and in the outline associated with 'The Bidding of the Minstrel' Eärendel was conceived to be an old man when he journeyed into the firmament.

No other 'connected' account of the *Tale of Eärendel* exists from the earliest period. There are however a number of separate notes, mostly in the form of single sentences, some found in the little notebook C, others jotted down on slips. I collect these references here more or less in the sequence of the tale.

(i) 'Dwelling in the Isle of Sirion in a house of snow-white stone.' – In C (p. 254) it is said that Eärendel dwelt with Tuor and Idril at Sirion's mouth by the sea 'on the Isles of Sirion'.

---

* This preface is found in all the texts of the poem save the earliest, and the versions of it differ only in name-forms: *Wingelot/Vingelot* and *Eglamar/Eldamar* (varying in the same ways as in the accompanying versions of the poem, see textual notes p. 272), and *Kôr* > *Tûn* in the third text, *Tûn* in the fourth. For *Egla* = *Elda* see I. 251 and II. 338, and for *Tûn* see p. 292.

(ii) 'The Oarni give to Eärendel a wonderful shining silver coat that wets not. They love Eärendel, in Ossë's despite, and teach him the lore of boat-building and of swimming, as he plays with them about the shores of Sirion.' – In the outlines are found references to the love of the Oarni for Eärendel (D, p. 259), the coming of the mermaids to him (E, p. 260), and to Ossë's enmity (C, p. 254).

(iii) Eärendel was smaller than most men but nimble-footed and a swift swimmer (but Voronwë could not swim).

(iv) 'Idril and Eärendel see Tuor's boat dropping into the twilight and a sound of song.' – In B Tuor's sailing is 'secret' (p. 253), in C 'Idril sees him too late' (p. 254), and in E Eärendel is present at Tuor's departure and thrusts the boat out: 'he hears a great song swelling from the sea' (p. 260).

(v) 'Death of Idril? – follows secretly after Tuor.' – That Idril died is denied in C: 'Tuor and Idril some say sail now in Swanwing . . .' (p. 255); in D Idril swam after him (p. 260).

(vi) 'Tuor has sailed back to Falasquil and so back up Ilbranteloth to Asgon where he sits playing on his lonely harp on the islanded rock.' – This is marked with a query and an 'X' implying rejection of the idea. There are curious references to the 'islanded rock' in Asgon in the outlines for Gilfanon's Tale (see I.238).

(vii) 'The fiord of the Mermaid: enchantment of his sailors. Mermaids are not Oarni (but are earthlings, or fays? – or both).' – In D (p. 259) Mermaids and Oarni are equated.

(viii) The ship Wingilot was built of wood from Falasquil with 'aid of the Oarni'. – This was probably said also in D: see p. 260.

(ix) Wingilot was 'shaped as a swan of pearls'.

(x) 'The doves and pigeons of Turgon's courtyard bring message to Valinor – only to Elves.' – Other references to the birds that flew from Gondolin also say that they came to the Elves, or to Kôr (pp. 253, 255, 257).

(xi) 'During his voyages Eärendel sights the white walls of Kôr gleaming afar off, but is carried away by Ossë's adverse winds and waves.' – The same is said in B (p. 253) of Eärendel's sighting of Tol Eressëa on his homeward voyage from Kôr.

(xii) 'The Sleeper in the Tower of Pearl awakened by Littleheart's gong: a messenger that was despatched years ago by Turgon and enmeshed in magics. Even now he cannot leave the Tower and warns them of the magic.' – In C there is a statement, rejected, that the Sleeper in the Tower of Pearl was Idril herself (see note 6).

(xiii) 'Ulmo's protection removed from Sirion in wrath at Eärendel's second attempt to Mandos, and hence Melko overwhelmed it.' – This note is struck through, with an 'X' written against it; but in D (p. 260) it is said that 'Ulmo forbade his quest but Eärendel would yet sail to find a passage to Mandos'. The meaning of this must be that it was contrary to Ulmo's purpose that Eärendel should seek to Mandos for his father, but must rather attempt to reach Kôr.

(xiv) 'Eärendel weds Elwing before he sets sail. When he hears of her loss he says that his children shall be "all such men hereafter as dare the great seas in ships".' – With this cf. *The Cottage of Lost Play* (I.13): 'even such a son of Eärendel as was this wayfarer', and (I.18): 'a man of great and excellent travel, a son meseems of Eärendel'. In an outline of Eriol's life (I.24) it is said that he was a son of Eärendel, born under his beam, and that if a beam from Eärendel fall on a child newborn he becomes 'a child of Eärendel' and a wanderer. In the early dictionary of Qenya there is an entry: *Eärendilyon* 'son of Eärendel (used of any mariner)' (I.251).

(xv) 'Eärendel goes even to the empty Halls of Iron seeking Elwing.' – Eärendel must have gone to Angamandi (empty after the defeat of Melko) at the same time as he went to the ruins of Gondolin (pp. 253, 255).

(xvi) The loss of the ship carrying Elwing and the Nauglafring took place on the voyage to Tol Eressëa with the exodus of the Elves from the Great Lands. – See my remarks, pp. 258–9. For the 'appeasing' of Mîm's curse by the drowning of the Nauglafring see the Appendix on Names, entry *Nauglafring*. The departure of the Elves to Tol Eressëa is discussed in the next chapter (p. 280).

(xvii) 'Eärendel and the northern tower on the Isle of Seabirds.' – In C (p. 255) Eärendel 'sets sail with Voronwë and dwells on the Isle of Seabirds in the northern waters (not far from Falasquil) – and there hopes that Elwing will return among the seabirds'; in B (p. 253) 'he sights the Isle of Seabirds "whither do all the birds of all waters come at whiles".' There is a memory of this in *The Silmarillion*, p. 250: 'Therefore there was built for [Elwing] a white tower northward upon the borders of the Sundering Seas; and thither at times all the seabirds of the earth repaired.'

(xviii) When Eärendel comes to Mandos he finds that Tuor is '*not* in Valinor, nor Erumáni, and neither Elves nor Ainu know where he is. (He is with Ulmo.)' – In C (p. 255) Eärendel, reaching the Halls of Mandos, learns that Tuor 'is gone to Valinor'. For the possibility that Tuor might be in Erumáni or Valinor see I.91 ff.

(xix) Eärendel 'returns from the firmament ever and anon with Voronwë to Kôr to see if the Magic Sun has been lit and the fairies have come back – but the Moon drives him back'. – On Eärendel's return from the firmament see (xxi) below; on the Rekindling of the Magic Sun see p. 286.

Two statements about Eärendel cited previously may be added here:

(xx) In the tale of *The Theft of Melko* (I.141) it is said that 'on the walls of Kôr were many dark tales written in pictured symbols, and runes of great beauty were drawn there too or carved upon stones, and Eärendel read many a wondrous tale there long ago'.

(xxi) The Name-list to *The Fall of Gondolin* has the following entry (cited on p. 215): '*Eärendel* was the son of Tuor and Idril and 'tis said the only being that is half of the kindred of the Eldalië and half of Men. He was the greatest and first of all mariners among Men, and saw regions that Men have not yet found nor gazed upon for all the multitude of their boats. He rideth now with Voronwë upon the winds of the firmament nor comes ever further back than Kôr, else would he die like other Men, so much of the mortal is in him.' – In the outline associated with the poem 'The Bidding of the Minstrel' Eärendel 'sets sail upon the sky and returns no more to earth' (p. 261); in the prose preface to 'The Shores of Faëry' 'to Eglamar he comes ever at plenilune when the Moon sails a-harrying beyond Taniquetil and Valinor' (p. 262); in outline C 'he cannot now return to the world or he will die' (p. 255); and in citation (xix) above he 'returns from the firmament ever and anon with Voronwë to Kôr'.

In *The Silmarillion* (p. 249) Manwë's judgement was that Eärendel and Elwing 'shall not walk ever again among Elves or Men in the Outer Lands'; but it is also said that Eärendel returned to Valinor from his 'voyages beyond the confines of the world' (*ibid.* p. 250), just as it is said in the Name-list to *The Fall of Gondolin* that he does not come ever further back than Kôr. The further statement in the Name-list, that if he did he would die like other Men, 'so much of the mortal is in him', was in some sense echoed long after in a letter of my father's written in 1967: '*Eärendil*, being in part descended from Men, was not allowed to set foot on Earth again, and became a star shining with the light of the Silmaril' (*The Letters of J. R. R. Tolkien* no. 297).

This brings to an end all the 'prose' materials that bear on the earliest form of the *Tale of Eärendel* (apart from a few other references to him that appear in the next chapter). With these outlines and notes we are at a very early stage of composition, when the conceptions were fluid and had not been given even preliminary narrative form: the myth was present in certain images that were to endure, but these images had not been articulated.

I have already noticed (p. 257) the remarkable fact that there is no hint of the idea that it was Eärendel who by his intercession brought aid out of the West; equally there is no suggestion that the Valar hallowed his ship and set him in the sky, nor that his light was that of the Silmaril. Nonetheless there were already present the coming of Eärendel to Kôr (Tirion) and finding it deserted, the dust of diamonds on his shoes, the changing of Elwing into a seabird, the passing of his ship through the Door of Night, and the sanction against his return to the lands east of the Sea. The raid on the Havens of Sirion appears in the early outlines, though that was an act of Melko's, not of the Fëanorians; and Tuor's departure also, but without Idril, whom he left behind. His ship was *Alqarámë*, Swanwing: afterwards it bore the name *Eärrámë*, with the meaning 'Sea-wing' (*The Silmarillion* p. 245), which retained, in form but not in meaning, the name of Eärendel's first ship *Eärámë* 'Eaglepinion' (pp. 253–4, and see note 9).

It is interesting to read my father's statement, made some half-century later (in the letter of 1967 referred to above), concerning the origins of Eärendil:

This name is in fact (as is obvious) derived from Anglo-Saxon *éarendel*. When first studying Anglo-Saxon professionally (1913– ) – I had done so as a boyish hobby when supposed to be learning Greek and Latin – I was struck by the great beauty of this word (or name), entirely coherent with the normal style of Anglo-Saxon, but euphonic to a peculiar degree in that pleasing but not 'delectable' language. Also its form strongly suggests that it is in origin a proper name and not a common noun. This is borne out by the obviously related forms in other Germanic languages; from which amid the confusions and debasements of late traditions it at least seems certain that it belonged to astronomical-myth, and was the name of a star or star-group. To my mind the Anglo-Saxon uses seem plainly to indicate that it was a star presaging the dawn (at any rate in English tradition): that is what we now call *Venus*: the morning star as it may be seen shining brilliantly in the dawn, before the actual rising of the Sun. That is at any rate how I took it. Before 1914 I wrote a 'poem' upon Eärendel who launched his ship like a bright spark from the havens of the Sun. I adopted him into my mythology – in which he became a prime figure as a mariner, and eventually as a herald star, and a sign of hope to men. *Aiya Eärendil Elenion Ancalima* ([The Lord of the Rings] II.329) 'hail Eärendil brightest of Stars' is derived at long remove from *Éalá Éarendel engla beorhtast*.* But the name could not be adopted just like that: it had to be accommodated to the Elvish linguistic situation, at the same time as a place for this person was made in legend. From this, far back in the history of 'Elvish', which was beginning, after many tentative starts in boyhood, to take definite shape at the time of the name's adoption, arose eventually (a) the C[ommon]E[lvish] stem *AYAR 'sea', primarily applied to the Great Sea of the West, lying between Middle-earth and Aman the Blessed Realm of the Valar; and (b) the element, or verbal base (N)DIL, 'to love, be devoted to' – describing the attitude of one to a person, thing, cause, or occupation to which one is devoted for its own sake. Eärendil became a character in the earliest written (1916–17) of the major legends: *The Fall of Gondolin*, the greatest of the *Pereldar* 'Half-elven', son of *Tuor* of the most renowned House of the Edain, and *Idril* daughter of the King of Gondolin.

My father did not indeed here say that his *Eärendel* contained from the beginning elements that in combination give a meaning like 'Sea-lover'; but it is in any case clear that at the time of the earliest extant writings on

---

* From the Old English poem *Crist*: *éalá! éarendel engla beorhtast ofer mid-dangeard monnum sended*.

the subject the name was associated with an Elvish word *ea* 'eagle' – see p. 265 on the name of Eärendel's first ship *Eärámë* 'Eaglepinion'. In the Name-list to *The Fall of Gondolin* this is made explicit: '*Earendl* [*sic*] though belike it hath some kinship to the Elfin *ea* and *earen* "eagle" and "eyrie" (wherefore cometh to mind the passage of Cristhorn and the use of the sign of the Eagle by Idril [see p. 193]) is thought to be woven of that secret tongue of the Gondothlim [see p. 165].'

★

I give lastly four early poems of my father's in which Eärendel appears.

I

### Éalá Éarendel Engla Beorhtast

There can be little doubt that, as Humphrey Carpenter supposes (*Biography* p. 71), this was the first poem on the subject of Eärendel that my father composed, and that it was written at Phoenix Farm, Gedling, Nottinghamshire, in September 1914.[10] It was to this poem that he was referring in the letter of 1967 just cited – 'I wrote a "poem" upon Eärendel who launched his ship like a bright spark': cf. line 5 'He launched his bark like a silver spark . . .'

There are some five different versions, each one incorporating emendations made in the predecessor, though only the first verse was substantially rewritten. The title was originally 'The Voyage of Éarendel the Evening Star', together with (as customarily) an Old English version of this: *Scipfæreld Éarendeles Æfensteorran*; this was changed in a later copy to *Éalá Éarendel Engla Beorhtast* 'The Last Voyage of Eärendel', and in still later copies the modern English name was removed. I give it here in the last version, the date of which cannot be determined, though the handwriting shows it to be substantially later than the original composition; together with all the divergent readings of the earliest extant version in footnotes.

> Éarendel arose where the shadow flows
>     At Ocean's silent brim;
> Through the mouth of night as a ray of light
>     Where the shores are sheer and dim                    4
> He launched his bark like a silver spark
>     From the last and lonely sand;
> Then on sunlit breath of day's fiery death
>     He sailed from Westerland.                            8

He threaded his path o'er the aftermath
    Of the splendour of the Sun,
And wandered far past many a star
    In his gleaming galleon.            12
On the gathering tide of darkness ride
    The argosies of the sky,
And spangle the night with their sails of light
    As the streaming star goes by.     16

Unheeding he dips past these twinkling ships,
    By his wayward spirit whirled
On an endless quest through the darkling West
    O'er the margin of the world;     20
And he fares in haste o'er the jewelled waste
    And the dusk from whence he came
With his heart afire with bright desire
    And his face in silver flame.     24

The Ship of the Moon from the East comes soon
    From the Haven of the Sun,
Whose white gates gleam in the coming beam
    Of the mighty silver one.     28
Lo! with bellying clouds as his vessel's shrouds
    He weighs anchor down the dark,
And on shimmering oars leaves the blazing shores
    In his argent-timbered bark.     32

*Readings of the earliest version:*
1–8    Eärendel sprang up from the Ocean's cup
        In the gloom of the mid-world's rim;
    From the door of Night as a ray of light
        Leapt over the twilight brim,
    And launching his bark like a silver spark
        From the golden-fading sand
    Down the sunlit breath of Day's fiery Death
        He sped from Westerland.

10    splendour] glory
11    wandered] went wandering
16    streaming] Evening
17    Unheeding] But unheeding
18    wayward] wandering
19    endless] magic    darkling] darkening
20    O'er the margin] Toward the margent
22    And the dusk] To the dusk
25    The Ship] For the Ship
31    blazing] skiey
32    timbered] orbéd

Then Éarendel fled from that Shipman dread
  Beyond the dark earth's pale,
Back under the rim of the Ocean dim,
  And behind the world set sail;                          36
And he heard the mirth of the folk of earth
  And the falling of their tears,
As the world dropped back in a cloudy wrack
  On its journey down the years.                          40

Then he glimmering passed to the starless vast
  As an isléd lamp at sea,
And beyond the ken of mortal men
  Set his lonely errantry,                                44
Tracking the Sun in his galleon
  Through the pathless firmament,
Till his light grew old in abysses cold
  And his eager flame was spent.                          48

There seems every reason to think that this poem preceded all the
outlines and notes given in this chapter, and that verbal similarities to
the poem found in these are echoes (e.g. 'his face is in silver flame',
outline C, p. 255; 'the margent of the world', outline E, p. 260).

In the fourth verse of the poem the Ship of the Moon comes forth from
the Haven of the Sun; in the tale of *The Hiding of Valinor* (I. 215) Aulë
and Ulmo built two havens in the east, that of the Sun (which was 'wide
and golden') and that of the Moon (which was 'white, having gates of
silver and of pearl') – but they were both 'within the same harbourage'.
As in the poem, in the *Tale of the Sun and Moon* the Moon is urged on
by 'shimmering oars' (I. 195).

## II

### The Bidding of the Minstrel

This poem, according to a note that my father scribbled on one of the
copies, was written at St. John's Street, Oxford (see I. 27) in the winter
of 1914; there is no other evidence for its date. In this case the earliest
workings are extant, and on the back of one of the sheets is the outline

33  Then] And
38  And the falling of] And hearkened to

46–8  And voyaging the skies
     Till his splendour was shorn by the birth of Morn
     And he died with the Dawn in his eyes.

account of Eärendel's great voyage given on p. 261. The poem was then much longer than it became, but the workings are exceedingly rough; they have no title. To the earliest finished text a title was added hastily later: this apparently reads 'The Minstrel renounces the song'. The title then became 'The Lay of Eärendel', changed in the latest text to 'The Bidding of the Minstrel, from the Lay of Eärendel'.

There are four versions following the original rough draft, but the changes made in them were slight, and I give the poem here in the latest form, noting only that originally the minstrel seems to have responded to the 'bidding' much earlier – at line 5, which read 'Then harken – a tale of immortal sea-yearning'; and that 'Eldar' in line 6 and 'Elven' in line 23 are emendations, made on the latest text, of 'fairies', 'fairy'.

'Sing us yet more of Eärendel the wandering,
Chant us a lay of his white-oared ship,
More marvellous-cunning than mortal man's pondering,
Foamily musical out on the deep.
Sing us a tale of immortal sea-yearning                          5
The Eldar once made ere the change of the light,
Weaving a winelike spell, and a burning
Wonder of spray and the odours of night;
Of murmurous gloamings out on far oceans;
Of his tossing at anchor off islets forlorn                     10
To the unsleeping waves' never-ending sea-motions;
Of bellying sails when a wind was born,
And the gurgling bubble of tropical water
Tinkled from under the ringéd stem,
And thousands of miles was his ship from those wrought her   15
A petrel, a sea-bird, a white-wingéd gem,
Gallantly bent on measureless faring
Ere she came homing in sea-laden flight,
Circuitous, lingering, restlessly daring,
Coming to haven unlooked for, at night.'                       20

'But the music is broken, the words half-forgotten,
The sunlight has faded, the moon is grown old,
The Elven ships foundered or weed-swathed and rotten,
The fire and the wonder of hearts is acold.
Who now can tell, and what harp can accompany              25
With melodies strange enough, rich enough tunes,
Pale with the magic of cavernous harmony,
Loud with shore-music of beaches and dunes,
How slender his boat; of what glimmering timber;
How her sails were all silvern and taper her mast,           30
And silver her throat with foam and her limber
Flanks as she swanlike floated past!

The song I can sing is but shreds one remembers
Of golden imaginings fashioned in sleep,
A whispered tale told by the withering embers                    35
Of old things far off that but few hearts keep.'


### III

*The Shores of Faëry*

This poem is given in its earliest form by Humphrey Carpenter, *Bio-graphy*, pp. 76–7.[11] It exists in four versions each as usual incorporating slight changes; my father wrote the date of its composition on three of the copies, viz. 'July 8–9, 1915'; 'Moseley and Edgbaston, Birmingham July 1915 (walking and on bus). Retouched often since – esp. 1924'; and 'First poem of my mythology, Valinor . . . . . . . . . . 1910'. This last cannot have been intended for the date of composition, and the illegible words preceding it may possibly be read as 'thought of about'. But it does not in any case appear to have been 'the first poem of the mythology': that, I believe, was *Éalá Éarendel Engla Beorhtast* – and my father's mention of this poem in his letter of 1967 (see p. 266) seems to suggest this also.

The Old English title was *Ielfalandes Strand* (The Shores of Elfland). It is preceded by a short prose preface which has been given above, p. 262. I give it here in the latest version (undateable), with all readings from the earliest in footnotes.

East of the Moon, west of the Sun
There stands a lonely hill;
Its feet are in the pale green sea,
Its towers are white and still,
Beyond Taniquetil                                   5
In Valinor.
Comes never there but one lone star
That fled before the moon;
And there the Two Trees naked are
That bore Night's silver bloom,                     10
That bore the globéd fruit of Noon
In Valinor.
There are the shores of Faëry

*Readings of the earliest version:*

1    East . . . . . west] West . . . . . East
7    No stars come there but one alone
8    fled before] hunted with.
9    For there the Two Trees naked grow
10   bore] bear        11 bore] bear

With their moonlit pebbled strand
Whose foam is silver music                                    15
On the opalescent floor
Beyond the great sea-shadows
On the marches of the sand
That stretches on for ever
To the dragonheaded door,                                     20
The gateway of the Moon,
Beyond Taniquetil
In Valinor.
West of the Sun, east of the Moon
Lies the haven of the star,                                   25
The white town of the Wanderer
And the rocks of Eglamar.
There Wingelot is harboured,
While Eärendel looks afar
O'er the darkness of the waters                               30
Between here and Eglamar –
Out, out, beyond Taniquetil
In Valinor afar.

There are some interesting connections between this poem and the tale
of *The Coming of the Elves and the Making of Kôr*. The 'lonely hill'
of line 2 is the hill of Kôr (cf. the tale, I. 122: 'at the head of this long creek
there stands a lonely hill which gazes at the loftier mountains'), while 'the
golden feet of Kôr' (a line replaced in the later versions of the poem) and
very probably 'the sand That stretches on for ever' are explained by the
passage that follows in the tale:

> Thither [i.e. to Kôr] did Aulë bring all the dust of magic metals that
> his great works had made and gathered, and he piled it about the foot
> of that hill, and most of this dust was of gold, and a sand of gold
> stretched away from the feet of Kôr out into the distance where the
> Two Trees blossomed.

18        marches] margent
• 20–21    To the dragonheaded door, The gateway of the Moon] From the golden feet of Kôr
24        West of the Sun, east of the Moon] O! West of the Moon, East of the Sun
27        rocks] rock
28        Wingelot] *Earliest text* Wingelot > Vingelot; *second text* Vingelot; *third text*
          Vingelot > Wingelot; *last text* Wingelot
30        O'er the darkness of the waters] On the magic and the wonder
31        Between] 'Tween

In the latest text *Elvenland* is lightly written over *Faëry* in line 13, and *Eldamar* against
*Eglamar* in line 27 (only); *Eglamar* > *Eldamar* in the second text.

With the 'dragonheaded door' (line 20) cf. the description of the Door of Night in *The Hiding of Valinor* (I. 215–16):

> Its pillars are of the mightiest basalt and its lintel likewise, but great dragons of black stone are carved thereon, and shadowy smoke pours slowly from their jaws.

In that description the Door of Night is not however 'the gateway of the Moon', for it is the Sun that passes through it into the outer dark, whereas 'the Moon dares not the utter loneliness of the outer dark by reason of his lesser light and majesty, and he journeys still beneath the world [i.e. through the waters of Vai]'.

## IV

### The Happy Mariners

I give lastly this poem whose subject is the Tower of Pearl in the Twilit Isles. It was written in July 1915,[12] and there are six texts preceding the version which was published (together with 'Why the Man in the Moon came down too soon') at Leeds in 1923* and which is the first of the two given here.

(1)

I know a window in a western tower
That opens on celestial seas,
And wind that has been blowing round the stars
Comes to nestle in its tossing draperies.
It is a white tower builded in the Twilight Isles,      5
Where Evening sits for ever in the shade;
It glimmers like a spike of lonely pearl
That mirrors beams forlorn and lights that fade;
And sea goes washing round the dark rock where it stands,
And fairy boats go by to gloaming lands      10
All piled and twinkling in the gloom
With hoarded sparks of orient fire

---

* *A Northern Venture:* see I. 204, footnote. Mr Douglas A. Anderson has kindly supplied me with a copy of the poem in this version, which had been very slightly altered from that published in *The Stapeldon Magazine* (Exeter College, Oxford), June 1920 (Carpenter, p. 268). – *Twilight* in line 5 of the Leeds version is almost certainly an error, for *Twilit*, the reading of all the original texts.

That divers won in waters of the unknown Sun –
And, maybe, 'tis a throbbing silver lyre,
Or voices of grey sailors echo up                               15
Afloat among the shadows of the world
In oarless shallop and with canvas furled;
For often seems there ring of feet and song
Or twilit twinkle of a trembling gong.

O! happy mariners upon a journey long                           20
To those great portals on the Western shores
Where far away constellate fountains leap,
And dashed against Night's dragon-headed doors,
In foam of stars fall sparkling in the deep.
While I alone look out behind the Moon                          25
From in my white and windy tower,
Ye bide no moment and await no hour,
But chanting snatches of a mystic tune
Go through the shadows and the dangerous seas
Past sunless lands to fairy leas                                30
Where stars upon the jacinth wall of space
Do tangle burst and interlace.
Ye follow Earendel through the West,
The shining mariner, to Islands blest;
While only from beyond that sombre rim                          35
A wind returns to stir these crystal panes
And murmur magically of golden rains
That fall for ever in those spaces dim.

In *The Hiding of Valinor* (I. 215) it is told that when the Sun was first made the Valar purposed to draw it beneath the Earth, but that

> it was too frail and lissom; and much precious radiance was spilled in their attempts about the deepest waters, and escaped to linger as secret sparks in many an unknown ocean cavern. These have many elfin divers, and divers of the fays, long time sought beyond the outmost East, even as is sung in the song of the Sleeper in the Tower of Pearl.

That 'The Happy Mariners' was in fact 'the song of the Sleeper in the Tower of Pearl' seems assured by lines 10–13 of the poem.

For 'Night's dragon-headed doors' see p. 273. The meaning of *jacinth* in 'the jacinth wall of space' (line 31) is 'blue'; cf. 'the deep-blue walls' in *The Hiding of Valinor* (I. 215).

Many years later my father rewrote the poem, and I give this version here. Still later he turned to it again and made a few further alterations (here recorded in footnotes); at this time he noted that the revised version dated from '1940?'.

### (2)

I know a window in a Western tower
that opens on celestial seas,
and there from wells of dark behind the stars
blows ever cold a keen unearthly breeze.
It is a white tower builded on the Twilit Isles,                5
and springing from their everlasting shade
it glimmers like a house of lonely pearl,
where lights forlorn take harbour ere they fade.

Its feet are washed by waves that never rest.
There silent boats go by into the West                        10
all piled and twinkling in the dark
with orient fire in many a hoarded spark
that divers won
in waters of the rumoured Sun.
There sometimes throbs below a silver harp,                   15
touching the heart with sudden music sharp;
or far beneath the mountains high and sheer
the voices of grey sailors echo clear,
afloat among the shadows of the world
in oarless ships and with their canvas furled,               20
chanting a farewell and a solemn song:
for wide the sea is, and the journey long.

O happy mariners upon a journey far,
beyond the grey islands and past Gondobar,
to those great portals on the final shores                    25
where far away constellate fountains leap,
and dashed against Night's dragon-headed doors
in foam of stars fall sparkling in the deep!
While I, alone, look out behind the moon
from in my white and windy tower,                             30
ye bide no moment and await no hour,
but go with solemn song and harpers' tune
through the dark shadows and the shadowy seas
to the last land of the Two Trees,
whose fruit and flower are moon and sun,                      35
where light of earth is ended and begun.

*Last revisions:*
3   and there *omitted*
4   blows ever cold] there ever blows
17   mountains] mountain
22   the journey] their journey
29   While I look out alone        30   imprisoned in the white and windy tower
31   ye] you        33–6   *struck through*

Ye follow Eärendel without rest,
the shining mariner, beyond the West,
who passed the mouth of night and launched his bark
upon the outer seas of everlasting dark.                    40
Here only comes at whiles a wind to blow
returning darkly down the way ye go,
with perfume laden of unearthly trees.
Here only long afar through window-pane
I glimpse the flicker of the golden rain               45
that falls for ever on the outer seas.

I cannot explain the reference (in the revised version only, line 24) to the journey of the mariners 'beyond the grey islands and past Gondobar'. *Gondobar* ('City of Stone') was one of the seven names of Gondolin (p. 158).

## NOTES

1 Falasquil was the name of Tuor's dwelling on the coast (p. 152); the Oarni, with the Falmariní and the Wingildi, are called 'the spirits of the foam and the surf of ocean' (I. 66).

2 *Irildë*: the 'Elvish' name corresponding to Gnomish *Idril*. See the Appendix on Names, entry *Idril*.

3 'Elwing of the *Gnomes* of Artanor' is perhaps a mere slip.

4 For the Swan-wing as the emblem of Tuor see pp. 152, 164, 172, 193.

5 The words 'Idril has vanished' replace an earlier reading: 'Sirion has been sacked and only Littleheart (Ilfrith) remained who tells the tale.' *Ilfrith* is yet another version of Littleheart's Elvish name (see pp. 201–2).

6 Struck out here: 'The Sleeper is Idril but he does not know.'

7 Cf. *Kortirion among the Trees* (I. 36, lines 129–30): 'I need not know the desert or red palaces Where dwells the sun'; lines retained slightly changed in the second (1937) version (I. 39).

8 This passage, from 'Eärendel distraught...', replaced the following: '[*illegible name, possibly* Orlon] is [?biding] there and tells him of the sack of Sirion and the captivity of Elwing. The faring of the Koreldar and the binding of Melko.' Perhaps the words 'The faring of the Koreldar' were struck out by mistake (cf. Outline B).

9 *Earum* is emended (at the first occurrence only) from *Earam*; and following it stood the name *Earnhama*, but this was struck out. *Earnhama* is Old English, 'Eagle-coat', 'Eagle-dress'.

37 Ye] You      40 outer *omitted*
41–3 *struck through*      46 the] those
*Line added at end:* beyond the country of the shining Trees.

10 The two earliest extant texts date it thus, one of them with the addition 'Ex[eter] Coll[ege] Essay Club Dec. 1914', and on a third is written 'Gedling, Notts., Sept. 1913 [error for 1914] and later'. My father referred to having read 'Eärendel' to the Essay Club in a letter to my mother of 27 November 1914.

11 But *rocks* in line 27 (26) should read *rock*.

12 According to one note it was written at 'Barnt Green [see *Biography* p. 36] July 1915 and Bedford and later', and another note dates it 'July 24 [1915], rewritten Sept. 9'. The original workings are on the back of an unsent letter dated from Moseley (Birmingham) July 11, 1915; my father began military training at Bedford on July 19.

# VI

# THE HISTORY OF ERIOL OR
# ÆLFWINE AND THE END OF THE
# TALES

In this final chapter we come to the most difficult (though not, as I hope
to show, altogether insoluble) part of the earliest form of the mythology:
its end, with which is intertwined the story of Eriol/Ælfwine – and with
that, the history and original significance of Tol Eressëa. For its elucidation we have some short pieces of connected narrative, but are largely
dependent on the same materials as those that constitute *Gilfanon's Tale*
and the story of Eärendel: scribbled plot-outlines, endlessly varying,
written on separate slips of paper or in the pages of the little notebook 'C'
(see p. 254). In this chapter there is much material to consider, and
for convenience of reference within the chapter I number the various
citations consecutively. But it must be said that no device of presentation
can much diminish the inherent complexity and obscurity of the matter.

The fullest account (bald as it is) of the March of the Elves of Kôr and
the events that followed is contained in notebook C, continuing on from
the point where I left that outline on p. 255, after the coming of the birds
from Gondolin, the 'counsels of the Gods and uproar of the Elves', and
the 'March of the Inwir and Teleri', with the Solosimpi only agreeing to
accompany the expedition on condition that they remain by the sea. The
outline continues:

(1)     Coming of the Eldar. Encampment in the Land of Willows of
        first host. Overwhelming of Noldorin and Valwë. Wanderings
        of Noldorin with his harp.
        Tulkas overthrows Melko in the battle of the Silent Pools. Bound
        in Lumbi and guarded by Gorgumoth the hound of Mandos.
        Release of the Noldoli. War with Men as soon as Tulkas and
        Noldorin have fared back to Valinor.
        Noldoli led to Valinor by Egalmoth and Galdor.

There have been previous references in the *Lost Tales* to a battle in
Tasarinan, the Land of Willows: in the *Tale of Turambar* (pp. 70, 140),
and, most notably, in *The Fall of Gondolin* (p. 154), where when
Tuor's sojourn in that land is described there is mention of events that
would take place there in the future:

Did not even after the days of Tuor Noldorin and his Eldar come there seeking for Dor Lómin and the hidden river and the caverns of the Gnomes' imprisonment; yet thus nigh to their quest's end were like to abandon it? Indeed sleeping and dancing here . . . they were whelmed by the goblins sped by Melko from the Hills of Iron and Noldorin made bare escape thence.

Valwë has been mentioned once before, by Lindo, on Eriol's first evening in Mar Vanwa Tyaliéva (I. 16): 'My father Valwë who went with Noldorin to find the Gnomes.' Of Noldorin we know also that he was the Vala Salmar, the twin-brother of Ómar-Amillo; that he entered the world with Ulmo, and that in Valinor he played the harp and lyre and loved the Noldoli (I. 66, 75, 93, 126).

An isolated note states:

(2)   Noldorin escapes from the defeat of the Land of Willows and takes his harp and goes seeking in the Iron Mountains for Valwë and the Gnomes until he finds their place of imprisonment. Tulkas follows. Melko comes to meet him.

The only one of the great Valar who is mentioned in these notes as taking part in the expedition to the Great Lands is Tulkas; but whatever story underlay his presence, despite the anger and sorrow of the Valar at the March of the Elves (see p. 257), is quite irrecoverable. (A very faint hint concerning it is found in two isolated notes: 'Tulkas gives – or the Elves take *limpë* with them', and '*Limpë* given by the Gods (Oromë? Tulkas?) when Elves left Valinor'; cf. *The Flight of the Noldoli* (I.166): 'no *limpë* had they [the Noldoli] as yet to bring away, for that was not given to the fairies until long after, when the March of Liberation was undertaken'.) According to (1) above Tulkas fought with and overthrew Melko 'in the battle of the Silent Pools'; and the Silent Pools are the Pools of Twilight, 'where Tulkas after fought with Melko's self' (*The Fall of Gondolin*, p. 195; the original reading here was 'Noldorin and Tulkas').

The name *Lumbi* is found elsewhere (in a list of names associated with the tale of *The Coming of the Valar*, I.93), where it is said to be Melko's third dwelling; and a jotting in notebook C, sufficiently mysterious, reads: 'Lumfad. Melko's dwelling after release. Castle of Lumbi.' But this story also is lost.

That the Noldoli were led back to Valinor by Egalmoth and Galdor, as stated in (1), is notable. This is contradicted in detail by a statement in the Name-list to *The Fall of Gondolin*, which says (p. 215) that Egalmoth was slain in the raid on the dwelling at the mouth of Sirion when Elwing was taken; and contradicted in general by the next citation to be given, which denies that the Elves were permitted to dwell in Valinor.

The only other statement concerning these events is found in the first of the four outlines that constitute *Gilfanon's Tale*, which I there called 'A' (I. 234). This reads:

**(3)**   March of the Elves out into the world.
The capture of Noldorin.
The camp in the Land of Willows.
Army of Tulkas at the Pools of Twilight . . . . . . and [?many] Gnomes, but Men fall on them out of Hisilómë.
Defeat of Melko.
Breaking of Angamandi and release of captives.
Hostility of Men. The Gnomes collect some of the jewels.
Elwing and most of the Elves go back to dwell in Tol Eressëa. The Gods will not let them dwell in Valinor.

This seems to differ from (1) in the capture of Noldorin and in the attack of Men from Hisilómë before the defeat of Melko; but the most notable statement is that concerning the refusal of the Gods to allow the Elves to dwell in Valinor. There is no reason to think that this ban rested only, or chiefly, on the Noldoli. The text, (3), does not refer specifically to the Gnomes in this connection; and the ban is surely to be related to 'the sorrow and wrath of the Gods' at the time of the March of the Elves (p. 253). Further, it is said in *The Cottage of Lost Play* (I. 16) that Ingil son of Inwë returned to Tol Eressëa with 'most of the fairest and the wisest, most of the merriest and the kindest, of all the Eldar', and that the town that he built there was named 'Koromas or "the Resting of the Exiles of Kôr".' This is quite clearly to be connected with the statement in (3) that 'Most of the Elves go back to dwell in Tol Eressëa', and with that given on p. 255: 'The wars with Men and the departure to Tol Eressëa (the Eldar unable to endure the strife of the world)'. These indications taken together leave no doubt, I think, that my father's original conception was of the Eldar of Valinor undertaking the expedition into the Great Lands against the will of the Valar; together with the rescued Noldoli they returned over the Ocean, but being refused re-entry into Valinor they settled in Tol Eressëa, as 'the Exiles of Kôr'. That some did return in the end to Valinor may be concluded from the words of Meril-i-Turinqi (I. 129) that Ingil, who built Kortirion, 'went long ago back to Valinor and is with Manwë'. But Tol Eressëa remained the land of the fairies in the early conception, the Exiles of Kôr, Eldar and Gnomes, speaking both *Eldarissa* and *Noldorissa*.

It seems that there is nothing else to be found or said concerning the original story of the coming of aid out of the West and the renewed assault on Melko.

★

The conclusion of the whole story as originally envisaged was to be rejected in its entirety. For it we are very largely dependent on the outline in notebook C, continuing on from citation (1) above; this is extremely rough and disjointed, and is given here in a very slightly edited form.

**(4)** After the departure of Eärendel and the coming of the Elves to Tol Eressëa (and most of this belongs to the history of Men) great ages elapse; Men spread and thrive, and the Elves of the Great Lands fade. As Men's stature grows theirs diminishes. Men and Elves were formerly of a size, though Men always larger.[1]

Melko again breaks away, by the aid of Tevildo (who in long ages gnaws his bonds); the Gods are in dissension about Men and Elves, some favouring the one and some the other. Melko goes to Tol Eressëa and tries to stir up dissension among the Elves (between Gnomes and Solosimpi), who are in consternation and send to Valinor. No help comes, but Tulkas sends privily Telimektar (Taimonto) his son.[2]

Telimektar of the silver sword and Ingil surprise Melko and wound him, and he flees and climbs up the great Pine of Tavrobel. Before the Inwir left Valinor Belaurin (Palúrien)[3] gave them a seed, and said that it must be guarded, for great tidings would one day come of its growth. But it was forgotten, and cast in the garden of Gilfanon, and a mighty pine arose that reached to Ilwë and the stars.[4]

Telimektar and Ingil pursue him, and they remain now in the sky to ward it, and Melko stalks high above the air seeking ever to do a hurt to the Sun and Moon and stars (eclipses, meteors). He is continually frustrated, but on his first attempt – saying that the Gods stole his fire for its making – he upset the Sun, so that Urwendi fell into the Sea, and the Ship fell near the ground, scorching regions of the Earth. The clarity of the Sun's radiance has not been so great since, and something of magic has gone from it. Hence it is, and long has been, that the fairies dance and sing more sweetly and can the better be seen by the light of the Moon – because of the death of Urwendi.

The 'Rekindling of the Magic Sun' refers in part to the Trees and in part to Urwendi.

Fionwë's rage and grief. In the end he will slay Melko.

'Orion' is only the image of Telimektar in the sky? [*sic*] Varda gave him stars, and he bears them aloft that the Gods may know he watches; he has diamonds on his sword-sheath, and this will go red when he draws his sword at the Great End.

But now Telimektar, and Gil[5] who follows him like a Blue Bee, ward off evil, and Varda immediately replaces any stars that Melko loosens and casts down.

Although grieved at the Gods' behest, the Pine is cut down; and

Melko is thus now out of the world – but one day he will find a way back, and the last great uproars will begin before the Great End.

The evils that still happen come about in this wise. The Gods can cause things to enter the hearts of Men, but not of Elves (hence their difficult dealings in the old days of the Exile of the Gnomes) – and though Melko sits without, gnawing his fingers and gazing in anger on the world, he can suggest evil to Men so inclined – but the lies he planted of old still grow and spread.

Hence Melko can now work hurt and damage and evil in the world only through Men, and he has more power and subtlety with Men than Manwë or any of the Gods, because of his long sojourn in the world and among Men.

In these early chartings we are in a primitive mythology, with Melko reduced to a grotesque figure chased up a great pine-tree, which is thereupon cut down to keep him out of the world, where he 'stalks high above the air' or 'sits without, gnawing his fingers', and upsets the Sun-ship so that Urwendi falls into the Sea – and, most strangely, meets her death.

That Ingil (Gil) who with Telimektar pursues Melko is to be identified with Ingil son of Inwë who built Kortirion is certain and appears from several notes; see the Appendix on Names to Vol. I, entries *Ingil, Telimektar*. This is the fullest statement of the Orion-myth, which is referred to in the *Tale of the Sun and Moon* (see I.182, 200):

of Nielluin [Sirius] too, who is the Bee of Azure, Nielluin whom still may all men see in autumn or winter burning nigh the foot of Telimektar son of Tulkas whose tale is yet to tell.

In the Gnomish dictionary it is said (I.256) that Gil rose into the heavens and 'in the likeness of a great bee bearing honey of flame' followed Telimektar. This presumably represents a distinct conception from that referred to above, where Ingil 'went long ago back to Valinor and is with Manwë' (I.129).

With the reference to Fionwë's slaying of Melko 'in the end' cf. the end of *The Hiding of Valinor* (I.219):

Fionwë Úrion, son of Manwë, of love for Urwendi shall in the end be Melko's bane, and shall destroy the world to destroy his foe, and so shall all things then be rolled away.

Cf. also the *Tale of Turambar*, p. 116, where it is said that Turambar 'shall stand beside Fionwë in the Great Wrack'.

For the prophecies and hopes of the Elves concerning the Rekindling of the Magic Sun see pp. 285–6.

The outline in C continues and concludes thus (again with some very slight and insignificant editing):

**(5)**   Longer ages elapse. Gilfanon is now the oldest and wisest Elf in Tol Eressëa, but is not of the Inwir – hence Meril-i-Turinqi is Lady of the Isle.

Eriol comes to Tol Eressëa. Sojourns at Kortirion. Goes to Tavrobel to see Gilfanon, and sojourns in the house of a hundred chimneys – for this is the last condition of his drinking *limpë*. Gilfanon bids him write down all he has heard before he drinks.

Eriol drinks *limpë*. Gilfanon tells him of things to be; that in his mind (although the fairies hope not) he believes that Tol Eressëa will become a dwelling of Men. Gilfanon also prophesies concerning the Great End, and of the Wrack of Things, and of Fionwë, Tulkas, and Melko and the last fight on the Plains of Valinor.

Eriol ends his life at Tavrobel but in his last days is consumed with longing for the black cliffs of his shores, even as Meril said.

The book lay untouched in the house of Gilfanon during many ages of Men.

The compiler of the Golden Book takes up the Tale: one of the children of the fathers of the fathers of Men. [*Against this is written*:] It may perhaps be much better to let Eriol himself see the last things and finish the book.

Rising of the Lost Elves against the Orcs and Nautar.[6] The time is not ready for the Faring Forth, but the fairies judge it to be necessary. They obtain through Ulmo the help of Uin,[7] and Tol Eressëa is uprooted and dragged near to the Great Lands, nigh to the promontory of Rôs. A magic bridge is cast across the intervening sound. Ossë is wroth at the breaking of the roots of the isle he set so long ago – and many of his rare sea-treasures grow about it – that he tries to wrench it back; and the western half breaks off, and is now the Isle of Íverin.

The Battle of Rôs: the Island-elves and the Lost Elves against Nautar, Gongs,[8] Orcs, and a few evil Men. Defeat of the Elves. The fading Elves retire to Tol Eressëa and hide in the woods.

Men come to Tol Eressëa and also Orcs, Dwarves, Gongs, Trolls, etc. After the Battle of Rôs the Elves faded with sorrow. They cannot live in air breathed by a number of Men equal to their own or greater; and ever as Men wax more powerful and numerous so the fairies fade and grow small and tenuous, filmy and transparent, but Men larger and more dense and gross. At last Men, or almost all, can no longer see the fairies.

The Gods now dwell in Valinor, and come scarcely ever to the world, being content with the restraining of the elements from utterly destroying Men. They grieve much at what they see; *but Ilúvatar is over all*.

On the page opposite the passage about the Battle of Rôs is written:

> A great battle between Men at the Heath of the Sky-roof (now the
> Withered Heath), about a league from Tavrobel. The Elves and the
> Children flee over the Gruir and the Afros.
> 'Even now do they approach and our great tale comes to its ending.'
> The book found in the ruins of the house of a hundred chimneys.

That Gilfanon was the oldest of the Elves of Tol Eressëa, though Meril
held the title of Lady of the Isle, is said also in the *Tale of the Sun and
Moon* (I.175): but what is most notable is that Gilfanon (not Ailios,
teller of the *Tale of the Nauglafring*, whom Gilfanon replaced, see
I.197 note 19 and 229ff.) appears in this outline, which must therefore
be late in the period of the composition of the *Lost Tales*.

Also noteworthy are the references to Eriol's drinking *limpë* at
Gilfanon's 'house of a hundred chimneys'. In *The Cottage of Lost Play*
(I.17) Lindo told Eriol that he could not give him *limpë* to drink:

> Turinqi only may give it to those not of the Eldar race, and those that
> drink must dwell always with the Eldar of the Island until such time as
> they fare forth to find the lost families of the kindred.

Meril-i-Turinqi herself, when Eriol besought her for a drink of *limpë*,
was severe (I.98):

> ↳f you drink this drink . . . even at the Faring Forth, should Eldar and
> Men fall into war at the last, still must you stand by us against the
> children of your kith and kin, but until then never may you fare away
> home though longings gnaw you . . .

In the text described in I.229ff. Eriol bemoans to Lindo the refusal to
grant him his desire, and Lindo, while warning him against 'thinking to
overpass the bounds that Ilúvatar hath set', tells him that Meril has not
irrevocably refused him. In a note to this text my father wrote: '. . . Eriol
fares to Tavrobel − after Tavrobel he drinks of *limpë*.'

The statement in this passage of outline C that Eriol 'in his last days is
consumed with longing for the black cliffs of his shores, even as Meril
said' clearly refers to the passage in *The Chaining of Melko* from which
I have cited above:

> On a day of autumn will come the winds and a driven gull, maybe, will
> wail overhead, and lo! you will be filled with desire, remembering the
> black coasts of your home. (I.96).

Lindo's reference, in the passage from *The Cottage of Lost Play* cited above, to the faring forth of the Eldar of Tol Eressëa 'to find the lost families of the kindred' must likewise relate to the mentions in (5) of the Faring Forth (though the time was not ripe), of the 'rising of the Lost Elves against the Orcs and Nautar', and of 'the Island-elves and the Lost Elves' at the Battle of Rôs. Precisely who are to be understood by the 'Lost Elves' is not clear; but in *Gilfanon's Tale* (I. 231) all Elves of the Great Lands 'that never saw the light at Kôr' (Ilkorins), whether or not they left the Waters of Awakening, are called 'the lost fairies of the world', and this seems likely to be the meaning here. It must then be supposed that there dwelt on Tol Eressëa only the Eldar of Kôr (the 'Exiles') and the Noldoli released from thraldom under Melko; the Faring Forth was to be the great expedition from Tol Eressëa for the rescue of those who had never departed from the Great Lands.

In (5) we meet the conception of the dragging of Tol Eressëa back eastwards across the Ocean to the geographical position of England – it becomes England (see I. 26); that the part which was torn off by Ossë, the Isle of Íverin, is Ireland is explicitly stated in the Qenya dictionary. The promontory of Rôs is perhaps Brittany.

Here also there is a clear definition of the 'fading' of the Elves, their physical diminution and increasing tenuity and transparency, so that they become invisible (and finally incredible) to gross Mankind. This is a central concept of the early mythology: the 'fairies', as now conceived by Men (in so far as they are rightly conceived), have *become* so. They were not always so. And perhaps most remarkable in this remarkable passage, there is the final and virtually complete withdrawal of the Gods (to whom the Eldar are 'most like in nature', I. 57) from the concerns of 'the world', the Great Lands across the Sea. They watch, it seems, since they grieve, and are therefore not wholly indifferent to what passes in the lands of Men; but they are henceforward utterly remote, hidden in the West.

Other features of (5), the Golden Book of Tavrobel, and the Battle of the Heath of the Sky-roof, will be explained shortly. I give next a separate passage found in the notebook C under the heading 'Rekindling of the Magic Sun. Faring Forth.'

(6) The Elves' prophecy is that one day they will fare forth from Tol Eressëa and on arriving in the world will gather all their fading kindred who still live in the world and march towards Valinor – through the southern lands. This they will only do with the help of Men. If Men aid them, the fairies will take Men to Valinor – those that wish to go – fight a great battle with Melko in Erumáni and open Valinor.[9] Laurelin and Silpion will be rekindled, and the mountain wall being destroyed then soft radiance will spread over all the world, and the Sun and Moon will be recalled. If Men oppose them and aid Melko the Wrack of the Gods and the ending of the fairies will result – and maybe the Great End.

On the opposite page is written:

> Were the Trees relit all the paths to Valinor would become clear to
> follow – and the Shadowy Seas open clear and free – Men as well as
> Elves would taste the blessedness of the Gods, and Mandos be emptied.

This prophecy is clearly behind Vairë's words to Eriol (I.19–20): '. . .
the Faring Forth, when if all goes well the roads through Arvalin to
Valinor shall be thronged with the sons and daughters of Men.'

Since 'the Sun and Moon will be recalled' when the Two Trees give
light again, it seems that here 'the Rekindling of the Magic Sun' (to which
the toast was drunk in Mar Vanwa Tyaliéva, I.17, 65) refers to the
relighting of the Trees. But in citation (4) above it is said that 'the
"Rekindling of the Magic Sun" refers in part to the Trees and in part to
Urwendi', while in the *Tale of the Sun and Moon* (I.179) Yavanna
seems to distinguish the two ideas:

> 'Many things shall be done and come to pass, and the Gods grow old,
> and the Elves come nigh to fading, ere ye shall see the rekindling of
> these trees or the Magic Sun relit', and the Gods knew not what she
> meant, speaking of the Magic Sun, nor did for a long while after.

Citation (xix) on p. 264 does not make the reference clear: Eärendel
'returns from the firmament ever and anon with Voronwë to Kôr to see if
the Magic Sun has been lit and the fairies have come back'; but in the
following isolated note the Rekindling of the Magic Sun explicitly means
the re-arising of Urwendi:

(7)  Urwendi imprisoned by Móru (upset out of the boat by Melko and
     only the Moon has been magic since). The Faring Forth and the
     Battle of Erumáni would release her and rekindle the Magic Sun.

This 'upsetting' of the Sun-ship by Melko and the loss of the Sun's
'magic' is referred to also in (4), where it is added that Urwendi fell into
the sea and met her 'death'. In the tale of *The Theft of Melko* it is said
(I.151) that the cavern in which Melko met Ungweliant was the place
where the Sun and Moon were imprisoned afterwards, for 'the primeval
spirit Móru' was indeed Ungweliant (see I.261). The Battle of Erumáni
is referred to also in (6), and is possibly to be identified with 'the last fight
on the plains of Valinor' prophesied by Gilfanon in (5). But the last part
of (5) shows that the Faring Forth came to nothing, and the prophecies
were not fulfilled.

There are no other references to the dragging of Tol Eressëa across the
Ocean by Uin the great whale, to the Isle of Íverin, or to the Battle
of Rôs; but a remarkable writing survives concerning the aftermath of

the 'great battle between Men at the Heath of the Sky-roof (now the Withered Heath), about a league from Tavrobel' (end of citation (5)). This is a very hastily pencilled and exceedingly difficult text titled *Epilogue*. It begins with a short prefatory note:

(8)   Eriol flees with the fading Elves from the Battle of the High Heath (Ladwen-na-Dhaideloth) and crosses the Gruir and the Afros.
      The last words of the book of Tales. Written by Eriol at Tavrobel before he sealed the book.

This represents the development mentioned as desirable in (5), that Eriol should 'himself see the last things and finish the book'; but an isolated note in C shows my father still uncertain about this even after the *Epilogue* was in being: 'Prologue by the writer of Tavrobel [*i.e., such a Prologue is needed*] telling how he found Eriol's writings and put them together. His epilogue after the battle of Ladwen Daideloth is written.'

The rivers Gruir and Afros appear also in the passage about the battle at the end of (5). Since it is said there that the Heath was about a league from Tavrobel, the two rivers are clearly those referred to in the *Tale of the Sun and Moon*: 'the Tower of Tavrobel beside the rivers' (I.174, and see I.196 note 2). In scattered notes the battle is also called 'the Battle of the Heaven Roof' and 'the Battle of Dor-na-Dhaideloth'.[10]

I give now the text of the *Epilogue*:

And now is the end of the fair times come very nigh, and behold, all the beauty that yet was on earth – fragments of the unimagined loveliness of Valinor whence came the folk of the Elves long long ago – now goeth it all up in smoke. Here be a few tales, memories ill-told, of all that magic and that wonder twixt here and Eldamar of which I have become acquaint more than any mortal man since first my wandering footsteps came to this sad isle.

Of that last battle of the upland heath whose roof is the wide sky – nor was there any other place beneath the blue folds of Manwë's robe so nigh the heavens or so broadly and so well encanopied – what grievous things I saw I have told.

Already fade the Elves in sorrow and the Faring Forth has come to ruin, and Ilúvatar knoweth alone if ever now the Trees shall be relit while the world may last. Behold, I stole by evening from the ruined heath, and my way fled winding down the valley of the Brook of Glass, but the setting of the Sun was blackened with the reek of fires, and the waters of the stream were fouled with the war of men and grime of strife. Then was my heart bitter to see the bones of the good earth laid bare with winds where the destroying hands of men had torn the heather and the fern and burnt them to make sacrifice to Melko and to lust of ruin; and the thronging places of the bees that all day hummed among the whins and whortlebushes long ago bearing rich honey down to Tavrobel – these were now become fosses and [?mounds] of stark red earth, and nought sang there nor danced but unwholesome airs and flies of pestilence.

Now the Sun died and behold, I came to that most magic wood where once the ageless oaks stood firm amid the later growths of beech and slender trees of birch, but all were fallen beneath the ruthless axes of unthinking men. Ah me, here was the path beaten with spells, trodden with musics and enchantment that wound therethrough, and this way were the Elves wont to ride a-hunting. Many a time there have I seen them and Gilfanon has been there, and they rode like kings unto the chase, and the beauty of their faces in the sun was as the new morning, and the wind in their golden hair like to the glory of bright flowers shaken at dawn, and the strong music of their voices like the sea and like trumpets and like the noise of very many viols and of golden harps unnumbered. And yet again have I seen the people of Tavrobel beneath the Moon, and they would ride or dance across the valley of the two rivers where the grey bridge leaps the joining waters; and they would fare swiftly as clad in dreams, spangled with gems like to the grey dews amid the grass, and their white robes caught the long radiance of the Moon . . . . . . . . . . . . . and their spears shivered with silver flames.

And now sorrow and . . . . . has come upon the Elves, empty is Tavrobel and all are fled, [?fearing] the enemy that sitteth on the ruined heath, who is not a league away; whose hands are red with the blood of Elves and stained with the lives of his own kin, who has made himself an ally to Melko and the Lord of Hate, who has fought for the Orcs and Gongs and the unwholesome monsters of the world – blind, and a fool, and destruction alone is his knowledge. The paths of the fairies he has made to dusty roads where thirst [?lags wearily] and no man greeteth another in the way, but passes by in sullenness.

So fade the Elves and it shall come to be that because of the encompassing waters of this isle and yet more because of their unquenchable love for it that few shall flee, but as men wax there and grow fat and yet more blind ever shall they fade more and grow less; and those of the after days shall scoff, saying Who are the fairies – lies told to the children by women or foolish men – who are these fairies? And some few shall answer: Memories faded dim, a wraith of vanishing loveliness in the trees, a rustle of the grass, a glint of dew, some subtle intonation of the wind; and others yet fewer shall say . . . . . 'Very small and delicate are the fairies now, yet we have eyes to see and ears to hear, and Tavrobel and Kortirion are filled yet with [?this] sweet folk. Spring knows them and Summer too and in Winter still are they among us, but in Autumn most of all do they come out, for Autumn is their season, fallen as they are upon the Autumn of their days. What shall the dreamers of the earth be like when their winter come.

Hark O my brothers, they shall say, the little trumpets blow; we

hear a sound of instruments unimagined small. Like strands of wind,
like mystic half-transparencies, Gilfanon Lord of Tavrobel rides out
tonight amid his folk, and hunts the elfin deer beneath the paling sky.
A music of forgotten feet, a gleam of leaves, a sudden bending of the
grass,[11] and wistful voices murmuring on the bridge, and they are
gone.

But behold, Tavrobel shall not know its name, and all the land be
changed, and even these written words of mine belike will all be lost;
and so I lay down the pen, and so of the fairies cease to tell.

Another text that bears on these matters is the prose preface to
*Kortirion among the Trees* (1915), which has been given in Part I
25–6, but which I repeat here:

**(9)**  Now on a time the fairies dwelt in the Lonely Isle after the great
wars with Melko and the ruin of Gondolin; and they builded a fair
city amidmost of that island, and it was girt with trees. Now this city
they called Kortirion, both in memory of their ancient dwelling of
Kôr in Valinor, and because this city stood also upon a hill and had
a great tower tall and grey that Ingil son of Inwë their lord let raise.

Very beautiful was Kortirion and the fairies loved it, and it
became rich in song and poesy and the light of laughter; but on a
time the great Faring Forth was made, and the fairies had rekindled
once more the Magic Sun of Valinor but for the treason and faint
hearts of Men. But so it is that the Magic Sun is dead and the
Lonely Isle drawn back unto the confines of the Great Lands,
and the fairies are scattered through all the wide unfriendly pathways of the world; and now Men dwell even on this faded isle, and
care nought or know nought of its ancient days. Yet still there be
some of the Eldar and the Noldoli of old who linger in the island,
and their songs are heard about the shores of the land that once was
the fairest dwelling of the immortal folk.

And it seems to the fairies and it seems to me who know that town
and have often trodden its disfigured ways that autumn and the
falling of the leaf is the season of the year when maybe here or there
a heart among Men may be open, and an eye perceive how is the
world's estate fallen from the laughter and the loveliness of old.
Think on Kortirion and be sad – yet is there not hope?

★

At this point we may turn to the history of Eriol himself. My father's
early conceptions of the mariner who came to Tol Eressëa are here again
no more than allusive outlines in the pages of the little notebook C, and
some of this material cannot be usefully reproduced. Perhaps the earliest
is a collection of notes headed 'Story of Eriol's Life', which I gave in Vol.

I. 23–4 but with the omission of some features that were not there relevant. I repeat it here, with the addition of the statements previously omitted.

(10)   Eriol's original name was Ottor, but he called himself *Wǽfre* (Old English: 'restless, wandering') and lived a life on the waters. His father was named Eoh (Old English: 'horse'); and Eoh was slain by his brother Beorn, either 'in the siege' or 'in a great battle'. Ottor Wǽfre settled on the island of Heligoland in the North Sea, and wedded a woman named Cwén; they had two sons named Hengest and Horsa 'to avenge Eoh'.

Then sea-longing gripped Ottor Wǽfre (he was 'a son of Eärendel', born under his beam), and after the death of Cwén he left his young children. Hengest and Horsa avenged Eoh and became great chieftains; but Ottor Wǽfre set out to seek, and find, Tol Eressëa (*se uncúpa holm*, 'the unknown island').

In Tol Eressëa he wedded, being made young by *limpë* (here also called by the Old English word *líp*), Naimi (Éadgifu), niece of Vairë, and they had a son named Heorrenda.

It is then said, somewhat inconsequentially (though the matter is in itself of much interest, and recurs nowhere else), that Eriol told the fairies of *Wóden, Þunor, Tíw*, etc. (these being the Old English names of the Germanic gods who in Old Scandinavian form are *Óðinn, Þórr, Týr*), and they identified them with Manweg, Tulkas, and a third whose name is illegible but is not like that of any of the great Valar.

Eriol adopted the name of *Angol*.

Thus it is that through Eriol and his sons the *Engle* (i.e. the English) have the true tradition of the fairies, of whom the *Íras* and the *Wéalas* (the Irish and Welsh) tell garbled things.

Thus a specifically English fairy-lore is born, and one more true than anything to be found in Celtic lands.

The wedding of Eriol in Tol Eressëa is never referred to elsewhere; but his son Heorrenda is mentioned (though not called Eriol's son) in the initial link to *The Fall of Gondolin* (p. 145) as one who 'afterwards' turned a song of Meril's maidens into the language of his people. A little more light will be shed on Heorrenda in the course of this chapter.

Associated with these notes is a title-page and a prologue that breaks off after a few lines:

(11)            The Golden Book of Heorrenda
                    being the book of the
                    Tales of Tavrobel

                    ―――――

            Heorrenda of Hægwudu

This book have I written using those writings that my father Wǽfre (whom the Gnomes named after the regions of his home Angol) did make in his sojourn in the holy isle in the days of the Elves; and much else have I added of those things which his eyes saw not afterward; yet are such things not yet to tell. For know

Here then the Golden Book was compiled from Eriol's writings by his son Heorrenda – in contrast to (5), where it was compiled by someone unnamed, and in contrast also to the *Epilogue* (8), where Eriol himself concluded and 'sealed the book'.

As I have said earlier (I. 24) *Angol* refers to the ancient homeland of the 'English' before their migration across the North Sea (for the etymology of *Angol/Eriol* 'ironcliffs' see I. 24, 252).

(12)    There is also a genealogical table accompanying the outline (10) and altogether agreeing with it. The table is written out in two forms that are identical save in one point: for Beorn, brother of Eoh, in the one, there stands in the other *Hasen of Isenóra* (Old English: 'iron shore'). But at the end of the table is introduced the cardinal fact of all these earliest materials concerning Eriol and Tol Eressëa: Hengest and Horsa, Eriol's sons by Cwén in Heligoland, and Heorrenda, his son by Naimi in Tol Eressëa, are bracketed together, and beneath their names is written:

conquered Íeg
('seo unwemmede Íeg')
now called Englaland
and there dwell the Angolcynn or Engle.

*Íeg* is Old English, 'isle'; *seo unwemmede Íeg* 'the unstained isle'. I have mentioned before (I. 25, footnote) a poem of my father's written at Étaples in June 1916 and called 'The Lonely Isle', addressed to England: this poem bears the Old English title *seo Unwemmede Íeg*.

(13)    There follow in the notebook C some jottings that make precise identifications of places in Tol Eressëa with places in England.

First the name *Kortirion* is explained. The element *Kôr* is derived from an earlier *Qorǎ*, yet earlier *Guorǎ*; but from *Guorǎ* was also derived (i.e. in Gnomish) the form *Gwâr*. (This formulation agrees with that in the Gnomish dictionary, see I. 257). Thus *Kôr* = *Gwâr*, and *Kortirion* = *\*Gwarmindon* (the asterisk implying a hypothetical, unrecorded form). The name that was actually used in Gnomish had the elements reversed, *Mindon-Gwar*. (*Mindon*, like *Tirion*, meant, and continued always to mean, 'tower'. The meaning of *Kôr/Gwâr* is not given here, but both in the tale of *The Coming of the Elves* (I. 122) and in the Gnomish dictionary (I. 257) the name is explained as referring to the *roundness* of the hill of Kôr.)

The note continues (using Old English forms): 'In Wíelisc *Caergwâr*, in Englisc *Warwíc*.' Thus the element *War-* in *Warwick* is derived from the same Elvish source as *Kor-* in *Kortirion* and *Gwar* in *Mindon-Gwar*.[12] Lastly, it is said that 'Hengest's capital was Warwick'.

Next, Horsa (Hengest's brother) is associated with *Oxenaford* (Old English: Oxford), which is given the equivalents Q[enya] *Taruktarna* and Gnomish *\*Taruithorn* (see the Appendix on Names, p. 347).

The third of Eriol's sons, Heorrenda, is said to have had his 'capital' at Great Haywood (the Staffordshire village where my parents lived in 1916−17, see I. 25); and this is given the Qenya equivalents *Tavaros*(*së*) and *Taurossë*, and the Gnomish *Tavrobel* and *Tavrost*; also 'Englisc [i.e. Old English] *Hægwudu se gréata, Gréata Hægwudu*'.[13]

These notes conclude with the statement that 'Heorrenda called Kôr or Gwâr "Tûn".' In the context of these conceptions, this is obviously the Old English word *tún*, an enclosed dwelling, from which has developed the modern word *town* and the place-name ending *-ton*. *Tûn* has appeared several times in the *Lost Tales* as a later correction, or alternative to *Kôr*, changes no doubt dating from or anticipating the later situation where the city was *Tûn* and the name *Kôr* was restricted to the hill on which it stood. Later still *Tûn* became *Túna*, and then when the city of the Elves was named *Tirion* the hill became *Túna*, as it is in *The Silmarillion*; by then it had ceased to have any connotation of 'dwelling-place' and had cut free from all connection with its actual origin, as we see it here, in Old English *tún*, Heorrenda's 'town'.

Can all these materials be brought together to form a coherent narrative? I believe that they can (granting that there are certain irreconcilable differences concerning Eriol's life), and would reconstruct it thus:

−   The Eldar and the rescued Noldoli departed from the Great Lands and came to Tol Eressëa.

−   In Tol Eressëa they built many towns and villages, and in Alalminórë, the central region of the island, Ingil son of Inwë built the town of Koromas, 'the Resting of the Exiles of Kôr' ('Exiles', because they could not return to Valinor); and the great tower of Ingil gave the town its name *Kortirion*. (See I. 16.)

−   Ottor Wǽfre came from Heligoland to Tol Eressëa and dwelt in the Cottage of Lost Play in Kortirion; the Elves named him *Eriol* or *Angol* after the 'iron cliffs' of his home.

−   After a time, and greatly instructed in the ancient history of Gods, Elves, and Men, Eriol went to visit Gilfanon in the village of Tavrobel, and there he wrote down what he had learnt; there also he at last drank *limpë*.

- In Tol Eressëa Eriol was wedded and had a son named Heorrenda (Half-elven!). (According to (5) Eriol died at Tavrobel, consumed with longing for 'the black cliffs of his shores'; but according to (8), certainly later, he lived to see the Battle of the Heath of the Sky-roof.)

- The Lost Elves of the Great Lands rose against the dominion of the servants of Melko; and the untimely Faring Forth took place, at which time Tol Eressëa was drawn east back across the Ocean and anchored off the coasts of the Great Lands. The western half broke off when Ossë tried to drag the island back, and it became the Isle of Íverin (= Ireland).

- Tol Eressëa was now in the geographical position of England.

- The great battle of Rôs ended in the defeat of the Elves, who retreated into hiding in Tol Eressëa.

- Evil men entered Tol Eressëa, accompanied by Orcs and other hostile beings.

- The Battle of the Heath of the Sky-roof took place not far from Tavrobel, and (according to (8)) was witnessed by Eriol, who completed the Golden Book.

- The Elves faded and became invisible to the eyes of almost all Men.

- The sons of Eriol, Hengest, Horsa, and Heorrenda, conquered the island and it became 'England'. They were not hostile to the Elves, and from them the English have 'the true tradition of the fairies'.

- Kortirion, ancient dwelling of the fairies, came to be known in the tongue of the English as Warwick; Hengest dwelt there, while Horsa dwelt at Taruithorn (Oxford) and Heorrenda at Tavrobel (Great Haywood). (According to (11) Heorrenda completed the Golden Book.)

This reconstruction may not be 'correct' in all its parts: indeed, it may be that any such attempt is artificial, treating all the notes and jottings as of equal weight and all the ideas as strictly contemporaneous and relatable to each other. Nonetheless I believe that it shows rightly in essentials how my father was thinking of ordering the narrative in which the *Lost Tales* were to be set; and I believe also that this was the conception that still underlay the *Tales* as they are extant and have been given in these books.

For convenience later I shall refer to this narrative as 'the *Eriol* story'. Its most remarkable features, in contrast to the later story, are the transformation of Tol Eressëa into England, and the early appearance of the mariner (in relation to the whole history) and his importance.

In fact, my father was exploring (before he decided on a radical transformation of the whole conception) ideas whereby his importance would be greatly increased.

**(14)** From very rough jottings it can be made out that Eriol was to be so tormented with home longing that he set sail from Tol Eressëa with his son Heorrenda, against the command of Meril-i-Turinqi (see the passage cited on p. 284 from *The Chaining of Melko*); but his purpose in doing so was also 'to hasten the Faring Forth', which he 'preached' in the lands of the East. Tol Eressëa was drawn back to the confines of the Great Lands, but at once hostile peoples named the *Guiðlin* and the *Brithonin* (and in one of these notes also the *Rúmhoth*, Romans) invaded the island. Eriol died, but his sons Hengest and Horsa conquered the Guiðlin. But because of Eriol's disobedience to the command of Meril, in going back before the time for the Faring Forth was ripe, 'all was cursed'; and the Elves faded before the noise and evil of war. An isolated sentence refers to 'a strange prophecy that a man of good will, yet through longing after the things of Men, may bring the Faring Forth to nought'.

Thus the part of Eriol was to become cardinal in the history of the Elves; but there is no sign that these ideas ever got beyond this exploratory stage.

★

I have said that I think that the reconstruction given above ('the *Eriol* story') is in essentials the conception underlying the framework of the *Lost Tales*. This is both for positive and negative reasons: positive, because he is there still named *Eriol* (see p. 300), and also because Gilfanon, who enters (replacing Ailios) late in the development of the *Tales*, appears also in citation (5) above, which is one of the main contributors to this reconstruction; negative, because there is really nothing to contradict what is much the easiest assumption. There is no explicit statement anywhere in the *Lost Tales* that Eriol came from England. At the beginning (I.13) he is only 'a traveller from far countries'; and the fact that the story he told to Vëannë of his earlier life (pp. 4–7) agrees well with other accounts where his home is explicitly in England does no more than show that the story remained while the geography altered – just as the 'black coasts' of his home survived in later writing to become the western coasts of Britain, whereas the earliest reference to them is the etymology of *Angol* 'iron cliffs' (his own name, = *Eriol*, from the land 'between the seas', Angeln in the Danish peninsula, whence he came: see I.252). There is in fact a very early, rejected, sketch of Eriol's life in which essential features of the same story are outlined – the attack on his father's dwelling (in this case the destruction of Eoh's castle by his brother Beorn, see citation (10)), Eriol's captivity and escape – and in this note it is said that Eriol afterwards 'wandered over the wilds of the Central Lands to the Inland Sea, *Wendelsæ* [Old English, the Mediterranean], and hence to the shores of the Western Sea', whence his father had originally come. The mention in the typescript text of the *Link* to the *Tale of Tinúviel* (p. 6) of wild men out of the Mountains of the East, *which the duke could see from his tower*, seems likewise to imply that at this time Eriol's original home was placed in some 'continental' region.

The only suggestion, so far as I can see, that this view might not be correct is found in an early poem with a complex history, texts of which I give here.

The earliest rough drafts of this poem are extant; the original title was 'The Wanderer's Allegiance', and it is not clear that it was at first conceived as a poem in three parts. My father subsequently wrote in subtitles on these drafts, dividing the poem into three: *Prelude*, *The Inland City*, and *The Sorrowful City*, with (apparently) an overall title *The Sorrowful City*; and added a date, March 16–18, 1916. In the only later copy of the whole poem that is extant the overall title is *The Town of Dreams and the City of Present Sorrow*, with the three parts titled: *Prelude* (Old English *Foresang*), *The Town of Dreams* (Old English *Þæt Slæpende Tún*), and *The City of Present Sorrow* (Old English *Seo Wépende Burg*). This text gives the dates 'March 1916, Oxford and Warwick; rewritten Birmingham November 1916'. 'The Town of Dreams' is Warwick, on the River Avon, and 'The City of Present Sorrow' is Oxford, on the Thames, during the First War; there is no evident association of any kind with Eriol or the *Lost Tales*.

## Prelude

In unknown days my fathers' sires
Came, and from son to son took root
Among the orchards and the river-meads
And the long grasses of the fragrant plain:
Many a summer saw they kindle yellow fires
Of iris in the bowing reeds,
And many a sea of blossom turn to golden fruit
In walléd gardens of the great champain.

★

There daffodils among the ordered trees
Did nod in spring, and men laughed deep and long
Singing as they laboured happy lays
And lighting even with a drinking-song.
There sleep came easy for the drone of bees
Thronging about cottage gardens heaped with flowers;
In love of sunlit goodliness of days
There richly flowed their lives in settled hours –
But that was long ago,

And now no more they sing, nor reap, nor sow,
And I perforce in many a town about this isle
Unsettled wanderer have dwelt awhile.

### The Town of Dreams

Here many days once gently past me crept
In this dear town of old forgetfulness;
Here all entwined in dreams once long I slept
And heard no echo of the world's distress
Come through the rustle of the elms' rich leaves,
While Avon gurgling over shallows wove
Unending melody, and morns and eves
Slipped down her waters till the Autumn came,
(Like the gold leaves that drip and flutter then,
Till the dark river gleams with jets of flame
That slowly float far down beyond our ken.)

For here the castle and the mighty tower,
More lofty than the tiered elms,
More grey than long November rain,
Sleep, and nor sunlit moment nor triumphal hour,
Nor passing of the seasons or the Sun
Wakes their old lords too long in slumber lain.

★

No watchfulness disturbs their splendid dream,
Though laughing radiance dance down the stream;
And be they clad in snow or lashed by windy rains,
Or may March whirl the dust about the winding lanes,
The Elm robe and disrobe her of a million leaves
Like moments clustered in a crowded year,
Still their old heart unmoved nor weeps nor grieves,
Uncomprehending of this evil tide,
Today's great sadness, or Tomorrow's fear:
Faint echoes fade within their drowsy halls
Like ghosts; the daylight creeps across their walls.

★

### The City of Present Sorrow

There is a city that far distant lies
And a vale outcarven in forgotten days –
There wider was the grass, and lofty elms more rare;
The river-sense was heavy in the lowland air.
There many willows changed the aspect of the earth and skies
Where feeding brooks wound in by sluggish ways,
And down the margin of the sailing Thames
Around his broad old bosom their old stems
Were bowed, and subtle shades lay on his streams
Where their grey leaves adroop o'er silver pools
Did knit a coverlet like shimmering jewels
Of blue and misty green and filtering gleams.

★

O agéd city of an all too brief sojourn,
I see thy clustered windows each one burn
With lamps and candles of departed men.
The misty stars thy crown, the night thy dress,
Most peerless magical thou dost possess
My heart, and old days come to life again;
Old mornings dawn, or darkened evenings bring
The same old twilight noises from the town.
Thou hast the very core of longing and delight,
To thee my spirit dances oft in sleep
Along thy great grey streets, or down
A little lamplit alley-way at night –
Thinking no more of other cities it has known,
Forgetting for a while the tree-girt keep,
And town of dreams, where men no longer sing.
For thy heart knows, and thou shedst many tears
For all the sorrow of these evil years.
Thy thousand pinnacles and fretted spires
Are lit with echoes and the lambent fires
Of many companies of bells that ring
Rousing pale visions of majestic days
The windy years have strewn down distant ways;
And in thy halls still doth thy spirit sing
Songs of old memory amid thy present tears,
Or hope of days to come half-sad with many fears.
Lo! though along thy paths no laughter runs
While war untimely takes thy many sons,
No tide of evil can thy glory drown
Robed in sad majesty, the stars thy crown.

★

In addition, there are two texts in which a part of *The City of Present Sorrow* is treated as a separate entity. This begins with 'O agéd city of an all too brief sojourn', and is briefer: after the line 'Thinking no more of other cities it has known' it ends:

> Forgetting for a while that all men weep
> It strays there happy and to thee it sings
> 'No tide of evil can thy glory drown,
> Robed in sad majesty, the stars thy crown!'

This was first called *The Sorrowful City*, but the title was then changed to *Winsele wéste, windge reste réte berofene* (*Beowulf* lines 2456–7, very slightly adapted: 'the hall of feasting empty, the resting places swept by the wind, robbed of laughter').

There are also two manuscripts in which *The Town of Dreams* is treated as a separate poem, with a subtitle *An old town revisited*; in one of these the primary title was later changed to *The Town of Dead Days*.

Lastly, there is a poem in two parts called *The Song of Eriol*. This is found in three manuscripts, the later ones incorporating minor changes made to the predecessor (but the third has only the second part of the poem).

### The Song of Eriol

Eriol made a song in the Room of the Tale-fire telling how his feet were set to wandering, so that in the end he found the Lonely Isle and that fairest town Kortirion.

I

> In unknown days my fathers' sires
> Came, and from son to son took root
> Among the orchards and the river-meads
> And the long grasses of the fragrant plain:
>
> Many a summer saw they kindle yellow fires
> Of flaglilies among the bowing reeds,
> And many a sea of blossom turn to golden fruit
> In walléd gardens of the great champain.
>
> There daffodils among the ordered trees
> Did nod in spring, and men laughed deep and long
> Singing as they laboured happy lays
> And lighting even with a drinking-song.

There sleep came easy for the drone of bees
Thronging about cottage gardens heaped with flowers;
In love of sunlit goodliness of days
There richly flowed their lives in settled hours –
    But that was long ago,
    And now no more they sing, nor reap, nor sow;
    And I perforce in many a town about this isle
    Unsettled wanderer have dwelt awhile.

2

Wars of great kings and clash of armouries,
Whose swords no man could tell, whose spears
Were numerous as a wheatfield's ears,
Rolled over all the Great Lands; and the Seas

Were loud with navies; their devouring fires
Behind the armies burned both fields and towns;
And sacked and crumbled or to flaming pyres
Were cities made, where treasuries and crowns,

Kings and their folk, their wives and tender maids
Were all consumed. Now silent are those courts,
Ruined the towers, whose old shape slowly fades,
And no feet pass beneath their broken ports.

★

There fell my father on a field of blood,
And in a hungry siege my mother died,
And I, a captive, heard the great seas' flood
Calling and calling, that my spirit cried

For the dark western shores whence long ago had come
Sires of my mother, and I broke my bonds,
Faring o'er wasted valleys and dead lands
Until my feet were moistened by the western sea,
Until my ears were deafened by the hum,
The splash, and roaring of the western sea –
    But that was long ago
    And now the dark bays and unknown waves I know,
    The twilight capes, the misty archipelago,
    And all the perilous sounds and salt wastes 'tween this isle
    Of magic and the coasts I knew awhile.

★

One of the manuscripts of *The Song of Eriol* bears a later note: 'Easington 1917–18' (Easington on the estuary of the Humber, see Humphrey Carpenter, *Biography*, p. 97). It may be that the second part of *The Song of Eriol* was written at Easington and added to the first part (formerly the *Prelude*) already in existence.

Little can be derived from this poem of a strictly narrative nature, save the lineaments of the same tale: Eriol's father fell 'on a field of blood', when 'wars of great kings . . . rolled over all the Great Lands', and his mother died 'in a hungry siege' (the same phrase is used in the *Link* to the *Tale of Tinúviel*, pp. 5–6); he himself was made a captive, but escaped, and came at last to the shores of the Western Sea (whence his mother's people had come).

The fact that the first part of *The Song of Eriol* is also found as the Prelude to a poem of which the subjects are Warwick and Oxford might make one suspect that the castle with a great tower overhanging a river in the story told by Eriol to Vëannë was once again Warwick. But I do not think that this is so. There remains in any case the objection that it would be difficult to accommodate the attack on it by men out of the Mountains of the East which the duke could see from his tower; but also I think it is plain that the original tripartite poem had been dissevered, and the *Prelude* given a new bearing: my father's 'fathers' sires' became Eriol's 'fathers' sires'. At the same time, certain powerful images were at once dominant and fluid, and the great tower of Eriol's home was indeed to become the tower of Kortirion or Warwick, when (as will be seen shortly) the structure of the story of the mariner was radically changed. And nothing could show more clearly than does the evolution of this poem the complex root from which the story rose.

Humphrey Carpenter, writing in his *Biography* of my father's life after he returned to Oxford in 1925, says (p. 169):

> He made numerous revisions and recastings of the principal stories in the cycle, deciding to abandon the original sea-voyager 'Eriol' to whom the stories were told, and instead renaming him 'Ælfwine' or 'elf-friend'.

That *Eriol* was (for a time) displaced by *Ælfwine* is certain. But while it may well be that at the time of the texts now to be considered the name *Eriol* had actually been rejected, in the first version of 'The Silmarillion' proper, written in 1926, *Eriol* reappears, while in the earliest *Annals of Valinor*, written in the 1930s, it is said that they were translated in Tol Eressëa 'by Eriol of Leithien, that is Ælfwine of the Angelcynn'. On the other hand, at this earlier period it seems entirely justifiable on the evidence to treat the two names as indicative of different narrative projections – 'the *Eriol* story' and 'the *Ælfwine* story'.

'Ælfwine', then, is associated with a new conception, *subsequent to* the writing of the *Lost Tales*. The mariner is Ælfwine, not Eriol, in the second 'Scheme' for the *Tales*, which I have called 'an unrealised project for the revision of the whole work' (see I.234). The essential difference may be made clear now, before citing the difficult evidence: *Tol Eressëa is now in no way identified with England*, and the story of the drawing back of the Lonely Island across the sea has been abandoned. England is indeed still at the heart of this later conception, and is named *Luthany*.[14] The mariner, Ælfwine, is an Englishman sailing westward from the coast of Britain; and his role is diminished. For whereas in the writings studied thus far he comes to Tol Eressëa *before* the dénouement and disaster of the Faring Forth, and either he himself or his descendants witness the devastation of Tol Eressëa by the invasion of Men and their evil allies (in one line of development he was even to be responsible for it, p. 294), in the later narrative outlines he does not arrive until all the grievous history is done. His part is only to learn and to record.[15]

I turn now to a number of short and very oblique passages, written on separate slips, but found together and clearly dating from much the same time.

(15)   Ælfwine of England dwelt in the South-west; he was of the kin of Ing, King of Luthany. His mother and father were slain by the sea-pirates and he was made captive.

He had always loved the fairies: his father had told him many things (of the tradition of Ing). He escapes. He beats about the northern and western waters. He meets the Ancient Mariner – and seeks for Tol Eressëa (*seo unwemmede íeg*), whither most of the unfaded Elves have retired from the noise, war, and clamour of Men.

The Elves greet him, and the more so when they learn of him who he is. They call him *Lúthien* the man of Luthany. He finds his own tongue, the ancient English tongue, is spoken in the isle.

The 'Ancient Mariner' has appeared in the story that Eriol told to Vëannë (pp. 5, 7), and much more will be told of him subsequently.

(16)   Ælfwine of Englaland, [*added later*: driven by the Normans,] arrives in Tol Eressëa, whither most of the fading Elves have withdrawn from the world, and there fade now no more.

Description of the harbour of the southern shore. The fairies greet him well hearing he is from Englaland. He is surprised to hear them speak the speech of Ælfred of Wessex, though to one another they spoke a sweet and unknown tongue.

The Elves name him Lúthien for he is come from Luthany, as they call it ('friend' and 'friendship'). Eldaros or Ælfhâm. He is sped to Rôs their capital. There he finds the Cottage of Lost Play, and Lindo and Vairë.

He tells who he is and whence, and why he has long sought for the isle (by reason of traditions in the kin of Ing), and he begs the Elves to come back to Englaland.

Here begins (as an explanation of why they cannot) the series of stories called the Book of Lost Tales.

In this passage (16) Ælfwine becomes more firmly rooted in English history: he is apparently a man of eleventh-century Wessex – but as in (15) he is of 'the kin of Ing'. The capital of the Elves of Tol Eressëa is not Kortirion but Rôs, a name now used in a quite different application from that in citation (5), where it was a promontory of the Great Lands.

I have been unable to find any trace of the process whereby the name *Lúthien* came to be so differently applied afterwards (*Lúthien Tinúviel*). Another note of this period explains the name quite otherwise: 'Lúthien or Lúsion was son of Telumaith (Telumektar). Ælfwine loved the sign of Orion, and made the sign, hence the fairies called him Lúthien (Wanderer).' There is no other mention of Ælfwine's peculiar association with Orion nor of this interpretation of the name Lúthien; and this seems to be a development that my father did not pursue.

It is convenient to give here the opening passage from the second Scheme for the *Lost Tales*, referred to above; this plainly belongs to the same time as the rest of these 'Ælfwine' notes, when the *Tales* had been written so far as they ever went within their first framework.

(17)   Ælfwine awakens upon a sandy beach. He listens to the sea, which is far out. The tide is low and has left him.

Ælfwine meets the Elves of Rôs; finds they speak the speech of the English, beside their own sweet tongue. Why they do so – the dwelling of Elves in Luthany and their faring thence and back. They clothe him and feed him, and he sets forth to walk along the island's flowery ways.

The scheme goes on to say that on a summer evening Ælfwine came to Kortirion, and thus differs from (16), where he goes to 'Rôs their capital', in which he finds the Cottage of Lost Play. The name Rôs seems to be used here in yet another sense – possibly a name for Tol Eressëa.

(18)   He is sped to Ælfhâm (Elfhome) Eldos where Lindo and Vairë tell him many things: of the making and ancient fashion of the world: of the Gods: of the Elves of Valinor: of Lost Elves and Men: of the Travail of the Gnomes: of Eärendel: of the Faring Forth and the Loss of Valinor: of the disaster of the Faring Forth and the war with evil Men. The retreat to Luthany where Ingwë was king.

Of the home-thirst of the Elves and how the greater number
sought back to Valinor. The loss of Elwing. How a new home was
made by the Solosimpi and others in Tol Eressëa. How the Elves
continually sadly leave the world and fare thither.

For the interpretation of this passage it is essential to realise (the key
indeed to the understanding of this projected history) that 'the Faring
Forth' does *not* here refer to the Faring Forth in the sense in which it has
been used hitherto – that from Tol Eressëa for the Rekindling of the
Magic Sun, which ended in ruin, but to the March of the Elves of Kôr
and the 'Loss of Valinor' that the March incurred (see pp. 253, 257,
280). It is not indeed clear why it is here called a 'disaster': but this is
evidently to be associated with 'the war with evil Men', and war between
Elves and Men at the time of the March from Kôr is referred to in
citations (1) and (3).

In 'the *Eriol* story' it is explicit that after the March from Kôr the Elves
departed from the Great Lands to Tol Eressëa; here on the other hand
'the war with evil Men' is followed by 'the retreat to Luthany where
Ingwë was king'. The (partial) departure to Tol Eressëa is from Luthany;
the loss of Elwing seems to take place on one of these voyages. As will be
seen, the 'Faring Forth' of 'the *Eriol* story' has disappeared as an event of
Elvish history, and is only mentioned as a prophecy and a hope.

Schematically the essential divergence of the two narrative structures
can be shown thus:

| (*Eriol* story) | (*Ælfwine* story) |
| --- | --- |
| March of the Elves of Kôr to the Great Lands | March of the Elves of Kôr to the Great Lands (called 'the Faring Forth') |
| War with Men in the Great Lands | War with Men in the Great Lands |
| Retreat of the Elves to Tol Eressëa (loss of Elwing) | Retreat of the Elves to Luthany (> England) ruled by Ingwë |
| | Departure of many Elves to Tol Eressëa (loss of Elwing) |
| Eriol sails from the East (North Sea region) to Tol Eressëa | Ælfwine sails from England to Tol Eressëa |
| The Faring Forth, drawing of Tol Eressëa to the Great Lands; ultimately Tol Eressëa > England | |

This is of course by no means a full statement of the *Ælfwine* story, and is
merely set out to indicate the radical difference of structure. Lacking
from it is the history of Luthany, which emerges from the passages that
now follow.

**(19)**  *Luthany* means 'friendship', *Lúthien* 'friend'. Luthany the only land where Men and Elves once dwelt an age in peace and love.

How for a while after the coming of the sons of Ing the Elves throve again and ceased to fare away to Tol Eressëa.

How Old English became the sole mortal language which an Elf will speak to a mortal that knows no Elfin.

**(20)**  Ælfwine of England (whose father and mother were slain by the fierce Men of the Sea who knew not the Elves) was a great lover of the Elves, especially of the shoreland Elves that lingered in the land. He seeks for Tol Eressëa whither the fairies are said to have retired.

He reaches it. The fairies call him Lúthien. He learns of the making of the world, . . . . . . . of Gods and Elves, of Elves and Men, down to the departure to Tol Eressëa.

How the Faring Forth came to nought, and the fairies took refuge in Albion or Luthany (the Isle of Friendship).

Seven invasions.

Of the coming of Men to Luthany, how each race quarrelled, and the fairies faded, until [?the most] set sail, after the coming of the Rúmhoth, for the West. Why the Men of the seventh invasion, the Ingwaiwar, are more friendly.

Ingwë and Eärendel who dwelt in Luthany before it was an isle and was [*sic*] driven east by Ossë to found the Ingwaiwar.

**(21)**  All the descendants of Ing were well disposed to Elves; hence the remaining Elves of Luthany spoke to [?them] in the ancient tongue of the English, and since some have fared . . . . . to Tol Eressëa that tongue is there understood, and all who wish to speak to the Elves, if they know not and have no means of learning Elfin speeches, must converse in the ancient tongue of the English.

In (20) the term 'Faring Forth' must again be used as it is in (18), of the March from Kôr. There it was called a 'disaster' (see p. 303), and here it is said that it 'came to nought': it must be admitted that it is hard to see how that can be said, if it led to the binding of Melko and the release of the enslaved Noldoli (see (1) and (3)).

Also in (20) is the first appearance of the idea of the Seven Invasions of Luthany. One of these was that of the Rúmhoth (mentioned also in (14)) or Romans; and the seventh was that of the Ingwaiwar, who were not hostile to the Elves.

Here something must be said of the name *Ing* (*Ingwë*, *Ingwaiar*) in these passages. As with the introduction of Hengest and Horsa, the association of the mythology with ancient English legend is manifest. But it would serve no purpose, I believe, to enter here into the obscure and speculative scholarship of English and Scandinavian origins: the

Roman writers' term *Inguaeones* for the Baltic maritime peoples from whom the English came; the name *Ingwine* (interpretable either as *Ing-wine* 'the friends of Ing' or as containing the same *Ingw-* seen in *Inguaeones*); or the mysterious personage *Ing* who appears in the Old English *Runic Poem*:

> Ing wæs ærest   mid East-Denum
> gesewen secgum   oþ he siþþan east
> ofer wæg gewat;   wæn æfter ran

– which may be translated: 'Ing was first seen by men among the East Danes, until he departed eastwards over the waves; his car sped after him.' It would serve no purpose, because although the connection of my father's *Ing*, *Ingwë* with the shadowy *Ing* (*Ingw-*) of northern historical legend is certain and indeed obvious he seems to have been intending no more than an *association* of his mythology with known traditions (though the words of the *Runic Poem* were clearly influential). The matter is made particularly obscure by the fact that in these notes the names *Ing* and *Ingwë* intertwine with each other, but are never expressly differentiated or identified.

Thus Ælfwine was 'of the kin of Ing, King of Luthany' (15, 16), but the Elves retreated 'to Luthany where Ingwë was king' (18). The Elves of Luthany throve again 'after the coming of the sons of Ing' (19), and the Ingwaiwar, seventh of the invaders of Luthany, were more friendly to the Elves (20), while Ingwë 'founded' the Ingwaiwar (20). This name is certainly to be equated with Inguaeones (see above), and the invasion of the Ingwaiwar (or 'sons of Ing') equally certainly represents the 'Anglo-Saxon' invasion of Britain. Can *Ing*, *Ingwë* be equated? So far as this present material is concerned, I hardly see how they can not be. Whether this ancestor-founder is to be equated with *Inwë* (whose son was *Ingil*) of the *Lost Tales* is another question. It is hard to believe that there is no connection (especially since *Inwë* in *The Cottage of Lost Play* is emended from *Ing*, I.22), yet it is equally difficult to see what that connection could be, since Inwë of the *Lost Tales* is an Elda of Kôr (Ingwë Lord of the Vanyar in *The Silmarillion*) while Ing(wë) of 'the *Ælfwine* story' is a Man, the King of Luthany and Ælfwine's ancestor. (In outlines for *Gilfanon's Tale* it is said that Ing King of Luthany was descended from Ermon, or from Ermon and Elmir (the first Men, I.236–7).)

The following outlines tell some more concerning Ing(wë) and the Ingwaiwar:

(22)   How Ing sailed away at eld [i.e. in old age] into the twilight, and Men say he came to the Gods, but he dwells on Tol Eressëa, and will guide the fairies one day back to Luthany when the Faring Forth takes place.*

* The term 'Faring Forth' is used here in a prophetic sense, not as it is in (18) and (20).

How he prophesied that his kin should fare back again and possess Luthany until the days of the coming of the Elves.

How the land of Luthany was seven times invaded by Men, until at the seventh the children of the children of Ing came back to their own.

How at each new war and invasion the Elves faded, and each loved the Elves less, until the Rúmhoth came – and they did not even believe they existed, and the Elves all fled, so that save for a few the isle was empty of the Elves for three hundred years.

(23)    How Ingwë drank *limpë* at the hands of the Elves and reigned ages in Luthany.

How Eärendel came to Luthany to find the Elves gone.

How Ingwë aided him, but was not suffered to go with him. Eärendel blessed all his progeny as the mightiest sea-rovers of the world.[16]

How Ossë made war upon Ingwë because of Eärendel, and Ing longing for the Elves set sail, and all were wrecked after being driven far east.

How Ing the immortal came among the Dani OroDáni Urdainoth East Danes.

How he became the half-divine king of the Ingwaiwar, and taught them many things of Elves and Gods, so that some true knowledge of the Gods and Elves lingered in that folk alone.

Part of another outline that does not belong with the foregoing passages but covers the same part of the narrative as (23) may be given here:

(24)    Eärendel takes refuge with [Ingwë] from the wrath of Ossë, and gives him a draught of *limpë* (enough to assure immortality). He gives him news of the Elves and the dwelling on Tol Eressëa.

Ingwë and a host of his folk set sail to find Tol Eressëa, but Ossë blows them back east. They are utterly wrecked. Only Ingwë rescued on a raft. He becomes king of the Angali, Euti, Saksani, and Firisandi,* who adopt the title of Ingwaiwar. He teaches them much magic and first sets men's hearts to seafaring westward. . . . . .

After a great [?age of rule] Ingwë sets sail in a little boat and is heard of no more.

It is clear that the intrusion of Luthany, and Ing(wë), into the conception has caused a movement in the story of Eärendel: whereas in the older version he went to Tol Eressëa after the departure of the Eldar and Noldoli from the Great Lands (pp. 253, 255), now he goes to

---

* Angles, Saxons, Jutes, and Frisians.

Luthany; and the idea of Ossë's enmity towards Eärendel (pp. 254, 263) is retained but brought into association with the origin of the Ingwaiwar.

It is clear that the narrative structure is:

- Ing(wë) King of Luthany.
- Eärendel seeks refuge with him (after [many of] the Elves have departed to Tol Eressëa).
- Ing(wë) seeks Tol Eressëa but is driven into the East.
- Seven invasions of Luthany.
- The people of Ing(wë) are the Ingwaiwar, and they 'come back to their own' when they invade Luthany from across the North Sea.

(25)    Luthany was where the tribes first embarked in the Lonely Isle for Valinor, and whence they landed for the Faring Forth,* whence [also] many sailed with Elwing to find Tol Eressëa.

That Luthany was where the Elves, at the end of the great journey from Palisor, embarked on the Lonely Isle for the Ferrying to Valinor, is probably to be connected with the statement in (20) that 'Ingwë and Eärendel dwelt in Luthany before it was an isle'.

(26)    There are other references to the channel separating Luthany from the Great Lands: in rough jottings in notebook C there is mention of an isthmus being cut by the Elves, 'fearing Men now that Ingwë has gone', and 'to the white cliffs where the silver spades of the Teleri worked'; also in the next citation.

(27)    The Elves tell Ælfwine of the ancient manner of Luthany, of Kortirion or Gwarthyryn (Caer Gwâr),[17] of Tavrobel.
        How the fairies dwelt there a hundred ages before Men had the skill to build boats to cross the channel – so that magic lingers yet mightily in its woods and hills.
        How they renamed many a place in Tol Eressëa after their home in Luthany. Of the Second Faring Forth and the fairies' hope to reign in Luthany and replant there the magic trees – and it depends most on the temper of the Men of Luthany (since they first must come there) whether all goes well.

Notable here is the reference to 'the Second Faring Forth', which strongly supports my interpretation of the expression 'Faring Forth' in (18), (20), and (25); but the prophecy or hope of the Elves concerning

_____

* In the sense of the March of the Elves from Kôr, as in (18) and (20).

the Faring Forth has been greatly changed from its nature in citation (6):
here, the Trees are to be replanted in Luthany.

(28)   How Ælfwine lands in Tol Eressëa and it seems to him like his own
       land made . . . . . . . clad in the beauty of a happy dream. How the
       folk comprehended [his speech] and learn whence he is come by
       the favour of Ulmo. How he is sped to Kortirion.

With these two passages it is interesting to compare (9), the prose preface
to *Kortirion among the Trees*, according to which Kortirion was a city
built by the Elves in Tol Eressëa; and when Tol Eressëa was brought
across the sea, becoming England, Kortirion was renamed in the tongue
of the English *Warwick* (13). In the new story, Kortirion is likewise an
ancient dwelling of the Elves, but with the change in the fundamental
conception it is in Luthany; and the Kortirion to which Ælfwine comes
in Tol Eressëa is the second of the name (being called 'after their home in
Luthany'). There has thus been a very curious transference, which may
be rendered schematically thus:

(I)    Kortirion, Elvish dwelling in Tol Eressëa.
       Tol Eressëa ———→ England.
       Kortirion = Warwick.

(II)   Kortirion, Elvish dwelling in Luthany (> England).
       Elves ———→ Tol Eressëa.
       Kortirion (2) in Tol Eressëa named after Kortirion (1)
       in Luthany.

On the basis of the foregoing passages, (15) to (28), we may attempt to
construct a narrative taking account of all the essential features:

– March of the Elves of Kôr (called 'the Faring Forth', or (by implica-
  tion in 27) 'the First Faring Forth') into the Great Lands, landing in
  Luthany (25), and the Loss of Valinor (18).
– War with evil Men in the Great Lands (18).
– The Elves retreated to Luthany (not yet an island) where Ing(wë)
  was king (18, 20).
– Many [but by no means all] of the Elves of Luthany sought back
  over the sea and settled in Tol Eressëa; but Elwing was lost (18, 25).
– Places in Tol Eressëa were named after places in Luthany (27).
– Eärendel came to Luthany, taking refuge with Ing(wë) from the
  hostility of Ossë (20, 23, 24).
– Eärendel gave Ing(wë) *limpë* to drink (24), *or* Ing(wë) received
  *limpë* from the Elves before Eärendel came (23).

- Eärendel blessed the progeny of Ing(wë) before his departure (23).

- Ossë's hostility to Eärendel pursued Ing(wë) also (23, 24).

- Ing(wë) set sail (with many of his people, 24) to find Tol Eressëa (23, 24).

- Ing(wë)'s voyage, through the enmity of Ossë, ended in shipwreck, but Ing(wë) survived, and far to the East [i.e. after being driven across the North Sea] he became King of the Ingwaiwar the ancestors of the Anglo-Saxon invaders of Britain (23, 24).

- Ing(wë) instructed the Ingwaiwar in true knowledge of the Gods and Elves (23) and turned their hearts to seafaring westwards (24). He prophesied that his kin should one day return again to Luthany (22).

- Ing(wë) at length departed in a boat (22, 24), and was heard of no more (24), or came to Tol Eressëa (22).

- After Ing(wë)'s departure from Luthany a channel was made so that Luthany became an isle (26); but Men crossed the channel in boats (27).

- Seven successive invasions took place, including that of the Rúmhoth or Romans, and at each new war more of the remaining Elves of Luthany fled over the sea (20, 22).

- The seventh invasion, that of the Ingwaiwar, was however not hostile to the Elves (20, 21); and these invaders were 'coming back to their own' (22), since they were the people of Ing(wë).

- The Elves of Luthany (now England) throve again and ceased to leave Luthany for Tol Eressëa (19), and they spoke to the Ingwaiwar in their own language, Old English (21).

- Ælfwine was an Englishman of the Anglo-Saxon period, a descendant of Ing(wë), who had derived a knowledge of and love of the Elves from the tradition of his family (15, 16).

- Ælfwine came to Tol Eressëa, found that Old English was spoken there, and was called by the Elves Lúthien 'friend', the Man of Luthany (the Isle of Friendship) (15, 16, 19).

I claim no more for this than that it seems to me to be the only way in which these *disjecta membra* can be set together into a comprehensive narrative scheme. It must be admitted even so that it requires some forcing of the evidence to secure apparent agreement. For example, there seem to be different views of the relation of the Ingwaiwar to Ing(wë): they are 'the sons of Ing' (19), 'his kin' (22), 'the children of the children of Ing' (22), yet he seems to have become the king and teacher of North Sea peoples who had no connection with Luthany or the Elves (23, 24). (Over whom did he rule when the Elves first retreated to Luthany (18, 23)?) Again, it is very difficult to fit the 'hundred ages' during which the

Elves dwelt in Luthany before the invasions of Men began (27) to the rest of the scheme. Doubtless in these jottings my father was thinking with his pen, exploring independent narrative paths; one gets the impression of a ferment of ideas and possibilities rapidly displacing one another, from which no one stable narrative core can be extracted. A complete 'solution' is therefore in all probability an unreal aim, and this reconstruction no doubt as artificial as that attempted earlier for 'the *Eriol* story' (see p. 293). But here as there I believe that this outline shows as well as can be the direction of my father's thought at that time.

There is very little to indicate the further course of 'the *Ælfwine* story' after his sojourn in Tol Eressëa (as I have remarked, p. 301, the part of the mariner is only to learn and record tales out of the past); and virtually all that can be learned from these notes is found on a slip that reads:

(29)    How Ælfwine drank of *limpë* but thirsted for his home, and went back to Luthany; and thirsted then unquenchably for the Elves, and went back to Tavrobel the Old and dwelt in the House of the Hundred Chimneys (where grows still the child of the child of the Pine of Belawryn) and wrote the Golden Book.

Associated with this is a title-page:

(30)                  The Book of Lost Tales
              and the History of the Elves of Luthany
                          [?being]
                 The Golden Book of Tavrobel
the same that Ælfwine wrote and laid in the House of a Hundred Chimneys at Tavrobel, where it lieth still to read for such as may.

These are very curious. Tavrobel the Old must be the original Tavrobel in Luthany (after which Tavrobel in Tol Eressëa was named, just as Kortirion in Tol Eressëa was named after Kortirion = Warwick in Luthany); and the House of the Hundred Chimneys (as also the Pine of Belawryn, on which see p. 281 and note 4) was to be displaced from Tol Eressëa to Luthany. Presumably my father intended to rewrite those passages in the 'framework' of the *Lost Tales* where the House of a Hundred Chimneys in Tavrobel is referred to; unless there was to be another House of a Hundred Chimneys in Tavrobel the New in Tol Eressëa.

Lastly, an interesting entry in the Qenya dictionary may be mentioned here: *Parma Kuluinen* 'the Golden Book — the collected book of legends, especially of Ing and Eärendel'.

★

In the event, of all these projections my father only developed the story of Ælfwine's youth and his voyage to Tol Eressëa to a full and polished form, and to this work I now turn; but first it is convenient to collect the passages previously considered that bear on it.

In the opening *Link* to the *Tale of Tinúviel* Eriol said that 'many years agone', when he was a child, his home was 'in an old town of Men girt with a wall now crumbled and broken, and a river ran thereby over which a castle with a great tower hung'.

> My father came of a coastward folk, and the love of the sea that I had never seen was in my bones, and my father whetted my desire, for he told me tales that his father had told him before. Now my mother died in a cruel and hungry siege of that old town, and my father was slain in bitter fight about the walls, and in the end I Eriol escaped to the shoreland of the Western Sea.

Eriol told then of

> his wanderings about the western havens, . . . of how he was wrecked upon far western islands until at last upon one lonely one he came upon an ancient sailor who gave him shelter, and over a fire within his lonely cabin told him strange tales of things beyond the Western Seas, of the Magic Isles and that most lonely one that lay beyond. . . .
> 'Ever after,' said Eriol, 'did I sail more curiously about the western isles seeking more stories of the kind, and thus it is indeed that after many great voyages I came myself by the blessing of the Gods to Tol Eressëa in the end . . .'

In the typescript version of this *Link* it is further told that in the town where Eriol's parents lived and died

> there dwelt a mighty duke, and did he gaze from the topmost battlements never might he see the bounds of his wide domain, save where far to east the blue shapes of the great mountains lay – yet was that tower held the most lofty that stood in the lands of Men.

The siege and sack of the town were the work of 'the wild men from the Mountains of the East'.

At the end of the typescript version the boy Ausir assured Eriol that 'that ancient mariner beside the lonely sea was none other than Ulmo's self, who appeareth not seldom thus to those voyagers whom he loves'; but Eriol did not believe him.

I have given above (pp. 294–5) reasons for thinking that in 'the *Eriol* story' this tale of his youth was not set in England.

Turning to the passages concerned with the later, *Ælfwine* story, we learn from (15) that Ælfwine dwelt in the South-west of England and that his mother and father were slain by 'the sea-pirates', and from (20) that they were slain by 'the fierce Men of the Sea'; from (16) that he was 'driven by the Normans'. In (15) there is a mention of his meeting with 'the Ancient Mariner' during his voyages. In (16) he comes to 'the harbour of the southern shore' of Tol Eressëa; and in (17) he 'awakens upon a sandy beach' at low tide.

I come now to the narrative that finally emerged. It will be observed, perhaps with relief, that Ing, Ingwë, and the Ingwaiwar have totally disappeared.

## ÆLFWINE OF ENGLAND

There are three versions of this short work. One is a plot-outline of less than 500 words, which for convenience of reference I shall call *Ælfwine A*; but the second is a much more substantial narrative bearing the title *Ælfwine of England*. This was written in 1920 or later: demonstrably not earlier, for my father used for it scraps of paper pinned together, and some of these are letters to him, all dated in February 1920.[18] The third text no doubt began as a fair copy in ink of the second, to which it is indeed very close at first, but became as it proceeded a complete rewriting at several points, with the introduction of much new matter, and it was further emended after it had been completed. It bears no title in the manuscript, but must obviously be called *Ælfwine of England* likewise.

For convenience I shall refer to the first fully-written version as *Ælfwine I* and to its rewriting as *Ælfwine II*. The relation of *Ælfwine A* to these is hard to determine, since it agrees in some respects with the one and in some with the other. It is obvious that my father had *Ælfwine I* in front of him when he wrote *Ælfwine II*, but it seems likely that he drew on *Ælfwine A* at the same time.

I give here the full text of *Ælfwine II* in its final form, with all noteworthy emendations and all important differences from the other texts in the notes (differences in names, and changes to names, are listed separately).

There was a land called England, and it was an island of the West, and before it was broken in the warfare of the Gods it was westernmost of all the Northern lands, and looked upon the Great Sea that Men of old called Garsecg;[19] but that part that was broken was called Ireland and many names besides, and its dwellers come not into these tales.

All that land the Elves named Lúthien[20] and do so yet. In Lúthien alone dwelt still the most part of the Fading Companies, the Holy Fairies that have not yet sailed away from the world, beyond the horizon of Men's knowledge, to the Lonely Island, or even to the Hill of Tûn[21] upon the Bay of Faëry that washes the western shores of the kingdom of the Gods. Therefore is Lúthien even yet a holy land, and a magic that is not otherwise lingers still in many places of that isle.

Now amidmost of that island is there still a town that is aged among Men, but its age among the Elves is greater far; and, for this is a book of the Lost Tales of Elfinesse, it shall be named in their tongue Kortirion, which the Gnomes call Mindon Gwar.[22] Upon the hill of Gwar dwelt in the days of the English a man and his name was Déor, and he came thither from afar, from the south of the island and from the forests and from the enchanted West, where albeit he was of the English folk he had long time wandered. Now the Prince of Gwar was in those days a lover of songs and no enemy of the Elves, and they lingered yet most of all the isle in those regions about Kortirion (which places they called Alalminórë, the Land of Elms), and thither came Déor the singer to seek the Prince of Gwar and to seek the companies of the Fading Elves, for he was an Elf-friend. Though Déor was of English blood, it is told that he wedded to wife a maiden from the West, from Lionesse as some have named it since, or Evadrien 'Coast of Iron' as the Elves still say. Déor found her in the lost land beyond Belerion whence the Elves at times set sail.

Mirth had Déor long time in Mindon Gwar, but the Men of the North, whom the fairies of the island called Forodwaith, but whom Men called other names, came against Gwar in those days when they ravaged wellnigh all the land of Lúthien. Its walls availed not and its towers might not withstand them for ever, though the siege was long and bitter.

There Éadgifu (for so did Déor name the maiden of the West, though it was not her name aforetime)[23] died in those evil hungry days; but Déor fell before the walls even as he sang a song of ancient valour for the raising of men's hearts. That was a desperate sally, and the son of Déor was Ælfwine, and he was then but a boy left fatherless. The sack of that town thereafter was very cruel, and whispers of its ancient days alone remained, and the Elves that had grown to love the English of the isle fled or hid themselves for a long time, and none of Elves or Men were left in his old halls to lament the fall of Óswine Prince of Gwar.

Then Ælfwine, even he whom the unfaded Elves beyond the waters of Garsecg did after name Eldairon of Lúthien (which is

Ælfwine of England), was made a thrall to the fierce lords of the
Forodwaith, and his boyhood knew evil days. But behold a
wonder, for Ælfwine knew not and had never seen the sea, yet
he heard its great voice speaking deeply in his heart, and its
murmurous choirs sang ever in his secret ear between wake and
sleep, that he was filled with longing. This was of the magic of
Éadgifu, maiden of the West, his mother, and this longing
unquenchable had been hers all the days that she dwelt in the
quiet inland places among the elms of Mindon Gwar – and
amidmost of her longing was Ælfwine her child born, and the
Foamriders, the Elves of the Sea-marge, whom she had known
of old in Lionesse, sent messengers to his birth. But now
Éadgifu was gone beyond the Rim of Earth, and her fair form
lay unhonoured in Mindon Gwar, and Déor's harp was silent,
but Ælfwine laboured in thraldom until the threshold of manhood, dreaming dreams and filled with longing, and at rare
times holding converse with the hidden Elves.

At last his longing for the sea bit him so sorely that he
contrived to break his bonds, and daring great perils and suffering many grievous toils he escaped to lands where the Lords of
the Forodwaith had not come, far from the places of Déor's
abiding in Mindon Gwar. Ever he wandered southward and to
the west, for that way his feet unbidden led him. Now Ælfwine
had in a certain measure the gift of elfin-sight (which was not
given to all Men in those days of the fading of the Elves and still
less is it granted now), and the folk of Lúthien were less faded
too in those days, so that many a host of their fair companies he
saw upon his wandering road. Some there were dwelt yet and
danced yet about that land as of old, but many more there were
that wandered slowly and sadly westward; for behind them all
the land was full of burnings and of war, and its dwellings ran
with tears and with blood for the little love of Men for Men – nor
was that the last of the takings of Lúthien by Men from Men,
which have been seven, and others mayhap still shall be. Men of
the East and of the West and of the South and of the North have
coveted that land and dispossessed those who held it before
them, because of its beauty and goodliness and of the glamour
of the fading ages of the Elves that lingered still among its trees
beyond its high white shores.[24]

Yet at each taking of that isle have many more of the most
ancient of all dwellers therein, the folk of Lúthien, turned
westward; and they have got them in ships at Belerion in the

West and sailed thence away for ever over the horizon of Men's knowledge, leaving the island the poorer for their going and its leaves less green; yet still it abides the richest among Men in the presence of the Elves. And it is said that, save only when the fierce fathers of Men, foes of the Elves, being new come under the yoke of Evil,[25] entered first that land, never else did so great a concourse of elfin ships and white-winged galleons sail to the setting sun as in those days when the ancient Men of the South set first their mighty feet upon the soil of Lúthien – the Men whose lords sat in the city of power that Elves and Men have called Rûm (but the Elves alone do know as Magbar).[26]

Now is it the dull hearts of later days rather than the red deeds of cruel hands that set the minds of the little folk to fare away; and ever and anon a little ship[27] weighs anchor from Belerion at eve and its sweet sad song is lost for ever on the waves. Yet even in the days of Ælfwine there was many a laden ship under elfin sails that left those shores for ever, and many a comrade he had, seen or half-unseen, upon his westward road. And so he came at last to Belerion, and there he laved his weary feet in the grey waters of the Western Sea, whose great roaring drowned his ears. There the dim shapes of Elvish[28] boats sailed by him in the gloaming, and many aboard called to him farewell. But he might not embark on those frail craft, and they refused his prayer – for they were not willing that even one beloved among Men should pass with them beyond the edge of the West, or learn what lies far out on Garsecg the great and measureless sea. Now the men who dwelt thinly about those places nigh Belerion were fishermen, and Ælfwine abode long time amongst them, and being of nature shaped inly thereto he learned all that a man may of the craft of ships and of the sea. He recked little of his life, and he set his ocean-paths wider than most of those men, good mariners though they were; and there were few in the end who dared to go with him, save Ælfheah the fatherless who was with him in all ventures until his last voyage.[29]

Now on a time journeying far out into the open sea, being first becalmed in a thick mist, and after driven helpless by a mighty wind from the East, he espied some islands lying in the dawn, but he won not ever thereto for the winds changing swept him again far away, and only his strong fate saved him to see the black coasts of his abiding once again. Little content was he with his good fortune, and purposed in his heart to sail some time again yet further into the West, thinking unwitting it was

the Magic Isles of the songs of Men that he had seen from afar.
Few companions could he get for this adventure. Not all men
love to sail a quest for the red sun or to tempt the dangerous seas
in thirst for undiscovered things. Seven such found he in the
end, the greatest mariners that were then in England, and Ulmo
Lord of the Sea afterward took them to himself and their names
are now forgotten, save Ælfheah only.[30] A great storm fell upon
their ship even as they had sighted the isles of Ælfwine's desire,
and a great sea swept over her; but Ælfwine was lost in the
waves, and coming to himself saw no sign of ship or comrades,
and he lay upon a bed of sand in a deep-walled cove. Dark and
very empty was the isle, and he knew then that these were not
those Magic Isles of which he had heard often tell.[31]

There wandering long, 'tis said, he came upon many hulls of
wrecks rotting on the long gloomy beaches, and some were
wrecks of many mighty ships of old, and some were treasure-
laden. A lonely cabin looking westward he found at last upon
the further shore, and it was made of the upturned hull of a
small ship. An ancient man dwelt there, and Ælfwine feared
him, for the eyes of the man were as deep as the unfathomable
sea, and his long beard was blue and grey; great was his stature,
and his shoes were of stone,[32] but he was all clad in tangled rags,
sitting beside a small fire of drifted wood.

In that strange hut beside an empty sea did Ælfwine long
abide for lack of other shelter or of other counsel, thinking his
ship lost and his comrades drowned. But the ancient man grew
kindly toward him, and questioned Ælfwine concerning his
coming and his goings and whither he had desired to sail before
the storm took him. And many things before unheard did
Ælfwine hear tell of him beside that smoky fire at eve, and
strange tales of wind-harried ships and harbourless tempests in
the forbidden waters. Thus heard Ælfwine how the Magic Isles
were yet a great voyage before him keeping a dark and secret
ward upon the edge of Earth, beyond whom the waters of
Garsecg grow less troublous and there lies the twilight of the
latter days of Fairyland. Beyond and on the confines of the
Shadows lies the Lonely Island looking East to the Magic
Archipelago and to the lands of Men beyond it, and West into
the Shadows beyond which afar off is glimpsed the Outer Land,
the kingdom of the Gods — even the aged Bay of Faëry whose
glory has grown dim. Thence slopes the world steeply beyond
the Rim of Things to Valinor, that is God-home, and to the

Wall and to the edge of Nothingness whereon are sown the stars. But the Lonely Isle is neither of the Great Lands or of the Outer Land, and no isle lies near it.

In his tales that aged man named himself the Man of the Sea, and he spoke of his last voyage ere he was cast in wreck upon this outer isle, telling how ere the West wind took him he had glimpsed afar off bosomed in the deep the twinkling lanterns of the Lonely Isle. Then did Ælfwine's heart leap within him, but he said to that aged one that he might not hope to get him a brave ship or comrades more. But that Man of the Sea said: 'Lo, this is one of the ring of Harbourless Isles that draw all ships towards their hidden rocks and quaking sands, lest Men fare over far upon Garsecg and see things that are not for them to see. And these isles were set here at the Hiding of Valinor, and little wood for ship or raft does there grow on them, as may be thought;[33] but I may aid thee yet in thy desire to depart from these greedy shores.'

Thereafter on a day Ælfwine fared along the eastward strands gazing at the many unhappy wrecks there lying. He sought, as often he had done before, if he might see perchance any sign or relic of his good ship from Belerion. There had been that night a storm of great violence and dread, and lo! the number of wrecks was increased by one, and Ælfwine saw it had been a large and well-built ship of cunning lines such as the Forodwaith then loved. Cast far up on the treacherous sands it stood, and its great beak carven as a dragon's head still glared unbroken at the land. Then went the Man of the Sea out when the tide began to creep in slow and shallow over the long flats. He bore as a staff a timber great as a young tree, and he fared as if he had no need to fear tide or quicksand until he came far out where his shoulders were scarce above the yellow waters of the incoming flood to that carven prow, that now alone was seen above the water. Then Ælfwine marvelled watching from afar, to see him heave by his single strength the whole great ship up from the clutches of the sucking sand that gripped its sunken stern; and when it floated he thrust it before him, swimming now with mighty strokes in the deepening water. At that sight Ælfwine's fear of the aged one was renewed, and he wondered what manner of being he might be; but now the ship was thrust far up on the firmer sands, and the swimmer strode ashore, and his mighty beard was full of strands of sea-weed, and sea-weed was in his hair.

When that tide again forsook the Hungry Sands the Man of
the Sea bade Ælfwine go look at that new-come wreck, and
going he saw it was not hurt; but there were within nine dead
men who had not long ago been yet alive. They lay abottom
gazing at the sky, and behold, one whose garb and mien still
proclaimed a chieftain of Men lay there, but though his locks
were white with age and his face was pale in death, still a proud
man and a fierce he looked. 'Men of the North, Forodwaith, are
they,' said the Man of the Sea, 'but hunger and thirst was their
death, and their ship was flung by last night's storm where she
stuck in the Hungry Sands, slowly to be engulfed, had not fate
thought otherwise.'

'Truly do you say of them, O Man of the Sea; and him I know
well with those white locks, for he slew my father; and long was
I his thrall, and Orm men called him, and little did I love him.'

'And his ship shall it be that bears you from this Harbourless
Isle,' said he; 'and a gallant ship it was of a brave man, for few
folk have now so great a heart for the adventures of the sea as
have these Forodwaith, who press ever into the mists of the
West, though few live to take back tale of all they see.'

Thus it was that Ælfwine escaped beyond hope from that
island, but the Man of the Sea was his pilot and steersman, and
so they came after few days to a land but little known.[34] And the
folk that dwell there are a strange folk, and none know how they
came thither in the West, yet are they accounted among the
kindreds of Men, albeit their land is on the outer borders of the
regions of Mankind, lying yet further toward the Setting Sun
beyond the Harbourless Isles and further to the North than is
that isle whereon Ælfwine was cast away. Marvellously skilled
are these people in the building of ships and boats of every kind
and in the sailing of them; yet do they fare seldom or never to
the lands of other folk, and little do they busy themselves with
commerce or with war. Their ships they build for love of that
labour and for the joy they have only to ride the waves in them.
And a great part of that people are ever aboard their ships, and
all the water about the island of their home is ever white with
their sails in calm or storm. Their delight is to vie in rivalry with
one another with their boats of surpassing swiftness, driven by
the winds or by the ranks of their long-shafted oars. Other
rivalries have they with ships of great seaworthiness, for with
these will they contest who will weather the fiercest storms (and
these are fierce indeed about that isle, and it is iron-coasted save

for one cool harbour in the North). Thereby is the craft of their shipwrights proven; and these people are called by Men the Ythlings,[35] the Children of the Waves, but the Elves call the island Eneadur, and its folk the Shipmen of the West.[36]

Well did these receive Ælfwine and his pilot at the thronging quays of their harbour in the North, and it seemed to Ælfwine that the Man of the Sea was not unknown to them, and that they held him in the greatest awe and reverence, hearkening to his requests as though they were a king's commands. Yet greater was his amaze when he met amid the throngs of that place two of his comrades that he had thought lost in the sea; and learnt that those seven mariners of England were alive in that land, but the ship had been broken utterly on the black shores to the south, not long after the night when the great sea had taken Ælfwine overboard.

Now at the bidding of the Man of the Sea do those islanders with great speed fashion a new ship for Ælfwine and his fellows, since he would fare no further in Orm's ship; and its timbers were cut, as the ancient sailor had asked, from a grove of magic oaks far inland that grew about a high place of the Gods, sacred to Ulmo Lord of the Sea, and seldom were any of them felled. 'A ship that is wrought of this wood,' said the Man of the Sea, 'may be lost, but those that sail in it shall not in that voyage lose their lives; yet may they perhaps be cast where they little think to come.'

But when that ship was made ready that ancient sailor bid them climb aboard, and this they did, but with them went also Bior of the Ythlings, a man of mighty sea-craft for their aid, and one who above any of that strange folk was minded to sail at times far from the land of Eneadur to West or North or South. There stood many men of the Ythlings upon the shore beside that vessel; for they had builded her in a cove of the steep shore that looked to the West, and a bar of rock with but a narrow opening made here a sheltered pool and mooring place, and few like it were to be found in that island of sheer cliffs. Then the ancient one laid his hand upon her prow and spoke words of magic, giving her power to cleave uncloven waters and enter unentered harbours, and ride untrodden beaches. Twin rudder-paddles, one on either side, had she after the fashion of the Ythlings, and each of these he blessed, giving them skill to steer when the hands that held them failed, and to find lost courses, and to follow stars that were hid. Then he strode away,

and the press of men parted before him, until climbing he came
to a high pinnacle of the cliffs. Then leapt he far out and down
and vanished with a mighty flurry of foam where the great
breakers gathered to assault the towering shores.

Ælfwine saw him no more, and he said in grief and amaze:
'Why was he thus weary of life? My heart grieves that he is
dead,' but the Ythlings smiled, so that he questioned some that
stood nigh, saying: 'Who was that mighty man, for meseems ye
know him well,' and they answered him nothing. Then thrust
they forth that vessel valiant-timbered[37] out into the sea, for no
longer would Ælfwine abide, though the sun was sinking to the
Mountains of Valinor beyond the Western Walls. Soon was her
white sail seen far away filled with a wind from off the land, and
red-stained in the light of the half-sunken sun; and those aboard
her sang old songs of the English folk that faded on the sailless
waves of the Western Seas, and now no longer came any sound
of them to the watchers on the shore. Then night shut down and
none on Eneadur saw that strong ship ever more.[38]

So began those mariners that long and strange and perilous
voyage whose full tale has never yet been told. Nought of their
adventures in the archipelagoes of the West, and the wonders
and the dangers that they found in the Magic Isles and in seas
and sound unknown, are here to tell, but of the ending of their
voyage, how after a time of years sea-weary and sick of heart
they found a grey and cheerless day. Little wind was there, and
the clouds hung low overhead; while a grey rain fell, and nought
could any of them descry before their vessel's beak that moved
now slow and uncertain over the long dead waves. That day had
they trysted to be the last ere they turned their vessel homeward
(if they might), save only if some wonder should betide or any
sign of hope. For their heart was gone. Behind them lay the
Magic Isles where three of their number slept upon dim strands
in deadly sleep, and their heads were pillowed on white sand
and they were clad in foam, wrapped about in the agelong spells
- of Eglavain. Fruitless had been all their journeys since, for ever
the winds had cast them back without sight of the shores of the
Island of the Elves.[39] Then said Ælfheah[40] who held the helm:
'Now, O Ælfwine, is the trysted time! Let us do as the Gods and
their winds have long desired — cease from our heart-weary
quest for nothingness, a fable in the void, and get us back if the
Gods will it seeking the hearths of our home.' And Ælfwine

yielded. Then fell the wind and no breath came from East or West, and night came slowly over the sea.

Behold, at length a gentle breeze sprang up, and it came softly from the West; and even as they would fill their sails therewith for home, one of those shipmen on a sudden said: 'Nay, but this is a strange air, and full of scented memories,' and standing still they all breathed deep. The mists gave before that gentle wind, and a thin moon they might see riding in its tattered shreds, until behind it soon a thousand cool stars peered forth in the dark. 'The night-flowers are opening in Faëry,' said Ælfwine; 'and behold,' said Bior,[41] 'the Elves are kindling candles in their silver dusk,' and all looked whither his long hand pointed over their dark stern. Then none spoke for wonder and amaze, seeing deep in the gloaming of the West a blue shadow, and in the blue shadow many glittering lights, and ever more and more of them came twinkling out, until ten thousand points of flickering radiance were splintered far away as if a dust of the jewels self-luminous that Fëanor made were scattered on the lap of the Ocean.

'Then is that the Harbour of the Lights of Many Hues,' said Ælfheah, 'that many a little-heeded tale has told of in our homes.' Then saying no more they shot out their oars and swung about their ship in haste, and pulled towards the never-dying shore. Near had they come to abandoning it when hardly won. Little did they make of that long pull, as they thrust the water strongly by them, and the long night of Faërie held on, and the horned moon of Elfinesse rode over them.

Then came there music very gently over the waters and it was laden with unimagined longing, that Ælfwine and his comrades leant upon their oars and wept softly each for his heart's half-remembered hurts, and memory of fair things long lost, and each for the thirst that is in every child of Men for the flawless loveliness they seek and do not find. And one said: 'It is the harps that are thrumming, and the songs they are singing of fair things; and the windows that look upon the sea are full of light.' And another said: 'Their stringéd violins complain the ancient woes of the immortal folk of Earth, but there is a joy therein.' 'Ah me,' said Ælfwine, 'I hear the horns of the Fairies shimmering in magic woods – such music as I once dimly guessed long years ago beneath the elms of Mindon Gwar.'

And lo! as they spoke thus musing the moon hid himself, and the stars were clouded, and the mists of time veiled the shore, and nothing could they see and nought more hear, save the sound of the surf of the seas in the far-off pebbles of the Lonely Isle; and soon the wind blew even that faint rustle far away. But Ælfwine stood forward with wide-open eyes unspeaking, and suddenly with a great cry he sprang forward into the dark sea, and the waters that filled him were warm, and a kindly death it seemed enveloped him. Then it seemed to the others that they awakened at his voice as from a dream; but the wind now suddenly grown fierce filled all their sails, and they saw him never again, but were driven back with hearts all broken with regret and longing. Pale elfin boats awhile they would see beating home, maybe, to the Haven of Many Hues, and they hailed them; but only faint echoes afar off were borne to their ears, and none led them ever to the land of their desire; who after a great time wound back all the mazy clue of their long tangled ways, until they cast anchor at last in the haven of Belerion, aged and wayworn men. And the things they had seen and heard seemed after to them a mirage, and a phantasy, born of hunger and sea-spells, save only to Bior of Eneadur of the Ship-folk of the West.

Yet among the seed of these men has there been many a restless and wistful spirit thereafter, since they were dead and passed beyond the Rim of Earth without need of boat or sail. But never while life lasted did they leave their sea-faring, and their bodies are all covered by the sea.[42]

★

The narrative ends here. There is no trace of any further continuation, though it seems likely that *Ælfwine of England* was to be the beginning of a complete rewriting of the *Lost Tales*. It would be interesting to know for certain when *Ælfwine II* was written. The handwriting of the manuscript is certainly changed from that of the rest of the *Lost Tales*; yet I am inclined to think that it followed *Ælfwine I* at no great interval, and the first version is unlikely to be much later than 1920 (see p. 312).

At the end of *Ælfwine II* my father jotted down two suggestions: (1) that Ælfwine should be made 'an early pagan Englishman who fled to the West'; and (2) that 'the Isle of the Old Man' should be cut out and all should be shipwrecked on Eneadur, the Isle of the Ythlings. The latter would (astonishingly) have entailed the abandonment of the foundered ship, with the Man of the Sea thrusting it to shore on the incoming tide, and the dead Vikings 'lying abottom gazing at the sky'.

In this narrative – in which the 'magic' of the early Elves is most intensely conveyed, in the seamen's vision of the Lonely Isle beneath 'the horned moon of Elfinesse' – Ælfwine is still placed in the context of the figures of ancient English legend: his father is Déor the Minstrel. In the great Anglo-Saxon manuscript known as the Exeter Book there is a little poem of 42 lines to which the title of *Déor* is now given. It is an utterance of the minstrel Déor, who, as he tells, has lost his place and been supplanted in his lord's favour by another bard, named Heorrenda; in the body of the poem Déor draws examples from among the great misfortunes recounted in the heroic legends, and is comforted by them, concluding each allusion with the fixed refrain *þæs ofereode; þisses swa mæg*, which has been variously translated; my father held that it meant 'Time has passed since then, this too can pass'.[43]

From this poem came both Déor and Heorrenda. In 'the *Eriol* story' Heorrenda was Eriol's son born in Tol Eressëa of his wife Naimi (p. 290), and was associated with Hengest and Horsa in the conquest of the Lonely Isle (p. 291); his dwelling in England was at Tavrobel (p. 292). I do not think that my father's Déor the Minstrel of Kortirion and Heorrenda of Tavrobel can be linked more closely to the Anglo-Saxon poem than in the names alone – though he did not take the names at random. He was moved by the glimpsed tale (even if, in the words of one of the poem's editors, 'the autobiographical element is purely fictitious, serving only as a pretext for the enumeration of the heroic stories'); and when lecturing on *Beowulf* at Oxford he sometimes gave the unknown poet a name, calling him *Heorrenda*.

Nor, as I believe, can any more be made of the other Old English names in the narrative: Óswine prince of Gwar, Éadgifu, Ælfheah (though the names are doubtless in themselves 'significant': thus *Óswine* contains *ós* 'god' and *wine* 'friend', and *Éadgifu éad* 'blessedness' and *gifu* 'gift'). The Forodwaith are of course Viking invaders from Norway or Denmark; the name Orm of the dead ship's captain is well-known in Norse. But all this is a mise-en-scène that is historical only in its bearings, not in its structure.

The idea of the seven invasions of Lúthien (Luthany) remained (p. 314), and that of the fading and westward flight of the Elves (which indeed was never finally lost),[44] but whereas in the outlines the invasion of the Ingwaiwar (i.e. the Anglo-Saxons) was the seventh (see citations (20) and (22)), here the Viking invasions are portrayed as coming upon the English – 'nor was that the last of the takings of Lúthien by Men from Men' (p. 314), obviously a reference to the Normans.

There is much of interest in the 'geographical' references in the story. At the very beginning there is a curious statement about the breaking off of Ireland 'in the warfare of the Gods'. Seeing that 'the *Ælfwine* story' does not include the idea of the drawing back of Tol Eressëa eastwards across the sea, this must refer to something quite other than the story in (5), p. 283, where the Isle of Íverin was broken off when Ossë tried to wrench back Tol Eressëa. What this was I do not know; but it seems conceivable that this is the first trace or hint of the great cataclysm at the end of the Elder Days, when Beleriand was drowned. (I have found no trace of any connection between the harbour of *Belerion* and the region of *Beleriand*.)

Kortirion (Mindon Gwar) is in this tale of course 'Kortirion the Old', the original Elvish dwelling in Lúthien, after which Kortirion in Tol Eressëa was named (see pp. 308, 310); in the same way we must suppose that the name Alalminórë (p. 313) for the region about it ('Warwickshire') was given anew to the midmost region of Tol Eressëa.

Turning to the question of the islands and archipelagoes in the Great Sea, what is said in *Ælfwine of England* may first be compared with the passages of geographical description in *The Coming of the Valar* (I.68) and *The Coming of the Elves* (I.125), which are closely similar the one to the other. From these passages we learn that there are many lands and islands in the Great Sea before the Magic Isles are reached; beyond the Magic Isles is Tol Eressëa; and beyond Tol Eressëa are the Shadowy Seas, 'whereon there float the Twilit Isles', the first of the Outer Lands. Tol Eressëa itself 'is held neither of the Outer Lands or of the Great Lands' (I.125); it is far out in mid-ocean, and 'no land may be seen for many leagues' sail from its cliffs' (I.121). With this account *Ælfwine of England* agrees closely; but to it is added now the archipelago of the Harbourless Isles.

As I have noted before (I.137), this progression from East to West of Harbourless Isles, Magic Isles, the Lonely Isle, and then the Shadowy Seas in which were the Twilit Isles, was afterwards changed, and it is said in *The Silmarillion* (p. 102) that at the time of the Hiding of Valinor

the Enchanted Isles were set, and all the seas about them were filled with shadows and bewilderment. And these isles were strung as a net in the Shadowy Seas from the north to the south, before Tol Eressëa, the Lonely Isle, is reached by one sailing west. Hardly might any vessel pass between them, for in the dangerous sounds the waves sighed for ever upon dark rocks shrouded in mist. And in the twilight a great weariness came upon mariners and a loathing of the sea; but all that ever set foot upon the islands were there entrapped, and slept until the Change of the World.

As a conception, the Enchanted Isles are derived primarily from the old Magic Isles, set at the time of the Hiding of Valinor and described in that Tale (I.211): 'Ossë set them in a great ring about the western limits of the mighty sea, so that they guarded the Bay of Faëry', and

all such as stepped thereon came never thence again, but being woven in the nets of Oinen's hair the Lady of the Sea, and whelmed in agelong slumber that Lórien set there, lay upon the margin of the waves, as those do who being drowned are cast up once more by the movements

of the sea; yet rather did these hapless ones sleep unfathomably and
the dark waters laved their limbs . . .

Here three of Ælfwine's companions

> slept upon dim strands in deadly sleep, and their heads were pillowed
> on white sand and they were clad in foam, wrapped about in the
> agelong spells of Eglavain (p. 320).

(I do not know the meaning of the name *Eglavain*, but since it clearly
contains *Egla* (Gnomish, = *Elda*, see I.251) it perhaps meant
'Elfinesse'.) But the Enchanted Isles derive also perhaps from the Twilit
Isles, since the Enchanted Isles were likewise in twilight and were set in·
the Shadowy Seas (cf. I.224); and from the Harbourless Isles as well,
which, as Ælfwine was told by the Man of the Sea (p. 317), were set at the
time of the Hiding of Valinor – and indeed served the same purpose as
did the Magic Isles, though lying far further to the East.

Eneadur, the isle of the Ythlings (Old English ýð 'wave'), whose life
is so fully described in *Ælfwine of England*, seems never to have been
mentioned again. Is there in Eneadur and the Shipmen of the West
perhaps some faint foreshadowing of the early Númenóreans in their
cliff-girt isle?

The following passage (pp. 316–17) is not easy to interpret:

> Thence [i.e. from the Bay of Faëry] slopes the world steeply beyond
> the Rim of Things to Valinor, that is God-home, and to the Wall and
> to the edge of Nothingness whereon are sown the stars.

In the *Ambarkanta* or 'Shape of the World' of the 1930s a map of the
world shows the surface of the Outer Land sloping steeply westwards
from the Mountains of Valinor. Conceivably it is to this slope that my
father was referring here, and the Rim of Things is the great mountain-
wall; but this seems very improbable. There are also references in
*Ælfwine of England* to 'the Rim of Earth', beyond which the dead pass
(pp. 314, 322); and in an outline for the *Tale of Eärendel* (p. 260)
Tuor's boat 'dips over the world's rim'. More likely, I think, the
expression refers to the rim of the horizon ('the horizon of Men's
knowledge', p. 313).

The expression 'the sun was sinking to the Mountains of Valinor
beyond the Western Walls' (p. 320) I am at a loss to explain according to
what has been told in the *Lost Tales*. A possible, though scarcely
convincing, interpretation is that the sun was sinking towards Valinor,
*whence it would pass* 'beyond the Western Walls' (i.e. through the
Door of Night, see I.215–16).

Lastly, the suggestion (p. 313) is notable that the Elves sailing west from Lúthien might go beyond the Lonely Isle and reach even back to Valinor; on this matter see p. 280.

★

Before ending, there remains to discuss briefly a matter of a general nature that has many times been mentioned in the texts, and especially in these last chapters: that of the 'diminutiveness' of the Elves.

It is said several times in the *Lost Tales* that the Elves of the ancient days were of greater bodily stature than they afterwards became. Thus in *The Fall of Gondolin* (p. 159): 'The fathers of the fathers of Men were of less stature than Men now are, and the children of Elfinesse of greater growth'; in an outline for the abandoned tale of Gilfanon (I. 235) very similarly: 'Men were almost of a stature at first with Elves, the fairies being far greater and Men smaller than now'; and in citation (4) in the present chapter: 'Men and Elves were formerly of a size, though Men always larger.' Other passages suggest that the ancient Elves were of their nature of at any rate somewhat slighter build (see pp. 142, 220).

The diminishing in the stature of the Elves of later times is very explicitly related to the coming of Men. Thus in (4) above: 'Men spread and thrive, and the Elves of the Great Lands fade. As Men's stature grows theirs diminishes'; and in (5): 'ever as Men wax more powerful and numerous so the fairies fade and grow small and tenuous, filmy and transparent, but Men larger and more dense and gross. At last Men, or almost all, can no longer see the fairies.' The clearest picture that survives of the Elves when they have 'faded' altogether is given in the *Epilogue* (p. 289):

> Like strands of wind, like mystic half-transparencies, Gilfanon Lord of Tavrobel rides out tonight amid his folk, and hunts the elfin deer beneath the paling sky. A music of forgotten feet, a gleam of leaves, a sudden bending of the grass, and wistful voices murmuring on the bridge, and they are gone.

But according to the passages bearing on the later '*Ælfwine*' version, the Elves of Tol Eressëa who had left Luthany were unfaded, or had ceased to fade. Thus in (15): 'Tol Eressëa, whither most of the unfaded Elves have retired from the noise, war, and clamour of Men'; and (16): 'Tol Eressëa, whither most of the fading Elves have withdrawn from the world, and there fade now no more'; also in *Ælfwine of England* (p. 313): 'the unfaded Elves beyond the waters of Garsecg'.

On the other hand, when Eriol came to the Cottage of Lost Play the doorward said to him (I. 14):

> Small is the dwelling, but smaller still are they that dwell here – for all who enter must be very small indeed, or of their own good wish become as very little folk even as they stand upon the threshold.

I have commented earlier (I. 32) on the oddity of the idea that the Cottage and its inhabitants were peculiarly small, in an island entirely inhabited by Elves. But my father, if he had ever rewritten *The Cottage of Lost Play*, would doubtless have abandoned this; and it may well be that he was in any case turning away already at the time of *Ælfwine II* from the idea that the 'faded' Elves were diminutive, as is suggested by his rejection of the word 'little' in 'little folk', 'little ships' (see note 27).

Ultimately, of course, the Elves shed all associations and qualities that would be now commonly considered 'fairylike', and those who remained in the Great Lands in Ages of the world at this time unconceived were to grow greatly in stature and in power: there was nothing filmy or transparent about the heroic or majestic Eldar of the Third Age of Middle-earth. Long afterwards my father would write, in a wrathful comment on a 'pretty' or 'ladylike' pictorial rendering of Legolas:

> He was tall as a young tree, lithe, immensely strong, able swiftly to draw a great war-bow and shoot down a Nazgûl, endowed with the tremendous vitality of Elvish bodies, so hard and resistant to hurt that he went only in light shoes over rock or through snow, the most tireless of all the Fellowship.

★

This brings to an end my rendering and analysis of the early writings bearing on the story of the mariner who came to the Lonely Isle and learned there the true history of the Elves. I have shown, convincingly as I hope, the curious and complex way in which my father's vision of the significance of Tol Eressëa changed. When he jotted down the synopsis (10), the idea of the mariner's voyage to the Island of the Elves was of course already present; but he journeyed out of the East and the Lonely Isle of his seeking was – England (though not yet the land of the English and not yet lying in the seas where England lies). When later the entire concept was shifted, England, as 'Luthany' or 'Lúthien', remained preeminently the Elvish land; and Tol Eressëa, with its meads and coppices, its rooks' nests in the elm-trees of Alalminórë, seemed to the English mariner to be remade in the likeness of his own land, which the Elves had lost at the coming of Men: for it was indeed a re-embodiment of Elvish Luthany far over the sea.

All this was to fall away afterwards from the developing mythology; but Ælfwine left many marks on its pages before he too finally disappeared.

Much in this chapter is necessarily inconclusive and uncertain; but I believe that these very early notes and projections are rightly disinterred. Although, as 'plots', abandoned and doubtless forgotten, they bear witness to truths of my father's heart and mind that he never abandoned. But these notes were scribbled down in his youth, when for him Elvish magic 'lingered yet mightily in the woods and hills of Luthany'; in his old age all was gone West-over-sea, and an end was indeed come for the Eldar of story and of song.

## NOTES

1 On this statement about the stature of Elves and Men see pp. 326–7.

2 For the form *Taimonto* (*Taimondo*) see I. 268, entry *Telimektar*.

3 *Belaurin* is the Gnomish equivalent of *Palúrien* (see I. 264).

4 A side-note here suggests that perhaps the Pine should not be in Tol Eressëa. – For *Ilwë*, the middle air, that is 'blue and clear and flows among the stars', see I. 65, 73.

5 *Gil* = *Ingil*. At the first occurrence of *Ingil* in this passage the name was written *Ingil* (*Gil*), but (*Gil*) was struck out.

6 The word *Nautar* occurs in a rejected outline for the *Tale of the Nauglafring* (p. 136), where it is equated with *Nauglath* (Dwarves).

7 *Uin*: 'the mightiest and most ancient of whales', chief among those whales and fishes that drew the 'island-car' (afterwards Tol Eressëa) on which Ulmo ferried the Elves to Valinor (I. 118–20).

8 *Gongs*: these are evil beings obscurely related to Orcs: see I. 245 note 10, and the rejected outlines for the *Tale of the Nauglafring* given on pp. 136–7.

9 A large query is written against this passage.

10 The likeness of this name to *Dor Daedeloth* is striking, but that is the name of the realm of Morgoth in *The Silmarillion*, and is interpreted 'Land of the Shadow of Horror'; the old name (whose elements are *dai* 'sky' and *teloth* 'roof') has nothing in common with the later except its form.

11 Cf. *Kortirion among the Trees* (I. 34, 37, 41): *A wave of bowing grass*.

12 The origin of *Warwick* according to conventional etymology is uncertain. The element *wic*, extremely common in English place-names, meant essentially a dwelling or group of dwellings. The earliest recorded form of the name is *Wæring wic*, and *Wæring* has been thought to be an Old English word meaning a dam, a derivative from *wer*, Modern English *weir*: thus 'dwellings by the weir'.

13 Cf. the title-page given in citation (11): *Heorrenda of Hægwudu*. – No forms of the name of this Staffordshire village are actually recorded from before the Norman Conquest, but the Old English form was undoubtedly *hæg-wudu* 'enclosed wood' (cf. the *High Hay*, the great hedge that protected Buckland from the Old Forest in *The Lord of the Rings*).

14 The name Luthany, of a country, occurs five times in Francis

Thompson's poem *The Mistress of Vision*. As noted previously (I. 29) my father acquired the Collected Poems of Francis Thompson in 1913–14; and in that copy he made a marginal note against one of the verses that contains the name *Luthany* – though the note is not concerned with the name. But whence Thompson derived *Luthany* I have no idea. He himself described the poem as 'a fantasy' (Everard Meynell, *The Life of Francis Thompson*, 1913, p. 237).

This provides no more than the origin of the name as a series of sounds, as with *Kôr* from Rider Haggard's *She*,\* or *Rohan* and *Moria* mentioned in my father's letter of 1967 on this subject (*The Letters of J. R. R. Tolkien*, pp. 383–4), in which he said:

> This leads to the matter of 'external history': the actual way in which I came to light on or choose certain sequences of sound to use as names, *before* they were given a place inside the story. I think, as I said, this is unimportant: the labour involved in my setting out what I know and remember of the process, or in the guess-work of others, would be far greater than the worth of the results. The spoken forms would simply be mere audible forms, and when transferred to the prepared linguistic situation in my story would receive meaning and significance according to that situation, and to the nature of the story told. It would be entirely delusory to refer to the sources of the sound-combination to discover any meanings overt or hidden.

15  The position is complicated by the existence of some narrative outlines of extreme roughness and near-illegibility in which the mariner is named Ælfwine and yet essential elements of 'the *Eriol* story' are present. These I take to represent an intermediate stage. They are very obscure, and would require a great deal of space to present and discuss; therefore I pass them by.

16  Cf. p. 264 (xiv).

17  *Caer Gwâr*: see p. 292.

18  It may be mentioned here that when my father read *The Fall of Gondolin* to the Exeter College Essay Club in the spring of 1920 the mariner was still *Eriol*, as appears from the notes for his preliminary remarks on that occasion (see *Unfinished Tales* p. 5). He said here, very strangely, that 'Eriol lights by accident on the Lonely Island'.

19  *Garsecg* (pronounced *Garsedge*, and so written in *Ælfwine* A) was one of the many Old English names of the sea.

20  In *Ælfwine I* the land is likewise named *Lúthien*, not *Luthany*. In *Ælfwine* A, on the other hand, the same distinction is made as in the outlines: 'Ælfwine of England (whom the fairies after named

---

\* There is no external evidence for this, but it can hardly be doubted. In this case it might be thought that since the African Kôr was a city built on the top of a great mountain standing in isolation the relationship was more than purely 'phonetic'.

Lúthien (friend) of Luthany (friendship)).' − At this first occurrence (only) of *Lúthien* in *Ælfwine II* the form *Leithian* is
pencilled above, but *Lúthien* is not struck out. *The Lay of Leithian*
was afterwards the title of the long poem of Beren and Lúthien
Tinúviel.

21  The *Hill of Tûn*, i.e. the hill on which the city of Tûn was built: see
p. 292.

22  *Mindon Gwar*: see p. 291.

23  *Éadgifu*: in 'the *Eriol* story' this Old English name (see p. 323) was
given as an equivalent to Naimi, Eriol's wife whom he wedded in
Tol Eressëa (p. 290).

24  In *Ælfwine I* the text here reads: 'by reason of her beauty and
goodliness, even as that king of the Franks that was upon a time
most mighty among men hath said . . .' [*sic*]. In *Ælfwine II* the
manuscript in ink stops at 'high white shores', but after these words
my father pencilled in: 'even as that king of the Franks that was
in those days the mightiest of earthly kings hath said . . .' [*sic*]. The
only clue in *Ælfwine of England* to the period of Ælfwine's life is
the invasion of the Forodwaith (Vikings); the mighty king of the
Franks may therefore be Charlemagne, but I have been unable
to trace any such reference.

25  *Evil* is emended from *Melko. Ælfwine I* does not have the phrase.

26  *Ælfwine I* has: 'when the ancient Men of the South from
Micelgeard the Heartless Town set their mighty feet upon the soil
of Lúthien.' This text does not have the reference to Rûm and
Magbar. The name *Micelgeard* is struck through, but *Mickleyard*
is written at the head of the page. *Micelgeard* is Old English (and
*Mickleyard* a modernisation of this in spelling), though it does
not occur in extant Old English writings and is modelled on Old
Norse *Mikligarðr* (Constantinople). − The peculiar hostility of
the Romans to the Elves of Luthany is mentioned by implication in
citation (20), and their disbelief in their existence in (22).

27  The application, frequent in *Ælwine I*, of 'little' to the fairies
(Elves) of Lúthien and their ships was retained in *Ælfwine II* as
first written, but afterwards struck out. Here the word is twice
retained, perhaps unintentionally.

28  *Elvish* is a later emendation of *fairy*.

29  This sentence, from 'save Ælfheah . . .', was added later in
*Ælfwine II*; it is not in *Ælfwine I*. − The whole text to this point
in *Ælfwine I* and *II* is compressed into the following in *Ælfwine A*:

Ælfwine of England (whom the fairies after named Lúthien
(friend) of Luthany (friendship)) born of Déor and Éadgifu.
Their city burned and Déor slain and Éadgifu dies. Ælfwine a
thrall of the Winged Helms. He escapes to the Western Sea
and takes ship from Belerion and makes great voyages. He is

seeking for the islands of the West of which Éadgifu had told him
in his childhood.

30  *Ælfwine I* has here: 'But three men could he find as his com-
    panions; and Ossë took them unto him.' *Ossë* was emended to
    *Neorth*; and then the sentence was struck through and rewritten:
    'Such found he only three; and those three Neorth after took unto
    him and their names are not known.' Neorth = Ulmo; see note 39.

31  *Ælfwine A* reads: 'He espies some islands lying in the dawn but
    is swept thence by great winds. He returns hardly to Belerion. He
    gathers the seven greatest mariners of England; they sail in spring.
    They are wrecked upon the isles of Ælfwine's desire and find
    them desert and lonely and filled with gloomy whispering
    trees.' This is at variance with *Ælfwine I* and *II* where Ælfwine
    is cast on to the island alone; but agrees with *II* in giving Ælfwine
    seven companions, not three.

32  A clue that this was Ulmo: cf. *The Fall of Gondolin* (p. 155): 'he
    was shod with mighty shoes of stone.'

33  In *Ælfwine A* they were 'filled with gloomy whispering trees'
    (note 31).

34  From the point where the Man of the Sea said: 'Lo, this is one of the
    ring of Harbourless Isles . . .' (p. 317) to here (i.e. the whole episode
    of the foundered Viking ship and its captain Orm, slayer of
    Ælfwine's father) there is nothing corresponding in *Ælfwine I*,
    which has only: 'but that Man of the Sea aided him in building a
    little craft, and together, guided by the solitary mariner, they fared
    away and came to a land but little known.' For the narrative in
    *Ælfwine A* see note 39.

35  At one occurrence of the name *Ythlings* (Old English *ýð* 'wave')
    in Ælfwine I it is written *Ythlingas*, with the Old English plural
    ending.

36  *The Shipmen of the West*: emendation from *Eneathrim*.

37  Cf. in the passage of alliterative verse in my father's *On Translating
    Beowulf* (*The Monsters and the Critics and Other Essays*, 1983,
    p. 63): *then away thrust her to voyage gladly valiant-timbered*.

38  The whole section of the narrative concerning the island of the
    Ythlings is more briefly told in *Ælfwine I* (though, so far as it goes,
    in very much the same words) with several features of the later story
    absent (notably the cutting of timber in the grove sacred to Ulmo,
    and the blessing of the ship by the Man of the Sea). The only actual
    difference of structure, however, is that whereas in *Ælfwine II*
    Ælfwine finds again his seven companions in the land of the
    Ythlings, and sails west with them, together with Bior of the
    Ythlings, in *Ælfwine I* they were indeed drowned, and he got seven
    companions from among the Ythlings (among whom Bior is not
    named).

39    The plot-outline *Ælfwine A* tells the story from the point where
Ælfwine and his seven companions were cast on the Isle of the Man
of the Sea (thus differing from *Ælfwine I* and *II*, where he came
there alone) thus:

They wander about the island upon which they have been cast
and come upon many decaying wrecks − often of mighty ships,
some treasure-laden. They find a solitary cabin beside a lonely
sea, built of old ship-wood, where dwells a solitary and strange
old mariner of dread aspect. He tells them these are the Harbourless Isles whose enchanted rocks draw all ships thither, lest men
fare over far upon Garsedge [*see note 19*] − and they were
devised at the Hiding of Valinor. Here, he says, the trees are
magical. They learn many strange things about the western world
of him and their desire is whetted for adventure. He aids them to
cut holy trees in the island groves and to build a wonderful
vessel, and shows them how to provision it against a long voyage
(that water that drieth not save when heart fails, &c.). This he
blesses with a spell of adventure and discovery, and then dives
from a cliff-top. They suspect it was Neorth Lord of Waters.

They journey many years among strange western islands hearing often many strange reports − of the belt of Magic Isles which
few have passed; of the trackless sea beyond where the wind
bloweth almost always from the West; of the edge of the twilight
and the far-glimpsed isle there standing, and its glimmering
haven. They reach the magic island [*read* islands?] and three
are enchanted and fall asleep on the shore.

The others beat about the waters beyond and are in despair −
for as often as they make headway west the wind changes and
bears them back. At last they tryst to return on the morrow if
nought other happens. The day breaks chill and dull, and they
lie becalmed looking in vain through the pouring rain.

This narrative differs from both *Ælfwine I* and *II* in that here
there is no mention of the Ythlings; and Ælfwine and his seven
companions depart on their long western voyage from the Harbourless Isle of the ancient mariner. It agrees with *Ælfwine I* in the
name Neorth; but it foreshadows *II* in the cutting of sacred trees
to build a ship.

40    In *Ælfwine I* Ælfheah does not appear, and his two speeches in
this passage are there given to one *Gelimer*. Gelimer (Geilamir) was
the name of a king of the Vandals in the sixth century.

41    In *Ælfwine I* Bior's speech is given to Gelimer (see note 40).

42    *Ælfwine I* ends in almost the same words as *Ælfwine II*, but with a
most extraordinary difference; Ælfwine does not leap overboard,
but returns with his companions to Belerion, and so never comes to

Tol Eressëa! 'Very empty thereafter were the places of Men for Ælfwine and his mariners, and of their seed have been many restless and wistful folk since they were dead . . .' Moreover my father seems clearly to have been going to say the same in *Ælfwine II*, but stopped, struck out what he had written, and introduced the sentence in which Ælfwine leapt into the sea. I cannot see any way to explain this.

*Ælfwine A* ends in much the same way as *Ælfwine II*:

As night comes on a little breath springs up and the clouds lift. They hoist sail to return – when suddenly low down in the dusk they see the many lights of the Haven of Many Hues twinkle forth. They row thither, and hear sweet music. Then the mist wraps all away and the others rousing themselves say it is a mirage born of hunger, and with heavy hearts prepare to go back, but Ælfwine plunges overboard and swims into the dark until he is overcome in the waters, and him seems death envelops him. The others sail away home and are out of the tale.

43 Literally, as he maintained: 'From that (grief) one moved on; from this in the same way one can move on.'

44 There are long roots beneath the words of *The Fellowship of the Ring* (I. 2): 'Elves . . . could now be seen passing westward through the woods in the evening, passing and not returning; but they were leaving Middle-earth and were no longer concerned with its troubles.' '"That isn't anything new, if you believe the old tales,"' said Ted Sandyman, when Sam Gamgee spoke of the matter.

I append here a synopsis of the structural differences between the three versions of *Ælfwine of England*.

| A | I | II |
|---|---|---|
| Æ. sails from Belerion and sees 'islands in the dawn'. | As in A | As in A, but his companion Ælfheah is named. |
| Æ. sails again with 7 mariners of England. They are shipwrecked on the isle of the Man of the Sea but all survive. | Æ. has only 3 companions, and he alone survives the shipwreck. | Æ. has 7 companions, and is alone on the isle of the Man of the Sea, believing them drowned. |
| The Man of the Sea helps them to build a ship but does not go with them. | The Man of the Sea helps Æ. to build a boat and goes with him. | Æ. and the Man of the Sea find a stranded Viking ship and sail away in it together. |

| A | I | II |
|---|---|---|
| The Man of the Sea dives into the sea from a cliff-top of his isle. | They come to the Isle of the Ythlings. The Man of the Sea dives from a cliff-top. Æ. gets 7 companions from the Ythlings. | As in I, but Æ. finds his 7 companions from England, who were not drowned; to them is added Bior of the Ythlings. |
| On their voyages 3 of Æ.'s companions are enchanted in the Magic Isles. | As in A, but in this case they are Ythlings. | As in A |
| They are blown away from Tol Eressëa after sighting it; Æ. leaps overboard, and the others return home. | They are blown away from Tol Eressëa, and all, including Æ., return home. | As in A |

## Changes made to names, and differences in names, in the texts of *Ælfwine of England*

*Lúthien*   The name of the land in I and II; in A *Luthany* (see note 20).

*Déor*   At the first occurrence only in I *Déor* < *Heorrenda*, subsequently *Déor*; A *Déor*.

*Evadrien*   In I < *Erenol*. *Erenol* = 'Iron Cliff'; see I. 252, entry *Eriol*.

*Forodwaith*   II has *Forodwaith* < *Forwaith* < *Gwasgonin*; I has *Gwasgonin or the Winged Helms*; A has *the Winged Helms*.

*Outer Land*   < *Outer Lands* at both occurrences in II (pp. 316–17).

*Ælfheah*   I has *Gelimer* (at the first occurrence only < *Helgor*).

*Shipmen of the West*   In II < *Eneathrim*.

# APPENDIX
## NAMES IN THE *LOST TALES* – PART II

This appendix is designed only as an adjunct and extension to that in Part One. Names that have already been studied in Part One are not given entries in the following notes, if there are entries under that name in Part One, e.g. *Melko, Valinor*; but if, as is often the case, the etymological information in Part One is contained in an entry under some other name, this is shown, e.g. '*Gilim* See I.260 (*Melko*)'.

Linguistic information from the Name-list to *The Fall of Gondolin* (see p. 148) incorporated in these notes is referred to 'NFG'. 'GL' and 'QL' refer to the Gnomish and Qenya dictionaries (see I.246ff.). *Qenya* is the term used in both these books and is strictly the name of the language spoken in Tol Eressëa; it does not appear elsewhere in the early writings, where the distinction is between 'Gnomish' on the one hand and 'Elfin', 'Eldar', or 'Eldarissa' on the other.

★

**Alqarámë**  For the first element Qenya *alqa* 'swan' see I.249 (*Alqaluntë*). Under root RAHA QL gives *râ* 'arm', *rakta* 'stretch out, reach', *ráma* 'wing', *rámavoitë* 'having wings'; GL has *ram* 'wing, pinion', and it is noted that Qenya *ráma* is a confusion of this and a word *róma* 'shoulder'.

**Amon Gwareth**  Under root AM(U) 'up(wards)' QL gives *amu* 'up(wards)', *amu-* 'raise', *amuntë* 'sunrise', *amun(d)* 'hill'; GL has *am* 'up(wards)', *amon* 'hill, mount', adverb 'uphill'.

GL gives the name as *Amon 'Wareth* 'Hill of Ward', also *gwareth* 'watch, guard, ward', from the stem *gwar-* 'watch' seen also in the name of *Tinfang Warble* (*Gwarbilin* 'Birdward', I.268). See *Glamhoth, Gwarestrin*.

**Angorodin**  See I.249 (*Angamandi*) and I.256 (*Kalormë*).

**Arlisgion**  GL gives *Garlisgion* (see I.265 (*Sirion*)), as also does NFG, which has entries '*Garlisgion* was our name, saith Elfrith, for the Place of Reeds which is its interpretation', and '*lisg* is a reed (*liskë*)'. GL has *lisg, lisc* 'reed, sedge', and QL *liskë* with the same meaning. For *gar* see I.251 (*Dor Faidwen*).

**Artanor**  GL has *athra* 'across, athwart', *athron* adverb 'further, beyond', *athrod* 'crossing, ford' (changed later to *adr(a), adron, adros*). With *athra, adr(a)* is compared Qenya *arta*. Cf. also the name *Dor Athro* (p. 41). It is clear that both *Artanor* and *Dor Athro* meant 'the Land Beyond'. Cf. *Sarnathrod*.

**Asgon**   An entry in NFG says: '*Asgon* A lake in the "Land of Shadows" Dor Lómin, by the Elves named *Aksan*.'

**Ausir**   GL gives *avos* 'fortune, wealth, prosperity,' *avosir*, *Ausir* 'the same (personified)'; also *ausin* 'rich', *aus(s)aith* or *avosaith* 'avarice'. Under root AWA in QL are *autë* 'prosperity, wealth; rich', *ausië* 'wealth'.

**Bablon**   See p. 214.

**Bad Uthwen**   Gnomish *uthwen* 'way out, exit, escape', see I. 251 (*Dor Faidwen*). The entry in NFG says: '*Bad Uthwen* [emended from *Uswen*] meaneth but "way of escape" and is in Eldarissa *Uswevandë*.' For *vandë* see I. 264 (*Qalvanda*).

**Balcmeg**   In NFG it is said that Balcmeg 'was a great fighter among the *Orclim* (*Orqui* say the Elves) who fell to the axe of Tuor – 'tis in meaning "heart of evil".' (For *-lim* in *Orclim* see *Gondothlim*.) The entry for *Balrog* in NFG says: '*Bal* meaneth evilness, and *Balc* evil, and *Balrog* meaneth evil demon.' GL has *balc* 'cruel': see I. 250 (*Balrog*).

**Bansil**   For the entry in NFG, where this name is translated 'Fairgleam', see p. 214; and for the elements of the name see I. 272 (*Vána*) and I. 265 (*Sil*).

**Belaurin**   See I. 264 (*Palúrien*).

**Belcha**   See I. 260 (*Melko*). NFG has an entry: '*Belca* Though here [i.e. in the Tale] of overwhelming custom did Bronweg use the elfin names, this was the name aforetime of that evil Ainu.'

**Beleg**   See I. 254 (*Haloisi Velikë*).

**Belegost**   For the first element see *Beleg*. GL gives *ost* 'enclosure, yard – town', also *oss* 'outer wall, town wall', *osta-* 'surround with walls, fortify', *ostor* 'enclosure, circuit of walls'. QL under root oso has *os(t)* 'house, cottage', *osta* 'homestead', *ostar* 'township', *ossa* 'wall and moat'.

**bo-**   A late entry in GL: '*bo* (*bon*) (cf. Qenya *vô*, *vondo* "son") as patronymic prefix, *bo- bon-* "son of"'; as an example is given *Tuor bo-Beleg*. There is also a word *bôr* 'descendant'. See *go-*, *Indorion*.

**Bodruith**   In association with *bod-* 'back, again' GL has the words *bodruith* 'revenge', *bodruithol* 'vengeful (by nature)', *bodruithog* 'thirsting for vengeance', but these were struck out. There is also *gruith* 'deed of horror, violent act, vengeance'. – It may be that Bodruith Lord of Belegost was supposed to have received his name from the events of the *Tale of the Nauglafring*.

**Cópas Alqalunten**   See I. 257 (*Kópas*) and I. 249 (*Alqaluntë*).

**Cris Ilbranteloth**   GL gives the group *crisc* 'sharp', *criss* 'cleft, gash, gully', *crist* 'knife', *crista-* 'slash, cut, slice'; NFG: '*Cris* meaneth much as doth *falc*, a cleft, ravine, or narrow way of waters with high walls'. QL under root KIRI 'cut, split' has *kiris* 'cleft, crack' and other words.

For *ilbrant* 'rainbow' see I.256 (*Ilweran*). The final element is *teloth* 'roofing, canopy': see I.267–8 (*Teleri*).

**Cristhorn** For *Cris* see *Cris Ilbranteloth*, and for *thorn* see I.266 (*Sorontur*). In NFG is the entry: '*Cris Thorn* is Eagles' Cleft or *Sornekiris*.'

**Cuilwarthon** For *cuil* see I.257 (*Koivië-néni*); the second element is not explained.

**Cûm an-Idrisaith** For *cûm* 'mound' see I.250 (*Cûm a Gumlaith*). *Idrisaith* is thus defined in GL: 'cf. *avosaith*, but that means avarice, money-greed, but *idrisaith* = excessive love of gold and gems and beautiful and costly things' (for *avosaith* see *Ausir*). Related words are *idra* 'dear, precious', *idra* 'to value, prize', *idri* (*îd*) 'a treasure, a jewel', *idril* 'sweetheart' (see *Idril*).

**Curufin** presumably contains *curu* 'magic'; see I.269 (*Tolli Kuruvar*).

**Dairon** GL includes this name but without etymological explanation: '*Dairon* the fluter (Qenya *Sairon*).' See *Mar Vanwa Tyaliéva* below.

**Danigwiel** In GL the Gnomish form is *Danigwethil*; see I.266 (*Taniquetil*). NFG has an entry: '*Danigwethil* do the Gnomes call *Taniquetil*; but seek for tales concerning that mountain rather in the elfin name.'

**(bo-)Dhrauthodavros** '(Son of) the weary forest'. Gnomish *drauth* 'weary, toilworn', *drauthos* 'toil, weariness', *drautha-* 'to be weary'; for the second element *tavros* see I.267 (*Tavari*).

**Dor Athro** See *Artanor, Sarnathrod*.

**Dor-na-Dhaideloth** For Gnomish *dai* 'sky' see I.268 (*Telimektar*), and for *teloth* 'roofing, canopy' see *ibid.* (*Teleri*); cf. *Cris Ilbranteloth*.

**Dramborleg** NFG has the following entry: '*Dramborleg* (or as it may be named *Drambor*) meaneth in its full form Thudder-sharp, and was the axe of Tuor that smote both a heavy dint as of a club and cleft as a sword; and the Eldar say *Tarambor* or *Tarambolaika*.' QL gives *Tarambor, Tarambolaike* 'Tuor's axe' under root TARA, TARAMA 'batter, thud, beat', with *taran, tarambo* 'buffet', and *taru* 'horn' (included here with a query: see *Taruithorn*). No Gnomish equivalents are cited in GL.

The second element is Gnomish *leg, lêg* 'keen, piercing', Qenya *laika*; cf. *Legolast* 'keen-sight', I.267 (*Tári-Laisi*).

**Duilin** NFG has the following entry: '*Duilin* whose name meaneth Swallow was the lord of that house of the Gondothlim whose sign was the swallow and was surest of the archers of the Eldalië, but fell in the fall of Gondolin. Now the names of those champions appear

but in Noldorissa, seeing that Gnomes they were, but his name
would be in Eldarissa *Tuilindo*, and that of his house (which the
Gnomes called *Nos Duilin*) *Nossë Tuilinda.*' *Tuilindo* '(spring-
singer), swallow' is given in QL, see I.269 (*Tuilérë*); GL has
*duilin(g)* 'swallow', with *duil, duilir* 'Spring', but these last were
struck through and in another part of the book appear *tuil, tuilir*
'Spring' (see I.269).

  For *nossë* 'kin, people' see I.272 (*Valinor*); GL does not give
*nos* in this sense, but has *nosta-* 'be born', *nost* 'birth; blood, high
birth; birthday', and *noss* (changed to *nôs*) 'birthday'. Cf. *Nost-
na-Lothion* 'the Birth of Flowers', *Nos Galdon, Nos nan Alwen*.

**Eärámë**  For *ea* 'eagle' see I.251 (*Eärendel*), and for *rámë* see
  *Alqarámë*. GL has an entry *Iorothram, -um* '= Qenya *Eärámë* or
  Eaglepinion, a name of one of Eärendel's boats'. For Gnomish *ior,
  ioroth* 'eagle' see I.251 (*Eärendel*), and cf. the forms *Earam,
  Earum* as the name of the ship (pp. 260, 276).
**Eärendel**  See pp. 266–7 and I.251.
**Eärendilyon**  See I.251 (*Eärendel*), and *Indorion*.
**Ecthelion**  Both GL and NFG derive this name from *ecthel*
  'fountain', to which corresponds Qenya *ektelë*. (This latter
  survived: cf. the entry *kel-* in the Appendix to *The Silmarillion*:
  'from *et-kelē* "issue of water, spring" was derived, with transposition of the consonants, Quenya *ehtelë*, Sindarin *eithel*'. A
  later entry in GL gives *aithil* (< *ektl*) 'a spring'.) – A form *kektelë*
  is also found in Qenya from root KELE, KELU: see I.257 (*Kelusindi*).
**Egalmoth**  NFG has the following entry: '*Egalmoth* is a great name,
  yet none know clearly its meaning – some have said its bearer was so
  named in that he was worth a thousand Elves (but Rúmil says nay)
  and others that it signifies the mighty shoulders of that Gnome, and
  so saith Rúmil, but perchance it was woven of a secret tongue of the
  Gondothlim' (for the remainder of this entry see p. 215). For
  Gnomish *moth* '1000' see I.270 (*Uin*).
  GL interprets the name as Rúmil did, deriving it from *alm*
  (< *alðam-*) 'the broad of the back from shoulder to shoulder, back,
  shoulders', hence *Egalmoth* = 'Broadshoulder'; the name in Qenya
  is said to be *Aikaldamor*, and an entry in QL of the same date
  gives *aika* 'broad, vast', comparing Gnomish *eg, egrin*. These
  in turn GL glosses as 'far away, wide, distant' and 'wide, vast,
  broad; far' (as in *Egla*; see I.251 (*Eldar*)).
**Eglamar**  See I.251 (*Eldamar*). NFG has the following entry: '*Egla*
  said the son of Bronweg was the Gnome name of the Eldar (now but
  seldom used) who dwelt in Kôr, and they were called *Eglothrim*
  [emended from *Eglothlim*] (that is *Eldalië*), and their tongue *Lam
  Eglathon* or *Egladrin*. Rúmil said these names *Egla* and *Elda* were
  akin, but Elfrith cared not overmuch for such lore and they seem not

over alike.' With this cf. I. 251 (*Eldar*). GL gives *lam* 'tongue', and *lambë* is found in QL: a word that survived into later Quenya. In QL it is given as a derivative of root LAVA 'lick', and defined 'tongue (of body, but also of land, or even = "speech")'.

**Eldarissa**  appears in QL ('the language of the Eldar') but without explanation of the final element. Possibly it was derived from the root ISI: *ista* 'know', *issë* 'knowledge, lore', *iswa, isqa* 'wise', etc.

**Elfrith**  See pp. 201–2, and I. 255 (*Ilverin*).

**Elmavoitë**  'One-handed' (Beren). See *Ermabwed*.

**Elwing**  GL has the following entry: '*Ailwing* older spelling of *Elwing* = "lake foam". As a noun = "white water-lily". The name of the maiden loved by Ioringli' (*Ioringli* = *Eärendel*, see I. 251). The first element appears in the words *ail* 'lake, pool', *ailion* 'lake', Qenya *ailo, ailin* – cf. later *Aelin-uial*. The second element is *gwing* 'foam': see I. 273 (*Wingilot*).

**Erenol**  See I. 252 (*Eriol*).

**Ermabwed**  'One-handed' (Beren). GL gives *mab* 'hand', *amabwed*, *mabwed* 'having hands', *mabwedri* 'dexterity', *mabol* 'skilful', *mablios* 'cunning', *mablad, mablod* 'palm of hand', *mabrin(d)* 'wrist'. A related word in Qenya was said in GL to be *mapa* (root MAPA) 'seize', but this statement was struck out. QL has also a root MAHA with many derivatives, notably *mā* (= *maha*) 'hand', *mavoitë* 'having hands' (cf. *Elmavoitë*).

**Faiglindra**  'Long-tressed' (Airin). Gnomish *faigli* 'hair, long tresses (especially used of women)'; *faiglion* 'having long hair', and *faiglim* of the same meaning, 'especially as a proper name', *Faiglim, Aurfaiglim* 'the Sun at noon'. With this is bracketed the word *faiglin(d)ra*.

**Failivrin**  Together with *fail* 'pale, pallid', *failthi* 'pallor', and *Failin* a name of the Moon, GL gives *Failivrin*: '(1) a maid beloved by Silmo; (2) a name among the Gnomes of many maidens of great beauty, especially Failivrin of the Rothwarin in the Tale of Turumart.' (In the Tale *Rothwarin* was replaced by *Rodothlim*.)

The second element is *brin*, Qenya *vírin*, 'a magic glassy substance of great lucency used in fashioning the Moon. Used of things of great and pure transparency.' For *vírin* see I. 192–3.

**Falasquil**  Three entries in NFG refer to this name (for *falas* see also I. 253 (*Falman*)):

'*Falas* meaneth (even as *falas* or *falassë* in Eldar) a beach.'

'*Falas-a-Gwilb* the "beach of peace" was *Falasquil* in Elfin where Tuor at first dwelt in a sheltered cove by the Great Sea.' -*a-Gwilb* is struck through and above is written, apparently, '*Wilb or Wilma*.

'*Gwilb* meaneth "full of peace", which is *gwilm*.'

GL gives *gwil, gwilm, gwilthi* 'peace', and *gwilb* 'quiet, peaceful'.

**Fangluin** 'Bluebeard'. See *Indrafang*. For *luin* 'blue' see I.262 (*Nielluin*).

**Foalókë** Under a root FOHO 'hide, hoard, store up' QL gives *foa* 'hoard, treasure', *foina* 'hidden', *fólë* 'secrecy, a secret', *fólima* 'secretive', and *foalókë* 'name of a serpent that guarded a treasure'. *lókë* 'snake' is derived from a root LOKO 'twine, twist, curl'.

GL originally had entries *fû, fûl, fûn* 'hoard', *fûlug* 'a dragon (who guards treasure)', and *ulug* 'wolf'. By later changes this construction was altered to *fuis* 'hoard', *fuithlug, -og* (the form that appears in the text, p. 70), *ulug* 'dragon' (cf. Qenya *lókë*). An entry in NFG reads: '*Lûg* is *lókë* of the Eldar, and meaneth "drake".'

**Fôs'Almir** (Earlier name of *Faskala-númen*; translated in the text (p. 115) 'the bath of flame'.) For *fôs* 'bath' see I.253 (*Faskalanúmen*). GL gives three names: '*Fôs Aura, Fôs'Almir*, and *Fôs na Ngalmir*, i.e. Sun's bath = the Western Sea.' For *Galmir, Aur*, names of the Sun, see I.254 and I.271 (*Ûr*).

**Fuithlug** See *Foalókë*.

**Galdor** For the entry in NFG concerning Galdor see p. 215; as first written *galdon* was there said to mean 'tree', and Galdor's people to be named *Nos Galdon*. *Galdon* is not in GL. Subsequently *galdon* > *alwen*, and *alwen* does appear in GL, as a word of poetic vocabulary: *alwen* '= *orn*'. – Cf. Qenya *alda* 'tree' (see I.249 (*Aldaron*)), and the later relationship Quenya *alda*, Sindarin *galadh*.

**Gar Thurion** NFG has the earlier form *Gar Furion* (p. 202), and GL has *furn, furion* 'secret, concealed', also *fûr* 'a lie' (Qenya *furu*) and *fur-* 'to conceal; to lie'. QL has *furin* and *hurin* 'hidden, concealed' (root FURU or HURU). With *Thurion* cf. *Thuringwethil* 'Woman of Secret Shadow', and *Thurin* 'the Secret', Finduilas' name for Túrin (*Unfinished Tales* pp. 157, 159).

**Gil** See I.256 (*Ingil*).

**Gilim** See I.260 (*Melko*).

**Gimli** GL has *gimli* '(sense of) hearing', with *gim-* 'hear', *gimriol* 'attentive' (changed to 'audible'), *gimri* 'hearkening, attention'. The hearing of Gimli, the captive Gnome in the dungeons of Tevildo, 'was the keenest that has been in the world' (p. 29).

**Glamhoth** GL defines this as 'name given by the Goldothrim to the Orcin: People of Dreadful Hate' (cf. 'folk of dreadful hate', p. 160). For *Goldothrim* see I.262 (*Noldoli*). The first element is *glâm* 'hatred, loathing'; other words are *glamri* 'bitter feud', *glamog* 'loathsome'. An entry in NFG says: '*Glam* meaneth "fierce hate" and even as *Gwar* has no kindred words in Eldar.'

For *hoth* 'folk' see I.264 (*orchoth* in entry *Orc*), and cf. *Goldothrim, Gondothlim, Rúmhoth, Thornhoth*. Under root HOSO QL gives *hos* 'folk', *hossë* 'army, band, troop', *hostar* 'tribe', *horma* 'horde, host'; also *Sankossi* 'the Goblins', equivalent of Gnomish *Glamhoth*, and evidently compounded of *sankë* 'hateful' (root SṆKṆ 'rend, tear') and *hossë*.

**Glend** Perhaps connected with Gnomish *glenn* 'thin, fine', *glendrin* 'slender', *glendrinios* 'slenderness', *glent*, *glentweth* 'thinness'; Qenya root LENE 'long', which developed its meaning in different directions: 'slow, tedious, trailing', and 'stretch, thin': *lenka* 'slow', *lenwa* 'long and thin, straight, narrow', *lenu-* 'stretch', etc.

**Glingol** For the entry in NFG, where the name is translated 'singing-gold', see p. 216; and see I. 258 (*Lindelos*). The second element is *culu* 'gold', for which see I. 255 (*Ilsaluntë*); another entry in NFG reads: '*Culu* or *Culon* is a name we have in poesy for *Glor* (and. Rúmil saith that it is the Elfin *Kulu*, and *-gol* in our *Glingol*).'

**Glorfalc** For *glor* see I. 258 (*Laurelin*). NFG has an entry: '*Glor* is gold and is that word that cometh in verse of the Kôr-Eldar *laurë* (so saith Rúmil).'

*Falc* is glossed in GL '(1) cleft, gash; (2) cleft, ravine, cliffs' (also given is *falcon* 'a great two-handed sword, twibill', which was changed to *falchon*, and so close to English *falchion* 'broadsword'). NFG has: '*Falc* is cleft and is much as *Cris*; being Elfin *Falqa*'; and under root FḶKḶ in QL are *falqa* 'cleft, mountain pass, ravine' and *falqan* 'large sword'. GL has a further entry: *Glorfalc* 'a great ravine leading out of Garioth'. *Garioth* is here used of Hisilómë; see I. 252 (*Eruman*). Cf. later *Orfalch Echor*.

**Glorfindel** For the entry in NFG, where the name is rendered 'Goldtress', see p. 216. For *glor* see I. 258 (*Laurelin*), and *Glorfalc*. GL had an entry *findel* 'lock of hair', together with *fith* (*fidhin*) 'a single hair', *fidhra* 'hairy', but *findel* was struck out; later entries are *finn* 'lock of hair' (see *fin-* in the Appendix to *The Silmarillion*) and *fingl* or *finnil* 'tress'. NFG: '*Findel* is "tress", and is the Elfin *Findil*.' Under root FIRI QL gives *findl* 'lock of hair' and *firin* 'ray of the sun'.

In another place in GL the name *Glorfindel* was given, and translated 'Goldlocks', but it was changed later to *Glorfinn*, with a variant *Glorfingl*.

**Glorund** For *glor* see I. 258 (*Laurelin*), and *Glorfalc*. GL gives *Glorunn* 'the great drake slain by Turumart'. Neither of the Qenya forms *Laurundo*, *Undolaurë* (p. 84) appear in QL, which gives an earlier name for 'the great worm', *Fentor*, together with *fent* 'serpent', *fenumë* 'dragon'. As this entry was first written it read 'the great worm slain by Ingilmo'; to this was added 'or Turambar'.

**Golosbrindi** (Earlier name of Hirilorn, rendered in the text (p. 51) 'Queen of the Forest'.) A word *goloth* 'forest' is given in GL, derived from *\*gwōloth*, which is itself composed of *aloth* (*alos*), a verse word meaning 'forest' (= *taur*), and the prefix *\*ngua* > *gwa*, unaccented *go*, 'together, in one', 'often used merely intensively'.

The corresponding word in Qenya is said to be *málos*, which does not appear in QL.

**Gondobar**  See *Gondolin*, and for *-bar* see I.251 (*Eldamar*). In GL the form *Gondobar* was later changed to *Gonthobar*.

**Gondolin**  To the entries cited in I.254 may be added that in NFG: '*Gond* meaneth a stone, or stone, as doth Elfin *on* and *ondo*.' For the statement about Gondolin (where the name is rendered 'stone of song') in NFG see p. 216; and for the latest formulation of the etymology of *Gondolin* see the Appendix to *The Silmarillion*, entry *gond*.

**Gondothlim**  GL has the following entry concerning the word *lim* 'many', Qenya *limbë* (not in QL): 'It is frequently suffixed and so becomes a second plural inflexion. In the singular it = English "many a", as *golda-lim*. It is however most often suffixed to the plural in those nouns making their plural in *-th*. It then changes to *-rim* after *-l*. Hence great confusion with *grim* "host" and *thlim* "race", as in *Goldothrim* ("the people of the Gnomes").' NFG has an entry: '*Gondothlim* meaneth "folk of stone" and (saith Rúmil) is *Gond* "stone", whereto be added *Hoth* "folk" and that *-lim* we Gnomes add after to signify "the many".' Cf. *Lothlim*, *Rodothlim*, and *Orclim* in entry *Balcmeg*; for *hoth* see *Glamhoth*.

**Gondothlimbar**  See *Gondolin*, *Gondothlim*, and for *-bar* see I.251 (*Eldamar*). In GL the form *Gondothlimbar* was later changed to '*Gonthoflimar or Gonnothlimar*'.

**go-**  An original entry in GL, later struck out, was: *gon- go-* 'son of, patronymic prefix (cf. suffix *ios/ion/io* and Qenya *yô, yondo*)'. The replacement for this is given above under *bo-*. See *Indorion*.

**Gon Indor**  See *go-*, *Indorion*.

**Gothmog**  See pp. 67, 216, and I.258 (*Kosomot*). GL has *mog-* 'detest, hate', *mogri* 'detestation', *mogrin* 'hateful'; Qenya root MOKO 'hate'. In addition to *goth* 'war, strife' (Qenya root KOSO 'strive') may be noted *gothwen* 'battle', *gothweg* 'warrior', *gothwin* 'Amazon', *gothriol* 'warlike', *gothfeng* 'war-arrow', *gothwilm* 'armistice'.

**Gurtholfin**  GL: *Gurtholfin* 'Urdolwen, a sword of Turambar's, Wand of Death'. Also given is *gurthu* 'death' (Qenya *urdu*; not in QL). The second element of the name is *olfin(g)* (also *olf*) 'branch, wand, stick' (Qenya *olwen(n)*).

It may be noted that in QL Turambar's sword is given as *Sangahyando* 'cleaver of throngs', from roots SANGA 'pack tight, press' (*sanga* 'throng') and HYARA 'plough through' (*hyar* 'plough', *hyanda* 'blade, share'). *Sangahyando* 'Throng-cleaver' survived to become the name of a man in Gondor (see the Appendix to *The Silmarillion*, entry *thang*).

**Gwar**  See I.257 (*Kôr*, *korin*).

**Gwarestrin**  Rendered in the Tale (p. 158) as 'Tower of Guard', and so also in NFG; GL glosses it 'watchtower (especially as a name of Gondolin)'. A late entry in GL gives *estirin, estirion, estrin* 'pinnacle', beside *esc* 'sharp point, sharp edge'. The second element of this word is *tiri(o)n*; see I.258 (*Kortirion*). For *gwar* see *Amon Gwareth*.

**Gwedheling** See I.273 (*Wendelin*).

**Heborodin** 'The Encircling Hills.' Gnomish preposition *heb* 'round about, around'; *hebrim* 'boundary', *hebwirol* 'circumspect'. For *orod* see I.256 (*Kalormë*).

**Hirilorn** GL gives *hiril* 'queen (a poetic use), princess; feminine of *bridhon*'. For *bridhon* see *Tevildo*. The second element is *orn* 'tree'. (It may be mentioned here that the word *neldor* 'beech' is found in QL; see the Appendix to *The Silmarillion*, entry *neldor*).

**Idril** For Gnomish *idril* 'sweetheart' see *Cûm an-Idrisaith*. There is another entry in GL as follows: *Idhril* 'a girl's name often confused with *Idril*. *Idril* = "beloved" but *Idhril* = "mortal maiden". Both appear to have been the names of the daughter of Turgon – or apparently *Idril* was the older and the Kor-eldar called her *Irildë* (= *Idhril*) because she married Tuor.' Elsewhere in GL appear *idhrin* 'men, earth-dwellers; especially used as a folk-name contrasted with *Eglath* etc.; cf. Qenya *indi*', and *Idhru, Idhrubar* 'the world, all the regions inhabited by Men; cf. Qenya *irmin*'. In QL these words *indi* and *irmin* are given under root IRI 'dwell?', with *irin* 'town', *indo* 'house', *indor* 'master of house' (see *Indor*), etc.; but *Irildë* does not appear. Similar words are found in Gnomish: *ind, indos* 'house, hall', *indor* 'master (of house), lord'.

After the entry in NFG on *Idril* which has been cited (p. 216) a further note was added: 'and her name meaneth "Beloved", but often do Elves say *Idhril* which more rightly compares with *Irildë* and that meaneth "mortal maiden", and perchance signifies her wedding with Tuor son of Men.' An isolated note (written in fact on a page of the *Tale of the Nauglafring*) says: 'Alter name of *Idril* to *Idhril*. The two were confused: *Idril* = "beloved", *Idhril* = "maiden of mortals". The Elves thought this her name and called her *Irildë* (because she married Tuor Pelecthon).'

**Ilbranteloth** See *Cris Ilbranteloth*.

**Ilfiniol, Ilfrith** See I.255 (*Ilverin*).

**Ilúvatar** An entry in NFG may be noticed here: '*En* do the mystic sayings of the Noldoli also name *Ilathon* [emended from *Âd Ilon*], who is Ilúvatar – and this is like the Eldar *Enu*.' QL gives *Enu*, the Almighty Creator who dwells without the world. For *Ilathon* see I.255–6 (*Ilwë*).

**Indor** (Father of Tuor's father Peleg). This is perhaps the word *indor* 'master (of house), lord' (see *Idril*) used as a proper name.

**Indorion**  See *go-.* QL gives *yô, yond-* as poetic words for 'son', adding: 'but very common as *-ion* in patronymics (and hence practically = "descendant")'; also *yondo* 'male descendant, usually (great) grandson' (cf. Eärendel's name *Gon Indor*). Cf. *Eärendilyon.*

**Indrafang**  GL has *indra* 'long (also used of time)', *indraluin* 'long ago'; also *indravang* 'a special name of the *nauglath* or dwarves', on which see p. 247. These forms were changed later to *in(d)ra, in(d)rafang, in(d)raluin/idhraluin.*

An original entry in GL was *bang* 'beard' = Qenya *vanga*, but this was struck out; and another word with the same meaning as *Indravang* was originally entered as *Bangasur* but changed to *Fangasur*. The second element of this is *súr* 'long, trailing', Qenya *sóra*, and a later addition here is *Surfang* 'a long-beard, a *naugla* or *inrafang*'. Cf. *Fangluin*, and later *Fangorn* 'Treebeard'.

**Irildë**  See *Idril.*

**Isfin**  NFG has this entry: '*Isfin* was the sister of Turgon Lord of Gondolin, whom Eöl at length wedded; and it meaneth either "snow-locks" or "exceeding-cunning".' Long afterwards my father, noting that *Isfin* was 'derived from the earliest (1916) form of *The Fall of Gondolin*', said that the name was 'meaningless'; but with the second element cf. *finn* 'lock of hair' (see *Glorfindel*) or *fim* 'clever', *finthi* 'idea, notion', etc. (see I. 253 (*Finwë*)).

**Iváre**  GL gives *Ior* 'the famous "piper of the sea"', Qenya *Iváre.*'

**Íverin**  A late entry in GL gives *Aivrin or Aivrien* 'an island off the west coast of Tol Eressëa, Qenya *Íwerin* or *Iverindor.*' QL has *Íverind-* 'Ireland'.

**Karkaras**  In GL this is mentioned as the Qenya form; the Gnomish name of 'the great wolf-warden of Belca's door' was *Carcaloth* or *Carcamoth*, changed to *Carchaloth, Carchamoth*. The first element is *carc* 'jag, point, fang'; QL under root KṚKṚ has *karka* 'fang, tooth, tusk', *karkassë, karkaras* 'row of spikes or teeth'.

**Kosmoko**  See *Gothmog.*

**Kurûki**  See I. 269 (*Tolli Kuruvar*).

**Ladwen-na-Dhaideloth**  'Heath of the Sky-roof'. See *Dor-na-Dhaideloth*. GL gives *ladwen* '(1) levelness, flatness; (2) a plain, heath; (3) a plane; (4) surface.' Other words are *ladin* 'level, smooth; fair, equable' (cf. *Tumladin*), *lad* 'a level' (cf. *mablad* 'palm of hand' mentioned under *Ermabwed*), *lada-* 'to smooth out, stroke, soothe, beguile', and *ladwinios* 'equity'. There are also words *bladwen* 'a plain' (see I. 264 (*Palúrien*)), and *fladwen* 'meadow' (with *flad* 'sward' and *Fladweth Amrod (Amrog)* 'Nomad's Green', 'a place in *Tol Erethrin* where Eriol sojourned a while; nigh to Tavrobel.' *Amrog, amrod* = 'wanderer', 'wandering', from *amra-* 'go up and down, live in the mountains, wander'; see *Amon Gwareth*).

**Laiqalassë** See I. 267 (*Tári-laisi*), I. 254 (*Gar Lossion*).

**Laurundo** See *Glorund*.

**Legolas** See *Laiqalassë*.

**Lindeloktë** See I. 258 (*Lindelos*).

**Linwë Tinto** See I. 269 (*Tinwë Linto*).

**Lókë** See *Foalókë*.

**Lôs** See I. 254 (*Gar Lossion*). The later form *loth* does not appear in GL (which has however *lothwing* 'foamflower'). NFG has '*Lôs* is a flower and in Eldarissa *lossë* which is a rose' (all after the word 'flower' struck out).

**Lósengriol** As with *lôs*, the later form *lothengriol* does not appear in GL. *Losengriol* is translated 'lily of the valley' in GL, which gives the Gnomish words *eng* 'smooth, level', *enga* 'plain, vale', *engri* 'a level', *engriol* 'vale-like; of the vale'. NFG says '*Eng* is a plain or vale and *Engriol* that which liveth or dwelleth therein', and translates *Lósengriol* 'flower of the vale or lily of the valley'.

**Los 'lóriol** (changed from *Los Glóriol*; the Golden Flower of Gondolin). See I. 254 (*Gar Lossion*), and for *glóriol* 'golden' see I. 258 (*Laurelin*).

**Loth, Lothengriol** See *Lôs, Lósengriol*.

**Lothlim** See *Lôs* and *Gondothlim*. The entry in NFG reads: '*Lothlim* being for *Loslim* meaneth folk of the flower, and is that name taken by the Exiles of Gondolin (which city they had called *Lôs* aforetime).'

**Mablung** For *mab* 'hand' see *Ermabwed*. The second element is *lung* 'heavy; grave, serious'; related words are *lungra-* 'weigh, hang heavy', *luntha* 'balance, weigh', *lunthang* 'scales'.

**Malkarauki** See I. 250 (*Balrog*).

**Mar Vanwa Tyaliéva** See I. 260 and add: a late entry in GL gives the Gnomish name, *Bara Dhair Haithin*, the Cottage of Lost Play; also *daira-* 'play' (with *dairwen* 'mirth', etc.), and *haim or haithin* 'gone, departed, lost' (with *haitha-* 'go, walk', etc.). Cf. *Dairon*.

**Mathusdor** (Aryador, Hisilómë). In GL are given *math* 'dusk', *mathrin* 'dusky', *mathusgi* 'twilight', *mathwen* 'evening'. See *Umboth-muilin*.

**Mavwin** A noun *mavwin* 'wish' in GL was struck out, but related words allowed to stand: *mav-* 'like', *mavra* 'eager after', *mavri* 'appetite', *mavrin* 'delightful, desirable', *mavros* 'desire', *maus* 'pleasure; pleasant'. Mavwin's name in Qenya, *Mavoinë*, is not in QL, unless it is to be equated with *maivoinë* 'great longing'.

**Meleth** A noun *meleth* 'love' is found in GL; see I. 262 (*Nessa*).

**Melian, Melinon, Melinir** None of these names occur in the glossaries, but probably all are derivatives of the stem *mel-* 'love'; see I.262 (*Nessa*). The later etymology of *Melian* derived the name from *mel-* 'love' (*Melyanna* 'dear gift').

**Meoita, Miaugion, Miaulë**    See *Tevildo*.

**Mindon-Gwar**    For *mindon* 'tower' see I.260 (*Minethlos*); and for *Gwar* see p. 291 and I.257 (*Kôr, korin*).

**Morgoth**    See p. 67 and *Gothmog*. For the element *mor-* see I.261 (*Mornië*).

**Mormagli, Mormakil**    See I.261 (*Mornië*) and I.259 (*Makar*).

**Nan Dumgorthin**    See p. 62. For *nan* see I.261 (*Nandini*).

**Nantathrin**    This name does not occur in the *Lost Tales*, where the Land of Willows is called *Tasarinan*, but GL gives it (see I.265 (*Sirion*)) and NFG has an entry: '*Dor-tathrin* was that Land of Willows of which this and many a tale tells.' GL has *tathrin* 'willow', and QL *tasarin* of the same meaning.

**Nauglafring**    GL has the following entry: '*Nauglafring* = *Fring na Nauglithon*, the Necklace of the Dwarves. Made for Ellu by the Dwarves from the gold of Glorund that Mîm the fatherless cursed and that brought ruin on Beren Ermabwed and Damrod his son and was not appeased till it sank with Elwing beloved of Eärendel to the bottom of the sea.' For Damrod (Daimord) son of Beren see pp. 139, 259, and for the loss of Elwing and the Nauglafring see pp. 255, 264. This is the only reference to the 'appeasing' of Mîm's curse. – Gnomish *fring* means 'carcanet, necklace' (Qenya *firinga*).

**Níniel**    Cf. Gnomish *nîn* 'tear', *ninios* 'lamentation', *ninna-* 'weep'; see I.262 (*Nienna*).

**Nínin-Udathriol**    ('Unnumbered Tears'). See *Níniel*. GL gives *tathn* 'number', *tathra-* 'number, count', *udathnarol, udathriol* 'innumerable'. *Ú-* is a 'negative prefix with any part of speech'. (QL casts no light on *Nieriltasinwa*, p. 84, apart from the initial element *nie* 'tear', see I.262 (*Nienna*).)

**Noldorissa**    See *Eldarissa*.

**Nos Galdon, Nos nan Alwen**    See *Duilin, Galdor*.

**Nost-na-Lothion**    See *Duilin*.

**Parma Kuluinen**    The Golden Book, see p. 310. This entry is given in QL under root PARA: *parma* 'skin, bark; parchment; book, writings'. This word survived in later Quenya (*The Lord of the Rings* III.401). For *Kuluinen* see *Glingol*.

**Peleg**    (Father of Tuor). GL has a common noun *peleg* 'axe', verb *pelectha-* 'hew' (QL *pelekko* 'axe', *pelekta-* 'hew'). Cf. Tuor's name *Pelecthon* in the note cited under *Idril*.

**Ramandur**    See I.259 (*Makar*).

**Rog**   GL gives an adjective *rôg, rog* 'doughty, strong'. But with the Orcs' name for Egnor Beren's father, Rog the Fleet, cf. *arog* 'swift, rushing', and *raug* of the same meaning; Qenya *arauka*.

**Rôs**   GL gives yet another meaning of this name: 'the Sea' (Qenya *Rása*).

**Rodothlim**   See *Rothwarin* (earlier form replaced by *Rodothlim*).

**Rothwarin**   GL has this name in the forms *Rothbarin, Rosbarin*: '(literally "cavern-dwellers") name of a folk of secret Gnomes and also of the regions about their cavernous homes on the banks of the river.' Gnomish words derived from the root ROTO 'hollow' are *rod* 'tube, stem', *ross* 'pipe', *roth* 'cave, grot', *rothrin* 'hollow', *rodos* 'cavern'; QL gives *rotsë* 'pipe', *róta* 'tube', *ronta, rotwa* 'hollow', *rotelë* 'cave'.

**Rúmhoth**   See *Glamhoth*.

**Rúsitaurion**   GL gives a noun *rûs (rôs)* 'endurance, longsuffering, patience', together with adjective *rô* 'enduring, longsuffering; quiet, gentle', and verb *rô-* 'remain, stay; endure'. For *taurion* see I.267 (*Tavari*).

**Sarnathrod**   Gnomish *sarn* 'a stone'; for *athrod* 'ford' see *Artanor*.

**Sarqindi**   ('Cannibal-ogres'). This must derive from the root SṚKṚ given in QL, with derivatives *sarko* 'flesh', *sarqa* 'fleshy', *sarkuva* 'corporeal, bodily'.

**Silpion**   An entry in NFG (p. 215) translates the name as 'Cherry-moon'. In QL is a word *pio* 'plum, cherry' (with *piukka* 'blackberry', *piosenna* 'holly', etc.), and also *Valpio* 'the holy cherry of Valinor'. GL gives *Piosil* and *Silpios*, without translation, as names of the Silver Tree, and also a word *piog* 'berry'.

**Taimonto**   See I.268 (*Telimektar*).

**Talceleb, Taltelepta**   (Name of *Idril/Irildë*, 'of the Silver Feet'.) The first element is Gnomish *tâl* 'foot (of people and animals)'; related words are *taltha* 'foot (of things), base, pedestal, pediment', *talrind, taldrin* 'ankle', *taleg, taloth* 'path' – another name for the Way of Escape into Gondolin was *Taleg Uthwen* (see *Bad Uthwen*). QL under root TALA 'support' gives *tala* 'foot', *talwi* (dual) 'the feet', *talas* 'sole', etc. For the second element see I.268 (*Telimpë*). QL gives the form *telepta* but without translation.

**Tarnin Austa**   For *tarn* 'gate' see I.261 (*Moritarnon*). GL gives *aust* 'summer'; cf. *Aur* 'the Sun', I.271 (*Ûr*).

**Taruithorn, Taruktarna**   (Oxford). GL gives *târ* 'horn' and *tarog* 'ox' (Qenya *taruku-*), *Taruithron* older *Taruitharn* 'Oxford'. Immediately following these words are *tarn* 'gate' and *taru* '(1) cross (2) crossing'. QL has *taru* 'horn' (see *Dramborleg*), *tarukka* 'horned', *tarukko, tarunko* 'bull', *Taruktarna* 'Oxford', and under root TARA *tara-* 'cross, go athwart', *tarna* 'crossing, passage'.

**Tasarinan**    See *Nantathrin*.

**Taurfuin**    See I. 267 (*Tavari*) and I. 253 (*Fui*).

**Teld Quing Ilon**    NFG has an entry: '*Cris a Teld Quing Ilon*
signifieth Gully of the Rainbow Roof, and is in the Eldar speech
*Kiris Iluqingatelda*'; a *Teld Quing Ilon* was struck out and
replaced by *Ilbranteloth*. Another entry reads: '*Ilon* is the
sky'; in GL *Ilon* (= Qenya *Ilu*) is the name of *Ilúvatar* (see I. 255
(*Ilwë*)). *Teld* does not appear in GL, but related words as *telm*
'roof' are given (see I. 267–8 (*Teleri*)); and *cwing* = 'a bow'.
QL has *iluqinga* 'rainbow' (see I. 256 (*Ilweran*)) and *telda*
'having a roof' (see I. 268 (*Telimektar*)). For *Cris, Kiris* see *Cris
Ilbranteloth*.

**Tevildo, Tifil**    For the etymology see I. 268, to which can be added that
the earlier Gnomish form *Tifil* (later *Tiberth*) is associated in GL
with a noun *tîf* 'resentment, ill-feeling, bitterness'.

    *Vardo Meoita* 'Prince of Cats': for *Vardo* see I. 273 (*Varda*).
QL gives *meoi* 'cat'.

    *Bridhon Miaugion* 'Prince of Cats': *bridhon* 'king, prince', cf.
*Bridhil*, Gnomish name of Varda (I. 273). Nouns *miaug, miog*
'tomcat' and *miauli* 'she-cat' (changed to *miaulin*) are given in GL,
where the Prince of Cats is called *Tifil Miothon or Miaugion*.
*Miaulë* was the name of Tevildo's cook (p. 28).

**Thorndor**    See I. 266 (*Sorontur*).

**Thornhoth**    See *Glamhoth*.

**Thorn Sir**    See I. 265 (*Sirion*).

**Tifanto**    This name is clearly to be associated with the Gnomish words
(*tif-, tifin*) given in I. 268 (*Tinfang*).

**Tifil**    See *Tevildo*.

**Tirin**    See I. 258 (*Kortirion*).

**Tôn a Gwedrin**    *Tôn* is a Gnomish word meaning 'fire (on a hearth)',
related to *tan* and other words given under *Tanyasalpë* (I. 266–7);
*Tôn a Gwedrin* 'the Tale-fire' in *Mar Vanwa Tyaliéva*. Cf. *Tôn
Sovriel* 'the fire lake of Valinor' (*sovriel* 'purification', *sovri*
'cleansing'; *sôn* 'pure, clean', *soth* 'bath', *sô-* 'wash, clean, bathe').

    *Gwedrin* belongs with *cwed-* (preterite *cwenthi*) 'say, tell',
*cweth* 'word', *cwent* 'tale, saying', *cwess* 'saying, proverb', *cwedri*
'telling (of tales)', *ugwedriol* 'unspeakable, ineffable'. In QL under
root QETE are *qet-* (*qentë*) 'speak, talk', *quent* 'word', *qentelë*
'sentence', *Eldaqet* = *Eldarissa*, etc. Cf. the Appendix to *The
Silmarillion*, entry *quen-* (*quet-*).

**Tumladin**    For the first element, Gnomish *tûm* 'valley', see I. 269
(*Tombo*), and for the second, *ladin* 'level, smooth' see *Ladwen na
Dhaideloth*.

**Turambar**    For the first element see I. 260 (*Meril-i-Turinqi*). QL gives
*amarto, ambar* 'Fate', and also (root MṚTṚ) *mart* 'a piece of luck',
*marto* 'fortune, fate, lot', *mart-* 'it happens' (impersonal). GL has

*mart* 'fate', *martion* 'fated, doomed, fey'; also *umrod* and *umbart* 'fate'.

**Turumart**   See *Turambar*.

**Ufedhin**   Possible connections of this name are Gnomish *uf* 'out of, forth from', or *fedhin* 'bound by agreement, ally, friend'.

**Ulbandi**   See I. 260 (*Melko*).

**Ulmonan**   The Gnomish name was *Ingulma(n)* (*Gulma* = *Ulmo*), with the prefix *in-* (*ind-*, *im-*) 'house of' (*ind* 'house', see *Idril*). Other examples of this formation are *Imbelca*, *Imbelcon* 'Hell (house of Melko)', *inthorn* 'eyrie', *Intavros* 'forest' (properly 'the forest palace of Tavros').

**Umboth-muilin**   Gnomish *umboth*, *umbath* 'nightfall'; *Umbathor* is a name of Garioth (see I. 252 (*Eruman*)). This word is derived from *\*mbaþ-*, related to *\*maþ-* seen in *math* 'dusk': see *Mathusdor*. The second element is *muil* 'tarn', Qenya *moilë*.

**Undolaurë**   See *Glorund*.

**Valar**   NFG has the following entry: '*Banin* [emended from *Banion*] or *Bandrim* [emended from *Banlim*]. Now these dwell, say the Noldoli, in *Gwalien* [emended from *Banien*] but they are spoken of ever by Elfrith and the others in their Elfin names as the *Valar* (or *Vali*), and that glorious region of their abode is *Valinor*.' See I. 272 (*Valar*).

# SHORT GLOSSARY OF OBSOLETE, ARCHAIC, AND RARE WORDS

Words that have been given in the similar glossary to Part I (such as *an* 'if', *fain, lief, meed, rede, ruth*) are not as a rule repeated here. Some words of current English used in obsolete senses are included.

**acquaint**   old past participle, superseded by *acquainted*, 287
**ardour**   burning heat, 38, 170 (modern sense 194)
**bested**   beset, 193
**bravely**   splendidly, showily, 75
**broidure**   embroidery, 163. Not recorded, but *broid-* varied with *broud-* etc. in Middle English, and *broudure* 'embroidery' is found.
**burg**   walled and fortified town, 175
**byrnie**   body-armour, corslet, coat-of-mail, 163
**carcanet**   ornamental collar or necklace, 227–8, 235, 238
**carle**   (probably) serving-man, 85; **house-carle** 190
**chain**   linear measure (a chain's length), sixty-six feet, 192
**champain**   level, open country, 295, 298
**clue**   thread, 322
**cot**   small cottage, 95, 141
**damasked**   224, **damascened** 173, 227, ornamentally inlaid with designs in gold and silver.
**diapered**   covered with a small pattern, 173
**dight**   arrayed, fitted out, 173
**drake**   dragon, 41, 46, 85–7, etc. (*Drake* is the original English word, Old English *draca*, derived from Latin; *dragon* was from French).
**drolleries**   comic plays or entertainments, 190
**enow**   enough, 241–2
**enthralled**   enslaved, 97, 163, 196, 198
**entreat**   treat, 26, 77, 87, 236 (modern sense 38)
**errant**   wandering, 42
**estate**   situation, 97
**ewer**   pitcher for water, 226
**eyot**   small island, 7
**fathom**   linear measure (six feet), formerly not used only of water, 78
**fell in dread**   fell into dread, 106
**force**   waterfall, 105 (Northern English, from Scandinavian).
**fordone**   overcome, 233
**fosses**   pits, 288
**fretted**   adorned with elaborate carving, 297

**glamour**   enchantment, spell, 314
**greaves**   armour for the lower leg, 163
**guestkindliness**   hospitality, 228. Apparently not recorded; used in I.175.
**haply**   perhaps, 13, 94, 99
**hie**   hasten; **hie thee**, hasten, 75
**high-tide**   festival, 231
**house-carle**   190, see **carle**.
**inly**   inwardly, 315
**jacinth**   blue, 274
**kempt**   combed, 75; **unkempt**, uncombed, 159
**kirtle**   long coat or tunic, 154
**knave**   male child, boy, 96 (the original sense of the word, long since lost).
**lair**   in **the dragon's lair**, 105, the place where the dragon was lying (i.e. happened at that time to be lying).
**lambent**   (of flame) playing lightly on a surface without burning, 297
**league**   about three miles, 171, 189, 201
**lealty**   loyalty, 185
**let**   desisted, 166; allowed, 181; **had let fashion**, had had fashioned, 174, **let seize**, had (him) seized, 225, **let kill**, had (them) killed, 235
**like**   please, 41; **good liking**, good will, friendly disposition, 169
**list**   wish, 85, 101; like, 236
**or ever**   before ever, 5–6, 38, 80, 110, 233–4, 240
**or ... or**   either ... or, 226
**pale**   boundary, 269
**ports**   gateways, 299
**prate**   chatter, speak to no purpose, 75
**puissance**   power, 168
**repair**   make one's way, go, 162
**runagate**   deserter, 15, 44 (the same word in origin as **renegade**, 15, 44, 224, 232)
**scathe**   hurt, harm, 99, 233
**scatterlings**   wanderers, stragglers, 182
**sconces**   brackets fastened on a wall, to carry candle or torch, 226
**scullion**   menial kitchen-servant, drudge, 17, 45
**shallop**   274. See I.275; but here the boat is defined as oarless.
**silvern**   silver, 270 (the original Old English adjective).
**slot**   track of an animal, 38, 96 (=**spoor** 38).
**stead**   farm, 89
**stricken**   in **the Stricken Anvil**, struck, beaten, 174, 179
**swinge**   stroke, blow, 194
**thews**   strength, bodily power, 33
**tilth**   cultivated (tilled) land, 4, 88, 101
**tithe**   tenth part, 188, 223, 227

**travail**    hardship, suffering, 77, 82, 239; toil, 168; **travailed**, toiled, 163; **travailing**, enduring hardship, 75

**trencher**    large dish or platter, 226

**uncouth**    85 perhaps has the old meaning 'strange', but elsewhere (13, 75, 115) has the modern sense.

**vambrace**    armour for the fore-arm, 163

**weird**    fate, 85–6, 111, 155, 239

**whin**    gorse, 287

**whortle**    whortleberry, bilberry; **whortlebush** 287

**withe**    withy, flexible branch of willow, 229

**worm**    serpent, dragon, 85–8, etc.

**wrack**    downfall, ruin, 116, 253, 283, 285

# INDEX

This index is made on the same basis as that to Part I, but selected references are given in rather more cases, and the individual *Lost Tales* are not included. In view of the large number of names that appear in Part II fairly full cross-references are provided to associated names (earlier and later forms, equivalents in different languages, etc.). As in the index to Part I, the more important names occurring in *The Silmarillion* are not given explanatory definitions; and references sometimes include passages where the person or place is not actually named.

243, 245–51, 283, 328; adjective *dwarven* 227, *dwarfen* 238. See especially 223–4, 247–8, and see *Indrafangs*, *Nauglath*, *Nauglafring*.

*Éadgifu* (Old English) (1) Ælfwine's wife, Elf of Tol Eressëa. 290. See *Naimi*. (2) Déor's wife, mother of Ælfwine. 313–14, 323, 330–1.

*Eagles* 58, 193, 211; King of Eagles, see *Ramandur*, *Sorontur*, *Thorndor*; *People of the Eagles*, see *Thornhoth*; *Eagles' Cleft*, see *Cleft of Eagles*; *Eagle-stream*, see *Thorn Sir*; the Eagle as emblem, 193, 267

*Éalá Éarendel engla beorhtast* (poem) 266–9, 271, 277

*Eärámë* 'Eaglepinion', Eärendel's first ship. 253–4, 261, 265, 267. *Earum* 260–1, 276, *Earam* 276. See *Earnhama*, *Eärrámë*.

*Eärendel* 130, 144–5, 149, 165, 167, 169–71, 174, 177–8, 185, 187–93, 196, 199–201, 213, 215–17, 219, 221, 242, 252–70, 272, 274, 276, 278, 281, 286, 290, 302, 304, 306–10; unnamed, in Ulmo's words to Tuor, 155, 205. See especially 266–7. *Lay of Eärendel* 270. Later form *Eärendil* 212, 265–6; *Earendl* 267

*Eärendilyon* 'Son of Eärendel', mariner. 264

*Earnhama* (Old English) 'Eagle-dress', see 276

*Eärrámë* 'Sea-wing', Tuor's ship. 265. See *Alqarámë*, *Eärámë*.

*East Danes* 305; *East-Denum* (Old English, dative case) 305

*Easterling Men, Easterlings* 120, 126, 204. See *Incomers*.

*Ecthelion* (1) Lord of the people of the Fountain in Gondolin; called *Ecthelion of the Fountain, Lord of the Fountain(s)*. 173, 175, 180–4, 191, 200, 211–13, 215–16. (2) Name of two Stewards of Gondor. 212

*Edain* 266

*Edda* (Old Norse) 125

*Egalmoth* (1) Lord of the people of the Heavenly Arch in Gondolin. 173, 175, 183, 192, 212, 215, 258, 278–9. (2) Steward of Gondor. 211

*Eglamar* =*Eldamar*. 262, 265, 272

*Eglavain* Elfinesse (?). 320, 325

*Egnor* Father of Beren; called 'the forester', 'the huntsman of the Elves, of the Gnomes', 'Elf of the greenwood'. 11, 15, 22–3, 28, 43–5, 49, 51–2, 61, 65–6, 71–2, 116, 139–40, 242, 248. *Egnor bo-Rimion* (> *go-Rimion*) 'son of Rimion' 22, 51. See *Rog* (1).

*Eithel Ivrin* 123; *Ivrin* 124

*Elbenil* Littleheart. 202. (Replaced by *Elwenil*.)

*Eldairon* Elvish name of Ælfwine: *Eldairon of Lúthien*, replacing *Lúthien of Luthany*. 313

*Eldalië* 9, 42–3, 115, 130, 136, 165, 167, 180, 199, 215, 219, 224, 241, 265

*Eldamar* 'Elfhome'. 261–2, 272, 287. See *Eglamar*.

*Eldar* Selected references: used of all Elves including Dark Elves 9, 64,

82; in reference to Noldoli 95, 149; distinct from Noldoli 153, 165,
178, 215, 218, 289. References to the language of the Eldar (as
opposed to Gnomish) 8, 70, 85, 148–9, 169, 192, 199, 215–16 (see
*Eldarissa, Elfin*); *Eldar* as adjective referring to the language 148.
See *Elves*.

*Eldarissa*   The language of the Eldar, as distinct from *Noldorissa*.
148–9, 280

*Eldaros*   = *Ælfhâm*, Elfhome. 301. *Eldos* 302

*Elder Days*   324

*Elenwë*   Wife of Turgon. 209

*Elf-friend*   141 (of Úrin), 313 (of Déor Ælfwine's father).

*Elfin*   References only to use as name of the language of the 'Eldar' (as
distinct from Gnomish). 42, 49, 149, 202, 267; probably used in
general sense 304. See *Eldar, Eldarissa*.

*Elfinesse*   21, 38, 43, 47, 59, 130, 240, 313, 321, 323, 325; *children of
Elfinesse* 159, 326, *daughter of Elfinesse* 164, 215

*Elf-march*   The expedition of the Elves of Kôr for the rescue of the
Gnomes in the Great Lands. 144, 221, 252; *March of the Elves*
253, 257–8, 278–80, 303–4, 307–8, *March of the Inwir and Teleri*
255, 278, *March of Liberation* 279. See *Faring Forth*.

*Elfriniel*   Littleheart. 148, 201, 214–16. (Replaced by *Elfrith*.) *Elfriniol*
50, 201. (Replaced by *Ilfiniol*.) See *Ilfiniol, Ilfrin*.

*Elfrith*   Littleheart. 148, 201–2, 216. (Replaced *Elfriniel*.) See *Ilfrith*.

*Ellon*   A (Gnomish) name of Tinwelint. 69, 116. See *Tinto'ellon,
Tinthellon*.

*Ellu*   (1) Name of Tinwelint in Eldarissa. 49–50, 69. (2) Lord of the
Solosimpi in Tinwelint's place (later Olwë). 50

*Elmavoitë*   'One-handed', name of Beren 'in the language of the Lonely
Isle.' 34. See *Ermabwed*.

*Elmir*   One of the two first Men (with Ermon). 305

*Eltas*   Teller of the *Tale of Turambar*. 69–70, 112, 116, 118–19,
135–7, 144–5, 242–3; see especially 119.

*Elu Thingol*   50

*Elvenfolk*   286, 297. *Elvenland* 272

*Elves*   Selected references (see also *Eldar, Fairies*). Used to include
Gnomes 22, 26, 35, 38, etc.; distinct from Gnomes 8, 45, 48–9,
216–17. Fate of the Elves 60, 250; stature of Elves and Men 73, 80,
142, 159, 198, 220, 281, 283, 326–7; references to 'fading' 240, 242,
250, 281, 283, 285–9, 293–4, 301, 304, 306, 312–14, 323, 326–7;
union with mortals, see *Men*; feud with the Dwarves 230; tongues
of 4, 148, 163; written characters 163; and Old English 301–2, 304,
309.

    *Wild Elves* 77, 95, 113, 128, 243. See *Brown, Dark, Green,
Grey-, Island-, Lost, Elves*; for *Hidden, Secret, Wood(land)
Elves* see *Woodland Elves*.

*Elwë Singollo*   Thingol. 50

*House of a (the) Hundred Chimneys*   The house of Gilfanon at
     Tavrobel. 283–4, 310
*Huan*   Called 'lord of the Hounds of Hisilomë' (47), 'Captain of Dogs'
     (21, 231), 'Huan of the Dogs'. 21–3, 26–7, 30–1, 34–6, 38–9, 41,
     47–8, 53–9, 62, 68, 231, 233–4, 239, 243
*Hungry Sands*   On the coast of the Isle of the Ancient Mariner. 318
*Hunthor*   Companion of Turambar in the attack on Glaurung. 133
*Huor*   214
*Húrin*   52, 118, 120, 126, 128, 131, 135, 137, 210, 216, 245. See *Úrin*.

*Iceland*   261
*I·Cuilwarthon*   The dead that live again. 41, 51, 245, 249. (Replaced
     *i·Guilwarthon*.)
*Icy Seas*   254
*Idril*   Wife of Tuor, mother of Eärendel. 130, 162, 164–5, 167–70, 174,
     177, 185–93, 199–201, 209–16, 219–20, 253–6, 260, 262–7, 276;
     *Idril Talceleb, Idril of the Silver Feet* 165, 199, 210, 216. See
     *Irildë*.
*I·Guilwarthon*   The dead that live again. 51, 233, 243, 245; *the
     Guilwarthon* 240. (Replaced by *i·Cuilwarthon*.)
*Ilbranteloth*   See *Cris Ilbranteloth*.
*Ilfiniol*   Littleheart. 5, 50, 144–5, 201, 221, 244. (Replaced *Elfriniol*,
     replaced by *Ilfrin*.)
*Ilfrin*   Littleheart. 7, 50, 201. (Replaced *Ilfiniol*.)
*Ilfrith*   Littleheart. 276
*Ilinsor*   Spirit of the Súruli, steersman of the Moon. 259
*Ilkorindi*   Elves 'not of Kôr' (see especially 64). 9, 64–5, 70; *Ilkorin(s)*
     74, 122, 285
*Ilúvatar*   8, 42, 163, 209, 219, 223, 247, 283–4, 287; *the Lord for
     Always* 163, 209
*Ilverin*   Littleheart. 201–2. (Replaced *Elwenildo*.)
*Ilwë*   The middle air that flows among the stars. 281, 328
*Incomers*   Easterlings. 126
*Indor*   Father of Peleg father of Tuor. 160, 217. See *Gon Indor*,
     *Indorildo*.
*Indorildo, Indorion*   Name of Eärendel, great-grandson of Indor.
     217. See *Gon Indor*.
*Indrafangs*   The Longbeard Dwarves of Belegost. 46, 68, 223, 230,
     232–5, 243, 247–8; *Indrafangin* 234, *Indravangs* 19, 68. See
     especially 247.
*Ing*   (1) *Ing, Ingwë* King of Luthany; many references are to his kin,
     sons, or descendants. 301–10, 312; on the relationship between *Ing*
     and *Ingwë* see 305. (2) Earlier name of Inwë. 305. (3) *Ing* in Old
     English legend. 305
*Ingil*   Son of Inwë. 5–6, 258, 280–2, 289, 292, 305, 328. See *Gil*.
*Inguaeones*   See 304–5.

Littleheart   Son of Bronweg (Voronwë), called 'the Gong-warden' (of Mar Vanwa Tyaliéva). 197, 201, 221, 228, 244, 252, 254, 256, 263, 276. For his Elvish names see 201–2, 276.

Lókë   Name in Eldarissa for the dragons of Melko. 85. See Foalókë, Fuithlug.

Lonely Isle, Lonely Island   4–5, 7, 34, 148, 253, 289, 298, 301, 307, 311, 313, 316–17, 322–4, 326–7, 329; the Isle 42, 144, 283–4; the holy isle 291; Island of the Elves 320, 327; Old English se uncúpa holm 290, seo unwemmede íeg 291, 301; speech of 34, 148; poem The Lonely Isle 291. See Tol Eressëa.

Longbeards   See Indrafangs.

Lord of the Rings, The   211, 247, 266, 328; The Fellowship of the Ring 333; The Two Towers 140; The Return of the King 67, 216

Lord of Wolves   Thû (the Necromancer). 54

Lords of the West   The Valar. 205

Lórien   8–9, 33, 42–3, 240, 324

Lôs   Earlier form of the name Loth of Gondolin. 202

Lósengriol   Earlier form of the name Lothengriol of Gondolin. 202

Los'lóriol   Name in Noldorissa of the Golden Flower (kindred of the Gondothlim); earlier Los Glóriol. 216

Lost Elves   Elves of the Great Lands. 9 (of Artanor), 40, 42, 283, 285, 293, 302; tongue of 22, 47. Lost Elves of Hisilómë 63–4, 249

Loth   'The Flower', one of the Seven Names of Gondolin. 158, 202. (Replaced Lôs.)

Lothengriol   'Flower of the Plain', one of the Seven Names of Gondolin. 158, 202. See I.172 and Flower of the Plain.

Lothlim   'People of the Flower', name taken by the survivors of Gondolin at the mouth of Sirion. 196, 201, 252, 259–60

Lug   Orc slain by Tuor in Gondolin. 181

Lumbi   A place where Melko dwelt after his defeat. 278–9

Lúsion   = Lúthien (2). 302

Luthany   England. 301–10, 323, 326–30, 334. See Lúthien (1) and (3), Leithian.

Lúthien   (1) 'Man of Luthany', name given to Ælfwine by the Elves of Tol Eressëa. 301, 304, 309; explained as meaning 'Wanderer', 302. (2) Son of Telumektar 302. (3) = Luthany (England). 312–15, 323–4, 326–7, 329–30, 334. (4) Tinúviel. 52–8, 66, 302, 330

Mablung   'The Heavy-hand(ed)', chief of the thanes of Tinwelint. 38–41, 49–50, 56, 59, 121, 128–30, 134, 231, 233, 243

Maeglin   Later form for Meglin. 210–12, 248

Magbar   Elvish name of Rome. 315, 330. See Rûm.

Magic Isles   5, 7, 254, 260, 311, 316, 320, 324–5, 332, 334; Magic Archipelago 316

Magic Sun   264, 281–2, 285–6, 289, 303; see especially 285–6

name among the Gnomes, though *makil* is an 'Eldar' form (I.259). 84, 86, 94, 112, 116, 118, 125, 128. See *Mormagli*, *Mormegil*.

*Mormegil* 'Black Sword', Túrin (later form of the name). 125, 128

*Morning Star* 266

*Móru* The 'Primeval Night' personified in the Great Spider. 286

*Morwen* 120–1, 126–8, 135, 139. (Replaced *Mavwin*.)

*Mound of Avarice* See *Cûm an-Idrisaith*.

*Mountain of the World* See *Taniquetil*.

*Mountains of Darkness* = *Mountains of Iron*. 162

*Mountains of Iron* See *Iron Mountains*.

*Mountains of Night* The mountains on which grew Taurfuin, the Forest of Night. 20, 46, 62

*Mountains of Shadow* 61–2, 122, 205, 217. See *Ered Wethrin*.

*Mountains of Terror* See *Ered Gorgoroth*.

*Mountains of the East* 6, 295, 300, 311

*Mountains of Valinor* 161, 171, 285, 320, 325

*Music of the Ainur* (not including references to the Tale) 146, 163, 209. See *Ainulindalë*.


*Naimi* Ælfwine's wife, Elf of Tol Eressëa. 290–1, 323, 330. See *Éadgifu* (1).

*Nan* A Giant. 19, 46, 67–8

*Nandorin* 122

*Nan Dumgorthin* 'The Land of the Dark Idols'. 35, 62, 68; *Nan Dungorthin* 62

*Nan Dungortheb* 'The Valley of Dreadful Death'. 62–3

*Nan Elmoth* 248

*Nan-tathren* 140, 214. See *Land of Willows*, *Tasarinan*.

*Nargothrond* 53–4, 56, 61, 123–6, 128–9, 131, 135, 137, 140–1, 205, 208, 245–6, 251; see especially 123–4

*Narn i Hîn Húrin* 119–22, 124, 126–35, 142

*Narog* 123, 132, 135, 141, 244. See *Aros*.

*Narthseg* The Elf who betrayed Artanor to the Dwarves. 231, 243

*Naugladur* Lord of the Dwarves of Nogrod. 225, 230–8, 243, 246–7 (called *king* 225).

*Nauglafring* The Necklace of the Dwarves (references include both names). 41, 59, 72, 136–7, 144, 221, 227–8, 231–2, 234–5, 237–41, 243, 245–7, 252–6, 259, 264; see especially 228

*Nauglath* The Dwarves of Nogrod. 68, 136–7, 223–6, 229, 233–4, 243, 247, 328; see especially 247

*Nautar* Apparently = *Nauglath*. 136, 247, 283, 285, 328

*Nazgûl* 327

*Necklace of the Dwarves* See *Nauglafring*.

*Necromancer, The* 53–5

*Nellas* Elf of Doriath who bore witness at the trial of Túrin. 121

*Oarni*   Spirits of the Sea (identified with 'mermaids' 259, identity denied 263). 253–4, 259–60, 263, 276. See *Mermaids*.
*Oikeroi*   A cat, thane of Tevildo, slain by Huan. 27–8, 30–2, 55–8
*Oinen*   See *Uinen*.
*Old English*   (including citations, words, titles of poems) 197, 200, 266–7, 271, 276, 290–2, 294–5, 298, 301, 304–5, 309, 323, 325, 328–31. Old English spoken by the Elves of Tol Eressëa 301–2, 304, 309
*Old Forest*   328
*Olórë Mallë*   'The Path of Dreams'. 48, 70, 119, 258. See *Way of Dreams*.
*Olwë*   Lord of the Solosimpi in Thingol's place. 50. See *Ellu* (2).
*Ómar*   Youngest of the great Valar, called also *Amillo*. 279
*Ónen*   Earlier name of Uinen. 51
*Orcobal*   Champion of the Orcs, slain by Ecthelion in Gondolin. 181
*Orcs*   Selected references: origin of 14, 159, 219; *children of Melko* 193; described 99, 159–60; sight and hearing of 78–9, 165–6; wolfriders 44, 67, 84, 190, 195; Orcs' blood in Meglin 165; *sons of the Orcs* 165; mercenaries of the Dwarves 230, 247. Singular *Ork* 202, plural *Orqui* 136, 202, 219. See *Goblins*.
*Orfalch Echor*   The great rift in the Encircling Mountains by which Gondolin was approached. 207, 211
*Orgof*   Elf of Artanor, slain by Túrin. 74–6, 122, 142
*Orion*   281–2, 302. See *Telimektar*.
*Orlin*   Man of Hisilómë, slain in Brodda's hall by Turambar. 90
*Orm*   Sea-captain of the Forodwaith, slayer of Déor Ælfwine's father. 318–19, 323, 331
*Orodreth*   Lord of the Rodothlim. 82–4, 98, 117, 123–4
*Oromë*   8, 42, 240, 279
*Orqui*   Earlier plural of *Orc* (*Ork*). See *Orcs*.
*Ossë*   150, 197, 254, 256, 263, 283, 285, 293, 304, 306–9, 323–4, 331
*Ossiriand*   249
*Ost Belegost*   See *Belegost*.
*Oswine*   Prince of Gwar (Kortirion). 313, 323
*Óðinn*   290. See *Wóden*.
*Othrod*   A lord of the Orcs, slain by Tuor in Gondolin. 181
*Ottor Wæfre*   Eriol. 290, 292; Wæfre 291
*Outer Dark*   273, 276
*Outer Land(s)*   (1) The Great Lands (Middle-earth). 254, 265. See *Lands Without*. (2) The lands West of the Great Sea. 316–17, 324–5, 334
*Outer Oceans, Outer Sea(s)*   154, 160, 276. See *Vai*.
*Oxford*   146, 269, 292–3, 295, 300, 323; (Old English) *Oxenaford* 292; poem *The City of Present Sorrow* 295–8. See *Taruithorn*, *Taruktarna*.
*Oxford English Dictionary*   69, 147

on 281, 286; dwelling of 255, 276; Sun-dwellers 261; beyond the Sun 162, West of the Sun 271–2; an emblem of the King's House in Gondolin 172. See *Magic Sun*, *Urwendi*.

*Sundering Seas*    264

*Swallow, The*    Name of one of the kindreds of the Gondothlim. 173, 176, 178–83, 193. See *Duilin* (2).

*Swan*    As emblem of Tuor and of his men in Gondolin (swanwings on helm and shield). 152, 164, 172, 193, 205, 210, 276; *house of the Swan* 160. See *Alqarámë*, *Swanwing*, *Wing*.

*Swanhaven*    258; *Haven of the Swans* 11, 65. See *Cópas Alqalunten*, *Kópas*.

*Swanwing*    Tuor's ship. 253–5, 260, 263, 265. See *Alqarámë*.

*Taimonto*    = *Telimektar*. 281, 328; *Taimondo* 328

*Talath Dirnen*    The Guarded Plain of Nargothrond. 61

*Talceleb*    See *Idril*.

*Tale-fire*    In Mar Vanwa Tyaliéva. 144–5, 197, 221, 252. See *Room of Logs*, *Tôn a Gwedrin*.

*Tale of Years*    208

*Taltelepta*    See *Irildë*.

*Tamar Lamefoot*    Son of Bethos of the Woodmen. 101, 103, 106, 108–11, 130, 132–4, 215. (Replaced by *Brandir*.)

*Taniquetil*    77, 141, 161, 163, 171, 202, 257, 262, 265, 271–2; *Mountain of the World* 77

*Tanyasalpë*    'Bowl of Fire'. 138. See *Fauri*, *Faskalan*, *Fôs 'Almir*.

*Tarnin Austa*    172. See *Gates of Summer*.

*Taruithorn, Taruktarna*    Gnomish and Eldarissa names of Oxford. 292–3

*Tasarinan*    The Land of Willows. 140, 225, 248, 278; *the Battle of Tasarinan* 70, 140, 154, 219–20, 278–9. See *Land of Willows*, *Nan-tathren*.

*Taurfuin*    The Forest of Night. 34–5, 47, 62, 78. Later form *Taur-nu-Fuin* 62, 123. See *Forest of Night*.

*Taurossë, Tavaros(së)*    Eldarissa forms for *Tavrobel*. 292

*Tavrobel*    145, 283–4, 287–9, 292–3, 307, 310, 323, 326; *Tavrobel the Old* 310, *the New* 310; tower of 287; bridge and joining rivers at 288–9; *Golden Book of* 285, 310; *Tales of* 290. See *Gilfanon*, *Great Haywood*, *Pine of Belaurin*.

*Tavrost*    = *Tavrobel*. 292

*Teiglin*    130, 132, 135, 140, 249; *Crossings of Teiglin* 127, 130, 132; ravines of 132–4

*Telchar*    Dwarf smith of Nogrod. 58, 129

*Teld Quing Ilon*    'Rainbow Roof', earlier name for *(Cris) Ilbranteloth*. 202

*Teleri*    The first kindred of the Elves (afterwards called Vanyar). 4, 253, 255, 278, 307

*West Wind* 261

*Wielisc* See *Wéalas.*

*Wing, The* Emblem of Tuor, see *Swan*; *White Wing* 172; *men, folk, guard, of the Wing* in Gondolin 174, 176–8, 180, 182, 190, 192

*Winged Helms* The Forodwaith. 330, 334. See *Gwasgonin.*

*Wingildi* Spirits of the sea-foam. 276

*Wingilot* 'Foam-flower', Eärendel's ship. 145, 253–4, 256, 260–1, 263; *Wingelot* 260, 262, 272; *Vingelot* 262, 272

*Wirilómë* 'Gloomweaver'. 260–1. See *Ungweliant(ë).*

*Withered Dale* Where Tevildo encountered Huan. 48, 56

*Withered Heath* Heath near Tavrobel, after the Battle of the Heath of the Sky-roof. 284, 287

*Wóden* Old English name of the Germanic god in Old Norse called *Óðinn*; by Eriol identified with Manwë. 290

*Wolfriders* See *Orcs.*

*Wolf-Sauron* 55

*Woodland Elves* Elves of Artanor. Also *Woodelves, Elves of the wood(land), of the forest*, etc. 11, 13, 18, 34–5, 37, 43, 45, 52, 63, 65–6, 69, 73–4, 78, 92, 142, 222–3, 228, 242–3, 245–6; *wood(land) fairies* 23, 35, 63; *hidden Elves* 10; *secret Elves* 11, 73, 123

*Woodmen* (later *Woodmen of Brethil*) Also *woodfolk, wood(land)-rangers*. 91, 100–8, 112–13, 125, 127, 130–5, 138, 141–2. See *Vettar.*

*Yavanna* 286. See *Belaurin, Palúrien.*

*Year of Lamentation* 120

*Ythlings* 'Children of the Waves'. 319–20, 322, 325, 331–2, 334; *Ythlingas* 331; described, 318. See *Eneathrim, Shipmen of the West.*

Far in the Northern hills of stone
in caverns black there was a throne
by flame encircled; there the smoke
in coiling columns rose to choke
the breath of life, and there in deep
and gasping dungeons lost would creep
to hopeless death all those who strayed
by doom beneath that ghastly shade.

A King there sat, most dark and fell
of all that under heaven dwell.
Than earth or sea, than moon or star
more ancient was he, mightier far
in mind abysmal than the thought
of Eldar or of Men, and wrought
of strength primeval; ere the stone
was hewn to build the world, alone
he walked in darkness, fierce and dire,
burned, as he wielded it, by fire.

He 'twas that laid in ruin black
the Blessed Realm and fled then back
to Middle-earth anew to build
beneath the mountains mansions filled
with misbegotten slaves of hate:
death's shadow brooded at his gate.
His host he armed with spears of steel
and brands of flame, and at their heel
the wolf walked and the serpent crept
with lidless eyes. Now forth they leapt,
his ruinous legions, kindling war
in field and fell and woodland hoar.
Where long the golden elanor
had gleamed amid the grass they bore
their banners black; where finch had sung
and harpers silver harps had wrung
now dark the ravens wheeled and cried
amid the reek, and far and wide
the swords of Morgoth dripped with red
above the hewn and trampled dead.

# THE LAYS OF BELERIAND

ᚠᛟ ᛒᚱᛟᚷᛈ ᛈᚾᛈ ᛏᛟ ᚻᛣ ᛈᛋᚠᛩ ᛖ ᛇᛏᛒᛟᛘ ᛏᛟ ᛏᚢᚻ ᛒᛖ ᛩᛏᛈᛘᛟᛁ
ᚪᚥᛟᛘ ᛈᚩᚪ ᚳᚳᚠᛚᛘ ᛦᛟᚻᛏᛈᛟ ᛦᛁᛚᛏ ᛈᛏᛩᛁᛘ ᚾᚻ ᛞᚳᛩ ᛖ ᚷᚠ

J. R. R. TOLKIEN

# The Lays
## of
# Beleriand

Christopher Tolkien

ᚥᛏ ᚾᚻ ᛈᚾᛈ ᛏᛟ ᛈᛏᛖ ᛒᛖ ᛈᚥᛟᛘ꞉ ᚾᚻ ᛏᛟ ᛚᛩᛘᛈᛟ ᛈᚾᛈ ᛖ ᛏᛟ ᛏᛖ
ᛏᛁᛒᛁᛘ ᛞᚳᛩ ᛖ ᛏᛟ ᚳᛩᚳᛈ ᛒᛖ ᛈᛣᚥᛘ ᛈᚪᚾ ᛏᛁᛒᛁᛘ ᛖ ᛒᚱᚪ ᛖ ᛏᛟ
ᛩᚪᛘᛈᛟ ᛒᛖ ᛈᛣᚥᛘ ᚾᚻᛏ ᛩᛏᚪᚪᚥᛒᚪ ᛈ ᛏᛟ ᛇᛩᚪᚻ ᛒᛖ ᛏᚾᛈᛘᚾᛏ

# CONTENTS

# PREFACE

This third part of 'The History of Middle-earth' contains the two major poems by J. R. R. Tolkien concerned with the legends of the Elder Days: the *Lay of the Children of Húrin* in alliterative verse, and the *Lay of Leithian* in octosyllabic couplets. The alliterative poem was composed while my father held appointments at the University of Leeds (1920–5); he abandoned it for the *Lay of Leithian* at the end of that time, and never turned to it again. I have found no reference to it in any letter or other writing of his that has survived (other than the few words cited on p. 3), and I do not recollect his ever speaking of it. But this poem, which though extending to more than 2000 lines is only a fragment in relation to what he once planned, is the most sustained embodiment of his abiding love of the resonance and richness of sound that might be achieved in the ancient English metre. It marks also an important stage in the evolution of the Matter of the Elder Days, and contains passages that strongly illumine his imagination of Beleriand; it was, for example, in this poem that the great redoubt of Nargothrond arose from the primitive caves of the Rodothlim in the *Lost Tales*, and only in this poem was Nargothrond described. It exists in two versions, the second being a revision and enlargement that proceeds much less far into the story, and both are given in this book.

My father worked on the *Lay of Leithian* for six years, abandoning it in its turn in September 1931. In 1929 it was read so far as it then went by C. S. Lewis, who sent him a most ingenious commentary on a part of it; I acknowledge with thanks the permission of C. S. Lewis PTE Limited to include this.

In 1937 he said in a letter that 'in spite of certain virtuous passages' the *Lay of Leithian* had 'grave defects' (see p. 366). A decade or more later, he received a detailed, and remarkably unconstrained, criticism of the poem from someone who knew and admired his poetry. I do not know for certain who this was. In choosing 'the staple octosyllabic couplet of romance,' he wrote, my father had chosen one of the most difficult of forms 'if one wishes to avoid monotony and sing-song in a very long poem. I am often astonished by your success, but it is by no means consistently maintained.' His strictures on the diction of the Lay included archaisms so archaic that they needed annotation, distorted order, use of emphatic *doth* or *did* where there is no emphasis, and language sometimes flat and conventional (in contrast to passages of 'gorgeous description'). There is no record of what my father thought of this criticism (written when *The Lord of the Rings* was already completed), but it must be associated in some way with the fact that in 1949 or 1950 he returned to the *Lay of Leithian* and began a revision that soon became virtually a new poem; and relatively little though he wrote of it, its advance on the old version in all those respects in which that had been censured is so great as to give it a sad prominence in the long list of his works that might have been. The new Lay is included in this book, and a page from a fine manuscript of it is reproduced as frontispiece.

The sections of both poems are interleaved with commentaries which are primarily concerned to trace the evolution of the legends and the lands they are set in.

The two pages reproduced from the *Lay of the Children of Húrin* (p. 15) are from the original manuscript of the first version, lines 297–317 and 318–33. For differences between the readings of the manuscript and those of the printed text see pp. 4–5. The page from the *Lay of Leithian* in Elvish script (p. 299) comes from the 'A' version of the original Lay (see pp. 150–1), and there are certain differences in the text from the 'B' version which is that printed. These pages from the original manuscripts are reproduced with the permission of the Bodleian Library, Oxford, and I thank the staff of the Department of Western Manuscripts at the Bodleian for their assistance.

The two earlier volumes in this series (the first and second parts of *The Book of Lost Tales*) are referred to as 'I' and 'II'. The fourth volume will contain the 'Sketch of the Mythology' (1926), from which the *Silmarillion* 'tradition' derived; the *Quenta Noldorinwa* or History of the Noldoli (1930); the first map of the North-west of Middle-earth; the *Ambarkanta* ('Shape of the World') by Rúmil, together with the only existing maps of the entire World; the earliest *Annals of Valinor* and *Annals of Beleriand*, by Pengolod the Wise of Gondolin; and the fragments of translations of the *Quenta* and *Annals* from Elvish into Anglo-Saxon by Ælfwine of England.

# I

# THE LAY OF THE
# CHILDREN OF HÚRIN

There exists a substantial manuscript (28 pages long) entitled 'Sketch of the Mythology with especial reference to "The Children of Húrin"'; and this 'Sketch' is the next complete narrative, in the *prose* tradition, after the *Lost Tales* (though a few fragmentary writings are extant from the intervening time). On the envelope containing this manuscript my father wrote at some later time:

> Original 'Silmarillion'. Form orig[inally] composed c. 1926–30 for R. W. Reynolds to explain background of 'alliterative version' of Túrin & the Dragon: then in progress (unfinished) (begun c. 1918).

He seems to have written first '1921' before correcting this to '1918'.

R. W. Reynolds taught my father at King Edward's School, Birmingham (see Humphrey Carpenter, *Biography*, p. 47). In a passage of his diary written in August 1926 he wrote that 'at the end of last year' he had heard again from R. W. Reynolds, that they had corresponded subsequently, and that he had sent Reynolds many of his poems, including *Tinúviel* and *Túrin* ('*Tinúviel* meets with qualified approval, it is too prolix, but how could I ever cut it down, and the specimen I sent of *Túrin* with little or none'). This would date the 'Sketch' as originally written (it was subsequently heavily revised) definitely in 1926, probably fairly early in the year. It must have accompanied the specimen of *Túrin* (the alliterative poem), the background of which it was written to explain, to Anacapri, where Reynolds was then living in retirement.

My father took up his appointment to the Professorship of Anglo-Saxon at Oxford in the winter term (October–December) of 1925, though for that term he had to continue to teach at Leeds also, since the appointments overlapped. There can be no doubt that at any rate the great bulk of the alliterative *Children of Húrin* (or *Túrin*) was completed at Leeds, and I think it virtually certain that he had ceased to work on it before he moved south: in fact there seems nothing to oppose to the natural assumption that he left 'Túrin' for 'Tinúviel' (the *Lay of Leithian*), which he began according to his diary in the summer of 1925 (see p. 159 and footnote).

For the date of its commencement we have only my father's later (and perhaps hesitant) statement that it was 'begun c. 1918'. A *terminus a quo* is provided by a page of the earliest manuscript of the poem, which is written on a slip from the Oxford English Dictionary bearing the printer's stamp *May 1918*. On the other hand the name *Melian* which occurs near the beginning of the earliest manuscript shows it to be later than the typescript version of the *Tale of Tinúviel*, where the Queen's name was *Gwenethlin* and only became *Melian* in the course of its composition (II. 51); and the manuscript version of that Tale which underlies the typescript seems itself to have been one of the last completed elements in the *Lost Tales* (see I. 204).

*The Children of Húrin* exists in two versions, which I shall refer to as I and II, both of them found in manuscript and later typescript (IA, IB; IIA, IIB). I do not think that the second is significantly later than the first; it is indeed possible, and would not be in any way uncharacteristic, that my father began work on II while he was still composing at a later point in I. II is essentially an expansion of I, with many lines, and blocks of lines, left virtually unchanged. Until the second version is reached it will be sufficient to refer simply to 'A' and 'B', the manuscript and typescript of the first version.

The manuscript A consists of two parts: first (a) a bundle of small slips, numbered 1–32. The poem is here in a very rough state with many alternative readings, and in places at least may represent the actual beginnings, the first words written down. This is followed by (b) a set of large sheets of examination paper from the University of Leeds, numbered 33 ff., where the poem is for the most part written out in a more finished form – the second stage of composition; but my father wrote in line-numbers continuously through (a) and (b) – lines 1–528 in (a), lines 528 ff. in (b). We have thus one sole text, not two, without any overlap; and if (a), the slips, ever existed in the form of (b), the examination sheets, that part has disappeared. In part (b) there are many later emendations in pencil.

Based on this manuscript is the typescript B. This introduces changes not found in A or its emendations; and it was itself emended both in ink and pencil, doubtless involving several movements of revision. To take a single line as exemplification: line 8 was written first in A:

> Lo! Thalion in the throng    of thickest battle

The line was emended, in two stages, to

> Lo! Thalion Húrin    in the throng of battle

and this was the form in B as typed; but B was emended, in two stages, to

> Lo! Húrin Thalion    in the hosts of war

It is obvious that to set this and a great many other similar cases out in a textual apparatus would be a huge task and the result impossibly complicated. The text that follows is therefore, so far as purely metrical-stylistic changes are concerned, that of B as *emended*, and apart from a few special cases there is no mention in the notes of earlier readings.

In the matter of names, however, the poem presents great difficulty; for changes were made at quite different times and were not introduced consistently throughout. If the latest form in any particular passage is made the principle of choice, irrespective of any other consideration, then the text will have *Morwin* at lines 105, 129, *Mavwin* 137 etc., *Morwen* 438, 472; *Ulmo* 1469, but *Ylmir* 1529 and subsequently; *Nirnaith Ornoth* 1448, but *Nirnaith Únoth* 1543. If the later *Nirnaith Ornoth* is adopted at 1543, it seems scarcely justifiable to intrude it at lines 13 and 218 (where the final form is *Ninin Unothradin*). I have decided finally to abandon overall consistency, and to treat individual names as seems best in the circumstances; for example, I give *Ylmir* rather than *Ulmo* at line 1469, for consistency with all the other occurrences, and while changing *Únoth* to *Ornoth* at line 1543 I retain *Ornoth* rather than the much later *Arnediad* at line 26 of the second version – similarly I prefer the earlier *Finweg* to *Fingon* (1975, second version 19, 520) and *Bansil, Glingol* to *Belthil, Glingal* (2027–8). All such points are documented in the notes.

A has no title. In B as typed the title was *The Golden Dragon*, but this was emended to *Túrin Son of Húrin & Glórund the Dragon*. The second version of the poem was first titled *Túrin*, but this was changed to *The Children of Húrin*, and I adopt this, the title by which my father referred to the poem in the 1926 'Sketch', as the general title of the work.

The poem in the first version is divided into a short prologue (Húrin and Morgoth) without sub-title and three long sections, of which the first two ('Túrin's Fostering' and 'Beleg') were only introduced later into the typescript; the third ('Failivrin') is marked both in A and in B as typed.

The detail of the typescript is largely preserved in the present text, but I have made the capitalisation rather more consistent, added in occasional accents, and increased the number of breaks in the text. The space between the half-lines is marked in the second part of the A-text and begins at line 543 in B.

I have avoided the use of numbered notes to the text, and all annotation is related to the line-numbers of the poem. This annotation (very largely concerned with variations of names, and comparisons with names in the *Lost Tales*) is found at the end of each of the three major parts, followed by a commentary on the matter of that part.

Throughout, the *Tale* refers to the *Tale of Turambar and the Foalókë* (II. 69 ff.); *Narn* refers to the *Narn i Hîn Húrin*, in *Unfinished Tales* pp. 57 ff.

★

# TÚRIN SON OF HÚRIN
## &
# GLÓRUND THE DRAGON

Lo! the golden dragon    of the God of Hell,
the gloom of the woods    of the world now gone,
the woes of Men,    and weeping of Elves
fading faintly    down forest pathways,
is now to tell,    and the name most tearful    5
of Níniel the sorrowful,    and the name most sad
of Thalion's son Túrin    o'erthrown by fate.

Lo! Húrin Thalion    in the hosts of war
was whelmed, what time    the white-clad armies
of Elfinesse    were all to ruin    10
by the dread hate driven    of Delu-Morgoth.
That field is yet    by the folk naméd
Nínin Unothradin,    Unnumbered Tears.
There the children of Men,    chieftain and warrior,
fled and fought not,    but the folk of the Elves    15
they betrayed with treason,    save that true man only,
Thalion Erithámrod    and his thanes like gods.
There in host on host    the hill-fiend Orcs
overbore him at last    in that battle terrible,
by the bidding of Bauglir    bound him living,    20
and pulled down the proudest    of the princes of Men.
To Bauglir's halls    in the hills builded,
to the Hells of Iron    and the hidden caverns
they haled the hero    of Hithlum's land,
Thalion Erithámrod,    to their thronéd lord,    25
whose breast was burnt    with a bitter hatred,
and wroth he was    that the wrack of war
had not taken Turgon    ten times a king,
even Finweg's heir;    nor Fëanor's children,
makers of the magic    and immortal gems.    30
For Turgon towering    in terrible anger
a pathway clove him    with his pale sword-blade
out of that slaughter –    yea, his swath was plain
through the hosts of Hell    like hay that lieth
all low on the lea    where the long scythe goes.    35
A countless company    that king did lead
through the darkened dales    and drear mountains

out of ken of his foes,    and he comes not more
in the tale; but the triumph    he turned to doubt
of Morgoth the evil,    whom mad wrath took.                    40
Nor spies sped him,    nor spirits of evil,
nor his wealth of wisdom    to win him tidings,
whither the nation    of the Gnomes was gone.
Now a thought of malice,    when Thalion stood,
bound, unbending,    in his black dungeon,                      45
then moved in his mind    that remembered well
how Men were accounted    all mightless and frail
by the Elves and their kindred;    how only treason
could master the magic    whose mazes wrapped
the children of Corthûn,    and cheated his purpose.           50

'Is it dauntless Hurin,'    quoth Delu-Morgoth,
'stout steel-handed,    who stands before me,
a captive living    as a coward might be?
Knowest thou my name,    or need'st be told
what hope he has    who is haled to Angband –                   55
the bale most bitter,    the Balrogs' torment?'

'I know and I hate.    For that knowledge I fought thee
by fear unfettered,    nor fear I now,'
said Thalion there,    and a thane of Morgoth
on the mouth smote him;    but Morgoth smiled:                  60
'Fear when thou feelest,    and the flames lick thee,
and the whips of the Balrogs    thy white flesh brand.
Yet a way canst win,    an thou wishest, still
to lessen thy lot    of lingering woe.
Go question the captives    of the accursed people             65
I have taken, and tell me    where Turgon is hid;
how with fire and death    I may find him soon,
where he lurketh lost    in lands forgot.
Thou must feign thee a friend    faithful in anguish,
and their inmost hearts    thus open and search.                70
Then, if truth thou tellest,    thy triple bonds
I will bid men unbind,    that abroad thou fare
in my service to search    the secret places
following the footsteps    of these foes of the Gods.'

'Build not thy hopes    so high, O Bauglir –                    75
I am no tool    for thy evil treasons;
torment were sweeter    than a traitor's stain.'

'If torment be sweet,    treasure is liever.
The hoards of a hundred    hundred ages,
the gems and jewels    of the jealous Gods,                   80
are mine, and a meed    shall I mete thee thence,
yea, wealth to glut    the Worm of Greed.'

'Canst not learn of thy lore    when thou look'st on a foe,
O Bauglir unblest?    Bray no longer
of the things thou hast thieved    from the Three Kindreds.    85
In hate I hold thee,    and thy hests in scorn.'

'Boldly thou bravest me.    Be thy boast rewarded,'
in mirth quod Morgoth,    'to me now the deeds,
and thy aid I ask not;    but anger thee nought
if little they like thee.    Yea, look thereon               90
helpless to hinder,    or thy hand to raise.'

Then Thalion was thrust    to Thangorodrim,
that mountain that meets    the misty skies
on high o'er the hills    that Hithlum sees
blackly brooding    on the borders of the north.             95
To a stool of stone    on its steepest peak
they bound him in bonds,    an unbreakable chain,
and the Lord of Woe    there laughing stood,
then cursed him for ever    and his kin and seed
with a doom of dread,    of death and horror.                100
There the mighty man    unmovéd sat;
but unveiled was his vision,    that he viewed afar
all earthly things    with eyes enchanted
that fell on his folk –    a fiend's torment.

# I

## TÚRIN'S FOSTERING

Lo! the lady Morwin    in the Land of Shadows            105
waited in the woodland    for her well-beloved;
but he came never    from the combat home.
No tidings told her    whether taken or dead,
or lost in flight    he lingered yet.
Laid waste his lands,    and his lieges slain,             110
and men unmindful    of his mighty lordship
dwelt in Dorlómin    and dealt unkindly

with his widowed wife;    and she went with child,
who a son must succour    now sadly orphaned,
Túrin Thaliodrin    of tender years.        115
Then in days of blackness    was her daughter born,
and was naméd Nienor,    a name of tears
that in language of eld    is Lamentation.
Then her thoughts turnéd    to Thingol the Elf-king,
and the dancer of Doriath,    his daughter Tinúviel,        120
whom the boldest of the brave,    Beren Ermabwed,
had won to wife.    He once had known
firmest friendship    to his fellow in arms,
Thalion Erithámrod –    so thought she now,
and said to her son,    'My sweetest child,        125
our friends are few,    and thy father comes not.
Thou must fare afar    to the folk of the wood,
where Thingol is throned    in the Thousand Caves.
If he remember Morwin    and thy mighty sire
he will fain foster thee,    and feats of arms        130
he will teach thee, the trade    of targe and sword,
and Thalion's son    no thrall shall be –
but remember thy mother    when thy manhood nears.'

Heavy boded the heart    of Húrin's son,
yet he weened her words    were wild with grief,        135
and he denied her not,    for no need him seemed.
Lo! henchmen had Morwin,    Halog and Gumlin,
who were young of yore    ere the youth of Thalion,
who alone of the lieges    of that lord of Men
steadfast in service    staid beside her:        140
now she bade them brave    the black mountains,
and the woods whose ways    wander to evil;
though Túrin be tender    and to travail unused,
they must gird them and go;    but glad they were not,
and Morwin mourned    when men saw not.        145

Came a summer day    when sun filtered
warm through the woodland's    waving branches.
Then Morwin stood    her mourning hiding
by the gate of her garth    in a glade of the woods.
At the breast she mothered    her babe unweaned,        150
and the doorpost held    lest she droop for anguish.
There Gumlin guided    her gallant boy,
and a heavy burden    was borne by Halog;

but the heart of Túrin    was heavy as stone
uncomprehending    its coming anguish.                                    155
He sought for comfort,    with courage saying:
'Quickly will I come    from the courts of Thingol;
long ere manhood    I will lead to Morwin
great tale of treasure,    and true comrades' –
for he wist not the weird    woven by Bauglir,                            160
nor the sundering sorrow    that swept between.
The farewells are taken:    their footsteps are turned
to the dark forest:    the dwelling fadeth
in the tangled trees.    Then in Túrin leapt
his awakened heart,    and he wept blindly,                               165
calling 'I cannot,    I cannot leave thee.
O Morwin, my mother,    why makest me go?
Hateful are the hills    where hope is lost.
O Morwin, my mother,    I am meshed in tears.
Grim are the hills,    and my home is gone.'                              170
And there came his cries    calling faintly
down the dark alleys    of the dreary trees,
and one who wept    weary on the threshold
heard how the hills said    'my home is gone.'

The ways were weary    and woven with deceit                             175
o'er the hills of Hithlum    to the hidden kingdom
deep in the darkness    of Doriath's forest;
and never ere now    for need or wonder
had children of Men    chosen that pathway,
and few of the folk    have followed it since.                           180
There Túrin and the twain    knew torment of thirst,
and hunger and fear    and hideous nights,
for wolfriders    and wandering Orcs
and the Things of Morgoth    thronged the woodland.
Magics were about them,    that they missed their ways                   185
and strayed steerless,    and the stars were hid.
Thus they passed the mountains,    but the mazes of Doriath
wildered and wayworn    in wanhope bound them.
They had nor bread nor water,    and bled of strength
their death they deemed it    to die forewandered,                       190
when they heard a horn    that hooted afar,
and baying dogs.    It was Beleg the hunter,
who farthest fared    of his folk abroad
ahunting by hill    and hollow valley,

who cared not for concourse    and commerce of men.          195
He was great of growth    and goodly-limbed,
but lithe of girth,    and lightly on the ground
his footsteps fell    as he fared towards them,
all garbed in grey    and green and brown –
a son of the wilderness    who wist no sire.          200

'Who are ye?' he asked.    'Outlaws, or maybe
hard hunted men    whom hate pursueth?'

'Nay, for famine and thirst    we faint,' saith Halog,
'wayworn and wildered,    and wot not the road.
Or hast not heard    of the hills of slain,          205
or the tear-drenchéd field    where the terror and fire
of Morgoth devoured    both Men and Elves?
There Thalion Erithámrod    and his thanes like gods
vanished from the earth,    and his valiant lady
weeps yet widowed    as she waits in Hithlum.          210
Thou lookest on the last    of the lieges of Morwin
and Thalion's son Túrin,    who to Thingol's court
are wending by the word    of the wife of Húrin.'

Then Beleg bade them    be blithe, and said:
'The Gods have guided you    to good keeping.          215
I have heard of the house    of Húrin the Steadfast –
and who hath not heard    of the hills of slain,
of Nínin Unothradin,    the Unnumbered Tears?
To that war I went not,    but wage a feud
with the Orcs unending,    whom mine arrows bitter          220
oft stab unseen    and strike to death.
I am the huntsman Beleg    of the Hidden People.'
Then he bade them drink,    and drew from his belt
a flask of leather    full filled with wine
that is bruised from the berries    of the burning South –          225
and the Gnome-folk know it,    and the nation of the Elves,
and by long ways lead it    to the lands of the North.
There bakéd flesh    and bread from his wallet
they had to their hearts' joy;    but their heads were mazed
by the wine of Dor-Winion    that went in their veins,          230
and they soundly slept    on the soft needles
of the tall pine-trees    that towered above.
Later they wakened    and were led by ways
devious winding    through the dark wood-realm

by slade and slope   and swampy thicket                    235
through lonely days   and long night-times,
and but for Beleg   had been baffled utterly
by the magic mazes   of Melian the Queen.
To the shadowy shores   he showed the way
where stilly that stream   strikes 'fore the gates           240
of the cavernous court   of the King of Doriath.
O'er the guarded bridge   he gained a passage,
and thrice they thanked him,   and thought in their hearts
'the Gods are good' –   had they guessed maybe
what the future enfolded   they had feared to live.          245

To the throne of Thingol   the three were come,
and their speech sped them;   for he spake them fair,
and held in honour   Húrin the steadfast,
Beren Ermabwed's   brother-in-arms.
Remembering Morwin,   of mortals fairest,                    250
he turned not Túrin   in contempt away;
said: 'O son of Húrin,   here shalt sojourn
in my cavernous court   for thy kindred's sake.
Nor as slave or servant,   but a second king's son
thou shalt dwell in dear love,   till thou deem'st it time   255
to remember thy mother   Morwin's loneliness.
Thou wisdom shalt win   unwist of Men
and weapons shalt wield   as the warrior Elves,
and Thalion's son   no thrall shall be.'

There tarried the twain   that had tended the child,          260
till their limbs were lightened   and they longed to fare
through dread and danger   to their dear lady.
But Gumlin was gone   in greater years
than Halog, and hoped not   to home again.
Then sickness took him,   and he stayed by Túrin,            265
while Halog hardened   his heart to go.
An Elfin escort   to his aid was given
and magics of Melian,   and a meed of gold.
In his mouth a message   to Morwin was set,
words of the king's will,   how her wish was granted;        270
how Thingol called her   to the Thousand Caves
to fare unfearing   with his folk again,
there to sojourn in solace,   till her son be grown;
for Húrin the hero   was held in mind,
and no might had Morgoth   where Melian dwelt.               275

Of the errand of the Elves    and that other Halog
the tale tells not,    save in time they came
to the threshold of Morwin,    and Thingol's message
was said where she sate    in her solitary hall.
But she dared not do    as was dearly bidden,                    280
for Nienor her nestling    was not yet weaned.
More, the pride of her people,    princes of Men,
had suffered her send    her son to Thingol
when despair sped her,    but to spend her days
as alms-guest of others,    even Elfin kings,                   285
it liked her little;    and there lived e'en now
a hope in her heart    that Húrin would come,
and the dwelling was dear    where he dwelt of old.
At night she would listen    for a knock at the doors,
or a footstep falling    that she fondly knew;                  290
so she fared not forth,    and her fate was woven.
Yet the thanes of Thingol    she thanked nobly,
and her shame she showed not,    how shorn of glory
to reward their wending    she had wealth too scant;
but gave them in gift    her golden things                      295
that last lingered,    and they led away
a helm of Húrin    that was hewn in war
when he battled with Beren    his brother-in-arms
against ogres and Orcs    and evil foemen;
'twas o'erwritten with runes    by wrights of old.              300
She bade Thingol receive it    and think of her.

Thus Halog her henchman    came home, but the Elves,
the thanes of Thingol,    thrust through the woods,
and the message of Morwin    in a month's journey,
so quick their coming,    to the king was said.                 305
Then was Melian    moved to ruth,
and courteously received    the king her gift,
who deeply delved    had dungeons filled
with Elfin armouries    of ancient gear,
but he handled the helm    as his hoard were scant;             310
said: 'High were the head    that upheld this thing
with that token crowned    of the towering dragon
that Thalion Erithámrod    thrice-renownéd
oft bore into battle    with baleful foes.'
Then a thought was thrust    into Thingol's heart,              315
and Túrin he called    and told when come

that Morwin his mother    a mighty thing
had sent to her son,    his sire's heirloom,
a helm that hammers    had hardened of old,
whose makers had mingled    a magic therein          320
that its worth was a wonder    and its wearer safe,
guarded from glaive    or gleaming axe –
'Lo! Húrin's helm    hoard thou till manhood
bids thee battle;    then bravely don it';
and Túrin touched it,    but took it not,          325
too weak to wield    that weight as yet,
and his mind mournéd    for Morwin's answer,
and the first of his sorrows    o'erfilled his soul.

Thus came it to pass    in the court of Thingol
that Túrin tarried    for twelve long years          330
with Gumlin his guardian,    who guided him thither
when but seven summers    their sorrows had laid
on the son of Thalion.    For the seven first
his lot was lightened,    since he learnt at whiles
from faring folk    what befell in Hithlum,          335
and tidings were told    by trusty Elves,
how Morwin his mother    was more at ease;
and they named Nienor    that now was growing
to the sweet beauty    of a slender maiden.
Thus his heart knew hope,    and his hap was fairer.          340
There he waxed wonderly    and won him praise
in all lands where Thingol    as lord was held
for the strength of his body    and stoutness of heart.
Much lore he learned,    and loved wisdom,
but fortune followed him    in few desires;          345
oft wrong and awry    what he wrought turnéd;
what he loved he lost,    what he longed for he won not;
and full friendship    he found not easily,
nor was lightly loved    for his looks were sad.
He was gloomy-hearted,    and glad seldom,          350
for the sundering sorrow    that seared his youth.

On manhood's threshold    he was mighty holden
in the wielding of weapons;    and in weaving song
he had a minstrel's mastery,    but mirth was not in it,
for he mourned the misery    of the Men of Hithlum.          355
Yet greater his grief    grew thereafter,
when from Hithlum's hills    he heard no more,

Two pages from the original manuscript of *The Lay of the Children of Húrin*

and no traveller told him    tidings of Morwin.
For those days were drawing    to the Doom of the Gnomes,
and the power of the Prince    of the People of Hell,                    360
of the grim Glamhoth,    was grown apace,
till the lands of the North    were loud with their noise,
and they fell on the folk    with flame and ruin
who bent not to Bauglir,    or the borders passed
of dark Dorlómin    with its dreary pines                                365
that Hithlum unhappy    is hight by Men.
There Morgoth shut them,    and the Shadowy Mountains
fenced them from Faërie    and the folk of the wood.
Even Beleg fared not    so far abroad
as once was his wont,    and the woods were filled                       370
with the armies of Angband    and evil deeds,
while murder walked    on the marches of Doriath;
only mighty magic    of Melian the Queen
yet held their havoc    from the Hidden People.

To assuage his sorrow    and to sate the rage                            375
and hate of his heart    for the hurts of his folk
then Húrin's son    took the helm of his sire
and weapons weighty    for the wielding of men,
and went to the woods    with warlike Elves;
and far in the fight    his feet led him,                                380
into black battle    yet a boy in years.
Ere manhood's measure    he met and slew
the Orcs of Angband    and evil things
that roamed and ravened    on the realm's borders.
There hard his life,    and hurts he got him,                           385
the wounds of shaft    and warfain sword,
and his prowess was proven    and his praise renowned,
and beyond his years    he was yielded honour;
for by him was holden    the hand of ruin
from Thingol's folk,    and Thû feared him –                            390
Thû who was thronéd    as thane most mighty
neath Morgoth Bauglir;    whom that mighty one bade
'Go ravage the realm    of the robber Thingol,
and mar the magic    of Melian the Queen.'

Only one was there    in war greater,                                    395
higher in honour    in the hearts of the Elves,
than Túrin son of Húrin    untamed in war –
even the huntsman Beleg    of the Hidden People,

the son of the wilderness    who wist no sire
(to bend whose bow    of the black yew-tree                    400
had none the might),    unmatched in knowledge
of the wood's secrets    and the weary hills.
He was leader beloved    of the light-armed bands,
the scouts that scoured,    scorning danger,
afar o'er the fells    their foemen's lairs;                   405
and tales and tidings    timely won them
of camps and councils,    of comings and goings –
all the movements of the might    of Morgoth the Terrible.
Thus Túrin, who trusted    to targe and sword,
who was fain of fighting    with foes well seen,               410
and the banded troops    of his brave comrades
were snared seldom    and smote unlooked-for.

Then the fame of the fights    on the far marches
were carried to the court    of the King of Doriath,
and tales of Túrin    were told in his halls,                  415
and how Beleg the ageless    was brother-in-arms
to the black-haired boy    from the beaten people.
Then the king called them    to come before him
ever and anon    when the Orc-raids waned;
to rest them and revel,    and to raise awhile                 420
the secret songs    of the sons of Ing.
On a time was Túrin    at the table of Thingol –
there was laughter long    and the loud clamour
of a countless company    that quaffed the mead,
amid the wine of Dor-Winion    that went ungrudged             425
in their golden goblets;    and goodly meats
there burdened the boards,    neath the blazing torches
set high in those halls    that were hewn of stone.
There mirth fell on many;    there minstrels clear
did sing to them songs    of the city of Tûn                   430
neath Tain-Gwethil,    towering mountain,
where the great gods sit    and gaze on the world
from the guarded shores    of the gulf of Faërie.
Then one sang of the slaying    at the Swanships' Haven
and the curse that had come    on the kindreds since:          435
all silent sat    and soundless harkened,
and waited the words    save one alone –
the Man among Elves    that Morwin bore.
Unheeding he heard    or high feasting

or lay or laughter,    and looked, it seemed,       440
to a deep distance    in the dark without,
and strained for sounds    in the still spaces,
for voices that vanished    in the veils of night.
He was lithe and lean,    and his locks were wild,
and woodland weeds    he wore of brown       445
and grey and green,    and gay jewel
or golden trinket    his garb knew not.

An Elf there was – Orgof –    of the ancient race
that was lost in the lands    where the long marches
from the quiet waters    of Cuiviénen       450
were made in the mirk    of the midworld's gloom,
ere light was lifted    aloft o'er earth;
but blood of the Gnomes    was blent in his veins.
He was close akin    to the King of Doriath –
a hardy hunter    and his heart was brave,       455
but loose his laughter    and light his tongue,
and his pride outran    his prowess in arms.
He was fain before all    of fine raiment
and of gems and jewels,    and jealous of such
as found favour    before himself.       460
Now costly clad    in colours gleaming
he sat on a seat    that was set on high
near the king and queen    and close to Túrin.
When those twain were at table    he had taunted him oft,
lightly with laughter,    for his loveless ways,       465
his haggard raiment    and hair unshorn;
but Túrin untroubled    neither turned his head
nor wasted words    on the wit of Orgof.
But this day of the feast    more deep his gloom
than of wont, and his words    men won harder;       470
for of twelve long years    the tale was full
since on Morwin his mother    through a maze of tears
he looked the last,    and the long shadows
of the forest had fallen    on his fading home;
and he answered few,    and Orgof nought.       475
Then the fool's mirth    was filled the more,
to a keener edge    was his carping whetted
at the clothes uncouth    and the uncombéd hair
of Túrin newcome    from the tangled forest.
He drew forth daintily    a dear treasure,       480

a comb of gold    that he kept about him,
and tendered it to Túrin;    but he turned not his eyes,
nor deigned to heed    or harken to Orgof,
who too deep drunken    that disdain should quell him:
'Nay, an thou knowest not    thy need of comb,                    485
nor its use,' quoth he,    'too young thou leftest
thy mother's ministry,    and 'twere meet to go
that she teach thee tame    thy tangled locks –
if the women of Hithlum    be not wild and loveless,
uncouth and unkempt    as their cast-off sons.'                    490

Then a fierce fury,    like a fire blazing,
was born of bitterness    in his bruiséd heart;
his white wrath woke    at the words of scorn
for the women of Hithlum    washed in tears;
and a heavy horn    to his hand lying,                    495
with gold adorned    for good drinking,
of his might unmindful    thus moved in ire
he seized and, swinging,    swiftly flung it
in the face of Orgof.    'Thou fool', he said,
'fill thy mouth therewith,    and to me no further                    500
thus witless prate    by wine bemused' –
but his face was broken,    and he fell backward,
and heavy his head    there hit upon the stone
of the floor rock-paved    mid flagons and vessels
of the o'erturned table    that tumbled on him                    505
as clutching he fell;    and carped no more,
in death silent.    There dumb were all
at bench and board;    in blank amaze
they rose around him,    as with ruth of heart
he gazed aghast    on his grievous deed,                    510
on his wine-stained hand,    with wondering eyes
half-comprehending.    On his heel then he turned
into the night striding,    and none stayed him;
but some their swords    half slipped from sheaths
– they were Orgof's kin –    yet for awe of Thingol                    515
they dared not draw    while the dazéd king
stonefacéd stared    on his stricken thane
and no sign showed them.    But the slayer weary
his hands laved    in the hidden stream
that strikes 'fore the gates,    nor stayed his tears:                    520
'Who has cast,' he cried,    'a curse upon me;

for all I do is ill,    and an outlaw now,
in bitter banishment    and blood-guilty,
of my fosterfather    I must flee the halls,
nor look on the lady    beloved again' –                              525
yea, his heart to Hithlum    had hastened him now,
but that road he dared not,    lest the wrath he draw
of the Elves after him,    and their anger alight
should speed the spears    in despite of Morgoth
o'er the hills of Hithlum    to hunt him down;                        530
lest a doom more dire    than they dreed of old
be meted his mother    and the Maid of Tears.

In the furthest folds    of the Forest of Doriath,
in the darkest dales    on its drear borders,
in haste he hid him,    lest the hunt take him;                       535
and they found not his footsteps    who fared after,
the thanes of Thingol;    who thirty days
sought him sorrowing,    and searched in vain
with no purpose of ill,    but the pardon bearing
of Thingol throned    in the Thousand Caves.                         540
He in council constrained    the kin of Orgof
to forget their grief    and forgiveness show,
in that wilful bitterness    had barbed the words
of Orgof the Elf;    said 'his hour had come
that his soul should seek    the sad pathway                         545
to the deep valley    of the Dead Awaiting,
there a thousand years    thrice to ponder
in the gloom of Gurthrond    his grim jesting,
ere he fare to Faërie    to feast again.'
Yet of his own treasure    he oped the gates,                        550
and gifts ungrudging    of gold and gems
to the sons he gave    of the slain; and his folk
well deemed the deed.    But that doom of the King
Túrin knew not,    and turned against him
the hands of the Elves    he unhappy believed,                       555
wandering the woodland    woeful-hearted;
for his fate would not    that the folk of the caves
should harbour longer    Húrin's offspring.

★

# NOTES

(Throughout the Notes statements such as '*Delimorgoth* A, and B as typed' (line 11) imply that the reading in the printed text (in that case *Delu-Morgoth*) is a later emendation made to B).

8  *Húrin* is *Úrin* in the *Lost Tales* (and still when this poem was begun, see note to line 213), and his name *Thalion* 'Steadfast', found in *The Silmarillion* and the *Narn*, does not occur in them (though he is called 'the Steadfast').

11  *Delimorgoth* A, and B as typed. *Morgoth* occurs once only in the *Lost Tales*, in the typescript version of the *Tale of Tinúviel* (II.44); see note to line 20.

13  *Nínin Udathriol* A, and B as typed; this occurs in the *Tale* (II.84; for explanation of the name see II.346). When changing *Udathriol* to *Unothradin* my father wrote in the margin of B: 'or *Nirnaithos Unothradin*'.

17  Above *Erithámrod* is pencilled in A *Urinthalion*.

20  B as typed had *Belcha*, which was then changed through *Belegor, Melegor*, to *Bauglir*. (A has a different reading here: *as a myriad rats  in measureless army / might pull down the proudest . . .*) *Belcha* occurs in the typescript version of the *Tale of Tinúviel* (II.44), where *Belcha Morgoth* are said to be Melko's names among the Gnomes. *Bauglir* is found as a name of Morgoth in *The Silmarillion* and the *Narn*.

22  *Melko's* A; *Belcha's* B as typed, then the line changed to *To the halls* of *Belegor* (> *Melegor*), and finally to the reading given. See note to line 20.

25  Above *Erithámrod* in A is written *UrinThalion* (see note to line 17); *Úrin* > *Húrin*, and a direction to read *Thalion Húrin*.

29  *Finweg's son* A, and B as typed; the emendation is a later one, and at the same time my father wrote in the margin of B 'he was Fingolfin's son', clearly a comment on the change of *son* to *heir*. *Finweg* is *Finwë Nólemë* Lord of the Noldoli, who in the *Lost Tales* was Turgon's father (I.115), not as he afterwards became his grandfather.

50  *Kor* > *Cor* A, *Cor* B as typed. When emending *Cor* to *Corthûn* my father wrote in the margin of B: '*Corthun* or *Tûn*'.

51  *Thalion* A, and B as typed.
    *Delimorgoth* A, and B as typed (as at line 11).

73  In B there is a mark of insertion between lines 72 and 73. This probably refers to a line in A, not taken up into B: *bound by the* (> *my*) *spell  of bottomless* (> *unbroken*) *might*.

75  *Belcha* A, and B as typed; the same chain of emendations in
     B as at lines 20 and 22.

84  *Bauglir*: as at line 75.

105 *Mavwin* A, and B as typed; in B then emended to *Mailwin*,
     and back to *Mavwin*; *Morwin* written later in the margin of
     B. Exactly the same at 129, and at 137 though here without
     *Morwin* in the margin; at 145 *Mavwin* unemended, but
     *Morwin* in the margin. Thereafter *Mavwin* stands un-
     emended and without marginal note, as far as 438 (see note).
     For consistency I read *Morwin* throughout the first version
     of the poem. – *Mavwin* is the form in the *Tale*; *Mailwin* does
     not occur elsewhere.

117 On the variation *Nienóri/Nienor* in the *Tale* see II. 118–19.

120 *Tinúviel* A, *Tinwiel* B unemended but with *Tinúviel* in the
     margin. *Tinwiel* does not occur elsewhere.

121 *Ermabwed* 'One-handed' is Beren's title or nickname in the
     *Lost Tales*.

137 *Gumlin* is named in the *Tale* (II. 74, etc.); the younger of the
     two guardians of Túrin on his journey to Doriath (here called
     *Halog*) is not.

160 *Belcha* A, and B as typed, emended to *Bauglir*. Cf. notes to
     lines 20, 22, 75.

213 *Urin* > *Húrin* A; but *Húrin* A in line 216.

218 *Nínin Udathriol* A, and B as typed; cf. line 13.

226 The distinction between 'Gnomes' and 'Elves' is still made;
     see I. 43–4.

230 *Dorwinion* A.

306 *For Mavwin was Melian        moved to ruth* A, and B as
     typed, with *Then was Melian moved* written in the margin.
     The second half-line has only three syllables unless *moved* is
     read *movéd*, which is not satisfactory. The second version of
     the poem has here *For Morwen Melian        was moved to
     ruth*. Cf. lines 494, 519.

333 *Túrin Thaliodrin* A (cf. line 115), emended to *the son of
     Thalion*.

361 *Glamhoth* appears in *The Fall of Gondolin* (II. 160), with
     the translation 'folk of dreadful hate'.

364 *Belcha* A, and B as typed; then > *Melegor* > *Bauglir* in B.

392 *Bauglir*: as at line 364.

408 *Morgoth Belcha* A, and B as typed.

430 *Kor* > *Cor* A, *Cor* B as typed. Cf. line 50.

431 *Tengwethil* A, and B as typed. In the early Gnomish dic-
     tionary and in the Name-list to *The Fall of Gondolin* the
     Gnomish name of Taniquetil is *Danigwethil* (I. 266,
     II. 337).

438 *Mavwin* A, and B as typed, but *Mavwin* > *Morwen* a later

emendation in B. I read *Morwin* throughout the first version of the poem (see note to line 105).

450   *Cuinlimfin* A, and B as typed; *Cuiviénen* a later emendation in B. The form in the *Lost Tales* is *Koivië-Néni*; *Cuinlimfin* occurs nowhere else.

461–3   These lines bracketed and marked with an X in B.

471   This line marked with an X in B.

472   *Mavwin* > *Morwen* B; see line 438.

494   *all washed in tears* A, *washed in tears* B (half-line of three syllables), with an X in the margin and an illegible word written in pencil before *washed*. Cf. lines 306, 519. The second version of the poem does not reach this point.

514–16   Against these lines my father wrote in the margin of B: 'Make Orgof's kin set on him and T. fight his way out.'

517   *stonefacéd stared*: the accent on *stonefacéd* was put in later and the line marked with an X. – In his essay *On Translating Beowulf* (1940; *The Monsters and the Critics and Other Essays* (1983) p. 67) my father gave *stared stonyfaced* as an example of an Old English metrical type.

519   *his hands laved*: the line is marked with an X in B. Cf. lines 306, 494.

528   With the half-line *and their anger alight* the second, more finished, part of the manuscript A begins; see p. 4.

529   *Belcha* A, *Morgoth* B as typed.

548   *Guthrond* A, and B as typed.

## Commentary on the *Prologue* and *Part I 'Túrin's Fostering'*

The opening section or 'Prologue' of the poem derives from the opening of the *Tale* (II. 70–1) and in strictly narrative terms there has been little development. In lines 18–21 (and especially in the rejected line in A, *as a myriad rats in measureless army / might pull down the proudest*) is clearly foreshadowed the story in *The Silmarillion* (p. 195):

> . . . they took him at last alive, by the command of Morgoth, for the Orcs grappled him with their hands, which clung to him though he hewed off their arms; and ever their numbers were renewed, until at last he fell buried beneath them.

On the other hand the motive in the later story for capturing him alive (Morgoth knew that Húrin had been to Gondolin) is necessarily not present, since Gondolin in the older phases of the legends was not discovered till Turgon retreated down Sirion after the Battle of Unnumbered Tears (II. 120, 208). That he was taken alive by Morgoth's command is however already stated in the poem (line 20), though it is not explained why. In the *Tale* Morgoth's interest in Húrin as a tool for the discovery of Turgon arose from his knowledge that

> the Elves of Kôr thought little of Men, holding them in scant fear or suspicion for their blindness and lack of skill

– an idea that is repeated in the poem (46–8); but this idea seems only to have arisen in Morgoth's mind when he came to Húrin in his dungeon (44 ff.).

The place of Húrin's torment (in the *Tale* 'a lofty place of the mountains') is now defined as *a stool of stone* on the steepest peak of Thangorodrim; and this is the first occurrence of that name.

In the change of *son* to *heir* in line 29 is seen the first hint of a development in the kingly house of the Noldoli, with the appearance of a second generation between Finwë (Finweg) and Turgon; but by the time that my father pencilled this change on the text (and noted 'He was Fingolfin's son') the later genealogical structure was already in being, and this is as it were a casual indication of it.

In 'Túrin's Fostering' there is a close relationship between the *Tale* and the poem, extending to many close similarities of wording – especially abundant in the scene in Thingol's hall leading to the death of Orgof; and some phrases had a long life, surviving from the *Tale*, through the poem, and into the *Narn i Hîn Húrin*, as

> rather would she dwell poor among Men than live sweetly as an almsguest among the woodland Elves                    (II. 73)

> but to spend her days
> as alms-guest of others,    even Elfin kings,                    (284–6)
> it liked her little

> she would not yet humble her pride to be an alms-guest, not even of a king                    (*Narn* p. 70)

– though in the *Narn* the 'alms-guest' passage occurs at a different point, before Túrin left Hithlum (Morwen's hope that Húrin would come back is in the *Narn* her reason for not journeying to Doriath with her son, not for refusing the later invitation to her to go).

Of Morwen's situation in Dor-lómin after the Battle of Unnumbered Tears there are a few things to say. In the poem (111–13)

> men unmindful    of his mighty lordship
> dwelt in Dorlómin    and dealt unkindly
> with his widowed wife

– echoing the *Tale*: 'the strange men who dwelt nigh knew not the dignity of the Lady Mavwin', but there is still no indication of who these men were or where they came from (see II. 126). As so often, the narrative situation was prepared but its explanation had not emerged. The unclarity of the *Tale* as to where Úrin dwelt before the great Battle (see II. 120) is no longer present: *the dwelling was dear where he dwelt of old* (288). Nienor was born before Túrin left (on the contradiction in the *Tale* on this point see II. 131); and the chronology of Túrin's childhood is still that of the *Tale* (see II. 142): seven years old when he left Hithlum (332), seven years in Doriath while tidings still came from Morwen (333), twelve years since he came to Doriath when he slew Orgof (471). In the later story the last figure remained unchanged, which suggests that the X (mark of dissatisfaction) placed against line 471 had some other reason.

There are several references in the poem to Húrin and Beren having been friends and fellows-in-arms (122–4, 248–9, 298). In the *Tale* it was said originally (when Beren was a Man) that Egnor Beren's father was akin to Mavwin; this was replaced by a different passage (when Beren had become a Gnome) according to which Egnor was a friend of Úrin ('and Beren Ermabwed son of Egnor he knew'); see II. 71–2, 139. In the later version of the *Tale of Tinúviel* (II. 44) Úrin is named as the 'brother in arms' of Egnor; this was emended to make Úrin's relationship with Beren himself – as in the poem. In *The Silmarillion* (p. 198) Morwen thought to send Túrin to Thingol 'for Beren son of Barahir was her father's kinsman, and he had been moreover a friend of Húrin, ere evil befell'. There is no mention of the fact in the *Narn* (p. 63): Morwen merely says: 'Am I not now kin of the king [Thingol]? For Beren son of Barahir was grandson of Bregor, as was my father also.'

That Beren was still an Elf, not a Man, (deducible on other grounds) is apparent from lines 178–9:

> and never ere now    for need or wonder
> had children of Men    chosen that pathway

– cf. the *Tale* (II. 72): 'and Túrin son of Úrin was the first of Men to tread that way', changed from the earlier reading 'and Beren Ermabwed was the first of Men . . .'

In the parting of Túrin from his mother comparison with the *Tale* will show some subtle differences which need not be spelled out here. The younger of Túrin's guardians is now named, Halog (and it is said that Gumlin and Halog were the only 'henchmen' left to Morwen).

Some very curious things are said of Beleg in the poem. He is twice (200, 399) called 'a (the) son of the wilderness who wist no sire', and at line 416 he is 'Beleg the ageless'. There seems to be a mystery about him, an otherness that sets him apart (as he set himself apart, 195) from the Elves of Thingol's lordship (see further p. 127). It may be that there is still a trace of this in the 1930 'Silmarillion', where it is said that none went from Doriath to the Battle of Unnumbered Tears save Mablung, and Beleg 'who obeyed no man' (in the later text this becomes 'nor any out of Doriath save Mablung and Beleg, who were unwilling to have no part in these great deeds. To them Thingol gave leave to go . . .'; *The Silmarillion* p. 189). In the poem (219) Beleg says expressly that he did not go to the great Battle. – His great bow of black yew-wood (so in *The Silmarillion*, p. 208, where it is named *Belthronding*) now appears (400): in the *Tale* he is not particularly marked out as a bowman (II. 123).

Beleg's *The gods have guided you* (215) and Turin's guardians' thought *the gods are good* (244) accord with references in the *Lost Tales* to the influence of the Valar on Men and Elves in the Great Lands: see II. 141.

The potent wine that Beleg carried and gave to the travellers from his flask (223 ff.) is notable – brought from *the burning South* and *by long ways* carried *to the lands of the North* – as is the name of the land from which it came: *Dor-Winion* (230, 425). The only other places in my father's writings where this name occurs (so far as I know) are in *The Hobbit*, Chapter IX *Barrels out of Bond*: 'the heady vintage of the great gardens of Dorwinion', and 'the wine of Dorwinion brings deep and pleasant dreams'.* See further p. 127.

The curious element in Thingol's message to Morwen in the *Tale*, explaining why he did not go with his people to the Battle of Un-numbered Tears (II. 73), has now been rejected; but with Morwen's response to the messengers out of Doriath there enters the legend the Dragon-helm of Dor-lómin (297 ff.). As yet little is told of it (though more is said in the second version of the poem, see p. 126): Húrin often bore it in battle (in the *Narn* it is denied that he used it, p. 76); it magically protected its wearer (as still in the *Narn*, p. 75); and it was *with that token crowned of the towering dragon, and o'er-written with runes by wrights of old* (cf. the *Narn*: 'on it were graven runes of victory'). But nothing is here said of how Húrin came by it, beyond the fact that it was his *heirloom*. Very notable is the passage (307 ff.) in which is described Thingol's handling of the helm *as his hoard were scant*, despite his possession of *dungeons filled / with Elfin armouries of ancient gear*. I have commented previously (see II. 128–9, 245–6) on the early emphasis on the poverty of Tinwelint (Thingol): here we have the first appearance of the idea of his wealth (present also at the beginning of the *Lay of Leithian*). Also notable is the close echoing of the lines of the poem in the words of the *Narn*, p. 76:

---

*\**Dorwinion* is marked on the decorated map by Pauline Baynes, as a region on the North-western shores of the Sea of Rhûn. It must be presumed that this, like other names on that map, was communicated to her by my father (see *Unfinished Tales* p. 261, footnote), but its placing seems surprising.

Yet Thingol handled the Helm of Hador as though his hoard were scanty, and he spoke courteous words, saying: 'Proud were the head that bore this helm, which the sires of Húrin bore.'

There is also a clear echo of lines 315–18

> Then a thought was thrust into Thingol's heart,
> and Túrin he called and told when come
> that Morwin his mother a mighty thing
> had sent to her son, his sire's heirloom

in the prose of the *Narn*:

> Then a thought came to him, and he summoned Túrin, and told him that Morwen had sent to her son a mighty thing, the heirloom of his fathers.

Compare also the passages that follow in both works, concerning Túrin's being too young to lift the Helm, and being in any case too unhappy to heed it on account of his mother's refusal to leave Hithlum. This was *the first of his sorrows* (328); in the *Narn* (p. 75) the second.

The account of Túrin's character in boyhood (341 ff.) is very close to that in the *Tale* (II. 74), which as I have noted before (II. 121) survived into the *Narn* (p. 77): the latter account indeed echoes the poem ('he learned much lore', 'neither did he win friendship easily'). In the poem it is now added that *in weaving song/he had a minstrel's mastery, but mirth was not in it*.

An important new element in the narrative enters with the companionship of Beleg and Túrin (wearing the Dragon-helm, 377) in warfare on the marches of Doriath:

> how Beleg the ageless was brother-in-arms
> to the black-haired boy from the beaten people. (416–17)

Of this there is no mention in the *Tale* at all (II. 74). Cf. my Commentary, II. 122:

> Túrin's prowess against the Orcs during his sojourn in Artanor is given a more central or indeed unique importance in the tale ('he held the wrath of Melko from them for many years'), especially as Beleg, his companion-in-arms in the later versions, is not here mentioned.

In the poem the importance to Doriath of Túrin's warfare is not diminished, however:

> for by him was holden the hand of ruin
> from Thingol's folk, and Thû feared him (389–90)

We meet here for the first time Thû, *thane most mighty/neath*

*Morgoth Bauglir*. It is interesting to learn that Thû knew of Túrin and feared him, also that Morgoth ordered Thû to assault Doriath: this story will reappear in the *Lay of Leithian*.

In the story of Túrin and Orgof the verses are very clearly following the prose of the *Tale*, and there are many close likenesses of wording, as already noted. The relation of this scene to the later story has been discussed previously (II. 121–2). Orgof still has Gnome-blood, which may imply the continuance of the story that there were Gnomes among Thingol's people (see II. 43). The occasion of Túrin's return from the forest to the Thousand Caves (a name that first occurs in the poem) becomes, as it seems, a great feast, with songs of Valinor – quite unlike the later story, where the occasion is in no way marked out and Thingol and Melian were not in Menegroth (*Narn* p. 79); and Túrin and Orgof were *set on high / near the king and queen* (i.e. presumably on the dais, at the 'high table'). Whether it was a rejection of this idea that caused my father to bracket lines 461–3 and mark them with an X I cannot say. *The secret songs of the sons of Ing* referred to in this passage (421) are not indeed songs of the sons of Ing of the Ælfwine history (II. 301 ff.); this Ing is the Gnomish form of Ingwë, Lord of the First Kindred of the Elves (earlier Inwë Lord of the Teleri).*

The lines concerning Orgof dead are noteworthy:

> his hour had come
> that his soul should seek     the sad pathway
> to the deep valley     of the Dead Awaiting,
> there a thousand years     thrice to ponder
> in the gloom of Gurthrond     his grim jesting,
> ere he fare to Faërie     to feast again.          (544–9)

With this compare the tale of *The Coming of the Valar and the Building of Valinor* (I. 76):

There [in the hall of Vê] Mandos spake their doom, and there they waited in the darkness, dreaming of their past deeds, until such time as he appointed when they might again be born into their children, and go forth to laugh and sing again.

The name *Gurthrond* (< *Guthrond*) occurs nowhere else; the first element is doubtless *gurth* 'death', as in the name of Túrin's sword *Gurtholfin* (II. 342).

---

*That *Ing* is the Gnomish form of *Ingwë* appears from the 1926 'Sketch of the Mythology' and the 1930 'Silmarillion'. *Ing* was replaced by *Inwë* in *The Cottage of Lost Play*, but there the Gnomish name of Inwë is *Inwithiel*, changed from *Gim Githil* (I. 16, 22).

There remain a few particular points concerning names. At line 366 *Hithlum* is explained as the name of Dorlómin among Men:

> of dark Dorlómin    with its dreary pines
> that Hithlum unhappy    is hight by Men.

This is curious. In the *Lost Tales* the name of the land among Men was *Aryador*; so in the *Tale of Turambar* (II. 70):

> In those days my folk dwelt in a vale of Hisilómë and that land did Men name Aryador in the tongues they then used.

In the 1930 'Silmarillion' it is specifically stated that *Hithlum* and *Dorlómin* were Gnomish names for *Hisilómë*, and there seems every reason to suppose that this was always the case. The answer to the puzzle may however lie in the same passage of the *Tale of Turambar*, where it is said that

> often was the story of Turambar and the Foalókë in their [i.e. Men's] mouths – but rather after the fashion of the Gnomes did they say Turumart and the Fuithlug.

Perhaps then the meaning of line 366 is that Men called Hisilómë *Hithlum* because they used the Gnomish name, not that it was the name in their own tongue.

In the following lines (367–8)

> the Shadowy Mountains
> fenced them from Faërie    and the folk of the wood.

This is the first occurrence of the name *Shadowy Mountains*, and it is used as it was afterwards (*Ered Wethrin*); in the *Lost Tales* the mountains forming the southern fence of Hithlum are called the Iron Mountains or the Bitter Hills (see II. 61).

The name *Cuinlimfin* of the Waters of Awakening (note to line 450) seems to have been a passing idea, soon abandoned.

Lastly, at line 50 occurs (by emendation in B from *Côr*) the unique compound name *Corthûn*, while at 430 *the city of Côr* was emended to *the city of Tún*; see II. 292.

★

II

BELEG

Long time alone    he lived in the hills
a hunter of beast    and hater of Men,                         560
or Orcs, or Elves,    till outcast folk

there one by one,   wild and reckless
around him rallied;   and roaming far
they were feared by both foe   and friend of old.
For hot with hate   was the heart of Túrin,                          565
nor a friend found him   such folk of Thingol
as he wandering met   in the wood's fastness.

There Beleg the brave   on the borders of Doriath
they found and fought   – and few were with him –
and o'erborne by numbers   they bound him at last,            570
till their captain came   to their camp at eve.
Afar from that fight   his fate that day
had taken Túrin   on the trail of the Orcs,
as they hastened home   to the Hills of Iron
with the loot laden   of the lands of Men.                          575
Then soon was him said   that a servant of Thingol
they had tied to a tree –   and Túrin coming
stared astonied   on the stern visage
of Beleg the brave   his brother in arms,
of whom he learned the lore   of leaping blades,              580
and of bended bow   and barbéd shaft,
and the wild woodland's   wisdom secret,
when they blent in battle   the blood of their wounds.

Then Túrin's heart   was turned from hate,
and he bade unbind   Beleg the huntsman.                        585
'Now fare thou free!   But, of friendship aught
if thy heart yet holds   for Húrin's son,
never tell thou tale   that Túrin thou sawst
an outlaw unloved   from Elves and Men,
whom Thingol's thanes   yet thirst to slay.                        590
Betray not my trust   or thy troth of yore!'
Then Beleg of the bow   embraced him there –
he had not fared to the feast   or the fall of Orgof –
there kissed him kindly   comfort speaking:
'Lo! nought know I   of the news thou tellest;                  595
but outlawed or honoured   thou ever shalt be
the brother of Beleg,   come bliss come woe!
Yet little me likes   that thy leaping sword
the life should drink   of the leaguered Elves.
Are the grim Glamhoth   then grown so few,                      600
or the foes of Faërie   feeble-hearted,
that warlike Men   have no work to do?

Shall the foes of Faërie    be friends of Men?
Betrayest thou thy troth    whom we trusted of yore?'

'Nor of arméd Orc,    nor [of] Elf of the wood,                    605
nor of any on earth    have I honour or love,
O Beleg the bowman.    This band alone
I count as comrades,    my kindred in woe
and friendless fate –    our foes the world.'

'Let the bow of Beleg    to your band be joined;              610
and swearing death    to the sons of darkness
let us suage our sorrow    and the smart of fate!
Our valour is not vanquished,    nor vain the glory
that once we did win    in the woods of old.'

Thus hope in the heart    of Húrin's offspring              615
awoke at those words;    and them well likéd
of that band the boldest,    save Blodrin only –
Blodrin Bor's son,    who for blood and for gold
alone lusted,    and little he recked
whom he robbed of riches    or reft of life,                    620
were it Elf or Orc;    but he opened not
the thoughts of his heart.    There throbbed the harp,
where the fires flickered,    and the flaming brands
of pine were piled    in the place of their camp;
where glad men gathered    in good friendship              625
as dusk fell down    on the drear woodland.
Then a song on a sudden    soaring loudly –
and the trees up-looming    towering harkened –
was raised of the Wrack    of the Realm of the Gods;
of the need of the Gnomes    on the Narrow Crossing;        630
of the fight at Fangros,    and Fëanor's sons'
oath unbreakable.    Then up sprang Beleg:
'That our vaunt and our vows    be not vain for ever,
even such as they swore,    those seven chieftains,
an oath let us swear    that is unchanging                      635
as Tain-Gwethil's    towering mountain!'
Their blades were bared,    as blood shining
in the flame of the fires    while they flashed and touched.
As with one man's voice    the words were spoken,
and the oath uttered    that must unrecalled                  640
abide for ever,    a bond of truth
and friendship in arms,    and faith in peril.

Thus war was waked    in the woods once more
for the foes of Faërie,    and its fame widely,
and the fear of that fellowship,    now fared abroad;                645
when the horn was heard    of the hunting Elves
that shook the shaws    and the sheer valleys.
Blades were naked    and bows twanging,
and shafts from the shadows    shooting wingéd,
and the sons of darkness    slain and conquered;                    650
even in Angband    the Orcs trembled.
Then the word wandered    down the ways of the forest
that Túrin Thalion    was returned to war;
and Thingol heard it,    and his thanes were sped
to lead the lost one    in love to his halls –                      655
but his fate was fashioned    that they found him not.
Little gold they got    in that grim warfare,
but weary watches    and wounds for guerdon;
nor on robber-raids    now rode they ever,
who fended from Faërie    the fiends of Hell.                       660
But Blodrin Bor's son    for booty lusted,
for the loud laughter    of the lawless days,
and meats unmeasured,    and mead-goblets
refilled and filled,    and the flagons of wine
that went as water    in their wild revels.                         665
Now tales have told    that trapped as a child
he was dragged by the Dwarves    to their deep mansions,
and in Nogrod nurtured,    and in nought was like,
spite blood and birth,    to the blissful Elves.
His heart hated    Húrin's offspring                                670
and the bowman Beleg;    so biding his while
he fled their fellowship    and forest hidings
to the merciless Orcs,    whose moon-pallid
cruel-curvéd blades    to kill spare not;
than whose greed for gold    none greater burns                     675
save in hungry hearts    of the hell-dragons.
He betrayed his troth;    traitor made him
and the forest fastness    of his fellows in arms
he opened to the Orcs,    nor his oath heeded.
There they fought and fell    by foes outnumbered,                  680
by treachery trapped    at a time of night
when their fires faded    and few were waking –
some wakened never,    not for wild noises,
nor cries nor curses,    nor clashing steel,

swept as they slumbered    to the slades of death.          685
But Túrin they took,    though towering mighty
at the Huntsman's hand    he hewed his foemen,
as a bear at bay    mid bellowing hounds,
unheeding his hurts;    at the hest of Morgoth
yet living they lapped him,    his limbs entwining,          690
with hairy hands    and hideous arms.
Then Beleg was buried    in the bodies of the fallen,
as sorely wounded    he swooned away;
and all was over,    and the Orcs triumphed.
The dawn over Doriath    dimly kindled          695
saw Blodrin Bor's son    by a beech standing
with throat thirléd    by a thrusting arrow,
whose shaven shaft,    shod with poison,
and feather-wingéd,    was fast in the tree.
He bargained the blood    of his brothers for gold:          700
thus his meed was meted –    in the mirk at random
by an orc-arrow    his oath came home.

From the magic mazes    of Melian the Queen
they haled unhappy    Húrin's offspring,
lest he flee his fate;    but they fared slowly          705
and the leagues were long    of their laboured way
over hill and hollow    to the high places,
where the peaks and pinnacles    of pitiless stone
looming up lofty    are lapped in cloud,
and veiled in vapours    vast and sable;          710
where Eiglir Engrin,    the Iron Hills, lie
o'er the hopeless halls    of Hell upreared
wrought at the roots    of the roaring cliffs
of Thangorodrim's    thunderous mountain.
Thither led they laden    with loot and evil;          715
but Beleg yet breathed    in blood drenchéd
aswoon, till the sun    to the South hastened,
and the eye of day    was opened wide.
Then he woke and wondered,    and weeping took him,
and to Túrin Thalion    his thoughts were turned,          720
that o'erborne in battle    and bound he had seen.
Then he crawled from the corpses    that had covered him over,
weary, wounded,    too weak to stand.
So Thingol's thanes    athirst and bleeding
in the forest found him:    his fate willed not          725

that he should drink the draught    of death from foes.
Thus they bore him back    in bitter torment
his tidings to tell    in the torchlit halls
of Thingol the king;    in the Thousand Caves
to be healéd whole    by the hands enchanted                          730
of Melian Mablui,    the moonlit queen.

Ere a week was outworn    his wounds were cured,
but his heart's heaviness    those hands of snow
nor soothed nor softened,    and sorrow-laden
he fared to the forest.    No fellows sought he                      735
in his hopeless hazard,    but in haste alone
he followed the feet    of the foes of Elfland,
the dread daring,    and the dire anguish,
that held the hearts    of Hithlum's men
and Doriath's doughtiest    in a dream of fear.                      740
Unmatched among Men,    or magic-wielding
Elves, or hunters    of the Orc-kindred,
or beasts of prey    for blood pining,
was his craft and cunning,    that cold and dead
an unseen slot    could scent o'er stone,                           745
foot-prints could find    on forest pathways
that lightly on the leaves    were laid in moons
long waned, and washed    by windy rains.
The grim Glamhoth's    goblin armies
go cunning-footed,    but his craft failed not                      750
to tread their trail,    till the lands were darkened,
and the light was lost    in lands unknown.
Never-dawning night    was netted clinging
in the black branches    of the beetling trees;
oppressed by pungent    pinewood's odours,                          755
and drowsed with dreams    as the darkness thickened,
he strayed steerless.    The stars were hid,
and the moon mantled.    There magic foundered
in the gathering glooms,    there goblins even
(whose deep eyes drill    the darkest shadows)                      760
bewildered wandered,    who the way forsook
to grope in the glades,    there greyly loomed
of girth unguessed    in growth of ages
the topless trunks    of trees enchanted.
That fathomless fold    by folk of Elfland                          765
is Taur-na-Fuin,    the Trackless Forest
of Deadly Nightshade.    dreadly naméd.

Abandoned, beaten,    there Beleg lying
to the wind harkened    winding, moaning
in bending boughs;    to branches creaking                    770
up high over head,    where huge pinions
of the pluméd pine-trees    complained darkly
in black foreboding.    There bowed hopeless,
in wit wildered,    and wooing death,
he saw on a sudden    a slender sheen                          775
shine a-shimmering    in the shades afar,
like a glow-worm's lamp    a-gleaming dim.
He marvelled what it might be    as he moved softly;
for he knew not the Gnomes    of need delving
in the deep dungeons    of dark Morgoth.                       780
Unmatched their magic    in metal-working,
who jewels and gems    that rejoiced the Gods
aforetime fashioned,    when they freedom held,
now swinking slaves    of ceaseless labour
in Angband's smithies,    nor ever were suffered              785
to wander away,    warded always.
But little lanterns    of lucent crystal
and silver cold    with subtlest cunning
they strangely fashioned,    and steadfast a flame
burnt unblinking    there blue and pale,                      790
unquenched for ever.    The craft that lit them
was the jewel-makers'    most jealous secret.
Not Morgoth's might,    nor meed nor torment
them vowed, availed    to reveal that lore;
yet lights and lamps    of living radiance,                   795
many and magical,    they made for him.
No dark could dim them    the deeps wandering;
whose lode they lit    was lost seldom
in groundless grot,    or gulfs far under.

'Twas a Gnome he beheld    on the heaped needles              800
of a pine-tree pillowed,    when peering wary
he crept closer.    The covering pelt
was loosed from the lamp    of living radiance
by his side shining.    Slumber-shrouded
his fear-worn face    was fallen in shade.                    805
Lest in webs woven    of unwaking sleep,
spun round by spells    in those spaces dark,
he lie forlorn    and lost for ever,
the Hunter hailed him    in the hushed forest –

to the drowsy deeps    of his dream profound                    810
fear ever-following    came falling loud;
as the lancing lightning    he leapt to his feet
full deeming that dread    and death were upon him,
Flinding go-Fuilin    fleeing in anguish
from the mines of Morgoth.   Marvelling he heard        815
the ancient tongue    of the Elves of Tûn;
and Beleg the Bowman    embraced him there,
and learnt his lineage    and luckless fate,
how thrust to thraldom    in a throng of captives,
from the kindred carried    and the cavernous halls        820
of the Gnomes renowned    of Nargothrond,
long years he laboured    under lashes and flails
of the baleful Balrogs,    abiding his time.
A tale he unfolded    of terrible flight
o'er flaming fell    and fuming hollow,                          825
o'er the parchéd dunes    of the Plains of Drouth,
till his heart took hope    and his heed was less.
'Then Taur-na-Fuin    entangled my feet
in its mazes enmeshed;    and madness took me
that I wandered witless,    unwary stumbling              830
and beating the boles    of the brooding pines
in idle anger –    and the Orcs heard me.
They were camped in a clearing,    that close at hand
by mercy I missed.   Their marching road
is beaten broad    through the black shadows              835
by wizardry warded    from wandering Elves;
but dread they know    of the Deadly Nightshade,
and in haste only    do they hie that way.
Now cruel cries    and clamorous voices
awoke in the wood,    and winged arrows                    840
from horny bows    hummed about me;
and following feet,    fleet and stealthy,
were padding and pattering    on the pine-needles;
and hairy hands    and hungry fingers
•in the glooms groping,    as I grovelled fainting          845
till they cowering found me.   Fast they clutched me
beaten and bleeding,    and broken in spirit
they laughing led me,    my lagging footsteps
with their spears speeding.   Their spoils were piled,
and countless captives    in that camp were chained,      850
and Elfin maids    their anguish mourning.

But one they watched,    warded sleepless,
was stern-visaged, strong,    and in stature tall
as are Hithlum's men    of the misty hills.
Full length he lay    and lashed to pickets          855
in baleful bonds,    yet bold-hearted
his mouth no mercy    of Morgoth sued,
but defied his foes.    Foully they smote him.
Then he called, as clear    as cry of hunter
that hails his hounds    in hollow places,          860
on the name renowned    of that noblest king –
but men unmindful    remember him little –
Húrin Thalion,    who Erithámrod hight,
the Unbending,    for Orc and Balrog
and Morgoth's might    on the mountain yet          865
he defies fearless,    on a fangéd peak
of thunder-riven    Thangorodrim.'

In eager anger    then up sprang Beleg,
crying and calling,    careless of Flinding:
'O Túrin, Túrin,    my troth-brother,          870
to the brazen bonds    shall I abandon thee,
and the darkling doors    of the Deeps of Hell?'

'Thou wilt join his journey    to the jaws of sorrow,
O bowman crazéd,    if thy bellowing cry
to the Orcs should come;    their ears than cats'          875
are keener whetted,    and though the camp from here
be a day distant    where those deeds I saw,
who knows if the Gnome    they now pursue
that crept from their clutches,    as a crawling worm
on belly cowering,    whom they bleeding cast          880
in deathly swoon    on the dung and slough
of their loathsome lair.    O Light of Valinor!
and ye glorious Gods!    How gleam their eyes,
and their tongues are red!'    'Yet I Túrin will wrest
from their hungry hands,    or to Hell be dragged,          885
or sleep with the slain    in the slades of Death.
Thy lamp shall lead us,    and my lore rekindle
and wise wood-craft!'    'O witless hunter,
thy words are wild –    wolves unsleeping
and wizardry ward    their woeful captives;          890
unerring their arrows;    the icy steel
of their curvéd blades    cleaves unblunted

the meshes of mail;    the mirk to pierce
those eyes are able;    their awful laughter
the flesh freezes!    I fare not thither,                                895
for fear fetters me    in the Forest of Night:
better die in the dark    dazed, forwandered,
than wilfully woo    that woe and anguish!
I know not the way.'    'Are the knees then weak
of Flinding go-Fuilin?    Shall free-born Gnome              900
thus show himself    a shrinking slave,
who twice entrapped    has twice escaped?
Remember the might    and the mirth of yore,
the renown of the Gnomes    of Nargothrond!'

Thus Beleg the bowman    quoth bold-hearted,                 905
but Flinding fought    the fear of his heart,
and loosed the light    of his lamp of blue,
now brighter burning.    In the black mazes
enwound they wandered,    weary searching;
by the tall tree-boles    towering silent                        910
oft barred and baffled;    blindly stumbling
over rock-fast roots    writhing coiléd;
and drowsed with dreams    by the dark odours,
till hope was hidden.    'Hark thee, Flinding;
viewless voices    vague and distant,                            915
a muffled murmur    of marching feet
that are shod with stealth    shakes the stillness.'

'No noise I hear',    the Gnome answered,
'thy hope cheats thee.'    'I hear the chains
clinking, creaking,    the cords straining,                      920
and wolves padding    on worn pathways.
I smell the blood    that is smeared on blades
that are cruel and crooked;    the croaking laughter –
now, listen! louder    and louder comes,'
the hunter said.    'I hear no sound',                            925
quoth Flinding fearful.    'Then follow after!'
with bended bow    then Beleg answered,
'my cunning rekindles,    my craft needs not
thy lamp's leading.'    Leaping swiftly
he shrank in the shadows;    with shrouded lantern      930
Flinding followed him,    and the forest-darkness
and drowsy dimness    drifted slowly
unfolding from them    in fleeing shadows,

and its magic was minished,    till they marvelling saw
they were brought to its borders.    There black-gaping          935
an archway opened.    By ancient trunks
it was framed darkly,    that in far-off days
the lightning felled,    now leaning gaunt
their lichen-leprous    limbs uprooted.
There shadowy bats    that shrilled thinly          940
flew in and flew out    the air brushing
as they swerved soundless.    A swooning light
faint filtered in,    for facing North
they looked o'er the leagues    of the lands of mourning,
o'er the bleak boulders,    o'er the blistered dunes          945
and dusty drouth    of Dor-na-Fauglith;
o'er that Thirsty Plain,    to the threatening peaks,
now glimpséd grey    through the grim archway,
of the marching might    of the Mountains of Iron,
and faint and far    in the flickering dusk          950
the thunderous towers    of Thangorodrim.
But backward broad    through the black shadows
from that darkling door    dimly wandered
the ancient Orc-road;    and even as they gazed
the silence suddenly    with sounds of dread          955
was shaken behind them,    and shivering echoes
from afar came fleeting.    Feet were tramping;
trappings tinkling;    and the troublous murmur
of viewless voices    in the vaulted gloom
came near and nearer.    'Ah! now I hear',          960
said Flinding fearful;    'flee we swiftly
from hate and horror    and hideous faces,
from fiery eyes    and feet relentless!
Ah! woe that I wandered    thus witless hither!'

Then beat in his breast,    foreboding evil,          965
with dread unwonted    the dauntless heart
of Beleg the brave.    With blanchéd cheeks
in faded fern    and the feathery leaves
of brown bracken    they buried them deep,
where dank and dark    a ditch was cloven          970
on the wood's borders    by waters oozing,
dripping down to die    in the drouth below.
Yet hardly were they hid    when a host to view
round a dark turning    in the dusky shadows

came swinging sudden    with a swift thudding          975
of feet after feet    on fallen leaves.
In rank on rank    of ruthless spears
that war-host went;    weary stumbling
countless captives,    cruelly laden
with bloodstained booty,    in bonds of iron          980
they haled behind them,    and held in ward
by the wolf-riders    and the wolves of Hell.
Their road of ruin    was a-reek with tears:
many a hall and homestead,    many a hidden refuge
of Gnomish lords    by night beleaguered          985
their o'ermastering might    of mirth bereft,
and fair things fouled,    and fields curdled
with the bravest blood    of the beaten people.

To an army of war    was the Orc-band waxen
that Blodrin Bor's son    to his bane guided          990
to the wood-marches,    by the welded hosts
homeward hurrying    to the halls of mourning
swiftly swollen    to a sweeping plague.
Like a throbbing thunder    in the threatening deeps
of cavernous clouds    o'ercast with gloom          995
now swelled on a sudden    a song most dire,
and their hellward hymn    their home greeted;
flung from the foremost    of the fierce spearmen,
who viewed mid vapours    vast and sable
the threefold peaks    of Thangorodrim,          1000
it rolled rearward,    rumbling darkly,
like drums in distant    dungeons empty.
Then a werewolf howled;    a word was shouted
like steel on stone;    and stiffly raised
their spears and swords    sprang up thickly          1005
as the wild wheatfields    of the wargod's realm
with points that palely    pricked the twilight.
As by wind wafted    then waved they all,
and bowed, as the bands    with beating measured
moved on mirthless    from the mirky woods,          1010
from the topless trunks    of Taur-na-Fuin,
neath the leprous limbs    of the leaning gate.

Then Beleg the bowman    in bracken cowering,
on the loathly legions    through the leaves peering,
saw Túrin the tall    as he tottered forward          1015

neath the whips of the Orcs    as they whistled o'er him;
and rage arose    in his wrathful heart,
and piercing pity    outpoured his tears.
The hymn was hushed;    the host vanished
down the hellward slopes    of the hill beyond;                    1020
and silence sank    slow and gloomy
round the trunks of the trees    of Taur-na-Fuin,
and nethermost night    drew near outside.

'Follow me, Flinding,    from the forest curséd!
Let us haste to his help,    to Hell if need be                    1025
or to death by the darts    of the dread Glamhoth!':
and Beleg bounded    from the bracken madly,
like a deer driven    by dogs baying
from his hiding in the hills    and hollow places;
and Flinding followed    fearful after him                        1030
neath the yawning gate, ·    through yew-thickets,
through bogs and bents    and bushes shrunken,
till they reached the rocks    and the riven moorlands
and friendless fells    falling darkly
to the dusty dunes    of Dor-na-Fauglith.                         1035
In a cup outcarven    on the cold hillside,
whose broken brink    was bleakly fringed
with bended bushes    bowed in anguish
from the North-wind's knife,    beneath them far
the feasting camp    of their foes was laid;                      1040
the fiery flare    of fuming torches,
and black bodies    in the blaze they saw
crossing countlessly,    and cries they heard
and the hollow howling    of hungry wolves.

Then a moon mounted    o'er the mists riding,                     1045
and the keen radiance    of the cold moonshine
the shadows sharpened    in the sheer hollows,
and slashed the slopes    with slanting blackness;
in wreaths uprising    the reek of fires
was touched to tremulous    trails of silver.                     1050
Then the fires faded,    and their foemen slumbered
in a sleep of surfeit.    No sentinel watched,
nor guards them girdled –    what good were it
to watch wakeful    in those withered regions
neath Eiglir Engrin,    whence the eyes of Bauglir                1055
gazed unclosing    from the gates of Hell?

Did not werewolves' eyes   unwinking gleam
in the wan moonlight –   the wolves that sleep not,
that sit in circles   with slavering tongues
round camp or clearing   of the cruel Glamhoth?      1060
Then was Beleg a-shudder,   and the unblinking eyes
nigh chilled his marrow   and chained his flesh
in fear unfathomed,   as flat to earth
by a boulder he lay.   Lo! black cloud-drifts
surged up like smoke   from the sable North,      1065
and the sheen was shrouded   of the shivering moon;
the wind came wailing   from the woeful mountains,
and the heath unhappy   hissed and whispered;
and the moans came faint   of men in torment
in the camp accursed.   His quiver rattled      1070
as he found his feet   and felt his bow,
hard horn-pointed,   by hands of cunning
of black yew wrought;   with bears' sinews
it was stoutly strung;   strength to bend it
had nor Man nor Elf   save the magic helped him      1075
that Beleg the bowman   now bore alone.
No arrows of the Orcs   so unerring wingéd
as his shaven shafts   that could shoot to a mark
that was seen but in glance   ere gloom seized it.
Then Dailir he drew,   his dart beloved;      1080
howso far fared it,   or fell unnoted,
unsought he found it   with sound feathers
and barbs unbroken   (till it broke at last);
and fleet bade he fly   that feather-pinioned
snaketonguéd shaft,   as he snicked the string      1085
in the notch nimbly,   and with naked arm
to his ear drew it.   The air whistled,
and the tingling string   twanged behind it,
soundless a sentinel   sank before it –
there was one of the wolves   that awaked no more.      1090
Now arrows after   he aimed swiftly
that missed not their mark   and meted silent
death in the darkness   dreadly stinging,
till three of the wolves   with throats piercéd,
and four had fallen   with fleet-wingéd      1095
arrows a-quivering   in their quenchéd eyes.
Then great was the gap   in the guard opened,
and Beleg his bow   unbent, and said:

'Wilt come to the camp,     comrade Flinding,
or await me watchful?   If woe betide                            1100
thou might win with word    through the woods homeward
to Thingol the king    how throve my quest,
how Túrin the tall     was trapped by fate,
how Beleg the bowman     to his bane hasted.'
Then Flinding fiercely,     though fear shook him:              1105
'I have followed thee far,   O forest-walker,
nor will leave thee now    our league denying!'
Then both bow and sword    Beleg left there
with his belt unbound    in the bushes tangled
of a dark thicket    in a dell nigh them,                        1110
and Flinding there laid    his flickering lamp
and his nailéd shoes,    and his knife only
he kept, that uncumbered    he might creep silent.

Thus those brave in dread    down the bare hillside
towards the camp clambered    creeping wary,                     1115
and dared that deed    in days long past
whose glory has gone    through the gates of earth,
and songs have sung    unceasing ringing
wherever the Elves    in ancient places
had light or laughter    in the later world.                     1120
With breath bated    on the brink of the dale
they stood and stared    through stealthy shadows,
till they saw where the circle    of sleepless eyes
was broken; with hearts    beating dully
they passed the places    where pierced and bleeding            1125
the wolves weltered    by wingéd death
unseen smitten;    as smoke noiseless
they slipped silent    through the slumbering throngs
as shadowy wraiths    shifting vaguely
from gloom to gloom,    till the Gods brought them              1130
and the craft and cunning    of the keen huntsman
to Túrin the tall    where he tumbled lay
with face downward    in the filthy mire,
and his feet were fettered,    and fast in bonds
anguish enchained    his arms behind him.                        1135
There he slept or swooned,    as sunk in oblivion
by drugs of darkness    deadly blended;
he heard not their whispers;    no hope stirred him
nor the deep despair    of his dreams fathomed;

to awake his wit    no words availed.                        1140
No blade would bite    on the bonds he wore,
though Flinding felt    for the forgéd knife
of dwarfen steel,    his dagger prizéd,
that at waist he wore    awake or sleeping,
whose edge would eat    through iron noiseless            1145
as a clod of clay    is cleft by the share.
It was wrought by wrights    in the realms of the East,
in black Belegost,    by the bearded Dwarves
of troth unmindful;    it betrayed him now
from its sheath slipping    as o'er shaggy slades        1150
and roughhewn rocks    their road they wended.

'We must bear him back    as best we may,'
said Beleg, bending    his broad shoulders.
Then the head he lifted    of Húrin's offspring,
and Flinding go-Fuilin    the feet claspéd;              1155
and doughty that deed,    for in days long gone
though Men were of mould    less mighty builded
ere the earth's goodness    from the Elves they drew,
though the Elfin kindreds    ere old was the sun
were of might unminished,    nor the moon haunted         1160
faintly fading    as formed of shadows
in places unpeopled,    yet peers they were not
in bone and flesh    and body's fashioning,
and Túrin was tallest    of the ten races
that in Hithlum's hills    their homes builded.           1165
Like a log they lifted    his limbs mighty,
and straining staggered    with stealth and fear,
with bodies bending    and bones aching,
from the cruel dreaming    of the camp of dread,
where spearmen drowsed    sprawling drunken              1170
by their moon-blades keen    with murder whetted
mid their shaven shafts    in sheaves piléd.

Now Beleg the brave    backward led them,
but his foot fumbled    and he fell thudding
with Túrin atop of him,    and trembling stumbled         1175
Flinding forward;    there frozen lying
long while they listened    for alarm stirring,
for hue and cry,    and their hearts cowered;
but unbroken the breathing    of the bands sleeping,
as darkness deepened    to dead midnight,                1180

and the lifeless hour    when the loosened soul
oft sheds the shackles    of the shivering flesh.
Then dared their dread    to draw its breath,
and they found their feet    in the fouléd earth,
and bent they both    their backs once more                    1185
to their task of toil,    for Túrin woke not.
There the huntsman's hand    was hurt deeply,
as he groped on the ground,    by a gleaming point –
'twas Dailir his dart    dearly prizéd
he had found by his foot    in fragments twain,               1190
and with barbs bended:    it broke at last
neath his body falling.    It boded ill.

As in dim dreaming,    and dazed with horror,
they won their way    with weary slowness,
foot by footstep,    till fate them granted                    1195
the leaguer at last    of those lairs to pass,
and their burden laid they,    breathless gasping,
on bare-bosméd earth,    and abode a while,
ere by winding ways    they won their path
up the slanting slopes    with silent labour,                  1200
with spended strength    sprawling to cast them
in the darkling dell    neath the deep thicket.
Then sought his sword,    and songs of magic
o'er its eager edge    with Elfin voice
there Beleg murmured,    while bluely glimmered               1205
the lamp of Flinding    neath the lacéd thorns.
There wondrous wove he    words of sharpness,
and the names of knives    and Gnomish blades
he uttered o'er it:    even Ogbar's spear
and the glaive of Gaurin    whose gleaming stroke             1210
did rive the rocks    of Rodrim's hall;
the sword of Saithnar,    and the silver blades
of the enchanted children    of chains forgéd
in their deep dungeon;    the dirk of Nargil,
the knife of the North    in Nogrod smithied;                 1215
the sweeping sickle    of the slashing tempest,
the lambent lightning's    leaping falchion
even Celeg Aithorn    that shall cleave the world.

Then whistling whirled he    the whetted sword-blade
and three times three    it threshed the gloom,               1220
till flame was kindled    flickering strangely

like licking firelight    in the lamp's glimmer
blue and baleful    at the blade's edges.
Lo! a leering laugh    lone and dreadful
by the wind wafted    wavered nigh them;                    1225
their limbs were loosened    in listening horror;
they fancied the feet    of foes approaching,
for the horns hearkening    of the hunt afoot
in the rustling murmur    of roving breezes.
Then quickly curtained    with its covering pelt           1230
was the lantern's light,    and leaping Beleg
with his sword severed    the searing bonds
on wrist and arm    like ropes of hemp
so strong that whetting;    in stupor lying
entangled still    lay Túrin moveless.                      1235
For the feet's fetters    then feeling in the dark
Beleg blundering    with his blade's keenness
unwary wounded    the weary flesh
of wayworn foot,    and welling blood
bedewed his hand –    too dark his magic:                   1240
that sleep profound    was sudden fathomed;
in fear woke Túrin,    and a form he guessed
o'er his body bending    with blade naked.
His death or torment    he deemed was come,
for oft had the Orcs    for evil pastime                    1245
him goaded gleeful    and gashed with knives
that they cast with cunning,    with cruel spears.
Lo! the bonds were burst    that had bound his hands:
his cry of battle    calling hoarsely
he flung him fiercely    on the foe he dreamed,             1250
and Beleg falling    breathless earthward
was crushed beneath him.    Crazed with anguish
then seized that sword    the son of Húrin,
to his hand lying    by the help of doom;
at the throat he thrust;    through he pierced it,          1255
that the blood was buried    in the blood-wet mould;
ere Flinding knew    what fared that night,
all was over.    With oath and curse
he bade the goblins    now guard them well,
or sup on his sword:    'Lo! the son of Húrin               1260
is freed from his fetters.'    His fancy wandered
in the camps and clearings    of the cruel Glamhoth.
Flight he sought not    at Flinding leaping

with his last laughter,   his life to sell
amid foes imagined;   but Fuilin's son                          1265
there stricken with amaze,   starting backward,
cried: 'Magic of Morgoth!   A! madness damned!
with friends thou fightest!' –   then falling suddenly
the lamp o'erturned   in the leaves shrouded
that its light released   illumined pale                         1270
with its flickering flame   the face of Beleg.
Then the boles of the trees   more breathless rooted
stone-faced he stood   staring frozen
on that dreadful death,   and his deed knowing
wildeyed he gazed   with waking horror,                         1275
as in endless anguish   an image carven.
So fearful his face   that Flinding crouched
and watched him, wondering   what webs of doom
dark, remorseless,   dreadly meshed him
by the might of Morgoth;   and he mourned for him,              1280
and for Beleg, who bow   should bend no more,
his black yew-wood   in battle twanging –
his life had winged   to its long waiting
in the halls of the Moon   o'er the hills of the sea.

Hark! he heard the horns   hooting loudly,                       1285
no ghostly laughter   of grim phantom,
no wraithlike feet   rustling dimly –
the Orcs were up;   their ears had hearkened
the cries of Túrin;   their camp was tumult,
their lust was alight   ere the last shadows                     1290
of night were lifted.   Then numb with fear
in hoarse whisper   to unhearing ears
he told his terror;   for Túrin now
with limbs loosened   leaden-eyed was bent
crouching crumpled   by the corse moveless;                      1295
nor sight nor sound   his senses knew,
and wavering words   he witless murmured,
'A! Beleg,' he whispered,   'my brother-in-arms.'
Though Flinding shook him,   he felt it not:
had he comprehended   he had cared little.                       1300
Then winds were wakened   in wild dungeons
where thrumming thunders   throbbed and rumbled;
storm came striding   with streaming banners
from the four corners   of the fainting world;

then the clouds were cloven    with a crash of lightning,      1305
and slung like stones    from slings uncounted
the hurtling hail    came hissing earthward,
with a deluge dark    of driving rain.
Now wafted high,    now wavering far,
the cries of the Glamhoth    called and hooted,      1310
and the howl of wolves    in the heavens' roaring
was mingled mournful:    they missed their paths,
for swollen swept there    swirling torrents
down the blackening slopes,    and the slot was blind,
so that blundering back    up the beaten road      1315
to the gates of gloom    many goblins wildered
were drowned or drawn    in Deadly Nightshade
to die in the dark;    while dawn came not,
while the storm-riders    strove and thundered
all the sunless day,    and soaked and drenched      1320
Flinding go-Fuilin    with fear speechless
there crouched aquake;    cold and lifeless
lay Beleg the bowman;    brooding dumbly
Túrin Thalion    neath the tangled thorns
sat unseeing    without sound or movement.      1325

The dusty dunes    of Dor-na-Fauglith
hissed and spouted.    Huge rose the spires
of smoking vapour    swathed and reeking,
thick-billowing clouds    from thirst unquenched,
and dawn was kindled    dimly lurid      1330
when a day and night    had dragged away.
The Orcs had gone,    their anger baffled,
o'er the weltering ways    weary faring
to their hopeless halls    in Hell's kingdom;
no thrall took they    Túrin Thalion –      1335
a burden bore he    than their bonds heavier,
in despair fettered    with spirit empty
in mourning hopeless    he remained behind.

★

## NOTES

617    *Blodrin*: *Bauglir* A, and B as typed. See line 618.
618    *Bauglir Ban's son* A, and B as typed (*Bauglir > Blodrin*

carefully-made early change, *Ban* > *Bor* hasty and later).
See lines 661, 696, 990.

631  *Fangair* A, *Fangros* B as typed.

636  *Tengwethiel* [*sic*] A, *Tain-Gwethil* B as typed. Cf. line 431.

653  *Túrin Thaliodrin* A, and B as typed. Cf. lines 115, 333, 720.

661, 696  As at line 618.

711  *Aiglir-angrin* A, *Aiglir Angrin* B as typed, emended
roughly in pencil to *Eiglir Engrin*; cf. line 1055. In the *Tale
of Turambar* occurs *Angorodin* (the Iron Mountains),
II.77.

711–14  These lines read in A (and as typed in B, with *of Hell is
reared* for *of the Hells of Iron*):

> where Aiglir-angrin    the Iron Hills lie
> and Thangorodrim's    thunderous mountain
> o'er the hopeless halls    of the Hells of iron
> wrought at the roots    of the ruthless hills.

718  Cf. Bilbo's second riddle to Gollum.

720  As at line 653.

780  *Delimorgoth* A, *Delu-Morgoth* B as typed, *dark Morgoth* a late pencilled emendation. At lines 11 and 51 *Delu-
Morgoth* is an emendation of *Delimorgoth* in B.

816  *Tûn* also in A; see lines 50, 430.

818–20  Against these lines my father wrote in the margin of B:
'Captured in battle at gates of Angband.'

826  *o'er the black boulders    of the Blasted Plain* A (marked
with query).

834  *mercy: magic* A, and B as typed; *mercy* in pencil and not
quite certain.

946  *Daideloth* A emended at time of writing to *Dor-na-
Maiglos*, *Dor-na-Fauglith* B as typed. In margin of A is
written: 'a plateau from *Dai* "high", *Deloth* "plain"'; contrast II. 337, entry *Dor-na-Dhaideloth*.

990  *Blodrin Ban's son* A, and B as typed; *Ban's* > *Bor's* later
in B. At lines 617–18, 661, 696 A, and B as typed, had
*Bauglir*, changed to *Blodrin* in B.

1055  *Aiglir Angrin* A, and B as typed; see line 711.
*Bauglir* A and B.

1098  This line is emended in B, but the reading is uncertain:
apparently *Then his bow unbending    Beleg asked him:*

1137  In the margin of B is written *r*?, i.e. *dreadly* for *deadly*.

1147  *East: South* A, and B as typed.

1198  *bosméd* (bosomed) written thus in both A and B.

1214  *Nargil: Loruin* A, with *Nargil* added as an alternative.

1324  *Túrin Thaliodrin* A, and B as typed; see lines 653, 720.

1335  *Thalion-Túrin* A, and B as typed.

## Commentary on *Part II 'Beleg'*

In this part of the poem there are some narrative developments of much interest. The poem follows the *Tale* (II. 76) in making Beleg become one of Turin's band on the marches of Doriath not long after Túrin's departure from the Thousand Caves, and with no intervening event – in *The Silmarillion* (p. 200) Beleg came to Menegroth, and after speaking to Thingol set out to seek Túrin, while in the *Narn* (pp. 82–5) there is the 'trial of Túrin', and the intervention of Beleg bringing Nellas as witness, before he set out on Túrin's trail. In the poem it is explicit that Beleg was not searching for him, and indeed knew nothing whatever of what had passed in the Thousand Caves (595). But Túrin's band are no longer the 'wild spirits' of the *Tale*; they are hostile to all comers, whether Orcs or Men or Elves, including the Elves of Doriath (560–1, 566), as in *The Silmarillion*, and in far greater detail in the *Narn*, where the band is called *Gaurwaith*, the Wolf-men, 'to be feared as wolves'.

The element of Beleg's capture and maltreatment by the band now appears, and also that of Túrin's absence from the camp at the time. Several features of the story in the *Narn* are indeed already present in the poem, though absent from the more condensed account in *The Silmarillion*: as Beleg's being tied to a tree by the outlaws (577, *Narn* pp. 92–3), and the occasion of Túrin's absence – he was

> on the trail of the Orcs,
> as they hastened home    to the Hills of Iron
> with the loot laden    of the lands of Men

just as in the *Narn* (pp. 91–2), where however the story is part of a complex set of movements among the Woodmen of Brethil, Beleg, the Gaurwaith, and the Orcs.

Whereas in the *Tale* it was only now that Beleg and Túrin became companions-in-arms, we have already seen that the poem has the later story whereby they had fought together on the marches of Doriath before Túrin's flight from the Thousand Caves (p. 27); and we now have also the development that Túrin's altered mood at the sight of Beleg tied to the tree (*Then Túrin's heart    was turned from hate*, 584), and Beleg's own reproaches (*Shall the foes of Faërie    be friends of Men?* 603), led to the band's turning their arms henceforth only against *the foes of Faërie* (644). Of the great oath sworn by the members of the band, explicitly echoing that of the Sons of Fëanor (634) – and showing incidentally that in that oath the holy mountain of Taniquetil (Tain-Gwethil) was taken in witness (636), there is no trace in *The Silmarillion* or the *Narn*: in the latter, indeed, the outlaws are not conceived in such a way as to make such an oath-taking at all probable.

Lines 643 ff., describing the prowess of the fellowship in the forest, are the ultimate origin of the never finally achieved story of the Land of Dor-Cúarthol (*The Silmarillion* p. 205, *Narn* pp. 152–4); lines 651–4

> even in Angband    the Orcs trembled.
> Then the word wandered    down the ways of the forest
> that Túrin Thalion    was returned to war;
> and Thingol heard it . . .

lead in the end to

In Menegroth, and in the deep halls of Nargothrond, and even in the hidden realm of Gondolin, the fame of the deeds of the Two Captains was heard; and in Angband also they were known.

But in the later story Túrin was hidden under the name Gorthol, the Dread Helm, and it was his wearing of the Dragon-helm that revealed him to Morgoth. There is no suggestion of this in the earlier phase of the legend; the Dragon-helm makes no further appearance here in the poem.
    A table may serve to clarify the development:

| *Tale* | *Lay* | *Silmarillion* and *Narn* |
|---|---|---|
| Túrin's prowess on the marches of Doriath (Beleg not mentioned). | Túrin and Beleg companions-in-arms on the marches of Doriath; Túrin wears the Dragon-helm. | As in the poem. |
| Death of Orgof. | Death of Orgof. | Death of Saeros. |
| Túrin leaves Doriath; a band forms round him which includes Beleg. | Túrin leaves Doriath; a band of outlaws forms round him which attacks all comers. | Túrin leaves Doriath and joins a band of desperate outlaws. |
|  | The band captures Beleg (who knows nothing of Túrin's leaving Doriath) and ties him to a tree. | The band captures Beleg (who is searching for Túrin bearing Thingol's pardon) (and ties him to a tree, *Narn*). |
|  | Túrin has him set free; suffers a change of heart; Beleg joins the band; all swear an oath. | Túrin has him set free; suffers a change of heart; but Beleg will not join the band and departs. (No mention of oath.) |
| Great prowess of the band. | Great prowess of the band against the Orcs. | (Later Beleg returns and joins the band:) Land of Dor-Cúarthol. |

Before leaving this part of the story, it may be suggested that lines 605 ff., in which Túrin declares to Beleg that *This band alone / I count as comrades*, contain the germ of Túrin's words to him in the *Narn*, p. 94:

> The grace of Thingol will not stretch to receive these companions of my fall, I think; but I will not part with them now, if they do not wish to part with me, &c.

The traitor, who betrayed the band to the Orcs, now first appears. At first he is called *Bauglir* both in A and in B as originally typed; and it might be thought that the name had much too obviously an evil significance. The explanation is quite clearly, however, that *Bauglir* became *Blodrin* at the same time as *Bauglir* replaced *Belcha* as a name of Morgoth. (By the time my father reached line 990 *Blodrin* is the name as first written in both A and B; while similarly at line 1055 *Bauglir* is Morgoth's name, not *Belcha*, both in A and B as first written.) The change of *Ban* (father of Blodrin) to *Bor* was passing; he is *Ban* in the 1926 'Sketch of the Mythology', and so remained until, much later, he disappeared.

Blodrin's origin is interesting:

>                                     trapped as a child
> he was dragged by the Dwarves    to their deep mansions,
> and in Nogrod nurtured,    and in nought was like,
> spite blood and birth,    to the blissful Elves.          (666–9)

Thus Blodrin's evil nature is explicitly ascribed to the influence of *the bearded Dwarves / of troth unmindful* (1148–9); and Blodrin follows Ufedhin of the *Tale of the Nauglafring* as an example of the sinister effect of Elvish association with Dwarves – not altogether absent in the tale of Eöl and Maeglin as it appears in *The Silmarillion*. Though the nature – and name – of the traitor in Túrin's band went through Protean mutations afterwards, it is not inconceivable that recollection of the Dwarvish element in Blodrin's history played some part in the emergence of Mîm in this rôle. On the early hostile view of the Dwarves see II. 247. The words of the poem just cited arise from the 'betrayal' of Flinding by his dwarvish knife, which slipped from its sheath; so later, in the *Lay of Leithian*, when Beren attempted to cut a second Silmaril from the Iron Crown (lines 4160–2)

> The dwarvish steel of cunning blade
> by treacherous smiths of Nogrod made
> ˌsnapped . . .

The idea expressed in the *Tale* (II. 76) that Túrin was taken alive by Morgoth's command 'lest he cheat the doom that was devised for him' reappears in the poem: *lest he flee his fate* (705).

The rest of the story as told in the poem differs only in detail from that in the *Tale*. The survival of Beleg in the attack by Orcs and his swift recovery from his grievous wounds (II. 77), present in much changed circumstances in *The Silmarillion* (p. 206), is here made perhaps more comprehensible, in that Elves from Doriath, who were searching for Túrin (654–5), found Beleg and took him back to be healed by Melian in the Thousand Caves (727–31). In the account of Beleg's meeting with Flinding in Taur-na-Fuin, led to him by his blue lamp, the poem is following the *Tale* very closely.* My father's painting of the scene (*Pictures by J. R. R. Tolkien* no. 37) was almost certainly made a few years later, when the Elf lying under the tree was still called Flinding son of Fuilin (in the *Tale bo-Dhuilin*, earlier *go-Dhuilin*, son of Duilin; the patronymic prefix has in the poem (814, 900) reverted to the earlier form *go-*, see II. 119).

In the *Tale* it is only said (II. 81) that Flinding was of the people of the Rodothlim 'before the Orcs captured him'; from the poem (819–21) it seems that he was carried off, with many others, from Nargothrond, but this can scarcely be the meaning, since *nought yet knew they* [the Orcs] *of Nargothrond* (1578). The marginal note in B against these lines 'Captured in battle at gates of Angband' refers to the later story, first appearing in the 1930 'Silmarillion'.

The poem follows the *Tale* in the detail of Flinding's story to Beleg, except that in the poem he was recaptured by the Orcs in Taur-na-Fuin (846 ff.) and escaped again (*crept from their clutches as a crawling worm*, 879), whereas in the *Tale* he was not recaptured but 'fled heedlessly' (II. 79). The notable point in the *Tale* that Flinding 'was overjoyed to have speech with a free Noldo' reappears in the poem: *Marvelling he heard / the ancient tongue of the Elves of Tûn*. The detail of their encountering of the Orc-host is slightly different: in the *Tale* the Orcs had changed their path, in the poem it seems that Beleg and Flinding merely came more quickly than did the Orcs to the point where the Orc-road emerged from the edge of the forest. In the *Tale* it seems indeed that the Orcs had not left the forest when they encamped for the night: the eyes of the wolves 'shone like points of red light among the trees', and Beleg and Flinding laid Túrin down after his rescue 'in the woods at no great distance from the camp'. The *cup outcarven on the cold hillside* of the poem (1036), where the Orcs made their bivouac, is the 'bare dell' of *The Silmarillion*.

In contrast to the *Tale* (see p. 26) Beleg is now frequently called *Beleg the bowman*, his great bow (not yet named) is fully described, and his unmatched skill as an archer (1071 ff.). There is also in the poem the feature of the arrow Dailir, unfailingly found and always unharmed (1080 ff.), until it broke when Beleg fell upon it while carrying Túrin (1189–92): of this there is never a mention later. The element of Beleg's

*The element of the blue lamp is lacking from the account in *The Silmarillion*; see *Unfinished Tales* p. 51 note 2.

archery either arose from, or itself caused, the change in the story of the entry of Beleg and Flinding into the Orc-camp that now appears: in the *Tale* they merely 'crept between the wolves at a point where there was a great gap between them', whereas in the poem Beleg performed the feat of shooting seven wolves in the darkness, and only so was 'a great gap opened' (1097). But the words of the *Tale*, 'as the luck of the Valar had it Túrin was lying nigh', are echoed in

> till the Gods brought them
> and the craft and cunning    of the keen huntsman
> to Túrin the tall    where he tumbled lay            (1130–2)

The lifting and carrying of Túrin by the two Elves, referred to in the *Tale* as 'a great feat', 'seeing that he was a Man and of greater stature than they' (II. 80), is expanded in the poem (1156 ff.) into a comment on the stature of Men and Elves in the ancient time, which agrees with earlier statements on this topic (see I. 235, II. 142, 220). The notable lines

> though Men were of mould    less mighty builded
> ere the earth's goodness    from the Elves they drew (1157–8)

are to be related to the statements cited in II. 326: 'As Men's stature grows [the Elves'] diminishes', and 'ever as Men wax more powerful and numerous so the fairies fade and grow small and tenuous, filmy and transparent, but Men larger and more dense and gross'. The mention here (1164) of *the ten races* of Hithlum occurs nowhere else, and it is not clear whether it refers to all the peoples of Men and Elves who in one place or another in the *Lost Tales* are set in Hithlum, which as I have remarked 'seems to have been in danger of having too many inhabitants' (see II. 249, 251).

The *Tale* has it that it was Beleg's knife that had slipped from him as he crept into the camp; in the poem it is Flinding's (1142 ff.). In the *Tale* Beleg returned to fetch his sword from the place where he had left it, since they could carry Túrin no further; in the poem they carried Túrin all the way up to the *dark thicket in a dell* whence they had set out (1110, 1202). The 'whetting spell' of Beleg over his (still unnamed) sword is an entirely new element (and without trace later); it arises in association with line 1141, *No blade would bite    on the bonds he wore*. In style it is reminiscent of Lúthien's 'lengthening spell' in Canto V of the *Lay of Leithian*; but of the names in the spell, of *Ogbar*, *Gaurin, Rodrim, Saithnar, Nargil, Celeg Aithorn*, there seems to be now no other trace.

There now occurs in the poem the mysterious *leering laugh* (1224), to which it seems that the *ghostly laughter    of grim phantom* in line 1286 refers, and which is mentioned again in the next part of the poem (1488–90). The narrative purpose of this is evidently to cause the covering of the lamp and to cause Beleg to work too quickly in the darkness at the cutting of the bonds. It may be also that the wounding of

Beleg's hand when he put it on the point of Dailir his arrow (1187) accounts for his clumsiness; for every aspect of this powerful scene had been pondered and refined.

In the poem the great storm is introduced: first presaged in lines 1064 ff., when Beleg and Flinding were at the edge of the dell (as it is in *The Silmarillion*):

> Lo! black cloud-drifts
> surged up like smoke    from the sable North,
> and the sheen was shrouded    of the shivering moon;
> the wind came wailing    from the woeful mountains,
> and the heath unhappy    hissed and whispered

and bursting at last after Beleg's death (1301 ff.), to last all through the following day, during which Túrin and Flinding crouched on the hillside (1320, 1330–1). On account of the storm the Orcs were unable to find Túrin, and departed, as in *The Silmarillion*; in the *Tale* Flinding roused Túrin to flee as soon as the shouts of discovery were heard from the Orc-camp, and nothing more is said of the matter. But in the poem it is still, as in the *Tale*, the sudden uncovering of Flinding's lamp as he fell back from Túrin's assault that illumined Beleg's face; in the last account that my father wrote of this episode he was undecided whether it was the cover falling off the lamp or a great flash of lightning that gave the light, and in the published work I chose the latter.

There remain a few isolated points, mostly concerning names. In this part of the poem we meet for the first time:

*Nargothrond* 821, 904;

*Taur-na-Fuin* (for *Taur Fuin* of the *Lost Tales*) 766, 828; called also *Deadly Nightshade* 767, 837, 1317, and *Forest of Night* 896;

*Dor-na-Fauglith* 946, 1035, 1326, called also *the Plains of Drouth* 826, *the Thirsty Plain* 947 (and in A, note to 826, *the Blasted Plain*). The name *Dor-na-Fauglith* arose during the composition of the poem (see note to 946). By this time the story of the blasting of the great northern plain, so that it became a dusty desert, in the battle that ended the Siege of Angband, must have been conceived, though it does not appear in writing for several years.

Here also is the first reference to the triple peaks of Thangorodrim (1000), called *the thunderous towers* (951), though in the 'Prologue' to the poem it is said that Húrin was set *on its steepest peak* (96); and from lines 713–14 (as rewritten in the B-text) we learn that Angband was *wrought at the roots* of the great mountain.

The name *Fangros* (631; *Fangair* A) occurs once elsewhere, in a very obscure note, where it is apparently connected with the burning of the ships of the Noldoli.

Melian's name *Mablui – by the hands enchanted of Melian*

*Mablui*, 731 – clearly contains *mab* 'hand', as in *Mablung, Ermabwed* (see II. 339).

That the Dwarves were said in A and originally in B to dwell in the South (1147, emended in B to *East*) is perhaps to be related to the statement in the *Tale of the Nauglafring* that Nogrod lay '*a very long journey southward* beyond the wide forest on the borders of those great heaths nigh Umboth-muilin the Pools of Twilight' (II. 225).

I cannot explain the reference in line 1006 to *the wild wheatfields of the wargod's realm*; nor that in the lines concerning Beleg's fate after death to the long waiting of the dead *in the halls of the Moon* (1284).

★

## III

## FAILIVRIN

Flinding go-Fuilin    faithful-hearted
the brand of Beleg    with blood stainéd                          1340
lifted with loathing    from the leafy mould,
and hid it in the hollow    of a huge thorn-tree;
then he turned to Túrin    yet tranced brooding,
and softly said he:    'O son of Húrin,
unhappy-hearted,    what helpeth it                               1345
to sit thus in sorrow's    silent torment
without hope or counsel?'    But Húrin's son,
by those words wakened,    wildly answered:
'I abide by Beleg;    nor bid me leave him,
thou voice unfaithful.    Vain are all things.                    1350
O Death dark-handed,    draw thou near me;
if remorse may move thee,    from mourning loosed
crush me conquered    to his cold bosom!'
Flinding answered,    and fear left him
for wrath and pity:    'Arouse thy pride!                         1355
Not thus unthinking    on Thangorodrim's
heights enchainéd    did Húrin speak.'
'Curse thy comfort!    Less cold were steel.
If Death comes not    to the death-craving,
I will seek him by the sword.    The sword – where lies it?       1360
O cold and cruel,    where cowerest now,
murderer of thy master?    Amends shalt work,
and slay me swift,    O sleep-giver.'
'Look not, luckless,    thy life to steal,

nor sully anew   his sword unhappy      1365
in the flesh of the friend   whose freedom seeking
he fell by fate,   by foes unwounded.
Yea, think that amends   are thine to make,
his wrongéd blade   with wrath appeasing,
its thirst cooling   in the thrice-abhorred      1370
blood of Bauglir's   baleful legions.
Is the feud achieved   thy father's chains
on thee laid, or lessened   by this last evil?
Dream not that Morgoth   will mourn thy death,
or thy dirges chant   the dread Glamhoth –      1375
less would like them   thy living hatred
and vows of vengeance;   nor vain is courage,
though victory seldom   be valour's ending.'

Then fiercely Túrin   to his feet leaping
cried new-crazéd:   'Ye coward Orcs,      1380
why turn ye tail?   Why tarry ye now,
when the son of Húrin   and the sword of Beleg
in wrath await you?   For wrong and woe
here is vengeance ready.   If ye venture it not,
I will follow your feet   to the four corners      1385
of the angry earth.   Have after you!'
Fainting Flinding   there fought with him,
and words of wisdom   to his witless ears
he breathless spake:   'Abide, O Túrin,
for need hast thou now   to nurse thy hurt,      1390
and strength to gather   and strong counsel.
Who flees to fight   wears not fear's token,
and vengeance delayed   its vow achieves.'
The madness passed;   amazed pondering
neath the tangled trees   sat Túrin wordless      1395
brooding blackly   on bitter vengeance,
till the dusk deepened   on his day of waking,
and the early stars   were opened pale.

Then Beleg's burial   in those bleak regions
did Flinding fashion;   where he fell sadly      1400
he left him lying,   and lightly o'er him
with long labour   the leaves he poured.
But Túrin tearless   turning suddenly
on the corse cast him,   and kissed the mouth
cold and open,   and closed the eyes.      1405

His bow laid he    black beside him,
and words of parting    wove about him:
'Now fare well, Beleg,    to feasting long
neath Tengwethil    in the timeless halls
where drink the Gods,    neath domes golden          1410
o'er the sea shining.'    His song was shaken,
but the tears were dried    in his tortured eyes
by the flames of anguish    that filled his soul.
His mind once more    was meshed in darkness
as heaped they high    o'er the head beloved          1415
a mound of mould    and mingled leaves.
Light lay the earth    on the lonely dead;
heavy lay the woe    on the heart that lived.
That grief was graven    with grim token
on his face and form,    nor faded ever:              1420
and this was the third    of the throes of Túrin.

Thence he wandered witless    without wish or purpose;
but for Flinding the faithful    he had fared to death,
or been lost in the lands    of lurking evil.
Renewed in that Gnome    of Nargothrond              1425
was heart and valour    by hatred wakened,
that he guarded and guided    his grim comrade;
with the light of his lamp    he lit their ways,
and they hid by day    to hasten by night,
by darkness shrouded    or dim vapours.              1430

The tale tells not    of their travel weary,
how roamed their road    by the rim of the forest,
whose beetling branches,    black o'erhanging,
did greedy grope    with gloomy malice
to ensnare their souls    in silent darkness.          1435
Yet west they wandered    by ways of thirst
and haggard hunger,    hunted often,
and hiding in holes    and hollow caverns,
by their fate defended.    At the furthest end
of Dor-na-Fauglith's    dusty spaces                  1440
to a mighty mound    in the moon looming
they came at midnight:    it was crowned with mist,
bedewed as by drops    of drooping tears.
'A! green that hill    with grass fadeless,
where sleep the swords    of seven kindreds,          1445
where the folk of Faërie    once fell uncounted.

There was fought the field    by folk naméd
Nirnaith Ornoth,    Unnùmbered Tears.
'Twas built with the blood    of the beaten people;
neath moon nor sun    is it mounted ever                    1450
by Man nor Elf;    not Morgoth's host
ever dare for dread    to delve therein.'
Thus Flinding faltered,    faintly stirring
Túrin's heaviness,    that he turned his hand
toward Thangorodrim,    and thrice he cursed               1455
the maker of mourning,    Morgoth Bauglir.

Thence later led them    their lagging footsteps
o'er the slender stream    of Sirion's youth;
not long had he leapt    a lace of silver
from his shining well    in those shrouded hills,          1460
the Shadowy Mountains    whose sheer summits
there bend humbled    towards the brooding heights
in mist mantled,    the mountains of the North.
Here the Orcs might pass him;    they else dared not
o'er Sirion swim,    whose swelling water                  1465
through moor and marsh,    mead and woodland,
through caverns carven    in the cold bosom
of Earth far under,    through empty lands
and leagues untrodden,    beloved of Ylmir,
fleeting floweth,    with fame undying                     1470
in the songs of the Gnomes,    to the sea at last.
Thus reached they the roots    and the ruinous feet
of those hoary hills    that Hithlum girdle,
the shaggy pinewoods    of the Shadowy Mountains.
There the twain enfolded    phantom twilight               1475
and dim mazes    dark, unholy,
in Nan Dungorthin    where nameless gods
have shrouded shrines    in shadows secret,
more old than Morgoth    or the ancient lords
the golden Gods    of the guarded West.                    1480
But the ghostly dwellers    of that grey valley
hindered nor hurt them,    and they held their course
with creeping flesh    and quaking limb.
Yet laughter at whiles    with lingering echo,
as distant mockery    of demon voices                      1485
there harsh and hollow    in the hushed twilight
Flinding fancied,    fell, unwholesome

as that leering laughter    lost and dreadful
that rang in the rocks    in the ruthless hour
of Beleg's slaughter. ''Tis Bauglir's voice          1490
that dogs us darkly    with deadly scorn'
he shuddering thought;    but the shreds of fear
and black foreboding    were banished utterly
when they clomb the cliffs    and crumbling rocks
that walled that vale    of watchful evil,          1495
and southward saw    the slopes of Hithlum
more warm and friendly.    That way they fared
during the daylight    o'er dale and ghyll,
o'er mountain pasture,    moor and boulder,
over fell and fall    of flashing waters          1500
that slipped down to Sirion,    to swell his tide
in his eastward basin    onward sweeping
to the South, to the sea,    to his sandy delta.

After seven journeys    lo! sleep took them
on a night of stars    when they nigh had stridden          1505
to those lands beloved    that long had known
Flinding aforetime.    At first morning
the white arrows    of the wheeling sun
gazed down gladly    on green hollows
and smiling slopes    that swept before them.          1510
There builded boles    of beeches ancient
marched in majesty    in myriad leaves
of golden russet    greyly rooted,
in leaves translucent    lightly robéd;
their boughs up-bending    blown at morning          1515
by the wings of winds    that wandered down
o'er blossomy bent    breathing odours
to the wavering water's    winking margin.
There rush and reed    their rustling plumes
and leaves like lances    louted trembling          1520
green with sunlight.    Then glad the soul
of Flinding the fugitive;    in his face the morning
there glimmered golden,    his gleaming hair
was washed with sunlight.    'Awake from sadness,
Túrion Thalion,    and troublous thoughts!          1525
On Ivrin's lake    is endless laughter.
Lo! cool and clear    by crystal fountains
she is fed unfailing,    from defilement warded

by Ylmir the old,    who in ancient days,
wielder of waters,    here worked her beauty.                1530
From outmost Ocean    yet often comes
his message hither    his magic bearing,
the healing of hearts    and hope and valour
for foes of Bauglir.    Friend is Ylmir
who alone remembers    in the Lands of Mirth            1535
the need of the Gnomes.    Here Narog's waters
(that in tongue of the Gnomes    is 'torrent' naméd)
are born, and blithely    boulders leaping
o'er the bents bounding    with broken foam
swirl down southward    to the secret halls              1540
of Nargothrond    by the Gnomes builded
that death and thraldom    in the dreadful throes
of Nirnaith Ornoth,    a number scanty,
escaped unscathed.    Thence skirting wild
the Hills of the Hunters,    the home of Beren          1545
and the Dancer of Doriath    daughter of Thingol,
it winds and wanders    ere the willowy meads,
Nan-Tathrin's land,    for nineteen leagues
it journeys joyful    to join its flood
with Sirion in the South.    To the salt marshes        1550
where snipe and seamew    and the sea-breezes
first pipe and play    they press together
sweeping soundless    to the seats of Ylmir,
where the waters of Sirion    and the waves of the sea
murmurous mingle.    A marge of sand                    1555
there lies, all lit    by the long sunshine;
there all day rustles    wrinkled Ocean,
and the sea-birds call    in solemn conclave,
whitewingéd hosts    whistling sadly,
uncounted voices    crying endlessly.                    1560
There a shining shingle    on that shore lieth,
whose pebbles as pearl    or pale marble
by spray and spindrift    splashed at evening
in the moon do gleam,    or moan and grind
when the Dweller in the Deep    drives in fury          1565
the waters white    to the walls of the land;
when the long-haired riders    on their lathered horses
with bit and bridle    of blowing foam,
in wrack wreathéd    and ropes of seaweed,
to the thunder gallop    of the thudding of the surf.'   1570

Thus Flinding spake    the spell feeling
of Ylmir the old    and unforgetful,
which hale and holy    haunted Ivrin
and foaming Narog,    so that fared there never
Orc of Morgoth,    and that eager stream                          1575
no plunderer passed.    If their purpose held
to reach the realms    that roamed beyond
(nought yet knew they    of Nargothrond)
they harried o'er Hithlum    the heights scaling
that lay behind    the lake's hollow,                             1580
the Shadowy Mountains    in the sheen mirrored
of the pools of Ivrin.    Pale and eager
Túrin hearkened    to the tale of Flinding:
the washing of waters    in his words sounded,
an echo as of Ylmir's    awful conches                           1585
in the abyss blowing.    There born anew
was hope in his heart    as they hastened down
to the lake of laughter.    A long and narrow
arm it reaches    that ancient rocks
o'ergrown with green    girdle strongly,                         1590
at whose outer end    there open sudden
a gap, a gateway    in the grey boulders;
whence thrusteth thin    in threadlike jets
newborn Narog,    nineteen fathoms
o'er a flickering force    falls in wonder,                      1595
and a glimmering goblet    with glass-lucent
fountains fills he    by his freshets carven
in the cool bosom    of the crystal stones.

There deeply drank    ere day was fallen
Túrin the toilworn    and his true comrade;                      1600
hurt's ease found he,    heart's refreshment,
from the meshes of misery    his mind was loosed,
as they sat on the sward    by the sound of water,
and watched in wonder    the westering sun
o'er the wall wading    of the wild mountains,                   1605
whose peaks empurpled    pricked the evening.
Then it dropped to the dark    and deep shadows
up the cliffs creeping    quenched in twilight
the last beacons    leashed with crimson.
To the stars upstanding    stony-mantled                         1610
the mountains waited    till the moon arose

o'er the endless East,    and Ivrin's pools
dreaming deeply    dim reflected
their pallid faces.    In pondering fast
woven, wordless,    they waked no sound,                    1615
till cold breezes    keenly breathing
clear and fragrant    curled about them;
then sought they for sleep    a sand-pavéd
cove outcarven;    there kindled fire,
that brightly blossomed    the beechen faggots               1620
in flowers of flame;    floated upward
a slender smoke,    when sudden Túrin
on the firelit face    of Flinding gazed,
and wondering words    he wavering spake:
'O Gnome, I know not    thy name or purpose                  1625
or father's blood –    what fate binds thee
to a witless wayworn    wanderer's footsteps,
the bane of Beleg,    his brother-in-arms?'

Then Flinding fearful    lest fresh madness
should seize for sorrow    on the soul of Túrin,             1630
retold the tale    of his toil and wandering;
how the trackless folds    of Taur-na-Fuin,
Deadly Nightshade,    dreadly meshed him;
of Beleg the bowman    bold, undaunted,
and that deed they dared    on the dim hillside,             1635
that song has since    unceasing wakened;
of the fate that fell,    he faltering spake,
in the tangled thicket    neath the twining thorns
when Morgoth's might    was moved abroad.
Then his voice vanished    veiled in mourning,              1640
and lo! tears trickled    on Túrin's face
till loosed at last    were the leashed torrents
of his whelming woe.    Long while he wept
soundless, shaken,    the sand clutching
with griping fingers    in grief unfathomed.                1645
But Flinding the faithful    feared no longer;
no comfort cold    he kindly found,
for sleep swept him    into slumber dead.
There a singing voice    sweetly vexed him
and he woke and wondered:    the watchfire faded;           1650
the night was aging,    nought was moving
but a song upsoaring    in the soundless dark

went strong and stern    to the starlit heaven.
'Twas Túrin that towering    on the tarn's margin,
up high o'er the head    of the hushed water        1655
now falling faintly,    let flare and echo
a song of sorrow    and sad splendour,
the dirge of Beleg's    deathless glory.
There wondrous wove he    words enchanted,
that woods and water    waked and answered,        1660
the rocks were wrung    with ruth for Beleg.
That song he sang    is since remembered,
by Gnomes renewed    in Nargothrond
it widely has wakened    warfain armies
to battle with Bauglir –    'The Bowman's Friendship'.        1665

'Tis told that Túrin    then turned him back
and fared to Flinding,    and flung him down
to sleep soundless    till the sun mounted
to the high heavens    and hasted westward.
A vision he viewed    in the vast spaces        1670
of slumber roving:    it seemed he roamed
up the bleak boulders    of a bare hillside
to a cup outcarven    in a cruel hollow,
whose broken brink    bushes limb-wracked
by the North-wind's knife    in knotted anguish        1675
did fringe forbidding.    There black unfriendly
was a dark thicket,    a dell of thorn-trees
with yews mingled    that the years had fretted.
The leafless limbs    they lifted hopeless
were blotched and blackened,    barkless, naked,        1680
a lifeless remnant    of the levin's flame,
charred chill fingers    changeless pointing
to the cold twilight..    There called he longing:
'O Beleg, my brother,    O Beleg, tell me
where is buried thy body    in these bitter regions?' –        1685
and the echoes always    him answered 'Beleg';
yet a veiléd voice    vague and distant
he caught that called    like a cry at night
o'er the sea's silence:    'Seek no longer.
My bow is rotten    in the barrow ruinous;        1690
my grove is burned    by grim lightning;
here dread dwelleth,    none dare profane
this angry earth,    Orc nor goblin;

none gain the gate    of the gloomy forest
by this perilous path;    pass they may not,                    1695
yet my life has winged    to the long waiting
in the halls of the Moon    o'er the hills of the sea.
Courage be thy comfort,    comrade lonely!'

Then he woke in wonder;    his wit was healed,
courage him comforted,    and he called aloud                  1700
Flinding go-Fuilin,    to his feet striding.
There the sun slanted    its silver arrows
through the wild tresses    of the waters tumbling
roofed with a radiant    rainbow trembling.
'Whither, O Flinding,    our feet now turn we,                 1705
or dwell we for ever    by the dancing water,
by the lake of laughter,    alone, untroubled?'
'To Nargothrond    of the Gnomes, methinks,'
said Flinding, 'my feet    would fain wander,
that Celegorm and Curufin,    the crafty sons                  1710
of Fëanor founded    when they fled southward;
there built a bulwark    against Bauglir's hate,
who live now lurking    in league secret
with those five others    in the forests of the East,
fell unflinching    foes of Morgoth.                           1715
Maidros whom Morgoth    maimed and tortured
is lord and leader,    his left wieldeth
his sweeping sword;    there is swift Maglor,
there Damrod and Díriel    and dark Cranthir,
the seven seekers    of their sire's treasure.                 1720
Now Orodreth rules    the realms and caverns,
the numbered hosts    of Nargothrond.
There to woman's stature    will be waxen full
frail Finduilas    the fleet maiden
his daughter dear,    in his darkling halls                    1725
a light, a laughter,    that I loved of yore,
and yet love in longing,    and love calls me.'

Where Narog's torrent    gnashed and spouted
down his stream bestrewn    with stone and boulder,
swiftly southward    they sought their paths,                  1730
and summer smiling    smoothed their journey
through day on day,    down dale and wood
where birds blithely    with brimming music
thrilled and trembled    in thronging trees.

No eyes them watched    onward wending                       1735
till they gained the gorge    where Ginglith turns
all glad and golden    to greet the Narog.
There her gentler torrent    joins his tumult,
and they glide together    on the guarded plain
to the Hunters' Hills    that high to southward          1740
uprear their rocks    robed in verdure.
There watchful waited    the Wards of Narog,
lest the need of the Gnomes    from the North should come,
for the sea in the South    them safe guarded,
and eager Narog    the East defended.                     1745
Their treegirt towers    on the tall hilltops
no light betrayed    in the trees lurking,
no horns hooted    in the hills ringing
in loud alarm;    a leaguer silent
unseen, stealthy,    beset the stranger,                   1750
as of wild things wary    that watch moveless,
then follow fleetly    with feet of velvet
their heedless prey    with padding hatred.
In this fashion fought they,    phantom hunters
that wandering Orc    and wild foeman                      1755
unheard harried,    hemmed in ambush.
The slain are silent,    and silent were the shafts
of the nimble Gnomes    of Nargothrond,
who word or whisper    warded sleepless
from their homes deep-hidden,    that hearsay never       1760
was to Bauglir brought.    Bright hope knew they,
and east over Narog    to open battle
no cause or counsel    had called them yet,
though of shield and shaft    and sheathéd swords,
of warriors wieldy    now waxed their host                1765
to power and prowess,    and paths afar
their scouts and woodmen    scoured in hunting.

Thus the twain were tracked    till the trees thickened
and the river went rushing    neath a rising bank,
in foam hastened    o'er the feet of the hills.           1770
In a gloom of green    there they groped forward;
there his fate defended    from flying death
Túrin Thalion –    a twisted thong
of writhing roots    enwrapped his foot;
as he fell there flashed,    fleet, whitewingéd,          1775

a shrill-shafted arrow    that shore his hair,
and trembled sudden    in a tree behind.
Then Flinding o'er the fallen    fiercely shouted:
'Who shoots unsure    his shafts at friends?
Flinding go-Fuilin    of the folk of Narog            1780
and the son of Húrin    his sworn comrade
here flee to freedom    from the foes of the North.'

His words in the woods    awoke no echo;
no leaf there lisped,    nor loosened twig
there cracked, no creak    of crawling movement      1785
stirred the silence.    Still and soundless
in the glades about    were the green shadows.
Thus fared they on,    and felt that eyes
unseen saw them,    and swift footsteps
unheard hastened    behind them ever,              1790
till each shaken bush    or shadowy thicket
they fled furtive    in fear needless,
for thereafter was aimed    no arrow wingéd,
and they came to a country    kindly tended;
through flowery frith    and fair acres            1795
they fared, and found    of folk empty
the leas and leasows    and the lawns of Narog,
the teeming tilth    by trees enfolded
twixt hills and river.    The hoes unrecked
in the fields were flung,    and fallen ladders     1800
in the long grass lay    of the lush orchards;
every tree there turned    its tangled head
and eyed them secretly,    and the ears listened
of the nodding grasses;    though noontide glowed
on land and leaf,    their limbs were chilled.      1805
Never hall or homestead    its high gables
in the light uplifting    in that land saw they,
but a pathway plain    by passing feet
was broadly beaten.    Thither bent their steps
Flinding go-Fuilin,    whose feet remembered        1810
that white roadway.    In a while they reached
to the acres' end,    that ever narrowing
twixt wall and water    did wane at last
to blossomy banks    by the borders of the way.
A spuming torrent,    in spate tumbling            1815
from the highest hill    of the Hunters' Wold

clove and crossed it;    there of carven stone
with slim and shapely    slender archway
a bridge was builded,    a bow gleaming
in the froth and flashing    foam of Ingwil,         1820
that headlong hurried    and hissed beneath.
Where it found the flood,    far-journeyed Narog,
there steeply stood    the strong shoulders
of the hills, o'erhanging    the hurrying water;
there shrouded in trees    a sheer terrace,         1825
wide and winding,    worn to smoothness,
was fashioned in the face    of the falling slope.
Doors there darkly    dim gigantic
were hewn in the hillside;    huge their timbers,
and their posts and lintels    of ponderous stone.         1830

They were shut unshakeable.    Then shrilled a trumpet
as a phantom fanfare    faintly winding
in the hill from hollow    halls far under;
a creaking portal    with clangour backward
was flung, and forth    there flashed a throng,         1835
leaping lightly,    lances wielding,
and swift encircling    seized bewildered
the wanderers wayworn,    wordless haled them
through the gaping gateway    to the glooms beyond.
Ground and grumbled    on its great hinges         1840
the door gigantic;    with din ponderous
it clanged and closed    like clap of thunder,
and echoes awful    in empty corridors
there ran and rumbled    under roofs unseen;
the light was lost.    Then led them on         1845
down long and winding    lanes of darkness
their guards guiding    their groping feet,
till the faint flicker    of fiery torches
flared before them;    fitful murmur
as of many voices    in meeting thronged         1850
they heard as they hastened.    High sprang the roof.
Round a sudden turning    they swung amazed,
and saw a solemn    silent conclave,
where hundreds hushed    in huge twilight
neath distant domes    darkly vaulted         1855
them wordless waited.    There waters flowed
with washing echoes    winding swiftly

amid the multitude,     and mounting pale
for fifty fathoms     a fountain sprang,
and wavering wan,     with winking redness          1860
flushed and flickering     in the fiery lights,
it fell at the feet     in the far shadows
of a king with crown     and carven throne.

A voice they heard     neath the vault rolling,
and the king them called:     'Who come ye here     1865
from the North unloved     to Nargothrond,
a Gnome of bondage     and a nameless Man?
No welcome finds here     wandering outlaw;
save his wish be death     he wins it not,
for those that have looked     on our last refuge     1870
it boots not to beg     other boon of me.'
Then Flinding go-Fuilin     freely answered:
'Has the watch then waned     in the woods of Narog,
since Orodreth ruled     this realm and folk?
Or how have the hunted     thus hither wandered,     1875
if the warders willed it not     thy word obeying;
or how hast not heard     that thy hidden archer,
who shot his shaft     in the shades of the forest,
there learned our lineage,     O Lord of Narog,
and knowing our names     his notched arrows     1880
loosed no longer?'     Then low and hushed
a murmur moved     in the multitude,
and some were who said:     ''Tis the same in truth:
the long looked-for,     the lost is found,
the narrow path he knew     to Nargothrond     1885
who was born and bred here     from babe to youth';
and some were who said:     'The son of Fuilin
was lost and looked for     long years agone.
What sign or token     that the same returns
have we heard or seen?     Is this haggard fugitive     1890
with back bended     the bold leader,
the scout who scoured,     scorning danger,
most far afield     of the folk of Narog?'
'That tale was told us,'     returned answer
the Lord Orodreth,     'but belief were rash.     1895
That alone of the lost,     whom leagues afar
the Orcs of Angband     in evil bonds
have dragged to the deeps,     thou darest home,

by grace or valour,    from grim thraldom,
what proof dost thou proffer?   What plea dost show          1900
that a Man, a mortal,    on our mansions hidden
should look and live,    our league sharing?'

Thus the curse on the kindred    for the cruel slaughter
at the Swans' Haven    there swayed his heart,
but Flinding go-Fuilin    fiercely answered:                1905
'Is the son of Húrin,    who sits on high
in a deathless doom    dreadly chainéd,
unknown, nameless,    in need of plea
to fend from him the fate    of foe and spy?
Flinding the faithful,    the far wanderer,                 1910
though form and face    fires of anguish
and bitter bondage,    Balrogs' torment,
have seared and twisted,    for a song of welcome
had hoped in his heart    at that home-coming
that he dreamed of long    in dark labour.                  1915
Are these deep places    to dungeons turned,
a lesser Angband    in the land of the Gnomes?'

Thereat was wrath aroused    in Orodreth's heart,
and the muttering waxed    to many voices,
and this and that    the throng shouted;                    1920
when sweet and sudden    a song awoke,
a voice of music    o'er that vast murmur
mounted in melody    to the misty domes;
with clear echoes    the caverned arches
it filled, and trembled    frail and slender,               1925
those words weaving    of welcome home
that the wayweary    had wooed from care
since the Gnomes first knew    need and wandering.
Then hushed was the host;    no head was turned,
for long known and loved    was that lifted voice,          1930
and Flinding knew it    at the feet of the king
like stone graven    standing silent
with heart laden;    but Húrin's son
was waked to wonder    and to wistful thought,
and searching the shadows    that the seat shrouded,        1935
the kingly throne,    there caught he thrice
a gleam, a glimmer,    as of garments white.
'Twas frail Finduilas,    fleet and slender,
to woman's stature,    wondrous beauty,

now grown in glory,    that glad welcome                    1940
there raised in ruth,    and wrath was stilled.
Locked fast the love    had lain in her heart
that in laughter grew    long years agone
when in the meads merrily    a maiden played
with fleet-footed    Fuilin's youngling.                    1945
No searing scars    of sundering years
could blind those eyes    bright with welcome,
and wet with tears    wistful trembling
at the grief there graven    in grim furrows
on the face of Flinding.    'Father,' said she,            1950
'what dream of doubt    dreadly binds thee?
'Tis Flinding go-Fuilin,    whose faith of yore
none dared to doubt.    This dark, lonely,
mournful-fated    Man beside him
if his oath avows    the very offspring                    1955
of Húrin Thalion,    what heart in this throng
shall lack belief    or love refuse?
But are none yet nigh us    that knew of yore
that mighty of Men,    mark of kinship
to seek and see    in these sorrow-laden                   1960
form and features?    The friends of Morgoth
not thus, methinks,    through thirst and hunger
come without comrades,    nor have countenance
thus grave and guileless,    glance unflinching.'

Then did Túrin's heart    tremble wondering              1965
at the sweet pity    soft and gentle
of that tender voice    touched with wisdom
that years of yearning    had yielded slow;
and Orodreth, whose heart    knew ruth seldom,
yet loved deeply    that lady dear,                        1970
gave ear and answer    to her eager words,
and his doubt and dread    of dire treachery,
and his quick anger,    he quelled within him.
No few were there found    who had fought of old
where Finweg fell    in flame of swords,                   1975
and Húrin Thalion    had hewn the throngs,
the dark Glamhoth's    demon legions,
and who called there looked    and cried aloud:
"'Tis the face of the father    new found on earth,
and his strong stature    and stalwart arms;               1980

though such care and sorrow    never claimed his sire,
whose laughing eyes    were lighted clear
at board or battle,    in bliss or in woe.'
Nor could lack belief    for long the words
and faith of Flinding    when friend and kin        1985
and his father hastening    that face beheld.
Lo! sire and son    did sweet embrace
neath trees entwining    tangled branches
at the dark doorways    of those deep mansions
that Fuilin's folk    afar builded,        1990
and dwelt in the deep    of the dark woodland
to the West on the slopes    of the Wold of Hunters.
Of the four kindreds    that followed the king,
the watchtowers' lords,    the wold's keepers
and the guards of the bridge,    the gleaming bow        1995
that was flung o'er the foaming    froth of Ingwil,
from Fuilin's children    were first chosen,
most noble of name,    renowed in valour.

In those halls in the hills    at that homecoming
mirth was mingled    with melting tears        2000
for the unyielding years    whose yoke of pain
the form and face    of Fuilin's son
had changed and burdened,    chilled the laughter
that leapt once lightly    to his lips and eyes.
Now in kindly love    was care lessened,        2005
with song assuaged    sadness of hearts;
the lights were lit    and lamps kindled
o'er the burdened board;    there bade they feast
Túrin Thalion    with his true comrade
at the long tables'    laden plenty,        2010
where dish and goblet    on the dark-gleaming
wood well-waxéd,    where the wine-flagons
engraven glistened    gold and silver.
Then Fuilin filled    with flowing mead,
dear-hoarded drink    dark and potent        2015
a carven cup    with curious brim,
by ancient art    of olden smiths
fairly fashioned,    filled with marvels;
there gleamed and lived    in grey silver
the folk of Faërie    in the first noontide        2020
of the Blissful Realms;    with their brows wreathéd

in garlands golden   with their gleaming hair
in the wind flying   and their wayward feet
fitful flickering,   on unfading lawns
the ancient Elves   there everlasting                    2025
danced undying   in the deep pasture
of the gardens of the Gods;   there Glingol shone
and Bansil bloomed   with beams shimmering,
mothwhite moonlight   from its misty flowers;
the hilltops of Tûn   there high and green              2030
were crowned by Côr,   climbing, winding,
town white-walléd   where the tower of Ing
with pale pinnacle   pierced the twilight,
and its crystal lamp   illumined clear
with slender shaft   the Shadowy Seas.                  2035
Through wrack and ruin,   the wrath of the Gods,
through weary wandering,   waste and exile,
had come that cup,   carved in gladness,
in woe hoarded,   in waning hope
when little was left   of the lore of old.              2040
Now Fuilin at feast   filled it seldom
save in pledge of love   to proven friend;
blithely bade he   of that beaker drink
for the sake of his son   that sate nigh him
Túrin Thalion   in token sure                           2045
of a league of love   long enduring.
'O Húrin's child   chief of Hithlum,
with mourning marred,   may the mead of the Elves
thy heart uplift   with hope lightened;
nor fare thou from us   the feast ended,                2050
here deign to dwell;   if this deep mansion
thus dark-dolven   dimly vaulted
displease thee not,   a place awaits thee.'
There deeply drank   a draught of sweetness
Túrin Thalion   and returned his thanks                 2055
in eager earnest,   while all the folk
with loud laughter   and long feasting,
with mournful lay   or music wild
of magic minstrels   that mighty songs
did weave with wonder,   there wooed their hearts       2060
from black foreboding;   there bed's repose
their guest was granted,   when in gloom silent
the light and laughter   and the living voices

were quenched in slumber.    Now cold and slim
the sickle of the Moon    was silver tilted                    2065
o'er the wan waters    that washed unsleeping,
nightshadowed Narog,    the Gnome-river.
In tall treetops    of the tangled wood
there hooted hollow    the hunting owls.

Thus fate it fashioned    that in Fuilin's house        2070
the dark destiny    now dwelt awhile
of Túrin the tall.    There he toiled and fought
with the folk of Fuilin    for Flinding's love;
lore long forgotten    learned among them,
for light yet lingered    in those leaguered places,        2075
and wisdom yet lived    in that wild people,
whose minds yet remembered    the Mountains of the West
and the faces of the Gods,    yet filled with glory
more clear and keen    than kindreds of the dark
or Men unwitting    of the mirth of old.                    2080

Thus Fuilin and Flinding    friendship showed him,
and their halls were his home,    while high summer
waned to autumn    and the western gales
the leaves loosened    from the labouring boughs;
the feet of the forest    in fading gold                    2085
and burnished brown    were buried deeply;
a restless rustle    down the roofless aisles
sighed and whispered.    Lo! the Silver Wherry,
the sailing Moon    with slender mast,
was filled with fires    as of furnace golden              2090
whose hold had hoarded    the heats of summer,
whose shrouds were shaped    of shining flame
uprising ruddy    o'er the rim of Evening
by the misty wharves    on the margin of the world.
Thus the months fleeted    and mightily he fared          2095
in the forest with Flinding,    and his fate waited
slumbering a season,    while he sought for joy
the lore learning    and the league sharing
of the Gnomes renowned    of Nargothrond.

The ways of the woods    he wandered far,                  2100
and the land's secrets    he learned swiftly
by winter unhindered    to weathers hardened,
whether snow or sleet    or slanting rain

from glowering heavens    grey and sunless
cold and cruel    was cast to earth,                              2105
till the floods were loosed    and the fallow waters
of sweeping Narog,    swollen, angry,
were filled with flotsam    and foaming turbid
passed in tumult;    or twinkling pale
ice-hung evening    was opened wide,                              2110
a dome of crystal    o'er the deep silence
of the windless wastes    and the woods standing
like frozen phantoms    under flickering stars.
By day or night    danger needless
he dared and sought for,    his dread vengeance               2115
ever seeking unsated    on the sons of Angband;
yet as winter waxed    wild and pathless,
and biting blizzards    the bare faces
lashed and tortured    of the lonely tors
and haggard hilltops,    in the halls more often             2120
was he found in fellowship    with the folk of Narog,
and cunning there added    in the crafts of hand,
and in subtle mastery    of song and music
and peerless poesy,    to his proven lore
and wise woodcraft;    there wondrous tales                   2125
were told to Túrin    in tongues of gold
in those mansions deep,    there many a day
to the hearth and halls    of the haughty king
did those friends now fare    to feast and game,
for frail Finduilas    her father urged                      2130
to his board and favour    to bid those twain,
and it grudging her granted    that grimhearted
king deep-counselled –    cold his anger,
his ruth unready,    his wrath enduring;
yet fierce and fell    by the fires of hate                  2135
his breast was burned    for the broods of Hell
(his son had they slain,    the swift-footed
Halmir the hunter    of hart and boar),
and kinship therein    the king ere long
in his heart discovered    for Húrin's son,                  2140
dark and silent,    as in dreams walking
of anguish and regret    and evergrowing
feud unsated.    Thus favour soon
by the king accorded    of the company of his board
he was member made,    and in many a deed                    2145

and wild venture    to West and North
he achieved renown    among the chosen warriors
and fearless bowmen;    in far battles
in secret ambush    and sudden onslaught,
where fell-tonguéd flew    the flying serpents,        2150
their shafts envenomed,    in valleys shrouded
he played his part,    but it pleased him little,
who trusted to targe    and tempered sword,
whose hand was hungry    for the hilts it missed
but dared never a blade    since the doom of Beleg      2155
to draw or handle.    Dear-holden was he,
though he wished nor willed it,    and his works were praised.
When tales were told    of times gone by,
of valour they had known,    of vanished triumph,
glory half-forgot,    grief remembered,        2160
then they bade and begged him    be blithe and sing
of deeds in Doriath    in the dark forest
by the shadowy shores    that shunned the light
where Esgalduin    the Elf-river
by root-fencéd pools    roofed with silence,        2165
by deep eddies    darkly gurgling,
flowed fleetly on    past the frowning portals
of the Thousand Caves.    Thus his thought recalled
the woodland ways    where once of yore
Beleg the bowman    had a boy guided        2170
by slade and slope    and swampy thicket
neath trees enchanted;    then his tongue faltered
and his tale was stilled.

            At Túrin's sorrow
one marvelled and was moved,    a maiden fair
the frail Finduilas    that Failivrin,        2175
the glimmering sheen    on the glassy pools
of Ivrin's lake    the Elves in love
had named anew.    By night she pondered
and by day wondered    what depth of woe
lay locked in his heart    his life marring;        2180
for the doom of dread    and death that had fallen
on Beleg the bowman    in unbroken silence
Túrin warded,    nor might tale be won
of Flinding the faithful    of their fare and deeds
in the waste together.    Now waned her love        2185

for the form and face    furrowed with anguish,
for the bended back    and broken strength,
the wistful eyes    and the withered laughter
of Flinding the faithful,    though filled was her heart
with deepwelling pity    and dear friendship.      2190
Grown old betimes    and grey-frosted,
he was wise and kindly    with wit and counsel,
with sight and foresight,    but slow to wrath
nor fiercely valiant,    yet if fight he must
his share he shirked not,    though the shreds of fear    2195
in his heart yet hung;    he hated no man,
but he seldom smiled,    save suddenly a light
in his grave face glimmered    and his glance was fired:
Finduilas maybe    faring lightly
on the sward he saw    or swinging pale,      2200
a sheen of silver    down some shadowy hall.*
Yet to Túrin was turned    her troublous heart
against will and wisdom    and waking thought:
in dreams she sought him,    his dark sorrow
with love lightening,    so that laughter shone    2205
in eyes new-kindled,    and her Elfin name
he eager spake,    as in endless spring
they fared free-hearted    through flowers enchanted
with hand in hand    o'er the happy pastures
of that land that is lit    by no light of Earth,    2210
by no moon nor sun,    down mazy ways
to the black abysmal    brink of waking.

From woe unhealed    the wounded heart
of Túrin the tall    was turned to her.
Amazed and moved,    his mind's secret    2215
half-guessed, half-guarded,    in gloomy hour
of night's watches,    when down narrow winding
paths of pondering    he paced wearily,
he would lonely unlock,    then loyal-hearted
shut fast and shun,    or shroud his grief    2220
in dreamless sleep,    deep oblivion
where no echo entered    of the endless war
of waking worlds,    woe nor friendship,
flower nor firelight    nor the foam of seas,

*Here the B-typescript ends, and the remainder of the text is manuscript. See the Note
on the Texts, p. 81.

a land illumined    by no light at all.                         2225

'O! hands unholy,    O! heart of sorrow,
O! outlaw whose evil    is yet unatonéd,
wilt thou, troth-breaker,    a treason new
to thy burden bind;    thy brother-in-arms,
Flinding go-Fuilin    thus foully betray,                       2230
who thy madness tended    in mortal perils,
to thy waters of healing    thy wandering feet
did lead at the last    to lands of peace,
where his life is rooted    and his love dwelleth?
O! stainéd hands    his hope steal not!'                        2235

Thus love was fettered    in loyal fastness
and coldly clad    in courteous word;
yet he would look and long    for her loveliness,
in her gentle words    his joy finding,
her face watching    when he feared no eye                      2240
might mark his mood.    One marked it all –
Failivrin's face,    the fleeting gleams,
like sun through clouds    sailing hurriedly
over faded fields,    that flickered and went out
as Túrin passed;    the tremulous smiles,                       2245
his grave glances    out of guarded shade,
his sighs in secret –    one saw them all,
Flinding go-Fuilin,    who had found his home
and lost his love    to the lying years,
he watched and wondered,    no word speaking,                   2250
and his heart grew dark    'twixt hate and pity,
bewildered, weary,    in the webs of fate.
Then Finduilas,    more frail and wan
twixt olden love    now overthrown
and new refused,    did nightly weep;                           2255
and folk wondered    at the fair pallor
of the hands upon her harp,    her hair of gold
on slender shoulders    slipped in tumult,
the glory of her eyes    that gleamed with fires
of secret thought    in silent deeps.                           2260

Many bosoms burdened    with foreboding vague
their glooms disowned    neath glad laughter.
In song and silence,    snow and tempest,
winter wore away;    to the world there came

a year once more    in youth unstained,                                    2265
nor were leaves less green,    light less golden,
the flowers less fair,    though in faded hearts
no spring was born,    though speeding nigh
danger and dread    and doom's footsteps
to their halls hasted.    Of the host of iron                               2270
came tale and tidings    ever treading nearer;
Orcs unnumbered    to the East of Narog
roamed and ravened    on the realm's borders,
the might of Morgoth    was moved abroad.
No ambush stayed them;    the archers yielded                              2275
each vale by vale,    though venomed arrows

Here both A and B end abruptly, and I think it is certain that no more of
the poem was ever written.

# NOTES

1409    *Tengwethil* B, *Taingwethil* A. This is the reverse of the
         previous occurrences; see lines 431, 636.
1417–18   These lines are bracketed in B, and line 1418 struck through;
         in the margin is a mark of deletion, but with a query
         beside it.
1448    *Nirnaith Únoth* A, and B as typed; emended in pencil in
         B to *Nirnaith Ornoth*. Earlier in the poem (lines 13, 218)
         the forms were *Nínin Udathriol* emended in B to *Nínin
         Unothradin* (also *Nirnaithos Unothradin* at line 13). Cf.
         line 1543.
1469    *Ulmo* A, and B as typed; in B *Ulmo* struck through in pencil
         and replaced by *Ylmir*, but this also struck through. I read
         *Ylmir*; see note to line 1529.
1525    *Túrin Thalion* A, and B as typed (not *Túrin Thaliodrin*, see
         note to line 1324).
1529    *Ylmir*: so already in A and B as typed; so also at lines 1534,
         1553, 1572, 1585. See note to line 1469.
1537    This line was struck through in pencil in B.
1542–3    These lines were bracketed in pencil in B, and *Not so* written
         in margin. Though *Únoth* was not here emended I read
         *Ornoth* (see note to line 1448).
1558    *the sea-birds call    in solemn conclave*: cf. the tale of *The
         Coming of the Elves and the Making of Kôr*, I. 124.
1673–6    Cf. lines 1036–9.

1696–7    Cf. lines 1283–4.

1710–11   Line 1710 is wholly and 1711 partly crossed out in B, with
          marginal additions to make 1711 read:

> [by] Felagund founded    flying southward

Also written in the margin is: '*before* Nirnaith Únoth'. At
line 1711 A has *found* for *founded*, but as the manuscript
was written very rapidly this may not be significant.

1713–20   These lines are bracketed in B, as if needing revision, and two
          lines are written in the margin for insertion after 1715:

> that home came never    to their halls of old
> since the field of tears    was fought and lost.

I have not included these lines (written, it seems, at the same
time as the other marginal comments in this passage) in the
text in view of the complexity of the 'historical background' at
this point; see the Commentary, pp. 84–5.
    Against this passage is written in the margin:

> but Nargothrond was founded by *Felagund* Finrod's son
> (whose brothers were Angrod Egnor & Orodreth). Curufin
> and Celegorm dwelt at Nargothrond.

1719      *Cranthor* A, *Cranthir* B as typed.

1724      *Finduilas*: *Failivrin* A, and B as typed; *Finduilas* written in
          pencil in the margin of B; so also at line 1938. See lines 2130,
          2175, 2199.

1938      *Finduilas*: as at line 1724.

1945      The word *youngling* is struck out in B and *Flinding* written
          against it, but the resulting *Fuilin's Flinding* (with alliter-
          ation in the second half-line) cannot possibly have been
          intended. Subsequently another word was written in the
          margin, but this is illegible.

1974–5    *Not so* written in the margin of B.

1975      *Finweg* A, and B as typed; late emendation to *Fingon* in B.
          I retain *Finweg* since that is still the name in the 1930
          'Silmarillion'.

1993–8    In A and in B as typed these lines were differently ordered:

> Of the four kindreds    that followed the king,
> most noble of name,    renowned in valour,
> the watchtowers' lords,    the wold's keepers
> from Fuilin's children    were first chosen,
> and the guards of the bridge,    the gleaming bow
> that was flung o'er the foaming    froth of Ingwil.

2027      *Glingol* A, and B as typed; late emendation to *Glingal* in B. I
          retain *Glingol*, the form in the *Lost Tales* and still in the 1930

'Silmarillion'; in the published work *Glingal* is the name of the golden tree of Gondolin.

2028   *Bansil* A, and B as typed; late emendation to *Belthil* in B. I retain *Bansil* for the same reason as *Glingol* in line 2027.

2030   *there high and green   the hill of Tûn* A, and B as typed; emended in pencil in B to the reading given; *was* 2031 not corrected to *were*, but that *hilltops* (plural) was intended is shown by the text C, see p. 82.

2130   I give *Finduilas*, though *Failivrin* was not so emended here in B, as it was at lines 1724, 1938. See notes to lines 2175. 2199.

2164   *Esgaduin* A, and B as typed; emended in pencil to *Esgalduin* in B.

2175   *the frail Finduilas   that Failivrin* as typed B; *the frail Failivrin* changed at the time of writing in A to *Findóriel* (sc. *the frail Findóriel   that Failivrin* &c.).

2199   *Finduilas* A and B; *Failivrin* written in the margin of A. At the subsequent occurrences (*Failivrin* 2242, *Finduilas* 2253) the names both in A and in B are as in the printed text.

*Note on the texts of the section 'Failivrin'*

B comes to an end as a typescript at line 2201, but continues as a well-written manuscript for a further 75 lines. This last part is written on the paper of good quality that my father used for many years in all his writing (University lectures, *The Silmarillion*, *The Lord of the Rings*, etc.) in ink or pencil (i.e. when not typing): this plain paper was supplied to him by the Examination Schools at Oxford University, being the unused pages of the booklets of paper provided for examination candidates. The change in paper does not show however that he had moved from Leeds to Oxford (cf. p. 3), since he acted as an external examiner at Oxford in 1924 and 1925; but it does suggest that the final work on the Lay (before *Leithian* was begun) dates from the latter part of the one year or the earlier part of the next. The conclusion of A is also written on this paper.

There is a further short text to be considered here, a well-written manuscript that extends from line 2005 to line 2225, which I will call 'C'. Textual details show clearly that C followed B – not, I think, at any long interval. Some emendations made to B were made to C also. I give here a list of the more important differences of C from B (small changes of punctuation and sentence-connection are not noticed).

C bears the title *Túrin in the House of Fuilin and his son Flinding*. It is not clear whether this was to be the title of a fourth section of the poem, but it seems unlikely, if the third section was to remain 'Failivrin'.

2005   *Now was care lessened   in kindly love* C
2020   *noontide*] *summer* pencil emendation in C

2027–8  *Glingol* > *Glingal* and *Bansil* > *Belthil* pencil emendations in C as in B

2029   The original reading of B and C was *like magic moonlight from its mothwhite flowers*; this was differently emended in C, to *like moths of pearl   in moonlit flowers*.

2030–2  C as written was exactly as the text of B after emendation (with *were* for *was* 2031); these lines were then crossed out and the following substituted:

> there high and green    that hill by the sea
> was crowned by Tûn,    climbing, winding
> in tall walls of white,    where the tower of Ing

2036–53  are omitted in C (with *Thence* for *There* 2054).

2069   After *hunting owls* C has lines of omission dots, and the text takes up again at line 2081.

2083   *waned to autumn*] *waned towards winter* pencil emendations in C

2090   *as of furnace golden*] *as a furnace of gold* C

2114–16  are omitted in C.

2123–8  C omits 2124, 2125b–7, and reads:

> and in subtle mastery    of song and music
> to his wise woodcraft    and wielding of arms.
> To the hearth and halls    of the haughty king

2135–8  C omits these lines (referring to Orodreth's son Halmir, slain by Orcs) and reads:

> his ruth unready,    his wrath enduring.
> But kinship of mood    the king ere long

2142b–2143a  C omits these lines, and reads:

> of anguish and regret.    Thus was honour granted
> by the king to Túrin;    of the company of his board

2158   *were told*] *men told* emendation in C.

2164   *Esgalduin* C as written; see note to this line above.

## Commentary on *Part III 'Failivrin'*

In this very remarkable section of the poem a great development has taken place in the story since the *Tale of Turambar* (if there was an intervening stage there is now no trace of it); while concurrently the history of the exiled Noldoli was being deepened and extended from its representation in the outlines for *Gilfanon's Tale* – a factor that complicates the presentation of the poems, since statements about that history were often superseded during the long process of composition.

Most notable of all in this part of the poem is the description of Nargothrond, unique in the Lay. In all the later rewritings and restructurings of the Túrin saga this part was never touched, apart from the development of the relations between Túrin, Gwindor, and Finduilas which I have given in *Unfinished Tales*, pp. 155–9. In this there is a parallel to Gondolin, very fully described in the tale of *The Fall of Gondolin*, but never again. As I said in the introduction to *Unfinished Tales* (p. 5):

> It is thus the remarkable fact that the only full account that my father ever wrote of the story of Tuor's sojourn in Gondolin, his union with Idril Celebrindal, the birth of Eärendil, the treachery of Maeglin, the sack of the city, and the escape of the fugitives – a story that was a central element in his imagination of the First Age – was the narrative composed in his youth.

Gondolin and Nargothrond were each made once, and not remade. They remained powerful sources and images – the more powerful, perhaps, because never remade, and never remade, perhaps, because so powerful. Both *Tuor* and *Túrin* were indeed to receive written form outside the condensed *Silmarillion* as long prose narratives, and what my father achieved of this intention I have given in the first two sections of *Unfinished Tales*; but though he set out to remake Gondolin he never reached the city again: after climbing the endless slope of the Orfalch Echor and passing through the long line of heraldic gates he paused with Tuor at the vision of Gondolin amid the plain, and never recrossed Tumladen. The remaking of *Túrin* went much further, but here too he skirted the imaginative focus of Nargothrond.

## The founding of Nargothrond

I shall discuss first the 'background' history, which centres on the complex question of the founding of Nargothrond. In the *Tale* (II. 81–2) Nargothrond is not named, and is represented by the Caves of the Rodothlim; as in the poem, Orodreth was the chief of these Gnomes, but he was then an isolated figure, and not yet associated in kinship with other princes. Nothing is said there of the origin of the redoubt, but that it was imagined to have arisen (like Gondolin) after the Battle of Unnumbered Tears is, I think, certain, since in the earliest phase of the legends, as I remarked in commenting on *Gilfanon's Tale* (I. 242),

> the entire later history of the long years of the Siege of Angband, ending with the Battle of Sudden Flame (Dagor Bragollach), of the passage of Men over the Mountains into Beleriand and their taking service with the Noldorin Kings, had yet to emerge; indeed these outlines give the effect of only a brief time elapsing between the

coming of the Noldoli from Kôr and their great defeat [in the Battle of Unnumbered Tears].

In the poem, this idea is still clearly present in lines 1542–4:

> the secret halls
> of Nargothrond by the Gnomes builded
> that death and thraldom in the dreadful throes
> of Nirnaith Ornoth, a number scanty,
> escaped unscathed.

Against this passage my father wrote 'Not so'; and this comment obviously means 'Nargothrond was *not* founded after the Battle of Unnumbered Tears', as is further shown by his note to lines 1710–11:

> (to Nargothrond)
> that Celegorm and Curufin, the crafty sons
> of Fëanor founded when they fled southward

against which he wrote: '*before* Nirnaith Únoth'. When, then, was it founded? The 'Sketch of the Mythology', certainly later than the poem (the background of which it was written to explain), already in its earliest form knows of the Leaguer of Angband and of Morgoth's breaking of the Leaguer – though described in the barest possible way, without any reference to the battle that ended it; and it is said there that at that time 'Gnomes and Ilkorins and Men are scattered . . . Celegorm and Curufin found the realm of Nargothrond on the banks of Narog in the south of the Northern lands.' The 'Sketch' (again, in its earliest, unrevised, form) also states that Celegorm and Curufin despatched a host from Nargothrond to the Battle of Unnumbered Tears, that this host joined with that of Maidros and Maglor, but 'arrived too late for the main battle'. 'They are beaten back and driven into the South-east, where they long time dwelt, and did not go back to Nargothrond. There Orodreth ruled the remnant.'

The problem is to explain how it comes about in the earlier story, as found in the poem (Nargothrond founded by Celegorm and Curufin *after* the Battle of Unnumbered Tears), that Celegorm and Curufin are no longer there when Túrin comes, and Orodreth is king. Why do they *live now lurking . . . in the forests of the East* with their five brothers (1713–14)?

The only explanation that I can put forward is as follows. When my father wrote lines 1542–4 his view was that Nargothrond was founded after the Battle of Unnumbered Tears (this is quite explicit). But when he wrote lines 1710–15

> (to Nargothrond)
> that Celegorm and Curufin, the crafty sons          1710
> of Fëanor founded when they fled southward;
> there built a bulwark against Bauglir's hate,

> who live now lurking    in league secret
> with those five others    in the forests of the East
> fell unflinching    foes of Morgoth                                1715

the later story was already present. (There would be nothing uncharacteristic about this; in the *Lay of Leithian* the story changes from one
Canto to the next.) Thus *when they fled southward* refers to the flight
of Celegorm and Curufin from the battle that ended the Leaguer of
Angband; *they live now lurking . . . in the forests of the East* refers to
the period after the Battle of Unnumbered Tears, when 'they did not go
back to Nargothrond' and 'Orodreth ruled the remnant', as stated in the
'Sketch'.* On this view, my father's note against lines 1710–11 ('*before*
Nirnaith Únoth') was mistaken – he took the lines to refer to the old story
(as 1542–4 certainly do), whereas in fact they refer to the later. This
explanation may seem far-fetched, but it is less so than the demonstrably
correct solutions to other puzzles in the history of 'The Silmarillion', and
I see no other way out of the difficulty. – The two additional lines to
follow 1715:

> that home came never    to their halls of old
> since the field of tears    was fought and lost

refer (I think) to Celegorm and Curufin, and reinforce the reference to
the later story (i.e. that after the Battle of Unnumbered Tears they did
not return to Nargothrond).

The change of lines 1710–11 to make the passage read

> (to Nargothrond)
> by Felagund founded    flying southward

and the marginal note against 1713–20 'but Nargothrond was founded by
*Felagund* Finrod's son' etc., reflect of course a further stage, though a
stage that came in soon after the 'Sketch' was first written. The essential
shifts in the history of Nargothrond to this point are certainly thus:

(1)    Orodreth ruled the Rodothlim in their caves, first inhabited after
       the Battle of Unnumbered Tears.

(2)    Celegorm and Curufin founded Nargothrond after the Battle of
       Unnumbered Tears.

(3)    Celegorm and Curufin founded Nargothrond after the breaking of
       the Leaguer of Angband; they went with a host to the Battle of
       Unnumbered Tears and did not return, but remained in the East;
       Orodreth ruled the remnant of the Gnomes of Nargothrond.

(4)    Felagund son of Finrod and his brothers Angrod, Egnor, and

---

*Cf. lines 1873–4:
> Has the watch then waned    in the woods of Narog
> *since Orodreth ruled    this realm and folk?*

Orodreth founded Nargothrond after the breaking of the Leaguer of Angband; Celegorm and Curufin dwelt there.

Another sign of development in the history and genealogy of the Gnomish princes is the mention of *Finweg*, later emended in the B-text to *Fingon*, who *fell in flame of swords* at the Battle of Unnumbered Tears (1975). *Finweg* has appeared early in the poem (line 29), but there as a spelling or form of Finwë (Nólemë), founder of the line; this *Finweg* appears in the 'Sketch', as originally written, as the son of Fingolfin.

The Sons of Fëanor have previously all been named only in the *Tale of the Nauglafring* (II. 241); now (1716 ff.), with *Cranthir* (emended from *Cranthor* in B), and *Díriel* for earlier *Dinithel* (?*Durithel*), they reach the forms they long retained. Characteristic epithets appear: Maglor is 'swift', Cranthir 'dark', and Curufin's 'craftiness', already appearing in the *Tale of the Nauglafring*, extends here to Celegorm. Maidros' wielding his sword with his left hand is mentioned, which clearly implies that the story that Morgoth had him hung from a cliff by his right hand, and that Finweg (> Fingon) rescued him, was already present, as it is in the 'Sketch'. His torment and maiming was mentioned in the outlines for *Gilfanon's Tale* (I. 238, 240), but not described.

To turn now to the foreground narrative of this part of the poem. The poem advances on the *Tale* by mentioning the disposal of Beleg's sword, not mentioned in the *Tale*; but here Flinding hides it in the hollow of a tree (1342), and it plays no further part in the story. If the poem had gone further Túrin would have received his black sword in Nargothrond in gift from Orodreth, as happens in the *Tale* (II. 83). In the *Tale* it is said that Túrin 'had not wielded a sword since the slaying of Beleg, but rather had he been contented with a mighty club'; in the poem this reappears with the implication made explicit (2155–6):

> dared never a blade    since the doom of Beleg
> to draw or handle.

The burial of Beleg now appears, with his great bow beside him (1399 ff.), and Túrin's kiss survives from the *Tale*; that the mark of his grief over the death of Beleg (called the third of his sorrows, 1421) never left his face was an enduring feature of the legend.

*Geography*

In the *Tale* (II. 80–1) very little is made of the journey of Flinding and Túrin from the place of Beleg's death to Nargothrond: by the light of Flinding's lamp they 'fared by night and hid by day and were lost in the hills, and the Orcs found them not'. In the poem, on the other hand, the journey is quite fully described, and contains some noteworthy features; moreover there is nothing in the description that contradicts the earliest

'Silmarillion' map (to be given in the next volume), which dates from this period and may have been made originally in association with this poem. The wanderers pass at midnight by the Mound of Slain, looming up under the moon *at the furthest end / of Dor-na-Fauglith's dusty spaces* (1439–40); this feature does not recur again in the story of Túrin. The only previous reference to the great burial-mound is in the outlines for *Gilfanon's Tale*, where it is called the Hill of Death, and was raised by the Sons of Feanor (I. 241). It is said in the poem that Túrin despite his heavy listlessness *turned his hand / toward Thangorodrim* at Flinding's words concerning the Mound, and cursed Morgoth thrice – as did Fëanor in the hour of his death after the Battle-under-Stars (*The Silmarillion* p. 107); the one was doubtless the precursor of the other. The inviolability of the Mound now appears (1450–2).

Túrin and Flinding now crossed Sirion not far from his source in the Shadowy Mountains, where the river was fordable (1457 ff.); this is the first reference to Sirion's Well. Sirion's great journey to the Sea is described, with references to his passage underground (1467; cf. II. 195, 217) and through lands *beloved of Ylmir* (Ulmo). The travellers then find themselves in Nan Dungorthin, which was mentioned in the *Tale of Tinúviel* (see II. 35, 62–3): Huan found Beren and Tinúviel after their escape from Angband in 'that northward region of Artanor that was called afterward Nan Dumgorthin, the land of the dark idols', 'even then a dark land and gloomy and foreboding, and dread wandered beneath its lowering trees'. My father hesitated long about the placing of this land: in the Gnomish dictionary it was east of Artanor (II. 62), in the *Tale of Tinúviel* a 'northward region of Artanor', while here it is west of Sirion, in a valley of the southern slopes of the Shadowy Mountains. In the earliest 'Silmarillion' map Nan Dungorthin was first likewise placed west of Sirion (west of the Isle of Werewolves), before being returned once more to the region north of Doriath, where it remained.

It is said that when Túrin and Flinding climbed out of the vale of Nan Dungorthin they *southward saw the slopes of Hithlum / more warm and friendly* (1496–7). At first sight this seems difficult to understand, but I think that the meaning is: they were indeed on *the slopes of Hithlum* at the time (i.e. below the southern faces of the Shadowy Mountains that fenced Hithlum), but looking southward (actually southwestward) they saw more agreeable regions further along the foothills, towards Ivrin. This is the first appearance of Ivrin, source of the Narog, and it is seen very clearly. The line (1537) giving the meaning of *Narog* (Gnomish, 'torrent') was struck out, but this (I think) was because my father felt that it was intrusive, not that the etymology was rejected. In this connection it may be mentioned that in a list of Old English equivalents of Elvish names, composed some years after the time of the present poem and associated with Ælfwine's translations of Elvish texts into his own language, occur *Narog*: *Hlýda* and *Nargothrond*: *Hlýdingaburg*. Hlýda was the name in Old English of March ('the noisy

month of wind'; cf. the Quenya name *Súlimë* and the Sindarin name
*Gwaeron*); related words are *hlúd* (Modern English *loud*), *hlýd*
'sound', *hlýdan* 'make a sound'. The meaning is here undoubtedly 'the
loud one'; it lies behind the English stream-name *Lydbrook*.

Following the course of the Narog southward from Ivrin, the travellers

> gained the gorge    where Ginglith turns
> all glad and golden    to greet the Narog.
> There her gentler torrent    joins his tumult,
> and they glide together    on the guarded plain
> to the Hunters' Hills    that high to southward
> uprear their rocks    robed in verdure.          (1736–41)

A little earlier Flinding has described to Túrin how Narog, passing
Nargothrond, 'thence skirted wild the Hills of the Hunters, the home of
Beren and the Dancer of Doriath' (1544–6). In these verses are the first
appearances of the river Ginglith, the Guarded Plain, and the Hills of the
Hunters (all shown on the earliest map), though the hills themselves are
described without being named in the *Tale*, II. 96. On the map Nargothrond is shown near the northern extremity of the Hills of the Hunters,
which extend far to the southward, falling down to the coast of the Sea
west of Sirion's mouths. Various things are said of these hills. In the
*Tale* they are 'high and tree-grown'; in the poem they *uprear their
rocks    robed in verdure*; in *The Silmarillion* (p. 122), where they are
called *Taur-en-Faroth* or *the High Faroth*, they are 'great wooded
highlands'; in the *Narn* (p. 116) they are 'brown and bare'. In the poem
they are also called *the Hunters' Wold* (1816), *the Wold of Hunters*
(1992), where the word is probably used in the old sense of 'forest,
wooded uplands'. If we judge by my father's unfinished watercolour of
the Doors of Nargothrond, painted in all probability in 1928 (see *Pictures by J. R. R. Tolkien* no. 33), he saw the hills as great rocky heights
standing up from thick forest on their lower slopes. At line 1746 the
Wards of Narog look out from *their treegirt towers    on the tall
hilltops*; these watchtowers were in the north of the Hills of the Hunters
and looking northwards (1743–5), and it may not be casual therefore that
on the earliest map the northern end (only) of the hills is shown as
heavily forested.

As Túrin and Flinding came south down the west bank of Narog the
river *hastened o'er the feet of the hills* (1770), and the fields and
orchards through which they passed

>                   ever narrowing
>    twixt wall and water    did wane at last
> to blossomy banks    by the borders of the way          (1812–14)

The map likewise shows the Narog drawing steadily closer to the
northeastern edge of the Hills of the Hunters. Here the travellers crossed
the foaming Ingwil, falling down from the hills, by a slender bridge; this

is the first appearance of this stream (cf. *The Silmarillion* p. 122: 'the short and foaming stream Ringwil tumbled headlong into Narog from the High Faroth'), and the bridge over it is mentioned nowhere else.

The Land of the Dead that Live (Beren and Tinúviel after their return) is now placed in the Hills of the Hunters (1545–6), where it was originally placed also on the map. This land was moved even more often than was Nan Dungorthin. In the *Tale of the Nauglafring* it was in Hisilómë (but with a note on the manuscript saying that it must be placed in 'Doriath beyond Sirion', II. 249); in the *Tale of Tinúviel* Beren and Tinúviel 'became mighty fairies in the lands about the north of Sirion' (II. 41). From the Hills of the Hunters it would subsequently be moved several times more.

Before leaving the Narog, we meet here for the first time in narrative writing the name *Nan-Tathrin* (1548), in the *Lost Tales* always called by its name in Eldarissa, *Tasarinan* (but *Nantathrin* occurs in the Gnomish dictionary, I. 265, entry *Sirion* and *Dor-tathrin* in the Name-list to *The Fall of Gondolin*, II. 346).

Far fuller than in any later account is the story in the poem of the sojourn of Túrin and his companion at Ivrin, and much that lies behind the passage in *The Silmarillion* (p. 209) is here revealed. In *The Silmarillion* Túrin drank from the water of Ivrin and was at last able to weep, and his madness passed; then he made a song for Beleg (*Laer Cú Beleg*, the Song of the Great Bow), 'singing it aloud heedless of peril'; and then he asked Gwindor who he was. In the Lay all these features of the story are present, somewhat differently ordered. Flinding describes to Túrin the courses of Narog and Sirion and the protection of Ulmo, and Túrin feels some return of hope (1586–7); they hasten down to the lake and drink (1599–1600); and *from the meshes of misery his mind was loosed* (1602). In the early night, as they sat beside their fire by the pools of Ivrin, Túrin asked Flinding his name and fate, and it was Flinding's reply that led Túrin at last to weep. Flinding fell asleep, but woke towards the end of the night to hear Túrin singing the dirge of Beleg by the edge of the lake (and here the song is called 'the Bowman's Friendship'). Túrin then himself fell asleep, and in his sleep he returned to the terrible place on the edge of Taur-na-Fuin where he slew Beleg, seeking the place of his burial and the lightning-blackened trees, and heard the voice of Beleg far off telling him to seek no longer but to take comfort in courage.

> Then he woke in wonder;   his wit was healed,
> courage him comforted,   and he called aloud
> Flinding go-Fuilin,   to his feet striding.   (1699–1701)

The structure of the episode in the Lay is firm and clear, the images strong and enduring. I said in the introduction to *Unfinished Tales* that it was grievous that my father went no further, in the later Tale of Tuor,

than the coming of Tuor and Voronwë to the last gate and Tuor's sight of
Gondolin across the plain. It is no less grievous that he never retold, in
his later prose, the story of Túrin and Gwindor at the Lake of Ivrin. The
passage in *The Silmarillion* is no substitute; and it is only from this poem
that we can fully grasp the extremity of the disaster for Túrin, that he had
killed his friend.

The description in the poem of the stealth and secrecy of the defenders
of Nargothrond is derived, in concept, from the *Tale* (II. 81). In the *Tale*

the spies and watchers of the Rodothlim . . . gave warning of their
approach, and the folk withdrew before them, such as were abroad
from their dwelling. Then they closed their doors and hoped that the
strangers might not discover their caves . . .

When Flinding and Túrin came to the mouths of the caves,

the Rodothlim sallied and made them prisoners and drew them within
their rocky halls, and they were led before the chief, Orodreth.

All this is taken up into the poem and greatly elaborated; there is also the
incident of Túrin's stumbling on a root and thus being missed by the
arrow aimed at him, and Flinding's cry of reproach to the unseen archers,
after which they were not further molested. It is perhaps not so clear in
the poem as in the *Tale* that the farmlands and orchards of Nargothrond
were deserted lest the travellers should find the entrance to the caves,
especially since a *pathway plain    by passing feet/was broadly
beaten* (1808–9) – though it is said that the throng in the great hall of
Nargothrond was waiting for them (1856). Moreover, in the *Tale* they
were not attacked. As the story is told in the poem, one might wonder
why the hidden archers in the woods, if they believed Flinding's cry
sufficiently to withhold their arrows, did not emerge at that point and
conduct them as prisoners to the caves. The new element of the arrow
shot in the woods has not, I think, been altogether assimilated to the old
account of the timorous withdrawal of the Rodothlim in the hope that
Túrin and Flinding would not find the entrance. But the passage describing the 'home-fields' of Nargothrond is of great interest in itself, for
rarely are there references to the agriculture of the peoples of Middle-
earth in the Elder Days.

The great Doors of Nargothrond are here first described – the triple
doors of timber as my father imagined them are seen in his drawing of the
entrance made in Dorset in the summer of 1928, and (in a different
conception) *their posts and lintels    of ponderous stone* (1830) in
the watercolour of the same period referred to above (*Pictures* nos 33,
34).

In the *Tale* the fear and suspicion among the Rodothlim of Noldoli
who had been slaves is attributed to 'the evil deeds of the Gnomes at
Cópas Alqalunten', and this element reappears in the poem (1903–4).

Nevertheless, there is no suggestion in the *Tale* of any serious questioning of the identity and goodwill of Flinding, greatly changed in aspect though he was, so that 'few knew him again'. In the poem, on the other hand, Orodreth emerges as hostile and formidable, and his character is carefully outlined: he is quick to anger (1973) but his wrath is cold and long-enduring (2133–4), he is seldom moved to pity (1969, 2134), grim-hearted and deep-counselled (2132–3), but capable of deep love (1970) as also of fierce hate (2135). Afterwards, as the legends developed, Orodreth underwent a steady decline into weakness and insignificance, which is very curious. Many years later, when meditating the development of the Túrin saga, my father noted that Orodreth was 'rather a weak character'; cf. the *Narn*, p. 160: 'he turned as he ever did to Túrin for counsel'. Ultimately he was to be displaced as the second King of Nargothrond (*Unfinished Tales* p. 255, note 20). But all this is a far cry from the hard and grim king in his underground hall depicted in the poem; Felagund had not yet emerged, nor the rebellious power of Celegorm and Curufin in Nargothrond (see further p. 246).

The killing of Orodreth's son Halmir the hunter by Orcs (2137–8; omitted in the C-text, p. 82) is a new element, which will reappear, though not found in *The Silmarillion*, where the name *Halmir* is borne by a ruler of the People of Haleth.

In the *Tale*, as I noticed in my commentary (II. 124),

> Failivrin is already present, and her unrequited love for Túrin, but the complication of her former relation with Gwindor is quite absent, and she is not the daughter of Orodreth the King but of one Galweg (who was to disappear utterly).

In the poem Galweg has already disappeared, and Failivrin has become Orodreth's daughter, loved by Flinding and returning his love before his captivity; and it is her plea to her father before the assembled multitude that sways the king and leads to the admission of Flinding and Túrin to Nargothrond. Of this intervention there is probably a trace in the very condensed account in *The Silmarillion* (p. 209):

> At first his own people did not know Gwindor, who went out young and strong, and returned now seeming as one of the aged among mortal Men, because of his torments and his labours; but Finduilas daughter of Orodreth the King knew him and welcomed him, for she had loved him before the Nirnaeth, and so greatly did Gwindor love her beauty that he named her Faelivrin, which is the gleam of the sun on the pools of Ivrin.

In the poem she is called *Failivrin* in A and B as written, emended or not in B to *Finduilas* (1724, 1938, 2130), but the name *Finduilas* emerges towards the end in the texts as first written (2175, 2199), and *Failivrin (the glimmering sheen on the glassy pools / of Ivrin's lake)* is the name by which the Elves renamed *Finduilas*.

In the Lay as in the *Tale* there is no hiding of Túrin's identity, as there is in *The Silmarillion*, where he checked Gwindor, when Gwindor would declare his name, saying that he was Agarwaen, the Bloodstained, son of Úmarth, Ill-fate (p. 210). Finduilas (Failivrin) asks:

> But are none yet nigh us    that knew of yore
> that mighty of Men [Húrin],    mark of kinship
> to seek and see    in these sorrow-laden
> form and features?                              (1958–61)

and then

> No few were there found    who had fought of old
> where Finweg fell    in flame of swords
> and Húrin Thalion    had hewn the throngs,
> the dark Glamhoth's    demon legions          (1974–7)

and they declared that Turin's face was *the face of the father new found on earth*. Against the second of these passages my father wrote in the margin: 'Not so.' This is a comment on the idea that there were many Gnomes in Nargothrond who had fought in the Battle of Unnumbered Tears (see pp. 84–5); according to the later story scarcely any went from Nargothrond, and of the small company that did none came back, save Flinding/Gwindor himself. – In *The Silmarillion* (p. 210) Túrin is not said to be the image of his father; on the contrary,

> he was in truth the son of Morwen Eledhwen to look upon: dark-haired and pale-skinned, with grey eyes.

Cf. also the *Narn*, p. 161, where Túrin said to Arminas:

> But if my head be dark and not golden, of that I am not ashamed. For I am not the first of sons in the likeness of his mother.

Húrin himself was

> shorter in stature than other men of his kin; in this he took after his mother's people, but in all else he was like Hador his grandfather, fair of face and golden-haired, strong in body and fiery of mood (*Narn* p. 57).

But Túrin was already conceived to be dark-haired in the Lay:

> the black-haired boy    from the beaten people          (417)

and in the second version of the poem Húrin also has *dark tresses* (p. 97, line 88).

At the feast of welcome in the house of Fuilin Flinding's father, deep in the woods on the slopes of the Hunters' Wold (1989–92), Fuilin filled with mead a great ancient silver cup that had come from Valinor:

> carved in gladness,
> in woe hoarded,    in waning hope
> when little was left    of the lore of old.    (2038–40)

It was of such things as that cup, carved with images of *the folk of Faërie in the first noontide / of the Blissful Realms*, of the Two Trees, and of the tower of Ing on the hill of Côr, that my father was thinking when he wrote of the treasures that Finrod Felagund brought out of Tirion (*The Silmarillion* p. 114); 'a solace and a burden on the road' (*ibid*. p. 85). – This is the first reference to the tower of Ing (Ingwë, see p. 28) in the Elvish city, whose

> pale pinnacle    pierced the twilight,
> and its crystal lamp    illumined clear
> with slender shaft    the Shadowy Seas    (2033–5)

as afterwards the silver lamp of the Mindon Eldaliéva 'shone far out into the mists of the sea' (*The Silmarillion* p. 59).

According to the readings of the A and B texts at lines 2030–2 the hill on which the Elvish city was built, figured on Fuilin's cup, is *Tûn*, crowned by the white-walled city of Côr; and this is anomalous, since the name *Tûn* certainly arose as the name of the city (see II. 292), and in the 'Sketch of the Mythology' and the 1930 'Silmarillion' Kôr is the hill and Tûn the city. In the C-text of the poem, however, these lines were changed, and the city is named Tûn (p. 82).

The elaboration at the end of the relationship of Túrin and Finduilas is an indication of the large scale on which this work was planned: seeing how much in bare narrative terms is yet to come (the fall of Nargothrond, the Dragon, the loss of Finduilas, Túrin's journey to Dor-lómin, Morwen and Nienor in Doriath and the journey to Nargothrond, the enspelling of Nienor, Túrin and Nienor among the Woodmen, the coming and death of the Dragon, and the deaths of Nienor and Túrin) it must have run to many more thousands of lines.

There remain a few isolated matters. The name *Esgalduin* now first appears, but the form in A and B as typed (2164), *Esgaduin*, is the original name. The C-text has *Esgalduin* (p. 82).

The Moon is seen in lines 2088–94 as a ship, the Silver Wherry, with mast, hold, and shrouds, sailing from wharves on the margin of the world; but the imagery has no real point of contact with the Ship of the Moon in the *Tale of the Sun and Moon* (I. 192–3).

Ulmo is now called *Ylmir* (first appearing by emendation in B at line 1469, but thereafter in both A and B as first written); in the 'Sketch' he first appears as *Ulmo (Ylmir)*, thereafter as *Ylmir*, suggesting that at this time *Ylmir* was the Gnomish form of his name (in the Gnomish dictionary it was *Gulma*, I. 270). He is also called *the Dweller in the Deep* at line

1565, as he is in the later *Tuor* (*Unfinished Tales* pp. 22, 28). Flinding mentions messages from Ulmo that are heard at Ivrin, and says that Ulmo *alone remembers in the Lands of Mirth / the need of the Gnomes* (1531 ff.); cf. the *Tale*, II. 77.

Lastly may be noticed Túrin's words of parting to Beleg at his burial (1408–11), in which he foresees for him an afterlife in Valinor, in the halls of the Gods, and does not speak of a time of 'waiting'; cf. lines 1283–4, 1696–7.

———

# THE SECOND VERSION
# OF
# THE CHILDREN OF HÚRIN

This version of the poem (II) is extant in a bundle of very rough manuscript notes (IIA), which do not constitute a complete text, and a typescript (IIB) – the twin of the typescript (IB) of the first version, done with the same distinctive purple ribbon – based on IIA. That II is a later work than I is obvious from a casual scrutiny – to give a single example, the name *Morwen* appears thus both in IIA and IIB. As I have said (p. 4), I do not think that II is significantly later than I, and may indeed have been composed before my father ceased work on I.* Towards the end of II the amount of expansion and change from I becomes very much less, but it seems best to give II in full.

The text of the opening of the second version is complicated by the existence of two further texts, both extending from lines II. 1–94. The earlier of these is another typescript (IIC), which takes up emendations made to IIB and is itself emended: the second is a manuscript (IID) written on 'Oxford' paper (see p. 81), which takes up the changes made to IIC and introduces yet further changes. At the beginning of the poem, therefore, we have lines that exhibit a continuous development through six different texts, as for example line 18 in the first version, which is line 34 in the second:

IA   Yet in host upon host    the hillfiends, the orcs *emended in the manuscript to*:

     Yet in host upon host    the hillfiend orcs

IB   There in host on host    the hill-fiend Orcs

---

*The only external evidence for date (other than the physical nature of the texts, which were clearly made at Leeds, not at Oxford) is the fact that a page of IIA is written on the back of a formal letter from *The Microcosm* (a Leeds literary quarterly, in which my father published the poem *The City of the Gods* in the Spring 1923 issue, see I. 136) acknowledging receipt of a subscription for 1922; the letter was evidently written in 1923.

IIA    but in host on host     from the hills of darkness (*with* from the
       hills swarming *as an alternative*)

IIB    but in host on host     from the hills swarming

IIC    *as IIB but emended on the typescript to*:

       and in host on host     from the hills swarming

IID    In host upon host     from the hills swarming

The majority of the changes throughout the successive texts of the poem
were made for metrical reasons – in the later revisions, especially for the
removal of 'little words', to achieve an effect nearer to that of Old English
lines, and to get rid of metrical aids such as -*éd* pronounced as a separate
syllable; and as I have said, the provision of a full apparatus would be
exceedingly lengthy and complex (and in places scarcely possible, for the
actual texts are often more obscure than appears in print). For the second
version of the poem, therefore, I give the text of IID (the last one) to its
end at line 94 (since the changes from IIB though pervasive are extremely
minor), and continue thereafter with IIB (the major typescript of the
second version); and as before purely verbal/metrical alterations that
have no bearing on the story or on names are not cited in the notes.

IIA has no title; in IIB it was TÚRIN, then THE CHILDREN OF
HÚRIN, which is also the title in IIC and IID.

The 'Prologue', greatly expanded in the second version, is still given
no subheading, except that in IIC it is marked 'I'; in IIB *Túrin's
Fostering* is a section-heading, to which my father afterwards added 'II'.

# THE CHILDREN OF HÚRIN

## I

Ye Gods who girt     your guarded realms
with moveless pinnacles,     mountains pathless,
o'er shrouded shores     sheer uprising
of the Bay of Faëry     on the borders of the World!
Ye Men unmindful     of the mirth of yore,                          5
wars and weeping     in the worlds of old,
of Morgoth's might     remembering nought!
Lo! hear what Elves     with ancient harps,
lingering forlorn     in lands untrodden,
fading faintly     down forest pathways,                           10
in shadowy isles     on the Shadowy Seas,

sing still in sorrow    of the son of Húrin,
how his webs of doom    were woven dark
with Níniel's sorrow:    names most mournful.

A! Húrin Thalion    in the hosts of battle          15
was whelmed in war,    when the white banners
of the ruined king    were rent with spears,
in blood beaten;    when the blazing helm
of Finweg fell    in flame of swords,
and his gleaming armies'    gold and silver         20
shields were shaken,    shining emblems
in darkling tide    of dire hatred,
the cruel Glamhoth's    countless legions,
were lost and foundered –    their light was quenched!
That field yet now    the folk name it            25
Nirnaith Ornoth,    Unnumbered Tears:
the seven chieftains    of the sons of Men
fled there and fought not,    the folk of the Elves
betrayed with treason.    Their troth alone
unmoved remembered    in the mouths of Hell      30
Thalion Erithámrod    and his thanes renowned.
Torn and trampled    the triple standard
of the house of Hithlum    was heaped with slain.
In host upon host    from the hills swarming
with hideous arms    the hungry Orcs           35
enmeshed his might,    and marred with wounds
pulled down the proud    Prince of Mithrim.
At Bauglir's bidding    they bound him living;
to the halls of Hell    neath the hills builded,
to the Mountains of Iron,    mournful, gloomy,      40
they led the lord    of the Lands of Mist,
Húrin Thalion,    to the throne of hate
in halls upheld    with huge pillars
of black basalt.    There bats wandered,
worms and serpents    enwound the columns;      45
there Bauglir's breast    was burned within
with blazing rage,    baulked of purpose:
from his trap had broken    Turgon the mighty,
Fingolfin's son;    Fëanor's children,
the makers of the magic and immortal gems.        50
For Húrin standing    storm unheeding,
unbent in battle,    with bitter laughter

his axe wielded –    as eagle's wings
the sound of its sweep,    swinging deadly;
as livid lightning    it leaped and fell,                              55
as toppling trunks    of trees riven
his foes had fallen.    Thus fought he on,
where blades were blunted    and in blood foundered
the Men of Mithrim;    thus a moment stemmed
with sad remnant    the raging surge                               60
of ruthless Orcs,    and the rear guarded,
that Turgon the terrible    towering in anger
a pathway clove    with pale falchion
from swirling slaughter.    Yea! his swath was plain
through the hosts of Hell,    as hay that is laid              65
on the lea in lines,    where long and keen
goes sweeping scythe.    Thus seven kindreds,
a countless company,    that king guided
through darkened dales    and drear mountains
out of ken of his foes –    he comes no more                  70
in the tale of Túrin.    Triumph of Morgoth
thus to doubt was turned,    dreams of vengeance,
thus his mind was moved    with malice fathomless,
thoughts of darkness,    when the Thalion stood
bound, unbending,    in his black dungeon.                    75

Said the dread Lord of Hell:    'Dauntless Húrin,
stout steel-handed,    stands before me
yet quick a captive,    as a coward might be!
Then knows he my name,    or needs be told
what hope he has    in the halls of iron?                        80
The bale most bitter,    Balrogs' torment!'

Then Húrin answered,    Hithlum's chieftain –
his shining eyes    with sheen of fire
in wrath were reddened:    'O ruinous one,
by fear unfettered    I have fought thee long,               85
nor dread thee now,    nor thy demon slaves,
fiends and phantoms,    thou foe of Gods!'
His dark tresses,    drenched and tangled,
that fell o'er his face    he flung backward,
in the eye he looked    of the evil Lord –                       90
since that day of dread    to dare his glance
has no mortal Man    had might of soul.
There the mind of Húrin    in a mist of dark

neath gaze unfathomed    groped and foundered,*
yet his heart yielded not    nor his haughty pride.                    95
But Lungorthin    Lord of Balrogs
on the mouth smote him,    and Morgoth smiled:
'Nay, fear when thou feelest,    when the flames lick thee
and the whistling whips    thy white body
and wilting flesh    weal and torture!'                               100
Then hung they helpless    Húrin dauntless
in chains by fell    enchantments forged
that with fiery anguish    his flesh devoured,
yet loosed not lips    locked in silence
to pray for pity.    Thus prisoned saw he                            105
on the sable walls    the sultry glare
of far-off fires    fiercely burning
down deep corridors    and dark archways
in the blind abysses    of those bottomless halls;
there with mourning mingled    mighty tumult                         110
the throb and thunder    of the thudding forges'
brazen clangour;    belched and spouted
flaming furnaces;    there faces sad
through the glooms glided    as the gloating Orcs
their captives herded    under cruel lashes.                         115
Many a hopeless glance    on Húrin fell,
for his tearless torment    many tears were spilled.

Lo! Morgoth remembered    the mighty doom,
the weird of old,    that the Elves in woe,
in ruin and wrack    by the reckless hearts                          120
of mortal Men    should be meshed at last;
that treason alone    of trusted friend
should master the magic    whose mazes wrapped
the children of Côr,    cheating his purpose,
from defeat fending    Fingolfin's son,                              125
Turgon the terrible,    and the troth-brethren
the sons of Fëanor,    and secret, far,
homes hid darkly    in the hoar forest
where Thingol was throned    in the Thousand Caves.

Then the Lord of Hell    lying-hearted                               130
to where Húrin hung    hastened swiftly,

---

*Here the latest text IID ends, and IIB is followed from this point; see p. 95.

and the Balrogs about him    brazen-handed
with flails of flame    and forgéd iron
there laughed as they looked    on his lonely woe;
but Bauglir said:    'O bravest of Men,                    135
'tis fate unfitting    for thus fellhanded
warrior warfain    that to worthless friends
his sword he should sell,    who seek no more
to free him from fetters    or his fall avenge.
While shrinking in the shadows    they shake fearful    140
in the hungry hills    hiding outcast
their league belying,    lurking faithless,
he by evil lot    in everlasting
dungeons droopeth    doomed to torment
and anguish endless.    That thy arms unchained    145
I had fainer far    should a falchion keen
or axe with edge    eager flaming
wield in warfare    where the wind bloweth
the banners of battle –    such a brand as might
in my sounding smithies    on the smitten anvil    150
of glowing steel    to glad thy soul
be forged and fashioned,    yea, and fair harness
and mail unmatched –    than that marred with flails
my mercy waiving    thou shouldst moan enchained
neath the brazen Balrogs'    burning scourges:    155
who art worthy to win    reward and honour
as a captain of arms    when cloven is mail
and shields are shorn,    when they shake the hosts
of their foes like fire    in fell onset.
Lo! receive my service;    forswear hatred,    160
ancient enmity    thus ill-counselled –
I am a mild master    who remembers well
his servants' deeds.    A sword of terror
thy hand should hold,    and a high lordship
as Bauglir's champion,    chief of Balrogs,    165
to lead o'er the lands    my loud armies,
whose royal array    I already furnish;
on Turgon the troll    (who turned to flight
and left thee alone,    now leaguered fast
in waterless wastes    and weary mountains)    170
my wrath to wreak,    and on redhanded
robber-Gnomes, rebels,    and roaming Elves,
that forlorn witless    the Lord of the World

defy in their folly –   they shall feel my might.
I will bid men unbind thee,   and thy body comfort!          175
Go follow their footsteps   with fire and steel,
with thy sword go search   their secret dwellings;
when in triumph victorious   thou returnest hither,
I have hoards unthought-of' –   but Húrin Thalion
suffered no longer   silent wordless;          180
through clenchéd teeth   in clinging pain,
'O accursed king',   cried unwavering,
'thy hopes build not   so high, Bauglir;
no tool am I   for thy treasons vile,
who tryst nor troth   ever true holdest –          185
seek traitors elsewhere.'

                    Then returned answer
Morgoth amazed   his mood hiding:
'Nay, madness holds thee;   thy mind wanders;
my measureless hoards   are mountains high
in places secret   piled uncounted          190
agelong unopened;   Elfin silver
and gold in the gloom   there glister pale;
the gems and jewels   once jealous-warded
in the mansions of the Gods,   who mourn them yet,
are mine, and a meed   I will mete thee thence          195
of wealth to glut   the Worm of Greed.'

Then Húrin, hanging,   in hate answered:
'Canst not learn of thy lore   when thou look'st on a foe,
O Bauglir unblest?   Bray no longer
of the things thou hast thieved   from the Three Kindreds!          200
In hate I hold thee.   Thou art humbled indeed
and thy might is minished   if thy murderous hope
and cruel counsels   on a captive sad
must wait, on a weak   and weary man.'
To the hosts of Hell   his head then he turned:          205
'Let thy foul banners   go forth to battle,
ye Balrogs and Orcs;   let your black legions
go seek the sweeping   sword of Turgon.
Through the dismal dales   you shall be driven wailing
like startled starlings   from the stooks of wheat.          210
Minions miserable   of master base,
your doom dread ye,   dire disaster!
The tide shall turn;   your triumph brief

and victory shall vanish.    I view afar
the wrath of the Gods    roused in anger.'                    215

Then tumult awoke,    a tempest wild
in rage roaring    that rocked the walls;
consuming madness    seized on Morgoth,
yet with lowered voice    and leering mouth
thus Thalion Erithámrod    he threatened darkly:         220
'Thou hast said it! See    how my swift purpose
shall march to its mark    unmarred of thee,
nor thy aid be asked,    overweening
mortal mightless.    I command thee gaze
on my deeds of power    dreadly proven.                   225
Yet if little they like thee,    thou must look thereon
helpless to hinder    or thy hand to raise,
and thy lidless eyes    lit with anguish
shall not shut for ever,    shorn of slumber
like the Gods shall gaze    there grim, tearless,         230
on the might of Morgoth    and the meed he deals
to fools who refuse    fealty gracious.'

To Thangorodrim    was the Thalion borne,
that mountain that meets    the misty skies
on high over the hills    that Hithlum sees               235
blackly brooding    on the borders of the North.
There stretched on the stone    of steepest peak
in bonds unbreakable    they bound him living;
there the lord of woe    in laughter stood,
there cursed him for ever    and his kindred all           240
that should walk and wander    in woe's shadow
to a doom of death    and dreadful end.
There the mighty man    unmovéd sat,
but unveiled was his vision    that he viewed afar
with eyes enchanted    all earthly things,                 245
and the weird of woe    woven darkly
that fell on his folk –    a fiend's torment.

★

# NOTES

14   After this line IIB had the following:

> how the golden dragon    of the God of darkness
> wrought wrack and ruin    in realms now lost –
> only the mighty of soul,    of Men or Elves,
> doom can conquer,    and in death only.

These lines were struck out in IIB, and do not appear in IIC, IID.

19   Cf. I. 1975:

> where Finweg fell    in flame of swords

with *Finweg* > *Fingon* a later pencilled change in IB. All the
texts of II have *Finweg* (IIA *Fingweg*), but *Fingon* appears in a
late pencilled emendation to IID.

26   *Nirnaith Únoth* IIB, IIC; *Nirnaith Ornoth* IID, emended in
pencil to *Nirnaith Arnediad*. For *Únoth*, *Ornoth* in the first version
see p. 79, notes to lines 1448, 1542–3. I read *Ornoth* here, since
*Arnediad* is a form that arose much later.

27   All the texts of II have *the chosen chieftains   of the children
of Men*, but IID is emended in pencil to *the seven chieftains   of
the sons of Men*.

49   *Fingolfin's son*: see p. 21, note to line 29.
*Fëanor's children* IID; *and Fëanor's children* IIA, B, C.

76   *'Is it dauntless Húrin,'   quoth Delu-Morgoth* IIB, as in IB
(line 51).

157   *as a captain among them* IIB as typed. Cf line 165.

## Commentary on Part I
## of the second version

This part has been expanded to two and a half times its former length,
partly through the introduction of descriptions of Angband (42–5,
105–15) – to be greatly enlarged some years later in the *Lay of Leithian*,
and of Húrin's last stand (51–61), but chiefly through the much extended account of Morgoth's dealings with Húrin, his attempted seduc-
tion of 'the Thalion', and his great rage (not found at all in the first
version) at his failure to break his will. The rewritten scene is altogether
fiercer, the sense of lying, brutality, and pain (and the heroic power of
Húrin's resistance) much stronger.

There are some interesting details in this opening section. Húrin's
dark hair (88) has been referred to above (p. 92). The *thane of Morgoth* who smote him on the mouth (version I, 59) now becomes *Lungorthin, Lord of Balrogs* (96) – which is probably to be interpreted as 'a

Balrog lord', since Gothmog, Lord or Captain of the Balrogs in *The Fall of Gondolin*, soon reappears in the 'Silmarillion' tradition. Notable is the passage (88–94) in which Húrin, thrusting back his long hair, looked into Morgoth's eye, and his mind *in a mist of dark . . . groped and foundered*: the originator of the power of the eye of Glórund his servant, which this poem did not reach.

A line that occurs much later in the first version (1975)

> where Finweg [> Fingon] fell    in flame of swords

is introduced here (19), and there is mention also of his *white banners . . . in blood beaten*, and his *blazing helm*: this is ultimately the origin of the passage in *The Silmarillion* (pp. 193–4):

> a white flame sprang up from the helm of Fingon as it was cloven . . .
> they beat him into the dust with their maces, and his banner, blue and
> silver, they trod into the mire of his blood.

At line 26 is the first occurrence of *Nirnaith Arnediad*, but this is a hasty pencilled change to the last text (IID) and belongs to a later phase of nomenclature.

It is said that Turgon guided *seven kindreds* (67) out of the battle; in the tale of *The Fall of Gondolin* there were twelve kindreds of the Gondothlim.

Húrin is named the Prince of Mithrim (37), and his men the Men of Mithrim (59). This may suggest that the meaning of Mithrim, hitherto the name of the lake only, was being extended to the region in which the lake lay; on the earliest 'Silmarillion' map, however, this is not suggested. *The land of Mithrim* occurs at line 248, but the phrase was changed.

The passage in the first version (46–50) saying that Morgoth

> remembered well
> how Men were accounted    all mightless and frail
> by the Elves and their kindred;    how only treason
> could master the magic    whose mazes wrapped
> the children of Corthûn

is changed in the second (118–24) to

> Lo! Morgoth remembered    the mighty doom,
> the weird of old,    that the Elves in woe,
> in ruin and wrack    by the reckless hearts
> of mortal Men    should be meshed at last;
> that treason alone    of trusted friend
> should master the magic    whose mazes wrapped
> the children of Côr

There has been no reference in the *Lost Tales* to any such ancient 'doom' or 'weird'. It is possible that the reference to 'treason' is to the 'Prophecy of the North', spoken by Mandos or his messenger as the host of the

Noldor moved northward up the coast of Valinor after the Kinslaying
(*The Silmarillion* pp. 87–8); in the earliest version of this, in the tale of
*The Flight of the Noldoli* (I. 167), there is no trace of the idea, but it is
already explicit in the 1930 'Silmarillion' that the Gnomes should pay for
the deeds at Swanhaven in 'treachery and the fear of treachery among
their own kindred'. On the other hand, to *the mighty doom, the weird
of old* is ascribed also the ultimate ruin of the Elves which is to come to
pass through Men; and this is not found in any version of the Prophecy of
the North. This passage in the revised version of the poem is echoed in
the same scene in the 1930 'Silmarillion':

> Afterward Morgoth remembering that treachery or the fear of it, and
> especially the treachery of Men, alone would work the ruin of the
> Gnomes, came to Húrin . . .

★

# II

## TÚRIN'S FOSTERING

Lo! the lady Morwen    in the land of shadow
waited in the woodland    for her well-beloved,
but he came never    to clasp her nigh                          250
from that black battle.    She abode in vain;
no tidings told her    whether taken or dead
or lost in flight    he lingered yet.
Laid waste his lands    and his lieges slain,
and men unmindful    of that mighty lord                        255
in Dorlómin dwelling    dealt unkindly
with his wife in widowhood;    she went with child,
and a son must succour    sadly orphaned,
Túrin Thalion    of tender years.
In days of blackness    was her daughter born,                 260
and named Nienor,    a name of tears
that in language of eld    is Lamentation.
Then her thoughts were turned    to Thingol the Elf,
and Lúthien the lissom    with limbs shining,
his daughter dear,    by Dairon loved,                         265
who Tinúviel was named    both near and far,
the Star-mantled,    still remembered,
who light as leaf    on linden tree
had danced in Doriath    in days agone,
on the lawns had lilted    in the long moonshine,              270

while deftly was drawn    Dairon's music
with fingers fleet    from flutes of silver.
The boldest of the brave,    Beren Ermabwed,
to wife had won her,    who once of old
had vowed fellowship    and friendly love                    275
with Húrin of Hithlum,    hero dauntless
by the marge of Mithrim's    misty waters.
Thus to her son she said:    'My sweetest child,
our friends are few;    thy father is gone.
Thou must fare afar    to the folk of the wood,               280
where Thingol is throned    in the Thousand Caves.
If he remember Morwen    and thy mighty sire
he will foster thee fairly,    and feats of arms,
the trade he will teach thee    of targe and sword,
that no slave in Hithlum    shall be son of Húrin.            285
A! return my Túrin    when time passeth;
remember thy mother    when thy manhood cometh
or when sorrows snare thee.'    Then silence took her,
for fears troubled    her trembling voice.
Heavy boded the heart    of Húrin's son,                      290
who unwitting of her woe    wondered vaguely,
yet weened her words    were wild with grief
and denied her not;    no need him seemed.

Lo! Mailrond and Halog,    Morwen's henchmen,
were young of yore    ere the youth of Húrin,                 295
and alone of the lieges    of that lord of Men
now steadfast in service    stayed beside her:
now she bade them brave    the black mountains
and the woods whose ways    wander to evil;
though Túrin be tender,    to travail unused,                 300
they must gird them and go.    Glad they were not,
but to doubt the wisdom    dared not openly
of Morwen who mourned    when men saw not.

Came a day of summer    when the dark silence
of the towering trees    trembled dimly                       305
to murmurs moving    in the milder airs
far and faintly;    flecked with dancing
sheen of silver    and shadow-filtered
sudden sunbeams    were the secret glades
where winds came wayward    wavering softly                   310
warm through the woodland's    woven branches.

Then Morwen stood,   her mourning hidden,
by the gate of her garth   in a glade of Hithlum;
at her breast bore she   her babe unweaned,
crooning lowly   to its careless ears                            315
a song of sweet   and sad cadence,
lest she droop for anguish.   Then the doors opened,
and Halog hastened   neath a heavy burden,
and Mailrond the old   to his mistress led
her gallant Túrin,   grave and tearless,                        320
with heart heavy as stone   hard and lifeless,
uncomprehending   his coming torment.
There he cried with courage,   comfort seeking:
'Lo! quickly will I come   from the courts afar,
I will long ere manhood   lead to Morwen                        325
great tale of treasure   and true comrades.'
He wist not the weird   woven of Morgoth,
nor the sundering sorrow   that them swept between,
as farewells they took   with faltering lips.
The last kisses   and lingering words                           330
are over and ended;   and empty is the glen
in the dark forest,   where the dwelling faded
in trees entangled.   Then in Túrin woke
to woe's knowledge   his bewildered heart,
that he wept blindly   awakening echoes                         335
sad resounding   in sombre hollows,
as he called: 'I cannot,   I cannot leave thee.
O! Morwen my mother,   why makest me go?
The hills are hateful,   where hope is lost;
O! Morwen my mother,   I am meshed in tears,                    340
for grim are the hills   and my home is gone.'
And there came his cries   calling faintly
down the dark alleys   of the dreary trees,
that one there weeping   weary on the threshold
heard how the hills said   'my home is gone.'                   345

                    *        *        *

The ways were weary   and woven with deceit
o'er the hills of Hithlum   to the hidden kingdom
deep in the darkness   of Doriath's forest,
and never ere now   for need or wonder
had children of Men   chosen that pathway,                      350
save Beren the brave   who bounds knew not

to his wandering feet    nor feared the woods
or fells or forest    or frozen mountain,
and few had followed    his feet after.
There was told to Túrin    that tale by Halog          355
that in the Lay of Leithian,    Release from Bonds,
in linkéd words    has long been woven,
of Beren Ermabwed,    the boldhearted;
how Lúthien the lissom    he loved of yore
in the enchanted forest    chained with wonder –          360
Tinúviel he named her,    than nightingale
more sweet her voice,    as veiled in soft
and wavering wisps    of woven dusk
shot with starlight,    with shining eyes
she danced like dreams    of drifting sheen,          365
pale-twinkling pearls    in pools of darkness;
how for love of Lúthien    he left the woods
on that quest perilous    men quail to tell,
thrust by Thingol    o'er the thirst and terror
of the Lands of Mourning;    of Lúthien's tresses,          370
and Melian's magic,    and the marvellous deeds
that after happened    in Angband's halls,
and the flight o'er fell    and forest pathless
when Carcharoth    the cruel-fangéd,
the wolf-warden    of the Woeful Gates,          375
whose vitals fire    devoured in torment
them hunted howling    (the hand of Beren
he had bitten from the wrist    where that brave one held
the nameless wonder,    the Gnome-crystal
where light living    was locked enchanted,          380
all hue's essence.    His heart was eaten,
and the woods were filled    with wild madness
in his dreadful torment,    and Doriath's trees
did shudder darkly    in the shrieking glens);
how the hound of Hithlum,    Huan wolf-bane,          385
to the hunt hasted    to the help of Thingol,
and as dawn came dimly    in Doriath's woods
was the slayer slain,    but silent lay
there Beren bleeding    nigh brought to death,
till the lips of Lúthien    in love's despair          390
awoke him to words,    ere he winged afar
to the long awaiting;    thence Lúthien won him,
the Elf-maiden,    and the arts of Melian,

her mother Mablui    of the moonlit hand,
that they dwell for ever    in days ageless                    395
and the grass greys not    in the green forest
where East or West    they ever wander.
Then a song he made them    for sorrow's lightening,
a sudden sweetness    in the silent wood,
that is 'Light as Leaf    on Linden' called,                  400
whose music of mirth    and mourning blended
yet in hearts does echo.    This did Halog sing them:*

    The grass was very long and thin,
        The leaves of many years lay thick,
    The old tree-roots wound out and in,                     405
        And the early moon was glimmering.
    There went her white feet lilting quick,
        And Dairon's flute did bubble thin,
    As neath the hemlock umbels thick
        Tinúviel danced a-shimmering.                         410

    The pale moths lumbered noiselessly,
        And daylight died among the leaves,
    As Beren from the wild country
        Came thither wayworn sorrowing.
    He peered between the hemlock sheaves,                    415
        And watched in wonder noiselessly
    Her dancing through the moonlit leaves
        And the ghostly moths a-following.

    There magic took his weary feet,
        And he forgot his loneliness,                         420
    And out he danced, unheeding, fleet,
        Where the moonbeams were a-glistening.
    Through the tangled woods of Elfinesse
        They fled on nimble fairy feet,
    And left him to his loneliness                           425
        In the silent forest listening,

    Still hearkening for the imagined sound
        Of lissom feet upon the leaves,

*For the textual history of this poem's insertion into the Lay see the Note on pp. 120–2.

For music welling underground
    In the dim-lit caves of Doriath.           430
But withered are the hemlock sheaves,
    And one by one with mournful sound
Whispering fall the beechen leaves
    In the dying woods of Doriath.

He sought her wandering near and far        435
    Where the leaves of one more year were strewn,
By winter moon and frosty star
    With shaken light a-shivering.
He found her neath a misty moon,
    A silver wraith that danced afar,        440
And the mists beneath her feet were strewn
    In moonlight palely quivering.

She danced upon a hillock green
    Whose grass unfading kissed her feet,
While Dairon's fingers played unseen       445
    O'er his magic flute a-flickering;
And out he danced, unheeding, fleet,
    In the moonlight to the hillock green:
No impress found he of her feet
    That fled him swiftly flickering.        450

And longing filled his voice that called
    'Tinúviel, Tinúviel,'
And longing sped his feet enthralled
    Behind her wayward shimmering.
She heard as echo of a spell        455
    His lonely voice that longing called
'Tinúviel, Tinúviel':
    One moment paused she glimmering.

And Beren caught that elfin maid
    And kissed her trembling starlit eyes,    460
Tinúviel whom love delayed
    In the woods of evening morrowless.
Till moonlight and till music dies
    Shall Beren by the elfin maid
Dance in the starlight of her eyes      465
    In the forest singing sorrowless.

Wherever grass is long and thin,
　　And the leaves of countless years lie thick,
And ancient roots wind out and in,
　　As once they did in Doriath,                    470
Shall go their white feet lilting quick,
　　But never Dairon's music thin
Be heard beneath the hemlocks thick
　　Since Beren came to Doriath.

This for hearts' uplifting    did Halog sing them        475
as the frowning fortress    of the forest clasped them
and nethermost night    in its net caught them.
There Túrin and the twain    knew torture of thirst
and hunger and fear,    and hideous flight
from wolfriders    and wandering Orcs                480
and the things of Morgoth    that thronged the woods.
There numbed and wetted    they had nights of waking
cold and clinging,    when the creaking winds
summer had vanquished    and in silent valleys
a dismal dripping    in the distant shadows             485
ever splashed and spilt    over spaces endless
from rainy leaves,    till arose the light
greyly, grudgingly,    gleaming thinly
at drenching dawn.    They were drawn as flies
in the magic mazes;    they missed their ways           490
and strayed steerless,    and the stars were hid
and the sun sickened.    Sombre and weary
had the mountains been;    the marches of Doriath
bewildered and wayworn    wound them helpless
in despair and error,    and their spirits foundered.    495
Without bread or water    with bleeding feet
and fainting strength    in the forest straying
their death they deemed it    to die forwandered,
when they heard a horn    that hooted afar
and dogs baying.    Lo! the dreary bents                500
and hushed hollows    to the hunt wakened,
and echoes answered    to eager tongues,
for Beleg the bowman    was blowing gaily,
who furthest fared    of his folk abroad
by hill and by hollow    ahunting far,                  505
careless of comrades    or crowded halls,
as light as a leaf,    as the lusty airs

as free and fearless   in friendless places.
He was great of growth   with goodly limbs
and lithe of girth,   and lightly on the ground          510
his footsteps fell   as he fared towards them
all garbed in grey   and green and brown.

'Who are ye?' he asked.   'Outlaws, maybe,
hiding, hunted,   by hatred dogged?'

'Nay, for famine and thirst   we faint,' said Halog,          515
'wayworn and wildered,   and wot not the road.
Or hast not heard   of the hills of slain,
field tear-drenchéd   where in flame and terror
Morgoth devoured   the might and valour
of the hosts of Finweg   and Hithlum's lord?          520
The Thalion Erithámrod   and his thanes dauntless
there vanished from the earth,   whose valiant lady
yet weeps in widowhood   as she waits in Hithlum.
Thou lookest on the last   of the lieges of Morwen,
and the Thalion's child   who to Thingol's court          525
now wend at the word   of the wife of Húrin.'

Then Beleg bade them   be blithe, saying:
'The Gods have guided you   to good keeping;
I have heard of the house   of Húrin undaunted,
and who hath not heard   of the hills of slain,          530
of Nirnaith Ornoth,   Unnumbered Tears!
To that war I went not,   yet wage a feud
with the Orcs unending,   whom mine arrows fleeting
smite oft unseen   swift and deadly.
I am the hunter Beleg   of the hidden people;          535
the forest is my father   and the fells my home.'
Then he bade them drink   from his belt drawing
a flask of leather   full-filled with wine
that is bruised from the berries   of the burning South –
the Gnome-folk know it,   from Nogrod the Dwarves          540
by long ways lead it   to the lands of the North
for the Elves in exile   who by evil fate
the vine-clad valleys   now view no more
in the land of Gods.   There was lit gladly
a fire, with flames   that flared and spluttered,          545
of wind-fallen wood   that his wizard's cunning
rotten, rain-sodden,   to roaring life

there coaxed and kindled    by craft or magic;
there baked they flesh    in the brands' embers;
white wheaten bread    to hearts' delight                       550
he haled from his wallet    till hunger waned
and hope mounted,    but their heads were mazed
by that wine of Dor-Winion    that went in their veins,
and they soundly slept    on the soft needles
of the tall pinetrees    that towered above.                    555
Then they waked and wondered,    for the woods were light,
and merry was the morn    and the mists rolling
from the radiant sun.    They soon were ready
long leagues to cover.    Now led by ways
devious winding    through the dark woodland,                   560
by slade and slope    and swampy thicket,
through lonely days,    long-dragging nights,
they fared unfaltering,    and their friend they blessed,
who but for Beleg    had been baffled utterly
by the magic mazes    of Melian the Queen.                      565
To those shadowy shores    he showed the way
where stilly the stream    strikes before the gates
of the cavernous court    of the King of Doriath.
Over the guarded bridge    he gained them passage,
and thrice they thanked him,    and thought in their hearts     570
'the Gods are good' –    had they guessed, maybe,
what the future enfolded,    they had feared to live.

To the throne of Thingol    were the three now come;
there their speech well sped,    and he spake them fair,
for Húrin of Hithlum    he held in honour,                      575
whom Beren Ermabwed    as a brother had loved
and remembering Morwen,    of mortals fairest,
he turned not Túrin    in contempt away.
There clasped him kindly    the King of Doriath,
for Melian moved him    with murmured counsel,                  580
and he said: 'Lo, O son    of the swifthanded,
the light in laughter,    the loyal in need,
Húrin of Hithlum,    thy home is with me,
and here shalt sojourn    and be held my son.
In these cavernous courts    for thy kindred's sake             585
thou shalt dwell in dear love,    till thou deemest it time
to remember thy mother    Morwen's loneliness;
thou shalt wisdom win    beyond wit of mortals,

and weapons shalt wield    as the warrior-Elves,
nor slave in Hithlum    shall be son of Húrin.'                    590

There the twain tarried    that had tended the child,
till their limbs were lightened    and they longed to fare
through dread and danger    to their dear lady,
so firm their faith.    Yet frore and grey
eld sat more heavy    on the aged head                             595
of Mailrond the old,    and his mistress' love
his might matched not,    more marred by years
than Halog he hoped not    to home again.
Then sickness assailed him    and his sight darkened:
'To Túrin I must turn    my troth and fealty,'                     600
he said and he sighed,    'to my sweet youngling';
but Halog hardened    his heart to go.
An Elfin escort    to his aid was given,
and magics of Melian,    and a meed of gold,
and a message to Morwen    for his mouth to bear,                  605
words of gladness    that her wish was granted,
and Túrin taken    to the tender care
of the King of Doriath;    of his kindly will
now Thingol called her    to the Thousand Caves
to fare unfearing    with his folk again,                          610
there to sojourn in solace    till her son be grown;
for Húrin of Hithlum    was holden in mind
and no might had Morgoth    where Melian dwelt.

Of the errand of the Elves    and of eager Halog
the tale tells not,    save in time they came                      615
to Morwen's threshold.    There Thingol's message
was said where she sat    in her solitary hall,
but she dared not do    as was dearly bidden,
who Nienor her nursling    yet newly weaned
would not leave nor be led    on the long marches                  620
to adventure her frailty    in the vast forest;
the pride of her people,    princes ancient,
had suffered her send    a son to Thingol
when despair urged her,    but to spend her days
an almsguest of others,    even Elfin kings,                       625
it little liked her;    and lived there yet
a hope in her heart    that Húrin would come,
and the dwelling was dear    where he dwelt of old;
at night she would listen    for a knock at the doors

or a footstep falling    that she fondly knew.                    630
Thus she fared not forth;    thus her fate was woven.
Yet the thanes of Thingol    she thanked nobly,
nor her shame showed she,    how shorn of glory
to reward their wending    she had wealth too scant,
but gave them in gift    those golden things                      635
that last lingered,    and led they thence
a helm of Húrin    once hewn in wars
when he battled with Beren    as brother and comrade
against ogres and Orcs    and evil foes.
Grey-gleaming steel,    with gold adorned                         640
wrights had wrought it,    with runes graven
of might and victory,    that a magic sat there
and its wearer warded    from wound or death,
whoso bore to battle    brightly shining
dire dragon-headed    its dreadful crest.                         645
This Thingol she bade    and her thanks receive.

Thus Halog her henchman    to Hithlum came,
but Thingol's thanes    thanked her lowly
and girt them to go,    though grey winter
enmeshed the mountains    and the moaning woods,                  650
for the hills hindered not    the hidden people.
Lo! Morwen's message    in a month's journey,
so speedy fared they,    was spoken in Doriath.
For Morwen Melian    was moved to ruth,
but courteously the king    that casque received,                 655
her golden gift,    with gracious words,
who deeply delved    had dungeons filled
with elvish armouries    of ancient gear,
yet he handled that helm    as his hoard were scant:
'That head were high    that upheld this thing                    660
with the token crowned,    the towering crest
to Dorlómin dear,    the dragon of the North,
that Thalion Erithámrod    the thrice renowned
oft bore into battle    with baleful foes.
Would that he had worn it    to ward his head                     665
on that direst day    from death's handstroke!'
Then a thought was thrust    into Thingol's heart,
and Túrin was called    and told kindly
that his mother Morwen    a mighty thing
had sent to her son,    his sire's heirloom,                      670

o'er-written with runes    by wrights of yore
in dark dwarfland    in the deeps of time,
ere Men to Mithrim    and misty Hithlum
o'er the world wandered;    it was worn aforetime
by the father of the fathers    of the folk of Húrin,          675
whose sire Gumlin    to his son gave it
ere his soul severed    from his sundered heart –
"Tis Telchar's work    of worth untold,
its wearer warded    from wound or magic,
from glaive guarded    or gleaming axe.          680
Now Húrin's helm    hoard till manhood
to battle bids thee,    then bravely don it,
go wear it well!'    Woeful-hearted
did Túrin touch it    but take it not,
too weak to wield    that mighty gear,          685
and his mind in mourning    for Morwen's answer
was mazed and darkened.

                    Thus many a day
it came to pass    in the courts of Thingol
for twelve years long    that Túrin lived.
But seven winters    their sorrows had laid          690
on the son of Húrin    when that summer to the world
came glad and golden    with grievous parting;
nine years followed    of his forest-nurture,
and his lot was lightened,    for he learned at whiles
from faring folk    what befell in Hithlum,          695
and tidings were told    by trusty Elves
how Morwen his mother    knew milder days
and easement of evil,    and with eager voice
all Nienor named    the Northern flower,
the slender maiden    in sweet beauty          700
now graceful growing.    The gladder was he then
and hope yet haunted    his heart at whiles.
He waxed and grew    and won renown
in all lands where Thingol    as lord was held
for his stoutness of heart    and his strong body.          705
Much lore he learned    and loved wisdom,
but fortune followed him    in few desires;
oft wrong and awry    what he wrought turnéd,
what he loved he lost,    what he longed for failed,
and full friendship    he found not with ease,          710

nor was lightly loved,    for his looks were sad;
he was gloomy-hearted    and glad seldom
for the sundering sorrow    that seared his youth.

On manhood's threshold    he was mighty-thewed
in the wielding of weapons;    in weaving song          715
he had a minstrel's mastery,    but mirth was not in it,
for he mourned the misery    of the Men of Hithlum.
Yet greater his grief    grew thereafter
when from Hithlum's hills    he heard no more
and no traveller told him    tidings of Morwen.          720
For those days were drawing    to the doom of the Gnomes
and the power of the Prince    of the pitiless kingdom,
of the grim Glamhoth,    was grown apace,
till the lands of the North    were loud with their noise,
and they fell on the folk    with fire and slaughter          725
who bent not to Bauglir    or the borders passed
of dark Dorlómin    with its dreary pines
that Hithlum was called    by the unhappy people.
There Morgoth shut them    in the Shadowy Mountains,
fenced them from Faërie    and the folk of the wood.          730
Even Beleg fared not    so far abroad
as once was his wont,    for the woods were filled
with the armies of Angband    and with evil deeds,
and murder walked    on the marches of Doriath;
only the mighty magic    of Melian the Queen          735
yet held their havoc    from the hidden people.

To assuage his sorrow    and to sate his rage,
for his heart was hot    with the hurts of his folk,
then Húrin's son    took the helm of his sire
and weapons weighty    for the wielding of men,          740
and he went to the woods    with warrior-Elves,
and far in the forest    his feet led him
into black battle    yet a boy in years.
Ere manhood's measure    he met and he slew
Orcs of Angband    and evil things          745
that roamed and ravened    on the realm's borders.
There hard his life,    and hurts he lacked not,
the wounds of shaft    and the wavering sheen
of the sickle scimitars,    the swords of Hell,
the bloodfain blades    on black anvils          750
in Angband smithied,    yet ever he smote

unfey, fearless,    and his fate kept him.
Thus his prowess was proven    and his praise was noised
and beyond his years    he was yielded honour,
for by him was holden    the hand of ruin                              755
from Thingol's folk,    and Thû feared him,
and wide wandered    the word of Túrin:
'Lo! we deemed as dead    the dragon of the North,
but high o'er the host    its head uprises,
its wings are spread!    Who has waked this spirit              760
and the flame kindled    of its fiery jaws?
Or is Húrin of Hithlum    from Hell broken?'
And Thû who was throned    as thane mightiest
neath Morgoth Bauglir,    whom that master bade
'go ravage the realm    of the robber Thingol                      765
and mar the magic    of Melian the Queen',
even Thû feared him,    and his thanes trembled.

One only was there    in war greater,
more high in honour    in the hearts of the Elves
than Túrin son of Húrin,    tower of Hithlum,                      770
even the hunter Beleg    of the hidden people,
whose father was the forest    and the fells his home;
to bend whose bow,    Balthronding named,
that the black yewtree    once bore of yore,
had none the might;    unmatched in knowledge              775
of the woods' secrets    and the weary hills.
He was leader beloved    of the light companies
all garbed in grey    and green and brown,
the archers arrowfleet    with eyes piercing,
the scouts that scoured    scorning danger                        780
afar o'er the fells    their foemen's lair,
and tales and tidings    timely won them
of camps and councils,    of comings and goings,
all the movements of the might    of Morgoth Bauglir.
Thus Túrin, who trusted    to targe and sword,                    785
who was fain of fighting    with foes well seen,
where shining swords    made sheen of fire,
and his corslet-clad    comrades-in-arms
were snared seldom    and smote unlooked-for.

Then the fame of the fights    on the far marches              790
was carried to the courts    of the king of Doriath,
and tales of Túrin    were told in his halls,

of the bond and brotherhood  of Beleg the ageless
with the blackhaired boy  from the beaten people.
Then the king called them  to come before him                    795
did Orc-raids lessen  in the outer lands
ever and often  unasked to hasten,
to rest them and revel  and to raise awhile
in songs and lays  and sweet music
the memory of the mirth  ere the moon was old,            800
when the mountains were young  in the morning of the world.

On a time was Túrin  at his table seated,
and Thingol thanked him  for his thriving deeds;
there was laughter long  and the loud clamour
of a countless company  that quaffed the mead                805
and the wine of Dor-Winion  that went ungrudged
in their golden goblets;  and goodly meats
there burdened the boards  neath blazing torches
in those high halls set  that were hewn of stone.
There mirth fell on many;  there minstrels clear            810
did sing them songs  of the city of Côr
that Taingwethil  towering mountain
o'ershadowed sheerly,  of the shining halls
where the great gods sit  and gaze on the world
from the guarded shores  of the gulf of Faërie.              815
One sang of the slaying  at the Swans' Haven
and the curse that had come  on the kindreds since

Here the typescript IIB ends abruptly, in the middle of a page; the
manuscript IIA has already ended at line 767.

## NOTES

The first page of the typescript of this section of the poem, covering lines
248–95, is duplicated, the one version (b) taking up changes made to the
other (a) and itself receiving further changes. There is no corresponding
text of IIA until line 283.

248   *in the land of Mithrim* (a), and (b) as typed. The emendation
in (b) reverts to the reading of the first version (105), *in the
Land of Shadows*.

265    *Dairon's sister* (a), and (b) as typed.

266–8    These three lines were inserted in (b), with change of *who had danced* 269 to *had danced*. See below, *Note on the poem 'Light as Leaf on Lindentree'*.

273    *Ermabweth* (a), and (b) as typed. The emendation in (b) to *Ermabwed* reverts to the form of the name in the *Lost Tales* and in the first version of the poem (121).

274–8    As typed, (a) was virtually identical with the first version lines 122–5. This was then changed to read:

> did win her to wife,    who once of old
> fellowship had vowed    and friendly love
> Elf with mortal,    even Egnor's son
> with Húrin of Hithlum,    hunting often
> by the marge of Mithrim's    misty waters.
> Thus said she to her son . . .

This passage was then typed in (b), with change of *hunting often* to *hero dauntless*. Subsequently the line *Elf with mortal,  even Egnor's son* was struck out, and other minor changes made to give the text printed.

294    *Mailrond*: *Mailgond* IIA, IIB; I read *Mailrond* in view of the emendations at lines 319, 596.

319    *Mailrond*: *Mailgond* IIA, and IIB as typed, emended in pencil to *Mailrond*; similarly at line 596.

356    *Release from Bondage* IIB as typed (the change to *Release from Bonds* was made for metrical reasons). The reference to the *Lay of Leithian* is not in IIA, but the manuscript is here so scrappy and disjointed as to be of no service.

358–66    These nine lines are typed on a slip pasted into IIB, replacing the following which were struck out:

> how Lúthien the lissom    he loved of yore
> in the enchanted forest    chained with wonder
> as she danced like dreams    of drifting whiteness
> of shadows shimmering    shot with moonlight;

In the first line (358) of the inserted slip *the boldhearted* is an emendation of *brave undaunted*; and above *Ermabwed* is written (later, in pencil) *Er(h)amion*.

374    *Carcharoth*: *Carcharolch* IIA, and IIB as typed.

398–402    These five lines are typed on a slip pasted into IIB at the same time as that giving lines 358–66, but in this case there was nothing replaced in the original typescript. Line 400 as typed read:

> that 'Light as Leaf    on Lind' is called

emended to the reading given.

Beneath the five typed lines my father wrote: 'Here follow verses "Light as leaf on linden-tree".'

*Note on the poem 'Light as Leaf on Lindentree'*
Lines 266–8 (see note above) were clearly added to the typescript at the same time as the two pasted-in slips (giving lines 358–66 and 398–402), in view of line 268 *who light as leaf   on linden tree.*

This poem, here to be inset into the *Lay of the Children of Húrin*, is found in three typescripts, here referred to as (a), (b), and (c), together with a small manuscript page giving reworkings of the penultimate stanza. These typescripts were made with the same purple ribbon used for the texts IB and IIB of the Lay and obviously belong to the same period.

(a), earliest of the three, had no title as typed: the title *Light as leaf on lind* was written in in ink, and before the poem begins there is written also in ink:

> 'Light was Tinúviel as leaf on lind
> light as a feather in the laughing wind.'
>         Tinúviel! Tinúviel!

On this typescript my father wrote some notes on the poem's dating: 'first beginnings Oxford 1919–20 Alfred St.', 'Leeds 1923, retouched 1924'. (a) is the 1923 version; it differs from the later (1924) only in the penultimate stanza, on which see note to lines 459–66 below.

(b) again has no title as typed, but *As Light as Leaf on Lindentree* was written in ink. This begins with 15 lines of alliterative verse:

> In the Lay of Leithian,   Release from Bondage
> in linkéd words   has long been wrought
> of Beren Ermabwed,   brave, undaunted;
> how Lúthien the lissom   he loved of yore
> in the enchanted forest   chained in wonder.         5
> Tinúviel he named her,   than nightingale
> more sweet her voice,   as veiled in soft
> and wavering wisps   of woven dusk
> shot with starlight,   with shining eyes
> she danced like dreams   of drifting sheen,         10
> pale-twinkling pearls   in pools of darkness.
>     And songs were raised   for sorrow's lightening,
> a sudden sweetness   in a silent hour,
> that 'Light as Leaf   on Linden-tree'
> were called – here caught   a cadent echo.         15

(c) has the typed title *As Light as Leaf on Lind*, the last word emended to *Linden-tree*. This has only the text of the poem, without the alliterative introduction; and the text is identical to that of (b).

It will be seen that of the alliterative verses in (b) lines 1–2 are very close to lines 356–7 of the Lay (which were original lines in the typescript, not inserted later):

(There was told to Túrin    that tale by Halog)
that in the Lay of Leithian,    Release from Bonds
                                   [< Bondage],
in linkéd words    has long been woven

while lines 3–11 are identical with those on the first pasted-in slip, 358–66 (as typed: *the boldhearted* in line 358 is an emendation from *brave undaunted*). Further, lines 12–15 are close to those on the second pasted-in slip, 398–402:

Then a song he made them    for sorrow's lightening,
a sudden sweetness    in a silent hour,
that is 'Light as Leaf    on Linden' called,
whose music of mirth    and mourning blended
yet in hearts does echo.    This did Halog sing them:

The order of events is very difficult to determine, but the key is probably to be found in the fact that lines 356–7 are found in IIB as originally typed, not in the pasted-in insertion. I think (or perhaps rather guess) that my father composed an alliterative continuation of 13 lines (beginning *of Beren Ermabwed, brave undaunted*) as an introduction to the poem *Light as Leaf on Lindentree*; and then, at the same time as he typed text (b) of this poem, with the alliterative head-piece, he added them to the typescript of the Lay already in existence.

*Light as Leaf on Lindentree* was published in *The Gryphon* (Leeds University), New Series, Vol. VI, no. 6, June 1925, p. 217. It is here preceded by nine lines of alliterative verse, beginning

'Tis of Beren Ermabwed brokenhearted

and continuing exactly as in (b) above (and in the text of the Lay) as far as *in pools of darkness*; the last four lines do not appear. In his cutting from *The Gryphon* my father changed *broken-hearted* (which is obviously a mere printer's error) to *the boldhearted* (as in the Lay, 358); changed the title to *As Light as Leaf on Lindentree*; and wrote *Erchamion* above *Ermabwed* (see note to lines 358–66).

The text of the inserted poem given in the body of the Lay is that published, which is identical to that of the typescripts (b) and (c). My father made a very few changes to (c) afterwards (i.e. after the poem had been printed) and these are given in the notes that follow, as also are the earlier forms of the penultimate verse.

It may finally be observed that if my deductions are correct the introduction in the Lay of the reference to the *Lay of Leithian* and the outline of the story told by Halog preceded the publication *of Light as Leaf on Lindentree* in June 1925.

───────

419    *magic > wonder*, later emendation made to the typescript (c) of *Light as Leaf on Lindentree* after the poem was published.

424    *fairy > elvish*, see note to 419.

459, 464    *elfin > elvish*, see note to 419.

459–66    In the typescript (a) this penultimate stanza reads as follows:

> And Beren caught the elfin maid
>    And kissed her trembling starlit eyes:
> The elfin maid that love delayed
>    In the days beyond our memory.
> Till moon and star, till music dies,
>    Shall Beren and the elfin maid
> Dance to the starlight of her eyes
>    And fill the woods with glamoury.

The single manuscript page (bearing the address 'The University, Leeds') has two versions of the stanza intermediate between that in (a) and the final form. The first of these reads:

> Ere Beren caught the elfin maid
>    And kissed her trembling starlit eyes
> Tinúviel, whom love delayed
>    In the woven woods of Nemoric
>    In the tangled trees of Tramorie.
> Till music and till moonlight dies
>    Shall Beren by the elfin maid
> Dance in the starlight of her eyes
>    And fill the woods with glamoury.

Other variants are suggested for lines 4 and 8:

> In the woven woods of Glamoury
>
> . . .
>
> O'er the silver glades of Amoury

and

> Ere the birth of mortal memory
>
> . . .
>
> And fill the woods with glamoury.

I can cast no light on these names.

The second version advances towards the final form, with for lines 4 and 8 of the stanza:

> In the land of laughter sorrowless
> \> In spells enchanted sorrowless
>
> . . .
>
> In eve unending morrowless

The lines finally achieved are also written here. This rewriting of the penultimate stanza is unquestionably the 1924 'retouching' referred to in the note on typescript (a) (see p. 120).

475   *did Halog sing them*: *did Halog recall* IIB as typed. The emendation was made at the same time as the insertion of *Light as Leaf on Lindentree*; as originally written the line followed on 397, at the end of Halog's story.

520   *Finweg* IIB unemended; see note to second version line 19.

531   *Nirnaith Únoth* IIA, and IIB as typed. See note to second version line 26.

551   *haled* underlined in IIB and an illegible word substituted, perhaps *had*.

576   *Ermabweth* IIA, and IIB as typed. Cf. line 273.

596   *Mailrond*: see note to line 319.

658   *elfin* IIA, *elvish* IIB as typed.

767   The manuscript IIA ends here.

811   *Côr* emended in pencil to *Tûn*, but *Tûn* later struck out. In the first version (IB, line 430) the same, but there the emendation *Tûn* not struck out.

812   *Taingwethil*: *Tengwethil* as typed. In the first version IB introduces *Tain-* for *Ten-* at lines 431, 636, but at line 1409 IB has *Ten-* for IA *Tain-*.

A later pencilled note here says: 'English *Tindbrenting*' (see Commentary, p. 127).

## Commentary on Part II
## of the second version
### 'Túrin's Fostering'

### (i)   References to the story of Beren and Lúthien

In this second part of the second version the major innovation is of course the introduction of the story of Beren and Lúthien, told to Túrin by his guardian Halog when they were lost in the forest, at once reminiscent of Aragorn's telling of the same story to his companions on Weathertop before the attack of the Ringwraiths (*The Fellowship of the Ring* I. 11); and with the further introduction of the poem *Light as Leaf on Lindentree*, the original form of the very song that Aragorn chanted on Weathertop, we realise that the one scene is actually the precursor of the other.

At line 264 (an original, not an interpolated line) is the first appearance of the name *Lúthien* for Thingol's daughter, so that Tinúviel becomes her acquired name (given to her by Beren, line 361). The suggestion of the interpolated lines 266–7 is that Tinúviel meant 'Starmantled', which seems likely enough (see I. 269, entry *Tinwë Linto*; the Gnomish dictionary, contemporary with the *Lost Tales*, rather surprisingly gives no indication of the meaning of *Tinúviel*). On the other hand, in the interpolated line 361 the suggestion is equally clear that it meant 'Nightingale'. It is difficult to explain this.*

The original reading at line 265, *Dairon's sister*, goes back to the *Tale of Tinúviel*, where Dairon was the son of Tinwelint (II. 10).

I noted earlier (p. 25) that lines 178–9 in the first version

> and never ere now    for need or wonder
> had children of Men    chosen that pathway

show that Beren was still an Elf, not a Man; but while these lines are retained without change in the second version (349–50) their meaning is reversed by the new line that immediately follows – *save Beren the brave*, which shows equally clearly that Beren was a Man, not an Elf. At this time my father was apparently in two minds on this subject. At lines 273 ff. of the second version (referring to Beren's friendship with Húrin) he originally repeated lines 122–5 of the first, which make no statement on the matter; but in the first revision of this passage (given in the note to lines 274–8) he explicitly wrote that Beren was an Elf:

---

* A possible if rather finespun explanation is that lines 266–8 were not in fact written in to the text at the same time as the two pasted-in slips (giving lines 358–66 and 398–402), as I have supposed (p. 120), but were earlier. On this view, when 266–8 were written *Tinúviel* was not yet Beren's name for Lúthien, but was her common *soubriquet*, known *both near and far* (266), and meant 'Star-mantled'. Later, when 358–66 were added, it had become the name given to her by Beren (361), and meant 'Nightingale'. If this were so, it could also be supposed that line 268, *who light as leaf   on linden tree*, gave rise to the title of the poem.

> (Beren)    who once of old
> fellowship had vowed    and friendly love
> Elf with mortal,    even Egnor's son
> with Húrin of Hithlum . . .

Since this is a rewriting of the original text of IIB it is presumably a withdrawal from the idea (that Beren was a Man) expressed in lines 349–50; while the further rewriting of this passage, getting rid of the line *Elf with mortal, even Egnor's son*, presumably represents a return to it.

In Halog's recounting of the story of Beren and Lúthien there are some apparent differences from that told in the *Tale of the Nauglafring* and the *Lay of Leithian*. The reference to *Melian's magic* in line 371 is presumably to Melian's knowledge of where Beren was; cf. the *Tale of Tinúviel* II. 17: "'O Gwendeling, my mother,' said she, 'tell me *of thy magic*, if thou canst, how doth Beren fare . . .'" A probable explanation of the mention later in this passage of *the arts of Melian* (393), in association with Lúthien's winning Beren back from death, will be given later. But in no other version of the story is there any suggestion that Carcharoth 'hunted' Beren and Lúthien (377) after he had devoured Beren's hand holding the Silmaril – indeed, the reverse: from the *Tale of Tinúviel* (II. 34) 'Then did Tinúviel and Beren flee like the wind from the gates, *yet was Karkaras far before them*' to *The Silmarillion* (p. 181) 'Howling he fled before them'. (The form *Carcharoth* now first appears, by emendation of *Carcharolch*, which occurs nowhere else; in the *Tale of Tinúviel* the forms are *Karkaras* and (in the second version) *Carcaras*.)

More important, lines 395–7

> that they dwell for ever    in days ageless
> and the grass greys not    in the green forest
> where East or West    they ever wander

seems to represent a conception of the second lives of Beren and Lúthien notably different from that in the *Tale of the Nauglafring* (II. 240), where the doom of mortality that Mandos had spoken fell swiftly upon them (as also in *The Silmarillion*, p. 236):

> nor this time did those twain fare the road together, but when yet was the child of those twain, Dior the Fair, a little one, did Tinúviel slowly fade . . . and she vanished in the woods, and none have seen her dancing ever there again. But Beren searched all the lands of Hithlum and Artanor ranging after her; and never has any of the Elves had more loneliness than his, or ever he too faded from life . . .

However this matter is to be interpreted, the lines in the Lay are clearly to be associated with the end of *Light as Leaf on Lindentree*:

> Till moonlight and till music dies
> Shall Beren by the elfin maid
> Dance in the starlight of her eyes
> In the forest singing sorrowless.

Compare the end of the song that Aragorn sang on Weathertop:

> The Sundering Seas between them lay,
> And yet at last they met once more,
> And long ago they passed away
> In the forest singing sorrowless.


### (ii)  *The Dragon-helm and Húrin's ancestors*

The elder of Túrin's guardians, still Gumlin in the first version, is now named (Mailgond >) Mailrond; and Gumlin becomes the name of Húrin's father, who has not been even mentioned before (other than in the reference in the first version to the Dragon-helm being Húrin's *heirloom*, 318). In the second version the Dragon-helm

> was worn aforetime
> by the father of the fathers    of the folk of Húrin,
> whose sire Gumlin    to his son gave it
> ere his soul severed    from his sundered heart.       (674–7)

The last line suggests that a story of Húrin's father had already come into existence; and line 675 suggests a long line of ancestors behind Húrin – as also does line 622, *the pride of her people,   princes ancient*, behind Morwen. It is hard to know how my father at this time conceived the earlier generations of Men; and the question must be postponed.

The Dragon-helm itself now begins to gather a history: it was made

> in dark dwarfland    in the deeps of time,
> ere Men to Mithrim    and misty Hithlum
> o'er the world wandered                              (672–4)

and was the work of Telchar (678), now named for the first time. But there is still no indication of the significance attaching to the dragon-crest.

Lines 758–62 (*Lo! we deemed as dead   the dragon of the North . . . Or is Húrin of Hithlum   from Hell broken?*), to which there is nothing corresponding in the first version, clearly foreshadows the *Narn*, p. 79:

> and word ran through the woods, and was heard far beyond Doriath, that the Dragon-helm of Dor-lómin was seen again. Then many wondered, saying: 'Can the spirit of Hador or of Galdor the Tall return from death; or has Húrin of Hithlum escaped indeed from the pits of Angband?'

### (iii)   *Miscellaneous Matters*

The curious references to Beleg in the first version ('son of the wilderness who wist no sire', see p. 25) reappear in the second, but in a changed form, and at one of the occurrences put into Beleg's own mouth: *the forest is my father* 536, cf. 772. *Beleg the ageless* is retained in the second version (793), and at lines 544 ff. he shows a Gandalf-like quality of being able to make fire in wet wood, with *his wizard's cunning* (cf. *The Fellowship of the Ring* II. 3).

The great bow of Beleg is now at last named: *Balthronding* (773; later *Belthronding*).

We learn now that the strong wine of Dor-Winion that Beleg gave to the travellers and which was drunk at the fateful feast in the Thousand Caves was brought to the Northern lands from Nogrod by Dwarves (540–1); and also that there was viticulture in Valinor (543–4), though after the accounts of life in the halls of Tulkas and Oromë in the tale of *The Coming of the Valar* (I. 75) this causes no surprise – indeed it is said that Nessa wife of Tulkas bore 'goblets of the goodliest wine', while Meássë went among the warriors in her house and 'revived the fainting with strong wine' (I. 78).

An interesting detail in the second account of Túrin's reception in Doriath, not found again, is that Melian played a part in the king's graciousness:

> for Melian moved him     with murmured counsel.        (580)

From the feast at which Túrin slew Orgof *the songs of the sons of Ing* of the first version (line 421) have now disappeared.

The chronology of Túrin's youth is slightly changed in the second version. In the first, as in the *Tale* (see p. 25), Túrin spent seven years in Doriath while tidings still came from Morwen (line 333); this now becomes nine years (line 693), as in *The Silmarillion* (p. 199).

Lastly, at line 812 a pencilled note against the name *Taingwethil* (Taniquetil) says 'English *Tindbrenting*'. This name is found in notes on the Old English forms of Elvish names (see p. 87), *Tindbrenting þe þa Brega Taniquetil nemnað* ('Tindbrenting which the Valar name Taniquetil'; Old English *bregu* 'king, lord, ruler' = 'Vala'). The name is perhaps to be derived from Old English *tind* 'projecting spike' (Modern English *tine*) and *brenting* (a derivative of *brant* 'steep, lofty'), here used in an unrecorded sense (*brenting* occurs only once in recorded Old English, in *Beowulf*, where it means 'ship').

### Verses associated with *The Children of Húrin*

There is a poem found in three manuscripts, all on 'Oxford' paper (see p. 81), in which my father developed elements in the passage lines

2082–2113 in *The Children of Húrin* to a short independent work. The
first text has no title, and reads:

<pre>
                    The high summer
        waned to autumn,    and western gales
        the leaves loosened    from labouring boughs.
        The feet of the forest    in fading gold
        and burnished brown    were buried deeply;                5
        a restless rustle    down the roofless aisles
        sighed and whispered.    The Silver Wherry,
        the sailing moon    with slender mast
        was filled with fires    as of furnace hot;
        its hold hoarded    the heats of summer,                 10
        its shrouds were shaped    of shining flame
        uprising ruddy    o'er the rim of Evening
        by the misty wharves    on the margin of the world.
        Then winter hastened    and weathers hardened,
        and sleet and snow    and slanting rain                  15
        from glowering heaven,    grey and sunless,
        whistling whiplash    whirled by tempest,
        the lands forlorn    lashed and tortured:
        floods were loosened,    the fallow waters
        sweeping seaward,    swollen, angry,                     20
        filled with flotsam,    foaming, turbid
        passed in tumult.    The tempest failed:
        frost descended    from the far mountains,
        steel-cold and still.    Stony-glinting
        icehung evening    was opened wide,                      25
        a dome of crystal    over deep silence,
        the windless wastes,    the woods standing
        frozen phantoms    under flickering stars.
</pre>

Against *deeply* in line 5 is given *thickly* as an alternative reading, and
against *Wherry* in line 7 is given *vessel*.

    The first 13 lines of this are almost identical to 2082–94 in the Lay,
with only a few slight changes (mostly for the common purpose in my
father's revisions of his alliterative verse of making the lines more taut).
Then follow in lines 14–16 adaptations of 2102–4; 17 is a new line; 18
contains a part of 2119; 19–22a are based on 2106–9a; 22b–24 are new;
and 25–8 are almost the same as 2110–13.

The second version of the poem bears the title *Storm over Narog*, and is
much developed. This version as written retained lines 14–15 from the
first, but they were changed and expanded to three; and the third text,
entitled *Winter comes to Nargothrond*, is a copy of the second with
this alteration and one or two other very slight changes. I give the third
text here.

*Winter comes to Nargothrond*

The summer slowly     in the sad forest
waned and faded.     In the west arose
winds that wandered     over warring seas.
Leaves were loosened     from labouring boughs:
fallow-gold they fell,     and the feet buried          5
of trees standing     tall and naked,
rustling restlessly     down roofless aisles,
shifting and drifting.
                    The shining vessel
of the sailing moon     with slender mast,
with shrouds shapen     of shimmering flame,          10
uprose ruddy     on the rim of Evening
by the misty wharves     on the margin of the world.
With winding horns     winter hunted
in the weeping woods,     wild and ruthless;
sleet came slashing,     and slanting hail          15
from glowering heaven     grey and sunless,
whistling whiplash     whirled by tempest.
The floods were freed     and fallow waters
sweeping seaward,     swollen, angry,
filled with flotsam,     foaming, turbid,          20
passed in tumult.     The tempest died.
Frost descended     from far mountains
steel-cold and still.     Stony-glinting
icehung evening     was opened wide,
a dome of crystal     over deep silence,          25
over windless wastes     and woods standing
as frozen phantoms     under flickering stars.

★

On the back of *Winter comes to Nargothrond* are written the following verses, which arose from lines 1554–70 of the Lay. The poem has no
title.

With the seething sea     Sirion's waters,
green streams gliding     into grey furrows,
murmurous mingle.     There mews gather,
seabirds assemble     in solemn council,
whitewingéd hosts     whining sadly          5
with countless voices     in a country of sand:
plains and mountains     of pale yellow
sifting softly     in salt breezes,
sere and sunbleached.     At the sea's margin

a shingle lies,    long and shining                          10
with pebbles like pearl    or pale marble:
when the foam of waves    down the wind flieth
in spray they sparkle;    splashed at evening
in the moon they glitter;    moaning, grinding,
in the dark they tumble;    drawing and rolling,          15
when strongbreasted storm    the streams driveth
in a war of waters    to the walls of land.
When the Lord of Ocean    his loud trumpets
in the abyss bloweth    to battle sounding,
longhaired legions    on lathered horses                  20
with backs like whales,    bridles spuming,
charge there snorting,    champing seaweed;
hurled with thunder    of a hundred drums
they leap the bulwarks,    burst the leaguer,
through the sandmountains    sweeping madly           25
up the river roaring    roll in fury.

The last three lines were later placed within brackets.

It may be mentioned here that there exists a poem in rhyming couplets
entitled *The Children of Húrin*. This extends only to 170 lines and
breaks off abruptly, after a short prologue based on the opening of the
later version of the alliterative Lay and an incomplete second section
titled 'The Battle of Unnumbered Tears and Morgoth's Curse'. This
poem comes however from a rather later period – approximately the time
of the abandonment of the *Lay of Leithian* in the same metre, in the
early 1930s, and I do not give it here.

# II
# POEMS EARLY ABANDONED

During his time at the University of Leeds my father embarked on five distinct poetical works concerned with the matter of the mythology; but three of these went no further than the openings. This chapter treats each of them in turn.

## (i)  The Flight of the Noldoli

There do not seem to be any certain indications of the date of this brief poem in alliterative verse in relation to *The Children of Húrin* (though it is worth noticing that already in the earliest of the three texts of *The Flight of the Noldoli* Fëanor's son Cranthir is so named, whereas this form only arose by emendation of Cranthor in the typescript text of the Lay (line 1719)). However, both from its general air and from various details it can be seen that it comes from the same time; and since it seems unlikely that (on the one hand) my father would have embarked on a new poem in alliterative verse unless he had laid the other aside, or that (on the other) he would have returned to this mode once he was fully engaged on a long poem in rhyming couplets, I think it very probable that *The Flight of the Noldoli* comes from the earlier part of 1925 (see pp. 3, 81).

Each of the three manuscripts of the poem (A, B, and C) is differently titled: A has *The Flight of the Gnomes as sung in the Halls of Thingol*; B (pencilled in later) *Flight of the Gnomes*; C *The Flight of the Noldoli from Valinor*. A has emendations that are taken up in the text of B, and B has emendations taken up in C; almost all are characteristic metrical/verbal rearrangements, as for example in line 17:

A *in anguish mourning*, emended to the reading of B;
B *and in anguish mourn*, emended to the reading of C;
C *mourning in anguish*.

As generally in this book, earlier variants that have no bearing on names or story are not cited. Each text ends at the same point, but three further lines are roughly written in the margin of A (see note to line 146). I give now the text of the third version, C.

# THE FLIGHT OF THE NOLDOLI
## FROM VALINOR

A! the Trees of Light,    tall and shapely,
gold and silver,    more glorious than the sun,
than the moon more magical,    o'er the meads of the Gods
their fragrant frith    and flowerladen
gardens gleaming,    once gladly shone.                          5
In death they are darkened,    they drop their leaves
from blackened branches    bled by Morgoth
and Ungoliant the grim    the Gloomweaver.
In spider's form    despair and shadow
a shuddering fear    and shapeless night                       10
she weaves in a web    of winding venom
that is black and breathless.    Their branches fail,
the light and laughter    of their leaves are quenched.
Mirk goes marching,    mists of blackness,
through the halls of the Mighty    hushed and empty,           15
the gates of the Gods    are in gloom mantled.

Lo! the Elves murmur    mourning in anguish,
but no more shall be kindled    the mirth of Côr
in the winding ways    of their walled city,
towercrownèd Tûn,    whose twinkling lamps                     20
are drowned in darkness.    The dim fingers
of fog come floating    from the formless waste
and sunless seas.    The sound of horns,
of horses' hooves    hastening wildly
in hopeless hunt,    they hear afar,                           25
where the Gods in wrath    those guilty ones
through mournful shadow,    now mounting as a tide
o'er the Blissful Realm,    in blind dismay
pursue unceasing.    The city of the Elves
is thickly thronged.    On threadlike stairs                   30
carven of crystal    countless torches
stare and twinkle,    stain the twilight
and gleaming balusters    of green beryl.
A vague rumour    of rushing voices,
as myriads mount    the marble paths,                          35
there fills and troubles    those fair places
wide ways of Tûn    and walls of pearl.

Of the Three Kindreds    to that clamorous throng

are none but the Gnomes    in numbers drawn.
The Elves of Ing    to the ancient halls                               40
and starry gardens    that stand and gleam
upon Timbrenting    towering mountain
that day had climbed    to the cloudy-domed
mansions of Manwë    for mirth and song.
There Bredhil the Blessed    the bluemantled,              45
the Lady of the heights    as lovely as the snow
in lights gleaming    of the legions of the stars,
the cold immortal    Queen of mountains,
too fair and terrible    too far and high
for mortal eyes,    in Manwë's court                          50
sat silently    as they sang to her.

The Foam-riders,    folk of waters,
Elves of the endless    echoing beaches,
of the bays and grottoes    and the blue lagoons,
of silver sands    sown with moonlit,                         55
starlit, sunlit,    stones of crystal,
paleburning gems    pearls and opals,
on their shining shingle,    where now shadows groping
clutched their laughter,    quenched in mourning
their mirth and wonder,    in amaze wandered            60
under cliffs grown cold    calling dimly,
or in shrouded ships    shuddering waited
for the light no more    should be lit for ever.

But the Gnomes were numbered    by name and kin,
marshalled and ordered    in the mighty square          65
upon the crown of Côr.    There cried aloud
the fierce son of Finn.    Flaming torches
he held and whirled    in his hands aloft,
those hands whose craft    the hidden secret
knew, that none    Gnome or mortal                           70
hath matched or mastered    in magic or in skill.
'Lo! slain is my sire    by the sword of fiends,
his death he has drunk    at the doors of his hall
and deep fastness,    where darkly hidden
the Three were guarded,    the things unmatched       75
that Gnome and Elf    and the Nine Valar
can never remake    or renew on earth,
recarve or rekindle    by craft or magic,
not Fëanor Finn's son    who fashioned them of yore –

the light is lost    whence he lit them first,                    80
the fate of Faërie    hath found its hour

Thus the witless wisdom    its reward hath earned
of the Gods' jealousy,    who guard us here
to serve them, sing to them    in our sweet cages,
to contrive them gems    and jewelled trinkets,              85
their leisure to please    with our loveliness,
while they waste and squander    work of ages,
nor can Morgoth master    in their mansions sitting
at countless councils.    Now come ye all,
who have courage and hope!    My call harken            90
to flight, to freedom    in far places!
The woods of the world    whose wide mansions
yet in darkness dream    drowned in slumber,
the pathless plains    and perilous shores
no moon yet shines on    nor mounting dawn              95
in dew and daylight    hath drenched for ever,
far better were these    for bold footsteps
than gardens of the Gods    gloom-encircled
with idleness filled    and empty days.
Yea! though the light lit them    and the loveliness      100
beyond heart's desire    that hath held us slaves
here long and long.    But that light is dead.
Our gems are gone,    our jewels ravished;
and the Three, my Three,    thrice-enchanted
globes of crystal    by gleam undying                          105
illumined, lit    by living splendour
and all hues' essence,    their eager flame –
Morgoth has them    in his monstrous hold,
my Silmarils.    I swear here oaths,
unbreakable bonds    to bind me ever,                        110
by Timbrenting    and the timeless halls
of Bredhil the Blessed    that abides thereon –
may she hear and heed –    to hunt endlessly
unwearying unwavering    through world and sea,
through leaguered lands,    lonely mountains,            115
over fens and forest    and the fearful snows,
till I find those fair ones,    where the fate is hid
of the folk of Elfland    and their fortune locked,
where alone now lies    the light divine.'

Then his sons beside him,    the seven kinsmen,          120

crafty Curufin,    Celegorm the fair,
Damrod and Díriel    and dark Cranthir,
Maglor the mighty,    and Maidros tall
(the eldest, whose ardour    yet more eager burnt
than his father's flame,    than Fëanor's wrath;                    125
him fate awaited    with fell purpose),
these leapt with laughter    their lord beside,
with linkëd hands    there lightly took
the oath unbreakable;    blood thereafter
it spilled like a sea    and spent the swords                    130
of endless armies,    nor hath ended yet:

'Be he friend or foe    or foul offspring
of Morgoth Bauglir,    be he mortal dark
that in after days    on earth shall dwell,
shall no law nor love    nor league of Gods,                    135
no might nor mercy,    not moveless fate,
defend him for ever    from the fierce vengeance
of the sons of Fëanor,    whoso seize or steal
or finding keep    the fair enchanted
globes of crystal    whose glory dies not,                    140
the Silmarils.    We have sworn for ever!'

Then a mighty murmuring    was moved abroad
and the harkening host    hailed them roaring:
'Let us go! yea go    from the Gods for ever
on Morgoth's trail    o'er the mountains of the world                    145
to vengeance and victory!    Your vows are ours!'

The poem ends here (but see note to line 146).

★

# NOTES

41    *starry gardens* C, *starlit domes* A, B.

42    *Tengwethil's* A (with *Timbrenting* written in margin), *Timbrenting's* B, *Timbrenting* C (with *Taingwethil* written in margin). See note to *The Children of Húrin* (second version) line 812.

45    *Bridhil* A, B, C, emended in C to *Bredhil*; so also at line 112.

107    *and all hues' essence*: this half-line (in the form *all hue's*

*essence*) occurs also in the second version of *The Children of Húrin*, line 381, where it is said of the Silmaril of Beren.

111  *Tengwethil* A, *Timbrenting* B, C.

134  *that in after days   on earth shall dwell*: this line bracketed later in pencil in C.

146  There are three roughly-written lines in the margin of the last page of A which were not taken up in B and C, but which presumably follow on line 146:

> But Finweg cried    Fingolfin's son
> when his father found    that fair counsel,
> that wit and wisdom    were of worth no more:
> 'Fools

## Commentary on *The Flight of the Noldoli*

Sad as it is that this poem was abandoned so soon – when in full mastery of the alliterative line my father might have gone on to recount the Kinslaying of Alqualondë, the Prophecy of the North, the crossing of the Helcaraxë, and the burning of the ships, there is nonetheless in its few lines much of interest for the study of the development of the legend. Most notably, there here appears the earliest version of the actual words of the Fëanorian Oath. The Oath was first referred to in the outlines for *Gilfanon's Tale* (I. 238, 240):

> The Seven Sons of Fëanor swore their terrible oath of hatred for ever against all, Gods or Elves or Men, who should hold the Silmarils

but it was there sworn after the coming of the Elves from Valinor, and after the death of Fëanor. In the present poem is the first appearance of the story that the Oath was taken in Valinor before the departure of the Gnomes. It has also been referred to in *The Children of Húrin*, lines 631 ff. of the first version, where it is implied that the mountain of Tain-Gwethil was taken in witness – as it was in *The Silmarillion* (p. 83): here (line 111) Fëanor himself swears by Timbrenting that he will never cease to hunt for the Silmarils.

I cannot explain why line 134

> that in after days   on earth shall dwell

was bracketed (always a mark of exclusion or at least of doubtful retention) in the C-text. The line reappears in identical form in the *Lay of Leithian* (Canto VI, 1636); cf. *The Silmarillion* 'Vala, Demon, Elf or Man as yet unborn'.

The fixed epithets of certain of the Sons of Fëanor are changed from those in *The Children of Húrin* (see p. 86): Celegorm is now 'the fair' and Maidros 'the tall', as they remained; Maglor is 'the mighty' (in *The Silmarillion* 'the mighty singer'). The line concerning Maidros him fate awaited   with fell purpose       (126)

may show that a form of the story of his end was already in being (in the *Tale of the Nauglafring* he survived the attack on Dior the Fair but nothing more is told of him), but I think it much more likely that it refers to his capture and maiming by Morgoth.

    In Fëanor's speech occur two interesting references: to *the Nine Valar*, and to his father *Finn*. The number of the Valar is nowhere stated in the *Lost Tales* (where in any case the name includes lesser divine beings; cf. e.g. I. 65–6 'With them came many of those lesser Vali . . . the Mánir and the Súruli, the sylphs of the airs and of the winds'); but 'the Nine Valar' are referred to in the 'Sketch of the Mythology' (1926) and named in the 1930 'Silmarillion': Manwë, Ulmo, Ossë, Aulë, Mandos, Lórien, Tulkas, Oromë, and Melko.

    Fëanor's father has not been named since the tale of *The Theft of Melko and the Darkening of Valinor* (I. 145 ff.), where he was called Bruithwir, slain by Melko. In *The Children of Húrin* there is no indication that Fëanor was akin to other princes of the Gnomes – though there can be no doubt that by that time he in fact was so. But the essential features of the Noldorin royal house as it had now emerged and as it was to remain for many years can now be deduced. In the first version of *The Children of Húrin* (line 29 and note) Turgon was the son of Finwë (actually spelt *Finweg*), as he had been in the *Lost Tales* (I. 115), but this was changed to Finwë's heir, with the note 'he was Fingolfin's son'; and in the second version *Turgon the mighty, / Fingolfin's son* is found in the text as written (48–9). We thus have:

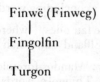

Finwë (Finweg)

|

Fingolfin

|

Turgon

Further, *Finweg* appears in *The Children of Húrin* (first version 1975, second version 19, 520) as the King of the Gnomes who died in the Battle of Unnumbered Tears; in two of these cases the name was later changed to *Fingon*. In the lines added at the end of the A-text of *The Flight of the Noldoli* (note to line 146) Finweg is Fingolfin's son. We can therefore add:

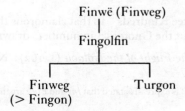

Finwë (Finweg)

|

Fingolfin

                 |

Finweg          Turgon
(> Fingon)

Now in *The Flight of the Noldoli* Fëanor is called Finn's son; and in the
'Sketch of the Mythology' Finn is given as an alternative to Finwë:

> The Eldar are divided into three hosts, one under Ingwë (Ing) . . ., one
> under Finwë (Finn) after called the Noldoli . . .*

Thus Fëanor has become Fingolfin's brother:

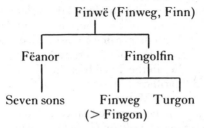

Finwë (Finweg, Finn)

Fëanor        Fingolfin

Seven sons      Finweg    Turgon
               (> Fingon)

(Only in a later note to lines 1713–20 of *The Children of Húrin* has
Finwë's third son Finrod appeared, father of Felagund, Angrod, Egnor,
and Orodreth.)

Fëanor's speech also contains a curious foreknowledge of the making
of the Sun and Moon (92–6):

> The woods of the world    whose wide mansions
> yet in darkness dream    drowned in slumber,
> the pathless plains    and perilous shores
> no moon yet shines on    nor mounting dawn
> in dew and daylight    hath drenched for ever

Very notable are Fëanor's concluding words (117–18):

> till I find those fair ones,    where the fate is hid
> of the folk of Elfland    and their fortune locked

Cf. *The Silmarillion*, p. 67: 'Mandos foretold that the fates of Arda lay
locked within them', and Thingol's words to Beren (*ibid.* p. 167):
'though the fate of Arda lie within the Silmarils, yet you shall hold me
generous'. It is clear that the Silmarils had already gained greatly in
significance since the earliest period of the mythology (see I. 156, 169
note 2; II. 259).

In no other version is Fëanor seen on this occasion holding flaming
torches in his hands and whirling them aloft.

The lines (38–9)

> Of the Three Kindreds    to that clamorous throng
> are none but the Gnomes    in numbers drawn

go back to the tale of *The Flight of the Noldoli* (I. 162): 'Now when . . .

---

* In the 1930 'Silmarillion' it is expressly stated that *Ing* and *Finn* are the Gnomish forms
of *Ingwë* and *Finwë*.

Fëanor sees that far the most of the company is of the kin of the Noldor', on which I noted (I. 169) 'It is to be remembered that in the old story the Teleri (i.e. the later Vanyar) had not departed from Kôr.' Later evidence shows that the old story had not been changed; but the fact that in the present poem *the Elves of Ing* (Ingwë) were on Timbrenting (Taniquetil) in the mansions of Manwë and Varda shows the entry of the later narrative (found in the 'Sketch') of the destruction of the Trees. In the old tale of *The Theft of Melko and the Darkening of Valinor* (I. 143 ff. and commentary I. 157) the great festival was the occasion of Melko's attack on the place of the Gnomes' banishment northward in Valinor, the slaying of Fëanor's father, and the theft of the Silmarils; and the destruction of the Trees followed some time afterwards. Now however the festival is the occasion of the attack on the Trees; the First Kindred are on Taniquetil but most of the Gnomes are not.

The name by which Varda is here called, Bridhil the Blessed (changed in C to Bredhil), is found in the old Gnomish dictionary, and also Timbridhil (I. 269, 273, entries *Tinwetári, Varda*). On *Timbrenting* see p. 127, where the form *Tindbrenting* occurring in *The Children of Húrin* (in a note to second version line 812) is discussed. Both forms are found in the 'Sketch':

Timbrenting or Tindbrenting in English, Tengwethil in Gnomish, Taniquetil in Elfin.

The form with -*m*- is therefore evidently due to a change of pronunciation in English, *ndb* > *mb*.

In line 41 the earlier reading *starlit domes*, changed to *starry gardens*, is probably to be related to the account in the tale of *The Coming of the Valar and the Building of Valinor* of Manwë's abode on Taniquetil (I. 73):

That house was builded of marbles white and blue and stood amid the fields of snow, and its roofs were made of a web of that blue air called *ilwë* that is above the white and grey. This web did Aulë and his wife contrive, but Varda spangled it with stars, and Manwë dwelt thereunder.

This idea of a roof lit with stars was never lost and appears in a changed form long after, though it is not mentioned in *The Silmarillion*.
The lines (21–3)

The dim fingers

of fog came floating     from the formless waste
and sunless seas

find an echo in *The Silmarillion* (p. 76):

it blew chill from the East in that hour, and the vast shadows of the sea were rolled against the walls of the shore.

The lines at the end of the A-text (note to line 146) show that Fingolfin has taken Finwë Nólemë's place as the voice of reason and moderation amid the revolutionary enthusiasm of the Noldoli in the great square of Kôr (see I. 162, 171).

Lastly may be noticed the term 'Foam-riders' used (line 52) of the Third Kindred (the Solosimpi of the *Lost Tales*, later the Teleri); this has been used once before, in *Ælfwine of England* (II. 314), where it is said of Ælfwine's mother Éadgifu that when he was born

> the Foamriders, the Elves of the Sea-marge, whom she had known of old in Lionesse, sent messengers to his birth.

### *Analysis of the metre of the poem*

At the end of the second text (B) of *The Flight of the Noldoli* my father made an analysis of the metrical forms of the first 20 and certain subsequent lines. For his analysis and explanation of the Old English metre see *On Translating Beowulf*, in *The Monsters and the Critics and Other Essays*, 1983, pp. 61 ff. The letters A, + A, B, C, D, E on the left-hand side of the table refer to the 'types' of Old English half-line; the letters beneath the analyses of 'lifts' and 'dips' are the alliterations employed in each line, with O used for any vowel (since all vowels 'alliterate' with each other) and X for a consonant beginning a lift but not forming part of the alliterative scheme of the line; the words 'full', 'simple', etc. refer to the nature of the alliterative pattern in each case.

| 1 | B | A | ∪∪ ∕T ∪∕X | ‖ | ∕T ∪∕X ∪ | simple |
|---|---|---|---|---|---|---|
| 2 | A | B | ∕G ∪∕S ∪ | ‖ | ∪∕G(∪)∪∪∪ ∕S | crossed |
| 3 | +A | B | ∪∪∣∕M ∪⌢∕M ∪ | ‖ | ∪∪ ∕M ∪∪ ∕X | full |
| 4 | B | C | ∪∕F ∪∕F | ‖ | ∪∕F ∕X ∪ | full |
| 5 | A | B | ∕G ∪∕G ∪ | ‖ | ∪∕G ∪∕X | full |
| 6 | +A | B | ∪∣∕D ∪∕D ∪ | ‖ | ∪∕D ∪∕X | full |
| 7 | C | A | ∪ ⌢∕B ∕B ∪ | ‖ | ∕B ∪∕X ∪ | full |
| 8 | B | C | ∪∪ ⌢∕G ∪∪∕G | ‖ | ∪∕G ∕X ∪ | full |
| 9 | B | B | ∪∕Sp ∪∕X | ‖ | ∪∕Sp ∪⌢∕X | simple |
| 10 | B | B | ∪⌢∕Sh ∪∕X | ‖ | ∪∕Sh ∪∕X | simple |
| 11 | B | B | ∪∕W ∪∪∕W | ‖ | ∪∕W ∪⌢∕X | full |
| 12 | C | B | ∪∪ ⌢∕B ∕B ∪ | ‖ | ∪∕B ∪∕X | full |
| 13 | +A | B | ∪∣∕L ∪∕L ∪ | ‖ | ∪∪∕L ∪∕X | full |

| 14 | A A | | full |
| 15 | +A A | | simple |
| 16 | B C | | full |
| 17 | C A | | double |
| 18 | +A B | | crossed |
| 19 | B C · | | full |
| 20 | E B | | full |
| 37 | E B | | simple + |
| 51 | D B | | full |
| 57 | E A | | simple |
| 61 | B A | | full |
| 67 | +E A | | full |
| 79 | +A B | | full |
| 107 | +A B | | full |

It may be noticed that the scansion of the first half of line 8 (with the first lift *-goli-*) shows that the primary stress fell on the second syllable of *Ungóliant*; and that *sp* can only alliterate with *sp* (lines 9, 130), as in Old English (the same is of course true of *sh*, which is a separate consonant).

★

## (ii) *Fragment of an alliterative Lay of Eärendel*

There exists one other piece of alliterative verse concerned with the matter of the *Lost Tales*, the opening of a poem that has no title and does not extend far enough to make clear what its subject was to be. The fall of Gondolin, the escape of the fugitives down the secret tunnel, the fight at Cristhorn, and the long wandering in the wilds thereafter, are passed over rapidly in what were to be the introductory lines, and the subject seems about to appear at the end of the fragment:

> all this have others    in ancient stories
> and songs unfolded,    but say I further . . .

and the concluding lines refer to the sojourn of the fugitives in the Land of Willows. But at the end of the text my father wrote several times in different scripts 'Earendel', 'Earendel son of Fengel', 'Earendel Fengelsson'; and I think it extremely likely, even almost certain, that this poem was to be a Lay of Eärendel. (On Fengel see the next section.)

The text is in the first stage of composition and is exceedingly rough, but it contains one line of the utmost interest for the history of Eärendel. It is written on examination paper from the University of Leeds and clearly belongs in time with *The Lay of the Children of Húrin* and *The Flight of the Noldoli*: more than that seems impossible to say.

> Lo! the flame of fire     and fierce hatred
> engulfed Gondolin     and its glory fell,
> its tapering towers     and its tall rooftops
> were laid all low,     and its leaping fountains
> made no music more     on the mount of Gwareth,                    5
> and its whitehewn walls     were whispering ash.
> { But Wade of the Helsings     wearyhearted }
> { Tûr the earthborn     was tried in battle }
> from the wrack and ruin     a remnant led
> women and children     and wailing maidens
> and wounded men     of the withered folk                          10
> down the path unproven     that pierced the hillside,
> neath Tumladin he led them     to the leaguer of hills
> that rose up rugged     as ranged pinnacles
> to the north of the vale.     There the narrow way
> of Cristhorn was cloven,     the Cleft of Eagles,                  15
> through the midmost mountains.     And more is told
> in lays and in legend     and lore of others
> of that weary way     of the wandering folk;
> how the waifs of Gondolin     outwitted Melko,
> vanished o'er the vale     and vanquished the hills,               20
> how Glorfindel the golden     in the gap of the Eagles
> battled with the Balrog     and both were slain:
> one like flash of fire     from fangéd rock,
> one like bolted thunder     black was smitten
> to the dreadful deep     digged by Thornsir.                       25
> Of the thirst and hunger     of the thirty moons
> when they sought for Sirion     and were sore bestead
> by plague and peril;     of the Pools of Twilight
> and Land of Willows;     when their lamentation
> was heard in the halls     where the high Gods sate               30
> veiled in Valinor     . . the Vanished Isles;
> all this have others     in ancient stories
> and songs unfolded,     but say I further
> how their lot was lightened,     how they laid them down
> in long grasses     of the Land of Willows.                       35
> There sun was softer,     . . . the sweet breezes
> and whispering winds,     there wells of slumber
> and the dew enchanted

★

# NOTES

25    The next lines are

> where stony-voicéd    that stream of Eagles
> runs o'er the rocky

but the second of these is struck out and the first left without
continuation.

31    The second half-line was written *in the Vanished Isles*, but *in* was
struck out and replaced by a word that I cannot interpret.

36    The second half-line was written *and the sweet breezes*, but *and*
was struck out and replaced by some other word, possibly *then*.

## Commentary

For the form *Tûr* see II. 148, 260.

In the tale of *The Fall of Gondolin* Cristhorn, the Eagles' Cleft, was in
the Encircling Mountains south of Gondolin, and the secret tunnel led
southwards from the city (II. 167–8 etc.); but from line 14 of this
fragment it is seen that the change to the north had already entered the
legend.

Lines 26–7 (*the thirty moons    when they sought for Sirion*) go
back to the *Fall of Gondolin*, where it is said that the fugitives wandered
'a year and more' in the wastes (see II. 195, 214).

The reading of line 7 as first written (it was not struck out, but *Tûr the
earthborn    was tried in battle* was added in the margins):

> But Wade of the Helsings    wearyhearted

is remarkable. It is taken directly from the very early Old English poem
*Widsith*, where occurs the line *Wada Hælsingum*, sc. *Wada* [*weold*]
*Hælsingum*, 'Wada ruled the Hælsingas'. One may well wonder why the
mysterious figure of Wade should appear here in Tuor's place, and
indeed I cannot explain it: but whatever the reason, the association of
Wade with Tuor is not casual. Of the original story of Wade almost
nothing is known; but he survived in popular recollection through the
Middle Ages and later – he is mentioned by Malory as a mighty being,
and Chaucer refers to 'Wade's boat' in *The Merchant's Tale*; in *Troilus
and Crisyede* Pandare told a 'tale of Wade'. R. W. Chambers (*Widsith*,
Cambridge 1912, p. 95) said that Wade was perhaps 'originally a sea-
giant, dreaded and honoured by the coast tribes of the North Sea and the
Baltic'; and the tribe of the Hælsingas over which he is said to have ruled
in *Widsith* is supposed to have left its name in Helsingör (Elsinore) in
Denmark and in Helsingfors in Finland. Chambers summed up what
few generalities he thought might be made from the scattered references
in English and German as follows:

We find these common characteristics, which we may assume belonged to their ancient prototype, Wada of the Hælsingas:

(1) Power over the sea.
(2) Extraordinary strength – often typified by superhuman stature.
(3) The use of these powers to help those whom Wade favours.

. . . Probably he grew out of the figure, not of a historic chief, but of a supernatural power, who had no story all his own, and who interested mortal men only when he interfered in their concerns. Hence he is essentially a helper in time of need; and we may be fairly confident that already in the oldest lays he possessed this character.

Most interesting, however, is the fact that in Speght's annotations to Chaucer (1598) he said:

Concerning Wade and his bote *Guingelot*, as also his strange exploits in the same, because the matter is long and fabulous, I passe it over.

The likeness of *Guingelot* to *Wingelot* is sufficiently striking; but when we place together the facts that Wingelot was Eärendel's ship,* that Eärendel was Tuor's son, that Tuor was peculiarly associated with the sea, and that here 'Wade of the Helsings' stands in the place of Tuor, coincidence is ruled out. *Wingelot* was derived from Wade's boat *Guingelot* as certainly, I think, as was Eärendel from the Old English figure (this latter being a fact expressly stated by my father, II. 309).

Why my father should have intruded 'Wade of the Helsings' into the verses at this point is another question. It may conceivably have been unintentional – the words *Wada Hælsingum* were running in his mind (though in that case one might expect that he would have struck the line out and not merely written another line against it as an alternative): but at any rate the reason why they were running in his mind is clear, and this possibility in no way diminishes the demonstrative value of the line that *Wingelot* was derived from *Guingelot*, and that there was a connection of greater significance than the mere taking over of a name – just as in the case of Eärendel.

(iii)   *The Lay of the Fall of Gondolin*

This was the title that late in his life my father wrote on the bundle of papers constituting the abandoned beginning of this poem; but it seems that it was not conceived on a large scale, since the narrative had reached

---

*In which he undertook 'fabulous exploits'. It is conceivable that there was some connection between Eärendel's great world-girdling voyage and the travels of Wade as described by the twelfth-century English writer Walter Map, who tells how *Gado* (sc. Wade) journeyed in his boat to the furthest Indies.

the dragon-fire arising over the northern heights already within 130 lines. That he composed it while at the University of Leeds is certain, but I strongly suspect that it was the first versification of matter from the *Lost Tales* undertaken, before he turned to the alliterative line. The story, so far as it goes, has undergone virtually no development from the prose tale of *The Fall of Gondolin*, and the closeness of the Lay to the Tale can be seen from this comparison (though the passage is exceptional):

(Tale, II. 158)
> Rejoice that ye have found it, for behold before you the City of Seven Names where all who war with Melko may find hope.'
> Then said Tuor: 'What be those names?' And the chief of the Guard made answer: "'Tis said and 'tis sung: "Gondobar am I called and Gondothlimbar, City of Stone and City of the Dwellers in Stone, &c.

(Lay)
> Rejoice that ye have found it and rest from endless war,
> For the seven-naméd city 'tis that stands upon the hill,
> Where all who strive with Morgoth find hope and valour still.'
> 'What be those names,' said Tuor, 'for I come from long afar?'
> "'Tis said and 'tis sung,' one answered, '"My name is Gondobar
> And Gondothlimbar also, the City hewn of Stone,
> The fortress of the Gnome-folk who dwell in Halls of Stone, &c.

I do not give this poem *in extenso* here, since it does not, so far as the main narrative is concerned, add anything to the Tale; and my father found, as I think, the metrical form unsuitable to the purpose. There are, however, several passages of interest for the study of the larger development of the legends.

In the *Tale*, Tuor was the son of Peleg (who was the son of Indor, II. 160), but here he is the son of Fengel; while on a scrap of paper giving rough workings of the passage cited above* Tuor himself is called Fengel – cf. 'Eärendel son of Fengel' at the end of the fragment of an Eärendel Lay, p. 141. Long afterwards Fengel was the name of the fifteenth King of Rohan in the Third Age, grandfather of Théoden, and there it is the Old English noun *fengel* 'king, prince'.

There are some puzzling statements made concerning Fingolfin, whose appearance here, I feel certain, is earlier than those in the alliterative poems; and the passage in which he appears introduces also the story of Isfin and Eöl.

---

*This is the page referred to in *Unfinished Tales* p. 4: 'some lines of verse in which appear the Seven Names of Gondolin are scribbled on the back of a piece of paper setting out "the chain of responsibility in a battalion".' Not knowing at that time where this isolated scrap came from I took this as an indication of very early date, but this is certainly mistaken: the paper must have survived and been used years later for rough writing.

Lo, that prince of Gondobar [Meglin]
dark Eöl's son whom Isfin, in a mountain dale afar
in the gloom of Doriath's forest, the white-limbed maiden bare,
the daughter of Fingolfin, Gelmir's mighty heir.
'Twas the bent blades of the Glamhoth that drank Fingolfin's life
as he stood alone by Fëanor; but his maiden and his wife
were wildered as they sought him in the forests of the night,
in the pathless woods of Doriath, so dark that as a light
of palely mirrored moonsheen were their slender elfin limbs
straying among the black holes where only the dim bat skims
from Thû's dark-delvéd caverns. There Eöl saw that sheen
and he caught the white-limbed Isfin, that she ever since hath been
his mate in Doriath's forest, where she weepeth in the gloam;
for the Dark Elves were his kindred that wander without home.
Meglin she sent to Gondolin, and his honour there was high
as the latest seed of Fingolfin, whose glory shall not die;
a lordship he won of the Gnome-folk who quarry deep in the earth,
seeking their ancient jewels; but little was his mirth,
and dark he was and secret and his hair as the strands of night
that are tangled in Taur Fuin* the forest without light.

In the *Lost Tales* Finwë Nólemë, first Lord of the Noldoli, was the
father of Turgon (and so of Isfin, who was Turgon's sister), I. 115;
Finwë Nólemë was slain in the Battle of Unnumbered Tears and his
heart cut out by Orcs, but Turgon rescued the body and heart of his
father, and the Scarlet Heart became his grim emblem (I. 241, II. 172).
Finwë Nólemë is also called Fingolma (I. 238–9, II. 220).

In the alliterative poems Fingolfin is the son of Finwë (Finweg) and
the father of Turgon, and also of Finweg (> Fingon), as he was to remain
(see p. 137).     Thus:

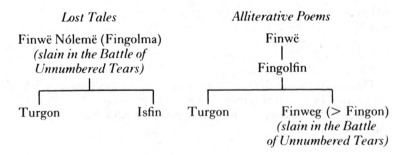

| *Lost Tales* | *Alliterative Poems* |
|---|---|

Finwë Nólemë (Fingolma)                         Finwë
    *(slain in the Battle of*                           |
    *Unnumbered Tears)*                            Fingolfin

Turgon          Isfin          Turgon          Finweg (> Fingon)
                                                              *(slain in the Battle*
                                                              *of Unnumbered Tears)*

But whereas in the *Lay of the Fall of Gondolin* Fingolfin has

---

*Taur Fuin* is the form in the *Lost Tales*; it was here emended later to *Taur-na-Fuin*,
which is the form from the first in *The Children of Húrin*.

emerged and stepped into Finwë's place as the father of Turgon and Isfin, he is not here the son of Finwë but of one *Gelmir*:

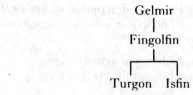

Gelmir
|
Fingolfin

Turgon    Isfin

In an early prose text – one of the very few scraps (to be given in the next volume) that bridge the gap in the prose history between the *Lost Tales* and the 'Sketch of the Mythology' – Gelmir appears as the King of the Noldoli at the time of the flight from Valinor, and one of his sons is there named *Golfin*.

There is too little evidence extant (if there ever was any more written down) to penetrate with certainty the earliest evolution of the Noldorin kings. The simplest explanation is that this Gelmir, father of Golfin/ Fingolfin = Fingolma/Finwë Nólemë, father of Fingolfin. But it is also said in this passage that Fingolfin was slain by the Glamhoth 'as he stood alone by Fëanor', and whatever story lies behind this is now vanished (for the earliest, very obscure, references to the death of Fëanor see I. 238–9).

This passage from the *Lay of the Fall of Gondolin* contains the first account of the story of Eöl the Dark Elf, Isfin sister of Turgon, and their son Meglin (for a very primitive form of the legend see II. 220). In the prose tale of *The Fall of Gondolin* the story is dismissed in the words 'that tale of Isfin and Eöl may not here be told', II. 165. In the Lay, Fingolfin's wife and daughter (Isfin) *were seeking for him* when Isfin was taken by Eöl. Since in the 'Sketch' Isfin was lost in Taur-na-Fuin after the Battle of Unnumbered Tears and there trapped by Eöl, it is possible that at this stage Fingolfin was the Elvish king who died (beside Fëanor?) in the great battle. It is also possible that we see here the genesis of the idea of Isfin's wandering in the wilds, although of course with subsequent shifts, whereby Fingolfin died in duel with Morgoth after the Battle of Sudden Flame and Fingon (Isfin's brother) was the Noldorin king slain in the Battle of Unnumbered Tears, the story that she was seeking her father was abandoned. What this passage does certainly show is that the story of Isfin's sending her son to Gondolin is original, but that originally Isfin remained with her captor Eöl and never escaped from him.

Eöl here dwells 'in a mountain dale afar in the gloom of Doriath's forest', 'in the forests of the night', 'where only the dim bat skims from Thû's dark-delvéd caverns'. This must be the earliest reference to Thû, and at any rate in connected writing the earliest to Doriath (Artanor of the *Lost Tales*). I have suggested (II. 63) that in the *Tale of Tinúviel*

'Artanor was conceived as a great region of forest in the heart of which was Tinwelint's cavern', and that the zone of the Queen's protection 'was originally less distinctly bordered, and less extensive, than "the Girdle of Melian" afterwards became'. Here the description of Eöl's habitation in a forest without light (where Thû lives in caverns) suggests rather the forest of Taur-na-Fuin, where

> Never-dawning night   was netted clinging
> in the black branches   of the beetling trees

and where

>                                  goblins even
> (whose deep eyes drill   the darkest shadows)
> bewildered wandered
>           (*The Children of Húrin*, p. 34, lines 753 ff.)

The passage also contains an interesting reference to the purpose of the miners of Gondolin: 'seeking their ancient jewels.'

Earlier in this Lay some lines are given to the coming of Tuor to the hidden door beneath the Encircling Mountains:

> Thither Tuor son of Fengel came out of the dim land
> that the Gnomes have called Dor-Lómin, with Bronweg at his hand,
> who fled from the Iron Mountains and had broken Melko's chain
> and cast his yoke of evil, of torment and bitter pain;
> who alone most faithful-hearted led Tuor by long ways
> through empty hills and valleys by dark nights and perilous days,
> till his blue lamp magic-kindled, where flow the shadowy rills
> beneath enchanted alders, found that Gate beneath the hills,
> the door in dark Dungorthin that only the Gnome-folk knew.

In a draft for this passage the name here is *Nan Orwen*, emended to *Dungorthin*. In *The Children of Húrin* (lines 1457 ff.) Túrin and Flinding came to this 'grey valley' after they had passed west over Sirion, and reached the roots of the Shadowy Mountains 'that Hithlum girdle'. For earlier references to Nan Dungorthin and different placings of it see p. 87; the present passage seems to indicate yet another, with the hidden door of Gondolin opening into it.

A few other passages may be noticed. At the beginning there is a reference to old songs telling

> how the Gods in council gathered on the outmost rocky bars
> of the Lonely Island westward, and devised a land of ease
> beyond the great sea-shadows and the shadowy seas;
> how they made the deep gulf of Faërie with long and lonely shore . . .

That the Gods were ferried on an island by Ossë and the Oarni at the time of the fall of the Lamps is told in the tale of *The Coming of the Valar*

(I. 70), and that this isle was afterwards that of the Elves' ferrying (becoming Tol Eressëa) is told in *The Coming of the Elves* (I. 118). When Gondolin was built the people cried 'Côr is built anew!' and the guard who told Tuor the seven names said:

> Loth, the Flower, they name me, saying 'Côr is born again,
> even in Loth-a-ladwen,* the Lily of the Plain.'

I have noticed earlier (II. 208) that whereas it is explicit in *The Silmaril-lion* that Turgon devised the city to be 'a memorial of Tirion upon Túna', and it became 'as beautiful as a memory of Elven Tirion', this is not said in *The Fall of Gondolin*: Turgon was born in the Great Lands after the return of the Noldoli from Valinor, and had never known Kôr: 'One may feel nonetheless that the tower of the King, the fountains and stairs, the white marbles of Gondolin embody a recollection of Kôr as it is described in *The Coming of the Elves and the Making of Kôr* (I. 122–3).'

There is also a reference to Eärendel

> who passed the Gates of Dread,
> half-mortal and half-elfin, undying and long dead.

The Gates of Dread are probably the gates of the Door of Night, through which Eärendel passed (II. 255).

---

*This is the only point in which the Seven Names differ from their forms in the *Tale* (II. 158). In the *Tale* the name of the city as 'Lily of the Valley' is *Lothengriol*. For *ladwen* 'plain' see II. 344. In a draft of the passage in the lay the name was *Loth Barodrin*.

# III
# THE LAY OF LEITHIAN

My father wrote in his diary that he began 'the poem of Tinúviel' during the period of the summer examinations of 1925 (see p. 3), and he abandoned it in September 1931 (see below), when he was 39. The rough workings for the whole poem are extant (and 'rough' means very rough indeed); from them he wrote a fair copy, which I shall call 'A'.*

On this manuscript A my father most uncharacteristically inserted dates, the first of these being at line 557 (August 23, 1925); and he composed the last hundred-odd lines of the third Canto (ending at line 757) while on holiday at Filey on the Yorkshire coast in September 1925. The next date is two and a half years and 400 lines later, 27–28 March 1928 written against line 1161; and thereafter each day for a further nine days, till 6 April 1928, is marked, during which time he wrote out no less than 1768 lines, to 2929.

Since the dates refer to the copying of verses out fair in the manuscript, not to their actual composition, it might be thought that they prove little; but the rough workings of lines 2497–2504 are written on an abandoned letter dated 1 April 1928, and these lines were written in the fair copy A on 4 April – showing that lines 2505–2929 were actually composed between 1 and 6 April. I think therefore that the dates on A can be taken as effectively indicating the time of composition.

The date November 1929 (at line 3031) is followed by a substantial amount of composition in the last week of September 1930, and again in the middle of September 1931; the last date is 17 September of that year against line 4085 very near the point where the Lay was abandoned. Details of the dates are given in the Notes.

There is also a typescript text ('B') made by my father, of which the last few hundred lines are in manuscript, and this text ends at precisely the same point as does A. This typescript was begun quite early, since my father mentioned in his diary for 16 August 1926 having done 'a little typing of part of *Tinúviel*'; and before the end of 1929 he gave it to C. S. Lewis to read. On 7 December of that year Lewis wrote to him about it, saying:

> I sat up late last night and have read the *Geste* as far as to where Beren and his gnomish allies defeat the patrol of orcs above the sources of the

---

*This was written on the backs of examination-scripts, tied together and prepared as a blank manuscript: it was large enough to last through the six years, and a few scripts at the end of the bundle remained unused.

Narog and disguise themselves in the *rēaf* [Old English: 'garments, weapons, taken from the slain']. I can quite honestly say that it is ages since I have had an evening of such delight: and the personal interest of reading a friend's work had very little to do with it. I should have enjoyed it just as well as if I'd picked it up in a bookshop, by an unknown author. The two things that come out clearly are the sense of reality in the background and the mythical value: the essence of a myth being that it should have no taint of allegory to the maker and yet should suggest incipient allegories to the reader,

Lewis had thus reached in his reading about line 2017. He had evidently received more; it may be that the typescript by this time extended to the attack on Lúthien and Beren by Celegorm and Curufin fleeing from Nargothrond, against which (at line 3031) is the date November 1929 in the manuscript. Some time after this, probably early in 1930, Lewis sent my father 14 pages of detailed criticism, as far as line 1161 (if there was any more it has not survived). This criticism he contrived as a heavily academic commentary on the text, pretending to treat the Lay as an ancient and anonymous work extant in many more or less corrupt manuscripts, overlaid by scribal perversions in antiquity and the learned argumentation of nineteenth-century scholars; and thus entertainingly took the sting from some sharply expressed judgements, while at the same time in this disguise expressing strong praise for particular passages. Almost all the verses which Lewis found wanting for one reason or another are marked for revision in the typescript B if not actually rewritten, and in many cases his proposed emendations, or modifications of them, are incorporated into the text. The greater part of Lewis's commentary is given on pp. 315 ff., with the verses he criticised and the alterations made as a result.

My father abandoned the Lay at the point where the jaws of Carcharoth *crashed together like a trap* on Beren's hand and the Silmaril was engulfed, but though he never advanced beyond that place in the narrative, he did not abandon it for good. When *The Lord of the Rings* was finished he returned to the Lay again and recast the first two Cantos and a good part of the third, and small portions of some others.

To summarise the elements of this history:

(1)   Rough workings of the whole poem, composed 1925–31.
(2)   Manuscript A of the whole poem, written out progressively during 1925–31.
(3)   Typescript B of the whole poem (ending in manuscript), already in progress in 1926.

     This typescript given to C. S. Lewis towards the end of 1929, when it extended probably to about line 3031.

(4)    Recasting of the opening Cantos and parts of some others (after
the completion of *The Lord of the Rings*).

---

The manuscript A was emended, both by changes and insertions, at
different times, the majority of these alterations being incorporated in
the typescript B; while in B, as typed, there are further changes not
found in A.

The amount of emendation made to B varies very greatly. My father
used it as a basis for the later rewritings, and in these parts the old
typescript is entirely covered with new verses; but for long stretches – by
far the greater part of the poem – the text is untouched save for very
minor and as it were casual modifications to individual lines here and
there.

After much experimentation I have concluded that to make a single
text, an amalgam derived from the latest writing throughout the poem,
would be wholly mistaken. Quite apart from the practical difficulty of
changed names in the rewritten parts that do not scan in the old lines, the
later verse in its range and technical accomplishment is too distinct; too
much time had passed, and in the small amount that my father rewrote of
the *Lay of Leithian* after *The Lord of the Rings* we have fragments of a
new poem: from which we can gain an idea of what might have been. I
have therefore excised these parts, and give them subsequently and
separately (Chapter IV).

A further reason for doing so lies in the purpose of this book, which
includes the consideration of the Lays as important stages in the evolution of the legends. Some of the revisions to the *Lay of Leithian* are at
least 30 years later than the commencement of the poem. From the point
of view of the 'history', therefore, the abandonment of the poem in or
soon after September 1931 constitutes a terminal point, and I have
excluded emendations to names that are (as I believe) certainly later than
that, but included those which are earlier.* In a case like that of
*Beleriand*, for instance, which was *Broseliand* for much of the poem in
B and always later emended to *Beleriand*, but had become *Beleriand* as
first written by line 3957, I give *Beleriand* throughout. On the other
hand I retain *Gnomes* since my father still used this in *The Hobbit*.

The many small changes made for metrical/stylistic reasons, however,
constitute a problem in the attempt to produce a '1931 text', since it
is often impossible to be sure to which 'phase' they belong. Some are

---

*This leads to inconsistent treatment of certain names as between the two long Lays, e.g.
*Finweg* son of Fingolfin in *The Children of Húrin* but *Fingon* in the *Lay of Leithian*.
*Finweg* survived into the 1930 version of 'The Silmarillion' but was early emended to
*Fingon*.

demonstrably very early – e.g. *candle flowers* emended to *flowering candles* (line 516), since C. S. Lewis commented on the latter – while others are demonstrably from many years later, and strictly speaking belong with the late rewritings; but many cannot be certainly determined. In any case, such changes – very often made to get rid of certain artifices employed as metrical aids, most notably among these the use of emphatic tenses with *doth* and *did* simply in order to obtain a syllable – such changes have no repercussions beyond the improvement of the individual line; and in such cases it seems a pity, through rigid adherence to the textual basis, to lose such small enhancements, or at any rate to hide them in a trail of tedious textual notes, while letting their less happy predecessors stand in the text. I have thought it justifiable therefore to be frankly inconsistent in these details, and while for example retaining *Gnomes* (for *Elves* or other substitution) or *Thû* (for *Gorthû* or *Sauron*), to introduce small changes of wording that are certainly later than these.

As in the *Lay of the Children of Húrin* there are no numbered notes to the text; the annotation, related to the line-numbers of the poem, is very largely restricted to earlier readings, and these earlier readings are restricted to cases where there is some significant difference, as of name or motive. Citations from the manuscript A are always citations from that text *as first written* (in very many cases it was emended to the reading found in B).

It is to be noticed that while the *Lay of Leithian* was in process of composition the 'Sketch of the Mythology' was written (first in 1926) and rewritten, leading directly into the version of 'The Silmarillion' that I ascribe to 1930, in which many of the essentials, both in narrative and language, of the published work were already present. In my commentaries on each Canto I attempt to take stock of the development in the legends *pari passu* with the text of the poem, and only refer exceptionally to the contemporary prose works.

The A-text has no title, but on the covering page of the bundle of rough workings is written *Tinúviel*, and in his early references to the poem my father called it thus, as he called the alliterative poem *Túrin*. The B-text bears this title:

The
GEST
of
BEREN son of BARAHIR
and
LÚTHIEN the FAY
called
TINÚVIEL the NIGHTINGALE
or the
LAY OF LEITHIAN
Release from Bondage

The 'Gest of Beren and Lúthien' means a narrative in verse, telling of the deeds of Beren and Lúthien. The word *gest* is pronounced as Modern English *jest*, being indeed the 'same word' in phonetic form, though now totally changed in meaning.

My father never explained the name *Leithian* 'Release from Bondage', and we are left to choose, if we will, among various applications that can be seen in the poem. Nor did he leave any comment on the significance – if there is a significance – of the likeness of *Leithian* to *Leithien* 'England'. In the tale of *Ælfwine of England* the Elvish name of England is *Lúthien* (which was earlier the name of Ælfwine himself, England being *Luthany*), but at the first occurrence (only) of this name the word *Leithian* was pencilled above it (II. 330, note 20). In the 'Sketch of the Mythology' England was still *Lúthien* (and at that time Thingol's daughter was also *Lúthien*), but this was emended to *Leithien*, and this is the form in the 1930 version of 'The Silmarillion'. I cannot say (i) what connection if any there was between the two significances of *Lúthien*, nor (ii) whether *Leithien* (once *Leithian*) 'England' is or was related to *Leithian* 'Release from Bondage'. The only evidence of an etymological nature that I have found is a hasty note, impossible to date, which refers to a stem *leth-* 'set free', with *leithia* 'release', and compares *Lay of Leithian*.

## The GEST of BEREN and LÚTHIEN

### I

A king there was in days of old:
ere Men yet walked upon the mould
his power was reared in cavern's shade,
his hand was over glen and glade.
His shields were shining as the moon,                    5
his lances keen of steel were hewn,
of silver grey his crown was wrought,
the starlight in his banners caught;
and silver thrilled his trumpets long
beneath the stars in challenge strong;                    10
enchantment did his realm enfold,
where might and glory, wealth untold,
he wielded from his ivory throne
in many-pillared halls of stone.

There beryl, pearl, and opal pale, 15
and metal wrought like fishes' mail,
buckler and corslet, axe and sword,
and gleaming spears were laid in hoard –
all these he had and loved them less
than a maiden once in Elfinesse; 20
for fairer than are born to Men
a daughter had he, Lúthien.

Such lissom limbs no more shall run
on the green earth beneath the sun;
so fair a maid no more shall be 25
from dawn to dusk, from sun to sea.
Her robe was blue as summer skies,
but grey as evening were her eyes;
'twas sewn with golden lilies fair,
but dark as shadow was her hair. 30
Her feet were light as bird on wing,
her laughter lighter than the spring;
the slender willow, the bowing reed,
the fragrance of a flowering mead,
the light upon the leaves of trees, 35
the voice of water, more than these
her beauty was and blissfulness,
her glory and her loveliness;
and her the king more dear did prize
than hand or heart or light of eyes. 40

They dwelt amid Beleriand,
while Elfin power yet held the land,
in the woven woods of Doriath:
few ever thither found the path;
few ever dared the forest-eaves 45
to pass, or stir the listening leaves
with tongue of hounds a-hunting fleet,
with horse, or horn, or mortal feet.
To North there lay the Land of Dread,
whence only evil pathways led 50
o'er hills of shadow bleak and cold
or Taur-na-Fuin's haunted hold,
where Deadly Nightshade lurked and lay
and never came or moon or day;
to South the wide earth unexplored; 55

to West the ancient Ocean roared,
unsailed and shoreless, wide and wild;
to East in peaks of blue were piled
in silence folded, mist-enfurled,
the mountains of the Outer World,                    60
beyond the tangled woodland shade,
thorn and thicket, grove and glade,
whose brooding boughs with magic hung
were ancient when the world was young.

There Thingol in the Thousand Caves,                 65
whose portals pale that river laves
Esgalduin that fairies call,
in many a tall and torchlit hall
a dark and hidden king did dwell,
lord of the forest and the fell;                     70
and sharp his sword and high his helm,
the king of beech and oak and elm.

There Lúthien the lissom maid
would dance in dell and grassy glade,
and music merrily, thin and clear,                   75
went down the ways, more fair than ear
of mortal Men at feast hath heard,
and fairer than the song of bird.
When leaves were long and grass was green
then Dairon with his fingers lean,                   80
as daylight melted into shade,
a wandering music sweetly made,
enchanted fluting, warbling wild,
for love of Thingol's elfin child.

There bow was bent and shaft was sped,               85
the fallow deer as phantoms fled,
and horses proud with braided mane,
with shining bit and silver rein,
went fleeting by on moonlit night,
as swallows arrow-swift in flight;                   90
a blowing and a sound of bells,
a hidden hunt in hollow dells.
There songs were made and things of gold,
and silver cups and jewels untold,
and the endless years of Faëry land                  95

rolled over far Beleriand,
until a day beneath the sun,
when many marvels were begun.

## NOTES

The opening of the poem in B is complicated by the fact that my father
partly rewrote, and retyped, the first Canto – a rewriting entirely distinct
from the later fundamental recasting that the early part of the poem
underwent. This first rewriting of the opening Canto was done while the
original composition of the poem was still proceeding, but was fairly far
advanced. The second version was typed in exactly the same form as that
it replaced, whereas the last part of the B-text is not typed; but the name
*Beleriand* appears in it, as typed, and not as an emendation, whereas
elsewhere in B the form is *Broseliand*, always emended in ink to
*Beleriand*.* Moreover it was the first version of Canto I in the B-text that
C. S. Lewis read on the night of 6 December 1929, and I think it very
probable that it was Lewis's criticism that led my father to rewrite the
opening (see pp. 315–16). In the following notes the first version of B is
called B(1), the rewritten text given above being B(2).

1–30  A:   A king was in the dawn of days:
             his golden crown did brightly blaze
             with ruby red and crystal clear;
             his meats were sweet, his dishes dear;
             red robes of silk, an ivory throne,         5
             and ancient halls of archéd stone,
             and wine and music lavished free,
             and thirty champions and three,
             all these he had and heeded not.
             His daughter dear was Melilot:         10
             from dawn to dusk, from sun to sea,
             no fairer maiden found could be.
             Her robe was blue as summer skies,
             but not so blue as were her eyes;
             'twas sewn with golden lilies fair,         15
             but none so golden as her hair.

An earlier draft, after line 12 *found could be*, has the couplet:

        from England unto Eglamar
        o'er folk and field and lands afar.

*Once near the very end (line 3957), in the manuscript conclusion of the B-text, the form
as written is *Beleriand*, not *Broseliand*.

B(1):   A king there was in olden days:
          &c. as A to line 6

      and hoarded gold in gleaming grot,
      all these he had and heeded not.
      But fairer than are born to Men
      a daughter had he, Lúthien:
        &c. as B(2)

14–18  These lines were used afterwards in Gimli's song in Moria
(*The Fellowship of the Ring* II. 4); see the Commentary by
C. S. Lewis, p. 316.

41–4  A:      They dwelt in dark Broceliand
          while loneliness yet held the land.

B(1):   They dwelt beyond Broseliand
          while loneliness yet held the land,
          in the forest dark of Doriath.
          Few ever thither found the path;

In B(1) *Ossiriande* is pencilled above *Broseliand*. As noted
above, B(2) has *Beleriand* as typed.

48   After this line A and B(1) have:

      Yet came at whiles afar and dim
      beneath the roots of mountains grim
      a blowing and a sound of bells,
      a hidden hunt in hollow dells.

The second couplet reappears at a later point in B(2), lines
91–2.

49–61  A and B(1):

      To North there lay the Land of Dread,
      whence only evil pathways led
      o'er hills of shadow bleak and cold;
      to West and South the oceans rolled
      unsailed and shoreless, wild and wide;
      to East and East the hills did hide
      beneath the tangled woodland shade,

65–6  A:      There Celegorm his ageless days
          doth wear amid the woven ways,
          the glimmering aisles and endless naves
          whose pillared feet that river laves

67   *Esgalduin* A, but *Esgaduin* in the rough workings, which is
the form in *The Children of Húrin* (p. 76, line 2164) before
correction.

73    A:        There Melilot the lissom maid

79–84  Not in A.

85–93  A and B(1) (with one slight difference):

> There bow was bent and shaft was sped
> and deer as fallow phantoms fled,
> and horses pale with harness bright
> went jingling by on moonlit night;
> there songs were made and things of gold

See note to line 48.

96    A:        rolled over dark Broceliand,
      B(1):     rolled over far Broseliand,
      In B(1) *Ossiriande* is pencilled against *Broseliand*, as at line 41.

## Commentary on Canto I

An extraordinary feature of the A-version is the name *Celegorm* given to the King of the woodland Elves (Thingol); moreover in the next Canto the rôle of Beren is in A played by *Maglor*, son of Egnor. The only possible conclusion, strange as it is, is that my father was prepared to abandon *Thingol* for *Celegorm* and (even more astonishing) *Beren* for *Maglor*. Both *Celegorm* and *Maglor* as sons of Fëanor have appeared in the *Tale of the Nauglafring* and in the *Lay of the Children of Húrin*.

The name of the king's daughter in A, *Melilot*, is also puzzling (and is it the English plant-name, as in Melilot Brandybuck, a guest at Bilbo Baggins' farewell party?). Already in the second version of *The Children of Húrin* Lúthien has appeared as the 'true' name of Tinúviel (see p. 119, note to 358–66). It is perhaps possible that my father in fact began the *Lay of Leithian* before he stopped work on *The Children of Húrin*, in which case *Melilot* might be the first 'true' name of Tinúviel, displaced by *Lúthien*; but I think that this is extremely unlikely.* In view of *Beren* > *Maglor*, I think *Lúthien* > *Melilot* far more probable. In any event, *Beren* and *Lúthien* soon appear in the original drafts of the *Lay of Leithian*.

It is strange also that in A the king's daughter was blue-eyed and golden-haired, for this would not accord with the robe of darkness that

---

*My father expressly stated in his diary that he began *Tinúviel* in the summer of 1925; and it is to be noted that a reference to the *Lay of Leithian* appears in the alliterative head-piece to one of the typescripts of *Light as Leaf on Lindentree* – which was actually published in June 1925 (see pp. 120–1). Thus the reference in the second version of *The Children of Húrin* to the *Lay of Leithian* (p. 107 line 356) is not evidence that he had in fact begun it.

she spun from her hair: in the *Tale of Tinúviel* her hair was 'dark' (II.20).

The name *Broceliand* that appears in A (*Broseliand* B) is remarkable, but I can cast no light on my father's choice of this name (the famous Forest of Broceliande in Brittany of the Arthurian legends).* It would be interesting to know how *Broseliand* led to *Beleriand*, and a clue may perhaps be found on a page of rough working for the opening of the Lay, where he jotted down various names that must be possibilities that he was pondering for the name of the land. The fact that *Ossiriand* occurs among them, while it is also pencilled against *Broseliand* at lines 41 and 96 in B(1), may suggest that these names arose during the search for a replacement of *Broseliand*. The names are:

> *Golodhinand, Noldórinan, Geleriand, Bladorinand, Belaurien, Arsiriand, Lassiriand, Ossiriand.*

*Golodhinand* is incidentally interesting as showing *Golodh*, the later Sindarin equivalent of Quenya *Noldo* (in the old Gnomish dictionary *Golda* was the Gnomish equivalent of 'Elvish' *Noldo*, I.262). *Geleriand* I can cast no light on; but *Belaurien* is obviously connected with *Belaurin*, the Gnomish form of *Palúrien* (I.264), and *Bladorinand* with Palúrien's name *Bladorwen* 'the wide earth, Mother Earth' (*ibid.*). It seems at least possible that *Belaurien* lies behind *Beleriand* (which was afterwards explained quite differently).

Another curious feature is the word *beyond* in *They dwelt beyond Broseliand*, the reading of B(1) at line 41, where A has *in* and B(2) has *amid*.

*Esga(l)duin, Taur-na-Fuin* (for *Taur Fuin* of the *Lost Tales*), and the Thousand Caves have all appeared in *The Children of Húrin*; but in the mountains that

> to East in peaks of blue were piled
> in silence folded, mist-enfurled

– lines that are absent from A and B(1) – we have the first appearance of the Blue Mountains (*Ered Luin*) of the later legends: fencing Beleriand, as it seems, from *the Outer World*.

In all the texts of the first Canto the King of the woodland Elves is presented as possessing great wealth. This conception appears already in *The Children of Húrin* (see p. 26), in the most marked contrast to all that is told in the *Lost Tales*: cf. the *Tale of Turambar* (II.95) 'the folk of Tinwelint were of the woodlands and had scant wealth', 'his riches were small', and the *Tale of the Nauglafring* (II.227) 'A golden crown

---

* On the earliest 'Silmarillion' map it is said that 'all the lands watered by Sirion south of Gondolin are called *in English* "Broseliand" '.

they [the Dwarves] made for Tinwelint, who yet had worn nought but a
wreath of scarlet leaves.'

## II

Far in the North neath hills of stone
in caverns black there was a throne          100
by fires illumined underground,
that winds of ice with moaning sound
made flare and flicker in dark smoke;
the wavering bitter coils did choke
the sunless airs of dungeons deep            105
where evil things did crouch and creep.
There sat a king: no Elfin race
nor mortal blood, nor kindly grace
of earth or heaven might he own,
far older, stronger than the stone           110
the world is built of, than the fire
that burns within more fierce and dire;
and thoughts profound were in his heart:
a gloomy power that dwelt apart.

Unconquerable spears of steel                115
were at his nod. No ruth did feel
the legions of his marshalled hate,
on whom did wolf and raven wait;
and black the ravens sat and cried
upon their banners black, and wide           120
was heard their hideous chanting dread
above the reek and trampled dead.
With fire and sword his ruin red
on all that would not bow the head
like lightning fell. The Northern land       125
lay groaning neath his ghastly hand.

But still there lived in hiding cold
undaunted, Barahir the bold,
of land bereaved, of lordship shorn,
who once a prince of Men was born             130
and now an outlaw lurked and lay
in the hard heath and woodland grey,

and with him clung of faithful men
but Beren his son and other ten.
Yet small as was their hunted band                    135
still fell and fearless was each hand,
and strong deeds they wrought yet oft,
and loved the woods, whose ways more soft
them seemed than thralls of that black throne
to live and languish in halls of stone.               140
King Morgoth still pursued them sore
with men and dogs, and wolf and boar
with spells of madness filled he sent
to slay them as in the woods they went;
yet nought hurt them for many years,                  145
until, in brief to tell what tears
have oft bewailed in ages gone,
nor ever tears enough, was done
a deed unhappy; unaware
their feet were caught in Morgoth's snare.            150

   Gorlim it was, who wearying
of toil and flight and harrying,
one night by chance did turn his feet
o'er the dark fields by stealth to meet
with hidden friend within a dale,                     155
and found a homestead looming pale
against the misty stars, all dark
save one small window, whence a spark
of fitful candle strayed without.
Therein he peeped, and filled with doubt              160
he saw, as in a dreaming deep
when longing cheats the heart in sleep,
his wife beside a dying fire
lament him lost; her thin attire
and greying hair and paling cheek                     165
of tears and loneliness did speak.
'A! fair and gentle Eilinel,
whom I had thought in darkling hell
long since emprisoned! Ere I fled
I deemed I saw thee slain and dead                    170
upon that night of sudden fear
when all I lost that I held dear':
thus thought his heavy heart amazed

outside in darkness as he gazed.
But ere he dared to call her name,                    175
or ask how she escaped and came
to this far vale beneath the hills,
he heard a cry beneath the hills!
There hooted near a hunting owl
with boding voice. He heard the howl                    180
of the wild wolves that followed him
and dogged his feet through shadows dim.
Him unrelenting, well he knew,
the hunt of Morgoth did pursue.
Lest Eilinel with him they slay                    185
without a word he turned away,
and like a wild thing winding led
his devious ways o'er stony bed
of stream, and over quaking fen,
until far from the homes of men                    190
he lay beside his fellows few
in a secret place; and darkness grew,
and waned, and still he watched unsleeping,
and saw the dismal dawn come creeping
in dank heavens above gloomy trees.                    195
A sickness held his soul for ease,
and hope, and even thraldom's chain
if he might find his wife again.
But all he thought twixt love of lord
and hatred of the king abhorred                    200
and anguish for fair Eilinel
who drooped alone, what tale shall tell?

        Yet at the last, when many days
of brooding did his mind amaze,
he found the servants of the king,                    205
and bade them to their master bring
a rebel who forgiveness sought,
if haply forgiveness might be bought
with tidings of Barahir the bold,
and where his hidings and his hold                    210
might best be found by night or day.
And thus sad Gorlim, led away
unto those dark deep-dolven halls,
before the knees of Morgoth falls,

and puts his trust in that cruel heart                    215
wherein no truth had ever part.
Quoth Morgoth: 'Eilinel the fair
thou shalt most surely find, and there
where she doth dwell and wait for thee
together shall ye ever be,                                220
and sundered shall ye sigh no more.
This guerdon shall he have that bore
these tidings sweet, O traitor dear!
For Eilinel she dwells not here,
but in the shades of death doth roam                      225
widowed of husband and of home –
a wraith of that which might have been,
methinks, it is that thou hast seen!
Now shalt thou through the gates of pain
the land thou askest grimly gain;                         230
thou shalt to the moonless mists of hell
descend and seek thy Eilinel.'

Thus Gorlim died a bitter death
and cursed himself with dying breath,
and Barahir was caught and slain,                         235
and all good deeds were made in vain.
But Morgoth's guile for ever failed,
nor wholly o'er his foes prevailed,
and some were ever that still fought
unmaking that which malice wrought.                       240
Thus men believed that Morgoth made
the fiendish phantom that betrayed
the soul of Gorlim, and so brought
the lingering hope forlorn to nought
that lived amid the lonely wood;                          245
yet Beren had by fortune good
long hunted far afield that day,
and benighted in strange places lay
far from his fellows. In his sleep
he felt a dreadful darkness creep                         250
upon his heart, and thought the trees
were bare and bent in mournful breeze;
no leaves they had, but ravens dark
sat thick as leaves on bough and bark,
and croaked, and as they croaked each neb                 255

let fall a gout of blood; a web
unseen entwined him hand and limb,
until worn out, upon the rim
of stagnant pool he lay and shivered.
There saw he that a shadow quivered                    260
far out upon the water wan,
and grew to a faint form thereon
that glided o'er the silent lake,
and coming slowly, softly spake
and sadly said: 'Lo! Gorlim here,                      265
traitor betrayed, now stands! Nor fear,
but haste! For Morgoth's fingers close
upon thy father's throat. He knows
your secret tryst, your hidden lair',
and all the evil he laid bare                          270
that he had done and Morgoth wrought.
Then Beren waking swiftly sought
his sword and bow, and sped like wind
that cuts with knives the branches thinned
of autumn trees. At last he came,                      275
his heart afire with burning flame,
where Barahir his father lay;
he came too late. At dawn of day
he found the homes of hunted men,
a wooded island in the fen,                            280
and birds rose up in sudden cloud –
no fen-fowl were they crying loud.
The raven and the carrion-crow
sat in the alders all a-row;
one croaked: 'Ha! Beren comes too late',              285
and answered all: 'Too late! Too late!'
There Beren buried his father's bones,
and piled a heap of boulder-stones,
and cursed the name of Morgoth thrice,
but wept not, for his heart was ice.                   290

Then over fen and field and mountain
he followed, till beside a fountain
upgushing hot from fires below
he found the slayers and his foe,
the murderous soldiers of the king.                    295
And one there laughed, and showed a ring

he took from Barahir's dead hand.
'This ring in far Beleriand,
now mark ye, mates,' he said, 'was wrought.
Its like with gold could not be bought,                    300
for this same Barahir I slew,
this robber fool, they say, did do
a deed of service long ago
for Felagund. It may be so;
for Morgoth bade me bring it back,                         305
and yet, methinks, he has no lack
of weightier treasure in his hoard.
Such greed befits not such a lord,
and I am minded to declare
the hand of Barahir was bare!'                             310
Yet as he spake an arrow sped;
with riven heart he crumpled dead.
Thus Morgoth loved that his own foe
should in his service deal the blow
that punished the breaking of his word.                    315
But Morgoth laughed not when he heard
that Beren like a wolf alone
sprang madly from behind a stone
amid that camp beside the well,
and seized the ring, and ere the yell                      320
of wrath and rage had left their throat
had fled his foes. His gleaming coat
was made of rings of steel no shaft
could pierce, a web of dwarvish craft;
and he was lost in rock and thorn,                         325
for in charméd hour was Beren born;
their hungry hunting never learned
the way his fearless feet had turned.

As fearless Beren was renowned,
as man most hardy upon ground,                             330
while Barahir yet lived and fought;
but sorrow now his soul had wrought
to dark despair, and robbed his life
of sweetness, that he longed for knife,
or shaft, or sword, to end his pain,                       335
and dreaded only thraldom's chain.
Danger he sought and death pursued,

and thus escaped the fate he wooed,
and deeds of breathless wonder dared
whose whispered glory widely fared, 340
and softly songs were sung at eve
of marvels he did once achieve
alone, beleaguered, lost at night
by mist or moon, or neath the light
of the broad eye of day. The woods 345
that northward looked with bitter feuds
he filled and death for Morgoth's folk;
his comrades were the beech and oak,
who failed him not, and many things
with fur and fell and feathered wings; 350
and many spirits, that in stone
in mountains old and wastes alone,
do dwell and wander, were his friends.
Yet seldom well an outlaw ends,
and Morgoth was a king more strong 355
than all the world has since in song
recorded, and his wisdom wide
slow and surely who him defied
did hem and hedge. Thus at the last
must Beren flee the forest fast 360
and lands he loved where lay his sire
by reeds bewailed beneath the mire.
Beneath a heap of mossy stones
now crumble those once mighty bones,
but Beren flees the friendless North 365
one autumn night, and creeps him forth;
the leaguer of his watchful foes
he passes – silently he goes.
No more his hidden bowstring sings,
no more his shaven arrow wings, 370
no more his hunted head doth lie
upon the heath beneath the sky.
The moon that looked amid the mist
upon the pines, the wind that hissed
among the heather and the fern 375
found him no more. The stars that burn
about the North with silver fire
in frosty airs, the Burning Briar
that Men did name in days long gone,

were set behind his back, and shone                           380
o'er land and lake and darkened hill,
forsaken fen and mountain rill.

His face was South from the Land of Dread,
whence only evil pathways led,
and only the feet of men most bold                            385
might cross the Shadowy Mountains cold.
Their northern slopes were filled with woe,
with evil and with mortal foe;
their southern faces mounted sheer
in rocky pinnacle and pier,                                   390
whose roots were woven with deceit
and washed with waters bitter-sweet.
There magic lurked in gulf and glen,
for far away beyond the ken
of searching eyes, unless it were                             395
from dizzy tower that pricked the air
where only eagles lived and cried,
might grey and gleaming be descried
Beleriand, Beleriand,
the borders of the faëry land.                                400

★

## NOTES

128    A:   a lord of Men undaunted, bold
134    A:   Maglor his son and other ten.
141    A:   But the king Bauglir did hunt them sore
177–9  Earlier reading:
             to this far vale among the hills
             a haggard hungry people tills,
             there hooted nigh a hunting owl
205    *found*: earlier reading *sought*
209–10 A:   with tidings of Lord Egnor's band,
             and where their hidings in the land
235    A:   and Egnor was betrayed and slain
246    A:   yet Maglor it was by fortune good
             who hunting &c.
272    A:   till Maglor waking swiftly sought
277    A:   to where his father Egnor lay;
297    A:   he took from Egnor's slaughtered hand:

298 *Broceliand* A, *Broseliand* B emended to *Beleriand*
301 A:   for this same Egnor that I slew
304 *Celegorm* A, emended to *Felagoth* and then to *Felagund*
310 A:   I found the hand of Egnor bare!'
313–16 These four lines were bracketed, and *that* at line 317 changed to *Then*, before the B-text went to C. S. Lewis (my father's numbering of the lines excludes these four, and Lewis's line-references agree). Lewis did not concur with the exclusion of 313–14, and I have let all four lines stand. See pp. 318–19.
317, 329 *Maglor* A, *Beren* B
326 A:   and deep ghylls in the mountains torn.
331–3 A:   ere Egnor in the wilderness
             was slain; but now his loneliness,
             grief and despair, did rob his life
360 A:   proud Maglor fled the forest fast
       (*fast* is used in the sense 'secure against attack'; cf. *fastness*).
365 *Maglor* A, *Beren* B
377–81 A:   about the North with silver flame
             in frosty airs, that men did name
             Timbridhil in the days long gone,
             he set behind his back, and shone
             that sickle of the heavenly field
             that Bridhil Queen of stars did wield
             o'er land and lake and darkened hill,
       The fifth and sixth lines are bracketed, with *and shone* in the fourth changed to *It shone*.
383–4 Cf. lines 49–50.
399 *Broceliand* A, *Broseliand* B emended to *Beleriand*.

## Commentary on Canto II

In this second Canto the story of the betrayal of the outlaw band is already in A close to its final form in essentials; but there is no trace of the story in any form earlier than the first drafts of the *Lay of Leithian*, composed in the summer of 1925 (see p. 150). In commenting on the *Tale of Tinúviel* I noted (II. 52):

> It seems clear that at this time the history of Beren and his father (Egnor) was only very sketchily devised; there is in any case no hint of the story of the outlaw band led by his father and its betrayal by Gorlim the Unhappy before the first form of the *Lay of Leithian*.

There are indeed differences in the plot of the Lay from the story told in *The Silmarillion* (pp. 162 ff.): thus the house where Gorlim saw the phantom of Eilinel was not in the Lay his own; his treachery was far deeper and more deliberate, in that he sought out the servants of Morgoth with the intention of revealing the hiding-place of the outlaws; and he came before Morgoth himself (not Thû-Sauron). But these differences are much outnumbered by the similarities, such as the absence of Maglor-Beren on the fatal day, the apparition of Gorlim coming to him in dream across the water of the lake, the carrion-birds in the alder-trees, the cairn, the seizing of the ring, his friendship with birds and beasts.

As regards the names in the A-text: *Gorlim* and *Eilinel* were to remain. Maglor-Beren has already been discussed (p. 159). *Egnor* was still his father, as in the *Lost Tales* (the emendation to *Barahir* in the second version of the *Tale of Tinúviel*, II. 43, was a change made casually years later). *Bauglir* (which entered during the composition of *The Children of Húrin*, see p. 52) is changed throughout to *Morgoth*, but this seems not to have been a rejection of the name, since it appears later in the B-text of the Lay, and survives in *The Silmarillion*.

In A Varda is called *Bridhil* (note to lines 377–81), as she is also in the alliterative poem *The Flight of the Noldoli* (pp. 135, 139); but it is puzzling that the constellation of the Great Bear is in the same passage called *Timbridhil*, for that according to the old Gnomish dictionary is the title of Varda herself (as one would expect: cf. *Tinwetári*, I. 269). The 'Sickle of the Gods' (*Valacirca*) is here the 'sickle of the heavenly field' wielded by Bridhil Queen of Stars. I can cast no light at all on the name *Burning Briar* that appears in B (line 378); it reappears in the 1930 version of 'The Silmarillion':

Many names have these [the Seven Stars] been called, but in the old days of the North both Elves and Men called them the Burning Briar, and some the Sickle of the Gods.

For the earliest myth of the Great Bear see I. 114, 133.

Indications of geography are sparse, and not increased in the B-text. Taur-na-Fuin has been named earlier in B (line 52), but it is not actually said in the present Canto to be the region where the outlaws lurked, though there is no reason to doubt that this is where my father placed it. Coming southwards Maglor-Beren crossed 'the Shadowy Mountains cold' (386). The Shadowy Mountains were named several times in *The Children of Húrin*, where they are the mountains fencing Hithlum, mirrored in the pools of Ivrin, as they are in *The Silmarillion*. But it would obviously be impossible for Beren to cross the Shadowy Mountains in this application of the name if he were coming out of Taur-na-Fuin and moving south towards Doriath. In the 'Sketch of the Mythology' Beren likewise 'crosses the Shadowy Mountains and after grievous hardships comes to Doriath', and similarly in the 1930 version; in this latter, however, 'Mountains of Shadow' was emended to 'Mountains of Terror'. It is then clear that in the *Lay of Leithian* my father was using 'Shadowy Mountains' in a different sense from that in *The Children of Húrin*, and that the Shadowy Mountains of the present

Canto are the first mention of Ered Gorgoroth, the Mountains of Terror, 'the precipices in which Dorthonion [Taur-nu-Fuin] fell southward' (*The Silmarillion* p. 95); but the other meaning reappears (p. 234).

The lake where Egnor-Barahir and his band dwelt in hiding, in *The Silmarillion* (p. 162) *Tarn Aeluin*, is not named in the Lay, where the hiding-place was 'a wooded island in the fen' (280). That the Orc-camp was beside a spring (also unnamed) appears in the Lay, and it is here a hot spring (292–3); in *The Silmarillion* (p. 163) it was *Rivil's Well* above the Fen of Serech.

Most notable of the features of this Canto so far as the development of the legends is concerned, the rescue of Felagund by Barahir in the Battle of Sudden Flame (*The Silmarillion* p. 152) makes its first appearance in the 'service' done to Celegorm by Egnor in A (lines 301–4, where B has Felagund and Barahir). 'Celegorm' has already ceased its brief life as a replacement of Thingol (see p. 159), and is now again that of one of the sons of Fëanor, as it was in *The Children of Húrin*. When these lines in A were written the story was that Celegorm (and Curufin) founded Nargothrond after the breaking of the Leaguer of Angband – a story that seems to have arisen in the writing of *The Children of Húrin*, see pp. 83–5; and it was Celegorm who was rescued by Egnor-Barahir in that battle, and who gave Egnor-Barahir his ring. In the B-text the story has moved forward again, with the emergence of (Felagoth >) Felagund as the one saved by Barahir and the founder of Nargothrond, thrusting Celegorm and Curufin into a very different rôle.

In A Egnor and his son Maglor (Beren) are Men (e.g. Egnor was 'a lord of Men', note to line 128). In the first version of *The Children of Húrin* Beren was still an Elf, while in the second version my father seems to have changed back and forth on this matter (see pp. 124–5). He had not even now, as will appear later, finally settled the question.

# III

There once, and long and long ago,
before the sun and moon we know
were lit to sail above the world,
when first the shaggy woods unfurled,
and shadowy shapes did stare and roam     405
beneath the dark and starry dome
that hung above the dawn of Earth,
the silences with silver mirth
were shaken; the rocks were ringing,

the birds of Melian were singing,                    410
the first to sing in mortal lands,
the nightingales with her own hands
she fed, that fay of garments grey;
and dark and long her tresses lay
beneath her silver girdle's seat                     415
and down unto her silver feet.

She had wayward wandered on a time
from gardens of the Gods, to climb
the everlasting mountains free
that look upon the outmost sea,                      420
and never wandered back, but stayed
and softly sang from glade to glade.
Her voice it was that Thingol heard,
and sudden singing of a bird,
in that old time when new-come Elves                 425
had all the wide world to themselves.
Yet all his kin now marched away,
as old tales tell, to seek the bay
on the last shore of mortal lands,
where mighty ships with magic hands                  430
they made, and sailed beyond the seas.
The Gods them bade to lands of ease
and gardens fair, where earth and sky
together flow, and none shall die.
But Thingol stayed, enchanted, still,                435
one moment to hearken to the thrill
of that sweet singing in the trees.
Enchanted moments such as these
from gardens of the Lord of Sleep,
where fountains play and shadows creep,              440
do come, and count as many years
in mortal lands. With many tears
his people seek him ere they sail,
while Thingol listens in the dale.
There after but an hour, him seems,                  445
he finds her where she lies and dreams,
pale Melian with her dark hair
upon a bed of leaves. Beware!
There slumber and a sleep is twined!
He touched her tresses and his mind                  450

was drowned in the forgetful deep,
and dark the years rolled o'er his sleep.

Thus Thingol sailed not on the seas
but dwelt amid the land of trees,
and Melian he loved, divine, 455
whose voice was potent as the wine
the Valar drink in golden halls
where flower blooms and fountain falls;
but when she sang it was a spell,
and no flower stirred nor fountain fell. 460
A king and queen thus lived they long,
and Doriath was filled with song,
and all the Elves that missed their way
and never found the western bay,
the gleaming walls of their long home 465
by the grey seas and the white foam,
who never trod the golden land
where the towers of the Valar stand,
all these were gathered in their realm
beneath the beech and oak and elm. 470

In later days when Morgoth first,
fleeing the Gods, their bondage burst,
and on the mortal lands set feet,
and in the North his mighty seat
founded and fortified, and all 475
the newborn race of Men were thrall
unto his power, and Elf and Gnome
his slaves, or wandered without home,
or scattered fastnesses walled with fear
upraised upon his borders drear, 480
and each one fell, yet reigned there still
in Doriath beyond his will
Thingol and deathless Melian,
whose magic yet no evil can
that cometh from without surpass. 485
Here still was laughter and green grass,
and leaves were lit with the white sun,
and many marvels were begun.

In sunshine and in sheen of moon,
with silken robe and silver shoon, 490

the daughter of the deathless queen
now danced on the undying green,
half elven-fair and half divine;
and when the stars began to shine
unseen but near a piping woke,                    495
and in the branches of an oak,
or seated on the beech-leaves brown,
Dairon the dark with ferny crown
played with bewildering wizard's art
music for breaking of the heart.                  500
Such players have there only been
thrice in all Elfinesse, I ween:
Tinfang Gelion who still the moon
enchants on summer nights of June
and kindles the pale firstling star;              505
and he who harps upon the far
forgotten beaches and dark shores
where western foam for ever roars,
Maglor whose voice is like the sea;
and Dairon, mightiest of the three.               510

Now it befell on summer night,
upon a lawn where lingering light
yet lay and faded faint and grey,
that Lúthien danced while he did play.
The chestnuts on the turf had shed                515
their flowering candles, white and red;
there darkling stood a silent elm
and pale beneath its shadow-helm
there glimmered faint the umbels thick
of hemlocks like a mist, and quick                520
the moths on pallid wings of white
with tiny eyes of fiery light
were fluttering softly, and the voles
crept out to listen from their holes;
the little owls were hushed and still;            525
the moon was yet behind the hill.
Her arms like ivory were gleaming,
her long hair like a cloud was streaming,
her feet atwinkle wandered roaming
in misty mazes in the gloaming;                   530
and glowworms shimmered round her feet,

and moths in moving garland fleet
above her head went wavering wan –
and this the moon now looked upon,
uprisen slow, and round, and white,                    535
above the branches of the night.
Then clearly thrilled her voice and rang;
with sudden ecstasy she sang
a song of nightingales she learned
and with her elvish magic turned                    540
to such bewildering delight
the moon hung moveless in the night.
And this it was that Beren heard,
and this he saw, without a word,
enchanted dumb, yet filled with fire                    545
of such a wonder and desire
that all his mortal mind was dim;
her magic bound and fettered him,
and faint he leaned against a tree.
Forwandered, wayworn, gaunt was he,                    550
his body sick and heart gone cold,
grey in his hair, his youth turned old;
for those that tread that lonely way
a price of woe and anguish pay.
And now his heart was healed and slain                    555
with a new life and with new pain.

He gazed, and as he gazed her hair
within its cloudy web did snare
the silver moonbeams sifting white
between the leaves, and glinting bright                    560
the tremulous starlight of the skies
was caught and mirrored in her eyes.
Then all his journey's lonely fare,
the hunger and the haggard care,
the awful mountains' stones he stained                    565
with blood of weary feet, and gained
only a land of ghosts, and fear
in dark ravines imprisoned sheer –
there mighty spiders wove their webs,
old creatures foul with birdlike nebs                    570
that span their traps in dizzy air,
and filled it with clinging black despair,

and there they lived, and the sucked bones
lay white beneath on the dank stones –
now all these horrors like a cloud                          575
faded from mind. The waters loud
falling from pineclad heights no more
he heard, those waters grey and frore
that bittersweet he drank and filled
his mind with madness – all was stilled.                    580
He recked not now the burning road,
the paths demented where he strode
endlessly... and ever new
horizons stretched before his view,
as each blue ridge with bleeding feet                       585
was climbed, and down he went to meet
battle with creatures old and strong
and monsters in the dark, and long,
long watches in the haunted night
while evil shapes with baleful light                        590
in clustered eyes did crawl and snuff
beneath his tree – not half enough
the price he deemed to come at last
to that pale moon when day had passed,
to those clear stars of Elfinesse,                          595
the hearts-ease and the loveliness.

Lo! all forgetting he was drawn
unheeding toward the glimmering lawn
by love and wonder that compelled
his feet from hiding; music welled                          600
within his heart, and songs unmade
on themes unthought-of moved and swayed
his soul with sweetness; out he came,
a shadow in the moon's pale flame –
and Dairon's flute as sudden stops                          605
as lark before it steeply drops,
as grasshopper within the grass
listening for heavy feet to pass.
'Flee, Lúthien!', and 'Lúthien!'
from hiding Dairon called again;                            610
'A stranger walks the woods! Away!'
But Lúthien would wondering stay;
fear had she never felt or known,

till fear then seized her, all alone,
seeing that shape with shagged hair 615
and shadow long that halted there.
Then sudden she vanished like a dream
in dark oblivion, a gleam
in hurrying clouds, for she had leapt
among the hemlocks tall, and crept 620
under a mighty plant with leaves
all long and dark, whose stem in sheaves
upheld an hundred umbels fair;
and her white arms and shoulders bare
her raiment pale, and in her hair 625
the wild white roses glimmering there,
all lay like spattered moonlight hoar
in gleaming pools upon the floor.
Then stared he wild in dumbness bound
at silent trees, deserted ground; 630
he blindly groped across the glade
to the dark trees' encircling shade,
and, while she watched with veiléd eyes,
touched her soft arm in sweet surprise.
Like startled moth from deathlike sleep 635
in sunless nook or bushes deep
she darted swift, and to and fro
with cunning that elvish dancers know
about the trunks of trees she twined
a path fantastic. Far behind 640
enchanted, wildered and forlorn
Beren came blundering, bruised and torn:
Esgalduin the elven-stream,
in which amid tree-shadows gleam
the stars, flowed strong before his feet. 645
Some secret way she found, and fleet
passed over and was seen no more,
and left him forsaken on the shore.
'Darkly the sundering flood rolls past!
To this my long way comes at last — 650
a hunger and a loneliness,
enchanted waters pitiless.'

A summer waned, an autumn glowed,
and Beren in the woods abode,

as wild and wary as a faun                               655
that sudden wakes at rustling dawn,
and flits from shade to shade, and flees
the brightness of the sun, yet sees
all stealthy movements in the wood.
The murmurous warmth in weathers good,                    660
the hum of many wings, the call
of many a bird, the pattering fall
of sudden rain upon the trees,
the windy tide in leafy seas,
the creaking of the boughs, he heard;                     665
but not the song of sweetest bird
brought joy or comfort to his heart,
a wanderer dumb who dwelt apart;
who sought unceasing and in vain
to hear and see those things again:                       670
a song more fair than nightingale,
a wonder in the moonlight pale.

An autumn waned, a winter laid
the withered leaves in grove and glade;
the beeches bare were gaunt and grey,                     675
and red their leaves beneath them lay.
From cavern pale the moist moon eyes
the white mists that from earth arise
to hide the morrow's sun and drip
all the grey day from each twig's tip.                    680
By dawn and dusk he seeks her still;
by noon and night in valleys chill,
nor hears a sound but the slow beat
on sodden leaves of his own feet.

The wind of winter winds his horn;                        685
the misty veil is rent and torn.
The wind dies; the starry choirs
leap in the silent sky to fires,
whose light comes bitter-cold and sheer
through domes of frozen crystal clear.                    690

A sparkle through the darkling trees,
a piercing glint of light he sees,
and there she dances all alone
upon a treeless knoll of stone!

Her mantle blue with jewels white 695
caught all the rays of frosted light.
She shone with cold and wintry flame,
as dancing down the hill she came,
and passed his watchful silent gaze,
a glimmer as of stars ablaze. 700
And snowdrops sprang beneath her feet,
and one bird, sudden, late and sweet,
shrilled as she wayward passed along.
A frozen brook to bubbling song
awoke and laughed; but Beren stood 705
still bound enchanted in the wood.
Her starlight faded and the night
closed o'er the snowdrops glimmering white.

    Thereafter on a hillock green
he saw far off the elven-sheen 710
of shining limb and jewel bright
often and oft on moonlit night;
and Dairon's pipe awoke once more,
and soft she sang as once before.
Then nigh he stole beneath the trees, 715
and heartache mingled with hearts-ease.

    A night there was when winter died;
then all alone she sang and cried
and danced until the dawn of spring,
and chanted some wild magic thing 720
that stirred him, till it sudden broke
the bonds that held him, and he woke
to madness sweet and brave despair.
He flung his arms to the night air,
and out he danced unheeding, fleet, 725
enchanted, with enchanted feet.
He sped towards the hillock green,
the lissom limbs, the dancing sheen;
he leapt upon the grassy hill
his arms with loveliness to fill: 730
his arms were empty, and she fled;
away, away her white feet sped.
But as she went he swiftly came
and called her with the tender name
of nightingales in elvish tongue, 735

that all the woods now sudden rung:
'Tinúviel! Tinúviel!'
And clear his voice was as a bell;
its echoes wove a binding spell:
'Tinúviel! Tinúviel!'                                    740
His voice such love and longing filled
one moment stood she, fear was stilled;
one moment only; like a flame
he leaped towards her as she stayed
and caught and kissed that elfin maid.                   745

    As love there woke in sweet surprise
the starlight trembled in her eyes.
A! Lúthien! A! Lúthien!
more fair than any child of Men;
O! loveliest maid of Elfinesse,                          750
what madness does thee now possess!
A! lissom limbs and shadowy hair
and chaplet of white snowdrops there;
O! starry diadem and white
pale hands beneath the pale moonlight!                   755
She left his arms and slipped away
just at the breaking of the day.

★

## NOTES

439    Original reading of B:

        from gardens of the God of Sleep,

457    Original reading of B:

        the Gods drink in their golden halls

467–8    Original reading of B:

        who never passed the golden gate
        where doorwards of the Gods do wait,

These three changes are late, and their purpose is to remove
the word *Gods*. The change in line 468 also gets rid of the
purely metrical *do* in *do wait*; similarly *did build and fortify*
> *founded and fortified* 475 and *did raise* > *upraised* 480
look as if they belong to the same time. On the other hand *did*

*flutter* > *were fluttering* 523 and *did waver* > *went wavering* 533 seem to belong with the early emendations (see C. S. Lewis's commentary, pp. 320–1). I mention these changes here to illustrate my remarks on this subject, pp. 152–3.

493  *elfin-* B, emended to *elven-*. Here and subsequently this belongs with the early changes, as does *elfin* to *elvish* at 540, etc.

503  *Tinfang Warble* A, and B as typed; *Gelion* an early change in B.

508  After this line A has a couplet omitted in B:

> from England unto Eglamar
> on rock and dune and sandy bar,

The first of these lines occurs also in an early draft for the opening of the poem, see p. 157, note to lines 1–30.

509  *Maglor* A, B; in the rough draft of this passage *Ivárë* (with *Maglor* written beside it).

527–30  Marked in B with an X (i.e. in need of revision), but with no other verses substituted.

557  This line begins a new page in the A manuscript; at the top of the page is written the date '23/8/25'.

558  *golden* A, and B as typed (no doubt an oversight), early emended to *cloudy*. See note to lines 1–30, and pp. 159–60.

648  After this line the bundle of examination-scripts on which the A manuscript is written (p. 150) is interleaved with other pages, which carry the poem to the end of Canto III. At the bottom of the first of these pages is written *Filey 1925*, where my father was on holiday in September of that year.

743  The couplet lacks its second line. The passage 741–5 is a hasty revision, based on a criticism of Lewis's; see his commentary, p. 325.

### Commentary on Canto III

In this Canto there are many things that derive from the *Tale of Tinúviel* (II. 10 ff.): the chestnut trees, the white moths, the moon rising, the sudden ceasing of Dairon's piping, Tinúviel's unwillingness to flee, her hiding under the hemlocks *like spattered moonlight* (cf. II. 11 'like a spatter of moonlight shimmering'), Beren's touching her arm, her darting between the tree-trunks, and afterwards the 'treeless knoll' where she danced in the winter. But the Canto is also related to the poem *Light as Leaf on Lindentree* (see pp. 108–10, 120–2), which had been published in June 1925, while this part of the *Lay of Leithian* was written a little later in the same year. Echoes of the one poem are heard in the other, and more than an echo in the line *and out he danced unheeding, fleet*, which is found in both (p. 109, line 447; p. 179, line 725).

The aberrant names in the first two Cantos of A have now disappeared from the text. In the second Canto my father had already given back the name *Celegorm* to the son of Fëanor (note to line 304), and now *Thingol* appears in A; *Lúthien* replaces *Melilot*; and *Beren* replaces *Maglor*. *Morgoth* now replaces *Bauglir* in A (see p. 170).

In both texts *Tinúviel* is now explicitly the Elvish word for 'nightingale' (line 735; see p. 124); and *Maglor*, again in both texts, is the name of one of the three greatest singers of Elfinesse:

> he who harps upon the far
> forgotten beaches and dark shores
> where western foam for ever roars,
> Maglor whose voice is like the sea          (506–9)

In the rough draft of this passage the name of this minstrel is however *Ivárë* (though *Maglor* is written beside it), and Ivárë was named in the *Tale of Tinúviel* (II. 10), with Tinfang and Dairon, as one of 'the three most magic players of the Elves', who 'plays beside the sea'. This is the first hint of the after-history of Maglor son of Fëanor, who in the *Tale of the Nauglafring* (II. 241) was slain, as also was Celegorm, in the attack on Dior. The lines in A, omitted in B (note to line 508), are interesting:

> from England unto Eglamar
> on rock and dune and sandy bar

The form *Eglamar* (Gnomish, = *Eldamar*) occurs in the very early poem *The Shores of Faëry* and its prose preface (II. 262, 272); and the same line *from England unto Eglamar* is found in the rough workings of the beginning of the Lay (note to lines 1–30). The mention of *England* is a reminder that at this time the association of the legends with Eriol/Ælfwine was still very much alive, though there is no other indication of it in the *Lay of Leithian*.

*Tinfang Warble* reappears from the *Lost Tales* at line 503, changed to *Tinfang Gelion*; the meaning of *Gelion* is not explained.

In one respect only does the narrative content of the Canto depart in any significant way from the common 'tradition' of the texts, but this is sufficiently remarkable: the Elves departed over the sea to Valinor at the end of the Great Journey in a fleet of ships!

> Yet all his kin now marched away,
> as old tales tell, to seek the bay
> on the last shore of mortal lands,
> where mighty ships with magic hands
> they made, and sailed beyond the seas.          (427–31)

This is very strange (and I am at a loss to account for it, except by the obvious explanation of a passing shift), in that the story of the 'island-car' (Tol Eressëa), which goes back to the *Lost Tales* (I. 118–20), is present in all the versions of 'The Silmarillion'. The Elves are here presented, on the other hand, as great shipbuilders in the beginning of their days. – With the reference in the passage just cited to the *bay* whence the Elves set sail cf. *The Silmarillion* p. 57, where it is told that Ulmo anchored the 'island-car' in the Bay of Balar (and that the eastern horn of the island, breaking off, was the Isle of Balar).

In the description of Beren's journey to Doriath in lines 563 ff. is the first account of the Ered Gorgoroth, the Mountains of Terror (called 'the Shadowy Mountains' in Canto II, see pp. 170–1), with their spiders and their waters that drove mad those who drank from them (cf. *The Silmarillion* p. 121; and with lines 590–1 *evil shapes with baleful light / in clustered eyes* cf. *ibid.* p. 164: 'monsters . . . hunting silently with many eyes').

★

# IV

He lay upon the leafy mould,
his face upon earth's bosom cold,
aswoon in overwhelming bliss,    760
enchanted of an elvish kiss,
seeing within his darkened eyes
the light that for no darkness dies,
the loveliness that doth not fade,
though all in ashes cold be laid.    765
Then folded in the mists of sleep
he sank into abysses deep,
drowned in an overwhelming grief
for parting after meeting brief;
a shadow and a fragrance fair    770
lingered, and waned, and was not there.
Forsaken, barren, bare as stone,
the daylight found him cold, alone.

    'Where art thou gone? The day is bare,
the sunlight dark, and cold the air!    775
Tinúviel, where went thy feet?
O wayward star! O maiden sweet!
O flower of Elfland all too fair
for mortal heart! The woods are bare!

The woods are bare!' he rose and cried.                    780
'Ere spring was born, the spring hath died!'
And wandering in path and mind
he groped as one gone sudden blind,
who seeks to grasp the hidden light
with faltering hands in more than night.                    785

And thus in anguish Beren paid
for that great doom upon him laid,
the deathless love of Lúthien,
too fair for love of mortal Men;
and in his doom was Lúthien snared,                         790
the deathless in his dying shared;
and Fate them forged a binding chain
of living love and mortal pain.

Beyond all hope her feet returned
at eve, when in the sky there burned                        795
the flame of stars; and in her eyes
there trembled the starlight of the skies,
and from her hair the fragrance fell
of elvenflowers in elven-dell.

Thus Lúthien, whom no pursuit,                              800
no snare, no dart that hunters shoot,
might hope to win or hold, she came
at the sweet calling of her name;
and thus in his her slender hand
was linked in far Beleriand;                                805
in hour enchanted long ago
her arms about his neck did go,
and gently down she drew to rest
his weary head upon her breast.
A! Lúthien, Tinúviel,                                       810
why wentest thou to darkling dell
with shining eyes and dancing pace,
the twilight glimmering in thy face?
Each day before the end of eve
she sought her love, nor would him leave,                   815
until the stars were dimmed, and day
came glimmering eastward silver-grey.
Then trembling-veiled she would appear
and dance before him, half in fear;

there flitting just before his feet 820
she gently chid with laughter sweet:
'Come! dance now, Beren, dance with me!
For fain thy dancing I would see.
Come! thou must woo with nimbler feet,
than those who walk where mountains meet 825
the bitter skies beyond this realm
of marvellous moonlit beech and elm.'

In Doriath Beren long ago
new art and lore he learned to know;
his limbs were freed; his eyes alight, 830
kindled with a new enchanted sight;
and to her dancing feet his feet
attuned went dancing free and fleet;
his laughter welled as from a spring
of music, and his voice would sing 835
as voices of those in Doriath
where paved with flowers are floor and path.
The year thus on to summer rolled,
from spring to a summertime of gold.

Thus fleeting fast their short hour flies, 840
while Dairon watches with fiery eyes,
haunting the gloom of tangled trees
all day, until at night he sees
in the fickle moon their moving feet,
two lovers linked in dancing sweet, 845
two shadows shimmering on the green
where lonely-dancing maid had been.
'Hateful art thou, O Land of Trees!
May fear and silence on thee seize!
My flute shall fall from idle hand 850
and mirth shall leave Beleriand;
music shall perish and voices fail
and trees stand dumb in dell and dale!'

It seemed a hush had fallen there
upon the waiting woodland air; 855
and often murmured Thingol's folk
in wonder, and to their king they spoke:
'This spell of silence who hath wrought?
What web hath Dairon's music caught?

It seems the very birds sing low;                          860
murmurless Esgalduin doth flow;
the leaves scarce whisper on the trees,
and soundless beat the wings of bees!'

This Lúthien heard, and there the queen
her sudden glances saw unseen.                             865
But Thingol marvelled, and he sent
for Dairon the piper, ere he went
and sat upon his mounded seat –
his grassy throne by the grey feet
of the Queen of Beeches, Hirilorn,                         870
upon whose triple piers were borne
the mightiest vault of leaf and bough
from world's beginning until now.
She stood above Esgalduin's shore,
where long slopes fell beside the door,                    875
the guarded gates, the portals stark
of the Thousand echoing Caverns dark.
There Thingol sat and heard no sound
save far off footsteps on the ground;
no flute, no voice, no song of bird,                       880
no choirs of windy leaves there stirred;
and Dairon coming no word spoke,
silent amid the woodland folk.
Then Thingol said: 'O Dairon fair,
thou master of all musics rare,                            885
O magic heart and wisdom wild,
whose ear nor eye may be beguiled,
what omen doth this silence bear?
What horn afar upon the air,
what summons do the woods await?                           890
Mayhap the Lord Tavros from his gate
and tree-propped halls, the forest-god,
rides his wild stallion golden-shod
amid the trumpets' tempest loud,
amid his green-clad hunters proud,                         895
leaving his deer and friths divine
and emerald forests? Some faint sign
of his great onset may have come
upon the Western winds, and dumb
the woods now listen for a chase                           900

that here once more shall thundering race
beneath the shade of mortal trees.
Would it were so! The Lands of Ease
hath Tavros left not many an age,    905
since Morgoth evil wars did wage,
since ruin fell upon the North
and the Gnomes unhappy wandered forth.
But if not he, who comes or what?'
And Dairon answered: 'He cometh not!    910
No feet divine shall leave that shore,
where the Shadowy Seas' last surges roar,
till many things be come to pass,
and many evils wrought. Alas!
the guest is here. The woods are still,    915
but wait not; for a marvel chill
them holds at the strange deeds they see,
but kings see not – though queens, maybe,
may guess, and maidens, maybe, know.
Where one went lonely two now go!'

'Whither thy riddle points is plain'    920
the king in anger said, 'but deign
to make it plainer! Who is he
that earns my wrath? How walks he free
within my woods amid my folk,
a stranger to both beech and oak?'    925
But Dairon looked on Lúthien
and would he had not spoken then,
and no more would he speak that day,
though Thingol's face with wrath was grey.
Then Lúthien stepped lightly forth:    930
'Far in the mountain-leaguered North,
my father,' said she, 'lies the land
that groans beneath King Morgoth's hand.
Thence came one hither, bent and worn
in wars and travail, who had sworn    935
undying hatred of that king;
the last of Bëor's sons, they sing,
and even hither far and deep
within thy woods the echoes creep
through the wild mountain-passes cold,    940
the last of Bëor's house to hold

a sword unconquered, neck unbowed,
a heart by evil power uncowed.
No evil needst thou think or fear
of Beren son of Barahir!                              945
If aught thou hast to say to him,
then swear to hurt not flesh nor limb,
and I will lead him to thy hall,
a son of kings, no mortal thrall.'

    Then long King Thingol looked on her          950
while hand nor foot nor tongue did stir,
and Melian, silent, unamazed,
on Lúthien and Thingol gazed.
'No blade nor chain his limbs shall mar'
the king then swore. 'He wanders far,                 955
and news, mayhap, he hath for me,
and words I have for him, maybe!'
Now Thingol bade them all depart
save Dairon, whom he called: 'What art,
what wizardry of Northern mist                        960
hath this illcomer brought us? List!
Tonight go thou by secret path,
who knowest all wide Doriath,
and watch that Lúthien – daughter mine,
what madness doth thy heart entwine,                  965
what web from Morgoth's dreadful halls
hath caught thy feet and thee enthralls! –
that she bid not this Beren flee
back whence he came. I would him see!
Take with thee woodland archers wise.                 970
Let naught beguile your hearts or eyes!'

    Thus Dairon heavyhearted did,
and the woods were filled with watchers hid;
yet needless, for Lúthien that night
led Beren by the golden light                         975
of mounting moon unto the shore
and bridge before her father's door;
and the white light silent looked within
the waiting portals yawning dim.

    Downward with gentle hand she led              980
through corridors of carven dread
whose turns were lit by lanterns hung

or flames from torches that were flung
on dragons hewn in the cold stone
with jewelled eyes and teeth of bone. 985
Then sudden, deep beneath the earth
the silences with silver mirth
were shaken and the rocks were ringing,
the birds of Melian were singing;
and wide the ways of shadow spread 990
as into archéd halls she led
Beren in wonder. There a light
like day immortal and like night
of stars unclouded, shone and gleamed.
A vault of topless trees it seemed, 995
whose trunks of carven stone there stood
like towers of an enchanted wood
in magic fast for ever bound,
bearing a roof whose branches wound
in endless tracery of green 1000
lit by some leaf-emprisoned sheen
of moon and sun, and wrought of gems,
and each leaf hung on golden stems.
    Lo! there amid immortal flowers
the nightingales in shining bowers 1005
sang o'er the head of Melian,
while water for ever dripped and ran
from fountains in the rocky floor.
There Thingol sat. His crown he wore
of green and silver, and round his chair 1010
a host in gleaming armour fair.
Then Beren looked upon the king
and stood amazed; and swift a ring
of elvish weapons hemmed him round.
Then Beren looked upon the ground, 1015
for Melian's gaze had sought his face,
and dazed there drooped he in that place,
and when the king spake deep and slow:
'Who art thou stumblest hither? Know
that none unbidden seek this throne 1020
and ever leave these halls of stone!'
no word he answered, filled with dread.
But Lúthien answered in his stead:
'Behold, my father, one who came

pursued by hatred like a flame!                              1025
Lo! Beren son of Barahir!
What need hath he thy wrath to fear,
foe of our foes, without a friend,
whose knees to Morgoth do not bend?'

'Let Beren answer!' Thingol said.                            1030
'What wouldst thou here? What hither led
thy wandering feet, O mortal wild?
How hast thou Lúthien beguiled
or darest thus to walk this wood
unasked, in secret? Reason good                              1035
'twere best declare now if thou may,
or never again see light of day!'
Then Beren looked in Lúthien's eyes
and saw a light of starry skies,
and thence was slowly drawn his gaze                         1040
to Melian's face. As from a maze
of wonder dumb he woke; his heart
the bonds of awe there burst apart
and filled with the fearless pride of old;
in his glance now gleamed an anger cold.                     1045
'My feet hath fate, O king,' he said,
'here over the mountains bleeding led,
and what I sought not I have found,
and love it is hath here me bound.
Thy dearest treasure I desire;                               1050
nor rocks nor steel nor Morgoth's fire
nor all the power of Elfinesse
shall keep that gem I would possess.
For fairer than are born to Men
A daughter hast thou, Lúthien.'                              1055

Silence then fell upon the hall;
like graven stone there stood they all,
save one who cast her eyes aground,
and one who laughed with bitter sound.
Dairon the piper leant there pale                            1060
against a pillar. His fingers frail
there touched a flute that whispered not;
his eyes were dark; his heart was hot.
'Death is the guerdon thou hast earned,
O baseborn mortal, who hast learned                          1065

in Morgoth's realm to spy and lurk
like Orcs that do his evil work!'
'Death!' echoed Dairon fierce and low,
but Lúthien trembling gasped in woe.
'And death,' said Thingol, 'thou shouldst taste,      1070
had I not sworn an oath in haste
that blade nor chain thy flesh should mar.
Yet captive bound by never a bar,
unchained, unfettered, shalt thou be
in lightless labyrinth endlessly                      1075
that coils about my halls profound
by magic bewildered and enwound;
there wandering in hopelessness
thou shalt learn the power of Elfinesse!'
'That may not be!' Lo! Beren spake,                   1080
and through the king's words coldly brake.
'What are thy mazes but a chain
wherein the captive blind is slain?
Twist not thy oaths, O elvish king,
like faithless Morgoth! By this ring –                1085
the token of a lasting bond
that Felagund of Nargothrond
once swore in love to Barahir,
who sheltered him with shield and spear
and saved him from pursuing foe                       1090
on Northern battlefields long ago –
death thou canst give unearned to me,
but names I will not take from thee
of baseborn, spy, or Morgoth's thrall!
Are these the ways of Thingol's hall?'                1095
Proud are the words, and all there turned
to see the jewels green that burned
in Beren's ring. These Gnomes had set
as eyes of serpents twined that met
beneath a golden crown of flowers,                    1100
that one upholds and one devours:
the badge that Finrod made of yore
and Felagund his son now bore.

    His anger was chilled, but little less,
and dark thoughts Thingol did possess,                1105
though Melian the pale leant to his side
and whispered: 'O king, forgo thy pride!

Such is my counsel. Not by thee
shall Beren be slain, for far and free
from these deep halls his fate doth lead,                    1110
yet wound with thine. O king, take heed!'
But Thingol looked on Lúthien.
'Fairest of Elves! Unhappy Men,
children of little lords and kings
mortal and frail, these fading things,                       1115
shall they then look with love on thee?'
his heart within him thought. 'I see
thy ring,' he said, 'O mighty man!
But to win the child of Melian
a father's deeds shall not avail,                            1120
nor thy proud words at which I quail.
A treasure dear I too desire,
but rocks and steel and Morgoth's fire
from all the powers of Elfinesse
do keep the jewel I would possess.                           1125
Yet bonds like these I hear thee say
affright thee not. Now go thy way!
Bring me one shining Silmaril
from Morgoth's crown, then if she will,
may Lúthien set her hand in thine;                           1130
then shalt thou have this jewel of mine.'

      Then Thingol's warriors loud and long
they laughed; for wide renown in song
had Fëanor's gems o'er land and sea,
the peerless Silmarils; and three                            1135
alone he made and kindled slow
in the land of the Valar long ago,
and there in Tûn of their own light
they shone like marvellous stars at night,
in the great Gnomish hoards of Tûn,                          1140
while Glingal flowered and Belthil's bloom
yet lit the land beyond the shore
where the Shadowy Seas' last surges roar,
ere Morgoth stole them and the Gnomes
seeking their glory left their homes,                        1145
ere sorrows fell on Elves and Men,
ere Beren was or Lúthien,
ere Fëanor's sons in madness swore

their dreadful oath. But now no more
their beauty was seen, save shining clear          1150
in Morgoth's dungeons vast and drear.
His iron crown they must adorn,
and gleam above Orcs and slaves forlorn,
treasured in Hell above all wealth,
more than his eyes; and might nor stealth          1155
could touch them, or even gaze too long
upon their magic. Throng on throng
of Orcs with reddened scimitars
encircled him, and mighty bars
and everlasting gates and walls,                   1160
who wore them now amidst his thralls.
      Then Beren laughed more loud than they
in bitterness, and thus did say:
'For little price do elven-kings
their daughters sell – for gems and rings          1165
and things of gold! If such thy will,
thy bidding I will now fulfill.
On Beren son of Barahir
thou hast not looked the last, I fear.
Farewell, Tinúviel, starlit maiden!                1170
Ere the pale winter pass snowladen,
I will return, not thee to buy
with any jewel in Elfinesse,
but to find my love in loveliness,
a flower that grows beneath the sky.'              1175
Bowing before Melian and the king
he turned, and thrust aside the ring
of guards about him, and was gone,
and his footsteps faded one by one
in the dark corridors. 'A guileful oath            1180
thou sworest, father! Thou hast both
to blade and chain his flesh now doomed
in Morgoth's dungeons deep entombed,'
said Lúthien, and welling tears
sprang in her eyes, and hideous fears              1185
clutched at her heart. All looked away,
and later remembered the sad day
whereafter Lúthien no more sang.
Then clear in the silence the cold words rang
of Melian: 'Counsel cunning-wise,                  1190

O king!' she said. 'Yet if mine eyes
lose not their power, 'twere well for thee
that Beren failed his errantry.
Well for thee, but for thy child
a dark doom and a wandering wild.'                    1195

'I sell not to Men those whom I love'
said Thingol, 'whom all things above
I cherish; and if hope there were
that Beren should ever living fare
to the Thousand Caves once more, I swear          1200
he should not ever have seen the air
or light of heaven's stars again.'
But Melian smiled, and there was pain
as of far knowledge in her eyes;
for such is the sorrow of the wise.                    1205

★

## NOTES

The opening of this Canto is extant in two typescripts (to line 863), the
second version being substantially expanded; it was the first of them that
C. S. Lewis received – indeed, it is clear that the rewriting was in part
due to his criticism.

758–863   The rough drafts for this portion of the Lay (much briefer
          than the later text here printed) were written on the backs of
          booksellers' invoices dated 31 December 1925 and 2 February
          1926.
    761   In this Canto *elvish* rather than *elfin* is found already in A,
          but still *elfin* in both texts at 1164 (emended in B to *elven-*).
          *elven-* 799 occurs in a line found only in the later rewriting,
          B(2).
762–73   These lines are not in A; the B(1) version, severely criticised
          by C. S. Lewis, is given with his commentary, p. 326.
781–841   A:   and the bare woods nor moved nor sighed.
                   Yet ever after when star or moon
               shone clear or misty then came she soon
               just after day before the eve
               and found him, nor his side did leave               5
               until night waned and starlight ceased
               and day came pale o'er the pathless east.
               And there in far Broseliand

> he learned the touches of her hand;
> his feet grew swift as unseen airs,                   10
> his laughter soft, and far his cares,
> his voice like those in Doriath
> that wander where there runs no path.
> Thus days of golden spring did rise
> while Dairon watched with fiery eyes        15

The spelling *Broseliand* with *s* has now entered the A-text.

B(1) is as A, except that between lines 7 and 8 above were inserted ten lines that my father retained in the much longer B(2) text, 818–27 (*Then trembling-veiled*, &c.)

805    *Broseliand* B(2), emended to *Beleriand.*

849–51    These verses are an emendation to B(2)', with *Beleriand* thus written. For the B(1) version criticised by C. S. Lewis and the B(2) version before emendation see Lewis's commentary, p. 327.

891, 904    *Tavros* was emended in B to *Tauros*, but this seems to have been a much later change. The rough workings here had first the name (*Ormain* >) *Ormaid*, then *Tavros*.

937    Original reading of B: the last of Men, as songs now sing (with *like echoes* 939)

941    Original reading of B: the last of Men alone to hold

983–5    These lines are marked with an X on the B-text, and the words *on dragons* underlined and marked with an X – presumably because the creatures of Morgoth were not carved on the walls of the Thousand Caves.

987–9    These lines are repeated from Canto III, lines 408–10.

1010    *silver*: original reading of B *gold.*

1059–63    These lines are marked with an X on the B-text, as also are lines 1068–9. It may be that my father wished to represent Dairon as less unequivocally hostile to Beren, and also as ashamed of his words to Thingol (909–19).

1087    A:   that Celegorm of Nargothrond
with *Celegorm* emended first to *Felagoth* and then to *Felagund* (as at line 304).

1098    *Gnomes*: in the margin of B is written *Elves/smiths*. This is clearly a late change intended simply to get rid of the word *Gnomes* (see I. 43–4).

1102–3    A:   the badge that Fëanor made of yore
and Celegorm his son now bore.
*Celegorm* is not emended here as it is at line 1087, but the couplet is enclosed within brackets in the manuscript.

1141    *Glingal, Belthil*: original readings of B *Glingol, Bansil.* The same changes were made in *The Children of Húrin* (pp. 80–1, notes to lines 2027–8), where I retain the earlier forms.

1144-5   These lines are marked with an X on the B-text, perhaps
         simply because of the word *Gnomes* which here occurs in
         rhyme and cannot be easily replaced (see note to 1098); but
         C. S. Lewis criticised the word *their* in line 1145 as obscure
         in its reference (see his commentary, p. 329).

1151     A: in Morgoth Bauglir's dungeons drear. See p. 182.

1161     Here is written in the margin of the A manuscript: 'Mar. 27,
         28 1928'.

1175     This line was not originally in A but was pencilled in with
         queried indications to place it either after 1172 or (with
         irregular rhyming) after 1174, as it is in B.

### Commentary on Canto IV

Comparison of this Canto with the *Tale of Tinúviel* shows that the
narrative has undergone a deepening of significance, and this is largely
brought about by the cardinal change of Beren's being no longer an Elf
but a mortal Man (see p. 171). The story told in the poem is that of
*The Silmarillion* (pp. 165-8); for the prose version, close to the Lay in
every feature large and small, and indeed in many actual phrases, was
based directly on the verses, and in this Canto the verses underwent no
significant later revision. There are some elements in the poem that were
not taken up into the prose version, such as the description of the
Thousand Caves (980 ff.), whose splendour and beauty now first appear
(cf. my remarks on Thingol's wealth, pp. 160-1) – but a description of
Thingol's dwelling is given earlier in *The Silmarillion*, p. 93. In the
original text of the *Silmarillion* version Daeron's part was in fact entirely
excluded, though obviously only for the sake of compression (it was
reintroduced into the published work*). The loud laughter of Thingol's
warriors at Thingol's demand that Beren fetch him a Silmaril is not in the
prose account, and was perhaps deliberately excluded. This feature
harks back rather to the scene in the *Tale of Tinúviel* (II. 13), where
Thingol 'burst into laughter' at the aspect of Beren as suitor for his
daughter, and where the courtiers smiled when Thingol requested a
Silmaril as the bride-price, seeing that he 'treated the matter as an
uncouth jest'. Cf. my commentary on the Tale, II. 53:

> The tone is altogether lighter and less grave than it afterwards became;
> in the jeering laughter of Thingol, who treats the matter as a jest and
> Beren as a benighted fool, there is no hint of what is quite explicit in
> the later story: 'Thus he wrought the doom of Doriath, and was
> ensnared within the curse of Mandos.'

Canto III was in being by the autumn of 1925; while against Canto IV

─────────

*On pp. 166, 172; but the passage concerning Daeron on p. 183 is original. My father
apparently intended to insert references to Daeron's betrayals of Lúthien, but did not do so.

line 1161 in A there stands the date 27–8 March, 1928. The rough drafts for the opening of IV (lines 758–863) are written on the backs of invoices dated December 1925 and February 1926, but this does not show very much. In any case it seems to me most improbable that my father was writing lines 758–1161 over a period of two and a half years (September 1925 to March 1928): it is far more likely that there was a long gap, and that this fourth Canto was written pretty much at one time. Other evidence in fact suggests that he paused. There exist three pages of notes written on the backs of booksellers' invoices dated February, March, and May 1926, and these pages are of great interest for the development of the legend, for they contain a rapidly-composed plot-outline in which my father is seen working out the narrative of the next Cantos of the Lay.

This outline I will refer to as 'Synopsis I'. I give here its content as far as the end of Canto IV. Contractions used for names are expanded, and passages struck out (done at the time of writing) are included.

Beren and Tinúviel dance in the woods.
Dairon reports to the king.
Beren taken captive to the king.
Dairon will have him slain.
The king will shut him in his dungeons.
Tinúviel pleads.
Melian [*struck out*: says that he must not be slain, and that] refuses to advise but warns Thingol darkly that Beren must not be slain by him, and his coming was not without fate.
Thingol sends him for the Silmaril.
Beren's speech.
Melian says [*struck out*: this was better than his death, but] it were better for Thingol if Beren succeeded not.
Thingol said he would not send him if [he] were going to succeed. Melian smiles.
Flight of Beren.

In the *Tale of Tinúviel* Beren was led by Tinúviel into Thingol's caves (II. 13), and as I noted (II. 52–3):

The betrayal of Beren to Thingol by Daeron . . . has no place in the old story – there is nothing to betray; and indeed it is not shown in the tale that Dairon knew anything whatsoever of Beren before Tinúviel led him into the cave, beyond having once seen his face in the moonlight.

Moreover, in the *Tale* Dairon was Tinúviel's brother (II. 10; see p. 124). In the Lay (lines 909 ff.) Dairon utters strong hints concerning the strange quietness of the forest, which lead directly to a declaration by Lúthien of Beren's presence, and a demand that her father shall not harm him; Thingol swears that he will not, but sends Dairon with archers to prevent Beren's escape – needlessly, for Lúthien brings him that same night to Thingol's hall. This first part of Synopsis I suggests ideas that were never given form. Thus Dairon speaks to Thingol of Beren, as in the Lay, but Beren is actually apprehended and taken to the king as a prisoner; moreover (while it is of course impossible to be certain of the precise articulation of the plot from such an extremely compressed outline) Dairon seems more actively to seek Beren's death than he does in the poem (despite line 1068), and Tinúviel pleads against her father's policy.

For explanation of the references in A to Celegorm (notes to lines 1087, 1102–3) see p. 171. According to the earlier story seen in A the ring given to Barahir was made by Fëanor, Celegorm's father. In B the later story is present, and the badge of the entwined serpents is that of Felagund's father Finrod (Finarfin in *The Silmarillion*) who now first appears (other than in a later note to *The Children of Húrin*, see pp. 80, 138). Barahir now first replaces Egnor as Beren's father in A; and by later emendation to B (lines 937, 941) Bëor appears, who at this time, as is seen from the prose texts, was Barahir's father. With exceedingly complex genealogical and chronological restructuring of the houses of the Elf-friends in later years Bëor came to be removed from Barahir by many generations.

The name *Tavros* given to Oromë (891, 904) has occurred long before in the Gnomish dictionary, defined as the 'chief wood-fay, the Blue Spirit of the Woods' (I. 267, entry *Tavari*). With his *tree-propped halls* (892) compare the description of Oromë's dwelling in Valmar in the tale of *The Coming of the Valar and the Building of Valinor*, I. 75–6. At line 893 is the first mention of the golden hooves of Oromë's horse.

# V

So days drew on from the mournful day;
the curse of silence no more lay
on Doriath, though Dairon's flute
and Lúthien's singing both were mute.
The murmurs soft awake once more                    1210
about the woods, the waters roar
past the great gates of Thingol's halls;
but no dancing step of Lúthien falls
on turf or leaf. For she forlorn,
where stumbled once, where bruised and torn,          1215

with longing on him like a dream,
had Beren sat by the shrouded stream
Esgalduin the dark and strong,
she sat and mourned in a low song:
'Endless roll the waters past!                    1220
To this my love hath come at last,
enchanted waters pitiless,
a heartache and a loneliness.'

The summer turns. In branches tall
she hears the pattering raindrops fall,           1225
the windy tide in leafy seas,
the creaking of the countless trees;
and longs unceasing and in vain
to hear one calling once again
the tender name that nightingales                 1230
were called of old. Echo fails.
'Tinúviel! Tinúviel!'
the memory is like a knell,
a faint and far-off tolling bell:
'Tinúviel! Tinúviel!'                             1235

'O mother Melian, tell to me
some part of what thy dark eyes see!
Tell of thy magic where his feet
are wandering! What foes him meet?
O mother, tell me, lives he still                 1240
treading the desert and the hill?
Do sun and moon above him shine,
do the rains fall on him, mother mine?'

'Nay, Lúthien my child, I fear
he lives indeed in bondage drear.                 1245
The Lord of Wolves hath prisons dark,
chains and enchantments cruel and stark,
there trapped and bound and languishing
now Beren dreams that thou dost sing.'

'Then I alone must go to him                      1250
and dare the dread in dungeons dim;
for none there be that will him aid
in all the world, save elven-maid
whose only skill were joy and song,
and both have failed and left her long.'         1255

Then nought said Melian thereto,
though wild the words. She wept anew,
and ran through the woods like hunted deer
with her hair streaming and eyes of fear.
Dairon she found with ferny crown                    1260
silently sitting on beech-leaves brown.
On the earth she cast her at his side.
'O Dairon, Dairon, my tears,' she cried,
'now pity for our old days' sake!
Make me a music for heart's ache,                    1265
for heart's despair, and for heart's dread,
for light gone dark and laughter dead!'

'But for music dead there is no note,'
Dairon answered, and at his throat
his fingers clutched. Yet his pipe he took,          1270
and sadly trembling the music shook;
and all things stayed while that piping went
wailing in the hollows, and there intent
they listened, their business and mirth,
their hearts' gladness and the light of earth        1275
forgotten; and bird-voices failed
while Dairon's flute in Doriath wailed.
Lúthien wept not for very pain,
and when he ceased she spoke again:
'My friend, I have a need of friends,                1280
as he who a long dark journey wends,
and fears the road, yet dare not turn
and look back where the candles burn
in windows he has left. The night
in front, he doubts to find the light                1285
that far beyond the hills he seeks.'
And thus of Melian's words she speaks,
and of her doom and her desire
to climb the mountains, and the fire
and ruin of the Northern realm                       1290
to dare, a maiden without helm
or sword, or strength of hardy limb,
where magic founders and grows dim.
His aid she sought to guide her forth
and find the pathways to the North,                  1295
if he would not for love of her

go by her side a wanderer.

    'Wherefore,' said he, 'should Dairon go
into direst peril earth doth know
for the sake of mortal who did steal                    1300
his laughter and joy? No love I feel
for Beren son of Barahir,
nor weep for him in dungeons drear,
who in this wood have chains enow,
heavy and dark. But thee, I vow,                    1305
I will defend from perils fell
and deadly wandering into hell.'

    No more they spake that day, and she
perceived not his meaning. Sorrowfully
she thanked him, and she left him there.                    1310
A tree she climbed, till the bright air
above the woods her dark hair blew,
and straining afar her eyes could view
the outline grey and faint and low
of dizzy towers where the clouds go,                    1315
the southern faces mounting sheer
in rocky pinnacle and pier
of Shadowy Mountains pale and cold;
and wide the lands before them rolled.
But straightway Dairon sought the king                    1320
and told him his daughter's pondering,
and how her madness might her lead
to ruin, unless the king gave heed.
Thingol was wroth, and yet amazed;
in wonder and half fear he gazed                    1325
on Dairon, and said: 'True hast thou been.
Now ever shall love be us between,
while Doriath lasts; within this realm
thou art a prince of beech and elm!'
He sent for Lúthien, and said:                    1330
'O maiden fair, what hath thee led
to ponder madness and despair
to wander to ruin, and to fare
from Doriath against my will,
stealing like a wild thing men would kill                    1335
into the emptiness outside?'
'The wisdom, father,' she replied;

nor would she promise to forget,
nor would she vow for love or threat
her folly to forsake and meek                            1340
in Doriath her father's will to seek.
This only vowed she, if go she must,
that none but herself would she now trust,
no folk of her father's would persuade
to break his will or lend her aid;                       1345
if go she must, she would go alone
and friendless dare the walls of stone.

    In angry love and half in fear
Thingol took counsel his most dear
to guard and keep. He would not bind                     1350
in caverns deep and intertwined
sweet Lúthien, his lovely maid,
who robbed of air must wane and fade,
who ever must look upon the sky
and see the sun and moon go by.                          1355
But close unto his mounded seat
and grassy throne there ran the feet
of Hirilorn, the beechen queen.
Upon her triple boles were seen
no break or branch, until aloft                          1360
in a green glimmer, distant, soft,
the mightiest vault of leaf and bough
from world's beginning until now
was flung above Esgalduin's shores
and the long slopes to Thingol's doors.                  1365
    Grey was the rind of pillars tall
and silken-smooth, and far and small
to squirrels' eyes were those who went
at her grey feet upon the bent.
Now Thingol made men in the beech,                       1370
in that great tree, as far as reach
their longest ladders, there to build
an airy house; and as he willed
a little dwelling of fair wood
was made, and veiled in leaves it stood                  1375
above the first branches. Corners three
it had and windows faint to see,
and by three shafts of Hirilorn

in the corners standing was upborne.

There Lúthien was bidden dwell,                    1380
until she was wiser and the spell
of madness left her. Up she clomb
the long ladders to her new home
among the leaves, among the birds;
she sang no song, she spoke no words.              1385
White glimmering in the tree she rose,
and her little door they heard her close.
The ladders were taken and no more
her feet might tread Esgalduin's shore.

Thither at whiles they climbed and brought         1390
all things she needed or besought;
but death was his, whoso should dare
a ladder leave, or creeping there
should set one by the tree at night;
a guard was held from dusk to light                1395
about the grey feet of Hirilorn
and Lúthien in prison and forlorn.
There Dairon grieving often stood
in sorrow for the captive of the wood,
and melodies made upon his flute                   1400
leaning against a grey tree-root.
Lúthien would from her windows stare
and see him far under piping there,
and she forgave his betraying word
for the music and the grief she heard,             1405
and only Dairon would she let
across her threshold foot to set.

Yet long the hours when she must sit
and see the sunbeams dance and flit
in beechen leaves, or watch the stars              1410
peep on clear nights between the bars
of beechen branches. And one night
just ere the changing of the light
a dream there came, from the Gods, maybe,
or Melian's magic. She dreamed that she            1415
heard Beren's voice o'er hill and fell
'Tinúviel' call, 'Tinúviel.'
And her heart answered: 'Let me be gone
to seek him no others think upon!'

She woke and saw the moonlight pale                    1420
through the slim leaves. It trembled frail
upon her arms, as these she spread
and there in longing bowed her head,
and yearned for freedom and escape.

   Now Lúthien doth her counsel shape;                 1425
and Melian's daughter of deep lore
knew many things, yea, magics more
than then or now know elven-maids
that glint and shimmer in the glades.
She pondered long, while the moon sank                 1430
and faded, and the starlight shrank,
and the dawn opened. At last a smile
on her face flickered. She mused a while,
and watched the morning sunlight grow,
then called to those that walked below.                1435
And when one climbed to her she prayed
that he would in the dark pools wade
of cold Esgalduin, water clear,
the clearest water cold and sheer
to draw for her. 'At middle night,'                    1440
she said, 'in bowl of silver white
it must be drawn and brought to me
with no word spoken, silently.'
Another she begged to bring her wine
in a jar of gold where flowers twine –                 1445
'and singing let him come to me
at high noon, singing merrily.'
Again she spake: 'Now go, I pray,
to Melian the queen, and say:
"thy daughter many a weary hour                         1450
slow passing watches in her bower;
a spinning-wheel she begs thee send."'
Then Dairon she called: 'I prithee, friend,
climb up and talk to Lúthien!'
And sitting at her window then,                         1455
she said: 'My Dairon, thou hast craft,
beside thy music, many a shaft
and many a tool of carven wood
to fashion with cunning. It were good,
if thou wouldst make a little loom                      1460

to stand in the corner of my room.
My idle fingers would spin and weave
a pattern of colours, of morn and eve,
of sun and moon and changing light
amid the beech-leaves waving bright.'  1465
This Dairon did and asked her then:
'O Lúthien, O Lúthien,
What wilt thou weave? What wilt thou spin?'
'A marvellous thread, and wind therein
a potent magic, and a spell  1470
I will weave within my web that hell
nor all the powers of Dread shall break.'
Then Dairon wondered, but he spake
no word to Thingol, though his heart
feared the dark purpose of her art.  1475

    And Lúthien now was left alone.
A magic song to Men unknown
she sang, and singing then the wine
with water mingled three times nine;
and as in golden jar they lay  1480
she sang a song of growth and day;
and as they lay in silver white
another song she sang, of night
and darkness without end, of height
uplifted to the stars, and flight  1485
and freedom. And all names of things
tallest and longest on earth she sings:
the locks of the Longbeard dwarves; the tail
of Draugluin the werewolf pale;
the body of Glómund the great snake;  1490
the vast upsoaring peaks that quake
above the fires in Angband's gloom;
the chain Angainor that ere Doom
for Morgoth shall by Gods be wrought
of steel and torment. Names she sought,  1495
and sang of Glend the sword of Nan;
of Gilim the giant of Eruman;
and last and longest named she then
the endless hair of Uinen,
the Lady of the Sea, that lies  1500
through all the waters under skies.

Then did she lave her head and sing
a theme of sleep and slumbering,
profound and fathomless and dark
as Lúthien's shadowy hair was dark –                    1505
each thread was more slender and more fine
than threads of twilight that entwine
in filmy web the fading grass
and closing flowers as day doth pass.

Now long and longer grew her hair,                      1510
and fell to her feet, and wandered there
like pools of shadow on the ground.
Then Lúthien in a slumber drowned
was laid upon her bed and slept,
till morning through the windows crept                  1515
thinly and faint. And then she woke,
and the room was filled as with a smoke
and with an evening mist, and deep
she lay thereunder drowsed in sleep.
Behold! her hair from windows blew                      1520
in morning airs, and darkly grew
waving about the pillars grey
of Hirilorn at break of day.

Then groping she found her little shears,
and cut the hair about her ears,                        1525
and close she cropped it to her head,
enchanted tresses, thread by thread.
Thereafter grew they slow once more,
yet darker than their wont before.
And now was her labour but begun:                       1530
long was she spinning, long she spun;
and though with elvish skill she wrought,
long was her weaving. If men sought
to call her, crying from below,
'Nothing I need,' she answered, 'go!                     1535
I would keep my bed, and only sleep
I now desire, who waking weep.'

Then Dairon feared, and in amaze
he called from under; but three days
she answered not. Of cloudy hair                        1540
she wove a web like misty air
of moonless night, and thereof made

a robe as fluttering-dark as shade
beneath great trees, a magic dress
that all was drenched with drowsiness,　　　1545
enchanted with a mightier spell
than Melian's raiment in that dell
wherein of yore did Thingol roam
beneath the dark and starry dome
that hung above the dawning world.　　　1550
And now this robe she round her furled,
and veiled her garments shimmering white;
her mantle blue with jewels bright
like crystal stars, the lilies gold,
were wrapped and hid; and down there rolled　　　1555
dim dreams and faint oblivious sleep
falling about her, to softly creep
through all the air. Then swift she takes
the threads unused; of these she makes
a slender rope of twisted strands　　　1560
yet long and stout, and with her hands
she makes it fast unto the shaft
of Hirilorn. Now, all her craft
and labour ended, looks she forth
from her little window facing North.　　　1565

　　Already the sunlight in the trees
is drooping red, and dusk she sees
come softly along the ground below,
and now she murmurs soft and slow.
Now chanting clearer down she cast　　　1570
her long hair, till it reached at last
from her window to the darkling ground.
Men far beneath her heard the sound;
but the slumbrous strand now swung and swayed
above her guards. Their talking stayed,　　　1575
they listened to her voice and fell
suddenly beneath a binding spell.

　　Now clad as in a cloud she hung;
now down her ropéd hair she swung
as light as squirrel, and away,　　　1580
away, she danced, and who could say
what paths she took, whose elvish feet
no impress made a-dancing fleet?

★

## NOTES

1222-3  At lines 651–2 these lines were transposed on C. S. Lewis's suggestion (see p. 323); and *heartache* was emended to *hunger*.

1226    Cf. line 664.

1231    Original reading of B: *are called in elfland. Echo fails.* The change was probably simply to get rid of 'elfland'.

1249    *now*: uncertain (original reading *doth Beren dream* emended to *?now Beren dreams*).

1253    Throughout this Canto *elven-* and *elvish* are emendations of *elfin* made on the B-text.

1260-1  Cf. lines 497–8.

1308-10 Marked *revise* on the B-text.

1312    *her dark hair*: so also in A. See note to line 558.

1316-17 Cf. lines 389–90. The *Shadowy Mountains* (1318) are the Mountains of Terror (Ered Gorgoroth): see pp. 170–1.

1323    This line is marked with an X on the B-text.

1329    As line 1323.

1358    Against *Hirilorn* in A is written *Hiradorn*, and so also at lines 1396, 1523. At line 1563 *Hiradorn* is the form in the text of A.

1362-3  Cf. lines 872–3.

1370    *men* > *them* A. At 1390, where B has *they*, A had *men* > *they*; at 1533, 1573 *men* was not changed in either text.

1414-17 Marked with a line on the B-text; in the margin some new verses are written, but so faint and rapid as to be quite illegible.

1488    *locks* B] *beards* A

1489    A:    of Carcharas the wolf-ward pale;
        In the original draft the spelling is *Carcaras* as in the typescript version of the *Tale of Tinúviel* (manuscript version *Karkaras*). In the second version of *The Children of Húrin* (p. 107 line 374) the form is *Carcharoth* (emended from *Carcharolch*).

1490    *Glómund* B] *Glórund* A (as in the *Lost Tales*, but there always without accent).

1493    *Angainor* A, B] *Engainor* in the original draft.

1496    *Nan* B] *Nann* A (but *Nan* in the original draft).

1549-50 Cf. lines 406–7.

1563    *Hirilorn* B] *Hiradorn* A. See note to line 1358.

## Commentary on Canto V

The plot-outline 'Synopsis I' covering the narrative of this Canto is very slight:

Mourning of Tinúviel.
Treachery of Dairon.
Building of the Tree House in Hirilorn.
Escape of Tinúviel.
[*Added in*: Repentance, wandering, and loss of Dairon.]

The wandering and loss of Dairon goes back to the *Tale of Tinúviel* (II. 20–1) and survived into *The Silmarillion* (p. 183), but there is no other mention of his 'repentance' (though this is perhaps implied in the Lay, lines 1398 ff.)

In my commentary on the passage in the *Tale of Tinúviel* corresponding to this Canto I remarked (II. 54) that

> the story of her imprisonment in the house in Hirilorn and her escape from it never underwent any significant change. The passage in *The Silmarillion* (p. 172) is indeed very brief, but its lack of detail is due to compression rather than to omission based on dissatisfaction; the *Lay of Leithian*, from which the prose account in *The Silmarillion* directly derives, is in this passage so close, in point of narrative detail, to the *Tale of Tinúviel* as to be almost identical with it.

There is little to add to this here. In one respect the narrative of the Lay is at variance with the story told in *The Silmarillion*. What was 'the curse of silence' (1207)? It was due to Dairon (848–53). In a preliminary, soon abandoned draft for the 'Silmarillion' version, where the story was to be told far more amply (by following the Lay more closely) the matter is made more explicit:

> But Dairon haunted the trees and watched them from afar; and he cried aloud in the bitterness of his heart: 'Hateful is now become the land that I loved, and the trees misshapen. No more shall music here be heard. Let all voices fail in Doriath, and in every dale and upon every hill let the trees stand silent!' And there was a hush and a great stillness; and Thingol's folk were filled with wonder. And they spoke to their king, asking what was the reason of the silence.

Dairon's 'curse' was lifted after Beren's departure, although Lúthien no longer sang and Dairon no longer piped. This is in contrast to *The Silmarillion* (p. 168), where after Beren went

> Lúthien was silent, and from that hour she sang not again in Doriath. *A brooding silence fell upon the woods*.

For the names in the 'lengthening spell' see II. 67–8. A new element among the 'longest things' is introduced in the version in the Lay, the peaks above Angband (1491–2); and in B the name of the great Dragon becomes *Glómund*. The chain with which Morgoth was bound, *Angaino/Angainu* in the *Lost Tales*, becomes *Angainor*; but it is curious that in the Lay it is only spoken of as a punishment awaiting

Morgoth in the future (*ere Doom*, 1493), whereas in the old story of *The Chaining of Melko* (I. 104) it was the shackle with which he was taken prisoner in the original war that led to his captivity in Valinor, and this survived in *The Silmarillion* (p. 51): at the end of the Elder Days 'he was bound with the chain Angainor which he had worn aforetime' (*ibid.* p. 252).

New elements in the story that have yet to appear in the actual narrative of the Lay are seen in *Draugluin*, replacing in B *Carcharas* of A in the 'lengthening spell' (thus Carcharas is no longer the 'father of wolves', see II. 68), and in Melian's reference to Beren's lying in the dungeons of the Lord of Wolves (1246).

Lúthien's dream in which she heard Beren's voice far off is still ascribed, as it was in the *Tale*, to the Gods, if less positively (*a dream there came, from the Gods, maybe, / or Melian's magic*, 1414–15); see II. 19, 68. But the passage is marked in B, perhaps indicating dissatisfaction with the idea.

There is curious detail in a marginal note to the B-text. At some time (as I think) long afterwards someone unknown wrote against lines 1331–6: 'Thingol is here being rather obtuse'; and against this remark my father scribbled: 'But he could not believe she *loved* Beren – unless some evil spell had somehow been laid on her.'

# VI

When Morgoth in that day of doom
had slain the Trees and filled with gloom                    1585
the shining land of Valinor,
there Fëanor and his sons then swore
the mighty oath upon the hill
of tower-crownéd Tûn, that still
wrought wars and sorrow in the world.                       1590
From darkling seas the fogs unfurled
their blinding shadows grey and cold
where Glingal once had bloomed with gold
and Belthil bore its silver flowers.
The mists were mantled round the towers                     1595
of the Elves' white city by the sea.
There countless torches fitfully
did start and twinkle, as the Gnomes
were gathered to their fading homes,

and thronged the long and winding stair 1600
that led to the wide echoing square.

There Fëanor mourned his jewels divine,
the Silmarils he made. Like wine
his wild and potent words them fill;
a great host harkens deathly still. 1605
But all he said both wild and wise,
half truth and half the fruit of lies
that Morgoth sowed in Valinor,
in other songs and other lore
recorded is. He bade them flee 1610
from lands divine, to cross the sea,
the pathless plains, the perilous shores
where ice-infested water roars;
to follow Morgoth to the unlit earth
leaving their dwellings and olden mirth; 1615
to go back to the Outer Lands
to wars and weeping. There their hands
they joined in vows, those kinsmen seven,
swearing beneath the stars of Heaven,
by Varda the Holy that them wrought 1620
and bore them each with radiance fraught
and set them in the deeps to flame.
Timbrenting's holy height they name,
whereon are built the timeless halls
of Manwë Lord of Gods. Who calls 1625
these names in witness may not break
his oath, though earth and heaven shake.

Curufin, Celegorm the fair,
Damrod and Díriel were there,
and Cranthir dark, and Maidros tall 1630
(whom after torment should befall),
and Maglor the mighty who like the sea
with deep voice sings yet mournfully.
'Be he friend or foe, or seed defiled
of Morgoth Bauglir, or mortal child 1635
that in after days on earth shall dwell,
no law, nor love, nor league of hell,
not might of Gods, not moveless fate
shall him defend from wrath and hate
of Fëanor's sons, who takes or steals 1640

or finding keeps the Silmarils,
the thrice-enchanted globes of light
that shine until the final night.'

The wars and wandering of the Gnomes
this tale tells not. Far from their homes      1645
they fought and laboured in the North.
Fingon daring alone went forth
and sought for Maidros where he hung;
in torment terrible he swung,
his wrist in band of forgéd steel,      1650
from a sheer precipice where reel
the dizzy senses staring down
from Thangorodrim's stony crown.
The song of Fingon Elves yet sing,
captain of armies, Gnomish king,      1655
who fell at last in flame of swords
with his white banners and his lords.
They sing how Maidros free he set,
and stayed the feud that slumbered yet
between the children proud of Finn.      1660
Now joined once more they hemmed him in,
even great Morgoth, and their host
beleaguered Angband, till they boast
no Orc nor demon ever dare
their leaguer break or past them fare.      1665
Then days of solace woke on earth
beneath the new-lit Sun, and mirth
was heard in the Great Lands where Men,
a young race, spread and wandered then.
That was the time that songs do call      1670
the Siege of Angband, when like a wall
the Gnomish swords did fence the earth
from Morgoth's ruin, a time of birth,
of blossoming, of flowers, of growth;
but still there held the deathless oath,      1675
and still the Silmarils were deep
in Angband's darkly-dolven keep.

An end there came, when fortune turned,
and flames of Morgoth's vengeance burned,
and all the might which he prepared      1680
in secret in his fastness flared

and poured across the Thirsty Plain;
and armies black were in his train.
  The leaguer of Angband Morgoth broke;
his enemies in fire and smoke                            1685
were scattered, and the Orcs there slew
and slew, until the blood like dew
dripped from each cruel and crooked blade.
Then Barahir the bold did aid
with mighty spear, with shield and men,                  1690
Felagund wounded. To the fen
escaping, there they bound their troth,
and Felagund deeply swore an oath
of friendship to his kin and seed,
of love and succour in time of need.                     1695
But there of Finrod's children four
were Angrod slain and proud Egnor.
Felagund and Orodreth then
gathered the remnant of their men,
their maidens and their children fair;                   1700
forsaking war they made their lair
and cavernous hold far in the south.
On Narog's towering bank its mouth
was opened; which they hid and veiled,
and mighty doors, that unassailed                        1705
till Túrin's day stood vast and grim,
they built by trees o'ershadowed dim.
And with them dwelt a long time there
Curufin, and Celegorm the fair;
and a mighty folk grew neath their hands                 1710
in Narog's secret halls and lands.

  Thus Felagund in Nargothrond
still reigned, a hidden king whose bond
was sworn to Barahir the bold.
And now his son through forests cold                      1715
wandered alone as in a dream.
Esgalduin's dark and shrouded stream
he followed, till its waters frore
were joined to Sirion, Sirion hoar,
pale silver water wide and free                           1720
rolling in splendour to the sea.
  Now Beren came unto the pools,

wide shallow meres where Sirion cools
his gathered tide beneath the stars,
ere chafed and sundered by the bars                    1725
of reedy banks a mighty fen
he feeds and drenches, plunging then
into vast chasms underground,
where many miles his way is wound.
Umboth-Muilin, Twilight Meres,                         1730
those great wide waters grey as tears
the Elves then named. Through driving rain
from thence across the Guarded Plain
the Hills of the Hunters Beren saw
with bare tops bitten bleak and raw                    1735
by western winds; but in the mist
of streaming rains that flashed and hissed
into the meres he knew there lay
beneath those hills the cloven way
of Narog, and the watchful halls                       1740
of Felagund beside the falls
of Ingwil tumbling from the wold.
An everlasting watch they hold,
the Gnomes of Nargothrond renowned,
and every hill is tower-crowned,                       1745
where wardens sleepless peer and gaze
guarding the plain and all the ways
between Narog swift and Sirion pale;
and archers whose arrows never fail
there range the woods, and secret kill                 1750
all who creep thither against their will.
    Yet now he thrusts into that land
bearing the gleaming ring on hand
of Felagund, and oft doth cry:
'Here comes no wandering Orc or spy,                    1755
but Beren son of Barahir
who once to Felagund was dear.'
    So ere he reached the eastward shore
of Narog, that doth foam and roar
o'er boulders black, those archers green                1760
came round him. When the ring was seen
they bowed before him, though his plight
was poor and beggarly. Then by night
they led him northward, for no ford

nor bridge was built where Narog poured          1765
before the gates of Nargothrond,
and friend nor foe might pass beyond.
    To northward, where that stream yet young
more slender flowed, below the tongue
of foam-splashed land that Ginglith pens          1770
when her brief golden torrent ends
and joins the Narog, there they wade.
Now swiftest journey thence they made
to Nargothrond's sheer terraces
and dim gigantic palaces.                         1775
    They came beneath a sickle moon
to doors there darkly hung and hewn
with posts and lintels of ponderous stone
and timbers huge. Now open thrown
were gaping gates, and in they strode             1780
where Felagund on throne abode.

    Fair were the words of Narog's king
to Beren, and his wandering
and all his feuds and bitter wars
recounted soon. Behind closed doors               1785
they sat, while Beren told his tale
of Doriath; and words him fail
recalling Lúthien dancing fair
with wild white roses in her hair,
remembering her elven voice that rung             1790
while stars in twilight round her hung.
He spake of Thingol's marvellous halls
by enchantment lit, where fountain falls
and ever the nightingale doth sing
to Melian and to her king.                        1795
The quest he told that Thingol laid
in scorn on him; how for love of maid
more fair than ever was born to Men,
of Tinúviel, of Lúthien,
he must essay the burning waste,                  1800
and doubtless death and torment taste.

    This Felagund in wonder heard,
and heavily spake at last this word:
'It seems that Thingol doth desire
thy death. The everlasting fire                   1805

of those enchanted jewels all know
is cursed with an oath of endless woe,
and Fëanor's sons alone by right
are lords and masters of their light.
He cannot hope within his hoard                    1810
to keep this gem, nor is he lord
of all the folk of Elfinesse.
And yet thou saist for nothing less
can thy return to Doriath
be purchased? Many a dreadful path                 1815
in sooth there lies before thy feet —
and after Morgoth, still a fleet
untiring hate, as I know well,
would hunt thee from heaven unto hell.
Fëanor's sons would, if they could,                1820
slay thee or ever thou reached his wood
or laid in Thingol's lap that fire,
or gained at least thy sweet desire.
Lo! Celegorm and Curufin
here dwell this very realm within,                 1825
and even though I, Finrod's son,
am king, a mighty power have won
and many of their own folk lead.
Friendship to me in every need
they yet have shown, but much I fear               1830
that to Beren son of Barahir
mercy or love they will not show
if once thy dreadful quest they know.'

    True words he spake. For when the king
to all his people told this thing,                 1835
and spake of the oath to Barahir,
and how that mortal shield and spear
had saved them from Morgoth and from woe
on Northern battlefields long ago,
then many were kindled in their hearts             1840
once more to battle. But up there starts
amid the throng, and loudly cries
for hearing, one with flaming eyes,
proud Celegorm with gleaming hair
and shining sword. Then all men stare              1845
upon his stern unyielding face,

and a great hush falls upon that place.

'Be he friend or foe, or demon wild
of Morgoth, Elf, or mortal child,
or any that here on earth may dwell,                    1850
no law, nor love, nor league of hell,
no might of Gods, no binding spell,
shall him defend from hatred fell
of Fëanor's sons, whoso take or steal
or finding keep a Silmaril.                             1855
These we alone do claim by right,
our thrice enchanted jewels bright.'

Many wild and potent words he spoke,
and as before in Tûn awoke
his father's voice their hearts to fire,               1860
so now dark fear and brooding ire
he cast on them, foreboding war
of friend with friend; and pools of gore
their minds imagined lying red
in Nargothrond about the dead,                         1865
did Narog's host with Beren go;
or haply battle, ruin, and woe
in Doriath where great Thingol reigned,
if Fëanor's fatal jewel he gained.
And even such as were most true                        1870
to Felagund his oath did rue,
and thought with terror and despair
of seeking Morgoth in his lair
with force or guile. This Curufin
when his brother ceased did then begin                 1875
more to impress upon their minds;
and such a spell he on them binds
that never again till Túrin's day
would Gnome of Narog in array
of open battle go to war.                              1880
With secrecy, ambush, spies, and lore
of wizardry, with silent leaguer
of wild things wary, watchful, eager,
of phantom hunters, venomed darts,
and unseen stealthy creeping arts,                     1885
with padding hatred that its prey
with feet of velvet all the day

followed remorseless out of sight
and slew it unawares at night –
thus they defended Nargothrond,                    1890
and forgot their kin and solemn bond
for dread of Morgoth that the art
of Curufin set within their heart.

So would they not that angry day
King Felagund their lord obey,                     1895
but sullen murmured that Finrod
nor yet his son were as a god.
Then Felagund took off his crown
and at his feet he cast it down,
the silver helm of Nargothrond:                    1900
'Yours ye may break, but I my bond
must keep, and kingdom here forsake.
If hearts here were that did not quake,
or that to Finrod's son were true,
then I at least should find a few                  1905
to go with me, not like a poor
rejected beggar scorn endure,
turned from my gates to leave my town,
my people, and my realm and crown!'

Hearing these words there swiftly stood            1910
beside him ten tried warriors good,
men of his house who had ever fought
wherever his banners had been brought.
One stooped and lifted up his crown,
and said: 'O king, to leave this town              1915
is now our fate, but not to lose
thy rightful lordship. Thou shalt choose
one to be steward in thy stead.'
Then Felagund upon the head
of Orodreth set it: 'Brother mine,                 1920
till I return this crown is thine.'
Then Celegorm no more would stay,
and Curufin smiled and turned away.

★

# NOTES

1593–4    Original readings of B *Glingol*, *Bansil*, as at line 1141.

1598–9    Couplet marked for revision, partly on account of *did start*, partly on account of *Gnomes*. I do not record further instances of this sort, which occur casually throughout.

1619    Here is written on the B-text: '∧ see the Qenta.' This is the 'Silmarillion' version of 1930, and presumably refers to the form of the Oath as it appears there.

1620    *Varda the Holy* is written in the margin of the B-text, which like A has *Bridhil the Blessed*. *Bridhil* occurs earlier in A (note to lines 377–81), where B has a different reading.

1632–3    Cf. lines 506–9.

1647    *Finweg* A, and B as typed, early emended in B to *Fingon*.

1654    As line 1647.

1656    Cf. *The Children of Húrin*, first version line 1975, second version line 19, from which the words (referring to Finweg/Fingon) *fell in flame of swords* are derived; in the second version occur also the king's *white banners*.

1710–11    A:   a great people were gathered of the Gnomes
                 in these new-builded secret homes.

1736    Against the words *by western winds* is written (in such a way as to show that this was the point reached, not the starting-point) the date '29 Mar. 1928', the previous date being 27–28 March 1928 at line 1161.

1859    *Tûn* B] *Côr* A

1866    A:   if Felagund should with Beren go;

1891    A:   and forgot their blood and kinship's bond

1900    *helm* is an emendation in B for *crown*.

1920    An X is written against this line, probably long after when Orodreth was moved from his place as Felagund's brother (see p. 91).

1921    *crown* B] *realm* A

## Commentary on Canto VI

The plot-outline 'Synopsis I' continues thus:

Beren goes to Celegorm, who disguises him [*struck out*: and gives him a magic knife. Beren and his Gnomish guides* are captured by Orcs: and a few survivors taken before (Melko >) Morgoth. Beren tells M. he is a 'trapper of the woods'.]

---

*This phrase was changed to: 'Beren gets lost and separated from his Gnomish guides'; and was then struck out with the rest of the passage.

They go and seek to break into Angband disguised as Orcs, but are captured [*struck out*: and set in chains, and killed one by one. Beren lies wondering which will be his turn.] by the Lord of Wolves, and set in bonds, and devoured one by one.

It is interesting here to see how the relevant features of the story are treated in the 'Sketch of the Mythology' of 1926, as originally written. In this account Beren's father is Barahir, and he 'had been a friend of Celegorm of Nargothrond'. After Thingol's demand that Beren get him a Silmaril:

Beren sets out to achieve this, is captured, and set in dungeon in Angband, but conceals his real identity, and is given as a slave to Thû the hunter.

This passage is evidently earlier than 'Synopsis I' (at the earliest, the end of May 1926, the date of the latest of the three invoices on which it is written), since the 'Sketch' contains no reference to Celegorm's aid, Beren's companions, their disguising as Orcs, and their capture by the Lord of Wolves. On the contrary, Beren goes to Angband alone just as he did in the *Tale of Tinúviel*, and – most notably – is given to 'Thû the hunter' as a slave, just as in the *Tale* he was given to Tevildo Prince of Cats as a slave. In Synopsis I we see, I think, the very point at which the story of Beren's Gnomish companions came into being, of their disguise as Orcs, and of their deaths one by one in the dungeons of the Lord of Wolves. (Thû appears first in the fragment of the *Lay of the Fall of Gondolin* (p. 146), and in *The Children of Húrin* as Morgoth's most mighty thane: first version line 391, second version line 763).

But already at lines 296 ff. in the A-text of the *Lay of Leithian* (summer 1925) there is a reference to the 'deed of service' done by Egnor Beren's father to Celegorm, and the gift of the ring: while in the 'Sketch' Barahir 'had been a friend of Celegorm of Nargothrond'. Thus:

| | |
|---|---|
| *Lay of Leithian*<br>Canto II<br>(summer 1925) | Egnor Beren's father performed a service for Celegorm, from whom he received a ring. |
| *Sketch of the*<br>*Mythology*<br>(early in 1926,<br>see p. 3) | Barahir Beren's father was a friend of Celegorm of Nargothrond.<br><br>Beren sets out alone and is captured and imprisoned in Angband, but is given as a slave to Thû the hunter. |
| *Synopsis I*<br>(after May 1926) | Beren goes to Celegorm who aids him (story of the Gnomish companions appears). |

The rather surprising conclusion must be that the association of Egnor/Barahir with Celegorm and the gift of the ring *preceded* the emergence of the story of Beren's going to Celegorm for aid.

In the rejected part of Synopsis I here we see a last survival from the

*Tale of Tinúviel*: Beren tells Morgoth that he is a trapper of the woods; cf. the *Tale* (II. 15): 'Beren said therewith that he was a great trapper of small animals and a snarer of birds' – and it was indeed this explanation of Beren's to Melko that got him his post in Tevildo's kitchens. The mention in this rejected passage of a magic knife given to Beren by Celegorm was clearly a passing idea to account for the knife with which Beren would cut the Silmaril from the Iron Crown, since the kitchen-knife with which he did the deed in the *Tale* (II. 33) had been abandoned with the kitchens.

Other loose papers in addition to Synopsis I show the further development of the narrative. The first of these I will refer to as 'Synopsis II'; it begins with the beginning of Canto VI and I cite it here as far as the end of the Canto.

Beren comes to Felagund at Nargothrond; who receives him well, but warns him of the oath of the sons of Fëanor, and that Curufin and Celegorm dwelling with him have great power in his realm.

Curufin and Celegorm learn of Beren's purpose, and recalling their oath forbid the Gnomes to aid Beren to get the Silmaril for Thingol. The Gnomes fearing war in Nargothrond, or war against Thingol, and in [any] case despairing utterly of reaching the depths of Angband by force or guile will not support Felagund. Felagund mindful of his own oath hands his kingdom over to Orodreth, and with only his own faithful followers of his household (ten in number) goes forth with Beren.

In the *Lay of Leithian* the 'Nargothrond Element' in the story had by this time (the spring of 1928) evolved further (see p. 171). The major figure of (Felagoth >) Felagund, son of Finwë's third son Finrod, had emerged (see p. 91), and by Canto VI was present also in the A-text; it was he, not Celegorm, who was rescued in the battle that ended the Siege of Angband and who then went south with his brother Orodreth to found Nargothrond, and Celegorm with his brother Curufin have been shifted by the movement of the legend into the rôle of Felagund's overpowerful 'guests' (it is not made explicit in the Lay why they were there, though it could be guessed that they also had fled from 'the Northern battlefields'). In the passage from Synopsis II just given my father is seen working out the narrative from this point and on this narrative basis, and many of the motives that are important in the final version now appear: on account of their oath Celegorm and Curufin are the cause of the refusal of the Elves of Nargothrond to support Felagund in the aiding of Beren; Felagund gives the crown to Orodreth; and only ten of Felagund's people go with him.* I think it certain that Synopsis II was written as, and did in fact provide, the outline narrative for this and the following Cantos.

* An intermediate stage is seen in a rewritten passage of the 1926 'Sketch of the Mythology', to be given in Vol. IV, where Celegorm has already been displaced by Felagoth (not yet Felagund) but where Celegorm only learns the errand of Felagoth and Beren *after* their departure from Nargothrond, and they leave with a large force.

In Canto VI we meet for the first time several central features of the earlier history of the Gnomes in Beleriand and the North, though these are not necessarily their first occurrences in my father's writings. Thus the story of the rescue of Maidros by (Finweg >) Fingon from his torment on Thangorodrim, where he was hanged by his right hand, is almost certainly implied in *The Children of Húrin*, where it is said that Maidros wielded his sword with his left (see p. 86); and it is fully told in the 'Sketch' as first written early in 1926, some two years before the date of the present Canto (see note to line 1736). Here also are references to the long years of the Siege of Angband after the healing of the feud among the Gnomish princes (the cause of which we do not yet know); and to the bursting of Morgoth's *armies black* (cf. *The Silmarillion* p. 151: 'the black armies of the Orcs') across *the Thirsty Plain* (for which see p. 55). Here we meet for the first time (apart from a later note to *The Children of Húrin*, p. 80) Angrod and Egnor, sons of Finrod and brothers of Felagund and Orodreth, who meet their deaths in the battle; and here it is said that Felagund was wounded (line 1691), and that his rescuers withdrew 'to the fen' – very probably the 'mighty fen' of Sirion referred to at line 1726.

For Finweg > Fingon, and Finn (line 1660) = Finwë, see p. 137–8. The genealogy of the princes of the Gnomes as it had emerged in the 1920s is now complete:

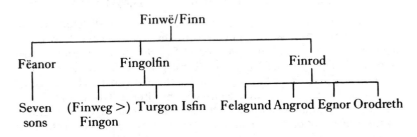

The earliest version of the Fëanorian Oath is found in alliterative verse in *The Flight of the Noldoli* (see pp. 135–6), and that in the *Lay of Leithian* (lines 1634–43) follows it quite closely despite its being in rhyming couplets, with many of the same phrases. Further variations are introduced in Celegorm's version (lines 1848–57). On the name *Timbrenting* of Taniquetil (taken in witness of the Oath) see pp. 127, 139.

Most of the geographical references and names in this Canto are amply explained by Part III 'Failivrin' of *The Children of Húrin*. For the Hills of the Hunters, the rivers Ginglith and Ingwil, and the Guarded Plain see pp. 88–9. It is now made clear that Umboth-Muilin, the Twilight Meres, were north of Sirion's fall and passage underground (to which there is a reference in *The Children of Húrin*, line 1467), whereas in the

*Lost Tales* the reverse was the case (see II. 217); and also that Esgalduin was a tributary of Sirion (lines 1717–20). In the verses describing Nargothrond the *Lay of Leithian* looks back to and echoes *The Children of Húrin*; compare

> Doors there darkly    dim gigantic
> were hewn in the hillside;    huge their timbers
> and their posts and lintels    of ponderous stone
>
> (p. 68, 1828–30)

with

> Nargothrond's sheer terraces
> and dim gigantic palaces                          (1774–5)

and

> doors there darkly hung and hewn
> with posts and lintels of ponderous stone
> and timbers huge.                                   (1777–9)

I have mentioned earlier (pp. 88, 90) the drawing and watercolour of the entrance to Nargothrond. The drawing is inscribed 'Lyme 1928' (a summer holiday at Lyme Regis in Dorset) and the watercolour was very likely done at the same time: thus a few months after the writing of Canto VI of the *Lay of Leithian*. In both are seen the bare Hills of the Hunters beyond (*with bare tops bitten bleak and raw*, 1735), and in the watercolour *Nargothrond's sheer terraces* (1774); but neither picture suggests that the entrance was *hid and veiled* (1704), *by trees o'er-shadowed dim* (1707) – a feature of the description that goes back to the *Tale of Turámbar* ('the doors of the caves . . . were cunningly concealed by trees', II. 81).

I noticed in my commentary on the *Tale of Turambar* (II. 124 and footnote) that 'the policy of secrecy and refusal of open war pursued by the Elves of Nargothrond was always an essential element', but that from *The Silmarillion* p. 168 'it seems that when Beren came to Nargothrond the "secret" policy was already pursued under Felagund', whereas from p. 170 'it seems that it came into being from the potent rhetoric of Curufin after Beren went there'. From this Canto it is seen that this contradiction, if contradiction it is, has its source in the two passages lines 1743–51 and 1877–93.

In this latter passage there are again strong echoes of *The Children of Húrin*; compare

> a leaguer silent
> unseen, stealthy,    beset the stranger,
> as of wild things wary    that watch moveless,
> then follow fleetly    with feet of velvet
> their heedless prey    with padding hatred (p. 66, 1749–53)

with

> with silent leaguer
> of wild things wary, watchful, eager,
> of phantom hunters, venomed darts,
> and unseen stealthy creeping arts,
> with padding hatred that its prey
> with feet of velvet all the day
> followed remorseless . . .                          (1882–8)

There remain a couple of points concerning names. The Great Lands are still so called (1668); but at 1616 the expression 'Outer Lands' occurs. This was used in *The Cottage of Lost Play* as first written in the sense of the Great Lands, but was subsequently applied to the lands beyond the Western Sea (see I. 21, 81–2). 'Outer Lands' = Middle-earth is frequent in *The Silmarillion*.

The name of the river, Narog, is used, as often later, to refer to the realm of Nargothrond: the King of Nargothrond is the King of Narog (see lines 1782, 1866).

★

# VII

Thus twelve alone there ventured forth
from Nargothrond, and to the North                    1925
they turned their silent secret way,
and vanished in the fading day.
No trumpet sounds, no voice there sings,
as robed in mail of cunning rings
now blackened dark with helmets grey                  1930
and sombre cloaks they steal away.
    Far-journeying Narog's leaping course
they followed till they found his source,
the flickering falls, whose freshets sheer
a glimmering goblet glassy-clear                       1935
with crystal waters fill that shake
and quiver down from Ivrin's lake,
from Ivrin's mere that mirrors dim
the pallid faces bare and grim
of Shadowy Mountains neath the moon.                   1940

    Now far beyond the realm immune
from Orc and demon and the dread

of Morgoth's might their ways had led.
In woods o'ershadowed by the heights
they watched and waited many nights,                    1945
till on a time when hurrying cloud
did moon and constellation shroud,
and winds of autumn's wild beginning
soughed in the boughs, and leaves went spinning
down the dark eddies rustling soft,                    1950
they heard a murmur hoarsely waft
from far, a croaking laughter coming;
now louder; now they heard the drumming
of hideous stamping feet that tramp
the weary earth. Then many a lamp                    1955
of sullen red they saw draw near,
swinging, and glistening on spear
and scimitar. There hidden nigh
they saw a band of Orcs go by
with goblin-faces swart and foul.                    1960
Bats were about them, and the owl,
the ghostly forsaken night-bird cried
from trees above. The voices died,
the laughter like clash of stone and steel
passed and faded. At their heel                    1965
the Elves and Beren crept more soft
than foxes stealing through a croft
in search of prey. Thus to the camp
lit by flickering fire and lamp
they stole, and counted sitting there                    1970
full thirty Orcs in the red flare
of burning wood. Without a sound
they one by one stood silent round,
each in the shadow of a tree;
each slowly, grimly, secretly                    1975
bent then his bow and drew the string.

Hark! how they sudden twang and sing,
when Felagund lets forth a cry;
and twelve Orcs sudden fall and die.
Then forth they leap casting their bows.                    1980
Out their bright swords, and swift their blows!
The stricken Orcs now shriek and yell
as lost things deep in lightless hell.

Battle there is beneath the trees
bitter and swift; but no Orc flees;                          1985
there left their lives that wandering band
and stained no more the sorrowing land
with rape and murder. Yet no song
of joy, or triumph over wrong,
the Elves there sang. In peril sore                         1990
they were, for never alone to war
so small an Orc-band went, they knew.
Swiftly the raiment off they drew
and cast the corpses in a pit.
This desperate counsel had the wit                         1995
of Felagund for them devised:
as Orcs his comrades he disguised.

    The poisoned spears, the bows of horn,
the crooked swords their foes had borne
they took; and loathing each him clad                       2000
in Angband's raiment foul and sad.
They smeared their hands and faces fair
with pigment dark; the matted hair
all lank and black from goblin head
they shore, and joined it thread by thread                  2005
with Gnomish skill. As each one leers
at each dismayed, about his ears
he hangs it noisome, shuddering.
    Then Felagund a spell did sing
of changing and of shifting shape;                          2010
their ears grew hideous, and agape
their mouths did start, and like a fang
each tooth became, as slow he sang.
Their Gnomish raiment then they hid,
and one by one behind him slid,                             2015
behind a foul and goblin thing
that once was elven-fair and king.

    Northward they went; and Orcs they met
who passed, nor did their going let,
but hailed them in greeting; and more bold                  2020
they grew as past the long miles rolled.
    At length they came with weary feet
beyond Beleriand. They found the fleet
young waters, rippling, silver-pale

of Sirion hurrying through that vale 2025
where Taur-na-Fuin, Deadly Night,
the trackless forest's pine-clad height,
falls dark forbidding slowly down
upon the east, while westward frown
the northward-bending Mountains grey 2030
and bar the westering light of day.

An isléd hill there stood alone
amid the valley, like a stone
rolled from the distant mountains vast
when giants in tumult hurtled past. 2035
Around its feet the river looped
a stream divided, that had scooped
the hanging edges into caves.
There briefly shuddered Sirion's waves
and ran to other shores more clean. 2040
An elven watchtower had it been,
and strong it was, and still was fair;
but now did grim with menace stare
one way to pale Beleriand,
the other to that mournful land 2045
beyond the valley's northern mouth.
Thence could be glimpsed the fields of drouth,
the dusty dunes, the desert wide;
and further far could be descried
the brooding cloud that hangs and lowers 2050
on Thangorodrim's thunderous towers.

Now in that hill was the abode
of one most evil; and the road
that from Beleriand thither came
he watched with sleepless eyes of flame. 2055
(From the North there led no other way,
save east where the Gorge of Aglon lay,
and that dark path of hurrying dread
which only in need the Orcs would tread
through Deadly Nightshade's awful gloom 2060
where Taur-na-Fuin's branches loom;
and Aglon led to Doriath,
and Fëanor's sons watched o'er that path.)

Men called him Thû, and as a god

in after days beneath his rod                          2065
bewildered bowed to him, and made
his ghastly temples in the shade.
Not yet by Men enthralled adored,
now was he Morgoth's mightiest lord,
Master of Wolves, whose shivering howl       2070
for ever echoed in the hills, and foul
enchantments and dark sigaldry
did weave and wield. In glamoury
that necromancer held his hosts
of phantoms and of wandering ghosts,          2075
of misbegotten or spell-wronged
monsters that about him thronged,
working his bidding dark and vile:
the werewolves of the Wizard's Isle.

From Thû their coming was not hid;            2080
and though beneath the eaves they slid
of the forest's gloomy-hanging boughs,
he saw them afar, and wolves did rouse:
'Go! fetch me those sneaking Orcs,' he said,
'that fare thus strangely, as if in dread,         2085
and do not come, as all Orcs use
and are commanded, to bring me news
of all their deeds, to me, to Thû.'

From his tower he gazed, and in him grew
suspicion and a brooding thought,             2090
waiting, leering, till they were brought.
Now ringed about with wolves they stand,
and fear their doom. Alas! the land,
the land of Narog left behind!
Foreboding evil weights their mind,           2095
as downcast, halting, they must go
and cross the stony bridge of woe
to Wizard's Isle, and to the throne
there fashioned of blood-darkened stone.

'Where have ye been? What have ye seen?'      2100

'In Elfinesse; and tears and distress,
the fire blowing and the blood flowing,
these have we seen, there have we been.
Thirty we slew and their bodies threw

in a dark pit. The ravens sit                                          2105
and the owl cries where our swath lies.'

  'Come, tell me true, O Morgoth's thralls,
what then in Elfinesse befalls?
What of Nargothrond? Who reigneth there?
Into that realm did your feet dare?'                                   2110

  'Only its borders did we dare.
There reigns King Felagund the fair.'

  'Then heard ye not that he is gone,
that Celegorm sits his throne upon?'

  'That is not true! If he is gone,                                    2115
then Orodreth sits his throne upon.'

  'Sharp are your ears, swift have they got
tidings of realms ye entered not!
What are your names, O spearmen bold?
Who your captain, ye have not told.'                                   2120

  'Nereb and Dungalef and warriors ten,
so we are called, and dark our den
under the mountains. Over the waste
we march on an errand of need and haste.
Boldog the captain awaits us there                                     2125
where fires from under smoke and flare.'

  'Boldog, I heard, was lately slain
warring on the borders of that domain
where Robber Thingol and outlaw folk
cringe and crawl beneath elm and oak                                   2130
in drear Doriath. Heard ye not then
of that pretty fay, of Lúthien?
Her body is fair, very white and fair.
Morgoth would possess her in his lair.
Boldog he sent, but Boldog was slain:                                  2135
strange ye were not in Boldog's train.
  Nereb looks fierce, his frown is grim.
Little Lúthien! What troubles him?
Why laughs he not to think of his lord
crushing a maiden in his hoard,                                        2140
that foul should be what once was clean,
that dark should be where light has been?

Whom do ye serve, Light or Mirk?
Who is the maker of mightiest work?
Who is the king of earthly kings,                    2145
the greatest giver of gold and rings?
Who is the master of the wide earth?
Who despoiled them of their mirth,
the greedy Gods? Repeat your vows,
Orcs of Bauglir! Do not bend your brows!             2150
Death to light, to law, to love!
Cursed be moon and stars above!
May darkness everlasting old
that waits outside in surges cold
drown Manwë, Varda, and the sun!                     2155
May all in hatred be begun,
and all in evil ended be,
in the moaning of the endless Sea!'

But no true Man nor Elf yet free
would ever speak that blasphemy,                     2160
and Beren muttered: 'Who is Thû
to hinder work that is to do?
Him we serve not, nor to him owe
obeisance, and we now would go.'

Thû laughed: 'Patience! Not very long               2165
shall ye abide. But first a song
I will sing to you, to ears intent.'
Then his flaming eyes he on them bent,
and darkness black fell round them all.
Only they saw as through a pall                      2170
of eddying smoke those eyes profound
in which their senses choked and drowned.
He chanted a song of wizardry,
of piercing, opening, of treachery,
revealing, uncovering, betraying.                    2175
Then sudden Felagund there swaying
sang in answer a song of staying,
resisting, battling against power,
of secrets kept, strength like a tower,
and trust unbroken, freedom, escape;                 2180
of changing and of shifting shape,
of snares eluded, broken traps,
the prison opening, the chain that snaps.

Backwards and forwards swayed their song.
Reeling and foundering, as ever more strong          2185
Thû's chanting swelled, Felagund fought,
and all the magic and might he brought
of Elfinesse into his words.
Softly in the gloom they heard the birds
singing afar in Nargothrond,                         2190
the sighing of the sea beyond,
beyond the western world, on sand,
on sand of pearls in Elvenland.

Then the gloom gathered: darkness growing
in Valinor, the red blood flowing                    2195
beside the sea, where the Gnomes slew
the Foamriders, and stealing drew
their white ships with their white sails
from lamplit havens. The wind wails.
The wolf howls. The ravens flee.                     2200
The ice mutters in the mouths of the sea.
The captives sad in Angband mourn.
Thunder rumbles, the fires burn,
a vast smoke gushes out, a roar –
and Felagund swoons upon the floor.                  2205

Behold! they are in their own fair shape,
fairskinned, brighteyed. No longer gape
Orclike their mouths; and now they stand
betrayed into the wizard's hand.
Thus came they unhappy into woe,                     2210
to dungeons no hope nor glimmer know,
where chained in chains that eat the flesh
and woven in webs of strangling mesh
they lay forgotten, in despair.

Yet not all unavailing were                          2215
the spells of Felagund; for Thû
neither their names nor purpose knew.
These much he pondered and bethought,
and in their woeful chains them sought,
and threatened all with dreadful death,              2220
if one would not with traitor's breath
reveal this knowledge. Wolves should come
and slow devour them one by one

> before the others' eyes, and last
> should one alone be left aghast,                    2225
> then in a place of horror hung
> with anguish should his limbs be wrung,
> in the bowels of the earth be slow
> endlessly, cruelly, put to woe
> and torment, till he all declared.                  2230
>
> Even as he threatened, so it fared.
> From time to time in the eyeless dark
> two eyes would grow, and they would hark
> to frightful cries, and then a sound
> of rending, a slavering on the ground,              2235
> and blood flowing they would smell.
> But none would yield, and none would tell.

★

## NOTES

1943   Against the end of this line is written the date 'March 30 1928'. The previous date was 29 March 1928 at line 1736.

2023   (and subsequently) *Broseliand* A, and B as typed.

2026   *Deadly Night*] *Tangled Night* A, and B as typed. Cf. *Deadly Nightshade* as a name of Taur-na-Fuin in *The Children of Húrin* (p. 55) and at line 2060 in the present Canto.

2047   *fields of drouth*: the expression *Plains of Drouth* occurs in *The Children of Húrin*, p. 36, line 826.

2056–63   These lines are marked with an X and a sign for deletion in the B-text, probably not on account of anything in their content but because my father felt them to be intrusive.

2064–6   Emended in B to:

> Gnomes called him Gorthû, as a god
> in after days beneath his rod
> bewildered they bowed to him, and made

(*Sauron* was first substituted for *Thû*. *Men* is written beside *they* in line 2066.) *Thû* > *Gorthû* at all subsequent occurrences in this Canto, or the name avoided by substitution of pronoun or article; thus 2088 *of all their deeds to me, Gorthû*; 2161–2 *Doth Gorthû / now hinder work*; 2165 *He laughed*; 2186 *the chanting*; etc.

This change is difficult to date, but was made when *Gnomes* was still employed (2064). In Canto VIII *Thû* was left unchanged, and subsequently, until 3290, which was emended to *where Gorthû reigned*; at the end of the poem (3947, 3951) *Thû* was changed to *Sauron*.

2100–6   On the changed metre of these lines see the Commentary.

2114   After this line is written the date 'March 31st' (i.e. 1928). The previous date was 30 March 1928 at line 1943.

2121   *Nereb and Dungalef*: emended in B to *Wrath and Hate*, at the same time as *Thû > Gorthû*.

2137   *Nereb looks fierce*: emended in B to *Fierce is your chief*.

2155   *Bridhil* A, and B as typed; the change to *Varda* made at the same time as *Thû* to *Gorthû*. Cf. note to line 1620.

2175–7   The three rhyming lines go back through A to the original draft.

2193   *Elvenland* is an emendation to B *Fairyland*.

## Commentary on Canto VII

The plot-outline 'Synopsis I' for the narrative in this Canto has already been given (pp. 219–20). 'Synopsis II' continues from the point reached on p. 221.

They ambush an Orc-band, and disguising themselves in the raiment and fashion of the slain, march on Northward. Between the Shadowy Mountains and the Forest of Night, where the young Sirion flows in the narrowing valley, they come upon the *werewolves*, and the host of Thû Lord of Wolves. They are taken before Thû, and after a contest of riddling questions and answers are revealed as spies, but Beren is taken as a Gnome, and that Felagund is King of Nargothrond remains hidden.

They are placed in a deep dungeon. Thû desires to discover their purpose and real names and vows death, one by one, and torment to the last one, if they will not reveal them. From time to time a great werewolf [*struck through*: Thû in disguise] comes and devours one of the companions.

This is obviously the narrative basis for Canto VII, and the story here reaches its final form. There may seem to be a difference between the outline and the Lay, in that the former says that 'after a contest of riddling questions and answers they are revealed as spies', whereas in the latter Felagund is overcome by song of greater power. In fact, the riddling contest is present, but seems not to have been fully developed. In the original draft my father scribbled the following note before he wrote the passage lines 2100 ff.:

Riddling questions. Where have you been, who have you slain? Thirty men. Who reigns in Nargothrond? Who is captain of Orcs? Who wrought the world? Who is king &c. They show Elfin [?bias] and too little knowledge of Angband, too much of Elfland. Thû and Felagund . . . . . enchantments against one another and Thû's slowly win, till they stand revealed as Elves.

Lines 2100–6 are in a changed metre, especially suitable to a riddle contest, and their content (the reply to Thû's question 'Where have ye been? What have ye seen?') is riddling ('misleading accuracy'). But after this the verse returns to the common metre, and the riddling element disappears (except in *dark our den / under the mountains*). The name *Dungalef* (2121), though it sounds Orcish enough, was an oddly transparent device, since *Felagund* had just been mentioned; but it succeeded (2217). No doubt Thû's ponderings on the matter were too subtle.

This is the first full portrait of Thû, who emerges as a being of great power, far advanced in sorcery, and is indeed here called 'necromancer' (2074). Here also is the first suggestion that his history would extend far beyond the tale of Beren and Lúthien, when 'in after days' Men would worship him, and build 'his ghastly temples in the shade'.

It is in this Canto, also, that the island in the river Sirion (not actually mentioned in Synopsis II) makes its first appearance, together with a mention of the origin of the fortress:

> An elven watchtower had it been,
> and strong it was, and still was fair.          (2041–2)

My father's drawing (*Pictures by J. R. R. Tolkien*, no. 36) was made at Lyme Regis in Dorset in July 1928, less than four months after these lines were written; and in the drawing the caves scooped by the waters in the edges of the island (lines 2037–8) can be seen.

The Shadowy Mountains referred to in Synopsis II and in the poem are no longer the Mountains of Terror (Ered Gorgoroth), as they were at lines 386, 1318 (see pp. 170–1). In Synopsis II it is said that the young Sirion flows in the narrowing valley between the Shadowy Mountains and the Forest of Night (Taur-na-Fuin), and in the poem Ivrin's lake mirrors

> the pallid faces bare and grim
> of Shadowy Mountains neath the moon          (1939–40)

as in *The Children of Húrin* (p. 62, lines 1581–2). Thus the term now reverts to its meaning in the alliterative poem, a meaning that it would henceforward retain. It is also to be noted that this mountain-range is 'northward-bending' (2030).

The lines concerning Ivrin in *The Children of Húrin* (1594–7):

> newborn Narog,     nineteen fathoms
> o'er a flickering force     falls in wonder,

> and a glimmering goblet    with glass-lucent
> fountains fills he    by his freshets carven

are echoed in *The Lay of Leithian* (1934–6):

> the flickering falls, whose freshets sheer
> a glimmering goblet glassy-clear
> with crystal waters fill . . .

A new feature of the northern lands appears in this Canto: the Gorge of Aglon (2057), already placed (as other evidence shows) at the eastern end of Taur-na-Fuin; and line 2063 gives the first indication that this region was the territory of the Fëanorians.

The raid of the Orc-captain Boldog into Doriath, seeking to capture Lúthien for Morgoth, was an important element in the history of this time, though later it disappeared and there is no trace of it in *The Silmarillion*. Discussion of it is postponed till later in the *Lay of Leithian*, but it may be noticed here that an early reference to it is found in *The Children of Húrin* (p. 16 lines 392–4, p. 117 lines 764–6). There it was Thû himself who was bidden by Morgoth *go ravage the realm    of the robber Thingol*.

The term *Foamriders*, used of the Third Kindred of the Elves in line 2197, is found earlier in the alliterative *Flight of the Noldoli* (see p. 140).

★

# VIII

> Hounds there were in Valinor
> with silver collars. Hart and boar,
> the fox and hare and nimble roe                    2240
> there in the forests green did go.
> Oromë was the lord divine
> of all those woods. The potent wine
> went in his halls and hunting song.
> The Gnomes anew have named him long                    2245
> Tavros, the God whose horns did blow
> over the mountains long ago;
> who alone of Gods had loved the world
> before the banners were unfurled
> of Moon and Sun; and shod with gold                    2250
> were his great horses. Hounds untold
> baying in woods beyond the West

of race immortal he possessed:
grey and limber, black and strong,
white with silken coats and long,                    2255
brown and brindled, swift and true
as arrow from a bow of yew;
their voices like the deeptoned bells
that ring in Valmar's citadels,
their eyes like living jewels, their teeth            2260
like ruel-bone. As sword from sheath
they flashed and fled from leash to scent
for Tavros' joy and merriment.

    In Tavros' friths and pastures green
had Huan once a young whelp been.                     2265
He grew the swiftest of the swift,
and Oromë gave him as a gift
to Celegorm, who loved to follow
the great God's horn o'er hill and hollow.
    Alone of hounds of the Land of Light,            2270
when sons of Fëanor took to flight
and came into the North, he stayed
beside his master. Every raid
and every foray wild he shared,
and into mortal battle dared.                         2275
Often he saved his Gnomish lord
from Orc and wolf and leaping sword.
A wolf-hound, tireless, grey and fierce
he grew; his gleaming eyes would pierce
all shadows and all mist, the scent                   2280
moons old he found through fen and bent,
through rustling leaves and dusty sand;
all paths of wide Beleriand
he knew. But wolves, he loved them best;
he loved to find their throats and wrest             2285
their snarling lives and evil breath.
The packs of Thû him feared as Death.
    No wizardry, nor spell, nor dart,
no fang, nor venom devil's art
could brew had harmed him; for his weird             2290
was woven. Yet he little feared
that fate decreed and known to all:
before the mightiest he should fall,

before the mightiest wolf alone
that ever was whelped in cave of stone.          2295

Hark! afar in Nargothrond,
far over Sirion and beyond,
there are dim cries and horns blowing,
and barking hounds through the trees going.
  The hunt is up, the woods are stirred.          2300
Who rides to-day? Ye have not heard
that Celegorm and Curufin
have loosed their dogs? With merry din
they mounted ere the sun arose,
and took their spears and took their bows.          2305
The wolves of Thû of late have dared
both far and wide. Their eyes have glared
by night across the roaring stream
of Narog. Doth their master dream,
perchance, of plots and counsels deep,          2310
of secrets that the Elf-lords keep,
of movements in the Gnomish realm
and errands under beech and elm?

  Curufin spake: 'Good brother mine,
I like it not. What dark design          2315
doth this portend? These evil things,
we swift must end their wanderings!
And more, 'twould please my heart full well
to hunt a while and wolves to fell.'
And then he leaned and whispered low          2320
that Orodreth was a dullard slow;
long time it was since the king had gone,
and rumour or tidings came there none.
  'At least thy profit it would be
to know whether dead he is or free;          2325
to gather thy men and thy array.
"I go to hunt" then thou wilt say,
and men will think that Narog's good
ever thou heedest. But in the wood
things may be learned; and if by grace,          2330
by some blind fortune he retrace
his footsteps mad, and if he bear
a Silmaril – I need declare
no more in words; but one by right

is thine (and ours), the jewel of light;                    2335
another may be won – a throne.
The eldest blood our house doth own.'

    Celegorm listened. Nought he said,
but forth a mighty host he led;
and Huan leaped at the glad sounds,                    2340
the chief and captain of his hounds.
    Three days they ride by holt and hill
the wolves of Thû to hunt and kill,
and many a head and fell of grey
they take, and many drive away,                    2345
till nigh to the borders in the West
of Doriath a while they rest.

    There were dim cries and horns blowing,
and barking dogs through the woods going.
The hunt was up. The woods were stirred,                    2350
and one there fled like startled bird,
and fear was in her dancing feet.
She knew not who the woods did beat.
Far from her home, forwandered, pale,
she flitted ghostlike through the vale;                    2355
ever her heart bade her up and on,
but her limbs were worn, her eyes were wan.
    The eyes of Huan saw a shade
wavering, darting down a glade
like a mist of evening snared by day                    2360
and hasting fearfully away.
He bayed, and sprang with sinewy limb
to chase the shy thing strange and dim.
On terror's wings, like a butterfly
pursued by a sweeping bird on high,                    2365
she fluttered hither, darted there,
now poised, now flying through the air –
in vain. At last against a tree
she leaned and panted. Up leaped he.
No word of magic gasped with woe,                    2370
no elvish mystery she did know
or had entwined in raiment dark
availed against that hunter stark,
whose old immortal race and kind
no spells could ever turn or bind.                    2375

Huan alone that she ever met
she never in enchantment set
nor bound with spells. But loveliness
and gentle voice and pale distress
and eyes like starlight dimmed with tears          2380
tamed him that death nor monster fears.

Lightly he lifted her, light he bore
his trembling burden. Never before
had Celegorm beheld such prey:
'What hast thou brought, good Huan say!          2385
Dark-elvish maid, or wraith, or fay?
Not such to hunt we came today.'

''Tis Lúthien of Doriath,'
the maiden spake. 'A wandering path
far from the Wood-Elves' sunny glades          2390
she sadly winds, where courage fades
and hope grows faint.' And as she spoke
down she let slip her shadowy cloak,
and there she stood in silver and white.
Her starry jewels twinkled bright          2395
in the risen sun like morning dew;
the lilies gold on mantle blue
gleamed and glistened. Who could gaze
on that fair face without amaze?
Long did Curufin look and stare.          2400
The perfume of her flower-twined hair,
her lissom limbs, her elvish face,
smote to his heart, and in that place
enchained he stood. 'O maiden royal,
O lady fair, wherefore in toil          2405
and lonely journey dost thou go?
What tidings dread of war and woe
In Doriath have betid? Come tell!
For fortune thee hath guided well;
friends thou hast found,' said Celegorm,          2410
and gazed upon her elvish form.

In his heart him thought her tale unsaid
he knew in part, but nought she read
of guile upon his smiling face.
'Who are ye then, the lordly chase          2415

that follow in this perilous wood?'
she asked; and answer seeming-good
they gave. 'Thy servants, lady sweet,
lords of Nargothrond thee greet,
and beg that thou wouldst with them go                    2420
back to their hills, forgetting woe
a season, seeking hope and rest.
And now to hear thy tale were best.'

So Lúthien tells of Beren's deeds
in northern lands, how fate him leads                    2425
to Doriath, of Thingol's ire,
the dreadful errand that her sire
decreed for Beren.. Sign nor word
the brothers gave that aught they heard
that touched them near. Of her escape                    2430
and the marvellous mantle she did shape
she lightly tells, but words her fail
recalling sunlight in the vale,
moonlight, starlight in Doriath,
ere Beren took the perilous path.                    2435
    'Need, too, my lords, there is of haste!
No time in ease and rest to waste.
For days are gone now since the queen,
Melian whose heart hath vision keen,
looking afar me said in fear                    2440
that Beren lived in bondage drear.
The Lord of Wolves hath prisons dark,
chains and enchantments cruel and stark,
and there entrapped and languishing
doth Beren lie – if direr thing                    2445
hath not brought death or wish for death':
then gasping woe bereft her breath.

To Celegorm said Curufin
apart and low: 'Now news we win
of Felagund, and now we know                    2450
wherefore Thû's creatures prowling go',
and other whispered counsels spake,
and showed him what answer he should make.
    'Lady,' said Celegorm, 'thou seest
we go a-hunting roaming beast,                    2455
and though our host is great and bold,

'tis ill prepared the wizard's hold
and island fortress to assault.
Deem not our hearts or wills at fault.
Lo! here our chase we now forsake     2460
and home our swiftest road we take,
counsel and aid there to devise
for Beren that in anguish lies.'

To Nargothrond they with them bore
Lúthien, whose heart misgave her sore.     2465
Delay she feared; each moment pressed
upon her spirit, yet she guessed
they rode not as swiftly as they might.
Ahead leaped Huan day and night,
and ever looking back his thought     2470
was troubled. What his master sought,
and why he rode not like the fire,
why Curufin looked with hot desire
on Lúthien, he pondered deep,
and felt some evil shadow creep     2475
of ancient curse o'er Elfinesse.
His heart was torn for the distress
of Beren bold, and Lúthien dear,
and Felagund who knew no fear.

In Nargothrond the torches flared     2480
and feast and music were prepared.
Lúthien feasted not but wept.
Her ways were trammelled; closely kept
she might not fly. Her magic cloak
was hidden, and no prayer she spoke     2485
was heeded, nor did answer find
her eager questions. Out of mind,
it seemed, were those afar that pined
in anguish and in dungeons blind
in prison and in misery.     2490
Too late she knew their treachery.
It was not hid in Nargothrond
that Fëanor's sons her held in bond,
who Beren heeded not, and who
had little cause to wrest from Thû     2495
the king they loved not and whose quest
old vows of hatred in their breast

had roused from sleep. Orodreth knew
the purpose dark they would pursue:
King Felagund to leave to die,                                    2500
and with King Thingol's blood ally
the house of Fëanor by force
or treaty. But to stay their course
he had no power, for all his folk
the brothers had yet beneath their yoke,                          2505
and all yet listened to their word.
Orodreth's counsel no man heard;
their shame they crushed, and would not heed
the tale of Felagund's dire need.

   At Lúthien's feet there day by day                 2510
and at night beside her couch would stay
Huan the hound of Nargothrond;
and words she spoke to him soft and fond:
'O Huan, Huan, swiftest hound
that ever ran on mortal ground,                                   2515
what evil doth thy lords possess
to heed no tears nor my distress?
Once Barahir all men above
good hounds did cherish and did love;
once Beren in the friendless North,                               2520
when outlaw wild he wandered forth,
had friends unfailing among things
with fur and fell and feathered wings,
and among the spirits that in stone
in mountains old and wastes alone                                 2525
still dwell. But now nor Elf nor Man,
none save the child of Melian,
remembers him who Morgoth fought
and never to thraldom base was brought.'

   Nought said Huan; but Curufin                     2530
thereafter never near might win
to Lúthien, nor touch that maid,
but shrank from Huan's fangs afraid.
   Then on a night when autumn damp
was swathed about the glimmering lamp                             2535
of the wan moon, and fitful stars
were flying seen between the bars
of racing cloud, when winter's horn

already wound in trees forlorn,
lo! Huan was gone. Then Lúthien lay                    2540
fearing new wrong, till just ere day,
when all is dead and breathless still
and shapeless fears the sleepless fill,
a shadow came along the wall.
Then something let there softly fall                    2545
her magic cloak beside her couch.
Trembling she saw the great hound crouch
beside her, heard a deep voice swell
as from a tower a far slow bell.

Thus Huan spake, who never before                    2550
had uttered words, and but twice more
did speak in elven tongue again:
'Lady beloved, whom all Men,
whom Elfinesse, and whom all things
with fur and fell and feathered wings                    2555
should serve and love – arise! away!
Put on thy cloak! Before the day
comes over Nargothrond we fly
to Northern perils, thou and I.'
And ere he ceased he counsel wrought                    2560
for achievement of the thing they sought.
There Lúthien listened in amaze,
and softly on Huan did she gaze.
Her arms about his neck she cast –
in friendship that to death should last.                    2565

# NOTES

2246   *Tavros* not emended, nor at lines 2263–4 (see p. 195, note to
       lines 891, 904).
2248   *of Gods had loved* B] *of Valar loved* A
2283   *Beleriand*] *Broseliand* A, and B as typed.
2385   After this line is written the date 'April 2nd'. The previous
       date was 31 March 1928 at line 2114.
2423   After this line is written the date 'April 3rd'. The previous
       date was 2 April 1928 at line 2385.
2442–4   Cf. lines 1246–8.

2484–5   The reference to the hiding of Lúthien's cloak is not in A.
2522–6   Cf. lines 349–53. Line 2523 is repeated at 2555.
  2551   *But twice more* emendation in B; *nor ever more* A, *but once more* B as typed.
  2552   *elven*: *elfin* B, but since *elfin* is changed at almost every occurrence I have done so here.

## Commentary on Canto VIII

The development of the narrative of this Canto from the *Tale of Tinúviel* to *The Silmarillion* can be followed step by step. The first stage is seen in the very brief words of the 'Sketch', following on the passage given on p. 220.

> Lúthien is imprisoned by Thingol, but escapes and goes in search of Beren. With the aid of Huan lord of dogs she rescues Beren [i.e. from 'Thû the hunter'], and gains entrance to Angband . . .

This is too compressed to reveal what ideas underlay it; but at least it is clear that Huan was still independent of any master. In the earliest map Huan is assigned a territory (south and east of Ivrin), and this clearly belongs with the old conception.

Synopsis I, a little later than the 'Sketch' (see p. 220), continues from the point reached on pp. 219–20:

> Tinúviel flies in her magic robe, she meets Celegorm out hunting, and is pursued by him and captured by Huan his dog and hurt. [*Struck out*: In redress he offers to help] He offers redress – but cannot help; he lent his Gnomes to Beren and all perished, and so must Beren. Huan goes with her.

A little later in the outline it is said:

> It was written in the fate of Huan that he could only be slain by a wolf.

At this stage, where Celegorm was the ruler of Nargothrond to whom Beren went in his trouble, Celegorm 'lent his Gnomes' to Beren;* Lúthien fleeing from Doriath was pursued by Celegorm while out hunting and was hurt by Huan, who now first appears as Celegorm's hound. Here there is no suggestion of evil behaviour towards her (and no mention of Curufin); Celegorm is unable to assist her, further than he has already assisted Beren, but Huan goes with her on her quest: was this the 'redress' for her hurt that Celegorm offered her? It is not said. It is clear that the position of the ruler of Nargothrond as a son of Fëanor,

---

* If the previous passage of Synopsis I (p. 219) is strictly interpreted Celegorm went with Beren from Nargothrond, but this is obviously not meant: my father must have struck out more than he intended to. It is now clear that in this form of the story Celegorm disguised Beren and gave him guides.

bound by the Oath, must have developed quite differently if this form of the story had been retained, since he was also sworn to aid the kin of Barahir (see below, p. 247).

In Synopsis II, given on p. 233 to the point equivalent to the end of Canto VII, the plot reaches almost to its development in the present Canto of the Lay; but this was achieved in stages, and the original text of the outline was so much changed and extended by later alterations that it would be extremely difficult to follow if set out as hitherto. I give it therefore in two forms. As first written it read:

Curufin and Celegorm go hunting with all their hounds. Huan the sleepless is the chief. He is proof against magic sleep or death – it is his fate to be slain only by the 'greatest wolf'. They espy Lúthien who flees, but is caught by Huan whom she cannot enchant. The hound bears her to Celegorm, who learns her purpose. Hearing who she is, and falling in love with her he takes away her magic cloak, and holds her captive.

At last he yields to her tears to let her free and give her back her cloak, but he will not aid her because of his oath. Nor does he desire to rescue Felagund, since he is now all-powerful in Nargothrond. She departs from Celegorm. But Huan has become devoted to her, and goes with her.

At this stage, the hunting evidently had no significance in itself: it was the device by which Huan (already in Synopsis I the hound of Celegorm, and with a peculiar fate) was to be brought to accompany Lúthien, an essential feature going back to the *Tale of Tinúviel*. There is no mention of her being hurt by Huan, as there is in Synopsis I (and so no question of 'redress'); and here Celegorm falls in love with her and therefore holds her captive. But this is only for a time; he yields to her prayer and gives her back her cloak, though because of his oath he will not aid her; and the evil motive of his desiring to let Felagund perish so that he may retain power in Nargothrond appears. Lúthien leaves Celegorm; Huan goes with her, as in Synopsis I, but the motive is now explicitly the hound's love for her.

After emendation the outline read as follows:

Because of the disguise of Felagund Thû is suspicious and his wolves fare far abroad. Celegorm seizes pretext for a wolfhunt.

Curufin and Celegorm go wolf-hunting guilefully (really to intercept Felagund*) with all their hounds. Huan the sleepless is the chief. (Huan came with him [i.e. Celegorm] from Tavros' halls.) He is proof against magic sleep or death – it is his fate to be slain only by the

---

*i.e., if he should return to Nargothrond; see lines 2330ff.

'greatest wolf'. They espy Lúthien who flees, but is caught by Huan whom she cannot enchant. The hound bears her to Celegorm, who learns her purpose. Hearing who she is, and falling in love with her, Curufin takes away her magic cloak, and holds her captive. Although she tells him Melian's words and that Felagund and Beren are in Thû's power he won't attempt a rescue even of Felagund. (*Marginal note*: It is Curufin who put evil into Celegorm's heart.)

In spite of her tears to let her free and give her back her cloak he will not aid her because of his oath and love. Nor does he desire to rescue Felagund, since he is now all-powerful in Nargothrond. But Huan has become devoted to her, and aids her to escape *without her cloak*.

The hunting of Celegorm and Curufin is now given a sinister import, and is related to the wolves of Thû who 'fare far abroad'. Huan's Valinórean ancestry appears; and Curufin becomes the evil genius of the brothers, and also the lover of Lúthien. Lúthien is now held prisoner in Nargothrond until she escapes by the aid of Huan – but she does not get back her cloak.

Which of the brothers is referred to in the latter part of the emended outline is not clear: as originally written it was Celegorm throughout, but by the change of 'falling in love with her he takes away her magic cloak' to 'falling in love with her Curufin takes away her magic cloak' Curufin becomes the antecedent to all that follows. Whether my father really intended this is hard to say.

When he came to write Canto VIII, on the basis of this emended outline, some further change took place – notably, the return to Lúthien by Huan of her cloak before they left Nargothrond; and the element added to the outline 'It is Curufin who put evil into Celegorm's heart' is expanded. It is now Curufin who suggests the wolfhunt, with its secret intention, and line 2453 shows him as the subtler and more longheaded schemer, standing behind his brother and prompting him – it is clear from lines 2324 ff. that Celegorm has some authority – or is felt by Curufin to have some authority – that Curufin lacks.

Curufin expresses his contempt for Orodreth ('a dullard slow', 2321), and this is the first hint of that weakening of Orodreth's character to which I referred earlier (p. 91). Of course the emergence of Felagund pushed him in any case into a subordinate rôle, as the younger brother of the founder of Nargothrond, and the concomitant development whereby Celegorm and Curufin remained in Nargothrond as powerful interlopers weakened his position still further. It may be that the position imposed on him by the movements in the legend led to the conclusion that he cannot have been made of very stern stuff.

These subtleties in the relationship between Celegorm and Curufin are passed over in the prose version (*The Silmarillion* pp. 172–3), and there is no suggestion that Curufin was the more sinister of the pair, and the prime mover in their machinations. Celegorm recovers his earlier rôle as the one who was enamoured of Lúthien. In the Lay appears the motive, not mentioned in Synopsis II, of the intention of Celegorm and Curufin to ally themselves with 'King Thingol's blood' by the forced marriage of Lúthien (lines 2498–2503); and this reappears in *The Silmarillion*, where it is to Celegorm that Thingol is to be compelled to give her.

The process whereby the legends of Beren and Lúthien on the one hand and of Nargothrond on the other became entwined is now (to this point in the story) almost complete, and this is a convenient point to recapitulate the main shifts in its evolution.

In the *Lost Tales* Orodreth was lord of the Rodothlim, a people of the Gnomes, in the caves that were to become Nargothrond, but Beren had no connection with the Rodothlim (and Huan had no master). Then Celegorm appeared as the Gnomish prince rescued by Beren's father (Egnor > Barahir) in the battle that afterwards became the Battle of Sudden Flame, to whom he swore an oath of abiding friendship and aid; and Celegorm and Curufin became the founders of Nargothrond after the battle (p. 84). It was to Celegorm that Beren therefore came seeking aid; and Celegorm plays the later role of Felagund in Synopsis I to the extent that he gives him Gnomish guides. Lúthien fleeing from Doriath is caught by Huan, now the hound of Celegorm, and hurt, but this has no outcome beyond the departure of Lúthien in Huan's company (Synopsis I).

The most major change came with the emergence of Felagund and his taking over Celegorm's part both as founder of Nargothrond and as the one rescued by Barahir. Orodreth became his younger brother, the only other son of Finrod to survive the battle in which the Siege of Angband ended. But Celegorm's association with Nargothrond was not abandoned; and his powerful presence there together with that of his brother Curufin – again as a result of the battle – introduces the motive of conflict between the Fëanorians and the King, each held by their own oaths. This conflict had been present in the earlier plot, but there it was a conflict within Celegorm's mind alone, since he had sworn both oaths; there is however no real evidence as to how my father would have treated this, unless we assume from his giving Gnomish guides to Beren in Synopsis I that he gave precedence to his oath to Barahir.

When Lúthien is captured by Huan and taken to Nargothrond she is caught up in the ambitions of Celegorm and Curufin, and indeed her capture itself is made to come about from their evil intentions towards Felagund and determination to prevent his return.

Of Huan it is told in the Lay that he was the only hound of Valinor to come east over the sea (2270). His fate that he should meet death only when 'he encountered the mightiest wolf that would ever walk the world'

(*The Silmarillion* p. 173) appears (already referred to in Synopsis II, pp. 245–6), but it is not said as it is in *The Silmarillion* that this was because as the hound of Celegorm he came under the Doom of the Noldor. In the A-text of the Lay (note to line 2551) he spoke only once in his life, in the B-text twice; but this was emended to three times, as still in *The Silmarillion*.

The statement in lines 2248–50 that Oromë

> alone of Gods had loved the world
> before the banners were unfurled
> of Moon and Sun

seems to forget Yavanna: see the tale of *The Chaining of Melko* (I. 98–9) and *The Silmarillion* pp. 40–1.

The *dim cries and horns blowing, / and barking hounds through the trees going* (lines 2298–9, repeated with variations in lines 2348–9) derive from the Middle English Lay of Sir Orfeo:

> With dim cri & bloweing
> & houndes also wiþ him berking.*

## IX

> In Wizard's Isle still lay forgot,
> enmeshed and tortured in that grot
> cold, evil, doorless, without light,
> and blank-eyed stared at endless night
> two comrades. Now alone they were.            2570
> The others lived no more, but bare
> their broken bones would lie and tell
> how ten had served their master well.
>
>     To Felagund then Beren said:
> "Twere little loss if I were dead,            2575
> and I am minded all to tell,
> and thus, perchance, from this dark hell
> thy life to loose. I set thee free

---

* Auchinleck manuscript lines 285–6 (ed. A. J. Bliss, Oxford 1954, p. 26); cf. my father's translation (*Sir Gawain and the Green Knight, Pearl, and Sir Orfeo*, 1975):

> with blowing far and crying dim
> and barking hounds that were with him

from thine old oath, for more for me
hast thou endured than e'er was earned.'        2580

'A! Beren, Beren hast not learned
that promises of Morgoth's folk
are frail as breath. From this dark yoke
of pain shall neither ever go,
whether he learn our names or no,               2585
with Thû's consent. Nay more, I think
yet deeper of torment we should drink,
knew he that son of Barahir
and Felagund were captive here,
and even worse if he should know                2590
the dreadful errand we did go.'

A devil's laugh they ringing heard
within their pit. 'True, true the word
I hear you speak,' a voice then said.
''Twere little loss if he were dead,             2595
the outlaw mortal. But the king,
the Elf undying, many a thing
no man could suffer may endure.
Perchance, when what these walls immure
of dreadful anguish thy folk learn,              2600
their king to ransom they will yearn
with gold and gem and high hearts cowed;
or maybe Celegorm the proud
will deem a rival's prison cheap,
and crown and gold himself will keep.            2605
Perchance, the errand I shall know,
ere all is done, that ye did go.
The wolf is hungry, the hour is nigh;
no more need Beren wait to die.'

The slow time passed. Then in the gloom          2610
two eyes there glowed. He saw his doom,
Beren, silent, as his bonds he strained
beyond his mortal might enchained.
Lo! sudden there was rending sound
of chains that parted and unwound,               2615
of meshes broken. Forth there leaped
upon the wolvish thing that crept
in shadow faithful Felagund,

careless of fang or venomed wound.
There in the dark they wrestled slow,                    2620
remorseless, snarling, to and fro,
teeth in flesh, gripe on throat,
fingers locked in shaggy coat,
spurning Beren who there lying
heard the werewolf gasping, dying.                       2625
Then a voice he heard: 'Farewell!
On earth I need no longer dwell,
friend and comrade, Beren bold.
My heart is burst, my limbs are cold.
Here all my power I have spent                           2630
to break my bonds, and dreadful rent
of poisoned teeth is in my breast.
I now must go to my long rest
neath Timbrenting in timeless halls
where drink the Gods, where the light falls             2635
upon the shining sea.' Thus died the king,
as elvish singers yet do sing.

There Beren lies. His grief no tear,
his despair no horror has nor fear,
waiting for footsteps, a voice, for doom.               2640
Silences profounder than the tomb
of long-forgotten kings, neath years
and sands uncounted laid on biers
and buried everlasting-deep,
slow and unbroken round him creep.                      2645

The silences were sudden shivered
to silver fragments. Faint there quivered
a voice in song that walls of rock,
enchanted hill, and bar and lock,
and powers of darkness pierced with light.              2650
He felt about him the soft night
of many stars, and in the air
were rustlings and a perfume rare;
the nightingales were in the trees,
slim fingers flute and viol seize                       2655
beneath the moon, and one more fair
than all there be or ever were
upon a lonely knoll of stone
in shimmering raiment danced alone.

Then in his dream it seemed he sang,                    2660
and loud and fierce his chanting rang,
old songs of battle in the North,
of breathless deeds, of marching forth
to dare uncounted odds and break
great powers, and towers, and strong walls shake; 2665
and over all the silver fire
that once Men named the Burning Briar,
the Seven Stars that Varda set
about the North, were burning yet,
a light in darkness, hope in woe,                    2670
the emblem vast of Morgoth's foe.

'Huan, Huan! I hear a song
far under welling, far but strong;
a song that Beren bore aloft.
I hear his voice, I have heard if oft                    2675
in dream and wandering.' Whispering low
thus Lúthien spake. On the bridge of woe
in mantle wrapped at dead of night
she sat and sang, and to its height
and to its depth the Wizard's Isle,                    2680
rock upon rock and pile on pile,
trembling echoed. The werewolves howled,
and Huan hidden lay and growled
watchful listening in the dark,
waiting for battle cruel and stark.                    2685

Thû heard that voice, and sudden stood
wrapped in his cloak and sable hood
in his high tower. He listened long,
and smiled, and knew that elvish song.
'A! little Lúthien! What brought                    2690
the foolish fly to web unsought?
Morgoth! a great and rich reward
to me thou wilt owe when to thy hoard
this jewel is added.' Down he went,
and forth his messengers he sent.                    2695

Still Lúthien sang. A creeping shape
with bloodred tongue and jaws agape
stole on the bridge; but she sang on
with trembling limbs and wide eyes wan.

The creeping shape leaped to her side,                    2700
and gasped, and sudden fell and died.
    And still they came, still one by one,
and each was seized, and there were none
returned with padding feet to tell
that a shadow lurketh fierce and fell                      2705
at the bridge's end, and that below
the shuddering waters loathing flow
o'er the grey corpses Huan killed.
    A mightier shadow slowly filled
the narrow bridge, a slavering hate,                       2710
an awful werewolf fierce and great:
pale Draugluin, the old grey lord
of wolves and beasts of blood abhorred,
that fed on flesh of Man and Elf
beneath the chair of Thû himself.                          2715

No more in silence did they fight.
Howling and baying smote the night,
till back by the chair where he had fed
to die the werewolf yammering fled.
'Huan is there' he gasped and died,                        2720
and Thû was filled with wrath and pride.
'Before the mightiest he shall fall,
before the mightiest wolf of all',
so thought he now, and thought he knew
how fate long spoken should come true.                     2725
    Now there came slowly forth and glared
into the night a shape long-haired,
dank with poison, with awful eyes
wolvish, ravenous; but there lies
a light therein more cruel and dread                       2730
than ever wolvish eyes had fed.
More huge were its limbs, its jaws more wide,
its fangs more gleaming-sharp, and dyed
with venom, torment, and with death.
The deadly vapour of its breath                            2735
swept on before it. Swooning dies
the song of Lúthien, and her eyes
are dimmed and darkened with a fear,
cold and poisonous and drear.

    Thus came Thû, as wolf more great                      2740

than e'er was seen from Angband's gate
to the burning south, than ever lurked
in mortal lands or murder worked.
Sudden he sprang, and Huan leaped
aside in shadow. On he swept                    2745
to Lúthien lying swooning faint.
To her drowning senses came the taint
of his foul breathing, and she stirred;
dizzily she spake a whispered word,
her mantle brushed across his face.             2750
He stumbled staggering in his pace.
Out leaped Huan. Back he sprang.
Beneath the stars there shuddering rang
the cry of hunting wolves at bay,
the tongue of hounds that fearless slay.        2755
Backward and forth they leaped and ran
feinting to flee, and round they span,
and bit and grappled, and fell and rose.

   Then suddenly Huan holds and throws
his ghastly foe; his throat he rends,           2760
choking his life. Not so it ends.
From shape to shape, from wolf to worm,
from monster to his own demon form,
Thû changes, but that desperate grip
he cannot shake, nor from it slip.              2765
No wizardry, nor spell, nor dart,
no fang, nor venom, nor devil's art
could harm that hound that hart and boar
had hunted once in Valinor.

   Nigh the foul spirit Morgoth made            2770
and bred of evil shuddering strayed
from its dark house, when Lúthien rose
and shivering looked upon his throes.

   'O demon dark, O phantom vile
of foulness wrought, of lies and guile,         2775
here shalt thou die, thy spirit roam
quaking back to thy master's home
his scorn and fury to endure;
thee he will in the bowels immure
of groaning earth, and in a hole                2780
everlastingly thy naked soul

shall wail and gibber – this shall be,
unless the keys thou render me
of thy black fortress, and the spell
that bindeth stone to stone thou tell,                 2785
and speak the words of opening.'

    With gasping breath and shuddering
he spake, and yielded as he must,
and vanquished betrayed his master's trust.

    Lo! by the bridge a gleam of light,                2790
like stars descended from the night
to burn and tremble here below.
There wide her arms did Lúthien throw,
and called aloud with voice as clear
as still at whiles may mortal hear                     2795
long elvish trumpets o'er the hill
echo, when all the world is still.
    The dawn peered over mountains wan,
their grey heads silent looked thereon.
The hill trembled; the citadel                         2800
crumbled, and all its towers fell;
the rocks yawned and the bridge broke,
and Sirion spumed in sudden smoke.
    Like ghosts the owls were flying seen
hooting in the dawn, and bats unclean                  2805
went skimming dark through the cold airs
shrieking thinly to find new lairs
in Deadly Nightshade's branches dread.
The wolves whimpering and yammering fled
like dusky shadows. Out there creep                    2810
pale forms and ragged as from sleep,
crawling, and shielding blinded eyes:
the captives in fear and in surprise
from dolour long in clinging night
beyond all hope set free to light.                     2815

    A vampire shape with pinions vast
screeching leaped from the ground, and passed,
its dark blood dripping on the trees;
and Huan neath him lifeless sees
a wolvish corpse – for Thû had flown                   2820

to Taur-na-Fuin, a new throne
and darker stronghold there to build.
  The captives came and wept and shrilled
their piteous cries of thanks and praise.
But Lúthien anxious-gazing stays.                    2825
Beren comes not. At length she said:
'Huan, Huan, among the dead
must we then find him whom we sought,
for love of whom we toiled and fought?'
  Then side by side from stone to stone      2830
o'er Sirion they climbed. Alone
unmoving they him found, who mourned
by Felagund, and never turned
to see what feet drew halting nigh.
'A! Beren, Beren!' came her cry,            2835
'almost too late have I thee found?
Alas! that here upon the ground
the noblest of the noble race
in vain thy anguish doth embrace!
Alas! in tears that we should meet          2840
who once found meeting passing sweet!'

  Her voice such love and longing filled
he raised his eyes, his mourning stilled,
and felt his heart new-turned to flame
for her that through peril to him came.      2845

  'O Lúthien, O Lúthien,
more fair than any child of Men,
O loveliest maid of Elfinesse,
what might of love did thee possess
to bring thee here to terror's lair!         2850
O lissom limbs and shadowy hair,
O flower-entwinéd brows so white,
O slender hands in this new light!'

  She found his arms and swooned away
just at the rising of the day.               2855

★

## NOTES

| | |
|---|---|
| 2637 | *elfin* B, not here emended, but it is clear that the intention was to change *elfin* to *elvish (elven)* in all cases. |
| 2666–7 | Cf. lines 377–9 and note. In the present passage A's reading is as B. |
| 2699 | Line marked with an X on the B-text. |
| 2712–13 | These lines (referring to Draugluin) not in A. |
| 2722–3 | Cf. lines 2293–4. |
| 2755 | Line marked with an X on the B-text. |
| 2766–7 | Cf. lines 2288–9. |
| 2769 | After this line is written the date 'April 4th'. The previous date was 3 April 1928 at line 2423. |
| 2842 | Cf. line 741. |
| 2854–5 | Cf. the ending of Canto III, lines 756–7. |

### Commentary on Canto IX

Synopsis I continues from the point reached on p. 244:

Huan goes with her. She goes to the castle of the Lord of Wolves and sings for him. The captives in the dungeons hear her.

It was written in the fate of Huan that he could only be slain by a wolf.

She tells (by arrangement) of the sickness of Huan and so induces the Lord of Wolves to go werewolf and seek him. The wolf-battle of the glade. The 'words of opening' wrung from the Lord of Wolves and the castle broken. Rescue of Beren.

Synopsis II is here less affected by later changes and can be given in a single text (taking it up from the point reached on p. 246).

But Huan has become devoted to her, and aids her to escape *without her cloak*. [*Bracketed*: He trails Beren and Felagund to the House of Thû.]

At last only Felagund and Beren remain. It is Beren's turn to be devoured. But Felagund bursts his bonds and wrestles with the were-wolf and slays him, but is killed. Beren is reserved for torment.

Lúthien sings outside the house [*added*: on the bridge of woe] of Thû and Beren hears her voice, and his answering song comes up from underground to Huan's ears.

Thû takes her inside. She tells him a twisted tale – by the desire of Huan, and because without her cloak she cannot enchant him. She tells of her bondage to Celegorm and her capture by Huan of whom she feigns hatred. Of all things in the world Thû hates Huan most. His weird to be slain only by the 'greatest wolf' is known. Lúthien says Huan is lying sick in the woods. Thû disguises himself as a mighty werewolf and is led by her to where Huan is lying in ambush. [*Added*: But he purposes to make her a thrall.]

There follows the battle of the werewolf. Huan slays Thû's companions and with his teeth in Thû's throat wrests in return for life 'the words of opening' from him. The house of Thû is broken, and the captives set free. Beren is found [*struck out*: and borne back to Nargothrond.]

There is also to be considered now another outline, 'Synopsis III', very hastily written and not entirely legible. This outline begins here and I follow it to the end of the narrative in this Canto.

Thû lies choking under Huan. Lúthien arouses. She says 'thou phantom made of foulness by Morgoth, thou shalt die and thy spirit go back in fear to Angband to meet thy master's scorn and languish in the dark bosom of the world, if the "spoken keys" of thy fortress are not yielded.'

With his gasping breath he says them. Lúthien standing on the bridge with her arms spread calls them aloud. The dawn comes pale over the mountains. The hill quivers and gapes, the towers fall, the bridge falls and block[s] Sirion on one side, the dungeons gape. The owls flee away like phantoms in the first light, great bats are seen skimming away to Taur-na-Fuin shrieking thinly. [*Added*: and one as large as an eagle leads them. The spirit of Thû. His body has a ... ..... .... a wolf.] The wolves flee whimpering and yammering. Pale captives blinking in the light creep and crawl into the light. [*Struck out*: Beren comes forth.] No Beren. They seek for him and find him sitting beside Felagund.

These outlines are of great interest, since they show very clearly an intermediate stage in the evolution of the legend, between the original story of Tevildo Prince of Cats in the *Tale of Tinúviel* and the story of Thû in the *Lay of Leithian*. Still present is Lúthien's untrue tale that Huan is lying sick in the woods (see II. 26), and in Synopsis II Thû retains the (originally feline) Tevildo-trait of hating Huan more than any other creature in the world (II. 21). The old element of Tinúviel's entering the castle alone in order to inveigle Tevildo out of it, so that he may be attacked by Huan, was not yet abandoned – but in Synopsis II she does not have her cloak, and so cannot enchant Thû, whereas in the *Tale* the drowsiness which came upon the doorkeeper cat Umuiyan, and afterwards on Tevildo himself, is ascribed to her 'robe of sable mist' (II. 24–5). In the Lay, as in the account in *The Silmarillion* based on the Lay, Lúthien's sleep-bearing cloak has come back into the story at this juncture, since Huan retrieved it before they left Nargothrond, and she used it against Thû in the battle on the bridge.

A new element enters in Synopsis I with the singing of Lúthien before Thû, and the captives in the dungeons hearing her; in the old *Tale*

Tinúviel merely spoke very loudly so that Beren might hear her in the kitchen where he toiled. In Synopsis II this element is developed to the final form, with Lúthien singing on the bridge leading to the Wizard's Isle; but she still enters the castle by herself, before 'the battle of the werewolf'.

The sentence added in Synopsis II saying that Thû 'purposes to make her a thrall' goes back to the *Tale* (II. 26), and survived into the Lay and *The Silmarillion* ('he thought to make her captive and hand her over to the power of Morgoth, for his reward would be great').

The statement in II that 'Huan slays Thû's companions' doubtless proceeds from the story in the *Tale*, where when Tevildo set out to find Huan he was accompanied by two of his 'thanes', though in the *Tale* only Oikeroi was slain by Huan, and the other (unnamed) cat fled up a tree, as also did Tevildo himself (II. 28). In II, and in more detail in III, Thû is at Huan's mercy on the ground. In neither I nor II (III only takes up after this point) is there any suggestion of the wolves coming out from the castle and being slain by Huan one by one and silently, until at last Draugluin came forth; but as I noted in my commentary on the *Tale* (II. 54–5) 'the killing of the cat Oikeroi is the germ of Huan's fight with Draugluin – the skin of Huan's dead opponent is put to the same use in either case'. This element of the procession of wolves before Thû comes only enters with the poem. The verses naming Draugluin as the last and greatest of them (2712–13) are not in A, but in Lúthien's 'lengthening spell' *Draugluin the werewolf pale* is named in B (1489), where A has *Carcharas*.

Most interesting of all the features of this part of the story is that of the 'words of opening' or 'spoken keys', which goes back to the *Tale* (II. 28–9). I have discussed there (II. 55) the implications of this element in the enlarged context (the fortress of Thû had been an Elvish watchtower): the consequent 'displacement' of the spell that held the stones together.

In Synopsis III appear other features of the final story: the flight of Thû as a great bat; the finding of Beren sitting beside the body of Felagund. The pale captives who creep blinking into the light go back ultimately to the host of cats, reduced by the breaking of Tevildo's spell to puny size, who came forth from the castle in the *Tale* (II. 29, 55).

In Canto IX the story reaches its final form, and the passage in *The Silmarillion* derives from it closely, with only minor differences – the chief being the omission of all mention of Thû's voice in the dungeon, which is only found in the poem (lines 2592–2609). The old element still present in Synopsis II of Lúthien entering the castle alone has at last disappeared.

There remain a few matters of interest apart from the development of the story. Felagund's dying words (2633–6):

> I now must go to my long rest
> neath Timbrenting in timeless halls
> where drink the Gods, where the light falls
> upon the shining sea

are closely similar to Túrin's words of parting to Beleg dead (p. 58, 1408–11):

> Now fare well, Beleg,   to feasting long
> neath Tengwethil   in the timeless halls
> where drink the Gods,   neath domes golden
> o'er the sea shining.

As I have said (p. 94), Túrin foresees for Beleg an afterlife in Valinor, in the halls of the Gods, and does not speak, as does Beleg himself in Túrin's dream, of a time of 'waiting':

> my life has winged   to the long waiting
> in the halls of the Moon   o'er the hills of the sea.
>
> (p. 65, 1696–7)

Very notable are the words about Thû: 'the foul spirit Morgoth *made*' (line 2770).

In the passage (2666–71) referring to the constellation of the Great Bear is the first suggestion of the idea that Varda set the Seven Stars in the sky as an emblem of hope against Morgoth. Cf. *The Silmarillion* (p. 174):

[Beren] sang a song of challenge that he had made in praise of the Seven Stars, the Sickle of the Valar that Varda hung above the North as a sign for the fall of Morgoth.

# X

> Songs have recalled the Elves have sung
> in old forgotten elven tongue
> how Lúthien and Beren strayed
> by the banks of Sirion. Many a glade
> they filled with joy, and there their feet          2860
> passed by lightly, and days were sweet.
> Though winter hunted through the wood,
> still flowers lingered where she stood.
> Tinúviel! Tinúviel!
> the birds are unafraid to dwell                     2865

and sing beneath the peaks of snow
where Beren and where Lúthien go.

The isle in Sirion they left behind;
but there on hill-top might one find
a green grave, and a stone set,                              2870
and there there lie the white bones yet
of Felagund, of Finrod's son –
unless that land is changed and gone,
or foundered in unfathomed seas,
while Felagund laughs beneath the trees                      2875
in Valinor, and comes no more
to this grey world of tears and war.

To Nargothrond no more he came;
but thither swiftly ran the fame
of their king dead, of Thû o'erthrown,                       2880
of the breaking of the towers of stone.
For many now came home at last,
who long ago to shadow passed;
and like a shadow had returned
Huan the hound, and scant had earned                         2885
or praise or thanks of master wroth;
yet loyal he was, though he was loath.
The halls of Narog clamours fill
that vainly Celegorm would still.
There men bewailed their fallen king,                        2890
crying that a maiden dared that thing
which sons of Fëanor would not do.
'Let us slay these faithless lords untrue!'
the fickle folk now loudly cried
with Felagund who would not ride.                            2895
Orodreth spake: 'The kingdom now
is mine alone. I will allow
no spilling of kindred blood by kin.
But bread nor rest shall find herein
these brothers who have set at nought                        2900
the house of Finrod.' They were brought.
Scornful, unbowed, and unashamed
stood Celegorm. In his eye there flamed
a light of menace. Curufin
smiled with his crafty mouth and thin.                       2905

'Be gone for ever – ere the day
shall fall into the sea. Your way
shall never lead you hither more,
nor any son of Fëanor;
nor ever after shall be bond                          2910
of love twixt yours and Nargothrond.'

'We will remember it,' they said,
and turned upon their heels, and sped,
and took their horses and such folk
as still them followed. Nought they spoke        2915
but sounded horns, and rode like fire,
and went away in anger dire.

Towards Doriath the wanderers now
were drawing nigh. Though bare the bough,
though cold the wind, and grey the grasses        2920
through which the hiss of winter passes,
they sang beneath the frosty sky
uplifted o'er them pale and high.
They came to Mindeb's narrow stream
that from the hills doth leap and gleam            2925
by western borders where begin
the spells of Melian to fence in
King Thingol's land, and stranger steps
to wind bewildered in their webs.

There sudden sad grew Beren's heart:               2930
'Alas, Tinúviel, here we part
and our brief song together ends,
and sundered ways each lonely wends!'

'Why part we here? What dost thou say,
just at the dawn of brighter day?'                  2935

'For safe thou'rt come to borderlands
o'er which in the keeping of the hands
of Melian thou wilt walk at ease
and find thy home and well-loved trees.'

'My heart is glad when the fair trees              2940
far off uprising grey it sees
of Doriath inviolate.
Yet Doriath my heart did hate,
and Doriath my feet forsook,

my home, my kin. I would not look                    2945
on grass nor leaf there evermore
without thee by me. Dark the shore
of Esgalduin the deep and strong!
Why there alone forsaking song
by endless waters rolling past                       2950
must I then hopeless sit at last,
and gaze at waters pitiless
in heartache and in loneliness?'

'For never more to Doriath
can Beren find the winding path,                     2955
though Thingol willed it or allowed;
for to thy father there I vowed
to come not back save to fulfill
the quest of the shining Silmaril,
and win by valour my desire.                         2960
"Not rock nor steel nor Morgoth's fire
nor all the power of Elfinesse,
shall keep the gem I would possess":
thus swore I once of Lúthien
more fair than any child of Men.                     2965
My word, alas! I must achieve,
though sorrow pierce and parting grieve.'

'Then Lúthien will not go home,
but weeping in the woods will roam,
nor peril heed, nor laughter know.                   2970
And if she may not by thee go
against thy will thy desperate feet
she will pursue, until they meet,
Beren and Lúthien, love once more
on earth or on the shadowy shore.'                   2975

'Nay, Lúthien, most brave of heart,
thou makest it more hard to part.
Thy love me drew from bondage drear,
but never to that outer fear,
that darkest mansion of all dread,                   2980
shall thy most blissful light be led.'

'Never, never!' he shuddering said.
But even as in his arms she pled,
a sound came like a hurrying storm.

There Curufin and Celegorm 2985
in sudden tumult like the wind
rode up. The hooves of horses dinned
loud on the earth. In rage and haste
madly northward they now raced
the path twixt Doriath to find 2990
and the shadows dreadly dark entwined
of Taur-na-Fuin. That was their road
most swift to where their kin abode
in the east, where Himling's watchful hill
o'er Aglon's gorge hung tall and still. 2995

They saw the wanderers. With a shout
straight on them swung their hurrying rout,
as if neath maddened hooves to rend
the lovers and their love to end.
But as they came the horses swerved 3000
with nostrils wide and proud necks curved;
Curufin, stooping, to saddlebow
with mighty arm did Lúthien throw,
and laughed. Too soon; for there a spring
fiercer than tawny lion-king 3005
maddened with arrows barbéd smart,
greater than any hornéd hart
that hounded to a gulf leaps o'er,
there Beren gave, and with a roar
leaped on Curufin; round his neck 3010
his arms entwined, and all to wreck
both horse and rider fell to ground;
and there they fought without a sound.
Dazed in the grass did Lúthien lie
beneath bare branches and the sky; 3015
the Gnome felt Beren's fingers grim
close on his throat and strangle him,
and out his eyes did start, and tongue
gasping from his mouth there hung.
Up rode Celegorm with his spear, 3020
and bitter death was Beren near.
With elvish steel he nigh was slain
whom Lúthien won from hopeless chain,
but baying Huan sudden sprang
before his master's face with fang 3025

white-gleaming, and with bristling hair,
as if he on boar or wolf did stare.
    The horse in terror leaped aside,
and Celegorm in anger cried:
'Curse thee, thou baseborn dog, to dare          3030
against thy master teeth to bare!'
But dog nor horse nor rider bold
would venture near the anger cold
of mighty Huan fierce at bay.
Red were his jaws. They shrank away,             3035
and fearful eyed him from afar:
nor sword nor knife, nor scimitar,
no dart of bow, nor cast of spear,
master nor man did Huan fear.

    There Curufin had left his life,             3040
had Lúthien not stayed that strife.
Waking she rose and softly cried
standing distressed at Beren's side:
'Forbear thy anger now, my lord!
nor do the work of Orcs abhorred;                3045
for foes there be of Elfinesse
unnumbered, and they grow not less,
while here we war by ancient curse
distraught, and all the world to worse
decays and crumbles. Make thy peace!'            3050

    Then Beren did Curufin release;
but took his horse and coat of mail,
and took his knife there gleaming pale,
hanging sheathless, wrought of steel.
No flesh could leeches ever heal                 3055
that point had pierced; for long ago
the dwarves had made it, singing slow
enchantments, where their hammers fell
in Nogrod ringing like a bell.
Iron as tender wood it cleft,                    3060
and sundered mail like woollen weft.
But other hands its haft now held;
its master lay by mortal felled.
Beren uplifting him, far him flung,
and cried 'Begone!', with stinging tongue;       3065
'Begone! thou renegade and fool,

and let thy lust in exile cool!
Arise and go, and no more work
like Morgoth's slaves or curséd Orc;
and deal, proud son of Fëanor,                    3070
in deeds more proud than heretofore!'
Then Beren led Lúthien away,
while Huan still there stood at bay.

'Farewell,' cried Celegorm the fair.
'Far get you gone! And better were                3075
to die forhungered in the waste
than wrath of Fëanor's sons to taste,
that yet may reach o'er dale and hill.
No gem, nor maid, nor Silmaril
shall ever long in thy grasp lie!                 3080
We curse thee under cloud and sky,
we curse thee from rising unto sleep!
Farewell!' He swift from horse did leap,
his brother lifted from the ground;
then bow of yew with gold wire bound              3085
he strung, and shaft he shooting sent,
as heedless hand in hand they went;
a dwarvish dart and cruelly hooked.
They never turned nor backward looked.
Loud bayed Huan, and leaping caught               3090
the speeding arrow. Quick as thought
another followed deadly singing;
but Beren had turned, and sudden springing
defended Lúthien with his breast.
Deep sank the dart in flesh to rest.              3095
He fell to earth. They rode away,
and laughing left him as he lay;
yet spurred like wind in fear and dread
of Huan's pursuing anger red.
Though Curufin with bruised mouth laughed,        3100
yet later of that dastard shaft
was tale and rumour in the North,
and Men remembered at the Marching Forth,
and Morgoth's will its hatred helped.

Thereafter never hound was whelped                3105
would follow horn of Celegorm
or Curufin. Though in strife and storm,

though all their house in ruin red
went down, thereafter laid his head
Huan no more at that lord's feet,                    3110
but followed Lúthien, brave and fleet.
Now sank she weeping at the side
of Beren, and sought to stem the tide
of welling blood that flowed there fast.
The raiment from his breast she cast;                3115
from shoulder plucked the arrow keen;
his wound with tears she washed it clean.

Then Huan came and bore a leaf,
of all the herbs of healing chief,
that evergreen in woodland glade                     3120
there grew with broad and hoary blade.
The powers of all grasses Huan knew,
who wide did forest-paths pursue.
Therewith the smart he swift allayed,
while Lúthien murmuring in the shade                 3125
the staunching song, that Elvish wives
long years had sung in those sad lives
of war and weapons, wove o'er him.

The shadows fell from mountains grim.
Then sprang about the darkened North                 3130
the Sickle of the Gods, and forth
each star there stared in stony night
radiant, glistering cold and white.
But on the ground there is a glow,
a spark of red that leaps below:                     3135
under woven boughs beside a fire
of crackling wood and sputtering briar
there Beren lies in drowsing deep,
walking and wandering in sleep.
Watchful bending o'er him wakes                      3140
a maiden fair; his thirst she slakes,
his brow caresses, and softly croons
a song more potent than in runes
or leeches' lore hath since been writ.
Slowly the nightly watches flit.                     3145
The misty morning crawleth grey
from dusk to the reluctant day.

Then Beren woke and opened eyes,

and rose and cried: 'Neath other skies,
in lands more awful and unknown,                    3150
I wandered long, methought, alone
to the deep shadow where the dead dwell;
but ever a voice that I knew well,
like bells, like viols, like harps, like birds,
like music moving without words,                    3155
called me, called me through the night,
enchanted drew me back to light!
Healed the wound, assuaged the pain!
Now are we come to morn again,
new journeys once more lead us on –                 3160
to perils whence may life be won,
hardly for Beren; and for thee
a waiting in the wood I see,
beneath the trees of Doriath,
while ever follow down my path                      3165
the echoes of thine elvish song,
where hills are haggard and roads are long.'

   'Nay, now no more we have for foe
dark Morgoth only, but in woe,
in wars and feuds of Elfinesse                      3170
thy quest is bound; and death, no less,
for thee and me, for Huan bold
the end of weird of yore foretold,
all this I bode shall follow swift,
if thou go on. Thy hand shall lift                  3175
and lay in Thingol's lap the dire
and flaming jewel, Fëanor's fire,
never, never! A why then go?
Why turn we not from fear and woe
beneath the trees to walk and roam                  3180
roofless, with all the world as home,
over mountains, beside the seas,
in the sunlight, in the breeze?'

   Thus long they spoke with heavy hearts;
and yet not all her elvish arts,                    3185
nor lissom arms, nor shining eyes
as tremulous stars in rainy skies,
nor tender lips, enchanted voice,
his purpose bent or swayed his choice.

Never to Doriath would he fare                                    3190
save guarded fast to leave her there;
never to Nargothrond would go
with her, lest there came war and woe;
and never would in the world untrod
to wander suffer her, worn, unshod,                               3195
roofless and restless, whom he drew
with love from the hidden realms she knew.
'For Morgoth's power is now awake;
already hill and dale doth shake,
the hunt is up, the prey is wild:                                 3200
a maiden lost, an elven child.
Now Orcs and phantoms prowl and peer
from tree to tree, and fill with fear
each shade and hollow. Thee they seek!
At thought thereof my hope grows weak,                            3205
my heart is chilled. I curse mine oath,
I curse the fate that joined us both
and snared thy feet in my sad doom
of flight and wandering in the gloom!
Now let us haste, and ere the day                                 3210
be fallen, take our swiftest way,
till o'er the marches of thy land
beneath the beech and oak we stand
in Doriath, fair Doriath
whither no evil finds the path,                                   3215
powerless to pass the listening leaves
that droop upon those forest-eaves.'

     Then to his will she seeming bent.
Swiftly to Doriath they went,
and crossed its borders. There they stayed                        3220
resting in deep and mossy glade;
there lay they sheltered from the wind
under mighty beeches silken-skinned,
and sang of love that still shall be,
though earth be foundered under sea,                              3225
and sundered here for evermore
shall meet upon the Western Shore.

     One morning as asleep she lay
upon the moss, as though the day
too bitter were for gentle flower                                 3230

to open in a sunless hour,
Beren arose and kissed her hair,
and wept, and softly left her there.
   'Good Huan,' said he, 'guard her well!     3235
In leafless field no asphodel,
in thorny thicket never a rose
forlorn, so frail and fragrant blows.
Guard her from wind and frost, and hide
from hands that seize and cast aside;
keep her from wandering and woe,     3240
for pride and fate now make me go.'

   The horse he took and rode away,
nor dared to turn; but all that day
with heart as stone he hastened forth
and took the paths toward the North.     3245

## NOTES

2877    Against this line is written the date 'April 5th'. The previous
date was 4 April 1928 at line 2769.

2929    At the end of this line is written the date 'April 6th'.

2950–3    Cf. lines 649–52, 1220–3.

2998    Against this line is written the date 'April 27th 1928'.

3031    Before this line is written the date 'Nov. 1929'. This date may
refer forward or backward; but both it and the text that
follows are written with a slightly finer nib than that used for
the preceding portion of the poem. The previous date was 27
April 1928 at line 2998.

3076–84    Against these seven lines, as first written in the margin of the
manuscript A, is the date 'Sept. 1930'.

3119    Against this line my father wrote in the margin of the B-text
the word *athelas*. In *The Fellowship of the Ring* (I. 12)
Aragorn said that it was brought to Middle-earth by the
Númenóreans.

3220    After the word *borders* is written the date '25 September
1930'.

3242–5    These last four lines of the Canto are only found in A, but I
suspect that they were omitted inadvertently.

## Commentary on Canto X

The development of the story in this Canto can again be followed step by step in the outlines. In the *Tale of Tinúviel* (II. 30–1) Beren and Tinúviel wandered away with Huan after the defeat of Tevildo, and it was her desire to return to Artanor but unwillingness to part from Beren that led to their resolve to try to gain a Silmaril. The catskin of Oikeroi, thane of Tevildo, was carried by Huan as a trophy, and they begged it from him; it was in the guise of a cat that Beren went to Angband. Synopsis I says no more of this part of the narrative than 'Tinúviel and Beren disguised as a werewolf go to Angband', and apart from the fact that the skin was that of a werewolf and not of a cat there had probably been no development from the *Tale*.

Synopsis II continues from the point reached on p. 257 as follows:

> Lúthien tends Beren in the wood. Huan brings news to Nargothrond. The Gnomes drive forth Curufin and Celegorm, grieving for Felagund, and send the cloak back to Lúthien. Lúthien takes her cloak again and led by Huan they go to Angband. By his guidance and her magic they escape capture. Huan dare not come any further. Beren is disguised as a werewolf. They enter Angband.

The sentences 'and send the cloak back to Lúthien. Lúthien takes her cloak again' were changed at the time of writing to read: 'and send to succour Beren and Lúthien. Huan brings Lúthien back her cloak again.' (This outline was written of course before my father reached Canto VIII, at the end of which Huan brought Lúthien her cloak before she escaped from Nargothrond.)

Here Synopsis II ends. At the bottom of the page is written very roughly:

> Celegorm's embassy to Thingol so that Thingol knows or thinks he knows Beren dead and Lúthien in Nargothrond.
> Why Celegorm and Curufin hated by Thingol . .   . . . . .
> The loss of Dairon.

While the expulsion of Celegorm and Curufin from Nargothrond is now first mentioned, it is clear that the story of their attack on Beren and Lúthien did not exist. Huan brings the news of the destruction of the Wizard's Tower, but it seems that he does not leave Nargothrond with Celegorm and brings back the cloak to Lúthien independently.

Synopsis III has been given on p. 257 to the point where Lúthien and Huan find Beren 'sitting beside Felagund'. I give the next portion of this outline as it was first written:

> They hallow the isle and bury Felagund on its top, and no wolf or evil creature will ever come there again. Beren is led into the woods. [*The following sentence was bracketed with a marginal direction that it should come later*: Morgoth hearing of the breaking of

the Wizard's Tower sends out an army of Orcs; finding the wolves are slain with . . . . . . throats he thinks it is Huan and fashions a vast wolf – Carcharas – mightiest of all wolves to guard his door.]

They hide in Taur-na-Fuin careful not to lose sight of light at edge. Lúthien bids Beren desist. He cannot, he says, return to Doriath. Then, she says, she will live in the woods with Beren and Huan. But he has spoken his word; he has vowed not to fear Morgoth . . . hell. Then she says [that she] fears that their lives will all be forfeit. But life perchance lies after death. Where Beren goes she goes. This gives him pause. They ask Huan. He speaks for second and last time. 'No more may Huan go with you – what you see at the gate, he will see later – his fate does not lead to Angband. Perchance, though his eyes are dim, [?thy] paths lead out of it again.' He goes to Nargothrond. They will not return to Nargothrond with him.

Lúthien and Beren leave Taur-na-Fuin and wander about together a while. Longing to look on Doriath seizes her and Beren thinks of the quest unaccomplished. Beren offers to lead her to the borders of Doriath, but they cannot bear to part.

They go to the Wizard's Isle and take a 'wolf-ham' and a bat-robe. Thus they trembling inwardly set forth. The journey to Angband over Dor-na-Fauglith and into the dark ravines of the hills.

Here first appears the burial of Felagund on the summit of the isle, and its hallowing. This outline makes no mention of the events in Nargothrond, and concentrates exclusively on Beren and Lúthien. They are in Taur-na-Fuin, and Huan is with them; and we have the first version of Huan's counsel to them, and his foreseeing that what they meet at the Gate of Angband he will himself see later. Since the attack by Celegorm and Curufin had still not been devised, the story is briefer than it was to become; thus Huan speaks to them in Taur-na-Fuin soon after the destruction of the Wizard's Tower, and then departs to Nargothrond, while they after a while go to the Isle and take the 'wolf-ham' ('wolf-hame' in *The Silmarillion* p. 178, Old English *hama*) and 'bat-robe', which now first appear (though the 'wolf-hame' derives from the catskin of Oikeroi in the *Tale*). From the words 'They will not return to Nargothrond with him' and from the fact that as the outline was written he is not mentioned again, it is clear that Huan was now out of the story (until his reappearance in a later episode). His speech is here called 'the second and last time' that he spoke with words. Afterwards the story was changed in this point, for he spoke to Beren a third time at his death (see note to line 2551).

Pencilled changes were made to this passage of Synopsis III, and these move the narrative a long way to the final version:

They hallow the isle and bury Felagund on its top, and no wolf or evil creature will ever come there again.

Lúthien and Beren leave Taur-na-Fuin and wander about together a while. Longing to look on Doriath seizes her and Beren thinks of the quest unaccomplished. Beren offers to lead her to the borders of Doriath, but they cannot bear to part.

News by captives and Huan is brought to Nargothrond. Celegorm and Curufin in a revulsion of feeling the Nargothronders wish to slay them. Orodreth will not. They are exiled and all Fëanorians from Nargothrond for ever. They ride off. Assault of Celegorm and Curufin in wood on Beren and Lúthien. Rescue by Huan. Beren wrestles with Curufin and gets his magic knife – [eight further words illegible]

Huan brings them a wolf-ham. Thus they trembling inwardly set forth. Huan speaks for last time and says farewell. He will not come. The journey to Angband, &c.

Here more is told of the expulsion of Celegorm and Curufin from Nargothrond, and Orodreth's refusal to allow them to be slain, and here at last is mention – probably written here at the very time of its devising – of the attack on Beren and Lúthien as the Fëanorians rode from Nargothrond. The desertion of Celegorm by Huan is implied; Beren gets Curufin's knife, which is to replace the knife from Tevildo's kitchens as the implement with which Beren cut the Silmaril from the Iron Crown; and it is Huan who gets the wolfskin, and then utters his parting speech.

An extremely difficult page in pencil ('Synopsis IV') shows these new elements being developed further:

Beren's heart grows sad. He says he has led Tinúviel back to the border of her land where she is safe. Alas for their second parting. She says but from this land she herself escaped and fled only to be with him – yet she admits that her heart longs for Doriath and Melian too, but not Doriath without him. He quotes his own words to Thingol: 'Not Morgoth's fire &c.' – and says he cannot (even if Thingol would allow) return emptyhanded. . . . . . she will not go back. She will wander in the woods – and if he will not take her with him she will follow his feet against his will. He protests – at this moment Celegorm and Curufin ride up seeking the way North [struck out at time of writing: round Doriath by the Gorgoroth] between Doriath and Taur-na-Fuin to the Gorge of Aglon and their own kin.

They ride straight on and seek to ride Beren down. Curufin stoops and lifts Lúthien to his saddle. Beren leaps aside and leaps at Curufin's neck [?hurling] him down. Celegorm with his spear rides up to slay Beren. Huan intervenes scattering the [?brothers'] folk and dogs and holds Celegorm at bay while Beren wrestles with Curufin and chokes him senseless. Beren takes his weapons – especially his magic knife, and bids him get on horse and be gone. They ride off. Huan stays with Beren and Lúthien and forsakes his master [?for ever]. Celegorm suddenly turns and shoots an arrow at Huan which of course falls harmless from him, but Curufin shoots at Beren (and Lúthien) [*changed to*: shoots at Lúthien] and wounds Beren.

Lúthien heals Beren. They tell Huan of their doubts and debate and he goes off and brings the wolfham and batskin from the Wizard's Isle. Then he speaks for the last time.

They prepare to go to Angband.

This was certainly prepared as an outline for Canto 10 of the Lay, for the section of the synopsis that follows is headed '11'.

There is here the further development that Beren and Lúthien have come to the borders of Doriath; but the solitary departure of Beren after his healing, leaving Lúthien with Huan, has still not emerged. There are a few differences in the account of the fight with Celegorm and Curufin from the final form, but for the most part the detail of the events was never changed from its first writing down (as I believe it to be) on this page. There is here no mention of Beren's taking Curufin's horse, on which he was later to ride north by himself to Anfauglith; and the detail of the shooting is different – in the synopsis Celegorm aimed at Huan, and Curufin (who seems to have retained his bow, though Beren took all his weapons) at (Beren and) Lúthien. There is also mention of 'folk' accompanying the brothers on their journey from Nargothrond.

In this outline is the first occurrence of the name *Gorgoroth*.

There is one further outline ('Synopsis V'), consisting of four pages that are the concluding part of a text of which the beginning has disappeared: it begins with a heading '10 continued', which is certainly a Canto number, though the content extends much beyond the end of Canto X in the Lay.* The text takes up with the healing of Beren's wound.

Huan brings a herb of healing, and Lúthien and the hound tend Beren in the forest, building a hut of boughs. Beren mending will still go on his quest. But Lúthien foretells that all their lives will be forfeit if they pursue. Beren will not go back to Doriath otherwise. Nor will he or Huan go to Nargothrond, or keep Lúthien in Thingol's despite, for war would certainly arise twixt Elf and Elf, [?even] if Orodreth harboured them. 'Then why shall we not dwell here in the wood?' saith Lúthien. Because of danger outside Doriath, and the Orcs, and the knowledge Morgoth must now possess of Lúthien's wandering.

One morning early Beren steals away on Curufin's horse and reaches the eaves of Taur-na-Fuin.

Here at last is the element of Beren's solitary departure.

---

* It is also possible that '10 continued' means only that my father began Synopsis V at this point, i.e. he had already reached about line 3117 in the actual composition of the Lay when he began the outline.

The casting out of Celegorm and Curufin from Nargothrond in the
Lay is very closely followed in *The Silmarillion* (even to phrases, as
'neither bread nor rest'); in the Lay, however, there are some who will go
with them (lines 2914–15), a detail found in Synopsis IV, whereas in *The
Silmarillion* it is explicit that they went alone.*

The debate between Beren and Lúthien which was interrupted by the
coming of Celegorm and Curufin (lines 2930–82) is clearly based on the
scheme of it given in Synopsis IV (p. 272); in *The Silmarillion* it
reappears, though much reduced and changed. The fight with Celegorm
and Curufin is likewise derived from Synopsis IV, and is followed in the
prose of *The Silmarillion* – with such detail as the cursing of Beren
'under cloud and sky', and Curufin's knife that would cut iron as if it were
green wood, hanging sheathless by his side. In the Lay the knife becomes
a dwarf-made weapon from Nogrod, though neither it nor its maker is yet
named. In the Lay the shooter of the treacherous shafts is Celegorm; in
*The Silmarillion* it is Curufin, using Celegorm's bow, and the vile act is
settled on the wickeder (as he was certainly also the cleverer) of the
brothers – in this Canto he is given the proper visage of a cunning villain:
'with his crafty mouth and thin' (2905). The reference of line 3103 'and
Men remembered at the Marching Forth' is to the Union of Maidros
before the Battle of Unnumbered Tears.

The second debate between Beren and Lúthien after his recovery from
the wound is derived from Synopsis V; it is not present at all in *The
Silmarillion*, though it is not without its importance in its representation
of Beren's utter determination in the face of Lúthien's persuasions to
abandon the quest.

Two new elements in the geography appear in this Canto: the Hill of
Himling (later Himring) rising to the east of the Gorge of Aglon (2994),
and the river Mindeb: lines 2924–5 (and the rewritten verses given on
p. 360) seem to be the only description of it anywhere.

The curious element of Morgoth's particular interest in Lúthien (so
that he sent the Orc-captain Boldog to Doriath to capture her, lines
2127–36) reappears in this Canto (3198–3201).

At the beginning of the Canto the burial of Felagund leads to a further
reference to his fate after death without mention of Mandos (see p. 259):

> while Felagund laughs beneath the trees
> in Valinor, and comes no more
> to this grey world of tears and war.

---

*The reference in *The Silmarillion* to Celebrimbor son of Curufin remaining in Nargothrond at this time and renouncing his father was a much later development.

## XI

Once wide and smooth a plain was spread,
where King Fingolfin proudly led
his silver armies on the green,
his horses white, his lances keen;
his helmets tall of steel were hewn,　　　　　3250
his shields were shining as the moon.

　　There trumpets sang both long and loud,
and challenge rang unto the cloud
that lay on Morgoth's northern tower,
while Morgoth waited for his hour.　　　　　3255

　　Rivers of fire at dead of night
in winter lying cold and white
upon the plain burst forth, and high
the red was mirrored in the sky.
From Hithlum's walls they saw the fire,　　　3260
the steam and smoke in spire on spire
leap up, till in confusion vast
the stars were choked. And so it passed,
the mighty field, and turned to dust,
to drifting sand and yellow rust,　　　　　3265
to thirsty dunes where many bones
lay broken among barren stones.

　　Dor-na-Fauglith, Land of Thirst,
they after named it, waste accurst,
the raven-haunted roofless grave　　　　　3270
of many fair and many brave.
Thereon the stony slopes look forth
from Deadly Nightshade falling north,
from sombre pines with pinions vast,
black-plumed and drear, as many a mast　　3275
of sable-shrouded ships of death
slow wafted on a ghostly breath.

　　Thence Beren grim now gazes out
across the dunes and shifting drought,
and sees afar the frowning towers　　　　　3280
where thunderous Thangorodrim lowers.

　　The hungry horse there drooping stood,
proud Gnomish steed; it feared the wood;
upon the haunted ghastly plain

no horse would ever stride again.                    3285
'Good steed of master ill,' he said,
'farewell now here! Lift up thy head,
and get thee gone to Sirion's vale,
back as we came, past island pale
where Thû once reigned, to waters sweet     3290
and grasses long about thy feet.
And if Curufin no more thou find,
grieve not! but free with hart and hind
go wander, leaving work and war,
and dream thee back in Valinor,              3295
whence came of old thy mighty race
from Tavros' mountain-fencéd chase.'

  There still sat Beren, and he sang,
and loud his lonely singing rang.
Though Orc should hear, or wolf a-prowl,     3300
or any of the creatures foul
within the shade that slunk and stared
of Taur-na-Fuin, nought he cared,
who now took leave of light and day,
grim-hearted, bitter, fierce and fey.        3305

  'Farewell now here, ye leaves of trees,
your music in the morning-breeze!
Farewell now blade and bloom and grass
that see the changing seasons pass;
ye waters murmuring over stone,              3310
and meres that silent stand alone!
Farewell now mountain, vale, and plain!
Farewell now wind and frost and rain,
and mist and cloud, and heaven's air;
ye star and moon so blinding-fair            3315
that still shall look down from the sky
on the wide earth, though Beren die –
though Beren die not, and yet deep,
deep, whence comes of those that weep
no dreadful echo, lie and choke             3320
in everlasting dark and smoke.
  'Farewell sweet earth and northern sky,
for ever blest, since here did lie,
and here with lissom limbs did run,
beneath the moon, beneath the sun,           3325

Lúthien Tinúviel
more fair than mortal tongue can tell.
Though all to ruin fell the world,
and were dissolved and backward hurled
unmade into the old abyss,                                    3330
yet were its making good, for this –
the dawn, the dusk, the earth, the sea –
that Lúthien on a time should be!'

His blade he lifted high in hand,
and challenging alone did stand                              3335
before the threat of Morgoth's power;
and dauntless cursed him, hall and tower,
o'ershadowing hand and grinding foot,
beginning, end, and crown and root;
then turned to stride forth down the slope                  3340
abandoning fear, forsaking hope.

'A, Beren, Beren!' came a sound,
'almost too late have I thee found!
O proud and fearless hand and heart,
not yet farewell, not yet we part!                           3345
Not thus do those of elven race
forsake the love that they embrace.
A love is mine, as great a power
as thine, to shake the gate and tower
of death with challenge weak and frail                      3350
that yet endures, and will not fail
nor yield, unvanquished were it hurled
beneath the foundations of the world.
Beloved fool! escape to seek
from such pursuit; in might so weak                          3355
to trust not, thinking it well to save
from love thy loved, who welcomes grave
and torment sooner than in guard
of kind intent to languish, barred,
wingless and helpless him to aid                             3360
for whose support her love was made!'

Thus back to him came Lúthien:
they met beyond the ways of Men;
upon the brink of terror stood
between the desert and the wood.                             3365

He looked on her, her lifted face
beneath his lips in sweet embrace:
'Thrice now mine oath I curse,' he said,
'that under shadow thee hath led!
But where is Huan, where the hound          3370
to whom I trusted, whom I bound
by love of thee to keep thee well
from deadly wandering unto hell?'

'I know not! But good Huan's heart
is wiser, kinder than thou art,          3375
grim lord, more open unto prayer!
Yet long and long I pleaded there,
until he brought me, as I would,
upon thy trail – a palfrey good
would Huan make, of flowing pace:          3380
thou wouldst have laughed to see us race,
as Orc on werewolf ride like fire
night after night through fen and mire,
through waste and wood! But when I heard
thy singing clear – (yea, every word          3385
of Lúthien one rashly cried,
and listening evil fierce defied) –,
he set me down, and sped away;
but what he would I cannot say.'

Ere long they knew, for Huan came,          3390
his great breath panting, eyes like flame,
in fear lest her whom he forsook
to aid some hunting evil took
ere he was nigh. Now there he laid
before their feet, as dark as shade,          3395
two grisly shapes that he had won
from that tall isle in Sirion:
a wolfhame huge – its savage fell
was long and matted, dark the spell
that drenched the dreadful coat and skin,          3400
the werewolf cloak of Draugluin;
the other was a batlike garb
with mighty fingered wings, a barb
like iron nail at each joint's end –
such wings as their dark cloud extend          3405
against the moon, when in the sky

from Deadly Nightshade screeching fly
Thû's messengers.

　　　　　　'What hast thou brought,
good Huan? What thy hidden thought?
Of trophy of prowess and strong deed, 3410
when Thû thou vanquishedst, what need
here in the waste?' Thus Beren spoke,
and once more words in Huan woke:
his voice was like the deeptoned bells
that ring in Valmar's citadels: 3415

'Of one fair gem thou must be thief,
Morgoth's or Thingol's, loath or lief;
thou must here choose twixt love and oath!
If vow to break is still thee loath,
then Lúthien must either die 3420
alone, or death with thee defie
beside thee, marching on your fate
that hidden before you lies in wait.
Hopeless the quest, but not yet mad,
unless thou, Beren, run thus clad 3425
in mortal raiment, mortal hue,
witless and redeless, death to woo.
　'Lo! good was Felagund's device,
but may be bettered, if advice
of Huan ye will dare to take, 3430
and swift a hideous change will make
to forms most curséd, foul and vile,
of werewolf of the Wizard's Isle,
of monstrous bat's envermined fell
with ghostly clawlike wings of hell. 3435
　'To such dark straits, alas! now brought
are ye I love, for whom I fought.
Nor further with you can I go –
whoever did a great hound know
in friendship at a werewolf's side 3440
to Angband's grinning portals stride?
Yet my heart tells that at the gate
what there ye find, 'twill be my fate
myself to see, though to that door
my feet shall bear me nevermore. 3445
Darkened is hope and dimmed my eyes,

I see not clear what further lies;
yet maybe backwards leads your path
beyond all hope to Doriath,
and thither, perchance, we three shall wend,          3450
and meet again before the end.'

They stood and marvelled thus to hear
his mighty tongue so deep and clear;
then sudden he vanished from their sight
even at the onset of the night.          3455

His dreadful counsel then they took,
and their own gracious forms forsook;
in werewolf fell and batlike wing
prepared to robe them, shuddering.
With elvish magic Lúthien wrought,          3460
lest raiment foul with evil fraught
to dreadful madness drive their hearts;
and there she wrought with elvish arts
a strong defence, a binding power,
singing until the midnight hour.          3465

Swift as the wolvish coat he wore,
Beren lay slavering on the floor,
redtongued and hungry; but there lies
a pain and longing in his eyes,
a look of horror as he sees          3470
a batlike form crawl to its knees
and drag its creased and creaking wings.
Then howling under moon he springs
fourfooted, swift, from stone to stone,
from hill to plain – but not alone:          3475
a dark shape down the slope doth skim,
and wheeling flitters over him.

Ashes and dust and thirsty dune
withered and dry beneath the moon,
under the cold and shifting air          3480
sifting and sighing, bleak and bare;
of blistered stones and gasping sand,
of splintered bones was built that land,
o'er which now slinks with powdered fell
and hanging tongue a shape of hell.          3485
Many parching leagues lay still before

when sickly day crept back once more;
many choking miles yet stretched ahead
when shivering night once more was spread
with doubtful shadow and ghostly sound     3490
that hissed and passed o'er dune and mound.
    A second morning in cloud and reek
struggled, when stumbling, blind and weak,
a wolvish shape came staggering forth
and reached the foothills of the North;     3495
upon its back there folded lay
a crumpled thing that blinked at day.

    The rocks were reared like bony teeth,
and claws that grasped from opened sheath,
on either side the mournful road     3500
that onward led to that abode
far up within the Mountain dark
with tunnels drear and portals stark.
    They crept within a scowling shade,
and cowering darkly down them laid.     3505
Long lurked they there beside the path,
and shivered, dreaming of Doriath,
of laughter and music and clean air,
in fluttered leaves birds singing fair.
    They woke, and felt the trembling sound,     3510
the beating echo far underground
shake beneath them, the rumour vast
of Morgoth's forges; and aghast
they heard the tramp of stony feet
that shod with iron went down that street:     3515
the Orcs went forth to rape and war,
and Balrog captains marched before.

    They stirred, and under cloud and shade
at eve stepped forth, and no more stayed;
as dark things on dark errand bent     3520
up the long slopes in haste they went.
Ever the sheer cliffs rose beside,
where birds of carrion sat and cried;
and chasms black and smoking yawned,
whence writhing serpent-shapes were spawned;   3525
until at last in that huge gloom,
heavy as overhanging doom,

that weighs on Thangorodrim's foot
like thunder at the mountain's root,
they came, as to a sombre court                        3530
walled with great towers, fort on fort
of cliffs embattled, to that last plain
that opens, abysmal and inane,
before the final topless wall
of Bauglir's immeasurable hall,                        3535
whereunder looming awful waits
the gigantic shadow of his gates.

★

## NOTES

3249–53  Cf. the opening of the Lay, lines 5–10.

3267  Against this line is written the date 'Sep. 26 1930'. The previous date was 25 Sept. 1930 at line 3220.

3297  *Tavros* > *Tauros* B: see notes to lines 891, 904; 2246.

3303  *Taur-na-Fuin* > *Taur-nu-Fuin* B (a late change).

3401  *Draugluin* appears here in the A-text (see p. 258).

3414–15  Cf. lines 2258–9.

3419–23  The shift from *thee* to *your* and *you* is intentional, and indicates that Huan now refers to both Beren and Lúthien.

3478  Against this line is written the date 'Sep. 27 1930'.

### Commentary on Canto XI

The earliest version of the narrative of this Canto describes Tinúviel's sewing of Beren into the catskin of Oikeroi and teaching him some aspects of feline behaviour; she herself was not disguised. Very little is made of the journey to Angamandi, but the approach to the gates is described:

> At length however they drew near to Angamandi, as indeed the rumblings and deep noises, and the sound of mighty hammerings of ten thousand smiths labouring unceasingly, declared to them. Nigh were the sad chambers where the thrall-Noldoli laboured bitterly under the Orcs and goblins of the hills, and here the gloom and darkness was great so that their hearts fell . . . (II.31).

Synopses I and II have virtually nothing here beyond the bare event (p. 270). In its emended form Synopsis III comes near to the final story of the 'wolfhame' and the parting from Huan (p. 272); and this outline continues:

Thangorodrim towers above them. There are rumblings, steam and vapours burst from fissures in the rock. Ten thousand smiths are hammering – they pass the vaults where the thrall-Gnomes are labouring without rest. The gloom sinks into their hearts.

This is remarkably close to the passage cited above from the *Tale of Tinúviel*.

Synopsis IV (p. 273) adds no more, for after 'They prepare to go to Angband' it continues with events in Doriath and the embassy to Thingol from Celegorm, which at this stage my father was going to introduce before the Angband adventure, and in this outline virtually nothing is said of that.

There remains Synopsis V, whose outline for Canto '10' has been given on p. 273 as far as 'One morning early Beren steals away on Curufin's horse and reaches the eaves of Taur-na-Fuin', and it is here that Beren's solitary departure first enters. This outline continues, still under the heading 'Canto 10':

There he looks upon Thangorodrim and sings a song of farewell to earth and light, and to Lúthien. In the midst up come Lúthien and Huan! With the hound's aid she has followed him; and moreover from the Wizard's Isle Huan has brought a wolf-ham and a bat-coat. [*Struck through at time of writing*: Beren sets Lúthien upon the horse and they ride through Taur-na-Fuin.\*] Beren sets Curufin's horse to gallop free and he speeds away. Now Beren takes the shape of werewolf and Tinúviel of bat. Then Huan bids farewell. And speaks. No hound can walk with werewolf – more peril should I be than help in Morgoth's land. Yet what ye shall see at Angband's gate I perchance too shall see, though my fate doth not lead to those doors. Darkened is all hope, and dimmed my eyes, yet perchance I see thy paths leading from that place once more. Then he vanishes. They make a grievous journey. Thangorodrim looms over them, . . . . . . . . in its smoky foothills.

This ends the outline for 'Canto 10' in Synopsis V.

There is a notable difference in the structure of the story in the Lay from that in *The Silmarillion* (pp. 178–9): in the Lay Huan is absent (gone to the Wizard's Isle for the wolfcoat and batskin) when Lúthien finds Beren – she does not know where he has gone – but he comes up a little later; whereas in the prose account Huan and Lúthien came together, and they were clad in 'the ghastly wolf-hame of Draugluin and the bat-fell of Thuringwethil' – an apparition that filled Beren with

---

\* Beren must in fact have been on the northern edge of Taur-na-Fuin when Lúthien and Huan came up with him, since 'he looks upon Thangorodrim'.

dismay. The story in *The Silmarillion* is a reversion, at least in so far as Huan and Lúthien arrive together, to that of Synopsis V ('In the midst up come Lúthien and Huan', p. 283).

In the Lay the bat-wings are only said to be such as bear up Thû's messengers, and are not associated with a particular or chief messenger (Thuringwethil, 'messenger of Sauron').

But the prose version in other respects follows that of the Lay closely, with as before retention of phrases ('between the desert and the wood', 'Thrice now I curse my oath', 'fingered wings . . . barbed at each joint's end', 'the bat wheeled and flittered above him'); and the speech of Huan is closely modelled on that in the Lay.

From Beren's words to the horse (3288–90)

> get thee gone to Sirion's vale,
> back as we came, past island pale
> where Thû once reigned

it is clear that as in *The Silmarillion* 'he rode northward again with all speed to the Pass of Sirion, and coming to the skirts of Taur-nu-Fuin he looked out across the waste of Anfauglith'. It is not said in the Lay how Lúthien and Huan came there, but in *The Silmarillion* 'clad in these dreadful garments' they 'ran through Taur-nu-Fuin, and all things fled before them'.

The Battle of Sudden Flame (lines 3256 ff.) has been described earlier in the Lay (lines 1678 ff.), but it has not been actually stated before that the northern plain was once green and grassy (3246–8), and became a desert after the 'rivers of fire . . . upon the plain burst forth'.

With Beren's words to Curufin's horse (3295–7):

> dream thee back in Valinor,
> whence came of old thy mighty race

cf. *The Silmarillion* p. 119, where it is told that 'many of the sires' of the horses of the Noldor of Hithlum who rode on Ard-galen came from Valinor.

# XII

> In that vast shadow once of yore
> Fingolfin stood: his shield he bore
> with field of heaven's blue and star        3540
> of crystal shining pale afar.
> In overmastering wrath and hate
> desperate he smote upon that gate,

the Gnomish king, there standing lone,
while endless fortresses of stone 3545
engulfed the thin clear ringing keen
of silver horn on baldric green.
His hopeless challenge dauntless cried
Fingolfin there: 'Come, open wide,
dark king, your ghastly brazen doors! 3550
Come forth, whom earth and heaven abhors!
Come forth, O monstrous craven lord,
and fight with thine own hand and sword,
thou wielder of hosts of banded thralls,
thou tyrant leaguered with strong walls, 3555
thou foe of Gods and elvish race!
I wait thee here. Come! Show thy face!'

Then Morgoth came. For the last time
in those great wars he dared to climb
from subterranean throne profound, 3560
the rumour of his feet a sound
of rumbling earthquake underground.
Black-armoured, towering, iron-crowned
he issued forth; his mighty shield
a vast unblazoned sable field 3565
with shadow like a thundercloud;
and o'er the gleaming king it bowed,
as huge aloft like mace he hurled
that hammer of the underworld,
Grond. Clanging to ground it tumbled 3570
down like a thunder-bolt, and crumbled
the rocks beneath it; smoke up-started,
a pit yawned, and a fire darted.

Fingolfin like a shooting light
beneath a cloud, a stab of white, 3575
sprang then aside, and Ringil drew
like ice that gleameth cold and blue,
his sword devised of elvish skill
to pierce the flesh with deadly chill.
With seven wounds it rent his foe, 3580
and seven mighty cries of woe
rang in the mountains, and the earth quook,
and Angband's trembling armies shook.
Yet Orcs would after laughing tell

of the duel at the gates of hell;                                     3585
though elvish song thereof was made
ere this but one – when sad was laid
the mighty king in barrow high,
and Thorndor, Eagle of the sky,
the dreadful tidings brought and told                                 3590
to mourning Elfinesse of old.
Thrice was Fingolfin with great blows
to his knees beaten, thrice he rose
still leaping up beneath the cloud
aloft to hold star-shining, proud,                                    3595
his stricken shield, his sundered helm,
that dark nor might could overwhelm
till all the earth was burst and rent
in pits about him. He was spent.
His feet stumbled. He fell to wreck                                   3600
upon the ground, and on his neck
a foot like rooted hills was set,
and he was crushed – not conquered yet;
one last despairing stroke he gave:
the mighty foot pale Ringil clave                                     3605
about the heel, and black the blood
gushed as from smoking fount in flood.

  Halt goes for ever from that stroke
great Morgoth; but the king he broke,
and would have hewn and mangled thrown                                3610
to wolves devouring. Lo! from throne
that Manwë bade him build on high,
on peak unscaled beneath the sky,
Morgoth to watch, now down there swooped
Thorndor the King of Eagles, stooped,                                 3615
and rending beak of gold he smote
in Bauglir's face, then up did float
on pinions thirty fathoms wide
bearing away, though loud they cried,
the mighty corse, the Elven-king;                                     3620
and where the mountains make a ring
far to the south about that plain
where after Gondolin did reign,
embattled city, at great height
upon a dizzy snowcap white                                            3625
in mounded cairn the mighty dead

he laid upon the mountain's head.
Never Orc nor demon after dared
that pass to climb, o'er which there stared
Fingolfin's high and holy tomb,                            3630
till Gondolin's appointed doom.

Thus Bauglir earned the furrowed scar
that his dark countenance doth mar,
and thus his limping gait he gained;
but afterward profound he reigned                          3635
darkling upon his hidden throne;
and thunderous paced his halls of stone,
slow building there his vast design
the world in thraldom to confine.
Wielder of armies, lord of woe,                            3640
no rest now gave he slave or foe;
his watch and ward he thrice increased,
his spies were sent from West to East
and tidings brought from all the North,
who fought, who fell; who ventured forth,                  3645
who wrought in secret; who had hoard;
if maid were fair or proud were lord;
well nigh all things he knew, all hearts
well nigh enmeshed in evil arts.

Doriath only, beyond the veil                              3650
woven by Melian, no assail
could hurt or enter; only rumour dim
of things there passing came to him.
A rumour loud and tidings clear
of other movements far and near                            3655
among his foes, and threat of war
from the seven sons of Fëanor,
from Nargothrond, from Fingon still
gathering his armies under hill
and under tree in Hithlum's shade,                         3660
these daily came. He grew afraid
amidst his power once more; renown
of Beren vexed his ears, and down
the aisléd forests there was heard
great Huan baying.

                              Then came word                3665
most passing strange of Lúthien

wild-wandering by wood and glen,
and Thingol's purpose long he weighed,
and wondered, thinking of that maid
so fair, so frail. A captain dire,                    3670
Boldog, he sent with sword and fire
to Doriath's march; but battle fell
sudden upon him: news to tell
never one returned of Boldog's host,
and Thingol humbled Morgoth's boast.                  3675
Then his heart with doubt and wrath was burned:
new tidings of dismay he learned,
how Thû was o'erthrown and his strong isle
broken and plundered, how with guile
his foes now guile beset; and spies                   3680
he feared, till each Orc to his eyes
was half suspect. Still ever down
the aisléd forests came renown
of Huan baying, hound of war
that Gods unleashed in Valinor.                       3685

Then Morgoth of Huan's fate bethought
long-rumoured, and in dark he wrought.
Fierce hunger-haunted packs he had
that in wolvish form and flesh were clad,
but demon spirits dire did hold;                      3690
and ever wild their voices rolled
in cave and mountain where they housed
and endless snarling echoes roused.
From these a whelp he chose and fed
with his own hand on bodies dead,                     3695
on fairest flesh of Elves and Men,
till huge he grew and in his den
no more could creep, but by the chair
of Morgoth's self would lie and glare,
nor suffer Balrog, Orc, nor beast                     3700
to touch him. Many a ghastly feast
he held beneath that awful throne,
rending flesh and gnawing bone.
There deep enchantment on him fell,
the anguish and the power of hell;                    3705
more great and terrible he became
with fire-red eyes and jaws aflame,

with breath like vapours of the grave,
than any beast of wood or cave,
than any beast of earth or hell                     3710
that ever in any time befell,
surpassing all his race and kin,
the ghastly tribe of Draugluin.

    Him Carcharoth, the Red Maw, name
the songs of Elves. Not yet he came                 3715
disastrous, ravening, from the gates
of Angband. There he sleepless waits;
where those great portals threatening loom
his red eyes smoulder in the gloom,
his teeth are bare, his jaws are wide;              3720
and none may walk, nor creep, nor glide,
nor thrust with power his menace past
to enter Morgoth's dungeon vast.

    Now, lo! before his watchful eyes
a slinking shape he far descries                    3725
that crawls into the frowning plain
and halts at gaze, then on again
comes stalking near, a wolvish shape
haggard, wayworn, with jaws agape;
and o'er it batlike in wide rings                   3730
a reeling shadow slowly wings.
Such shapes there oft were seen to roam,
this land their native haunt and home;
and yet his mood with strange unease
is filled, and boding thoughts him seize.           3735

    'What grievous terror, what dread guard
hath Morgoth set to wait, and barred
his doors against all entering feet?
Long ways we have come at last to meet
the very maw of death that opes                     3740
between us and our quest! Yet hopes
we never had. No turning back!'
Thus Beren speaks, as in his track
he halts and sees with werewolf eyes
afar the horror that there lies.                    3745
Then onward desperate he passed,
skirting the black pits yawning vast,

where King Fingolfin ruinous fell
alone before the gates of hell.

Before those gates alone they stood,                    3750
while Carcharoth in doubtful mood
glowered upon them, and snarling spoke,
and echoes in the arches woke:
'Hail! Draugluin, my kindred's lord!
'Tis very long since hitherward                         3755
thou camest. Yea, 'tis passing strange
to see thee now: a grievous change
is on thee, lord, who once so dire,
so dauntless, and as fleet as fire,
ran over wild and waste, but now                        3760
with weariness must bend and bow!
'Tis hard to find the struggling breath
when Huan's teeth as sharp as death
have rent the throat? What fortune rare
brings thee back living here to fare –                  3765
if Draugluin thou art? Come near!
I would know more, and see thee clear.'

'Who art thou, hungry upstart whelp,
to bar my ways whom thou shouldst help?
I fare with hasty tidings new                           3770
to Morgoth from forest-haunting Thû.
Aside! for I must in; or go
and swift my coming tell below!'

Then up that doorward slowly stood,
eyes shining grim with evil mood,                       3775
uneasy growling: 'Draugluin,
if such thou be, now enter in!
But what is this that crawls beside,
slinking as if 'twould neath thee hide?
Though wingéd creatures to and fro                      3780
unnumbered pass here, all I know.
I know not this. Stay, vampire, stay!
I like not thy kin nor thee. Come, say
what sneaking errand thee doth bring,
thou wingéd vermin, to the king!                        3785
Small matter, I doubt not, if thou stay
or enter, or if in my play

I crush thee like a fly on wall,
or bite thy wings and let thee crawl.'

   Huge-stalking, noisome, close he came.    3790
In Beren's eyes there gleamed a flame;
the hair upon his neck uprose.
Nought may the fragrance fair enclose,
the odour of immortal flowers
in everlasting spring neath showers    3795
that glitter silver in the grass
in Valinor. Where'er did pass
Tinúviel, such air there went.
From that foul devil-sharpened scent
its sudden sweetness no disguise    3800
enchanted dark to cheat the eyes
could keep, if near those nostrils drew
snuffling in doubt. This Beren knew
upon the brink of hell prepared
for battle and death. There threatening stared    3805
those dreadful shapes, in hatred both,
false Draugluin and Carcharoth
when, lo! a marvel to behold:
some power, descended from of old,
from race divine beyond the West,    3810
sudden Tinúviel possessed
like inner fire. The vampire dark
she flung aside, and like a lark
cleaving through night to dawn she sprang,
while sheer, heart-piercing silver, rang    3815
her voice, as those long trumpets keen
thrilling, unbearable, unseen
in the cold aisles of morn. Her cloak
by white hands woven, like a smoke,
like all-bewildering, all-enthralling,    3820
all-enfolding evening, falling
from lifted arms, as forth she stepped,
across those awful eyes she swept,
a shadow and a mist of dreams
wherein entangled starlight gleams.    3825

   'Sleep, O unhappy, tortured thrall!
Thou woebegotten, fail and fall
down, down from anguish, hatred, pain,

from lust, from hunger, bond and chain,
to that oblivion, dark and deep,                    3830
the well, the lightless pit of sleep!
For one brief hour escape the net,
the dreadful doom of life forget!'

His eyes were quenched, his limbs were loosed;
he fell like running steer that noosed             3835
and tripped goes crashing to the ground.
Deathlike, moveless, without a sound
outstretched he lay, as lightning stroke
had felled a huge o'ershadowing oak.

★

# NOTES

3554    *banded* A, B; > *branded* B, but I think that the *r* was
written in by somebody else.

3589    *Thorndor* emended to *Thorondor* in B, but I think that this
was a late correction.

3606    *pinned it to earth* A, B; *about the heel* apparently a late
emendation to B.

3615    *Thorndor* later emended to *Thorondor* in B, see 3589.

3623    *after* > *secret* B, a late emendation when Gondolin's foundation had been made much earlier.

3638–9    A:   nor ever again to war came forth
until the last battle of the North,
but builded slow his mighty thought
of pride and lust unfathomed wrought.

3650    Against this line is written the date 'Sep. 28'. The previous
date was 27 Sept. 1930 against line 3478.

3658    *Finweg* A, B, emended to *Fingon* B, as at lines 1647, 1654.

3712–13    This couplet not in A, as originally written.

3714    A (as originally written):

Him Carcharos, the Knife-fang, name

*Carcharos* then > *Carcharas*, and then > *Carcharoth* (see
notes to lines 3751, 3807). In the margin of A is written *Red
Maw*, and *Caras* with another, illegible, word beginning
*Car-*; also *Gargaroth*; and *Fearphantom Draugluin is his
name*. This may mean that my father was thinking of using
the name *Draugluin* for the Wolf of Angband, though

*Drauglun* had by now appeared in the A-text (3401) for the great wolf of the Wizard's Isle.

3751    *Carcharas* A, not emended to *Carcharoth* (see note to 3714).

3790    Against this line is written the date 'Sep. 30 1930'. The previous date was 28 Sept. 1930 against line 3650.

3807    *Carcharoth* A (rhyming with *both*); see notes to 3714, 3751.

## Commentary on Canto XII

The greater part of this Canto is retrospective: beginning with the death of Fingolfin in combat with Morgoth, it passes to Morgoth's doubts and fears and his rearing of Carcharoth. By this time (September 1930) a large part, at any rate, of the prose 'Silmarillion' developed out of the 'Sketch of the Mythology' had been written, as I hope to demonstrate later, and it seems certain that the story of Fingolfin's duel with Morgoth as it appears in this Canto followed the prose version, though we meet it here for the first time (together with the names *Grond*, the Hammer of the Underworld, and *Ringil*, Fingolfin's sword). The text in *The Silmarillion* (pp. 153–4) was largely based on the Lay, which it follows in the structure of the account and from which derive many phrases;* but independent traces of the 'prose tradition' are also present. The account in the poem gives no indication of when the duel took place, or of what led Fingolfin to challenge Morgoth. For the much earlier mention of Fingolfin's death (now very obscure, but certainly quite differently conceived) see pp. 146–7.

The further mention in this Canto of Boldog's raid (lines 3665–75) will be discussed at the end of the poem (pp. 310–13).

Turning to the 'foreground' narrative, a passage in Synopsis III already given (pp. 270–1) bears on the content of Canto XII: it was bracketed and marked 'Later'.

> Morgoth hearing of the breaking of the Wizard's Tower sends out an army of Orcs; finding the wolves are slain with . . . . . . throats he thinks it is Huan and fashions a vast wolf – Carcharas – mightiest of all wolves to guard his door.

Synopsis III continues from the point reached on p. 283:

> The hideous gates of Angband. There lay *Carcharoth knifefang*. He gets slowly to his feet and bars the gate. 'Growl not O Wolf for I go to seek Morgoth with news of Thû.' He approached to snuff the air of

---

*For example: 'the rumour of his feet' (cf. line 3561); Morgoth 'like a tower, iron-crowned' (cf. 3563); he swung Grond down 'like a bolt of thunder' (cf. 3571); 'smoke and fire darted' (cf. 3572–3); 'the blood gushed forth black and smoking' (cf. 3606–7); &c.

her, for faint suspicion moved in his wicked heart, and he fell into
slumber.

The interpretation of the wolf's name as 'Knife-fang' goes back to the
*Tale of Tinúviel* and survived into the A-text of the Lay (see note to line
3714), but was replaced in B by the translation 'Red Maw'. The words
'red maw' are used of Karkaras in the *Tale*, but not as his name (II. 34).

The idea of Carcharoth's approaching Lúthien 'to snuff the air of her'
is also derived, in these same words, from the *Tale* (II. 31).

Synopsis IV does not here concern us (see p. 283); Synopsis V, after
the point reached on p. 283, now has a heading '11', and is clearly the
basis for the story in Canto XII of the Lay:

[*Added in pencil*: Battle of Morgoth and Fingolfin.]

Morgoth hears of the ruin of Thû's castle. His mind is filled with
misgiving and anger. The gates of Angband strengthened; because of
the rumour of Huan he [*struck out at time of writing*: fashions the
greatest] chooses the fiercest wolf from all the whelps of his packs, and
feeds him on flesh of Men and Elves, and enchants him so that he
becomes the most great and terrible of all beasts that ever have been –
Carcharos.

Beren and Lúthien approach. [*Added in pencil*: the pitted plain of
Fingolfin's fight.] The enchanting of Carcharos.

# XIII

Into the vast and echoing gloom,                    3840
more dread than many-tunnelled tomb
in labyrinthine pyramid
where everlasting death is hid,
down awful corridors that wind
down to a menace dark enshrined;                    3845
down to the mountain's roots profound,
devoured, tormented, bored and ground
by seething vermin spawned of stone;
down to the depths they went alone.
    The arch behind of twilit shade                 3850
they saw recede and dwindling fade;
the thunderous forges' rumour grew,
a burning wind there roaring blew
foul vapours up from gaping holes.

Huge shapes there stood like carven trolls          3855
enormous hewn of blasted rock
to forms that mortal likeness mock;
monstrous and menacing, entombed,
at every turn they silent loomed
in fitful glares that leaped and died.              3860
There hammers clanged, and tongues there cried
with sound like smitten stone; there wailed
faint from far under, called and failed
amid the iron clink of chain
voices of captives put to pain.                     3865

Loud rose a din of laughter hoarse,
self-loathing yet without remorse;
loud came a singing harsh and fierce
like swords of terror souls to pierce.
Red was the glare through open doors                3870
of firelight mirrored on brazen floors,
and up the arches towering clomb
to glooms unguessed, to vaulted dome
swathed in wavering smokes and steams
stabbed with flickering lightning-gleams.           3875
To Morgoth's hall, where dreadful feast
he held, and drank the blood of beast
and lives of Men, they stumbling came:
their eyes were dazed with smoke and flame.
The pillars, reared like monstrous shores           3880
to bear earth's overwhelming floors,
were devil-carven, shaped with skill
such as unholy dreams doth fill:
they towered like trees into the air,
whose trunks are rooted in despair,                 3885
whose shade is death, whose fruit is bane,
whose boughs like serpents writhe in pain.
Beneath them ranged with spear and sword
stood Morgoth's sable-armoured horde:
the fire on blade and boss of shield                3890
was red as blood on stricken field.
Beneath a monstrous column loomed
the throne of Morgoth, and the doomed
and dying gasped upon the floor:
his hideous footstool, rape of war.                 3895

About him sat his awful thanes,
the Balrog-lords with fiery manes,
redhanded, mouthed with fangs of steel;
devouring wolves were crouched at heel.
And o'er the host of hell there shone          3900
with a cold radiance, clear and wan,
the Silmarils, the gems of fate,
emprisoned in the crown of hate.

Lo! through the grinning portals dread
sudden a shadow swooped and fled;              3905
and Beren gasped – he lay alone,
with crawling belly on the stone:
a form bat-wingéd, silent, flew
where the huge pillared branches grew,
amid the smokes and mounting steams.           3910
And as on the margin of dark dreams
a dim-felt shadow unseen grows
to cloud of vast unease, and woes
foreboded, nameless, roll like doom
upon the soul, so in that gloom                3915
the voices fell, and laughter died
slow to silence many-eyed.
A nameless doubt, a shapeless fear,
had entered in their caverns drear,
and grew, and towered above them cowed,        3920
hearing in heart the trumpets loud
of gods forgotten. Morgoth spoke,
and thunderous the silence broke:
'Shadow, descend! And do not think
to cheat mine eyes! In vain to shrink          3925
from thy Lord's gaze, or seek to hide.
My will by none may be defied.
Hope nor escape doth here await
those that unbidden pass my gate.
Descend! ere anger blast thy wing,             3930
thou foolish, frail, bat-shapen thing,
and yet not bat within! Come down!'

Slow-wheeling o'er his iron crown,
reluctantly, shivering and small,
Beren there saw the shadow fall,               3935
and droop before the hideous throne,

a weak and trembling thing, alone.
And as thereon great Morgoth bent
his darkling gaze, he shuddering went,
belly to earth, the cold sweat dank 3940
upon his fell, and crawling shrank
beneath the darkness of that seat,
beneath the shadow of those feet.

Tinúviel spake, a shrill, thin, sound
piercing those silences profound: 3945
'A lawful errand here me brought;
from Thû's dark mansions have I sought,
from Taur-na-Fuin's shade I fare
to stand before thy mighty chair!'

'Thy name, thou shrieking waif, thy name! 3950
Tidings enough from Thû there came
but short while since. What would he now?
Why send such messenger as thou?'

'Thuringwethil I am, who cast
a shadow o'er the face aghast 3955
of the sallow moon in the doomed land
of shivering Beleriand.'

'Liar art thou, who shalt not weave
deceit before mine eyes. Now leave
thy form and raiment false, and stand 3960
revealed, and delivered to my hand!'

There came a slow and shuddering change:
the batlike raiment dark and strange
was loosed, and slowly shrank and fell
quivering. She stood revealed in hell. 3965
About her slender shoulders hung
her shadowy hair, and round her clung
her garment dark, where glimmered pale
the starlight caught in magic veil.
Dim dreams and faint oblivious sleep 3970
fell softly thence, in dungeons deep
an odour stole of elven-flowers
from elven-dells where silver showers
drip softly through the evening air;
and round there crawled with greedy stare 3975
dark shapes of snuffling hunger dread.

With arms upraised and drooping head
then softly she began to sing
a theme of sleep and slumbering,
wandering, woven with deeper spell                    3980
than songs wherewith in ancient dell
Melian did once the twilight fill,
profound, and fathomless, and still.

The fires of Angband flared and died,
smouldered into darkness; through the wide            3985
and hollow halls there rolled unfurled
the shadows of the underworld.
All movement stayed, and all sound ceased,
save vaporous breath of Orc and beast.
One fire in darkness still abode:                     3990
the lidless eyes of Morgoth glowed;
one sound the breathing silence broke:
the mirthless voice of Morgoth spoke.

'So Lúthien, so Lúthien,
a liar like all Elves and Men!                        3995
Yet welcome, welcome, to my hall!
I have a use for every thrall.
What news of Thingol in his hole
shy lurking like a timid vole?
What folly fresh is in his mind,                      4000
who cannot keep his offspring blind
from straying thus? or can devise
no better counsel for his spies?'

She wavered, and she stayed her song.
'The road,' she said, 'was wild and long,            4005
but Thingol sent me not, nor knows
what way his rebellious daughter goes.
Yet every road and path will lead
Northward at last, and here of need
I trembling come with humble brow,                    4010
and here before thy throne I bow;
for Lúthien hath many arts
for solace sweet of kingly hearts.'

'And here of need thou shalt remain
now, Lúthien, in joy or pain –                        4015
or pain, the fitting doom for all,

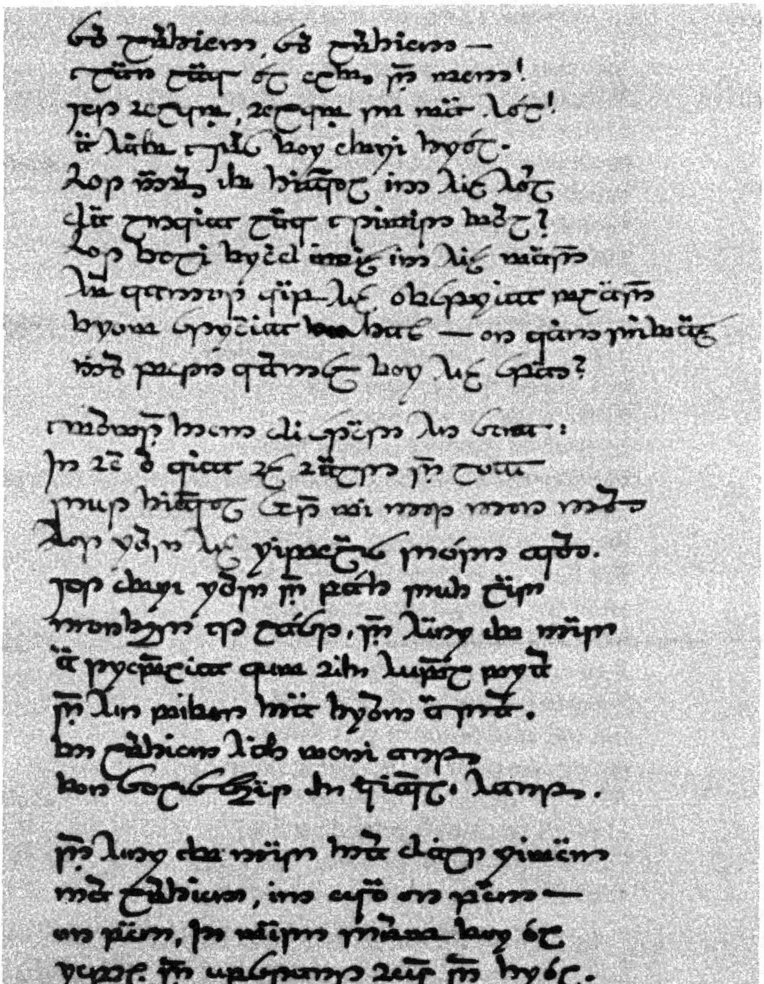

*The Lay of Leithian*, lines 3994–4027

for rebel, thief, and upstart thrall.
Why should ye not in our fate share
of woe and travail? Or should I spare
to slender limb and body frail                        4020
breaking torment? Of what avail
here dost thou deem thy babbling song
and foolish laughter? Minstrels strong
are at my call. Yet I will give
a respite brief, a while to live,                     4025
a little while, though purchased dear,
to Lúthien the fair and clear,
a pretty toy for idle hour.
In slothful gardens many a flower
like thee the amorous gods are used                   4030
honey-sweet to kiss, and cast then bruised,
their fragrance loosing, under feet.
But here we seldom find such sweet
amid our labours long and hard,
from godlike idleness debarred.                       4035
And who would not taste the honey-sweet
lying to lips, or crush with feet
the soft cool tissue of pale flowers,
easing like gods the dragging hours?
A! curse the Gods! O hunger dire,                     4040
O blinding thirst's unending fire!
One moment shall ye cease, and slake
your sting with morsel I here take!'

In his eyes the fire to flame was fanned,
and forth he stretched his brazen hand.               4045
Lúthien as shadow shrank aside.
'Not thus, O king! Not thus!' she cried,
'do great lords hark to humble boon!
For every minstrel hath his tune;
and some are strong and some are soft,                4050
and each would bear his song aloft,
and each a little while be heard,
though rude the note, and light the word.
But Lúthien hath cunning arts
for solace sweet of kingly hearts.                    4055
Now hearken!' And her wings she caught
then deftly up, and swift as thought

slipped from his grasp, and wheeling round,
fluttering before his eyes, she wound
a mazy-wingéd dance, and sped                                4060
about his iron-crownéd head.
Suddenly her song began anew;
and soft came dropping like a dew
down from on high in that domed hall
her voice bewildering, magical,                             4065
and grew to silver-murmuring streams
pale falling in dark pools in dreams.

She let her flying raiment sweep,
enmeshed with woven spells of sleep,
as round the dark void she ranged and reeled.              4070
From wall to wall she turned and wheeled
in dance such as never Elf nor fay
before devised, nor since that day;
than swallow swifter, than flittermouse
in dying light round darkened house                        4075
more silken-soft, more strange and fair
than sylphine maidens of the Air
whose wings in Varda's heavenly hall
in rhythmic movement beat and fall.
Down crumpled Orc, and Balrog proud;                       4080
all eyes were quenched, all heads were bowed;
the fires of heart and maw were stilled,
and ever like a bird she thrilled
above a lightless world forlorn
in ecstasy enchanted borne.                                4085
All eyes were quenched, save those that glared
in Morgoth's lowering brows, and stared
in slowly wandering wonder round,
and slow were in enchantment bound.
Their will wavered, and their fire failed,                 4090
and as beneath his brows they paled,
the Silmarils like stars were kindled
that in the reek of Earth had dwindled
escaping upwards clear to shine,
glistening marvellous in heaven's mine.                    4095

Then flaring suddenly they fell,
down, down upon the floors of hell.
The dark and mighty head was bowed;

like mountain-top beneath a cloud
the shoulders foundered, the vast form          4100
crashed, as in overwhelming storm
huge cliffs in ruin slide and fall;
and prone lay Morgoth in his hall.
His crown there rolled upon the ground,
a wheel of thunder; then all sound          4105
died, and a silence grew as deep
as were the heart of Earth asleep.

Beneath the vast and empty throne
the adders lay like twisted stone,
the wolves like corpses foul were strewn;          4110
and there lay Beren deep in swoon:
no thought, no dream nor shadow blind
moved in the darkness of his mind.
    'Come forth, come forth! The hour hath knelled,
and Angband's mighty lord is felled!          4115
Awake, awake! For we two meet
alone before the aweful seat.'
This voice came down into the deep
where he lay drowned in wells of sleep;
a hand flower-soft and flower-cool          4120
passed o'er his face, and the still pool
of slumber quivered. Up then leaped
his mind to waking; forth he crept.
The wolvish fell he flung aside
and sprang unto his feet, and wide          4125
staring amid the soundless gloom
he gasped as one living shut in tomb.
There to his side he felt her shrink,
felt Lúthien now shivering sink,
her strength and magic dimmed and spent,          4130
and swift his arms about her went.

Before his feet he saw amazed
the gems of Fëanor, that blazed
with white fire glistening in the crown
of Morgoth's might now fallen down.          4135
To move that helm of iron vast
no strength he found, and thence aghast
he strove with fingers mad to wrest
the guerdon of their hopeless quest,

till in his heart there fell the thought 4140
of that cold morn whereon he fought
with Curufin; then from his belt
the sheathless knife he drew, and knelt,
and tried its hard edge, bitter-cold,
o'er which in Nogrod songs had rolled 4145
of dwarvish armourers singing slow
to hammer-music long ago.
Iron as tender wood it clove
and mail as woof of loom it rove.
The claws of iron that held the gem, 4150
it bit them through and sundered them;
a Silmaril he clasped and held,
and the pure radiance slowly welled
red glowing through the clenching flesh.
Again he stooped and strove afresh 4155
one more of the holy jewels three
that Fëanor wrought of yore to free.
But round those fires was woven fate:
not yet should they leave the halls of hate.
The dwarvish steel of cunning blade 4160
by treacherous smiths of Nogrod made
snapped; then ringing sharp and clear
in twain it sprang, and like a spear
or errant shaft the brow it grazed
of Morgoth's sleeping head, and dazed 4165
their hearts with fear. For Morgoth groaned
with voice entombed, like wind that moaned
in hollow caverns penned and bound.
There came a breath; a gasping sound
moved through the halls, as Orc and beast 4170
turned in their dreams of hideous feast;
in sleep uneasy Balrogs stirred,
and far above was faintly heard
an echo that in tunnels rolled,
a wolvish howling long and cold. 4175

★

## NOTES

3840    At the beginning of the Canto is written the date 'Oct. 1 1930'.
        The previous date was 30 Sept. 1930 at line 3790.

3860    With this line the B typescript comes to an end, and the text
        continues to the end in fine manuscript.

3881    This line is dated 'Sept. 14 1931'. The previous date was 1 Oct.
        1930 at line 3840.

3887    This line is dated 'Sept. 15' (1931).

3947    Late change in B: *from Sauron's mansions have I sought*. See
        p. 232, note to lines 2064–6.

3951    Late change in B: *Tidings enough from Sauron came*.

3954    In the margin of B is written against *Thuringwethil*, at the
        time of the writing out of the text, 'sc. she of hidden shadow'.

3957    *Beleriand* A and B (i.e. not *Broseliand* emended).

3962    This line is dated 'Sep. 16 1931'.

3969    *magic* > *elvish* in B, but this is doubtless a late change, when
        my father no longer used this once favourite word.

4029    Against this line is written the date 'Sep. 14', duplicating that
        given to line 3881.

4045    Against this line is written the date 'Sep. 16', duplicating that
        given to line 3962.

4085    After this line is written the last date in the A manuscript,
        'Sept. 17 1931'.

4092–3  These lines were written in the margin of B, but the original
        lines:

> the Silmarils were lit like stars
> that fume of Earth upreeking mars

        were not struck out.

4163–6  A:    in twain it sprang; and quaking fear
              fell on their hearts, for Morgoth groaned

### Commentary on Canto XIII

There is not much to be learnt from the Synopses concerning this part of
the narrative, but the Angband scene was never greatly changed from its
original form in the *Tale of Tinúviel* (II. 31 ff.). Synopsis I is at the end
reduced to mere headings, II has given out, and IV does not deal with the
entry into Angband. III, given on pp. 293–4 as far as the enchantment of
Carcharoth, continues:

After endless wanderings in corridors they stumble into the presence of Morgoth. Morgoth speaks. 'Who art thou that flittest about my
halls as a bat, but art not a bat? Thou dost not belong here, nor wert
thou summoned. Who has ever come here unsummoned? None!' 'But

I was summoned. I am Lúthien daughter of Thingol.' Then Morgoth
laughed, but he was moved with suspicion, and said that her accursed
race would get no soft words or favour in Angband. What could she do
to give him pleasure, and save herself from the lowest dungeons? He
reached out his mighty brazen hand but she shrank away. He is angry
but she offers to dance.

[*The remainder of the outline is in pencil and in places indecipherable*:] She lets fall her bat-garb. Her hair falls about. The
lights of Angband die. Impenetrable dark falls: only the eyes of
Morgoth and the faint glimmer of Tinúviel . . . . . . . . . . . . . Her
fragrance causes all to draw near greedily. Tinúviel flies [?in at] door
leaving Beren struck with horror. . . . . . . . . . . .

Here this outline ends. Morgoth's words 'Who art thou that flittest about
my halls as a bat' occur also in the *Tale of Tinúviel* (II. 32) – this outline
several times adopts directly the wording of the *Tale*, see pp. 283, 294.
This is a curious point, for in the *Tale* Tinúviel was not attired in a
bat-skin, whereas in Synopsis III she was. It is conceivable that Melko's
words actually gave rise to this element in the story.

In the *Tale* Tinúviel lied to Melko, saying that Tinwelint her father
had driven her out, and in reply he said that she need not hope for 'soft
words'– this too is a phrase that recurs in Synopsis III. But the remainder
of this outline does not relate closely to the *Tale*.

Synopsis V is here very brief. After 'the enchanting of Carcharos'
(p. 294) it has only (still under the heading '11'):

> The cozening of Morgoth and the rape of the Silmaril.
> The dwarvish knife of Curufin breaks.

It is clear that the concluding passage of Synopsis III, given above,
was a direct precursor of Canto XIII; but some elements – and actual
wording – in the scene go back to the *Tale* without being mentioned in
the Synopsis. Lúthien's words 'his rebellious daughter' (4007) seem to
echo 'he is an overbearing Elf and I give not my love at his command'
(II. 32); there is a clear relation between the words of the *Tale* (*ibid.*):

> Then did Tinúviel begin such a dance as neither she nor other sprite or
> fay or elf danced ever before or has done since

and lines 4072–3

> in dance such as never Elf nor fay
> before devised, nor since that day;

and with 'the adders lay like twisted stone' (4109) cf. 'Beneath his chair
the adders lay like stones.' It is interesting to see the idea of the shard of
the knife-blade striking Morgoth's brow (in *The Silmarillion* his cheek)
emerging in the composition of this Canto; as first written (see note to
lines 4163–6) it seems to have been the sound of the knife snapping that

disturbed the sleepers, as it was expressly in the *Tale* (II. 33). With the 'treacherous smiths of Nogrod' (4161) who made Curufin's knife cf. the passage in *The Children of Húrin* concerning *the bearded Dwarves of troth unmindful* who made the knife of Flinding that slipped from its sheath (p. 44, lines 1142 ff.): that was made by the Dwarves of Belegost, and like Curufin's

> [its] edge would eat    through iron noiseless
> as a clod of clay    is cleft by the share.

The account in *The Silmarillion* (pp. 180–1) is clearly based on Canto XIII, from which it derives many features, though it is reduced, notably by compressing the two episodes of Lúthien singing (3977 ff., 4062 ff.) into one; and the prose here owes less to the verses than in other places.

Lúthien's naming herself *Thuringwethil* to Morgoth (line 3954) is notable. In *The Silmarillion* (p. 178) the bat-fell which Huan brought from Tol-in-Gaurhoth was that of Thuringwethil: 'she was the messenger of Sauron, and was wont to fly in vampire's form to Angband'; whereas in the Lay (lines 3402 ff.), as I have noticed (p. 284), 'the bat-wings are only said to be such as bear up Thû's messengers, and are not associated with a particular or chief messenger'. It seems possible that in the Lay Lúthien devised this name ('she of hidden shadow') as a riddling description of herself, and that this led to the conception of the bat-messenger from the Wizard's Isle to Angband named Thuringwethil; but there is no proof of this.

With the

> sylphine maidens of the Air
> whose wings in Varda's heavenly hall
> in rhythmic movement beat and fall                    (4077–9)

cf. the tale of *The Coming of the Valar and the Building of Valinor* (I. 65–6), where it is said that with Manwë and Varda there entered the world 'many of those lesser Vali who loved them and had played nigh them and attuned their music to theirs, and these are the Mánir and the Súruli, *the sylphs of the airs and of the winds*'.

# XIV

> Up through the dark and echoing gloom
> as ghosts from many-tunnelled tomb,
> up from the mountains' roots profound
> and the vast menace underground,
> their limbs aquake with deadly fear,                    4180

terror in eyes, and dread in ear,
together fled they, by the beat
affrighted of their flying feet.

　　At last before them far away
they saw the glimmering wraith of day,　　　　4185
the mighty archway of the gate –
and there a horror new did wait.
Upon the threshold, watchful, dire,
his eyes new-kindled with dull fire,
towered Carcharoth, a biding doom:　　　　4190
his jaws were gaping like a tomb,
his teeth were bare, his tongue aflame;
aroused he watched that no one came,
no flitting shade nor hunted shape,
seeking from Angband to escape.　　　　4195
Now past that guard what guile or might
could thrust from death into the light?

　　He heard afar their hurrying feet,
he snuffed an odour strange and sweet;
he smelled their coming long before　　　　4200
they marked the waiting threat at door.
His limbs he stretched and shook off sleep,
then stood at gaze. With sudden leap
upon them as they sped he sprang,
and his howling in the arches rang.　　　　4205
　　Too swift for thought his onset came,
too swift for any spell to tame;
and Beren desperate then aside
thrust Lúthien, and forth did stride
unarmed, defenceless to defend　　　　4210
Tinúviel until the end.
With left he caught at hairy throat,
with right hand at the eyes he smote –
his right, from which the radiance welled
of the holy Silmaril he held.　　　　4215
As gleam of swords in fire there flashed
the fangs of Carcharoth, and crashed
together like a trap, that tore
the hand about the wrist, and shore
through brittle bone and sinew nesh,　　　　4220
devouring the frail mortal flesh;

> and in that cruel mouth unclean
> engulfed the jewel's holy sheen.

### The Unwritten Cantos

There was virtually no change in the narrative from the *Tale* to the Lay in the opening passage of Canto XIV, but the account in *The Silmarillion* differs, in that there Beren did not strike at the eyes of the wolf with his right hand holding the Silmaril, but held the jewel up before Carcharoth to daunt him. My father intended to alter the Lay here, as is seen from a marginal direction to introduce the element of 'daunting'.

*The Lay of Leithian* ends here, in both the A and B texts, and also in the pages of rough draft, but an isolated sheet found elsewhere gives a few further lines, together with variants, in the first stage of composition:

> Against the wall then Beren reeled
> but still with his left he sought to shield
> fair Lúthien, who cried aloud
> to see his pain, and down she bowed
> in anguish sinking to the ground.

There is also a short passage, found on a separate sheet at the end of the B-text, which is headed 'a piece from the end of the poem':

> Where the forest-stream went through the wood,
> and silent all the stems there stood
> of tall trees, moveless, hanging dark
> with mottled shadows on their bark
> above the green and gleaming river,      5
> there came through leaves a sudden shiver,
> a windy whisper through the still
> cool silences; and down the hill,
> as faint as a deep sleeper's breath,
> an echo came as cold as death:      10
> 'Long are the paths, of shadow made
> where no foot's print is ever laid,
> over the hills, across the seas!
> Far, far away are the Lands of Ease,
> but the Land of the Lost is further yet,      15
> where the Dead wait, while ye forget.
> No moon is there, no voice, no sound
> of beating heart; a sigh profound
> once in each age as each age dies
> alone is heard. Far, far it lies,      20

> the Land of Waiting where the Dead sit,
> in their thought's shadow, by no moon lit.

With the last lines compare the passage at the end of the tale of Beren and Lúthien in *The Silmarillion* (p. 186):

> But Lúthien came to the halls of Mandos, which are the appointed places of the Eldalië, beyond the mansions of the West upon the confines of the world. There those that wait sit in the shadow of their thought.

There is nothing else, and I do not think that there ever was anything else. All my father's later work on the poem was devoted to the revision of what was already in existence; and the *Lay of Leithian* ends here.

★

Of the five synopses that have been given in sections in previous pages, only the fifth bears on the escape of Beren and Lúthien from Angband. This outline was last quoted on p. 305 ('the dwarvish knife of Curufin breaks'). It continues:

> Beren and Lúthien flee in fear. Arousing of Carcharos. Beren's hand is bitten off in which he holds the Silmaril. Madness of Carcharos. Angband awakes. Flight of Beren and Lúthien towards the waters of Sirion. Canto [i.e. Canto 11, see p. 305] ends as they hear the pursuing wolves behind. Wrapped in Lúthien's cloak they flit beneath the stars.

Thus the rescue of Beren and Lúthien by Thorondor and his vassals was not yet present, and the story was still in this respect unchanged from the *Tale of Tinúviel* (II. 34); cf. especially:

> Tinúviel wrapped part of her dark mantle about Beren, and so for a while flitting by dusk and dark amid the hills they were seen by none.

The first record of the changed story of the escape from Angband is found on an isolated slip, written hastily in pencil and very difficult to decipher:

> Carcharoth goes mad and drives all [?orcs] before him like a wind. The sound of his awful howling causes rocks to split and fall. There is an earthquake underground. Morgoth's wrath on waking. The gateway [?falls] in and hell is blocked, and great fires and smokes burst from Thangorodrim. Thunder and lightning. Beren lies dying before the gate. Tinúviel's song as she kisses his hand and prepares to die. Thorondor comes down and bears them amid the lightning that [?stabs] at them like spears and a hail of arrows from the battlements. They pass above Gondolin and Lúthien sees the white city far below, [?gleaming] like a lily in the valley. Thorondor sets her down in Brethil.

This is very close in narrative structure to the story in *The Silmarillion* (p. 182), with the earthquake, fire and smoke from Thangorodrim, Beren's lying near death at the Gate, Lúthien's kissing his hand (staunching the wound), the descent of Thorondor, and the passage of the eagle(s) over Gondolin. This last shows that this brief outline is relatively late, since Gondolin was already in existence before the Battle of Unnumbered Tears (II. 208). But in this text they are set down in Brethil (a name that does not appear in the works until several years later); in *The Silmarillion* they are set down 'upon the borders of Doriath', in 'that same dell whence Beren had stolen in despair and left Lúthien asleep'. – On the reference to Gondolin as 'a lily in the valley' see I. 172.

Synopsis V has more to tell subsequently of the wanderings of Beren and Lúthien before they returned to Doriath, but I now set out the remaining materials in their entirety before commenting on them. First it is convenient to cite the end of Synopsis II, which has been given already (p. 270):

> Celegorm's embassy to Thingol so that Thingol knows or thinks he knows Beren dead and Lúthien in Nargothrond.
> Why Celegorm and Curufin hated by Thingol . . . . . . . .
> The loss of Dairon.

Synopsis IV has been given (p. 273) only as far as 'They prepare to go to Angband', since the outline then turns away from the story of Beren and Lúthien themselves, according to my father's projection at that time for the further course of the Lay, and continues as follows:

II

> Doriath. The hunt for Lúthien and the loss of Dairon. War on the borders. Boldog slain. So Thingol knows Lúthien not yet dead is caught, but fears that Boldog's raid means that Morgoth has got wind of her wandering. Actually it means no more than the legend of her beauty.
> An embassy comes from Celegorm. Thingol learns that Beren is dead, and Lúthien at Nargothrond. He is roused to wrath by the hints of the letter that Celegorm will leave Felagund to die, and will usurp the throne of Nargothrond. And so Thingol had better let Lúthien stay where she is.
> Thingol prepares an army to go against Nargothrond, but learns that Lúthien has left, and Celegorm and Curufin have fled to Aglon. He sends an embassy to Aglon. It is routed and put to flight by the sudden onslaught of Carcharas. Mablung escapes to tell the tale. The devastation of Doriath by Carcharas.

12

The rape of the Silmaril and the home-coming of Beren and Lúthien.

13

The wolf-hunt and death of Huan and Beren.

14

The recall of Beren and Huan.

Synopsis V continues as a more substantial preparation for the end of the poem never to be written, which my father at this stage conceived in three further Cantos.

12

Sorrow in Doriath at flight of Lúthien. Thingol's heart hardened against Beren, despite words of Melian. A mighty hunt is made throughout the realm, but many of the folk strayed north and west and south of Doriath beyond the magic of Melian and were lost. Dairon became separated from his comrades and wandered away into the East of the world, where some say he pipes yet seeking Lúthien in vain.

The embassy of Celegorm tells Thingol that Beren and Felagund are dead, that Celegorm will make himself king of Narog, and while telling him that Lúthien is safe in Nargothrond and treating for her hand, hints that she will not return: it also warns him to trouble not the matter of the Silmarils. Thingol is wroth – and is moved to think better of Beren, while yet blaming [him] for the woes that followed his coming to Doriath, and most for loss of Dairon.

Thingol arms for war against Celegorm. Melian says she would forbid this evil war of Elf with Elf, but that never shall Thingol cross blade with Celegorm. Thingol's army meets with the host of Boldog on the borders of Doriath. Morgoth has heard of the beauty of Lúthien, and the rumour of her wandering. He has ordered Thû and the Orcs to capture her. A battle is fought and Thingol is victorious. The Orcs are driven into Taur-na-Fuin or slain. Thingol himself slays Boldog. Mablung Heavyhand was Thingol's chief warrior and fought at his side; Beleg was the chief of his scouts. Though victorious Thingol is filled with still more disquiet at Morgoth's hunt for Lúthien. Beleg goes forth from the camp on Doriath's borders and journeys, unseen by the archers, to Narog. He brings tidings of the flight of Lúthien, the rescue of Beren, and the exile of Celegorm and Curufin. He [*read* Thingol] goes home and sends an embassy to Aglon to demand recompense, and aid in the rescue of Lúthien. He renews his vow to imprison Beren for ever if he does not return with a Silmaril, though Melian warns him that he knows not what he says.

The embassy meets the onslaught of Carcharos who by fate or the power of the Silmaril bursts into Doriath. All perish save Mablung who brings the news. Devastation of the woods. The wood-elves flee to the caves.

## 13

Beren and Lúthien escape to the Shadowy Mountains, but become lost and bewildered in the dreads of Nan Dungorthin, and are hunted by phantoms, and snared at last by the great spiders. Huan rescues them, and guides them down Sirion, and so they reach Doriath from the south, and find the woods silent and empty till they come to the guarded bridge.

Huan, Beren, and Lúthien come before Thingol. They tell their tale; yet Thingol will not relent. The brave words of Beren, revealing the mystery of Carcharos. Thingol relents. The wolf-hunt is prepared. Huan, Thingol, Beren, and Mablung depart. Lúthien abides with Melian in foreboding. Carcharos is slain, but slew Huan who defended Beren. Yet Beren is mortally hurt, though he lived to place the Silmaril on Thingol's hand which Mablung cut from the wolf's belly.

The meeting and farewell of Beren and Tinúviel beneath Hirilorn. Burial of Huan and Beren.

## 14

Fading of Lúthien. Her journey to Mandos. The song of Lúthien in Mandos' halls, and the release of Beren. They dwelt long in Broseliand, but spake never more to mortal Men, and Lúthien became mortal.

This concludes all the material in the outlines. For the references to Boldog's raid, and Morgoth's interest in Lúthien, in the Lay itself see lines 2127–36, 2686–94, 3198–3201, and 3665–75.

In Synopsis IV (p. 310) Boldog's raid takes place earlier in the story, before the coming of Celegorm's embassy to Thingol, but its narrative value is obscure. It is not clear why the raid must inform Thingol that 'Lúthien not yet dead is caught', nor why he should conclude that 'Morgoth has got wind of her wandering'. Moreover the statement that 'actually it means no more than the legend of her beauty' can only mean (if Morgoth had *not* heard of her wandering forth from Doriath) that he sent out Boldog's warband with the express intention of seizing her from the fastness of the Thousand Caves.

In Synopsis V the raid was moved to a later point, and the host out of Doriath that destroyed Boldog was actually moving against Nargothrond. In *The Silmarillion* the embassy from Celegorm survived, but of Boldog's raid there is no hint, and Thingol does no more than 'think to make war' on Nargothrond:

But Thingol learned that Lúthien had journeyed far from Doriath, for messages came secretly from Celegorm, . . . saying that Felagund was dead, and Beren was dead, but Lúthien was in Nargothrond, and that Celegorm would wed her. Then Thingol was wrathful, and he sent forth spies, thinking to make war upon Nargothrond; and thus he learned that Lúthien was again fled, and that Celegorm and Curufin were driven from Nargothrond. Then his counsel was in doubt, for he had not the strength to assail the seven sons of Fëanor; but he sent messengers to Himring to summon their aid in seeking for Lúthien, since Celegorm had not sent her to the house of her father, nor had he kept her safely (pp. 183–4).

The 'spies' of this passage were derived from Beleg's secret mission to Nargothrond in Synopsis V (p. 311). It seems probable that my father actually discarded Boldog's raid; and with it went all suggestion that Lúthien's wandering had been reported to Morgoth (cf. lines 3665 ff.) and that Thû was given orders to capture her (Synopsis V). The passage in Canto IX of the Lay (2686–94) where Thû recognised Lúthien's voice – or, at least, knew that it must be she who was singing – does not, indeed, at all suggest that Thû was actively seeking her. These lines were the source for the passage in *The Silmarillion*, where Sauron standing in the tower of Tol-in-Gaurhoth

smiled hearing her voice, for he knew that it was the daughter of Melian. The fame of the beauty of Lúthien, and the wonder of her song had long gone forth from Doriath; and he thought to make her captive and hand her over to the power of Morgoth, for his reward would be great.

But the idea that the beauty and singing of Lúthien had come to the ears of Sauron survives from the stage when Morgoth's interest in her was an important motive.

As noticed earlier (p. 209), the wandering and loss of Dairon goes back to the *Tale of Tinúviel* (II. 20–1) and survived into *The Silmarillion* (p. 183), where it is said that Daeron passed over the Blue Mountains 'into the East of Middle-earth, where for many ages he made lament beside dark waters for Lúthien'. Less is made in the later story of the great hunt for Lúthien, and nothing is said of the changing moods and intentions of Thingol towards Beren referred to in Synopsis V. The 'political' element of the ambitions of Celegorm and Curufin and the attempted browbeating and blackmail of Thingol is of course a new element that first appears in the Synopses (other than the earlier reference in the Lay, 2501–3, to the brothers' intentions in this regard), since the 'Nargothrond Element' is wholly absent from the *Tale of Tinúviel*; and similarly the interception of the embassy from Thingol to Aglon by Carcharoth, from which Mablung alone survived. This also remains in *The Silmarillion*.

In Synopsis V, where the bearing away of Beren and Lúthien from Angband by Thorondor is not yet present, they flee from Angband 'towards the waters of Sirion' (p. 309), and (p. 312) 'escape to the Shadowy Mountains, but become lost and bewildered in the dreads of Nan Dungorthin, and are hunted by phantoms, and snared at last by the great spiders. Huan rescues them, and guides them down Sirion . . .' In the *Tale* likewise (II. 34–5), Huan rescued them from 'Nan Dumgorthin'. This is a point of geography and shifting nomenclature of great perplexity. I have shown (pp. 170–1, 234) that the meaning of 'Shadowy Mountains' changes in the course of the *Lay of Leithian*: whereas at first (lines 386, 1318) the reference is to the Mountains of Terror (Ered Gorgoroth), subsequently (line 1940) it is to Ered Wethrin, the range fencing Hithlum. The Mountains of Terror, with the great spiders, are described in lines 563 ff.

In the present passage of Synopsis V the statements that Beren and Lúthien escaping from Angband fled towards Sirion, and that Huan rescuing them from Nan Dungorthin guided them down Sirion, very strongly suggests that the Shadowy Mountains are here again, as might be expected, Ered Wethrin. Nan Dungorthin must then be placed as in *The Children of Húrin*, west of Sirion, in a valley of the southern slopes of the Shadowy Mountains. But this means that the great spiders are found in both places.

It is difficult to suggest a satisfactory explanation of this. A possibility is that when Beren crossed the Mountains of Terror and encountered the spiders (lines 569–74) 'Nan Dungorthin' was placed in that region, though it is not named; in Synopsis V however it is again placed, with its spiders, west of Sirion.

In the later story the eagles set Beren and Lúthien down on the borders of Doriath, and Huan came to them there.

In the conclusion of Synopsis V there is very little that is at variance with the story of the wolf-hunt and the death of Beren in *The Silmarillion*, so far as can be seen from the very compressed outline; but Beleg was not present at the hunt in the Synopsis, as he was not in the *Tale* (II. 38).

The sentence that concludes Synopsis IV is curious: 'The recall of Beren and Huan' (p. 311). 'Recall' obviously refers to the return from Mandos (the last heading of Synopsis I is 'Tinúviel goes to Mandos and recalls Beren'); in which case my father must have intended to have Huan return from the dead with Beren and Lúthien. In the *Tale of Tinúviel* Huan was not slain (II. 39), and there was no prophecy concerning his fate to fall before the mightiest wolf that should ever walk the world; but he became the companion of Mablung (II. 41), and in the *Tale of the Nauglafring* he returned to Beren and Lúthien in the land of i·Guilwarthon after the death of Thingol and the sack of the Thousand Caves.

# APPENDIX

## C. S. Lewis's Commentary on the Lay of Leithian

I give here the greater part of this commentary, for which see pp. 150–1.*
Lewis's line-references are of course changed throughout to those in this
book. The letters H, J, K, L, P, R refer to the imaginary manuscripts of
the ancient poem.

For the text criticised in the first entry of the commentary see
pp. 157–8, i.e. text B(1).

4    *Meats were sweet.* This is the reading of PRK. Let
     any one believe if he can that our author gave such a
     cacophany. J *His drink was sweet his dishes dear.*
     L *His drink was sweet his dish was dear.* (Many
     scholars have rejected lines 1–8 altogether as un-
     worthy of the poet. 'They were added by a later hand
     to supply a gap in the archtype,' says Peabody; and
     adds 'The more melodious movement and surer nar-
     rative stride of the passage beginning with line 9 [*But
     fairer than are born to Men*] should convince the
     dullest that here, and here only, the authentic work of
     the poet begins.' I am not convinced that H, which
     had better be quoted in full, does not give the true
     opening of the *Geste*.

          *That was long since in ages old*
          *When first the stars in heaven rolled,*
          *There dwelt beyond Broseliand,*
          *While loneliness yet held the land,*
          *A great king comely under crown,*
          *The gold was woven in his gown,*
          *The gold was clasped about his feet,*
          *The gold about his waist did meet.*
          *And in his many-pillared house*
          *Many a gold bee and ivory mouse*
          *And amber chessmen on their field*
          *Of copper, many a drinking horn*
          *Dear purchased from shy unicorn*
          *Lay piled, with gold in gleaming grot.*
          *All these he had* etc.)

---

* An account of it, with some citation, has been given by Humphrey Carpenter in *The
Inklings*, pp. 29–31, where the view expressed in his *Biography*, p. 145, that 'Tolkien did
not accept any of Lewis's suggestions', is corrected.

[It seems virtually certain that it was Lewis's criticism that led my father to rewrite the opening (the B (2) text, p. 154). If the amber chessmen and ivory mice found no place in the new version, it is notable that in Lewis's lines occur the words 'And in his many-pillared house'. These are not derived from the B(1) text which Lewis read, but in B(2) appears the line (14) *in many-pillared halls of stone*. It seems then that Durin's *many-pillared* halls in Gimli's song in Moria were originally so called by C. S. Lewis, thinking of the halls of Thingol in Doriath.]

40    The description of Lúthien has been too often and too justly praised to encourage the mere commentator in intruding.

68    *tall*. Thus PRKJH. L *vast*. Schick's complimentary title of 'internal rime' for these cacophanies does not much mend matters. 'The poet of the *Geste* knew nothing of internal rime, and its appearance (so called) is an infallible mark of corruption' (Pumpernickel). But cf. 209, 413.

71–2    The reader who wishes to acquire a touchstone for the true style of the *Geste* had better learn by heart this faultless and characteristic distych.

77    HL    *Of mortal men at feast has heard*

[The line in B(1) was *of mortal feaster ever heard*. With *hath* for *has* Lewis's line was adopted.]

99–150    This is considered by all critics one of the noblest passages in the *Geste*.

112    Notice the double sense of within (macrocosmic and microcosmic). That the original poet may have been unconscious of this need not detract from our pleasure.

[Lewis was clearly right to suspect that the original poet had no such double sense in mind.]

117        H   *The legions of his marching hate*

[Lewis was criticising the original line in B *his evil legions' marshalled
hate*. With retention of *marshalled* for *marching* Lewis's line was
adopted.]

[In the following comment the reading criticised was:

> *swift ruin red of fire and sword*
> *leapt forth on all denied his word,*
> *and all the lands beyond the hills*        125
> *were filled with sorrow and with ills.*]

124    The relative understood. I suspect both the construction and the word *denied*, neither of which has the
true ring. H reads:

> *And ruin of red fire and sword*
> *To all that would not hail him lord*
> *Came fast, and far beyond the hills*
> *Spread Northern wail and iron ills.*
> *And therefore in wet woods and cold* etc.

130    'A weak line' (Peabody).

[The original reading in B which Lewis criticised was *who had this king
once held in scorn*, changed to *who once a prince of Men was born*]

137    Some emend. The rhythm, however, is good, and
probably would occur more often if the syllabic
prudery of scribes had not elsewhere 'emended' it.

172    LH   *When I lost all*

[No alteration made to the text.]

173–4    L   *Thus, out of wet night while he gazed,*
                      *he thought, with heavy heart amazed*

[No alteration made to the text.]

[In the following comment the reading criticised was:

> *But ere he dared to call her name*
> *or ask how she escaping came*]

175–6   *she escaping.* A Latinised phrase, at once betraying very late corruption. The ugly assonance *ere . . . dared* confirms my suspicion of the distych. No satisfactory emendation has been proposed.

[*she escaping came* was changed to *she escaped and came*]

196   H   *Whining, his spirit ached for ease.* Peabody observes of the whole passage: 'The combination of extreme simplicity, with convincing truth of psychology, and the pathos which, without comment, makes us aware that Gorlim is at once pardonable and unpardonable, render this part of the story extremely affecting.'

[No alteration made to line 196]

208   *haply.*   LH   *chance.*

[No alteration made to the text.]

209–10   One of the few passages in which Schick's theory of deliberate internal rime finds some support.

[See the comment on line 68.]

215   *that.*   H   *the.*

[No alteration made to the text.]

[The lines 313–16 referred to in the following comment had been bracketed for exclusion, and *that* at 317 changed to *Then*, before the text went to Lewis.]

313   H reads   *Thus Morgoth loved that his own foe*
             *Should in his service deal the blow.*
             *Then Beren . . .*

'Our scribe is right in his erasure of the second distych, but wrong in his erasure of the first' (Peabody). The first erased couplet certainly deserves to remain in the text; indeed its loss seriously impairs the reality of Morgoth. I should print as in H, enclosing *Thus . . . blow* in brackets or dashes.

[My father ticked the first two lines (313–14), which may show that he accepted this suggestion. I have let all four stand in the text.]

400    Of Canto 2 as a whole Peabody writes: 'If this is not good romantic narrative, I confess myself ignorant of the meaning of the words.'

401    et seq. A more philosophical account of the period is given in the so called *Poema Historiale*, probably contemporary with the earliest MSS of the *Geste*. The relevant passage runs as follows:

> *There was a time before the ancient sun*
> *And swinging wheels of heaven had learned*
>     *to run*
> *More certainly than dreams; for dreams*
>     *themselves*
> *Had bodies then and filled the world with elves.*
> *The starveling lusts whose walk is now*
>     *confined*
> *To darkness and the cellarage of the mind,*
> *And shudderings and despairs and shapes of sin*
> *Then walked at large, and were not cooped*
>     *within.*
> *Thought cast a shadow: brutes could speak:*
>     *and men*
> *Get children on a star. For spirit then*
> *Kneaded a fluid world and dreamed it new*
> *Each moment. Nothing yet was false or true.*

[Humphrey Carpenter, who cites these verses in *The Inklings*, says (p. 30): 'Sometimes Lewis actually suggested entirely new passages to replace lines he thought poor, and here too he ascribed his own versions to supposedly historical sources. For example, he suggested that the lines about the "elder days" [401 ff.] could be replaced by the following stanza of his own, which he described as "the so called *Poema Historiale* [&c.]".' But he cannot have intended these lines, which not only, as Humphrey Carpenter says, show 'how greatly Lewis's poetic imagination differed from Tolkien's', but are in a different metre, as a replacement; see Lewis's comment on lines 438–42.]

413    Another instance where the 'internal rime' theory is justified.

438–42    Almost certainly spurious. This abstract philosophical statement – which would not surprise us in the scholastic verse of the period, such as the *Poema Historiale* – is quite foreign to the manner of the *Geste*. L reads:

> *. . . singing in the wood*
> *And long he stood and long he stood*
> *Till, many a day, with hound and hail*
> *His people seek him ere they sail,*
> *Then, finding not, take ship with tears.*
> *But after a long tale of years*
> *(Though but an hour to him it seemed)*
> *He found her where she lay and dreamed.*

[My father marked lines 438 ff. in the typescript, but made no change to the text.]

516    *Flowering candles.* The reader should notice how the normally plain style of the *Geste* has yet the power of rising into such expressions as this without losing its unity.

[In the following comment the reading criticised was:

> *the silent elms stood dark and tall,*
> *and round their boles did shadows fall*    518
> *where glimmered faint . . .*]

518    *did* PRK, *let* JL. Though neither is good, PRK seems the better reading. Its slight clumsiness may be passed over by a reader intent on the story: the 'neat' evasion *let*, with its purely formal attribution of an active rôle to the trees, is much worse, as cheap scenery is worse than a plain backcloth. H reads:

> *The silent elms stood tall and grey*
> *And at the roots long shadows lay*

519–42    'This passage', Peabody observes, 'amply atones for the poet's lapse (*dormitat Homerus*) in 518. *Ipsa mollities.*'

[I do not understand why Lewis picked particularly on *did* at line 518: the

use of *did* as a metrical aid was very common in the B-text as Lewis saw it
– it occurred twice, for instance, in the passage here praised: *did flutter*
523, *did waver* 533, both subsequently changed.]

555–6   '*O si sic omnia!* Does not our poet show glimpses of
the true empyrean of poesy, however, in his work-
manlike humility, he has chosen more often to
inhabit the milder and aerial (not aetherial) middle
heaven?' (Pumpernickel). Some have seen in the
conception of death-into-life a late accretion. But cf.
the very early lyric preserved in the MS N3057, now
in the public library at Narrowthrode (the ancient
*Nargothrond*), which is probably as early as the *Geste*,
though like all the scholastic verse it strikes a more
modern note:

> *Because of endless pride*
> *Reborn with endless error,*
> *Each hour I look aside*
> *Upon my secret mirror,*
> *And practice postures there*
> *To make my image fair.*

> *You give me grapes, and I,*
> *Though staring, turn to see*
> *How dark the cool globes lie*
> *In the white hand of me,*
> *And stand, yet gazing thither,*
> *Till the live clusters wither.*

> *So should I quickly die*
> *Narcissus-like for want,*
> *Save that betimes my eye*
> *Sees there such shapes as haunt*
> *Beyond nightmare and make*
> *Pride humble for pride's sake.*

> *Then, and then only, turning*
> *The stiff neck round, I grow*
> *A molten man all burning*
> *And look behind, and know*
> *Who made the flaw, what light makes dark,*
>     *what fair*

> *Makes foul my shadowy form reflected there,*
> *That self-love, big with love, dying, its child*
> *may bear.*

[It is a matter for speculation, what the author of Nargothrond thought of the public library at Narrowthrode. – This poem, with some alterations, was included in *The Pilgrim's Regress* (1933).]

563–92 *Sic* in all MSS. The passage is, of course, genuine, and truly worthy of the *Geste*. But surely it must originally have stood at 391 or 393? The artificial insertion of Beren's journey in its present place – where it appears as retrospect not as direct narrative, though defensible, belongs to a kind of art more sophisticated than that of the *Geste*: it is just such a transposition as a late Broseliandic literary redactor would make under the influence of the classical epic.

[A quarter of a century later, or more, my father rewrote this part of the poem; and he took Lewis's advice. See p. 352.]

[The original reading of B criticised in the next comment (lines 629 ff.) was:

> *Then stared he wild in dumbness bound*
> *at silent trees, deserted ground;*
> *the dizzy moon was twisted grey*
> *in tears, for she had fled away.*]

629–30 Thus in PRKJ. The Latinised adverbial use of the adjective in *wild* and the omitted articles in the next line are suspicious.

  L *But wildly Beren gazed around*
   *On silent trees (and)\* empty ground.*
   *The dizzy moon etc.*

 \*Peabody supplies *and*. But the monosyllabic foot is quite possible. Cf. 687.

  H *But wildly Beren gazed around.*
   *Emptied the tall trees stood. The ground*
   *Lay empty. A lonely moon looked grey*
   *Upon the untrodden forest way.*

> I prefer H because it gets rid of the conceit (it is little
> more) about the moon. (This sort of half-hearted
> personification is, of course, to be distinguished from
> genuine mythology.)

[Against this my father scribbled on Lewis's text: 'Not so!! The moon
was dizzy and twisted because of the tears in his eyes.' Nonetheless he
struck the two lines out heavily in the typescript, and I have excluded
them from the text.]

635-6   An excellent simile.

641     Peabody, though a great friend to metrical resol-
        utions in general, finds this particular resolution
        (*Bewildered enchanted*) 'singularly harsh'. Per-
        haps the original text read *wildered*.

[The reading in B was *bewildered, enchanted and forlorn*. My father
then changed *bewildered* to *wildered* and placed it after *enchanted*.]

651-2   JHL transpose.

[This was done. Cf. lines 1222-3, where these lines are repeated but left
in the original sequence.]

[After line 652 B had:

> *Thus thought his heart. No words would come*
> *from his fast lips, for smitten dumb*
> *a spell lay on him, as a dream*
> *in longing chained beside the stream.*

After seeing Lewis's comment my father marked this passage 'revise',
and also with a deletion mark, on which basis I have excluded the four
lines from the text.]

> Only in PR. Almost undoubtedly spurious. 'The latest redac-
> tors', says Pumpernickel, 'were always needlessly amplifying,
> as if the imagination of their readers could do nothing for itself,
> and thus blunting the true force and energy of the *Geste*. . . .'
> Read:
>
> > *A heartache and a loneliness*
> > *– Enchanted waters pitiless.'*
> > *A summer waned* etc.

[*heartache* was the original reading of B at 651, changed later to *hunger*, but retained at 1223.]

653–72    Of this admirable passage Peabody remarks: 'It is as if the wood itself were speaking.'

677–9    LH    *From her dim cave the damp moon eyed*
*White mists that float from earth to hide*
*The sluggard morrow's sun and drip*

[No alteration made to the text.]

683    *Beat*, which is utterly inappropriate to the sound described, must be a corruption. No plausible emendation has been suggested.

[My father scribbled in a hesitant substitute for *beat* and a different form for line 684 (*of his own feet on leafy* . . . .) but I cannot read the rhyming words.]

685–708    In praise of this passage I need not add to the innumerable eulogies of my predecessors.

710    Bentley read *saw far off*, to avoid the ugliness that always results from w-final followed by an initial vowel in the next word.

[The reading criticised was *saw afar*, and the line was changed as suggested.]

715    *Stole he* PRK. *He stole* JHL. PRK looks like the metrical 'improvement' of a scribe: dearly bought by a meaningless inversion.

•[The reading criticised was *Then stole he nigh*, changed to *Then nigh he stole*.]

727–45    This passage, as it stands, is seriously corrupt, though the beauty of the original can still be discerned.

[See the following notes.]

[The original reading of B in lines 729–30 was:

> *the hillock green he leapt upon –*
> *the elfin loveliness was gone*;]

729    Intolerable bathos and prose in a passage of such
         tension.

[The original reading of B in line 739 was:

> *its echoes wove a halting spell*:]

739    Why *halting*? 'Let the amanuensis take back his
         rubbish' (Bentley).

[Against this my father wrote 'A spell to halt anyone', but in the margin
of B he wrote *staying/binding*, and I have adopted *binding* in the
text.]

[The original reading of B in lines 741–5 was:

> *His voice such love and longing fill*          741
> *one moment stood she, touched and still;*
> *one moment only, but he came*
> *and all his heart was burned with flame.*          744]

741–2    The historic present is always to be suspected. The
           second verse is hopelessly corrupt. *Touched* in this
           sense is impossible in the language of the *Geste*: and
           if the word were possible, the conception is fitter for a
           nineteenth century drawing-room in Narrowthrode
           than for the loves of heroes. HL read:

> *And clear his voice came as a bell*
> *Whose echoes wove a wavering spell*
> *Tinúviel. Tinúviel.*
> *Such love and longing filled his voice*
> *That, one moment, without choice,*
> *One moment without fear or shame,*
> *Tinúviel stood; and like a flame*
> *He leapt towards her as she stayed*
> *And caught and kissed that elfin maid.*

[My father marked the passage 'revise', and very roughly corrected it
(adopting the concluding verses of Lewis's version) to the form which I
have given in the text, despite the defective couplet.]

[The original reading of B was:

> *aswoon in mingled grief and bliss,*
> *enchantment of an elvish kiss.*]

760–1 L  *Aswoon with grief, aswoon with bliss,*
*Enchanted of an elvish kiss.*

[*enchanted* for *enchantment* was adopted.]

[The original reading – the text B(1) seen by Lewis, see p. 194 – of lines 762–73 was:

> *and saw within his blinded eyes*
> *a light that danced like silver flies*
> *a starlit face of tenderness*
> *crowned by the stars of Elfinesse.*
> *A mist was in his face like hair,*                                5
> *and laughing whispers moved the air –*
> *'O! dance with me now, Beren. Dance!' –*
> *a silver laugh, a mocking glance:*
> *'Come dance the wild and headlong maze*
> *those dance, we're told, beyond the ways*          10
> *who dwell that lead to lands of Men!*
> *Come teach the feet of Lúthien!'*
> *The shadows wrapped her. Like a stone*
> *the daylight found him cold and lone.*

On line 8 of this passage Lewis commented:]

L  *a silver laughter, an arch glance*

'Whether *mocking* or *arch* is the more intolerably miss-ish I care not to decide' (Peabody).

[The line was abandoned in the B(2) version. On lines 9–12 Lewis commented:]

JHL omit. Is not the whole passage [from the beginning of the Canto to the end of the passage from B(1) given above] unworthy of the poet?

[It is clear that this severe criticism led to the rewriting of the opening of the Canto.]

775  The chiasmus is suspiciously classical. H gives *Dark is the sun, cold is the air.*

[Against this my father scribbled: 'But classics did not invent chiasmus! – it is perfectly natural.' (*Chiasmus*: a grammatical figure by which the order of words in one of two parallel clauses is inverted in the other.)]

[The passage criticised by Lewis in the following comment was:

> *Hateful art thou, O Land of Trees!*
> *My flute shall finger no more seize;*
> *may music perish* etc.]

849    Clearly corrupt. HJL *Oh hateful land of trees be mute! My fingers, now forget the flute!*

[Against this my father wrote: 'Frightful 18th century!!!' But he re-ordered the second line to: *my fingers the flute shall no more seize*, and subsequently rewrote the passage to the form given in the text, lines 849–52.]

849–83    'These lines are very noble' (Pumpernickel).

909    *cometh.* HJL *comes.* HJL is certainly the more emphatic rhythm.

[No alteration made to the text.]

[The original reading of B at line 911 was:

> *. . . those shores,*
> *those white rocks where the last tide roars*]

911    'Where *eight* dull words oft creep in one low line.' Lines of monosyllables are often to be found in the *Geste*, but rarely so clustered with consonants as this. No satisfactory emendation has been suggested. I suspect this is a garbled version of 1142–3: our scribes do not always accept or understand epic repetition.

[The emendation made to B and given in the text is derived from lines 1142–3 as Lewis suggested. His reference is to Pope, *An Essay on Criticism*, line 347: *And ten low words oft creep in one dull line.*]

978–9    In *Gestestudien* Vol. XIII pp. 9–930 the reader will find a summary of the critical war that has raged

round the possibility of the assonance (or rime) of
*within-dim*. Perhaps a great deal of ink would have
been saved if the scholars of the last century had been
familiar with the L reading *Where out of yawning
arches came A white light like unmoving flame*.
'My own conclusion is that *if* the assonance in the
*textus receptus* is correct, the same phenomenon
must originally have occurred often, and have been
suppressed elsewhere by the scribes. Editorial effort
might profitably be devoted to restoring it' (Schuffer).
But cf. 1140–1.

[The original reading of B in lines 980–1 was:

> With gentle hand there she him led
> down corridors etc.]

980   J   *Downward with gentle hand she him led*,
which explains the corruption. The verse originally ran *Downward with gentle hand she led*.
The scribe of J, wrongly believing an object to be
needed, inserted *him*. *Vulg.* then 'emends' the
metre by dropping *Downward* and inserting
*there*: thus giving a clumsy line.

[In this note *Vulg.* = *Vulgate*, the common or usual form of a literary
work. My father wrote in Lewis's line on the B-text with his initials, and
made the consequent change of *down* to *through* in line 981.]

[The original reading of B was: *as into archéd halls was led*]

991   HJL   *she led*

996   L   *in old stone carven stood*
[No alteration made to the text.]

[The original reading in B was: *while waters endless dripped and
ran*]

1007   H   *While water forever dript and ran*

[The original reading in B was: *in lightless labyrinths endlessly*]

1075 *Labyrinths.* HJL *Labyrinth.*

[Lewis corrected his spelling to *Laborynth(s)*, against which my father queried: 'Why this spelling?']

980–1131 The whole of this passage has always been deservedly regarded as one of the gems of the *Geste*.

1132–61 I suspect that this passage has been greatly expanded by the late redactors who found their audience some- times very ignorant of the myths. It is, as it stands, far from satisfactory. On the one hand it is too long an interruption of the action: on the other it is too succinct for a reader who knows nothing of the myth- ology. It is also obscure: thus in 1145 few readers can grasp that *their* means 'the Silmarils'. The shorter version of H and L, though not good, may in some respects be nearer the original:

> *Then Thingol's warriors loud and long*
> *Laughed: for wide renown in song*
> *Had Fëanor's gems o'er land and sea,*
> *The Silmarils, the shiners three,*
> *Three only, and in every one*
> *The light that was before the sun*
> *And moon, shone yet. But now no more*
> *Those leavings of the lights of yore*
> *Were seen on earth's back: in the drear*
> *Abysm of Morgoth blazing clear*
> *His iron crown they must adorn*
> *And glitter on orcs and slaves forlorn* etc.

[My father put an exclamation mark against *the shiners three*; and he wrote an X against lines 1144–5 (see note to these lines).]

★

Here C. S. Lewis's commentary on *The Gest of Beren and Lúthien* ends, and no more is recorded of the opinions of Peabody, Pumpernickel, Schuffer and Schick in the volumes of *Gestestudien* – nor indeed, on this subject, of those of their generous-minded inventor.

# IV
# THE LAY OF LEITHIAN
# RECOMMENCED

When my father began the *Lay of Leithian* again from the beginning, he did not at first intend much more, perhaps, than a revision, an improvement of individual lines and short passages, but all on the original plan and structure. This, at least, is what he did with Canto I; and he carried out the revisions on the old B typescript. But with Canto II he was quickly carried into a far more radical reconstruction, and was virtually writing a new poem on the same subject and in the same metre as the old. This, it is true, was partly because the story of Gorlim had changed, but it is also clear that a new impulse had entered, seeking a new rather than merely altered expression. The old typescript was still used at least as a physical basis for the new writing, but for a long stretch the typed verses were simply struck through and the new written on inserted pages and slips.

The old Canto II of just over 300 lines was expanded to 500, and divided into new Cantos 2 and 3 (the old and the new can be conveniently distinguished by Roman and Arabic numerals).

The rewriting on the old typescript continues for a short distance into Canto III (new Canto 4) and then stops. On the basis of this now extremely chaotic text my father wrote out a fine, decorated manuscript, 'C', inevitably introducing some further changes; and this stops only a few lines short of the point where the rewriting on the B-text stops. Subsequently, an amanuensis typescript ('D') was made, in two copies, apparently with my father's supervision, but for the moment nothing need be said of this beyond noticing that he made certain changes to these texts at a later time.

The rewriting on the B-text was no doubt a secondary stage, of which the preliminary workings no longer exist; for in the case of the new Canto 4 such preliminary drafts are extant. On one of these pages, and quite obviously done at the same time as the verse-drafts, my father drew a floor-plan of part of the house 99 Holywell Street, Oxford, to which he removed in 1950. He doubtless drew the plan shortly before moving house, while pondering its best arrangement. It is clear then that a new start on the *Lay of Leithian* was one of the first things that he turned to when *The Lord of the Rings* was complete.

I give below the text of the manuscript C in its final form (that is, after certain changes had been made to it) so far as it goes (line 624), incor-

porating one or two very minor alterations made later to the D type-
script(s), followed by a further short section (lines 625–60) found only in
draft before being added to D. Brief Notes and Commentary are given on
pp. 348 ff.

# THE LAY OF LEITHIAN

## I.   OF THINGOL IN DORIATH

A king there was in days of old:
ere Men yet walked upon the mould
his power was reared in caverns' shade,
his hand was over glen and glade.
Of leaves his crown, his mantle green,      5
his silver lances long and keen;
the starlight in his shield was caught,
ere moon was made or sun was wrought.
   In after-days, when to the shore
of Middle-earth from Valinor      10
the Elven-hosts in might returned,
and banners flew and beacons burned,
when kings of Eldamar went by
in strength of war, beneath the sky
then still his silver trumpets blew      15
when sun was young and moon was new.
Afar then in Beleriand,
in Doriath's beleaguered land,
King Thingol sat on guarded throne
in many-pillared halls of stone:      20
there beryl, pearl, and opal pale,
and metal wrought like fishes' mail,
buckler and corslet, axe and sword,
and gleaming spears were laid in hoard:
all these he had and counted small,      25
for dearer than all wealth in hall,
and fairer than are born to Men,
a daughter had he, Lúthien.

## OF LÚTHIEN THE BELOVED

Such lissom limbs no more shall run
on the green earth beneath the sun;      30

so fair a maid no more shall be
from dawn to dusk, from sun to sea.
Her robe was blue as summer skies,
but grey as evening were her eyes;
her mantle sewn with lilies fair,                                35
but dark as shadow was her hair.
Her feet were swift as bird on wing,
her laughter merry as the spring;
the slender willow, the bowing reed,
the fragrance of a flowering mead,                               40
the light upon the leaves of trees,
the voice of water, more than these
her beauty was and blissfulness,
her glory and her loveliness.

She dwelt in the enchanted land                                  45
while elven-might yet held in hand
the woven woods of Doriath:
none ever thither found the path
unbidden, none the forest-eaves
dared pass, or stir the listening leaves.                        50
To North there lay a land of dread,
Dungorthin where all ways were dead
in hills of shadow bleak and cold;
beyond was Deadly Nightshade's hold
in Taur-nu-Fuin's fastness grim,                                 55
where sun was sick and moon was dim.
To South the wide earth unexplored;
to West the ancient Ocean roared,
unsailed and shoreless, wide and wild;
to East in peaks of blue were piled,                             60
in silence folded, mist-enfurled,
the mountains of the outer world.

Thus Thingol in his dolven hall
amid the Thousand Caverns tall
of Menegroth as king abode:                                      65
to him there led no mortal road.
Beside him sat his deathless queen,
fair Melian, and wove unseen
nets of enchantment round his throne,
and spells were laid on tree and stone:                          70
sharp was his sword and high his helm,

the king of beech and oak and elm.
When grass was green and leaves were long,
when finch and mavis sang their song,
there under bough and under sun                              75
in shadow and in light would run
fair Lúthien the elven-maid,
dancing in dell and grassy glade.

### OF DAIRON MINSTREL OF THINGOL

When sky was clear and stars were keen,
then Dairon with his fingers lean,                           80
as daylight melted into eve,
a trembling music sweet would weave
on flutes of silver, thin and clear
for Lúthien, the maiden dear.

There mirth there was and voices bright;                     85
there eve was peace and morn was light;
there jewel gleamed and silver wan
and red gold on white fingers shone,
and elanor and niphredil
bloomed in the grass unfading still,                         90
while the endless years of Elven-land
rolled over far Beleriand,
until a day of doom befell,
as still the elven-harpers tell.

★

### 2.  OF MORGOTH & THE SNARING OF GORLIM

Far in the Northern hills of stone                           95
in caverns black there was a throne
by flame encircled; there the smoke
in coiling columns rose to choke
the breath of life, and there in deep
and gasping dungeons lost would creep                        100
to hopeless death all those who strayed
by doom beneath that ghastly shade.
   A king there sat, most dark and fell

of all that under heaven dwell.
Than earth or sea, than moon or star                105
more ancient was he, mightier far
in mind abysmal than the thought
of Eldar or of Men, and wrought
of strength primeval; ere the stone
was hewn to build the world, alone               110
he walked in darkness, fierce and dire,
burned, as he wielded it, by fire.

He 'twas that laid in ruin black
the Blessed Realm and fled then back
to Middle-earth anew to build                    115
beneath the mountains mansions filled
with misbegotten slaves of hate:
death's shadow brooded at his gate.
His hosts he armed with spears of steel
and brands of flame, and at their heel           120
the wolf walked and the serpent crept
with lidless eyes. Now forth they leapt,
his ruinous legions, kindling war
in field and frith and woodland hoar.
Where long the golden elanor                     125
had gleamed amid the grass they bore
their banners black, where finch had sung
and harpers silver harps had wrung
now dark the ravens wheeled and cried
amid the reek, and far and wide                  130
the swords of Morgoth dripped with red
above the hewn and trampled dead.
Slowly his shadow like a cloud
rolled from the North, and on the proud
that would not yield his vengeance fell;          135
to death or thraldom under hell
all things he doomed: the Northern land
lay cowed beneath his ghastly hand.

But still there lived in hiding cold
Bëor's son, Barahir the bold,                    140
of land bereaved and lordship shorn
who once a prince of Men was born,
and now an outlaw lurked and lay
in the hard heath and woodland grey.

## OF THE SAVING OF KING INGLOR FELAGUND BY THE XII BËORINGS

Twelve men beside him still there went,                145
still faithful when all hope was spent.
Their names are yet in elven-song
remembered, though the years are long
since doughty Dagnir and Ragnor,
Radhruin, Dairuin and Gildor,                          150
Gorlim Unhappy, and Urthel,
and Arthad and Hathaldir fell;
since the black shaft with venomed wound
took Belegund and Baragund,
the mighty sons of Bregolas;                           155
since he whose doom and deeds surpass
all tales of Men was laid on bier,
fair Beren son of Barahir.
For these it was, the chosen men
of Bëor's house, who in the fen                        160
of reedy Serech stood at bay
about King Inglor in the day
of his defeat, and with their swords
thus saved of all the Elven-lords
the fairest; and his love they earned.                 165
And he escaping south, returned
to Nargothrond his mighty realm,
where still he wore his crownëd helm;
but they to their northern homeland rode,
dauntless and few, and there abode                     170
unconquered still, defying fate,
pursued by Morgoth's sleepless hate.

### OF TARN AELUIN THE BLESSED

Such deeds of daring there they wrought
that soon the hunters that them sought
at rumour of their coming fled.                        175
Though price was set upon each head
to match the weregild of a king,
no soldier could to Morgoth bring
news even of their hidden lair;
for where the highland brown and bare                  180
above the darkling pines arose
of steep Dorthonion to the snows

and barren mountain-winds, there lay
a tarn of water, blue by day,
by night a mirror of dark glass                              185
for stars of Elbereth that pass
above the world into the West.
Once hallowed, still that place was blest:
no shadow of Morgoth, and no evil thing
yet thither came; a whispering ring                          190
of slender birches silver-grey
stooped on its margin, round it lay
a lonely moor, and the bare bones
of ancient Earth like standing stones
thrust through the heather and the whin;                     195
and there by houseless Aeluin
the hunted lord and faithful men
under the grey stones made their den.

### OF GORLIM UNHAPPY

Gorlim Unhappy, Angrim's son,
as the tale tells, of these was one                          200
most fierce and hopeless. He to wife,
while fair was the fortune of his life,
took the white maiden Eilinel:
dear love they had ere evil fell.
To war he rode; from war returned                            205
to find his fields and homestead burned,
his house forsaken roofless stood,
empty amid the leafless wood;
and Eilinel, white Eilinel,
was taken whither none could tell,                           210
to death or thraldom far away.
Black was the shadow of that day
for ever on his heart, and doubt
still gnawed him as he went about
in wilderness wandring, or at night                          215
oft sleepless, thinking that she might
ere evil came have timely fled
into the woods: she was not dead,
she lived, she would return again
to seek him, and would deem him slain.                        220
Therefore at whiles he left the lair,

and secretly, alone, would peril dare,
and come to his old house at night,
broken and cold, without fire or light,
and naught but grief renewed would gain,          225
watching and waiting there in vain.

     In vain, or worse – for many spies
had Morgoth, many lurking eyes
well used to pierce the deepest dark;
and Gorlim's coming they would mark                230
and would report. There came a day
when once more Gorlim crept that way,
down the deserted weedy lane
at dusk of autumn sad with rain
and cold wind whining. Lo! a light                 235
at window fluttering in the night
amazed he saw; and drawing near,
between faint hope and sudden fear,
he looked within. 'Twas Eilinel!
Though changed she was, he knew her well.          240
With grief and hunger she was worn,
her tresses tangled, raiment torn;
her gentle eyes with tears were dim,
as soft she wept: 'Gorlim, Gorlim!
Thou canst not have forsaken me.                   245
Then slain, alas! thou slain must be!
And I must linger cold, alone,
and loveless as a barren stone!'

     One cry he gave – and then the light
blew out, and in the wind of night                 250
wolves howled; and on his shoulder fell
suddenly the griping hands of hell.
There Morgoth's servants fast him caught
and he was cruelly bound, and brought
to Sauron captain of the host,                     255
the lord of werewolf and of ghost,
most foul and fell of all who knelt
at Morgoth's throne. In might he dwelt
on Gaurhoth Isle; but now had ridden
with strength abroad, by Morgoth bidden            260
to find the rebel Barahir.
He sat in dark encampment near,

and thither his butchers dragged their prey.
There now in anguish Gorlim lay:
with bond on neck, on hand and foot,                    265
to bitter torment he was put,
to break his will and him constrain
to buy with treason end of pain.
But naught to them would he reveal
of Barahir, nor break the seal                          270
of faith that on his tongue was laid;
until at last a pause was made,
and one came softly to his stake,
a darkling form that stooped, and spake
to him of Eilinel his wife.                             275
   'Wouldst thou,' he said, 'forsake thy life,
who with few words might win release
for her, and thee, and go in peace,
and dwell together far from war,
friends of the King? What wouldst thou more?'          280
And Gorlim, now long worn with pain,
yearning to see his wife again
(whom well he weened was also caught
in Sauron's net), allowed the thought
to grow, and faltered in his troth.                     285
Then straight, half willing and half loath,
they brought him to the seat of stone
where Sauron sat. He stood alone
before that dark and dreadful face,
and Sauron said: 'Come, mortal base!                    290
What do I hear? That thou wouldst dare
to barter with me? Well, speak fair!
What is thy price?' And Gorlim low
bowed down his head, and with great woe,
word on slow word, at last implored                     295
that merciless and faithless lord
that he might free depart, and might
again find Eilinel the White,
and dwell with her, and cease from war
against the King. He craved no more.                    300

   Then Sauron smiled, and said: 'Thou thrall!
The price thou askest is but small
for treachery and shame so great!

I grant it surely! Well, I wait:
Come! Speak now swiftly and speak true!'      305
Then Gorlim wavered, and he drew
half back; but Sauron's daunting eye
there held him, and he dared not lie:
as he began, so must he wend
from first false step to faithless end:      310
he all must answer as he could,
betray his lord and brotherhood,
and cease, and fall upon his face.

    Then Sauron laughed aloud. 'Thou base,
thou cringing worm! Stand up,      315
and hear me! And now drink the cup
that I have sweetly blent for thee!
Thou fool: a phantom thou didst see
that I, I Sauron, made to snare
thy lovesick wits. Naught else was there.      320
Cold 'tis with Sauron's wraiths to wed!
Thy Eilinel! She is long since dead,
dead, food of worms less low than thou.
And yet thy boon I grant thee now:
to Eilinel thou soon shalt go,      325
and lie in her bed, no more to know
of war – or manhood. Have thy pay!'

    And Gorlim then they dragged away,
and cruelly slew him; and at last
in the dank mould his body cast,      330
where Eilinel long since had lain
in the burned woods by butchers slain.
    Thus Gorlim died an evil death,
and cursed himself with dying breath,
and Barahir at last was caught      335
in Morgoth's snare; for set at naught
by treason was the ancient grace
that guarded long that lonely place,
Tarn Aeluin: now all laid bare
were secret paths and hidden lair.      340

★

### 3. OF BEREN SON OF BARAHIR & HIS ESCAPE

Dark from the North now blew the cloud;
the winds of autumn cold and loud
hissed in the heather; sad and grey
Aeluin's mournful water lay.
'Son Beren', then said Barahir,     345
'Thou knowst the rumour that we hear
of strength from the Gaurhoth that is sent
against us; and our food nigh spent.
On thee the lot falls by our law
to go forth now alone to draw     350
what help thou canst from the hidden few
that feed us still, and what is new
to learn. Good fortune go with thee!
In speed return, for grudgingly
we spare thee from our brotherhood,     355
so small: and Gorlim in the wood
is long astray or dead. Farewell!'
As Beren went, still like a knell
resounded in his heart that word,
the last of his father that he heard.     360

Through moor and fen, by tree and briar
he wandered far: he saw the fire
of Sauron's camp, he heard the howl
of hunting Orc and wolf a-prowl,
and turning back, for long the way,     365
benighted in the forest lay.
In weariness he then must sleep,
fain in a badger-hole to creep,
and yet he heard (or dreamed it so)
nearby a marching legion go     370
with clink of mail and clash of shields
up towards the stony mountain-fields.
He slipped then into darkness down,
until, as man that waters drown
strives upwards gasping, it seemed to him     375
he rose through slime beside the brim
of sullen pool beneath dead trees.
Their livid boughs in a cold breeze
trembled, and all their black leaves stirred:
each leaf a black and croaking bird,     380

whose neb a gout of blood let fall.
He shuddered, struggling thence to crawl
through winding weeds, when far away
he saw a shadow faint and grey
gliding across the dreary lake.                                385
Slowly it came, and softly spake:
'Gorlim I was, but now a wraith
of will defeated, broken faith,
traitor betrayed. Go! Stay not here!
Awaken, son of Barahir,                                         390
and haste! For Morgoth's fingers close
upon thy father's throat; he knows
your trysts, your paths, your secret lair.'

　　Then he revealed the devil's snare
in which he fell, and failed; and last                          395
begging forgiveness, wept, and passed
out into darkness. Beren woke,
leapt up as one by sudden stroke
with fire of anger filled. His bow
and sword he seized, and like the roe                           400
hotfoot o'er rock and heath he sped
before the dawn. Ere day was dead
to Aeluin at last he came,
as the red sun westward sank in flame;
but Aeluin was red with blood,                                  405
red were the stones and trampled mud.
Black in the birches sat a-row
the raven and the carrion crow;
wet were their nebs, and dark the meat
that dripped beneath their griping feet.                        410
One croaked: 'Ha, ha, he comes too late!'
'Ha, ha!' they answered, 'ha! too late!'

　　There Beren laid his father's bones
in haste beneath a cairn of stones;
no graven rune nor word he wrote                                415
o'er Barahir, but thrice he smote
the topmost stone, and thrice aloud
he cried his name. 'Thy death', he vowed,
'I will avenge. Yea, though my fate
should lead at last to Angband's gate.'                         420
And then he turned, and did not weep:
too dark his heart, the wound too deep.

Out into night, as cold as stone,
loveless, friendless, he strode alone.

Of hunter's lore he had no need                    425
the trail to find. With little heed
his ruthless foe, secure and proud,
marched north away with blowing loud
of brazen horns their lord to greet,
trampling the earth with grinding feet.            430
Behind them bold but wary went
now Beren, swift as hound on scent,
until beside a darkling well,
where Rivil rises from the fell
down into Serech's reeds to flow,                  435
he found the slayers, found his foe.
From hiding on the hillside near
he marked them all: though less than fear,
too many for his sword and bow
to slay alone. Then, crawling low                  440
as snake in heath, he nearer crept.
There many weary with marching slept,
but captains, sprawling on the grass,
drank and from hand to hand let pass
their booty, grudging each small thing            445
raped from dead bodies. One a ring
held up, and laughed: 'Now, mates,' he cried
'here's mine! And I'll not be denied,
though few be like it in the land.
For I 'twas wrenched it from the hand              450
of that same Barahir I slew,
the robber-knave. If tales be true,
he had it of some elvish lord,
for the rogue-service of his sword.
No help it gave to him – he's dead.                455
They're parlous, elvish rings, 'tis said;
still for the gold I'll keep it, yea
and so eke out my niggard pay.
Old Sauron bade me bring it back,
and yet, methinks, he has no lack                  460
of weightier treasures in his hoard:
the greater the greedier the lord!
So mark ye, mates, ye all shall swear

the hand of Barahir was bare!'
And as he spoke an arrow sped                           465
from tree behind, and forward dead
choking he fell with barb in throat;
with leering face the earth he smote.

Forth, then as wolfhound grim there leapt
Beren among them. Two he swept                         470
aside with sword; caught up the ring;
slew one who grasped him; with a spring
back into shadow passed, and fled
before their yells of wrath and dread
of ambush in the valley rang.                          475
Then after him like wolves they sprang,
howling and cursing, gnashing teeth,
hewing and bursting through the heath,
shooting wild arrows, sheaf on sheaf,
at trembling shade or shaken leaf.                     480

In fateful hour was Beren born:
he laughed at dart and wailing horn;
fleetest of foot of living men,
tireless on fell and light on fen,
elf-wise in wood, he passed away,                      485
defended by his hauberk grey
of dwarvish craft in Nogrod made,
where hammers rang in cavern's shade.

As fearless Beren was renowned:
when men most hardy upon ground                        490
were reckoned folk would speak his name,
foretelling that his after-fame
would even golden Hador pass
or Barahir and Bregolas;
but sorrow now his heart had wrought                   495
to fierce despair, no more he fought
in hope of life or joy or praise,
but seeking so to use his days
only that Morgoth deep should feel
the sting of his avenging steel,                       500
ere death he found and end of pain:
his only fear was thraldom's chain.
Danger he sought and death pursued,
and thus escaped the doom he wooed,

and deeds of breathless daring wrought            505
alone, of which the rumour brought
new hope to many a broken man.
They whispered 'Beren', and began
in secret swords to whet, and soft
by shrouded hearths at evening oft                510
songs they would sing of Beren's bow,
of Dagmor his sword: how he would go
silent to camps and slay the chief,
or trapped in his hiding past belief
would slip away, and under night                  515
by mist or moon, or by the light
of open day would come again.
Of hunters hunted, slayers slain
they sang, of Gorgol the Butcher hewn,
of ambush in Ladros, fire in Drûn,                520
of thirty in one battle dead,
of wolves that yelped like curs and fled,
yea, Sauron himself with wound in hand.
Thus one alone filled all that land
with fear and death for Morgoth's folk;           525
his comrades were the beech and oak
who failed him not, and wary things
with fur and fell and feathered wings
that silent wander, or dwell alone
in hill and wild and waste of stone               530
watched o'er his ways, his faithful friends.

  Yet seldom well an outlaw ends;
and Morgoth was a king more strong
than all the world has since in song
recorded: dark athwart the land                   535
reached out the shadow of his hand,
at each recoil returned again;
two more were sent for one foe slain.
New hope was cowed, all rebels killed;
quenched were the fires, the songs were stilled,  540
tree felled, heath burned, and through the waste
marched the black host of Orcs in haste.
  Almost they closed their ring of steel
round Beren; hard upon his heel
now trod their spies; within their hedge          545

of all aid shorn, upon the edge
of death at bay he stood aghast
and knew that he must die at last,
or flee the land of Barahir,
his land beloved. Beside the mere          550
beneath a heap of nameless stones
must crumble those once mighty bones,
forsaken by both son and kin,
bewailed by reeds of Aeluin.

   In winter's night the houseless North    555
he left behind, and stealing forth
the leaguer of his watchful foe
he passed – a shadow on the snow,
a swirl of wind, and he was gone,
the ruin of Dorthonion,                     560
Tarn Aeluin and its water wan,
never again to look upon.
No more shall hidden bowstring sing,
no more his shaven arrows wing,
no more his hunted head shall lie           565
upon the heath beneath the sky.
The Northern stars, whose silver fire
of old Men named the Burning Briar,
were set behind his back, and shone
o'er land forsaken: he was gone.            570

   Southward he turned, and south away
his long and lonely journey lay,
while ever loomed before his path
the dreadful peaks of Gorgorath.
Never had foot of man most bold             575
yet trod those mountains steep and cold,
nor climbed upon their sudden brink,
whence, sickened, eyes must turn and shrink
to see their southward cliffs fall sheer
in rocky pinnacle and pier                  580
down into shadows that were laid
before the sun and moon were made.
In valleys woven with deceit
and washed with waters bitter-sweet
dark magic lurked in gulf and glen;         585
but out away beyond the ken

of mortal sight the eagle's eye
from dizzy towers that pierced the sky
might grey and gleaming see afar,
as sheen on water under star,                           590
Beleriand, Beleriand,
the borders of the Elven-land.


★


4.    OF THE COMING OF BEREN TO DORIATH; BUT FIRST IS TOLD OF
         THE MEETING OF MELIAN AND THINGOL

There long ago in Elder-days
ere voice was heard or trod were ways,
the haunt of silent shadows stood                       595
in starlit dusk Nan Elmoth wood.
In Elder-days that long are gone
a light amid the shadows shone,
a voice was in the silence heard:
the sudden singing of a bird.                           600
There Melian came, the Lady grey,
and dark and long her tresses lay
beneath her silver girdle-seat
and down unto her silver feet.
The nightingales with her she brought,                  605
to whom their song herself she taught,
who sweet upon her gleaming hands
had sung in the immortal lands.
    Thence wayward wandering on a time
from Lórien she dared to climb                           610
the everlasting mountain-wall
of Valinor, at whose feet fall
the surges of the Shadowy Sea.
Out away she went then free,
to gardens of the Gods no more                          615
returning, but on mortal shore,
a glimmer ere the dawn she strayed,
singing her spells from glade to glade.
    A bird in dim Nan Elmoth wood
trilled, and to listen Thingol stood                    620
amazed; then far away he heard

a voice more fair than fairest bird,
a voice as crystal clear of note
as thread of silver glass remote.

Here the manuscript C ends. Of the next short section there are no less
than five rough drafts, with endless small variations of wording (and the
first ten lines of it were written onto the B-text). The final form was then
added, in type, to the D typescript:

Of folk and kin no more he thought;                    625
of errand that the Eldar brought
from Cuiviénen far away,
of lands beyond the Seas that lay
no more he recked, forgetting all,
drawn only by that distant call                        630
till deep in dim Nan Elmoth wood
lost and beyond recall he stood.
And there he saw her, fair and fay:
Ar-Melian, the Lady grey,
as silent as the windless trees,                       635
standing with mist about her knees,
and in her face remote the light
of Lórien glimmered in the night.
No word she spoke; but pace by pace,
a halting shadow, towards her face                      640
forth walked the silver-mantled king,
tall Elu Thingol. In the ring
of waiting trees he took her hand.
One moment face to face they stand
alone, beneath the wheeling sky,                        645
while starlit years on earth go by
and in Nan Elmoth wood the trees
grow dark and tall. The murmuring seas
rising and falling on the shore
and Ulmo's horn he heeds no more.                       650

    But long his people sought in vain
their lord, till Ulmo called again,
and then in grief they marched away,
leaving the woods. To havens grey
upon the western shore, the last                        655
long shore of mortal lands, they passed,
and thence were borne beyond the Sea

in Aman, the Blessed Realm, to be
by evergreen Ezellohar
in Valinor, in Eldamar.                                    660

★

52    On one of the copies of D *Dungorthin* was changed to
*Dungortheb*, but this belongs to a later layer of nomenclature and I have not introduced it into the text.

55    *Taur-nu-Fuin* C: the line as written on the B-text still had
*Taur-na-Fuin*.

140   *Bëor's son*: changed on one of the copies of D to *the
Bëoring*, i.e. a man of Bëor's house. This was a change made
when the genealogy had been greatly extended and Barahir
was no longer Bëor's son but his remote descendant (see
p. 198).

249–330   In this section of the Canto the rewriting on (or inserted into)
the B-text exists in two versions, one the immediate forerunner of the other. The difference between them is that in
the earlier Gorlim was still, as in the earlier Lay, taken to
Angband and to Morgoth himself. Thus the passage in the
first rewriting corresponding to lines 255–66 reads:

> to Angband and the iron halls
> where laboured Morgoth's hopeless thralls;
> and there with bonds on hand and foot
> to grievous torment he was put

In what follows the two versions are the same, except that
in the first it is Morgoth, not Sauron: precisely the same lines
are used of each. But at lines 306–11 the first version has:

> Then Gorlim wavered, and he drew
> half back; but Morgoth's daunting eyes
> there held him. To the Lord of Lies
> 'tis vain in lies the breath to spend:
> as he began, so he must end,
> and all must answer as he could

and at lines 318–21 Morgoth says:

> Thou fool! A phantom thou didst see
> that Sauron my servant made to snare
> thy lovesick wits. Naught else was there.
> Cold 'tis with Sauron's wraiths to wed!

547   The word *aghast* is marked with an X in C (because Beren
was not aghast).

567–8    At first the passage in B (p. 167, lines 369–82) beginning *No more his hidden bowstring sings* was scarcely changed in the rewriting, but as first written C had (old lines 376–9):

> found him no more. The stars that burn
> about the North with silver fire
> that Varda wrought, the Burning Briar
> as Men it called in days long gone

Old lines 373–5 were then cut out and 376–9 rewritten:

> The stars that burn with silver fire
> about the North, the Burning Briar
> that Varda lit in ages gone

This was in turn changed to the text given, lines 567–8.

581    In one of the copies of D an X is placed against this line. I think this was probably very late and marks my father's changed ideas concerning the making of the Sun and Moon.

596    *Nan Elmoth*: in the preliminary draft the name of the wood was first *Glad-uial*, emended to *Glath-uial*; then *Gilammoth*, emended to *Nan Elmoth*. It was here that the name *Nan Elmoth* emerged.

627    In one of the drafts of this passage the line is *from Waking Water far away*.

634    In one of the drafts of this passage *Tar-Melian* stands in the margin as an alternative.

## Commentary on lines 1–660

A strictly chronological account of the evolution of the legends of the Elder Days would have to consider several other works before the revisions to the *Lay of Leithian* were reached. By treating the Lay revised and unrevised as an entity and not piecemeal I jump these stages, and names which had in fact emerged a good while before appear here for the first time in this 'History'. I do little more than list them:

65    *Menegroth*

89    *elanor* and *niphredil*. At line 125 is a reference to *the golden elanor*.

115    *Middle-earth*

149 ff.    The names of the men of Barahir's band, beside Beren and Gorlim: *Dagnir, Ragnor, Radhruin, Dairuin, Gildor, Urthel, Arthad, Hathaldir; Belegund* and *Baragund*.

    Belegund and Baragund are the sons of *Bregolas* (Barahir's brother); and Gorlim is the son of *Angrim* (199).

    All these names appear in *The Silmarillion* (pp. 155, 162).

161  'the fen of reedy *Serech.*' Beren came on the Orcs at the well of *Rivil*, which 'rises from the fell / down into Serech's reeds to flow' (434–5).

162  Felagund is called *Inglor* (*Inglor Felagund* in the sub-title, p. 335).

182, 560  *Dorthonion*

186  *Elbereth*

196, etc.  (*Tarn*) *Aeluin*

255, etc.  *Sauron*

259, 347  *Gaurhoth.* Cf. *Tol-in-Gaurhoth* 'Isle of Werewolves' in *The Silmarillion.*

434  *Rivil*

493  *Hador*

512  *Dagmor.* Beren's sword is named nowhere else.

519  *Gorgol the Butcher.* He is named nowhere else.

520  *Ladros* (the lands to the north-east of Dorthonion that were granted by the Noldorin kings to the Men of the House of Bëor).

520  *Drûn.* This name is marked on the later of the 'Silmarillion' maps (that on which the published map was based) as north of Aeluin and west of Ladros, but is named in no other place.

574  *Gorgorath.* This has occurred in the prose outline for Canto X of the Lay, but in the form *Gorgoroth* (p. 272).

596, etc.  *Nan Elmoth.* See note to line 596.

634  *Ar-Melian (Tar-Melian).* The name is not found elsewhere with either prefix.

659  *Ezellohar* (the Green Mound of the Two Trees in Valinor).

In addition may be noted here *Dungorthin* (52), where the new version changes the old lines 49–50

> To North there lay the Land of Dread
> whence only evil pathways led

to

> To North there lay a land of dread,
> Dungorthin where all ways were dead

In the old version 'the Land of Dread' clearly meant, simply, 'the land of Morgoth'. Here Dungorthin is placed as it is in *The Silmarillion* (p. 121), between the Mountains of Terror and the northern bound of the Girdle of Melian; see p. 314.

In the revised Lay the story of Gorlim was greatly developed. In the old (see pp. 162–4, 169–70), Gorlim left his companions and went 'to meet / with hidden friend within a dale'; he found 'a homestead looming pale', and within it he saw a phantom of Eilinel. He left the house, in fear of Morgoth's hunters and wolves, and returned to his companions; but after some days he deliberately sought out Morgoth's servants and offered to betray his fellows. He was taken to the halls of Morgoth – who does not say that the wraith was set to decoy Gorlim:

> a wraith of that which might have been,
> methinks, it is that thou hast seen!

(But in lines 241–2 it is said that 'men believed that Morgoth made/the fiendish phantom'.)

There is also a remarkable development in the revised Lay, in that 'the XII Bëorings' (one would expect XIII, including Barahir himself) of Dorthonion were the very men who saved King Felagund in the Battle of Sudden Flame:

> For these it was, the chosen men
> of Bëor's house, who in the fen
> of reedy Serech stood at bay
> about King Inglor in the day
> of his defeat . . .                                    (159–63)

In *The Silmarillion* the story is that 'Morgoth pursued [Barahir] to the death, until at last there remained to him only twelve companions' (p. 162): there is no suggestion that these survivors were a picked band, already joined as companions in an earlier heroic deed.

Felagund (Inglor) is now said to have *returned* to Nargothrond (lines 166–7) after his rescue by Barahir and his men (see pp. 85–6).

From this point onwards substantial rewriting of the poem is restricted to a few sections.

## Canto III continued

From the end of the rewritten opening of the poem (line 660 above) the D typescript continues as a copy of B to the end of the poem, but though it was certainly made under my father's supervision it is of very minor textual value in itself.

The passage in the original text (p. 173) lines 453 (*Thus Thingol sailed not on the seas*) to 470 was left unchanged; but for lines 471 (*In later days when Morgoth first*) to approximately 613 my father substituted 142 lines of new verse (omitting the long retrospective passage lines 563 ff. concerning Beren's journey over the Mountains of Terror), in which there is very little of the old Lay, and as the passage proceeds progressively less. There is no doubt that these lines are (relatively) very late: an apparently contemporaneous piece of rewriting in Canto X is

certainly post-1955 (see p. 360), and they may well be considerably later
than that. There is a quantity of rough draft material in manuscript, but
also a typescript made by my father of the first 103 lines, inserted into the
D-text.

In later days, when Morgoth fled
from wrath and raised once more his head
and Iron Crown, his mighty seat
beneath the smoking mountain's feet
founded and fortified anew,                                    5
then slowly dread and darkness grew:
the Shadow of the North that all
the Folk of Earth would hold in thrall.
    The lords of Men to knee he brings,
the kingdoms of the Exiled Kings                              10
assails with ever-mounting war:
in their last havens by the shore
they dwell, or strongholds walled with fear
defend upon his borders drear,
till each one falls. Yet reign there still                    15
in Doriath beyond his will
the Grey King and immortal Queen.
No evil in their realm is seen;
no power their might can yet surpass:
there still is laughter and green grass,                      20
there leaves are lit by the white sun,
and many marvels are begun.

    There went now in the Guarded Realm
beneath the beech, beneath the elm,
there lightfoot ran now on the green                          25
the daughter of the king and queen:
of Arda's eldest children born
in beauty of their elven-morn
and only child ordained by birth
to walk in raiment of the Earth                               30
from Those descended who began
before the world of Elf and Man.

    Beyond the bounds of Arda far
still shone the Legions, star on star,
memorials of their labour long,                               35
achievement of Vision and of Song;

and when beneath their ancient light
on Earth below was cloudless night,
music in Doriath awoke,
and there beneath the branching oak,                    40
or seated on the beech-leaves brown,
Daeron the dark with ferny crown
played on his pipes with elvish art
unbearable by mortal heart.

No other player has there been,                          45
no other lips or fingers seen
so skilled, 'tis said in elven-lore,
save Maelor* son of Fëanor,
forgotten harper, singer doomed,
who young when Laurelin yet bloomed                      50
to endless lamentation passed
and in the tombless sea was cast.†
But Daeron in his heart's delight
yet lived and played by starlit night,
until one summer-eve befell,                             55
as still the elven harpers tell.
Then merrily his piping trilled;
the grass was soft, the wind was stilled,
the twilight lingered faint and cool
in shadow-shapes upon the pool‡                          60
beneath the boughs of sleeping trees
standing silent. About their knees
a mist of hemlocks glimmered pale,
and ghostly moths on lace-wings frail
went to and fro. Beside the mere                         65
quickening, rippling, rising clear
the piping called. Then forth she came,
as sheer and sudden as a flame
of peerless white the shadows cleaving,
her maiden-bower on white feet leaving;                  70
and as when summer stars arise

---

*Both *Maglor* and *Maelor* appear in the draft manuscripts of this passage. The final
typescript has *Maelor*, changed to *Maglor*, but not I think by my father.

†In *The Silmarillion* (p. 254) it is not said that Maglor ended his life in the sea: he cast
the Silmaril into the sea, 'and thereafter he wandered ever upon the shores, singing in pain
and regret beside the waves'.

‡There is no other reference to a 'pool' or 'mere' at the place in the woods where Beren
came upon Lúthien.

radiant into darkened skies,
her living light on all was cast
in fleeting silver as she passed.
    There now she stepped with elven pace,    75
bending and swaying in her grace,
as half-reluctant; then began
to dance, to dance: in mazes ran
bewildering, and a mist of white
was wreathed about her whirling flight.    80
Wind-ripples on the water flashed,
and trembling leaf and flower were plashed
with diamond-dews, as ever fleet
and fleeter went her wingéd feet.

    Her long hair as a cloud was streaming    85
about her arms uplifted gleaming,
as slow above the trees the Moon
in glory of the plenilune
arose, and on the open glade
its light serene and clear was laid.    90
Then suddenly her feet were stilled,
and through the woven wood there thrilled,
half wordless, half in elven-tongue,
her voice upraised in blissful song
that once of nightingales she learned    95
and in her living joy had turned
to heart-enthralling loveliness,
unmarred, immortal, sorrowless.

*Ir Ithil ammen Eruchín*
   *menel-vîr síla díriel*    100
*si loth a galadh lasto dîn!*
   *A Hîr Annûn gilthoniel,*
*le linnon im Tinúviel!*

The typescript ends here, but the final manuscript draft continues:

    O elven-fairest Lúthien
what wonder moved thy dances then?    105
That night what doom of Elvenesse
enchanted did thy voice possess?
Such marvel shall there no more be
on Earth or west beyond the Sea,

at dusk or dawn, by night or noon                    110
or neath the mirror of the moon!
On Neldoreth was laid a spell;
the piping into silence fell,
for Daeron cast his flute away,
unheeded on the grass it lay,                         115
in wonder bound as stone he stood
heart-broken in the listening wood.
And still she sang above the night,
as light returning into light
upsoaring from the world below                       120
when suddenly there came a slow
dull tread of heavy feet on leaves,
and from the darkness on the eaves
of the bright glade a shape came out
with hands agrope, as if in doubt                    125
or blind, and as it stumbling passed
under the moon a shadow cast
bended and darkling. Then from on high
as lark falls headlong from the sky
the song of Lúthien fell and ceased;                 130
but Daeron from the spell released
awoke to fear, and cried in woe:
'Flee Lúthien, ah Lúthien go!
An evil walks the wood! Away!'
Then forth he fled in his dismay                     135
ever calling her to follow him,
until far off his cry was dim
'Ah flee, ah flee now, Lúthien!'
But silent stood she in the glen
unmoved, who never fear had known,                   140
as slender moonlit flower alone,
white and windless with upturned face
waiting

Here the manuscript comes to an end.


Canto IV

A small section of this Canto was partly rewritten at some late date. Lines
884 ff. were changed to:

> Then Thingol said: 'O Dairon wise,
> with wary ears and watchful eyes,
> who all that passes in this land
> dost ever heed and understand,
> what omen doth this silence bear?

This was written rapidly on the B-text and was primarily prompted, I think, by the wish to get rid of the word 'magic' at line 886, which is underlined and marked with an X on the D typescript. At the same time 'wild stallion' at 893 was changed to 'great stallion', and *Tavros* to *Tauros* at 891. A little further on, lines 902–19 were changed, also at this time:

> beneath the trees of Ennorath.*
> Would it were so! An age now hath
> gone by since Nahar trod this earth
> in days of our peace and ancient mirth,
> ere rebel lords of Eldamar
> pursuing Morgoth from afar
> brought war and ruin to the North.
> Doth Tauros to their aid come forth?
> But if not he, who comes or what?'
> And Dairon said: 'He cometh not!
> No feet divine shall leave that shore
> where the Outer Seas' last surges roar,
> till many things be come to pass,
> and many evils wrought. Alas!
> the guest is here. The woods are still,
> but wait not; for a marvel chill
> them holds at the strange deeds they see,
> though king sees not – yet queen, maybe,
> can guess, and maiden doubtless knows
> who ever now beside her goes.'

Lines 926–9 were rewritten:

> But Dairon looked on Lúthien's face
> and faltered, seeing his disgrace
> in those clear eyes. He spoke no more,
> and silent Thingol's anger bore.

But these rewritings were hasty, at the level of rough draft, and in no way comparable to what has preceded.

---

*Ennorath*: 'Middle-earth'; cf. *The Lord of the Rings*, Appendix E (III. 393, footnote 1).

## Cantos V–IX

There is no later recasting in these Cantos save for four lines in Canto IX: the dying words of Felagund to Beren (2633 ff.):

> I now must go to my long rest
> in Aman, there beyond the shore
> of Eldamar for ever more
> in memory to dwell.' Thus died the king,
> as still the elven harpers sing.

At this point my father wrote on one of the copies of the D-text: 'He should give ring back to Beren' (for the later history of the ring see *Unfinished Tales* p. 171 note 2, and *The Lord of the Rings* Appendix A, III. 322 note 1 and 338). But in fact it is nowhere said that Beren had returned the ring to Felagund.

## Canto X

With the beginning of this Canto a substantial passage of new writing begins, at first written on the B-text, and then, with further change, in a typescript made by my father, to all appearance at the same time as that given on pp. 352–5 (but in this case the new verse was retyped as part of the D-text).

> Songs have recalled, by harpers sung
> long years ago in elven tongue,
> how Lúthien and Beren strayed
> in Sirion's vale; and many a glade
> they filled with joy, and there their feet          5
> passed by lightly, and days were sweet.
> Though winter hunted through the wood,
> still flowers lingered where they stood.
> Tinúviel! Tinúviel!
> Still unafraid the birds now dwell          10
> and sing on boughs amid the snow
> where Lúthien and Beren go.
>
> From Sirion's Isle they passed away,
> but on the hill alone there lay
> a green grave, and a stone was set,          15
> and there there lie the white bones yet
> of Finrod fair, Finarfin's son,

unless that land be changed and gone,
or foundered in unfathomed seas,
while Finrod walks beneath the trees          20
in Eldamar* and comes no more
to the grey world of tears and war.

To Nargothrond no more he came
but thither swiftly ran the fame
of their dead king and his great deed,        25
how Lúthien the Isle had freed:
the Werewolf Lord was overthrown,
and broken were his towers of stone.
For many now came home at last
who long ago to shadow passed;               30
and like a shadow had returned
Huan the hound, though scant he earned
or praise or thanks of Celegorm.
There now arose a growing storm,
a clamour of many voices loud,                35
and folk whom Curufin had cowed
and their own king had help denied,
in shame and anger now they cried:
'Come! Slay these faithless lords untrue!
Why lurk they here? What will they do,        40
but bring Finarfin's kin to naught,
treacherous cuckoo-guests unsought?
Away with them!' But wise and slow
Orodreth spoke: 'Beware, lest woe
and wickedness to worse ye bring!             45
Finrod is fallen. I am king.
But even as he would speak, I now
command you. I will not allow
in Nargothrond the ancient curse
from evil unto evil worse                     50
to work. With tears for Finrod weep
repentant! Swords for Morgoth keep!
No kindred blood shall here be shed.
Yet here shall neither rest nor bread
the brethren find who set at naught           55

---

*Eldamar: earlier reading *the Blessed Realm*. – With these lines cf. the revised version
of Felagund's dying words in Canto IX (p. 357).

Finarfin's house. Let them be sought,
unharmed to stand before me! Go!
The courtesy of Finrod show!'

In scorn stood Celegorm, unbowed,
with glance of fire in anger proud                    60
and menacing; but at his side
smiling and silent, wary-eyed,
was Curufin, with hand on haft
of his long knife. And then he laughed,
and 'Well?' said he. 'Why didst thou call            65
for us, Sir Steward? In thy hall
we are not wont to stand. Come, speak,
if aught of us thou hast to seek!'

Cold words Orodreth answered slow:
'Before the king ye stand. But know,                 70
of you he seeks for naught. His will
ye come to hear, and to fulfil.
Be gone for ever, ere the day
shall fall into the sea! Your way
shall never lead you hither more,                    75
nor any son of Fëanor;
of love no more shall there be bond
between your house and Nargothrond!'

'We will remember it,' they said,
and turned upon their heels, and sped,               80
saddled their horses, trussed their gear,
and went with hound and bow and spear,
alone; for none of all the folk
would follow them. No word they spoke,
but sounded horns, and rode away                     85
like wind at end of stormy day.

The typescript made by my father ends here, but the revision written on
the B-text continues (and was incorporated in the D typescript).

Towards Doriath the wanderers now
were drawing nigh. Though bare was bough,
and winter through the grasses grey
went hissing chill, and brief was day,               90
they sang beneath the frosty sky

above them lifted clear and high.
They came to Mindeb swift and bright
that from the northern mountains' height
to Neldoreth came leaping down                        95
with noise among the boulders brown,
but into sudden silence fell,
passing beneath the guarding spell
that Melian on the borders laid
of Thingol's land. There now they stayed;            100
for silence sad on Beren fell.
Unheeded long, at last too well
he heard the warning of his heart:
alas, beloved, here we part.
'Alas, Tinúviel,' he said,                           105
'this road no further can we tread
together, no more hand in hand
can journey in the Elven-land.'
        'Why part we here? What dost thou say,
even at dawn of brighter day?'                       110

From lines 2936 to 2965 no further changes were made (except
*Elfinesse* to *Elvenesse* at 2962). In the preceding passage, Inglor
Felagund son of Finrod has become Finrod Felagund son of Finarfin,
which dates the revision to, at earliest, 1955, for the change had not been
made in the first edition of *The Lord of the Rings*.

A further short stretch of rewriting begins at 2966, returning to the
original text two lines later:

My word, alas! I now must keep,
and not the first of men must weep
for oath in pride and anger sworn.
Too brief the meeting, brief the morn,
too soon comes night when we must part!               5
All oaths are for breaking of the heart,
with shame denied, with anguish kept.
Ah! would that now unknown I slept
with Barahir beneath the stone,
and thou wert dancing still alone,                    10
unmarred, immortal, sorrowless,
singing in joy of Elvenesse.'

        'That may not be. For bonds there are
stronger than stone or iron bar,

more strong than proudly spoken oath.          15
Have I not plighted thee my troth?
Hath love no pride nor honour then?
Or dost thou deem then Lúthien
so frail of purpose, light of love?
By stars of Elbereth above!          20
If thou wilt here my hand forsake
and leave me lonely paths to take,
then Lúthien will not go home . . .

At the same time line 2974 was changed to

beyond all hope in love once more

and 2988 ff. to

                    In rage and haste
thus madly eastward they now raced,
to find the old and perilous path
between the dreadful Gorgorath
and Thingol's realm. That was their road
most swift to where their kin abode
far off, where Himring's watchful hill
o'er Aglon's gorge hung tall and still.

          They saw the wanderers. With a shout
straight on them turned their steeds about . . .

### Cantos XI–XIII

There is no rewriting in Cantos XI and XII, but a little towards the end
of XIII. Lines 4092–5 were replaced by:

the Silmarils with living light
were kindled clear, and waxing bright
shone like the stars that in the North
above the reek of earth leap forth.

Lines 4150–9 were replaced by:

In claws of iron the gem was caught;
the knife them rent, as they were naught

but brittle nails on a dead hand.
Behold! the hope of Elvenland,
the fire of Fëanor, Light of Morn                          5
before the sun and moon were born,
thus out of bondage came at last,
from iron to mortal hand it passed.
There Beren stood. The jewel he held,
and its pure radiance slowly welled                       10
through flesh and bone, and turned to fire
with hue of living blood. Desire
then smote his heart their doom to dare,
and from the deeps of Hell to bear
all three immortal gems, and save                         15
the elven-light from Morgoth's grave.
Again he stooped; with knife he strove;
through band and claw of iron it clove.
But round the Silmarils dark Fate
was woven: they were meshed in hate,                      20
and not yet come was their doomed hour
when wrested from the fallen power
of Morgoth in a ruined world,
regained and lost, they should be hurled
in fiery gulf and groundless sea,                         25
beyond recall while Time shall be.


### Canto XIV

Lines 4184–90 were rewritten:

At last before them far away
they saw a glimmer, faint and grey
of ghostly light that shivering fell
down from the yawning gates of Hell.
Then hope awoke, and straightway died –
the doors were open, gates were wide;
but on the threshold terror walked.
{ The dreadful wolf awake there stalked }
{ The wolf awake there watchful stalked }
and in his eyes the red fire glowered;
there Carcharoth in menace towered,
a waiting death, a biding doom:

Lines 4208–11 were rewritten:

> and Beren in despair then strode
> past Lúthien to bar the road,
> unarmed, defenceless, to defend
> the elven-maid until the end.

Of the original Lay scarcely more than a sixth is represented in the rewriting, and the proportion of new verse to old is less than a quarter; so that Humphrey Carpenter's statement in *The Inklings*, p. 31, that 'Eventually, indeed, he came to rewrite the whole poem' must, alas, be corrected.

# Note on the original submission of the
## *Lay of Leithian* and *The Silmarillion*
### in 1937

In the wake of the immediate success of *The Hobbit*, which was published on 21 September 1937, Stanley Unwin, the chairman of George Allen & Unwin, was naturally anxious that my father should produce a sequel or successor – about hobbits. The result of the first meeting between them, not long after the publication of the book, was that my father sent in various manuscripts, among them the *Lay of Leithian* (referred to in the correspondence of that time as the *Gest(e) of Beren and Lúthien*) and *The Silmarillion*.

Humphrey Carpenter says in his *Biography* (p. 183) that 'the manuscript [of *The Silmarillion*] – or rather, the bundle of manuscripts – had arrived in a somewhat disordered state, and the only clearly continuous section seemed to be the long poem "The Gest of Beren and Lúthien".' Rayner Unwin has told me that in the record kept by Allen & Unwin of incoming manuscripts the works delivered on 15 November 1937 were listed as:

1   Farmer Giles of Ham
2   Long Poem
3   Mr Bliss
4   The Gnomes Material
5   The Lost Road

Notes of my father's show that together with *The Silmarillion* 'proper' he sent at this time *Ainulindalë* (The Music of the Ainur), *Ambarkanta* (The Shape of the World), and *The Fall of the Númenoreans*. I think that this is why the fourth item in the record book was written down as 'The Gnomes Material'. It may be that the different manuscripts were not very clearly differentiated, while the title-pages of the different works would certainly seem obscure; and 'The Gnomes Material' was a convenient covering phrase.* But perhaps one may detect in it a note of helplessness as well, apparent also in the description of item 2 as a 'Long Poem'. – On the other hand, it should be mentioned that the text of *The Silmarillion* was at that time a fine, simple, and very legible manuscript.

---

*There is no question that *The Silmarillion* itself did go to Allen & Unwin at this time. My father made a note while it was gone about changes to be made to it when it came back to him, and he specifically acknowledged the return of it (*Letters* p. 27): 'I have received safely . . . the *Geste* (in verse) and the *Silmarillion* and related fragments.'

There is no evidence that *The Silmarillion* and the other Middle-earth prose works were submitted to the publishers' reader. In his report on the poem he referred only to 'a few pages' and 'some pages' in prose, and Stanley Unwin, when he returned the manuscripts on 15 December 1937, mentioned 'the pages of a prose version' which accompanied the poem. Humphrey Carpenter seems certainly right in his suggestion (*Biography* p. 184) that these pages were attached 'for the purpose of completing the story, for the poem itself was unfinished'; they were pages from the story of Beren and Lúthien as told in *The Silmarillion*. But it is also obvious from the reader's report that he saw nothing else of *The Silmarillion*. He headed his report: '*The Geste of Beren and Lúthien* (Retold in Verse by ? )', and began:

I am rather at a loss to know what to do with this – it doesn't even seem to have an author! – or any indication of sources, etc. Publishers' readers are rightly supposed to be of moderate intelligence and reading; but I confess my reading has not extended to early Celtic Gestes, and I don't even know whether this is a famous Geste or not, or, for that matter, whether it is authentic. I presume it is, as the unspecified versifier has included some pages of a prose-version (which is far superior).

By the last sentence he meant, I think, that the *story*, as represented in what he took to be a close prose translation, was authentic 'Celtic Geste', and that 'the unspecified versifier' had proceeded to make a poem out of it.

However, he was a critic positive in his taste, and he contrasted the poem, greatly to its disadvantage, with 'the few pages of (presumably) prose transcript from the original'. In the poem, he said, 'the primitive strength is gone, the clear colours are gone' – a notable conclusion, even if the actual evolution of the Matter of Beren and Lúthien was thus turned onto its head.

It may seem odd that the reader who was given the poem should have had so little to go on; even odder, that he wrote with some enthusiasm about the fragment of prose narrative that accompanied it, yet never saw the work from which the fragment came, though that was the most important manuscript sent in by the author: he had indeed no reason to suspect its existence. But I would guess that my father had not made it sufficiently clear at the outset what the Middle-earth prose works were and how they related to each other, and that as a result 'the Gnomes Material' had been set aside as altogether too peculiar and difficult.

At the bottom of the reader's report Charles Furth of Allen & Unwin wrote: 'What do we do?'; and it was left to the tact of Stanley Unwin to devise a way. When he returned the manuscripts to my father he said:

As you yourself surmised, it is going to be a difficult task to do anything with the *Geste of Beren and Lúthien* in verse form, but our reader is much impressed with the pages of a prose version that accompanied it

– and he quoted from the report *only* the approving (if misdirected) remarks which the reader had made about the *Silmarillion* fragment, and which Humphrey Carpenter quotes – 'It has something of that mad, bright-eyed beauty that perplexes all Anglo-Saxons in the face of Celtic art,' &c. But Stanley Unwin then went on to say:

> The Silmarillion contains plenty of wonderful material; in fact it is a mine to be explored in writing further books like *The Hobbit* rather than a book in itself.

These words effectively show in themselves that *The Silmarillion* had not been given to a reader and reported on. At that time it was an extremely coherent work, though unfinished in that version.* Beyond question, Stanley Unwin's object was to save my father's feelings, while (relying on the reader's report – which concerned the poem) rejecting the material submitted, and to persuade him to write a book that would continue the success of *The Hobbit*. But the result was that my father was entirely misled; for in his reply of 16 December 1937 (given in full in *Letters* pp. 26–7) – three days before he wrote saying that he had completed the first chapter, 'A Long-expected Party', of 'a new story about Hobbits' – he said:

> My chief joy comes from learning that the Silmarillion is not rejected with scorn . . . I do not mind about the verse-form [i.e. the verse-form of the tale of Beren and Lúthien, the *Lay of Leithian*] which in spite of certain virtuous passages has grave defects, for it is only for me the rough material.† But I shall certainly now hope one day to be able, or to be able to afford, to publish the Silmarillion!

He was quite obviously under the impression that *The Silmarillion* had been given to a reader and reported on (no doubt he saw no significance in Stanley Unwin's phrase '*the pages of* a prose version'); whereas so far as the existing evidence goes (and it seems sufficiently complete) this was not the case at all. He thought it had been read and rejected, whereas it had merely been rejected. The reader had certainly rejected the *Lay of Leithian*; he had not rejected *The Silmarillion*, of which he had only seen a few pages (not knowing what they were), and in any case enjoyed them – granting the difficulties that an Anglo-Saxon finds in appreciating Celtic art.

---

*There was not in fact a great deal more to be done in reworking the 1930 text: the new version extended (in some 40,000 words) to part way through Chapter XXI, *Of Túrin Turambar*.

†This may seem a rather surprising thing to say; but it is to be remembered that he had abandoned the poem six years before, and was at this time absorbed in the perfecting of the prose *Silmarillion*.

It is strange to reflect on what the outcome might conceivably have been if *The Silmarillion* actually had been read at that time, and if the reader had maintained the good opinion he formed from those few pages; for while there is no necessary reason to suppose even so that it would have been accepted for publication, it does not seem absolutely out of the question. And if it had been? My father wrote long after (in 1964, *Letters* p. 346):

I then [after the publication of *The Hobbit*] offered them the legends of the Elder Days, but their readers turned that down. They wanted a sequel. But I wanted heroic legends and high romance. The result was *The Lord of the Rings*.

# GLOSSARY OF OBSOLETE, ARCHAIC, AND RARE WORDS AND MEANINGS

In this list words occurring in the *Lay of the Children of Húrin* (H, and the second version H ii) and in the *Lay of Leithian* (L, and the continuous part of the later rewriting L ii) are referenced to the lines; words from other poems or passages are referenced to the pages on which they occur.

Both Lays, but especially *The Children of Húrin*, make use of some totally lost words (and lost meanings), but the list includes also a good many that remain well-known literary archaisms, and some words that are neither but are of very limited currency.

**an**   if, H 63, 485
**as**   as if, H 310, ii. 659
**astonied**   astounded, H 578
**bade**   H ii. 646. If *This Thingol she bade* means 'This she *offered* to Thingol' the word is used in two senses within the line: she *bade* (offered) him the helm, and *bade* (asked) him to receive her thanks'; but more probably the line means 'she asked him to receive it, and her thanks' (cf. H 301).
**bale**   evil, woe, torment, H 56, ii. 81
**balusters**   the pillars of a balustrade, p. 132
**bated**   restrained, held in, H 1121
**bent**   open place covered with grass, H 1032, 1517, 1539, ii. 500; L 1369, 2281
**betid**   come to pass, L 2408
**blent**   mingled, H 453, 583; L ii. 317
**boots**   in **it boots not**, it is of no use, H 1871
**bosmed**   (in **bare-bosmed**) bosomed, H 1198
**brand**   blade, sword, H 1340, ii. 149
**carping**   talk, chatter, H 477; **carped** H 506
**casque**   helmet, H ii. 655
**chaplet**   garland, L 753
**chase**   hunting-grounds, L 3297
**clomb**   old past tense of *climb*, H 1494; L 1382, 3872
**corse**   corpse, H 1295, 1404; L 3620
**cozening**   beguiling or defrauding, p. 305
**croft**   enclosed plot of arable land, L 1968
**dear**   precious, valuable, H 480
**dolour**   suffering, L 2814
**dolven**   (also in **dark(ly)-**, **deep-dolven**) delved, dug, H 2052; L 213, 1677, ii. 63

**dreed** endured, suffered, H 531

**drouth** (the same word in origin as *drought*) dryness, H 946, 972; **(plains of, fields of) drouth**, thirst, H 826; L 2047

**eld** old age, H ii. 595; **of eld**, of old, H 118, ii. 262

**enfurled** (in **mist-enfurled**) enveloped, swathed (in something twisted or folded), L 59, ii. 61. The word is not recorded with the prefix *en-*. Cf. **furled**, wrapped, L 1551, **unfurled**, opened out, L 404, 1591, 3986

**enow** enough, L 1304

**error** (probably) wandering, H ii. 495

**fain** gladly, H 130; L 823; glad, L ii. 368; **fain of** eager for, or well-pleased with, H 410, 458, ii. 786; **warfain** eager for war, H 386, 1664, ii. 137, **bloodfain** ii. 750; **I had fainer** I would like it better, H ii. 146

**falchion** (broad) sword, H 1217, ii. 63, 146

**fallow** golden brown, H 2106; pp. 128–9; **fallow-gold** p. 129; **fallow deer** L 86. (A distinct word from *fallow* of ground.)

**fare** journeying, H 2184

**fast** fixedly, unmovingly, H 1614 (or perhaps adjective qualifying *pondering*, deep, unbroken, cf. *fast asleep*); secure against attack, L 360

**fell** hide, L 2344, 3398, 3458, 3484, 3941, 4124, ii. 528

**fey** death-bound, L 3305; see **unfey**.

**flittermouse** bat, L 4074

**fold** land, H 765; **folds** H 533, 1632 probably the same, but perhaps 'windings'.

**force** waterfall, H 1595

**forhungered** starved, L 3076

**forwandered** worn out by wandering, H 190, 897, ii. 498; L 550, 2354

**freshets** small streams of fresh water, H 1597; L 1934

**frith** wood, woodland, H 1795; p. 132; L 896, 2264, ii. 124

**frore** frosty, H ii. 594; very cold, L 578, 1718

**garth** enclosed ground beside a house, garden, yard, H 149, ii. 313

**ghyll** deep rocky ravine, H 1498

**glaive** lance, or sword, H 322, 1210, ii. 680

**glamoury** magic, enchantment, pp. 122–3; L 2073

**gloam** twilight, p. 146

**grasses** plants, herbs, L 3122

**guerdon** recompense, H 658; L 222, 1064, 4139

**haggard** (of clothes) ragged, disordered, H 466; (of hills) wild, H 2120, L 3167; modern meaning H 1890, L 3720 (in transferred sense, **haggard hunger**, **haggard care** H 1437, L 564)

**haled** drew, pulled out, H ii. 551

**hap** fortune, lot, condition, H 340

**hest** command, H 86, 689

**hie**    hasten, H 838

**hight**    called, named, H 366, 863

**hold**    fastness, stronghold, L 52, 1702, 2457; p. 134 (or perhaps 'grasp'); refuge, L 210

**holt**    wood, copse, L 2342

**inane**    empty, void, L 3533

**keep**    central part of the stronghold, L 1677

**lambent**    of flame, playing on a surface without burning, H 1217

**lapped**    hemmed in, H 690; enfolded, H 709

**lea**    grassland, H 35, 1797, ii. 66

**leasows**    meadows, H 1797

**leeches**    physicians, L 3055, 3144

**let**    hinder, L 2019

**levin**    lightning, H 1681

**lief**    willing, L 3417; **liever** better, more delightful, H 78

**like**    please, H 90, 286, 598, 1376, ii. 226, 626 (but 'like' H 616)

**lind**    linden, lime-tree, p. 120

**loath**    hateful to, L 3419; unwilling, L 3417

**lode**    path, road, H 798

**louted**    bent, bowed, H 1520

**march**    borderland, H ii. 493; L 3672

**marge**    margin, H 1555

**mavis**    song-thrush, L ii. 74

**meed**    reward, requital, H 81, 268, 701, 793, ii. 195, 231, 604

**meet**    fitting, H 487

**mete**    deal out (used in the construction *I shall mete thee a meed, his meed was meted*) H 81, 532, 701, 1092, ii. 195

**mews**    seagulls, p. 129; **seamew** H 1551

**neb**    beak, bill, L 255, 570, ii. 381, 409

**nesh**    soft, tender, L 4220

**opes**    opens, L 3740; **oped** H 550

**or ever**    before ever, L 1821

**or . . . or**    either . . . or, H 439–40; L 54, 2886; p. 359

**outer**    utter, uttermost (?), L 2979

**palfrey**    small saddle-horse, L 3379

**parlous**    perilous, dangerous, L ii. 456

**pled**    old past tense of *plead*, L 2983

**plenilune**    full moon, p. 354

**prate**    chatter, talk to no purpose, H 501

**quick**    living, alive, H ii. 78

**quod**    (quoth), said, H 88

**quook**    old past tense of *quake*, L 3582

**recked**    cared, H 619; L ii. 629; **unrecked** unheeded, disregarded, H 1799

**redeless**    without resource, devoid of counsel, L 3427

**rive**    cleave, H 1211; past tense **rove**, L 4149

**roamed**   wandered, went (of a path or journey), H 1432; extended (?) (of regions), H 1577. (These usages appear to be unrecorded.)

**rout**   company, troop, band, L 2997

**rove**   see **rive**.

**ruel-bone**   some kind of ivory, L 2261 (cf. J. R. R. Tolkien, *Sir Gawain, Pearl, and Sir Orfeo*, translation of *Pearl* stanza 18: *And her hue as rewel ivory wan*).

**ruth**   pity, compassion, H 306, 1941, 1969, 2134, ii. 654; L 116; remorse, H 509; sorrow, H 1661

**shaws**   woods, thickets, H 647 (cf. the *Trollshaws* west of Rivendell).

**sheer**   (of light) bright, L 689; (of water) clear and pure, L 1439

**shoon**   old plural of *shoe*, L 490

**shores**   supports, props, L 3880

**sigaldry**   sorcery, L 2072 (cf. stanza 3 of the poem *Errantry*, in J. R. R. Tolkien, *The Adventures of Tom Bombadil*, 1962).

**slade**   valley, dell, H 235, 1150, 2171, ii. 561; **slades of death** H 685, 886

**slot**   track, trail (of a hunted creature), H 745, 1314

**slough**   mire, mud, H 881

**sped**   availed (attained his purpose), H 41; prospered (transitive), H 247, (intransitive) ii. 574; pressed, urged on, H 284; sent with haste, H 654

**stared**   (probably) shone, L 3132, a meaning of the verb found in the mediaeval alliterative poems: cf. J. R. R. Tolkien, *Sir Gawain, Pearl, and Sir Orfeo*, translation of *Pearl* stanza 10: *stars stare in the welkin in winter night*, where the original has *staren* with this meaning.

**strikes**   runs, flows, H 240, 520, ii. 567

**suage**   assuage, relieve, H 612

**sued**   petitioned for, appealed for, H 857

**swath**   'the space covered by a sweep of the mower's scythe' (O.E.D.), H 33, ii. 64; L 2106

**swinking**   toiling, H 784

**sylphine**   of the nature of a sylph (spirit inhabiting the air, see p. 306), L 4077. (This adjective to *sylph* is not recorded.)

**tale**   count, amount, sum, H 159, 471, ii. 326. Cf. **untold** uncounted, H ii. 678, L 12, 2251

**targe**   shield, H 131, 409, 2153, ii. 284, 785

**thewed**   in **mighty-thewed**, of great strength, with mighty sinews, H ii. 714

**thirled**   pierced, H 697

**tilth**   cultivated land, H 1798

**tors**   rocky hill-tops, H 2119

**travail**   hardship (as endured on a journey, i.e. both *travail* and *travel*), H 143, ii. 300

**unfey**   not 'fey', not fated to die, H ii. 752 (or possibly the meaning is 'not feeble, not timid', reversing another sense of *fey*). This word is apparently not recorded in English, but *ú-feigr* 'unfey' is found in Old Norse.

**unkempt**   uncombed, H 490

**unrecked**   see **recked**.

**wading**   going, passing, H 1605

**waiving**   refusing, rejecting, H ii. 154

**wallet**   bag for provisions, H 228, ii. 551

**wan**   dark, L 261, ii. 561

**wanhope**   despair, H 188

**web**   woven fabric, L 1471; used of ring-mail L 324, and of the 'weavings' of fate H ii. 13

**weeds**   clothes, H 445

**weft**   woven fabric, L 3061

**weird**   fate, doom, H 160, ii. 119, 246, 327; L 2290, 3173

**weregild**   the price to be paid in compensation for the killing of a man, varying according to his rank, L ii. 177

**whin**   gorse, L ii. 195

**wieldy**   (capable of easily wielding body or weapon), vigorous, agile, H 1765

**wildered**   lost, H 188, 204, 1316, ii. 516; p. 146; bewildered, H 774; L 641 (see p. 323).

**winding**   (1) of the motion of wind or water (without any necessary suggestion of twisting), H 769, 1857. (2) (of trumpet) blowing, H 1832

**wist**   see **wot**.

**wold**   forested hills or uplands (see p. 88), H 1816, 1992, 1994; L 1742

**wolfham(e)**   wolfskin, L 3398; pp. 271–3, 283 (see p. 271).

**woof**   woven fabric, L 4149

**wot**   (present tense of verb *wit*), know, H 204, ii. 516; past tense **wist** knew, H 160, 200, 399, ii. 327; past participle **unwist** unknown, H 257

**wrack**   (1) ruin, disaster, destruction, H 27, 629, 2036, ii. 120; p. 142. (2) seaweed, H 1569

**wrights**   craftsmen, H 300, 1147, ii. 641, 671

# INDEX

This index is made on the same lines as those to *The Book of Lost Tales* Parts I and II, and like them it is intended to provide (with only a few exceptions) complete references to all entries, and includes occasional references to passages where the person or place is not actually named. The note on the submission of the *Lay of Leithian* and *The Silmarillion* in 1937 is not indexed.

*Drûn*   Region north of Tarn Aeluin. 344, 350

*Duilin*   Father of Flinding, in the *Tale of Turambar*; with patronymic prefix *go-* > *bo-Dhuilin* 'son of Duilin'. 53. (Replaced by *Fuilin*.)

*Dungalef*   Riddling reversal of *Felagund* (replaced by *Hate*, 233). 229, 233–4

*Dungorthin, Dungortheb*   See *Nan Dungorthin*.

*Durin*   316

*Dwarves*   32, 44, 52, 56, 111, 127, 161, 264, 306 (see especially 52, 306); *dwarfland* 115, 126; adjective *dwarfen* 44, elsewhere *dwarvish*. See *Longbeard Dwarves*.

*Dweller in the Deep*   See *Ulmo*.

*Éadgifu*   Mother of Ælfwine. 140

*Eagles' Cleft*   See *Cristhorn*.

*Eärendel*   141–2, 144–5, 149; son of Fengel 141, 145. Later form *Eärendil* 83

*Eglamar*   =*Eldamar*. 157, 181–2

*Egnor*   (1) Beren's father (replaced by *Barahir*). 25, 119, 125, 159, 168–71, 198, 220, 247. (2) Son of Finrod (later Aegnor son of Finarfin), slain in the Battle of Sudden Flame. 80, 85, 138, 213, 222

*Eiglir Engrin*   The Iron Mountains. 33, 41, 49. (Replaced *Aiglir Angrin*.)

*Eilinel*   Wife of Gorlim the Unhappy; called 'the white'. 162–4, 169–70, 336–9, 350

*elanor*   Plant with golden flowers that grew in Beleriand. 333–4, 349

*Elbereth*   Sindarin name of Varda. 336, 350, 361

*Eldalië*   309

*Eldamar*   'Elfhome'. 182, 331, 348, 356–8. See *Eglamar*.

*Eldar*   138, 334, 347

*Eldarissa*   The language of the Eldar (in the period of the *Lost Tales*). 89

*Elder Days*   90, 210, 346, 349

*Eledhwen*   Name of Morwen. 92

*Elf-friends*   198

*Elfin*   As name of the language of the Eldar (opposed to Gnomish). 139. (Other uses of *elfin*, replaced by *elven* and *elvish*, are not given.)

*Elfinesse*   6, 108, 155, 174, 176, 180, 182, 190–3, 216, 228–9, 231, 241, 243, 255, 262, 264, 267, 286, 326, 360; later form *Elvenesse* 354, 360

*Elfland*   34, 134, 138, 183, 208, 234. See *Elvenland*.

*Elu (Thingol)*   Sindarin form of *Elwë (Singollo)*. 347

*Elvenesse*   See *Elfinesse*.

*Elvenland*   231, 233, 333, 346, 360, 362. See *Elfland*.

*Elves*   Selected references. Distinguished from Gnomes 11, 22; estimation of Men 7, 24; stature, and diminishment in relation to Men 44, 54; ruin of the Elves to be brought about by Men 98, 103–4; fate

*Hador* 92, 126, 343, 350; *Helm of Hador* 27 (see *Dragon-helm*).

*Haleth*, People of 91

*Halmir* (1) Son of Orodreth, slain by Orcs; called 'the hunter'. 75, 82, 91. (2) A ruler of the People of Haleth. 91

*Halog* The younger of Túrin's guardians on the journey to Doriath. 9, 11–12, 22, 25, 105–8, 110–11, 113–14, 121–5

*Hathaldir* One of the twelve companions of Barahir on Dorthonion. 335, 349

*Helcaraxë* 136

*Hells of Iron* Angband. 6, 49

*Helm of Húrin* 114–15. See *Dragon-helm*.

*Helsings* Germanic tribe ruled by Wada (Wade). 142–4; Old English *Hælsingas* 143–4

*Hidden Kingdom* Doriath. 10, 106

*Hidden People* The Elves of Doriath. 11, 16, 111, 114, 116–17. See *Woodland Elves*.

*High Faroth* See *Hills of the Hunters*.

*Hill of Death* The mound raised by the Sons of Fëanor after the Battle of Unnumbered Tears. 87. See *Mound of Slain*.

*Hills of Iron* See *Iron Hills*.

*Hills of the Hunters* The highlands west of the river Narog. 61, 88–9, 214, 222–3; *Hunters' Hills* 66, 88; *Wold of Hunters* 72, 89, *Hunters' Wold* 67, 88, 92; later names *High Faroth* 88–9, *Taur-en-Faroth* 88. The Land of the Dead that Live in the Hills of the Hunters, 61, 89

*Himling* Great height east of the Gorge of Aglon. 263, 274; later form *Himring* 274, 313, 361

*Hiradorn* =*Hirilorn*. 208

*Hirilorn* 'Queen of Beeches' in Doriath. 186, 202–3, 206–9, 312

*Hisilómë* 28, 89. See *Hithlum*.

*Hithlum* 6, 8, 10–11, 14, 16, 19–20, 24–5, 27, 29, 34, 37, 44, 54, 59–60, 62, 73, 87, 96–7, 101, 105–7, 111–17, 119, 125–6, 148, 170, 274, 284, 287, 314. See *Aryador, Dorlómin, Hisilómë, Land of Shadows, Lands of Mist*.

*Hlýda, Hlýdingaburg* (Old English) Narog, Nargothrond. 87

*Huan* 87, 107, 236, 238–9, 241–8, 251–8, 260, 263–7, 269–73, 278–9, 283–4, 287–8, 290, 294, 306, 311–12, 314, 358; *the hound of Hithlum, Huan wolf-bane* 107

*Hunters' Wold* See *Hills of the Hunters*.

*Húrin* 4, 7, 11–14, 21–7, 37, 55–6, 71, 92, 96–8, 100, 102–5, 111–15, 117, 119, 125–6 (references to Túrin as *son of Húrin* etc. are included under *Túrin*). Called *the Steadfast* 11–12; *Prince of Mithrim* 96, 103; *Lord of the Lands of Mist* 96; and see *Erithámrod, Thalion*. Earlier form *Urin* 21–2, 25 (*Urinthalion* 21).

*niphredil*    A white flower that bloomed in Doriath. 333, 349

*Nirnaith Arnediad*    'Unnumbered Tears'. 5, 102–3; later form *the Nirnaeth*. 91. (Replaced *Nirnaith Ornoth*.)

*Nirnaith Ornoth*    'Unnumbered Tears'. 5, 59, 61, 79, 84, 96, 102, 111. (Replaced by *Nirnaith Arnediad*.)

*Nirnaith Únoth*    'Unnumbered Tears'. 5, 79–80, 84–5, 102, 123. (Replaced by *Nirnaith Ornoth*.)

*Nogrod*    City of the Dwarves. 32, 45, 52, 56, 111, 127, 264, 274, 303, 306, 343

*Noldoli*    21, 24, 55, 82, 84, 90, 138, 140, 146–7, 149, 282; singular *Noldo* 53, 160. See *Noldor, Gnomes*.

*Noldor*    104, 139, 284; *Doom of the Noldor* 248; adjective *Noldorin* 83, 137, 147, 350. See *Noldoli, Gnomes*.

*Noldórinan*    Rejected name for Beleriand. 160

*Númenóreans*    269

*Oarni*    Spirits of the sea. 148

*Oath of the Fëanorians*    31, 50, 135–6 (in alliterative verse), 193, 210, 211–12 (in rhyming couplets), 216, 217 (as spoken by Celegorm), 219, 221–2, 245

*Ogbar*    Unknown; named in Beleg's 'whetting spell'. 45, 54

*Oikeroi*    A cat, thane of Tevildo, slain by Huan. 258, 270–1, 282

*Old English*    23, 87, 95, 127, 140–1 (metre), 143–5, 151, 271

*Orcs*    Passim. See *Glamhoth, Goblins, Wolfriders*. *Orc-road*, see *Taur-na-Fuin*.

*Orfalch Echor*    The ravine through the Encircling Mountains about Gondolin. 83

*Orgof*    Elf of Doriath, slain by Túrin. 18–20, 23–5, 28, 30, 51, 127

*Ormaid*    Rejected name for Tavros (Oromë), changed from *Ormain*. 195

*Orodreth*    King of Nargothrond. 65, 69–71, 75, 80, 82–6, 90–1, 138, 213, 218–19, 221–2, 229, 237, 242, 246–7, 260, 272–3, 358–9; see especially 91, 246

*Oromë*    127, 137, 198, 235–6, 248. See *Ormaid, Tauros, Tavros*.

*Ossë*    137, 148

*Ossiriand(e)*    Rejected name for Beleriand. 158–60

*Outer Lands*    The Great Lands (Middle-earth). 211, 224

*Outer Seas*    356; *outmost sea* 172

*Outer World*    The lands east of the Blue Mountains. 156, 160, 332

*Oxford*    3, 81, 94, 120, 127, 330

*Palúrien*    Yavanna. 160; Aulë's wife 139

*Peleg*    Father of Tuor in the *Lost Tales*. 145. See *Fengel* (1).

*Plains of Drouth*    Dor-na-Fauglith. 36, 55, 232; *fields of drouth* 227, 232

*Pools of Twilight*    56, 142. See *Twilight Meres, Umboth-Muilin*.

# THE SHAPING OF MIDDLE-EARTH

J. R. R. TOLKIEN

# The Shaping of Middle-earth

### THE QUENTA, THE AMBARKANTA
### AND THE ANNALS

together with
the earliest 'Silmarillion' and the first Map

Christopher Tolkien

# The Shaping of Middle-earth

# CONTENTS

# CONTENTS

# PREFACE

This book brings the 'History of Middle-earth' to some time in the 1930s: the cosmographical work *Ambarkanta* and the earliest *Annals of Valinor* and *Annals of Beleriand*, while later than the *Quenta Noldorinwa* – the 'Silmarillion' version that was written, as I believe, in 1930 – cannot themselves be more precisely dated.

This is the stage at which my father had arrived when *The Hobbit* was written. Comparison of the *Quenta* with the published *Silmarillion* will show that the essential character of the work was now fully in being; in the shape and fall of sentences, even of whole passages, the one is constantly echoed in the other; and yet the published *Silmarillion* is between three and four times as long.

After the hasty 'Sketch of the Mythology' (chapter II in this book), the *Quenta Noldorinwa* was in fact the only complete version of 'The Silmarillion' that my father ever made. Towards the end of 1937 he interrupted work on a new version, *Quenta Silmarillion*, which extended to part way through the story of Túrin Turambar, and began *The Lord of the Rings* (see *The Lays of Beleriand* pp. 364–7). When after many years he returned to the First Age, the vast extension of the world that had now come into being meant that the *Quenta Silmarillion*, which had been stopped in full flight, could not be taken up from where it fell; and though he undertook exceedingly complex revisions and enlargements of the earlier parts during the following years, he never achieved again a complete and coherent structure. Especially in its concluding chapters the *Quenta Noldorinwa* is thus one of the primary elements in the study of the work as a whole.

In the *Annals of Valinor* and the *Annals of Beleriand* are seen the beginnings of the chronological structure which was to become a central preoccupation. The Annals would develop into a separate 'tradition', parallel to and overlapping but distinct from 'The Silmarillion' proper, and (after intervening versions) emerging in the years following the completion of *The Lord of the Rings* in two chief works of the Matter of Middle-earth, the *Annals of Aman* and the *Grey Annals of Beleriand* (see pp. 262, 294). With the *Quenta* and with these earliest versions of the *Annals* I give the brief texts in Anglo-Saxon feigned to have been made by Ælfwine (Eriol) from the works that he studied in Tol Eressëa, the Lonely Isle.

The commentaries are largely concerned to relate geography, names, events, relationships and motives to what preceded and what followed; inevitably this entails a great deal of reference back to the previous books, and the text of the commentaries is hardly enticing (though being in smaller print they can be readily distinguished from the original works). My object is to try to show, and not merely impressionistically, how Middle-earth and its history was built up gradually and delicately, and how a long series of small shifts or combinations would often lead to the emergence of new and unforeseen structures – as for example in the story of Gwindor of Nargothrond (p. 180).

The arrangement of the texts of the 'Sketch of the Mythology' and the *Quenta*, split into numbered sections comparable from one text to the other, is explained on p. 11. The earlier volumes in the series are referred to as I (*The Book of Lost Tales Part I*), II (*The Book of Lost Tales Part II*), and III (*The Lays of Beleriand*).

The maps and diagrams in the book are reproduced with the permission of the Bodleian Library, Oxford, and I thank the staff of the Department of Western Manuscripts at the Bodleian for their assistance.

The fifth volume will contain my father's unfinished 'time-travel' story, *The Lost Road*, together with the earliest forms of the legend of Númenor, which were closely related to it; the *Lhammas* or Account of Tongues; the *Etymologies*; and all the writings concerned with the First Age up to the time when *The Lord of the Rings* was begun.

# I

# PROSE FRAGMENTS FOLLOWING
# THE LOST TALES

Before giving the 'Sketch of the Mythology', the earliest form of the prose
'Silmarillion', there are some brief prose texts that can be conveniently
collected here.

## (i)

Among loose papers there is an early piece, soon abandoned, entitled
*Turlin and the Exiles of Gondolin*. It will be seen that it relates closely
to the beginning of the tale of *The Fall of Gondolin* (II. 149) but at the
same time contains much that is new. That it was the beginning of a later
version of the tale is clear at once from the name *Mithrim*, for this only
replaced *Asgon* by emendation in the final text of *The Fall of Gondolin*
(II.202). This brief text reads as follows. At the first three occurrences of
the name *Turlin* in the narrative (but not in the title) it was emended to
*Turgon*; at the fourth and fifth *Turgon* was so written from the first. I
give *Turgon* throughout.

'Then' said Ilfiniol son of Bronweg 'know that Ulmo Lord of
Waters forgot never the sorrows of the Elfin kindreds beneath the
power of Melko, but he might do little because of the anger of the
other Gods who shut their hearts against the race of the Gnomes,
and dwelt behind the veiled hills of Valinor heedless of the Outer
World, so deep was their ruth and regret for the death of the Two
Trees. Nor did any save Ulmo only dread the power of Melko that
wrought ruin and sorrow over all the Earth; but Ulmo desired that
Valinor should gather all its might to quench his evil ere it be too
late, and him seemed that both purposes might perchance be
achieved if messengers from the Gnomes should win to Valinor
and plead for pardon and for pity upon the Earth; for the love of
Palúrien and Oromë her son for those wide realms did but slumber
still. Yet hard and evil was the road from the Outer Earth to
Valinor, and the Gods themselves had meshed the ways with
magic and veiled the encircling hills. Thus did Ulmo seek unceasingly to stir the Gnomes to send messengers unto Valinor, but
Melko was cunning and very deep in wisdom, and unsleeping was

his wariness in all things that touched the Elfin kindreds, and their messengers overcame not the perils and temptations of that longest and most evil of all roads, and many that dared to set forth were lost for ever.

Now tells the tale how Ulmo despaired that any of the Elfin race should surpass the dangers of the way, and of the deepest and the latest design that he then fashioned, and of those things which came of it.

In those days the greater part of the kindreds of Men dwelt after the Battle of Unnumbered Tears in that land of the North that has many names, but which the Elves of Kôr have named Hisilómë which is the Twilit Mist, and the Gnomes, who of the Elf-kin know it best, Dor-Lómin the Land of Shadows. A people mighty in numbers were there, dwelling about the wide pale waters of Mithrim the great lake that lies in those regions, and other folk named them Tunglin or folk of the Harp, for their joy was in the wild music and minstrelsy of the fells and woodlands, but they knew not and sang not of the sea. Now this folk came into those places after the dread battle, being too late summoned thither from afar, and they bore no stain of treachery against the Elfin kin; but indeed many among them clung to such friendship with the hidden Gnomes of the mountains and Dark Elves as might be still for the sorrow and mistrust born of those ruinous deeds in the Vale of Niniach. Turgon was a man of that folk, son of Peleg, son of Indor, son of [Ear >] Fengel who was their chief and hearing the summons had marched out of the deeps of the East with all his folk. But Turgon dwelt not much with his kindred, and loved rather solitude and the friendship of the Elves whose tongues he knew, and he wandered alone about the long shores of Mithrim, now hunting in its woods, now making sudden music in the rocks upon his rugged harp of wood strung with the sinews of bears. But he sang not for the ears of Men, and many hearing the power of his rough songs came from afar to hearken to his harping; [?but] Turgon left his singing and departed to lonely places in the mountains.

Many strange things he learned there, broken tidings of far off things, and longing came upon him for deeper lore, but as yet his heart turned not from the long shores, and the pale waters of Mithrim in the mists. Yet was he not fated to dwell for ever in those places, for 'tis said that magic and destiny led him on a day to a cavernous opening in the rocks down which a hidden river flowed from Mithrim. And Turgon entered that cavern seeking to learn its secret, but having entered the waters of Mithrim drave him forward into the heart of the rock and he might not win back into the light. This men have said was not without the will of Ulmo, at whose prompting may be the Gnomes had fashioned that deep and hidden way. Then came the Gnomes to Turgon and guided him along the dark passages amid the mountains until he came out once more into the light.

The text ends here (though manuscript pages written at the same time continue on another subject, see (ii) below).

*Turlin* must have been a passing shift from *Tuor* (cf. the form *Tûr* that appears in texts of *The Fall of Gondolin*, II. 148), and *Turgon* likewise; in the Tale *Turgon* is of course the name of the King of Gondolin. This curious passing transference of a primary name in the legends may be compared with the brief substitution of *Celegorm* for *Thingol* and *Maglor* for *Beren* in the *Lay of Leithian* (III. 159).

Particularly interesting is the account here of the origins of Tuor's people: they came out of the East to the Battle of Unnumbered Tears, but they came too late. This can hardly be wholly unconnected with the coming of the Easterlings before the battle in the later story. The genealogy of Tuor (Turlin, Turgon) is here 'son of Peleg son of Indor son of Fengel'. In *The Fall of Gondolin* he is 'son of Peleg son of Indor' (II. 160); in the fragment of the *Lay of the Fall of Gondolin* he is the son of Fengel, and in associated notes Tuor is himself called *Fengel* (III. 145). His people are here the *Tunglin*, the folk of the Harp, whereas in *The Fall of Gondolin* (*ibid.*) he belongs to 'the house of the Swan of the sons of the Men of the North'.

Also noteworthy is the opening of the present text where Ulmo's desires and devisings are described: his unceasing attempts to persuade the Gnomes to send messengers to Valinor, his isolation from the other Valar, his wish that the power of Valinor should go against Melko in time. There does not appear to be any other mention of Ulmo's attempting to arouse the Gnomes to send messages to Valinor; and though his isolation in his pity for the Gnomes in the Great Lands appears strongly at the beginning of the tale of *The Hiding of Valinor* (I. 209), there Manwë and Varda beside Ulmo were opposed to the withdrawal of Valinor from the fate of 'the world'.

Lastly, 'the Vale of Niniach' must be the site of the Battle of Unnumbered Tears; cf. 'the Vale (Valley) of Weeping Waters' in the outlines for *Gilfanon's Tale* (I. 239–40). *Niniach* never occurs again in this application, though the way by which Tuor went down to the sea came to be called *Cirith Ninniach*, the Rainbow Cleft.

(ii)

The manuscript *Turlin and the Exiles of Gondolin* continues (the paper and the handwriting are identical, and all were placed together) with a further text of great interest, since it represents the first step towards the later story of the coming of the Noldor to Middle-earth since the outlines for *Gilfanon's Tale* (I. 237 ff.). This was hastily pencilled and is in places difficult to make out.

Then Gelmir king of the Gnomes marshalled his unhappy folk and he said to them: 'We are come at last to the Great Lands and have set our feet upon the Earth, and not even Elf-wisdom may yet say what shall come of it; but the torment and the pain and the tears that we have borne in the way hither shall be sung in song and told in tale by all the folk of the Elfin race hereafter; yea and even among other children of Ior shall some remember it.'

Long time did the Gnome-folk dwell nigh those westward shores in the northern regions of the Earth; and their anguish was lessened. Some were there that fared far afield and gained know-ledge of the lands about, and they sought ever to know whither Melko had fled, or where was hidden the gems and treasury of Valinor. [*Struck out*: Then did Gelmir marshal his hosts and three great armies had he, and Golfin his son was captain of the one, and Delin his son of a second, [Oleg >] Lúthien his son of the third, but Gelmir was lord and king.] Thereafter did all the folk move onward to the East and somewhat South, and all the armies of Golfin and of Delin moved ahead unhampered. Now the ice melted, and the snow [?thinned], and the trees grew deep upon the hills, and their hearts knew comfort, till their harps and elfin pipes awoke once more. Then did the rocks ring with the sweet music of the Elves, and countless [?coming] of their many feet; new flowers sprang behind those armies as they trod, for the earth was glad of the coming of the Gnomes, nor had the sun or the white moon yet seen fairer things in those places than their moving field of glinting spears and their goldwrought elfin armoury. But the women and the Gnome-maids and Gnome-children sang as they journeyed after, and no such clear song of hope have the lands heard since, yet was it sad and boding beside that singing that was heard upon [Kôr >] the hill of Tûn while the Two Trees blossomed still.

Of all those scouts and scattered hosts that went far ahead or upon either side of the marching Gnomes none were more eager or burnt with greater fire than Fëanor the gem-smith and his seven sons; but nothing did they discover yet, and came the Gnomes at length unto that magic northern land of which tales often speak, and by reason of its dark woods and grey mountains and its deep mists the Gnomes named Dor Lómin land of shadows. There lies a lake, Mithrim whose mighty waters reflect a pale image of the encircling hills. Here did the Gnomes rest once more a great while, and Gelmir let build dwellings for the folk about the shores and shoreland woods, but there too he numbered and marshalled all his hosts both of spearmen, and bowmen, and of swordsmen, for no lack of arms did the Gnomes bring out of Valinor and the armouries of Makar to their war with Melko. And three great armies had Gelmir under his lordship, and Golfin his son was captain of one, and Delin his son of another, and Lúthien (not that Lúthien of the Roses who is of another and a later tale) of a third; and Golfin's might was in swordsmen, and Delin had more of those who bore the long . . . . elfin spears, but Lúthien's joy was in the number and . . . . . of his bowmen – and the bow has ever been the weapon wherein the Elf-kin has had the most wondrous skill. Now the colours of the Gnomes were gold and white in those ancient days in memory of the Two Trees, but Gelmir's standard bore upon a silver field a crown of gold, and each captain had a fair banner; and the sign of Golfin in those days was upon gold a silver sword, and of Delin a green beech leaf upon silver diapered with golden flowers, and of Lúthien a golden swallow that winged through an azure field as it were the sky set with silver stars, and the sons of Fëanor wrought that standard and those banners, and they shone by sunlight and by mist and by moonlight and by starless dark by the light of the Gnome-wrought gems that sewed them [sic].

Now it happened on a while that Fëanor got him beyond to the hills that girt Dor Lómin in those parts [northward of >] beyond Artanor where there were open empty lands and treeless hills, and he had no small company and three of his sons were with him. Thus came they on a day nigh evening to a hilltop, and afar off descried a red light leaping in a vale open on that side that looked toward [?them]. Then Fëanor wondered what this fire might be, and he and his folk marched in the still night swiftly thereto, so that ere dawn they looked down into that vale. There saw they an armed company no less than their own, and they sat around a mighty fire of wood. The most were asleep, but some few stirred, and Fëanor stood then up and called in his clear voice so that the dark vale rang: 'Who be ye; men of the Gnomes or other what – say swiftly for 'tis best for [you to] know the children of Fëanor compass you around.'

Then a great clamour broke forth in the vale and the folk of

Fëanor knew full soon that here were no elfin folk, by reason of their harsh voices and unlovely cries, and many arrows came winging in the dark towards that voice, but Fëanor was no longer there. Swiftly had he gone and drawn the most of his folk before the vale's mouth whence a stream issued forth tree-hung

Here the text ends abruptly and near the top of a new page; it is clear that no more was written.

The Noldorin house has still not emerged, but we have a king *Gelmir* of the Gnomes, with his sons *Golfin, Delin, Lúthien* (the last emended from *Oleg*), captains of his three armies. There is no suggestion that Fëanor and his sons were associated with these in any sort of close kinship. In the fragment of the *Lay of the Fall of Gondolin* (see III. 146–7) there appears – for the first time – *Fingolfin*, who steps into Finwë Nólemë's place as the father of Turgon and Isfin, but is not the son of Finwë, rather of *Gelmir*. I have suggested there that this Gelmir, father of Golfin/Fingolfin, is to be identified with Finwë, father of Fingolfin in the alliterative poems and later; and it may be that the name *Gelmir* is formally connected with *Fin-golma*, which in the outlines for *Gilfanon's Tale* is another name for Finwë Nólemë (I. 238–9, and see I. 263, entry *Nólemë*). It is to be remembered that Finwë Nóleme was not in the earliest legend the father of Fëanor and was not slain by Melko in Valinor, but came to the Great Lands. – Of the other sons of Gelmir named in the present text, Delin and Lúthien, there is no trace elsewhere.

It is certainly clear that *Golfin* here is the first appearance of Fingolfin, and by the same token that this text preceded the abandoned beginning of the *Lay of the Fall of Gondolin*. On the other hand, the obscure story of the death of Fëanor in the earliest outlines (I. 238–9) has disappeared, and though the present text breaks off too soon for certainty it seems extremely probable that, had my father continued it a little further, we should have learned of Fëanor's death in battle with the Orcs whom he and his companions had aroused in the valley where they were encamped. It may be, too, that we should have had an explanation of the puzzling lines of the Lay (III. 146):

'Twas the bent blades of the Glamhoth that drank Fingolfin's life as he stood alone by Fëanor.

We are in any case here still a long way from the story of the divided hosts and the treachery of Fëanor.

The encampment of Mithrim (Asgon) is referred to already in the early outlines, but in the later of these there is mention (I. 239) of the first devising of weapons by the Gnomes at this time, whereas in the present text they are said to have brought great store of arms 'out of Valinor and the armouries of Makar'. Here also appears the earliest form of the idea of the flowers springing beneath the marching feet of the Gnomish host.

A characteristic heraldry appears in the armies led by Gelmir's sons, all in gold and silver, in memory of the Two Trees – the banners made (curiously enough) by the sons of Fëanor. In the 'Sketch of the Mythology' the banners of Fingolfin were in blue and silver, as they remained (p. 22).

The name *Ior*, which occurs at the beginning of the text in the expression 'among other children of Ior' (as opposed to 'the Elfin race') and seems therefore to refer to Ilúvatar, occurs elsewhere only in a quite different reference: it is given in the early Gnomish dictionary as the equivalent of Qenya *Ivárë*, 'the famous "piper of the sea"'.

## (iii)

Thirdly and lastly, an isolated slip of paper contains a most curious trace of a stage in development between *The Flight of the Noldoli* in the *Lost Tales* and the 'Sketch of the Mythology'.

The Trees stand dark. The Plain is full of trouble. The Gnomes gather by torchlight in Tûn or Côr; Fëanor laments Bruithwir (Felegron) [*emended to* (Feleor)] his father, bids Gnomes depart & seek Melko and their treasures – he longs for the Silmarils – Finweg & Fingolfin speak against him. The Gnomes shout and prepare to depart. The Solosimpi refuse: the wise words of Ethlon (Dimlint). Foamriders [?beaches]. The threats of Fëanor to march to Cú nan Eilch. The arch, the lamplit quays; they seize the boats. One Gilfanon sees his mighty swanwinged swan-feather boat with red oars [?going] & he & his sons run to the arch and threaten the Gnomes. The fight on the arch & Gilfanon's [?curse] ere they throw him into the waves. The Gnomes reach Fangros & repent – burn the boats.

Here Bruithwir (with the additional name Felegron > Feleor) is still the father of Fëanor as in the *Lost Tales*; but Fingolfin and Finweg have emerged, and speak against Fëanor (it is not clear whether Finweg here is Fingolfin's father (Finwë) or Fingolfin's son (later Fingon): see III. 137–8, 146). Narrative features that were never taken up in the later development of 'The Silmarillion' here make their only appearance. What lay behind 'the wise words of Ethlon (Dimlint)' and 'the threats of Fëanor to march to Cú nan Eilch' has now vanished without trace. The name *Fangros* appears once elsewhere, in the alliterative *Children of Húrin*, III. 31 line 631 (earlier *Fangair*), where there is a reference to a song, or songs, being sung

> of the fight at Fangros,    and Fëanor's sons'
> oath unbreakable

(the fight and the oath need not be in any way connected). But whatever happened at Fangros is lost beyond recall; and nowhere later is there any suggestion that the burning of the ships arose from repentance. In the *Lost Tales* (I. 168) the Gnomes 'abandoned their stolen ships' when they made the passage of the Ice; Sorontur reported to Manwë (I. 177) that he had seen 'a fleet of white ships that drifted empty in the gales, and some were burning with bright fires'; and Manwë 'knew thereby that the Noldoli were gone for ever and their ships burned or abandoned'.

Lastly, *Gilfanon* appears as an Elf of Alqualondë, one of those hurled by the Gnomes into the sea, though it is not said that he was drowned. Gilfanon of Tavrobel was a Gnome (I. 174–5); and it seems virtually certain that the two Gilfanons were not the same. In that case it is most probable that the Elf of Tavrobel had ceased to be so named; though he had not, as I think, ceased to exist (see p. 274).

# II
# THE EARLIEST 'SILMARILLION'
## (The 'Sketch of the Mythology')

I have earlier (III. 3) given an account of this text, but I repeat the essentials of it here. On the envelope containing the manuscript my father wrote at some later time:

> Original 'Silmarillion'. Form orig[inally] composed c. 1926–30 for R. W. Reynolds to explain background of 'alliterative version' of Túrin & the Dragon: then in progress (unfinished) (begun c. 1918).

The 'Sketch' represents a new starting-point in the history of 'The Silmarillion'; for while it is a quite brief synopsis, the further written development of the prose form proceeded from it in a direct line. It is clear from details that need not be repeated here that it was originally written in 1926 (after the *Lay of the Children of Húrin* had been abandoned, III. 3); but it was afterwards revised, in places very heavily, and this makes it a difficult text to present in a way that is both accurate and readily comprehensible. The method I have adopted is to give the text exactly as it was first written (apart from a very few slight alterations of expression in no way affecting the narrative, which are adopted silently into the text), but to break it up into short sections, following each with notes giving the later changes made in that section. I must emphasize that there is no manuscript warrant for the 19 divisions so made: it is purely a matter of convenience of presentation. This method has certain advantages: the later changes can be readily compared with the original text immediately preceding; and since the following version of 'The Silmarillion', the *Quenta*, has been treated in the same way and divided into corresponding numbered sections, passages of the one can be easily related to those in the other.

The later changes are referenced by numbers that begin with 1 in each section. The commentary follows at the end of the complete text, and is related to the numbered sections.

## Sketch of the mythology with especial reference to the 'Children of Húrin'

### 1

After the despatch of the Nine Valar for the governance of the world Morgoth (Demon of Dark) rebels against the overlordship of Manwë, overthrows the lamps set up to illumine the world, and floods the isle where the Valar (or Gods) dwelt. He fortifies a palace of dungeons in the North. The Valar remove to the uttermost West, bordered by the Outer Seas and the final Wall, and eastward by the towering Mountains of Valinor which the Gods built. In Valinor they gather all light and beautiful things, and build their mansions, gardens, and city, but Manwë and his wife Bridhil have halls upon the highest mountain (Timbrenting or Tindbrenting in English, Tengwethil in Gnomish, Taníquetil in Elfin) whence they can see across the world to the dark East. Ifan Belaurin[1] plants the Two Trees in the middle of the plain of Valinor outside the gates of the city of Valmar. They grow under her songs, and one has dark green leaves with shining silver beneath, and white blossoms like the cherry from which a dew of silver light falls; the other has golden-edged leaves of young green like the beech and yellow blossom like the hanging blossoms of laburnum which give out heat and blazing light. Each tree waxes for seven[2] hours to full glory and then wanes for seven; twice a day therefore comes a time of softer light when each tree is faint and their light is mingled.

1   *Yavanna Palúrien* added in the margin.
2   At both occurrences of *seven* in this sentence my father first wrote *six*, but changed it in the act of writing the manuscript.

## 2

The Outer Lands are in darkness. The growth of things was checked when Morgoth quenched the lamps. There are forests of darkness, of yew and fir and ivy. There Oromë sometimes hunts, but in the North Morgoth and his demonic broods (Balrogs) and the Orcs (Goblins, also called Glamhoth or people of hate) hold sway. Bridhil looks on the darkness and is moved, and taking all the hoarded light of Silpion (the white tree) she makes and strews the stars.

At the making of the stars the children of Earth awake – the Eldar (or Elves). They are found by Oromë dwelling by the star-lit pool (Cuiviénen, water of awakening) in the East. He rides home to Valinor filled with their beauty and tells the Valar, who are reminded of their duty to the Earth, since they came thither knowing that their office was to govern it for the two races of Earth who should after come each in appointed time. There follows an expedition to the fortress of the North (Angband, Iron-hell), but this is now too strong for them to destroy. Morgoth is nonetheless taken captive, and consigned to the halls of Mandos who dwelt in the North of Valinor.

The Eldalië (people of the Elves) are invited to Valinor for fear of the evil things of Morgoth that still wandered in the dark. A great march is made by the Eldar from the East led by Oromë on his white horse. The Eldar are divided into three hosts, one under Ingwë (Ing) after called the Quendi (or Elves proper, or Light-elves), one under Finwë (Finn) after called the Noldoli (Gnomes or Deep-elves), one under Elwë (Elu) after called the Teleri (Sea-elves, or Solosimpi, the Shoreland Pipers or Foam-riders). Many of them are lost upon the march and wander in the woods of the world, becoming after the various hosts of Ilkorindi (Elves who never dwelt in Côr in Valinor). The chief of these was Thingol, who heard Melian and her nightingales singing and was enchanted and fell asleep for an age. Melian was one of the divine maidens of the Vala Lórien who sometimes wandered into the outer world. Melian and Thingol became Queen and King of woodland Elves in Doriath, living in a hall called the Thousand Caves.

## 3

The other Elves came to the ultimate shores of the West. In the North these in those days sloped westward in the North until only a narrow sea divided them from the land of the Gods, and this narrow sea was filled with grinding ice. But at the point to which the Elf-hosts came a wide dark sea stretched west.

There were two Valar of the Sea. Ulmo (Ylmir), the mightiest of all Valar next to Manwë, was lord of all waters, but dwelt often in Valinor, or in the 'Outer Seas'. Ossë and the lady Óin,[1] whose tresses lay through all the sea, loved rather the seas of the world that washed the shores beneath the Mountains of Valinor. Ylmir uprooted the half-sunk island where the Valar had first dwelt, and embarking on it the Noldoli and Qendi, who arrived first, bore them to Valinor. The Teleri dwelt some time by the shores of the sea awaiting him, and hence their love of it. While they were being also transported by Ylmir, Ossë in jealousy and out of love for their singing chained the island to the sea-bottom far out in the

Bay of Faërie whence the Mountains of Valinor could dimly be seen. No other land was near it, and it was called the Lonely Isle. There the Teleri dwelt a long age becoming different in tongue, and learning strange music of Ossë, who made the sea-birds for their delight.

The Gods gave a home in Valinor to the other Eldar. Because they longed even among the Tree-lit gardens of Valinor for a glimpse of the stars, a gap was made in the encircling mountains, and there in a deep valley a green hill, Côr, was built. This was lit from the West by the Trees, to the East it looked out onto the Bay of Faërie and the Lonely Isle, and beyond to the Shadowy Seas. Thus some of the blessed light of Valinor filtered into the Outer Lands, and falling on the Lonely Isle caused its western shores to grow green and fair.

On the top of Côr the city of the Elves was built and called Tûn. The Qendi became most beloved by Manwë and Bridhil, the Noldoli by Aulë (the Smith) and Mandos the wise. The Noldoli invented gems and made them in countless numbers, filling all Tûn with them, and all the halls of the Gods.[2]

The greatest in skill and magic of the Noldoli was Finn's second son Fëanor. (His elder son Fingolfin[3] whose son was Finnweg comes into the tale later.) He contrived three jewels (Silmarils) wherein a living fire combined of the light of the Two Trees was set, they shone of their own light, impure hands were burned by them.

The Teleri seeing afar the light of Valinor were torn between desire to rejoin their kindred and to dwell by the sea. Ylmir taught them craft of boat-building. Ossë yielding gave them swans, and harnessing many swans to their boats they sailed to Valinor, and dwelt there on the shores where they could see the light of the Trees, and go to Valmar if they wished, but could sail and dance in the waters touched to light by the radiance that came out past Côr. The other Eldar gave them many gems, especially opals and diamonds and other pale crystals which were strewn upon the beaches of the Bay of Faërie. They themselves invented pearls. Their chief town was Swanhaven upon the shores northward of the pass of Côr.

★

1  *Uinen* pencilled against *Óin*.
2  The following passage was afterwards added here:

Since the Gnomes or Noldoli afterwards came back into the Great Lands, and these tales deal mostly with them, it may here be said that Lord or King of the Noldoli was Finn. His sons were Fëanor, Fingolfin, and Finrod. Of whom Fëanor was the most skilful, the deepest in lore, Fingolfin the mightiest and most valiant, Finrod the fairest, and the most wisehearted and gentle. The seven sons of Fëanor were Maidros the tall; Maglor a musician and mighty singer whose voice carried far over hill and sea; Curufin the crafty who inherited most of his father's skill; Celegorm the fair; Cranthir the dark; and Damrod and Díriel who after were great hunters. The sons of Fingolfin were Finweg who was after the king of the Noldoli in the North of the world, and Turgon of Gondolin; and his daughter was Isfin the white. The sons of Finrod were Orodreth, Felagoth, Anrod, and Egnor.

In the last sentence *Felagoth* > *Felagund*, and *Orodreth* moved to stand after *Felagund*.

3  *Finn's second son Fëanor* and *His elder son Fingolfin* > *Finn's elder son Fëanor* and *His second son Fingolfin* (an early change, quite possibly made at the time of the writing of the manuscript).

## 4

The Gods were now beguiled by Morgoth, who having passed seven ages in the prisons of Mandos in gradually lightened pain came before the conclave of the Gods in due course. He looks with greed and malice upon the Eldar, who also sit there about the knees of the Gods, and lusts especially after the jewels. He dissembles his hatred and desire for revenge. He is allowed a humble dwelling in Valinor, and after a while goes freely about Valinor, only Ylmir foreboding ill, while Tulcas the strong who first captured him watches him. Morgoth helps the Eldar in many deeds, but slowly poisons their peace with lies.

He suggests that the Gods brought them to Valinor out of jealousy, for fear their marvellous skill, and magic, and beauty, should grow too strong for them outside in the world. The Qendi and Teleri are little moved, but the Noldoli, the wisest of the Elves, become affected. They begin at whiles to murmur against the Gods and their kindred; they are filled with vanity of their skill.[1]

Most of all does Morgoth fan the flames of the heart of Fëanor, but all the while he lusts for the immortal Silmarils, although Fëanor has cursed for ever anyone, God or Elf or mortal that shall come hereafter, who touches them. Morgoth lying tells Fëanor that Fingolfin and his son Finnweg are plotting to usurp the leadership of the Gnomes from Fëanor and his sons, and to gain the Silmarils. A quarrel breaks out between the sons of Finn. Fëanor is summoned before the Gods, and the lies of Morgoth laid bare. Fëanor is banished from Tûn, and with him goes Finn who loves Fëanor best of his sons, and many of the Gnomes. They build a treasury Northward in Valinor in the hills near Mandos' halls. Fingolfin rules the Gnomes that are left in Tûn. Thus Morgoth's words seem justified and the bitterness he sowed goes on after his words are disproved. .

Tulcas is sent to put Morgoth in chains once more, but he escapes through the pass of Côr into the dark region beneath the feet of Timbrenting called Arvalin, where the shadow is thickest in all the world. There he finds Ungoliant, Gloomweaver, who dwells in a cleft of the mountains, and sucks up light or shining things to spin them out again in webs of black and choking darkness, fog, and gloom. With her he plots revenge. Only a terrible reward will bring her to dare the dangers of Valinor or the sight of the Gods. She weaves a dense gloom about her to protect her and swings on cords from pinnacle to pinnacle till she has scaled the highest peak of the mountains in the south of Valinor (little guarded because of their height and their distance from the old fortress of Morgoth). She makes a ladder that Morgoth can scale. They creep into Valinor. Morgoth stabs the Trees and Ungoliant sucks up their juices, belching forth clouds of blackness. The Trees succumb slowly to the poisoned sword, and to the venomous lips of Ungoliant.

The Gods are dismayed by a twilight at midday, and vapours of black float in about the ways of the city. They are too late. The Trees die while they wail about them. But Tulcas and Oromë and many others hunt on horseback in the gathering gloom for Morgoth. Wherever Morgoth goes there the confusing darkness is greatest owing to the webs of Ungoliant. Gnomes from the treasury of Finn come in and report that Morgoth is assisted by a spider of darkness. They had seen them making for the North. Morgoth had stayed his flight at the Treasury, slain Finn and many of his men, and carried off the Silmarils and a vast hoard of the most splendid jewels of the Elves.

In the meanwhile Morgoth escapes by Ungoliant's aid northward and crosses the Grinding Ice. When he has regained the northern regions of the world Ungoliant summons him to pay the other half of her reward. The first half was the sap of the Trees of

Light. Now she claims one half of the jewels. Morgoth yields them up and she devours them. She is now become monstrous, but he will not give her any share in the Silmarils. She enmeshes him in a black web, but he is rescued by the Balrogs with whips of flame, and the hosts of the Orcs; and Ungoliant goes away into the uttermost South.

Morgoth returns to Angband, and his power and the numbers of his demons and Orcs becomes countless. He forges an iron crown and sets therein the Silmarils, though his hands are burned black by them, and he is never again free from the pain of the burning. The crown he never leaves off for a moment, and he never leaves the deep dungeons of his fortress, governing his vast armies from his deep throne.

★

1 Added here:

which Morgoth flatters. The Gods knew also of the coming of mortals or Men that was to be. They had not yet told the Elves, for the time was not near, nor explained what was to be the realm of each race, and their relations. Morgoth tells of Men, and suggests that the Gods are keeping the Elves captive, so that weaker Men shall be controlled more easily by the Gods, and the Elves defrauded of their kingdoms.

This was an early addition, probably not materially later than the writing of the manuscript.

## 5

When it became clear that Morgoth had escaped the Gods assemble about the dead Trees and sit in the darkness stricken and dumb for a long while, caring about nothing. The day which Morgoth chose for his attack was a day of festival throughout Valinor. Upon this day it was the custom of the chief Valar and many of the Elves, especially the people of Ing (the Quendi), to climb the long winding paths in endless procession to Manwë's halls upon Timbrenting. All the Quendi and some of the Noldoli (who under Fingolfin dwelt still in Tûn) had gone to Timbrenting, and were singing upon its topmost height when the watchers from afar descried the fading of the Trees. Most of the Noldoli were in the plain, and the Teleri upon the shore. The fogs and darkness drift in now off the seas through the pass of Côr as the Trees die. Fëanor summons the Gnomes to Tûn (rebelling against his banishment).[1]

There is a vast concourse on the square on the summit of Côr about the tower of Ing, lit by torches. Fëanor makes a violent speech, and though his wrath is for Morgoth his words are in part the fruit of Morgoth's lies.[2] He bids the Gnomes fly in the darkness while the Gods are wrapped in mourning, to seek freedom in the world and to seek out Morgoth, now Valinor is no more blissful than the earth outside.[3] Fingolfin and Finweg speak against him.[4] The assembled Gnomes vote for flight, and Fingolfin and Finweg yield; they will not desert their people, but they retain command over a half of the people of the Noldoli.[5]

The flight begins.[6] The Teleri will not join. The Gnomes cannot escape without boats, and do not dare to cross the Grinding Ice. They attempt to seize the swan-ships in Swanhaven, and a fight ensues (the first between the races of the Earth) in which many Teleri are slain, and their ships carried off. A curse is pronounced upon the Gnomes, that they shall after suffer often from treachery and the fear of treachery among their own kindred in punishment for the blood spilled at Swanhaven.[7] They sail North along the coast of Valinor. Mandos sends an emissary, who speaking from a high cliff hails them as they sail by, and warns them to return, and when they will not speaks the 'Prophecy of Mandos' concerning the fate of after days.[8]

The Gnomes come to the narrowing of the seas, and prepare to sail. While they are encamped upon the shore Fëanor and his sons and people sail off taking with them all the boats, and leave Fingolfin on the far shore treacherously, thus beginning the Curse of Swanhaven. They burn the boats as soon as they land in the East of the world, and Fingolfin's people see the light in the sky. The same light also tells the Orcs of the landing.

Fingolfin's people wander miserably. Some under Fingolfin return to Valinor[9] to seek the Gods' pardon. Finweg leads the main host North, and over the Grinding Ice. Many are lost.

1   As originally written, this sentence began *Finn and Fëanor summon* &c. This was a mere slip, since Finn's death has already been mentioned in the text as first written (§4), and my father later struck out *Finn and*. He left the plural verb *summon* and *their banishment*; this I have changed to *his banishment*, since it is not said of

the Gnomes who accompanied Fëanor that they left Tûn under
banishment (though this is not said of Finn either). The *Quenta* has
*his banishment* in this passage (p. 94).

2   Added here hastily in pencil:

He claims the lordship as eldest son now Finn is dead, in spite of
the Gods' decree.

[Except for the later pencilled alteration given in note 5, all the changes
noted below, mostly concerned to introduce the part of Finrod in the
events, were made at the same time, in red ink. Finrod, the third son of
Finn/Finwë, appears in the interpolated passage given in §3 note 2.]

3   Added here:

Fëanor and his sons take the unbreakable oath by Timbrenting and
the names of Manwë and Briðil to pursue anyone, Elf, Mortal, or
Orc, who holds the Silmarils.

4   Added here:

Finrod tries to calm their conflicting anger, but his sons Orodreth,
Anrod, and Egnor side with the sons of Fëanor.

5   *a half of the people of the Noldoli* > *a half of the Noldoli of Tûn*
(later pencilled change).

6   Added here but then struck out (see note 7):

Finrod does not go, but bids Felagoth (and his other sons) go and
cherish the Gnomes of his [?house].

7   Added here:

Finrod is slain at Swanhaven in trying to stay the violence.

This was also struck out (see note 6) and a third version of Finrod's
part entered:

Finrod and his sons were not at Swanhaven. They leave Tûn
reluctantly, and more than the others carry away memories of it,
and even many fair things made there by hands.

8   Added here:

and the curse of war against one another because of Swanhaven.

9   This passage, from *Fingolfin's people wander*, changed to read:

Finrod and his people arrive. The people of Finrod and Fingolfin
wander miserably. Some under Finrod return to Valinor, &c.

## 6

In the meanwhile Manwë summons Ifan Belaurin to the council. Her magic will not avail to cure the Trees. But Silpion under her spells bears one last great silver bloom, and Laurelin one great golden fruit. The Gods fashion the Moon and Sun from these and set them to sail appointed courses from West to East, but afterwards they find it safer to send them in Ylmir's care through the caverns and grottoes beneath the Earth, to rise in the East and come home again high in the air over the mountains of the West, to sink after each journey into the waters of the Outer Seas.

The light of Valinor is henceforth not much greater than that now scattered over the Earth, save that here the ships of Sun and Moon come nearer to Earth, and rest for a while close to Valinor. The Gods and Elves look forward to a future time when the 'magic sun and moon' of the Trees may be rekindled and the old beauty and bliss renewed. Ylmir foretells[1] that it will only be achieved with the aid of the second race of earth. But the Gods, even Manwë, pay little heed to him. They are wroth and bitter because of the slaying at Swanhaven[2] and they fortify all Valinor making the mountains impenetrable, save at Côr which the remaining Elves are commanded to guard, ceaselessly and for ever, and let no bird or beast or Elf or Man land on the shores of Faëry. The magic isles, filled with enchantment, are strung across the confines of the Shadowy Seas, before the Lonely Isle is reached sailing West, to entrap any mariners and wind them in everlasting sleep and enchantment.[3] The Gods sit now behind the mountains and feast, and dismiss the rebel and fugitive Noldoli from their hearts. Ylmir alone remembers them, and gathers news of the outer world through all the lakes and rivers.

At the rising of the first Sun the younger children of earth awoke in the far East. No god came to guide them, but the messages of Ylmir little understood came at whiles to them. They meet Ilkorindi and learn speech and other things of them, and become great friends of the Eldalië. They spread through the earth, wandering West and North.

1    *Ylmir foretells* changed at the time of writing from *Bridhil foretells*

2    Added here (hastily in pencil):

    and the flight and ingratitude of the Gnomes

3   Added here:

> Thus the many emissaries of the Gnomes in after days never reach Valinor.

# 7

Now begins the time of the great wars of the powers of the North (Morgoth and his hosts against Men, Ilkorins, and the Gnomes from Valinor). Morgoth's cunning and lies, and the curse of Swanhaven (as well as the oaths of the sons of Fëanor who swore the unbreakable oath by Timbrenting to treat all as foes who had the Silmarils in keeping) in these wars do the greatest injury to Men and Elves.

These stories only tell a part of the deeds of those days, especially such as relate to the Gnomes and the Silmarils, and the mortals who became entangled in their fates. In the early days Eldar and Men were of nearly equal stature and power of body, but the Eldar were blessed with greater wit, skill, and beauty; and those (the Gnomes) who had dwelt in Côr (Koreldar) as much surpassed the Ilkorins as they surpassed mortals. Only in the realm of Doriath, whose queen was of divine race, did the Ilkorins equal the Koreldar. The Elves were immortal, and free from all sickness.[1] But they might be slain with weapons in those days,[2] and then their spirits went back to the halls of Mandos and awaited a thousand years, or the pleasure of the Gods, before they were recalled to free life.[3] Men from the first though slightly bigger were more frail, more easily slain, subject to ills, and grew old and died, if not slain. What happened to their spirits was not known to the Eldalië. They did not go to the halls of Mandos, and many thought their fate was not in the hands of the Valar after death. Though many, associating with Eldar, believed that their spirits went to the western land, this was not true. Men were not born again.[4]

In after days when owing to the triumph of Morgoth Men and Elves became estranged the Eldalië living in the world faded, and Men usurped the sunlight. The Eldar wandered, such as remained in the Outer Lands, took to the moonlight and starlight, the woods and caves.

★

1  *free from all sickness* > *free from death by sickness* (early change, made at the same time as that given in note 4).

2   Added (rough pencilled insertion): *or waste away of sorrow,*
3   Added at the same time as the insertion given in note 2: *and they were reborn in their children, so that the number grows not.*
4   This passage, from *They did not go to the halls of Mandos*, was struck out and replaced by the following:

> They went to the halls of Mandos, but not the same as the halls of awaiting where the Elves were sent. There they too waited, but it was said that only Mandos knew whither they went after the time in his halls – they were never reborn on Earth, and none ever came back from Mandos, save only Beren son of Barahir, who thereafter spoke not to mortal Men. Their fate after death was perchance not in the hands of the Valar.

# 8

But in these days they were kindred and allies. Before the rising of the Sun and Moon Fëanor and his sons marched into the North and sought for Morgoth. A host of Orcs aroused by the burning ships resisted them and was defeated in the First Battle with such loss that Morgoth pretended to treat with them. Fëanor refused, but he was wounded in the fight by a Balrog chief (Gothmog), and died. Maidros the tall, the elder son, induced the Gnomes to meet Morgoth (with as little intent of faith on his side as on Morgoth's). Morgoth took Maidros captive and tortured him, and hung him from a rock by his right hand. The six remaining sons of Fëanor (Maglor, Celegorm, Curufin, Damrod, Díriel, and Cranthir) are encamped about the lake Mithrim in Hisilómë (Hithlum, or Dorlómin, the land of shadows in the North-west), when they hear of the march of Finweg and his men[1] who have crossed the Grinding Ice. The Sun rises as they march, their blue and silver banners are unfurled, flowers spring beneath the feet of their armies. The Orcs dismayed at the light retreat to Angband. But there is little love between the two hosts of Gnomes encamped now on opposite shores of Mithrim. Vast smokes and vapours are made and sent forth from Angband, and the smoking top of Thangorodrim (the highest of the Iron Mountains around Morgoth's fortress) can be seen from far away. The North shakes with the thunder under the earth. Morgoth is forging armouries. Finweg resolves to heal the feud. Alone he goes in search of Maidros. Aided by the vapours, which are now floating down and filling Hithlum, and by the withdrawal of Orcs and Balrogs to Angband, he finds him, but cannot release him.

Manwë, to whom birds bring news upon Timbrenting of all things which his farsighted eyes do not see upon earth, fashions the race of eagles, and sends them under their king Thorndor to dwell in the crags of the North and watch Morgoth. The eagles dwell out of reach of Orc and Balrog, and are great foes of Morgoth and his people. Finweg meets Thorndor who bears him to Maidros. There is no releasing the enchanted bond upon his wrist. In his agony he begs to be slain, but Finweg cuts off his hand, and they are both borne away by Thorndor, and come to Mithrim. The feud is healed by the deed of Finweg (except for the oath of the Silmarils).

1  *the march of Finweg and his men* > *the march of Fingolfin and his sons and his men and Felagoth and the sons of Finrod* (This change belongs with those made in red ink in §5 and concerns the shift from Fingolfin to Finrod as the Gnomish lord who returned to Valinor, see §5 note 9.)

## 9

The Gnomes march forward and beleaguer Angband. They meet Ilkorins and Men. At that time Men already dwelt in the woods of the North, and Ilkorins also. They long warred with Morgoth.[1] Of Ilkorin race was Barahir and his son Beren. Of mortal race was Húrin son of Gumlin, whose wife was Morwen;[2] they lived in the woods upon the borders of Hithlum. These come after into the tales.

Morgoth sends out his armies and breaks the leaguer of Angband, and from that time the fortunes of his enemies decline.[3] Gnomes and Ilkorins and Men are scattered, and Morgoth's emissaries go among them with lying promises and false suggestions of the greed and treachery of each to each. Because of the curse of Swanhaven these often are believed by the Gnomes.

Celegorm and Curufin found the realm of Nargothrond on the banks of the Narog in the south of the Northern lands.[4] Many Gnomes take service with Thingol and Melian of the Thousand Caves in Doriath. Because of the divine magic of Melian Doriath is the safest from the raids of the Orcs, and it is prophesied that only treachery from within will cause the realm to fall.

★

[This section was substantially interpolated and altered (all in red ink, see §5, except for the change given in note 2).]

1   Added here:

> This is the time of Morgoth's retreat, and the growth and prosperity of Men, a time of growth and birth and flowering known as the 'Siege of Angband'.

2   This passage, from *Of Ilkorin race*, was emended to read:

> In later times of mortal race was Barahir and his son Beren. Of mortal race also were Húrin and Huor sons of Gumlin. Húrin's wife was Morwen, &c.

3   Here was added *The men of Barahir rescue Celegorm*, but this was struck out and the following insertion made:

> In the Leaguer of Angband Fingolfin's host guards the North-west on borders of Hithlum; Felagoth [> Felagund] and the sons of Finrod the South and the [?plains] of Sirion (or Broseliand); the sons of Fëanor the East. Fingolfin is slain when Morgoth breaks the leaguer. Felagoth [> Felagund] is saved by Barahir the Bold a mortal and escapes south to found Nargothrond, swearing a vow of friendship to the race of Barahir. The sons of Fëanor live a wild and nomad life in the East, warring with Dwarves and Orcs and Men. Fingolfin's sons Finweg and Turgon still hold out in the North.

4   This sentence was changed to read:

> Felagoth [> Felagund] and his brothers found the realm of Nargothrond on the banks of Narog in the south of the Northern lands. They are aided by Celegorm and Curufin who long while dwelt in Nargothrond.

## 10

The power of Morgoth begins to spread once more. One by one he overthrows Men and Elves in the North. Of these a famous chieftain of Ilkorindi[1] was Barahir, who had been a friend of Celegorm of Nargothrond. Barahir is driven into hiding, his hiding betrayed, and Barahir slain; his son Beren after a life outlawed flees south, crosses the Shadowy Mountains, and after grievous hardships comes to Doriath. Of this and his other adventures are told in the Lay of Leithian. He gains the love of Tinúviel 'the nightingale' – his own name for Lúthien – the daughter of Thingol. To win her Thingol, in mockery, requires a Silmaril from the crown of Morgoth. Beren sets out to achieve this, is captured, and set in dungeon in Angband, but conceals his real identity and is given as a slave to Thû the hunter.[2] Lúthien is imprisoned by Thingol, but escapes and goes in search of Beren. With the aid of Huan lord of dogs she rescues Beren, and gains entrance to Angband where Morgoth is enchanted and finally wrapped in slumber by her dancing. They get a Silmaril and escape, but are barred at gates of Angband by Carcaras the Wolf-ward. He bites off Beren's hand which holds the Silmaril, and goes mad with the anguish of its burning within him.

They escape and after many wanderings get back to Doriath. Carcaras ravening through the woods bursts into Doriath. There follows the Wolf-hunt of Doriath, in which Carcaras is slain, and Huan is killed in defence of Beren. Beren is however mortally wounded and dies in Lúthien's arms. Some songs say that Lúthien went even over the Grinding Ice, aided by the power of her divine mother, Melian, to Mandos' halls and won him back; others that Mandos hearing his tale released him. Certain it is that he alone of mortals came back from Mandos and dwelt with Lúthien and never spoke to Men again, living in the woods of Doriath and in the Hunters' Wold, west of Nargothrond.[3]

In the days of his outlawry Beren had been befriended by Húrin of Hithlum, son of Gumlin. In the woods of Hithlum Húrin still remains unbowed to the yoke of Morgoth.

1 *a famous chieftain of Ilkorindi* > *a famous chieftain of Men* (cf. §9 note 2).

2 This sentence, following *Beren sets out to achieve this*, was struck through and replaced by the following (in red ink):

(Beren sets out to achieve this,) and seeks the aid of Felagoth in Nargothrond. Felagoth warns him of the oath of the sons of Fëanor, and that even if he gets the Silmaril they will not, if they can prevent it, allow him to take it to Thingol. But faithful to his own oath he gives him aid. The kingdom is given to Orodreth, and Felagoth and Beren march North. They are overcome in battle. Felagoth and Beren and a small band escape, and creeping back despoil the dead. Disguising themselves as Orcs they get as far as the house of the Lord of Wolves. There they are discovered, and placed in prison – and devoured one by one.

Celegorm discovered what was the secret mission of Felagoth and Beren. He gathers his dogs and hunters and goes a-hunting. He finds the traces of battle. Then he finds Lúthien in the woods.

She flies but is overtaken by Huan the chief of Celegorm's dogs, who is sleepless, and she cannot enchant him. He bears her off. Celegorm offers redress.

From the second sentence *Felagoth warns him of the oath* . . . this entire passage was then struck through and *See tale of Lúthien* written across it; *Felagoth* in the surviving sentence at the beginning was changed to *Felagund*; and *They fall in the power of the Lord of Wolves (Thû)* was added.

3   Here was added, perhaps at the time of the writing of the manuscript:

(But Mandos in payment exacted that Lúthien should become mortal as Beren.)

# 11

Maidros forms now a league against Morgoth seeing that he will destroy them all, one by one, if they do not unite. The scattered Ilkorins and Men are gathered together. Curufin and Celegorm despatch a host (but not all they could gather, thus breaking their word) from Nargothrond. The Gnomes of Nargothrond refuse to be led by Finweg, and go in search of the hosts of Maidros and Maglor. Men march up from South and East and West and North. Thingol will not send from Doriath.[1] Some say out of selfish policy, others because of the wisdom of Melian and of fate which decreed that Doriath should become the only refuge of the Eldar from Morgoth afterwards. Part was certainly due to the Silmaril, which Thingol now possessed, and which Maidros had demanded with haughty words. The *Gnomes* of Doriath are allowed[2] nonetheless to join the league.

Finweg advances into the Plain of Thirst (Dor-na-Fauglith) before the Iron Mountains and defeats an Orc-army, which falls back. Pursuing he is overwhelmed by countless hordes suddenly loosed on him from the deeps of Angband, and there is fought the field of Unnumbered Tears, of which no elfin songs tell except in lamentation.

The mortal armies, whose leaders had mostly been corrupted or bribed by Morgoth, desert or flee away: all except Húrin's kin. From that day Men and Elves have been estranged, save the descendants of Húrin. Finweg falls, his blue and silver banner is destroyed. The Gnomes attempt to fall back towards the hills and Taur-na-Fuin (forest of night). Húrin holds the rearguard, and all his men are slain, so that not a single man escapes to bring news to

Hithlum. By Morgoth's orders Húrin, whose axe had slain a thousand Orcs, is taken alive. By Húrin alone was Turgon (Finweg's brother) son of Fingolfin enabled to cut his way back into the hills with a part of his people. The remainder of the Gnomes and Ilkorins would have been all slain or taken, but for the arrival of Maidros, Curufin and Celegorm – too late for the main battle.

They are beaten back and driven into the South-east, where they long time dwelt, and did not go back to Nargothrond. There Orodreth ruled over the remnant.[3] Morgoth is utterly triumphant. His armies range all the North, and press upon the borders of Doriath and Nargothrond. The slain of his enemies are piled into a great hill upon Dor-na-Fauglith, but there the grass comes and grows green where all else is desert, and no Orc dare tread upon that hill where the Gnomish swords rust.

Húrin is taken to Angband and defies Morgoth. He is chained in torment. Afterward Morgoth offers him a high captaincy in his forces, a wealth of jewels, and freedom, if he will lead an army against Turgon. None knew whither Turgon had departed save Húrin. Húrin refused and Morgoth devised a torture. He set him upon the highest peak of Thangorodrim and cursed him with never-sleeping sight like the Gods, and he cursed his seed with a fate of ill-hap, and bade Húrin watch the working of it.

★

1   This passage, from *Curufin and Celegorm despatch a host*, was altered by hastily made changes and additions:

> Curufin and Celegorm come from their wandering; but Orodreth because of Felagund his brother will not come: Thingol also sends but few of his folk. The Gnomes of Fëanor's sons refuse to be led by Finweg, and the battle is divided into two hosts, one under Maidros and Maglor, and one under Finweg and Turgon. Men march up from South and East and West and North. Thingol sends but few from Doriath.

2   Added here: *by Thingol*

3   This passage was changed to read:

> They are beaten back and driven into the South-east, where they long time dwelt. In Nargothrond Orodreth ruled still.

## 12

Morwen wife of Húrin was left alone in the woods. Her son Túrin was a young boy of seven, and she was with child. Only two old men Halog and Mailgond remained faithful to her. The men of Hithlum were slain, and Morgoth breaking his words had driven all men, who had not escaped (as few did) away South, into Hithlum. Now most of these were faithless men who had deserted the Eldar in the battle of Unnumbered Tears. Yet he penned them behind the Shadowy Mountains, nonetheless, and slew such as wandered forth, desiring to keep them from fellowship with Elves. But little love all the same did they show to Húrin's wife. Wherefore it came into her heart to send Túrin to Thingol, because of Beren Húrin's friend who had wedded Lúthien. The 'Children of Húrin' tells of his fate, and how Morgoth's curse pursued him, so that all he did turned out unhappily against his will.

He grew up in Thingol's court, but after a while as Morgoth's power grew no news from Hithlum came and he heard no more of Morwen or of his sister Nienor whom he had not seen. Taunted by Orgof, of the kin of King Thingol, he unwitting of his growing strength killed him at the king's table with a drinking horn. He fled the court thinking himself an outlaw, and took to war against all, Elves, Men, and Orcs, upon the borders of Doriath, gathering a wild band of hunted Men and Elves about him.

One day in his absence his men captured Beleg the bowman, who had befriended Túrin of old. Túrin released him, and is told how Thingol had forgiven his deed long ago. Beleg brings him to abandon his war against Elves, and to assuage his wrath upon the Orcs. The fame of the deeds upon the marches and the prowess of Beleg the Gnome and Túrin son of Húrin against the Orcs is brought to Thingol and to Morgoth. One only of Túrin's band, Blodrin Ban's son, hates the new life with little plunder and harder fighting. He betrays the secret place of Túrin to the Orcs. Their camp is surprised, Túrin is taken and dragged to Angband (for Morgoth has begun to fear he will escape his curse through his valour and the protection of Melian); Beleg is left for dead under a heap of slain. He is found by Thingol's men come to summon them to a feast at the Thousand Caves. Melian heals him, and he sets out to track the Orcs. Beleg is the most skilled in tracking of all who have lived, but the mazes of Taur-na-Fuin bewilder him. There in despair he sees the lamp of Flinding son of Fuilin, a

Gnome of Nargothrond who was captured by Orcs and had long been a thrall in the mines of Morgoth, but escaped.

Of Flinding he learns news of the Orc-band that captured Túrin. They hide and watch the host go by laden with spoil along the Orc-road through the heart of the forest, which the Orcs use when in need of haste. They dread the forest beyond the road as much as Elf or Man. Túrin is seen dragged along and whipped. The Orcs leave the forest and descend the slopes toward Dor-na-Fauglith, and encamp in a dale in sight of Thangorodrim. Beleg shoots the wolf-sentinels and steals with Flinding into the camp. With the greatest difficulty and direst peril they carry the senseless Túrin away and lay him in a dell of thick thorn-trees. In striking off his bonds Beleg pricks Túrin's foot; he is roused, and demented thinks the Orcs are tormenting him, he leaps on Beleg and kills him with his own sword. The covering of Flinding's lamp falls off and seeing Beleg's face he is turned to stone. The Orcs roused by his cries as he leaped upon Beleg discover his escape but are driven far and wide by a dreadful storm of thunder and deluge. In the morning Flinding sees them marching over the steaming waste of Dor-na-Fauglith. Beleg is buried with his bow in the dell.

Flinding leads the dazed unwitting Túrin towards safety. His wits return by Ivrin's lake where are the sources of Narog, and he weeps a great while, and makes a song for Beleg, the 'Bowman's Friendship', which afterwards became a battle-song of the enemies of Morgoth.

# 13

Flinding leads Túrin to Nargothrond. There Túrin gains the love and loves against his will Finduilas daughter of Orodreth, who had been betrothed before his captivity to Flinding. He fights against his love out of loyalty to Flinding, but Flinding seeing that Finduilas loves Túrin becomes embittered.

Túrin leads the Gnomes of Nargothrond to forsake their secrecy and hidden warfare, and fights the Orcs more openly.[1] He has Beleg's sword forged anew, into a black blade with shining edges, and he is from this given the name of 'Mormakil' or black-sword. The fame of Mormakil reaches even to Thingol. Túrin adopts the name instead of 'Túrin'. For a long while Túrin and the Gnomes of Narog are victorious and their realm reaches to the sources of Narog, and from the western sea to the confines of Doriath. There is a stay in the might of Morgoth.

Morwen and Nienor are able to journey to Thingol leaving their goods in the care of Brodda who had wedded a kinswoman of Morwen. They learn at Thingol's court of the loss of Túrin. News comes to them of the fall of Nargothrond. Morgoth had suddenly loosed a great army on them, and with them one of the first and mightiest[2] of those Dragons that bred in his deep places and for a long while troubled the Northern lands of Men and Elves.[3]

The host of Narog is overwhelmed. Flinding wounded refuses Túrin's succour and dies reproaching him. Túrin hastes back to Nargothrond but the Dragon and Orcs come thither before he can put it in defence, and all the fair halls beneath the earth are plundered, and all the women and maidens of Narog herded as slaves in captivity. Túrin seeks to slay the Dragon, but is held immovable by the spell of his eyes, while the Dragon Glórung[4] taunts him. Glórung then offers him freedom either to follow seeking to rescue his 'stolen love' Finduilas, or to do his duty and go to the rescue of his mother and sister who are living (as he lying says) in great misery in Hithlum. Túrin forsakes Finduilas against his heart (which if he had obeyed his uttermost fate would not have befallen him) and believing the serpent goes to seek Hithlum. Glórung lies in the caves of Narog and gathers beneath him all the gold and silver and gems there hoarded.

Túrin after long wandering goes to Hithlum. But Morwen and Nienor are in Thingol's court, when survivors tell of the fall of Nargothrond, and of Túrin, and some say Túrin escaped alive, and some say he was turned to stone by the eyes of the serpent and lived still in bondage in Nargothrond. Morwen and Nienor at last get Thingol to give them men to go against Glórung, or to spy out his lair at least.

Túrin slays Brodda in his hall, in his anger when he finds Morwen's hall and lands empty and despoiled. Repenting his deed he flies from Hithlum again, and seeks no more after his kin. Desiring to forget his past he takes the name of Turambar (Turmarth) 'Conqueror of Fate', and gathers a new people, 'Men of the Woods', east of Narog, whom he rules, and lives in peace.

The expedition of Thingol, with whom ride Morwen and Nienor, views Narog from a hill-top. The Elves ride down towards the lair,[5] but Glórung coming out lies into the stream and a huge hissing and great vapour goes up, so that their horses turn and fly. Morwen's horse and Nienor's are also panic-stricken and gallop wildly in the mist. When the mist clears Nienor finds herself face to face with the Dragon, whose eye holds her, and a spell of darkness and utter forgetfulness comes upon her. She wanders witless in the woods. At last her senses return but she remembers little.[6] Orcs see her and chase her, but are driven off by a band of 'Woodmen' under Turambar, who lead her to their pleasant homes.

As they pass the falls of Silver Bowl a shivering touches her. She lives amid the woodfolk and is loved by Tamar the Lame, but at last weds Turambar, who calls her Níniel 'the Tearful' since he first found her weeping.

Glórung begins to raid across Narog, and Orcs gather to him. The woodmen slay many of them, and Glórung hearing of their dwelling comes crawling and filled with fire over Narog and through the woods against them. He leaves a blasted track behind him. Turambar ponders how the horror can be warded from his land. He marches with his men, and Níniel foreboding evil rides with him,[7] till they can see the burning track of Glórung, and the smoking place where he lies. Between them runs a stream in a deep-cloven ravine after falling over the high falls of Silver Bowl. Turambar asks for volunteers and obtains six only to lie in the ravine over which the Dragon must pass. The seven depart. They climb the far side of the ravine at evening and cling near its edge in the trees. The next morning all have slunk away and Turambar is alone.

Glórung creeps over. Turambar transfixes him with Gurtholfin[8] 'Wand of Death', his black sword. Glórung coils back in anguish and lies dying. Turambar comes forth to retrieve his sword, and places his foot upon Glórung and exults. But the venom of Glórung gushes out as he tugs out his sword, and he falls in a swoon. The watchers see that Glórung is slain, but Túrin does not return. Níniel goes in search of him and finds him lying beside Glórung. As she is tending him, Glórung opens his eyes and speaks, and tells her who Turambar is, and lifts his spell from off her. Then she knows who she is, and knows his tale true from things Turambar has told her. Filled with horror and anguish she flies and casts herself over Silver Bowl and none ever found her body again. Tamar followed her and heard her lament.

Túrin comes back in triumph. He asks for Níniel, but none dare tell him. Then Tamar comes and tells him. Túrin slays him, and taking Gurtholfin bids it slay him. The sword answers that his blood is sweet as any other's, and pierces him to the heart. Túrin is buried beside Silver Bowl, and his name carved in characters of Nargothrond upon a rock. Beneath is written Níniel.

Some say Morwen released from spell by Glórung's death came that way and read the stone.

★

1   Added here: *At his advice Narog is bridged* (cf. note 5).
2   *one of the first and mightiest* > *that first and mightiest*
3   Added here: *even Glómund, who was at the Battle of Tears* (see note 4).
4   *Glórung* > *Glómund* here and subsequently, except at the last occurrence.
5   *towards the lair* > *towards the bridge leading to the lair* (cf. note 1).
6   *she remembers little* > *she remembers not even her name.*
7   Added here: *though she is with child,*
8   *Gurtholfin* > *Gurtholfir* at both occurrences.

# 14

Húrin was released by Morgoth after the end of Túrin and Nienor, for Morgoth thought still to use him. He accused Thingol's faint heart and ungentleness of Túrin's unhappiness, and Húrin wandering bowed with grief pondered his words and was embittered by them.

Húrin and outlaws come to Nargothrond, whom none dare plunder for dread of the spirit of Glórung[1] or even of his memory. They slay Mîm the Dwarf who had taken possession and enchanted all the gold. Húrin casts the gold at Thingol's feet with reproaches. Thingol will not have it, and bears with Húrin, until goaded too far he bids him begone. Húrin wanders away and seeks Morwen, and many for ages after related that they met them together in the woods lamenting their children.

The enchanted gold lays its spell on Thingol. He summons the Dwarves of Nogrod and Belegost to come and fashion it into beautiful things, and to make a necklace of great wonder whereon the Silmaril shall hang. The Dwarves plot treachery, and Thingol bitter with the curse of the gold denies them their reward. After their smithying they are driven away without payment. The Dwarves come back; aided by treachery of some Gnomes who also were bitten by the lust of the gold, they surprise Thingol on a hunt, slay him, and surprise the Thousand Caves and plunder them. Melian they cannot touch. She goes away to seek Beren and Lúthien.

The Dwarves are ambushed at a ford by Beren and the brown and green Elves of the wood, and their king slain, from whose neck Beren takes the 'Nauglafring'[2] or necklace of the Dwarves, with its Silmaril. It is said that Lúthien wearing that jewel is the most beautiful thing that eyes have ever seen outside Valinor. But Melian warned Beren of the curse of the gold and of the Silmaril. The rest of the gold is drowned in the river.

But the 'Nauglafring'[3] remains hoarded secretly in Beren's keeping. When Mandos let Beren return with Lúthien, it was only at the price that Lúthien should become as shortlived as Beren the mortal. Lúthien now fades, even as the Elves in later days faded as Men grew strong and took the goodness of earth (for the Elves needed the light of the Trees). At last she vanished, and Beren was lost, looking in vain for her, and his son Dior ruled after him. Dior re-established Doriath and grew proud, and wore the 'Nauglafring', and the fame of the Silmaril went abroad. After vain bargaining the sons of Fëanor made war on him (the second slaying of Elf by Elf) and destroyed him, and took the 'Nauglafring'. They quarrelled over it, owing to the curse of the gold, until only Maglor was left. But Elwing daughter of Dior was saved and carried away to the mouth of the river Sirion.[4]

★

1  The name *Glórung* is not here emended, as in §13, to *Glómund*, but a *d* is written over the *g*, sc. *Glórund* (the earliest form of the name of the Dragon).
2  At the first occurrence only of *Nauglafring*, *th* is pencilled above, i.e. *Nauglathring* or *Nauglathfring*.
3  Above Nauglafring here my father wrote *Dweorgmene* [Old English, 'Dwarf-necklace']; this was struck out, and *Glingna Nauglir* substituted.
4  The conclusion of this section was changed very soon after it was written, since in §17 already as first written the Nauglafring is with Elwing at the mouth of Sirion:

> After vain bargaining the sons of Fëanor made war on him (the second slaying of Elf by Elf) and destroyed him. But Elwing daughter of Dior, Beren's son, escaped, and was carried away by faithful servants to the mouth of the river Sirion. With her went the Nauglafring.

## 15

The great river Sirion flowed through the lands South-west; at its mouth was a great delta, and its lower course ran through wide green and fertile lands, little peopled save by birds and beasts because of the Orc-raids; but they were not inhabited by Orcs, who preferred the northern woods, and feared the power of Ylmir – for Sirion's mouth was in the Western Seas.

Turgon Fingolfin's son had a sister Isfin. She was lost in Taur-na-Fuin after the Battle of Unnumbered Tears. There she was trapped by the Dark Elf Eöl. Their son was Meglin. The people of Turgon escaping aided by the prowess of Húrin were lost from the knowledge of Morgoth, and indeed of all in the world save Ylmir. In a secret place in the hills their scouts climbing to the tops discovered a broad valley entirely encircled by the hills in rings ever lower as they came towards the centre. Amid this ring was a wide land without hills, except for one rocky hill that stuck up from the plain, not right at the centre, but nearest to that part of the outer wall which marched close to the edge of Sirion.[1]

Ylmir's messages come up Sirion bidding them take refuge in this valley, and teaching them spells of enchantment to place upon all the hills about, to keep off foes and spies. He foretells that their fortress shall stand longest of all the refuges of the Elves against Morgoth, and like Doriath never be overthrown – save by treachery from within. The spells are strongest near to Sirion, although here the encircling mountains are lowest. Here the Gnomes dig a mighty winding tunnel under the roots of the mountains, that issues at last in the Guarded Plain. Its outer entrance is guarded by the spells of Ylmir; its inner is watched unceasingly by the Gnomes. It is set there in case those within ever need to escape, and as a way of more rapid exit from the valley for scouts, wanderers, and messages, and also as an entrance for fugitives escaping from Morgoth.

Thorndor King of Eagles removes his eyries to the Northern heights of the encircling mountains and guards them against Orc-spies.[2] On the rocky hill, Amon Gwareth, the hill of watching, whose sides they polish to the smoothness of glass, and whose top they level, the great city of Gondolin with gates of steel is built. The plain all about is levelled as flat and smooth as a lawn of clipped grass to the feet of the hills, so that nothing can creep over it unawares. The people of Gondolin grows mighty, and their armouries are filled with weapons. But Turgon does not march to

the aid of Nargothrond, or Doriath, and after the slaying of Dior
he has no more to do with the son of Fëanor (Maglor).³ Finally he
closes the vale to all fugitives, and forbids the folk of Gondolin to
leave the valley. Gondolin is the only stronghold of the Elves left.
Morgoth has not forgotten Turgon, but his search is in vain.
Nargothrond is destroyed; Doriath desolate; Húrin's children
dead; and only scattered and fugitive Elves, Gnomes and Ilkorins,
left, except such as work in the smithies and mines in great
numbers. His triumph is nearly complete.

★

1   Added here roughly in pencil: *The hill nearest to Angband was
    guarded by Fingolfin's cairn* (cf. note 2).
2   Added here at the same time as the addition given in note 1: *sitting
    upon Fingolfin's cairn*.
3   *the son of Fëanor (Maglor)* > *the sons of Fëanor* (this goes with
    the change at the end of §14, note 4).

## 16

Meglin son of Eöl and Isfin sister of Turgon was sent by his
mother to Gondolin, and there received,¹ although half of Ilkorin
blood, and treated as a prince.

Húrin of Hithlum had a brother Huor. The son of Huor was
Tuor, younger than Túrin² son of Húrin. Rían, Huor's wife,
sought her husband's body among the slain on the field of Unnumbered Tears, and died there. Her son remaining in Hithlum
fell into the hands of the faithless men whom Morgoth drove into
Hithlum after that battle, and he was made a thrall. Growing wild
and rough he fled into the woods, and became an outlaw, and a
solitary, living alone and communing with none save rarely with
wandering and hidden Elves. On a time Ylmir contrived that he
should be led to a subterranean river-course leading out of
Mithrim into a chasmed river that flowed at last into the Western
Sea. In this way his going was unmarked by Man, Orc, or spy, and
unknown of Morgoth. After long wanderings down the western
shores he came to the mouths of Sirion, and there fell in with the
Gnome Bronweg, who had once been in Gondolin. They journey
secretly up Sirion together. Tuor lingers long in the sweet land
Nan Tathrin 'Valley of Willows'; but there Ylmir himself comes
up the river to visit him, and tells him of his mission. He is to bid

Turgon prepare for battle against Morgoth; for Ylmir will turn
the hearts of the Valar to forgive the Gnomes and send them
succour. If Turgon will do this, the battle will be terrible, but the
race of Orcs will perish and will not in after ages trouble Elves and
Men. If not, the people of Gondolin are to prepare for flight to
Sirion's mouth, where Ylmir will aid them to build a fleet and
guide them back to Valinor. If Turgon does Ylmir's will Tuor is to
abide a while in Gondolin and then go back to Hithlum with a
force of Gnomes and draw Men once more into alliance with the
Elves, for 'without Men the Elves shall not prevail against the Orcs
and Balrogs'. This Ylmir does because he knows that ere seven[3]
full years are passed the doom of Gondolin will come through
Meglin.[4]

Tuor and Bronweg reach the secret way,[5] and come out upon
the guarded plain. Taken captive by the watch they are led before
Turgon. Turgon is grown old[6] and very mighty and proud, and
Gondolin so fair and beautiful, and its people so proud of it and
confident in its secret and impregnable strength, that the king and
most of the people do not wish to trouble about the Gnomes and
Elves without, or care for Men, nor do they long any more for
Valinor. Meglin approving, the king rejects Tuor's message in
spite of the words of Idril the far-sighted (also called Idril Silver-
foot, because she loved to walk barefoot) his daughter, and the
wiser of his counsellors. Tuor lives on in Gondolin, and becomes a
great chieftain. After three years he weds Idril – Tuor and Beren
alone of all mortals ever wedded Elves, and since Elwing daughter
of Dior Beren's son wedded Eärendel son of Tuor and Idril of
them alone has come the strain of Elfinesse into mortal blood.

Not long after this Meglin going far afield over the mountains is
taken by Orcs, and purchases his life when taken to Angband by
revealing Gondolin and its secrets. Morgoth promises him the
lordship of Gondolin, and possession of Idril. Lust for Idril led
him the easier to his treachery, and added to his hatred of Tuor.

Morgoth sends him back to Gondolin. Eärendel is born, having
the beauty and light and wisdom of Elfinesse, the hardihood and
strength of Men, and the longing for the sea which captured Tuor
and held him for ever when Ylmir spoke to him in the Land of
Willows.

At last Morgoth is ready, and the attack is made on Gondolin
with dragons, Balrogs, and Orcs. After a dreadful fight about the
walls the city is stormed, and Turgon perishes with many of the
most noble in the last fight in the great square. Tuor rescues Idril

and Eärendel from Meglin, and hurls him from the battlements. He then leads the remnant of the people of Gondolin down a secret tunnel previously made by Idril's advice which comes out far in the North of the plain. Those who would not come with him but fled to the old way of escape are caught by the dragon sent by Morgoth to watch that exit.

In the fume of the burning Tuor leads his company into the mountains into the cold pass of Cristhorn (Eagles' Cleft). There they are ambushed, but saved by the valour of Glorfindel (chief of the house of the Golden Flower of Gondolin, who dies in a duel with a Balrog upon a pinnacle) and the intervention of Thorndor. The remnant reaches Sirion and journeys to the land at its mouth – the Waters of Sirion. Morgoth's triumph is now complete.

★

[All the changes in this section except that given in note 3 were late alterations made roughly and hastily.]

1  Added against this sentence: *last of the fugitives from without*
2  *younger than Túrin > cousin of Túrin*
3  *seven* early changed to *twelve*
4  Added here: *if they sit still in their halls*.
5  Added here: *which they find by the grace of Ylmir*
6  The word *old* circled for removal.

# 17

To Sirion's mouth Elwing daughter of Dior comes, and is received by the survivors of Gondolin.[1] These become a seafaring folk, building many boats and living far out on the delta, whither the Orcs dare not come.

Ylmir reproaches the Valar, and bids them rescue the remnants of the Noldoli and the Silmarils in which alone now lives the light of the old days of bliss when the Trees were shining.

The sons of the Valar led by Fionwë Tulcas' son lead forth a host, in which all the Qendi march, but remembering Swanhaven few of the Teleri go with them. Côr is deserted.

Tuor growing old[2] cannot forbear the call of the sea, and builds Eärámë and sails West with Idril and is heard of no more. Eärendel weds Elwing. The call of the sea is born also in him. He builds Wingelot and wishes to sail in search of his father. Ylmir bids him to sail to Valinor.[3] Here follow the marvellous adventures of Wingelot in the seas and isles, and of how Eärendel slew Ungoliant in the South. He returned home and found the Waters of Sirion desolate. The sons of Fëanor learning of the dwelling of Elwing and the Nauglafring had come down on the people of Gondolin. In a battle all the sons of Fëanor save Maidros[4] were slain, but the last folk of Gondolin destroyed or forced to go away and join the people of Maidros.[5] Elwing cast the Nauglafring into the sea and leapt after it,[6] but was changed into a white sea-bird by Ylmir, and flew to seek Eärendel, seeking about all the shores of the world.

Their son (Elrond) who is half-mortal and half-elfin,[7] a child, was saved however by Maidros. When later the Elves return to the West, bound by his mortal half he elects to stay on earth. Through him the blood of Húrin[8] (his great-uncle) and of the Elves is yet among Men, and is seen yet in valour and in beauty and in poetry.

Eärendel learning of these things from Bronweg, who dwelt in a hut, a solitary, at the mouth of Sirion, is overcome with sorrow. With Bronweg he sets sail in Wingelot once more in search of Elwing and of Valinor.

He comes to the magic isles, and to the Lonely Isle, and at last to the Bay of Faërie. He climbs the hill of Côr, and walks in the deserted ways of Tûn, and his raiment becomes encrusted with the dust of diamonds and of jewels. He dares not go further into Valinor. He builds a tower on an isle in the northern seas, to which all the seabirds of the world repair. He sails by the aid of their wings even over the airs in search of Elwing, but is scorched by the Sun, and hunted from the sky by the Moon, and for a long while he wanders the sky as a fugitive star.[9]

[In this section again most of the changes (not those in notes 2 and 4) were hastily made in pencil.]

1   This sentence was changed to read:

     At Sirion's mouth Elwing daughter of Dior dwelt, and received the survivors of Gondolin.

2   *growing old* struck out.
3   *Ylmir bids him to sail to Valinor* struck out.
4   *Maidros > Maidros and Maglor*
5   Written in the margin: *Maglor sat and sang by the sea in repentance.*

6  My father first wrote *Elwing cast herself into the sea with the Nauglafring*, but changed it to *Elwing cast the Nauglafring into the sea and leapt after it* in the act of writing.

7  This sentence was changed to read:

Their son (Elrond) who is part mortal and part elfin and part of the race of Valar,

8  *Húrin* struck out, and *Huor and of Beren* written above, together with some illegible words. One might expect *Through him the blood of Huor and of Beren his great-grandfathers*, but the illegible words do not seem to be these. (Húrin was in fact Elrond's great-great-uncle.)

9  The last sentence (*He sails by the aid of their wings . . .*) is an addition, but I think an addition made at the time of writing.

# 18

The march of Fionwë into the North is then told, and of the Terrible or Last Battle. The Balrogs are all destroyed, and the Orcs destroyed or scattered. Morgoth himself makes a last sally with all his dragons; but they are destroyed, all save two which escape, by the sons of the Valar, and Morgoth is overthrown and bound[1] and his iron crown is made into a collar for his neck. The two Silmarils are rescued. The Northern and Western parts of the world are rent and broken in the struggle.[2]

The Gods and Elves release Men from Hithlum, and march through the lands summoning the remnants of the Gnomes and Ilkorins to join them. All do so except the people of Maidros. Maidros aided by many men[3] prepares to perform his oath, though now at last weighed down by sorrow because of it. He sends to Fionwë reminding him of the oath and begging for the Silmarils. Fionwë replies that he has lost his right to them because of the evil deeds of Fëanor, and of the slaying of Dior, and of the plundering of Sirion. He must submit, and come back to Valinor; in Valinor only and at the judgement of the Gods shall they be handed over.

Maidros and Maglor[4] submit. The Elves set sail from Lúthien (Britain or England) for Valinor.[5] Thence they ever still from time [to time] set sail leaving the world ere they fade.

On the last march Maglor says to Maidros that there are two sons of Fëanor now left, and two Silmarils; one is his. He steals it, and flies, but it burns him so that he knows he no longer has a right to it. He wanders in pain over the earth, and casts himself into a pit.[6] One Silmaril is now in the sea, and one in the earth.[7]

The Gnomes and many of the Ilkorins and Teleri and Qendi repeople the Lonely Isle. Some go back to live upon the shores of Faëry and in Valinor, but Côr and Tûn remain desolate.

★

1   Added here: *by the chain Angainor*
2   Added here: *and the fashion of their lands altered* (late pencilled addition).
3   *aided by many men* struck out.
4   *and Maglor* circled in pencil.
5   This sentence was changed to read:

> The Elves march to the Western shore, and begin to set sail from Leithien (Britain or England) for Valinor.

6   *casts himself into a pit* > *casts it into a fiery pit.*
7   Added here: *Maglor sings now ever in sorrow by the sea.*

## 19

The judgement of the Gods takes place. The earth is to be for Men, and the Elves who do not set sail for the Lonely Isle or Valinor shall slowly fade and fail. For a while the last dragons and Orcs shall grieve the earth, but in the end all shall perish by the valour of Men.

Morgoth is thrust through the Door of Night into the outer dark beyond the Walls of the World, and a guard set for ever on that Door. The lies that he sowed in the hearts of Men and Elves do not die and cannot all be slain by the Gods, but live on and bring much evil even to this day. Some say also that secretly Morgoth or his black shadow and spirit in spite of the Valar creeps back over the Walls of the World in the North and East and visits the world, others that this is Thû his great chief who escaped the Last Battle and dwells still in dark places, and perverts Men to his dreadful worship. When the world is much older, and the Gods weary, Morgoth will come back through the Door, and the last battle of all will be fought. Fionwë will fight Morgoth on the plain of Valinor, and the spirit of Túrin shall be beside him; it shall be Túrin who with his black sword will slay Morgoth, and thus the children of Húrin shall be avenged.

In those days the Silmarils shall be recovered from sea and earth and air, and Maidros shall break them and Belaurin[1] with their fire rekindle the Two Trees, and the great light shall come forth again, and the Mountains of Valinor shall be levelled so that it goes out over the world, and Gods and Elves and Men[2] shall grow young again, and all their dead awake.[3]

And thus it was that the last Silmaril came into the air. The Gods adjudged the last Silmaril to Eärendel – 'until many things shall come to pass' – because of the deeds of the sons of Fëanor. Maidros is sent to Eärendel and with the aid of the Silmaril Elwing is found and restored. Eärendel's boat is drawn over Valinor to the Outer Seas, and Eärendel launches it into the outer darkness high above Sun and Moon. There he sails with the Silmaril upon his brow and Elwing at his side, the brightest of all stars, keeping watch upon Morgoth.[4] So he shall sail until he sees the last battle gathering upon the plains of Valinor. Then he will descend.

And this is the last end of the tales of the days before the days, in the Northern regions of the Western World. These tales are some of those remembered and sung by the fading Elves, and most by the vanished Elves of the Lonely Isle. They have been told by Elves to Men of the race of Eärendel, and most to Eriol who alone of mortals of later days sailed to the Lonely Isle, and yet came back to Lúthien,[5] and remembered things he had heard in Cortirion, the town of the Elves in Tol Eressëa.

1   Against *Belaurin* was written *Palúrien* (cf. §1 note 1).
2   *and Men* struck out.
3   Added here:

> But of Men in that last Day the prophecy speaks not, save of Túrin only.

4   Added here: *and the Door of Night* (late pencilled addition).
5   *Lúthien* > *Leithien* (cf. §18 note 5).

## Commentary on the 'Sketch of the Mythology'

While the 'Sketch' is a good and clear manuscript, as it had to be (since it was to be read by R. W. Reynolds), it will be apparent that my father composed it extremely rapidly: I think it quite possible and even probable that he wrote it without consulting the earlier prose tales.

Very great advances have been made towards the form of the story as it appears in the published work; but there is no trace of a prose narrative even in fragmentary or note form that bridges the gap between the *Lost Tales* and this synopsis in the 'Valinórean' part of the mythology (i.e. to the flight of the Noldoli and the making of the Sun and Moon). This is not to say, of course, that none such ever existed, though the fact that my father did undoubtedly preserve a very high proportion of all that he ever wrote leads me to doubt it. I think it far more likely that while working on other things (during his time at Leeds) he had developed his ideas, especially on the 'Valinórean' part, without setting them to paper; and since the prose *Tales* had been set aside a good many years before, it may be that certain narrative shifts found in the 'Sketch' were less fully intended, less conscious, than such shifts in the later development of 'The Silmarillion', where he always worked on the basis of existing writings.

It is in any case often extremely difficult, or impossible, to judge whether features in the *Tales* that are not present in the 'Sketch' were omitted simply for the sake of compression, or whether they had been definitively abandoned. Thus while Eriol – not Ælfwine, see II. 300 – is mentioned at the end, and his coming to Kortirion in Tol Eressëa, there is no trace of the Cottage of Lost Play: the entire narrative framework of the *Lost Tales* has disappeared. But this does not by any means demonstrate that my father had actually rejected it at this time.

The Commentary that follows is divided according to the 19 sections into which I have divided the narrative.

The 'Sketch of the Mythology' is referred to throughout the rest of this book by the abbreviation 'S'.

# 1

S (the 'Sketch'), which makes no reference to the Creation and the Music of the Ainur, begins with the coming of the Nine Valar 'for the governance of the world': the Nine Valar have been referred to in the alliterative poem *The Flight of the Noldoli* (see III. 133, 137). There now appears the isle (later called Almaren) on which the Gods dwelt after the making of the Lamps, the origin of which is probably to be seen in the tale of *The Coming of the Valar* I. 69–70, where it is said that when the Lamps fell the Valar were gathered on the Twilit Isles, and that 'that island whereon stood the Valar' was dragged westward by Ossë. It might seem that the story of Melko's making the pillars of the Lamps out of ice that melted had been abandoned, but it reappears again later, in the *Ambarkanta* (p. 238).

The use of the word 'plant' of the Two Trees is curious, and might be dismissed simply as a hasty expression if it did not appear in the following version of 'The Silmarillion', the *Quenta* (p. 80). In the old tale, as in the published work, the Trees rose from the ground under the chanted spells of Yavanna. The silver undersides of the leaves of the White Tree now appear, and its flowers are likened to those of a cherry: *Silpion* is translated 'Cherry-moon' in the Name-list to *The Fall of Gondolin* (II. 215). The mention of the White Tree first may imply that it had now become the Elder Tree, as it is explicitly in the *Quenta*.

As S was first written the Trees had periods of twelve hours, as in the *Lost Tales* (see I. 88 and footnote), but with emendation from 'six' to 'seven' (allowing for the time of 'mingled light') the period becomes fourteen hours. This was a movement towards the formulation in *The Silmarillion* (p. 38), where each Tree 'waxed to full and waned again to naught' in seven hours; but in *The Silmarillion* 'each day of the Valar in Aman contained twelve hours', whereas in S each day was double that length.

The Gnomish name of Varda, *Bridhil*, occurs in the alliterative *Flight of the Noldoli* (changed to *Bredhil*), the *Lay of Leithian*, and the early Gnomish dictionary (I. 273, entry *Varda*). On *Timbrenting*, *Tindbrenting* see III. 127, 139; *Tengwethil* (varying with *Taingwethil*) is found in the *Lay of the Children of Húrin*. For *Ifan Belaurin* see I. 273, entry *Yavanna*; in the Gnomish dictionary the Gnomish form is *Ifon*, *Ivon*.

## 2

The description in S of the 'Outer Lands' (now used of the Great Lands, see III. 224), where growth was checked at the downfall of the Lamps, but where there are forests of dark trees in which Oromë goes hunting at times, moves the narrative at this point in one step to its structure in *The Silmarillion*; of the very different account in the *Lost Tales* I noticed in my commentary on *The Chaining of Melko* (I. 111): 'In this earliest narrative there is no mention of the beginning of growth during the time when the Lamps shone, and the first trees and low plants appeared under Yavanna's spells in the twilight after their overthrow.'

Whereas in the *Lost Tales* the star-making of Varda took place after the awakening of the Elves (I. 113), here they awake 'at the making of the stars'.

In commenting on the *Lost Tales* I noticed (I. 111, 131) that the Gods sought out Melko on account of his renewed cosmic violence, before the awakening of the Elves and without respect to them in any way; and that the release of Melko from Mandos took place before the coming of the Eldar to Valinor, so that he played a part in the debate concerning their summons. In S the later story (that the discovery of the Elves led directly to the assault of the Valar on the fortress of Morgoth) is already present, and moreover a motive is ascribed to the intervention of the Valar that is not found in *The Silmarillion*: they are 'reminded of their duty to the Earth, since they came thither knowing that their office was to govern it for the two races of Earth who should after come each in appointed time'. It seems clear also that the old story of the coming of the Elves being known to Manwë independently of their discovery by Oromë (see I. 131) had been abandoned.

In the *Lost Tales* Melko's first fortress was Utumna, and though it was not wholly destroyed to its foundations (I. 104) after his escape back into the Great Lands he was 'busy making himself new dwellings', as Sorontur told Manwë, for 'never more will Utumna open unto him' (I. 176). This second fortress was Angband (Angamandi). In S, on the other hand, the first fortress is Angband, and after his escape Morgoth is able to return to it (§4), for it was too strong for the Gods to destroy (§2). The name Utumna (Utumno) has thus disappeared.

In the passage describing the three hosts of the Elves on the great march from Cuiviénen (which occurs, by emendation, in the *Lay of the Children of Húrin*, III. 18, 23) there appears the later use of *Teleri* for the third kindred (who however still retain the old name *Solosimpi*, the Shoreland Pipers), while the first kindred (the *Teleri* of the *Lost Tales*) now acquire the name *Quendi* (subsequently spelt in S both *Quendi* and *Qendi*). Thus:

| *Lost Tales* | *'Sketch'* | *The Silmarillion* |
|---|---|---|
| Teleri | Q(u)endi | Vanyar |
| Noldoli | Noldoli | Noldor |
| Solosimpi | Teleri, Solosimpi | Teleri |

The formulation at the time of the *Lost Tales* (see I. 235) was that *Qendi* was the original name of all the Elves, and *Eldar* the name given by the Gods and adopted by the Elves of Valinor; those who remained in the Great Lands (Ilkorins) preserved the old name, *Qendi*. There also appear now the terms 'Light-elves', 'Deep-elves', and 'Sea-elves' (as in *The Hobbit*, chapter 8); the meaning of 'the Elves proper', applied to the first kindred, is clear from the *Quenta* (p. 85): 'the Quendi . . . who sometimes are alone called Elves.'

*Inwë* of the *Lost Tales* now becomes *Ingwë*, with the Gnomish equivalent *Ing* which appears in the alliterative poems, as does Gnomish *Finn* (in *The Flight of the Noldoli*). *Elwë (Elu)* is in the rôle of the later Olwë, leader of the third kindred after the loss of Thingol. In the *Tale of Tinúviel* Tinwelint (Thingol) was indeed originally called *Tinto Ellu* or *Ellu*, but in the tales of *The Coming of the Elves* and *The Theft of Melko*, by later changes, *Ellu* becomes the name of the second lord of the Solosimpi chosen in Tinwelint's place; see II. 50.

Notably absent from the account in S are the initial coming of the three Elvish ambassadors to Valinor, and the Elves who did not leave the Waters of Awakening, referred to in *Gilfanon's Tale* (I. 231): the

Ilkorins are here defined as those who were lost on the great march into the West. On these omissions see the commentary on §2 in the *Quenta*, p. 168.

Other omissions in S are the two starmakings of Varda (see p. 168) and the chain Angainor with which Morgoth was bound (see S §18 note 1).

## 3

In the tale of *The Coming of the Elves* the island on which the Gods were drawn to the western lands at the time of the fall of the Lamps was the island on which the Elves were afterwards ferried, becoming Tol Eressëa (see I. 118, 134); now, the isle on which the Gods dwelt (see the commentary on §1) is again the isle of the Elves' ferrying. But in *The Silmarillion* there is no connection between the Isle of Almaren and Tol Eressëa.

In the story of the ferrying features of the final narrative emerge in S: the first two kindreds to arrive at the shores of the sea are ferried together on this island, not separately as in the tale; and the love of the sea among the Teleri (Solosimpi) began during their waiting for Ulmo's return. On the other hand the old story of Ossë's rebellious anchoring of Tol Eressëa still survives (see I. 134); but the position of the island after its anchoring has now shifted westwards, to the Bay of Faërie, 'whence the Mountains of Valinor could dimly be seen': contrast the account in the tale, where Ulmo had traversed 'less than half the distance' across the Great Sea when Ossë waylaid it, and where 'no land may be seen for many leagues' sail from its cliffs' (see I. 120-1, and my discussion of this change, I. 134). In the tale, Ossë seized and anchored Tol Eressëa before its journey was done because he 'deemed himself slighted that his aid was not sought in the ferrying of the Elves, but his own island taken unasked' (I. 119); in S his jealousy is indeed mentioned, but also his love of the singing of the Teleri, which was afterwards a prominent motive. Ossë's making of the seabirds for the Teleri (Solosimpi) was retained, though afterwards lost.

In the tale the gap in the Mountains of Valinor was not made by the Valar for the sake of the Elves, nor was the hill of Kôr raised for them: they had existed since distant days, when 'in the trouble of the ancient seas a shadowy arm of water had groped in toward Valinor' (I. 122). In the passage in S can be seen the origin of that in *The Silmarillion* (p. 59). Here in S Côr is the hill and Tûn is the city built upon it (though in §2 there is a reference to Elves dwelling 'in Côr'); see III. 93.

On the 'invention' of gems by the Noldoli see I. 138. The especial love of Mandos 'the wise' for the Noldoli is found neither in the *Lost Tales* nor in *The Silmarillion*, and may seem an improbable attribute of that Vala: cf. *The Coming of the Elves*, I. 117: 'Mandos and Fui were cold to the Eldar as to all else.'

The passage concerning the Noldorin princes, added to the text of S (though probably after no great interval), is the origin of the passage in *The Silmarillion* (p. 60) which begins in the same way: 'The Noldor afterwards came back to Middle-earth, and this tale tells mostly of their deeds . . .' For the details of names and relations in this passage see the Note at the end of this section of the commentary.

The story of the coming of the Teleri (Solosimpi) to Valinor from Tol Eressëa comes in S, in essentials, almost to the form in *The Silmarillion* (p. 61); for the very different account in the tale see I. 124–6. In S, however, it was Ylmir (Ulmo) not Ossë who taught them the craft of shipbuilding, and this of course reflects the difference still underlying: for here Ylmir was still, as in the tale, eager for the coming of the Third Kindred to Valinor, whereas in *The Silmarillion* he had himself bidden Ossë make fast the island to the sea-bottom, and afterwards only 'submitted to the will of the Valar'. – The name *Ylmir* – almost certainly the Gnomish form – appears in the *Lay of the Children of Húrin*, see III. 93; but the form *Óin* for Uinen is not found elsewhere.

### Note on the Noldorin princes

Fingolfin as the son of Finwë (Finn) and father of Turgon emerges first in the *Lay of the Fall of Gondolin* (III. 146–7), and is present in the second version of the *Lay of the Children of Húrin* (only by emendation in the first) (III. 137). That Fëanor was Fingolfin's brother is deducible from the alliterative *Flight of the Noldoli (ibid.)*, but from S, as originally written in this section, it is seen that Fëanor was at first the second, not the elder son. Here in S Finwë's third son Finrod first emerges: the mention of him, and his sons, in a note to the *Lay of the Children of Húrin* (III. 80) is certainly later, as is his first appearance in the *Lay of Leithian* (III. 191, 195).

The seven sons of Fëanor with the same name-forms as here in S have appeared in the *Lay of the Children of Húrin* (III. 65, 86); the naming of Damrod and Díriel together in S suggests that they were already twin brothers.

Of the sons of Fingolfin Turgon of course goes back to the *Lost Tales*, where he was the son, not the grandson, of Finwë; the other son Finweg appears in the *Lay of the Children of Húrin*, where the emendation to Fingon (see III. 5, 80) is later than S – and the *Quenta*, where he was still Finweg in the text as first written.

The sons of Finrod first emerge here, and as the inserted passage in S was first written Orodreth was apparently the eldest son; Angrod was Anrod; and Felagund was Felagoth. Felagoth occurs as an intervening stage between Celegorm and Felagund in the A-text of the *Lay of Leithian* (III. 169, 195).

# 4

In this section again S moves at a step close to the essential structure of the narrative in *The Silmarillion*, though there are important features not yet present. I have discussed previously (I. 156–8) the radical differences between the tale of *The Theft of Melko* and the story in *The Silmarillion*, and it will be seen that it was with S that almost all these differences entered: there is thus no need to repeat the comparison again here. But various more minor matters may be noticed.

The quarrel of the Noldorin princes has as yet none of the complexity and subtlety that entered into it afterwards with the history of Míriel, the first wife of Finwë and mother of Fëanor; the quarrel is in any case treated with great brevity.

It is said here that 'Fëanor has cursed for ever anyone, God or Elf or mortal that shall come hereafter, who touches [the Silmarils]'. In §5, by a later interpolation, the oath is taken by Fëanor and his sons at the time of the torchlit concourse in Tûn, but the statement in §4 my father allowed to stand, clearly because he overlooked it. In the alliterative fragment *The Flight of the Noldoli*, however, which on general grounds I assume to belong to the earlier part of 1925 (III. 131), the oath is sworn by Fëanor and his sons as in the interpolation in S §5, 'in the mighty square upon the crown of Côr' (see III. 136). I incline to think that the statement here in §4 was a slip of memory.

The events immediately following the council of the Gods in which Morgoth's lies were disclosed and Fëanor banished from Tûn (in S the banishment is not said to be limited to a term of years) are not yet given the form they have in *The Silmarillion*. The entire story of Morgoth's going to Formenos (not yet so named) and his speech with Fëanor before the doors (*The Silmarillion* pp. 71–2) has yet to appear. Morgoth's northward movement up the coast in feint is also absent; rather he comes at once to Arvalin 'where the shadow is thickest in all the world', as is said in *The Silmarillion* (p. 73) of Avathar.

In the story of Morgoth's encounter with Ungoliant and the destruction of the Trees details of the final version appear, as Ungoliant's ascent of the great mountain (later named Hyarmentir) 'from pinnacle to pinnacle', and the ladder made for Morgoth to climb. There is no mention of the great festival, but it appears in §5: it looks as if my father omitted to include it earlier and brought it in a bit further on as an afterthought.

In the tale of *The Theft of Melko* Ungoliant fled south at once after the destruction of the Trees (I. 154), and of Melko's subsequent movements after his crossing of the Ice it is only told (by Sorontur to Manwë, I. 176) that he was busy building himself a new dwelling-place in the region of the Iron Mountains. But in S the story of 'the Thieves' Quarrel' and Morgoth's rescue by the Balrogs emerges suddenly fully-formed.

## 5

From the account of the great festival (see commentary on §4) is absent both the original occasion for holding it (commemoration of the coming of the Eldar to Valinor, I. 143) and that given in *The Silmarillion* (the autumn feast: pp. 74–5). The later feature that the Teleri were not present appears (see I. 157); but there is no suggestion of the important elements of Fëanor coming alone to the festival from Formenos, the formal reconciliation with Fingolfin, and Fëanor's refusal to surrender the Silmarils before he heard the news of his father's death and the theft of the jewels (*The Silmarillion* pp. 75, 78–9).

In the later emendations to the text of S we see the growth of the story of the divided counsels of the Gnomes, with the introduction of the attempt of Finrod (later Finarfin) to calm the conflicting factions – though this element was present in the tale of *The Flight of the Noldoli*, where Finwë Nólemë plays the part of the appeaser (I. 162). After a good deal of further shifting in this passage in later texts, and the introduction of Galadriel, the alignment, and the motives, of the princes as they appear in *The Silmarillion* are more complex (pp. 83–4); but the element is already present that only one of Finrod's sons sided with him (here Felagund, in *The Silmarillion* Orodreth).

The emendation making Fingolfin and Finweg (Fingon) rule over 'a half of the Noldoli of Tûn' must be incorrect; my father probably intended the revised text to read 'over the Noldoli of Tûn'.

The rapid shifting in the part of Finrod (Finarfin) in these events can be observed in the successive interpolations made in S. It seems that in the original text he did not appear at all (the first mention of him is in the interpolated passage in §3, p. 15). He is said not to have left Tûn; then he is said to have been slain at Swanhaven; and finally it is told that he and his sons were not at Swanhaven, but left Tûn reluctantly, carrying with them many things of their making. Finrod was then introduced as only arriving with his people in the far North after the burning of the ships by the Fëanorians on the other side of the strait. As S was originally written Fingolfin, deserted and shipless, returned to Valinor, and it was his son Finweg (Fingon) who led the main host over the Grinding Ice; but with the introduction of Finrod he becomes the one who returned. (Finweg as the leader of the host was not then changed to Fingolfin, but this was obviously an oversight.)

In the account of the northward journey of the Noldoli after the battle of Swanhaven it seems that all the host was embarked in the ships of the Teleri, since Mandos' emissary hails them from a high cliff 'as they sail by'; but this may be merely due to compression, since in the *Tale* (I. 166) some marched along the shore while 'the fleet coasted beside them not far out to sea', and the same is told in *The Silmarillion* ('some by ship and some by land', p. 87). The storm raised by Uinen is not mentioned.

It is curious that the curse upon the Gnomes, that they should suffer from treachery and the fear of treachery among their own kindred, is separated from the Prophecy of Mandos; but it is not said by whom this curse was pronounced. Nothing is told in S as originally written of the content of the Prophecy of Mandos, save that it concerned 'the fate of after days', but my father subsequently added that it told of 'the curse of war against one another because of Swanhaven', thus bringing the 'curse' into the content of the 'Prophecy', as in *The Silmarillion*. There is no trace of the old prophecies concerning Turgon and Gondolin (I. 167, 172), but nor is there any suggestion of the nature of the doom of the Noldor as it is stated in *The Silmarillion*.

For the original story of the crossing of the Grinding Ice by the Gnomes, where there is no element of treachery (though the blaming of Fëanor was already present), see I. 167–9.

# 6

The making of the Sun and Moon is here compressed into a couple of phrases. Virtually all of the extremely elaborate account in the old *Tale of the Sun and Moon* has disappeared: the tears of Vána leading to the last fruit of Laurelin, the breaking of the 'Fruit of Noon', the Bath of the Setting Sun where the Sun-maiden and her ship were drawn on coming out of the East, the song of Lórien leading to the last flower of Silpion, the fall of the 'Rose of Silpion' which caused the markings on the Moon, the refusal to allow Silmo to steer the ship of the Moon and the task given instead to Ilinsor, a spirit of the Súruli, Lake Irtinsa where the ship of the Moon was refreshed, and much else. But while it is impossible to say how much of all this my father had 'privately' rejected at this time (see my remarks, I. 200), some elements at least were suppressed for the purposes of this 'Sketch', which is after all only an outline, for they will reappear.

The change in the celestial plan now takes place because the Gods 'find it safer to send [the Sun and Moon] in Ylmir's care through the caverns and grottoes beneath the Earth'. This is wholly different from the old story (I. 215), in which the *original* plan of the Gods was that the Sun and Moon should be drawn beneath the earth; this plan was changed when they found that the Sun-ship 'might not safely come beneath the world' – the very reverse of what is said in S. Though the Moon continued to pass beneath the earth, the Gods now made the Door of Night in the West and the Gates of Morn in the East, through which the Sun passed thenceforward, going into and returning from the Outer Dark (I. 216). The astronomical aspect of the mythology has thus undergone a profound shift, an entire re-making.

The reference to the rekindling of the 'Magic Sun' (here with extension to the Moon, not found in the earliest writings) is a noteworthy survival; and the meaning is explicitly the rebirth of the Trees (see

II. 286). Very remarkable is Ulmo's foretelling to the Valar that the
rekindling of the Two Trees and the return of 'the bliss and glory of old'
would only come to pass by the aid of Men. It is possible that this is a
reference to his own deep designs laid through Turgon, Tuor, and
Eärendel; but it is nowhere suggested that these designs issued or were
intended to issue in such a way. Perhaps we should see here rather
the continued existence in some form of the old prophecy given in
II. 285:

> The Elves' prophecy is that one day they will fare forth from Tol
> Eressëa and on arriving in the world will gather all their fading kindred
> who still live in the world and march towards Valinor. . . This they will
> only do with the help of Men. If Men aid them, the fairies will take
> Men to Valinor – those that wish to go – fight a great battle with Melko
> in Erumáni and open Valinor. Laurelin and Silpion will be rekindled,
> and the mountain wall being destroyed then soft radiance will spread
> over all the world, and the Sun and Moon will be recalled.

In the account of the Hiding of Valinor we move in S from the *Lost
Tales* to *The Silmarillion*: I have observed (I. 223) the total absence in
the latter of the bitter divisions among the Valar, of Manwë's disgusted
withdrawal, of Ulmo's vain pleading for pity on the Noldor – and of my
father's explicit view in the tale of *The Hiding of Valinor* that the actions
of the Valar at this time, and their failure to make war upon Morgoth,
were a profound error arising from indolence and fear. The fear of
Morgoth does indeed remain, and is the only motive offered in *The
Silmarillion* for the Hiding of Valinor; but the author makes no comment on it. In S however the element of divine anger against the Noldoli
is still present (though neither here nor later is there any reference to the
peculiar anger of Aulë against them (see I. 176), save that in the *Annals
of Valinor* (p. 267) when Finrod and others returned to Valinor after
hearing the Doom of Mandos 'Aulë their ancient friend smiled on them
no more').

There are differences and omissions in the later versions of the story of
the Hiding of Valinor in relation to that in the tale which have been
sufficiently discussed already (I. 223–4); but it may be noticed that in S
no reason is given for keeping open the pass of Kôr, neither that in the
tale nor that in *The Silmarillion*.

It is very clear that with the 'Sketch' the structure of the Valinórean
part of the mythology, though not of course the detail, had quite largely
reached the stage of development of the published version; and it can be
understood why my father wrote on the envelope containing S the words
*Original 'Silmarillion'*. It is here that 'The Silmarillion' begins.

# 7

It will be seen that in this passage S has already the structure and some even of the phrases of the last three paragraphs of chapter 12 ('Of Men') in *The Silmarillion*.

The Fëanorian oath (ascribed here to the sons only) is embodied in the text as written, which probably shows that the interpolated passage, introducing the oath, in §5 (p. 19) was inserted while S was still in process of composition.

The words of S, 'in the early days Eldar and Men were of nearly equal stature and power of body', are echoed in *The Silmarillion*: 'Elves and Men were of like stature and strength of body'; for statements on this matter in earlier writings see II. 326.

The 'higher culture' that my father came to ascribe to the Elves of Doriath (or more widely to the Grey-elves of Beleriand) is now established ('Only in the realm of Doriath . . . did the Ilkorins equal the Koreldar'); contrast the description of the Ilkorins of Tinwelint's following in the old *Tale of Tinúviel* ('eerie they were and strange beings, knowing little of light or loveliness or of musics. . .'), concerning which I noted that Tinwelint's people are there described in terms applicable rather to the wild Avari of *The Silmarillion* (see II. 9, 64). It is however said in this passage of the tale that 'Different indeed did they become when the Sun arose.'

The ideas expressed here concerning the nature of the immortality of the Elves go back largely to the *Lost Tales*; cf. the description of the hall of Mandos in *The Coming of the Valar* (I. 76):

> Thither in after days fared the Elves of all the clans who were by illhap slain with weapons or did die of grief for those that were slain – and only so might the Eldar die, and then it was only for a while. There Mandos spake their doom, and there they waited in the darkness, dreaming of their past deeds, until such time as he appointed when they might again be born into their children, and go forth to laugh and sing again.

Similarly in *The Music of the Ainur* (I. 59) it is said that 'the Eldar dwell till the Great End unless they be slain or waste in grief (for to both of these deaths are they subject)', and 'dying they are reborn in their children, so that their number minishes not, nor grows'. But in the early texts death by sickness is not mentioned, and this appears for the first time in S: where by emendation there is a modification of the idea, from freedom from all sickness to freedom from death by sickness. Moreover in the early texts rebirth in their own children seems to be represented as the universal fate of the Eldar who die; whereas in S they are said to return from Mandos 'to free life'. Rebirth is mentioned in S very briefly and only in a later interpolation.

In S my father's conception of the fate of Men after death is seen evolving (for the extremely puzzling account in the *Lost Tales* see I. 77, 90–3). As he first wrote S, there was an explicit assertion that Men did not go to Mandos, did not pass to the western land: this was an idea derived from contact with the Eldar. But he changed this, and wrote instead that Men do indeed go to their own halls in Mandos, for a time; none know whither they go after, save Mandos himself.

On the 'fading' of the Elves who remained 'in the world' see II. 326.

# 8

Neither the brief outlines for what was to have been Gilfanon's tale of *The Travail of the Noldoli* (I. 237–41) nor the subsequent abandoned narrative given on pp. 6–8 bear much relation to what came after. Enduring features were the camp by Asgon-Mithrim, the death of Fëanor, the first affray with the Orcs, the capture and maiming of Maidros; but these elements had different motivations and concomitants in the earliest writing, already discussed (I. 242–3). With the 'Sketch', however, most of the essentials of the later story appear fully-formed, and the distance travelled from the *Lost Tales* is here even more striking than hitherto.

The first battle of the Gnomes with the forces of Morgoth is not clearly placed in S (cf. *Gilfanon's Tale*, I. 238, 240, where the battle was fought 'in the foothills of the Iron Mountains' or in 'the pass of the Bitter Hills') – but the idea is already present that the Orcs were aroused by the burning of the ships (cf. §5: 'The same light also tells the Orcs of the landing'.)

There now emerge the death of Fëanor at the hand of Gothmog the Balrog, the parley with the enemy and the faithless intentions on both sides, the arrival of the second host, unfurling their blue and silver banners (see p. 9) under the first Sunrise, and the dismay of the Orcs at the new light, the hostile armies of the Gnomes encamped on opposite sides of Lake Mithrim, the 'vast smokes and vapours' rising from Angband. The only important structural element in the narrative that has yet to appear is that of Fingolfin's march to Angband immediately on arrival in Middle-earth and his beating on the doors.

The earlier existence of the story of the rescue of Maidros by Finweg (Fingon) is implied by a reference in the *Lay of the Children of Húrin* (see III. 65, 86) – that in the *Lay of Leithian* is some two years later than S (III. 222). A curious point arises in the account in S: it seems that it was only at this juncture that Manwë brought into being the race of Eagles. In the tale of *The Theft of Melko* Sorontur (the 'Elvish' form of Gnomish Thorndor) had already played a part in the story before the departure of the Noldoli from Valinor: he was the emissary of the Valar to Melko before the destruction of the Trees, and because Melko tried to slay the Eagle between that evil one and Sorontur has there ever since been hate and war, and that was most bitter when Sorontur and his folk fared to the Iron Mountains and there abode, watching all that Melko did (I. 149).

It may be noted that Lake Mithrim is placed in Hisilómë/Hithlum/Dorlómin; see III. 103.

# 9

For this section of the narrative the earliest materials are so scanty that we may almost say that the 'Sketch' is the starting-point. In an outline for *Gilfanon's Tale* (I. 238) there is mention of a meeting between Gnomes and Ilkorins, and it was with the guidance of these Ilkorins that Maidros led an army to Angamandi, whence they were driven back with slaughter leaving Maidros a captive; and this was followed by Melko's southward advance and the Battle of Unnumbered Tears. As I have noted (I. 242):

> The entire later history of the long years of the Siege of Angband, ending with the Battle of Sudden Flame (Dagor Bragollach), of the passage of Men over the Mountains into Beleriand and their taking service with the Noldorin Kings, had yet to emerge; indeed these outlines give the effect of only a brief time elapsing between the coming of the Noldoli from Kôr and their great defeat.

In another outline (I. 240) there is a slight suggestion of a longer period, in the reference to the Noldoli 'practising many arts'. In this outline the meeting of Gnomes and Ilkorins takes place at 'the Feast of Reunion' (where Men were also present). But beyond this there is really nothing of the later story to be found in these projections. Nor indeed had S (as originally written) made any very remarkable advances. Men 'already dwelt in the woods of the North', which is sufficiently strange, since according to S Men awoke at the first rising of the Sun (§6), when also Fingolfin marched into Middle-earth (§8), and far too little time had elapsed, one would think, for Men to have journeyed out of 'the far East' (§6) and become established in 'the woods of the North'. Moreover there is no suggestion (even allowing for the brief and concentrated nature of the 'Sketch') that the Leaguer of Angband lasted any great length of time, nor is the breaking of the Leaguer particularly character-ised: Morgoth 'sends out his armies', and 'Gnomes and Ilkorins and Men are scattered'; that is all. But the breaking of the Leaguer was already seen as a turning-point in the history of the Elves of Beleriand. It is perfectly possible that much of the new material that appears at this place in the *Quenta* (see pp. 104 ff.) was already in my father's mind when he wrote S (i.e., S was a précis, but a précis of an unwritten story); for instance, the blasting of the great grassy northern plain in the battle that ended the siege (not even mentioned in S) was already present when the *Lay of the Children of Húrin* was written (III. 55).

With the later interpolations in S enters the idea of the Siege of Angband as an epoch, 'a time of growth and birth and flowering'; and also the disposition of the Gnomish princes, with the essentials of the later history already present – Fingolfin in Hithlum, the Fëanorians in the East (where they afterwards warred with Dwarves, Orcs, and Men), and Felagund guarding the entry into the lands of Sirion. (The reference to *Broseliand* in this passage is noteworthy: the form of the name spelt with -s- first appears in the A-text of Canto IV of the *Lay of Leithian* – probably early 1928; III. 195, 197). 'Fingolfin is slain when Morgoth breaks the leaguer' may or may not imply the story of his duel with Morgoth before Angband.

Gumlin father of Húrin has appeared in the second version of the *Lay of the Children of Húrin* (III. 115, 126); but Huor, named as Húrin's brother in the rewriting of S, here makes his first appearance in the legends.

The complexities of the history of Barahir and Beren and the founding of Nargothrond are best discussed together with what is said in §10; see the commentary on the next section.

# 10

In §9 as first written Barahir already appears as the father of Beren, replacing Egnor; and they are here Ilkorin Elves, not Men, though this was changed when the passage was revised. In the first version of the *Lay of the Children of Húrin* Beren was still an Elf, while in the second version my father shifted back and forth between Man and Elf (III. 124–5); in the opening cantos of the A-text of the *Lay of Leithian* (in being by the autumn of 1925) Egnor and his son were Men (III. 171); now here in S (early 1926) they are again Elves, though Egnor has become Barahir. Perplexingly, in §10 as first written, while Barahir is 'a famous chieftain of Ilkorindi', on the same page of the manuscript and quite certainly written at the same time Beren 'alone of *mortals* came back from Mandos'. It may well be that the statements in S that Barahir and Beren were Ilkorins were an inadvertent return to the former idea, after the decision that they were Men (seen in the A-text of the *Lay of Leithian*) had been made. (Later in the original text of S, §14, Beren is a mortal.)

The reference in §9 to the founding of Nargothrond by Celegorm and Curufin and in §10 to Barahir having been 'a friend of Celegorm of Nargothrond' belong to the phase of the swiftly-evolving legend represented by alterations to the text of the *Lay of the Children of Húrin* (see III. 83–5), when it was Celegorm and Curufin who founded Nargothrond after the breaking of the Leaguer of Angband and Felagund had not yet emerged; similarly in the A-text of the *Lay of Leithian* (III. 171).

The alterations to S in these sections move the story on to the form

found in the B-text of the *Lay of Leithian*, with Felagund as the one
saved by Barahir and the founder of Nargothrond – though here it is said
specifically that Felagund *and his brothers* founded the realm, with the
aid of Celegorm and Curufin; it seems therefore that the deaths of
Angrod and Egnor in the battle that ended the Leaguer had not yet arisen
(see III. 221, 247).

The very early form of the story of Beren (the first stage of development from the *Tale of Tinúviel*) in S §10 as first written has been
discussed in III. 219–20, 244. There remains an interesting point to
mention in the end of this version: the sentence 'Some songs say that
Lúthien went even over the Grinding Ice, aided by the power of her
divine mother, Melian, to Mandos' halls and won him back.' There is no
suggestion here that Lúthien herself died at the time of Beren's death;
and the same idea seems likely to underlie the lines of the second version
of the *Lay of the Children of Húrin* (III.107):

> ere he winged afar
> to the long awaiting;    thence Lúthien won him,
> the Elf-maiden,    *and the arts of Melian* . . .

In the *Tale of Tinúviel*, on the other hand, it is said (II. 40) that

> Tinúviel crushed with sorrow and finding no comfort or light in all the
> world followed him swiftly down those dark ways that all must tread
> alone

– and this seems quite clear in its meaning.

Beren and Lúthien are here said to have lived, after Beren's return, 'in
the woods of Doriath and in the Hunters' Wold, west of Nargothrond'.
The Land of the Dead that Live was placed in the Hunters' Wold (Hills
of the Hunters) in the *Lay of the Children of Húrin*; see III. 89, where
the previous history of its placing is given.

That Beren and Húrin were friends and fellows-in-arms is stated in the
*Lay of the Children of Húrin*, and earlier (see III. 25), but it has not
been said before that this relationship arose during the time of Beren's
outlawry.·

For the use of 'Shadowy Mountains' to mean the Mountains of Terror
see III. 170–1.

In the rewritten passage (pp. 25–6) the story is seen at an earlier stage
than that in the 'Synopsis II' for Cantos VI and VII of the *Lay of Leithian*
(1928), the text of which is given in III. 221, 233. Celegorm has been
displaced by Felagoth (not yet Felagund); but Celegorm 'discovered
what was the secret mission of Felagoth and Beren' *after* their departure
from Nargothrond, and thus the element of the intervention of Celegorm
and Curufin, turning the Elves of Nargothrond against their king, was
not yet present. Moreover in the northward journey of Beren and his
companions from Nargothrond there is a battle with Orcs, from which
only a small band of the Elves escapes, afterwards returning to the

battlefield to despoil the dead and disguise themselves as Orcs. These two elements are clearly interconnected: Celegorm (and Curufin) do not know why Beren and Felagoth are setting out, and thus there is no reason why the king should not set out with a strong force. When my father wrote 'Synopsis II' he had brought in the element of the intervention of the Fëanorian brothers against Felagund and Beren, and with it the small band that was all they had as companions from their first departure from Nargothrond.

The sequence is thus clearly: S – Synopsis I – interpolation in S – Synopsis II; and in the revision of S here we have an interesting stage in which Felagund (Felagoth) has emerged as the lord of Nargothrond, but the 'Fëanorian intervention' has not, and Celegorm still 'offers redress' to Lúthien, as he did in Synopsis I (III. 244) – for his dog Huan had hurt her.

## 11

The earliest form of this part of the story (apart from that which relates to Húrin) is extant only in the compressed outlines for *Gilfanon's Tale*. In my comparison of those early outlines with the narrative of *The Silmarillion* I noted (I.242) as essential features of the story that were to survive:

- A mighty battle called the Battle of Unnumbered Tears is fought between Elves and Men and the hosts of Melko;
- Treachery of Men, corrupted by Melko, at that battle;
- But the people of Úrin (Húrin) are faithful, and do not survive it;
- The leader of the Gnomes is isolated and slain;
- Turgon and his host cut their way out, and go to Gondolin;
- Melko is wrathful because he cannot discover where Turgon has gone;
- The Fëanorians come late to the battle;
- A great cairn is piled.

There is no evidence for any narrative of the Battle of Unnumbered Tears in its own right between the outlines for *Gilfanon's Tale* and the 'Sketch'; thus §11 in S shows at a step a very great advance. This is not however to be regarded as a direct evolution from the outlines, for many elements – such as the stories of Beren and Tinúviel, and of Nargothrond – had been developed 'collaterally' in the meantime. As S was originally written in §11, the old 'pre-Felagund' story was present ('Curufin and Celegorm despatch a host from Nargothrond', see commentary on §10), and although the failure of the Union of Maidros to gather together all the Elves of Beleriand into a united force already appears, the alignments were for this reason quite different: the Gnomes of Nargothrond (ruled by Celegorm and Curufin) will not serve under Finweg (Fingon). But with the rewriting of S, made after the emergence of the Felagund-story, an essential element of the later narrative comes into being: Orodreth will not join the league on account of Felagund his brother (cf. *The Silmarillion* p. 188: 'Orodreth would not march forth at the word of any son of Fëanor, because of the deeds of Celegorm and Curufin.') That Thingol sent few (emended from none) out of Doriath is a very old element, appearing already in the *Tale of Turambar* (II. 73), where Tinwelint said to Mavwin, in words echoed in the present passage of S:

> not for love nor for fear of Melko but of the wisdom of my heart and the fate of the Valar did I not go with my folk to the Battle of Unnumbered Tears, who am now become a safety and a refuge . . .

A new factor in Thingol's policy now appears, however, in that he resented the 'haughty words' addressed to him by Maidros, demanding the return of the Silmaril – those 'haughty words' and their effect on the Union of Maidros survived into *The Silmarillion* (p. 189). That Thingol here allows 'the *Gnomes* of Doriath' to join the league is to be related to the statement in S §9: 'Many Gnomes take service with Thingol and Melian' (after the breaking of the Siege of Angband). (In the *Tale of Tinúviel* there were Noldoli in Tinwelint's service: it was they indeed who built the bridge before his doors. II. 9, 43.)

As S was rewritten, the division of the opponents of Morgoth into two hosts was due to the refusal of the Fëanorians to be led by Finweg (Fingon), whereas in *The Silmarillion* account there was good agreement between Himring and Eithel Sirion, and the assault from East and West of the Fëanorians and the Noldor of Hithlum a matter of strategy ('they thought to take the might of Morgoth as between anvil and hammer, and break it to pieces').

The Battle of Unnumbered Tears is still in S in a simple form, but the advance of the Elves of Hithlum into Dor-na-Fauglith in pursuit of a defeated Orc-army, so that they fall prey to much greater hosts loosed from Angband, moves towards the plan of the later narrative; the late arrival of the Fëanorians goes back to an outline for *Gilfanon's Tale* (see above). No detail is given in S concerning the treachery of Men at the battle, nor is any reason suggested for the late coming of the Eastern Noldor.

Finweg (Fingon) had taken the place of Finwë (Nólemë) as the Gnomish king slain in the battle already in the *Lay of the Children of Húrin* (III. 86), and so the story of the Scarlet Heart, emblem of Turgon (I. 241, II. 172), had disappeared; in the second version of the Lay there is mention of his *white banners . . . in blood beaten* (III. 96). In S Turgon is a leader, with his brother Finweg (Fingon), of the Western Noldor from the outset, and was clearly conceived to be dwelling at this time in Hithlum (cf. the interpolation in §9: 'Fingolfin's sons Finweg and Turgon still hold out in the North', i.e. after the ending of the Siege of Angband); and the discovery of the secret valley and the founding of Gondolin follows from the retreat from the disaster of the Battle of Unnumbered Tears. The 'sacrifice of Mablon the Ilkorin' (I.239, 241) has disappeared.

The great mound of the slain on Dor-na-Fauglith, the first trace of which appears in an outline for *Gilfanon's Tale* (I.241, 243), had been described in the *Lay of the Children of Húrin* (III. 58–9), where Flinding said to Túrin as they passed by it in the moonlight:

> A! green that hill    with grass fadeless
> where sleep the swords    of seven kindreds . . .
>
> neath moon nor sun    is it mounted ever
> by Man nor Elf;    not Morgoth's host
> ever dare for dread    to delve therein.

The story of Húrin at the Battle of Unnumbered Tears – his holding of the rearguard with his men while Turgon escaped southwards, his capture, defiance of Morgoth, and torture – had already been told in the *Tale of Turambar* (II.70–1) and in the *Lay of the Children of Húrin* (see III. 23–4, 102). In all these sources Morgoth's concern with Húrin, his attempts to seduce him, and his great rage when defied, arise from his desire to find Turgon; but the element is still of course lacking in S that Húrin had previously visited Gondolin, which at this stage in the development of the legend did not exist as a Noldorin fastness until after the Battle. As the story evolved, this fact, known to Morgoth, gave still more ugency to his wish to take Húrin alive, and to use him against Turgon.

## 12

It is immediately obvious that S was based on the second version of the *Lay of the Children of Húrin*, so far as it goes – which in relation to the whole narrative is not far: no further than the feast at which Túrin slew Orgof. This is already evident from the preceding portion of S, describing Morgoth's treatment of Húrin in Angband; while in the present section the guardians of Túrin on the journey to Doriath bear the later names Halog and Mailgond (emended in the Lay to Mailrond, III. 119), not Halog and Gumlin.

It is not to be expected that the synopsis of the story in S should show any substantial alteration of that in the first version of the Lay; there is some development nonetheless. It is now explicit that the Men who in the Lay *dwelt in Dorlómin and dealt unkindly* with Húrin's wife, and of whom I noted (III. 24) that 'there is still no indication of who these men were or where they came from', are now explicitly 'faithless men who had deserted the Eldar in the Battle of Unnumbered Tears', penned in Hithlum because Morgoth 'desired to keep them from fellowship with Elves'. The question of whether Nienor was born before Túrin left Hithlum is now resolved: he had never seen her. For the uncertainty on this point in the *Tale of Turambar* see II. 131; in the Lay she was born before Túrin left (III. 9).

Whereas in the Lay Beleg, who was not searching for Túrin when he was captured by the outlaw band, knew nothing of what had happened in the Thousand Caves (see III. 50), in S 'Túrin released Beleg, and is told how Thingol had forgiven his deed long ago'. Blodrin is now again the son of Ban, not of Bor (see III. 52).

There is an interesting note in S that Túrin was taken alive to Angband 'for Morgoth has begun to fear he will escape his curse through his valour and the protection of Melian'. This idea is seen in the words of the Lay (III. 33) *they haled unhappy    Húrin's offspring / lest he flee his fate*, and goes back to the *Tale of Turambar* (II. 76):

Túrin was overborne and bound, for such was the will of Melko that he be brought to him alive; for behold, dwelling in the halls of Linwë [*i.e.* Tinwelint] about which had that fay Gwedheling the queen woven much magic and mystery . . . Túrin had been lost out of his sight, and he feared lest he cheat the doom that was devised for him.

There is little else to note in this section beyond the new detail that the Orcs feared Taur-na-Fuin no less than Elves or Men, and only went that way when in haste, and the ancestor of the phrase 'Gwindor saw them marching away over the steaming sands of Anfauglith' (*The Silmarillion* p. 208) in 'Flinding sees them marching over the steaming waste of Dor-na-Fauglith' (cf. the Lay, III. 48: *The dusty dunes    of Dor-na-Fauglith / hissed and spouted*). A very great deal is of course omitted in the synopsis.

# 13

With the second paragraph of this section, 'Túrin leads the Gnomes of Nargothrond to forsake their secrecy and hidden warfare', S reaches the point where the *Lay of the Children of Húrin* stops, and certain advances made on the *Tale of Turambar* (II. 83 ff.) can be observed. The re-forging of Beleg's sword for Túrin in Nargothrond now appears. In the Lay Flinding put the sword in the hollow of a tree after Beleg's death (III. 56); as I noted (III. 86): 'if the poem had gone further Túrin would have received his black sword in Nargothrond in gift from Orodreth, as happens in the *Tale*'. S thus shows a development from the plot implicit in the Lay. The bridging of Narog by Túrin's counsel enters the story only as a pencilled marginal note. The extent of the victories and reconquest of territory by the Gnomes of Nargothrond at this time is made explicit, and the realm is much as described in *The Silmarillion* (p. 211):

> The servants of Angband were driven out of all the land between Narog and Sirion eastward, and westward to the Nenning and the desolate Falas

(where however its northern border along the southern feet of the Shadowy Mountains is not mentioned; in S 'their realm reaches to the sources of Narog').

The later addition to the text of S, 'even Glómund, who was at the Battle of Tears', is to be related to the absence of any mention of the Dragon in S's account of the battle (§11). As S was first written, the Dragon was named *Glórung*, a change from *Glórund* of the *Lost Tales*; the series was thus *Glórund* > *Glórung* > *Glómund* > *Glaurung*. In the *Lay of Leithian Glómund* replaces *Glórund* (III. 208–9).

The sentence 'Flinding wounded refuses Túrin's succour and dies reproaching him' shows the later form of the story, as in *The Silmarillion* pp. 212–13; for discussion of the substantial change from the *Tale* see II. 124. It is said in S that Túrin forsook Finduilas 'against his heart (which if he had obeyed his uttermost fate would not have befallen him)', and this is no doubt to be related to the passage in the *Tale* (II. 87):

> And truly is it said: 'Forsake not for anything thy friends – nor believe those who counsel thee to do so' – for of his abandoning of Failivrin in danger that he himself could see came the very direst evil upon him and all he loved.

For discussion of this see II. 125.

Of Túrin's return to Hithlum there is little to note, for the synopsis is here very compressed; and I have earlier discussed fully the relationship between the *Tale* and the later story (II. 126–7). The Woodmen with whom Túrin lives after his flight from Hithlum are now given a more definite location 'east of Narog' (see II. 140–1). In S it is made clear that Túrin did not join himself to a people already existing, but 'gathered a new people'. This is in contradiction, strangely enough, both to the *Tale* (II. 91, 102), where they had a leader (Bethos) when Túrin joined them, and to the later story. Túrin now takes the name *Turambar* at this point in the narrative, not as in the *Tale* before the Dragon outside the caves of the Rodothlim (II. 86, 125).

Turning now to the expedition from Doriath to Nargothrond, the only important structural difference from the *Tale* that emerges in the brief account in S is that Morwen (Mavwin) was evidently no longer present at the conversation between Nienor and the Dragon (II. 98–9, 129); on the other hand, it is said at the end of this section that 'Some say Morwen *released from spell by Glórung's death* came that way and read the stone.'

When Nienor-Níniel came to the falls of the Silver Bowl a fit of shivering came on her, as in the later narrative, whereas in the *Tale* it is only said that she was filled with dread (II. 101, 130). Very notably, the statement that Níniel was with child by Turambar was added to S later, just as it was in the *Tale* (see II. 117 note 25, 135).

In the foregoing I have only picked out points that seem to show quite clearly a different conception of the events in S from that in the *Tale*. I have not mentioned the many slight differences (including the very many omissions) that are probably or certainly due to compression.

# 14

Of this section of the narrative there exists in earlier writing only the conclusion of the *Tale of Turambar* (II. 112–16) and the *Tale of the Nauglafring* (II. 221 ff.) in which the story is continued. The opening passage of S follows the end of the *Tale of Turambar* in Melko's accusation against Thingol of faintheartedness, Húrin's embitterment from the pondering of Melko's words, the gathering to him of a band of outlaws, the fear of the spirit of the dead Dragon that prevented any from plundering Nargothrond, the presence there of Mîm, Húrin's reproaches and the casting of the gold at Thingol's feet, and Húrin's departure. The words of S concerning the fate of Húrin derive from the *Tale*, where however he died in Hithlum and it was his 'shade' that 'fared into the woods seeking Mavwin, and long those twain haunted the woods about the fall of Silver Bowl bewailing their children'.

From this point the source for S (or perhaps more accurately, the previous written form of the narrative) is the *Tale of the Nauglafring*. It is here impossible to say for certain how much of the complex story in the *Tale* had by this time been abandoned.

It is not made clear whether Mîm's presence in Nargothrond goes back to the time of the Dragon (see II. 137), nor whether the outlaws of Húrin's band were Men or Elves (in the *Tale* the text was emended to convert them from Men to Elves); and there is no indication of how the gold was brought to Doriath. The outlaws disappear in S after the slaying of Mîm, and there is no suggestion of the fighting in the Thousand Caves that in the *Tale* led to the mound made over the slain, Cûm an-Idrisaith, the Mound of Avarice.

The next part of the *Tale* (Ufedhin the renegade Gnome and the complex dealings of Thingol with him and with the Dwarves of Nogrod, II. 223–9) is reduced to a few lines in S, which could possibly stand as an extremely abbreviated account of the old story, even though Ufedhin is here not even mentioned. The making of the Necklace was not in the *Tale*, as it is in S, part of the king's request: the idea of it was indeed hatched by

Ufedhin during his captivity as a lure 'for the greater ensnaring of the king' (II. 226); but this also could be set down to compression. I think it is more probable, however, that my father had in fact decided to reduce and simplify the narrative, and that Ufedhin had been abandoned.

The problem of the entry of the Dwarvish army into Doriath, defended by the Girdle of Melian, is still solved by the device – the too simple device, see II. 250 – of 'some treacherous Gnomes' (in the *Tale* there was only one traitor); the slaying of Thingol while hunting remains, and as in the *Tale* Melian, inviolable, left the Thousand Caves seeking Beren and Lúthien. Though it is not so stated, it seems likely that in this version it was Melian who brought the news and the warning to Beren (this is the story in the *Quenta*, p. 134). In the *Tale* it was Huan who brought word to Beren and Lúthien of the assault on Artanor and the death of Tinwelint, and it was Ufedhin, fleeing from the Dwarf-host (after his abortive attempt to slay Naugladur and steal the Nauglafring, and his killing of Bodruith lord of Belegost), who revealed the course that the Dwarves were taking and made possible the ambush at the Stony Ford; but Huan has in S been slain in the Wolf-hunt (§10), and Ufedhin has (as I think) been eliminated.

The ambush at the ford is made by 'Beren and the brown and green Elves of the wood', which goes back to 'the brown Elves and the green', the 'elfin folk all clad in green and brown' ruled by Beren and afterwards by Dior in Hithlum, in the *Tale of the Nauglafring*. But of the vigorous account of the battle at the ford in the *Tale* – the laughter of the Elves at the misshapen Dwarves running with their long white beards torn by the wind, the duel of Beren and Naugladur, whose forge-hammer blows would have overcome Beren had not Naugladur stumbled and Beren swung him off his feet by catching hold of the Nauglafring – there is nothing in S: though equally, nothing to contradict the old story. There is however no mention of the two Dwarf-lords, Naugladur of Nogrod and Bodruith of Belegost, and though both Dwarf-cities are named the Dwarves are treated as an undivided force, with, as it seems, one king (slain at the ford): Thingol summoned those of Belegost as well as those of Nogrod to Doriath for the fashioning of the gold, whereas in the *Tale* (II. 230) the former only enter the story after the humiliating expulsion of the Dwarves of Nogrod, in order to aid them in their revenge. Of the old story of the death of Bodruith and the feud and slaughter among the two kindreds (brought about by Ufedhin) there is no trace.

The drowning of the treasure in the river goes back to the *Tale*; but there however the suggestion is not that the treasure was deliberately sunk: rather it fell into the river with the bodies of the Dwarves who bore it:

> those that waded in the ford cast their golden burdens in the waters and sought affrighted to either bank, but many were stricken with those pitiless darts and fell with their gold into the currents (II. 237).

It is not said in the *Tale* that any of the gold was drowned by the Elves. There, Gwendelin came to Beren and Tinúviel *after* the battle of the Stony Ford, and found Tinúviel already wearing the Nauglafring; there is mention of the greatness of her beauty when she wore it. Gwendelin's warning is only against the Silmaril (the rest of the treasure being drowned), and indeed her horror at seeing the Necklace of the Dwarves on Tinúviel was so great that Tinúviel put it off. This was to Beren's displeasure, and he kept it (II. 239–40). In S the drowning seems to be carried out in response to Melian's warning of the curse upon it, and the story seems to be thus: Melian comes to Beren and Lúthien and warns them of the approach of the Dwarf-host returning out of Doriath; after the battle Lúthien wears the Nauglafring and becomes immeasurably beautiful; but Melian warns them of the curse on the gold and on the Silmaril and they drown the treasure, though Beren keeps the Necklace secretly.

The fading of Lúthien follows immediately on the statement that the Necklace was kept, but no connection is made. In the *Tale* such a connection is explicit: the doom of mortality that Mandos had spoken 'fell swiftly' –

and in this perhaps did the curse of Mîm have [?potency] in that it came more soon upon them (II. 240).

Moreover in a synopsis for a projected revision of the *Lost Tales* it is said that the Nauglafring 'brought sickness to Tinúviel' (II. 246).

The reference to the fading of Lúthien in S retains the words of the *Tale*: Tinúviel slowly faded 'even as the Elves of later days have done'; and, again as in the *Tale*, Lúthien 'vanished'. In the *Tale* Beren was an Elf, and it is said of him that after searching all Hithlum and Artanor for Tinúviel in terrible loneliness 'he too faded from life'. In my discussion of this I said (II. 250):

Since this fading is here quite explicitly the mode in which 'that doom of mortality that Mandos had spoken' came upon them, it is very notable that it is likened to, and even it seems identified with, the fading of 'the Elves of later days throughout the world' – as though in the original idea Elvish fading was a form of mortality.

The passage in S, retaining this idea in respect of Lúthien, but now with the later conception that Beren was a mortal Man, not an Elf, is changed in that Beren is no longer said to have faded: he 'was lost', looking in vain for Lúthien. It is also said here that the price of Beren's return from Mandos was 'that Lúthien should become as shortlived as Beren the mortal'; and in §10, where the story of Beren and Lúthien is briefly told, it is not in fact said that Lúthien died when Beren died in Doriath (see the commentary on that section, p. 55). There is also a sentence added to the MS in §10: 'But Mandos in payment exacted that Lúthien should become mortal as Beren.'

It is possible to conclude from this that, in the conception as it was when S was written, Beren died, as a mortal dies; Lúthien went to Valinor as a living being; and Mandos allowed Beren to return to a second mortal span, but Lúthien now became subject to the same shortness of span as he. In this sense she became 'mortal'; but being an Elf she 'faded' – this was the manner of her death: as it was also the manner of the death of the fading Elves of later ages. Part of the difficulty in all this undoubtedly lies in the ambiguous nature of the words 'mortal' and 'immortal' applied to the Elves: they are 'immortal', both in the sense that they need not die, it is not in their essential nature to die, 'in the world', and also in the sense that, if they did, they did not 'leave the world', did not go to 'a fate beyond the world'; and they are 'mortal' in that they might nonetheless die 'in the world' (by wounds or by grief, but not from sickness or age). Lúthien became 'mortal' in that, although an Elf, she *must* die – she *must* fade.

It may be noted that the words 'as Men grew strong and took the goodness of earth' derive from the *Lay of the Children of Húrin* (III. 44, 54):

> for in days long gone
> . . . Men were of mould    less mighty builded
> ere the earth's goodness    from the Elves they drew.

Cf. *The Silmarillion*, p. 105: 'In after days, when because of the triumph of Morgoth Elves and Men became estranged, as he most wished, those of the Elven-race that lived still in Middle-earth waned and faded, and Men usurped the sunlight.'

Lastly, in the story of Dior and the ruin of Doriath as told in S, there are various developments. The son of Dior, Auredhir (II. 240) has disappeared. The 'vain bargaining' between Dior and the Sons of Fëanor perhaps refers to the passage in the *Tale* (II. 241) where Dior asserts that to return the Silmaril the Nauglafring must be broken, and Curufin (the messenger of the Fëanorians) retorts that in that case the Nauglafring must be given to them unbroken. In the *Tale* Maglor, Díriel, Celegorm, and Cranthir (or the earlier equivalents of their names) were killed in the battle (which there took place in Hithlum, where Dior ruled after his father); but in S, as first written, the story takes a very strange turn, in that the Fëanorians did get their hands on the Nauglafring, but then so quarrelled over it that in the end 'only Maglor was left'. How the story would have gone in this case is impossible to discern.

## 15 and 16

The two sections describing Gondolin and its fall are discussed together in the following commentary.

At the beginning of §15 the brief reference to the story of Isfin and Eöl shows development from what was said in the *Lay of the Fall of Gondolin* (III. 146): for in the poem Isfin was seeking, together with her mother, for her father Fingolfin when she was entrapped by Eöl in the dark forest. The larger history has evolved since then, and now Isfin 'was lost in Taur-na-Fuin after the Battle of Unnumbered Tears'. We can only surmise how she came to be there. Either she left Gondolin soon after its settlement bent on some purpose unrecorded, or else she was lost in the retreat from the battle. (It is, incidentally, a curious aspect of the earlier conception of Gondolin's foundation that there were women and children to people it as well as warriors; for one would suppose that Turgon had left the old men, the women, and the children of his people in Hithlum – why should he do otherwise? But in the outlines for *Gilfanon's Tale* there are references to Turgon's having 'rescued a part of the women and children', and having 'gathered women and children from the camps' as he fled south down Sirion (I. 239, 241).) Meglin is still, as in the poem, 'sent by his mother to Gondolin', while she remained with her captor.

In the account of Gondolin and its history S is fairly close to the tale of *The Fall of Gondolin*, but there are some developments, if mostly of a minor kind. There is first a notable statement that 'Ylmir's messages come up Sirion bidding them [i.e. the host of Turgon retreating from the battle] take refuge in this valley'; this is unlike the *Tale*, where Tuor speaking the words of Ulmo in Gondolin says: 'There have come to the ears of Ulmo whispers of your dwelling and your hill of vigilance against the evil of Melko, and he is glad' (II. 161, 208). Here in S we have the first appearance of the idea that the foundation of Gondolin was a part of Ulmo's design. But Tuor's journey is as in the old story, and the visitation of Ulmo is in Nan Tathrin, not at Vinyamar. The bidding of Ulmo offers Turgon similar choices, to prepare for war, or, if he will not, then to send people of Gondolin down Sirion to the sea, to seek for Valinor. Here, however, there are differences. In the *Tale*, Ulmo offers scarcely more than a slender hope that such sailors from Gondolin would reach Valinor, and if they did, that they would persuade the Valar to act:

> [The Gods] hide their land and weave about it inaccessible magic that no evil come to its shores. Yet still might thy messengers win there and turn their hearts that they rise in wrath and smite Melko . . . (II. 161–2).

In S, on the other hand, the people of Gondolin, if they will not go to war against Morgoth, are to desert their city ('the people of Gondolin are to prepare for flight') – cf. *The Silmarillion* p. 240: '[Ulmo] bade him depart, and abandon the fair and mighty city that he had built, and go down Sirion to the sea' – and at the mouths of Sirion Ylmir will not only aid them in the building of a fleet but will himself guide them over the ocean. But if Turgon will accept Ylmir's counsel, and prepare for war, then Tuor is to go to Hithlum with Gnomes from Gondolin and 'draw Men once more into alliance with the Elves, for "without Men the Elves shall not prevail against the Orcs and Balrogs".' Of this strange bidding there is no trace in the *Tale*; nor is it said there that Ulmo knew of Meglin, and knew that this treachery would bring about the end of Gondolin at no distant time. These features are absent also from *The Silmarillion*; Ulmo does indeed foresee the ruin of the city, but his foreseeing is not represented as being so precise: 'Thus it may come to pass that the curse of the Noldor shall find thee too ere the end, and treason awake within thy walls. Then they shall be in peril of fire' (p. 126).

The description of the Vale of Gondolin in S is essentially as in the *Tale*, with a few added details. As in the *Tale*, the rocky height of Amon Gwareth was not in the centre of the plain but nearest to Sirion – that is, nearest to the Way of Escape (II. 158, 177). In S, the level top of the hill is said to have been achieved by the people of Gondolin themselves, who also 'polished its sides to the smoothness of glass'. The Way of Escape is still, as in the *Tale* (II. 163), a tunnel made by the Gnomes – the Dry River and the Orfalch Echor have not yet been conceived; and the meaning of the name 'Way of Escape' is made very clear: both a way of escape from Gondolin, if the need should ever arise, and a way of escape from the outer world and from Morgoth. In the *Tale* (*ibid.*) it is said only that there had been divided counsels concerning its delving, 'yet pity for the enthralled Noldoli had prevailed in the end to its making'. The 'Guarded Plain' into which the Way of Escape issued is the Vale of Gondolin. An additional detail in S is that the hills were lower in the region of the Way of Escape, and the spells of Ylmir there strongest (because nearest to Sirion).

The cairn of Fingolfin, added in pencil in S, is an element that entered the legends in the *Quenta* (p. 107) and the *Lay of Leithian* (III. 286–7); the duel of Fingolfin with Morgoth does not appear in S (p. 54). – Here in S it is said that Thorndor 'removed his eyries to the Northern heights of the encircling mountains'. In the *Tale* the eyries in Cristhorn, the Eagles' Cleft, were in the mountains south of Gondolin, but in S Cristhorn is in the northern heights: this is already the case in the Fragment of an alliterative *Lay of Eärendel* (III. 143). Thorndor had come there from Thangorodrim (stated in the *Quenta*, p. 137); cf. the 'later *Tuor*' in *Unfinished Tales* (p. 43 and note 25): 'the folk of Thorondor, who dwelt once even on Thangorodrim ere Morgoth grew so mighty, and dwell now in the Mountains of Turgon since the fall of Fingolfin.' This goes back to the tale of *The Theft of Melko*, where there is a reference (I. 149) to the time 'when Sorontur and his folk fared to the Iron Mountains and there abode, watching all that Melko did'.

Some other points concerning the story of Gondolin may be noticed. The escort of Noldoli, promised to Tuor by Ulmo in the Land of Willows, of whom Voronwë (in S given the Gnomish form of the name, Bronweg) was the only one who did not desert him (II. 155–6), has disappeared; and 'Bronweg had once been in Gondolin', which is not the case in the *Tale* (II. 156–7). – In the *Tale* Tuor wedded Idril when he 'had dwelt among the Gondothlim many years' (II. 164); in S this took place three years after his coming to the hidden city, in *The Silmarillion* seven years after (p. 241). – In the *Tale* there is no mention of Meglin's support of Turgon's rejection of Ulmo's bidding (cf. *The Silmarillion* p. 240: 'Maeglin spoke ever against Tuor in the councils of the King'), nor of the opposition of Idril to her father (this is not in *The Silmarillion*). – The closing of Gondolin to all fugitives and the forbidding of the people to leave the valley is mentioned in S but not explained.

The sentence 'Meglin . . . purchases his life when taken to Angband *by revealing Gondolin* and its secrets' shows almost certainly, I think, that an important structural change in the story of the fall of the city had now entered. In the *Tale* Melko had discovered Gondolin *before* Meglin was captured, and his treachery lay in his giving an exact account of the structure of the city and the preparations made for its defence (see II. 210–11); but the words 'by revealing Gondolin' strongly suggest the later story, in which Morgoth did not know where it lay.

Lastly, there is a development in the early history of Tuor: that he became a slave of 'the faithless men' in Hithlum after the Battle of Unnumbered Tears. Moreover Tuor's parentage is now finally established. Huor has been mentioned in a rewritten passage of S (§9), but not named as father of Tuor; and this is the first occurrence of his mother Rían, and so of the story that she died seeking Huor's body on the battlefield. It cannot be said whether the story of Tuor's birth in the wild and his fostering by Elves had yet arisen.

# 17

In commenting on the conclusion of the mythology in S, here comprised in the three sections 17–19, I point to features that derive from or contradict those outlines and notes from an earlier period that are collected in Vol. II chapter V and the earlier part of Chapter VI. S is here an extremely abbreviated outline, composed very rapidly – my father was indeed changing his conceptions as he wrote.

For the narrative of §17 the primary extant early sources are the 'schemes' or plot-outlines which I have called 'B' and 'C', in the passages given in II. 253 and 254–5 respectively.

At the beginning of this section, before emendation, the survivors of Gondolin were already at the Mouths of Sirion when Elwing came there; and this goes back to B and C ('Elwing . . . flees to them [i.e. Tuor and Idril] with the Nauglafring', II. 254). But earlier in S (§15) the destruction of Dior took place before the fall of Gondolin; hence the revision here, to make Elwing 'receive the survivors of Gondolin'. (In the *Tale of the Nauglafring*, II. 242, the fall of Gondolin and the attack on Dior took place on the same day.)

Following this, there is a major development in S. In the early outlines there is the story, only glimpsed, of the March of the Elves of Valinor into the Great Lands; and in B (only) there is a reference to 'the sorrow and wrath of the Gods', of which I said in my discussion of these outlines (II. 257): 'the meaning can surely only be that the March of the Elves from Valinor was undertaken in direct opposition to the will of the Valar, that the Valar were bitterly opposed to the intervention of the Elves of Valinor in the affairs of the Great Lands.' On the other hand, the bare hints of what happened when the assault on Melko took place show that greater powers than the Eldar alone were present: Noldorin (the Vala Salmar, who entered the world with Ulmo, and loved the Noldoli), and Tulkas himself, who overthrew Melko in the Battle of the Silent Pools (outline C, II. 278). The only hint in the outlines of Ulmo's intervention is his saving of Eärendel from shipwreck, bidding him sail to Kôr with the words 'for this hast thou been brought out of the Wrack of Gondolin' (B, similarly in C). The March of the Eldar from Valinor was brought about by the coming of the birds from Gondolin.

In S, on the other hand, it is Ulmo (Ylmir) who directly brings about the intervention from the West by his reproaches to the Valar, bidding them rescue the remnants of the Noldoli and the Silmarils; and the host is led by 'the sons of the Valar', commanded by Fionwë – who is here the son of Tulkas! Fionwë is frequently named in the *Lost Tales* as the son of Manwë, while the son of Tulkas was Telimektar (who became the constellation Orion). The naming Fionwë son of Tulkas may have been a simple slip, though the same is said in the *Quenta* as first written (p. 149); subsequently Fionwë again becomes the son of Manwë (p. 154).

'Remembering Swanhaven few of the Teleri go with them': in the outline B the presence of the Solosimpi on the March is referred to without comment, while in C they only agreed to accompany the expedition on condition that they remained by the sea (see II. 258), and this was in some way associated with their remembrance of the Kinslaying.

The desertion of Kôr at this time is referred to in the outlines, but only in connection with Eärendel's coming there and finding it empty; I noted (II. 257) that 'it seems at least strongly implied that Kôr was empty because the Elves of Valinor had departed into the Great Lands', and this is now seen to be certain.

The narrative in S now turns to Tuor. The statement that he grew old at Sirion's mouths – a statement that was struck out – goes back to the old schemes. His ship is now *Eärámë*, untranslated; previously it was *Alqarámë* 'Swanwing', while *Eärámë* was Eärendel's earlier ship, translated 'Eaglepinion', which foundered. In *The Silmarillion* Tuor's ship is *Eärrámë*, as in S, with the meaning 'Sea-Wing'.

In S, Idril departs in company with Tuor. This is different from the original schemes, where Tuor leaves alone, and Idril 'sees him too late', 'laments', and afterwards 'vanishes'. But in the outline C it seems that she found him, for 'Tuor and Idril some say sail now in Swanwing and may be seen going swift down the wind at dawn and dusk'.

In S, the earlier history of Eärendel's ship-building and shipwrecks in the Fiord of the Mermaid and at Falasquil has, apparently, been abandoned entirely, and Wingelot is his first and only ship; but there remains the motive that Eärendel wishes to seek for his father, whereas Ylmir bids him sail to Valinor (this last being afterwards struck out). His adventures in Wingelot are referred to in S but not otherwise indicated, save for the slaying of Ungoliant 'in the South'; there is no mention of the Sleeper in the Tower of Pearl. In C the long voyage of Eärendel, accompanied by Voronwë, that finally took them to Kôr, included an encounter with Ungweliantë, though this was after his southern voyage: 'Driven west. Ungweliantë. Magic Isles. Twilit Isle. Littleheart's gong awakes the Sleeper in the Tower of Pearl.' In another outline Eärendel encounters Wirilómë (Gloomweaver) in the South (II. 260). In the account in S he does not on this great voyage come to Kôr, though from it, as in B and C, he returns to 'the Waters of Sirion' (the delta) and finds the dwellings there desolate. Now however enters the motive of the last desperate attempt of the Fëanorians to regain the Silmaril of Beren and Lúthien, their descent on the Havens of Sirion, and their destruction. Thus the raid on the Havens has remained, but it is no longer the work of Melko (see II. 258) and is brought into the story of the Oath of Fëanor. As S was first written only Maidros survived; but Maglor was added. (In §14, as written, all the Sons of Fëanor save Maglor were slain at the time of the attack on Dior, though this passage was afterwards struck out. In *The Silmarillion* Celegorm, Curufin, and Caranthir were slain at that time, and Amrod and Amras (later names of Damrod and Díriel) were slain in the attack on the Havens of Sirion, so that only Maidros and Maglor were left.)

In the old outlines Elwing was taken captive (as is to be deduced, by Melko); there is no mention of her release from captivity, and she next appears in references to the sinking of her ship (on the way to Tol Eressëa) and the loss of the Nauglafring; after which she becomes a seabird to seek Eärendel. Eärendel returning from his long voyage and finding the dwellings at Sirion's mouth sacked, goes with Voronwë to the ruins of Gondolin, and in an isolated note (II. 264, xv) he 'goes even to the empty Halls of Iron seeking Elwing'.

All this has disappeared in S, with the new story of Elwing casting herself and the Nauglafring into the sea, except that she still becomes a seabird (thus changed by Ulmo) and flies to seek Eärendel about all the shores of the world. The early outlines are then at variance: in C it is said that Eärendel dwelt on the Isle of Seabirds and hoped that Elwing would come to him, 'but she is seeking him wailing along all the shores' – yet 'he will find Elwing at the Faring Forth', while in the short outline E (II. 260) she came to him as a seamew on the Isle of Seabirds. But in S Elwing is further mentioned only as being sought by Eärendel when he sets sail again, until she reappears at the end (§19) and is restored to Eärendel.

The introduction of Elrond in S is of great interest. He has no brother as yet; and he is saved by Maidros (in *The Silmarillion*, p. 247, Elrond and Elros were saved by Maglor). When the Elves return into the West he elects to stay 'on earth', being 'bound by his mortal half'. It is most remarkable that although the idea of a choice of fate for the Half-elven is already present, it takes a curiously different form from that which it was to take afterwards, and which became of great importance in *The Lord of the Rings*; for afterwards, Elrond, unlike his brother Elros Tar-Minyatur, elected to remain an Elf – yet his later choice derives in part from the earlier conception, for he elected also not to go into the West. In S, to choose his 'elfin half' seems to have meant to choose the West; afterwards, it meant to choose Elvish immortality.

Eärendel learnt what had happened at the Mouths of Sirion from Bronweg (earlier it was Littleheart son of Bronweg who survived the sack of the havens, II. 276 note 5), and with Bronweg he sails again in Wingelot and comes to Kôr, which he finds deserted, and his raiment becomes encrusted with the dust of diamonds; not daring to go further into Valinor he builds a tower on an isle in the northern seas, 'to which all the sea-birds of the world repair'. Bronweg is not further mentioned. Almost all of this, other than the statement that Eärendel did not dare venture further into Valinor, goes back to the outline C. The tower on the Isle of Seabirds, which survives in *The Silmarillion* (p. 250), is mentioned in an isolated note on the Eärendel story (II. 264, xvii).

In the early outlines Eärendel now set out on his last voyage. In B, which is here very brief, his sailing to the Isle of Seabirds is followed by 'his voyage to the firmament'. In C he sails with Voronwë to the halls of Mandos seeking for tidings of Tuor, Idril, and Elwing; he 'reaches the bar at the margin of the world and sets sail on the oceans of the firmament in order to gaze over the Earth. The Moon mariner chases him for his brightness and he dives through the Door of Night.' In the outline E (II. 260) 'Elwing as a seamew comes to him. He sets sail over the margent of the world.' In the early note associated with the poem 'The Bidding of the Minstrel' (II. 261) he 'sails west again to the lip of the world, just as the Sun is diving into the sea', and 'sets sail upon the sky'; and in the preface to 'The Shores of Faëry' (II. 262) he

sat long while in his old age upon the Isle of Seabirds in the Northern Waters ere he set forth upon a last voyage. He passed Taniquetil and even Valinor, and drew his bark over the bar at the margin of the world, and launched it on the Oceans of the Firmament. Of his ventures there no man has told, save that hunted by the orbed Moon he fled back to Valinor, and mounting the towers of Kôr upon the rocks of Eglamar he gazed back upon the Oceans of the World.

The passage in S is different from all of these, in that here Eärendel's voyage into the sky is achieved with the aid of the wings of seabirds, and it introduces the idea of his being scorched by the Sun as well as hunted by the Moon. I suggested (II. 259) that Eärendel originally sailed into the sky in continuing search for Elwing, and this is now corroborated.

## 18 and 19

The story in S now leaves Eärendel, wandering the sky 'as a fugitive star', and comes to the march of Fionwë and the Last Battle (a term that is used in S both of the Last Battle in the mythological record, in which the hosts of Valinor overthrew Morgoth, and of the Last Battle of the world, declared in prophecy, when Morgoth will come back through the Door and Fionwë will fight him on the plains of Valinor). Almost all of this now enters the mythology for the first time; and almost all of what very little survives from the earliest period on the subject of the March of the Elves of Valinor (II. 278–80) has disappeared. There is no mention of Tulkas, of his battle with Melko, of Noldorin, of the hostility of Men; virtually the only point in common is that after the overthrow of Morgoth Elves depart into the West. In the old story the Silmarils play no part at the end (cf. the jotting 'What became of the Silmarils after the capture of Melko?' II. 259); but now in S there appear the lineaments of a story concerning their fate. Now also we have the first mention anywhere of the breaking of the Northwestern world in the struggle to overthrow Morgoth; and (in an addition to the text) the chain Angainor appears from the *Lost Tales*. (Angainor is not named in the earlier passage in S (§2) concerning the binding of Morgoth. It appears (later) in the *Lay of Leithian*, in a puzzling reference to 'the chain Angainor that *ere Doom*/for Morgoth *shall by Gods be wrought*'; see III. 205, 209–10.)

In the story of the fate of the Silmarils, Maglor says to Maidros that there are two sons of Fëanor now left, and two Silmarils. Does this imply that the Silmaril of Beren was lost when Elwing cast herself into the sea with the Nauglafring (unlike the later story)? The answer is certainly yes; the story in S is not comprehensible otherwise. Thus when Maglor casts himself (changed to casts the jewel) into the fiery pit, having stolen one of the Silmarils of the Iron Crown from Fionwë, 'one Silmaril is now in the sea, and one in the earth'. The third was the Silmaril that remained in Fionwë's keeping; and it was that one that was bound to Eärendel's brow. We thus have a remarkable stage of transition, in which the Silmarils have at last achieved primary importance, but where the fate of each has not arrived at the final form; and the conclusion, seen to be inevitable once reached, that it was the Silmaril regained by Beren and Lúthien that became the Evening Star, has not been achieved. In S, Eärendel becomes a star before receiving the Silmaril; but originally, as I have said (II. 265), 'there is no suggestion that the Valar hallowed his ship and set him in the sky, nor that his light was that of the Silmaril'. In this respect also S is transitional, for at the end the later story appears.

The Elves of the Outer Lands (Great Lands), after the conquest of Morgoth, set sail from Lúthien (later emended to Leithien), explained as 'Britain or England'. For the forms *Luthany*, *Lúthien*, *Leithian*, *Leithien* and the texts in which they occur see III. 154. It is remarkable that as S was originally written *Lúthien* is both the name of Thingol's daughter and the name of England.

It is further said in S that the Elves 'ever still from time to time set sail [from Lúthien] leaving the world ere they fade'. 'The Gnomes and many of the Ilkorins and Teleri and Qendi repeople the Lonely Isle. Some go back to live upon the shores of Faëry and in Valinor, but Côr and Tûn remain desolate.' Some of this can be brought into relation with the old outlines (see II. 308–9), but how much more was retained in mind, beyond 'The Elves retreated to Luthany' and 'Many of the Elves of Luthany sought back west over the sea and settled in Tol Eressëa', cannot be determined. That even this much was retained is however very instructive. The peculiar relation of the Elves to England keeps a foot-hold, as it were, in the actual articulation of the narrative; as also the idea that if they remained in 'the world' they would fade (see II. 326).

It is not made clear why 'Côr and Tûn' remained desolate, since some of the Elves 'go back to live upon the shores of Faëry and in Valinor'. In the original conception (as I have argued its nature, II. 280) the Eldar of Valinor, when they returned from the Great Lands where they had gone against the will of the Valar, were forbidden to re-enter Valinor and therefore settled in Tol Eressëa, as 'the Exiles of Kôr' (although some did return in the end to Valinor, since Ingil son of Inwë, according to Meril-i-Turinqi (I. 129), 'went long ago back to Valinor and is with Manwë'). But in the story as told in S the idea that the March of the Eldar was against the will of the Valar, and aroused them to wrath, has been abandoned, and 'the sons of the Valar' now lead the hosts out of the West; why then should the Elves of Tûn not return there? And we have the statement in S that Tol Eressëa was repeopled not only by Gnomes (and nothing at all is said of their pardon) and Ilkorins, but also by Qendi (= the later Vanyar) and Teleri, Elves who came from Valinor for the assault on Morgoth. I cannot explain this; and must conclude that my father was only noting down the chief points of his developing conceptions, leaving much unwritten.

There now appears the idea that the Gods thrust Morgoth through the

Door of Night 'into the outer dark beyond the Walls of the World';* and there is the first reference to the escape of Thû (Sauron) in the Last Battle. There is also a prophecy concerning the ultimate battle, when the world is old and the Gods weary, and Morgoth will come back through the Door of Night; then Fionwë with Túrin beside him shall fight Morgoth on the plain of Valinor, and Túrin shall slay him with his black sword. The Silmarils shall be recovered, and their light released, the Trees rekindled, the Mountains of Valinor levelled so that the light goes out over all the world, and Gods and Elves shall grow young again. Into this final resolution of the evil in the world it would prove unprofitable, I think, to enquire too closely. References to it have appeared in print in *Unfinished Tales*, pp. 395–6, in the remarks on Gandalf: 'Manwë will not descend from the Mountain until the Dagor Dagorath, and the coming of the End, when Melkor returns', and in the alliterative poem accompanying this, 'until Dagor Dagorath and the Doom cometh'. The earliest references are probably in the outline C (II. 282), where (when the Pine of Belaurin is cut down) 'Melko is thus now out of the world – but one day he will find a way back, and the last great uproars will begin before the Great End'. In the *Lost Tales* there are many references to the Great End, most of which do not concern us here; but at the end of the tale of *The Hiding of Valinor* is told (I. 219) of 'that great foreboding that was spoken among the Gods when first the Door of Night was opened':

For 'tis said that ere the Great End come Melko shall in some wise contrive a quarrel between Moon and Sun, and Ilinsor shall seek to follow Urwendi through the Gates, and when they are gone the Gates of both East and West will be destroyed, and Urwendi and Ilinsor shall be lost. So shall it be that Fionwë Úrion, son of Manwë, of love for Urwendi shall in the end be Melko's bane, and shall destroy the world to destroy his foe, and so shall all things then be rolled away.

(Cf. the outline C, II. 281: 'Fionwë's rage and grief [at the death of Urwendi]. In the end he will slay Melko.') Whether any of this prophecy underlies the idea of the ultimate return of Morgoth through the Door of Night I cannot say. At the end of the *Tale of Turambar*, after the account of the 'deification' of Túrin and Nienor, there is a prophecy (II. 116) that

Turambar indeed shall stand beside Fionwë in the Great Wrack, and Melko and his drakes shall curse the sword of Mormakil.

But there is no indication in S of how 'the spirit of Túrin' will survive to slay Morgoth in the ultimate battle on the plain of Valinor.

*See the commentary on the *Ambarkanta*, p. 252.

That the Mountains of Valinor shall be levelled, so that the light of the rekindled Trees goes out over all the world, is also found in the earliest texts; cf. the isolated passage in C (II.285) where is told the Elves' prophecy of the (second) Faring Forth:

Laurelin and Silpion will be rekindled, and the mountain wall being destroyed then soft radiance will spread over all the world, and the Sun and Moon will be recalled.

But this prophecy is associated with other conceptions that had clearly been abandoned.

At the end, with the aid of the Silmaril Elwing is found and restored, but there is no indication of how the Silmaril was used to this purpose. Elwing in this account sails with Eärendel, who bears the third Silmaril, and so he shall sail until he sees 'the last battle gathering upon the plains of Valinor'.

On the reappearance of the name *Eriol* at the very end of S see II.300.

I do not intend here to relate this version to that in the published work, but will conclude this long discussion of the concluding sections 17–19 with a brief summary. As I have said, S is here extremely condensed, and it is here even harder than elsewhere to know or guess what of the old material my father had suppressed and what was still 'potentially' present. But in any case nothing of the old layer that is not present in S was ever to reappear.

In the present version, Eärendel has still not come to his supreme function as the Messenger who spoke before the Powers on behalf of the Two Kindreds, though the birds of Gondolin have been abandoned as the bringers of tidings to Valinor, and Ulmo becomes the sole agent of the final assault on Morgoth out of the West. The voyages of Eärendel have been simplified: he now has the one great voyage – without Voronwë – in Wingelot, in which he slew Ungoliant, and the second voyage, with Voronwë, which takes him to Kôr – and the desertion of Kôr (Tûn) still depends on the March of the Eldar, which has already taken place when he comes there. His voyage into the sky is now achieved by the wings of birds; and the Silmaril still plays no part in his becoming a star, for the Silmaril of Beren and Lúthien was drowned with the Nauglafring at the Mouths of Sirion. But the Silmarils at last become central to the final acts of the mythological drama, and – unlike the later story – only one of the two Silmarils that remained in the Iron Crown is made away with by a son of Fëanor (Maglor); the second is given to Eärendel by the Gods, and the later story is visible at the end of S, where his boat 'is drawn over Valinor to the Outer Seas' and launched into the Outer Dark, where he sails with the Silmaril on his brow, keeping watch on Morgoth.

The destruction of the people of Sirion's Mouths now becomes the final evil of the Oath of Fëanor. Elrond appears, with a remarkable reference to the choice given to him as half-elven. The coming of the hosts of the West to the overthrow of Morgoth is now an act of the Valar, and the hosts are led by the Sons of the Valar. England, as Lúthien (Leithien), remains as the land from which the Elves of the Great Lands set sail at the end for Tol Eressëa; but I suspect that virtually all the highly complex narrative which I attempted to reconstruct (II. 308–9) had gone – Eärendel and Ing(wë) and the hostility of Ossë, the Ingwaiwar, the seven invasions of Luthany.

The original ideas of the conclusion of the Eldar Days (Melko's climbing of the Pine of Belaurin, the cutting down of the Pine, the warding of the sky by Telimektar and Ingil (Orion and Sirius), II. 281–2) have disappeared; in S, Morgoth is thrust through the Door of Night, and Eärendel becomes its guardian and guarantee against Morgoth's return, until the End. And lastly, and most pregnant for the future, Thû escapes the Last Battle when Morgoth was overcome, 'and dwells still in dark places'.

# III

# THE QUENTA

This work is extant in a typescript (made by my father) for which there is no trace of any preliminary notes or drafts. That the *Quenta*, or at any rate the greater part of it, was written in 1930 seems to me to be certainly deducible (see the commentary on §10, pp. 177–8). After a quite different initial section (which is the origin of the *Valaquenta*) this text becomes a reworking and expansion of the 'Sketch of the Mythology'; and it quickly becomes evident that my father had S (the 'Sketch') in front of him when he wrote the *Quenta* (which I shall refer to as 'Q'). The latter moves towards *The Silmarillion* in its published form, both in structure and in language (indeed already in S the first forms of many sentences can be perceived).

Eriol (as in S; not Ælfwine) is mentioned both in the title of Q and at the end of the work, and his coming to Kortirion, but (again as in S) there is no trace of the Cottage of Lost Play. As I have said of its absence from S (p. 42), this does not demonstrate that my father had rejected the conception in its entirety: in S he may have omitted it because his purpose was solely to recount the history of the Elder Days in condensed form, while in the title of Q it is said that the work was 'drawn from the Book of Lost Tales which Eriol of Leithien wrote'. At least then, we may think, some venue in which the *Lost Tales* were told to Eriol in Kortirion still existed.*

The title makes it very plain that while Q was written in a finished manner, my father saw it as a compendium, a 'brief history' that was 'drawn from' a much longer work; and this aspect remained an important element in his conception of 'The Silmarillion' properly so called. I do not know whether this idea did indeed arise from the fact that the starting point of the second phase of the mythological narrative was a condensed synopsis (S); but it seems likely enough, from the step by step continuity that leads from S through Q to the version that was interrupted towards its end in 1937.

It seems very probable that the greater number of the extensions and elaborations found in Q arose in the course of its composition, and that while Q contains features, omitted in S, which go back to the earliest version, these features argue only a recollection of the *Lost Tales* (to be

---

* It is said at the end of the *Quenta* that Eriol 'remembered things that he had heard in fair Cortirion'. But this Book of Lost Tales was composed by Eriol (according to the title) out of a 'Golden Book' which he *read* in Kortirion. (Previously the Golden Book of Tavrobel was written either by Eriol (Ælwine) himself, or by his son Heorrenda, or by some other person unnamed long after; see II. 291.)

assumed in any case! – and doubtless a very clear recollection), not a close derivation from the actual text. If that had been the case, one might expect to find the re-emergence of actual phrasing here and there; but that seems to be markedly lacking.

The history of the typescript becomes rather complex towards the end (from §15), where my father expanded and retyped portions of the text (though the discarded pages were not destroyed). But I see no reason to think that much time elapsed between the two versions; for near the very end (§19) the original typescript gives out, and only the second version continues to the conclusion of the *Quenta*, which strongly suggests that the revisions belong to the same time as the original text.

Subsequently the whole text was revised throughout, the corrections being made carefully in ink; these changes though frequent are mostly small, and very often no more than slight alterations of expression. This 'layer' of emendation was clearly the first;* afterwards further changes were made at different times, often very hastily and not always legibly in pencil. To present the text as first typed with annotation of every small stylistic improvement is obviously quite unnecessary, and would in any case require the introduction into the text of a forest of reference numbers to the notes. The text given here *includes*, therefore, without annotation, all minor changes that in no way affect the course of the narrative or alter its implications. Those emendations that are not taken up into the text but recorded in the notes are marked as 'late changes' if they are clearly distinguishable, as is not always the case, from the first 'layer' described above.

I have divided the text into the same 19 divisions made in S (see p. 11); but since the opening of Q has nothing corresponding in S this section is not given a number.

# THE QUENTA

### herein is

## QENTA NOLDORINWA

### or

## Pennas-na-Ngoelaidh

### This is the brief History of the Noldoli
### or Gnomes, drawn from the Book of Lost Tales

---

*The occurrence of *Beleriand* in the original typescript, first in §13, note 10, not as previously by emendation in ink from typescript *Broseliand*, shows that some of this 'layer' was carried out while the typescript was still in process of composition.

which Eriol of Leithien wrote, having read
the *Golden Book*, which the Eldar call *Parma
Kuluina*,* in Kortirion in Tol Eressëa, the
Lonely Isle.

After the making of the World by the Allfather, who in Elvish
tongue is named Ilúvatar, many of the mightiest spirits that dwelt
with him came into the world to govern it, because seeing it afar
after it was made they were filled with delight at its beauty. These
spirits the Elves named the Valar, which is the Powers, though
Men have often called them Gods. Many spirits[1] they brought in
their train, both great and small, and some of these Men have
confused with the Eldar or Elves: but wrongly, for they were
before the world, but Elves and Men awoke first in the world after
the coming of the Valar. Yet in the making of Elves and Men and
in the giving to each of their especial gifts Ilúvatar alone had part;
wherefore they are called the Children of the World or of Ilúvatar.

The chieftains of the Valar were nine. These were the names of
the Nine Gods in Elvish tongue as it was spoken in Valinor,
though other or altered names they have in the speech of the
Gnomes, and their names among Men are manifold. Manwë was
the Lord of the Gods and Prince of the airs and winds and the ruler
of the sky. With him dwelt as spouse the immortal lady of the
heights, Varda the maker of the stars. Next in might and closest in
friendship to Manwë was Ulmo Lord of Waters, who dwells alone
in the Outer Seas, but has in government all waves and waters,
rivers, fountains and springs, throughout the earth. Subject to
him, though he is often of rebellious mood, is Ossë the master of
the seas of the lands of Men, whose spouse is Uinen the Lady of
the Sea. Her hair lies spread through all the waters under skies. Of
might nigh equal to Ulmo was Aulë. He was a smith and a master
of crafts, but his spouse was Yavanna, the lover of fruits and all the
growth of the soil. In might was she next among the ladies of the
Valar to Varda. Very fair was she, and often the Elves named her
Palúrien, the Bosom of the Earth.

The Fanturi were called those brothers Mandos and Lórien.
Nefantur the first was also called, the master of the houses of the
dead, and the gatherer of the spirits of the slain. Olofantur was the
other, maker of visions and of dreams; and his gardens in the land

---

*The Elvish name of the Golden Book in the early dictionary of Qenya is *Parma
Kuluinen* (II. 310).

of the Gods were the fairest of all places in the world and filled with many spirits of beauty and power.

Strongest of all the Gods in limbs and greatest in all feats of prowess and valour was Tulkas, for which reason he was surnamed Poldórëa, the Strong One,[2] and he was the enemy and foe of Melko. Oromë was a mighty lord and little less in strength than Tulkas. He was a hunter, and trees he loved (whence he was called Aldaron and by the Gnomes Tavros,[3] Lord of Forests), and delighted in horses and in hounds. He hunted even in the dark earth before the Sun was lit, and loud were his horns, as still they are in the friths and pastures that Oromë possesses in Valinor. Vana was his spouse, the Queen of Flowers, the younger sister of Varda and Palúrien, and the beauty both of heaven and of earth is in her face and in her works. Yet mightier than she is Nienna who dwells with Nefantur Mandos. Pity is in her heart, and mourning and weeping come to her, but shadow is her realm and night her throne.

Last do all name Melko. But the Gnomes, who most have suffered from his evil, will not speak his name (Moeleg) in their own tongue's form, but call him Morgoth Bauglir, the Black God Terrible. Very mighty was he made by Ilúvatar, and some of the powers of all the Valar he possessed, but to evil uses did he turn them. He coveted the world and the lordship of Manwë, and the realms of all the Gods; and pride and jealousy and lust grew ever in his heart, till he became unlike his wise and mighty brethren. Violence he loved and wrath and destruction, and all excess of cold and flame. But darkness most he used for his works and turned it to evil and a name of horror among Elves and Men.

1  *Many spirits > Many lesser spirits* (late change).
2  *the Strong One > the Valiant* (late change).
3  *Tavros > Tauros* (late change).

Accents were put in throughout the work in ink (the typewriter did not possess them), and in addition short marks were put in on certain names in this section: *Fantŭri, Ŏlŏfantur, Ŏrŏmë, Aldăron, Vănă.*

# 1

In the beginning of the overlordship of the Valar they saw that the world was dark, and light was scattered over the airs and lands and seas. Two mighty lamps they made for the lighting of the world and set them on vast pillars in the North and South. They dwelt upon an island in the seas while they were labouring at their first tasks in the ordering of the earth. But Morgoth contested with them and made war. The lamps he overthrew, and in the confusion of darkness he aroused the sea against their island. Then the Gods removed into the West, where ever since their seats have been, but Morgoth escaped, and in the North he built himself a fortress and great caverns underground. And at that time the Valar could not overcome him or take him captive. Therefore they built then in the uttermost West the land of Valinor. It was bordered by the Outer Sea, and the Wall of the World beyond that fences out the Void and the Eldest Dark; but eastward they built the Mountains of Valinor, that are highest upon earth. In Valinor they gathered all light and all things of beauty, and built their many mansions, their gardens, and their towers. Amidmost of the plain was the city of the Gods, Valmar the beautiful of many bells. But Manwë and Varda have halls upon the highest of the Mountains of Valinor, whence they can look across the world even into the East. Taniquetil the Elves named that holy height, and the Gnomes Taingwethil, which in the tongue of this island of old was Tindbrenting.

In Valinor Yavanna planted two trees in the wide plain not far from the gates of Valmar the blessed. Under her songs they grew, and of all the things which the Gods made most renown have they, and about their fate all the stories of the world are woven. Dark-green leaves had one, that beneath were shining silver, and white blossoms like the cherry it bore, from which a dew of silver light was ever falling. Leaves of young green like the new-opened beech the other had. Their edges were of shining gold. Yellow flowers swung upon its boughs like the hanging blossom of the merry trees Men now call Golden Rain. But from those flowers there issued warmth and blazing light. For seven hours each tree waxed to full glory, and for seven hours it waned.[1] Each followed each, and so twice every day in Valinor there came an hour of softer light, when each tree was faint and their gold and silver radiance was mingled; for when white Silpion for six hours had been in bloom, then golden Laurelin awoke. But Silpion was the elder of the Trees, and the first hour that ever it shone the Gods did not count into the tale of hours, and called it the Hour of Opening, and from that hour dated the beginning of their reign in Valinor; and so at the sixth hour of the first of days Silpion ceased its first time of flower, and at the twelfth was the first blossoming of Laurelin at an end. These Trees the Gnomes called in after times Bansil and Glingol; but Men have no names for them, for their light was slain before the coming of the younger children of Ilúvatar upon earth.[2]

★

1 This sentence was emended to read: *In seven hours each tree waxed to full glory and waned*. Before this emendation, the text was confused, since periods of both fourteen and seven hours are attributed to the Trees; but the following sentence, beginning *Each followed each . . .*, was retyped over erasures that cannot be read, and this no doubt explains the confusion, which was rectified later by the emendation.

2 The typescript page beginning with the words *Sea, and the Wall of the World beyond* and continuing to the end of the section was replaced by another. As far as the end of the first paragraph the replacement is almost identical with the first, but with these differences: Manwë and Varda *had* halls, whence they *could* look out; and new names appear for Taniquetil:

> Taniquetil the Elves named that holy height, and Ialassë the Everlasting Whiteness, and Tinwenairin crowned with stars, and many names beside; and the Gnomes spake of it in their later tongue as Amon-Uilas; and in the language of this island of old Tindbrenting was its name.

The replacement page then continues:

> In Valinor Yavanna hallowed the mould with mighty song, and Nienna watered it with tears. The Gods were gathered in silence upon their thrones of council in the Ring of Doom nigh unto the golden gates of Valmar the Blessed; and Yavanna Palúrien sang before them, and they watched. From the earth came forth two slender shoots; and silence was over all the world save for the slow chanting of Palúrien. Under her songs two fair trees uprose and grew. Of all things which the Gods made most renown have they, and about their fate all the tales of the world are woven. Dark-green leaves had the one, that beneath were as silver shining, and he bore white blossoms like the cherry, from which a dew of silver light was ever falling, and earth was dappled with the dark and dancing shadows of his leaves amid the pools of gleaming radiance. Leaves of young green like the new-opened beech the other bore; their edges were of glittering gold. Yellow flowers swung upon her boughs like the hanging blossoms of the merry trees Men now call Golden-rain; and from those flowers there came forth warmth and a great light.

In seven hours the glory of each tree waxed to full and waned again to nought; and each awoke to life an hour before the other ceased to shine. Thus in Valinor twice each day there came a gentle hour of softer light, when both Trees were faint, and their gold and silver radiances mingled. Silpion was the elder of the Trees, and came first to full stature and to bloom, and that first hour wherein he shone, the white glimmer of a silver dawn, the Gods reckoned not into the tale of hours, but named it the Opening Hour, and counted therefrom the ages of their reign in Valinor. Wherefore at the sixth hour of the First of Days, and all the joyous days thereafter until the Darkening, Silpion ceased his time of flower; and at the twelfth Laurelin her blossoming. These Trees the Gnomes called in after days Bansil and Glingol; but Men have no names for them, for their light was slain before the coming of the younger children of the world.

On the next page, and obviously associated with this replacement text, is a typed table here represented. At the bottom of the replaced page, and clearly associated with the emendation given in note 1 above, is a simpler table of precisely similar significance, with the note:

'Day' ends every second waning to nought of Laurelin or at end of second hour of mingling of light.

## 2

In all this time, since Morgoth overthrew the lamps, the Outer[1] Lands east of the Mountains of Valinor were without light. While the lamps had shone growth began therein, which now was checked because of the darkness. But the oldest of all things already grew upon the world: the great weeds of the sea, and on the earth the dark shade of yew and fir and ivy, and small things faint and silent at their feet.[2] In such forests did Oromë sometimes hunt, but save Oromë and Yavanna the Valar went not out of Valinor, while in the North Morgoth built his strength, and gathered his demon broods about him, whom the Gnomes knew after as the Balrogs with whips of flame. The hordes of the Orcs he made of stone, but their hearts of hatred. Glamhoth, people of hate, the Gnomes have called them. Goblins may they be called, but in ancient days they were strong and cruel and fell. Thus he held sway. Then Varda looked on the darkness and was moved. The silver light that dripped from the boughs of Silpion she hoarded, and thence she made the stars. Wherefore she is called Tinwetári, Queen of Stars, and by the Gnomes Tim-Bridhil. The

Hour
of
Open-
ing

1 . 2 . 3 . 4 . 5 . 6 . 7

Silpion in bloom

Mingling
of
Light

1 . 2 . 3 . 4 . 5 . 6 . 7 . 8 . 9 . 10 . 11 . 12

The First of Days

Laurelin in bloom

Mingling
of
Light

1 . 2 . 3 . 4 . 5 . 6 . 7

Silpion in bloom

X

unlit skies she strewed with these bright globes of silver flame, and high above the North, a challenge unto Morgoth, she set the crown of Seven mighty Stars to swing, the emblem of the Gods, and sign of Morgoth's doom. Many names have these been called; but in the old days of the North both Elves and Men called them the Burning Briar, and some the Sickle of the Gods.

It is said that at the making of the stars the children of the earth awoke: the elder children of Ilúvatar. Themselves they named the Eldar, whom we call the Elves, but in the beginning mightier and more strong were they, yet not more fair. Oromë it was that found them, dwelling by a star-lit mere, Cuiviénen,[3] Water of Awakening, far in the East. Swift he rode home to Valinor filled with the thought of their beauty. When the Valar heard his tidings they pondered long, and they recalled their duty. For they came into the world knowing that their office was to govern it for the children of Ilúvatar who should after come, each in the appointed time.

Thus came it that because of the Elves the Gods made an assault upon the fortress of Morgoth in the North; and this he never forgot. Little do the Elves or Men know of that great riding of the power of the West against the North and of the war and tumult of the battle[4] of the Gods. Tulkas it was who overthrew Morgoth and bound him captive, and the world had peace for a long age. But the fortress which Morgoth had built was hidden with deceit in dungeons and caverns far beneath the earth, and the Gods did not destroy it utterly, and many evil things of Morgoth lingered there still, or dared to roam in the secret pathways of the world.

Morgoth the Gods drew back to Valinor in chains, and he was set in prison in the great halls of Mandos, from which none, God, Elf, nor Man has ever escaped save by the will of the Valar. Vast they are and strong, and built in the North of the land of Valinor. The Eldalië,[5] the people of the Elves, the Gods invited to Valinor, for they were in love with the beauty of that race, and because they feared for them in the starlit dusk, and knew not what deceits and evil wrought by Morgoth still wandered there.

Of their own free will, yet in awe of the power and majesty of the Gods, the Elves obeyed. A great march therefore they prepared from their first homes in the East. When all was ready Oromë rode at their head upon his white horse shod with gold. Into three hosts were the Eldalië arrayed. The first to march forth were led by that most high of all the elfin race, whose name was Ingwë, Lord of Elves. Ing the Gnomes now make his name, but never came he back into the Outer Lands until these tales were near their end.[6] The Quendi[7] were his own folk called, who sometimes are alone called Elves; they are the Light-elves and the beloved of Manwë and his spouse. Next came the Noldoli. The Gnomes we may call them, a name of wisdom; they are the Deep-elves, and on that march their lord was the mighty Finwë, whom his own folk in their tongue later changed call Finn.[8] His kindred are renowned in elfin song, and of them these tales have much to tell, for they warred and laboured long and sore in the Northern lands of old. Third came the Teleri. The Foam-riders may they be called; they are the Sea-elves, and the Solosimpi[9] they were named in Valinor, the pipers of the shores.[10] Elwë (or Elu) was their lord.[11]

Many of the elfin race were lost upon the long dark roads, and they wandered in the woods and mountains of the world, and never came to Valinor, nor saw the light of the Two Trees. Therefore they are called Ilkorindi, the Elves that dwelt never in Côr,[12] the city of the Eldar in the land of the Gods. The Dark-elves are they, and many are their scattered tribes, and many are their tongues.

Of the Dark-elves the chief in renown was Thingol. For this reason he came never to Valinor. Melian was a fay. In the gardens of Lórien she dwelt, and among all his fair folk none were there that surpassed her beauty, nor none more wise, nor none more skilled in magical and enchanting song. It is told that the Gods would leave their business, and the birds of Valinor their mirth, that Valmar's bells were silent, and the fountains ceased to flow, when at the mingling of the light Melian sang in the gardens of the God of Dreams. Nightingales went always with her, and their song she taught them. But she loved deep shadow, and often strayed on long journey into the Outer Lands, and there filled the silence of the dawning world with her voice and the voices of her birds.

The nightingales of Melian Thingol heard and was enchanted, and left his folk. Melian he found beneath the trees and was cast into a dream and a great slumber, so that his people sought him in vain. In after days Melian and Thingol became Queen and King of the woodland Elves of Doriath; and Thingol's halls were called the Thousand Caves.

★

1 At all three occurrences of *Outer Lands* in this section *Hither* is written above *Outer* (which is not struck out).

2   After *at their feet* is added: *and in their thickets dark creatures,*
    *old and strong.*
3   *Cuiviénen > Kuiviénen*
4   *the battle > the first battle*
5   Written against *Eldalië: Quendi* (late change).
6   This sentence, beginning *Ing the Gnomes now make his name,*
    was changed to read:

> He entered into Valinor and sits at the feet of the Powers, and all
> Elves revere his name, but he hath come never back into the
> Outer Lands.

7   *Quendi > Lindar* (late change).
8   *whom his own folk in their tongue later changed call Finn >*
    *wisest of all the children of the world.*
9   *Solosimpi > Soloneldi*
10  *the pipers of the shores > for they made music beside the*
    *breaking waves.*
11  *Elwë (or Elu) was their lord > Elwë was their lord, and his hair*
    *was long and white.*
12  *Côr > Kôr*

Short marks were written in on the names *Eldălië, Tĕlĕri.*


# 3

In time the hosts of the Eldar came to the last shores of the
West.[1] In the North these shores in the ancient days sloped ever
westward, until in the northernmost parts of the Earth only a
narrow sea divided the land of the Gods from the Outer[2] Lands;
but this narrow sea was filled with grinding ice, because of the
violence of the frosts of Morgoth. At that place where the elfin
hosts first looked upon the sea in wonder a wide dark ocean
stretched between them and the Mountains of Valinor. Over the
waves they gazed waiting; and Ulmo, sent by the Valar, uprooted
the half-sunk island upon which the Gods had first had their
dwelling, and drew it to the western shores. Thereon he embarked
the Quendi[3] and the Noldoli, for they had arrived first, but the
Teleri were behind and did not come until he had gone. The
Quendi and the Noldoli he bore thus to the long shores beneath the
Mountains of Valinor, and they entered the land of the Gods, and
were welcomed to its glory and its bliss. The Teleri thus dwelt long
by the shores of the sea awaiting Ulmo's return, and they grew to
love the sea, and made songs filled with the sound of it. And Ossë

loved them and the music of their voices, and sitting upon the rocks he spoke to them. Great therefore was his grief when Ulmo returned at length to take them to Valinor. Some he persuaded to remain on the beaches of the world, but the most embarked upon the isle and were drawn far away. Then Ossë followed them, and in rebellion, it is said, he seized the isle and chained it to the sea-bottom far out in the Bay of Faërie, whence the Mountains of Valinor could but dimly be descried, and the light of the realms beyond that filtered through the passes of the hills. There it stood for many an age. No other land was near to it, and it was called Tol-Eressëa, or the Lonely Isle. There long the Teleri dwelt, and learned strange music of Ossë, who made the seabirds for their delight. Of this long sojourn apart came the sundering of the tongue of the Foamriders and the Elves of Valinor.

To the other Elves the Valar gave a home and dwelling. Because even among the Tree-lit gardens of the Gods they longed at whiles to see the stars, a gap was made in the encircling mountains, and there in a deep valley that ran down to the sea the green hill of Côr[4] was raised. From the West the Trees shone upon it; to the East it looked out to the Bay of Faërie and the Lonely Isle and the Shadowy Seas. Thus some of the blessed light of Valinor came into the lands without, and fell upon the Lonely Isle, and its western shore grew green and fair. There bloomed the first flowers that ever were east of the mountains of the Gods.

On the top of Côr the city of the Elves was built, the white walls and towers and terraces of Tûn. The highest of those towers was the tower of Ing,[5] whose silver lamp shone far out into the mists of the sea, but few are the ships of mortals that have ever seen its marvellous beam. There dwelt the Elves and Gnomes. Most did Manwë and Varda love the Quendi, the Light-elves,[6] and holy and immortal were all their deeds and songs. The Noldoli, the Deep-elves, that Men call Gnomes, were beloved of Aulë, and of Mandos the wise; and great was their craft, their magic and their skill, but ever greater their thirst for knowledge, and their desire to make things wonderful and new. In Valinor of their skill they first made gems, and they made them in countless myriads, and filled all Tûn with them, and all the halls of the Gods were enriched.[7]

Since the Noldoli afterwards came back into the Great[8] Lands, and these tales tell mostly of them, here may be said, using the names in form of Gnomish tongue as it long was spoken on the earth, that King of the Gnomes was Finn.[9] His sons were Fëanor,

Fingolfin, and Finrod. Of these Fëanor was the most skilful, the deepest in lore of all his race; Fingolfin the mightiest and most valiant; Finrod the fairest and most wise of heart. The seven sons of Fëanor were Maidros the tall; Maglor, a musician and mighty singer whose voice carried far over hill and sea; Celegorm the fair, Curufin the crafty, the heir of well nigh all his father's skill, and Cranthir the dark; and last Damrod and Díriel, who after were great hunters in the world, though not more than Celegorm the fair, the friend of Oromë. The sons of Fingolfin were Finweg,[10] who was after king of the Gnomes in the North of the world, and Turgon of Gondolin; and his daughter was Isfin the White. The sons of Finrod were Felagund, Orodreth, Angrod, and Egnor.

In those far days Fëanor began on a time a long and marvellous labour, and all his power and all his subtle magic he called upon, for he purposed to make a thing more fair than any of the Eldar yet had made, that should last beyond the end of all. Three jewels he made, and named them Silmarils. A living fire burned within them that was blended of the light of the Two Trees; of their own radiance they shone even in the dark; no mortal flesh impure could touch them, but was withered and was scorched. These jewels the Elves prized beyond all the works of their hands, and Manwë hallowed them, and Varda said: 'The fate of the Elves is locked herein, and the fate of many things beside.' The heart of Fëanor was wound about the things he himself had made.

Now it must be told that the Teleri seeing afar the light of Valinor were torn between desire to see again their kindred and to look upon the splendour of the Gods, and love of the music of the sea. Therefore Ulmo taught them the craft of shipbuilding, and Ossë, yielding to Ulmo at last, brought to them as his last gift the strong-winged swans. Their fleet of white ships they harnessed to the swans of Ossë, and thus were drawn without help of the winds to Valinor. There they dwelt upon the long shores of Fairyland, and could see the light of the Trees, and could visit the golden streets of Valmar, and the crystal stairs of Tûn, if they wished – but most they sailed the waters of the Bay of Faërie and danced in those bright waves whose crests gleamed in the light beyond the hill. Many jewels the other Eldar gave to them, opals and diamonds and pale crystals that they strewed upon the pools and sands. Many pearls they made, and halls of pearl, and of pearls were the mansions of Elwë at the Haven of the Swans. That was their chief town, and their harbour. A marvellous arch of living rock sea-carven was its gate, and it lay upon the confines of Fairyland, north of the pass of Côr.

1   *the last shores of the West* > *the last western shores of the Hither Lands*

2   *Hither* written above *Outer* (see §2 note 1).

3   *Quendi* > *Lindar* at all three occurrences (late change; cf. §2 note 7).

4   *Côr* > *Kôr* at both occurrences (as in §2).

5   *Ing* > *Ingwë* (see §2 note 6).

6   *Light-elves* > *High-elves*, and later to *Fair-elves*.

7   On a separate slip is the following passage in manuscript without precise direction for its insertion, but which seems best placed here:

> But the love of the outer earth and stars remained in the hearts of the Noldoli, and they abode there ever and in the hills and valleys about the city. But the Lindar after a while grew to love rather the wide plains and the full light of Valinor, and they forsook Tûn, and came seldom back; and the Noldoli became a separate folk and their king was Finwë. Yet none dwelt in the tower of Ingwë nor . . . . . save such as tended that unfailing lamp, and Ingwë was held ever as high-king of all the Eldalië.

8   *Hither* written above *Great*.

9   *Finn* > *Finwë* (see §2 note 8).

10   *Finweg* > *Fingon*

## 4

Now it may be told how the Gods were beguiled by Morgoth. This was the high tide of the glory and the bliss of Gods and Elves, the noontide of the Blessed Realm. Seven[1] ages as the Gods decreed had Morgoth dwelt in the halls of Mandos, each age in lightened pain. When seven ages had passed, as they had promised, he was brought before their conclave. He looked upon the glory of the Valar, and greed and malice was in his heart; he looked upon the fair children of the Eldalië that sat at the knees of the Gods, and hatred filled him; he looked upon their wealth of jewels and lusted for them; but his thoughts he hid and his vengeance he postponed.

There Morgoth humbled himself before the feet of Manwë and sought for pardon; but they would not suffer him to depart from their sight and watchfulness. A humble dwelling he was granted in

Valinor within the gates of the city, and so fair-seeming were all his deeds and words that after a while he was allowed to go freely about all the land. Only Ulmo's heart misgave him, and Tulkas clenched his hands whenever he saw Morgoth his foe go by. Never has Tulkas the strong forgotten or forgiven a wrong done to himself or his. Most fair of all was Morgoth to the Elves, and he aided them in many works, if they would let him. The people of Ing,[2] the Quendi,[3] held him in suspicion, for Ulmo had warned them and they had heeded his words. But the Gnomes took delight in the many things of hidden and secret wisdom that he could tell to them, and some harkened to things which it had been better that they had never heard. And when he saw his chance he sowed a seed of lies and suggestions of evil among such as these. Bitterly did the folk of the Noldoli atone for it in after days. Often he would whisper that the Gods had brought the Eldar to Valinor but out of jealousy, for fear their marvellous skill and beauty and their magic should grow too strong for them, as they waxed and spread over the wide lands of the world. Visions he would set before them of the mighty realms they might have ruled in power and freedom in the East. In those days, moreover, the Valar knew of the coming of Men that were to be; but the Elves knew nought of this, for the Gods had not revealed it, and the time was not yet near. But Morgoth spoke in secret to the Elves of mortals, though little of the truth he knew or cared. Manwë alone knew aught clearly of the mind of Ilúvatar concerning Men, and ever has he been their friend. Yet Morgoth whispered that the Gods kept the Eldar captive so that Men coming should defraud them of their kingdoms, for the weaker race of mortals would be more easily swayed by them. Little truth was there in this, and little have the Valar ever prevailed to sway the wills or fates of Men, and least of all to good. Yet many of the Elves believed or half-believed his evil words. Gnomes were the most of these. Of the Teleri there were none.

Thus, ere the Gods were aware, the peace of Valinor was poisoned. The Gnomes began to murmur against the Valar and their kindred, and they became filled with vanity, and forgot all that the Gods had given them and taught them. Most of all did Morgoth fan the flames of the fierce and eager heart of Fëanor, though all the while he lusted for the Silmarils. These Fëanor at great feasts wore on brow and breast, but at other times, locked fast in the hoards of Tûn, they were guarded close, though there were no thieves in Valinor, as yet. Proud were the sons of Finn,[4] and the proudest Fëanor. Lying Morgoth said to him that Fingolfin

and his sons were plotting to usurp the leadership of Fëanor and
his sons, and supplant them in the favour of their father and of the
Gods. Of these words were quarrels born between the children of
Finn, and of those quarrels came the end of the high days of
Valinor and the evening of its ancient glory.[5]

Fëanor was summoned before the council of the Gods, and
there were the lies of Morgoth laid bare for all to see who had the
will. By the judgement of the Gods Fëanor was banished from
Tûn. But with him went Finn his father who loved him more than
his other sons, and many other Gnomes. Northward in Valinor in
the hills near the halls of Mandos they built a treasury and a
stronghold; but Fingolfin ruled the Noldoli in Tûn. Thus might
Morgoth's words seem justified, and the bitterness he sowed went
on, though his lies were disproved, and long after it lived still
between the sons of Fingolfin and of Fëanor.[6]

Straight from the midst of their council the Gods sent Tulkas to
lay hands on Morgoth and bring him before them in chains once
more. But he escaped through the pass of Côr,[7] and from the tower
of Ing the Elves saw him pass in thunder and in wrath.

Thence he came into that region that is called Arvalin, which
lies south of the Bay of Faërie, and beneath the very eastern feet of
the mountains of the Gods, and there are the shadows the thickest
in all the world. There secret and unknown dwelt Ungoliant,
Gloomweaver, in spider's form. It is not told whence she is, from
the outer darkness, maybe, that lies beyond the Walls of the
World. In a ravine she lived, and spun her webs in a cleft of the
mountains, and sucked up light and shining things to spin them
forth again in nets of black and choking gloom and clinging fog.
Ever she hungered for more food. There Morgoth met her, and
with her plotted his revenge. But terrible was the reward that he
must promise her, ere she would dare the perils of Valinor or the
power of the Gods.

A great darkness she wove about her to protect her, and then
from pinnacle to pinnacle she swung on her black ropes, until she
had scaled the highest places of the mountains. In the south of
Valinor was this, for there lay the wild woods of Oromë, and there
was little watch, since, far from the old fortress of Morgoth in the
North, the great walls there looked on untrodden lands and empty
sea. On a ladder that she made Morgoth climbed, and he looked
down upon the shining plain, seeing afar off the domes of Valinor
in the mingling of the light; and he laughed as he sped down the
long western slopes with ruin in his heart.

So came evil into Valinor. Silpion was waning fast and Laurelin but just begun to glow, when protected by fate Morgoth and Ungoliant crept unawares into the plain. With his black sword Morgoth stabbed each tree to its very core, and as their juices spouted forth Ungoliant sucked them up, and poison from her foul lips went into their tissues and withered them, leaf and branch and root. Slowly they succumbed, and their light grew dim, while Ungoliant belched forth black clouds and vapours as she drank their radiance. To monstrous form she swelled.

Then fell wonder and dismay on all in Valmar, when twilight and mounting gloom came on the land. Black vapours floated about the ways of the city. Varda looked down from Taniquetil and saw the trees and towers all hidden as in a mist. Too late they ran from hill and gate. The Trees died and shone no more, while wailing throngs stood round them and called on Manwë to come down. Out upon the plain the horses of Oromë thundered with a hundred hooves, and fire started in the gloom about their feet. Swifter than they ran Tulkas on before, and the light of the anger of his eyes was as a beacon. But they found not what they sought. Wherever Morgoth went a darkness and confusion was around him that Ungoliant made, so that feet were bewildered and search was blind.

This was the time of the Darkening of Valinor. In that day there stood before the gates of Valmar Gnomes that cried aloud. Bitter were their tidings. They told how Morgoth had fled North and with him was a great black shape, a spider of monstrous form it had seemed in the gathering night. Sudden he had fallen on the treasury of Finn. There he slew the king of the Gnomes before his doors, and spilled the first elfin blood and stained the land of Valinor. Many others too he slew, but Fëanor and his sons were not there. Bitterly they cursed the chance, for Morgoth took the Silmarils and all the wealth of the jewels of the Noldoli that were hoarded there.

Little is known of the paths or journeys of Morgoth after that terrible deed; but this is known to all, that escaping from the hunt he came at last with Ungoliant over the Grinding Ice and so into the northern lands of this world. There Ungoliant summoned him to give her the promised reward. The half of her pay had been the sap of the Trees of Light. The other half was a full share in the plundered jewels. Morgoth yielded these up, and she devoured them, and their light perished from the earth, and still more huge grew Ungoliant's dark and hideous form. But no share in the

Silmarils would Morgoth give. Such was the first thieves' quarrel.

So mighty had Ungoliant become that she enmeshed Morgoth in her choking nets, and his awful cry echoed through the shuddering world. To his aid came the Orcs and Balrogs that lived yet in the lowest places of Angband. With their whips of flame the Balrogs smote the webs asunder, but Ungoliant was driven away into the uttermost South, where she long dwelt.

Thus came Morgoth back to Angband, and there countless became the number of the hosts of his Orcs and demons.[8] He forged for himself a great crown of iron, and he called himself the king of the world. In sign of this he set the three Silmarils in his crown. It is said that his evil hands were burned black with the touch of those holy and enchanted things, and black they have ever been since, nor was he ever afterward free from the pain of the burning, and the anger of the pain. That crown he never took from his head, and it never was his wont to leave the deep dungeons of his fortress, but he governed his vast armies from his northern throne.

1   *Nine* written above *Seven* but then struck out.
2   *Ing > Ingwë* at both occurrences, as previously.
3   *Quendi > Lindar*, as previously (late change).
4   *Finn > Finwë* at all occurrences (except once where overlooked), as previously.
5   The following was added here later faintly in pencil:

> And Fëanor spoke words of rebellion against the Gods and plotted to depart from Valinor back into the outer world and deliver the Gnomes, as he said, from thraldom.

6   The following was added here in the same way and at the same time as the passage given in note 5:

> But Morgoth hid himself and none knew whither he had gone. And while the Gods were in council, for they feared that the shadows should lengthen in Valinor, a messenger came and brought tidings that Morgoth was in the North of the land, journeying towards the house of Finwë.

7   *Côr > Kôr*, as previously.

8   Written here later is the direction: *Here mention making of Orcs (p. 4)*. Page 4 of the typescript contains the sentence (p. 82) *The hordes of the Orcs he made of stone, but their hearts of hatred.* See p. 295.

## 5

When it became at last all too clear that Morgoth had escaped, the Gods assembled about the dead Trees and sat there in darkness for a long while in dumb silence, and mourned in their hearts. Now that day which Morgoth chose for this assault was a day of high festival throughout Valinor. On this day it was the custom of the chief Valar, all save Ossë who seldom came thither, and of many of the Elves, especially the people of Ing,[1] to climb the long winding paths in white-robed procession to Manwë's halls on the summit of Tindbrenting. All the Quendi[2] and many of the Gnomes, who under Fingolfin still lived in Tûn, were therefore on Tindbrenting's height and were singing before the feet of Varda, when the watchers from afar beheld the fading of the Trees. But most of the Gnomes were in the plain, and all the Teleri, as was their wont, were on the shore. The fogs and darkness now drifted in from off the sea through the pass of Côr,[3] as the Trees died. A murmur of dismay ran through all Elfland, and the Foamriders wailed beside the sea.

Then Fëanor rebelling against his banishment summoned all the Gnomes to Tûn. A vast concourse gathered in the great square on the top of the hill of Côr, and it was lit by the light of many torches which each one that came bore in hand.

Fëanor was a great orator with a power of moving words. A very wild and terrible speech he made before the Gnomes that day, and though his anger was most against Morgoth, yet his words were in great part the fruit of Morgoth's lies. But he was distraught with grief for his father and wrath for the rape of the Silmarils. He now claimed the kingship of all the Gnomes, since Finn[4] was dead, in spite of the decree of the Gods. 'Why should we obey the jealous Gods any longer,' he asked, 'who cannot even keep their own realm from their foe?' He bade the Gnomes prepare for flight in the darkness, while the Valar were still wrapped in mourning; to seek freedom in the world and of their own prowess to win there a new realm, since Valinor was no longer more bright and blissful than the lands outside; to seek out Morgoth and war with him for ever until they were avenged. Then he swore a terrible oath. His seven sons leaped to his side and took the selfsame vow together, each with drawn sword. They swore the unbreakable oath, by the name of Manwë and Varda and the holy mountain,[5] to pursue with hate and vengeance to the ends of the world Vala, Demon, Elf, or Man, or Orc who hold or take or keep a Silmaril against their will.

Fingolfin and his son Finweg[6] spake against Fëanor, and wrath and angry words came near to blows; but Finrod spoke and sought to calm them, though of his sons only Felagund was on his side. Orodreth, Angrod, and Egnor took the part of Fëanor. In the end it was put to the vote of the assembly, and moved by the potent words of Fëanor the Gnomes decided to depart. But the Gnomes of Tûn would not renounce the kingship of Fingolfin, and as two divided hosts therefore they set forth: one under Fingolfin who with his sons yielded to the general voice against their wisdom, because they would not desert their people; the other under Fëanor. Some remained behind. Those were the Gnomes who were with the Quendi upon Tindbrenting. It was long ere they came back into this tale of the wars and wanderings of their people.

The Teleri would not join that flight. Never had they listened to Morgoth. They desired no other cliffs nor beaches than the strands of Fairyland. But the Gnomes knew that they could not escape without boats and ships, and that there was no time to build. They must cross the seas far to the North where they were narrower, but further still feared to venture; for they had heard of Helkaraksë, the Strait of the Grinding Ice, where the great frozen hills ever shifted and broke, sundered and clashed together. But their white ships with white sails the Teleri would not give, since they prized them dearly, and dreaded moreover the wrath of the Gods.

Now it is told that the hosts of Fëanor marched forth first along the coast of Valinor; then came the people of Fingolfin less eager, and in the rear of this host were Finrod and Felagund and many of the noblest and fairest of the Noldoli. Reluctantly they forsook the walls of Tûn, and more than others they carried thence memories of its bliss and beauty, and even many fair things made there by hands. Thus the people of Finrod had no part in the dreadful deed that then was done, and not all of Fingolfin's folk shared in it; yet all the Gnomes that departed from Valinor came under the curse that followed. When the Gnomes came to the Haven of the Swans they attempted to seize by force the white fleets that lay anchored there. A bitter affray was fought upon the great arch of the gate and on the lamplit quays and piers, as is sadly told in the song of the Flight of the Gnomes. Many were slain on either side, but fierce and desperate were the hearts of the people of Fëanor, and they won the battle; and with the help beside of many even of the Gnomes of Tûn they drew away the ships of the Teleri, and manned their oars as best they might, and took them north along the coast.

After they had journeyed a great way and were come to the northern confines of the Blessed Realm, they beheld a dark figure standing high upon the cliffs. Some say it was a messenger, others that it was Mandos himself. There he spoke in a loud dread voice the curse and prophecy that is called the Prophecy of Mandos,[7] warning them to return and seek for pardon, or in the end to return only at last after sorrow and endless misery. Much he foretold in dark words, which only the wisest of them understood, of things that after befell; but all heard the curse he uttered upon those that would not stay, because they had at Swanhaven spilled the blood of their kindred, and fought the first battle between the children of earth unrighteously. For that they should suffer in all their wars and councils from treachery and from the fear of treachery among their own kindred. But Fëanor said: 'He saith not that we shall suffer from cowardice, from cravens or the fear of cravens', and that proved true.[8]

All too soon did the evil begin to work. They came at last far to the North and saw the first teeth of the ice that floated in the sea. Anguish they had of the cold. Many of the Gnomes murmured, especially of those that followed less eagerly under the banners of Fingolfin. So it came into the heart of Fëanor and his sons to sail off suddenly with all the ships, of which they had the mastery, and 'leave the grumblers to grumble, or whine their way back to the cages of the Gods'. Thus began the curse of the slaying at Swanhaven. When Fëanor and his folk landed on the shores in the West of the northern world, they set fire in the ships and made a great burning terrible and bright; and Fingolfin and his people saw the light of it in the sky. Thereafter those left behind wandered miserably, and were joined by the companies of Finrod that marched up after.

In the end in woe and weariness Finrod led some back to Valinor and the pardon of the Gods – for they were not at Swanhaven – but the sons of Finrod and Fingolfin[9] would not yield, having come so far. They led their host far into the bitterest North, and dared at last the Grinding Ice. Many were lost there wretchedly, and there was small love for the sons of Fëanor in the hearts of those that came at last by this perilous passage into the Northern lands.

★

1　*Ing* > *Ingwë*, as previously.
2　At neither of the occurrences of *Quendi* is the name changed, as previously, to *Lindar*, clearly through oversight.

3   *Côr* > *Kôr* at both occurrences, as previously.
4   *Finn* not emended to *Finwë* as previously, through oversight.
5   This sentence was rewritten:

> They swore an oath which none shall break, and none should take,
> by the name of the Allfather, calling the Everlasting Dark upon
> them, if they kept it not, and Manwë they named in witness, and
> Varda, and the Holy Mount, vowing

6   *Finweg* > *Fingon*, as in §3, note 10.
7   *Prophecy of Mandos* > *Prophecy of the North*
8   Here is written lightly in pencil: *Finrod returned*.
9   *the sons of Finrod and Fingolfin* > *Fingolfin and the sons of Finrod*. (This emendation was made, I think, simply for clarity, the original text having been intended to mean 'the sons of Finrod, together with Fingolfin': for Fingolfin, not his son Finweg/Fingon, has become the leader of the hosts across the Grinding Ice, since Finrod is now the one who returned to Valinor – see the commentary on S §5, p. 48.)

# 6

When the Gods heard of the flight of the Gnomes they were aroused from their grief. Manwë summoned then to his council Yavanna; and she put forth all her power, but it availed not to heal the Trees. Yet beneath her spells Silpion bore at last one great and single silver bloom, and Laurelin a great golden fruit. Of these, as is said in the song of the Sun and Moon, the Gods fashioned the great lamps of heaven, and set them to sail appointed courses above the world. Rána they named the Moon, and Úr the Sun; and the maiden who guided the galleon of the sun was Úrien,[1] and the youth who steered the floating island of the Moon was Tilion. Úrien was a maiden who had tended the golden flowers in the gardens of Vana, while still joy was in the Blissful Realm, and Nessa daughter of Vana[2] danced on the lawns of never-fading green. Tilion was a hunter from the company of Oromë, and he had a silver bow. Often he wandered from his course pursuing the stars upon the heavenly fields.

At first the Gods purposed that the Sun and Moon should sail from Valinor to the furthest East, and back again, each following the other to and fro across the sky. But because of the waywardness of Tilion and his rivalry with Úrien, and most because of the words of Lórien and Nienna, who said that they had banished all sleep and night and peace from the earth, they changed their design. The Sun and Moon were drawn by Ulmo or his chosen spirits through the caverns and grottoes at the roots of the world, and mounted then in the East, and sailed back to Valinor, into which the Sun descended each day at time of Evening. And so is Evening the time of greatest light and joy in the land of the Gods, when the Sun sinks down to rest beyond the rim of earth upon the cool bosom of the Outer Sea. Tilion was bidden not to mount until Úrien was fallen from the sky, or far had journeyed to the West, and so it is that they are now but seldom seen in the heaven together.

Still therefore is the light of Valinor more great and fair than that of other lands, because there the Sun and Moon together rest a while before they go upon their dark journey under the world, but their light is not the light which came from the Trees before ever Ungoliant's poisonous lips touched them. That light lives now only in the Silmarils. Gods and Elves therefore look forward yet to a time when the Magic Sun and Moon, which are the Trees, may be rekindled and the bliss and glory of old return. Ulmo foretold to them that this would only come to pass by the aid, frail though it might seem, of the second race of earth, the younger children of Ilúvatar. Little heed did they pay to him at that time. Still were they wroth and bitter because of the ingratitude of the Gnomes, and the cruel slaying at the Haven of the Swans. Moreover for a while all save Tulkas feared the might and cunning of Morgoth. Now therefore they fortified all Valinor, and set a sleepless watch upon the wall of hills, which they now piled to a sheer and dreadful height – save only at the pass of Côr.[3] There were the remaining Elves set to dwell, and they went now seldom to Valmar or Tindbrenting's height, but were bidden to guard the pass ceaselessly that no bird nor beast nor Elf nor Man, nor anything beside that came from the lands without, should approach the shores of Faërie, or set foot in Valinor. In that day, which songs call the Hiding of Valinor, the Magic Isles were set, filled with enchantment, and strung across the confines of the Shadowy Seas, before the Lonely Isle is reached sailing West, there to entrap mariners and wind them in everlasting sleep. Thus it was that the many emissaries of the Gnomes in after days came never back to Valinor – save one, and he came too late.[4]

The Valar sit now behind the mountains and feast, and dismiss the exiled Noldoli from their hearts, all save Manwë and Ulmo. Most in mind did Ulmo keep them, who gathers news of the outer world through all the lakes and rivers that flow into the sea.

At the first rising of the Sun over the world the younger children of earth awoke in the land of Eruman[5] in the East of East.[6] But of Men little is told in these tales, which concern the oldest days before the waning of the Elves and the waxing of mortals, save of those who in the first days of Sunlight and Moonsheen wandered into the North of the world. To Eruman there came no God to guide Men or to summon them to dwell in Valinor. Ulmo none-theless took thought for them, and his messages came often to them by stream and flood, and they loved the waters but under-stood little the messages. The Dark-elves they met and were aided by them, and were taught by them speech and many things beside, and became the friends of the children of the Eldalië who had never found the paths to Valinor, and knew of the Valar but as a rumour and a distant name. Not long was then Morgoth come back into the earth, and his power went not far abroad, so that there was little peril in the lands and hills where new things, fair and fresh, long ages ago devised in the thought of Yavanna, came at last to their budding and their bloom.

West, North, and South they spread and wandered, and their joy was the joy of the morning before the dew is dry, when every leaf is green.

★

1  *Úrien > Árien* at all occurrences.
2  *daughter of Vana* struck out. See p. 275.
3  *Côr > Kôr*, as previously.
4  *and he came too late > the mightiest mariner of song.*
5  At the first occurrence the name *Eruman* was later underlined in pencil, as if for correction, but not at the second.
6  Added here:

> for measured time had come into the world, and the first of days; and thereafter the lives of the Eldar that remained in the Hither Lands were lessened, and their waning was begun.

# 7

Now began the times of the great wars of the powers of the North, when the Gnomes of Valinor and Ilkorins and Men strove against the hosts of Morgoth Bauglir, and went down in ruin. To this end the cunning lies of Morgoth that he sowed amongst his foes, and the curse that came of the slaying at the Haven of the

Swans, and the oath of the sons of Fëanor, were ever at work; the greatest injury they did to Men and Elves.

Only a part do these tales tell of the deeds of those days, and most they tell concerning the Gnomes and the Silmarils and the mortals that became entangled in their fate. In the early days Eldar and Men were of little different stature and bodily might; but the Eldar were blessed with greater skill, beauty, and wit, and those who had come from Valinor as much surpassed the Ilkorins in these things as they in turn surpassed the people of mortal race. Only in the realm of Doriath, whose queen Melian was of the kindred of the Valar, did the Ilkorins come near to match the Elves of Côr.[1] Immortal were the Elves, and their wisdom waxed and grew from age to age, and no sickness or pestilence brought them death. But they could be slain with weapons in those days, even by mortal Men, and some waned and wasted with sorrow till they faded from the earth. Slain or fading their spirits went back to the halls of Mandos to wait a thousand years, or the pleasure of Mandos[2] according to their deserts, before they were recalled to free life in Valinor, or were reborn,[3] it is said, into their own children.[4] More frail were Men, more easily slain by weapon or mischance, subject to ills, or grew old and died. What befell their spirits the Eldalië knew not. The Eldar said that they went to the halls of Mandos, but that their place of waiting was not that of the Elves, and Mandos under Ilúvatar knew alone whither they went after the time in his wide halls beyond the western sea. They were never reborn on earth, and none ever came back from the mansions of the dead, save only Beren son of Barahir, who after spoke never to mortal Men. Maybe their fate after death was not in the hands of the Valar.

In after days, when because of the triumphs of Morgoth Elves and Men became estranged, as he most wished, those of the Eldalië that lived still in the world faded, and Men usurped the sunlight. Then the Eldar wandered in the lonelier places of the Outer[5] Lands, and took to the moonlight and to the starlight, and to the woods and caves.[6]

★

1    *Côr > Kôr*, as previously.
2    *Mandos > Nefantur*
3    *or were reborn > or sometimes were reborn*
4    Added here:

And of like fate were those fair offspring of Elf and mortal, Eärendel, and Elwing, and Dior her father, and Elrond her child.

5   *Hither* written above *Outer*, but *Outer* not struck out.
6   Added at the end:

and became as shadows, wraiths and memories, such as set not sail unto the West and vanished from the world, as is told ere the tale's ending.

## 8

But in these days Elves and Men were kindred and allies. Before the rising of the Sun and Moon Fëanor and his sons marched into the North seeking for Morgoth. A host of Orcs aroused by the light of the burning ships came down on them, and there was battle on the plain renowned in song. Yet young and green it stretched[1] to the feet of the tall mountains upreared over Morgoth's halls; but afterward it became burnt and desolate, and is called the Land of Thirst, Dor-na-Fauglith in the Gnomish tongue. There was the First Battle.[2] Great was the slaughter of the Orcs and Balrogs, and no tale can tell the valour of Fëanor or of his sons. Yet woe entered into that first great victory. For Fëanor was wounded to the death by Gothmog Lord of Balrogs, whom Ecthelion after slew in Gondolin. Fëanor died in the hour of victory, looking upon the gigantic peaks of Thangorodrim, the greatest of hills of the world;[3] and he cursed the name of Morgoth, and laid it on his sons never to treat or parley with their foe. Yet even in the hour of his death there came to them an embassy from Morgoth acknowledging his defeat, and offering to treat, and tempting them with a Silmaril. Maidros the tall persuaded the Gnomes to meet Morgoth at the time and place appointed, but with as little thought of faith on his side as there was on the part of Morgoth. Wherefore each embassy came in far greater force than they had sworn, but Morgoth brought the greater, and they were Balrogs. Maidros was ambushed and most of his company was slain; but Maidros was taken alive by the command of Morgoth, and carried to Angband and tortured, and hung from the face of a sheer precipice upon Thangorodrim by his right wrist alone.

Then the six sons of Fëanor dismayed drew off and encamped by the shores of Lake Mithrim, in that northern land which was after called Hisilómë, Hithlum or Dorlómin by the Gnomes, which is the Land of Mist. There they heard of the march of

Fingolfin and Finweg[4] and Felagund, who had crossed the Grinding Ice.

Even as these came the first Sun arose; their blue and silver banners were unfurled, and flowers sprang beneath their marching feet. The Orcs dismayed at the uprising of the great light retreated to Angband, and Morgoth thwarted pondered a long while in wrathful thought.

Little love was there between the two hosts encamped upon the opposing shores of Mithrim, and the delay engendered by their feud did great harm to the cause of both.

Now vast vapours and smokes were made in Angband and sent forth from the smoking tops of the Mountains of Iron, which even afar off in Hithlum could be seen staining the radiance of those earliest mornings. The vapours fell and coiled about the fields and hollows, and lay on Mithrim's bosom dark and foul.

Then Finweg the valiant resolved to heal the feud. Alone he went in search of Maidros. Aided by the very mists of Morgoth, and by the withdrawal of the forces of Angband, he ventured into the fastness of his enemies, and at last he found Maidros hanging in torment. But he could not reach him to release him; and Maidros begged[5] him to shoot him with his bow.

Manwë to whom all birds are dear, and to whom they bring news upon Tindbrenting of all things which his farsighted eyes do not see, sent[6] forth the race of Eagles. Thorndor was their king. At Manwë's command they dwelt in the crags of the North and watched Morgoth and hindered his deeds, and brought news of him to the sad ears of Manwë.

Even as Finweg sorrowing bent his bow, there flew down from the high airs Thorndor king of eagles. He was the mightiest of all birds that ever have been. Thirty feet[7] was the span of his outstretched wings. His beak was of gold. So the hand of Finweg was stayed, and Thorndor bore him to the face of the rock where Maidros hung. But neither could release the enchanted bond upon the wrist, nor sever it nor draw it from the stone. Again in agony Maidros begged them to slay him, but Finweg cut off his hand above the wrist, and Thorndor bore them to Mithrim, and Maidros' wound was healed, and he lived to wield sword with his left hand more deadly to his foes than his right had been.

Thus was the feud healed for a while between the proud sons of Finn[8] and their jealousy forgotten, but still there held the oath of the Silmarils.

★

1  *Yet young and green* > *Yet dark beneath the stars* (and later *it stretched* > *the plain stretched*). (This change was made no doubt because the Sun had not yet risen; but it destroys the force of the antithesis with *but afterward it became burnt and desolate*.)

2  Added here: *the Battle under Stars*.

3  *the world* > *the hither world*

4  *Finweg* > *Fingon*, as previously, at all occurrences.

5  The typescript had present tenses, *finds*, *cannot*, *begs*, early emended to *found*, *could not*, *begged*; an indication that my father was closely following the S manuscript. Present tenses are occasionally found later in Q as originally typed.

6  *sent* > *had sent*

7  *feet* > *fathoms*

8  *Finn* > *Finwë*, as previously.

# 9

Then the Gnomes marched forward and beleaguered Angband from West, South, and East. In Hithlum and on its borders in the West lay the hosts of Fingolfin. The South was held by Felagund son of Finrod and his brethren. A tower they had on an island in the river Sirion, which guarded the valley between the northward bending mountains on the borders of Hithlum and the slopes where the great pine-forest grew, which Morgoth after filled with such dread and evil that not even the Orcs would go through it, save by a single road and in great need and haste, and the Gnomes came to call it Taur-na-Fuin, which is Deadly Nightshade. But in those days it was wholesome, if thick and dark,[1] and the people of Orodreth, of Angrod and Egnor, ranged therein and watched from its eaves the plain below, that stretched to the Mountains of Iron. Thus they guarded the plain of Sirion, most fair of rivers in elfin song, most loved of Ulmo, and all that wide land of beech and elm and oak and flowering mead that was named Broseliand.[2]

In the east lay the sons of Fëanor. Their watchtower was the high hill of Himling, and their hiding place the Gorge of Aglon, cloven deep between Himling and Taur-na-Fuin, and watered by the river of Esgalduin the dark and strong, which came out of secret wells in Taur-na-Fuin and flowed into Doriath and past the doors of Thingol's halls. But they needed little a hiding place in those days, and ranged far and wide, even to the walls of Angband in the North, and east to the Blue Mountains,[3] which are the borders of the lands of which these tales tell. There they made war upon[4] the Dwarves of Nogrod and Belegost; but they did not discover whence that strange race came, nor have any since. They are not friend of Valar[5] or of Eldar or of Men, nor do they serve Morgoth; though they are in many things more like his people, and little did they love the Gnomes.[6] Skill they had well-nigh to rival that of the Gnomes, but less beauty was in their works, and iron they wrought rather than gold and silver, and mail and weapons were their chief craft. Trade and barter was their delight and the winning of wealth of which they made little use. Long were their beards and short and squat their stature. Nauglir the Gnomes called them, and those who dwelt in Nogrod they called Indrafangs, the Longbeards, because their beards swept the floor before their feet. But as yet little they troubled the people of earth, while the power of the Gnomes was great.

This was the time that songs call the Siege of Angband. The swords of the Gnomes then fenced the earth from the ruin of Morgoth, and his power was shut behind the walls of Angband. The Gnomes boasted that never could he break their leaguer, and that none of his folk could ever pass to work evil in the ways of the world.

A time of solace it was beneath the new Sun and Moon, a time of birth and blossoming. In those days befell the first meeting of the Gnomes with the Dark-elves, and the Feast of Meeting that was held in the Land of Willows was long recalled in after days of little joy. In those days too Men came over the Blue Mountains into Broseliand[7] and Hithlum,[8] the bravest and fairest of their race. Felagund it was that found them, and he ever was their friend. On a time he was the guest of Celegorm in the East, and rode a-hunting with him. But he became separated from the others,[9] and at a time of night he came upon a dale in the western foothills of the Blue Mountains. There were lights in the dale and the sound of rugged song. Then Felagund marvelled, for the tongue of those songs was not the tongue of Eldar or of Dwarves.[10] Nor was it the tongue of Orcs, though this at first he feared. There were camped the people of Bëor, a mighty warrior of Men, whose son was Barahir the bold. They were the first of Men to come into Broseliand. After them came Hador the tall, whose sons were Haleth and Gumlin, and the sons of Gumlin Huor and Húrin,[11] and the son of Huor Tuor, and the son of Húrin Túrin. All these were tangled in the fates of the Gnomes and did mighty deeds which the Elves still remember among the songs of the deeds of their own lords and kings.

But Hador was not yet seen in the camps of the Gnomes. That

night Felagund went among the sleeping men of Bëor's host and sat by their dying fires where none kept watch, and he took a harp which Bëor had laid aside, and he played music on it such as mortal ear had never heard, having learned the strains of music from the Dark-elves alone. Then men woke and listened and marvelled, for great wisdom was in that song, as well as beauty, and the heart grew wiser that listened to it. Thus came it that Men called Felagund, whom they met first of the Noldoli, Wisdom;[12] and after him they called his race the Wise, whom we call the Gnomes.[13]

Bëor lived till death with Felagund, and Barahir his son was the greatest friend of the sons of Finrod.[14] But the sons of Hador were allied to the house of Fingolfin, and of these Húrin and Túrin were the most renowned. The realm of Gumlin was in Hithlum, and there afterward Húrin dwelt and his wife Morwen Elfsheen, who was fair as a daughter of the Eldalië.[15]

Now began the time of the ruin of the Gnomes. It was long before this was achieved, for great was their power grown, and they were very valiant, and their allies were many and bold, Dark-elves and Men.

But the tide of their fortune took a sudden turn. Long had Morgoth prepared his forces in secret. On a time of night at winter he let forth great rivers of flame that poured over all the plain before the Mountains of Iron and burned it to a desolate waste. Many of the Gnomes of Finrod's sons perished in that burning, and the fumes of it wrought darkness and confusion among the foes of Morgoth. In the train of the fire[16] came the black armies of the Orcs in numbers such as the Gnomes had never before seen or imagined. In this way Morgoth broke the leaguer of Angband and slew by the hands of the Orcs a great slaughter of the bravest of the besieging hosts. His enemies were scattered far and wide, Gnomes, Ilkorins, and Men. Men he drove for the most part back over the Blue Mountains, save the children of Bëor and of Hador who took refuge in Hithlum beyond the Shadowy Mountains, where as yet the Orcs came not in force. The Dark-elves fled south to Broseliand[17] and beyond, but many went to Doriath, and the kingdom and power of Thingol grew great in that time, till he became a bulwark and a refuge of the Elves. The magics of Melian that were woven about the borders of Doriath fenced evil from his halls and realm.

The pine-forest Morgoth took and turned it to a place of dread as has been told, and the watchtower of Sirion he took and made it into a stronghold of evil and of menace. There dwelt Thû the chief servant of Morgoth, a sorcerer of dreadful power, the lord of wolves.[18] Heaviest had the burden of that dreadful battle, the second battle and the first defeat[19] of the Gnomes, fallen upon the sons of Finrod. There were Angrod and Egnor slain. There too would Felagund have been taken or slain, but Barahir came up with all his men and saved the Gnomish king and made a wall of spears about him; and though grievous was their loss they fought their way from the Orcs and fled to the fens of Sirion to the South. There Felagund swore an oath of undying friendship and aid in time of need to Barahir and all his kin and seed, and in token of his vow he gave to Barahir his ring.

Then Felagund went South,[20] and on the banks of Narog established after the manner of Thingol a hidden and cavernous city, and a realm. Those deep places were called Nargothrond. There came Orodreth after a time of breathless flight and perilous wanderings, and with him Celegorm and Curufin, the sons of Fëanor, his friends. The people of Celegorm swelled the strength of Felagund, but it would have been better if they had gone rather to their own kin, who fortified the hill of Himling[21] east of Doriath and filled the Gorge of Aglon with hidden arms.

Most grievous of the losses of that battle was the death of Fingolfin mightiest of the Noldoli. But his own death he sought in rage and anguish seeing the defeat of his people. For he went to the gates of Angband alone and smote upon them with his sword, and challenged Morgoth to come out and fight alone. And Morgoth came. That was the last time in those wars that he left the gates of his strong places, but he could not deny the challenge before the faces of his lords and chieftains. Yet it is said that though his power and strength is the greatest of the Valar and of all things here below, at heart he is a craven when alone, and that he took not the challenge willingly. The Orcs sing of that duel at the gates, but the Elves do not, though Thorndor looked down upon it and has told the tale.

High Morgoth towered above the head of Fingolfin, but great was the heart of the Gnome, bitter his despair and terrible his wrath. Long they fought. Thrice was Fingolfin beaten to his knees and thrice arose. Ringil was his sword, as cold its blade and as bright as the blue ice, and on his shield was the star on a blue field that was his device. But Morgoth's shield was black without a blazon and its shadow was like a thundercloud. He fought with a mace like a great hammer of his forges. Grond the Orcs called it, and when it smote the earth as Fingolfin slipped aside, a pit yawned and smoke came forth. Thus was Fingolfin overcome, for the earth was broken about his feet, and he tripped and fell, and Morgoth put his foot, that is heavy as the roots of hills, upon his neck. But this was not done before Ringil had given him seven wounds, and at each he had cried aloud. He goes halt in his left foot for ever, where in his last despair Fingolfin pierced it through and pinned it to the earth.[22] But the scar upon his face Fingolfin did not give. This was the work of Thorndor. For Morgoth took the body of Fingolfin to hew it and give it to his wolves. But Thorndor swept down from on high amid the very throngs of Angband that watched the fight, and smote his claw[23] into the face of Morgoth and rescued the body of Fingolfin, and bore it to a great height. There he set his cairn upon a mountain, and that mountain looks down upon the plain of Gondolin, and over the Mount of Fingolfin no Orc or demon ever dared to pass for a great while, till treachery was born among his kin.

But Finweg[24] took the kingship of the Gnomes, and held yet out, nighest of the scattered Gnomes to the realm of their foe, in Hithlum and the Shadowy Mountains of the North that lie South and East of the Land of Mist, between it and Broseliand and the Thirsty Plain. Yet each of their strongholds Morgoth took one by one, and ever the Orcs growing more bold wandered far and wide, and numbers of the Gnomes and Dark-elves they took captive and carried to Angband and made thralls, and forced them to use their skill and magic in the service of Morgoth, and to labour unceasingly in tears in his mines and forges.[25] And Morgoth's emissaries went ever among the Dark-elves and the thrall-Gnomes and Men (to whom in those days he feigned the greatest friendship while they were out of his power), and lying promises they made and false suggestions of the greed and treachery of each to each; and because of the curse of the slaying at Swanhaven often were the lies believed; and the Gnomes feared greatly the treachery of those of their own kin who had been thralls of Angband, so that even if they escaped and came back to their people little welcome they had, and wandered often in miserable exile and despair.[26]

★

1  Added here: *and it was called Taur Danin* (late change).
2  *Broseliand* > *Beleriand* (see note 7), and the following added:

in Gnomish tongue; and Noldórien has it been called,
[Geleithian>] Geleidhian, the kingdom of the Gnomes, and
Ingolondë the fair and sorrowful.

3   *east to the Blue Mountains* > *east unto Erydluin, the Blue
    Mountains.* Against *Erydluin* was pencilled later *Eredlindon.*
4   *made war upon* > *had converse with* (late change).
5   This sentence was emended to read: *Little friendship was there
    between Elf and Dwarf, for these are not friend of Valar,* &c.
    (late change).
6   *and little did they love the Gnomes* bracketed for exclusion (late
    change).
7   *Broseliand* > *Beleriand* at all occurrences (see note 2).
8   *and Hithlum* struck out.
9   Added here: *and passed into Ossiriand* (late change).
10  Almost illegible words were pencilled above *Eldar or of Dwarves:
    the [?Valar] or of [?Doriath] nor yet of the Green Elves.*
11  This sentence was emended to read: *After them came Hador the
    Golden-haired, whose sons were Gundor and Gumlin, and the
    sons of Gumlin Húrin and Huor,* &c. (late change).
    At the bottom of the page, without direction for its insertion, is
    written: *Haleth the hunter, and little later*
12  *Wisdom* > *Gnome that is Wisdom* > *Gnome or Wisdom*
13  Added here: *Took F[elagund] to be a god* (late change).
14  Added here: *but he abode in Dorthonion* (late change).
15  Written here, with mark of insertion: *Dagor Aglareb and the
    Foreboding of the Kings* (late addition).
16  *In the train of the fire* > *In the front of that fire came Glómund
    the golden, the father of dragons, and in his train*
17  Above *Beleriand* (emended from *Broseliand*, see note 7) is pen-
    cilled *Geleidhian* (see note 2).
18  Scribbled against this: *Sauron his servant in Valinor whom he
    suborned.*
19  *the second battle and the first defeat* > *the Second Battle, the
    Battle of Sudden Flame, and the first defeat* (and later *Second
    > Third*).
20  Added here: *and West*
21  *Himling* > *Himring* (late change; at the first two occurrences of the
    name, near the beginning of this section, it was not emended).
22  *and pinned it to the earth* struck through (late change).
23  *claw* > *bill*
24  *Finweg* > *Fingon*, as previously.
25  In this sentence *magic* > *craft* and *in tears in his mines and
    forges* to an uncertain reading, probably *and tears and torment
    were their wages* (late changes).

26 A page of the typescript ends here, and at the bottom of the page is written *Turgon* (late addition).

# 10

In these days of doubt and fear, after the Second[1] Battle, many dreadful things befell of which but few are here told. It is told that Bëor was slain and Barahir yielded not to Morgoth, but all his land was won from him and his people scattered, enslaved or slain, and he himself went in outlawry with his son Beren and ten faithful men. Long they hid and did secret and valiant deeds of war against the Orcs. But in the end, as is told in the beginning of the lay of Lúthien and Beren, the hiding place of Barahir was betrayed, and he was slain and his comrades, all save Beren who by fortune was that day hunting afar. Thereafter Beren lived an outlaw alone, save for the help he had from birds and beasts which he loved; and seeking for death in desperate deeds found it not, but glory and renown in the secret songs of fugitives and hidden enemies of Morgoth, so that the tale of his deeds came even to Broseliand,[2] and was rumoured in Doriath. At length Beren fled south from the ever-closing circle of those that hunted him, and crossed the dreadful Mountains of Shadow,[3] and came at last worn and haggard into Doriath. There in secret he won the love of Lúthien daughter of Thingol, and he named her Tinúviel, the nightingale, because of the beauty of her singing in the twilight beneath the trees; for she was the daughter of Melian.

But Thingol was wroth and he dismissed him in scorn, but did not slay him because he had sworn an oath to his daughter. But he desired nonetheless to send him to his death. And he thought in his heart of a quest that could not be achieved, and he said: If thou bring me a Silmaril from the crown of Morgoth, I will let Lúthien wed thee, if she will. And Beren vowed to achieve this, and went from Doriath to Nargothrond bearing the ring of Barahir. The quest of the Silmaril there aroused the oath from sleep that the sons of Fëanor had sworn, and evil began to grow from it. Felagund, though he knew the quest to be beyond his power, was willing to lend all his aid to Beren, because of his own oath to Barahir. But Celegorm and Curufin dissuaded his people and roused up rebellion against him. And evil thoughts awoke in their hearts, and they thought to usurp the throne of Nargothrond, because they were sons of the eldest line. Rather than a Silmaril should be won and given to Thingol, they would ruin the power of Doriath and Nargothrond.

So Felagund gave his crown to Orodreth and departed from his people with Beren and ten faithful men of his own board. They waylaid an Orc-band and slew them and disguised themselves by the aid of Felagund's magic as Orcs. But they were seen by Thû from his watchtower, which once had been Felagund's own, and were questioned by him, and their magic was overthrown in a contest between Thû and Felagund. Thus they were revealed as Elves, but the spells of Felagund concealed their names and quest. Long they were tortured in the dungeons of Thû, but none betrayed the other.

In the meanwhile Lúthien learning by the far sight of Melian that Beren had fallen into the power of Thû sought in her despair to fly from Doriath. This became known to Thingol, who imprisoned her in a house in the tallest of his mighty beeches far above the ground. How she escaped and came into the woods, and was found there by Celegorm as they hunted on the borders of Doriath, is told in the lay of Lúthien. They took her treacherously to Nargothrond, and Curufin the crafty became enamoured of her beauty. From her tale they learned that Felagund was in the hands of Thû; and they purposed to let him perish there, and keep Lúthien with them, and force Thingol to wed Lúthien to Curufin,[4] and so build up their power and usurp Nargothrond and become the mightiest of the princes of the Gnomes. They did not think to go in search of the Silmarils, or suffer any others to do so, until they had all the power of the Elves beneath themselves and obedient to them. But their designs came to nought save estrangement and bitterness between the kingdoms of the Elves.

Huan was the name of the chief of the hounds of Celegorm. He was of immortal race from the hunting-lands of Oromë. Oromë gave him to Celegorm long before in Valinor, when Celegorm often rode in the train of the God and followed his horn. He came into the Great[5] Lands with his master, and dart nor weapon, spell nor poison, could harm him, so that he went into battle with his lord and saved him many times from death. His fate had been decreed that he should not meet death save at the hands of the mightiest wolf that should ever walk the world.

Huan was true of heart, and he loved Lúthien from the hour that he first found her in the woods and brought her to Celegorm. His heart was grieved by his master's treachery, and he set Lúthien free and went with her to the North.

There Thû slew his captives one by one, till only Felagund and Beren were left. When the hour for Beren's death came Felagund put forth all his power, and burst his bonds, and wrestled with the werewolf that came to slay Beren; and he killed the wolf, but was himself slain in the dark. There Beren mourned in despair, and waited for death. But Lúthien came and sang outside the dungeons. Thus she beguiled Thû to come forth, for the fame of the loveliness of Lúthien had gone through all lands and the wonder of her song. Even Morgoth desired her, and had promised the greatest reward to any who could capture her. Each wolf that Thû sent Huan slew silently, till Draugluin the greatest of his wolves came. Then there was fierce battle, and Thû knew that Lúthien was not alone. But he remembered the fate of Huan, and he made himself the greatest wolf that had yet walked the world, and came forth. But Huan overthrew him, and won from him the keys and the spells that held together his enchanted walls and towers. So the stronghold was broken and the towers thrown down and the dungeons opened. Many captives were released, but Thû flew in bat's form to Taur-na-Fuin. There Lúthien found Beren mourning beside Felagund. She healed his sorrow and the wasting of his imprisonment, but Felagund they buried on the top of his own island hill, and Thû came there no more.

Then Huan returned to his master, and less was the love between them after. Beren and Lúthien wandered careless in happiness, until they came nigh to the borders of Doriath once more. There Beren remembered his vow, and bade Lúthien farewell, but she would not be sundered from him. In Nargothrond there was tumult. For Huan and many of the captives of Thû brought back the tidings of the deeds of Lúthien, and the death of Felagund, and the treachery of Celegorm and Curufin was laid bare. It is said they had sent a secret embassy to Thingol. ere Lúthien escaped, but Thingol in wrath had sent their letters back by his own servants to Orodreth.[6] Wherefore now the hearts of the people of Narog turned back to the house of Finrod, and they mourned their king Felagund whom they had forsaken, and they did the bidding of Orodreth. But he would not suffer them to slay the sons of Fëanor as they wished. Instead he banished them from Nargothrond, and swore that little love should there be between Narog and any of the sons of Fëanor thereafter. And so it was.

Celegorm and Curufin were riding in haste and wrath through the woods to find their way to Himling,[7] when they came upon Beren and Lúthien, even as Beren sought to part from his love.

They rode down on them, and recognizing them tried to trample Beren under their hooves. But Curufin swerving lifted Lúthien to his saddle. Then befell the leap of Beren, the greatest leap of mortal Men. For he sprang like a lion right upon the speeding horse of Curufin, and grasped him about the throat, and horse and rider fell in confusion upon the earth, but Lúthien was flung far off and lay dazed upon the ground. There Beren choked Curufin, but his death was very nigh from Celegorm, who rode back with his spear. In that hour Huan forsook the service of Celegorm, and sprang upon him so that his horse swerved aside, and no man for fear of the terror of the great hound dared go nigh. Lúthien forbade the death of Curufin, but Beren despoiled him of his horse and weapons, chief of which was his famous knife, made by the Dwarves. It would cut iron like wood. Then the brothers rode off, but shot back at Huan treacherously and at Lúthien. Huan they did not hurt, but Beren sprang before Lúthien and was wounded, and Men remembered that wound against the sons of Fëanor, when it became known.

Huan stayed with Lúthien, and hearing of their perplexity and the purpose Beren had still to go to Angband, he went and fetched them from the ruined halls of Thû a werewolf's coat and a bat's. Three times only did Huan speak with the tongue of Elves or Men. The first was when he came to Lúthien in Nargothrond. This was the second, when he devised the desperate counsel for their quest. So they rode North, till they could no longer go on horse in safety. Then they put on the garments as of wolf and bat, and Lúthien in guise of evil fay rode upon the werewolf.

In the lay of Lúthien is all told how they came to Angband's gate, and found it newly guarded, for rumour of he knew not what design abroad among the Elves had come to Morgoth. Wherefore he fashioned the mightiest of all wolves, Carcharas[8] Knife-fang, to sit at the gates.[9] But Lúthien set him in spells, and they won their way to the presence of Morgoth, and Beren slunk beneath his chair. Then Lúthien dared the most dreadful and most valiant deed that any of the women of the Elves have ever dared; no less than the challenge of Fingolfin is it accounted, and may be greater, save that she was half-divine. She cast off her disguise and named her own name, and feigned that she was brought captive by the wolves of Thû. And she beguiled Morgoth, even as his heart plotted foul evil within him; and she danced before him, and cast all his court in sleep; and she sang to him, and she flung the magic robe she had woven in Doriath in his face, and she set a binding dream upon him – what song can sing the marvel of that deed, or the wrath and humiliation of Morgoth, for even the Orcs laugh in secret when they remember it, telling how Morgoth fell from his chair and his iron crown rolled upon the floor.

Then forth leaped Beren casting aside the wolvish robe, and drew out the knife of Curufin. With that he cut forth a Silmaril. But daring more he essayed to gain them all. Then the knife of the treacherous Dwarves snapped, and the ringing sound of it stirred the sleeping hosts and Morgoth groaned. Terror seized the hearts of Beren and Lúthien, and they fled down the dark ways of Angband. The doors were barred by Carcharas, now aroused from the spell of Lúthien. Beren set himself before Lúthien, which proved ill; for ere she could touch the wolf with her robe or speak word of magic, he sprang upon Beren, who now had no weapon. With his right he smote at the eyes of Carcharas, but the wolf took the hand into his jaws and bit it off. Now that hand held the Silmaril. Then was the maw of Carcharas burned with a fire of anguish and torment, when the Silmaril touched his evil flesh; and he fled howling from before them, so that all the mountains shuddered, and the madness of the wolf of Angband was of all the horrors that ever came into the North[10] the most dire and terrible. Hardly did Lúthien and Beren escape, ere all Angband was aroused.

Of their wanderings and despair, and of the healing of Beren, who ever since has been called Beren Ermabwed the One-handed, of their rescue by Huan, who had vanished suddenly from them ere they came to Angband, and of their coming to Doriath once more, here there is little to tell.[11] But in Doriath many things had befallen. Ever things had gone ill there since Lúthien fled away. Grief had fallen on all the people and silence on their songs when their hunting found her not. Long was the search, and in searching Dairon the piper of Doriath was lost, who loved Lúthien before Beren came to Doriath. He was the greatest of the musicians of the Elves, save Maglor son of Fëanor, and Tinfang Warble.[12] But he came never back to Doriath and strayed into the East of the world.[13]

Assaults too there were on Doriath's borders, for rumours that Lúthien was astray had reached Angband. Boldog captain of the Orcs was there slain in battle by Thingol, and his great warriors Beleg the Bowman and Mablung Heavyhand were with Thingol in that battle. Thus Thingol learned that Lúthien was yet free of Morgoth, but that he knew of her wandering; and Thingol was filled with fear. In the midst of his fear came the embassy of Celegorm in secret, and said that Beren was dead, and Felagund, and Lúthien was at Nargothrond. Then Thingol found it in his heart to regret the death of Beren, and his wrath was aroused at the hinted treachery of Celegorm to the house of Finrod, and because he kept Lúthien and did not send her home. Wherefore he sent spies into the land of Nargothrond and prepared for war. But he learned that Lúthien had fled and that Celegorm and his brother were gone to Aglon. So now he sent an embassy to Aglon, since his might was not great enough to fall upon all the seven brethren, nor was his quarrel with others than Celegorm and Curufin. But this embassy journeying in the woods met with the onslaught of Carcharas. That great wolf had run in madness through all the woods of the North, and death and devastation went with him. Mablung alone escaped to bear the news of his coming to Thingol. Of fate, or the magic of the Silmaril that he bore to his torment, he was not stayed by the spells of Melian, but burst into the inviolate woods of Doriath, and far and wide terror and destruction was spread.

Even as the sorrows of Doriath were at their worst came Lúthien and Beren and Huan back to Doriath. Then the heart of Thingol was lightened, but he looked not with love upon Beren in whom he saw the cause of all his woes. When he had learned how Beren had escaped from Thû he was amazed, but he said: 'Mortal, what of thy quest and of thy vow?' Then said Beren: 'Even now I have a Silmaril in my hand.' 'Show it to me,' said Thingol. 'That I cannot,' said Beren, 'for my hand is not here.' And all the tale he told, and made clear the cause of the madness of Carcharas, and Thingol's heart was softened by his brave words, and his for-bearance, and the great love that he saw between his daughter and this most valiant Man.

Now therefore did they plan the wolf-hunt of Carcharas. In that hunt was Huan and Thingol and Mablung and Beleg and Beren and no more. And here the sad tale of it must be short, for it is elsewhere told more fully. Lúthien remained behind in fore-boding, as they went forth; and well she might, for Carcharas was slain, but Huan died in the same hour, and he died to save Beren.[14] Yet Beren was hurt to the death, but lived to place the Silmaril in the hands of Thingol, when Mablung had cut it from the belly of the wolf. Then he spoke not again, until they had borne him with Huan at his side back to the doors of Thingol's halls. There beneath the beech, wherein before she had been imprisoned,

Lúthien met them, and kissed Beren ere his spirit departed to the halls of awaiting. So ended the long tale of Lúthien and Beren. But not yet was the lay of Leithian, release from bondage, told in full. For it has long been said that Lúthien failed and faded swiftly and vanished from the earth, though some songs say that Melian summoned Thorndor, and he bore her living unto Valinor. And she came to the halls of Mandos, and she sang to him a tale of moving love so fair that he was moved to pity, as never has befallen since. Beren he summoned, and thus, as Lúthien had sworn as she kissed him at the hour of death, they met beyond the western sea. And Mandos suffered them to depart, but he said that Lúthien should become mortal even as her lover, and should leave the earth once more in the manner of mortal women, and her beauty become but a memory of song. So it was, but it is said that in recompense Mandos gave to Beren and to Lúthien thereafter a long span of life and joy, and they wandered knowing thirst nor cold in the fair land of Broseliand, and no mortal Man thereafter spoke to Beren or his spouse.[15] Yet he came back into these tales when one more sad than his was done.

1  *Second > Third* (late change); see §9 note 19.
2  *Broseliand > Beleriand*, as previously.
3  *Mountains of Shadow > Mountains of Terror* (see III.170–1).
4  *Curufin* struck through and *Cele[gorm]* written above (late change).
5  *Great > Hither* (cf. §3 note 8).
6  This sentence, from *Thingol in wrath*, emended to: *Thingol was wroth, and would have gone to war with them as is later told.*
7  *Himling > Himring*, as in §9 note 21 (late change).
8  *Carcharas > Carcharoth* at all occurrences.
9  Added here: *Dire and dreadful was that beast; and songs have also named him Borosaith, Everhungry, and Anfauglin, Jaws of Thirst.*
10  Added here: *ere Angband's fall*
11  Late addition in the margin: *Thorndor bore them over Gondolin to Brethil.*
12  *save Maglor son of Fëanor, and Tinfang Warble > and Maglor son of Fëanor and Tinfang Gelion alone are named with him.*
13  Added here: *where long he made secret music in memory of Lúthien.*
14  Added here: *and he bade him farewell, and that was the third and last time Huan spoke.*

15  This sentence emended to: *and they wandered knowing neither thirst nor cold upon the confines of Geleidhian in fair Ossiriand, Land of Seven Streams, Gwerth-i-cuina, the Living Dead; and no mortal Man thereafter*, &c.

# 11

Now[1] it must be told that Maidros son of Fëanor perceived that Morgoth was not unassailable after the deeds of Huan and Lúthien and the breaking of the towers of Thû,[2] but that he would destroy them all one by one, if they did not form again a league and council. This was the Union of Maidros and wisely planned. The scattered Ilkorins and Men were gathered together, while the forces of Maidros made ever fiercer assaults from Himling,[3] and drove back the Orcs and took their spies. The smithies of Nogrod and Belegost were busy in those days making mail and sword and spear for many armies, and much of the wealth and jewelry of Elves and Men they got into their keeping in that time, though they went not themselves to war. 'For we do not know the rights of this quarrel,' they said, 'and we are friends of neither side – until it hath the mastery.' Thus great and splendid was the army of Maidros, but the oath and the curse did injury to his design.

All the hosts of Hithlum, Gnomes and Men, were ready to his summons, and Finweg[4] and Turgon and Huor and Húrin were their chiefs.[5] Orodreth would not march from Narog at the word of Maidros, because of the death of Felagund, and the deeds of Curufin and Celegorm.[6] Yet he suffered a small company of the bravest, who would not endure to be idle when the great war was afoot, to go North. Their leader was the young Flinding son of Fuilin, most daring of the scouts of Nargothrond; but they took the devices of the house of Finweg and went beneath his banners, and came never back, save one.[7]

From Doriath none came.[8] For Maidros and his brethren had before sent unto Doriath and reminded Thingol with exceedingly haughty words of their oath, and summoned him to yield up the ·Silmaril. This Melian counselled him to do, and maybe he would have done, but their words were overproud, and he thought how the jewel had been gained by the sorrows of Thingol's people,[9] and despite the crooked deeds of the sons of Fëanor; and greed[10] too, it may be, had some part in the heart of Thingol, as afterwards was shown. Wherefore he sent the messengers of Maidros back in scorn. Maidros said nought, for at that time he was beginning to ponder[11] the reunion of the forces of the Elves. But Celegorm and Curufin vowed aloud to slay Thingol or any of his folk they should ever see, by night or day, in war or peace.[12]

For this reason Thingol went not forth,[13] nor any out of Doriath save Mablung, and Beleg who obeyed no man.

Now came the day when Maidros sent forth his summons and the Dark-elves, save out of Doriath, marched to his banner, and Men from East and South. But Finweg and Turgon and the Men of Hithlum were gathered in the West upon the borders of the Thirsty Plain, waiting for the signal of the advancing standards from the East. It may be that Maidros delayed too long gathering his forces; certain it is that secret emissaries of Morgoth went among the camps, thrall-Gnomes or things in elfin form, and spread foreboding and thoughts of disunion. To Men they went most, and the fruit of their words was later seen.

Long the army waited in the West, and fear of treachery fell upon them, when Maidros came not, and the hot hearts of Finweg and Turgon became impatient.[14] They sent their heralds across the plain and their silver trumpets rang; and they summoned the hosts of Morgoth to come out. Then Morgoth sent forth a force, great and yet not too great. And Finweg was moved to attack from the woods at the feet of the Shadowy Mountains where he lay hid. But Húrin spoke against it.

Then Morgoth led forth one of the heralds of Finweg that he had wrongfully taken prisoner and slew him upon the plain, so that the watchers from afar might see – for far and clear do the eyes of the Gnomes behold things in bright air. Then the wrath of Finweg burst its bonds and his army leaped forth to sudden onslaught. This was as Morgoth designed, but it is said that he reckoned not the true number of their array, nor knew yet the measure of their valour, and well nigh his plan went ill. Ere his army could be succoured they were overwhelmed, and that day there was a greater slaughter of the servants of Morgoth than there yet had been, and the banners of Finweg were raised before the walls of Angband.

Flinding, it is said, and the men of Nargothrond burst even within the gates; and fear came on Morgoth on his throne. But they were slain or taken, for no help came.[15] By other secret gates Morgoth let issue forth the main host that he had kept in waiting, and Finweg and the Men of Hithlum were beaten back from the walls.

Then in the plain began the Battle of Unnumbered Tears,[16] of which no song or tale tells the full, for the voice of the teller is whelmed in lamentation. The host of the Elves was surrounded. Yet in that hour there marched up at last the banners of Maidros and his allies from the East. Even yet the Elves might have won the day, for the Orcs wavered. But as the vanguard of Maidros came upon the Orcs, Morgoth let loose his last forces, and all Angband was empty. There came wolves and serpents, and there came Balrogs like fire, and there came the first of all the dragons, the eldest of all the Worms of Greed. Glómund was his name and long had his terror been noised abroad, though he was not come to his full growth and evil, and seldom had he been seen.[17] Thus Morgoth strove to hinder the joining of the hosts of the Elves, but this the Eldar say he would not even so have achieved, had not the captains of Men in the hosts of Maidros turned and fled, and their number was very great. Treachery or cowardice or both was the cause of that grievous wrong. But worse is to tell, for the swart Men, whom Uldor the Accursed led, went over to the foe and fell upon Maidros' flank. From that day were Elves estranged from Men, unless it be from the children of the children of Hador.[18]

There Finweg fell in flame of swords, and a fire it is said burst from his helm when it was cloven; but he was beaten to the earth and his white banners were trodden under foot. Then the army of the West, sundered from Maidros, fell back as best it could win its way, step by step, towards the Shadowy Mountains or even the dreadful fringes of Taur-na-Fuin. But Húrin did not retreat,[19] and he held the rearguard, and all the Men of Hithlum and his brother Huor were there slain about him in a heap, so that not one came back with tidings to their home. The valiant stand of Húrin is still remembered by the Elves, for by it was Turgon enabled to cleave his way from the field and save part of his battle, and rescue his people from the hills, and escape southward to Sirion. Renowned in song is the axe of Húrin that slew a hundred Orcs, but the magic helm that Gumlin his sire bequeathed him he did not wear that day. Thereon was set in mockery the image of the head of Glómund, and oft it had gone into victory, so that the Men of Hithlum said: We have a dragon of more worth than theirs. It was Telchar's work, the great smith of Belegost, but it would not have availed Húrin on that field, for by the command of Morgoth he was taken alive, grasped by the hideous arms of the uncounted Orcs, till he was buried beneath them.

Maidros and the sons of Fëanor wrought great slaughter on Orc and Balrog and traitor Man that day, but the dragon they did not slay and the fire of his breath was the death of many. And they were driven in the end far away, and the Gorge of Aglon was filled with Orcs and the hill of Himling with the people of Morgoth. But the seven sons of Fëanor, though each was wounded, were not slain.[20]

Great was the triumph of Morgoth. The bodies of his enemies that were slain were piled in a mound like a great hill upon Dor-na-Fauglith, but there the grass came and grew green in that place alone in all the desert, and no Orc thereafter trod upon the earth beneath which the Gnomish swords crumbled into rust. The realm of Finweg was no more, the sons of Fëanor wandered in the East, fugitives in the Blue Mountains.[21] The armies of Angband ranged all the North. To Hithlum Morgoth sent Men who were his servants or afraid of him. South and East his Orcs went in plunder and ruin; well nigh all Broseliand[22] they overran. Doriath yet held where Thingol lived, and Nargothrond. But he heeded these not much as yet, maybe because he knew little of them. But one thing grievously marred his triumph, and great was his wrath when he thought of it. This was the escape of Turgon, and in no way could he learn whither that king had gone.[23]

Húrin was now brought before Morgoth and defied him. He was chained in torment. Afterward Morgoth remembering that treachery or the fear of it, and especially the treachery of Men, alone would work the ruin[24] of the Gnomes, came to Húrin and offered him honour and freedom and a wealth of jewels, if he would lead an army against Turgon, or even tell him whither that king had gone; for he knew that Húrin was close in the counsels of the sons of Fingolfin. But Húrin mocked him. Therefore Morgoth devised a cruel punishment. Upon the highest peak of Thangorodrim he set him chained upon a chair of stone, and he cursed him with a curse of never-sleeping sight like unto the Gods, but his kin and seed he cursed with a fate of sorrow and ill-chance, and bade Húrin sit there and watch the unfolding of it.

★

The first part of this section was heavily but hastily and roughly emended, on top of the careful alterations that belong to an earlier 'layer'. In three of the following notes (7, 14, 15) I give the final text of the passages that were most changed.

1   Scribbled in the margin is *Swarthy Men*, apparently with a mark of
insertion to this point in the narrative.

2   *the towers of Thû > Sauron's tower* (late change).

3   This sentence emended to read: *The Dark-elves were summoned
again from afar, and Men of the East were gathered together;
and the forces of Maidros sallied forth from Himling* (late
change). *Himling > Himring* subsequently.

4   *Finweg > Fingon* throughout, as previously.

5   Added here: *Yet less was the aid that Maidros had of Men than
should have been, because of the wounding of Beren in the
wood; and (Orodreth would not march, &c.)*

6   *Celegorm > Celegorn* at both occurrences (this change has not
been made previously).

7   This paragraph, after the changes given in notes 4–6, was rewritten
later (introducing the later story of the foundation of Gondolin),
thus:

All the hosts of Hithlum, Gnomes and Men, were ready to his
summons; and Fingon and Huor and Húrin were their chiefs.
And Turgon himself deeming that haply the hour of deliverance
was at hand came forth himself unlooked for, and he brought a
great army, and they encamped before the West Pass in sight of
the walls of Hithlum, and there was joy among the people of
Fingon his brother. [*An addition here was struck out, no
doubt at the time of writing, and replaced by a different
statement about the folk of Haleth below*: The folk of Haleth
made ready in the forest of Brethil.] Yet less was the aid that
Maidros had of Men than should have b̈een, because of the
wounding of Beren in the wood; for the folk of Haleth abode in
the forest, and few came to war. Orodreth, moreover, would not
march from Narog at the word of Maidros, because of the death of
Felagund, and the deeds of Curufin and Celegorn. Yet he suffered
a small company of the bravest, who would not endure to be idle
when great war was afoot, to go North. Their leader was Gwindor
son of Guilin, a very valiant prince; but they took the devices of
the house of Fingon and went beneath his banners, and came
never back, save one.

8   *From Doriath none came > From Doriath too came scanty aid.*

9   Added here: *and the anguish of Lúthien*

10  *greed > covetice*

11  *beginning to ponder > already beginning to devise* (late
change).

12  This sentence changed to read: *vowed aloud to slay Thingol, and
destroy his folk, if they came victorious from war, and the
jewel were not yielded of free-will.*

13 *Thingol went not forth* > *Thingol fortified his realm, and went not forth*

14 From the beginning of the preceding paragraph (*Now came the day* . . .) the text was extensively rewritten in the later 'layer' of change:

> At length having gathered at last all the strength that he might Maidros appointed a day, and sent word to Fingon and Turgon. Now for a while the Gnomes had victory, and the Orcs were driven out of Beleriand, and hope was renewed; but Morgoth was aware of all that was done, and he took counsel against their uprising, and he sent forth his spies and emissaries among Elves and Men, but especially did these come unto the Swarthy Men, and to the sons of Ulfang. Upon the East under the banner of Maidros were all the folk of the sons of Fëanor, and they were many; and the Dark-elves coming from the South were with him, and the battalions of the Easterlings, with the sons of Bor and Ulfang. But Fingon and Turgon and the Men of Hithlum and such as came from the Falas and from Nargothrond were gathered ready in the West upon the borders of the Thirsty Plain, waiting under the banner of Fingon for the signal of the advancing standards from the East. But Maidros was delayed upon the road by the machinations of Uldor the Accursed son of Ulfang, and ever the secret emissaries of Morgoth went among the camps, thrall-Gnomes or things in elvish form, and spread foreboding and thoughts of treason.
>
> Long the army waited in the West, and fear of treachery grew in their thought, when Maidros came not. Then the hot hearts of Fingon and Turgon became impatient.

15 This passage, from *Flinding, it is said*, was changed by late emendation to read:

> Gwindor son of Guilin, it is said, and the men of Nargothrond were in the forefront of the battle and burst within the gates; and they slew the Orcs in the very halls of Morgoth, and fear came on Morgoth on his throne. But at the last Gwindor and his men were all slain or taken, for no help came to them.

16 Added here: *Nirnaith Arnediad* (late change).

17 Added here: *since the second battle of the North*.

18 Added here: *and of Bëor* (late change).

19 *But Húrin did not retreat* > *But there Húrin turned to bay*

20 The following passage was added here:

> But their arms were scattered, and their folk minished and dispersed and their league broken; and they took to a wild and woodland life, beneath the feet of Eryd-luin [*later* > Ered-luin],

mingling with the Dark-elves, and forgetting their power and glory of old.

21   *wandered in the East, fugitives in the Blue Mountains* > *wandered as leaves before the wind.*

22   *Broseliand* > *Beleriand*, as previously.

23   The following passage was added here:

and his anger was the greater, for it is said that of all the Gnomes he feared and hated most the house and people of Fingolfin, who had harkened never to his lies and blandishments, and came into the North, as has been told, only out of loyalty to their kin.

24   *the ruin* > *the final ruin*


# 12

Morwen[1] the wife of Húrin was left in Hithlum and with her were but two old men too old for war, and maidens and young boys. One of these was Húrin's child, Túrin son of Húrin renowned in song. But Morwen was with child once more, and so she stayed and mourned in Hithlum, and went not like Rían wife of Huor to seek for tidings of her lord. The Men[2] of the faithful race were slain, and Morgoth drove thither in their stead those who had betrayed the Elves, and he penned them behind the Shadowy Mountains, and slew them if they wandered to Broseliand[3] or beyond; and such was all they got of the love and rewards he had promised them. Yet their hearts were turned to evil, and little love they showed to the women and children of the faithful who had been slain, and most of them they enslaved. Great was the courage and majesty of Morwen, and many were afraid of her, and whispered that she had learned black magics of the Gnomes.[4] But she was poor and well nigh alone, and was succoured in secret by her kinswoman Airin whom Brodda, one of the incoming Men, and mighty among them, had taken to wife. Wherefore it came into her heart to send Túrin, who was then seven years of age, to Thingol, that he might not grow up a churl or servant; for Húrin and Beren had been friends of old. The fate of Túrin is told in the 'Children of Húrin', and it need not in full be told here, though it is wound with the fates of the Silmarils and the Elves. It is called the Tale of Grief, for it is very sorrowful, and in it are seen the worst of the deeds of Morgoth Bauglir.

Túrin grew up in Thingol's court, but after a while as Morgoth's power grew news came no more from Hithlum, for it was a long

and perilous road, and he heard no more of Nienor his sister who
was born after he left his home, nor of Morwen his mother; and his
heart was dark and heavy. He was often in battle on the borders of
the realm where Beleg the Bowman was his friend, and he came
little to the court, and wild and unkempt was his hair and his
attire, though sweet his voice and sad his song. On a time at the
table of the king he was taunted by a foolish Elf, Orgof by name,
with his rough garb and strange looks. And Orgof in jest slighted
the maidens and wives of the Men of Hithlum. But Túrin unwitting
of his growing strength slew Orgof with a drinking vessel at the
king's board.

He fled then the court, and thinking himself an outlaw took to
war against all, Elves, Men, or Orcs, that crossed the path of the
desperate band he gathered upon the borders of the kingdom,
hunted Men and Ilkorins and Gnomes. One day, when he was not
among them, his men captured Beleg the Bowman and tied him to
a tree, and would have slain him; but Túrin returning was smitten
with remorse, and released Beleg and forswore war or plunder
against all save the Orcs. From Beleg he learned that Thingol had
pardoned his deed the day that it was done. Still he went not back
to the Thousand Caves; but the deeds that were done on the
marches of Doriath by Beleg and Túrin were noised in Thingol's
halls, and in Angband they were known.

Now one of Túrin's band was Blodrin son of Ban, a Gnome,[5]
but he had lived long with the Dwarves and was of evil heart and
joined Túrin for the love of plunder. He loved little the new life in
which wounds were more plentiful than booty. In the end he
betrayed the hiding-places of Túrin[6] to the Orcs, and the camp of
Túrin was surprised. Blodrin was slain by a chance arrow of his
evil allies in the gloom, but Túrin was taken alive, as Húrin had
been, by the command of Morgoth. For Morgoth began to fear
that in Doriath behind the mazes of Melian, where his deeds were
hidden from him, save by report,[7] Túrin would cheat the doom
that he had devised. Beleg was left for dead beneath a heap of
slain. There he was found by Thingol's messengers who came to
summon them to a feast in the Thousand Caves. Taken back
thither he was healed by Melian, and set off alone to track Túrin.
Beleg was the most marvellous of all woodsmen that have ever
been, and his skill was little less than Huan in the following of a
trail, though he followed by eye and cunning not by scent. Nonetheless he was bewildered in the mazes of Deadly Nightshade and
wandered there in despair, until he saw the lamp of Flinding

Fuilin's son,[8] who had escaped from the mines of Morgoth, a bent and timid shadow of his former shape and mood. From Flinding he learned news of the Orc-band that had captured Túrin; and it had delayed long in the lands plundering East among Men, but was now come in great haste, owing to the angry message of Morgoth, and was passing along the Orc-road through Taur-na-Fuin itself.

Near the issuing of this road, where it reaches the edge of the forest upon the face of the steep[9] slopes that lie to the south of the Thirsty Plain, Flinding and Beleg lay and watched the Orcs go by. When the Orcs left the forest and went far down the slopes to camp in a bare dale in sight of Thangorodrim, Beleg and his companion followed them. At night Beleg shot the wolf-sentinels of the Orc-camp, and stole with Flinding into its midst. With the greatest difficulty and direst peril they lifted Túrin, senseless in a sleep of utter weariness, and brought him out of the camp and laid him in a dell of thick thorn trees high up on the hillside. In striking[10] off the bonds Beleg pricked Túrin's foot; and he, roused in sudden fear and anger, for the Orcs had often tormented him, found himself free. Then in his madness he seized Beleg's sword, and slew his friend thinking him a foe. The covering of Flinding's lamp fell off at that moment, and Túrin saw Beleg's face; and his madness left him and he was turned as to stone.

The Orcs, awakened by his cries as he leaped on Beleg, discovered the escape of Túrin, but were scattered by a terrible storm of thunder and a deluge of rain. In the morning Flinding saw them marching away over the steaming sands of Dor-na-Fauglith. But through all the storm Túrin sat without movement; and scarcely could he be roused to help in the burying of Beleg and his bow in the dell of thorns. Flinding afterwards led him, dazed and unwitting, towards safety; and his mind was healed when he drank of the spring of Narog by Ivrin's lake. For his frozen tears were loosed, and he wept, and after his weeping made a song for Beleg, the Bowman's Friendship, which became a battle song of the foes of Morgoth.

1   Written in the margin against the opening of this section is *Take in Helm of Gumlin from page 34*. Page 34 in the typescript contains the passage concerning the Helm in §11, p. 118.
2   *The Men > Most of the Men*

3  *Broseliand* > *Beleriand*, as previously.
4  *whispered that she had learned black magics of the Gnomes* >
   *whispered that she was a witch* (late change).
5  *a Gnome* > *a Gnome of Fëanor's house*
6  *the hiding-places of Túrin* > *the hiding-places of Túrin beyond the
   eaves of Doriath*
7  *save by report* > *or upon its borders whence came but uncertain
   report*
8  *Flinding Fuilin's son* > *Gwindor son of Guilin*, and subsequently *Flinding* > *Gwindor* (late changes; see §11 note 15).
9  *steep* > *long*
10 Added after *high up on the hillside*:

> Then Beleg drew his renowned sword, made of iron that fell from
> heaven as a blazing star, and it would cut all earth-dolven iron.
> But fate was that day more strong, for in striking, &c.

## 13

Flinding[1] led Túrin in the end to Nargothrond. There in days
long gone[2] Flinding had loved Finduilas daughter of Orodreth,
and he called her Failivrin, which is the gleam on the waters of the
fair lake whence Narog comes. But her heart was turned against
her will to Túrin, and his to her. Out of loyalty[3] he fought against
his love and Finduilas grew wan and pale, but Flinding perceiving
their hearts grew bitter.

Túrin grew great and mighty in Nargothrond, but he loved not
their secret manner of fighting and ambush, and began to long for
brave strokes and battle in the open. Then he caused to be forged
anew the sword of Beleg, and the craftsmen of Narog made thereof
a black blade with shining edges of pale fire; from which sword he
became known among them as Mormaglir.[4]

With this sword he thought to avenge the death of Beleg the
Bowman, and with it he did many mighty deeds; so that the fame
of Mormaglir, the Black-sword of Nargothrond, came even unto
Doriath and to the ears of Thingol, but the name of Túrin was not
heard. And long victory dwelt with Mormaglir and the host of the
Gnomes of Nargothrond who followed him; and their realm
reached even to the sources of Narog, and from the western sea to
the marches of Doriath; and there was a stay in the onset of
Morgoth.

In this time of respite and hope Morwen arose, and leaving her
goods in the care of Brodda, who had to wife[5] her kinswoman

Airin, she took with her Nienor her daughter, and adventured the long journey to Thingol's halls. There did new grief await her, for she learnt of the loss and vanishing of Túrin; and even as she dwelt a while as the guest of Thingol, in sorrow and in doubt, there came to Doriath the tidings of the fall of Nargothrond; whereat all folk wept.

Biding his hour Morgoth had loosed upon the folk of Narog at unawares a great army that he had long prepared, and with the host came that father of the dragons, Glómund, who wrought ruin in the Battle of Unnumbered Tears. The might of Narog was overwhelmed upon the Guarded Plain, north of Nargothrond; and there fell Flinding son of Fuilin,[6] mortally wounded, and dying he refused the succour of Túrin, reproaching him, and bidding him, if he would amend the evil he had wrought his friend, to hasten back to Nargothrond to rescue even with his life, if he could, Finduilas whom they loved, or to slay her else.

But the Orc-host and the mighty dragon came upon Nargothrond before Túrin could put it in defence, and they overthrew Orodreth and all his remaining folk, and the great halls beneath the earth were sacked and plundered, and all the women and maidens of the folk of Narog were herded as slaves and taken into Morgoth's thraldom. Túrin only they could not overcome, and the Orcs fell back before him in terror and amaze, and he stood alone. Thus ever did Morgoth achieve the downfall of men by their own deeds; for but little would men have accounted the woe of Túrin had he fallen in brave defence before the mighty doors of Nargothrond.

Fire was in the eyes of Túrin, and the edges of his sword shone as with flame, and he strode to battle even with Glómund, alone and unafraid. But it was not his fate that day to rid the world of that creeping evil; for he fell under the binding spell of the lidless eyes of Glómund, and he was halted moveless; but Glómund[7] taunted him, calling him deserter of his kin, friend-slayer, and love-thief. And the dragon offered him his freedom either to follow seeking to rescue his 'stolen love' Finduilas, or to do his duty and go to the rescue of his mother and sister, who were living in great misery in Hithlum (as he said and lied) and nigh to death. But he must swear to abandon one or the other.

Then Túrin in anguish and in doubt forsook Finduilas against his heart, and against his last word to Flinding[8] (which if he had obeyed, his uttermost fate had not befallen him), and believing the words of the serpent whose spell was upon him, he left the realm of Narog and went to Hithlum. And it is sung that he stopped in vain his ears to keep out the echo of the cries of Finduilas calling on his name as she was borne away; and that sound hunted him through the woods. But Glómund, when Túrin had gone, crept back to Nargothrond and gathered unto himself the greater part of its wealth of gold and gems, and he lay thereon in its deepest hall, and desolation was about him.

It is said that Túrin came at length to Hithlum, and he found not his mother or his kin; for their hall was empty and their land despoiled, and Brodda had added their goods unto his own. In his wooden hall at his own board Túrin slew Brodda; and fought his way from the house, but must needs afterward flee from Hithlum.[9]

There was a dwelling of free Men in the wood, the remnant of the people of Haleth, son of Hador and brother of Gumlin the grandsire of Túrin. They were the last of the Men that were Elf-friends to linger in Beleriand,[10] neither subdued by Morgoth, nor penned in Hithlum beyond the Shadowy Mountains. They were small in numbers, but bold, and their houses were in the green woods about the River Taiglin that enters the land of Doriath ere it joins with the great waters of Sirion, and maybe some magic of Melian had yet protected them. Down from the sources of Taiglin that issues from the Shadowy Mountains Túrin came seeking for the trail of the Orcs that had plundered Nargothrond and must pass that water on their road back to the realm of Morgoth.

Thus he came upon the woodmen and learned tidings of Finduilas; and then he thought that he had tasted his fill of woe, yet it was not so. For the Orcs had marched nigh to the borders of the woodmen, and the woodmen had ambushed them, and come near to rescuing their captives. But few had they won away, for the Orc-guards had slain most of them cruelly; and among them Finduilas had been pierced with spears,[11] as those few who had been saved told him amid their tears. So perished the last of the race of Finrod fairest of Elven-kings, and vanished from the world of Men.

Grim was the heart of Túrin and all the deeds and days of his life seemed vile; yet the courage of the race of Hador was as a core of unbent steel. There Túrin vowed to renounce his past, his kin, his name, and all that had been his, save hatred of Morgoth; and he took a new name, Turambar (Turumarth[12] in the forms of Gnomish speech), which is Conqueror of Fate; and the woodmen gathered to him, and he became their lord, and ruled a while in peace.

Tidings came now more clear to Doriath of the fall of Orodreth and the destruction of all the folk of Narog, though fugitives no more than could be counted on the hands came ever into safety there, and uncertain was their report. Yet thus was it known to Thingol and to Morwen that Mormaglir was Túrin; and yet too late; for some said that he had escaped and fled,[13] and some told that he had been turned to stone by the dreadful eyes of Glómund and lived still enthralled in Nargothrond.

At last Thingol yielded so far to the tears and entreaties of Morwen that he sent forth a company of Elves toward Nargothrond to explore the truth. With them rode Morwen, for she might not be restrained; but Nienor was bidden to remain behind. Yet the fearlessness of her house was hers, and in evil hour, for love and care of her mother, she disguised herself as one of the folk of Thingol, and went with that ill-fated riding.

They viewed Narog afar from the summit of the tree-clad Hill of Spies to the east of the Guarded Plain, and thence they rode down greatly daring towards the banks of Narog. Morwen remained upon the hill with scanty guard and watched them from afar. Now in the days of victory when the folk of Narog had gone forth once more to open war, a bridge had been built across the river before the doors of the hidden city (and this had proved their undoing). Towards this bridge the Elves of Doriath now came, but Glómund was aware of their coming, and he issued forth on a sudden and lay into the stream, and a vast and hissing vapour arose and engulfed them. This Morwen saw from the hill-top, and her guards would not stay longer but fled back to Doriath taking her with them.

In that mist the Elves were overwhelmed, and their horses were stricken with panic, and they fled hither and thither and could not find their fellows; and the most part returned never back to Doriath. But when the mist cleared Nienor found that her wandering had taken her only back unto the banks of Narog, and before her lay Glómund, and his eye was upon her. Dreadful was his eye, like to the eye of Morgoth his master who had made him; and as she gazed perforce upon it a spell of darkness and utter forgetfulness fell upon her mind. Thence she wandered witless in the woods, as a wild creature without speech or thought.

When her madness left her, she was far from the borders of Nargothrond, she knew not where; and she remembered not her name or home. Thus was she found by a band of Orcs and pursued as a beast of the woods; but she was saved by fate. For a party of the woodmen of Turambar in whose land they were fell upon the Orcs and slew them; and Turambar himself placed her upon his horse and bore her to the woodmen's pleasant homes. He named her Níniel, Tear-maiden, for he had first seen her weeping. There is a narrow gorge and a high and foaming fall in the river Taiglin, that the woodmen called the Falls of Silver-bowl;[14] and this fair place they passed as they rode home, and would camp there as they were wont; but Níniel would not stay, for a chill and a mortal shivering took her in that place.

Yet afterwards she found some peace in the dwellings of the woodmen, who treated her with kindliness and honour. There she won the love of Brandir, son of Handir, son of Haleth; but he was lame of foot, being wounded by an Orc-arrow as a child, and uncomely and of less might than many, wherefore he had yielded the rule to Túrin at the choice of the woodfolk. He was gentle of heart and wise of thought, and great was his love, and he was ever true to Turambar; yet bitter was his soul when he might not win the love of Níniel. For Níniel would not be parted ever from the side of Turambar, and great love was ever between those twain from the hour of their first meeting. Thus Túrin Turambar thinking to cast off his ancient woes was wed to Nienor Níniel, and fair was the feast in the woods of Taiglin.

Now the power and malice of Glómund waxed apace and well-nigh all the realm of Nargothrond of old he laid waste, both west of Narog and beyond it to the east; and he gathered Orcs to him and ruled as a dragon-king; and there were battles on the marches of the woodmen's land, and the Orcs fled. Wherefore learning of their dwelling, Glómund issued from Nargothrond, and came crawling, filled with fire, over the lands and to the borders of the woods of Taiglin, leaving behind him a trail of burning. But Turambar pondered how the horror could be warded from his people; and he marched forth with his men, and Níniel rode with them, her heart foreboding ill, until they could descry afar the blasted track of the dragon and the smoking place where he now lay, west of the deep-cloven bed of Taiglin. Between them lay the steep ravine of the river, whose waters had in that spot fallen, but a little way before, over the foaming fall of Silver-bowl.

There Turambar thought of a desperate counsel, for he knew but too well the might and malice of Glómund. He resolved to lie in wait in the ravine over which the dragon must pass, if he would reach their land. Six of his boldest men begged to come with him; and at evening they climbed up the further side of the ravine and clung in hiding among the bushes at its brink. In the night the great dragon moved nigh to the river, and the rumour of his approach filled them with fear and loathing. Indeed in the morning all had slunk away leaving Turambar only.

The next evening, when Turambar was now nearly spent, Glómund began the passage of the ravine, and his huge form passed over Turambar's head. There Turambar transfixed Glómund with Gurtholfin, Wand-of-Death, his black sword; and Glómund coiled back in anguish and lay dying nigh to the river's brink and came not into the woodmen's land. But he wrested the sword from Turambar's grasp in his throes, and Turambar came now forth from hiding, and placed his foot upon Glómund and in exultation drew out his sword. Greedy was that blade and very fast in the wound, and as Turambar wrenched it with all his might, the venom of the dragon spouted on his hand and in the anguish of its burning he fell in a swoon.

So it was that the watchers from afar perceived that Glómund had been slain, yet Turambar did not return. By the light of the moon Níniel went forth without a word to seek him, and ere she had long gone Brandir missed her and followed after. But Níniel found Turambar lying as one dead beside the body of Glómund. There as she wept beside Turambar and sought to tend him, Glómund opened his eyes for the last time, and spake, telling her the true name of Turambar; and thereafter he died, and with his death the spell of forgetfulness was lifted from Níniel, and she remembered her kin. Filled with horror and anguish, for she was with child, she fled and cast herself over the heights of Silver-bowl, and none ever found her body. Her last lament ere she cast herself away was heard only by Brandir; and his back was bowed and his head turned grey in that night.

In the morn Túrin awoke and found that one had tended his hand. Though it pained him grievously, he returned in triumph filled with joy for the death of Glómund, his ancient foe; and he asked for Níniel, but none dared tell him, save Brandir. And Brandir distraught with grief reproached him; wherefore Túrin slew him, and taking Gurtholfin red with blood bade it slay its master; and the sword answered that his blood was as sweet as any other, and it pierced him to the heart as he fell upon it.

Túrin they buried nigh to the edge of Silver-bowl, and his name Túrin Turambar was carved there upon a rock. Beneath was written Nienor Níniel. Men changed the name of that place thereafter to Nen-Girith, the Shuddering Water.

So ended the tale of Túrin the unhappy; and it has ever been held the worst of the works of Morgoth in the ancient world. Some have said that Morwen, wandering woefully from Thingol's halls, when she found Nienor not there on her return, came on a time to that stone and read it, and there died.

★

1  *Flinding > Gwindor* at all occurrences, as previously (late changes).
2  *in days long gone > in days before* (late change).
3  *Out of loyalty > Out of loyalty to Gwindor* (late change).
4  Added here: *but the sword he named Gurtholfin, Wand-of-Death.*
5  The words *Brodda, who had to wife* struck through (late change), so the sentence reads *leaving her goods in the care of her kinswoman Airin*
6  *Flinding son of Fuilin > Gwindor son of Guilin* (late change).
7  This passage, from *and he was halted moveless*, was extended:

    and long time he stood there as one graven of stone silent before the dragon, until they two alone were left before the doors of Nargothrond. Then Glómund taunted him, &c.

8  *and against his last word to Flinding* struck through.
9  This sentence rewritten to read:

    Then Túrin knew the lie of Glómund, and in his anguish and in his wrath for the evil that had been done to his mother he slew Brodda at his own board and fought his way from the house; and in the night, a hunted man, he fled from Hithlum.

10  *Belèriand* here as originally typed, not emended from *Broseliand*; and subsequently.
11  *and among them Finduilas had been pierced > and Finduilas they fastened to a tree and pierced*
12  *Turumarth > Turamarth*
13  This passage, from *came ever into safety there*, was altered thus:

    . . . came ever into safety in Doriath. Thus was it known to Thingol and to Morwen that Mormaglir was Túrin himself; and yet too late they learned this; for some said that he was slain, and some told, &c.

14  *Falls of Silver-bowl > Falls of Celebros, Foam-silver*; and subsequently *Silver-bowl > Celebros*.

## 14

But after the death of Túrin and Nienor, Húrin was released by Morgoth, for Morgoth thought still to use him; and he accused Thingol of faint heart and ungentleness, saying that only thus had his purpose been brought about; and Húrin distraught, wandering bowed with grief, pondered these words, and was embittered by them, for such is the way of the lies of Morgoth.

Húrin gathered therefore a few outlaws of the woods unto him, and they came to Nargothrond, which as yet none, Orc, Elf, or Man, had dared to plunder, for dread of the spirit of Glómund and his very memory. But one Mîm the Dwarf they found there. This is the first coming of the Dwarves into these tales[1] of the ancient world; and it is said that Dwarves first spread west from Erydluin,[2] the Blue Mountains, into Beleriand after the Battle of Unnumbered Tears. Now Mîm had found the halls and treasure of Nargothrond unguarded; and he took possession of them, and sat there in joy fingering the gold and gems, and letting them run ever through his hands; and he bound them to himself with many spells. But the folk of Mîm were few, and the outlaws filled with the lust of the treasure slew them, though Húrin would have stayed them; and at his death Mîm cursed the gold.

And the curse came upon the possessors in this wise. Each one of Húrin's company died or was slain in quarrels upon the road; but Húrin went unto Thingol and sought his aid, and the folk of Thingol bore the treasure to the Thousand Caves. Then Húrin bade cast it all at the feet of Thingol, and he reproached the Elf-king with wild and bitter words. 'Receive thou,' said he, 'thy fee for thy fair keeping of my wife and kin.'

Yet Thingol would not take the hoard, and long he bore with Húrin; but Húrin scorned him, and wandered forth in quest of Morwen his wife, but it is not said that he found her ever upon the earth; and some have said that he cast himself at last into the western sea, and so ended the mightiest of the warriors of mortal Men.

Then the enchantment of the accursed dragon gold began to fall even upon the king of Doriath, and long he sat and gazed upon it, and the seed of the love of gold that was in his heart was waked to growth. Wherefore he summoned the greatest of all craftsmen that now were in the western world, since Nargothrond was no more (and Gondolin was not known), the Dwarves of Nogrod and Belegost, that they might fashion the gold and silver and the gems (for much was yet unwrought) into countless vessels and fair things; and a marvellous necklace of great beauty they should make, whereon to hang the Silmaril.

But the Dwarves coming were stricken at once with the lust and desire of the treasure, and they plotted treachery. They said one to another: 'Is not this wealth as much the right of the Dwarves as of the elvish king, and was it not wrested evilly from Mîm?' Yet also they lusted for the Silmaril.

And Thingol, falling deeper into the thraldom of the spell, for his part scanted his promised reward for their labour; and bitter words grew between them, and there was battle in Thingol's halls. There many Elves and Dwarves were slain, and the howe wherein they were laid in Doriath was named Cûm-nan-Arasaith, the Mound of Avarice. But the remainder of the Dwarves were driven forth without reward or fee.

Therefore gathering new forces in Nogrod and in Belegost they returned at length, and aided by the treachery of certain Elves on whom the lust of the accursed treasure had fallen they passed into Doriath secretly. There they surprised Thingol upon a hunt with but small company of arms; and Thingol was slain, and the fortress of the Thousand Caves taken at unawares and plundered; and so was brought well nigh to ruin the glory of Doriath, and but one stronghold of the Elves against Morgoth now remained, and their twilight was nigh at hand.

Queen Melian the Dwarves could not seize or harm, and she went forth to seek Beren and Lúthien. Now the Dwarf-road to Nogrod and Belegost in the Blue Mountains passed through East Beleriand and the woods about the River Ascar,[3] where aforetime were the hunting grounds of Damrod and Díriel, sons of Fëanor. To the south of those lands between the river and the mountains lay the land of Assariad, and there[4] lived and wandered still in peace and bliss Beren and Lúthien, in that time of respite which Lúthien had won, ere both should die; and their folk were the Green Elves of the South, who were not of the Elves of Côr,[5] nor of Doriath, though many had fought at the Battle of Unnumbered Tears. But Beren went no more to war, and his land was filled with loveliness and a wealth of flowers; and while Beren was and Lúthien remained Men called it oft Cuilwarthien,[6] the Land of the Dead that Live.

To the north of that region is a ford across the river Ascar, near to its joining with Duilwen[7] that falls in torrents from the mountains; and that ford is named Sarn-athra,[8] the Ford of Stones. This ford the Dwarves must pass ere they reached their homes;[9] and there Beren fought his last fight, warned of their approach by Melian. In that battle the Green Elves took the Dwarves unawares as they were in the midst of their passage, laden with their plunder; and the Dwarvish chiefs were slain, and well nigh all their host. But Beren took the Nauglafring,[10] the Necklace of the Dwarves, whereon was hung the Silmaril; and it is said and sung that Lúthien wearing that necklace and that immortal jewel on her white breast was the vision of greatest beauty and glory that has ever been seen outside the realms of Valinor, and that for a while the Land of the Dead that Live became like a vision of the land of the Gods, and no places have been since so fair, so fruitful, or so filled with light.

Yet Melian warned them ever of the curse that lay upon the treasure and upon the Silmaril. The treasure they had drowned indeed in the river Ascar, and named it anew Rathlorion,[11] Golden-Bed, yet the Silmaril they retained. And in time the brief hour of the loveliness of the land of Rathlorion departed. For Lúthien faded as Mandos had spoken, even as the Elves of later days faded, when Men waxed strong and usurped the goodness of the earth; and she vanished from the world; and Beren died, and none know where their meeting shall be again.[12]

Thereafter was Dior Thingol's heir, child of Beren and Lúthien, king in the woods, most fair of all the children of the world, for his race was threefold: of the fairest and goodliest of Men, and of the Elves, and of the spirits divine of Valinor; yet it shielded him not from the fate of the oath of the sons of Fëanor. For Dior went back to Doriath and for a time a part of its ancient glory was raised anew, though Melian no longer dwelt in that place, and she departed to the land of the Gods beyond the western sea, to muse on her sorrows in the gardens whence she came.

But Dior wore the Silmaril upon his breast and the fame of that jewel went far and wide; and the deathless oath was waked once more from sleep. The sons of Fëanor, when he would not yield the jewel unto them, came[13] upon him with all their host; and so befell the second slaying of Elf by Elf, and the most grievous. There fell Celegorm and Curufin and dark Cranthir, but Dior was slain,[14] and Doriath was destroyed and never rose again.

Yet the sons of Fëanor gained not the Silmaril; for faithful servants fled before them and took with them Elwing the daughter of Dior, and she escaped, and they bore with them the Nauglafring, and came in time to the mouth of the river Sirion by the sea.

★

1    *This is the first coming of the Dwarves into these tales* > *Now for the
     first time did the Dwarves take part in these tales*

2    *Eryd-luin* > *Ered-luin* (late change).

3    *Ascar* > *Flend* > *Gelion* at the first two occurrences, but left
     unchanged at the third.

4    This sentence emended to read: *To the south of those lands between
     the river Flend* [> *Gelion*] *and the mountains lay the land of
     Ossiriand, watered by seven streams, Flend* [> *Gelion*], *Ascar,
     Thalos, Loeglin* [> *Legolin*], *Brilthor, Duilwen, Adurant. There
     lived, &c.*

     (The rivers were first written *Flend, Ascar, Thalos, Loeglin,
     Brilthor, Adurant*. *Duilwen* was then added between *Thalos* and
     *Loeglin*; then *Legolin* replaced *Loeglin* and *Duilwen* was moved to
     stand between *Brilthor* and *Adurant*.)

5    *Côr* > *Kôr*, as previously.

6    *Men called it oft Cuilwarthien* > *Elves called it oft Gwerth-i-cuina*
     (see §10 note 15).

7    *Duilwen* > *Ascar* (see p. 232, entry *Dwarf-road*).

8    *Sarn-athra* > *Sarn-athrad*.

9    *ere they reached their homes* > *ere they reached the mountain passes
     that led unto their homes*

10   *Nauglafring* > *Nauglamír* at both occurrences (late changes).

11   *Rathlorion* > *Rathloriel* at both occurrences (late changes).

12   Added here:

     Yet it hath been sung that Lúthien alone of Elves hath been
     numbered among our race, and goeth whither we go to a fate
     beyond the world.

     A large pencilled X is made in the margin against the sentence in the
     typescript beginning *For Lúthien faded . . .*; in my father's
     manuscripts this always implies that there is some misstatement in
     the text that requires revision.

13   The words *The sons of Fëanor, when* were struck out, and the
     sentence enlarged thus:

     For while Lúthien wore that peerless gem no Elf would dare assail
     her, and not even Maidros dared ponder such a thought. But now
     hearing of the renewal of Doriath and Dior's pride, the seven
     gathered again from wandering; and they sent unto Dior to claim
     their own. But he would not yield the jewel unto them; and they
     came, &c.

14   Added here: *and his young sons Eldûn and Elrûn* (late change).

# 15

[For much of this section there exist two typescript texts, the later of the
two being longer. Subsequently there is a lot more of such replacement,

and I shall call the earlier 'Q I', the later 'Q II'. Q II is given after the notes to Q I.]

Here must be told of Gondolin. The great river Sirion, mightiest in elvish song, flowed through all the land of Beleriand and its course was south-west; and at its mouth was a great delta and its lower course ran through green and fertile lands, little peopled save by birds and beasts. Yet the Orcs came seldom there, for it was far from the northern woods and fells, and the power of Ulmo waxed ever in that water, as it drew nigh to the sea; for the mouths of that river were in the western sea, whose uttermost borders are the shores of Valinor.

Turgon, Fingolfin's son, had a sister, Isfin the white-handed. She was lost in Taur-na-Fuin after the Battle of Unnumbered Tears. There she was captured by the Dark-elf Eöl, and it is said that he was of gloomy mood, and had deserted the hosts ere the battle; yet he had not fought on Morgoth's side. But Isfin he took to wife, and their son was Meglin.

Now the people of Turgon escaping from the battle, aided by the prowess of Húrin, as has been told, escaped from the knowledge of Morgoth and vanished from all men's eyes; and Ulmo alone knew whither they had gone. Their scouts climbing the heights had come upon a secret place in the mountains: a broad valley[1] entirely circled by the hills, ringed about it in a fence unbroken, but falling ever lower as they came towards the middle. In the midmost of this marvellous ring was a wide land and a green plain, wherein was no hill, save for a single rocky height. This stood up dark upon the plain, not right at its centre, but nearest to that part of the outer wall that marched close to the borders of Sirion. Highest were the Encircling Mountains towards the North and the threat of Angband, and on their outer slopes to East and North began the shadow of dread Taur-na-Fuin; but they were crowned with the cairn of Fingolfin, and no evil came that way, as yet.

In this valley the Gnomes took refuge,[2] and spells of hiding and enchantment were set on all the hills about, that foes and spies might never find it. In this Turgon had the aid of the messages of Ulmo, that came now up the river Sirion; for his voice is to be heard in many waters, and some of the Gnomes had yet the lore to harken. In those days Ulmo was filled with pity for the exiled Elves in their need, and in the ruin that had now almost overwhelmed them. He foretold that the fortress of Gondolin should stand longest of all the refuges of the Elves against the might of Morgoth,[3] and like Doriath never be overthrown save by treachery from within. Because of his protecting might the spells of concealment were strongest in those parts nearest to Sirion, though there the Encircling Mountains were at their lowest. There the Gnomes dug a great winding tunnel under the roots of the hills, and its issue was in the steep side, tree-clad and dark, of a gorge through which Sirion ran, at that point still a young stream flowing strongly through the narrow vale between the shoulders of the Encircling Mountains and the Shadowy Mountains, in whose northern heights it took its rise.

The outer entrance of that passage, which they made at first to be a way of secret issue for themselves and for their scouts and spies, and for a way of return to safety for fugitives, was guarded by their magic and the power of Ulmo,[4] and no evil thing found it; yet its inner gate which looked upon the vale of Gondolin was guarded unceasingly by the Gnomes.[5]

Thorndor King of Eagles removed his eyries from Thangorodrim to the northward heights of the Encircling Mountains, and there he kept watch, sitting upon the cairn of King Fingolfin. But on the rocky hill amid the vale, Amon Gwareth, the Hill of Watch, whose sides they polished to the smoothness of glass, and whose top they levelled, the Gnomes built the great city of Gondolin with gates of steel, whose fame and glory is greatest of all dwellings of the Elves in the Outer Lands. The plain all about they levelled, that it was as smooth and flat as a lawn of grass until nigh unto the feet of the hills; and nothing might walk or creep across unseen.

In that city the folk waxed mighty, and their armouries were filled with weapons and with shields, for they purposed yet to come forth to war when the hour was ripe. But as the years drew on they grew to love that place, and desired no better, and few ever issued forth;[6] they shut them behind their impenetrable and enchanted hills, and suffered none to enter, fugitive or foe, and tidings of the outer world came but faint and far, and they heeded them little, and forgot the messages of Ulmo. They succoured not Nargothrond or Doriath, and the wandering Elves knew not how to find them; and when Turgon learned of the slaying of Dior, he vowed never to march with any son of Fëanor, and closed his realm, forbidding any of his folk to go ever forth.[7]

Gondolin now alone remained of all the strongholds of the Elves. Morgoth forgot not Turgon, and knew that without knowledge of that king his triumph could not be achieved; yet his search unceasing was in vain. Nargothrond was void, Doriath desolate, the sons of Fëanor driven away to a wild woodland life in the South and East, Hithlum was filled with evil men, and Taur-na-Fuin was a place of nameless dread; the race of Hador was at an end, and the house of Finrod; Beren came no more to war, and Huan was slain; and all Elves and Men bowed to his will, or laboured as slaves in the mines and smithies of Angband, save only the wild and wandering, and few there were of these save far in the East of once fair Beleriand. His triumph was near complete, and yet was not quite full.[8]

★

1   This sentence was rewritten thus:

> Ulmo alone knew whither they had gone; for they returned to the hidden city of Gondolin that Turgon had built. In a secret place in the mountains there was a broad valley, &c.

2   *the Gnomes took refuge > Turgon had taken refuge*
3   At this point the replacement text Q II begins.
4   *the power of Ulmo > the power of Sirion beloved of Ulmo*
5   The following passage was added in pencil in the margin without direction for insertion. For its place in Q II, where it is embodied in the text, see below.

> For Turgon deemed after the Battle of Unnumbered Tears that Morgoth had grown too mighty for Elves and Men, and that it were better to ask the forgiveness and aid of the Valar ere all was lost. Wherefore some of his folk would at whiles go down Sirion, and a small and secret haven they there made, whence ever and anon ships would set forth into the West. Some came back driven by contrary winds, but many never returned; and none reached Valinor.

6   Added here: *and they sent no more messengers into the West*;
7   Here the replacement text Q II ends.
8   Added at the end: *In this wise came the fall of Gondolin.*

### §15 in the Q II version
*(see note 3 above)*

and like Doriath never be overthrown save by treachery from within. Because of his protecting might the spells of concealment were strongest in those parts nearest to Sirion, though there the

Encircling Mountains were at their lowest. In that region the
Gnomes dug a great winding tunnel under the roots of the hills,
and its issue was in the steep side, tree-clad and dark, of a gorge
through which the blissful river ran. There he was still a young
stream, but strong, flowing down the narrow vale that lies
between the shoulders of the Encircling Mountains and the
Mountains of Shadow, Eryd-Lómin,[1] the walls of Hithlum, in
whose northern heights he took his rise.[2]

That passage they made at first to be a way of return for
fugitives and for such as escaped from the bondage of Morgoth;
and most as an issue for their scouts and messengers. For Turgon
deemed, when first they came into that vale after the dreadful
battle,[3] that Morgoth Bauglir had grown too mighty for Elves and
Men, and that it were better to seek the forgiveness and aid of the
Valar, if either might be got, ere all was lost. Wherefore some of
his folk went down the river Sirion at whiles, ere the shadow of
Morgoth yet stretched into the uttermost parts of Beleriand, and a
small and secret haven they made at his mouth; thence ever and
anon ships would set forth into the West bearing the embassy of
the Gnomish king. Some there were that came back driven by
contrary winds; but the most never returned again, and none
reached Valinor.

The issue of that Way of Escape was guarded and concealed by
the mightiest spells they could contrive, and by the power that
dwelt in Sirion beloved of Ulmo, and no thing of evil found it; yet
its inner gate, which looked upon the vale of Gondolin, was
watched unceasingly by the Gnomes.

In those days Thorndor[4] King of Eagles removed his eyries from
Thangorodrim, because of the power of Morgoth, and the stench
and fumes, and the evil of the dark clouds that lay now ever upon
the mountain-towers above his cavernous halls. But Thorndor
dwelt upon the northward heights of the Encircling Mountains,
and he kept watch and saw many things, sitting upon the cairn of
King Fingolfin. And in the vale below dwelt Turgon Fingolfin's
son. Upon Amon Gwareth, the Hill of Defence, the rocky height
amidst the plain, was built Gondolin the great, whose fame and
glory is mightiest in song of all dwellings of the Elves in these
Outer Lands. Of steel were its gates and of marble were its walls.
The sides of the hill the Gnomes polished to the smoothness of
dark glass, and its top they levelled for the building of their town,
save amidmost where stood the tower and palace of the king.
Many fountains there were in that city, and white waters fell

shimmering down the glistening sides of Amon Gwareth. The plain all about they smoothed till it became as a lawn of shaven grass from the stairways before the gates unto the feet of the mountain wall, and nought might walk or creep across unseen.

In that city the folk waxed mighty, and their armouries were filled with weapons and with shields; for they purposed at first to come forth to war, when the hour was ripe. But as the years drew on, they grew to love that place, the work of their hands, as the Gnomes do, with a great love, and desired no better. Then seldom went any forth from Gondolin on errand of war or peace again. They sent no messengers more into the West, and Sirion's haven was desolate. They shut them behind their impenetrable and enchanted hills, and suffered none to enter, though he fled from Morgoth hate-pursued; tidings of the lands without came to them faint and far, and they heeded them little; and their dwelling became as a rumour, and a secret no man could find. They succoured not Nargothrond nor Doriath, and the wandering Elves sought them in vain; and Ulmo alone knew where the realm of Turgon could be found. Tidings Turgon heard of Thorndor concerning the slaying of Dior, Thingol's heir, and thereafter he shut his ear to word of the woes without; and he vowed to march never at the side of any son of Fëanor; and his folk he forbade ever to pass the leaguer of the hills.

*Changes made to this passage*

1  *Eryd-Lómin* > *Eredwethion*
2  *in whose northern heights he took his rise* struck through.
3  This sentence marked with an X in the margin.
4  *Thorndor* > *Thorondor* throughout.

## 16

[A substantial part of this section is again extant both in the original typescript (Q I) and in a replacement text (Q II).]

On a time Eöl was lost in Taur-na-Fuin, and Isfin came through great peril and dread unto Gondolin, and after her coming none entered until the last messenger of Ulmo, of whom the tales speak more ere the end. With her came her son Meglin, and he was there received by Turgon his mother's brother,[1] and though he was half of Dark-elfin[2] blood he was treated as a prince of Fingolfin's line.

He was swart but comely, wise and eloquent, and cunning to win men's hearts and minds.

Now Húrin of Hithlum had a brother Huor. The son of Huor was Tuor. Rían Huor's wife sought her husband among the slain upon the field of Unnumbered Tears, and there bewailed him, ere she died. Her son was but a child, and remaining in Hithlum fell into the hands of the faithless Men whom Morgoth drove into that land after the battle; and he became a thrall. Growing of age, and he was fair of face and great of stature, and despite his grievous life valiant and wise, he escaped into the woods, and he became an outlaw and a solitary, living alone and communing with none save rarely wandering and hidden Elves.[3]

On a time Ulmo contrived, as is told in the *Tale of the Fall of Gondolin*, that he should be led to a river-course that flowed underground from Lake Mithrim in the midst of Hithlum into a great chasm, Cris-Ilfing,[4] the Rainbow-cleft, through which a turbulent water ran at last into the western sea. And the name of this chasm was so devised by reason of the rainbow that shimmered ever in the sun in that place, because of the abundance of the spray of the rapids and the waterfalls.

In this way the flight of Tuor was marked by no Man nor Elf; neither was it known to the Orcs or any spy of Morgoth, with whom the land of Hithlum was filled.

Tuor wandered long by the western shores, journeying ever South; and he came at last to the mouths of Sirion, and the sandy deltas peopled by many birds of the sea. There he fell in with a Gnome, Bronweg,[5] who had escaped from Angband, and being of old of the people of Turgon, sought ever to find the path to the hidden places of his lord, of which rumour ran among all captives and fugitives. Now Bronweg had come thither by far and wandering paths to the East, and little though any step back nigher to the thraldom from which he had come was to his liking, he purposed now to go up Sirion and seek for Turgon in Beleriand. Fearful and very wary was he, and he aided Tuor in their secret march, by night and twilight, so that they were not discovered by the Orcs.

They came first into the fair Land of Willows, Nan-Tathrin which is watered by the Narog and by Sirion; and there all things were yet green, and the meads were rich and full of flowers, and there was song of many birds; so that Tuor lingered there as one enchanted, and it seemed sweet to him to dwell there after the grim lands of the North and his weary wandering.

There Ulmo came and appeared before him, as he stood in the long grass at evening; and the might and majesty of that vision is told of in the song of Tuor that he made for his son Eärendel. Thereafter the sound of the sea and the longing for the sea was ever in Tuor's heart and ear; and an unquiet was on him at whiles that took him at last into the depths of the realm of Ulmo.⁶ But now Ulmo bade him make all speed to Gondolin, and gave him guidance for the finding of the hidden door; and words were set in his mouth to bear to Turgon, bidding him prepare for battle with Morgoth ere all was lost, and promising that Ulmo would win the hearts of the Valar to send him succour. That would be a mortal and a terrible strife, yet if Turgon would dare it, Morgoth's power should be broken and his servants perish and never after trouble the world. But if Turgon would not go forth to this war, then he must abandon Gondolin and lead his people down Sirion, ere Morgoth could oppose him, and at Sirion's mouth Ulmo would befriend him, and lend his aid to the building of a mighty fleet wherein the Gnomes should sail back at last to Valinor, but then grievous would be the fate of the Outer Lands. Tuor's part if Turgon should accept the counsels of Ulmo, would be to go forth when Turgon marched to war and lead a force into Hithlum and draw its Men once more into alliance with the Elves, for 'without Men the Elves shall not prevail against the Orcs and Balrogs'.

This errand did Ulmo himself perform out of his love of Elves and of the Gnomes, and because he knew that ere twelve years were passed the doom of Gondolin would come, strong though it seemed, if its people sat still behind their walls.

Obedient to Ulmo Tuor and Bronweg journeyed North, and came to the hidden door; and passing down the tunnel neath the hills they came to the inner gate and looked upon the vale of Gondolin, the city of seven names, shining white flushed with the rose of dawn upon the plain. But there they were made captive by the guard of the gate and led before the king. Tuor spoke his embassy to Turgon in the great square of Gondolin before the steps of his palace; but the king was grown proud and Gondolin so fair and beautiful and he was so trustful of its secret and impregnable strength, that he and the most of his folk wished no longer to trouble with the Gnomes and Men without, nor did they long more to return to the lands of the Gods.

Meglin spake against Tuor in the councils of the king, and Turgon rejected the bidding of Ulmo, and neither did he go forth to war nor seek to fly to the mouths of Sirion; but there were some of his wiser counsellors who were filled with disquiet, and the king's daughter spake ever for Tuor. She was named Idril, one of the fairest of the maidens of the Elves of old, and folk called her Celebrindal, Silver-foot, for the whiteness of her slender feet, and she walked and danced ever unshod.

Thereafter Tuor sojourned in Gondolin, and grew a mighty man in form and in wisdom, learning deeply of the lore of the Gnomes; and the heart of Idril was turned to him, and his to her. At which Meglin ground his teeth, for he loved Idril, and despite his close kinship purposed to wed her; indeed already he was planning in his heart to oust Turgon and to seize the throne, but Turgon loved and trusted him. Tuor wedded Idril nonetheless, for he had become beloved by all the Gnomes of Gondolin, even Turgon the proud, save only Meglin and his secret following. Tuor and Beren alone of mortal Men ever wedded Elves of old, and since Elwing daughter of Dior son of Beren after wedded Eärendel son of Tuor and Idril, of them alone has come the elfin blood into mortal Men. But yet Eärendel was an infant; and he was a child surpassing fair: a light was in his face as of heaven, and he had the beauty and the wisdom of Elfinesse[7] and the strength and hardihood of the Men of old; and the sea spoke ever in his ear and heart, even as with Tuor his father.

On a time when Eärendel was yet young, and the days of Gondolin were full of joy and peace (and yet Idril's heart misgave her, and foreboding crept upon her spirit like a cloud), Meglin was lost. Now Meglin loved mining and quarrying after metals above other craft; and he was master and leader of the Gnomes who worked in the mountains distant from the city, seeking for metals for their smithying of things both of peace and war. But often Meglin went with few of his folk beyond the leaguer of the hills, though the king knew not that his bidding was defied; and so it came to pass, as fate willed, that Meglin was taken prisoner by the Orcs and taken before Morgoth. Meglin was no weakling or craven, but the torment wherewith he was threatened cowed his soul, and he purchased his life and freedom by revealing unto Morgoth the place of Gondolin and the ways whereby it might be found and assailed. Great indeed was the joy of Morgoth; and to Meglin he promised the lordship of Gondolin, as his vassal, and the possession of Idril, when that city should be taken. Lust for Idril and hatred of Tuor led Meglin the easier to his foul treachery. But Morgoth sent him back to Gondolin, lest men should suspect the betrayal, and so that Meglin should aid the assault from within when the hour came; and Meglin abode in the halls of the king with a smile on his face and evil in his heart, while the gloom gathered ever deeper upon Idril.

At last, and Eärendel was then seven years of age, Morgoth was ready, and he loosed upon Gondolin his Orcs and his Balrogs and his serpents; and of these, dragons of many and dire shapes were new devised for the taking of the city. The host of Morgoth came over the Northern hills where the height was greatest and the watch less vigilant, and it came at night at a time of festival, when all the folk of Gondolin were upon the walls to wait upon the rising sun and sing their songs at its uplifting; for the morrow was the feast which they named the Gates of Summer. But the red light mounted the hills in the North and not in the East; and there was no stay in the advance of the foe until they were beneath the very walls of Gondolin, and Gondolin was beleaguered without hope.

Of the deeds of desperate valour there done, by the chieftains of the noble houses and their warriors, and not least by Tuor, is much told in *The Fall of Gondolin*; of the death of Rog without the walls; and of the battle of Ecthelion of the Fountain with Gothmog lord of Balrogs in the very square of the king, where each slew the other; and of the defence of the tower of Turgon by the men of his household, until the tower was overthrown; and mighty was its fall and the fall of Turgon in its ruin.

Tuor sought to rescue Idril from the sack of the city, but Meglin had laid hands upon her and Eärendel; and Tuor fought on the walls with him, and cast him down to death. Then Tuor and Idril led such remnants of the folk of Gondolin as they could gather in the confusion of the burning down a secret way that Idril had let prepare in the days of her foreboding. This was not yet complete, but its issue was already far beyond the walls and in the North of the plain where the mountains were long distant from Amon Gwareth. Those who would not come with them, but fled to the old Way of Escape that led into the gorge of Sirion, were caught and destroyed by a dragon that Morgoth had sent to watch that gate, being apprised of it by Meglin. But of the new passage Meglin had not heard, and it was not thought that fugitives would take a path towards the North and the highest parts of the mountains and the nighest to Angband.

The fume of the burning, and the steam of the fair fountains of Gondolin withering in the flame of the dragons of the North, fell upon the vale in mournful mists; and thus was the escape of Tuor and his company aided, for there was still a long and open road to follow from the tunnel's mouth to the foothills of the mountains. They came nonetheless into the mountains, in woe and misery, for the high places were cold and terrible, and they had among them many women and children and many wounded men.

There is a dreadful pass, Cristhorn[8] was it named, the Eagle's Cleft, where beneath the shadow of the highest peaks a narrow path winds its way, walled by a precipice to the right and on the left a dreadful fall leaps into emptiness. Along that narrow way their march was strung, when it was ambushed by an outpost of Morgoth's power; and a Balrog was their leader. Then dreadful was their plight, and hardly would it have been saved by the deathless valour of yellow-haired Glorfindel, chief of the House of the Golden Flower of Gondolin, had not Thorndor[9] come timely to their aid.

Songs have been sung of the duel of Glorfindel with the Balrog upon a pinnacle of rock in that high place; and both fell to ruin in the abyss. But Thorndor bore up Glorfindel's body and he was buried in a mound of stones beside the pass, and there came after a turf of green and small flowers like yellow stars bloomed there amid the barrenness of stone. And the birds of Thorndor stooped upon the Orcs and drove them shrieking back; and all were slain or cast into the deeps, and rumour of the escape from Gondolin came not until long after to Morgoth's ears.

Thus by weary and dangerous marches the remnant of Gondolin came unto Nan-Tathrin and there rested a while, and were healed of their hurts and weariness, but their sorrow could not be cured. There they made feast in memory of Gondolin and those that had perished, fair maidens, wives, and warriors and their king; but for Glorfindel the well-beloved many and sweet were the songs they sang. And there Tuor in song spoke to Eärendel his son of the coming of Ulmo aforetime, the sea-vision in the midst of the land, and the sea-longing awoke in his heart and in his son's. Wherefore they removed with the most part of the people to the mouths of Sirion by the sea, and there they dwelt, and joined their folk to the slender company of Elwing daughter of Dior, that had fled thither little while before.

Then Morgoth thought in his heart that his triumph was fulfilled, recking little of the sons of Fëanor, and of their oath, which had harmed him never and turned always to his mightiest aid. And in his black thought he laughed, regretting not the one Silmaril he had lost, for by it he deemed the last shreds of the elvish race should vanish yet from the earth and trouble it no more. If he knew of the dwelling by the waters of Sirion he made no sign, biding his time, and waiting upon the working of oath and lie.

★

1 *mother's brother* > *sister-son*; no doubt *as his sister-son* was intended.
2 *Dark-elfin* > *Dark-elven*
3 This paragraph was largely struck out, as well as some hasty emendations that had been made to it (introducing the idea of Tuor's being born 'in the wild' and fostered by Dark-elves, and Rían's dying on the Hill of Slain – which is here called *Amon Dengin*). The passage was then rewritten:

> Now Húrin of Hithlum had a brother Huor, and as has been told Rían his wife went forth into the wild and there her son Tuor was born, and he was fostered by the Dark-elves; but Rían laid herself down and died upon the Hill of Slain. But Tuor grew up in the woods of Hithlum, and he was fair of face and great of stature, and valiant and wise; and he walked and hunted alone in the woods, and he became a solitary, living alone and communing with none save rarely wandering and hidden Elves.

4 *Cris-Ilfing* > *Kirith Helvin*
5 *Bronweg* > *Bronwë* at the first two occurrences, but not at the third, which occurs in the part replaced by the Q II text.
6 At this point the replacement text Q II begins.
7 Here the replacement text Q II ends.
8 *Cristhorn* > *Kirith-thoronath*
9 *Thorndor* > *Thorondor*, as previously.

## §16 in the Q II version
*(see note 6 above)*

But now Ulmo bade him make all speed to Gondolin, and gave him guidance for the finding of the hidden door; and a message he gave him to bear from Ulmo, friend of Elves, unto Turgon, bidding him to prepare for war, and battle with Morgoth ere all was lost; and to send again his messengers into the West. Summons too should he send into the East and gather, if he might, Men (who were now multiplying and spreading on the earth) unto his banners; and for that task Tuor was most fit. 'Forget,' counselled Ulmo, 'the treachery of Uldor the accursed, and remember Húrin; for without mortal Men the Elves shall not

prevail against the Balrogs and the Orcs.' Nor should the feud
with the sons of Fëanor be left unhealed; for this should be the last
gathering of the hope of the Gnomes, when every sword should
count. A terrible and mortal strife he foretold, but victory if
Turgon would dare it, the breaking of Morgoth's power, and the
healing of feuds, and friendship between Men and Elves, whereof
the greatest good should come into the world, and the servants of
Morgoth trouble it no more. But if Turgon would not go forth to
this war, then he should abandon Gondolin and lead his people
down Sirion, and build there his fleets and seek back to Valinor
and the mercy of the Gods. But in this counsel there was danger
more dire than in the other, though so it might not seem; and
grievous thereafter would be the fate of the Outer[1] Lands.

This errand Ulmo performed out of his love of the Elves, and
because he knew that ere many years were passed the doom of
Gondolin would come, if its people sat still behind its walls; not
thus should anything of joy or beauty in the world be preserved
from Morgoth's malice.

Obedient to Ulmo Tuor and Bronweg[2] journeyed North, and
came at last to the hidden door; and passing down the tunnel
reached the inner gate, and were taken by the guard as prisoners.
There they saw the fair vale Tumladin[3] set like a green jewel amid
the hills; and amidst Tumladin Gondolin the great, the city of
seven names, white, shining from afar, flushed with the rose of
dawn upon the plain. Thither they were led and passed the gates
of steel, and were brought before the steps of the palace of the
king. There Tuor spake the embassy of Ulmo, and something of
the power and majesty of the Lord of Waters his voice had caught,
so that all folk looked in wonder on him, and doubted that this
were a Man of mortal race as he declared. But proud was Turgon
become, and Gondolin as beautiful as a memory of Tûn, and he
trusted in its secret and impregnable strength; so that he and the
most part of his folk wished not to imperil it nor leave it, and they
desired not to mingle in the woes of Elves and Men without; nor
did they any longer desire to return through dread and danger to
the West.

Meglin spoke ever against Tuor in the councils of the king, and
his words seemed the more weighty in that they went with
Turgon's heart. Wherefore Turgon rejected the bidding of Ulmo;
though some there were of his wisest counsellors who were filled
with disquiet. Wise-hearted even beyond the measure of the
daughters of Elfinesse was the daughter of the king, and she spoke

ever for Tuor, though it did not avail, and her heart was heavy. Very fair and tall was she, well nigh of warrior's stature, and her hair was a fountain of gold. Idril was she named, and called Celebrindal, Silver-foot, for the whiteness of her foot; and she walked and danced ever unshod in the white ways and green lawns of Gondolin.

Thereafter Tuor sojourned in Gondolin, and went not to summon the Men of the East, for the blissfulness of Gondolin, the beauty and wisdom of its folk, held him enthralled. And he grew high in the favour of Turgon; for he became a mighty man in stature and in mind, learning deeply of the lore of the Gnomes. The heart of Idril was turned to him, and his to her; at which Meglin ground his teeth, for he desired Idril, and despite his close kinship purposed to possess her; and she was the only heir of the king of Gondolin. Indeed in his heart he was already planning how he might oust Turgon and seize his throne; but Turgon loved and trusted him. Nonetheless Tuor took Idril to wife; and the folk of Gondolin made merry feast, for Tuor had won their hearts, all save Meglin and his secret following. Tuor and Beren alone of mortal Men had Elves to wife, and since Elwing daughter of Dior son of Beren after wedded Eärendel son of Tuor and Idril of Gondolin, of them alone has come the elfin[4] blood into mortal race. But as yet Eärendel was a little child: surpassing fair was he, a light was in his face as the light of heaven, and he had the beauty and the wisdom of Elfinesse

*Changes made to this passage*

1   *Outer > Hither*
2   *Bronweg > Bronwë* (see note 5 above).
3   *Tumladin > Tumladen*
4   *elfin > elven*

## 17

[The whole of this section is extant in the two typescript versions Q I and Q II.]

Yet by Sirion there grew up an elfin folk, the gleanings of Doriath and Gondolin, and they took to the sea and to the making of fair ships, and they dwelt nigh unto its shores and under the shadow of Ulmo's hand.

But in Valinor Ulmo spake grievous words unto the Valar and unto the Elves the kinsfolk of the exiled and ruined Gnomes, and he called on them to forgive, and to rescue the world from the overmastering might of Morgoth, and win back the Silmarils wherein alone now bloomed the light of the days of ancient bliss when the Two Trees still shone. And the sons of the Valar prepared for battle, and Fionwë son of Tulcas was the captain of the host. With him marched the host of the Quendi, the Light-elves, the folk of Ingwë, and among them such of the race of the Gnomes [as] had not left Valinor; but remembering Swan Haven the Teleri came not forth. Tûn was deserted and the hill of Côr knew no more the feet of the elder children of the world.

In those days Tuor felt old age creep upon him, and he could not forbear the longing that possessed him for the sea; wherefore he built a great ship Eärámë, Eagle's Pinion, and with Idril he set sail into the sunset and the West, and came no more into any tale. But Eärendel the shining became the lord of the folk of Sirion and took to wife fair Elwing; and yet he could not rest. Two thoughts were in his heart blended as one: the longing for the wide sea; and he thought to sail thereon following after Tuor and Idril Celebrindal who returned not, and he thought to find perhaps the last shore and bring ere he died a message to the Gods and Elves of the West, that should move their hearts to pity on the world and the sorrows of Mankind.

Wingelot he built, fairest of the ships of song, the Foam-flower; white were its timbers as the argent moon, golden were its oars, silver were its shrouds, its masts were crowned with jewels like stars. In the Lay of Eärendel is many a thing sung of his adventures in the deep and in lands untrod, and in many seas and many isles; and most of how he fought and slew Ungoliant in the South and her darkness perished, and light came to many places which had yet long been hid. But Elwing sat sorrowing at home.

Eärendel found not Tuor, nor came he ever on that journey to the shores of Valinor; and at last he was driven by the winds back East, and he came at a time of night to the havens of Sirion, unlooked for, unwelcomed, for they were desolate. Bronweg alone sat there in sorrow, the companion of his father of old, and his tidings were filled with new woe.

The dwelling of Elwing at Sirion's mouth, where still she possessed the Nauglafring and the glorious Silmaril, became known to the sons of Fëanor; and they gathered together from their wandering hunting-paths. But the folk of Sirion would not yield that jewel which Beren had won and Lúthien had worn, and for which fair Dior had been slain. And so befell the last and cruellest slaying of Elf by Elf, the third woe achieved by the accursed oath; for the sons of Fëanor came down upon the exiles of Gondolin and the remnant of Doriath, and though some of their folk stood aside and some few rebelled and were slain upon the other part aiding Elwing against their own lords, yet they won the day. Damrod was slain and Díriel, and Maidros and Maglor alone now remained of the Seven; but the last of the folk of Gondolin were destroyed or forced to depart and join them to the people of Maidros. And yet the sons of Fëanor gained not the Silmaril; for Elwing cast the Nauglafring into the sea, whence it shall not return until the End; and she leapt herself into the waves, and took the form of a white sea-bird, and flew away lamenting and seeking for Eärendel about all the shores of the world.

But Maidros took pity upon her child Elrond, and took him with him, and harboured and nurtured him, for his heart was sick and weary with the burden of the dreadful oath.

Learning these things Eärendel was overcome with sorrow; and with Bronweg he set sail once more in search of Elwing and of Valinor. And it is told in the Lay of Eärendel that he came at last unto the Magic Isles, and hardly escaped their enchantment, and found again the Lonely Isle, and the Shadowy Seas, and the Bay of Faërie on the borders of the world. There he landed on the immortal shore alone of living Men, and his feet clomb the marvellous hill of Côr; and he walked in the deserted ways of Tûn, where the dust upon his raiment and his shoes was a dust of diamonds and gems. But he ventured not into Valinor. He came too late to bring messages to the Elves, for the Elves had gone.[1]

He built a tower in the Northern Seas to which all the sea-birds of the world might at times repair, and ever he grieved for fair Elwing looking for her return to him. And Wingelot was lifted on their wings and sailed now even in the airs searching for Elwing; marvellous and magical was that ship, a starlit flower in the sky. But the Sun scorched it and the Moon hunted it in heaven, and long Eärendel wandered over Earth, glimmering as a fugitive star.

★

1    At the foot of the page is written very quickly and faintly in pencil:

Make *Eärendel* move the Gods. And it is said that there were Men of Hithlum repentant of their evil in that day, and that so were fulfilled Ulmo's words, for by Eärendel's embassy and the aid of valiant Men the Orcs and Balrogs were destroyed, yet not as utterly as might have been.

At the top of the next page is written: *Men turned the* [*tide*] (the last word is illegible).

## §17 in the Q II version

·Yet by Sirion and the sea there grew up an elfin[1] folk, the gleanings of Gondolin and Doriath, and they took to the waves and to the making of fair ships, dwelling ever nigh unto the shores and under the shadow of Ulmo's hand.

In Valinor Ulmo spoke unto the Valar of the need of the Elves, and he called on them to forgive and send succour unto them and rescue them from the overmastering might of Morgoth, and win back the Silmarils wherein alone now bloomed the light of the days of bliss when the Two Trees still were shining. Or so it is said, among the Gnomes, who after had tidings of many things from their kinsfolk the Quendi, the Light-elves beloved of Manwë, who ever knew something of the mind of the Lord of the Gods. But as yet Manwë moved not, and the counsels of his heart what tale shall tell? The Quendi have said that the hour was not yet come, and that only one speaking in person for the cause of both Elves and Men, pleading for pardon upon their misdeeds and pity on their woes, might move the counsels of the Powers; and the oath of Fëanor perchance even Manwë could not loose, until it found its end, and the sons of Fëanor relinquished the Silmarils, upon which they had laid their ruthless claim. For the light which lit the Silmarils the Gods had made.

In those days Tuor felt old age creep upon him, and ever a longing for the deeps of the sea grew stronger in his heart. Wherefore he built a great ship Eärámë, Eagle's Pinion,[2] and with Idril he set sail into the sunset and the West, and came no more into any tale or song.[3] Bright Eärendel was then lord of the folk of Sirion and their many ships; and he took to wife Elwing the fair, and she bore him Elrond Half-elfin.[4] Yet Eärendel could not rest, and his voyages about the shores of the Outer[5] Lands eased not his unquiet. Two purposes grew in his heart, blended as one in longing for the wide sea: he sought to sail thereon, seeking after Tuor and Idril Celebrindal who returned not; and he thought to find perhaps the last shore and bring ere he died the message of Elves and Men unto the Valar of the West, that should move the hearts of Valinor and of the Elves of Tûn to pity on the world and the sorrows of Mankind.

Wingelot[6] he built, fairest of the ships of song, the Foam-flower; white were its timbers as the argent moon, golden were its oars, silver were its shrouds, its masts were crowned with jewels like stars. In the Lay of Eärendel is many a thing sung of his adventures in the deep and in lands untrodden, and in many seas and many isles. Ungoliant[7] in the South he slew, and her darkness was destroyed, and light came to many regions which had yet long been hid. But Elwing sat sorrowing at home.

Eärendel found not Tuor nor Idril, nor came he ever on that journey to the shores of Valinor, defeated by shadows and enchantment, driven by repelling winds, until in longing for Elwing he turned him homeward toward the East. And his heart bade him haste, for a sudden fear was fallen on him out of dreams, and the winds that before he had striven with might not now bear him back as swift as his desire.

Upon the havens of Sirion new woe had fallen. The dwelling of Elwing there, where still she possessed the Nauglafring[8] and the glorious Silmaril, became known unto the remaining sons of Fëanor, Maidros and Maglor and Damrod and Díriel; and they gathered together from their wandering hunting-paths, and messages of friendship and yet stern demand they sent unto Sirion. But Elwing and the folk of Sirion would not yield that jewel which Beren had won and Lúthien had worn, and for which Dior the Fair was slain; and least of all while Eärendel their lord was in the sea, for them seemed that in that jewel lay the gift of bliss and healing that had come upon their houses and their ships.

And so came in the end to pass the last and cruellest of the slayings of Elf by Elf; and that was the third of the great wrongs achieved by the accursed oath. For the sons of Fëanor came down upon the exiles of Gondolin and the remnant of Doriath and destroyed them. Though some of their folk stood aside, and some few rebelled and were slain upon the other part aiding Elwing against their own lords (for such was the sorrow and confusion of the hearts of Elfinesse in those days), yet Maidros and Maglor won the day. Alone they now remained of the sons of Fëanor, for in that battle Damrod and Díriel were slain; but the folk of Sirion perished or fled away, or departed of need to join the people of Maidros, who claimed now the lordship of all the Elves of the

Outer Lands. And yet Maidros gained not the Silmaril, for Elwing
seeing that all was lost and her child Elrond[9] taken captive, eluded
the host of Maidros, and with the Nauglafring upon her breast she
cast herself into the sea, and perished as folk thought.

But Ulmo bore her up and he gave unto her the likeness of a
great white bird, and upon her breast there shone as a star the
shining Silmaril, as she flew over the water to seek Eärendel her
beloved. And on a time of night Eärendel at the helm saw her come
towards him, as a white cloud under moon exceeding swift, as a
star over the sea moving in strange course, a pale flame on wings of
storm. And it is sung that she fell from the air upon the timbers of
Wingelot, in a swoon, nigh unto death for the urgency of her
speed, and Eärendel took her unto his bosom. And in the morn
with marvelling eyes he beheld his wife in her own form beside
him with her hair upon her face; and she slept.

But great was the sorrow of Eärendel and Elwing for the ruin of
the havens of Sirion, and the captivity of their son, for whom they
feared death, and yet it was not so. For Maidros took pity on
Elrond, and he cherished him, and love grew after between them,
as little might be thought; but Maidros' heart was sick and weary[10]
with the burden of the dreadful oath. Yet Eärendel saw now no
hope left in the lands of Sirion, and he turned again in despair and
came not home, but sought back once more to Valinor with
Elwing at his side. He stood now most oft at the prow, and the
Silmaril he bound upon his forehead; and ever its light grew
greater as they drew unto the West. May be it was due in part to
the puissance of that holy jewel that they came in time to the
waters that as yet no vessels save those of the Teleri had known;
and they came unto the Magic Isles and escaped their magic;[11] and
they came into the Shadowy Seas and passed their shadows; and
they looked upon the Lonely Isle and they tarried not there; and
they cast anchor in the Bay of Faërie[12] upon the borders of the
world. And the Teleri saw the coming of that ship and were
amazed, gazing from afar upon the light of the Silmaril, and it was
very great.

But Eärendel landed on the immortal shores alone of living
Men; and neither Elwing nor any of his small company would he
suffer to go with him, lest they fell beneath the wrath of the Gods,
and he came at a time of festival even as Morgoth and Ungoliant
had in ages past, and the watchers upon the hill of Tûn were few,
for the Quendi were most in the halls of Manwë on Tinbrenting's[13]
height.[14]

The watchers rode therefore in haste to Valmar, or hid them in the passes of the hills; and all the bells of Valmar pealed; but Eärendel clomb the marvellous hill of Côr[15] and found it bare, and he entered into the streets of Tûn and they were empty; and his heart sank. He walked now in the deserted ways of Tûn and the dust upon his raiment and his shoes was a dust of diamonds, yet no one heard his call. Wherefore he went back unto the shores and would climb once more upon Wingelot his ship; but one came unto the strand and cried unto him: 'Hail Eärendel, star most radiant, messenger most fair![16] Hail thou bearer of light before the Sun and Moon, the looked-for that comest unawares, the longed-for that comest beyond hope! Hail thou splendour of the children of the world, thou slayer of the dark! Star of the sunset hail! Hail herald of the morn!'

And that was Fionwë the son of Manwë, and he summoned Eärendel before the Gods; and Eärendel went unto Valinor and to the halls of Valmar, and came never again back into the lands of Men.[17] But Eärendel spake the embassy of the two races[18] before the faces of the Gods, and asked for pardon upon the Gnomes and pity for the exiled Elves and for unhappy Men, and succour in their need.

Then the sons of the Valar prepared for battle, and the captain of their host was Fionwë son of Manwë. Beneath his white banner marched also the host of the Quendi, the Light-elves, the folk of Ingwë, and among them such of the Gnomes of old as had never departed from Valinor;[19] but remembering Swan Haven the Teleri went not forth save very few, and these manned the ships wherewith the most of that army came into the Northern lands; but they themselves would set foot never on those shores.

Eärendel was their guide; but the Gods would not suffer him to return again, and he built him a white tower upon the confines of the outer world in the Northern regions of the Sundering Seas; and there all the sea-birds of the earth at times repaired. And often was Elwing in the form and likeness of a bird; and she devised wings for the ship of Eärendel, and it was lifted even into the oceans of the air. Marvellous and magical was that ship, a starlit flower in the sky, bearing a wavering and holy flame; and the folk of earth beheld it from afar and wondered, and looked up from despair, saying surely a Silmaril is in the sky, a new star is risen in the West. Maidros said unto Maglor:[20] 'If that be the Silmaril that riseth by some power divine out of the sea into which we saw it fall, then let us be glad, that its glory is seen now by many.' Thus hope arose and a promise of betterment; but Morgoth was filled with doubt. Yet it is said that he looked not for the assault that came upon him from the West. So great was his pride become that he deemed none would ever again come against him in open war; moreover he thought that he had estranged the Gnomes for ever from the Gods and from their kin, and that content in their Blissful Realm the Valar would heed no more his kingdom in the world without. For heart that is pitiless counteth not the power that pity hath, of which stern anger may be forged and a lightning kindled before which mountains fall.

1  elfin > elven
2  Eärámë, Eagle's Pinion > Eärrámë, Sea-wing
3  Added here:

> But Tuor alone of mortal Men was numbered among the elder race, and joined with the Noldoli whom he loved, and in after time dwelt still, or so it hath been said, [struck out: in Tol Eressëa] ever upon his ship voyaging the seas of Fairyland [> the Elven-lands], or resting a while in the harbours of the Gnomes of Tol Eressëa; and his fate is sundered from the fate of Men.

4  and she bore him Elrond Half-elfin > and she bore him Elros and Elrond, who are called the Halfelven.
5  Outer > Hither at both occurrences.
6  Wingelot > Vingelot at all three occurrences; at the first only, Vingelot later > Wingilot
7  Ungoliant > Ungoliantë at both occurrences.
8  Nauglafring > Nauglamír at both occurrences (cf. §14 note 10).
9  her child Elrond > her children Elros and Elrond
10 This passage was rewritten thus:

> But great was the sorrow of Eärendel and Elwing for the ruin of the havens of Sirion, and the captivity of their sons; and they feared that they would be slain. But it was not so. For Maglor took pity on Elros and Elrond, and he cherished them, and love grew after between them, as little might be thought; but Maglor's heart was sick and weary, &c.

11  and they came unto the Magic Isles and escaped their magic > and they came to the Enchanted Isles and escaped their enchantment
12  Bay of Faërie > Bay of Elvenhome
13  Tinbrenting's > Tindbrenting's

14  This paragraph was emended at different times, and it is not perfectly clear what was intended. The first change was the addition, after *lest they fell beneath the wrath of the Gods*, of: *And he bade farewell to all whom he loved upon the last shore, and was taken from them for ever.* Subsequently *nor any of his small company* seems to have been removed, with the result: *and he would not suffer Elwing to go with him, lest she fell beneath the wrath of the Gods*: but the previous addition was not struck out.

15  *Côr > Kôr*, as previously.

16  This passage was altered to read:

> Wherefore he turned back towards the shores thinking to set sail once more upon Vingelot his ship; but one came unto him and cried: 'Hail Eärendel, radiant star, messenger most fair!

17  *came never again back into the lands of Men* > *never again set foot upon the lands of Men*

18  *races > kindreds*

19  Added here: *and Ingwiel son of Ingwë was their chief;*

20  This passage, from the beginning of the paragraph, was extensively rewritten:

> In those days the ship of Eärendel was drawn by the Gods beyond the edge of the world, and it was lifted even into the oceans of the air. Marvellous and magical was that ship, a starlit flower in the sky, bearing a wavering and holy flame; and the folk of Earth beheld it from afar and wondered, and looked up from despair, saying surely a Silmaril is in the sky, a new star is risen in the West. But Elwing mourned for Eärendel yet found him never again, and they are sundered till the world endeth. Therefore she built a white tower upon the confines of the outer world in the Northern regions of the Sundering Seas; and there all the sea-birds of the earth at times repaired. And Elwing devised wings for herself, and desired to fly to Eärendel's ship. But [?she fell back] . . . . . . . . But when the flame of it appeared on high Maglor said unto Maidros:

## 18

[The whole of this section is again extant in the two typescript versions Q I and Q II.]

Of the march of Fionwë to the North little is said, for in that host there were none of the Elves who had dwelt and suffered in the Outer Lands, and who made these tales; and tidings only long after did they learn of these things from their distant kinsfolk the

Elves of Valinor. The meeting of the hosts of Fionwë and of Morgoth in the North is named the Last Battle, the Battle Terrible, the Battle of Wrath and Thunder. Great was Morgoth's amaze when this host came upon him from the West, and all Hithlum was ablaze with its glory, and the mountains rang; for he had thought that he had estranged the Gnomes for ever from the Gods and from their kin, and that content in their blissful realm the Gods would heed no further his kingdom in the world without. For heart that is pitiless counts not the power that pity hath; nor foresees that of gentle ruth for anguish and for valour overthrown stern anger may be forged, and a lightning kindled before which mountains fall.[1]

There was marshalled the whole power of the Throne of Hate, and well nigh measureless had it become, so that Dor-na-Fauglith might by no means contain it, and all the North was aflame with war. But it availed not. All the Balrogs were destroyed, and the uncounted hosts of the Orcs perished like straw in fire, or were swept away like shrivelled leaves before a burning wind. Few remained to trouble the world thereafter. And Morgoth himself came forth, and all his dragons were about him; and Fionwë for a moment was driven back. But the sons of the Valar in the end overthrew them all, and but two escaped. Morgoth escaped not. Him they threw down, and they bound him with the chain Angainor, wherewith Tulkas had chained him aforetime, and whence in unhappy hour the Gods had released him; but his iron crown they beat into a collar for his neck, and his head was bowed unto his knees. The Silmarils Fionwë took and guarded them.

Thus perished the power and woe of Angband in the North and its multitude of captives came forth into the light again beyond all hope, and looked upon a world all changed. Thangorodrim was riven and cast down, and the pits of Morgoth uncovered, roofless and broken, never to be rebuilt; but so great was the fury of those adversaries that all the Northern and Western parts of the world were rent and gaping, and the sea roared in in many places; the rivers perished or found new paths, the valleys were upheaved and the hills trod down; and Sirion was no more. Then Men fled away, such as perished not in the ruin of those days, and long was it ere they came back over the mountains to where Beleriand once had been, and not till the tale of those days had faded to an echo seldom heard.

But Fionwë marched through the lands summoning the remnants of the Gnomes and the Dark-elves that never yet had looked on Valinor to join with the captives released from Angband, and depart; and with the Elves should those of the race of Hador and Bëor alone be suffered to depart, if they would. But of these only Elrond was now left, the Half-elfin; and [he] elected to remain, being bound by his mortal blood in love to those of the younger race; and of Elrond alone has the blood of the elder race and of the seed divine of Valinor come among mortal Men.

But Maidros would not obey the call, preparing to fulfil even yet the obligation of his oath, though with weary loathing and despair. For he would have given battle for the Silmarils, if they were withheld from him, though he should stand alone in all the world save for Maglor his brother alone. And he sent unto Fionwë and bade him yield up those jewels which of old Morgoth stole from Fëanor. But Fionwë said that the right that Fëanor and his sons had in that which they had made, had perished, because of the many and evil deeds they had wrought blinded by their oath, and most of all the slaying of Dior and the assault upon Elwing. To Valinor must Maidros and Maglor return and abide the judgement of the Gods, by whose decree alone would he yield the jewels to any keeping other than his own.

Maidros was minded to submit, for he was sad at heart, and he said: 'The oath decrees not that we shall not bide our time, and maybe in Valinor all shall be forgiven and forgot, and we shall be vouchsafed our own.' But Maglor said that if once they returned and the favour of the Gods was not granted them, then would their oath still remain, and be fulfilled in despair yet greater; 'and who can tell to what dreadful end we shall come if we disobey the Powers in their own land, or purpose ever to bring war into their Guarded Realm again?' And so came it that Maidros and Maglor crept into the camps of Fionwë, and laid hands on the Silmarils; and they took to their weapons when they were discovered. But the sons of the Valar arose in wrath and prevented them, and took Maidros prisoner; and yet Maglor eluded them and escaped.

Now the Silmaril that Maidros held – for the brothers had agreed each to take one, saying that two brethren alone now remained, and but two jewels – burned the hand of Maidros, and he had but one hand as [has] been before told, and he knew then that his right thereto had become void, and that the oath was vain. But he cast the Silmaril upon the ground, and Fionwë took it; and for the anguish of his pain and the remorse of his heart he took his own life, ere he could be stayed.

It is told too of Maglor that he fled far, but he too could not endure the pain with which the Silmaril tormented him; and in an agony he cast it from him into a yawning gap filled with fire, in the rending of the Western lands, and the jewel vanished into the bosom of the Earth. But Maglor came never back among the folk of Elfinesse, but wandered singing in pain and in regret beside the sea.

In those days there was a mighty building of ships on the shores of the Western Sea, and most upon the great isles, which in the disruption of the Northern world were fashioned of old Beleriand. Thence in many a fleet the survivors of the Gnomes, and of the Western companies of the Dark-elves, set sail into the West and came no more into the lands of weeping and of war; and the Light-elves marched back beneath the banners of their king following in the train of Fionwë's victory. Yet not all returned, and some lingered many an age in the West and North, and especially in the Western Isles. Yet ever as the ages drew on and the Elf-folk faded on the Earth, they would still set sail at eve from our Western shores; as still they do, when now there linger few anywhere of the lonely companies.

But in the West the Gnomes returned rehabited for the most part the Lonely Isle that looks both East and West; and with them were mingled the Dark-elves, especially such as had once belonged to Doriath. And some returned even to Valinor, and were welcomed amid the bright companies of the Quendi, and admitted to the love of Manwë and the pardon of the Gods; and the Teleri forgave their ancient bitterness, and the curse was laid to rest. But Tûn was never again inhabited; and Côr stands still a hill of silent and untrodden green.

1    The content of this passage, from *Great was Morgoth's amaze . . .*, has been given at the end of §17 in the Q II version, since it appears there before the words *Of the march of the host of Fionwë* with which I begin §18.

## §18 in the Q II version

Of the march of the host of Fionwë to the North little is said, for in his armies came none of those Elves who had dwelt and suffered in the Outer[1] Lands, and who made these tales; and tidings only long after did they learn of these things from their kinsfolk the Light-elves of Valinor. But Fionwë came, and the challenge of his trumpets filled the sky, and he summoned unto him all Men and Elves from Hithlum unto the East; and Beleriand was ablaze with the glory of his arms, and the mountains rang.

The meeting of the hosts of the West and of the North is named the Great Battle, the Battle Terrible, the Battle of Wrath and Thunder. There was marshalled the whole power of the Throne of Hate, and well nigh measureless had it become, so that Dor-na-Fauglith could not contain it, and all the North was aflame with war. But it availed not. All the Balrogs were destroyed, and the uncounted hosts of the Orcs perished like straw in fire, or were swept like shrivelled leaves before a burning wind. Few remained to trouble the world thereafter. And it is said that there many Men of Hithlum repentant of their evil servitude did deeds of valour, and many beside of Men new come out of the East;[2] and so were fulfilled in part the words of Ulmo; for by Eärendel son of Tuor was help brought unto the Elves, and by the swords of Men were they strengthened on the fields of war.[3] But Morgoth quailed and he came not forth; and he loosed his last assault, and that was the winged dragons.[4] So sudden and so swift and ruinous was the onset of that fleet, as a tempest of a hundred thunders winged with steel, that Fionwë was driven back; but Eärendel came and a myriad of birds were about him, and the battle lasted all through the night of doubt. And Eärendel slew Ancalagon the black and the mightiest of all the dragon-horde, and cast him from the sky, and in his fall the towers of Thangorodrim were thrown down. Then the sun rose of the second day and the sons[5] of the Valar prevailed, and all the dragons were destroyed save two alone; and they fled into the East. Then were all the pits of Morgoth broken and unroofed, and the might of Fionwë descended into the deeps of the Earth, and there Morgoth was thrown down. He was bound[6] with the chain Angainor, which long had been prepared, and his iron crown they beat into a collar for his neck, and his head was bowed unto his knees. But Fionwë took the two Silmarils that remained and guarded them.

Thus perished the power and woe of Angband in the North, and its multitude of thralls came forth beyond all hope into the light of day, and they looked upon a world all changed; for so great was the fury of those adversaries that the Northern regions of the Western world were rent and riven, and the sea roared in through many chasms, and there was confusion and great noise; and the rivers perished or found new paths, and the valleys were upheaved and the hills trod down; and Sirion was no more. Then Men fled away, such as perished not in the ruin of those days, and long was it ere they came back over the mountains to where Beleriand once had been, and not until the tale of those wars had faded to an echo seldom heard.

But Fionwë marched through the Western lands summoning the remnants of the Gnomes, and the Dark-elves that had yet not looked on Valinor, to join with the thralls released and to depart. But Maidros would not harken, and he prepared, though with weary loathing and despair, to perform even yet the obligation of his oath. For Maidros and Maglor would have given battle for the Silmarils, were they withheld, even against the victorious host of Valinor, and though they stood alone in all the world. And they sent unto Fionwë and bade him yield now up those jewels which of old Morgoth stole from Fëanor. But Fionwë said that the right to the work of their hands which Fëanor and his sons had formerly possessed now had perished, because of their many and evil deeds blinded by their oath, and most of all the slaying of Dior and the assault upon Elwing; the light of the Silmarils should go now to the Gods whence it came, and to Valinor must Maidros and Maglor return and there abide the judgement of the Gods, by whose decree alone would Fionwë yield the jewels from his charge.

Maglor was minded to submit, for he was sad at heart, and he said: 'The oath says not that we may not bide our time, and maybe in Valinor all shall be forgiven and forgot, and we shall come into our own.' But Maidros said that if once they returned and the favour of the Gods were withheld from them, then would their oath still remain, to be fulfilled in despair yet greater; 'and who can tell to what dreadful doom we shall come, if we disobey the Powers in their own land, or purpose ever to bring war again into their Guarded Realm?' And so it came that Maidros and Maglor crept into the camps of Fionwë, and laid hands on the Silmarils, and slew the guards; and there they prepared to defend themselves to the death. But Fionwë stayed his folk; and the brethren departed and fled far away.

Each took a single Silmaril, saying that one was lost unto them and two remained, and but two brethren. But the jewel burned the hand of Maidros in pain unbearable (and he had but one hand as has before been told); and he perceived that it was as Fionwë had said, and that his right thereto had become void, and that the oath was vain. And being in anguish and despair he cast himself into a gaping chasm filled with fire, and so ended; and his Silmaril was taken into the bosom of the Earth.

And it is told also of Maglor that he could not bear the pain with which the Silmaril tormented him; and he cast it at last into the sea, and thereafter wandered ever upon the shore singing in pain and regret beside the waves; for Maglor was the mightiest of the singers of old, but he came never back among the folk of Elfinesse.

In those days there was a mighty building of ships on the shores of the Western Sea, and especially upon the great isles, which in the disruption of the Northern world were fashioned of ancient Beleriand. Thence in many a fleet the survivors of the Gnomes and of the Western companies of the Dark-elves set sail into the West and came not again into the lands of weeping and of war; but the Light-elves marched back beneath the banners of their king following in the train of Fionwë's victory, and they were borne back in triumph unto Valinor.[7] But in the West the Gnomes and Dark-elves rehabited for the most part the Lonely Isle, that looks both East and West; and very fair did that land become, and so remains. But some returned even unto Valinor, as all were free to do who willed; and the Gnomes were admitted again to the love of Manwë and the pardon of the Valar, and the Teleri forgave their ancient grief, and the curse was laid to rest.

Yet not all would forsake the Outer Lands where they had long suffered and long dwelt; and some lingered many an age in the West and North, and especially in the western isles and the lands of Leithien. And among these were Maglor as has been told; and with him Elrond the Half-elfin,[8] who after went among mortal Men again, and from whom alone the blood of the elder race[9] and the seed divine of Valinor have come among Mankind (for he was son of Elwing, daughter of Dior, son of Lúthien, child of Thingol and Melian; and Eärendel his sire was son of Idril Celebrindal, the fair maid of Gondolin). But ever as the ages drew on and the Elf-folk faded on the Earth, they would still set sail at eve from our Western shores; as still they do, when now there linger few anywhere of their lonely companies.

★

1   *Hither* written above or replacing *Outer* at both occurrences.

2   In this sentence, in the first 'layer' of emendation, *many Men* > *some few Men* and *many beside of Men* > *some beside of Men*. Later the sentence was rewritten rapidly in pencil:

> And it is said that all that were left of the three Houses of the Fathers of Men fought for Fionwë, and to them were joined some of the Men of Hithlum who repenting of their evil servitude did deeds of valour against the Orcs; and so were fulfilled, &c. ·

See note 3.

3   Added here at the same time as the rewriting given in note 2:

> But most Men, and especially those new come out of the East, were on the side of the Enemy.

4   Added here:

> for as yet had none of these creatures of his cruel thought assailed the air.

5   *sons* > *children* (late change).

6   *and there Morgoth was thrown down* altered and expanded thus:

> and there Morgoth stood at last at bay; and yet not valiant. He fled unto the deepest of his mines and sued for peace and pardon. But his feet were hewn from under him, and he was hurled upon his face. Then was he bound, &c.

7   Added here:

> Yet little joy had they in their return, for they came without the Silmarils, and these could not be again found, unless the world was broken and re-made anew.

8   *Half-elfin* > *Half-elven* (cf. §17 in the Q II version, note 4).

9   *the elder race* > *the Firstborn*

## 19

[Q I comes to an end soon after the beginning of this section.]

Thus did the Gods adjudge when Fionwë and the sons of the Valar returned unto Valmar: the Outer Lands should thereafter be for Men, the younger children of the world; but to the Elves alone should the gateways of the West stand ever open; but if they would not come thither and tarried in the world of Men, then should they slowly fade and fail. And so hath it been; and this is the most grievous of the fruits of the works and lies of Morgoth.

For a while his Orcs and Dragons breeding again in dark places troubled and affrighted the world, as in far places they do yet; but ere the End all shall perish by the valour of mortal Men. But Morgoth the Gods thrust through the Door of Timeless Night into the Void beyond the Walls of the World; and a guard is set for ever on that door. Yet the lies that

[Here the Q I text gives out, at the foot of a typescript page, but Q II continues to the end.]

This was the judgement of the Gods, when Fionwë and the sons of the Valar had returned unto Valmar: thereafter the Outer Lands should be for Mankind, the younger children of the world; but to the Elves alone should the gateways of the West stand ever open; and if they would not come thither and tarried in the world of Men, then they should slowly fade and fail. This is the most grievous of the fruits of the lies and works that Morgoth wrought, that the Eldalië should be sundered and estranged from Men. For a while his Orcs and his Dragons breeding again in dark places affrighted the world, and in sundry regions do so yet; but ere the End all shall perish by the valour of mortal Men.

But Morgoth the Gods thrust through the Door of Timeless Night into the Void, beyond the Walls of the World; and a guard is set for ever on that door, and Eärendel keeps watch upon the ramparts of the sky. Yet the lies that Melko,[1] Moeleg the mighty and accursed, Morgoth Bauglir the Dark Power Terrible, sowed in the hearts of Elves and Men have not all died, and cannot by the Gods be slain, and they live to work much evil even to this later day. Some say also that Morgoth at whiles secretly as a cloud that cannot be seen or felt, and yet is, and the poison is,[2] creeps back surmounting the Walls and visiteth the world; but others say that this is the black shadow of Thû, whom Morgoth made, and who escaped from the Battle Terrible, and dwells in dark places and perverts Men[3] to his dreadful allegiance and his foul worship.

After the triumph of the Gods Eärendel sailed still in the seas of heaven, but the Sun scorched him and the Moon hunted him in the sky, [and he departed long behind the world voyaging the Outer Dark a glimmering and fugitive star.][4] Then the Valar drew his white ship Wingelot[5] over the land of Valinor, and they filled it with radiance and hallowed it, and launched it through the Door of Night. And long Eärendel set sail into the starless vast, Elwing at his side,[6] the Silmaril upon his brow, voyaging the Dark behind the world, a glimmering and fugitive star. And ever and anon he returns and shines behind the courses of the Sun and Moon above the ramparts of the Gods, brighter than all other stars, the mariner of the sky, keeping watch against Morgoth upon the confines of the world. Thus shall he sail until he sees the Last Battle fought upon the plains of Valinor.

Thus spake the prophecy of Mandos, which he declared in Valmar at the judgement of the Gods, and the rumour of it was whispered among all the Elves of the West: when the world is old and the Powers grow weary, then Morgoth shall come back through the Door out of the Timeless Night; and he shall destroy the Sun and the Moon, but Eärendel shall come upon him as a white flame and drive him from the airs. Then shall the last battle be gathered on the fields of Valinor. In that day Tulkas shall strive with Melko, and on his right shall stand Fionwë and on his left Túrin Turambar, son of Húrin, Conqueror of Fate;[7] and it shall be the black sword of Túrin that deals unto Melko his death and final end; and so shall the children of Húrin and all Men be avenged.

Thereafter shall the Silmarils[8] be recovered out of sea and earth and air; for Eärendel shall descend and yield up that flame that he hath had in keeping. Then Fëanor shall bear the Three and yield them unto Yavanna Palúrien; and she will break them and with their fire rekindle the Two Trees, and a great light shall come forth; and the Mountains of Valinor shall be levelled, so that the light goes out over all the world. In that light the Gods will again grow young, and the Elves awake and all their dead arise, and the purpose of Ilúvatar be fulfilled concerning them. But of Men in that day the prophecy speaks not, save of Túrin only, and him it names among the Gods.[9]

*Such is the end of the tales of the days before the days in the Northern regions of the Western world. Some of these things are sung and said yet by the fading Elves; and more still are sung by the vanished Elves that dwell now on the Lonely Isle. To Men of the race of Eärendel have they at times been told, and most to Eriol,[10] who alone of the mortals of later days, and yet now long ago, sailed to the Lonely Isle, and came back to the land of Leithien[11] where he lived, and remembered things that he had heard in fair Cortirion, the city of the Elves in Tol Eressëa.*

★

1  *Melko* > *Melkor* (but only at the first occurrence).
2  *and yet is, and the poison is* > *and yet is venomous*
3  This sentence was rewritten:

>  but others say that this is the black shadow of Sauron, who served
>  Morgoth and became the greatest and most evil of his underlings;
>  and Sauron escaped from the Great Battle, and dwelt in dark
>  places and perverted Men, &c.

4  This sentence survives from an earlier point in the narrative in Q I
   (end of §17, p. 150); in Q II the latter part of it, *and he departed*
   *long behind the world voyaging the Outer Dark a glimmering and*
   *fugitive star*, was struck out, since it recurs immediately below.
5  *Wingelot* not here emended (as in §17 in the Q II version, note 6) to
   *Vingelot*.
6  *Elwing at his side* struck out.
7  Added here in pencil: *coming from the halls of Mandos*
8  *Thereafter shall the Silmarils* > *Thereafter Earth shall be broken*
   *and re-made, and the Silmarils*
9  *among the Gods* emended in pencil to *among the sons of the Gods*
10  Apparently changed, in pencil, to *Ereol*.
11  *Leithien* emended in pencil to *Britain*.

## Commentary on the *Quenta*

### Opening Section

This passage, to which there is nothing corresponding in S, may be
compared with the *Lost Tales* I. 58, 66–7 on the one hand and with
the *Valaquenta* (*The Silmarillion* pp. 25 ff.) on the other. This
opening section of Q is the origin and precursor of the *Valaquenta*, as
may be seen from the fall of its sentences and from many details of
wording; while brief as it is it offers no actual contradictions to the text of
the *Lost Tales*, save in a few details of names. The Nine Valar, referred to
in S§1 and in the alliterative *Flight of the Noldoli* (III. 133), are now for
the first time identified. This number was to remain in the Eight *Aratar*
(eight, because 'one is removed from their number', *The Silmarillion*
p. 29), though there was much shifting in the composition of the number
in later writings; in the *Lost Tales* there were 'four great ones' among the
Valar, Manwë, Melko, Ulmo, Aulë (I. 58).
    The name of Mandos in the *Lost Tales*, Vefántur 'Fantur of Death',
who 'called his hall with his own name Vê' (I. 66, 76), now becomes
*Nefantur*. Nowhere is there any indication of the meaning of the first
element; but the new name bears a curious resemblance to the Old
English name of Mandos found in a list of such names of the Valar
(p. 208): *Néfréa* (Old English *né(o)* 'corpse', *fréa* 'lord'). The late change

of *Tavros* to *Tauros* is made also to the B-text of the *Lay of Leithian* (III. 195, 282).

Vána (here specifically given as *Văna*) is now the younger sister of Varda and Palúrien (in the *Lost Tales* these goddesses are not said to be 'related'); in *The Silmarillion* Vána remains the younger sister of Yavanna. We meet here the Gnomish name of Melko, *Moeleg*, which the Gnomes will not use; cf. the *Valaquenta* (p. 31): 'the Noldor, who among the Elves suffered most from his malice, will not utter it [Melkor], and they name him Morgoth, the Dark Enemy of the World'. The original Gnomish form was *Belcha* (II. 44, 67).

## 1

In this section of Q, before the replacement page (see note 2) was written, the only important developments from S are the reduction of the periods of the Trees from fourteen hours to seven (and this only came in with an alteration to the typescript, see note 1), and the explicit statement that Silpion was the elder of the Trees, and shone alone for a time (the Opening Hour). It is also said that the Gnomes afterwards called the Trees *Bansil* and *Glingol*. In the tale of *The Fall of Gondolin* these names were expressly those of the Trees of Gondolin (see II. 214–16), but (especially since *Glingol* occurs in a rejected reading in *The Cottage of Lost Play* (I. 22) as a name of the Golden Tree of Valinor) it seems clear that they were the Gnomish names of the original Trees, which were transferred to their scions in Gondolin; in the *Lay of the Children of Húrin* and in the *Lay of Leithian*, as here in Q, Glingol and Bansil (later emended to *Glingal* and *Belthil*) are the Trees of Valinor. But in *The Silmarillion* Glingal and Belthil are the particular names of Turgon's images of the Trees in Gondolin.

With the replacement page in this section (note 2) there are several further developments, and the passage describing the periods of the Trees and the mingling of the lights is effectively the final form, only differing from that in *The Silmarillion* (pp. 38–9) in some slight rhythmical changes in the sentences. Yavanna no longer 'plants' the Trees, and Nienna is present at their birth (replacing Vána of the *Lost Tales*, I. 71–2); the Valar sit upon their 'thrones of council' in the Ring of Doom near the golden gates of Valmar; and the moving shadows of Silpion's leaves, not mentioned in S or in Q as first written, reappear from the *Lost Tales* (see I. 88). Here also appear the names of Taniquetil, *Ialassë* 'Everlasting Whiteness', Gnomish *Amon-Uilas*, and *Tinwenairin* 'crowned with stars'; cf. *The Silmarillion* p. 37:

> Taniquetil the Elves name that holy mountain, and Oiolossë Everlasting Whiteness, and Elerrína Crowned with Stars, and many names beside; but the Sindar spoke of it in their later tongue as Amon Uilos.

'Elves' is still used here in contradistinction to 'Gnomes'; on this usage see p. 44.

## 2

Q remains close to S in this section. I have noticed in commenting on S the absence of certain features that are found both in the *Lost Tales* and in *The Silmarillion*: (1) the coming of the three Elvish ambassadors to Valinor, (2) the Elves who did not leave the Waters of Awakening, (3) the two starmakings of Varda, and (4) the chain Angainor with which Morgoth was bound; and there is still no mention of them. As I have said (p. 76), the *Quenta* though written in a finished manner is still very much an outline, and the absence of these elements may be thought to be due merely to its compressed nature. Against this, however, in respect of (1), is the statement in Q that Thingol 'came never to Valinor', whereas in the old story (I. 115) as in *The Silmarillion* (p. 52) Tinwelint/Thingol was one of the three original ambassadors; and in respect of (3), Varda is said in Q to have strewn 'the unlit skies' with stars. As regards (4), it is said later in Q (§18) that Morgoth was bound after the Last Battle 'with the chain Angainor, wherewith Tulkas had chained him aforetime'.

The constellation of the Great Bear is called the Burning Briar, and the Sickle of the Gods, in the *Lay of Leithian*.

It is said here that the Elves named themselves *Eldar*, in contrast both to the old idea (I. 235) that *Eldar* was the name given to them by the Gods, and to *The Silmarillion* (p. 49), where Oromë 'named them in their own tongue Eldar, the people of the stars'.

The original statement in Q that Ingwë 'never came back into the Outer Lands until these tales were near their end' is a reference to his leadership of the March of the Elves of Valinor in the second assault on Morgoth, in which he perished (I. 129). The revised statement given in note 6, saying that Ingwë never came back from the West, is virtually the same as that in *The Silmarillion* (p. 53); see the Commentary on §17. The Gnomish forms of the names of the three leaders, *Ing*, *Finn*, and *Elu*, are removed by the rewritings given in notes 6, 8, and 11; and the use of *Quendi* for the First Kindred ('who sometimes are alone called Elves', see p. 44) is displaced by *Lindar* in a late emendation (note 7), while *Quendi* reappears (note 5) as the name for all the Elves. These late changes belong to a new nomenclature that came in after the *Quenta* was completed.

## 3

While Q again follows S very closely here, there is one important narrative development: the first appearance of the story of Ossë's sitting on the rocks of the seashore and instructing the Teleri, and of his persuading some to remain 'on the beaches of the world' (the later Elves of the Havens of Brithombar and Eglarest, ruled by Círdan the Shipwright). And with the late addition given in note 7 there appears the removal of the First Kindred (here called the Lindar) from Tûn, and their sunderance from the Gnomes; here there is a detail not taken up into subsequent texts (probably because it was overlooked), that the Noldoli of Tûn left the tower of Ingwë uninhabited, though they tended the lamp.

As in §2, *Finn* was emended to *Finwë* (and *Ing* to *Ingwë*), although the names of the Noldorin princes are said to be given in Gnomish form, and *Ylmir* found in S is not taken up in Q (similarly *Óin* in S§3, but *Uinen* in the opening section of Q).

In the passage on the Noldorin princes (a later addition to S) Celegorm becomes 'the friend of Oromë' (a development arising from the later story of Huan, see §10); Finrod's third son, *Anrod* in S, becomes *Angrod*. On the change *Finweg* > *Fingon* see p. 46.

# 4

Many touches found in the story in *The Silmarillion* now make their appearance in Q (as Fëanor's wearing the Silmarils at great feasts, Morgoth's sight of the domes of Valmar far off in the mingling of the lights, his laugh 'as he sped down the long western slopes', his great cry that echoed through the world as Ungoliant's webs enmeshed him). I have noticed in my commentary on S that 'the entire story of Morgoth's going to Formenos (not yet so named) and his speech with Fëanor before the doors has yet to appear', and it has not done so in Q; but the late interpolation given in note 6, stating that a messenger came to the Gods in council with tidings that Morgoth was in the North of Valinor and journeying to the house of Finwë, is the first hint of this element. In *The Silmarillion* (p. 72) messengers came to the Valar from Finwë at Formenos telling of Morgoth's first coming there, and this is followed by the news from Tirion that he had passed through the Calacirya – a movement that appears at this point in S and Q ('he escaped through the pass of Kôr, and from the tower of Ingwë the Elves saw him pass in thunder and in wrath').

There is no mention in S§4 of the great festival at this point in the narrative, and its appearance in §5 looks like an afterthought (see p. 47); that the same is still true in Q shows the close dependence of the later version on the earlier at this stage in the work.

# 5

In this section Q as usual contains many details and enduring phrases not found in S, such as the wailing of the Foamriders beside the sea,

Fëanor's contempt for the Valar 'who cannot even keep their own realm from their foe', the drawn swords of the oath-takers, the fighting on 'the great arch of the gate and on the lamplit quays and piers' of Swanhaven, and the suggestion that the speaker of the Prophecy may have been Mandos himself. There was no mention in S of the Gnomes who did not join the Flight (they being those who were on Taniquetil celebrating the festival): this now reappears from the *Lost Tales* (I. 176); nor was it said that not all Fingolfin's people shared in the Kinslaying at Swanhaven.

The reference to 'the song of the Flight of the Gnomes' may be to the alliterative poem *The Flight of the Noldoli* (III. 131 ff.), though that was abandoned at the Fëanorian Oath: perhaps my father still thought to continue it one day, or to write a new poem on the subject.*

The pencilled addition 'Finrod returned' (note 8) indicates the later story, according to which Finarfin (Finrod) left the march of the Noldor after hearing the Prophecy of the North (*The Silmarillion* p. 88); in S as emended (note 9) and in Q Finrod only came up with Fingolfin after the burning of the ships by the Fëanorians, and only after that did Finrod return to Valinor.

*Helkaraksë* reappears in Q from the *Lost Tales*, but is now rendered 'the Strait of the Grinding Ice', whereas its original meaning was 'Ice-fang', and referred to the narrow neck of land which 'ran out from the western land almost to the eastern shores' and was separated from the Great Lands by the Qerkaringa or Chill Gulf (I. 166–7 and note 5).

# 6

If there ever was a 'song of the Sun and Moon' (called in *The Silmarillion* p. 99 by an Elvish name, *Narsilion*) it has disappeared. The account in Q scarcely expands the extremely cursory passage in S; but the reason now given for the change in the divine plan is not that the Gods 'find it safer' to send the Sun and Moon beneath the Earth: rather it is changed on account of 'the waywardness of Tilion and his rivalry with Úrien', and still more because of the complaints of Lórien and Nienna against the unceasing light. This element re-emerges from the *Tale of the Sun and Moon* (I. 189–90), where the Valar who protested were Mandos and Fui Nienna, Lórien, and Vána. Likewise the names *Rána* and *Úr* given by the Gods to the Moon and Sun go back to the old story, where however *Úr* is said to be the Elvish name: the Gods named the Sun *Sári* (I. 186–7).

The Sun-maiden is now named *Úrien*, emended to *Árien* (her name in *The Silmarillion*), replacing *Urwendi* (< *Urwen*); she is said to have

---

* Later this becomes a reference to 'that lament which is named *Noldolantë*, the Fall of the Noldor, that Maglor made ere he was lost' (*The Silmarillion* p. 87); but I have found no trace of this.

'tended the golden flowers in the gardens of Vana', which clearly derives from the tending of Laurelin by Urwen(di) in the *Lost Tales* (I. 73).

Tilion, the hunter with the silver bow from the company of Oromë, not Ilinsor, is now the steersman of the Moon; but as I noted in I. 88, Tilion, who in *The Silmarillion* 'lay in dream by the pools of Estë [Lórien's wife], in Telperion's flickering beams', perhaps owes something to the figure of Silmo in the *Lost Tales*, the youth whom Lórien loved and who was given the task of 'watering' Silpion. The words of Q concerning Tilion, 'often he wandered from his course pursuing the stars upon the heavenly fields', and the reference to his rivalry with Úrien (Árien), clearly derive from the passage in the old tale (I. 195) where it is told of Ilinsor that he was 'jealous of the supremacy of the Sun' and that 'often he set sail in chase of [the stars]'.

A trace of the old conception of the Moon survives in the reference to 'the floating island of the Moon', a phrase still found in *The Silmarillion* (see I. 202).

The occurrence of the name *Eruman* of the land where Men awoke (*Murmenalda* in *Gilfanon's Tale*, 'far to the east of Palisor', I. 232–3, *Hildórien* in *The Silmarillion*, 'in the eastward regions of Middle-earth') is strange, and can only be regarded as a passing application of it in a wholly different meaning, for it was in fact retained in a refinement of its original sense – the land between the mountains and the sea south of Taniquetil and Kôr, also in the *Lost Tales* called *Arvalin* (which is the name given to it in S and Q): *Eruman* (> *Araman*) afterwards became the wasteland between the mountains and the sea north of Taniquetil (see I. 82–3).

Though the phrase in Q 'the oldest days before the waning of the Elves and the waxing of mortals' was retained in *The Silmarillion* (p. 103), a later addition to Q (note 6), not retained, is more explicit: 'for measured time had come into the world, and the first of days; and thereafter the lives of the Eldar that remained in the Hither Lands were lessened, and their waning was begun.' The meaning of this is undoubtedly that measured time had come into the Great or Hither Lands, for the phrase 'thus measured time came into the Hither Lands' is found in the earliest *Annals of Beleriand* (p. 295). This seems to relate the waning of the Elves to the coming of 'measured time', and may in turn be associated with the following passage from *The Silmarillion* (p. 103):

From this time forth were reckoned the Years of the Sun. Swifter and briefer are they than the long Years of the Trees in Valinor. In that time the air of Middle-earth became heavy with the breath of growth and mortality, and the changing and ageing of all things was hastened exceedingly.

In the earlier writings the waning or fading of the Elves is always, clearly if mysteriously, a necessary concomitant of the waxing of Men.* Since Men came into the world at the rising of the Sun it may be that the conceptions are not fundamentally at variance: Men, and measured time, arose in the world together, and were the sign for the declining of the Elves. But it must be remembered that the doom of 'waning' was, or became, a part of the Prophecy of the North (*The Silmarillion* p. 88):

And those that endure in Middle-earth and come not to Mandos shall grow weary of the world as with a great burden, and shall wane, and become as shadows of regret before the younger race that cometh after.

On the phrase used of Eärendel: 'he came too late', see II. 257; and cf. Q§17: 'He came too late to bring messages to the Elves, for the Elves had gone.'

# 7

In this section Q does scarcely more than polish the text of S and embody the later alterations made to it, and the content has been discussed in the commentary on S. In the sentence added to the end of Q (note 6) there is a clear echo of the old idea of the fading Elves of Luthany, and the Elves of Tol Eressëa who have withdrawn from the world 'and there fade now no more' (see II. 301, 326).

# 8

Q provides here new details but otherwise follows S closely. The site of the First Battle (by later interpolation called 'The Battle under Stars') is now in the great Northern plain, still unnamed before its desolation, when it became Dor-na-Fauglith; in *The Silmarillion* (p. 106) the Orcs attacked through the passes of the Mountains of Shadow and the battle was fought 'on the grey fields of Mithrim'. Fëanor's sight of Thangorodrim as he died now appears, and his cursing of the name of Morgoth as he gazed on the mountain – transferred from Túrin, who did the same after the death of Beleg in the *Lay of the Children of Húrin* (III. 87).

A very minor structural change is found in the story of the feigned offer of a peace-treaty by Morgoth. In S this was made before the death of Fëanor, and Fëanor indeed refused to treat; after his death Maidros 'induced the Gnomes to meet Morgoth'. In Q 'even in the hour of his death there came to [his sons] an embassy from Morgoth acknowledging

---

*See II. 326. In one place it was said that the Elves 'cannot live in an air breathed by a number of Men equal to their own or greater' (II. 283). In the *Lay of the Children of Húrin* (see III. 54) appears the idea of 'the goodness of the earth' being usurped by Men, and this reappears in §14 in both S and Q (in S with the added statement that 'the Elves needed the light of the Trees').

his defeat, and offering to treat, and tempting them with a Silmaril'. The greater force sent by Morgoth is now referred to; and it is seen that the numbers of the Balrogs were still conceived to be very great: 'but Morgoth brought the greater, *and they were Balrogs*' (contrast *The Silmarillion*: 'but Morgoth sent the more, *and there were Balrogs*').

In the story of the rescue of Maidros by Finweg (Fingon) the explicit and puzzling statement of S that it was only now that Manwë 'fashioned the race of eagles' is changed to a statement that it was now that he sent them forth; by the later change of 'sent' to 'had sent' the final text is reached. In Q are found the details that Finweg (Fingon) climbed to Maidros unaided but could not reach him, and of the thirty fathoms of Thorndor's outstretched wings, the staying of Finweg's hand from his bow, the twice repeated appeal of Maidros that Finweg slay him, and the healing of Maidros so that he lived to wield his sword better with his left hand than he had with his right – cf. the *Lay of the Children of Húrin* (III. 65): *his left wieldeth / his sweeping sword*. But there are of course still many elements in the final story that do not appear: as the former close friendship of Maidros and Fingon, the song of Fingon and Maidros' answer, Fingon's prayer to Manwë, and Maidros' begging of forgiveness for the desertion in Araman and waiving of his claim to kingship over all the Noldor.

# 9

In this section of the narrative Q shows an extraordinary and unexpected expansion of S, much greater than has been the case hitherto, and many elements of the history in the published *Silmarillion* appear here (notably still absent are the entire story of Thingol's cold welcome to the new-come Noldor, and of course the origin at this time of Nargothrond and Gondolin); but S, as emended and interpolated, was still the basis. A few of the new features had in fact already emerged in the poems: thus the Elvish watchtower on Tol Sirion first appears in Canto VII of the *Lay of Leithian* (early 1928); the deaths of Angrod and Egnor in the battle that ended the Siege of Angband, called the Battle of Sudden Flame in one of the earlier additions in this section (note 19), in Canto VI of the Lay (see p. 55); the Gorge of Aglon in Canto VII and Himling in Canto X (both passages written in 1928); Esgalduin already in the *Lay of the Children of Húrin* (but its source in 'secret wells in Taur-na-Fuin' has not been mentioned before). But much of the content of Q in this section introduces wholly new elements into the legends.

The later pencilled alterations and additions given in the notes were put in a good while afterwards, and the names thus introduced (*Taur Danin, Eredlindon, Ossiriand*–which was *Assariad* in Q§14, *Dorthonion, Sauron*) belong to later phases. But it may be noticed here that the change of *Second Battle* to *Third Battle* (note 19) is explained by the development of the Glorious Battle (*Dagor Aglareb*, a late addition given in note 15), so that the Battle of Sudden Flame became the third of the Battles of Beleriand. With 'the Foreboding of the Kings' in note 15 cf. *The Silmarillion* p. 115: 'A victory it was, and yet a warning'; or the reference may be to the foreboding dreams of Turgon and Felagund (*ibid.* p. 114).

The names of Beleriand given in one of the earlier additions (note 2), *Noldórien*, *Geleidhian*, and *Ingolondë* 'the fair and sorrowful', are interesting. With these may be compared the list of names given in III. 160, which include *Noldórinan* and *Golodhinand*, the latter showing *Golodh*, the Sindarin equivalent of Quenya *Noldo*; *Geleidhian* obviously contains the same element (cf. *Annon-in-Gelydh*, the Gate of the Noldor). *Ingolondë* occurs again in the next version of 'The Silmarillion' (the version nearing completion in 1937, see I. 8):

> And that region was named of old in the language of Doriath *Beleriand*, but after the coming of the Noldor it was called also in the tongue of Valinor *Ingolondë*, the fair and sorrowful, the Kingdom of the Gnomes.

If *Ingolondë* means 'the Kingdom of the Gnomes', this name also should probably be associated with the stem seen in *Noldo*, *Golodh*. In much later writing my father gave the original form of the word as *ngolodō*, whence Quenya *ñoldo*, Sindarin *golodh*, noting that *ñ* = 'the Fëanorian letter for the back nasal, the *ng* of *king*'. He also said that the mother-name of Finrod (= Felagund) was *Ingoldo*: this was 'a form of *ñoldo* with syllabic *n*, and being in full and more dignified form is more or less equivalent to "*the* Noldo", one eminent in the kindred'; and he noted that 'the name was never Sindarized (the form would have been *Angoloð*)'.

How significant is the likeness of *Ingolondë* to *England*? I cannot certainly answer this; but it seems plain from the conclusion of Q that England was one of the great isles that remained after the destruction of Beleriand (see the commentary on §18).

The territory of the other sons of Finrod (Finarfin), Orodreth, Angrod, and Egnor, is now set in the pineclad highlands which afterwards were Taur-na-Fuin.

Quite new in Q is the passage concerning the Dwarves, with the notable statement that the Fëanorians 'made war upon' the Dwarves of Nogrod and Belegost, changed afterwards to 'had converse with' them; this led ultimately to the picture in *The Silmarillion* (p. 113) of Caranthir's contemptuous but highly profitable traffic with the Dwarves in Thargelion. The older view of the Dwarves (see II. 247) was still present when my father wrote the *Quenta*: though 'they do not serve Morgoth', 'they are in many things more like his people' (a hard saying indeed); they were naturally hostile to the Gnomes, who as naturally made war on them. The Dwarf-cities of Nogrod and Belegost go back to the *Tale of the Nauglafring*, where the Dwarves are called *Nauglath* (*Nauglir* in Q, *Naugrim* in *The Silmarillion*); but in the *Tale* the Indrafangs are the Dwarves of Belegost.

The Feast of Reunion, which goes back to *Gilfanon's Tale* (I. 240) but is not mentioned in S (where there is only a reference to the 'meeting' of the Gnomes with Ilkorins and Men), reappears in Q ('The Feast of Meeting'); it is held in the Land of Willows, not as in *The Silmarillion* near the pools of Ivrin. The presence of Men at the feast has been excised, and there now enters the story of the passage of Men over the Blue Mountains (called in an addition *Erydluin*, note 3) and the encounter of Felagund, hunting in the East with Celegorm, and Bëor. This passage in Q is the forerunner of that in *The Silmarillion* (p. 140), with the strangeness of the tongue of Men in Felagund's ears, his taking up Bëor's harp, the wisdom that was in Felagund's song, so that Men called him 'Gnome or Wisdom' (note 12). It is interesting to observe that after my father abandoned the use of the word 'Gnome' (see I. 43–4) he retained Nóm as the word for 'wisdom' in the language of the people of Bëor (*The Silmarillion* p. 141). The abiding of Bëor with Felagund until his death is mentioned (and in a late addition the dwelling of the Bëorians on Dorthonion, note 14).

Hador, called the Tall and by a later change (note 11) the Golden-haired, now first enters, and he is one of the two leaders of Men to cross the Mountains into Beleriand. Later, whereas in the House of Bëor the original leader remained, and new generations were introduced beneath him, in the case of the House of Hador the original leader was moved downwards and replaced by Marach; but the two Houses remained known as the House of Bëor and the House of Hador.

Hador has, beside Gumlin (who appeared in the second version of the *Lay of the Children of Húrin* as Húrin's father, III. 115, 126), another son Haleth; and this occurrence of Haleth is not merely an initial application of the name without particular significance, but implies that originally the 'Hadorian' and 'Halethian' houses of the Elf-friends were one and the same: the affinity of the names *Ha*dor, *Ha*leth (though Haleth ultimately became the Lady Haleth) goes back to their origin as father and son. The pencilled words 'Haleth the hunter, and little later' (note 11) were very probably intended to go after the words 'After them came', i.e.

They were the first of Men to come into Beleriand. After them came Haleth the hunter, and little later Hador, &c.

This shows of course the development of the third house of the Elf-friends, later called the Haladin; and with the removal of Haleth to independent status as the leader of a third people the other son of Hador became Gundor (note 11). Thus:

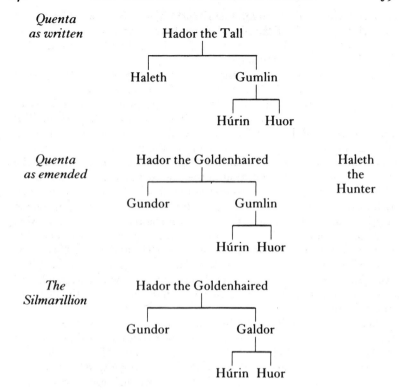

*Quenta as written*

Hador the Tall
— Haleth  Gumlin
Gumlin — Húrin  Huor

*Quenta as emended*

Hador the Goldenhaired
— Gundor  Gumlin
Gumlin — Húrin  Huor

Haleth the Hunter

*The Silmarillion*

Hador the Goldenhaired
— Gundor  Galdor
Galdor — Húrin  Huor

Morwen now gains the name 'Elfsheen', and the association of the House of Hador with Fingolfin in Hithlum appears.

The battle that ended the Siege of Angband had already been described in Canto VI (III. 212–13) of the *Lay of Leithian* (March 1928); a second description of it is found in Canto XI of the Lay (III. 275; September 1930). By later additions the name 'The Battle of Sudden Flame' (note 19) and Glómund's presence in it (note 16) are introduced (on the name *Glómund* see p. 60). Here also is the flight of many Dark-elves (not Gnomes as in S) to Doriath, to the increase of Thingol's power.

It is now suggested that Celegorm and Curufin came to Nargothrond after the Battle of Sudden Flame as to a refuge already in being, and with them came Orodreth their friend; this is to be related to the earlier passage in Q (§5): 'Orodreth, Angrod, and Egnor took the part of Fëanor' (in the debate before the Flight of the Noldoli). That Thingol's halls in Doriath were the inspiration for Nargothrond is also suggested.

With the account here of the challenge of Fingolfin and his death compare the *Lay of Leithian* Canto XII. This dates from late September 1930, and is later than this section of Q (see the commentary on §10), as is seen by the reference to Thorndor's 'beak of gold' (line 3616, found already in the A-text of the Lay), in contrast to his 'claw' in Q, emended to 'bill' (note 23).*

# 10

This version of the legend of Beren and Lúthien is unlike previous sections of the *Quenta*: for whereas hitherto it has been an independent extension of S, here (for a good part of its length) it is a compression of the *Lay of Leithian*. Very slight differences between Q and the Lay are not in my opinion significant, but are merely the result of précis.

At the end of the fight with Celegorm and Curufin, however, Q and the Lay diverge. In the Lay Beren's healing (not mentioned in Q) is followed by debate between him and Lúthien (3148ff.), their return to the borders of Doriath, and Beren's departure alone on Curufin's horse, leaving Huan to guard Lúthien (3219ff.). The narrative in Canto XI begins with Beren's reaching Dor-na-Fauglith and his Song of Parting; then follows (3342ff.) Lúthien's overtaking of Beren, having ridden after him on Huan, Huan's coming to them shortly after with the wolfcoat and batskin from the Wizard's Isle, and his counsel to them. In Q, on the other hand, the story is essentially different, and the difference cannot be explained by compression (admittedly at this point severe): for Huan went off to the Wizard's Isle for the wolfcoat and batskin and *then* Beren and Lúthien rode North together *on horseback*, until they came to a point where they must put on the disguises. This is clearly the form of the story given in Synopsis IV for this part of the Lay (III. 273):

Lúthien heals Beren. They tell Huan of their doubts and debate and he goes off and brings the wolfham and batskin from the Wizard's Isle. Then he speaks for the last time.
They prepare to go to Angband.

But Q is later than Synopsis IV, for the idea had already emerged that Huan spoke thrice, the third time at his death.

It seems at least extremely probable, then, that Q§10 was written when the *Lay of Leithian* extended to about the point where the narrative turns to the events following the routing of Celegorm and Curufin and Huan's desertion of his master. Now against line 3031 is written the date November 1929, probably referring forwards (see the note to this line), and the next date, against line 3220 (the return of Beren and Lúthien to Doriath), is 25 September 1930. In the last week of September of that year my father composed the small amount remaining of Canto X, and Cantos XI and XII, taking the story from Beren's solitary departure on Curufin's horse to the enspelling of Carcharoth at the gates of Angband;

---

*Cf. also 'thirty feet' as the span of Thorndor's wings emended to 'thirty fathoms' in Q§8 (note 7), 'thirty fathoms' in the Lay (line 3618).

and this part had not, according to the analysis above, been composed when Q§10 was written.* These considerations make 1930 a virtually certain date for the composition of Q or at least the major part of it; and this fits well with my father's statement (see p. 11) that the 'Sketch' was written 'c. 1926–30', for we have seen that the original writing of S dates from 1926 (III. 3), and the interpolations and emendations to it, which were taken up into Q, would belong to the following years. The statement in Q that 'in the lay of Lúthien is all told how they came to Angband's gate' must be an anticipation of further composition of the Lay that my father was at this time premeditating.

From here on there are minor narrative divergences between Q and the Lay. Thus in the prose Morgoth 'fashioned' (rather than bred) Carcharoth (cf. Synopsis III 'fashions', Synopsis V 'fashions' > 'chooses', III. 293–4). The wolf's names Borosaith, Everhungry, and Anfauglin, Jaws of Thirst (an addition given in note 9), are not found in the Synopses or the Lay, but the latter, in the form Anfauglir, reappears in The Silmarillion (p. 180) with the same meaning.

In the prose Lúthien is praised for casting off her disguise and naming her own name, feigning 'that she was brought captive by the wolves of Thû', whereas in the Lay she claims at first to be Thuringwethil, sent to Morgoth by Thû as a messenger, and it seems that her bat-raiment falls from her at Morgoth's command (lines 3959–65), and that he divines who she is without her naming her name. In these features Q agrees rather with Synopsis III, where she does say who she is, and 'lets fall her bat-garb' (III. 305). It is not said in the Lay that 'she flung the magic robe in his face' (but in The Silmarillion p. 181 'she cast her cloak before his eyes'), and there is in the prose the notable detail of the Orcs' secret laughter at Morgoth's fall from his throne. In Q Beren leaps forth, casting aside the wolfcoat, when Morgoth falls, whereas in the Lay Lúthien must rouse him from his swoon. The ascription of the snapping of Curufin's knife to dwarvish 'treachery' agrees however with the verse ('by treacherous smiths of Nogrod made', line 4161) – this feature is not found in The Silmarillion, of course; while the arousing of the sleepers by the sound of its breaking agrees with the A-text of the Lay (lines 4163–6), not with the revised version of B, where the shard struck Morgoth's brow.

From the point where the Lay ends, with the biting off of Beren's hand by the Wolf, the Q account can be compared with the Synopses. The 'wanderings and despair' of Beren and Lúthien and 'their rescue by Huan' clearly associate Q with Synopsis V (III. 312), and the marginal addition (note 11) concerning their rescue by Thorndor, their flight over Gondolin, and their setting down in Brethil, belongs with the brief late outline given in III. 309. The structure of events in Doriath, with

---

*Cf. also the internal evidence given in the commentary on §9 that the Fall of Fingolfin in Canto XII is later than Q's account.

Boldog's raid preceding the embassy from Celegorm to Thingol, agrees with Synopsis IV (III.310) rather than with Synopsis V (III.311), where Thingol's host moving against Nargothrond meets Boldog; but Q agrees with Synopsis V in many details, such as the presence of Beleg and Mablung in the battle with Boldog, and Thingol's changed view of Beren.

At the end of this section the Land of the Dead that Live reaches, in the emendation given in note 15, its final placing in Ossiriand, and the name *Gwerth-i-Cuina* appears for the Dead that Live (later in Q as originally written, §14, the names are *Assariad* and *Cuilwarthien*, cf. *i·Cuilwarthon* of the *Lost Tales*). On the name *Geleidhian* for Broseliand/Beleriand, occurring in this emendation, see the commentary on §9.

On the statements at the end of this section concerning Lúthien's fate, and the 'long span of life and joy' granted to Beren and Lúthien by Mandos, see the commentary on §14.

A matter unconcerned with the story of Beren and Lúthien arises at the beginning of this section, where it is said that Bëor was slain in the Battle of Sudden Flame; in §9, on the other hand, 'Bëor lived till death with Felagund'. This can be interpreted to mean that he died in Felagund's service at the time that his son Barahir rescued Felagund, but such an explanation is forced (especially since in the later form of his legend his death was expressly of old age, and was a source of great wonder to the Elves who witnessed it, *The Silmarillion* p. 149). It seems more likely that there is here an inconsistency within Q, admittedly surprising since the two passages are not widely separated.

For the emendation of 'Second Battle' to 'Third Battle' (note 1) see the commentary on §9; and with the change of *Tinfang Warble* to *Tinfang Gelion* (note 12) cf. line 503 in the *Lay of Leithian*, where the same change was made.

## 11

In this section the *Quenta* becomes, both in structure and in much of its actual wording, the first draft of Chapter 20 ('Of the Fifth Battle') of *The Silmarillion*.

There appears now the unwise and premature demonstration of his gathering strength by Maidros, warning Morgoth of what was afoot among his enemies and allowing him time to send out his emissaries among the Men from the East – though this is less clear and explicit in Q as originally written than it becomes with the rewriting given in note 14, and even then the two phases of the war are not clearly distinguished. Some further development in this had still to come: in *The Silmarillion* the coming of the Easterlings into Beleriand is told at an earlier point (p. 157; cf. note 1 to this section in Q), and it is said that some of them, though not all, 'were already secretly under the dominion of Morgoth, and came at his call'; the entry of his 'spies and workers of treason' was made easier 'for the faithless Men of his secret allegiance were yet deep in the secrets of the sons of Fëanor' (p. 189). Though these agents of Morgoth are said in Q (as rewritten, note 14) to have gone especially to the sons of Ulfang, and though Bor and his sons are mentioned, there is no suggestion here of the good faith of the sons of Bor, who slew Ulfast and Ulwarth in the midst of the battle (*The Silmarillion* p. 193).

The Dwarves now play a part in these events, though only as furnishers of weapons; but in Q they are shown as calculating and indeed cynical ('we are friends of neither side – until it has won'), actuated solely by desire for gain. In *The Silmarillion* the Dwarves actually entered the war on Maedhros' side, and 'won renown': Azaghâl Lord of Belegost wounded Glaurung as the dragon crawled over him (p. 193). But at this time I do not think that my father would have conceived of the Dwarves of the mountains taking any active part in the wars of the Elves.

Whereas in S (as emended, §11 note 1) it is only said that 'Orodreth because of Felagund his brother will not come', there now appears in Q the small company out of Nargothrond who went to the war under the banners of Finweg (Fingon) 'and came never back, save one'; the leader is Flinding son of Fuilin, who comes out of the old *Tale of Turambar* and the *Lay of the Children of Húrin*, and who is thus given a fuller history before he fled from the Mines of Melko to meet Beleg in the Forest of Night. In the tale as in the poem (see III. 53) it is only said that he had been of the people of the Rodothlim (of Nargothrond) and that he was captured by Orcs. By later change in Q (note 7) he becomes Gwindor son of Guilin. But it is notable that although the wild onrush of the Gnomes of Nargothrond, that carried them even into Angband and made Morgoth tremble on his throne, was led by Flinding/Gwindor, his heroic fury had as yet no special cause: for the herald of Finweg/Fingon who was murdered on Dor-na-Fauglith in order to provoke the Elves of Hithlum to attack Morgoth's decoy force is not named.* The next and final stage was for the herald to become Gelmir of Nargothrond, Gwindor's brother, who had been captured in the Battle of Sudden Flame: it was indeed grief for the loss of Gelmir that had brought Gwindor out of Nargothrond against the will of Orodreth (*The Silmarillion* p. 188). Thus Flinding/Gwindor, devised long before for a different story, ends by being, in his earlier life, the involuntary cause of the loss of the great battle and the ruin of the kingdoms of the Noldor in Middle-earth.

The account of the behaviour of the people of Haleth in the rewritten passage given in note 7 shows my father in doubt: they made ready for

---

*The statement that 'Morgoth led forth one of the heralds . . . and slew him upon the plain' certainly does not mean, I think, that Morgoth himself came forth and did the deed; rather 'Morgoth' here stands for 'the servants of Morgoth, obeying his command'.

war, then they abode in the forest and few came forth 'because of the wounding of Beren in the wood' (cf. 'Men remembered that wound against the sons of Fëanor', Q§10; 'Men remembered at the Marching Forth', the *Lay of Leithian* line 3103). In the event, the former idea prevailed: 'In the forest of Brethil Halmir, lord of the People of Haleth, gathered his men, and they whetted their axes', and in the battle 'fell most of the Men of Brethil, and came never back to their woods' (*The Silmarillion* pp. 189, 192).

In this same rewritten passage the later story of the foundation of Gondolin *before* the Battle of Unnumbered Tears is present, with Turgon coming forth 'unlooked for' with a great host. It is perhaps strange that in the subsequent passage of rewriting (note 14) Maidros 'appointed a day, and sent word to Fingon *and Turgon*', and 'Fingon *and Turgon* and the Men of Hithlum . . . were gathered ready in the West upon the borders of the Thirsty Plain', which does not at all suggest that Turgon had just arrived, but seems rather to revert to the earlier story (in S, note 1, and in Q as originally written) according to which he was one of the leaders of the Western Elves from the beginning of the preparations for war ('all the hosts of Hithlum . . . were ready to his summons, and Finweg and Turgon and Huor and Húrin were their chiefs'). It seems that the emended narrative in Q represents an intermediate stage: Turgon now emerges from Gondolin already long since in existence, but he does not march up in the nick of time, on the day itself, as in the later story: he comes, certainly unexpected, but in time to take part in the final strategic preparations.

The challenge to Morgoth, summoning by silver trumpets his host to come forth, was afterwards abandoned, but Morgoth's decoying force, 'great and yet not too great', survived, as did Húrin's warning against premature attack. The uncontrollable bursting forth of the Elves of Hithlum and their allies is brought about in the same way as in the later story, even though there is still lacking in Q the fine point that the one slaughtered before their eyes was the brother of Gwindor of Nargothrond; and there is present in the Q narrative the initial success of the hosts of Hithlum, the near-miscarriage of Morgoth's plans, the sweeping of the banners of Finweg (Fingon) over the plain to the very walls of Angband. The final stages of the battle are less fully treated in Q, but all the essential structure is there; several features are indeed still absent, as the death of Fingon at the hands of Gothmog (but the flame from his helm as it was cloven is mentioned, a feature that goes back to the *Lay of the Children of Húrin*, and from which the words *Finweg (Fingon) fell in flame of swords* derive, see III. 103), the fall of the Men of Brethil in the rearguard (see above), the presence of the Dwarves of Belegost (with the death of Azaghâl and the wounding of the dragon), the fateful words between Huor and Turgon that were overheard by Maeglin (*The Silmarillion* p. 194).

Glómund's presence at the Battle of Unnumbered Tears was intro-

duced in a later addition to the text of S (§13, note 3) and is now
incorporated in the Q narrative; his earlier appearance at the Battle of
Sudden Flame enters with an addition to Q§9 (note 16), and is referred
to again here (note 17) – 'the second battle of the North', because the
Glorious Battle, Dagor Aglareb, which became the second battle, had
not yet been developed. But according to Q the dragon 'was not yet come
to his full growth' at the Battle of Unnumbered Tears; later, he was
already full grown at the Battle of Sudden Flame (*The Silmarillion*
p. 151), and his first, immature emergence from Angband was placed
still further back (*ibid*. pp. 116–17).

The Dragon-helm of Dor-lómin here reappears from the *Lay of the
Children of Húrin* (see III. 26, 126), where in the second version it is said
that it was the work of Telchar, and

Would that he [Húrin] had worn it    to ward his head
on that direst day    from death's handstroke!    (665–6)

But only now does the dragon-crest become the image of Glómund.
Afterwards the history of the helm was much enlarged: in the *Narn i Hîn
Húrin* (*Unfinished Tales* p. 75) it is told that Telchar (of Nogrod, not as
in Q of Belegost) made it for Azaghâl of Belegost, and that it was given by
him to Maedhros, by Maedhros to Fingon, and by Fingon to Hador,
whence it descended to Hador's grandson Húrin. In the *Narn* it is said
that Húrin never in fact wore it; and also that the people of Hithlum said
'Of more worth is the Dragon of Dorlómin than the gold-worm of
Angband!' – which originated in this passage of Q, 'We have a dragon of
more worth than theirs'. A pencilled direction against the beginning of
§12 in Q (note 1) postpones the introduction of the Helm to the point
where Morwen sends it to Thingol, as it is placed in *The Silmarillion*
(p. 199).

Some other minor features now enter, as Melian's counsel to restore
the Silmaril to the sons of Fëanor (*The Silmarillion* p. 189), and in
additions to the text the presence of Elves of the Falas among the Western
hosts at the great battle (note 14), and the especial hatred and fear felt by
Morgoth of the House of Fingolfin (note 23; *The Silmarillion* p. 196,
where however the reasons for it are their friendship with Ulmo and the
wounds that Fingolfin had given him – and Turgon, Fingolfin's son). In
emendations to Q (note 6) the name *Celegorm* begins a long uncertainty
between that form and *Celegorn*.

The mention of 'Dark-elves, *save out of Doriath*' marching to Maidros'
banners shows that my father still naturally used this term of Thingol's
people; cf. the Index to *The Silmarillion*, entry *Dark Elves*.

## 12

It is immediately apparent, from many actual repetitions of wording,
that when my father composed the Q version of the tale of Túrin

Turambar he had the 'Sketch' in front of him; while many of the phrases that occur in *The Silmarillion* version are first found here. There are also features in Q's narrative that derive from the *Lay of the Children of Húrin* but which were omitted in S. The statement in Q, repeated from S, that 'the fate of Túrin is told in the "Children of Húrin"' no doubt shows that my father had not yet given up all thought of completing that poem some day.

In this first of the two sections into which the tale of Túrin is here divided there are only minor points to be noticed. Q, though much fuller than S, is still expressly a synopsis, and the entire element of the Dragonhelm is omitted (see note 1 and the commentary on §11), together with the guiding of Túrin by the two old men and the return of one of them to Morwen: the guides (Halog and Mailgond in S) are here not named. Rían Huor's wife has already appeared in S at a later point (§16).

Airin, wife of Brodda and kinswoman of Morwen, re-enters from the old *Tale* (she is mentioned in S§13 but not named),* and the aid she gives to Morwen is secret, which perhaps suggests a movement towards the worsening of Brodda's character as tyrant and oppressor (see II. 127), though later in Q it is still told that Morwen entrusted her goods to him when she left her home (the text was subsequently altered here, §13 note 5). We meet here the expression 'the incoming Men', surviving in the term 'Incomers' used in the *Narn*, and also the element that the Easterlings were afraid of Morwen, whispering that she was a witch skilled in Elvish magic.

There has been virtually no further development in the story of Túrin in Doriath, the slaying of Orgof, and the outlaw band. Blodrin the traitor is now described as a Gnome, and by a later addition (note 5) a member of the House of Fëanor; in the Lay (as in S) it is not made clear who he was, beyond the fact that he was an Elf who had been turned to evil during his upbringing among the Dwarves (III. 52).

In the passage concerned with Taur-na-Fuin there is the new detail that the Orc-band that captured Túrin 'had delayed long in the lands plundering East among Men', which is found in *The Silmarillion* (p. 206): the Orcs 'had tarried on their road, hunting in the lands and fearing no pursuit as they came northward'. This feature clearly arose from a feeling that Beleg would never have caught up with the Orcs if they had returned swiftly to Angband, but in both S and Q they were moving in haste through Taur-na-Fuin, and in Q this is explained by 'the angry message of Morgoth'.

The addition concerning Beleg's sword (note 10) is the first indication that it was of a strange nature; the phrase 'made of iron that fell from heaven as a blazing star, and it would cut all earth-dolven iron' is found in

---

*In the *Tale* Airin was Morwen's friend (II.93); in S and Q she was Morwen's kinswoman; in *The Silmarillion* (p. 198) and the *Narn* (p. 69) she was Húrin's kinswoman.

*The Silmarillion* at a different point (p. 201), where the origin of the sword is more fully told.

## 13

There are several substantial developments in the latter part of the story of Túrin in Q. Finduilas' name *Failivrin* is now ascribed to Flinding (Gwindor); in the Lay occur the lines

> the frail Finduilas    that Failivrin,
> the glimmering sheen    on the glassy pools
> of Ivrin's lake    the Elves in love
> had named anew.    (III. 76, lines 2175–8)

In Nargothrond Túrin, as the Black Sword, is *Mormaglir*, not as in S *Mormakil* (cf. the *Tale of Turambar*, II. 84: 'Hence comes that name of Túrin's among the Gnomes, calling him Mormagli or Mormakil according to their speech'). The final form was *Mormegil*. It is now expressly stated that though rumour of the Black Sword of Nargothrond reached Thingol 'the name of Túrin was not heard'; but there is still no suggestion that Túrin deliberately concealed his identity.

The place where the Gnomes of Nargothrond were defeated is not said to be between the rivers Ginglith and Narog (*The Silmarillion* p. 212), but 'upon the Guarded Plain, north of Nargothrond', and as will be seen later the battlefield at this time was east of Narog, not in the triangle of land between it and Ginglith. The impression is given that the reproaches of Flinding (Gwindor) as he died were on account of Finduilas. There is indeed no suggestion here that Túrin's policy of open war was opposed in Nargothrond, nor that it was this policy that revealed Nargothrond to Morgoth; but since these elements were fully present in the *Tale of Turambar* (II. 83–4) their absence from Q must be set down to compression. There is also no mention at this point in Q of the bridge over the Narog (see S§13 notes 1 and 5), but it is referred to later in this section as having proved the undoing of the Elves of Nargothrond. Orodreth was slain at Nargothrond, and not as in *The Silmarillion* on the battlefield.

In an alteration to Q (note 9) a shift is implied in the motive of Túrin's slaying of Brodda. In the *Tale* Túrin struck Brodda's head off in explicit vengeance on 'the rich man who addeth the widow's little to his much' (II. 90); in the revised passage in Q (as afterwards in *The Silmarillion*, p. 215, and most clearly in the *Narn*, pp. 107–8) Túrin's action sprang in part from the fury and agony of his realisation that the dragon had cheated him.*

Whereas in S the Woodmen are placed 'east of Narog', in Q they are

---

*In the *Narn* it is not made clear that Túrin actually intended to kill Brodda when he hurled him across the table.

said to dwell 'in the green woods about the River Taiglin that enters the land of Doriath ere it joins with the great waters of Sirion' – these being the first occurrences of Taiglin and 'Doriath beyond Sirion' in the texts (though both are marked on the earliest 'Silmarillion' map, see pp. 222, 224). I noted in connection with the passage in S that it is strange that whereas in the *Tale* the Woodmen had a leader (Bethos) when Túrin joined them, as also in the later story, in S Túrin 'gathered a new people'. Now in Q the Woodmen have an identity, 'the remnant of the people of Haleth', Haleth being at this time the son of Hador and uncle of Húrin, and the 'Hadorian' and 'Halethian' houses one and the same, as already in §9; but still as in S Túrin at once becomes their ruler. Brandir the Lame, son of Handir son of Haleth, does indeed emerge here, replacing Tamar (son of Bethos the ruler) of the *Tale of Turambar*, who is still present in S, and it is said that Brandir had 'yielded the rule to Túrin at the choice of the woodfolk'; but in the later story it is an important element that Brandir remained the titular ruler until his death, though disregarded by Túrin.

Here is the first mention of Túrin's vain seeking for Finduilas when he came down from Hithlum, and the first account of Finduilas' fate; in the *Tale* and in S there is no suggestion of what became of her. Finduilas is 'the last of the race of Finrod' (later Finarfin) because Galadriel had not yet emerged.

The narrative of Q also advances to the later form in making Nienor accompany the expedition from Doriath in disguise (see II. 128); and the 'high place . . . covered with trees' of the *Tale* and the 'hill-top' of S now becomes 'the tree-clad Hill of Spies'. But in Q it was only Morwen who was set for safety on the Hill of Spies: there is no mention of what Nienor did until she was confronted by Glómund on the banks of Narog (not, as later, on the Hill). This is a movement away both from the *Tale* and from the later story, where Morwen and Nienor remained together until the dragon-fog arose; but towards the later story in that Nienor met the dragon alone (on the treatment of this in S see the commentary). We must suppose that at this stage in the development of the legend Nienor's presence was never revealed, either to her mother or to anyone else save the dragon; in the later story she was discovered at the passage of the Twilit Meres (*The Silmarillion* p. 217, *Narn* pp. 114–15). The 'Mablung-element' is still wholly absent; and it is to be noted that Morwen was taken back in safety to the Thousand Caves, whence she afterwards wandered away when she found that Nienor was gone. – The bridge over Narog seems to have been still standing after the sack (in *The Silmarillion* Glaurung broke it down, p. 214).

By emendation in Q (note 14) appears for the first time the name *Celebros*, translated 'Foam-silver', for Silver-bowl; but in Q (as in S) the falls are still in the Taiglin itself (see II. 132). Later, *Celebros* became the name of the tributary stream in which were the falls; and the falls were named *Dimrost*, the Rainy Stair.

In the story of the slaying of the dragon, the six (not as afterwards two) companions of Turambar still survive through S from the *Tale* (II. 106); though in Q they were not so much the only companions that Turambar could find but rather 'begged to come with him'. In the *Tale* the band of seven clambered up the far side of the ravine in the evening and stayed there all night; at dawn of the second day, when the dragon moved to cross, Turambar saw that he had now only three companions, and when they had to climb back down to the stream-bed to come up under Glórund's belly these three had not the courage to go up again. Turambar slew the dragon by daylight; Níniel went down to the ravine on the *second* evening, and threw herself over the falls at sunrise of the *third* day; and Turambar slew himself in the afternoon of that day. In S the only indication of time is that all six of Turambar's companions deserted him during the night spent clinging to the further lip of the ravine. In Q the six all deserted Turambar during the first night, as in S, but he spent the whole of the following day clinging to the cliff; Glómund moved to pass over the ravine on the *second* night (my father clearly wished to make the dragon-slaying take place in darkness, but achieved this at first by extending the time Turambar spent in the gorge). But Níniel went down and found him, and threw herself over the falls, on that same night. Thus in Q the story has moved closer to that of *The Silmarillion* and the *Narn*, and needed only the contraction of the time before the dragon crossed the ravine, so that all took place in a single night and the following morning. – It seems to be suggested in Q that Glómund in his death-throes hurled himself back on to the bank from which he was coming: he '*coiled back in anguish* . . . and came not into the woodmen's land'. If this is so Níniel must have crossed the ravine to reach Turambar. In the *Tale* (II. 107) it is explicit that 'almost had [the dragon] crossed the chasm when Gurtholfin pierced him, and now he cast himself upon its farther bank', as also in the later versions.

That Níniel was with child by Turambar is now stated in the text as written (in the *Tale* and in S this appears only in later additions).

In the *Tale* (II. 111) Turambar slew himself in the glade of Silver Bowl; it is not said in S or in Q where he died, though in both he was buried beside Silver Bowl. – At the very end appears in Q the name *Nen-Girith*, its first occurrence: 'Men changed the name of that place thereafter to Nen-Girith, the Shuddering Water.' In *The Silmarillion* (p. 220) it is said, in the passage describing the great fit of shuddering that came on Nienor at Dimrost, the falls of Celebros, that – on account of this – 'afterwards that place was called Nen Girith'; and in the *Narn* (p. 123) that 'after that day' it was called Nen Girith. These passages can be taken to mean that the falls of Celebros were renamed Nen Girith simply on account of Nienor's shivering when she first came there. But this is surely absurd; the event was, in itself and without aftermath, far too slight for a renaming – too slight, indeed for narrative mention or legendary recollection, if it had no aftermath: places are not renamed in legend because a person, however important, caught a chill there. Obviously the prophetic element is the whole point, and it goes back to the *Tale*, where before ever the name Nen Girith was devised Nienor 'not knowing why was filled with a dread and could not look upon the loveliness of that foaming water' (II. 101), and in the original story both Nienor and Turambar died in that very place (see II. 134–5). I think that the phrase in the *Narn*, 'after that day', must be interpreted to mean 'after that time', 'after the events which are now to be described had come to pass'. I noted in *Unfinished Tales* (p. 149, note 24):

> One might suppose that it was only when all was over, and Túrin and Nienor dead, that her shuddering fit was recalled and its meaning seen, and Dimrost renamed Nen Girith; but in the legend Nen Girith is used as the name throughout.

Almost certainly, the use of the name 'Nen Girith' in the later narratives *before* the account of the events that must have given rise to the name is to be explained in the same way as that proposed by my father for *Mablung*: concerning which he observed in a very late essay that when Mablung took the Silmaril from the belly of Carcharoth

> the hand [of Beren] and jewel seemed to have so great a weight that Mablung's own hand was dragged earthward and forced open, letting the other fall to the ground. It was said that Mablung's name ('with weighted hand') was prophetic; but it may have been a title derived from the episode *that afterwards became the one that the hero was chiefly remembered by in legend*.

I have no doubt that the story in Q shows the original idea: Nienor shivered with prophetic but unconscious fear when she came to the falls of Celebros; there both she and her brother died horrifyingly; and after their deaths the falls were renamed Nen Girith, the Shuddering Water, because the meaning was understood. 'Afterwards', 'After that day', this became the name of the falls; but in the legendary history, when all was well-known both to the historian and to his audience, the later name became generalised, like that of Mablung.

## 14

At the beginning of this section it is made clear that Mîm's presence in Nargothrond did not go back to the time of the dragon, since he 'had found the halls and treasure of Nargothrond unguarded'. In the *Lost Tales* my father doubtless saw no particular need to 'explain' Mîm; he was simply there, a feature of the narrative situation, like Andvari the Dwarf in the Norse Völsung legend. But in Q the first step is taken to relate him to the developing conception of the Dwarves of Middle-earth: they spread into Beleriand from the Blue Mountains after the Battle of

Unnumbered Tears. (Ultimately the need to 'explain' Mîm led to the conception of the Petty-dwarves.) But Q's statement that the Dwarves only now enter the tales of the ancient world seems at variance with earlier passages: with §9, where it is said that the Fëanorians made war on the Dwarves of Nogrod and Belegost, and with §11, concerning the furnishing of weapons by the Dwarves to the armies of the Union of Maidros.

Here Mîm has some companions, slain with him by the outlaws of Húrin's band, whom Húrin 'would have stayed'; in the *Tale of Turambar* (II. 113) Mîm was alone, and it was Úrin himself who gave him his death-blow. Whereas in the *Tale* Úrin's band – large enough to be called a host – brought the treasure of Nargothrond to the caves of Tinwelint in a mass of sacks and rough boxes (while in S there is no indication whatsoever of how the treasure came to Doriath, and the outlaws are not further mentioned after the slaying of Mîm), in Q Húrin's outlaws are as conveniently got rid of as they were conveniently come by – 'each one died or was slain in quarrels upon the road', deaths ascribed to Mîm's curse; and since Húrin now goes alone to Doriath and gets Thingol's help in the transportation of the treasure the outlaw-band seems to serve very little narrative purpose. The fight in the halls of Tinwelint between the woodland Elves and the outlaws, not mentioned in S, has now therefore been expunged (the emergence in Q of a new fight in the halls, between the Elves and the Dwarves, would demand its removal in any case, if Menegroth were not to appear a permanent shambles).

But the problem remained: how did the gold come to Doriath? It was an essential idea that Húrin, destroyed by what he had seen (or by what Morgoth allowed him to see) and tormented by bitterness and grief, should cast the treasure of Nargothrond at Thingol's feet in a gesture of supreme scorn of the craven and greedy king, as he conceived him to be; but the new story in Q is obviously unsatisfactory – it ruins the gesture, if Húrin must get the king himself to send for the gold with which he is *then* to be humiliated, and it is difficult to imagine the conversation between Húrin and Thingol when Húrin first appeared in Doriath, announcing that the treasure had become available.

However this may be, the gold comes to Doriath, and in all versions Húrin departs: but now in Q, to drown himself in the western sea, without ever finding Morwen again.

I have said in commenting on the corresponding section in S that I think it probable that my father had already decided to simplify the involved story in the *Tale of the Nauglafring* concerning the gold of Nargothrond. In Q, which is a fully articulated narrative, if brief, the absence of Ufedhin can be taken as a clear indication that he had been abandoned, and with him, necessarily, many of the complexities of the king's dealings with the Dwarves. The story has become, then, quite simple. Thingol desires the unwrought gold brought by Húrin to be worked; he sends for the greatest craftsmen on earth, the Dwarves of

Nogrod and Belegost; and they coming desire the treasure for themselves, the Silmaril also, and plot to gain it. The argument that they use –
that the treasure belonged in right to the Dwarves, since it was taken
from Mîm – reappears from the *Tale of the Nauglafring*, where it occurs
in a different context (II. 230: an argument used by Naugladur lord of
Nogrod to support his intention to attack Tinwelint).

The relative wealth or otherwise of Thingol has not been touched on in
Q, but his riches are recounted in the *Lay of the Children of Húrin* (see
III. 26) and in the *Lay of Leithian* (III. 160–1); and this is no doubt the
force of the word 'even' in 'Then the enchantment of the accursed dragon
gold began to fall *even* upon the king of Doriath.'

In S the king drives the Dwarves away without any payment; there is
no mention of any strife at this point, and one would think that even the
most severe compression could hardly have avoided mentioning it. But
in Q the narrative now takes a quite different turn. Thingol 'scanted his
promised reward', and this led to fighting in the Thousand Caves, with
many slain on both sides; and 'the Mound of Avarice', which in the *Tale
of the Nauglafring* covered the bodies of the slain Elves of Artanor after
the battle with the outlaws of Húrin's band, now covers those of the
Dwarves and Elves; the form of the Elvish name is changed from *Cûm
an-Idrisaith* (II. 223) to *Cûm-nan-Arasaith*.

As in S, the sack of Menegroth by the Dwarves is still treated in Q with
the utmost brevity, and central features of the story in the *Tale of the
Nauglafring* do not recur, nor ever would. But (in addition to the loss of
Ufedhin) it seems likely that the 'great host' of Orcs, paid and armed by
Naugladur of Nogrod (II. 230), would by now have been abandoned. Of
course the whole story arose in terms of, and continues to depend on, the
hostile view of the Dwarves which is so prominent in the early writings.

The much emended geographical passage that follows now in Q is best
understood in relation to the first 'Silmarillion' map, and I postpone
discussion of the rivers of Ossiriand and the Dwarf-road to Chapter IV,
pp. 230ff. It is sufficient to notice here that the courses of the six
tributary rivers of Gelion (here called Ascar,* before emendation to
*Flend* and then to *Gelion*, note 3) are drawn on that map in precisely
the same form as they have on that published in *The Silmarillion*, and the
first map names them in order of the original emendation to Q (note 4)
before that was itself changed: i.e., Ascar, Thalos, Duilwen, Loeglin,
Brilthor, Adurant.

It is now made explicit that it was Melian who warned Beren of the
approach of the Dwarves (see p. 62); and the removal of the Land of
the Dead that Live from 'the woods of Doriath and the Hunters' Wold,
west of Nargothrond', where it is still placed in S (§10), to Assariad

---

*It seems probable that the first two occurrences of *Ascar* in this section were mere slips,
for *Flend* (> *Gelion*). At the third occurrence the name is used, as it is on the map, for the
northernmost of the rivers coming down out of the Blue Mountains, afterwards renamed
*Rahlorion* (> *Rathloriel*).

(Ossiriand) in the East makes the interception of the Dwarves far simpler and more natural: the Stony Ford (which goes back to the *Tale of the Nauglafring* and is there called *Sarnathrod*) now lies on the river that bounds that very land. The geographical shift and development has made the whole organisation of the story here much easier.

Beren's people now at last become 'the Green Elves' (see p. 62); but the story of the ambush at the ford is passed over in Q as sketchily as it was in S: there is now no mention even of the taking of the Nauglafring (> Nauglamír) from the slain king. The story of the drowning of the treasure remains much the same as in S, but there are suggestions of wider implications in the wearing of the Nauglafring: that the Land of the Dead that Live became itself so fruitful and so fair because of the presence of Lúthien wearing the Silmaril. This passage is retained almost word for word in *The Silmarillion* (p. 235). It is clearly to be associated with a later passage, found both in Q (p. 152) and in *The Silmarillion* (p. 247), where the people dwelling at the Havens of Sirion after the fall of Gondolin would not surrender the Silmaril to the Fëanorians 'for it seemed to them that in the Silmaril lay the healing and the blessing that had come upon their houses and their ships'. But the Silmaril was cursed (and this may seem a sufficiently strange conception), and Melian warned Beren and Lúthien against it. In Q it is not said, as it is in S, that the Silmaril was kept secretly by Beren, merely that he and Lúthien 'retained' it. In both texts the fading of Lúthien follows immediately; but while Q again makes no actual connection (see p. 63) the very ordering of its sentences suggests that such a connection was there: 'the Land of the Dead that Live became like a vision of the land of the Gods . . . Yet Melian warned them ever of the curse . . . yet the Silmaril they retained. And in time the brief hour of the loveliness of the land of Rathlorion departed. For Lúthien faded as Mandos had spoken . . .'

The statements made in S§§10 and 14 on the fates of Beren and Lúthien have been discussed at some length (pp. 63–4). When we turn to Q, we find that in the earlier passage (§10, where the first death of Beren and Lúthien's pleading with Mandos is recounted), while there is mention of songs that say that Lúthien was borne living to Valinor by Thorndor, these are discounted, and 'it has long been said that Lúthien failed and faded swiftly and vanished from the earth', and thus came to Mandos: she had died, as Elves might die, of grief (cf. the old *Tale of Tinúviel*, II. 40). And the dispensation of Mandos exacted that 'Lúthien should become mortal even as her lover, *and should leave the earth once more in the manner of mortal women*'. This seems precise: it can surely only mean that Lúthien had become, not an Elf with a peculiar destiny, but a mortal woman. Her nature had changed.[*]

[*]The further judgement of Mandos in §10, that 'in recompense' he 'gave to Beren and Lúthien thereafter a long span of life and joy', seems at variance with what is implied here in Q. See III. 125.

Yet Q retains the conception in the present passage of Lúthien's fading – her second fading. I think it can now be seen why my father wrote an X against this sentence (note 12); and note also the marginal addition at this point: 'Yet it hath been sung that Lúthien *alone of Elves hath been numbered among our race,** and goeth whither we go to a fate beyond the world*' (cf. *The Silmarillion* p. 236: 'Beren Erchamion and Lúthien Tinúviel had died indeed, and gone where go the race of Men to a fate beyond the world').

Coming lastly to the story of Dior and the end of Doriath, it is now Celegorm, Curufin, and Cranthir who were slain, as in *The Silmarillion* (p. 236); and by a late addition to the text (note 14) Dior has sons, Eldûn and Elrûn, who were killed with their father. In *The Silmarillion* they were Eluréd and Elurín, who were left by the servants of Celegorm to starve in the forest.

## 15

In this version of the story of Eöl and Isfin it is told that Eöl 'was of gloomy mood, and had deserted the hosts ere the battle [of Unnumbered Tears]'. Nothing has been said before of how Eöl came to be dwelling in the terrible forest (and later his earlier history was to be wholly changed again: *The Silmarillion* p. 132).

The general description of the plain and city of Gondolin in Q is obviously closely based on S, and shows little more than stylistic development. But Thorndor is here said to have dwelt on Thangorodrim before he moved his eyries to the Encircling Mountains (see p. 66); and there is an interesting reference to the original intention of the people of Gondolin to go to war again when the time was ripe. The most important alteration here is the pencilled addition (note 5), taken up into the Q II text, telling that Turgon after the Battle of Unnumbered Tears sent at times Elves down Sirion to the sea, where they built a small haven and set sail, in vain, for Valinor. This is the forerunner of the passage in *The Silmarillion* (p. 159), where however the building of ships by the Gondolindrim and the setting sail for Valinor 'to ask for pardon and aid of the Valar' is placed after the Dagor Bragollach and the breaking of the Leaguer of Angband (for the foundation of Gondolin took place centuries before the Battle of Unnumbered Tears). But in *The Silmarillion* (p. 196) there was also a further attempt by Turgon to reach Valinor in the time after the great battle, when Círdan of the Falas built for him seven ships, of which the only survivor was Voronwë. The origin of this idea of the fruitless voyages of the Gondolindrim is to be found in the tale of *The Fall of Gondolin* (II. 162), where Ulmo by the mouth of Tuor counselled Turgon to make such voyages, and Turgon replied that he had done so 'for years untold', and would do so now no more.

*'our race': the *Quenta*, according to its title (pp. 77-8), was 'drawn from the Book of Lost Tales which Eriol of Leithien wrote'.

In the replacement text Q II (pp. 138–40), where the old story of the foundation of Gondolin is still present, there is very little to record in narrative development, except that the sending of Elves to Sirion's mouth and the sailing of ships from a secret haven is now incorporated in the text; and it is said that as the years drew on these sailings ceased and the haven was abandoned. It is now explained why it was that Thorndor (> Thorondor) moved his eyries from Thangorodrim.

The passage of time is left entirely vague in these narratives. There is no indication of how many years elapsed between the Battle of Unnumbered Tears or its immediate aftermath – when in the first years of Gondolin Turgon was trying to get his messages to Valinor – and the coming of Tuor, by which time the haven at Sirion's mouth was desolate, none could enter Gondolin from the outside world, and neither the king nor the most part of his people wished any more for return to Valinor (p. 142). But the change in feeling in Gondolin – and all the mighty works of levelling and tunnelling – must imply a long lapse of time ('as the years drew on', pp. 137, 140). This conception goes back to the original *Fall of Gondolin* (see my remarks, II. 208); but at that time Tuor had no associations that would tie him into a chronological framework. Already in S (§16), however, Huor, brother of Húrin, had become Tuor's father, and Huor was slain in the Battle of Unnumbered Tears. Clearly there was a major narrative-chronological difficulty lurking here, and it was not long before my father moved the founding of Gondolin (and with it that of Nargothrond) to a far earlier point in the history. Unhappily, as I have mentioned before (II. 208, footnote), the *Quenta* account was the last that my father ever wrote of the story of Gondolin from Tuor's coming to its destruction; and therefore, though the revised chronological structure is perfectly clear, the latest actual formed narrative retains the old story of the founding of Gondolin after the Battle of Unnumbered Tears. Against the words in the Q II replacement 'For Turgon deemed, *when first they came into that vale after the dreadful battle*' my father wrote an X (note 3); but in all the years that followed he never turned to it again.*

The name *Eryd-Lómin* occurs for the first time† in the Q II replacement text, but its reference is to the Mountains of Shadow fencing Hithlum, and it was later emended (note 1) to *Eredwethion* (*Ered Wethrin* in *The Silmarillion*). The name *Eryd-Lómin* did at this time mean 'Shadowy Mountains', just as *Dor-lómin* meant 'Land of Shadows' (see I. 112, and I. 255 entry *Hisilómë*). Subsequently *Eryd-Lómin*, *Ered*

---

*The passage in *The Silmarillion* (p. 240) is an editorial attempt to use the old narrative within the later structure.

†For the first time in the narrative texts. The actual first occurrence is probably in the caption to my father's painting of Tol Sirion (*Pictures by J. R. R. Tolkien* no. 36) of July 1928, which though it cannot be made out in the reproduction reads: 'The Vale of Sirion, looking upon Dor-na-Fauglith, with Eryd Lómin (the Shadowy Mountains) on the left and the eaves of Taur-na-Fuin on the right.'

*Lómin* was changed both in meaning ('Shadowy Mountains' to 'Echoing Mountains', with *lóm* 'echo', as also in *Dor-lómin* 'Land of Echoes') and in application, becoming the name of the coastal range to the west of Hithlum.

## 16

At the beginning of this section we find the first beginnings of the later story of the coming of Isfin and Meglin (Aredhel and Maeglin) to Gondolin, rather than (as still in S) the sending of Meglin by his mother; Eöl was lost in Taur-na-Fuin, and his wife and son came to Gondolin in his absence. There was much further development to come (the story of Maeglin in *The Silmarillion* is one of the latest elements in the book). In the rewritten passage given in note 3 the birth of Tuor 'in the wild' appears (see p. 67); the implication is no doubt that as in *The Silmarillion* (p. 198) and with more detail in the 'later *Tuor*' (*Unfinished Tales* p. 17) he was born in the wilds of Hithlum, and that it was after his birth that Rían went east to the Hill of Slain (in the rough rewriting of the passage in Q I now first given an Elvish name, *Amon Dengin*). But it is odd that in the rewriting Tuor's servitude among 'the faithless Men', found in S and in Q as first written, is excluded.

In the account of Tuor's flight from Hithlum the name of the Rainbow Cleft as originally written was *Cris-Ilfing* (in the tale of *The Fall of Gondolin* it was *Cris Ilbranteloth* or *Glorfalc*), emended to *Kirith Helvin* (*Cirith Ninniach* in *The Silmarillion*).

Tuor's journey remains unchanged. It was already said in S that Bronweg 'had once been in Gondolin'; now it is added that he had escaped from Angband, and had reached Sirion after long wanderings in the East. That he had been in Angband appears in fact already in the *Lay of the Fall of Gondolin* (III. 148), and is implied in the *Tale* (II. 156–7). The story of his lone survival from the last of the ships sent out on Turgon's orders had not yet arisen; and his escape from Angband makes him a rather obvious parallel to Flinding (Gwindor), or at least points a general likeness between the stories of Túrin and Tuor at this point. In each case a Man is guided by an Elf escaped from Angband to the hidden city of which the Elf was a citizen in the past. – The visitation of Ulmo to Tuor 'as he stood in the long grass at evening' in the Land of Willows goes back to the *Tale*, where he stood 'knee-deep in the grass' (II. 155). This was an essential element never abandoned; see II. 205. The song of Tuor that he made for his son Eärendel is extant, and is given in Appendix 2 to this chapter (p. 213).

Ulmo's instructions to Tuor in Q remain the same as in S; but in the Q II replacement there are important differences. Here, the great war between Gondolin and Angband foreseen by Ulmo is given a larger scope, and its succesful outcome made to seem more plausible: Tuor's errand to Hithlum, where he was to draw the ('evil' and 'faithless') Men of Hithlum (a land full of Morgoth's spies) into alliance with the Elves, a task it would seem of the utmost hopelessness, is now abandoned, and Tuor is to journey into the East and rouse the new nations of Men; the feud with the Fëanorians is to be healed. But in the contrary case, Ulmo no longer makes any promise to aid the people of Gondolin in the building of a fleet. His foreknowledge of the approaching doom of Gondolin is made progressively less precise: in S he knows that it will come through Meglin in seven (> twelve) years, in Q I that it will come in twelve years, but without mention of Meglin, in Q II only that it will come before many years are passed, if nothing is done.

In the story of Meglin's treachery in Q it is expressly stated (as it is not in S, though it is almost certainly implied) that he revealed the actual situation of Gondolin, of which Morgoth was until then ignorant.

There are strong suggestions in this compressed account that Gondolin's rich heraldry of houses and emblems was only in abeyance, not abandoned. The seven names of Gondolin are referred to, though not given, and Ecthelion of the Fountain and Glorfindel of the House of the Golden Flower are named. Indeed so many old features reappear – the Gates of Summer, the 'death of Rog without the walls'* – that it does not need the reference in the text to *The Fall of Gondolin* to show that my father had the *Tale* very fully in mind. In the reference to the 'devising' (rather than 'breeding') of new dragons by Morgoth for the assault on the city there is even a suggestion of the (apparently) inanimate constructions of the *Tale* (see II.213).

The relation between the present short version of the escape of the fugitives and the ambush in Cristhorn (> Kirith-thoronath), which is effectively that in *The Silmarillion* (p. 243), and that in the *Tale* has been discussed in II.213–14. The absence from *The Silmarillion* of the fugitives who went to the Way of Escape and were there destroyed by the dragon lying in wait, an element present in S and Q, is due to editorial excision, based on evidence in a much later text that the old entrance to Gondolin had been blocked up. That text is the basis for the passage in *The Silmarillion* (p. 228) where Húrin after his release from Thangorodrim came to the feet of the Encircling Mountains:

> he looked about him with little hope, standing at the foot of a great fall of stones beneath a sheer rock-wall; and he knew not that this was all that was now left to see of the old Way of Escape: the Dry River was blocked, and the arched gate was buried.

The sentence in *The Silmarillion* p. 240 'Therefore in that time the very entrance to the hidden door in the Encircling Mountains was caused to be blocked up' was an editorial addition.

In Q reappears from the *Tale* the sojourn of the survivors of Gondolin

---

*For the absence of Rog from the passage in *The Silmarillion* (p. 242) see II.211, second footnote.

in the Land of Willows, and the return of the 'sea-longing' to Tuor, leading to the departure from Nan-Tathrin down Sirion to the Sea.

Lastly may be noticed the description of Idril Celebrindal in Q II (p. 148) – tall, 'well nigh of warrior's stature', with golden hair: the prototype of Galadriel (see especially the description of her in *Unfinished Tales* pp. 229–30).

## 17

In the original Q text in this section the structure of S is closely followed, and in many respects the story is still unchanged where change was very soon to take place.

All trace of Ulmo's urging Eärendel to undertake the voyage to Valinor has disappeared (see S §17 note 3); but it is still Ulmo's 'grievous words' to the Valar that lead to the coming forth of the Sons of the Valar against Morgoth, and still Eärendel 'came too late to bring messages to the Elves, for the Elves had gone' (cf. Q§6: 'he came too late'). There now appears, on the other hand, Eärendel's *wish* to bring 'a message to the Gods and Elves of the West, that should move their hearts to pity on the world', even though, when he came, there were none in Kôr to whom to deliver it. But the ultimate story is noted on the text in pencil (note 1).

In the account of the host that came from Valinor Fionwë is still the son of Tulkas (see p. 68); but now none of the Teleri leave Valinor, while on the other hand there is mention of the Gnomes who had not left Valinor at the time of the Rebellion – cf. the earlier passage in Q (§5): 'Some remained behind . . . It was long ere they came back into this tale of the wars and wanderings of their people.'

Bronweg is still present as in S living alone at Sirion's mouth after the attack by the Fëanorians, and he still sails with Eärendel on the second voyage of Wingelot that brought them to Kôr. Eärendel still at this point in the story builds the Tower of Seabirds; his ship is raised, as in S, on the wings of birds, as he searches for Elwing from the sky, whence he is hunted by the Moon and wanders over the earth as a fugitive star. Elwing still casts the Silmaril into the sea and leaps after it, taking the form of a seabird to seek Eärendel 'about all the shores of the world'. Minor developments are the dissension among the Fëanorians, so that some stood aside and others aided Elwing; the deaths of Damrod and Díriel (see p. 69); the explanation of Maidros' pity for the child Elrond ('for his heart was sick and weary with the burden of the dreadful oath'); and the description of Wingelot. The name of Tuor's ship *Eärámë* is translated 'Eagle's Pinion' (the old explanation of the name, when it was Eärendel's ship), not 'Sea-wing' (see p. 69). The passage in S concerning the choice of Elrond Halfelven is here omitted, but the matter reappears in §18.

With this section the rewriting of Q (as 'Q II') becomes continuous to the end of the work, and the original text ('Q I') in fact gives out before the end. Since substantial stretches of Q I remain unchanged in Q II, I do not suppose that much time elapsed between them; but certain major new strokes are introduced into the legend in the rewriting.

These major developments in the present section are, first, that Ulmo's words to the Valar did *not* achieve the war against Morgoth ('Manwë moved not'); second, that Elwing, borne up as a seabird, *bore the Silmaril on her breast*, and came to Eärendel, returning from his first voyage in Wingelot: so that the Silmaril of Beren was not lost, but became the Evening Star; and third, that Eärendel, voyaging to Valinor *with Elwing*, came before the Valar, and it was his 'embassy of the two kindreds' that led to the assault on Morgoth.*

But there are also many changes of a less structural character in Q II, as: Eärendel's earlier voyages about the shores of the Outer Lands before he built Wingelot; his warning dreams to return in haste to the Mouths of Sirion, which in the event he never came back to, being intercepted by the coming of Elwing as a seabird and her tidings of what had happened there in his absence— hence the disappearance of Bronweg from the story; the healing power of the Silmaril on the people of Sirion (see p. 190); the great light of the Silmaril as Wingelot approached Valinor, and the suggestion that it was the power of the jewel that brought the ship through the enchantments and the shadows; Eärendel's refusal to allow any of those that travelled with him to come with him into Valinor; the new explanation of the desertion of Tûn upon Kôr (for the story still endured that the city of the Elves was empty of its inhabitants when Eärendel came there); the greeting of Eärendel by Fionwë (now again the son of Manwë) as the Morning and Evening Star; the manning by the Teleri of the ships that bore the hosts of the West; and the sighting of the Silmaril in the sky by Maidros and Maglor and the people of the Outer Lands.

By subsequent emendation to Q II some further elements enter. To Tuor is ascribed a fate (note 3) hardly less astonishing than that of his cousin Túrin Turambar. Elrond's brother Elros appears (notes 4 and 9); and Maglor takes over Maidros' rôle as their saviour, and as the less ruthless and single-minded of the two brothers (note 10; see the commentary on §18). The addition in note 19 stating that the leader of the Gnomes who had never departed from Valinor was Ingwiel son of Ingwë is at first sight surprising: one would expect Finrod (> Finarfin), as in *The Silmarillion* (p. 251). I think however that this addition was imperfectly accommodated to the text: the meaning intended was that Ingwiel was the chief of the Quendi (the Light-elves, the Vanyar) among whom the Gnomes of Valinor marched.† In a revision to Q§2 (note 6) the

---

*The first appearance of this central idea is in a hasty pencilled note to Q I (note 1): 'Make *Eärendel* move the Gods.'

†In the final version of this passage my father noticed the (apparent) error, and changed *Ingwiel son of Ingwë* to *Finarfin son of Finwë* (hence the reading in *The Silmarillion*). The result is that whereas in Q II only the leader of the First Kindred is named, Ingwiel, in the final version only the leader of the Noldor of Valinor is named, Finarfin; but the one should not, I think, have replaced the other – rather both should have been named.

original text, saying that Ingwë never came back into the Outer Lands 'until these tales were near their end', was changed to a statement that he never returned. Ingwiel replaces Ingil son of Inwë of the *Lost Tales*, who built Ingil's Tower in Tol Eressëa (I. 16) after his return from the Great Lands.

As Q II was first written

> Eärendel was their guide [i.e. of the fleet of the hosts of Valinor]; but the Gods would not suffer him to return again,* and he built him a white tower upon the confines of the outer world in the Northern regions of the Sundering Seas, and there all the sea-birds of the earth at times repaired.

The Tower of Seabirds thus survives in the same place in the narrative as in S and Q, where Eärendel builds the tower after his fruitless visit to Kôr. At the end of this section in S Eärendel

> sails by the aid of [the seabirds'] wings even over the airs in search of Elwing, but is scorched by the Sun, and hunted from the sky by the Moon, and for a long while he wanders the sky as a fugitive star.

Virtually the same is said at the end of the section in Q I. In Q II, however, as first written, Elwing was with Eärendel at this time,† in the form of a bird, and it was she who devised wings for his ship, so that 'it was lifted even into the oceans of the air'.

In S and Q I Eärendel does not yet bear a Silmaril when he wanders the sky 'as a fugitive star' (for the Silmaril of Beren is drowned with the Nauglafring, and the others are still in the Iron Crown of Morgoth); whereas in Q II it is at this time that the Silmaril appears in the sky and gives hope to the people of the Outer Lands.

With the revision to Q II given in note 20 enters the idea that it was the Gods themselves who set Eärendel and his ship in the sky. It is now Elwing who builds the Tower of Seabirds, devising wings for herself in order to try to reach him, in vain; *and they are sundered till the end of the world*. This no doubt goes with the revision to Q II given in note 14: 'And he bade farewell to all whom he loved upon the last shore, and was taken from them for ever.'

In *The Silmarillion* the element of a small ship's company remains: the three mariners Falathar, Erellont, and Aerandir (p. 248). These, and Elwing, Eärendil refused to allow to set foot on the shore of Aman; but Elwing leapt into the sea and ran to him, saying: 'Then would our paths be sundered for ever.' There Eärendil and Elwing 'bade farewell to the companions of their voyage, and were taken from them for ever'; but

---

*Cf. the letter of 1967 cited in II.265: '*Eärendil*, being in part descended from Men, was not allowed to set foot on Earth again.'

†It is not actually said in Q II that Elwing returned to Eärendel after being bidden by him to remain behind when he landed on 'the immortal shores' and went to Kôr; but it is evident that she did, from her having devised wings for his ship.

Elwing did not even so accompany Eärendil to Tirion. She sojourned
among the Teleri of Alqualondë, and Eärendil came to her there after he
had 'delivered the errand of the Two Kindreds' before the Valar; and
they went then together to Valmar and heard Manwë's decree, and the
choice of fate that was given to them and to their children,

A curious point arises in the account in Q II of the voyage of Eärendel
and Elwing that brought them to the coast of Valinor. Whereas in Q I it
is said that Eärendel 'found again the Lonely Isle, and the Shadowy
Seas', in Q II 'they came into the Shadowy Seas *and passed their
shadows*; and they looked upon the Lonely Isle . . .' This suggests that
the Shadowy Seas had become a region of the Great Sea lying to the east
of Tol Eressëa; and the same idea seems to be present in §6 both in S and
in Q, for it is said there that at the Hiding of Valinor 'the Magic Isles were
. . . strung across the confines of the Shadowy Seas, *before the Lonely Isle
is reached* sailing West'. Quite different is the account in the *Lost Tales*,
where '*beyond Tol Eressëa* [lying west of the Magic Isles] is the misty
wall and those great sea glooms beneath which lie the Shadowy Seas'
(I. 125); and the Shadowy Seas extend to the coasts of the western land
(I. 68). Conceivably, this development is related to the changed position
of Tol Eressëa – anchored in the Bay of Faërie within far sight of the
Mountains of Valinor, and not as in the *Lost Tales* in mid-Ocean: a
change that entered the geography in S§3.

In emendations to Q II the Magic Isles become the Enchanted Isles
(note 11; see II. 324–5) and the Bay of Faërie becomes the Bay of Elvenhome (note 12); also the name *Eärámë* of Tuor's ship becomes *Eärrámë*,
with the later interpretation 'Sea-wing' (note 2).

# 18

There are several interesting developments in the story of the Last
Battle and its aftermath as told in the original Q I text of this section. The
very brief account in S is here greatly expanded, and much of the final
version appears, if still with many differences (notably the absence of
Eärendel). That Morgoth had been bound long before by Tulkas in the
chain Angainor now re-emerges from the *Lost Tales* (this feature is
absent in Q§2; see pp. 71, 168).

The passage describing the rending of Beleriand survives almost
unchanged in *The Silmarillion* (p. 252), which in fact adds nothing else.
There is a notable statement (retained in Q II) that

Men fled away, such as perished not in the ruin of those days, and long
was it ere they came back over the mountains to where Beleriand once
had been, and not till the tale of those days had faded to an echo seldom
heard.

I do not know certainly what this refers to (see below, p. 200). Unhappily the evidence for the development of the conception of the

drowning of Beleriand is extremely scanty. Later, it was only a small region (Lindon) that remained above the sea west of the Blue Mountains; but this need not by any means yet have been the case. It is also said in Q (again retained in Q II) that

> there was a mighty building of ships on the shores of the Western Sea, and most upon the great isles, which in the disruption of the Northern world were fashioned of old Beleriand.

Of the size and number of these 'great isles' we are not told. On one of my father's sketchmaps made for *The Lord of the Rings* there is the island of Himling, i.e. the summit of the Hill of Himring, and also Tol Fuin, i.e. the highest part of Taur-na-Fuin (see *Unfinished Tales* pp. 13–14); and in *The Silmarillion* (p. 230) it is said that the stone of the Children of Húrin and the grave of Morwen above Cabed Naeramarth stands on Tol Morwen 'alone in the water beyond the new coasts that were made in the days of the wrath of the Valar'. But it seems obvious that my father was at this time imagining far larger islands than these, since it was on them that the great fleets were built at the end of the War of Wrath. Lúthien (> Leithien) as the land from which the Elves set sail, named in S §18 and explained as 'Britain or England', is not named in Q; but the words that follow in S: 'Thence they ever still from time to time set sail leaving the world ere they fade', are clearly reflected in Q:

> Yet not all returned, and some lingered many an age in the West and North, and especially in the Western Isles. Yet ever as the ages drew on and the Elf-folk faded on the Earth, they would still set sail at eve from our Western shores; as still they do, when now there linger few anywhere of the lonely companies.

The relation between these passages strongly suggests that the 'Western Isles' were the British Isles,* and that England still had a place in the actual mythological geography, as is explicitly so in S. In this connection the opening of *Ælfwine of England*, in the final text *Ælfwine II* (II. 312–13), is interesting:

> There was a land called England, and it was an island of the West, and before it was broken in the warfare of the Gods it was westernmost of all the Northern lands, and looked upon the Great Sea that Men of old called Garsecg; but that part that was broken was called Ireland and many names besides, and its dwellers come not into these tales.
>
> All that land the Elves named Lúthien and do so yet. In Lúthien alone dwelt still the most part of the Fading Companies, the Holy Fairies that have not yet sailed away from the world, beyond the

---

*This may seem to be rendered less likely by the form of the passage in Q II, where the first sentence is expanded: 'and especially in the western isles *and the lands of Leithien*'. But I do not think that this phrase need be taken too precisely, and believe that the equation holds.

horizon of Men's knowledge, to the Lonely Island, or even to the Hill of Tûn upon the Bay of Faëry that washes the western shores of the kingdom of the Gods.

It is possible, as I suggested (II. 323–4), that this passage refers to the cataclysm, and its aftermath, that is otherwise first mentioned in S §18. *Ælfwine II* cannot be dated, but *Ælfwine I* on which it was based was probably written in 1920 or not much later. It is also conceivable, if no more, that the meaning of the words in Q, that it was long before Men came back over the mountains to where Beleriand once had been, refers to the bloody invasions of England in later days described in *Ælfwine II*; for there is very little in that text that cannot be readily accommodated to the present passage in S and Q, with the picture of the fading Elves of Lúthien 'leaving our Western shores'.* But a serious difficulty with this idea lies in the coming of Men 'over the mountains' to where Beleriand once had been.

Certainly the most remarkable, even startling, feature of the aftermath of the Last Battle in Q (I) is the statement that when Fionwë marched through the lands summoning the Gnomes and the Dark-elves to leave the Outer Lands, the Men of the Houses of Hador and Bëor were 'suffered to depart, if they would'. But only Elrond was left; and of his choice, as Half-elven, the same is told as in S §17. The implications of this passage are puzzling. It is obvious that 'the race of Hador and Bëor' means those directly descended from Hador and Bëor; afterwards the conception of these Houses became much enlarged – they became clans. But since of the direct descendants only Elrond was left, what does this permission mean? Is it a (very curious) way of offering the choice of departure to the Half-elven, if he (they) wished? – because the Half-elven had only come into existence in the Houses of Hador and Bëor. But this seems too legalistic and contorted to be at all probable. Then does it imply that, if there had in fact been other descendants – if, for example, Gundor son of Hador had had children – they would have been permitted to depart? And what then? Would they have ended their days as mortal Men on Tol Eressëa? The permission seems very obscure on either interpretation; and it was removed from Q II. Nonetheless it represents, as I think, the first germ of the story of the departure of the survivors of the Elf-friends to Númenor.

---

*Two small likenesses may be noticed: in *Ælfwine II* the ships of the Elves weigh anchor from the western haven 'at eve' (II. 315), as in Q; and with 'the lonely companies' of Q cf. 'the Fading Companies' of *Ælfwine II* in the passage cited above.

A further attractive deduction, that this was the origin of the haven of *Belerion* in *Ælfwine of England*, the western harbour 'whence the Elves at times set sail' (a survival of the old name *Beleriand* among the Men of later days when its original reference was forgotten, and 'the tale of those days had faded to an echo seldom heard'), cannot be sustained: for *Ælfwine II* was certainly written long before the earliest occurrences of *Beleriand* (rather than *Broseliand*).

The story of the fate of the Silmarils in Q I advances on S, and here reaches an interesting transitional stage between S and Q II, where the final resolution is achieved. Maidros remains as in S the less fiercely resolute of the two surviving sons of Fëanor in the fulfilment of the oath: in S it is Maglor alone who steals a Silmaril from Fionwë's keeping, and in Q I it is Maidros who is 'minded to submit', but is argued down by Maglor. In Q II the arguments remain, but the parts of Maidros and Maglor are reversed, just as in §17 (by later emendation to Q II, note 10) Maglor becomes the one who saved Elrond and Elros. In Q I both brothers go to steal the Silmarils from Fionwë, as in the final version of the legend; but, as in S, only Maglor carries his away – for in the new story Maidros is captured. Yet, whereas as in S only one of the two remaining Silmarils is consigned to the deep places by the act of one of the brothers (Maglor), and the other is retained by Fionwë and ultimately becomes Eärendel's star – Maidros playing, so far as can be seen, no further part in its fate, in Q I the burning of the unrighteous hand, and the realisation that the right of the sons of Fëanor to the Silmarils is now void, becomes that of Maidros; and, a prisoner of Fionwë, he slays himself, casting the Silmaril on the ground (and though the text of Q I does not go so far as this, the logic of the narrative must lead to the giving of this Silmaril to Eärendel, as in S). The emended version in S (notes 6 and 7), that Maglor casts his Silmaril into a fiery pit and thereafter wanders singing in sorrow by the sea (rather than that he casts himself also into the pit), is taken up into Q I.

In Q II the story has shifted again, to the final harmonious and symmetrical structure: the Silmaril of Beren is not lost, and becomes the star of Eärendel: both Maglor and Maidros take a Silmaril from the camp of Fionwë, and both cast them down into inaccessible places. Maidros still takes his own life, but does so by casting himself into the fiery pit – and this is a return to the original story of Maglor told in S. Maglor now casts his Silmaril into the sea – and thus the Silmarils of earth, sea, and sky are retained, but they are different Silmarils; for in the earlier versions it was one of those from the Iron Crown of Morgoth that became the Evening Star.

This extraordinarily complex but highly characteristic narrative evolution can perhaps be shown more clearly in a table:

| S | Q I | Q II |
|---|---|---|
| The Silmaril of Beren is cast into the sea by Elwing and lost | As in S | The Silmaril of Beren is brought by Elwing to Eärendel on Wingelot; with it he goes to Valinor |
| — | *Maidros* is minded to submit, but *Maglor* argues against him | *Maglor* is minded to submit, but *Maidros* argues against him |

| S | Q I | Q II |
|---|-----|------|
| *Maglor* alone steals a Silmaril from Fionwë, and escapes | *Maidros* and *Maglor* together steal both Silmarils from Fionwë, but *Maidros* is captured | As in Q I, but both *Maidros* and *Maglor* are permitted to depart bearing the Silmarils |
| *Maglor* knows from the pain of the Silmaril that he no longer has a right to it | *Maidros* knows from the pain of the Silmaril that he no longer has a right to it | As in Q I |
| *Maglor* casts himself and the Silmaril into a fiery pit<br>> He casts the Silmaril into a pit and wanders by the shores | *Maidros* casts his Silmaril on the ground and takes his life<br><br>*Maglor* casts his Silmaril into a fiery pit and wanders by the shores | *Maidros* casts himself and his Silmaril into a fiery pit<br><br>*Maglor* casts his Silmaril into the sea and wanders by the shores |
| *Maidros'* Silmaril is adjudged by the Gods to Eärendel | [As in S, though this point not reached in Q I] | The Silmaril of Beren, never lost, is retained by Eärendel |

We find still in both versions of Q, as in S, the statement that some of the returning Elves went beyond Tol Eressëa and dwelt in Valinor ('as all were free to do who willed', Q II) – and it is made clear in the Q texts that these included some of the exiled Noldoli, 'admitted to the love of Manwë and the pardon of the Gods'. Also retained in Q I (but not in Q II) is the statement that Tûn remained deserted, again without explanation given (see p. 72). But whereas in S Tol Eressëa was repeopled by 'the Gnomes and many of the Ilkorins and Teleri and Qendi', in the Q-texts Teleri and Quendi are not mentioned here, only Gnomes and Dark-elves ('especially such as had once belonged to Doriath', Q I).

In a hasty pencilled note to Q I (§17 note 1) there is a reference to some Men of Hithlum being repentant, and to the fulfilment of Ulmo's foretelling (i.e. 'without Men the Elves shall not prevail against the Orcs and Balrogs', §16): both by the valour of the Men of Hithlum, and by the embassy of Eärendel to the Valar. This is taken up into Q II in the present section, with the addition that many Men new come out of the East fought against Morgoth; but further revision (notes 2 and 3) altered this to say that most Men and especially these newcomers from the East fought on the side of the Enemy, and also that in addition to the repentant Men of Hithlum 'all that were left of the three Houses of the Fathers of Men fought for Fionwë'. This latter phrase indicates both that the house of Hador had now been divided (see the commentary on §9), and also that the houses of the Elf-friends are now enlarged, so that they are not restricted to those descendants of the Fathers who have been mentioned in the narrative. The strange permission of Fionwë to the Men of the houses of Hador and Bëor to depart into the West has disappeared in Q II.

Other developments in Q II are the failure of Morgoth to come forth at the end; the coming of the winged dragons, of which the greatest was Ancalagon the black; the slaying of Ancalagon by Eärendel descending out of the skies with countless birds about him; and the destruction of Thangorodrim by the fall of Ancalagon.

## 19

In this concluding section the narrative, almost entirely now in the Q II text only, returns again to Eärendel; and, very curiously, the scorching of him by the Sun and the hunting of him by the Moon, and his voyaging as 'a fugitive star', reappears *after* the Last Battle and overthrow of Morgoth; in S and Q this is said of his first uprising into the heavens, at the end of §17. It is only now that

> the Valar drew his white ship Wingelot over the land of Valinor, and they filled it with radiance and hallowed it, and launched it through the Door of Night.

It seems plain that in this account this act of the Valar was to protect Eärendel, by setting him to sail in the Void, above the courses of the Sun and Moon and stars (see the diagram in the *Ambarkanta*, p. 243), where also he could guard the Door against Morgoth's return. And in Q II Elwing was beside him in his journeys 'into the starless vast' (this being later struck out, note 6).

We have in fact already encountered, in the rewritten passage given in note 20 to §17 in Q II, the final story, that Wingelot was hallowed by the Gods and set in the heavens *before* the departure of the hosts of the West; but this postdates the writing of the conclusion of Q II. In this passage Elwing herself builds the Tower of Seabirds, devising wings in order to try to reach Eärendel, but they never meet again; and thus the element of the seabirds is removed from any direct association with Eärendel. In the account of the Last Battle in Q II §18 Eärendel descends out of the sky accompanied by 'a myriad of birds', but this of course belongs with the story in Q II §17 that it was Eärendel who built the Tower, and Elwing who devised wings for his ship. One might have expected that the birds that descended with Eärendel on Ancalagon the black would disappear in the later story, where it is the Valar who raise Wingelot, and the bird-wings by which it was formerly lifted up are rejected; but in the final version of the story of 'the last things' they are still present, and so in *The Silmarillion* (p. 252).

I give (p. 204) a table that may serve to show the development of the story of Eärendel and Elwing in these texts more clearly.

The final version of the story is further changed in that Elwing remained with Eärendel in Valinor; the Tower of Seabirds was built for her, and from it she would fly to meet Eärendel as his ship returned to Valinor (*The Silmarillion* p. 250).

| S and Q | Q II | Revisions to Q II |
|---|---|---|
| Eärendel (with Bronweg) visits Kôr fruitlessly, for the Elves have already gone (§17) | Eärendel (with Elwing, and bearing the Silmaril) goes to Valinor, and forbidding Elwing to accompany him further declares 'the embassy of the Two Kindreds' (§17) | Eärendel bids farewell to Elwing for ever on the shore of Valinor (§17 note 14) |
| He builds the Tower where all seabirds come (Q: and grieves for the loss of Elwing) (§17) | He guides the fleet out of the West; he builds the Tower of Seabirds, and Elwing is with him (§17) | Eärendel's ship is hallowed by the Valar and set in the sky (§17 note 20) |
| By birds' wings Wingelot is lifted into the sky (§17) | Elwing devises wings for Wingelot (§17) | Elwing builds the Tower and devises bird-wings for herself, but cannot reach Eärendel, and they are sundered for ever (§17 note 20) |
| He is scorched by the Sun and hunted by the Moon, and wanders as a fugitive star. He has no Silmaril. (§17) | He sails the sky bearing the Silmaril (?with Elwing), and the star is seen by the people of the Outer Lands (§17) | (Elwing is not with him) |
| | He descends from the sky to the Last Battle with countless birds about him, and slays Ancalagon (§18) | |
| After the Last Battle the Silmaril of Maidros is given to Eärendel and Elwing is restored to him; he sails into the Outer Dark with Elwing, bearing the Silmaril (§19) [The Q I text ends before this point is reached] | He is scorched by the Sun and hunted by the Moon, and sails as a fugitive star (§19) His ship is hallowed by the Valar and launched through the Door of Night. Elwing is with him (§19) | (Elwing is not with him; §19 note 6) |

Apart from the passage concerning Eärendel, Q II follows S (presumably now the immediate precursor) fairly closely, in its account of the belief that Morgoth comes back in secret from time to time, whereas others declare that it is Thû (> Sauron), who survived the Last Battle; and in the content of the prophecy of the Last Things – which is now given formal existence as 'the Prophecy of Mandos', which Mandos declared in Valmar at the judgement of the Gods. There are however certain changes and developments in the Prophecy: Morgoth when he returns will destroy the Sun and Moon (which must surely contain at least a reminiscence of the passage from the tale of *The Hiding of Valinor* cited on p. 73); Tulkas is now named as the chief antagonist of Melko in the final battle on the plains of Valinor, together with Fionwë and Túrin Turambar; Eärendel will yield up his Silmaril, and Fëanor will bear the Three to Yavanna to break them (in S they are to be broken by Maidros); and with the awakening of the Elves and the rising of their dead the purpose of Ilúvatar will be fulfilled concerning them. The appearance of Túrin at the end remains profoundly mysterious; and here it is said that the Prophecy names him among the Gods, which is clearly to be related to the passage in the old *Tale of Turambar* (II. 116), where it is said that Túrin and Nienor 'dwelt as shining Valar among the blessed ones', after they had passed through Fôs'Almir, the bath of flame. In changes to the text of Q II it is said that Túrin is named among 'the sons of the Gods', rather than among the Gods, and also that he comes 'from the halls of Mandos' to the final battle; about which I can say no more than that Túrin Turambar, though a mortal Man, did not go, as do the race of Men, to a fate beyond the world.

★

# APPENDIX 1

### Fragment of a translation of the Quenta Noldorinwa
### into Old English, made by Ælfwine or Eriol;
### together with Old English equivalents
### of Elvish names

There are extant fragments of Old English (Anglo-Saxon) versions of the *Annals of Valinor* (three), the *Annals of Beleriand*, and *Quenta Noldorinwa*. All begin at the beginning of the respective works and only one, a version of the *Annals of Valinor*, constitutes a substantial text. The Old English version of the *Quenta* which is given here had no title, but my father later inserted in pencil the title *Pennas*; cf. *Qenta Noldorinwa or Pennas-na-Ngoelaidh*, p. 77. In a brief detached list of Elvish names and words that belongs to this period occurs this entry:

*Quenta* story, tale (*quete-* 'say'). N[oldorin] *pent*.
*pennas* history (*quentassë*).

At this time *Eriol* and *Ælfwine* reappear together as the Elvish and
English names of the mariner who came to Tol Eressëa and there
translated various Elvish works into his own language: in the preamble to
the *Annals of Valinor* (p. 263) he is 'Eriol of Leithien, that is Ælfwine of
the Angelcynn', and in one of the Old English versions of these *Annals*
the work is said (p. 281) to have been translated by 'Ælfwine, whom the
Elves named Eriol'. (On the earlier relations of the two names see
II. 300–1.)

The Old English version of the *Quenta* is a very close equivalent of the
Modern English text from its opening 'After the making of the World by
the Allfather' to 'shadow is her realm and night her throne' (pp.
78–9), where the Old English ends. It is a manuscript in ink, obviously a
first draft, with pencilled emendations (mostly small alterations of word-
order and suchlike) which I take up into the text; the last paragraph is
written in pencil, very rapidly. Acute accents on long vowels were put in
rather sporadically and I have made the usage consistent, as with the Old
English texts throughout.

## Pennas

Æfter þám þe Ealfæder, se þe on elfisc Ilúuatar hátte, þás
worolde geworhte, þá cómon manige þá mihtegostan gǽstas
þe mid him wunodon hire to stíeranne; for þon þe hí híe
feorran ofsáwon fægre geworhte and hí lustfollodon on hire
wlitignesse. þás gǽstas nemdon þá Elfe *Valar*, þæt is þá        5
Mægen, þe men oft siððan swápéah nemdon Godu. Óþre
gǽstas manige hæfdon hí on hira folgoðe, ge máran ge
lǽssan, 7 þára sume tealdon men siþþan gedwollice mid þǽm
Elfum; ac híe lugon, for þám þe ǽr séo worold geworht wǽre
hí wǽron, 7 Elfe and Fíras (þæt sindon men) onwócon ǽrest   10
on worolde æfter þára Valena cyme. Ealfæder ána geworhte
Elfe and Fíras ond ǽgþerum gedǽlde hira ágene gifa; þý
hátað hí woroldbearn oþþe Ealfæderes bearn.
     þara Valena ealdoras nigon wǽron. þus hátað þá nigon
godu on elfiscum gereorde swá swá þa elfe hit on Valinóre   15
sprǽcon, þéah þe hira naman sind óþre 7 onhwerfede on
nold-elfisc, and missenlice sind hira naman mid mannum.
*Manwe* wæs goda hláford, and winda and wedera wealdend
and heofones stýrend. Mid him wunede to his geféran séo
undéadlice héanessa hlǽfdige, úprodera cwén, *Varda*     20

tunglawyrhte. Him se nyxta on mægene, and on fréondscipe
se cúðesta, wæs *Ulmo* ágendfréa ealra wætera, se þe ána
wunað on Útgársecge, 7 stýreð swáþéah eallum wǽgum 7
wæterum, éam 7 stréamum, wyllum ond ǽwelmum geond
eorðan ymbhwyrfte. Him underþýded, þéah he him oft       25
unhold bið, is *Osse*, se þe manna landa sǽm stýreð, 7 his
geféra is *Uinen* merehlǽfdige. Hire feax líþ gesprǽdd geond
ealle sǽ under heofenum.

On mægene wæs *Aule* Ulmo swíðost gelíc. He wæs smiþ
and cræftiga, 7 *Yavanna* wæs his geféra, séo þe ofet and       30
hærfest and ealle eorðan wæstmas lufode. Nyxt wæs héo on
mægene þára Valacwéna Vardan. Swíþe wlítig wæs héo, and
híe þá Elfe nemdon oft *Palúrien* þæt is 'eorþan scéat'.

þá gebróþru *Mandos* 7 *Lórien* hátton *Fanturi*. *Nefantur*
háteð se ǽresta, neoærna hláford, and wælcyriga, se þe       35
samnode ofslægenra manna gǽstas. *Olofantur* háteð se óðer,
swefna wyrhta 7 gedwimora; 7 his túnas on goda landum
wǽron ealra stówa fægroste on worolde 7 wǽron gefylde mid
manigum gǽstum wlitigum and mihtigum.

Ealra goda strengest 7 leoþucræftigost and foremǽrost       40
ellendǽdum wæs *Tulkas*; þý háteð he éac þon *Poldórea* se
ellenrófa (se dyhtiga); and he wæs Melkoes unwine and his
wiþerbroca.

*Orome* wæs mihtig hláford and lýtle lǽssa maegenes þonne
Tulkas sylf. Orome wæs hunta 7 tréowcynn lufode – þý hátte       45
he *Aldaron*, 7 þá noldielfe hine *Tauros* nemdon, þæt is
Wealdafréa – 7 him wǽron léofe hors and hundas. Húru he
éode on huntoð þurh þá deorce land ǽr þám þe séo sunne
wurde gýt atend /onǽled; swíþe hlúde wǽron his hornas, 7
swá béoð gíet on friðum and feldum þe Orome áh on       50
Valinóre. *Vana* hátte his geféra, séo wæs gingra sweostor
hira Vardan 7 Palúrienne, 7 séo fægernes ge heofenes ge
eorðan bið on hire wlite and hire weorcum. Hire mihtigre
swáþéah bið *Nienna*, séo þe mid Nefantur Mandos eardað.
Mildheort bið héo, hire bið geómor sefa, murnende mód;       55
sceadwa bið hire scír 7 hire þrymsetl þéostru.

## NOTES

6 *Mægen* ('Powers') was emended to *Reg*.. (?*Regen* ?*Regin*). Old
English *regn*- in compounds 'great, mighty', related to Old Norse
*regin* 'Gods' (occurring in *Ragnarök*).

10    *Fíras* is an emendation of *Elde* (both are old poetic words for 'men').
At line 12 *Fíras* is written beside *Elde*, which was emended to *Ælde*
(and *Elfe* apparently to *Ælfe*).

11    *Valena* genitive plural is an emendation from *Vala*; also in line 14.

23    *on Útgársecge*: *Út-gársecg* 'the Outer Seas'. *Gársecg*, one of many
Old English names of the sea, is used frequently in *Ælfwine of
England* of the Great Sea of the West (in one of the texts spelt
*Garsedge* to represent the pronunciation).

35    *wælcyriga*: 'chooser of the slain (*wæl*)', the Old English equivalent
of Old Norse *valkyrja* (Valkyrie).

49    *atend, onæled*: these words are alternatives, but neither is marked
for rejection.

55    Cf. *Beowulf* lines 49–50: *him wæs geómor sefa, murnende mód* ('sad
was their heart and mourning in their soul').

★

Associated with the Old English texts are several lists of Elvish names
with Old English equivalents, some of which are of much interest for the
light they cast on the meaning of Elvish names; though many are not in
fact translations, as will be seen.
There is firstly a list of the Valar:

### The chief gods are Fréan. ós (ése)

[O.E. *fréa* 'ruler, lord'; *ós* 'god' (in proper names as *Oswald*), with
mutated vowel in the plural.]

**Manwë is Wolcenfréa** [O.E. *wolcen* 'sky'; cf. Modern English *welkin*.]

**Ulmo is Gársecges fréa, & ealwæter-fréa** [For *Gársecg* see note to
line 23 of the O.E. *Quenta*. In that text Ulmo is called *ágendfréa ealra
wœtera* 'Lord of Waters' (literally 'owning lord of all waters').]

**Aulë is Cræftfréa**

**Tulkas is Afoðfréa** [O.E. *afoð, eafoð* 'might, strength'.]

**Oromë is Wáðfréa and Huntena fréa** [O.E. *wáð* 'hunting'; 'Hunting
Lord and Lord of Hunters'. In the O.E. *Quenta* he is *Wealdafréa*
'Lord of Forests', translating *Tauros*.]

**Mandos is Néfréa** [O.E. *né(o)* 'corpse'; cf. *néoœrna hláford* 'master of
the houses of the dead' in the O.E. *Quenta*. On the Elvish name
*Nefantur* see p. 166.]

**Lórien is Swefnfréa** [O.E. *swefn* 'dream'.]

**Melko is Mánfréa, Bolgen, Malscor** [O.E. *mán* 'evil, wickedness'; *bolgen* 'wrathful'. An O.E. verbal noun *malscrung* is recorded, with the meaning 'bewildering, bewitching'; see the Oxford English Dictionary s.v. *Masker* (verb), 'bewilder'.]

**Ossë is Sæfréa**

There are also several lists of Old English equivalents of Elvish names of persons and places, and since they all obviously belong to the same period I combine them and give them in alphabetical order:

**Aldaron: Béaming** [O.E. *béam* 'tree'.]

**Amon Uilas: Sinsnáw, Sinsnæwen** [O.E. *sin-* 'perpetual'; *snáw* 'snow', *snǽwen* (not recorded) 'snowy'. *Amon Uilas* appears in the *Quenta*, p. 81 note 2.]

**Ancalagon: Anddraca** [O.E. *and-* as the first element in compounds denotes opposition, negation (*anda* 'enmity, hatred, envy'); *draca* 'dragon' (see II. 350).]

**Angband: Engbend, Irenhell** [*Engbend* contains O.E. *enge* 'narrow, strait, oppressive, cruel' and *bend* 'bond, fetter'; it is thus not a translation but a word-play between the two languages.]

**Asgar: Bǽning** [This river, *Ascar* in Q as in *The Silmarillion*, is also *Asgar* in the *Annals of Beleriand* (p. 307). I cannot interpret *Bǽning*. If a derivative of O.E. *bán* 'bone' (cf. *bǽnen* 'of bone') it might have some meaning like 'the place (i.e. the river) filled with bones', with reference to the Dwarves who were drowned in the river at the battle of the Stony Ford; but this does not seem at all probable.]

**Balrog: Bealuwearg, Bealubróga** [O.E. *bealu* 'evil', cf. Modern English *bale(ful)*; *wearg* 'felon, outlaw, accursed being' (Old Norse *vargr* 'wolf, outlaw', whence the *Wargs*); *bróga* 'terror'. These O.E. names are thus like *Engbend* ingenious sound-correspondences contrived from O.E. words.]

**Bansil: Béansíl, Béansigel** [The second element is O.E. *sigel* 'sun, jewel' (cf. J. R. R. Tolkien, *Sigelwara land*, in *Medium Ævum III*, June 1934, p. 106); the first is presumably *béam* 'tree'. This is another case where Ælfwine used Old English words to give a likeness of sound (with of course a suitable meaning), rather than a translation. – In the Name-list to *The Fall of Gondolin Bansil* is translated 'Fair-gleam', II. 214.]

**Baragund, Barahir: Beadohun, Beadomær** [O.E. *beadu* 'battle'.]

**Bauglir: Bróga** [O.E. *bróga* 'terror'.]

**Beleg: Finboga** [O.E. *boga* 'bow'.]

**Belegar: Ingársecg, Westsǽ, Wídsǽ** [The Gnomish name of the Great Sea has not yet appeared in the texts. *Ingársecg* = *Gársecg*; *Útgársecg* is the Outer Sea (see note to line 23 of the O.E. *Quenta*).]

**Belegost: Micelburg** ['Great fortress', the original meaning (see II.336).]

**Blodrin Ban's son: Blodwine Banan sunu** [*Blodwine* presumably contains O.E. *blód* 'blood'; while *bana* is 'slayer'.]

**Doriath: Éaland, Folgen(fold), Infolde, Wudumǽraland** [O.E. *éaland*, land by water or by a river – doubtless with reference to the rivers Sirion and Esgalduin. *Folgen(fold)*: O.E. *folgen* is the past participle of *féolan* 'penetrate, make one's way, get to', but the cognate verbs in Gothic and Old Norse have the meaning 'hide', and it may be that *folgen* is here given the sense of Old Norse *fólginn* 'hidden', i.e. 'the hidden (land)'. Gondolin is called *Folgenburg. Infolde*, a word not recorded, perhaps has some meaning like 'the inner land', 'the land within'. *Wudumǽraland* no doubt contains *mǽre* 'boundary, border'.]

**Dor-lómen: Wómanland** [See *Ered-lómen*.]

**Drengist: Nearufléot** [*Drengist* has not yet appeared in the texts. O.E. *nearu* 'narrow', *fléot* 'arm of the sea, estuary, firth'.]

**Ered-lómen: Wómanbeorgas** [O.E. *wóma* 'sound, noise', *beorg* 'mountain'; sc. the Echoing Mountains, and similarly *Wómanland* for Dor-lómen, Land of Echoes. This is the later etymology of these names; see pp. 192–3.]

**Gelion: Glæden** [*Gelion* appears by emendation of *Flend* in the *Quenta* §14. O.E. *glædene* 'iris, gladdon', as in the Gladden Fields and Gladden River in *The Lord of the Rings*.]

**Gondolin: Stángaldor(burg), Folgenburg, Galdorfæsten** [O.E. *stán* 'stone'; *galdor* 'spell, enchantment'; *fæsten* 'fastness, fortress'. For *Folgenburg* (? 'the hidden city') see *Doriath*.]

**Hithlum: Hasuglóm, Hasuland (Hasulendingas)** [O.E. *hasu* 'grey'; *glóm* 'gloaming, twilight'. *Hasulendingas* 'the people of Hasuland'.]

**Laurelin: Gleng(g)old** [O.E. *gleng* 'ornament, splendour'; *Glengold* is not a translation but a sound-imitation of *Glingol* ('Singing-gold', II.216.]

**Mithrim: Mistrand, Mistóra** [O.E. *óra* 'bank, shore', and *rand* of the same meaning.]

**Nargothrond: Hlýdingaburg, Stángaldor(burg)** [*Hlýdingaburg* is the city of the *Illýdingas*, the people of Narog (*Hlýda*). *Stángaldor (burg)* is also given as an O.E. name for Gondolin.]

**Narog: Hlýda** [*Illýda* 'the loud one' (O.E. *hlúd* 'loud'; see III. 87–8).]

**Silmaril: Sigel, Sigelmǽrels** [For *sigel* see *Bansil* above. O.E. *mǽrels* 'rope'; *Sigelmǽrels* is another case of imitation – but it refers to the Necklace of the Dwarves.]

**Sirion: Fléot (Fléwet), Scírwendel** [*Fléot* must here have the meaning 'river', which is scarcely evidenced in Old English, though it is the general meaning of the word in cognate languages (cf. *Drengist* above). *Scírwendel*: O.E. *scír* 'bright'; *wendel* does not occur, but certainly refers to the windings of a river's course – cf. *Withywindle*, the river in the Old Forest, concerning which my father noted: '*-windle* does not actually occur (*Withywindle* was modelled on *withywind*, a name of the convolvulus or bindweed)' (*Guide to the Names in The Lord of the Rings*, in *A Tolkien Compass*, p. 196).]

**Taur-na-Danion: Furhweald** [In an addition to the *Quenta* §9 (note 1) *Taur Danin* is given as the former name of Taur-na-Fuin, when it was still 'wholesome, if thick and dark'; *Taur-na-Danion* here was changed to *Taur-na-Donion*, precursor of *Dorthonion* 'Land of Pines'. O.E. *furh* 'fir, pine', *weald* 'forest'.]

**Taur-na-Fuin: Nihtsceadu, Nihtsceadwesweald, Atol Nihtegesa, Nihthelm unfǽle** [O.E. *sceadu* 'shadow'; *weald* 'forest'; *atol* 'dire, terrible'; *egesa* 'terror'; *niht-helm* 'cover of night', a poetic compound found in *Beowulf* and other poems; *unfǽle* 'evil'. Cf. the Modern English translation, found in the long Lays and in the *Quenta*, 'Forest of Deadly Nightshade'.]

**Tindbrenting þe þa Brega Taniquetil nemnað** ['Tindbrenting which the Valar name Taniquetil': see III. 127, and for *Brega* see *Vala*.]

**Vala: Bregu** [O.E. *bregu* 'ruler, lord', plural (unrecorded) *brega*. Two other words were added to the list: *Mægen* 'Powers', which is used in the O.E. *Quenta* line 6, and *Ése* (see p. 208).]

**Valinor: Breguland, Godéðel** [O.E. *éðel* 'country, native land'.]

**Valmar: Godaburg, Bregubold** [O.E. *bold* 'dwelling'.]

Another page gives Old English equivalents of the names of the Kindreds of the Elves, and of the princes of the Noldoli arranged in a genealogical table. This page is headed:

**Fíras. Includes both Men and Elves.**

This contradicts the use of *Fíras* in the O.E. *Quenta*, where it appears as an emendation of *Elde* (lines 10 and 12), used in distinction to *Elfe*.

Then follows:

### Fíra bearn

§1. þæt eldre cyn: *Elfe* oþþe *Wine*

1. *Ingwine*: *lyftelfe*, *héahelfe*, *hwítelfe*, *Líxend*.  *Godwine*
2. *Éadwine*: *goldelfe*, *eorðelfe*, *déopelfe*, *Rǽdend*.  *Finningas*
3. *Sǽwine*: *sǽelfe*, *mereþyssan*, *flotwine*, *Nówend*.  *Elwingas*

*Wine* can only be O.E. *wine* (old plural *wine*) 'friend' (a word used of equals, of superiors, and of inferiors); but its use here as a general term equivalent to *Elfe* is curious. Of the names given to the First Kindred, *lyftelfe* contains O.E. *lyft* 'sky, air'; *Líxend* 'Shining Ones'. The Second Kindred: *Éad-* in the context of the Noldoli is in no doubt to be interpreted 'riches'. I am not sure of the meaning of *Rǽdend*, though it clearly refers to the knowledge and desire for knowledge of the Noldoli in some aspect. *Finningas* 'the people of Finn' (*Ing* and *Finn* as the Gnomish forms of Ingwë and Finwë were still found in Q §2, though removed by later changes to the text). The Third Kindred: O.E. *mereþyssa* 'sea-rusher' (used in recorded O.E. poetry of ships); *flotwine* contains O.E. *flot* 'sea'; *Nówend* 'mariners, shipmasters'.

In the genealogical table that follows Fëanor is given the Old English name *Finbrós Gimwyrhta* ('Jewel-wright'); since his sons are here called *Brósingas* (from *Brósinga mene* 'the necklace of the Brósings' in *Beowulf*, line 1199) *-brós* is presumably a back-formation from *Brósingas*. They are also called *Yrfeloran*: an unrecorded compound, 'those bereft of their inheritance', the Dispossessed. The *Brósingas* or sons of Fëanor are given thus:

1. *Dǽgred Winsterhand* [O.E. *dǽgred* 'daybreak, dawn'; *winsterhand* 'left-handed' (for the right hand of Maidros was cut off in his rescue from Thangorodrim, Q §8). I can cast no light on the O.E. equivalent *Dǽgred* for Maidros, unless an extremely late note on Maidros (Maedhros) is relevant (for ideas long buried so far as written record goes might emerge again many years later): according to this he inherited 'the rare red-brown hair of Nerdanel's kin' (Nerdanel was the wife of Fëanor, *The Silmarillion* p. 64), and was called 'by his brothers and other kin' *Russandol* 'copper-top'.]

2. *Dǽgmund Swinsere* [I cannot explain *Dǽgmund* for Maglor. O.E. *mund* is 'hand', also 'protection'; *swinsere* (not recorded) 'musician, singer' (cf. *swinsian* 'make music').]

3.  *Cynegrim Fægerfeax* [Celegorm 'Fairfax', i.e. fair-haired. *Cynegrim* is probably the substitution of an O.E. name with some similarity of sound.]

4.  *Cyrefinn Fácensearo* [Curufin the Crafty. O.E. *cyre* 'choice'; *fácen* 'deceit, guile, wickedness' (a word of wholly bad meaning); *searu* 'skill, cunning' (also with bad meaning, 'plot, snare, treachery'); *fácensearu* 'treachery'.]

5.  *Colþegn Nihthelm* [Cranthir the Dark. O.E. *col* 'coal'; for *nihthelm* see under *Taur-na-Fuin* above.]

6.  *Déormód*  
7.  *Tirgeld* } *huntan* [Damrod and Díriel the hunters. O.E. *déormód* 'brave-hearted'; *tír* 'glory'; *-geld* (*-gild*) in names, 'of worth'.]

Fingolfin appears as *Fingold Fengel* (O.E. *fengel* 'king, prince'; cf. III. 145), and his sons are *Finbrand* (i.e. Finweg/Fingon) and *Finstán* (i.e. Turgon); the element *stán* 'stone' presumably showing that *-gon* in Turgon is *gond* (*gonn*) 'stone', see I. 254. Fingolfin's daughter is *Finhwít* (i.e. Isfin), and Eöl is *Éor*; Meglin is *Mánfrið* (an unrecorded compound of *mán* 'evil deed, wickedness' and *frið* 'peace').

*Finbrand* (i.e. Finweg/Fingon) here has a son, *Fingár*; and the daughter of *Finstán* (i.e. Turgon) is *Ideshild Silfrenfót* (i.e. Idril Celebrindal).

*Finrod* (i.e. the later Finarfin) is called *Finred Felanóþ* (*felanóþ* 'very bold'), and his sons are *Ingláf Felahrór* (i.e. Felagund; *felahrór* has the same meaning as *felanóþ*), *Ordred* (i.e. Orodreth), *Angel* (i.e. Angrod), and *Eangrim* (i.e. Egnor).

*Ordred* (i.e. Orodreth) has two sons, *Ordhelm* and *Ordláf*; his daughter is *Friþuswiþ Fealuléome* (i.e. Finduilas Failivrin; *fealuléome* perhaps 'golden light').

Lastly, there is a fourth child of Finwë given in this table: *Finrún Felageómor* (*felageómor* 'very sorrowful').

The name given to Felagund, *Ingláf Felahrór*, is notable; for *Felagund* was to become his 'nickname', and his true name *Inglor* (as it remained until replaced long afterwards by Finrod, when the original Finrod became Finarfin); see p. 341.

★

## APPENDIX 2

### The Horns of Ylmir

This poem is unquestionably that referred to in the *Quenta*, p. 142: 'the might and majesty of that vision is told of in the song of Tuor that he made for his son Eärendel.' It is extant in three versions and five texts.

The first version, found only in one manuscript, consists of 40 lines, beginning:

> I sat on the ruined margin of the deep-voiced echoing sea

and ending:

> and I wake to silent caverns, and empty sands, and peace

(lines 15 and 66 in the text given below). To the manuscript in ink my father added in pencil the title *The Tides*, together with the notes *Dec. 4 1914* and *On the Cornish Coast*. For his visit to the Lizard Peninsula in Cornwall in the summer of 1914 see Humphrey Carpenter, *Biography*, pp. 70–1. But although I have found nothing earlier than this text it is clear from my father's notes to subsequent versions that he remembered the origin of the poem to be earlier than that time.

The second version bears the title *Sea Chant of an Elder Day* (and Old English *Fyrndaga Sǽléoþ*), and is extant in two manuscripts which differ only in small details. The second has some minor emendations, and the date: *Mar. 1915 < Dec. 1914 < 1912*, also *Essay Club* [of Exeter College, Oxford] *March 1915*. This version begins:

> In a dim and perilous region, down whose great tempestuous ways
> I heard no sound of men's voices; in those eldest of the days,
> I sat on the ruined margin of the deep-voiced echoing sea . . .

(i.e. it begins at line 13 in the text, p. 216) and contains two further lines after 'and empty sands, and peace' (where *The Tides* ends):

> In a lovely sunlit region down whose old chaotic ways
> Yet no sound of men's voices echoed in those eldest of all days.

It is from this version, not that of 1914, that Humphrey Carpenter cites the first six lines (*ibid*. pp. 73–4). The *Sea Chant* differs from *The Tides* both by extension (it has 50 lines as against 40) and in the reconstruction of many verses.

Against the second text of the *Sea Chant* my father wrote in pencil:

> This is the song that Tuor told to Eärendel his son what time the Exiles of Gondolin dwelt awhile in Dor Tathrin the Land of Willows after the burning of their city. Now Tuor was the first of Men to see the Great Sea, but guided by Ulmo towards Gondolin he had left the shores of the Ocean and passing through the Land of Willows became enamoured of its loveliness, forgetting both his quest and his former love of the sea. Now Ulmo lord of Vai coming in his deep-sea car sat at twilight in the reeds of Sirion and played to him on his magic flute of

hollow shells. Thereafter did Tuor hunger ever after the sea and had no peace in his heart did he dwell in pleasant inland places.*

This very evidently belongs with the tale of *The Fall of Gondolin* (see especially II. 153–6), and was no doubt added at the time of the composition of the tale (and of the third version of the poem), since the *Sea Chant* has no point of contact with the Tuor legend, nor indeed with any feature of the mythology.

The third version, entitled *The Horns of Ulmo*, is extant in a manuscript and in a typescript taken directly from it, and it is only now that the references to Ulmo and Ossë (and to the rending of the Earth by the Gods in the primeval darkness) appear in the poem. A note on the MS, written at the same time as the poem, reads:

1910–11–12 rewr[itten] & recast often. Present shape due to rewriting and adding introd[uction] & ending in a lonely house near Roos, Holderness (Thistle Bridge Camp) Spring 1917

(For Roos see Humphrey Carpenter, *Biography*, p. 97.) A further pencilled note adds: 'poem to "The Fall of Gondolin".'

Thus the absorption of the poem into the legend of Tuor and Eärendel took place at much the same time as the writing of the tale of *The Fall of Gondolin* (see I. 203, II. 146); it should have been given in *The Book of Lost Tales Part II*.

A few small emendations were made to the MS of *The Horns of Ulmo*, notably *Ulmo > Ylmir* (the latter being the Gnomish form, found in the *Lay of the Children of Húrin* and in the 'Sketch'), and the second reference to Ossë (lines 41–2, replacing two earlier verses). The typescript is essentially the same as the manuscript (with the words 'from "The Fall of Gondolin"' added beneath the title), but it has some small alterations made in red ball-point pen, which therefore belong to a much later time. These late changes are not incorporated in the text given here, but are given in notes following the poem.

The Horns of Ylmir
from
'The Fall of Gondolin'

'Tuor recalleth in a song sung to his son Eärendel
the visions that Ylmir's conches once called before
him in the twilight in the Land of Willows.'

---

*Dor Tathrin* occurs in the Name-list to *The Fall of Gondolin*, II. 346, and Ulmo's 'deep-sea car' in the tale of *The Chaining of Melko*, I. 101.

'Twas in the Land of Willows where the grass is long and green –
I was fingering my harp-strings, for a wind had crept unseen
And was speaking in the tree-tops, while the voices of the reeds
Were whispering reedy whispers as the sunset touched the meads,
5   Inland musics subtly magic that those reeds alone could weave –
'Twas in the Land of Willows that once Ylmir came at eve.

In the twilight by the river on a hollow thing of shell
He made immortal music, till my heart beneath his spell
Was broken in the twilight, and the meadows faded dim
10   To great grey waters heaving round the rocks where sea-birds swim.

I heard them wailing round me where the black cliffs towered high
And the old primeval starlight flickered palely in the sky.
In that dim and perilous region in whose great tempestuous ways
I heard no sound of men's voices, in those eldest of the days,
15   I sat on the ruined margin of the deep-voiced echoing sea
Whose roaring foaming music crashed in endless cadency
On the land besieged for ever in an aeon of assaults
And torn in towers and pinnacles and caverned in great vaults;
And its arches shook with thunder and its feet were piled with shapes
20   Riven in old sea-warfare from those crags and sable capes.

Lo! I heard the embattled tempest roaring up behind the tide
When the trumpet of the first winds sounded, and the grey sea sang
        and cried
As a new white wrath woke in him, and his armies rose to war
And swept in billowed cavalry toward the walled and moveless shore.
25   There the windy-bannered fortress of those high and virgin coasts
Flung back the first thin feelers of the elder tidal hosts;
Flung back the restless streamers that like arms of a tentacled thing
Coiling and creeping onward did rustle and suck and cling.
Then a sigh arose and a murmuring in that stealthy-whispering van,
30   While, behind, the torrents gathered and the leaping billows ran,
Till the foam-haired water-horses in green rolling volumes came –
A mad tide trampling landward – and their war-song burst to flame.

Huge heads were tossed in anger and their crests were towers of froth
And the song the great seas were singing was a song of unplumbed
        wrath,
35   For through that giant welter Ossë's trumpets fiercely blew,
That the voices of the flood yet deeper and the High Wind louder
        grew;
Deep hollows hummed and fluted as they sucked the sea-winds in;
Spumes and great white spoutings yelled shrilly o'er the din;
Gales blew the bitter tresses of the sea in the land's dark face
40   And wild airs thick with spindrift fled on a whirling race
From battle unto battle, till the power of all the seas

Gathered like one mountain about Ossë's awful knees,
And a dome of shouting water smote those dripping black facades
And its catastrophic fountains smashed in deafening cascades.

\*          \*          \*

45 · Then the immeasurable hymn of Ocean I heard as it rose and fell
To its organ whose stops were the piping of gulls and the
   thunderous swell;
Heard the burden of the waters and the singing of the waves
Whose voices came on for ever and went rolling to the caves,
Where an endless fugue of echoes splashed against wet stone
50 And arose and mingled in unison into a murmuring drone –
'Twas a music of uttermost deepness that stirred in the profound,
And all the voices of all oceans were gathered to that sound;
'Twas Ylmir, Lord of Waters, with all-stilling hand that made
Unconquerable harmonies, that the roaring sea obeyed,
55 That its waters poured off and Earth heaved her glistening
   shoulders again
Naked up into the airs and the cloudrifts and sea-going rain,
Till the suck and suck of green eddies and the slap of ripples was all
That reached to mine isléd stone, save the old unearthly call
Of sea-birds long-forgotten and the grating of ancient wings.

60 Thus murmurous slumber took me mid those far-off eldest things
(In a lonely twilit region down whose old chaotic ways
I heard no sound of men's voices, in those eldest of the days
When the world reeled in the tumult as the Great Gods tore the
   Earth
In the darkness, in the tempest of the cycles ere our birth),
65 Till the tides went out, and the Wind died, and did all sea musics
   cease
And I woke to silent caverns and empty sands and peace.

Then the magic drifted from me and that music loosed its bands –
Far, far-off, conches calling – lo! I stood in the sweet lands,
And the meadows were about me where the weeping willows grew,
70 Where the long grass stirred beside me, and my feet were drenched
   with dew.
Only the reeds were rustling, but a mist lay on the streams
Like a sea-roke drawn far inland, like a shred of salt sea-dreams.
'Twas in the Land of Willows that I heard th'unfathomed breath
Of the Horns of Ylmir calling – and shall hear them till my death.

## NOTES

The following are the late changes made to the typescript, referred to on p. 215:

1 and 6  *'Twas* to *It was*
16     The line changed to: *Whose endless roaring music crashed in foaming harmony*, and marked with an X
21     *roaring* to *rolling*
28     The line marked with an X, probably primarily on account of the use of *did* (cf. III. 153)
65     The line changed to: *Till the tides went out, and the Wind ceased, and all sea musics died* (but this destroys the rhyme).

---

72     'sea-roke': *roke* is a medieval English word surviving until recent times in dialect meaning 'mist, fog, drizzling rain'.

# IV

# THE FIRST 'SILMARILLION' MAP

This map was made on a sheet of examination paper from the University
of Leeds (as was most of the A-text of the *Lay of the Children of Hurin*,
III.4), which suggests that it originated in association with the Lay, or
perhaps rather with the 'Sketch of the Mythology' which was written to
accompany it (p. 11). On the other hand, some names which seem to
belong with the first making of the map do not appear in the texts before
the *Quenta*. Though it was not drawn initially in a way that would
suggest that my father intended it to endure, it was his working map for
several years, and it was much handled and much altered. Names were
emended and places re-sited; the writing is in red ink, black ink, green
ink, pencil, and blue crayon, often overlaying each other. Lines
representing contours and others representing streams tangle with lines
for redirection and lines cancelling other lines. But it is striking that the
river-courses as drawn on this first map were scarcely changed at all
afterwards.

Associated with the map are two supplementary sheets, giving an
Eastern and a Western extension to the main or central map; these are
reproduced and annotated subsequently (pp. 227ff.). The main map is
on a single sheet but is here reproduced in two halves, Northern and
Southern. Names in red ink all seem to belong to the original 'layer' of
names, as do some (e.g. *Huan, Mavwin, Turgon*) of those in black ink;
but *Taiglin, Geleidhian*, in red, do not otherwise occur before the
*Quenta*. Those in green ink are few: *Broseliand*; *Gnomes* on the
Northern half beside Gondolin, and on the Southern half beside
Nargothrond; and *Wandering Gnomes* in the South-east.

In the following alphabetically-ordered list I take each half in turn*
and comment on almost every item, noticing especially where the name
in question first appears in the narrative texts.

## The Northern Half of the Map

*Aglon, Gorge of*   The name itself is a hasty later addition. The Gorge of
   Aglon first occurs in the *Lay of Leithian* (lines 2062, 2995, passages
   composed in 1928). In the Lay and in Q (§§9, 10) the Gorge is the

---

*The list of names for the northern half includes names as far south as the fold in the
original map, which can be seen in the reproductions; thus *Ginglith, Esgalduin, Thousand
Caves* appear in the first list, but *Doriath beyond Sirion, Aros* in the second.

dwelling of the Sons of Fëanor, who are placed on the map to the North of it (and circled with an arrow directing to the East).

*Angband*  The placing of Angband in relation to Thangorodrim shows how my father saw them at the time of the long Lays and the 'Sketch'. In the *Lay of the Children of Húrin* (lines 712–14) the 'hopeless halls of Hell' are

> wrought at the roots   of the roaring cliffs
> of Thangorodrim's   thunderous mountain.

In the *Lay of Leithian* (lines 3526ff.) Angband's gate seems clearly to lie beneath Thangorodrim; and in S (§8) Thangorodrim is 'the highest of the Iron Mountains around Morgoth's fortress'. See further the commentary on the *Ambarkanta*, p. 260.

*Angeryd*  The Iron Mountains. Cf. *Angorodin* in the *Tale of Turambar* (II. 77).

*Angrin Aiglir*  *Aiglir Angrin* occurs twice in the *Lay of the Children of Húrin* (lines 711, 1055), emended later to *Eiglir Engrin* (in *The Silmarillion Ered Engrin*).

*Aryador*  This name reappears, rather surprisingly, from the *Lost Tales*, as a third name of Hithlum. In the tale of *The Coming of the Elves* (I. 119) Aryador is said to be the name among Men for Hisilómë; see also I. 249.

*Battle of Unnumbered Tears*  The Mound of Slain is placed in the *Lay of the Children of Húrin* (lines 1439 ff.) 'at the furthest end of Dor-na-Fauglith's dusty spaces' (Flinding and Túrin were wandering westward, line 1436); cf. also Q§11 'Finweg and Turgon and the Men of Hithlum were gathered in the West upon the borders of the Thirsty Plain.'

*Beleg and Túrin*  These names mark the north march of Doriath, where Beleg and Túrin fought together against the Orcs, an element that first entered the story in the *Lay of the Children of Húrin* (see III. 27).

*Cristhorn*  Placed in the mountains north (not as originally south) of Gondolin, as already in the fragment of the alliterative *Lay of Eärendel* (III. 143).

*Deadly Nightshade, Forest of*  See *Taur-na-Fuin*.

*Dorlómin*  See *Hithlum*.

*Dor-na-Fauglith*  This name arose during the composition of the *Lay of the Children of Húrin* (see III. 55), where also the *Thirsty Plain* is found. On the map this is an emendation of *The Black Plain*.

*Dwarf-road to Belegost and Nogrod in the South*  It is interesting that the Dwarf-road is shown as leading all the way from Nogrod and

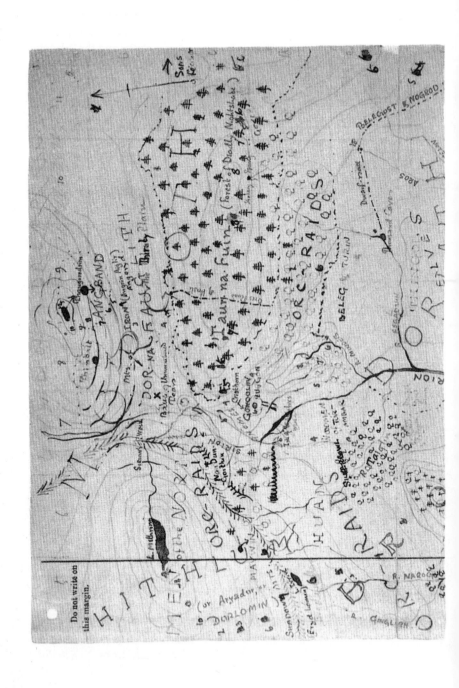

The Northern Half
of the First 'Silmarillion' Map

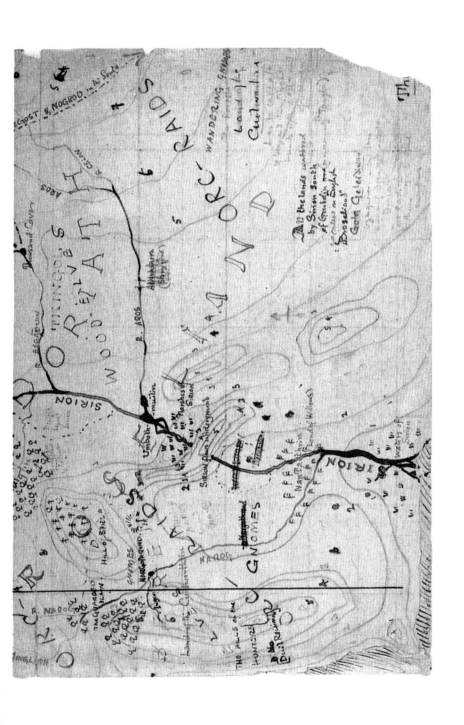

**The Southern Half
of the First 'Silmarillion' Map**

Belegost in the far South to the very doors of the Thousand Caves. It is possible, if not very likely, that the 'Dwarf-road' on the map merely indicates the path that the Dwarves did in fact take when summoned to Doriath, rather than a beaten track.

*Eredwethion*    A later replacement of *Eryd Lómin*, as also in Q II §15 (note 1).

*Eryd Lómin*    This name occurs in the caption to the painting of Tol Sirion of July 1928, where, as on the map and in Q II §15, it refers to the Shadowy Mountains; see pp. 192–3.

*Esgalduin*    First found in the *Lay of the Children of Húrin* (III.93). It is said in Q (§9) that it 'came out of secret wells in Taur-na-Fuin'; see *Shadowy Spring*. The course of Esgalduin was not afterwards changed.

*Ginglith*    First occurs in the *Lay of the Children of Húrin* (III.88). Its course was never changed.

*Gondolin*    Placed as it was to remain. The lines running south and west from the Encircling Mountains perhaps represent the hidden 'Way of Escape'.

*Hithlum*    Obviously Hithlum was not intended to extend south of the Shadowy Mountains, despite the placing of the M. The contour lines show that the Mountains of Mithrim did not yet exist. *Dorlómin* is given as an alternative name, as it is in S and Q (§8), where Lake Mithrim is placed in Hisilómë/Hithlum/Dorlómin; on the map *Mithrim* is simply and solely the name of the lake (cf. III. 103).

*Huan*    That a territory, south and east of Ivrin, is assigned to Huan shows a very early stage in the legend of Beren and Lúthien, when Huan was independent of any master (see III. 244).

*Isle of the Werewolves*    The Isle first appears in the *Lay of Leithian* in a passage written in March 1928 (see III.234). Originally marked on the map S.W. of Gondolin, and with the river Sirion dividing quite broadly and enclosing a large island, this site was struck out, and an arrow directs from here to a more northerly position, not far south of the battlefield of Unnumbered Tears. The later map brought it somewhat southward again.

*Ivrin, Lake*    First occurs in the *Lay of the Children of Húrin* (line 1526); it is placed on the map in the position that I think is indicated in the Lay (see III. 87), and where it remained.

*Land of Dread*    Occurs twice in the *Lay of Leithian* (lines 49, 383) of the realm of Morgoth.

*Mavwin*    It is curious that the map retains the old name, which goes back to the *Tale of Turambar*, for *Morwen* is found already in the second version of the *Lay of the Children of Húrin* (III.94) and in S. In S (§9) Húrin and Morwen 'lived in the woods upon the borders of Hithlum'.

*Mindeb*   First occurs in the *Lay of Leithian*, line 2924 (April 1928).

*Mithrim, Lake*   See *Hithlum*.

*Mountains of Iron*   See *Angeryd, Angrin Aiglir*.

*Nan Dun-Gorthin*   As the map was originally drawn this was placed west of Sirion, S.W. of Gondolin and very close to the Isle of the Werewolves (as that was originally placed). This cannot be the same placing as in the *Lay of the Fall of Gondolin* (III.148), where the hidden door of Gondolin was actually 'in dark Dungorthin'.

Subsequently *Nan-Dungorthin* was struck out and the name written again further north, still west of Sirion, but close beneath the Shadowy Mountains. This position is clearly that of the *Lay of the Children of Húrin*, where Túrin and Flinding passed the site of the Battle of Unnumbered Tears, crossed Sirion not far from his source, and came to 'the roots . . . of the Shadowy Mountains', where they entered the valley of Nan Dungorthin (see III. 59, 87).

Later again, an arrow was drawn moving Nan Dungorthin to a position east of Sirion and north of Doriath, and so more or less into the position of Nan Dungorthin (Nan Dungortheb) on the later map.

*Orcs' Road of Haste*   Cf. S §12: 'the Orc-road . . . which the Orcs use when in need of haste.'

*Shadowy Mountains*   First occurs in the *Lay of the Children of Húrin* (see III. 29). See *Eryd Lómin*.

*Shadowy Spring*   It is notable that the rivers Aros and Esgalduin arise at the same place, in the *Shadowy Spring* (not previously named in the texts; see *Esgalduin*). In the later map, on which mine in the published *Silmarillion* was based, this is still the case, and my map, showing the two sources as separate, is regrettably in error.

*Silver Bowl*   Shown in the Taiglin itself (not as later in the tributary stream Celebros), as in the *Tale of Turambar* and still in S and Q (§13).

*Sirion*   The course of the river was never changed; in the later map my father followed the earlier precisely.

*Sirion's Well*   This is referred to in the *Lay of the Children of Húrin* (line 1460). Its site remained unchanged.

*Sons of Fëanor*   See *Aglon*.

*Taiglin*   This looks like an original element on the map, although the name does not otherwise occur until the *Quenta*, §13 (see p. 185).

*Taur-na-Fuin*   This name (for *Taur Fuin* of the *Lost Tales*) and its translation *Deadly Nightshade* first occur in the *Lay of the Children of Húrin* (III. 55).

*Thangorodrim*   See *Angband*.

*Thimbalt*   This name occurs nowhere else. It is not clear from the map what it represents, but since an area marked out by dots surrounds Angband, and a similar area surrounds Thimbalt, it seems likely that this was another fortress. Thimbalt was struck out in pencil.

*Thirsty Plain*   See *Dor-na-Fauglith*. *Thirsty* is an emendation in black ink of *Black* in red ink.

*Thousand Caves*   First occurs in the *Lay of the Children of Húrin*. It is here placed as it was to remain, where Esgalduin bends westward towards Sirion.

*Woodmen of Turambar*   This is the second and later placing of the Woodmen on the map; see notes on the southern half.

## The Southern Half of the Map

*Aros, River*   *Aros* has only been named hitherto in the *Tale of the Nauglafring*, where after the sack of Artanor (Doriath) the Dwarves journeying thence to their homes in the South (II.225) had to pass the 'fierce stream' Aros at Sarnathrod, the Stony Ford (II.236). It is also said in the same place that Aros, nearer to its spring, ran past the doors of the Caves of the Rodothlim, though against this my father later noted (II.244 note 15) 'No [?that] is Narog'; while in the *Tale of Turambar* it is said (II.81) that the Caves were above a stream that 'ran down to feed the river Sirion'. I am not sure how to interpret this. If it is assumed that the Stony Ford in the *Tale of the Nauglafring* was on the (later) Aros, then the Caves of the Rodothlim were on that river also, which is most improbable. On the other hand, if Aros was simply the earlier name of Narog, the question arises why the Dwarves fleeing out of Artanor should have been going in this direction.

On the whole I am inclined to think that the phrase in the *Tale of the Nauglafring* saying that Aros ran past the Caves of the Rodothlim was a momentary confusion in a text written at very great speed (II.221), and that the Stony Ford (but *not* the Caves) was always on the Aros, this river having always borne this name. If this is so, this is still the geography on the map (as originally marked in this detail), where *Athrasarn* (*Stony Ford*) was placed on the Aros halfway between Umboth-muilin and the inflowing of Celon. At this time the Land of the Cuilwarthin was in the North of the Hills of the Hunters; and therefore in the story implied by the map Beren and his Elves crossed Sirion from his land and ambushed the Dwarves on the southern confines of Doriath. It is not clear why the Dwarves were not taking the Dwarf-road from the Thousand Caves, which crossed the Aros much higher up; on this point see the note on the Dwarf-road in the northern half of the map.

Before the first map was laid aside the idea had changed, and when the Land of the Cuilwarthin was moved eastward (see note on *Beren*) the Stony Ford was moved eastward also; for the later history see under the Eastward Extension of this map.

*Athrasarn* (*Stony Ford*)     See *Aros*.

*Beren*     The first placing of *Beren* and *Land of the Cuilwarthin* (Land of the Dead that Live), in the North of the Hills of the Hunters and in the proximity of Nargothrond, agrees with the *Lay of the Children of Húrin* lines 1545–6 (see III.89), and so still in S (§10). In the *Lost Tales* the Dead that Live Again were *(i·)Guilwarthon*, changed in the *Tale of Tinúviel* (II.41) to *i·Cuilwarthon*; in Q (§14) the land is called *Cuilwarthien*, changed to *Gwerth-i-Cuina*.

Subsequently *Beren* and *Land of the Cuilwarthin* were struck out in this position, and *Land of the Cuilwarthin* re-entered much further to the East, in the empty lands between Sirion and Gelion. This was again struck out, in pencil, with the note 'Lies to the east of this and beyond the Great Lands of the East and of wild men' (on which see *Beren and Lúthien* and *Great Lands* under the Eastward Extension of the map). In Q (§14) the Land of the Dead that Live is in Assariad (>Ossiriand), 'between the river [Gelion] and the [Blue] mountains'.

*Broseliand*     This name occurs first in the *Lay of Leithian*, with the spelling *Broceliand* (III.158–9, 169); *Beleriand* first appears (i.e. as originally typed, not as an emendation of *Broseliand*) in Q §13, and in the *Lay of Leithian* at line 3957. *Broseliand* occurs also in the note in red ink in the south-east corner of the map; this is given together with the later alterations to it at the end of these notes on the southern half.

*Celon, River*     This has not occurred in any text. The course of Celon is the same as on the later map, the river rising (in the Eastward Extension of the present map) in Himling.

*Cuilwarthin, Land of the*     See *Beren*.

*Doriath*     The bounds of Doriath are represented, I think, by Mindeb, by the dotted line (above 'Beleg and Túrin') between Mindeb and Aros, then by Aros and Sirion to the dotted line encircling 'Doriath beyond Sirion', and so back to Mindeb.

*Doriath beyond Sirion*     It is said in Q (§13) that the Taiglin 'enters the land of Doriath *ere it joins with* the great waters of Sirion'. As a name,

'Doriath beyond Sirion' has only occurred in a note on the MS of the *Tale of the Nauglafring* (II. 249).

*Duil Rewinion*   This name of the Hills of the Hunters (also on the Westward Extension of the map) is not found elsewhere.

*Dwarf-road*   See *Aros*.

*Geleidhian*   This occurs in the note in the corner of the map, as the Gnomish name of Broseliand. It is found in additions to Q, §9 (note 2) and §10 (note 15); see p. 174.

*Guarded Plain, The*   First occurs in the *Lay of the Children of Húrin* (III. 88). On the later map the name is written over a much larger area further to the North-east, and outside the boundaries of the realm of Nargothrond as shown on that map (see *Realm of Narog beyond Narog*).

*Hill of Spies*   This first appears in Q §13 (see p. 185). If, as would seem natural, the Hill of Spies is the eminence marked by radiating lines a little north of east from Nargothrond, the name itself is placed oddly distant from it, and seems rather to refer to the highland rising N.E. of Nargothrond, between Narog and Taiglin.

*Hills of the Hunters, The*   First named in the *Lay of the Children of Húrin*, though they had been described without being named in the *Tale of Turambar*; see my discussion, III. 88. On the map the Hills of the Hunters are shown as extending far southwards towards the coast of the Sea, with the Narog bending south-eastwards along the line of the Hills; and there is an outlying eminence above the unnamed cape in the S.W. corner of the map (later Cape Balar).

*Ingwil*   First occurs in the *Lay of the Children of Húrin* (III. 88–9).

*Lúthien caught by Celegorm*   In the *Lay of Leithian* (lines 2342–7) Celegorm and Curufin hunting out of Nargothrond with Huan on the occasion when Lúthien was captured rode for 'three days',

> till nigh to the borders in the West
> of Doriath a while they rest.

*Marshes of Sirion*   On the later map called 'Fens of Sirion'.

*Nan Tathrin (Land of Willows)*   For the name *Nan Tathrin* see III. 89. It was already placed essentially thus in the tale of *The Fall of Gondolin* (see II. 153, 217), and in Q §16 Nan-Tathrin 'is watered by the Narog and by Sirion'.

*Nargothrond*   Nargothrond was placed first further to the South and nearer to the confluence with Sirion; the second site is where it remained – but it is curious that in both sites it is marked as lying on the east side of the river: in the *Lay of the Children of Húrin* it was on the western side (cf. line 1762), and, I would think, always had been. (On the Westward Extension map this is corrected.)

In Q §9, after the Battle of Sudden Flame Barahır and Felagund 'fled to the fens of Sirion to the South'; and after swearing his oath to Barahir Felagund 'went South' (emended to 'South and West') and founded Nargothrond. This would in fact point to the first site of Nargothrond on the map; since the later site is due West from the fens.

*Narog*    First occurs in the *Lay of the Children of Húrin*. The course of the river was scarcely changed subsequently.

*Realm of Narog beyond Narog*    This was hastily added to the map in blue crayon, together with the broken line indicating its boundaries. On the later map the 'Realm of Nargothrond beyond the river' covers a much larger territory to the North-east (see *Guarded Plain*).

*Sirion*    See notes on the northern half.

*Sirion flows underground*    See *Umboth-muilin*. Sirion's fall is also referred to in the *Lay of the Children of Húrin*, lines 1467–8.

*Umboth-muilin*    The name goes back to the *Tale of the Nauglafring* (II.225). It emerges from the *Lay of Leithian* (lines 1722 ff.) that the Twilight Meres were north of Sirion's fall and passage underground, whereas in the tale of *The Fall of Gondolin* the reverse was the case (see II.217, III.222–3).

*Waters of Sirion*    Cf. S §16 'The remnant reaches Sirion and journeys to the land at its mouth – the Waters of Sirion', and §17 'He returned home and found the Waters of Sirion desolate.'

*Woodmen of Turambar*    The Woodmen were first placed a long way away from their later location – south of Sirion's passage underground and north of Nan Tathrin, with their land (shown by a dotted line) extending on both sides of the river. This position is quite at variance with what was said in the *Tale of Turambar* (II.91): 'that people had houses . . . in lands that *were not utterly far from Sirion* or the grassy hills of that river's *middle course*', which as I said (II.141) 'may be taken to agree tolerably with the situation of the Forest of Brethil'. The first placing of the name was struck out, and the second agrees with Q (§13): 'their houses were in the green woods about the River Taiglin that enters the land of Doriath ere it joins with the great waters of Sirion.'

Note on the south-east corner of the map, in red ink with later pencilled additions:

All the lands watered by Sirion south of Gondolin [*added*: or more usually R. Taiglin] are called in English 'Broseliand', *Geleidhian* by the gnomes. [*Added*: – but this usually does *not* include Doriath. Its east boundary is not shown. It is the Blue Mountains.]

It is interesting that *Broseliand* is said to be the English name; and that Doriath is not usually included in Broseliand.

Lastly, it may be mentioned that of the highlands rising on the eastern side of the lower course of Sirion there is no trace on the later map.

## THE WESTWARD AND EASTWARD EXTENSIONS TO THE MAP

These supplementary maps were drawn in relation to the main or central map and substantially overlapping it: they are in close accord with it in all features where they overlap. These sheets were carefully laid out, but the actual markings were done extremely rapidly in soft pencil, and are now very faint; the paper is thin and the maps are battered. Some alterations and additions were made in ink (some of the rivers of Ossiriand are written in ink and some in pencil).

The notes on these supplementary maps include almost all names that do not occur on the main map, and a few that occur on both which have features of interest on the extensions.

## The Westward Extension

*Bridge of Ice*    The words in the N.W. corner 'Far north lies the bridge of Ice' refer to the Helkaraksë, but the meaning of the word 'bridge' is only explained in the *Ambarkanta* (see p. 238).

*Brithombar* (and *Eldorest*)    This is the first occurrence of the Havens of the Falas. That Ossë persuaded some of the Teleri to remain 'on the beaches of the world' is mentioned in Q §3; and in a later rewriting of a passage in Q §11 (note 14) the presence of Elves 'from the Falas' before the Battle of Unnumbered Tears is referred to.

*Brithon, River*    The first occurrence of the name, as of *Brithombar* the haven at its mouth. The later imposition on the coast-line as originally drawn of the river-mouth and the long cape giving protection to the haven can be seen.

*Celegorm and Curufin*    They are shown as being lords of a 'fief' N.W. of the Hills of the Hunters, with *Felagund* ruling in Nargothrond.

*Eldor, River*    The first occurrence of the name. This river was later named *Eglor, Eglahir*, and finally *Nenning*, its course remaining unchanged.

*Eldorest, Haven of Eldorest*    The first occurrence of the name (see *Brithombar*). The haven at the mouth of the Eldor became *Eglorest*

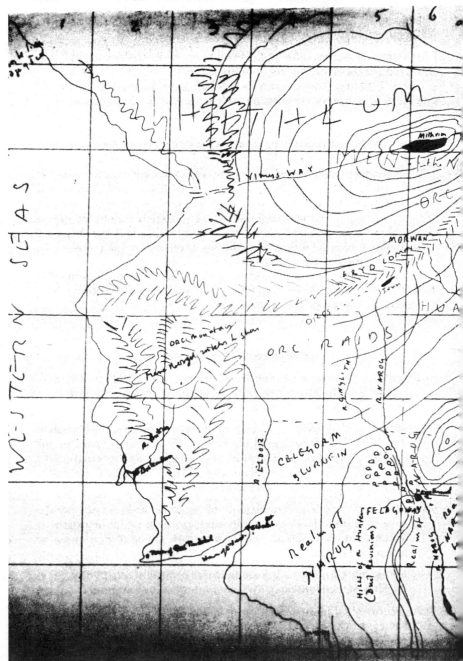

The Westward Extension

when the river became the *Eglor*, and so remained (*Eglarest* in *The Silmarillion*) when the river was again renamed *Nenning*.

**Felagund** See *Celegorm* and *Curufin*.

**Hithlum** The mountain-range fencing Hithlum on the West (later *Ered Lómin* when that name was transferred from the Shadowy Mountains, see pp. 192–3) is shown.

**Morwen** This is written over *Mavwin* (see this entry under the main map).

**Nargothrond** is now placed on the west bank of Narog.

**Orc-Mountains** Extensive highlands cover the entire region between Brithombar and the range forming the southern fence of what was later called Nevrast. On the later map these highlands are retained in the region between the sources of the Brithon and the Eldor (Nenning), and are too little represented on my map in the published *Silmarillion*.

Here *Morgoth reaches the shores* is probably a reference to the story that has not yet emerged in the texts, that in the year after the Battle of Unnumbered Tears 'Morgoth sent great strength over Hithlum and Nevrast, and they came down the rivers Brithon and Nenning and ravaged all the Falas' (*The Silmarillion* p. 196).

**Realm of Narog** Of the three occurrences, that in the centre between the Hills of the Hunters and the river was put in at the time of the making of the map; the other two (*Realm of Narog* in the West, and *Realm of Narog beyond Narog* to the East of the river) were entered in blue crayon at the same time as *Realm of Narog beyond Narog* on the main map, as also was the continuation of the broken line, marking the northern boundary, as far as the river Eldor.

**Tower of Tindobel** This stands where on the later map is Barad Nimras (the tower raised by Felagund 'to watch the western sea', *The Silmarillion* pp. 120, 196). *Tindobel* is first mentioned in the *Annals of Beleriand* (later than the *Quenta*), p. 331.

**Ylmir's Way** *Ylmir*, almost certainly the Gnomish form of *Ulmo*, is found in the *Lay of the Children of Húrin* (III.93) and regularly in S. With 'Ylmir's Way' cf. the tale of *The Fall of Gondolin* (II.149–50):

Thereafter 'tis said that magic and destiny led [Tuor] on a day to a cavernous opening down which a hidden river flowed from Mithrim. And Tuor entered that cavern seeking to learn its secret, but the waters of Mithrim drove him forward into the heart of the rock and he might not win back into the light. And this, 'tis said, was the will of Ulmo Lord of Waters at whose prompting the Noldoli had made that hidden way.

It is not clear from this passage at what point the river out of Lake Mithrim went underground. In the story of Tuor written long afterwards and given in *Unfinished Tales* Tuor followed 'a sudden spring of water in the hills' (p. 21), and

> he came down from the tall hills of Mithrim and passed out into the northward plain of Dor-lómin; and ever the stream grew as he followed it westward, until after three days he could descry in the west the long grey ridges of Ered Lómin . . . (p. 20).

The Gate of the Noldor, where the stream went underground, was in the eastern foothills of Ered Lómin.

Ylmir's Way issues in a firth that is unnamed on the map (*Drengist* has hitherto only occurred in the list of Old English names, p. 210).

It will be seen that the western coastline is closely similar to that on the later map.

## The Eastward Extension

*Adurant, River*   The most southerly of the tributaries of Gelion, named in an addition to Q §14 (note 4). Its course and relation to the mountains and the other rivers was not changed.

*Ascar, River*   The name of the northernmost of the tributaries of Gelion occurs in Q §14 (see entry *Flend* below). Its course and relation to the mountains and the other rivers was not changed.

*Beren and Lúthien*   *Here dwelt Beren and Lúthien before destruction of Doriath in Land of Cuilwarthin.*   On the main map the second placing of this land, between Sirion and Gelion, was rejected with the note: 'Lies to the east of this and beyond the Great Lands of the East and of wild men.' This must mean that my father was moving the Land of the Dead that Live far away into unknown regions (see the entry *Great Lands*); but the Eastward Extension map places it in the final position, in the region of the Seven Rivers: see *Gweirth-i-cuina*.

*Blue Mountains*   These were first named in Q §9.

*Brilthor, River*   This, the fifth of the tributaries of Gelion, is named in an addition to Q §14 (note 4); later emendation to Q moved Duilwen further south and brought Brilthor into the fourth place.

*Broseliand*   *Here is end of Broseliand*, written between the rivers Ascar and Thalos, and against the western feet of the Blue Mountains. Cf. the addition to the note in the corner of the main map (p. 227): 'Its east boundary is not shown. It is the Blue Mountains.'

*Cuilwarthin*   See *Beren and Lúthien*, *Gweirth-i-cuina*.

**The Eastward Extension**

*Damrod and Díriel*   The note above the name *Díriel* reads: 'Here is a wide forest where many fugitive gnomes wander. Orcs come seldom.' Cf. Q §14: 'the woods about the River [Flend/Gelion], where aforetime were the hunting grounds of Damrod and Díriel.' The note below the name *Díriel* reads: 'Here also are many Ilkorins who do not live in Doriath but fought at Nirnaith Únoth.' *Nirnaith Únoth* occurs in the *Lay of the Children of Húrin*, replaced by *Nirnaith Ornoth* (III.79, 102, 123). On Dark-elves at the Battle of Unnumbered Tears see S and Q §11.

*Dolm, Mt.*   This is the first appearance of the mountain afterwards named *Dolmed*, placed as on the later map.

*Duilwen*   This, the third of the tributaries of Gelion, is named in an addition to Q §14 (note 4), where it is placed as on the map between Thalos and Loeglin. Later emendation to Q gave the final order; with Duilwen moved south to become the fifth tributary.

*Dwarf-road and Sarn Athra*   As the Dwarf-road was first marked on this map, after crossing Aros it bent south-east and ran in that direction in a straight line across East Broseliand, crossing (Flend) Gelion at Sarn Athra, which (having been moved from its position on the main map, where it was on the Aros) was now placed at the confluence of the third tributary river (here Duilwen). The line of the road goes off the map in the south-east corner, with the direction: 'Southward in East feet of Blue Mountains are Belegost and Nogrod.' This site for Sarn Athra agrees with Q §14, where the ford is near the confluence of (Flend) Gelion and Duilwen.

A later route for the Dwarf-road is also marked on this map. Here the road bears more nearly east in the land of Damrod and Díriel and so crosses (Flend) Gelion further north: Sarn Athra is now placed just below the confluence of Ascar with Gelion (this is the reason for the emendation of Duilwen to Ascar in Q §14, note 7). It then follows the course of Ascar on the southern side, crosses the mountains by a pass below Mount Dolm, and then turns sharply south and goes away on the eastern side of the mountains.

On the later map Sarn Athra is placed just *above* the confluence of Ascar and Gelion, and the road therefore goes along the northern bank of Ascar, but still crosses the mountains south of Mount Dolmed; the Dwarf-cities are now placed in the eastern side of the mountains not far from Mount Dolmed.

*East Broseliand*   The term *East Beleriand* occurs in Q §14.

*Flend*   In Q §14 the great river of East Beleriand was first named *Ascar*, but since *Ascar* was already in Q the name of the northernmost of the tributaries from the Blue Mountains I think that this was a mere slip (see p. 189 and footnote) for *Flend*, to which it was emended. *Flend* then > *Gelion*, as on the map. The course of Gelion was not changed afterwards, but the map does not show the later eastern tributary arm ('Greater Gelion').

*Gelion*   See *Flend*.

*Great Lands*   The note down the right hand side of the map reads: 'Here lie the Great Lands of the East where Ilkorins (dark-elves) and Wild Men live, acknowledging Morgoth as God and King.' This use of *Great Lands* for the lands of Middle-earth *east of the Blue Mountains* is notable; it is used also on the main map, where the third site of the Land of the Dead that Live is said to lie 'beyond the Great Lands of the East and of wild men' (see *Beren and Lúthien*). In the *Lost Tales* the term *Great Lands* always means the lands between the Seas (i.e. the whole of the later *Middle-earth*); in S and Q *Outer Lands* (which in the *Lost Tales* meant the Western Lands) is used of Middle-earth, with later emendation to *Hither Lands* in Q.

The statement here that in the Great Lands of the East both Wild Men and Dark-elves acknowledged Morgoth as God and King is significant for the future. Cf. the emendation to Q II §18, note 3: 'But most Men, and especially those new come out of the East, were on the side of the Enemy.' The corruption of certain Men in the beginning of their days appears in very early synopses (for *Gilfanon's Tale*); see I. 236.

*Gweirth-i-cuina*   This name, in which *Gweirth-* is apparently emended from *Gwairth-*, is written over *Cuilwarthin*. *Gwerth-i-cuina* (not *Gweirth-* as on the map) has appeared in two emended passages in Q: §10 (note 15) 'they wandered . . . upon the confines of Geleidhian in fair Ossiriand, Land of Seven Streams, Gwerth-i-cuina, the Living Dead' (where the name seems to be used of Beren and Lúthien themselves); and §14 (note 6) 'Elves called it oft Gwerth-i-cuina', where it is used of the land, as on the map.

*Himling*   The first occurrence is in the *Lay of Leithian* lines 2994-5 (April 1928):

where Himling's watchful hill<br>o'er Aglon's gorge hung tall and still.

*Loeglin*   As the fourth of the tributaries of Gelion this is named in an addition to Q §14 (note 4). Later emendation moved Duilwen further south and brought Loeglin (> Legolin) into the third place.

*Nirnaith Únoth*   See *Damrod and Díriel*.

*Ossiriath (of the Seven rivers)*   This form is not found elsewhere. It is written over *Assariad*, which occurs in Q §14, later emended to *Ossiriand* (note 4). *Ossiriand(e)* is found as a rejected alternative to *Broseliand* in Canto I of the *Lay of Leithian* (III.158-60). The placing of the name, between the sixth and seventh rivers, is odd, but in view of 'of the Seven rivers' probably not significant.

*Rathlorion*    This is the form of the new name of Ascar found in Q (§14), later emended to *Rathloriel*.

*Sarn Athra*    See *Dwarf-road*. In Q §14 *Sarn-athra*, emended to *Sarn-athrad* (note 8).

*Sons of Fëanor*    See entry *Aglon* to the northern half of the main map.

*Thalos*    This, the second of the tributaries of Gelion, is named in an addition to Q §14 (note 4). Its course and relation to the mountains and the other rivers was not changed.

# V

# THE AMBARKANTA

This very short work, of cardinal interest (and not least in the associated maps), is entitled at the beginning of the text 'Of the Fashion of the World'; on a title-page loose from but obviously belonging with the work is written:

*Ambarkanta*

The Shape of the World

Rúmil

together with the word *Ambarkanta* in tengwar. This is the first appearance of Rúmil since the *Lost Tales*; but he is not mentioned in the text itself.

That the *Ambarkanta* is later than the *Quenta* (perhaps by several years) cannot be doubted. The reappearance of the name *Utumna* is an advance on Q, where also the term 'Middle-earth' does not appear; *Eruman* is (aberrantly) the name in Q of the land where Men awoke (pp. 99, 171), whereas in the *Ambarkanta* its name is for the first time *Hildórien*; and there are several cases where the *Ambarkanta* has names and details that are only found in Q by emendation (for example, *Elvenhome* p. 236, but *Bay of Faërie* > *Bay of Elvenhome* in Q (II), p. 155 note 12).

The text consists of six pages of fine manuscript in ink, with very little emendation; I give the final forms throughout, with all rejected readings in the notes that follow the text. Closely associated with the work and here reproduced from the originals are three diagrams of the World, here numbered I, II, and III, and two maps, numbered IV and V. On the pages facing these reproductions I note changes made to names. The text begins with a list of cosmographical words, with explanations; this I give on pp. 240–1.

### OF THE FASHION OF THE WORLD

About all the World are the Ilurambar, or Walls of the World. They are as ice and glass and steel, being above all imagination of the Children of Earth cold, transparent, and hard. They cannot be seen, nor can they be passed, save by the Door of Night.

Within these walls the Earth is globed: above, below, and upon all sides is Vaiya, the Enfolding Ocean. But this is more like to sea below the Earth and more like to air above the Earth. In Vaiya below the Earth dwells Ulmo. Above the Earth lies the Air, which is called Vista,[1] and sustains birds and clouds. Therefore it is called above Fanyamar, or Cloudhome; and below Aiwenórë[2] or Bird-land. But this air lies only upon Middle-earth and the Inner Seas, and its proper bounds are the Mountains of Valinor in the West and the Walls of the Sun in the East. Therefore clouds come seldom in Valinor, and the mortal birds pass not beyond the peaks of its mountains. But in the North and South, where there is most cold and darkness and Middle-earth extends nigh to the Walls of the World, Vaiya and Vista and Ilmen[3] flow together and are confounded.

Ilmen is that air that is clear and pure being pervaded by light though it gives no light. Ilmen lies above Vista, and is not great in depth, but is deepest in the West and East, and least in the North and South. In Valinor the air is Ilmen, but Vista flows in at times especially in Elvenhome, part of which is at the eastern feet of the Mountains; and if Valinor is darkened and this air is not cleansed by the light of the Blessed Realm, it takes the form of shadows and grey mists. But Ilmen and Vista will mingle being of like nature, but Ilmen is breathed by the Gods, and purified by the passage of the luminaries; for in Ilmen Varda ordained the courses of the stars, and later of the Moon and Sun.

From Vista there is no outlet nor escape save for the servants of Manwë, or for such as he gives powers like to those of his people, that can sustain themselves in Ilmen or even in the upper Vaiya, which is very thin and cold. From Vista one may descend upon the Earth. From Ilmen one may descend into Valinor. Now the land of Valinor extends almost to Vaiya, which is most narrow in the West and East of the World, but deepest in the North and South. The Western shores of Valinor are therefore not far from the Walls of the World. Yet there is a chasm which sunders Valinor from Vaiya, and it is filled with Ilmen, and by this way one may come from Ilmen above the earth to the lower regions, and to the Earthroots, and the caves and grottoes that are at the foundations of the lands and seas. There is Ulmo's abiding-place. Thence are derived the waters of Middle-earth. For these waters are compounded of Ilmen and Vaiya and Ambar[4] (which is Earth), since Ulmo blends Ilmen and Vaiya and sends them up through the veins of the World to cleanse and refresh the seas and rivers, the lakes and the fountains of Earth. And running water thus possesses the memory of the deeps and the heights, and holds somewhat of the wisdom and music of Ulmo, and of the light of the luminaries of heaven.

In the regions of Ulmo the stars are sometimes hidden, and there the Moon often wanders and is not seen from Middle-earth. But the Sun does not tarry there. She passes under the earth in haste, lest night be prolonged and evil strengthened; and she is drawn through the nether Vaiya by the servants of Ulmo, and it is warmed and filled with life. Thus days are measured by the courses of the Sun, which sails from East to West through the lower Ilmen, blotting out the stars; and she passes over the midst of Middle-earth and halts not, and she bends her course northward or southward, not waywardly but in due procession and season. And when she rises above the Walls of the Sun it is Dawn, and when she sinks behind the Mountains of Valinor it is evening.

But days are otherwise in Valinor than in Middle-earth. For there the time of greatest light is Evening. Then the Sun comes down and rests for a while in the Blessed Land, lying upon the bosom of Vaiya. And when she sinks into Vaiya it is made hot and glows with rosecoloured fire, and this for a long while illumines that land. But as she passes toward the East the glow fades, and Valinor is robbed of light, and is lit only with stars; and the Gods mourn then most for the death of Laurelin. At dawn the dark is deep in Valinor, and the shadows of their mountains lie heavy on the mansions of the Gods. But the Moon does not tarry in Valinor, and passeth swiftly o'er it to plunge in the chasm of Ilmen,[5] for he pursues ever after the Sun, and overtakes her seldom, and then is consumed and darkened in her flame. But it happens at times that he comes above Valinor ere the Sun has left it, and then he descends and meets his beloved, and Valinor is filled with mingled light as of silver and gold; and the Gods smile remembering the mingling of Laurelin and Silpion long ago.

The Land of Valinor slopes downward from the feet of the Mountains, and its western shore is at the level of the bottoms of the inner seas. And not far thence, as has been said, are the Walls of the World; and over against the westernmost shore in the midst of Valinor is Ando Lómen[6] the Door of Timeless Night that pierceth the Walls and opens upon the Void. For the World is set amid Kúma, the Void, the Night without form or time. But none can pass the chasm and the belt of Vaiya and come to that Door,

save the great Valar only. And they made that Door when Melko
was overcome and put forth into the Outer Dark; and it is guarded
by Eärendel.

The Middle-earth lies amidst the World, and is made of land
and water; and its surface is the centre of the world from the
confines of the upper Vaiya to the confines of the nether. Of old its
fashion was thus. It was highest in the middle, and fell away on
either side into vast valleys, but rose again in the East and West
and again fell away to the chasm at its edges. And the two valleys
were filled with the primeval water, and the shores of these ancient
seas were in the West the western highlands and the edge of the
great land, and in the East the eastern highlands and the edge of
the great land upon the other side. But at the North and South it
did not fall away, and one could go by land from the uttermost
South and the chasm of Ilmen to the uttermost North and the
chasm of Ilmen. The ancient seas lay therefore in troughs, and
their waters spilled not to the East or to the West; but they had no
shores either at the North or at the South, and they spilled into the
chasm, and their waterfalls became ice and bridges of ice because
of the cold; so that the chasm of Ilmen was here closed and
bridged, and the ice reached out into Vaiya, and even unto the
Walls of the World.

Now it is said that the Valar coming into the World descended
first upon Middle-earth at its centre, save Melko who descended in
the furthest North. But the Valar took a portion of land and made
an island and hallowed it, and set it in the Western Sea and abode
upon it, while they were busied in the exploration and first
ordering of the World. As is told they desired to make lamps, and
Melko offered to devise a new substance of great strength and
beauty to be their pillars. And he set up these great pillars north
and south of the Earth's middle yet nearer to it than the chasm;
and the Gods placed lamps upon them and the Earth had light for
a while.

But the pillars were made with deceit, being wrought of ice; and
they melted, and the lamps fell in ruin, and their light was spilled.
But the melting of the ice made two small inland seas, north and
south of the middle of Earth, and there was a northern land and a
middle land and a southern land. Then the Valar removed into the
West and forsook the island; and upon the highland at the western
side of the West Sea they piled great mountains, and behind them

made the land of Valinor. But the mountains of Valinor curve backward, and Valinor is broadest in the middle of Earth, where the mountains march beside the sea; and at the north and south the mountains come even to the chasm. There are those two regions of the Western Land which are not of Middle-earth and are yet outside the mountains: they are dark and empty. That to the North is Eruman, and that to the South is Arvalin; and there is only a narrow strait between them and the corners of Middle-earth, but these straits are filled with ice.

For their further protection the Valar thrust away Middle-earth at the centre and crowded it eastward, so that it was bended, and the great sea of the West is very wide in the middle, the widest of all waters of the Earth. The shape of the Earth in the East was much like that in the West, save for the narrowing of the Eastern Sea, and the thrusting of the land thither. And beyond the Eastern Sea lies the Eastern Land, of which we know little, and call it the Land of the Sun; and it has mountains, less great than those of Valinor, yet very great, which are the Walls of the Sun. By reason of the falling of the land these mountains cannot be descried, save by highflying birds, across the seas which divide them from the shores of Middle-earth.

And the thrusting aside of the land caused also mountains to appear in four ranges, two in the Northland, and two in the Southland; and those in the North were the Blue Mountains in the West side, and the Red Mountains in the East side; and in the South were the Grey Mountains and the Yellow. But Melko fortified the North and built there the Northern Towers, which are also called the Iron Mountains, and they look southward. And in the middle land there were the Mountains of the Wind, for a wind blew strongly there coming from the East before the Sun; and Hildórien the land where Men first awoke lay between these mountains and the Eastern Sea. But Kuiviénen where Oromë found the Elves is to the North beside the waters of Helkar.[7]

But the symmetry of the ancient Earth was changed and broken in the first Battle of the Gods, when Valinor went out against Utumno,[8] which was Melko's stronghold, and Melko was chained. Then the sea of Helkar (which was the northern lamp) became an inland sea or great lake, but the sea of Ringil (which was the southern lamp) became a great sea flowing north-eastward and joining by straits both the Western and Eastern Seas.

And the Earth was again broken in the second battle, when

Melko was again overthrown, and it has changed ever in the wearing and passing of many ages.[9] But the greatest change took place, when the First Design was destroyed, and the Earth was rounded, and severed from Valinor. This befell in the days of the assault of the Númenóreans upon the land of the Gods, as is told in the Histories. And since that time the world has forgotten the things that were before, and the names and the memory of the lands and waters of old has perished.

## NOTES

1   *Vista*: at all seven occurrences the original name *Wilwa* was changed, first in pencil then in ink, to *Vista*; so also on the world-diagrams I and II, and on the diagram III (the World Made Round).

2   Original reading *Aiwenor*; so also on diagram I.

3   *Ilmen*: at all the many occurrences the original name *Silma* was carefully erased and changed to *Ilma* (the same change on the map IV); *Ilma* was then itself altered to *Ilmen* (the same succession of changes on diagrams I and II).

4   *Ambar* is an emendation but the underlying word is wholly erased (so also on diagram II; written in later on I).

5   In the margin is written *Ilmen-assa*, changed from *Ilman-assa*.

6   *Ando Lómen* is interpolated into the text, but in all probability not significantly later than the original writing of the MS.

7   The last two sentences of this paragraph (from 'And in the middle land . . .') were added, but to all appearance belong in time with the original writing of the MS.

8   *Utumno* is emended from *Utumna*.

9   The original MS ends here; what follows, concerning the Earth Made Round at the time of the assault of the Númenóreans, was added later (see p. 261).

I give now the list of cosmological words accompanying the *Ambarkanta*. My father made several changes to this list, but since the alterations were mostly made over erasures and the additions belong to the same period it is impossible to know the original form of the list in all points. The changes in the list are however much the same as those made in the text of the *Ambarkanta* and on the world-diagrams; thus *Silma* > *Ilma* > *Ilmen*, *Wilwa* > *Vista*, *Aiwenor* > *Aiwenórë*; *ava, ambar, Endor* over erasures; *Avakúma, & Elenarda Stellar Kingdom* additions. The translation of *Ilmen* as 'Place of light' is an emendation from 'sheen'.

*Ilu*  The World                                    World
  *Ilurambar*  The Walls of the World;
  *ramba*  wall

*Kúma*  darkness, void                              Dark
  *ava*  outer, exterior; *Avakúma*

*Vaiya*  fold, envelope. In nature like             Outer Sea, or Encircling
  to water, but less buoyant than air,              Ocean, or Enfolding Ocean
  and surrounding  The Outer Sea.*

*Ilmen*  Place of light. The region above           Sky. Heaven
  the air, than which it is thinner and
  more clear. Here only the stars and
  Moon and Sun can fly. It is called
  also *Tinwë-mallë* the Star-street, &
  *Elenarda* Stellar Kingdom.

*Vista*  air. Wherein birds may fly and             Air
  clouds sail. Its upper region is
  *Fanyamar* or Cloudhome, and its
  lower *Aiwenórë* or Birdland.

*ambar*  Earth. *ambar-endya* or                    Earth
  Middle Earth of which *Endor* is
  the midmost point.

*ëar*  water; sea.                                  Sea
  The roots of the Earth are
  *Mar-talmar*, or *Talmar Ambaren*.

*ando*  door, gate.

*lómë*  Night. *Ando Lómen* the Door of
  Night, through which Melko was
  thrust after the Second War of the
  Gods.

All that land that lies above water, between the Seas of the West and East
and the Mountains of North and South is *Pelmar*, the Enclosed
Dwelling.

## Commentary on the *Ambarkanta*

This elegant universe, while certainly in many respects an evolution
from the old cosmology of the *Lost Tales*, shows also radical shifts and
advances in essential structure.

*This is very confusing, since Vaiya is apparently said to *surround* the Outer Sea
(though in the right-hand column it is itself defined as 'Outer Sea'). But the word 'The' in
'The Outer Sea' has a capital T; and I think that my father left the preceding sentence
unfinished, ending with 'surrounding', and that he added 'The Outer Sea' afterwards as a
definition of Vaiya, without noticing that the preceding phrase was incomplete.

## Diagram I

Some of the names on this diagram were written in over erasures, and in most of the cases only the fact of correction can be seen:

*Ilmen* (replacing *Ilma* and *Silma*, see note 3 to the text of the *Ambarkanta*); *Vista* (replacing *Wilwa*, see note 1); *Ava-* (in *Ava-kúma*); *Ambarendya*; *Endor*; *Martalmar*. The letter A in the centre, of obscure significance, is also written over an erasure.

Additions are: *Elenarda* or; *-e* added to *Aiwenor* (see note 2); *Ambar* (see note 4).

Much later pencilled changes and additions are: *Ilurambar* to *Earambar* at one only of the occurrences; *Hidden Half* added above the lower occurrence of *Vaiya*; *Ilu* to *Arda* in the title. The note at the right-hand bottom corner is too faint to make out after the words 'Alter story of Sun'; that on the left reads: 'Make world *always a globe* but larger than now. Mountains of East and West prevent anyone from going to Hidden Half.'

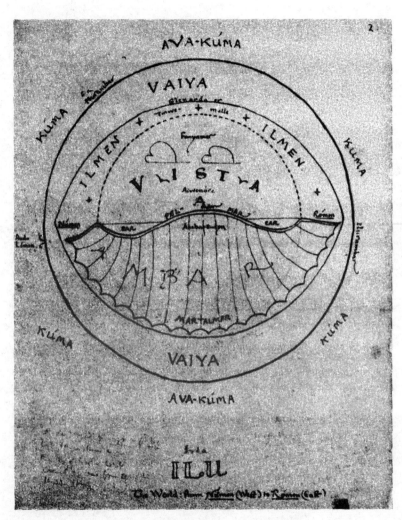

## Diagram II

As in diagram I some names were written in over erasures:

*Ilmen* (from *Ilma* and *Silma*); *Vista* (from *Wilwa*); *Ambar*; *Endor*; *Martalmar*; *Formen* (from *Tormen*) in the title.

Late pencilled changes are: *Ilurambar* to *Earambar* at one of the occurrences, as on diagram I; *Harmen* to *Hyarmen* both on the diagram and in the title; *Tormen* > *Formen* on the diagram.

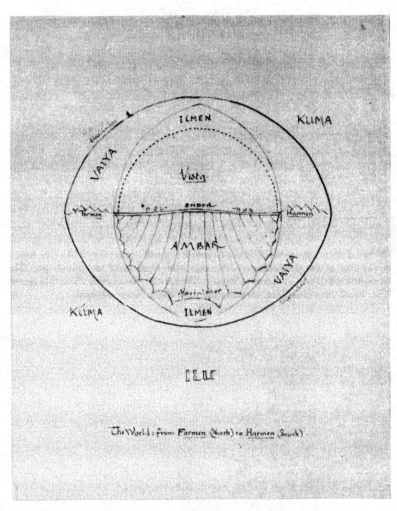

The World: from Formen (North) to Harmen (South)

II

## Diagram III

On this diagram the name *Wilwa* was struck out and replaced by *Vista* (see note 1 to the text of the *Ambarkanta*). Names other than those in capitals are: *The Straight Path* (twice), *Valinor, Eressëa, Old Lands, New Lands*. The title reads: 'The World after the Cataclysm and the ruin of the Númenoreans'.

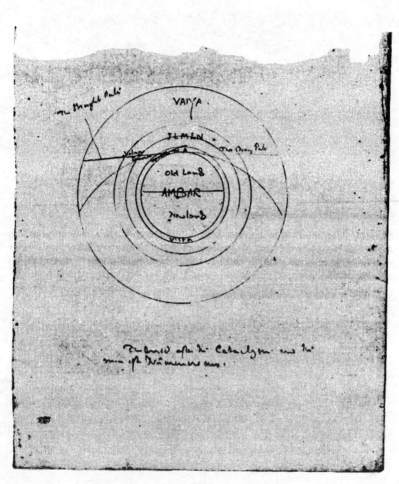

III

Map IV

Changes made to this map were:

*Silma* to *Ilma* at all three occurrences, and at one only *Ilma* later in pencil to *Ilmen* (see note 3 to the text of the *Ambarkanta*); *Endor* to *Endon* (but *Endor* written again above in pencil); and *Tormen* > *Formen, Harmen* > *Hyarmen*, as on diagram II.

V.Y. 500 = Valian Year 500; see p. 263.

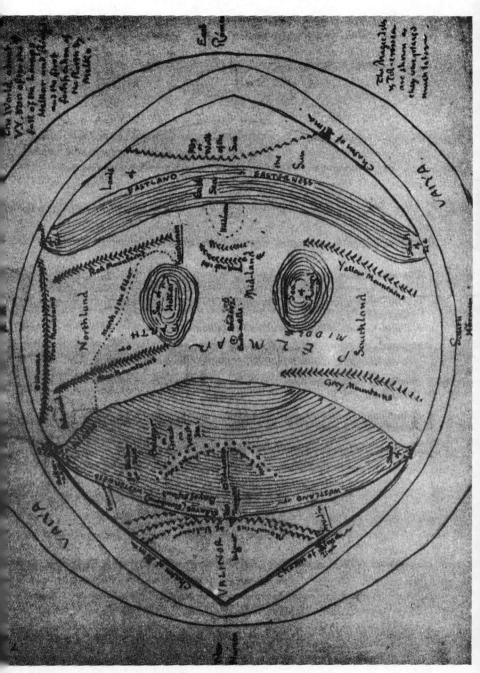

IV

## Map V

Some of the names on this map are not easy to read, and I list here all that appear on it:

The West: *Outer Seas, Utgarsecg*
   *Eruman* (written above this later: *Araman*); *Outer Lands* (*Valinor*); *Alflon*; *Two Trees*; *Tún*; *Valmar*; *Taniquetil*; *Bay of Faery*; *Arvalin* (changed from *Eruman*).
   Lightly pencilled later across the Western Land: *Aman*

The Western Sea: in the extreme North: *Helkaraksë*.
   *Great Seas*; *The G[rea]t Gulf*; *Beleglo[rn?]*; *(Belegar)*; *Ingarsecg*

The North-west of Middle-earth: *Hithlum*; *Angband*; *Thangorodrim*; *Daidelos*; *Beleriand*

Central regions: *Hither Lands*; *Inland Sea*; *Straits of the World; East Sea*; *Dark Land (South Land)*

The East: *Walls of the Sun*; *Burnt Land of the Sun*; *Outer Seas*

Note in the upper right-hand corner: *After the War of the Gods*
   *(Arvalin was cast up by the Great Sea at the foot of the Mts.* See pp. 260–1.

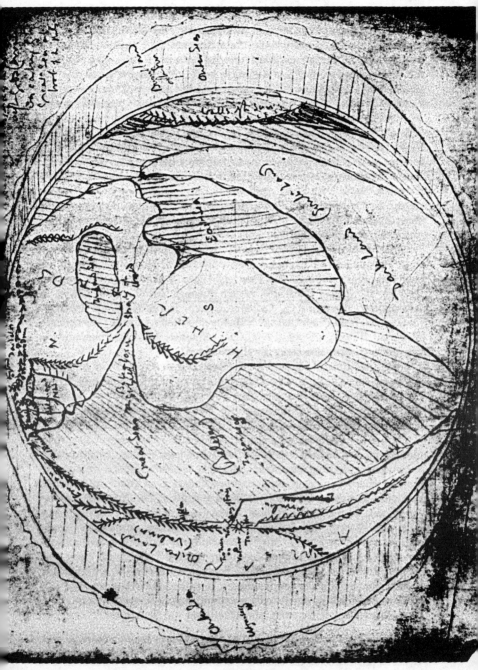

To begin from the Outside: beyond the Walls of the World lies 'the Void, the Night without form or time', *Kúma* (*Ava-kúma*); and this is of course an aboriginal conception, 'the outer dark', 'the limitless dark', 'the starless vast' of the tale of *The Hiding of Valinor* (I.216). The Walls of the World, *Ilurambar*,* are the unbroken, uninterrupted shell of a vast globe; they are cold, invisible, and impassable save by *Ando Lómen*, the Door of Night. This Door was made by the Valar 'when Melko was overcome and put forth into the Outer Dark'; and Eärendel guards it.

Already in S (§19) it was said that 'Morgoth is thrust through the Door of Night into the outer dark beyond the Walls of the World, and a guard set for ever on that Door'; this is repeated in the corresponding passage in Q, where the same expressions are used as in the *Ambarkanta*, 'the Door of Timeless Night', 'the Void', and where Eärendel, sailing in the Void, is named as the guardian (see pp. 164–5, 203). It is not however said in these texts that the Door of Night was made *when Melko was overcome*, at the end of the Great Battle.

I have remarked earlier (p. 49) on the great shift in the astronomical myth introduced in S by the passage of the Sun beneath the Earth, rather than departure through the Door of Night followed by the journey through the Outer Dark and return through the Gates of Morn, as described in *The Hiding of Valinor*; in that account the Gods made the Door of Night in order that the Sunship should not have to pass beneath the Earth. Thus the Door of Night has remained, but its purpose and the time of its making have been totally changed.

The conception of a great Wall surrounding the 'World' and fencing it against an outer Emptiness and Darkness goes back to the beginning; in *The Hiding of Valinor* it is called 'the Wall of Things', and Ulmo instructs the Valar that 'Vai runneth from the Wall of Things unto the Wall of Things whithersoever you may fare' (I.214). I have discussed earlier (I.86) the possibility that already in the early cosmology Vaitya (the outermost of the three 'airs') and Vai (the Outer Ocean) constituted 'a continuous enfolding substance', and that the *Ambarkanta* 'only makes explicit what was present but unexpressed in the *Lost Tales*'; and pointed to the difficulties in this idea. In the first draft of *The Hiding of Valinor* (see I.221 note 16) the Wall of Things was evidently imagined, as I have said (I.227), 'like the walls of terrestrial cities, or gardens – walls with a top: a "ring-fence"'; the Walls were lower in the East, so that there was no Door there corresponding to the Door of Night in the West, and the Sun *rode over* the Eastern Wall. In the second draft (I.216) the idea of the Gates of Morn was introduced; but the nature and extent of the Walls was still left obscure, and indeed nothing else is said of them in the *Lost Tales* beyond the statement that they are 'deep-blue' (I.215). A

---

*\**Ilu* is 'the World' in diagrams I and II, and is so defined in the list of words (p. 241); for its early meaning see I.255, entry *Ilwë*. – The changes to *Earambar* in diagrams I and II, like the pencilled note at the bottom of I, were made very much later and do not concern us here.

remarkable sentence in the original tale of *The Music of the Ainur* (I. 56) declares that 'the Ainur marvelled to see how *the world was globed amid the void* and yet separated from it'. How this is to be interpreted in the context of the *Lost Tales* I do not know; but the sentence was retained through all the rewritings of the *Ainulindalë* (cf. *The Silmarillion* p. 17), and·so became a precise description of the world of the *Ambarkanta*, whatever my father's original meaning may have been.

In view of the close similarity of wording between Q and the *Ambarkanta* on the subject of the expulsion of Melko through the Door of Night, mentioned above, it is very puzzling that in the same passage of Q (p. 164) it is said that some think that he 'creeps back *surmounting the Walls* and visiteth the world'. The fact that this is only a surmise ('Some say . . .'), and that the Prophecy of Mandos which immediately follows declares that when Morgoth does return it will be through the Door of Night, hardly explains how the idea of his 'surmounting the Walls' (in inescapable contradiction to the *Ambarkanta*, and negating the purpose of Eärendel's guard) could arise.*

It is not indeed explained in the *Ambarkanta* how the Valar entered the world at its beginning, passing through the impassable Walls, and perhaps we should not expect it to be. But the central idea at this time is clear: from the Beginning to the Great Battle in which Melko was overthrown, the world with all its inhabitants was inescapably bounded; but at the very end, in order to extrude Melko into the Void, the Valar were able to pierce the Walls by a Door.

Wholly new is the conception of Ilmen as the pure air that is breathed in Valinor, and whose bounds are the Mountains of Valinor and the mountains called the Walls of the Sun, beyond the Eastern Sea, though 'Vista flows in at times especially in Elvenhome'. In Ilmen journey the Sun, Moon, and Stars, so that this region is called also *Tinwë-mallë*† and *Elenarda* (translated 'Star-street' and 'Stellar Kingdom' in the list of words, p. 241). This partly corresponds to the cosmology of the *Lost Tales*, where the Moon-ship 'saileth in the lower folds of Ilwë threading a white swathe among the stars', and the stars 'could not soar into the dark and tenuous realm of Vaitya that is outside all', but where the Sun 'voyageth even above Ilwë and beyond the stars' (I. 181, 193). The lowest air, Vista, in which are *Fanyamar* 'Cloudhome' and *Aiwenórë* 'Bird-land', retains the characteristic nature of the earlier Vilna; cf. I.65 'Vilna that is grey and therein may the birds fly safely'. But there is an important corollary to the frontier between Ilmen and

---

*This conception of the Walls reappears much later, and is found in *The Silmarillion* (p. 36): Melkor, returning to Arda after his expulsion by Tulkas into the outer darkness, 'passed over the Walls of the Night with his host, and came to Middle-earth far in the north'. But this is an aspect of intractable problems arising in the later cosmology that cannot be entered into here.

†See I. 269 (entry *Tinwë Linto*) and 263 (entry *Olórë Mallë*).

Vista in the West: 'clouds come seldom in Valinor, and the mortal birds pass not beyond the peaks of its mountains'.

An aspect of the cosmology that seems puzzling at first sight arises from the statements in the *Ambarkanta* (1) that 'in the North and South . . . Middle-earth extends nigh to the Walls of the World' (p. 236), and (2) that Vaiya is 'most narrow in the West and East of the World, but deepest in the North and South' (*ibid.*). This apparent contradiction is to be explained by the passage (p. 238) describing how the Inner Seas have no shores at North and South, but spilling into the Chasm of Ilmen form ice bridges*that close the chasm, and the ice extends out into Vaiya and even to the Walls of the World. This ice is represented by the mountain-like peaks above the words *Tormen* and *Harmen* in diagram II. Of all this there is no trace in the *Lost Tales*; but it will be found that the *Ambarkanta* here greatly illumines the passage in *The Silmarillion* (p. 89) describing the Helcaraxë:

> For between the land of Aman that in the north curved eastward, and the east-shores of Endor (which is Middle-earth) that bore westward, there was a narrow strait, through which the chill waters of the Encircling Sea and the waves of Belegaer flowed together, and there were vast fogs and mists of deathly cold, and the sea-streams were filled with clashing hills of ice and the grinding of ice deep-sunken.

The passage of the Sun beneath the Earth seems to be differently conceived in the *Ambarkanta* from that of the Moon; for while both pass from East to West through Ilmen, the Sun 'sinks into Vaiya' and is 'drawn through the nether Vaiya by the servants of Ulmo', whereas the Moon plunges into the Chasm of Ilmen.†

Turning now to the surface of the Earth, we meet for the first time the name *Endor*, which does not occur in the text of the *Ambarkanta* itself, but which is defined in the word-list as 'the midmost point' of *Ambarendya* or Middle-earth. *Endor* is marked in also on the 'World-diagrams' I and II, and also on the map IV, where it is shown as a point, the 'Earth-middle', and subsequently changed to *Endon*. The name *Endor* occurs once in *The Silmarillion* (in the passage just cited), but there it is a name of Middle-earth, not of the midmost point of Middle-earth; so also in *The*

---

*Cf. 'Far north lies the bridge of Ice' in the N.W. corner of the Westward Extension of the first 'Silmarillion' map, pp. 227–8.

†The statement in *The Silmarillion* (p. 101) that Tilion (steersman of the Moon) 'would pass swiftly over the western land . . . and plunge in *the Chasm beyond the Outer Sea*' cannot in any way be brought into harmony with the *Ambarkanta*, where the Chasm of Ilmen is reached before Vaiya, and must be so by virtue of the fundamental ideas of the cosmology.

The passage in the 'Silmarillion' version that followed Q and was interrupted at the end of 1937 has: 'But Tilion . . . passes swiftly over the western land . . . and plunges into the chasm between the shores of the Earth and the Outer Sea.' The passage in the published *Silmarillion* derives from a later version written in all probability in 1951–2; but though I retained it I am at a loss to explain it.

*Lord of the Rings* (Appendix E): Quenya *Endóre*, Sindarin *Ennor* 'Middle-earth'. *Ambar-endya* seems to be synonymous with *Pelmar*, since in the word-list the former is defined as 'Middle-earth', while on map IV the region between the two seas of East and West is called 'Pelmar or Middle-earth'; but in diagram I they are marked as if different in reference. Possibly, *Pelmar* (translated in the list of words as 'the Enclosed Dwelling') means strictly the habitable surface, *Ambar-endya* the central raised part of *Ambar*, the Earth.*

The lines drawn downwards from the surface of the Earth to *Martalmar* 'the roots of the Earth' in diagrams I and II are 'the veins of the World' (p. 236); and this passage is important in understanding Ulmo's power and benign influence exerted through the waters of the world (cf. *The Silmarillion* pp. 27, 40, in both of which passages the expression 'the veins of the world' is used).

In the East of the world are the Walls of the Sun, which is a great mountain range symmetrically answering the Mountains of Valinor in the West, as shown on map IV. Of this range there is no mention in the *Lost Tales*, where almost all that is said of the East is contained in Oromë's words to the Valar: 'In the East beyond the tumbled lands there is a silent beach and a dark and empty sea' (I.214); in the East also was the great mountain Kalormë (I.212), and there Aulë and Ulmo 'builded great havens [of the Sun and Moon] beside the soundless sea' (I.215). In the *Ambarkanta* the Gates of Morn, through which the Sun returns from the Outer Dark in the *Lost Tales*, have disappeared.

In the description of evening and dawn in Valinor in the *Ambarkanta* there is an echo of the *Lost Tales*: 'Valinor is filled with mingled light as of silver and gold; and the Gods smile remembering the mingling of Laurelin and Silpion long ago'; cf. I.216 'Then smile the Gods wistfully and say: "It is the mingling of the lights once more."'

The extremely close symmetry of the Eastern and Western lands as displayed on map IV is striking; the chief departure from symmetry being the difference in shape of the great Seas, and this was due to the eastward thrusting or 'crowding' of Middle-earth – 'so that it was bended' – at the time of the making of Valinor and the raising of its protective mountain-chain. This more than Titanic crushing of the new-made world was the origin of the great mountain ranges of Middle-earth, the Blue, the Red, the Yellow, and the Grey. Cf. *The Silmarillion* p. 37:

> And the shape of Arda and the symmetry of its waters and its lands was marred in that time, so that the first designs of the Valar were never after restored.

*For the first element in *Pelmar* see the Appendix to *The Silmarillion*, entry *pel-*. Neither this name nor *Ambar, Ambar-endya* occur in *The Silmarillion*, but *Ambar-metta* 'world-ending' is found in *The Return of the King* (VI.5). – *Middle-earth* is first found in the *Ambarkanta* and in the *Annals of Valinor*, which belong to the same period but cannot be dated relative to one another. – *Rómen* 'East' appears for the first time in diagram I, and *Hyarmen* 'South' and *Formen* 'North' (< *Harmen, Tormen*) in diagram II.

But in *The Silmarillion* this loss of symmetry is not attributed to the deliberate act of the Valar themselves, who in the *Ambarkanta* are ready to contort the very structure of *Ambar* for the sake of their own security. There are some interesting points in the *Ambarkanta* account of the first days of the Valar in the world. Here it is said for the first time that Melko 'descended in the furthest North', whereas the Valar, coming to Middle-earth at its centre, made their island from 'a portion of land' and set it in the Western Sea. The old story of Melko's treacherous assistance of the Valar in their works by devising the pillars of the Lamps out of ice is still present, despite the wording of S, and still more of Q (§1): 'Morgoth contested with them and. made war. The lamps he overthrew . . .', which seems to suggest that it had been abandoned. In the tale of *The Coming of the Valar* the name *Ringil* was given (by Melko!) to the northern pillar, and *Helkar* to the southern (I.69); in the *Ambarkanta* the names are applied to the Lamps rather than the pillars, and *Ringil* becomes that of the southern, *Helkar* that of the northern. In the tale there is no mention of the formation of Inland Seas at the time of the fall of the Lamps; rather 'great floods of water poured from [the Lamps] into the Shadowy Seas', and 'so great was their thaw that whereas those seas were at first of no great size but clear and warm, now were they black and wide and vapours lay upon them and deep shades, for the great cold rivers that poured into.them' (I.70). Later the names of the Lamps were changed more than once, but *Helcar* remained the name of the Inland Sea 'where aforetime the roots of the mountain of Illuin [the northern Lamp] had been' (*The Silmarillion* p. 49), and it is seen from the *Ambarkanta* that the idea of the sea being formed where the Lamp once stood owed its origin to the melting pillar of ice, although the actual story of Melko's devising of the pillars was abandoned when it became impossible to represent Melko as co-operative, even in seeming, with the Valar. There is no mention in *The Silmarillion* of a southern sea where the other Lamp had stood.

Kuiviénen is said in the *Ambarkanta* to be 'to the North beside the waters of Helkar', as shown on map IV. In the *Lost Tales* (I.115, 117) Koivië-néni was a lake (with 'bare margin', set in a vale 'surrounded by pine-clad slopes') in Palisor, the midmost region; in *The Silmarillion* it is 'a bay in the Inland Sea of Helcar' (p. 49). In the same passage Oromë, on that ride that led him to the finding of the Elves, 'turned north by the shores of Helcar and passed under the shadows of the Orocarni, the Mountains of the East', and this agrees perfectly with map IV (*Orocarni* 'Red Mountains', see the Appendix to *The Silmarillion* entry *caran*). The Blue Mountains oppose them symmetrically in the West; and in the South are the Grey Mountains and the Yellow, again symmetrically opposed both to each other and to the northern ranges. The track of the March of the Elves as marked on map IV is again in complete agreement with *The Silmarillion* (p. 53): 'passing northward about the Sea of Helcar they turned towards the west'; but of the Misty Mountains

(*Hithaeglir*) and the Great River (*Anduin*) where many Elves of the Third Host turned away South (*ibid.* p. 54) there is no sign. In *The Hobbit* and *The Lord of the Rings* the Grey Mountains (*Ered Mithrin*) are a range beyond Mirkwood in the North of Middle-earth.

It seems that Beleriand, to judge by the placing and size of the lettering of the name on map IV, was relatively a very small region; and the Elves reached the Sea to the south of it, at the *Falassë* (later the *Falas* of Beleriand). But my father circled 'Beleriand' in pencil and from the circle drew an arrow to the point where the track of the March reached the Sea, which probably implies that he wished to show that this was in fact within the confines of Beleriand.

The name *Hildórien* of the land where Men awoke (implying *Hildor*, the Aftercomers) now first appears; for the curious use of the name *Eruman* for this land in Q see pp. 99, 171. Hildórien is a land lying between the Mountains of the Wind and the Eastern Sea; in *The Silmarillion* (p. 103) it is placed, more vaguely, 'in the eastward regions of Middle-earth'.

The placing of *Utumna* (in the *Ambarkanta* emended to *Utumno*, note 8) on map IV is notable, as is also the occurrence of the name itself. Whereas in the *Lost Tales* Melko's first fortress was *Utumna*, and his second *Angband* (see I.198), in S and Q the original fortress is *Angband*, to which Melko returned after the destruction of the Trees (see p. 44), and *Utumna* is not mentioned in those texts. My father had now reverted to *Utumna* (*Utumno*) as the name of Melko's ancient and original dwelling in Middle-earth (see further below, pp. 259–60).

The archipelagoes in the Western Sea have undergone the great change and simplification that distinguishes the account in *The Silmarillion* from that in the *Lost Tales* (see II.324–5); there is no sign on the map of the Harbourless Isles or the Twilit Isles, and instead we have 'The Enchanted or Magic Isles' – in Q II §17 *Magic Isles* is emended to *Enchanted Isles* (note 11). The 'Shadowy Isles' lying to the northward of the Enchanted Isles on the map seem to be a new conception.

The name *Eldaros* (not *Eldamar*, see I.251) appears on map IV with the meaning 'Elvenhome'. *Eldaros* has occurred once previously, in one of the 'Ælfwine' outlines (II.301): 'Eldaros or Ælfhâm', where the reference is unclear, but seems to be to Tol Eressëa. The words 'Bay of Elfland' are written on the map but no bay is indicated.

In the West the symmetrically formed lands of Eruman and Arvalin between the Mountains and the Sea now appear; for the earlier history see I.83. *Tún* lies a little to the north of Taniquetil; and the position of *Valmar* is as it was on the little ancient map given in I. 81.

In the *Ambarkanta* something is said of the vast further changes in the shape of the lands and seas that took place in 'the first Battle of the Gods', when Melko was taken captive, concerning which there is nothing in Q (§2) beyond a reference to the 'tumult'. In *The Silmarillion* (p. 51) this is called 'the Battle of the Powers'; and

In that time the shape of Middle-earth was changed, and the Great Sea that sundered it from Aman grew wide and deep; and it broke in upon the coasts and made a deep gulf to the southward. Many lesser bays were made between the Great Gulf and Helcaraxë far in the north, where Middle-earth and Aman came nigh together. Of these the Bay of Balar was the chief; and into it the mighty river Sirion flowed down from the new-raised highlands northwards: Dorthonion, and the mountains about Hithlum.

The text of the *Ambarkanta* does not mention the Great Gulf or the Bay of Balar, but speaks rather of the vast extension of the sea of Ringil and its joining to the Eastern and Western Seas (it is not clear why it is said that the sea of Helkar 'became an inland sea or great lake', since it was so already). But on the back of the map IV is another map (V) that illustrates all the features of both accounts. This map is however a very rapid pencil sketch, and is in places difficult to interpret, from uncertainty as to the meaning of lines, more especially in the Western Lands (Outer Lands). It is very hard to say how precisely this map should be interpreted in relation to map IV. For example, in map IV the Grey Mountains are very widely separated from the Blue, whereas in map V there is only a narrow space at the head of the Great Gulf between them; the Inland Sea (Helkar) is further to the North; and so on. Again, many features are absent (such as the Straits of Ice), and in such cases one cannot be sure whether their absence is casual or intentional; though the failure to mark in Tol Eressëa or the Enchanted Isles suggests the former. I am inclined to think that map V is a very rough sketch not to be interpreted too strictly.

The narrow ring between the Earth and the Outer Seas clearly represents the Chasm of Ilmen.

In relation to Beleriand in the North-west, and bearing in mind the whole underlying history of Eriol-Ælfwine and Leithien (England), the southern part of the Hither Lands, below the Great Gulf, bears an obvious resemblance to the continent of Africa; and in a vaguer way the Inland Sea could be interpreted as the Mediterranean and the Black Sea. But I can offer nothing on this matter that would not be the purest speculation.

The sea marked 'East Sea' on map V is the former sea of Ringil; cf. the *Ambarkanta*: 'the sea of Ringil . . . became a great sea flowing north-eastward and joining by straits both the Western and Eastern Seas.'

In the North-west the ranges of Eredlómin and Eredwethrin (not named; see pp. 192–3) enclosing Hithlum (which is named) are shown, and the western extension of Eredwethrin that was the southern fence of later Nevrast.* In the version of 'The Silmarillion' that followed Q it is said that in the War of the Gods the Iron Mountains 'were broken and distorted at their western end, and of their fragments were made Eredwethrin and Eredlómin', and that the Iron Mountains 'bent back northward'; and map V, in relation to map IV, agrees well with this. The first 'Silmarillion' map (after p. 220), on the other hand, shows the Iron Mountains curving back strongly to the North-east (it is conceivable that the hasty zigzag lines to the east of Thangorodrim were intended to rectify this).

In the version of 'The Silmarillion' just referred to it is also said that 'beyond the River Gelion the land narrowed suddenly, for the Great Sea ran into a mighty gulf reaching almost to the feet of Eredlindon, and there was a strait of mountainous land between the gulf and the inland sea of Helcar, by which one might come into the vast regions of the south of Middle-earth'. Again, these features are clearly seen on map V, where the 'strait of mountainous land' is called the 'Straits of the World'. The enclosed areas to the east of Eredwethrin and south-east of Thango-rodrim clearly represent the Encircling Mountains about Gondolin and the highlands of Taur-na-Fuin; we see what was later called the Gap of Maglor between those highlands and the Blue Mountains, and the rivers Gelion (with its tributaries, the rivers of Ossiriand), Sirion, and Narog.† With this part of map V compare the first 'Silmarillion' map and its Eastward extension.

Particularly notable is the closeness of Hithlum on map V to the edge of the world (the Chasm of Ilmen).

Angband is placed in very much the same position on map V as is Utumna on map IV: very near to the Chasm of Ilmen and well behind the mountain-wall, in the land that on map V is called *Daidelos* (later *Dor Daedeloth*).‡ As noted above, Utumna had now been resurrected from the *Lost Tales* as Melko's original fortress; and it emerges clearly from later texts that the story now was that when Melko returned to Middle-earth after the destruction of the Trees *he returned to the ruins of Utumna and built there his new fortress, Angband*. This, I think, is why the fortress is called Angband, not Utumna, on map V.

The history was therefore as follows:

| | | |
|---|---|---|
| *Lost Tales* | { *Utumna* | Melko's original fortress |
| | { *Angband* | His dwelling when he returned |

---

*This range is seen also on the Westward Extension of the first 'Silmarillion' map, p. 228.

†All these north-western features are drawn in ink, whereas the rest of map V is in pencil; but the mountain-ranges (though not the rivers) are inked in over pencil.

‡Similar forms but with different application have occurred earlier: in the *Epilogue* to the *Lost Tales* the High Heath in Tol Eressëa where the battle was fought is *Ladwen-na-Dhaideloth*, *Dor-na-Dhaideloth* ('Sky-roof'), II.287; and in line 946 of the *Lay of the Children of Húrin* Dor-na-Fauglith was first called *Daideloth* ('High plain'), III.49.

S, Q          *Angband*    Melko's original fortress to which he
returned

*Ambarkanta*    { *Utumna*    Melko's original fortress
maps           { *Angband*    His second fortress built on the site of
Utumna when he returned

Much later, Utumno and Angband were both ancient fortresses of
Morgoth, and Angband was that to which he returned (*The Silmarillion*
pp. 47, 81).
Thangorodrim is shown on map V as a point, set slightly out from the
Iron Mountains. This represents a change in the conception of
Thangorodrim from that on the first 'Silmarillion' map, which illustrates
the words of S (§8) that Thangorodrim is 'the highest of the Iron
Mountains around Morgoth's fortress'. The marking of Thangorodrim
on *Ambarkanta* map V shows the later conception, seen in *The Silmarillion* p. 118, where it is said expressly that Melkor made a tunnel
under the mountains which issued south of them, that Thangorodrim
was piled above the gate of issue, and that Angband was behind the
mountain-wall: thus Thangorodrim stood out somewhat from the main
range.

There are extremely puzzling features in the Western Land on map V.
There is now a mountain chain (for so the herring-bone markings must
be interpreted, since that is their meaning elsewhere on the map)
extending up the western coast northwards from Taniquetil to the
Helkaraksë and (as it seems) rising out of the sea, as well as the old
westward curve of the Mountains of Valinor (bending back to the Chasm
of Ilmen) seen on map IV; thus Eruman (with the first occurrence of the
name *Araman* pencilled above it afterwards) is not represented as a
coastal wasteland between the mountains and the sea but is walled in by
mountains both on the East and on the West. I do not understand this;
in any case *The Silmarillion* has the geography shown on map IV.
Equally puzzling is the representation of the lands south of Tûn and
Taniquetil. Here there are herring-bone lines continuing the main line of
mountains southwards from Taniquetil, with again the old westward
curve back to the Chasm; but the area symmetrically corresponding to
Eruman in the North is here left unnamed, and *Arvalin* (emended
from *Eruman*) is shown as a substantial land extending east even of the
'new' mountains, from the southern shore of the Bay of Faëry to the
extreme South of the world. The Bay of Faëry, which is clearly shown on
this map (in contrast to map IV), is in fact partly formed by this 'new'
Arvalin. In a corner of the map is written:

After the War of the Gods (Arvalin was cast up by the Great Sea at the
foot of the Mts.

Though the brackets are not closed after 'Mts.', I think that the first words may have been intended as a title, indicating the period represented by the map. But the following words, coupled with the absence of Arvalin from its expected place on the map, seem to imply that it was only now that Arvalin came into being.

The Old English names *Ingarsecg*, *Utgarsecg* are found in the Old English texts (pp. 207, 210). *Alflon* on the coast north of Tûn is Alqualondë (later Sindarin *alph*, *lond* (*lonn*): see the Appendix to *The Silmarillion*, entries *alqua*, *londë*). The names *Aman*, *Araman* were added to map V many years later (as also *Arda*, *Earambar* on the diagrams).

If this map shows the vastness of the cataclysm that my father conceived as having taken place at the time of the breaking of Utumno and the chaining of Melko, at the end of the *Ambarkanta* he added (see note 9) a passage concerning the far greater cataclysm that took place 'in the days of the assault of the Númenóreans upon the land of the Gods'. This may have been added much later; but the passage is written carefully in ink, not scribbled in pencil, and is far more likely to be contemporary, since the story of Númenor arose about this time. In support of this is the diagram III, 'the World after the Cataclysm and the ruin of the Númenóreans'; for on this diagram the inner air was originally marked *Wilwa* and only later changed to *Vista*. In the *Ambarkanta* and the accompanying list of words, as in diagrams I and II, *Vista* is likewise an emendation from *Wilwa*; it seems therefore that diagram III belongs to the same period.

# VI

# THE EARLIEST ANNALS
# OF VALINOR

I refer to this work as the 'earliest' *Annals of Valinor* because it was followed later in the 1930s by a second version, and then, after the completion of *The Lord of the Rings* and very probably in 1951–2, by a third, entitled *The Annals of Aman*, which though still a part of the continuous evolution of these *Annals* is a major new work, and which contains some of the finest prose in all the Matter of the Elder Days. These earliest *Annals of Valinor* are comprised in a short manuscript of nine pages written in ink. There is a good deal of emendation and interpolation, some changes being made in ink and probably not much if any later than the first writing of the text, while a second layer of change consists of alterations in faint and rapid pencil that are not always legible. These latter include two quite substantial passages (given in notes 14 and 18) which introduce wholly new material concerning events in Middle-earth.

The text that follows is that of the *Annals* as originally written, apart from one or two insignificant alterations of wording that are taken up silently, and all later changes are given in the numbered notes, other than those made to dates. These are many and complex and are dealt with all together, separately, at the end of the notes.

It is certain that these *Annals* belong to the same period as the *Quenta*, but also that they are later than the *Quenta*. This is seen from the fact that whereas in Q Finrod (= the later Finarfin) returned to Valinor out of the far North after the burning of the ships, and the later story of his return earlier, after the Prophecy of the North, is only introduced in a marginal note (§5 note 8 and commentary p. 170), in the *Annals* the later story is already embodied in the text (Valian Year 2993). The Annals have *Beleriand*, whereas Q, as far as §12, had *Broseliand* emended to *Beleriand*; they have several names that do not occur in Q, e.g. *Bladorion, Dagor-os-Giliath, Drengist, Eredwethion* (this only by later emendation in Q); and *Eredlómin* has its later sense of the Echoing Mountains, not as in Q and on the first map of the Shadowy Mountains (see pp. 192–3). I see no way of showing that the *Annals* are later, or earlier, than the *Ambarkanta*, but the matter seems of no importance; the two texts certainly belong to very much the same time.

Following my commentary on the *Annals*, which I shall refer to as 'AV', I give the Old English versions in an appendix.

## ANNALS OF VALINOR

(These and the *Annals of Beleriand* were written by
Pengolod the Wise of Gondolin, before its fall, and after
at Sirion's Haven, and at Tavrobel in Toleressëa after
his return unto the West, and there seen and translated
by Eriol of Leithien, that is Ælfwine of the Angelcynn.)

### Here begin the Annals of Valinor

0 At the beginning Ilúvatar, that is 'Allfather', made all
things, and the Valar, that is the 'Powers', came into the
World. These are nine, Manwë, Ulmo, Aulë, Oromë,
Tulkas, Ossë, Mandos, Lórien, and Melko. Of these
Manwë and Melko were most puissant and were brethren, and Manwë was lord of the Valar and holy; but
Melko turned to lust and pride and violence and evil,
and his name is accursed, and is not uttered, but he is
called Morgoth. The spouses of the Valar were Varda,
and Yavanna, who were sisters; and Vana; and the sister
of Oromë, Nessa the wife of Tulkas;[1] and Uinen lady of
the Seas; and Nienna sister of Manwë and Melko; and
Estë. No spouse hath Ulmo or Melko.[2] With them came
many lesser spirits, their children, or beings of their own
kind but of less might; these are the Valarindi.

Time was counted in the world before the Sun and
Moon by the Valar according to ages, and a Valian age
hath 100 of the years of the Valar, which are each as ten
years are now.

In the Valian Year **500**: Morgoth destroyed by deceit
the Lamps[3] which Aulë made for the lighting of the
World, and the Valar, save Morgoth, retired to the West
and built there Valinor between the Outer Seas that
surround the Earth and the Great Seas of the West, and
on the shores of these they piled great mountains. But
the symmetry of land and sea was first broken in those
days.[4]

In the Valian Year **1000**, after the building of Valinor,
and Valmar the city of the Gods, the Valar brought into
being the Two Trees of Silver and of Gold, whose
bloom gave light unto Valinor.

But all this while Morgoth had dwelt in the Middle-earth and made him a great fortress in the North of the World; and he broke and twisted the Earth much in that time.[5]

A thousand Valian Years of bliss and glory followed in Valinor, but growth that began on Middle-earth at the lighting of the Lamps was checked. To Middle-earth came only Oromë to hunt in the dark woods of the ancient Earth, and sometimes Yavanna walked there.

The Valian Year 2000 is accounted the Noontide of the Blessed Realm, and the full season of the mirth of the Gods. Then did Varda make the stars[6] and set them aloft, and thereafter some of the Valarindi strayed into the Middle-earth, and among them was Melian, whose voice was renowned in Valmar. But she returned not thither for many ages, and the nightingales sang about her in the dark woods of the Western Lands.

At the first shining of the Sickle of the Gods which Varda set[7] above the North as a threat to Morgoth and an omen of his fall, the elder children of Ilúvatar awoke in the midmost of the World: they are the Elves.[8] Oromë found them and befriended them; and the most part under his guidance marched West and North to the shores of Beleriand, being bidden by the Gods to Valinor.

But first Morgoth in a great war was bound and made captive and imprisoned in Mandos. There he was confined in punishment for nine ages (900 Valian Years)[9] until he sought for pardon. In that war the lands were rent and sundered anew.[10]

The Quendi[11] and the Noldoli were the first to reach Valinor, and upon the hill of Kôr nigh to the strand they built the city of Tûn. But the Teleri who came after abode an age (100 Valian Years) upon the shores of Beleriand, and some never departed thence. Of these most renowned was Thingol (Sindingul)[12] brother of Elwë, lord of the Teleri, whom Melian enchanted. Her he after wedded and dwelt as a king in Beleriand, but this was after the departure of most of the Teleri, drawn by Ulmo upon Toleressëa.[13] This is the Valian Years 2000 to 2100.

From **2100** to **2200** the Teleri dwelt on Toleressëa in the Great Sea within sight of Valinor; in **2200** they came in their ships to Valinor, and dwelt upon its eastern strands, and there they made the town and haven of Alqalondë or 'Swan-haven', so called because there were moored their swan-shaped boats.

About **2500** the Noldoli invented and began the fashioning of gems; and after a while Fëanor the smith, eldest son of Finwë chief of the Noldoli, devised the thrice-renowned Silmarils, concerning the fates of which these tales tell. They shone of their own light, being filled with the radiance of the Two Trees, the holy light of Valinor, blended to a marvellous fire.[14]

In **2900** Morgoth sued for pardon, and at the prayers of Nienna his sister, and by the clemency of Manwë his brother, but against the wish of Tulkas and Aulë, he was released, and feigned humility and repentance, obeisance to the Valar, and love and friendship for the Elves, and dwelt in Valinor in ever-increasing freedom. But he lied and dissembled, and most he cozened the Noldoli, for he had much to teach, and they had an over-mastering desire to learn; but he coveted their gems and lusted for the Silmarils.

**2900** During two more ages[15] Valinor abode yet in bliss, yet a shadow of foreboding began to gather in many hearts; for Morgoth was at work with secret whisperings and cunning lies; and most he worked, alas, upon the Noldoli, and sowed the seeds of dissension between the sons of Finwë, Fëanor, Fingolfin, and Finrod, and of distrust between Noldoli and Valar. **2950** By the doom of the Gods Fëanor, eldest son of Finwë, and his household and following was deposed from the leadership of the Noldoli – wherefore the house of Fëanor was after called the Dispossessed, for this and because Morgoth after robbed them of their treasure – and the Gods sent also to apprehend Morgoth. But he fled into hiding in Arvalin, and plotted evil.[16]

**2990–1** Morgoth now completed his designs and with the aid of Ungoliantë out of Arvalin stole back into Valinor, and destroyed the Trees, escaping in the gathering dark northward, where he sacked the dwellings of Fëanor, and carried off a host of jewels, among them the Silmarils; and he slew Finwë and many Elves and thus defiled Valinor and began slaughter in the World.[17] Though hunted by the Valar he escaped into the North of the Hither Lands and re-established there his stronghold, and bred and gathered once more his evil servants, Orcs and Balrogs.[18]

**2991** Valinor lay now in great gloom, and darkness, save only for the stars, fell on all the World. But Fëanor against the will of the Valar returned to Tûn and claimed the kingship of the Noldoli after Finwë, and he summoned to Tûn all the people of that kindred. And Fëanor spoke to them, and his words were filled with the lies of Morgoth, and distrust of the Valar, even though his heart was hot with hate for Morgoth, slayer of his father and robber of his gems.

The most of the Noldoli[19] he persuaded to follow him out of Valinor and recover their realms on earth, lest they be filched by the younger children of Ilúvatar, Men (herein he echoed Morgoth unwitting); and war for ever on Morgoth seeking to recover their treasure. At that meeting Fëanor and his sons swore their dreadful oath to slay or pursue any soever that held a Silmaril against their will.

**2992** The march began, though the Gods forbade (and yet hindered not), but under divided leadership, for Fingolfin's house held him for king. Long was the people preparing. Then it came into Fëanor's heart that never should that great host, both warriors and other, and store of goods make the vast leagues unto the North (for Tûn beneath Taniquetil is upon the Girdle of the Earth, where the Great Seas are measurelessly wide) save with the help of ships. But the Teleri alone had ships, and they would not yield or lend them against the will of the Valar.

Thus about **2992** of Valian Years befell the dreadful battle about Alqalondë, and the Kin-slaying evilly renowned in song, where the Noldoli distraught furthered Morgoth's work. But the Noldoli overcame the Teleri and took their ships, and fared slowly north along the rocky coasts in great peril and hardship and amid dissensions.

In 2993 it is said they came to a place where a high rock stands above the shores, and there stood either Mandos or his messenger and spoke the Doom of Mandos. For the kin-slaying he cursed the house of Fëanor, and to a less degree all who followed them or shared in their emprise, unless they would return to abide the doom and pardon of the Valar. But if they would not, then should evil fortune and disaster befall them, and ever from treachery of kin towards kin; and their oath should turn against them; and a measure of mortality should visit them, that they should be lightly slain with weapons, or torments, or sorrow, and in the end fade and wane before the younger race. And much else he foretold darkly that after befell, warning them that the Valar would fence Valinor against their return.[20]

But Fëanor hardened his heart and held on, and so also but reluctantly did Fingolfin's folk, feeling the constraint of their kindred and fearing for the doom of the Gods (for not all of Fingolfin's house had been guiltless of the kin-slaying). Felagund and the other sons of Finrod went forward also, for they had aforetime great fellowship, Felagund with the sons of Fingolfin, and Orodreth, Angrod, and Egnor with Celegorm and Curufin sons of Fëanor. Yet the lords of this third house were less haughty and more fair than the others, and had had no part in the kin-slaying, and many with Finrod himself returned unto Valinor and the pardon of the Gods. But Aulë their ancient friend smiled on them no more, and the Teleri were estranged.

2994    The Noldoli came to the bitter North, and further they would not dare, for there is a strait between the Western Land (whereon Valinor is built) that curveth east, and the Hither Lands which bear west, and through this the chill waters of the Outer Seas and the waves of the Great Sea flow together, and there are vast mists of deathly cold, and the streams are filled with clashing hills of ice and with the grinding of ice submerged. This strait was named Helkaraksë.
But the ships that remained, many having been lost,

were too few to carry all across, and dissensions awoke between Fëanor and Fingolfin. But Fëanor seized the ships and sailed east;[21] and he said: 'Let the murmurers whine their way back to the shadows of Valinor.' And he burned the ships upon the eastern shore, and so great was its fire that the Noldoli left behind saw its redness afar off.

Thus about **2995** Fëanor came unto Beleriand and the shores beneath Eredlómin the Echoing Mountains, and their landing was at the narrow inlet Drengist that runs into Dorlómen. And they came thence into Dorlómen and about the north of the mountains of Mithrim, and camped in the land of Hithlum in that part that is named Mithrim and north of the great lake that hath the same name.

**2996**    And in the land of Mithrim they fought an army of Morgoth aroused by the burning and the rumour of their advance; and they were victorious and drove away the Orcs with slaughter, and pursued them beyond Eredwethion (the Shadowy Mountains) into Bladorion. And that battle is the First Battle of Beleriand, and is called Dagor-os-Giliath, the Battle under Stars; for all was as yet dark. But the victory was marred by the death of Fëanor, who was wounded mortally by Gothmog, lord of Balrogs, when he advanced unwarily too far upon Bladorion;[22] and Fëanor was borne back to Mithrim and died there, reminding his sons of their oath. To this they now added an oath of vengeance for their father.

**2997**    But Maidros eldest son of Fëanor was caught in the snares of Morgoth. For Morgoth feigned to treat with him, and Maidros feigned to be willing, and either purposed evil to the other, and came with force to the parley; but Morgoth with the more, and Maidros was made captive.

Then Morgoth held him as hostage, and swore only to release him if the Noldoli would march away either to Valinor, if they could, or from Beleriand and away to the far South; and if they would not he would torment Maidros.

But the Noldoli trusted not that he would release

Maidros if they departed, nor were they willing to do so whatever he might do. Wherefore in **2998** Morgoth hung Maidros by the right wrist in a band of hellwrought steel above a precipice upon Thangorodrim, where none could reach him.

Now it is told that Fingolfin and the sons of Finrod[23] won their way at last with grievous losses and with minished might into the North of the World. And they came perforce over Helkaraksë, being unwilling to retrace their way to Valinor, and having no ships; but their agony in that crossing was very great and their hearts were filled with bitterness against Fëanor.

And even as they came the First Ages of the World were ended;[24] and these are reckoned as 30000 years or **3000** years of the Valar; whereof the first Thousand was before the Trees, and Two Thousand save nine were Years of the Trees or of the Holy Light, which lived after and lives yet only in the Silmarils. And the Nine are the Years of Darkness or the Darkening of Valinor.

But towards the end of this time as is elsewhere told the Gods made the Sun and Moon and sent them forth over the World, and light came unto the Hither Lands.[25] And Men awoke in the East of the World even at the first Dawn.[26]

But with the first Moonrise Fingolfin set foot upon the North; for the Moonrise came ere the Dawn, even as Silpion of old bloomed ere Laurelin and was the elder of the Trees. But the first Dawn shone upon Fingolfin's march, and his banners blue and silver were unfurled, and flowers sprang beneath his marching feet, for a time of opening and growth was come into the Earth, and good of evil as ever happens.

But Fingolfin marched through the very fastness of Morgoth's land, Dor-Daideloth[27] the Land of Dread, and the Orcs fled before the new light amazed, and hid beneath the earth; and the Elves smote upon the gates of Angband and their trumpets echoed in Thangorodrim's towers.

They came thus south unto Mithrim, and little love[28] was there between them and the house of Fëanor; and the folk of Fëanor removed and camped upon the southern shores, and the lake lay between the peoples. And from this time are reckoned the Years of the Sun, and these things happened in the first year. And after came measured time into the World, and the growth and change and ageing of all things was thereafter more swift even in Valinor, but most in the Hither Lands,[29] the mortal regions between the Seas of East and West. And what else happened is recorded in the *Annals of Beleriand*, and in the *Pennas* or *Qenta*, and in many songs and tales.

## NOTES

1   Added here in pencil: *daughter of Yavanna*.
2   This passage, from *and Nienna* . . ., was emended in pencil to read: *and Vairë; and Estë. No spouse hath Ulmo or Melko or Nienna, Manwë's sister and Melko's*.
3   Cf. the title to the *Ambarkanta* map IV (p. 249): *The World about V.Y. 500 after the fall of the Lamps*.
4   *But the symmetry of land and sea was first broken in those days* is an addition, but was probably made at the time of writing of the text. Cf. pp. 255–6 and the citation from *The Silmarillion* given there.
5   *and he broke and twisted the Earth much in that time* is another addition probably made at the time of writing.
6   The paragraph to this point was emended in ink to read: *But on a time (1900) Varda began the making of the stars* . . . The sentence *The Valian Year 2000 is accounted the Noontide of the Blessed Realm, and the full season of the mirth of the Gods* was removed to a later point: see note 10.
7   Added here in ink: *last and* (i.e. *the Sickle of the Gods which Varda set last and above the North*)
8   Added here in ink: *Hence are they called the children of the stars*.
9   *nine ages (900 Valian Years)* emended in ink to *seven ages (700 Valian Years)*.
10   At this point the sentence *The Valian Year 2000* . . . was reintroduced (see note 6).
11   *Quendi > Lindar* in pencil.
12   *Sindingul > Tindingol* in pencil.
13   Added here in pencil: *His folk looked for him in vain, and his sleep lasted till they had gone*.
14   Added here in pencil:

2700   Here the Green-elves or Laiqi or Laiqeldar came to Ossiriand at length after many wanderings and long sojourns in diverse places. It is told that a company of the Noldoli under Dan forsook the host of Finwë early in the march and turned south, but again finding the lands barren and dark turned north, and they came about 2700 over Eredlindon under Denithor son of Dan, and dwelt in Ossiriand, and they were allies of Thingol.

The name *Denithor* is an emendation, probably of *Denilos* (see note 18).

15 This second entry for 2900 was written after the first was changed to 2700 (see note 9, and the note on dates below).

16 This passage was emended and extended thus in pencil:

... robbed them of their treasure. But Morgoth hid himself in the North of the land, as was known only to Finwë and Fëanor, who dwelt now apart.

2950    The Gods sent to apprehend Morgoth, but he fled over the mountains into Arvalin, and plotted evil for a long while, gathering the strength of darkness into him.

The date 2950 earlier in the paragraph was struck out at the same time.

17 Added here in pencil: *This reward got Finwë for his friendship.*

18 Added here in ink:

Then fear came into Beleriand, and Thingol made his mansions in Menegroth, and Melian wove magics of the Valar about the land of Doriath, and the most of the Elves of Beleriand withdrew within its protection, save some that lingered in the western havens, Brithombar and Eglorest, beside the Great Seas.

To this was added, in faint and hasty pencil:

and the remnant of the Green-elves of Ossiriand behind the rivers and the might of Ulmo. But Thingol with his ally Denilos of the Green-elves kept the Orcs for a while from the South. But at length Denilos son of Dan was slain, and Thingol

Here the pencilled note ends abruptly. Above -*los* of *Denilos* at the first occurrence is an alternative reading, illegible, but in view of *Denithor* probably < *Denilos* in note 14, no doubt -*thor*.

19 *Noldoli* emended from *Gnomes* at the time of writing.

20 Added here in pencil: *Here endeth that which Rúmil wrote.* See pp.1292–3.

21 Added here in ink: *with all his folk and no others save Orodreth, Angrod, and Egnor, whom Celegorm and Curufin loved*;

22 Added here in pencil: *but he . . . . . . . . . duel and Fëanor fell wrapped in fire.*

23 *Fingolfin and the sons of Finrod* emended in ink to *Fingolfin and Felagund* (cf. note 21).

24 Added here in pencil: *for they had tarried long in despair upon the shores of the West.* The next sentence begins: *And these . . .*

25  Added here in pencil: *But the Moon was the first to set sail.*
26  *Sun-rise* written in pencil above *Dawn*.
27  *Dor-Daideloth* is an emendation in ink of (almost certainly) *Dor-Daidelos*; cf. the *Ambarkanta* map V, and p. 259.
28  This sentence emended in pencil to read: *Then being wary of the wiles of Morgoth they turned unto Mithrim, that the Shadowy Mountains should be their guard. But little love . . .*
29  Added in pencil: *of Middle-earth.*

### Note on changes made to the dates

### (i)  Dates in the period up to the Valian Year 2200

The mention of the Noontide of the Blessed Realm was displaced (notes 6 and 10) in order to date the starmaking and other events earlier than 2000. The beginning of the starmaking was then dated 1900 (note 6), and against *At the first shining of the Sickle of the Gods* was written in the date 1950. Against the march of the Elves led by Oromë was written in 1980–1990; and against the arrival of the Quendi (Lindar) and Noldoli in Valinor 2000.

In the sentence *But the Teleri who came after abode an age (100 Valian Years) upon the shores of Beleriand* the words *an age* were struck out, *100* changed to *10*, and the dates 2000–2010 written in. In the sentence *This is the Valian Years 2000 to 2100* the second date was likewise changed to 2010.

In the concluding part of the period, by pencilled changes perhaps later than the foregoing, the dates of the dwelling of the Teleri on Tol Eressëa, originally 2100 to 2200, were changed to 2010 to 2110; and the coming of the Teleri to Valinor in 2200 was changed to 2111. The result of these changes may be shown in a table:

| Original Annals | After changes | |
| --- | --- | --- |
| 2000 | 1900 | Making of the stars by Varda begun |
| | 1950 | Making of the Sickle of the Gods (end of the starmaking) |
| | 1980–1990 | March of the Elves |
| 2000 | 2000 | Noontide of the Blessed Realm |
| | 2000 | Coming of the first two kindreds of the Elves to Valinor |
| 2000–2100 | 2000–2010 | Teleri on the shores of Beleriand |
| 2100–2200 | 2010–2110 | Teleri dwelling in Tol Eressëa |
| 2200 | 2111 | Coming of the Teleri to Valinor |

(ii)   *Dates in the period from the Valian Year 2900*

The year 2900, in which Morgoth sued for pardon, was changed to 2700, following the change in the length of his imprisonment from nine to seven ages (900 to 700 Valian Years) made earlier (note 9). These changes must have been made while the *Annals* were in progress, in view of the second entry for 2900 that follows in the text as written, *During two more ages Valinor abode yet in bliss*, i.e. two more ages from the *emended* date, 2700, when Morgoth sued for pardon and was released.

For the shifting of the date 2950 see note 16.

Almost all the dates from 2990–1 to the end were emended in pencil, and the results are best set out in a table. (The dates given in the text as 2992 to 2995 are themselves emendations in ink, apparently in each case advancing the date by one year from that originally written.)

The sentence *Thus about 2992 of Valian Years* (p. 266) was changed to *Thus in the dread Year of the Valar 2999 (29991 S.Y.)*, where S.Y. = Sun Year; cf. the opening of the *Annals*, where it is explained that a Valian Year was equal to ten years 'now', i.e. of the Sun.

It will be seen that the effect of the later pencilled changes given in the table below was to speed up events from the Battle of Alqualondë to the landing of Fingolfin in Middle-earth, so that they extend over only a single Valian Year. In the passage giving the reckoning of the First Ages of the World (p. 269), over *nine* in *Two Thousand save nine were Years of the Trees* my father wrote *one*; this one year is *the dread Year of the Valar 2999*.

In this table, only actual pencilled changes made to the dates are recorded. The change of 2991 to 2998–3000 is intended to cover all that follows, or refers only to the beginning of the entry: *Valinor now lay in great gloom, and darkness . . . fell on all the World.*

| Original Annals | | After changes | |
|---|---|---|---|
| *(Valian Years)* | | *(Valian Years)* | *(Sun Years)* |
| 2990–1 | Destruction of the Trees and escape of Morgoth | 2998 | |
| 2991 | Rebellion of Fëanor | 2998–3000 | |
| 2992 | Preparation for the Flight of the Noldoli | 2999 | |
| 2992 | The Battle of Alqualondë | 2999 | 29991 |
| 2993 | The Doom of Mandos | | 29992 |
| 2994 | The Noldoli in the far North; the burning of the ships | | 29994 |

| Original Annals | | After changes | |
|---|---|---|---|
| (Valian Years) | | (Valian Years) | (Sun Years) |
| 2995 | The landing of the Fëanorians and the encampment in Mithrim | | 29995 |
| 2996 | The Battle under Stars and the death of Fëanor | | Date struck out |
| 2997 | Capture of Maidros | | 29996 |
| 2998 | Maidros hung from Thangorodrim | | |
| 3000 | Landing of Fingolfin | | |

## Commentary on the Annals of Valinor

In the preamble to the *Annals of Valinor* (AV) we meet one Pengolod the Wise of Gondolin, who dwelt at Tavrobel in Tol Eressëa 'after his return unto the|West'. Pengolod (or Pengoloð) often appears later, but nothing more is told of his history (the reference to Sirion's Haven shows that he was one of those who escaped from Gondolin with Tuor and Idril). I am much inclined to think that his literary origin is to be found in Gilfanon of the *Lost Tales*, who also lived at Tavrobel (which now first emerges again); there Eriol stayed in his house ('the house of a hundred chimneys'), and Gilfanon bade him write down all that he had heard (II.283), while in the preamble to AV Eriol saw Pengolod's book at Tavrobel and translated it there. Moreover Gilfanon was of the Noldoli, and though in the *Lost Tales* he is not associated with Gondolin he was an Elf of Kôr, 'being indeed one of the oldest of the fairies and the most aged that now dwelt in the isle', and had lived long in the Great Lands (I.175); while Pengolod was also an Elf whose life began in Valinor, since he 'returned' into the West.

It is not clear whether the ascription of both sets of *Annals* to Pengolod of Tavrobel, where Ælfwine/Eriol translated them, is a departure from or is congruent with the title of the *Quenta* (pp. 77–8), in which Eriol is said to have read the Golden Book (*Parma Kuluina*) in Kortirion. In the early notes and outlines there are different conceptions of the Golden Book: see II.287, 290–1, 310. On the explicit equation of *Ælfwine* and *Eriol* in the preamble to AV see p. 206.

On the later addition to AV (note 20) 'Here endeth that which Rúmil wrote' see pp. 292–3. Rúmil re-emerges from the *Lost Tales* also as the author of the *Ambarkanta* (p. 235).

In the opening passage of AV, and in the later alterations made to it, there are some developments in the composition and relations of the

Valar. The Nine Valar are the same as the nine 'chieftains of the Valar' or the 'Nine Gods' of the opening section in Q; and the association of the Valar with their spouses has undergone little change from the *Lost Tales*: Manwë and Varda; Aulë and Yavanna; Oromë and Vana;· Tulkas and Nessa; Ossë and Uinen; Mandos and Nienna. But now Estë first appears, the spouse of Lórien (as is implied here by the arrangement of the passage, and as is expressly stated in the Old English version of AV, p. 285). .

The '*consanguinity*' *of the Valar*. In the *Lost Tales* Aulë and Yavanna Palúrien were the parents of Oromë (I.67), and Nessa was Oromë's sister (I.75). In the addition to AV given in note 1 Nessa is still the daughter of Yavanna;* as will appear subsequently (p. 293) Oromë was the son of Yavanna, but not of Aulë. In *The Silmarillion* (p. 29) Oromë and Nessa remain brother and sister, though their parentage is not stated.

Varda and Yavanna are said to be sisters in Q, as in AV; in Q Vana is a third sister, though apparently not so in AV, and she remains the younger sister of Yavanna in *The Silmarillion* (*ibid.*).

Manwë and Melko are said in AV to be 'brethren' (cf. *The Silmarillion* p. 26: 'Manwë and Melkor were brethren in the thought of Ilúvatar'), and Nienna is their sister; in *The Silmarillion* (p. 28) she is the sister of the Fëanturi, Mandos and Lórien.

If these sources are combined the fullest extension of the genealogy is therefore:

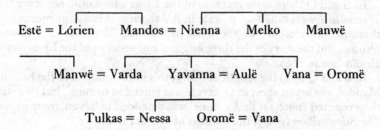

Only the sea-gods, Ulmo, and Ossë with Uinen, are not brought in.

By the emendation given in note 2 Vairë appears, and is clearly by the arrangement of the passage the spouse of Mandos, as she remained; and Nienna now becomes solitary, again as she remained. Of course it is altogether unclear what is really meant by the terms 'brother', 'sister', 'mother', 'son', 'children' in the context of the great Valar.

The term *Valarindi* has not occurred before; see further p. 293.

In what follows I relate my remarks to the dates of the *Annals*. In most respects this text (as originally written) is in harmony with the *Quenta*,

---

*In Q §6 (p. 99) Nessa is the daughter of Vana, though this statement was struck out (note 2).

and I notice only the relatively few and for the most part minor points in which they are not, or in which the *Annals* offer some detail that is absent from the *Quenta* (a great deal is of course found in the much longer *Quenta* that is omitted in the brief *Annals*).

*Valian Year 500*   The words 'Morgoth destroyed *by deceit* the Lamps' indicates the story of his devising the pillars out of ice, as in the *Ambarkanta* (see pp. 238, 256).

*Valian Year 2000 (later 1900, 1950)*   The making of the stars seems still to be thought of as accomplished by Varda at one and the same period, as in Q §2 (see p. 168). A later addition in AV (note 7) makes the Sickle of the Gods the last of Varda's works in the heavens, and thus the Elves awoke when the starmaking was concluded, as in *The Silmarillion* (p. 48); in S and Q they awoke 'at the making of the stars'. The addition given in note 8 telling that the Elves were for this reason called 'the children of the stars' is interesting; but later evidence shows that this was not yet the meaning of the name *Eldar*.

The Elves are said to have awoken 'in the midmost of the World'; in S and Q Cuiviénen is 'in the East', 'far in the East', as in *The Silmarillion*. But I doubt that this is significant, in view of the placing of Kuiviénen on the *Ambarkanta* map IV (p. 249), which could be referred to either as 'in the East' or as 'in the midmost of the World'.

In S and Q there is no mention of the Elves who would not leave the Waters of Awakening (see p. 44); in AV there is at least a suggestion of them in the reference to 'the most part' of the Elves having followed Oromë. But the story of the three original ambassadors of the Elves is still absent (see p. 168).

In S and Q (§ 4) the length of Morgoth's imprisonment in the halls of Mandos was seven ages; in Q 'seven' was emended to 'nine', but this was then rejected (note 1); in AV 'nine' was emended to 'seven' (note 9). In *The Silmarillion* (p. 65) the number of ages is three.

The rending and sundering of the lands in the war that ended in the captivity of Morgoth is described in the *Ambarkanta* (see pp. 239, 257–9).

The term *Quendi* for the First Kindred is still used in AV as in Q, and as in Q was later changed to *Lindar*. The addition in note 13 makes it explicit that Thingol did not awake from his enchanted sleep until his people had passed over the Sea; so in the *Tale of Tinúviel*, II.9: 'Now when he awoke he thought no more of his people (and indeed it had been vain, for long now had those reached Valinor).' He is now the brother of Elwë Lord of the Teleri (cf. I.120).

*Valian Year 2200 (later 2111)*   The name *Alqalondë* (not in S and Q, where only the English name, Swanhaven or Haven of the Swans, is used) reappears from *(Kópas) Alqaluntë* of the *Lost Tales*; cf. *Alflon* on the *Ambarkanta* map V (pp. 251, 261).

It is to be noticed that while the changing of the dates (p. 272) greatly reduced the time during which the Teleri dwelt on the coast of Beleriand (from 100 Valian Years to 10), it does not affect the length of their sojourn in Tol Eressëa, 100 Valian Years, equivalent to 1000 Years of the Sun (cf. Q §3: 'Of this long sojourn apart came the sundering of the tongue of the Foamriders and the Elves of Valinor').

*Valian Year 2500*   Wholly new is the matter of the pencilled addition given in note 14. My father was here working out the chronology at large, for there is no reason for this story to appear in Annals of Valinor.* It agrees with what is told in *The Silmarillion* (p. 54), save that Denethor's father is there Lenwë not Dan, and that these Elves came from the third host, the Teleri, not from the Noldor.

This is the first indication of the origin of the Green-elves, who have hitherto only appeared in association with Beren (see p. 62, and Q §14), and the first appearance of their Elvish names *Laiqi* or *Laiqeldar* (later *Laiquendi*). For earlier forms of Ossiriand see p. 233; the final form occurs also in emendations to Q (§§9, 10, 14). *Eredlindon* appears in a late addition to Q §9, note 3.

*Valian Year 2900 (later 2700)*   In S and Q it is Tulkas and Ulmo who are opposed to the release of Morgoth, as in *The Silmarillion* (p. 66); in AV it is Tulkas and Aulë. In AV appears the intercession of Nienna on Morgoth's behalf, and this was retained in *The Silmarillion* (p. 65), though Nienna is no longer his sister.

*Valian Year 2950*   'The Dispossessed', the name given to the House of Fëanor, has appeared in the Old English name *Yrfeloran*, p. 212.

I have noticed in my commentary on Q §4 that the later interpolation (note 6), telling that a messenger came to the Gods in council with tidings that Morgoth was in the North of Valinor and journeying to the house of Finwë, is the first hint of the story of Morgoth's going to Formenos and his speech with Fëanor before the doors. In AV also, as originally written, the northward movement of Morgoth was absent (he fled at once into Arvalin after the council of the Gods in which they deposed Fëanor and sent to apprehend Morgoth); but in the pencilled interpolation given in note 16 Morgoth 'hid himself in the North of the land, as was known only to Finwë and Fëanor, who dwelt now apart'. It was then that the Gods sent to apprehend him, though no explanation is given of how they knew where he was; but the story now becomes

---

*It remained in the 'tradition' of these Annals, however, and is still present in the much later *Annals of Aman* (though there with a direction to transfer it to the *Annals of Beleriand*).

structurally the same as that in *The Silmarillion* (p. 72), where it was only when Finwë sent messengers to Valmar saying that Morgoth had come to Formenos that Oromë and Tulkas went after him.

*Valian Years 2990–1*   The addition given in note 17, 'This reward got Finwë for his friendship', refers, I think, to the relations between Morgoth and the Noldoli before his exposure. This seems much more likely than that Morgoth actually succeeded in cozening the Noldoli in exile in the North of Valinor, that they formed an alliance with him.

It is remarkable that according to the revised dating no less than 48 Valian Years (2950–2998), that is 480 Years of the Sun, elapsed between Morgoth's flight into Arvalin and the destruction of the Trees.

The insertion (in two instalments) given in note 18 introduces further new history of the 'Dark Ages' of Middle-earth. The Havens on the coast of Beleriand were marked in later on the Westward Extension of the first map (p. 228), where they are named *Brithombar* and *Eldorest* (see p. 227). Now appears also the withdrawal of the Elves of Beleriand behind the Girdle of Melian; cf. *The Silmarillion*, pp. 96–7: '[Thingol] withdrew all his people that his summons could reach within the fastness of Neldoreth and Region.' The name *Menegroth* of the Thousand Caves has not occurred before.

The incomplete pencilled addition is the first hint of the battle of the Elves of Beleriand with the Orcs after Morgoth's return ('the first battle in the Wars of Beleriand', *The Silmarillion* p. 96), in which Denethor was slain.

*Valian Year 2992 (later 2999)*   In the account of the Flight of the Noldoli there is a suggestion, in the words 'The march began, though the Gods forbade (and yet hindered not)', of the speech of the messenger of Manwë as the march began in *The Silmarillion* (p. 85): 'Go not forth! . . . No aid will the Valar lend you in this quest, but neither will they hinder you.'

*Valian Year 2993 (later Sun Year 29992)*   More is now told of the content of the Prophecy of Mandos, in particular as it concerns the altered fate of the Noldoli who would not turn back from their rebellion. In Q (§5) nothing is said of this, and the curse, as reported, is restricted to the doom of treachery and the fear of treachery among themselves; but in a later passage (§7), which goes back to S and indeed to the *Lost Tales* (see p. 51), it is told that

Immortal were the Elves, and . . . no sickness or pestilence brought them death. But they could be slain by weapons in those days . . . and some waned and wasted with sorrow till they faded from the earth.

In AV the Doom of Mandos foretells that

a measure of mortality should visit them [the House of Fëanor and those who followed them], that they should be lightly slain with weapons, or torments, or sorrow, and in the end fade and wane before the younger race.

At first sight this seems at odds with the story as it stands, where Finwë and many other Elves had already been slain by Morgoth, who thus 'began slaughter in the world'; 'a measure of mortality' was their fate in any case. But it may be that the word 'lightly' is to be given full weight, and that the meaning is that the Noldoli will be less resistant to death that comes in these ways. In *The Silmarillion* (p. 88) Mandos or his emissary said:

For though Eru appointed you to die not in Eä, and no sickness may assail you, yet slain ye may be, and slain ye shall be: by weapon and by torment and by grief.

This I take to mean, in effect: 'Do not forget that, though you are immortal in that you cannot die through sickness, you can nonetheless be slain in other ways; and you will indeed now die in such ways abundantly.'

The waning of the Elves now becomes an element in the Doom of Mandos; on this see p. 172.

The statement in AV that when Finrod and many others returned to Valinor and were pardoned by the Gods 'Aulë their ancient friend smiled on them no more' is interesting. It does not appear in *The Silmarillion*, where nothing is said of the reception of Finarfin (Finrod) and those who came with him on their return beyond the fact that 'they received the pardon of the Valar, and Finarfin was set to rule the remnant of the Noldor in the Blessed Realm' (p. 88); but it is to be related to a passage in the old *Tale of the Sun and Moon* (I. 176) in which Aulë's peculiar anger against the Noldoli for their ingratitude and for the Kinslaying is described.

The alliances and friendships between the princes of the Noldoli in the third generation have been touched on in S and Q §5, where Orodreth, Angrod, and Egnor, sons of Finrod, sided with the Fëanorians in the debate in Tûn before the Flight of the Noldoli; in AV this becomes a friendship especially with Celegorm and Curufin, and is no doubt to be related to the evolution of the Nargothrond legend.

*Valian Year 2994 (later Sun Year 29994)* The friendship of Celegorm and Curufin with Orodreth, Angrod, and Egnor just referred to leads to the remarkable development (in the addition given in note 21) that these three sons of Finrod were actually allowed passage in the ships by the Fëanorians, and that only Felagund came over the Helkaraksë with Fingolfin (note 23). This story if adhered to would presumably have affected the further evolution of the history of the Noldor in Beleriand.

In *The Silmarillion* the only especial relationship of friendship between any of the sons of Fëanor and their cousins (apart from that with Aredhel Fingolfin's daughter) is that between Maedhros and Fingon; and Maedhros, not perceiving that his father meant to burn the ships, proposed that Fingon be among the first of the other Noldor to be brought over in a second journey (p. 90).

*Valian Year 2995 (later Sun Year 29995)*    Here the firth of *Drengist* is named for the first time in the narrative texts (it occurs in the list of Old English names, p. 210, but is not named on the Westward Extension of the first map); *Eredlómin* has the later sense of the Echoing Mountains (see pp. 192–3, 221); and *Mithrim* is used not only of the Lake but of the region about the Lake, and the *Mountains of Mithrim* are mentioned for the first time (see p. 221, entry *Hithlum*). The encampment of the Fëanorians by Lake Mithrim now precedes the Battle under Stars.

*Valian Year 2996 (date later struck out)*    The first battle of the returning Noldor with the Orcs is now fought in Mithrim, not on the Northern plain (Q §8), and the plain at last receives an Elvish name, *Bladorion*, referring to the time when it was still grassland (with *Bladorion* perhaps compare *Bladorwen* 'the wide earth', a name of Yavanna given in the old Gnomish dictionary, I.264, entry *Palúrien*). The Orcs are pursued into Bladorion and Fëanor is wounded there, but dies in Mithrim. The name *Battle under Stars* is added in Q §8, note 2, but this is the first occurrence of an Elvish name, *Dagor-os-Giliath* (later *Dagor-nuin-Giliath*). *Eredwethion* replaces, in the text as written, *Eredlómin* as the Elvish name of the Shadowy Mountains (previously it is found only in later alterations, Q II§15, note 1, and on the first map, p. 221).

*Valian Year 2997 (later Sun Year 29996)*    A new element in AV is the condition which Morgoth proposed for the release of Maidros.

*Valian Year 3000*    Here is introduced the story that Fingolfin after landing in Middle-earth marched even to Angband and beat on the gates, but (in the emendation given in note 28) being prudent retreated to Mithrim; and although in S and Q §8 it is already told that the two hosts of the Noldor were encamped on opposing shores of Lake Mithrim, it is now added that the Fëanorians removed to the southern shore when Fingolfin came.

On the phrase 'after came measured time into the World' see Q §6 note 6, and pp. 171–2.

With 'the *Pennas* or *Qenta*' cf. the title of Q (p. 77): *Qenta Noldorinwa or Pennas-na-Ngoelaidh*.

# APPENDIX

### Old English versions of the Annals of Valinor, made by Ælfwine or Eriol

The first version given here is certainly the oldest, and is perhaps earlier than the Modern English *Annals*. A few late pencilled alterations or suggestions are given in the notes.

## I

þéos gesegen wearþ ǽrest on bócum gesett of Pengolode
þám Úþwitan of Gondoline ǽr þám þe héo abrocen
wurde, 7 siþþan æt Sirigeones Hýþe, 7 æt Tafrobele on
Toleressean (þæt is Ánetíge), æfter þám þe he eft west
cóm; 7 héo wearþ þær gerǽdd and geþíedd of Ælfwine,   5
þám þe ielfe Eriol genemdon.

**Frumsceaft** Hér ǽrest worhte Ilúfatar, þæt is Ealfæder
oþþe Heofonfæder oþþe Beorhtfæder, cal þing.

**D** géara þára Falar (þæt is þára Mihta oþþe Goda): án géar
þára Goda bið swá lang swá tíen géar béoð nú on þǽre   10
worolde arímed æfter þǽre sunnan gange. Melco (þæt is
Orgel) oþþe Morgoþ (þæt is Sweart-ós) oferwearp þára
Goda Blácern, 7 þá Godu west gecirdon híe, and híe
þær Valinor þæt is Godéþel geworhton.

**M** Hér þá Godu awehton þá Twégen Béamas, Laurelin   15
(þæt is Goldléoþ) 7 Silpion (þæt is Glisglóm).

**MM** Godéðles Middæg oþþe Héahþrymm. Hér bléowon þá
Béamas þúsend géara; ond Varda (héo wæs gydena
æþelust) steorran geworhte; for þám hátte héo
Tinwetári Steorrena Hlǽfdige. Hér onwócon Ielfe on   20
Éastlandum; 7 se Melco wearð gefangen 7 on clústre
gebunden; 7 siððan cómon ielfa sume on Godéðel.

**MM** oþ **MMC** Hér wearð Tún, séo hwíte burg, atimbred
on munte Córe. þá Telere gewunodon gíet on þam
weststrandum þára Hiderlanda; ac se Teler þingol   25
wearð on wuda begalen.

**MMC** oþ **MMCC** Wunodon þá Telere on Ánetíge.

**MMCC** Hér cómon þá Telere oþ Godéðel.

**MMD**   Hér þurh searucræftas apóhton and beworhton þá
Nold-ielfe gimmas missenlice, 7 Féanor Noldena          30
hláford worhte þá Silmarillas, þæt wǽron
Eorclanstánas.

**MM** oþ **MMDCCCC**   Hæftnýd Morgoðes.

**MMDCCCC**   Hér wearð Morgoþ alýsed, 7 he wunode on
Godéðle,, 7 lícette þæt he hold wǽre Godum 7 Ielfum.    35

**MMDCCCCXCIX**   Hér ofslóh Morgoð þá Béamas ond
opfléah, 7 ætferede mid him þára Elfa gimmas 7 þá
Eorclanstánas. Siþþan forléton þá Noldelfe hiera hyldo,
and éodon on elþéodignes, 7 gefuhton wið þá Telere æt
Elfethýðe 7 sige námon 7 ætferedon þa Teleriscan        40
scipu.
Hér wearð micel gesweorc 7 genipu on Godéðle 7
ofer ealne middangeard. þá hwíle edníwede Morgoð his
ealde fæsten on þám Norþdǽlum, and getrymede
micle, and orcas gegaderode, and þa Eorclanstánas on    45
his irenhelme befæste.
þá fór Féanor mid his seofon sunum and micelre
fierde norþ 7 þá siglde on Teleriscum scipum to þám
Weststrandum, and þǽr forbærndon híe þa scipu ond
aswicon hiera geféran þe on lást síðodon.               50
Hér gefeaht Féanores fierd wiþ þam orcum 7 sige
námon 7 þá orcas gefliemdon oþ Angband (þæt is
Irenhelle); ac Goðmog, Morgoðes þegn, ofslóh Féanor,
and Mǽgdros gewéold siþþan Féanores folc. þis gefeoht
hátte Tungolgúð.                                        55

## NOTES

### Textual Notes to Version I

All the following changes, except that in line 9, were made very quickly
in pencil and without striking out the original forms; they belong to a
much later period, as is shown by the fact that *Melkor* for *Melko* was not
introduced until 1951.

1   *Pengolode* > *Pengoloðe*
2   *Gondoline* > *Gondolinde*
3   *Taþrobele* > (probably) *Taþrobele* (see p. 288 note to line 7, and
    p. 291 note to line 7).

6  *Eriol* > *Ereol*
9  *Falar* is an emendation in ink of *Valar.*
11  *Melco* > *Melcor* (but not at line 21)
13  *Blácern* > *Léohtfatu*
14  *Godépel* > *Ésa-eard* (*ésa* genitive plural of *ós*, see p. 208)

## Old English Names in Version I

Far less use is made of Old English equivalents than is provided for in
the lists given on pp. 208–13; so we have *Gondoline* with an Old English
inflectional ending (not *Stángaldorburg*, etc.), *Nold(i)elfe*, also genitive
plural *Noldena* (not *Déopelfe*, etc.), *Féanor*, *Mægdros*, *Goðmog*, *on
munte Córe*. Old English equivalents, used or only mentioned, are
mostly actual translations. Thus *Melco* is *Orgel* ('Pride'); *Morgoð* is
*Sweart-ós* ('Black God', 'Dark God', see II.67); *Laurelin* is *Goldléoþ*
('Gold-song', 'Song of Gold' – cf. the translation 'singing-gold' in
the name-list to *The Fall of Gondolin*, II.216, and contrast *Glengold*
imitating *Glingol*, p. 210); *Silpion* is *Glisglóm* (of which the elements are
evidently the stem *glis-* seen in the verbs *glisian, glisnian* 'shine, glitter',
and *glóm* 'twilight'); *Alqalondë* is *Elfethýð* ('Swan-haven')*; *Tol Eressëa*
is *Ánetig* ('Solitary Isle'); the Battle-under-Stars is *Tungolgúð* ('Star-
battle'). *Irenhell* for *Angband* and *Godéðel* ('Land of the Gods') for
*Valinor* are found in the list of Old English names.

The Silmarils are *Eorclanstánas* (also treated as an Old English noun
with plural *Silmarillas*). There are several different forms of this Old
English word: *eorclan-*, *eorcnan-*, *earcnan-*, and *eorcan-* from which is
derived the 'Arkenstone' of the Lonely Mountain. The first element may
be related to Gothic *airkns* 'holy'. With *middangeard* line 43 cf. my
father's note in *Guide to the Names in The Lord of the Rings*, in *A Tolkien
Compass*, p. 189: 'The sense is "the inhabited lands of (Elves and) Men",
envisaged as lying between the Western Sea and that of the Far East (only
known in the West by rumour). *Middle-earth* is a modern alteration of
medieval *middel-erde* from Old English *middan-geard*.'

Varda's name *Tinwetári*, Queen of the Stars, goes back to the tale of
*The Chaining of Melko* (I.100), and is found also in Q §2.

## Dates in Version I

The date MMDCCCCXCIX (written with M for MM, as also the two
occurrences of MMDCCCC, but these are obviously mere slips without
significance), 2999, does not agree with that in the Modern English
version for the destruction of the Two Trees and the rape of the
Silmarils, which are there given under 2990–1.

---

*This Old English name (with variant initial vowel, *Ielfethýþ*) is found long before in a
marginal note to *Kópas Alqaluntë* in the tale of *The Flight of the Noldoli*, I.164, footnote.

## II

This text relates very closely indeed to the Modern English version. There are slight differences of substance between them here and there, and some of the emendations made to the modern version are embodied in the Old English text; these points are mentioned in the notes, as also are some details concerning the dates and some features of the names.

The text was lightly emended in pencil, but these changes are almost without exception modifications of word-order or other slight syntactical changes, and all such I take into the text silently. It breaks off abruptly at the beginning of the annal entry equivalent to 2991 with the words 'Valinor lay now'; these are not at the foot of a page, and none of the text has been lost.

At first sight it is puzzling that in the preamble the *Annals of Valinor* are called *Pennas*, since the *Pennas* or *Quenta* (see pp. 205-6) is clearly intended to represent a different literary tradition from the *Annals*, or at least a different mode of presenting the material. The preamble goes on to say, however, that this book *Pennas* is divided into three parts: the first part is *Valinórelúmien*, that is *Godéðles géargetœl* (i.e. Annals of Valinor); the second is *Beleriandes géargetœl* (i.e. Annals of Beleriand); and the third is *Quenta Noldorinwa* or *Pennas nan Goeliỡ*, that is *Noldelfaracu* (the History of the Noldorin Elves). Thus, here at any rate, *Pennas* (*Quenta*) is used in both a stricter and a wider sense: the whole opus that Ælfwine translated in Tol Eressëa is the *Pennas* (*Quenta*), 'the History', but the term is also used more narrowly of the *Pennas nan Goeliỡ* or *Quenta Noldorinwa*, which may be thought of as 'the Silmarillion proper', as opposed to the 'Annals'. In fact, in an addition to the very brief Old English version III of the *Annals of Valinor* (p. 291, note to line 5) it is expressly said: 'This third part is also called *Silmarillion*, that is the history of the *Eorclanstánas* [*Silmarils*].'

Her onginneð séo bóc þe man *Pennas* nemneð, 7 héo is
on þréo gedæled; se forma dæl is *Valinórelúmien* þæt is
Godéðles géargetæl, 7 se óþer is Beleriandes géargetæl,
7 se þridda *Quenta Noldorinwa* oþþe *Pennas nan
Goeliỡ* þæt is Noldelfaracu. þás ærest awrát Pengolod se        5
Úþwita of Gondoline, ær þám þe héo abrocen wurde, 7
siþþan æt Siriones hýþe 7 æt Tavrobele in Toleressean
(þæt is Ánetége), þá he eft west cóm. And þás béc
Ælfwine of Angelcynne geseah on Ánetége, þá þá he æt
sumum cerre funde híe; 7 he geleornode híe swa he        10
betst mihte 7 eft geþéodde 7 on Englisc ásette.

## I

Hér onginneð Godéðles géargetæl.

On frumsceafte Ilúuvatar, þæt is Ealfæder, gescóp
eal þing, 7 þá Valar, þæt is þá Mihtigan (þe sume menn
siþþan for godu héoldon) cómon on þás worolde.
Híe sindon nigon: Manwe, Ulmo, Aule, Orome, Tulkas,   15
Mandos, Lórien, Melko. þára wǽron Manwe 7 Melko
his bróþor ealra mihtigoste, ac Manwe wæs se yldra, 7
wæs Vala-hláford 7 hálig, 7 Melko béah to firenlustum
and úpahæfennesse and oferméttum and wearþ yfel and
unmǽðlic, and his nama is awergod and unasprecenlic,   20
ac man nemneð hine Morgoð in Noldelfisc-gereorde.

þa Valacwéne hátton swá: Varda 7 Geauanna, þe
gesweostor wǽron, Manwes cwén 7 Aules cwén; 7 Vana
Oromes cwén; 7 Nessa Tulkases cwén (séo wæs
Oromes sweostor); 7 Uinen, merecwén, Osses wíf; 7   25
Vaire Mandosses cwén, 7 Este Lóriendes cwén. Ac
Ulmo 7 Melko næfdon cwéne, 7 Nienna séo geómore
næfde wer.

Mid þissum geférum cómon micel héap lǽsra
gesceafta, Valabearn, oþþe gǽstas Valacynnes þe lǽsse   30
mægen hæfdon. þás wæron Valarindi.

And þá Valar ǽr þám þe Móna 7 Sunne wurden
gerímdon tíde be langfirstum oþþe ymbrynum, þe
wǽron hund Valagéara on geteald; 7 án Valagéar wæs
efne swá lang swá tén géar sindon nú on worolde.   35

D       On þám Valagéare D mid searucræfte fordyde
Morgoþ þá blácern, þe Aule smiþode, þætte séo weorold
mid sceolde onleohted weorðan; 7 þá Valar, búton
Morgoþe ánum, gecerdon híe West, and þær
getimbredon Valinor (þæt is Godéðel) be sǽm   40
twéonum (þæt is betwuh Útgársecge þe ealle eorðan
bebúgeð, and séo micle Westsǽ, þæt is Gársecg, oþþe
Ingársecg, oþþe Belegar on Noldelfisce; 7 on Westsǽs
strandum gehéapodon hie micle beorgas. And
middangear[d]es rihtgesceap wearþ on þám dagum   45
ǽrest of Morgoðe onhwerfed.

M       Hér, æfter þám þe Valinor wearð getimbrod, 7
Valmar þæt is Godaburg, gescópon 7 onwehton þá
Valar þá Twégen Béamas, óþerne of seolfre óþerne of
golde geworhtne, þe hira léoma onléohte Valinor. Ac   50
Morgoþ búde on middangearde and geworhte him þǽr

micel fæsten on norþdælum; and on þǽre tíde forbræc
he and forsceóp he micle eorðan 7 land. Siþþan wearþ'
þúsend géara blǽd 7 bliss on Godéþle, ac on
middangearde þá wæstmas, þe be þára blácerna      55
ontendnesse ǽr ongunnon úpaspringan, amerde
wurdon. To middangearde cóm þára Vala nán bútan
Orome, þe oft wolde huntian on þǽre firnan eorðan be
deorcum wealdum, 7 Iauannan þe hwílum fór þider.

MM   þis géar biþ Valaríces Middæg oþþe Heahþrymm      60
geteald, 7 þá wæs Goda myrgþu gefullod. þá geworhte
Varda steorran 7 sette híe on lyfte (7 þý hátte héo
Tinwetári, þæt is Tungolcwén), and sóna æfter þám of
Godéþle wandrodon Valarindi sume 7 cómon on
middangeard, and þára gefrǽgost wearð Melian, þe      65
wæs ǽr Lóriendes híredes, 7 hire stefn wæs mǽre mid
Godum: ac héo ne cóm eft to Godabyrig ǽr þon þe fela
géara oferéodon and fela wundra gelumpon, ac
nihtegalan wǽron hire geféran 7 sungon ymb híe be
þám deorcum wudum on westdǽlum.                  70
      þá þá þæt tungol, þe gefyrn Godasicol oþþe
Brynebrér hátte, líxte ǽrest forþ on heofonum, for þám
þe Varda hit asette Morgoþe on andan him his hryre to
bodianne, þá onwócon þá yldran Ealfæderes bearn on
middan worolde: þæt sindon Elfe. Híe funde Orome      75
and wearþ him fréondhald, and þára se mǽsta dǽl
siþþan West fóron him on láste and mid his
latteowdóme sóhton Beleriandes weststrand, for þám
þe Godu híe laþodon on Valinor.
      þá wearþ Morgoþ ǽr mid micle heregange forhergod      80
and gebunden and siþþan æt Mandosse on cwearterne
gedón. þǽr wearð he wítefæst seofon firstmearce (þæt is
seofon hund Valagéara) oþ þæt he dǽdbétte and him
forgifennesse bǽde. On þám gefeohtum éac wurdon
eorðan land eft forbrocen swíðe 7 forscapen.      85

      þá Cwendi (þæt wǽron Léohtelfe) and þá Noldelfe
sóhton ǽrest to lande on Valinor, 7 on þám grénan hylle
Córe þám sǽriman néah getimbrodon híe Tún þá hwítan
Elfaburg; ac þá Teleri, þe síþ cómon on Beleriand,
gebidon áne firstmearce þǽr be strande, and sume híe      90
ne fóron þanon siþþan nǽfre. þára wæsþingol gefrǽgost,
Elwes bróðor, Teleria hláfordes: hine Melian begól.

Híe hæfde he siþþan to wífe, and cyning wearð on
Beleriande; ac þæt gelamp æfter þám þe Ulmo ofládde
Teleria þone mǽstan dǽl on Ánetíge, and bróhte híe 95
swá to Valinore. Þás þing wurdon on þám Valagéarum
MM oþ MMC.

Of MMC oþ MMCC wunodon þá Teleri on
Toleressean onmiddum Ingársecge, þanon híe mihton
Valinor feorran ofséon; on MMCC cómon híe mid 100
micelre scipferde to Valinore, and þǽr gewunodon on
éastsǽriman Valinores, and geworhton þǽr burg and
hýþe, and nemdon híe Alqualonde, þæt is Elfethýþ, for
þǽm þe híe þǽr hira scipu befæston, 7 þá wǽron
ielfetum gelíc. 105

þæs ymb þréo hund sumera, oþþe má oþþe lǽs,
apóhton þá Noldelfe gimmas and ongunnon híe
asmiþian, and siþþan Féanor se smiþ, Finwes yldesta
sunu Nol[d]elfa hláfordes, apóhte and geworhte þá
felamǽran Silmarillas, þe þéos gesǽgen fela áh to 110
secganne be hira wyrdum. Híe lixton mid hira ágenum
léohte, for þám þe híe wǽron gefylde þára twégra
Béama léomum, þe wurdon þǽroninnan geblanden and
to hálgum and wundorfyllum fýre gescapen.

MMDCC Hér Morgoþ dǽdbétte and him forgefennesse 115
bæd; ond be Niennan þingunga his sweostor him
Manwe his bróðor áre getéah, Tulkases unþance and
Aules, and hine gelésde; 7 he lícette þæt he hréowsode 7
éaðmód wǽre, and þám Valum gehérsum and þám
elfum swíþe hold; ac he léah, and swíþost he bepǽhte þá 120
Noldelfe, for þám þe he cúþe fela uncúþra þinga lǽran;
he gítsode swáþéah hira gimma and hine langode þá
Silmarillas.

MMCM þurh twá firstmearce wunode þá gíet Valinor on
blisse, ac twéo 7 inca awéox swáþéah manigum on 125
heortan swulce nihtsceadu náthwylc, for þám þe Morgoþ
fór mid dernum rúnungum and searolicum lygum, and
yfelsóþ is to secganne, swíþost he onbryrde þá Noldelfe
and unsibbe awehte betwux Finwes sunum, Féanor
and Fingolfin and Finrod, and ungeþwǽrnes betwux 130
Godum 7 elfum.

**MMCMD**  Be Goda dóme wearþ Féanor, Finwes yldesta
sunu, mid his hírede 7 folgoþe adón of Noldelfa
ealdordóme – þý hátte sippan Féanores cynn þá
Erfeloran, for þám dóme 7 for þý þe Morgoþ beréafode  135
híe hira máþma – 7 þá Godu ofsendon Morgoþ to
démanne hine; ac he ætfléah 7 darode on Arualine and
beþóhte hine yfel.

**MMCMD** –  Hér Morgoþ fullfremede his searowrencas
**MMCMDI**  sóhte Ungoliante on Arualine and bæd híe  140
fultumes.  þa bestǽlon híe eft on Valinor 7 þá Béamas
forspildon,  and  sippan  ætburston  under  þám
weaxendum sceadum and fóron norþ and þǽr hergodon
Féanores eardunge and ætbǽron gimma unrím and þá
Silmarillas mid ealle, 7 Morgoþ ofslóh þǽr Finwe 7  145
manige his elfe mid him and awídlode swá Valinor ǽrest
mid blódgyte and morþor astealde on worolde.  He þá
fléame generede his feorh, þéah þe þá Godu his éhton
wíde  landes,  sippan  becóm  he  on  middangeardes
norþdǽlas and geedstaðelode þǽr his fæsten, and fédde  150
and samnode on níwe his yfele þéowas, ge Balrogas ge
orcas.  þá cóm micel ege on Beleriand, 7 þingol his
burgfæsten getrymede on Menegroþ þæt is þúsend
þéostru, and Melian séo cwén mid Vala-gealdrum begól
þæt land Doriaþ and bewand hit ymbútan, and sippan  155
sóhton se mǽsta dǽl þára deorc-elfa of Beleriande
þingoles munde.

**MMCMI**  Hér læg Valinor on

## NOTES TO VERSION II

5  *Noldelfaracu* emended in ink from *Noldelfagesægen*.

7  *Tavrobele* > (probably) *Tafrobele*, in pencil. In version I
*Tafrobele* probably > *Taþrobele*, and in version III
*Taþrobele* as written, but in this case the emendation seems
clearly to be to *f*; this would be a mere spelling-correction (*f*
being the Old English spelling for the voiced consonant [v] in
this position).

13–14  This phrase (*þe sume menn sippan for godu héoldon*) is not in the
Modern English version, but cf. the opening section of Q
(p. 78): 'These spirits the Elves named the Valar, which is the
Powers, though Men have often called them Gods.'

15 Ossë has been inadvertently omitted.

17 It is not said in the Modern English version that Manwë was the elder.

22 *Geauanna*: this spelling would represent 'Yavanna' in Old English. At line 59 the name is spelt *Iauanna(n)*, and in the Old English version of the *Quenta* (p. 207) *Yavanna*; in version III *Geafanna* (p. 291).

26–8 The text here embodies the sense of the pencilled emendation to the Modern English version (p. 270 note 2) whereby Vairë enters as the spouse of Mandos and Nienna becomes solitary. At line 28, after *næfde wer*, was added in pencil: *Séo wæs Manwes sweostor 7 Morgoðes*; this is stated in the Modern English version as written.

41–3 *Útgársecg, Gársecg, Ingársecg*: see pp. 208, 210. – *Belegar*: see pp. 210, 249–51.

45 *middangeardes*: see p. 283.

48 Valmar is *Godaburg* in the list of Old English names, p. 211.

60–2 The changes made to the text of the Modern English version, in order to date the Starmaking and the Awakening of the Elves before 2000 (see p. 270, notes 6 and 10), are not embodied in the Old English.

65–6 The statement that Melian was of Lórien's people is not in the Modern English version, but is found in S and Q (§2) and goes back to the *Tale of Tinúviel* (II. 8): '[Wendelin] was a sprite that escaped from Lórien's gardens before even Kôr was built.'

72 *Brynebrér* ('Burning Briar'): this name for the Great Bear, not found in the Modern English version, occurs in Q (§2) and in the *Lay of Leithian*.

82 *seofon firstmearce*, not 'nine ages' as first written in the Modern English version (p. 270 note 9). *firstmearce* ('spaces of time') is an emendation made at the time of writing from *langfirstas* (one of the words used for Valian 'ages' earlier, line 33).

86 *Cwendi* emended in pencil first to *Eldar* and then to *Lindar*; *Quendi* > *Lindar* also in Q (§2 and subsequently) and in the modern version. – *Léohtelfe* is not one of the Old English names of the First Kindred given in the list on p. 212, but they are called *Light-elves* in S and Q (§2; see p. 44).

95 *Ánetíge* spelt thus, as in version I line 4; *Ánetége* lines 8 and 9.

99 *Ingársecge* < *Gársecge* (see lines 42–3).

115 For the date 2700 see note to line 82 above, and the note on dates, p. 273.

135 *Erfeloran* ('the Dispossessed'), with variant initial vowel *Yrfeloran*, is found in the list of Old English names of the Fëanorians, p. 212.

139 These dates are presumably to be interpreted as 2950–1: in the

previous entry (line 132) MMCMD corresponds to 2950 in the
Modern English version. My father was here using D = 50, not
500. But 2950-1 does not correspond to the Modern English
version, which has 2990-1. The discrepancy is perhaps no more
than a mere error of writing (though version I is also discrepant
in this date, having 2999); the date of the next entry, MMCMI
(2901), is obviously an error, from its place in the chronological
series.

152-7    This sentence represents part of the passage added to the
Modern English version (p. 271 note 18), but omits the
reference to the Elves who remained in Brithombar and
Eglorest.


III

This version, on a single manuscript page, gives a slightly different
form of the first twenty-odd lines of version II. It is much later than II, as
is shown by *Melkor*, not *Melko* (see p. 282), but was nonetheless taken
directly from it, as is shown by the continued absence of Ossë from the
list of the Valar (see note to line 15 in version II). Later changes pencilled
on version I are here embodied in the text (*Pengoloð* for *Pengolod*,
*Taþrobele* for *Tafrobele*, *Melkor* for *Melko*).

Version III is cast in a different form of Old English, that of ninth
century Mercia (some of the forms are peculiarly characteristic of the
Mercian dialect represented by the interlinear glosses on the Vespasian
Psalter). A few pencilled emendations are not included in the text, but
recorded in the notes that follow.


Hér onginneð séo bóc þe man *Pennas* nemneð on ælfisc, 7 hío
is on þréo gedǽled: se forma dǽl is *Ualinórelúmien* þæt is
Godoeðles gérgetæl; 7 se óðer dǽl is Beleriandes gérgetæl; 7
se þridda *Quenta Noldorinwa* oððe *Pennas na Ngoeloeð*, þæt
is Noldælfaracu. þás bóc ǽrest awrát Pengoloð se úðwita on        5
Gondoline ǽr þám þe héo abrocen wurde 7 seoððan æt
Siriones hýðe 7 æt Taþrobele on Tol-eressean (þæt is
Ánetége), þá he eft west cóm. And þás béc Ælfwine of
Ongulcynne gesæh on Ánetége ða ða he æt sumum cerre þæt
land funde; 7 he ðær liornode híe swá he betst mæhte 7 eft       10
geþéodde 7 on englisc gereord ásette.


Hér onginneð Godoeðles gérgetæl, 7 spriceð ǽrest of
weorulde gescefte. On frumscefte gescóp Ilúuatar þæt is

Allfeder all þing, 7 þá þá séo weoruld ǽrest weorðan ongon þá
cómun hider on eorðan þá Ualar (þæt is þá Mehtigan þe sume 15
men seoððan for godu héoldun). Hí earun nigun on ríme:
Manwe, Ulmo, Aule, Orome, Tulcas, Mandos, Lórien,
Melkor. þeara wérun Manwe 7 Melcor his bróður alra
mehtigoste, ac Manwe wes se ældra 7 is Uala-hláfard 7 hálig,
7 Melcor béh to firenlustum 7 to úpahefennisse 7 ofer- 20
moettum 7 wearð yfel 7 unméðlic, 7 his noma is awergod 7
unasproecenlic, for þám man nemneð hine Morgoþ on Nold-
ælfiscgereorde. Orome 7 Tulcas wérun gingran on Alfeadur
geþóhte acende ǽr þere weorulde gescepennisse þonne óðre
fífe. þá Uala-cwéne háttun swé: Uarda Manwes cwén, 7 .25
Geafanna Aules cwén (þá þá he and híe wurdon to sinhíwan
æfter þám þe Ualar hider cómon on weorulde).

## NOTES TO VERSION III

2-4 *Ualinórelúmien þæt is* and *Quenta Noldorinwa oððe* are circled
 in pencil as if for exclusion.
5 Added in pencil here: 'and þes þridda dǽl man éac nemneð
 *Silmarillion* þæt is Eorclanstána gewyrd.' See p. 284.
5-6 *on Gondoline* is an emendation in ink from *of Gondoline*, i.e.
 Pengoloð began the work in Gondolin; but this is implied in the
 preambles to versions I and II, which have *of Gondoline* here. –
 *Gondoline* > *Gondolinde* in pencil, as in version I (note to
 line 2).
7 *Taþrobele* is very clearly written with þ; see p. 288 note to line 7.
17 Ossë is left out following version II.
18 *Melkor* > *Melcor* in ink at the second occurrence, no doubt at the
 time of writing, since *Melcor* is written at line 20.
23-5 The statement that Oromë and Tulkas 'were younger in the
 thought of Ilúvatar' is absent from the other versions (cf. *The
 Silmarillion* p. 26: 'Manwë and Melkor were brethren in the
 thought of Ilúvatar'). – *óðre fífe*: i.e. the other Valar with the
 exclusion of Manwë and Melkor. See p. 293, Old English text
 lines 1-4.
26 *Geafanna*: see p. 289, note to line 22.
26-7 It is very notable that Aulë and Yavanna are here (alone) said to
 have become husband and wife (*wurdon to sinhíwan*) after the
 Valar came into the world. In *The Silmarillion* the only union
 among the Valar that is said to have taken place after the entry
 into Arda is that of Tulkas and Nessa; and Tulkas came late to
 Arda (pp. 35-6). See further p. 293.

IV

This is not a version, but a single page of manuscript with, first, a different beginning to the *Annals of Valinor* in Modern English, and then ten lines, written very rapidly, in Old English. Both contain interesting features. The first reads as follows:

## Annals of Valinor

These were written first by Rúmil the Elfsage of Valinor, and after by Pengolod the Wise of Gondolin, who made also the Annals of Beleriand, and the *Pennas* that are set forth below. These also did Ælfwine of the Angelcynn turn into speech of his land.

Here beginneth the Annals of Valinor and the foundations of the world.

### Of the Valar and their kindred

At the beginning Ilúvatar, that is Allfather, made all things, and the Valar, or Powers, came into the world. These are nine: Manwë, Ulmo, Aulë, Oromë, Tulkas, Ossë, Lórien, Mandos, and Melko.

*Pennas* is here used in the narrow sense of 'The History of the Gnomes' (*Quenta Noldorinwa, Silmarillion*): see p. 284. Here Rúmil appears as author, and in view of the interpolation in AV (note 20) 'Here endeth that which Rúmil wrote' it is clear that the words of this preamble 'These were written first by Rúmil . . . and after by Pengolod' mean that Pengolod completed what Rúmil began. The next version of the *Annals of Valinor* in fact makes this explicit, for after 'Here endeth that which Rúmil wrote' the later text has 'Here followeth the continuation of Pengolod'; and the two interpolations in AV (notes 14 and 18) concerning events in Middle-earth before the Return of the Noldoli are embodied in the second version as additions by Pengolod: 'This have I, Pengolod, added here, *for it was not known unto Rúmil.*'

In the original tale of *The Music of the Ainur* (I.47–8) Rúmil was a Noldo of Kôr,* but he also spoke to Eriol of his 'thraldom under Melko'. From the reference here to Rúmil as 'the Elfsage of Valinor', however, and from his ignorance of events in Middle-earth, it seems clear that in the later conception he never left Valinor. It might be suggested that his part in the *Annals* ends where it does (p. 267 and note 20) because he was

---

*As he remained; cf. *The Silmarillion* p. 63: 'Then it was that the Noldor first bethought them of letters, and Rúmil of Tirion was the name of the loremaster who first achieved fitting signs for the recording of speech and song.'

one of those who returned to Valinor with Finrod after hearing the Doom of Mandos. This is admittedly pure speculation, but it is perhaps significant that in the next version of the *Annals* the end of Rúmil's part in the work was moved on to the end of the entry for the Valian Year 2993, after the words 'But Aulë their ancient friend smiled on them no more, and the Teleri were estranged'; thus his part ends with the actual record of Finrod's return, and of the reception that he and those with him received.

The passage in Old English that follows begins with virtually the same phrase, concerning Oromë and Tulkas, as that in version III lines 23–5; but this manuscript has a curious, uninterpretable sign between *Orome* and the plural verb *wǽron*, which in view of the other text I expand to mean 7 *Tulkas*.

Orome [7 Tulkas] wǽron gingran on Ealfæderes geþóhtum acende ǽr þǽre worolde gescepennisse þonne óþre fífe, 7 Orome wearð Iafannan geboren, séo þe wyrð æfter nemned, ac he nis Aules sunu.

Mid þissum mihtigum cómon manige lǽssan gǽstas þæs ilcan cynnes 7 cnéorisse, þeah lǽssan mægnes. þás sindon þá Vanimor, þá Fægran. Mid him éac þon wurdon getealde hira bearn, on worolde acende, þá wǽron manige and swíþe fægre. Swylc wæs Fionwe Manwes sunu

There follow a few more words that are too uncertain to reproduce. Here Oromë, younger in the thought of Ilúvatar than the other great Valar 'born before the making of the world', is declared to be the son of Yavanna but not of Aulë, and this must be connected with the statement in the Old English version III that Yavanna and Aulë became *sinhíwan* after the entry of the Valar into the world (see p. 291, note to lines 26–7).

In what is said here concerning the lesser spirits of Valarin race there are differences from AV (p. 263) and the Old English version II (p. 285). In this present fragment these spirits are not called *Valarindi* but *Vanimor*, 'the Fair'.* The Children of the Valar, 'who were many and very beautiful', are counted among the *Vanimor*, but, in contradiction to AV, they were *on worolde acende*, 'born in the world'. At this time, it seems, my father was tending to emphasize the generative powers of the great Valar, though afterwards all trace of the conception disappeared.

---

*The word *Vanimor* has not occurred before, but its negative *Úvanimor* is defined in the tale of *The Coming of the Valar* (I.75) as 'monsters, giants, and ogres', and elsewhere in the *Lost Tales* Úvanimor are creatures bred by Morgoth (I.236–7), and even Dwarves (II.136).

# VII

# THE EARLIEST ANNALS
# OF BELERIAND

As with the *Annals of Valinor*, these are the 'earliest' *Annals of Beleriand* because they were followed by others, the last being called the *Grey Annals*, companion to the *Annals of Aman* and belonging to the same time (p. 262). But unlike the *Annals of Aman*, the *Grey Annals* were left unfinished at the end of the story of Túrin Turambar; and both as prose narrative and still more as definitive history of the end of the Elder Days from the time of *The Lord of the Rings* their abandonment is grievous.

The earliest *Annals of Beleriand* ('AB') are themselves found in two versions, which I shall call AB I and AB II. AB I is a complete text to the end of the First Age; AB II is quite brief, and though it begins as a fair copy of the much-emended opening of I it soon becomes strongly divergent. In this chapter I give both texts separately and in their entirety, and in what follows I refer only to the earlier, AB I.

This is a good, clear manuscript, but the style suggests very rapid composition. For much of its length the entries are in the present tense and often staccato, even with such expressions as 'the Orcs got between them' (annal 172), though by subsequent small expansions and alterations here and there my father slightly modified this character. I think that his primary intention at this time was the consolidation of the historical structure in its internal relations and chronology – the *Annals* began, perhaps, in parallel with the *Quenta* as a convenient way of driving abreast, and keeping track of, the different elements in the ever more complex narrative web. Nonetheless major new developments enter here.

The manuscript was fairly heavily emended, though much less so towards the end, and from the nature of the changes, largely concerned with dating, it has become a complicated document. To present it in its original form, with all the later changes recorded in notes, would make it quite unnecessarily difficult to follow, and indeed would be scarcely possible, since many alterations were made either at the time of writing or in its immediate context. A later 'layer' of pencilled emendation, very largely concerned with names, is easily separable. The text given here, therefore, is that of the manuscript *after all the earlier changes and additions (in ink) had been made to it*, and these are only recorded in the notes in certain cases. The later pencilled alterations are fully registered.

That AB I is earlier than the comparable portion of AV is easily shown. Thus in AB I, as in Q (§8), there is no mention of Fingolfin's march to

Angband immediately on his arrival, whereas it appears in AV (p. 269); again as in Q and in contrast to AV (p. 268) the Battle under Stars was fought, and Fëanor died, before the encampment in Mithrim. Further, the names *Dagor-os-Giliath* and *Eredwethion* are added in pencil in AB I, whereas in AV they appear in the text as first written, and *Erydlómin* still means the Shadowy Mountains (see p. 280). That AB I is later than Q is shown by a multiplicity of features, as will be seen from the Commentary. There follows the text of AB I.

## ANNALS OF BELERIAND

Morgoth flees from Valinor with the Silmarils, the magic gems of Fëanor, and returns into the Northern World and rebuilds his fortress of Angband beneath the Black Mountain, Thangorodrim. He devises the Balrogs and the Orcs. The Silmarils are set in Morgoth's iron crown.

The Gnomes of the eldest house, the Dispossessed, come into the North under Fëanor and his seven sons, with their friends Orodreth, Angrod, and Egnor, sons of Finrod.[1] They burn the Telerian ships.

*First of the Battles* with Morgoth,[2] the Battle under Stars. Fëanor defeats the Orcs, but is mortally wounded by Gothmog captain of Balrogs, and dies. Maidros, his eldest son, is ambushed and captured and hung on Thangorodrim. The sons of Fëanor camp about Lake Mithrim in the North-west, behind the Shadowy Mountains.[3]

**Year 1**  Here Sun and Moon, made by the Gods after the death of the Two Trees of Valinor, appear. Thus measured time came into the Hither Lands. Fingolfin leads the second house of the Gnomes over the straits of Grinding Ice into the Hither Lands. With him came the son of Finrod, Felagund,[4] and part of the third or youngest house. They march from the North as the Sun rises, and unfurl their banners; and they come to Mithrim, but there is feud[5] between them and the sons of Fëanor. Morgoth at coming of Light retreats into his deepest dungeons, but smithies in secret, and sends forth black clouds.

**2**  Fingon son of Fingolfin heals the feud by rescuing Maidros.

**1–100**   The Gnomes explore and settle Beleriand, and all the vale of Sirion from[6] the Great Sea to the Blue Mountains,[7] except for Doriath in the centre where Thingol and Melian reign.

**20**   Feast and Games of Reuniting were held in Nan Tathrin, the Land of Willows, near the delta of Sirion, between the Elves of Valinor returning and the Dark-elves, both those of the Western Havens (Brithombar and Eldorest)[8] and the scattered Wood-elves of the West, and ambassadors of Thingol. A time of peace followed.[9]

**50**   Morgoth's might begins to move once more. Earthquakes in the North. Orc-raids begin. Turgon son of Fingolfin is great in friendship with Felagund son of Finrod; but Orodreth, Angrod, and Egnor, sons of Finrod, are friends of the sons of Fëanor, especially Celegorm and Curufin.

**50**   Turgon and Felagund are troubled by dreams and forebodings. Felagund finds the caves of Narog and establishes his armouries there.[10] Turgon alone discovers the hidden vale of Gondolin. Being still troubled in heart he gathers folk about him and departs from Hithlum, the Land of Mist about Mithrim, where his brother Fingon remains.

**51**   The Gnomes drive back the Orcs again, and the Siege of Angband is laid. The North has great peace and quiet again. Fingolfin holds the North-west and all Hithlum, and is overlord of the Dark-elves west of Narog. His might is gathered on the slopes of Erydlómin[11] the Shadowy Mountains and thence watches and traverses the great plains of Bladorion up to the walls of Morgoth's mountains in the North. Felagund holds the vale of Sirion save Doriath, and has his seat[12] beside Narog in the South, but his might is gathered in the North guarding the access to Sirion's vale between Erydlómin and the mountainous region of Taur-na-Danion, the forest of pines. He has a fortress on a rocky isle in the midst of Sirion, Tolsirion. His brothers dwell in the centre about Taur-na-Danion and scour Bladorion thence, and join in the East with the sons of Fëanor. The fortress of the sons of Fëanor is upon Himling, but they roam and hunt all the woods of East Beleriand even up to the Blue Mountains. Thither at times many of the Elf-lords go for hunting. But none get tidings of Turgon and his folk.

**70** Bëor born in the East.

**88. 90** Haleth, and Hádor the Goldenhaired, born in the East.

**100** Felagund hunting in the East comes upon Bëor the mortal and his Men who have wandered into Beleriand. Bëor becomes a vassal of Felagund and goes west with him. Bregolas son of Bëor born.

**102** Barahir son of Bëor born.

**120** Haleth comes into Beleriand; also Hádor the Goldenhaired and his great companies of Men. Haleth remains in Sirion's vale, but Hádor becomes a vassal of Fingolfin and strengthens his armies and is given lands in Hithlum.

113 Hundor son of Haleth born. 117 Gundor son of Hádor born. 119 Gumlin son of Hádor born.[13]

**122** The strength of Men being added to the Gnomes, Morgoth is straitly enclosed. The Gnomes deem the siege of Angband cannot be broken, but Morgoth ponders new devices, and bethinks him of Dragons. The Men of the three houses grow and multiply, and are gladly subject to the Elf-lords, and learn many crafts of the Gnomes. The Men of Bëor were dark or brown of hair but fair of face, with grey eyes; of shapely form, of great courage and endurance, but little greater than the Elves of that day. The folk of Hádor were yellow-haired and blue-eyed and of great stature and strength. Like unto them but somewhat shorter and more broad were the folk of Haleth.

**124. 128** Baragund and Belegund, sons of Bregolas son of Bëor, born.

**132** Beren, after named the Ermabwed[14] or One-handed,[15] son of Barahir, born.

**141**  Húrin the Steadfast, son of Gumlin, born. Handir son of Hundor son of Haleth born.

**144**  Huor Húrin's brother born.

**145**  Morwen Elfsheen, daughter of Baragund, born.

**150**  Rían daughter of Belegund, mother of Tuor, born.[16] Bëor the Old, Father of Men, dies of old age in Beleriand. The Elves see for the first time the death of weariness, and sorrow over the short span allotted to Men. Bregolas rules the house of Bëor.

★  **155**  Morgoth unlooses his might, and seeks to break into Beleriand. The Battle begins on a sudden on a night of mid-winter and falls first most heavily on the sons of Finrod and their folk. This is the Battle of Sudden Fire.[17] Rivers of fire flow from Thangorodrim. Glómund the golden, Father of Dragons, appears.[18] The plains of Bladorion are turned into a great desert without green, and called after Dor-na-Fauglith, Land of Gasping Thirst.

Here were Bregolas slain, and the greater part of the warriors of Bëor's house. Angrod and Egnor sons of Finrod fell. Barahir and his chosen champions saved Felagund and Orodreth, and Felagund swore a great oath of friendship to his kin and seed. Barahir rules the remnant of the house of Bëor.

**155**  Fingolfin and Fingon marched to the aid of their kin, but were driven back with great loss. Hádor, now aged, fell defending his lord Fingolfin, and with him Gundor his son. Gumlin took the lordship of Hádor's house.

The sons of Fëanor were not slain, but Celegorm and Curufin were defeated and fled with Orodreth son of Finrod. Maidros the left-handed did deeds of great prowess, and Morgoth did not take Himling as yet, but he broke into the passes east of Himling and ravaged into East Beleriand and scattered the Gnomes of Fëanor's house.

Turgon was not at that battle, nor Haleth or any but few of his folk. It is said that Húrin was at foster with Haleth, and that Haleth and Húrin hunting in Sirion's vale came upon some of Turgon's folk, and were brought into the secret vale of Gondolin, whereof of those outside none yet knew save Thorndor King of Eagles; for Turgon had messages and dreams sent by the God Ulmo, Lord of Waters, up Sirion warning him that help of Men was necessary for him. But Haleth and Húrin swore oaths of secrecy and never revealed Gondolin, but Haleth learned something of the counsels of Turgon, and told them after to Húrin. Great liking had Turgon for the boy Húrin, and would keep him in Gondolin, but the grievous tidings of the great battle came and they departed. Turgon sends secret messengers to Sirion's mouths and begins a building of ships. Many set sail for Valinor, but none return.[19]

Fingolfin seeing the ruin of [the] Gnomes and the defeat of all their houses was filled with wrath and despair, and rode alone to the gates of Angband and challenged Morgoth to single combat. Fingolfin was slain, but Thorndor rescued his body, and set it in a cairn on the mountains north of Gondolin to guard that valley, and so came the tidings thither. Fingon ruled the royal house of [the] Gnomes.

157 Morgoth took Tolsirion and pierced the passes into West Beleriand. There he set Thû the wizard, and Tolsirion became a place of evil.[20] Felagund and Orodreth, together with Celegorm and Curufin, retreated to Nargothrond, and made there a great hidden palace after the fashion of Thingol in[21] the Thousand Caves in Doriath.

Barahir will not retreat and holds out still in Taurna-Danion. Morgoth hunts them down and turns Taur-na-Danion into a region of great dread, so that it was after called Taur-na-Fuin, the Forest of Night, or Math-Fuin-delos[22] Deadly Nightshade. Only Barahir and his son Beren, and his nephews Baragund and Belegund sons of Bregolas and a few men remain.[23] The wives of Baragund and Belegund and their young daughters Morwen and Rían were sent[24] into Hithlum to the keeping of Gumlin.

158 Haleth and his folk lead a woodland life in the woods about Sirion on the west marches of Doriath and harry the Orc-bands.[25]

**160**  Barahir was betrayed by Gorlim, and all his company is slain by the Orcs save Beren who was hunting alone. Beren pursues the Orcs and slays his father's slayer and retakes the ring which Felagund gave to Barahir. Beren becomes a solitary outlaw.

**162**  Renewed assaults of Morgoth. Thẹ Orc-raids encompass Doriath, protected by the magic of Melian the divine, west down Sirion and east beyond Himling. Beren is driven south and comes hardly into Doriath. Gumlin slain in an assault upon the fortress of Fingon at Sirion's Well[26] in the west of Erydlómin.[27] Húrin his son is mighty in strength. He is summoned to Hithlum and comes there hardly. He rules the house of Hádor and serves Fingon.

**163**  The Swarthy Men first come into East Beleriand. They were short, broad, long and strong in the arm, growing much hair on face and breast, and this was dark as were their eyes; their skins were sallow or dark, but most were not uncomely. Their houses were many, and many had liking rather for the[28] Dwarves of the mountains, of Nogrod and Belegost, than for the Elves. Of the Dwarves the Elves first learned in these days, and their friendship was small. It is not known whence they are, save that they are not of Elf-kin, nor of mortal, nor of Morgoth.[29] But Maidros seeing the weakness of the Gnomes and the waxing power of the armies of Morgoth made alliance with the new-come Men, and with the houses of Bor and of Ulfand.[30] The sons of Ulfand were Uldor, after called the Accursed, and Ulfast, and Ulwar; and by Cranthir son of Fëanor were they most beloved, and they swore fealty to him.

**163–4**  The great geste of Beren and Lúthien.[31] King Felagund of Nargothrond dies in Tolsirion[32] in the dungeons of Thû. Orodreth rules Nargothrond and breaks friendship with Celegorm and Curufin who are expelled.[33] Lúthien and Huan overthrow Thû. Beren and Lúthien go to Angband and recover a Silmaril. Carcharoth the great wolf of Angband with the Silmaril in his belly bursts into Doriath. Beren and the hound Huan are slain by Carcaroth, but Huan slays Carcharoth and the Silmaril is regained.

Beren was recalled from the dead by Lúthien and dwelt with her[34] in the Land of Seven Rivers, Ossiriand, out of the knowledge of Men and Elves.[35]

164 Húrin weds Morwen.

165 Túrin son of Húrin born in winter with sad omens.[36]

165–70 *The Union of Maidros.* Maidros enheartened by the deeds of Beren and Lúthien plans a reuniting of forces for the driving back of Morgoth. But because of the deeds of Celegorm and Curufin he receives no help from Thingol, and only small support from Nargothrond, where the Gnomes attempt to guard themselves by stealth and secrecy. He gathers and arms all the Gnomes of Fëanor's house, and multitudes of the Dark-elves, and of Men, in East Beleriand. He gets help in smithying of the Dwarves, and summons yet more Men over the mountains out of the East.

Tidings come to Turgon the hidden king and he prepares in secret for war, for his people who were not at the Second Battle will not be restrained.

167 Dior the Beautiful born to Beren and Lúthien in Ossiriand.

168 Haleth, last of the Fathers of Men, dies. Hundor rules his folk. The Orcs are slowly driven back out of Beleriand.

171 Isfin daughter of Turgon strays out of Gondolin and is taken to wife by Eöl a Dark-elf.

★ 172 *The year of sorrow.* Maidros plans an assault upon Angband, from West and East. Fingon is to march forth as soon as Maidros' main host gives the signal in the East of Dor-na-Fauglith. Huor son of Hádor[37] weds Rían daughter of Belegund on the eve of battle and marches with Húrin his brother in the army of Fingon.

*The Battle of Unnumbered Tears,*[38] the third battle of the Gnomes and Morgoth, was fought upon the plains of Dor-na-Fauglith before the pass in which the young waters of Sirion enter Beleriand between Erydlómin[39] and Taur-na-Fuin. The place was long marked by a great hill in which the slain, Elves and Men, were piled. Grass grew there alone in Dor-na-Fauglith. The Elves and Men were utterly defeated and their ruin accomplished.

Maidros was hindered on the road by the machinations of Uldor the Accursed whom Morgoth's spies had bought. Fingon attacked without waiting and drove in Morgoth's feinted attack, even to Angband. The companies from Nargothrond burst into his gates, but they and their leader Flinding son of Fuilin[40] were all taken; and Morgoth now released a countless army and drove the Gnomes back with terrible slaughter. Hundor son of Haleth and the Men of the wood were slain in the retreat across the sands. The Orcs got between them and the passes into Hithlum, and they retreated towards Tolsirion.

Turgon and the army of Gondolin sound their horns and issue out of Taur-na-Fuin. Fortune wavers and the Gnomes begin to gain ground. Glad meeting of Húrin and Turgon.

The trumpets of Maidros heard in the East, and the Gnomes take heart. The Elves say victory might have been theirs yet but for Uldor. But Morgoth now sent forth all the folk of Angband and Hell was emptied. There came afresh a hundred thousand Orcs and a thousand Balrogs, and in the forefront came Glómund the Dragon, and Elves and Men withered before him. Thus the union of the hosts of Fingon and Maidros was broken. But Uldor went over to Morgoth and fell on the right flank of the sons of Fëanor.

Cranthir slew Uldor, but Ulfast and Ulwar slew Bor and his three sons and many Men who were faithful, and the host of Maidros was scattered to the winds and fled far into hiding into East Beleriand and the mountains there.

Fingon fell in the West, and it is said flame sprang from his helm as he was smitten down by the Balrogs. Húrin and the Men of Hithlum of Hádor's house, and Huor his brother, stood firm, and the Orcs could not pass into Beleriand. The stand of Húrin is the most renowned deed of Men among the Elves. He held the rear while Turgon with part of his battle, and some of the remnant of Fingon's host, escaped into the dales and mountains. They vanished and were not again found by Elf or by spy of Morgoth until Tuor's day. Thus was Morgoth's victory marred and he was greatly angered.

Húrin fought on after Huor fell pierced with a venomed arrow, and until he alone was left. He threw away his shield and fought with an axe and slew a hundred Orcs.

Húrin was taken alive by Morgoth's command and dragged to Angband where Morgoth cursed him and his kin, and because he would not reveal where Turgon was gone chained him with enchanted sight on Thangorodrim to see the evil that befell his wife and children. His son Túrin was nigh three years old,[41] and his wife Morwen was again with child.

The Orcs piled the slain and entered Beleriand to ravage. Rían sought for Huor, for no tidings came to Hithlum of the battle, and her child Tuor son of Huor was born to her in the wild. He was taken to nurture by Dark-elves, but Rían went to the Mound of Slain[42] and laid her down to die there.[43]

173 Morgoth took all Beleriand or filled it with roving bands of Orcs and wolves, but there held still Doriath. Of Nargothrond he heard little, of Gondolin he could discover nothing. In Beleriand outside these three places only scattered Elves and Men lived in outlawry, and among them the remnant of Haleth's folk under Handir, son of Hundor, son of Haleth.[44]

Morgoth broke his pledges to the sons of Ulfand,[45] and drove the evil Men into Hithlum, without reward, save that they there ill-treated and enslaved the remnants of Hádor's house, the old men and the women and children. The remnants of the Elves of Hithlum also he mostly enslaved and took to the mines of Angband, and others he forbade to leave Hithlum, and they were slain if Orcs found them east or south of the Shadowy Mountains.[46] Nienor the sorrowful, daughter of Húrin and Morwen, born in Hithlum in the beginning of the year.

Tuor grew up wild in the woods among fugitive Elves nigh the shores of Mithrim;[47] but Morwen sent Túrin to Doriath begging for Thingol's fostering and aid, for she was of Beren's kindred. They have a desperate journey, the boy of seven and his two guides.[48]

181   The power of Morgoth waxes and Doriath is cut off and no tidings of the outer world reach it. Túrin though not fully grown takes to war on the marches in company of Beleg.

184   Túrin slays Orgof, kinsman of the royal house, and flees from Thingol's court.

184–7   Túrin an outlaw in the woods. He gathers a desperate band, and plunders on the marches of Doriath and beyond.

187   Túrin's companions capture Beleg. But Túrin releases him and they renew their fellowship, and make war on the Orcs, adventuring far beyond Doriath.[49]

189   Blodrin Ban's son betrays their hiding place, and Túrin is taken alive. Beleg healed of his wounds follows in pursuit. He comes upon Flinding son of Fuilin,[50] who escaped from Morgoth's mines; together they rescue Túrin from the Orcs. Túrin slays Beleg by misadventure.

190   Túrin healed of his madness by Ivrin's well,[51] and is brought at last by Flinding to Nargothrond. They are admitted on the prayer of Finduilas daughter of Orodreth, who had before loved Flinding.

190–5   The sojourn of Túrin in Nargothrond. Beleg's sword is reforged and Túrin rejects his ancient name and is renowned as Mormegil (Mormakil)[52] 'Black-Sword'. He calls his sword Gurtholfin 'Wand of Death'. Finduilas forgets her love of Flinding, and is beloved of Túrin, who will not reveal his love out of faithfulness to Flinding; nonetheless Flinding is embittered. Túrin becomes a great captain. He leads the Gnomes of Nargothrond to victory and their ancient secrecy is broken. Morgoth learns of the growing strength of the

stronghold,[53] but the Orcs are driven out of all the land
between Narog and Sirion and Doriath to the East, and
West to the Sea, and North to Erydlómin.[54] A bridge is
built over Narog. The Gnomes ally them with Haleth's
folk under Handir.

192   Meglin comes to Gondolin and is received by Turgon
as his sister's child.

194   In this time of betterment Morwen and Nienor leave
Hithlum and seek tidings of Túrin in Doriath. There
many speak of the prowess of Mormakil,[55] but of Túrin
none know tidings.

195   Glómund with a host of Orcs comes over Erydlómin
and defeats the Gnomes between Narog and Taiglin.
Handir is slain. Flinding dies refusing succour of
Túrin. Túrin hastens back to Nargothrond but it is
sacked ere his coming. He is deceived and spellbound
by Glómund. Finduilas and the women of Nargothrond are taken as thralls, but Túrin deceived by
Glómund goes to Hithlum to seek Morwen.
News comes to Doriath that Nargothrond is taken
and Mormakil is Túrin.
Tuor was led out of Hithlum by a secret way under
Ulmo's guidance, and journeyed along the coast past
the ruined havens of Brithombar and Eldorest[56] and
reached Sirion's mouth.[57]

195–6  Túrin goes to Hithlum and finds his mother gone. He
slays Brodda and escapes. He joins the Woodmen and
becomes their lord, since Brandir son of Handir is
lame from childhood. He takes name of Turambar
(Turumarth)[58] 'Conqueror of Fate'.

196   Here Tuor meets Bronweg at Sirion's mouth. Ulmo
himself appears to him in Nan-tathrin; and Tuor and
Bronweg guided by Ulmo find Gondolin. They are
received after questioning, and Tuor speaks the
embassy of Ulmo. Turgon does not now harken to it,
partly because of the urging of Meglin. But Tuor for
his kindred's sake is held in great honour.
Morwen goes to Nargothrond, whither Glómund
has returned and lies on the treasure of Felagund. She

seeks for tidings of Túrin. Nienor against her bidding rides in disguise with her escort of Elves of the folk of Thingol.

Glómund lays a spell on the company and disperses it. Morwen vanishes in the woods; and a great darkness of mind comes on Nienor.

Túrin found Nienor hunted by the Orcs. He names her Níniel, the tearful, since she knew not her name, and himself Turambar.

**197–8** Nienor Níniel dwells with the Woodfolk and is beloved by Túrin Turambar and Brandir the lame.

**198** Túrin weds Nienor.

**199** Glómund seeks out the dwellings of Túrin. Túrin slays him with Gurtholfin his sword; but falls aswoon beside him. Nienor finds him, but Glómund ere death releases her from the spell and declares her kindred. Nienor casts herself away over the waterfall in that place.[59] Brandir reveals the truth to Túrin and is slain by him. Túrin bids Gurtholfin slay him, and he dies. So ended the worst of Morgoth's evil; but Húrin was released from Angband, bowed as with age, and sought for Morwen.

Tuor weds Idril Celebrindal daughter of [Turgon of] Gondolin, and earns the secret hate of Meglin.

**200** Here was born Eärendel the Bright, the star of the Two Kindreds, unto Tuor and Idril in Gondolin. Here was born also Elwing the White, fairest of women save Lúthien, unto Dior in Ossiriand.

Húrin gathers men unto him. They find the treasure of Nargothrond and slay Mîm the Dwarf who had taken it to himself. The treasure is cursed. The treasure is brought to Thingol. But Húrin departs from Doriath with bitter words, but of his fate and of Morwen's after no certain tidings are known.

**201** Thingol employs the Dwarves to smithy his gold and silver and the treasure of Narog, and they make the renowned Nauglafring,[60] the Dwarf-necklace, whereon is hung the Silmaril. Enmity awakes[61] between the Elves and Dwarves, and the Dwarves are driven away.

**202** Here the Dwarves invaded Doriath aided by treachery, for many Elves were smitten with the accursed lust of the treasure. Thingol was slain and the Thousand Caves sacked. But Melian the divine could not be taken and departed to Ossiriand.

Beren[62] summoned by Melian overthrew the Dwarves at Sarn-Athra[63] and cast the gold into the River Asgar, which afterwards was called Rathlorion[64] the Golden-bed; but the Nauglafring and the Silmaril he took. Lúthien wore the necklace and the Silmaril on her breast. Here Beren and Lúthien depart out of men's knowledge and their deathday is not known; save that at night a messenger brought the necklace unto Dior in Doriath, and the Elves said: 'Lúthien and Beren are dead as Mandos doomed.'

Dior son of Lúthien and Beren, Thingol's heir, returned unto Doriath and for a while re-established it, but Melian went back to Valinor and he had no longer her protection.

**203** The necklace came to Dior; he wore it on his breast.

**205** The sons of Fëanor hear tidings of the Silmaril in the East, and gather from wandering and hold council. They summon Dior to give up the jewel.

**206** Here Dior fought the sons of Fëanor on the east marches of Doriath, but he was slain. Celegorm and Curufin and Cranthir fell in battle. The young sons of Dior, Elboron and Elbereth, were slain by the evil men of Maidros' host, and Maidros bewailed the foul deed. The maiden Elwing was saved by faithful Elves and taken to Sirion's mouth, and with them they took the jewel and the necklace.

Meglin was taken in the hills and betrayed Gondolin to Morgoth.

**207** Here Morgoth loosed a host of dragons over the mountains from the North and Gondolin's vale was taken and the city besieged. The Orcs sacked Gondolin and destroyed the king and most of his people; but Ecthelion of the Fountain slew there Gothmog lord of Balrogs ere he fell.

Tuor slew Meglin. Tuor, Idril, and Eärendel

escaped by a secret way devised by Idril and came to Cristhorn, Eagles' Cleft, a high pass beneath Fingolfin's cairn in the North. Glorfindel was there slain in an ambush, but Thorndor saved the remnant of Gondolin, and they escaped at last into the vale of Sirion. The ruin of the Elves was now well-nigh complete, and no refuge or strong place or realm remained to them.

208 Here the wanderers from Gondolin reached the mouths of Sirion and joined with the slender company of Elwing. The Silmaril brings blessing upon them and they multiply, and build ships and a haven, and dwell upon the delta amid the waters. Fugitives gather to them.

210 Maidros hears of the upspringing of Sirion's Haven and that a Silmaril is there, but he forswears his oath.

224 The unquiet of Ulmo comes upon Tuor and he builds the ship Earámë, Eagle's Pinion, and departs with Idril into the West and is heard of no more. Eärendel weds Elwing and is lord of the folk of Sirion.

225 Torment of Maidros and his brothers because of their oath. Damrod and Díriel resolve to win the Silmaril if Eärendel will not yield it.

Here unquiet came upon Eärendel and he voyaged the seas afar seeking Tuor, and seeking Valinor, but he found neither. The marvels that he did and saw were very many and renowned. Elrond Half-elfin, son of Eärendel, was born.

The folk of Sirion refused to give up the Silmaril in Eärendel's absence, and they thought their joy and prosperity came of it.

229 Here Damrod and Díriel ravaged Sirion, and were slain. Maidros and Maglor gave reluctant aid. Sirion's folk were slain or taken into the company of Maidros. Elrond was taken to nurture by Maglor. Elwing cast herself with the Silmaril into the sea, but by Ulmo's aid in the shape of a bird flew to Eärendel and found him returning.

230  Eärendel binds the Silmaril on his brow and with Elwing sails in search of Valinor.

233  Eärendel comes unto Valinor and speaks on behalf of both races.

240  Maglor, Maidros, and Elrond with few free Elves, the last of the Gnomes, live[65] in hiding from Morgoth, who rules all Beleriand and the North, and thrusts ever East and South.

233–43  The sons of the Gods[66] under Fionwë son of Manwë prepare for war. The Light-elves arm, but the Teleri do not leave Valinor, though they built a countless host of ships.

247  Fionwë's host draws nigh to the Hither Lands and his trumpets from the sea ring in the western woods. Here was fought the Battle of Eldorest,[67] where Ingwil[68] son of Ingwë made a landing. Great war comes into Beleriand, and Fionwë summons all Elves, and Dwarves, and Men, and beasts, and birds to his standards, who do not elect to fight for Morgoth. But the power and dread of Morgoth was very great, and many did not obey.

★  250  Here Fionwë fought the last battle of the ancient North, the Great or Terrible Battle. Morgoth came forth, and the hosts were arrayed on either side of Sirion. But the host of Morgoth were driven as leaves and the Balrogs destroyed utterly, and Morgoth fled to Angband pursued by the hosts of Fionwë.

He loosed thence all the winged Dragons, and Fionwë was driven back upon Dor-na-Fauglith, but Eärendel came in the sky and overthrew Ancalagon the Black Dragon, and in his fall Thangorodrim was broken.[69]

The sons of the Gods wrestled with Morgoth in his dungeons and the earth shook and all Beleriand was shattered and changed and many perished, but Morgoth was bound.

Fionwë departed to Valinor with the Light-elves and many of the Gnomes and the other Elves of the Hither Lands, but Elrond Half-elfin remained and ruled in the

West of the world. Maidros and Maglor perished in [70] a last endeavour to seize the Silmarils which Fionwë took from Morgoth's crown.[71] So ended the First Age of the World and Beleriand was no more.

## NOTES

1   This sentence, *with their friends Orodreth, Angrod, and Egnor, sons of Finrod*, was an early addition; cf. the addition made to AV, note 21.

2   Later addition: *Dagor-os-Giliath*, which is found in AV as first written, entry Valian Year 2996.

3   Later addition: *(Eredwethion)*, which is found in AV as first written, entry Valian Year 2996. – Pencilled in the margin against this passage, but then struck out, is: *The passage of the Gnomes into Mithrim occupied equivalent of 10 years of later time or 1 Valinorian year.* Cf. AV, p. 268.

4   This is an early alteration, going with that given in note 1, of *With him come the sons of Finrod*; cf. the alteration made to AV, note 23.

5   An early alteration from: *They march to Mithrim as the Sun rises, and unfurl their banners; but there is feud . . .*

6   Later addition: *Belegar*. This name occurs in the Old English version II of AV, p. 285 line 43.

7   Later addition: *Eredlindon*. This name occurs in late additions to Q (§9 note 3) and AV (note 14).

8   *Eldorest > Eglarest > Eglorest* (cf. notes 56, 67). On the Westward extension of the first map (see pp. 227–8) the name is *Eldorest*; in an interpolation to AV (note 18) it is *Eglorest*; in *The Silmarillion* it is *Eglarest*.

9   The conclusion of this annal (very probably changed at the time of composition) was originally: *A time of peace and growth. Before the Sun were only the pines and firs and dark . . . . .*

10   Later addition: *at Nargothrond*.

11   *Erydlómin > Eredwethion* (twice; later changes). See note 3, and pp. 192–3, 221.

12   Later addition: *at Nargothrond*.

13   These three annals are placed here and written thus in the manuscript, and enclosed in square brackets. The brackets perhaps only indicate that the annals are an addition (Gumlin's birth was first placed in the annal 122, but struck out probably at the time of writing, and the mention of the birth of Handir son of Hundor was an early addition to annal 141).

14   Later change: *Ermabwed > Ermabuin*. *Ermabwed* is the form in the *Lay of the Children of Húrin* and in Q (§10).

15 Later addition: *or Mablosgen the Empty-handed*.

16 Most of the birth-dates from 124 to 150 were changed by a year or two, but since the figures were overwritten the underlying dates cannot all be made out with certainty. The entry for the birth of Rían was first given a separate entry under the year 152: *Rían the sorrowful, daughter of Belegund, born*.

17 Later addition: *Dagor Hurbreged*.

18 Later addition: *in full might*.

19 These two sentences were an addition, though a very early one: hence the change of tense.

20 Later addition: *Tol-na-Gaurhoth, Isle of Werewolves*.

21 Later addition: *Menegroth*. This name occurs in an interpolation to AV (note 18) and in the Old English version II, p. 288 line 153.

22 *Math-Fuin-delos* > *Gwath-Fuin-daidelos* (late change). On *delos, daidelos* see p. 259 third footnote and p. 272 note 27.

23 Later addition: *Gorlim, Radros, Dengar, & 7 others*. Above *Dengar* is written (later) *Dagnir*.

24 This sentence was struck through in pencil and the following replacement written in: *Their wives and children were captured or slain by Morgoth, save Morwen Eledwen Elfsheen (daughter of Baragund) and Rían (daughter of Belegund), who were sent*, &c.

25 Following this the original text had: *Haleth, last of the Fathers of Men, dies in the woods. Hundor his son rules his folk*. This was struck out while the *Annals* were in course of composition, for it reappears later, and not as an insertion (year 168).

26 *Sirion's Well* > *Eithyl Sirion* (later change). *Eithyl* (of which the *y* is uncertain) replaces an earlier form, probably *Eothlin*.

27 *Erydlómin* > *Eredwethion* (later change; cf. note 11).

28 Later addition: *nauglar or* (i.e. *for the nauglar or Dwarves*). *nauglar* seems to have been changed from *nauglir*, the form in Q.

29 These two sentences, from *Of the Dwarves* . . ., bracketed in pencil; see pp. 335–6.

30 *Ulfand* is an early emendation from *Ulband*, and so also in the next sentence.

31 Later addition: *Tinúviel, daughter of Thingol of Doriath*. – For the word *geste* see III. 154.

32 *Tolsirion* > *Tol-na-Gaurhoth* (later change; cf. note 20).

33 Later addition: *Nargothrond is hidden*.

34 Later addition: *among the Green-elves*.

35 *Elves* > *Gnomes* (later change, depending on that given in note 34).

36 These two entries, for the years 164 and 165, are early replacements of essentially the same entries originally placed under 169 and 170: *Húrin son of Hádor weds Morwen Elfsheen daughter of Baragund son of Bëor*, and *Túrin son of Húrin born*. The first of these contains two errors, which cannot be other than the merest slips in rapid

composition, for *son of Gumlin son of Hádor* and *son of Bregolas son of Bëor*. Similarly in the entry for 172 Huor is called *son of Hádor*.

37  *Huor son of Hádor:* an error; see note 36.

38  Later addition: *Nirnaith Irnoth*, changed to *Nirnaith Dirnoth*. In the *Lay of the Children of Húrin* there are many different forms of the Elvish name of the Battle of Unnumbered Tears, one replacing another: the last are *Nirnaith Únoth* replaced by *Nirnaith Ornoth* (the final form *Nirnaith Arnediad* is also found in the poem, written in at a later period, as in Q §11, note 16).

39  *Erydlómin > Erydwethion* (later change; cf. notes 11, 27).

40  *Flinding* first *> Findor*; then *Flinding son of Fuilin > Gwindor son of Guilin* (later changes).

41  *Túrin was nigh three years old* depends on the earlier date of his birth in the year 170: see note 36.

42  Later addition: *Cûm-na-Dengin*. The name *Amon Dengin* is found in a late rewriting of a passage in Q §16, note 3.

43  This passage replaced, at the time of writing, the original: *Rían sought for Huor and died beside his body*. See note 46.

44  The date 173 was added subsequently, though early, to this passage. It remains in its original place, not struck out though not included here, at the beginning of the next passage, *Morgoth broke his pledges . . .*

45  *Ulfand* early *< Ulband*, as previously (note 30).

46  The original text had here: *Tuor son of Huor was born in sorrow*, which was struck out at the time of writing when the additional passage concerning Tuor at the end of annal 172 was written in (note 43). The sentence concerning Nienor that follows was an early addition.

47  This sentence is roughly marked for transference to between the annals 184 and 184–7.

48  This paragraph, from *Tuor grew up . . .*, was dated 177, but the date was struck out. As the *Annals* were first written, Túrin's birth was placed in the year 170, but this entry was rejected and replaced under 165 (note 36). When the present passage was dated 177, therefore, Túrin was 7 when he went to Doriath; but with the striking out of this date the passage belongs under 173, and the years of Túrin's life in Hithlum become 165–73, which may or may not signify a change in his age when he went to Doriath. In *The Silmarillion* (p. 198) he was eight; but the statement here that he was seven is left unchanged.

49  After this annal another was inserted in the later, pencilled layer of emendation: *188. Halmir son of Orodreth trapped and hung to a tree by Orcs*.

50  *Flinding son of Fuilin > Gwindor son of Guilin* (later change; cf. note 40). *Flinding > Gwindor* at all occurrences of the name in annals 190, 190–5, 195.

51 *Ivrin's well* > *the well of Ivrineithil* (later change).
52 *Mormegil (Mormakil)* > *Mormael (Q. Mormakil)* (later change).
   This is the first occurrence of the form *Mormegil*; for earlier forms
   see p. 184.
53 *Morgoth learns of the growing strength of the stronghold* is an early
   ·change from *Morgoth learns of the stronghold*.
54 *Erydlómin* > *Erydwethion*, as previously (later change); again in
   annal 195.
55 *Mormakil* > *Mormael (Mormakil)* (later change; cf. note 52).
56 *Eldorest* > *Eglorest* (later change; cf. note 8).
57 This entry, from *Tuor was led out of Hithlum* . . ., originally dated
   196, was changed (early) to 195, but left where it was, with its date,
   after that for 195–6. A pencilled direction places it in the position in
   which it is printed here.
58 The *h* of *Turumarth* circled in pencil for deletion. The sentence is
   an early addition.
59 Later addition: *Silver Bowl (Celebrindon)*. This was struck out and
   the following substituted: *which was called Celebros Silver Foam,
   but after Nen Girith Shuddering Water*.
60 *Nauglafring* > *Nauglamír* (later change); again in annal 202.
61 *Enmity awakes* is an early change from *War ensues*.
62 Later addition: *and the Green-elves* (cf. note 34).
63 *Sarn-Athra* > *Sarn-Athrad* (later change). The same change is
   made in Q (§14, note 8).
64 *Rathlorion* > *Rathloriel* (later change). The same change is made in
   Q (§14, note 11).
65 Later addition: *upon Amon Ereb the Lonely Hill in East Beleriand*.
   Above *East Beleriand* is written *in the South*.
66 *the Gods* > *the Valar that is the Gods* (later change).
67 *Eldorest* > *Eglarest* > *Eglorest* (later changes; cf. notes 8, 56).
68 *Ingwil* > *Ingwiel* (later change). *Ingwiel* is the form in an addition to
   Q (Q II, §17, note 19).
69 Written hastily in the margin against this paragraph: *This great war
   lasted 50 years*.
70 *perished in* > *made* (later change).
71 Later addition: *but Maidros perished and his Silmaril went into the
   bosom of the earth, and Maglor cast his into the sea, and wandered
   for ever on the shores of the world*.

Commentary on the *Annals of Beleriand* (text AB I)

   This commentary follows the annal-sections of the text (in some cases
groups of annals).

**Opening section (before the rising of the Sun).** Morgoth 'rebuilds his
fortress of Angband'. This is as in S and Q, before *Utumna* reappeared,

as it does in the *Ambarkanta* (see pp. 257, 259–60); AV is not explicit, merely saying (p. 266) that he 're-established his stronghold'. Angband is 'beneath the Black Mountain, Thangorodrim'; on this see pp. 220, 260. There is here the remarkable statement that Morgoth 'devises the Balrogs and the Orcs', implying that it was only now that they came into being. In Q (§2), following S, they originated (if the Balrogs were not already in existence) in the ancient darkness after the overthrow of the Lamps, and when Morgoth returned to Angband 'countless became the number of the hosts of his Orcs and demons' (§4); similarly in AV (p. 266) he 'bred and gathered *once more* his evil servants, Orcs and Balrogs'. A note written against the passage in Q §4 directs, however, that the making of the Orcs should be brought in here rather than earlier (note 8); and in the version of 'The Silmarillion' that followed Q (later than these *Annals*) this was in fact done: when Morgoth returned,

countless became the hosts of his beasts and demons; and *he brought into being the race of the Orcs*, and they grew and multiplied in the bowels of the earth.

(The subsequent elaboration of the origin of the Orcs is extremely complex and cannot be entered into here.) It is clear, therefore, that these words in AB I, despite the fact of its being evidently earlier than AV, look forward to the later idea (itself impermanent) that the Orcs were not made until after Morgoth's return from Valinor.

According to AV Morgoth escaped in the course of the Valian Years 2990–1; some century and a half of later time elapsed, then, between the first making of the Orcs and the beginning of their raids, referred to under the first of the annals dated 50.

On the addition (notes 1 and 4) that Orodreth, Angrod, and Egnor came to Middle-earth in the ships with the Fëanorians, while Felagund crossed the Grinding Ice with Fingolfin, see the commentary on AV, p. 279.

**Annal 1**  The reason for the alteration in note 5 is not clear to me; unless the purpose was to emphasize that the second host of the Noldoli came 'from the North', i.e. from the Grinding Ice, not from Drengist.

**Annals 20 to 51**  The 'Feast of Reuniting' is the later name, as in *The Silmarillion* (p. 113); in Q (§9) it is the 'Feast of Meeting'. But it is still held in the Land of Willows (see p. 175). Now appear at the Feast ambassadors out of Doriath, and Elves from the Western Havens Brithombar and Eldorest (> Eglorest); for the growth of the idea of the Havens see p. 227, entry *Brithombar*. Whereas in Q the Feast took place within the period of the Siege of Angband, it now preceded the laying of the Siege, which in the later story began after the Glorious Battle (*Dagor Aglareb*) – of which the earthquakes and the Orc-raids of the years 50–51 are the first suggestion.

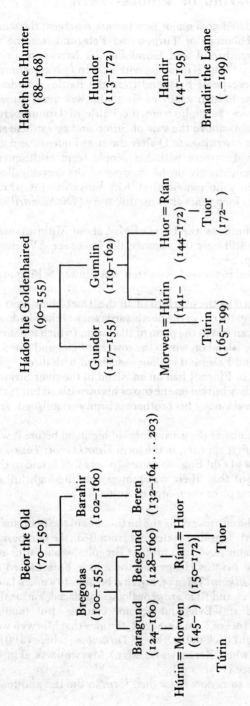

Bregolas, Hádor, and Gundor were slain in the Battle of Sudden Fire (155); Barahir, Baragund, and Belegund were slain as outlaws on Taur-na-Danion (160); Gumlin was slain at the fortress of Sirion's Well (162); Huor and Hundor were slain in the Battle of Unnumbered Tears (172); Handir was slain at the Fall of Nargothrond (195).

(See p. 317)

In the second annal dated 50 a major new feature emerges: the story of the dreams and forebodings of Turgon and Felagund, leading to the foundation of Nargothrond and Gondolin. (A later note in Q refers to 'the Foreboding of the Kings', §9 note 15.) In Q Nargothrond was founded after the escape of Felagund from the Battle of Sudden Flame (p. 106), and the hidden valley of Gondolin was never known until Turgon's scouts, in the flight from the Battle of Unnumbered Tears, climbed the heights above the vale of Sirion and saw it beneath them (§15, p. 136; later rewritings to Q alter the story: notes 1 and 2). But in AB I Turgon's departure with his people from Hithlum to Gondolin took place immediately on his finding of the secret valley, whereas in the later story he remained still in Vinyamar (of which there is as yet no sign) for long years after his discovery (*The Silmarillion* pp. 115, 125–6).

The definition of Hithlum as 'the Land of Mist about Mithrim' may imply that *Mithrim* was still only the name of the Lake: see AV, entry 2995, and commentary p. 280.

Fingon is now so named in the text as written, not Finweg > Fingon as in Q.

Fingolfin is now named as the overlord of all the 'Dark-elves' west of Narog, and his power is gathered in the northward range of the Shadowy Mountains, whence he can watch the plain of Bladorion (which is named in AV, entry 2996). The island on which the tower of Felagund stood is now named *Tolsirion*, and Felagund is alone associated with it (cf. Q §9 'A tower they [the sons of Finrod] had on an island in the river Sirion', but also §10 'Felagund they buried on the top of his own island hill'); the pre-eminence of Felagund among his brothers is firmly established, and his isolation from them.

In Q §9, note 1, the name of the great pineclad highland before it was turned to a place of evil first appears, in the form *Taur Danin*; *Taur-na-Danion* occurs in the list of Old English names (p. 211). It is said of the sons of Fëanor in Q (§9) that 'their watchtower was the high hill of Himling, and their hiding place the Gorge of Aglon'.

**Annals 70 to 150**     In the entries giving the birth-dates of the Bëorians is seen the emergence of an elder line of descent from Bëor the Old beside Barahir and Beren: Barahir now has a brother Bregolas, whose sons are Baragund and Belegund (in this History all three have been named in rewriting of the *Lay of Leithian*, III.335, but that belongs to a much later time). In this line Morwen and Rían are genealogically placed, and as the daughters of Baragund and Belegund become cousins. But though nothing has been said before of Rían's kindred, the idea that Morwen was related to Beren goes right back to the *Tale of Turambar*, where (as that text was first written, when Beren was a Man) Mavwin was akin to Egnor, Beren's father (see II.71, 139).

The Bëorian house is thus now in its final form in the last and most important generations, though Barahir and Bregolas were later to be removed by many steps from Bëor with the lengthening of the years of Beleriand from the rising of the Sun.

By this genealogical development, too, Túrin and Tuor are descended both from the house of Bëor and from the house of Hador; and they become cousins on both sides.

Haleth, who in Q was the son of Hador, now becomes independent, a 'Father of Men'; cf. the pencilled alterations to Q §9 (note 11 and p. 175), where Haleth 'the Hunter' enters Beleriand shortly before Hador – as is implied also in AB I. The account of the physical characters of the Men of the Three Houses of the Elf-friends is the origin of that in *The Silmarillion* (p. 148); but at this stage the people of Haleth are likened to those of Hador rather than to the Bëorians, and this is undoubtedly a reflection of the fact that the 'Hadorian' and 'Halethian' houses had only just been divided (see pp. 175–6).

In Q (§13, p. 129), Brandir the Lame was the son of Handir, son of Haleth; but now in AB I a new generation is introduced in the person of Hundor, by early addition to the text (see note 13).

In the house of Hador the removal of Haleth as Hador's elder son leads to the appearance of Gundor, as seen already in the later alteration to Q §9 (note 11 and pp. 175–6). In AB I *Hador* is spelt both *Hádor* and *Hador*, and on the assumption that the accent must be intended whereas its absence may not I have extended the form *Hádor* throughout.

The genealogies of the Three Houses of the Elf-friends, together with their dates as given in AB I (after revision), are now therefore as shown on p. 315.

That Hádor became a vassal of Fingolfin (annal 120) is extended from the statement in Q §9, 'the sons of Hador were allied to the house of Fingolfin', with the addition that he was given lands in Hithlum. That his grandson Húrin had his house in Hithlum is of course an ancient feature of the legends.

Beren's name *Mablosgen*, the Empty-handed (note 15) first appears here (*Camlost* in *The Silmarillion*).

The sadness of the Elves who witnessed it at Bëor's death 'of weariness' (annal 150) foreshadows the passage in *The Silmarillion*, p. 149.

**Annals 155 to 157**   In these annals (to be compared with Q §9) are many new details and one major development. In a later addition (note 17) the Battle of Sudden Fire (itself appearing, as the Battle of Sudden Flame, in a later addition to Q, note 19) receives the Elvish name *Dagor Hurbreged*; and Glómund is present at the battle – by another later addition (note 18) now in his 'full might'. At each stage, in addition to S, in Q, in addition to Q, in AB, and in addition to AB, the history of Glómund is pushed further back; for the details see pp. 181–2. In *The Silmarillion* p. 151 the same expression 'in his full might' is used of Glaurung at the Battle of Sudden Flame, where the statement has the point that at his first appearance (p. 116) he was not yet full-grown; see pp. 336–7.

The death of Bregolas and the greater part of the warriors of Bëor's house is recorded (cf. *The Silmarillion* pp. 151–2), as also is the death of Hádor 'now aged' and his son Gundor, defending Fingolfin (in *The Silmarillion* they fell at Eithel Sirion). Orodreth as well as Felagund is said to have been rescued by Barahir: this is not at all suggested in Q, where he came to Nargothrond with Celegorm and Curufin only 'after a time of breathless flight and perilous wanderings', and it seems natural to suppose that he had escaped from Taur-na-Danion (Taur-na-Fuin) when his brothers Angrod and Egnor were slain. On this matter see further below, annal 157.

Whereas in Q Himling is said to have been 'fortified' by the sons of Fëanor at this time (p. 106; previously it was their 'watchtower', p. 103), in AB it has been said earlier (annal 51) that Himling was their 'fortress', and it is now told that through the prowess of Maidros it was not lost to them. The passage of Orcs through 'the passes east of Himling' into East Beleriand, and the scattering of 'the Gnomes of Fëanor's house', are now first mentioned: in *The Silmarillion* (p. 153) this is much amplified.

Much the most important and interesting development in these annals is the sojourn of Húrin in Gondolin, of which there has been no hint hitherto; but there are many differences from the story in *The Silmarillion* (p. 158). In AB it was Haleth and his fosterling Húrin (a boy of fourteen) who were brought to Gondolin, having been found by some of Turgon's people in the vale of Sirion; and it is suggested that this was done because Turgon had been warned by messages from Ulmo that 'the help of Men was necessary for him' – this being an element in Ulmo's message to Turgon by the mouth of Tuor at a much later time in Q: 'without Men the Elves shall not prevail against the Orcs and Balrogs' (pp. 142, 146–7). In this earliest version of the story Haleth and Húrin left Gondolin because of the tidings of the Battle of Sudden Fire. In the later legend, on the other hand, it was Húrin and his brother Huor who were brought (by the Eagles) to Gondolin, and this happened during the battle itself; they left the city because they desired to return to the world outside, and they were permitted to go (despite Maeglin) because, having been brought by the Eagles, they did not know the way. This was an important element in the later story, since Húrin could not reveal the secret of Gondolin whether he would or no. The messages and dreams sent by Ulmo, which caused Turgon to receive Húrin and Huor well when he found them in his city, counselled him expressly 'to deal kindly with the sons of the house of Hador, from whom help should come to him at need'. Of course the essential element of Turgon's leaving arms at Vinyamar on Ulmo's command was not yet present. The story in AB has however the liking of Turgon for Húrin and his desire to keep him in Gondolin, the oath of secrecy, and the fostering of Húrin among the people of Haleth (with whom, however, the 'Hadorians' were not yet allied by intermarriage). Now too appears Turgon's sending of messages to Sirion's mouths and the building of ships for vain embassage to Valinor (*The Silmarillion* p. 159).

The annal 157 introduces the interval of two years between the Battle of Sudden Fire and the taking of Tolsirion, which thenceforward was the Isle of Werewolves (and by the later addition given in note 20 receives the Elvish name *Tol-na-Gaurhoth*); cf. *The Silmarillion* p. 155. But in this annal it is said that not only Orodreth and Celegorm and Curufin retreated to Nargothrond at this time, but Felagund also, and that they made there a great hidden palace. It is difficult to know what to make of this, since in the entry for the year 50 it is said that Felagund 'established his armouries' in the caves of Narog, and in that for 51 'he has his seat beside Narog in the South' (though his power is centred on Tolsirion). Possibly the meaning is that though Nargothrond had existed for more than a hundred years as a Gnomish stronghold it was not until the Battle of Sudden Fire that it was made into a great subterranean dwelling or 'palace', and the centre of Felagund's power. Even so, the story still seems very confused. In annal 155 'Barahir and his chosen champions saved Felagund and Orodreth', but also 'Celegorm and Curufin were defeated and fled with Orodreth'; while two years later, in 157, 'Felagund and Orodreth, together with Celegorm and Curufin, retreated to Nargothrond'.

The implication of the last two of these statements is surely that Celegorm and Curufin fled west with Orodreth after Taur-na-Danion was overrun and took refuge with Felagund on Tolsirion; and when Tolsirion was taken two years later all four went south to Narog. If this is so, it seems to contradict the first statement, that Barahir saved Felagund and Orodreth at the Battle of Sudden Fire in 155. Perhaps the fact that the annal heading 155 is written twice hints at an explanation. The second heading is written at the top of a manuscript page (which finishes at the end of the entry for 157); and it may be that this page is a revision which was not properly integrated into the narrative.

In the second paragraph of 157 various new elements appear: the sending of Morwen and Rían to Hithlum (cf. *The Silmarillion* p. 155); Morwen's name *Eledwen* (note 24; she is called 'Elfsheen' in Q §9 and in annal 145); the presence of Baragund and Belegund in Barahir's band, and (by later addition, note 23) the names of two others (in addition to Gorlim): Radros and Dengar (> Dagnir). Dagnir remains in *The Silmarillion*; Radros became Radhruin.

It may be noticed here that while my father subsequently greatly expanded the duration of Beleriand from the rising of the Sun to the end of the Elder Days, this expansion was not achieved by a general, proportionate enlargement of the intervals between major events. Rather, he increased (in successive versions of the *Annals*) the lapse of time in the earlier part of the period, the Siege of Angband being enormously extended; and the relative dating of the later events remained little affected. Thus in AB I the Battle of Sudden Fire took place in the year 155, the attack on the fortress of Sirion's Well in 162, and the Fall of Nargothrond in 195; in *The Silmarillion* the dates are 455 (p. 150), 462 (p. 160), and 495 (p. 211).

**Annal 162**   The renewed assault of Morgoth seven years after the Battle of Sudden Fire, and the death of Gumlin at Sirion's Well, are referred to in *The Silmarillion*, p. 160 (with Galdor for Gumlin). Sirion's Well is referred to in the *Lay of the Children of Húrin* (line 1460) and marked on the map (p. 222): but 'in the west of (the Shadowy Mountains)' in this annal must be a slip for 'east'. The Elvish name *Eithyl Sirion* (note 26) here first occurs.

Húrin was 'summoned to Hithlum', clearly, because he was at that time still with his fosterfather Haleth in the vale of Sirion.

**Annal 163**   The Swarthy Men were referred to somewhat obliquely in Q §11, as first written: 'Men from East and South' came to Maidros' banner (p. 117), and 'the swart Men, whom Uldor the Accursed led, went over to the foe' (p. 118). In a later interpolation (note 14) the Men from the East are 'the Swarthy Men' and 'the Easterlings', and 'the sons of Bor and Ulfang' are referred to, Uldor the Accursed being the son of Ulfang. It is not made clear in Q when these Men came out of the East. In AB they entered Beleriand in the year following the attack on Eithel Sirion, while in *The Silmarillion* their coming is put somewhat earlier (p. 157); but the description of them in AB is preserved closely in *The Silmarillion*, with the mention of their liking (clearly boding no good) for the Dwarves of the mountains. The interpolation in Q has the final form *Ulfang*, whereas in AB he is *Ulfand* (< *Ulband*, notes 30, 45);* his sons are *Uldor*, *Ulfast*, whose names were not afterwards changed, and *Ulwar*, who became *Ulwarth*. The association of Cranthir (Caranthir) with these Men also now appears. With the words of AB concerning the Dwarves cf. Q §9, p. 104.

**Annal 163–4**   On the Green-elves of Ossiriand, appearing in a later interpolation (note 34, and again subsequently, note 62), see AV note 14, and p. 277.

**Annal 165–70**   There is some slight difference in the accounts in Q §11 and in AB: thus the deeds of Celegorm and Curufin are here made the reason for Thingol's refusal to join the Union of Maidros, and the reluctance of the Elves of Nargothrond is due to their strategy of stealth and secrecy, whereas in Q (as in *The Silmarillion*, pp. 188–9) Thingol's

---

*My father doubtless had both Q and AB in front of him as working texts for a considerable time, and some emendations to Q are later than some emendations to AB.

motive is the demand made on him by the Fëanorians for the return of the Silmaril, and it is the deeds of Celegorm and Curufin that determine Orodreth's policy. There is possibly a suggestion in the words 'for his people will not be restrained' that the emergence of the host of Gondolin was against Turgon's wisdom; in Q §11 as rewritten (in note 7, where the story of the much earlier foundation of Gondolin had entered) Turgon 'deemed that the hour of deliverance was at hand'.

**Annal 168**   'The Orcs are slowly driven back out of Beleriand': cf. the rewritten passage in Q §11, note 14, 'Now for a while the Gnomes had victory, and the Orcs were driven out of Beleriand.' But this comes *after* 'having gathered at last all the strength that he might Maidros appointed a day': as I noted (p. 179), the two phases of the war are not clearly distinguished – or else it is only with the *Annals* that the first successes against the Orcs are moved back, with the concomitant idea that Maidros 'made trial of his strength too soon, ere his plans were full-wrought' (*The Silmarillion* p. 189).

**Annal 171**   In Q §15 Isfin was lost *after* the Battle of Unnumbered Tears, and Eöl 'had deserted the hosts ere the battle'.

**Annal 172**   In this account of the Battle of Unnumbered Tears, with which is to be compared that in Q §11, the *Annals* introduce many new details that were to endure. Thus it is now told that Huor wedded Rían 'on the eve of battle'; and that there was to be a visible signal from Maidros to the hosts waiting in the West. The doubt concerning the part of the people of Haleth (see pp. 180–1) is now resolved, and 'Hundor son of Haleth and the Men of the wood were slain in the retreat across the sands'; the 'glad meeting of Húrin and Turgon' now arises out of the story first told in annal 155; Balrogs smote down Fingon, though Gothmog is not yet named as his slayer; Turgon took with him in his retreat a remnant of Fingon's host (so in *The Silmarillion* p. 194); Huor died of a venomed arrow (*ibid.*); Húrin threw away his shield (*ibid.* p. 195).

The change of *Flinding son of Fuilin* to *Gwindor son of Guilin* (note 40), which is made also in Q, clearly occurs for the first time in AB, since *Flinding* here became *Findor* before he became *Gwindor*.

In a few points AB differs from the later story. Here, Turgon's host descended out of Taur-na-Fuin, whereas in Q (as rewritten, note 7) 'they encamped before the West Pass in sight of the walls of Hithlum', just as in *The Silmarillion* (p. 192) the host of Gondolin 'had been stationed southward guarding the Pass of Sirion'. The loyalty of Bór and his sons, not mentioned in Q, now appears, but whereas in the later story Maglor slew Uldor, and the sons of Bór slew Ulfast and Ulwarth 'ere they themselves were slain', in AB Cranthir slew Uldor, and Ulfast and Ulwar slew Bór and his three sons. The number of a thousand Balrogs who came from Angband when 'Hell was emptied' shows once again (see II.212–13 and p. 173), and more clearly than ever, that Morgoth's demons of fire were not conceived as rare or peculiarly terrible – unlike the Dragon.

The passage at the end of annal 172 concerning Rían and Tuor, with the further reference to Tuor in annal 173, follows the rewriting of Q §16, note 3; and here as there there is no mention of Tuor's slavery among the Easterlings, which was however referred to in Q as first written.

**Annal 173**   The words 'others [Morgoth] forbade to leave Hithlum, and they were slain if Orcs found them east or south of the Shadowy Mountains' must refer to those Elves who were not enslaved in Angband; but this is surprising. Cf. Q §12, where it is told that Morgoth penned the Easterlings behind the Shadowy Mountains in Hithlum 'and slew them if they wandered to Broseliand or beyond'; similarly in *The Silmarillion* (p. 195) it was the Easterlings that Morgoth would not permit to leave.

In Q §12, as in S, and as in *The Silmarillion* (pp. 198–9), Túrin left his home before his sister Nienor was born (see p. 59). The entry in AB for Nienor's birth is an early addition and certainly belongs with the revised dating of Túrin's birth (i.e. in the year 165, not 170, see note 36) and of his journey to Doriath (i.e. in 173 not 177, see note 48); thus Túrin left *after* his sister's birth.

**Annals 181 to 199**   In the legend of the Children of Húrin there is virtually no development from its form in the *Quenta*, from which the *Annals* doubtless derive it direct. The compression is very great, and AB was obviously not intended as an independent composition – thus Túrin's slaying of Brodda is recorded in the annal 195–6 without any indication of the cause, and Brodda has not even been mentioned. The passage in the entry for 196: 'Glómund lays a spell on the company and disperses it. Morwen vanishes in the woods; and a great darkness of mind comes on Nienor' is hardly recognisable as an account of the events known from the *Tale*, S, Q, and *The Silmarillion*; but the general concurrence of all these other versions shows that the wording of AB is the result of severe compression of the narrative, composed very rapidly (see p. 294). It is here, however, that the only development in the story appears: Morwen 'vanishes in the woods', and is not, as in Q §13, led back in safety to Doriath.

The dates in these annals are of much interest as indicating my father's conception of the duration and intervals of time in the legend, concerning which the other early texts give very little idea. Thus Túrin's life as an outlaw after his flight from Doriath and until the capture of Beleg lasted three years, and a further two until the band was betrayed by Blodrin; he spent five years in Nargothrond, and was thirty years old at the time of its fall. Nienor dwelt among the Woodmen for some three years; she was twenty-six years old when she died, and Túrin Turambar was thirty-four.

**Annal 181**    The first sentence of this annal refers to the time when tidings of Morwen ceased – seven years after Túrin's arrival in Doriath according to the *Tale of Turambar* (II.74) and the first version of the *Lay of the Children of Húrin* (line 333), nine according to the second version of the Lay (line 693) and in *The Silmarillion* (p. 199). In AB it is eight years since his coming to Doriath.

**Annal 184**    Túrin, born in 165, was thus nineteen when he slew Orgof, as in the *Tale of Turambar* and the *Lay of the Children of Húrin*; see II.142.

**Annal 188**    In the entry for this year added later in pencil (note 49) the story of the slaying of Orodreth's son Halmir by Orcs re-emerges from the *Lay of the Children of Húrin*, lines 2137–8, where Orodreth's hatred for 'the broods of Hell' is explained:

> his son had they slain,    the swift-footed
> Halmir the hunter    of hart and boar.

This disappeared again later, and the name *Halmir* came to be borne by one of the Lords of Brethil, when that line was much changed and extended. (In the list of Old English names of the Noldorin princes (p. 213) Orodreth has two sons, *Ordhelm* and *Ordlaf*, without Elvish equivalents given.)

**Annal 190**    The added Elvish name *Ivrineithil* (note 51) first occurs here (*Eithel Ivrin* in *The Silmarillion*).
     'They are admitted on the prayer of Finduilas' is a reminiscence of the Lay (lines 1950ff.).

**Annal 190–195**    In this annal is the first occurrence of the form *Mormegil* (*Mormaglir* in Q), though here corrected later (notes 52, 55) to *Mormael*.
     The early emendation given in note 53 is curious: from 'Morgoth learns of the stronghold' to 'Morgoth learns of the growing strength of the stronghold'. It looks as if this change was made in order to get rid of the idea that the loss of the 'ancient secrecy' of the Elves of Nargothrond in Túrin's time led to Morgoth's discovery of its site. I have said in my commentary on Q §13 (p. 184) that while there is no suggestion that Túrin's policy of open war revealed Nargothrond to Morgoth, this element goes back to the *Tale of Turambar* and its absence from Q must be due to compression (earlier in Q, at the end of §11, it is said that after the Battle of Unnumbered Tears Morgoth paid little heed to Doriath and Nargothrond 'maybe because he knew little of them'). In *The Silmaril-*

*lion* it is said (p. 211) 'Thus Nargothrond was revealed to the wrath and hatred of Morgoth', and this is an important element in the contention over policy between Túrin and Gwindor in a late passage that was not fully assimilated to the *Narn i Hîn Húrin* (*Unfinished Tales* p. 156):

You speak of secrecy, and say that therein lies the only hope; but could you ambush and waylay every scout and spy of Morgoth to the last and least, so that none came ever back with tidings to Angband, yet from that he would learn that you lived and guess where.

The alliance of the Gnomes of Nargothrond with the people of Handir (Haleth's grandson) is not found in *The Silmarillion*. In AB (annal 195) Handir was slain in the battle of the fall of Nargothrond; in *The Silmarillion* (p. 212) he was slain in the year of the fall, but before it, when Orcs invaded his land.

**Annal 192**   Cf. the beginning of Q §16, and note 1.

**Annal 195**   'Glómund with a host of Orcs comes over Erydlómin (> Erydwethion, note 54) and defeats the Gnomes between Narog and Taiglin' shows that, as in Q, the battle before the sack of Nargothrond was not fought at the later site, between Ginglith and Narog; see|p. 184.

That Glómund passed over the Shadowy Mountains implies that he came from Angband by way of Hithlum, and it seems strange that he should not have entered Beleriand by the Pass of Sirion; but in the next major version of the *Annals of Beleriand* it is said expressly that he 'passed into Hithlum and did great evil' before moving south over the mountains. There is no indication of why Morgoth commanded, or permitted, this.

In the redating of the entry (196 > 195, see note 57) concerning Tuor's journey from Hithlum to the sea and along the coast to the mouths of Sirion there is a foreshadowing of the situation in *The Silmarillion*, where (p. 238) 'Tuor dwelt in Nevrast alone, and the summer of that year passed, and the doom of Nargothrond drew near'; thus it was that Tuor and Voronwë on their journey to Gondolin saw at Ivrin, defiled by the passage of Glaurung on his way to Nargothrond, a tall man hastening northwards and bearing a black sword, though 'they knew not who he was, nor anything of what had befallen in the south' (p. 239).

Why were the havens of Brithombar and Eldorest (> Eglorest) 'ruined'? Nothing has been said anywhere of the destruction of the Havens. In the next version of the *Annals of Beleriand* the same remains true, and the Havens are again said, in the corresponding passage, to be in ruins. Later, the Havens were besieged and destroyed in the year after the Battle of Unnumbered Tears (*The Silmarillion* p. 296), and I have suggested (p. 229) that the statement on the Westward extension of the first map 'Here Morgoth reaches the shores' may be a reference to this story: it seems then that it was present, though my father neglected to refer to it until much later.

**Annal 195–6**   If the *h* of *Turumarth* was to be deleted (note 58) this was a reversion to the form in the *Tale of Turambar* (II. 70, 86). In Q §13 *Turumarth* was later changed to *Turamarth* (note 12).

**Annal 199**   The addition *Silver Bowl (Celebrindon)* (note 59) is another case, like that of *Flinding > Gwindor* in annal 172, where the alteration to AB preceded that made to Q. This is shown by the first, rejected form *Celebrindon*, whereas in the addition to Q (§13, note 14) there is only *Celebros* (translated, as here, 'Foam-silver').

Tuor entered Gondolin in 196, and thus dwelt there for three years before he wedded Idril. This agrees with S (§16, see p. 67); in Q nothing is said on the subject.

**Annal 200**   Húrin's band is now composed of Men, not Elves (see II. 137; in Q §14 they are only described as 'outlaws of the woods'); but the story as very briefly given in AB does not advance matters at this difficult point (see my discussion, p. 188). Húrin's fate, and Morwen's, is now unknown; in Q 'some have said that he cast himself at last into the western sea', and (at the end of §13) 'some have said that Morwen, wandering woefully from Thingol's halls . . . came on a time to that stone and read it, and there died'.

**Annals 201 and 202**   In the story of the Nauglafring (> Nauglamír, note 60) there is very little narrative development from Q (§14); but the change from 'War ensues between the Elves and Dwarves' to 'Enmity awakes' (note 61) suggests that my father was revising the story at this point. The 'war' is the fighting in the Thousand Caves which first enters the narrative in Q, and of which the slain were buried in Cûm-nan-Arasaith, the Mound of Avarice.

The name of the river in which the gold was drowned, *Asgar*, is found also in the list of Old English names (p. 209); in Q, and on the Eastward extension of the map, as in *The Silmarillion*, the form is *Ascar*.

It is made clear that Lúthien died as a mortal (see pp. 190–1), and the suggestion is that she and Beren died at the same time. It is seen from the dates that they lived on only a very brief while after the coming of the Silmaril to Ossiriand; cf. Q 'the brief hour of the loveliness of the land of Rathlorion departed'. Here is first mentioned the bringing of the Silmaril to Dior in Doriath by night.

**Annal 206**   A minor addition to the story in Q (§14) is that the battle between the Elves of the renewed Doriath and the Fëanorians took place on the eastern marches of the realm; and the young sons of Dior were slain 'by the evil men of Maidros' host' – which does not necessarily mean that the Fëanorians came upon Doriath with mortal allies, since 'men' is used in the sense 'male Elves'. The sons of Dior, named Eldûn and Elrûn in an addition to Q (note 14), here bear the names Elboron and Elbereth;

the latter must be the first occurrence of *Elbereth* in my father's writings. It is seen from the next version of the *Annals of Beleriand* that the names *Eldûn* and *Elrûn* replaced those given here.

**Annal 207**    As with the legend of the Necklace of the Dwarves, the extremely abbreviated account of the Fall of Gondolin in AB shows no change from that in Q §16.

**Annals 208 to 233**    In annal 210 it is said that Maidros actually forswore his oath (although in the final annal he still strives to fulfil it); and this is clearly to be related to his revulsion at the killing of Dior's sons in the annal for 206. Damrod and Díriel now emerge as the most ferocious of the surviving sons of Fëanor, and it is on them that the blame for the assault on the people of Sirion is primarily laid: Maidros and Maglor only 'gave reluctant aid'. This develops further an increasing emphasis in these texts on the weariness and loathing felt by Maidros and Maglor for the duty they felt bound to.

In annal 229 Maglor, rather than Maidros as in Q §17, becomes the saviour of Elrond; this change is made also in a late rewriting of Q II (§17 note 10), where however Elrond's brother Elros also emerges, as is not the case in AB.

The story of Elwing and Eärendel follows that in Q II: Elwing bearing the Silmaril is borne up out of the sea by Ulmo in the form of a bird and comes to Eärendel as he returns in his ship, and they voyage together in search of Valinor; and it is Eärendel's 'embassy of the two kindreds' that leads to the assault on Morgoth (see p. 196).

**Annal 240**    This is the first mention of any kind of the life of the few surviving Gnomes who remained free after the destruction of the people of Sirion; and in a later addition (note 65) is the first appearance of Amon Ereb, the Lonely Hill in East Beleriand, where they lurked.

**Annal 233–43**    The refusal of the Teleri to leave Valinor at all (though they built a great number of ships) seems to be a reversion to the story in Q I §17 (p. 149); in Q II (p. 154) 'they went not forth save very few', and those that did manned the fleet that bore the hosts of Valinor. But AB may here be simply very compressed.

**Annals 247 and 250**    In the account of the assault on Morgoth from the West there are some additions to the narrative in Q (§17): the Battle of Eldorest (> Eglorest), where Ingwil (> Ingwiel) landed in Middle-earth (*Ingwiel* is the form in an addition to Q II, note 19; the form *Ingwil* in AB preceded this), the summons of Fionwë to all Elves, Dwarves, Men, beasts and birds to come to his banners, and the array of the hosts of West and North on either side of Sirion.

The statement (subsequently corrected, notes 70–1) that both Maglor

and Maidros 'perished in a last endeavour to seize the Silmarils' seems
to suggest a passing movement to yet another formulation of the story
(see the table on p. 202); but may well have been a slip due to hasty
composition and compression. It remains to notice the chronology of the last years of Beleriand that
now emerges. Tuor wedded Idril in the year (199) of the deaths of Túrin
and Nienor; and both Eärendel and Elwing were born in the following
year, five years after the Fall of Nargothrond (195). Dior's re-establish-
ment of Thingol's realm lasted no more than four years (202–6), and the
Fall of Gondolin followed only one year after the final ruin of Doriath (in
the old *Tale of the Nauglafring*, II. 242, the two events took place on the
very same day), and one year after the capture of Meglin in the hills.
Eärendel was seven years old at the Fall of Gondolin (as stated in Q §16),
and thirty-three years old when he came to Valinor. The settlement at the
delta of Sirion lasted twenty-three years from Elwing's coming there.
    The shortness of the time as my father at this period conceived it is
very remarkable, the more so in comparison with the later lavish
millennia of the Second and Third Ages, not to mention the aeons
allowed to the ages before the rising of the Sun and Moon. The history of
Men in Beleriand is comprised in 150 years before the beginning of the
Great Battle; Nargothrond, Doriath, and Gondolin were all destroyed
within thirteen years; and the entire history from the rising of the Sun
and Moon and the coming of the exiled Noldoli to the destruction of
Beleriand and the end of the Elder Days covers two and half centuries (or
three according to the addition given in note 69: 'This great war lasted
fifty years').

### The second version of the earliest Annals of Beleriand

    This brief text, 'AB II', is in the first annals closely based on AB I, with
some minor developments, but from the entry for the year 51 becomes a
new work, and an important step in the evolution of the legendary
history. The text was lightly emended in pencil, and these few changes
are given in the notes, apart from one or two small alterations of wording
or sentence-order that are taken up silently. As to its date, it was later
than AV if one judges from the fact that the crossing to Middle-earth of
Orodreth, Angrod, and Egnor in the ships with the Fëanorians is
embodied in the text, whereas in AV it is an insertion (note 21).

ANNALS OF BELERIAND

## Translation of Ælfwine

**Before the Uprising of the Sun**  Morgoth fled from Valinor
with the Silmarils the magic gems of Fëanor, and returned into the
Northern regions and rebuilt his fortress of Angband beneath the

Black Mountains, where is their highest peak Thangorodrim. He devised the Balrogs and the Orcs; and he set the Silmarils in his iron crown.

The Gnomes of the eldest house, the Dispossessed, came into the North under Fëanor and his seven sons, with their friends Orodreth, Angrod, and Egnor, sons of Finrod. They burned the Telerian ships. They fought soon after the First Battle with Morgoth, that is Dagor-os-Giliath, or the 'Battle-under-Stars'; and Fëanor defeated the Orcs, but was mortally wounded by Gothmog, captain of Balrogs, and died after in Mithrim.

Maidros, his eldest son, was ambushed and captured by Morgoth, and hung on Thangorodrim; but the other sons of Fëanor camped about Lake Mithrim behind Eredwethion, that is the 'Shadowy Mountains'.

### Years of the Sun

1 Here the Moon and Sun, made by the Gods after the death of the Two Trees of Valinor, first appeared. Thus measured time came into the Hither Lands.[1] Fingolfin (and with him came Felagund son of Finrod) led the second house of the Gnomes over the straits of Grinding Ice into the Hither Lands. They came into the North even with the first Moonrise, and the first dawn shone upon their march and their unfurled banners. And Morgoth at the coming of Light withdrew dismayed into his deepest dungeons, but there he smithied in secret, and sent forth black smokes. But Fingolfin blew his trumpets in defiance before the gates of Angband, and came south to Mithrim; but the sons of Fëanor withdrew to its south shores, and there was feud between the houses, because of the burning of the ships, and the lake lay between them.

2 Here Fingon son of Fingolfin healed the feud, by rescuing Maidros with the help of Thorndor, king of Eagles.

1–50 Here the Gnomes wandered far and wide over Beleriand exploring it, and settling it in many places, from the Great Sea, Belegar, to the Eredlindon, that is the 'Blue Mountains', and all Sirion's vale, save Doriath in the middle, which Thingol and Melian held.

20 Here the 'Feast and Games of Reuniting' (that is in

Gnomish Mereth Aderthad) were held in Nan Tathrin, the 'Land of Willows', near the delta of Sirion, and there were the Elves of Valinor, of the three houses of the Gnomes, and the Dark-elves, both those of the Western Havens, Brithombar and Eglorest,[2] and the scattered Wood-elves of the West, and ambassadors of Thingol. But Thingol would not open his kingdom, or remove the magic that fenced it, and trusted not in the restraint of Morgoth to last long. Yet a time of peace, of growth and blossoming, and of prosperous mirth followed.

50  Here unquiet and troubled dreams came upon Turgon son of Fingolfin and Felagund, his friend, son of Finrod, and they sought for places of refuge, lest Morgoth burst from Angband as their dreams foreboded. And Felagund found the caves of Narog and began there to establish a strong place and armouries, after the fashion of Thingol's abode at Menegroth; and he called it Nargothrond. But Turgon journeying alone discovered by the grace of Ulmo the hidden vale of Gondolin, and he told no man as yet.

51  Now Morgoth's might began suddenly to move once more; there were earthquakes in the North, and fire came from the mountains, and the Orcs raided into Beleriand. But Fingolfin and Maidros gathered their forces, and many of the Dark-elves, and they destroyed all the Orcs that were without Angband, and they fell upon an army that gathered upon Bladorion, and before it could retreat to Morgoth's walls they destroyed it utterly; and this was the 'Second Battle', Dagor Aglareb, 'the Glorious Battle'. And afterward they laid the Siege of Angband which lasted more than two[3] hundred years; and Fingolfin boasted that Morgoth could never burst from his leaguer, though neither could they take Angband nor recover the Silmarils. But war never ceased utterly in all this time, for Morgoth was secretly arming, and ever and anon would try the strength and watchfulness of his foes.[4]

But Turgon being still troubled in heart took a third part of the Gnomes of Fingolfin's house, and their goods, and their womenfolk, and departed south and vanished, and none knew whither he was gone; but he came to Gondolin and built a city and fortified the surrounding hills.

But the rest beleaguered Angband in this wise. In the West, were Fingolfin and Fingon, and they dwelt in Hithlum, and their chief fort was at 'Sirion's Well' (Eithel Sirion), on the east of Eredwethion, and all Eredwethion they manned, and watched Bladorion thence and rode often upon that plain, even to the feet of the mountains of Morgoth; and their horses multiplied for the grass was good. Of those horses many of the sires came from Valinor. But the sons of Finrod held the land from Eredwethion to the eastern end of Taur-na-Danion the Forest of Pines, from whose northern slopes also they guarded Bladorion. But Fingolfin was overlord of the Dark-elves as far south as Eglorest⁵ and west of Eglor; and he was King of Hithlum, and Lord of the Falas or Western Shore; and Felagund was King of Narog, and his brothers were the Lords of Taur-na-Danion, and his vassals; and Felagund was lord of the lands east and west of Narog as far south as Sirion's mouths, from Eglor to Sirion, save for part of Doriath that lay west of Sirion between Taiglin and Umboth-Muilin. But between Sirion and Mindeb no man dwelt; and in Gondolin, south-west of Taur-na-Danion, was Turgon, but that was not known.

And King Felagund had his seat at Nargothrond far to the South, but his fort and strong place was in the North, in the pass into Beleriand between Eredwethion and Taur-na-Danion, and it was upon an isle in the waters of Sirion, that was called Tolsirion. South of Taur-na-Danion was a wide space untenanted between the fences of Melian and the regions of Finrod's sons, who held most to the northern borders of the wooded mountains. Easternmost dwelt Orodreth, nighest to his friends the sons of Fëanor. And of these Celegorm and Curufin held the land between Aros and Celon even from the borders of Doriath to the Pass of Aglon between Taur-na-Danion and the Hill of Himling, and this pass and the plains beyond they guarded. But Maidros had a strong place upon the Hill of Himling, and the lower hills that lie from the Forest even to

Eredlindon were called the Marches of Maidros, and he was much in the plains to the North, but held also the woods south between Celon and Gelion; and to the East Maglor held the land even as far as Eredlindon; but Cranthir ranged in the wide lands between Gelion and the Blue Mountains; and all East Beleriand behind was wild and little tenanted save by scattered Dark-elves, but it was under the overlordship of Maidros from Sirion's mouths to Gelion (where it joins with Brilthor), and Damrod and Díriel were there, and came not much to war in the North. But Ossiriand was not subject to Maidros or his brethren, and there dwelt the Green-elves between Gelion and Ascar and Adurant, and the mountains. Into East Beleriand many of the Elf-lords even from afar came at times for hunting in the wild woods.

**51–255⁶** This time is called the Siege of Angband and was a time of bliss, and the world had peace and light, and Beleriand became exceedingly fair, and Men waxed and multiplied and spread, and had converse with the Dark-elves of the East, and learned much of them, and they heard rumours of the Blessed Realms of the West and of the Powers that dwelt there, and many in their wanderings moved slowly thither.

In this time Brithombar and Eglorest were builded to fair towns and the Tower of Tindobel was set up upon the cape west of Eglorest to watch the Western Seas; and some went forth and dwelt upon the great isle of Balar that lieth in the Bay of Balar into which Sirion flows. And in the East the Gnomes clomb Eredlindon and gazed afar, but came not into the lands beyond; but in those mountains they met the Dwarves, and there was yet no enmity between them and nonetheless little love. For it is not known whence the Dwarves came, save that they are not of Elf-kin or mortal kind or of Morgoth's breed. But in those regions the Dwarves dwelt in great mines and cities in the East of Eredlindon and far south of Beleriand, and the chief of these were Nogrod and Belegost.

**102** About this time the building of Nargothrond and of Gondolin was wellnigh complete.

**104**   About this time Cranthir's folk first met the Dwarves as
is told above; for the Dwarves had of old a road into the
West that came up along Eredlindon to the East and
passed westward in the passes south of Mount Dolm and
down the course of [the] R[iver] Ascar and over Gelion
at the ford Sarn Athrad and so to Aros.[7]

**105**   Morgoth endeavoured to take Fingolfin at unawares
and an army, but a small one, marched south, west of
Eredlómin, but were destroyed and passed not into
Hithlum, but the most were driven into the sea in the
firth at Drengist; and this is not reckoned among the
great battles, though the slaughter of Orcs was great.

After this was peace a long while, save that Glómund
the first of Dragons came forth from Angband's gate at
night in 155 and he was yet young. And the Elves fled to
Eredwethion and Taur-na-Danion, but Fingon with his
horsed archers rode up and Glómund could not yet
withstand their darts, and fled back and came not forth
again for a long time.

**170**   Here Bëor was born east of Eredlindon.

**188**   Here Haleth was born east of Eredlindon.

**190**   Here Hádor the Goldenhaired was born east of Eredlindon.

**200**   Meeting of Felagund and Bëor. Bregolas born.

**202**   War on east marches. Bëor and Felagund there. Barahir
born.

**220**   Unfriendliness of sons of Fëanor to Men – because of lies
of Morgoth: – hence tragedy of their treaty in end of
need to the worst Men, and their betrayal by them.[8]

## NOTES

1   Added in pencil: *At this time Men first awoke in the midst* [emended
to *east*] *of the world. In the meantime (Fingolfin,* &c.) In the second
sentence *led* was changed to *had led.*

2   *Eglorest* is an early change in ink from *Eglarest*; cf. AB I, notes 8, 67.

3   *two* was changed from *one* while these *Annals* were in process of
composition; see note 6.

4 This sentence was an early addition, probably made when my father was writing the annal for 105.

5 *Eglorest* < *Eglarest*, as in note 2. At the occurrences of the name in the annal 51–255 it was written *Eglorest*.

6 255 is a change in pencil from 155, but it obviously belongs with the change given in note 3, made while the *Annals* were being written, as can be seen from the reference in annal 105 to Glómund's emergence in 155, which took place during the Siege. My father must have overlooked the need to change the date, and put it in later when he noticed it.

7 Added in pencil: *But they came not into Beleriand after the coming of the Gnomes, until the power of Maidros and Fingon fell in the Third (Fourth) Battle.*

8 At the end the text was written at increasing speed and the last few lines are a scrawl. The unfilled annal 220 was to be the entry of Haleth and Hádor into Beleriand. In the final sentence 'tragedy' replaced 'justice' at the time of writing.

### Commentary on the *Annals of Beleriand* (text AB II)

*The revised dates.* The period of the Siege of Angband is extended by a hundred years, and now lasts from 51 (as in AB I) to 255 (notes 3 and 6). The birth dates of Bëor, Haleth, Hádor, Bregolas, and Barahir, and the meeting of Felagund with Bëor, are all increased pari passu with the lengthening of the Siege by a hundred years from AB I.

This commentary again follows the annal-sections of the text. The many cases where names pencilled on the AB I manuscript are embodied in the text of AB II can be noticed together: *Dagor-os-Giliath*, *Eredwethion*, *Belegar*, *Eredlindon*, *Eglorest* (< *Eglarest*), *Eithel Sirion*, *Sarn Athrad* (for *Sarn Athra*). *Menegroth* in annal 50 occurs in an addition to AV (note 18) and in the Old English version II (p. 288).

**Opening section and Annals 1 to 51** As I have said, while AB II is here closely based on AB I, there are some minor developments. Where in AB I Thangorodrim is called 'the Black Mountain', it is now the highest peak of 'the Black Mountains'. Whether the story of the Battle-under-Stars had yet shifted is not clear; the statement that the sons of Fëanor encamped about Lake Mithrim *after* the capture of Maidros belongs to the older story (see p. 295), whereas Fëanor's death 'in Mithrim' (which shows that Mithrim was a region and not only the name of the lake) suggests the later. Fingolfin's defiance before Angband is now present, and the removal of the Fëanorians to the southern shores of the lake when Fingolfin's people arrived, as they are in AV (pp. 269–70). In annal 20 the Elvish name *Mereth Aderthad* for the Feast of Reuniting now appears for the first time; and a little more is said of Thingol's policies at this time (a passage that reappears in *The Silmarillion*, p. 111), though nothing of his hostility to the Gnomes.

In AB I Turgon's departure to Gondolin is given under the year 50, but in AB II it was in this year that he discovered it ('by the grace of Ulmo'), and in 51 he departed from Hithlum (with a third of the Gnomes of the second house: so also in *The Silmarillion*, p. 126). Under 102 it is stated that the building of Gondolin was 'wellnigh complete'; and this (relative) dating survived into *The Silmarillion* (p. 125), where Gondolin was 'full-wrought after two and fifty years of secret toil' – though in the final story it was only then that Turgon himself abandoned his halls of Vinyamar.

**Annal 51**    The Glorious Battle, of which there is only a suggestion in AB I (under the years 50–51), now becomes a determinate event with a name (and the Elvish *Dagor Aglareb* appears), and the driving back of the Orcs becomes the destruction of an Orc-host on Bladorion; cf. *The Silmarillion* p. 115. Fingolfin's boast that Morgoth could never break the Siege goes back to Q §9: 'The Gnomes boasted that never could he break their leaguer.'

In AB II the passage concerning the disposition of the Gnomish princes during the years of the Siege is greatly expanded, with much new detail (later appearing in *The Silmarillion* in chapter 14, *Of Beleriand and its Realms*). It was clearly composed very rapidly.

We now hear of the horses of the Lords of Hithlum that pastured on Bladorion, many of whose sires came from Valinor (cf. *The Silmarillion* p. 119). In AB I Fingolfin was overlord of 'the Dark-elves west of Narog' (which no doubt implies the relatively small importance of Nargothrond before the Battle of Sudden Flame), but here his authority is over the Dark-elves west of the river Eglor (*Eldor* on the Westward extension of the first map, pp. 227–8), and he is 'Lord of the Falas' (cf. *Falassë* on the *Ambarkanta* map IV, pp. 249, 257); while Felagund is lord of the whole territory between Eglor and Sirion except for Doriath-beyond-Sirion. In *The Silmarillion* (p. 120) Felagund (there called Finrod) likewise 'became the overlord of all the Elves of Beleriand between Sirion and the sea, save only in the Falas'; but the Falas were ruled by Círdan the Shipwright, of whom there is still no trace. Felagund's brothers have now become his vassals, as they are in *The Silmarillion* (p. 120).

Between Sirion and Mindeb (see p. 222) is a land where 'no man dwelt', but it is not named; in *The Silmarillion* (p. 121) it is 'the empty land of Dimbar'. 'A wide space untenanted' lay between the Girdle of Melian in the North and Taur-na-Danion, but Nan Dungorthin (see p. 222) is not named. Orodreth's land is now specifically in the east of the great pine-forested highlands, where he is near to his friends Celegorm and Curufin, whose territory between Aros and Celon (afterwards called

Himlad) and extending up through the Pass of Aglon is now made definite, and as it was to remain.

The territories of the other sons of Fëanor are also given clearer bounds, with mention for the first time of the Marches of Maidros, of Maglor's land in the East 'even as far as Eredlindon' (afterwards 'Maglor's Gap'), of Cranthir's (not yet called Thargelion) between Gelion and the mountains, and of the territory of Damrod and Díriel in the South of East Beleriand. I do not know why Maidros' overlordship is said to extend from Sirion's mouths to Gelion 'where it joins with Brilthor'. At this time Brilthor was the fifth (not as later the fourth) of the tributaries of Gelion coming down from the mountains, the sixth and most southerly being Adurant (pp. 230–1).

**Annal 51–255**  With the opening paragraph of this annal cf. Q §6:

The Dark-elves they met and were aided by them, and were taught by them speech and many things beside, and became the friends of the children of the Eldalië who had never found the paths to Valinor, and knew of the Valar but as a rumour and a distant name.

The reference to the building of Brithombar and Eglorest 'to fair towns' is found in *The Silmarillion* (p. 120), but there with the addition of the word 'anew'; this is because in the later narrative the Havens of the Falas had long existed under the lordship of Círdan, and were rebuilt with the aid and skill of the Noldor of Felagund's following. In the same passage it is said that Felagund 'raised the tower of Barad Nimras to watch the western sea', and also that some of the Elves of Nargothrond 'went forth and explored the great Isle of Balar', though 'it was not their fate that they should ever dwell there'. The present annal is the first occurrence of the Isle and Bay of Balar. The Tower of Tindobel, forerunner of Barad Nimras, is marked on the Westward extension of the first map, p. 228.

The climbing of Eredlindon by the Gnomes and their meeting with the Dwarves is in *The Silmarillion* (pp. 112–13) ascribed specifically to Caranthir's people settled in Thargelion. The Dwarf-cities are in AB II still placed 'far south of Beleriand', as on the Eastward extension of the map (pp. 231–2). The view of the Gnomes' relations with the Dwarves, and of the Dwarves themselves, though very briefly expressed, is much as in the passage of Q §9 on the subject – as emended (note 4) from 'There they made war upon the Dwarves of Nogrod and Belegost' to 'There they had converse with' them: there is no suggestion here that there was fighting between the peoples, though there is also no mention of traffic between them, which is much emphasized in the passage that 'structurally' corresponds in *The Silmarillion* (p. 113).

**Annal 104**  In AB I it is not until annal 163 that the Elves' first encounter with the Dwarves is mentioned; this passage was bracketed (note 29), obviously because the matter was to be introduced earlier. The description of the Dwarf-road agrees precisely with the later course of the road on the Eastward extension of the map (see pp. 231–2). Mount Dolm, which is marked on the map, is here first named in the narrative texts. It is notable that the Dwarves are here said to have had this road 'of old'; and the pencilled interpolation given in note 7 certainly means that they *no longer* came into Beleriand after the return of the Noldoli. In Q §14 it is recorded that 'Dwarves first spread west from Eryd-luin, the Blue Mountains, into Beleriand after the Battle of Unnumbered Tears'. In *The Silmarillion* (p. 91) Dwarves entered Beleriand and its history very long before: 'It came to pass during the second age of the captivity of Melkor that Dwarves came over the Blue Mountains of Ered Luin into Beleriand', and it was Dwarves of Belegost who devised the mansions of Thingol, the Thousand Caves. 'And when the building of Menegroth was achieved . . . the Naugrim yet came ever and anon over the mountains and went in traffic about the lands.' Annal 104 in AB II must be the first sign of this important structural change in the history; and it is probably significant that the reference is to the first encounter of the Gnomes (not of Elves in general) with the Dwarves.

The next version of the *Annals of Beleriand* makes it clear that the reference in the interpolated passage (note 7) to 'the Third (Fourth) Battle' is to the Battle of Sudden Flame, despite the naming of Fingon rather than Fingolfin. In AB II the first battle is Dagor-os-Giliath, the second Dagor Aglareb, and the third (though AB II did not reach it) the Battle of Sudden Flame. This interpolation shows my father already thinking of what became the First Battle of Beleriand, in which Denethor of the Green-elves was slain, and which is first hinted at in a pencilled addition to AV (note 18); after the inclusion of this battle in the great Battles of Beleriand, that of Sudden Flame became the fourth.

**Annal 105**    In this annal are described for the first time Morgoth's tests of the strength and watchfulness of the besiegers, referred to in annal 51, and which remain in *The Silmarillion* (p. 116). The first of these is there said to have taken place nearly a hundred years since Dagor Aglareb, not as here fifty-four; but the route taken by Morgoth's host is the same in both accounts, southwards down the coast between Ered Lómin and the sea to the Firth of Drengist. The story of the emergence of Glómund, not yet full-grown, from the gates of Angband by night, the flight of the Elves to Eredwethion and Taur-na-Danion, and the rout of Glómund by Fingon's horsed archers, is very close to the account in *The Silmarillion*, where however it took place a hundred years after the attack that ended at Drengist: in AB II, again, the time was only half as long. These differences are associated with further great lengthening of the duration of the Siege.

The addition 'in full might' (of Glómund at the Battle of Sudden Flame) made to AB I (note 18) clearly depends on this final stage in the backward movement of Glómund's entries into the history: see pp. 317–18. Some lines of Old English verse accompanying the lists of Old English names refer to Fingon's victory over the Dragon:

> þá cóm of Mistóran    méare rídan
> Finbrand felahrór    flánas scéotan;
> Glómundes gryre    grimmum strǽlum
> forþ áflíemde.

*Finbrand* is given as Ælfwine's rendering of Fingon (p. 213); *Mistóra* is Mithrim (p. 210).

The concluding, hastily scrawled, sentence of AB II is interesting. In *The Silmarillion* the Haladin (the 'People of Haleth') dwelt in the south of Thargelion after crossing the Blue Mountains, and there 'the people of Caranthir paid little heed to them' (p. 143); after their brave defence of their homes Caranthir 'looked kindly upon Men', and 'seeing, over late, what valour there was in the Edain' offered them free lands to dwell in further North under the protection of the Eldar: an offer which was refused. This is the only reference in *The Silmarillion* to 'unfriendliness' on the part of the Fëanorians towards Men (though one could well imagine it); but it is noteworthy, in respect of the last words of these *Annals*, that it was to Cranthir (Caranthir) that the treacherous sons of Ulfang were allied (AB I annal 163, *The Silmarillion* p. 157).

★

## APPENDIX

### Old English version of the Annals of Beleriand made by Ælfwine or Eriol

This is the only further fragment of Ælfwine's work in Tol Eressëa in his own language. Its relation to the Modern English version is puzzling, since, though it largely corresponds closely to AB II, it also has features of the AB I text. For instance, the defiance of Fingolfin before Angband and the withdrawal of the Fëanorians to the southern shore of the lake is absent from annal I; the date 'I–C' follows AB I; while *Mereth Aderthad* in annal XX agrees with AB II the annal is otherwise as AB I; and annal L is a confused mixture. The simple explanation that my father made the Old English version after AB I but before AB II (and hence the headnote to AB II 'Translation of Ælfwine') comes up against the difficulty that in the Old English the Siege of Angband lasted *tú hund géara oððe má* (line 81), whereas AB II has 'one hundred' emended to 'two hundred'. But the matter is not of importance.

Like version II of the Old English *Annals of Valinor*, the text breaks off in mid-sentence. My father composed these annals, like the others, fluently and rapidly (hence such variations as *Mægdros, Mægedros, Maidros*); but he was interrupted, no doubt, and never took them up again. I suspect that Ælfwine's version of the *Annals of Beleriand* was the last.

## Beleriandes Géargesægen

**Fore sunnan úpgange:** Morgoþ gefléah Godéðel þæt is Falinor, ond genóm þá eorclanstánas Féanóres, and þa cóm he eft on Norþdǽlas ond getimbrode þǽr on níwan his fæsten Angband (þæt is Irenhell) under þám Sweartbeorgum. He of searucræfte gescóp þá Balrogas       5
ond þá orcas; ond þá eorclanstánas sette he on his isernan helme. þá cómon þá Noldielfe þǽre yldestan mǽgþe, þe Ierfeloran hátton, ond sóhton to lande, and gelǽdde híe Féanor and his seofon suna. þǽ:
forbærndon híe þá Teleriscan scipu; and híe gefuhton     10
siþþan wiþ Morgoþes here and geflíemde hine: þæt wæs þæt ǽreste gefeoht, and hátte on noldisce Dagor-os-Giliað, þæt is on Englisc gefeoht under steorrum oþþe Tungolgúþ. þær Féanor gewéold wælstówe ond adrǽfde þá orcas, ac wearð self forwundod þearle of     15
Goþmoge Balroga heretoga, Morgoþes þegne, and swealt siþþan on Miþrime. þá wearð Mægdros his yldesta sunu of Morgoþe beswicen, and wearð gefangen, and Morgoþ hét hine ahón be þǽre rihthande on þangorodrim. þá gedydon þá óþere suna Féanóres     20
ymb Miþrim þone mere on Northwestweardum landum, behindan Scúgebeorge (Eredweþion).

## Æfter sunnan úpgange

**Sunnan géar I**   Hér ætíewdon on ǽrest se móna 7 séo     25
sunne, and þa Godu scópon híe æfter þám þe Morgoþ fordyde þá Béamas, for þon þe híe næfdon léoht. Swá cóm gemeten Tíd on middangeard. Fingolfin gelǽdde þá óþere mǽgþe þára Noldielfa on Norþdǽlas ofer Ísgegrind oþþe Helcarakse on þá Hiderland; ond þá fór     30
Felagund mid sume þǽre þriddan mǽgþe. þá fóron híe ealle norþan mid þám þe séo sunne arás, and þá onbrugdon híe hira gúþfanan, and cómon siþþan mid micle þrymme on Miþrim. þær wæs þá gíet him fǽhþ betwux þǽre mǽgþe Féanóres ond þám óþrum.     35

Morgoþ mid þý þe léoht ætíewde béah on his déopestan
gedelf, ac siþþan smiþode þǽr fela þinga dearnunga and
sende forþ sweartne smíc.

**II** Hér Fingon Fingolfines sunu sibbe geníwode betwux
þám mǽgþum for þám þe he áhredde Mǽgedros. 40

**I–C** Hér geondférdon and gescéawodon þá Noldelfe
Beleriand and gesǽton hit missenlice ond eal Sirigeones
dene of Gársecge (þe Noldelfe Belegar hátað) oþ
Hǽwengebeorg (þæt sind Eredlindon), butan Doriaðe
on middan þám lande þe þingol and Melian áhton. 45

**XX** Hér wearð se gebéorscipe and se fréolsdæg and se plega
þe Noldelfe Mereþ Aderþad nemnað (þæt is
Sibbegemótes fréols) on Wiligwangas gehealden, þe
Noldielfe Nanta riþ hátað, néah Sirigeones múþum,
and þǽr wurdon gesamnode ge elfe of Godéðle ge 50
deorcelfe ge éac sume þá elfe of þám Westhýþum and of
Doriaðe of þingole gesende. þá wearð long sibbtíd.

**L** Hér wearþ eft unfriðu aweht of Morgoþe, ond wurdon
micle eorþdynas on Norðdǽlum, ond þá orcas
hergodon floccmǽlum on Beleriand ond þé elfe híe 55
fuhton wið.

Hér wurdon Turgon Fingolfines sunu 7 Inglor Felagund Finrodes sunu his fréond 7 mǽg yfelum swefnum
geswencte, 7 híe fæsten 7 friþstówa gesóhton ǽr þon þe
Morgoþ ǽtburste swá hira swefn him manodon. þá 60
funde Felagund þá déopan scrafu be Naroge stréame,
7 he þǽr ongann burg gestaðelian and wǽpenhord
samnian, æfter þǽre wísan þe þingol búde Menegroþ, 7
he þæt heald Nargoþrond nemnde. Ac Turgon ána
férde 7 be Ulmoes láre funde Gondoelin þá díeglan 65
dene, ne sægde nánum menn þá gíet.

Hér ongann Morgoþ eft his mægen styrian; 7 wearþ
oft unfriðu aweht on Beleriandes gemǽrum. Micle
eorðdynas wurdon on norðdǽlum, 7 þá orcas hergodon
floccmǽlum on Beleriand, ac þá elfe fuhton híe wið 7 70
híe geflíemdon.

**LI** Hér gegaderode Morgoð medmicelne here, and fýr
ábærst of þám norðernum beorgum; ac Fingolfin 7
Maidros fierda gesamnodon and manige þára deorcelfa

mid, 7 híe fordydon þone orchere to nahte, and áslógon     75
ealle þe híe útan Angbande gemétton, and híe éhton þæs
heriges geond þone feld Bladorion, þæt nán eft to
Angbandes durum cómon. Þis gefeoht hátte siððan
Dagor Aglareb, þæt is Hrépgúþ on Englisc. Siþþan
gesetton híe 'Angbandes Ymbsetl', and þæt gelǽston     80
híe tú hund géara oððe má, 7 Fingolfin béotode þæt
Morgoþ nǽfre from þám ymbhagan ætberstan mihte.
He ne mihte self swáþéah Angband ábrecan ne þá
Silmarillan áhreddan. Unfriðu wearð nǽfre eallunga
áswefed on þisse langan tíde, for þǽm þe Morgoþ     85
d. . .lice hine gewæpnode 7 ǽfre ymbe stunde wolde
fandian þǽre strengu and þǽre wæcene his gefána.
Turgon cyning swáþéah

## NOTES

1–17    Another, earlier, Old English account of these events is found at
the end of version I of the *Annals of Valinor*, p. 282.

2    *eorclanstánas*: see p. 283. As in the Old English version I of AV
the name *Silmaril* is also treated as an Old English noun, with
plural *Silmarillan* (line 84) (in the AV version *Silmarillas*).

8    *Ierfeloran*: with variant vowels *Erfeloran*, *Yrfeloran* in the Old
English version II of AV (line 135), and in the list of Old English
names, p. 212.

14    *Tungolgúþ* occurs also in the Old English version I of AV,
line 55.

32    *sunne*: *sunnan* MS.

48    *Wiligwangas* is a pencilled correction from *Wiligléagas*.

51    *þám*: *þá* MS.

53–71    The text of this annal is confused. The first paragraph follows
the beginning of the first entry numbered 50 in AB I; the second
paragraph corresponds closely to AB II annal 50; and the third
repeats the first.

65    *Gondoelin* is clearly written thus.

86    The illegible word is not *dirnlice* 'secretly'.

New Old English names in this text are:

*Sweartbeorgas* (line 5) 'Black Mountains' (O.E. *sweart* 'black,
dark');

*Scúgebeorg* (line 22) = *Eredwethion* (O.E. *scúa* 'shadow');

*Ísgegrind* (line 30) = *Helcaraksë* (O.E. *gegrind* 'grinding
together, clashing');

*Hæwengebeorg* (line 44) = *Eredlindon* (O.E. *hæwen* 'blue'); *Wiligwangas* (line 48) = *Nan Tathrin* (O.E. *wilig* 'willow'; *wang* 'meadow, flat place' (cf. *Wetwang* in *The Lord of the Rings*); the rejected name *Wiligléagas* contains *léah*, Modern English *lea*).

*Westhýþum* (line 51, dative plural) = Western Havens (cf. *Elfethýð* = Swanhaven, p. 283; Modern English *hithe*).

*Hréþgúþ* (line 79) = *Dagor Aglareb* (O.E. *hréþ* 'glory').

The most notable name here is *Inglor Felagund* (line 57). This is the first occurrence of *Inglor*, which remained his 'true' name for many years, though its existence is indicated by the Old English equivalent *Ingláf Felahrór* (p. 213).

# INDEX

This Index, like those of the previous volumes, attempts both to provide an almost complete register and to give some indication of the interrelations of names for the same places, persons, and events; but from the nature of this book the range of such variation is here particularly large, and some names appear in complicated relations (and several languages), so that inconsistency in the arrangement of the material has been hard to avoid.

In general, Modern English names are not given separate entries when they occur solely in association with an Elvish name, but are included under the latter.

Page-references include the occurrences of names in Ælfwine's works in Old English ('O.E.'), but these are not distinguished as such unless the name has a distinctive Old English form; and in such cases the Old English name is not given a separate entry, but included under the original name (as *Elfethýð* under *Alqualondë*).

Names that occur on the first 'Silmarillion' map and its Eastward and Westward extensions are not referenced to the reproductions themselves, but those on the *Ambarkanta* maps and diagrams are (including the emended names that are noticed on the facing pages, as *Silma* > *Ilma* > *Ilmen*): all these references are preceded by an asterisk.

References to the published *Silmarillion* are not included, and those to the individual tales of *The Book of Lost Tales* are collected under the entry *Lost Tales*.

So many variant arrangements of capitalisation and hyphenation are found in compound names in the texts (as *Sarn-athrad*, *Sarn-Athrad*, *Sarn Athrad*) that I have adopted a single form for the purposes of the Index.

*Grinding Ice* (Also *the Ice*). 10, 13, 16, 18, 22, 25, 47–9, 55, 86, 92, 95–7, 102, 170, 295, 314, 328. See *Bridge(s) of Ice, Straits of Ice, Helkaraksë*.

*Grond* The great mace of Morgoth. 107

*Guarded Plain* (1) Of Gondolin (= *Tumladen*). 34, 36, 66. (2) North of Nargothrond. 126, 128, 184, 225

*Guarded Realm* Valinor. 158, 161

*Guilin* (Only referred to as the father of Gwindor) 120–1, 125, 131, 180, 312, 321. (Replaced *Fuilin*.)

*Gumlin* (1) The elder of Túrin's guardians on the journey to Doriath. 58. (Replaced by *Mailgond*.) (2) Son of Hador and father of Húrin and Huor. 23–5, 54, 104–5, 108, 118, 124, 127, 175–6, 297–300, 310, 312, 315, 320; *Helm of Gumlin* 124. (Replaced by *Galdor*.)

*Gundor* Son of Hador and brother of Gumlin (2). 108, 175–6, 200, 297–8, 315, 317–18

*Gurtholfin* 'Wand of Death', Túrin's sword. 31–2, 130–1, 186, 304, 306; *Gurtholfir* 32

*Gwath-Fuin-daidelos* 'Deadly Nightshade', Taur-na-Fuin. 311. (Replaced *Math-Fuin-delos*.)

*Gwedheling* Name of Melian in the *Tale of Turambar*. 59

*Gwendelin* Name of Melian in the *Tale of the Nauglafring*. 63

*Gwerth-i-cuina* (Also *Gwairth-, Gweirth-* 233.) The Dead that Live Again, and their land. 116, 135, 179, 224, 233

*Gwindor of Nargothrond* 59, 120–1, 125, 131, 180–1, 184, 193, 312, 321, 324–5. (Replaced *Flinding*.)

*Hador* Called 'the Tall', and 'the Golden-haired'. (Also *Hádor*: see 317.) References include those to the house, son(s), people, etc. of Hador. 104–5, 108, 118, 127, 138, 158, 175–6, 182, 185, 200, 202, 297–8, 300–3, 311–12, 315, 317–18, 332–3; the people described 297, 317

*Haladin* Later name for the People of Haleth. 175, 337

*Haleth* (1) Originally the son of Hador, later one of the Fathers of Men (see 175, 317); called 'the Hunter' (108, 175). References include those to the people of Haleth. 104, 108, 120, 127, 129, 175–6, 180–1, 185, 297–9, 301–3, 305, 311, 315, 317–18, 320–1, 324, 332–3, 337; the people described 297, 317. See *Woodmen*. (2) The Lady Haleth. 175

*Half-elfin, Half-elven* 38–9, 70, 75, 151, 155, 158, 162–3, 195, 200, 308–9 (*Half-elfin >Half-elven* 155, 163). See especially 38, 70, 158, and see *Elrond, Elros*.

*Halls of Awaiting* 22, 115

*Halls of Iron* Angband. 69

*Halmir* (1) Son of Orodreth, hanged by Orcs. 312, 323. (2) (later) Lord of the People of Haleth at the time of the Union of Maidros. 181, 323

# THE LOST ROAD

## AND OTHER WRITINGS

# J. R. R. TOLKIEN

# The Lost Road

## AND OTHER WRITINGS

Language and Legend before
'The Lord of the Rings'

Christopher Tolkien

# CONTENTS

## APPENDIX

# PREFACE

This fifth volume of *The History of Middle-earth* completes the presentation and analysis of my father's writings on the subject of the First Age up to the time at the end of 1937 and the beginning of 1938 when he set them for long aside. The book provides all the evidence known to me for the understanding of his conceptions in many essential matters at the time when *The Lord of the Rings* was begun; and from the *Annals of Valinor*, the *Annals of Beleriand*, the *Ainulindalë*, and the *Quenta Silmarillion* given here it can be quite closely determined which elements in the published *Silmarillion* go back to that time, and which entered afterwards.

To make this a satisfactory work of reference for these purposes I have thought it essential to give the texts of the later 1930s in their entirety, even though in parts of the *Annals* the development from the antecedent versions was not great; for the curious relations between the *Annals* and the *Quenta Silmarillion* are a primary feature of the history and here already appear, and it is clearly better to have all the related texts within the same covers. Only in the case of the prose form of the tale of Beren and Lúthien have I not done so, since that was preserved so little changed in the published *Silmarillion*; here I have restricted myself to notes on the changes that were made editorially.

I cannot, or at any rate I cannot yet, attempt the editing of my father's strictly or narrowly linguistic writings, in view of their extraordinary complexity and difficulty; but I include in this book the general essay called *The Lhammas* or Account of Tongues, and also the *Etymologies*, both belonging to this period. The latter, a kind of etymological dictionary, provides historical explanations of a very large number of words and names, and enormously increases the known vocabularies of the Elvish tongues – as they were at that time, for like everything else the languages continued to evolve as the years passed. Also hitherto unknown except by allusion is my father's abandoned 'time-travel' story *The Lost Road*, which leads primarily to Númenor, but also into the history and legend of northern and western Europe, with the associated poems *The Song of Ælfwine* (in the stanza of *Pearl*) and *King Sheave* (in alliterative verse). Closely connected with *The Lost Road* were the earliest forms of the legend of the

Drowning of Númenor, which are also included in the book, and
the first glimpses of the story of the Last Alliance of Elves and
Men.

In the inevitable *Appendix* I have placed three works which are
not given complete: the *Genealogies*, the *List of Names*, and the
second 'Silmarillion' Map, all of which belong in their original
forms to the earlier 1930s. The *Genealogies* only came to light
recently, but they add in fact little to what is known from the
narrative texts. The *List of Names* might have been better
included in Vol. IV, but this was again a work of reference which
provides very little new matter, and it was more convenient to
postpone it and then to give just those few entries which offer new
detail. The second Map is a different case. This was my father's
sole 'Silmarillion' map for some forty years, and here I have
redrawn it to show it as it was when first made, leaving out all the
layer upon layer of later accretion and alteration. The *Tale of
Years* and the *Tale of Battles*, listed in title-pages to *The Silmarillion* as elements in that work (see p. 202), are not included,
since they were contemporary with the later *Annals* and add
nothing to the material found in them; subsequent alteration of
names and dates was also carried out in a precisely similar way.

In places the detailed discussion of dating may seem excessive,
but since the chronology of my father's writings, both 'internal'
and 'external', is extremely difficult to determine and the evidence
full of traps, and since the history can be very easily and very
seriously falsified by mistaken deductions on this score, I have
wished to make as plain as I can the reasons for my assertions.

In some of the texts I have introduced paragraph-numbering.
This is done in the belief that it will provide a more precise and
therefore quicker method of reference in a book where the discussion of its nature moves constantly back and forth.

As in previous volumes I have to some degree standardized
usage in respect of certain names: thus for example I print *Gods*,
*Elves*, *Orcs*, *Middle-earth*, etc. with initial capitals, and *Kôr*,
*Tûn*, *Eärendel*, *Númenórean*, etc. for frequent *Kôr*, *Tûn*,
*Earendel*, *Numenórean* of the manuscripts.

The earlier volumes of the series are referred to as I (*The Book of
Lost Tales Part I*), II (*The Book of Lost Tales Part II*), III (*The
Lays of Beleriand*), and IV (*The Shaping of Middle-earth*).
The sixth volume now in preparation will concern the evolution of
*The Lord of the Rings*.

The tables illustrating *The Lhammas* are reproduced with the permission of the Bodleian Library, Oxford, who kindly supplied photographs.

I list here for convenience the abbreviations used in the book in reference to various works (for a fuller account see pp. 107–8).

*Texts in Vol. IV:*

S    The *Sketch of the Mythology* or 'earliest Silmarillion'.

Q    The *Quenta* ('*Quenta Noldorinwa*'), the second version of 'The Silmarillion'.

AV 1    The earliest *Annals of Valinor*.

AB 1    The earliest *Annals of Beleriand* (in two versions, the second early abandoned).

*Texts in Vol. V:*

FN    *The Fall of Númenor* (**FN I** and **FN II** referring to the first and second texts).

AV 2    The second version of the *Annals of Valinor*.

AB 2    The second version (or strictly the third) of the *Annals of Beleriand*.

QS    The *Quenta Silmarillion*, the third version of 'The Silmarillion', nearing completion at the end of 1937.

Other works (*Ambarkanta*, *Ainulindalë*, *Lhammas*, *The Lost Road*) are not referred to by abbreviations.

In conclusion, I take this opportunity to notice and explain the erroneous representation of the Westward Extension of the first 'Silmarillion' Map in the previous volume (*The Shaping of Middle-earth* p. 228). It will be seen that this map presents a strikingly different appearance from that of the Eastward Extension on p. 231. These two maps, being extremely faint, proved impossible to reproduce from photographs supplied by the Bodleian Library, and an experimental 'reinforcement' (rather than re-drawing) of a copy of the Westward Extension was tried out. This I rejected, and it was then found that my photocopies of the originals gave a result sufficiently clear for the purpose. Unhappily, the rejected 'reinforced' version of the Westward Extension map was substituted for the photocopy. (Photocopies were also used for diagram III on p. 247 and map V on p. 251, where the originals are in faint pencil.)

# PART ONE

---

## THE FALL OF
## NÚMENOR

### AND

## THE LOST ROAD

# I
# THE EARLY HISTORY OF THE LEGEND

In February 1968 my father addressed a commentary to the authors of an article about him (*The Letters of J. R. R. Tolkien* no. 294). In the course of this he recorded that 'one day' C. S. Lewis said to him that since 'there is too little of what we really like in stories' they would have to try to write some themselves. He went on:

We agreed that he should try 'space-travel', and I should try 'time-travel'. His result is well known. My effort, after a few promising chapters, ran dry: it was too long a way round to what I really wanted to make, a new version of the Atlantis legend. The final scene survives as *The Downfall of Númenor*.*

A few years earlier, in a letter of July 1964 (*Letters* no. 257), he gave some account of his book, *The Lost Road*:

When C. S. Lewis and I tossed up, and he was to write on space-travel and I on time-travel, I began an abortive book of time-travel of which the end was to be the presence of my hero in the drowning of Atlantis. This was to be called *Númenor*, the Land in the West. The thread was to be the occurrence time and again in human families (like Durin among the Dwarves) of a father and son called by names that could be interpreted as Bliss-friend and Elf-friend. These no longer understood are found in the end to refer to the Atlantid-Númenórean situation and mean 'one loyal to the Valar, content with the bliss and prosperity within the limits prescribed' and 'one loyal to friendship with the High-elves'. It started with a father-son affinity between Edwin and Elwin of the present, and was supposed to go back into legendary time by way of an Eädwine and Ælfwine of circa A.D.918, and Audoin and Alboin of Lombardic legend, and so to the traditions of the North Sea concerning the coming of corn and culture heroes, ancestors of kingly lines, in boats (and their departure in funeral ships). One such Sheaf, or Shield Sheafing, can actually be made out as one of the remote ancestors of the present Queen. In my tale we were to come at last to Amandil and Elendil leaders of the loyal party in Númenor, when it fell under the domination of Sauron. Elendil 'Elf-friend' was the founder of the Exiled kingdoms in Arnor and Gondor. But I found my real

---

*This is *Akallabêth, The Downfall of Númenor*, posthumously published in *The Silmarillion*, pp. 259–82.

interest was only in the upper end, the *Akallabêth* or *Atalantie**
('Downfall' in Númenórean and Quenya), so I brought all the stuff I
had written on the originally unrelated legends of Númenor into
relation with the main mythology.

I do not know whether evidence exists that would date the conversation
that led to the writing of *Out of the Silent Planet* and *The Lost Road*, but
the former was finished by the autumn of 1937, and the latter was
submitted, so far as it went, to Allen and Unwin in November of that
year (see III.364).

The significance of the last sentence in the passage just cited is not
entirely clear. When my father said 'But I found my real interest was only
in the upper end, the *Akallabêth* or *Atalantie*' he undoubtedly meant that
he had not been inspired to write the 'intervening' parts, in which the
father and son were to appear and reappear in older and older phases of
Germanic legend; and indeed *The Lost Road* stops after the introductory
chapters and only takes up again with the Númenórean story that was to
come at the end. Very little was written of what was planned to lie
between. But what is the meaning of '*so I brought all the stuff I had
written on the originally unrelated legends of Númenor* into relation with
the main mythology'? My father seems to be saying that, having found
that he only wanted to write about Númenor, he therefore and only then
(abandoning *The Lost Road*) appended the Númenórean material to 'the
main mythology', thus inaugurating the Second Age of the World. But
what was this material? He cannot have meant the Númenórean matter
contained in *The Lost Road* itself, since that was already fully related to
'the main mythology'. It must therefore have been something else, already
existing when *The Lost Road* was begun, as Humphrey Carpenter assumes
in his *Biography* (p. 170): 'Tolkien's legend of Númenor... was probably
composed some time before the writing of "The Lost Road", perhaps in
the late nineteen-twenties or early thirties.' But, in fact, the conclusion
seems to me inescapable that my father erred when he said this.

The original rough workings for *The Lost Road* are extant, but they are
very rough, and do not form a continuous text. There is one complete
manuscript, itself fairly rough and heavily emended in different stages;
and a professional typescript that was done when virtually all changes
had been made to the manuscript.† The typescript breaks off well before

---

*It is a curious chance that the stem *talat* used in Q[uenya] for 'slipping,
sliding, falling down', of which *atalantie* is a normal (in Q) noun-formation,
should so much resemble Atlantis. [Footnote to the letter.] – See the
*Etymologies*, stem TALÁT. The very early Elvish dictionary described in I.246 has
a verb *talte* 'incline (transitive), decline, shake at foundations, make totter, etc.'
and an adjective *talta* 'shaky, wobbly, tottering – sloping, slanting.'

†This typescript was made at Allen and Unwin, as appears from a letter from
Stanley Unwin dated 30th November 1937: '*The Lost Road*: We have had this
typed and are returning the original herewith. The typed copy will follow when
we have had an opportunity of reading it.' See further p. 73 note 14.

the point where the manuscript comes to an end, and my father's emendations to it were very largely corrections of the typist's errors, which were understandably many; it has therefore only slight textual value, and the manuscript is very much the primary text.

The Lost Road breaks off finally in the course of a conversation during the last days of Númenor between Elendil and his son Herendil; and in this Elendil speaks at length of the ancient history: of the wars against Morgoth, of Eärendel, of the founding of Númenor, and of the coming there of Sauron. The Lost Road is therefore, as I have said, entirely integrated with 'the main mythology' – and this is true already in the preliminary drafts.

Now as the papers were found, there follows immediately after the last page of The Lost Road a further manuscript with a new page-numbering, but no title. Quite apart from its being so placed, this text gives a strong physical impression of belonging to the same time as The Lost Road; and it is closely associated in content with the last part of The Lost Road, for it tells the story of Númenor and its downfall – though this second text was written with a different purpose, to be a complete if very brief history: it is indeed the first fully-written draft of the narrative that ultimately became the Akallabêth. But it is earlier than The Lost Road; for where that has Sauron and Tarkalion this has Sûr and Angor.

A second, more finished manuscript of this history of Númenor followed, with the title (written in afterwards) The Last Tale: The Fall of Númenor. This has several passages that are scarcely different from passages in The Lost Road, but it seems scarcely possible to show for certain which preceded and which followed, unless the evidence cited on p. 74, note 25, is decisive that the second version of The Fall of Númenor was the later of the two; in any case, a passage rewritten very near the time of the original composition of this version is certainly later than The Lost Road, for it gives a later form of the story of Sauron's arrival in Númenor (see pp. 26–7).

It is therefore clear that the two works were intimately connected; they arose at the same time and from the same impulse, and my father worked on them together. But still more striking is the existence of a single page that can only be the original 'scheme' for The Fall of Númenor, the actual first writing down of the idea. The very name Númenor is here only in process of emergence. Yet in this primitive form of the story the term Middle-earth is used, as it never was in the Quenta: it did not appear until the Annals of Valinor and the Ambarkanta. Moreover the form Ilmen occurs, which suggests that this 'scheme' was later than the actual writing of the Ambarkanta, where Ilmen was an emendation of Ilma (earlier Silma): IV.240, note 3.

I conclude therefore that 'Númenor' (as a distinct and formalised conception, whatever 'Atlantis-haunting', as my father called it, lay behind) arose in the actual context of his discussions with C. S. Lewis in (as seems probable) 1936. A passage in the 1964 letter can be taken to say precisely that: 'I began an abortive book of time-travel of which the end was to be the presence of my hero in the drowning of Atlantis. *This was to be called Númenor*, the Land in the West.' Moreover, 'Númenor' was from the outset conceived in full association with 'The Silmarillion'; there never was a time when the legends of Númenor were 'unrelated to the main mythology'. My father erred in his recollection (or expressed himself obscurely, meaning something else); the letter cited above was indeed written nearly thirty years later.

# II

# THE FALL OF NÚMENOR

## (i)

### *The original outline*

The text of the original 'scheme' of the legend, referred to in the previous chapter, was written at such speed that here and there words cannot be certainly interpreted. Near the beginning it is interrupted by a very rough and hasty sketch, which shows a central globe, marked *Ambar*, with two circles around it; the inner area thus described is marked *Ilmen* and the outer *Vaiya*. Across the top of *Ambar* and cutting through the zones of *Ilmen* and *Vaiya* is a straight line extending to the outer circle in both directions. This must be the forerunner of the diagram of the World Made Round accompanying the *Ambarkanta*, IV.247. The first sentence of the text, concerning Agaldor (on whom see pp. 78–9), is written separately from the rest, as if it were a false start, or the beginning of a distinct outline.

Agaldor chieftain of a people who live upon the N.W. margin of the Western Sea.

The last battle of the Gods. Men side largely with Morgoth. After the victory the Gods take counsel. Elves are summoned to Valinor. [*Struck out*: Faithful men dwell in the Lands] Many men had not come into the old Tales. They are still at large on earth. The Fathers of Men are given a land to dwell in, raised by Ossë and Aulë in the great Western Sea. The Western Kingdom grows up. *Atalantë*. [*Added in margin*: Legend so named it afterward (the old name was *Númar* or *Númenos*) *Atalantë* = The Falling.] Its people great mariners, and men of great skill and wisdom. They range from Tol-eressëa to the shores of Middle-earth. Their occasional appearance among Wild Men, where Faithless Men also [?ranged corrupting them]. Some become lords in the East. But the Gods will not allow them to land in Valinor – and though they become long-lived because many have been bathed in the radiance of Valinor from Tol-eressëa – they are mortal and their span brief. They murmur against this decree. Thû comes to Atalantë, heralded [*read* heralding] the approach of Morgoth. But Morgoth cannot come except as a spirit, being doomed to *dwell* outside the Walls of Night. The Atalanteans fall, and rebel. They make a temple to Thû-Morgoth. They build an armament and assail the shores of the Gods with thunder.

The Gods therefore sundered Valinor from the earth, and an awful rift appeared down which the water poured and the armament of Atalantë was drowned. They globed the whole earth so that however far a man sailed he could never again reach the West, but came back to his starting-point. Thus new lands came into being beneath the Old World; and the East and West were bent back and [?water flowed all over the round] earth's surface and there was a time of flood. But Atalantë being near the rift was utter[ly] thrown down and submerged. The remnant of [*struck out at time of writing*: Númen the Lie-númen] the Númenóreans in their ships flee East and land upon Middle-earth. [*Struck out*: Morgoth induces many to believe that this is a natural cataclysm.]

The [?longing] of the Númenóreans. Their longing for life on earth. Their ship burials, and their great tombs. Some evil and some good. Many of the good sit upon the west shore. These also seek out the Fading Elves. How [*struck out at time of writing*: Agaldor] Amroth wrestled with Thû and drove him to the centre of the Earth and the Iron-forest.

The old line of the lands remained as a plain of air upon which only the Gods could walk, and the Eldar who faded as Men usurped the sun. But many of the Númenórië could see it or faintly see it; and tried to devise ships to sail on it. But they achieved only ships that would sail in Wilwa or lower air. Whereas the Plain of the Gods cut through and traversed Ilmen [in] which even birds cannot fly, save the eagles and hawks of Manwë. But the fleets of the Númenórië sailed round the world; and Men took them for gods. Some were content that this should be so.

As I have said, this remarkable text documents the beginning of the legend of Númenor, and the extension of 'The Silmarillion' into a Second Age of the World. Here the idea of the World Made Round and the Straight Path was first set down, and here appears the first germ of the story of the Last Alliance, in the words 'These also seek out the Fading Elves. How [Agaldor >] Amroth wrestled with Thû and drove him to the centre of the Earth' (at the beginning of the text Agaldor is named as the chief of a people living on the North-west coasts of Middle-earth). The longevity of the Númenóreans is already present, but (even allowing for the compression and distortion inherent in such 'outlines' of my father's, in which he attempted to seize and dash onto paper a bubbling

up of new ideas) seems to have far less significance than it would
afterwards attain; and is ascribed, strangely, to 'the radiance of Valinor',
in which the mariners of Númenor were 'bathed' during their visits to
Tol-eressëa, to which they were permitted to sail. Cf. the *Quenta*,
IV.98: 'Still therefore is the light of Valinor more great and fair than that
of other lands, because there the Sun and Moon together rest a while
before they go upon their dark journey under the world'; but this does
not seem a sufficient or satisfactory explanation of the idea (see further
p. 20). The mortuary culture of the Númenóreans does indeed appear,
but it arose among the survivors of Númenor in Middle-earth, after the
Downfall; and this remained into more developed forms of the legend, as
did the idea of the flying ships which the exiles built, seeking to sail on the
Straight Path through *Ilmen*, but achieving only flight through the lower
air, *Wilwa*.*

The sentence 'Thû comes to Atalantë, herald[ing] the approach of
Morgoth' certainly means that Thû *prophesied* Morgoth's return, as in
subsequent texts. The meaning of 'But Morgoth cannot come except as a
spirit' is made somewhat clearer in the next version, §5.

(ii)

### The first version of The Fall of Númenor

The preliminary outline was the immediate precursor of a first full
narrative – the manuscript described above (p. 9), placed with *The
Lost Road*. This was followed by further versions, and I shall refer to the
work as a whole (as distinct from the *Akallabêth*, into which it was
afterwards transformed) as *The Fall of Númenor*, abbreviated 'FN'; the
first text has no title, but I shall call it 'FN I'.

FN I is rough and hasty, and full of corrections made at the time of
composition; there are also many others, mostly slight, made later and
moving towards the second version FN II. I give it as it was written,
without the second layer of emendations (except in so far as these make
small necessary corrections to clarify the sense). As explained in the
Preface, here as elsewhere I have introduced paragraph numbers into the
text to make subsequent reference and comparison easier. A commentary, following the paragraphing of the text, follows at its end.

§1   In the Great Battle when Fionwë son of Manwë overthrew Morgoth and rescued the Gnomes and the Fathers of Men,
many mortal Men took part with Morgoth. Of these those that
were not destroyed fled into the East and South of the World, and
the servants of Morgoth that escaped came to them and guided

---

*Although this text has the final form *Ilmen*, beside *Silma* > *Ilma* > *Ilmen* in
the *Ambarkanta*, *Wilwa* was replaced in the *Ambarkanta* by *Vista*.

them; and they became evil, and they brought evil into many places where wild Men dwelt at large in the empty lands. But after their victory, when Morgoth and many of his captains were bound, and Morgoth was thrust again into the Outer Darkness, the Gods took counsel. The Elves were summoned to Valinor, as has been told, and many obeyed, but not all. But the Fathers of Men, who had served the Eldar, and fought against Morgoth, were greatly rewarded. For Fionwë son of Manwë came among them and taught them, and gave them wisdom, power and life stronger than any others of the Second Kindred.

§2    And a great land was made for them to dwell in, neither part of Middle-earth nor wholly separate from it. This was raised by Ossë out of the depths of Belegar, the Great Sea, and established by Aulë, and enriched by Yavanna. It was called Númenor, that is Westernesse, and Andúnië or the Sunsetland, and its chief city in the midmost of its western coasts was in the days of its might called Númar or Númenos; but after its fall it was named in legend Atalantë, the Ruin.

§3    For in Númenórë a great people arose, in all things more like the First Kindred than any other races of Men that have been, yet less fair and wise than they, though greater in body. And above all their arts the people of Númenor nourished shipbuilding and sea-craft, and became mariners whose like shall never be again, since the world was diminished. They ranged from Tol-eressëa, where for many ages they still had converse and dealings with the Gnomes, to the shores of Middle-earth, and sailed round to the North and South, and glimpsed from their high prows the Gates of Morning in the East. And they appeared among the wild Men, and filled them with wonder and also with fear. For many esteemed them to be Gods or sons of Gods out of the West, and evil men had told them lies concerning the Lords of the West. But the Númenóreans tarried not long yet in Middle-earth, for their hearts hungered ever westward for the undying bliss of ·Valinor. And they were restless and pursued with desire even at the height of their glory.

§4    But the Gods forbade them to sail beyond the Lonely Isle, and would not permit any save their kings (once in each life before he was crowned) to land in Valinor. For they were mortal Men, and it was not in the power and right of Manwë to alter their fate. Thus though the people were long-lived, since their land was more nigh than other lands to Valinor, and many had looked long on the radiance of the Gods that came faintly to Tol-eressëa, they remained mortal, even their kings, and their span brief in the eyes of the Eldar. And they murmured against this decree. And a great discontent grew among them; and their masters of lore sought unceasingly for the secrets that should prolong their lives, and they sent spies to seek these in Valinor. And the Gods were angered.

§5   And in time it came to pass that Sûr (whom the Gnomes called Thû) came in the likeness of a great bird to Númenor and preached a message of deliverance, and he prophesied the second coming of Morgoth. But Morgoth did not come in person, but only in spirit and as a shadow upon the mind and heart, for the Gods shut him beyond the Walls of the World. But Sûr spake to Angor the king and Istar his queen, and promised them undying life and lordship of the Earth. And they believed him and fell under the shadow, and the greatest part of the people of Númenor followed them. Angor raised a great temple to Morgoth in the midst of the land, and Sûr dwelt there.

§6   But in the passing of the years Angor felt the oncoming of old age, and he was troubled; and Sûr said that the gifts of Morgoth were withheld by the Gods, and that to obtain plenitude of power and undying life he must be master of the West. Wherefore the Númenóreans made a great armament; and their might and skill had in those days become exceedingly great, and they had moreover the aid of Sûr. The fleets of the Númenóreans were like a great land of many islands, and their masts like a forest of mountain-trees, and their banners like the streamers of a thunderstorm, and their sails were black. And they moved slowly into the West, for all the winds were stilled and the world lay silent in the fear of that time. And they passed Tol-eressëa, and it is said that the Elves mourned and grew sick, for the light of Valinor was cut off by the cloud of the Númenóreans. But Angor assailed the shores of the Gods, and he cast bolts of thunder, and fire came upon the sides of Taniquetil.

§7   But the Gods were silent. Sorrow and dismay were in the heart of Manwë, and he spoke to Ilúvatar, and took power and counsel from the Lord of All; and the fate and fashion of the world was changed. For the silence of the Gods was broken suddenly, and Valinor was sundered from the earth, and a rift appeared in the midst of Belegar east of Tol-eressëa, and into this chasm the great seas plunged, and the noise of the falling waters filled all the earth and the smoke of the cataracts rose above the tops of the everlasting mountains. But all the ships of Númenor that were west of Tol-eressëa were drawn down into the great abyss and drowned, and Angor the mighty and Istar his queen fell like stars into the dark, and they perished out of all knowledge. And the mortal warriors that had set foot in the land of the Gods were buried under fallen hills, where legend saith that they lie imprisoned in the Forgotten Caves until the day of Doom and the Last Battle. And the Elves of Tol-eressëa passed through the gates of death, and were gathered to their kindred in the land of the Gods, and became as they; and the Lonely Isle remained only as a shape of the past.

§8    But Ilúvatar gave power to the Gods, and they bent back the edges of the Middle-earth, and they made it into a globe, so that however far a man should sail he could never again reach the true West, but came back weary at last to the place of his beginning. Thus New Lands came into being beneath the Old World, and all were equally distant from the centre of the round earth; and there was flood and great confusion of waters, and seas covered what was once the dry, and lands appeared where there had been deep seas. Thus also the heavy air flowed round all the earth in that time, above the waters; and the springs of all waters were cut off from the stars.

§9    But Númenor being nigh upon the East to the great rift was utterly thrown down and overwhelmed in sea, and its glory perished. But a remnant of the Númenóreans escaped the ruin in this manner. Partly by the device of Angor, and partly of their own will (because they revered still the Lords of the West and mistrusted Sûr) many had abode in ships upon the east coast of their land, lest the issue of war be evil. Wherefore protected for a while by the land they avoided the draught of the sea, and a great wind arose blowing from the gap, and they sped East and came at length to the shores of Middle-earth in the days of ruin.

§10    There they became lords and kings of Men, and some were evil and some were of good will. But all alike were filled with desire of long life upon earth, and the thought of Death was heavy upon them; and their feet were turned east but their hearts were westward. And they built mightier houses for their dead than for their living, and endowed their buried kings with unavailing treasure. For their wise men hoped ever to discover the secret of prolonging life and maybe the recalling of it. But it is said that the span of their lives, which had of old been greater than that of lesser races, dwindled slowly, and they achieved only the art of preserving uncorrupt for many ages the dead flesh of men. Wherefore the kingdoms upon the west shores of the Old World became a place of tombs, and filled with ghosts. And in the fantasy of their hearts, and the confusion of legends half-forgotten concerning that which had been, they made for their thought a land of shades, filled with the wraiths of the things of mortal earth. And many deemed this land was in the West, and ruled by the Gods, and in shadow the dead, bearing the shadows of their possessions, should come there, who could no more find the true West in the body. For which reason in after days many of their descendants, or men taught by them, buried their dead in ships and set them in pomp upon the sea by the west coasts of the Old World.

§11    For the blood of the Númenóreans was most among the men of those lands and coasts, and the memory of the primeval world remained most strongly there, where the old paths to the West had of old set out from Middle-earth. And the spell that lay there was not wholly vain. For the old line of the world remained in the mind of the Gods and in the memory of the world as a shape and a plan that has been changed, but endures. And it has been likened to a plain of air, or to a straight vision that bends not to the hidden curving of the earth, or to a level bridge that rises imperceptibly but surely above the heavy air of earth. And of old many of the Númenóreans could see or half see the paths to the True West, and believed that at times from a high place they could descry the peaks of Taniquetil at the end of the straight road, high above the world.

§12    But the most, that could not see this, scorned them, and trusted in ships upon the water. But they came only to the lands of the New World, and found them to be as those of the Old; and they reported that the world was round. But upon the straight road only the Gods and the vanished Elves could walk, or such as the Gods summoned of the fading Elves of the round earth, who became diminished in substance as Men usurped the sun. For the Plain of the Gods being straight, whereas the surface of the world was bent, and the seas that lay upon it, and the heavy airs that lay above, cut through the air of breath and flight, and traversed Ilmen, in which no flesh can endure. And it is said that even those of the Númenóreans of old who had the straight vision did not all comprehend this, and they tried to devise ships that would rise above the waters of the world and hold to the imagined seas. But they achieved only ships that would sail in the air of breath. And these ships flying came also to the lands of the New World and to the East of the Old World; and they reported that the world was round. And many abandoned the Gods, and put them out of their legends, and even out of their dreams. But Men of Middle-earth looked on them with wonder and great fear, and took them to be gods; and many were content that this should be so.

§13   But not all the hearts of the Númenóreans were crooked; and the lore of the old days descending from the Fathers of Men, and the Elf-friends, and those instructed by Fionwë, was preserved among some. And they knew that the fate of Men was not bounded by the round path of the world, nor destined for the straight path. For the round is crooked and has no end but no escape; and the straight is true, but has an end within the world, and that is the fate of the Elves. But the fate of Men, they said, is neither round nor ended, and is not within the world. And they remembered from whence the ruin came, and the cutting off of Men from their just portion of the straight path; and they avoided the shadow of Morgoth according to their power, and hated Thû. And they assailed his temples and their servants, and there were wars of allegiance among the mighty of this world, of which only the echoes remain.

§14   But there remains still a legend of Beleriand: for that land in the West of the Old World, although changed and broken, held still in ancient days to the name it had in the days of the Gnomes. And it is said that Amroth was King of Beleriand; and he took counsel with Elrond son of Eärendel, and with such of the Elves as remained in the West; and they passed the mountains and came into inner lands far from the sea, and they assailed the fortress of Thû. And Amroth wrestled with Thû and was slain; but Thû was brought to his knees, and his servants were dispelled; and the peoples of Beleriand destroyed his dwellings, and drove him forth, and he fled to a dark forest, and hid himself. And it is said that the war with Thû hastened the fading of the Eldar, for he had power beyond their measure, as Felagund King of Nargothrond had found in the earliest days; and they expended their strength and substance in the assault upon him. And this was the last of the services of the older race to Men, and it is held the last of the deeds of alliance before the fading of the Elves and the estrangement of the Two Kindreds. And here the tale of the ancient world, as the Elves keep it, comes to an end.

*Commentary on the first version of The Fall of Númenor*

§1   As Q §18 was first written (IV. 158), it was permitted by Fionwë that 'with the Elves should those of the race of Hador and Bëor alone be suffered to depart, if they would. But of these only Elrond was now left . . .' On this extremely puzzling passage see the commentary, IV. 200, where I suggested that obscure as it is it represents 'the first germ of the story of the departure of the Elf-friends to Númenor.' It was removed in the rewriting, Q II §18, where there appears a reference to Men of Hithlum who 'repentant of their evil servitude did deeds of valour, and many beside of Men new come out of the East', but now no mention of the Elf-friends. A final hasty revision of the passage (IV. 163, notes 2 and 3) gave:

And it is said that *all that were left of the three Houses of the Fathers of Men* fought for Fionwë, and to them were joined some of the Men of Hithlum who repenting of their evil servitude did deeds of valour . . . But most Men, and especially those new come out of the East, were on the side of the Enemy.

This is very close to, and no doubt belongs in fact to the same time as, the corresponding passage in the following version of 'The Silmarillion' (QS*, p. 328 §16), which however omits the reference to the Men of Hithlum. I have little doubt that this development came in with the emergence of Númenor.

§2 Here first appear the names *Andúnië* (but as a name of the island, translated 'the Sunsetland'), and *Númenor* itself (which does not occur in the preliminary outline, though the people are there called *Númenórië* and *Númenóreans*). The chief city is called *Númar* or *Númenos*, which in the outline were the names of the land. The name *Belegar* was emended later, here and in §7, to *Belegaer*.

After the words *enriched by Yavanna* the passage concerning names was early replaced as follows:

It was called by the Gods Andor, the Land of Gift, but by its own folk Vinya, the Young; but when the men of that land spake of it to the men of Middle-earth they named it Númenor, that is Westernesse, for it lay west of all lands inhabited by mortals. Yet it was not in the true West, for there was the land of the Gods. The chief city of Númenor was in the midmost of its western coasts, and in the days of its might it was called Andúnië, because it faced the sunset; but after its fall it was named in the legends of those that fled from it Atalantë the Downfall.

Here first appears *Andor*, Land of Gift, and also the name given to the land by the Númenóreans, *Vinya*, the Young, which did not survive in the later legend (cf. *Vinyamar, Vinyalondë*, Index to *Unfinished Tales*); *Andúnië* now becomes the name of the chief city. In the text as originally written the name *Atalantë* could refer either to the land or the city, but in the rewriting it can only refer to the city. It seems

---

*Throughout this book the abbreviation 'QS' (*Quenta Silmarillion*) is used for the version interrupted near the end of 1937; see pp. 107–8.

unlikely that my father intended this; see the corresponding passage in FN II and commentary.

§3    The permission given to the Númenóreans to sail as far west as Toleressëa, found already in the original outline, contrasts with the *Akallabêth* (pp. 262–3), where it is told that they were forbidden 'to sail so far westward that the coasts of Númenor could no longer be seen', and only the most keen-sighted among them could descry far off the tower of Avallónë on the Lonely Isle.

The *Gates of Morning* reappear, remarkably, from the *Lost Tales* (I. 216). In the original astronomical myth the Sun passed into the Outer Dark by the Door of Night and re-entered by the Gates of Morn; but with the radical transformation of the myth that entered with the *Sketch of the Mythology* (see IV. 49), and is found in the *Quenta* and *Ambarkanta*, whereby the Sun is drawn by the servants of Ulmo beneath the roots of the Earth, the Door of Night was given a different significance and the Gates of Morn no longer appear (see IV. 252, 255). How the reference to them here (which survives in the *Akallabêth*, p. 263) is to be understood I am unable to say.

In this paragraph is the first occurrence of the expression *The Lords of the West*.

§4    The words *save their kings (once in each life before he was crowned)* were early placed in square brackets. In the conclusion of QS (p. 326 §§8–9) the prohibition appears to be absolute, not to be set aside for any mortal; there Mandos says of Eärendel 'Now he shall surely die, for he has trodden *the forbidden shores*', and Manwë says 'To Eärendel I remit *the ban*, and the peril that he took upon himself.' Later (as noted under §3 above) the Ban extended also, and inevitably, to Toleressëa ('easternmost of the Undying Lands', the *Akallabêth*, p. 263).

The ascription of the longevity of the Númenóreans to the light of Valinor appeared already in the original outline, and I cited (p. 13) the passage from the *Quenta* where it is said that the light of Valinor was greater and fairer than in the other lands 'because there the Sun and Moon together rest a while.' But the wording here, 'the radiance of the Gods that came faintly to Tol-eressëa', surely implies a light of a different nature from that of the Sun and Moon (which illumine the whole world). Conceivably, the further idea that appears in the corresponding passage in QS (§79) is present here: 'moreover the Valar store the radiance of the Sun in many vessels, and in vats and pools for their comfort in times of dark.' The passage was later enclosed in brackets, and it does not appear in FN II; but at a subsequent point in the narrative (§6) the Elves of Tol-eressëa mourned 'for the light of Valinor was cut off by the cloud of the Númenóreans', and this was not rejected. Cf. the *Akallabêth* (p. 278): 'the Eldar mourned, for *the light of the setting sun* was cut off by the cloud of the Númenóreans.'

§5    With what is said here of Morgoth's not returning 'in person', for he was shut beyond the Walls of the World, 'but only in spirit and as a shadow upon the mind and heart', cf. the *Quenta* (IV. 164): 'Some say also that Morgoth at whiles secretly as a cloud that cannot be seen or felt . . . creeps back surmounting the Walls and visiteth the world' (a passage that survived in QS, pp. 332–3 §30).

§7 · The concluding sentence concerning the Elves of Tol-eressëa was an addition, but one that looks as if it belongs with the writing of the text. It is very hard to interpret. The rift in the Great Sea appeared *east* of Tol-eressëa, but the ships that were *west* of the isle were drawn down into the abyss; and it might be concluded from this that Tol-eressëa also was swallowed up and disappeared: so the Elves who dwelt there 'passed through the gates of death, and were gathered to their kindred in the land of the Gods', and 'the Lonely Isle remained only as a shape of the past.' But this would be very strange, for it would imply the abandonment of the entire story of Ælfwine's voyage to Tol-eressëa in ages after; yet Ælfwine as recorder and pupil was still present in my father's writings after the completion of *The Lord of the Rings*. On the diagram of the World Made Round accompanying the *Ambarkanta* (IV. 247) Tol-eressëa is marked as a point on the Straight Path. Moreover, much later, in the *Akallabêth* (pp. 278–9), the same is told of the great chasm: it opened 'between Númenor and the Deathless Lands', and all the fleets of the Númenóreans (which had passed on to Aman and so were west of Tol-eressëa) were drawn down into it; but 'Valinor and Eressëa were taken from [the world] into the realm of hidden things.'

§8    The concluding sentence ('Thus also the heavy air . . .') is a marginal addition which seems certainly to belong with the original text. It has no mark for insertion, but must surely be placed here.

§10    The desire to prolong life was already a mark of the Númenóreans (§4), but the dark picture in the *Akallabêth* (p. 266) of a land of tombs and embalming, of a people obsessed with death, was not present. At this stage in the evolution of the legend, as already in the preliminary outline, the tomb-culture arose among the Númenóreans who escaped the Downfall and founded kingdoms in the 'Old World': whether of good or evil disposition 'all alike were filled with desire of long life upon earth, and the thought of Death was heavy upon them'; and it was the life-span of the Exiles, as it appears, that slowly dwindled. There are echoes of the present passage in the *Akallabêth* account of Númenor after the Shadow fell upon it in the days of Tar-Atanamir (cf. *Unfinished Tales* p. 221); but in the very different context of the original story, when this culture arose among those who survived the Cataclysm and their descendants, other elements were present: for the Gods were now removed into the realm of the unknown and unseen, and they became the 'explanation' of the mystery of death, their dwelling-place in the far West the region to which the dead passed with their possessions.

In 'The Silmarillion' the Gods are 'physically' present, because (whatever the actual mode of their own being) they inhabit the same physical world, the realm of the 'seen'; if, after the Hiding of Valinor, they could not be reached by the voyages sent out in vain by Turgon of Gondolin, they were nonetheless reached by Eärendel, sailing from Middle-earth in his ship Wingelot, and their physical intervention of arms changed the world for ever through the physical destruction of the power of Morgoth. Thus it may be said that in 'The Silmarillion' there is no 'religion', because the Divine is present and has not been 'displaced'; but with the physical removal of the Divine from the World Made Round a religion arose (as it had arisen in Númenor under the teachings of Thû concerning Morgoth, the banished and absent God), and the dead were despatched, for religious reasons, in burial ships on the shores of the Great Sea.

§12  'But upon the straight road only the Gods and the vanished Elves could walk, or such as the Gods summoned of the fading Elves of the round earth, who became diminished in substance as Men usurped the sun.' Cf. the *Quenta*, IV. 100–1, as emended (a passage that goes back to the *Sketch of the Mythology*, IV. 21):

> In after days, when because of the triumph of Morgoth Elves and Men became estranged, as he most wished, those of the Eldalië that still lived in the world faded, and Men usurped the sunlight. Then the Eldar wandered in the lonelier places of the Outer Lands, and took to the moonlight and to the starlight, and to the woods and caves, and became as shadows, wraiths and memories, such as set not sail unto the West and vanished from the world.

This passage survived very little changed in QS (§87).

I believe that the story of the flying ships built by the exiled Númenóreans, found already in the preliminary draft (p. 12), is the sole introduction of aerial craft in all my father's works. No hint is given of the means by which they rose and were propelled; and the passage did not survive into the later legend.

§13  It is a curious feature of the original story of Númenor that there is no mention of what befell Thû at the Downfall (cf. the *Akallabêth* p. 280); but he reappears here as a master of temples (cf. the *Lay of Leithian* lines 2064–7), dwelling in a fortress (§14), an object of hatred to those of the survivors of Númenor who retained something of the ancient knowledge.

§14  In the *Quenta* (IV. 160–1) it is told that in the Great Battle

> the Northern regions of the Western world were rent and riven, and the sea roared in through many chasms, and there was confusion and great noise; and the rivers perished or found new paths, and the valleys were upheaved and the hills trod down, and Sirion was no more. Then Men fled away . . . and long was it ere they came back over the mountains to where Beleriand once had been.

The last words of the earliest *Annals of Beleriand* (IV. 310) are 'So ended the First Age of the World and Beleriand was no more.' It is also said in the *Quenta* (IV. 162) that after the War was ended 'there was a mighty building of ships on the shores of the Western Sea, and especially upon the great isles, which in the disruption of the Northern world were fashioned of ancient Beleriand.'

In FN a rather different conception is suggested. Though Beleriand had been 'changed and broken', it is spoken of as 'that land', it was still called *Beleriand*, and it was peopled by Men and Elves, able to form an alliance against Thû. I would suggest (though hesitantly) that with the emergence, here first glimpsed, of a Second Age of Middle-earth consequent on the legend of Númenor, the utter devastation of Beleriand, suitable to the finality of the conclusion of the earlier conception, had been diminished.* Moreover it seems that at this time my father did not conceive of any further destruction of Beleriand at the time of the Downfall of Númenor, as he would do later (see p. 32).

At this stage there is no mention of a first and founder king of Númenor. Elrond was still the only child of Eärendel and Elwing; his brother Elros has appeared only in late additions to the text of Q (IV. 155), which were inserted after the Númenórean legend had begun to develop. In the oldest conception in the *Sketch of the Mythology* (IV. 38) Elrond 'bound by his mortal half elects to stay on earth' (i.e. in the Great Lands), and in Q (IV. 158) he 'elected to remain, being bound by his mortal blood in love to those of the younger race'; see my remarks on the Choice of the Half-elven, IV. 70. Elrond is here, as it seems, a leader of the Elves of Beleriand, in alliance with Amroth, predecessor of Elendil. The Last Alliance leading to the overthrow of Thû is seen as the last intervention of the Elves in the affairs of the World of Men, in itself hastening their inevitable fading. The 'dark forest' to which Thû fled (cf. the 'Iron-forest' in the original outline) is doubtless Mirkwood. In *The Hobbit* all that had been told of the Necromancer was that he dwelt in a dark tower in the south of Mirkwood.†

(iii)

*The second version of The Fall of Númenor*

FN II is a clear manuscript, made by my father with FN I before him and probably soon after it. It has many emendations made in the act of

---

*The passages cited here from Q were rather surprisingly retained almost unaltered in QS: see p. 337.

†Cf. *Letters* no. 257, referring to *The Hobbit*: 'the (originally) quite casual reference to the Necromancer, whose function was hardly more than to provide a reason for Gandalf going away and leaving Bilbo and the Dwarves to fend for themselves, which was necessary for the tale.'

composition, and none that seem to have been made after any significant interval, apart from the title, which was inserted later in pencil, and the rejection of a sentence in §7. In contrast to my father's common tendency to begin a new text keeping close to the antecedent but then to diverge ever more strongly as he proceeded, in this case the earlier part is much changed and expanded whereas the latter is scarcely altered, other than in very minor improvements to the run of sentences, until the end is reached. To give the whole of FN II is therefore unnecessary. Retaining the paragraph numbering of FN I, I give §§1–5 and 14 in full, and of the remainder only such short passages as were significantly altered.

### THE LAST TALE: THE FALL OF NÚMENOR

§1　In the Great Battle when Fionwë son of Manwë overthrew Morgoth and rescued the Exiles, the three houses of the Men of Beleriand fought against Morgoth. But most Men were allies of the Enemy; and after the victory of the Lords of the West those that were not destroyed fled eastward into Middle-earth; and the servants of Morgoth that escaped came to them, and enslaved them. For the Gods forsook for a time the Men of Middle-earth, because they had disobeyed their summons and hearkened to the Enemy. And Men were troubled by many evil things that Morgoth had made in the days of his dominion: demons and dragons and monsters, and Orcs, that are mockeries of the creatures of Ilúvatar; and their lot was unhappy. But Manwë put forth Morgoth, and shut him beyond the world in the Void without; and he cannot return again into the world, present and visible, while the Lords are enthroned. Yet his Will remaineth, and guideth his servants; and it moveth them ever to seek the overthrow of the Gods and the hurt of those that obey them.

But when Morgoth was thrust forth, the Gods held council. The Elves were summoned to return into the West, and such as obeyed dwelt again in Eressëa, the Lonely Island, which was renamed Avallon: for it is hard by Valinor. But Men of the three faithful houses and such as had joined with them were richly rewarded. For Fionwë son of Manwë came among them and taught them; and he gave them wisdom, power, and life stronger than any others have of the mortal race.

§2　And a great land was made for them to dwell in, neither part of Middle-earth nor wholly separate from it. It was raised by Ossë out of the depths of the Great Sea, and established by Aulë and enriched by Yavanna; and the Eldar brought thither flowers and fountains out of Avallon and wrought gardens there of great beauty, in which the Gods themselves at times would walk. That land was called by the Valar Andor, the Land of Gift, and by its own folk it was at first called Vinya, the Young; but in the days of its pride they named it Númenor, that is Westernesse, for it lay west of all lands inhabited by mortals; yet it was far from the true West, for that is Valinor, the land of the Gods. But its glory fell and its name perished; for after its ruin it was named in the legends of those that fled from it Atalantë, the Downfallen. Of old its chief city and haven was in the midst of its western coasts, and it was called Andúnië, because it faced the sunset. But the high place of its king was at Númenos in the heart of the land. It was built first by Elrond son of Eärendel, whom the Gods and Elves chose to be the lord of that land; for in him the blood of the houses of Hador and Bëor was mingled, and with it some part of that of the Eldar and Valar, which he drew from Idril and from Lúthien. But Elrond and all his folk were mortal; for the Valar may not withdraw the gift of death, which cometh to Men from Ilúvatar. Yet they took on the speech of the Elves of the Blessed Realm, as it was and is in Eressëa, and held converse with the Elves, and looked afar upon Valinor; for their ships were suffered to sail to Avallon and their mariners to dwell there for a while.

§3    And in the wearing of time the people of Númenor grew great and glorious, in all things more like the Firstborn than any other races of Men that have been; yet less fair and wise than the Elves, though greater in stature. For the Númenóreans were taller even than the tallest of the sons of Men in Middle-earth. Above all their arts they nourished shipbuilding and sea-craft, and became mariners whose like shall never be again, since the world has been diminished. They ranged from Eressëa in the West to the shores of Middle-earth, and came even into the inner seas; and they sailed about the North and the South, and glimpsed from their high prows the Gates of Morning in the East. And they appeared among the wild Men and filled them with wonder and dismay, and some esteemed them to be Gods or the sons of Gods out of the West; and the Men of Middle-earth feared them, for they were under the shadow of Morgoth, and believed the Gods to be terrible and cruel. The Númenóreans taught them such of the truth as they could comprehend, but it became only as a distant rumour little understood; for as yet the Númenóreans came seldom to Middle-earth and did not tarry there long. Their hearts were set westward, and they began to hunger for the undying bliss of Valinor; and they were restless and pursued by desire as their power and glory grew.

§4    For the Gods forbade them to sail beyond the Lonely Isle, and would not permit any to land in Valinor, because the Númenóreans were mortal; and though the Lords had rewarded them with long life, they could not take from them the weariness of the world that cometh at last; and they died, even their kings of the seed of Eärendel, and their span was brief in the eyes of the Elves. And they began to murmur against this decree; and a great discontent grew among them. Their masters of knowledge sought unceasingly for secrets that should prolong their lives; and they sent spies to seek forbidden lore in Avallon. But the Gods were angered.

§5    And it came to pass that Sauron, servant of Morgoth, grew mighty in Middle-earth; and the mariners of Númenor brought rumour of him. Some said that he was a king greater than the King of Númenor; some said that he was one of the Gods or their sons set to govern Middle-earth. A few reported that he was an evil spirit, perchance Morgoth himself returned. But this was held to be only a foolish fable of the wild Men. Tar-kalion was King of Númenor in those days, and he was proud; and believing that the Gods had delivered the dominion of the earth to the Númenóreans, he would not brook a king mightier than himself in any land. Therefore he purposed to send his servants to summon Sauron to Númenor, to do homage before him. The Lords sent messages to the king and spake through the mouths of wise men and counselled him against this mission; for they said that Sauron would work evil if he came; but he could not come to Númenor unless he was summoned and guided by the king's messengers. But Tar-kalion in his pride put aside the counsel, and he sent many ships.

Now rumour of the power of Númenor and its allegiance to the Gods came also to Sauron, and he feared lest the Men of the West should rescue those of Middle-earth from the Shadow; and being cunning and filled with malice he plotted in his heart to destroy Númenor, and (if he might) to bring grief upon the Gods. Therefore he humbled himself before the messengers, and came by ship to Númenor. But as the ships of the embassy drew nigh to the land an unquiet came upon the sea, and it arose like a mountain and cast the ships far inland; and the ship whereon Sauron stood was set upon a hill. And Sauron stood upon the hill and preached a message of deliverance from death to the Númenóreans; and he beguiled them with signs and wonders. And little by little he turned their hearts toward Morgoth, his master; and he prophesied that ere long he would come again into the world. And

Sauron spake to Tar-kalion the king, and to Tar-ilien his queen, and promised them life unending and the dominion of the earth, if they would turn unto Morgoth. And they believed him, and fell under the Shadow, and the greatest part of their people followed them. And Tar-kalion raised a great temple to Morgoth upon the Mountain of Ilúvatar in the midst of the land; and Sauron dwelt there and all Númenor was under his vigilance.

[The greater part of §5 was replaced by the following shorter version:]

And it came to pass that Sauron, servant of Morgoth, grew strong in Middle-earth; and he learned of the power and glory of the Númenóreans, and of their allegiance to the Gods, and he feared lest coming they should wrest the dominion of the East from him and rescue the Men of Middle-earth from the Shadow. And the king heard rumour of Sauron; and it was said that he was a king greater than the King of Númenor. Wherefore, against the counsel of the Gods, the king sent his servants to Sauron, and bade him come and do homage. And Sauron, being filled with cunning and malice, humbled himself and came; and he beguiled the Númenóreans with signs and wonders. But little by little Sauron turned their hearts towards Morgoth; and he prophesied that ere long he would come again into the world. And Sauron spake to Tar-kalion King of Númenor and to Tar-ilien his queen . . .

For the remainder of FN II, until the final paragraph, I note only the few differences from FN I that are of any substance. The changes of *Súr*, *Angor*, and *Istar* to *Sauron*, *Tar-kalion*, and *Tar-ilien* are not noticed.

§6 'And they passed Tol-eressëa' > 'And they encompassed Avallon'; 'fire came upon the sides of Taniquetil' > 'fire came upon Kôr and smokes rose about Taniquetil.'

§7 In FN II the paragraph opens: 'But the Gods made no answer. Then many of the Númenóreans set foot upon the forbidden shores, and they camped in might upon the borders of Valinor.'
'Angor the mighty and Istar his queen' > 'Tar-kalion the golden and bright Ilien his queen'; 'the Forgotten Caves' > 'the Caves of the Forgotten'.
The mysterious concluding sentence concerning the Elves of Eressëa (see the commentary on FN I) was retained but struck out later in pencil.

§8 The concluding sentence does not appear; see the commentary on FN I.

§9 'Partly by the [desire >] command of Tar-kalion, and partly by their own will (because some still revered the Gods and would not go with war into the West) many had remained behind, and sat in their ships . . .'

There is now no mention of the great wind that arose.

§10   The paragraph now opens: 'There, though shorn of their former power, and few in number and scattered, they after became lords and kings of Men. Some were evil and forsook not Sauron in their hearts; and some were of good will and retained memory of the Gods. But all alike . . .'

In 'the span of their lives, which had of old been greater than that of the lesser races' the words 'greater than' > 'thrice'.

The concluding sentence reads: 'For which reason in after days they would bury their dead in ships, or set them in pomp . . .'

§11   'And the spell that lay there was not wholly vain' > 'And this was not wholly fantasy', but this was struck out.

'For the ancient line of the world remained in the mind of Ilúvatar and in the thought of the Gods, and in the memory of the world . . .'

At the end of the paragraph is added: 'Therefore they built very high towers in those days.'

§12   The paragraph now begins: 'But most, who could not see this or conceive it in thought, scorned the builders of towers, and trusted to ships that sailed upon water. But they came only to the lands of the New World, and found them like to those of the Old, and subject to death; and they reported that the world was round. But upon the Straight Road only the Gods could walk, and only the ships of the Elves of Avallon could journey. For the Road being straight, whereas the surface of the earth was bent . . .'

The paragraph concludes: 'Therefore many abandoned the Gods, and put them out of their legends. But Men of Middle-earth looked up with wonder upon them, and with great fear, for they descended out of the air; and they took the Númenóreans to be Gods, and some were content that this should be so.'

§13   The paragraph begins: 'But not all the hearts of the Númenóreans were crooked; and the knowledge of the days before the ruin, descending from their fathers and the Elf-friends, and those that had held converse with the Gods, was long preserved among the wise. And they said that the fate of Men . . .'

'But the fate of Men . . . is not complete within the world.'

'there were wars of faith among the mighty of Middle-earth'

§14   But there remains still a legend of Beleriand: for that land in the West of the North of the Old World, where Morgoth had been overthrown, was still in a measure blessed and free from his shadow; and many of the exiles of Númenor had come thither. Though changed and broken it retained still in ancient days the name that it had borne in the days of the Gnomes. And it is said that in Beleriand there arose a king, who was of Númenórean race, and he was named Elendil, that is Elf-friend. And he took counsel with the Elves that remained in Middle-earth (and these abode then mostly in Beleriand); and he made a league with Gil-galad the Elf-king who was descended from Fëanor. And their armies were joined, and passed the mountains and came into inner lands far from the Sea. And they came at last even to Mordor the Black Country, where Sauron, that is in the Gnomish tongue named Thû, had rebuilt his fortresses. And they encompassed the stronghold, until Thû came forth in person, and Elendil and Gil-galad wrestled with him; and both were slain. But Thû was thrown down, and his bodily shape destroyed, and his servants were dispelled, and the host of Beleriand destroyed his dwelling; but Thû's spirit fled far away, and was hidden in waste places, and took no shape again for many ages. But it is sung sadly by the Elves that the war with Thû hastened the fading of the Eldar, decreed by the Gods; for Thû had power beyond their measure, as Felagund, King of Nargothrond, had found aforetime; and the Elves expended their strength and substance in the assault upon him. And this was the last of the services of the Firstborn to Men, and it is held the last of the deeds of alliance before the fading of the Elves and the estrangement of the Two Kindreds. And here endeth the tale of the ancient world as it is known to the Elves.

### Commentary on the second version of The Fall of Númenor

§1    On 'Orcs, that are mockeries of the creatures of Ilúvatar' see QS §18 and commentary. – It was said in FN I §5 that Morgoth 'did not come in person, but only in spirit, and as a shadow upon the mind and heart.' Now the idea of his 'return' in any sense seems to be denied; but there appears the concept of his malevolent and guiding Will that remains always in the world.

'such as obeyed dwelt again in Eressëa': in FN I 'the Elves were summoned to Valinor, as has been told, and many obeyed, but not all.' In the *Quenta* (IV. 162) 'the Gnomes and Dark-elves rehabited for the most part the Lonely Isle . . . But some returned even unto Valinor, as all were free to do who willed' (retained in QS, pp. 331–2 §27). The name *Avallon* ('for it is hard by Valinor') appears, but as a new name for Tol Eressëa; afterwards, in the form *Avallónë* ('for it is of all cities the nearest to Valinor'), it became the name of a haven in the isle: *Akallabêth* p. 260.

§2    At first my father preserved exactly the rewriting of FN I given in the commentary on FN I §2, whereby *Atalantë* is the name of the city Andúnië after the Downfall. I have suggested that he did not in fact intend this; at any rate he corrected it here, so that *Atalantë* again becomes the name of Númenor drowned. *Númenos* now reappears from FN I §2 as originally written, where it -was the name of the western city, but becomes the name of the high place of the king in the centre of the land (afterwards *Armenelos*).

Elrond (see the commentary on FN I §14) now becomes the first King of Númenor and the builder of Númenos; his brother Elros has still not emerged.

The statement here that the Númenóreans 'took on the speech of the Elves of the Blessed Realm, as it was and is in Eressëa' suggests that they abandoned their own Mannish tongue; and that this is the meaning is shown in *The Lost Road* (p. 68). In the *Lhammas* it is said (p. 179) that 'already even in [Húrin's father's] day Men in Beleriand forsook the daily use of their own tongue and spoke and gave even names unto their children in the language of the Gnomes.' The words 'as it was and is in Eressëa' would contradict any idea that the Lonely Isle was destroyed in the Downfall (see the commentary on FN I §7). But the difficult passage which suggests it was preserved in the present text, §7 (though subsequently struck out).

§4     The association of the longevity of the Númenóreans with the radiance of Valinor (see the commentary on FN I §4) is abandoned, and is attributed solely to the gift of the Valar.

§5     In all probability the name *Sauron* (replacing *Sûr* of FN I) first occurs here or in the closely related passage in *The Lost Road* (p. 66). Its first occurrence in the 'Silmarillion' tradition is in QS §143. The story of Sauron's coming to Númenor is changed from that in FN I, and it is explicit that he could not have come had he not been summoned. The story as told in the first version here, in which the ships returning from Middle-earth were cast upon Númenor far inland by a great wave, and Sauron stood upon a hill and 'preached a message of deliverance', is told in more detail in *The Lost Road*; but the second version in FN II, omitting the element of the great wave, looks as if it were substituted for the first almost immediately (on the significance of this see p. 9).

The temple to Morgoth is now raised upon the Mountain, of Ilúvatar in the midst of the land, and this (or in *The Lost Road*) is the first appearance of the Meneltarma. The story was later rejected: in the *Akallabêth* 'not even Sauron dared to defile the high place', and the temple was built in Armenelos (pp. 272–3).

§11     The addition in FN II, 'Therefore they built very high towers in those days', must be the first reference to the White Towers on Emyn Beraid, the Tower Hills. Cf. *The Lord of the Rings* Appendix A (I. iii), where it is told of the *palantír* of Emyn Beraid that 'Elendil set it there so that he could look back with "straight sight" and see Eressëa in the vanished West; but the bent seas below covered Númenor for ever.' Cf. also *Of the Rings of Power* in *The Silmarillion*, p. 292. But when the present text was written the *palantíri* had not (so far as one can tell) been conceived.

§14   The rewriting of the passage concerning Beleriand reinforces the suggestion in FN I that it remained a country less destroyed after the Great Battle than is described in the other texts: it was 'still in a measure blessed' – and moreover the Elves who remained in Middle-earth 'abode mostly in Beleriand'. Here Elendil 'Elf-friend' appears, displacing Amroth of FN I. It might be thought from the words 'in Beleriand there arose a king, who was of Númenórean race' that he was not a survivor of the Downfall; but this is clearly not the case. In *The Lost Road*, closely connected with FN II, Elendil (the father in the Númenórean incarnation of 'Elwin-Edwin') is a resolute foe of Sauron and his dominance in Númenor; and though *The Lost Road* breaks off before the sailing of Tar-kalion's fleet, Elendil must have been among those who 'sat in their ships upon the east coast of the land' (FN §9) and so escaped the Downfall.

Here is certainly the first appearance of Gil-galad, the Elf-king in Beleriand, descended from Fëanor (it would be interesting to know his parentage), and the story of the Last Alliance moves a stage further; and there seems no question but that it was in this manuscript that the name *Mordor*, the Black Country, first emerged in narrative.

(iv)

*The further development of The Fall of Númenor*

FN II was followed by a typescript made on my father's typewriter of that period, but not typed by him. This is seen from its being an exact copy of FN II after all corrections had been made to it, and from two or three misreadings of the manuscript. I have no doubt that the typescript was made soon afterwards. In itself it has no textual value, but my father used it as the basis for certain further changes.

Associated with it is a loose manuscript page bearing passages that relate closely to changes made to the typescript. There is here a textual development that has important bearings on the dating in general.

Two passages are in question. The first concerns §8 (which had remained unchanged from FN I, apart from the omission in FN II of the concluding sentence). The loose page has here two forms of a new version of the paragraph, of which the first, which was struck through, reads as follows:

Then Ilúvatar cast back the Great Sea west of Middle-earth and the Barren Land east of Middle-earth and made new lands and new seas where aforetime nought had been but the paths of the Sun and Moon. And the world was diminished; for Valinor and Eressëa were taken into the Realm of Hidden Things, and thereafter however far a man might sail he could never again reach the True West. For all lands old and new were equally distant from the centre of the earth. There was [flood and great confusion of waters, and seas covered what once was dry, and lands appeared where there had been deep seas,] and Beleriand fell into the sea in that time, all save the land where Beren and Lúthien had dwelt for a while, the land of Lindon beneath the western feet of the [*struck out*: Ered] Lunoronti.

(The section enclosed in square brackets is represented in the manuscript by a mark of omission, obviously meaning that the existing text was to be followed.) Here the words '[the Gods] bent back the edges of the Middle-earth' have disappeared; it is the Great Sea in the West and 'the Barren Land' in the East that are 'cast back' by Ilúvatar. It is now said that the new lands and new seas came into being 'where aforetime nought had been but the paths of the Sun and Moon' (i.e. at the roots of the world, see the *Ambarkanta* diagrams IV. 243, 245). This was in turn lost in the further rewriting (below), where the final and very brief statement found in the *Akallabêth* (p. 279) is reached.

This passage is very notable, since the drowning of all Beleriand west of Lindon is here ascribed to the cataclysm of the Downfall of Númenor; see the commentaries on FN I and II, §14. The name *Lunoronti* of the Blue Mountains has not occurred previously (but see the *Etymologies*, stem LUG²); and this is perhaps the first occurrence of the name *Lindon* for the ancient Ossiriand, or such of it as remained above the sea (see the commentary on QS §108).

The second form of this revised version of §8 follows immediately in the manuscript:

Then Ilúvatar cast back the Great Sea west of Middle-earth, and the Empty Land east of it, and new lands and new seas were made; and the world was diminished: for Valinor and Eressëa were taken from it into the realm of hidden things. And thereafter however a man might sail, he could never again reach the True West, but would come back weary at last to the place of his beginning; for all lands and seas were equally distant from the centre of the earth, and all roads were bent. There was flood and great confusion of waters in that time, and sea covered much that in the Elder Days had been dry, both in the West and East of Middle-earth.

Thus the passage concerning the drowning of Beleriand at the time of the Númenórean cataclysm and the survival of Lindon was again removed. In this form my father then copied it onto the typescript, with change of *Empty Land* to *Empty Lands*. (If this region, called in the first version *the Barren Land*, is to be related to the *Ambarkanta* map V (IV. 251) it must be what is there called *the Burnt Land of the Sun*; perhaps also *the Dark Land*, which is there shown as a new continent, formed from the southern part of *Pelmar* or Middle-earth (map IV) after the vast extension of the former inland sea of Ringil at the time of the breaking of

Utumno). – The expression *Elder Days* is not found in any writing of my father's before this.

The second passage is the concluding paragraph in FN II §14, concerning Beleriand and the Last Alliance. Here a few pencilled changes were made to the typescript: *Thû* was changed to *Sauron* except in the sentence 'that is in the Gnomish tongue named Thû', where *Thû* > *Gorthû* (see p. 338); 'in Beleriand there arose a king' > 'in Lindon . . .'; and Gil-galad is descended from Finrod, not Fëanor. The passage in the typescript was then struck through, with a direction to introduce a substitute. This substitute is found on the reverse of the loose page giving the two forms of the rewriting of §8, and was obviously written at the same time as those. It reads as follows:

But there remains a legend of Beleriand. Now that land had been broken in the Great Battle with Morgoth; and at the fall of Númenor and the change of the fashion of the world it perished; for the sea covered all that was left save some of the mountains that remained as islands, even up to the feet of Eredlindon. But that land where Lúthien had dwelt remained, and was called Lindon. A gulf of the sea came through it, and a gap was made in the Mountains through which the River Lhûn flowed out. But in the land that was left north and south of the gulf the Elves remained, and Gil-galad son of Felagund son of Finrod was their king. And they made Havens in the Gulf of Lhûn whence any of their people, or any other of the Elves that fled from the darkness and sorrow of Middle-earth, could sail into the True West and return no more. In Lindon Sauron had as yet no dominion. And it is said that the brethren Elendil and Valandil escaping from the fall of Númenor came at last to the mouths of the rivers that flowed into the Western Sea. And Elendil (that is Elf-friend), who had aforetime loved the folk of Eressëa, came to Lindon and dwelt there a while, and passed into Middle-earth and established a realm in the North. But Valandil sailed up the Great River Anduin and established another realm far to the South. But Sauron dwelt in Mordor the Black Country, and that was not very distant from Ondor the realm of Valandil; and Sauron made war against all Elves and all Men of Westernesse or others that aided them, and Valandil was hard pressed. Therefore Elendil and Gil-galad seeing that unless some stand were made Sauron would become lord of [?all] Middle-earth they took counsel together, and they made a great league. And Gil-galad and Elendil marched into the Middle-earth [?and gathered force of Men and Elves, and they assembled at Imladrist].

Towards the end the text degenerates into a scribble and the final words are a bit doubtful. If the name *Imladrist* is correctly interpreted there is certainly a further letter after the *s*, which must be a *t*. Cf. *The Tale of*

*Years* in *The Lord of the Rings* (Appendix B): Second Age 3431 'Gilgalad and Elendil march east to Imladris.'

All this passage was in turn struck through, and not copied into the typescript. It will be seen that it brings in the new matter concerning Beleriand and Lindon which appeared in the first form of the revision of §8 but was then removed (pp. 31–2); and in addition many important new elements have entered. Gil-galad is the son of Felagund; it is now explicit that Elendil was one of the survivors of Númenor, and he has a brother named Valandil (the name of his father in *The Lost Road*); the river Lhûn appears, and its gulf, and the gap in the Blue Mountains through which it flowed; the Elves of Lindon built havens on the Gulf of Lhûn; Elendil established a kingdom in the North, east of the mountains, and Valandil, sailing up the Anduin, founded his realm of Ondor not far from Mordor.

Now there is no question that the entire conception of Gondor arose in the course of the composition of *The Lord of the Rings*. Moreover my father pencilled the following notes (also struck through) at the end of the typescript:

> More of this is told in *The Lord of the Rings*
> Only alteration required is this:
> (1) Many Elves remained behind
> (2) Beleriand was all sunk except for a few islands = mountains, and part of Ossiriand (called Lindon) where Gil-galad dwelt.
> (3) Elrond remained with Gil-galad. Or else sailed back to Middle-earth. The Half-elven.

The second of these is decisive, since the passage last given clearly contains a working-up of this note; and it is clear that all the rewritings of the second version of *The Fall of Númenor* considered here come from several years later. FN II represents the form of the work at the time when *The Lord of the Rings* was begun. On the other hand, these revisions come from a time when it was a long way from completion, as is seen by the form *Ondor*, and by the brothers Elendil and Valandil, founders of the Númenórean kingdoms in Middle-earth.

Apart from these major passages of revision there were few other changes made to the typescript copy of FN II, and those very minor, save for the substitution of *Elros* for *Elrond* at both occurrences in §2. This belongs to the pre-*Lord of the Rings* period, as is seen from the appearance of Elros in the conclusion of QS (see p. 337, commentary on §28).\*

---

\*The third 'alteration' required (in the notes on the typescript of FN II), that 'Elrond remained with Gil-galad, or else sailed back to Middle-earth', presumably takes account of this change, and means that my father had not yet determined whether or not Elrond originally went to Númenor with his brother Elros.

My father next wrote a fine new manuscript incorporating the changes made to the typescript of FN II – but now wholly omitting the concluding passage (§14) concerning Beleriand and the Last Alliance, and ending with the words 'there were wars among the mighty of Middle-earth, of which only the echoes now remain.' This version, improved and altered in detail, shows however very little further advance in narrative substance, and clearly belongs to the same period as the revisions studied in this section.

# III

# THE LOST ROAD

## (i)

### *The opening chapters*

For the texts of *The Lost Road* and its relation to *The Fall of Númenor* see pp. 8–9. I give here the two completed chapters at the beginning of the work, following them with a brief commentary.

### Chapter I

### *A Step Forward. Young Alboin**

'Alboin! Alboin!'

There was no answer. There was no one in the play-room.

'Alboin!' Oswin Errol stood at the door and called into the small high garden at the back of his house. At length a young voice answered, sounding distant and like the answer of someone asleep or just awakened.

'Yes?'

'Where are you?'

'Here!'

'Where is "here"?'

'Here: up on the wall, father.'

Oswin sprang down the steps from the door into the garden, and walked along the flower-bordered path. It led after a turn to a low stone wall, screened from the house by a hedge. Beyond the stone wall there was a brief space of turf, and then a cliff-edge, beyond which outstretched, and now shimmering in a calm evening, the western sea. Upon the wall Oswin found his son, a boy about twelve years old, lying gazing out to sea with his chin in his hands.

'So there you are!' he said. 'You take a deal of calling. Didn't you hear me?'

'Not before the time when I answered,' said Alboin.

'Well, you must be deaf or dreaming,' said his father. 'Dream-

*The title was put in afterwards, as was that of Chapter II; see p. 78.

ing, it looks like. It is getting very near bed-time; so, if you want any story tonight, we shall have to begin at once.'

'I am sorry, father, but I was thinking.'

'What about?'

'Oh, lots of things mixed up: the sea, and the world, and Alboin.'

'Alboin?'

'Yes. I wondered why Alboin. Why am I called Alboin? They often ask me "Why Alboin?" at school, and they call me All-bone. But I am not, am I?'

'You look rather bony, boy; but you are not all bone, I am glad to say. I am afraid I called you Alboin, and that is why you are called it. I am sorry: I never meant it to be a nuisance to you.'

'But it is a *real* name, isn't it?' said Alboin eagerly. 'I mean, it means something, and *men* have been called it? It isn't just invented?'

'Of course not. It is just as real and just as good as Oswin; and it belongs to the same family, you might say. But no one ever bothered me about Oswin. Though I often used to get called Oswald by mistake. I remember how it used to annoy me, though I can't think why. I was rather particular about my name.'

They remained talking on the wall overlooking the sea; and did not go back into the garden, or the house, until bed-time. Their talk, as often happened, drifted into story-telling; and Oswin told his son the tale of Alboin son of Audoin, the Lombard king; and of the great battle of the Lombards and the Gepids, remembered as terrible even in the grim sixth century; and of the kings Thurisind and Cunimund, and of Rosamunda. 'Not a good story for near bed-time,' he said, ending suddenly with Alboin's drinking from the jewelled skull of Cunimund.

'I don't like that Alboin much,' said the boy. 'I like the Gepids better, and King Thurisind. I wish they had won. Why didn't you call me Thurisind or Thurismod?'

'Well, really mother had meant to call you Rosamund, only you turned up a boy. And she didn't live to help me choose another name, you know. So I took one out of that story, because it seemed to fit. I mean, the name doesn't belong only to that story, it is much older. Would you rather have been called Elf-friend? For that's what the name means.'

'No-o,' said Alboin doubtfully. 'I like names to mean something, but not to say something.'

'Well, I might have called you Ælfwine, of course; that is the

Old English form of it. I might have called you that, not only after
Ælfwine of Italy, but after all the Elf-friends of old; after Ælfwine,
King Alfred's grandson, who fell in the great victory in 937, and
Ælfwine who fell in the famous defeat at Maldon, and many other
Englishmen and northerners in the long line of Elf-friends. But I
gave you a latinized form. I think that is best. The old days of the
North are gone beyond recall, except in so far as they have been
worked into the shape of things as we know it, into Christendom.
So I took Alboin; for it is not Latin and not Northern, and that is
the way of most names in the West, and also of the men that bear
them. I might have chosen Albinus, for that is what they sometimes turned the name into; and it wouldn't have reminded your
friends of bones. But it is too Latin, and means something in
Latin. And you are not white or fair, boy, but dark. So Alboin you
are. And that is all there is to it, except bed.' And they went in.

But Alboin looked out of his window before getting into bed;
and he could see the sea beyond the edge of the cliff. It was a late
sunset, for it was summer. The sun sank slowly to the sea, and
dipped red beyond the horizon. The light and colour faded
quickly from the water: a chilly wind came up out of the West, and
over the sunset-rim great dark clouds sailed up, stretching huge
wings southward and northward, threatening the land.

'They look like the eagles of the Lord of the West coming upon
Númenor,' Alboin said aloud, and he wondered why. Though it
did not seem very strange to him. In those days he often made up
names. Looking on a familiar hill, he would see it suddenly
standing in some other time and story: 'the green shoulders of
Amon-ereb,' he would say. 'The waves are loud upon the shores of
Beleriand,' he said one day, when storm was piling water at the
foot of the cliff below the house.

Some of these names were really made up, to please himself
with their sound (or so he thought); but others seemed 'real', as if
they had not been spoken first by him. So it was with Númenor. 'I
like that,' he said to himself. 'I could think of a long story about the
land of Númenor.'

But as he lay in bed, he found that the story would not be
thought. And soon he forgot the name; and other thoughts
crowded in, partly due to his father's words, and partly to his own
day-dreams before.

'Dark Alboin,' he thought. 'I wonder if there is any Latin in me.
Not much, I think. I love the western shores, and the real sea – it

is quite different from the Mediterranean, even in stories. I wish there was no other side to it. There were darkhaired people who were not Latins. Are the Portuguese Latins? What is Latin? I wonder what kind of people lived in Portugal and Spain and Ireland and Britain in old days, very old days, before the Romans, or the Carthaginians. Before anybody else. I wonder what the man thought who was the first to see the western sea.'

Then he fell asleep, and dreamed. But when he woke the dream slipped beyond recall, and left no tale or picture behind, only the feeling that these had brought: the sort of feeling Alboin connected with long strange names. And he got up. And summer slipped by, and he went to school and went on learning Latin.

Also he learned Greek. And later, when he was about fifteen, he began to learn other languages, especially those of the North: Old English, Norse, Welsh, Irish. This was not much encouraged – even by his father, who was an historian. Latin and Greek, it seemed to be thought, were enough for anybody; and quite old-fashioned enough, when there were so many successful modern languages (spoken by millions of people); not to mention maths and all the sciences.

But Alboin liked the flavour of the older northern languages, quite as much as he liked some of the things written in them. He got to know a bit about linguistic history, of course; he found that you rather had it thrust on you anyway by the grammar-writers of 'unclassical' languages. Not that he objected: sound-changes were a hobby of his, at the age when other boys were learning about the insides of motor-cars. But, although he had some idea of what were supposed to be the relationships of European languages, it did not seem to him quite all the story. The languages he liked had a definite flavour – and to some extent a similar flavour which they shared. It seemed, too, in some way related to the atmosphere of the legends and myths told in the languages.

One day, when Alboin was nearly eighteen, he was sitting in the study with his father. It was autumn, and the end of summer holidays spent mostly in the open. Fires were coming back. It was the time in all the year when book-lore is most attractive (to those who really like it at all). They were talking 'language'. For Errol encouraged his boy to talk about anything he was interested in; although secretly he had been wondering for some time whether Northern languages and legends were not taking up more time and energy than their practical value in a hard world justified. 'But I had better know what is going on, as far as any father can,' he thought. 'He'll go on anyway, if he really has a bent – and it had better not be bent inwards.'

Alboin was trying to explain his feeling about 'language-atmosphere'. 'You get echoes coming through, you know,' he said, 'in odd words here and there – often very common words in their own language, but quite unexplained by the etymologists; and in the general shape and sound of all the words, somehow; as if something was peeping through from deep under the surface.'

'Of course, I am not a philologist,' said his father; 'but I never could see that there was much evidence in favour of ascribing language-changes to a *substratum*. Though I suppose underlying ingredients do have an influence, though it is not easy to define, on the final mixture in the case of peoples taken as a whole, different national talents and temperaments, and that sort of thing. But races, and cultures, are different from languages.'

'Yes,' said Alboin; 'but very mixed up, all three together. And after all, language goes back by a continuous tradition into the past, just as much as the other two. I often think that if you knew the living faces of any man's ancestors, a long way back, you might find some queer things. You might find that he got his nose quite clearly from, say, his mother's great-grandfather; and yet that something about his nose, its expression or its set or whatever you like to call it, really came down from much further back, from, say, his father's great-great-great-grandfather or greater. Anyway I like to go back – and not with race only, or culture only, or language; but with all three. I wish I could go back with the three that are mixed in us, father; just the plain Errols, with a little house in Cornwall in the summer. I wonder what one would see.'

'It depends how far you went back,' said the elder Errol. 'If you went back beyond the Ice-ages, I imagine you would find nothing in these parts; or at any rate a pretty beastly and uncomely race, and a tooth-and-nail culture, and a disgusting language with no echoes for you, unless those of food-noises.'

'Would you?' said Alboin. 'I wonder.'

'Anyway you can't go back,' said his father; 'except within the limits prescribed to us mortals. You can go back in a sense by honest study, long and patient work. You had better go in for archaeology as well as philology: they ought to go well enough together, though they aren't joined very often.'

'Good idea,' said Alboin. 'But you remember, long ago, you said I was not *all-bone*. Well, I want some mythology, as well. I want myths, not only bones and stones.'

'Well, you can have 'em! Take the whole lot on!' said his father laughing. 'But in the meanwhile you have a smaller job on hand. Your Latin needs improving (or so I am told), for school purposes. And scholarships are useful in lots of ways, especially for folk like you and me who go in for antiquated subjects. Your first shot is this winter, remember.'

'I wish Latin prose was not so important,' said Alboin. 'I am really much better at verses.'

'Don't go putting any bits of your *Eressëan*, or *Elf-latin*, or whatever you call it, into your verses at Oxford. It might scan, but it wouldn't pass.'

'Of course not!' said the boy, blushing. The matter was too private, even for private jokes. 'And don't go blabbing about *Eressëan* outside the partnership,' he begged; 'or I shall wish I had kept it quiet.'

'Well, you did pretty well. I don't suppose I should ever have heard about it, if you hadn't left your note-books in my study. Even so I don't know much about it. But, my dear lad, I shouldn't dream of blabbing, even if I did. Only don't waste too much time on it. I am afraid I am anxious about that schol[arship], not only from the highest motives. Cash is not too abundant.'

'Oh, I haven't done anything of that sort for a long while, at least hardly anything,' said Alboin.

'It isn't getting on too well, then?'

'Not lately. Too much else to do, I suppose. But I got a lot of jolly new words a few days ago: I am sure *lōmelindë* means *nightingale*, for instance, and certainly *lōmë* is *night* (though not *darkness*). The verb is very sketchy still. But –' He hesitated. Reticence (and uneasy conscience) were at war with his habit of what he called 'partnership with the pater', and his desire to unbosom the secret anyway. 'But, the real difficulty is that another language is coming through, as well. It seems to be related but quite different, much more – more Northern. *Alda* was a *tree* (a word I got a long time ago); in the new language it is *galadh*, and *orn*. The Sun and Moon seem to have similar names in both: *Anar* and *Isil* beside *Anor* and *Ithil*. I like first one, then the other, in different moods. *Beleriandic* is really very attractive; but it complicates things.'

'Good Lord!' said his father, 'this is serious! I will respect unsolicited secrets. But do have a conscience as well as a heart, and – moods. Or get a Latin and Greek mood!'

'I do. I have had one for a week, and I have got it now; a Latin one luckily, and Virgil in particular. So here we part.' He got up. 'I am going to do a bit of reading. I'll look in when I think you ought to go to bed.' He closed the door on his father's snort.

As a matter of fact Errol did not really like the parting shot. The affection in it warmed and saddened him. A late marriage had left him now on the brink of retirement from a schoolmaster's small pay to his smaller pension, just when Alboin was coming of University age. And he was also (he had begun to feel, and this year to admit in his heart) a tired man. He had never been a strong man. He would have liked to accompany Alboin a great deal further on the road, as a younger father probably would have done; but he did not somehow think he would be going very far. 'Damn it,' he said to himself, 'a boy of that age ought not to be thinking such things, worrying whether his father is getting enough rest. Where's my book?'

Alboin in the old play-room, turned into junior study, looked out into the dark. He did not for a long time turn to books. 'I wish life was not so short,' he thought. 'Languages take such a time, and so do all the things one wants to know about. And the pater, he is looking tired. I want him for years. If he lived to be a hundred I should be only about as old as he is now. and I should still want him. But he won't. I wish we could stop getting old. The pater could go on working and write that book he used to talk about, about Cornwall; and we could go on talking. He always plays up, even if he does not agree or understand. Bother *Eressëan*. I wish he hadn't mentioned it. I am sure I shall dream tonight; and it is so exciting. The Latin-mood will go. He is very decent about it, even though he thinks I am making it all up. If I were, I would stop it to please him. But it comes, and I simply can't let it slip when it does. Now there is Beleriandic.'

Away west the moon rode in ragged clouds. The sea glimmered palely out of the gloom, wide, flat, going on to the edge of the world. 'Confound you, dreams!' said Alboin. 'Lay off, and let me do a little patient work at least until December. A schol[arship] would brace the pater.'

He found his father asleep in his chair at half past ten. They went up to bed together. Alboin got into bed and slept with no shadow of a dream. The Latin-mood was in full blast after breakfast; and the weather allied itself with virtue and sent torrential rain.

## Chapter II
### *Alboin and Audoin*

Long afterwards Alboin remembered that evening, that had marked the strange, sudden, cessation of the Dreams. He had got a scholarship (the following year) and had 'braced the pater'. He had behaved himself moderately well at the university – not too many side-issues (at least not what he called too many); though neither the Latin nor the Greek mood had remained at all steadily to sustain him through 'Honour Mods.' They came back, of course, as soon as the exams were over. They would. He had switched over, all the same, to history, and had again 'braced the pater' with a 'first-class'. And the pater had needed bracing. Retirement proved quite different from a holiday: he had seemed just to slip slowly out. He had hung on just long enough to see Alboin into his first job: an assistant lecturership in a university college.

Rather disconcertingly the Dreams had begun again just before 'Schools', and were extraordinarly strong in the following vacation – the last he and his father had spent together in Cornwall. But at that time the Dreams had taken a new turn, for a while.

He remembered one of the last conversations of the old pleasant sort he had been able to have with the old man. It came back clearly to him now.

'How's the Eressëan Elf-latin, boy?' his father asked, smiling, plainly intending a joke, as one may playfully refer to youthful follies long atoned for.

'Oddly enough,' he answered, 'that hasn't been coming through lately. I have got a lot of different stuff. Some is beyond me, yet. Some might be Celtic, of a sort. Some seems like a very old form of Germanic; pre-runic, or I'll eat my cap and gown.'

The old man smiled, almost raised a laugh. 'Safer ground, boy, safer ground for an historian. But you'll get into trouble, if you let your cats out of the bag among the philologists – unless, of course, they back up the authorities.'

'As a matter of fact, I rather think they do,' he said.

'Tell me a bit, if you can without your note-books,' his father slyly said.

'*Westra lage wegas rehtas, nu isti sa wraithas.*' He quoted that, because it had stuck in his mind, though he did not understand it. Of course the mere sense was fairly plain: *a straight road lay westward, now it is bent.* He remembered waking up, and feeling it was somehow very significant. 'Actually I got a bit of plain Anglo-Saxon last night,' he went on. He thought Anglo-Saxon would please his father; it was a real historical language, of which the old man had once known a fair amount. Also the bit was very fresh in his mind, and was the longest and most connected he had yet had. Only that very morning he had waked up late, after a dreamful night, and had found himself saying the lines. He jotted them down at once, or they might have vanished (as usual) by breakfast-time, even though they were in a language he knew. Now waking memory had them secure.

> 'Thus cwæth Ælfwine Wídlást:
> Fela bith on Westwegum werum uncúthra
> wundra and wihta, wlitescéne land,
> eardgeard elfa, and ésa bliss.
> Lýt ænig wát hwylc his longath síe
> thám the eftsíthes eldo getwǽfeth.'

His father looked up and smiled at the name Ælfwine. He translated the lines for him; probably it was not necessary, but the old man had forgotten many other things he had once known much better than Anglo-Saxon.

'Thus said Ælfwine the far-travelled: "There is many a thing in the West-regions unknown to men, marvels and strange beings, a land fair and lovely, the homeland of the Elves, and the bliss of the Gods. Little doth any man know what longing is his whom old age cutteth off from return."'

He suddenly regretted translating the last two lines. His father looked up with an odd expression. 'The old know,' he said. 'But age does not cut us off from going away, from – from *forthsith*. There is no *eftsith*: we can't go back. You need not tell me that. But good for Ælfwine-Alboin. You could always do verses.'

Damn it – as if he would make up stuff like that, just to tell it to the old man, practically on his death-bed. His father had, in fact, died during the following winter.

On the whole he had been luckier than his father; in most ways, but not in one. He had reached a history professorship fairly early; but he had lost his wife, as his father had done, and had been left with an only child, a boy, when he was only twenty-eight.

He was, perhaps, a pretty good professor, as they go. Only in a small southern university, of course, and he did not suppose he would get a move. But at any rate he wasn't tired of being one; and history, and even teaching it, still seemed interesting (and fairly important). He did his duty, at least, or he hoped so. The boundaries were a bit vague. For, of course, he had gone on with the other things, legends and languages – rather odd for a history professor. Still there it was: he was fairly learned in such book-lore, though a lot of it was well outside the professional borders.

And the Dreams. They came and went. But lately they had been getting more frequent, and more – absorbing. But still tantalizingly linguistic. No tale, no remembered pictures; only the feeling that he had seen things and heard things that he wanted to see, very much, and would give much to see and hear again – and these fragments of words, sentences, verses. *Eressëan* as he called it as a boy – though he could not remember why he had felt so sure that that was the proper name – was getting pretty complete. He had a lot of Beleriandic, too, and was beginning to understand it, and its relation to Eressëan. And he had a lot of unclassifiable fragments, the meaning of which in many cases he did not know, through forgetting to jot it down while he knew it. And odd bits in recognizable languages. Those might be explained away, of course. But anyway nothing could be done about them: not publication or anything of that sort. He had an odd feeling that they were not essential: only occasional lapses of forgetfulness which took a linguistic form owing to some peculiarity of his own mental make-up. The real thing was the feeling the Dreams brought more and more insistently, and taking force from an alliance with the ordinary professional occupations of his mind. Surveying the last thirty years, he felt he could say that his most permanent mood, though often overlaid or sup-pressed, had been since childhood the desire *to go back*. To walk in Time, perhaps, as men walk on long roads; or to survey it, as men may see the world from a mountain, or the earth as a living map beneath an airship. But in any case to see with eyes and to hear with ears: to see the lie of old and even forgotten lands, to behold ancient men walking, and hear their languages as they spoke them, in the days before the days, when tongues of for-gotten lineage were heard in kingdoms long fallen by the shores of the Atlantic.

But nothing could be done about that desire, either. He used to be able, long ago, to talk about it, a little and not too seriously, to his father. But for a long while he had had no one to talk to about that sort of thing. But now there was Audoin. He was growing up. He was sixteen.

He had called his boy Audoin, reversing the Lombardic order. It seemed to fit. It belonged anyway to the same name-family, and went with his own name. And it was a tribute to the memory of his father – another reason for relinquishing Anglo-Saxon Eadwine, or even commonplace Edwin. Audoin had turned out remarkably like Alboin, as far as his memory of young Alboin went, or his penetration of the exterior of young Audoin. At any rate he seemed interested in the same things, and asked the same questions; though with much less inclination to words and names, and more to things and descriptions. Unlike his father he could draw, but was not good at 'verses'. Nonetheless he had, of course, eventually asked why he was called Audoin. He seemed rather glad to have escaped Edwin. But the question of meaning had not been quite so easy to answer. Friend of fortune, was it, or of fate, luck, wealth, blessedness? Which?

'I like *Aud*,' young Audoin had said – he was then about thirteen – 'if it means all that. A good beginning for a name. I wonder what Lombards looked like. Did they all have Long Beards?'

Alboin had scattered tales and legends all down Audoin's childhood and boyhood, like one laying a trail, though he was not clear what trail or where it led. Audoin was a voracious listener, as well (latterly) as a reader. Alboin was very tempted to share his own odd linguistic secrets with the boy. They could at least have some pleasant private fun. But he could sympathize with his own father now – there was a limit to time. Boys have a lot to do.

Anyway, happy thought, Audoin was returning from school tomorrow. Examination-scripts were nearly finished for this year for both of them. The examiner's side of the business was decidedly the stickiest (thought the professor), but he was nearly unstuck at last. They would be off to the coast in a few days, together.

There came a night, and Alboin lay again in a room in a house by the sea: not the little house of his boyhood, but the same sea. It was a calm night, and the water lay like a vast plain of chipped and polished flint, petrified under the cold light of the Moon. The path of moonlight lay from the shore to the edge of sight.

Sleep would not come to him, although he was eager for it. Not for rest – he was not tired; but because of last night's Dream. He hoped to complete a fragment that had come through vividly that morning. He had it at hand in a note-book by his bed-side; not that he was likely to forget it once it was written down.

*ar     sauron   tūle   nahamna* ... *lantier   turkildi*
and      ?      came      ?    ... they-fell    ?

*unuhuine* ... *tarkalion   ohtakāre   valannar* ...
under-Shadow ...  ?      war-made    on-Powers ...

*herunūmen   ilu   terhante* ... *ilūvatāren* ... *ëari*
Lord-of-West world broke ... of-Ilúvatar ... seas

*ullier   kilyanna* ... *nūmenōre   ataltane* ...
poured   in-Chasm ... Númenor   down-fell ...

Then there had seemed to be a long gap.

... *malle   tēra   lende   nūmenna   ilya   sī   maller*
... road   straight went Westward all   now   roads

*raikar* ..... *turkildi   rōmenna* ... *nuruhuine   mel-lumna*
bent  ..... ?    eastward ... Death-shadow us-is-heavy

... *vahāya   sin   atalante.*
... far-away now    ?

There were one or two new words here, of which he wanted to discover the meaning: it had escaped before he could write it down this morning. Probably they were names: *tarkalion* was almost certainly a king's name, for *tār* was common in royal names. It was curious how often the remembered snatches harped on the theme of a 'straight road'. What was *atalante*? It seemed to mean *ruin* or *downfall*, but also to be a name.

Alboin felt restless. He left his bed and went to the window. He stood there a long while looking out to sea; and as he stood a chill wind got up in the West. Slowly over the dark rim of sky and water's meeting clouds lifted huge heads, and loomed upwards, stretching out vast wings, south and north.

'They look like the eagles of the Lord of the West over Númenor,' he said aloud, and started. He had not purposed any words. For a moment he had felt the oncoming of a great disaster long foreseen. Now memory stirred, but could not be grasped. He shivered. He went back to bed and lay wondering. Suddenly the old desire came over him. It had been growing again for a long time, but he had not felt it like this, a feeling as vivid as hunger or thirst, for years, not since he was about Audoin's age.

'I wish there was a "Time-machine",' he said aloud. 'But Time is not to be conquered by machines. And I should go back, not forward; and I think backwards would be more possible.'

The clouds overcame the sky, and the wind rose and blew; and in his ears, as he fell asleep at last, there was a roaring in the leaves of many trees, and a roaring of long waves upon the shore. 'The storm is coming upon Númenor!' he said, and passed out of the waking world.

In a wide shadowy place he heard a voice. 'Elendil!' it said. 'Alboin, whither are you wandering?'
'Who are you?' he answered. 'And where are you?'
A tall figure appeared, as if descending an unseen stair towards him. For a moment it flashed through his thought that the face, dimly seen, reminded him of his father.
'I am with you. I was of Númenor, the father of many fathers before you. I am Elendil, that is in Eressëan "Elf-friend", and many have been called so since. You may have your desire.'
'What desire?'
'The long-hidden and the half-spoken: to go back.'
'But that cannot be, even if I wish it. It is against the law.'
'It is against the *rule*. Laws are commands upon the will and are binding. Rules are conditions; they may have exceptions.'
'But are there ever any exceptions?'
'Rules may be strict, yet they are the means, not the ends, of government. There are exceptions; for there is that which governs and is above the rules. Behold, it is by the chinks in the wall that light comes through, whereby men become aware of the light and therein perceive the wall and how it stands. The veil is woven, and each thread goes an appointed course, tracing a design; yet the tissue is not impenetrable, or the design would not be guessed; and if the design were not guessed, the veil would not be perceived, and all would dwell in darkness. But these are old parables, and I came not to speak such things. The world is not a machine that makes other machines after the fashion of Sauron. To each under the rule some unique fate is given, and he is excepted from that which is a rule to others. I ask if you would have your desire?'
'I would.'
'You ask not: how or upon what conditions.'
'I do not suppose I should understand how, and it does not seem to me necessary. We go forward, as a rule, but we do not know how. But what are the conditions?'
'That the road and the halts are prescribed. That you cannot return at your wish, but only (if at all) as it may be ordained. For

you shall not be as one reading a book or looking in a mirror, but as one walking in living peril. Moreover you shall not adventure yourself alone.'

'Then you do not advise me to accept? You wish me to refuse out of fear?'

'I do not counsel, yes or no. I am not a counsellor. I am a messenger, a permitted voice. The wishing and the choosing are for you.'

'But I do not understand the conditions, at least not the last. I ought to understand them all clearly.'

'You must, if you choose to go back, take with you Herendil, that is in other tongue Audoin, your son; for you are the ears and he is the eyes. But you may not ask that he shall be protected from the consequences of your choice, save as your own will and courage may contrive.'

'But I can ask him, if he is willing?'

'He would say yes, because he loves you and is bold; but that would not resolve your choice.'

'And when can I, or we, go back?'

'When you have made your choice.'

The figure ascended and receded. There was a roaring as of seas falling from a great height. Alboin could still hear the tumult far away, even after his waking eyes roamed round the room in the grey light of morning. There was a westerly gale blowing. The curtains of the open window were drenched, and the room was full of wind.

He sat silent at the breakfast-table. His eyes strayed continually to his son's face, watching his expressions. He wondered if Audoin ever had any Dreams. Nothing that left any memory, it would appear. Audoin seemed in a merry mood, and his own talk was enough for him, for a while. But at length he noticed his father's silence, unusual even at breakfast.

'You look glum, father,' he said. 'Is there some knotty problem on hand?'

'Yes – well no, not really,' answered Alboin. 'I think I was thinking, among other things, that it was a gloomy day, and not a good end to the holidays. What are you going to do?'

'Oh, I say!' exclaimed Audoin. 'I thought you loved the wind. I do. Especially a good old West-wind. I am going along the shore.'

'Anything on?'

'No, nothing special – just the wind.'

'Well, what about the beastly wind?' said Alboin, unaccountably irritated.

The boy's face fell. 'I don't know,' he said. 'But I like to be in it, especially by the sea; and I thought you did.' There was a silence.

After a while Audoin began again, rather hesitatingly: 'Do you remember the other day upon the cliffs near Predannack, when those odd clouds came up in the evening, and the wind began to blow?'

'Yes,' said Alboin in an unencouraging tone.

'Well, you said when we got home that it seemed to remind you of something, and that the wind seemed to blow through you, like, like, a legend you couldn't catch. And you felt, back in the quiet, as if you had listened to a long tale, which left you excited, though it left absolutely no *pictures* at all.'

'Did I?' said Alboin. 'I can remember feeling very cold, and being glad to get back to a fire.' He immediately regretted it, and felt ashamed. For Audoin said no more; though he felt certain that the boy had been making an opening to say something more, something that was on his mind. But he could not help it. He could not talk of such things to-day. He felt cold. He wanted peace, not wind.

Soon after breakfast Audoin went out, announcing that he was off for a good tramp, and would not be back at any rate before tea-time. Alboin remained behind. All day last night's vision remained with him, something different from the common order of dreams. Also it was (for him) curiously unlinguistic – though plainly related, by the name Númenor, to his language dreams. He could not say whether he had conversed with Elendil in Eressëan or English.

He wandered about the house restlessly. Books would not be read, and pipes would not smoke. The day slipped out of his hand, running aimlessly to waste. He did not see his son, who did not even turn up for tea, as he had half promised to do. Dark seemed to come unduly early.

In the late evening Alboin sat in his chair by the fire. 'I dread this choice,' he said to himself. He had no doubt that there was really a choice to be made. He would have to choose, one way or another, however he represented it to himself. Even if he dismissed the Dream as what is called 'a mere dream', it would be a choice – a choice equivalent to *no*.

'But I cannot make up my mind to *no*,' he thought. 'I think, I am almost sure, Audoin would say *yes*. And he will know of my choice sooner or later. It is getting more and more difficult to hide my thoughts from him: we are too closely akin, in many ways besides blood, for secrets. The secret would become unbearable, if I tried to keep it. My desire would become doubled through feeling that *I might have*, and become intolerable. And Audoin would probably feel I had robbed him through funk.

'But it is dangerous, perilous in the extreme – or so I am warned. I don't mind for myself. But for Audoin. But is the peril any greater than fatherhood lets in? It is perilous to come into the world at any point in Time. Yet I feel the shadow of this peril more heavily. Why? Because it is an exception to the rules? Or am I experiencing a choice backwards: the peril of fatherhood repeated? Being a father twice to the same person would make one think. Perhaps I am already moving back. I don't know. I wonder. Fatherhood is a choice, and yet it is not wholly by a man's will. Perhaps this peril is my choice, and yet also outside my will. I don't know. It is getting very dark. How loud the wind is. There is storm over Númenor.' Alboin slept in his chair.

He was climbing steps, up, up on to a high mountain. He felt, and thought he could hear, Audoin following him, climbing behind him. He halted, for it seemed somehow that he was again in the same place as on the previous night; though no figure could be seen.

'I have chosen,' he said. 'I will go back with Herendil.'

Then he lay down, as if to rest. Half-turning: 'Good night!' he murmured. 'Sleep well, Herendil! We start when the summons comes.'

'You have chosen,' a voice said above him. 'The summons is at hand.'

Then Alboin seemed to fall into a dark and a silence, deep and absolute. It was as if he had left the world completely, where all silence is on the edge of sound, and filled with echoes, and where all rest is but repose upon some greater motion. He had left the world and gone out. He was silent and at rest: a point.

He was poised; but it was clear to him that he had only to will it, and he would move.

'Whither?' He perceived the question, but neither as a voice from outside, nor as one from within himself.

'To whatever place is appointed. Where is Herendil?'

'Waiting. The motion is yours.'

'Let us move!'

Audoin tramped on, keeping within sight of the sea as much as he could. He lunched at an inn, and then tramped on again, further than he had intended. He was enjoying the wind and the rain, yet he was filled with a curious disquiet. There had been something odd about his father this morning.

'So disappointing,' he said to himself. 'I particularly wanted to have a long tramp with him to-day. We talk better walking, and I really must have a chance of telling him about the Dreams. I can talk about that sort of thing to my father, if we both get into the mood together. Not that he is usually at all difficult – seldom like to-day. He usually takes you as you mean it: joking or serious; doesn't mix the two, or laugh in the wrong places. I have never known him so frosty.'

He tramped on. 'Dreams,' he thought. 'But not the usual sort, quite different: very vivid; and though never quite repeated, all gradually fitting into a story. But a sort of phantom story with no explanations. Just pictures, but not a sound, not a word. Ships coming to land. Towers on the shore. Battles, with swords glinting but silent. And there is that ominous picture: the great temple on the mountain, smoking like a volcano. And that awful vision of the chasm in the seas, a whole land slipping sideways, mountains rolling over; dark ships fleeing into the dark. I want to tell someone about it, and get some kind of sense into it. Father would help: we could make up a good yarn together out of it. If I knew even the name of the place, it would turn a nightmare into a story.'

Darkness began to fall long before he got back. 'I hope father will have had enough of himself and be chatty to-night,' he thought. 'The fireside is next best to a walk for discussing dreams.' It was already night as he came up the path, and saw a light in the sitting-room.

He found his father sitting by the fire. The room seemed very still, and quiet – and too hot after a day in the open. Alboin sat, his head rested on one arm. His eyes were closed. He seemed asleep. He made no sign.

Audoin was creeping out of the room, heavy with disappointment. There was nothing for it but an early bed, and perhaps better luck tomorrow. As he reached the door, he thought he heard the chair creak, and then his father's voice (far away and rather strange in tone) murmuring something: it sounded like *herendil*.

He was used to odd words and names slipping out in a murmur

from his father. Sometimes his father would spin a long tale round them. He turned back hopefully.

'Good night!' said Alboin. 'Sleep well, Herendil! We start when the summons comes.' Then his head fell back against the chair. 'Dreaming,' thought Audoin. 'Good night!'

And he went out, and stepped into sudden darkness.

### Commentary on Chapters I and II

Alboin's biography sketched in these chapters is in many respects closely modelled on my father's own life – though Alboin was not an orphan, and my father was not a widower. Dates pencilled on the covering page of the manuscript reinforce the strongly biographical element: Alboin was born on February 4, (1891 >) 1890, two years earlier than my father. Audoin was born in September 1918.

'Honour Mods.' (i.e. 'Honour Moderations'), referred to at the beginning of Chapter II, are the first of the two examinations taken in the Classical languages at Oxford, after two years (see Humphrey Carpenter, *Biography*, p. 62); 'Schools', in the same passage, is a name for the final Oxford examinations in all subjects.

Alboin's father's name *Oswin* is 'significant': *ós* 'god' and *wine* 'friend' (see IV. 208, 212); Elendil's father was *Valandil* (p. 60). That *Errol* is to be associated in some way with *Eriol* (the Elves' name for Ælfwine the mariner, IV. 206) must be allowed to be a possibility.*

### The Lombardic legend

The Lombards ('Long-beards': Latin *Langobardi*, Old English *Long-beardan*) were a Germanic people renowned for their ferocity. From their ancient homes in Scandinavia they moved southwards, but very little is known of their history before the middle of the sixth century. At that time their king was *Audoin*, the form of his name in the *Historia Langobardorum* by the learned Paul the Deacon, who died about 790. *Audoin* and Old English *Éadwine* (later *Edwin*) show an exact correspondence, are historically the same name (Old English *éa* derived from the original diphthong *au*). On the meaning of *éad* see p. 46, and cf. *Éadwine* as a name in Old English of the Noldor, IV. 212.

Audoin's son was *Alboin*, again corresponding exactly to Old English *Ælfwine* (*Elwin*). The story that Oswin Errol told his son (p. 37) is known from the work of Paul the Deacon. In the great battle between the Lombards and another Germanic people, the Gepids, Alboin son of Audoin slew Thurismod, son of the Gepid king Thurisind, in single combat; and when the Lombards returned home after their victory they

---

*It is worth mentioning that Oswin Errol's frequent address to Alboin as 'boy' is not intended to suggest an aloofly schoolmasterish tone. My father frequently used it to his sons as a term of friendship and affection.

asked Audoin to give his son the rank of a companion of his table, since it was by his valour that they had won the day. But this Audoin would not do, for, he said, 'it is not the custom among us that the king's son should sit down with his father before he has first received weapons from the king of some other people.' When Alboin heard this he went with forty young men of the Lombards to king Thurisind to ask this honour from him. Thurisind welcomed him, invited him to the feast, and seated him at his right hand, where his dead son Thurismod used to sit.

But as the feast went on Thurisind began to think of his son's death, and seeing Alboin his slayer in his very place his grief burst forth in words: 'Very pleasant to me is the seat,' he said, 'but hard is it to look upon him who sits in it.' Roused by these words the king's second son Cunimund began to revile the Lombard guests; insults were uttered on both sides, and swords were grasped. But on the very brink Thurisind leapt up from the table, thrust himself between the Gepids and the Lombards, and threatened to punish the first man who began the fight. Thus he allayed the quarrel; and taking the arms of his dead son he gave them to Alboin, and sent him back in safety to his father's kingdom.

It is agreed that behind this Latin prose tale of Paul the Deacon, as also behind his story of Alboin's death, there lies a heroic lay: as early a vestige of such ancient Germanic poetry as we possess.

Audoin died some ten years after the battle, and Alboin became king of the Lombards in 565. A second battle was fought against the Gepids, in which Alboin slew their king Cunimund and took his daughter Rosamunda captive. At Easter 568 Alboin set out for the conquest of Italy; and in 572 he was murdered. In the story told by Paul the Deacon, at a banquet in Verona Alboin gave his queen Rosamunda wine to drink in a cup made from the skull of king Cunimund, and invited her to drink merrily with her father ('and if this should seem to anyone impossible,' wrote Paul, 'I declare that I speak the truth in Christ: I have seen [Radgisl] the prince holding the very cup in his hand on a feastday and showing it to those who sat at the table with him.')

Here Oswin Errol ended the story, and did not tell his son how Rosamunda exacted her revenge. The outcome of her machinations was that Alboin was murdered in his bed, and his body was buried 'at the going up of the stairs which are near to the palace,' amid great lamentation of the Lombards. His tomb was opened in the time of Paul the Deacon by Gislbert *dux Veronensium*, who took away Alboin's sword and other gear that was buried with him; 'wherefore he used to boast to the ignorant with his usual vanity that he has seen Alboin face to face.'

The fame of this formidable king was such that, in the words of Paul, 'even down to our own day, among the Bavarians and the Saxons and other peoples of kindred speech, his open hand and renown, his success and courage in war, are celebrated in their songs.' An extraordinary testimony to this is found in the ancient English poem *Widsith*, where occur the following lines:

Swylce ic wæs on Eatule mid Ælfwine:
se hæfde moncynnes mine gefræge
leohteste hond lofes to wyrcenne,
heortan unhneaweste hringa gedales,
beorhta beaga, bearn Eadwines.

(I was in Italy with Alboin: of all men of whom I have heard he had the hand most ready for deeds of praise, the heart least niggard in the giving of rings, of shining armlets, the son of Audoin.)*

In my father's letter of 1964 (given on pp. 7–8) he wrote as if it had been his intention to find one of the earlier incarnations of the father and son in the Lombard story: 'It started with a father-son affinity between Edwin and Elwin of the present, and was supposed to go back into legendary time by way of an Eädwine and Ælfwine of circa A.D. 918, *and Audoin and Alboin of Lombardic legend* . . .' But there is no suggestion that at the time this was any more than a passing thought; see further pp. 77–8.

*The two Englishmen named Ælfwine* (p. 38). King Alfred's youngest son was named Æthelweard, and it is recorded by the twelfth century historian William of Malmesbury that Æthelweard's sons Ælfwine and Æthelwine both fell at the battle of Brunanburh in 937.

Years later my father celebrated the Ælfwine who died at Maldon in *The Homecoming of Beorhtnoth*, where Torhthelm and Tídwald find his corpse among the slain: 'And here's Ælfwine: barely bearded, and his battle's over.'

*Oswin Errol's reference to a 'substratum'* (p. 40). Put very simply, the *substratum* theory attributes great importance, as an explanation of linguistic change, to the influence exerted on language when a people abandons their own former speech and adopts another; for such a people will retain their habitual modes of articulation and transfer them to the new language, thus creating a *substratum* underlying it. Different *substrata* acting upon a widespread language in different areas is therefore regarded as a fundamental cause of divergent phonetic change.

*The Old English verses of Ælfwine Wídlást* (p. 44). These verses, in identical form except for certain features of spelling, were used in the title-pages to the *Quenta Silmarillion* (p. 203); see also p. 103.

*The generous heart of Alboin, the hand ready for deeds of praise, made a different impression on the stricken population of Italy in the sixth century. From the walls of Rome Pope Gregory the Great watched men being led away by 'the unspeakable Lombards', tied together at the neck to be sold as slaves; and in one of his letters he welcomed the advent of bubonic plague, for 'when we consider the way in which other men have died we find a solace in reflecting on the form of death that threatens us. What mutilations, what cruelties we have seen inflicted upon men, for which death is the only cure, and in the midst of which life is a torture!'

*Names and words in the Elvish languages.* Throughout, the term *Eressëan* was a replacement of *Númenórean.* Perhaps to be compared is FN II, §2: 'Yet they [the Númenóreans] took on the speech of the Elves of the Blessed Realm, as it was and is in Eressëa.' The term 'Elf-latin', applied by Alboin to 'Eressëan' (pp. 41, 43), is found in the *Lhammas* (p. 172). There it refers to the archaic speech of the First Kindred of the Elves (the Lindar), which 'became early fixed . . . as a language of high speech and of writing, and as a common speech among all Elves; and all the folk of Valinor learned and knew this language.' It was called *Qenya*, the Elvish tongue, *tarquesta* high-speech, and *parmalambë* the book-tongue. But it is not explained in *The Lost Road* why Alboin should have called the language that 'came through' to him by this term.

*Amon-ereb* (p. 38): the rough draft of this passage had *Amon Gwareth*, changed more than once and ending with *Amon Thoros*. *Amon Ereb* (the Lonely Hill) is found in the *Annals of Beleriand* (p. 143, annal 340) and in QS §113.

'The shores of *Beleriand*' (p. 38): the draft has here 'the rocks of the *Falassë*.' The form *Falassë* occurs on the *Ambarkanta* map IV (IV. 249).

'*Alda* was a *tree* (a word I got a long time ago)' (p. 41). *Alda* 'tree' is found in the very early 'dictionary' (I. 249), where also occurs the word *lómë*, which Alboin also refers to here, with the meanings 'dusk, gloom, darkness' (I. 255).

*Anar, Isil*, and *Anor, Ithil* (p. 41): in QS §75 the names of the Sun and Moon given by the Gods are *Úrin* and *Isil*, and by the Elves *Anar* and *Rana* (see the commentary on that passage).

The Eressëan fragment concerning the Downfall of Númenor and the Straight Road (p. 47) is slightly different in the draft text:

> Ar Sauron lende nûmenorenna...lantie nu huine...ohtakárie valannar...manwe ilu terhante.  eari lantier kilyanna nûmenor atalante...malle tēra lende nûmenna, ilya si maller raikar. Turkildi rómenna...nuruhuine me lumna.
> And Sauron came to-Númenor...fell under Shadow...war-made on-Powers...  ?  ? broke.  seas fell into-Chasm.  Númenor down-fell.  road straight went westward, all now roads bent.  ? eastward.  Death-shadow us is-heavy.

The name *Tar-kalion* is here not present, but *Sauron* is (see p. 9), and is interpreted as being a name. Most notably, this version has *manwe* (which Alboin could not interpret) for *herunúmen* 'Lord-of-West' of the later; on this see p. 75.

On the name *Herendil* (= Audoin, Eadwine) see the *Etymologies*, stem KHER.

(ii)

*The Númenórean chapters*

My father said in his letter of 1964 on the subject that 'in my tale *we were to come at last* to Amandil and Elendil leaders of the loyal party in Númenor, when it fell under the domination of Sauron.' It is nonetheless plain that he did not reach this conception until *after* the extant narrative had been mostly written, or even brought to the point where it was abandoned. At the end of Chapter II the Númenórean story is obviously just about to begin, and the Númenórean chapters were originally numbered continuously with the opening ones. On the other hand the decision to postpone Númenor and make it the conclusion and climax to the book had already been taken when *The Lost Road* went to Allen and Unwin in November 1937.

Since the Númenórean episode was left unfinished, this is a convenient point to mention an interesting note that my father presumably wrote while it was in progress. This says that when the first 'adventure' (i.e. Númenor) is over 'Alboin is still precisely in his chair and Audoin just shutting the door.'

With the postponement of Númenor the chapter-numbers were changed, but this has no importance and I therefore number these 'III' and 'IV'; they have no titles. In this case I have found it most convenient to annotate the text by numbered notes.

## Chapter III

Elendil was walking in his garden, but not to look upon its beauty in the evening light. He was troubled and his mind was turned inward. His house with its white tower and golden roof glowed behind him in the sunset, but his eyes were on the path before his feet. He was going down to the shore, to bathe in the blue pools of the cove beyond his garden's end, as was his custom at this hour. And he looked also to find his son Herendil there. The time had come when he must speak to him.

He came at length to the great hedge of *lavaralda*[1] that fenced the garden at its lower, western, end. It was a familiar sight, though the years could not dim its beauty. It was seven twelves of years[2] or more since he had planted it himself when planning his garden before his marriage; and he had blessed his good fortune. For the seeds had come from Eressëa far westward, whence ships came seldom already in those days, and now they came no more. But the spirit of that blessed land and its fair people remained still in the trees that had grown from those seeds: their long green leaves were golden on the undersides, and as a breeze off the water stirred them they whispered with a sound of many soft voices, and glistened like sunbeams on rippling waves. The flowers were pale with a yellow flush, and laid thickly on the branches like a sunlit snow; and their odour filled all the lower garden, faint but clear. Mariners in the old days said that the scent of *lavaralda* could be felt on the air long ere the land of Eressëa could be seen, and that it brought a desire of rest and great content. He had seen the trees in flower day after day, for they rested from flowering only at rare intervals. But now, suddenly, as he passed, the scent struck him with a keen fragrance, at once known and utterly strange. He seemed for a moment never to have smelled it before: it pierced the troubles of his mind, bewildering, bringing no familiar content, but a new disquiet.

'Eressëa, Eressëa!' he said. 'I wish I were there; and had not been fated to dwell in Númenor³ half-way between the worlds. And least of all in these days of perplexity!'

He passed under an arch of shining leaves, and walked swiftly down rock-hewn steps to the white beach. Elendil looked about him, but he could not see his son. A picture rose in his mind of Herendil's white body, strong and beautiful upon the threshold of early manhood, cleaving the water, or lying on the sand glistening in the sun. But Herendil was not there, and the beach seemed oddly empty.

Elendil stood and surveyed the cove and its rocky walls once more; and as he looked, his eyes rose by chance to his own house among trees and flowers upon the slopes above the shore, white and golden, shining in the sunset. And he stopped and gazed: for suddenly the house stood there, as a thing at once real and visionary, as a thing in some other time and story, beautiful, beloved, but strange, awaking desire as if it were part of a mystery that was still hidden. He could not interpret the feeling.

He sighed. 'I suppose it is the threat of war that maketh me look upon fair things with such disquiet,' he thought. 'The shadow of fear is between us and the sun, and all things look as if they were already lost. Yet they are strangely beautiful thus seen. I do not know. I wonder. A Númenórë! I hope the trees will blossom on your hills in years to come as they do now; and your towers will stand white in the Moon and yellow in the Sun. I wish it were not hope, but assurance – that assurance we used to have before the Shadow. But where is Herendil? I must see him and speak to him, more clearly than we have spoken yet. Ere it is too late. The time is getting short.'

'Herendil!' he called, and his voice echoed along the hollow shore above the soft sound of the light-falling waves. 'Herendil!' And even as he called, he seemed to hear his own voice, and to mark that it was strong and curiously melodious. 'Herendil!' he called again.

At length there was an answering call: a young voice very clear came from some distance away – like a bell out of a deep cave.

'*Man-ie, atto, man-ie?*'

For a brief moment it seemed to Elendil that the words were strange. '*Man-ie, atto?* What is it, father?' Then the feeling passed.

'Where art thou?'

'Here!'

'I cannot see thee.'

'I am upon the wall, looking down on thee.'

Elendil looked up; and then swiftly climbed another flight of stone steps at the northern end of the cove. He came out upon a flat space smoothed and levelled on the top of the projecting spur of rock. Here there was room to lie in the sun, or sit upon a wide stone seat with its back against the cliff, down the face of which there fell a cascade of trailing stems rich with garlands of blue and silver flowers. Flat upon the stone with his chin in his hands lay a youth. He was looking out to sea, and did not turn his head as his father came up and sat down on the seat.

'Of what art thou dreaming, Herendil, that thy ears hear not?'

'I am thinking; I am not dreaming. I am a child no longer.'

'I know thou art not,' said Elendil; 'and for that reason I wished to find thee and speak with thee. Thou art so often out and away, and so seldom at home these days.'

He looked down on the white body before him. It was dear to him, and beautiful. Herendil was naked, for he had been diving from the high point, being a daring diver and proud of his skill. It seemed suddenly to Elendil that the lad had grown over night, almost out of knowledge.

'How thou dost grow!' he said. 'Thou hast the makings of a mighty man, and have nearly finished the making.'

'Why dost thou mock me?' said the boy. 'Thou knowest I am dark, and smaller than most others of my year. And that is a trouble to me. I stand barely to the shoulder of Almáriel, whose hair is of shining gold, and she is a maiden, and of my own age. We hold that we are of the blood of kings, but I tell thee thy friends' sons make a jest of me and call me *Terendul*⁴ – slender and dark;

and they say I have Eressëan blood, or that I am half-Noldo. And that is not said with love in these days. It is but a step from being called half a Gnome to being called Godfearing; and that is dangerous.'⁵

Elendil sighed. 'Then it must have become perilous to be the son of him that is named *elendil*; for that leads to Valandil, God-friend, who was thy father's father.'⁶

There was a silence. At length Herendil spoke again: 'Of whom dost thou say that our king, Tarkalion, is descended?'

'From Eärendel the mariner, son of Tuor the mighty who was lost in these seas.'⁷

'Why then may not the king do as Eärendel from whom he is come? They say that he should follow him, and complete his work.'

'What dost thou think that they mean? Whither should he go, and fulfil what work?'

'Thou knowest. Did not Eärendel voyage to the uttermost West, and set foot in that land that is forbidden to us? He doth not die, or so songs say.'

'What callest thou Death? He did not return. He forsook all whom he loved, ere he stepped on that shore.⁸ He saved his kindred by losing them.'

'Were the Gods wroth with him?'

'Who knoweth? For he came not back. But he did not dare that deed to serve Melko, but to defeat him; to free men from Melko, not from the Lords; to win us the earth, not the land of the Lords. And the Lords heard his prayer and arose against Melko. And the earth is ours.'

'They say now that the tale was altered by the Eressëans, who are slaves of the Lords: that in truth Eärendel was an adventurer, and showed us the way, and that the Lords took him captive for that reason; and his work is perforce unfinished. Therefore the son of Eärendel, our king, should complete it. They wish to do what has been long left undone.'

'What is that?'

'Thou knowest: to set foot in the far West, and not withdraw it. To conquer new realms for our race, and ease the pressure of this peopled island, where every road is trodden hard, and every tree and grass-blade counted. To be free, and masters of the world. To escape the shadow of sameness, and of ending. We would make our king Lord of the West: *Nuaran Númenóren*.⁹ Death comes here slow and seldom; yet it cometh. The land is only a cage gilded to look like Paradise.'

'Yea, so I have heard others say,' said Elendil. 'But what knowest thou of Paradise? Behold, our wandering words have come unguided to the point of my purpose. But I am grieved to find thy mood is of this sort, though I feared it might be so. Thou art my only son, and my dearest child, and I would have us at one in all our choices. But choose we must, thou as well as I – for at thy last birthday thou became subject to arms and the king's service. We must choose between Sauron and the Lords (or One Higher). Thou knowest, I suppose, that all hearts in Númenor are not drawn to Sauron?'

• 'Yes. There are fools even in Númenor,' said Herendil, in a lowered voice. 'But why speak of such things in this open place? Do you wish to bring evil on me?'

'I bring no evil,' said Elendil. 'That is thrust upon us: the choice between evils: the first fruits of war. But look, Herendil! Our house is one of wisdom and guarded learning; and was long revered for it. I followed my father, as I was able. Dost thou follow me? What dost thou know of the history of the world or Númenor? Thou art but four twelves,[10] and wert but a small child when Sauron came. Thou dost not understand what days were like before then. Thou canst not choose in ignorance.'

'But others of greater age and knowledge than mine – or thine – have chosen,' said Herendil. 'And they say that history confirmeth them, and that Sauron hath thrown a new light on history. Sauron knoweth history, all history.'

'Sauron knoweth, verily; but he twisteth knowledge. Sauron is a liar!' Growing anger caused Elendil to raise his voice as he spoke. The words rang out as a challenge.

'Thou art mad,' said his son, turning at last upon his side and facing Elendil, with dread and fear in his eyes. 'Do not say such things to me! They might, they might ...'

'Who are they, and what might they do?' said Elendil, but a chill fear passed from his son's eyes to his own heart.

'Do not ask! And do not speak – so loud!' Herendil turned away, and lay prone with his face buried in his hands. 'Thou knowest it is dangerous – to us all. Whatever he be, Sauron is mighty, and hath ears. I fear the dungeons. And I love thee, I love thee. *Atarinya tye-meláne.*'

*Atarinya tye-meláne*, my father, I love thee: the words sounded strange, but sweet: they smote Elendil's heart. '*A yonya inye tye-méla*: and I too, my son, I love thee,' he said, feeling each syllable strange but vivid as he spoke it. 'But let us go within! It is too late to bathe. The sun is all but gone. It is bright there westwards in the gardens of the Gods. But twilight and the dark are coming here, and the dark is no longer wholesome in this land. Let us go home. I must tell and ask thee much this evening – behind closed doors, where maybe thou wilt feel safer.' He looked towards the sea, which he loved, longing to bathe his body in it, as though to wash away weariness and care. But night was coming.

The sun had dipped, and was fast sinking in the sea. There was fire upon far waves, but it faded almost as it was kindled. A chill wind came suddenly out of the West ruffling the yellow water off shore. Up over the fire-lit rim dark clouds reared; they stretched out great wings, south and north, and seemed to threaten the land.

Elendil shivered. 'Behold, the eagles of the Lord of the West are coming with threat to Númenor,' he murmured.

'What dost thou say?' said Herendil. 'Is it not decreed that the king of Númenor shall be called Lord of the West?'

'It is decreed by the king; but that does not make it so,' answered Elendil. 'But I meant not to speak aloud my heart's foreboding. Let us go!'

The light was fading swiftly as they passed up the paths of the garden amid flowers pale and luminous in the twilight. The trees were shedding sweet night-scents. A *lómelindë* began its thrilling bird-song by a pool.

Above them rose the house. Its white walls gleamed as if moonlight was imprisoned in their substance; but there was no moon yet, only a cool light, diffused and shadowless. Through the clear sky like fragile glass small stars stabbed their white flames. A voice from a high window came falling down like silver into the pool of twilight where they walked. Elendil knew the voice: it was the voice of Fíriel, a maiden of his household, daughter of Orontor. His heart sank, for Fíriel was dwelling in his house because Orontor had departed. Men said he was on a long voyage. Others said that he had fled the displeasure of the king. Elendil knew that he was on a mission from which he might never return, or return too late.[11] And he loved Orontor, and Fíriel was fair.

Now her voice sang an even-song in the Eressëan tongue, but made by men, long ago. The nightingale ceased. Elendil stood still to listen; and the words came to him, far off and strange, as some melody in archaic speech sung sadly in a forgotten twilight in the beginning of man's journey in the world.

*Ilu Ilúvatar en káre eldain a firimoin*
*ar antaróta mannar Valion: númessier.....*

The Father made the World for elves and mortals, and he gave
it into the hands of the Lords, who are in the West.

So sang Fíriel on high, until her voice fell sadly to the question
with which that song ends: *man táre antáva nin Ilúvatar,*
*Ilúvatar, enyáre tar i tyel íre Anarinya qeluva?* What will
Ilúvatar, O Ilúvatar, give me in that day beyond the end, when
my Sun faileth?'[12]
'*E man antaváro?* What will he give indeed?' said Elendil; and
stood in sombre thought.

'She should not sing that song out of a window,' said Herendil,
breaking the silence. 'They sing it otherwise now. Melko cometh
back, they say, and the king shall give us the Sun forever.'

'I know what they say,' said Elendil. 'Do not say it to thy father,
nor in his house.' He passed in at a dark door, and Herendil,
shrugging his shoulders, followed him.

### Chapter IV

Herendil lay on the floor, stretched at his father's feet upon a
carpet woven in a design of golden birds and twining plants with
blue flowers. His head was propped upon his hands. His father sat
upon his carved chair, his hands laid motionless upon either arm
of it, his eyes looking into the fire that burned bright upon the
hearth. It was not cold, but the fire that was named 'the heart of
the house' (*hon-maren*)[13] burned ever in that room. It was moreover a protection against the night, which already men had begun
to fear.

But cool air came in through the window, sweet and flower-
scented. Through it could be seen, beyond the dark spires of still
trees, the western ocean, silver under the Moon, that was now
swiftly following the Sun to the gardens of the Gods. In the night-
silence Elendil's words fell softly. As he spoke he listened, as if to
another that told a tale long forgotten.[14]

'There[15] is Ilúvatar, the One; and there are the Powers, of
whom the eldest in the thought of Ilúvatar was Alkar the Radiant;[16]
and there are the Firstborn of Earth, the Eldar, who perish not
while the World lasts; and there are also the Afterborn, mortal
Men, who are the children of Ilúvatar, and yet under the rule of
the Lords. Ilúvatar designed the World, and revealed his design

to the Powers; and of these some he set to be Valar, Lords of the World and governors of the things that are therein. But Alkar, who had journeyed alone in the Void before the World, seeking to be free, desired the World to be a kingdom unto himself. Therefore he descended into it like a falling fire; and he made war upon the Lords, his brethren. But they established their mansions in the West, in Valinor, and shut him out; and they gave battle to him in the North, and they bound him, and the World had peace and grew exceeding fair.

'After a great age it came to pass that Alkar sued for pardon; and he made submission unto Manwë, lord of the Powers, and was set free. But he plotted against his brethren, and he deceived the Firstborn that dwelt in Valinor, so that many rebelled and were exiled from the Blessed Realm. And Alkar destroyed the lights of Valinor and fled into the night; and he became a spirit dark and terrible, and was called Morgoth, and he established his dominion in Middle-earth. But the Valar made the Moon for the Firstborn and the Sun for Men to confound the Darkness of the Enemy. And in that time at the rising of the Sun the Afterborn, who are Men, came forth in the East of the world; but they fell under the shadow of the Enemy. In those days the exiles of the Firstborn made war upon Morgoth; and three houses of the Fathers of Men were joined unto the Firstborn: the house of Bëor, and the house of Haleth, and the house of Hador. For these houses were not subject to Morgoth. But Morgoth had the victory, and brought all to ruin.

'Eärendel was son of Tuor, son of Huor, son of Gumlin, son of Hador; and his mother was of the Firstborn, daughter of Turgon, last king of the Exiles. He set forth upon the Great Sea, and he came at last unto the realm of the Lords, and the mountains of the West. And he renounced there all whom he loved, his wife and his child, and all his kindred, whether of the Firstborn or of Men; and he stripped himself.[17] And he surrendered himself unto Manwë, Lord of the West; and he made submission and supplication to him. And he was taken and came never again among Men. But the Lords had pity, and they sent forth their power, and war was renewed in the North, and the earth was broken; but Morgoth was overthrown. And the Lords put him forth into the Void without.

'And they recalled the Exiles of the Firstborn and pardoned them; and such as returned dwell since in bliss in Eressëa, the Lonely Isle, which is Avallon, for it is within sight of Valinor and the light of the Blessed Realm. And for the men of the Three Houses they made Vinya, the New Land, west of Middle-earth in the midst of the Great Sea, and named it Andor, the Land of Gift; and they endowed the land and all that lived thereon with good beyond other lands of mortals. But in Middle-earth dwelt lesser men, who knew not the Lords nor the Firstborn save by rumour; and among them were some who had served Morgoth of old, and were accursed. And there were evil things also upon earth, made by Morgoth in the days of his dominion, demons and dragons and mockeries of the creatures of Ilúvatar.[18] And there too lay hid many of his servants, spirits of evil, whom his will governed still though his presence was not among them. And of these Sauron was the chief, and his power grew. Wherefore the lot of men in Middle-earth was evil, for the Firstborn that remained among them faded or departed into the West, and their kindred, the men of Númenor, were afar and came only to their coasts in ships that crossed the Great Sea. But Sauron learned of the ships of Andor, and he feared them, lest free men should become lords of Middle-earth and deliver their kindred; and moved by the will of Morgoth he plotted to destroy Andor, and ruin (if he might) Avallon and Valinor.[19]

'But why should we be deceived, and become the tools of his will? It was not he, but Manwë the fair, Lord of the West, that endowed us with our riches. Our wisdom cometh from the Lords, and from the Firstborn that see them face to face; and we have grown to be higher and greater than others of our race – those who served Morgoth of old. We have knowledge, power, and life stronger than they. We are not yet fallen. Wherefore the dominion of the world is ours, or shall be, from Eressëa to the East. More can no mortals have.'

'Save to escape from Death,' said Herendil, lifting his face to his father's. 'And from sameness. They say that Valinor, where the Lords dwell, has no further bounds.'

'They say not truly. For all things in the world have an end, since the world itself is bounded, that it may not be Void. But Death is not decreed by the Lords: it is the gift of the One, and a gift which in the wearing of time even the Lords of the West shall envy.[20] So the wise of old have said. And though we can perhaps no longer understand that word, at least we have wisdom enough to know that we cannot escape, unless to a worse fate.'

'But the decree that we of Númenor shall not set foot upon the shores of the Immortal, or walk in their land – that is only a decree of Manwë and his brethren. Why should we not? The air there giveth enduring life, they say.'

'Maybe it doth,' said Elendil; 'and maybe it is but the air which those need who already have enduring life. To us perhaps it is death, or madness.'

'But why should we not essay it? The Eressëans go thither, and yet our mariners in the old days used to sojourn in Eressëa without hurt.'

'The Eressëans are not as we. They have not the gift of death. But what doth it profit to debate the governance of the world? All certainty is lost. Is it not sung that the earth was made for us, but we cannot unmake it, and if we like it not we may remember that we shall leave it. Do not the Firstborn call us the Guests? See what this spirit of unquiet has already wrought. Here when I was young there was no evil of mind. Death came late and without other pain than weariness. From Eressëans we obtained so many things of beauty that our land became well nigh as fair as theirs; and maybe fairer to mortal hearts. It is said that of old the Lords themselves would walk at times in the gardens that we named for them. There we set their images, fashioned by Eressëans who had beheld them, as the pictures of friends beloved.

'There were no temples in this land. But on the Mountain we spoke to the One, who hath no image. It was a holy place, untouched by mortal art. Then Sauron came. We had long heard rumour of him from seamen returned from the East. The tales differed: some said he was a king greater than the king of Númenor; some said that he was one of the Powers, or their offspring set to govern Middle-earth. A few reported that he was an evil spirit, perchance Morgoth returned; but at these we laughed.[21]

'It seems that rumour came also to him of us. It is not many years — three twelves and eight[22] — but it seems many, since he came hither. Thou wert a small child, and knew not then what was happening in the east of this land, far from our western house. Tarkalion the king was moved by rumours of Sauron, and sent forth a mission to discover what truth was in the mariners' tales. Many counsellors dissuaded him. My father told me, and he was one of them, that those who were wisest and had most knowledge of the West had messages from the Lords warning them to beware. For the Lords said that Sauron would work evil; but he could not come hither unless he were summoned.[23] Tarkalion was grown proud, and brooked no power in Middle-earth greater than his own. Therefore the ships were sent, and Sauron was summoned to do homage.

'Guards were set at the haven of Moriondë in the east of the land,[24] where the rocks are dark, watching at the king's command without ceasing for the ships' return. It was night, but there was a bright Moon. They descried ships far off, and they seemed to be sailing west at a speed greater than the storm, though there was little wind. Suddenly the sea became unquiet; it rose until it became like a mountain, and it rolled upon the land. The ships were lifted up, and cast far inland, and lay in the fields. Upon that ship which was cast highest and stood dry upon a hill there was a man, or one in man's shape, but greater than any even of the race of Númenor in stature.

'He stood upon the rock[25] and said: "This is done as a sign of power. For I am Sauron the mighty, servant of the Strong" (wherein he spoke darkly). "I have come. Be glad, men of Númenor, for I will take thy king to be my king, and the world shall be given into his hand."

'And it seemed to men that Sauron was great; though they feared the light of his eyes. To many he appeared fair, to others terrible; but to some evil. But they led him to the king, and he was humble before Tarkalion.

'And behold what hath happened since, step by step. At first he revealed only secrets of craft, and taught the making of many things powerful and wonderful; and they seemed good. Our ships go now without the wind, and many are made of metal that sheareth hidden rocks, and they sink not in calm or storm; but they are no longer fair to look upon. Our towers grow ever stronger and climb ever higher, but beauty they leave behind upon earth. We who have no foes are embattled with impregnable fortresses – and mostly on the West. Our arms are multiplied as if for an agelong war, and men are ceasing to give love or care to the making of other things for use or delight. But our shields are impenetrable, our swords cannot be withstood, our darts are like thunder and pass over leagues unerring. Where are our enemies? We have begun to slay one another. For Númenor now seems narrow, that was so large. Men covet, therefore, the lands that other families have long possessed. They fret as men in chains.

'Wherefore Sauron hath preached deliverance; he has bidden our king to stretch forth his hand to Empire. Yesterday it was over the East. To-morrow – it will be over the West.

'We had no temples. But now the Mountain is despoiled. Its trees are felled, and it stands naked; and upon its summit there is a Temple. It is of marble, and of gold, and of glass and steel, and is wonderful, but terrible. No man prayeth there. It waiteth. For long Sauron did not name his master by the name that from old is accursed here. He spoke at first of the Strong One, of the Eldest Power, of the Master. But now he speaketh openly of Alkar,[26] of Morgoth. He hath prophesied his return. The Temple is to be his house. Númenor is to be the seat of the world's dominion. Meanwhile Sauron dwelleth there. He surveys our land from the Mountain, and is risen above the king, even proud Tarkalion, of the line chosen by the Lords, the seed of Eärendel.

'Yet Morgoth cometh not. But his shadow hath come; it lieth upon the hearts and minds of men. It is between them and the Sun, and all that is beneath it.'

'Is there a shadow?' said Herendil. 'I have not seen it. But I have heard others speak of it; and they say it is the shadow of Death. But Sauron did not bring that; he promiseth that he will save us from it.'

'There is a shadow, but it is the shadow of the fear of Death, and the shadow of greed. But there is also a shadow of darker evil. We no longer see our king. His displeasure falleth on men, and they go out; they are in the evening, and in the morning they are not. The open is insecure; walls are dangerous. Even by the heart of the house spies may sit. And there are prisons, and chambers underground. There are torments; and there are evil rites. The woods at night, that once were fair – men would roam and sleep there for delight, when thou wert a babe – are filled now with horror. Even our gardens are not wholly clean, after the sun has fallen. And now even by day smoke riseth from the temple: flowers and grass are withered where it falleth. The old songs are forgotten or altered; twisted into other meanings.'

'Yea: that one learneth day by day,' said Herendil. 'But some of the new songs are strong and heartening. Yet now I hear that some counsel us to abandon the old tongue. They say we should leave Eressëan, and revive the ancestral speech of Men. Sauron teacheth it. In this at least I think he doth not well.'

'Sauron deceiveth us doubly. For men learned speech of the Firstborn, and therefore if we should verily go back to the beginnings we should find not the broken dialects of the wild men, nor the simple speech of our fathers, but a tongue of the Firstborn. But the Eressëan is of all the tongues of the Firstborn the fairest, and they use it in converse with the Lords, and it linketh their varied kindreds one to another, and them to us. If we forsake it, we should be sundered from them, and be impoverished.[27] Doubtless that is what he intendeth. But there is no end to his malice. Listen now, Herendil, and mark well. The time is nigh when all this evil shall bear bitter fruit, if it be not cut down. Shall we wait until the fruit be ripe, or hew the tree and cast it into the fire?'

Herendil got suddenly to his feet, and went to the window. 'It is cold, father,' he said; 'and the Moon is gone. I trust the garden is empty. The trees grow too near the house.' He drew a heavy embroidered cloth across the window, and then returned, crouching by the fire, as if smitten by a sudden chill.

Elendil leant forward in his chair, and continued in a lowered voice. 'The king and queen grow old, though all know it not, for they are seldom seen. They ask where is the undying life that Sauron promised them if they would build the Temple for Morgoth. The Temple is built, but they are grown old. But Sauron foresaw this, and I hear (already the whisper is gone forth) that he declareth that Morgoth's bounty is restrained by the Lords, and cannot be fulfilled while they bar the way. To win life Tarkalion must win the West.[28] We see now the purpose of the towers and weapons. War is already being talked of – though they do not name the enemy. But I tell thee: it is known to many that the war will go west to Eressëa: and beyond. Dost thou perceive the extremity of our peril, and the madness of the king? Yet this doom draws swiftly near. Our ships are recalled from the [?corners] of the earth. Hast thou not marked and wondered that so many are absent, especially of the younger folk, and in the South and West of our land both works and pastimes languish? In a secret haven to the North there is a building and forging that hath been reported to me by trusty messengers.'

'Reported to thee? What dost thou mean, father?' asked Herendil as if in fear.

'Even what I say. Why dost thou look on me so strangely? Didst thou think the son of Valandil, chief of the wise men of Númenor, would be deceived by the lies of a servant of Morgoth? I would not break faith with the king, nor do I purpose anything to his hurt. The house of Eärendel hath my allegiance while I live. But if I must choose between Sauron and Manwë, then all else must come after. I will not bow unto Sauron, nor to his master.'

'But thou speakest as if thou wert a leader in this matter – woe is me, for I love thee; and though thou swearest allegiance, it will not save thee from the peril of treason. Even to dispraise Sauron is held rebellious.'

'I am a leader, my son. And I have counted the peril both for myself and for thee and all whom I love. I do what is right and my right to do, but I cannot conceal it longer from thee. Thou must choose between thy father and Sauron. But I give thee freedom of choice and lay on thee no obedience as to a father, if I have not convinced thy mind and heart. Thou shalt be free to stay or go, yea even to report as may seem good to thee all that I have said. But if thou stayest and learnest more, which will involve closer counsels and other [?names] than mine, then thou wilt be bound in honour to hold thy peace, come what may. Wilt thou stay?'

'*Atarinya tye-meláne*,' said Herendil suddenly, and clasping his father's knees he laid his [?head there] and wept. 'It is an evil hour that [?putteth] such a choice on thee,' said his father, laying a hand on his head. 'But fate calleth some to be men betimes. What dost thou say?'

'I stay, father.'

The narrative ends here. There is no reason to think that any more was ever written. The manuscript, which becomes increasingly rapid towards the end, peters out in a scrawl.

### Notes on the Númenórean chapters of The Lost Road

1 *Lavaralda* (replacing *lavarin*) is not mentioned in *A Description of Númenor* (*Unfinished Tales* p. 167) among the trees brought by the Eldar from Tol-eressëa.

2 *seven twelves of years* is an emendation of *four score of years* (first written *three score of years*); see note 10.

3 *Vinya* is written above *Númenor* in the manuscript; it occurs again in a part of the text that was rewritten (p. 64), rendered 'the New Land'. The name first appeared in an emendation to FN I (p. 19, §2).

4 For *Terendul* see the *Etymologies*, stem TER, TERES.

5 As the text was originally written there followed here:
   Poldor called me *Eärendel* yesterday.'
   Elendil sighed. 'But that is a fair name. I love the story above others; indeed I chose thy name because it recalleth his. But I did not presume to give his name even to thee, nor to liken myself to Tuor the mighty, who first of Men sailed these seas. At least thou canst answer thy foolish friends that Eärendel was the chief of mariners, and surely that is still held worthy of honour in Númenor?'
   'But they care not for Eärendel. And neither do I. We wish to do what he left undone.'
   'What dost thou mean?'
   'Thou knowest: to set foot in the far West . . .' (&c. as on p. 60).

6   This is the earliest appearance of a Númenórean named *Valandil*. In later rewriting of FN II Valandil is Elendil's brother, and they are the founders of the Númenórean kingdoms in Middle-earth (pp. 33–4). The name was afterwards given to both an earlier Númenórean (the first Lord of Andúnië) and a later (the youngest son of Isildur and third King of Arnor): Index to *Unfinished Tales*, entries *Valandil* and references.

7   In the *Quenta* (IV. 151) it is not told that Tuor was 'lost'. When he felt old age creeping on him 'he built a great ship Eärámë, Eagle's Pinion, and with Idril he set sail into the sunset and the West, and came no more into any tale or song.' Later the following was added (IV. 155): 'But Tuor alone of mortal Men was numbered among the elder race, and joined with the Noldoli whom he loved, and in after time dwelt still, or so it hath been said, ever upon his ship voyaging the seas of the Elven-lands, or resting a while in the harbours of the Gnomes of Tol Eressëa; and his fate is sundered from the fate of Men.'

8   This is the final form in the *Quenta* of the story of Eärendel's landing in Valinor, where in emendations made to the second text Q II (IV. 156) Eärendel 'bade farewell to all whom he loved upon the last shore, and was taken from them for ever,' and 'Elwing mourned for Eärendel yet found him never again, and they are sundered till the world endeth.' Later Elendil returns more fully to the subject (p. 64). In QS the story is further changed, in that Elwing entered Valinor (see pp. 324–5 §§1–2, and commentary).

9   *Nuaran Númenóren*: the letters *ór* were scratched out in the type-script (only).

10   *Thou art but four twelves* replaced *Thou art scarce two score and ten*. As in the change recorded in note 2, a duodecimal counting replaces a decimal; but the number of years is in either case very strange. For Herendil has been called a 'boy', a 'lad', and a 'youth', and he is 'upon the threshold of early manhood' (p. 58); how then can he be forty-eight years old? But his age is unequivocally stated, and moreover Elendil says later (p. 66) that it is 44 years since Sauron came and that Herendil was then a small child; it can only be concluded therefore that at this time the longevity of the Númenóreans implied that they grew and aged at a different rate from other men, and were not fully adult until about fifty years old. Cf. *Unfinished Tales* pp. 224–5.

11   Orontor's mission, from which he might never return, seems like a premonition of the voyage of Amandil into the West, from which he never returned (*Akallabêth* pp. 275–6).

12   The manuscript (followed by the typescript) is here confused, since in addition to the text as printed the whole song that Fíriel sang is given as well, with translation; thus the two opening and the two closing lines and their translations are repeated. It is clear however from pencilled markings on the manuscript that my father moved at

once to a second version (omitting the greater part of the song)
without striking out the first.

The text of the song was emended in three stages. Changes made
probably very near the time of writing were *Valion númenyaron*
(translated 'of the Lords of the West') > *Valion: númessier* in line 2,
and *hondo-ninya* > *indo-ninya* in line 9; *Vinya* was written above
*Númenor* as an alternative in line 8 (cf. note 3). Before the later
emendations the text ran thus:

Ilu Ilúvatar en kárę eldain a fírimoin
ar antaróta mannar Valion: númessier.
Toi aina, mána, meldielto – enga morion:
talantie. Mardello Melko lende: márie.
Eldain en kárier Isil, nan hildin Úr-anar.
Toi írimar. Ilqainen antar annar lestanen
Ilúvatáren. Ilu vanya, fanya, eari,
i-mar, ar ilqa ímen. Írima ye Númenor.
Nan úye sére indo-ninya símen, ullume;
ten sí ye tyelma, yéva tyel ar i-narqelion,
írę ilqa yéva nótina, hostainiéva, yallume:
ananta úva táre fárea, ufárea!
Man táre antáva nin Ilúvatar, Ilúvatar
enyárę tar i tyel, írę Anarinya qeluva?

The Father made the World for Elves and Mortals, and he gave it
into the hands of the Lords. They are in the West. They are holy,
blessed, and beloved: save the dark one. He is fallen. Melko has
gone from Earth: it is good. For Elves they made the Moon, but
for Men the red Sun; which are beautiful. To all they gave in
measure the gifts of Ilúvatar. The World is fair, the sky, the seas,
the earth, and all that is in them. Lovely is Númenor. But my
heart resteth not here for ever; for here is ending, and there will
be an end and the Fading, when all is counted, and all numbered
at last, but yet it will not be enough, not enough. What will the
Father, O Father, give me in that day beyond the end when my
Sun faileth?

Subsequently *Mardello Melko* in line 4 was changed to *Melko
Mardello*, and lines 5–6 became

En kárielto eldain Isil, hildin Úr-anar.
Toi írimar. Ilyain antalto annar lestanen

Then, after the typescript was made, *Melko* was changed to *Alkar*
in text and translation; see note 15.

The thought of lines 5–6 of the song reappears in Elendil's words
to Herendil later (p. 64): 'But the Valar made the Moon for the
Firstborn and the Sun for Men to confound the Darkness of the
Enemy.' Cf. QS §75 (*The Silmarillion* p. 99): 'For the Sun was set
as a sign for the awakening of Men and the waning of the Elves; but
the Moon cherishes their memory.'

13  For *hon-maren* 'heart of the house' see the *Etymologies*, stem KHO-N.
14  Here the typescript made at Allen and Unwin (p. 8, footnote) ends.
The publishers' reader (see p. 97) said that 'only the preliminary
two chapters . . . and one of the last chapters . . . are written.' It
might be supposed that the typescript ended where it does because
no more had been written at that time, but I do not think that this
was the reason. At the point where the typescript breaks off (in the
middle of a manuscript page) there is no suggestion at all of any
interruption in the writing, and it seems far more likely that the
typist simply gave up, for the manuscript here becomes confused
and difficult through rewriting and substitutions.
   In the previous parts of *The Lost Road* I have taken up all
corrections to the manuscript, however quickly and lightly made,
since they all appear in the typescript. From this point there is no
external evidence to show when the pencilled emendations were
made; but I continue to take these up into the text as before.
15  Elendil's long tale to Herendil of the ancient history, from 'There is
Ilúvatar, the One' to 'and ruin (if he might) Avallon and Valinor' on
p. 65, is a replacement of the original much briefer passage. This
replacement must be later than the submission of *The Lost Road* to
Allen and Unwin, for Morgoth is here called *Alkar* as the text was
first written, not *Melko*, whereas in the song sung by Fíriel in the
previous chapter *Melko* was only changed in pencil to *Alkar*, and
this was not taken up into the typescript. The original passage read
thus:

>   He spoke of the rebellion of Melko [*later* > Alkar *and sub-
> sequently*], mightiest of the Powers, that began at the making of
> the World; and of his rejection by the Lords of the West after he
> had wrought evil in the Blessed Realm and caused the exile of the
> Eldar, the firstborn of the earth, who dwelt now in Eressëa. He
> told of Melko's tyranny in Middle-earth, and how he had enslaved
> Men; of the wars which the Eldar waged with him, and were
> defeated, and of the Fathers of Men that had aided them; how
> Eärendel brought their prayer to the Lords, and Melko was
> overthrown and thrust forth beyond the confines of the World.
>   Elendil paused and looked down on Herendil. He did not move
> or make a sign. Therefore Elendil went on. 'Dost thou not
> perceive then, Herendil, that Morgoth is a begetter of evil, and
> brought sorrow upon our fathers? We owe him no allegiance
> except by fear. For his share of the governance of the World was
> forfeit long ago. Nor need we hope in him: the fathers of our race
> were his enemies; wherefore we can look for no love from him or
> any of his servants. Morgoth doth not forgive. But he cannot
> return into the World in present power and form while the Lords
> are enthroned. He is in the Void, though his Will remaineth and
> guideth his servants. And his will is to overthrow the Lords, and

return, and wield dominion, and have vengeance on those who obey the Lords.

'But why should we be deceived . . .' (&c. as on p. 65).

The closing sentences ('But he cannot return into the World . . .') closely echo, or perhaps rather are closely echoed by (see note 25) a passage in FN II (§1).

16  In QS §10 it is said that Melko was 'coëval with Manwë'. The name *Alkar* 'the Radiant' of Melko occurs, I believe, nowhere outside this text.

17  See note 8. The reference to Eärendel's *child* shows that Elros had not yet emerged, as he had not in FN II (p. 34).

18  'mockeries of the creatures of Ilúvatar': cf. FN II §1 and commentary.

19  Here the long replacement passage ends (see note 15), though as written it continued in much the same words as did the earlier form ('For Morgoth cannot return into the World while the Lords are enthroned . . .'); this passage was afterwards struck out.

20  The words 'a gift which in the wearing of time even the Lords of the West shall envy' were a pencilled addition to the text, and are the first appearance of this idea: a closely similar phrase is found in a text of the *Ainulindalë* written years later (cf. *The Silmarillion* p. 42: 'Death is their fate, the gift of Ilúvatar, which as Time wears even the Powers shall envy.')

21  Cf. FN II §5: 'Some said that he was a king greater than the King of Númenor; some said that he was one of the Gods or their sons set to govern Middle-earth. A few reported that he was an evil spirit, perchance Morgoth himself returned. But this was held to be only a foolish fable of the wild Men.'

22  This duodecimal computation is found in the text as written; see note 10.

23  Cf. FN II §5: 'for [the Lords] said that Sauron would work evil if he came; but he could not come to Númenor unless he was summoned and guided by the king's messengers.'

24  The name *Moriondë* occurs, I think, nowhere else. This eastern haven is no doubt the forerunner of Rómenna.

25  This is the story of the coming of Sauron to Númenor found in FN II §5, which was replaced soon after by a version in which the lifting up of the ships by a great wave and the casting of them far inland was removed; see pp. 9, 26-7. In the first FN II version the sea rose like a *mountain*, the ship that carried Sauron was set upon a *hill*, and Sauron stood upon the hill to preach his message to the Númenóreans. In *The Lost Road* the sea rose like a *hill*, changed in pencil to *mountain*, Sauron's ship was cast upon a *high rock*, changed in pencil to *hill*, and Sauron spoke standing on the rock (left unchanged). This is the best evidence I can see that of these two companion works (see notes 15, 21, 23) *The Lost Road* was written first.

26  *Alkar*: pencilled alteration of *Melko*: see note 15.

27  On Eressëan ('Elf-latin', Qenya), the common speech of all Elves, see p. 56. The present passage is the first appearance of the idea of a linguistic component in the attack by the Númenórean 'government' on Eressëan culture and influence; cf. *The Line of Elros* in *Unfinished Tales* (p. 222), of Ar-Adûnakhôr, the twentieth ruler of Númenor: 'He was the first King to take the sceptre with a title in the Adûnaic tongue . . . In this reign the Elven-tongues were no longer used, nor permitted to be taught, but were maintained in secret by the Faithful'; and of Ar-Gimilzôr, the twenty-third ruler: 'he forbade utterly the use of the Eldarin tongues' (very similarly in the *Akallabêth*, pp. 267–8). But of course at the time of *The Lost Road* the idea of Adûnaic as one of the languages of Númenor had not emerged, and the proposal is only that 'the ancestral speech of Men' should be 'revived'.

28  This goes back to FN I §6: 'Sûr said that the gifts of Morgoth were withheld by the Gods, and that to obtain plenitude of power and undying life he [the king Angor] must be master of the West.'

There are several pages of notes that give some idea of my father's thoughts – at a certain stage – for the continuation of the story beyond the point where he abandoned it. These are in places quite illegible, and in any case were the concomitant of rapidly changing ideas: they are the vestiges of thoughts, not statements of formulated conceptions. More important, some at least of these notes clearly preceded the actual narrative that was written and were taken up into it, or replaced by something different, and it may very well be that this is true of them all, even those that refer to the latter part of the story which was never written. But they make it very clear that my father was concerned above all with the relation between the father and the son, which was cardinal. In Númenor he had engendered a situation in which there was the potentiality of anguishing conflict between them, totally incommensurate with the quiet harmony in which the Errols began – or ended. The relationship of Elendil and Herendil was subjected to a profound menace. This conflict could have many narrative issues within the framework of the known event, the attack on Valinor and the Downfall of Númenor, and in these notes my father was merely sketching out some solutions, none of which did he develop or return to again.

An apparently minor question was the words 'the Eagles of the Lord of the West': what did they mean, and how were they placed within the story? It seems that he was as puzzled by them as was Alboin Errol when he used them (pp. 38, 47). He queries whether 'Lord of the West' means the King of Númenor, or Manwë, or whether it is the title properly of Manwë but taken in his despite by the King; and concludes 'probably the latter'. There follows a 'scenario' in which Sorontur King of Eagles is sent by Manwë, and Sorontur flying against the sun casts a great shadow on the ground. It was then that Elendil spoke the phrase, but he was overheard, informed upon, and taken before Tarkalion, who declared that the title was his. In the story as actually written Elendil speaks the words to Herendil (p. 62), when he sees clouds rising out of the West in the evening sky and stretching out 'great wings' – the same spectacle as made Alboin Errol utter them, and the men of Númenor in the *Akallabêth* (p. 277); and Herendil replies that the title has been decreed to belong to the King. The outcome of Elendil's arrest is not made clear in the notes, but it is said that Herendil was given command of one of the ships, that Elendil himself joined in the great expedition because he followed Herendil, that when they reached Valinor Tarkalion set Elendil as a hostage in his son's ship, and that when they landed on the shores Herendil was struck down. Elendil rescued him and set him on shipboard, and 'pursued by the bolts of Tarkalion' they sailed back east. 'As they approach Númenor the world bends; they see the land slipping towards them'; and Elendil falls into the deep and is drowned.* This group of notes ends with references to the coming of the Númenóreans to Middle-earth, and to the 'later stories'; 'the flying ships', 'the painted caves', 'how Elf-friend walked on the Straight Road'.

Other notes refer to plans laid by the 'anti-Saurians' for an assault on the Temple, plans betrayed by Herendil 'on condition that Elendil is spared'; the assault is defeated and Elendil captured. Either associated with this or distinct from it is a suggestion that Herendil is arrested and imprisoned in the dungeons of Sauron, and that Elendil renounces the Gods to save his son.

My guess is that all this had been rejected when the actual narrative was written, and that the words of Herendil that conclude it show that my father had then in mind some quite distinct solution, in which Elendil and his son remained united in the face of whatever events overtook them.†

In the early narratives there is no indication of the duration of the realm of Númenor from its foundation to its ruin; and there is only one named king. In his conversation with Herendil, Elendil attributes all the evils that have befallen to the coming of Sauron: they have arisen therefore in a quite brief time (forty-four years, p. 66); whereas in the *Akallabêth*, when a great extension of Númenórean history had taken

---

*It would be interesting to know if a tantalisingly obscure note, scribbled down in isolation, refers to this dimly-glimpsed story: 'If either fails the other they perish and do not return. Thus at the last moment Elendil must prevail on Herendil to hold back, otherwise they would have perished. At that moment he sees himself as Alboin: and realises that Elendil and Herendil had perished.'

†I have suggested (p. 31) that since Elendil of Númenor appears in FN II (§14) as king in Beleriand he must have been among those who took no part in the expedition of Tar-kalion, but 'sat in their ships upon the east coast of the land' (FN §9).

place, those evils began long before, and are indeed traced back as far as the twelfth ruler, Tar-Ciryatan the Shipbuilder, who took the sceptre nearly a millennium and a half before the Downfall (*Akallabêth* p. 265, *Unfinished Tales* p. 221).

From Elendil's words at the end of *The Lost Road* there emerges a sinister picture: the withdrawal of the besotted and aging king from the public view, the unexplained disappearance of people unpopular with the 'government', informers, prisons, torture, secrecy, fear of the night; propaganda in the form of the 'rewriting of history' (as exemplified by Herendil's words concerning what was now said about Eärendel, p. 60); the multiplication of weapons of war, the purpose of which is concealed but guessed at; and behind all the dreadful figure of Sauron, the real power, surveying the whole land from the Mountain of Númenor. The teaching of Sauron has led to the invention of ships of metal that traverse the seas without sails, but which are hideous in the eyes of those who have not abandoned or forgotten Tol-eressëa; to the building of grim fortresses and unlovely towers; and to missiles that pass with a noise like thunder to strike their targets many miles away. Moreover, Númenor is seen by the young as over-populous, boring, 'over-known': 'every tree and grass-blade is counted', in Herendil's words; and this cause of discontent is used, it seems, by Sauron to further the policy of 'imperial' expansion and ambition that he presses on the king. When at this time my father reached back to the world of the first man to bear the name 'Elf-friend' he found there an image of what he most condemned and feared in his own.

(iii)

*The unwritten chapters*

It cannot be shown whether my father decided to alter the structure of the book by postponing the Númenórean story to the end before he abandoned the fourth chapter at Herendil's words 'I stay, father'; but it seems perfectly possible that the decision in fact led to the abandonment. At any rate, on a separate sheet he wrote: '*Work backwards* to Númenor and make that last', adding a proposal that in each tale a man should utter the words about the Eagles of the Lord of the West, but only at the end would it be discovered what they meant (see pp. 75–6). This is followed by a rapid jotting down of ideas for the tales that should intervene between Alboin and Audoin of the twentieth century and Elendil and Herendil in Númenor, but these are tantalisingly brief: 'Lombard story?'; 'a Norse story of ship-burial (Vinland)'; 'an English story – of the man who got onto the Straight Road?'; 'a Tuatha-de-Danaan story, or Tir-nan-Og' (on which see pp. 81–3); a story concerning 'painted caves'; 'the Ice Age – great figures in ice', and 'Before the Ice Age: the Galdor story'; 'post-Beleriand and the Elendil and Gil-galad story of the assault on Thû'; and finally 'the Númenor story'. To one of these, the 'English story of the man who got onto the Straight Road', is attached a more extended note, written at great speed:

But this would do best of all for introduction to the Lost Tales: How Ælfwine sailed the Straight Road. They sailed on, on, on over the sea; and it became very bright and very calm, – no clouds, no wind. The water seemed thin and white below. Looking down Ælfwine suddenly saw lands and mt [*i.e.* mountains *or* a mountain] down in the water shining in the sun. Their breathing difficulties. His companions dive overboard one by one. Ælfwine falls insensible when he smells a marvellous fragrance as of land and flowers. He awakes to find the ship being drawn by people walking in the water. He is told very few men there in a thousand years can breathe air of Eressëa (which is Avallon), but *none* beyond. So he comes to Eressëa and is told the Lost Tales.

Pencilled later against this is 'Story of Sceaf or Scyld'; and it was only here, I think, that the idea of the Anglo-Saxon episode arose (and this was the only one of all these projections that came near to getting off the ground).

This note is of particular interest in that it shows my father combining the old story of the voyage of Ælfwine to Tol-eressëa and the telling of the *Lost Tales* with the idea of the World Made Round and the Straight Path, which entered at this time. With the words about the difficulty of breathing cf. FN §12, where it is said that the Straight Path 'cut through the air of breath and flight [Wilwa, Vista], and traversed Ilmen, in which no flesh can endure.'

My father then (as I judge) roughed out an outline for the structure of the book as he now foresaw it. Chapter III was to be called *A Step Backward: Ælfwine and Eadwine** – the Anglo-Saxon incarnation of the father and son, and incorporating the legend of King Sheave; Chapter IV 'the Irish legend of Tuatha-de-Danaan – and oldest man in the world'; Chapter V 'Prehistoric North: old kings found buried in the ice': Chapter VI 'Beleriand'; Chapter VIII (presumably a slip for VII) 'Elendil and Herendil in Númenor'. It is interesting to see that there is now no mention of the Lombard legend as an ingredient: see p. 55.

This outline structure was sent to Allen and Unwin with the manu-, script and was incorporated in the typescript made there.

Apart from the Anglo-Saxon episode, the only scrap of connected writing for any of the suggested tales is an extremely obscure and roughly-written fragment that appears to be a part of 'the Galdor story' (p. 77). In this, one *Agaldor* stands on a rocky shore at evening and sees great clouds coming up, 'like the very eagles of the Lord of the West'. He is filled with a formless foreboding at the sight of these clouds; and he.

---

*I think it almost certain that the titles of Chapters I and II were put in at this time: as the manuscript was written they had no titles.

turns and climbs up the beach, passing down behind the land-wall to the houses where lights are already lit. He is eyed doubtfully by men sitting at a door, and after he has gone by they speak of him.

'There goes Agaldor again, from his speech with the sea: earlier than usual,' said one. 'He has been haunting the shores more than ever of late.' 'He will be giving tongue soon, and prophesying strange things,' said another; 'and may the Lords of the West set words more comforting in his mouth than before.' 'The Lords of the West will tell him naught,' said a third. 'If ever they were on land or sea they have left this earth, and man is his own master from here to the sunrise. Why should we be plagued with the dreams of a twilight-walker? His head is stuffed with them, and there let them bide. One would think to hear him talk that the world had ended in the last age, not new begun, and we were living in the ruins.'

'He is one of the old folk, and well-nigh the last of the long-lived in these regions,' said another. 'Those who knew the Eldar and had seen even the Sons of the Gods had a wisdom we forget.' 'Wisdom I know not,' said the other, 'but woe certainly in abundance if any of their tales are true. I know not (though I doubt it). But give me the Sun. That is glory . . . I would that the long life of Agaldor might be shortened. It is he that holds [??nigh] this sea-margin – too near the mournful water. I would we had a leader to take us East or South. They say the land is golden in the [??domains] of the Sun.'

Here the fragment ends. Agaldor has appeared in the original outline for *The Fall of Númenor*: 'Agaldor chieftain of a people who live upon the N.W. margin of the Western Sea' (p. 11), and later in that text it was Agaldor who wrestled with Thû, though the name was there changed at the time of writing to Amroth (p. 12). That this is a fragment of 'the Galdor story' seems to be shown by a pencilled and partly illegible scrawl at the head of the page, where *Galdor* appears; but the story is here significantly different.

Galdor is a good man [?among] the exiles (not a Númenórean) – not a long-liver but a prophet. He prophesies [?coming] of Númenóreans and [?salvation] of men. Hence holds his men by sea. This foreboding passage heralds the Ruin and the Flood. How he escapes in the flood . . . . . of land. The Númenóreans come – but appear no longer as good but as rebels against the Gods. They slay Galdor and take the chieftainship.

There is very little to build on here, and I shall not offer any speculations. The story was abandoned without revealing how the Ælfwine-Eadwine element would enter.

Turning now to 'the Ælfwine story', there are several pages of very rough notes and abandoned beginnings. One of these pages consists of increasingly rapid and abbreviated notes, as follows:

Ælfwine and Eadwine live in the time of Edward the Elder, in North
Somerset. Ælfwine ruined by the incursions of Danes. Picture opens
with the attack (c. 915) on *Portloca* (Porlock) and *Wæced*. Ælfwine is
awaiting Eadwine's return at night. (The attack actually historically
took place in autumn, *æt hærfest*).
    Conversation of Ælfwine and Eadwine. Eadwine is sick of it. He
says the Danes have more sense; always pressing on. They go *west*.
They pass round and go to Ireland; while the English sit like *Wealas*
waiting to be made into slaves.
    Eadwine says he has heard strange tales from Ireland. A land in the
North-west filled with ice, but fit for men to dwell – holy hermits have
been driven out by Norsemen. Ælfwine has Christian objections.
Eadwine says the holy Brendan did so centuries ago – and lots of
others, [as] Maelduin. And they came back – not that he would want
to. *Insula Deliciarum* – even Paradise.
    Ælfwine objects that Paradise cannot be got to by ship – there are
deeper waters between us than Garsecg. *Roads are bent*: you come
back in the end. No escape by ship.
    Eadwine says he does not think it true – and hopes it isn't. At any
rate their ancestors had won new lands by ship. Quotes story of *Sceaf*.
    In the end they go off with ten neighbours. Pursued by Vikings off
Lundy. Wind takes them out to sea, and persists. Eadwine falls sick
and says odd things. Ælfwine dreams too. Mountainous seas.
    The Straight Road . . . . . water (island of Azores?) . . . . . off.
Ælfwine [?restores ?restrains] Eadwine. Thinks it a vision of delirium.
The vision of Eressëa and the sound of voices. Resigns himself to die
but prays for Eadwine. Sensation of falling. They come down in
[?real] sea and west wind blows them back. Land in Ireland (implication is they *settle* there, and this leads to Finntan).

I add some notes on this far-ranging outline. Edward the Elder, eldest
son of King Alfred, reigned from 900 to 924. In the year 914 a large
Viking fleet, coming from Brittany, appeared in the Bristol Channel, and
began ravaging in the lands beyond the Severn. According to the *Anglo-
Saxon Chronicle* the leaders were two *jarls* ('earls') named Ohtor
and Hroald. The Danes were defeated at Archenfield (Old English
*Ircingafeld*) in Herefordshire and forced to give hostages in pledge of
their departure. King Edward was in arms with the forces of Wessex on
the south side of the Severn estuary, 'so that', in the words of the
*Chronicle*, 'they did not dare to attack the land anywhere on that side.
Nonetheless they twice stole inland by night, on one occasion east of
Watchet and on the other at Porlock (*æt oprum cierre be eastan Wæced,
and æt oprum cierre æt Portlocan*). Each time they were attacked and
only those escaped who swam out to the ships; and after that they were
out on the island of Steepholme, until they had scarcely any food, and
many died of hunger. From there they went to Dyfed [South Wales] and

from there to Ireland; and that was in the autumn (*and þis wæs on hærfest*).'

Porlock and Watchet are on the north coast of Somerset; the island of Steepholme lies to the North-east, in the mouth of the Severn. My father retained this historical mise-en-scène in the draft of a brief 'Ælfwine' narrative given below, pp. 83–4, and years later in *The Notion Club Papers* (1945).

*Wealas*: the British (as distinct from the English or Anglo-Saxons); in Modern English *Wales*, the name of the people having become the name of the land.

'A land in the North-west filled with ice, but fit for men to dwell – holy hermits have been driven out by Norsemen.' It is certain that by the end of the eighth century (and how much earlier cannot be said) Irish voyagers had reached Iceland, in astounding journeys achieved in their boats called *curachs*, made of hides over a wooden frame. This is known from the work of an Irish monk named Dicuil, who in his book *Liber de Mensura Orbis Terrae* (written in 825) recorded that

It is now thirty years since certain priests who lived in that island from the first day of February to the first day of August told me that not only at the summer solstice, but also in the days before and after, the setting sun at evening hides itself as if behind a little hill, so that it does not grow dark even for the shortest period of time, but whatever task a man wishes to perform, even picking the lice out of his shirt, he can do it just as if it were broad daylight.

When the first Norsemen came to Iceland (about 860) there were Irish hermits living there. This is recorded by the Icelandic historian Ari the Learned (1067–1148), who wrote:

At that time Christian men whom the Norsemen call *papar* dwelt here; but afterwards they went away, because they would not live here together with heathen men, and they left behind them Irish books, bells, and croziers; from which it could be seen that they were Irishmen.

Many places in the south of Iceland, such as Papafjörðr and the island of Papey, still bear names derived from the Irish *papar*. But nothing is known of their fate: they fled, and they left behind their precious things.

*Brendan; Maelduin; Insula Deliciarum.* The conception of a 'blessed land' or 'fortunate isles' in the Western Ocean is a prominent feature of the old Irish legends: *Tir-nan-Og*, the land of youth; *Hy Bresail*, the fortunate isle; *Insula Deliciosa*; etc. *Tir-nan-Og* is mentioned as a possible story for *The Lost Road*, p. 77.

*The holy Brendan* is Saint Brendan called the Navigator, founder of the Abbey of Clonfert in Galway, and the subject of the most famous of the tales of seavoyaging (*imrama*) told of early Irish saints. Another is the *Imram Maelduin*, in which Maelduin and his companions set out from Ireland in a *curach* and came in their voyaging to many islands in succession, where they encountered marvel upon marvel, as did Saint Brendan.

My father's poem *Imram*, in which Saint Brendan at the end of his life recalls the three things that he remembers from his voyage, was published in 1955, but it originally formed a part of *The Notion Club Papers*. Many years before, he had written a poem (*The Nameless Land*) on the subject of a paradisal country 'beyond the Shadowy Sea', in which Brendan is named. This poem and its later forms are given in a note at the end of this chapter, pp. 98 ff.; to the final version is attached a prose note on Ælfwine's voyage that relates closely to the end of the present outline.

*Garsecg:* the Ocean. See II. 312 and note 19; also the Index to Vol. IV, entry *Belegar*.

*Sceaf:* see pp. 7, 78, and 85 ff.

*Lundy:* an island off the west coast of Devon.

It is unfortunate that the last part of this outline is so illegible. The words following 'The Straight Road' could be interpreted as 'a world like water'. After the mysterious reference to the Azores the first word is a noun or name in the plural, and is perhaps followed by 'driven'.

*Finntan:* An isolated note elsewhere among these papers reads: 'See Lit. Celt. p. 137. Oldest man in the world *Finntan* (*Narkil* White Fire).' The reference turns out to be to a work entitled *The Literature of the Celts*, by Magnus Maclean (1906). In the passage to which my father referred the author wrote of the history of Ireland according to mediaeval Irish annalists:

Forty days before the Flood, the Lady Cæsair, niece or granddaughter of Noah – it is immaterial which – with fifty girls and three men came to Ireland. This, we are to understand, was the first invasion or conquest of that country. All these were drowned in the Deluge, except Finntan, the husband of the lady, who escaped by being cast into a deep sleep, in which he continued for a year, and when he awoke he found himself in his own house at Dun Tulcha. . . . At Dun Tulcha he lived throughout many dynasties down to the sixth century of our era, when he appears for the last time with eighteen companies of his descendants engaged in settling a boundary dispute. Being the oldest man in the world, he was *ipso facto* the best informed regarding ancient landmarks.

After the Flood various peoples in succession stepped onto the platform of Irish history. First the Partholans, then the Nemedians, Firbolgs, Tuatha de Danaan, and last of all the Milesians, thus carrying the chronology down to the time of Christ. From the arrival of the earliest of these settlers, the Fomorians or 'Sea Rovers' are represented as fighting and harassing the people. Sometimes in conjunction with the plague, at other times with the Firbolgs and Gaileoin and Fir-Domnann, they laid waste the land. The Partholans and Nemedians were early disposed of. And then appeared from the north of Europe, or from heaven, as one author says, the Tuatha de Danann, who at the great battle of Moytura South overcame the Firbolgs, scattering them to the islands of Aran, Islay, Rathlin, and the Hebrides, and afterwards defeating the Fomorians at Moytura North, thus gaining full possession of the land. The Tuatha de Danann are twice mentioned (pp. 77–8) as a possible narrative element in *The Lost Road*.

The only actual narrative concerning Ælfwine from this time (apart from some beginnings abandoned after a few lines) is brief and roughly scrawled; but it was to be used afterwards, and in places quite closely followed, in *The Notion Club Papers*.

Ælfwine awoke with a start – he had been dozing on a bench with his back to a pillar. The voices poured in on him like a torrent. He felt he had been dreaming; and for a moment the English speech about him sounded strange, though mostly it was the soft speech of western Wessex. Here and there were men of the Marches, and a few spoke oddly, using strange words after the manner of those among whom the Danes dwelt in the eastern lands. He looked down the hall, looking for his son Eadwine. He was due on leave from the fleet, but had not yet come.

There was a great crowd in the hall, for King Edward was here. The fleet was in the Severn sea, and the south shore was in arms. The jarls had been defeated far north at Irchenfield, but the Danish ships were still at large on the Welsh coast; and the men of Somerset and Devon were on guard.

Ælfwine looked down the hall. The faces of the men, some old and careworn, some young and eager, were dim, not only because the torchlight was wavering and the candles on the high table were guttering. He looked beyond them. There was a wind blowing, surging round the house; timbers creaked. The sound brought back old longings to him that he had thought were long buried. He was born in the year the Danes wintered in Sheppey, and he had sailed many seas and heard many winds since then. The sound of the west wind and the fall of seas on the beaches had always been a challenging music to him. Especially in spring. But now it was autumn, and also he was growing old. And the seas were wide, beyond the power of man to cross – to unknown shores: wide and dangerous. The faces of the men about him faded and the clamour of their voices was changed. He heard the crash of waves on the black cliffs and the sea-birds diving and crying; and snow and hail fell. Then the seas opened pale and wide; the sun shone on the land and the sound and smell of it fell far behind. He was alone going west towards the setting sun with fear and longing in his heart, drawn against his will.

His dream was broken by calls for the minstrel. 'Let Ælfwine sing!' men were crying. The king had sent to bid him sing something. He lifted up his voice and chanted aloud, but as one speaking to himself alone:

> Monað modes lust mid mereflode
> forð to feran, þæt ic feor heonan
> ofer hean holmas, ofer hwæles eðel
> elþeodigra eard gesece.
> Nis me to hearpan hyge ne to hringþege
> ne to wife wyn ne to worulde hyht
> ne ymb owiht elles nefne ymb yða gewealc.

'The desire of my spirit urges me to journey forth over the flowing sea, that far hence across the hills of water and the whale's country I may seek the land of strangers. No mind have I for harp, nor gift of ring, nor delight in women, nor joy in the world, nor concern with aught else save the rolling of the waves.'

Then he stopped suddenly. There was some laughter, and a few jeers, though many were silent, as if feeling that the words were not spoken to their ears – old and familiar as they were, words of the old poets whom most men had heard often. 'If he has no mind to the harp he need expect no [?wages],' said one. 'Is there a mortal here who has a mind?' 'We have had enough of the sea,' said another. 'A spell of Dane-hunting would cure most men's love of it.' 'Let him go rolling on the waves,' said another. 'It is no great sail to the . . . Welsh country, where folk are strange enough – and the Danes to talk to as well.'

'Peace!' said an old man sitting near the threshold. 'Ælfwine has sailed more seas than you have heard of; and the Welsh tongue is not strange to him . . . . . His wife was of Cornwall. He has been to Ireland and the North, and some say far to the west of all living lands. Let him say what his mood bids.' There was a short silence.

The text ends here. The historical situation is slightly filled out, with mention of the Viking *jarls* and their defeat at *Irchenfield* (Archenfield), on which see p. 80. Ælfwine 'was born in the year the Danes wintered in Sheppey' (the isle of Sheppey off the north coast of Kent). The *Anglo-Saxon Chronicle* records under the year 855: *Her hæþne men ærest on Sceapige ofer winter sætun* (In this year heathen men for the first time stayed in Sheppey ['Sheep-isle'] over the winter); but an earlier wintering on Thanet is recorded under 851. These winterings by Vikings were ominous of what was to come, a sign of the transition from isolated raids followed by a quick departure to the great invasions in the time of Æthelred and Alfred. – Ælfwine was therefore approaching sixty at this time.

The verses that Ælfwine chanted are derived from the Old English poem known as *The Seafarer*, with the omission of five lines from the original after line 4, and some alterations of wording. The third line is an addition (and is enclosed, both in the Old English and in the translation, in square brackets in the manuscript).

With the reference to Ælfwine's wife who came from Cornwall cf. the old tale of *Ælfwine of England*, where his mother came 'from the West, from Lionesse' (II. 313).

It seems to me certain that what was to follow immediately on the end of this brief narrative was the legend of *King Sheave*, which in one of the three texts is put into Ælfwine's mouth (and which follows here in *The Notion Club Papers*, though it is not there given to Ælfwine). There is both a prose and a verse form of *King Sheave*; and it may well be that the prose version, which I give first, belongs very closely with the Ælfwine narrative; there is no actual link between them, but the two manuscripts are very similar.

To the shore the ship came and strode upon the sand, grinding upon the broken shingle. In the twilight as the sun sank men came down to it, and looked within. A boy lay there, asleep. He was fair of face and limb, dark-haired, white-skinned, but clad in gold. The inner parts of the boat were gold-adorned, a vessel of gold filled with clear water was at his side, [*added*: at his right was a harp,] beneath his head was a sheaf of corn, the stalks and ears of which gleamed like gold in the dusk. Men knew not what it was. In wonder they drew the boat high upon the beach, and lifted the boy and bore him up, and laid him sleeping in a wooden house in their burh. They set guards about the door.

In the morning the chamber was empty. But upon a high rock men saw the boy standing. The sheaf was in his arms. As the risen sun shone down, he began to sing in a strange tongue, and they were filled with awe. For they had not yet heard singing, nor seen such beauty. And they had no king among them, for their kings had perished, and they were lordless and unguided. Therefore they took the boy to be king, and they called him *Sheaf*; and so is his name remembered in song. For his true name was hidden and is forgotten. Yet he taught men many new words, and their speech was enriched. Song and verse-craft he taught them, and rune-craft, and tillage and husbandry, and the making of many things; and in his time the dark forests receded and there was plenty, and corn grew in the land; and the carven houses of men were filled with gold and storied webs. The glory of King Sheaf sprang far and wide in the isles of the North. His children were many and fair, and it is sung that of them are come the kings of men of the North Danes and the West Danes, the South Angles and the East Gothfolk. And in the time of the Sheaf-lords there was peace in the isles, and ships went unarmed from land to land bearing treasure and rich merchandise. And a man might cast a golden ring upon the highway and it would remain until he took it up again.

Those days songs have called the golden years, while the great mill of Sheaf was guarded still in the island sanctuary of the North; and from the mill came golden grain, and there was no want in all the realms.

But it came to pass after long years that Sheaf summoned his friends and counsellors, and he told them that he would depart. For the shadow of old age was fallen upon him (out of the East) and he would return whence he came. Then there was great mourning. But Sheaf laid him upon his golden bed, and became as one in deep slumber; and his lords obeying his commands while he yet ruled and had command of speech set him in a ship. He lay beside the mast, which was tall, and the sails were golden. Treasures of gold and of gems and fine raiment and costly stuffs were laid beside him. His golden banner flew above his head. In this manner he was arrayed more richly than when he came among them; and they thrust him forth to sea, and the sea took him, and the ship bore him unsteered far away into the uttermost West out of the sight or thought of men. Nor do any know who received him in what haven at the end of his journey. Some have said that that ship found the Straight Road. But none of the children of Sheaf went that way, and many in the beginning lived to a great age, but coming under the shadow of the East they were laid in great tombs of stone or in mounds like green hills; and most of these were by the western sea, high and broad upon the shoulders of the land, whence men can descry them that steer their ships amid the shadows of the sea.

This is a first draft, written at speed and very roughly; but the form in alliterative verse is very finished, so far as it goes (it does not extend to the departure of Sheaf, or Sheave, and was not added to for its inclusion in *The Notion Club Papers*). There are two texts of the verse form: (i) a clear manuscript in which the poem is written out as prose, and (ii) a more hasty text in which it is written out in verse-lines. It is hard to

decide which of the two came first, but the poem is in any case almost
identical in the two versions, which were obviously closely contemporary. I print it here in lines, with breaks introduced from the paragraphs
of the 'prose' form. Version (i) has a formal title, *King Sheave*; (ii) has a
short narrative opening, which could very well follow the words 'There
was a short silence' on p. 84.

Suddenly Ælfwine struck a note on his harp. 'Lo!' he cried,
loud and clear, and men stiffened to attention. 'Lo!' he cried, and
began to chant an ancient tale, yet he was half aware that he was
telling it afresh, adding and altering words, not so much by
improvisation as after long pondering hidden from himself, catching at the shreds of dreams and visions.

> In days of yore out of deep Ocean
> to the Longobards, in the land dwelling
> that of old they held amid the isles of the North,
> a ship came sailing, shining-timbered
> without oar and mast, eastward floating.
> The sun behind it sinking westward
> with flame kindled the fallow water.
> Wind was wakened. Over the world's margin
> clouds greyhelméd climbed slowly up
> wings unfolding wide and looming,   10
> as mighty eagles moving onward
> to eastern Earth omen bearing.
> Men there marvelled, in the mist standing
> of the dark islands in the deeps of time:
> laughter they knew not, light nor wisdom;
> shadow was upon them, and sheer mountains
> stalked behind them stern and lifeless,
> evilhaunted. The East was dark.
>
> The ship came shining to the shore driven
> and strode upon the strand, till its stem rested  20
> on sand and shingle. The sun went down.
> The clouds overcame the cold heavens.
> In fear and wonder to the fallow water
> sadhearted men swiftly hastened
> to the broken beaches the boat seeking,
> gleaming-timbered in the grey twilight.
> They looked within, and there laid sleeping
> a boy they saw breathing softly:
> his face was fair, his form lovely,

his limbs were white, his locks raven                    30
golden-braided.   Gilt and carven
with wondrous work was the wood about him.
In golden vessel gleaming water
stood beside him; strung with silver
a harp of gold neath his hand rested;
his sleeping head was soft pillowed
on a sheaf of corn shimmering palely
as the fallow gold doth from far countries
west of Angol.   Wonder filled them.

The boat they hauled and on the beach moored it        40
high above the breakers; then with hands lifted
from the bosom its burden. The boy slumbered.
On his bed they bore him to their bleak dwellings
darkwalled and drear in a dim region
between waste and sea.   There of wood builded
high above the houses was a hall standing
forlorn and empty.   Long had it stood so,
no noise knowing, night nor morning,
no light seeing.   They laid him there,
under lock left him lonely sleeping              50
in the hollow darkness.   They held the doors.
Night wore away.   New awakened
as ever on earth early morning;
day came dimly.   Doors were opened.
Men strode within, then amazed halted;
fear and wonder filled the watchmen.
The house was bare, hall deserted;
no form found they on the floor lying,
but by bed forsaken the bright vessel
dry and empty in the dust standing.              60

The guest was gone.   Grief o'ercame them.
In sorrow they sought him, till the sun rising
over the hills of heaven to the homes of men
light came bearing.   They looked upward
and high upon a hill hoar and treeless
the guest beheld they: gold was shining
in his hair, in hand the harp he bore;
at his feet they saw the fallow-golden
cornsheaf lying.   Then clear his voice
a song began, sweet, unearthly,                  70

words in music woven strangely,
in tongue unknown.   Trees stood silent
and men unmoving marvelling hearkened.

Middle-earth had known for many ages
neither song nor singer; no sight so fair
had eyes of mortal, since the earth was young,
seen when waking in that sad country
long forsaken.   No lord they had,
no king nor counsel, but the cold terror
that dwelt in the desert, the dark shadow                    80
that haunted the hills and the hoar forest.
Dread was their master.   Dark and silent,
long years forlorn, lonely waited
the hall of kings, house forsaken
without fire or food.

         Forth men hastened
from their dim houses.   Doors were opened
and gates unbarred.   Gladness wakened.
To the hill they thronged, and their heads lifting
on the guest they gazed.   Greybearded men
bowed before him and blessed his coming                     90
their years to heal; youths and maidens,
wives and children welcome gave him.
His song was ended.   Silent standing
he looked upon them.   Lord they called him;
king they made him, crowned with golden
wheaten garland, white his raiment,
his harp his sceptre.   In his house was fire,
food and wisdom; there fear came not.
To manhood he grew, might and wisdom.

Sheave they called him, whom the ship brought them,   100
a name renowned in the North countries
ever since in song.   For a secret hidden
his true name was, in tongue unknown
of far countries where the falling seas
wash western shores beyond the ways of men
since the world worsened.   The word is forgotten
and the name perished.

         Their need he healed,
and laws renewed long forsaken.

Words he taught them wise and lovely –
their tongue ripened in the time of Sheave                    110
to song and music.   Secrets he opened
runes revealing.   Riches he gave them,
reward of labour, wealth and comfort
from the earth calling, acres ploughing,
sowing in season seed of plenty,
hoarding in garner golden harvest
for the help of men.   The hoar forests
in his days drew back to the dark mountains;
the shadow receded, and shining corn,
white ears of wheat, whispered in the breezes               120
where waste had been.   The woods trembled.

Halls and houses hewn of timber,
strong towers of stone steep and lofty,
golden-gabled, in his guarded city
they raised and roofed.   In his royal dwelling
of wood well-carven the walls were wrought;
fair-hued figures filled with silver,
gold and scarlet, gleaming hung there,
stories boding of strange countries,
were one wise in wit the woven legends               130
to thread with thought.   At his throne men found
counsel and comfort and care's healing,
justice in judgement.   Generous-handed
his gifts he gave.   Glory was uplifted.
Far sprang his fame over fallow water,
through Northern lands the renown echoed
of the shining king, Sheave the mighty.

At the end of (ii) occur eight lines which seem to have been added to the text; they were also inserted in pencil to the 'prose' text (i), here written in as verse-lines, with a further eight lines following (the whole passage of sixteen lines was struck through, but it was used afterwards in *The Notion Club Papers*, in the form of an addition to the poem proper).

Seven sons he begat, sires of princes,
men great in mind, mighty-handed
and high-hearted.   From his house cometh               140
the seeds of kings, as songs tell us,
fathers of the fathers, who before the change
in the Elder Years the earth governed,
Northern kingdoms named and founded,

shields of their peoples: Sheave begat them:
Sea-danes and Goths, Swedes and Northmen,
Franks and Frisians, folk of the islands,
Swordmen and Saxons, Swabes and English,
and the Langobards who long ago
beyond Myrcwudu a mighty realm                    150
and wealth won them in the Welsh countries
where Ælfwine Eadwine's heir
in Italy was king.   All that has passed.

### Notes on King Sheave

References in the following notes are given to the lines of the poem.

1–3    On the association of Sheave with the Longobards (Lombards)
       see p. 93.

7      The word *fallow* ('golden, golden-brown') is used several times
       in this poem of water, and once of gold (38); the corn sheaf is
       fallow-golden (68). See III. 369.

8–12   The 'eagle-clouds' that precede Sheave's coming in the poem
       do not appear in the prose version.

39     *Angol*: the ancient home of the English before their migration
       across the North Sea. See I. 24, 252 (entry *Eriol*).

142–3  I am at a loss to say what is referred to in these lines, where the
       'fathers of the fathers' who founded kingdoms in the North, the
       descendants of Sheave, 'governed the earth *before the change
       in the Elder Years*'.

148    *Swordmen*: it is evident that this is intended as the name of a
       people, but it is not clear to me which people. Conceivably, my
       father had in mind the *Brondingas*, ruled by Breca, Beowulf's
       opponent in the swimming-match, for that name has been
       interpreted to contain the word *brond* (*brand*) 'sword'.
       *Swabes*: this reading seems clear (*Swabians* in *The Notion
       Club Papers*). The Old English form was *Swæfe*: thus in
       *Widsith* is found *Engle ond Swæfe*, and *Mid Englum ic wæs
       ond mid Swæfum*. The *Suevi* of Roman historians, a term used
       broadly to cover many Germanic tribes, but here evidently
       used as in *Widsith* to refer particularly to Swabians dwelling in
       the North and neighbours of the Angles.

150    *Myrcwudu* (Old English): 'Mirkwood'. This was an ancient
       Germanic legendary name for a great dark boundary-forest,
       found in various quite different applications. The reference
       here is to the Eastern Alps (see note to line 151).

151    *Welsh*: 'foreign' (Roman). My father used the word here in the
       ancient sense. The old Germanic word *walhoz* meant 'Celtic or
       Roman foreigner'; whence in the plural the Old English *Walas*

(modern *Wales*), the Celts of Britain. So in *Widsith* the Romans are called *Rūm-walas*, and Caesar ruled over the towns and riches of *Wala rice*, the realm of the *Walas*. A line in *King Sheave* rejected in favour of 150–1 reads *Wide realms won them beyond the Welsh Mountains*, and these are the Alps. The ancient meaning survives in the word *walnut*, 'nut of the Roman lands'; also in *Wallace, Walloon*.

152–3    See pp. 54–5.

The roots of *King Sheave* lie far back in Northern Germanic legend. There are three primary sources: *Beowulf*, and the statements of two later chroniclers writing in Latin, Æthelweard (who died about the year 1000), and William of Malmesbury (who died in 1143). I give those of the historians first.

In Æthelweard's Chronicle the genealogy of the English kings ends with the names *Beo – Scyld – Scef* (which mean Barley, Shield, and Sheaf; Old English *sc* = 'sh'); and of *Scef* he says:

This Scef came in a swift boat, surrounded by arms, to an island of the ocean called Scani, and he was a very young boy, and unknown to the people of that country; but he was taken up by them, and they watched over him attentively as one of their own kin, and afterwards chose him to be their king.

William of Malmesbury (a writer notable for his drawing on popular stories and songs) has likewise in his genealogy the three figures *Beowius – Sceldius – Sceaf*, and he tells this of *Sceaf*:

He, as they say, was brought as a child in a boat without any oarsman to Scandza, a certain island of Germany. . . . He was asleep, and by his head was placed a handful of corn, on which account he was called 'Sheaf'. He was regarded as a marvel by the people of that country, and carefully fostered; when he was grown he ruled in the town which was then called Slaswic, but now Haithebi. That region is called Old Anglia, whence the Angli came to Britain.

The prologue, or as my father called it the *exordium*, to *Beowulf*, I give from his prose translation of the poem.

Lo! the glory of the kings of the people of the Spear-Danes in days of old we have heard tell, how those princes deeds of valour wrought. Oft Scyld Scefing robbed the hosts of foemen, many peoples of the seats where they drank their mead, laid fear upon men, who first was found in poverty; comfort for that he lived to know, mighty grew under heaven, throve in honour, until all that dwelt nigh about over the sea where the whale rides must hearken to him and yield him tribute – a good king was he!

To him was an heir afterwards born, a young child in his courts whom God sent for the comfort of the people: perceiving the dire need which they long while endured aforetime being without a prince. To him therefore the Lord of Life who rules in glory granted honour among men: Beowulf was renowned, far and wide his glory sprang – the heir of Scyld in Scedeland. Thus doth a young man bring it to pass with good deed and gallant gifts, while he dwells in his father's bosom, that after in his age there cleave to him loyal knights of his table, and the people stand by him when war shall come. By worthy deeds in every folk is a man ennobled.

Then at his allotted hour Scyld the valiant passed into the keeping of the Lord; and to the flowing sea his dear comrades bore him, even as he himself had bidden them while yet their prince he ruled them with his words – beloved lord of the land, long was he master. There at the haven stood with ringéd prow, ice-hung, eager to be gone, the prince's bark; they laid then their beloved king, giver of rings, in the bosom of the ship, in glory by the mast. There were many precious things and treasures brought from regions far away; nor have I heard tell that men ever in more seemly wise arrayed a boat with weapons of war and harness of battle; on his lap lay treasures heaped that now must go with him far into the dominion of the sea. With lesser gifts no whit did they adorn him, with treasures of that people, than did those that in the beginning sent him forth alone over the waves, a little child. Moreover, high above his head they set a golden standard and gave him to Ocean, let the sea bear him. Sad was their heart and mourning in their soul. None can report with truth, nor lords in their halls, nor mighty men beneath the sky, who received that load.

There is also a reference to a king named Sheaf (*Sceafa*) in *Widsith*, where in a list of rulers and the peoples they ruled occurs *Sceafa* [*weold*] *Longbeardum*, 'Sheaf ruled the Lombards'; at the beginning of the poem *King Sheave* it is to the Lombards that the boat bearing the child comes.

This is obviously not the place to enter into elaborate discussion of so intricate a subject as that of *Scyld Scefing*: 'a most astonishing tangle', my father called it. His lectures at Oxford during these years devote many pages to refined analysis of the evidences, and of competing theories concerning them. The long-fought argument concerning the meaning of 'Shield Sheafing' in *Beowulf* – does 'Sheafing' mean 'with a sheaf' or 'son of Sheaf', and is 'Shield' or 'Sheaf' the original ancestor king? – could in my father's opinion be settled with some certainty. In a summarising statement of his views in another lecture (here very slightly edited) he said:

*Scyld* is the eponymous ancestor of the *Scyldingas*, the Danish royal house to which Hrothgar King of the Danes in this poem belongs. His name is simply 'Shield': and he is a 'fiction', that is a name derived from the 'heraldic' family name *Scyldingas* after they became famous. This process was aided by the fact that the Old English (and Germanic) ending -*ing*, which could mean 'connected with, associated with, provided with', etc., was also the usual patronymic ending. The invention of this eponymous 'Shield' was probably Danish, that is actually the work of Danish dynastic historians (*þylas*) and alliterative poets (*scopas*) in the lifetime of the kings of whom we hear in *Beowulf*, the certainly historical Healfdene and Hrothgar.

As for *Scēfing*, it can thus, as we see, mean 'provided with a sheaf, connected in some way with a sheaf of corn', or son of a figure called Sheaf. In favour of the latter is the fact that there *are* English traditions of a *mythical* (not the same as eponymous and fictitious) ancestor called *Sceaf*, or *Sceafa*, belonging to ancient culture-myths of the North; and of his special association with Danes. In favour of the former is the fact that Scyld comes out of the unknown, a babe, and the name of his father, if he had any, could not be known by him or the Danes who received him. But such poetic matters are not strictly logical. Only in *Beowulf* are the two divergent traditions about the Danes blended in this way, the heraldic and the mythical. I think the poet meant (Shield) Sheafing as a patronymic. He was blending the vague and fictitious warlike glory of the eponymous ancestor of the conquering house with the more mysterious, far older and more poetical myths of the mysterious arrival of the babe, the corn-god or the culture-hero his descendant, at the beginning of a people's history, and adding to it a mysterious Arthurian departure, *back into the unknown*, enriched by traditions of ship-burials in the not very remote heathen past – to make a magnificent and suggestive *exordium*, and background to his tale.

*Beowulf*, son of Scyld Scefing, who appears in the *exordium* (to every reader's initial confusion, since he is wholly unconnected with the hero of the poem) my father held to be a corruption of *Beow* ('Barley') – which is the name found in the genealogies (p. 92).

To my mind it is overwhelmingly probable [he wrote] that the *Beowulf* name properly belongs *only* to the story of the bear-boy (that is of Beowulf the Geat); and that it is a fairy-tale name, in fact a 'kenning' for *bear*: 'Bee-wolf', that is 'honey-raider'. Such a name would be very unlikely to be transferred to the Scylding line by the poet, or at any time while the stories and legends which are the main fabric of the poem had any existence independent of it. I believe that *Beow* was turned into *Beowulf* after the poet's time, in the process of scribal tradition, either deliberately (and unhappily), or merely casually and erroneously.

Elsewhere he wrote:

A complete and entirely satisfactory explanation of the peculiarities of the *exordium* has naturally never been given. Here is what seems to me the most probable view.

The exordium is poetry, not (in intent) history. It was composed for its present place, and its main purpose was to glorify Scyld and his family, and so enhance the background against which the struggle of Grendel and Beowulf takes place. The choice of a marvellous legend, rather than a mere dynastic invention, was therefore natural. That our author was working principally on the blended form: *Beow* < *Scyld* < *Sceaf* [found in the genealogies, see p. 92] is shown by his retention of the patronymic *Scefing*. This title has indeed little point in his version, and certainly would not have appeared, had he really drawn on a story in which it was *Scyld* that came in a boat; while certain points in his account (the little destitute child) belong clearly to the Sheaf-Barley legends.

Why then did he make *Scyld* the child in the boat? – plainly his own device: it occurs nowhere else. Here are some probable reasons: (a) He was concentrating all the glamour on *Scyld* and the *Scylding* name.

(b)  A departure over sea – a sea-burial – was already associated with northern chieftains in old poems and lore, possibly already with the name of Scyld. This gains much in power and suggestiveness, if the same hero arrives and departs in a boat. The great heights to which Scyld climbed is also emphasized (explicitly) by the contrast thus made with his forlorn arrival.

(c)  Older and even more mysterious traditions may well still have been current concerning Danish origins: the legend of Ing who came and went back over the waves [see II. 305]. Our poet's *Scyld* has (as it were) replaced *Ing*.

Sheaf and Barley were after all in origin only rustic legends of no great splendour. But their legend here catches echoes of heroic traditions of the North going back into a remote past, into what philologists would call Primitive Germanic times, and are at the same time touched with the martial glories of the House of the Shield. In this way the poet contrives to clothe the lords of the golden hall of Hart with a glory and mystery, more archaic and simple but hardly less magnificent than that which adorns the king of Camelot, Arthur son of Uther. This is our poet's way throughout, seen especially in the exaltation among the great heroes that he has achieved for the Bear-boy of the old fairy-tale, who becomes in his poem Beowulf last king of the Geatas.

I give a final quotation from my father's lectures on this subject, where in discussing the concluding lines of the *exordium* he wrote of

the suggestion – it is hardly more; the poet is not explicit, and the idea was probably not fully formed in his mind – that Scyld went back to some mysterious land whence he had come. He came out of the Unknown beyond the Great Sea, and returned into It: a miraculous intrusion into history, which nonetheless left real historical effects: a new Denmark, and the heirs of Scyld in Scedeland. Such must have been his feeling.

In the last lines 'Men can give no certain account of the havens where that ship was unladed' we catch an echo of the 'mood' of pagan times in which ship-burial was practised. A mood in which the *symbolism* (what we should call the *ritual*) of a departure over the sea

whose further shore was unknown; and an actual belief in a magical
land or otherworld located 'over the sea', can hardly be distinguished –
and for neither of these elements or motives is conscious symbolism, or
real belief, a true description. It was a *murnende mōd*, filled with
doubt and darkness.

There remains to notice an element in my father's legend of Sheaf which
was not derived from the English traditions. This is found only in the
prose version (p. 86), where in the account of the great peace in the
Northern isles in the time of 'the Sheaf-lords' (so deep a peace that a gold
ring lying on the highway would be left untouched) he wrote of 'the great
mill of Sheaf', which 'was guarded still in the island sanctuary of the
North.' In this he was drawing on (and transforming) the Scandinavian
traditions concerned with Freyr, the god of fruitfulness, and King Fróthi
the Dane.

I cite here the story told by the Icelander Snorri Sturluson (c. 1179–
1241) in his work known as the *Prose Edda*, which is given to explain the
meaning of the 'kenning' *mjöl Fróða* ('Fróthi's meal') for 'gold'. According to Snorri, Fróthi was the grandson of *Skjöldr* (corresponding to Old
English *Scyld*).

Fróthi succeeded to the kingdom after his father, in the time when
Augustus Caesar imposed peace on the whole world; in that time
Christ was born. But because Fróthi was the mightiest of all kings in
the Northlands the peace was named after him wherever the Danish
tongue was spoken, and men call it the Peace of Fróthi. No man
injured another, even though he met face to face with the slayer of his
father or of his brother, free or bound; and there was no thief or robber
in those days, so that a gold ring lay long on *Ialangrsheiði* [in
Jutland]. King Fróthi went to a feast in Sweden at the court of a king
named Fjölnir. There he bought two bondwomen called Fenia and
Menia; they were big and strong. At that time there were in Denmark
two millstones so huge that no man was strong enough to turn them;
and the nature of these stones was such that whatever he who turned
them asked for was ground out by the mill. This mill was called Grótti.
King Fróthi had the bondwomen led to the mill, and he bade them
grind gold; and they did so, and at first they ground gold and peace and
happiness for Fróthi. Then he gave them rest or sleep no longer than
the cuckoo was silent or a song could be sung. It is said that they sang
the song which is called the Lay of Grótti, and this is its beginning:

> Now are come to the king's house
> The two foreknowing ones, Fenia and Menia;
> They are by Fróthi, son of Frithleif,
> The mighty maidens, as bondslaves held.

And before they ended their song they ground out a host against Fróthi, so that on that very night the sea-king named Mýsing came, and slew Fróthi, and took much plunder; and then the Peace of Fróthi was ended.

Elsewhere it is said that while the Danes ascribed the peace to Fróthi the Swedes ascribed it to Freyr; and there are close parallels between them. Freyr (which itself means 'the Lord') was called *inn Fróði*, which almost certainly means 'the Fruitful One'. The legend of the great peace, which in my father's work is ascribed to the time of Sheaf and his sons, goes back to very ancient origins in the worship of a divinity of fruitfulness in the great sanctuaries of the North: that of Freyr the Fruitful Lord at the great temple of Uppsala, and (according to an extremely plausible theory) that on the island of Zealand (Sjælland). Discussion of this would lead too far and into evidences too complex for the purpose of this book, but it may be said at least that it seems beyond question that Heorot, hall of the Danish kings in *Beowulf*, stood where is now the village of Leire, about three miles from the sea on the north coast of Zealand. At Leire there are everywhere huge grave mounds; and according to an eleventh-century chronicler, Thietmar of Merseburg, there was held at Leire in every ninth year (as also at Uppsala) a great gathering, in which large numbers of men and animals were sacrificed. A strong case can be made for supposing that the famous sanctuary described by Tacitus in his *Germania* (written near the end of the first century A.D.) where the goddess Nerthus, or *Mater Terra*, was worshipped 'on an island in the ocean', was indeed on Zealand. When Nerthus was present in her sanctuary it was a season of rejoicing and peace, when 'every weapon is laid aside.'*

In my father's legend of Sheaf these ancient echoes are used in new ways and with new bearings; and when Sheaf departed on his last journey his ship (as some have said) found the Straight Road into the vanished West.

A brief but perceptive report on *The Lost Road*, dated 17 December 1937, was submitted by a person unknown invited by Allen and Unwin to read the text. It is to be remembered that the typescript that had been made extended only to the beginning of the fourth chapter (p. 73 note 14) – and also, of course, that at this time nothing concerning the history of Middle-earth, of the Valar and Valinor, had been published. The reader described it as 'immensely interesting as a revelation of the personal enthusiasms of a very unusual mind', with 'passages of beautiful descriptive prose'; but found it 'difficult to imagine this novel when completed receiving any sort of recognition except in academic circles.' Stanley

---

*In Norse mythology the name of the goddess Nerthus survives in that of the god Njörth, father of Freyr. Njörth was especially associated with ships and the sea; and in very early writing of my father's *Neorth* briefly appears for Ulmo (II. 375, entry *Neorth*).

Unwin, writing to my father on 20 December 1937, said gently that he had no doubt of its being a *succès d'estime*, but while he would 'doubtless want to publish it' when complete, he could not 'hold out any hope of commercial success as an inducement to you to give the finishing of it prior claim upon your time.' He wrote this on the day after my father had written to say that he had finished the first chapter of 'a new story about Hobbits' (see III. 366).

With the entry at this time of the cardinal ideas of the Downfall of Númenor, the World Made Round, and the Straight Road, into the conception of 'Middle-earth', and the thought of a 'time-travel' story in which the very significant figure of the Anglo-Saxon Ælfwine would be both 'extended' into the future, into the twentieth century, and 'extended' also into a many-layered past, my father was envisaging a massive and explicit linking of his own legends with those of many other places and times: all concerned with the stories and the dreams of peoples who dwelt by the coasts of the great Western Sea. All this was set aside during the period of the writing of *The Lord of the Rings*, but not abandoned: for in 1945, before indeed *The Lord of the Rings* was completed, he returned to these themes in the unfinished *Notion Club Papers*. Such as he sketched out for these parts of *The Lost Road* remain, as it seems to me, among the most interesting and instructive of his unfinished works.

*Note on the poem 'The Nameless Land' and its later form*

*The Nameless Land* * is written in the form of the mediaeval poem *Pearl*, with both rhyme and alliteration and partial repetition of the last line of one stanza in the beginning of the next. I give it here in the form in which it was published; for *Tir-nan-Og* the typescripts have *Tír na nÓg*.

## THE NAMELESS LAND

There lingering lights do golden lie
    On grass more green than in gardens here,
On trees more tall that touch the sky
    With silver leaves a-swinging clear:
By magic dewed they may not die
    Where fades nor falls the endless year,
Where ageless afternoon goes by
    O'er mead and mound and silent mere.

---

* *The Nameless Land* was published in *Realities: an Anthology of Verse*, edited by G. S. Tancred (Leeds, at the Swan Press; London, Gay and Hancock Ltd.; 1927). A note on one of the typescripts states that it was written in May 1924 in the house at Darnley Road, Leeds (Carpenter, *Biography*, p. 107), and was 'inspired by reading *Pearl* for examination purposes'.

There draws no dusk of evening near,
  Where voices move in veiléd choir,
Or shrill in sudden singing sheer.
  And the woods are filled with wandering fire.

The wandering fires the woodland fill,
  In glades for ever green they glow,
In dells that immortal dews distill
  And fragrance of all flowers that grow.
There melodies of music spill,
  And falling fountains plash and flow,
And a water white leaps down the hill
  To seek the sea no sail doth know.
Its voices fill the valleys low,
  Where breathing keen on bent and briar
The winds beyond the world's edge blow
  And wake to flame a wandering fire.

That wandering fire hath tongues of flame
  Whose quenchless colours quiver clear
On leaf and land without a name
  No heart may hope to anchor near.
A dreamless dark no stars proclaim,
  A moonless night its marches drear,
A water wide no feet may tame,
  A sea with shores encircled sheer.
A thousand leagues it lies from here,
  And the foam doth flower upon the sea
'Neath cliffs of crystal carven clear
  On shining beaches blowing free.

There blowing free unbraided hair
  Is meshed with light of moon and sun,
And tangled with those tresses fair
  A gold and silver sheen is spun.
There feet do beat and white and bare
  Do lissom limbs in dances run,
Their robes the wind, their raiment air –
  Such loveliness to look upon
  Nor Bran nor Brendan ever won,
Who foam beyond the furthest sea
Did dare, and dipped behind the sun
  On winds unearthly wafted free.

Than Tir-nan-Og more fair and free,
  Than Paradise more faint and far,
O! shore beyond the Shadowy Sea,
  O! land forlorn where lost things are,

O! mountains where no man may be!
  The solemn surges on the bar
Beyond the world's edge waft to me;
  I dream I see a wayward star,
Than beacon towers in Gondobar
  More fair, where faint upon the sky
On hills imagineless and far
  The lights of longing flare and die.

My father turned again later to *The Nameless Land*, and altered the
title first to *Ælfwine's Song calling upon Eärendel* and then to *The Song of
Ælfwine (on seeing the uprising of Eärendel)*. There are many texts, both
manuscript and typescript, of *The Song of Ælfwine*, forming a continuous
development. That development, I feel certain, did not all belong to the
same time, but it seems impossible to relate the different stages to
anything external to the poem. On the third text my father wrote
afterwards 'Intermediate Version', and I give this here; my guess is – but
it is no more than a guess – that it belongs to about the time of *The Lost
Road*. Following it are two further texts which each change a few lines,
and then a final version with more substantial changes (including the loss
of a whole stanza) and an extremely interesting prose note on Ælfwine's
voyage. This is certainly relatively late: probably from the years after
*The Lord of the Rings*, though it might be associated with the *Notion Club
Papers* of 1945 – with the fifth line of the last verse (a line that entered
only in this last version) 'The white birds wheel; there flowers the Tree!'
compare the lines in the poem *Imram* (see p. 82), of the Tree full of birds
that Saint Brendan saw:

The Tree then shook, and flying free
  from its limbs the leaves in air
as white birds rose in wheeling flight,
  and the lifting boughs were bare.

Of course the *imrama* of Brendan and Ælfwine are in any case closely
associated. – There follow the texts of the 'intermediate' and final
versions.

## THE SONG OF ÆLFWINE

(on seeing the uprising of Eärendel)

There lingering lights still golden lie
  on grass more green than in gardens here,
On trees more tall that touch the sky
  with swinging leaves of silver clear.
While world endures they will not die,
  nor fade nor fall their timeless year,

As morn unmeasured passes by
　o'er mead and mound and shining mere.
When endless eve undimmed is near,
　o'er harp and chant in hidden choir
A sudden voice upsoaring sheer
　in the wood awakes the Wandering Fire.

The Wandering Fire the woodland fills:
　in glades for ever green it glows,
In dells where immortal dew distils
　the Flower that in secret fragrance grows.
There murmuring the music spills,
　as falling fountain plashing flows,
And water white leaps down the hills
　to seek the Sea that no sail knows.
Through gleaming vales it singing goes,
　where breathing keen on bent and briar
The wind beyond the world's end blows
　to living flame the Wandering Fire.

The Wandering Fire with tongues of flame
　with light there kindles quick and clear
The land of long-forgotten name:
　no man may ever anchor near;
No steering star his hope may aim,
　for nether Night its marches drear,
And waters wide no sail may tame,
　with shores encircled dark and sheer.
Uncounted leagues it lies from here,
　and foam there flowers upon the Sea
By cliffs of crystal carven clear
　on shining beaches blowing free.

There blowing free unbraided hair
　is meshed with beams of Moon and Sun,
And twined within those tresses fair
　a gold and silver sheen is spun,
As fleet and white the feet go bare,
　and lissom limbs in dances run,
Shimmering in the shining air:
　such loveliness to look upon
No mortal man hath ever won,
　though foam upon the furthest sea
He dared, or sought behind the Sun
　for winds unearthly flowing free.

O! Shore beyond the Shadowy Sea!
　O! Land where still the Edhil are!

O! Haven where my heart would be!
   the waves that beat upon thy bar
For ever echo endlessly,
   when longing leads my thought afar,
And rising west of West I see
   beyond the world the wayward Star,
Than beacons bright in Gondobar
   more clear and keen, more fair and high:
O! Star that shadow may not mar,
   nor ever darkness doom to die!

In the final version of the poem that now follows the prose note concerning Ælfwine's voyage is linked by an asterisk to the name *Ælfwine* in the title.

## THE SONG OF ÆLFWINE
### on seeing the uprising of Eärendil

Eressëa! Eressëa!

There elven-lights still gleaming lie
   On grass more green than in gardens here,
On trees more tall that touch the sky
   With swinging leaves of silver clear.
While world endures they will not die,
   Nor fade nor fall their timeless year,
As morn unmeasured passes by
   O'er mead and mount and shining mere.
When endless eve undimmed is near,
   O'er harp and chant in hidden choir
A sudden voice up-soaring sheer
   In the wood awakes the wandering fire.

With wandering fire the woodlands fill:
   In glades for ever green it glows;
In a dell there dreaming niphredil
   As star awakened gleaming grows,
And ever-murmuring musics spill,
   For there the fount immortal flows:
Its water white leaps down the hill,
   By silver stairs it singing goes
To the field of the unfading rose,
   Where breathing on the glowing briar
The wind beyond the world's end blows
   To living flame the wandering fire.

The wandering fire with quickening flame
   Of living light illumines clear

That land unknown by mortal name
Beyond the shadow dark and drear
And waters wild no ship may tame.
No man may ever anchor near,
To haven none his hope may aim
Through starless night his way to steer.
Uncounted leagues it lies from here:
In wind on beaches blowing free
Neath cliffs of carven crystal sheer
The foam there flowers upon the Sea.

O Shore beyond the Shadowy Sea!
O Land where still the Edhil are!
O Haven where my heart would be!
The waves still beat upon thy bar,
The white birds wheel; there flowers the Tree!
Again I glimpse them long afar
When rising west of West I see
Beyond the world the wayward Star,
Than beacons bright in Gondobar
More fair and keen, more clear and high.
O Star that shadow may not mar,
Nor ever darkness doom to die.

Ælfwine (Elf-friend) was a seaman of England of old who, being driven out to sea from the coast of Erin [*ancient name of Ireland*], passed into the deep waters of the West, and according to legend by some strange chance or grace found the 'straight road' of the Elvenfolk and came at last to the Isle of Eressëa in Elvenhome. Or maybe, as some say, alone in the waters, hungry and athirst, he fell into a trance and was granted a vision of that isle as it once had been, ere a West-wind arose and drove him back to Middle-earth. Of no other man is it reported that he ever beheld Eressëa the fair. Ælfwine was never again able to rest for long on land, and sailed the western seas until his death. Some say that his ship was wrecked upon the west shores of Erin and there his body lies; others say that at the end of his life he went forth alone into the deeps again and never returned.

It is reported that before he set out on his last voyage he spoke these verses:

Fela bið on Westwegum werum uncúðra
wundra and wihta, wlitescýne lond,
eardgeard Ylfa and Ésa bliss.
Lýt ǽnig wát hwylc his longað sý
þám þe eftsíðes yldu getwǽfeð.

'Many things there be in the West-regions unknown to Men, many wonders and many creatures: a land lovely to behold, the homeland of the Elves and the bliss of the Valar. Little doth any man understand what the yearning may be of one whom old age cutteth off from returning thither.'

Here reappears the idea seen at the end of the outline for the Ælfwine story in *The Lost Road* (p. 80), that after seeing a vision of Eressëa he was blown back again by a wind from the West. At the time when the outline was written the story that Ælfwine actually came to Tol-eressëa and was there told 'the Lost Tales' was also present (p. 78), and in the same way it seems from the present passage that there were the two stories. The idea that Ælfwine never in fact reached the Lonely Isle is found in a version of the old tale of *Ælfwine of England*, where he did not leap overboard but returned east with his companions (II. 332–3).

The verses that he spoke before his last voyage are those that Alboin Errol spoke and translated to his father in *The Lost Road* (p. 44), and which were used also in the title-pages to the *Quenta Silmarillion* (p. 203).

The retention of the name *Gondobar* right through from *The Nameless Land* is notable. It is found in the late version of the poem *The Happy Mariners*, which my father afterwards dated '1940?' (II. 274–5): 'O happy mariners upon a journey far, / beyond the grey islands and past Gondobar'. Otherwise *Gondobar* 'City of Stone' is one of the Seven Names of Gondolin (II. 158, 172; III. 145–6).

# PART TWO

---

## VALINOR AND MIDDLE-EARTH BEFORE THE LORD OF THE RINGS

# I
## THE TEXTS AND THEIR RELATIONS

In the fourth volume of this History were given the *Quenta Noldorinwa* (**Q**) or History of the Gnomes, which can be ascribed to the year 1930 (IV. 177–8); the earliest *Annals of Beleriand* (**AB**), which followed Q but is not itself dateable to a year, and the beginning of a new version (AB II); the earliest *Annals of Valinor* (**AV**), which followed the first version of AB but preceded the second (IV. 327); and the *Ambarkanta* or Shape of the World. The *Lay of Leithian*, given in Vol. III, was abandoned when far advanced in 1931.

I have described in III. 364 ff. how in November 1937 a new though unfinished version of 'The Silmarillion' was delivered to Allen and Unwin; while the first draft of the first chapter of *The Lord of the Rings* was written between 16 and 19 December 1937. Between 1930 and the end of 1937 must be placed the texts following Q in Vol. IV, and in addition these others which are given in this book (as well as *The Fall of Númenor* and *The Lost Road*):

(1) *Ainulindalë*, a new version of the original 'Lost Tale' of *The Music of the Ainur*. This is certainly later than AV, since in it the First Kindred of the Elves is named *Lindar*, not *Quendi*, and the old name *Noldoli* has given place to *Noldor*.

(2) A new version of the *Annals of Valinor*, again with the forms *Lindar* and *Noldor*. This version I shall call the *Later Annals of Valinor*, referring to it by the abbreviation **AV 2**, while the earliest version given in Vol. IV will be **AV 1**.

(3) A new version of the *Annals of Beleriand*, which looks to be a close companion text to AV 2. This I shall refer to similarly as **AB 2**, the *Later Annals of Beleriand*. In this case there are two antecedent versions, mentioned above, and called in Vol. IV AB I and AB II. These, to keep the parallel with the *Annals of Valinor*, can be referred to collectively as **AB 1** (since in writing AB 2 my father followed AB II so far as it went and then followed AB I).

(4) The *Lhammas* or Account of Tongues. This, extant in three versions, seems to have been closely related to the composition of the *Quenta Silmarillion*.

(5) The new version of 'The Silmarillion' proper, a once very fine manuscript whose making was interrupted when the material went to the publishers. To distinguish this version from its predecessor the *Quenta*

*Noldorinwa* or simply the *Quenta*, I use throughout the abbreviation
**QS**, i.e. *Quenta Silmarillion* or History of the Silmarils.

These five works form a later group (though I do not mean to imply
that there was any significant gap in time between them and the earlier);
a convenient defining mark of this is that they have *Noldor* where the
earlier have *Noldoli*.

Although I have said (IV. 262) that there seems no way of showing
whether the *Ambarkanta* was earlier or later than the earliest version of
the *Annals of Valinor*, it now seems clear to me that the *Ambarkanta*
belongs with the later group of texts. This is shown, I think, by the fact
that its title-page is closely similar in form to those of the *Ainulindalë* and
the *Lhammas* (all three bear the Elvish name of the work in *tengwar*);
moreover the reappearance in the *Ambarkanta* of *Utumna* as the name of
Melko's original fortress (see IV. 259–60) seems to place it later than
AB 2, which still names it *Angband* (but AV 2 has *Utumna*).

On the whole, I would be inclined to place these texts in the sequence
AB 2, AV 2, *Lhammas*, QS; the *Ambarkanta* at any rate after AB 2, and
the *Ainulindalë* demonstrably before QS. *The Fall of Númenor* was
later than the *Ambarkanta* (see p. 9 and IV. 261). But a definitive and
demonstrable sequence seems unattainable on the evidence; and the
attempt may in any case be somewhat unreal, for my father did not
necessarily complete one before beginning another. Certainly he had
them all before him, and as he progressed he changed what he had
already written to bring it into line with new developments in the stories
and in the names.

# II

# THE LATER ANNALS OF
# VALINOR

The second version of the *Annals of Valinor* (AV 2) is a fluent and legible manuscript in my father's ordinary handwriting of that time, with very little alteration during composition and very few subsequent changes in the early period – as opposed to wholesale rewriting of the earlier annals in the time after *The Lord of the Rings* : this being the initial drafting of the major later work, the *Annals of Aman*, and at almost all points clearly distinct from the emendations made many years before.

AV 2 shows no great narrative evolution from AV 1 (IV. 262 ff.), as that text was emended; on the other hand there are some noteworthy developments in names and conceptions. A curious feature is the retention of the original dates between the destruction of the Trees and the rising of the Sun and Moon, which in AV 1 were greatly accelerated by later pencilled changes: see IV. 273–4 and the commentary on annal 2992 below. Thus for example in AV 1 as originally written, and in AV 2, some ten years of the Sun (one Valian Year) elapsed between the Battle of Alqualondë and the utterance of the Prophecy of the North, whereas in AV 1 as emended only one year of the Sun passed between the two events.

In the brief commentary I treat AV 1 as including the emendations to it, fully recorded in IV. 270–4, and discussed in the commentary on that text. Later changes of the early period are recorded in the notes; these are few, mostly aspects of the progressive movement of names, and are merely referred forward to the place where they appear in original writing. Towards the end AV 2 becomes scarcely more than a fair copy of AV 1, but I give the text in full in order to provide within the same covers complete texts of the *Annals* and *Quenta* 'traditions' as they were when *The Lord of the Rings* was begun.

AV 2 is without any preamble concerning authorship, but there is a title-page comprising this and the closely similar later version of the *Annals of Beleriand* (AB 2):

*The Silmarillion*
2   Annals of Valinor
3   Annals of Beleriand

With this compare the title-pages given on p. 202, where 'The Silmarillion' is the comprehensive title of the tripartite (or larger) work.

# SILMARILLION

## II

### ANNALS OF VALINOR

Here begin the Annals of Valinor and speak of the foundation of the World.

At the beginning Ilúvatar, that is Allfather, made all things. Afterwards the Valar, or Powers, came into the world. These are nine: Manwë, Ulmo, Aulë, Oromë, Tulkas, Ossë, Mandos, Lórien, and Melko. Of these Manwë and Melko were most puissant, and were brethren; and Manwë is lord of the Valar, and holy. But Melko turned to lust and pride, and to violence and evil, and his name is accursed, and is not uttered, but he is called Morgoth. Oromë, Tulkas, Ossë, and Lórien were younger in the thought of Ilúvatar, ere the world's devising, than the other five; and Oromë was born of Yavanna, who is after named, but he is not Aulë's son.

The queens of the Valar were Varda, Manwë's spouse, and Yavanna, whom Aulë espoused after in the world, in Valinor; Vana the fair was the wife of Oromë; and Nessa the sister of Oromë was Tulkas' wife; and Uinen, the lady of the seas, was wife of Ossë; Vairë the weaver dwelt with Mandos, and Estë the pale with Lórien. No spouse hath Ulmo or Melko. No lord hath Nienna the mournful, queen of shadows, Manwë's sister and Melko's.

With these great ones came many lesser spirits, beings of their own kind but of smaller might; these are the Vanimor, the Beautiful. And with them also were later numbered their children, begotten in the world, but of divine race, who were many and fair; these are the Valarindi.

Of the beginning of the reckoning of Time and the foundation of Valinor.

Time was not measured by the Valar, until the building of Valinor was ended; but thereafter they counted time by the ages of Valinor, whereof each hath 100 years of the Valar, and each Valian year is as ten years of the Sun now are.

**Valian Years 500**   It is said that the Valar came into the world 30,000 Sun-years ere the first rising of the Moon, that is thirty ages ere the beginning of our time; and that Valinor was built five ages after their coming. In the long time before the fortifying of the West, Aulë made great lamps for the lighting of the world and set them upon pillars wrought by Morgoth. But Morgoth was already moved with hatred and jealousy and his pillars were made with deceit. Wherefore the Lamps fell and growth that had begun with the gathering of light was arrested; but the Gods assailed by many waters withdrew into the West. There they began the building of their land and mansions, between the Encircling Sea and the Great Sea of the West, upon whose shore they piled high mountains. But Morgoth departed to the North of the world. The symmetry of earth and water was first broken in those days.

**V.Y.1000** In this Valian Year, after Valinor was made, and Valmar built, the city of the Gods, the Valar brought into being the Two Trees, Laurelin and Silpion, of gold and silver, whose bloom gave light to Valinor. All this while Morgoth dwelt in Middle-earth, and he made his fortress at Utumna in the North; but he held sway with violence and the lands were yet more broken in that time.

**V.Y.1000–2000** A thousand Valian Years of bliss and splendour followed the kindling of the Trees in Valinor, but Middle-earth was in darkness. Thither came Yavanna at times, and the slow growth of the forests was begun. Of the Valar only Oromë came ever there, and he hunted in the dark woods of the ancient earth, when he was weary of the shining lands. Morgoth withdrew before his horn.

**V.Y.1900** Yavanna often reproached the Valar for their neglected stewardship; wherefore on a time Varda began the fashioning of the stars, and she set them aloft. Thereafter the night of the world was beautiful, and some of the Vanimor strayed into Middle-earth. Among these was Melian, whose voice was renowned in Valmar. She was of Lórien's house, but she returned not thither for many years, and the nightingales sang about her in the dark woods of the western lands.

**V.Y.1950** The mightiest of the works of Varda, lady of the stars, was that constellation which is called by the Elves the Sickle of the Gods, but by Men of the ancient North it was named the Burning Briar, and by later Men it has been given many names beside. This sign of the sickle Varda hung above the North as a threat to Morgoth and an omen of his fall. At its first shining the Elder Children of Ilúvatar awoke in the midmost of Middle-earth. They are the Elves.[1] Hence they are called also the children of the stars.[2]

**V.Y.1980–1990** Oromë found the Elves and befriended them; and the most part of that folk marched under his guidance west and north to the shores of Beleriand, being bidden by the Gods to Valinor. But first Morgoth was overcome with war and bound and led captive and imprisoned under Mandos. In that war of the Gods the lands were rent anew.

**V.Y.2000** From this time was counted the imprisonment of Morgoth. By the doom of Manwë he should be confined in punishment for seven ages, 700 Valian Years, after which time he should be given grace of repentance and atonement.

The Valian Year 2000 from the entry of the Gods into the world, and 1000 from the kindling of the Trees, is accounted the Noontide of the Blessed Realm, and the full season of the mirth of Valinor. In that time all the earth had peace.

In that year the first kindreds of the Elves came to the Western Shore and entered into the light of the Gods. The Eldar are all those Elves called who obeyed the summons of Oromë. Of these there are three kindreds, the Lindar, the Noldor, and the Teleri. The Lindar and the Noldor came first to Valinor, and they built the hill of Kôr in a pass of the mountains nigh to the sea-shore, and upon it upraised the city of Tûn³ and the tower of Ingwë their king.

**V.Y.2000–2010** But the Teleri, who came after them, waited in the meanwhile for ten Valian Years upon the shores of Beleriand, and some never departed thence. Wherefore they were called Ilkorindi, for they came never unto Kôr. Of these most renowned was Tindingol or Thingol,⁴ brother of Elwë, lord of the Teleri. Melian enchanted him in the woods of Beleriand; and he after wedded her and dwelt as a king in the western twilight. But while he slept under the spells of Melian his people sought him in vain, and ere he awoke most of the Teleri had departed. For they were drawn upon an island by Ulmo and so passed the sea as the Lindar and Noldor had done before.

[It is told that a company of the Noldor, whose leader was Dan, forsook the host of Finwë, lord of the Noldor, early upon the westward march, and turned south. But they found the lands barren and dark, and turned again north, and marched west once more with much wandering and grief. Of these some, under Denithor⁵ son of Dan, came at last, about the year of the Valar 2700, over Eredlindon, and dwelt in Ossiriand, and were allies of

Thingol.⁶ This have I, Pengolod, added here, for it was not known unto Rúmil.]

**V.Y.2010–2110**  By the deeds of Ossë, as is elsewhere recounted, the Teleri came not at once into Valinor, but during this time dwelt upon Tol-eressëa, the Lonely Isle, in the Great Sea, within sight of Valinor.

**V.Y.2111**  In this year the Teleri came in their ships to Valinor, and dwelt upon its eastern strands; and there they made the town and haven of Alqualondë, that is Swanhaven, thus named because they moored there their swans, and their swan-shaped boats.⁷

**V.Y.2500**  The Noldor had at this time invented gems, and they fashioned them in many myriads. At length, about five ages after the coming of the Noldor to Valinor, Fëanor the Smith, eldest son of Finwë, chief of the Noldor, devised the thrice-renowned Silmarils, about whose fate these tales are woven. They shone of their own light, being filled with the radiance of the Two Trees, the holy light of Valinor, which was blended therein to a marvellous fire.

**V.Y.2700**  In this time Morgoth sued for pardon; and at the prayers of Nienna his sister, and by the clemency of Manwë his brother, but against the wish of Tulkas and Aulë and Oromë, he was released; and he feigned humility and repentance, obeisance to the Valar, and love and friendship for the Elves, and dwelt in Valinor in ever-increasing freedom. He lied and dissembled, and most he cozened the Noldor, for he had much to teach, and they had an overmastering desire to learn; but he coveted their gems and lusted for the Silmarils.⁸

**V.Y.2900**  During two more ages the bliss of Valinor remained, yet a shadow began to gather in many hearts; for Morgoth was at work with secret whisperings and crooked counsels. Most he prevailed upon the Noldor, and he sowed the seeds of dissension between the proud sons of Finwë, lord of Gnomes, Fëanor, Fingolfin, and Finrod, and distrust was born between Noldor and Valar.

About this time, because of the feuds that began to awake, the Gods held council, and by their doom Fëanor, eldest son of Finwë, and his household and following, were deprived of the leadership of the Gnomes. Wherefore the house of Fëanor was after called the Dispossessed, for this, and because Morgoth later robbed them of their treasure. Finwë and Fëanor departed from the city of Tûn and dwelt in the north of Valinor; but Morgoth hid himself, and appeared only to Fëanor in secret, feigning friendship.

**V.Y.2950** The Gods heard tidings of Morgoth, and sent to apprehend him, but he fled over the mountains into the shadows of Arvalin, and abode there long, plotting evil, and gathering the strength of darkness unto him.

**V.Y.2990** Morgoth now completed his designs, and with the aid of Ungoliantë out of Arvalin he stole back into Valinor, and destroyed the Trees. Thence he escaped in the gathering dark northward, and he sacked the dwellings of Finwë and Fëanor, and carried off a host of jewels, and stole the Silmarils. There he slew Finwë before his doors, and many Elves, and defiled thus Valinor and began murder in the world. This reward had Finwë and Fëanor for their friendship.

Morgoth was hunted by the Valar, but he escaped into the North of Middle-earth, and re-established there his strong places, and bred and gathered once more his evil servants, Orcs and Balrogs.

[Then fear came into Beleriand, which for many ages had dwelt in starlit peace. But Thingol with his ally Denithor of Ossiriand for a long while held back the Orcs from the South. But at length Denithor son of Dan was slain, and Thingol made his deep mansions in Menegroth, the Thousand Caves, and Melian wove magic of the Valar about the land of Doriath; and most of the Elves of Beleriand withdrew within its protection, save some that lingered about the western havens, Brithombar and Eglorest beside the Great Sea, and the Green-elves of Ossiriand who dwelt still behind the rivers of the East, wherein the power of Ulmo ran. This have I, Pengolod, added to the words of Rúmil of Valinor.]

**V.Y.2990-3000** Of the last years before the Hiding of Valinor.

**V.Y.2991** Valinor lay now in great gloom, and darkness, save only for the stars, fell on all the western world. Then Fëanor, against the will of the Valar, returned to Tûn, and claimed the kingship of the Noldor after Finwë; and he summoned all that people unto Kôr. There Fëanor spoke unto them. Fëanor was the mightiest Gnome of all that have been, wordcrafty and hand-crafty, fair and strong and tall, fiery of mood and thought, hardtempered, undaunted, master of the wills of others. Songs have been made of his deeds that day. His speech was like to flame. Though his heart was hot with hatred for the slayer of his father and the robber of his gems, and he spoke much of vengeance, yet he echoed Morgoth unwitting, and his words were strong with the lies of Morgoth, and rebel[lion] against Manwë. The most part of the Noldor he persuaded that day to follow him out of Valinor and recover their realms on earth, lest they be filched by the Younger Children of Ilúvatar. At that assembly Fëanor and his seven sons swore their dreadful oath to slay or pursue with hate any so ever that held a Silmaril against their will.

**V.Y.2992** The great march of the Gnomes was long preparing. The Gods forbade but did not hinder, for Fëanor had accused them of keeping the Elves captive against their wills. At length the host set out, but under divided leadership, for Fingolfin's house held him for king.

The host had not gone far, ere it came into Fëanor's heart that all these mighty companies, both warriors and others, and great store of goods, would never make the vast leagues unto the North save with the help of ships. Now they went north both because they purposed to come at Morgoth, and because northward the Sundering Seas grew narrow; for Tûn beneath Taniquetil is upon the girdle of the earth, where the Great Sea is measurelessly wide. But the Teleri alone had ships, and they would not give them up, nor lend them, against the will of the Valar.

Thus befell in this year of dread the grievous battle about Alqualondë, and the kinslaying evilly renowned in song, wherein the Noldor distraught furthered Morgoth's work. But the Noldor overcame the Teleri, and took their ships, and fared thence slowly along the rocky coasts in great peril, and amid dissensions. Many marched on foot, and others manned the vessels.

**V.Y.2993** About this time the Noldor came unto a place, nigh unto the northern confines of Valinor, where a high rock stands above the shore, and there stood either Mandos himself or his messenger, and spoke the Doom of Mandos. For the kinslaying he cursed the house of Fëanor, and to a less degree all those who followed them or shared in their enterprise, unless they would return to abide the doom of the Valar. But if they would not, then should evil fortune and disaster befall them, and ever should this come most to pass through treachery of kin towards kin; and their oath should turn against them, hindering rather than aiding the recovery of the jewels. A measure of mortality should visit the Noldor, and they should be slain with weapons, and with torments, and with sorrow, and in the long end they should fade upon Middle-earth and wane before the younger race. Much else he foretold darkly that after befell, and he warned them that the Valar would fence Valinor against their return.

But Fëanor hardened his heart and held on, and with him went still, but reluctantly, Fingolfin's folk, feeling the constraint of their kinship and of the will of Fëanor; they feared also the doom of the Gods, for not all of Fingolfin's people had been guiltless of the kinslaying. Inglor (who was after surnamed Felagund, Lord of Caves) and the other sons of Finrod went forward also; for they had aforetime had great friendship, Inglor with the sons of Fingolfin, and his brothers Orodreth, Angrod, and Egnor with Celegorm and Curufin, sons of Fëanor.[9] But the lords of the house of Finrod were less grim and of kinder mood than the others, and they had no part in the kinslaying; yet they did not escape its curse who now refused to turn back. Finrod himself returned and many of his people with him, and came at last once more unto Valinor and received the pardon of the Gods. But Aulë their ancient friend smiled on them no more, and the Teleri were estranged.

Here endeth that which Rúmil wrote.

Here followeth the continuation of Pengolod.

**V.Y.2994**   The Noldor came at length into the bitter North, and further along the land they could not go by ship; for there is a strait between the Westworld, whereon Valinor is built, that curveth eastward, and the coast of Middle-earth, which beareth westward, and through these narrows the chill waters of the Encircling Sea and the waves of the Great Sea flow together, and there are vast mists of deathly cold, and the sea-streams are filled with clashing hills of ice, and the grinding of ice submerged. This strait was named Helkaraksë.

The ships that remained, many having been lost, were too few to carry all across, save with many a passage and return. But none were willing to abide upon the coast, while others sailed away, for trust was not full between the leaders, and quarrel arose between Fëanor and Fingolfin.

Fëanor and his folk seized all the ships and sailed east across the sea, and they took none of the other companies save Orodreth,[10] Angrod, and Egnor, whom Celegorm and Curufin loved. And

Fëanor said: 'Let the murmurers whine their way back to the shadows of Valmar!' And he burned the ships upon the eastern shore, and so great was its fire that the Noldor[11] left behind saw the redness afar off.

**V.Y.2995** In this year of the Valar Fëanor came unto Beleriand and the shores beneath Eredlómin, the Echoing Mountains; and his landing was at the narrow inlet, Drengist, that runs into Dorlómen. The Gnomes came thence into Dorlómen and about the north of the Mountains of Mithrim, and camped in the land of Hithlum in that part that is named Mithrim, and north of the great lake that hath the same name:

In the land of Mithrim they fought the first of the battles of the long war of the Gnomes and Morgoth. For an army of Orcs came forth aroused by the burning of the ships and the rumour of their advance; but the Gnomes were victorious and drove away the Orcs with slaughter, and pursued them beyond Eredwethion into the plain of Bladorion. That battle is the First Battle of Beleriand, and is called Dagor-os-Giliath,[12] the Battle under Stars; for all was yet dark.

But the victory was marred by the fall of Fëanor. He advanced unwarily upon Bladorion, too hot in pursuit, and was surrounded when the Balrogs turned to bay in the rearguard of Morgoth. Very great was the valour of Fëanor, and he was wrapped in fire; but at length he fell mortally wounded by the hand of Gothmog, Lord of Balrogs. But his sons bore him back to Mithrim, and he died there, reminding them of their oath. To this they added now an oath of vengeance for their father.

**V.Y.2996** Maidros, eldest son of Fëanor, was caught in the snares of Morgoth. For Morgoth feigned to treat with him, and Maidros feigned to be willing, and either purposed evil to the other; and each came with force to the parley, but Morgoth with the more, and Maidros was made captive.

Morgoth held Maidros as a hostage, and swore only to release him if the Noldor would march away, either to Valinor if they could, or else from Beleriand and away to the South of the world. But if they would not, he would torment Maidros. But the sons of Fëanor believed not that he would release their brother, if they departed, nor were they willing to depart, whatever he might do.

**V.Y.2997** Morgoth hung Maidros by the right wrist in a band of hellwrought steel above a precipice upon Thangorodrim, where none could reach him.

**V.Y.2998–3000** Now Fingolfin and Inglor, son of Finrod, won their way at last with grievous losses and with minished might into the North of Middle-earth. This is accounted among the most valiant and desperate of the deeds of the Gnomes; for they came perforce over Helkaraksë, being unwilling to retrace their way to Valinor, and having no ships. But their agony in that crossing was very great, and their hearts were filled with bitterness.

Even as Fingolfin set foot in Middle-earth the First Ages of the World were ended, for they had tarried long in despair upon the shores of the West, and long had been their bitter journey.

The First Ages are reckoned as 30000 years, or 3000 years of the Valar; whereof the first Thousand was before the Trees, and Two thousand save nine were the Years of the Trees or of the Holy Light, which lived after, and lives yet, only in the Silmarils; and the nine are the Years of Darkness, or the Darkening of Valinor.

Towards the end of these nine years, as is elsewhere told, the Gods made the Moon and Sun, and sent them forth over the world, and light came into the Hither Lands. The Moon was the first to go forth.

Men, the Younger Children of Ilúvatar, awoke in the East of the world at the first Sunrise;[13] hence they are also called the Children of the Sun. For the Sun was set as a sign of the waning of the Elves, but the Moon cherisheth their memory.

With the first Moonrise Fingolfin set foot upon the North, for the Moonrise came ere the Dawn, even as Silpion of old bloomed ere Laurelin and was the elder of the Trees.

**Year of the Sun 1** But the first Dawn shone upon Fingolfin's march, and his blue and silver banners were unfurled, and flowers sprang under his marching feet; for a time of opening and growth, sudden, swift, and fair, was come into the world, and good of evil, as ever happens.

Then Fingolfin marched through the fastness of Morgoth's land, that is Dor-Daideloth,[14] the Land of Dread; and the Orcs fled before the new light, amazed, and hid beneath the earth; and the Elves smote upon the gates of Angband, and their trumpets echoed in Thangorodrim's towers.

Now, being wary of the wiles of Morgoth, Fingolfin withdrew from the doors of hell and turned unto Mithrim, so that the Shadowy Mountains, Eredwethion, might be his guard, while his folk rested. But there was little love between Fingolfin's following and the house of Fëanor; and the sons of Fëanor removed and camped upon the southern shore, and the lake lay between the peoples.

From this time are reckoned the Years of the Sun, and these things happened in the first year. Now measured time came into the world, and the growth, changing, and ageing of all things was hereafter more swift, even in Valinor, but most swift in the Hither Lands upon Middle-earth, the mortal regions between the seas of East and West. And all living things spread and multiplied in those days, and the Elves increased, and Beleriand was green and filled with music. There many things afterward came to pass, as is recorded in the *Annals of Beleriand*, and in the *Quenta*, and in other songs and tales.

## NOTES

All the changes to the original text recorded here belong certainly to the 'early period', as distinct from alterations made after the completion of *The Lord of the Rings*.

1   *They are the Elves* > *They are the Quendi or Elves*. See *Lhammas* §1 and commentary.

2   *the children of the stars* > *Eldar, the children of the stars*. See *Lhammas* §2 and commentary.

3   *Tûn* > *Túna* (and in annals 2900 and 2992). See *Lhammas* §5, QS §39, and commentaries.

4   *Tindingol or Thingol* > *Sindo the Grey, later called Thingol*. See *Lhammas* §6 and commentary.

5   *Denithor* > *Denethor* (and in annal 2990). See *Lhammas* §7 and commentary.

6   Added here: *These were the Green-elves*.

7   The words *swans, and their* are a careful addition, probably made at the time of writing; but it seems odd, since my father can hardly have wished to say that the Teleri 'moored' their swans at Alqualondë.

8   Added here, perhaps at the time of composition of the *Annals*: [*Here the Danians came over Eredlindon and dwelt in Ossiriand.*] On the term *Danians* see commentary on *Lhammas* §7.

9   This sentence changed to read: *for they had aforetime had great friendship, Inglor and Orodreth with the sons of Fingolfin, and his brothers Angrod and Egnor with Celegorn and Curufin, sons of Fëanor*. See QS §42 and commentary. – *Celegorm* > *Celegorn* again in annal 2994; see commentary on QS §41.

10   *Orodreth* struck out; see note 9, and QS §73 and commentary.

11   *Noldor* was changed from *Noldoli*: see commentary on annal 2000.

12   *Dagor-os-Giliath* > *Dagor-nuin-Giliath*. See QS §88 and commentary.

13  *Men . . . awoke in the East of the world at the first Sunrise* > *At the Sunrise Men . . . awoke in Hildórien in the midmost regions of the world.* See QS §82 and commentary.

14  *Dor-Daideloth* > *Dor-Daedeloth.* See QS §91 and commentary.

### Commentary on the Later Annals of Valinor

**Opening section**  The mixture of tenses, already present in AV 1, becomes now slightly more acute with *Manwë is* for *Manwë was* lord of the Valar; see p. 208.

The sentence concerning Oromë, Tulkas, Ossë, and Lórien, who were 'younger in the thought of Ilúvatar, ere the world's devising' than the other five Valar, is not in AV 1, nor is anything similar said in any text of the *Quenta* tradition (though there does appear in QS §6 the statement that Mandos was the *elder* and Lórien the *younger* of the Fanturi; cf. also *The Lost Road* p. 63, where Alkar (Melko) is called 'the *éldest* in the thought of Ilúvatar'). The statements in AV 2 that 'Aulë espoused Yavanna after in the world, in Valinor', and that Oromë is Yavanna's son but not Aulë's, are likewise absent from AV 1 and from the whole *Quenta* tradition.

Two of the fragments of Ælfwine's Old English translations of the *Annals* given in Vol. IV bear on this. In the brief version III (IV. 291) the statement concerning the relative 'youth' of certain of the Valar appears, but it is confined to Tulkas and Oromë; and there also it is said, as here, that Aulë and Yavanna became husband and wife (*wurdon to sinhíwan*) after the Valar entered the world. That this text derives from the post-*Lord of the Rings* period is suggested but not proved by the form *Melkor*, not *Melko* (on this point see p. 338, commentary on §30). The other Old English passage in question, a hastily-written scrap (IV. 293), has the statement found in AV 2 that Oromë was not Aulë's son, but lacks that concerning the later union of Yavanna and Aulë.*

The opening of AV 2 was long after extensively changed and re-written; but one alteration in the present passage looks as if it were made during the earlier time. The sentence 'and Oromë was born of Yavanna, who is after named, but he is not Aulë's son' was changed to this notable statement:

and Oromë was the offspring of Yavanna, who is after named, but not as the Children of the Gods born in this world, for he came of her thought ere the world was made.

This is associated with development in the idea of the lesser beings who came into the world with the Valar, which underwent several changes (ultimately emerging into the conception of the Maiar). In Q (IV. 78)

---

*The uninterpretable mark following the name Oromë in this passage, which I explained to mean 'and Tulkas', may in fact be a shorthand for 'Oromë, Tulkas, Ossë, and Lórien', as in AV 2, with which this Old English fragment evidently belongs.

these spirits are mentioned but not given any name, and the same remains the case in QS (§2). In AV 1 (IV. 263) a distinction is made between the children of the Valar on the one hand and 'beings of their own kind but of less might' on the other; but all entered the world with the Valar, and all are called *Valarindi*. In AV 2 the distinction is enlarged: the lesser spirits, 'beings of their own kind but of smaller might', who came with the Valar, are the *Vanimor*, 'the Beautiful', and the Children of the Valar, who did not enter the world with them but were *begotten in the world*, are the *Valarindi*; these were 'later numbered with' the *Vanimor*. In the Old English fragment referred to above the same is said, though the name *Valarindi* is not there given to the Children of the Valar (IV. 293).

**Annal 500**  The story (going back to the *Lost Tales*) that Morgoth devised the pillars of the Lamps out of ice is told in the *Ambarkanta* (IV. 238) and indicated in AV 1 (IV. 263: 'Morgoth destroyed *by deceit* the Lamps which Aulë made'). In the other tradition, QS (§11) retains the wording of Q (IV. 80), in which it is only said that Morgoth overthrew the Lamps, and does not suggest the story of his deceit.

**Annal 1000**  On the appearance here of *Utumna*, a reversion to the *Lost Tales*, as the name of Melko's original fortress see p. 108. This is an indication that AV 2 followed AB 2, where (in the opening passage in both texts) *Angband* was retained.

**Annal 1000–2000**  The phrase 'and the slow growth of the forests was begun' is surprising. In S and Q (IV. 12, 82) the primaeval forests already grew in Middle-earth at the time of the downfall of the Lamps, and this is repeated in QS (§18). The present passage seems at variance with that under V.Y.500 ('the Lamps fell and growth that had begun with the gathering of light was arrested'), and to revert to the old story of the *Lost Tales*: cf. the commentary on the tale of *The Chaining of Melko* (I. 111): 'In this earliest narrative there is no mention of the beginning of growth during the time when the Lamps shone, and the first trees and low plants appeared under Yavanna's spells in the twilight after their overthrow.'

**Annal 1900**  This is the first appearance of the idea that the Valar, withdrawn behind their mountain-wall, 'neglected their stewardship' of Middle-earth, and that it was the reproaches of Yavanna that led to Varda's making of the stars. The idea of the two starmakings was not yet present.

For *Vanimor* AV 1 has *Valarindi*: see the commentary on the opening section.

**Annal 2000**  The form *Noldor* for *Noldoli* first occurs in these Annals and in AB 2 (in that for V.Y. 2994 my father still inadvertently wrote *Noldoli* before changing it to *Noldor*); and in the present passage is the first appearance of the name *Lindar* of the First Kindred, replacing earlier *Quendi* of S, Q, and AV 1 (*Lindar* occurs in the earlier texts by emendation at this later time). This change implies also that the application of *Quendi* had shifted, to its final meaning of 'all Elves' (this being in fact a reversion to a nomenclature that appeared briefly long before, I. 234–5); and indeed by an early change to the manuscript (note 1 above) 'They are the Elves' became 'They are the Quendi or Elves'. With this shift went the narrowing of meaning, first found here, of the term *Eldar* to those Elves who obeyed the summons of Oromë (although in the early change given in note 2 *Eldar* seems to be used as a simple equivalent of *Quendi*); see the commentary on *Lhammas* §2.

**Annal 2000–2010**  This is the first indication of a new meaning given to *Ilkorindi*, narrowing it from the old sense of 'Dark-elves' in general (IV. 85) to those of the Teleri who remained in Beleriand; see the commentary on *Lhammas* §2.

The conclusion of the annal is enclosed in square brackets in the manuscript, and this is no doubt original. It closely followed the pencilled addition to AV 1 (IV. 270–1), where it is not however said that this was an addition by Pengolod to Rúmil's work; for the preamble to AV 1 states that the *Annals of Valinor* were written in their entirety by Pengolod. This had now been changed, with Pengolod becoming the continuator of Rúmil's annals. See the commentary on annals 2990 and 2993. – The coming of the 'Danians' over Eredlindon in V.Y.2700 is referred to again in an addition to the annal for that year (note 8).

**Annal 2700**  Oromë is not named in the other texts as opposed to the release of Melko. In Q (IV. 90) and in QS (§48) it was Ulmo and Tulkas who doubted its wisdom; in AV 1 Aulë and Tulkas are named as opposers.

**Annal 2900**  On the evolution of the story of Morgoth's movements at this time see IV. 277–8.

**Annal 2990**  On the probable meaning of the sentence 'This reward had Finwë and Fëanor for their friendship' see IV. 278.

The phrase 'bred and gathered once more his evil servants, Orcs and Balrogs', retained from AV 1, shows the conception still present that the Orcs were first brought into being long before Morgoth's return to Middle-earth, in contrast to the opening of AB 2.

The conclusion of this annal, like that in annal 2000–2010, is enclosed in square brackets in the manuscript, and like the former passage is closely based on (though re-ordered from) interpolations to AV 1 (IV. 271), but with the addition attributing it to Pengolod.

**Annal 2992**  The accusation of Fëanor against the Valar is not in AV 1. – As first written AV 1 has 'Thus about 2992 of Valian Years befell . . .', which was changed to 'Thus in the dread Year of the Valar 2999 (Sun

Year 29991)' (IV. 273). The fact that my father partially adopted the revised phrasing ('the dread Year', 'this year of dread') suggests perhaps that the revised dating in AV 1, greatly accelerating the succession of events, was before him, and he rejected it.

That some went on foot up the coast while others manned the ships is not told in AV 1, but goes back to the *Lost Tales* (see IV. 48).

**Annal 2993**   In the phrase in the Doom of Mandos 'they should be slain with weapons' my father first put 'they should be lightly slain', as in AV 1, but struck out the word *lightly* as he wrote; see IV. 278-9.

After 'warned them that the Valar would fence Valinor against their return' he put 'Here endeth that which Rúmil wrote' (words added in pencil at this point in AV 1, IV. 271 note 20), but at once struck them out and set them at the end of the annal, as printed in the text. While the preamble to AV 1 states that the Annals were the work of Pengolod alone, a second version of the preamble (IV. 292) says that they 'were written first by Rúmil the Elfsage of Valinor, and after by [i.e. continued by] Pengolod the Wise of Gondolin'; and I have suggested (IV. 292-3) that Rúmil was one of the Noldor who returned to Valinor with Finrod, and that this would explain why the end of his part in the Annals was moved further on in AV 2 – 'his part ends with the actual record of Finrod's return, and of the reception that he and those with him received.' Cf. the passages in annals 2000-2010 and 2990 where insertions are made by Pengolod into Rúmil's text.

In this annal (and in AB 2 annal 50) *Felagund* is for the first time rendered 'Lord of Caves'. He was called *Inglor Felagund* in the Old English version of AB (IV. 339, 341).

**Annal 2998-3000**   With the words 'For the Sun was set as a sign of the waning of the Elves, but the Moon cherisheth their memory' (repeated in QS §75) cf. *The Lost Road*, p. 72 (note 12).

# III

# THE LATER ANNALS OF BELERIAND

The manuscript of this version, **AB 2**, of the *Annals of Beleriand* is closely similar to that of AV 2, and obviously belongs to very much the same time. As with AV 2, the manuscript was in its earlier part heavily corrected and overwritten years later – the first stage in the development of the final version of these chronicles, the *Grey Annals*. In this case, however, there was far more revision in the earlier period than with AV 2, and in some places it is hard to separate the 'early' from the 'late'; reference to QS will usually decide the point, but doubt remains in cases where QS was itself altered at an indeterminable time.

I give the text as it was originally written (admitting a few additions or corrections that were clearly made at or very soon after the time of composition), but make an exception in the case of dates. Here it is less confusing and easier for subsequent reference to give the emended dates in square brackets after the original ones. These major alterations in the chronology took place during the writing of QS, and are discussed on pp. 257–8. Changes others than those to dates, where I feel sufficiently certain that they belong to the pre-*Lord of the Rings* period, are recorded in the notes; the great majority of them reflect movement of names and narrative that had come in when QS was written (or in some cases entered in the course of the writing of QS), and I do not discuss them in the commentary on AB 2.

As already noted (p. 107), the two earlier versions of these Annals given in Vol. IV (AB I and AB II) are here referred to as **AB 1**; as far as annal 220 the comparison being with AB II, and after that point with AB I. As with AV 2, in the commentary I treat AB 1 as including the emendations made to those manuscripts (fully recorded in IV. 310–13, 332–3), and do not take up again points discussed in the commentaries in Vol. IV.

In content AB 2 remains in general close to AB 1, but it is not only fuller in matter but also more finished in manner; the *Annals of Beleriand* was becoming an independent work, and less (as I described AB 1 in IV. 294) a 'consolidation of the historical structure in its internal relations and chronology' in support of the *Quenta* – but it is still annalistic, retaining the introductory *Here* of the year-entries (derived from the *Anglo-Saxon Chronicle*), and lacking connection of motive between events. And since, most unhappily, my father abandoned the *Grey Annals* at the end of the story of Túrin, the conclusion of AB 2 contains the last account in the *Annals* tradition of the fourth (becoming the sixth) century of the Sun and of the Great Battle. Both AV 2 and AB 2 only came to light very recently (I was not aware of their existence when *The Silmarillion* was prepared for publication).

# SILMARILLION

## III

## ANNALS OF BELERIAND

**Before the uprising of the Sun**    Morgoth fled from the land of the Valar and carried off the Silmarils, the holy gems of Fëanor. He returned into the northern regions of the West of Middle-earth, and rebuilt his fortress of Angband, beneath the black Mountains of Iron, where their highest peak Thangorodrim towers. He brought forth Orcs and Balrogs; and set the Silmarils in his iron crown. Thingol and Denithor[1] resisted the inroads of the Orcs, but Denithor was slain, and Thingol withdrew to Menegroth, and Doriath was closed.

Here the Dispossessed came into the North, and Fëanor led them, and with him came his seven sons, Maidros, Maglor, Celegorm,[2] Curufin, Cranthir, Damrod, and Díriel, and with them their friends, the younger sons of Finrod. They burned the Telerian ships upon the coast, where it is since called Losgar, nigh to the outlet of Drengist. Soon after they fought that battle with the host of Morgoth that is named Dagor-os-Giliath;[3] and Fëanor had the victory, but he was mortally wounded by Gothmog, and died in Mithrim.

Maidros, Fëanor's son, was ambushed and captured by Morgoth, and hung upon Thangorodrim; but his brethren were camped about Lake Mithrim, behind Eredwethion, the Shadowy Mountains.

**Years of the Sun**

1    Here the Moon and Sun, made by the Valar after the death of the Two Trees, first appeared. At this time the Fathers of Men awoke first in the East of the world. Here Fingolfin, and with him Inglor son of Finrod, led the second host of the Gnomes over Helkaraksë, the Grinding Ice, into the Hither Lands. With the first Moonrise they set foot upon Middle-earth, and the first Sunrise shone upon their march.

At the coming of Day Morgoth withdrew, dismayed, into his deepest dungeons; and there he smithied in secret, and sent forth black smoke. Fingolfin blew his trumpets in defiance before the gates of Angband, and came thence into Mithrim; but the sons of Fëanor withdrew to the southern shore, and there was feud between the houses, because of the burning of the ships, and the lake lay between them.

2 [5]　Here Fingon, Fingolfin's son, healed the feud; for he sought after Maidros, and rescued him with the help of Thorndor,[4] King of Eagles.

1–50　Now the Gnomes wandered far and wide over Beleriand, exploring the land, and settling it in many places, from the great sea Belegar unto Eredlindon, that is the Blue Mountains; and they took all Sirion's vale to dwell in, save Doriath in the midmost of the land, which Thingol and Melian held, both the forest of Region and the forest of Neldoreth on either side of Esgalduin.

20　Here was held the Feast of Reuniting, that is Mereth-Aderthad in Gnomish speech. In Nan-Tathrin,[5] the Vale of Willows, near the mouths of Sirion, were gathered the Elves of Valinor, of the three houses of the Gnomes, and many of the Dark-elves, both those of the woods and of the havens of the West, and some of the Green-elves of Ossiriand; and Thingol sent ambassadors from Doriath. But Thingol came not himself, nor would he open his kingdom, nor remove the enchantment that fenced it in, for he trusted not in the restraint of Morgoth to last long. Yet a time of peace, of growth and blossoming, and of prosperous mirth followed.

50　Here unquiet and troubled dreams came upon Turgon son of Fingolfin, and Inglor his friend, son of Finrod; and they sought in the land for places of strength and refuge, lest Morgoth burst from Angband, as their dreams foreboded. Inglor found the caves of Narog, and began there to establish a stronghold and armouries, after the fashion of Thingol's abode in Menegroth; and he called his deep halls Nargothrond. Wherefore the Gnomes called him anew Felagund, lord of caverns, and that name he bore till death.
　　But Turgon journeyed alone, and by the grace of Ulmo discovered the hidden valley of Gondolin, but of this he told no one as yet.

51 [60]　Here Morgoth made trial of the strength and watchfulness of the Noldor. His might was moved once more on a sudden, and there were earthquakes in the North, and fire came from the mountains, and the Orcs raided Beleriand, and bands of

robbers were abroad far and wide in the land. But Fingolfin and Maidros gathered great force of their own folk, and of the Dark-elves, and they destroyed all the wandering Orcs; and they pursued the main host unto Bladorion, and there surrounded it, and destroyed it utterly within sight of Angband. This was the Second Battle, Dagor Aglareb, the Glorious Battle.

Now was set the Siege of Angband,[6] and it lasted more than two [> four] hundred years; and Fingolfin boasted that Morgoth could never burst again from the leaguer of his foes. Yet neither could the Gnomes take Angband or regain the Silmarils. But war never ceased utterly in all this time, for Morgoth was secretly forging new weapons, and ever anon he would make trial of his enemies; moreover he was not encircled upon the uttermost North.

52    Here[7] Turgon was troubled anew and yet more grievously in sleep; and he took a third part of the Gnomes of Fingolfin's people, and their goods and their womenfolk, and departed south, and vanished, and none knew whither he was gone; but he came to Gondolin and built there a city and fortified the surrounding hills.

In this fashion the other chieftains beleaguered Angband. In the West were Fingolfin and Fingon, and they dwelt in Hithlum, and their chief fortress was at Sirion's Well, Eithel Sirion, where the river hath its source on the eastern slopes of Eredwethion. And all Eredwethion they manned and watched Bladorion thence, and their cavalry rode upon the plain even to the feet of the mountains of Morgoth, and their horses multiplied, for the grass was good. Of those horses many of the sires came from Valinor, and were given back to Fingolfin by the sons of Fëanor at the settlement of the feud.[8]

The sons of Finrod held the land from Eredwethion unto the eastern end of the Taur-na-Danion,[9] the Forest of Pines, from the northward slopes of which they also held watch over Bladorion. Here were Angrod and Egnor, and Orodreth was nighest to the sons of Fëanor in the East.[10] Of these Celegorm and Curufin held the land between the rivers Aros and Celon, from the borders of Doriath to the pass of Aglon, that is between Taur-na-Danion and the Hill of Himling;[11] and this pass and the plain beyond they guarded. Maidros had his stronghold upon Himling, and those lower hills that lie from the Forest of Pines unto the foothills of Eredlindon were called the Marches of Maidros. Thence he rode often into East Bladorion, the plains to the north, but he held also the woods south between Celon and Gelion. Maglor lay to the east again about the upper waters of Gelion, where the hills are low or fail; and Cranthir ranged beneath the shadows of the Blue Mountains. And all the folk of Fëanor kept watch by scout and outrider towards the North-east.

To the south the fair land of Beleriand, west and east of Sirion, was apportioned in this manner. Fingolfin was King of Hithlum, and he was Lord of the Falas or Western Shore, and overlord of the Dark-elves as far south as Eglorest and west of the river Eglor. Felagund, lord of caverns, was King of Narog, and his brothers were the lords of Taur-na-Danion and his vassals;[12] and he possessed the lands both east and west of the river Narog, as far south as the mouths of Sirion, from Eglor's banks in the West, east to the banks of Sirion, save only for a portion of Doriath that lay west of Sirion, between the river Taiglin and Umboth-Muilin.[13] But between Sirion and the river Mindeb no one dwelt; and in Gondolin, to the south-west of Taur-na-Danion, was Turgon, but that was not yet known.

Now King Felagund had his seat in Nargothrond far to the south, but his fort and place of battle was in the north, in the wide pass between Eredwethion and Taur-na-Danion, through which Sirion flows to the south. There was an isle amid the waters of Sirion, and it was called Tolsirion, and there Felagund built a mighty watchtower.[14]

South of Taur-na-Danion was a wide space untenanted, between the precipices into which those highlands fall, and the fences of Melian, and here many evil things fled that had been nurtured in the dark of old, and sought refuge now in the chasms and ravines. South of Doriath and east, between Sirion and Aros and Gelion, was a wide land of wood and plain; this was East Beleriand, and it was wild and wide. Here few came and seldom, save Dark-elves wandering, but this land was held to be under the lordship of the sons of Fëanor, and Damrod and Díriel hunted in its borders and came seldom to the affrays in the northern siege. Ossiriand, the Land of Seven Rivers, that lies between Eredlindon and the river Gelion, and is watered by the streams of Ascar, Thalos, Legolin, Brilthor, Duilwen, and Adurant, was not subject to Maidros. Here dwelt the Green-elves, but they took no king after the death of Denithor, until Beren came among them. Into East Beleriand the Elf-lords, even from afar, would ride at times for hunting in the wild woods; but none passed east over Eredlindon, save only the Green-elves, for they had kindred that were yet in the further lands.

**52–255** [60–455] The time of the Siege of Angband was a time of bliss, and the world had peace under the new light. Beleriand became exceedingly fair, and was filled with beasts and birds and flowers. In this time Men waxed and multiplied, and spread; and they had converse with the Dark-elves of the East, and learned much of them. From them they took the first beginnings of the many tongues of Men. Thus they heard rumour of the Blessed Realms of the West and the Powers that dwelt there, and many of the Fathers of Men in their wanderings moved ever westward.

**65** Here Brithombar and Eglorest were built to fair towns, and the Tower of Tindobel was set up upon the cape west of Eglorest, to watch the Western Sea. Here some of the folk of Nargothrond built new ships with the help of the people of the havens, and they went forth and dwelt upon the great isle of Balar that lieth in the Bay of Balar into which Sirion flows.

**102** About this time the building of Nargothrond and of Gondolin was complete.

**104** [154] About this time the Gnomes climbed Eredlindon and gazed eastward, but they did not pass into the lands beyond. In those mountains the folk of Cranthir came first upon the Dwarves, and there was yet no enmity between them, and nonetheless little love. It was not known in those days whence the Dwarves had origin, save that they were not of Elf-kin or of mortal kind, nor yet of Morgoth's breeding. But it is said by some of the wise in Valinor, as I have since learned,[15] that Aulë made the Dwarves long ago, desiring the coming of the Elves and of Men, for he wished to have learners to whom he could teach his crafts of hand, and he could not wait upon the designs of Ilúvatar. But the Dwarves have no spirit indwelling, as have the Children of the Creator, and they have skill but not art; and they go back into the stone of the mountains of which they were made.[16]

In those days and regions the Dwarves had great mines and cities in the east of Eredlindon, far south of Beleriand, and the chief of these cities were Nogrod and Belegost. But the Elves went not thither, and the Dwarves trafficked into Beleriand; and they made a great road, which came north, east of the mountains, and thence it passed under the shoulders of Mount Dolm,[17] and followed thence the course of Ascar, and crossed Gelion at the ford Sarn-Athrad, and so came unto Aros. But the Dwarves came

that way seldom after the coming of the Gnomes, until the power
of Maidros fell in the Third Battle.

**105** [155]   Here Morgoth endeavoured to take Fingolfin at
unawares, and he sent forth an army into the white North, and it
turned then west, and again south, and came by the coast west of
Eredlómin. But it was destroyed and passed not into Hithlum,
and the most part was driven into the sea at Drengist. This is not
reckoned among the great battles. Thereafter there was peace for
many years, and no Orcs issued forth to war. But Morgoth took
new counsel in his heart, and thought of Dragons.

**155** [260]   Here Glómund the first of Dragons came forth
from Angband's gate by night; and he was yet young and but half
grown. But the Elves fled before him to Eredwethion and Taur-
na-Danion in dismay, and he defiled Bladorion. Then Fingon,
prince of Gnomes, rode up against him with his horsed archers,
and Glómund could not yet withstand their darts, being not yet
come to his full armoury; and he fled back to hell, and came not
forth again for a long time.

**170** [370]   Here Bëor, Father of Men, was born in the East.

**188** [388]   Here Haleth the Hunter was born.

**190** [390]   Here was born Hádor[18] the Goldenhaired.

**200** [400]   Here Felagund hunting in the East with the sons of
Fëanor came upon Bëor and his men, new come into Beleriand.
Bëor became a vassal of Felagund, and went back with him into
the West.[19] In East Beleriand was born Bregolas son of Bëor.

**202** [402]   Here there was war on the East Marches, and Bëor
was there with Felagund. Barahir son of Bëor was born.

**213** [413]   Hundor son of Haleth was born.

**217** [417]   Gundor son of Hádor was born.

**219** [419]   Gumlin son of Hádor was born, beneath the
shadows of Eredlindon.[20]

**220** [420]   Here Haleth the Hunter came into Beleriand. In
the same year came also Hádor the Goldenhaired, with his great
companies of men. Haleth remained in Sirion's vale, and his folk
wandered much, owning allegiance to none, but they held most to
the woods[21] between Taiglin and Sirion. Hádor became a vassal of
Fingolfin, and he strengthened much the armies of the king, and

was given lands in Hithlum. There was great love between Elves and the Men of Hádor's house, and the folk of Hádor abandoned their own tongue and spoke with the speech of the Gnomes.

222 [422]   In this time the strength of Men being added to the Gnomes hope grew high, and Morgoth was straitly enclosed. Fingolfin pondered an assault upon Angband, for he knew that they lived in danger while Morgoth was free to labour in the dark; but because the land was so fair most of the Gnomes were content with matters as they were, and his designs came to naught.

The Men of the three houses grew now and multiplied, and they learned wisdom and crafts of the Gnomes, and were gladly subject to the Elf-lords. The Men of Bëor were dark or brown of hair, but fair of face, with grey eyes; of shapely form, having courage and endurance, yet they were little greater in stature than the Elves of that day. The people of Hádor were yellow-haired and blue-eyed, for the most part (not so was Túrin, but his mother was of Bëor's house), and of greater strength and stature. Like unto them were the woodmen of Haleth, but somewhat less tall and more broad.

224 [424]   Baragund, son of Bregolas son of Bëor, was born in Taur-na-Danion.

228 [428]   Belegund his brother was born.

232 [432]   Beren, after surnamed Ermabuin, the One-handed, or Mablosgen, the Empty-handed, son of Barahir son of Bëor, was born.[22]

241 [441]   Húrin the Steadfast, son of Gumlin son of Hádor, was born in Hithlum. In the same year was born Handir, son of Hundor son of Haleth.

244 [444]   Huor, brother of Húrin, was born.

245 [445]   Morwen Eledwen[23] (Elfsheen) was born to Baragund. She was the fairest of all mortal maidens.

250 [450]   Rian, daughter of Belegund, mother of Tuor, was born. In this year Bëor the Old, Father of Men, died of old age. The Elves saw then for the first time the death of weariness, and they sorrowed over the short span allotted to Men. Bregolas thereafter ruled the people of Bëor.

★   255 [455]   Here came an end of peace and mirth. In the winter of this year Morgoth unloosed his long-prepared forces, and he sought to break into Beleriand and destroy the wealth of the

Gnomes. The battle began suddenly on a night of mid-winter, and
fell first most heavily on the sons of Finrod. This is Dagor Húr-
Breged,[24] the Battle of Sudden Fire. Rivers of flame ran from
Thangorodrim. Here Glómund the Golden, father of Dragons,
came forth in his full might. The green plains of Bladorion were
turned into a great desert without growing thing; and thereafter
they were called Dor-na-Fauglith, Land of Gasping Thirst. In
this war Bregolas was slain and a great part of the warriors of
Bëor's folk. Angrod and Egnor, sons of Finrod, fell. But Barahir
son of Bëor with his chosen companions saved King Felagund and
Orodreth, and Felagund swore an oath of help and friendship in
all need to Barahir and his kin and seed. Barahir ruled the remnant
of the house of Bëor.

256 [456]   Fingolfin and Fingon marched to the aid of Felagund and his folk, but they were driven back with grievous loss.
Hádor now aged fell defending his lord Fingolfin, and with him
fell Gundor his son. Gumlin took the lordship of the house of
Hádor.

The sons of Fëanor were not slain, but Celegorm and Curufin
were defeated, and fled unto Orodreth in the west of Taur-na-
Danion.[25] Maidros did deeds of valour, and Morgoth could not as
yet take the heights of Himling, but he broke through the passes[26]
to the east and ravaged far into East Beleriand, and the Gnomes of
Fëanor's house, for the most part, fled before him. Maglor joined
Maidros, but Cranthir, Damrod, and Díriel fled into the South.

Turgon was not in that battle, nor Haleth, nor any but few of
Haleth's folk. It is said that about this time[27] Húrin son of Gumlin
was being fostered by Haleth, and that Haleth and Húrin hunting
in Sirion's vale came upon some of Turgon's folk, and espied their
secret entrance into the valley of Gondolin. But they were taken
and brought before Turgon, and looked upon the hidden city,
whereof of those outside none yet knew save Thorndor King of
Eagles. Turgon welcomed them, for messages and dreams sent by
Ulmo Lord of Waters up the streams of Sirion warned him that
the aid of mortal Men was necessary for him. But Haleth and
Húrin swore oaths of secrecy, and never revealed Gondolin; yet at
this time they learned something of the counsels of Turgon,
though they kept them hidden in their hearts. It is said that
Turgon had great liking for the boy Húrin, and wished to keep
him in Gondolin; but grievous tidings of the great battle came,
and they departed to the succour of their folk.

When Turgon learned of the breaking of the leaguer he sent

secret messengers to the mouths of Sirion and to the Isle of Balar, and there was a building of swift ships. Many a messenger set sail thence seeking for Valinor, there to ask for aid and pardon, but none reached the West, or none returned.[28]

Fingolfin saw now the ruin of the Gnomes and the defeat of all their houses, and he was filled with wrath and despair; and he rode alone to the gates of Angband, and in his madness challenged Morgoth to single combat. Morgoth slew Fingolfin, but Thorndor recovered his body, and set it under a cairn on the mountains north of Gondolin. There was sorrow in Gondolin when those tidings were brought by Thorndor, for the folk of the hidden city were of Fingolfin's folk. Fingon now ruled the royal house of the Gnomes.

**257 [457]** Morgoth attacked now the west passes, and pierced them, and passed into the Vale of Sirion; and he took Tolsirion and made it into his own watchtower, and set there Thû the Wizard, his most evil servant, and the isle became a place of dread, and was called Tol-na-Gaurhoth, Isle of Werewolves. But Felagund and Orodreth retreated, and went unto Nargothrond, and strengthened it and dwelt in hiding. With them were Celegorm and Curufin.[29]

Barahir would not retreat but defended still the remnant of his lands in Taur-na-Danion. But Morgoth hunted his people down, and he turned all that forest into a region of great dread and dark enchantment, so that it was after called Taur-na-Fuin, which is Forest of Night, or Gwathfuin-Daidelos,[30] which is Deadly Nightshade. At length only Barahir and his son Beren, and his nephews Baragund and Belegund, sons of Bregolas, were left, with a few men yet faithful. Of these Gorlim, Radros,[31] Dagnir and Gildor are named. They were a desperate band of outlaws, for their dwellings were destroyed, and their wives and children were captured or slain, save Morwen Eledwen daughter of Baragund and Rian daughter of Belegund. For the wives of the sons of Bregolas were of Hithlum, and were sojourning there when war broke out, and Hithlum was not yet overthrown. But no help now came thence, and Barahir and his men were hunted like wild beasts.

**258 [458]** Haleth and his folk dwelt now on the west marches cf Doriath, and fought with the Orcs that came down Sirion. Here with the help of Beleg of Doriath they took an Orc-legion at unawares, and were victorious, and the Orcs came not afterwards for a long while into the land between Taiglin and Sirion: that is the forest of Brethil.[32]

**261** [460]    There was a high lake in the midst of Taur-na-Fuin, and here there was much heath, and there were many tarns; but the ground was full of deceit, and there was much fen and bog. In this region Barahir made his lair; but Gorlim betrayed him, and he was surprised and slain with all his company, save Beren only. Beren pursued the Orcs, and slew his father's murderer, and regained the ring of Felagund. Beren became now a solitary outlaw, and did many deeds of singlehanded daring, and Morgoth put a great price on his head.

**262** [462]    Here Morgoth renewed his assaults; and the invasion of the Orcs encompassed Doriath, both west down Sirion, and east through the passes beyond Himling. And Morgoth went against Hithlum, but was driven back as yet; but Gumlin was slain in the siege of the fortress of Fingon at Eithel Sirion. Húrin his son was new come to manhood, but he was mighty in strength, and he ruled now the house of Hádor, and served Fingon. In this time Beren was driven south and came hardly into Doriath.

**263** [463]    Here the Swarthy Men first came into Beleriand in the East. They were short and broad, long and strong in the arm, growing much hair on face and breast, and their locks were dark, as were their eyes; their skins were swart, yet their countenances were not uncomely for the most part, though some were grim-looking and illfavoured. Their houses were many, and some had liking rather for the Dwarves of the mountains, of Nogrod and Belegost, than for the Elves. But Maidros seeing the weakness of the Noldor, and the growing power of the armies of Morgoth, made alliance with these Men, and with their chieftains Bor and Ulfand.[33] The sons of Bor were Borlas and Boromir and Borthandos, and they followed Maidros and Maglor and were faithful. The sons of Ulfand the Swart were Uldor the Accursed, and Ulfast, and Ulwar,[34] and they followed Cranthir the Dark and swore allegiance to him, and proved faithless.

**263-4** [463-4]    Here began the renowned deeds of Beren and Lúthien Tinúviel, Thingol's daughter, of Doriath.

**264** [464]    Here King Felagund and Beren son of Barahir were emprisoned in Tol-na-Gaurhoth by Thû, and King Felagund was slain in combat with Draugluin the Werewolf; but Lúthien and

Huan, the hound of Valinor, slew Draugluin and overthrew Thû, who fled to Taur-na-Fuin. Orodreth took now the kingship of Nargothrond and broke friendship with Celegorm and Curufin, who fled to their kinsfolk in the East; but Nargothrond was closely hidden.

Húrin son of Gumlin wedded Morwen Elfsheen of the house of Bëor in Hithlum.

**265 [465]**   Beren and Lúthien went unto Angband and took a Silmaril from the crown of Morgoth. This is the most renowned deed of these wars. Carcharoth, the wolfwarden of the gate, bit off Beren's hand, and with the Silmaril in his belly burst in madness into Doriath. Then there was made the Wolfhunt, and Huan slew Carcharoth and the Silmaril was regained, but Carcharoth slew both Huan and Beren.

Beren was recalled from the Dead by Lúthien, and they passed from the knowledge of Men and Gnomes, and dwelt a while by the green waters of Ossiriand, Land of Seven Rivers. But Mandos foretold that Lúthien should be subject hereafter to death, together with Beren, whom she rescued for a time.

In the winter of this year Túrin son of Húrin was born with sad omens.

**265-70 [465-70]**   In this time was begun the Union of Maidros; for Maidros, taking heart from the deeds of Beren and Lúthien, planned the reuniting of the Elvish forces and the liberation of Beleriand. But because of the deeds of Celegorm and Curufin, Thingol would not aid him, and small help came from Nargothrond. There the Gnomes sought to guard their dwelling by stealth and secrecy. But Maidros had the help of the Dwarves in the smithying of many weapons, and there was much traffick between Beleriand and the mountains in the East; and he gathered again all the Gnomes of Fëanor's house, and he armed them; and many Dark-elves were joined to him; and the men of Bor and Ulfand were marshalled for war, and summoned yet more of their kindred out of the East.

Fingon prepared for war in Hithlum; and tidings came also to Turgon the hidden king, and he prepared for war in secret. Haleth's folk gathered also in the woods of Brethil, and made ready for battle.

**267 [467]**   Dior the Beautiful was born to Beren and Lúthien in Ossiriand.

**268** [468]   Now the Orcs were driven back once more out of Beleriand, east and west, and hope was renewed; but Morgoth took counsel against the uprising of the Elves, and he sent spies and secret emissaries far and wide among Elves and Men. Here Haleth, last of the Fathers of Men, died in the woods; and Hundor his son ruled over his folk.

**271** [471]   Here Isfin, sister of Turgon, strayed out of Gondolin, and was lost; but Eöl the Dark-elf took her to wife.

★ **272** [472]   This is the Year of Sorrow. Maidros planned now an assault upon Angband from West and East. With the main host he was to march from the East across Dor-na-Fauglith, and as soon as he gave the signal then Fingon should come forth from Eredwethion; for they thought to draw the host of Morgoth from its walls and take it between their two armies.

Huor son of Hádor wedded Rian daughter of Belegund upon the eve of battle, and marched with Húrin his brother in the army of Fingon.

Here was fought the Fourth Battle, Nirnaith Dirnoth,[35] Unnumbered Tears, upon the plains of Dor-na-Fauglith, before the pass of Sirion. The place was long marked by a great hill in which the slain were piled, both Elves and Men. Grass grew there alone in Dor-na-Fauglith. There Elves and Men were utterly defeated, and the ruin of the Gnomes was accomplished. For Maidros was hindered on the road by the machinations of Uldor the Accursed, whom the spies of Morgoth had bought. Fingon attacked without waiting, and he drove in Morgoth's feinted onslaught, and came even unto Angband. The companies of Nargothrond, such as Orodreth suffered to depart to the aid of Fingon, were led by Gwindor son of Guilin, a very valiant prince, and they were in the forefront of battle; and Gwindor and his men burst even within Angband's gates, and their swords slew in the halls of Morgoth. But they were cut off, and all were taken captive; for Morgoth released now a countless host that he had withheld, and he drove back the Gnomes with terrible slaughter.

Hundor son of Haleth, and most of the Men of the woods, were slain in the rearguard in the retreat across the sands of Dor-na-Fauglith.[36] But the Orcs came between Fingon and the passes of Eredwethion that led into Hithlum, and they withdrew towards Tolsirion.

Then Turgon and the army of Gondolin sounded their horns, and issued out of Taur-na-Fuin. They were delayed by the deceit and evil of the forest, but came now as help unlooked for. The meeting between Húrin and Turgon was very joyful, and they drove back the Orcs.

Now the trumpets of Maidros were heard in the East, and hope was renewed. It is said that the Elves would yet have had the victory, but for the deeds of Uldor; but very mighty was Glómund. For Morgoth sent forth now all the dwellers in Angband, and hell was emptied. There came a hundred thousand Orcs, and a thousand Balrogs, and in the van was Glómund the Dragon; and Elves and Men withered before him. Thus did Morgoth prevent the union of the forces of Maidros and Fingon. And Uldor went over to Morgoth with most of the Men of Ulfand, and they fell upon the right flank of the sons of Fëanor.

Cranthir slew Uldor, but Ulfast and Ulwar slew Bor and his three sons, and many faithful Men; and the host of Maidros was scattered to the winds, and the remnant fled far into hiding into East Beleriand and the South, and wandered there in sorrow.

Fingon fell in the West, surrounded by a host of foes, and flame sprang from his helm, as he was smitten down by the Balrogs. But Húrin, and Huor his brother, and the Men of the house of Hádor, stood firm, and the Orcs could not yet gain the pass of Sirion. The stand of Húrin is the most renowned deed of Men among the Elves; for Húrin held the rear, while Turgon with part of his battle, and some of the remnants of the host of Fingon, escaped down Sirion into the dales and mountains. They vanished once more, and were not found again by Elf or Man or spy of Morgoth, until Tuor's day. Thus was the victory of Morgoth marred, and his anger was very great.

Huor fell pierced with a venomed arrow, but Húrin fought until he alone was left. He threw away his shield, and wielded an axe, and he slew well nigh a hundred Orcs; but he was taken alive by Morgoth's command, and dragged to Angband. But Húrin would not reveal whither Turgon was gone, and Morgoth cursed him, and he was chained upon Thangorodrim; and Morgoth gave him sight to see the evil that befell his kindred in the world. Morwen his wife went with child, but his son Túrin was now well nigh seven years old.

The Orcs now piled the slain, and poured into Beleriand. No tidings came to Hithlum of the battle, wherefore Rian went forth, and her child Tuor was born to her in the wild. He was taken to nurture by Dark-elves; but Rian went to the Mound of Slain[37] and laid her there and died.

**273** [473]   Morgoth was now lord of Beleriand, save Doriath, and he filled it with roving bands of Orcs and wolves. But he went not yet against the gates of Nargothrond in the far South, and of Gondolin he could discover nothing. But the northern kingdom was no more. For Morgoth broke his pledges to the sons of Ulfand, and denied them the reward of their treachery; and he drove these evil Men into Hithlum, and forbade them to wander from that land. But they oppressed the remnant of the folk of Hádor, and took their lands and goods and their womenfolk, and enslaved their children. Such as remained of the Elves of Hithlum Morgoth took to the mines of Angband, and they became his thralls, save few that lived perilously in the woods.

In the beginning of this year Nienor the Sorrowful was born in Hithlum, daughter of Húrin and Morwen; but Morwen sent Túrin to Doriath, begging for Thingol's fostering and aid; for she was of Beren's kindred. Two old men she had, Gethron and Grithron, and they undertook the journey, as Túrin's guides. They came through grievous hardship and danger, and were rescued on the borders of Doriath by Beleg. Gethron died in Doriath, but Grithron returned to Morwen.

**281** [481]   The power of Morgoth grew now very great, and Doriath was cut off, and no tidings of the lands without came thither. Túrin was now but in his sixteenth year; but he took to war, and fought against the Orcs on the marches of Doriath in the company of Beleg.

**284** [484]   Here Túrin slew Orgof, kinsman of Thingol, at the king's board, and fled from Menegroth. He became an outlaw in the woods, and gathered a desperate band, and plundered on the marches of Doriath.

**287** [487]   Here Túrin's companions captured Beleg, but Túrin released him, and renewed his fellowship with him, and they adventured together beyond Doriath, making war upon the Orcs.

Tuor son of Huor came unto Hithlum seeking his kindred, but they were no more, and he lived as an outlaw in the woods about Mithrim.

**288** [488]   Here Halmir[38] Orodreth's son of Nargothrond was trapped and hung on a tree by Orcs.

**289** [489]   Here Gwindor son of Guilin escaped from the mines of Angband. Blodrin Ban's son betrayed the camp of Túrin and Beleg, and Túrin was taken alive, but Beleg was left for dead. Beleg was healed of his wounds by Melian, and followed the trail of the captors of Túrin. He came upon Gwindor bewildered in Taur-na-Fuin, and together they rescued Túrin; but Túrin slew Beleg by misadventure.

290 [490]   Túrin was healed of his madness at Ivrineithel, and was brought at last by Gwindor to Nargothrond. They were admitted to the secret halls at the prayer of Finduilas, daughter of Orodreth, who had before loved Gwindor.

290–5 [490–5]   During this time Túrin dwelt in Nargothrond. Beleg's sword, wherewith he was slain, was reforged for Túrin; and Túrin rejected his former name, and he called himself Mormael, Black-sword, but his sword he named Gurtholfin,[39] Wand of Death. Finduilas forgot her love of Gwindor and loved Túrin, and he loved her, but spoke not, for he was faithful to Gwindor. Túrin became a captain of the host of Nargothrond, and persuaded the Gnomes to abandon stealth and ambush and make open war. He drove the Orcs out of all the land between Narog and Sirion and Doriath to the east, and west to Eglor and the sea, and north to Eredwethion; and he let build a bridge over Narog. The Gnomes of Nargothrond allied themselves with Handir of Brethil and his men. Thus Nargothrond was revealed to the wrath of Morgoth.

292 [492]   Meglin son of Eöl was sent by Isfin to Gondolin, and was received as his sister's son by Turgon.

294 [494]   In this time when the power of Morgoth was stayed in the West, Morwen and Nienor departed from Hithlum and came to Doriath, seeking tidings of Túrin. There many spake of the prowess of Mormael, but of Túrin no man had heard, since the Orcs took him.

★ 295 [495]   Here Glómund passed into Hithlum and did great evil, and he came over Eredwethion with a host of Orcs, and came into the realm of Narog. And Orodreth and Túrin and Handir went up against him, and they were defeated in the field of Tum-halad between Narog and Taiglin; and Orodreth was slain, and Handir; and Gwindor died, and refused the succour of Túrin. Túrin gathered the remnants of the Gnomes and hastened to Nargothrond, but it was sacked ere his coming; and Túrin was deceived and bound in spell by Glómund. Finduilas and the women of Nargothrond were taken as thralls, but Túrin forsook them, and deceived by the lies of Glómund went to Hithlum to seek Morwen.

Tidings of the fall of Nargothrond came to Doriath, and Mormael was revealed as Túrin.

Tuor son of Huor departed from Hithlum by a secret way under the leading of Ulmo, and journeying down the coast he passed the ruined havens of Brithombar and Eglorest, and came to the mouths of Sirion.

**295–6** [495–6]    Túrin found that Morwen had departed from Hithlum. He slew Brodda in his hall and escaped from Hithlum. He took now the name of Turambar, Conqueror of Fate,[40] and joined the remnant of the Woodmen in Brethil; and he became their lord, since Brandir son of Handir was lame from childhood.

**296** [496]    Here Tuor met the Gnome Bronweg at the mouths of Sirion. Ulmo himself appeared to Tuor in Nantathrin, and Tuor went thence up Sirion, and guided by Ulmo found the entrance to Gondolin. There Tuor spake the embassy of Ulmo; but Turgon would not now harken to it, and Meglin urged him to this against Tuor. But Tuor was held in honour in Gondolin for his kindred's sake.

Glómund returned unto Nargothrond, and lay upon the treasure of Felagund in the caves.

Morwen Eledwen went to Nargothrond seeking tidings of Túrin, and Nienor against her bidding rode in disguise among her escort of Elves. But Glómund laid a spell upon the company and dispersed it, and Morwen was lost in the woods; and a great darkness of mind came upon Nienor.

Turambar found Nienor hunted by Orcs. He named her Níniel the tearful, since she knew not her own name.

**297–8** [497–8]    Níniel dwelt with the Woodmen, and was loved both by Turambar and by Brandir the Lame.

**298** [498]    Turambar wedded Níniel.

**299** [499]    Glómund sought out the dwelling of Túrin Turambar; but Túrin smote him mightily with Gurtholfin, and fell aswoon beside him. There Níniel found him; but Glómund ere death released her from spells and declared her kindred. Nienor cast herself over the waterfall in that place which was then called Celebros, Silver Rain, but afterwards Nen-girith, Shuddering Water.

Brandir brought the tidings to Túrin, and was slain by him, but Túrin bade Gurtholfin slay him; and he died there.

Húrin was released from Angband, and he was bowed as with great age; but he departed and sought for Morwen.

Tuor wedded Idril Celebrindal, Turgon's daughter, of Gondolin; and Meglin hated him.

**300** [500]    Here was born Eärendel the Bright, star of the Two Kindreds, unto Tuor and Idril in Gondolin. In this year was born also Elwing the White, fairest of all women save Lúthien, unto Dior son of Beren in Ossiriand.

Húrin gathered men unto him, and they came to Nargothrond, and slew the dwarf Mîm, who had taken the treasure unto himself. But Mîm cursed the treasure. Húrin brought the gold to Thingol in Doriath, but he departed thence again with bitter words, and of his fate and the fate of Morwen thereafter no sure tidings were ever heard.

**301** [501]    Thingol employed Dwarvish craftsmen to fashion his gold and silver and the treasure of Nargothrond; and they made the renowned Nauglamír, the Dwarf-necklace, whereon was hung the Silmaril. Enmity awoke between Dwarves and Elves, and the Dwarves were driven away unrewarded.

**302** [502]    Here the Dwarves[41] came in force from Nogrod and from Belegost and invaded Doriath; and they came within by treachery, for many Elves were smitten with the accursed lust of the gold. Thingol was slain and the Thousand Caves were plundered; and there hath been war between Elf and Dwarf since that day. But Melian the Queen could not be slain or taken, and she departed to Ossiriand.

Beren and the Green-elves overthrew the Dwarves at Sarn-Athrad as they returned eastward, and the gold was cast into the river Ascar, which was after called Rathloriel, the Bed of Gold. But Beren took the Nauglamír and the Silmaril. Lúthien wore the Silmaril upon her breast. Dior their son ruled over the remnants of the Elves of Doriath.

**303** [503]    Here Beren and Lúthien departed out of the knowledge of Elves and Men, and their deathday is not known; but at night a messenger brought the necklace to Dior in Doriath, and the Elves said: 'Lúthien and Beren are dead as Mandos doomed.'

**304** [504]    Dior son of Beren, Thingol's heir, was now king in Doriath, and he re-established it for a while. But Melian went back to Valinor and Doriath had no longer her protection. Dior wore the Nauglamír and the Silmaril upon his breast.

**305** [505]   The sons of Fëanor heard tidings of the Silmaril in the East, and they gathered from wandering, and held council together. Maidros sent unto Dior and summoned him to give up the jewel.

**306** [506]   Here Dior Thingol's heir fought the sons of Fëanor on the east marches of Doriath, but he was slain. This was the second kinslaying, and the fruit of the oath. Celegorm fell in that battle, and Curufin, and Cranthir. The young sons of Dior, Elboron and Elbereth,[42] were taken captive by the evil men of Maidros' following, and they were left to starve in the woods; but Maidros lamented the cruel deed, and sought unavailingly for them.

The maiden Elwing was saved by faithful Elves, and they fled with her to the mouths of Sirion, and they took with them the jewel and the necklace, and Maidros found it not.

Meglin was taken in the hills, and he betrayed Gondolin to Morgoth.

**307** [507]   Here Morgoth loosed a host of dragons over the mountains from the North and they overran the vale of Tumladin, and besieged Gondolin. The Orcs sacked Gondolin, and destroyed King Turgon and most of his people; but Ecthelion of the Fountain slew there Gothmog, Lord of Balrogs, ere he fell.

Tuor slew Meglin. Tuor escaped with Idril and Eärendel by a secret way devised before by Idril, and they came with a company of fugitives to the Cleft of Eagles, Cristhorn, which is a high pass beneath the cairn of Fingolfin in the north of the surrounding mountains. They fell into an ambush there, and Glorfindel of the house of the Golden Flower of Gondolin was slain, but they were saved by Thorndor, and escaped at last into the vale of Sirion.

**308** [508]   Here the wanderers from Gondolin reached the mouths of Sirion and joined there the slender company of Elwing. The Silmaril brought blessing upon them, and they were healed, and they multiplied, and built a haven and ships, and dwelt upon the delta amid the waters. Many fugitives gathered unto them.

**310** [510]   Maidros learned of the upspringing of Sirion's Haven, and that the Silmaril was there, but he forswore his oath.

**324** [524]   Here the unquiet of Ulmo came upon Tuor, and he built the ship Eärámë, Eagle's wing, and he departed with Idril into the West, and was heard of no more. Eärendel wedded Elwing the White, and was lord of the folk of Sirion.

**325** [525] Torment fell upon Maidros and his brethren, because of their unfulfilled oath. Damrod and Díriel resolved to win the Silmaril, if Eärendel would not give it up willingly. But the unquiet had come also upon Eärendel, and he set sail in his ship Wingelot, Flower of the Foam, and he voyaged the far seas seeking Tuor, and seeking Valinor. But he found neither; yet the marvels that he did were many and renowned.[43] Elrond the Half-elfin,[44] son of Eärendel, was born while Eärendel was far at sea.

The folk of Sirion refused to surrender the Silmaril, both because Eärendel was not there, and because they thought that their bliss and prosperity came from the possession of the gem.

**329** [529] Here Damrod and Díriel ravaged Sirion, and were slain. Maidros and Maglor were there, but they were sick at heart. This was the third kinslaying. The folk of Sirion were taken into the people of Maidros, such as yet remained; and Elrond was taken to nurture by Maglor. But Elwing cast herself with the Silmaril into the sea, and Ulmo bore her up, and in the shape of a bird she flew seeking Eärendel, and found him returning.

**330** [530] Eärendel bound the Silmaril upon his brow, and with Elwing he sailed in search of Valinor.

**333** [533] Eärendel came unto Valinor, and spake on behalf of the two races, both Elves and Men.

**340** [540] Maidros and Maglor, sons of Fëanor, dwelt in hiding in the south of Eastern Beleriand, about Amon Ereb, the Lonely Hill, that stands solitary amid the wide plain. But Morgoth sent against them, and they fled to the Isle of Balar. Now Morgoth's triumph was complete, and all that land was in his hold, and none were left there, Elves or Men, save such as were his thralls.

**333–343** [533–543] Here the sons of the Gods prepared for war, and Fionwë son of Manwë was their leader. The Light-elves marched under his banners, but the Teleri did not leave Valinor; but they built a countless multitude of ships.

**347** [547] Here the host of Fionwë was seen shining upon the sea afar, and the noise of his trumpets rang over the waves and echoed in the western woods. Thereafter was fought the battle of Eglorest, where Ingwiel son of Ingwë, prince of all the Elves, made a landing, and drove the Orcs from the shore.

Great war came now into Beleriand, and Fionwë drove the Orcs and Balrogs before him; and he camped beside Sirion, and his tents were as snow upon the field. He summoned now all Elves, Men, Dwarves, beasts and birds unto his standard, who did not elect to fight for Morgoth. But the power and dread of Morgoth was very great and many did not obey the summons.

★ **350** [550]    Here Fionwë fought the last battle of the ancient world, the Great or Terrible Battle. Morgoth himself came forth from Angband, and passed over Taur-na-Fuin, and the thunder of his approach rolled in the mountains. The waters of Sirion lay between the hosts; and long and bitterly they contested the passage. But Fionwë crossed Sirion and the hosts of Morgoth were driven as leaves, and the Balrogs were utterly destroyed; and Morgoth fled back to Angband pursued by Fionwë.

From Angband Morgoth loosed the winged dragons, which had not before been seen; and Fionwë was beaten back upon Dor-na-Fauglith. But Eärendel came in the sky and overthrew Ancalagon the Black Dragon, and in his fall Thangorodrim was broken.

The sons of the Gods wrestled with Morgoth in his dungeons, and the earth shook, and gaped, and Beleriand was shattered and changed, and many perished in the ruin of the land. But Morgoth was bound.

This war lasted fifty years from the landing of Fionwë.

**397** [597]    In this year Fionwë departed and went back to Valinor with all his folk, and with them went most of the Gnomes that yet lived and the other Elves of Middle-earth. But Elrond the Half-elfin remained, and ruled in the West of the world.

Now the Silmarils were regained, for one was borne in the airs by Eärendel, and the other two Fionwë took from the crown of Melko; and he beat the crown into fetters for his feet. Maidros and Maglor driven by their oath seized now the two Silmarils and fled; but Maidros perished, and the Silmaril that he took went into the bosom of the earth, and Maglor cast his into the sea, and wandered ever after upon the shores of the world in sorrow.

Thus ended the wars of the Gnomes, and Beleriand was no more.

## NOTES

From the end of annal 257 (457) the manuscript was very little changed, either before *The Lord of the Rings* or after, and while the addition of 200 years to every date was carried through to the end the alteration of names became more superficial, and instances were ignored or missed. This is obviously of no significance, but in the notes that follow I refer only to the first occurrence of the change.

1   *Denithor > Denethor* (as in AV 2, note 5).
2   *Celegorm > Celegorn* (as in AV 2, note 9).
3   *Dagor-os-Giliath > Dagor-nuin-Giliath* (as in AV 2, note 12).
4   *Thorndor > Thorondor.* See commentary on QS §§96–7.
5   *Nan-Tathrin > Nan-Tathren.* See commentary on QS §109.
6   *Now was set the Siege of Angband > But after this the chieftains of the Gnomes took warning, and drew closer their leaguer, and strengthened their watch; and they set the Siege of Angband*
7   This first paragraph of annal 52 was struck out; see note 8.
8   New matter was added here, taking up that of the cancelled first paragraph of annal 52 (note 7). The date of Dagor Aglareb was at the same time changed from 51 to 60.

> But Turgon held the land of Nivros [> Nivrost], between Eredwethion and the sea, south of Drengist; and his folk were many. But the unquiet of Ulmo was upon him, and a few years after the Dagor Aglareb he gathered his folk together, even to a third of the Gnomes of Fingolfin's house, and their goods and wives, and departed eastward in secret, and vanished from his kindred. And none knew whither he was gone; but he came to Gondolin and built there a hidden city.

Against this is written the date 64. On *Nivros(t)* see QS §100 and commentary; and on the changed chronology, as throughout, see pp. 257–8.

9   *Taur-na-Danion > Taur-na-Thanion > Dorthanion > Dorthonion.*
*Taur-na-Danion* is emended at every occurrence, but hardly ever in the same way; in addition, *Taur-na-Donion* and *Taur-na-Thonion* are found (see IV. 211). The precise details are scarcely material, and I do not notice these competing forms any further.

10  The sentence beginning *Here were Angrod and Egnor* changed to read:

> Inglor and Orodreth held the pass of Sirion, but Angrod and Egnor held the northern slopes of Dorthanion, as far as Aglon where the sons of Fëanor lay.

See note 14 and commentary on QS §117.

11  *Himling > Himring.* This change is found also in late emendations to Q.

12  The passage beginning *Fingolfin was King of Hithlum* changed to read:

Fingolfin was King of Hithlum and Nivrost, and overlord of all
the Gnomes. Felagund, lord of caverns, was King in Nargothrond, and his brothers Angrod and Egnor were the lords of
Dorthanion and his vassals; By this change Fingolfin ceases to be Lord of the Western Havens;
see note 13.

13  Added here (see commentary on QS §109):
And he was held also to be overlord of the Falas, and of the Dark-
elves of the havens of Brithombar and Eglorest.

14  Added after *a mighty watchtower*:
Inglormindon; but after the founding of Nargothrond this was in
the keeping of Orodreth.
Subsequently *Inglormindon* > *Minnastirith*, and that in turn to
*Minastirith*. See QS §117 and commentary.

15  *as I have since learned* > *as we have since learned*. See commentary on QS §123.

16  The passage beginning *But the Dwarves* changed to read:
And the Noldor believed that the Dwarves have no spirit indwelling, as have the Children of the Creator, and they have skill
but not art; and that they go back into the stone of the mountains
of which they were made. Yet others say that Aulë cares for them,
and that Ilúvatar will accept from him the work of his desire, so
that the Dwarves shall not perish.
See the *Lhammas* §9 and QS §123, and commentaries.

17  *a great road, which came north, east of the mountains, and thence it
passed under the shoulders of Mount Dolm* > *a great road, which
passed under the shoulders of Mount Dolmed*. At the same time, no
doubt, the words *far south of Beleriand* earlier in the paragraph were
struck out; see commentary on QS §122.

18  *Hádor* > *Hador* or *Hădor* sporadically, where noticed; see IV. 317.

19  Annal 200 to this point changed to read:
400  Here Felagund hunting in the East with the sons of Fëanor
passed into Ossiriand, and came upon Bëor and his men, new
come over the mountains. Bëor became a vassal of Felagund, and
went back with him into the West, and dwelt with him until
death. But Barahir his son dwelt in Dorthanion.

20  The three annals recording the births of Hundor, Gundor, and
Gumlin were misplaced after annal 220, as in AB 1, but a direction
moves them to their proper place, as I have done in the text printed.
*Gundor* > *Gumlin the Tall; Gumlin* > *Gundor*. See QS §140 and
commentary.

21  *the woods* > *the woods of Brethil*. *Brethil* occurs under the year 258
in the text as written (and subsequently); see the commentary on
that annal.

22  *Ermabuin* > *Erchamion* (but first to *Erchamui*), and *Mablosgen* >
*Camlost*. See p. 405. After this annal a new one was added:

436   Hundor son of Haleth wedded Glorwendel daughter of
Hador. On this see p. 310 (§13) and note 36 below.

23   *Eledwen > Eledhwen.*

24   *Dagor Húr-breged > Dagor Vregedúr.* The latter occurs in QS §134.

25   *Celegorm and Curufin were defeated, and fled unto Orodreth in the
west of Taur-na-Danion > Celegorn and Curufin were defeated,
and fled south and west, and took harbour at last with Orodreth in
Nargothrond.* See commentary on QS §§117, 141.

26   *the passes > the passes of Maglor.*

27   *about this time > in the autumn before the Sudden Fire.* Cf. QS
§153.

28   *or none returned > and few returned.* Cf. QS §154.

29   The passage from *But Felagund and Orodreth retreated* changed to
read:
   Orodreth, brother of Felagund, who commanded Minnastirith,
   escaped hardly and fled south. There Felagund had taken refuge
   in the stronghold he had prepared against the evil day; and he
   strengthened it, and dwelt in secret. Thither came Celegorn and
   Curufin.
See commentary on QS §§117, 141.

30   *Gwathfuin-Daidelos > Deldúwath.* See QS §138.

31   *Radros > Radruin.* In QS §139 the name is spelt *Radhruin.*

32   Added here:
   Húrin of Hithlum was with Haleth; but he departed afterward
   since the victory had made the journey possible, and returned to
   his own folk.
See QS §§153 and 156 (footnote to the text). Subsequently *afterward > soon after*, and the words *since the victory had made the
journey possible* removed.

33   *Bor > Bór*, and *Ulfand > Ulfang.* See QS §151 and commentary.

34   *Ulwar > Ulwarth.* See QS §151 and commentary.

35   *Nirnaith Dirnoth > Nirnaith Arnediad.* See IV. 312 note 38.

36   Added here: *Glorwendel his wife died in that year of grief.* See
note 22.

37   *the Mound of Slain > Cûm-na-Dengin the Mound of Slain.* See IV.
312 note 42.

38   *Halmir > Haldir* (the name of Orodreth's son in the *Etymologies*,
stem SKAL¹).

39   *Gurtholfin > Gurtholf.* See p. 406.

40   *Conqueror of Fate > Master of Fate.*

41   *Dwarves > Dwarfs* (the only occurrence of the change in the text).
See commentary on QS §122.

42   *Elboron and Elbereth > Elrún and Eldún* (a hasty pencilled
change). See IV. 325–6 and the *Etymologies*, stem BARATH.

43   Added here: *Chief of these was the slaying of Ungoliantë.* See the
commentary on annal 325.

44  *Elrond the Half-elfin* > *Elrond Beringol, the Half-elven.* See the commentary on annal 325.

## Commentary on the Later Annals of Beleriand

**Before the uprising of the Sun**    I take the words 'rebuilt his fortress of Angband' to mean that that was the name of Melko's original stronghold; see the commentary on AV 2, annal 1000.

The statement that Melko 'brought forth Orcs and Balrogs' after his return to Middle-earth is retained from AB 1 (where the word *devised* was used), in contrast to AV 1 and 2, where 'he bred and gathered *once more* his evil servants, Orcs and Balrogs'; see my discussion of this, IV. 314.

The sentence concerning Thingol and Denithor enters from the AV tradition (annal 2990).

The name *Losgar* of the place where the Telerian ships were burnt occurs here for the first time (and the only time in the texts of this period). The name had been used long before in the old tale of *The Cottage of Lost Play*, where it meant 'Place of Flowers', the Gnomish name of *Alalminórë* 'Land of Elms' in Tol-eressëa, and where it was replaced by *Gar Lossion* (I. 16, 21).

**Annal 1–50**    Here are the first occurrences of the names *Region* and *Neldoreth* (which were also marked in on the initial drawing of the Second Map, p. 409).

**Annal 20**    The presence of Green-elves at Mereth Aderthad is not mentioned in AB 1.

**Annal 52**    In AB 1 (IV. 329) the departure of Turgon to Gondolin is placed in annal 51 (as is all that follows concerning the regions over which the Noldorin princes ruled during the Siege).

The return of the horses to Fingolfin at the settlement of the feud is a new element in the story.

In the third paragraph of this annal is a clear reference to 'Maglor's Gap' (unnamed). The region where 'the hills are low or fail', shown clearly on the Second Map (though the name was never written in), is implied by the lines on the Eastward Extension of the First Map (IV. 231).

In the passage at the end of the annal concerning the Green-elves new elements in their history appear: that they were kingless after the death of Denithor, and that they had kindred who remained east of the Blue Mountains. The speech of the two branches of this people will have an important place in the linguistic history expounded in the *Lhammas*.

**Annal 52–255**    The earliest references in my father's writings to the origin of speech among Men are in outlines for *Gilfanon's Tale*, I. 236–7, where it is told that the Dark Elf Nuin 'Father of Speech', who awakened the first Men, taught them 'much of the Ilkorin tongue'. In S (IV. 20) and Q (IV. 99) it is told, as here, that the first Men learned speech from the Dark-elves.

The reference to '*many of* the Fathers of Men' wandering westward suggests a different application of the term, which elsewhere seems always to be used specifically of Bëor, Hador, and Haleth; so in annal 268, recording the death of Haleth, he is 'last of the Fathers of Men'.

**Annal 65** The matter of this entry is not dated to a separate year in AB 1 (IV. 331), but is contained in the annal 51–255, of the Siege of Angband. It is said there only that 'some went forth and dwelt upon the great isle of Balar.'

**Annal 104** In this annal (combining matter concerning the Dwarves from the old entries 51–255 and 104) is the first emergence of the legend of Aulë's making of the Dwarves, forestalling the plan of Ilúvatar, in longing to have those whom he might teach; but the old hostile view of them (see IV. 174) finds expression in the remarkable assertion that they 'have no spirit indwelling, as have the Children of the Creator, and they have skill but not art.' With the words 'they go back into the stone of the mountains of which they were made' cf. the reference in Appendix A (III) to *The Lord of the Rings* to 'the foolish opinion among Men . . . that the Dwarves "grow out of stone".'

**Annal 105** The phrase 'sent forth an army into the white North, and it turned then west', which is not in the earlier form of the annal, makes the route of this army clearer; see QS §103, and the note on the northern geography pp. 270–1.

**Annal 220** The second version of AB 1 comes to an end with the beginning of this annal – a hasty note concerning the unfriendliness of the sons of Fëanor towards Men, which was not taken up into AB 2. We here go back to the earlier version of AB 1 (IV. 297), the dates in AB 2 being of course a hundred years later.

There is here the first mention of the abandonment of their own tongue by the Men of Hador's house; cf. the *Lhammas*, §10. Afterwards the idea became important that they retained their own language; in *The Silmarillion* (p. 148), whereas in the house of Hador 'only the Elven-tongue was spoken', 'their own speech was not forgotten, and from it came the common tongue of Númenor' (see further *Unfinished Tales*, p. 215 note 19). But at this time the large linguistic conception did not include the subsequent development of Adûnaic. In the second version of *The Fall of Númenor* (§2) the Númenóreans 'took on the speech of the Blessed Realm, as it was and is in Eressëa', and in *The Lost Road* (p. 68) there is talk in Númenor of 'reviving the ancestral speech of Men'.

**Annal 222** With this allusion to Túrin's dark hair, not in AB 1, cf. the *Lay of the Children of Húrin* (III. 17): *the black-haired boy / from the beaten people.*

**Annal 255**   On the story repeated from AB 1, that Barahir rescued Orodreth as well as Felagund in the Battle of Sudden Fire see under Annal 256.

**Annal 256**   In AB 1 the date 155 is repeated here (see IV. 319). The date 256 in AB 2 is presumably because the Battle of Sudden Fire began at midwinter of the year 255.

The confusion in the story of Orodreth at this point is not less than that in the earlier *Annals*. In AB 1 Orodreth with his brothers Angrod and Egnor dwelt in Taur-na-Danion (in the second version, IV. 330, Orodreth is specifically placed furthest east and nearest to the sons of Fëanor); thus when Celegorm and Curufin were defeated in the Battle of Sudden Fire they 'fled with Orodreth' (annal 155), which must mean that they took refuge with Felagund on Tol Sirion, for two years later, when Morgoth captured Tol Sirion, all four went south to Nargothrond (annal 157). Obviously in contradiction to this story, however, is the statement earlier in 155 that Barahir and his men rescued Felagund *and Orodreth* in the Battle of Sudden Fire; see my discussion, IV. 319.

In AB 2 (annal 255) it is again said that Barahir rescued Orodreth as well as Felagund, apparently contradicting the statement in annal 52 that Orodreth dwelt furthest east on Taur-na-Danion. But where AB 1 says that Celegorm and Curufin, defeated, 'fled with Orodreth', in AB 2 (annal 256) they 'fled *unto* Orodreth in the *west* of Taur-na-Danion' (the word *west* being perfectly clear). In annal 257 AB 2 agrees with AB 1 that all four retreated together to Nargothrond. It does not seem possible to deduce a coherent narrative from AB 2. Alterations to the manuscript given in notes 10, 14, 25 and 29 show the later story.

The story of the sojourn of Haleth and Húrin in Gondolin scarcely differs from that in AB 1, except in the point that in the older version the men 'came upon some of Turgon's folk, and were brought into the secret vale of Gondolin', whereas here they 'espied their secret entrance'.

It is not said in AB 1 that Turgon's messengers went also to the Isle of Balar (where, according to annal 65 in AB 2, Elves from Nargothrond dwelt), nor that the messengers were to ask for 'aid and pardon'.

**Annal 257**   The puzzling statement in AB 1, that 'Felagund and Orodreth, together with Celegorm and Curufin, retreated to Nargothrond, and made there a great hidden palace', is now clarified, or anyway made consistent with the earlier annals. I suggested (IV. 319) that the meaning might be that 'though Nargothrond had existed for more than a hundred years as a Gnomish stronghold it was not until the Battle of Sudden Fire that it was made into a great subterranean dwelling or "palace", and the centre of Felagund's power'; and the words of AB 2 here ('went unto Nargothrond, and strengthened it') support this.

The named members of Barahir's band are now increased by *Gildor*, who was not included in the addition to AB 1 (IV. 311 note 23).

The concluding sentences of this annal introduce the story that

Morwen and Rian only escaped because they were staying in Hithlum at the time, with their mothers' people; for the wives of Baragund and Belegund were of Hador's house. In AB 1 they were sent into Hithlum at the taking of Taur-na-Danion by Morgoth.

**Annal 258** This is the first appearance of the story (*The Silmarillion* p. 157) of the defeat of the Orcs in Brethil by the people of Haleth and Beleg of Doriath; and this is the first occurrence of *Brethil* in a text as written.

**Annal 261** To this corresponds in AB 1 annal 160, not 161; but when (in the course of writing QS) my father lengthened the Siege of Angband by a further 200 years, and then entered the revised dates on the AB 2 manuscript, he changed 261 to 460, not 461.

**Annal 263** AB 1 does not name the sons of Bor, nor state that they followed Maidros and Maglor. Bor's son Boromir is the first bearer of this name. Afterwards the Boromir of the Elder Days was the father of Bregor father of Bregolas and Barahir.

**Annal 263–4** The matter of the much longer annal 163–4 in AB 1 is in AB 2 distributed into annals 264 and 265.

**Annal 264** It is strange that my father should have written here that Felagund was slain by Draugluin (who himself survived to be slain by Huan). Of this there is no suggestion elsewhere – it is told in the *Lay of Leithian* that Felagund slew the wolf that slew him in the dungeon (III. 250, line 2625), and still more emphatically in the prose tale: 'he wrestled with the werewolf, and slew it with his hands and teeth' (*The Silmarillion* p. 174).

**Annal 273** *Gethron* and *Grithron*: the two old men are not named in Q or AB 1; in S (IV. 28) they are Halog and Mailgond, their names in the second version of the *Lay of the Children of Húrin*. Later their names were *Gethron* and *Grithnir*, and it was Grithnir who died in Doriath, Gethron who went back (*Unfinished Tales* pp. 73–4).

**Annal 287** It might seem from the statement here (not found in AB 1) that Tuor '*came unto Hithlum* seeking his kindred' that he was born after Rian had crossed the mountains, wandering towards the battlefield, and that fifteen years later he came back; but there is no suggestion of this anywhere else. In AB 1, annal 173, it is said that 'Tuor grew up wild among fugitive Elves nigh the shores of Mithrim', and though this is omitted in AB 2 the idea was undoubtedly present; the explanation of the words 'came unto Hithlum' is then that Mithrim and Hithlum were distinct lands, even if the one is comprised within the other (cf. QS §§88, 106).

**Annal 290–5** As AB 1 was first written here, it was as a result of the loss of the 'ancient secrecy' of Nargothrond in Túrin's time that Morgoth 'learned of the stronghold'; but this was early changed (IV. 313 note 53) to 'learned of the growing strength of the stronghold', which looks as if my father was retreating from the idea that Nargothrond had till then been wholly concealed from Morgoth. AB 2 is explicit that Nargothrond was 'revealed' to him by Túrin's policy of open war. See IV. 323–4.

**Annal 292**   In Q (IV. 140) Isfin and Meglin went to Gondolin together. AB 1 is not explicit: 'Meglin comes to Gondolin'. AB 2 reverts to the old story in S (IV. 35), that Meglin was sent to Gondolin by his mother.

**Annal 295**   It is now said expressly, what is implied in AB 1, that Glómund approached Nargothrond by way of Hithlum, with the addition that he 'did great evil' there; see IV. 324. Here first appears the name *Tum-halad*, but the site of the battle, to which the name refers, was still east of Narog, not between Narog and Ginglith.

For an explanation of why the havens of Brithombar and Eglorest were in ruins see IV. 324.

**Annal 296**   It was said also in AB 1 that Glómund returned to Nargothrond in the year following the sack, though I did not there remark on it. I cannot explain this. There is no suggestion elsewhere that after Túrin had departed on his journey to Hithlum Glómund did other than crawl back into the halls of Nargothrond and lie down upon the treasure.

**Annal 299**   *Celebros*, here rendered 'Silver Rain', has previously been translated 'Foam-silver', 'Silver Foam'; see the *Etymologies*, stem ROS[1].

**Annal 325**   The early addition made to this annal (note 43), 'Chief of these was the slaying of Ungoliantë', is notable. This story goes back through S and Q (§17) to the very beginning (II. 254, etc.), but it does not appear again. It is told in S and Q (§4) that when Morgoth returned with Ungoliantë to Middle-earth she was driven away by the Balrogs 'into the uttermost South', with the addition in Q (and QS §62) 'where she long dwelt'; but in the recasting and expansion of this passage made long after it is reported as a legend that 'she ended long ago, when in her uttermost famine she devoured herself at last' (*The Silmarillion* p. 81).

The surname given to Elrond in another addition (note 44), *Beringol*, is not found again, but the form *Peringol* appears in the *Etymologies*, stem PER, of which *Beringol* is a variant (see p. 298, note on *Gorgoroth*). It is convenient to notice here a later, hastily pencilled change, which altered the passage to read thus:

The *Peringiul*, the Half-elven, were born of Elwing wife of Eärendel, while Eärendel was at sea, the twin brethren Elrond and Elros.

The order was then inverted to 'Elros and Elrond'. No doubt at the same time, in annal 329 'Elrond was taken' was changed to 'Elros and Elrond were taken'. Elros has appeared in late additions to the text of Q (IV. 155), which were inserted after the arising of the legend of Númenor, and by emendation to the second version of *The Fall of Númenor* (p. 34), where he replaces Elrond as the first ruler.

**Annal 340** It is not told in AB 1 that Maidros and Maglor and their people fled in the end from Amon Ereb to the Isle of Balar. In Q nothing is told of the actual habitation of Maidros and Maglor during the final years.

**Annal 350** Some new (and unique) elements appear in the account in AB 2 of the invasion out of the West. The camp of Fionwë beside Sirion (annal 347) does not appear in AB 1 (nor in Q or QS, where nothing is said of the landing of Fionwë or of the Battle of Eglorest), nor is it said there that Morgoth crossed Taur-na-Fuin and that there was a long battle on the banks of Sirion where the host of Valinor attempted to cross; in the second version of the story in Q §18 (repeated in QS, p. 329) it is indeed strongly suggested that Morgoth never left Angband until he was dragged out in chains.

After the words 'many perished in the ruin of the land' my father pencilled in the following sentence:

and the sea roared in and covered all but the tops of the mountains, and only part of Ossiriand remained.

This addition is of altogether uncertain date, but it bears on matters discussed earlier in this book and may be conveniently considered here.

What little was ever told of the Drowning of Beleriand is very difficult to interpret; the idea shifted and changed, but my father never at any stage clearly expounded it. In the *Quenta* (cited on p. 22) and the *Annals* there is a picture of cataclysmic destruction brought about by 'the fury of the adversaries' in the Great Battle between the host of Valinor and the power of Morgoth. The last words of the *Annals*, retained in AB 2, are 'Beleriand was no more' (which could however be interpreted to mean that Beleriand as the land of the Gnomes and the scene of their heroic wars had no further history); in Q there remained 'great isles', where the fleets were built in which the Elves of Middle-earth set sail into the West – and these may well be the British Isles (see IV. 199). In the concluding passage (§14) of *The Fall of Númenor* the picture is changed (see p. 23), for there it is said (most fully in the second version, p. 28) that the name *Beleriand* was preserved, and that it remained a land 'in a measure blessed'; it was to Beleriand that many of the Númenórean exiles came, and there that Elendil ruled and made the Last Alliance with the Elves who remained in Middle-earth ('and these abode then mostly in Beleriand'). There is no indication here of the extent of Beleriand remaining above the sea – and no mention of islands; all that is said is that it had been 'changed and broken' in the war against Morgoth. Later (at some time during the writing of *The Lord of the Rings*) my father rewrote this passage (see pp. 33–4), and there had now entered the idea that the Drowning of Beleriand took place at the fall of Númenor and the World Made Round – a far more overwhelming cataclysm, surely, than even the battle of the divine adversaries:

Now that land had been broken in the Great Battle with Morgoth; and *at the fall of Númenor and the change of the fashion of the world it perished*; for the sea covered *all that was left* save some of the mountains that remained as islands, even up to the feet of Eredlindon. But that land where Lúthien had dwelt remained, and was called Lindon.

Into these successive phases of the idea it is extremely difficult to find a place for the sentence added to this annal in AB 2. On the one hand, it describes the Drowning in the same way as does the later passage just cited – a part of Ossiriand and some high mountains alone left above the surface of the sea; on the other, it refers not to the time of the fall of Númenor and the World Made Round, but to the Great Battle against Morgoth. Various explanations are possible, but without knowing when the sentence was written they can only be extremely speculative and fine-spun, and I shall not rehearse them. It is in any case conceivable that this addition is an example of the casual, disconnected emendations that my father sometimes made when looking through an earlier manuscript – emendations that were not part of a thoroughgoing preparation for a new version, but rather isolated pointers to the need for revision. It may be that he jotted down this sentence long after – perhaps when considering the writing of the *Grey Annals* after *The Lord of the Rings* was completed, and that its real reference is not to the Great Battle at all but to the time after the fall of Númenor.

**Annal 397**   It is not said in AB 1 that the Iron Crown was beaten into fetters. In Q (§18) it was made into a collar for Morgoth's neck.

# IV

# AINULINDALË

In all the works given in this history so far, there has been only one account of the Creation of the World, and that is in the old tale of *The Music of the Ainur*, written while my father was at Oxford on the staff of the Dictionary in 1918–20 (I. 45). The 'Sketch of the Mythology' (S) makes no reference to it (IV. 11); Q and AV 1 only mention in their opening sentences 'the making of the World', the making of 'all things' by Ilúvatar (IV. 78, 263); and AV 2 adds nothing further. But now, among the later writings of the 1930s (see pp. 107–8), he turned again to the tale told by Rúmil to Eriol in the garden of Mar Vanwa Tyaliéva in Kortirion, and wrote a new version; and it is remarkable that in this case he went back to the actual text of the original *Music of the Ainur*. The new version was composed with the 'Lost Tale' in front of him, and indeed he followed it fairly closely, though rephrasing it at every point – a great contrast to the apparent jump between the rest of the 'Valinórean' narrative in the *Lost Tales* and the 'Sketch', where it seems possible that he wrote out the condensed synopsis without re-reading them (cf. IV. 41–2).

The 'cosmogonical myth', as he called it long after (I. 45), was thus already, as it would remain, a separate work, independent of 'The Silmarillion' proper; and I believe that its separation can be attributed to the fact that there was no mention of the Creation in S, where the *Quenta* tradition began, and no account of it in Q. But QS has a new opening, a brief passage concerning the Great Music and the Creation of the World, and this would show that the *Ainulindalë* was already in existence, even were this not demonstrable on other grounds (see note 20).

But the *Ainulindalë* consists in fact of two separate manuscripts. The first, which simply for the purposes of this chapter I will call 'A', is extremely rough, and is full of changes made at the time of composition – these being for the most part readings from the old *Lost Tales* version which were written down but at once struck out and replaced. There is neither title-page nor title, but at the beginning my father later scribbled *The Music of the Ainur*. The second text, which I will here call 'B', is a fair copy of the first, and in its original form a handsome manuscript, without hesitations or changes in the act of writing; and although there are a great many differences between the two the great majority of them are minor stylistic alterations, improvements of wording and the fall of sentences. I see no reason to think that there was any interval between them; and I think therefore that A can be largely passed over here, and comparison of the substance made directly between the very finished second text B and the original *Tale of the Music of the Ainur*; noting however that in many details of expression A was closer to the old *Tale*. More substantial differences between A and B are given in the notes.

B has a title-page closely associated in form with those of the *Ambarkanta* and the *Lhammas*, works also ascribed to Rúmil; see p. 108.

*Ainulindalë*
The Music of the Ainur
This was written by Rúmil of Tûn

I give now the text of this version as it was originally written (the manuscript became the vehicle of massive rewriting many years later, when great changes in the cosmological conception had entered).

### The Music of the Ainur
### and the Coming of the Valar

These are the words that Rúmil spake to Ælfwine concerning the beginning of the World.[1]

There was Ilúvatar, the All-father, and he made first the Ainur, the holy ones, that were the offspring of his thought, and they were with him before Time. And he spoke to them, propounding to them themes of music, and they sang before him, and he was glad. But for a long while they sang only each alone, or but few together, while the rest hearkened; for each comprehended only that part of the mind of Ilúvatar from which he came, and in the understanding of their brethren they grew but slowly. Yet ever as they listened they came to deeper understanding, and grew in unison and harmony.

And it came to pass that Ilúvatar called together all the Ainur, and declared to them a mighty theme, unfolding to them things greater and more wonderful than he had yet revealed; and the glory of its beginning and the splendour of its end amazed the Ainur, so that they bowed before Ilúvatar and were silent.

Then said Ilúvatar: 'Of the theme that I have declared to you, but only incomplete and unadorned, I desire now that ye make in harmony together a great music. And since I have kindled you with the Fire, ye shall exercise your powers in adorning this theme, each with his own thoughts and devices. But I will sit and hearken and be glad that through you great beauty has been wakened into song.'

Then the voices of the Ainur, like unto harps and lutes, and pipes and trumpets, and viols and organs, and like unto countless choirs singing with words, began to fashion the theme of Ilúvatar to a great music; and a sound arose of endless interchanging melodies, woven in harmonies, that passed beyond hearing both in the depths and in the heights, and the places of the dwelling of Ilúvatar were filled to overflowing, and the music and the echo of the music went out into the Void, and it was not void. Never was there before, nor has there since been, a music so immeasurable, though it has been said that a greater still shall be made before Ilúvatar by the choirs of the Ainur and the Children of Ilúvatar after the end of days.[2] Then shall the themes of Ilúvatar be played aright, and take being in the moment of their playing, for all shall then understand his intent in their part, and shall know the comprehension each of each, and Ilúvatar shall give to their thoughts the secret Fire, being well pleased.

But now the All-father sat and hearkened, and for a great while it seemed good to him, for the flaws in the music were few. But as the theme progressed, it came into the heart of Melko[3] to interweave matters of his own imagining that were not in accord with the theme of Ilúvatar; for he sought therein to increase the power and glory of the part assigned to himself. To Melko among the Ainur had been given the greatest gifts of power and knowledge, and he had a share in all the gifts of his brethren;[4] and he had gone often alone into the void places seeking the secret Fire that gives life. For desire grew hot within him to bring into being things of his own, and it seemed to him that Ilúvatar took no thought for the Void, and he was impatient of its emptiness.[5] Yet he found not the Fire, for it is with Ilúvatar, and he knew it not. But being alone he had begun to conceive thoughts of his own unlike those of his brethren.

Some of these he now wove into his music, and straightway discord arose about him, and many that sang nigh him grew despondent and their thought was disturbed and their music faltered; but some began to attune their music to his rather than to the thought which they had at first. And the discord of Melko spread ever wider and the music darkened, for the thought of Melko came from the outer dark whither Ilúvatar had not yet turned the light of his face. But Ilúvatar sat and hearkened, until all that could be heard was like unto a storm, and a formless wrath that made war upon itself in endless night.

Then Ilúvatar was grieved, but he smiled, and he lifted up his left hand, and a new theme began amid the storm, like and yet unlike the former theme, and it gathered power and had new sweetness. But the discord of Melko arose in uproar against it, and there was again a war of sound in which music was lost. Then Ilúvatar smiled no longer, but wept, and he raised his right hand; and behold, a third theme grew amid the confusion, and it was unlike the others, and more powerful than all. And it seemed at last that there were two musics progressing at one time before the seat of Ilúvatar, and they were utterly at variance. One was deep and wide and beautiful, but slow and blended with unquenchable sorrow, from which its beauty chiefly came. The other had grown now to a unity and system, yet an imperfect one, save in so far as it derived still from the eldest theme of Ilúvatar; but it was loud, and vain, and endlessly repeated, and it had little harmony, but rather a clamorous unison as of many trumpets braying upon one note. And it essayed to drown the other music by the violence of its voice, but it seemed ever that its most triumphant notes were taken by the other and woven into its pattern.[6]

In the midst of this strife, whereat the halls of Ilúvatar shook and a tremor ran through the dark places, Ilúvatar raised up both his hands, and in one chord, deeper than the abyss, higher than the firmament, more glorious than the sun, piercing as the light of the eye of Ilúvatar, the music ceased.

Then said Ilúvatar: 'Mighty are the Ainur, and mightiest among them is Melko; but that he may know, and all the Ainur, that I am Ilúvatar, those things that ye have sung and played, lo! I have caused to be. Not in the musics that ye make in the heavenly regions, as a joy to me and a play unto yourselves, but rather to have shape and reality, even as have ye Ainur. And behold I shall love these things that are come of my song even as I love the Ainur who are of my thought. And thou, Melko, shalt see that no theme may be played that has not its uttermost source in me, nor can any alter the music in my despite. For he that attempts this shall but aid me in devising things yet more wonderful, which he himself has not imagined. Through Melko have terror as fire, and sorrow like dark waters, wrath like thunder, and evil as far from my light as the uttermost depths of the dark places come into the design. In the confusion of sound were made pain and cruelty, devouring flame and cold without mercy, and death without hope. Yet he shall see that in the end this redounds only to the glory of the world, and this world shall be called of all the deeds of Ilúvatar the mightiest and most lovely.'

Then the Ainur were afraid, and understood not fully what was said; and Melko was filled with shame and with the anger of shame. But Ilúvatar arose in splendour and went forth from the fair regions that he had made for the Ainur and came into the dark places; and the Ainur followed him.[7]

But when they came into the midmost Void they beheld a sight of surpassing beauty, where before had been emptiness. And Ilúvatar said: 'Behold your music! For of my will it has taken shape, and even now the history of the world is beginning. Each will find contained within the design that is mine the adornments that he himself devised; and Melko will discover there those things which he thought to bring out new from his own heart, and will see them to be but a part of the whole, and tributary to its glory. But I have given being unto all.'[8] And lo! the secret Fire burned in the heart of the World.

Then the Ainur marvelled seeing the world globed amid the Void, and it was sustained therein, but not of it. And looking upon light they were joyful, and seeing many colours their eyes were filled with delight; but because of the roaring of the sea they felt a great unquiet. And they observed the air and winds, and the matters whereof the middle-earth was made,[9] of iron and stone and silver and gold and many substances: but of all these water they most greatly praised. And it is said that in water there lives yet the echo of the Music of the Ainur more than in any substance else that is in the world; and many of the Children of Ilúvatar hearken still unsated to the voices of the sea, and yet know not for what they listen.

Now of water had that Ainu whom we call Ulmo mostly thought, and of all most deeply was he instructed by Ilúvatar in music. But of the airs and winds Manwë most had pondered, who was the noblest of the Ainur. Of the fabric of earth had Aulë thought, to whom Ilúvatar had given skill and knowledge scarce less than to Melko; but the delight and pride of Aulë was in the process of making, and in the thing made, and not in possession nor in himself, wherefore he was a maker and teacher and not a master, and none have called him lord.[10]

Now Ilúvatar spake to Ulmo and said: 'Seest thou not how Melko has made war upon thy realm? He has bethought him of biting cold without moderation, and has not destroyed the beauty of thy fountains, nor of thy clear pools. Behold the snow, and the cunning work of frost! Behold the towers and mansions of ice! Melko has devised heats and fire without restraint, and has not dried up thy desire, nor utterly quelled the music of the sea. Behold rather the height and glory of the clouds, and the ever-changing mists and vapours, and listen to the fall of rain upon the earth. And in these clouds thou art drawn yet nearer to thy brother Manwë whom thou lovest.'[11]

Then Ulmo answered: 'Yea, truly, water is become now fairer than my heart imagined, neither had my secret thought conceived the snow-flake, nor in all my music was contained the falling of the rain. Lo! I will seek Manwë, that he and I may make melodies for ever and ever to thy delight!' And Manwë and Ulmo have from the beginning been allied, and in all things served most faithfully the purpose of Ilúvatar.

And even as Ilúvatar spake to Ulmo, the Ainur beheld the unfolding of the world, and the beginning of that history which Ilúvatar had propounded to them as a theme of song. Because of their memory of the speech of Ilúvatar and the knowledge that each has of the music which he played the Ainur know much of what is to come, and few things are unforeseen by them. Yet some things there are that they cannot see, neither alone nor taking counsel together. But even as they gazed, many became enamoured of the beauty of the world, and engrossed in the history which came there to being, and there was unrest among them. Thus it came to pass that some abode still with Ilúvatar beyond the world, and those were such as had been content in their playing with the thought of the All-father's design, caring only to set it forth as they had received it. But others, and among them were many of the wisest and fairest of the Ainur, craved leave of Ilúvatar to enter into the world and dwell there, and put on the form and raiment of Time.[12] For they said: 'We desire to have the guidance of the fair things of our dreams, which thy might has made to have a life apart, and we would instruct both Elves and Men in their wonder and uses, when the times come for thy Children to appear upon earth.' And Melko feigned that he desired to control the violence and turmoils, of heat and of cold, that he had caused within the world, but he intended rather to usurp the realms of all the Ainur and subdue to his will both Elves and Men; for he was jealous of the gifts with which Ilúvatar purposed to endow them.

For Elves and Men were devised by Ilúvatar alone, nor, since they comprehended not fully that part of the theme when it was propounded to them, did any of the Ainur dare in their music to add anything to their fashion; and for that reason these races are called the Children of Ilúvatar, and the Ainur are rather their elders and their chieftains than their masters. Wherefore in their meddling with Elves and Men the Ainur have endeavoured at times to force them, when they would not be guided, but seldom to good result, were it of good or evil intent. The dealings of the Ainur have been mostly with the Elves, for Ilúvatar made the Elves most like in nature to the Ainur, though less in might and stature; but to Men he gave strange gifts.

Knowing these things and seeing their hearts, Ilúvatar granted the desire of the Ainur, and it is not said that he was grieved. Then those that wished descended, and entered into the world. But this condition Ilúvatar made, or it is the necessity of their own love (I know not which), that their power should thenceforth be contained and bounded by the world, and fail with it; and his purpose with them afterward Ilúvatar has not revealed.

Thus the Ainur came into the world, whom we call the Valar, or the Powers, and they dwelt in many places: in the firmament, or in the deeps of the sea, or upon earth, or in Valinor upon the borders of earth. And the four greatest were Melko and Manwë and Ulmo and Aulë.

Melko for a long while walked alone, and he wielded both fire and frost, from the Walls of the World to the deepest furnaces that are under it, and whatsoever is violent or immoderate, sudden or cruel, is laid to his charge, and for the most part justly. Few of the divine race went with him, and of the Children of Ilúvatar none have followed him since, save as slaves, and his companions were of his own making: the Orcs and demons that long troubled the earth, tormenting Men and Elves.[13]

Ulmo has dwelt ever in the Outer Ocean, and governed the flowing of all waters, and the courses of all rivers, the replenishment of springs and the distilling of rain and dew throughout the world. In the deep places he gives thought to music great and terrible; and the echo thereof runs through all the veins of the world, and its joy is as the joy of a fountain in the sun whose wells are the wells of unfathomed sorrow at the foundations of the world.[14] The Teleri learned much of him, and for this reason their music has both sadness and enchantment. Salmar came with him, who made the conches of Ulmo;[15] and Ossë and Uinen, to whom he gave control of waves and of the inner seas; and many other spirits beside.

Aulë dwelt in Valinor, in the making of which he had most part, and he wrought many things both openly and in secret. Of him comes the love and the knowledge of the substances of earth, both tillage and husbandry, and the crafts of weaving and of beating metals and of shaping wood. Of him comes the science of earth and its fabric and the lore of its elements, their blending and mutation.[16] Of him the Noldor learned much in after days, and they are the wisest and most skilled of the Elves. But they added much to his teaching and delighted much in tongues and alphabets and in the figures of broidery, of drawing and carving. For art was the especial gift of the Children of Ilúvatar.[17] And the Noldor achieved the invention of gems, which were not in the world before them; and the fairest of all gems were the Silmarils, and they are lost.

But the highest and holiest of the Valar was Manwë Súlimo, and he dwelt in Valinor, sitting in majesty upon his throne; and his throne was upon the pinnacle of Taniquetil, which is the highest of the mountains of the world, and stands upon the borders of Valinor. Spirits in the shape of hawks and of eagles flew ever to and from his house, whose eyes could see to the depths of the sea and could pierce the hidden caverns under the world, whose wings could bear them through the three regions of the firmament beyond the lights of heaven to the edge of darkness;[18] and they brought word to him of well nigh all that passed: yet some things are hid even from the eyes of Manwë.

With him was Varda the most beautiful. Now the Ainur that came into the world took shape and form, such even as have the Children of Ilúvatar who were born of the world; but their shape and form is greater and more lovely and it comes of the knowledge and desire of the substance of the world rather than of that substance itself, and it cannot always be perceived, though they be present. And some of them, therefore, took form and temper as of female, and some as of male.[19] But Varda was the Queen of the Valar, and was the spouse of Manwë; and she wrought the stars, and her beauty is high and aweful, and she is named in reverence. The children of Manwë and Varda are Fionwë Úrion their son and Ilmar their daughter; and these are the eldest of the Children of the Gods.[20] They dwell with Manwë, and with them are a great host of fair spirits in great happiness. Elves and Men love Manwë most of all the Valar,[21] for he is not fain of his own honour, nor jealous of his own power, but ruleth all to peace. The Lindar[22] he loved most of all the Elves, and of him they received song and poesy; for poesy is the delight of Manwë, and the song of words is his music. Behold the raiment of Manwë is blue, and blue is the fire of his eyes, and his sceptre is of sapphire; and he is the king in this world of Gods and Elves and Men, and the chief defence against Melko.

After the departure of the Valar there was silence for an age, and Ilúvatar sat alone in thought. Then Ilúvatar spake, and he said: 'Behold I love the world, and it is a mansion for Elves and Men. But the Elves shall be the fairest of earthly creatures, and they shall have and shall conceive more beauty than all my children, and they shall have greater bliss in this world. But to Men I will give a new gift.'

Therefore he willed that the hearts of Men should seek beyond the world and find no rest therein; but they should have a virtue to fashion their life, amid the powers and chances of the world, beyond the Music of the Ainur, which is as fate to all things else. And of their operation everything should be, in shape and deed, completed, and the world fulfilled unto the last and smallest. Lo! even we, Elves, have found to our sorrow that Men have a strange power for good or ill, and for turning things aside from the purpose of Valar or of Elves; so that it is said among us that Fate is not master of the children of Men; yet are they blind, and their joy is small, which should be great.

But Ilúvatar knew that Men, being set amid the turmoils of the powers of the world, would stray often, and would not use their gift in harmony; and he said: 'These too, in their time, shall find that all they do redounds at the end only to the glory of my work.' Yet the Elves say that Men are often a grief even unto Manwë, who knows most of the mind of Ilúvatar.[23] For Men resemble Melko most of all the Ainur, and yet have ever feared and hated him.[24] It is one with this gift of freedom that the children of Men dwell only a short space in the world alive, and yet are not bound to it, nor shall perish utterly for ever. Whereas the Eldar remain until the end of days, and their love of the world is deeper, therefore, and more sorrowful. But they die not, till the world dies, unless they are slain or waste in grief – for to both these seeming deaths are they subject – nor does age subdue their strength, unless one grow weary of ten thousand centuries; and dying they are gathered in the halls of Mandos in Valinor, whence often they return and are reborn in their children. But the sons of Men die indeed. Yet it is said that they will join in the Second Music of the Ainur,[25] whereas

Ilúvatar has not revealed what he purposes for Elves and Valar after the world's end; and Melko has not discovered it.

## NOTES

1 There is nothing corresponding to this prefatory sentence in the draft text A. It is notable that Ælfwine still heard the story of the Music of the Ainur from Rúmil's own lips in Tol-eressëa, as he did in the *Lost Tales*.

2 The *Tale* has here: 'by the choirs of both Ainur *and the sons of Men* after the Great End.' Both texts of the new version have: 'by the choirs of the Ainur *and the Children of Ilúvatar* after the end of days.' On this see I. 63, where I suggested that the change in the present version may have been unintentional, in view of the last sentence of the text.

3 A has here: 'sitting upon the left hand of Ilúvatar'.

4 The *Tale* has here: '*some of the greatest* gifts of power and wisdom and knowledge'; A has '*many of the greatest* gifts of power and knowledge'. The statement in B that Melko had '*the greatest* gifts of power and knowledge' is the first unequivocal statement of the idea that Melko was the mightiest of all the Ainur; although in the *Tale* (I. 54) Ilúvatar says that 'among them [the Ainur] is Melko the most powerful in knowledge' (where the new version has 'mightiest among them is Melko' (p. 158)). In Q it is said (IV. 79) that 'Very mighty was he made by Ilúvatar, and some of the powers of all the Valar he possessed' (cf. QS §10). In *The Lost Road* (p. 63) he was 'the eldest in the thought of Ilúvatar', whereas in QS §10 he was 'coëval with Manwë'.

5 This sentence, from 'and it seemed to him', is not in A.

6 From this point a page is lost from the A manuscript. See note 7.

7 Here A takes up again after the missing page. It will be seen that in this passage B is very close to the *Tale* (I. 54–5), and A may be supposed to have been even closer.

8 The *Tale* has here: 'One thing only have I added, the fire that giveth Life and Reality'; A has: 'But this I have added: life.'

9 A has 'a middle-earth' (in the *Tale* 'the Earth'). The use of 'middle-earth' (which probably first appears in AV 1, IV. 264) here is curious and I cannot account for it; there seems no reason to specify the middle lands, between the seas, to the exclusion of the lands of the West and East. But the reading survived through the post-*Lord of the Rings* versions of the *Ainulindalë*; the change in *The Silmarillion* (p. 19) to 'the matters of which Arda was made' was editorial.

10 This sentence, from 'but the delight and pride of Aulë', is not in A.

11 Both A and B have Ilúvatar speak to Ulmo of 'thy brother Manwë'.

12 The words 'and put on the form and raiment of Time' are not in A.

13  This notable sentence ('Few of the divine race . . .') is not in A.

14  A still closely echoed the passage in the *Tale*: 'In the deeps he bethinks him of music great and strange, and yet full of sorrow (and in this he has aid from Manwë).' – On 'the veins of the world' see IV. 255.

15  Salmar appears here in the original *Music of the Ainur* and elsewhere in the *Lost Tales*, but in no subsequent text until now. This is the first mention of his being the maker of the conches of Ulmo.

16  This sentence is not in A.

17  A has here: 'For art was the especial gift of the Eldar.' The term *Eldar* is presumably used here in the old sense, i.e. 'Elves', as again also in the last paragraph of the text; cf. AV 2, annal 2000 and commentary.

18  This sentence, from 'whose wings could bear them', is not in A. For the three regions of the firmament (*Vista, Ilmen, Vaiya*) see the diagrams accompanying the *Ambarkanta*, IV. 243, 245.

19  This passage replaces the following briefer wording of A: 'Now the Ainur that came into the world took shape and form, such even as the Children of Ilúvatar who were born in the world; but greater and more beautiful, and some were in form and mind as women and some as men.' This is the first statement in my father's writings concerning the 'physical' (or rather 'perceptible') form of the Valar, and the meaning of gender as applied to them.

20  Fionwë *Urion* reappears from the *Lost Tales*; in the previous texts of the 1930s he is Fionwë simply, as also in QS (§4). On his 'parentage' see IV. 68. – Where B has *Ilmar* A has *Ild Merildë Ildumë Ind Estë*, struck out one after the other, and then *Ilmar* (*Ild* and *Ind* are perhaps uncompleted names). This was obviously where the name *Ilmar(ë)* arose (replacing *Erinti* of the *Lost Tales*), and it is thus shown that the *Ainulindalë* preceded QS, which has *Ilmarë* as first written (§4). A final -*e* was added, probably early, to *Ilmar* in B. The occurrence of *Estë* among the rejected names in A is curious, since Estë already appears in the certainly earlier AV 1 as the wife of Lórien; presumably my father was momentarily inclined to give the name another application.

The statements that Fionwë and Ilmar(ë) are the eldest of the Children of the Gods, and that they dwell with Manwë, are not in A.

21  A has: 'and Men love Manwë most of all the Valar' (not 'Elves and Men').

22  A has: 'The Lindar whom Ingwë ruled'; cf. the *Tale*: 'The Teleri whom Inwë ruled.'

23  A has: 'Yet the Eldar say that the thought of Men is often a grief to Manwë, and even to Ilúvatar.'

24  After 'feared and hated him' A (deriving closely from the *Tale*) has: 'And if the gift of freedom was the envy and amazement of the Ainur, the patience of Ilúvatar is beyond their understanding.'

25 This passage is somewhat different in A: 'whereas the Eldar remain until the end of days, unless they are slain or waste in grief – for to both these deaths they are subject – nor does age subdue their strength, unless one grow weary in a thousand centuries; and dying they are gathered in the halls of Mandos in Valinor, and some are reborn in their children. But the sons of Men will it is said join in the Second Music of the Ainur,' &c. In changing 'a thousand centuries' to 'ten thousand centuries' my father was going back to the *Tale* (I. 59).

On the mention specifically of Men at the Second Music of the Ainur, which goes back to the *Tale*, see note 2.

It will be seen that while every sentence of the original *Tale of the Music of the Ainur* was rewritten, and many new elements entered, the central difference between the oldest version and that in the published *Silmarillion* still survived at this time: 'the Ainur's first sight of the World was in its actuality, not as a Vision that was taken away from them and only given existence in the words of Ilúvatar: *Eä! Let these things Be!*' (I. 62).

# V

# THE LHAMMAS

There are three versions of this work, all good clear manuscripts, and I think that all three were closely associated in time. I shall call the first *Lhammas A*, and the second, developed directly from it, *Lhammas B*; the third is distinct and very much shorter, and bears the title *Lammasethen*. *Lhammas A* has now no title-page, but it seems likely that a rejected title-page on the reverse of that of *B* in fact belonged to it. This reads:

The *Lammas*
Or 'Account of Tongues' that Pengolod of Gondolin wrote afterward in Tol-eressëa, using in part the work of Rúmil the sage of Kôr

The title-page of *Lhammas B* reads:

The *'Lhammas'*
This is the 'Account of Tongues' which Pengoloð of Gondolin wrote in later days in Tol-eressëa, using the work of Rúmil the sage of Tûn. This account Ælfwine saw when he came into the West

At the head of the page is written: '3. *Silmarillion'*. At this stage the *Lhammas*, together with the *Annals*, was to be a part of 'The Silmarillion' in a larger sense (see p. 202).

The second version relates to the first in a characteristic way; closely based on the first, but with a great many small shifts of wording and some rearrangements, and various more or less important alterations of substance. In fact, much of *Lhammas B* is too close to *A* to justify the space required to give both, and in any case the essentials of the linguistic history are scarcely modified in the second version; I therefore give *Lhammas B* only, but interesting points of divergence are noticed in the commentary. The separate *Lammasethen* version is also given in full.

In order to make reference to the very packed text easier I divide it, without manuscript authority, into numbered sections (as with the *Quenta* in Vol. IV), and the commentary follows these divisions.

Associated with the text of *Lhammas A* and *B* respectively are two 'genealogical' tables, *The Tree of Tongues*, both of which are reproduced here (pp. 169–70). The later form of the *Tree* will be found to agree in almost all particulars with the text printed; differing features in the earlier form are discussed in the commentary.

Various references are made in the text to 'the Quenta'. In §5 the reference (made only in *Lhammas A*, see the commentary) is associated with the name *Kalakilya* (the Pass of Light), and this name occurs in QS but not in Q. Similarly in §6 'It is elsewhere told how Sindo brother of Elwë, lord of the Teleri, strayed from his kindred': the story of Thingol's disappearance and enchantment by Melian has of course been told elsewhere, but in Q he is not named Sindo, whereas in QS he is. It seems therefore that these references to the *Quenta* are to QS rather than to Q, though they do not demonstrate that my father had reached these passages in the actual writing of QS when he was composing the *Lhammas*; but that question is not important, since the new names themselves had already arisen, and therefore associate the *Lhammas* with the new version of 'The Silmarillion'.

There follows now the text of *Lhammas B*. The manuscript was remarkably little emended subsequently. Such few changes as were made are introduced into the body of the text but shown as such.

### Of the Valian Tongue and its Descendants

#### 1

From the beginning the Valar had speech, and after they came into the world they wrought their tongue for the naming and glorifying of all things therein. In after ages at their appointed time the *Qendi* (who are the Elves) awoke beside Kuiviénen, the Waters of Awakening, under the stars in the midst of Middle-earth.

There they were found by Oromë, Lord of Forests, and of him they learned after their capacity the speech of the Valar; and all the tongues that have been derived thence may be called Oromian or Quendian. The speech of the Valar changes little, for the Valar do not die; and before the Sun and Moon it altered not from age to age in Valinor. But when the Elves learned it, they changed it from the first in the learning, and softened its sounds, and they added many words to it of their own liking and devices even from the beginning. For the Elves love the making of words, and this has ever been the chief cause of the change and variety of their tongues.

#### 2

Now already in their first dwellings the Elves were divided into three kindreds, whose names are now in Valinorian form: the *Lindar* (the fair), the *Noldor* (the wise), and the *Teleri* (the last, for these were the latest to awake). The Lindar dwelt most

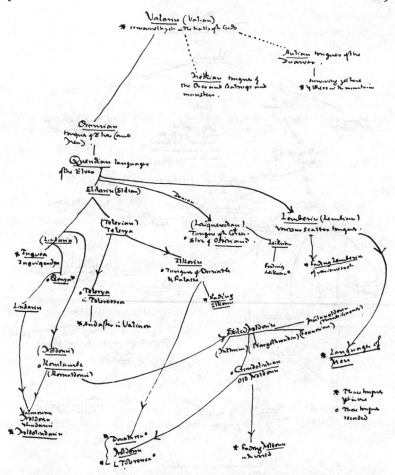

The Tree of Tongues (earlier form)

westerly; and the Noldor were the most numerous; and the Teleri
who dwelt most easterly were scattered in the woods, for even
from their awakening they were wanderers and lovers of freedom.
When Oromë led forth the hosts of the Elves on their march
westward, some remained behind and desired not to go, or heard
not the call to Valinor. These are named the *Lembi*, those that
lingered, and most were of Telerian race. / But those that followed
Oromë are called the *Eldar*, those that departed. [*This sentence
struck out and carefully emended to read:* But Oromë named the
Elves *Eldar* or 'star-folk', and this name was after borne by all that

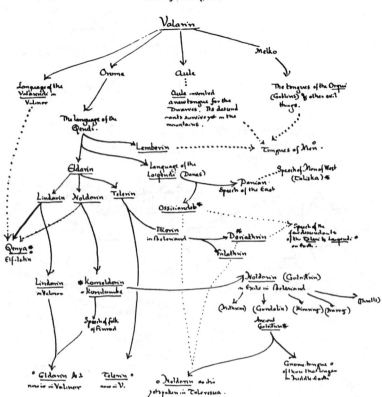

The Tree of Tongues (later form)

followed him, both the *Avari* (or 'departing') who forsook Middle-
earth, and those who in the end remained behind (*changed from*
who in the end remained in Beleriand, the Ilkorindi of Doriath
and the Falas).] But not all of the Eldar came to Valinor or to the
city of the Elves in the land of the Gods upon the hill of Kôr. For
beside the Lembi, that came never into the West of the Hither
Lands until ages after, there were the folk of the Teleri that
remained in Beleriand as is told hereafter, and the folk of the
Noldor that strayed upon the march and came also later into the

east of Beleriand. These are the *Ilkorindi* that are accounted among the Eldar, but came not beyond the Great Seas to Kôr while still the Two Trees bloomed. Thus came the first sundering of the tongues of the Elves, into *Eldarin* and *Lemberin*; for the Eldar and Lembi did not meet again for many ages, nor until their languages were wholly estranged.

## 3

On the march to the West the Lindar went first, and the chief house among them was the house of Ingwë, high-king of the Eldalië, and the oldest of all Elves, for he first awoke. His house and people are called the *Ingwelindar* or *Ingwi*. The march began when the Elves had dwelt for about thirty Valian years in the Hither Lands, and ten more Valian years passed, ere the first companies of the Lindar reached the Falassë, that is the western shores of the Hither Lands, where Beleriand lay of old. Now each Valian year in the days of the Trees was as ten years now are, but before the making of the Sun and Moon the change and growth of all living things was slow, even in the Hither Lands. Little difference, therefore, was found yet in the speeches of the three kindreds of the Eldalië. In the year 1950 of the Valar the Qendi awoke, and in the year 1980 they began their march, and in the year 1990 the Lindar came over the mountains into Beleriand; and in the year 2000 of the Gods the Lindar and the Noldor came over the seas unto Valinor in the west of the world and dwelt in the light of the Trees. But the Teleri tarried on the march, and came later, and they were left behind in Beleriand for ten Valian years, and lived upon the Falassë and grew to love the sea above all else. And thereafter, as is told in the *Quenta*, they dwelt, because of the deeds of Ossë, an age, which is 100 years of the Valar, on Toleressëa, the Lonely Isle, in the Bay of Faërie, before at last they sailed in their swan-ships to the shores of Valinor. The tongue of the Teleri became therefore sundered somewhat from that of the Noldor and Lindar, and it has ever remained apart though akin.

### Of the tongues of the Elves in Valinor

## 4

For nine ages, which is nine hundred Valian years, the Lindar and Noldor dwelt in Valinor, ere its darkening; and for eight of those ages the Teleri dwelt nigh them, yet separate, upon the shores and about the havens of the land of the Gods, while Morgoth was in captivity and vassalage. Their tongues therefore changed in the slow rolling of the years, even in Valinor, for the Elves are not as the Gods, but are children of Earth. Yet they changed less than might be thought in so great a space of time; for the Elves in Valinor did not die, and in those days the Trees still flowered, and the changeful Moon was not yet made, and there was peace and bliss.

Nonetheless the Elves much altered the tongue of the Valar, and each of their kindreds after their own fashion. The most beautiful and the least changeful of these speeches was that of the Lindar, and especially the tongue of the house and folk of Ingwë.*

It grew therefore to be a custom in Valinor, early in the days of the abiding there of the Elves, for the Gods to use this speech in converse with the Elves, and Elves of different kindred one with another; and for long this language was chiefly used in inscriptions or in writings of wisdom or poetry. Thus an ancient form of Lindarin speech became early fixed, save for some later adoptions of words and names from other dialects, as a language of high speech and of writing, and as a common speech among all Elves; and all the folk of Valinor learned and knew this language. It was called by the Gods and Elves 'the Elvish tongue', that is *Qenya*, and such it is usually now named, though the Elves call it also *Ingwiqenya*, especially in its purest and highest form, and also *tarquesta* high-speech, and *parmalambë* the book-tongue. This is the Elf-latin, and it remains still, and all Elves know it, even such as linger still in the Hither Lands. But the speech of daily converse among the Lindar has not remained as Qenya, but has changed therefrom, though far less than have Noldorin or even Telerin from their own tongues in the ancient days of the Trees.

The Noldor in the days of their exile brought the knowledge of the Elf-latin into Beleriand, and, though they did not teach it to Men, it became used among all the Ilkorindi. The names of the Gods were by all the Eldar preserved and chiefly used only in Qenya form; although most of the Valar had titles and by-names, different in different tongues, by which in daily use their high

*(*Footnote, added after the writing of the main text:*) But the Lindar were soft-spoken, and at first altered the Elvish speech more than the other peoples by the softening and smoothing of its sounds, especially the consonants; yet in words [*struck out:* and forms] they were, as is said, less changeful, and their grammar and vocabulary remained more ancient than those of any other Elvish folk.

names were usually supplanted, and they were seldom heard save in solemn oath and hymn. It was the Noldor who in the early days of their sojourn in Valinor devised letters, and the arts of cutting them upon stone or wood, and of writing them with brush or pen; for rich as are the minds of the Elves in memory, they are not as the Valar, who wrote not and do not forget. But it was long ere the Noldor themselves wrote in books with their own tongue, and though they carved and wrote in those days many things in monument and document, the language they used was Qenya, until the days of Fëanor's pride.

# 5

Now in this way did the daily speeches of the Lindar and Noldor draw apart. At first, though they saw and marvelled at the light and bliss of Valinor, the Elves forgot not Middle-earth and the starlight whence they came, and they longed at times to look upon the stars and walk a while in shadow. Wherefore the Gods made that cleft in the mountain-wall which is called the Kalakilya the Pass of Light. Therein the Elves piled the green hill of Kôr, and built thereon the city of Tûn [> Túna],* and highest amid the city of Tûn [> Túna] was the white tower of Ingwë. And the thought of the lands of earth was deepest in the hearts of the Noldor, who afterward returned thither, and they abode in that place whence the outer shadows could be seen, and among the vales and mountains about Kalakilya was their home. But the Lindar grew soon to love more the tree-lit gardens of the Gods, and the wide and fertile plains, and they forsook Tûn [> Túna], and dwelt far away and returned seldom; and though Ingwë was ever held the high-king of all the Eldar, and none used his white tower, save such as kept aflame the everlasting lamp that burned there, the Noldor were ruled by Finwë, and became a people apart, busy with the making of many things, and meeting with their kin only at such times as they journeyed into Valinor for feast or council. Their converse was rather with the Teleri of the neighbouring shores than with the Lindar, and the tongues of Teleri and Noldor drew somewhat together again in those days.

Now as the ages passed and the Noldor became more numerous and skilled and proud, they took also to the writing and using in books of their own speech beside the Qenya; and the form in

---

*(*Marginal note added at the same time as the change of Tûn to Túna:*) Which the Gods called *Eldamar.*

which it was earliest written and preserved is the ancient Noldorin or *Kornoldorin*, which goes back to the days of the gem-making of Fëanor son of Finwë. But this Noldorin never became fixed, as was Qenya, and was used only by the Noldor, and its writing changed in the course of years with the change of speech and with the varying devices of writing among the Gnomes. For this old Noldorin, the *Korolambë* (tongue of Kôr) or *Kornoldorin*, besides its change by reason of passing time, was altered much by new words and devices of language not of Valian origin, nor common to all the Eldar, but invented anew by the Noldor. The same may be said of all the tongues of the Qendi, but in the invention of language the Noldor were the chief, and they were restless in spirit, even before Morgoth walked among them, though far more so afterwards, and changeful in invention. And the fruit of their spirit were many works of exceeding beauty, and also much sorrow and great grief.

Thus in Valinor, ere the end of the days of Bliss, there was the Elf-latin, the written and spoken Qenya, which the Lindar first made, though it is not the same as their own daily speech; and there was Lindarin the language of the Lindar; and Noldorin the language, both written and spoken, of the Noldor (which is in its ancient form named *Korolambë* or *Kornoldorin*); and the tongue of the Teleri. And over all was the *Valya* or *Valarin*, the ancient speech of the Gods, that changed not from age to age. But that tongue they used little save among themselves in their high councils, and they wrote it not nor carved it, and it is not known to mortal Men.

*Of the tongues of the Elves in Middle-earth, and of the Noldorin that returned thither*

**6**

It is elsewhere told how Sindo brother of Elwë, lord of the Teleri, strayed from his kindred and was enchanted in Beleriand by Melian and came never to Valinor, and he was after called Thingol and was king in Beleriand of the many Teleri who would not sail with Ulmo for Valinor but remained on the Falassë, and of others that went not because they tarried searching for Thingol in the woods. And these multiplied and were yet at first scattered far and wide between Eredlindon and the sea; for the land of Beleriand is very great, and the world was then still dark. In the course of ages the tongues and dialects of Beleriand became altogether estranged from those of the other Eldar in Valinor, though the learned in such lore may perceive that they were anciently sprung from Telerian. These were the Ilkorin speeches of Beleriand, and they are also different from the tongues of the Lembi, who came never thither.

In after days the chief of the languages of Beleriand was the tongue of Doriath and of the folk of Thingol. Closely akin thereto was the speech of the western havens Brithombar and Eglorest, which is *Falassian*, and of other scattered companies of the Ilkorindi that wandered in the land, but all these have perished; for in the days of Morgoth only such of the Ilkorindi survived as were gathered under the protection of Melian in Doriath. The speech of Doriath was much used in after days by Noldor and Ilkorindi alike, / for Thingol was a great king, and his queen Melian divine [*emended to:* among the survivors at Sirion's mouth, for Elwing their queen and many of their folk came from Doriath.]

## 7

About the year of the Valar 2700, and nearly 300 years of the Valar ere the return of the Gnomes, while the world was still dark, the Green-elves, that were called / in their own tongue *Danas* [*written over heavily struck out: Danyar (. . . Qenya Nanyar*)], the followers of Dan, came also into eastern Beleriand, and dwelt in that region which is called Ossiriand, the Land of Seven Rivers, beneath the western slopes of Eredlindon. This folk was in the beginning of Noldorin race, but is not counted among the Eldar, nor yet among the Lembi. For they followed Oromë at first, yet forsook the host of Finwë ere the great march had gone very far, and turned southwards. But finding the lands dark and barren, for in the eldest days the South was never visited by any of the Valar, and its sky was scanty in stars, this folk turned again north. Their first leader was Dan, whose son was Denethor; and Denethor led many of them at last over the Blue Mountains in the days of Thingol. For though they had turned back, the Green-elves had yet heard the call to the West, and were still drawn thither at times in unquiet and restlessness; and for this reason they are not among the Lembi. Nor was their tongue like the tongues of the Lembi, but was of its own kind, different from the tongues of Valinor and of Doriath and of the Lembi [*emended to:* different from the tongues of Valinor and of the Lembi, and most like that of Doriath, though not the same.]

But the speech of the Green-elves in Ossiriand became some-what estranged from that of their own kindred that remained east of Eredlindon, being much affected by the tongue of Thingol's people. Yet they remained apart from the Telerian Ilkorins and remembered their kin beyond the mountains, with whom they had still some intercourse, and named themselves in common with these *Danas*. But they were called by others Green-elves, *Laiqendi*, because they loved the green wood, and green lands of fair waters; and the house of Denethor loved green above all colours, and the beech above all trees. They were allied with Thingol but not subject to him, until the return of Morgoth to the North, when after Denethor was slain many sought the protection of Thingol. But many dwelt still in Ossiriand, until the final ruin, and held to their own speech; and they were without a king, until Beren came unto them and they took him for lord. But their speech has now vanished from the earth, as have Beren and Lúthien.* Of their kindred that dwelt still east of the mountains few came into the history of Beleriand, and they remained in the Hither Lands after the ruin of the West in the great war, and have faded since or become merged among the Lembi. Yet in the overthrow of Morgoth they were not without part, for they sent many of their warriors to answer the call of Fionwë.

Of the tongues of the Lembi nought is known from early days, since these Dark-elves wrote not and preserved little; and now they are faded and minished. And the tongues of those that linger still in the Hither Lands show now little kinship one to another, save that they all differ from Eldarin tongues, whether of Valinor and Kôr or of lost Beleriand. But of Lembian tongues are come in divers ways, as is later said, the manifold tongues of Men, save only the eldest Men of the West.

## 8

Now we speak again of the Noldor; for these came back again from Valinor and dwelt in Beleriand for four hundred years of the Sun. In all about 500 years of our time passed from the darkening of Valinor and the rape of the Silmarils until the rescue of the remnant of the exiled Gnomes, and the overthrow of Morgoth by the sons of the Gods. For nigh 10 Valian years (which is 100 of our

---

*(*Footnote to the text:*) Yet this tongue was recorded in Gondolin, and it is not wholly forgotten, for it was known unto Elwing and Eärendel.

time) passed during the flight of the Noldor, five ere the burning of the ships and the landing of Fëanor, and five more until the reunion of Fingolfin and the sons of Fëanor; and thereafter wellnigh 400 years of warfare with Morgoth followed. And after the rising of the Sun and Moon and the coming into the Hither Lands of measured time, which had before lain under the moveless stars without night or day, growth and change were swift for all living things, most swift outside Valinor, and most swift of all in the first years of the Sun. The daily tongue of the Noldor changed therefore much in Beleriand, for there was death and destruction, woe and confusion and mingling of peoples; and the speech of the Gnomes was influenced also much by that of the Ilkorins of Beleriand, and somewhat by tongues of the eldest Men, and a little even by the speech of Angband and of the Orcs.

Though they were never far estranged, there came thus also to be differences in speech among the Noldor themselves, and the kinds are accounted five: the speech of Mithrim and of Fingolfin's folk; and the speech of Gondolin and the people of Turgon; the speech of Nargothrond and the house and folk of Felagund and his brothers; and the speech of Himring and the sons of Fëanor; and the corrupted speech of the thrall-Gnomes, spoken by the Noldor that were held captive in Angband, or compelled to the service of Morgoth and the Orcs. Most of these perished in the wars of the North, and ere the end was left only *múlanoldorin* [> *mólanoldorin*], or the language of the thralls, and the language of Gondolin, where the ancient tongue was kept most pure. But the folk of Maidros son of Fëanor remained, though but as a remnant, almost until the end; and their speech was mingled with that of all the others, and of Ossiriand, and of Men.

The Noldorin that lives yet is come in the most part from the speech of Gondolin. There the ancient tongue was preserved, for it was a space of 250 years from the founding of that fortress until its fall in the year of the Sun 307, and during most of that time its people held little converse with Men or Elves, and they dwelt in peace. Even after its ruin something was preserved of its books and traditions, and has survived unto this day, and in its most ancient form this is called *Gondolic* (*Gondolindeb* [> *Gondolindren*]) or Old [> Middle] Noldorin. But this tongue was the speech of the survivors of Gondolin at Sirion's mouth, and it became the speech of all the remnants of the free Elves in Beleriand, and of such as joined with the avenging hosts of Fionwë. But it suffered thus, after the fall of Gondolin, admixture from Falassian, and from Doriathrin most (for Elwing was there with the fugitives of Menegroth), and somewhat from Ossiriand, for Dior, father of Elwing, was the last lord of the Danas of Ossiriand.

Noldorin is therefore now the speech of the survivors of the wars of Beleriand that returned again to the West with Fionwë, and were given Tol-eressëa to dwell in. But still in the Hither Lands of the West there linger the fading remnants of the Noldor and the Teleri, and hold in secret to their own tongues; for there were some of those folk that would not leave the Middle-earth or the companionship of Men, but accepted the doom of Mandos that they should fade even as the younger Children of Ilúvatar waxed, and remained in the world, and are now, as are all those of Quendian race, but faint and few.

## 9

Of other tongues than the Oromian speeches, which have yet some relationship therewith, little will here be said. *Orquin*, or *Orquian*, the language of the Orcs, the soldiers and creatures of Morgoth, was partly itself of Valian origin, for it was derived from the Vala Morgoth. But the speech which he taught he perverted wilfully to evil, as he did all things, and the language of the Orcs was hideous and foul and utterly unlike the languages of the Qendi. But Morgoth himself spoke all tongues with power and beauty, when so he wished.

Of the language of the Dwarves little is known to us, save that its origin is as dark as is the origin of the Dwarvish race itself; and their tongues are not akin to other tongues, but wholly alien, and they are harsh and intricate, and few have essayed to learn them. (Thus saith Rúmil in his writings concerning the speeches of the earth of old, but I, Pengolod, have heard it said by some that Aulë first made the Dwarves, longing for the coming of Elves and Men, and desiring those to whom he could teach his crafts and wisdom. And he thought in his heart that he could forestall Ilúvatar. But the Dwarves have no spirit indwelling, as have Elves and Men, the Children of Ilúvatar, and this the Valar cannot give. Therefore the Dwarves have skill and craft, but no art, and they make no poetry.* Aulë devised a speech for them afresh, for his

---

*These two sentences were rewritten later, but very roughly; see the commentary on §9.

delight [is] in invention, and it has therefore no kinship with others; and they have made this harsh in use. Their tongues are, therefore, Aulian; and survive yet in a few places with the Dwarves in Middle-earth, and besides that the languages of Men are derived in part from them.)

But the Dwarves in the West and in Beleriand used, as far as they could learn it, an Elf-tongue in their dealings with the Elves, especially that of Ossiriand, which was nearest to their mountain homes; for the Elves would not learn Dwarvish speech.

## 10

The languages of Men were from their beginning diverse and various; yet they were for the most part derived remotely from the language of the Valar. For the Dark-elves, various folk of the Lembi, befriended wandering Men in sundry times and places in the most ancient days, and taught them such things as they knew. But other Men learned also wholly or in part of the Orcs and of the Dwarves; while in the West ere they came into Beleriand the fair houses of the eldest Men learned of the Danas, or Green-elves. But nought is preserved of the most ancient speeches of Men, save of the tongue of the folk of Bëor and Haleth and Hádor. Now the language of these folk was greatly influenced by the Green-elves, and it was of old named *Taliska*, and this tongue was known still to Tuor, son of Huor, son of Gumlin, son of Hádor, and it was in part recorded by the wise men of Gondolin, where Tuor for a while abode. Yet Tuor himself used this tongue no longer, for already even in Gumlin's day Men in Beleriand forsook the daily use of their own tongue and spoke and gave even names unto their children in the language of the Gnomes. Yet other Men there were, it seems, that remained east of Eredlindon, who held to their speech, and from this, closely akin to Taliska, are come after many ages of change languages that live still in the North of the earth. But the swarthy folk of Bor, and of Uldor the accursed, were not of this race, and were different in speech, but that speech is lost without record other than the names of these men.

## 11

From the great war and the overthrow of Morgoth by Fionwë and the ruin of Beleriand, which is computed to have happened about the year 397 of the Sun, are now very many ages passed; and the tongues of the waning Elves in different lands have changed beyond recognition of their kinship one to another, or to the languages of Valinor, save in so far as the wise among them use still Qenya, the Elf-latin, which remains in knowledge among them, and by means of which they yet at whiles hold converse with emissaries from the West. For many thousands of years have passed since the fall of Gondolin. Yet in Tol-eressëa, by the power of the Valar and their mercy, the old is preserved from fading, and there yet is Noldorin spoken, and the language of Doriath and of Ossiriand is held in mind; and in Valinor there flower yet the fair tongues of the Lindar and the Teleri; but the Noldor that returned and went not to war and suffering in the world are no longer separate and speak as do the Lindar. And in Kôr and in Tol-eressëa may still be heard and read the accounts and histories of things that befell in the days of the Trees, and of the Silmarils, ere these were lost.

[*The following passage was added to the manuscript:*]

The names of the Gnomes in the *Quenta* are given in the Noldorin form as that tongue became in Beleriand, for all those after *Finwë* father of the Noldor, whose name remains in ancient form. Likewise all the names of Beleriand and the regions adjacent (many of which were first devised by the Gnomes) dealt with in the histories are given in Noldorin form. Though many are not Noldorin in origin and only adjusted to their tongue, but come from Beleriandic, or from Ossiriandic or the tongues of Men. Thus from Beleriandic is the name *Balar*, and *Beleriand*, and the names *Brithombar*, *Eglorest*, *Doriath*, and most of the names of lakes and rivers.

### Commentary on the Lhammas

#### 1

The use of *Quendi* to signify 'all Elves' has appeared in a correction to AV 2, and is in any case implied by the name *Lindar* which is used in AV 2 for the First Kindred, formerly called *Quendi*; see the commentary on annal 2000.

For much earlier references to the language of the Valar see I. 235. In the small part of *Gilfanon's Tale* that was written it is said expressly (I. 232) that 'the Eldar or Qendi had the gift of speech direct from Ilúvatar'. Now, in the *Lhammas*, the origin of all Elvish speech is the speech of the Valar (in both forms of the *Tree of Tongues* called *Valarin*, and in §5 also *Valya*), communicated to the Elves by the instruction of Oromë.

## 2

There is no mention in Q of Elves who would not leave the Waters of Awakening: the Ilkorindi or Dark-elves are there (§2) defined as those who were lost on the Great March. But in AV (both versions) it was only 'the most part' of the Elvenfolk who followed Oromë, and there are very early references to those who would not or did not leave Palisor (see I. 234, II. 64). These Elves are here for the first time given a name: the *Lembi*, those that lingered, opposed to the *Eldar*, those that departed – and at this stage the old term *Eldar* was to bear, not merely this reference, but this actual meaning: 'those that departed' (see p. 344). The latter part of this section differs in *Lhammas A*:

> These are called the *Lembi*, or those that were left. But the others were called the *Eldar*, those that departed. Thus came the first sundering of tongues, for the Eldar and Lembi met not again for many ages. With the Lembi were merged and are reckoned such of the three kindreds of the Eldar as fell out by the way, or deserted the host, or were lost in the darkness of the ancient world; save only the remnants of the Teleri and the folk of Thingol that lingered in Beleriand. These also are called Eldar, but surnamed *Ilkorindi*, for they came never to Valinor or the city of the Elves in the land of the Gods upon the hill of Kôr. The tongue of the Ilkorindi of Beleriand showed still in after ages its kinship with Telerian, and thus Quendian was divided into three: Eldarin, and Ilkorin, and Lemberin; but the last was scattered and diverse and never one.

This is very clear. The term *Eldar* has acquired its later significance of the Elves of the Great Journey (only), and it is not restricted to those who in the end went to Valinor, but includes the Elves of Beleriand: the *Eldar* are those who completed the journey from Kuiviénen to the country between Eredlindon and the Sea. On the other hand all Elves who did depart from Kuiviénen but who did not complete that journey are numbered among the *Lembi*. The term *Ilkorindi* is now used in a much narrower sense than previously: specifically the Eldar of Beleriand – the later *Sindar*, or Grey-elves. (These new meanings have in fact appeared, without elaboration, in AV 2 (annals 2000 and 2000–2010), where 'The Eldar are all those Elves called who obeyed the summons of Oromë', and where the Teleri who remained in Beleriand are called *Ilkorindi*.) Thus whereas in Q there is the simple scheme:

Eldar (all Elves)

Quendi      Noldoli      Teleri

Those lost on the Journey
Ilkorindi (Dark-elves)

in *Lhammas A* we have:

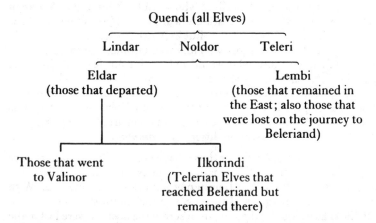

In *Lhammas B* (leaving aside for a moment the important emendation made to the text) there is now no mention of Elves who though they set out from Kuiviénen were lost on the road, and were merged with the Lembi; on the other hand, in addition to the Telerian Elves of Beleriand another people is included among the Ilkorindi – 'the folk of the Noldor that strayed upon the march and came also later into the east of Beleriand': the Green-elves of Ossiriand. It is also added in *Lhammas B* that most of the Lembi were of Telerian race (a statement not in fact consonant with what was said in one of the outlines for *Gilfanon's Tale* (I. 234), that the Elves who remained in Palisor were of the people of the Teleri, for the Teleri in the *Lost Tales* were the First Kindred, not the Third). The table just given for *Lhammas A* is changed to this extent, therefore:

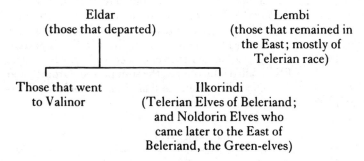

See further the commentaries on §§6, 7.

With the emendation made to *Lhammas B* we meet at last the ideas that it was Oromë who named the Elves *Eldar*, that *Eldar* meant 'Starfolk', and that Oromë's name was given to the Elves as a whole when he first found them, though it was only applied afterwards to those who set out on the Great Journey following him. (It is said in AV 2, annal 1950, that the Elves are called 'the children of the stars' on account of their awakening at the making of the stars, and this was later changed to '*Eldar*, the children of the stars'.) Here also appears for the first time the name *Avari*, taking over from *Eldar* the meaning 'Departing' (later, with the meaning changed to 'Unwilling', *Avari* was to replace *Lembi*). These movements are reflected in the *Etymologies* (see p. 344). The table must therefore now be further changed:

Eldar 'Star-folk', name given
to all Elves (Quendi) by Oromë

| Eldar | Lembi |
|---|---|
| (name restricted to those that followed Oromë) | |

| Avari | Ilkorindi |
|---|---|
| 'the Departing' | of Beleriand |

The further change made to the emended passage, from 'remained in Beleriand, the Ilkorindi of Doriath and the Falas' to 'remained behind', was perhaps introduced because my father wished to allow for the Green-elves, who were Ilkorindi (and therefore Eldar), not Lembi.

We find here the first explanation of the name *Teleri* that has appeared ('the last, for these were the latest to awake'); see I. 267, entries *Telelli*, *Teleri*. Another new element in this section is the idea that the Three Kindreds were geographically separated in their first homes beside Kuiviénen – and the Noldor the most numerous of the three.

The fact that in *Lhammas B* the fundamental division of Elvish speech is twofold, *Eldarin* and *Lemberin*, whereas in *A* it is threefold, *Eldarin* and *Ilkorin* and *Lemberin*, does not, I think, represent any real difference in the linguistic conception. The primary division was twofold, for Eldarin and Lemberin speech began to move apart on separate paths from the time when the Eldar left Kuiviénen; but the division became threefold when the Ilkorindi were left behind in Beleriand.

3

The terms *Ingwi* and *Ingwelindar*, used here of the chief house of the Lindar, have not occurred before; but in the *Lost Tales* (see especially I. 115) the *Inwir* are the royal clan, the house of Inwë, among the First Kindred. It is now told that Ingwë was not only the high-king of the Eldalië, but was 'the oldest of all Elves, for he first awoke.'

The dates in this section agree precisely with the dates in AV 2 (which are those of AV 1 after emendation, IV. 272–3).

The form *Falassë* is found on the *Ambarkanta* map IV (IV. 249).

With what is said here about the slowness of change ('even in the Hither Lands') before the making of the Sun and Moon cf. the conclusion of AV 2:*

Now measured time came into the world, and the growth, changing and ageing of all things was hereafter more swift, even in Valinor, but most swift in the Hither Lands upon Middle-earth, the mortal regions between the seas of East and West.

The reference to the *Quenta* at the end of this section, if to Q, is to IV. 87; if to QS, to §37. On this point see p. 168.

The two texts have no significant difference in this section, except that *Lhammas* A ends thus:

The tongue of the Teleri on Tol-eressëa became therefore somewhat sundered from the speech of the Lindar and Noldor, and they adhered to their own tongue after; though dwelling many ages later in friendship nigh to the Lindar and Noldor the tongue of the Teleri progressed, in such changes as befell in Valinor, alike with its kindred, and became sundered far from the Telerian speech in Beleriand (where moreover outside Valinor change was swifter).

### 4

In writing 'nine ages' and 'eight ages' (found in both versions) at the beginning of this section my father seems for some reason to have been counting only to V.Y.2900; for the Lindar and Noldor dwelt in Valinor for 990 years (2000–2990) or nearly ten ages, and the Teleri dwelt on the shores for 880 years (2111–2990) or nearly nine ages, before the Darkening.

The complex linguistic development described in this section may be summarised thus:

| Lindar: | |
|---|---|
| – *their early speech preserved* ('Elf-latin') | Brought to |
| – called *Qenya* (also *tarquesta, parmalambë*) | Middle-earth |
| – also called ('especially in its purest and highest form') *Ingwiqenya* | by the Noldor and used by |
| – used for *writing*, and also for converse with Elves of different speech and with the Gods | all the Ilkorindi |

Lindar: – *Lindarin*, later daily speech of the Lindar, changed from Qenya

The section in *Lhammas B* was changed in structure and substantially rewritten from that in A, but there is very little that materially changes

---

*Reference to the *Annals* is made to AV 2 and AB 2, the texts in this book, as being more convenient, whether or not the matter cited is found in the earlier versions given in Vol. IV.

the linguistic history as set out in the earlier version. At the end of the second paragraph, however, *Lhammas A* says of the speech of the Lindar:

Least changed was the language of the Lindar, for they were closest to the Valar and most in their company; and most like Valian was the speech of Ingwë and his household.

In the next paragraph *A* makes no mention of *Ingwiqenya* (see the commentary on §5); and states that it was the Gods who called the 'Elf-latin' by the name *Qendya* (so spelt), 'Elfspeech', whereas the Elves called it *Eldarin*. This is an application of the term *Eldarin* different from its earlier use in *A* (see the commentary on §2) and from its use in *B* and in both versions of the *Tree of Tongues*.

Alboin Errol used the term 'Elf-latin' (or *Eressëan*, in contrast to *Beleriandic*); see p. 56. 'Elven-latin' is used of Quenya in Appendix F to *The Lord of the Rings*.

## 5

*Lhammas A* contains a reference to the *Quenta* which is omitted in *B*: 'wherefore, as is said in the *Qenta*, the Gods made that cleft in the mountain-wall which is Kalakilya the Pass of Light'; see p. 168.

The removal of the Lindar from Tûn is told in very similar terms in an addition to Q (IV. 89 note 7), where appears also the story that the Tower of Ingwë was not used afterwards except by those that tended the lamp – a story that was not told in later texts of 'The Silmarillion'.

*Lhammas B* follows the earlier version closely in this section, but there are one or two differences to be remarked. In the concluding paragraph, summarising all the tongues of Valinor, *Lhammas A* adds a reference to 'the noble dialect' of the speech of the Lindar, called *Ingwelindarin*, *Ingwëa*, or *Ingwiqendya* (see the commentary on §4); in *B* §4, on the other hand, *Ingwiqenya* is the 'purest and highest form' of the 'Elf-latin', *Qenya*. The earlier form of the *Tree of Tongues* illustrates the account of the matter in *Lhammas A*; the later form does not have any representation of it, nor does it mention the name *Ingwiqenya*.

In *Lhammas A* this section ends:

And over all was *Valya* or *Valarin*, the Valian language, the pure speech of the Gods, and that changed little from age to age (and yet it did change, and swifter after the death of the Trees, for the Valar are not of the earth, yet they are in the world). But that tongue they used little save among themselves, for to Elves, and to such Men as knew it, they spoke the Qenya, and they wrote not nor carved in any letters the things which they spoke.

By emendations to *B* (as also in AV 2, note 3) *Tûn* becomes *Túna* – but it is still the name of the city, on the hill of Kôr; afterwards *Túna* was the hill, *Tirion* the city. In the added marginal note 'which the Gods called *Eldamar*' is the first occurrence of *Eldamar* since the *Lost Tales* (but the form *Eglamar* is found twice in drafts of the *Lay of Leithian*, in the line *from England unto Eglamar*, III. 157, 181). This was one of the original, foundation names of the mythology, occurring in the poem *The Shores of Faëry* (1915) and its prose preface (II. 262, 272). In the *Lost Tales* the name occurs very frequently, almost always with reference to the shores, or rocks, or bay of Eldamar. Now it becomes a name of the Elvish city itself, rather than of the regions in which the Elves dwelt and in which was situated their city on the hill. See QS §39 and commentary.

This is a convenient place to mention an element in the second *Tree of Tongues* which is not explained by anything in the text of the *Lhammas*. An unbroken line is drawn from *Valarin* to *Language of the Valarindi in Valinor*, and from there a dotted line to *Qenya*. The *Valarindi* are the Children of the Valar; see pp. 110, 121. The meaning of the dotted and unbroken lines is defined in a note to a *Tree of Tongues* made later on: the dotted lines 'indicate lines of strong influence of one language upon another' [e.g. that of French upon English], while the unbroken lines 'denote inheritance and direct descent' [e.g. from Latin to French].

A dotted line (originally drawn as unbroken) also runs from *Noldorin* to *Qenya*. This presumably illustrates the statement in the text (§4) that 'an ancient form of Lindarin speech became early fixed [i.e. as Qenya], save for some later adoptions of words and names from other dialects.'

6

In the *Lost Tales* (I. 120) the people of Tinwë Linto (Thingol) sought for him long when he was enchanted by Wendelin (Melian), but

it was in vain, and he came never again among them. When therefore they heard the horn of Oromë ringing in the forest great was their joy, and gathering to its sound soon are they led to the cliffs, and hear the murmur of the sunless sea.

In Q (IV. 87) appears first the story that some of the Teleri were persuaded by Ossë 'to remain on the beaches of the world'; of Thingol's people all that is said in Q (IV. 85) is that 'they sought him in vain', and no more is added in QS (§32).

With the reference here to the scattered Ilkorindi of Beleriand (i.e. those other than the folk of the Havens and Thingol's people) being gathered into Doriath at the time of Morgoth's return, cf. AV 2 (annal 2990, recounting the withdrawal after the fall of Denithor):

Melian wove magic of the Valar about the land of Doriath; and most of the Elves of Beleriand withdrew within its protection, save some that lingered about the western havens, Brithombar and Eglorest beside the Great Sea, and the Green-elves of Ossiriand who dwelt still behind the rivers of the East.

The reference to 'Sindo brother of Elwë, lord of the Teleri' is not in *Lhammas A*, which introduces the subject of the language of Beleriand differently:

Now in the courts of Thingol Valarin was known, for Melian was of the Valar; but it was used only by the king and queen and few of their household. For the tongue of Beleriand was the Eldarin speech of the Telerian Ilkorins, being the language of those that in the end would not sail with Ulmo, etc.

*Sindo the Grey* appears in AV 2, but as a correction of *Tindingol* (note 4); in QS §30 (again as *Sindo the Grey*) the name is present in the text from the first, as here in *Lhammas B*. With this name cf. *Singoldo* in the *Tale of Tinúviel* (II. 41), and *Sindingul* (> *Tindingol*) in AV 1 (IV. 264).

Where *Lhammas B* has 'These were the Ilkorin speeches of Beleriand, and they are also different from the tongues of the Lembi, who came never thither', *Lhammas A* has: 'These were the Ilkorin speeches of Beleriand, and they retained tokens of their kinship with Telerian, and they were different from the languages of the Lembi, for they saw none of these, until the Green-elves came from the East, as is later told.' That the Green-elves are reckoned as Lembi has been explicitly contradicted in *Lhammas B* §2, where they are Ilkorindi and counted among the Eldar; see the commentaries on §§2 and 7.

The emendation to *Lhammas B* at the end of the section modifies the linguistic history, but the implications of the change are not clear to me. As a result of it, it is no longer said that the Noldor and Ilkorindi in Beleriand used the speech of Doriath 'because Thingol was a great king', but, on the contrary, that the speech of Doriath was much used at Sirion's Haven. In §8 it was the Noldorin speech of Gondolin that was the speech of the Haven, influenced by that of Doriath because of the presence there of Elwing and fugitives from the Thousand Caves.

## 7

While the passage concerning the Green-elves very largely follows what has already been told in AV, there are some interesting details. It was said in AV that the Green-elves under their leader Dan found the southward lands barren and dark; but the barrenness and darkness are now explained: the Valar had neglected the South, and the skies had been less bountifully strewn with stars. The South was a dark region in the original myths: in the *Tale of the Sun and Moon* (I. 182) Manwë appointed the course of the Sun between East and West 'for Melko held the North and Ungweliant the South' – which as I noted (I. 200) 'seems to give Ungweliant a great importance and also a vast area subject to her power of absorbing light.'

It has not been told before that many of the Green-elves passed into Doriath after Morgoth's return; among these, much later, Túrin's enemy Saeros would be notorious (*Unfinished Tales* p. 77).

Other elements in the account in the *Lhammas* have already appeared in AB 2 (annal 52): that after the fall of Denethor the Green-elves had no king 'until Beren came among them', and also that they had kindred who remained east of Eredlindon, and whom they visited at times. In an early addition to annal 2700 in AV 2 (note 8) 'the *Danians* came over Eredlindon', and these Elves, on either side of the mountain-range, are called *Danians* also in *Lhammas A* (where *B* has *Danas*), with the further information that those who remained in the East were called *Leikvir*. In the earlier *Tree of Tongues* appears *Leikvian* where the later has *Danian speech of the East*.

In AV 1 the name of the Green-elves is *Laiqi* or *Laiqeldar* (IV. 270); in AV 2 no Elvish name is given; in *Lhammas A* they are *Laiqi* or *Laiqendi*, *Laiqendi* in *B*.

In *Lhammas A* the name *Denethor* is written over another name, very probably *Denilos*; in AV 1 *Denilos* > *Denithor* (IV. 271), in AV 2 *Denithor* > *Denethor* (note 5). In this connection there are some interesting pencilled alterations and additions in *Lhammas A* that were not taken up into *B* (or not made to it: it is not clear when these annotations were made):

> *ndan-* backwards, back. The turners-back. Thence the folk *ndāni.*
> *ndani-thārō* saviour of the Dani. Q[enya] *Nanisáro.* T[elerin]
> *Daintáro.* N[oldorin] *Dainthor.* D[oriathrin] *Denipor.*

(With this cf. the *Etymologies*, stems DAN, NDAN). At the same time, in 'This folk was in the beginning of Noldorin race' *Noldorin* was changed to *Lindarin*, and 'the host of Finwë' to 'the host of Ingwë'; cf. the conclusion of the *Lammasethen*.

The question again arises of whether the *Danas* were reckoned to be Eldar or not. *Lhammas A* is explicit that they were not Eldar but Lembi (commentary on §6); and again in the present section it is said in A that 'This folk was in the beginning of Noldorin race, but is not counted among the Eldar' – because they forsook the Great March. In *Lhammas B* on the other hand they are Ilkorindi and are counted among the Eldar (§2); yet in the present section the passage in *A* asserting that they were not Eldar reappears – with the addition that they were not Lembi either, because, although they turned back from the March, they were none-theless still drawn towards the West. I presume that my father changed his mind on this rather refined question as he wrote, and did not alter what he had written earlier. In any case, the Danas are sufficiently characterised as Elves of the Great March who abandoned it early on but who still felt a desire for the West, and the suggestion in *B* is clearly that it was this that ultimately brought a part of the people over the mountains. Their position is anomalous, and might equally well be classified either as Eldarin or as not Eldarin.

As a result, they introduce the possibility of a very distinct linguistic type among the Quendian tongues (it will be seen that in both forms of the *Tree of Tongues* their language is shown as branching from the Quendian line of descent between Lemberin and Eldarin). This type is characterised in an emendation to *B* as similar to the Ilkorin speech of Doriath (whereas in the text as first written it was said to be distinct from

Eldarin of Valinor, from Lemberin, and from the speech of Doriath). This emendation is rather puzzling. Why should the Danas show any particular linguistic affinity with the Elves of Doriath, who had completed the journey to Beleriand so very long before (some 700 Valian Years before)? Of course it is said immediately afterwards that the speech of the Danas *in Ossiriand* was 'much affected by the tongue of Thingol's people', but the emendation 'and most like that of Doriath, though not the same' presumably refers to this 'Danian' tongue in its original nature. See further the *Lammasethen* and commentary.

The sharp distinction made at the end of this section between all the Lemberin tongues on the one hand and all the Eldarin tongues (including those of the Ilkorindi of Beleriand) on the other is notable. It is implicit that long years of the Great Journey, followed by the utter separation of the Elves of Beleriand from those who remained in the East, rendered the Ilkorin speech at once quite isolated in development from any Lemberin tongue but also recognisably akin to Telerin of Valinor (at least to those 'learned in such lore', §6).

## 8

In this section *Lhammas B* followed *A* very closely, but one divergent passage in the earlier version may be cited. After the reference to *mūlanoldorin* and the language of Gondolin as being the only forms of Noldorin speech in Middle-earth that survived 'ere the end', *A* has:

> First perished Fingolfin's folk, whose tongue was pure, save for some small influence from Men of the house of Hádor; and afterward Nargothrond. But the folk of Maidros son of Fëanor remained almost until the end, as also did the thrall-Noldor whose tongue was heard not only in Angband, but later in Mithrim and widely elsewhere. The tongue of Fëanor's sons was influenced largely by Men and by Ossiriand, but it has not survived. The Noldorin that lives yet, etc.

With the account in the first paragraph of the swiftness of change after the rising of the Sun and Moon cf. the commentary on §3. The reference here to 'the moveless stars' is reminiscent of the old *Tale of the Sun and Moon*, where it is said that certain of the stars 'abode where they hung and moved not': see I. 182, 200. – In the second paragraph the form *Himring* (for *Himling* in *Lhammas A*) appears for the first time other than by later emendation. – At the end of the third paragraph, 'somewhat from Ossiriand' in *B* should probably be 'somewhat from Ossiriandeb', as here in *A* and on the later form of the *Tree of Tongues*. – In the last paragraph the languages of those Eldarin Elves who remained in Middle-earth are in *A* called *Fading Noldorin* and *Fading Ilkorin*, terms that appear on the earlier *Tree of Tongues* (together with *Fading Leikvian*: see the commentary on §7).

The later dating pencilled into the manuscript AV 1 (whereby the events from the Battle of Alqualondë to the arrival of Fingolfin in

Middle-earth were contracted into a single Valian Year, IV. 273–4), not adopted in AV 2, was not adopted in the *Lhammas* either. The dates of the Sun-years are those of AB 2 (before they were changed), with the fall of Gondolin in 307 and the Great Battle at the end of the fourth century of the Sun.

The most noticeable feature of this section of the *Lhammas* in relation to the later conception is the absence of the story that a ban was placed by Thingol on the speech of the Noldor throughout his realm. In *The Silmarillion* it is said (p. 113) that already at the Feast of Reuniting in the year 20 'the tongue of the Grey-elves was most spoken even by the Noldor, for they learned swiftly the speech of Beleriand, whereas the Sindar were slow to master the tongue of Valinor'; and (p. 129) that after Thingol's ban 'the Exiles took the Sindarin tongue in all their daily uses, and the High Speech of the West was spoken only by the lords of the Noldor among themselves.' In the *Lhammas* it is indeed said (at the end of §6, before emendation) that 'the speech of Doriath was much used in after days by Noldor and Ilkorindi alike', and in the present section that 'the speech of the Gnomes was influenced much by that of the Ilkorins of Beleriand'; but it was Noldorin (from Gondolin) that was the language (influenced by other tongues) of Sirion's Haven and afterwards of Tol-eressëa. In its essential plan, therefore, though now much more complex, the linguistic evolution still derives from that in the *Lost Tales*; as I remarked in I. 51,

> In *The Silmarillion* the Noldor brought the Valinórean tongue to Middle-earth but abandoned it (save among themselves), and adopted instead the language of Beleriand, *Sindarin* of the Grey-elves who had never been to Valinor . . . In the *Lost Tales*, on the other hand, the Noldor still brought the Elvish speech of Valinor to the Great Lands, but they retained it, and there it itself changed and became wholly different ['Gnomish'].

There is no reference at the end of this section to any Gnomes returning to Valinor (as opposed to Tol-eressëa), as there is in Q (IV. 159, 162: 'But some returned even unto Valinor, as all were free to do who willed'; this is retained in QS, p. 332 §27). For those who did not depart into the West – the speakers of 'Fading Noldorin' and 'Fading Ilkorin' in *Lhammas A* – see the same passages in Q, again repeated in QS.

## 9

There appears here the first account of the origin of the Orc-speech: a wilful perversion of Valian speech by Morgoth. The further remarkable statement that Morgoth 'spoke all tongues with power and beauty, when so he wished' is not found in *Lhammas A*.

The legend of Aulë's making of the Dwarves has appeared in AB 2 (annal 104), in a passage strikingly similar to the present, and containing the same phrase 'the Dwarves have no spirit indwelling'. The passage in AB 2 was later modified (note 16) to make this not an assertion by the writer but a conception of the Dwarves entertained by the Noldor, and not the only opinion on the subject; in the *Lhammas* the passage was also changed, very hastily, and quite differently, thus:

But the Dwarves derive their thought etc. (see *Quenta*). Therefore the works of the Dwarves have great skill and craft, but small beauty.

This reference to the *Quenta* is not to Q, which has nothing corresponding, but to QS, in which there is a chapter concerning the Dwarves. Here occurs the following (§123):

Yet they *derive their thought* and being after their measure from only one of the Powers, whereas Elves and Men, to whomsoever among the Valar they chiefly turn, have kinship with all in some degree. Therefore the works of the Dwarfs *have great skill, but small beauty*, save where they imitate the arts of the Eldar . . .

Where *Lhammas B* has 'Of the language of the Dwarves little is known to us' *A* has 'known to me' (i.e. Rúmil).

## 10

In *Lhammas A* the origin and early history of the tongues of Men is somewhat differently described:

For the Dark-elves . . . befriended wandering Men . . . and taught them such as they knew; and in the passing of the years the manifold tongues of Men developed from these beginnings, altered by time, and the invention of Men, and owning also the influence both of Dwarves and Orcs. But nought is preserved of the most ancient speech of Men, save [*struck out*: some words of] the tongues of Men of the West, who earliest came into Beleriand and spoke with the Elves, as is recorded in annals and accounts of those days by the Gnomes. Now the language of the three houses of Bëor, of Haleth, and of Hador, was *Taliska*, and this tongue was remembered still by Tuor, and recorded by the wise men of Gondolin. Yet Tuor himself used it no longer, for already ere [> in] his father Huor's day Men in Beleriand forsook the daily use of their own tongue, and spoke Noldorin, retaining some few words and names.

At the end of the section in *Lhammas A* my father added rapidly in pencil: 'But Taliska seems to have been derived largely from Danian'; see the commentary on the *Lammasethen*.

In the earlier *Tree of Tongues* the languages of Men are derived solely from Lemberin, agreeing with *Lhammas A* ('the manifold tongues of Men developed from these beginnings'), whereas the later *Tree* shows 'influence' (dotted lines) from Dwarf-speech, from Orc-speech, and from Lemberin (but no direct 'descent'), and 'influence' from the 'Danian speech of the East' on Taliska.

That the people of Hador abandoned their own language and adopted that of the Gnomes is told in AB 2 (annal 220). The account in *The Silmarillion* of the survival of the original tongue of the Edain, here called *Taliska*,* is quite different: see the commentary on AB 2 *ibid*.

The statement at the end of this section that the speech of the Swarthy Men 'is lost without record other than the names of these men' is not in accord with the *Etymologies* (stems BOR, ÚLUG), where the names of Bór and Ulfang and their sons are Elvish, given to them by the Noldor.

**11**

In the words of Rúmil here that 'many thousands of years have passed since the fall of Gondolin' an obliterated reading lies beneath 'many thousands of'; this was very probably '10,000', which is the reading of *Lhammas A*.

The statement in this section that 'the Noldor that returned [i.e. after hearing the Prophecy of the North] and went not to war and suffering in the world are no longer separate and speak as do the Lindar' is not in *Lhammas A*, but the earlier *Tree of Tongues* shows *Noldolindarin* as a coalescence of 'Valinorian Noldorin and Lindarin'; the later *Tree* similarly shows the 'speech of the folk of Finrod' (who returned to Valinor) coalescing with Lindarin, and becoming 'Eldarin as it now is in Valinor'.

The words '*in* Kôr' are not a simple slip, despite 'the Elves piled the green hill of Kôr, and built thereon the city of Tûn' in §5; see QS §29.

As regards the passage added at the end of *Lhammas B*, it may be noted that in Q (IV. 87) the names of the princes of the Noldoli are said to be given 'in form of Gnomish tongue as it long was spoken on the earth', and that there *Finn* (the form in S) was emended to *Finwë*. Of the place-names cited here as Beleriandic names accommodated to Noldorin, *Balar*, *Beleriand*, *Brithombar* and *Eglorest* appear in the *Etymologies* (stems BAL, BIRÍT, ELED) as Ilkorin names, but *Doriath* is Noldorin (stem GAT(H)).

## LAMMASETHEN

I give now the third, very short *Lhammas* text, which is I think certainly the latest of the three. At the head of it my father wrote in pencil *Sketch of a corrected version*, but then erased it. Its brief history is largely in agreement with that of *Lhammas B*, but it introduces a completely changed account of the origin of Quenya (so spelt).

The shorter account of Pengolod: or *Lammasethen*
Of the Elvish Tongues

The original Elvish or Quendian languages were derived from Oromë, and so from Valarin. But the Elves not only, already in the

---

*An historical grammar of *Taliska* is in existence.

brief period common to all, but especially in Eldarin, modified
and softened the sounds, especially the consonants, of Valarin,
but they began swiftly to invent new words and word-shapes, and
developed a language of their own.

Apart from new inventions their language changed slowly. This
was especially so in Valinor, but was true of all the tongues, for the
Elves do not die. In this way it will be seen that Telerin, the last to
leave Middle-earth, and isolated for an age and ten years of the
Valar, first in Beleriand and after in Tol Eressëa, changed more
than Koreldarin, but being after rejoined to its kindred in Valinor,
remained closely akin to Noldorin and Lindarin. But its branch,
spoken by the Teleri left in Beleriand for nearly 1000 Valian
Years, changed more than the tongues of Valinor, and became
very different from them. In some ways it grew like the Danian
branch in Ossiriand.

Now the tongue of Noldor and Lindar was at first most akin.
But the Lindar ceased after a time to dwell in Tûn or in close
consort with the Noldor, and association was closer between
Noldor and Teleri. Moreover the Lindar used a form of language
which they took *afresh* from the Valar themselves in Valmar; and
though they softened and altered this again it was in many ways
quite different from the old Elvish or Quendian derived from
Oromë. The Lindarin, which was a form of Quendian or
Oromian, they used only among themselves, and never wrote. But
their new tongue (Valinorian) became used by the Lindar in
converse with the Gods, and in all their books of poetry, history,
and wisdom. Moreover it was the first Elf-tongue to be written,
and remained always the tongue used most in writing by Lindar,
Teleri, and Noldor. It was used also by all Elves much in
converse, especially among those of different kindred and dialect.
The Gods, too, used this tongue, not pure Valarin, in their speech
with all Elves. This tongue they called *Quenya* (that is *Elvish*).
Quenya is the Elf-latin, and this name is given to its common form
as used and written by all Elves. Therein are mixed some forms
and words derived from other Elvish (Oromian) tongues. But a
purer and more archaic form is used by Ingwë High-king of the
Elves and his court and household, who never use the common
Oromian Lindarin: this is *Ingwiqenya*.

Now ancient Noldorin, as first used, and written in the days of
Fëanor in Tûn, remained spoken by the Noldor that did not leave
Valinor at its darkening, and it abides still there, not greatly
changed, and not greatly different from Lindarin. It is called

*Kornoldorin*, or *Finrodian* because Finrod and many of his folk returned to Valinor and did not go to Beleriand. But most of the Noldor went to Beleriand, and in the 400 years of their wars with Morgoth their tongue changed greatly. For three reasons: because it was not in Valinor; because there was war and confusion, and much death among the Noldor, so that their tongue was subject to vicissitudes similar to those of mortal Men; and because in all the world, but especially in Middle-earth, change and growth was very great in the first years of the Sun. Also in Beleriand the tongue and dialects of the Telerian Ilkorins was current, and their king Thingol was very mighty; and Noldorin in Beleriand took much from Beleriandic especially of Doriath. Most of the names and places in that land were given in Doriathrin form. Noldorin returned, after the overthrow of Morgoth, into the West, and lives still in Tol-eressëa, where it changes now little; and this tongue is derived mainly from the tongue of Gondolin, whence came Eärendel; but it has much of Beleriandic, for Elwing his wife was daughter of Dior, Thingol's heir; and it has somewhat of Ossiriand, for Dior was son of Beren who lived long in Ossiriand.

In Tol-eressëa are kept records of the ancient tongue of Ossiriand, which is no more; and also the tongue of the Western Men, the Elf-friends, whence came the mortal kindred of Eärendel. But this tongue is no more, and already in ancient days the Elf-friends spake mostly Noldorin, or Beleriandic; their own tongue was itself of Quendian origin, being learned east of the Mountains from a branch of the Danians, kindred of those Elves of Ossiriand which were called the Green-elves.

These are the Elvish tongues which are yet spoken, or of which writings are preserved.

Valinorian     { Ingwiqenya          } Valarin
               { Qenya (Elf-latin)   }

Oromian (a)  [ Lindarin                          ]
             [ Kornoldorin———Noldorin  ] Eldarin
             [ Telerin                          ]
        (b)  [ Doriathrin                       ]                ]
        (c)    Danian———Ossiriandic           } Ilkorin
                        Taliskan (mortals)     ]
        (d)    Lembian (many scattered dialects)   Lemberin

The Danians were of the Lindar [> Noldor] and began the march, but turned south and strayed, long ere Beleriand was reached. They did not come unto Beleriand, and then but in part, for many ages. Some reckon them Eldarin, some Lembian. In truth they are neither and have a middle place.

## Commentary on the Lammasethen

A further *Tree of Tongues* illustrates the *Lammasethen*, and is reproduced on p. 196. The starred languages are 'yet in use'.

The meaning of the passage concerning Quenya in this text is clearly that Quenya only arose after the separation of the Lindar from the Noldor, when the Noldor remained in Tûn but the Lindar retired into Valinor. There the Lindar retained their own spoken Eldarin tongue, not much different from the 'Finrodian' Noldorin of Tûn (*Kornoldorin*); but they also adopted and adapted a form of the Valarin language, and this 'Valinorian' tongue became *Quenya*. Much that is said of Quenya in the other versions is repeated in the *Lammasethen* – it was used by the Gods in converse with the Elves, by Elves in converse with Elves of different speech, and as the chief *written* language. The effect of this new conception is to withdraw Quenya from the various forms of Elvish (Quendian, Oromian) speech in Valinor and make it a language apart. *Ingwiqenya* remains as it became in *Lhammas B*, an especially pure and archaic form of Quenya used in the household of Ingwë; but it is now a pure and archaic form of 'Valinorian'. The differences between the conceptions are thus:

*Lhammas A* (commentary on §5):
- Early Lindarin speech preserved, and fixed as a high speech, a Common Speech, and a written tongue: *Quenya*
- *Later speech of the Lindar: Lindarin*
  'the noble dialect' of this: *Ingwiqendya* (*Ingwëa, Ingwelindarin*)
*Lhammas B* (§4):
- Early Lindarin speech preserved, and fixed as a high speech, a Common Speech, and a written tongue: *Quenya*
  Also called ('especially in its purest and highest form') *Ingwiqenya*
- Later speech of the Lindar: *Lindarin*
*Lammasethen:*
- The Lindar, after removal from Tûn, adopted anew the Valarin tongue; this 'Valinorian', a high speech, a Common Speech, and a written tongue, is *Quenya*
  A pure and archaic form of 'Valinorian': *Ingwiqenya*
- Original ('Quendian') speech of the Lindar, retained among themselves: *Lindarin*

There are a few other points to be noticed in the *Lammasethen*. The stage of *Koreldarin*, before the departure of the Lindar from Tûn upon Kôr, is marked on the third *Tree of Tongues*. – The Telerin speech of Beleriand (the speech of the Elves of Doriath and of the Havens of the Falas) is said to have 'grown like' (in some ways) the Danian tongue in

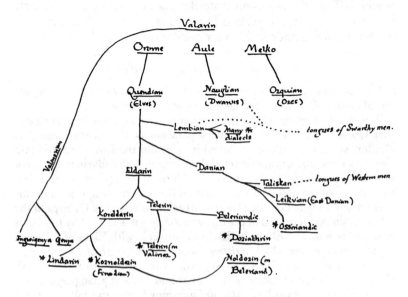

The Tree of Tongues (illustrating the *Lammasethen*)

Ossiriand; cf. the emendation in *Lhammas B* (§7) (the tongue of the
Danians was 'most like that of Doriath, though not the same'), and my
remarks on this in the commentary. – The Danians are said, as in
*Lhammas B* §7, to be neither Eldar nor Lembi: they 'have a middle
place'; though some will say one, and some the other. – The late
emendation to *Lhammas A* (commentary on §7), making the Danians an
originally Lindarin people, was adopted in the *Lammasethen*, but then
rejected and replaced again by Noldorin.

Taliskan is said in the *Lammasethen* to be 'of Quendian origin',
learned by the forefathers of the Western Men from Danian Elves east
of Eredlindon; and in the list of tongues at the end of the text it is classed
as an Ilkorin speech. In *B* (§10) the statements concerning Taliska are
not perfectly clear: the Western Men 'learned of the Danas, or Green-
elves', and their language was 'greatly influenced by the Green-elves'. In
the third *Tree of Tongues* Taliskan is shown as deriving directly from
Danian; cf. the addition to *Lhammas A* (commentary on §10): 'But
Taliska seems to have been derived largely from Danian.' It is not clear to
me why a dotted line (representing 'influence') leads from Taliskan to the
'tongues of Western Men'.

In the third *Tree* the name *Leikvian* reappears from the first, for the
tongue of the Danians who remained east of Eredlindon (the *Leikvir* in

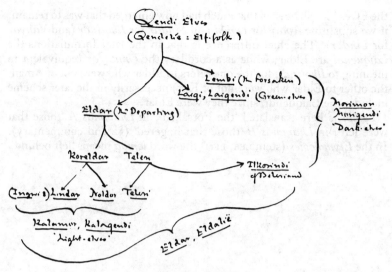

The Peoples of the Elves

*Lhammas A*, commentary on §7). The name *Nauglian* for the tongues of the Dwarves, used in the third *Tree*, does not appear in the *Lhammas* texts; in §9 they are called *Aulian*, as in the first *Tree*.

In conclusion, there is an interesting table of *the Elvish peoples* associated with the *Lhammas* papers, reproduced above. When my father made this table the *Eldar* were 'the Departing', as still in *Lhammas B* §2 before the emendation. The Green-elves, here *not* Eldar, are shown as a branch of the Quendi between Lembi and Eldar, just as in all three versions of the *Tree of Tongues* the language of the Green-elves (Danian) is shown as a branch from Quendian between Lemberin (Lembian) and Eldarin. The Lindar, Noldor, and Teleri are here placed as subdivisions of the Eldar, rather than as subdivisions of the Quendi before the Great Journey: in contrast to my table on p. 182, which is based on the express statement in *Lhammas A* and *B* (§2) that 'already in their first dwellings the Elves were divided into three kindreds, the Lindar, the Noldor, and the Teleri.'

An important new distinction appears in this table: *Morimor, Moriqendi* 'Dark-elves', and *Kalamor, Kalaqendi* 'Light-elves'. The Light-elves (a term formerly applied to the First Kindred) are now all those Elves who went to Valinor and saw the Light of the Trees; and the important overlap of nomenclature is introduced whereby the Ilkorindi of Beleriand are Eldar but also Dark-elves. The terms *Moriquendi* and *Calaquendi* of *The Silmarillion* here first appear. If this table is compared with that which I made for *The Silmarillion* ('The Sundering of the Elves') it will be seen that much had now emerged that was to remain, if we substitute *Avari* for *Lembi* and *Sindar* for *Ilkorindi* (and *Vanyar* for *Lindar*). The chief difference is that in the later formulations the *Laiquendi* are Eldar; while as a corollary the *Úmanyar* (equivalent in meaning to *Ilkorindi*, for the one refers to Eldar who were not of Aman, the other to Eldar who were not of Kôr) necessarily in the later scheme includes the Laiquendi, since they were Eldar.

*Lembi* is here translated 'the Forsaken'; in *Lhammas A* 'those that were left', in *Lhammas B* 'those that lingered' (§2 and commentary). In the *Etymologies* (stem LEB, LEM) the word *lemba* means 'left behind'.

# VI

# QUENTA SILMARILLION

As originally written, the *Quenta Silmarillion* (QS) was a beautiful and elegant manuscript; and when the first changes were made to it they were made with great care, usually by writing over erasures. It seems highly improbable that my father could have achieved this form without any intermediate texts developing it from the *Quenta Noldorinwa* (Q), and here and there in QS it appears in any case that he was copying, for words necessary to the sense were missed out and then put in above the line. But there is now, remarkably, no trace of any such material, until the tale of Beren and Lúthien is reached: from that point preliminary drafts do exist.

The manuscript became afterwards the vehicle of massive revisions, and was changed into a chaotic palimpsest, with layer upon layer of correction and wholesale rewriting, of riders and deletions. The great mass of this alteration and revision is firmly dateable to the period after the completion of *The Lord of the Rings*; but there is also an earlier phase of emendation in pencil to the opening chapters, which is in places substantial. From the manuscript thus emended my father made a typescript which was for most of its length almost an exact copy, but giving to the work a new title in addition to *Silmarillion*: *I·Eldanyárë*, 'The History of the Elves'. This new version did not proceed very far, however – no further in fact than the end of the chapter here numbered 3 (c). In order to understand the state of 'The Silmarillion' during the years when *The Lord of the Rings* was being written it is necessary to try to determine when it was made. It is in any case clear at once that it long preceded the major revision after *The Lord of the Rings* – the typescript, so far as it went, was indeed used for that revision, and was reduced to a shambles in the course of it.

In my father's letter to Stanley Unwin of 16 December 1937 – the day on which he received back the QS manuscript and other writings which he had submitted – he was still only 'promising to give thought and attention' to the question of 'a sequel or successor to *The Hobbit*' (*Letters* no. 19); but no more than three days later, on 19 December, he reported that he had written 'the first chapter of a new story about Hobbits – "A long expected party"' (*Letters* no. 20). It is certain, then, that he began work on the 'new story' at the very time that the QS manuscript came back into his possession; and I feel certain that when it did so he abandoned (for good, as it turned out) the new 'Silmarillion' narrative at

the point he had reached (for he had continued it in rougher form while
the manuscript was away, see pp. 293–4). But it is also clear that he did
not as yet abandon the work entirely. This is shown by some notes on a
scrap of paper to which my father fortunately and uncharacteristically
added a date:

Nov. 20 1937
*Note* when material returns
*Avari* are to be non-Eldarin = old *Lembi*
*Lembi* are to be Ilkorin Teleri
*Danians   Pereldar*
*Ilkorin*  :  *Alkorin* [struck out]
*hyarmen* for *harmen* south

The fact that the first three of these changes are among the early revisions
made to the QS manuscript (for their significance see pp. 218–19\*)
shows that he did do some further detailed work on it 'when the material
returned', i.e. after *The Lord of the Rings* was begun. It does not of course
show more precisely when that work was done or when the '*Eldanyárë*'
typescript was made, but here a second note with a date attached
provides evidence:

Feb. 3 1938
*Tintallë* Kindler can stand – but *tinwë* in Q[uenya] only = spark
(*tinta-* to kindle)
Therefore *Tinwerína* > *Elerína*
          *Tinwerontar* > *Elentári* (or *Tar-Ellion*)

Now the alterations of *Tinwerína* to *Elerína* and *Tinwerontar* to *Elentári*
were not made to the QS manuscript and do not appear in the typescript
(they were written in subsequently on the latter, only). This shows that
the typescript was made before 3 February 1938 – or more strictly, it had
at least reached the point where the name *Tinwerontar* occurs (chapter
3 (a), §19).

I conclude therefore that it was precisely at this crucial time (December
1937 – January 1938) that my father – entirely characteristically –
turned back again to the beginning of the *Quenta Silmarillion*, revising
the opening chapters and starting a new text in typescript ('*Eldanyárë*').
This soon petered out; and from that time the 'Silmarillion' narrative
remained unchanged for some thirteen years.

This conclusion determines the way in which the text of the first part
of the *Quenta Silmarillion* is presented in this book. In order to make the
contrast between 'The Silmarillion' of the earlier period and 'The
Silmarillion' after the major post-*Lord of the Rings* revision as clear in this
history as it was in fact, I give the text of the first five chapters (1 to 3 (c))
as it was *after* the first revision – which is the form of the typescript text as

---

\*For *Alkorin* beside *Ilkorin* see the *Etymologies*, stems AR², LA; for *Harmen*
> *Hyarmen* see p. 345.

it was originally made;* but important developments from the original form are given in the commentaries following each chapter. A great deal of this first rewriting was in fact a matter of improved expression rather than of narrative substance.

Although there are two texts for the first part of the work, I use the single abbreviation QS, distinguishing the manuscript and the typescript when necessary.

This is the title-page of the QS manuscript:

The
Quenta Silmarillion
Herein
is *Qenta Noldorinwa* or *Pennas inGeleidh*
or
History of the Gnomes

This is a history in brief drawn from many older tales; for all the matters that it contains were of old, and still are among the Eldar of the West, recounted more fully in other histories and songs. But many of these were not recalled by Eriol, or men have again lost them since his day. This Account was composed first by Pengolod of Gondolin, and Ælfwine turned it into our speech as it was in his time, adding nothing, he said, save explanations of some few names.

In this title, *inGeleidh* is an emendation made carefully over an erasure: the erased form was probably *na-Ngoelaidh* as in Q (IV. 77). The word *Silmarillion* was an addition; at first there stood simply *The Quenta*, as in Q.

In the preamble to Q only Eriol is named, and there is no mention of Pengolod; but in the preamble to AV 1 (IV. 263) it is said that both sets of *Annals*
were written by Pengolod the Wise of Gondolin, before its fall, and after at Sirion's Haven, and at Tavrobel in Toleressëa after his return unto the West, and there seen and translated by Eriol of Leithien, that is Ælfwine of the Angelcynn.

The preamble to the QS manuscript is decisively different in its representation of the literary history from that of Q; for in Q the abridgement which that work is declared to be was *drawn from the Book of Lost Tales which Eriol wrote* after he had read the Golden Book in Kortirion, whereas in QS it was *written by Pengolod and translated by Eriol* (like

---

*Here and there my father made further very small alterations in wording as he typed (i.e. beyond changes marked on the manuscript), and these are of course included in the text given here. The relation between manuscript and typescript changes in chapter 3 (c); see p. 220.

the *Annals*) – the work being conceived by Pengolod as an epitome on a small scale against a background of 'histories and songs' in which the matters were recounted at greater length (but many of these are lost to us).

Associated with the QS typescript are no less than five sheets of title and preamble. The first of these is in manuscript, and reads thus:

### The Silmarillion

The history of the Three Jewels, the
Silmarils of Fëanor, in which is told
in brief the history of the Elves from
their coming until the Change of the
World

1.  *Qenta Silmarillion*, or *Pennas Hilevril*
    To which is appended
    The houses of the princes of Men and Elves
    The tale of years
    The tale of battles

2.  *The Annals of Valinor     Nyarna Valinóren*

3.  *The Annals of Beleriand     Nyarna Valarianden*

4.  The *Lhammas* or Account of Tongues

This manuscript page was then copied in typescript, with these differences: above *The Silmarillion* at the head stands *Eldanyárë*, and the *Lhammas* is not included. In both manuscript and typescript *Nyarna Valinóren* was changed to *Yénië Valinóren or Inias Valannor*; and *Nyarna Valarianden* to *Inias Veleriand*. (In Old English versions of the *Annals of Valinor* the Elvish name is *Valinórelúmien*, IV. 284, 290). Subsequently, in the typescript only, *Pennas Hilevril* > *Pennas Silevril*; *Inias Valannor* > *Inias Balannor*; *Inias Veleriand* > *Inias Beleriand*.

   The next item is an elaborate and elegant page in red, blue, and black inks, which in its content is virtually the same as the typescript page just described; but here the name *I·Eldanyárë*, translated 'The History of the Elves', is explicitly an alternative: '*I·Eldanyárë* or *Silmarillion*'. The Elvish names of the *Annals* are the emended forms of the previous two pages: *Yénië Valinóren or Inias Valannor*, and *Inias Veleriand*, with the same later alterations of *Hilevril*, *Valannor*, and *Veleriand* to *Silevril*, *Balannor*, and *Beleriand* found on the typescript. On all three title-pages *Silmarillion* is a comprehensive title comprising within it not only the *Quenta Silmarillion* but also the two sets of *Annals*; cf. p. 109. The name *Qenta Noldorinwa* is not used.

   Following these title-pages is a preamble comprising a note by

Ælfwine and a note by the Translator. Five lines of Old English verse by Ælfwine are the selfsame lines that Alboin Errol 'dreamed', and translated for his father, in *The Lost Road* (p. 44); they would reappear again once more in association with the poem *The Song of Ælfwine* (p. 103). This preamble is found both in manuscript and typescript. The manuscript form reads:

### Silmarillion

*Ælfwine's note*
These histories were written by Pengolod the Wise of Gondolin, both in that city before its fall, and afterwards at Tathrobel in the Lonely Isle, Toleressëa, after the return unto the West. In their making he used much the writings of Rúmil the Elfsage of Valinor, chiefly in the annals of Valinor and the account of tongues, and he used also the accounts that are preserved in the Golden Book. The work of Pengolod I learned much by heart, and turned into my tongue, some during my sojourn in the West, but most after my return to Britain.

þus cwæþ Ælfwine Wídlást:
Fela bið on Westwegum werum uncúðra,
wundra ond wihta, wlitescyne lond,
eardgeard ylfa ond ésa bliss.
Lýt ænig wát hwylc his longað síe
þám þe eftsíðes yldu getwæfeð.

*Translator's note*
The histories are here given in English of this day, translated from the version of Eriol of Leithien, as the Gnomes called him, who was Ælfwine of Angelcynn. Such other matters as Ælfwine took direct from the Golden Book, together with his account of his voyage, and his sojourn in Toleressëa, are given elsewhere.

*Eriol* was altered to *Ereol* (cf. IV. 166, 283); and there is a pencilled annotation against the *Translator's note*:
Specimens (not here) are extant
  (a) of the original Eressëan form and script
  (b) of the annals as written by Ælfwine in ancient English
*Ælfwine's note* here is a development from the preamble to AV 1 (cited above p. 201); cf. also the second version of that preamble and my remarks about Rúmil's part in the *Annals* (p. 123). There is now no mention of Pengolod's having continued his work at Sirion's Haven after the fall of Gondolin. The form *Tathrobel* for *Tavrobel* occurs in Old English versions of AV 1 (IV. 282, 290). For the Golden Book see IV. 78, 274.
The typescript version of the preamble has some differences. The

page is headed *Eldanyárë*, not *Silmarillion*, and *Ælfwine's note* is changed: the passage beginning 'after the return unto the West' reads here:

> after the Elves had returned into the West. In their making he used much the writings of Rúmil the Elf-sage of Valinor concerning other matters than the wars of Beleriand; and he used also the accounts that are preserved by the Elves of Eressëa in the Golden Book. The work of Pengolod I learned by heart . . .

In the *Translator's note* the spelling is *Ereol* and the words *that is now England* are added after *Angolcynn* (so spelt).

I give now the text of the *Quenta Silmarillion* as I think it stood when it was for long laid aside. As with *The Fall of Númenor* I have numbered the paragraphs, the numbers running continuously through the text; the paragraphing of the original is very largely retained. A commentary, related to the paragraphs, follows each chapter.

# QUENTA SILMARILLION*

Here begins the *Silmarillion* or history of the Silmarils

## 1   OF THE VALAR

§1   In the beginning the All-father, who in Elvish tongue is named Ilúvatar, made the Ainur of his thought; and they made music before him. Of this music the World was made; for Ilúvatar gave it being, and set it amid the Void, and he set the secret fire to burn at the heart of the World; and he showed the World to the Ainur. And many of the mightiest of them became enamoured of its beauty, and desired to enter into it; and they put on the raiment of the World, and descended into it, and they are in it.

§2   These spirits the Elves name the Valar, which is the Powers, and Men have often called them Gods. Many lesser spirits of their own kind they brought in their train, both great and small; and some of these Men have confused with the Elves, but wrongly, for they were made before the World, whereas Elves and Men awoke first in the World, after the coming of the Valar. Yet in the making of Elves and of Men, and in the giving to each of their especial gifts, none of the Valar had any part. Ilúvatar alone was their author; wherefore they are called the Children of Ilúvatar.

§3   The chieftains of the Valar were nine. These were the

---

*In the manuscript (only) the word *Silmarillion* was an addition, as on the title-page (p. 201); but the heading 'Here begins the *Silmarillion* . . .' is original.

names of the Nine Gods in the Elvish tongue as it was spoken in Valinor; though they have other or altered names in the speech of the Gnomes, and their names among Men are manifold: Manwë and Melko, Ulmo, Aulë, Mandos, Lórien, Tulkas, Ossë, and Oromë.

§4    Manwë and Melko were brethren in the thought of Ilúvatar and mightiest of those Ainur who came into the World. But Manwë is the lord of the Gods, and prince of the airs and winds, and ruler of the sky. With him dwells as wife Varda the maker of the stars, immortal lady of the heights, whose name is holy. Fionwë and Ilmarë* are their son and daughter. Next in might and closest in friendship to Manwë is Ulmo, lord of waters, who dwells alone in the Outer Seas, but has the government of all water, seas and rivers, fountains and springs, throughout the earth. Subject to him, though he has often rebelled, is Ossë, the master of the seas about the lands of Men; and his wife is Uinen, the lady of the sea. Her hair lies spread through all the waters under skies.

*Marginal note to the text: Ilma is in the Quendian tongue starlight.

§5    Aulë has might but little less than Ulmo. He is the lord of earth. He is a smith and a master of crafts; and his spouse is Yavanna, the giver of fruits and lover of all things that grow. In majesty she is next to Varda among the queens of the Valar. She is fair and tall; and often the Elves name her Palúrien, the Lady of the Wide Earth.

§6    The Fanturi were brethren, and are named Mandos and Lórien. Nurufantur the elder was also called, the master of the houses of the dead, and the gatherer of the spirits of the slain. He forgets nothing, and knows all that shall be, save only what Ilúvatar has hidden, but he speaks only at the command of Manwë. He is the doomsman of the Valar. Vairë the weaver is his wife, who weaves all things that have been in time in her storied webs, and the halls of Mandos, that ever widen as the ages pass, are clothed therewith. Olofantur the younger of these brethren was also named, maker of visions and of dreams. His gardens in the land of the Gods are the fairest of all places in the world, and filled with many spirits. Estë the pale is his wife, who walks not by day, but sleeps on an island in the dark lake of Lórien. Thence his fountains bring refreshment to the folk of Valinor.

§7    Strongest of limb, and greatest in deeds of prowess, is

Tulkas, who is surnamed Poldórëa, the Valiant. He is unclothed in his disport, which is much in wrestling; and he rides no steed, for he can outrun all things that go on feet, and he is tireless. His hair and beard are golden, and his flesh ruddy; his weapons are his hands. He recks little of either past or future, and is of small avail as a counsellor, but a hardy friend. He has great love for Fionwë son of Manwë. His wife is Nessa, sister of Oromë, who is lissom of limb and fleet of foot, and dances in Valinor upon lawns of never-fading green.

§8   Oromë was a mighty lord, and little less in strength than Tulkas, though slower in wrath. He loved the lands of earth, while they were still dark, and he left them unwillingly and came last to Valinor; and he comes even yet at times east over the mountains. Of old he was often seen upon the hills and plains. He is a hunter, and he loves all trees; for which reason he is called Aldaron, and by the Gnomes Tauros, the lord of forests. He delights in horses and in hounds, and his horns are loud in the friths and woods that Yavanna planted in Valinor; but he blows them not upon the Middle-earth since the fading of the Elves, whom he loved. Vana is his wife, the queen of flowers, who has the beauty both of heaven and of earth upon her face and in all her works; she is the younger sister of Varda and Palúrien.

§9   But mightier than she is Nienna, Manwë's sister and Melko's. She dwells alone. Pity is in her heart, and mourning and weeping come to her; shadow is her realm and her throne hidden. For her halls are west of West, nigh to the borders of the World and the Darkness, and she comes seldom to Valmar, the city of the Gods, where all is glad. She goes rather to the halls of Mandos, which are nearer and yet more northward; and all those who go to Mandos cry to her. For she is a healer of hurts, and turns pain to medicine and sorrow to wisdom. The windows of her house look outward from the Walls of the World.

§10   Last do all name Melko. But the Gnomes, who suffered most from his evil deeds, will not speak his name, and they call him Morgoth, the Black God, and Bauglir, the Constrainer. Great might was given to him by Ilúvatar, and he was coëval with Manwë, and part he had of all the powers of the other Valar; but he turned them to evil uses. He coveted the world and all that was in it, and desired the lordship of Manwë and the realms of all the Gods; and pride and jealousy and lust grew ever in his heart, till he became unlike his brethren. Wrath consumed him, and he begot violence and destruction and excess. In ice and fire was his delight. But darkness he used most in all his evil works, and turned it to fear and a name of dread among Elves and Men.

## Commentary on Chapter 1

§1   There is nothing in Q concerning the Music of the Ainur; but the new version of that work was now in existence (see note 20 to the *Ainulindalë*).

§4   Though written in afterwards on the typescript, the marginal note clearly belongs either with the original writing of the manuscript or with the earliest changes. In the *Lhammas* (§1) *Quendian* is the term for all the Elvish languages, derived from Oromë, as a group. In the *Ambarkanta* (and on the diagrams associated with it) the 'middle air' was *Ilma*, replaced throughout by *Ilmen* (the form in the early Númenórean writings, pp. 9, 13); in the *Etymologies* both *Ilma* and *Ilmen* appear, under the stem GIL: *'Ilma* starlight (cf. *Ilmare*)', *'Ilmen* region above air where stars are'.

The children of Manwë and Varda are not mentioned here in Q: see note 20 to the *Ainulindalë*.

§5   *Lady of the Wide Earth* was a carefully made alteration over an erasure, the original reading being *Bosom of the Earth*, as in Q.

§6   *Nurufantur* was another early change like that in §5; here the erased form was *Nefantur*, as in Q. This is the first appearance of these elements in the character of Mandos: his knowledge of past and future, and his speaking only when commanded so to do by Manwë (cf. I. 90, 111). Here also are the first characterisations of Vairë and of Estë, who in AV are no more than names.

§7   This description of Tulkas, now first appearing, was largely retained in the ultimate form of this chapter, the *Valaquenta*, which like the *Ainulindalë* became a separate and distinct element in the whole work (see *The Silmarillion* pp. 28–9); but his great love for Fionwë is not mentioned there. – The original reading in the manuscript was *He had great love for Fionwë*; see the remarks on tenses at the end of this commentary.

§9   In AV Nienna had become the sister of Manwë and Melko, as still here; in the *Valaquenta* (p. 28) she is 'sister of the Fëanturi'.

The passage beginning 'For her halls are west of West' to the end of the paragraph, not in Q, is retained in the *Valaquenta*. In the *Lost Tales* the hall of Vefántur and Fui Nienna was 'beneath the roots of the most cold and northerly of the Mountains of Valinor' (I. 76). I do not certainly understand the statement that the windows of Nienna's house 'look outward from the Walls of the World'; for if her house is in the extreme West of Valinor her windows must surely look into the Chasm of Ilmen and through Vaiya *to* the Walls of the World (see the *Ambarkanta* diagram and map IV. 243, 249, and cf. QS §12). But an interpretation, admittedly rather forced, might be that from the windows of her house the gaze passes unhindered through Ilmen and Vaiya, and the invisible Walls of the World, and in this sense 'looks outward from the Walls'.

§10   In Q Bauglir is translated 'Terrible'. In the published *Silmarillion* the name is not interpreted in the text; in the Index I translated it 'Constrainer' as here. In the *Etymologies*, stem MBAW, it is rendered 'tyrant, oppressor'.

### Past and Present Tense in Chapter 1

In Q the past tense is used throughout in the account of the Valar, but with exceptions in the cases of Ossë, Uinen, and Nienna. These present tenses would probably not have occurred had not my father been imposing the past tense on thought that was not in fact so definite. In the opening section of AV 1 there is a mixture of present and past which is slightly increased in that of AV 2. In QS the present tense is used, with very few exceptions, and of these 'Manwë and Melko *were* brethren' and 'The Fanturi *were* brethren' were probably fully intended (sc. they were brethren 'in the thought of Ilúvatar'). Tulkas '*had* great love for Fionwë' was early corrected (§7); and only 'Oromë *was* a mighty lord' remains – a repetition of the phrase in Q. – In §2 the manuscript has 'the Elves *named* the Valar'; the typescript has *name*.

### 2   OF VALINOR AND THE TWO TREES

§11   In the beginning of the overlordship of the Valar they saw that the World was dark, and that light was scattered over the airs and lands and seas. They made therefore two mighty lamps for the lighting of the World, and set them upon lofty pillars in the South and North of the Middle-earth. But most of the Valar dwelt upon an island in the seas, while they laboured at their first tasks in the ordering of the World. And Morgoth contested with them, and made war. He overthrew the lamps, and in the confusion of darkness he roused the seas against their island.

§12   Then the Gods removed into the West, where ever since their seats have been; but Morgoth escaped from their wrath, and in the North he built himself a fortress, and delved great caverns underground.* At that time the Valar could not overcome him or take him captive. Therefore they made their home in the uttermost West, and fortified it, and built many mansions in that land

*Marginal note to the text:* Melko builds Utumno.

upon the borders of the World which is called Valinor. It is bounded on the hither side by the Great Sea, and on the further side by the Outer Sea, which the Elves call Vaiya; and beyond that the Walls of the World fence out the Void and the Eldest Dark. Eastwards on the shores of the inner sea the Valar built the mountains of Valinor, that are highest upon earth.

§13   In that land they gathered all light and all fair things, and there are their houses, their gardens and their towers. In the midst of the plain beyond the mountains was the city of the Gods, Valmar the beautiful of many bells. But Manwë and Varda had halls upon the loftiest of the mountains of Valinor, whence they could look out across the earth even into the furthest East. Taniquetil the Elves name that holy mountain; and Oiolossë Everlasting Whiteness; Elerína Crowned with Stars; and many names beside. And the Gnomes spake of it in their later tongue as Amon Uilos; and in the language of this island of old Tindbrenting was its name, among those few that had ever descried it afar off.

§14   In Valinor Yavanna hallowed the mould with mighty song, and Nienna watered it with tears. In that time the Gods were gathered together, and they sat silent upon their thrones of council in the Ring of Doom nigh unto the golden gates of Valmar the Blessed; and Yavanna Palúrien sang before them and they watched.

§15   From the earth there came forth two slender shoots; and silence was over all the world in that hour, nor was there any other sound save the slow chanting of Palúrien. Under her song two fair trees uprose and grew. Of all things which the Gods made they have most renown, and about their fate all the tales of the Eldar are woven. The one had leaves of a dark green that beneath were as shining silver; and he bore white blossoms like the cherry, from which a dew of silver light was ever falling, so that the earth beneath was dappled with the dark dancing shadows of his leaves and the flickering white radiance of his flowers. The other bore leaves of young green like the new-opened beech; their edges were of glittering gold. Yellow flowers swung upon her branches like the hanging blossom of those trees Men now call Golden-rain; and from those flowers came forth warmth and a great light.

§16   Silpion the one was called in Valinor, and Telperion and Ninquelótë and many names in song beside; but the Gnomes name him Galathilion. Laurelin the other was called, and

Kulúrien and Malinalda, and many other names; but the Gnomes name her Galadlóriel.*

§17   In seven hours the glory of each tree waxed to full and waned again to nought; and each awoke again to life an hour before the other ceased to shine. Thus in Valinor twice every day there came a gentle hour of softer light, when both Trees were faint, and their gold and silver beams were mingled. Silpion was the elder of the Trees, and came first to full stature and to bloom; and that first hour in which he shone alone, the white glimmer of a silver dawn, the Gods reckoned not into the tale of hours, but named it the Opening Hour, and counted therefrom the ages of their reign in Valinor. Therefore at the sixth hour of the First Day, and of all the joyous days afterward until the Darkening, Silpion ceased his time of flower; and at the twelfth hour Laurelin her blossoming. And each day of the Gods in Valinor contained, therefore, twelve hours, and ended with the second mingling of the lights, in which Laurelin was waning but Silpion was waxing.

### Commentary on Chapter 2

§12   The marginal note, with Utumno (not Angband) as the name of Melko's original fortress as in the *Ambarkanta* and AV 2, is an early addition, since in §§62, 105 *Utumno* is an early change from *Utumna*, whereas this is not the case in the note.

§13   The manuscript has 'named that holy mountain', but the typescript 'name'; cf. the note on tenses in the commentary on Chapter 1. In §16 both texts have 'the Gnomes name him', 'the Gnomes name her'.

*Elerína* is a change made to the typescript, which had *Tinwerína*, but it belongs to the earlier period (1938): see p. 200. The names *Oiolossë, Tinwerína, Amon Uilos* are replacements over erasures, the erased names being those found in Q (IV. 81), *Ialassë* (or perhaps rather *Iolossë*, see the *Etymologies*, stem EY), *Tinwenairin, Amon-Uilas*.

*Footnote to the text:* Other names of Silpion among the Gnomes are Silivros glimmering rain (which in Elvish form is Silmerossë), Nimloth pale blossom, Celeborn tree of silver; and the image that Turgon made of him in Gondolin was called Belthil divine radiance. Other names of Laurelin among the Gnomes are Glewellin (which is the same as Laurelin song of gold), Lhasgalen green of leaf, Melthinorn tree of gold; and her image in Gondolin was named Glingal hanging flame.

§16   *Names of the Trees*. This is the first occurrence in the texts of *Telperion*, as also of *Ninquelótë*, *Kulúrien*, and *Malinalda*. The names *Galathilion* and *Galadlóriel* are replacements over erasures – i.e. of *Bansil* and *Glingol*, as in Q, or of *Belthil* and *Glingal*, as in the footnote. The footnote was almost certainly added at the same time as these changes. In this note *Silmerossë* is called the 'Elvish' form as distinct from the Gnomish *Silivros*; later in QS (§25) the phrase 'The Lindar . . . who sometimes are alone called Elves' survived from Q (IV. 85), though it was struck out and does not appear in the typescript; in the present note, on the other hand, this old distinction between 'Elvish' and 'Gnomish' was retained in the typescript.

*Nimloth*, which now first appears, later became the name of the White Tree of Númenor, a seedling of the White Tree of Tol-eressëa. *Celeborn*, also now first appearing, was later the Tree of Tol-eressëa, derived from the Tree of Tirion. With *Lhasgalen* 'green of leaf' cf. *Eryn Lasgalen* 'Wood of Greenleaves', name of Mirkwood after the War of the Ring (*The Lord of the Rings*, Appendix B, III. 375).

*Belthil* and *Glingal* appear as late emendations of *Bansil* and *Glingol* in both the 'Lays of Beleriand' (III. 80–2, 195), where they are the names of the Trees of Valinor. The particular association of these names (in the earlier forms) with the Trees of Gondolin goes back to the old tale of *The Fall of Gondolin*, where however these Trees were not images but scions of the Trees of Valinor; but in Q (and in QS before the changes to *Galathilion* and *Galadlóriel*) they are the Gnomish names of Silpion and Laurelin. The present note is the first indication that the Trees of Gondolin were *images* made by Turgon.

§17   At the end of the chapter in the manuscript is a simplified form of the table of the periods of the Trees given in Q (IV. 83).


3 (a)   OF THE COMING OF THE ELVES

[In the QS manuscript the third chapter ('Of the Coming of the Elves') extends all the way through Chapters 3, 4 ('Of Thingol and Melian'), and 5 ('Of Eldamar and the Princes of the Eldalië') in the published work, though there is a sub-heading 'Thingol'. In the typescript text there are two emphatic breaks and subheadings, 'Of Thingol' and 'Of Kôr and Alqualondë' (which became 'Of Eldamar and the Princes of the Eldalië'), but they have no chapter-numbers; and after 'Of Kôr and Alqualondë' the typescript text comes to an end. It is convenient to treat the three parts here as separate chapters, numbering them 3 (a), 3 (b), and 3 (c).]

§18   In all this time, since Morgoth overthrew the lamps, the Middle-earth east of the Mountains of Valinor was without light. While the lamps were shining, growth began there, which now was checked, because all was again dark. But already the oldest living things had arisen: in the sea the great weeds, and on the earth the shadow of dark trees. And beneath the trees small things faint and silent walked, and in the valleys of the night-clad hills there were dark creatures old and strong. In such lands and forests Oromë would often hunt; and there too at times Yavanna came, singing sorrowfully; for she was grieved at the darkness of the Middle-earth and ill content that it was forsaken. But the other Valar came seldom thither; and in the North Morgoth built his strength, and gathered his demons about him. These were the first made of his creatures: their hearts were of fire, and they had whips of flame. The Gnomes in later days named them Balrogs. But in that time Morgoth made many monsters of divers kinds and shapes that long troubled the world; yet the Orcs were not made until he had looked upon the Elves, and he made them in mockery of the Children of Ilúvatar. His realm spread now ever southward over the Middle-earth.

§19   Varda looked out upon the darkness, and was moved. Therefore she took the silver dew that dripped from Silpion and was hoarded in Valinor, and therewith she made the stars. And for this reason she is called Tintallë, the Star-kindler, and Elentári, Queen of Stars. She strewed the unlit skies with these bright vessels, filled with silver flame; but high in the North, a challenge unto Morgoth, she set the crown of seven mighty stars to swing, the emblem of the Gods, and the sign of doom. Many names have these been called; but in the old days of the North both Elves and Men called them the Burning Briar, and some the Sickle of the Gods.

§20   It is told that at the opening of the first stars the children of the earth awoke, the Elder Children of Ilúvatar. Themselves they named the Quendi, whom we call Elves; but Oromë named them Eldar, Star-folk, and that name has since been borne by all that followed him upon the westward road. In the beginning they were greater and more strong than they have since become; but not more fair, for though the beauty of the Eldar in the days of their youth was beyond all other beauty that Ilúvatar has caused to be, it has not perished, but lives in the West, and sorrow and wisdom have enriched it. And Oromë looking upon the Elves was filled with love and wonder; for their coming was not in the Music of the Ainur, and was hidden in the secret thought of Ilúvatar. But Oromë came upon them by chance in his wandering, while they dwelt yet silent beside the starlit mere, Kuiviénen, Water of

Awakening, in the East of the Middle-earth. For a while he abode with them, and taught them the language of the Gods, from whence afterwards they made the fair Elvish speech, which was sweet in the ears of the Valar. Then swiftly Oromë rode back over land and sea to Valinor, filled with the thought of the beauty of the Elves, and he brought the tidings to Valmar. And the Gods were amazed, all save Manwë, to whom the secret thought of Ilúvatar was revealed in all matters that concern this world. Manwë sat now long in thought, and at length he spoke to the Valar, revealing to them the mind of the Father; and he bade them to return now to their duty, which was to govern the world for the Children of Ilúvatar, when they should appear, each kindred in its appointed time.

§21    Thus it came to pass that after long council the Gods resolved to make an assault upon the fortress of Morgoth in the North.* Morgoth did not forget that the Elves were the cause of his downfall. Yet they had no part in it; and little do they know of the riding of the power of the West against the North in the beginning of their days, and of the war and tumult of the first Battle of the Gods. In those days the shape of the Middle-earth was changed and broken and the seas were moved. It was Tulkas who at last wrestled with Morgoth and overthrew him, and bound him with the chain Angainor, and led him captive; and the world had peace for a long age. But the fortress of Morgoth had many vaults and caverns hidden with deceit far under earth, and these the Gods did not utterly destroy, and many evil things still lingered there; and others were dispersed and fled into the dark and roamed in the waste places of the world.

§22    The Gods drew Morgoth back to Valinor bound hand and foot and blindfold, and he was cast into prison in the halls of Mandos, from whence none have ever escaped save by the will of Mandos and of Manwë, neither Vala, nor Elf, nor Man. Vast are those halls and strong, and built in the North of Valinor.

§23    Then the Quendi, the people of the Elves, were summoned by the Gods to Valinor, for the Valar were filled with love of their beauty, and feared for them in the dangerous world amid the deceits of the starlit dusk; but the Gods as yet withheld the living light in Valinor. In this many have seen the cause of woes that after befell, holding that the Valar erred, and strayed from the

*Marginal note to the text: Utumno.

purpose of Ilúvatar, albeit with good intent. Yet such was the fate of the World, which cannot in the end be contrary to Ilúvatar's design. Nonetheless the Elves were at first unwilling to hearken to the summons; wherefore Oromë was sent unto them, and he chose from among them three ambassadors, and he brought them to Valmar. These were Ingwë and Finwë and Elwë, who after were kings of the Three Kindreds of the Eldar; and coming they were filled with awe by the glory and majesty of the Valar, and desired the light and splendour of Valinor. Therefore they returned and counselled the Elves to remove into the West, and the greater part of the people obeyed their counsel. This they did of their own free will, and yet were swayed by the power of the Gods, ere their wisdom was full grown. The Elves that obeyed the summons and followed the three princes are called the Eldar, by the name that Oromë gave them; for he was their guide, and led them at the last (save some that strayed upon the march) unto Valinor. Yet there were many who preferred the starlight and the wide spaces of the earth to the rumour of the glory of the Trees, and remained behind; and these are called the Avari, the Unwilling.

§24   The Eldar prepared now a great march from their first homes in the East. When all was ready, Oromë rode at their head upon his white horse shod with gold; and behind him the Eldalië was arrayed in three hosts.

§25   The first to take the road were led by Ingwë, the most high lord of all the Elvish race. He entered into Valinor, and sits at the feet of the Powers, and all Elves revere his name; but he never returned nor looked again upon the Middle-earth. The Lindar were his folk, the fairest of the Quendi; they are the High Elves, and the beloved of Manwë and Varda, and few among Men have spoken with them.

§26   Next came the Noldor. The Gnomes we may call them, a name of wisdom; they are the Deep Elves, and the friends of Aulë. Their lord was Finwë, wisest of all the children of the world. His kindred are renowned in song, and of them these tales have much to tell, for they fought and laboured long and grievously in the Northern lands of old.

§27   Third came the Teleri, for they tarried, and were not wholly of a mind to forsake the dusk; they are the Sea Elves, and the Soloneldi they were after named in Valinor, for they made music beside the breaking waves. Elwë was their lord, and his hair was long and white.

§28    The hindmost of the Noldor forsook the host of Finwë, repenting of the march, and they turned southward, and wandered long, and became a people apart, unlike their kin. They are not counted among the Eldar, nor yet among the Avari. Pereldar they are called in the tongue of the Elves of Valinor, which signifies Half-eldar. But in their own tongue they were called Danas, for their first leader was named Dân. His son was Denethor, who led them into Beleriand ere the rising of the Moon.

§29    And many others of the Eldar that set out upon the march were lost upon the long road, and they wandered in the woods and mountains of the world, and never came to Valinor nor saw the light of the Two Trees. Therefore they are called the Lembi, that is the Lingerers. And the Lembi and the Pereldar are called also the Ilkorindi, because though they began the journey they never dwelt in Kôr, the city which the Elves after built in the land of the Gods; yet their hearts were ever turned towards the West. But the Ilkorindi and the Avari are called the Dark Elves, because they never beheld the light of the Two Trees ere it was dimmed; whereas the Lindar and the Noldor and the Teleri are named the Light Elves, and remember the light that is no more.*

§30    The Lembi were for the most part of the race of the Teleri, and the chief of these were the Elves of Beleriand, in the West of the Middle-earth. Most renowned among them was that Elf who first was named Sindo, the Grey, brother of Elwë, but is called now Thingol in the language of Doriath.

*Footnote to the text*: Other names in song and tale are given to these folk. The Lindar are the Blessed Elves, and the Spear-elves, and the Elves of the Air, the Friends of the Gods, the Holy Elves, and the Immortal, and the Children of Ingwë; they are the Fair Folk and the White. The Noldor are the Wise and the Golden, the Valiant, the Sword-elves, the Elves of the Earth, the Foes of Melko, the Skilled of Hand, the Lovers of Jewels, the Companions of Men, the Followers of Finwë. The Teleri are the Foam-riders, Musicians of the Shore, the Free, the Wanderers, and the Elves of the Sea, the Sailors, the Arrow-elves, Ship-friends, the Lords of the Gulls, the Blue Elves, the Pearl-gatherers, and the People of Elwë. The Danas are the Elves of the Woods, the Hidden Elves, the Green Elves, the Elves of the Seven Rivers, the Lovers of Lúthien, the Lost Folk of Ossiriand, for they are now no more.

## Commentary on Chapter 3 (a)

[The names of the divisions of the Elves underwent extremely complicated changes on the QS manuscript to reach the form in the typescript text printed here, since the same names were moved into different references and given different meanings. I do not refer to the original names in the notes that follow, since the individual changes would be extremely hard to follow if given piecemeal, but attempt an explanation in a general note at the end of this commentary.]

§18    The original text of the passage concerning the demons of Morgoth ran as follows:

> . . . in the North Morgoth built his strength, and gathered his demon-broods about him, whom the Gnomes after knew as Balrogs: they had whips of flame. The Úvanimor he made, monsters of divers kinds and shapes; but the Orcs were not made until he had looked upon the Elves.

The term *Úvanimor* occurs in the *Lost Tales*, I. 75 ('monsters, giants, and ogres'), etc.; cf. *Vanimor* 'the Beautiful', p. 110. – On the question of when the Orcs first came into being see p. 148 and commentary on QS §62. It is said in *The Fall of Númenor* II (§1) that the Orcs are 'mockeries of the creatures of Ilúvatar' (cf. also *The Lost Road*, p. 65). In QS §62 the idea that the Orcs were mockeries of the Elves is found in the text as originally written.

§19    *Elentári* was changed on the typescript from *Tinwerontar*, but the alteration belongs to the earlier period, like *Elerína* > *Tinwerína* in §13; see p. 200. – *Tintallë* 'the Kindler' is found in *The Silmarillion* (p. 48) – and in *The Lord of the Rings* – but is there the name of Varda 'out of the deeps of time': the name 'Queen of the Stars' (*Elentári*) was given in reference to the second star-making, at the time of the awakening of the Elves. This second star-making of *The Silmarillion* was still in QS, as in AV 2 (annal 1900), the first.

§20    The sentence beginning 'but Oromë named them Eldar, "Starfolk" . . .' is a footnote in the manuscript, a very early addition; in the typescript it was taken up into the text. See the note on names at the end of this commentary.

The whole paragraph, from the words 'but not more fair', was greatly extended and altered in the first rewriting to give the text printed. As originally written it was almost an exact repetition of Q (IV. 84):

> . . . yet not more fair. Oromë it was that found them, dwelling by the star-lit mere, Kuiviénen, Water of Awakening, in the East of Middle-earth. Swiftly he rode to Valinor filled with the thought of their beauty. When the Valar heard his tidings, they pondered long, and they recalled their duty. For they came into the world knowing that their office was to govern it for the Children of Ilúvatar, who should afterward come, each in the appointed time.

In addition to the statement in the rewriting that Oromë taught the Elves 'the language of the Gods' (see the *Lhammas* §1), the new passage introduces an extraordinary development into the thought of the *Ainulindalë*: the coming of the Children of Ilúvatar *was not in the Music of the Ainur*, the Valar were amazed at the news brought by Oromë, and Manwë then revealed to them the mind of Ilúvatar. What in the original text was their known duty ('For they came into the world knowing that their office was to govern it for the Children of Ilúvatar') is now (it seems) presented to them as a duty indeed, but one of which they had until then been ignorant. In the *Ainulindalë* version of this period (pp. 160–1) it is said:

For Elves and Men were devised by Ilúvatar alone, nor, since they comprehended not fully that part of the theme when it was propounded to them, did any of the Ainur dare in their music to add anything to their fashion.

In the later, post-*Lord of the Rings* versions, while the conception is changed and the idea introduced of the Vision seen by the Ainur before the act of Creation, it is explicit that the Children of Ilúvatar 'came with the Third Theme' of the Music, and that the Ainur saw in the Vision the arising of Elves and Men.

§21    As originally written QS had 'symmetry' for 'shape', showing that my father had in mind the passage in the *Ambarkanta*: 'But the symmetry of the ancient Earth was changed and broken in the first Battle of the Gods' (IV. 239 and the map IV. 251).

§23    The passage from 'In this many have seen the cause of woes that after befell' is an addition to the original text, which had simply 'Oromë brought their ambassadors to Valmar.' Here the story of the three ambassadors, curiously absent from S and Q (IV. 168), re-emerges from the *Lost Tales* (I. 115–17); and the suggestion, first appearing in the rewriting of QS, that the Valar erred in summoning the Elves is also hinted at in the old tale: 'Maybe indeed had the Gods decided otherwise the world had been a fairer place and the Eldar a happier folk' (I. 117).

*Elwë* here, confusingly, is *not* Thingol, whose Quenya name is *Elwë* in *The Silmarillion*. In the *Lost Tales* Tinwelint (Thingol) was one of the three ambassadors; but the leader of the Third Kindred on the Great March (after the loss of Tinwelint) was 'one Ellu' (I. 120). In QS Thingol was *not* one of the ambassadors, and he never went to Valinor; the ambassador and the leader of the Third Host was Elwë (who was however the brother of Thingol). In *The Silmarillion* Thingol (Elwë Singollo) was again one of the ambassadors, while the leader of the Third Host (after the loss of Thingol) was his brother Olwë – a return therefore to the *Lost Tales*, with the addition that the two were brothers.

The original text of the passage following 'These were Ingwë and

Finwë and Elwë, who after were kings of the Three Kindreds of the Eldar' was thus:

And returning they counselled that the Elves should remove into the West. This they did of their own free will, yet in awe of the power and majesty of the Gods. Most of the Elves obeyed the summons, and these are they who afterward came unto Valinor (save some who strayed), and are called the Eldar, the Departing.

This explanation of the name *Eldar* is the same as that in the *Lhammas* (§2 and commentary), and in both works it was overtaken by the translation 'Star-folk', the name given by Oromë: see under §20 above and the note on names at the end of this commentary.

§25   After 'The Lindar were his folk, the fairest of the Quendi' the original text added: 'who sometimes are alone called Elves'; see the commentary on §16.

*High Elves*: Q had here 'Light-elves'; subsequently (IV. 89 note 6) 'Light-elves' was emended to 'High-elves', and that in turn to 'Fair-elves'. The term 'Light Elves' was now differently employed: see §29, and p. 197.

§27   This is the first appearance of the idea that the Teleri were the last of the Three Kindreds because 'they tarried, and were not wholly of a mind to forsake the dusk'. In the *Lhammas* (§2) they were the last because they were 'the latest to awake'.

§28   For 'Pereldar they are called in the tongue of the Elves of Valinor, which signifies Half-eldar' the original reading was: 'No name had they in the tongue of Valinor.' See the note on names below.

§29   The words 'they never dwelt in Kôr, the city which the Elves after built' are a reversion to the original meaning of the name, the more puzzling in view of §39: 'On the top of the hill of Kôr the city of the Elves was built, the white walls and terraces of Tûn [> Túna]'. Similarly in the *Lhammas* §11 the words 'in Kôr' contradict the reference in §5 to Kôr as the hill on which Tûn [> Túna] was built.

§30   It is said also in the *Lhammas* (§2) that the Lembi were for the most part of Telerian race, but the meaning there is not precisely the same, since in the *Lhammas* the name *Lembi* still meant the Elves who never left the lands of their awakening. – On *Sindo the Grey* see the commentary on *Lhammas* §6.

### Note on the names of the divisions of the Elves

Several of the changes referred to below are found in the list of proposed alterations dated 20 November 1937 (p. 200).

As this chapter was originally written, the classification was:

(§23)   *Eldar* 'the Departing', opposed to *Lembi* 'the Lingerers', those that remained behind. (This is the same formulation as in the *Lhammas* §2, before emendation.)

(§28)   Those of the Noldor who repented of the journey and turned south, the *Danas*, are counted neither as *Eldar* or *Lembi*. (This agrees with the statement in the *Lhammas* §7 (but not with that in §2: on the contradictory views see p. 188 and the *Lammasethen*, pp. 194-5).

(§29)   Those of the Eldar who set out but 'were lost upon the long road' and never came to Kôr are called *Ilkorindi*. (This agrees with the *Lhammas* §2, except that there the Danas are included among the Ilkorindi.)

The earliest changes to the QS manuscript then brought in the ideas that *Eldar* meant 'Star-folk' and was a name given to all Elves by Oromë, but also that this name was 'borne by all that followed him upon the westward road'. The distinction was also introduced that those who actually crossed the Sea were called *Avari*, 'the Departing'. This new formulation was written in also to *Lhammas* §2 (see the commentary), doubtless at the same time.

The third layer of early change to this passage in the QS manuscript, giving the text printed, is not represented in the *Lhammas*. These are the changes referred to in the notes dated 20 November 1937. *Avari* was changed to mean 'the Unwilling', and replaced *Lembi* as the name for those who remained behind in the East (§23); the Danas were given the name 'in the tongue of Valinor' of *Pereldar* 'Half-eldar' (§28);* *Lembi* was now given to the Eldar who were lost on the road and never came to Kôr (§29); and while the name *Ilkorindi* was retained (an alternative to *Lembi*) it now included also the Danas (*Pereldar*) (§29) – to that extent agreeing with *Lhammas* §2. Thus (in contrast to the table on p. 183):

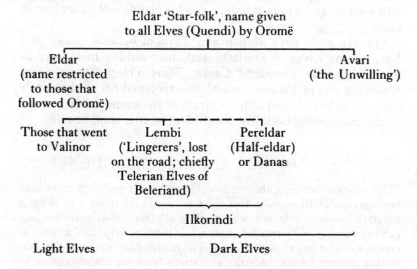

Eldar 'Star-folk', name given
to all Elves (Quendi) by Oromë

Eldar
(name restricted
to those that
followed Oromë)

Avari
('the Unwilling')

Those that went
to Valinor

Lembi
('Lingerers', lost
on the road; chiefly
Telerian Elves of
Beleriand)

Pereldar
(Half-eldar)
or Danas

Ilkorindi

Light Elves                    Dark Elves

*In *The Lord of the Rings* the Sindarin form *Peredhil* has a totally different application: 'The sons of Eärendil were Elros and Elrond, the *Peredhil* or Half-elven', Appendix A I (i). An earlier name was *Peringol, Peringiul*: see the commentary on AB 2, annal 325.

## 3 (b)  OF THINGOL

§31    For this reason Thingol abode in Beleriand and came not to Valinor. Melian was a fay, of the race of the Valar. She dwelt in the gardens of Lórien, and among all his fair folk there were none more beautiful than she, nor more wise, nor more skilled in songs of magic and enchantment. It is told that the Gods would leave their business, and the birds of Valinor their mirth, that the bells of Valmar were silent, and the fountains ceased to flow, when at the mingling of the light Melian sang in the gardens of the God of dreams. Nightingales went always with her, and she taught them their song. She loved deep shadow, but she was akin, before the World was made, unto Yavanna, and often strayed from Valinor on long journey into the Hither Lands, and there she filled the silence of the dawning earth with her voice and with the voices of her birds.

§32    Thingol heard the song of the nightingales of Melian and a spell was laid upon him, and he forsook his folk, and was lost, following their voices amid the shadows of the trees. He came at last upon a glade open to the stars; and there Melian stood, and the light of Valinor was in her face. Nought she said, but being filled with love Thingol came to her and took her hand, and he was cast into a dream and a long slumber, and his people looked for him in vain.

§33    In after days Melian and Thingol became Queen and King of the Elves of Doriath, and their hidden halls were in Menegroth, the Thousand Caves. Thus Thingol came never across the Sea to Valinor, and Melian returned not thither while their realm lasted; and of her a strain of the immortal race of the Gods came among both Elves and Men, as after shall be told.

## 3 (c)  OF KÔR AND ALQUALONDË

[The relation between the manuscript and the typescript texts here becomes quite different, in that the manuscript (in which this is not a separate chapter or in any way marked off from what precedes, see p. 211) was scarcely emended at all, while the typescript has, already as typed, a great many changes from it. The explanation is presumably that in this case my father made the alterations from the manuscript as he typed without pencilling them in on the manuscript first. There is not in fact a great deal in the second text that seriously alters the narrative or nomenclature of the first, though certain new elements do enter. As hitherto, I follow the typescript text and record significant differences from the manuscript in the commentary. With *Of Kôr and Alqualondë* the typescript ceases.]

§34   In time the hosts of the Eldar came to the last western shores of the Hither Lands. In the North these shores, in the ancient days after the Battle of the Gods, sloped ever westward, until in the northernmost parts of the earth only a narrow sea divided the Outer Land, upon which Valinor was built, from the Hither Lands; but this narrow sea was filled with grinding ice, because of the violence of the frosts of Melko. Therefore Oromë did not lead the Eldar into the far North, but brought them to the fair lands about the River Sirion that afterwards were named Beleriand; and from those shores whence first the hosts of the Eldar looked in fear and wonder on the sea there stretched an ocean, wide and dark and deep, between them and the Mountains of Valinor.

§35   There they waited and gazed upon the dark waves. But Ulmo came from the Valar; and he uprooted the half-sunken island, upon which the Gods had dwelt in the beginning, but which now long had stood alone amid the sea, far from either shore; and with the aid of his servants he moved it, as it were a mighty ship, and anchored it in the bay into which Sirion pours his water.* Thereon he embarked the Lindar and the Noldor, for they had already assembled. But the Teleri were behind, being slower and less eager upon the march, and they were delayed also by the loss of Thingol; and they did not come until Ulmo had departed.

§36   Therefore Ulmo drew the Lindar and the Noldor over the sea to the long shores beneath the Mountains of Valinor, and they entered the land of the Gods and were welcomed to its bliss. But the Teleri dwelt long by the shores of the western sea, awaiting Ulmo's return; and they grew to love the sound of the waves, and they made songs filled with the music of water. Ossë heard them, and came thither; and he loved them, delighting in the music of their voices. Sitting upon a rock nigh to the margin of the sea he spoke to them and instructed them. Great therefore was his grief when Ulmo returned at length to bear them away to Valinor. Some he persuaded to remain on the beaches of the Middle-earth,

---

*Footnote to the text:* And some have told that the great isle of Balar, that lay of old in that bay, was the eastern horn of the Lonely Isle, that broke asunder and remained behind, when Ulmo removed that land again into the West.

and these were the Elves of the Falas that in after days had dwellings at the havens of Brithombar and Eglorest in Beleriand; but most of the Teleri embarked upon the isle and were drawn far away.

§37   Ossë followed them, and when they were come near to their journey's end he called to them; and they begged Ulmo to halt for a while, so that they might take leave of their friend and look their last upon the sky of stars. For the light of the Trees, that filtered through the passes of the hills, filled them with awe. And Ulmo was wroth with them, yet he granted their request, and left them for a while. Then Ossë seized the isle and chained it to the sea-bottom, far out in the Bay of Elvenhome, whence the Mountains of Valinor could only dimly be descried. And when Ulmo returned the island could not be moved or uprooted without peril to the Teleri; and it was not moved, but stood alone for many an age. No other land was near it, and it was called Tol Eressëa, or the Lonely Isle. There the Teleri long dwelt, and of Ossë they learned strange musics and sea-lore; and he made the sea-birds for their delight. By this long sojourn of the Teleri apart in the Lonely Isle was caused the sundering of their speech from the language of the Lindar and Noldor.

§38   To these the Valar had given a home and a dwelling. Even among the radiant flowers of the Tree-lit gardens of the Gods they longed still to see the stars at times. Therefore a gap was made in the encircling mountains, and there in a deep valley that ran down to the sea the green hill of Kôr was raised. From the West the light of the Trees fell upon it, and its shadow lay ever eastward, and to the East it looked towards the Bay of Elvenhome, and the Lonely Isle, and the Shadowy Seas. The light of the Blessed Realm streamed forth, kindling the waves with gleams of gold and silver, and it touched the Lonely Isle, and its western shore grew green and fair. There bloomed the first flowers that ever were east of the Mountains of the Gods.

§39   On the top of the hill of Kôr the city of the Elves was built, the white walls and terraces of Túna, and the highest of the towers of that city was the Tower of Ingwë, the Ingwemindon, whose silver lamp shone far out into the mists of the sea. Few are the ships of mortal Men that have seen its slender beam. In Túna* dwelt the Lindar and the Noldor.

*Footnote to the text: That is the Hill-city. This city the Gods called Eldamar (that is Elvenhome), and the Gnomes in their later speech Tûn or Eledûn. But the regions where the Elves dwelt, and whence

§40  Manwë and Varda loved most the Lindar, the High Elves, and holy and immortal were all their deeds and songs. The Noldor, the Gnomes, were beloved of Aulë, and of Mandos the wise; and great became their knowledge and their skill. Yet ever greater was their thirst for more knowledge, and their desire to make things wonderful and new. They were changeful in speech, for they had great love of words, and sought ever to find names more fit for all things that they knew or imagined. In Valinor they first contrived the fashioning of gems, and they made them of many kinds and hues in countless myriads; and they filled all Túna with them, and the halls of the Gods were enriched.

§41  The Noldor afterwards came back to the Middle-earth, and this tale tells mostly of their deeds; therefore the names and kinship of their princes may here be told, in that form which these names after had in the tongue of the Gnomes as it was in Beleriand upon the Middle-earth. Finwë was King of the Noldor. His sons were Fëanor, Fingolfin, and Finrod. Of these Fëanor was the mightiest in skill of word and of hand, more learned in lore than his brethren; in his heart his spirit burned as flame. Fingolfin was the strongest, the most steadfast, and the most valiant. Finrod was the fairest, and the most wise of heart. The seven sons of Fëanor were Maidros the tall; Maglor a musician and a mighty singer, whose voice carried far over land and sea; Celegorn the fair, and Cranthir the dark; and Curufin the crafty, who inherited most of his father's skill of hand; and the youngest Damrod and Díriel, who were twin brethren alike in mood and face. They afterwards were great hunters in the woods of the Middle-earth. A hunter also was Celegorn, who in Valinor was a friend of Oromë and followed oft the great god's horn.

§42  The sons of Fingolfin were Fingon, who was after King of the Gnomes in the North of the world; and Turgon of Gondolin; and their sister was Isfin the White. The sons of Finrod were Inglor the faithful (who afterwards was named Felagund, Lord of Caves), and Orodreth, and Angrod, and Egnor. Inglor and Orodreth were close in love, and they were friends of the sons of Fingolfin; but Angrod and Egnor were friends of the sons of Fëanor.

§43  Here must be told how the Teleri came at last to Valinor.

---

the stars could be seen, were called Elendë or Eldanor, that is Elfland. The pass through the mountains which led to Elendë was named the Kalakilya, Pass of Light.

For nigh on one hundred of the years of Valinor, which were each as ten of the years of the Sun that were after made, they dwelt in Tol Eressëa. But slowly their hearts were moved, and were drawn towards the light that flowed out over the sea unto their isle; and they were torn between the love of the music of the waves upon their shores, and desire to see again their kindred and to look upon the splendour of the Gods. Yet in the end desire of the light was the stronger. Therefore Ulmo taught them the craft of ship-building; and Ossë, submitting to Ulmo, brought them as his farewell gift the strong-winged swans. These they harnessed to their fleet of white ships, and thus they were drawn without the help of the winds to Valinor.

§44 There they dwelt upon the long shores of Elvenhome, and if they wished they could see the light of the Trees, and could visit the golden streets of Valmar and the crystal stairs of Túna upon Kôr. But most they sailed upon the waters of the Bay of Elvenhome, or danced in the waves with their hair gleaming in the light beyond the hill. Many jewels the Noldor gave them, opals and diamonds and pale crystals, which they strewed upon the shores and scattered in the pools. Marvellous were the beaches of Elendë in those days. And many pearls they won for themselves from the sea, and their halls were of pearl, and of pearl were the mansions of Elwë at the Haven of the Swans, lit with many lamps. For Alqualondë, the Haven of the Swans, was their chief town, and the harbour of their ships; and these were fashioned in the likeness of swans, white, and their beaks were of gold with eyes of gold and jet. The gate of that harbour was an arch of living rock sea-carven, and it lay upon the confines of Elfland, north of the Kalakilya, which is the Pass of Light wherein stood the hill of Kôr.

§45 As the ages passed the Lindar grew to love the land of the Gods and the full light of the Trees, and they forsook the city of Túna, and dwelt upon the mountain of Manwë, or about the plains and woods of Valinor, and became sundered from the Gnomes. But remembrance of the earth under stars remained in the hearts of the Noldor, and they abode in the Kalakilya, and in the hills and valleys within sound of the western sea; and though many of them went oft about the land of the Gods, making far journeys in search of the secrets of land and water and all living things, yet their intercourse was more with the Teleri than with the Lindar; and the tongues of Túna and Alqualondë drew together in those days. Finwë was King of Túna and Elwë of

Alqualondë; but Ingwë was ever held High-king of all the Elves. He dwelt at the feet of Manwë upon Taniquetil. Fëanor and his sons abode seldom in one place for long. They travelled far and wide within the confines of Valinor, going even to the borders of the Dark and the cold shores of the Outer Sea, seeking the unknown. Often they were guests in the halls of Aulë; but Celegorn went rather to the house of Oromë, and there he got great knowledge of all birds and beasts, and all their tongues he knew. For all living things that are or have been on this earth, save only the fell and evil creatures of Melko, lived then in Valinor; and there were many other creatures beautiful and strange that have not yet been seen upon the Middle-earth, and perchance never now shall be, since the fashion of the World was changed.

### Commentary on Chapter 3 (c)

§34   It is not told in the manuscript version where Oromë came to the coast of the Great Sea; but cf. the *Ambarkanta* map (IV. 249) on which the track of the March of the Elves is shown (and see IV. 257).

§35   The manuscript does not have the sentence 'and with the aid of his servants . . .' nor the footnote. The story of the origin of the Isle of Balar has not been told before.

   In the last sentence of the paragraph the manuscript has only 'but the Teleri were behind and came not until he had gone.' In the typescript version enters the story that the loss of Thingol was one cause of the late arrival of the Teleri on the shores (though this idea was possibly present already in the original tale of *The Coming of the Elves*, I. 120); that they were less eager in any case has been said earlier in QS (§27).

§36   It has not been said expressly before that the Elves who were persuaded to remain by Ossë were the Elves of Brithombar and Eglorest.

§37   The story told here shows an interesting stage between Q and *The Silmarillion* (pp. 58–9). In QS, as in S and Q, the old story of Ossë's rebellious anchoring of Tol Eressëa still survives (see I. 120, 134; IV. 45); but there is now the element, found in *The Silmarillion*, that the Teleri hearing Ossë calling to them begged Ulmo to stay the voyage, and he did so, though in QS he was 'wroth with them'. In the final form of the story, however, not only did Ulmo do so willingly, but it was he himself who ordered Ossë to root the island to the sea-bottom, for he was opposed to the summoning of the Quendi to Valinor.

§39   The name *Ingwemindon* has not been used before. – The name *Tûn* in the body of the text was carefully altered to *Túna* in the manuscript at both occurrences in §39 and again in §§40, 44 (but not in §45: see the commentary), and the footnote clearly belongs to the same time. The name *Eldamar* is now used of the city itself, while the new names *Elendë* and *Eldanor* are given to the region. This is another case where my father altered the *Lhammas* in the same way and no doubt at the same time as he altered QS: in §5 *Tûn* was changed to *Túna*, with a marginal note 'which the Gods called Eldamar' (on the history of the name see the commentary on that section).

§40  The sentence about the changefulness of speech among the Noldor is not in the manuscript. Cf. the passage on this subject in the *Lhammas* §5.

§41  With the opening sentence concerning the form in which the names of the Noldorin princes are given cf. the passage added at the end of the *Lhammas* (§11): 'The names of the Gnomes in the *Quenta* are given in the Noldorin form as that tongue became in Beleriand, for all those after Finwë father of the Noldor, whose name remains in ancient form.' The manuscript has 'using the names in the form of the Gnomish tongue as it long was spoken on the earth', as in Q (IV. 87).

For 'in his heart his spirit burned as flame' the manuscript has 'he had a heart of fire'. Cf. the later interpretation of *Fëanáro* as 'Spirit of Fire', *The Silmarillion* p. 63 (in the *Etymologies*, stem PHAY, the name is translated 'radiant sun'). – *Celegorn* here and throughout QS until §141 was an early change on the manuscript from *Celegorm*, as also in AV 2 and AB 2. – The statement (not found in the manuscript version) that Damrod and Díriel were twins is now first made, though it is possible that they had always been conceived to be so (IV. 46).

§42  In AV 2 (annal 2993) the earlier idea of the alliances between the Noldorin princes still survived, with Inglor Felagund a friend of Fingon and Turgon, sons of Fingolfin, and his brothers Orodreth, Angrod, and Egnor friends especially of Celegorm and Curufin. This was changed in AV 2 to the story in QS, Orodreth becoming associated with Inglor in friendship with the sons of Fingolfin.

§44  The manuscript has 'Many pearls they made', as in Q (IV. 88). – The description of the ships of the Teleri is not in the manuscript; in the typescript text it re-emerges from the *Lost Tales*, I. 124-5.

§45  *Tûn* was not here emended to *Túna* in the manuscript, where there is a footnote to the text, added no doubt at the same time as that to §39: 'Which is therefore called hereafter by its name in the speech of the Gnomes' (i.e. because the Lindar had departed).

The conclusion of this chapter was much developed from the form in the manuscript, which has no mention of the drawing together of the tongues of Túna and Alqualondë after the departure of the Lindar (cf. the *Lhammas* §5), nor of Celegorn's knowledge of the tongues of birds and beasts, and it does not have the very curious concluding passage concerning the existence in Valinor of all living things that have ever been on earth, save only the creatures of Melko.

# 4  OF THE SILMARILS AND THE DARKENING OF VALINOR

[From this point, where the typescript version comes to an end, there seems to have been scarcely any emendation to the manuscript until the major revision was undertaken many years later. A few corrections, however, certainly belong to the early period, while some points are doubtful in this respect.]

§46    From this time, when the three kindreds of the Eldar were gathered at last in Valinor, began the Noontide of the Blessed Realm and its fullness of bliss and glory, which lasted many ages. In that time, five ages after the coming of the Noldor, when they had become full-grown in knowledge and skill, Fëanor, son of Finwë, began a long and marvellous labour; and he summoned all his lore, and power, and subtle skill; for he purposed to make things more fair than any of the Eldar had yet made, that should last beyond the end of all. Three jewels he made, and named them Silmarils. A living fire burned within them that was blended of the light of the Two Trees. Of their own radiance they shone even in the dark; yet all lights that fell upon them, however faint, they took and reflected in marvellous hues to which their own inner fire gave a surpassing loveliness. No mortal flesh, nor flesh unclean, could touch them, but was scorched and withered. These jewels the Elves prized beyond all their works, and Manwë hallowed them; but Varda foretold that the fate of the World was locked within them. And the heart of Fëanor was bound fast to these things that he himself had made.

§47    For two ages more the noontide of the glory of Valinor endured. For seven ages then, as the Gods had decreed, Melko had dwelt in the halls of Mandos, each age in lightened pain. When these ages were past, as they had promised, he was brought before their conclave. He looked upon the glory of the Valar, and greed and malice were in his heart; he looked upon the fair Children of Ilúvatar that sat at the feet of the Gods, and hatred filled him; he looked upon the wealth of gems and lusted for them; but he hid his thoughts and postponed his vengeance.

§48    Before the gates of Valmar Melko humbled himself at the feet of Manwë and sued for pardon, and Nienna his sister aided his prayer. But the Gods would not suffer him to depart from their sight and vigilance. He was given a humble dwelling within the gates of the city; but so fair-seeming were all his deeds and words that after a while he was permitted to go freely about all the land,

and both Gods and Elves had much help and profit from him. Yet Ulmo's heart misgave him, and Tulkas clenched his hands whenever he saw Morgoth, his foe, go by. For Tulkas is quick to wrath and slow to forgiveness.

§49   Most fair of all was Morgoth to the Elves, and he aided them in many works, if they would let him. The Lindar, the people of Ingwë, held him in suspicion; for Ulmo had warned them, and they heeded his words. But the Gnomes took delight in the many things of hidden knowledge that he could reveal to them, and some hearkened to words that it would have been better that they had never heard.* And when he saw his chance he sowed a seed of lies and suggestions of evil among such as these. Bitterly did the folk of the Noldor atone for their folly in after-days.

§50   Often Morgoth would whisper that the Gods had brought the Eldar to Valinor because of their jealousy, fearing that their marvellous skill and beauty and their magic would grow too strong for the Valar to control, as the Elves waxed and spread over the wide lands of the world. Visions he would conjure in their hearts of the mighty realms they might have ruled in power and freedom in the East. In those days, moreover, though the Valar knew of the coming of Men that were to be, the Elves knew yet nought of it; for the Gods had not revealed it, and the time was not yet near. But Morgoth spake to the Elves in secret of mortal Men, though he knew little of the truth. Manwë alone knew aught clearly of the mind of Ilúvatar concerning Men, and he has ever been their

*Footnote to the text: It is said that among other matters Melko spoke of weapons and armour to the Gnomes, and of the power they give to him who is armed to defend his own (as he said). The Elves had before possessed only weapons of the chase, spears and bows and arrows, and since the chaining of Melko the armouries of the Gods had been shut. But the Gnomes now learned the fashioning of swords of tempered steel, and the making of mail; and they made shields in those days and emblazoned them with silver, gold, and gems. And Fëanor became greatly skilled in this craft, and he made store of weapons secretly, as jealousy grew between him and Fingolfin. Thus it was that the Noldor were armed in the days of their Flight. Thus, too, the evil of Melko was turned against him, for the swords of the Gnomes did him more hurt than anything under the Gods upon this earth. Yet they had little joy of Morgoth's teaching; for all the sorrows of the Gnomes came from their swords, both from the unjust battle at Alqualondë, and from many ill deeds afterwards. Thus wrote Pengolod.

friend. Yet Morgoth whispered that the Gods kept the Eldar captive, so that Men coming should defraud them of the kingdoms of Middle-earth; for the weaker and short-lived race the Valar saw would more easily be swayed by them. Small truth was there in this, and little have the Valar ever prevailed to sway the wills or fates of Men, and least of all to good. But many of the Elves believed, or half-believed, the evil words. Most of these were Gnomes.

§51    Thus, ere the Gods were aware, the peace of Valinor was poisoned. The Gnomes began to murmur against the Valar and their kindred; and many became filled with vanity, forgetting all that the Gods had given them and taught them. Most of all Morgoth fanned the flames of the eager heart of Fëanor, though all the while he lusted for the Silmarils. These Fëanor at great feasts wore on brow and breast, but at other times they were guarded close, locked in the deep hoards of Tûn, for though there were no thieves in Valinor, as yet, Fëanor loved the Silmarils with a greedy love, and began to grudge the sight of them to all save himself and his sons.

§52    The sons of Finwë were proud, but proudest was Fëanor. Lying Morgoth said to him that Fingolfin and his sons were plotting to usurp the leadership of Fëanor and his elder house, and to supplant him in the favour of their father and of the Gods. Of these lies quarrels were born among the children of Finwë, and of these quarrels came the end of the high days of Valinor and the evening of its ancient glory; for Fëanor spake words of rebellion against the Valar, and plotted to depart from Valinor back to the world without, and deliver, as he said, the Gnomes from thraldom.

§53    Fëanor was summoned before the Valar to the Ring of Doom, and there the lies of Morgoth were laid bare for all those to see who had the will. By the judgement of the Gods Fëanor was banished for a while from Tûn, since he had disturbed its peace. But with him went Finwë his father, who loved him more than his other sons, and many other Gnomes. Northward in Valinor in the hills near to the halls of Mandos they built a strong place and a treasury; and they gathered there a multitude of gems. But Fingolfin ruled the Noldor in Tûn; and thus in part Morgoth's words seemed justified (though Fëanor had wrought their fulfilment by his own deeds), and the bitterness that he sowed went on, though the lies were revealed, and long afterwards it lived still between the sons of Fëanor and Fingolfin.

§54   Straight from the midst of their council the Valar sent
Tulkas to lay hands on Morgoth and bring him again to judgement, but Morgoth hid himself, and none could discover whither
he had gone; and the shadows of all standing things seemed to
grow longer and darker in that time. It is said that for a great while
none saw Morgoth, until he appeared privily to Fëanor, feigning
friendship with cunning argument, and urging him to his former
thought of flight. But Fëanor shut now his doors, if not his
heart; and Finwë sent word to Valmar, but Morgoth departed in
anger.

§55   Now the Gods were sitting in council before their gates
fearing the lengthening of the shadows, when the messenger came
from Finwë, but ere Tulkas could set forth others came that
brought tidings from Tûn. For Morgoth had fled over the passes
of the mountains, and from Kôr the Elves saw him pass in wrath as
a thunder-cloud. Thence he came into that region that is called
Arvalin, which lies south of the Bay of Elfland, and is a narrow
land beneath the eastern feet of the Mountains of Valinor. There
the shadows are deepest and thickest in the world. In that land,
secret and unknown, dwelt Ungoliantë, Gloomweaver, in spider's
form. It is not told whence she came; from the Outer Darkness,
maybe, that lies beyond the Walls of the World. In a ravine she
lived, and spun her webs in a cleft of the mountains; for she
sucked up light and shining things to spin them forth again in
black nets of choking gloom and clinging fog. She hungered ever
for more food.

§56   Morgoth met Ungoliantë in Arvalin, and with her
he plotted his revenge; but she demanded a great and terrible
reward, ere she would dare the perils of Valinor and the power of
the Gods. She wove a great darkness about her for their protection, and black spider-ropes she span, and cast from rocky peak to
peak; and in this way she scaled at last the highest pinnacle of the
mountains south of Taniquetil. In this region the vigilance of the
Valar was less, because the wild woods of Oromë lay in the south
of Valinor, and the walls of the mountains looked there eastward
upon untrodden land and empty seas; and the Gods held guard
rather against the North where of old Morgoth had raised his
throne and fortress.

§57   Now Ungoliantë made a ladder of woven ropes, and upon
this Morgoth climbed, and sat beside her; and he looked down
upon the shining plain, seeing afar off the domes of Valmar
glittering in the mingling of the light. Then Morgoth laughed;

and swiftly he sped down the long western slopes with Ungoliantë at his side, and her darkness was about them.

§58   It was a day of festival, and most of the people of Valinor were upon the mountain of Manwë, singing before him in his halls, or playing in the upland pleasaunces upon the green slopes of Taniquetil. The Lindar were there and many of the Noldor. Valmar's streets were fallen silent, and few feet passed upon the stairs of Tûn; only upon the shores of Elvenhome the Teleri still sang and played, recking little of times or seasons or the fate that should befall. Silpion was waning and Laurelin had just begun to glow, when protected by fate Morgoth and Ungoliantë crept into the plain. With his black spear Morgoth stabbed each tree to its very core, and as their juices spouted forth Ungoliantë sucked them up; and the poison from her foul lips went into their tissues and withered them, leaf and branch and root. Ungoliantë belched forth black vapours as she drank their radiance; and she swelled to monstrous form.

§59   Then wonder and dismay fell on Valinor, when a sudden twilight and a mounting gloom came upon the land. Black clouds floated about the towers of Valmar, and darkness drifted down its streets. Varda looked down from Taniquetil and saw the trees drowned and hidden in a mist. Too late they ran from hill and gate. The Two Trees died and shone no more, while wailing throngs stood round them and called on Manwë to come down. Out upon the plain the horses of Oromë thundered with a thousand hooves, and fire started in the gloom about their feet. Swifter than they Tulkas ran before them, and the light of the anger of his eyes was as a beacon. But they found not what they sought. Wherever Morgoth went, a darkness and confusion was around him woven by Ungoliantë, so that their feet strayed and their eyes were blind, and Morgoth escaped the hunt.

### Commentary on Chapter 4

§46   The danger of the Silmarils to Men is increased: for the words of Q (IV. 88) 'no mortal flesh impure could touch them' are changed to 'no mortal flesh, nor flesh unclean, could touch them'.

§49   The long footnote on Gnomish arms (the content of which is entirely novel), if not written at the same time as the main text, was certainly an early addition. 'Thus wrote Pengolod' seems to have been written at the same time as the rest of the note, which is difficult to explain, if Pengolod was the author of the Quenta Silmarillion anyway; on this question see the commentary on §123.

§50   The words 'though the Valar knew of the coming of Men that were to be' are not at variance with the rewritten text of §20; for although it is said there that the coming of the Elves was not in the Music of the Ainur and was unknown to the Valar save Manwë, it is also told that at the awakening of the Elves Manwë 'spoke to the Valar, revealing to them the mind of the Father; and he bade them to return now to their duty, which was to govern the world for the Children of Ilúvatar, when they should appear, each kindred in its appointed time.'

§54   'But Feanor shut now his doors . . .': the story of Morgoth's going to the stronghold of Finwë and Fëanor at this juncture moves further towards the final form (see AV 2, annal 2900).

§55   'Bay of Elfland': in §§37–8, 44 the manuscript has 'Bay of Elfland' where the typescript has 'Bay of Elvenhome'.

§58   'With his black spear': 'With his black sword' Q (§4); cf. the story in the *Lost Tales*, I. 153.

# 5   OF THE FLIGHT OF THE NOLDOR

§60   This was the time of the Darkening of Valinor. In that day there stood before the gates of Valmar Gnomes that cried aloud, bearing evil tidings. For they told that Morgoth had fled northward, and with him went a thing before unseen that in the gathering night had seemed to be a spider of monstrous form. Suddenly they had fallen upon the treasury of Finwë. There Morgoth slew the King of the Noldor before his doors, and spilled the first Elvish blood that stained the earth. Many others he slew also, but Fëanor and his sons were not there. The Silmarils Morgoth took, and all the wealth of the jewels of the Noldor that were hoarded in that place. Great was the grief of Fëanor, both for his father and not less for the Silmarils, and bitterly he cursed the chance that had taken him on that evil day to Taniquetil, thinking in his folly that with his own hands and his sons he might have withstood the violence of Morgoth.

§61   Little is known of the paths of Morgoth after his dreadful deeds in Valinor. But it is told that escaping from the hunt he came at last with Ungoliantë over the Grinding Ice and so into the northern regions of the Middle-earth once more. Then Ungoliantë summoned him to give her the promised reward. The half of her pay had been the sap of the Trees. The other half was a full share in the plundered jewels. Morgoth yielded these, and she devoured them, and their light perished from the earth, but Ungoliantë grew yet darker and more huge and hideous in form. But Morgoth would give her no share in the Silmarils. That was the first thieves' quarrel.

§62  So great had Ungoliantë become that she enmeshed Morgoth in her choking nets, and his awful cry echoed through the shuddering world. To his aid there came the Balrogs that lived yet in the deepest places of his ancient fortress, Utumno in the North. With their whips of flame the Balrogs smote the webs asunder, and drove away Ungoliantë into the uttermost South, where she long remained. Thus Morgoth came back to his ancient habitation, and he built anew his vaults and dungeons and great towers, in that place which the Gnomes after knew as Angband. There countless became the hosts of his beasts and demons; and he brought into being the race of the Orcs, and they grew and multiplied in the bowels of the earth. These Orcs Morgoth made in envy and mockery of the Elves, and they were made of stone, but their hearts of hatred. Glamhoth, the hosts of hate, the Gnomes have called them. Goblins they may be called, but in ancient days they were strong and fell.

§63  And in Angband Morgoth forged for himself a great crown of iron, and he called himself the King of the World. In token of this he set the three Silmarils in his crown. It is said that his evil hands were burned black by the touch of those holy jewels; and black they have ever been since; nor was he ever afterward free from the pain of the burning, and the anger of the pain. That crown he never took from his head, though its weight was a deadly weariness; and it was never his wont to leave the deep places of his fortress, but he governed his vast armies from his northern throne.

§64  When it became at last clear that Morgoth had escaped, the Gods assembled about the dead Trees, and sat there in darkness for a long while silent, and they were filled with grief. Since the people of the Blessed Realm had been gathered for festival, all the Valar and their children were there, save Ossë who came seldom to Valinor, and Tulkas who would not leave the unavailing hunt; and with them the Lindar, the folk of Ingwë, stood and wept. But most of the Noldor returned to Tûn and mourned for the darkening of their fair city. Fogs and shadows now drifted in from the sea through the pass of Kôr, and all shapes were confused, as the light of the Trees perished. A murmur was heard in Elfland, and the Teleri wailed beside the sea.

§65  Then Fëanor appeared suddenly amid the Noldor and called on all to come to the high square upon the top of the hill of

Kôr beneath the tower of Ingwë; but the doom of banishment from Tûn which the Gods had laid upon him was not yet lifted, and he rebelled against the Valar. A vast concourse gathered swiftly, therefore, to hear what he would say, and the hill, and all the stairs and streets that climbed upon it, were lit with the light of many torches that each one that came bore in hand.

§66    Fëanor was a great orator with a power of moving words. That day he made before the Gnomes a mighty speech that has ever been remembered. Fierce and fell were his words and filled with wrath and pride, and they stirred the people to madness like the fumes of potent wine. His anger was most against Morgoth, yet most that he said was drawn from the very lies of Morgoth himself; but he was distraught with grief for the slaying of his father, and anguish for the rape of the Silmarils. He now claimed the kingship of all the Noldor, since Finwë was dead, and mocked the decree of the Valar. 'Why should we longer obey the jealous Gods,' he asked, 'who cannot keep us, nor their own realm, safe from their foe? And is not Melko the accursed one of the Valar?'

§67    He bade the Gnomes prepare for flight in the darkness, while the Valar were still wrapped in idle mourning; to seek freedom in the world, and of their own prowess to win there a new realm, since Valinor was no longer more bright and blissful than the lands outside; to pursue Morgoth and war with him for ever until they were avenged. 'And when we have regained the Silmarils,' he said, 'we shall be masters of the enchanted light, and lords of the bliss and beauty of the world.' Then he swore a terrible oath. His seven sons leaped straightway to his side and took the selfsame vow together, each with drawn sword. They swore an oath which none shall break, and none should take, by the name of the Allfather, calling the Everlasting Dark upon them, if they kept it not; and Manwë they named in witness, and Varda, and the Holy Mount, vowing to pursue with vengeance and hatred to the ends of the world Vala, Demon, Elf, or Man as yet unborn, or any creature great or small, good or evil, that time should bring forth unto the end of days, whoso should hold or take or keep a Silmaril from their possession.

§68    Fingolfin and his son Fingon spake against Fëanor, and there was wrath and angry words that came near to blows. But Finrod spake gently and persuasively, and sought to calm them, urging them to pause and ponder, ere deeds were done that could not be undone. But of his own sons Inglor alone spake with him; Angrod and Egnor took the part of Fëanor, and Orodreth stood aside. In the end it was put to the vote of the assembled people, and they being moved by the potent words of Fëanor, and filled with desire for the Silmarils, decided to depart from Valinor. Yet the Noldor of Tûn would not now renounce the kingship of Fingolfin; and as two divided hosts, therefore, they at length set forth upon their bitter road. The greater part marched behind Fingolfin, who with his sons yielded to the general voice against their wisdom, because they would not desert their people; and with Fingolfin were Finrod and Inglor, though they were loth to go. In the van marched Fëanor and his sons with lesser host, but they were filled with reckless eagerness. Some remained behind: both some that had been upon Taniquetil on the day of fate, and sat now with the Lindar at the feet of the Gods partaking of their grief and vigil; and some that would not forsake the fair city of Tûn and its wealth of things made by cunning hands, though the darkness had fallen upon them. And the Valar learning of the purpose of the Noldor sent word that they forbade the march, for the hour was evil and would lead to woe, but they would not hinder it, since Fëanor had accused them, saying that they held the Eldar captive against their will. But Fëanor laughed hardening his heart, and he said that sojourn in Valinor had led through bliss to sorrow; they would now try the contrary, to find joy at last through woe.

§69   Therefore they continued their march, and the house of Fëanor hastened ahead along the coast of Valinor, and they did not turn their eyes back to look upon Tûn. The hosts of Fingolfin followed less eagerly, and at the rear came sorrowing Finrod and Inglor and many of the noblest and fairest of the Noldor; and they looked often backward, until the lamp of Ingwë was lost in the gathering tide of gloom; and more than others they carried thence memories of the glory of their ancient home, and some even of the fair things there made with hands they took with them. Thus the folk of Finrod had no part in the dreadful deed that then was done; yet all the Gnomes that departed from Valinor came under the shadow of the curse that followed it. For it came soon into the heart of Fëanor that they should persuade the Teleri, their friends, to join with them; for thus in his rebellion he thought that the bliss of Valinor might be further diminished, and his power for war upon Morgoth be increased; moreover he desired ships. As his mind cooled and took counsel, he saw that the Noldor might hardly escape without many vessels; but it would need long to build so great a fleet, even were there any among the Noldor skilled in that craft. But there were none, and he brooked no delay, fearing lest many should desert him. Yet they must at some time cross the seas, albeit far to the North where they were narrower; for further still, to those places where the western land and Middle-earth touched nigh, he feared to venture. There he knew was Helkaraksë, the Strait of Grinding Ice, where the frozen hills ever broke and shifted, sundering and clashing again together.

§70  But the Teleri would not join the Noldor in flight, and sent back their messengers. They had never lent ear to Morgoth nor welcomed him among them. They desired now no other cliffs nor beaches than the strands of Elvenhome, nor other lord than Elwë, prince of Alqualondë; and he trusted that Ulmo and the great Valar would yet redress the sorrow of Valinor. And their white ships with their white sails they would neither give nor sell, for they prized them dearly, nor did they hope ever again to make others so fair and swift. But when the host of Fëanor came to the Haven of the Swans they attempted to seize by force the white fleets that lay anchored there, and the Teleri resisted them. Weapons were drawn and a bitter fight was fought upon the great arch of the Haven's gate, and upon the lamplit quays and piers, as is sadly told in the song of the Flight of the Gnomes. Thrice the folk of Fëanor were driven back, and many were slain upon either side; but the vanguard of the Noldor were succoured by the foremost of the people of Fingolfin, and the Teleri were overcome, and most of those that dwelt at Alqualondë were slain or cast into the sea. For the Noldor were become fierce and desperate, and the Teleri had less strength, and were armed mostly with slender bows. Then the Gnomes drew away the white ships of the Teleri, and manned their oars as best they could, and took them north along the coast. And the Teleri cried to Ossë, and he came not, for he had been summoned to Valmar to the vigil and council of the Gods, and it was not decreed by fate nor permitted by the Valar that the flight of the Noldor should be waylaid. But Uinen wept for the slain of the Teleri; and the sea roared against the Gnomes, so that many of the ships were wrecked and those in them drowned.

§71  But most of them escaped and continued their journey, some by ship and some by foot; but the way was long and ever more evil going as they went on. After they had marched for a great while, and were come at length to the northern confines of the Blessed Realm – and they are mountainous and cold and look upon the empty waste of Eruman – they beheld a dark figure standing high upon a rock that looked down upon the shore. Some say it was the herald of the Gods, others that it was Mandos himself. There he spake in a loud voice, solemn and terrible, the curse and prophecy which is called the Prophecy of the North, warning them to return and ask for pardon, or in the end return only at last after sorrow and unspeakable misery. Much he foretold in dark words, which only the wisest of them understood, concerning things that after befell. But all heard the curse he uttered upon those that would not stay or seek the doom and pardon of the Valar, for the spilling of the blood of their kindred at Alqualondë and fighting the first battle between the children of earth unrighteously. For this the Noldor should taste death more often and more bitterly than their kindred, by weapon and by torment and by grief; and evil fortune should pursue the house of Fëanor, and their oath should turn against them, and all who now followed them should share their lot. And evil should come most upon them through treachery of kin to kin, so that in all their wars and councils they should suffer from treason and the fear of treason among themselves. But Fëanor said: 'He saith not that we shall suffer from cowardice, from cravens or the fear of cravens'; and that proved true also.

§72    Then Finrod and a few of his household turned back, and they came at last to Valinor again, and received the pardon of the Valar; and Finrod was set to rule the remnant of the Noldor in the Blessed Realm. But his sons went not with him; for Inglor and Orodreth would not forsake the sons of Fingolfin, nor Angrod and Egnor their friends Celegorn and Curufin; and all Fingolfin's folk went forward still, being constrained by the will of Fëanor and fearing also to face the doom of the Gods, since not all of them had been guiltless of the kinslaying at Alqualondë. Then all too swiftly the evil that was foretold began its work.

§73    The Gnomes came at last far to the North, and saw the first teeth of the ice that floated in the sea. They began to suffer anguish from the cold. Then many of them murmured, especially those that followed Fingolfin, and some began to curse Fëanor and name him as the cause of all the woes of the Eldar. But the ships were too few, many having been lost upon the way, to carry all across together, yet none were willing to abide upon the coast while others were transported; already fear of treachery was awake. Therefore it came into the heart of Fëanor and his sons to sail off on a sudden with all the ships, of which they had retained the mastery since the battle of the Haven; and they took with them only such as were faithful to their house, among whom were Angrod and Egnor. As for the others, 'we will leave the murmurers to murmur', said Fëanor, 'or to whine their way back to the cages of the Valar.' Thus began the curse of the kinslaying. When Fëanor and his folk landed on the shores in the west of the northern regions of Middle-earth, they set fire in the ships and made a great burning, terrible and bright; and Fingolfin and his people saw the light of it afar off red beneath the clouds. They saw then they were betrayed, and left to perish in Eruman or return; and they wandered long in misery. But their valour and endurance grew with hardship, for they were a mighty folk, but new come from the Blessed Realm, and not yet weary with the weariness of the earth, and the fire of their minds and hearts was young. Therefore led by Fingolfin, and Fingon, Turgon, and Inglor, they ventured into the bitterest North; and finding no other way they dared at last the terror of the Grinding Ice. Few of the deeds of the Gnomes after surpassed the perilous crossing in hardihood or in woe. Many there perished miserably, and it was with lessened host that Fingolfin set foot at last upon the northern lands. Small love for Fëanor or his sons had those that marched at last behind him, and came unto Beleriand at the rising of the sun.

### Commentary on Chapter 5

§60 Here first appears the story that Fëanor went to the festival, of which there is no suggestion in Q (IV. 92).

§62 Q has 'To his aid came the Orcs and Balrogs that lived yet in the lowest places of Angband', but Orcs are absent here in QS. Here and again in §105 Utumno is an early change from Utumna; see the commentary on §12. That the slightly ambiguous sentence 'he built anew . . .' means that he built Angband on the ruins of Utumno is seen from §105: 'Melko coming back into Middle-earth made the endless dungeons of Angband, the hells of iron, where of old Utumno had been.' See IV. 259–60.

In Q the passage about Morgoth's making of the Orcs, precursor of this in QS, is placed earlier (IV. 82), before the making of the stars and the awakening of the Elves; at the corresponding place in QS (§18) it is said that 'the Orcs were not made until he had looked upon the Elves.' In Q, at the place (IV. 93) corresponding to the present passage in QS, it is said that 'countless became the number of the hosts of his Orcs and demons' – i.e. the Orcs were already in existence before Morgoth's return (and so could come to his aid when they heard his cry); but there is a direction in Q at this point (IV. 93 note 8) to bring in the making of the Orcs here rather than earlier (the reason for this being the idea that the Orcs were made 'in mockery of the Children of Ilúvatar').

§68   That Orodreth 'stood aside', taking the part neither of Finrod and Inglor nor of Angrod and Egnor and the Fëanorians, is a new element in the story; see under §73 below.

§70   The account in QS of the Battle of Alqualondë, and of Fëanor's calculations before it, is given a better progression and is substantially expanded from that in Q (IV. 95), while the concluding passage of §70, recounting the calling of the Teleri upon Ossë and the storm raised by Uinen, is altogether absent from the earlier versions.

§71   *Eruman* is not used of this region in Q (where the name is applied to the land where Men first awoke in the East, IV. 99, 171), but it is found in this sense in the *Ambarkanta* (IV. 239; also on the maps, IV. 249, 251).

Some elements in this version of the Prophecy of the North not in Q (IV. 96) are found in AV annal 2993 (virtually the same in both versions), as 'their oath should turn against them', and 'they should be slain with weapons, and with torments, and with sorrow'. On the other hand the AV version has an element not in QS, the prophecy that the Noldor should 'in the long end fade upon Middle-earth and wane before the younger race' (see IV. 171-2).

§73   In AV 2 annal 2994 the story still went that Orodreth, as well as Angrod and Egnor, were taken by the Fëanorians in the ships; but with the separation of Orodreth from Angrod and Egnor in QS, making him instead a close associate of his brother Inglor Felagund (§42), his name was struck from the annal (AV 2 note 10). It is notable here that Orodreth is not named among the leaders in the passage of the second host across the Grinding Ice. This is to be associated, I think, with his 'standing aside' during the dissensions before the Flight of the Noldor (see §68); suggestions of the decline in his significance which I have described in III. 91, 246.

In QS §91 the first sun is said to have risen as Fingolfin marched into Mithrim; thus 'Beleriand' is here used in a very extended sense (as also in AV annal 2995: 'Fëanor came unto Beleriand and the shores beneath Eredlómin', repeated in QS §88). Similarly the Battle-under-Stars, fought in Mithrim, was the First Battle of Beleriand. But in QS §108 Beleriand 'was bounded upon the North by Nivrost and Hithlum and Dorthonion'.


# 6   OF THE SUN AND MOON AND THE HIDING OF VALINOR

§74   When the Gods learned that the Noldor had fled, and were come at last back into Middle-earth, they were aroused from their grief, and took counsel for the redress of the injuries of the world. And Manwë bade Yavanna to put forth all her power of growth and healing; and she put forth all her power upon the Trees, but it availed not to heal their mortal wounds. Yet even as the Valar listened in the gloom to her singing, Silpion bore at last upon a leafless bough one great silver bloom, and Laurelin a single golden fruit. These Yavanna took, and the Trees then died, and their lifeless stems stand yet in Valinor, a memorial of vanished joy. But the fruit and flower Yavanna gave to Aulë, and Manwë hallowed them, and Aulë and his folk made vessels to hold them and preserve their radiance, as is said in the song of the Sun and Moon. These vessels the Gods gave to Varda, that they might become lamps of heaven, outshining the ancient stars; and she gave them power to traverse the region of the stars, and set them to sail appointed courses above the earth. These things the Valar did, recalling in their twilight the darkness of the lands outside, and they resolved now to illumine Middle-earth, and with light to hinder the deeds of Melko; for they remembered the Dark-elves, and did not utterly forsake the exiled Gnomes; and Manwë knew that the hour of Men was drawing nigh.

§75    Isil the Sheen the Gods of old named the Moon in Valinor, and Úrin the Fiery they named the Sun; but the Eldar named them Răna, the wayward, the giver of visions, and Anar, the heart of flame, that awakens and consumes. For the Sun was set as a sign for the awakening of Men and the waning of the Elves; but the Moon cherishes their memory. The maiden chosen from among their own folk by the Valar to guide the ship of the Sun was named Arien; and the youth who steered the floating island of the Moon was Tilion.* In the days of the Trees Arien had tended the golden flowers in the gardens of Vana and watered them with the radiant dew of Laurelin. Tilion was a young hunter of the company of Oromë, and he had a silver bow. He loved Arien, but she was a holier spirit of greater power, and wished to be ever virgin and alone; and Tilion pursued her in vain. Tilion forsook then the woods of Oromë, and dwelt in the gardens of Lórien, sitting in dream beside the pools lit by the flickering light of Silpion.

§76    Răna was first wrought and made ready, and first rose into the region of the stars, and was the elder of the lights, as was Silpion of the Trees. Then for a while the world had moonlight,

---

*Marginal note to the text* : hyrned Æ.

and many creatures stirred and woke that had waited long in the dark; but many of the stars fled affrighted, and Tilion the bowman wandered from his path pursuing them; and some plunged in the chasm and sought refuge at the roots of the earth. The servants of Melko were amazed; and it is told that Fingolfin set foot upon the northern lands with the first moonrise, and the shadows of his host were long and black. Tilion had traversed the heaven seven times, and was thus in the furthest East when the ship of Arien was ready. Then Anar rose in glory and the snow upon the mountains glowed with fire, and there was the sound of many waterfalls; but the servants of Melko fled to Angband and cowered in fear, and Fingolfin unfurled his banners.

§77   Now Varda purposed that the two vessels should sail the sky and ever be aloft, but not together: each should journey from Valinor into the East and back, the one issuing from the West as the other turned from the East. Thus the first days were reckoned after the manner of the Trees from the mingling of the lights when Arien and Tilion passed above the middle of the earth. But Tilion was wayward and uncertain in speed, and held not to his appointed course; and at times he sought to tarry Arien, whom he loved, though the flame of Anar withered the sheen of Silpion's bloom, if he drew too nigh, and his vessel was scorched and darkened. Because of Tilion, therefore, and yet more because of the prayers of Lórien and Nienna, who said that all night and sleep and peace had been banished from the earth, Varda changed her design, and allowed a time wherein the world should still have shadow and half-light. The Sun rested, therefore, a while in Valinor, lying upon the cool bosom of the Outer Sea. So Evening, which is the time of the descent and resting of the Sun, is the hour of greatest light and joy in Valinor. But soon the Sun is drawn down into Vaiya by the servants of Ulmo, and brought in haste to the East, and mounts the sky again, lest night be overlong and evil strengthened. But the waters of Vaiya are made hot and glow with coloured fires, and Valinor has light for a while after the passing of Arien; yet as she goes under the earth and draws towards the East the glow fades and Valinor is dim, and the Gods mourn then most for the death of Laurelin. At dawn the shadows of their mountains of defence lie heavy on the land of the Valar.

§78   Varda commanded the Moon to rise only after the Sun had left heaven, but he travels with uncertain pace, and still pursueth her, so that at times they both are in the sky together, and still at times he draws nigh to her, and there is a darkness amid the day. But Tilion tarries seldom in Valinor, loving rather the great lands; and mostly he passes swiftly over the western land, either Arvalin or Eruman or Valinor, and plunges into the chasm between the shores of the earth and the Outer Sea, and pursues his way alone among the grots at the roots of the earth. There sometimes he wanders long, and stars that have taken hiding there flee before him into the upper air. Yet it happens at times that he comes above Valinor while the Sun is still there, and he descends and meets his beloved, for they leave their vessels for a space; then there is great joy, and Valinor is filled with silver and gold, and the Gods laugh recalling the mingling of the light long ago, when Laurelin flowered and Silpion was in bud.

§79    Still therefore the light of Valinor is greater and fairer than upon Middle-earth, because the Sun resteth there, and the lights of heaven draw nearer to the land in that region; moreover the Valar store the radiance of the Sun in many vessels, and in vats and pools for their comfort in times of dark. But the light is not the light which came from the Trees before the poisoned lips of Ungoliantë touched them. That light lives now only in the Silmarils. Gods and Elves, therefore, look forward yet to a time when the Elder Sun and Moon, which are the Trees, may be rekindled and the ancient joy and glory return. Ulmo foretold to them that this would only come to pass through the aid, frail though it might seem, of the second race of earth, the Younger Children of Ilúvatar. But Manwë alone heeded his words at that time; for the Valar were still wroth because of the ingratitude of the Noldor, and the cruel slaying at the Haven of the Swans. Moreover all save Tulkas for a while were in doubt, fearing the might and cunning of Morgoth. Therefore at this time they fortified all Valinor anew, and set a sleepless watch upon the mountain-walls, which now they raised, east, north, and south, to sheer and dreadful height. Their outer sides were dark and smooth, without ledge or foothold for aught save birds, and fell in precipices with faces hard as glass; their tops were crowned with ice. No pass led through them save only at the Kalakilya wherein stood the mound of Kôr. This they could not close because of the Eldar who were faithful; for all those of Elvish race must breathe at whiles the outer air of Middle-earth, nor could they wholly sunder the Teleri from their kin. But the Eldar were set to guard that pass unceasingly: the fleet of the Teleri kept the shore, the remnant of the Gnomes dwelt ever in the deep cleft of the mountains, and upon the plain of Valmar, where the pass issues into Valinor, the Lindar were camped as sentinels, that no bird nor beast nor Elf nor Man, nor any creature beside that came from Middle-earth could pass the leaguer.

§80    In that time, which songs call the Hiding of Valinor, the Enchanted Isles were set, and filled with shadows and bewilderment, and all the seas about were filled with shadows; and these isles were strung across the Shadowy Seas from north to south before Tol Eressëa, the Lonely Isle, is reached, sailing west; and hardly might any vessel come between them in the gloom or win through to the Bay of Elvenhome. For a great weariness comes upon mariners in that region, and a loathing of the sea; but all such as set foot upon those islands are there entrapped and wound in everlasting sleep. Thus it was that the many emissaries of the Gnomes in after days never came to Valinor – save one, the mightiest mariner of song or tale.

### Commentary on Chapter 6

§74    In the extremely brief account in Q (IV. 97) there is no mention of Aulë as having played any part in the making of the Sun and Moon, and QS reverts in this to the original story in the *Lost Tales* (I. 185–6, 191–2).

Of the passage beginning 'These vessels the Gods gave to Varda' there is only a trace in Q. Varda appears as the deviser of the motions of the Sun and Moon in the *Ambarkanta* (IV. 236).

§75    In Q the Moon is called *Rána* (without translation), and this name is said to have been given by the Gods (so also in the *Lost Tales*, I. 192). In QS the Gods' name is *Isil* 'the Sheen' (cf. the Elves' name *Sil* 'the Rose' in the *Lost Tales*, ibid.) and *Rǎna* 'the wayward' that of the Eldar. – In Q the name of the Sun, given by the Gods, is *Úr* (in the *Lost Tales*, I. 187, this was the Elvish name, meaning 'fire'; the Gods called the Sun *Sári*). In QS the Gods' name is *Úrin* 'the Fiery', and the Eldarin name *Anar*. – In *The Lost Road* (p. 41) the names of the Sun and Moon that 'came through' to Alboin Errol were *Anar* and *Isil* (and also *Anor* and *Ithil* in 'Beleriandic' – which presumably here means Exilic Noldorin: see the *Etymologies*, stems ANÁR and SIL).

Almost the same words of the Sun and Moon in relation to Men and Elves are used in AV 2 (annal 2998–3000 and commentary).

In Q the Sun-maiden was named *Úrien*, emended throughout to *Árien*. As QS was first written the name was still spelt *Árien*, but changed throughout to *Árien, Arien*. This seems to have been a very early change and I therefore read *Arien* in the text.

On 'the floating island of the Moon' see IV. 171. The marginal gloss by Ælfwine (see the preamble to QS on p. 201) is certainly contemporary with the writing of the manuscript. Old English *hyrned* 'horned'; cf. the *Etymologies*, stem TIL.

From 'He loved Arien, but she was a holier spirit of greater power' to the end of §76 there is nothing corresponding in Q, except the reference (IV. 97) to Tilion's pursuit of the stars. In Q Tilion is rather the rival of Arien, as was Ilinsor in the *Lost Tales* (I. 195); but cf. the *Ambarkanta* (where Arien and Tilion are not referred to): 'it happens at times that he [the Moon] comes above Valinor ere the Sun has left it, and then he descends and meets his beloved' (IV. 237) – a passage closely echoed in QS §78.

§76  'plunged in the chasm': the Chasm of Ilmen (see the *Ambarkanta*, IV. 236). – This is the first appearance of the image of the long shadows cast by Fingolfin's host as the Moon rose in the West behind them. – In this sentence the word *amazed* is used in an archaic and much stronger sense: overwhelmed with wonder and fear.

§77  'his vessel was scorched and darkened': no explanation is offered in Q for the markings on the Moon (for the old story concerning this see I. 191, 194). It is said in the *Ambarkanta* that the Moon 'pursues ever after the Sun, and overtakes her seldom, and then is consumed and darkened in her flame.'

§§77–8  While a great deal of the description of the motions of the Sun and Moon in these paragraphs is not found in Q, a passage in the *Ambarkanta* (IV. 237), while briefer and without any reference to the change in the divine plan, corresponds quite closely to QS in many features. The QS account introduces an explanation of solar eclipses ('still at times he draws nigh to her, and there is a darkness amid the day'), and of meteors ('stars that have taken hiding there flee before him into the upper air') – cf. the old conception in the *Lost Tales*, I. 216.

§79  The storing of the light of the Sun in vats and pools in Valinor reflects an idea found long before in Kulullin, the great cauldron of golden light in Valinor: the Gods gathered that light 'in the great vat Kulullin to the great increase of its fountains, or in other bright basons and wide pools about their courts, for the health and glory of its radiance was very great' (I. 181). Afterwards the idea emerged again in relation to the Two Trees: 'the dews of Telperion and the rain that fell from Laurelin Varda hoarded in great vats like shining lakes, that were to all the land of the Valar as wells of water and of light' (*The Silmarillion* p. 39).

The passage beginning 'Gods and Elves, therefore, look forward yet . . .' has survived through S and Q from the earliest conceptions. In the phrase 'the Elder Sun and Moon' the word 'Elder' is written over an erasure, and the obliterated word was certainly 'Magic' – the last occurrence of the old 'Magic Sun'. On the mysterious foretelling of Ulmo see IV. 50.

The account of the raising of the mountain-wall and the reason for not closing the Pass of Kôr is much enlarged from the corresponding passage in Q.

It will be seen that at the time when my father began *The Lord of the Rings* the conceptions of the *Ambarkanta* were still fully in being, and that the story of the making of the Sun and Moon from the last fruit and the last flower of the dying Trees was still quite unshadowed by doubt of its propriety in the whole structure of the mythology.

## 7  OF MEN

§81  The Valar sat now behind the mountains and feasted, and all save Manwë and Ulmo dismissed the exiled Noldor from their thought; and having given light to Middle-earth they left it for long untended, and the lordship of Morgoth was uncontested save by the valour of the Gnomes. Most in mind Ulmo kept them, who gathered news of the earth through all the waters.

§82  At the first rising of the Sun above the earth the younger children of the world awoke in the land of Hildórien in the uttermost East of Middle-earth that lies beside the eastern sea; for measured time had come upon earth, and the first of days, and the long awaiting was at an end. Thereafter the vigour of the Quendi that remained in the inner lands was lessened, and their waning was begun; and the air of Middle-earth became heavy with the breath of growth and mortality. For there was great growth in that time beneath the new Sun, and the midmost lands of Middle-earth were clothed in a sudden riot of forest and they were rich with leaves, and life teemed upon the soil and in the waters. But the first sun arose in the West, and the opening eyes of Men were turned thitherward, and their feet as they wandered over earth for the most part strayed that way.

§83  Of Men* little is told in these tales, which concern the eldest days before the waxing of mortals and the waning of the Elves, save of those Fathers of Men who in the first years of Moonsheen and Sunlight wandered into the North of the world. To Hildórien there came no God to guide Men or to summon them to dwell in Valinor; and Men have feared the Valar, rather than loved them, and have not understood the purposes of the Powers, being at variance with them, and at strife with the world.

*Footnote to the text:* The Eldar called them Hildi, the followers; whence Hildórien, the place of the birth of the Hildi, is named. And many other names they gave to them: Engwar the sickly, and Fírimor the mortals; and named them the Usurpers, the Strangers, and the Inscrutable, the Self-cursed, the Heavyhanded, the Nightfearers, the Children of the Sun.

Ulmo nonetheless took thought for them, aiding the counsel and will of Manwë; and his messages came often to them by stream and flood. But they have not skill in such matters, and still less had they in those days ere they had mingled with the Elves. Therefore they loved the waters, and their hearts were stirred, but they understood not the messages. Yet it is told that ere long they met the Dark-elves in many places, and were befriended by them. And the Dark-elves taught them speech, and many other things; and Men became the companions and disciples in their childhood of these ancient folk, wanderers of the Elf-race who had never found the paths to Valinor, and knew of the Valar but as a rumour and a distant name.

§84  Not long had Morgoth then come back into the Middle-earth, and his power went not far abroad, and was moreover checked by the sudden coming of great light. There was little peril, therefore, in the lands and hills; and there new things, fair and fresh, devised long ages before in the thought of Yavanna, and sown as seed in the dark, came at last to their budding and their bloom. West, north, and south the children of Men spread and wandered, and their joy was the joy of the morning before the dew is dry, when every leaf is green.

§85  But the dawn is brief and day full often belies its promise; and now time drew on to the great wars of the powers of the North, when Gnomes and Dark-elves and Men strove against the hosts of Morgoth Bauglir, and went down in ruin. To this end the cunning lies of Morgoth that he sowed of old, and sowed ever anew among his foes, and the curse that came of the slaying at Alqualondë, and the oath of Fëanor, were ever at work: the greatest injury they did to Elves and Men. Only a part is here told of the deeds of those days, and most is said of the Gnomes, and the Silmarils, and the mortals that became entangled in their fate. In those days Elves and Men were of like stature and strength of body; but Elves were blessed with greater wit, and skill, and beauty; and those who had dwelt in Valinor and looked upon the Gods as much surpassed the Dark-elves in these things as they in turn surpassed the people of mortal race. Only in the realm of Doriath, whose queen Melian was of divine race, did the Ilkorins come near to match the Elves of Kôr. Immortal were the Elves, and their wisdom waxed from age to age, and no sickness nor pestilence brought death to them. Yet their bodies were of the stuff of earth and could be destroyed, and in those days they were more like to the bodies of Men, and to the earth, since they had not so long been inhabited by the fire of the spirit, which consumeth them from within in the courses of time. Therefore they could perish in the tumults of the world, and stone and water had power over them, and they could be slain with weapons in those days, even by mortal Men. And outside Valinor they tasted bitter grief, and some wasted and waned with sorrow, until they faded from the earth. Such was the measure of their mortality foretold in the Doom of Mandos spoken in Eruman. But if they were slain or wasted with grief, they died not from the earth, and their spirits went back to the halls of Mandos, and there waited, days or years, even a thousand, according to the will of Mandos and their deserts. Thence they are recalled at length to freedom, either as spirits, taking form according to their own thought, as the lesser folk of the divine race; or else, it is said, they are at times re-born into their own children, and the ancient wisdom of their race does not perish or grow less.

§86   More frail were Men, more easily slain by weapons or mischance, and less easily healed; subject to sickness and many ills; and they grew old and died. What befell their spirits after death the Elves know not. Some say that they too go to the halls of Mandos; but their place of waiting there is not that of the Elves; and Mandos under Ilúvatar alone save Manwë knows whither they go after the time of recollection in those silent halls beside the Western Sea. They are not reborn on earth, and none have ever come back from the mansions of the dead, save only Beren son of Barahir, whose hand had touched a Silmaril; but he never spoke afterward to mortal Men. The fate of Men after death, maybe, is not in the hands of the Valar, nor was all foretold in the Music of the Ainur.

§87   In after days, when because of the triumph of Morgoth Elves and Men became estranged, as he most wished, those of the Elf-race that lived still in the Middle-earth waned and faded, and Men usurped the sunlight. Then the Quendi wandered in the lonelier places of the great lands and the isles, and took to the moonlight and the starlight, and to the woods and caves, becoming as shadows and memories, such as did not ever and anon set sail into the West, and vanished from the earth, as is here later told. But in the dawn of years Elves and Men were allies and held themselves akin, and there were some among Men that learned the wisdom of the Eldar, and became great and valiant and renowned among the captains of the Gnomes. And in the glory and beauty of the Elves, and in their fate, full share had the fair offspring of Elf and Mortal, Eärendel and Elwing, and Elrond their child.

Commentary on Chapter 7

§82  *Hildórien* as the name of the land where Men awoke (replacing
*Eruman* of Q) has appeared in the *Ambarkanta*: between the
Mountains of the Wind and the Eastern Sea (IV. 239). The name was
written into AV 2 (note 13): 'Hildórien in the midmost regions of the
world' – whereas in QS it lay 'in the uttermost East of Middle-earth'.
There is here only an appearance of contradiction, I think. Hildórien
was in the furthest east of *Middle-earth*, but it was in the middle
regions of the world; see *Ambarkanta* map IV, on which Hildórien is
marked (IV. 249). – My note in IV. 257 that the name *Hildórien*
implies *Hildor* needs correction: the footnote to the text in §83 shows
that the form at this time was *Hildi* (cf. also the *Etymologies*, stem
KHIL).

§83  The footnote on Elvish names for Men belongs with the original
writing of the manuscript.

§85  There are some important differences in the passage concerning
the fate of the Elves from that in Q (IV. 100) on which this is based. Q
has nothing corresponding to the statement that Elvish bodies were
then more like mortal bodies, more terrestrial, less 'consumed' by 'the
fire of their spirit', than they afterwards became. Nor is there in Q the
reference to the Doom of Mandos – which in any case does not in Q
refer to the subject of Elvish mortality. This first appears in the
account of the Doom in AV (annal 2993), where the phrase 'a measure
of mortality should visit them' is used, echoed here in QS: 'Such was
the measure of their mortality foretold in the Doom of Mandos'; see
IV. 278–9. Another, and remarkable, development lies in the idea of
the Elves, returning at length out of Mandos, 'taking form according to
their thought, as the lesser folk of the divine race' (i.e. no longer as
corporeal beings, but as spirits that could 'clothe' themselves in a
perceptible form).

§86  The 'Western Sea' is here the Outer Sea, Vaiya. This may well be
no more than a slip, for Q has 'his wide halls *beyond* the western sea';
my father corrected it at some later time to 'Outer Sea'.

§87  With 'the great lands and the isles' cf. Q (IV. 162): 'the great isles,
which in the disruption of the Northern world were fashioned of
ancient Beleriand' (retained in QS, p. 331, §26).

It is clear from the last sentence of the chapter that at this time Elros
had not yet emerged, as he had not in *The Fall of Númenor* and *The
Lost Road* (pp. 30, 74); on the other hand, he is present in the
concluding portion of QS, p. 332, §28.


# 8  OF THE SIEGE OF ANGBAND

§88  Before the rising of the Moon Fëanor and his sons
marched into the North; they landed on the northern shores of

Beleriand beneath the feet of Ered-lómin, the Echoing Mountains, at that place which is called Drengist. Thence they came into the land of Dor-lómen and about the north of the Mountains of Mithrim, and camped in Hithlum, the realm of mist, in that region that is named Mithrim, north of the great lake that has the same name. There a host of Orcs, aroused by the light of the burning ships, and the rumour of their march, came down upon them, and there was fought the first battle upon Middle-earth; and it is renowned in song, for the Gnomes were victorious, and drove away the Orcs with great slaughter, and pursued them beyond Eredwethion into the plain of Bladorion. This was the first battle of Beleriand, and is called the Battle-under-Stars.* Great was the valour of Fëanor and his sons, and the Orcs ever feared and hated them after; yet woe soon followed upon triumph. For Fëanor advanced unwarily upon Bladorion, pursuing the Orcs northward, and he was surrounded, when his own folk were far behind, but the Balrogs in the rearguard of Morgoth turned suddenly to bay. Fëanor fought undismayed, but he was wrapped in fire, and fell at length wounded mortally by the hand of Gothmog, lord of Balrogs, whom Ecthelion after slew in Gondolin. But his sons coming rescued him and bore him back to Mithrim. There he died, but was not buried; for so fiery was his spirit that his body fell to ash as his spirit sped; and it has never again appeared upon earth nor left the realm of Mandos. And Fëanor with his last sight saw afar the peaks of Thangorodrim, greatest of the hills of Middle-earth, that towered above the fortress of Morgoth; and he cursed the name of Morgoth thrice, and he laid it on his sons never to treat or parley with their foe.

§89   Yet even in the hour of his death an embassy came to them from Morgoth, acknowledging defeat, and offering terms, even to the surrender of a Silmaril. Then Maidros the tall, the eldest son, persuaded the Gnomes to feign to treat with Morgoth, and to meet his emissaries at the place appointed; but the Gnomes had as little thought of faith as had Morgoth. Wherefore each embassy came with greater force than was agreed, but Morgoth sent the greater and they were Balrogs. Maidros was ambushed, and all his company was slain, but he himself was taken alive by the command of Morgoth, and brought to Angband and tortured.

§90   Then the six brethren of Maidros drew back and fortified a great camp in Hithlum; but Morgoth held Maidros as hostage,

*Marginal note to the text:* Dagor-nui-Ngiliath.

and sent word to Maglor that he would only release his brother if the Noldor would forsake their war, returning either to Valinor, or else departing from Beleriand and marching to the South of the world. But the Gnomes could not return to Valinor, having burned the ships, and they did not believe that Morgoth would release Maidros if they departed; and they were unwilling to depart, whatever he might do. Therefore Morgoth hung Maidros from the face of a precipice upon Thangorodrim, and he was caught to the rock by the wrist of his right hand in a band of steel.

§91 Now rumour came to the camp in Hithlum of the march of Fingolfin and his sons, and Inglor the son of Finrod, who had crossed the Grinding Ice. And all the world lay then in new wonder at the coming of the Moon; for even as the Moon first rose Fingolfin set foot upon Middle-earth, and the Orcs were filled with amazement. But even as the host of Fingolfin marched into Mithrim the Sun rose flaming in the West; and Fingolfin unfurled his blue and silver banners, and blew his horns, and flowers sprang beneath his marching feet. For a time of opening and growth, sudden, swift, and fair, was come into the world, and good was made of evil, as happens still. Then the Orcs dismayed at the uprising of the great light fled unto Angband, and Morgoth was afraid, pondering long in wrathful thought. But Fingolfin marched through the fastness of the realm of Morgoth, that is Dor-Daedeloth, the Land of Dread, and his foes hid beneath the earth; but the Elves smote upon the gates of Angband, and the challenge of their trumpets shook the towers of Thangorodrim.

§92 But Fingolfin doubted the wiles of Morgoth, and he withdrew from the doors of hell, and turned back unto Mithrim, so that Eredwethion, the Shadow Mountains, might shelter his folk while they rested. But there was little love between those that followed Fingolfin and the house of Fëanor; for the agony of those that had endured the crossing of the ice had been great, and their hearts were filled with bitterness. The numbers of the host of Tûn had been diminished upon that grievous road, but yet was the army of Fingolfin greater than that of the sons of Fëanor. These therefore removed and camped upon the southern shore of Mithrim, and the lake lay between the peoples. In this the work of the curse was seen, for the delay wrought by their feud did great harm to the fortunes of all the Noldor. They achieved nothing while Morgoth hesitated and the dread of light was new and strong upon the Orcs.

§93 Then Morgoth arose from thought, and seeing the

division of his foes he laughed. And he let make vast vapours and great smoke in the vaults of Angband, and they were sent forth from the reeking tops of the Iron Mountains, and afar off these could be seen in Hithlum, staining the bright airs of those earliest of mornings. The North shook with the thunder of Morgoth's forges under ground. A wind came, and the vapours were borne far and wide, and they fell and coiled about the fields and hollows, dark and poisonous.

§94   Then Fingon the valiant resolved to heal the feud. Of all the children of Finwë he is justly most renowned: for his valour was as a fire and yet as steadfast as the hills of stone; wise he was and skilled in voice and hand; troth and justice he loved and bore good will to all, both Elves and Men, hating Morgoth only; he sought not his own, neither power nor glory, and death was his reward. Alone now, without counsel of any, he went in search of Maidros, for the thought of his torment troubled his heart. Aided by the very mists that Morgoth put abroad, he ventured unseen into the fastness of his enemies. High upon the shoulders of Thangorodrim he climbed, and looked in despair upon the desolation of the land. But no passage nor crevice could he find through which he might come within Morgoth's stronghold. Therefore in defiance of the Orcs, who cowered still in the dark vaults beneath the earth, he took his harp and played a fair song of Valinor that the Gnomes had made of old, ere strife was born among the sons of Finwë; and his voice, strong and sweet, rang in the mournful hollows that had never heard before aught save cries of fear and woe.

§95   Thus he found what he sought. For suddenly above him far and faint his song was taken up, and a voice answering called to him. Maidros it was that sang amid his torment. But Fingon climbed to the foot of the precipice where his kinsman hung, and then could go no further; and he wept when he saw the cruel device of Morgoth. Maidros, therefore, being in anguish without hope, begged Fingon to shoot him with his bow; and Fingon strung an arrow, and bent his bow. And seeing no better hope he cried to Manwë, saying: 'O King to whom all birds are dear, speed now this feathered shaft, and recall some pity for the banished Gnomes!'

§96   Now his prayer was answered swiftly. For Manwë to whom all birds are dear, and to whom they bring news upon Taniquetil from Middle-earth, had sent forth the race of Eagles. Thorondor was their king. And Manwë commanded them to dwell in the crags of the North, and keep watch upon Morgoth; for Manwë still had pity for the exiled Elves. And the Eagles brought news of much that passed in these days to the sad ears of Manwë; and they hindered the deeds of Morgoth. Now even as Fingon bent his bow, there flew down from the high airs Thorondor, King of Eagles; and he stayed Fingon's hand.

§97   Thorondor was the mightiest of all birds that have ever been. The span of his outstretched wings was thirty fathoms. His beak was of gold. He took up Fingon and bore him to the face of the rock where Maidros hung. But Fingon could not release the hell-wrought bond upon his wrist, nor sever it, nor draw it from the stone. Again, therefore, in his pain Maidros begged that he would slay him; but Fingon cut off his hand above the wrist, and Thorondor bore them both to Mithrim.

§98   There Maidros in time was healed; for the fire of life was hot within him, and his strength was of the ancient world, such as those possessed who were nurtured in Valinor. His body recovered from its torment and became hale, but the shadow of his pain was in his heart; and he lived to wield his sword with left hand more deadly than his right had been. By this deed Fingon won great renown, and all the Noldor praised him; and the feud was healed between Fingolfin and the sons of Fëanor. But Maidros begged forgiveness for the desertion in Eruman, and gave back the goods of Fingolfin that had been borne away in the ships; and he waived his claim to kingship over all the Gnomes. To this his brethren did not all in their hearts agree. Therefore the house of Fëanor were called the Dispossessed, because of the doom of the Gods which gave the kingdom of Tûn to Fingolfin, and because of the loss of the Silmarils. But there was now a peace and a truce to jealousy; yet still there held the binding oath.

§99   Now the Gnomes being reunited marched forth from the land of Hithlum and drove the servants of Morgoth before them, and they beleaguered Angband from west and south and east. And there followed long years of peace and happiness; for this was the age which songs name the Siege of Angband, and it lasted more than four hundred years of the Sun, while the swords of the Gnomes fenced the earth from the ruin of Morgoth, and his power was shut behind his gates. In those days there was joy beneath the new Sun and Moon, and there was birth and blossoming of many things; and the lands of the West of Middle-earth where now the Noldor dwelt became exceeding fair. And that region was named of old in the language of Doriath Beleriand, but after the coming of the Noldor it was called also in the tongue of Valinor Ingolondë, the fair and sorrowful, the Kingdom of the Gnomes. And behind the guard of their armies in the North the Gnomes began now to wander far and wide over the land, and they built there many fair habitations, and established realms; for save in Doriath and in Ossiriand (of which more is after said) there were few folk there before them. These were Dark-elves of Telerian race, and the Noldor met them in gladness, and there was joyful meeting as between kinsfolk long sundered. And Fingolfin made a great feast, and it was held in the South far from the threat of Morgoth, in the Land of Willows beside the waters of Sirion. The joy of that feast was long remembered in later days of sorrow; and it was called Mereth Aderthad, the Feast of Reuniting, and it was held in spring. Thither came all of the three houses of the Gnomes that could be spared from the northern guard; and great number of the Dark-elves, both the wanderers of the woods, and the folk of the havens from the land of the Falas; and many also came of the Green-elves from Ossiriand, the Land of Seven Rivers, afar off under the walls of the Blue Mountains. And from Doriath there came ambassadors, though Thingol came not himself, and he would not open his kingdom, nor remove its girdle of enchantment; for wise with the wisdom of Melian he trusted not that the restraint of Morgoth would last for ever. But the hearts of the Gnomes were high and full of hope, and it seemed to many of them that the words of Fëanor had been justified, bidding them seek freedom and fair kingdoms in Middle-earth.

§100   But on a time Turgon left Nivrost where he dwelt and went to visit Inglor his friend, and they journeyed southward along Sirion, being weary for a while of the northern mountains; and as they journeyed night came upon them beyond the Meres of Twilight beside the waters of Sirion, and they slept upon his banks beneath the summer stars. But Ulmo coming up the river laid a profound sleep upon them and heavy dreams; and the trouble of the dreams remained after they awoke, but neither said aught to the other, for their memory was not clear, and each deemed that Ulmo had sent a message to him alone. But unquiet was upon them ever after and doubt of what should befall, and they wandered often alone in unexplored country, seeking far and wide for places of hidden strength; for it seemed to each that he was bidden to prepare for a day of evil, and to establish a retreat, lest Morgoth should burst from Angband and overthrow the armies of the North.

§101   Thus it came to pass that Inglor found the deep gorge of Narog and the caves in its western side; and he built there a stronghold and armouries after the fashion of the deep mansions of Menegroth. And he called this place Nargothrond, and made there his home with many of his folk; and the Gnomes of the North, at first in merriment, called him on this account Felagund, or Lord of Caverns, and that name he bore thereafter until his end. But Turgon went alone into hidden places, and by the guidance of Ulmo found the secret vale of Gondolin; and of this he said nought as yet, but returned to Nivrost and his folk.

§102   And even while Turgon and Felagund were wandering abroad, Morgoth seeing that many Gnomes were dispersed over the land made trial of their strength and watchfulness. He shook the North with sudden earthquake, and fire came from the Iron Mountains; and the Orcs poured forth across the plain of Bladorion, and invaded Beleriand through the pass of Sirion in the West, and burst through the land of Maglor in the East; for there is a gap in that region between the hills of Maidros and the outliers of the Blue Mountains. But Fingolfin and Maidros gathered great force, and while others sought out and destroyed all the Orcs that strayed in Beleriand and did great evil, they came upon the main host from the other side, even as it was assaulting Dorthonion, and they defeated the servants of Morgoth, and pursued the remnant across Bladorion, and destroyed them utterly within sight of Angband's gates. This was the second great battle of these wars and was named Dagor Aglareb, the Glorious Battle; and for a long while after none of the servants of Morgoth would venture from his gates; for they feared the kings of the Gnomes. And many reckoned from that day the peace of the Siege of Angband. For the chieftains took warning from that assault and drew their leaguer closer, and set such watch upon Angband that Fingolfin boasted Morgoth could never again escape nor come upon them unawares.

§103   Yet the Gnomes could not capture Angband, nor could they regain the Silmarils; and the stronghold of Morgoth was never wholly encircled. For the Iron Mountains, from the southernmost point of whose great curving wall the towers of Thangorodrim were thrust forward, defended it upon either side, and were impassable to the Gnomes, because of their snow and ice. Thus in his rear and to the North Morgoth had no foes, and by that way his spies at times went out and came by devious routes into Beleriand. And the Orcs multiplied again in the bowels of the earth, and Morgoth began after a time to forge in secret new weapons for the destruction of his enemies. But only twice in all the years of the Siege did he give sign of his purpose. When nearly a hundred years had run since the Second Battle, he sent forth an army to essay the northern ways; and they passed into the white North. Many there perished, but the others turning west round the outer end of the Iron Mountains reached the shores of the sea, and came south along the coast by the route which Fingolfin followed from the Grinding Ice. Thus they endeavoured to invade Hithlum from the rear. But Fingon fell upon them by the firth of Drengist, and drove them into the sea, and none returned to Morgoth. This was not reckoned among the great battles, for the Orcs were not in great number, and only part of the folk of Hithlum fought there.

§104   Again after a hundred years Glómund, the first of Dragons, issued at night from the gates of Angband, by the command of Morgoth; for he was unwilling, being yet young and but half-grown. But the Elves fled before him in dismay, and abandoned the fields of Bladorion, and Glómund defiled them. But Fingon, prince of Gnomes, rode up against him with horsed archers; and Glómund could not withstand their darts, being not yet come to his full armoury, and he fled back to hell. And Fingon won great praise, and the Gnomes rejoiced; for few foresaw the full meaning and threat of this new thing. But they had not seen the last of Glómund.

### Commentary on Chapter 8

§88   In the opening passage my father was closely following AV annal 2995 (virtually the same in the two versions). The account of the Battle-under-Stars, placing it in Mithrim, followed by pursuit of the Orcs into the plain of Bladorion, likewise derives from AV; in Q the battle was fought on the (still unnamed) plain itself. Comparison of the texts will show that in the story of the pursuit of the Orcs and the mortal wounding of Fëanor he had both Q and AV in front of him when he wrote it. I shall not point further to the way in which he used Q and AV, and then AB, in this chapter (while at the same time introducing new narrative elements), for these interrelations are readily traced.

The marginal note *Dagor-nui-Ngiliath* is contemporary with the writing of the manuscript. The earlier form *Dagor-os-Giliath* was corrected to *Dagor-nuin-Giliath* in AV 2 (note 12) and AB 2 (note 3).

Fëanor's death and fate as described here may be compared with what is said in §85; the meaning is no doubt that Fëanor was never reborn, nor ever left Mandos in the manner described in the earlier passage. – His cursing of the name of Morgoth as he died was transferred, or extended, from Túrin (IV. 172), who did the same after the death of Beleg in the *Lay of the Children of Húrin*; but in the Lay Túrin cursed Morgoth thrice, as is not said of Fëanor in Q, and 'thrice' now reappears.

§89   The words 'and they were Balrogs', deriving from Q, show that at this time Balrogs were still conceived to exist in large numbers (see IV. 173); so also 'a host of Balrogs' in §143, and 'Balrogs one thousand' in the Battle of Unnumbered Tears (p. 310 §15).

§91   *Dor-Daedeloth* was altered from *Dor-Daideloth*; this looks to be an early change (the same in AV 2, note 14).

§92   It is not said in the earlier sources that Fingolfin's host remained the greater.

§93   'The North shook with the thunder of Morgoth's forges under ground' reappears from S (IV. 22): 'The North shakes with the thunder under the earth'; it is not found in Q, nor in AB.

§§96–7   *Thorondor* was an early change from *Thorndor*; but *Thorondor* appears later in QS (§147) as the manuscript was originally written.

§98   Maidros' asking of forgiveness for the desertion in Eruman, his returning of the goods of Fingolfin, the waiving of his claim to the kingship, and the secret disavowal of this among his brothers, are all new elements in the narrative (see IV. 173).

§99   The entire passage that in Q (§9) follows 'beleaguered Angband from west and south and east', concerning the dispositions of the Noldorin lords in Middle-earth and their relations with the Dwarves, is omitted here in QS, where the text now jumps on to IV. 104, 'This was the time that songs call the Siege of Angband'; similarly no use is made here of the long passage in AB on this subject (annal 52). The reason for this is the introduction of the new chapter (9) in QS, *Of Beleriand and its Realms*.

In 'it lasted more than four hundred years of the Sun' the word 'four' was an early emendation over an erased word, obviously 'two'; see the note on chronology at the end of this commentary.

With the statement that Beleriand was a Doriathrin name cf. the passage added at the end of the *Lhammas* (§11): 'from Beleriandic is the name *Balar*, and *Beleriand*'. In an addition to Q (IV. 107 note 2) *Beleriand* was said to be Gnomish; and in the same place occurs *Ingolondë the fair and sorrowful*: see IV. 174 and the *Etymologies*, stem ÑGOLOD.

With 'Dark-elves of Telerian race' cf. the earlier passage in QS (§30): 'The Lembi were for the most part of the race of the Teleri, and the chief of these were the Elves of Beleriand.'

§100   This is the first occurrence (other than in corrections to AB 2) of the name *Nivrost* (later *Nevrast*). It was in fact written *Nivros*, here and subsequently, but the final *t* was added carefully in each case, clearly soon after the writing of the manuscript (so also in the annal for

the year 64 added in to AB 2, note 8; *Nivrost* in the *Etymologies*, stems
NIB and ROS²).

The story of the discovery of Nargothrond by Inglor and of
Gondolin by Turgon derives from AB (annal 50), but it is not said
there that they journeyed together and slept by Sirion, that the
foreboding dreams were laid on them by Ulmo, or that neither spoke
to the other of his dream.

§101   Though *Felagund* has several times been rendered 'Lord of
Caves' or 'Lord of Caverns', it has not been said that it was at first a
laughing nickname given to him by the Noldor.

On the date of Turgon's actual departure to Gondolin see the note
on chronology at the end of this commentary.

§102   QS adds to the account of the Dagor Aglareb in AB 2, annal 51:
the Orc-hosts came through the Pass of Sirion and through Maglor's
Gap (see the commentary on AB 2 annal 52), and Fingolfin and
Maidros defeated the main host as it was assaulting Dorthonion. Here
and subsequently the form first written was *Dorthanion*, but the
change to *Dorthonion* was made early. For the many forms preceding
*Dorthonion* see note 9 to AB 2.

§103   On the relation of Angband to Thangorodrim and the Iron
Mountains see the commentary on the *Ambarkanta*, IV. 260, where I
noted that 'Thangorodrim is shown on map V as a point, set slightly
out from the Iron Mountains.' See also the beginning of Chapter 9 in
QS (§105).

In 'When nearly a hundred years had run since the Second Battle', 'a
hundred' was an early emendation from 'fifty'; see the note on chronology below.

On the route of the Orc-army that left Angband by the unguarded
northern exit (described also in AB 2, annal 105) see the note on the
northern geography, pp. 270–2.

§104   Here again (as in §103) 'a hundred' was an early change from
'fifty'; see the note on chronology below.

It is not said in AB 2 (annal 155) either that Glómund's first issuing
from Angband was by Morgoth's command, or that he was unwilling
to venture forth.

### Note on the chronology

This is a convenient place to discuss the chronology of the years of the
Siege of Angband in chapters 8 to 10.

In the chronology of AB 2 as originally written the Siege of Angband
lasted a little more than two hundred years; and important dates for the
present purpose are:

    50   Turgon discovered Gondolin
    51   Dagor Aglareb and the beginning of the Siege of Angband
    52   Turgon departed to Gondolin
    105   Orc-raid down the west coast

155    First emergence of Glómund
255    Battle of Sudden Fire and the end of the Siege

By corrections to the manuscript of AB 2 (given in parentheses in that text) these dates were changed as follows:

(50    Turgon discovered Gondolin; unchanged)
60    Dagor Aglareb and the beginning of the Siege of Angband
64    Turgon departed to Gondolin (additional annal, given in note 8 to AB 2)
155    Orc-raid down the west coast
260    First emergence of Glómund
455    Battle of Sudden Fire and the end of the Siege

Thus the Siege lasted nearly four hundred years; on this final extension of the chronology of the first centuries of the Sun, reaching that in the published *Silmarillion*, see IV. 319–20.

The dates in QS before emendation were:

- The Siege of Angband 'lasted more than two hundred years' (§99);
- The western Orc-raid took place 'nearly fifty years' after the Dagor Aglareb (§103) – which does not perfectly agree with the earlier chronology of the *Annals*, where 54 years elapsed between the two events);
- Glómund's first emergence from Angband was 'again after fifty years' (§104).

These dates were all emended at an early stage, to give 'more than four hundred years' for the Siege, 'nearly a hundred years' from the Dagor Aglareb to the Orc-raid, and a further hundred years to Glómund's coming forth. This agrees, if not quite precisely, with the revised chronology in AB 2 (i.e. 60 to 455; 60 to 155; and 155 to 260).

In QS chapter 10 the new chronology was already in being as the manuscript was written; thus in §125 the Orc-raid that ended at Drengist is stated to have occurred in 155, and this was 105 years before the appearance of Glómund; and after that, i.e. from the year 260, there were 'well nigh two hundred years' of peace, i.e. till the Battle of Sudden Fire in 455. Here also it is said that the encounter of the Noldor with the Dwarves in the Blue Mountains took place about the time of the Orc-raid, agreeing with the altered dating in AB 2, where the meeting with the Dwarves, first given in the year 104, was changed to 154.

In QS therefore, though the date of Turgon's departure to Gondolin is not precisely indicated, he left Nivrost in 64, 'a few years' (§116) after the Second Battle, as in AB 2 revised.

# 9    OF BELERIAND AND ITS REALMS

§105    This is the fashion of the lands into which the Gnomes came, in the North of the western regions of Middle-earth, in the ancient days. In the North of the world Melko reared Ered-engrin the Iron Mountains; and they stood upon the regions of ever-lasting cold, in a great curve from East to West, but falling short of the sea upon either side. These Melko built in the elder days as a fence to his citadel, Utumno, and this lay at the western end of his northern realm. In the war of the Gods the mountains of Melko were broken and distorted in the West, and of their fragments were made Eredwethion and Eredlómin; but the Iron Mountains bent back northward and there was a hundred leagues between them and the frozen straits at Helkaraksë. Behind their walls Melko coming back into Middle-earth made the endless dungeons of Angband, the hells of iron, where of old Utumno had been. But he made a great tunnel under them, which issued south of the mountains; and there he made a mighty gate. But above this gate, and behind it even to the mountains, he piled the thunderous towers of Thangorodrim; and these were made of the ash and slag of his subterranean furnaces, and the vast refuse of his tun-nellings. They were black and desolate and exceedingly lofty; and smoke issued from their tops, dark and foul upon the northern sky. Before the gates of Angband filth and desolation spread southward for many miles. There lay the wide plain of Bladorion. But after the coming of the Sun rich grass grew there, and while Angband was besieged and its gates shut, there were green things even among the pits and broken rocks before the doors of hell.

§106    To the West of Thangorodrim lay Hithlum, the land of mist, for so it was named by the Gnomes because of the clouds that Morgoth sent thither during their first encampment; and it became a fair land while the Siege lasted, although its air was cool and winter there was cold. It was bounded in the West by Eredlómin, the Echoing Mountains that march near the sea; and in the East and South by the great curve of Eredwethion, the Shadowy Mountains that looked across Bladorion, and across the vale of Sirion. In the East that corner which lay between Eredwethion and the Mountains of Mithrim was called the land of Mithrim, and most of Fingolfin's folk dwelt there about the shores of the great lake. West of Mithrim lay Dor-lómen, and was assigned to Fingon son of Fingolfin. West again lay Nivrost* beyond the Echoing Mountains, which below the Firth of Drengist marched inland. Here at first was the realm of Turgon, bounded by the sea, and Eredlómin, and the hills which continue

*Marginal note to the text: Which is West Vale in the tongue of Doriath.

the walls of Eredwethion westward to the sea, from Ivrin to Mount Taras which standeth upon a promontory. And Nivrost was a pleasant land watered by the wet winds from the sea, and sheltered from the North, whereas the rest of Hithlum was open to the cold winds. To the East of Hithlum lay Bladorion, as has been said; and below that the great highland that the Gnomes first named Dorthonion.* This stretched for a hundred leagues from West to East and bore great pine forests, especially upon its northern and western sides. For it arose by gentle slopes from Bladorion to a bleak and lofty land, where lay many tarns at the feet of bare tors whose heads were higher than the peaks of Eredwethion. But southward where it looked towards Doriath it fell suddenly in dreadful precipices. Between Dorthonion and the Shadowy Mountains there was a narrow vale with sheer walls clad with pines; but the vale itself was green, for the river Sirion flowed through it, hastening towards Beleriand.

§107   Now the great and fair country of Beleriand lay on either side of this mighty river Sirion, renowned in song, which rose at Eithel Sirion in the east of Eredwethion, and skirted the edge of Bladorion, ere he plunged through the pass, becoming ever fuller with the streams of the mountains. Thence he flowed down south, one hundred and twenty-one leagues, gathering the waters of many tributaries, until with a mighty flood he reached his many mouths and sandy delta in the Bay of Balar. And the chief of the tributaries of Sirion were in the West: Taiglin, and Narog the mightiest; and in the East: Mindeb, and Esgalduin the enchanted river that flowed through the midst of Doriath; and Aros, with its tributary Celon, that flowed into Sirion at the Meres of Twilight upon the confines of Doriath.

§108   Thus Beleriand was bounded upon the North by Nivrost and Hithlum and Dorthonion; and beyond Dorthonion by the hills of Maidros, son of Fëanor; and upon the West it was bounded by the Great Sea; and upon the East by the towers of Eredlindon, the Blue Mountains, one of the chief ranges of the ancient world; and by Ossiriand between these mountains and the river Gelion. And in the South it was held by some to be bounded by Gelion, that turning westward sought the sea far beyond the mouths of Sirion. Beyond the river Gelion the land narrowed suddenly, for the Great Sea ran into a mighty gulf reaching almost to the feet of Eredlindon, and there was a strait of mountainous

*Marginal note to the text: Ilkorin name.

land between the gulf and the inland sea of Helkar, by which one might come into the vast regions of the South of Middle-earth. But the land between the mouths of Sirion and Gelion was little visited by the Gnomes, a tangled forest in which no folk went save here and there a few Dark-elves wandering; and beyond Gelion the Gnomes seldom came, nor ever east of Eredlindon while that land lasted.

§109 Following Sirion from North to South there lay upon the right hand West Beleriand, at its widest seventy leagues from river to sea: first the Forest of Brethil between Sirion and Taiglin, and then the realm of Nargothrond, between Sirion and Narog. And the river Narog arose in the falls of Ivrin in the southern face of Dorlómen, and flowed some eighty leagues ere he joined Sirion in the Nan-tathren, the land of willows, south of Nargothrond. But the realm of Nargothrond extended also west of Narog, even to the sea, save only in the country of the Falas (or Coast), south of Nivrost. There dwelt the Dark-elves of the havens, Brithombar and Eglorest, and they were of ancient Telerian race; but they took Felagund, lord of Nargothrond, to be their king. And south of Nan-tathren was a region of fair meads filled with many flowers, where few folk dwelt; and beyond lay the marshes and isles of reeds about the mouths of Sirion, and the sands of his delta empty of all living things save birds of the sea.

§110 But upon the left hand of Sirion lay East Beleriand, at its widest a hundred leagues from Sirion to Gelion and the borders of Ossiriand: first the empty lands under the faces of the southern precipices of Dorthonion, Dimbar between Sirion and Mindeb, and Nan-dungorthin between Mindeb and the upper waters of Esgalduin; and these regions were filled with fear by the enchantments of Melian, as a defence of Doriath against the North, and after the fall of the Gnomes they became places of terror and evil. Beyond them to the East lay the north-marches of Beleriand, where the sons of Fëanor dwelt. Next southward lay the kingdom of Doriath; first its northern and lesser part, the Forest of Neldoreth, bounded east and south by the dark river Esgalduin, which bent westward in the midst of Doriath; and then the denser and greater woods of Region, between Esgalduin and Aros. And Menegroth the halls of Thingol were built upon the south bank of Esgalduin, where he turned westward; and all Doriath lay east of Sirion, save for a narrow region of woodland between the meeting of Taiglin and Sirion and the Meres of Twilight. And this wood which the folk of Doriath called Nivrim, or the West-march, was very fair, and oak-trees of great beauty grew there; and it was included in the girdle of Melian, so that some portion of Sirion which she loved in reverence of Ulmo should be wholly under the power of Thingol.

§111   Beyond Doriath to the East lay wide woods between Celon and Gelion; here few folk dwelt, but Damrod and Díriel took it as their realm and hunting-ground; and beyond, between Gelion and the Blue Mountains, was the wide land of Thargelion,* where Cranthir dwelt of old. But in the southern corner of Doriath, where Aros flowed into Sirion, lay a region of great pools and marshes on either side of the river, which halted there in his course and strayed in many channels. This region the Elves of Doriath named Umboth Muilin,† the Twilight Meres, for there were many mists, and the enchantment of Doriath lay over them.

§112   For all the northern half of Beleriand sloped southward to this point and then for a while was plain, and the flood of Sirion was stayed. But south of Umboth Muilin the land again fell suddenly and steeply, though in no wise with so great a fall as in the North. Yet all the lower plain of Sirion was divided from the upper plain by this sudden fall, which looking North appeared as an endless chain of hills running from Eglorest beyond Narog in the West to Amon Ereb in the East, within far sight of Gelion. Narog came south through a deep gorge, and flowed over rapids but had no fall, and on its west bank the land rose into great wooded highlands, Taur-na-Faroth, which stretched far southward. On the west side of this gorge under Taur-na-Faroth, where the short and foaming stream Ingwil tumbles headlong from the highlands into Narog, Inglor established Nargothrond.

§113   But some seventy miles east of the gorge of Nargothrond Sirion fell from the North in a mighty fall below the meres, and then he plunged suddenly underground into great tunnels that the weight of his falling waters delved; and he issued again three leagues southward with great noise and smoke through rocky arches at the foot of the hills which were called the Gates of Sirion. But this dividing fall was named Andram, or the Long Wall, from Nargothrond to Ramdal, or Wall's End, in East Beleriand. And in the East the wall became ever less sheer, for the vale of Gelion sloped ever southward steadily, and Gelion had neither fall nor

---

*Marginal note to the text:* or Radhrost.

†*Footnote to the text:* But the Gnomish names were Hithliniath the pools of mist or Aelin-uial Lakes of Twilight.

rapids throughout his course, but was ever swifter than was Sirion. But between Ramdal and Gelion there stood a single hill, of great extent and gentle slopes, but seeming loftier than it was, for it stood alone; and this hill was named Amon Ereb, and Maidros dwelt there after the great defeat. But until that time all the wide forests of East Beleriand south of Andram and between Sirion and Gelion were little inhabited, and the Gnomes came there seldom.

§114    And east of this wild land lay the country of Ossiriand, between Gelion and Eredlindon. Gelion was a great river, and it arose in two sources, and had at first two branches: Little Gelion that came from the hill of Himring, and Greater Gelion that came from Mount Rerir, an outlier of Eredlindon; and between these branches was the land of Maglor, son of Fëanor. Then joining his two arms Gelion flowed south, a swift river but of small volume, until he found his tributaries some forty leagues south of the meeting of his arms. Ere he found the sea Gelion was twice as long as Sirion, but ever less wide and full; for more rain fell in Hithlum and Dorthonion, whence Sirion drew his waters, than in the East. From Eredlindon flowed the tributaries of Gelion. These were six: Ascar (that was after renamed Rathlóriel), Thalos, Legolin, Brilthor, Duilwen, and Adurant; they were swift and turbulent, falling steeply from the mountains, but going southward each was longer than the one before, since Gelion bent ever away from Eredlindon. Between Ascar in the North and Adurant in the South, and between Gelion and the mountains, lay Ossiriand, the Land of Seven Rivers, filled with green woods wide and fair.

§115    There dwelt the Danian Elves, who in the beginning were of Gnomish race, but forsook the march from Kuiviénen, and came never to Valinor, and only after long wanderings came over the mountains in the dark ages; and some of their kindred dwelt still east of Eredlindon. Of old the lord of Ossiriand was Denethor, friend of Thingol; but he was slain in battle when he marched to the aid of Thingol against Melko, in the days when the Orcs were first made and broke the starlit peace of Beleriand. Thereafter Doriath was fenced with enchantment, and many of the folk of Denethor removed to Doriath and mingled with the Elves of Thingol; but those that remained in Ossiriand had no king, and lived in the protection of their rivers. For after Sirion Ulmo loved Gelion above all the waters of the western world. But the woodcraft of the Elves of Ossiriand was such that a stranger might pass through their land from end to end and see none of them. They were clad mostly in green in spring and in summer, and hence were called the Green-elves; and they delighted in song, and the sound of their singing could be heard even across the waters of Gelion, as if all their land was filled with choirs of birds whose fair voices had taken thought and meaning.

§116   In this way the chieftains of the Gnomes held their lands and the leaguer upon Morgoth after his defeat in the Second Battle. Fingolfin and Fingon his son held Hithlum, and their chief fortress was at Eithel Sirion in the east of Eredwethion, whence they kept watch upon Bladorion; and their cavalry rode upon that plain even to the shadow of Thangorodrim, and their horses multiplied for the grass was good. Of those horses many of the sires came from Valinor. But Turgon the wise, second son of Fingolfin, held Nivrost until the Second Battle, and returned thither afterward, and his folk were numerous. But the unquiet of Ulmo increased upon him, and after a few years he arose and took with him a great host of Gnomes, even to a third of the people of Fingolfin, and their goods and wives and children, and departed eastward. His going was by night and his march swift and silent, and he vanished out of knowledge of his kindred. But he came to Gondolin, and built there a city like unto Tûn of Valinor, and fortified the surrounding hills; and Gondolin lay hidden for many years.

§117   The sons of Finrod held the northern march from the pass of Sirion between Hithlum and Dorthonion unto the eastern end of Dorthonion, where is the deep gorge of Aglon. And Inglor held the pass of Sirion, and built a great watchtower, Minnastirith, upon an isle in the midst of the river; but after the founding of Nargothrond this fortress he committed mostly to the keeping of his brother Orodreth. But Angrod and Egnor watched Bladorion from the northern slopes of Dorthonion; and their folk was not great for the land was barren, and the great highlands behind were deemed to be a bulwark that Morgoth would not lightly seek to cross.

§118   But east of Dorthonion the marches of Beleriand were more open to attack, and only hills of no great height guarded the vale of Gelion from the North. Therefore the sons of Fëanor with many folk, well nigh half of the people of the Gnomes, dwelt in that region, upon the Marches of Maidros, and in the lands behind; and the riders of the folk of Fëanor rode often upon the vast northern plain, Lothland the wide and empty, east of Bladorion, lest Morgoth attempted any sortie towards East

Beleriand. And the chief citadel of Maidros was upon the hill of Himring, the Ever-cold; and this was wide-shouldered, bare of trees, and flat upon the summit, and surrounded by many lesser hills. Its name it bore because there was a pass, exceeding steep upon the west, between it and Dorthonion, and this was the pass of Aglon, and was a gate unto Doriath, and a bitter wind blew ever through it from the North. But Celegorn and Curufin fortified Aglon, and manned it with great strength, and they held all the land southward between the river Aros that arose in Dorthonion and his tributary Celon that came from Himring. And between Celon and Little Gelion was the ward of Damrod and Díriel. And between the arms of Gelion was the ward of Maglor, and here in one place the hills failed altogether; and here it was that the Orcs came into East Beleriand before the Second Battle. Therefore the Gnomes held much cavalry in the plains at that place; and the people of Cranthir fortified the mountains to the east of Maglor's Gap. For Mount Rerir, and about it many lesser heights, stood out from the main range of Eredlindon westward; and in the angle between Rerir and Eredlindon there was a lake, shadowed by mountains on all sides save the south. This was Lake Helevorn, deep and dark, and beside it Cranthir had his abode; but all the great land between Gelion and Eredlindon, and between Rerir and the river Ascar, was called by the Gnomes Thargelion (that is the land beyond Gelion), or Dor Granthir the land of Cranthir; and it was here that the Gnomes first met the Dwarves.*

§119    Thus the sons of Fëanor under the leadership of Maidros were lords of East Beleriand, but their folk was in that time mostly in the north of the land; and southward they rode only to hunt, and to seek solitude for a while. And thither for like purpose the other Elflords would sometimes come, for the land was wild but very fair; and of these Inglor came most often, for he had great love of wandering, and he came even into Ossiriand and won friendship of the Green-elves. But Inglor was King of Nargothrond and overlord of the Dark-elves of the western havens; and with his aid Brithombar and Eglorest were rebuilt and became fair towns, recalling somewhat the havens of the Elves upon the shores of Valinor.

§120    And Inglor let build the tower of Tindobel upon a cape west of Eglorest to watch the Western Sea; and some of the folk of

*Marginal note to the text:* But Dor Granthir was before called by the Dark-elves Radhrost, the East Vale.

Nargothrond with the aid of the Teleri of the havens built new ships, and they went forth and explored the great isle of Balar, thinking here to prepare an ultimate refuge, if evil came. But it was not their fate that they should ever dwell there. And Inglor's realm ran north to Tolsirion the isle in the river aforesaid, and his brothers held Dorthonion and were his vassals. Thus his realm was far the greatest, though he was the youngest of the great lords of the Gnomes, Fingolfin, Fingon, and Maidros, and Inglor Felagund. But Fingolfin was held overlord of all the Gnomes, and Fingon after him, though their own realm was but the northern lands of Nivrost and Hithlum. Yet were their folk the most hardy and valiant, and the most feared by the Orcs and most hated by Morgoth.

§121 And in Doriath abode Thingol, the hidden king, and into his realm none passed save by his will, and when summoned thither; and mighty though the Kings of the Noldor were in those days, and filled with the fire and glory of Valinor, the name of Thingol was held in awe among them.

### Commentary on Chapter 9

§105 This is the first occurrence of the final form *Ered-engrin* (for earlier *Eiglir Engrin*, IV. 220). The description of the Iron Mountains here agrees with the *Ambarkanta* map IV (IV. 249), where they are shown as a great wall across the North, slightly bowed southwards, and where, as stated in QS, they do not extend to the shores of either the Western or the Eastern Seas. I have discussed in IV. 258–60 the relation of the *Ambarkanta* map V to the description here of the changes in the northern mountains and of Angband and Thangorodrim.

§106 Hithlum is called 'Land(s) of Mist' in the *Lay of the Children of Húrin*, in Q, and in AB 1, 'realm of mist' in QS §88, but this explanation of the name has not been given before. It is interesting to look back to the original idea (I. 112): '*Dor Lómin* or the "Land of Shadow" was that region named of the Eldar *Hisilómë* (and this means "Shadowy Twilights") . . . and it is so called by reason of the scanty sun which peeps little over the Iron Mountains [i.e. the Mountains of Shadow] to the east and south of it.'

*Nivrost*, always early changed from *Nivros*, is now placed geographically in the previously unnamed region which appears already on the first Map (IV. 228), and it is here explicitly reckoned a part of Hithlum (but in §120 there is a reference to 'the northern lands of Nivrost and Hithlum'). The marginal note translating the name as 'West Vale' ('West-dales' in the *Etymologies*, stem NIB) is contemporary with the writing of the manuscript (in *The Silmarillion* the later form *Nevrast* is translated 'Hither Shore', p. 119). On Hithlum's exposure to the North see the note on the geography of the far North, pp. 270–2.

This is the first occurrence of *Taras*, but the great mountain was clearly marked out on the second Map as originally drawn, and before the name was inserted (p. 408, square D2).

The marginal note defining *Dorthonion* as an Ilkorin name (in agreement with the *Etymologies*, stem THŌN) looks as if it belongs with the original writing of the manuscript, although it contradicts the statement in the text: 'the great highland that the Gnomes first named Dorthonion.'

§108  At the first occurrence of *Eredlindon* in this paragraph there is a footnote to the text added after the writing of the manuscript:

> Which signifieth the Mountains of Ossiriand; for the Gnomes called that land Lindon, the region of music, and they first saw these mountains from Ossiriand. But their right name was Eredluin the Blue Mountains, or Luindirien the Blue Towers.

I have not included this in the text printed, feeling uncertain of its date. In the passages of revision to the second version of *The Fall of Númenor* the name *Lindon* appears. I have shown that these revisions come from a time during the writing of *The Lord of the Rings* (see pp. 31–4) – although that does not necessarily imply that *Lindon* had not arisen earlier. Originally *Eredlindon* certainly meant 'Blue Mountains': see IV. 328, 341; and in the *List of Names* (p. 405) a word *lind* 'blue' is adduced (cf. the *Etymologies*, stem GLINDI).

With the account of the extent of Beleriand cf. the legend on the first Map (IV. 226–7). – The present passage is the first statement about the lower course of Gelion; on the *Ambarkanta* map V (IV. 251) the river (unnamed) is shown turning west and flowing into the sea in another great bay south of Balar. Also shown on map V is the 'Great Gulf', and 'the strait of mountainous land' (there called the 'Straits of the World') 'between the gulf and the inland sea of Helkar' (see IV. 258–9).

§109  *Nan-tathren* was changed from *Nan-tathrin*, as in AB 2 (note 5). – In AB 2 (annal 52) Fingolfin was 'Lord of the Falas or Western Shore, and overlord of the Dark-elves as far south as Eglorest and west of the river Eglor', while Felagund possessed the lands east of Eglor (between Eglor and Sirion). Changes made to that manuscript (notes 12 and 13) altered the text to say that it was Felagund who was 'held to be overlord of the Falas, and of the Dark-elves of the havens of Brithombar and Eglorest'; and here in QS the Elves of the Havens 'took Felagund to be their king'.

§110  Here is the first occurrence of the name *Dimbar*. Cf. AB 2, annal 52: 'between Sirion and the river Mindeb no one dwelt.' On *Nan-dungorthin* see IV. 222. Here also is the first occurrence of *Nivrim*, 'the West-march'. On the second Map, as on the first, the region is marked as 'Doriath beyond Sirion'; see IV. 224, 330.

§111   *Thargelion*, here first appearing, was an early change from *Targelion* (but in §122 *Thargelion* is original in the manuscript). The marginal note 'or Radhrost' was probably a subsequent addition, but certainly belongs to the early period; see under §118 below. The second footnote is certainly original. While *Umboth Muilin* goes back to the *Lost Tales* (see II. 225, 349), neither *Hithliniath* nor *Aelin-uial* have occurred before.

§112   Here first appears the name *Taur-na-Faroth* of the highlands previously called in the *Lays of Beleriand* 'the Hills of the Hunters', 'the Hunters' Wold', and on the first Map *Duil Rewinion* (IV. 225), where these hills are shown extending far to the south of Nargothrond.

§113   This account of the Slope of Beleriand and the great dividing fall is entirely new, as are the names *Andram* 'the Long Wall' and *Ramdal* 'Wall's End' (both written at both occurrences over other names that were wholly obliterated). Ancient features of the rivers of Beleriand – the torrential Narog, the Pools of Twilight, the plunging of Sirion underground – are now related in a comprehensive geographical conception. The 'Gates of Sirion' are new both as name and conception (though marked and named on the second Map as originally drawn, p. 410): nothing has been said hitherto of the issuing of the river from its subterranean passage.

§114   The two tributary branches of Gelion are shown on the second Map but are here first named; and now occurs for the first time *Mount Rerir*, where Greater Gelion rose. The form *Himring* has already appeared in *Lhammas B*, p. 189 (but it was still *Himling* on the second Map as originally drawn).

At the name *Adurant* there is a footnote to the text added after the writing of the manuscript:

And at a point nearly midway in its course the stream of Adurant divided and joined again, enclosing a fair island; and this was called Tolgalen, the Green Isle. There Beren and Lúthien dwelt after their return.

Like the footnote to §108, I have not included this in the text because of uncertainty as to when the addition was made. The second Map does not show the island formed by the divided course of Adurant; on the other hand an addition to the stem AT(AT) in the *Etymologies* explains the actual meaning of *Adurant* precisely from the divided course (Ilkorin *adu*, *ado* 'double'). This is the first occurrence of the name *Tolgalen*, and of this precise placing of the dwelling of Beren and Lúthien after their return. On the first Map 'the Land of the Dead that Live' was moved several times, the final placing being in Ossiriand (IV. 224, 230), as in Q (IV. 133).

§115   With 'when the Orcs were first made' cf. QS §62: 'he brought into being the race of the Orcs' (i.e. when Morgoth came back to Middle-earth).

This account of the Green-elves ('Danian Elves') will be found to be in good agreement with the *Lhammas* §7. It is not told there that they were called Green-elves because they were clad in green in spring and summer (but 'the house of Denethor loved green above all colours'); and there is now the first mention of their singing, which led to their land being named *Lindon* (see the commentary on §108, but also the *Etymologies*, stem LIN²).

§116   From the beginning of this paragraph the text is derived, with much alteration and expansion, from AB 2, annal 52.

On the lapse of time between Turgon's discovery of the hidden valley of Gondolin and his final departure from Nivrost see pp. 257–8. In AB 2 he 'departed south', i.e. from Hithlum, later changed (note 8) to agree with QS, where he 'departed eastward', i.e. from Nivrost. This is the first mention of the likeness of Gondolin to the city of the Elves in Valinor, although, as I have suggested (II. 208), it was perhaps an old underlying idea.

§117   The name *Minnastirith* is written over a total erasure, but the obliterated name was clearly *Inglormindon*, which appears in an addition to AB 2 (note 14), changed there also to *Minnastirith* (and then to *Minastirith*).

Another element in the changed history of Orodreth now enters, an aspect of his association with Inglor Felagund rather than with Angrod and Egnor (see the commentary on §73): he no longer has land in the east of Dorthonion, near to his friends Celegorn and Curufin, but is the warden of Inglor's tower on Tol Sirion. This new story was introduced into AB 2 by later corrections (notes 10, 25, 29).

§118   The account of the defences of Beleriand in the North-east and the lands of the Fëanorian princes does not differ in essentials from that in AB 2, but is fuller and more precise in detail. The name *Lothland* first appears here, and this is the first time that Himring (Himling) has been described, or an interpretation given for either form. The territory of Damrod and Díriel is made more definite, and apparently more northward (earlier in this chapter, §111, its limits are 'between Celon and Gelion'). Lake *Helevorn*, beside which Cranthir dwelt, is now first mentioned (the name being written over an erasure, perhaps of *Elivorn*, see p. 405); it is not shown on the second Map as originally drawn.

The words 'by the Gnomes Thargelion (that is the land beyond Gelion) or Dor Granthir' were an addition, together with the marginal note on the Dark-elvish name *Radhrost*, but made very carefully at an earlier time. On *Granthir* beside *Cranthir* see the note on *Gorgoroth*, p. 298. The encounter of Cranthir's people with the Dwarves in Eredlindon is given in AB 2 under the year 104 (> 154), but the account of the Dwarves at this point in the *Annals* is in QS reserved for the new chapter that follows.

§§119–20   It is not said in AB 2 (annal 65) that Felagund aided the Elves of the Falas in the rebuilding of their Havens, nor that it was he who raised the Tower of Tindobel: for Fingolfin was still Lord of the Falas (see under §109 above). The name was first written here *Tindabel*, as also on the second Map: I read *Tindobel* on the assumption that this was an early change, a reversion to the form on the first Map and in AB 1 and 2.

### Note on the geography of the furthest North

I have remarked (IV. 259) when discussing the *Ambarkanta* maps that it is interesting to see how near Hithlum is placed on Map V to the edge of the world, the Chasm of Ilmen; and this is a convenient place to consider a further aspect of the matter. In QS §105 it is said:

In the war of the Gods the mountains of Melko were broken and distorted in the West, and of their fragments were made Eredwethion and Eredlómin; but the Iron Mountains bent back northward and there was a hundred leagues between them and the frozen straits at Helkaraksë.

Though very cramped and hastily sketched in, Map V seems to agree well with this. I attempt here to enlarge and clarify the depiction of these regions on the map, adding letters to make reference to it plainer.

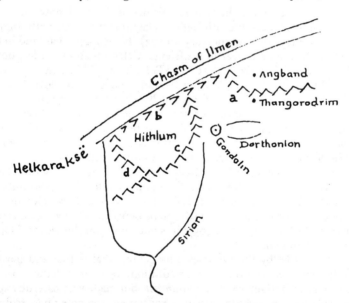

The western end of the Iron Mountains (marked *a* on the sketch) now turns in fairly sharply northwards to the Chasm of Ilmen; Eredwethion (*c*) and Eredlómin (*d*) are clearly identifiable. The herring-bone line (*b*) that runs along the edge of the Chasm is in pencil, whereas the other ranges are inked over pencil, but it is not clear whether this has any significance. The statement in QS just cited that there were a hundred leagues between the end of the Iron Mountains and the Helkaraksë suggests that there were no great heights between Hithlum and the Chasm – and cf. QS §106: 'Nivrost was sheltered from the North' (by Eredlómin), whereas 'Hithlum was open to the cold winds'.

On the other hand, earlier in QS (§103) the army sent out by Morgoth to test the defences of the Noldor 'turning west round the outer end of the Iron Mountains reached the shores of the sea', endeavouring 'to invade Hithlum from the rear'. This army came south along the coast and was destroyed by Fingon at the Firth of Drengist. Does this imply that the Orc-host could not invade Hithlum from the North owing to defensible heights between Hithlum and the Chasm of Ilmen? In which case some configuration after this fashion might be supposed:

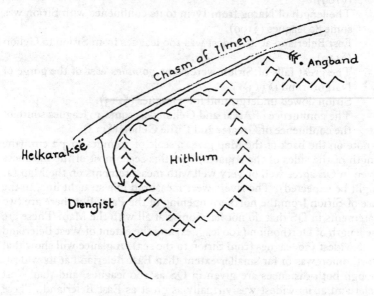

But the evidence does not seem to allow of a certain answer; and the second Map gives no help – indeed it presents a further problem in the representation of Thangorodrim (p. 409). Here the colossal triple peaks of Thangorodrim are surrounded by a closed circle of lesser heights, and there is no suggestion of the 'great curving wall' of the Iron Mountains from which 'the towers of Thangorodrim were thrust forward' (QS §103). I am at a loss to explain this; but in all the years during which my father used this map he never made any mark on it suggesting that the picture should be changed.

At this time Thangorodrim was conceived to be quite near: the second Map agrees closely with the *Ambarkanta* map V in this. In post-*Lord of the Rings* writing it is said that 'the gates of Morgoth were but one hundred and fifty leagues distant from the bridge of Menegroth' (*The Silmarillion* p. 96); whereas according to the scale of the second Map (see below) the distance was scarcely more than seventy.

### Note on distances

I list here the definitions of distance that are given in Chapter 9:

- 100 leagues between the end of the Iron Mountains in the West and the Helkaraksë (§105).
- Dorthonion stretched for 100 leagues (§106).
- The length of Sirion from the Pass to the Delta was 121 leagues (§107).
- West Beleriand at its widest was 70 leagues from Sirion to the sea (§109).
- The length of Narog from Ivrin to its confluence with Sirion was some 80 leagues (§109).
- East Beleriand at its widest was 100 leagues from Sirion to Gelion (§110).
- The great falls of Sirion were some 70 *miles* east of the gorge of Nargothrond (§113).
- Sirion flowed underground for 3 leagues (§113).
- The confluence of Ascar and Gelion was some 40 leagues south of the confluence of Greater and Little Gelion (§114).

A note on the back of the Map gives a scale of 50 miles to 3·2 cm. (the length of the sides of the squares). On this scale most of the distances given in QS agree well or very well with measurements on the Map (as might be expected). The rivers were measured in a straight line, in the case of Sirion from the northern opening of the Pass. But there are two statements in QS that do not harmonise at all with the Map. These are the length of Dorthonion (100 leagues) and the extent of West Beleriand at its widest (70 leagues from Sirion to the sea). A glance will show that Dorthonion was of far smaller extent than East Beleriand at its widest, though both distances are given in QS as 100 leagues, and that West Beleriand at its widest was virtually as great as East Beleriand. These statements are, I think, simply errors, without further significance; and they were in fact corrected (long after), the length of Dorthonion becoming 60 leagues, and West Beleriand at its widest 99 leagues, harmonising with the Map.

## 10   OF MEN AND DWARFS

§122   Now in time the building of Nargothrond was complete, and Gondolin had been raised in secret. But in the days of the Siege of Angband the Gnomes had yet small need of hiding places, and they ranged far and wide between the Western Sea and the

Blue Mountains in the East. It is said that they climbed Ered-lindon and looked eastward in wonder, for the lands of Middle-earth seemed wild and wide; but they did not pass the mountains, while Angband lasted. In those days the folk of Cranthir came first upon the Dwarfs, whom the Dark-elves named Naug-rim; for the chief dwellings of that race were then in the mountains east of Thargelion, the land of Cranthir, and were digged deep in the eastern slopes of Eredlindon. Thence they journeyed often into Beleriand, and were admitted at times even into Doriath. There was at that time no enmity between Elves and Dwarfs, but nonetheless no great love. For though the Dwarfs did not serve Morgoth, yet they were in some things more like to his people than to the Elves.

§123    The Naugrim were not of the Elf-race nor of mortal kind, nor yet of Morgoth's breeding; and in those days the Gnomes knew not whence they came. [But* it is said by the wise in Valinor, as we have learned since, that Aulë made the Dwarfs while the world was yet dark, desiring the coming of the Children of Ilúvatar, that he might have learners to whom he could teach his lore and craft, and being unwilling to await the fulfilment of the designs of Ilúvatar. Wherefore the Dwarfs are like the Orcs in this, that they come of the wilfulness of one of the Valar; but they were not made out of malice and mockery, and were not begotten of evil purpose. Yet they derive their thought and being after their measure from only one of the Powers, whereas Elves and Men, to whomsoever among the Valar they chiefly turn, have kinship with all in some degree. Therefore the works of the Dwarfs have great skill, but small beauty, save where they imitate the arts of the Eldar; and the Dwarfs return unto the earth and the stone of the hills of which they were fashioned.]†

§124    Iron they wrought rather than gold and silver, and the making of weapons and of mail was their chief craft. They aided

---

*Marginal note against the bracketed passage: quoth Pengolod.

†Footnote to the text: Aulë, in his love of invention, devised a new speech for the Dwarfs, and their tongues have no kinship with others; in use they have made them harsh and intricate, and few have essayed to learn them. In their converse with the Elves of old they used according to their ability the language of the Dark-elves of Doriath. But their own tongues they maintained in secret, and they survive still in Middle-earth, and in some part certain of the languages of Men are derived from them. Against this is written in the margin: So, the Lhammas.

the Gnomes greatly in their war with the Orcs of Morgoth; but it is not thought that they would have refused to smithy also for Morgoth, if he had had need of their work, or had been open to their trade. For buying and selling and exchange was their delight, and the winning of wealth. But this they gathered rather to hoard than to use, or to spend save in commerce. Their stature was short and squat; they had strong arms and sturdy legs, and their beards were long. Themselves they named Khuzûd, but the Gnomes called them Neweg, the stunted, and those who dwelt in Nogrod they called Enfeng, the Longbeards, because their beards swept the floor before their feet. Their chief cities in those days were Khazaddûm and Gabilgathol, which the Elves of Beleriand called, according to their meaning in the language of Doriath, Nogrod, the Dwarfmine, and Belegost, the Great Fortress. But few of the Elves, save Meglin of Gondolin, went ever thither, and the Dwarfs trafficked into Beleriand, and made a great road, passing under the shoulders of Mount Dolmed, which followed thence the course of Ascar, and crossed Gelion at Sarn-athrad. There battle later befell, but as yet the Dwarfs troubled the Elves little, while the power of the Gnomes lasted.

§125 It is reckoned that the first meeting of Gnomes and Dwarfs befell in the land of Cranthir about the time when Fingolfin destroyed the Orcs at Drengist, one hundred and fifty-five years after the crossing of the Ice, and one hundred and five before the first coming of Glómund the Dragon. After his defeat there was long peace, and it lasted for well nigh two hundred years of the Sun. During this time the fathers of the houses of the Men of Beleriand, that is of the Elf-friends of old, were born in the lands of Middle-earth, east of the mountains; Bëor the Vassal, Haleth the Hunter, and Hador the Goldenhaired.

§126 Now it came to pass, when some four hundred years were gone since the Gnomes came to Beleriand, that Felagund journeyed east of Sirion and went hunting with the sons of Fëanor. But he became separated from his companions, and passed into Ossiriand, and wandered there alone. At a time of night he came upon a valley in the western foothills of Eredlindon, and he saw lights in the valley and heard from afar the sound of uncouth song; and he wondered greatly, for the Green-elves of that land lit no fires and sang not by night. And the language of the song, which he heard as he drew nigh, was not that of the Eldar, neither of the Dark-elves nor of the Gnomes, nor was it that of the Dwarfs. Therefore he feared lest a raid of the Orcs had escaped the leaguer of the North, but he found that this was not so. For he spied upon the camp beneath the hills, and there he beheld a strange people. Tall they were, and strong, and fair of face, but rude and little clad.

§127  Now these were the people of Bëor, a mighty warrior among Men, whose son was Barahir the bold that was after born in the land of the Gnomes. They were the first of Men that wandering west from far Hildórien passed over Eredlindon and came into Beleriand. After Bëor came Haleth father of Hundor, and again somewhat later came Hador the Goldenhaired, whose children are renowned in song. For the sons of Hador were Gumlin and Gundor, and the sons of Gumlin were Húrin and Huor, and the son of Húrin was Túrin the bane of Glómund, and the son of Huor Tuor father of Eärendel the blessed. All these were caught in the net of the fate of the Gnomes and wrought great deeds which the Elves remember still among the deeds of their lords and kings of old. But Haleth and Hador at that time were yet in the wild lands east of the mountains.

§128  Felagund drew nigh among the trees to the camp of Bëor and he remained hidden, until all had fallen asleep. Then he went among the sleeping men, and sat beside their dying fire, where none kept watch; and he took a rude harp which Bëor had laid aside, and he played music upon it such as mortal ear had never heard. For Men had as yet had no masters in such arts, save only the Dark-elves in the wild lands. Now men awoke and listened to Felagund as he harped and sang; and they marvelled, for wisdom was in that song as well as beauty, so that the heart grew wiser that hearkened to it. Thus it was that Men called King Felagund, whom they met first of all the Noldor, Gnome or Wisdom;* and after him they named his race the Wise, whom we call the Gnomes. At first they deemed that Felagund was one of the Gods, of whom they had heard rumour that they dwelt far in the West. But Felagund taught them true lore, and they loved him and became his followers; and thus Bëor the Vassal got his name among the Gnomes.

*Footnote to the text: It is recorded that the word in the ancient speech of these Men, which they afterwards forsook in Beleriand for the tongue of the Gnomes, so that it is now mostly forgotten, was *Widris*. *Against this is written in the margin:* quoth Pengolod. *Added to this:* & Ælfwine.

§129   Bëor lived in the service of Felagund while his life lasted; and Barahir his son served also the sons of Finrod, but he dwelt mostly on the north marches with Angrod and Egnor. The sons of Hador were allied to the house of Fingolfin, and the lordship of Gumlin was in Hithlum; and there afterwards his son Húrin dwelt, whose wife was Morwen of the house of Bëor. She was surnamed Eledhwen, the Eflsheen, for her beauty was like unto the beauty of the daughters of the Eldalië. But Haleth and his folk took no service and dwelt in the woods upon the confines of Doriath in that forest that was called Brethil.

§130   In this time the strength of Men was added to the Gnomes, and the folk of the three houses grew and multiplied. Greatest was the house of Hador, and most beloved by the Elves. His folk were yellow-haired and blue-eyed for the most part; though Túrin was dark of hair, for his mother Morwen was from Bëor's people. They were of greater strength and stature in body than the Elves; quick to wrath and laughter, fierce in battle, generous to friends, swift in resolve, fast in loyalty, young in heart, the Children of Ilúvatar in the youth of mankind. Like to them were the woodland folk of Haleth, but they were not so tall; their backs were broader and their legs shorter and less swift. Less fiery were their spirits; slower but more deep was the movement of their thought; their words were fewer, for they had joy in silence, wandering free in the greenwood, while the wonder of the world was new upon them. But the people of Bëor were dark or brown of hair; their eyes were grey, and their faces fair to look upon; shapely they were of form, yet hardy and long-enduring. Their height was no greater than that of the Elves of that day, and they were most like to the Gnomes; for they were eager of mind, cunning-handed, swift of understanding, long in memory. But they were short-lived, and their fates were unhappy, and their joy was blended with sorrow.

§131   Bëor died when he had lived but eighty years, for fifty of which he had served Felagund; and it is said that when he lay dead of no weapon or sickness, but stricken by age, the Elves saw then for the first time the death of weariness, and they grieved for the short span allotted to mankind. Nonetheless these Men of old, being of races young and eager, learned swiftly of the Elves all such art and knowledge as they would teach; and in their skill and wisdom they far surpassed all others of their kind, who dwelt still east of the mountains, and knew not the Eldar of the West, ere ruin befell Beleriand.

*Commentary on Chapter 10*

§122   The transient use in this chapter and subsequently of the plural form *Dwarfs* is curious (*Dwarves*, which goes back to the beginning, and was the form in *The Hobbit*, is used in the previous chapter, §118). In AB 2 *Dwarves* was at one occurrence only (note 41) changed to *Dwarfs*. The form *Naugrim* first occurs here; the Dwarves were *Nauglath* in the *Lost Tales*, *Nauglir* in Q. In the third Tree of Tongues (p. 196) their language is *Nauglian*.

In AB 2 (annal 104) 'the Dwarves had great mines and cities in the east of Eredlindon, *far south of Beleriand*, and the chief of these cities were Nogrod and Belegost', as in the direction on the first Map (Eastward Extension), IV. 231–2; but the Dwarf-cities are now placed in QS as they were to remain, in the mountains east of Thargelion, and AB 2 was corrected correspondingly (note 17). That the Dwarves 'were admitted at times even into Doriath' has not been said before, but the idea that they were already well-known to the Dark-elves of Beleriand when the Gnomes first encountered them in the Blue Mountains appeared in the second version of AB 1 (see IV. 332, 336), and their ancient road is there said to have extended to the river Aros, i.e. to the confines of Doriath.

It is remarkable that at this time the statement that the Dwarves were 'in some things more like to Morgoth's people than to the Elves' still survived from Q (IV. 104); but this is now palliated by what is said in §123, where the likeness of the Dwarves to the Orcs is represented only as an analogous limitation of natural powers consequent on their origins.

§123   This is the third account of the legend of the origin of the Dwarves, following those in AB 2 (annal 104) and in the *Lhammas* §9, both of which contain the remarkable assertion that the Dwarves have 'no spirit indwelling'; see the commentaries on those passages. Both versions were modified in respect of this; the *Lhammas* text was roughly emended with a specific direction to follow the passage here in QS beginning 'Yet they derive their thought and being after their measure from only one of the Powers . . .' But this passage in QS is itself written over something else wholly erased. Very likely, then, QS also had here a phrase concerning the absence of a 'spirit indwelling' in the Dwarves, and my father corrected both QS and the *Lhammas* at the same time, as he did elsewhere. Moreover, the account of the fate of the Dwarves given here, their return 'unto the earth and the stone of the hills of which they were fashioned', is taken from the same passage in AB 2 (it is absent from that in the *Lhammas*), and this is surely a concomitant of the conception that 'the Dwarves have no spirit indwelling'.

The square brackets enclosing this passage can be seen to belong with the writing of the manuscript; they evidently show to what portion of the text the marginal 'quoth Pengolod' refers. The question again arises (see §49) why Pengolod appears as annotator if he were the author, as he certainly appears to be in the preamble to the *Quenta Silmarillion* given on p. 201: 'This Account was composed first by Pengolod of Gondolin'. A possible explanation is to be found in the other forms of preamble on pp. 203–4. From the first of these it can be concluded that the reference is to 'The Silmarillion' in the larger sense (i.e. as including the *Annals* and the *Lhammas*), since it is said that Pengolod 'used much the writings of Rúmil . . . *chiefly in the annals of Valinor and the account of tongues*'. The second (typescript) form of this preamble makes the wording less precise: 'he used much the writings of Rúmil . . . concerning other matters than the wars of Beleriand'. Both versions also say that he used the accounts preserved in the Golden Book, though there is no indication of what matter the Golden Book contained. In either case there is no statement one way or the other specifically about the *Quenta Silmarillion*. It may be therefore that my father now regarded Pengolod as redactor or compiler rather than as author, at any rate in certain parts of the book, and in these Pengolod marked off his own contributions and named himself as authority for them – just as he did in the *Annals of Valinor* and the *Lhammas*. Thus here, as in the *Lhammas* §9, the passage concerning the origin of the Dwarves is an addition by Pengolod to older material (in this case writing by Rúmil).

The footnote on Dwarvish language, making specific reference to the *Lhammas*, certainly belongs with the original writing of the manuscript.

§124  *Khuzûd*: the first appearance of this name, or of any Dwarvish name for Dwarves. Cf. *The Lord of the Rings*, Appendix F: '*Khazad-dûm*, the Mansion of the Khazad; for such is their own name for their own race, and has been so, since Aulë gave it to them at their making in the deeps of time.'

*Enfeng*: cf. Q (IV. 104): 'those who dwelt in Nogrod they called Indrafangs, the Longbeards, because their beards swept the floor before their feet.' The name *Enfeng* here first appears. Originally the Longbeards were the Dwarves of Belegost (II. 247).

*Khazaddûm* is the first occurrence of the celebrated name. It is interesting to observe that it existed – but as the Dwarvish name of Nogrod – already at this time. Later the Dwarvish name of Nogrod was *Tumunzahar* (*The Silmarillion* p. 91); *Gabilgathol*, now first appearing, remained as the Dwarvish name of Belegost.

In this paragraph is the first reference to Meglin's association with the Dwarves. – *Dolmed* now replaces *Dolm* (and AB 2 was corrected correspondingly, note 17).

§125  In QS §103 it is said that it was Fingon who destroyed the Orcs at Drengist. – On the new dating, now present from the first writing of the manuscript, see the note on chronology, pp. 257–8.

§126  Parallel with the extension of the Siege of Angband by two hundred years, the meeting of Felagund and Bëor, originally dated in the year 200 in AB 2, undergoes a corresponding postponement.

§128  The footnote to the text is original. Whereas in *The Silmarillion* the word in the language of the people of Bëor for 'Wisdom' was *Nóm* (see IV. 175), here it is *Widris*, and it can hardly be doubted that this is to be related to the Indo-European stem seen, for instance, in Sanskrit *veda* 'I know'; Greek *idein* (from *\*widein*) 'to see' and *oida* (from *\*woida*) '(I have seen >) I know'; Latin *vidēre* 'to see'; Old English *witan* 'to know' and *wāt* 'I know' (> archaic *I wot*), and the words that still survive, *wit*, *wise*, *wisdom*. Cf. the *Lhammas* §10: 'Yet other Men there were, it seems, that remained east of Eredlindon, who held to their speech, and from this, closely akin to Taliska, are come after many ages of change languages that live still in the North of the earth.' – On the abandonment of their own tongue by Men in Beleriand see the *Lhammas* §10 and commentary; and on the ascription of the footnote to Pengolod see commentary on §123 above.

'Thus Bëor the Vassal got his name among the Gnomes': in the *Etymologies* the name *Bëor* 'follower, vassal' is a Noldorin name (stem BEW), whereas in *The Silmarillion* (p. 142) it is said that 'Bëor signified "Vassal" in the tongue of his people'.

§131  According to the original dating of AB 2 Bëor was born in the year 170 and died in 250; with the altered chronology he was born in 370 and died in 450.

## 11    OF THE RUIN OF BELERIAND AND THE FALL OF FINGOLFIN

§132  Now Fingolfin, King of the North, and High-king of the Noldor, seeing that his folk were become numerous and strong, and that the Men allied to them were many and valiant, pondered once more an assault upon Angband. For he knew that they all lived in danger while the circle of the siege was incomplete, and Morgoth was free to labour in the dark beneath the earth. This counsel was wise according to the measure of his knowledge; for the Gnomes did not yet comprehend the fullness of the power of Morgoth, nor understand that their unaided war upon him was without final hope, whether they hasted or delayed. But because the land was fair and their kingdoms wide, most of the Noldor were grown content with things as they were, trusting them to last. Therefore they were little disposed to hearken to Fingolfin, and the sons of Fëanor at that time least of all. Among the chieftains of the Gnomes Angrod and Egnor alone were of like mind with the King; for they dwelt in regions whence Thangorodrim could be descried, and the threat of Morgoth was present to their thought. So the designs of Fingolfin came to naught, and the land had peace yet for a while.

§133    But when the sons of the sons of the Fathers of Men were but newly come to manhood, it being then four hundred years and five and fifty since the coming of Fingolfin, the evil befell that he had long dreaded, and yet more dire and sudden than his darkest fear. For Morgoth had long prepared his force in secret, while ever the malice of his heart grew greater, and his hatred of the Gnomes more bitter; and he desired not only to end his foes but to destroy also and defile the lands that they had taken and made fair. And it is said that his hate overcame his counsel, so that if he had but endured to wait longer, until his designs were full, then the Gnomes would have perished utterly. But on his part he esteemed too lightly the valour of the Elves, and of Men he took yet no account.

§134    There came a time of winter, when night was dark and without moon; and the wide plain of Bladorion stretched dim beneath the cold stars from the hill-forts of the Gnomes to the feet of Thangorodrim. The watchfires burned low, and the guards were few; and on the plain few were waking in the camps of the horsemen of Hithlum. Then suddenly Morgoth sent forth great rivers of flame that poured, swifter than the cavalry of the Balrogs, over all the plain; and the Mountains of Iron belched forth fires of many colours, and the fume stank upon the air and was deadly. Thus Bladorion perished, and fire devoured its grasses; and it became a burned and desolate waste, full of a choking dust, barren and lifeless; and its name was changed, and ever after was called the Land of Thirst, Dor-na-Fauglith in the Gnomish tongue. Many charred bones had there their roofless grave. For many Gnomes perished in that burning, who were caught by the running flame and could not fly to the hills. The heights of Dorthonion and of Eredwethion held back the fiery torrents, but their woods upon the slopes that looked toward Angband were all kindled, and the smoke wrought confusion among the defenders. This was the Third of the great Battles, Dagor Vreged-úr, the Battle of Sudden Fire.

§135    In the front of that fire came Glómund the golden, the father of dragons, and in his train were Balrogs, and behind them came the black armies of the Orcs in multitudes such as the Gnomes had never before seen or imagined. And they assaulted the fortresses of the Gnomes, and broke the leaguer about

Angband, and slew wherever they found them both the Gnomes and their allies, Dark-elves and Men. Many of the stoutest of the foes of Morgoth were destroyed in the first days of that war, bewildered and dispersed and unable to muster their strength. War ceased not wholly ever again in Beleriand; but the Battle of Sudden Fire is held to have ended with the coming of spring, when the onset of Morgoth grew less. For he saw now that he had not assembled sufficient strength, nor rightly measured the valour of the Gnomes. Moreover his captains and spies brought him tidings of the Elf-friends, the Men of Beleriand, and of their strength in arms; and a new anger possessed his heart, and he turned to thoughts of further evil.

§136 Thus ended the Siege of Angband; and the foes of Morgoth were scattered and sundered one from another. The Dark-elves fled south and forsook the northern war. Many were received into Doriath, and the kingdom and strength of Thingol grew greater in that time; for the power of the queen Melian was woven about his borders and evil could not yet enter that hidden realm. Others took refuge in the fortresses by the sea, or in Nargothrond; but most fled the land and hid in Ossiriand, or passing the mountains wandered homeless in the wild. And rumour of the war and the breaking of the siege reached the ears of Men in Middle-earth.

§137 The sons of Finrod bore most heavily the brunt of the assault, and Angrod and Egnor were slain; and Bregolas son of Bëor, who was lord of that house of Men after his father's death, was slain beside them. In that battle King Inglor Felagund was cut off from his folk and surrounded by the Orcs, and he would have been slain or taken, but Barahir son of Bëor came up with his men and rescued him, and made a wall of spears about him; and they cut their way out of the battle with great loss. Thus Felagund escaped and went south to Nargothrond, his deep fortress prepared against the evil day; but he swore an oath of abiding friendship and aid in every need unto Barahir and all his kin and seed, and in token of his vow he gave to Barahir his ring.

§138 Barahir was now by right lord of the remnant of the folk of Bëor; but most of these fled now from Dorthonion and took refuge among the people of Hador in the fastness of Hithlum. But Barahir would not flee, and remained contesting the land foot by foot with the servants of Morgoth. But Morgoth pursued his people to the death, until few remained; and he took all the forest and the highland of Dorthonion, save the highest and inmost region, and turned it little by little to a place of such dread and lurking evil that even the Orcs would not enter it unless need drove them. Therefore it was after called by the Gnomes Taur-na-Fuin, which is Mirkwood, and Deldúwath, Deadly Nightshade; for the trees that grew there after the burning were black and grim, and their roots were tangled, groping in the dark like claws; and those who strayed among them became lost and blind, and were strangled or pursued to madness by phantoms of terror.

§139   At length only twelve men remained to Barahir: Beren his son, and Baragund and Belegund, sons of Bregolas, his nephews, and nine faithful servants of his house whose names are yet remembered by the Gnomes: Radhruin and Dairuin they were, Dagnir and Ragnor, Gildor and Gorlim the unhappy, Arthod and Urthel, and Hathaldir the young. Outlaws they became, a desperate band that could not escape and would not yield; for their dwellings were destroyed, and their wives and children captured or slain, save only Morwen Eledhwen daughter of Baragund and Rian daughter of Belegund. For the wives of the sons of Bregolas were of Hithlum, and were sojourning there among their kinsfolk when the flame of war broke forth. But from Hithlum there came now neither news nor help, and Barahir and his men were hunted like wild beasts, and Morgoth sent many wolves against them; and they retreated to the barren highland above the forest, and wandered among the tarns and rocky moors of that region, furthest from the spies and spells of Morgoth. Their bed was the heather and their roof the cloudy sky.

§140   So great was the onslaught of Morgoth that Fingolfin and Fingon could not come to the succour of Felagund and his brethren; and the hosts of Hithlum were driven back with great loss to the fortresses of Eredwithion, and these they hardly defended against the Orcs. Hador the golden-haired, prince of Men, fell in battle before the walls defending the rearguard of his lord Fingolfin, being then sixty and six years of age, and with him fell Gundor his younger son; and they were mourned by the Elves. But Gumlin took the lordship of his father. And because of the strength and height of the Shadowy Mountains, which withstood the torrent of fire, and by the valour of the Elves and Men of the North, which neither Orc nor Balrog could yet overcome, Hithlum remained yet unconquered, a threat upon the flank of Morgoth's attack. But Fingolfin was sundered by a sea of foes from his kinsmen.

§141   For the war had gone ill with the sons of Fëanor, and well nigh all the east marches were taken by assault. The pass of Aglon was forced, though with great cost to Morgoth; and Celegorn and Curufin being defeated fled south and west by the marches of Doriath and came at last to Nargothrond, and sought harbour with their friend Orodreth. Thus it came to pass that the people of Celegorn swelled the strength of Felagund, but it would have been better, as after was seen, if they had remained in the East among their own kin. Maidros the chief of Fëanor's sons did deeds of surpassing valour, and the Orcs could not endure the light of his face; for since his torment upon Thangorodrim his spirit burned like a white fire within, and he was as one that returneth from the dead, keen and terrible; and they fled before him. Thus his citadel upon the hill of Himring could not at that time be taken, and many of the most valiant that remained, both of the folk of Dorthonion and of the east marches rallied there to Maidros; and for a while he closed once more the pass of Aglon, so that the Orcs could not enter Beleriand by that road.

§142  But they overwhelmed the riders of the folk of Fëanor upon Lothland, for Glómund came thither, and passed through Maglor's Gap, and destroyed all the land between the arms of Gelion. And the Orcs took the fortress upon the west slopes of Mount Rerir, and ravaged all Thargelion, the land of Cranthir; and they defiled Lake Helevorn. Thence they passed over Gelion with fire and terror and came far into East Beleriand. Maglor joined Maidros upon Himring; but Cranthir fled and joined the remnant of his people to the scattered folk of the hunters, Damrod and Díriel, and they retreated and passed Rhamdal in the South. Upon Amon Ereb they maintained a watch and some strength of war, and they had aid of the Green-elves; and the Orcs came not yet into Ossiriand or the wild of South Beleriand.

§143  For nearly two years the Gnomes still defended the west pass about the sources of Sirion, for the power of Ulmo was in that water, and Glómund would not yet adventure that way, for the time of his full strength was not come; and Minnastirith withstood the Orcs. But at length after the fall of Fingolfin, which is told hereafter, Sauron came against Orodreth, the warden of the tower, with a host of Balrogs. Sauron was the chief servant of the evil Vala, whom he had suborned to his service in Valinor from among the people of the Gods. He was become a wizard of dreadful power, master of necromancy, foul in wisdom, cruel in strength, mis-shaping what he touched, twisting what he ruled, lord of werewolves: his dominion was torment. He took Minnastirith by assault, the tower of Inglor upon the isle of Sirion, for a dark cloud of fear fell upon those that defended it; and he made it a stronghold of evil, and a menace;* for no living creature could pass through that vale that he did not espy from the tower where he sat. And Morgoth held now also the western pass and his terror filled the fields and woods of Beleriand.

§144   *The death of Fingolfin.* It came to pass that news came to Hithlum that Dorthonion was lost and the sons of Finrod overthrown, and that the sons of Fëanor were driven from their lands. Then Fingolfin saw that the ruin of the Gnomes was at hand, and he was filled with wrath and despair, and a madness came upon him. And he rode alone to the gates of Angband, and he sounded his horn and smote upon the brazen gates and challenged Morgoth to come forth to single combat. And Morgoth came. That was the last time in these wars that he passed the doors of his stronghold, and it is said that he took not the challenge willingly; for though his might is greatest of all things in this world, alone of the Valar he knows fear. But he could not now deny the challenge before the face of his captains; for the rocks rang with the shrill music of the silver horn of Fingolfin and his voice came keen and clear down into the depths of Angband; and Fingolfin named Morgoth craven, and lord of slaves. Therefore Morgoth came, climbing slowly from his subterranean throne, and the rumour of his feet was like thunder underground. And he issued forth clad in black armour; and he stood before the king like a tower, iron-crowned, and his vast shield, sable unblazoned, cast a shadow over him like a storm cloud. But Fingolfin gleamed beneath it like a star; for his mail was overlaid with silver, and his blue shield was set with crystals; and he drew his sword Ringil, and it glittered like ice, cold and grey and deadly.

§145   Then Morgoth hurled aloft as a mace Grond, the hammer of the Underworld, and swung it down like a bolt of thunder. But Fingolfin sprang aside, and Grond rent a mighty pit in the earth, whence smoke and fire darted. Many times Morgoth essayed to smite him, and each time Fingolfin leaped away, as a lightning shoots from under a dark cloud; and he wounded Morgoth with seven wounds, and seven times Morgoth gave a cry of anguish, whereat the rocks shivered, and the hosts of Angband fell upon their faces in dismay.

*\*Footnote to the text:* And it became called Tol-na-Gaurhoth, the Isle of Werewolves.

§146   But at last the king grew weary, and Morgoth bore down his shield upon him. Thrice he was crushed to his knees, and thrice arose again and bore up his broken shield and stricken helm. But the earth was all rent and pitted about him, and he stumbled and fell backward before the feet of Morgoth; and Morgoth set his left foot upon his neck, and the weight of it was like a fallen hill. Yet with his last and desperate stroke Fingolfin hewed the foot with Ringil, and the blood gushed forth black and smoking and filled the pits of Grond.

§147   Thus died Fingolfin, High-king of the Gnomes, most proud and valiant of the Elven-kings of old. The Orcs make no boast of that duel at the gate; neither do the Elves sing of it, for sorrow; but the tale of it is remembered, for Thorondor, king of eagles, brought the tidings to Gondolin, and to Hithlum. For Morgoth took the body of the Elven-king and broke it, and would hew it asunder and cast it to his wolves; but Thorondor came hasting from his eyrie among the peaks of Gochressiel, and he stooped upon Morgoth, and smote his golden beak into his face. The rushing of his wings was like the noise of the winds of Manwë, and he seized the body in his mighty talons, and soaring suddenly above the darts of the Orcs he bore the Elven-king away. And he laid him upon a mountain-top that looked from the North upon the hidden valley of Gondolin; and Turgon coming built a high cairn over him. Neither Orc nor Balrog dared ever after to pass over the mount of Fingolfin or draw nigh his tomb, until the doom of Gondolin was come and treachery was born among his kin. Morgoth goes ever halt of one foot since that day, and the pain of his wounds cannot be healed; and in his face is the scar that Thorondor made.

§148   There was lamentation in Hithlum when the fall of Fingolfin became known; but Fingon took the kingship of the Noldor, and he maintained still his realm behind the Shadowy Mountains in the North. But beyond Hithlum Morgoth pursued his foes relentlessly, and he searched out their hiding-places and took their strongholds one by one. And the Orcs growing ever bolder wandered at will far and wide, coming down Sirion in the West and Celon in the East, and they encompassed Doriath; and they harried the lands, so that beast and bird fled before them, and silence and desolation spread steadily from the North. Great numbers of the Gnomes, and of the Dark-elves, they took captive and led to Angband, and made thralls, forcing them to use their skill and knowledge in the service of Morgoth. They laboured without rest in his mines and forges, and torment was their wage.

§149   Yet Morgoth sent also his spies and emissaries among the Dark-elves and the thrall-Gnomes, and among the free; and they were clad in false forms and deceit was in their speech, and they made lying promises of reward, and with cunning words sought to arouse fear and jealously among the peoples, accusing their kings and chieftains of greed, and of treachery one to another. And because of the curse of the kin-slaying at Alqualondë, these lies were often believed; and indeed as the times darkened they had a measure of truth, for the hearts and minds of the Elves of Beleriand became clouded with despair and fear. And most the Gnomes feared the treachery of their own kin, who had been thralls in Angband; for Morgoth used some of these for his evil purposes, and feigning to give them liberty sent them abroad, but their wills were chained to his, and strayed only to come back to him again. Therefore if any of the captives escaped in truth, and returned to their own people, they had little welcome, and wandered alone outlawed and desperate.

§150   *Of the Swarthy Men.*  To Men Morgoth feigned pity, if any would hearken to his messages, saying that their woes came only of their servitude to the rebel Gnomes, but at the hands of the rightful lord of earth they would get honour and a just reward of valour, if they would leave rebellion. But of the Three Houses few men would give ear to him, not even were they brought to the torment of Angband. Therefore he pursued them with hatred, but he sent his messengers east over the mountains. And it is said that at this time the Swarthy Men came first into Beleriand; and some were already secretly under the dominion of Morgoth, and came at his call; but not all, for the rumour of Beleriand, of its lands and waters, of its wars and riches, went now far and wide, and the wandering feet of Men were ever set westward in those days. And Morgoth was glad of their coming, for he thought they would prove more pliable to his service, and that through them he might yet work great injury to the Elves.

§151   Now the Easterlings or Rómenildi, as the Elves named these newcomers, were short and broad, long and strong in the arm; their hair was black, and grew much also upon their face and breast; their skins were swart or sallow, and their eyes brown; yet their countenances were for the most part not uncomely, though some were grim and fierce. Their houses and tribes were many, and some had greater liking for the Dwarfs of the mountains than for the Elves. But the sons of Fëanor, seeing the weakness of the

Noldor, and the growing power of the armies of Morgoth, made alliances with these men, and gave their friendship to the greatest of their chieftains, Bór and Ulfang. And Morgoth was well content; for this was as he had designed. The sons of Bór were Borlas and Boromir and Borthandos; and they followed Maidros and Maglor, and cheated the hope of Morgoth, and were faithful. The sons of Ulfang the Black were Ulfast and Ulwarth and Uldor the Accursed; and they followed Cranthir and swore allegiance to him, and proved faithless.

§152   There was small love between the Three Houses and the Swarthy Men; and they met seldom. For the newcomers abode long in East Beleriand; but the people of Hador were shut in Hithlum, and Bëor's house was well nigh destroyed. Yet Haleth and his men remained still free; for they had been at first untouched by the northern war, since they dwelt to the southward in the woods by Sirion. There now there was war between them and the invading Orcs; for they were stout-hearted men and would not lightly forsake the woods they loved. And amid the tale of defeats of this time their deeds are remembered with honour: for after the taking of Minnastirith the Orcs came through the western pass, and would maybe have ravaged even unto the mouths of Sirion; but Haleth sent swift word to Thingol, being friendly with many of the Elves that guarded the borders of Doriath. And Thingol sent Beleg the bowman, chief of his march-wardens, to his aid with many archers; and Haleth and Beleg took an Orc-legion at unawares in the forest, and destroyed it; and the advance of the power of Morgoth southward down the course of Sirion was stayed. Thus the folk of Haleth dwelt yet for many years in watchful peace in the forest of Brethil; and behind their guard the kingdom of Nargothrond had respite and mustered anew its strength.

§153   It is said that Húrin son of Gumlin, son of Hador, of Hithlum was with Haleth in that battle, and he was then seventeen years of age; and this was his first deed of arms, but not his last. For Húrin son of Gumlin was fostered for a while in boyhood by Haleth, according to the custom of Men and Elves in that time. And it is recorded that in the autumn of the year of Sudden Fire Haleth took Húrin, then newcome from his father's house, and they went hunting northward up the vale of Sirion; and by chance or the will of Ulmo they came upon the secret entrance to the hidden valley of Tumladin, where Gondolin was built. But they were taken by the guards, and brought before Turgon; and they

looked upon the forbidden city, whereof none of those outside yet
knew aught, save Thorondor king of eagles. Turgon welcomed
them; for messages and dreams had come to him up Sirion from
the sea, from Ulmo, Lord of Waters, warning him of woe to come
and foretelling that the aid of mortal men would be necessary, if he
would save any of the Gnomes from their doom. But Turgon
deemed that Gondolin was strong, and the time not ripe for its
revealing; and he would not suffer the men to depart. It is said that
he had great liking for the boy Húrin, and love was joined to
policy; for he desired to keep Húrin at his side in Gondolin. But
tidings came of the great battle, and the need of Gnomes and Men;
and Haleth and Húrin besought Turgon for leave to go to the aid
of their own folk. Turgon then granted their prayer, but they
swore deep oaths to him, and never revealed his secret; and such
of the counsels of Turgon as Húrin had learned he kept hidden in
his heart.

§154   Turgon would not as yet suffer any of his own folk to
issue forth to war, and Haleth and Húrin departed from Gondolin
alone. But Turgon, rightly deeming that the breaking of the Siege
of Angband was the beginning of the downfall of the Noldor,
unless aid should come, sent secret messengers to the mouths of
Sirion, and to the Isle of Balar. There they built ships, and many
set sail thence, seeking for Valinor, to ask for help and pardon.
And they besought the birds of the sea to guide them. But the seas
were wild and wide, and shadow and enchantment lay upon them,
and Valinor was hidden. Therefore none of the messengers of
Gondolin came ever unto the West at that time; and many were
lost and few returned; but the doom of Gondolin drew nearer.

§155   Rumour came to Morgoth of these things, and he was
unquiet amid his victories; and he desired greatly to learn tidings
of Felagund and Turgon. For they had vanished out of knowledge, and yet were not dead; and he feared what they might yet
accomplish against him. Of Nargothrond he knew indeed the
name, but neither its place nor its strength; but of Gondolin he
knew naught, and the thought of Turgon troubled him the more.
Therefore he sent forth ever more spies into Beleriand; but he
recalled the main hosts of his Orcs and mustered again his forces.
And it is said that he was dismayed to find how great had been
their loss, perceiving that he could not yet make a final and
victorious battle, until he had gathered new strength. Thus
Beleriand in the South had a semblance of peace again for a few
brief years; but the forges of Angband were full of labour.

§156   *Siege of Eithel Sirion and Fall of Gumlin.* Nor did the assault upon the northern strongholds cease. Himring Morgoth besieged so close that no help might come from Maidros, and he threw suddenly a great force against Hithlum. The Orcs won many of the passes, and some came even into Mithrim; but Fingon drove them in the end with heavy slaughter from the land, and pursued them far across the sands of Fauglith. Yet sorrow marred his victory, for Gumlin son of Hador was slain by an arrow in the siege of the fortress of Fingon at Eithel Sirion. Húrin his son was then new-come to manhood, but he was great in strength both of mind and body; and he ruled now the house of Hador and served Fingon.* And in this time also the outlaws of Dorthonion were destroyed, and Beren son of Barahir alone escaping came hardly into Doriath.

### Commentary on Chapter 11

§132   This paragraph is developed from the first part of annal 222 in AB 2 (there is nothing of it in the earlier sources).

§133   'The sons of the sons of the Fathers of Men' are the second generation after Bëor, Hador, and Haleth (Baragund, Belegund, Beren; Húrin, Huor; Handir), whose birthdates, according to the revised chronology in AB 2, fall between 424 (Baragund) and 444 (Huor).

§138   The application of *Mirkwood* to Taur-na-Fuin is interesting. Cf. the reverse case in *Unfinished Tales*, p. 281, where (long after) in a note to *The Disaster of the Gladden Fields* my father wrote: 'the shadow of Sauron spread through Greenwood the Great, and changed its name from Eryn Galen to Taur-nu-Fuin (translated Mirkwood).'

§139   The only names of the men of Barahir's band given in AB 2 (annal 257), other than his son and nephews, are Gorlim, Radros (> Radruin), Dagnir, and Gildor. – On the story that Morwen and Rian were of Hithlum, and were staying there at the time of the Battle of Sudden Fire, see AB 2 annal 257 and commentary.

§140   According to the revised dating, Hador was born in 390, and he died with Gundor in 456. As AB 2 was originally written, Gundor was the elder son, but he became the younger (note 20), born in 419 'beneath the shadows of Eredlindon' (i.e. before Hador crossed the mountains into Beleriand).

§141   *Celegorn*, not *Celegorm*, was here the form first written (see commentary on §41). – It is said in QS §117 that after the founding of

*Footnote to the text:* For he returned unto his own folk after the victory in the woods of Brethil, while the ways north to Hithlum were passable because of the defeat of the Orcs at that time.

Nargothrond Inglor Felagund committed the tower of Minnastirith to Orodreth; and later in the present chapter (§143) it is recounted how Sauron came against Orodreth and took the tower by assault (the fate of the defenders is not there mentioned). The statement here that Celegorn and Curufin 'sought harbour with their friend Orodreth' – rather than 'sought harbour with Felagund' – is found also in an emendation to AB 2 (note 25); the implication is that Orodreth reached Nargothrond before them, and that their friendship with him was the motive for their going to Nargothrond. This friendship survived the change of Orodreth's lordship from the east of Dorthonion ('nighest to the sons of Fëanor', AB 2 annal 52 as originally written) to the wardenship of the tower on Tol Sirion. The sentence 'the people of Celegorn swelled the strength of Felagund, but it would have been better . . . if they had remained in the East among their own kin' goes back to Q (IV. 106), though in Q Celegorm and Curufin came to Nargothrond together with Orodreth.

§142  The fortress on the west slopes of Mount Rerir is here first mentioned.

§143  On the shifting representation of the growth of the great Dragon to his full power and terror see IV. 181–2, 317–18. The statement in AB 2 annal 255 that Glómund was 'in his full might' at the Battle of Sudden Fire was not taken up in QS §135, and in the present passage 'the time of his full strength was not come'. In *The Silmarillion* (p. 151) Glaurung was again 'in his full might' at the time of the battle: this was taken from the final version of the *Annals* (the *Grey Annals*).

This is the first occurrence of the name *Sauron* in the 'Silmarillion' tradition; but its actual first occurrence (in a text as first written) is probably either in *The Lost Road* or in the second version of *The Fall of Númenor* (see the commentary on FN II §5). The statement that Morgoth suborned Sauron *in Valinor* from among the people of the Gods' is notable. The implication must be that at this period my father conceived Sauron to have followed Morgoth when he fled to Middle-earth accompanied by Ungoliantë.

With the words 'a host of Balrogs' cf. the commentary on §89.

§§144–7  The account of the death of Fingolfin in QS was largely based on the *Lay of Leithian* Canto XII (see III. 293) – which in turn had followed the prose version in Q (IV. 176–8).

§147  In Q §9 (IV. 106) 'The Orcs sing of that duel at the gates', and in the *Lay of Leithian* (lines 3584–5) 'Yet Orcs would after laughing tell / of the duel at the gates of hell.'

The name *Thorondor* (for *Thorndor*) appears now in this form as first written (see commentary on §§96–7).

*Gochressiel*: this name (on which see the *Etymologies*, stem KHARÁS) was afterwards changed to *Crisaegrim*. In Q §15 Thorndor dwelt on Thangorodrim until the Battle of Unnumbered Tears, when he

removed his eyries 'to the northward heights of the Encircling Moun-
tains', and kept watch there 'sitting upon the cairn of King Fingolfin'.
This goes back to S (§15; see IV. 66). Afterwards the *Crissaegrim*
'abode of eagles' were expressly stated to be the peaks to the south of
Gondolin, and the name was so marked in on the second Map; but
*Gochressiel* in QS need not have had this narrower significance.

In Q §9 it was Thorndor who 'set' Fingolfin's cairn on the mountain-
top, just as in the *Lay of Leithian* (lines 3626-7) 'in mounded cairn the
mighty dead / he laid upon the mountain's head'; but in QS, with the
changed story of the foundation of Gondolin, it is Turgon who comes
up from the city in the valley beneath and builds his father's tomb.

§150  The earlier sources have nothing of the content of this paragraph,
in which first appears the important development that some of the
Swarthy Men were already under Morgoth's dominion before they
entered Beleriand (see IV. 179-80).

§151  In the description of the Swarthy Men, or *Rómenildi* ('Eastern
Men', Easterlings) as they are called here, my father was following
AB 2 annal 263 (463), the year of their first coming into East
Beleriand. The form *Bór* was changed from *Bor* subsequent to the
writing of the manuscript, as in AB 2 (note 33); but *Ulfang* and
*Ulwarth* (appearing only by emendation in AB 2) are original.

§152  There is here the explicit assertion that the house of Bëor was
'well nigh destroyed'; earlier in this chapter (§138) it was said that after
the Battle of Sudden Fire 'Barahir was now by right lord of the
remnant of the folk of Bëor; but most of these fled from Dorthonion
and took refuge among the people of Hador in the fastness of Hithlum.'

The passage concerning the people of Haleth and the destruction of
the Orcs in Brethil by Haleth and Beleg with archers out of Doriath is
derived from annal 258 in AB 2, and much expanded.

§153  The story of Húrin's sojourn in Gondolin is found in AB 2 (annal
256) in very much the same form as it is told here. The statement in the
opening sentence of the paragraph that Haleth and Húrin (then
seventeen years old) were 'in that battle' refers to the destruction of the
Orcs in Brethil in the year 458; Húrin was born in 441. See note 32 to
AB 2.

§154  The account of the vain attempt of Turgon to send messengers
over the ocean to Valinor is developed from that in annal 256 in AB 2.

§156  The attack on Hithlum took place in the year 462, the year in
which Beren fled from Dorthonion. – The name *Fauglith* was written
*Dor-na-Fauglith*, but changed at the time of writing.

With the footnote (contemporary with the writing of the
manuscript) cf. the addition to AB 2 annal 258 (note 32): 'Húrin
of Hithlum was with Haleth; but he departed afterward since the
victory [in Brethil] had made the journey possible, and returned to
his own folk.'

## 12–15  OF BEREN AND TINÚVIEL

The *Quenta Silmarillion* came to an end not abruptly but raggedly. The textual history now becomes very complex, but since it bears strongly on the question of how matters stood when *The Lord of the Rings* was begun I give here an account of it. Since, as I believe, the story of what happened, and when, can be put together with a high degree of probability, I set it out on the basis of my reconstruction and in the order of events that I deduce, since this will be briefer and clearer than to give all the evidences first and only then to draw conclusions.

I have noticed earlier (p. 199) that there is now no trace of any rough drafts underlying the polished and beautiful QS manuscript (though they must have existed) until the tale of Beren and Lúthien is reached; but at this point they appear abundantly. The first of them is a very rough manuscript which I shall call 'QS(A)', or simply 'A'; this represents, I feel sure, the first essay at a prose version of the tale since the original *Tale of Tinúviel*, a prose 'saga' to be told on a far more ample scale than the brief account in Q (§10). The treachery of Gorlim, the surprising of Barahir's lair on Dorthonion, and Beren's recapture of the ring from the Orcs, are fully told; and in some two and a half thousand words this text only reaches the words of Thingol's people when the woods of Doriath fell silent (the *Lay of Leithian* lines 861–2).

On the basis of A (or perhaps of a further draft version now lost) my father then continued QS in fine script through chapter 12 and into 13, giving a general heading *Of Beren and Tinúviel* to both but entitling the individual chapters *Of the Meeting of Beren and Lúthien Tinúviel* and *The Quest of the Silmaril*. Here too the story was told very fully, but less so than in the rough draft A; for the story of Gorlim and the betrayal of Barahir is dealt with in less than a page, and Dairon is entirely excluded from the narrative. At the point where Inglor Felagund gave the crown of Nargothrond to Orodreth, the text ends. It is convenient to call this – just for the purpose of this discussion – 'QS I'.

QS I ends here because my father saw that it was going to be too long, overbalancing the whole work. He had taken more than 4000 words to reach the departure of Beren and Felagund from Nargothrond – and this did not include the story of Lúthien's imprisonment in the tree-house and her escape from it, which in the Lay precedes the account of Beren in Nargothrond. (That QS I was originally simply the continuation of QS is obvious from the fact that in the course of it there is the new chapter-heading numbered 13.) He therefore set it aside, and began anew on a less ample version, though still by no means severely compressed (this version reaches the departure of Beren and Felagund from Nargothrond in some 1800 words); but he retained the first page of QS I, which he considered to be sufficiently 'compressed'. This page takes the story to the words [*Beren*] *swore upon it an oath of vengeance* (*The Silmarillion* p. 163). For this reason QS I, as it now stands, has no beginning, but takes up at the head of the second page with the words *First therefore he pursued the Orcs that had slain his father*.

As a basis for the projected 'short' version of the tale, my father now made a draft version of the whole. This manuscript, 'QS(B)' or 'B', starts out clearly enough but rapidly declines into a scrawl. It begins, on page 1, with the words *First therefore he pursued the Orcs that had slain his father* – because the first page of QS I, extending precisely to this point, was retained for the new version.

From text B was derived the 'short' form of the story ('QS II') in the QS manuscript, written in the same fine script. This retains the chapter division 12/13 at the same point as it had been made in QS I, where Beren left Doriath; chapter 13 ends with the burial of Felagund on Tol Sirion; and chapter 14 is entitled *The Quest of the Silmaril 2*. Near the end of this chapter the script changes, slightly but noticeably, from one page to the next. The first script, extraordinarily uniform right through the manuscript from the beginning, ends at the foot of page 91 with the words *but the jewel suffered his touch* (*The Silmarillion* p. 181), and the new begins at the head of page 92 with *and hurt him not*, continuing to the end of chapter 14 a few lines down page 93 at *for the power of the Silmaril was hidden within him*. I feel certain that it was at the foot of page 91 that my father broke off when the QS manuscript went to Allen and Unwin on 15 November 1937.

But he was reluctant to set his work (the development of the rough text B into the finished narrative QS II) suddenly aside. He therefore at once began on an intermediate manuscript, 'QS(C)' or 'C', in a less fine and time-consuming form (intending to copy this into the QS manuscript when it came back to him). This I deduce from the fact that the first page of text C is numbered 92 and begins with the words *and hurt him not*, just as does the portion of QS II in the changed script.

When QS came back from the publishers on 16 December 1937 my father began immediately (see III. 366) on 'a new story about Hobbits', and I do not think that after that time he extended the narrative of the *Quenta Silmarillion* any further. But while the QS manuscript was away, he had extended the text C for a good distance, completing the story of Beren and Lúthien through a final chapter (15) entitled *The Quest of the Silmaril 3: The Wolf-hunt of Carcharoth*, writing a further chapter (16) *Of the Fourth Battle: Nirnaith Arnediad*, and commencing 17 *Of Túrin the Hapless*. By this stage the manuscript had as usual degenerated into a scrawl, and he left it at Túrin's putting on the Dragon-helm and becoming the companion of Beleg on the north marches of Doriath.

Still (if I am right) before the return of the QS manuscript, however, he followed text C in this leap-frogging fashion with a further and clearer manuscript, 'QS(D)' or 'D', which took up from C in the middle of chapter 16 (*Of the Fourth Battle*) at the point where it is told that Maidros was delayed by the machinations of Uldor the Accursed (*The Silmarillion* p. 190), and continued somewhat further into chapter 17 (here called *Of Túrin Turamarth or Túrin the Hapless*), as far as the words (referring to Túrin's outlaw band) *and their hands were turned against all who came in their path, Elves, Men, or Orcs* (*The Silmarillion* p. 200). Here the *Quenta Silmarillion* comes to a stop; and it may well be that these last words were written on the 16th of December 1937, and *When Bilbo, son of Bungo of the family of Baggins, prepared to celebrate his seventieth birthday* on the following day.*

When the short passage in changed script at the end of chapter 14 in the QS manuscript (see p. 293) was copied in from text C cannot be determined; my father may have put it in when the manuscript came back to him. But with the beginning of chapter 15 (*The Wolf-hunt of Carcharoth*) the writing in the manuscript changes again and strikingly, to a heavier, more ornate form with a thicker nib; this third script completes the chapter and the story of Beren and Lúthien, and this is effectively the conclusion of the manuscript (a small portion was added later in yet a fourth script).

In fact, chapter 15 was added to the QS manuscript long afterwards, in the time following the completion of *The Lord of the Rings*. I base this assertion on various evidences; in the first place on the script itself, which has close affinity with that of manuscripts undoubtedly belonging to the later time. Further, the draft text C, begun when the QS manuscript went to the publishers, received important additions and alterations which can be dated, for at the end of chapter 15 in C my father noted: 'revised so far, 10 May 1951'. Among these 1951 revisions is the phrase (*The Silmarillion* p. 187) 'the Two Kindreds that were made by Ilúvatar to dwell *in Arda, the Kingdom of Earth amid the innumerable stars.*' This phrase is found also in the later *Ainulindalë*, where a cosmology decisively different from that of the *Ambarkanta* had entered; moreover a note of my father's gives a brief list of 'Alterations in last revision 1951', which includes *Arda* ('Elvish name of Earth = our world'). On this list see p. 338. It was the text of C *with these revisions* that was copied into the QS manuscript; and thus he at last fulfilled (though only to this point) his intention of fourteen years before.

The story can be summarised thus:

(1) A rough draft 'A', in which the telling of the tale of Beren and Lúthien was very amply conceived, was soon abandoned.

(2) The QS-manuscript version of the tale was begun, again in a very full form but less so than in A, and was in turn abandoned quite early in the tale ('QS I').

(3) A rough draft 'B' for the whole story of Beren and Lúthien was completed, and this was the basis for:

---

*As will be seen subsequently (pp. 323–4) a rewriting of the end of the 'Silmarillion' narrative in Q also belongs to this time, and it is possible, though I think it less likely, that this was the last work that my father did before beginning 'the new story about Hobbits'.

(4) A second, more compressed version to stand in the QS manuscript ('QS II'); this was interrupted towards the end of the tale when the manuscript went to the publishers.

(5) An intermediate text 'C', taking up from this point, was continued as a substitute while the QS manuscript was gone, and this completed the story of Beren and Lúthien, extended through the chapter on the Battle of Unnumbered Tears, and went some way into the story of Túrin.

(6) When C became very rough, it was taken over by a text 'D', which beginning in the course of the chapter on the Battle of Unnumbered Tears extended somewhat further into the story of Túrin; this was abandoned when the QS manuscript returned in December 1937.

(7) In 1951 the conclusion of the tale of Beren and Lúthien (chapter 15) was at last added to the QS manuscript.

On a covering page to the 'fuller' version QS I my father wrote: *Fragment of a fuller form of the Geste of Beren and Lúthien told as a separate tale;* and in a letter of November 1949 he said:

> The original intention was to tell certain of the included Tales at greater length, whether within the Chronicle [i.e. the *Quenta Silmarillion*], or as additions. A specimen of what was intended will be seen in the Tale of Lúthien . . .

But, as I have shown, the 'fragment of a fuller form' only became so when it had been rejected as unsuitable in its scale to stand as the version of the story in QS. This is not to say, however, that my father never did really intend to tell the tale as a long prose 'saga'; on the contrary, he greatly wished to. The abandoned draft A and the abandoned QS I are testimony to his reluctance to compress: the story kept overflowing the bounds. When at the end of 1937 he had finally completed a prose version, he must still have felt that even if one day he could get 'The Silmarillion' published, the story would still not be told as he wished to tell it. Thus at the time when he turned again to the *Lay of Leithian* (see III. 330), *The Lord of the Rings* being finished but its publication very doubtful, he embarked also once more on a prose 'saga' of Beren and Lúthien. This is a substantial text, though the story goes no further than the betrayal by Dairon to Thingol of Beren's presence in Doriath, and it is so closely based on the rewritten form of the Lay as to read in places almost as a prose paraphrase of the verse. It was written on the verso pages of the text AB 2 of the *Annals of Beleriand*, and was not known to me when *The Silmarillion* was prepared for publication.

To present these texts would take many pages and involve a great deal of pure repetition in relation to the published version, and I restrict myself here therefore to remarking particular features and to indicating the genesis of chapter 19 in *The Silmarillion*. Essentially, the published text was based on the 'fuller' form, QS I, so far as it goes, and then follows the 'shorter', complete form, QS II. The story was also told, briefly, in the final version of the *Annals of Beleriand*, the *Grey Annals*, and some passages in the published version are derived from that source.

I have mentioned above that the opening page of QS I, the commencement of chapter 12, was retained as the opening of QS II, and I give here the text of that page, for it was much modified and expanded in the published work (pp. 162–3).

Among the tales of sorrow and ruin that come down to us from the darkness of those days there are yet some that are fair in memory, in which amid weeping there is a sound of music, and amid the tears joy, and under the shadow of death light that endureth. And of these histories most fair still in the ears of the Elves is the tale of Beren and Lúthien; for it is sad and joyous, and touches upon mysteries, and it is not ended.*

Of their lives was made the *Lay of Leithian*, Release from Bondage, which is the longest save one of the songs of the Noldor concerning the world of old; but here the tale must be told in fewer words and without song. When [Bëor >] Bregolas was slain, as has been recounted, Barahir his [son >] brother saved King Felagund, and received his ring in token of never-failing friendship. But Barahir would not forsake Dorthonion, and there Morgoth pursued him to the death. At last there remained to him only twelve companions, Beren his son, and the sons of Bregolas, and nine other men. Of these Gorlim son of Angrim was one, a man of valour. But Gorlim was caught by the guile of Sauron the wizard, as the lay tells, and Morgoth wrung from him knowledge of the hiding-place of Barahir; but Gorlim he rewarded with death. Thus Morgoth drew his net about Barahir, and he was taken by surprise and slain with all his companions, save one. For by fortune Beren was not with them at that time, but was hunting alone in the woods, as often was his custom, for thus he gained news of the movement of their foes. But Beren was warned by a vision of Gorlim the unhappy that appeared to him in sleep, and he returned in haste, and yet too late. For his father was already slain, and the carrion-birds arose from the ground as Beren drew near, and sat in the alder-trees, and croaked in mockery. For there was a high tarn among the moors, and beside it Barahir had made his lair.

---

*For the meaning of the words 'and it is not ended' (which should not have been omitted in *The Silmarillion*) see p. 304: the thought underlying the last sentence of the tale is much more explicit in the draft text B.

There Beren buried his father's bones, and raised a cairn of boulders over him, and swore upon it an oath of vengeance.

Gorlim's father Angrim now appears. The words first written 'When Bëor was slain . . . Barahir his son saved King Felagund' are puzzling. The original draft manuscript A had here likewise 'When Bëor and Bregolas were slain . . .' It was said in Q §9 that 'Bëor lived till death with Felagund', but in §10 that Bëor was slain in the Battle of Sudden Fire; this I took to be a (surprising) inconsistency within Q (IV. 179). In QS §131 (and in AB 2, annal 250) Bëor died of old age, five years before the Battle of Sudden Fire, and in his death 'the Elves saw for the first time the death of weariness, and they grieved for the short span allotted to mankind'; thus the inconsistency appears again and still more surprisingly in this version. But the corrections to QS here were made, almost certainly, at the time of composition.

It is said here that 'Gorlim was caught by the guile of Sauron the wizard, as the lay tells, and Morgoth wrung from him knowledge of the hiding-place of Barahir.' In the much fuller draft A the story was still almost exactly as in the *Lay of Leithian* (III. 162-4): Gorlim was all but caught as he looked through the window of the house at the figure of his wife Eilinel, he returned to his companions but said nothing, and finally, with a far more deliberate treachery than in the later story, yielded himself to the servants of Morgoth, who took him to Angband. A minor development is that whereas in the Lay the house in which he thought he saw Eilinel was not his own, it is now told that he went often to his own deserted home, and Morgoth's spies knew this (cf. the *Lay of Leithian Recommenced*, III. 337). More important, in A Morgoth 'revealed to Gorlim that he had seen but a phantom devised by the wizardry of Sauron to entrap him', which again advances the story to that of the rewritten Lay, where the phantom was expressly made by Sauron (III. 339, and see III. 348). I see no reason to think that the brief sentence which is all that is told of Gorlim in the QS version reflects a story different in any way from that in A. Years later, when as mentioned above (p. 295) my father once more attempted a full prose version of the story, he went back to A and emended it in preparation for this new work. The story now entered that Gorlim was captured on the first occasion that he saw the image of Eilinel through the window; but he was still taken to Angband, and addressed by Morgoth himself. This stage is represented in the first version of the rewritten Lay at this point (see III. 348). Finally, pencilled alterations to A changed Angband to Sauron's camp, and Morgoth to Sauron, and so reached the final story, as in the second version of the rewritten Lay.

When I composed the text of the opening of chapter 19 in *The Silmarillion* I did not at all foresee the possibility of the publication of the *Lay of Leithian*, and I wished to include the story of Gorlim, which is virtually excluded from QS. The second paragraph of the chapter, from

'Now the forest of Dorthonion rose southward into mountainous moors', was taken from the *Grey Annals*; and for the story of Gorlim that follows I used the text of A – in its final form, as just described.

In the story of Beren's solitary life on Dorthonion, his flight south over the Mountains of Terror, and his meeting with Lúthien – as far as 'though the time was brief', *The Silmarillion* p. 166 – the two QS versions are not in fact greatly different in length, and here I interwove some elements from the 'shorter' version, QS II; but from the point where Thingol learns of Beren's presence in the forest QS I was followed to its end at the words 'and Celegorm and Curufin said nothing, but they smiled and went from the halls' (*The Silmarillion* p. 170), for all of this narrative is in QS II compressed into two paragraphs. Thereafter QS II was followed to the end of the story.

The QS version(s) of 'Beren and Lúthien' are thus to be found in chapter 19 of the published work, and are not given here; but significant points in which the QS text(s) were altered editorially must be mentioned. I list these in order of their occurrence, with references to the pages of *The Silmarillion* (hardback edition).

*Tarn Aeluin* (pp. 162–3): introduced from later sources (*Grey Annals*, rewritten Lay, etc.)

*Rivil's Well* and the *Fen of Serech* (p. 163): introduced from later sources.

*Noldor* for *Gnomes* (p. 164 and throughout, wherever *Gnomes* appears in QS).

*Gorgoroth*, *Ered Gorgoroth* (p. 164). In QS I the latter is *Ered-orgoroth*, and in A and QS II *Ered-'orgoroth* (beside *Gorgoroth* standing alone). As I understand the matter, this variation is due to the phenomenon in 'Exilic Noldorin' (i.e. the language of the Noldor in Middle-earth, in exile from Valinor) called 'Initial Variation of Consonants', whereby a consonant at the beginning of the second element of a compounded word (or of the second word in two words standing in a very close syntactic relation, as noun and article) underwent the same change as it would when standing in ordinary medial position. For example, the original voiceless stops *p, t, k* remained in Exilic Noldorin unchanged initially before vowels, but were voiced to *b, d, g* medially; so *tâl* 'foot' but *i·dâl* 'the foot', or *Thorondor* (*thoron* + *taur* 'king'). Medially, original voiced stop -*g*- became 'opened' to -ʒ-, which then weakened and disappeared; in this case therefore the 'initial variation' is between *g* and nil, the lost consonant being represented by a sign called *gasdil* ('stopgap', see the *Etymologies*, stem DIL), transcribed as '. Thus *galaðʒ* 'tree', *i·alað* 'the tree'; *Gorgoroth*, *Ered-'orgoroth*. (This was an old linguistic conception, as is seen from forms given in the original 'Gnomish dictionary', as *Balrog* but *i'Malrog*, from an initial consonant combination *mb*- (I. 250).) In post-*Lord of the Rings* texts the form is *Ered Orgoroth* (-*ath*), beside *Gorgoroth* (-*ath*), but in a couple of cases the form after *Ered* was apparently emended to *Gorgoroth*.

*the rising of the Moon* (p. 164) is an error; all the texts have *raising*.

*Dungortheb* (p. 164): later form for QS *Dungorthin*; again on p. 176.

*Ungoliant* (p. 164): introduced for agreement with the occurrence of the name in *The Lord of the Rings*; QS *Ungoliantë*.

*And he passed through the mazes that Melian wove about the kingdom of Thingol, for a great doom lay upon him* (pp. 164–5). QS I has here: 'he could not have found the way, if his fate had not so decreed. Neither could he have passed the mazes that Melian wove about Doriath, unless she had willed it; but she foresaw many things that were hidden from the Elves.' QS II is similar. The reason for the change in *The Silmarillion* is Melian's earlier foretelling to Galadriel that 'one of Men, even of Bëor's house, shall indeed come, and the Girdle of Melian shall not restrain him, for doom greater than my power shall send him' (*ibid.* p. 144), a passage introduced from the *Grey Annals*; the sentence cited above was taken from the same source.

*in the Grey-elven tongue* (p. 165). QS I has 'in the speech of Beleriand', with a marginal note 'quoth Ælfwine'.

*But Daeron the minstrel also loved Lúthien, and he espied her meetings with Beren, and betrayed them to Thingol* (p. 166). As noticed earlier, Dairon was omitted from QS I (he appears in QS II but much later in the story). In view however of a pencilled note on QS I: *Dairon*, with a mark of insertion, I introduced this sentence (derived from the *Grey Annals*). QS I has here simply: 'But it came to pass that the coming of Beren became known to Thingol, and he was wroth'; similarly in QS II.

*'Who are you,' said the King* (p. 166). Here and subsequently throughout, 'you', 'your' is substituted for QS 'thou', 'thy' (and 'ye' plural), except in Lúthien's words to Sauron, p. 175.

*the badge of Finarfin* (p. 167): QS *the badge of Finrod*.

*the fate of Arda* (p. 167): QS *the fate of the world*.

*Talath Dirnen* (p. 168): later form for QS *Dalath Dirnen* – the first occurrence of the Elvish name of the Guarded Plain.

*Taur-en-Faroth* (p. 168): later form for QS *Taur-na-Faroth*.

*Finrod Felagund* (p. 169): QS *Felagund*; again on p. 174.

*and he knew that the oath he had sworn was come upon him for his death, as long before he had foretold to Galadriel* (p. 169). Added from the *Grey Annals*; the reference is to *The Silmarillion* p. 130, where Felagund said to Galadriel: 'An oath I too shall swear, and must be free to fulfil it, and go into darkness' (also derived from the *Grey Annals*).

*Celegorm* (p. 169): QS *Celegorn*, and subsequently.

*Finarfin's son* (p. 169): QS *Finrod's son*; again on p. 170.

*Then Celegorm arose amid the throng* (p. 169). In QS this is followed by 'golden was his long hair'. In the Lay at this point (line 1844) Celegorm has 'gleaming hair'; his Old English name was *Cynegrim*

*Fœgerfeax* ('Fair-hair'), IV. 213. The phrase was removed in *The Silmarillion* text on account of the dark hair of the Noldorin princes other than in 'the golden house of Finarfin' (see I. 44); but he remains 'Celegorm the fair' in *The Silmarillion* p. 60.

*Edrahil* (p. 170). This name was taken from the *Grey Annals*; in QS the chief of those faithful to Felagund is *Enedrion*.

*Taur-nu-Fuin* (p. 170): later form for QS *Taur-na-Fuin* (and subsequently).

Citation from the *Lay of Leithian* (p. 171). QS (where the narrative is now only that of the 'shorter' version, QS II) has: 'Sauron had the mastery, and he stripped from them their disguise.' The introduction of a passage from the Lay was justified, or so I thought, by the passage cited later in QS (p. 178).

*Tol-in-Gaurhoth* (p. 172): later form for QS *Tol-na-Gaurhoth*.

*but she sought the aid of Daeron, and he betrayed her purpose to the King* (p. 172). An addition, derived like that on p. 166 from the *Grey Annals*; QS has only 'Thingol discovering her thought was filled with fear and wonder.'

*the mountains of Aman* (p. 174): QS *the Mountains of the Gods*.

*the fates of our kindreds are apart* (p. 174). In QS this is followed by: 'Yet perchance even that sorrow shall in the end be healed.'

*in Tol-in-Gaurhoth, whose great tower he himself had built* (p. 174) was an editorial addition.

*fairest and most beloved of the house of Finwë* (p. 174) was added from the *Grey Annals*.

*Ered Wethrin* (p. 175): later form for QS *Eredwethion*.

*unless thou yield to me the mastery of thy tower* (p. 175). In QS this is followed by: 'and reveal the spell that bindeth stone to stone.' A little further on, the words *and the spell was loosed that bound stone to stone* were an addition to the QS text. This rearrangement was mistaken. (The draft text B has here: 'Then lest he be forced from the body unwillingly, which is a dire pain to such spirits, he yielded himself. And Lúthien and Huan wrested from him the keys of the tower, and the spell that bound stone to stone.')

*and it was clean again* (p. 176). The passage following this in *The Silmarillion* was an editorial rewriting of QS, which has:

and it was clean again, and ever after remained inviolate; for Sauron came never back thither. There lies still the green grave of Inglor, Finrod's son, fairest of all the princes of the Elves, unless that land is changed and broken, or foundered under destroying seas. But Inglor walks with Finrod his father among his kinsfolk in the light of the Blessed Realm, and it is not written that he has ever returned to Middle-earth.

Cf. the *Lay of Leithian* lines 2871–7; and for 'the trees of Eldamar' in the rewriting see the rewritten Lay, III. 358 lines 20–1.

*In that time Celebrimbor the son of Curufin repudiated the deeds of his father, and remained in Nargothrond* (p. 176). This was an editorial addition derived from a late note.

*Maedhros* (p. 176): later form for QS *Maidros*. After 'where Maidros their brother dwelt' QS has: 'In the days of the Siege the high road had run that way, and it was still passable with speed, since it lay close,' &c. I do not now recollect why this change was made. This is the first reference to a highroad running from East to West.

*Anfauglith* (p. 178): QS *Fauglith*.

*There Beren slunk in wolf's form beneath his throne* (p. 180): an addition, taken from the *Grey Annals* ; cf. the Lay, lines 3939–43.

*She was not daunted by his eyes* (p. 180). QS has: 'she alone of all things in Middle-earth could not be daunted by his eyes.'

*with wings swifter than the wind* (p. 182). The draft text B (see p. 293) has at this point: 'Thorondor led them, and the others were Lhandroval (Wide-wing) and Gwaewar his vassal.' In the following text C, also of 1937, this became: 'Thorondor was their leader; and with him were his mightiest vassals, wide-winged Lhandroval, and Gwaewar lord of the wind.' This was emended (in 1951, see p. 294) to 'Gwaihir the lord of storm', and in this form the passage is found in the QS manuscript. It was omitted in *The Silmarillion* on account of the passage in *The Return of the King* (VI. 4): 'There came Gwaihir the Windlord, and Landroval his brother . . . *mightiest of the descendants of old Thorondor*, who built his eyries in the inaccessible peaks of the Encircling Mountains when Middle-earth was young.' At the time, I did not understand the nature and dating of the end of QS. It now appears that there was no reason to suppress the names; in fact, it seems that *Gwaewar* was changed to *Gwaihir* to bring it into accord with *The Lord of the Rings* – however this is to be interpreted.

*Gondolin the fair where Turgon dwelt* (p. 182). This is followed in QS by: 'But it is said in song that her tears falling from on high as she passed came like silver raindrops on the plain, and there a fountain sprang to life: the Fountain of Tinúviel, Eithel Nínui, most healing water until it withered in the flame.' This passage, found already in the draft text C, should not have been omitted.

*Crissaegrim* (p. 182). The draft texts B and C, and also the QS manuscript as it was written, have here *Gochressiel* (see QS §147 and commentary); in QS it was emended (as also in QS §147) to *Crisaegrim*.

*Daeron* (p. 183). *Dairon* (so spelt) here first appears in the QS version.

*and among the great in Arda* (p. 184). An addition, taken from the *Grey Annals*.

*Beren Erchamion* (p. 185): QS *Beren Gamlost; Beren Camlost* (p. 186): QS *Beren Gamlost;* but at the occurrence on p. 184, where the name stands alone, QS also has *Camlost*. The C/G variation is found also in the drafts B and C, and is another example of the 'initial variation of consonants' referred to in the note on *Gorgoroth* above (original voiceless stop *k* > *g* medially). But here also, as in the case of *Ered Orgoroth*, late changes altered *Beren Gamlost* to *Beren Camlost*. – *Erchamion* is original (and appears already in the draft B) at its occurrence on p. 183, and is the first appearance of the name other than by later emendation.

*They bore back Beren Camlost* (p. 186). At this point my father entered (later) a new chapter-heading in the QS manuscript: 16 *The Song of Lúthien in Mandos*. In C chapter 16 is *Of the Fourth Battle*.

*the Two Kindreds that were made by Ilúvatar to dwell in Arda, the Kingdom of Earth amid the innumerable stars* (p. 187). This is original, deriving from QS as revised in 1951 (see p. 294).

*Because of her labours and her sorrow* (p. 187): QS 'because she was the daughter of Melian, and because of her labours and her sorrow'; see pp. 304–5.

This is not an exhaustive list of all the alterations made to the QS version(s) in the published text, but it includes all changes in names, and all omissions and additions of any substance. I shall not here go into the question of the justifiability of constructing a text from different sources. I hope that it will be possible later to present the major texts from the post-*Lord of the Rings* period, on the basis of which and in relation to what has thus far been published almost every detail of the 'constructed' text will be determinable. The tale of Beren and Lúthien is only a small and relatively very simple element in that construction, and is far from providing sufficient evidence on which to judge either it or its justification. I will say, however, that I now regret certain of the changes made to this tale.

It is proper to mention that here as elsewhere almost every substantial change was discussed with Guy Kay, who worked with me in 1974–5 on the preparation of *The Silmarillion*. He indeed made many suggestions for the construction of the text (such as, in the tale of Beren and Lúthien, the introduction of a passage from the *Lay of Leithian*), and proposed solutions to problems arising in the making of a composite narrative – in some cases of major significance to the structure, as will I hope be shown in a later book. The responsibility for the final published form rests of course wholly with me.

The more important differences between the narratives of the *Lay of Leithian* and *The Silmarillion* have been sufficiently discussed in Vol. III, and I make no further general analysis here. Many other small divergences will be seen in a close comparison of the two works. There are however certain particular points in the QS version and the preparatory drafts that remain to be mentioned.

In QS I, Lúthien's song at the birth of spring (*The Silmarillion* p. 165) is likened to the song of the lark that 'rises from the gates of night and pours its voice among the dying stars, *seeing the sun behind the walls of the world.*' This self-evidently contradicts the *Ambarkanta*; but a possible explanation is that my father was in fact thinking, not of the *Ilurambar* beyond which is the Void, but of the Walls of the Sun, the mountain-range in the furthest East answering to the Mountains of Valinor in the West: see the *Ambarkanta*, IV. 236-7, 239, and the map of the world, IV. 249. The lark flying high in the early dawn sees the unrisen sun beyond the eastern mountains. On the other hand this is not the only place where the expression 'the Walls of the World' is used in a way that seems anomalous in relation to the *Ambarkanta*: see IV. 253, and the commentary on QS §9.

In Q (IV. 113), when the knife (unnamed) which Beren took from Curufin snapped as he tried to cut a second Silmaril from the Iron Crown, it is called 'the knife of the treacherous Dwarves'; cf. the Lay, lines 4160-1: 'The dwarvish steel of cunning blade / by treacherous smiths of Nogrod made'. The absence of this in QS may be significant, but it is more likely due merely to compression. In the draft B 'the knife of the Dwarfs snapped', which hints at the idea; C has simply 'the knife snapped'. – The name *Angrist* of the knife is found in B, but it is not there ascribed to Telchar; this is first found in QS (*The Silmarillion* p. 177), where also Telchar becomes a Dwarf of Nogrod, not of Belegost as in Q (named as the maker of the Dragon-helm, IV. 118).

Of much interest is the development of the conclusion of the tale (*The Silmarillion* pp. 186-7, from 'Thus ended the Quest of the Silmaril; but the Lay of Leithian, Release from Bondage, does not end.') The original draft B, written in a rapid scrawl, was already near to the final form as far as 'Manwë sought counsel in his inmost thought, where the will of Ilúvatar was revealed.' Text C, almost an exact copy of B to this point, was emended long after (1951) to produce the form in the QS manuscript, but a footnote to the sentence beginning 'But the spirit of Lúthien fell down into darkness' belongs to the earlier time (and was not taken up into the final text):

Though some have said that Melian summoned Thorondor and bade him bear Lúthien living to Valinor, claiming that she had a part in the divine race of the Gods.

With this cf. S §10 (IV. 25): 'Some songs say that Lúthien went even over the Grinding Ice, aided by the power of her divine mother, Melian, to Mandos' halls and won him back', and Q §10 (IV. 115): 'though some songs say that Melian summoned Thorndor, and he bore [Lúthien] living unto Valinor.' – The text of B continues:

And this was the choice that he decreed for Beren and Lúthien. They should dwell now in Valinor until the world's end in bliss, but in the end Beren and Lúthien must each go unto the fate appointed to their kind, when all things are changed: and of the mind of Ilúvatar concerning Men Manwë kn[ows] not. Or they might return unto Middle-earth without certitude of joy or life; then Lúthien should become mortal even as Beren, and subject to a second death, and in the end she should leave the earth for ever and her beauty become only a memory of song. And this doom they chose, that thus, whatsoever sorrow might lie before them, their fates might be joined, and their paths lead together beyond the confines of the world. So it was that alone of the Eldalië Lúthien died and left the world long ago: yet by her have the Two Kindreds been joined, and she is the foremother of many. For her line is not yet extinguished, though the world is changed, and the Eldalië honour still the children of Men. And though these are grown proud and strong, and often are blind, but the Elves are diminished, they cease not to haunt the paths of Men, or to seek converse with those that go apart, for haply such are descended from Lúthien, whom they have lost.

We meet here the conception of the 'choice of fate' by Beren and Lúthien before Mandos. In the earlier accounts there was no choice. In the old *Tale of Tinúviel* – where Beren was an Elf – the fate of Beren and Lúthien was the simple decree of Mandos (II. 40); and in Q (IV. 115) it is the same, though the decree is different, since Beren was now a Man. I have discussed the meaning of these passages at some length (II. 59–60; IV. 63–4, 190–1). In the present text, if the first choice were accepted Beren and Lúthien must finally part, even though that parting is cast into a future indefinitely remote – the end of the world; and that parting would proceed from the different principles of their being, leading inevitably to a different final destiny or doom. Beren could not *finally* escape the necessity imposed upon by him his 'kind', the necessity of leaving the Circles of the World, the Gift of Ilúvatar that cannot be refused, though he may dwell – by unheard-of privilege, as an unheard-of reward – in Valinor until the End. The union of Beren and Lúthien 'beyond the world' could only be achieved by acceptance of the second choice, whereby Lúthien herself should be permitted to change her 'kind', and 'die indeed'.

In the following text C this passage was entirely recast, virtually to the form in which it was afterwards written into the QS manuscript. Here the choices are imposed on Lúthien alone (in the margin of QS is written *The Choices of Lúthien*), and they are changed; for the possibility of Beren accompanying Lúthien to the Blessed Realm is not open. The choice becomes therefore in a sense simpler: Lúthien may leave Beren *now*, and their fates be sundered for ever, *now*; or she may remain with him 'for ever', by becoming mortal, changing her nature and her destiny.

The form of the first choice begins in C: 'She, being the daughter of Melian, and because of her sorrow, should be released from Mandos', becoming in QS: 'She, because she was the daughter of Melian, and because of her labours and her sorrow, should be released from Mandos.' This takes up the idea in the footnote to C cited above (p. 303): Melian claimed that Lúthien 'had a part in the divine race of the Gods'. The words 'because she was the daughter of Melian' were regrettably omitted from the *Silmarillion* text.

One other point may be noticed in the passage cited from the B text (p. 303). It is said there that 'of the mind of Ilúvatar concerning Men Manwë knows not.' With this cf. QS §86: 'Mandos under Ilúvatar alone *save Manwë* knows whither they [Men] go after the time of recollection in those silent halls beside the Western Sea.' In the passage of Q from which this derives (IV. 100) it is said that 'Mandos under Ilúvatar knew *alone* whither they went.'

Text B continues on from 'Lúthien, whom they have lost' as follows:

But yet Beren and Lúthien abode together for a while, as living man and woman; and Mandos gave unto them a long span of life. But they dwelt not in Doriath, and taking up their mortal forms they departed and wandered forth, knowing neither thirst nor hunger, and came beyond the river into Ossiriand, Land of Seven Streams. There they abode, and Gwerth-i-Cuina the Gnomes named their dwelling, the Land of the Dead that Live, and thereafter no mortal man spoke with Beren son of Barahir.

In C this passage becomes the opening paragraph of chapter 16, *Of the Fourth Battle* (and is so treated in *The Silmarillion*, where it opens chapter 20, *Of the Fifth Battle*), but it was not altered from B in any significant way. In the QS manuscript it was entered on a final page, in yet a fourth script, careful but much less ornate, and here it is again the conclusion of the previous chapter and the end of the tale of Beren and Lúthien. In QS it takes this form:

It is said that Beren and Lúthien returned to the northern lands of Middle-earth, and dwelt together for a time as living man and woman; for taking up again their mortal form in Doriath, they went forth alone, fearing neither thirst nor hunger, and they passed beyond the rivers into Ossiriand, and abode there in the green isle, Tol-galen, in the midst of Adurant, until all tidings of them ceased. Therefore the Noldor afterwards called that land Gyrth-i-Guinar, the country of the Dead that Live, and no mortal man spoke ever again with Beren son of Barahir; and whether the second span of his life was brief or long is not known to Elves or Men, for none saw Beren and Lúthien leave the world or marked where at last their bodies lay.

The longer form that appears in *The Silmarillion* was 'integrated' with the text of the *Grey Annals*. In QS, chapter 16 then opens, with the title *Of the Union of Maedros* (despite the insertion of a chapter-heading 16 *The Song of Lúthien in Mandos*, p. 302); but after the words 'In those days Maedros son of Fëanor lifted up his heart' my father laid down his pen, and the manuscript ends there.

In B and C it is said, as it had been in Q (IV. 115), that the span of the second lives of Beren and Lúthien was long.* In the *Annals of Beleriand* the first death of Beren took place, according to the latest chronology, in 465, and the final departure of Beren and Lúthien is recorded under the year 503. This date is found again in post-*Lord of the Rings* versions of the *Tale of Years*; and on this account the words 'whether the second span of his life was brief or long is not known to Elves or Men' were omitted from *The Silmarillion*. But they should not have been. It is also said in the annal for 503 that *their deathday is not known*: the annal records as fact the coming of the messenger to Dior in Doriath by night, bearing the Silmaril on the Necklace of the Dwarves, but as surmise the saying of the Elves that Beren and Lúthien must be dead, else the Silmaril would not have come to their son. I think now that this is how the words of QS are to be interpreted; the belief that the coming of the Silmaril to Dior was a sign of their deaths is simply not referred to.

The name *Gwerth-i-Cuina* has appeared in later emendations to Q, and in an emendation to the Eastward Extension of the first Map (IV. 233). The placing of the dwelling of Beren and Lúthien after their return on the isle of Tol-galen in the river Adurant appears in an addition to QS §114 (see the commentary).

## 16  OF THE FOURTH BATTLE:
## NÍRNAITH ARNEDIAD

The two manuscripts of this chapter have been described on pp. 293–4: the first, QS(C), was the intermediate text begun while QS was away in November–December 1937, and this gives the whole of chapter 16, while the second, QS(D), of the same period, begins some way through it. To the point where D takes up, therefore, C (rough but legible) is the only text. As noted above, in C the chapter opens with the paragraph concerning the second lives of Beren and Lúthien, whereas the QS manuscript includes it at the end of chapter 15 and begins 16 with the Union of Maidros, breaking off after the first words. I recommence the paragraph-numbers here from §1.

### The Union of Maidros

§1  'Tis said that Beren and Lúthien returned into the lands of the North, and abode together for a while, as living man and

---

*In another passage of Q (IV. 134) the land where they dwelt after their return had only a 'brief hour of loveliness', just as in the *Tale of the Nauglafring* (II. 240) 'upon Beren and Tinúviel fell swiftly that doom of mortality that Mandos had spoken.'

woman; and the span of their second life was long. But they did
not dwell in Doriath; for taking up their mortal form they
departed thence and went forth alone, fearing neither thirst nor
hunger. And they passed beyond the rivers into Ossiriand, the
Land of Seven Streams, and dwelt among the Green-elves
secretly. Therefore the Gnomes called that land Gwerth-i-Cuina,
the Land of the Dead that Live; and thereafter no mortal man
spoke with Beren son of Barahir.

§2    But in those days Maidros son of Fëanor lifted up his heart,
perceiving that Morgoth was not unassailable; for the deeds of
Beren and Lúthien and the breaking of the towers of Sauron were
sung in many songs throughout Beleriand. Yet Morgoth would
destroy them all, one by one, if they could not again unite, and
make a new league and common council. Therefore he planned
the Union of Maidros, and he planned wisely.

§3    For he renewed friendship with Fingon in the West, and
they acted thereafter in concert. Maidros summoned again to his
aid the Dark-elves from the South, and the Swarthy Men were
gathered together, and he sallied from Himring in force. At the
same time Fingon issued from Hithlum. For a while the Gnomes
had victory again, and the Orcs were driven out of the northward
regions of Beleriand, and hope was renewed. Morgoth withdrew
before them and called back his servants; for he was aware of all
that was done, and took counsel against the uprising of the
Gnomes. He sent forth many spies and emissaries, secret or
disguised, among Elves and Men, and especially they came to the
Easterlings, the Swarthy Men, and to the sons of Ulfang. The
smithies of Nogrod and Belegost were busy in those days, making
mail and sword and spear for many armies; and the Dwarfs in that
time became possessed of much of the wealth and jewelry of Elves
and Men, though they went not to war themselves. 'For we do not
know the right causes of this quarrel,' they said, 'and we favour
neither side – until one hath the mastery.'

§4    Great and well-armed was the host of Maidros in the East.
In the West all the strength of Hithlum, Gnomes and Men, were
ready to his summons: Fingon and Huor and Húrin were their
chiefs. Then Turgon, thinking that maybe the hour of deliverance
was at hand, came forth himself unlooked for from Gondolin; and
he brought a great army and encamped upon the plain before the
opening of the western pass in sight of the walls of Hithlum. There
was joy among the people of Fingon his brother, seeing their
kinsfolk that had long been hidden.

§5 Yet the oath of Fëanor and the evil deeds that it had wrought did injury to the design of Maidros, and he had less aid than should have been. Orodreth would not march from Nargothrond at the word of any son of Fëanor, because of the deeds of Celegorn and Curufin. Thence came only a small company, whom Orodreth suffered to go, since they could not endure to be idle when their kinsfolk were gathering for war. Gwindor was their leader, son of Guilin, a very valiant prince; but they took the badge of the house of Fingolfin, and marched beneath the banners of Fingon, and came never back, save one.

§6 From Doriath came little help. For Maidros and his brethren, being constrained by their oath, had before sent to Thingol and reminded him with haughty words of their claim, summoning him to yield to them the Silmaril, or become their enemy. Melian counselled him to surrender the jewel, and perchance he would have done so, but their words were proud and threatening, and he was wroth, thinking of the anguish of Lúthien and the blood of Beren whereby the jewel had been won, despite the malice of Celegorn and Curufin. And every day that he looked upon the jewel, the more his heart desired to keep it for ever. Such was its power. Therefore he sent back the messengers of Maidros with scornful words. Maidros answered naught, for he had now begun to devise the league and union of the Elves; but Celegorn and Curufin vowed openly to slay Thingol and destroy his folk, if they came victorious from war, and the jewel were not surrendered of free will. For this reason Thingol fortified the marches of his realm, and went not to war, nor any out of Doriath save Mablung, and Beleg who could not be restrained.

§7 The treacherous shaft of Curufin that wounded Beren was remembered among Men. Therefore of the folk of Haleth that dwelt in Brethil only the half came forth, and they went not to join Maidros, but came rather to Fingon and Turgon in the West.

§8 Having gathered at length all the strength that he could, Maidros appointed a day, and sent word to Fingon and Turgon. Upon the East was raised the standard of Maidros, and to it came all the folk of Fëanor, and they were many; and the Dark-elves of the South; and of the Green-elves of Ossiriand many companies; and the tribes and battalions of the Easterlings with the sons of Bór and Ulfang. Upon the West was the standard of Fingon, and to it were gathered the armies of Hithlum, both Gnomes and Men; and Turgon with the host of Gondolin; to which was added such strength as came from the Falas, and from Brethil, and from

Nargothrond; and they waited upon the borders of Dor-na-Fauglith, looking for the signal of the advancing banners from the East.

[At this point the manuscript D takes up, and is followed here. It is a very close reworking of C, taking up the preparatory emendations made to the earlier text but scarcely developing it except in small stylistic detail.]

§9     But Maidros was delayed upon the road by the machinations of Uldor the Accursed, son of Ulfang; and continually the emissaries of Morgoth went among the camps: and there were thrall-Gnomes or things in Elvish form, and they spread foreboding of evil and the suspicion of treason among all who would listen to them.

§10     Long the armies waited in the West, and fear of treachery grew in their thoughts when Maidros tarried. The hot hearts of Fingon and Turgon became impatient. Therefore they sent their heralds forth upon the plain of Fauglith, and their silver trumpets were blown, and they summoned the hosts of Morgoth to come out.

§11     Then Morgoth sent a force, great and yet not too great. Fingon was minded to attack it from the woods at the feet of Erydwethion, where the most of his strength was hid. But Húrin spake against it. Therefore Morgoth, seeing that they wavered, led forth the herald of Fingon that he had wrongfully taken prisoner, and he slew him upon the plain, and sent back the others with his head. Thereupon the wrath of Fingon was kindled to flame, and his army leaped forth in sudden onslaught; and ere Turgon could restrain them, a great part also of his host joined in the battle. The light of the drawing of the swords of the Noldor was like a sudden fire kindled in a field of reeds.

§12     This was indeed as Morgoth designed; but it is said that he had not reckoned the true number of his enemies' array, nor measured rightly their valour, and almost his plan went astray. Ere the army that he sent forth could be strengthened, it was overwhelmed; for it was assailed suddenly from West and South; and that day there was a greater slaughter of the servants of Morgoth than had yet been achieved. Loud rang the trumpets. The banners of Fingon were raised before the very walls of Angband. It is told that Gwindor son of Guilin and the folk of Nargothrond were in the front of the battle, and they burst through the gates, and slew the Orcs upon the stairs of Angband, and fear came upon Morgoth on his deep throne. But in the end

Gwindor and his men were taken or slain, for no help came to them. By other secret doors in the mountains of Thangorodrim Morgoth had let issue forth his main host that he had held in waiting; and Fingon and the army of Hithlum were beaten back from the walls.

§13    Then in the plain there began that Battle which is called Nírnaith Arnediad, Unnumbered Tears, for no song or tale can contain all the grief of that day, and the voices of those that sing of it are turned to mourning. The host of Fingon retreated with great loss over the sands of Dor-na-Fauglith, and Hundor son of Haleth was slain in the rearguard, and with him fell most of the Men of Brethil and came never back to the woods. And Glorwendil, daughter of Hador and wife of Hundor, died of grief in that unhappy year. But the Orcs came between Fingon and the passes of Erydwethion that led into Hithlum; therefore he withdrew towards the vale of Sirion. Before the entrance of that valley, upon the borders of Taur-na-Fuin, there remained still in hiding a great part of the host of Turgon; and Turgon now sounded his horns, and came forth in might with help unlooked for, and many of the Orcs, being caught between the two armies, were destroyed.

§14    Then hope was renewed in the hearts of the Elves. And in that hour the trumpets of Maidros were heard coming from the East, and the banners of the Sons of Fëanor and their allies came up on the flank of the Enemy. And some have said that even now the Elves might have won the day, had all been faithful; for the Orcs wavered, and their onslaught was stayed, and already some were turning in flight.

§15    But even as the vanguard of Maidros came upon the Orcs, Morgoth let loose his last strength, and hell was emptied. There came wolves and serpents, and there came Balrogs one thousand, and there came Glómund the Father of Dragons. And the strength and terror of the Worm were now grown very great; and Elves and Men withered before him. Thus Morgoth hindered the joining of the hosts of the Elves; yet he would not have achieved this, neither with Balrog nor Dragon, had the captains of the Easterlings remained true. Many of these men now turned and fled; but the sons of Ulfang went over to the side of Morgoth, and they fell upon the rear of Maidros and wrought confusion. From that day the hearts of the Elves were estranged from Men, save only from those of the Three Houses, the peoples of Hador, and Bëor, and Haleth; for the sons of Bór, Boromir, Borlas, and Borthandos, who alone among the Easterlings proved true at need, all perished in that battle, and they left no heirs. But the sons of Ulfang reaped not the reward that Morgoth had promised them; for Cranthir slew Uldor the Accursed, the leader in treason, and Ulfast and Ulwarth were slain by the sons of Bór, ere they themselves fell.

§16   Thus the design of Morgoth was fulfilled in a manner after his own heart; for Men took the lives of Men, and betrayed the Elves, and fear and hatred were aroused among those who should have been united against him. And the host of Maidros, assailed in front and rear, was dispersed and was driven from the battle eastward; and the Gorge of Aglon was filled with Orcs, and the Hill of Himring garrisoned by the soldiers of Angband, and the gates of the land were in the power of Morgoth. But fate saved the Sons of Fëanor, and though all were wounded none were slain. Yet their arms were scattered, and their people diminished, and their league broken; and they took to a wild and woodland life beneath the feet of Eredlindon, mingling with the Dark-elves, bereft of their power and glory of old.

§17   In the west of the battle Fingon fell, and flame sprang from his helm when it was cloven. He was overborne by the Balrogs and beaten to the earth, and his white banners were trodden underfoot. But Húrin and Huor his brother, and the men of the House of Hador, stood firm, and the Orcs could not yet gain the pass of Sirion. Thus was the treachery of Uldor redressed. The last stand of Húrin is the most renowned of the deeds of Men among the Elves; for he held the rear while the remnant of the hosts of the West withdrew from the battle. Few came ever back over Eredwethion to Hithlum; but Turgon mustered all that remained of the folk of Gondolin, and such of Fingon's folk as he could gather; and he escaped down Sirion into the dales and mountains, and was hidden from the eyes of Morgoth. Neither Elf nor Man nor spy of Angband knew whither he had gone, nor found the hidden stronghold until the day of Tuor son of Huor. Thus the victory of Morgoth was marred, and he was wroth.

§18   But the Orcs now surrounded the valiant Men of Hithlum like a great tide about a lonely rock. Huor fell pierced with a venomed arrow, and all the children of Hador were slain about him in a heap, until Húrin alone was left. Then he cast away his shield and wielded his axe two-handed; and it is said that standing alone he slew one hundred of the Orcs. At length he was taken alive by Morgoth's command, for in this way Morgoth thought to do him more evil than by death. Therefore his servants grasped

Húrin with their hands, and though he slew them, their numbers were ever renewed, until at last he fell buried beneath them, and they clung to him like leeches. Then binding him they dragged him with mockery to Angband.

§19   Great was the triumph of Morgoth. The bodies of his enemies that were slain he let pile in a great mound in the midst of the plain; and it was named Hauð-na-Dengin, the Hill of Slain. But grass came there and grew green upon that hill alone in all the desert that Morgoth made; and no Orc thereafter trod upon the earth beneath which the swords of the Gnomes crumbled into rust. The realm of Fingon was no more, and the Sons of Fëanor wandered as leaves before the wind. To Hithlum none of the men of Hador's house returned, nor any tidings of the battle and the fate of their lords. But Morgoth sent thither Men who were under his dominion, swarthy Easterlings; and he shut them in that land and forbade them to leave it, and such was all the reward that he gave them: to plunder and harass the old and the children and women-folk of Hador's people. The remnant of the Elves of Hithlum he took to the mines of Angband, and they became his thralls, save some few that eluded him and wandered wild in the woods.

§20   But the Orcs went freely through all the North and came ever further southward into Beleriand. Doriath yet remained, and Nargothrond was hidden; but Morgoth gave small heed to them, either because he knew little of them, or because their hour was not yet come in the deep purposes of his malice. But the thought of Turgon troubled him greatly; for Turgon came of the mighty house of Fingolfin and was now by right the lord of all the Gnomes. And Morgoth feared and hated most the house of Fingolfin, both because they had scorned him in Valinor, and because of the wounds that Fingolfin had given him in battle.

§21   Húrin was now brought before Morgoth, and defied him; and he was chained and set in torment. But Morgoth remembered that treachery, and the fear of treachery, alone would work the final ruin of the Gnomes, and he thought to make use of Húrin. Therefore he came to him where he lay in pain, and he offered to him honour and freedom and both power and wealth, if he would accept service in his armies and would lead a host against Turgon, or even if he would reveal where that king had his secret stronghold. For he had learned that Húrin knew the secret of Turgon, but kept it silent under oath. But Húrin the Steadfast mocked him.

§22   Then Morgoth devised a cruel punishment; and taking Húrin from prison he set him in a chair of stone upon a high place of Thangorodrim. There he was bound by the power of Morgoth, and Morgoth standing beside him cursed him with a curse of unsleeping sight like unto the Gods, but upon his kin and seed he laid a doom of sorrow and dark mischance.

§23   'Sit now there,' said Morgoth, 'and behold the working of the doom that I have appointed. For thou shalt see with my eyes, and know with my thought, all things that befall those whom thou lovest. But never shalt thou move from this place until all is fulfilled unto its bitter end.' As so it came to pass; for Morgoth kept life in Húrin. But it is not said that Húrin ever spoke in pleading, either for death or for mercy upon himself or his children.

### Commentary on Chapter 16

A comparison with Q §11 and AB 2 annal (272>) 472 will show that the present text is very largely derived from these two sources, which are interwoven. In the treatment of the part played by Turgon and the people of Gondolin in the Battle of Unnumbered Tears the result of this combination is (surprisingly) not entirely coherent, and this is discussed in a note at the end of the Commentary.

§1   On the development of this paragraph see pp. 305–6. In the sentence *dwelt among the Green-elves secretly*, the word *secretly* was struck out and replaced by *in Tol-galen the Green Isle*; and *Gwerth-i-Cuina* was changed to *Gwerth-i-Guinar*. These may have been much later changes preparatory to the inclusion of the paragraph as the final instalment of the QS manuscript (which has however *Gyrth-i-Guinar*).

§3   It is not said elsewhere that 'Fingon issued from Hithlum' during the initial period of warfare under the Union of Maidros in which the Noldor were victorious.

The passage concerning the cynical and calculating Dwarves derives closely from Q (IV. 116). Against it my father scribbled 'Not true of Dwarvish attitude'; this, I feel sure, was put in long after. The plural form *Dwarfs* associates the text with QS chapters 10 and 11 (see the commentary on §122). It was used also in the manuscript QS(B) of the tale of Beren and Lúthien (p. 303).

§7   The wounding of Beren by Curufin, not mentioned in the *Annals* in connection with the response of the Men of Brethil to the Union of Maidros, reappears (see IV. 180–1), and 'only the half' of Haleth's people came to the war, although in §13 (as in AB 2) 'most of the Men of Brethil' were slain.

§8    Neither in Q nor in the *Annals* are the Green-elves of Ossiriand mentioned among the forces of Maidros.

§11    That the heralds were sent back bearing the head of the one who had been executed is a new detail.

§13    The retreat of the western host towards the Pass of Sirion, and the destruction of the Men of Brethil in the rearguard, is derived from the *Annals*, not from Q.

An addition to AB 2 (note 22) gives a new annal: '436. Hundor son of Haleth wedded Glorwendel daughter of Hador', and an addition to the annal describing the Battle of Unnumbered Tears states: 'Glorwendel his wife died in that year of grief.' These are the first allusions to this union between the House of Hador and the People of Haleth. In *The Silmarillion* Hador's daughter is *Glóredhel*.

§15    The number of a thousand Balrogs (found in both versions of the *Annals*) was still present (see the commentary on §89). – After 'all perished in that battle' the earlier text (C) has the addition 'defending Maglor against the assault of Uldor', but this was not taken up in D. It is not said in the *Annals* that Ulfast and Ulwar(th) were slain by the sons of Bór ('ere they themselves fell'), but the reverse.

§17    Text D has *Erydwethion* in §§11 and 13, but *Eredwethion* here; C has *Eredwethion* throughout.

§18    In Q the Dragon-helm, reappearing from the *Lay of the Children of Húrin*, is first described at this point in the narrative (for Húrin was not wearing it at the battle); but a note to Q postpones it to the tale of Túrin, as is done in this version.

§19    *Hauð-na-Dengin:* C had *Cûm-na-Dengin* (see note 37 to AB 2), changed to *Amon Dengin* (see IV. 146), with *Hauð na* written above *Amon*. This is the first occurrence of *Hauð-na-Dengin* (the form in text D); cf. *Hauð i Ndengin* in the *Etymologies*, stems KHAG, NDAK.

### Turgon's part in the Battle of Unnumbered Tears

As noted above, the combination of Q and the *Annals* produced here a most uncharacteristic incoherence. Turgon came forth from Gondolin unlooked for and encamped on the plain before the western pass in sight of the walls of Hithlum (§4); when the day was appointed 'Maidros sent word to Fingon and Turgon', and the host of Gondolin was arrayed under the standard of Fingon (§8); Turgon and Fingon became impatient and sent their heralds out onto the plain of Fauglith (§10). In all this my father was closely following Q as emended (IV. 120-1, notes 7 and 14), where, as I suggested (IV. 181), there seems to be a stage intermediate between the original story (in which Turgon was one of the leaders of the Western Elves from the beginning of the preparations for war) and that in *The Silmarillion*: 'Turgon now emerges from Gondolin already long since in existence, but he does not march up in the nick of time, on the day itself, as in the later story: he comes, certainly unexpected, but in time to take part in the final strategic preparations.'

Then, in the present account, 'a great part' of Turgon's host joined in the premature assault, though he would have restrained them if he could (§11). This is not in Q, which only further mentions Turgon as escaping down Sirion. But *then*, Turgon 'sounded his horns', and 'a great part' of his host that had remained in hiding before the Pass of Sirion and on the borders of Taur-na-Fuin came forth unlooked for, so that many Orcs were destroyed, caught between Turgon's army and that of Fingon retreating southwards (§13). It seems that at this point my father went over to the *Annals*; but they (both AB 1 and AB 2) tell a different story from that in Q. In the *Annals*, 'tidings came to Turgon' long before the battle, and 'he prepared for war in secret' (annal 465–70, according to the final dating); there is no suggestion of his playing any part at all until Fingon, cut off from the passes of Eredwethion, retreated towards Sirion – and then 'Turgon and the army of Gondolin sounded their horns, and issued out of Taur-na-Fuin': they had been 'delayed by the deceit and evil of the forest, but came now as help unlooked for.' There now took place, in the *Annals*, the joyful meeting between Turgon and Húrin (the story of Húrin's sojourn in Gondolin had not emerged when Q was written). This meeting does not take place in the present account; for they would have met again much earlier (when 'there was joy among the people of Fingon, seeing their kinsfolk that had long been hidden', §4).

This chapter appears in subsequent amanuensis typescripts, but my father never changed them or corrected them in any way.

## 17   OF TÚRIN TURAMARTH OR TÚRIN THE HAPLESS

The two manuscripts QS (C) and QS (D) continue into one further chapter, and D extends somewhat further in it than does C (see pp. 293–4). C is here extremely rough, and the text given is that of D, since it followed C very closely and scarcely deviated from it save in small points of expression. D was substantially corrected and added to, and the concluding pages struck out in their entirety, but I believe that all this belongs to a much later phase of work on the "Túrinssaga', and I give the text as it was originally written.

This version of the story, so far as it goes, shows a huge expansion on the very brief account in Q §12 – and would have run into the same problem of length as did the QS version of the tale of Beren and Lúthien. The primary source for this chapter was in fact the *Lay of the Children of Húrin* in the section *Túrin's Fostering* (III. 8 ff., and in the revised form of the poem III. 104 ff.), which in turn derived quite closely from the original story, the *Tale of Turambar*. The later evolution of the 'Túrinssaga' is as tangled as Taur-na-Fuin, and need not be in any way considered here; but it may be noticed that the present chapter is not (apart from a few phrases) the antecedent of the opening of chapter 21 in

*The Silmarillion*. On the other hand, it will be found that much of the chapter is in fact preserved embedded in the *Narn i Hîn Húrin* in *Unfinished Tales* (from 'Now Túrin was made ready for the journey', p. 73), despite the introduction of several major new elements (the history of the Dragon-helm, Nellas the friend of Túrin's childhood, the changed story of Orgof/Saeros, etc.)

The dependence of the new version on the Lay is in places close, extending even to actual wording here and there; on the other hand some features of the Lay are changed (as for example the taunting of Orgof), reduced (as the account of Orgof and his character), or omitted (as the avenging wrath of Orgof's kinsmen and Thingol's placating gifts). But the comparison between the two is now easily made, and I restrict the commentary to a few particular points. The relation between the Lay and the *Narn* is in any case studied in the commentary on the Lay (III. 24–8).

§24 Rían, daughter of Belegund, was the wife of Huor. When no tidings came of her lord, she went forth, and her child Tuor was born of her in the wild. He was taken to nurture by Dark-elves; but Rían went to Hauð-na-Dengin and laid her there and died. But Morwen daughter of Baragund was wife of Húrin, and she abode in Hithlum, for her son Túrin was then seven years old, and she went again with child. With her there remained only old men, too aged for war, and maidens and young boys. Those days were evil; for the Easterlings dealt cruelly with the people of Hador and robbed them of all that they possessed and enslaved them. But so great was the beauty and majesty of the Lady Morwen that they were afraid and whispered among themselves, saying that she was perilous and a witch skilled in magic and in league with the Elves. Yet she was now poor and without aid, save that she was succoured secretly by her kinswoman Airin, whom Brodda had taken to wife. Brodda was mighty among the in-coming Men, and wealthy (such as wealth was reckoned in that time of ruin); for he had taken for his own many of the lands and cattle of Húrin.

§25 Morwen could see no hope for her child Túrin son of Húrin but to become a churl or a servant of the Easterlings. Therefore it came into her heart to send him away in secret and to beg King Thingol to harbour him. For Beren son of Barahir was her father's cousin, and had been, moreover, a friend of Húrin ere evil befell. But she herself did not at that time venture forth from Hithlum, for the road was long and perilous, and she was with child. Also her heart still cheated her with hope, and she would not yet leave the house in which she had dwelt with Húrin; and she listened for the sound of his feet returning in the watches of the night, for her inmost thought foreboded that he was not dead. And though she was willing that her son might be fostered in the halls of another after the manner of that time, if boys were left fatherless, she would not humble her pride to be an almsguest even of the King of Doriath. And thus was the fate of Túrin woven, which is full told in that lay which is called *iChúrinien*, the Children of Húrin, and is the longest of all the lays that speak of those days. Here that tale is told in brief, for it is woven in with the fate of the Silmarils and of the Elves; and it is called the Tale of Grief, for it is sorrowful, and in it are revealed the worst of the works of Morgoth Bauglir.

§26   It came to pass that on a day Túrin was made ready for the journey, and he understood not the purpose of his mother Morwen, nor the grief that he saw upon her face. But when his companions bade him turn and look upon the house of his father, then the anguish of parting smote him like a sword, and he cried: 'Morwen, Morwen, when shall I see thee again?', and he fell upon the grass. But Morwen standing on her threshold heard the echo of that cry in the wooded hills, and she clutched the post of the door so that her fingers were torn. This was the first of the sorrows of Túrin.

§27   After Túrin was gone Morwen gave birth to her child, and it was a maiden, and she named her Nienor, which is Mourning. But Túrin saw not his sister, for he was in Doriath when she was born. Long and evil was the road thither, for the power of Morgoth was ranging far abroad; but Túrin had as guides Gethron and Grithron, who had been young in the days of Gumlin; and albeit they were now aged, they were valiant, and they knew all the lands, for they had journeyed often through Beleriand in former times. Thus by fate and courage they passed over the Shadowy Mountains and came down into the vale of Sirion and so to the Forest of Brethil; and at last weary and haggard they reached the confines of Doriath. But there they became bewildered, and were enmeshed in the mazes of the Queen, and wandered lost amid the pathless trees, until all their food was spent. There they came near to death, but not so light was Túrin's doom. Even as they lay in despair they heard a horn sounded. Beleg the Bowman was hunting in that region, for he dwelt ever upon the marches of Doriath. He heard their cries and came to them, and when he had given them meat and drink he learned their names and whence they came, and he was filled with wonder and pity. And he looked with great liking upon Túrin, for he had the beauty of his mother Morwen Elfsheen and the eyes of his father, and was sturdy and strong of limb and showed a stout heart.

§28  'What boon wouldst thou have of King Thingol?' said Beleg to the boy. 'I would be a captain of his knights, and lead them against Morgoth and avenge my father,' said Túrin. 'That may well be when the years have increased thee,' said Beleg. 'For though thou art yet small, thou hast the makings of a valiant man, worthy to be the son of Húrin the Steadfast, if that were possible.' For the name of Húrin was held in honour in all the lands of the Elves. Therefore Beleg gladly became the guide of the wanderers, and he led them through the marches of the Hidden Kingdom, which no mortal man before had passed save Beren only.

§29  Thus Túrin came at last before Thingol and Melian; and Gethron spoke the message of Morwen. Thingol received them kindly, and he set Túrin upon his knee in honour of Húrin the mightiest of Men and of Beren his kinsman. And those that saw this marvelled, for it was a sign that Thingol took Túrin as foster-son, and this was not at that time done by kings. 'Here, O son of Húrin, shall thy home be,' said he; 'and thou shalt be held as my son, Man though thou art. Wisdom shall be given thee beyond the wit of mortals, and the weapons of the Elves shall be set in thy hands. Perchance the time may come when thou shalt regain the lands of thy father in Hithlum; but dwell now here in love.'

§30  Thus began the sojourn of Túrin in Doriath. With him for a while remained Gethron and Grithron his guardians, though they longed to return again to their lady, Morwen. Then age and sickness came upon Grithron and he stayed beside Túrin until he died; but Gethron departed, and Thingol sent with him an escort to guide him and guard him, and they brought words from Thingol to Morwen. They came at last to the house of Morwen, and when she learned that Túrin was received with honour in the halls of Thingol, her grief was lightened. And the Elves brought also rich gifts from Melian, and a message bidding her return with Thingol's folk to Doriath. For Melian was wise and foresighted, and she hoped thus to avert the evil that was prepared in the thought of Morgoth. But Morwen would not depart from her house, for her heart was yet unchanged and her pride still high; moreover Nienor was a babe in arms. Therefore she dismissed the Elves with her thanks, and gave them in gift the last small things of gold that remained to her, concealing her poverty; and she bade them take back to Thingol the helm of Gumlin. And behold! Túrin watched ever for the return of Thingol's messengers; and when they came back alone he fled into the woods and wept; for he knew of Melian's bidding and had hoped that Morwen would come. This was the second sorrow of Túrin.

§31 When the messengers brought Morwen's answer, Melian was moved with pity, perceiving her mind; and she saw that the fate which she foreboded could not lightly be set aside. The helm of Gumlin was given into Thingol's hands. It was made of grey steel adorned with gold, and thereon were graven runes of victory. A power was in it that guarded any who wore it from wound or death, for the sword that hewed it was broken, and the dart that smote it sprang aside. Upon this helm was set in mockery an image of the head of Glómund the dragon, and oft had Gumlin borne it to victory, for fear fell on those who looked upon it towering above the heads of Men in battle. But the Men of Hithlum said: 'We have a dragon of more worth than Angband hath.' This helm was wrought by Telchar the dwarf-smith of Belegost, whose works were renowned. But Húrin wore it not, in reverence of his father, lest it should suffer hurt or be lost, so greatly did he treasure the heirloom of Gumlin.

§32 Now Thingol had in Menegroth deep armouries filled with great wealth of weapons; metal wrought like fishes' mail and shining like water in the moon; swords and axes, shields and helms, wrought by Telchar himself or by his master Zirak the old, or by elven-wrights more skilful still. For many things he had received in gift that came out of Valinor and were wrought by Fëanor in his mastery, than whom no craftsman was greater in all the days of the world. Yet he handled the helm of Gumlin as though his hoard were scanty, and spoke courteous words saying: 'Proud were the head that bore this helm, which Gumlin bore, father of Húrin.'

§33 Then a thought came into his heart and he summoned Túrin, and he told him that Morwen had sent to her son a mighty thing, the heirloom of his grandsire. 'Take now the Dragonhead of the North,' he said, 'and when the time cometh, go wear it well!' But Túrin was yet too young to lift the helm, and he heeded it not because of the sorrow of his heart.

§34 For nine years Túrin lived in the halls of Thingol; and in that time his grief grew less; for Thingol gained tidings of Hithlum as he could, and messengers went at times between Morwen and her son. Thus Túrin learned that Morwen's plight was bettered, and that his sister Nienor grew in beauty, a flower among maidens in the grey North. Greatly he desired to see her.

§35   Meanwhile Túrin grew, until while yet a boy his stature was great among Men and surpassed that of the Elves of Doriath; and his strength and courage were renowned in the realm of Thingol. Much lore he learned, and was wise in word and crafty in hand; yet fortune favoured him little, and oft what he wrought went awry, and what he wished he did not gain. Neither did he win friendship easily, for sorrow sat upon him, and his youth was scarred. Now when he was seventeen years of age and upon the threshold of manhood he was strong of arm and skilled with all weapons, and in the weaving of words in song or tale he had a great craft, whether in the tongue of the Noldor or of Doriath; but mirth was not in his words or his works, and he brooded upon the downfall of the Men of Hithlum.

§36   Still deeper became his grief when after nine years tidings came no more from his home; for Morgoth's power was over the land of Hithlum, and doubtless he knew much of all the doings of Húrin's folk, and had not further molested them, so that his design might be fulfilled. But now in pursuit of this purpose he set a close watch upon all the passes in the mountains, so that none might come out of Hithlum or enter into it; and the Orcs swarmed about the sources of Narog and Taiglin and the upper waters of Sirion. Thus there came a time when the messengers of Thingol did not return, and he would send no more. He was ever loath to let any stray beyond the guarded borders, and in nothing had shown greater goodwill to Túrin than in sending his people through many perils to Morwen.

§37   Now the heart of Túrin grew grim and heavy, for he knew not what evil was afoot, or what dire fate had befallen Morwen and Nienor. Therefore he put on the helm of Gumlin, and taking mail and sword and shield he went to Thingol, and begged him to give him Elf-warriors for his companions; and he went to the marches of the land and made war upon the Orcs. Thus while yet a boy in years his valour was proved; for he did many daring deeds. His wounds were many by spear, or arrow, or the crooked blades of Angband; but his doom delivered him from death. And word ran through the woods that the Dragon-helm was seen again in battle; and Men said: 'Who hath waked from death the spirit of Gumlin, or hath Húrin of Hithlum indeed returned from the pits of hell?'

§38   One only was there mightier in war at that time than the boy Túrin, and that was Beleg the Bowman; and they became friends and companions in arms, and walked far and wide in the wild woods together. Túrin came seldom to the halls of Thingol, and he cared no longer for his looks or raiment, but was unkempt of hair and his mail was covered with a grey cloak stained with the weather. But on a time it chanced that Thingol summoned him to a feast, to do him some honour for his prowess; and Túrin came and sat at the table of the king. And at the same table sat one of the Dark-elves, Orgof by name, and he was proud and was no lover of Men, and thought that Túrin had slighted him; for Túrin would oft make no answer to words that others spoke to him, if sorrow or brooding were on him. And now as they sat and drank Orgof spoke across the board to Túrin, and Túrin heeded him not, for his thought was upon Beleg whom he had left in the woods. Then Orgof took out a golden comb and cast it towards Túrin, and he cried: 'Doubtless, Man of Hithlum, you came in great haste to this feast and may be excused thy ragged cloak; but there is no need to leave thy head untended like a thicket of brambles. And maybe if thy ears were uncovered thou wouldst hear somewhat better.'

§39    Then Túrin said nought but turned his eyes upon Orgof, and he being wroth was not warned by the light that was in them. And he said to one that sat nigh him: 'If the Men of Hithlum are so wild and fell, of what sort are women of that land? Do they run like the deer, clad only in their hair?'

§40    Then Túrin, unwitting of his growing strength, took up a drinking vessel and cast it in Orgof's face, and he fell backwards and died, for the vessel was heavy and his face was broken. But Túrin, grown suddenly cold, looked in dismay at the blood upon the board, and knowing that he had done grievous offence he rose straightway and went from the hall without a word; and none hindered him, for the king was silent and gave no sign. But Túrin went out into the darkness, and he fell into a grim mood, and deeming himself now an outlaw whom the king would pursue he fled far from Menegroth, and passing the borders of the realm he gathered to himself a company of such houseless and desperate folk as could be found in those evil days lurking in the wild; and their hands were turned against all whom came in their path, Elves, Men, or Orcs.

*Commentary on Chapter 17*

In the title of the chapter (which has in fact no number in either C or D) *Turamarth* is emended from *Turumarth*; the same change in Q (IV. 131 note 12).

§24  *Hauð-na-Dengin:* C has here *Amon Dengin*; cf. the commentary on chapter 16, §19.

§25  In Q it is said that the fate of Túrin is told in the 'Children of Húrin', which is certainly a reference to the alliterative Lay, though that had been abandoned several years before; now the Lay is expressly mentioned, and given the Elvish name *iChúrinien*. This form is a further example of the phenomenon of 'Initial Variation of Consonants' in Exilic Noldorin (see pp. 298, 301). The original aspirated stops *ph, th, kh* were 'opened', and *kh* became the spirant [x] (as in Scottish *loch*), represented as *ch*; this sound remained medially, but initially was reduced to [h]. Thus *aran Chithlum* 'King of Hithlum' (*Etymologies*, stem TĀ-), *iChúrinien*. It may be noted here that later *iChúrinien* was replaced by *Narn i Chîn Húrin*, which is so spelt at all occurrences, but was improperly changed by me to *Narn i Hîn Húrin* in *Unfinished Tales* (because I did not want *Chîn* to be pronounced like Modern English *chin*).

§27  *Gethron* and *Grithron* as the names of Túrin's guides appear in AB 2, annal (273>) 473. See under §30 below.

§28  Of the words between Beleg and Túrin (preserved in the *Narn*, p. 74) there is no suggestion in the Lay.

§30  In AB 2 it was Gethron who died in Doriath, Grithron who went back (see the commentary on annal 273). – The gifts of Melian to Morwen are not mentioned in the old versions.

§31  It is curious that whereas in the tale of Beren and Lúthien in QS Telchar is of Nogrod (p. 303), he now becomes a smith of Belegost, as he had been in Q (IV. 118). – A new element in this passage is the statement that Húrin never wore the Dragon-helm, and the reasons for this; in Q he did not wear it 'that day' (i.e. at the Battle of Unnumbered Tears), and in the Lay he often bore it into battle (line 314). In the much enlarged account of the Helm found in the *Narn* Húrin's reasons for not wearing it are quite different (*Unfinished Tales* p. 76).

§32  Here first appear Telchar's master Zirak, and the story that Thingol possessed many treasures that had come from Valinor (both preserved in the *Narn*).

§34  On the 'betterment' of Morwen's plight see II. 127.

§35  *Dates in Túrin's early life.* According to the (later) dating of AB 2, Túrin was born in the winter of 465, and departed for Doriath in 473, when he was seven years old (as is said here in §24); in 481 all tidings out of Hithlum ceased, and he being 'in his sixteenth year' went to war on the marches (his sixteenth birthday fell in the winter of that year). In the present text, however, the dates appear to be different by a year. The reference in §35 to his being seventeen is presumably made because it was then that he went out to fight; and in §§36–7 the ending of news from Hithlum and his going to the marches took place 'after nine years' (i.e. from his coming to Doriath).

The supposition must be that Túrin had acquired a knowledge of the Noldorin tongue from the Noldor in Hithlum – or perhaps rather from his father and mother – while he was a child.

§38  In the Tale and the Lay Túrin's peculiar gloominess on that night was caused by its being the twelfth anniversary of his departure from Hithlum.

## THE CONCLUSION OF THE
## *QUENTA SILMARILLION*

There remains one further text to be considered within the framework of the *Quenta Silmarillion*. This is a clear manuscript very similar in style to QS(D), which has been followed to its conclusion in the last chapter, and may conveniently be called 'QS(E)' or 'E'. The first page is numbered '55', and it begins in the middle of a sentence: 'and they looked upon the Lonely Isle and there they tarried not', which will be found in the second version of Q (Q II) §17, IV. 153. The passage describes the voyage of Eärendel and Elwing to Valinor:

they came to the Enchanted Isles and escaped their enchantment; and they came into the Shadowy Seas and passed their shadows; [here page 54 of the Q II typescript ends and page 55 begins] and they looked upon the Lonely Isle and they tarried not there . . .

This manuscript E is in fact a further version of the conclusion of Q: and the question arises, when was it written? A note on a page found with Q provides, I think, a clear answer. This says: '36–54 is still included in main version, being unrevised.' Now on p. 36 of the Q typescript occurs the sentence (IV. 123):

He fled then the court, and thinking himself an outlaw took to war against all, Elves, Men, or Orcs, that crossed the path of the desperate band he gathered upon the borders of the kingdom, hunted Men and Ilkorins and Gnomes.

This is the antecedent of the sentence which ends the QS(D) version of the tale of Túrin (p. 321); and at this point on the Q typescript a line is drawn across, separating what precedes from what follows.

By 'main version' my father probably meant the *Quenta Noldorinwa*, the implication being that the narrative from Túrin's outlawry to the voyage of Eärendel to Valinor (i.e. pages 36–54 in the Q typescript) had not been rewritten, and so was absent from the *Quenta Silmarillion* (QS) and still only found in the *Quenta Noldorinwa* (Q). I think therefore that it is certain that the text QS(E) now to be given belongs to the same period (i.e. immediately before the commencement of *The Lord of the Rings*) as the other chapters (the end of 'Beren and Tinúviel', the Battle of Unnumbered Tears, the beginning of 'Túrin') that belong with the QS manuscript but were not written into it (or, in the case of the last part of 'Beren and Tinúviel', not till long after).* Why my father should have jumped to the end in this way, taking up in mid-sentence, I cannot at all explain.

It is seen then that at the period with which this book is concerned the missing parts of the QS narrative were the greater part of the tale of Túrin, the destruction of Doriath, the fall of Gondolin, and the earlier part of the tale of Eärendel. But my father never returned to these tales (in the strictly 'Silmarillion' tradition: the Túrin story was of course enormously developed later, and some slight elaboration is found elsewhere for the other parts. The *Grey Annals* were abandoned at the end of the tale of Túrin, and the later tale of Tuor (given in *Unfinished Tales*) before Tuor came to Gondolin).

The manuscript E was emended, frequently but not radically, at different times: some changes were made at or very near the time of its original composition (and these are adopted silently into the text); others, made very roughly in pencil, are clearly from long after (and these are not mentioned here).

The text is closely related to Q II, §§17–19, and for substantial stretches, especially towards the end, the earlier work was followed with unusual fidelity: thus for example the Second Prophecy of Mandos, with its mysterious elements, was repeated virtually without change. Of course, the later emendations made to Q II and given in the notes to that text were, according to my father's usual practice, preparatory to the present version, and very likely belong to this time: the amount of change is therefore, to appearance, diminished, as between the material given in Vol. IV and the present chapter. It would have been possible to restrict the text printed here to those passages which differ significantly from Q II (as revised), but I have thought it best to give it in its entirety. The very fact that the end of 'The Silmarillion' still took this form when *The Lord of the Rings* was begun is sufficiently remarkable, and by its inclusion in full a complete view of the Matter of Middle-earth and Valinor at that time is provided.

The numbering of the paragraphs begins again here from §1.

§1    And they looked upon the Lonely Isle and there they tarried not; and at the last they cast anchor in the Bay of Elvenhome upon the borders of the world; and the Teleri saw the coming of that ship and were amazed, gazing from afar upon the light of the Silmaril, and it was very great. But Eärendel, alone of living Men, landed on the immortal shores; and he said to Elwing and to those that were with him, three mariners who had sailed all the seas beside him, and Falathar, Airandir, and Erellont were

---

*The existence of the rewritten conclusion should have been mentioned in the footnote to III. 366.

their names: 'Here shall none but myself set foot, lest you fall under the wrath of the Gods and the doom of death; for it is forbidden. But that peril I will take on myself for the sake of the Two Kindreds.'

§2   And Elwing answered: 'Then shall our paths be sundered for ever. Nay, all thy perils I will take on myself also!' And she leaped into the white foam and ran towards him; but Eärendel was sorrowful, for he deemed that they would now both die ere many days were past. And there they bade farewell to their companions and were taken from them for ever.

§3   And Eärendel said to Elwing: 'Await me here; for one only may bear the messages that I am charged with'; and he went up alone into the land, and it seemed to him empty and silent. For even as Morgoth and Ungoliantë came in ages past, so now Eärendel had come at a time of festival, and wellnigh all the Elvenfolk were gone to Valinor, or were gathered in the halls of Manwë upon Taniquetil, and few were left to keep watch upon the walls of Tûn.

§4   These watchers rode therefore in great haste to Valmar; and all the bells in Valmar pealed. But Eärendel climbed the great green hill of Kôr and found it bare; and he entered into the streets of Tûn and they were empty; and his heart was heavy, for he feared that some evil had come even to the Blessed Realm. He walked now in the deserted ways of Tûn, and the dust upon his raiment and his shoes was a dust of diamonds, and he shone and glistened as he climbed the long white stairs. And he called aloud in many tongues, both of Elves and Men, but there were none to answer him. Therefore he turned back at last towards the shores, thinking to set sail once more upon Vingelot his ship and abandon his errand, and live for ever upon the sea. But even as he took the shoreward road and turned his face away from the towers of Tûn one stood upon the hill and called to him in a great voice, crying: 'Hail Eärendel, radiant star, messenger most fair! Hail thou bearer of light before the Sun and Moon, the looked for that comest unawares, the longed for that comest beyond hope! Hail, splendour of the children of the world, slayer of the dark! Star of the sunset, hail! Hail, herald of the morn!'

§5   And that was the voice of Fionwë son of Manwë; and he came from Valmar and he summoned Eärendel to come before the Gods. And Eärendel went to Valinor and to the halls of Valmar, and never again set foot upon the lands of Men. There before the faces of the undying Gods he stood, and delivered the errand of the Two Kindreds. Pardon he asked for the Noldor and pity for their great sorrows, and mercy upon unhappy Men and succour in their need. And his prayers were granted.

§6 Then the sons of the Valar prepared for battle, and the captain of their host was Fionwë son of Manwë. Beneath his white banner marched also the Lindar, the Light-elves, the people of Ingwë; and among them were also those of the Noldor of old who had never departed from Valinor, and Ingwiel son of Ingwë was their chief. But remembering the slaying at the Swan-haven and the rape of their ships, few of the Teleri were willing to go forth to war; but Elwing went among them, and because she was fair and gentle, and was come also upon her father's side from Thingol who was of their own kindred, they harkened to her; and they sent mariners sufficient to man and steer the ships upon which most of that army was borne east oversea; but they stayed aboard their ships and none ever set foot upon the shores of the Hither Lands.

§7 And thus it was that Elwing came among the Teleri. Eärendel was long time gone and she became lonely and afraid; and she wandered along the margin of the sea, singing sadly to herself; and so she came to Alqualondë, the Swan-haven, where lay the Telerian fleets; and there the Teleri befriended her. When therefore Eärendel at last returned, seeking her, he found her among them, and they listened to her tales of Thingol and Melian and the Hidden Kingdom, and of Lúthien the fair, and they were filled with pity and wonder.

§8 Now the Gods took counsel concerning Eärendel, and they summoned Ulmo from the deeps; and when they were gathered together Mandos spoke, saying: 'Now he shall surely die, for he has trodden the forbidden shores.' But Ulmo said: 'For this he was born into the world. And say unto me: whether is he Eärendel Tuor's son of the line of Hador, or Idril's son Turgon's daughter of the Elven-house of Finwë? Or being half of either kindred, which half shall die?' And Mandos answered: 'Equally was it forbidden to the Noldor that went wilfully into exile to return hither.'

§9 Then Manwë gave judgement and he said: 'To Eärendel I remit the ban, and the peril that he took upon himself out of love for the Two Kindreds shall not fall on him; neither shall it fall upon Elwing who entered into peril for love of Eärendel: save only in this: they shall not ever walk again among Elves or Men in the Outer Lands. Now all those who have the blood of mortal Men, in whatever part, great or small, are mortal, unless other doom be granted to them; but in this matter the power of doom is given to me. This is my decree: to Eärendel and to Elwing and to their sons shall be given leave each to choose freely under which kindred they shall be judged.'

§10   Then Eärendel and Elwing were summoned, and this decree was declared to them. But Eärendel said to Elwing: 'Choose thou, for now I am weary of the world.' And she chose to be judged among the Firstborn, because of Lúthien, and for the sake of Elwing Eärendel chose alike, though his heart was rather with the kindred of Men and the people of his father.

§11   The Gods then sent Fionwë, and he came to the shore where the companions of Eärendel still remained, awaiting tidings. And Fionwë took a boat and set therein the three mariners, and the Gods drove them away East with a great wind. But they took Vingelot, and they hallowed it, and they bore it away through Valinor to the uttermost rim of the world, and there it [*added:* passed through the Door of Night and] was lifted up even into the oceans of heaven. Now fair and marvellous was that vessel made, and it was filled with a wavering flame, pure and bright; and Eärendel the mariner sat at the helm, glistening with dust of elven-gems; and the Silmaril was bound upon his brow. Far he journeyed in that ship, even into the starless voids; but most often was he seen at morning or at eve, glimmering in sunrise or sunset, as he came back to Valinor from voyages beyond the confines of the world.

§12   On those journeys Elwing did not go, for she had not the strength to endure the cold and pathless voids, and she loved rather the earth and the sweet winds that blow on sea and hill. Therefore she let build for her a white tower upon the borders of the outer world, in the northern region of the Sundering Seas; and thither all the sea-birds of the earth at times repaired. And it is said that Elwing learned the tongues and lore of birds, who had herself once worn their shape; and she devised wings for herself of white and silver-grey, and they taught her the craft of flight. And at whiles, when Eärendel returning drew near again to earth, she would fly to meet him, even as she had flown long ago, when she was rescued from the sea. Then the farsighted among the Elves that dwelt most westerly in the Lonely Isle would see her like a white bird, shining, rose-stained in the sunset, as she soared in joy to greet the coming of Vingelot to haven.

§13   Now when first Vingelot was set to sail on the seas of heaven, it rose unlooked-for, glittering and bright; and the folk of earth beheld it from afar and wondered, and they took it for a sign of hope. And when this new star arose in the West, Maidros said unto Maglor: 'Surely that is a Silmaril that shineth in the sky?' And Maglor said: 'If it be verily that Silmaril that we saw cast into the sea that riseth again by the power of the Gods, then let us be glad; for its glory is seen now by many, and is yet secure from all evil.' Then the Elves looked up, and despaired no longer; but Morgoth was filled with doubt.

§14  Yet it is said that Morgoth looked not for the assault that came upon him from the West. So great was his pride become that he deemed that none would ever again come up with open war against him. Moreover he thought that he had for ever estranged the Gnomes from the Gods and from their kin; and that content in their blissful Realm the Valar would heed no more his kingdom in the world without. For to him that is pitiless the deeds of pity are ever strange and beyond reckoning.

§15  Of the march of the host of Fionwë to the North little is said in any tale; for in his armies went none of those Elves who had dwelt and suffered in the Hither Lands, and who made the histories of those days that still are known; and tidings of these things they learned long afterward from their kinsfolk, the Light-elves of Valinor. But at the last Fionwë came up out of the West, and the challenge of his trumpets filled the sky; and he summoned unto him all Elves and Men from Hithlum unto the East; and Beleriand was ablaze with the glory of his arms, for the sons of the Gods were young and fair and terrible, and the mountains rang beneath their feet.

§16  The meeting of the hosts of the West and of the North is named the Great Battle, the Battle Terrible, and the War of Wrath. There was marshalled the whole power of the Throne of Morgoth, and it had become great beyond count, so that Dor-na-Fauglith could not contain it, and all the North was aflame with war. But it availed not. The Balrogs were destroyed, save some few that fled and hid themselves in caverns inaccessible at the roots of the earth. The uncounted legions of the Orcs perished like straw in a great fire, or were swept like shrivelled leaves before a burning wind. Few remained to trouble the world for long years after. And it is said that all that were left of the three Houses of the Elf-friends, Fathers of Men, fought for Fionwë; and they were avenged upon the Orcs in those days for Baragund and Barahir, Gumlin and Gundor, Huor and Húrin, and many others of their lords; and so were fulfilled in part the words of Ulmo, for by

Eärendel son of Tuor help was brought unto the Elves, and by the swords of Men they were strengthened on the fields of war. But the most part of the sons of Men, whether of the people of Uldor or others newcome out of the East, marched with the Enemy; and the Elves do not forget it.

§17   Then, seeing that his hosts were overthrown and his power dispersed, Morgoth quailed, and he dared not to come forth himself. But he loosed upon his foes the last desperate assault that he had prepared, and out of the pits of Angband there issued the winged dragons, that had not before been seen; for until that day no creatures of his cruel thought had yet assailed the air. So sudden and ruinous was the onset of that dreadful fleet that Fionwë was driven back; for the coming of the dragons was like a great roar of thunder, and a tempest of fire, and their wings were of steel.

§18   Then Eärendel came, shining with white flame, and about Vingelot were gathered all the great birds of heaven, and Thorondor was their captain, and there was battle in the air all the day and through a dark night of doubt. And ere the rising of the sun Eärendel slew Ancalagon the Black, the mightiest of the dragon-host, and he cast him from the sky, and in his fall the towers of Thangorodrim were thrown down. Then the sun rose, and the Children of the Valar prevailed, and all the dragons were destroyed, save two alone; and they fled into the East. Then all the pits of Morgoth were broken and unroofed, and the might of Fionwë descended into the deeps of the earth. And there Morgoth stood at last at bay, and yet unvaliant. He fled into the deepest of his mines and sued for peace and pardon; but his feet were hewn from under him and he was hurled upon his face. Then he was bound with the chain Angainor, which long had been prepared; and his iron crown they beat into a collar for his neck, and his head was bowed upon his knees. But Fionwë took the two Silmarils which remained and guarded them.

§19   Thus an end was made of the power of Angband in the North, and the evil realm was brought to nought; and out of the pits and deep prisons a multitude of thralls came forth beyond all hope into the light of day, and they looked upon a world all changed. For so great was the fury of those adversaries that the northern regions of the western world were rent asunder, and the sea roared in through many chasms, and there was confusion and great noise; and rivers perished or found new paths, and the valleys were upheaved and the hills trod down; and Sirion was no more. Then Men, such as had not perished in the ruin of those days, fled far away, and it was long ere any came back over Eredlindon to the places where Beleriand had been.

§20   But Fionwë marched through the western lands summoning the remnant of the Noldor, and the Dark-elves that had not yet looked on Valinor, to join with the thralls released and to depart from Middle-earth. But Maidros would not harken, and he prepared, though now with weariness and loathing, to attempt in despair the fulfilment of his oath. For Maidros would have given battle for the Silmarils, were they withheld, even against the victorious host of Valinor and the might and splendour of the sons of the Gods: even though he stood alone in all the world. And he sent a message unto Fionwë, bidding him yield up now those jewels which of old Fëanor made and Morgoth stole from him.

§21   But Fionwë said that the right to the work of their hands, which Fëanor and his sons formerly possessed, had now perished, because of their many and merciless deeds, being blinded by their oath, and most of all because of the slaying of Dior and the assault upon Elwing. The light of the Silmarils should go now to the Gods, whence it came in the beginning; and to Valinor must Maidros and Maglor return and there abide the judgement of the Valar, by whose decree alone would Fionwë yield the jewels from his charge.

§22   Maglor desired indeed to submit, for his heart was sorrowful, and he said: 'The oath says not that we may not bide our time, and maybe in Valinor all shall be forgiven and forgot, and we shall come into our own in peace.' But Maidros said that, if once they returned and the favour of the Gods were withheld from them, then their oath would still remain, but its fulfilment be beyond all hope. 'And who can tell to what dreadful doom we shall come, if we disobey the Powers in their own land, or purpose ever to bring war again into their holy realm?' And Maglor said: 'Yet if Manwë and Varda themselves deny the fulfilment of an oath to which we named them in witness, is it not made void?' And Maidros answered: 'But how shall our voices reach to Ilúvatar beyond the circles of the World? And by Him we swore in our madness, and called the Everlasting Darkness upon us, if we kept not our word. Who shall release us?' 'If none can release us,' said Maglor, 'then indeed the Everlasting Darkness shall be our lot, whether we keep our oath or break it; but less evil shall we do in the breaking.' Yet he yielded to the will of Maidros, and they took counsel together how they should lay hands on the Silmarils.

§23   And so it came to pass that they came in disguise to the camps of Fionwë, and at night they crept in to the places where the Silmarils were guarded, and they slew the guards, and laid hands upon the jewels; and then, since all the camp was roused against them, they prepared to die, defending themselves until the last. But Fionwë restrained his folk, and the brethren departed unfought, and fled far away. Each took a single Silmaril, for they said: 'Since one is lost to us, and but two remain, and two brethren, so is it plain that fate would have us share the heirlooms of our father.'

§24   But the jewel burned the hand of Maidros in pain unbearable (and he had but one hand, as has before been told); and he perceived that it was as Fionwë had said, and that his right thereto had become void, and that the oath was vain. And being in anguish and despair he cast himself into a gaping chasm filled with fire, and so ended; and the Silmaril that he bore was taken into the bosom of Earth.

§25   And it is told of Maglor that he could not endure the pain with which the Silmaril tormented him; and he cast it at last into the sea, and thereafter he wandered ever upon the shores singing in pain and regret beside the waves. For Maglor was the mightiest of the singers of old, but he came never back among the people of the Elves. And thus it came to pass that the Silmarils found their long homes: one in the airs of heaven, and one in the fires of the heart of the world, and one in the deep waters.

§26   In those days there was a great building of ships upon the shores of the Western Sea, and especially upon the great isles which, in the disruption of the northern world, were fashioned of ancient Beleriand. Thence in many a fleet the survivors of the Gnomes, and of the companies of the Dark-elves of Doriath and Ossiriand, set sail into the West and came never again into the lands of weeping and of war. But the Lindar, the Light-elves, marched back beneath the banners of their king, and they were borne in triumph unto Valinor. Yet their joy in victory was diminished, for they returned without the Silmarils and the light before the Sun and Moon, and they knew that those jewels could not be found or brought together again until the world was broken and re-made anew.

§27   And when they came into the West the Gnomes for the most part rehabited the Lonely Isle, that looks both West and

East; and that land became very fair, and so remains. But some returned even to Valinor, as all were free to do who willed; and there the Gnomes were admitted again to the love of Manwë and the pardon of the Valar; and the Teleri forgave their ancient grief, and the curse was laid to rest.

§28   Yet not all the Eldalië were willing to forsake the Hither Lands where they had long suffered and long dwelt; and some lingered many an age in the West and North, and especially in the western isles and in the Land of Leithien. And among these were Maglor, as hath been told; and with him for a while was Elrond Halfelven, who chose, as was granted to him, to be among the Elf-kindred; but Elros his brother chose to abide with Men. And from these brethren alone the blood of the Firstborn and the seed divine of Valinor have come among Mankind: for they were the sons of Elwing, Dior's daughter, Lúthien's son, child of Thingol and Melian; and Eärendel their sire was Idril's son Celebrindal, the fair maid of Gondolin. But ever as the ages drew on and the Elf-folk faded upon earth, they would set sail at eve from the western shores of this world, as still they do, until now there linger few anywhere of their lonely companies.

§29   This was the doom of the Gods, when Fionwë and the sons of the Valar returned to Valmar and told of all the things that had been done. Thereafter the Hither Lands of Middle-earth should be for Mankind, the younger children of the world; but to the Elves, the Firstborn, alone should the gateways of the West stand ever open. And if the Elves would not come thither and tarried in the lands of Men, then they should slowly fade and fail. This is the most grievous of the fruits of the lies and works that Morgoth wrought, that the Eldalië should be sundered and estranged from Men. For a while other evils that he had devised or nurtured lived on, although he himself was taken away; and Orcs and Dragons, breeding again in dark places, became names of terror, and did evil deeds, as in sundry regions they still do; but ere the End all shall perish. But Morgoth himself the Gods thrust through the Door of Night into the Timeless Void, beyond the Walls of the World; and a guard is set for ever on that door, and Eärendel keeps watch upon the ramparts of the sky.

§30   Yet the lies that Melkor, the mighty and accursed, Morgoth Bauglir, the Power of Terror and of Hate, sowed in the hearts of Elves and Men are a seed that doth not die and cannot by the Gods be destroyed; and ever and anon it sprouts anew, and bears dark fruit even to these latest days. Some say also that Morgoth himself has at times crept back, secretly as a cloud that cannot be seen, and yet is venomous, surmounting the Walls, and visiting the world to encourage his servants and set on foot evil when all seems fair. But others say that this is the black shadow of Sauron, whom the Gnomes named Gorthû, who served Morgoth even in Valinor and came with him, and was the greatest and most evil of his underlings; and Sauron fled from the Great Battle and escaped, and he dwelt in dark places and perverted Men to his dreadful allegiance and his foul worship.

§31   Thus spake Mandos in prophecy, when the Gods sat in judgement in Valinor, and the rumour of his words was whispered among all the Elves of the West. When the world is old and the Powers grow weary, then Morgoth, seeing that the guard sleepeth, shall come back through the Door of Night out of the Timeless Void; and he shall destroy the Sun and Moon. But Eärendel shall descend upon him as a white and searing flame and drive him from the airs. Then shall the Last Battle be gathered on the fields of Valinor. In that day Tulkas shall strive with Morgoth, and on his right hand shall be Fionwë, and on his left Túrin Turambar, son of Húrin, coming from the halls of Mandos; and the black sword of Túrin shall deal unto Morgoth his death and final end; and so shall the children of Húrin and all Men be avenged.

§32   Thereafter shall Earth be broken and re-made, and the Silmarils shall be recovered out of Air and Earth and Sea; for Eärendel shall descend and surrender that flame which he hath had in keeping. Then Fëanor shall take the Three Jewels and bear them to Yavanna Palúrien; and she will break them and with their fire rekindle the Two Trees, and a great light shall come forth. And the Mountains of Valinor shall be levelled, so that the Light shall go out over all the world. In that light the Gods will grow young again, and the Elves awake and all their dead arise, and the purpose of Ilúvatar be fulfilled concerning them. But of Men in that day the prophecy of Mandos doth not speak, and no Man it names, save Túrin only, and to him a place is given among the sons of the Valar.

§33   Here endeth *The Silmarillion*: which is drawn out in brief from those songs and histories which are yet sung and told by the fading Elves, and (more clearly and fully) by the vanished Elves that dwell now upon the Lonely Isle, Tol Eressëa, whither few mariners of Men have ever come, save once or twice in a long age when some man of Eärendel's race hath passed beyond the lands of mortal sight and seen the glimmer of the lamps upon the quays of Avallon, and smelt afar the undying flowers in the meads of Dorwinion. Of whom was Eriol one, that men named Ælfwine, and he alone returned and brought tidings of Cortirion to the Hither Lands.

### Commentary on the conclusion of the Quenta Silmarillion

[All references to Q are to the second version, Q II.]

§1   After 'landed on the immortal shores' my father wrote (following Q, IV. 153) 'and neither Elwing nor any of his three mariners would he suffer to go with him, lest they fall under the wrath of the Gods', but struck this out in the moment of composition and replaced it by the passage given. The three mariners were not named in Q, where it is only said that Eärendel had a 'small company'. Cf. *The Lost Road* p. 60 and note 8.

§2   The story here of Elwing's leaping into the surf in the Bay of Elvenhome, and (in §3) of Eärendel's command to her to stay by the shores and await his return, is changed from that found in revisions to the text of Q (IV. 156), where Elwing was sundered for ever from Eärendel (see IV. 197–8).

§6   It is notable that the Lindar are here (and again in §§15, 26) called the 'Light-elves', this being a reversion to the earlier application of the term. At the beginning of QS (§§25, 40) the Lindar are the 'High Elves', and 'the Lindar and the Noldor and the Teleri are named the Light Elves' (§29), thus distinguished from the 'Dark Elves' who never passed over the sea to Valinor.

   The words 'and Ingwiel son of Ingwë was their chief' first appear in an addition to Q (IV. 156 note 19). I suggested (IV. 196) that what my father really meant was that Ingwiel was the chief of the Lindar, among whom went the Noldor of Valinor; not that Ingwiel was the leader of the Noldor themselves – that was Finrod (later Finarfin).

§§6–7   A new element in the story is the sojourn of Elwing among the Teleri; the implication is clearly that the Teleri were influenced by her in providing their ships and mariners. Elwing was the great-grand-niece of Elwë Lord of Alqualondë. In AB 2 (annal 333–43), following AB 1, none of the Teleri left Valinor, though 'they built a countless multitude of ships.'

§§8–11   Wholly new is the matter of the council of the Gods, the decree of Manwë declared to Eärendel and Elwing, their choices of fate, and the despatch of the three mariners eastwards with a great wind. – On 'the forbidden shores' and the Ban of the Valar see the commentary on *The Fall of Númenor I*, §4.

§9   It is to be observed that according to the judgement of Manwë Dior

Thingol's Heir, son of Beren, was mortal irrespective of the choice of his mother.

§11    As Q II was originally written, Elwing devised wings for Eärendel's ship, whereby he sailed into the sky bearing the Silmaril (§17), but *after* the Great Battle and the expulsion of Morgoth through the Door of Night, because Eärendel was scorched by the Sun and hunted by the Moon, the Gods took his ship Wingelot and hallowed it, and launched it through the Door of Night (§19). In view of the statement in Q here that Eärendel 'set sail into *the starless vast* . . . voyaging *the Dark behind the world*', and in view also of the very explicit account of the Door in the *Ambarkanta* (IV. 237) – it 'pierceth the Walls and opens upon the Void' – I have supposed (IV. 203) that 'this act of the Valar was to protect Eärendel, by setting him to sail in the Void, above the courses of the Sun and Moon and stars, where also he could guard the Door against Morgoth's return.' In the same passage of the *Ambarkanta* it is said that the Valar made the Door of Night 'when Melko was overcome and put forth into the Outer Dark', and that it is 'guarded by Eärendel'.

The passage in Q §17 was, however, revised (IV. 156 note 20), and the launching of Wingelot by the Gods introduced at an earlier point in the narrative, before the Great Battle, and so before the making of the Door of Night (according to the *Ambarkanta*). It is not said in this revised passage that Eärendel passed through the Door, nor is it made explicit into what high regions he passed: his ship 'was lifted even into the oceans of the air'. This revision is taken up here in the present text, and again (as originally written) the Door of Night is not mentioned: the ship 'was lifted up even into the oceans of heaven' – and Eärendel journeyed far in it, 'even into the starless voids'. One could therefore possibly accommodate the revised story of the launching of Eärendel in Vingelot to the *Ambarkanta* by supposing that it was no longer my father's thought that he passed through the Door of Night (which was not yet in existence): he did not pass into Ava-kúma, the Outer Dark, but remained within 'the starless voids' of Vaiya. But this theory is undone by my father's addition of the very words in question, 'passed through the Door of Night', to the account. (This addition was not one of those made at the time of the writing of the manuscript, but it was made carefully in ink and does not belong with the rough alterations made much later.) In any case the words 'as he came back to Valinor from voyages *beyond the confines of the world*' suggest that he sailed into the Void. It seems therefore only possible to explain this on the assumption that the *Ambarkanta* conception had in this point been abandoned, and that the Door of Night was already in existence before Morgoth's great defeat.

§12    On the history of the white tower whither all the sea-birds of the world at times repaired see IV. 197. In Q II as originally written it was Eärendel who built the tower; by the revision (IV. 156 note 20) it was built by Elwing, who devised wings for herself in order to try to fly to him, but in vain: 'and they are sundered till the end of the world.' Now the story shifts again. Elwing still builds the tower, but it is added that she learns the tongues of the birds and from them the craft of flight; and she is not now parted for ever from Eärendel after his transformation into the Star: she rises to meet him from her tower as he returns from his voyages beyond the confines of the world.

§15    A substantial space is left in the text after §14, and §15 begins with an ornate initial, suggesting that my father foresaw the beginning of a new chapter here. This was in fact inserted at the time of the late, pencilled emendations: *Of the Great Battle and the War of Wrath*.

§§15–16    In the account of the Great Battle my father simply followed the opening of Q II §18, though the outline of a much fuller tale had appeared at the end of AB 2: the landing of Ingwiel at Eglorest, the Battle of Eglorest, Fionwë's camp by Sirion, the thunderous coming of Morgoth over Taur-na-Fuin (this, if not actually excluded, at least made to seem very improbable in Q and QS), and the long-contested passage of Sirion.

§16    In my view there is no question that the words (not in Q) 'save some few [Balrogs] that fled and hid themselves in caverns inaccessible at the roots of the earth' preceded by a good while the Balrog of Moria (there is in any case evidence that a Balrog was not my father's original conception of Gandalf's adversary on the Bridge of Khazad-dûm). It was, I believe, the idea – first appearing here – that some Balrogs had survived from the ancient world in the deep places of Middle-earth that led to the Balrog of Moria. In this connection a letter of my father's written in April 1954 (*Letters* no. 144, p. 180) is interesting:

[The Balrogs] were supposed to have been all destroyed in the overthrow of Thangorodrim . . . But it is here found . . . that one had escaped and taken refuge under the mountains of Hithaeglin [*sic*].

On the words 'all that were left of the three Houses of the Elf-friends, Fathers of Men' see the commentary on *The Fall of Númenor I*, §1.

§18    On the retention of the motive of the birds that accompanied Eärendel (which arose from an earlier form of the legend) see IV. 203. Thorondor as the captain of 'the great birds of heaven' is not named in Q, which has here 'a myriad of birds were about him.'

§20    A further heading was pencilled in against the beginning of this paragraph (see under §15 above): *Of the Last End of the Oath of Fëanor and his Sons*.

§22    The debate between Maglor and Maidros is articulated further than it was in Q, with the last and wisest word to Maglor, though the outcome is the same: for Maidros overbore him.

§26    A final heading was pencilled at the beginning of this paragraph: *Of the Passing of the Elves*.

§28    On the earlier accounts of Elrond's choice see p. 23. Now there appears both his changed decision, 'to be among the Elf-kindred', and the choice of his brother Elros 'to abide with Men'. Elros has been named in emendations to Q (IV. 155) and in later alterations to AB 2 (commentary on annal 325), and though these additions say nothing about him he was obviously introduced into these texts after the legend of Númenor had begun to develop. This is shown by the fact that still in the second text of *The Fall of Númenor* it was Elrond the mortal who was the first King of Númenor and the builder of Númenos (§2), and Elros only appears in his place by emendation.

In view of the presence here of Elros beside Elrond – whereas Elros is still absent in QS §87 – and the respective choices of the Half-elven, it is perhaps surprising that in §16 my father made no mention of the land of Númenor made for the Men of the T˙ ree Houses (see §§1–2 in both FN I and FN II); still more so, that he followed Q so closely in features where the 'intrusion' of Númenor had already introduced new conceptions. Thus he still wrote here in §19 that after the Great Battle 'Men . . . fled far away, and it was long ere any came back over Eredlindon to the places *where Beleriand had been*', and in §26 of 'the great building of ships upon the shores of the Western Sea, and especially upon the great isles which, in the disruption of the northern world, were fashioned of ancient Beleriand.'

It is not easy to trace the evolution of my father's conception of the survival of Beleriand (especially in relation to the destruction wrought at the Downfall of Númenor, see pp. 153–4); but in the FN texts there is clearly already a somewhat different view from that in Q. In FN II (where as noted above Elros had not yet emerged and which must therefore have preceded the present text) the story of the Last Alliance was already developed (§14): Elendil the Númenórean, a king in Beleriand,

> took counsel with the Elves that remained in Middle-earth (and these abode then mostly in Beleriand); and he made a league with Gil-galad the Elf-king . . . And their armies were joined, and passed the mountains and came into inner lands far from the Sea.

While the passages cited above from the present text are not in necessary or explicit contradiction to this, they are hardly congruent with it. The fact that my father later pencilled against §28 the names *Gilgalad* and *Lindon* could indeed be taken at first sight as showing that the conception of the undrowned land west of the Blue Mountains, and the alliance between Men and Elves who dwelt there, arose after it was written; but the evidence is decisive against this being the case.

I cannot offer any convincing explanation of this situation. It might be suggested that my father had the conscious intent to represent different and to some degree divergent 'traditions' concerning events after the overthrow of Morgoth and the great departure of Elves into the West; but this seems to me improbable. (On the name *Lindon* of the undrowned land see pp. 31–4 and the commentary on QS §108.)

*Idril's son Celebrindal* is an old idiom = Idril Celebrindal's son.

§30   Notable, and disconcerting to the editor, is the form *Melkor* (instead of *Melko*), which is quite certainly original here. I have said in IV. 282 that '*Melkor* for *Melko* was not introduced until 1951.' The evidence for this lies in the note referred to on p. 294, which gives a list of 'Alterations in last revision [i.e. of 'The Silmarillion'] 1951': these include *Aman*, *Arda*, *Atani* / *Edain*, *Eä*, *Eru*, *Melkor*, and a few less significant names. This important scrap of paper provides an external date – rare good fortune in this study – by which pre- and post-*Lord of the Rings* texts can often be distinguished; and the checks furnished by it are in complete harmony with what may be more tentatively deduced on other grounds. I have found nowhere any reason to suspect that *Aman*, *Arda*, etc. were ever used in the pre-*Lord of the Rings* period; and I therefore too readily assumed that the same was true of *Melkor* (which differs from the others in that it is not an entirely new name but only a new form), not having observed that it occurred in the present passage as an original form. It is to be noted that *Melko* was changed to *Melkor* on the Q-text at the same point (IV. 166 note 1).

No doubt the explanation of my father's including *Melkor* as an alteration made in 1951 when he had used it long before is in fact quite simple: he decided on *Melkor* at this time, and when he returned to 'The Silmarillion' after *The Lord of the Rings* was finished he used it in his revisions and rewritings of QS, and it was therefore an alteration of 1951. This is a good example of the traps that he most unwittingly laid, and which I cannot hope to have evaded in more significant matters than this.

The difficult passage concerning Morgoth's 'surmounting' the Walls of the World survives from Q (IV. 164): see IV. 253.

*Gorthû:* thus the name *Thû*, compounded *Gorthû*, reappears as the name of Sauron in the Noldorin tongue (see the *Etymologies*, stem THUS). *Gorthû* has occurred in emendations to the *Lay of Leithian* (III. 232–3), and in a change to the typescript text of FN II (p. 33). – With the statement that Sauron served Morgoth in Valinor cf. QS §143 and commentary ('Sauron was the chief servant of the evil Vala, whom he had suborned to his service in Valinor from among the people of the Gods'). In Q here 'others say that this is the black shadow of Thû, *whom Morgoth made*', changed (IV. 166 note 3) to a reading close to that of the present text.

§33   *The quays of Avallon.* At this time *Avallon* was a name of Tol Eressëa: 'the Lonely Island, which was renamed Avallon', FN II §1. *The meads of Dorwinion* must be in Tol Eressëa. The name has previously occurred as a land of vines in 'the burning South' in the *Lay of the Children of Húrin*, in the wine of Dorwinion in *The Hobbit*, and as marked on the map made by Pauline Baynes; see III. 26, which needs to be corrected by addition of a reference to this passage.

# PART THREE

---

# THE
# ETYMOLOGIES

# THE ETYMOLOGIES

The mode of my father's linguistic construction, which as is well known was carried on throughout his life and in very close relation to the evolution of the narratives, shows the same unceasing movement as do they: a quality fundamental to the art, in which (as I believe) finality and a system fixed at every point was not its underlying aim. But while his 'language' and his 'literature' were so closely interwoven, to trace the history of the literary process through many texts (even though the trail might be greatly obscured) is of its nature enormously much easier than to trace the astounding complexity of the phonological and grammatical evolution of the Elvish languages.

Those languages were conceived, of course, from the very beginning in a deeply 'historical' way: they were embodied in a history, the history of the Elves who spoke them, in which was to be found, as it evolved, a rich terrain for linguistic separation and interaction: 'a language requires a suitable habitation, and a history in which it can develop' (*Letters* no. 294, p. 375). Every element in the languages, every element in every word, is in principle historically 'explicable' – as are the elements in languages that are not 'invented' – and the successive phases of their intricate evolution were the delight of their creator. 'Invention' was thus altogether distinct from 'artificiality'. In his essay 'A Secret Vice' (*The Monsters and the Critics and Other Essays*, 1983, p. 198) my father wrote of his liking for Esperanto, a liking which, he said, arose 'not least because it is the creation ultimately of one man, not a philologist, and is therefore something like a "human language bereft of the inconveniences due to too many successive cooks" – which is as good a description of the ideal artificial language (in a particular sense) as I can give.' The Elvish languages are, in this sense, very inconvenient indeed, and they image the activities of countless cooks (unconscious, of course, of what they were doing to the ingredients they had come by): in other words, they image language not as 'pure structure', without 'before' and 'after', but as growth, in time.

On the other hand, the linguistic histories were nonetheless 'images', invented by an inventor, who was free to change those histories as he was free to change the story of the world in which they took place; and he did so abundantly. The difficulties inherent in the study of the history of any language or group of languages are here therefore compounded: for this history is not a datum of historical fact to be uncovered, but an unstable, shifting view of what the history was. Moreover, the alterations in the history were not confined to features of 'interior' linguistic development: the 'exterior' conception of the languages and their relations underwent change, even profound change; and it is not to be thought that the representation of the languages in letters, in *tengwar*, should be exempt.

It must be added that my father's characteristic method of work – elaborate beginnings collapsing into scrawls; manuscripts overlaid with layer upon layer of emendation – here find their most extreme expression; and also that the philological papers were left in the greatest disorder. Without external dating, the only way to determine sequence (apart from the very general and uncertain guide of changing hand-writing) is in the internal evidence of the changing philology itself; and that, of its nature, does not offer the sort of clues that lead through the maze of the literary texts. The clues it does offer are very much more elusive. It is also unfortunately true that hasty handwriting and ill-formed letters are here far more destructive; and a great deal of my father's late philological writing is, I think, strictly unusable.

It will be seen then that the philological component in the evolution of Middle-earth can scarcely be analysed, and most certainly cannot be presented, as can the literary texts. In any case, my father was perhaps more interested in the processes of change than he was in displaying the structure and use of the languages at any given time – though this is no doubt due to some extent to his so often starting again at the beginning with the primordial sounds of the Quendian languages, embarking on a grand design that could not be sustained (it seems indeed that the very attempt to write a definitive account produced immediate dissatisfaction and the desire for new constructions: so the most beautiful manuscripts were soon treated with disdain).

The most surprising thing, perhaps, is that he was so little concerned to make comprehensive vocabularies of the Elvish tongues. He never made again anything like the little packed 'dictionary' of the original Gnomish language on which I drew in the appendices to *The Book of Lost Tales*. It may be that such an undertaking was always postponed to the day, which would never come, when a sufficient finality had been achieved; in the meantime, it was not for him a prime necessity. He did not, after all, 'invent' new words and names arbitrarily: in principle, he devised them from within the historical structure, proceeding from the 'bases' or primitive stems, adding suffix or prefix or forming compounds, deciding (or, as he would have said, 'finding out') when the word came into the language, following through the regular changes of form that it would thus have undergone, and observing the possibilities of formal or semantic influence from other words in the course of its history. Such a word would then exist for him, and he would know it. As the whole system evolved and expanded, the possibilities for word and name became greater and greater.

The nearest he ever came to a sustained account of Elvish vocabulary is not in the form of nor intended to serve as a dictionary in the ordinary sense, but is an etymological dictionary of word-relationships: an alphabetically-arranged list of primary stems, or 'bases', with their derivatives (thus following directly in form from the original 'Qenya Lexicon' which I have described in I. 246). It is this work that is given here. My father wrote a good deal on the theory of *sundokarme* or 'base-structure' (see SUD and KAR in the *Etymologies*), but like everything else it was frequently elaborated and altered, and I do not attempt its presentation here. My object in giving the *Etymologies* * in this book is rather as an indication of the development, and mode of development, of the vocabularies of the Elvish languages at this period than as a first step in the elucidation of the linguistic history; and also because they form an instructive companion to the narrative works of this time.

It is a remarkable document, which must be reckoned among the most difficult of all the papers containing unique material which my father left. The inherent difficulties of the text are increased by the very bad condition of the manuscript, which for much of its length is battered, torn, crumpled at the edges, and discoloured (so that much that was very lightly pencilled is now barely visible and extremely hard to decipher). In some sections the maze of forms and cancellations is so dense, and for the most part made so quickly, that one cannot be sure what my father's final intention was: in these parts he was working out potential connections and derivations on the spot, by no means setting down already determined histories. There were many routes by which a name might have evolved, and the whole etymological system was like a kaleidoscope, for a decision in one place was likely to set up disturbing ripples in etymological relations among quite distinct groups of words. Moreover, complexity was (as it were) built in, for the very nature of the 'bases' set words on phonetic collision courses from their origin.

The work varies a great deal, however, between its sections (which are the groups of base-stems beginning with the same initial letter). The worst parts, both in their physical condition and in the disorganisation of their content, are the central letters of the alphabet, beginning with E. As the text proceeds the amount of subsequent alteration and addition, and resultant confusion, diminishes, and when P and R are reached the etymologies, though rough and hasty, are more orderly. With these groups my father began to use smaller sheets of paper which are much better preserved, and from S to the end the material does not present serious difficulty; while the concluding section (W) is written out very legibly in ink (in this book the last section is Y, but that is not so in the original: see p. 346). These relatively clear and orderly entries are found also in the A-stems, while the B-stems are distinct from all the rest in that they were written out as a very finished and indeed beautiful manuscript. The entries under D are in two forms: very rough material that was partly overwritten more legibly in ink, and then a second, much clearer and more ordered version on the smaller sheets.

---

*On a covering page to the manuscript is written *Etymologies*, and also *Beleriandic and Noldorin names and words: Etymologies*.

I have not been able to reach any certain interpretation of all this, or find an explanation that satisfies all the conditions in detail. On the whole I am inclined to think that the simplest is most likely to be right in essentials. I have little doubt that the dictionary was composed progressively, through the letters of the alphabet in succession; and it may be that the very making of such a dictionary led to greater certainty in the whole etymological system, and greater clarity and assurance in its setting-out, as the work proceeded – but this also led to much change in the earlier parts. Having reached the end of the alphabet, my father then turned back to the beginning, with the intention of putting into better order the sections which had been first made and had suffered the most alteration; but this impulse petered out after the entries under D. If this were so, the original A and B entries were subsequently destroyed or lost; whereas in the case of D both survive (and it is noticeable that the second version of the D-entries differs from the former chiefly in arrangement, rather than in further etymological development).

Turning now to the question of date, I give some characteristic examples of the evidence on which I think firm conclusions can be based.

The original entry ELED gave the meaning of the stem as 'depart', with a derivative Elda 'departed'. Since this was the interpretation of Eldar in the Lhammas §2 and in QS §23 as those works were originally written, and first appears in them, the original entries under E clearly belong to that time. This interpretation was replaced in both the Lhammas and QS by carefully made emendations changing the meaning to 'Star-folk', and introducing the term Avari, with the meaning 'Departing'. Now the meaning 'Star-folk' appears in a second entry ELED replacing the first (and to all appearance made not long after); while the stem AB, ABAR bore, as first written, the meaning 'depart', and the derivative Avari was defined as 'Elves who left Middle-earth'. Thus the original A-entries and some at least of the alterations under E belong to the phase of the earliest alterations to QS.

In QS the meaning of Avari was then changed to 'the Unwilling' (see p. 219), and at the same time the root-meaning of AB, ABAR in the Etymologies was changed to 'refuse, deny' and the interpretation of Avari to 'Elves who never left Middle-earth or began the march.' This change can be dated from the note of 20 November 1937 (given on p. 200) in which my father said that Avari was to replace Lembi as the name of the Elves who remained in the East, while Lembi were to be 'Ilkorin Teleri', i.e. the Eldar who remained in Beleriand (see QS §§29–30 and p. 219). These changes were incorporated in the typescript of QS, which seems to have been in being by the beginning of February 1938 (p. 200). (The additional entry LEB, LEM shows this development, since Lembi is there translated as 'Elves remaining behind = Telerin Ilkorins'.)

In the note dated 3 February 1938 (p. 200) my father said that while Tintallë 'Kindler' could stand as a name of Varda, Tinwerontar 'Queen of Stars' must be changed to Elentári, because 'tinwë in Qenya only =

spark (*tinta-* to kindle).' In the entry TIN the names *Tinwetar* and *Tinwerontar* of Varda were struck from the original material, and in the margin was written: '*Tintanië, Tintallë* Kindler = Varda; Q *tinta-* to kindle, make to spark'. Original T-entries can therefore be dated before February 1938.

Under the stem MEN appears the form *harmen* 'south', which was not subsequently changed, and again under the (additional) entry KHAR, but in this case the base-stem was afterwards changed to KHYAR and *harmen* to *hyarmen*. The insertion of *y* in this word was one of the alterations required in the note of 20 November 1937.

Putting these and a number of other similar evidences together, it seems to me clear that despite their very various appearance the *Etymologies* were not spread over a long period, but were contemporary with QS; and that some of the additions and corrections can be securely dated to the end of 1937 and the beginning of 1938, the time of the abandonment of QS and the beginning of *The Lord of the Rings*. How much longer my father kept the work in being with further additions and improvements is another question, but here also I think that an answer can be given sufficient for the purpose. This lies in the observations that there are relatively few names that belong specifically to *The Lord of the Rings*; that all of them are quite clearly additions to existing entries or introduce additional base-stems; that almost all were put in very hastily, mere memoranda, and not really accommodated to or explained in relation to the base-stems; and that the great majority come from the earlier part of *The Lord of the Rings* – before the breaking of the fellowship. Thus we find, for example, *Baranduin* (BARÁN); the imperative *daro!* 'stop!' (DAR; this was the sentry's command to the Company of the Ring on the borders of Lothlórien); *Hollin* added under ERÉK; the scrawled addition of a base ETER with the imperative *edro!* 'open!' (the word shouted by Gandalf before the doors of Moria); *Celebrimbor* (KWAR); *Caradras* (RAS; replacing in the original draft of the chapter *The Ring Goes South* the name *Taragaer*, itself found in the *Etymologies* under the added base TARÁK); *Celebrant* (RAT); *Imladris* (RIS). The words *caras* (KAR) and *naith* (SNAS), both of them additions, probably argue the existence of *Caras Galadon* and the *Naith* of Lothlórien, and the added *rhandir* 'pilgrim' under RAN, taken with the added *mith* 'grey' under MITH, shows *Mithrandir*. Clear cases of names from later in *The Lord of the Rings* do occur (so *Palantir* under PAL and TIR, *Dolbaran* under BARÁN), but they are very few.

I conclude therefore that while my father did for two or three years more make rather desultory entries in the *Etymologies* as new names emerged in *The Lord of the Rings*, he gave up even this as the new work proceeded; and that the *Etymologies* as given here illustrate the development of the Quenya and Noldorin (later > Sindarin) lexicons at the decisive period reached in this book, and provide in fact a remarkable point of vantage.

The *Etymologies*, then, reflect the linguistic situation in Beleriand envisaged in the *Lhammas* (see especially the third version, *Lammasethen*, p. 194), with Noldorin fully preserved as the language of the Exiles, though profoundly changed from its Valinorian form and having complex interrelations in respect of names with 'Beleriandic' (Ilkorin), especially the speech of Doriath. Afterwards my father developed the conception of a kind of amalgamation between Noldorin and the indigenous speech of Beleriand, though ultimately there emerged the situation described in *The Silmarillion* (p. 129): the Noldor abandoned their own tongue and adopted that of the Elves of Beleriand (Sindarin). So far-reaching was this reformation that the pre-existent linguistic structures themselves were moved into new historical relations and given new names; but there is no need here to enter that rather baffling territory.

The presentation of such a text as this can obviously not be exact: in the most chaotic parts a degree of personal interpretation of what was meant is altogether inevitable. There is in any case a great deal of inconsistency in detail between the different parts of the manuscript – for example, in the use of marks expressing length of vowel, which vary unceasingly between acute accent, macron (long mark), and circumflex. I have only 'standardized' the entries to a very limited extent, and only in so far as I have felt confident that I ran little risk of confusing the original intention. In particular, I have done nothing to bring divergent forms, as between one part of the *Etymologies* and another, into accord, seeing that the evolution of 'bases' and derivative words is an essential part of the history; and indeed in the most complex parts of the manuscript (initial letters E, G, K) I have attempted to distinguish the different 'layers' of accretion and alteration, though elsewhere I have been very selective in pointing out additions to the original list. I have 'standardized' the entries to the extent of giving the 'bases' always in capitals, and of using the acute accent to signify long vowels in all 'recorded' forms (as opposed to 'hypothetical' antecedent forms), with the circumflex for long vowels in stressed final syllables in Exilic Noldorin and Ilkorin, as is largely done in the original. I use *y* for *j* of the original throughout (e.g. KUY, DYEL for KUJ, DJEL), since this is less misleading and was my father's own practice elsewhere (found in fact here and there in the *Etymologies*); the stems with initial J, becoming Y, are moved forward from their original place before K to the end of the list. I print the back nasal (as in English *king*) with a Spanish *tilde* (ñ), again following my father's frequent practice, though in the *Etymologies* he used special forms of the letter *n*. His grammatical abbreviations are retained, as follows:

| | | | |
|---|---|---|---|
| *adj.* | adjective | *g.sg.* | genitive singular |
| *adv.* | adverb | *inf.* | infinitive |
| *cpd.* | compound | *intr.* | intransitive |
| *f.* | feminine | *m.* | masculine |

| *pa.t.* | past tense | *q.v.* | *quod vide,* 'which see' |
|---|---|---|---|
| *pl.* | plural | *sg.* | singular |
| *p.p.* | past participle | *tr.* | transitive |
| *prep.* | preposition | | |

The sign † means 'poetic or archaic'. The abbreviations used for the different languages are as follows (there is no explanatory list of them accompanying the manuscript):

| *Dan.* | Danian |
|---|---|
| *Dor.* | Doriathrin |
| *Eld.* | Eldarin |
| *EN* | Exilic Noldorin (also referred to as 'Exilic', but most often simply as N) |
| *Ilk.* | Ilkorin |
| *L* | Lindarin |
| *N* | Noldorin |
| *ON* | Old Noldorin (i.e. the *Korolambë* or *Kornoldorin*, see the *Lhammas* §5) |
| *Oss.* | Ossiriandeb (the name in the *Lhammas*, where however the form *Ossiriandic* is also found) |
| *PQ* | Primitive Quendian |
| *T* | Telerin |

An asterisk prefixed to a form means that it is 'hypothetical', deduced to have existed from later, recorded forms.

My own contributions are always enclosed within square brackets. A question mark standing within such brackets indicates doubt as to the correctness of my reading, but in other cases is original. Where I have found words totally illegible or can do no better than a guess (a very small proportion of the whole, in fact) I have usually omitted them silently, and so also with scattered jottings where no meaning is attached to forms, or where no clear connections are given. I have kept my own notes to a minimum, and in particular have very largely eschewed the temptation to discuss the etymologies in relation to earlier and later Elvish forms published elsewhere. On the other hand, while my father inserted many internal references to other stems, I have substantially increased the number (those due to me being enclosed within square brackets), since it is often difficult to find an element when it had been greatly changed from its ultimate 'base'. The Index to the book is further designed to assist in the tracing of name-elements that appear in the *Etymologies*.

# A

**AB-, ABAR-** refuse, deny, \**ábārŏ* refuser, one who does not go forth: Q *Avar* (or *Avaro*), pl. *Avari* = Elves who never left Middle-earth or began the march; N *Afor*, pl. *Efuir, Efyr* (ON *abóro*). Cf. AWA.
[This entry as first written gave the root-meaning as 'go away, depart',

translated *ábārŏ as 'departer, one who goes forth', and defined *Avari* as 'Elves who left Middle-earth' (see p. 344). An additional entry seems to allow for both developments from the root-meaning: 'AB-retreat, move back, refuse'.]

**AD-**  entrance, gate, *adnō: Q *ando* gate; N *annon*, pl. *ennyn* great gate, Q *andon* (pl. *andondi*).

**AIWĒ-**  (small) bird. Q *aiwe*, N *aew*. Cf. *Aiwenor* 'Birdland' = lower air. [For *Aiwenor(ë)* see the *Ambarkanta* and diagrams, IV. 236 etc.]

**AK-**  narrow, confined. *akrā: Q *arka* narrow; N *agr, agor*. Cf. N *Aglond, Aglon* defile, pass between high walls, also as proper name; cf. *lond, lonn* path [LOD]. Q *aksa* narrow path, ravine.

**AKLA-R-**  See KAL. Q *alka* ray of light; *alkar* or *alkare* radiance, brilliance; *alkarinqa* radiant, glorious. N *aglar* glory, *aglareb* glorious.

**ÁLAK-**  rushing. *álākō rush, rushing flight, wild wind: N *alag* rushing, impetuous; *alagos* storm of wind. Cf. *Anc-alagon* dragon-name [NAK]. Related to LAK[2].

*alk-wā swan: Q *alqa*; T *alpa*; ON *alpha*; N *alf*; Ilk. *alch*; Dan. *ealc*. Cf. *Alqalonde* Swan-road or Swan-haven, city of the Teleri [LOD].

**ÁLAM-**  elm-tree. Q *alalme*, also *lalme*; N *lalf (lelf)* or *lalven*, pl. *lelvin*; Ilk. *lalm*, pl. *lelmin*; Dan. *alm*. The stem is perhaps LÁLAM, q.v., but some hold it related to ALA since the elm was held blessed and beloved by the Eldar. [The end of this entry, from 'but some hold it', was an addition. Probably at the same time a stem AL- was added, with derivatives *alma* 'good fortune', *alya* 'rich', etc.; but this entry was struck out. The same derivative words are found under GALA.]

**ÁLAT-**  large, great in size. Q *alta [. . .] alat-* as in *Alataire* = *Belegoer* [AY].

**AM[1]-**  mother. Q *amil* or *amme* mother; Ilk. *aman*, pl. *emuin*. (N uses a different word, *naneth*, hypocoristic [pet-name form] *nana* [NAN]).

**AM[2]-**  up: usually in form *amba-*. Q prefix *am-* up; *amba* adv. up(wards); *amban* upward slope, hill-side; *ambapenda, ampenda* uphill (adj.); see PEN. N *am* up; *am-bend, amben* uphill; *amon* hill, pl. *emuin, emyn*; *am-rûn* uprising, sunrise, Orient = Q *ambaron* (g.sg. *ambarónen*) or *Ambaróne*.

**ANA[1]-**  Cf. NA[1]. to, towards. *anta-* to present, give: Q *anta-* give; *anna* gift; *ante* (f.), *anto* (m.) giver. Cf. *Yav-anna* [YAB]; *Aryante* [AR[1]]. N *anno* to give; *ant* gift. [Added:] Q *anta* face.

**ANA[2]-**  Cf. NA[2]. be, exist. [Added:] *anwa* real, actual, true.

**ÁNAD-, ANDA-**  *andā long: Q *anda*; N *and, ann*. Cf. names *Andram* long-wall [RAMBĀ], *Andfang, Anfang* Longbeard, one of the tribes of Dwarves (pl. *Enfeng*) [SPÁNAG].

**ÁNAK-**  Cf. NAK bite. Q *anca* jaw; N *anc*; cf. *Ancalagon* [ÁLAK].

**ANÁR-**  sun; derivative of NAR[1]. *anār-: Q *Anar* sun; EN *Anor*.

**ANGĀ-**  iron. Q *anga*; N *ang*. Q *angaina* of iron; N *angren*, pl. *engrin*.

**ANGWA-** or **ANGU-**   snake. Q *ango*, pl. *angwi*; N *am-* in *amlug* dragon: see LOK.

**AP-**   *apsa* cooked food, meat. N *aes*; Ilk. *ass*.

**AR¹-**   day. *\*ari*: Q *are*, pl. *ari*; N *ar-* only in names of week-days, as *Arvanwe* [see LEP]. Cf. name *Aryante* Day-bringer [ANA¹], N *Eriant*. Q *arin* morning, *arinya* morning, early; *arie* daytime; *ára* dawn; *Arien* the Sun-maiden. N *aur* day, morning; *arad* daytime, a day (= Q *arya* twelve hours, day).

**AR²-**   Q *ara* outside, beside; also prefix *ar-* as in *Arvalin* (= outside Valinor). In Q this is purely local in sense. So also in Ilkorin, cf. *Argad* place 'outside the fence', or *Argador* (in Falathrin dialect *Ariad*, *Ariador*) lands outside Doriath (in Ilkorin *Eglador*), especially applied to West Beleriand, where there was a considerable dwelling of Dark-elves. In N *ar-* developed a privative sense (as English *without*), probably by blending with *\*al*, which is only preserved in *Alchoron* = Q *Ilkorin* [LA]. Thus *arnediad* without reckoning, = numberless [NOT]. In this sense Q uses *ava-*, as *avanóte* (see AWA). Hence Q *ar* and.

**ÁS-AT-**   Q *asto* dust; N *ast*.

**ATA-**   father. PQ *\*atū*, *\*atar*: Q *atar*, pl. *atari*; hypocoristic *atto*. N *adar*, pl. *edeir*, *eder*; *ada*. Cf. *Ilúv-atar*. Ilk. *adar*, pl. *edrin*; *adda*.

**AT(AT)-**   again, back. Q *ata* again, *ata-*, *at-* back, again, re-; N *ad*. Cf. TAT, ATTA = two; Q *atta* two, N *tad*. N prefix *ath-* on both sides, across, is probably related; *athrad* ford, crossing (see RAT). Ilk. *adu*, *ado* double; cf. *Adurant*, a river in Ossiriand which for a distance has divided streams. [Ilk. *adu*, *ado* 'double' and the explanation of *Adurant* was an addition; this shows the conception of the island of Tol-galen (see the commentary on QS §114). Other additions made at different times to this entry were Q *atwa* double, and N *eden* new, begun again.]

**AWA-**   away, forth; out. Q *ava* outside; *Avakúma* [KUM] Exterior Void beyond the World; *au-*, *ava-* privative prefixes = N *ar* (see AR²), as *avanóte* without number, numberless [NOT]. [Added:] *Avalóna*, cf. *lóna* [LONO].

**AY-**   *\*ai-lin-* pool, lake: Q *ailin* (g.sg. *ailinen*); N *oel*, pl. *oelin*; cf. *Oelinuial* Pools of Twilight [LIN¹; YŪ, KAL].

**AYAR-, AIR-**   sea, only used of the inner seas of Middle-earth. Q *ear* (*earen*) and *aire* (*airen*); N *oear*, *oer*. Cf. *Earráme*, a Q name = Wings of the Sea, name of Tuor's ship. *Belegoer* 'great sea', name of Western Ocean between Beleriand and Valinor, Q *Alataire* (see ÁLAT).

**AYAK-**   sharp, pointed. Q *aika* sharp, *aikale* a peak; N *oeg* sharp, pointed, piercing, *oegas* (= Q *aikasse*) mountain peak. Cf. N *Oeges engrin* Peaks of Iron, *oeglir* range of mountain peaks. ?Related is Q *aiqa* steep, cf. Ilk. *taig* deep (blended with *tára*, see TĀ).

**AYAN-** See YAN. *ayan-* holy: Q *Ainu*, f. *Aini*, holy one, angelic spirit; *aina* holy; *Ainulindale* Music of the Ainur, Song of Creation.

# B

[On the distinctive manuscript of the B-entries see p. 343. The following entries were added in pencil: BAD, BARÁN, BARAT, BARATH, BEN, and at the same time certain changes were made to existing entries. In this section I give the original entries as they were written, and note the alterations.]

**BAD-** *bad-* judge. Cf. MBAD. Not in Q. N *bauð* *(bād-)* judgement; *badhor, baðron* judge. [Pencilled addition.]

**BAL-** *bálā:* Q *Vala* Power, God (pl. *Valar* or *Vali* = PQ *bal-ī* formed direct from stem, cf. *Valinor*); there is no special f. form, where necessary the cpd. *Valatári* 'Vala-queen' is used, f. of *Valatar* (g.sg. *Valatáren*) 'Vala-king', applied only to the nine chief Valar: Manwe, Ulmo, Aule, Mandos, Lorien, Tulkas, Osse, Orome, and Melko. The *Valatári* were Varda, Yavanna, Nienna, Vana, Vaire, Este, Nessa, Uinen. T *Bala*. ON *Bala*, and *Balano* m., *Balane* f.; EN *Balan* m. and f., pl. *Belein, Belen*. In Ilk. *tórin* 'kings' was used, or the cpd. *Balthor, Balthorin* (*bal'tar-*).

Q *valya* having (divine) authority or power; *valaina* of or belonging to the Valar, divine; *valasse* divinity. Q *Valinor*, for *bálī-ndŏre*, reformed after the simplex *nóre* 'land', also in form *Valinóre*, land of the Gods in the West; ON *Balandor* (*bala-ndore*), EN *Balannor*. Cf. also ON *Balthil* one of the names of the White Tree of Valinor, usually named in Q *Silpion*; EN *Belthil*, but this was usually applied to the image of the divine tree made in Gondolin, the tree itself being called *Galathilion*. Related is probably the name *Balar* of the large island at Sirion's mouth, where the Ilkorins long dwelt who refused to go West with Ulmo; from this is named *Beleriand* which they colonized from the island in the dark ages. *Balar* is probably from *bálāre*, and so called because here Ossë visited the waiting Teleri. [The explanation of *Balar, Beleriand* given here is not necessarily at variance with the story told in QS §35 that the Isle of Balar was 'the eastern horn of the Lonely Isle, that broke asunder and remained behind, when Ulmo removed that land again into the West'; but it can scarcely be brought into accord with the story (QS §36) that 'the Teleri dwelt long by the shores of the western sea, awaiting Ulmo's return', and that Ossë instructed the waiting Teleri 'sitting upon a rock nigh to the margin of the sea.' Moreover, the 'colonization' of Beleriand from Balar seems to take no account of Thingol, and those of his people 'that went not because they tarried searching for Thingol in the woods': 'and these multiplied and were yet scattered far and wide between

Eredlindon and the sea' (*Lhammas* §6). More must be meant than simply that Elves from Balar removed to the mainland, for this 'colonization' from Balar is here made the very basis of the name *Beleriand*.]

**BAN-** *\*bánā* : Q *Vana* name of the Vala, wife of Orome, and sister of Varda and Yavanna; ON and T *Bana*; in ON also called *Bana-wende*, whence EN *Banwend, Banwen* (see WEN). *\*bányā* : Q *vanya* beautiful; EN *bein*. Cf. Q *vanima* fair; *Vanimo*, pl. *Vanimor* 'the beautiful', children of the Valar; *Úvanimo* monster (creature of Melko); EN *úan* (*\*úbanō*) monster; *uanui* monstrous, hideous.

**BAR-** Original significance probably 'raise'; cf. BARÁD, MBAR. Hence uplift, save, rescue(?). *\*barnā́* : Q *varna* safe, protected, secure; [struck out: *varne* protection;] *varnasse* security. *\*baryá-*: Q *varya-* to protect; EN *berio* to protect. [The removal of *varne* 'protection' was due to the emergence of BARAN 'brown' with the derivative Q *varne* 'brown'.]

**BARÁD-** [Added: is blended with BARATH, q.v.] *\*barádā* lofty, sublime: [added: ON *barada*, EN *baradh*, steep;] Q *Varda*, chief of the Valatári, spouse of Manwe; T *Barada* [> *Baradis*]. [Struck out: ON *Bradil*, EN *Breðil*.(*\*b'radil-*).] *\*b'randā* lofty, noble, fine: T *branda*; ON *branda*, EN *brand, brann* (whence *brannon* lord, *brennil* lady); cf. name *Brandir* (*brand-dīr*: see DER).

**BARÁN-** Q *varne* (*varni-*) brown, swart, dark brown. ON *barane*, EN *baran*. Cf. river name *Baranduin, Branduin. Dolbaran*. [Pencilled addition. On *Dolbaran* (probably a further addition) see p. 345.]

**BARAS-** Stem only found in Noldorin: *\*barasā* hot, burning: ON *barasa, baraha*; EN *bara* fiery, also eager; frequent in masculine names as *Baragund, Barahir* [KHER], etc. *\*b'rás-sē* heat: ON *brasse*, white heat, EN *brass*: whence *brassen* white-hot.

**BARAT-** N *barad* tower, fortress. [Pencilled addition.]

**BARATH-** Probably related to BAR and BARÁD. *\*Barathī* spouse of Manwe, Queen of Stars: ON *Barathi(l)*; EN *Berethil* and *El-bereth*. Q *Varda*, T *Baradis* show influence of *barádā* lofty. [Pencilled addition. The application of the name *Elbereth* to Varda seems to have arisen in the hymn of the Elves to the Goddess in the original second chapter (*Three is Company*) of *The Lord of the Rings*, written early in 1938 (where in rough workings for the song the name appears as *Elberil*). Concomitant with this the Ilkorin names *Elbereth* (of different meaning) and *Elboron* were removed from the original entries BER and BOR. These were the names of Dior's sons in AB 1 and 2 (annal 206/306), replaced in AB 2 (note 42) by *Eldûn* and *Elrûn* (which were added also to Q §14); *Elrûn* appears in the *Etymologies* in an addition to stem RŌ.]

**BAT-** tread. *\*bátā* : ON *bata* beaten track, pathway; EN *bâd*. *\*battā́-* (with medial consonant lengthened in frequentative formation): ON *batthó-* trample, EN *batho*. ON *tre-batie* traverse, EN *trevedi* (pa.t. *trevant*) [see TER]. Cf. Q *vanta-* to walk, *vanta* a walk.

**BEL-**    strong. Cf. BAL(?). Stem not found in Q. T *belle* (physical) strength; *belda* strong. Ilk. *bel* (*\*belē*) strength; *Beleg* the Strong, name of Ilkorin bowman of Doriath. *\*bélek* : *\*béleka* : ON *beleka* mighty, huge, great; EN *beleg* great (n.b. this word is distinct in form from though related to Ilk. name *Beleg*); cf. EN *Beleg-ol* [GAWA] = Q Aule; *Belegoer* Great Sea [AY], name of sea between Middle-earth and the West; *Belegost* Great City [OS], name of one of the chief places of the Dwarves. T *belka* 'excessive' is possibly from ON; ON *belda* strong, *belle* strength (EN *belt* strong in body, *bellas* bodily strength) are possibly from T. Cf. name *Belthronding* of Beleg's yew-bow: see STAR, DING.

**BEN-**    corner (from inside), angle. N *bennas* angle [NAS]. [Pencilled addition.]

**BER-**    valiant. *\*bérya-* : Q *verya-* to dare; *verya* bold; *verie* boldness. ON *berina* bold, brave; *bértha-* to be bold; EN *beren* bold, *bertho* dare; cf. proper name *Beren*. Ilk. *ber* valiant man, warrior (*\*berō*); *bereth* valor; [struck out: cf. Ilk. name *El-bereth*.] Danian *beorn* man; this is probably blended with *\*besnō* : see BES. [On the removal of *El-bereth* see BARATH.]

**BERÉK-**    *\*berékā* : Q *verka* wild; EN *bregol* violent, sudden, cf. proper name *Bregolas* fierceness; *breged* violence, suddenness; *breitho* (*\*b'rekta-*) break out suddenly. Cf. *Dagor Vregedúr* [UR] Battle of Sudden Fire (EN *bregedur* wild-fire). [See MERÉK.]

**BERÉTH-**    T *bredele* beech-tree; Ilk. *breth* (*\*b'rethā*) beech-mast, but the beech was called *galbreth* [GALAD] in Falasse, and *neldor* in Doriath (see NEL). The beech-tree was probably originally called *\*phéren*, Q *feren* or *ferne* (pl. *ferni*), ON *pheren*; but in EN *fêr* pl. *ferin* was usually replaced by the Ilk. *breth* mast, whence EN *brethil* beech-tree; cf. *Brethiliand, -ian* 'Forest of Brethil' [see PHER].

**BES-**    wed. *\*besnō* husband: Q *verno*; ON *benno*, EN *benn* man, replacing in ordinary use the old word *dîr* (see DER); *hervenn, herven* husband (see KHER). Ilk. *benn* husband; Danian *beorn* man, blended with *\*ber(n)ō* : see BER.
   *\*bessē* wife: Q *vesse*; ON *besse*, EN *bess* woman, replacing old words *dî, dîs* (see NĪ¹, NDIS); *herves* wife (see KHER). In the f. the shift of sense in ON was assisted probably by blending with *\*dess* young woman, ON *dissa*.
   *\*besū* dual, husband and wife, married pair: Q *veru*. Cf. Q *Arveruen* third day (of the Valinorian week of 5 days) dedicated to Aule and Yavanna [LEP].
   *\*bestā* : Q *vesta* matrimony; *vesta-* to wed; *vestale* wedding.

**BEW-**    follow, serve. *\*beurō* follower, vassal: ON *biuro, bioro*, EN *bior, beor*; cf. proper name *Bëor*. *\*beuyā-* follow, serve: ON *buióbe*

to serve, follow, EN *buio* serve, hold allegiance to. T *búro* vassal, *búa-*
serve. [On the name *Bëor* see the commentary on QS §128.]

**BIRÍT-** Stem only found in Ilkorin. *\*b'rittē*: Ilk. *brith* broken stones,
gravel. Cf. river name *Brithon* (whence is named *Brithombar*)
'pebbly'. Late Exilic *brith* gravel is from Ilkorin.

**BOR-** endure. Q *voro* ever, continually; prefix *vor, voro-* as in *voro-*
*gandele* 'harping on one tune', continual repetition; *vorima* continual,
repeated. *\*bóron-*: ON *boron* (pl. *boroni*) steadfast, trusty man,
faithful vassal; EN *bór* and pl. *býr* for older *berein, beren*; Ilk. *boron*,
pl. *burnin*. Cf. N names given to the 'Faithful Men': *Bór, Borthandos,*
*Borlas, Boromir. Borthandos* = *Borth* (see below) [but this element is
not further mentioned] + *handos* (see KHAN). *Borlas* = *Bór* + *glass*
joy (see GALÁS). *Boromir* is an old N name of ancient origin also borne
by Gnomes: ON *Boronmíro, Boromíro*: see MIR. [Struck out: 'Cf.
also Ilk. *boron* in Dor. name *El-boron.*' On the removal of *El-boron* see
BARATH.]

**BORÓN-** extension of the above (originally a verbal form of the stem
seen in *\*bóron-* above). Q *voronwa* enduring, long-lasting; *voronwie*
endurance, lasting quality; cf. name *Voronwe* = ON *Bronwega*, EN
*Bronwe* [WEG]. ON *bronie* last, endure, survive; EN *bronio* endure,
*brono* last, survive; *bronadui* enduring, lasting. *\*b'rōnā*: ON *brūna*
that has long endured, old (only used of things, and implies that they
are old, but not changed or worn out); EN *brūn* old, that has long
endured, or been established, or in use.

**Brodda** Name of a man in Hithlum. He was not one of the Elf-friend
races, and his name is therefore probably not EN or Ilkorin.

**BUD-** jut out. Cf. MBUD.

# D

[A very rough pencilled list was for most of its length overwritten in
ink, and nearly all these entries appear in a second, pencilled list, the
differences between the two being largely a matter of arrangement; see
p. 343.]

**DAB-** give way, make room, permit, allow. Q *lav-* yield, allow, grant.
N *dâf* permission.

**DAL-** flat (variant or alteration of LAD). Q *lára* 'flat' may derive from
*\*dāla* or *\*lāda*. EN *dalw* flat; *dalaih* flat surface, plane, plain [see
TIR]. ON *dalma* (probably = *dal* + *mā* hand) palm of hand; EN *dalf*.
Ilk. *dôl* flat, lowlying vale.

**DAN-** Element found in names of the Green-elves, who called themselves *Danas* (Q *Nanar*, N *Danath*). Cf. *Dan, Denethor* and other
names. See NDAN?

**DAR-** stay, wait, stop, remain. N *deri*, imperative *daro!* stop, halt;
*dartha* wait, stay, last, endure.

**DARÁK-** *d'rāk : Q *ráka* wolf; EN *draug*; Dor. *drôg*.

**DARÁM-** beat, hew. EN *dramb*, *dram(m)* a heavy stroke, a blow (e.g. of axe); *dravo* to hew (pa.t. *drammen*, † *dramp*); *drafn* hewn log; *drambor* clenched fist, hence blow with fist (see KWAR); *gondrafn*, *gondram* hewn stone. [Cf. the name of Tuor's axe in the *Lost Tales*: *Drambor*, *Dramborleg*; see II. 337.]

**DAT-, DANT-** fall down. EN *dad* down, cf. *dadben* downhill (see PEN); *dath* (*dattā*) hole, pit, Q *latta*. Q *lanta* a fall, *lanta-* to fall; N *dant-* to fall, *dannen* fallen. Cf. *Atalante* 'the Fallen', and *lasselanta* 'leaf-fall', Autumn [see TALÁT].

**DAY-** shadow. Q *leo* (*daio*) shade, shadow cast by any object; *laime* shade; *laira* shady. EN *dae* shadow; cf. *Daeðelos* = Shadow of Fear. Dor., Ilk. *dair* shadow of trees; cf. names *Dairon* and *Nan-dairon*.

**DEM-** sad, gloomy. Ilk. *dimb* sad (cf. *Dimbar*); *dim* gloom, sadness (*dimbē*); *dem* sad, gloomy (*dimbā*).

**DEN-** hole; gap, passage. N *din* opening, gap, pass in mountains, as in *Din-Caradras*, *Din-Dûhir*, etc. [On the first list DEN was given the meaning 'hillside, slope', whence Q *nende* slope, *nenda* sloping; N *dend*, *denn*, sloping, *dadðenn* downhill, *amdenn* uphill. This entry was struck through and the material transformed and transferred to PEN (whence *dadbenn*, *ambenn*). Cf. AM²; the A-entries belong to the second phase, later than the first form of the D-entries (see pp. 343-4).]

**DER-** Adult male, man (elf, mortal, or of other speaking race). Q *nér*, pl. *neri*, with *n* partly due to NĪ, NIS woman, partly to strengthened stem *ndere* bridegroom, ON *daer* [see NDER]. ON *dîr*, EN † *dîr* surviving chiefly in proper names (as *Diriel* older *Dirghel* [GYEL], *Haldir*, *Brandir*) and as agental ending (as *ceredir* doer, maker). Owing to influence of *dîr* (and of strengthened *ndisi* bride) N goes the opposite way to Q and has *di* woman (see NDIS). In ordinary use EN has *benn* (properly = husband) [see BES].

**DIL-** stop up, fill up hole, etc. EN *dîl* stopper, stopping, stuffing, cf. *gasdil* stopgap [GAS]; *dilio* to stop up. [The rather unlikely word *gasdil* is mentioned because it was the name of a sign used to indicate that *g* had disappeared; see p. 298, note on *Gorgoroth*.]

**DING-** Onomatopoeic, var. of TING, TANG, q.v. Ilk. *ding*, *dang*, sound; cf. name *Bel-thron(d)-ding* [BEL, STAR].

**DO3, DÔ-** Q *ló* night, a night; *lóme* Night, night-time, shades of night. ON *dogme*, *dougme*, *doume*; EN *daw* night-time, gloom; *dû* (associated with NDŪ) nightfall, late evening – in EN night, dead of night is *fuin*; *Dú(w)ath* night-shade; *dûr* dark, sombre; cf. Q *lóna* dark. Ilk. *daum* = N *daw*. Cf. N *durion* a Dark-elf = *dureðel*. Q *lómelinde* nightingale; N *dúlind*, *dúlin(n)*. Cf. *Del-du-thling* [DYEL, SLIG.]

**DOMO-** Possibly related to the preceding (and certainly in some derivatives blended with it); faint, dim. *dōmi-* twilight in Q fell together with *doʒmē* from DOʒ in *lóme* night. Ilk. *dûm* twilight; Q *tindóme* starry twilight = Ilk. *tindum* = N *tinnu* (see TIN).

**DÓRON-** oak. Q *norno*; N *doron* (pl. *deren*); Dor., Ilk. *dorn*. Cf. Q *lindornea* adj. having many oak-trees [LI].

**DRING-** Noldorin stem = beat, strike. EN *dringo* to beat. Cf. sword-name *Glamdring*. [In *The Hobbit*, *Glamdring* is rendered 'Foe-hammer', called by the Orcs 'Beater'.]

**DUB-** lie, lie heavy, loom, hang over oppressively (of clouds). Q *lumna* lying heavy, burdensome, oppressive, ominous; *lumna-* to lie heavy. N *dofn* gloomy.

**DUI-** Ilk. *duin* water, river; cf. *Esgalduin*. Cf. *duil* river in *Duilwen*.

**DUL-** hide, conceal. N *doelio*, *delio*, and *doltha* conceal, pa.t. † *daul*, p.p. *dolen* hidden, secret. Cf. *Gondolind*, *-inn*, *-in* 'heart of hidden rock' [see ID]. Related is *\*ndulna* secret: Q *nulla*, *nulda*; N *doll* (*dolt*) obscure. Cf. name *Terendul*. [See NDUL, and for *Terendul* see TER.]

**DUN-** dark (of colour). Dor. *dunn* black; Dan. *dunna*; N *donn* swart, swarthy. Cf. Doriath place-name *(Nan) Dungorthin* = N *Nan Dongoroth*, or *Nann Orothvor* Vale of Black Horror [see ÑGOROTH].

**DYEL-** feel fear and disgust; abhor. EN *delos*, *deloth* (probably < *del* + *gos*, *goth*) abhorrence, detestation, loathing, cf. *Dor-deloth* Loathly Land; *deleb* horrible, abominable, loathsome; *delw* hateful, deadly, fell; cf. *Daedhelos* Shadow of Abomination, *Deldú(w)ath* Deadly Nightshade, a name of Taur-na-Fuin, *Delduthling*, N name of Ungoliantë [DAY, DOʒ]. Q *yelma* loathing, *yelwa* loathsome, *yelta-* to loathe.

# E

[The entries under E are particularly confused and difficult. A small number of original and clear entries were mostly struck through and the pages covered with faint pencilled notes often hard to interpret.]

**EK-, EKTE-** spear. Q *ehte* spear, *ehtar* spearman. N *aith* spear-point, *êg* thorn, cf. *Egthelion*, *Ecthelion* [STELEG]. [This original entry was retained, with change of EKTE to EKTI, Q *ehtar* to *ehtyar*, and the following additions:] [N] *ech* spear, Q *ekko*. Cf. *Eg-nor*.

**EL-** star. Q poetical *él* star (*elen*). Dor. *el*; N only in names, as *Elwing*. [This original entry received many changes:] **EL-** star, starry sky. Q poetical *elen* (*ellen* or *elena*) star. Dor *el*; N only in names, as *Elwing*, *Elbereth*. Cf. *Eled-* Starfolk, that is Elves. *Elrond* = starry-dome, sky [ROD]. [Added in margin:] Q *Elerína* star-crowned = Taniquetil; *Elentári* Star Queen = Varda; N *Elbereth* = Varda. [On *Elbereth* see note to BARATH; on *Elerína* and *Elentári* see p. 200.]

**ELED-**   go, depart, leave. Q *Elda* 'departed' Elf; N *eledh*. Q *lesta-* to leave, pa.t. *lende*. [This original entry was replaced by the following, written as carefully and clearly as the first:] **ÉLED-**   'Star-folk', Elf. Q *Elda* (*Eldamar* or *Elende* = Elvenhome, *Eldalie*, *Eldarin*); N *Eledh*, pl. *Elidh*, cf. *Eledhrim*, *Eledhwen* [Elf-fair >] Elf-maid, *Elennor* (*Eledandore* > *Eleðndor*). Dor. *Eld*, pl. *Eldin*. Dan. *Elda*. [The Dor. and Dan. forms were subsequently struck through and the following added:] In Dor. and Dan. transposed > *edel-* whence Dor. *Egla*, *Eglath* (cf. *Eglamar*, *Eglorest*); Dan. *Edel*. *Eglador* = Doriath in Doriathrin; *Ariador* = lands outside of Eglador. Cf. *Eglor* (Elf-river), Ilkorin name of a river in W. Beleriand. [On the earlier and later entries ELED see p. 344. Further faint pencillings show my father doubtful of the derivation of *Eldar* from a base meaning 'star', and suggesting that, although the name was so interpreted, it was probably in fact altered from *edela* 'eldest' – *eðel*, *eðil* being found also in Noldorin. A base EDE-, EDEL- 'precede, come forward' is proposed, with derivative *edela* (= *eleda*) 'firstborn', but this is struck out.]

**EN-**   element or prefix = over there, yonder. Q *en* there, look! yonder. Adj. *enta* that yonder. *Entar*, *Entarda* (*Enta* + *harda* [ᴈᴀʀ]) Thither Lands, Middle-earth, Outer Lands, East.

**ÉNED-**   centre. Q *endya*, *enya* middle; *ende* middle, centre. N *enedh*. [To this original entry was added:] *Endamar* Middle-earth. *Endor* centre of the world. [See ɴÉD.]

**ÉNEK-**   six. Q *enqe*; N *eneg*.

**ERE-**   be alone, deprived. Q *er* one, alone; *erya* single, sole; *eresse* solitude; *eressea* lonely. N *ereb* isolated (*\*ereqa*); *eriol* alone, single. Cf. *Tol-eressea*, *Amon Ereb*. Q *erume* desert, cf. *Eruman* desert N.E. of Valinor; N *eru* waste, desert.

**ERÉD-**   *\*ereðe* seed: Q *erde* seed, germ; N *eredh*; Ilk *erdh*. [See ʀED.]

**ERÉK-**   thorn. Q *erka* prickle, spine; *erka-* to prick; *erkasse* holly. N *ercho* to prick; *erch* a prickle; *ereg* (and *eregdos* [ᴛᴜS]) holly-tree, pl. *erig*. Cf. *Taur-nan-Erig* or *Eregion* = Dor. Forest of *Region*: Dor. *regorn* holly-tree (pl. *regin*, g.pl. *region*) [see OR-ɴí]. [Further addition:] *Regornion* = Hollin.

**ES-**   indicate, name. Q *esta* to name, *esse* a name.

**ESE-, ESET-**   precede. Q *esta* first; *esse* beginning; *essea* [?primary]; *Estanesse* the Firstborn. [Neither of these two entries were rejected, though they are certainly mutually exclusive, but the second was marked with a query.]

**ESEK-**   Ilk. *esg* sedge, *esgar* reed-bed. Cf. *Esgaroth* Reedlake, because of reed-banks in west.

**ET-**   forth, out. Q prefix *et-*, N *ed-*. Cf. *ehtele* under KEL. [To this original entry was added:] *etsiri*: Q *etsir* mouth of a river, N *ethir* [SIR]. *ette* outside; *ettele* outer lands; *ettelen* [?foreign].

**ETER-** Cf. ET out. open (come out, of flowers, sun, etc.). *edro!* open!

**EY-** everlasting. Q *aira* eternal; *aire* eternity; *ia (\*eyā)* ever. Cf. *Iolosse* ever-snow, N *Uiloss (\*Eigolosse)*. N *uir* eternity, *uireb* eternal. [This original entry was struck out, the material reappearing under GEY. *Iolosse* was probably the form underlying the early emendation to *Oiolosse* in QS §13. *Oiolosse* arose with the further transformation of this base to OY, q.v.]

**EZDĒ-** 'rest', name of the wife of Lórien. Q *Este*; ON *Ezde, Eide, Ide*; N *Idh*. See SED.

**EZGE-** rustle, noise of leaves. Q *eske*; Ilk. *esg*; cf. *Esgalduin*. [This, which may be one of the original entries, was struck out. Cf. ESEK, and for *Esgalduin* see SKAL¹.]

# G

[The entries under G present much the same appearance as those under E: an initial layer of a few clear entries in ink, and a mass of changes and additions put in very roughly afterwards.]

**GAL-** shine; variant of KAL.

**GALA-** thrive (prosper, be in health – be glad). Q *'al* in the following forms which are not confused with *ala-* 'not': *alya* prosperous, rich, abundant, blessed; *alma* good fortune, weal, wealth; *almie, almare* blessedness, 'blessings', good fortune, bliss; *almárea* blessed. Cf. name *Almáriel*. N *galw*; cf. names *Galadhor, Galdor* (later *Gallor*) – though these may contain GÁLAD. N *galas* growth, plant; *galo-* to grow. Possibly related are GÁLAD, GALÁS. [*Almáriel* is the name of a girl in Númenor in *The Lost Road*, p. 59.]

**GALAD-** tree. Q *alda*; N *galadh*. Cf. *Galadloriel (Galagloriel)*, *Galathilvion*. [*Galadlóriel* and *Galathilion* (not as here *Galathilvion*) appear in very early emendations to QS §16. The form *Galagloriel* is found in an early draft for the chapter *A Knife in the Dark* in *The Fellowship of the Ring*. – This, one of the original entries, was not struck out or altered (apart from *Galathilvion* > *Galathilion*), but a new entry for the stem was made:] **GÁLAD-** tree. Q *alda*; N *galadh*. Cf. names *Galadhor, Galdor*, etc. Q *Aldaron* name of Oromë. *Aldalemnar*, see LEP. Dor. *gald*, cf. *galbreth* beech [BERÉTH].

**GALÁS-** joy, be glad. N *glas* joy; cf. names as *Borlas*. Q *alasse* joy, merriment.

**GAP-** N *gamp* hook, claw; Q *ampa* hook.

**GAR-** hold, possess. N *gar-*. [An original entry, struck out; see 3AR.]

**GAS-** yawn, gape. *\*gassā*: N *gas* hole, gap; *gasdil* stopgap [DIL]; Q *assa* hole, perforation, opening, mouth. [Cf. *Ilmen-assa*, the Chasm of Ilmen, IV. 240. – This original entry was retained, but the following addition made:] *gāsa : ON gása = Q kúma ; EN gaw, Belego the Void.

**GAT-**   Q atsa catch, hook, claw; N gad-, gedi catch.

**GAT(H)-**   N gath (*gattā) cavern; Doriath 'Land of the Cave' is Noldorin name for Dor. Eglador = Land of the Elves. The Ilkorins called [?themselves] Eglath = Eldar. Rest of Beleriand was called Ariador 'land outside'. N gadr, gador prison, dungeon; gathrod cave. Another name is Garthurian = Fenced Realm = N Ardholen (which was also applied to Gondolin). [Added to this later:] Dor. gad fence; argad 'outside the fence', the exterior, the outside. Cf. Argador, Falathrin Ariador. [See AR², ÉLED, 3AR, LED.]

**GAWA-** or **GOWO-**   think out, devise, contrive. Q auta invent, originate, devise; aule invention, also as proper name of the god Aule, also called Martan : N Gaul usually called Belegol (= great Aule) or Barthan : see TAN, MBAR. N gaud device, contrivance, machine.

**GAY-**   Q aira red, copper-coloured, ruddy; N gaer, goer.

**GÁYAS-**   fear. *gais-: Q aista to dread; ON gaia dread; N gae. *gaisrā : ON gǣsra, gērrha ; N gaer dreadful.

**GENG-WĀ-**   Q engwa sickly. N gemb, gem ; cf. ingem 'year-sick' [YEN], suffering from old age (new word coined after meeting with Men). N iaur ancient [YA], ifant 'year-full' [YEN, KWAT] did not connote weakness. [Engwar 'the Sickly' is found in the list of Elvish names for Men in QS §83.]

**GEY-**   everlasting. Q ia ever (*geiā); iale everlasting; íra eternal; íre eternal [?read 'eternity']; Iolosse Everlasting Snow (*Geigolosse) = Taniquetil. N Guilos, Amon Uilos (guir eternity, guireb eternity [read 'eternal']). N Guir is confounded with Gui = Q Vaiya (*wāyā) [WAY]. [This note, replacing the rejected entry EY, was in its turn struck out and replaced by OY.]

**GIL-**   (cf. GAL, KAL; SIL, THIL; GUL, KUL) shine (white or pale). *gilya : N gîl star (pl. giliath). [This original entry was retained, with the addition to gîl: 'pl. geil, collective pl. giliath', and the following also added:] gael pale, glimmering; gilgalad starlight; Gilbrennil, Gilthoniel = Varda. Q Ilma starlight (cf. Ilmare), N [?Gilwen] or Gilith ; Ilmen region above air where stars are. [On Ilma and Ilmen see the commentary on QS §4.]

**GIR-**   quiver, shudder. N giri shudder; girith shuddering, horror.

**GLAM-**   N form of LAM, also influenced by ÑGAL(AM). N glamb, glamm shouting, confused noise; Glamhoth = 'the barbaric host', Orcs [KHOTH]. glambr, glamor echo; glamren echoing; cf. Eredlemrin = Dor. Lóminorthin. glavro to babble, glavrol babbling.

**GLAW(-R)-**   Q laure gold (properly the light of the Tree Laurelin); N glaur gold. The element glaur reduced in polysyllables to glor, lor appears in many names, as Glorfindel, Glaurfindel, Galadloriel. [This original entry was struck out and replaced by:] **GLAWAR-**   N alteration of LAWAR, q.v.

**GLIN-**   sing. Q *lin-*; N *glin-*. Q *linde* song, air, tune; N *glinn*. Cf. *Laurelin*. [Original entry, struck out. See LIN².]

**GLINDI-**   pale blue. N *glind*, *glinn*; Q *ilin*. [Original entry, struck out. Cf. the original meaning of *Eredlindon*, Blue Mountains, commentary on QS §108, and see LIN².]

**GLING-**   hang. Q *linga*; N *gling*. Cf. *Glingal*. [Original entry, struck out and replaced by:] **GLING-** N alteration of LING 'hang', q.v.

**GLIR-**   N form of LIR¹ sing. N *glîr* song, poem, lay; *glin* to sing, recite poem; *glær* long lay, narrative poem. Q *laire* poem, *lirin* I sing.

**GÓLOB-**   *golbā* branch: Q *olwa*; N *golf*. Cf. *Gurtholf* [> *Gurutholf*] [ÑGUR]. [For the form *Gurtholf* (earlier *Gurtholfin*) see p. 406.]

**GOLÓS-**   Q *olosse* snow, fallen snow; N *gloss* snow. Cf. *Uilos*. N *gloss* also adj. snow-white. [An original entry, this was retained with alteration of Q *olosse* to † *olos*, † *olosse* and the note: 'poetical only: confused with *losse* flower, see LOS which is perhaps originally connected.' The stem in question in fact appears as LOT(H).]

**GOND-**   stone. Q *ondo* stone (as a material); N *gonn* a great stone, or rock. [This original entry was retained, but the base was changed to GONOD-, GONDO-, and the following added:] Cf. *Gondolin* (see DUL); *Gondobar* (old *Gondambar*), *Gonnobar* = Stone of the World = Gondolin. Another name of Gondolin *Gondost* [OS], whence *Gondothrim*, *Gondothrimbar*. [Cf. *Gondothlim*, *Gondothlimbar* in the *Lost Tales* (II. 342).]

**GOR-**   violence, impetus, haste. Q *orme* haste, violence, wrath; *orna* hasty. N *gormh*, *gorf* impetus, vigour; *gorn* impetuous. [Apart from the removal of the form *gormh* this original entry was retained, with these additions:] Cf. *Celegorn* [KYELEK]; and cf. *Huor, Tuor* : *Khôgore* [KHŌ-N], *Tūgore* [TUG].

**GOS-, GOTH-**   dread. Q *osse* terror, as name *Osse*. Cf. *Mandos* (see MBAD). N has *Oeros* for *Osse* (\**Goss*). Cf. *Taur-os* [TÁWAR]. N *gost* dread, terror; *gosta-* fear exceedingly; cf. *Gothrog* = Dread Demon [RUK]; *Gothmog* [MBAW]. *Gostir* 'dread glance', dragon-name [THĒ].

**GŪ-**   Prefix *gū-* no, not, as in Q *ū-* not (with evil connotation); *Úvanimor* [BAN].

**GUL-**   glow, shine gold or red (cf. GIL); also *yul-* smoulder [YUL]. N *goll* red (\**guldā*). [This original entry was struck out. See KUL.]

**GWEN-**   (distinguish WEN(ED)). Q *wenya* green, yellow-green, fresh; *wên* greenness, youth, freshness (blended with *wende* maid). N *bein* fair, blended with BAN. Ilk. *gwên* greenness; *gwene* green; cf. *Duilwen* [DUI].

**GYEL-**   [< GEL-] Q *yello* [< *ello*] call, shout of triumph. N *gell* joy, triumph; *gellui* triumphant; *gellam* jubilation. Cf. *Diriel* [DER]. *Gelion* merry singer, surname of Tinfang. [*Tinfang Gelion* occurs in the *Lay of Leithian*: III. 174, 181–2.] *Gelion* shorter name of a great river in E. Beleriand; a Gnome interpretation (this would have been

*Dilion* in Ilkorin); cf. Ilk. *gelion* = bright, root GAL. [This rather perplexing note seems certain in its reading.]

**GYER-** *\*gyernā* old, worn, decrepit (of things): Q *yerna* old, worn; *yerya* to wear (out), get old. N *gern* worn, old (of things).


# 3

[The few entries under the initial back spirant 3 were struck out and replaced more legibly.]


**3AN-** male. Q *hanu* a male (of Men or Elves), male animal; ON *anu*, N *anw*; Dor. *ganu*. (The feminine is INI.)

**3AR-** Stems 3AR have, hold, and related GAR, GARAT, GARAD were much blended in Eldarin. From 3AR come: Q *harya-* possess; *harma* treasure, a treasured thing; *harwe* treasure, treasury; *haryon* (heir), prince; *haran* (pl. *harni*) king, chieftain (see TĀ). N *ardh* realm (but Q *arda* < GAR); *aran* king (pl. *erain*). Dor. *garth* realm, *Garthurian* (Fenced Realm = Doriath), *garon* lord, may come from 3AR or GAR.

From GAR: Q *arda* realm – often in names as *Elenarda* 'Star-kingdom', upper sky; *armar* pl. goods; *aryon* heir; *arwa* adj. (with genitive) in control of, possessing, etc., and as semi-suffix *-arwa*, as *aldarwa*, having trees, tree-grown. N *garo-* (*gerin*) I hold, have; *garn* 'own', property.

**GARAT-** Q *arta* fort, fortress. N *garth*: cf. *Garth(th)oren* 'Fenced Fort' = Gondolin – distinguish *Ardh-thoren* = Garthurian. [This note is the final form of two earlier versions, in which the Qenya words are all derived from 3AR. In one of these versions it is said that N *Arthurien* is a Noldorinized form of *Garthurian*, *Arthoren* a translation; in the other that N *Arthurien* is 'a half-translation = N *Arthoren*'; see THUR.]

**3ARAM-** Dor. *garm* wolf; N *araf*. [Struck out. Another version gave also Q *harma*, Dan. *garma*.]

**3EL-** sky. Q *helle*, ON *elle*, sky. In Noldorin and Telerin this is confused with EL star. Other derivatives: Q *helwa*, ON *elwa* (pale) blue, N *elw*; cf. name of *Elwe* King of the Teleri [WEG]; and names as *Elulind*, *Elwing*, *Elrond*. Q *helyanwe* 'sky-bridge', rainbow, ON *elyadme*, N *eilian(w)* [YAT]. Dor. *gell* sky, *gelu* sky-blue. [A later note directs that *Elwe* be transferred to EL star. *Elrond*, *Elwing* are also given under EL.]

**3Ŏ-** from, away, from among, out of. This element is found in the old partitive in Q *-on* (3ŏ + plural *m*). Q *ho* from; Ilk. *go*; N *o* from. In Ilk. *go* was used for patronymics, as *go-Thingol*.

# I

[The single page of entries under I consists only of very rough notes.]

I- that (deictic particle) in Q is indeclinable article 'the'. N *i*- 'the', plural *in* or *i*-.

I- intensive prefix where *i* is base vowel. ITHIL- Moon (THIL, SIL): Q *Isil*; N *Ithil*; Dor. *Istil*. INDIS- = *ndis* bride; *Indis* name of the goddess Nessa (see NDIS, NĪ). [*Ithil* occurs in *The Lost Road* (p. 41) as the 'Beleriandic' name of the Moon – i.e. the name in a language (Noldorin) perceived by Alboin Errol to be spoken in Beleriand.]

ID- *\*īdī*: heart, desire, wish. Q *íre* desire; *írima* lovely, desirable. Q *indo* heart, mood; cf. *Indlour, Inglor* (*Indo-klār* or *Indo-glaurē*). N *inn, ind* inner thought, meaning, heart; *idhren* pondering, wise, thoughtful; *idher* (*\*idrē*) thoughtfulness. Cf. *Idhril*; *Túrin(n)* [TUR], *Húrin(n)* [KHOR]. [The Q word *írima* occurs in the song in *The Lost Road* (p. 72): *Toi írimar*; *Írima ye Númenor*; cf. also *Írimor* 'Fair Ones', name of the Lindar in the Genealogies, p. 403. – For the original etymology of *Idril, Idhril* see II. 343.]

IL- all. Q *ilya* all, the whole. ILU- universe: Q *ilu, ilúve*: cf. *Ilúvatar, Ilurambar* Walls of the World. *Ilumíre* = Silmaril. *ilqa* everything.

ING- first, foremost. *inga* first. Element in Elfin and especially Lindarin names. Cf. *Ingwe* prince of Elves. QL [i.e. Qenya-Lindarin] form is always used (*Ingwe*): not *ngw* > *mb* [i.e. in Noldorin] because the L form persisted and also the composition was felt *ing* + *wege* [WEG]. Cf. *Ingil*. [Elfin at this date is a strange reversion to old usage.]

INI- female. See NĪ: Qenya *ní* female, woman. Q *hanwa* male, *inya* female; *hanuvoite, inimeite*. N *inw* after *anw* [see 3AN].

INK-, INIK-? Q *intya*- guess, suppose; *intya* guess, supposition, idea; *intyale* imagination. N *inc* guess, idea, notion.

IS- Q*`ista*- know (pa.t. *sinte*); *ista* knowledge; *istima* having knowledge, wise, learned, *Istimor* = Gnomes [cf. p. 403]. Q *istya* knowledge; *istyar* scholar, learned man. N *ist* lore, knowledge; *istui* learned; *isto* to have knowledge. Cf. *Isfin* (= *Istfin*) [PHIN].

# K

[The numerous entries under K are perhaps the most difficult in the work. A first layer of etymologies written carefully and clearly in ink was overlaid by a mass of rapid notes in pencil that are now in places almost invisible.]

KAB- hollow. Q *kambe* hollow (of hand); N *camb, cam* hand, cf. *Camlost* 'Emptyhand' [LUS] (= Dor. *Mablost*). *Erchamui* 'One-

362 THE LOST ROAD

handed'. [An earlier version of this entry gives also *Cambant* 'full hand'; see KWAT.]

**KAL-** shine (general word). Variant forms AKLA-, KALAR-, AKLAR-. Q *kala* light; *kalma* a light, lamp; *kalya* illuminate; *kalina* light (adj.). In N the variant GAL appears: *gail* (\**galyā*) bright light, *glaw* radiance (\**g'lā*, cf. Q *kala* < \**k'lā*). But in longer forms KAL also in N, as *aglar*, *aglareb*, see AKLA-R. Also *celeir* brilliant (\**kalaryā*); Q *kallo* noble man, hero (\**kalrō*), N *callon* (\**kalrondō*) hero; N poetical *claur* splendour, glory – often in names in form *-glor*. *gôl* light (\**gālœ-*) in *Thingol*. [Parts of this original entry were rejected: the etymology of *Thingol* (see THIN), and the idea that GAL was a Noldorin variant of KAL. It is not clear at this stage how these bases were related. The entry was covered with a maze of new forms, often rejected as soon as written. The following can be discerned:] N *calad* light (cf. *Gilgalad*); *calen* bright-coloured = green. Q *kalta-* shine; *Kalakilya*; *Kalaqendi*, N *Kalamor*; *Kalamando* = Manwe [see MBAD]. *Ankale* 'radiant one', Sun. *yúkale*, *yuale* twilight, N *uial* [YŪ].

**KALPA-** water-vessel. Q *kalpa*; N *calf*. Q *kalpa-* draw water, scoop out, bale out. [Added entry.]

**KAN-** dare. Q *káne* valour; N *caun*, *-gon* (cf. *Turgon*, *Fingon*). Q *kanya* bold. N *cann* (\**kandā*). *Eldakan* (name) = *Ælfnoþ*. [Added entry.]

**KÁNAT-** four. Q *kanta-*, *kan-*; N *canad*. [Added entry.]

**KAP-** leap. [Added:] N *cabr*, *cabor* frog.

**KAR-** make, do. Q *kar* (*kard-*) deed; N *carð*, *carth* deed, feat. Cf. KYAR cause. Q *karo* doer, actor, agent; *ohtakaro* warrior. [This stem was very roughly rewritten thus:] **KAR-** make, build, construct. Q *kar* (*kard-*) building, house; N *car* house, also *carð*. Q *karin*, *karne*, I make, build. Cf. **KYAR-** cause, do. Q *tyaro* doer, actor, agent; *ohtatyaro* warrior. N *caras* a city (built above ground).

**KARAK-** sharp fang, spike, tooth. Q *karakse* jagged hedge of spikes; cf. *Helkarakse*, N *elcharaes* [KHEL]. [This entry was retained, with KARAK > KÁRAK and *elcharaes* > *helcharaes*, and the following faintly visible additions made:] Q *karka* tooth, *karkane* row of teeth. N *carag* spike, tooth of rock; *carch* tooth, fang (*Carcharoth*).

**KARÁN-** red. Q *karne* (\**karani*) red; N *caran*. \**k'rannā*: N *crann* ruddy (of face), cf. *Cranthir* [THĒ], [?as noun] like Old English *rudu*, face, blush, the cheeks. [Added entry.]

**KARKA-** crow. Q *karko*; N *carach*. [This stem was changed thus:] **KORKA-** crow. Q *korko*; N *corch*.

**KAS-** head. Q *kár* (*kas-*); N *caw* top. [Added:] \**kas-sa*, \**kas-ma*: Q *cassa* helmet.

**KAT-** shape. Q *kanta* shaped, and as quasi-suffix, as in *lassekanta* leaf-shaped; *kanta-* to shape; N *cant*. [The meaning 'outline' was attributed to *cant*, and the following added:] \**katwā*: ON *katwe*

shaped, formed, N *cadw*, *-gadu*. *\*katwārā* shapely: N *cadwor*,
*cadwar*. N *echedi*, pa.t. *echant* (*\*et-kat*) fashion. [Cf. *Im Narvi hain
echant* above the Doors of Moria.]

**KAY-** lie down. Q *kaima* bed. N *caew* lair, resting-place; *cael* (Q
*kaila*) lying in bed, sickness; *caeleb* bedridden, sick: cf. Q *kaimasse*,
*kaimassea*.

**KAYAN-, KAYAR-** ten. Q *kainen*; N *caer*. [Added entry.]

**KEL-** go, run (especially of water). *\*et-kelē* spring, issue of water: Q
*ehtele*, N *eithel* (from metathesized [i.e. with transposed consonants]
form *\*ektele*). Q *kelume* stream, flow; N *celon* river; Q *kelma*
channel. Cf. KYEL run out, come to an end; KWEL fade away. [These
changes were made: 'N *celon* river' > 'Ilk. *celon* river, and as proper
name, *kelu+n*'; 'N *celw* spring, source' added.]

**KEM-** soil, earth. Q *kén* (*kemen*). N *coe* earth (indeclinable), *cef* soil,
pl. *ceif*. Q *kemina* of earth, earthen; [N] *cevn*. Q *kemnaro* potter.
[Added entry.]

**KEPER-** knob, head, top [changed to 'ridge'. This entry consists of
disconnected jottings, all struck out, but concerned with N *ceber* pl.
*cebir* and *Sern Gebir*, of which the meaning seems to be 'lone stones'.]

**KHAG-** *\*khagda* pile, mound; Q *hahta*; N *hauð* mound, grave,
tomb (cf. *Ilauð iNdengin*). [Added entry.]

**KHAL¹-** (small) fish. Q *hala*; cf. Q *halatir* 'fishwatcher', kingfisher, N
*heledir*. [Added entry. The same origin of *halatir* is found under TIR;
but here KHAL was changed to KHOL and the *-a-* of the Q forms to *-o-*,
before the entry was struck out with a reference to base SKAL – which (a
later addition to the S-stems) is clearly the later formulation.]

**KHAL²-** uplift. ON *khalla* noble, exalted (*\*khalnā́*); *orkhalla*
superior. N *hall* exalted, high; *orchel* [*e* uncertain] superior, lofty,
eminent. [Added entry.]

**KHAM-** sit. Q *ham-* sit. [The other derivatives are too chaotic and
unclear to present.]

**KHAN-** understand, comprehend. Q *hanya* understand, know about,
be skilled in dealing with; *hande* knowledge, understanding; *handa*
understanding, intelligent; *handele* intellect; *handasse* intelligence.
EN *henio* understand; *hann*, *hand* intelligent; *hannas* understanding,
intelligence. Cf. *Handir*, *Borthandos*. [Added entry.]

**KHAP-** enfold. N *hab-* clothe; *hamp* garment; *hamnia-* clothe;
*hammad* clothing.

**KHARÁS-** (cf. KARAK). *\*khrassē*: precipice: N *rhass* (*i-rass*, older
*i-chrass*); Dan. *hrassa*. Cf. *Gochressiel* [< *Gochrass*] a sheer
mountain-wall. [Added entry. For *Gochressiel* see QS §147 and
commentary.]

**KHAT-** hurl. N *hedi*, pa.t. *hennin*, *hant*; *hador* or *hadron* thrower (of
spears or darts), cf. *Hador*; *hadlath*, *haglath* a sling (see LATH).
[Added entry.]

**KHAW-** (= KAY, q.v.) N *haust* bed. [This original entry was enlarged

thus:] **KHAW-** rest, lie at ease (= KAY, q.v.) N *haust* bed (*\**khau-stā*,
literally 'rest-ing'). In N associated with *hauð* mound (see KHAG).
Cf. Q *hauta-* cease, take a rest, stop.

**KHAYA-** far, distant. Q *haira* adj. remote, far, [?also] *ekkaira*,
*avahaira*. *hāya* adv. far off, far away. [Added entry.]

**KHEL-** freeze. Q *helle* frost; N *hell*. **KHELEK-** ice. N *heleg* ice, *helch*
bitter cold; Q *helke* ice, *helk* ice-cold. [The base KHEL and derivatives
were struck out, but KHELEK and derivatives retained.]

**KHEN-D-E-** eye. Q *hen* (*hendi*); N *hent*, pl. *hinn* >*hent*, *hint*, or
*henn*, *hinn*. [N forms changed to *hên*, *hîn*.]

**KHER-** rule, govern, possess. Q *heru* master, *heri* lady; *héra* chief,
principal. ON *khéro* master, *khíril* lady; N *hîr*, *hiril*. N *herth* household, troop under a *hîr*; cf. *Bara-chir* [BARÁS]. Cf. N *hervenn*
husband, *hervess* wife [BES]. Q *heren* fortune (= governance), and so
what is in store for one and what one has in store; *herenya* fortunate,
wealthy, blessed, rich; cf. *Herendil* = Eadwine. [Added entry.
'*Herendil* = Eadwine' derives from *The Lost Road*: Herendil is
Audoin/Eadwine/Edwin in Númenor, son of Elendil. On the meaning
of Old English *éad* see *ibid.* p. 46, and cf. IV. 212.]

**KHIL-** follow. Q *hilya-* to follow; *hildi* followers = mortal men (cf.
*Hildórien*), also *-hildi* as suffix. In N *fir* was used [PHIR]. Cf. *Tarkil*
(*\**tāra-khil*). [Added entry. Cf. *Rómenildi* in QS §151.]

**KHIM-** stick, cleave, adhere. Q *himya-* to stick to, cleave to, abide by;
*himba* adhering, sticking. N *him* steadfast, abiding, and as adv.
continually. Cf. N *hîw* sticky, viscous (*\**khīmā*); *hæw* custom, habit
(*\**khaimē*) = Q *haime* habit. [Added entry.]

**KHIS-, KHITH-** mist, fog. *\**khīthi*: Q *híse*; N *hith*, cf. *Hithlum*
[LUM]. *\**khithme*: Q *hiswe*; N *hithw* fog. *\**khithwa*: Q *hiswa* grey; N
*hethw* foggy, obscure, vague; Dor. *heðu*. Cf. *Hithliniath* or *Eilinuial*
= Dor. *Umboth Muilin*. [Added entry. For *Hithliniath* 'pools of mist'
(LIN[1]) see QS §111.]

**KHŌ-N-** heart (physical). Q *hōn*; N *hûn*. Cf. *Hundor*. *Khō-gorē*, Q
*Huore*, N *Huor* 'heart-vigour', courage [GOR]. [Added entry.]

**KHOP-** Q *hópa* haven, harbour, small landlocked bay; *hopasse*
harbourage. N *hûb*; *hobas*, cf. *Alfobas* or *hobas in Elf* = *Alqalonde*
capital of the Teleri. [Added entry; see KOP.]

**KHOR-** set going, put in motion, urge on, etc. Q *horta-* send flying,
speed, urge, *hortale* speeding, urging; *horme* urgency (confused with
*orme* rushing [GOR]); *hóre* impulse, *hórea* impulsion. N *hûr* readi-
ness for action, vigour, fiery spirit; *hortha-* urge on, speed; *horn* driven
under compulsion, impelled; *hoeno*, *heno* begin suddenly and
vigorously. Cf. *Húr-ind*, *Húrin* [ID]. [Added entry.]

**KHOTH-** gather. *\**khotsē* assembly: N *hoth* host, crowd, frequent in
people-names as *Glamhoth*. Cf. *host* gross (144). Q *hosta* large
number, *hosta-* to collect. N *hûd* assembly.

**KHUGAN-** Q *huan* (*húnen*) hound; N *huan*. [This entry was changed to read thus:] **KHUG-** bark, bay. *\*khugan*: Q *huan* (*húnen*) hound; N *Huan* (dog-name); Q *huo* dog; N *hû*.

**KHYAR-** left hand. Q *hyarmen* south, *hyarmenya* southern; *hyarya* left, *hyarmaite* lefthanded [MA3]. N *heir* left (hand), *hargam* lefthanded [KAB]; *harad* south, *haradren*, *harn* southern. [Added entry. The -*y*- in the base-stem was a further addition, and at the same time the Q forms were changed from *har*- to *hyar*-; see p. 345.]

**KHYEL(ES)-** glass. Q *hyelle* (*\*khyelesē*); ON *khelesa*, *khelelia*; N *hele*, cf. *Helevorn* 'black-glass' [MOR], lake-name. Cf. KHELEK. [Added entry. *Helevorn* is written over an erasure in QS §118.]

**KIL-** divide (also SKIL). Q *kilya* cleft, pass between hills, gorge. [The base SKIL is not found in the *Etymologies*. To this entry was added:] N *cîl*. Cf. *Kalakilya* 'Pass of Light', in which Kôr was built. N *Cilgalad*; *Cilthoron* or *Cilthorondor*.

**KIR-** Q *kirya* ship; N *ceir*. [Added:] *cirdan* shipbuilder [TAN].

**KIRIK-** Q *kirka* sickle; N *cerch*. Q *Valakirka*, N *Cerch iMbelain* [BAL], Sickle of the Gods = Great Bear. N *critho* reap (*\*k'riktā*).

**KIRIS-** cut. Q *kirisse* slash, gash; N *criss* cleft, cut. [Added:] *Cristhoron* – g.sg. of *thôr* eagle. N *crist* a cleaver, sword. Cf. RIS.

**KOP-** Q *kópa* harbour, bay. [This entry was struck out; see KHOP.]

**KOR-** round. *\*kornā*: Q *korna* round, globed; *koron* (*kornen*) globe, ball; *koromindo* cupola, dome. *Kôr* round hill upon which Túna (Tûn) was built. N *corn*, *coron*, *Côr* (*koro*). [*Côr* > *Caur*, and the following added:] [Q] *korin* circular enclosure [cf. I. 257]; N *cerin*. N *rhin-gorn* circle [RIN]. Cf. Ilk. *basgorn* [sc. *bast-gorn* 'round bread', loaf: MBAS].

**KOT-** strive, quarrel. *\*okta* strife: Q *ohta* war. N *auth* war, battle; *cost* quarrel (*kot-t-*), Q *kosta-* quarrel. [The base was changed to **KOTH**, and the following added:] Q *kotumo* enemy, *kotya* hostile. [N] *coth* enmity, enemy; cf. *Morgoth* – but this may also contain GOTH. [See OKTĀ.]

**KRAB-** press. N *cramb*, *cram* cake of compressed flour or meal (often containing honey and milk) used on long journey. [Added entry.]

**KŪ-** *\*kukūwā* dove; Q *ku*, *kua*, ON *ku*, *kua*, (= *kūua*); N *cugu*. [Added entry. The base-stem is not given but is taken from a later etymological note.]

**KUB-** Q *kumbe* mound, heap; N *cumb*, *cum*. [Added entry.]

**KU3-** bow. > *kuw*: Q *kú* bow; N *cû* arch, crescent; *cúran* the crescent moon, see RAN. [Added:] *\*ku3nā*: N *cûn* bowed, bowshaped, bent; but Ilk. *\*kogna* >*coun*, *caun*, Dan. *cogn*.

**KUL-** gold (metal). Q *kulu*, N *côl*; Q *kuluinn* of gold. **KULU-** gold (substance). Q *kulo*. [This entry was struck out and the following roughly substituted:] **KUL-** golden-red. Q † *kullo* red gold; *kulda*, *kulina* flame-coloured, golden-red; *kuluina* orange; *kuluma* an orange; N *coll* red (*\*kuldā*).

**KUM-** void. Q *kúma* the Void; *kumna* empty; N *cûn* empty. [The Q forms were retained, but the Noldorin altered to read:] ON *kúma*, N *cofn*, *caun* empty, void, but in EN [the Void was] called *Gast*, *Belegast* [cf. GAS].

**KUNDŪ-**   prince. Q *kundu*; N *cunn*, especially in names as *Felagund*, *Baragund*. [Added entry.]

**KUR-**   craft. Q *kurwe* craft. N *curw*, *curu*; *curunir* wizard; cf. *Curufin* [PHIN]. Cf. N *crum* wile, guile; *corw* cunning, wily. [Added entry. N *crum* was rejected; see KURÚM.]

**KURÚM-**   N *crum* the left hand; *crom* left; *crumui* left-handed (\**krumbē*, *-ā*). [Added entry. Cf. KHYAR.]

**KUY-**   come to life, awake. Q *kuile* life, being alive; *kuina* alive; *kuive* (noun) awakening; *kuivea* (adj.) wakening; *kuivie* = *kuive*, cf. *Kuiviénen*. N *cuil* life; *cuin* alive; *echui(w)* awakening (\**et-kuiwē*), hence *Nen-Echui* = Q *Kuiviénen*. [The following additions were made:] N *cuino* to be alive; *Dor Firn i guinar* Land of the Dead that Live.

**KWAL-**   die in pain. Q·*qalme* agony, death; *qalin* dead; *unqale* agony, death. [Added entry. See WAN.]

**KWAM-**   Q *qáme* sickness; N *paw*; Ilk. *côm*. [Added entry.]

**KWAR-**   clutching hand, fist. Q *qár* hand (*qari*); N *paur* fist. [This stem was not struck out, but a second form of it was put in elsewhere in the list:] **KWAR-**  Q *qáre* fist; ON *póre*; N *paur*, *-bor*, cf. *Celebrimbor* Silver-fist.

**KWAT-**   Q *qanta* full; ON *panta*; N *pant* full, cf. *Cambant* [KAB]; *pathred* fullness; *pannod* or *pathro* fill. [Added entry.]

**KWEL-**   fade, wither. Cf. *Narqelion* fire-fading, autumn, N *lhasbelin* [LAS¹]. \**kwelett-* corpse: Q *qelet*, *qeletsi*.

**KWEN(ED)-**   Elf. \**kwenedē*: Q *qende* Elf; N *penedh*, pl. *penidh*; Dan. *cwenda*. Q *Qendelie*, N *Penedhrim*. The word *Eledh* is usually employed. [Added entry.]

**KWES-**   \**kwessē*: Q *qesse* feather; Ilk. *cwess* down; N *pesseg* pillow (Q *qesset*). [Added entry.]

**KWET-**  (and **PET-**)  say. \**kwetta*: N *peth* word. \**kwentā* tale: N *pent*, Q *qenta*; N *pennas* history. \**kwentro* narrator: Q *qentaro*; N *pethron*; Dor. *cwindor*. [Added:] Q *qetil* tongue, language; *qentale* account, history; *lúmeqentale* history [LU]. N *gobennas* history, *gobennathren* historical. Q *avaqet-* refuse, forbid [AWA]. [For *go-* prefix see WO.]

**KWIG-**   Cf. KUȝ. \**kwingā*: Q *qinga* bow (for shooting); N *peng*. [Added entry.]

**KYAB-**   taste. Q *tyavin* I taste.

**KYAR-**   cause (cf. KAR). Q *tyar-* cause.

**KYEL-**   come to an end. Q *tyel-* end, cease; *tyel* (*tyelde*) end; *tyelima* final. Cf. TELES. [Added entry.]

**KYELEK-**   swift, agile. Q *tyelka*; N *celeg*, cf. *Celegorn* [GOR].

**KYELEP-** and **TELEP-**   silver. N *celeb* silver; Q *telpe* and *tyelpe* silver; *telepsa* of silver = *telpina*, N *celebren*. Cf. *Irilde Taltelepsa* =

*Idhril Gelebrendal.* [*celebren, Gelebrendal* early changed from *celebrin, Celebrindal.* The entry was rewritten thus:] **KYELEP-** (and **TELEP?**) silver. ON *kelepe,* N *celeb,* silver; Q *telpe* and *tyelpe* silver; *telemna,* N *celefn, celevon* = *telpina,* N *celebren.* Cf. *Irilde Taltelemna* = *Idhril Gelebrendal.* T *telpe*; Ilk. *telf.* Q *telpe* may be Telerin form (Teleri specially fond of silver, as Lindar of gold), in which case all forms may refer to KYELEP. [For *Idril* (*Idhril*) see ID, and cf. *Irilde Taltelepta* in the *Lost Tales,* II. 216.]

# L

[The L-stems consist of lightly pencilled entries, in themselves hard to read, but not much changed subsequently.]

**LA-** no, not. Q *lá* and *lala,* also *lau, laume* (= *lá úme* [UGU]), no, no indeed not, on the contrary; also used for asking incredulous questions. As prefix *la-* > [vocalic] *l* > Q *il,* N *al,* as in *Ilkorin,* N *Alchoron,* pl. *Elcheryn.* Q *lala-* to deny. [See AR².]

**LAB-** lick. Q *lamba* tongue, N *lham(b).* Q *lavin* I lick, also *lapsa* to lick (frequentative). N *lhefi* (*lhâf*).

**LAD-** Cf. DAL, LAT. Q *landa* wide, N *lhand, lhann.* N *camland* palm of hand. Cf. *Lhothland, Lhothlann* (empty and wide), name of a region [LUS].

**LAG-** Q *lango* broad sword; also prow of a ship. N *lhang* cutlass, sword.

**LAIK-** keen, sharp, acute. Q *laike,* N *lhaeg.* Q *laike* acuteness, keenness of perception. Ilk. *laig* keen, sharp, fresh, lively (blended with *laikwa* [see LÁYAK]).

**LAK¹-** swallow; cf. LANK. Q *lanko* throat.

**LAK²-** swift (cf. ÁLAK). *lakra* : Q *larka* swift, rapid, also *alarka* ; N *lhagr, lhegin.*

**LÁLAM-** elm-tree. Q *alalme* ; N *lhalwen* (*lelwin*), *lhalorn* ; D *lalm.* [See ÁLAM.]

**LAM-** Q *lamya* to sound; *láma* ringing sound, echo; *lamma* a sound; *lámina* echoing; *nallama* echo. Dor. *lóm* echo, *lómen* echoing. Thus Dor. *Lómendor, Lóminorthin,* Noldorinized > *Dorlómen, Ered Lómin* ; pure N *Eredlemrin, Dorlamren.* See GLAM.

**LAN-** weave. Q *lanya* weave; *lanwa* loom; *lanat* weft; *lanne* tissue, cloth.

**LANK-** Q *lanko* throat; N *lhanc.* [This stem was first written LANG, with derivatives Q *lango* (**langwi*), N *lhang.* See LAK¹.]

**LAP-** Q *lapse* babe; N *lhaes.*

**LAS¹-** *lassē* leaf: Q *lasse,* N *lhass* ; Q *lasselanta* leaf-fall, autumn, N *lhasbelin* (**lassekwelēne*), cf. Q *Narqelion* [KWEL]. *Lhasgalen*

Greenleaf, Gnome name of Laurelin. (Some think this is related to the next and *lassē 'ear'. The Quendian ears were more pointed and leaf-shaped than [?human].)

**LAS²-**  listen. N *lhaw* ears (of one person), old dual *lasū* – whence singular *lhewig*. Q *lár, lasta-* listen; *lasta* listening, hearing – *Lastalaika* 'sharp-ears', a name, cf. N *Lhathleg*. N *lhathron* hearer, listener, eavesdropper (< *la(n)sro-ndo*); *lhathro* or *lhathrado* listen in, eavesdrop.

**LAT-**  lie open. Q *latin(a)* open, free, cleared (of land); cf. *Tumbolatsin*. Cf. *Tumladen* plain of Gondolin. N *lhaden*, pl. *lhedin* open, cleared; *lhand* open space, level; *lhant* clearing in forest. [Cf. LAD.]

**LATH-**  string, thong. Q *latta* strap; N *lhath* thong of [?leather]; cf. *hadlath, haglath* sling (KHAT).

**LAW-**  warm. *lauka* warm: Q *lauka*, N *lhaug*.

**LÁWAR-, N GLÁWAR-**  *laurē* (light of the golden Tree *Laurelin*) gold – the metal was properly *smalta*, see SMAL; Q *laure*, N *glaur*, Dor. Oss. *laur*. Hence N *glor-, lor-* in names, as *Glorfindel* [SPIN], *Inglor* [ID]. Cf. *Laurelin*, N *Galad-loriel*; *Rathloriel* [RAT]. N *glawar* sunlight, radiance of Laurelin; † *Glewellin*. [See GLAW(-R). Cf. QS §16: 'Glewellin (which is the same as Laurelin song of gold)'.]

**LÁYAK-**  *laik-wā*: Q *laiqa* green; N *lhoeb* fresh – 'green' only in Q *Laiqendi* Green-elves, N *Lhoebenidh* or *Lhoebelidh*. Ilk. *laig* is blended with *laika* [LAIK].

**LEB-, LEM-**  stay, stick, adhere, remain, tarry. Q *lemba* (*lebnā*) left behind, pl. *Lembi* Elves remaining behind = Telerin Ilkorins; N *lhevon, lhifnir*. [See p. 344.]

**LED-**  go, fare, travel. Cf. Q *lende* went, departed (*linna* go). ON *lende* fared; *etledie* go abroad, go into exile; N *egledhi* or *eglehio* go into exile, *egledhron* exile (ON *etledro*), *eglenn* exiled (ON *etlenna*). In N *egledhron* was often taken as the meaning of Ilk. *Eglath* = Eldar = Ilkorins [see ÉLED, GAT(H)].

**LEK-**  loose, let loose, release. N *lhein, lhain* free(d); *lheitho* to release, set free; *lheithian* release, freeing. Q *leuka, lehta* loose, slacken. Ilk. *legol* nimble, active, running free; cf. *Legolin*, a river-name. [A note on a slip accompanying these etymologies gives: '*Leth-* set free (cf. LED); EN *leithia* to release, *leithian* release; cf. *Lay of Leithian*.' I have referred to this note in III. 154, at which time I overlooked the present entry.]

**LEP-, LEPET**  finger. Q *lepse*; N *lhebed*.

Cf. **LEP- (LEPEN, LEPEK)** five. Q *lempe*; N *lheben*. Q *lemnar* week. The Valian week had five days, dedicated (1) to Manwe: *(Ar)Manwen*; (2) to Ulmo: *(Ar)Ulmon*; (3) to Aule and Yavanna: *(Ar)Veruen*, i.e. of the Spouses [BES]; (4) to Mandos and Lorien: *(Ar)Fanturion* [SPAN]; (5) to the three younger Gods, Osse, Orome, Tulkas, called *Nessaron* or *Neldion* [NETH, NEL]. The 73 weeks were divided into 12 months of 6 weeks. In the middle of the Year there was a separate week, Midyear week or week of the Trees, *Endien* [YEN] or *Aldalemnar*, N *Enedhim, Galadlevnar*.

N names: *Ar Vanwe*; *Ar Uiar* (Ulmo) [WAY]; *Ar Vedhwen* (*Bedū* + *ina*), or *Ar Velegol* (Aule [see GAWA]); *Ar Fennuir*; *Ar Nethwelein* = of the young Gods, or *Ar Neleduir* of the three kings.

. [The dual form 'husband and wife' is given as *besū* in the entry BES 'wed', not as here *bedū*; similarly under KHER, NDIS and NĪ reference is made in the original to BED, not BES. There is however no suggestion of any alteration in the entry BES itself. – For the element *Ar* see AR¹. In the Quenya names of the days *Ae* is written above *Ar*, but *Ar* is not struck out. – For the 'young Gods' see p. 120.]

**LI-**  many. Q *lie* people; *-li* pl. suffix, *lin-* prefix = many, as *lintyulussea* having many poplars [TYUL], *lindornea* having many oaks [DÓRON]. In N the ending *-lin* 'many' has been blended with *rhim* > *lim, rim*.

**LIB¹-**  drip. Q *limba* a drop; cf. *helkelimbe* [KHELEK].

**LIB²-**  *\*laibē*: Q *laive* ointment. N shows GLIB-: *glaew* salve. *\*libda*: Q *lipsa*; N [*lhúð* >] *glúð* soap.

**LILT-**  dance. Q *lilta-* dance.

**LIN¹-**  pool. Q *linya* pool; N *lhîn*; Ilk. *line*. Cf. *Ailin* [AY], *Taiglin*.

**LIN²-**  (originally GLIN) sing. Q *linde* air, tune; N *lhind, lhinn*. Q *lindo* singer, singing bird: cf. *tuilindo* swallow, N *tuilinn* [TUY], Q *lómelinde* nightingale, N *dúlinn*. Q *lindele* music. Cf. *Laurelin* (g.sg. *Laurelinden*), but this also taken as 'hanging-gold' (g.sg. *Laurelingen*): see LING. *Lindon, Lhinnon* Ilk. name of Ossiriand: 'musical land' (*\*Lindān-d*), because of water and birds; hence *Eredlindon*, = Mountains of Lindon.

[*tuilindo* ('spring-singer'): cf. I. 269. On the origin of *Lindon, Eredlindon* see commentary on QS §108. – See GLIN.]

**LIND-**  fair (especially of voice); in Q blended with *slindā* (see SLIN). Q *linda* fair, beautiful, cf. *Lindar*; N *lhend* tuneful, sweet; Ilk. *lind*.

**LING-**, N **GLING-**  hang. Q *linga-* hang, dangle; N *gling*. Cf. *Glingal* [and see LIN²].

**LINKWI-**  Q *linqe* wet. N *lhimp*; *lhimmid* moisten (pa.t. *lhimmint*).

**LIP-**  Q *limpe* (wine), drink of the Valar. [The first appearance of *limpe* since the *Lost Tales*, where it was the drink of the Elves; for the old etymology see I. 258.]

**LIR¹-**  sing, trill; in N *g-lir-* [see GLIR]. Q *lirin* I chant.

**LIR²-**  ON *líre* row, range, N *lhîr* row. Cf. *oeglir* range of mountain peaks.

**LIS-**  honey. Q *lis* (*lissen*); N *glî, g-lisi*. Cf. *megli* (*meglin* adj.) bear (*\*mad-lī* honey-eater [MAT], kenning for *brôg*, see MORÓK). Cf. *Meglivorn* = Blackbear.

**LIT-**  Q *litse* sand; ON *litse* > *litthe*, N *lith*; cf. *Fauglith* [PHAU].

**LIW-**  *\*liñwi* fish: Q *lingwe*; N *lhimb, lhim*; Dor. *líw*.

**LOD-** *londē* narrow path, strait, pass: N *lhonn* (cf. *Aglon*); cf. N *othlond, othlon* paved way (*ost* city + *lond*). Q *londe* road (in sea), entrance to harbour, cf. *Alqalonde*.

**LOK-** great serpent, dragon. Q *lóke* (*-ī*) dragon; *angulóke* dragon [ANGWA], *rámalóke* winged dragon [RAM], *urulóke* fire-dragon [UR], *fealóke* spark-dragon [PHAY], *lingwilóke* fish-dragon, sea-serpent [LIW]. Cf. N *lhûg, amlug, lhimlug*.

**LOKH-** Q *lokse* hair; N *lhaws, lhoch* (**lokko*) ringlet.

**LONO-** *lóna* island, remote land difficult to reach. Cf. *Avalóna* [AWA] = Tol Eressea = the outer isle. [Added to this is *A-val-lon*. *Avallon* first appears in the second version of *The Fall of Númenor* (§1) as a name of Tol Eressea with the explanation that 'it is hard by Valinor'.]

**LOS-** sleep. Q *olor* dream, cf. *Lórien* = N *Lhuien*. Q *lóre* slumber, *lorna* asleep. N *ôl* dream, *oltha* [to dream]. [See ÓLOS.]

**LOT(H)** flower. Q *lóte* (large single) flower; *losse* blossom (usually, owing to association with *olosse* snow, only used of white blossom [see GOLÓS]). N *lhoth* flower; *gwaloth* blossom, collection of flowers [WO]. Cf. *Wingelot, Wingelóte* Foamflower, N *Gwingeloth* [WIG]; *Nimloth* [NIK-W] = Galathilion.

**LU-** Q *lúme* time (cf. *lúmeqenta* history, chronological account, *lúmeqentale* history, *lúmeqentalea* historical); *lú* a time, occasion. N *lhû*. [See KWET.]

**LUG¹-** **lungā* heavy: Q *lunga*; N *lhong*; Dor. *lung*; cf. Dor. *Mablung* [MAP].

**LUG²-** **lugni* blue: Q *lúne*; N *lhûn* (Dor. *luin* pale, Dan. *lygn*). Cf. *Lúnoronti* Blue Mountains, N *Eredluin* (also *Lhúnorodrim, Lhúndirien* Blue Towers) = *Eredlindon* Mountains of Lindon (= Ossiriand). [For an occurrence of *Lunoronti* see p. 32. *Luindirien* Blue Towers occurs in a footnote added to QS §108 (commentary).]

**LUK-** magic, enchantment. N *lhûth* spell, charm; *lhútha* to enchant; *Lhúthien* enchantress (Dor. *Luithien*). Q *lúke* enchantment; *luhta* enchant. [The etymology of *Lúthien* changed to read thus:] Doriath *luth*, whence *Luthien* (Noldorized as *Lhúthien*): **luktiēnē*.

**LUM-** Q *lumbe* gloom, shadow; *Hísilumbe*, N *Hithlum* [KHIS]. In Q the form is usually *Hísilóme* by attraction of *lóme* night [DO3]. N *lhum* shade, *lhumren* shady.

**LUS-** N *lhost* empty, cf. [*Mablothren* >] *Camlost* [KAB], *Lothlann* [LAD]. Q *lusta* void, empty.

**LUT-** float, swim. Q *lunte* boat; N *lhunt*. N *lhoda* float.

# M

[The M-entries are faint and difficult to interpret, and some are very confused. My father made a beginning on a new list, writing the etymologies out afresh and clearly, but this petered out after he had treated the stems in MA- and a few others (MBAD, MBER, MEL).]

**MAD-** Q *marya* pale, fallow, fawn. N *meið*, *maið*, hence *Maidhros* (anglicized *Maidros*) = 'pale-glitter' [RUS].

**MA3-** hand. PQ *māʒ* (*maʒ-*) hand: Q *mā*; ON *mō* (pl. *mai*) usually replaced by *kamba* (N *camm*): see KAB. Hence *maʒiti* handy, skilled, Q *maite* (pl. *maisi*); ON *maite*, N *moed*. *maʒ-tā* to handle: Eld. *mahtā-*: Q *mahta-*, ON *matthō-be*, N *matho* stroke, feel, handle; wield (confused with *maktā*, see MAK).

Related is **MAG-** use, handle, in *magrā* useful, fit, good (of things): Q *mára*, N *maer*; *magnā* skilled: ON *magnā*, N *maen* skilled, clever, *maenas* craft, handicraft, art. [In the original form of this entry the name *Maidros* (see MAD) was placed under MAG: *Maedhros* < *Maenros*.]

**MAK-** sword, or as verb-stem: fight (with sword), cleave. *makla*: Q *makil* sword; N *magl*, *magol*. *maktā*: Q *mahta-* wield a weapon (blended with *maʒ-tā*, see MA3), fight: hence *mahtar* warrior = N *maethor*. N *maeth* battle, fight (not of general host but of two or a few), *maetha* to fight. Cf. *Maglaðûr* [cf. DO3?] or *Maglaðhonn* = Black-sword (as name). Q *Makalaure* = Gold-cleaver, name of fifth son of Feanor, N *Maglor*.

[In the original form of this entry the N forms of the noun 'sword' were *megil*, *magol*, and the name 'Black-sword' was *Megildur* (> *Magladhûr*, *Maglavorn*). If these forms were to replace *Mormakil*, *Mormegil* etc. as Túrin's name in Nargothrond they never appear in the texts.]

**MAN-** holy spirit (one who has not been born or who has passed through death). Q *manu* departed spirit; N *mān*. Cf. Q *Manwe* (also borrowed and used in N [see WEG]).

**MANAD-** doom, final end, fate, fortune (usually = final bliss). Q *manar*, *mande*. N *manað*. Cf. N *manathon*. In Q this stem is partly blended with MBAD, q.v. and cf. *Mandos*, *Kalamando*.

**MAP-** lay hold of with hand, seize. Q *mapa-* grasp, seize. ON *map-* seize, take away by force. Ilk. (Dor.) *mab* hand (*mapā*), cf. *Mablung* [LUG¹]. Ilk. *Ermab(r)in* one-handed (of Beren: cf. *Mablosgen* emptyhanded = N *Erchamron*, *Camlost*). [The forms *Ermab(r)in* and *Erchamron* are certain.]

**MASAG-** knead, make soft by rubbing, kneading, etc. *mazgā*: Q *maksa* pliant, soft; ON *mazga* > *maiga*, N *moe*, soft. *mazgē*: Q *makse* dough, N *moeas* dough. Ilk. *maig* dough.

**MAT-** eat. Q *mat-*; N *medi*. For *megli* bear see LIS.

**MBAD-** duress, prison, doom, hell. *mbanda*: N *band*, *bann* duress, prison; *Angband* Hell (Iron-prison) (Q *Angamanda*). Q *Mando* the Imprisoner or Binder, usually lengthened *Mand-os* (*Mandosse* = Dread Imprisoner, N *Bannos* [GOS]. Blended in Q with MAN –

hence *Kalamando* Light Mando = Manwe, *Morimando* Dark Mando = Mandos. MBAD is in turn related to BAD, q.v.

**MBAKH-** exchange. Q *manka-* trade; *makar* tradesman; *mankale* commerce. N *banc, banga*; *bachor* pedlar; *bach* article (for exchange), ware, thing (**mbakhā*).

**MBAL-** Q *malle* street; *ambal* shaped stone, flag.

**MBAR-** dwell, inhabit. Q *a-mbar* (*ambaron*) 'oikoumenē', Earth; *Endamar, Ambarenya* Middle-earth. N *ambar, amar* Earth; *Emmerein, Emerin* (*Ambarenya*) Middle-earth. *Martan(ō)* Earthbuilder = Aule (N *Barthan*) [TAN]. *Gondobar, Findobar* [PHIN]. [With the use of the Greek word *oikoumenē* here cf. *Letters* no. 154, p. 197. – *Ambarendya* occurs in the *Ambarkanta*, IV. 241–3. – With *Martan* cf. I. 266, entry *Talka Marda*. – *Findobar* was the son of Fingon (p. 403).]

**MBARAT-** Q *umbar* (*umbarten*) fate, doom; N *ammarth*. Q *marta* fey, fated; *maranwe* destiny; *martya-* destine. N *barad* doomed; *bartho* to doom. Cf. *Turamarth*, Q *Turambar* [apparently written thus over *Turumbar*].

**MBAS-** knead. Q *masta-* bake, *masta* bread. N *bast* bread; *basgorn* loaf [KOR].

**MBAW-** compel, force, subject, oppress. Q *mauya-* compel; *mausta* compulsion; *maure* need. N *baug* tyrannous, cruel, oppressive; *bauglo* to oppress; *bauglir* tyrant, oppressor; *bui* (**mauy-*) (impersonal); *baur* need. Cf. *Gothmog* (**Gothombauk-*) [GOS].

**MBER-** Q *meren* (*merend-*) or *merende* feast, festival; N *bereth*. Q *merya* festive; *meryale* holiday. N *beren* festive, gay, joyous. [This stem was first MER, and the N words *mereth, meren*; but a new stem MER was then introduced and the former MER changed to MBER, the N words becoming *bereth, beren*. The name *Mereth Aderthad* was never changed in the texts.]

**MBIRIL-** (compound of MIR and RIL, q.v.) Q *miril* (*mirilli*) shining jewel; *mirilya-* glitter. Ilk. *bril* glass, crystal; cf. *Brilthor* glittering torrent.

**MBOTH-** Dor. *moth* pool, *umboth* large pool. Cf. Q *motto* blot, N *both* puddle, small pool. Cf. *Umboth Muilin* [MUY] = N *Elinuial* or *Hithliniath*.

**MBUD-** project. **mbundu*: Q *mundo* snout, nose, cape; N *bund, bunn*. Cf. **andambundā* long-snouted, Q *andamunda* elephant, N *andabon, annabon* [ÁNAD].

**MEL-** love (as friend). Q *mel-*; *melin* dear, *melda* beloved, dear; *melme* love; *melisse* (f.), *melindo* (m.) lover; *melima* loveable, fair, *Melimar* = Lindar. Irregular vocalism: **mālō* friend, Q *málo*. N *meleth* love; *mell* dear; *mellon* friend; *meldir* friend, f. *meldis*; *melethron, melethril* lover. *mîl* love, affection; *milui* friendly, loving, kind.

**MEN-** Q *men* place, spot; *ména* region. Cf. *Númen, Rómen, Harmen* [see KHYAR], *Tormen* [which is the form in the *Ambarkanta*, IV. 244–5, 248–9, changed later to *Formen* (PHOR).]

**MER-** wish, desire, want. Q *mere*, pa.t. *merne*. [See MBER.]

**MERÉK-** [This entry was struck out, and the stem MBERÉK written against it. It was the same as the entry BERÉK, q.v., except that the Q form was here *merka* 'wild' for *verka*, a N form *brerg* 'wild, fierce' was given, and *bregol* was translated 'fierce'.]

**MET-** end. Q *mente* point, end; N *ment* point; *meth* end (*\*metta*); *methen* end. Q *metya-* put an end to.

**MI-** inside. Q *mi* in, within; *mir* and *minna* to the inside, into; *mitya* adj. interior.

**MIL-IK-** Q *milme* desire, greed; *maile* lust; *mailea* lustful; *milya-* long for; *milka* greedy; *Melko* (\**Mailikō*), N *Maeleg* (\**-kā*). N *melch* greedy; *mael* lust; *maelui* lustful. [The stem vowel *ae* in the N words was changed to *oe*: *Moeleg*, etc. The Gnomish name *Moeleg* of Melko occurs in Q (IV. 79, 164).]

**MINI-** stand alone, stick out. Q *mine* one; *minya* first; *minda* prominent, conspicuous; *mindo* isolated tower. N *min* one, *minei* (\**miniia*) single, distinct, unique; *minnas* tower, also *mindon* (\**minitaun*, cf. *tunn* [see TUN]).

**MINIK-W-** Q *minqe* eleven.

**MIR-** Q, ON *mîre*; N *mîr* jewel, precious thing, treasure. Cf. *Nauglamîr* (Doriathrin form). *Mirion* ordinary N name of the *Silevril* (*Silmarilli*), pl. *Miruin*; = N *Golo(ð)vir* or *Mîr in Geleið*, Dor. *Goldamir*. [The name *Borommiro* is scribbled in: see BOR.]

**MIS-** go free, stray, wander. Q *mirima* free; cf. *Mirimor* = the Teleri. *mista-* stray about. N *mist* error, wandering; *misto* to stray; *mistrad* straying, error. [In the long note to QS §29 giving names 'in song and tale' of the Kindreds of the Elves a name of the Teleri is 'the Free' (and another 'the Wanderers').]

**MISK-** Q *miksa* wet; N *mesg, mesc*.

**MITH-** N *mith* white fog, wet mist; cf. *Mithrim* [RINGI]. [Later addition: *mith* = grey.]

**MIW-** whine. Q *maiwe* gull, N *maew*. Q *miule* whining, mewing.

**MIZD-** \**mizdē*: Q *miste* fine rain; N *mídh* dew; Dor. *míd* moisture (adj. *méd* wet, \**mizdā*); Dan. *meord* fine rain. Cf. Dor. name *Dolmed* 'Wet-head' [NDOL]. [The stems MISK-, MITH-, MIZD- are evidently related, but it is scarcely possible to see from the changes on the manuscript what my father finally intended.]

**MŌ-** \**mōl-*: Q *mól* slave, thrall; N *mûl*. Q *móta-* labour, toil; N *mudo* (pa.t. *mudas*). [Cf. *Lhammas* §8: *múlanoldorin* > *mólanoldorin*, language of the Noldor enslaved by Morgoth.]

**MOR-** \**mori* black: Q *more* black (N †*môr*); *mordo* shadow, obscurity, stain; *móre* blackness, dark, night; *morna* gloomy, sombre; *morilinde* nightingale (Ilk. *murulind, myrilind*). N *maur* gloom; *moru* black. Ilk. *môr* night. *Meglivorn*: see LIS, MAT. *Morgoth* Black Foe

[ĸoт] = Melko. *Morimando* = Mandos [see MBAD]. *Moriqendi* Dark
Elves = *Morimor*, N *Duveledh* or *Dúrion* [DO3]. [This entry is
extremely confused through changes and afterthought additions, and
I have tried to arrange the material more sequentially. It is not clear,
however, that all the forms given were intended to stand.]

**MORÓK-** *\*moróko* bear: Q *morko*; N *brôg*; Ilk. *broga*. [See LIS.]

**MOY-** Q *moina* familiar, dear; ON *muina*, N *muin* dear. [See TOR.]

**MŪ-** not, no. [See UGU, UMU.]

**MUY-** Q *muina* hidden, secret; *muile* secrecy. Dor. *muilin* secret,
veiled; *Umboth Muilin* veiled pool = N *Lhîn Uial* or *Eilinuial*. Dor.
*muil* twilight, shadow, vagueness. (Not in N because it became
identical with *moina* [MOY].)


# N

[There was no new start made on the N-entries, which remain in their
extremely difficult original form. The stems with an initial back nasal
consonant (followed by the stop *g*), represented in the manuscript by a
special form of the latter *n*, are here printed Ŋ̄G-.]

**NĀ¹-** [Cf. ANA¹] Q *an, ana, na* to, towards, prefix *ana-*. N *na* with,
by, prefix *an-*. Also used as genitive sign.

**NĀ²-** [Cf. ANA²] be. Stem of verb 'to be' in Q. Cf. *nat* thing, N *nad*.

**NAD-** Q *nanda* water-mead, watered plain. N *nand, nann* wide
grassland; *naðor, naðras* pasture. Dor. *nand* field, valley. Cf.
*Nandungorthin, Nan Tathren.*

**NAK-** [Cf. ÁNAK] bite. Q *nak-* bite; N *nag-*. Q *nahta* a bite; N *naeth*
biting, gnashing of teeth [see NAY]. N *naew* (*\*nakma*), Q *nangwa*
jaw. Cf. *\*an-kā* jaw, row of teeth: Q *anka*, N *anc*; *Anc-alagon*
'Biting-Storm', dragon-name [ÁLAK].

**NAN-** N *nana* (hypocoristic) mother; *naneth*. [See AM¹.]

**NAR¹-** flame, fire. Q *nár* and *náre* flame, cf. *Anar* Sun; *narwā* fiery
red. N *naur* flame; *Anar* Sun; *narw, naru* red. Cf. *Egnor* [EK], etc.;
for *Feanor* see PHAY. Q *narqelion* 'fire-fading', autumn [KWEL].
[The N form *Anar* is clear. See ANÁR.]

**NAR²-** (Q *nyar-*) tell, relate. Q *nyáre* tale, saga, history, *lumenyáre*
[LU]; *nyarin* I tell. ON *naróbe* he tells a story (pa. t. *narne*), *trenare*
he recounts, tells to end (inf. *trenarie*). N †*naro* tell; *treneri (nennar)*,
pa.t. *trenor, trener*; *trenarn* account, tale (ON *trenárna*); *narn* tale,
saga (Q *nyarna*). [For prefix *tre-* see TER.]

**NÁRAK-** tear, rend (tr. and intr.). *\*narāka* rushing, rapid, violent: Q
*naraka* harsh, rending, violent; N *narcha-* to rend, Q *narki*. N *Narog*
river-name; *Nar(o)gothrond* [OS] = fortress of Narog; *Narogardh* =
realm of Narog.

**NAS-** point, sharp end. Q *nasse* thorn, spike; *nasta-* prick, sting. N *nass* point, sharp end; angle or corner (cf. BEN); *nasta* prick, point, stick, thrust. Cf. SNAS, SNAT.

**NAT-** (cf. NUT) lace, weave, tie. Q *natse* web, net; N *nath* web; Dor. *nass*. N *nathron* weaver, webster; *gonathra-* entangle, enmesh, *gonathras* entanglement. [For prefix *go-* see wŏ.]

**NAUK-** Q *nauko* dwarf. N *naug*. Cf. *Nogrod* Dwarf-city [cf. ROD?]. Also in diminutive form *naugol* (*naugl-*). The name *Nauglamír* is strictly Doriathric, in which genitive in *-a(n)* preceded. The true N idiom is *mîr na Nauglin* or *Nauglvir > Nauglavir*.
[N *naug* was struck out and replaced by: 'N *nawag* (pl. *neweig*, *neweg*); Dor. *naugol*, whence EN *naugl*'; but the rest of the entry was allowed to stand. The stem NÁWAK was written beside NAUK.]

**NAY-** lament. *naeth* (*nakt-*) 'biting' is associated in N with this stem, and gets senses of gnashing teeth in grief: cf. *Nírnaeth Arnediad* (or *Aronoded*) [NOT]. Q *naire* lament, *naina-* lament. N *noer* adj. sad, lamentable; *nae* alas, Q *nai*. Q, ON *noi, nui* lament (**naye*); *Nuinoer*, *Nuinor*, name of Túrin's sister.

**NÁYAK-** (or perhaps NAYKA-, elaboration of NAK, q.v.) pain. Q *naike* sharp pain; *naikele*; *naikelea* painful. N *naeg* pain; *negro* to pain.

**NDAK-** slay. ON *ndakie* to slay, pa.t. *ndanke*; *ndagno* slain (as noun), corpse; *ndakro* slaughter, battle. N *degi* to slay; *daen* corpse; *dangen* slain, cf. *Hauð i Ndengin*; *dagr, dagor* battle; *dagro* to battle, make war. **ndākō* warrior, soldier: ON *ndóko*, N *daug* chiefly used of Orcs, also called *Boldog*. [*Boldog* is an Orc-captain in the *Lay of Leithian* and in Q §10. The meaning here is that *Boldog* was used beside *daug*; see ÑGWAL.]

**NDAM-** hammer, beat. Q *namba* a hammer, *namba-* to hammer. *Nambarauto* hammerer of copper, sixth son of Fëanor, N *Damrod* [RAUTĀ]. N *dam* a hammer, *damna-* to hammer (pa.t. *dammint*).

**NDAN-** back. (Cf. *Danas*; N *Dân*, pl. *Dein, Daðrin*). Q *nan-* (prefix) backwards. Dor. *dôn* back (noun). Cf. Q *nā, nān* but, on the contrary, on the other hand, *a-nanta* and yet, but yet. [See DAN, and commentary on *Lhammas* §7.]

**NDER-** strengthened form of *der* man (see DER). **ndēro* bridegroom > Eldarin *ndǣr*, Q *nér* man (blended with *dér*); ON *ndair*, N *doer* bridegroom. Cf. *Ender* surname of Tulkas (*Endero*), as *Indis* (see NDIS) of his wife.

**NDEW-** follow, come behind. Q *neuna* (**ndeuna*) second; **ndeuro* follower, successor: Q *neuro*, cf. Dor. *Dior* successor (i.e. of Thingol). The stem is confused with NDŪ 'sink' in N.

**NDIS-** Strengthening (parallel to NDER of DER) of NIS 'woman', itself elaborated from INI.

    **NDIS-SĒ/SĀ** Q *nisse* beside *nis* (see NIS, NĪ) woman. ON *ndissa* young woman (in N *dess* was blended with *bess*, properly 'wife'); **ndīse* bride > ON *ndîs*, N *dîs*. Intensive form **i-ndise* = Q *Indis* 'bride', name of the goddess Nessa.

**NDOL-**   Q *nóla* round head, knoll; N *dôl* (ON *ndolo*) head. Cf. Q *Andolat* hill-name, N *Dolad*. N *dolt* (pl. *dylt*) round knob, boss. Cf. Dor. *Ndolmed, Dolmed* = Wet Head, name of mountain in Eredlindon.

**NDOR-**   dwell, stay, rest, abide. Q *nóre* land, dwelling-place, region where certain people live, as *Vali-nóre* (*Valinor*). The long vowel in Q is due to confusion with *nóre* clan (NŌ; ONO). N *dor* (\**ndorē*); *dortho-* dwell, stay. Cf. *Endor* = *Endamar* Middle-earth. *Doriath*: see GATH. [Under ÉNED *Endor* is defined as 'centre of the world'. See IV. 254–5.]

**NDŪ-**   (see also NŬ) go down, sink, set (of Sun, etc). Associated in N with DO3 night, also with NDEW. Q *númen* west (see MEN), *númenya* western; *núta* set, sink (of Sun or Moon); *andūne* (\**ndūnē*) sunset. N *dûn* west, beside *annûn* used as opposite of *amrûn* (see AM); also *dúven* [?southern].
[Scribbled marginal notes give: '*Númenóre* and *Andúnie* = Land of Great Men (after the Last Battle). NDUR, NUR bow down, obey, serve; *núro* sunset; cf. *-dûr* in name *Isildur*.' In FN I (§2) *Andúnie* was likewise the name of the land of Númenor, not (as in FN II) of its chief town.]

**NDUL-**   See DUL. \**ndulla*: Q *nulla* dark, dusky, obscure; N *doll*, cf. *Terendul*.

**NÉD-**   See ÉNED. middle, centre. N *enedh* core, centre; Q *ende*. But N *nedh-* as prefix = mid-.

**NEI-**   tear. Q *níre, nie* tear; cf. *nieninqe* snowdrop [NIK-W], *Nienna*. N *nîr* tear, weeping; *nírnaeth* lamentation [NAY]; *nîn* (\**neinē*) tear, *nínim* snowdrop (*nifredil*). Q *níte* (\**neiti-*) moist, dewy; N *nîd* damp, wet; tearful. \**neiniel-*: N *niniel* tearful.

**NEL-**   three. **NÉL-ED-** three: Q *nelde*; N *neledh* later *neled* (after *canad* four). Prefix *nel-* tri-. *nelthil* triangle (*neltildi*) [TIL]. Doriathrin *neldor* beech. Cf. *Neldoreth* name of a forest in Doriath, properly name of *Hirilorn* the great beech of Thingol with three trunks = *neld-orn*? [see ÓR-NI]. The N name is *brethel*, pl. *brethil* (cf. Forest of Brethil); see BERÉTH [where *brethil* is given as the singular]. The proper Dor. name was *galdbreth* > *galbreth* [GALAD].

**NÉL-EK-**   tooth. Q *nelet, nelki*. ON *nele, neleki*; N *nêl, neleg*.

**NEN-**   Q *nén* (nen-) water; N *nen* (pl. *nîn*). Q *nelle* (\**nen-le*) brook; *nende* pool; *nenda* watery, wet. N *nend, nenn* watery. Cf. *Ui-nend*, Q *Uinen* [UY].

**NEŃ-WI-**   nose. Q *nengwe, nengwi*; *nengwea* nasal. N *nemb, nem*; Dor. *nîw*.

**NÊR-**   Q stem for PQ *der-* man, derived from influence of *ndere* and *nī, nis*: see NĪ, DER, NDER.

**NÉTER-**   nine. Q *nerte*; N *neder*.

**NETH-**   young. Q *Nessa* goddess, also called *Indis* (bride): see NĪ,

NDIS. *nessa* young (**neth-rā*); *nése* or *nesse* youth; *nessima* youthful. N *nîth* youth (**nēthē*); *neth* young (*nethra*); *Neth* or *Dineth* = Indis Nessa.

ÑGAL- / ÑGALAM- talk loud or incoherently. Q *ñalme* clamour; N *glamb, glamm* (**ngalámbe*, influenced by *lambe* [LAB]) barbarous speech; *Glamhoth* = Orcs. See LAM, GLAM. [The stem was changed subsequently to ÑGYAL- and Q *ñalme* to *yalme*.]

ÑGAN-, ÑGÁNAD- play (on stringed instrument). Q *ñande* a harp, *ñandelle* little harp; *ñandele* harping; *ñanda-* to harp; *ñandaro* harper. N *gandel, gannel* a harp; *gannado* or *ganno* play a harp; *talagant* [> *talagand*] harper (**tyalañgando*), cf. *Talagant* [> *Talagand*] of Gondolin [TYAL]. Ilk. *gangel, genglin*. [*Talagant* appears in no literary source, but cf. *Salgant* in the tale of *The Fall of Gondolin*, the cowardly but not wholly unattractive lord of the People of the Harp: II. 173, 190–1, etc.]

ÑGAR(A)M- Dor. *garm* wolf; N *garaf*; Q *ñarmo, narmo*.

ÑGAW- howl. N *gaur* werewolf; Q *ñauro*. N *gaul*, Q *naule* wolf-howl. N *gaw-* howl; *gawad* howling.

ÑGOL- wise, wisdom, be wise. Q *ñolwe* wisdom, secret lore; *ñóle* wisdom; *ñóla* wise, learned; †*ingole* deep lore, magic (N †*angol*). N †*golw* lore, *golwen* (**ngolwina*) wise, learned in deep arts; *goll* (**ngolda*) wise; *gollor* magician; *gûl* magic. Dor. *ngol, gôl* wise, magical; *(n)golo* magic, lore; *durgul, mor(n)gul* sorcery.

ÑGOLOD- one of the wise folk, Gnome. Q *ñoldo*; ON *ngolodo*, N *golodh*, pl. *goeloeidh, geleidh*, and *golodhrim*; T *golodo*, Dor. *(n)gold*; Dan. *golda*. Q *Ingolonde* Land of the Gnomes (Beleriand, but before applied to parts of Valinor); N *Angolonn* or *Geleidhien. Golovir* (*Mîr in Geleidh*) = Silmaril; Dor. *Goldamir*; Q *Noldomíre* [MIR].

ÑGOROTH- horror (cf. GOR; GOS, GOTH). N *Gorgoroth* deadly fear (**gor-ngoroth*), cf. (*Fuin*) *Gorgoroth*, later name of Dorthanion, also called *Taur-na-Fuin* or *Taur-na-Delduath*. Cf. Dor. name *Nan Dungorthin* (Dor. *ngorthin* horrible, *dunn* black); Dor. *ngorth* horror = N *goroth, Nan Dongoroth* or *Nann Orothvor* [see DUN].

ÑGUR- ON *nguru, ngurtu*; N *gûr* Death, also *guruth* [see WAN]. Q *nuru, Nuru* (personified) = Mandos; *Nurufantur* = Mandos *Gurfannor* [SPAN]. Cf. *Gurtholv* [> *Gurutholf*] 'Wand of Death', sword-name [GÓLOB].

ÑGWAL- torment. Q *ungwale* torture; *nwalya-* to pain, torment; *nwalka* cruel. N *balch* cruel; *baul* torment, cf. *Bal-* in *Balrog* or *Bolrog* [RUK], and Orc-name *Boldog* = Orc-warrior 'Torment-slayer' (cf. NDAK).

ÑGYÔ-, ÑGYON- grandchild, descendant. Q *indyo*; T *endo*; ON *ango* (not in N). Cf. YÔ, YON.

NĪ[1]- woman – related to ĪNI female, counterpart to 3AN male. In Q *ní* was archaic and poetic and usually replaced by *nis* pl. *nissi* or *nisse* pl. *nissi*. See NIS, NDIS. In Q, PQ *dēr* 'man' became *nér* (not *lér*) owing to blending with *ndǽr* 'bridegroom' and to influence of *nī*, *nis* (see DER, NDER).

In ON *nî* 'woman' later > *dî* through influence of *dîr* [see DER]; but *dî* was only rare and poetical ('bride, lady'): it was replaced in sense 'woman' by *bess* [see BES], and in sense 'bride' by cpd. *di-neth* (see NETH). *Dineth* is also N name for the goddess *Neth* = Q *Nessa*, and *Indis*.

**NI²-**  = I.

**NIB-**  face, front. N *nîf* (*\*nībe*) front, face. Dor. *nef* face; *nivra-* to face, go forward; *nivon* west, *Nivrim* West-march, *Nivrost* West-dales [ROS²]. [*Nivrim* 'West-march' occurs in QS §110, and *Nivrost* 'West Vale' in QS §106.]

**NID-**  lean against. *\*nidwō* bolster, cushion: Q *nirwa*; ON *nidwa*, N *nedhw*.

**NIK-W-**  Q *niqe* snow; *ninqe* white (*\*ninkwi*); *nieninqe* 'white tear' = snowdrop [NEI]; *ninqita-* shine white; *ninqitá-* whiten; *ninqisse* whiteness. *Taniqetil(de)* = High White Horn = N.*Nimdil-dor* (*\*Ninkwitil(de) Tára*). N *nimp* (*nim*) pale; *nifred* pallor, fear; *nimmid* to whiten (pa.t. *nimmint*); *nifredil* snowdrop; *nimred* (*nimpred*) pallor.

**NIL-, NDIL-**  friend. Q *nilda* friendly, loving; *nildo* (and *nilmo*), f. *nilde*, friend; *nilme* friendship. In names *-nil*, *-dil* = Old English *wine*, as *Elendil* (*\*Eled-nil*) = Ælfwine; *Herendil* = Eadwine [see KHER].

**NIN-DI-**  fragile, thin. Q *ninde* slender; N *ninn*.

**NIS-**  Probably an elaboration of INI, NĪ; feminine counterpart to DER 'man'. Q *nis*, *nissi* (see NĪ).

**NŌ-**  (cf. ONO) beget. Q *nóre* country, land, race (see NDOR). N *nûr* race; *noss* (= Q *nosse*) clan, family, 'house', as *Nos Finrod* House of Finrod. Q *onóro* brother, *onóne* sister. ON *wanúro*, N *gwanur* [wǒ].

**ÑOL-**  smell (intr.). Q, L *holme* odour. N *ûl* odour (*\*ñōle*); *angol* stench.

**NOROTH-**  Q *norsa* a giant.

**NOT-**  count, reckon. Q *not-* reckon, *onot-* count up; *nóte* number. N *noedia* count; *gonod-* count up, reckon, sum up; cf. *arnoediad*, *arnediad*, beside *aronoded*, innumerable, countless, endless; *gwanod* tale, number [see wǒ].

**NOWO-**  think, form idea, imagine. Q *noa* and *nó*, pl. *nówi*, conception; *nause* imagination (*\*nauþe*). N *naw*, pl. *nui*, idea; *nauth-* thought; *nautha-* conceive.

**NŪ-**  Cf. NDŪ. Q *nún* adv. down below, underneath; *no* prep. under. N *no* under, with article *nui* (*Dagor nuin Giliath*). *\*nūrā*, or separate stem NUR; Q *núra* deep; N *nûr*. Cf. *Nurqendi* = Gnomes; *Núron*, N name for Ulmo.

**NUT-**  tie, bind. Q *nutin* I tie; *núte* bond, knot; *nauta* bound, obliged. N *nud-*; *nûd* bond; *naud* bound.

**NYAD-** gnaw. *nyadrō : Q nyano rat; N nâr (< naðr).

**NYEL-** ring, sing, give out a sweet sound. Q nyello singer; nyelle bell; T Fallinel (Fallinelli) = Teleri [PHAL]. N nell bell; nella- sound bells; nelladel ringing of bells. Q Solonyeldi = Teleri (see SOL); in Telerin form Soloneldi.

# O

**OKTĀ-** See KOT. Q ohta war. N auth. Ilk. oth.

**ÓLOS-** dream. Q olor dream, Olofantur (s-f > f) = Lórien. N [olt >] ôl (pl. elei); oltha- to dream (*olsa-); Olfannor (= Olo(s)-fantur) [SPAN] = Lórien. [See LOS.]

**OM-** Q óma voice; óman, amandi vowel.

**ONO-** beget (see NŌ). Q onta- beget, create (pa.t. óne, ontane); onna creature; ontaro (ontáro) begetter, parent (f. ontare); ontani parents. N odhron parent (odhril); (*onrō) ed-onna beget; ûn creature.

**ORO-** up; rise; high; etc. (cf. RŌ). Q óre rising, anaróre sunrise; orta- rise, raise. N or prep. above; prefix or- as in orchall, orchel superior, eminent (see KHAL²); ON ortie, orie rise, ortóbe raise; N ortho raise (orthant); erio rise (†oronte arose).

**OROT-** height, mountain. Q oron (pl. oronti) mountain; orto mountain-top. ON oro, pl. oroti, beside oroto; N orod (pl. ereid, ered) mountain; orodrim range of mountains (see RIM). Dor. orth, pl. orthin. Cf. Orodreth; Eredwethion, Eredlindon, Eredlemrin, Eredengrin.

**ÓR-NI-** high tree. Q orne tree, high isolated tree. N, Dor. orn. In Doriath used especially of beech, but as suffix in regorn etc. used of any tree of any size. In N used of any large tree – holly, hawthorn, etc. were classed as toss (tussa) bush [TUS]: thus eregdos = holly [ERÉK]. N orn has pl. yrn.

**ÓROK-** *órku goblin: Q orko, pl. orqi. ON orko, pl. orkui; N orch, pl. yrch. Dor. urch, pl. urchin. Dan. urc, pl. yrc.

**ORÓM-** *Orōmē: Q Orome; ON Oroume, Araume > Exilic Araw, also called Tauros. See ROM.

**OS-** round, about. N o about, concerning, h before vowel as o Hedhil concerning Elves; os- prefix 'about', as esgeri cut round, amputate (3 sg. osgar). Q osto city, town with wall round. N ost; othrond fortress, city in underground caves = ost-rond (see ROD). Cf. Belegost, Nargothrond.

**OT- (OTOS, OTOK)** seven. Q otso; N odog. Q Otselen Seven Stars, N Edegil, = Great Bear or Valakirka Sickle of the Gods.

**OY-** ever, eternal. Q oi ever; oia (*oiyā) everlasting; oiale, oire everlasting [?age]; oira eternal. Oiolosse 'Everlasting snow' = Taniqetil = ON Uigolosse, N Uilos, Amon Uilos; uir eternity; uireb eternal. Q Oiakúmi = Avakúma. [This entry replaced that under GEY, which itself replaced EY.]

# P

**PAD-** Q *panda* enclosure. N in *cirban* haven; *pann* courtyard.

**PAL-** wide (open). Q *palla* wide, expansive; *palu-, palya-* open wide, spread, expand, extend; N *pelio* spread. Q *palme* surface; N *palath* surface. Q *palúre* surface, bosom, bosom of Earth (= Old English *folde*), hence *Palúrien* surname of Yavanna. [Later addition:] *palan-* far, distant, wide, to a great extent; *palantir* a far-seeing stone.

**PALAP-** Q *palpa-* to beat, batter. N *blebi* for *\*plebi* ; *blâb* flap, beat (wing, etc.)

**PAN-** place, set, fix in place (especially of wood). Q *panya-* fix, set; N *penio*. Q *pano* piece of shaped wood. *\*panō*: plank, fixed board, especially in a floor: ON *pano, panui,* N *pân, pein*; *panas* floor. Q *ampano* building (especially of wood), wooden hall.

**PAR-** compose, put together. *\*parmā*: Q *parma* book, ON *parma,* N *parf (perf)*. Q *parmalambe* book-language = Qenya. ON *parthóbi* arrange, compose.

**PÁRAK-** Q *parka* dry; ON *parkha,* N *parch.*

**PAT-** (cf. PATH) *\*pantā* open: Q *panta,* obsolete in ON owing to coalescence with *qanta* full. Q *panta-* to unfurl, spread out, open. N *panno* to open, enlarge; *pann (\*patnā)* wide.

**PATH-** *\*pathnā*: ON *pattha,* N *path* ; Q *pasta* smooth. *\*pathmā*: ON *pathwa,* N *pathw* level space, sward.

**PEG-** mouth. Q *pē*.

**PEL-** revolve on fixed point. Q *pel-* go round, revolve, return. *\*pel-takse*: Q *peltas,* pl. *peltaksi* pivot; ON *pelthaksa,* N *pelthaes* pivot (see TAK).

**PEL(ES)-** ON *pele* (pl. *pelesi, peleki*) [Old English] *'tūn',* fenced field. N *pel,* pl. *peli.* Q *peler; opele* walled house or village, 'town'; N *gobel,* cf. *Tavrobel* (village of Túrin in the forest of Brethil, and name of village in Tol Eressea) [TAM]; *Tindobel* = starlit village [TIN]. [On this remarkable reference to Tavrobel see pp. 412–13.]

**PEN-, PÉNED-** Q *pende* slope, downslope, declivity; *ampende* upward slope, *penda* sloping down, inclined. N *pend, penn* declivity; *ambenn* uphill; *dadbenn* downhill, inclined, prone [see AM², DAT]. N *pendrad* or *pendrath* passage up or down slope, stairway. [See note to DEN.]

**PER-** divide in middle, halve. Q *perya, perina* ; N *perin,* cf. *Peringol* = half-Elf, or Gnome. [Cf. *Beringol* and *Peringiul* 'Half-elven', commentary on AB 2 annal 325; also *Pereldar* 'Half-eldar', Danas, in QS §28. The puzzling words 'or Gnome' should perhaps be interpreted as if 'half-Elf, or rather half-Gnome *(perin + ñgol)'*.]

**PERES-** affect, disturb, alter. N *presto* to affect, trouble, disturb; *prestannen* 'affected', of vowel [i.e. 'mutated'] ; *prestanneth* 'affection' of vowels. ON *persōs* it affects, concerns. [This entry is found on a detached slip.]

**PHAL-, PHÁLAS-** foam. Q *falle* foam; *falma* (crested) wave; *falmar* or *falmarin* (*falmarindi*) sea-spirit, nymph; *falasse* beach; *Falanyel*, pl. *Falanyeldi* = *Solonel*, name of the Teleri, also in Telerin form *Fallinel* (see NYEL). N *falf* foam, breaker; *faltho* (ON *phalsóbe*) to foam; *falas* (pl. *feles*) beach, shore, as proper name *i Falas* west coast (of Beleriand), whence adj. *Falathren*. The variant SPÁLAS is seen in *espalass* foaming [?fall]; T *spalasta-* to foam, froth. [With *falmarin* 'sea-spirit' cf. *Falmaríni*, spirits of the foam, in the *Lost Tales*, I. 66. *Falmarindi* is used of the Teleri: p. 403.]

**PHAR-** reach, go all the way, suffice. Q *farya-* suffice (pa.t. *farne*); *fáre* sufficiency, plenitude, all that is wanted; *farea* enough, sufficient. EN *farn* enough; *far* adv. sufficient, enough, quite.

**PHAS-** Q *fasse* tangled hair, shaggy lock; *fasta-* tangle. ON *phasta* shaggy hair, EN *fast* (cf. *Ulfast* [ÚLUG]).

**PHAU-** gape. Q *fauka* open-mouthed, thirsty, parched; ON *phauka* thirsty, N *faug* thirsty; *Dor na Fauglith* (thirsty sand, see LIT).

**PHAY-** radiate, send out rays of light. Q *faina-* emit light; *faire* radiance; ON *phaire*. Cf. *\*Phay-anáro* 'radiant sun' > Q *Feanáro*, ON *Phayanór*, N *Feanoúr*, *Féanor*. Cf. N *foen* radiant, white. [See SPAN.]

**PHÉLEG-** cave. T *felga* cave; Q *felya*; ON *phelga*, N *fela*, pl. *fili*; cf. *Felagund* [KUNDŪ].

**PHEN-** Q *fenda* threshold; ON *phenda*, N *fend*, *fenn*.

**PHER-, PHÉREN-** beech. Q *feren* or *ferne* (pl. *ferni*) beech-tree; *ferna* mast, beechnuts; *ferinya* beechen. T *ferne*. ON *pheren* beech; *pherna* mast; Exilic *fêr* was usually replaced by *brethil* (see BERÉTH).

**PHEW-** feel disgust at, abhor. Q *feuya*; ON *phuióbe*, N *fuio*.

**PHI-** Q *fion* (*fioni*, *fiondi*) [. . . .] Cf. *Fionwe* son of Manwe [see WEG]. [The meaning of Q *fion* is unfortunately not certainly legible; the likeliest interpretation would be 'haste', but 'hawk' is a possibility.]

**PHILIK-** small bird. Q *filit*, pl. *filiki*; N *filig* pl., analogical singular *fileg* or *filigod*.

**PHIN-** nimbleness, skill. ON *phinde* skill, *phinya* skilled; *\*Phinderauto*, N *Finrod* [RAUTĀ]. Cf. Q *Finwe*, ON *Phinwe*, name of chief Gnome (Exilic *\*Finw* [see WEG]). *Find-* occurs also in names *Findabar* (*\*Phind-ambar*), *Fingon* (*\*Findekāno*) [KAN]; *phinya* or *-phini* occurs in *Fingolfin* (= *ngolfine* 'magic skill'), *Isfin* [IS], *Curufin* [KUR]; distinguish SPIN in *Glorfindel*. [On the absence of *Finw* in Exilic Noldorin see also the passage at the end of the *Lhammas* §11. – The name *Findabar* appears in the entry MBAR in the form *Findobar*, as also in the *Genealogies*, p. 403.]

**PHIR-** Q *firin* dead (by natural cause), *fírima* mortal; *fire* mortal man (*firi*); *firya* human; *Firyanor* = *Hildórien*; *ilfirin* (for *\*ilpirin*) immortal; *faire* natural death (as act). N *feir*, pl. *fir* mortals; *firen* human; *fern*, pl. *firn* dead (of mortals). *Dor firn i guinar* Land of the

Dead that Live [KUY]. *Firiel* = 'mortal maid', later name of Lúthien.

**PHOR-** right-hand. Q *forya* right; *formaite* righthanded, dexterous [MA3]. *formen* north, *formenya* northern [MEN]. N *foeir, feir* right (hand); *forgam* righthanded [KAB]; *forven* north, also *forod*; *forodren* northern. Cf. *Forodwaith* Northmen, Northerland [WEG]; *Forodrim*. \**phoroti* : Q *forte*. N *forn* right or north. (Cf. KHYAR.)

**PHUY-** Q *fuine, huine* deep shadow; *Fui, Hui* Night. ON *phuine* night, N *fuin*; cf. *Taur na Fuin* = *Taure Huinéva*.

**PIK-** ON *pika* small spot, dot; N *peg*. ON *pikina* tiny, N *pigen*.

**PÍLIM-** Q *pilin* (*pilindi*) arrow.

**PIS-** Q *pirya* juice, syrup. N *peich* ; *pichen* juicy.

**PIW-** spit. Q *piuta* ; ON *puióbe*, N *puio*.

**POL-, POLOD-** physically strong. Q *polda* strong, burly. Cf. *poldore*, adj. *Poldórea*.

**POR-** \**pori* : Q *pore* flour, meal.

**POTŌ-** animal's foot. ON *poto, poti*, N *pôd, pŷd*.

**POY-** \**poikā* clean, pure: Q *poika* ; N *puig* clean, tidy, neat.

**PUS-** stop, halt, pause. Q *pusta-* to stop, put a stop to, and intr. cease, stop; *pusta* (noun) stop, in punctuation full stop. N *post* pause, halt, rest, cessation, respite. [An added entry gives PUT-, with Q *putta* stop (in punctuation), *pusta-* to stop, *punta* a stopped consonant; but the entry PUS- was not cancelled or changed.]

# R

**RAB-** \**rāba* wild, untamed: Q *ráva*, N *rhaw* wilderness. [Q *ráva* and N *rhaw* with wholly different meaning are also derivatives from stem RAMBĀ, and N *rhaw* appears in a third sense under RAW.]

**RAD-** back, return. Dor. *radhon* east (cf. *nivon* forward = west [NIB]); *Radhrim* East-march (part of Doriath); *Radhrost* East-vale, land of Cranthir under Blue Mountains [ROS²]. \**randā* cycle, age (100 Valian Years): Q, ON *randa* ; N *anrand*.

**RAG-** \**ragnā* : ON *ragna* crooked, N *rhaen*.

**RAK-** stretch out, reach. \**ranku* : Q *ranko* arm, pl. *ranqi* ; ON *ranko*, pl. *rankui* ; N *rhanc*, pl. (archaic) *rhengy*, usually *rhenc*, arm. \**rakmē* fathom: Q *rangwe* ; ON *ragme*, N *rhaew*.

**RAM-** \**rāmā* : Q *ráma* wing, cf. *Earráme* 'Sea-wing' [AY], name of Tuor's ship. N *rhenio* (\**ramya-*) fly, sail; wander (cf. RAN); *rhofal* pinion, great wing (of eagle), pl. *rhofel* (\**rāmalē*); *rhafn* wing (horn), extended point at side, etc. (\**ramna*). [With *rhofal* cf. 'wide-winged Lhandroval' in QS (p. 301); for the first element see LAD.]

**RAMBĀ-** Q *ramba* wall, cf. *Ilurambar*; N *rhamb, rham*, cf. *Andram* 'Long Walls' [ÁNAD] in Beleriand. Q *ráva* bank, especially of a river; N *rhaw* [see RAB, RAW].

**RAN-** wander, stray. *Ranā: Q *Rana* Moon, N *Rhân*. Q *ranya-* to stray, N *rhenio* (cf. RAM); Q *ráne* straying, wandering, *ránen* errant; N *rhaun*, [added later:] N *rhandir* wanderer, pilgrim.

**RAS-** stick up (intr.). Q *rasse* horn (especially on living animal, but also applied to mountains); N *rhaes, rhasg*; cf. *Caradras* = Redhorn [KARÁN]. [This entry was an addition at the end of the list. The N words and the reference to *Caradras* were scribbled in still later.]

**RÁSAT-** twelve. [No other forms are given.]

**RAT-** walk. *ratā: N *râd* path, track; *rado* to make a way, find a way; *ath-rado* to cross, traverse [AT(AT)]; *athrad* crossing, ford, cf. *Sarn Athrad*. *rattā̆: ON *rattha* course, river-bed, N *rath* (cf. *Rathloriel*) [LÁWAR]. *ostrad* a street. [Added:] *rant* lode, vein; *Celebrant* river-name. Ilk. *rant* flow, course of river.

**RAUTĀ-** metal. Q, ON *rauta*; N. *rhaud*, cf. *-rod* in names *Finrod*, *Angrod*, *Damrod* (see PHIN, ANGĀ, NDAM). [The original meaning of RAUTĀ was given as 'copper', changed to 'metal'; cf. *Nambarauto* (*Damrod*) 'hammerer of copper' under NDAM.]

**RAW-** *rāu: Q *rá* (pl. *rávi*) lion; ON *ró* (pl. *rówi*), N *rhaw* (pl. *rhui*). [Cf. I. 260, entry *Meássë*. – Distinct N words *rhaw* appear under RAB and RAMBĀ.]

**RÁYAK-** Q *raika* crooked, bent, wrong; N *rhoeg* wrong.

**RED-** (Cf. ERÉD) scatter, sow. Q *rerin* I sow, pa.t. *rende*; N *rheði* to sow. ? *reddā* 'sown', sown field, acre.

**REG-** edge, border, margin. Q *réna*. N *rhein, rhain* border; *edrein*.

**REP-** bend, hook. *rempa* crooked, hooked.

**RĪ-** Q *ríma* edge, hem, border. Dor. *rim* (as in *Nivrim* [NIB], *Radhrim* [RAD]); N *rhîf*.

**RIG-** Q *rie* crown (*rīgē); *rína* crowned (cf. *Tinwerína*); ON *ríge*, N *rhî* crown. Cf. *Rhian* name of a woman, = 'crown-gift', *ríg-anna* [ANA¹]; N *rhîn* crowned; *rhîs* queen. [*Elerína*, which was substituted for *Tinwerína* in a note dated February 1938 (p. 200), appears in a marginal addition to entry EL.]

**RIK(H)-** jerk, sudden move, flirt. Q *rihta-* jerk, give quick twist or move, twitch. *rinki: Q *rinke* flourish, quick shake. N *rhitho* jerk, twitch, snatch; *rhinc* twitch, jerk, trick, sudden move.

**RIL-** glitter (cf. SIL, THIL, GIL). Q *rilma* glittering light; *rilya* glittering, brilliance. Cf. *Silmarille, Silmaril* (pl. *Silmarilli*), N *Silevril* (*silimarille*).

**RIM-** *rimbā: Q *rimba* frequent, numerous; ON *rimba*, N *rhemb*, *rhem*. *rimbē crowd, host; Q, ON *rimbe*, N *rhimb, rhim* – often as pl. *-rim* [see LI].

**RIN-** Q *rinde* circle, *rinda* circular. N *rhind, rhinn* circle; *iðrind*, *iðrin* year [YEN]; *rhinn* circular; *rhingorn* circle [KOR].

**RINGI-** cold. Q *ringe*; ON *ringe*, N *rhing*; cf. *Ringil* name of one of the great Lamps (pillared on ice), also of Fingolfin's sword. Q *ringe* cold pool or lake (in mountains); Dor. *ring*, N *rhimb, rhim*, as in *Mith-rim*.

**RIP-** rush, fly, fling. Q *rimpa* rushing, flying; N *rhib-, rhimp, rhimmo* to flow like a [?torrent]; river-name *Rhibdath, Rhimdath* 'Rushdown'. [This entry was a hasty scribbled addition at the end of the R-stems.]

**RIS-** slash, rip. ON *rista-* rend, rip; N *risto*. Cf. *Orchrist* sword-name. [This entry was left unchanged, but a second form of it was added later without reference to the first:]

**RIS-** Cf. KIRÍS; cut, cleave. *\*rista-*: Q *rista-* cut; *rista* a cut; N *rhisto, rhest*; Ilk. *rest*, cf. *Eglorest*, ghyll or ravine made by the river *Eglor* [see ELED] at its mouth, name of town there. *\*risse-*: N *rhis, rhess* a ravine, as in *Imladris*.

**RŌ-** (form of ORO, q.v.) rise. Q *rómen* (see MEN) east, *rómenya* eastern; *róna* east; contrast NDŪ 'down'. ON *róna* east, N *rhûn, amrûn* (cf. *dûn, annûn*); †*rhufen* east. Cf. name *El-rûn*. [*El-rûn* was an addition. See note to BARATH.]

**ROD-** cave. Q *rondo* cave; N *rhond, rhonn*, cf. *Nargothrond, othrond* (see OS). Dor. *roth*, pl. *rodhin*, as in *Meneg-roth* is probably from *rōda* > *rōdh* > *rōth*. Cf. ON *rauda* hollow, cavernous, N *rhauð*. ON *rostóbe* to hollow out, excavate, N *rosto*. In Ilkorin *rond* = domed roof, hence *Elrond* (vault of heaven) [EL], name of Eärendel's son.

**ROK-** Q *rokko* horse; N *roch* horse.

**ROM-** (Cf. ORÓM and *Orome, Araw*) loud noise, horn-blast, etc. Q *romba* horn, trumpet; ON *romba*, N *rhom*. Q *róma* loud sound, trumpet-sound; ON *rúma*, N †*rhû* in *rhomru* sound of horns.

**ROS¹-** distil, drip. Q *rosse* fine rain, dew. N *rhoss* rain, cf. name *Celebros* Silver-rain of a waterfall. *Silivros* = Q *Silmerosse*, name of Silpion. [Both *Silivros* and *Silmerosse* are found in the list of the names of the Trees in QS §16. *Celebros* is translated 'Silver Rain' in AB 2 annal 299 (previously 'Foam-silver', 'Silver Foam').]

**ROS²-** Dor. *rost* plain, wide land between mountains; cf. *Nivrost* [NIB], *Radhrost* [RAD].

**ROY¹-** chase. *\*ronyō* 'chaser', hound of chase: Q *ronyo*, N *rhŷn*. Q *roita-* pursue; *raime* hunt, hunting; N *rhui(w)*.

**ROY²-** (N GROJ-) ruddy, red. Q *roina* ruddy; N *gruin*. [This second stem ROY was put in very rapidly at the end of the R-stems and without any reference to the former.]

**RUD-** *\*rundā*: Q *runda* rough piece of wood; ON *runda*, N *grond* club; cf. *Grond* name of Melko's mace, and name *Celebrond* 'Silver-mace'.

**RUK-** demon. Q *rauko* demon, *malarauko* (*\*ñgwalaraukō*, cf. ÑGWAL); N *rhaug, Balrog*.

**RUN-** flat of hand or sole of foot. Q *runya* slot, footprint; *tallune* (*\*talrunya*) sole of foot, N *telloein, tellen* [TAL]. N *rhoein, rhein* slot, spoor, track, footprint.

**RUS-** flash, glitter of metal. Q *russe* corruscation, †sword-blade; ON *russe* polished metal (N †*rhoss* chiefly found in names as *Maedhros* [MAD], *Findros*, *Celebros* etc., owing to coalescence with ROS¹).

**RUSKĀ-** ON *ruska*, N *rhosc* brown.

# S

**S-** demonstrative stem. *sŭ*, *sŏ* he (cf. *-so* inflexion of verbs); *sĭ*, *sĕ* she (cf. *-se* inflexion of verbs). Cf. N *ho*, *hon*, *hono* he; *he*, *hen*, *hene* she; *ha*, *hana* it; plurals *huin*, *hîn*, *hein*.

**SAB-** Q *sáva* juice; ON *sóba*, N *saw* (pl. *sui*).

**SAG-** *\*sagrā* : Q *sára* bitter; N *saer*. *\*sagmā* : Q *sangwa* poison; N *saew*.

**SALÁK-(WĒ)** Q *salqe* grass; Ilk. *salch*. ON *salape* herb, green food plant, N *salab* (pl. *seleb*) herb.

**SÁLAP-** lick up. Q *salpa-* lick up, sup, sip; ON *salpha* liquid food, soup, broth; N *salf* broth.

**SAM-** unite, join. *samnar* diphthongs. [Hasty later addition; see SUD and SUS.]

**SAR-** Q *sar*, pl. *sardi* stone (small); *sarna* of stone; *sarne* strong place. N *sarn* stone as a material, or as adj.; cf. *Sarnathrad*.

**SAY-** know, understand. *saira-* wise; *sairon* wizard.

**SED-** rest (cf. EZDĒ 'rest', Q *Este*, ON *Ezda*, wife of Lórien). Q *sére* rest, repose, peace; *senda* resting, at peace; *serin* I rest. N *sîdh* peace.

**SEL-D-** daughter [see YEL]. Q *selde*. In N *iell* (poetic *sell* girl, maid) with *i* from *iondo* son [YŌ]; a change assisted by the loss of *s* in cpds. and patronymics: cf. *Tinnúviel* (*\*tindōmiselde*, Q *Tindómerel*), see TIN. [The meaning 'daughter' was later changed to 'child', with Q forms *seldo*, *selda* added.]

**SER-** love, be fond of (of liking, friendship). Q suffix *-ser* friend; *sermo* friend (f. *serme*), also *seron*. Cf. name *Elesser* (*Eleðser*) = Ælfwine.

**SI-** this, here, now. Q *sí*, *sin* now; *sinya* new. N *sein* (pl. *sîn*) new; *siniath* news, tidings; *sinnarn* novel tale [NAR²].

**SIK-** Q *sikil* dagger, knife; N *sigil*.

**SIL-** variant of THIL; 'shine silver'. These in Q cannot be distinguished normally, but Q *Isil* Moon, N †*Ithil* has *th*. *s-* appears in *\*silimē* 'light of Silpion', †silver, Q *silme* (cf. *Silmerosse*, N *Silivros*), N *\*silif*. *\*silimā* silver, shining white (adj.): Q *silma*, N *\*silef*, cf. *Silevril*, Q *Silmaril* (see RIL). In N *Belthil* (see BAL) *s* or *th* may be present. The Q name of the Elder Tree is *Silpion* (see below).

Cf. Dor *istel*, *istil* silver light, applied by the Ilkorins to starlight, probably a Q form learned from Melian. For *\*silif* N has *silith*, by assimilation to or from influence of †*Ithil*.

Related is **SÍLIP** whence Q *Silpion* (N *\*Silfion*, not used).

**SIR-** flow. Q *sir-*, ON *sirya-*, N *sirio* flow. Q, ON *síre*, N *sîr* river (cf. *Sirion*); Q *siril* rivulet.

**SIW-**   excite, egg on, urge. Q *siule* incitement; ON *hyúle*, N *húl* cry of encouragement in battle.

**SKAL¹-**   screen, hide (from light). Q *halya-* veil, conceal, screen from light; *halda* (*\*skalnā*) veiled, hidden, shadowed, shady (opposed to *helda* stripped bare, see SKEL). ON *skhalia-, skhalla* ; N *hall* ; *haltha-* to screen. Ilk. *esgal* screen, hiding, roof of leaves. Dan. *sc(i)ella* shade, screen. Derivative name *Haldir* 'hidden hero' [DER] (son of Orodreth); also Ilk. *Esgalduin* 'River under Veil' (of [?leaves]). [There seems to be a query before the bracketed words at the end of the entry.]

**SKAL²-**   small fish. Q *hala* ; *halatir(no)* 'fishwatcher', kingfisher; N *heledir*. [This stem was a later addition; see KHAL¹, TIR.]

**SKAR-**   *\*skarwē* : Q *harwe* wound; N *harw*. Cf. Ilk. *esgar*. *\*skarnā* : Q *harna* wounded; N *harn* ; *harno* to wound (Q *harna-*). Root sense: tear, rend; cf. *\*askarā* tearing, hastening: N *asgar, ascar* violent, rushing, impetuous. Ilk. *ascar* (cf. river-name *Askar*).

**SKAT-**   break asunder. Q *hat-*, pa.t. *hante; terhat-* break apart.

**SKEL-**   *\*skelmā* : Q *helma* skin, fell. N *helf* fur, *heleth* fur, fur-coat. *\*skelnā* naked: Q *helda* ; ON *skhella*, N *hell*. *helta* (*skelta-*) strip.

**SKWAR-**   crooked. Q *hwarin* crooked; *hwarma* crossbar. Dan. *swarn* perverse, obstructive, hard to deal with.

**SKYAP-**   *\*skyapat-* shore: Q *hyapat* ; ON *skhapa*, pl. *skhapati* ; N *habad* shore (pl. *hebeid*).

**SLIG-**   *\*slignē*, *\*slingē* : N *thling* spider, spider's web, cobweb. Q *líne* cobweb; N *thlingril* [*r* uncertain] spider. Q *lia* fine thread, spider filament (*\*ligā*); N *thlê* ; Q *liante* spider. Cf. *Ungoliante* [UÑG], N *Deldu-thling* [DO3, DYEL].

**SLIN-**   *\*slindi* fine, delicate. Q *linda* 'fair' is blended with *\*lindā* sweet-sounding [see LIND]. N *thlinn, thlind* fine, slender; *thlein* (pl. *thlîn*) = *\*slinyā* lean, thin, meagre.

**SLIW-**   sickly. *\*slīwē* sickness: Q *líve*, ON *slíwe, thlíwe*, N *thliw* later *fliw*. *\*slaiwā* sickly, sick, ill; Q *laiwa*, ON *slaiwa, thlaiwa*, N *thlaew* [> *thloew*] later *flaew*.

**SLUK-**   swallow. [No forms given.]

**SLUS-, SRUS-**   whisper. N *thloss* (*floss*) or *thross* a whisper or rustling sound; Q *lusse* a whispering sound, *lussa-* to whisper.

**SMAG-**   soil, stain. N *maw* (*\*māgā*) soil, stain, *mael* (*\*magla*) stain and adj. stained. [N *maw* and *mael* changed to *hmas* and *hmael*; see note to SMAL.]

**SMAL-**   yellow. *\*smalinā* : Q, ON *malina* yellow, N *malen* (pl. *melin*). *\*smaldā* : Q *malda* gold (as metal), ON *malda*, N *malt* ; N *malthen* (analogical for *mallen*) of gold. Cf. *Melthinorn*, older *Mellinorn*. *\*smalu* pollen, yellow powder: Q *malo*, ON *malo* (pl. *malui*), N *mâl*, pl. *meil* or *mely*. *\*smalwā* fallow, pale: Q *malwa*, N *malw*.

   *\*asmalē*, *\*asmalindē* yellow bird, 'yellow hammer': Q *ammale*, *ambale* ; ON *ammale, ammalinde*, N *em(m)elin, emlin*.

[I give this entry as it was before it became confused by later changes in the phonology of initial *sm-* (ON retained *sm-*, and the N words have *(h)m-*); these were not carried through consistently. – *Melthinorn* 'tree of gold' is found in the list of names of the Trees in QS §16.]

**SNAR-**  tie. Q *narda* knot; N *narð*.

**SNAS-, SNAT-**  ? Q *nasta* spear-head, point, gore, triangle (cf. NAS); Dan. *snǽs*. N *naith* (*natsai* pl. ? ) gore. [Cf. the Naith of Lothlórien. The question-mark is followed by a drawing of an arrow-head.]

**SNEW-**  entangle. Q *neuma* snare; ON *núma*, N *nû* noose, snare. [The N forms were changed to *sniuma* and *snýma*; *hniof* (pl. *hnyf*) and *hnuif*. See note to SMAL.]

**SNUR-**  twist. N *norn* twisted, knotted, crabbed, contorted; *norð* cord.

**SOL-**  Q *solor* (*solos*) surf, cf. *Solonel*, pl. *Soloneldi* = Teleri. This is a Telerin form, cf. *Fallinel*, and cf. pure Q *Solonyeldi* [see NYEL].

**SPAL-, SPALAS-**  variants of PHAL, PHALAS, q.v.

**SPAN-**  white. Q *fanya*, *fána* cloud. N *fein* white, *faun* cloud (*spāna*); T *spania*; Dan. *spenna*. Cf. *Fanyamar* upper air; *Span-turo* 'lord of cloud', Q *Fantur* surname of Mandos (*Nurufantur*, N *Gurfannor* 'lord of Death-cloud') and of his brother Lórien (*Olofantur*, N *Olfannor* 'lord of Dream-cloud'); N pl. *i-Fennyr* or *Fennir* = Lórien and Mandos [see ÑGUR, OLOS]. (Confused in N with PHAY, q.v.) [The beginning of this entry was first written '*fanya* cloud'; 'cloud' was struck through, and *fána* added, with meanings 'white' and 'cloud', but it is not clear how they are to be applied. – For *Fanyamar* see the *Ambarkanta*, IV. 236 etc. – I do not think that this association of the Fanturi with 'cloud' is found anywhere else.]

**SPÁNAG-**  *spangā*: Q *fanga*; T *spanga*; ON *sphanga* beard; N *fang*, cf. *An(d)fang* [ÁNAD] Longbeard, one of the tribes of Dwarves (pl. *Enfeng*). Cf. *Tinfang* 'Starbeard', name of an Elvish piper; *Ulfang* [ÚLUG].

**SPAR-**  hunt, pursue. ON *(s)pharóbe* hunt, *(s)pharasse* hunt(ing); EN *faras* hunting (cf. *Taur-na-Faras*); *feredir* hunter (pl. *faradrim*); *faro* to hunt. *Elfaron* 'star-hunter', Moon. [With *Taur-na-Faras* (the Hills of the Hunters or Hunters' Wold) cf. *Taur-na-Faroth* in QS §112, and with the name 'Star-hunter' of the Moon cf. QS §76.]

**SPAY-**  despise, contemn. Q *faika* contemptible, mean. N *foeg* mean, poor, bad.

**SPIN-**  *spindē* tress, braid of hair: Q *finde*, ON *sphinde* lock of hair; *sphindele* (braided) hair; N *findel*, *finnel*, cf. *Glorfindel*. Cf. *spinē* larch, Q *fine*.

**SRIP-**  scratch. N *thribi* to scratch.

**STAB-**  *stabnē*, *stambē*: Q *sambe* room, chamber; *samna* wooden post. ON *stabne*, *sthamine*; N *thafn* post, wooden pillar; *tham*, *thamb* hall. Q *kaimasan*, pl. *kaimasambi* bedchamber [KAY]. N *thambas*, *thamas* great hall. **stabnō*, **stabrō* carpenter, wright, builder: Q *samno*; ON *sthabro(ndo)*, N *thavron*; Ilk. *thavon*.

**STAG-** press, compress. **stangā*: Q *sanga* crowd, throng, press; N *thang* compulsion, duress, need, oppression; cf. *Thangorodrim* (the mountains of duress). Cf. *sangahyando* 'throng-cleaver' (sword-name), N **haðathang*, dissimilated to *havathang*, *haðafang* [see SYAD].

**STAK-** split, insert. **stankā*, **staknā*: Q *sanka* cleft, split; ON *sthanka*, N *thanc*, cf. *Lhamthanc* 'forked tongue', serpent-name [LAB]. ON *nestak-* insert, stick in, EN *nestegi*, pa.t. *nestanc*.

**STAL-** steep. Ilk. *thall* (**stalrē*) steep, falling steeply (of river); *thalos* torrent (also a proper name) [the river *Thalos* in Ossiriand].

**STÁLAG-** **stalga* stalwart, steady, firm: T *stalga*; ON *sthalga*, N *thala*, cf. *thalion* (**stalgondō*) hero, dauntless man (pl. *thelyn*), especially as surname of Húrin *Thalion*.

**STAN-** fix, decide. Cf. Q *sanda* firm, true, abiding; N *thenid*, *thenin*. Q *sanye* rule, law; *sanya* regular, law-abiding, normal.

**STAR-** stiff. Q *sara* stiff dry grass, bent; N *thâr* stiff grass; *tharas* hassock, footstool; *gwa-star* hummock [wǒ]. ON *stharna* sapless, stiff, rigid, withered; N *tharn*; not in Q since it would coalesce with **sarnā* of stone [SAR].

**STARAN-** Cf. Ilk. *thrôn* stiff, hard (**starāna*); cf. *thron-ding* in *Balthronding* name of Beleg's bow. [Under stems BEL and DING the name is written *Bel-*.]

**STELEG-** N *thela* point (of spear); *egthel*, *ecthel*, cf. *Ecthelion* (see EK). [An illegible word after *ecthel* may read 'same', i.e. the same meaning as *thela*.]

**STINTĀ-** short. Q *sinta*; ON *sthinta*, N *thent*. N *thinnas* 'shortness', name of mark indicating short quality of vowel.

**SUD-** base, ground. *sundo* base, root, root-word. [A hasty later addition.]

**SÚLUK-** Q *sulka*; ON *sulkha*, N *solch* root (especially as edible).

**SUK-** drink. Q *sukin* I drink. N *sogo*, 3 sg. *sôg*, pa.t. *sunc*, *asogant* (*sogennen*); N *sûth* draught, Q *suhto*; N *sautha-* drain. **sukmā* drinking-vessel; Q *sungwa*; Ilk. *saum*.
Variant **SUG-** in **suglu*: Q *súlo* goblet, N *sûl*.

**SUS-** hiss. *surya* spirant consonant. [Later addition with SUD and SAM.]

**SWAD-** **swanda*: Q *hwan* (*hwandi*) sponge, fungus; N *chwand*, *chwann*, *hwand*.

**SWES-** noise of blowing or breathing. **swesta-*: Q *hwesta-* to puff; *hwesta* breath, breeze, puff of air; ON *hwesta*, N *chwest* puff, breath, breeze.

**SWIN-** whirl, eddy. Q *hwinya-* to swirl, eddy, gyrate; *hwinde* eddy, whirlpool. N *chwinio* twirl, whirl, eddy; *chwind*, *chwinn* adj.; *chwîn* giddiness, faintness; *chwiniol* whirling, giddy, fantastic.

**SYAD-** shear through, cleave. Q *hyarin* I cleave. *\*syadnō*, *\*syandō* 'cleaver', sword; cf. *\*stangasyandō* = Q *sangahyando* 'throng-cleaver' (sword-name) (see STAG). In N lost owing to coalescence with KHAD [a stem not given in the *Etymologies*], except in †*hâð* [. . . .] (*\*syadā*), cf. *haðafang* (for *haðathang*) = Q *sangahyando*; *hasto* hack through, from *hast* axe-stroke (*\*syad-ta*). Cf. Q *hyatse* cleft, gash (*\*syadsē* > *syatsē*), and N *hathel* (*\*syatsĕla*) broadsword-blade, or axe-blade. [The illegible word would most naturally be interpreted as 'throng', but this obviously cannot be the case (or cannot have been intended.).]

**SYAL-** *\*syalmā*: Q *hyalma* shell, conch, horn of Ulmo. N *half* seashell.

# T

**TA-** demonstrative stem 'that'. Q *ta* that, it; *tana* that (anaphoric); *tar* thither (*\*tad*), ON *tó*.

**TĀ-, TA3-** high, lofty; noble. *\*tārā* lofty: Q *tára*, ON *tára* absorbed in N by *taur* from PQ *\*taurā* (see TÁWAR, TUR). N poetic only or in ancient titles *taur*; often found in names, as *Tor-, -dor*. The latter was blended with *tāro* king and *turo* master: cf. *Fannor* [SPAN].

*\*tāro* king: only used of the legitimate kings of the whole tribes, as Ingwe of the Lindar, Finwe of the Noldor (and later Fingolfin and Fingon of all the exiled Gnomes). The word used of a lord or king of a specified region was *aran* (*âr*), Q *haran* [see 3AR]. Thus *Fingolfin taur egledhriur* 'King of the Exiles' [see LED], but *Fingolfin aran Chithlum* 'King of Hithlum'. Q *tár* (pl. *tári*). N †*taur*, Ilk. *tôr*, only used of Thingol: *Tor Thingol* = King Thingol.

*\*tārī* queen, wife of a *\*tāro*: Q *tári*, but especially used in Q of Varda (*Tinwetári* Queen of Stars) – but in cpds. and titles the sexless cpd. form -*tar* was used: *Tinwetar, Tinwerontar* Queen of Stars = Varda; *Sorontar* King of Eagles (name of a great eagle). The word survived in Ilk. only in form *tóril* = Melian. In N *rhien, rhîn* was used – 'crowned lady': see RIG.

Base stem TĀ appears in Q *Taniqetil* (see NIK-W, TIL), where N substitutes following adj.: *Nimdil-dor*. But the Q form is possibly reduction of *tān-nig* with adjectival *tāna* < *\*taȝna*. The latter is suggested by N *taen* height, summit of high mountain, especially in *Taen-Nimdil*, Manwe's hall. Cf. also *tarqendi* = Lindar, 'High-elves'; *tarqesta* = Lindarin, or Qenya 'high-speech'. [On *Tinwetar, Tinwerontar* see TIN and note.]

**TAK-** fix, make fast. Q *take* he fastens, pa.t. *tanke*; *tanka* firm, fixed, sure. N *taetho* fasten, tie; *tanc* firm; *tangado* to make firm, confirm, establish. Ilk. *taga* he fixes, constructs, makes; *tâch* firm, stiff, solid.

*\*tankla* pin, brooch: Q *tankil*; Ilk. *tangol*; N *tachl, tachol*. *\*taksē*

nail: Q *takse*; N *taes*; Ilk. *tass* pin. Cf. Q *peltas* (*peltaksi*) pivot, N *pelthaes* [PEL]. *\*takmā* 'thing for fixing': Q *tangwa* hasp, clasp; N *taew* holder, socket, hasp, clasp, staple; Ilk. *taum*. *\*atakwē* construction, building: Q *ataqe*; N *adab* building, house (pl. *edeb*).

TAL-   foot. Q *tál* (g.sg. *talen*); N *tâl*, pl. *teil*; Ilk. *tal*, pl. *tel*. Related is TALAM floor, base, ground: Q *talan* (*talami*) floor, ground; *talma* base, foundation, root (cf. *Martalmar*). N *talaf* ground, floor, pl. *teleif*; Ilk. *talum*, pl. *telmin*. *tal-* is often used for 'end, lower end': so *Rhamdal* 'Wall's-end', name of a place in East Beleriand [RAMBĀ]. – Q *tallune* (*\*talrunya*) sole of foot; N *tellein, tellen* (see RUN). [For *Martalmar* (also *Talmar Ambaren*) see the *Ambarkanta*, IV. 241–5.]

TALÁT-   to slope, lean, tip. Q *talta-* to slope; *talta* adj. sloping, tilted, leaning; *talta* an incline. N *talad* an incline, slope. *atland* sloping, tilted; *atlant* oblique, slanting; *atlanno* to slope, slant.
[The entry was first written thus. A first addition to it was 'Cf. *Atalante* (see LANT).' Subsequently the reference to LANT was changed to DAT (under which stem (DAT, DANT) are given Q *lanta* a fall, *lanta-* to fall, and *Atalante* the Fallen); but either at the same time or later this addition was made: '*Atalante* (*a*-prefix = complete) downfall, overthrow, especially as name of the land of Númenor.' Cf. the statement on this subject in my father's letter of July 1964, cited on p. 8 (footnote). – Other additions to this entry extended the meaning of Q *talta-* ('slope, slip, slide down') and added Q *atalta* 'collapse, fall in' and N *talt* 'slipping, falling, insecure.']

TAM-   (cf. NDAM) knock. *\*tamrō* 'woodpecker' (= knocker): Q *tambaro*; N *tafr* (= *tavr*), *tavor*, cf. *Tavr-obel* [PEL(ES)]. N *tamno* to knock (*\*tambā*); Q *tamin* I tap, pa.t. *tamne*; *tamba-* to knock, keep on knocking.

TAN-   make, fashion. *\*tanō*: Q *tano* craftsman, smith; *Martano* or *Martan*, surname of Aule (Earth-smith), N *Barthan* [MBAR]. Q *tanwe* craft, thing made, device, construction. Q *kentano* potter; N *cennan*. [*Certhan* >] *C(e)irdan* shipbuilder. *Tintánie* star-maker = Varda (Elbereth); N *Gilthonieth* or *Gilthoniel*. [The latter part of this entry, from Q *kentano*, was an addition. Under KEM a Q word *kemnaro* 'potter' is given. The form *Gilthonieth* appears in the first draft of the hymn to Elbereth in the original second chapter (*Three is Company*) of *The Lord of the Rings*.]

TAP-   stop. Q *tápe* he stops, blocks (pa.t. *tampe*); *tampa* stopper.

TÁRAG-   *\*targā* tough, stiff; Q *tarya*; ON *targa*, N *tara*, *tar-*; Ilk. *targ*. N *tarlanc* stiff-necked, obstinate; *tarias* [*s* uncertain] stiffness, toughness, difficulty. [There must be a connection between *tarlanc* 'stiff-necked' (LANK) and *Tarlang's Neck* (*The Return of the King* V.2), concerning which my father noted (*Nomenclature of The Lord of the Rings*, published in Lobdell, *A Tolkien Compass*, p. 193) that it was originally the name of a long ridge of rock but was later taken as a personal name.]

**TARÁK-** horn (of animals). Q *tarka* horn; N *tarag* horn, also used of steep mountain path, cf. *Tarag(g)aer* = Ruddihorn [GAY]. [This entry was additional to the main list. On *Taragaer* see p. 345.]

**TARAS-** ON *tarsa* trouble, N *tars*, *tass* labour, task. *trasta-* to harass, trouble.

**TATA-** (cf. ATA, ATTA). N *tâd* two, *tadol* double. Q *tatya-* to double, repeat; *tanta* double. [An earlier entry, struck out, was as follows: 'TAT- oldest form AT(AT)? two. Q *atta* again, *atta-* back again, re-'. See AT(AT).]

**TATHAR-** *\*tathar*, *\*tatharē*, *\*tathrē* willow-tree: Q *tasar*, *tasare*; N *tathor* (= *\*tathrē*), adj. *tathren* of willow; cf. *Nan-tathren*.

**TÁWAR-** wood, forest. *\*taurē* great wood, forest: Q *taure*; N *taur*; Ilk. *taur*. N *Tauros* 'Forest-Dread' [GOS], usual N by-name of Orome (N Araw). *\*tawar* wood (material): Q *tavar* wood, *taurina* of wood; N *tawar* often used = *taur*; *tawaren* wooden (pl. *tewerin*). Ilk. *taur* wood (place and material). *\*tawarŏ/ē* dryad, spirit of woods: Q *tavaro* or *tavaron*, f. *tavaril* [cf. the old name *Tavari*, I. 66, 267.]

Note: N adj. *taur* mighty, vast, overwhelming, huge, awful, is blend of *\*tārā* (= Q *tára* lofty), *\*taurā* masterful, mighty (TUR). It affected the sense of *taur* forest (only used of huge forests).

**TAY-** extend, make long(er). Q *taina* lengthened, extended; *taita* to prolong; *taile* lengthening, extension. N *taen* long (and thin).

**TE3-** line, direction. Q *tie* path, course, line, direction, way (*\*teȝē*), N *tê* line, way. Q *téra*, N *tîr* straight, right. [This stem was changed to TEÑ, and the ulterior form of Q *téra*, N *tîr* given as *\*teñrā*. There is also a very rough additional entry TEÑ (see below).]

**TEK-** make a mark, write or draw (signs or letters). Q *teke* writes; *tehta* a mark (in writing), sign, diacritic – as *andatehta* 'long-mark'. *\*tekla*: Q *tekil* pen. *\*tekmē* letter, symbol: Q *tengwa* letter, *tengwanda* alphabet; *tengwe* writing, *tengwesta* grammar. N *teitho* write; *teith* mark (as *andeith*, ON *andatektha*); *tîw* letter (*\*tekmē*); *tegl*, *tegol* pen. Q *tenkele* writing system, spelling; *tekko* stroke of pen or brush (') when not used as long mark.

**TEL-, TELU-** *\*telmă, -ĕ* hood, covering. Q *telme* (cf. *telmello telmanna* from hood to base [sic], from crown to foot, top to bottom); *telta-* to canopy, overshadow, screen; *telume* dome, (especially) dome of heaven. Cf. *Telumehtar* 'warrior of the sky', name of Orion. N *telu* dome, high roof; *daedelu* canopy (see DAY); *ortheli* roof, screen above, *orthelian* canopy. [*Telumehtar* reappears from the *Lost Tales* (*Telimektar*, *Telumektar*).]

**TÉLEK-** stalk, stem, leg. Q *telko* leg, analogical pl. *telqi*; N *telch* (pl. *tilch*) stem.

**TELEP-** silver; see KYELEP.

**TELES-** elf, sea-elf, third tribe of the Eldar. Q *Teler*, pl. *Teleri*; *Telerin* Telerian; general pl. *Telelli*, *Telellie* 'Teler-folk'. Originally the sense was 'hindmost, tarrier'; cf. Q *tella* hindmost, last, *telle* rear

(\**télesā*); N *tele* end, rear, hindmost part (pl. *telei*); *adel* behind, in rear (of). Some forms show blending with KYEL, q.v. [On the meaning of *Teleri* see the *Lhammas* §2 and QS §27.]

TEÑ- N *tî* line, row (< \**teñe*); *tær* (\**tenrā*) straight. Q *téma* row, series, line; *tea* straight line, road. [See stem TE3 (changed to TEÑ), where the derivative words are different formations.]

TER-, TERES- pierce. \**terēwā* piercing, keen: Q *tereva* fine, acute; N *trîw* fine, slender; Ilk. *trêw*. Cf. Q *tere*, *ter* through; N *trî* through, and as prefix *tre-*, *tri*; ON *tre* unstressed prefix, see BAT, NAR; prep. *trí*. \**terēn(ē)*: Q *teren* (*terene*) slender; *Terendul*, name ('slender-dark') [DUL, NDUL]. [The name *Terendul* occurs in *The Lost Road* (p. 59).]

THAR- across, beyond. *Thar-gelion*; *Thar-bad* [?Crossway]. [Scribbled additional entry.]

THĒ- look (see or seem). N *thîr* (\**thērē*) look, face, expression, countenance; cf. *Cranthir* Ruddy-face [KARÁN], *Gostir* older *Gorsthir* 'dread-glance', dragon-name [GOS]. N *thio* to seem, *thia* it appears.

THEL-, THELES- sister (cf. *tor*, *toron*- brother [TOR]). ON *wathel* sister, associate, N *gwathel*, pl. *gwethil*. N *thêl*, *thelei* sister, also *muinthel*, pl. *muinthil* [see MOY]. Q *seler*, pl. *selli* sister; ON *thele*, *thelehi* (*thelesi*); Q *oselle* [see WŎ] sister, associate. Usually used of blood-kin in Q was *onóne*, see NŌ, ONO; cf. ON *wanúre* kinswoman, N *gwanur* kinsman or kinswoman [WŎ].

THIL- (variant of SIL, q.v.) N *Ithil* poetic name of the Moon (*Rhân*) = Q *Isil* 'the Sheen'; *thilio* to glister. Cf. *Belthil*, *Galathilion*, names of the Elder of the Two Trees – but these may contain the variant SIL.

THIN- (cf. TIN). \**thindi* pallid, grey, wan: Q *sinde* grey. *Sindo* name of Elwe's brother, in Telerian form *Findo*, Ilk. *Thind*, later in Doriath called *Thingol* (i.e. *Thind* + *gôl* wise, see ÑGOL) or *Torthingol* [TĀ] King Thingol, also with title *Tor Tinduma* 'King of Twilight' [TIN], N *Aran Dinnu*. N *thind*, *thinn* grey, pale; Ilk. *thind*. Q *sinye* evening (N †*thin*); N *thinna*. Q *sinta-* fade (*sintane*), ON *thintha*.

THŌN- Ilk. *thôn* pine-tree. N *thaun* pl. *thuin* is probably an early loan-word, with Ilk. *ō* treated as ON *ō* < *ā*. Ilk. *Dor-thonion* 'Land of Pines', name of mountainous forest N. of Doriath and afterwards becoming *Taur-na-Fuin*, a punning alteration of *Dor-na-Thuin* (Noldorin translation of Ilk. *Dor-thonion*).

THOR-, THORON- Q *soron* (and *sorne*), pl. *sorni* eagle; N *thôr* and *thoron*, pl. *therein* – *thoron* is properly old gen. sg. = ON *thoronen*, Q *sornen*, appearing in names as *Cil-thoron*, or *Cil-thorondor* [KIL]. Ilk. *thorn*, pl. *thurin*. Q *Sorontar* (name of) King of Eagles, N *Thorondor*, Ilk. *Thorntor* = *Torthurnion*. [Added:] Cf. name *Elthor(o)n* = eagle of sky.

[The following was added in hastily above the entry THOR, THORON:

'THOR- = come swooping down; cf. *Brilthor*. Adj. *thôr* swooping, leaping down; *thórod* torrent.' I take this to be an indication of the root-sense of THOR eagle.]

THŪ- puff, blow. Q *súya*- breathe; *súle* breath. Cf. *Súlimo* surname of Manwe (wind-god). N *thuio* breathe; *thûl* breath.

THUR- surround, fence, ward, hedge in, secrete. Ilk. *thúren* guarded, hidden. Cf. Ilk. *Garthurian* Hidden Realm (= Doriath), sc. *garð-thurian*; Noldorinized as *Arthurien*, more completely as *Ar(ð)-thoren*: *thoren* (*\*tháurēnā*) pp. of *thoro*- fence [see 3AR]. *Thuringwethil* (woman of) secret shadow, Doriathren name (N *Dolwethil*) assumed by Tinúviel as a bat-shaped fay [WATH]. [Cf. the *Lay of Leithian* line 3954, where a marginal note explains *Thuringwethil* as 'she of hidden shadow' (III. 297, 304). The present entry retains the story of the Lay: it was Lúthien who called herself by this name before Morgoth (see III. 306).]

THUS- (related to THŪ?) *\*thausā*: Q *saura* foul, evil-smelling, putrid. N *thaw* corrupt, rotten; *thû* stench, as proper name *Thû* chief servant of Morgoth, also called *Mor-thu*, Q *Sauro* or *Sauron* or *Súro* = *Thû*. [In the original draft for the chapter *A Knife in the Dark* in *The Lord of the Rings* Frodo (but not there called Frodo) cries *Elbereth! Gilthoniel! Gurth i Morthu!*]

TIK- (cf. PIK) Q *tikse* dot, tiny mark, point; *amatikse, nuntikse* [indicated in the manuscript to mean dots or points placed above (*amatikse*) or below (*nuntikse*) the line of writing. Added entry.]

TIL- point, horn. Q *tilde* point, horn; cf. *Ta-niqe-til* (g.sg. *tilden*); N *tild, till* horn. Q *Tilion* 'the Horned', name of the man in the Moon; N *Tilion*. Q *neltil* (*neltildi*), N *nelthil* triangle (see NEL). [Cf. QS §75: marginal note by Ælfwine to the name *Tilion*: '*hyrned*' (Old English, 'horned'). It is strange that Tilion is here 'the man in the Moon': in QS (as in Q, IV. 97) he was 'a young hunter of the company of Oromë'. Is the implication that in later ages the myth of Tilion became the story of the Man in the Moon? (see I. 202).]

TIN- (variant of (?) and in any case affected by THIN, q.v.) sparkle, emit slender (silver, pale) beams. Q *tine* it glints, *tintina* it sparkles; *\*tinmē* sparkle, glint: Q *tinwe* sparkle (star), [struck out: cf. *Tin-wetar, Tinwerontar* star-queen, title of Varda;] *tin-dóme* starlit dusk (see DOMO); *tingilya, tingilinde* a twinkling star (see GIL).

N *tinno* to glint; *tinw* spark, small star; *tint* spark; *gildin* silver spark (see GIL); *\*tindumh, tindu, tinnu* dusk, twilight, early night (without moon). Cf. *Aran Dinnu* King of Twilight, name given by Gnomes to Thingol, called by Ilkorins *Tor Tinduma*. Ilk. *tim* spark, star; *tingla*- sparkle; *tindum* starlight, twilight. Q *tinda* glinting, silver; *tinde* a glint.

N *Tindúmhiell, Tinnúviel, Tinúviel* = 'daughter of twilight', a kenning of the nightingale, Q *Tindómerel* (see SEL-D: *\*Tin-dómiselde*), name given by Beren to Lúthien daughter of Thingol. N

ordinary name of nightingale is *dúlind*, *dúlin* [DO3, LIN²]; Q
*lómelinde*; Ilk. *mur(i)lind*, *myr(i)lind* (see MOR). N *moerilind*,
*merilin* was Noldorinized from Ilk. *murilind*, since *mori* did not =
'night' in N.
   The 'twilight' sense was largely due to THIN, q.v.
[Against this entry is written in the margin: '*Tintanie, Tintalle*
Kindler = Varda; Q *tinta-* to kindle, make to spark': see pp. 344–5.
Other marginal notes are: 'cf. *Timbreðil*', which thus reappears from
Q, IV. 82 (see BARATH); '*Tindubel* twilit city' (see PEL(ES).]

**TING-, TANG-**   onomatopoeic (cf. DING). Q *tinge, tango*, twang;
*tinga-*; N *tang* bowstring.

**TINKŌ-**   metal. Q *tinko*; N *tinc*.

**TIR-**   watch, guard. Q *tirin* I watch, pa.t. *tirne*; N *tiri* or *tirio*, pa.t.
*tiriant*. Q *tirion* watch-tower, tower. N *tirith* watch, guard; cf.
*Minnas-tirith* [MINI]. Cf. Q *halatir (-tirnen)*, PQ *\*khalatirnŏ*
'fish-watcher', N *heledirn* = kingfisher; *Dalath Dirnen* 'Guarded
Plain'; *Palantir* 'Far-seer'. [For the etymology of 'kingfisher' see
KHAL¹, SKAL². – *Palantir* was a later addition, as also under
PAL.]

**TIT-**   Q *titta* little, tiny; N *tithen* (pl. *tithin*).

**TIW-**   fat, thick. *\*tiukā* : Q *tiuka* thick, fat; ON *túka*, N *tûg*; Ilk. *tiog*.
*\*tiukō* thigh: Q *tiuko*. Q *tiuya-* swell, grow fat; ON *tuio-*, N *tuio* to
swell (associated with TUY).

**TOL¹-OTH/OT**   eight. Q *tolto*; N *toloth*. ·

**TOL²-**   *tollo* island: Q *tol*, pl. *tolle*; N *toll*, pl. *tyll*; cf. *Tol-eressea*, N
*Toll-ereb*.

**TOP-**   cover, roof. *\*tōp-*: Q *tópa* roof; *tópa-* to roof; *tope* covers (pa.t.
*tompe*). N *tobo* cover, roof over; *tobas* roofing.

**TOR-**   brother (cf. THEL- sister). ON *wator* brother (*wa* = together),
especially used of those not brothers by blood, but sworn brothers or
associates; N *gwador (gwedeir)*. ON *toron* brother, pl. *toroni*. N †*tôr*,
*terein* ; usually used was the cpd. *muindor* with analogical pl. *muindyr*
(see MOY, *moina*). Q *toron, torni* brother; *otorno* sworn brother,
associate [WŎ]; *otornasse* brotherhood; but usually of the blood-
kinship was used *onóro* (*\*wa-nōrō* = of one kin, see WŎ, NŌ) = ON
*wanúro*, N *gwanur* kinsman.

**TOW-**   Q *tō* wool; *toa* of wool, woollen; N *taw*.

**TUB-**   *\*tumbu* deep valley, under or among hills: Q *tumbo*, N *tum*. Cf.
*Tumladen* 'the level vale' [LAT], the vale of Gondolin. *\*tubnā* deep:
Q *tumna* lowlying, deep, low; N *tofn*; Ilk. *tovon*. *\*Utubnu* name of
Melko's vaults in the North: Q *Utumno*; N *Udun*; Ilk. *Uduvon*; Dan.
*Utum*.

**TUG-**   *\*tūgu* : Q *tuo*; ON *túgo*, N *tû*; Ilk. *tûgh, tû*; muscle, sinew;
vigour, physical strength. Cf. name *Tuor* (older *tūghor* = *tū-gor*
'strength-vigour', see GOR). *\*tungā* : Q *tunga* taut, tight (of strings,
resonant); N *tong*; Ilk. *tung*.

**TUK-** draw, bring. Q *tukin* I draw; N *tegi* (3 sg. *tôg*) to lead, bring; Ilk. *toga* he brings.

**TUL-** come, approach, move towards (point of speaker). Q *tulin* I come; N *teli* to come, *tôl* he comes. *tultā* make come: Q *tulta-* send for, fetch, summon; N *toltho* fetch; Ilk. *tolda* he fetches.

**TULUK-** Q *tulka* firm, strong, immoveable, steadfast; cf. *Tulkas* (*Tulkatho, Tulkassen*). *tulko* (*tulku*) support, prop. EN *tolog* stalwart, trusty. *tulu* (*tulukmē*, ON *tulugme*) support, prop. Tulkas was also called *Ender* (see NDER), EN *Enner*.

**TUMPU-** hump. Q *tumpo*; N *tump*.

**TUN-** *tundu*: Q *tundo*; N *tund, tunn* hill, mound. *tundā*: Q *tunda* tall; N *tond, tonn*; Ilk. *tund*. *Tūnǎ*: Q *Tún, Túna* Elf-city in Valinor; ON *Túna*, N *Tûn*. Cf. N *mindon* isolated hill (*minitunda*), especially a hill with a watch-tower. [Under MINI N *mindon* is derived from *minitaun*. – I cannot explain why *Tún* appears here as a Q form: see QS §39, and commentary on §§39, 45.]

**TUP-** *tupsē*: Q *tupse* thatch; N *taus*; Ilk. *tuss*.

**TUR-** power, control, mastery, victory. *tūrē* mastery, victory: Q *túre*; N *tûr*. Cf. name *Turambar*, N *Túramarth* 'Master of Fate', name taken in pride by *Túrin* (Q *Turindo*) – which contains the same element *tūr* victory, + *indo* mood (see ID).

*tūrō* and in cpds. *turo, tur*, master, victor, lord: cf. Q *Fantur*, N *Fannor*. Q *turin* I wield, control, govern, pa.t. *turne*; N *ortheri*, 3 sg. *orthor* (*ortur-*) master, conquer; *tortho* to wield, control. *taurā*: Q *taura* mighty; N *taur* vast, mighty, overwhelming, awful – also high, sublime (see TÁWAR). [Added:] *Turkil*, cf. *Tarkil* = Númenórean [KHIL].

**TURÚM-** *turumā*: Q *turma* shield; *turúmbē*: T *trumbe* shield; Ilk. *trumb, trum*.

**TUS-** *tussā*: Q *tussa* bush, N *toss* low-growing tree (as maple, hawthorn, blackthorn, holly, etc.): e.g. *eregdos* = holly-tree. See ERÉK, ÓR-NI.

**TUY-** spring, sprout (cf. TIW grow fat, swell?). Q *tuia* sprouts, springs; N *tuio*. *tuilē*: Q *tuile* spring-time; also used = dayspring, early morn = *artuile* [AR¹]. Cf. *tuilindo* (for *tuilelindō* 'spring-singer') swallow, N *tuilind, tuilin* [LIN²]. *tuimā*: Q *tuima* a sprout, bud; N *tuiw, tui*.

**TYAL-** play. Q *tyalie* sport, play, game; *tyalin* I play. N *telio, teilio* (*tyaliā-*) to play. Cf. *tyalañgandō* = harp-player (Q *tyalangan*): N *Talagand*, one of the chiefs of Gondolin (see ÑGAN). N *te(i)lien* sport, play.

**TYUL-** stand up (straight). *tyulmā* mast: Q *tyulma*. *tyulussē* poplar-tree: Q *tyulusse*, N *tulus* (pl. *tylys*) [see LI].

# U

**UB-** abound. Q *úvea* abundant, in very great number, very large; *úve* abundance, great quantity. N *ofr (ovr)*, *ovor* abundant (*\*ubrā*); *ovras* crowd, heap, etc.; *ovro* to abound.

**UGU-** and **UMU-** negative stems: Q *uin* and *umin* I do not, am not; pa.t. *úme*. Q prefix *ú* (< *ugu*, or *gū*) not, un-, in- (usually with bad sense), as *vanimor* fair folk = (men and) elves, *úvanimor* monsters. Cf. GŪ, MŪ. [Under BAN the *Vanimor* are the Children of the Valar; see pp. 403–4. – This entry was first written, like all others in this part of the manuscript, in pencil, but then overwritten in ink; it was struck out, in pencil, but this may have been done before it was overwritten. Apparently later pencilled additions are: [Q] *úmea* evil, [N] *um* bad, evil.]

**ULU-** pour, flow. Q *ulya-* pour (intr. pa.t. *ulle*, tr. *ulyane*); *ulunde* flood; *úlea* pouring, flooding, flowing. *\*Ulumō* name of the Vala of all waters: Q *Ulmo*; N *Ulu*, usually called *Guiar* (see WAY). N *oeil, eil* it is raining (*\*ulyā*); *\*ulda* torrent, mountain-stream, EN *old, oll*.

**ÚLUG-** T *ulga*, Ilk. *olg* hideous, horrible; *\*ulgundō* monster, deformed and hideous creature: Q *ulundo*; T *ulgundo*, Ilk. *ulgund*, *ulgon, ulion*; N *ulund, ulun*. Also **ÚLGU**: cf. *Ul-* in *Ulfang, Uldor, Ulfast, Ulwarth*, names of Swartmen. [These names of the Easterlings were of course given to them by the Elves (as is specifically stated of those with the element BOR); but cf. the *Lhammas* §10, where this is not so.]

**UŊG-** *\*uŋgwē*: Q *ungwe* gloom; *ungo* cloud, dark shadow. Cf. *Ungweliante, Ungoliante* the Spider, ally of Morgoth (cf. SLIG). Ilk. *ungol* darkness, *ungor* black, dark, gloomy. In N not used except in name *Ungoliant*, which is really taken from Q. The name of the Spider in N is *Delduthling* (see DYEL, DO3).

**UNU-** (cf. NŬ, NDŪ). *undu* a parallel form in Q made to equal *ama, amba* up [AM²]: down, under, beneath.

**UNUK-** Q *unqe* hollow; *unka-* hollow out; *unqa* adj. hollow.

**UR-** be hot. Q *úr* fire, N *ûr*. Q *Úrin* f. (g.sg. *Úrinden*) name of the Sun. Q *uruite, úruva* fiery. Cf. *Dagor Vreged-úr* Battle of Sudden Fire [BERÉK]. Q *urya-* blaze. [This entry was struck through, and beside it the following written very roughly:] **UR-** wide, large, great. *Úrion*. Q *úra* large; N *ûr* wide.

**USUK-** *\*us(u)k-wē*: Q *usqe* reek; N *osp*; Ilk. *usc* smoke.

**UY-** Q *uile* long trailing plant, especially seaweed; *earuile* seaweed [AY]; *Uinen (Uinenden)* wife of Osse, ON *Uinenda*, EN *Uinend, Uinen* (cf. NEN); [N] *uil* seaweed, *oeruil*.

# W

[The stems in W- form the concluding entries in the manuscript, and unlike those that precede were carefully written in ink, with some pencilled changes and additions.]

**WÃ-, WAWA-, WAIWA-** blow. Q *vaiwa, waiwa* wind; N *gwaew*; Ilk. *gwau*.

**WA3-** stain, soil. *\*wa3rã*: Q *vára* soiled, dirty; N *gwaur* (ON *wóra*); Ilk. *gôr*. *\*wahtã-* to soil, stain: Q *vahta*; N *gwatho* (ON *wattóbe*); Ilk. *góda-*. *\*wahtē* a stain: ON *watte*, N *gwath* coalescing with *\*wath*, q.v. [WATH]; Ilk. *gôd* dirtiness, filth. *\*wahsē*: Q *vakse* stain; ON *wasse*, N *gwass*. Cf. *Iarwath* 'Blood-stain' [YAR], surname of Túrin.

**WAN-** depart, go away, disappear, vanish. Q *vanya-* go, depart, disappear, pa.t. *vanne*; *vanwa* gone, departed, vanished, lost, past; *vanwie* the past, past time. This stem in N replaced KWAL in application to death (of elves by fading, or weariness): thus *gwanw* (*\*wanwē*) death; *gwanath* death; *gwann* (*\*wannã*) departed, dead. Note: *gwanw, gwanath* are the 'act of dying', not 'death, Death' as a state or abstract: that is *guru* (see ÑGUR). N *gwanno* (*wanta-*) depart, die. [The stem WAN was changed in pencil to VAN.]

**WA-N-** goose: Q *vãn, wãn* (pl. *vãni*) goose; N *gwaun*, pl. *guin*.

**WAR-** give way, yield, not endure, let down, betray. ON *warie* betray, cheat; *awarta* forsake, abandon. EN *gwerio* betray; *gwarth* betrayer; *awartha* forsake; *awarth* abandonment. Cf. *Ulwarth*. [This entry was an addition in pencil. On *Ulwarth* see ÚLUG and note.]

**WATH-** shade. ON *watha*, N *gwath*; Ilk. *gwath*. Cf. Ilk. *Urthin* (> N *Eredwethion*). [This entry was an addition in pencil. Above *Urthin* was written *Gwethion*.]

**WAY-** enfold. *\*wāyã* envelope, especially of the Outer Sea or Air enfolding the world within the Ilurambar or world-walls: Q *w- vaia, w- vaiya*; ON *\*wōia, uia*, N *ui*. *\*Vāyārō* name of Ulmo, lord of Vaiya: Q *Vaiaro*, N *Uiar* the usual N name of Ulmo. [The stem WAY was changed in pencil to VAY. Under ULU it is said that Ulmo was usually called *Guiar* in N.]

**WED-** bind. *\*wedã*: ON *weda* bond, N *gweð*; Ilk. *gweð*. N *gwedi*, pa.t. *gwend, gwenn* later *gweðant*, bind. N *angweð* 'iron-bond', chain. *\*wǣdē* bond, troth, compact, oath: Q *vére*; ON *waide*, N *gwaeð*. *\*wed-tã*: Q *vesta-* swear (to do something), contract, make a compact; *vesta* contract; *vestale* oath. N *gwest* oath; *gwesto* to swear; *gowest* contract, compact, treaty, Q *ovesta* [wǒ]. [The Q words derived from *\*wed-tã* were struck out in pencil, with the note that they 'all fell with derivatives of BES'. These same words, with different meaning, are found under BES: *vesta* matrimony, *vesta-* to wed;

*vestale* wedding. The reference in the original here is to BES (not as previously to BED: see note to LEP).]

**WEG-** (manly) vigour. Q *vie* manhood, vigour (*\*weʒē*); *vea* adult, manly, vigorous; *veaner* (adult) man [NĒR]; *veasse* vigour. *veo* (*\*wegō*) man. The latter in compound form *\*-wego* is frequent in masculine names, taking Q form *-we* (< *weg*). This can be distinguished from *-we* (*-wē* abstract suffix) by remaining *-we* in N, from ON *-wega*. The abstract suffix occurs in the names *Manwe, Fionwe, Elwe, Ingwe, Finwe*. These names do not occur in Exilic forms *\*Manw, \*Fionw, \*Elw, \*Finw* – since Finwe for instance remained in Valinor [see PHIN]. These names were used even by Gnomes in Qenya form, assisted by the resemblance to *-we* in other names, as *Bronwe*, ON *Bronwega* (see BORÓN). In N otherwise this stem only survives in *gweth* manhood, also used = man-power, troop of able-bodied men, host, regiment (cf. *Forodweith* Northmen). *\*weg-tē* [This entry, the last under W as the manuscript was originally written, was left unfinished. – Under PHOR the form is equally clearly *Forodwaith*.]

**WEN-, WENED-** maiden. Q *wende, vende*; N *gwend, gwenn*. Often found in feminine names, as *Morwen, Eleðwen*: since the latter show no *-d* even in archaic spelling, they probably contain a form *wen-*: cf. Ilk. *gwen* girl; Q *wéne, véne* and *venesse* virginity; N *gweneth* virginity. [Added:] Some names, especially those of men, may contain *gwend* bond, friendship: see WED. [The N noun *gwend* is not given under WED. – Against this entry is written: 'Transfer to GWEN'. – In the narrative texts (QS §129, AB 2 annal 245) the name *Eledhwen* was interpreted as 'Elfsheen' – and this survived much later in the *Grey Annals*; on the other hand under ELED the translation was changed from 'Elf-fair' to 'Elf-maid'.]

**WEY-** wind, weave. Q, owing to change *wei* > *wai*, confused this with WAY; but cf. *Vaire* (*\*weirē*) 'Weaver', name of the doom-goddess, wife of Mandos: N *Gwîr*. N *gwî* net, web. [The stem WEY was changed in pencil to VEY.]

**WIG-** *\*wingē*: Q *winge* foam, crest of wave, crest. Cf. *wingil* nymph; *Wingelot, Wingelóte* 'foam-flower', Earendel's boat (N *Gwingloth*) [LOT(H)]. N, Ilk. *gwing* spindrift, flying spray. [This entry was an addition in pencil. – With *wingil* cf. the old name *Wingildi*, I. 66, 273.]

**WIL-** fly, float in air. *\*wilwā* air, lower air, distinct from the 'upper' of the stars, or the 'outer' (see WAY): Q *wilwa* > *vilwa*; N *gwelw* air (as substance); *gwelwen* = Q *vilwa*; Ilk. *gwelu, gwelo*. Q *vilin* I fly, pa.t. *ville*. N *gwilith* 'air' as a region = Q *vilwa*; cf. *gilith* = Q *ilmen* (see GIL). Q *wilwarin* (pl. *wilwarindi*) butterfly; T *vilverin*; N *gwilwileth*; Ilk. *gwilwering*. [The name *Wilwa* of the lower air is found also in the preparatory outline for *The Fall of Númenor* (p. 12), whereas *Wilwa* in the *Ambarkanta* was changed throughout to Vista, and so also on the accompanying world-diagrams (IV. 240–7). By sub-

sequent pencilled changes the forms *wilwā, Q wilwa were changed to
*wilmā, Q wilma; Q wilwa > vilwa was struck out; and Q vilin was
changed to wilin. A new stem WIS with derivative Q vista (see below)
was introduced, either at the same time or later, but the stem WIL was
allowed to stand.]

**WIN-, WIND-** *windi blue-grey, pale blue or grey: Q vinde, N gwind,
gwinn. *winyā: Q winya, vinya evening; N gwein, pl. gwîn; Ilk.
gwini, gwine. *winta- fade: Q vinta-, pa.t. vinte, vintane; ON
wintha it fades, advesperascit ['evening approaches'], N gwinna.
[This entry was struck out, and 'see THIN' written against it. The
following pencilled addition may have been made either before or after
the original entry was rejected, since it is not itself struck through:]
*windiā pale blue: Q win(d)ya, vinya; N gwind.

**WIS-** Q vista air as substance. [See note to WIL.]

**WŌ-** together. The form wŏ would if stressed > wa in Eldarin. In Q
the form wō, and the unstressed wŏ, combined to produce prefix ŏ-
'together': as in o-torno (see TOR), o-selle (see THEL), and many other
words, e.g. ovesta (see WED). In N we have gwa- when stressed, as in
gwanur (= Q onóro) [TOR], gwastar (see STAR), and frequently, but
only in old cpds. The living form was go-, developed from gwa- in
unstressed positions – originally mainly in verbs, but thence spreading
to verbal derivatives as in gowest (see WED). In many words this had
become a fixed element. Thus not- count, nut- tie coalesced in Exilic
*nod-; but 'count' was always expressed by gonod- unless some other
prefix was added, as in arnediad [AR²]. In Ilk. owing to coalescence of
gwo, ʒo (in go) this prefix was lost [see ʒŏ].

# Y

[As already mentioned (p. 346) I have changed the representation of the
'semi-vowel' j to y, and therefore give these stems here, at the end of the
alphabet. The section belongs however among the entirely 'unrecon-
structed' parts of the work, and consists, like the I-stems, only of very
rough and difficult notes.]

**YA-** there, over there; of time, ago, whereas en yonder [EN] of time
points to the future. Q yana that (the former); yá formerly, ago:
yenya last year [YEN]; yára ancient, belonging to or descending from
former times; yáre former days; yalúme former times [LU]; yasse,
yalúmesse, yáresse once upon a time; yárea, yalúmea olden. N iaur
ancient, old(er); io (ia?) ago. 'Old' (in mortal sense, decrepit) is ingem
of persons, 'yearsick'; 'old' (decrepit, worn) of things is gem [GENG-
WĀ]. See GYER.

**YAB-** fruit. Q yáve fruit; N iau corn. Yavanna Fruit-giver (cf.
ANA¹), N Ivann.

**YAG-**    yawn, gape. *\*yagu-* gulf: N *ia*, chiefly in place-names like *Moria* = Black Gulf. *\*yagwē* : Q *yáwe* ravine, cleft, gulf; N *iau*. Q *yanga-* to yawn.

**YAK-**    *\*yakta-*: Q *yat* (*yaht-*) neck; N *iaeth*. Q *yatta* narrow neck, isthmus.

**YAN-**    Cf. AYAN. Q *yána* holy place, fane, sanctuary; N *iaun*.

**YAR-**    blood. Q *yár* (*yaren*); N *iâr*; *Iarwath* Blood-stained (see WA3), surname of Túrin. Ilk. *ôr* blood; *arn* red; cf. *Aros* (= N *iaros*) name of river with reddish water.

**YAT-**    join. *\*yantā* yoke, beside *\*yatmā* : Q *yanta* yoke; *yanwe* bridge, joining, isthmus. N *iant* yoke; *ianw* bridge (*eilianw* 'sky-bridge', rainbow, see 3EL).

**YAY-**    mock. Q *yaiwe*, ON *yaiwe*, mocking, scorn; N *iaew*.

**YEL-**    daughter. Q *yelde* ; N *iell, -iel*. [This entry was removed with the change of etymology of N *iell*: see SEL-D and YŌ, YON. A new formulation of the stem YEL was introduced, but was in turn rejected. This gave:] **YEL-**    friend: Q *yelda* friendly, dear as friend; *yelme* ; *-iel* in names = [Old English] *-wine* (distinguish N *-iel* derived from *selda*).

**YEN-**    year. Q *yén* (*yen-*); *linyenwa* old, having many years [LI]. Last day of year = *qantien*, N *penninar* [KWAT]; first year, first day *minyen* [MINI]. *Endien* Midyear [ÉNED] was a week outside the months, between the sixth and seventh months, [?dedicated] to the Trees: [also called] *Aldalemnar*, see LEP. N *în* year; *ínias* annals; *iðrin* year (= *ien-rinde*, see RIN); *edinar* (*at-yēn-ar*) anniversary day; *ennin* = Valian Year; *ingem* 'year-sick' = old (mortally) [GENG-WĀ]; *ifant* aged, long-lived (= *yen-panta* > *impanta* > *in-fant*) [KWAT]. [The word *Inias* 'Annals' occurs in the title-pages given on p. 202.]

**YES-**    desire. Q *yesta* desire; N *iest* wish.

**YŌ, YON-**    son. Q *yondo, -ion* ; N *ionn, -ion*. [The following was added when the entry YEL had been removed:] feminine *yēn, yend* = daughter; Q *yende, yen*.

**YŬ-**    two, both. N *ui-* twi-, as *uial* twilight [KAL]. Q *yūyo* both.

**YUK-**    employ, use. N *iuith* use, *iuitho* [?enjoy].

**YUL-**    smoulder. Q *yúla* ember, smouldering wood; *yulme* red [?heat], smouldering heat; *yulma* brand. ON *iolf* brand; *iûl* embers.

**YUR-**    run. ON *yurine* I run, *yura* course; N *iôr* course.

# APPENDIX

---

# THE GENEALOGIES
# THE LIST OF
# NAMES

### AND

# THE SECOND
# 'SILMARILLION'
# MAP

# I THE GENEALOGIES

These belong essentially with the earliest *Annals of Beleriand*, but though I knew of their existence (since they are referred to in the *List of Names*) I presumed them lost, and only recently discovered this small manuscript, after the work on Vol. IV was completed. It consists of genealogical tables of the Elvish princes, of the three houses of the Fathers of Men, and of the houses of the Eastern Men. There is no need to reproduce these tables, but only to mention certain details that are not found elsewhere. In the first of them are some additional persons:

Elwë, Lord of the Teleri (who is called 'Lord of Ships'), has a son *Elulindo*;

Fingon has a son *Findobar* (this name, simply as a name, occurs in the *Etymologies* under the stems PHIN (written *Findabar*) and MBAR);

Orodreth, in addition to his son Halmir, has a younger son *Orodlin*.

The genealogies of Men have dates of birth and death. These were a good deal emended, changing them by a year or two, but in the result are almost exactly as in the earlier version of AB 1. The following are however not given in the *Annals* in any version (if they had been they would of course have been extended in two steps, first by a hundred years and then by two hundred years).

*Elboron* son of Dior born 192; *Elbereth* his brother born 195 (they were thus fourteen and eleven years old at their deaths, AB 2 annal 306);

*Húrin* died in '?200' (in annal 200 in AB 1, repeated in AB 2, 'of his fate no certain tidings are known');

*Ulfand the Swart* born 100, died 170; *Uldor the Accursed* born 125, *Ulfast* born 128, *Ulwar* born 130;

*Bor the Faithful* born 120; *Borlas* born 143; *Boromir* born 145; *Borthandos* born 147.

In addition to the genealogical tables there is also a table of the divisions of the Qendi which is almost the same as that given with the *Lhammas* on p. 197, and together with this table is a list of the many names by which the Lindar, Noldor, and Teleri were known. This list is a first form of that in QS §29 (note to the text), and all the names found here are found also in the longer list in QS; but there are here also many Elvish names which (apart from *Soloneldi*) are not found in QS:

The Lindar are named also *Tarqendi* 'High-elves', *Vanimor* 'the Beautiful' [> *Írimor* 'the Fair Ones'], and *Ninqendi* 'White-elves';

The Noldor are named also *Nurqendi* 'Deep-elves', *Ainimor* [written above: *Istimor*] 'the Wise', and *Kuluqendi* 'Golden-elves';

The Teleri are named also *Falmarindi* 'Foam-riders', *Soloneldi* 'Musicians of the shore', and *Veaneldar* 'Sea-elves'.

The name *Vanimor* is used in AV 2 of the lesser spirits of Valarin race, among whom were 'later numbered' also the *Valarindi*, the Children of the Valar (pp. 110, 121); the latter are the *Vanimor* in the *Etymologies*, stem BAN, but under the negative stems UGU, UMU the name is translated 'fair folk = (men and) elves'. Some other of these names also appear in the *Etymologies*: *Tarqendi* (TĀ), *Nurqendi* (NŪ), *Istimor* (IS), *Falmarindi* (PHAL), *Soloneldi* (SOL). With *Irimor* cf. *Irima ye Númenor* in *The Lost Road* (p. 72), and see stem ID.

# II   THE LIST OF NAMES

During the 1930s my father began the task of making an alphabetic list, with definitions, of all the names in his works concerned with the legends of the Elder Days. A list of sources is attached to this list, and the entries are accompanied by full references to sources (by page-number or annal-date) – but these references are almost entirely confined to the *Annals of Beleriand* and the *Genealogies* : the only others are a few to the first pages of the *Qenta Noldorinwa* (Q) and two to the *Map*. In the list of sources 'Annals of Beleriand' and 'Genealogies' are marked with a tick; it is clear then that my father had indexed these and made a beginning on Q when he stopped.

As the List of Names was originally written the references are only to the first version of AB 1 (but include additions made to that text subsequently and given in the notes in IV. 310–13). But after the list was abandoned as a methodical work of reference my father added to it more haphazardly, without references, and these later additions show use of the second version of AB 1, as well as some names that do not appear in any of the texts; entries were also substantially modified and extended.

The majority of the entries do not in fact add anything in their definitions to what is available in the sources, and it is quite unnecessary to give the work in full. There follows here a small selection from the material, this being restricted to those entries or parts of entries which have some particular feature of interest (mostly concerning names or name-forms).

*Aldaron*   The Noldorin equivalent is given as *Galaðon*, which does not appear elsewhere.

*Balrog*   is said to be an Orc-word with no pure Qenya equivalent: 'borrowed *Malaroko-*'; contrast the *Etymologies*, stems ÑGWAL, RUK.

*Beleriand*   'Originally land about southern Sirion, named by the Elves of the Havens from Cape *Balar*, and Bay of *Balar* into which Sirion flowed; extended to all lands south of Hithlum and Taur-na-Danion, and west of Eredlindon. Its southern borders undefined. Sometimes includes Doriath and Ossiriand.' With this statement of the extent of Beleriand cf. QS §108; and with the derivation of the name *Beleriand* from Cape *Balar*, Bay of *Balar*, cf. the *Etymologies*, stem BAL. This is the first occurrence of Cape Balar, which was however marked in on the second Map as originally drawn and lettered.

*Beren* The surnames of Beren were first given as *Mablosgen* 'Empty-handed' and *Ermabuin* 'One-handed' (as in AB 2 annal 232). The former was changed to *Mablothren* and then to *Camlost* (and in a separate entry *Mablosgen* > *Mablost*); the latter to *Erchamui* and then to *Erchamion* (again as in AB 2, note 22). From the *Etymologies* (stems KAB, MAP) it appears that the names containing the element *mab* are Ilkorin (Doriathrin) names, while those containing *cam*, *cham* are Noldorin.

*Cinderion* 'Gnomish name = Hither Lands'. This name has no reference to a source; it is found nowhere else, nor any form at all like it.

*Cristhorn* was emended first to *Cil-thorn* and then to *Cil-thor(o)ndor*, with the definition 'Eagle-cleft of Thorondor King of Eagles'. The forms *Cilthoron* and *Cilthorondor* are found in the *Etymologies* (stem KIL), as also is *Cristhoron* (KIRIS).

*Dagor Delothrin* 'The Last Battle, "the Terrible Battle", in which Fionwë overcame Morgoth.' The reference given is to AB 1 annal 250, where however no Elvish name is found. In a cross-reference in the list to the Last Battle it is called also 'the Long Battle' (for it lasted fifty years).

*Dagor Nirnaith* is given as a name of the Battle of Unnumbered Tears.

*Dark-elves* 'Translation of *Moreldar* (also called *Ilkorindi*, those who came not to Kôr), the name of all the Elves who remained wandering in the Hither Lands . . .' The term *Moreldar* is not found elsewhere. The nomenclature here is of course that of Q (§2), where *Eldar* = 'all Elves' and the *Ilkorindi* or Dark-elves are those who were lost on the Great March.

*Dor-deloth*, or *Dor-na-Daideloth* '"Land of Dread" or "Land of the Shadow of Dread", those regions east of Eredwethion and north of Taur-na-Danion which Morgoth ruled; but its borders were ever increased southward, and early it included Taur-na-Fuin.'

*Dorthanion* is stated to be a Doriathrin name: *thanion* = 'of pines' (*than*). See the *Etymologies*, stem THŌN.

*Dwarves* 'Called by the Dark-elves (and so by the Gnomes) *Nauglar* (singular *Naugla*).' *Nauglar* appears in an addition to AB 1 (IV. 311); the QS form is *Naugrim*.

*Elivorn* 'Lake-Black in Dor Granthir.' This was a latter addition to the list and has no source-reference. *Elivorn* may well have been the form erased and replaced by *Helevorn* in QS §118. *Dor Granthir* is found in the same passage in QS.

*Eredlindon* '"Blue Mountains" (*lind* blue), eastern bounds of Beleriand.' See the commentary on QS §108.

*Eredlúmin* '"Gloomy Mountains", mountains to east [*read* west] of Hithlum, overlooking the Seas.' As the list was originally made, *Eredlómin* was at both occurrences written *Ered-lúmin*. I have noted (IV.

192–3) that both the meaning of the name and its application were changed, so that *Ered-lómin* 'Shadowy Mountains', to the east and south of Hithlum, as in Q, became *Ered-lómin* 'Echoing Mountains', the coastal range west of Hithlum; and at the same time the meaning of *Dor-lómin* changed from 'Land of Shadows' to 'Land of Echoes'. In the List of Names as originally made the new name for the mountains east and south of Hithlum, *Eredwethion* 'Shadowy Mountains', already appears (with the etymology *gwath* 'shadow'), and there is here therefore a halfway stage, when *Ered-lómin* (*-lúmin*) had become the name of the coastal range but did not yet have the significance 'Echoing'. There is no doubt an etymological halfway stage also, which I take to be the explanation of the *lúmin* form (found also in *Dor-lúmin* on the second Map): the source was now the stem LUM, given in the *Etymologies* as the source of *Hith-lum* (and of Q *Hísilumbe*, changed to *Hísilóme* under the influence of *lóme* 'night': Q *lumbe* 'gloom, shadow'). Hence the translation here 'Gloomy Mountains', which is not found elsewhere. Finally the interpretation 'Echoing' arose, with derivation of *-lómin* from the stem LAM.

*Fingolfin*   The cairn of Fingolfin is called *Sarnas Fingolfin*.

*Fuin Daidelos*   'Night of Dread's Shadow' or 'Deadly Nightshade' is given as a name of Taur-na-Fuin.

*Gothmog*   '= Voice of *Goth* (Morgoth), an Orc-name.' Morgoth is explained at its place in the list as 'formed from his Orc-name *Goth* "Lord or Master", with *mor* "dark or black" prefixed.' These entries in the List of Names have been discussed in II. 67. In the *Etymologies* the element *goth* is differently explained in *Gothmog* (GOS, GOTH) and in *Morgoth* (KOT, but with a suggestion that the name 'may also contain GOTH').

*Gurtholfin*   was subsequently changed to *Gurtholvin* and then to *Gurtholf*. *Gurtholfin* > *Gurtholf* also in AB 2, note 39; see the *Etymologies*, stems GÓLOB and NGUR.

*Hithlum*   is translated 'Mist-and-Dusk'; see the *Etymologies*, stems KHIS and LUM.

*Kuiviénen*   The Noldorin name *Nen Echui* is given; this is found in the *Etymologies*, stem KUY.

*Morgoth*   See *Gothmog*.

*Orcs*   'Gnomish *orch*, pl. *eirch, erch* ; Qenya *ork, orqui* borrowed from Gnomish. A folk devised and brought into being by Morgoth to war on Elves and Men; sometimes translated "Goblins", but they were of nearly human stature.' See the entry ÓROK in the *Etymologies*.

*Sarn Athrad*   is translated 'Stone of Crossing'.

*Sirion*   The length of Sirion is given as 'about 900 miles' from Eithil Sirion to the Delta. In QS §107 the length of the river from the Pass of Sirion to the Delta is 121 leagues, which if measured in a straight line from the northern opening of the Pass agrees with the scale on the second Map of 3·2 cm. = 50 miles (see p. 272). But the List of Names and the original drawing of the second Map were associated, and two of the references given in the list are made to the Map, so that the figure of 900 miles (300 leagues) is hard to account for.

*Sirion's Haven*: '(*Siriombar*), the settlement of Tuor and the remnants of Doriath at *Eges-sirion*; also called *Sirion*.' The name *Siriombar* only occurs here; cf. *Brithombar*.

*Mouths of Sirion*: '(*Eges-sirion*), the various branches of Sirion at its delta, also the region of the delta.' Above the second *s* of *Eges-sirion* (a name not found elsewhere) is written an *h*, showing the change of original *s* to *h* in medial position.

*Sirion's Well*: '(*Eithil* or *Eithil Sirion*), the sources of Sirion, and the fortress of Fingolfin and Fingon near the spring.'

*Tol Thû*   is another name for *Tol-na-Gaurhoth*.

*Tulkas*   'The youngest and strongest of the nine Valar.' The reference is to Q, IV. 79, but it is not said there that Tulkas was the youngest of the Valar.

## III   THE SECOND 'SILMARILLION' MAP

The second map of Middle-earth west of the Blue Mountains in the Elder Days was also the last. My father never made another; and over many years this one became covered all over with alterations and additions of names and features, not a few of them so hastily or faintly pencilled as to be more or less obscure. This was the basis for my map in the published 'Silmarillion'.

The original element in the map can however be readily perceived from the fine and careful pen (all subsequent change was roughly done); and I give here on four successive pages a reproduction of the map *as it was originally drawn and lettered*. I have taken pains to make this as close a copy of the original as I could, though I do not guarantee the exact correspondence of every tree.

It is clear that this second map, developed from that given in Vol. IV, belonged in its original form with the earlier work of the 1930s: it was in fact closely associated with the List of Names – which in two cases (*Eglor* and *Eredlúmin*, although *Eredlúmin* is not marked on the map) gives 'Map' as the source-reference – as is shown by certain name-forms common to both, e.g. *Dor-deloth*, *Dor-lúmin*, *Eithil Sirion*, and by the occurrence in both of *Cape Balar* (see the entry *Beleriand* in the List of Names). Moreover the date in 'Realm of Nargothrond Beyond the river (until 195)' on the map associates it with the original *Annals of Beleriand*, where the fall of the redoubt took place in that year (IV. 305), as does the river-name *Rathlorion* (later *Rathloriel*).

The map is on four sheets, originally pasted together but now separate, in which the map-squares do not entirely coincide with the sheets. In my reproductions I have followed the squares rather than the

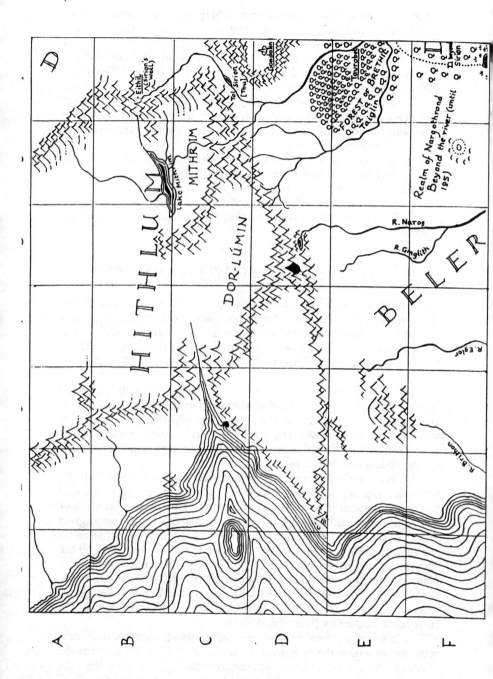

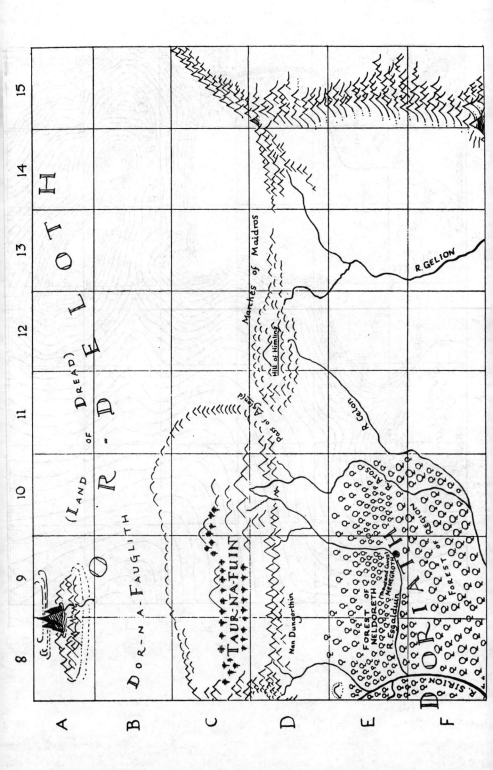

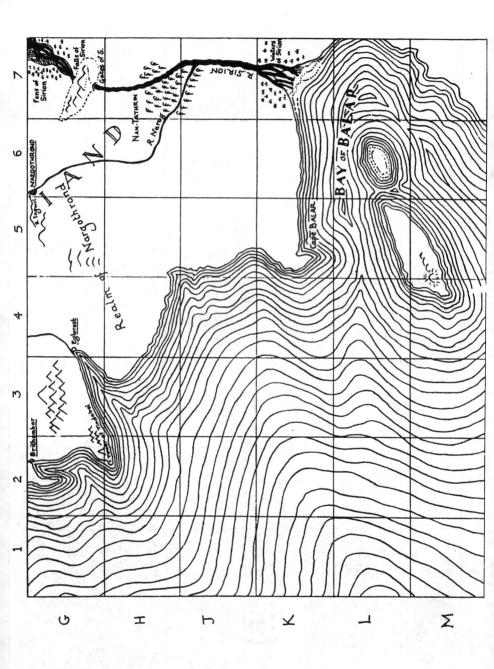

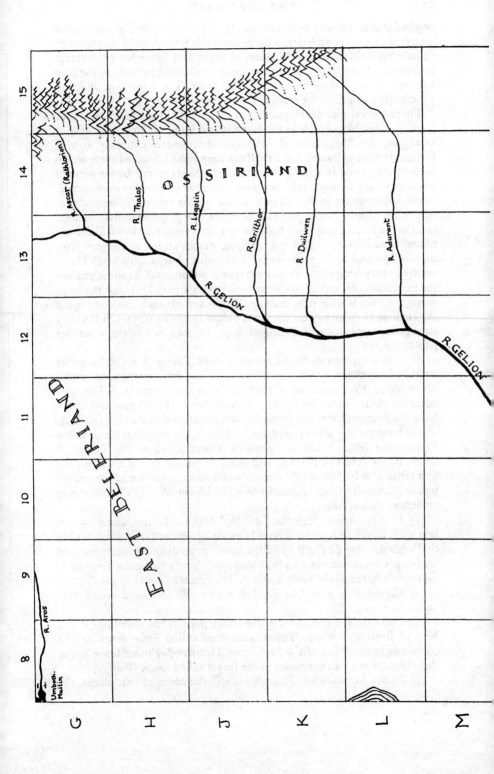

original sheets. I have numbered the squares horizontally right across the map from 1 to 15, and lettered them vertically from A to M, so that each square has a different combination of letter and figure for subsequent reference. I hope later to give an account of all changes made to the map afterwards, using these redrawings as a basis. The scale is 50 miles to 3·2 cm. (the length of the sides of the squares); see p. 272.

There are various developments in the physical features of the lands from the first Map (such as the large island lying off the coast west of Drengist; the Mountains of Mithrim; the eastern tributary arm of Gelion; the isle of Balar), but I shall not here make a detailed comparison between the two. It will be seen that at this stage my father entered remarkably few names on the new map – far fewer than were in existence, in marked contrast to the old one, which names Ivrin, Thangorodrim, Angband, Mount Dolm, the Hill of Spies, the great mountain-chains, etc. On the second map such features as Lake Ivrin and Mount Dolm are nonetheless shown, and of course some names added in roughly later may well go back to the early period; but as this is impossible to tell I have omitted everything in the redrawing that is not original. I cannot explain the mountain blacked-in to the west of Ivrin (square D5), nor the large mound, if that is what it is, between Sirion and Mindeb (E8), nor again the curious circular bay on the coast below Drengist (C3). On the very strange representation of Thangorodrim, isolated in a circle of smaller peaks, see p. 271.

Especially interesting is the appearance of Tavrobel in the Forest of Brethil. In the literary texts of this period Tavrobel is named only in the preamble to AV 1 (cited on p. 201), as Pengolod's home in Tol Eressëa 'after his return unto the West', where Ælfwine (Eriol) saw and translated the Annals; from this preamble was developed that to QS (p. 203), where however the name is written *Tathrobel*. On the other hand, in the *Etymologies* (stem PEL(ES)) *Tavrobel* is mentioned as the 'village of Túrin in the forest of Brethil, and name of village in Tol Eressëa'; the first element is Noldorin *tafr*, *tavor*, 'woodpecker' (TAM), and the second means '(fenced) village' (Qenya *opele*, Noldorin *gobel*). The following evidences thus appear:

(1) In the earliest legends *Tavrobel* (originally translated 'woodhome', I. 267) had likewise a double meaning: it was Great Haywood in Staffordshire in England, and it bore, according to complex and changing conceptions by this time long since lost, a particular relation to Gilfanon's home of the same name in Tol Eressëa (see II. 292–3, 310).

(2) *Haywood* was in Old English *hæg-wudu* 'enclosed wood' (II. 328).

(3) Later (in the post-*Lord of the Rings* period) the dwellings of the Men of Brethil to whom Túrin came were called *Ephel Brandir* 'the encircling fence of Brandir' (*ephel* derived from *et-pel* 'outer fence'), and this village was on an eminence in the forest called *Amon Obel*.

(4) In the *Etymologies*, *Tavrobel* is still the name of two places, the

village of the Woodmen in Brethil, and a village in Tol Eressëa, where (in the preambles to AV 1 and QS) Pengolod (successor, as I have argued in IV. 274, to Gilfanon) dwelt.

But there is no indication at all why Tavrobel should still be used twice in this way. It may be thought that my father did not wish finally to abandon this old and deep association of his youth; and it is tempting therefore to see his bestowal at this time of the name *Tavrobel* in this way and in this place as an echo of Great Haywood, and perhaps not entirely fanciful to wonder whether he was influenced by the confluence of the two rivers, Taiglin and Sirion, not wholly unlike, in their relative courses here, that of the Sow and the Trent at Great Haywood (I. 196).*

*Gilfanon's house, the House of the Hundred Chimneys, stood near the bridge of Tavrobel (I. 174–5), where two rivers, Gruir and Afros, joined (II. 284, 287). I noted (I. 196 note 5) the possibility that there was, or is, a house that gave rise to Gilfanon's; and it has been pointed out to me by Mr G. L. Elkin, Acting Director of the Shugborough Estate, who has kindly supplied me with photographs and a detailed map, that Shugborough Hall, the home of the Earls of Lichfield and now the property of the National Trust, is near the end of the old packhorse bridge (called the Essex Bridge) which crosses the rivers at their confluence, and that the chimneys of the mansion are a prominent feature. It seems very likely that it was my father's sight of the great house through the trees and its smoking chimneys as he stood on the bridge that lies, in some sense, behind the House of the Hundred Chimneys in the old legend. Mr Elkin has further suggested that the High Heath or Heath of the Sky-roof, where the great battle was fought, so that it became the Withered Heath (II. 284, 287–8), might be Hopton Heath (where a battle of the Civil War was fought in 1643), which lies a few miles to the North-west.

# INDEX

The vast array of forms contained in Part III of this book constitutes a problem in respect of the Index. In the first place, a large number of names found in the *Etymologies* do not occur elsewhere in the book, and in many cases names are registered in greatly varying forms according to the divergent phonetic development in the different languages. In the second place, discussion of the history of names and the isolation of their elements makes the distinction between 'name' and 'common word' unreal; for the purposes of this 'etymological dictionary' *Alqualondë* illustrates *alqua* 'swan' and *londë* 'harbour-entrance, roads'. But to list alphabetically even a proportion of these Elvish 'common words' in Part III would be preposterous, since (quite apart from the practical consideration of length) it would mean rewriting the 'dictionary' in such a way as to conceal the historical relation between words which it is the object of the work to display.

I have in fact excluded the whole content of the Etymologies from normal representation in the Index, but I have attempted to assist reference to them in the following ways. (1) In the page-references to names that do occur elsewhere in the book I include also pages in the *Etymologies* where these names are explained – all such references being printed in *italics*. As a general rule I restrict these references to actual occurrence in the *Etymologies* of the name in question, but I have departed from this rule where it seemed useful to provide a reference to an element in a name that only appears in the *Etymologies* as a 'common word' (e.g. *nyárë* 'tale, saga, history' under *Eldanyárë*). (2) Where the *Etymologies* give names for persons, peoples, or places that are different from those found elsewhere in the book these are mentioned in the Index but not given separate entries; e.g. the Noldorin names *Mirion* and *Núron* are given under *Silmarils* and *Ulmo*. By these means, the great majority of names in the *Etymologies* are at least indicated in the Index. But beyond this, the many curiosities of the work – such as the structure of the Valinorian year and the names of the days in the Valinorian 'week', or the etymology of *cram* – emerge only from the study of it.

From the large number of names that occur in or in association with *The Lost Road* I have excluded some of the more casual and insignificant. References are not given for names on the tables accompanying the *Lhammas* or on the reproductions of the second Map.

As before, I have adopted a single form of capitalisation and hyphenation for the purposes of the Index.

80, 282–5, 290, 308, 312, *381, 389* (his titles *Taur Egledhriur* 'King of the Exiles', *Aran Chithlum* 'King of Hithlum'), 407; *High-king of the Noldor, King of Hithlum and Nivrost, Lord of the Falas,* etc. 128, 145–6, 266–7, 270, 279, 285. The cairn of Fingolfin (*Sarnas Fingolfin*) 133, 142, 285, 291, 406, *mount of Fingolfin* 285; speech of his people 177, 189

Fingon  126–7, 130, 132–7, 223, 226, 234, 238, 251–2, 255, 259, 264, 266, 271, 278, 282, 285, 289, 307–15, *362, 381,* 403, 407; *Overlord of all the Gnomes* 266

Finn  = *Finwë.* 192

Finntan  See 80, 82

Finrod  (1) Third son of Finwë; later *Finarfin.* 113, 116, 123, 194, 223, 234–5, 237, 239, 299–300, 334, *381, 383*; son(s), house, people of Finrod 33, 116, 118, 125–7, 131, 192, 194, 223, 235, 237, 250, 264, 276, 281, 284, 299–300. (2) *Finrod Felagund,* son of Finarfin (later name of *Inglor Felagund*) 299

Finrodian  (speech) = *Kornoldorin.* 194–5

Finwë  112–14, 122, 173–5, 180, 188, 192, 214–15, 218, 223–4, 227, 229–30, 232, 234, 251, 300, 326, *381, 398*; *Father of the Noldor* 180, 226, *King of Túna* 224. The *Followers of Finwë,* a name of the Noldor, 215

Fionwë  13–14, 18–19, 24, 143–4, 153, 165, 176–9, 205–8, 325–33, 336, *381, 398,* 405; *Fionwë Urion* 162, 165, *396*

Fíriel  Daughter of Orontor of Númenor. 62–3, 71, 73, and see *382*

Fírimor  'The Mortals', an Elvish name for Men. 63, 72 (*firimoin*), 245, *381*

First Age(s) of the World  23, 118

First Battle of Beleriand  The Battle-under-Stars. 117, 239, 249. See *Dagor-os-Giliath.*

Firstborn, The  The Elves. 25, 29, 63–6, 68, 72–3, 327, 332; cf. *Estanessë* 'the Firstborn' *356*

First Kindred  (1) The Elves. 14. (2) The First Kindred of the Elves (see *Lindar, Qendi, Vanyar*) 56, 107, 122, 180, 182–3, 197

Flying ships  (of the Númenóreans after the Downfall) 12–13, 17, 22, 76

Foam-riders  A name of the Teleri. 215, 403. See *Falmarindi.*

Forest of Night  See *Taur-na-Fuin*; *Forest of Pines,* see *Taur-na-Danion.*

Forgotten Caves  See *Caves of the Forgotten.*

Fourth Battle of Beleriand  The Battle of Unnumbered Tears (afterwards the Fifth Battle, 305). 136, 293, 302, 305. See *Nirnaith Arnediad, Nirnaith Dirnoth.*

Franks  91

Free, The  A name of the Teleri (cf. 169 and *Mirimor 373*). 215

Freyr  God of fruitfulness in ancient Scandinavia. 96–7

Frisians  91

*Qendi, Quendi* (1) The First Kindred of the Elves (replaced by *Lindar*). 107, 122, 180–1. (2) All Elves. 119, 122, 168, 171, 174, 178, 180, 182–3, 197, 212–14, 218–19, 225, 246, 247, *366* (also *Qendië*, Noldorin *Penedhrim*), 403

*Qenta, Quenta* (References in the texts themselves) 119, 171, 180, 185, 191, 201–2, 226, *366*. See *Pennas*.

*Qenya, Quenya* 'The Elvish Tongue'. 8, 56, 75, 172–5, 180, 184–6, 188, 192–5, 200, 217, 343–5, 404, 406, 412; *Qendya* 185. See *Elflatin, Parmalambë, Tarquesta*.

*Quendian* Languages derived from Oromë (= *Oromian*). 168, 181, 188, 192–7, 205, 207, 342, 347; *Quendian race* 178

*Radhrost* 'East Vale', Dark-elvish name of Thargelion. 262, 265, 268–9, *382, 384*

*Radhruin* Companion of Barahir. 147, 282; *Radruin* 147, 289. (Replaced *Radros*.)

*Radros* Companion of Barahir. 133, 147, 289. (Replaced by *Rad(h)ruin*.)

*Ragnor* Companion of Barahir. 282

*Ramdal* 'Wall's End' in East Beleriand. 262–3, 268; *Rhamdal* 283, *390*

*Rana* 'The Wayward', the Moon. 56, 240, 243, *383* (also Noldorin *Rhân*). See *Isil, Ithil*.

*Rathloriel, River* 'Bed of Gold'. 141, 263, *368, 383*, 407; earlier form *Rathlorion* 407

*Region* The forest forming the southern part of Doriath. 126, 148, 261, *356* (also *Eregion, Taur-nan-Erig*)

*Rerir, Mount* Outlier of Eredlindon, on which was a fortress of the Noldor. 263, 265, 268, 283, 290

[*Rhibdath, Rhimdath* River Rushdown. 384. This name only appears in the *Etymologies*, but it should have been mentioned there that the Rushdown is the river that flowed from the Misty Mountains to join Anduin north of the Carrock.]

*Rian* Mother of Tuor. 131, 133, 136–7, 151, 282, 289, *383* (*Rhian*); *Rían* 316

*Ringil* (1) The Sea of Ringil, formed from the fall of the Lamp Ringil. 32, *383*. (2) Fingolfin's sword. 284–5, *383*

*Ring of Doom* The council-place of the Valar. 209, 229

*Rivil's Well* 298

*Rome* 55; *Roman(s)* 39, 91–2; Old English *Walas, Rūm-walas* 92

*Rómenildi* Easterlings. 286, 291, (*364*)

*Rómenna* Haven in the east of Númenor. 74

*Rosamunda* Wife of Alboin the Lombard. 37, 54

*Rúmil* 113–14, 116, 122–3, 155–6, 164, 167, 178, 191–2, 203–4, 278; called *the sage of Kôr, of Tûn* 167, *the Elf-sage of Valinor* 123, 203–4

*Saeros* Elf of Doriath, slain by Túrin. 187, 316. (Replaced *Orgof*.)

*Sailors, The* A name of the Teleri. 215